FICTION 100

SECOND EDITION

AN ANTHOLOGY OF

FICTION

100

SHORT STORIES

James H. Pickering

MICHIGAN STATE UNIVERSITY

MACMILLAN PUBLISHING CO., INC.
NEW YORK

MACMILLAN PUBLISHING CO., INC.
866 Third Avenue, New York, New York 10022

COLLIER MACMILLAN CANADA, LTD.

Library of Congress Cataloging in Publication Data

Pickering, James H   comp.
  Fiction 100

  1. Short stories. I. Title.
PZ1.P587Fi5   [PN6014]   808.83'1   76-50594
ISBN 0-02-395330-6

Printing: 1 2 3 4 5 6 7 8   Year: 8 9 0 1 2 3

For Pat

Preface to the First Edition

FICTION 100 is an anthology of short stories designed for use in introductory fiction courses or in any other college courses in which short stories are studied. The stories appear alphabetically by author; any other superimposed order has been rejected to ensure that the instructor may enjoy the most flexibility.

Every anthology, no matter how large its table of contents, presents its editor with the difficult decision of what selections to include. *Fiction 100* has proved to be no exception. In a very real sense the problem of choice is only multiplied by size, and the larger the book, the greater the need for a principle of selection. The stories in *Fiction 100* were chosen, above all, because they are inherently interesting and because they have literary merit. A dozen years of teaching the short story to college-age readers has persuaded me that any story, if it is to "work" in the classroom, must engage the curiosity and imagination of the student and provide him with an experience in pleasurable reading. Fortunately, there are many, many excellent stories that do just that. Further, I have tried to assemble a collection, international in scope, of stories that represent a wide variety of subject matter, theme, literary technique, and style and that, at the same time, serve to illustrate the development of short fiction, its continuity and tradition, from its identifiable beginnings in the early years of the nineteenth century to the present. The collection represents a mixture of the new and the familiar. Roughly a third of the anthology is composed of older, well-established stories, the so-called classics. They are offered anew to the current generation of college readers without apology, for a good story, no matter how often anthologized, is a source of endless pleasure and discovery that no amount of critical analysis and rereading can ever exhaust. On the other hand, *Fiction 100* also presents a selection of newer and contemporary stories (many seldom, if ever, anthologized) to suggest the direction in which short fiction is moving in the latter half of the twentieth century.

A number of authors—Borges, Chekhov, Faulkner, Hawthorne, James, Joyce, Kipling, and Flannery O'Connor—are represented by three stories, Edgar Allan Poe by two. Of course, the reason for the inclusion of more than a single story by an author is to encourage comparison, to provide the opportunity for studying to some degree an author and his work together, and to allow the reader to test generalizations about an author's theme, style, or view of life in a manner simply not possible with only one example of the writer's work.

Editorial apparatus has been kept to a minimum to make *Fiction 100* usable in as many kinds of short story courses as possible. However, each story is followed by a series of study questions. They are, by intent, neither complete nor comprehensive. Rather, the questions are designed to be suggestive, to help guide the student in his own literary response, and to serve as a springboard for the classroom discussion to follow. At the end of the book in the section entitled "Biographical Notes" a brief biographical sketch and the major published works of each author are given to aid the student's own further explorations.

My particular thanks go to Lynn Altenbernd, University of Illinois; John H. Bens, Merritt College; Blaze O. Bonazza, California State College, Long Beach; Lila Chalpin, Massachusetts College of Art; Paul Davis, University of New Mexico; Robert J. Frank, Oregon State University; Donald W. Good, The Ohio State University; James L. Green, Arizona State University; David B. Haley, University of Minnesota; Jay Jernigan, Eastern Michigan University; William T. Lenehan, University of Wisconsin; Peter Lindblom, Miami-Dade Junior College; Dorothea Nudelman, Foothill College; Jacqueline Stark, formerly Los Angeles Valley College; and Donald H. Stevenson, San Diego Mesa College. Their constructive suggestions added much to my own experience and fostered many improvements to the original plan. The failings that remain are my own. I also owe a debt to E. Fred Carlisle, William A. Johnsen, Stephen Judy, Jay B. Ludwig, Virgil Scott, and John A. Yunck, my colleagues in the Department of English at Michigan State University, for their encouragement, advice, and very tangible help in tracking down needed materials. Each of the above has helped make *Fiction 100* a better book. Finally, special gratitude goes to D. Anthony English and Ray Schultz, my editors at Macmillan, for the part they played in making the past months enjoyable in the extreme.

J. H. P.

Michigan State University

Preface to the Second Edition

MY AIM in the second edition of *Fiction 100* is precisely what it was in the first: to provide the student with a large body of good short fiction at a reasonable price. Twenty-four of the stories are new, among them a number of additional examples of detective fiction, science fiction, and humor. Eight authors are once again represented by three stories to encourage comparison: Chekhov, Faulkner, Hawthorne, James, Joyce, Flannery O'Connor, Poe, and Welty. I have also added a glossary of literary terms as an appendix.

Once again there are debts, now including an indebtedness to the many students who have bought and read *Fiction 100*, especially my own. I also wish to thank the following individuals who took the time to evaluate the first edition. Their comments and suggestions have proven invaluable. They include K. Gerald Balls, Illinois State University; Joseph M. Blimm, Villanova University; Carley Bogarad, State University of New York at New Paltz; Drury H. Cargill, Dutchess Community College; Janet M. Carnesi, State University of New York Agricultural and Technical College; Sam Colman, Broome County Community College; Diana Culbertson, Kent State University; F. Alan Ehmann, University of Texas at El Paso; H. Ramsey Fowler, Memphis State University; Jewell A. Friend, Southern Illinois University; Byron Koh, Springfield College; Robert G. Kraft, Eastern Michigan University; Mary M. Lago, University of Missouri; Katie Letcher Lyle, Southern Seminary; Charlotte S. McClure, Georgia State University; H. Ray McKnight, California State University, Fresno; William J. Maroldo, Texas Lutheran College; Herbert Michaels, Holyoke Community College; Donn Rawlings, University of Denver; Peter J. Reed, University of Minnesota; Alexander G. Rose, University of Baltimore; Harriet Stolorow, Jackson Community College; Barbara Stout, Montgomery College; Maureen P. Taylor, Kalamazoo Valley Community College; Neil H. Timm, Lafayette College; Robert G. Weaver, Pennsylvania State University; Ulrich Wicks, University of Maine at Orono; R. Ora Williams, California State University, Long Beach, and Christian K. Zacher, The Ohio State University. To Albert Drake, Stephen Judy, Michael Koppisch, William P. Mooney, and John Yunck, my colleagues at Michigan State University, I also owe a debt of gratitude. I extend my special thanks to authors Albert Drake and Harlan Ellison who helped to annotate their own stories. And I am continuingly grateful to my editors at Macmillan, Anthony English and Hurd Hutchins, for their many good offices.

J. H. P.

Michigan State University

Contents

CONTENTS

FICTION 100

ILSE AICHINGER

The Bound Man

SUNLIGHT on his face woke him, but made him shut his eyes again; it streamed unhindered down the slope, collected itself into rivulets, attracted swarms of flies, which flew low over his forehead, circled, sought to land, and were overtaken by fresh swarms. When he tried to whisk them away he discovered that he was bound. A thin rope cut into his arms. He dropped them, opened his eyes again, and looked down at himself. His legs were tied all the way up to his thighs; a single length of rope was tied round his ankles, criss-crossed all the way up his legs, and encircled his hips, his chest, and his arms. He could not see where it was knotted. He showed no sign of fear or hurry, though he thought he was unable to move, until he discovered that the rope allowed his legs some free play, and that round his body it was almost loose. His arms were tied to each other but not to his body, and had some free play too. This made him smile, and it occurred to him that perhaps children had been playing a practical joke on him.

He tried to feel for his knife, but again the rope cut softly into his flesh. He tried again, more cautiously this time, but his pocket was empty. Not only his knife, but the little money that he had on him, as well as his coat, were missing. His shoes had been pulled from his feet and taken too. When he moistened his lips he tasted blood, which had flowed from his temples down his cheeks, his chin, his neck, and under his shirt. His eyes were painful; if he kept them open for long he saw reddish stripes in the sky.

He decided to stand up. He drew his knees up as far as he could, rested his hands on the fresh grass and jerked himself to his feet. An elder-branch stroked his cheek, the sun dazzled him, and the rope cut into his flesh. He collapsed to the ground again, half out of his mind with pain, and then tried again. He went on trying until the blood started flowing from his hidden weals. Then he lay still again for a long while, and let the sun and the flies do what they liked.

When he awoke for the second time the elder-bush had cast its shadow over him, and the coolness stored in it was pouring from between its branches. He must have been hit on the head. Then they must have laid him down carefully, just as a mother lays her baby behind a bush when she goes to work in the fields.

His chances all lay in the amount of free play allowed him by the rope. He dug his elbows into the ground and tested it. As soon as the rope tautened he stopped, and tried again more cautiously. If he had been able to reach the branch over his head he could have used it to drag himself to his feet, but he could not reach it. He laid his head back on the grass, rolled over, and struggled to his knees. He tested the ground with his toes, and then managed to stand up almost without effort.

A few paces away lay the path across the plateau, and among the grass were wild pinks and thistles in bloom. He tried to lift his foot to avoid trampling on them, but the rope round his ankles prevented him. He looked down at himself.

The rope was knotted at his ankles, and ran round his legs in a kind of playful pattern. He carefully bent and tried to loosen it, but, loose though it seemed to be, he could not make it any looser. To avoid treading on the thistles with his bare feet he hopped over them like a bird.

The cracking of a twig made him stop. People in this district were very prone to laughter. He was alarmed by the thought that he was in no position to defend himself. He hopped on until he reached the path. Bright fields stretched far below. He could see no sign of the nearest village, and, if he could move no faster than this, night would fall before he reached it.

He tried walking, and discovered that he could put one foot before another if he lifted each foot a definite distance from the ground and then put it down again before the rope tautened. In the same way he could actually swing his arms a little.

After the first step he fell. He fell right across the path, and made the dust fly. He expected this to be a sign for the long-suppressed laughter to break out, but all remained quiet. He was alone. As soon as the dust had settled he got up and went on. He looked down and watched the rope slacken, grow taut, and then slacken again.

When the first glow-worms appeared he managed to look up. He felt in control of himself again, and his impatience to reach the nearest village faded.

Hunger made him light-headed, and he seemed to be going so fast that not even a motor-cycle could have overtaken him; alternatively he felt as if he were standing still and that the earth was rushing past him, like a river flowing past a man swimming against the stream. The stream carried branches which had been bent southwards by the north wind, stunted young trees, and patches of grass with bright, long-stalked flowers. It ended by submerging the bushes and the young trees, leaving only the sky and the man above water-level. The moon had risen, and illuminated the bare, curved summit of the plateau, the path, which was overgrown with young grass, the bound man making his way along it with quick, measured steps, and two hares, which ran across the hill just in front of him and vanished down the slope. Though the nights were still cool at this time of the year, before midnight the bound man lay down at the edge of the escarpment and went to sleep.

In the light of morning the animal-tamer who was camping with his circus in the field outside the village saw the bound man coming down the path, gazing thoughtfully at the ground. The bound man stopped and bent down. He held out one arm to help keep his balance and with the other picked up an empty wine-bottle. Then he straightened himself and stood erect again. He moved slowly, to avoid being cut by the rope, but to the circus proprietor what he did suggested the voluntary limitation of an enormous swiftness of movement. He was enchanted by its extraordinary gracefulness, and while the bound man looked about for a stone on which to break the bottle, so that he could use the splintered neck to cut the rope, the animal-tamer walked across the field and approached him. The first leaps of a young panther had never filled him with such delight.

"Ladies and gentlemen, the bound man!" His very first movements let loose a storm of applause, which out of sheer excitement caused the blood to rush to the cheeks of the animal-tamer standing at the edge of the arena. The bound man rose to his feet. His surprise whenever he did this was like that of a four-footed animal which has managed to stand on its hind-legs. He knelt, stood up, jumped, and turned cart-wheels. The spectators found it as astonishing as if they had seen a bird which voluntarily remained earth-bound, and confined itself to hopping. The bound man became an enormous draw. His absurd steps and little jumps, his elementary exercises in movement, made the rope-dancer superfluous. His fame grew from village to village, but the motions he went through were few and always the same; they were really quite ordinary motions, which he had continually to practise in the day-time in the half-dark tent in order to retain his shackled freedom. In that he remained entirely within the limits set by his rope he was free of it, it did not confine him, but gave him wings and endowed his leaps and jumps with purpose; just as the flights of birds of passage have purpose when they take wing in the warmth of summer and hesitantly make small circles in the sky.

All the children of the neighbourhood started playing the game of "bound man". They formed rival gangs, and one day the circus people found a little girl lying bound in a ditch, with a cord tied round her neck so that she could hardly breathe. They released her, and at the end of the performance that night the bound man made a speech. He announced briefly that there was no sense in being tied up in such a way that you could not jump. After that he was regarded as a comedian.

Grass and sunlight, tent-pegs driven into the ground and then pulled up again, and on to the next village. "Ladies and gentlemen, the bound man!" The summer mounted towards its climax. It bent its face deeper over the fish-ponds in the hollows, taking delight in its dark reflection, skimmed the surface of the rivers, and made the plain into what it was. Everyone who could walk went to see the bound man.

Many wanted a close-up view of how he was bound. So the circus proprietor announced after each performance that anyone who wanted to satisfy himself that the knots were real and the rope not made of rubber was at liberty to do so. The bound man generally waited for the crowd in the area outside the tent. He laughed or remained serious, and held out his arms for inspection. Many took the opportunity to look him in the face, others gravely tested the rope, tried the knots on his ankles, and wanted to know exactly how the lengths compared with the length of his limbs. They asked him how he had come to be tied up like that, and he answered patiently, always saying the same thing. Yes, he had been tied up, he said, and when he awoke he found that he had been robbed as well. Those who had done it must have been pressed for time, because they had tied him up somewhat too loosely for someone who was not supposed to be able to move and somewhat too tightly for someone who was expected to be able to move. But he did move, people pointed out. Yes, he replied, what else could he do?

Before he went to bed he always sat for a time in front of the fire. When the circus proprietor asked him why he didn't make up a better story, he always answered that he hadn't made up that one, and blushed. He preferred staying in the shade.

The difference between him and the other performers was that when the show was over he did not take off his rope. The result was that every movement that he made was worth seeing, and the villagers used to hang about the camp for hours, just for the sake of seeing him get up from in front of the fire and roll himself in his blanket. Sometimes the sky was beginning to lighten when he saw their shadows disappear.

The circus proprietor often remarked that there was no reason why he should not be untied after the evening performance and tied up again next day. He pointed out that the rope-dancers, for instance, did not stay on their rope over night. But no-one took the idea of untying him seriously.

For the bound man's fame rested on the fact that he was always bound, that whenever he washed himself he had to wash his clothes too and *vice versa*, and that his only way of doing so was to jump in the river just as he was every morning when the sun came out, and that he had to be careful not to go too far for fear of being carried away by the stream.

The proprietor was well aware that what in the last resort protected the bound man from the jealousy of the other performers was his helplessness; he deliberately left them the pleasure of watching him groping painfully from stone to stone on the river bank every morning with his wet clothes clinging to him. When his wife pointed out that even the bed clothes would not stand up indefinitely to such treatment (and the bound man's clothes were by no means of the best) he replied curtly that it was not going to last for ever. That was his answer to all objections—it was for the summer season only. But when he said this he was not being serious; he was talking like a gambler who has no intention of giving up his vice. In reality he would have been prepared cheerfully to sacrifice his lions and his rope-dancers for the bound man.

He proved this on the night when the rope-dancers jumped over the fire. Afterwards he was convinced that they did it, not because it was midsummer's day, but because of the bound man, who as usual was lying and watching them, with that peculiar smile that might have been real or might have been only the effect of the glow on his face. In any case no-one knew anything about him, because he never talked about anything that had happened to him before he emerged from the wood that day.

But that evening two of the performers suddenly picked him up by the arms and legs, carried him to the edge of the fire and started playfully swinging him to and fro, while two others held out their arms to catch him on the other side. In the end they threw him, but too short. The two men on the other side drew back—they explained afterwards that they did so the better to take the shock. The result was that the bound man landed at the very edge of the flames and would have been burned if the circus proprietor had not seized his arms and quickly dragged him away to save the rope which was starting to get singed. He was certain that the object had been to burn the rope. He sacked the four men on the spot.

A few nights later the proprietor's wife was awakened by the sound of footsteps on the grass, and went outside just in time to prevent the clown from playing his last practical joke. He was carrying a pair of scissors. When he was asked for an explanation he insisted that he had had no intention of taking the bound man's life, but only wanted to cut his rope, because he felt sorry for him. But he was sacked too.

These antics amused the bound man, because he could have freed himself if he had wanted to whenever he liked, but perhaps he wanted to learn a few new jumps first. The children's rhyme: "We travel with the circus, we travel with the circus" sometimes occurred to him while he lay awake at night. He could hear the voices of spectators on the opposite bank who had been driven too far downstream on the way home. He could see the river gleaming in the moonlight, and the young shoots growing out of the thick tops of the willow trees, and did not think about autumn yet.

The circus proprietor dreaded the danger involved for the bound man by sleep. Attempts were continually made to re-

lease him while he slept. The chief culprits were sacked rope-dancers, or children who were bribed for the purpose. But measures could be taken to safeguard against these. A much bigger danger was that which he represented to himself. In his dreams he forgot his rope, and was surprised by it when he woke in the darkness of morning. He would angrily try to get up, but lose his balance and fall back again. The previous evening's applause was forgotten, sleep was still too near, his head and neck too free. He was just the opposite of a hanged man—his neck was the only part of him that was free. You had to make sure that at such moments no knife was within his reach. In the early hours of the morning the circus proprietor sometimes sent his wife to see whether the bound man was all right. If he was asleep she would bend over him and feel the rope. It had grown hard from dirt and damp. She would test the amount of free play it allowed him, and touch his tender wrists and ankles.

The most varied rumours circulated about the bound man. Some said he had tied himself up and invented the story of having been robbed, and towards the end of the summer that was the general opinion. Others maintained that he had been tied up at his own request, perhaps in league with the circus proprietor. The hesitant way in which he told of his story, his habit of breaking off when the talk got round to the attack on him, contributed greatly to these rumours. Those who still believed in the robbery-with-violence story were laughed at. Nobody knew what difficulties the circus proprietor had in keeping the bound man, and how often he said he had had enough and wanted to clear off, for too much of the summer had passed.

Later, however, he stopped talking about clearing off. When the proprietor's wife brought him his food by the river and asked him how long he proposed to stay with them, he did not answer. She thought he had got used, not to being tied up, but to not forgetting for a moment that he was tied up—the only thing that anyone in his position could get used to. She asked him whether he did not think it ridiculous to be tied up all the time, but he answered that he did not. Such a variety of people—clowns, freaks, and comics, to say nothing of elephants and tigers—travelled with circuses that he did not see why a bound man should not travel with a circus too. He told her about the movements he was practising, the new ones he had discovered, and about a new trick that had occurred to him while he was whisking flies from the animals' eyes. He described to her how he always anticipated the effect of the rope and always restrained his movements in such a way as to prevent it from ever tautening; and she knew that there were days when he was hardly aware of the rope when he jumped down from the wagon and slapped the flanks of the horses in the morning, as if he were moving in a dream. She watched him vault over the bars almost without touching them, and saw the sun on his face, and he told her that sometimes he felt as if he were not tied up at all. She answered that if he were prepared to be untied there would never be any need for him to feel tied up. He agreed that he could be untied whenever he felt like it.

The woman ended by not knowing whether she were more concerned with the man or with the rope that tied him. She told him that he could go on travelling with the circus without his rope, but she did not believe it. For what would be the point of his antics without his rope, and what would he amount to without it? Without his rope he would leave them, and the happy days would be over. She would no longer be able to sit beside him on the stones by the river without rousing suspicion, and she knew that his continued presence, and her conversations with him, of which the rope was the only subject, depended on it. Whenever she agreed that the rope had its advantages he would start talking about how troublesome it was, and whenever he started talking about its advantages she would urge him to get rid of it. All this seemed as endless as the summer itself.

At other times she was worried at the thought that she was herself hastening the end by her talk. Sometimes she would get up in the middle of the night and run across the grass to where he slept. She wanted to shake him, wake him up and ask him to keep the rope. But then she would see him lying there; he had thrown off his blanket, and there he lay like a corpse, with his legs outstretched and his arms close together, with the rope tied round them. His clothes had suffered from the heat and the water, but the rope had grown no thinner. She felt that he would go on travelling with the circus until the flesh fell from him and exposed the joints. Next morning she would plead with him more ardently than ever to get rid of his rope.

The increasing coolness of the weather gave her hope. Autumn was coming, and he would not be able to go on jumping into the river with his clothes on much longer. But the thought of losing his rope, about which he had felt indifferent earlier in the season, now depressed him.

The songs of the harvesters filled him with foreboding. "Summer has gone, summer has gone." But he realized that soon he would have to change his clothes, and he was certain that when he had been untied it would be impossible to tie him up again in exactly the same way. About this time the proprietor started talking about travelling south that year.

The heat changed without transition into quiet, dry cold, and the fire was kept in all day long. When the bound man jumped down from the wagon he felt the coldness of the grass under his feet. The stalks were bent with ripeness. The horses dreamed on their feet and the wild animals, crouching to leap even in their sleep, seemed to be collecting gloom under their skins which would break out later.

On one of these days a young wolf escaped. The circus proprietor kept quiet about it, to avoid spreading alarm, but the wolf soon started raiding cattle in the neighbourhood. People at first believed that the wolf had been driven to these parts by the prospect of a severe winter, but the circus soon became suspect. The proprietor could not conceal the loss of the animal from his own employees, so the truth was bound to come out before long. The circus people offered their aid in tracking down the beast to the burgomasters of the neighbouring villages, but all their efforts were vain. Eventually the circus was openly blamed for the damage and the danger, and spectators stayed away.

The bound man went on performing before half-empty seats without losing anything of his amazing freedom of movement. During the day he wandered among the surrounding hills under the thin-beaten silver of the autumn sky, and, whenever he could, lay down where the sun shone longest. Soon he found a place which the twilight reached last of all, and when at last it reached him he got up most unwillingly from the withered grass. In coming down the hill he had to pass through a little wood on its southern slope, and one evening he saw the gleam of two little green lights. He knew that they came from no church window, and was not for a moment under any illusion about what they were.

He stopped. The animal came towards him through the thinning foliage. He could make out its shape, the slant of its neck, its tail which swept the ground, and its receding head. If he had not been bound, perhaps he would have tried to run away, but as it was he did not even feel fear. He stood calmly with dangling arms and looked down at the wolf's bristling coat, under which the muscles played like his own underneath the rope. He thought the evening wind was still between him and the wolf when the beast sprang. The man took care to obey his rope.

Moving with the deliberate care that he had so often put to the test, he seized the wolf by the throat. Tenderness for a fellow-creature arose in him, tenderness for the upright being concealed in the four-footed. In a movement that resembled the drive of a great bird—he felt a sudden awareness that flying would be possible only if one were tied up in a special way—he flung himself at the animal and brought it to the ground. He felt a slight elation at having lost the fatal advantage of free limbs which causes men to be worsted.

The freedom he enjoyed in this struggle was having to adapt every movement of his limbs to the rope that tied him—the freedom of panthers, wolves, and the wild flowers that sway in the evening breeze. He ended up lying obliquely down the slope, clasping the animal's hind-legs between his own bare feet and its head between his hands. He felt the gentleness of the faded foliage stroking the back of his hands, and he felt his own grip almost effortlessly reaching its maximum, and he felt too how he was in no way hampered by the rope.

As he left the wood light rain began to fall and obscured the setting sun. He stopped for a while under the trees at the edge of the wood. Beyond the camp and the river he saw the fields where the cattle grazed, and the places where they crossed. Perhaps he would travel south with the circus after all. He laughed softly. It was against all reason. Even if he went on putting up with his joints' being covered with sores, which opened and bled when he made certain movements, his clothes would not stand up much longer to the friction of the rope.

The circus proprietor's wife tried to persuade her husband to announce the death of the wolf without mentioning that it had been killed by the bound man. She said that even at the time of his greatest popularity people would have refused to believe him capable of it, and in their present angry mood, with the nights getting cooler, they would be more incredulous than ever. The wolf had attacked a group of children at play that day, and nobody would believe that it had really been killed; for the circus proprietor had many wolves, and it was easy enough for him to hang a skin on the rail and allow free entry. But he was not to be dissuaded. He thought that the announcement of the bound man's act would revive the triumphs of the summer.

That evening the bound man's movements were uncertain. He stumbled in one of his jumps, and fell. Before he managed to get up he heard some low whistles and catcalls, rather like birds calling at dawn. He tried to get up too quickly, as he had done once or twice during the summer, with the result that he tautened the rope and fell back again. He lay still to regain his calm, and listened to the boos and catcalls growing into an uproar. "Well, bound man, and how did you kill the wolf?" they shouted, and: "Are you the man who killed the wolf?" If he had been one of them he would not have believed it himself. He thought they had a perfect right to be angry: a circus at this time of year, a bound man, an escaped wolf, and all ending up with this. Some groups of spectators started arguing with others, but the greater part of the audience thought the whole thing a bad joke. By the time he had got to his feet there was such a hubbub that he was barely able to make out individual words.

He saw people surging up all around him, like faded leaves raised by a whirlwind in a circular valley at the centre of which all was yet still. He thought of the golden sunsets of the last few days; and the cemetery light which lay over the blight of all that he had built up during so many nights, the gold frame which the pious hang round dark, old pictures, this sudden collapse of everything, filled him with anger.

They wanted him to repeat his battle with the wolf. He said that such a thing had no place in a circus performance, and the proprietor declared that he did not keep animals to have them slaughtered in front of an audience. But the mob stormed the ring and forced them towards the cages. The proprietor's wife made her way between the seats to the exit and managed to get round to the cages from the other side. She pushed aside the attendant whom the crowd had forced to open a cage door, but the spectators dragged her back and prevented the door from being shut.

"Aren't you the woman who used to lie with him by the river in the summer?" they called out. "How does he hold you in his arms?" She shouted back at them that they needn't believe in the bound man if they didn't want to, [that] they had never deserved him—painted clowns were good enough for them.

The bound man felt as if the bursts of laughter were what he had been expecting ever since early May. What had smelt so sweet all through the summer now stank. But, if they insisted, he was ready to take on all the animals in the circus. He had never felt so much at one with his rope.

Gently he pushed the woman aside. Perhaps he would travel south with them after all. He stood in the open doorway of the cage, and he saw the wolf, a strong young animal, rise to its feet, and he heard the proprietor grumbling again about the loss of his exhibits. He clapped his hands to attract the animal's attention, and when it was near enough he turned to slam the cage door. He looked the woman in the face. Suddenly he remembered the proprietor's warning to suspect of murderous intentions anyone near him who had a sharp instrument in his hand. At the same moment he felt the blade on his wrists, as cool as the water of the river in autumn, which during the last few weeks he had been barely able to stand. The rope curled up in a tangle beside him while he struggled free. He pushed the woman back, but there was no point in anything he did now. Had he been insufficiently on his guard against those who wanted to release him, against the sympathy in which they wanted to lull him? Had he lain too long on the river bank? If she had cut the cord at any other moment it would have been better than this.

He stood in the middle of the cage, and rid himself of the rope like a snake discarding its skin. It amused him to see the spectators shrinking back. Did they realise that he had no choice now? Or that fighting the wolf now would prove nothing whatever? At the same time he felt all his blood rush to his feet. He felt suddenly weak.

The rope, which fell at its feet like a snare, angered the wolf more than the entry of a stranger into its cage. It crouched to spring. The man reeled, and grabbed the pistol that hung ready at the side of the cage. Then, before anyone could stop him, he shot the wolf between the eyes. The animal reared, and touched him in falling.

On the way to the river he heard the footsteps of his pursuers—spectators, the rope-dancers, the circus proprietor, and the proprietor's wife, who persisted in the chase longer than anyone else. He hid in a clump of bushes and listened to them hurrying past, and later on streaming in the opposite direction back to the camp. The moon shone on the meadow; in that light its colour was that of both growth and death.

When he came to the river his anger died away. At dawn it seemed to him as if lumps of ice were floating in the water, and as if snow had fallen, obliterating memory.

[1954]

QUESTIONS FOR STUDY

1. As an allegory, "The Bound Man" can profitably be compared with Kafka's "A Hunger Artist" printed elsewhere in this anthology. To what extent is the bound man an artist? In what sense is art a form of bondage? What other allegorical or symbolic interpretations of the story suggest themselves?

2. How do the bound man's attitudes toward his confinement change?

3. What is his relationship to the rest of society? How does this relationship change and why?

4. What is the significance of the following sentence: "In that he remained entirely within the limits set by his rope he was free of it, it did not confine him, but gave him wings and endowed his leaps and jumps with purpose. . . ."?

5. What special insight accompanies his struggle with the wolf?

6. Why does the proprietor's wife cut the rope? What does she fail to understand?

7. What is the reason for the man's flight?

SHERWOOD ANDERSON

I Want to Know Why

W E GOT up at four in the morning, that first day in the East. On the evening before, we had climbed off a freight train at the edge of town and with the true instinct of Kentucky boys had found our way across town and to the race track and the stables at once. Then we knew we were all right. Hanley Turner right away found a nigger we knew. It was Bildad Johnson, who in the winter works at Ed Becker's livery barn in our home town, Beckersville. Bildad is a good cook as almost all our niggers are and of course he, like everyone in our part of Kentucky who is anyone at all, likes the horses. In the spring Bildad begins to scratch around. A nigger from our country can flatter and wheedle anyone into letting him do most anything he wants. Bildad wheedles the stable men and the trainers from the horse farms in our country around Lexington. The trainers come into town in the evening to stand around and talk and maybe get into a poker game. Bildad gets in with them. He is always doing little favors and telling about things to eat, chicken browned in a pan, and how is the best way to cook sweet potatoes and corn bread. It makes your mouth water to hear him.

When the racing season comes on and the horses go to the races and there is all the talk on the streets in the evenings about the new colts, and everyone says when they are going over to Lexington or to the spring meeting at Churchill Downs or to Latonia, and the horsemen that have been down to New Orleans or maybe at the winter meeting at Havana in Cuba come home to spend a week before they start out again, at such a time when everything talked about in Beckersville is just horses and nothing else and the outfits start out and horse racing is in every breath of air you breathe, Bildad shows up with a job as cook for some outfit. Often when I think about it, his always going all season to the races and working in the livery barn in the winter where horses are and where men like to come and talk about horses, I wish I was a nigger. It's a foolish thing to say, but that's the way I am about being around horses, just crazy. I can't help it.

Well, I must tell you about what we did and let you in on what I'm talking about. Four of us boys from Beckerville, all whites and sons of men who live in Beckersville regular, made up our minds we were going to the races, not just to Lexington or Louisville, I don't mean, but to the big Eastern track we were always hearing our Beckersville men talk about, to Saratoga. We were all pretty young then. I was just turned fifteen and I was the oldest of the four. It was my scheme. I admit that, and I talked the others into trying it. There was Hanley Turner and Henry Rieback and Tom Tumberton and myself. I had thirty-seven dollars I had earned during the winter working nights and Saturdays in Enoch Myer's grocery. Henry Rieback had eleven dollars and the others, Hanley and Tom, had only a dollar or two each. We fixed it all up and laid low until the Kentucky spring meetings were over and some of our men, the sportiest ones, the ones we envied the most, had cut out. Then we cut out too.

I won't tell you the trouble we had beating our way on freights and all. We went through Cleveland and Buffalo and other cities and saw Niagara Falls. We bought things there, souvenirs and spoons and cards and shells with pictures of the falls on them for our sisters and mothers, but thought we had better not send any of the things home. We didn't want to put the folks on our trail and maybe be nabbed.

We got into Saratoga as I said at night and went to the track. Bildad fed us up. He showed us a place to sleep in hay over a shed and promised to keep still. Niggers are all right about things like that. They won't squeal on you. Often a white man you might meet, when you had run away from home like that, might appear to be all right and give you a quarter or a half dollar or something, and then go right and give you away. White men will do that, but not a nigger. You can trust them. They are squarer with kids. I don't know why.

At the Saratoga meeting that year there were a lot of men from home. Dave Williams and Arthur Mulford and Jerry Myers and others. Then there was a lot from Louisville and Lexington Henry Rieback knew but I didn't. They were professional gamblers and Henry Rieback's father is one too. He is what is called a sheet writer and goes away most of the year to tracks. In the winter when he is home in Beckersville he don't stay there much but goes away to cities and deals faro. He is a nice man and generous, is always sending Henry presents, a bicycle and a gold watch and a boy scout suit of clothes and things like that.

My own father is a lawyer. He's all right, but don't make much money and can't buy me things, and anyway I'm getting so old now I don't expect it. He never said nothing to me against Henry, but Hanley Turner and Tom Tumberton's fathers did. They said to their boys that money so come by is no good and they didn't want their boys brought up to hear gamblers' talk and be thinking about such things and maybe embrace them.

That's all right and I guess the men know what they are talking about, but I don't see what it's got to do with Henry or with horses either. That's what I'm writing this story about. I'm puzzled. I'm getting to be a man and want to think straight and be O. K., and there's something I saw at the race meeting at the Eastern track I can't figure out.

I can't help it, I'm crazy about thoroughbred horses. I've always been that

way. When I was ten years old and saw I was growing to be big and couldn't be a rider I was so sorry I nearly died. Harry Hellinfinger in Beckersville, whose father is Postmaster, is grown up and too lazy to work, but likes to stand around in the street and get up jokes on boys like sending them to a hardware store for a gimlet to bore square holes and other jokes like that. He played one on me. He told me that if I would eat a half a cigar I would be stunted and not grow any more and maybe could be a rider. I did it. When father wasn't looking I took a cigar out of his pocket and gagged it down some way. It made me awful sick and the doctor had to be sent for, and then it did no good. I kept right on growing. It was a joke. When I told what I had done and why, most fathers would have whipped me, but mine didn't.

Well, I didn't get stunted and didn't die. It serves Harry Hellinfinger right. Then I made up my mind I would like to be a stableboy, but had to give that up too. Mostly niggers do that work and I knew father wouldn't let me go into it. No use to ask him.

If you've never been crazy about thoroughbreds, it's because you've never been around where they are much and don't know any better. They're beautiful. There isn't anything so lovely and clean and full of spunk and honest and everything as some race horses. On the big horse farms that are all around our town Beckersville there are tracks, and the horses run in the early morning. More than a thousand times I've got out of bed before daylight and walked two or three miles to the tracks. Mother wouldn't of let me go, but father always says, "Let him alone." So I got some bread out of the breadbox and some butter and jam, gobbled it and lit out.

At the tracks you sit on the fence with men, whites and niggers, and they chew tobacco and talk, and then the colts are brought out. It's early and the grass is covered with shiny dew and in another field a man is plowing and they are frying things in a shed where the track niggers sleep, and you know how a nigger can giggle and laugh and say things that make you laugh. A white man can't do it and some niggers can't, but a track nigger can every time.

And so the colts are brought out and some are just galloped by stableboys, but almost every morning on a big track owned by a rich man who lives maybe in New York, there are always, nearly every morning, a few colts and some of the old race horses and geldings and mares that are cut loose.

It brings a lump up into my throat when a horse runs. I don't mean all horses, but some. I can pick them nearly every time. It's in my blood like in the blood of race track niggers and trainers. Even when they just go slop-jogging along with a little nigger on their backs, I can tell a winner. If my throat hurts and it's hard for me to swallow, that's him. He'll run like Sam Hill when you let him out. If he don't win every time it'll be a wonder and because they've got him in a pocket behind another or he was pulled or got off bad at the post or something. If I wanted to be a gambler like Henry Rieback's father I could get rich. I know I could and Henry says so too. All I would have to do is to wait till that hurt comes when I see a horse and then bet every cent. That's what I would do if I wanted to be a gambler, but I don't.

When you're at the tracks in the morning—not the race tracks but the training tracks around Beckersville—you don't see a horse, the kind I've been talking about, very often, but it's nice anyway. Any thoroughbred, that is sired right and out of a good mare and trained by a man that knows how, can run. If he couldn't, what would he be there for and not pulling a plow?

Well, out of the stables they come and the boys are on their backs and it's lovely to be there. You hunch down on top of the fence and itch inside you. Over in the sheds the niggers giggle and sing. Bacon is being fried and coffee made. Everything smells lovely. Nothing smells better than coffee and manure and horses and niggers and bacon frying and pipes being smoked out of doors on a morning like that. It just gets you, that's what it does.

But about Saratoga. We was there six days and not a soul from home seen us and everything came off just as we wanted it to, fine weather and horses and races and all. We beat our way home and Bildad gave us a basket with fried chicken and bread and other eatables in, and I had eighteen dollars when we got back to Beckersville. Mother jawed and cried, but Pop didn't say much. I told everything we done, except one thing. I did and saw that alone. That's what I'm writing about. It got me upset. I think about it at night. Here it is.

At Saratoga we laid up nights in the hay in the shed Bildad had showed us and ate with the niggers early and at night when the race people had all gone away. The men from home stayed mostly in the grandstand and betting field and didn't come out around the places where the horses are kept except to the paddocks just before a race when the horses are saddled. At Saratoga they don't have paddocks under an open shed as at Lexington and Churchill Downs and other tracks down in our country, but saddle the horses right out in an open place under trees on a lawn as smooth and nice as Banker Bohon's front yard here in Beckersville. It's lovely. The horses are sweaty and nervous and shine and the men come out and smoke cigars and look at them and the trainers are there and the owners, and your heart thumps so you can hardly breathe.

Then the bugle blows for post and the boys that ride come running out with their silk clothes on and you run to get a place by the fence with the niggers.

I always am wanting to be a trainer or owner, and at the risk of being seen and caught and sent home I went to the paddocks before every race. The other boys didn't, but I did.

We got to Saratoga on a Friday, and on Wednesday the next week the big Mullford Handicap was to be run. Middlestride was in it and Sunstreak. The weather was fine and the track fast. I couldn't sleep the night before.

What had happened was that both these horses are the kind it makes my throat hurt to see. Middlestride is long and looks awkward and is a gelding. He belongs to

Joe Thompson, a little owner from home who only has a half dozen horses. The Mullford Handicap is for a mile and Middlestride can't untrack fast. He goes away slow and is always 'way back at the half, then he begins to run and if the race is a mile and a quarter he'll just eat up everything and get there.

Sunstreak is different. He is a stallion and nervous and belongs on the biggest farm we've got in our country, the Van Riddle place that belongs to Mr. Van Riddle of New York. Sunstreak is like a girl you think about sometimes but never see. He is hard all over and lovely too. When you look at his head you want to kiss him. He is trained by Jerry Tillford who knows me and has been good to me lots of times, lets me walk into a horse's stall to look at him close and other things. There isn't anything as sweet as that horse. He stands at the post quiet and not letting on, but he is just burning up inside. Then when the barrier goes up he is off like his name, Sunstreak. It makes you ache to see him. It hurts you. He just lays down and runs like a bird dog. There can't anything I ever see run like him except Middlestride when he gets untracked and stretches himself.

Gee! I ached to see that race and those two horses run, ached and dreaded it too. I didn't want to see either of our horses beaten. We had never sent a pair like that to the races before. Old men in Beckersville said so and the niggers said so. It was a fact.

Before the race, I went over to the paddocks to see. I looked a last look at Middlestride, who isn't such a much standing in a paddock that way, then I went to see Sunstreak.

It was his day. I knew when I see him. I forgot all about being seen myself and walked right up. All the men from Beckersville were there and no one noticed me except Jerry Tillford. He saw me and something happened. I'll tell you about that.

I was standing looking at that horse and aching. In some way, I can't tell how, I knew just how Sunstreak felt inside. He was quiet and letting the niggers rub his legs and Mr. Van Riddle himself put the saddle on, but he was just a raging torrent inside. He was like the water in the river at Niagara Falls just before it goes plunk down. That horse wasn't thinking about running. He don't have to think about that. He was just thinking about holding himself back till the time for the running came. I knew that. I could just in a way see right inside him. He was going to do some awful running and I knew it. He wasn't bragging or letting on much or prancing or making a fuss, but just waiting. I knew it and Jerry Tillford his trainer knew. I looked up, and then that man and I looked into each other's eyes. Something happened to me. I guess I loved the man as much as I did the horse because he knew what I knew. Seemed to me there wasn't anything in the world but that man and the horse and me. I cried and Jerry Tillford had a shine in his eyes. Then I came away to the fence to wait for the race. The horse was better than me, more steadier and, now I know, better than Jerry. He was the quietest and he had to do the running.

Sunstreak ran first of course and he busted the world's record for a mile. I've seen that if I never see anything more. Everything came out just as I expected. Middlestride got left at the post and was 'way back and closed up to be second, just as I knew he would. He'll get a world's record too some day. They can't skin the Beckersville country on horses.

I watched the race calm because I knew what would happen. I was sure. Hanley Turner and Henry Rieback and Tom Tumberton were all more excited than me.

A funny thing had happened to me. I was thinking about Jerry Tillford the trainer and how happy he was all through the race. I liked him that afternoon even more than I ever liked my own father. I almost forgot the horses thinking that way about him. It was because of what I had seen in his eyes as he stood in the paddocks beside Sunstreak before the race started. I knew he had been watching and working with Sunstreak since the horse was a baby colt, had taught him to run and be patient and when to let himself out and not to quit, never. I knew that for him it was like a mother seeing her child do something brave or wonderful. It was the first time I ever felt for a man like that.

After the race that night I cut out from Tom and Hanley and Henry. I wanted to be by myself and I wanted to be near Jerry Tillford if I could work it. Here is what happened.

The track in Saratoga is near the edge of town. It is all polished up and trees around, the evergreen kind, and grass and everything painted and nice. If you go past the track you get to a hard road made of asphalt for automobiles, and if you go along this for a few miles there is a road turns off to a little rummy-looking farmhouse set in a yard.

That night after the race I went along that road because I had seen Jerry and some other men go that way in an automobile. I didn't expect to find them. I walked for a ways and then sat down by a fence to think. It was the direction they went in. I wanted to be as near Jerry as I could. I felt close to him. Pretty soon I went up the side road—I don't know why —and came to the rummy farmhouse. I was just lonesome to see Jerry, like wanting to see your father at night when you are a young kid. Just then an automobile came along and turned in. Jerry was in it and Henry Rieback's father, and Arthur Bedford from home, and Dave Williams and two other men I didn't know. They got out of the car and went into the house, all but Henry Rieback's father who quarreled with them and said he wouldn't go. It was only about nine o'clock, but they were all drunk and the rummy-looking farmhouse was a place for bad women to stay in. That's what it was. I crept up along a fence and looked through a window and saw.

It's what give me the fantods. I can't make it out. The women in the house were all ugly mean-looking women, not nice to look at or be near. They were homely too, except one who was tall and looked a little like the gelding Middlestride, but not clean like him, but with a hard ugly mouth. She had red hair. I saw everything plain. I got up by an old rosebush by an open window and looked. The women had on loose dresses and sat around in chairs. The men came in and some sat on the women's laps. The place smelled rotten and there was rotten talk, the kind a kid hears around a livery stable in a town like Beckersville in the winter but don't ever expect to hear talked when there are women around. It was rotten. A nigger wouldn't go into such a place.

I looked at Jerry Tillford. I've told you how I had been feeling about him on account of his knowing what was going on inside of Sunstreak in the minute before he went to the post for the race in which he made a world's record.

Jerry bragged in that bad woman house as I knew Sunstreak wouldn't never have bragged. He said that he made that horse, that it was him that won the race and made the record. He lied and bragged like a fool. I never heard such silly talk.

And then, what do you suppose he did! He looked at the woman in there, the one that was lean and hard-mouthed and looked a little like the gelding Middlestride but not clean like him, and his eyes began to shine just as they did when he looked at me and at Sunstreak in the paddocks at the track in the afternoon. I stood there by the window—gee!—but I wished I hadn't gone away from the tracks, but had stayed with the boys and the niggers and the horses. The tall rotten-looking woman was between us just as Sunstreak was in the paddocks in the afternoon.

Then, all of a sudden, I began to hate that man. I wanted to scream and rush in the room and kill him. I never had such a feeling before. I was so mad clean through that I cried and my fists were doubled up so my fingernails cut my hands.

And Jerry's eyes kept shining and he waved back and forth, and then he went and kissed that woman and I crept away and went back to the tracks and to bed and didn't sleep hardly any, and then next day I got the other kids to start home with me and never told them anything I seen.

I been thinking about it ever since. I can't make it out. Spring has come again and I'm nearly sixteen and go to the tracks mornings same as always, and I see Sunstreak and Middlestride and a new colt named Strident I'll bet will lay them all out, but no one thinks so but me and two or three niggers.

But things are different. At the tracks the air don't taste as good or smell as good. It's because a man like Jerry Tillford, who knows what he does, could see a horse like Sunstreak run, and kiss a woman like that the same day. I can't make it out. Darn him, what did he want to do like that for? I keep thinking about it and it spoils looking at horses and smelling things and hearing niggers laugh and everything. Sometimes I'm so mad about it I want to fight someone. It gives me the fantods. What did he do it for? I want to know why.

[1921]

QUESTIONS FOR STUDY

1. *Why is the narrator's age at the time of the story significant? What aspects of adult society has he already begun to question?*
2. *What positive human values and qualities does the boy associate with horses?*
3. *Why is he so upset to discover Jerry Tillford at the "rummy farmhouse"? How does that discovery conflict with the earlier moment of perception at the paddock? Why is he so puzzled by the discovery? Is the moment at the window simply an innocent's discovery of evil, or is there something more to it than that?*
4. *Why do "things" seem so "different" now? Why has the boy's experience spoiled "looking at horses and smelling things and hearing niggers laugh and everything"?*
5. *Why is the use of first person point of view particularly effective in telling the story?*

JAMES BALDWIN

This Morning, This Evening, So Soon

"YOU ARE full of nightmares," Harriet tells me. She is in her dressing gown and has cream all over her face. She and my older sister, Louisa, are going out to be girls together. I suppose they have many things to talk about— they have *me* to talk about, certainly— and they do not want my presence. I have been given a bachelor's evening. The director of the film which has brought us such incredible and troubling riches will be along later to take me out to dinner.

I watch her face. I know that it is quite impossible for her to be as untroubled as she seems. Her self-control is mainly for my benefit—my benefit, and Paul's. Harriet comes from orderly and progressive Sweden and has reacted against all the advanced doctrines to which she has been exposed by becoming steadily and beautifully old-fashioned. We never fought in front of Paul, not even when he was a baby. Harriet does not so much believe in protecting children as she does in helping them to build a foundation on which they can build and build again, each time life's high-flying steel ball knocks down everything they have built.

Whenever I become upset, Harriet becomes very cheerful and composed. I think she began to learn how to do this over eight years ago, when I returned from my only visit to America. Now, perhaps, it has become something she could not control if she wished to. This morning, at breakfast, when I yelled at Paul, she averted Paul's tears and my own guilt by looking up and saying, "My God, your father is cranky this morning, isn't he?"

Paul's attention was immediately distracted from his wounds, and the unjust inflicter of those wounds, to his mother's laughter. He watched her.

"It is because he is afraid they will not like his songs in New York. Your father is an *artiste, mon chou*,[1] and they are very mysterious people, *les artistes.* Millions of people are waiting for him in New York, they are begging him to come, and they will give him a *lot* of money, but he is afraid they will not like him. Tell him he is wrong."

She succeeded in rekindling Paul's excitement about places he has never seen. I was also, at once, reinvested with all my glamour. I think it is sometimes extremely difficult for Paul to realize that the face he sees on record sleeves and in the newspapers and on the screen is nothing more or less than the face of his father—who sometimes yells at him. Of course, since he is only seven—going on eight, he will be eight years old this winter—he cannot know that I am baffled, too.

"Of course, you are wrong, you are silly," he said with passion—and caused me to smile. His English is strongly accented and is not, in fact, as good as his French, for he speaks French all day at school. French is really his first language, the first he ever heard. "You are the greatest singer in France"—sounding exactly as he must sound when he makes this pronouncement to his schoolmates—"the greatest *American* singer"—this concession was so gracefully made that it was not a concession at all, it added inches to my stature, America being only a glamorous word for Paul. It is the place from which his father came, and to which he now is going, a place which very few people have ever seen. But his aunt is one of them and he looked over at her. "Mme. Dumont says so, and she says he is a *great actor, too.*" Louisa nodded, smiling. "And

1 "My pet"—a term of endearment. (JHP)

she has seen *Les Fauves Nous Attendent* [2] —five times!" This clinched it, of course. Mme. Dumont is our concierge and she has known Paul all his life. I suppose he will not begin to doubt anything she says until he begins to doubt everything.

He looked over at me again. "So you are wrong to be afraid."

"I was wrong to yell at you, too. I won't yell at you any more today."

"All right." He was very grave.

Louisa poured more coffee. "He's going to knock them dead in New York. You'll see."

"*Mais bien sûr,*" [3] said Paul, doubtfully. He does not quite know what "knock them dead" means, though he was sure, from her tone, that she must have been agreeing with him. He does not quite understand this aunt, whom he met for the first time two months ago, when she arrived to spend the summer with us. Her accent is entirely different from anything he has ever heard. He does not really understand why, since she is my sister and his aunt, she should be unable to speak French.

Harriet, Louisa, and I looked at each other and smiled. "Knock them dead," said Harriet, "means *d'avoir un succès fou.* But you will soon pick up all the American expressions." She looked at me and laughed. "So will I."

"That's what he's afraid of." Louisa grinned. "We have *got* some expressions, believe me. Don't let anybody ever tell you America hasn't got a culture. Our culture is as thick as clabber milk."

"Ah," Harriet answered, "I know. I know."

"I'm going to be practicing later," I told Paul.

His face lit up. "*Bon.*" This meant that, later, he would come into my study and lie on the floor with his papers and crayons while I worked out with the piano and the tape recorder. He knew that I was offering this as an olive branch. All things considered, we got on pretty well, my son and I.

He looked over at Louisa again. She held a coffee cup in one hand and a cigarette in the other; and something about her baffled him. It was early, so she had not yet put on her face. Her short, thick, graying hair was rougher than usual, almost as rough as my own—later, she would be going to the hairdresser's; she is fairer than I, and better-looking; Louisa, in fact, caught all the looks in the family. Paul knows that she is my older sister and that she helped to raise me, though he does not, of course, know what this means. He knows that she is a school-teacher in the *American* South, which is not, for some reason, the same place as South America. I could see him trying to fit all these exotic details together into a pattern which would explain her strangeness—strangeness of accent, strangeness of manner. In comparison with the people he has always known, Louisa must seem, for all her generosity and laughter and affection, peculiarly uncertain of herself, peculiarly hostile and embattled.

I wondered what he would think of his Uncle Norman, older and much blacker than I, who lives near the Alabama town in which we were born. Norman will meet us at the boat.

Now Harriet repeats, "Nightmares, nightmares. Nothing ever turns out as badly as you think it will—in fact," she adds laughing, "I am happy to say that that would scarcely be possible."

Her eyes seek mine in the mirror—dark-blue eyes, pale skin, black hair. I had always thought of Sweden as being populated entirely by blondes, and I thought that Harriet was abnormally dark for a Swedish girl. But when we visited Sweden, I found out differently. "It is all a great racial salad, Europe, that is why I am sure that I will never understand your country," Harriet said. That was in the days when we never imagined that we would be going to it.

I wonder what she is really thinking. Still, she is right, in two days we will be on a boat, and there is simply no point in carrying around my load of apprehension. I sit down on the bed, watching her fix her face. I realize that I am going to miss this old-fashioned bedroom. For years, we've

2 "The Wild Beasts Await Us." (JHP)
3 "But of course,". . . (JHP)

talked about throwing out the old junk which came with the apartment and replacing it with less massive, modern furniture. But we never have.

"Oh, everything will probably work out," I say. "I've been in a bad mood all day long. I just can't sing any more." We both laugh. She reaches for a wad of tissues and begins wiping off the cream. "I wonder how Paul will like it, if he'll make friends—that's all."

"Paul will like any place where you are, where we are. Don't worry about Paul."

Paul has never been called any names, so far. Only, once he asked us what the word *métis* meant and Harriet explained to him that it meant mixed blood, adding that the blood of just about everybody in the world was mixed by now. Mme. Dumont contributed bawdy and detailed corroboration from her own family tree, the roots of which were somewhere in Corsica; the moral of the story, as she told it, was that women were weak, men incorrigible, and *le bon Dieu* 4 appallingly clever. Mme. Dumont's version is the version I prefer, but it may not be, for Paul, the most utilitarian.

Harriet rises from the dressing table and comes over to sit in my lap. I fall back with her on the bed, and she smiles down into my face.

"Now, don't worry," she tells me, "please try not to worry. Whatever is coming, we will manage it all very well, you will see. We have each other and we have our son and we know what we want. So, we are luckier than most people."

I kiss her on the chin. "I'm luckier than most men."

"I'm a very lucky woman, too."

And for a moment we are silent, alone in our room, which we have shared so long. The slight rise and fall of Harriet's breathing creates an intermittent pressure against my chest, and I think how, if I had never left America, I would never have met her and would never have established a life of my own, would never have entered my own life. For everyone's life begins on a level where races, armies, and churches stop. And yet everyone's life is

always shaped by races, churches, and armies; races, churches, armies menace, and have taken many lives. If Harriet had been born in America, it would have taken her a long time, perhaps forever, to look on me as a man like other men; if I had met her in America, I would never have been able to look on her as a woman like all other women. The habits of public rage and power would also have been our private compulsions, and would have blinded our eyes. We would never have been able to love each other. And Paul would never have been born.

Perhaps, if I had stayed in America, I would have found another woman and had another son. But that other woman, that other son are in the limbo of vanished possibilities. I might also have become something else, instead of an actor-singer, perhaps a lawyer, like my brother, or a teacher, like my sister. But no, I am what I have become and this woman beside me is my wife, and I love her. All the sons I might have had mean nothing, since I *have* a son, I named him, Paul, for my father, and I love him.

I think of all the things I have seen destroyed in America, all the things that I have lost there, all the threats it holds for me and mine.

I grin up at Harriet. "Do you love me?"

"Of course not. I simply have been madly plotting to get to America all these years."

"What a patient wench you are."

"The Swedes are very patient."

She kisses me again and stands up. Louisa comes in, also in a dressing gown.

"I hope you two aren't sitting in here yakking about the *subject*." She looks at me. "My, you are the sorriest-looking celebrity I've ever seen. I've always wondered why people like you hired press agents. Now I know." She goes to Harriet's dressing table. "Honey, do you mind if I borrow some of that *mad* nail polish?"

Harriet goes over to the dressing table. "I'm not sure I know *which* mad nail polish you mean."

Harriet and Louisa, somewhat to my surprise, get on very well. Each seems to find the other full of the weirdest and most delightful surprises. Harriet has been teaching Louisa French and Swedish expressions, and Louisa has been teaching Harriet some of the saltier expressions of the black South. Whenever one of them is not playing straight man to the other's accent, they become involved in long speculations as to how a language reveals the history and the attitudes of a people. They discovered that all the European languages contain a phrase equivalent to "to work like a nigger." ("Of course," says Louisa, "they've had black men working for them for a long time.") "Language is experience and language is power," says Louisa, after regretting that she does not know any of the African dialects. "That's what I keep trying to tell those dirty bastards down South. They get their own experience into the language, we'll have a great language. But, no, they all want to talk like white folks." Then she leans forward, grasping Harriet by the knee. "I tell them, honey,white folks ain't saying *nothing*. Not a thing are they saying—and *some* of them know it, they *need* what you got, the whole world needs it." Then she leans back, in disgust. "You think they listen to me? Indeed they do not. They just go right on, trying to talk like white folks." She leans forward again, in tremendous indignation. "You know some of them folks are *ashamed* of Mahalia Jackson? *Ashamed* of her, one of the greatest singers alive! They think she's common." Then she looks about the room as though she held a bottle in her hand and were looking for a skull to crack.

I think it is because Louisa has never been able to talk like this to any white person before. All the white people she has ever met needed, in one way or another, to be reassured, consoled, to have their consciences pricked but not blasted; could not, could not afford to hear a truth which would shatter, irrevocably, their image of themselves. It is astonishing the lengths to which a person, or a people, will go in order to avoid a truthful mirror. But Harriet's necessity is precisely the opposite: it is of the utmost importance that she learn everything that Louisa can tell her, and then learn more, much more. Harriet is really trying to learn from Louisa how best to protect her husband and her son. This is why they are going out alone to-

night. They will have, tonight, as it were, a final council of war. I may be moody, but they, thank God, are practical.

Now Louisa turns to me while Harriet rummages about on the dressing table. "What time is Vidal coming for you?"

"Oh, around seven-thirty, eight o'clock. He says he's reserved tables for us in some very chic place, but he won't say where." Louisa wriggles her shoulders, raises her eyebrows, and does a tiny bump and grind. I laugh. "That's right. And then I guess we'll go out and get drunk."

"I hope to God you do. You've been about as cheerful as a cemetery these last few days. And, that way, your hangover will keep you from bugging us tomorrow."

"What about *your* hangovers? I know the way you girls drink."

"Well, we'll be paying for our own drinks," says Harriet, "so I don't think we'll have that problem. But *you're* going to be feted, like an international movie star."

"You sure you don't want to change your mind and come out with Vidal and me?"

"We're sure," Louisa says. She looks down at me and gives a small, amused grunt. "An international movie star. And I used to change your diapers. I'll be damned." She is grave for a moment. "Mama'd be proud of you, you know that?" We look at each other and the air between us is charged with secrets which not even Harriet will ever know. "Now, get the hell out of here, so we can get dressed."

"I'll take Paul on down to Mme. Dumont's."

Paul is to have supper with her children and spend the night there.

"For the last time," says Mme. Dumont and she rubs her hand over Paul's violently curly black hair. *"Tu vas nous manquer, tu sais?"* 5 Then she looks up at me and laughs. "He doesn't care. He is only interested in seeing the big ship and all the wonders of New York. Children are never sad to make journeys."

---

5 "We're going to miss you, you know?" (JHP)

"I would be very sad to go," says Paul, politely, "but my father must go to New York to work and he wants me to come with him."

Over his head, Mme. Dumont and I smile at each other. *"Il est malin, ton gosse!"* 6 She looks down at him again. "And do you think, my little diplomat, that you will like New York?"

"We aren't only going to New York," Paul answers, "we are going to California, too."

"Well, do you think you will like California?"

Paul looks at me. "I don't know. If we don't like it, we'll come back."

"So simple. Just like that," says Mme. Dumont. She looks at me. "It is the best way to look at life. Do come back. You know, we feel that you belong to us, too, here in France."

"I hope you do," I say. "I hope you do. I have always felt—always felt at home here." I bend down and Paul and I kiss each other on the cheek. We have always done so—but will we be able to do so in America? American fathers never kiss American sons. I straighten, my hand on Paul's shoulder. "You be good. I'll pick you up for breakfast, or, if you get up first you come and pick me up and we can hang out together tomorrow, while your *Maman* and your Aunt Louisa finish packing. They won't want two men hanging around the house."

*D'accord.*7 Where shall we hang out?" On the last two words he stumbles a little and imitates me.

"Maybe we can go to the zoo, I don't know. And I'll take you to lunch at the Eiffel Tower, would you like that?"

"Oh, yes," he says, "I'd love that." When he is pleased, he seems to glow. All the energy of his small, tough, concentrated being charges an unseen battery and adds an incredible luster to his eyes, which are large and dark brown—like mine—and to his skin, which always reminds me of the colors of honey and the fires of the sun.

"OK, then." I shake hands with Mme. Dumont. *"Bonsoir, Madame,"* I ring for the elevator, staring at Paul. *"Ciao, Pauli."* 8

"Bonsoir, Papa."

And Mme. Dumont takes him inside.

Upstairs, Harriet and Louisa are finally powdered, perfumed, and jeweled, and ready to go: dry martinis at the Ritz, supper, "in some *very* expensive little place," says Harriet, and perhaps the Folies Bergère afterwards. "A real cornball, tourist evening," says Louisa. "I'm working on the theory that if I can get Harriet to act like an American now, she won't have so much trouble later."

"I very much doubt," Harriet says, "that I will be able to endure the Folies Bergère for three solid hours."

"Oh, then we'll duck across town to Harry's New York bar and drink mint juleps," says Louisa.

I realize that, quite apart from everything else, Louisa is having as much fun as she has ever had in her life. Perhaps she, too, will be sad to leave Paris, even though she has only known it for such a short time.

"Do people drink those in New York?" Harriet asks. I think she is making a list of the things people do or do not do in New York.

"Some people do." Louisa winks at me. "Do you realize that this Swedish chick's picked up an Alabama drawl?"

We laugh together. The elevator chugs to a landing.

"We'll stop and say goodnight to Paul," Harriet says. She kisses me. "Give our best to Vidal."

"Right. Have a good time. Don't let any Frenchmen run off with Louisa."

"I did not come to Paris to be protected, and if I had, this wild chick *you* married couldn't do it. I just *might* upset everybody and come home with a French count." She presses the elevator button and the cage goes down.

I walk back into our dismantled apartment. It stinks of departure. There are bags and crates in the hall which will be taken away tomorrow, there are no books in the bookcases, the kitchen looks as though we never cooked a meal there,

6 "He's a smart one, your kid." (JHP)
7 "Right." (JHP)

8 "So long, Pauli." (JHP)

never dawdled there, in the early morning or late at night, over coffee. Presently, I must shower and shave but now I pour myself a drink and light a cigarette and step out on our balcony. It is dusk, the brilliant light of Paris is beginning to fade, and the green of the trees is darkening.

I have lived in this city for twelve years. This apartment is on the top floor of a corner building. We look out over the trees and the roof tops to the Champ de Mars, where the Eiffel Tower stands. Beyond this field is the river, which I have crossed so often, in so many states of mind. I have crossed every bridge in Paris, I have walked along every *quai*. I know the river as one finally knows a friend, know it when it is black, guarding all the lights of Paris in its depths, and seeming, in its vast silence, to be communing with the dead who lie beneath it; when it is yellow, evil, and roaring, giving a rough time to tugboats and barges, and causing people to remember that it has been known to rise, it has been known to kill; when it is peaceful, a slick, dark, dirty green, playing host to rowboats and *les bateaux mouches* 9 and throwing up from time to time an extremely unhealthy fish. The men who stand along the *quais* all summer with their fishing lines gratefully accept the slimy object and throw it in a rusty can. I have always wondered who eats those fish.

And I walk up and down, up and down, glad to be alone.

It is August, the month when all Parisians desert Paris and one has to walk miles to find a barbership or a laundry open in some tree-shadowed, silent side street. There is a single person on the avenue, a paratrooper walking toward École Militaire. He is also walking, almost certainly, and rather sooner than later, toward Algeria. I have a friend, a good-natured boy who was always hanging around the clubs in which I worked in the old days, who has just returned from Algeria, with a recurring, debilitating fever, and minus one eye. The

9 Passenger steamers used primarily as sight-seeing boats along the Seine. (JHP)

government has set his pension at the sum, arbitrary if not occult, of fifty-three thousand francs every three months. Of course, it is quite impossible to live on this amount of money without working—but who will hire a half-blind invalid? This boy has been spoiled forever, long before his thirtieth birthday, and there are thousands like him all over France.

And there are fewer Algerians to be found on the streets of Paris now. The rug sellers, the peanut vendors, the postcard peddlers and money-changers have vanished. The boys I used to know during my first years in Paris are scattered—or corralled—the Lord knows where.

Most of them had no money. They lived three and four together in rooms with a single skylight, a single hard cot, or in buildings that seemed abandoned, with cardboard in the windows, with erratic plumbing in a wet, cobblestoned yard, in dark, dead-end alleys, or on the outer, chilling heights of Paris.

The Arab cafés are closed—those dark, acrid cafés in which I used to meet with them to drink tea, to get high on hashish, to listen to the obsessive, stringed music which has no relation to any beat, any time, that I have ever known. I once thought of the North Africans as my brothers and that is why I went to their cafés. They were very friendly to me, perhaps one or two of them remained really fond of me even after I could no longer afford to smoke Lucky Strikes and after my collection of American sport shirts had vanished—mostly into their wardrobes. They seemed to feel that they had every right to them, since I could only have wrested these things from the world by cunning—it meant nothing to say that I had had no choice in the matter; perhaps I had wrestled these things from the world by treason, by refusing to be identified with the misery of my people. Perhaps, indeed, I identified myself with those who were responsible for this misery.

And this was true. Their rage, the only note in all their music which I could not fail to recognize, to which I responded, yet had the effect of setting us more than ever at a division. They were perfectly prepared to drive all Frenchmen into the sea, and to level the city of Paris. But I could not hate the French, because they left me alone. And I love Paris, I will always love it, it is the city which saved my life. It saved my life by allowing me to find out who I am.

It was on a bridge, one tremendous April morning, that I knew I had fallen in love. Harriet and I were walking hand in hand. The bridge was the Pont Royal, just before us was the great *horloge,* high and lifted up, saying ten to ten; beyond this, the golden statue of Joan of Arc, with her sword uplifted. Harriet and I were silent, for we had been quarreling about something. Now, when I look back, I think we had reached that state when an affair must either end or become something more than an affair.

I looked sideways at Harriet's face, which was still. Her dark-blue eyes were narrowed against the sun, and her full, pink lips were still slightly sulky, like a child's. In those days, she hardly ever wore make-up. I was in my shirt sleeves. Her face made me want to laugh and run my hand over her short dark hair. I wanted to pull her to me and say, *Baby, don't be mad at me,* and at that moment something tugged at my heart and made me catch my breath. There were millions of people all around us, but I was alone with Harriet. She was alone with me. Never, in all my life, until that moment, had I been alone with anyone. The world had always been with us, between us, defeating the quarrel we could not achieve, and making love impossible. During all the years of my life, until that moment, I had carried the menacing, the hostile, killing world with me everywhere. No matter what I was doing or saying or feeling, one eye had always been on the world—that world which I had learned to distrust almost as soon as I learned my name, that world on which I knew one could never turn one's back, the white man's world. And for the first time in my life I was free of it; it had not existed for me; I had been quarreling with my girl. It was our quarrel, it was entirely between us, it had nothing to do with anyone else in the world. For the first time in my life I had not been afraid of the pa-

triotism of the mindless, in uniform or out, who would beat me up and treat the woman who was with me as though she were the lowest of untouchables. For the first time in my life I felt that no force jeopardized my right, my power, to possess and to protect a woman; for the first time, the first time, felt that the woman was not, in her own eyes or in the eyes of the world, degraded by my presence.

The sun fell over everything, like a blessing, people were moving all about us, I will never forget the feeling of Harriet's small hand in mine, dry and trusting, and I turned to her, slowing our pace. She looked up at me with her enormous blue eyes, and she seemed to wait. I said, *"Harriet. Harriet. Tu sais, il y a quelque chose de très grave qui m'est arrivé. Je t'aime. Je t'aime. Tu me comprends,* or shall I say it in English?" 10

This was eight years ago, shortly before my first and only visit home.

That was when my mother died. I stayed in America for three months. When I came back, Harriet thought that the change in me was due to my grief— I was very silent, very thin. But it had not been my mother's death which accounted for the change. I had known that my mother was going to die. I had not known what America would be like for me after nearly four years away.

I remember standing at the rail and watching the distance between myself and LeHavre increase. Hands fell, ceasing to wave, handerkerchiefs ceased to flutter, people turned away, they mounted their bicycles or got into their cars and rode off. Soon, Le Havre was nothing but a blur. I thought of Harriet, already miles from me in Paris, and I pressed my lips tightly together in order not to cry.

Then, as Europe dropped below the water, as the days passed and passed, as we left behind us the skies of Europe and the eyes of everyone on the ship began, so to speak, to refocus, waiting for the first glimpse of America, my apprehension began to give way to a secret joy, a

10 "Harriet, Harriet. You know, something very serious has happened to me. I love you. I love you. You understand me, or shall I say it in English?" (JHP)

checked anticipation. I thought of such details as showers, which are rare in Paris, and I thought of such things as rich, cold, American milk and heavy, chocolate cake. I wondered about my friends, wondered if I had any left, and wondered if they would be glad to see me.

The Americans on the boat did not seem to be so bad, but I was fascinated, after such a long absence from it, by the nature of their friendliness. It was a friendliness which did not suggest, and was not intended to suggest, any possibility of friendship. Unlike Europeans, they dropped titles and used first names almost at once, leaving themselves, unlike the Europeans, with nowhere thereafter to go. Once one had become "Pete" or "Jane" or "Bill" all that could decently be known was known and any suggestion that there might be further depths, a person, so to speak, behind the name, was taken as a violation of that privacy which did not, paradoxically, since they trusted it so little, seem to exist among Americans. They apparently equated privacy with the unspeakable things they did in the bathroom or the bedroom, which they related only to the analyst, and then read about in the pages of best sellers. There was an eerie and unnerving irreality about everything they said and did, as though they were all members of the same team and were acting on orders from some invincibly cheerful and tirelessly inventive coach. I was fascinated by it. I found it oddly moving, but I cannot say that I was displeased. It had not occurred to me before that Americans, who had never treated me with any respect, had no respect for each other.

On the last night but one, there was a gala in the big ballroom and I sang. It had been a long time since I had sung before so many Americans. My audience had mainly been penniless French students, in the weird, Left Bank bistros I worked in those days. Still, I was a great hit with them and by this time I had become enough of a drawing card, in the Latin Quarter and in St. Germain des Prés, to have attracted a couple of critics, to have had my picture in *France-soir*,

and to have acquired a legal work permit which allowed me to make a little more money. Just the same, no matter how industrious and brilliant some of the musicians had been, or how devoted my audience, they did not know, they could not know, what my songs came out of. They did not know what was funny about it. It was impossible to translate: It damn well better be funny, or Laughing to keep from crying, or What did *I* do to be so black and blue?

The moment I stepped out on the floor, they began to smile, something opened in them, they were ready to be pleased. I found in their faces, as they watched me, smiling, waiting, an artless relief, a profound reassurance. Nothing was more familiar to them than the sight of a dark boy, singing, and there were few things on earth more necessary. It was under cover of darkness, my own darkness, that I could sing for them of the joys, passions, and terrors they smuggled about with them like steadily depreciating contraband. Under cover of the midnight fiction that I was unlike them because I was black, they could stealthily gaze at those treasures which they had been mysteriously forbidden to possess and were never permitted to declare.

I sang *I'm Coming, Virginia,* and *Take This Hammer,* and *Precious Lord.* They wouldn't let me go and I came back and sang a couple of the oldest blues I knew. Then someone asked me to sing *Swanee River,* and I did, astonished that I could, astonished that this song, which I had put down long ago, should have the power to move me. Then, if only, perhaps, to make the record complete, I wanted to sing *Strange Fruit,* but, on this number, no one can surpass the great, tormented Billie Holiday. So I finished with *Great Getting-Up Morning* and I guess I can say that if I didn't stop the show I certainly ended it. I got a big hand and I drank at a few tables and I danced with a few girls.

After one more day and one more night, the boat landed in New York. I woke up, I was bright awake at once, and

I thought, *We're here.* I turned on all the lights in my small cabin and I stared into the mirror as though I were committing my face to memory. I took a shower and I took a long time shaving and I dressed myself very carefully. I walked the long ship corridors to the dining room, looking at the luggage piled high before the elevators and beside the steps. The dining room was nearly half empty and full of a quick and joyous excitement which depressed me even more. People ate quickly, chattering to each other, anxious to get upstairs and go on deck. Was it my imagination or was it true that they seemed to avoid my eyes? A few people waved and smiled, but let me pass; perhaps it would have made them uncomfortable, this morning, to try to share their excitement with me; perhaps they did not want to know whether or not it was possible for me to share it. I walked to my table and sat down. I munched toast as dry as paper and drank a pot of coffee. Then I tipped my waiter, who bowed and smiled and called me "sir" and said that he hoped to see me on the boat again. "I hope so, too," I said.

And was it true, or was it my imagination, that a flash of wondering comprehension, a flicker of wry sympathy, then appeared in the waiter's eyes? I walked upstairs to the deck.

There was a breeze from the water but the sun was hot and made me remember how ugly New York summers could be. All of the deck chairs had been taken away and people milled about in the space where the deck chairs had been, moved from one side of the ship to the other, clambered up and down the steps, crowded the rails, and they were busy taking photographs—of the harbor, of each other, of the sea, of the gulls. I walked slowly along the deck, and an impulse stronger than myself drove me to the rail. There it was, the great, unfinished city, with all its towers blazing in the sun. It came toward us slowly and patiently, like some enormous, cunning, and murderous beast, ready to devour, impossible to escape. I watched it come closer and I listened to the people around me, to their excitement and their pleasure. There was no doubt that it was real. I watched their shining faces and wondered if I were mad. For a moment I longed, with all my heart, to be able to feel whatever they were feeling, if only to know what such a feeling was like. As the boat moved slowly into the harbor, they were being moved into safety. It was only I who was being floated into danger. I turned my head, looking for Europe, but all that stretched behind me was the sky, thick with gulls. I moved away from the rail. A big, sandy-haired man held his daughter on his shoulders, showing her the Statue of Liberty. I would never know what this statue meant to others, she had always been an ugly joke for me. And the American flag was flying from the top of the ship, above my head. I had seen the French flag drive the French into the most unspeakable frenzies, I had seen the flag which was nominally mine used to dignify the vilest purposes: now I would never, as long as I lived, know what others saw when they saw a flag. "There's no place like home," said a voice close by, and I thought, *There damn sure isn't.* I decided to go back to my cabin and have a drink.

There was a cablegram from Harriet in my cabin. It said: Be good. Be quick. I'm waiting. I folded it carefully and put it in my breast pocket. Then I wondered if I would ever get back to her. How long would it take me to earn the money to get out of this land? Sweat broke out on my forehead and I poured myself some whiskey from my nearly empty bottle. I paced the tiny cabin. It was silent. There was no one down in the cabins now.

I was not sober when I faced the uniforms in the first-class lounge. There were two of them; they were not unfriendly. They looked at my passport, they looked at me. "You've been away a long time," said one of them.

"Yes," I said, "it's been a while."

"What did you do over there all that time?"—with a grin meant to hide more than it revealed, which hideously revealed more than it could hide.

I said, "I'm a singer," and the room

seemed to rock around me. I held on to what I hoped was a calm, open smile. I had not had to deal with these faces in so long that I had forgotten how to do it. I had once known how to pitch my voice precisely between curtness and servility, and known what razor's edge of a pickaninny's smile would turn away wrath. But I had forgotten all the tricks on which my life had once depended. Once I had been an expert at baffling these people, at setting their teeth on edge, and dancing just outside the trap laid for me. But I was not an expert now. These faces were no longer merely the faces of two white men, who were my enemies. They were the faces of two white people whom I did not understand, and I could no longer plan my moves in accordance with what I knew of their cowardice and their needs and their strategy. That moment on the bridge had undone me forever.

"That's right," said one of them, "that's what it says, right here on the passport. Never heard of you, though." They looked up at me. "Did you do a lot of singing over there?"

"Some."

"What kind—concerts?"

"No." I wondered what I looked like, sounded like. I could tell nothing from their eyes. "I worked a few nightclubs."

"Nightclubs, eh? I guess they liked you over there."

"Yes," I said, "they seemed to like me all right."

"Well"—and my passport was stamped and handed back to me—"let's hope they like you over here."

"Thanks." They laughed—was it at me, or was it my imagination? and I picked up the one bag I was carrying and threw my trench coat over one shoulder and walked out of the first-class lounge. I stood in the slow-moving, murmuring line which led to the gangplank. I looked straight ahead and watched heads, smiling faces, step up to the shadow of the gangplank awning and then swiftly descend out of sight. I put my passport back in my breast pocket— *Be quick. I'm waiting*—and I held my landing card in my hand. Then, suddenly, there I was, standing on the edge of the boat, staring

down the long ramp to the ground. At the end of the plank, on the ground, stood a heavy man in a uniform. His cap was pushed back from his gray hair and his face was red and wet. He looked up at me. This was the face I remembered, the face of my nightmares; perhaps hatred had caused me to know this face better than I would ever know the face of any lover. "Come on, boy," he cried, "come on, come on!"

And I almost smiled. I was home. I touched my breast pocket. I thought of a song I sometimes sang, *When will I ever get to be a man?* I came down the gangplank, stumbling a little, and gave the man my landing card.

Much later in the day, a customs inspector checked my baggage and waved me away. I picked up my bags and started walking down the long stretch which led to the gate, to the city.

And I heard someone call my name.

I looked up and saw Louisa running toward me. I dropped my bags and grabbed her in my arms and tears came to my eyes and rolled down my face. I did not know whether the tears were for joy at seeing her, or from rage, or both.

"How are you? How are you? You look wonderful, but, oh, haven't you lost weight? It's wonderful to see you again."

I wiped my eyes. "It's wonderful to see you, too, I bet you thought I was never coming back."

Louisa laughed. "I wouldn't have blamed you if you hadn't. These people are just as corny as ever, I swear I don't believe there's any hope for them. How's your French? Lord, when I think that it was I who studied French and now I can't speak a word. And you never went near it and you probably speak it like a native."

I grinned. *"Pas mal. Je me défends pas mal."* [11] We started down the wide steps into the street. "My God," I said. "New York." I was not aware of its towers now. We were in the shadow of the elevated highway but the thing which most struck me was neither light nor shade, but noise. It came from a million things at once, from trucks and tires and

11 "Not bad. I get along okay." (JHP)

clutches and brakes and doors; from machines shuttling and stamping and rolling and cutting and pressing; from the building of tunnels, the checking of gas mains, the laying of wires, the digging of foundations; from the chattering of rivets, the scream of the pile driver, the clanging of great shovels; from the battering down and the raising up of walls; from millions of radios and television sets and juke boxes. The human voices distinguished themselves from the roar only by their note of strain and hostility. Another fleshy man, uniformed and red faced, hailed a cab for us and touched his cap politely but could only manage a peremptory growl: "Right this way, miss. Step up, sir." He slammed the cab door behind us. Louisa directed the driver to the New Yorker Hotel.

"Do they take us there?"

She looked at me. "They got laws in New York, honey, it'd be the easiest thing in the world to spend all your time in court. But over at the New Yorker, I believe they've already got the message." She took my arm. "You see? In spite of all this chopping and booming, this place hasn't really changed very much. You still can't hear yourself talk."

And I thought to myself, Maybe that's the point.

Early the next morning we checked out of the hotel and took the plane for Alabama.

I am just stepping out of the shower when I hear the bell ring. I dry myself hurriedly and put on a bathrobe. It is Vidal, of course, and very elegant he is, too, with his bushy gray hair quite lustrous, his swarthy, cynical, gypsylike face shaved and lotioned. Usually he looks just any old way. But tonight his brief bulk is contained in a dark-blue suit and he has an ironical pearly stickpin in his blue tie.

"Come in, make yourself a drink. I'll be with you in a second."

"I am, *hélas!*, on time. I trust you will forgive me for my thoughtlessness."

But I am already back in the bathroom. Vidal puts on a record: Mahalia Jackson, singing *I'm Going to Live the Life I Sing About in My Song.*

When I am dressed, I find him sitting in a chair before the open window. The daylight is gone, but it is not exactly dark. The trees are black now against the darkening sky. The lights in windows and the lights of motorcars are yellow and ringed. The street lights have not yet been turned on. It is as though, out of deference to the departed day, Paris waited a decent interval before assigning her role to a more theatrical but inferior performer.

Vidal is drinking a whiskey and soda. I pour myself a drink. He watches me.

"Well. How are you, my friend? You are nearly gone. Are you happy to be leaving us?"

"No." I say this with more force than I had intended. Vidal raises his eyebrows, looking amused and distant. "I never really intended to go back there. I certainly never intended to raise my kid there—"

"*Mais, mon cher,*" Vidal says, calmly, "you are an intelligent man, you must have known that you would probably be returning one day." He pauses. "And, as for Pauli—did it never occur to you that he might wish one day to see the country in which his father and his father's fathers were born?"

"To do that, really, he'd have to go to Africa."

"America will always mean more to him than Africa, you know that."

"I don't know." I throw my drink down and pour myself another. "Why should he want to cross all that water just to be called a nigger? America never gave him anything."

"It gave him his father."

I look at him. "You mean, his father escaped."

Vidal throws back his head and laughs. If Vidal likes you, he is certain to laugh at you and his laughter can be very unnerving. But the look, the silence which follow this laughter can be very unnerving, too. And, now, in the silence, he asks me, "Do you really think that you have escaped anything? Come. I know you for a better man than that." He walks to the table which holds the liquor. "In that movie of ours which has made you so famous, and, as I now see, so troubled, what are you playing, after all? What is the tragedy of this half-breed troubadour if not, precisely, that he has taken all the possible roads to escape and that all these roads have failed him?" He pauses, with the bottle in one hand, and looks at me. "Do you remember the trouble I had to get a performance out of you? How you hated me, you sometimes looked as though you wanted to shoot me! And do you remember when the role of Chico began to come alive?" He pours his drink. "Think back, remember. I am a very great director, *mais pardon!* I could not have got such a performance out of anyone but you. And what were you thinking of, what was in your mind, what nightmare were you living with when you began, at last, to play the role—truthfully?" He walks back to his seat.

Chico, in the film, is the son of a Martinique woman and a French *colon* [12] who hates both his mother and his father. He flees from the island to the capital, carrying his hatred with him. This hatred has now grown, naturally, to include all dark women and all white men, in a word, everyone. He descends into the underworld of Paris, where he dies. *Les fauves*—the wild beasts—refers to the life he has fled and to the life which engulfs him. When I agreed to do the role, I felt that I could probably achieve it by bearing in mind the North Africans I had watched in Paris for so long. But this did not please Vidal. The blowup came while we were rehearsing a fairly simple, straightforward scene. Chico goes into a sleazy Pigalle dance hall to beg the French owner for a particularly humiliating job. And this Frenchman reminds him of his father.

"You are playing this boy as though you thought of him as the noble savage," Vidal said, icily. "*Ça vient d'où* [13]—all these ghastly mannerisms you are using all the time?"

Everyone fell silent, for Vidal rarely spoke this way. This silence told me that everyone, the actor with whom I was playing the scene and all the people in

the "dance hall," shared Vidal's opinion of my performance and were relieved that he was going to do something about it. I was humiliated and too angry to speak; but perhaps I also felt, at the very bottom of my heart, a certain relief, an unwilling respect.

"You are doing it all wrong," he said, more gently. Then, "Come, let us have a drink together."

We walked into his office. He took a bottle and two glasses out of his desk. "Forgive me, but you put me in mind of some of those English *lady* actresses who love to play *putain* as long as it is always absolutely clear to the audience that they are really ladies. So perhaps they read a book, not usually, *hélas!* [14] *Fanny Hill,* and they have their chauffeurs drive them through Soho once or twice—and they come to the stage with a performance so absolutely loaded with detail, every bit of it meaningless, that there can be no doubt that they are acting. It is what the British call a triumph." He poured two cognacs. "That is what you are doing. Why? Who do you think this boy is, what do you think he is feeling, when he asks for this job?" He watched me carefully and I bitterly resented his look. "You come from America. The situation is not so pretty there for boys like you. I know you may not have been as poor as—as some—but is it really impossible for you to understand what a boy like Chico feels? Have you never, yourself, been in a similar position?"

I hated him for asking the question because I knew he knew the answer to it. "I would have had to be a very lucky black man not to have been in such a position."

"You would have had to be a very lucky *man.*"

"Oh, God," I said, "please don't give me any of this equality-in-anguish business."

"It is perfectly possible," he said, sharply, "that there is not another kind."

Then he was silent. He sat down behind his desk. He cut a cigar and lit it, puffing up clouds of smoke, as though to prevent us from seeing each other too

---

12 In the context used, "colon" probably refers to a colonist or settler. (JHP)

13 "Where did you pick them up"—(JHP)

14 "alas" (JHP)

clearly. "Consider this," he said. "I am a French director who has never seen your country. I have never done you any harm, except, perhaps, historically—I mean, because I am white—but I cannot be blamed for that—"

"But *I* can be," I said, "and I am! I've never understood why, if *I* have to pay for the history written in the color of my skin, *you* should get off scot-free!" But I was surprised at my vehemence, I had not known I was going to say these things, and by the fact that I was trembling and from the way he looked at me I knew that, from a professional point of view anyway, I was playing into his hands.

"What makes you think I *do*?" His face looked weary and stern. "I am a Frenchman. Look at France. You think that I—we—are not paying for our history?" He walked to the window, staring out at the rather grim little town in which the studio was located. "If it is revenge that you want, well, then, let me tell you, you will have it. You will probably have it, whether you want it or not, our stupidity will make it inevitable." He turned back into the room. "But I beg you not to confuse me with the happy people of your country, who scarcely know that there is such a thing as history and so, naturally, imagine that they can escape, as you put it, scot-free. That is what you are doing, that is what I was about to say. I was about to say that I am a French director and I have never been in your country and I have never done you any harm—but you are not talking to that man, in this room, now. You are not talking to Jean Luc Vidal, but to some other white man, whom you remember, who has nothing to do with me." He paused and went back to his desk. "Oh, most of the time you are not like this, I know. But it is there all the time, it must be, because when you are upset, this is what comes out. So you are not playing Chico truthfully, you are lying about him, and I will not let you do it. When you go back, now, and play this scene again, I want you to remember what has just happened in this room. You brought your past into this room. That is what Chico does when he walks into the dance hall.

The Frenchman whom he begs for a job is not merely a Frenchman—he is the father who disowned and betrayed him and all the Frenchmen whom he hates." He smiled and poured me another cognac. "Ah! If it were not for *my* history, I would not have so much trouble to get the truth out of you." He looked into my face, half smiling. "And you, you are angry—are you not?—that I *ask* you for the truth. You think I have no right to ask." Then he said something which he knew would enrage me. "Who are you then, and what good has it done you to come to France, and how will you raise your son? Will you teach him never to tell the truth to anyone?" And he moved behind his desk and looked at me, as though from behind a barricade.

"You have no right to talk to me this way."

"Oh, yes, I do," he said. "I have a film to make and a reputation to maintain and I am going to get a performance out of you." He looked at his watch. "Let us go back to work."

I watch him now, sitting quietly in my living room, tough, cynical, crafty old Frenchman, and I wonder if he knows that the nightmare at the bottom of my mind, as I played the role of Chico, was all the possible fates of Paul. This is but another way of saying that I relived the disasters which had nearly undone me; but, because I was thinking of Paul, I discovered that I did not want my son ever to feel toward me as I had felt toward my own father. He had died when I was eleven, but I had watched the humiliations he had to bear, and I had pitied him. But was there not, in that pity, however painfully and unwillingly, also some contempt? For how could I *know* what he had borne? I knew only that I was his son. However he had loved me, whatever he had borne, I, his son, was despised. Even had he lived, he could have done nothing to prevent it, nothing to protect me. The best that he could hope to do was to prepare me for it; and even at that he had failed. How can one be prepared for the spittle in the face, all the tireless ingenuity which goes into the spite and fear of small, unutterably miserable people, whose greatest terror is the singular identity, whose joy, whose safety, is entirely dependent on the humiliation and anguish of others?

But for Paul, I swore it, such a day would never come. I would throw my life and my work between Paul and the nightmare of the world. I would make it impossible for the world to treat Paul as it had treated my father and me.

Mahalia's record ends. Vidal rises to turn it over. "Well?" He looks at me very affectionately. "Your nightmares, please!"

"Oh, I was thinking of that summer I spent in Alabama when my mother died." I stop. "You know, but when we finally filmed that bar scene, I was thinking of New York. I was scared in Alabama, but I almost went crazy in New York. I was sure I'd never make it back here—back here to Harriet. And I knew if I didn't, it was going to be the end of me." Now Mahalia is singing *When the Saints Go Marching In.* "I got a job in the town as an elevator boy, in the town's big department store. It was a special favor, one of my father's white friends got it for me. For a long time, in the South, we all—depended—on the—*kindness*—of white friends." I take out a handkerchief and wipe my face. "But this man didn't like me. I guess I didn't seem grateful enough, wasn't enough like my father, what he thought my father was. And I couldn't get used to the town again, I'd been away too long, I hated it. It's a terrible town, anyway, the whole thing looks as though it's been built around a jailhouse. There's a room in the courthouse, a room where they beat you up. Maybe you're walking along the street one night, it's usually at night, but it happens in the daytime, too. And the police car comes up behind you and the cop says, 'Hey, boy. Come on over here.' So you go on over. He says, 'Boy, I believe you're drunk.' And, you see, if you say, 'No, no sir,' he'll beat you because you're calling him a liar. And if you say anything else, unless it's something to make him laugh, he'll take you in and beat you, just for fun. The trick is to think of some way for them to have their fun without beating you up."

The street lights of Paris click on and turn all green leaves silver. "Or to go along with the ways *they* dream up. And they'll do anything, anything at all, to prove that you're no better than a dog and to make you feel like one. And they hated me because I'd been North and I'd been to Europe. People kept saying, I hope you didn't bring no foreign notions back here with you, boy. And I'd say, 'No sir,' or 'No ma'am,' but I never said it right. And there was a time, all of them remembered it, when I *had* said it right. But now they could tell that I despised them—I guess, no matter what, I wanted them to know that I despised them. But I didn't despise them any more than everyone else did, only the others never let it show. They knew how to keep the white folks happy, and it was easy—you just had to keep them feeling like they were God's favor to the universe. They'd walk around with great, big, foolish grins on their faces and the colored folks loved to see this, because they hated them so much. "Just look at So-and-So," somebody'd say. "His white is *on* him today." And when we didn't hate them, we pitied them. In America, that's usually what it means to have a white friend. You pity the poor bastard because he was born believing the world's a great place to be, and you know it's not, and you can see that he's going to have a terrible time getting used to this idea, if he *ever* gets used to it."

Then I think of Paul again, those eyes which still imagine that I can do anything, that skin, the color of honey and fire, his jet-black, curly hair. I look out at Paris again, and I listen to Mahalia. "Maybe it's better to have the terrible times first. I don't know. Maybe, then, you can have, *if* you live, a better life, a real life, because you had to fight so hard to get it away—you know?—from the mad dog who held it in his teeth. But then your life has all those tooth marks, too, all those tatters, and all that blood." I walk to the bottle and raise it. "One for the road?"

"Thank you," says Vidal.

I pour us a drink, and he watches me. I have never talked so much before, not about those things anyway. I know that Vidal has nightmares, because he knows so much about them, but he has never told me what his are. I think that he probably does not talk about his nightmares any more. I know that the war cost him his wife and his son, and that he was in prison in Germany. He very rarely refers to it. He has a married daughter who lives in England, and he rarely speaks of her. He is like a man who has learned to live on what is left of an enormous fortune.

We are silent for a moment.

"Please go on," he says, with a smile. "I am curious about the reality behind the reality of your performance."

"My sister, Louisa, never married," I say, abruptly, "because, once, years ago, she and the boy she was going with and two friends of theirs were out driving in a car and the police stopped them. The girl who was with them was very fair and the police pretended not to believe her when she said she was colored. They made her get out and stand in front of the headlights of the car and pull down her pants and raise her dress—they said that was the only way they could be sure. And you can imagine what they said, and what they did—and they were lucky, at that, that it didn't go any further. But none of the men could do anything about it. Louisa couldn't face that boy again, and I guess he couldn't face her." Now it is really growing dark in the room and I cross to the light switch. "You know, I know what that boy felt, I've felt it. They want you to feel that you're not a man, maybe that's the only way they can feel like men, I don't know. I walked around New York with Harriet's cablegram in my pocket as though it were some atomic secret, in *code*, and they'd kill me if they ever found out what it meant. You know, there's something wrong with people like that. And thank God Harriet was here, she *proved* that the world was bigger than the world they wanted me to live in, I *had* to get back here, get to a place where people were too busy with their own lives, *their private lives*, to make fantasies about mine, to set up walls around mine." I look at him. The light in the

room has made the night outside blue-black and golden and the great searchlight of the Eiffel Tower is turning in the sky. "That's what it's like in America, for me, anyway. I always feel that I don't exist there, except in someone else's—usually dirty—mind. I don't know if you know what that means, but I do, and I don't want to put Harriet through that and I don't want to raise Paul there."

"Well," he says at last, "you are not required to remain in America forever, are you? You will sing in that elegant club which apparently feels that it cannot, much longer, so much as open its doors without you, and you will probably accept the movie offer, you would be very foolish not to. You will make a lot of money. Then, one day, you will remember that airlines and steamship companies are still in business and that France still exists. *That* will certainly be cause for astonishment."

Vidal was a Gaullist before de Gaulle came to power. But he regrets the manner of de Gaulle's rise and he is worried about de Gaulle's regime. "It is not the fault of *mon général*," he sometimes says, sadly. "Perhaps it is history's fault. I *suppose* it must be history which always arranges to bill a civilization at the very instant it is least prepared to pay."

Now he rises and walks out on the balcony, as though to reassure himself of the reality of Paris. Mahalia is singing *Didn't It Rain?* I walk out and stand beside him.

"You are a good boy—Chico," he says. I laugh. "You believe in love. You do not know all the things love cannot do, but"—he smiles—"love will teach you that."

We go, after dinner, to a Left Bank discothèque which can charge outrageous prices because Marlon Brando wandered in there one night. By accident, according to Vidal. "Do you know how many people in Paris are becoming rich—to say nothing of those, *hélas!*, who are going broke—on the off chance that Marlon Brando will lose his way again?"

He has not, presumably, lost his way tonight, but the discothèque is crowded with those strangely faceless people who

are part of the night life of all great
cities, and who always arrive, moments,
hours, or decades late, on the spot made
notorious by an event or a movement or
a handful of personalities. So here are
American boys, anything but beardless,
scratching around for Hemingway; American girls titillating themselves with
Frenchmen and existentialism, while
waiting for the American boys to shave
off their beards; French painters, busily
pursuing the revolution which ended
thirty years ago; and the young, bored,
perverted, American *arrivistes* who are
buying their way into the art world via
flattery and liquor, and the production
of canvases as arid as their greedy little
faces. Here are boys, of all nations, one
step above the pimp, who are occasionally walked across a stage or trotted
before a camera. And the girls, their
enemies, whose faces are sometimes seen
in ads, one of whom will surely have a
tantrum before the evening is out.

In a corner, as usual, surrounded, as
usual, by smiling young men, sits the
drunken blonde woman who was once
the mistress of a famous, dead painter.
She is a figure of some importance in the
art world, and so rarely has to pay for
either her drinks or her lovers. An older
Frenchman, who was once a famous director, is playing *quatre cent ving-et-un* 15
with the woman behind the cash register.
He nods pleasantly to Vidal and me as
we enter, but makes no move to join us,
and I respect him for this. Vidal and I
are obviously cast tonight in the role
vacated by Brando: our entrance justifies
the prices and sends a kind of shiver
through the room. It is marvelous to
watch the face of the waiter as he approaches, all smiles and deference and
grace, not so much honored by our presence as achieving his reality from it;
excellence, he seems to be saying, gravi-
tates naturally toward excellence. We
order two whiskey and sodas. I know
why Vidal sometimes comes here. He is
lonely. I do not think that he expects
ever to love one woman again, and so he
distracts himself with many.

Since this is a discothèque, jazz is

15 A dice game. (JHP)

blaring from the walls and record sleeves
are scattered about with a devastating
carelessness. Two of them are mine and
no doubt, presently, someone will play
the recording of the songs I sang in the
film.

"I thought," says Vidal, with a malicious little smile, "that your farewell to
Paris would not be complete without a
brief exposure to the perils of fame. Perhaps it will help prepare you for America,
where, I am told, the populace is yet
more carnivorous than it is here."

I can see that one of the vacant models
is preparing herself to come to our table
and ask for an autograph, hoping, since
she is pretty—she has, that is, the usual
female equipment, dramatized in the
usual, modern way—to be invited for a
drink. Should the maneuver succeed, one
of her boy friends or girl friends will
contrive to come by the table, asking for
a light or a pencil or a lipstick, and it
will be extremely difficult not to invite
this person to join us, too. Before the
evening ends, we will be surrounded. I
don't, now, know what I expected of
fame, but I suppose it never occurred to
me that the light could be just as dangerous, just as killing, as the dark.

"Well, let's make it brief," I tell him.
"Sometimes I wish that you weren't
quite so fond of me."

He laughs. "There are some very interesting people here tonight. Look."

Across the room from us, and now
staring at our table, are a group of American Negro students, who are probably
visiting Paris for the first time. There are
four of them, two boys and two girls, and
I suppose that they must be in their late
teens or early twenties. One of the boys,
a gleaming, curly-haired golden-brown
type—the color of his mother's fried
chicken—is carrying a guitar. When they
realize we have noticed them, they smile
and wave—wave as though I were one of
their possessions, as, indeed, I am. Golden-brown is a mime. He raises his guitar,
drops his shoulders, and his face falls
into the lugubrious lines of Chico's face
as he approaches death. He strums a little
of the film's theme music, and I laugh
and the table laughs. It is as though we
were all back home and had met for a

moment, on a Sunday morning, say, before a church or a poolroom or a barbershop.

And they have created a sensation in the discothèque, naturally, having managed, with no effort whatever, to outwit all the gleaming boys and girls. Their table, which had been of no interest only a moment before, has now become the focus of a rather pathetic attention; their smiles have made it possible for the others to smile, and to nod in our direction.

"Oh," says Vidal, "he does that far better than you ever did. Perhaps I will make him a star."

"Feel free, *m'sieu, le bon Dieu,*16 I got mine." But I can see that his attention has really been caught by one of the girls, slim, tense, and dark, who seems, though it is hard to know how one senses such things, to be treated by the others with a special respect. And, in fact, the table now seems to be having a council of war, to be demanding her opinion or her cooperation. She listens, frowning, laughing; the quality, the force of her intelligence causes her face to keep changing all the time, as though a light played on it. And, presently, with a gesture she might once have used to scatter feed to chickens, she scoops up from the floor one of those dangling rag bags women love to carry. She holds it loosely by the drawstrings, so that it is banging somewhere around her ankle, and walks over to our table. She has an honest, forthright walk, entirely unlike the calculated, pelvic workout by means of which most women get about. She is small, but sturdily, economically, put together.

As she reaches our table, Vidal and I rise, and this throws her for a second. (It has been a long time since I have seen such an attractive girl.)

Also, everyone, of course, is watching us. It is really a quite curious moment. They have put on the record of Chico singing a sad, angry Martinique ballad; my own voice is coming at us from the walls as the girl looks from Vidal to me, and smiles.

"I guess you know," she says, "we

16 "Feel free, Mr. God the Father,". . . (JHP)

weren't *about* to let you get out of here without bugging you just a little bit. We've only been in Paris just a couple of days and we thought for sure that we wouldn't have a chance of running into you anywhere, because it's in all the papers that you're coming home."

"Yes," I say, "yes. I'm leaving the day after tomorrow."

"Oh!" She grins. "Then we really *are* lucky." I find that I have almost forgotten the urchin-like grin of a colored girl. "I guess, before I keep babbling on, I'd better introduce myself. My name is Ada Holmes."

We shake hands. "This is Monsieur Vidal, the director of the film."

"I'm very honored to meet you, sir."

"Will you join us for a moment? Won't you sit down?" And Vidal pulls a chair out for her.

But she frowns contritely. "I really ought to get back to my friends." She looks at me. "I really just came over to say, for myself and all the kids, that we've got your records and we've seen your movie, and it means so much to us" —and she laughs, breathlessly, nervously, it is somehow more moving than tears— "more than I can say. Much more. And we wanted to know if you and your friend"—she looks at Vidal—"your *director,* Monsieur Vidal, would allow us to buy you a drink? We'd be very honored if you would."

"It is we who are honored," says Vidal, promptly, "*and* grateful. We were getting terribly bored with one another, thank God you came along."

The three of us laugh, and we cross the room.

The three at the table rise, and Ada makes the introductions. The other girl, taller and paler than Ada, is named Ruth. One of the boys is named Talley —"short for Talliafero"—and Goldenbrown's name is Pete. "Man," he tells me, "I dig you the most. You tore me up, baby, tore me *up.*"

"You tore up a lot of people," Talley says, cryptically, and he and Ruth laugh. Vidal does not know, but I do, that Talley is probably referring to white people.

They are from New Orleans and Tallahassee and North Carolina; are college students, and met on the boat. They have been in Europe all summer, in Italy and Spain, but are only just getting to Paris.

"We meant to come sooner," says Ada, "but we could never make up our minds to leave a place. I thought we'd never pry Ruth loose from Venice."

"I resigned myself," says Pete, "and just sat in the Piazza San Marco, drinking gin fizz and being photographed with the pigeons, while Ruth had herself driven *all* up and down the Grand Canal." He looks at Ruth. "Finally, thank heaven, it rained."

"She was working off her hostilities," says Ada, with a grin. "We thought we might as well let her do it in Venice, the opportunities in North Carolina are really terribly limited."

"There are some very upset people walking around down there," Ruth says, "and a couple of tours around the Grand Canal might do them a world of good."

Pete laughs. "Can't you just see Ruth escorting them to the edge of the water?"

"I haven't lifted my hand in anger yet," Ruth says, "but, oh Lord," and she laughs, clenching and unclenching her fists.

"You haven't been back for a long time, have you?" Talley asks me.

"Eight years. I haven't really lived there for twelve years."

Pete whistles. "I fear you are in for some surprises, my friend. There have been some changes made." Then, "Are you afraid?"

"A little."

"We all are," says Ada, "that's why I was so glad to get away for a little while."

"Then you haven't been back since Black Monday," Talley says. He laughs. "That's how it's gone down in Confederate history." He turns to Vidal. "What do people think about it here?"

Vidal smiles, delighted. "It seems extraordinarily infantile behavior, even for Americans, from whom, I must say, I have never expected very much in the way of muturity." Everyone at the table laughs. Vidal goes on. "But I cannot really talk about it, I do not understand it. I have never really understood Ameri-

cans; I am an old man now, and I suppose I never will. There is something very nice about them, something very winning, but they seem so ignorant—so ignorant of life. Perhaps it is strange, but the only people from your country with whom I have ever made contact are black people —like my good friend, my discovery, here," and he slaps me on the shoulder. "Perhaps it is because we, in Europe, whatever else we do not know, or have forgotten, know about suffering. We have suffered here. You have suffered, too. But most Americans do not yet know what anguish is. It is too bad, because the life of the West is in their hands." He turns to Ada. "I cannot help saying that I think it is a scandal—and we may all pay very dearly for it—that a civilized nation should elect to represent it a man who is so simple that he thinks the world is simple." And silence falls at the table and the four young faces stare at him.

"Well," says Pete, at last, turning to me, "you won't be bored, man, when you get back there."

"It's much too nice a night," I say, "to stay cooped up in this place, where all I can hear is my own records." We laugh. "Why don't we get out of here, and find a sidewalk café?" I tap Pete's guitar. "Maybe we can find out if you've got any talent."

"Oh, talent I've got," says Pete, "but character, man, I'm lacking."

So, after some confusion about the bill, for which Vidal has already made himself responsible, we walk out into the Paris night. It is very strange to feel that, very soon now, these boulevards will not exist for me. People will be walking up and down, as they are tonight, and lovers will be murmuring in the black shadows of the plane trees, and there will be these same still figures on the benches or in the parks—but they will not exist for me, I will not be here. For a long while Paris will no longer exist for me, except in my mind; and only in the minds of some people will I exist any longer for Paris. After departure, only invisible things are left, perhaps the life of the world is held together by invisible chains of memory and loss and love. So many things, so many people, depart! And we can only repossess them in our minds. Perhaps this is what the old folks meant, what my mother and my father meant, when they counseled us to keep the faith.

We have taken a table at the Deux Magots and Pete strums on his guitar and begins to play this song:

Preach the word, preach the word,
    preach the word!
If I never, never see you any more.
Preach the word, preach the word.
And I'll meet you on Canaan's shore.

He has a strong, clear, boyish voice, like a young preacher's, and he is smiling as he sings his song. Ada and I look at each other and grin, and Vidal is smiling. The waiter looks a little worried, for we are already beginning to attract a crowd, but it is a summer night, the gendarmes on the corner do not seem to mind, and there will be time, anyway, to stop us.

Pete was not there, none of us were, the first time this song was needed; and no one now alive can imagine what that time was like. But the song has come down the bloodstained ages. I suppose this to mean that the song is still needed, still has its work to do.

The others are all, visibly, very proud of Pete; and we all join him, and people stop to listen:

Testify! Testify!
If I never, never see you any more!
Testify! Testify!
I'll meet you on Canaan's shore!

In the crowd that has gathered to listen to us, I see a face I know, the face of a North African prize fighter, who is no longer in the ring. I used to know him well in the old days, but have not seen him for a long time. He looks quite well, his face is shining, he is quite decently dressed. And something about the way he holds himself, not quite looking at our table, tells me that he has seen me, but does not want to risk a rebuff. So I call him. "Boona!"

And he turns, smiling, and comes loping over to our table, his hands in his pockets. Pete is still singing and Ada and Vidal have taken off on a conversation of their own. Ruth and Talley look curiously, expectantly, at Boona. Now that I have called him over, I feel somewhat uneasy. I realize that I do not know what he is doing now, or how he will get along with any of these people, and I can see in his eyes that he is delighted to be in the presence of two young girls. There are virtually no North African women in Paris, and not even the dirty, rat-faced girls who live, apparently, in cafés are willing to go with an Arab. So Boona is always looking for a girl, and because he is so deprived and because he is not Western, his techniques can be very unsettling. I know he is relieved that the girls are not French and not white. He looks briefly at Vidal and Ada. Vidal, also, though for different reasons, is always looking for a girl.

But Boona has always been very nice to me. Perhaps I am sorry that I called him over, but I did not want to snub him.

He claps one hand to the side of my head, as is his habit. *"Comment vas-tu, mon frère?"* [17] I have not see you, oh for long time." And he asks me, as in the old days, "You all right? Nobody bother you?" And he laughs. "Ah! *Tu as fait le chemin, toi!* [18] Now you are *vedette*, big star—wonderful!" He looks around the table, made a little uncomfortable by the silence that has fallen, now that Pete has stopped singing. "I have seen you in the movies—you know?—and I tell everybody, I know *him!*" He points to me, and laughs, and Ruth and Talley laugh with him. "That's right, man, you make me real proud, you make me cry!"

"Boona, I want you to meet some friends of mine." And I go round the table: "Ruth, Talley, Ada, Pete"—and he bows and shakes hands, his dark eyes gleaming with pleasure—*"et Monsieur Vidal, le metteur en scène du film qui t'a arraché des larmes."* [19]

"Enchanté." But his attitude toward Vidal is colder, more distrustful. "Of course I have heard of Monsieur Vidal. He is the director of many films, many of them made me cry." This last statement is utterly, even insolently, insincere.

But Vidal, I think, is relieved that I

[17] "How are you, my brother?" (JHP)
[18] "You have come a long way!" (JHP)
[19] "—and Mr. Vidal, the director of the film which made you cry." (JHP)

will now be forced to speak to Boona and will leave him alone with Ada.

"Sit down," I say, "have a drink with us, let me have your news. What's been happening with you, what are you doing with yourself these days?"

"Ah," he sits down, "nothing very brilliant, my brother." He looks at me quickly, with a little smile. "You know, we have been having hard times here."

"Where are you from?" Ada asks him.

His brilliant eyes take her in entirely, but she does not flinch. "I am from Tunis." He says it proudly, with a little smile.

"From Tunis. I have never been to Africa, I would love to go one day."

He laughs. "Africa is a big place. Very big. There are many countries in Africa, many"—he looks briefly at Vidal—"different kinds of people, many colonies."

"But Tunis," she continues, in her innocence, "is free? Freedom is happening all over Africa. That's why I would like to go there."

"I have not been back for a long time," says Boona, "but all the news I get from Tunis, from my people, is not good."

"Wouldn't you like to go back?" Ruth asks.

Again he looks at Vidal. "That is not so easy."

Vidal smiles. "You know what I would like to do? There's a wonderful Spanish place not far from here, where we can listen to live music and dance a little." He turns to Ada. "Would you like that?"

He is leaving it up to me to get rid of Boona, and it is, of course, precisely for this reason that I cannot do it. Besides, it is no longer so simple.

"Oh, I'd love that," says Ada, and she turns to Boona. "Won't you come, too?"

"Thank you, mam'selle," he says, softly, and his tongue flicks briefly over his lower lip, and he smiles. He is very moved, people are not often nice to him.

In the Spanish place there are indeed a couple of Spanish guitars, drums, castanets, and a piano, but the uses to which these are being put carry one back, as Pete puts it, to the levee. "These are the wailingest Spanish cats I ever heard," says Ruth. "They didn't learn how to do

this in Spain, no, they didn't, they been rambling. You ever hear anything like this going on in Spain?" Talley takes her out on the dance floor, which is already crowded. A very handsome Frenchwoman is dancing with an enormous, handsome black man, who seems to be her lover, who seems to have taught her how to dance. Apparently, they are known to the musicians, who egg them on with small cries of *"Olé!"* It is a very good-natured crowd, mostly foreigners, Spaniards, Swedes, Greeks. Boona takes Ada out on the dance floor while Vidal is answering some questions put to him by Pete on the entertainment situation in France. Vidal looks a little put out, and I am amused.

We are there for perhaps an hour, dancing, talking, and I am, at last, a little drunk. In spite of Boona, who is a very good and tireless dancer, Vidal continues his pursuit of Ada, and I begin to wonder if he will make it and I begin to wonder if I want him to.

I am still puzzling out my reaction when Pete, who has disappeared, comes in through the front door, catches my eye, and signals to me. I leave the table and follow him into the streets.

He looks very upset. "I don't want to bug you, man," he says, "but I fear your boy has goofed."

I know he is not joking. I think he is probably angry at Vidal because of Ada, and I wonder what I can do about it and why he should be telling me.

I stare at him, gravely, and he says, "It looks like he stole some money."

"Stole *money?* Who, Vidal?"

And then, of course, I get it, in the split second before he says, impatiently, "No, are you kidding? Your friend, the Tunisian."

I do not know what to say or what to do, and so I temporize with questions. All the time I am wondering if this can be true and what I can do about it if it is. The trouble is, I know that Boona steals, he would probably not be alive if he didn't, but I cannot say so to these children, who probably still imagine that everyone who steals is a thief. But he has never, to my knowledge, stolen from a friend. It seems unlike him. I have always thought of him as being better than that, and smarter than that. And so I cannot believe it, but neither can I doubt it. I do not know anything about Boona's life, these days. This causes me to realize that I do not really know much about Boona.

"Who did he steal it from?"

"From Ada. Out of her bag."

"How much?"

"Ten dollars. It's not an awful lot of money, but"—he grimaces—"none of us *have* an awful lot of money."

"I know." The dark side street on which we stand is nearly empty. The only sound on the street is the muffled music of the Spanish club. "How do you know it was Boona?"

He anticipates my own unspoken rejoinder. "Who else could it be? Besides—somebody *saw* him do it."

"Somebody saw him?"

"Yes."

I do not ask him who this person is, for fear that he will say it is Vidal.

"Well," I say, "I'll try to get it back." I think that I will take Boona aside and then replace the money myself. "Was it in dollars or in francs?"

"In francs."

I have no dollars and this makes it easier. I do not know how I can possibly face Boona and accuse him of stealing money from my friends. I would rather give him the benefit of even the faintest doubt. But, "Who saw him?" I ask.

"Talley. But we didn't want to make a thing about it—"

"Does Ada know it's gone?"

"Yes." He looks at me helplessly. "I know this makes you feel pretty bad, but we thought we'd better tell you, rather than"—lamely—"anybody else."

Now, Ada comes out of the club, carrying her ridiculous handbag, and with her face all knotted and sad. "Oh," she says, "I hate to cause all this trouble, it's not worth it, not for ten lousy dollars." I am astonished to see that she has been weeping, and tears come to her eyes now.

I put my arm around her shoulder. "Come on, now. You're not causing anybody any trouble and, anyway, it's nothing to cry about."

"It isn't your fault, Ada," Pete says, miserably.

"Oh, I ought to get a sensible handbag," she says, "like you're always telling me to do," and she laughs a little, then looks at me. "Please don't try to do anything about it. Let's just forget it."

"What's happening inside?" I ask her.

"Nothing. They're just talking. I think Mr. Vidal is dancing with Ruth. He's a great dancer, that little Frenchman."

"He's a great talker, too," Pete says.

"Oh, he doesn't mean anything," says Ada, "he's just having fun. He probably doesn't get a chance to talk to many American girls."

"He certainly made up for lost time tonight."

"Look," I say, "if Talley and Boona are alone, maybe you better go back in. We'll be in in a minute. Let's try to keep this as quiet as we can."

"Yeah," he says, "okay. We're going soon anyway, okay?"

"Yes," she tells him, "right away."

But as he turns away, Boona and Talley step out into the street, and it is clear that Talley feels that he has Boona under arrest. I almost laugh, the whole thing is beginning to resemble one of those mad French farces with people flying in and out of doors; but Boona comes straight to me.

"They say I stole money, my friend. You know me, you are the only one here who knows me, you know I would not do such a thing."

I look at him and I do not know what to say. Ada looks at him with her eyes full of tears and looks away. I take Boona's arm.

"We'll be back in a minute," I say. We walk a few paces up the dark, silent street.

"She say I take her money," he says. He, too, looks as though he is about to weep—but I do not know for which reason. "You know me, you know me almost twelve years, you think I do such a thing?"

Talley saw you, I want to say, but I cannot say it. Perhaps Talley only thought he saw him. Perhaps it is easy to see a boy who looks like Boona with his hand in an American girl's purse.

"If you not believe me," he says, "search me. Search me!" And he opens his arms wide, theatrically, and now there are tears standing in his eyes.

I do not know what his tears mean, but I certainly cannot search him. I want to say, I know you steal, I know you have to steal. Perhaps you took the money out of this girl's purse in order to eat tomorrow, in order not to be thrown into the streets tonight, in order to stay out of jail. This girl means nothing to you, after all, she is only an American, an American like me. Perhaps, I suddenly think, no girl means anything to you, or ever will again, they have beaten you too hard and kept you in the gutter too long. And I also think, if you would steal from her, then of course you would lie to me, neither of us means anything to you; perhaps, in your eyes, we are simply luckier gangsters in a world which is run by gangsters. But I cannot say any of these things to Boona. I cannot say, Tell me the truth, nobody cares about the money any more.

So I say, "Of course I will not search you." And I realize that he knew I would not.

"I think it is that Frenchman who say I am a thief. They think we all are thieves." His eyes are bright and bitter. He looks over my shoulder. "They have all come out of the club now."

I look around and they are all there, in a little dark knot on the sidewalk.

"Don't worry," I say. "It doesn't matter."

"You believe me? My brother?" And his eyes look into mine with a terrible intensity.

"Yes," I force myself to say, "yes, of course, I believe you. Someone made a mistake, that's all."

"You know, the way American girls run around, they have their sack open all the time, she could lost the money anywhere. Why she blame me? Because I come from Africa?" Tears are glittering on his face. "Here she come now."

And Ada comes up the street with her straight, determined walk. She walks straight to Boona and takes his hand. "I am sorry," she says, "for everything that happened. Please believe me. It isn't worth all this fuss. I'm sure you're a very nice person, and"—she falters—"I must have lost the money, I'm sure I lost it."

She looks at him. "It isn't worth hurting your feelings, and I'm terribly sorry about it."

"I no take your money," he says. "Really truly, I no take it. Ask him"— pointing to me, grabbing me by the arm, shaking me—"he know me for years, he will tell you that I never, never steal!"

"I'm sure," she says. "I'm sure."

I take Boona by the arm again. "Let's forget it. Let's forget it all. We're all going home now, and one of these days we'll have a drink again and we'll forget all about it, all right?"

"Yes," says Ada, "let us forget it." And she holds out her hand.

Boona takes it, wonderingly. His eyes take her in again. "You are a very nice girl. Really. A very nice girl."

"I'm sure you're a nice person, too." She pauses. "Goodnight."

"Goodnight," he says, after a long silence.

Then he kisses me on both cheeks. *"Au revoir, mon frère."* [20]

"Au revoir, Boona."

After a moment we turn and walk away, leaving him standing there.

"Did he take it?" asks Vidal.

"I tell you, I *saw* him," says Talley.

"Well," I say, "it doesn't matter now." I look back and see Boona's stocky figure disappearing down the street.

"No," says Ada, "it doesn't matter." She looks up. "It's almost morning."

"I would gladly," says Vidal, stammering, "gladly—"

But she is herself again. "I wouldn't think of it. We had a wonderful time tonight, a wonderful time, and I wouldn't think of it." She turns to me with that urchin-like grin. "It was wonderful meeting you. I hope you won't have too much trouble getting used to the States again."

"Oh, I don't think I will," I say. And then, "I hope you won't."

"No," she says, "I don't think anything they can do will surprise me any more."

"Which way are we all going?" asks Vidal. "I hope someone will share my taxi with me."

But he lives in the sixteenth arrondissement, which is not in anyone's direc-

20 "Good-bye, my brother." (JHP)

tion. We walk him to the line of cabs standing under the clock at Odéon.

And we look each other in the face, in the growing morning light. His face looks weary and lined and lonely. He puts both hands on my shoulders and then puts one hand on the nape of my neck. "Do not forget me, Chico," he says. "You must come back and see us, one of these days. Many of us depend on you for many things."

"I'll be back," I say. "I'll never forget you."

He raises his eyebrows and smiles. *"Alors, Adieu."* [21]

"Adieu, Vidal."

"I was happy to meet all of you," he says. He looks at Ada. "Perhaps we will meet again before you leave."

"Perhaps," she says. "Goodby, Monsieur Vidal."

"Goodby."

Vidal's cab drives away. "I also leave you now," I say. "I must go home and wake up my son and prepare for our journey."

I leave them standing on the corner, under the clock, which points to six. They look very strange and lost and determined, the four of them. Just before my cab turns off the boulevard, I wave to them and they wave back.

Mme. Dumont is in the hall, mopping the floor.

"Did all my family get home?" I ask. I feel very cheerful, I do not know why.

"Yes," she says, "they are all here. Paul is still sleeping."

"May I go in and get him?"

She looks at me in surprise. "Of course."

So I walk into her apartment and walk into the room where Paul lies sleeping. I stand over his bed for a long time.

Perhaps my thoughts traveled—travel through to him. He opens his eyes and smiles up at me. He puts a fist to his eyes and raises his arms. *"Bonjour, Papa."*

I lift him up. *"Bonjour.* How do you feel today?"

"Oh, I don't know yet," he says.

I laugh. I put him on my shoulder and walk out into the hall. Mme. Dumont looks up at him with her radiant, aging face.

"Ah," she says, "you are going on a journey! How does it feel?"

"He doesn't know yet," I tell her. I walk to the elevator door and open it, dropping Paul down to the crook of my arm.

She laughs again. "He will know later. What a journey! *Jusqu'au nouveau monde!"* [22]

I open the cage and we step inside. "Yes," I say, "all the way to the new world." I press the button and the cage, holding my son and me, goes up.

[1960]

21 "Well then, Adieu." (JHP)   22 "As far as the new world!" (JHP)

QUESTIONS FOR STUDY

1. *What are the sources of the narrator's anxieties as he contemplates leaving Paris? What are his regrets? How has his earlier visit to America—eight years before—been unsettling?*

2. *What lesson does Jean Luc Vidal communicate to the narrator in the course of making their movie?*

3. *Why does the episode with Boona and the American couples leave the narrator cheerful and optimistic? What has the narrator apparently discovered (or rediscovered) about his relationship to America?*

4. *What is the significance of the narrator's account of his relationship with the Algerian community in Paris? How does it serve to explain the later episode with Boona? How does it serve to clarify and explain the narrator's attitude at the end of the story?*

5. *What is the symbolism of the elevator or "cage," especially in the final scene of the story?*

JOHN BARTH

Title

BEGINNING: in the middle, past the middle, nearer three-quarters done, waiting for the end. Consider how dreadful so far: passionless, abstraction, pro, dis. And it will get worse. Can we possibly continue?

Plot and theme: notions vitiated by this hour of the world but as yet not successfully succeeded. Conflict, complication, no climax. The worst is to come. Everything leads to nothing: future tense; past tense; present tense. Perfect. The final question is, Can nothing be made meaningful? Isn't that the final question? If not, the end is at hand. Literally, as it were. Can't stand any more of this.

I think she comes. The story of our life. This is the final test. Try to fill the blank. Only hope is to fill the blank. Efface what can't be faced or else fill the blank. With words or more words, otherwise I'll fill in the blank with this noun here in my prepositional object. Yes, she already said that. And I think. What now. Everything's been said already, over and over; I'm as sick of this as you are; there's nothing to say. Say nothing.

What's new? Nothing.

Conventional startling opener. Sorry if I'm interrupting the Progress of Literature, she said, in a tone that adjective clause suggesting good-humored irony but in fact defensively and imperfectly making a taunt. The conflict is established though as yet unclear in detail. Standard conflict. Let's skip particulars. What do you want from me? What'll the story be this time? Same old story. Just thought I'd see if you were still around. Before. What? Quit right here. Too late. Can't we start over? What's past is past. On the contrary, what's forever past is eternally present. The future? Blank. All this is just fill in. Hang on.

Still around. In what sense? Among the gerundive. What is that supposed to mean? Did you think I meant to fill in the blank? Why should I? On the other hand, why not? What makes you think I wouldn't fill in the blank instead? Some conversation this is. Do you want to go on, or shall we end it right now? Suspense. I don't care for this either. It'll be over soon enough in any case. But it gets worse and worse. Whatever happens, the ending will be deadly. At least let's have just one real conversation. Dialogue or monologue? What has it been from the first? Don't ask me. What is there to say at this late date? Let me think; I'm trying to think. Same old story. Or. Or? Silence.

This isn't so bad. Silence. There are worse things. Name three. This, that, the other. Some choices. Who said there was a choice?

Let's try again. That's what I've been doing; I've been thinking while you've been blank. Story of Our Life. However, this may be the final complication. The ending may be violent. That's been said before. Who cares? Let the end be blank; anything's better than this.

It didn't used to be so bad. It used to be less difficult. Even enjoyable. For whom? Both of us. To do what? Complicate the conflict. I am weary of this. What, then? To complete this sentence, if I may bring up a sore subject. That never used to be a problem. Now it's impossible; we just can't manage it. You can't fill in the blank; I can't fill in the blank. Or won't. Is this what we're going to talk about, our obscene verbal problem? It'll be our last conversation. Why talk at all? Are you paying attention? I dare you to quit now! Never dare a desperate person. On with it, calmly, one sentence after another, like a recidivist. A what? A common noun. Or another common noun. Hold tight. Or a chronic forger, let's say; committed to the pen for life. Which is to say, death. The point, for pity's sake! Not yet. Forge on.

We're more than halfway through, as I remarked at the outset: youthful vigor, innocent exposition, positive rising action —all that is behind us. How sophisticated we are today. I'll ignore her, he vowed, and went on. In this dehuman, exhausted, ultimate adjective hour, when every humane value has become untenable, and not only love, decency, and beauty but even compassion and intelligibility are no more than one or two subjective complements to complete the sentence. . . .

This is a story? It's a story, he replied equably, or will be if the author can finish it. Without interruption I suppose you mean? she broke in. I can't finish anything; that is my final word. Yet it's these interruptions that make it a story. Escalate the conflict further. Please let me start over.

Once upon a time you were satisfied with incidental felicities and niceties of technique: the unexpected image, the refreshingly accurate word-choice, the memorable simile that yields deeper and subtler significance upon reflection, like a memorable simile. Somebody please stop me. Or arresting dialogue, so to speak. For example?

Why do you suppose it is, she asked, long participial phrase of the breathless variety characteristic of dialogue attributions in nineteenth-century fiction, that literate people such as we talk like characters in a story? Even supplying the dialogue-tags, she added with wry disgust. Don't put words in her mouth. The same old story, an old-fashioned one at that. Even if I should fill in the blank with my idle pen? Nothing new about that, to make a fact out of a figure. At least it's good for something. Every story is penned in red ink, to make a figure out of a fact. This whole idea is insane.

And might therefore be got away with.

No turning back now, we've gone too far. Everything's finished. Name eight. Story, novel, literature, art, humanism, humanity, the self itself. Wait: the story's not finished. And you and I, Howard? whispered Martha, her sarcasm belied by a hesitant alarm in her glance, flickering as it were despite herself to the blank instrument in his hand. Belied indeed; put that thing away! And what does flickering modify? A person who can't verb adverb ought at least to speak correctly.

A tense moment in the evolution of the story. Do you know, declared the narrator, one has no idea, especially nowadays, how close the end may be, nor will one necessarily be aware of it when it occurs. Who can say how near this universe has come to mere cessation? Or take two people, in a story of the sort it once was possible to tell. Love affairs, literary genres, third item in exemplary series, fourth—everything blossoms and decays, does it not, from the primitive and classical through the mannered and baroque to the abstract, stylized, dehumanized, unintelligible, blank. And you and I, Rosemary? Edward. Snapped! Patience. The narrator gathers that his audience no longer cherishes him. And conversely. But little does he know of the common noun concealed for months in her you name it, under her eyelet chemise. This is a slip. The point is the same. And she fetches it out nightly as I dream, I think. That's no slip. And she regards it and sighs, a quantum grimlier each night it may be. Is this supposed to be amusing? The world might end before this sentence, or merely someone's life. And/or someone else's. I speak metaphorically. Is the sentence ended? Very nearly. No telling how long a sentence will be until one reaches the stop It sounds as if somebody intends to fill in the blank. What *is* all this nonsense about?

It may not be nonsense. Anyhow it will presently be over. As the narrator was saying, things have been kaput for some time, and while we may be pardoned our great reluctance to acknowledge it, the fact is that the bloody century for example is nearing the three-quarter mark, and the characters in this little tale, for example, are similarly past their prime, as is the drama. About played out. Then God damn it let's ring the curtain. Wait wait. We're left with the following three possibilities, at least in theory. Horseshit. Hold onto yourself, it's too soon to fill in the blank. I hope this will be a short story.

Shorter than it seems. It seems endless. Be thankful it's not a novel. The novel is predicate adjective, as is the innocent anecdote of bygone days when life made a degree of sense and subject joined to complement by copula. No longer are these things the case, as you have doubtless remarked. There was I believe some mention of possibilities, three in number. The first is rejuvenation: having become an exhausted parody of itself, perhaps a form —Of what? Of anything—may rise neo-primitively from its own ashes. A tiresome prospect. The second, more appealing I'm sure but scarcely likely at this advanced date, is that moribund what-have-yous will be supplanted by vigorous new: the demise of the novel and short story, he went on to declare, needn't be the end of narrative art, nor need the dissolution of a used-up blank fill in the blank. The end of one road might be the beginning of another. Much good that'll do me. And you may not find the revolution as bloodless as you think, either. Shall we try it? Never dare a person who is fed up to the ears.

The final possibility is a temporary expedient, to be sure, the self-styled narrator of this so-called story went on to admit, ignoring the hostile impatience of his audience, but what is not, and every sentence completed is a step closer to the end. That is to say, every day gained is a day gone. Matter of viewpoint, I suppose. Go on. I am. Whether anyone's paying attention or not. The final possibility is to turn ultimacy, exhaustion, paralyzing self-consciousness and the adjective weight of accumulated history. . . . Go on. Go on. To turn ultimacy against itself to make something new and valid, the essence whereof would be the impossibility of making something new. What a nauseating notion. And pray how does it bear upon the analogy uppermost in everyone's mind? We've gotten this far, haven't we? Look how far we've come together. Can't we keep on to the end? I think not. Even another sentence is too many. Only if one believes the end to be a long way off; actually it might come at any moment; I'm

surprised it hasn't before now. Nothing does when it's expected to.

Silence. There's a fourth possibility, I suppose. Silence. General anesthesia. Self-extinction. Silence.

Historicity and self-awareness, he asseverated, while ineluctable and even greatly to be prized, are always fatal to innocence and spontaneity. Perhaps adjective period Whether in a people, an art, a love affair, on a fourth term added not impossibly to make the third less than ultimate. In the name of suffering humanity cease this harangue. It's over. And the story? Is there a plot here? What's all this leading up to?

No climax. There's the story. Finished? Not quite. Story of our lives. The last word in fiction, in fact. I chose the first person narrative viewpoint in order to reflect interest from the peculiarities of the technique (such as the normally unbearable self-consciousness, the abstraction, and the blank) to the nature and situation of the narrator and his companion, despite the obvious possibility that the narrator and his companion might be mistaken for the narrator and his companion. Occupational hazard. The technique is advanced, as you see, but the situation of the characters is conventionally dramatic. That being the case, may one of them, or one who may be taken for one of them, make a longish speech in the old-fashioned manner, charged with obsolete emotion. Of course.

I begin calmly, though my voice may rise as I go along. Sometimes it seems as if things could instantly be altogether different and more admirable. The times be damned, one still wants a man vigorous, confident, bold, resourceful, adjective, and adjective. One still wants a woman spirited, spacious of heart, loyal, gentle, adjective, adjective. That man and that woman are as possible as the ones in this miserable story, and a good deal realer. It's as if they live in some room of our house that we can't find the door to, though it's so close we can hear echoes of their voices. Experience has made them wise instead of bitter; knowledge has mellowed instead of souring them; in their forties and fifties, even in their sixties, they're gayer and stronger and more authentic than they were in their twenties; for the twenty-year-olds they have only affectionate sympathy. So? Why aren't the couple in this story that man and woman, so easy to imagine? God, but I am surfeited with clever irony! Ill of sickness! Parallel phrase to wrap up series! This last-resort idea, it's dead in the womb, excuse the figure. A false pregnancy, excuse the figure. God damn me though if that's entirely my fault. Acknowledge your complicity. As you see, I'm trying to do something about the present mess; hence this story. Adjective in the noun! Don't lose your composure. You tell me it's self-defeating to talk about it instead of just up and doing it; but to acknowledge what I'm doing while I'm doing it is exactly the point. Self-defeat implies a victor, and who do you suppose it is, if not blank? That's the only victory left. Right? Forward! Eyes open.

No. The only way to get out of a mirror-maze is to close your eyes and hold out your hands. And be carried away by a valiant metaphor, I suppose, like a simile.

There's only one direction to go in. Ugh. We must make something out of nothing. Impossible. Mystics do. Not only turn contradiction into paradox, but *employ* it, to go on living and working. Don't bet on it. I'm betting my cliché on it, yours too. What is that supposed to mean? On with the refutation; every denial is another breath, every word brings us closer to the end.

Very well: to write this allegedly ultimate story is a form of artistic fill in the blank, or an artistic form of same, if you like. I don't. What I mean is, same idea in other terms. The storyteller's alternatives, as far as I can see, are a series of last words, like an aging actress making one farewell appearance after another, or actual blank. And I mean literally fill in the blank. Is this a test? But the former is contemptible in itself, and the latter will certainly become so when the rest of the world shrugs its shoulders and goes on about its business. Just as people would do if adverbial clause of obvious analogical nature. The fact is, the narrator has narrated himself into a corner, a state of affairs more tsk-tsk than boo-hoo, and because his position is absurd he calls the world absurd. That some writers lack lead in their pencils does not make writing obsolete. At this point they were both smiling despite themselves. At this point they were both flashing hatred despite themselves. Every woman has a blade concealed in the neighborhood of her garters. So disarm her, so to speak, don't geld yourself. At this point they were both despite themselves. Have we come to the point at last? Not quite. Where there's life there's hope.

There's no hope. This isn't working. But the alternative is to supply an alternative. That's no alternative. Unless I make it one. Just try; quit talking about it, quit talking! Never dare a desperate man. Or woman. That's the one thing that can drive even the first part of a conventional metaphor to the second part of same. Talk, talk, talk. Yes yes, go on, I believe literature's not likely ever to manage abstraction successfully, like sculpture for example, is that a fact, what a time to bring up that subject, anticlimax, that's the point, do set forth the exquisite reason. Well, because wood and iron have a native appeal and first-order reality, whereas words are artificial to begin with, invented specifically to represent. Go on, please go on. I'm going. Don't you dare. Well, well, weld iron rods into abstract patterns, say, and you've still got real iron, but arrange words into abstract patterns and you've got nonsense. Nonsense is right. For example. On, God damn it; take the linear plot, take resolution of conflict, take third direct object, all that business, they may very well be obsolete notions, indeed they are, no doubt untenable at this late date, no doubt at all, but in fact we still lead our lives by clock and calendar, for example, and though the seasons recur our mortal human time does not; we grow old and tired, we think of how things used to be or might have been and how they are now, and in fact, and in fact we get exasperated and desperate and out of expedients and out of words.

Go on. Impossible. I'm going, too late now, one more step and we're done, you and I. Suspense. The fact is, you're driving me to it, the fact is that people still lead lives, mean and bleak and brief as they are, briefer than you think, and people have characters and motives that we divine more or less inaccurately from their appearance, speech, behavior, and the rest, you aren't listening, go on then, what do you think I'm doing, people still fall in love, and out, yes, in and out, and out and in, and they please each other, and hurt each other, isn't that the truth, and they do these things in more or less conventionally dramatic fashion, unfashionable or not, go on, I'm going, and what goes on between them is still not only the most interesting but the most important thing in the bloody murderous world, pardon the adjectives. And that my dear is what writers have got to find ways to write about in this adjective adjective hour of the ditto ditto same noun as above, or their, that is to say our, accursed self-consciousness will lead them,

that is to say us, to here it comes, say it straight out, I'm going to, say it in plain English for once, that's what I'm leading up to, me and my bloody anticlimactic noun, we're pushing each other to fill in the blank.

Goodbye. Is it over? Can't you read between the lines? One more step. Goodbye suspense goodbye.

Blank.

Oh God comma I abhor self-consciousness. I despise what we have come to; I loathe our loathesome loathing, our place our time our situation, our loathesome art, this ditto necessary story. The blank of our lives. It's about over. Let the *dénouement* be soon and unexpected, painless if possible, quick at least, above all soon. Now now! How in the world will it ever

[1968]

QUESTIONS FOR STUDY

1. *What does the narrator have to say about the demise of narrative fiction and human relationships, and the difficulty of sustaining both? What do these two problems seem to have in common?*
2. *Who are the "I" (or "he") and the "she" of the story's "dialogue"? What seems to be the nature of their relationship?*
3. *What three possibilities are suggested and then dismissed for rescuing fiction? What fourth alternative is proposed? How does the narrator answer his "final question": "Can nothing be made meaningful?"*
4. *Why is the final word of the story ("end") omitted?*
5. *Describe Barth's style. How is it appropriate to the story's thematic concerns?*
6. *To what extent does "Title" have a recognizable plot?*

DONALD BARTHELME

The Balloon

THE BALLOON, beginning at a point on Fourteenth Street, the exact location of which I cannot reveal, expanded northward all one night, while people were sleeping, until it reached the Park. There, I stopped it; at dawn the northernmost edges lay over the Plaza; the free-hanging motion was frivolous and gentle. But experiencing a faint irritation at stopping, even to protect the trees, and seeing no reason the balloon should not be allowed to expand upward, over the parts of the city it was already covering, into the "air space" to be found there, I asked the engineers to see to it. This expansion took place throughout the morning, soft imperceptible sighing of gas through the valves. The balloon then covered forty-five blocks north-south and an irregular area east-west, as many as six crosstown blocks on either side of the Avenue in some places. That was the situation, then.

But it is wrong to speak of "situations," implying sets of circumstances leading to some resolution, some escape of tension; there were no situations, simply the balloon hanging there—muted heavy grays and browns for the most part, contrasting with walnut and soft yellows. A deliberate lack of finish, enhanced by skillful installation, gave the surface a rough, forgotten quality; sliding weights on the inside, carefully adjusted, anchored the great, vari-shaped mass at a number of points. Now we have had a flood of original ideas in all media, works of singular beauty as well as significant milestones in the history of inflation, but at that moment there was only *this balloon,* concrete particular, hanging there.

There were reactions. Some people found the balloon "interesting." As a response this seemed inadequate to the immensity of the balloon, the suddenness of its appearance over the city; on the other hand, in the absence of hysteria or other societally-induced anxiety, it must be judged a calm, "mature" one. There was a certain amount of initial argumentation about the "meaning" of the balloon; this subsided, because we have learned not to insist on meanings, and they are rarely even looked for now, except in cases involving the simplest, safest phenomena. It was agreed that since the meaning of the balloon could never be known absolutely, extended discussion was pointless, or at least less purposeful than the activities of those who, for example, hung green and blue paper lanterns from the warm gray underside, in certain streets, or seized the occasion to write messages on the surface, announcing their availability for the performance of unnatural acts, or the availability of acquaintances.

Daring children jumped, especially at those points where the balloon hovered close to a building, so that the gap between balloon and building was a matter of a few inches, or points where the balloon actually made contact, exerting an ever-so-slight pressure against the side of a building, so that balloon and building seemed a unity. The upper surface was so structured that a "landscape" was presented, small valleys as well as slight knolls, or mounds; once atop the balloon, a stroll was possible, or even a trip, from one place to another. There was pleasure in being able to run down an incline, then up the opposing slope, both gently graded, or in making a leap from one side to the other. Bouncing was possible, because of the pneumaticity of the surface, and even falling, if that was your wish. That all these varied motions, as well as others, were within one's possibilities, in experiencing the "up" side of the balloon, was extremely exciting for children, accustomed to the city's flat, hard skin. But the purpose of the balloon was not to amuse children.

Too, the number of people, children and adults, who took advantage of the opportunities described was not so large as it might have been: a certain timidity, lack of trust in the balloon, was seen. There was, furthermore, some hostility. Because we had hidden the pumps, which fed helium to the interior, and because the surface was so vast that the authorities could not determine the point of entry—that is, the point at which the gas was injected—a degree of frustration was evidenced by those city officers into whose province such manifestations normally fell. The apparent purposelessness of the balloon was vexing (as was the fact that it was "there" at all). Had we painted, in great letters, "LABORATORY TESTS PROVE" or "18% MORE EFFECTIVE" on the sides of the balloon, this difficulty would have been circumvented. But I could not bear to do so. On the whole, these officers were remarkably tolerant, considering the dimensions of the anomaly, this tolerance being the result of, first, secret tests conducted by night that convinced them that little or nothing could be done in the way of removing or destroying the balloon, and, secondly, a public warmth that arose (not uncolored by touches of the aforementioned hostility) toward the balloon, from ordinary citizens.

As a single balloon must stand for a lifetime of thinking about balloons, so each citizen expressed, in the attitude he chose, a complex of attitudes. One man might consider that the balloon had to do with the notion *sullied,* as in the sentence *The big balloon sullied the otherwise clear and radiant Manhattan sky.* That is, the balloon was, in this man's view, an imposture, something inferior to the sky that had formerly been there, something interposed between the people and their "sky." But in fact it was January, the sky was dark and ugly; it was not a sky you could look up into, lying on your back in the street, with pleasure, unless pleasure, for you, proceeded from having been threatened, from having been misused. And the underside of the balloon was a pleasure to look up into, we had seen to that, muted grays and browns for the most part, contrasted with walnut and soft, forgotten yellows. And so, while this man was thinking *sullied,* still there was an admixture of pleasurable cognition in his thinking, struggling with the original perception.

Another man, on the other hand, might view the balloon as if it were part of a system of unanticipated rewards, as when one's employer walks in and says, "Here, Henry, take this package of money I have wrapped for you, because we have been doing so well in the business here, and I admire the way you bruise the tulips, without which bruising your department would not be a success, or at least not the success that it is." For this man the balloon might be a brilliantly heroic "muscle and pluck" experience, even if an experience poorly understood.

Another man might say, "Without the example of ————, it is doubtful that ———— would exist today in its present form," and find many to agree with him, or to argue with him. Ideas of "bloat" and "float" were introduced, as well as concepts of dream and responsibility. Others engaged in remarkably detailed fantasies having to do with a wish either to lose themselves in the balloon, or to engorge it. The private character of these wishes, of their origins, deeply buried and unknown, was such that they were not much spoken of; yet there is evidence that they were widespread. It was also argued that what was important was what you felt when you stood under the balloon; some people claimed that they felt sheltered, warmed, as never before, while enemies of the balloon felt, or reported feeling, constrained, a "heavy" feeling.

Critical opinion was divided:

"monstrous pourings"

"harp"

XXXXXXX "certain contrasts with darker portions"

"inner joy"

"large, square corners"

"conservative eclecticism that has so far governed modern balloon design"

::::::: "abnormal vigor"

"warm, soft, lazy passages"

"Has unity been sacrificed for a sprawling quality?"

"Quelle catastrophe!"

"munching"

People began, in a curious way, to locate themselves in relation to aspects of the balloon: "I'll be at that place where it dips down into Forty-seventh Street almost to the sidewalk, near the Alamo Chile House," or, "Why don't we go stand on top, and take the air, and maybe walk about a bit, where it forms a tight, curving line with the façade of the Gallery of Modern Art—" Marginal intersections offered entrances within a given time duration, as well as "warm, soft, lazy passages" in which . . . But it is wrong to speak of "marginal intersections," each intersection was crucial, none could be ignored (as if, walking there, you might not find someone capable of turning your attention, in a flash, from old exercises to new exercises, risks and escalations). Each intersection was crucial, meeting of balloon and building, meeting of balloon and man, meeting of balloon and balloon.

It was suggested that what was admired about the balloon was finally this: that it was not limited, or defined. Sometimes a bulge, blister, or subsection would carry all the way east to the river

on its own initiative, in the manner of an army's movements on a map, as seen in a headquarters remote from the fighting. Then that part would be, as it were, thrown back again, or would withdraw into new dispositions; the next morning, that part would have made another sortie, or disappeared altogether. This ability of the balloon to shift its shape, to change, was very pleasing, especially to people whose lives were rather rigidly patterned, persons to whom change, although desired, was not available. The balloon, for the twenty-two days of its existence, offered the possibility, in its randomness, of mislocation of the self, in contradistinction to the grid of precise, rectangular pathways under our feet. The amount of specialized training currently needed, and the consequent desirability of long-term commitments, has been occasioned by the steadily growing importance of complex machinery, in virtually all kinds of operations; as this tendency increases, more and more people will turn, in bewildered inadequacy, to solutions for which the balloon may stand as a prototype, or "rough draft."

I met you under the balloon, on the occasion of your return from Norway; you asked if it was mine; I said it was. The balloon, I said, is a spontaneous autobiographical disclosure, having to do with the unease I felt at your absence, and with sexual deprivation, but now that your visit to Bergen has been terminated, it is no longer necessary or appropriate. Removal of the balloon was easy; trailer trucks carried away the depleted fabric, which is now stored in West Virginia, awaiting some other time of unhappiness, sometime, perhaps, when we are angry with one another.

[1966]

QUESTIONS FOR STUDY

1. *Describe the story's point of view and tone, and explain how they contribute to the effectiveness of the story.*
2. *How much do we learn about the narrator and about his relationship to the balloon? Does it matter that we do not know more about him?*
3. *What does the balloon represent for the narrator? What does it represent for others? What is significant in the fact that although the*

balloon is "extremely exciting" for children, adults tend to react to
it with "hostility" and "lack of trust"? Why should the "apparent
purposelessness of the balloon" be so vexing?

4. What aspects of contemporary life does the story satirize? (Note,
for example, the words and phrases that Barthelme places within
quotation marks.)

SAUL BELLOW

Looking for Mr. Green

Whatsoever thy hand findeth to do,
do it with thy might. . . . 1

HARD work? No, it wasn't really so
hard. He wasn't used to walking
and stair-climbing, but the physical difficulty of his new job was not what
George Grebe felt most. He was delivering relief checks in the Negro district,
and although he was a native Chicagoan
this was not a part of the city he knew
much about—it needed a depression to
introduce him to it. No, it wasn't literally
hard work, not as reckoned in foot-
pounds, but yet he was beginning to feel
the strain of it, to grow aware of its peculiar difficulty. He could find the streets
and numbers, but the clients were not
where they were supposed to be, and he
felt like a hunter inexperienced in the
camouflage of his game. It was an unfavorable day, too—fall, and cold, dark
weather, windy. But, anyway, instead of
shells in his deep trenchcoat pocket he
had the cardboard of checks, punctured
for the spindles of the file, the holes reminding him of the holes in player-piano
paper. And he didn't look much like a
hunter, either; his was a city figure entirely, belted up in this Irish conspirator's
coat. He was slender without being tall,
stiff in the back, his legs looking shabby
in a pair of old tweed pants gone through
and fringy at the cuffs. With this stiffness,
he kept his head forward, so that his face
was red from the sharpness of the
weather; and it was an indoors sort of
face with gray eyes that persisted in some
kind of thought and yet seemed to avoid
definiteness of conclusion. He wore side-
burns that surprised you somewhat by
the tough curl of the blond hair and the

1 Ecclesiastes 9:10. (JHP)

effect of assertion in their length. He was
not so mild as he looked, nor so youthful; and nevertheless there was no effort
on his part to seem what he was not. He
was an educated man; he was a bachelor;
he was in some ways simple; without
lushing, he liked a drink; his luck had
not been good. Nothing was deliberately
hidden.

He felt that his luck was better than
usual today. When he had reported for
work that morning he had expected to
be shut up in the relief office at a clerk's
job, for he had been hired downtown as
a clerk, and he was glad to have, instead,
the freedom of the streets and welcomed,
at least at first, the vigor of the cold and
even the blowing of the hard wind. But
on the other hand he was not getting on
with the distribution of the checks. It
was true that it was a city job; nobody
expected you to push too hard at a city
job. His supervisor, that young Mr. Raynor, had practically told him that. Still,
he wanted to do well at it. For one thing,
when he knew how quickly he could deliver a batch of checks, he would know
also how much time he could expect to
clip for himself. And then, too, the
clients would be waiting for their money.
That was not the most important consideration, though it certainly mattered to
him. No, but he wanted to do well,
simply for doing-well's sake, to acquit
himself decently of a job because he so
rarely had a job to do that required just
this sort of energy. Of this peculiar energy he now had a superabundance; once
it had started to flow, it flowed all too
heavily. And, for the time being anyway,
he was balked. He could not find Mr.
Green.

So he stood in his big-skirted trenchcoat with a large envelope in his hand

and papers showing from his pocket, wondering why people should be so hard to locate who were too feeble or sick to come to the station to collect their own checks. But Raynor had told him that tracking them down was not easy at first and had offered him some advice on how to proceed. "If you can see the postman, he's your first man to ask, and your best bet. If you can't connect with him, try the stores and tradespeople around. Then the janitor and the neighbors. But you'll find the closer you come to your man the less people will tell you. They don't want to tell you anything."

"Because I'm a stranger."

"Because you're white. We ought to have a Negro doing this, but we don't at the moment, and of course you've got to eat, too, and this is public employment. Jobs have to be made. Oh, that holds for me too. Mind you, I'm not letting myself out. I've got three years of seniority on you, that's all. And a law degree. Otherwise, you might be back of the desk and I might be going out into the field this cold day. The same dough pays us both and for the same, exact, identical reason. What's my law degree got to do with it? But you have to pass out these checks, Mr. Grebe, and it'll help if you're stubborn, so I hope you are."

"Yes, I'm fairly stubborn."

Raynor sketched hard with an eraser in the old dirt of his desk, left-handed, and said, "Sure, what else can you answer to such a question. Anyhow, the trouble you're going to have is that they don't like to give information about anybody. They think you're a plain-clothes dick or an installment collector, or summons-server or something like that. Till you've been seen around the neighborhood for a few months and people know you're only from the relief."

It was dark, ground-freezing, pre-Thanksgiving weather; the wind played hob with the smoke, rushing it down, and Grebe missed his gloves, which he had left in Raynor's office. And no one would admit knowing Green. It was past three o'clock and the postman had made his last delivery. The nearest grocer, himself a Negro, had never heard the name Tulliver Green, or said he hadn't. Grebe was inclined to think that it was true, that he had in the end convinced the man that he wanted only to deliver a check. But he wasn't sure. He needed experience in interpreting looks and signs and, even more, the will not to be put off or denied and even the force to bully if need be. If the grocer did know, he had got rid of him easily. But since most of his trade was with reliefers, why should he prevent the delivery of a check? Maybe Green, or Mrs. Green, if there was a Mrs. Green, patronized another grocer. And was there a Mrs. Green? It was one of Grebe's great handicaps that he hadn't looked at any of the case records. Raynor should have let him read files for a few hours. But he apparently saw no need for that, probably considering the job unimportant. Why prepare systematically to deliver a few checks?

But now it was time to look for the janitor. Grebe took in the building in the wind and gloom of the late November day—trampled, frost-hardened lots on one side; on the other, an automobile junk yard and then the infinite work of Elevated frames, weak-looking, gaping with rubbish fires; two sets of leaning brick porches three stories high and a flight of cement stairs to the cellar. Descending, he entered the underground passage, where he tried the doors until one opened and he found himself in the furnace room. There someone rose toward him and approached, scraping on the coal grit and bending under the canvas-jacketed pipes.

"Are you the janitor?"

"What do you want?"

"I'm looking for a man who's supposed to be living here. Green."

"What Green?"

"Oh, you maybe have more than one Green?" said Grebe with new, pleasant hope. "This is Tulliver Green."

"I don't think I c'n help you, mister. I don't know any."

"A crippled man."

The janitor stood bent before him. Could it be that he was crippled? Oh, God! what if he was. Grebe's gray eyes sought with excited difficulty to see. But no, he was only very short and stooped. A head awakened from meditation, a strong-haired beard, low, wide shoulders. A staleness of sweat and coal rose from his black shirt and the burlap sack he wore as an apron.

"Crippled how?"

Grebe thought and then answered with the light voice of unmixed candor, "I don't know. I've never seen him." This was damaging, but his only other choice was to make a lying guess, and he was not up to it. "I'm delivering checks for the relief to shut-in cases. If he weren't crippled he'd come to collect himself. That's why I said crippled. Bedridden, chair-ridden—is there anybody like that?"

This sort of frankness was one of Grebe's oldest talents, going back to childhood. But it gained him nothing here.

"No suh. I've got four buildin's same as this that I take care of. I don' know all the tenants, leave alone the tenants' tenants. The rooms turn over so fast, people movin' in and out every day. I can't tell you."

The janitor opened his grimy lips but Grebe did not hear him in the piping of the valves and the consuming pull of air to flame in the body of the furnace. He knew, however, what he had said.

"Well, all the same, thanks. Sorry I bothered you. I'll prowl around upstairs again and see if I can turn up someone who knows him."

Once more in the cold air and early darkness he made the short circle from the cellarway to the entrance crowded between the brickwork pillars and began to climb to the third floor. Pieces of plaster ground under his feet; strips of brass tape from which the carpeting had been torn away marked old boundaries at the sides. In the passage, the cold reached him worse than in the street; it touched him to the bone. The hall toilets ran like springs. He thought grimly as he heard the wind burning around the building with a sound like that of the furnace, that this was a great piece of constructed shelter. Then he struck a match in the

gloom and searched for names and numbers among the writings and scribbles on the walls. He saw WHOODY-DOODY GO TO JESUS, and zigzags, caricatures, sexual scrawls, and curses. So the sealed rooms of pyramids were also decorated, and the caves of human dawn.

The information on his card was, TULLIVER GREEN—APT 3D. There were no names, however, and no numbers. His shoulders drawn up, tears of cold in his eyes, breathing vapor, he went the length of the corridor and told himself that if he had been lucky enough to have the temperament for it he would bang on one of the doors and bawl out "Tulliver Green!" until he got results. But it wasn't in him to make an uproar and he continued to burn matches, passing the light over the walls. At the rear, in a corner off the hall, he discovered a door he had not seen before and he thought it best to investigate. It sounded empty when he knocked, but a young Negress answered, hardly more than a girl. She opened only a bit, to guard the warmth of the room.

"Yes suh?"

"I'm from the district relief station on Prairie Avenue. I'm looking for a man named Tulliver Green to give him his check. Do you know him?"

No, she didn't; but he thought she had not understood anything of what he had said. She had a dream-bound, dream-blind face, very soft and black, shut off. She wore a man's jacket and pulled the ends together at her throat. Her hair was parted in three directions, at the sides and transversely, standing up at the front in a dull puff.

"Is there somebody around here who might know?"

"I jus' taken this room las' week."

He observed that she shivered, but even her shiver was somnambulistic and there was no sharp consciousness of cold in the big smooth eyes of her handsome face.

"All right, miss, thank you. Thanks," he said, and went to try another place.

Here he was admitted. He was grateful, for the room was warm. It was full of people, and they were silent as he entered—ten people, or a dozen, perhaps more, sitting on benches like a parliament. There was no light, properly speaking, but a tempered darkness that the window gave, and everyone seemed to him enormous, the men padded out in heavy work clothes and winter coats, and the women huge, too, in their sweaters, hats, and old furs. And, besides, bed and bedding, a black cooking range, a piano piled towering to the ceiling with papers, a dining-room table of the old style of prosperous Chicago. Among these people Grebe, with his cold-heightened fresh color and his smaller stature, entered like a schoolboy. Even though he was met with smiles and good will, he knew, before a single word was spoken, that all the currents ran against him and that he would make no headway. Nevertheless he began. "Does anybody here know how I can deliver a check to Mr. Tulliver Green?"

"Green?" It was the man that had let him in who answered. He was in short sleeves, in a checkered shirt, and had a queer, high head, profusely overgrown and long as a shako; 2 the veins entered it strongly from his forehead. "I never heard mention of him. Is this where he live?"

"This is the address they gave me at the station. He's a sick man, and he'll need his check. Can't anybody tell me where to find him?"

He stood his ground and waited for a reply, his crimson wool scarf wound about his neck and drooping outside his trenchcoat, pockets weighted with the block of checks and official forms. They must have realized that he was not a college boy employed afternoons by a bill collector, trying foxily to pass for a relief clerk, recognized that he was an older man who knew himself what need was, who had had more than an average seasoning in hardship. It was evident enough if you looked at the marks under his eyes and at the sides of his mouth.

"Anybody know this sick man?"

"No suh." On all sides he saw heads

2 A stiff military cap with a high crown. (JHP)

shaken and smiles of denial. No one knew. And maybe it was true, he considered, standing silent in the earthen, musky human gloom of the place as the rumble continued. But he could never really be sure.

"What's the matter with this man?" said shako-head.

"I've never seen him. All I can tell you is that he can't come in person for his money. It's my first day in this district."

"Maybe they given you the wrong number?"

"I don't believe so. But where else can I ask about him?" He felt that this persistence amused them deeply, and in a way he shared their amusement that he should stand up so tenaciously to them. Though smaller, though slight, he was his own man, he retracted nothing about himself, and he looked back at them, gray-eyed, with amusement and also with a sort of courage. On the bench some man spoke in his throat, the words impossible to catch, and a woman answered with a wild, shrieking laugh, which was quickly cut off.

"Well, so nobody will tell me?"

"Ain't nobody who knows."

"At least, if he lives here, he pays rent to someone. Who manages the building?"

"Greatham Company. That's on Thirty-ninth Street."

Grebe wrote it in his pad. But, in the street again, a sheet of wind-driven paper clinging to his leg while he deliberated what direction to take next, it seemed a feeble lead to follow. Probably this Green didn't rent a flat, but a room. Sometimes there were as many as twenty people in an apartment; the real-estate agent would know only the lessee. And not even the agent could tell you who the renters were. In some places the beds were even used in shifts, watchmen or jitney drivers or short-order cooks in night joints turning out after a day's sleep and surrendering their beds to a sister, a nephew, or perhaps a stranger, just off the bus. There were large numbers of newcomers in this terrific, blight-bitten portion of the city between Cottage Grove and Ashland, wandering from house to house and room to room. When you saw them, how could you know them? They didn't carry bundles on their backs or look picturesque. You only saw a man, a Negro, walking in the street or riding in the car, like everyone else, with his thumb closed on a transfer. And therefore how were you supposed to tell? Grebe thought the Greatham agent would only laugh at his question.

But how much it would have simplified the job to be able to say that Green was old, or blind, or consumptive. An hour in the files, taking a few notes, and he needn't have been at such a disadvantage. When Raynor gave him the block of checks he asked, "How much should I know about these people?" Then Raynor had looked as though he were preparing to accuse him of trying to make the job more important than it was. He smiled, because by then they were on fine terms, but nevertheless he had been getting ready to say something like that when the confusion began in the station over Staika and her children.

Grebe had waited a long time for this job. It came to him through the pull of an old schoolmate in the Corporation Counsel's office, never a close friend, but suddenly sympathetic and interested— pleased to show, moreover, how well he had done, how strongly he was coming on even in these miserable times. Well, he was coming through strongly, along with the Democratic administration itself. Grebe had gone to see him in City Hall, and they had had a counter lunch or beers at least once a month for a year, and finally it had been possible to swing the job. He didn't mind being assigned the lowest clerical grade, nor even being a messenger, though Raynor thought he did.

This Raynor was an original sort of guy and Grebe had taken to him immediately. As was proper on the first day, Grebe had come early, but he waited long, for Raynor was late. At last he darted into his cubicle of an office as though he had just jumped from one of those hurtling huge red Indian Avenue cars. His thin, rough face was wind-stung and he was grinning and saying something breathlessly to himself. In his hat, a small fedora, and his coat, the velvet collar a neat fit about his neck, and his silk muffler that set off the nervous twist of his chin, he swayed and turned himself in his swivel chair, feet leaving the ground; so that he pranced a little as he sat. Meanwhile he took Grebe's measure out of his eyes, eyes of an unusual vertical length and slightly sardonic. So the two men sat for a while, saying nothing, while the supervisor raised his hat from his miscombed hair and put it in his lap. His cold-darkened hands were not clean. A steel beam passed through the little makeshift room, from which machine belts once had hung. The building was an old factory.

"I'm younger than you; I hope you won't find it hard taking orders from me," said Raynor. "But I don't make them up, either. You're how old, about?"

"Thirty-five."

"And you thought you'd be inside doing paper work. But it so happens I have to send you out."

"I don't mind."

"And it's mostly a Negro load we have in this district."

"So I thought it would be."

"Fine. You'll get along. *C'est un bon boulot.* 3 Do you know French?"

"Some."

"I thought you'd be a university man."

"Have you been in France?" said Grebe.

"No, that's the French of the Berlitz School. I've been at it for more than a year, just as I'm sure people have been, all over the world, office boys in China and braves in Tanganyika. In fact, I damn well know it. Such is the attractive power of civilization. It's overrated, but what do you want? *Que voulez-vous?* 4 I get *Le Rire* 5 and all the spicy papers, just like in Tanganyika. It must be mystifying, out there. But my reason is that I'm aiming at the diplomatic service. I have a cousin who's a courier, and the way he describes it is awfully attractive. He rides in the *wagon-lits* 6 and reads

3 "It's a good job." (JHP)
4 "What do you want?" (JHP)
5 A humorous French periodical. (JHP)
6 Railroad sleeping cars. (JHP)

books. While we— What did you do before?"

"I sold."

"Where?"

"Canned meat at Stop and Shop. In the basement."

"And before that?"

"Window shades, at Goldblatt's."

"Steady work?"

"No, Thursdays and Saturdays. I also sold shoes."

"You've been a shoe-dog too. Well. And prior to that? Here it is in your folder." He opened the record. "Saint Olaf's College, instructor in classical languages. Fellow, University of Chicago, 1926–27. I've had Latin, too. Let's trade quotations—'*Dum spiro spero.*' " 7

" '*Da dextram misero.*' " 8

" '*Alea jacta est.*' " 9

" '*Excelsior.*' " 10

Raynor shouted with laughter, and other workers came to look at him over the partition. Grebe also laughed, feeling pleased and easy. The luxury of fun on a nervous morning.

When they were done and no one was watching or listening, Raynor said rather seriously, "What made you study Latin in the first place? Was it for the priesthood?"

"No."

"Just for the hell of it? For the culture? Oh, the things people think they can pull!" He made his cry hilarious and tragic. "I ran my pants off so I could study for the bar, and I've passed the bar, so I get twelve dollars a week more than you as a bonus for having seen life straight and whole. I'll tell you, as a man of culture, that even though nothing looks to be real, and everything stands for something else, and that thing for another thing, and that thing for a still further one—there ain't any comparison between twenty-five and thirty-seven dollars a week, regardless of the last reality. Don't you think that was clear to your

Greeks? They were a thoughtful people, but they didn't part with their slaves."

This was a great deal more than Grebe had looked for in his first interview with his supervisor. He was too shy to show all the astonishment he felt. He laughed a little, aroused, and brushed at the sunbeam that covered his head with its dust. "Do you think my mistake was so terrible?"

"Damn right it was terrible, and you know it now that you've had the whip of hard times laid on your back. You should have been preparing yourself for trouble. Your people must have been well off to send you to the university. Stop me, if I'm stepping on your toes. Did your mother pamper you? Did your father give in to you? Were you brought up tenderly, with permission to go and find out what were the last things that everything else stands for while everybody else labored in the fallen world of appearances?"

"Well, no, it wasn't exactly like that." Grebe smiled. *The fallen world of appearances!* no less. But now it was his turn to deliver a surprise. "We weren't rich. My father was the last genuine English butler in Chicago—"

"Are you kidding?"

"Why should I be?"

"In a livery?"

"In livery. Up on the Gold Coast." 11

"And he wanted you to be educated like a gentleman?"

"He did not. He sent me to the Armour Institute to study chemical engineering. But when he died I changed schools."

He stopped himself, and considered how quickly Raynor had reached him. In no time he had your valise on the table and all your stuff unpacked. And afterward, in the streets, he was still reviewing how far he might have gone, and how much he might have been led to tell if they had not been interrupted by Mrs. Staika's great noise.

But just then a young woman, one of Raynor's workers, ran into the cubicle

---

7 "While I breathe, I hope." (JHP)

8 "Give your right hand to the wretched." (JHP)

9 "The die is cast." (JHP)

10 "Higher." (JHP)

11 A fashionable residential area on Chicago's north side. (JHP)

exclaiming, "Haven't you heard all the fuss?"

"We haven't heard anything."

"It's Staika, giving out with all her might. The reporters are coming. She said she phoned the papers, and you know she did."

"But what is she up to?" said Raynor.

"She brought her wash and she's ironing it here, with our current, because the relief won't pay her electric bill. She has her ironing board set up by the admitting desk, and her kids are with her, all six. They never are in school more than once a week. She's always dragging them around with her because of her reputation."

"I don't want to miss any of this," said Raynor, jumping up. Grebe, as he followed with the secretary, said, "Who is this Staika?"

"They call her the 'Blood Mother of Federal Street.' She's a professional donor at the hospitals. I think they pay ten dollars a pint. Of course it's no joke, but she makes a very big thing out of it and she and the kids are in the papers all the time."

A small crowd, staff and clients divided by a plywood barrier, stood in the narrow space of the entrance, and Staika was shouting in a gruff, mannish voice, plunging the iron on the board and slamming it on the metal rest.

"My father and mother came in a steerage, and I was born in our house, Robey by Huron. I'm no dirty immigrant. I'm a U.S. citizen. My husband is a gassed veteran from France with lungs weaker'n paper, that hardly can he go to the toilet by himself. These six children of mine, I have to buy the shoes for their feet with my own blood. Even a lousy little white Communion necktie, that's a couple of drops of blood; a little piece of mosquito veil for my Vadja so she won't be ashamed in church for the other girls, they take my blood for it by Goldblatt. That's how I keep goin'. A fine thing if I had to depend on the relief. And there's plenty of people on the rolls —fakes! There's nothin' *they* can't get, that can go and wrap bacon at Swift and Armour any time. They're lookin' for

them by the Yards. They never have to be out of work. Only they rather lay in their lousy beds and eat the public's money." She was not afraid, in a predominantly Negro station, to shout this way about Negroes.

Grebe and Raynor worked themselves forward to get a closer view of the woman. She was flaming with anger and with pleasure at herself, broad and huge, a golden-headed woman who wore a cotton cap laced with pink ribbon. She was barelegged and had on black gym shoes, her Hoover apron was open and her great breasts, not much restrained by a man's undershirt, hampered her arms as she worked at the kid's dress on the ironing board. And the children, silent and white, with a kind of locked obstinacy, in sheepskins and lumberjackets, stood behind her. She had captured the station, and the pleasure this gave her was enormous. Yet her grievances were true grievances. She was telling the truth. But she behaved like a liar. The look of her small eyes was hidden, and while she raged she also seemed to be spinning and planning.

"They send me out college case workers in silk pants to talk me out of what I got comin'. Are they better'n me? Who told them? Fire them. Let 'em go and get married, and then you won't have to cut electric from people's budget."

The chief supervisor, Mr. Ewing, couldn't silence her and he stood with folded arms at the head of his staff, bald, bald-headed, saying to his subordinates like the ex-school principal he was, "Pretty soon she'll be tired and go."

"No she won't," said Raynor to Grebe. "She'll get what she wants. She knows more about the relief even then Ewing. She's been on the rolls for years, and she always gets what she wants because she puts on a noisy show. Ewing knows it. He'll give in soon. He's only saving face. If he gets bad publicity, the Commissioner'll have him on the carpet, downtown. She's got him submerged; she'll submerge everybody in time, and that includes nations and governments."

Grebe replied with his characteristic smile, disagreeing completely. Who would take Staika's orders, and what changes could her yelling ever bring about?

No, what Grebe saw in her, the power that made people listen, was that her cry expressed the war of flesh and blood, perhaps turned a little crazy and certainly ugly, on this place and this condition. And at first, when he went out, the spirit of Staika somehow presided over the whole district for him, and it took color from her; he saw her color, in the spotty curb fires, and the fires under the El, the straight alley of flamy gloom. Later, too, when he went into a tavern for a shot of rye, the sweat of beer, association with West Side Polish streets, made him think of her again.

He wiped the corners of his mouth with his muffler, his handkerchief being inconvenient to reach for, and went out again to get on with the delivery of his checks. The air bit cold and hard and a few flakes of snow formed near him. A train struck by and left a quiver in the frames and a bristling icy hiss over the rails.

Crossing the street, he descended a flight of board steps into a basement grocery, setting off a little bell. It was a dark, long store and it caught you with its stinks of smoked meat, soap, dried peaches, and fish. There was a fire wrinkling and flapping in the little stove, and the proprietor was waiting, an Italian with a long, hollow face and stubborn bristles. He kept his hands warm under his apron.

No, he didn't know Green. You knew people but not names. The same man might not have the same name twice. The police didn't know, either, and mostly didn't care. When somebody was shot or knifed they took the body away and didn't look for the murderer. In the first place, nobody would tell them anything. So they made up a name for the coroner and called it quits. And in the second place, they didn't give a goddamn anyhow. But they couldn't get to the bottom of a thing even if they wanted to. Nobody would get to know even a tenth of what went on among these people. They stabbed and stole, they did every crime and abomination you ever heard of, men and men, women and women, parents and children, worse than the animals. They carried on their own way, and the horrors passed off like a smoke. There was never anything like it in the history of the whole world.

It was a long speech, deepening with every word in its fantasy and passion and becoming increasingly senseless and terrible: a swarm amassed by suggestion and invention, a huge, hugging, despairing knot, a human wheel of heads, legs, bellies, arms, rolling through his shop.

Grebe felt that he must interrupt him. He said sharply, "What are you talking about! All I asked was whether you knew this man."

"That isn't even the half of it. I been here six years. You probably don't want to believe this. But suppose it's true?"

"All the same," said Grebe, "there must be a way to find a person."

The Italian's close-spaced eyes had been queerly concentrated, as were his muscles, while he leaned across the counter trying to convince Grebe. Now he gave up the effort and sat down on his stool. "Oh—I suppose. Once in a while. But I been telling you, even the cops don't get anywhere."

"They're always after somebody. It's not the same thing."

"Well, keep trying if you want. I can't help you."

But he didn't keep trying. He had no more time to spend on Green. He slipped Green's check to the back of the block. The next name on the list was FIELD, WINSTON.

He found the back-yard bungalow without the least trouble; it shared a lot with another house, a few feet of yard between. Grebe knew these two-shack arrangements. They had been built in vast numbers in the days before the swamps were filled and the streets raised, and they were all the same—a boardwalk along the fence, well under street level, three or four ball-headed posts for clotheslines, greening wood, dead shingles, and a long, long flight of stairs to the rear door.

A twelve-year-old boy let him into the

kitchen, and there the old man was, sitting by the table in a wheel chair.

"Oh, it's d' Government man," he said to the boy when Grebe drew out his checks. "Go bring me my box of papers." He cleared a space on the table.

"Oh, you don't have to go to all that trouble," said Grebe. But Field laid out his papers: Social Security card, relief certification, letters from the state hospital in Manteno, and a naval discharge dated San Diego, 1920.

"That's plenty," Grebe said. "Just sign."

"You got to know who I am," the old man said. "You're from the Government. It's not your check, it's a Government check and you got no business to hand it over till everything is proved."

He loved the ceremony of it, and Grebe made no more objections. Field emptied his box and finished out the circle of cards and letters.

"There's everything I done and been. Just the death certificate and they can close book on me." He said this with a certain happy pride and magnificence. Still he did not sign; he merely held the little pen upright on the golden-green corduroy of his thigh. Grebe did not hurry him. He felt the old man's hunger for conversation.

"I got to get better coal," he said. "I send my little gran'son to the yard with my order and they fill his wagon with screening. The stove ain't made for it. It fall through the grate. The order says Franklin County egg-size coal."

"I'll report it and see what can be done."

"Nothing can be done, I expect. You know and I know. There ain't no little ways to make things better, and the only big thing is money. That's the only sunbeams, money. Nothing is black where it shines, and the only place you see black is where it ain't shining. What we colored have to have is our own rich. There ain't no other way."

Grebe sat, his reddened forehead bridged levelly by his close-cut hair and his cheeks lowered in the wings of his collar—the caked fire shone hard within the isinglass-and-iron frames but the room was not comfortable—sat and listened while the old man unfolded his scheme. This was to create one Negro millionaire a month by subscription. One clever, good-hearted young fellow elected every month would sign a contract to use the money to start a business employing Negroes. This would be advertised by chain letters and word of mouth, and every Negro wage earner would contribute a dollar a month. Within five years there would be sixty milionaires.

"That'll fetch respect," he said with a throat-stopped sound that came out like a foreign syllable. "You got to take and organize all the money that gets thrown away on the policy wheel and horse race. As long as they can take it away from you, they got no respect for you. Money, that's d' sun of human kind!" Field was a Negro of mixed blood, perhaps Cherokee, or Natchez; his skin was reddish. And he sounded, speaking about a golden sun in this dark room, and looked, shaggy and slab-headed, with the mingled blood of his face and broad lips, the little pen still upright in his hand, like one of the underground kings of mythology, old judge Minos [12] himself.

And now he accepted the check and signed. Not to soil the slip, he held it down with his knuckles. The table budged and creaked, the center of the gloomy, heathen midden [13] of the kitchen covered with bread, meat, and cans, and the scramble of papers.

"Don't you think my scheme'd work?"

"It's worth thinking about. Something ought to be done, I agree."

"It'll work if people will do it. That's all. That's the only thing, any time. When they understand it in the same way, all of them."

"That's true," said Grebe, rising. His glance met the old man's.

"I know you got to go," he said. "Well, God bless you, boy, you ain't been sly with me. I can tell it in a minute."

He went back through the buried yard.

12 The mythical king and lawgiver of Crete who had the Labyrinth built. (JHP)
13 Refuse pile. (JHP)

Someone nursed a candle in a shed, where a man unloaded kindling wood from a sprawl-wheeled baby buggy and two voices carried on a high conversation. As he came up the sheltered passage he heard the hard boost of the wind in the branches and against the house fronts, and then, reaching the sidewalk, he saw the needle-eye red of cable towers in the open icy height hundreds of feet above the river and the factories—those keen points. From here, his view was obstructed all the way to the South Branch and its timber banks, and the cranes beside the water. Rebuilt after the Great Fire, this part of the city was, not fifty years later, in ruins again, factories boarded up, buildings deserted or fallen, gaps of prairie between. But it wasn't desolation that this made you feel, but rather a faltering of organization that set free a huge energy, an escaped, unattached, unregulated power from the giant raw place. Not only must people feel it but, it seemed to Grebe, they were compelled to match it. In their very bodies. He no less than others, he realized. Say that his parents had been servants in their time, whereas he was not supposed to be one. He thought that they had never done any service like this, which no one visible asked for, and probably flesh and blood could not even perform. Nor could anyone show why it should be performed; or see where the performance would lead. That did not mean that he wanted to be released from it, he realized with a grimly pensive face. On the contrary. He had something to do. To be compelled to feel this energy and yet have no task to do—that was horrible; that was suffering; he knew what that was. It was now quitting time. Six o'clock. He could go home if he liked, to his room, that is, to wash in hot water, to pour a drink, lie down on his quilt, read the paper, eat some liver paste on crackers before going out to dinner. But to think of this actually made him feel a little sick, as though he had swallowed hard air. He had six checks left, and he was determined to deliver at least one of these: Mr. Green's check.

So he started again. He had four or five dark blocks to go, past open lots, condemned houses, old foundations, closed schools, black churches, mounds, and he reflected that there must be many people alive who had once seen the neighborhood rebuilt and new. Now there was a second layer of ruins; centuries of history accomplished through human massing. Numbers had given the place forced growth; enormous numbers had also broken it down. Objects once so new, so concrete that it could have occurred to anyone they stood for other things, had crumbled. Therefore, reflected Grebe, the secret of them was out. It was that they stood for themselves by agreement, and were natural and not unnatural by agreement, and when the things themselves collapsed the agreement became visible. What was it, otherwise, that kept cities from looking peculiar? Rome, that was almost permanent, did not give rise to thoughts like these. And was it abidingly real? But in Chicago, where the cycles were so fast and the familiar died out, and again rose changed, and died again in thirty years, you saw the common agreement or covenant, and you were forced to think about appearances and realities. (He remembered Raynor and he smiled. Raynor was a clever boy.) Once you had grasped this, a great many things became intelligible. For instance, why Mr. Field should conceive such a scheme. Of course, if people were to agree to create a millionaire, a real millionaire would come into existence. And if you wanted to know how Mr. Field was inspired to think of this, why, he had within sight of his kitchen window the chart, the very bones of a successful scheme—the El with its blue and green confetti of signals. People consented to pay dimes and ride the crash-box cars, and so it was a success. Yet how absurd it looked; how little reality there was to start with. And yet Yerkes,[14] the great financier who built it, had known that he could get people to agree to do it. Viewed as itself, what a scheme of a scheme it seemed, how close to an appearance. Then why wonder at Mr. Field's idea?

[14] Charles T. Yerkes (1837–1905), the financier who built the Chicago railway system. (JHP)

He had grasped a principle. And then Grebe remembered, too, that Mr. Yerkes had established the Yerkes Observatory and endowed it with millions. Now how did the notion come to him in his New York museum of a palace or his Aegean-bound yacht to give money to astronomers? Was he awed by the success of his bizarre enterprise and therefore ready to spend money to find out where in the universe being and seeming were identical? Yes, he wanted to know what abides; and whether flesh is Bible grass; 15 and he offered money to be burned in the fire of suns. Okay, then, Grebe thought further, these things exist because people consent to exist with them—we have got so far—and also there is a reality which doesn't depend on consent but within which consent is a game. But what about need, the need that keeps so many vast thousands in position? You tell me that, you *private* little gentleman and *decent* soul—he used these words against himself scornfully. Why is the consent given to misery? And why so painfully ugly? Because there is *something* that is dismal and permanently ugly? Here he sighed and gave it up, and thought it was enough for the present moment that he had a real check in his pocket for a Mr. Green who must be real beyond question. If only his neighbors didn't think they had to conceal him.

This time he stopped at the second floor. He struck a match and found a door. Presently a man answered his knock and Grebe had the check ready and showed it even before he began. "Does Tulliver Green live here? I'm from the relief."

The man narrowed the opening and spoke to someone at his back.

"Does he live here?"

"Uh-uh. No."

"Or anywhere in this building? He's a sick man and he can come for his dough." He exhibited the check in the light, which was smoky— the air smelled of charred lard—and the man held off the brim of his cap to study it.

"Uh-uh. Never seen the name."

"There's nobody around here that uses crutches?"

15 See Isaiah 40:6. (JHP)

He seemed to think, but it was Grebe's impression that he was simply waiting for a decent interval to pass.

"No, suh. Nobody I ever see."

"I've been looking for this man all afternoon"—Grebe spoke out with sudden force—"and I'm going to have to carry this check back to the station. It seems strange not to be able to find a person to *give* him something when you're looking for him for a good reason. I suppose if I had bad news for him I'd find him quick enough."

There was a responsive motion in the other man's face. "That's right, I reckon."

"It almost doesn't do any good to have a name if you can't be found by it. It doesn't stand for anything. He might as well not have any," he went on, smiling. It was as much of a concession as he could make to his desire to laugh.

"Well, now, there's a little old knot-back man I see once in a while. He might be the one you lookin' for. Downstairs."

"Where? Right side or left? Which door?"

"I don't know which. Thin-face little knot-back with a stick."

But no one answered at any of the doors on the first floor. He went to the end of the corridor, searching by match-light, and found only a stairless exit to the yard, a drop of about six feet. But there was a bungalow near the alley, an old house like Mr. Field's. To jump was unsafe. He ran from the front door, through the underground passage and into the yard. The place was occupied. There was a light through the curtains, upstairs. The name on the ticket under the broken, scoop-shaped mailbox was Green! He exultantly rang the bell and pressed against the locked door. Then the lock clicked faintly and a long staircase opened before him. Someone was slowly coming down—a woman. He had the impression in the weak light that she was shaping her hair as she came, making herself presentable, for he saw her arms raised. But it was for support that they were raised; she was feeling her way downward, down the wall, stumbling. Next he wondered about the pressure of her feet on the treads; she did not seem to be wearing shoes. And it was a freezing stairway. His ring had got her out of bed, perhaps, and she had forgotten to put them on. And then he saw that she was not only shoeless but naked; she was entirely naked, climbing down while she talked to herself, a heavy woman, naked and drunk. She blundered into him. The contact of her breasts, though they touched only his coat, made him go back against the door with a blind shock. See what he had tracked down, in his hunting game!

The woman was saying to herself, furious with insult, "So I cain't—k, huh? I'll show that son-of-a-bitch kin I, cain't I."

What should he do now? Grebe asked himself. Why, he should go. He should turn away and go. He couldn't talk to this woman. He couldn't keep her standing naked in the cold. But when he tried he found himself unable to turn away.

He said, "Is this where Mr. Green lives?"

But she was still talking to herself and did not hear him.

"Is this Mr. Green's house?"

At last she turned her furious drunken glance on him. "What do you want?"

Again her eyes wandered from him; there was a dot of blood in their enraged brilliance. He wondered why she didn't feel the cold.

"I'm from the relief."

"Awright, what?"

"I've got a check for Tulliver Green."

This time she heard him and put out her hand.

"No, no, for *Mr.* Green. He's got to sign," he said. How was he going to get Green's signature tonight!

"I'll take it. He cain't."

He desperately shook his head, thinking of Mr. Field's precautions about identification. "I can't let you have it. It's for him. Are you Mrs. Green?"

"Maybe I is, and maybe I ain't. Who want to know?"

"Is he upstairs?"

"Awright. Take it up yourself, you goddamn fool."

Sure, he was a goddamn fool. Of course he could not go up because Green would probably be drunk and naked, too. And perhaps he would appear on the

landing soon. He looked eagerly upward. Under the light was a high narrow brown wall. Empty! It remained empty!

"Hell with you, then!" he heard her cry. To deliver a check for coal and clothes, he was keeping her in the cold. She did not feel it, but his face was burning with frost and self-ridicule. He backed away from her

"I'll come tomorrow, tell him."

"Ah, hell with you. Don' never come. What you doin' here in the nighttime? Don' come back." She yelled so that he saw the breadth of her tongue. She stood astride in the long cold box of the hall and held on to the banister and the wall. The bungalow itself was shaped something like a box, a clumsy, high box pointing into the freezing air with its sharp, wintry lights.

"If you are Mrs. Green, I'll give you the check," he said, changing his mind.

"Give here, then." She took it, took the pen offered with it in her left hand, and tried to sign the receipt on the wall. He looked around, almost as though to see whether his madness was being observed, and came near believing that someone was standing on a mountain of used tires in the auto-junking shop next door.

"But are you Mrs. Green?" he now thought to ask. But she was already climbing the stairs with the check, and it was too late, if he had made an error, if he was now in trouble, to undo the thing. But he wasn't going to worry about it. Though she might not be Mrs. Green, he was convinced that Mr. Green was upstairs. Whoever she was, the woman stood for Green, whom he was not to see this time. Well, you silly bastard, he said to himself, so you think you found him. So what? Maybe you really did find him —what of it? But it was important that there was a real Mr. Green whom they could not keep him from reaching because he seemed to come as an emissary from hostile appearances. And though the self-ridicule was slow to diminish, and his face still blazed with it, he had, nevertheless, a feeling of elation, too." "For after all," he said, "he *could* be found!"

[1951]

QUESTIONS FOR STUDY

1. *What essential information about George Grebe do we learn from his morning interview with Mr. Raynor? In what important ways do these two men seem to differ?*
2. *Each of the characters in the story—Grebe, Mr. Raynor, the janitor, Staika, the Italian grocer, Mr. Field—either explicitly or implicitly embodies a certain attitude toward life. Can you identify or characterize these attitudes?*
3. *Why does it become increasingly important to Grebe that there is "a real Mr. Green"?*
4. *What is the appropriateness of the story's setting? What symbolic importance does it come to assume in the course of the story?*
5. *What are we to make of the story's conclusion? Is it optimistic, pessimistic, or simply ambivalent and inconclusive?*
6. *What is the appropriateness of the story's biblical epigraph (Ecclesiastes 9:10)?*

AMBROSE BIERCE

Chickamauga

ONE SUNNY autumn afternoon a child strayed away from its rude home in a small field and entered a forest unobserved. It was happy in a new sense of freedom from control, happy in the opportunity of exploration and adventure; for this child's spirit, in bodies of its ancestors, had for thousands of years been trained to memorable feats of discovery and conquest—victories in battles whose critical moments were centuries, whose victors' camps were cities of hewn stone. From the cradle of its race it had conquered its way through two continents and passing a great sea had penetrated a third, there to be born to war and dominion as a heritage.

The child was a boy aged about six years, the son of a poor planter. In his younger manhood the father had been a soldier, had fought against naked savages and followed the flag of his country into the capital of a civilized race to the far South. In the peaceful life of a planter the warrior-fire survived; once kindled, it is never extinguished. The man loved military books and pictures and the boy had understood enough to make himself a wooden sword, though even the eye of his father would hardly have known it for what it was. This weapon he now bore bravely, as became the son of an heroic race, and pausing now and again in the sunny space of the forest assumed, with some exaggeration, the postures of aggression and defense that he had been taught by the engraver's art. Made reckless by the ease with which he overcame invisible foes attempting to stay his advance, he committed the common enough military error of pushing the pursuit to a dangerous extreme, until he found himself upon the margin of a wide but shallow brook, whose rapid waters barred his direct advance against the flying foe that had crossed with illogical ease. But the intrepid victor was not to be baffled; the spirit of the race which had passed the great sea burned unconquerable in that small breast and would not be denied. Finding a place where some bowlders in the bed of the stream lay but a step or a leap apart, he made his way across and fell again upon the rearguard of his imaginary foe, putting all to the sword.

Now that the battle had been won, prudence required that he withdraw to his base of operations. Alas; like many a mightier conqueror, and like one, the mightiest, he could not

> curb the lust for war,
> Nor learn that tempted Fate will leave
> the loftiest star.

Advancing from the bank of the creek he suddenly found himself confronted with a new and more formidable enemy: in the path that he was following, sat, bolt upright, with ears erect and paws suspended before it, a rabbit! With a startled cry the child turned and fled, he knew not in what direction, calling with inarticulate cries for his mother, weeping, stumbling, his tender skin cruelly torn by brambles, his little heart beating hard with terror—breathless, blind with tears—lost in the forest! Then, for more than an hour, he wandered with erring feet through the tangled undergrowth, till at last, overcome by fatigue, he lay down in a narrow space between two rocks, within a few yards of the stream and still grasping his toy sword, no longer a weapon but a companion, sobbed himself to sleep. The wood birds sang merrily above his head; the squirrels, whisking their bravery of tail, ran barking from tree to tree, unconscious of the pity of it, and somewhere far away was a strange, muffled thunder, as if the partridges were drumming in celebration of nature's victory over the son of her immemorial enslavers. And back at the little plantation, where white men and black were hastily searching the fields and hedges in alarm, a mother's heart was breaking for her missing child.

Hours passed, and then the little sleeper rose to his feet. The chill of the evening was in his limbs, the fear of the gloom in his heart. But he had rested, and he no longer wept. With some blind instinct which impelled to action he struggled through the undergrowth about him and came to a more open ground—on his right the brook, to the left a gentle acclivity studded with infrequent trees; over all, the gathering gloom of twilight. A thin, ghostly mist rose along the water. It frightened and repelled him; instead of recrossing, in the direction whence he had come, he turned his back upon it, and went forward toward the dark inclosing wood. Suddenly he saw before him a strange moving object which he took to be some large animal—a dog, a pig—he could not name it; perhaps it was a bear. He had seen pictures of bears, but knew of nothing to their discredit and had vaguely wished to meet one. But something in form or movement of this object —something in the awkwardness of its approach—told him that it was not a bear, and curiosity was stayed by fear. He stood still and as it came slowly on gained courage every moment, for he saw that at least it had not the long, menacing ears of the rabbit. Possibly his impressionable mind was half conscious of something familiar in its shambling, awkward gait. Before it had approached near enough to resolve his doubts he saw that it was followed by another and another. To right and to left were many more; the whole open space about him was alive with them—all moving toward the brook.

They were men. They crept upon their hands and knees. They used their hands only, dragging their legs. They used their knees only, their arms hanging idle at their sides. They strove to rise to their feet, but fell prone in the attempt. They did nothing naturally, and nothing alike, save only to advance foot by foot in the same direction. Singly, in pairs and in little groups, they came on through the gloom, some halting now and again while others crept slowly past them, then resuming their movement. They came by dozens and by hundreds; as far on either hand as one could see in the deepening gloom they extended and the black wood behind them appeared to be inexhaustible. The very ground seemed in motion toward the creek. Occasionally one who had paused did not again go on, but lay motionless. He was dead. Some, pausing, made strange gestures with their hands, erected their arms and lowered them again, clasped their heads; spread their palms upward, as men are sometimes seen to do in public prayer.

Not all of this did the child note; it is what would have been noted by an elder observer; he saw little but that these were men, yet crept like babes. Being men, they were not terrible, though unfamiliarly clad. He moved among them freely, going from one to another and peering into their faces with childish curiosity. All their faces were singularly white and many were streaked and gouted with red. Something in this—something too, perhaps, in their grotesque attitudes and movements —reminded him of the painted clown whom he had seen last summer in the circus, and he laughed as he watched them. But on and ever on they crept, these maimed and bleeding men, as heedless as he of the dramatic contrast between his laughter and their own ghastly gravity. To him it was a merry spectacle. He had seen his father's negroes creep upon their hands and knees for his amusement—had ridden them so, "making believe" they were his horses. He now approached one of these crawling figures from behind and with an agile movement mounted it astride. The man sank upon his breast, recovered, flung the small boy fiercely to the ground as an unbroken colt might have done, then turned upon him a face that lacked a lower jaw—from the upper teeth to the throat was a great red gap fringed with hanging shreds of flesh and splinters of bone. The unnatural prominence of nose, the absence of chin, the fierce eyes, gave this man the appearance of a great bird of prey crimsoned in throat and breast by the blood of its quarry. The man rose to his knees, the child to his feet. The man shook his fist at the child; the child, terrified at last, ran to a tree near by, got upon the farther side of it and took a more serious view of the situation. And so the clumsy multitude dragged itself slowly and painfully along in hideous pantomime —moved forward down the slope like a swarm of great black beetles, with never a sound of going—in silence profound, absolute.

Instead of darkening, the haunted landscape began to brighten. Through the belt of trees beyond the brook shone a strange red light, the trunks and branches of the trees making a black lacework against it. It struck the creeping figures and gave them monstrous shadows, which caricatured their movements on the lit grass. It fell upon their faces, touching their whiteness with a ruddy tinge, accentuating the stains with which so many of them were freaked and maculated. It sparkled on buttons and bits of metal in their clothing. Instinctively the child turned toward the growing splendor and moved down the slope with his horrible companions; in a few moments had passed the foremost of the throng—not much of a feat, considering his advantages. He placed himself in the lead, his wooden sword still in hand, and solemnly directed the march, conforming his pace to theirs and occasionally turning as if to see that his forces did not straggle. Surely such a leader never before had such a following.

Scattered about upon the ground now slowly narrowing by the encroachment of this awful march to water, were certain articles to which, in the leader's mind, were coupled no significant associations: an occasional blanket, tightly rolled lengthwise, doubled and the ends bound together with a string; a heavy knapsack here, and there a broken rifle—such things, in short, as are found in the rear of retreating troops, the "spoor" of men flying from their hunters. Everywhere near the creek, which here had a margin of lowland, the earth was trodden into mud by the feet of men and horses. An observer of better experience in the use of his eyes would have noticed that these footprints pointed in both directions; the ground had been twice passed over—in advance and in retreat. A few hours before, these desperate, stricken men, with their more fortunate and now distant comrades, had penetrated the forest in thousands. Their successive battalions, breaking into swarms and re-forming in lines, had passed the child on every side— had almost trodden on him as he slept. The rustle and murmur of their march had not awakened him. Almost within a stone's throw of where he lay they had fought a battle; but all unheard by him were the roar of the musketry, the shock of the cannon, "the thunder of the captains and the shouting." He had slept through it all, grasping his little wooden sword with perhaps a tighter clutch in unconscious sympathy with his martial environment, but as heedless of the grandeur of the struggle as the dead who had died to make the glory.

The fire beyond the belt of woods on the farther side of the creek, reflected to earth from the canopy of its own smoke, was now suffusing the whole landscape. It transformed the sinuous line of mist to the vapour of gold. The water gleamed with dashes of red, and red, too, were many of the stones protruding above the surface. But that was blood; the less desperately wounded had stained them in crossing. On them, too, the child now crossed with eager steps; he was going to the fire. As he stood upon the farther bank he turned about to look at the companions of his march. The advance was arriving at the creek. The stronger had already drawn themselves to the brink and plunged their faces into the flood. Three or four who lay without motion appeared to have no heads. At this the child's eyes expanded with wonder; even his hospitable understanding could not accept a phenomenon implying such vitality as that. After slaking their thirst these men had not had the strength to back away from the water, nor to keep their heads above it. They were drowned. In rear of these, the open spaces of the forest showed the leader as many formless figures of his grim command as at first; but not nearly so many were in motion. He waved his cap for their encouragement and smilingly pointed with his weapon in the direction of the guiding light—a pillar of fire to this strange exodus.

Confident of the fidelity of his forces, he now entered the belt of woods, passed through it easily in the red illumination, climbed a fence, ran across a field, turning now and again to coquet with his responsive shadow, and so approached the blazing ruin of a dwelling. Desolation everywhere! In all the wide glare not a living thing was visible. He cared nothing for that; the spectacle pleased, and he danced with glee in imitation of the wavering flames. He ran about, collecting fuel, but every object that he found was too heavy for him to cast in from the distance to which the heat limited his approach. In despair he flung in his sword—a surrender to the superior forces of nature. His military career was at an end.

Shifting his position, his eyes fell upon some outbuildings which had an oddly familiar appearance, as if he had dreamed of them. He stood considering them with wonder, when suddenly the entire plantation, with its inclosing forest, seemed to turn as if upon a pivot. His little world swung half around; the points of the compass were reversed. He recognized the blazing building as his own home!

For a moment he stood stupefied by the power of the revelation, then ran with stumbling feet, making a half-circuit of the ruin. There, conspicuous in the light of the conflagration, lay the dead body of a woman—the white face turned upward, the hands thrown out and clutched full of grass, the clothing deranged, the long dark hair in tangles and full of clotted blood. The greater part of the forehead was torn away, and from the jagged hole the brain protruded, overflowing the temple, a frothy mass of gray, crowned with clusters of crimson bubbles—the work of a shell.

The child moved his little hands, making wild, uncertain gestures. He uttered a series of inarticulate and indescribable cries—something between the chattering of an ape and the gobbling of a turkey—a startling, soulless, unholy sound, the language of a devil. The child was a deaf mute.

Then he stood motionless, with quivering lips, looking down upon the wreck.

[1891]

QUESTIONS FOR STUDY

1. *What is the purpose of the first two paragraphs? What is Bierce trying to tell the reader about the nature of man and his capacity for aggression? How is that statement a fitting commentary on the story that follows? How does it explain the boy's behavior?*

2. *How does Bierce's choice of a six-year-old deaf mute as the story's center of revelation increase its surrealistic horror? Why does Bierce withhold the fact until the very end of the story? Has this revelation been prepared for earlier?*

3. *What kind of imagery is used to describe the wounded and maimed soldiers? What does such imagery suggest about human nature? How is that suggestion reinforced and underscored by the imagery accompanying the boy's final recognition?*

4. *To what extent may the story be characterized as a moral fable?*

ARNA BONTEMPS

A Summer Tragedy

OLD Jeff Patton, the black share farmer, fumbled with his bow tie. His fingers trembled and the high, stiff collar pinched his throat. A fellow loses his hand for such vanities after thirty or forty years of simple life. Once a year, or maybe twice if there's a wedding among his kinfolks, he may spruce up, but generally fancy clothes do nothing but adorn the wall of the big room and feed the moths. That had been Jeff Patton's experience. He had not worn his stiff-bosomed shirt more than a dozen times in all his married life. His swallow-tailed coat lay on the bed beside him, freshly brushed and pressed, but it was as full of holes as the overalls in which he worked on weekdays. The moths had used it badly. Jeff twisted his mouth into a hideous toothless grimace as he contended with the obstinate bow. He stamped his good foot and decided to give up the struggle.

"Jennie," he called.

"What's that, Jeff?" His wife's shrunken voice came out of the adjoining room like an echo. It was hardly bigger than a whisper.

"I reckon you'll have to he'p me wid this heah bow tie, baby," he said meekly. "Dog if I can hitch it up."

Her answer was not strong enough to reach him, but presently the old woman came to the door, feeling her way with a stick. She had a wasted, dead-leaf appearance. Her body, as scrawny and gnarled as a string bean, seemed less than nothing in the ocean of frayed and faded petticoats that surrounded her. These hung an inch or two above the tops of her heavy unlaced shoes and showed little grotesque piles where the stockings had fallen down from her negligible legs.

"You oughta could do a heap mo' wid a thing like that'n me—beingst as you got yo' good sight."

"Looks like I oughta could," he admitted. "But my fingers is gone democrat on me. I get all mixed up in the looking glass an' can't tell wicha way to twist the devilish thing."

Jennie sat on the side of the bed, and old Jeff Patton got down on one knee while she tied the bow knot. It was a slow and painful ordeal for each of them in this position. Jeff's bones cracked, his knee ached, and it was only after a half dozen attempts that Jennie worked a semblance of a bow into the tie.

"I got to dress maself now," the old woman whispered. "These is ma old shoes an' stockings, and I ain't so much as unwrapped ma dress."

"Well, don't worry 'bout me no mo', baby," Jeff said. "That 'bout finishes me. All I gotta do now is slip on that old coat 'n ves' an' I'll be fixed to leave."

Jennie disappeared again through the dim passage into the shed room. Being blind was no handicap to her in that black hole. Jeff heard the cane placed against the wall beside the door and knew that his wife was on easy ground. He put on his coat, took a battered top hat from the bed post, and hobbled to the front door. He was ready to travel. As soon as Jennie could get on her Sunday shoes and her old black silk dress, they would start.

Outside the tiny log house, the day was warm and mellow with sunshine. A host of wasps were humming with busy excitement in the trunk of a dead sycamore. Gray squirrels were searching through the grass for hickory nuts, and blue jays were in the trees, hopping from branch to branch. Pine woods stretched away to the left like a black sea. Among them were scattered scores of log houses like Jeff's, houses of black share farmers. Cows and pigs wandered freely among the trees. There was no danger of loss. Each farmer knew his own stock and knew his neighbor's as well as he knew his neighbor's children.

Down the slope to the right were the cultivated acres on which the colored folks worked. They extended to the river, more than two miles away, and they were today green with the unmade cotton crop. A tiny thread of a road, which passed directly in front of Jeff's place, ran through these green fields like a pencil mark.

Jeff, standing outside the door, with his absurd hat in his left hand, surveyed the wide scene tenderly. He had been forty-five years on these acres. He loved them with the unexplained affection that others have for the countries to which they belong.

The sun was hot on his head, his collar still pinched his throat, and the Sunday clothes were intolerably hot. Jeff transferred the hat to his right hand and began fanning with it. Suddenly the whisper that was Jennie's voice came out of the shed room.

"You can bring the car round front whilst you's waitin'," it said feebly. There was a tired pause; then it added, "I'll soon be fixed to go."

"A'right, baby," Jeff answered. "I'll get it in a minute."

But he didn't move. A thought struck him that made his mouth fall open. The mention of the car brought to his mind with new intensity, the trip he and Jennie were about to take. Fear came into his eyes; excitement took his breath. Lord, Jesus!

"Jeff. . . . O Jeff," the old woman's whisper called.

He awakened with a jolt. "Hunh, baby?"

"What you doin'?"

"Nuthin. Jes studyin'. I jes been turnin' things round 'n round in ma mind."

"You could be gettin' the car," she said.

"Oh yes, right away, baby."

He started round to the shed, limping heavily on his bad leg. There were three frizzly chickens in the yard. All his other chickens had been killed or stolen recently. But the frizzly chickens had been saved somehow. That was fortunate indeed, for these curious creatures had a way of devouring "poison" from the yard and in that way protecting against conjure and black luck and spells. But even the frizzly chickens seemed now to be in a stupor. Jeff thought they had some ailment; he expected all three of them to die shortly.

The shed in which the old T-model Ford stood was only a grass roof held up by four corner poles. It had been built by tremulous hands at a time when the little rattletrap car had been regarded as a peculiar treasure. And, miraculously, despite wind and downpour, it still stood.

Jeff adjusted the crank and put his weight upon it. The engine came to life with a sputter and bang that rattled the old car from radiator to tail light. Jeff hopped into the seat and put his foot on the accelerator. The sputtering and banging increased. The rattling became more violent. That was good. It was good banging, good sputtering and rattling, and it meant that the aged car was still in running condition. She could be depended on for this trip.

Again Jeff's thought halted as if paralyzed. The suggestion of the trip fell into the machinery of his mind like a wrench. He felt dazed and weak. He swung the car out into the yard, made a half turn, and drove around to the front door. When he took his hands off the wheel, he noticed that he was trembling violently. He cut off the motor and climbed to the ground to wait for Jennie.

A few minutes later she was at the window, her voice rattling against the pane like a broken shutter.

"I'm ready, Jeff."

He did not answer, but limped into the house and took her by the arm. He led her slowly through the big room, down the step, and across the yard.

"You reckon I'd oughta lock the do'?" he asked softly.

They stopped and Jennie weighed the question. Finally she shook her head.

"Ne' mind the door'," she said. "I don't see no cause to lock up things."

"You right," Jeff agreed. "No cause to lock up."

Jeff opened the door and helped his wife into the car. A quick shudder passed over him. Jesus! Again he trembled.

"How come you shaking so?" Jennie whispered.

"I don't know," he said.

"You mus' be scairt, Jeff."

"No, baby, I ain't scairt."

He slammed the door after her and went around to crank up again. The motor started easily. Jeff wished that it had not been so responsive. He would have liked a few more minutes in which to turn things around in his head. As it was, with Jennie chiding him about being afraid, he had to keep going. He swung the car into the little pencil-mark road and started off toward the river, driving very slowly, very cautiously.

Chugging across the green countryside, the small battered Ford seemed tiny indeed. Jeff felt a familiar excitement, a thrill, as they came down the first slope to the immense levels on which the cotton was growing. He could not help reflecting that the crops were good. He knew what that meant, too; he had made forty-five of them with his own hands. It was true that he had worn out nearly a dozen mules, but that was the fault of old man Stevenson, the owner of the land. Major Stevenson had the old notion that one mule was all a share farmer needed to work a thirty-acre plot. It was an expensive notion, the way it killed mules from overwork but the old man held to it. Jeff thought it killed a good many share farmers as well as mules, but he had no sympathy for them. He had always been strong, and he had been taught to have no patience with weakness in men. Women or children might be tolerated if they were puny, but a weak man was a curse. Of course, his own children—

Jeff's thought halted there. He and Jennie never mentioned their dead children any more. And naturally, he did not wish to dwell upon them in his mind. Before he knew it, some remark would slip out of his mouth and that would make Jennie feel blue. Perhaps she would cry. A woman like Jennie could not easily throw off the grief that comes from losing five grown children within two years. Even Jeff was still staggered by the blow. His memory had not been much good recently. He frequently talked to himself.

And, although he had kept it a secret, he knew that his courage had left him. He was terrified by the least unfamiliar sound at night. He was reluctant to venture far from home in the daytime. And that habit of trembling when he felt fearful was now far beyond his control. Sometimes he became afraid and trembled without knowing what had frightened him. The feeling would just come over him like a chill.

The car rattled slowly over the dusty road. Jennie sat erect and silent with a little absurd hat pinned to her hair. Her useless eyes seemed very large, very white in their deep sockets. Suddenly Jeff heard her voice, and he inclined his head to catch the words.

"Is we passed Delia Moore's house yet?" she asked.

"Not yet," he said.

"You must be drivin' mighty slow, Jeff."

"We just as well take our time, baby."

There was a pause. A little puff of steam was coming out of the radiator of the car. Heat wavered above the hood. Delia Moore's house was nearly half a mile away. After a moment Jennie spoke again.

"You ain't really scairt, is you, Jeff?"

"Nah, baby, I ain't scairt."

"You know how we agreed—we gotta keep on goin'."

Jewels of perspiration appeared on Jeff's forehead. His eyes rounded, blinked, became fixed on the road.

"I don't know," he said with a shiver, "I reckon it's the only thing to do."

"Hm."

A flock of guinea fowls, pecking in the road, were scattered by the passing car. Some of them took to their wings; others hid under bushes. A blue jay, swaying on a leafy twig, was annoying a roadside squirrel. Jeff held an even speed till he came near Delia's place. Then he slowed down noticeably.

Delia's house was really no house at all, but an abandoned store building converted into a dwelling. It sat near a crossroads, beneath a single black cedar tree. There Delia, a cattish old creature of Jennie's age, lived alone. She had been there more years than anybody could remember, and long ago had won the disfavor of such women as Jennie. For in her young days Delia had been gayer, yellower, and saucier than seemed proper in those parts. Her ways with menfolks had been dark and suspicious. And the fact that she had had as many husbands as children did not help her reputation.

"Yonder's old Delia," Jeff said as they passed.

"What she doin'?"

"Jes sittin' in the do'," he said.

"She see us?"

"Hm," Jeff said. "Musta did."

That relieved Jennie. It strengthened her to know that her old enemy had seen her pass in her best clothes. That would give the old she-devil something to chew her gums and fret about, Jennie thought. Wouldn't she have a fit if she didn't find out? Old evil Delia! This would be just the thing for her. It would pay her back for being so evil. It would also pay her, Jennie thought, for the way she used to grin at Jeff—long ago, when her teeth were good.

The road became smooth and red, and Jeff could tell by the smell of the air that they were nearing the river. He could see the rise where the road turned and ran along parallel to the stream. The car chugged on monotonously. After a long silent spell, Jennie leaned against Jeff and spoke.

"How many bale o' cotton you think we got standin'?" she said.

Jeff wrinkled his forehead as he calculated.

" 'Bout twenty-five, I reckon."

"How many you make las' year?"

"Twenty-eight," he said. "How come you ask that?"

"I's jes thinkin'," Jennie said quietly.

"It don't make a speck o' difference though," Jeff reflected. "If we get much or if we get little, we still gonna be in debt to old man Stevenson when he gets through counting up agin us. It's took us a long time to learn that."

Jennie was not listening to these words. She had fallen into a trancelike meditation. Her lips twitched. She chewed her gums and rubbed her gnarled hands nervously. Suddenly, she leaned forward, buried her face in the nervous hands, and burst into tears. She cried aloud in a dry, cracked voice that suggested the rattle of fodder on dead stalks. She cried aloud like a child, for she had never learned to suppress a genuine sob. Her slight old frame shook heavily and seemed hardly able to sustain such violent grief.

"What's the matter, baby?" Jeff asked awkwardly. "Why you cryin' like all that?"

"I's jes thinkin'," she said.

"So you the one what's scairt now, hunh?"

"I ain't scairt, Jeff. I's jes thinkin' 'bout leavin' eve'thing like this—eve'thing we been used to. It's right sad-like."

Jeff did not answer, and presently Jennie buried her face again and cried.

The sun was almost overhead. It beat down furiously on the dusty wagon-path road, on the parched roadside grass and the tiny battered car. Jeff's hands, gripping the wheel, became wet with perspiration; his forehead sparkled. Jeff's lips parted. His mouth shaped a hideous grimace. His face suggested the face of a man being burned. But the torture passed and his expression softened again.

"You mustn't cry, baby," he said to his wife. "We gotta be strong. We can't break down."

Jennie waited a few seconds, then said, "You reckon we oughta do it, Jeff? You reckon we oughta go 'head an' do it, really?"

Jeff's voice choked; his eyes blurred. He was terrified to hear Jennie say the thing that had been in his mind all morning. She had egged him on when he had wanted more than anything in the world to wait, to reconsider, to think things over a little longer. Now she was getting cold feet. Actually, there was no need of thinking the question through again. It would only end in making the same painful decision once more. Jeff knew that. There was no need of fooling around longer.

"We jes as well to do like we planned," he said. "They ain't nothin' else for us now—it's the bes' thing."

Jeff thought of the handicaps, the near impossibility, of making another crop with his leg bothering him more and more each week. Then there was always the chance that he would have another stroke, like the one that had made him lame. Another one might kill him. The least it could do would be to leave him helpless. Jeff gasped—Lord Jesus! He could not bear to think of being helpless, like a baby, on Jennie's hands. Frail, blind Jennie.

The little pounding motor of the car worked harder and harder. The puff of steam from the cracked radiator became larger. Jeff realized that they were climbing a little rise. A moment later the road turned abruptly, and he looked down upon the face of the river.

"Jeff."

"Hunh?"

"Is that the water I hear?"

"Hm. Tha's it."

"Well, which way you goin' now?"

"Down this-a way," he said. "The road runs 'long 'side o' the water a lil piece."

She waited a while calmly. Then she said, "Drive faster."

"A'right, baby," Jeff said.

The water roared in the bed of the river. It was fifty or sixty feet below the level of the road. Between the road and the water there was a long smooth slope, sharply inclined. The slope was dry, the clay hardened by prolonged summer heat. The water below, roaring in a narrow channel, was noisy and wild.

"Jeff."

"Hunh?"

"How far you goin'?"

"Jes a lil piece down the road."

"You ain't scairt, is you, Jeff?"

"Nah, baby," he said trembling. "I ain't scairt."

"Remember how we planned it, Jeff. We gotta do it like we said. Brave-like."

"Hm."

Jeff's brain darkened. Things suddenly seemed unreal, like figures in a dream. Thoughts swam in his mind foolishly, hysterically, like little blind fish in a pool within a dense cave. They rushed again. Jeff soon became dizzy. He shuddered violently and turned to his wife.

"Jennie, I can't do it. I can't." His voice broke pitifully.

She did not appear to be listening. All the grief had gone from her face. She sat erect, her unseeing eyes wide open, strained and frightful. Her glossy black skin had become dull. She seemed as thin, as sharp and bony, as a starved bird. Now, having suffered and endured the sadness of tearing herself away from beloved things, she showed no anguish. She was absorbed with her own thoughts, and she didn't even hear Jeff's voice shouting in her ear.

Jeff said nothing more. For an instant there was light in his cavernous brain. The great chamber was, for less than a second, peopled by characters he knew and loved. They were simple, healthy creatures, and they behaved in a manner that he could understand. They had quality. But since he had already taken leave of them long ago, the remembrance did not break his heart again. Young Jeff Patton was among them, the Jeff Patton of fifty years ago who went down to New Orleans with a crowd of country boys to the Mardi Gras doings. The gay young crowd, boys with candy-striped shirts and rouged brown girls in noisy silks, was like a picture in his head. Yet it did not make him sad. On that very trip Slim Burns had killed Joe Beasley—the crowd had been broken up. Since then Jeff Patton's world had been the Greenbriar Plantation. If there had been other Mardi Gras carnivals, he had not heard of them. Since then there had been no time; the years had fallen on him like waves. Now he was old, worn out. Another paralytic stroke (like the one he had already suffered) would put him on his back for keeps. In that condition, with a frail blind woman to look after him, he would be worse off than if he were dead.

Suddenly Jeff's hands became steady. He actually felt brave. He slowed down the motor of the car and carefully pulled off the road. Below, the water of the stream boomed, a soft thunder in the deep channel. Jeff ran the car onto the clay slope, pointed it directly toward the stream, and put his foot heavily on the accelerator. The little car leaped furiously down the steep incline toward the water. The movement was nearly as swift and direct as a fall. The two old black folks, sitting quietly side by side, showed no excitement. In another instant the car hit the water and dropped immediately out of sight.

A little later it lodged in the mud of a shallow place. One wheel of the crushed and upturned little Ford became visible above the rushing water.

[1933]

QUESTIONS FOR STUDY

1. *What are the motives that lead Jeff and Jennie Patton to take their own lives?*
2. *How does the author go about enlisting the sympathies of the reader on behalf of the old couple? Why does he dwell on so many of the mundane, commonplace details of their daily life and spend what at first may seem an inordinate amount of time describing the opening scene in which they dress for their journey?*
3. *Why is Delia Moore included in the story? What function does she serve?*
4. *Why does Bontemps withhold the Pattons' destination until the very end of the story? Does it make the story more effective, or does the reader come to feel that he has somehow been imposed upon?*

JORGE LUIS BORGES

The Garden of Forking Paths

O N PAGE 22 of Liddell Hart's *History of World War I* you will read that an attack against the Serre-Montauban line by thirteen British divisions (supported by 1,400 artillery pieces) planned for the 24th of July, 1916, had to be postponed until the morning of the 29th. The torrential rains, Captain Liddell Hart comments, caused this delay, an insignificant one, to be sure.

The following statement, dictated, re-read and signed by Dr. Yu Tsun, former professor of English at the *Hochschule* at Tsingtao, throws an unsuspected light over the whole affair. The first two pages of the document are missing.

". . . and I hung up the receiver. Immediately afterwards, I recognized the voice that had answered in German. It was that of Captain Richard Madden. Madden's presence in Viktor Runeberg's apartment meant the end of our anxieties and—but this seemed, *or should have seemed*, very secondary to me—also the end of our lives. It meant that Runeberg had been arrested or murdered.[1] Before the sun set on that day, I would encounter the same fate. Madden was implacable. Or rather, he was obliged to be so. An Irishman at the service of England, a man accused of laxity and perhaps of treason, how could he fail to seize and be thankful for such a miraculous opportunity; the discovery, capture, maybe even the death of two agents of the German Reich? I went up to my room; absurdly I locked the door and threw myself on my back

---

[1] An hypothesis both hateful and odd. The Prussian spy Hans Rabener, alias Viktor Runeberg, attacked with drawn automatic the bearer of the warrant for his arrest, Captain Richard Madden. The latter, in self-defense, inflicted the wound which brought about Runeberg's death. (Editor's note.)

on the narrow iron cot. Through the window I saw the familiar roofs and the cloud-shaded six o'clock sun. It seemed incredible to me that that day without premonitions or symbols should be the one of my inexorable death. In spite of my dead father, in spite of having been a child in a symmetrical garden of Hai Feng, was I—now—going to die? Then I reflected that everything happens to a man precisely, precisely *now*. Centuries of centuries and only in the present do things happen; countless men in the air, on the face of the earth and the sea, and all that really is happening is happening to me . . . The almost intolerable recollection of Madden's horselike face banished these wanderings. In the midst of my hatred and terror (it means nothing to me now to speak of terror, now that I have mocked Richard Madden, now that my throat yearns for the noose) it occurred to me that that tumultuous and doubtless happy warrior did not suspect that I possessed the Secret. The name of the exact location of the new British artillery park on the River Ancre. A bird streaked across the gray sky and blindly I translated it into an airplane and that airplane into many (against the French sky) annihilating the artillery station with vertical bombs. If only my mouth, before a bullet shattered it, could cry out that secret name so it could be heard in Germany . . . My human voice was very weak. How might I make it carry to the ear of the Chief? To the ear of that sick and hateful man who knew nothing of Runeberg and me save that we were in Staffordshire and who was waiting in vain for our report in his arid office in Berlin, endlessly examining newspapers . . . I said out loud: *I must flee.* I sat up noiselessly, in a useless perfection of silence, as if

---

Madden were already lying in wait for me. Something—perhaps the mere vain ostentation of proving my resources were nil—made me look through my pockets. I found what I knew I would find. The American watch, the nickel chain and the square coin, the key ring with the incriminating useless keys to Runeberg's apartment, the notebook, a letter which I resolved to destroy immediately (and which I did not destroy), a crown, two shillings and a few pence, the red and blue pencil, the handkerchief, the revolver with one bullet. Absurdly, I took it in my hand and weighed it in order to inspire courage within myself. Vaguely I thought that a pistol report can be heard at a great distance. In ten minutes my plan was perfected. The telephone book listed the name of the only person capable of transmitting the message; he lived in a suburb of Fenton, less than a half hour's train ride away.

I am a cowardly man. I say it now, now that I have carried to its end a plan whose perilous nature no one can deny. I know its execution was terrible. I didn't do it for Germany, no. I care nothing for a barbarous country which imposed upon me the abjection of being a spy. Besides, I know of a man from England—a modest man—who for me is no less great than Goethe. I talked with him for scarcely an hour, but during that hour he was Goethe ... I did it because I sensed that the Chief somehow feared people of my race—for the innumerable ancestors who merge within me. I wanted to prove to him that a yellow man could save his armies. Besides, I had to flee from Captain Madden. His hands and his voice could call at my door at any moment. I dressed silently, bade farewell to myself in the mirror, went downstairs, scrutinized the peaceful street and went out. The station was not far from my home, but I judged it wise to take a cab. I argued that in this way I ran less risk of being recognized; the fact is that in the deserted street I felt myself visible and vulnerable, infinitely so. I remember that I told the cab driver to stop a short distance before the main entrance. I got out with voluntary, almost painful slowness; I was going to the village of Ashgrove but I bought a ticket for a more distant station. The train left within a very few minutes, at eight-fifty. I hurried; the next one would leave at nine-thirty. There was hardly a soul on the platform. I went through the coaches; I remember a few farmers, a woman dressed in mourning, a young boy who was reading with fervor the *Annals* of Tacitus, a wounded and happy soldier. The coaches jerked forward at last. A man whom I recognized ran in vain to the end of the platform. It was Captain Richard Madden. Shattered, trembling, I shrank into the far corner of the seat, away from the dreaded window.

From this broken state I passed into an almost abject felicity. I told myself that the duel had already begun and that I had won the first encounter by frustrating, even if for forty minutes, even if by a stroke of fate, the attack of my adversary. I argued that this slightest of victories foreshadowed a total victory. I argued (no less fallaciously) that my cowardly felicity proved that I was a man capable of carrying out the adventure successfully. From this weakness I took strength that did not abandon me. I foresee that man will resign himself each day to more atrocious undertakings; soon there will be no one but warriors and brigands; I give them this counsel: *The author of an atrocious undertaking ought to imagine that he has already accomplished it, ought to impose upon himself a future as irrevocable as the past.* Thus I proceeded as my eyes of a man already dead registered the elapsing of the day, which was perhaps the last, and the diffusion of the night. The train ran gently along, amid ash trees. It stopped, almost in the middle of the fields. No one announced the name of the station. "Ashgrove?" I asked a few lads on the platform. "Ashgrove," they replied. I got off.

A lamp enlightened the platform but the faces of the boys were in shadow. One questioned me, "Are you going to Dr. Stephen Albert's house?" Without waiting for my answer, another said, "The house is a long way from here, but you won't get lost if you take this road to the left and at every crossroads turn again to your left." I tossed them a coin (my last), descended a few stone steps and started down the solitary road. It went downhill slowly. It was of elemental earth; overhead the branches were tangled; the low, full moon seemed to accompany me.

For an instant, I thought that Richard Madden in some way had penetrated my desperate plan. Very quickly, I understood that that was impossible. The instructions to turn always to the left reminded me that such was the common procedure for discovering the central point of certain labyrinths. I have some understanding of labyrinths: not for nothing am I the great grandson of that Ts'ui Pên who was governor of Yunnan and who renounced worldly power in order to write a novel that might be even more populous than the *Hung Lu Meng* and to construct a labyrinth in which all men would become lost. Thirteen years he dedicated to the heterogeneous tasks, but the hand of a stranger murdered him—and his novel was incoherent and no one found the labyrinth. Beneath English trees I meditated on that lost maze: I imagined it inviolate and perfect at the secret crest of a mountain; I imagined it erased by rice fields or beneath the water; I imagined it infinite, no longer composed of octagonal kiosks and returning paths, but of rivers and provinces and kingdoms . . . I thought of a labyrinth of labyrinths, of one sinuous spreading labyrinth that would encompass the past and the future and in some way involve the stars. Absorbed in these illusory images, I forgot my destiny of one pursued. I felt myself to be, for an unknown period of time, an abstract perceiver of the world. The vague, living countryside, the moon, the remains of the day worked on me, as well as the slope of the road which eliminated any possibility of weariness. The afternoon was intimate, infinite. The road descended and forked among the now confused meadows. A high-pitched, almost syllabic music approached and receded in the shifting of the wind, dimmed by leaves and distance. I thought that a man can be an enemy of other men, of the moments of other men, but not of a country: not of fireflies, words, gardens, streams of water, sunset. Thus I arrived before a

tall, rusty gate. Between the iron bars I made out a poplar grove and a pavilion. I understood suddenly two things, the first trivial, the second almost unbelievable: the music came from the pavilion, and the music was Chinese. For precisely that reason I had openly accepted it without paying it any heed. I do not remember whether there was a bell or whether I knocked with my hand. The sparkling of the music continued.

From the rear of the house within a lantern approached: a lantern that the trees sometimes striped and sometimes eclipsed, a paper lantern that had the form of a drum and the color of the moon. A tall man bore it. I didn't see his face for the light blinded me. He opened the door and said slowly, in my own language: "I see that the pious Hsi P'êng persists in correcting my solitude. You no doubt wish to see the garden?"

I recognized the name of one of our consuls and I replied, disconcerted, "The garden?"

"The garden of forking paths."

Something stirred in my memory and I uttered with incomprehensible certainty, "The garden of my ancestor Ts'ui Pên."

"Your ancestor? Your illustrious ancestor? Come in."

The damp path zigzagged like those of my childhood. We came to a library of Eastern and Western books. I recognized bound in yellow silk several volumes of the Lost Encyclopedia, edited by the Third Emperor of the Luminous Dynasty but never printed. The record on the phonograph revolved next to a bronze phoenix. I also recall a *famille rose* vase and another, many centuries older, of that shade of blue which our craftsmen copied from the potters of Persia . . .

Stephen Albert observed me with a smile. He was, as I have said, very tall, sharp-featured, with gray eyes and a gray beard. He told me that he had been a missionary in Tientsin "before aspiring to become a Sinologist."

We sat down—I on a long, low divan, he with his back to the window and a tall circular clock. I calculated that my pursuer, Richard Madden, could not arrive for at least an hour. My irrevocable determination could wait.

"An astounding fate, that of Ts'ui Pên," Stephen Albert said. "Governor of his native province, learned in astronomy, in astrology and in the tireless interpretation of the canonical books, chess player, famous poet and calligrapher—he abandoned all this in order to compose a book and a maze. He renounced the pleasures of both tyranny and justice, of his populous couch, of his banquets and even of erudition—all to close himself up for thirteen years in the Pavilion of the Limpid Solitude. When he died, his heirs found nothing save chaotic manuscripts. His family, as you may be aware, wished to condemn them to the fire; but his executor—a Taoist or Buddhist monk—insisted on their publication."

"We descendants of Ts'ui Pên," I replied, "continue to curse that monk. Their publication was senseless. The book is an indeterminate heap of contradictory drafts. I examined it once: in the third chapter the hero dies, in the fourth he is alive. As for the other undertaking of Ts'ui Pên, his labyrinth . . ."

"Here is Ts'ui Pên's labyrinth," he said, indicating a tall lacquered desk.

"An ivory labyrinth!" I exclaimed. "A minimum labyrinth."

"A labyrinth of symbols," he corrected. "An invisible labyrinth of time. To me, a barbarous Englishman, has been entrusted the revelation of this diaphanous mystery. After more than a hundred years, the details are irretrievable; but it is not hard to conjecture what happened. Ts'ui Pên must have said once: I am withdrawing to write a book. And another time: I am withdrawing to construct a labyrinth. Every one imagined two works; to no one did it occur that the book and the maze were one and the same thing. The Pavilion of the Limpid Solitude stood in the center of a garden that was perhaps intricate; that circumstance could have suggested to the heirs a physical labyrinth. Hs'ui Pên died; no one in the vast territories that were his came upon the labyrinth; the confusion of the novel suggested to me that it was the maze. Two circumstances gave me the correct solution of the problem. One: the curious legend that Ts'ui Pên had planned to create a labyrinth which would be strictly infinite. The other: a fragment of a letter I discovered."

Albert rose. He turned his back on me for a moment; he opened a drawer of the black and gold desk. He faced me and in his hands he held a sheet of paper that had once been crimson, but was now pink and tenuous and cross-sectioned. The fame of Ts'ui Pên as a calligrapher had been justly won. I read, uncomprehendingly and with fervor, these words written with a minute brush by a man of my blood: *I leave to the various futures (not to all) my garden of forking paths.* Wordlessly, I returned the sheet. Albert continued:

"Before unearthing this letter, I had questioned myself about the ways in which a book can be infinite. I could think of nothing other than a cyclic volume, a circular one. A book whose last page was identical with the first, a book which had the possibility of continuing indefinitely. I remembered too that night which is at the middle of the Thousand and One Nights when Scheherazade (through a magical oversight of the copyist) begins to relate word for word the story of the Thousand and One Nights, establishing the risk of coming once again to the night when she must repeat it, and thus on to infinity. I imagined as well a Platonic, hereditary work, transmitted from father to son, in which each new individual adds a chapter or corrects with pious care the pages of his elders. These conjectures diverted me; but none seemed to correspond, not even remotely, to the contradictory chapters of Ts'ui Pên. In the midst of this perplexity, I received from Oxford the manuscript you have examined. I lingered, naturally, on the sentence: *I leave to the various futures (not to all) my garden of forking paths.* Almost instantly, I understood: 'the garden of forking paths' was the chaotic novel; the phrase 'the various futures (not to all)' suggested to me the forking in time, not in space. A broad rereading of the work confirmed the theory. In all fictional works, each time a man is confronted with several alternatives, he chooses one and eliminates the others; in the fiction of Ts'ui Pên, he chooses—simultaneously—all of them. *He creates*, in this way, diverse futures, diverse times which themselves also proliferate and fork. Here, then, is the explanation of the novel's contradictions. Fang, let us say, has a secret; a stranger calls at his door; Fang resolves to kill him. Naturally, there are several possible outcomes: Fang can kill the intruder, the intruder can kill Fang, they both can escape, they both can die, and so forth. In the work of Ts'ui Pên, all possible outcomes occur; each one is the point of departure for other forkings. Sometimes, the paths of this labyrinth converge: for example, you arrive at this house, but in one of the possible pasts you are my enemy, in another, my friend. If you will resign yourself to my incurable pronunciation, we shall read a few pages."

His face, within the vivid circle of the lamplight, was unquestionably that of an old man, but with something unalterable about it, even immortal. He read with slow precision two versions of the same epic chapter. In the first, an army marches to a battle across a lonely mountain; the horror of the rocks and shadows makes the men undervalue their lives and they gain an easy victory. In the second, the same army traverses a palace where a great festival is taking place; the resplendent battle seems to them a continuation of the celebration and they win the victory. I listened with proper veneration to these ancient narratives, perhaps less admirable in themselves than the fact that they had been created by my blood and were being restored to me by a man of a remote empire, in the course of a desperate adventure, on a Western isle. I remember the last words, repeated in each version like a secret commandment: *Thus fought the heroes, tranquil their admirable hearts, violent their swords, resigned to kill and to die.*

From that moment on, I felt about me and within my dark body an invisible, intangible swarming. Not the swarming of the divergent, parallel and finally coalescent armies, but a more inaccessible, more intimate agitation that they in some

manner prefigured. Stephen Albert continued:

"I don't believe that your illustrious ancestor played idly with these variations. I don't consider it credible that he would sacrifice thirteen years to the infinite execution of a rhetorical experiment. In your country, the novel is a subsidiary form of literature; in Ts'ui Pên's time it was a despicable form. Ts'ui Pên was a brilliant novelist, but he was also a man of letters who doubtless did not consider himself a mere novelist. The testimony of his contemporaries proclaims—and his life fully confirms—his metaphysical and mystical interests. Philosophic controversy usurps a good part of the novel. I know that of all problems, none disturbed him so greatly nor worked upon him so much as the abysmal problem of time. Now then, the latter is the only problem that does not figure in the pages of the *Garden*. He does not even use the word that signifies *time*. How do you explain this voluntary omission?"

I proposed several solutions—all unsatisfactory. We discussed them. Finally, Stephen Albert said to me:

"In a riddle whose answer is chess, what is the only prohibited word?"

I thought a moment and replied, "The word *chess*."

"Precisely," said Albert. "*The Garden of Forking Paths* is an enormous riddle, or parable, whose theme is time; this recondite cause prohibits its mention. To omit a word always, to resort to inept metaphors and obvious periphrases, is perhaps the most emphatic way of stressing it. That is the tortuous method preferred, in each of the meanderings of his indefatigable novel, by the oblique Ts'ui Pên. I have compared hundreds of manuscripts, I have corrected the errors that the negligence of the copyists has introduced, I have guessed the plan of this chaos, I have re-established—I believe I have re-established—the primordial organization, I have translated the entire work: it is clear to me that not once does he employ the word 'time.' The explanation is obvious: *The Garden of Forking Paths* is an incomplete, but not false, image of the universe as Ts'ui Pên conceived it. In contrast to Newton and Schopenhauer, your ancestor did not believe in a uniform, absolute time. He believed in an infinite series of times, in a growing, dizzying net of divergent, convergent and parallel times. This network of times which approached one another, forked, broke off, or were unaware of one another for centuries, embraces *all* possibilities of time. We do not exist in the majority of these times; in some you exist, and not I; in others I, and not you; in others, both of us. In the present one, which a favorable fate has granted me, you have arrived at my house; in another, while crossing the garden, you found me dead; in still another, I utter these same words, but I am a mistake, a ghost."

"In every one," I pronounced, not without a tremble to my voice, "I am grateful to you and revere you for your re-creation of the garden of Ts'ui Pên."

"Not in all," he murmured with a smile. "Time forks perpetually toward innumerable futures. In one of them I am your enemy."

Once again I felt the swarming sensation of which I have spoken. It seemed to me that the humid garden that surrounded the house was infinitely saturated with invisible persons. Those persons were Albert and I, secret, busy and multiform in other dimensions of time. I raised my eyes and the tenuous nightmare dissolved. In the yellow and black garden there was only one man; but this man was as strong as a statue . . . this man was approaching along the path and he was Captain Richard Madden.

"The future already exists," I replied, "but I am your friend. Could I see the letter again?"

Albert rose. Standing tall, he opened the drawer of the tall desk; for the moment his back was to me. I had readied the revolver. I fired with extreme caution. Albert fell uncomplainingly, immediately. I swear his death was instantaneous—a lightning stroke.

The rest is unreal, insignificant. Madden broke in, arrested me. I have been condemned to the gallows. I have won out abominably; I have communicated to Berlin the secret name of the city they must attack. They bombed it yesterday; I read it in the same papers that offered to England the mystery of the learned Sinologist Stephen Albert who was murdered by a stranger, one Yu Tsun. The Chief had deciphered this mystery. He knew my problem was to indicate (through the uproar of the war) the city called Albert, and that I had found no other means to do so than to kill a man of that name. He does not know (no one can know) my innumerable contrition and weariness.

[1941]

TRANSLATED BY
DONALD A. YATES

QUESTIONS FOR STUDY

1. *Why does Borges begin his story with the reference to Liddell Hart's military history? Is it functionally related to the rest of the story? What is the purpose of the sudden shift to Dr. Yu Tsun's statement, the first two pages of which are missing? And why does Borges choose to narrate his story backwards from a point in time immediately prior to Dr. Yu Tsun's execution?*

2. *What is Ts'ui Pên's* The Garden of Forking Paths?

3. *What comments does the story make about time, human decisions, and the nature of reality?*

4. *Is the rather conventional spy plot related to the story's theme?*

5. *Why does Dr. Yu Tsun speak at the end of the story of his "innumerable contrition and weariness"? Is this feeling related to his discovery of the meaning of* The Garden of Forking Paths, *to his assassination of Albert, to both, or to some other cause?*

ELIZABETH BOWEN

The Demon Lover

TOWARDS the end of her day in London Mrs. Drover went round to her shut-up house to look for several things she wanted to take away. Some belonged to herself, some to her family, who were by now used to their country life. It was late August; it had been a steamy, showery day; at the moment the trees down the pavement glittered in an escape of humid yellow afternoon sun. Against the next batch of clouds, already piling up ink-dark, broken chimneys and parapets stood out. In her once familiar street, as in any unused channel, an unfamiliar queerness had silted up; a cat wove itself in and out of railings, but no human eye watched Mrs. Drover's return. Shifting some parcels under her arm, she slowly forced round her latchkey in an unwilling lock, then gave the door, which had warped, a push with her knee. Dead air came out to meet her as she went in.

The staircase window having been boarded up, no light came down into the hall. But one door, she could just see, stood ajar, so she went quickly through into the room and unshuttered the big window in there. Now the prosaic woman, looking about her, was more perplexed than she knew by everything that she saw, by traces of her long former habit of life—the yellow smoke-stain up the white marble mantelpiece, the ring left by a vase on the top of the escritoire; the bruise in the wallpaper where, on the door being thrown open widely, the china handle had always hit the wall. The piano, having gone away to be stored, had left what looked like claw-marks on its part of the parquet. Though not much dust had seeped in, each object wore a film of another kind; and, the only ventilation being the chimney, the whole drawing-room smelled of the cold hearth. Mrs. Drover put down her parcels on the escritoire and left the room to proceed upstairs; the things she wanted were in a bedroom chest.

She had been anxious to see how the house was—the part-time caretaker she shared with some neighbours was away this week on his holiday, known to be not yet back. At the best of times he did not look in often, and she was never sure that she trusted him. There were some cracks in the structure, left by the last bombing, on which she was anxious to keep an eye. Not that one could do anything—

A shaft of refracted daylight now lay across the hall. She stopped dead and stared at the hall table—on this lay a letter addressed to her.

She thought first—then the caretaker *must* be back. All the same, who, seeing the house shuttered, would have dropped a letter in at the box? It was not a circular, it was not a bill. And the post office redirected, to the address in the country, everything for her that came through the post. The caretaker (even if he *were* back) did not know she was due in London today—her call here had been planned to be a surprise—so his negligence in the manner of this letter, leaving it to wait in the dusk and the dust, annoyed her. Annoyed, she picked up the letter, which bore no stamp. But it cannot be important, or they would know . . . She took the letter rapidly upstairs with her, without a stop to look at the writing till she reached what had been her bedroom, where she let in light. The room looked over the garden and other gardens: the sun had gone in; as the clouds sharpened and lowered, the trees and rank lawns seemed already to smoke with dark. Her reluctance to look again at the letter came from the fact that she felt intruded upon—and by someone contemptuous of her ways. However, in the tenseness preceding the fall of rain she read it: it was a few lines.

Dear Kathleen: You will not have forgotten that today is our anniversary, and the day we said. The years have gone by at once slowly and fast. In view of the fact that nothing has changed, I shall rely upon you to keep your promise. I was sorry to see you leave London, but was satisfied that you would be back in time. You may expect me, therefore, at the hour arranged. Until then . . . K.

Mrs. Dover looked for the date: it was today's. She dropped the letter on to the bed-springs, then picked it up to see the writing again—her lips, beneath the remains of lipstick, beginning to go white. She felt so much the change in her own face that she went to the mirror, polished a clear patch in it and looked at once urgently and stealthily in. She was confronted by a woman of forty-four, with eyes starting out under a hat-brim that had been rather carelessly pulled down. She had not put on any more powder since she left the shop where she ate her solitary tea. The pearls her husband had given her on their marriage hung loose round her now rather thinner throat, slipping in the V of the pink wool jumper her sister knitted last autumn as they sat round the fire. Mrs. Drover's most normal expression was one of controlled worry, but of assent. Since the birth of the third of her little boys, attended by a quite serious illness, she had had an intermittent muscular flicker to the left of her mouth, but in spite of this she could always sustain a manner that was at once energetic and calm.

Turning from her own face as precipitately as she had gone to meet it, she went to the chest where the things were, unlocked it, threw up the lid and knelt to search. But as rain began to come crashing down she could not keep from looking over her shoulder at the stripped bed on which the letter lay. Behind the blanket of rain the clock of the church that still stood struck six—with rapidly heightening apprehension she counted each of the slow strokes. 'The hour arranged . . . My God,' she said, *'what hour? How should I . . . ? After twenty-five years. . . .'*

The young girl talking to the soldier in the garden had not ever completely seen his face. It was dark; they were saying goodbye under a tree. Now and then —for it felt, from not seeing him at this intense moment, as though she had never seen him at all—she verified his presence for these few moments longer by putting out a hand, which he each time pressed, without very much kindness, and painfully, on to one of the breast buttons of his uniform. That cut of the button on the palm of her hand was, principally what she was to carry away. This was so near the end of a leave from France that she could only wish him already gone. It was August 1916. Being not kissed, being drawn away from and looked at intimidated Kathleen till she imagined spectral glitters in the place of his eyes. Turning away and looking back up the lawn she saw, through branches of trees, the drawing-room window alight: she caught a breath for the moment when she could go running back there into the safe arms of her mother and sister, and cry: 'What shall I do, what shall I do? He has gone.'

Hearing her catch her breath, her fiancé said, without feeling: 'Cold?'

'You're going away such a long way.'

'Not so far as you think.'

'I don't understand?'

'You don't have to,' he said. 'You will. You know what we said.'

'But that was—suppose you—I mean, suppose.'

'I shall be with you,' he said, 'sooner or later. You won't forget that. You need do nothing but wait.'

Only a little more than a minute later she was free to run up the silent lawn. Looking in through the window at her mother and sister, who did not for the moment perceive her, she already felt that unnatural promise drive down between her and the rest of all human kind. No other way of having given herself could have made her feel so apart, lost and foresworn. She could not have plighted a more sinister troth.

Kathleen behaved well when, some months later, her fiancé was reported missing, presumed killed. Her family not only supported her but were able to praise her courage without stint because they could not regret, as a husband for her, the man they knew almost nothing about. They hoped she would, in a year or two, console herself—and had it been only a question of consolation things might have gone much straighter ahead. But her trouble, behind just a little grief, was a complete dislocation from everything. She did not reject other lovers, for these failed to appear: for years she failed to attract men—and with the approach of her 'thirties she became natural enough to share her family's anxiousness on this score. She began to put herself out, to wonder; and at thirty-two she was very greatly relieved to find herself being courted by Willian Drover. She married him, and the two of them settled down in this quiet, arboreal part of Kensington: in this house the years piled up, her children were born and they all lived till they were driven out by the bombs of the next war. Her movements as Mrs. Drover were circumscribed, and she dismissed any idea that they were still watched.

As things were—dead or living the letter-writer sent her only a threat. Unable, for some minutes, to go on kneeling with her back exposed to the empty room, Mrs. Drover rose from the chest to sit on an upright chair whose back was firmly against the wall. The desuetude of her former bedroom, her married London home's whole air of being a cracked cup from which memory, with its reassuring power, had either evaporated or leaked away, made a crisis—and at just this crisis the letter-writer had, knowledgeably, struck. The hollowness of the house this evening cancelled years on years of voices, habits and steps. Through the shut windows she only heard rain fall on the roofs around. To rally herself, she said she was in a mood—and, for two

or three seconds shutting her eyes, told herself that she had imagined the letter. But she opened them—there it lay on the bed.

On the supernatural side of the letter's entrance she was not permitting her mind to dwell. Who, in London, knew she meant to call at the house today? Evidently, however, this had been known. The caretaker, *had* he come back, had had no cause to expect her: he would have taken the letter in his pocket, to forward it, at his own time, through the post. There was no other sign that the caretaker had been in—but, if not? Letters dropped in at doors of deserted houses do not fly or walk to tables in halls. They do not sit on the dust of empty tables with the air of certainty that they will be found. There is needed some human hand—but nobody but the caretaker had a key. Under circumstances she did not care to consider, a house can be entered without a key. It was possible that she was not alone now. She might be being waited for, downstairs. Waited for —until when? Until 'the hour arranged'. At least that was not six o'clock: six has struck.

She rose from the chair and went over and locked the door.

The thing was, to get out. To fly? No, not that: she had to catch her train. As a woman whose utter dependability was the keystone of her family life she was not willing to return to the country, to her husband, her little boys and her sister, without the objects she had come up to fetch. Resuming work at the chest she set about making up a number of parcels in a rapid, fumbling-decisive way. These, with her shopping parcels, would be too much to carry; these meant a taxi—at the thought of the taxi her heart went up and her normal breathing resumed. I will ring up the taxi now; the taxi cannot come too soon: I shall hear the taxi out there running its engine, till I walk calmly down to it through the hall. I'll ring up— But no: the telephone is cut off . . . She tugged at a knot she had tied wrong.

The idea of flight . . . He was never kind to me, not really. I don't remember him kind at all. Mother said he never considered me. He was set on me, that was what it was—not love. Not love, not meaning a person well. What did he do, to make me promise like that? I can't remember—But she found that she could.

She remembered with such dreadful acuteness that the twenty-five years since then dissolved like smoke and she instinctively looked for the weal left by the button on the palm of her hand. She remembered not only all that he said and did but the complete suspension of *her* existence during that August week. I was not myself—they all told me so at the time. She remembered—but with one white burning blank as where acid has dropped on a photograph: *under no conditions* could she remember his face.

So, wherever he may be waiting, I shall not know him. You have no time to run from a face you do not expect.

The thing was to get to the taxi before any clock struck what could be the hour. She would slip down the street and round the side of the square to where the square gave on the main road. She would return in the taxi, safe, to her own door, and bring the solid driver into the house with her to pick up the parcels from room to room. The idea of the taxi driver made her decisive, bold: she unlocked her door, went to the top of the staircase and listened down.

She heard nothing—but while she was hearing nothing the *passé* air of the staircase was disturbed by a draught that travelled up to her face. It emanated from the basement: down there a door or window was being opened by someone who chose this moment to leave the house.

The rain had stopped; the pavements steamily shone as Mrs. Drover let herself out by inches from her own front door into the empty street. The unoccupied houses opposite continued to meet her look with their damaged stare. Making towards the thoroughfare and the taxi,

she tried not to keep looking behind. Indeed, the silence was so intense—one of those creeks of London silence exaggerated this summer by the damage of war—that no tread could have gained on hers unheard. Where her street debouched on the square where people went on living, she grew conscious of, and checked, her unnatural pace. Across the open end of the square two buses impassively passed each other: women, a perambulator, cyclists, a man wheeling a barrow signalized, once again, the ordinary flow of life. At the square's most populous corner should be—and was—the short taxi rank. This evening, only one taxi—but this, although it presented its blank rump, appeared already to be alertly waiting for her. Indeed, without looking round the driver started his engine as she panted up from behind and put her hand on the door. As she did so, the clock struck seven. The taxi faced the main road: to make the trip back to her house it would have to turn—she had settled back on the seat and the taxi *had* turned before she, surprised by its knowing movement, recollected that she had not 'said where'. She leaned forward to scratch at the glass panel that divided the driver's head from her own.

The driver braked to what was almost a stop, turned round and slid the glass panel back: the jolt of this flung Mrs. Drover forward till her face was almost into the glass. Through the aperture driver and passenger, not six inches between them, remained for an eternity eye to eye. Mrs. Drover's mouth hung open for some seconds before she could issue her first scream. After that she continued to scream freely and to beat with her gloved hands on the glass all round as the taxi, accelerating without mercy, made off with her into the hinterland of deserted streets.

[1945]

QUESTIONS FOR STUDY

1. *Is "The Demon Lover" an authentic ghost story, or is it, as critic Douglas Hughes has argued, "a masterful dramatization of acute*

psychological delusion"? What evidence would you offer in support of your position?

2. *In what ways is the story's wartime setting appropriate?*

3. *What essential information about Mrs. Drover does the reader gradually come to learn?*

4. *What are some of the possible implications of the story's conclusion?*

KAY BOYLE

Astronomer's Wife

THERE is an evil moment on awakening when all things seem to pause. But for women, they only falter and may be set in action by a single move: a lifted hand and the pendulum will swing, or the voice raised and through every room the pulse takes up its beating. The astronomer's wife felt the interval gaping and at once filled it to the brim. She fetched up her gentle voice and sent it warily down the stairs for coffee, swung her feet out upon the oval mat, and hailed the morning with her bare arms' quivering flesh drawn taut in rhythmic exercise: left, left, left my wife and fourteen children, right, right, right in the middle of the dusty road.

The day would proceed from this, beat by beat, without reflection, like every other day. The astronomer was still asleep, or feigning it, and she, once out of bed, had come into her own possession. Although scarcely ever out of sight of the impenetrable silence of his brow, she would be absent from him all the day in being clean, busy, kind. He was a man of other things, a dreamer. At times he lay still for hours, at others he sat upon the roof behind his telescope, or wandered down the pathway to the road and out across the mountains. This day, like any other, would go on from the removal of the spot left there from dinner on the astronomer's vest to the severe thrashing of the mayonnaise for lunch. That man might be each time the new arching wave, and woman the undertow that sucked him back, were things she had been told by his silence were so.

In spite of the earliness of the hour, the girl had heard her mistress's voice and was coming up the stairs. At the threshold of the bedroom she paused, and said: "Madame, the plumber is here."

The astronomer's wife put on her white and scarlet smock very quickly and buttoned it at the neck. Then she stepped carefully around the motionless spread of water in the hall.

"Tell him to come right up," she said. She laid her hands on the bannisters and stood looking down the wooden stairway. "Ah, I am Mrs. Ames," she said softly as she saw him mounting. "I am Mrs. Ames," she said softly, softly down the flight of stairs. "I am Mrs. Ames," spoken soft as a willow weeping. "The professor is still sleeping. Just step this way."

The plumber himself looked up and saw Mrs. Ames with her voice hushed, speaking to him. She was a youngish woman, but this she had forgotten. The mystery and silence of her husband's mind lay like a chiding finger on her lips. Her eyes were gray, for the light had been extinguished in them. The strange dim halo of her yellow hair was still uncombed and sideways on her head.

For all of his heavy boots, the plumber quieted the sound of his feet, and together they went down the hall, picking their way around the still lake of water that spread as far as the landing and lay docile there. The plumber was a tough, hardy man; but he took off his hat when he spoke to her and looked her fully, almost insolently in the eye.

"Does it come from the wash-basin," he said, "or from the other . . . ?"

"Oh, from the other," said Mrs. Ames without hesitation.

In this place the villas were scattered out few and primitive, and although beauty lay without there was no reflection of her face within. Here all was awkward and unfit; a sense of wrestling with uncouth forces gave everything an austere countenance. Even the plumber, dealing as does a woman with matters under hand, was grave and stately. The mountains round about seemed to have cast them into the shadow of great dignity.

Mrs. Ames began speaking of their arrival that summer in the little villa, mourning each event as it followed on the other.

"Then, just before going to bed last night," she said, "I noticed something was unusual."

The plumber cast down a folded square of sackcloth on the brimming floor and laid his leather apron on it. Then he stepped boldly onto the heart of the island it shaped and looked long into the overflowing bowl.

"The water should be stopped from the meter in the garden," he said at last.

"Oh, I did that," said Mrs. Ames, "the very first thing last night. I turned it off at once, in my nightgown, as soon as I saw what was happening. But all this had already run in."

The plumber looked for a moment at her red kid slippers. She was standing just at the edge of the clear, pure-seeming tide.

"It's no doubt the soil lines," he said severely. "It may be that something has stopped them, but my opinion is that the water seals aren't working. That's the trouble often enough in such cases. If you had a valve you wouldn't be caught like this."

Mrs. Ames did not know how to meet this rebuke. She stood, swaying a little, looking into the plumber's blue relentless eye.

"I'm sorry—I'm sorry that my husband," she said, "is still—resting and cannot go into this with you. I'm sure it must be very interesting. . . ."

"You'll probably have to have the traps sealed," said the plumber grimly, and at the sound of this Mrs. Ames' hand flew in dismay to the side of her face. The plumber made no move, but the set of his mouth as he looked at her seemed to soften. "Anyway, I'll have a look from the garden end," he said.

"Oh, do," said the astronomer's wife in relief. Here was a man who spoke of action and object as simply as women did! But however hushed her voice had been, it carried clearly to Professor Ames who lay, dreaming and solitary, upon his bed. He heard their footsteps come down the hall, pause, and skip across the pool of overflow.

"Katherine!" said the astronomer in a ringing tone. "There's a problem worthy of your mettle!"

Mrs. Ames did not turn her head, but led the plumber swiftly down the stairs. When the sun in the garden struck her face, he saw there was a wave of color in it, but this may have been anything but shame.

"You see how it is," said the plumber, as if leading her mind away. "The drains run from these houses right down the hill, big enough for a man to stand upright in them, and clean as a whistle too." There they stood in the garden with the vegetation flowering in disorder all about. The plumber looked at the astronomer's wife. "They come out at the torrent on the other side of the forest beyond there," he said.

But the words the astronomer had spoken still sounded in her in despair. The mind of man, she knew, made steep and sprightly flights, pursued illusion, took foothold in the nameless things that cannot pass between the thumb and finger. But whenever the astronomer gave voice to the thoughts that soared within him, she returned in gratitude to the long expanses of his silence. Desert-like they stretched behind and before the articulation of his scorn.

Life, life is an open sea, she sought to explain it in sorrow, and to survive women cling to the floating débris on the tide. But the plumber had suddenly fallen upon his knees in the grass and had crooked his fingers through the ring of the drains' trap-door. When she looked down she saw that he was looking up into her face, and she saw too that his hair was as light as gold.

"Perhaps Mr. Ames," he said rather bitterly, "would like to come down with me and have a look around?"

"Down?" said Mrs. Ames in wonder.

"Into the drains," said the plumber brutally. "They're a study for a man who likes to know what's what."

"Oh, Mr. Ames," said Mrs. Ames in confusion. "He's still—still in bed, you see."

The plumber lifted his strong, weathered face and looked curiously at her. Surely it seemed to him strange for a man to linger in bed, with the sun pouring yellow as wine all over the place. The astronomer's wife saw his lean cheeks, his high, rugged bones, and the deep seams in his brow. His flesh was as firm and clean as wood, stained richly tan with the climate's rigor. His fingers were blunt, but comprehensible to her, gripped in the ring and holding the iron door wide. The backs of his hands were bound round and round with ripe blue veins of blood.

"At any rate," said the astronomer's wife, and the thought of it moved her lips to smile a little, "Mr. Ames would never go down there alive. He likes going up," she said. And she, in her turn, pointed, but impudently, towards the heavens. "On the roof. Or on the mountains. He's been up on the tops of them many times."

"It's matter of habit," said the plumber, and suddenly he went down the trap. Mrs. Ames saw a bright little piece of his hair still shining, like a star, long after the rest of him had gone. Out of the depths, his voice, hollow and dark with foreboding, returned to her. "I think something has stopped the elbow," was what he said.

This was speech that touched her flesh and bone and made her wonder. When her husband spoke of height, having no sense of it, she could not picture it nor hear. Depth or magic passed her by unless a name were given. But madness in a daily shape, as elbow stopped, she saw clearly and well. She sat down on the grasses, bewildered that it should be a man who had spoken to her so.

She saw the weeds springing up, and she did not move to tear them up from life. She sat powerless, her senses veiled, with no action taking shape beneath her hands. In this way some men sat for hours on end, she knew, tracking a single thought back to its origin. The mind of man could balance and divide, weed out, destroy. She sat on the full, burdened grasses, seeking to think, and dimly waiting for the plumber to return.

Whereas her husband had always gone up, as the dead go, she knew now that there were others who went down, like the corporeal being of the dead. That men were then divided into two bodies now seemed clear to Mrs. Ames. This knowledge stunned her with its simplicity and took the uneasy motion from her limbs. She could not stir, but sat facing the mountains' rocky flanks, and harking in silence to lucidity. Her husband was the mind, this other man the meat, of all mankind.

After a little, the plumber emerged from the earth: first the light top of his ʻhead, then the burnt brow, and then the blue eyes fringed with whitest lash. He braced his thick hands flat on the pavings of the garden-path and swung himself completely from the pit.

"It's the soil lines," he said pleasantly. "The gases," he said as he looked down upon her lifted face, "are backing up the drains."

"What in the world are we going to do?" said the astronomer's wife softly. There was a young and strange delight in putting questions to which true answers would be given. Everything the astronomer had ever said to her was a continuous query to which there could be no response.

"Ah, come, now," said the plumber, looking down and smiling. "There's a remedy for every ill, you know. Sometimes it may be that," he said as if speaking to a child, "or sometimes the other thing. But there's always a help for everything a-miss."

Things come out of herbs and make you young again, he might have been saying to her; or the first good rain will quench any drought; or time of itself will put a broken bone together.

"I'm going to follow the ground pipe out right to the torrent," the plumber was saying. "The trouble's between here and there and I'll find it on the way. There's nothing at all that can't be done over for the caring," he was saying, and his eyes were fastened on her face in insolence, or gentleness, or love.

The astronomer's wife stood up, fixed a pin in her hair, and turned around towards the kitchen. Even while she was calling the servant's name, the plumber began speaking again.

"I once had a cow that lost her cud," the plumber was saying. The girl came out on the kitchen-step and Mrs. Ames stood smiling at her in the sun.

"The trouble is very serious, very serious," she said across the garden. "When Mr. Ames gets up, please tell him I've gone down."

She pointed briefly to the open door in the pathway, and the plumber hoisted his kit on his arm and put out his hand to help her down.

"But I made her another in no time," he was saying, "out of flowers and things and what-not."

"Oh," said the astronomer's wife in wonder as she stepped into the heart of the earth. She took his arm, knowing that what he said was true.

[1936]

QUESTIONS FOR STUDY

1. *In what ways do the opening paragraphs prepare the reader for the story that follows? What insights do they provide into the character and personality of Mrs. Ames?*

2. *Define the relationship that exists between Mr. and Mrs. Ames. What alternative to that relationship is offered by the plumber? How does he differ from Mr. Ames?*

3. *What is the significance of the story's final sentence? Does it imply that Mrs. Ames has reached and passed through some turning point in her emotional life?*

4. *What symbolic details does Miss Boyle employ to reinforce the story's characterization, conflict, and theme?*

5. *What is the appropriateness of the comic tones that seem to color much of the story, particularly its ending?*

RAY BRADBURY

August 2002: Night Meeting

BEFORE going on up into the blue hills, Tomás Gomez stopped for gasoline at the lonely station.

"Kind of alone out here, aren't you, Pop?" said Tomás.

The old man wiped off the windshield of the small truck. "Not bad."

"How do you like Mars, Pop?"

"Fine. Always something new. I made up my mind when I came here last year I wouldn't expect nothing, nor ask nothing, nor be surprised at nothing. We've got to forget Earth and how things were. We've got to look at what we're in here, and how *different* it is. I get a hell of a lot of fun out of just the weather here. It's *Martian* weather. Hot as hell daytimes, cold as hell nights. I get a big kick out of the different flowers and different rain. I came to Mars to retire and I wanted to retire in a place where everything is different. An old man needs to have things different. Young people don't want to talk to him, other old people bore hell out of him. So I thought the best thing for me is a place so different that all you got to do is open your eyes and you're entertained. I got this gas station. If business picks up too much, I'll move on back to some other old highway that's not so busy, where I can earn just enough to live on and still have time to feel the *different* things here."

"You got the right idea, Pop," said Tomás, his brown hands idly on the wheel. He was feeling good. He had been working in one of the new colonies for ten days straight and now he had two days off and was on his way to a party.

"I'm not surprised at anything any more," said the old man. "I'm just looking. I'm just experiencing. If you can't take Mars for what she is, you might as well go back to Earth. Everything's crazy up here, the soil, the air, the canals, the natives (I never saw any yet, but I hear they're around), the clocks. Even my clock acts funny. Even *time* is crazy up here. Sometimes I feel I'm here all by myself, no one else on the whole damn planet. I'd take bets on it. Sometimes I feel about eight years old, my body squeezed up and everything else tall. Jesus, it's just the place for an old man. Keeps me alert and keeps me happy. You know what Mars is? It's like a thing I got for Christmas seventy years ago—don't know if you ever had one—they called them kaleidoscopes, bits of crystal and cloth and beads and pretty junk. You held it up to the sunlight and looked in through at it, and it took your breath away. All the patterns! Well, that's Mars. Enjoy it. Don't ask it to be nothing else but what it is. Jesus, you know that highway right there, built by the Martians, is over sixteen centuries old and still in good condition? That's one dollar and fifty cents, thanks and good night."

Tomás drove off down the ancient highway, laughing quietly.

It was a long road going into darkness and hills and he held to the wheel, now and again reaching into his lunch bucket and taking out a piece of candy. He had been driving steadily for an hour, with no other car on the road, no light, just the road going under, the hum, the roar, and Mars out there, so quiet. Mars was always quiet, but quieter tonight than any other. The deserts and empty seas swung by him, and the mountains against the stars.

There was a smell of Time in the air tonight. He smiled and turned the fancy in his mind. There was a thought. What did Time smell like? Like dust and clocks and people. And if you wondered what Time sounded like it sounded like water running in a dark cave and voices crying and dirt dropping down upon hollow box lids, and rain. And, going further, what did Time *look* like? Time looked like snow dropping silently into a black room or it looked like a silent film in an ancient theater, one hundred billion faces falling like those New Year balloons, down and down into nothing. That was how Time smelled and looked and sounded. And tonight—Tomás shoved a hand into the wind outside the truck—tonight you could almost *touch* Time.

He drove the truck between hills of Time. His neck prickled and he sat up, watching ahead.

He pulled into a little dead Martian town, stopped the engine, and let the silence come in around him. He sat, not breathing, looking out at the white buildings in the moonlight. Uninhabited for centuries. Perfect, faultless, in ruins, yes, but perfect, nevertheless.

He started the engine and drove on another mile or more before stopping again, climbing out, carrying his lunch bucket, and walking to a little promontory where he could look back at that dusty city. He opened his thermos and poured himself a cup of coffee. A night bird flew by. He felt very good, very much at peace.

Perhaps five minutes later there was a sound. Off in the hills, where the ancient highway curved, there was a motion, a dim light, and then a murmur.

Tomás turned slowly with the coffee cup in his hand.

And out of the hills came a strange thing.

It was a machine like a jade-green insect, a praying mantis, delicately rushing through the cold air, indistinct, countless green diamonds winking over its body, and red jewels that glittered with multi-faceted eyes. Its six legs fell upon the ancient highway with the sounds of a sparse rain which dwindled away, and from the back of the machine a Martian with melted gold for eyes looked down at Tomás as if he were looking into a well.

Tomás raised his hand and thought Hello! automatically but did not move his lips, for this *was* a Martian. But Tomás had swum in blue rivers on Earth, with strangers passing on the road, and eaten in strange houses with strange people, and

his weapon had always been his smile. He did not carry a gun. And he did not feel the need of one now, even with the little fear that gathered about his heart at this moment.

The Martian's hands were empty too. For a moment they looked across the cool air at each other.

It was Tomás who moved first.

"Hello!" he called.

"Hello!" called the Martian in his own language.

They did not understand each other.

"Did you say hello?" they both asked.

"What did you say?" they said, each in a different tongue.

They scowled.

"Who are you?" said Tomás in English.

"What are you doing here?" In Martian; the stranger's lips moved.

"Where are you going?" they said, and looked bewildered.

"I'm Tomás Gomez."

"I'm Muhe Ca."

Neither understood, but they tapped their chests with the words and then it became clear.

And then the Martian laughed. "Wait!" Tomás felt his head touched, but no hand had touched him. "There!" said the Martian in English. "That is better!"

"You learned my language, so quick!"

"Nothing at all!"

They looked, embarrassed with a new silence, at the steaming coffee he had in one hand.

"Something different?" said the Martian, eying him and the coffee, referring to them both, perhaps.

"May I offer you a drink?" said Tomás.

"Please."

The Martian slid down from his machine.

A second cup was produced and filled, steaming. Tomás held it out.

Their hands met and—like mist—fell through each other.

"Jesus Christ!" cried Tomás, and dropped the cup.

"Name of the Gods!" said the Martian in his own tongue.

"Did you see what happened?" they both whispered.

They were very cold and terrified.

The Martian bent to touch the cup but could not touch it.

"Jesus!" said Tomás.

"Indeed." The Martian tried again and again to get hold of the cup, but could not. He stood up and thought for a moment, then took a knife from his belt. "Hey!" cried Tomás. "You misunderstand, catch!" said the Martian, and tossed it. Tomás cupped his hands. The knife fell through his flesh. It hit the ground. Tomás bent to pick it up but could not touch it, and he recoiled, shivering.

Now he looked at the Martian against the sky.

"The stars!" he said.

"The stars!" said the Martian, looking, in turn, at Tomás.

The stars were white and sharp beyond the flesh of the Martian, and they were sewn into his flesh like scintillas swallowed into the thin, phosphorescent membrane of a gelatinous sea fish. You could see stars flickering like violet eyes in the Martian's stomach and chest, and through his wrists, like jewelry.

"I can see through you!" said Tomás.

"And I through you!" said the Martian, stepping back.

Tomás felt of his own body and, feeling the warmth, was reassured. *I am real*, he thought.

The Martian touched his own nose and lips. "*I have flesh*," he said, half aloud. "*I am alive.*"

Tomás stared at the stranger. "And if *I* am real, then you must be dead."

"No, you!"

"A ghost!"

"A phantom!"

They pointed at each other, with starlight burning in their limbs like daggers and icicles and fireflies, and then fell to judging their limbs again, each finding himself intact, hot, excited, stunned, awed, and the other, ah yes, that other over there, unreal, a ghostly prism flashing the accumulated light of distant worlds.

I'm drunk, thought Tomás. I won't tell anyone of this tomorrow, no, no.

They stood there on the ancient highway, neither of them moving.

"Where are you from?" asked the Martian at last.

"Earth."

"What is that?"

"There." Tomás nodded to the sky.

"When?"

"We landed over a year ago, remember?"

"No."

"And all of you were dead, all but a few. You're rare, don't you *know* that?"

"That's not true."

"Yes, dead. I saw the bodies. Black, in the rooms, in the houses, dead. Thousands of them."

"That's ridiculous. We're *alive!*"

"Mister, you're invaded, only you don't know it. You must have escaped."

"I haven't escaped; there was nothing to escape. What do you mean? I'm on my way to a festival now at the canal, near the Eniall Mountains. I was there last night. Don't you see the city there?" The Martian pointed.

Tomás looked and saw the ruins. "Why, that city's been dead thousands of years."

The Martian laughed. "Dead. I slept there yesterday!"

"And I was in it a week ago and the week before that, and I just drove through it now, and it's a heap. See the broken pillars?"

"Broken? Why, I see them perfectly. The moonlight helps. And the pillars are upright."

"There's dust in the streets," said Tomás.

"The streets are clean!"

"The canals are empty right there."

"The canals are full of lavender wine!"

"It's dead."

"It's alive!" protested the Martian, laughing more now. "Oh, you're quite wrong. See all the carnival lights? There are beautiful boats as slim as women, beautiful women as slim as boats, women the color of sand, women with fire flowers in their hands. I can see them, small, running in the streets there. That's where I'm going now, to the festival; we'll float on the waters all night long; we'll sing, we'll drink, we'll make love. Can't you *see* it?"

"Mister, that city is dead as a dried

lizard. Ask any of our party. Me, I'm on my way to Green City tonight; that's the new colony we just raised over near Illinois Highway. You're mixed up. We brought in a million board feet of Oregon lumber and a couple dozen tons of good steel nails and hammered together two of the nicest little villages you ever saw. Tonight we're warming one of them. A couple rockets are coming in from Earth, bringing our wives and girl friends. There'll be barn dances and whisky——"

The Martian was now disquieted. "You say it is over *that* way?"

"There are the rockets." Tomás walked him to the edge of the hill and pointed down. "See?"

"No."

"Damn it, there they *are!* Those long silver things."

"No."

Now Tomás laughed. "You're blind!"

"I see very well. You are the one who does not see."

"But you see the new *town,* don't you?"

"I see nothing but an ocean, and water at low tide."

"Mister, that water's been evaporated for forty centuries."

"Ah, now, now, that *is* enough."

"It's true, I tell you."

The Martian grew very serious. "Tell me again. You do not see the city the way I describe it? The pillars very white, the boats very slender, the festival lights—oh, I see them *clearly!* And listen! I can hear them singing. It's no space away at all."

Tomás listened and shook his head. "No."

"And I, on the other hand," said the Martian, "cannot see what you describe. Well."

Again they were cold. An ice was in their flesh.

"Can it be . . . ?"

"What?"

"You say 'from the sky'?"

"Earth."

"Earth, a name, nothing," said the Martian. "*But* . . . as I came up the pass an hour ago . . ." He touched the back of his neck. "I felt . . ."

"Cold?"

"Yes."

"And now?"

"Cold again. Oddly. There was a thing to the light, to the hills, the road," said the Martian. "I felt the strangeness, the road, the light, and for a moment I felt as if I were the last man alive on this world. . . ."

"So did I!" said Tomás, and it was like talking to an old and dear friend, confiding, growing warm with the topic.

The Martian closed his eyes and opened them again. "This can only mean one thing. It has to do with Time. Yes. You are a figment of the Past!"

"No, you are from the Past," said the Earth Man, having had time to think of it now.

"You are so *certain.* How can you prove who is from the Past, who from the Future? What year is it?"

"Two thousand and one!"

"What does that mean to *me?*"

Tomás considered and shrugged. "Nothing."

"It is as if I told you that it is the year 4462853 s.e.c. It is nothing and more than nothing! Where is the clock to show us how the stars stand?"

"But the ruins prove it! They prove that *I* am the Future, *I* am alive, *you* are dead!"

"Everything in me denies this. My heart beats, my stomach hungers, my mouth thirsts. No, no, not dead, not alive, either of us. More alive than anything else. Caught between is more like it. Two strangers passing in the night, that is it. Two strangers passing. Ruins, you say?"

"Yes. You're afraid?"

"Who wants to see the Future, who *ever* does? A man can face the Past, but to think—the pillars *crumbled,* you say? And the sea empty, and the canals dry, and the maidens dead, and the flowers withered?" The Martian was silent, but then he looked on ahead. "But there they *are. I see* them. Isn't that enough for me? They wait for me now, no matter *what* you say."

And for Tomás the rockets, far away, waiting for *him,* and the town and the women from Earth. "We can never agree," he said.

"Let us agree to disagree," said the Martian. "What does it matter who is Past or Future, if we are both alive, for what follows will follow, tomorrow or in ten thousand years. How do you know that those temples are not the temples of your own civilization one hundred centuries from now, tumbled and broken? You do not know. Then don't ask. But the night is very short. There go the festival fires in the sky, and the birds."

Tomás put out his hand. The Martian did likewise in imitation.

Their hands did not touch; they melted through each other.

"Will we meet again?"

"Who knows? Perhaps some other night."

"I'd like to go with you to that festival."

"And I wish I might come to your new town, to see this ship you speak of, to see these men, to hear all that has happened."

"Good-by," said Tomás.

"Good night."

The Martian rode his green metal vehicle quietly away into the hills. The Earth Man turned his truck and drove it silently in the opposite direction.

"Good lord, what a dream that was," sighed Tomás, his hands on the wheel, thinking of the rockets, the women, the raw whisky, the Virginia reels, the party.

How strange a vision was that, thought the Martian, rushing on, thinking of the festival, the canals, the boats, the women with golden eyes, and the songs.

The night was dark. The moons had gone down. Starlight twinkled on the empty highway where now there was not a sound, no car, no person, nothing. And it remained that way all the rest of the cool dark night.

[1950]

QUESTIONS FOR STUDY

1. *How does the opening conversation between Tomás and Pop serve to establish the story's mood and setting? In what way does it anticipate the story's theme?*
2. *What keeps Tomás and the Martian from touching one another and from seeing the same objects? What are they able to share in common?*
3. *Following their leave-taking why is neither man willing to accept the reality of their encounter?*
4. *In what ways are the setting in time and space essential ingredients of Bradbury's story?*

ALBERT CAMUS

The Guest

THE SCHOOLMASTER was watching the two men climb toward him. One was on horseback, the other on foot. They had not yet tackled the abrupt rise leading to the schoolhouse built on the hillside. They were toiling onward, making slow progress in the snow, among the stones, on the vast expanse of the high deserted plateau. From time to time the horse stumbled. Without hearing anything yet, he could see the breath issuing from the horse's nostrils. One of the men, at least, knew the region. They were following the trail although it had disappeared two days ago under a layer of dirty white snow. The schoolmaster calculated that it would take them half an hour to get onto the hill. It was cold; he went back into the school to get a sweater.

He crossed the empty, frigid classroom. On the blackboard the four rivers of France, drawn with four different colored chalks, had been flowing toward their estuaries for the past three days. Snow had suddenly fallen in mid-October after eight months of drought without the transition of rain, and the twenty pupils, more or less, who lived in the villages scattered over the plateau had stopped coming. With fair weather they would return. Daru now heated only the single room that was his lodging, adjoining the classroom and giving also onto the plateau to the east. Like the class windows, his window looked to the south too. On that side the school was a few kilometers from the point where the plateau began to slope toward the south. In clear weather could be seen the purple mass of the mountain range where the gap opened onto the desert.

Somewhat warmed, Daru returned to the window from which he had first seen the two men. They were no longer visible. Hence they must have tackled the rise. The sky was not so dark, for the snow had stopped falling during the night. The morning had opened with a dirty light which had scarcely become brighter as the ceiling of clouds lifted. At two in the afternoon it seemed as if the day were merely beginning. But still this was better than those three days when the thick snow was falling amidst unbroken darkness with little gusts of wind that rattled the double door of the classroom. Then Daru had spent long hours in his room, leaving it only to go to the shed and feed the chickens or get some coal. Fortunately the delivery truck from Tadjid, the nearest village to the north, had brought his supplies two days before the blizzard. It would return in forty-eight hours.

Besides, he had enough to resist a siege, for the little room was cluttered with bags of wheat that the administration left as a stock to distribute to those of his pupils whose families had suffered from the drought. Actually they had all been victims because they were all poor. Every day Daru would distribute a ration to the children. They had missed it, he knew, during these bad days. Possibly one of the fathers or big brothers would come this afternoon and he could supply them with grain. It was just a matter of carrying them over to the next harvest. Now shiploads of wheat were arriving from France and the worst was over. But it would be hard to forget that poverty, that army of ragged ghosts wandering in the sunlight, the plateaus burned to a cinder month after month, the earth shriveled up little by little, literally scorched, every stone bursting into dust under one's foot. The sheep had died then by thousands and even a few men, here and there, sometimes without anyone's knowing.

In contrast with such poverty, he who lived almost like a monk in his remote schoolhouse, nonetheless satisfied with the little he had and with the rough life, had felt like a lord with his whitewashed walls, his narrow couch, his unpainted shelves, his well, and his weekly provision of water and food. And suddenly this snow, without warning, without the foretaste of rain. This is the way the region was, cruel to live in, even without men—who didn't help matters either. But Daru had been born here. Everywhere else, he felt exiled.

He stepped out onto the terrace in front of the schoolhouse. The two men were now halfway up the slope. He recognized the horseman as Balducci, the old gendarme he had known for a long time. Balducci was holding on the end of a rope an Arab who was walking behind him with hands bound and head lowered. The gendarme waved a greeting to which Daru did not reply, lost as he was in contemplation of the Arab dressed in a faded blue jellaba, his feet in sandals but covered with socks of heavy raw wool, his head surmounted by a narrow, short *chèche*. They were approaching. Balducci was holding back his horse in order not to hurt the Arab, and the group was advancing slowly.

Within earshot, Balducci shouted: "One hour to do the three kilometers from El Ameur!" Daru did not answer. Short and square in his thick sweater, he watched them climb. Not once had the Arab raised his head. "Hello," said Daru when they got up onto the terrace. "Come in and warm up." Balducci painfully got down from his horse without letting go the rope. From under his bristling mustache he smiled at the schoolmaster. His little dark eyes, deep-set under a tanned forehead, and his mouth surrounded with wrinkles made him look attentive and studious. Daru took the bridle, led the horse to the shed, and came back to the two men, who were now waiting for him in the school. He led them into his room. "I am going to heat up the classroom," he said. "We'll be more comfortable there." When he entered the room again, Balducci was on the couch. He had undone the rope tying him to the Arab, who had squatted near the stove. His hands still bound, the *chèche* pushed back on his head, he was looking toward the window.

At first Daru noticed only his huge lips, fat, smooth, almost Negroid; yet his nose was straight, his eyes were dark and full of fever. The *chèche* revealed an obstinate forehead and, under the weathered skin now rather discolored by the cold, the whole face had a restless and rebellious look that struck Daru when the Arab, turning his face toward him, looked him straight in the eyes. "Go into the other room," said the schoolmaster, "and I'll make you some mint tea." "Thanks," Balducci said. "What a chore! How I long for retirement." And addressing his prisoner in Arabic: "Come on, you." The Arab got up and, slowly, holding his bound wrists in front of him, went into the classroom.

With the tea, Daru brought a chair. But Balducci was already enthroned on the nearest pupil's desk and the Arab had squatted against the teacher's platform facing the stove, which stood between the desk and the window. When he held out the glass of tea to the prisoner, Daru hesitated at the sight of his bound hands. "He might perhaps be untied." "Sure," said Balducci. "That was for the trip." He started to get to his feet. But Daru, setting the glass on the floor, had knelt beside the Arab. Without saying anything, the Arab watched him with his feverish eyes. Once his hands were free, he rubbed his swollen wrists against each other, took the glass of tea, and sucked up the burning liquid in swift little sips.

"Good," said Daru. "And where are you headed?"

Balducci withdrew his mustache from the tea. "Here, son."

"Odd pupils! And you're spending the night?"

"No. I'm going back to El Ameur. And you will deliver this fellow to Tinguit. He is expected at police headquarters."

Balducci was looking at Daru with a friendly little smile.

"What's this story?" asked the schoolmaster. "Are you pulling my leg?"

"No, son. Those are the orders."

"The orders? I'm not . . ." Daru hesitated, not wanting to hurt the old Corsican. "I mean, that's not my job."

"What! What's the meaning of that? In wartime people do all kinds of jobs."

"Then I'll wait for the declaration of war!"

Balducci nodded.

"O.K. But the orders exist and they concern you too. Things are brewing, it appears. There is talk of a forthcoming revolt. We are mobilized, in a way."

Daru still had his obstinate look.

"Listen, son," Balducci said. "I like you and you must understand. There's only a dozen of us at El Ameur to patrol throughout the whole territory of a small department and I must get back in a hurry. I was told to hand this guy over to you and return without delay. He couldn't be kept there. His village was beginning to stir; they wanted to take him back. You must take him to Tinguit tomorrow before the day is over. Twenty kilometers shouldn't faze a husky fellow like you. After that, all will be over. You'll come back to your pupils and your comfortable life."

Behind the wall the horse could be heard snorting and pawing the earth. Daru was looking out the window. Decidedly, the weather was clearing and the light was increasing over the snowy plateau. When all the snow was melted, the sun would take over again and once more would burn the fields of stone. For days, still, the unchanging sky would shed its dry light on the solitary expanse where nothing had any connection with man.

"After all," he said, turning around toward Balducci, "what did he do?" And, before the gendarme had opened his mouth, he asked: "Does he speak French?"

"No, not a word. We had been looking for him for a month, but they were hiding him. He killed his cousin."

"Is he against us?"

"I don't think so. But you can never be sure."

"Why did he kill?"

"A family squabble, I think: One owed the other grain, it seems. It's not at all clear. In short, he killed his cousin with a billhook. You know, like a sheep, *kreezk!*"

Balducci made the gesture of drawing a blade across his throat and the Arab, his attention attracted, watched him with

a sort of anxiety. Daru felt a sudden wrath against the man, against all men with their rotten spite, their tireless hates, their blood lust.

But the kettle was singing on the stove. He served Balducci more tea, hesitated, then served the Arab again, who, a second time, drank avidly. His raised arms made the jellaba fall open and the schoolmaster saw his thin, muscular chest.

"Thanks, kid," Balducci said. "And now, I'm off."

He got up and went toward the Arab, taking a small rope from his pocket.

"What are you doing?" Daru asked dryly.

Balducci, disconcerted, showed him the rope.

"Don't bother."

The old gendarme hesitated. "It's up to you. Of course, you are armed?"

"I have my shotgun."

"Where?"

"In the trunk."

"You ought to have it near your bed."

"Why? I have nothing to fear."

"You're crazy, son. If there's an uprising, no one is safe, we're all in the same boat."

"I'll defend myself. I'll have time to see them coming."

Balducci began to laugh, then suddenly the mustache covered the white teeth.

"You'll have time? O.K. That's just what I was saying. You have always been a little cracked. That's why I like you, my son was like that."

At the same time he took out his revolver and put it on the desk.

"Keep it; I don't need two weapons from here to El Ameur."

The revolver shone against the black paint of the table. When the gendarme turned toward him, the schoolmaster caught the smell of leather and horse-flesh.

"Listen, Balducci," Daru said suddenly, "every bit of this disgusts me, and first of all your fellow here. But I won't hand him over. Fight, yes, if I have to. But not that."

The old gendarme stood in front of him and looked at him severely.

"You're being a fool," he said slowly.

"I don't like it either. You don't get used to putting a rope on a man even after years of it, and you're even ashamed— yes, ashamed. But you can't let them have their way."

"I won't hand him over," Daru said again.

"It's an order, son, and I repeat it."

"That's right. Repeat to them what I've said to you: I won't hand him over."

Balducci made a visible effort to reflect. He looked at the Arab and at Daru. At last he decided.

"No, I won't tell them anything. If you want to drop us, go ahead; I'll not denounce you. I have an order to deliver the prisoner and I'm doing so. And now you'll just sign this paper for me."

"There's no need. I'll not deny that you left him with me."

"Don't be mean with me. I know you'll tell the truth. You're from hereabouts and you are a man. But you must sign, that's the rule."

Daru opened his drawer, took out a little square bottle of purple ink, the red wooden penholder with the "sergeant-major" pen he used for making models of penmanship, and signed. The gendarme carefully folded the paper and put it into his wallet. Then he moved toward the door.

"I'll see you off," Daru said.

"No," said Balducci. "There's no use being polite. You insulted me."

He looked at the Arab, motionless in the same spot, sniffed peevishly, and turned away toward the door. "Good-by, son," he said. The door shut behind him. Balducci appeared suddenly outside the window and then disappeared. His footsteps were muffled by the snow. The horse stirred on the other side of the wall and several chickens fluttered in fright. A moment later Balducci reappeared outside the window leading the horse by the bridle. He walked toward the little rise without turning around and disappeared from sight with the horse following him. A big stone could be heard bouncing down. Daru walked back toward the prisoner, who, without stirring, never took his eyes off him. "Wait," the schoolmaster said in Arabic and went toward the bedroom. As he was going through the door, he had a second thought, went to the desk, took the revolver, and stuck it in his pocket. Then, without looking back, he went into his room.

For some time he lay on his couch watching the sky gradually close over, listening to the silence. It was this silence that had seemed painful to him during the first few days here, after the war. He had requested a post in the little town at the base of the foothills separating the upper plateaus from the desert. There, rocky walls, green and black to the north, pink and lavender to the south, marked the frontier of eternal summer. He had been named to a post farther north, on the plateau itself. In the beginning, the solitude and the silence had been hard for him on these wastelands peopled only by stones. Occasionally, furrows suggested cultivation, but they had been dug to uncover a certain kind of stone good for building. The only plowing here was to harvest rocks. Elsewhere a thin layer of soil accumulated in the hollows would be scraped out to enrich paltry village gardens. This is the way it was: bare rock covered three quarters of the region. Towns sprang up, flourished, then disappeared; men came by, loved one another or fought bitterly, then died. No one in this desert, neither he nor his guest, mattered. And yet, outside this desert neither of them, Daru knew, could have really lived.

When he got up, no noise came from the classroom. He was amazed at the unmixed joy he derived from the mere thought that the Arab might have fled and that he would be alone with no decision to make. But the prisoner was there. He had merely stretched out between the stove and the desk. With eyes open, he was staring at the ceiling. In that position, his thick lips were particularly noticeable, giving him a pouting look. "Come," said Daru. The Arab got up and followed him. In the bedroom, the schoolmaster pointed to a chair near the table under the window. The Arab sat down without taking his eyes off Daru.

"Are you hungry?"

"Yes," the prisoner said.

Daru set the table for two. He took flour and oil, shaped a cake in a frying-pan, and lighted the little stove that functioned on bottled gas. While the cake was cooking, he went out to the shed to get cheese, eggs, dates, and condensed milk. When the cake was done he set it on the window sill to cool, heated some condensed milk diluted with water, and beat up the eggs into an omelette. In one of his motions he knocked against the revolver stuck in his right pocket. He set the bowl down, went into the classroom, and put the revolver in his desk drawer. When he came back to the room, night was falling. He put on the light and served the Arab. "Eat," he said. The Arab took a piece of the cake, lifted it eagerly to his mouth, and stopped short.

"And you?" he asked.

"After you. I'll eat too."

The thick lips opened slightly. The Arab hesitated, then bit into the cake determinedly.

The meal over, the Arab looked at the schoolmaster. "Are you the judge?"

"No, I'm simply keeping you until tomorrow."

"Why do you eat with me?"

"I'm hungry."

The Arab fell silent. Daru got up and went out. He brought back a folding bed from the shed, set it up between the table and the stove, perpendicular to his own bed. From a large suitcase which, upright in a corner, served as a shelf for papers, he took two blankets and arranged them on the camp bed. Then he stopped, felt useless, and sat down on his bed. There was nothing more to do or to get ready. He had to look at this man. He looked at him, therefore, trying to imagine his face bursting with rage. He couldn't do so. He could see nothing but the dark yet shining eyes and the animal mouth.

"Why did you kill him?" he asked in a voice whose hostile tone surprised him.

The Arab looked away.

"He ran away. I ran after him."

He raised his eyes to Daru again and they were full of a sort of woeful interrogation. "Now what will they do to me?"

"Are you afraid?"

He stiffened, turning his eyes away.

"Are you sorry?"

The Arab stared at him openmouthed. Obviously he did not understand. Daru's annoyance was growing. At the same time he felt awkward and self-conscious with his big body wedged between the two beds.

"Lie down there," he said impatiently. "That's your bed."

The Arab didn't move. He called to Daru:

"Tell me!"

The schoolmaster looked at him.

"Is the gendarme coming back tomorrow?"

"I don't know."

"Are you coming with us?"

"I don't know. Why?"

The prisoner got up and stretched out on top of the blankets, his feet toward the window. The light from the electric bulb shone straight into his eyes and he closed them at once.

"Why?" Daru repeated, standing beside the bed.

The Arab opened his eyes under the blinding light and looked at him, trying not to blink.

"Come with us," he said.

In the middle of the night, Daru was still not asleep. He had gone to bed after undressing completely; he generally slept naked. But when he suddenly realized that he had nothing on, he hesitated. He felt vulnerable and the temptation came to him to put his clothes back on. Then he shrugged his shoulders; after all, he wasn't a child and, if need be, he could break his adversary in two. From his bed he could observe him, lying on his back, still motionless with his eyes closed under the harsh light. When Daru turned out the light, the darkness seemed to coagulate all of a sudden. Little by little, the night came back to life in the window where the starless sky was stirring gently. The schoolmaster soon made out the body lying at his feet. The Arab still did not move, but his eyes seemed open. A faint wind was prowling around the schoolhouse. Perhaps it would drive away the clouds and the sun would reappear.

During the night the wind increased.

The hens fluttered a little and then were silent. The Arab turned over on his side with his back to Daru, who thought he heard him moan. Then he listened for his guest's breathing, become heavier and more regular. He listened to that breath so close to him and mused without being able to go to sleep. In this room where he had been sleeping alone for a year, the presence bothered him. But it bothered him also by imposing on him a sort of brotherhood he knew well but refused to accept in the present circumstances. Men who share the same rooms, soldiers or prisoners, develop a strange alliance as if, having cast off their armor with their clothing, they fraternized every evening, over and above their differences, in the ancient community of dream and fatigue. But Daru shook himself; he didn't like such musings, and it was essential to sleep.

A little later, however, when the Arab stirred slightly, the schoolmaster was still not asleep. When the prisoner made a second move, he stiffened, on the alert. The Arab was lifting himself slowly on his arms with almost the motion of a sleepwalker. Seated upright in bed, he waited motionless without turning his head toward Daru, as if he were listening attentively. Daru did not stir; it had just occurred to him that the revolver was still in the drawer of his desk. It was better to act at once. Yet he continued to observe the prisoner, who, with the same slithery motion, put his feet on the ground, waited again, then began to stand up slowly. Daru was about to call out to him when the Arab began to walk, in a quite natural but extraordinarily silent way. He was heading toward the door at the end of the room that opened into the shed. He lifted the latch with precaution and went out, pushing the door behind him but without shutting it. Daru had not stirred. "He is running away," he merely thought. "Good riddance!" Yet he listened attentively. The hens were not fluttering; the guest must be on the plateau. A faint sound of water reached him, and he didn't know what it was until the Arab again stood framed in the doorway, closed the door carefully, and came back to bed without

a sound. Then Daru turned his back on him and fell asleep. Still later he seemed, from the depths of his sleep, to hear furtive steps around the schoolhouse. "I'm dreaming! I'm dreaming!" he repeated to himself. And he went on sleeping.

When he awoke, the sky was clear; the loose window let in a cold, pure air. The Arab was asleep, hunched up under the blankets now, his mouth open, utterly relaxed. But when Daru shook him, he started dreadfully, staring at Daru with wild eyes as if he had never seen him and such a frightened expression that the schoolmaster stepped back. "Don't be afraid. It's me. You must eat." The Arab nodded his head and said yes. Calm had returned to his face, but his expression was vacant and listless.

The coffee was ready. They drank it seated together on the folding bed as they munched their pieces of the cake. Then Daru led the Arab under the shed and showed him the faucet where he washed. He went back into the room, folded the blankets and the bed, made his own bed and put the room in order. Then he went through the classroom and out onto the terrace. The sun was already rising in the blue sky; a soft, bright light was bathing the deserted plateau. On the ridge the snow was melting in spots. The stones were about to reappear. Crouched on the edge of the plateau, the schoolmaster looked at the deserted expanse. He thought of Balducci. He had hurt him, for he had sent him off in a way as if he didn't want to be associated with him. He could still hear the gendarme's farewell and, without knowing why, he felt strangely empty and vulnerable. At that moment, from the other side of the schoolhouse, the prisoner coughed. Daru listened to him almost despite himself and then, furious, threw a pebble that whistled through the air before sinking into the snow. That man's stupid crime revolted him, but to hand him over was contrary to honor. Merely thinking of it made him smart with humiliation. And he cursed at one and the same time his own people who had sent him this Arab and the Arab too who had dared to kill and not managed to get away. Daru got up, walked in a circle on the terrace, waited motionless, and then went back into the schoolhouse.

The Arab, leaning over the cement floor of the shed, was washing his teeth with two fingers. Daru looked at him and said: "Come." He went back into the room ahead of the prisoner. He slipped a hunting-jacket on over his sweater and put on walking-shoes. Standing, he waited until the Arab had put on his *chèche* and sandals. They went into the classroom and the schoolmaster pointed to the exit, saying: "Go ahead." The fellow didn't budge. "I'm coming," said Daru. The Arab went out. Daru went back into the room and made a package of pieces of rusk, dates, and sugar. In the classroom, before going out, he hesitated a second in front of his desk, then crossed the threshold and locked the door. "That's the way," he said. He started toward the east, followed by the prisoner. But, a short distance from the schoolhouse, he thought he heard a slight sound behind them. He retraced his steps and examined the surroundings of the house; there was no one there. The Arab watched him without seeming to understand. "Come on," said Daru.

They walked for an hour and rested beside a sharp peak of limestone. The snow was melting faster and faster and the sun was drinking up the puddles at once, rapidly cleaning the plateau, which gradually dried and vibrated like the air itself. When they resumed walking, the ground rang under their feet. From time to time a bird rent the space in front of them with a joyful cry. Daru breathed in deeply the fresh morning light. He felt a sort of rapture before the vast familiar expanse, now almost entirely yellow under its dome of blue sky. They walked an hour more, descending toward the south. They reached a level height made up of crumbly rocks. From there on, the plateau sloped down, eastward, toward a low plain where there were a few spindly trees and, to the south, toward outcroppings of rock that gave the landscape a chaotic look.

Daru surveyed the two directions. There was nothing but the sky on the horizon. Not a man could be seen. He turned toward the Arab, who was looking at him blankly. Daru held out the package to him. "Take it," he said. "There are dates, bread, and sugar. You can hold out for two days. Here are a thousand francs too." The Arab took the package and the money but kept his full hands at chest level as if he didn't know what to do with what was being given him. "Now look," the schoolmaster said as he pointed in the direction of the east, "there's the way to Tinguit. You have a two-hour walk. At Tinguit you'll find the administration and the police. They are expecting you." The Arab looked toward the east, still holding the package and the money against his chest. Daru took his elbow and turned him rather roughly toward the south. At the foot of the height on which they stood could be seen a faint path. "That's the trail across the plateau. In a day's walk from here you'll find pasture-lands and the first nomads. They'll take you in and shelter you according to their law." The Arab had now turned toward Daru and a sort of panic was visible in his expression. "Listen," he said. Daru shook his head: "No, be quiet. Now I'm leaving you." He turned his back on him, took two long steps in the direction of the school, looked hesitantly at the motionless Arab, and started off again. For a few minutes he heard nothing but his own step resounding on the cold ground and did not turn his head. A moment later, however, he turned around. The Arab was still there on the edge of the hill, his arms hanging now, and he was looking at the schoolmaster. Daru felt something rise in his throat. But he swore with impatience, waved vaguely, and started off again. He had already gone some distance when he again stopped and looked. There was no longer anyone on the hill.

Daru hesitated. The sun was now rather high in the sky and was beginning to beat down on his head. The schoolmaster retraced his steps, at first somewhat uncertainly, then with decision. When he reached the little hill, he was bathed in sweat. He climbed it as fast as he could and stopped, out of breath, at the top. The rock-fields to the south stood out sharply against the blue sky, but on the plain to the east a steamy heat was already rising. And in that slight haze, Daru, with heavy heart, made out the Arab walking slowly on the road to prison.

A little later, standing before the window of the classroom, the schoolmaster was watching the clear light bathing the whole surface of the plateau, but he hardly saw it. Behind him on the blackboard, among the winding French rivers, sprawled the clumsily chalked-up words he had just read: "You handed over our brother. You will pay for this." Daru looked at the sky, the plateau, and, beyond, the invisible lands stretching all the way to the sea. In this vast landscape he had loved so much, he was alone.

[1957]

TRANSLATED BY
JUSTIN O'BRIEN

QUESTIONS FOR STUDY

1. *What kind of man is Daru? What beliefs and attitudes does he have? Do they change in the course of the story? How do his attitudes differ from Balducci's?*

2. *What basic dilemma does Daru have to face? What conflicting claims is he called upon to reconcile?*

3. *How does Daru treat his Arab prisoner? Why does he derive "unmixed joy" at the thought that the Arab may have run away?*

4. *Why does Daru allow the Arab to make his own final decision? Is this an abdication of Daru's own responsibility? Is the accusation written on the blackboard just?*

5. *Why does the Arab choose the road to prison rather than the road to freedom?*

6. *Why does Camus continually emphasize Daru's aloneness? How is this aloneness reinforced by the story's setting?*

7. *"The Guest" takes place in Algeria following the end of World War II on the eve of the outbreak of the civil war between the Algerian nationalists and the French colonists. In what ways is this background important to Camus' story?*

JOHN CHEEVER

The Country Husband

To BEGIN at the beginning, the airplane from Minneapolis in which Francis Weed was traveling East ran into heavy weather. The sky had been a hazy blue, with the clouds below the plane lying so close together that nothing could be seen of the earth. Then mist began to form outside the windows, and they flew into a white cloud of such density that it reflected the exhaust fires. The color of the cloud darkened to gray, and the plane began to rock. Francis had been in heavy weather before, but he had never been shaken up so much. The man in the seat beside him pulled a flask out of his pocket and took a drink. Francis smiled at his neighbor, but the man looked away; he wasn't sharing his painkiller with anyone. The plane had begun to drop and flounder wildly. A child was crying. The air in the cabin was overheated and stale, and Francis' left foot went to sleep. He read a little from a paper book that he had bought at the airport, but the violence of the storm divided his attention. It was black outside the ports. The exhaust fires blazed and shed sparks in the dark, and, inside, the shaded lights, the stuffiness, and the window curtains gave the cabin an atmosphere of intense and misplaced domesticity. Then the lights flickered and went out. "You know what. I've always wanted to do?" the man beside Francis said suddenly. "I've always wanted to buy a farm in New Hampshire and raise beef cattle." The stewardess announced that they were going to make an emergency landing. All but the child saw in their minds the spreading wings of the Angel of Death. The pilot could be heard singing faintly, "I've got sixpence, jolly, jolly sixpence. I've got sixpence to last me all my life . . ." There was no other sound.

The loud groaning of the hydraulic valves swallowed up the pilot's song, and there was a shrieking high in the air, like automobile brakes, and the plane hit flat on its belly in a cornfield and shook them so violently that an old man up forward howled, "Me kidneys! Me kidneys!" The stewardess flung open the door, and someone opened an emergency door at the back, letting in the sweet noise of their continuing mortality—the idle splash and smell of heavy rain. Anxious for their lives, they filed out of the doors and scattered over the cornfield in all directions, praying that the thread would hold. It did. Nothing happened. When it was clear that the plane would not burn or explode, the crew and stewardess gathered the passengers together and led them to the shelter of a barn. They were not far from Philadelphia, and in a little while a string of taxis took them into the city. "It's just like the Marne," someone said, but there was surprisingly little relaxation of suspiciousness with which many Americans regard their fellow-travelers.

In Philadelphia, Francis Weed got a train to New York. At the end of that journey, he crossed the city and caught, just as it was about to pull out, the commuting train that he took five nights a week to his home in Shady Hill.

He sat with Trace Bearden. "You know, I was in that plane that just crashed outside Philadelphia," he said. "We came down in a field . . ." He had traveled faster than the newspapers or the rain, and the weather in New York was sunny and mild. It was a day in late September, as fragrant and shapely as an apple. Trace listened to the story, but how could he get excited? Francis had no powers that would let him re-create a brush with death—particularly in the atmosphere of a commuting train, journeying through a sunny countryside where already, in the slum gardens, there were signs of harvest. Trace picked up his newspaper, and Francis was left alone with his thoughts. He said good night to Trace on the platform at Shady Hill and drove in his secondhand Volkswagen up to the Blenhollow neighborhood, where he lived.

The Weeds' Dutch Colonial house was larger than it appeared to be from the driveway. The living room was spacious and divided like Gaul into three parts. Around an ell to the left as one entered from the vestibule was the long table, laid for six, with candles and a bowl of fruit in the center. The sounds and smells that came from the open kitchen door were appetizing, for Julia Weed was a good cook. The largest part of the living room centered around a fireplace. On the right were some bookshelves and a piano. The room was polished and tranquil, and from the windows that opened to the west there was some late-summer sunlight, brilliant and as clear as water. Nothing here was neglected; nothing had not been burnished. It was not the kind of household where, after prying open a stuck cigarette box, you would find an old shirt button and a tarnished nickel. The hearth was swept, the roses on the piano were reflected in the polish of the broad top, and there was an album of Schubert waltzes on the rack. Louisa Weed, a pretty girl of nine, was looking out the western windows. Her younger brother Henry was standing beside her. Her still younger brother, Toby, was studying the figures of some tonsured monks drinking beer on the polished brass of the wood box. Francis, taking off his hat and putting down his paper, was not consciously pleased with the scene; he was not that reflective. It was his element, his creation, and he returned to it with that sense of lightness and strength with which any creature returns to its home. "Hi, everybody," he said. "The plane from Minneapolis . . ."

Nine times out of ten, Francis would be greeted with affection, but tonight the children are absorbed in their own antagonisms. Francis has not finished his sentence about the plane crash before Henry plants a kick in Louisa's behind. Louisa swings around, saying, "*Damn* you!" Francis makes the mistake of scolding Louisa for bad language before he punishes Henry. Now Louisa turns on her father and accuses him of favoritism. Henry is always right; she is persecuted and lonely; her lot is hopeless. Francis turns to his son, but the boy has justification for the kick—she hit him first; she hit him on the ear, which is dangerous. Louisa agrees with this passionately. She hit him on the ear, and she *meant* to hit him on the ear, because he messed up her china collection. Henry says that this is a lie. Little Toby turns away from the wood box to throw in some evidence for Louisa. Henry claps his hand over little Toby's mouth. Francis separates the two boys but accidentally pushes Toby into the wood box. Toby begins to cry. Louisa is already crying. Just then, Julia Weed comes into that part of the room where the table is laid. She is a pretty, intelligent woman, and the white in her hair is premature. She does not seem to notice the fracas. "Hello, darling," she says serenely to Francis. "Wash your hands, everyone. Dinner is ready." She strikes a match and lights the six candles in this vale of tears.

This simple announcement, like the war cries of the Scottish chieftains, only refreshes the ferocity of the combatants. Louisa gives Henry a blow on the shoulder. Henry, although he seldom cries, has pitched nine innings and is tired. He bursts into tears. Little Toby discovers a splinter in his hand and begins to howl. Francis says loudly that he has been in a plane crash and that he is tired. Julia appears again, from the kitchen, and, still ignoring the chaos, asks Francis to go upstairs and tell Helen that everything is ready. Francis is happy to go; it is like getting back to headquarters company. He is planning to tell his oldest daughter about the airplane crash, but Helen is lying on her bed reading a *True Romance* magazine, and the first thing Francis does is to take the magazine from her hand and remind Helen that he has forbidden her to buy it. She did not buy it, Helen replies. It was given to her by her best friend,

Bessie Black. Everybody reads *True Romance*. Bessie Black's father reads *True Romance*. There isn't a girl in Helen's class who doesn't read *True Romance*. Francis expresses his detestation of the magazine and then tells her that dinner is ready—although from the sounds downstairs it doesn't seem so. Helen follows him down the stairs. Julia has seated herself in the candlelight and spread a napkin over her lap. Neither Louisa nor Henry has come to the table. Little Toby is still howling, lying face down on the floor. Francis speaks to him gently: "Daddy was in a plane crash this afternoon, Toby. Don't you want to hear about it?" Toby goes on crying. "If you don't come to the table now, Toby," Francis says, "I'll have to send you to bed without any supper." The little boy rises, gives him a cutting look, flies up the stairs to his bedroom, and slams the door. "Oh dear," Julia says, and starts to go after him. Francis says that she will spoil him. Julia says that Toby is ten pounds underweight and has to be encouraged to eat. Winter is coming, and he will spend the cold months in bed unless he has his dinner. Julia goes upstairs. Francis sits down at the table with Helen. Helen is suffering from the dismal feeling of having read too intently on a fine day, and she gives her father and the room a jaded look. She doesn't understand about the plane crash, because there wasn't a drop of rain in Shady Hill.

Julia returns with Toby, and they all sit down and are served. "Do I have to look at that big, fat slob?" Henry says, of Louisa. Everybody but Toby enters into this skirmish, and it rages up and down the table for five minutes. Toward the end, Henry puts his napkin over his head and, trying to eat that way, spills spinach all over his shirt. Francis asks Julia if the children couldn't have their dinner earlier. Julia's guns are loaded for this. She can't cook two dinners and lay two tables. She paints with lightning strokes that panorama of drudgery in which her youth, her beauty, and her wit have been lost. Francis says that he must be understood; he was nearly killed in an airplane crash, and he doesn't like to come home every

night to a battlefield. Now Julia is deeply committed. Her voice trembles. He doesn't come home every night to a battlefield. The accusation is stupid and mean. Everything was tranquil until he arrived. She stops speaking, puts down her knife and fork, and looks into her plate as if it is a gulf. She begins to cry. "Poor Mummy!" Toby says, and when Julia gets up from the table, drying her tears with a napkin, Toby goes to her side. "Poor Mummy," he says. "Poor Mummy!" And they climb the stairs together. The other children drift away from the battlefield, and Francis goes into the back garden for a cigarette and some air.

It was a pleasant garden, with walks and flower beds and places to sit. The sunset had nearly burned out, but there was still plenty of light. Put into a thoughtful mood by the crash and the battle, Francis listened to the evening sounds of Shady Hill. "Varmints! Rascals!" old Mr. Nixon shouted to the squirrels in his bird-feeding station. "Avaunt and quit my sight!" A door slammed. Someone was playing tennis on the Babcocks' court; someone was cutting grass. Then Donald Goslin, who lived at the corner, began to play the "Moonlight Sonata." He did this nearly every night. He threw the tempo out the window and played it *rubato* from beginning to end, like an outpouring of tearful petulance, lonesomeness, and self-pity—of everything it was Beethoven's greatness not to know. The music rang up and down the street beneath the trees like an appeal for love, for tenderness, aimed at some lonely housemaid—some fresh-faced, homesick girl from Galway, looking at old snapshots in her third-floor room. "Here, Jupiter, here, Jupiter," Francis called to the Mercers' retriever. Jupiter crashed through the tomato vines with the remains of a felt hat in his mouth.

Jupiter was an anomaly. His retrieving instincts and his high spirits were out of place in Shady Hill. He was as black as coal, with a long, alert, intelligent, rake-hell face. His eyes gleamed with mischief, and he held his head high. It was the fierce, heavily collared dog's head that appears in heraldry, in tapestry, and that used to appear on umbrella handles and walking sticks. Jupiter went where he pleased, ransacking wastebaskets, clotheslines, garbage pails, and shoe bags. He broke up garden parties and tennis matches, and got mixed up in the processional at Christ Church on Sunday, barking at the men in red dresses. He crashed through old Mr. Nixon's rose garden two or three times a day, cutting a wide swath through the Condesa de Sastagos, and as soon as Donald Goslin lighted his barbecue fire on Thursday nights, Jupiter would get the scent. Nothing the Goslins did could drive him away. Sticks and stones and rude commands only moved him to the edge of the terrace, where he remained, with his gallant and heraldic muzzle, waiting for Donald Goslin to turn his back and reach for the salt. Then he would spring onto the terrace, lift the steak lightly off the fire, and run away with the Goslins' dinner. Jupiter's days were numbered. The Wrightsons' German gardener or the Farquarsons' cook would soon poison him. Even old Mr. Nixon might put some arsenic in the garbage that Jupiter loved. "Here, Jupiter, Jupiter!" Francis called, but the dog pranced off, shaking the hat in his white teeth. Looking in at the windows of his house, Francis saw that Julia had come down and was blowing out the candles.

Julia and Francis Weed went out a great deal. Julia was well liked and gregarious, and her love of parties sprang from a most natural dread of chaos and loneliness. She went through her morning mail with real anxiety, looking for invitations, and she usually found some, but she was insatiable, and if she had gone out seven nights a week, it would not have cured her of a reflective look—the look of someone who hears distant music— for she would always suppose that there was a more brilliant party somewhere else. Francis limited her to two week-night parties, putting a flexible interpretation on Friday, and rode through the weekend like a dory in a gale. The day after the airplane crash, the Weeds were to have dinner with the Farquarsons.

Francis got home late from town, and

Julia got the sitter while he dressed, and then hurried him out of the house. The party was small and pleasant, and Francis settled down to enjoy himself. A new maid passed the drinks. Her hair was dark, and her face was round and pale and seemed familiar to Francis. He had not developed his memory as a sentimental faculty. Wood smoke, lilac, and other such perfumes did not stir him, and his memory was something like his appendix—a vestigial repository. It was not his limitation at all to be unable to escape the past; it was perhaps his limitation that he had escaped it so successfully. He might have seen the maid at other parties, he might have seen her taking a walk on Sunday afternoons, but in either case he would not be searching his memory now. Her face was, in a wonderful way, a moon face—Norman or Irish—but it was not beautiful enough to account for his feeling that he had seen her before, in circumstances that he ought to be able to remember. He asked Nellie Farquarson who she was. Nellie said that the maid had come through an agency, and that her home was Trénon, in Normandy—a small place with a church and a restaurant that Nellie had once visited. While Nellie talked on about her travels abroad, Francis realized where he had seen the woman before. It had been at the end of the war. He had left a replacement depot with some other men and taken a three-day pass in Trénon. On their second day, they had walked out to a crossroads to see the public chastisement of a young woman who had lived with the German commandant during the Occupation.

It was a cool morning in the fall. The sky was overcast, and poured down onto the dirt crossroads a very discouraging light. They were on high land and could see how like one another the shapes of the clouds and the hills were as they stretched off toward the sea. The prisoner arrived sitting on a three-legged stool in a farm cart. She stood by the cart while the mayor read the accusation and the sentence. Her head was bent and her face was set in that empty half smile behind which the whipped soul is suspended. When the mayor was finished, she undid her hair and let it fall across her back. A little man with a gray mustache cut off her hair with shears and dropped it on the ground. Then, with a bowl of soapy water and a straight razor, he shaved her skull clean. A woman approached and began to undo the fastening of her clothes, but the prisoner pushed her aside and undressed herself. When she pulled her chemise over her head and threw it on the ground, she was naked. The women jeered; the men were still. There was no change in the falseness or the plaintiveness of the prisoner's smile. The cold wind made her white skin rough and hardened the nipples of her breasts. The jeering ended gradually, put down by the recognition of their common humanity. One woman spat on her, but some inviolable grandeur in her nakedness lasted through the ordeal. When the crowd was quiet, she turned—she had begun to cry —and, with nothing on but a pair of worn black shoes and stockings, walked down the dirt road alone away from the village. The round white face had aged a little, but there was no question but that the maid who passed his cocktails and later served Francis his dinner was the woman who had been punished at the crossroads.

The war seemed now so distant and that world where the cost of partisanship had been death or torture so long ago. Francis had lost track of the men who had been with him in Vésey. He could not count on Julia's discretion. He could not tell anyone. And if he had told the story now, at the dinner table, it would have been a social as well as a human error. The people in the Farquarsons' living room seemed united in their tacit claim that there had been no past, no war— that there was no danger or trouble in the world. In the recorded history of human arrangements, this extraordinary meeting would have fallen into place, but the atmosphere of Shady Hill made the memory unseemly and impolite. The prisoner withdrew after passing the coffee, but the encounter left Francis feeling languid; it had opened his memory and his senses, and left them dilated. He and Julia drove home when the party ended, and Julia went into the house. Francis stayed in the car to take the sitter home.

Expecting to see Mrs. Henlein, the old lady who usually stayed with the children, he was surprised when a young girl opened the door and came out onto the lighted stoop. She stayed in the light to count her textbooks. She was frowning and beautiful. Now, the world is full of beautiful young girls, but Francis saw here the difference between beauty and perfection. All those endearing flaws, moles, birthmarks, and healed wounds were missing, and he experienced in his consciousness that moment when music breaks glass, and felt a pang of recognition as strange, deep, and wonderful as anything in his life. It hung from her frown, from an impalpable darkness in her face—a look that impressed him as a direct appeal for love. When she had counted her books, she came down the steps and opened the car door. In the light, he saw that her cheeks were wet. She got in and shut the door.

"You're new," Francis said.

"Yes. Mrs. Henlein is sick. I'm Anne Murchison."

"Did the children give you any trouble?"

"Oh, no, no." She turned and smiled at him unhappily in the dim dashboard light. Her light hair caught on the collar of her jacket, and she shook her head to set it loose.

"You've been crying."

"Yes."

"I hope it was nothing that happened in our house."

"No, no, it was nothing that happened in your house." Her voice was bleak. "It's no secret. Everybody in the village knows. Daddy's an alcoholic, and he just called me from some saloon and gave me a piece of his mind. He thinks I'm immoral. He called just before Mrs. Weed came back."

"I'm sorry."

"Oh, *Lord!*" She gasped and began to cry. She turned toward Francis, and he took her in his arms and let her cry on his shoulder. She shook in his embrace, and this movement accentuated his sense of the fineness of her flesh and bone. The layers of their clothing felt thin, and when her shuddering began to diminish, it was so much like a paroxysm of love that Francis lost his head and pulled her roughly against him. She drew away. "I live on Belleview Avenue," she said. "You go down Lansing Street to the railroad bridge."

"All right." He started the car.

"You. turn left at that traffic light. . . . Now you turn right here and go straight on toward the tracks."

The road Francis took brought him out of his own neighborhood, across the tracks, and toward the river, to a street where the near-poor lived, in houses whose peaked gables and trimmings of wooden lace conveyed the purest feelings of pride and romance, although the houses themselves could not have offered much privacy or comfort, they were all so small. The street was dark, and, stirred by the grace and beauty of the troubled girl, he seemed, in turning in to it, to have come into the deepest part of some submerged memory. In the distance, he saw a porch light burning. It was the only one, and she said that the house with the light was where she lived. When he stopped the car, he could see beyond the porch light into a dimly lighted hallway with an old-fashioned clothes tree. "Well, here we are," he said, conscious that a young man would have said something different.

She did not move her hands from the books, where they were folded, and she turned and faced him. There were tears of lust in his eyes. Determinedly—not sadly —he opened the door on his side and walked around to open hers. He took her free hand, letting his fingers in between hers, climbed at her side the two concrete steps, and went up a narrow walk through a front garden where dahlias, marigolds, and roses—things that had withstood the light frosts—still bloomed, and made a bittersweet smell in the night air. At the steps, she freed her hand and then turned and kissed him swiftly. Then she crossed the porch and shut the door. The porch light went out, then the light in the hall. A second later, a light went on upstairs at the side of the house, shining into a tree that was still covered with leaves. It took her only a few minutes to undress and get into bed, and then the house was dark.

Julia was asleep when Francis got home. He opened a second window and got into bed to shut his eyes on that night,

but as soon as they were shut—as soon as he had dropped off to sleep—the girl entered his mind, moving with perfect freedom through its shut doors and filling chamber after chamber with her light, her perfume, and the music of her voice. He was crossing the Atlantic with her on the old *Mauretania* and, later, living with her in Paris. When he woke from his dream, he got up and smoked a cigarette at the open window. Getting back into bed, he cast around in his mind for something he desired to do that would injure no one, and he thought of skiing. Up through the dimness in his mind rose the image of a mountain deep in snow. It was late in the day. Wherever his eyes looked, he saw broad and heartening things. Over his shoulder, there was a snow-filled valley, rising into wooded hills where the trees dimmed the whiteness like a sparse coat of hair. The cold deadened all sound but the loud, iron clanking of the lift machinery. The light on the trails was blue, and it was harder than it had been a minute or two earlier to pick the turns, harder to judge—now that the snow was all deep blue–the crust, the ice, the bare spots, and the deep piles of dry powder. Down the mountain he swung, matching his speed against the contours of a slope that had been formed in the first ice age, seeking with ardor some simplicity of feeling and circumstance. Night fell then, and he drank a Martini with some old friend in a dirty country bar.

In the morning, Francis' snow-covered mountain was gone, and he was left with his vivid memories of Paris and the *Mauretania*. He had been bitten gravely. He washed his body, shaved his jaws, drank his coffee, and missed the seven-thirty-one. The train pulled out just as he brought his car to the station, and the longing he felt for the coaches as they drew stubbornly away from him reminded him of the humors of love. He waited for the eight-two, on what was now an empty platform. It was a clear morning; the morning seemed thrown like a gleaming bridge of light over his mixed affairs. His spirits were feverish and high. The image of the girl seemed to put him into relationship to the world that was mysterious and enthralling. Cars were beginning to fill up the parking lot, and he noticed that those that had driven down from the high land above Shady Hill were white with hoarfrost. The first clear sign of autumn thrilled him. An express train—a night train from Buffalo or Albany—came down the tracks between the platforms, and he saw that the roofs of the foremost cars were covered with a skin of ice. Struck by the miraculous physicalness of everything, he smiled at the passengers in the dining car, who could be seen eating eggs and wiping their mouths with napkins as they traveled. The sleeping-car compartments, with their soiled bed linen, trailed through the fresh morning like a string of rooming-house windows. Then he saw an extraordinary thing: at one of the bedroom windows sat an unclothed woman of exceptional beauty, combing her golden hair. She passed like an apparition through Shady Hill, combing and combing her hair, and Francis followed her with his eyes until she was out of sight. Then old Mrs. Wrightson joined him on the platform and began to talk.

"Well, I guess you must be surprised to see me here the third morning in a row," she said, "but because of my window curtains I'm becoming a regular commuter. The curtains I bought on Monday, I returned on Tuesday, and the curtains I bought on Tuesday I'm returning today. On Monday, I got exactly what I wanted —it's a wool tapestry with roses and birds —but when I got them home, I found they were the wrong length. Well, I exchanged them yesterday, and when I got them home, I found they were still the wrong length. Now I'm praying to high Heaven that the decorator will have them in the right length, because you know my house, you *know* my living-room windows, and you can imagine what a problem they present. I don't know what to do with them."

"I know what to do with them," Francis said.

"What?"

"Paint them black on the inside, and shut up."

There was a gasp from Mrs. Wrightson, and Francis looked down at her to be sure that she knew he meant to be rude. She turned and walked away from him, so damaged in spirit that she limped. A wonderful feeling enveloped him, as if light were being shaken about him, and he thought again of Venus combing and combing her hair as she drifted through the Bronx. The realization of how many years had passed since he had enjoyed being deliberately impolite sobered him. Among his friends and neighbors, there were brilliant and gifted people—he saw that—but many of them, also, were bores and fools, and he had made the mistake of listening to them all with equal attention. He had confused a lack of discrimination with Christian love, and the confusion seemed general and destructive. He was grateful to the girl for this bracing sensation of independence. Birds were singing—cardinals and the last of the robins. The sky shone like enamel. Even the smell of ink from his morning paper honed his appetite for life, and the world that was spread out around him was plainly a paradise.

If Francis had believed in some hierarchy of love—in spirits armed with hunting bows, in the capriciousness of Venus and Eros—or even in magical potions, philters, and stews, in scapulae and quarters of the moon, it might have explained his susceptibility and his feverish high spirits. The autumnal loves of middle age are well publicized, and he guessed that he was face to face with one of these, but there was not a trace of autumn in what he felt. He wanted to sport in the green woods, scratch where he itched, and drink from the same cup.

His secretary, Miss Rainey, was late that morning—she went to a psychiatrist three mornings a week—and when she came in, Francis wondered what advice a psychiatrist would have for him. But the girl promised to bring back into his life something like the sound of music. The realization that this music might lead him straight to a trial for statutory rape at the county courthouse collapsed his happiness. The photograph of his four children laughing into the camera on the beach at Gay Head reproached him. On the letterhead of his firm there was a drawing of the Laocoön, and the figure of the priest and his sons in the coils of the snakes appeared to him to have the deepest meaning.

He had lunch with Pinky Trabert. At a conversational level, the mores of his friends were robust and elastic, but he knew that the moral card house would come down on them all—on Julia and the children as well—if he got caught taking advantage of a babysitter. Looking back over the recent history of Shady Hill for some precedent, he found there was none. There was no turpitude; there had not been a divorce since he lived there; there had not even been a breath of scandal. Things seemed arranged with more propriety even than in the Kingdom of Heaven. After leaving Pinky, Francis went to a jeweler's and bought the girl a bracelet. How happy this clandestine purchase made him, how stuffy and comical the jeweler's clerks seemed, how sweet the woman who passed at his back smelled! On Fifth Avenue, passing Atlas with his shoulders bent under the weight of the world, Francis thought of the strenuousness of containing his physicalness within the patterns he had chosen.

He did not know when he would see the girl next. He had the bracelet in his inside pocket when he got home. Opening the door of his house, he found her in the hall. Her back was to him, and she turned when she heard the door close. Her smile was open and loving. Her perfection stunned him like a fine day—a day after a thunderstorm. He seized her and covered her lips with his, and she struggled but she did not have to struggle for long, because just then little Gertrude Flannery appeared from somewhere and said, "Oh, Mr. Weed . . ."

Gertrude was a stray. She had been born with a taste for exploration, and she did not have it in her to center her life with her affectionate parents. People who did not know the Flannerys concluded from Gertrude's behavior that she was the child of a bitterly divided family, where drunken quarrels were the rule. This was not true. The fact that little Gertrude's clothing was ragged and thin was her own triumph over her mother's struggle to dress her warmly and neatly. Garrulous,

skinny, and unwashed, she drifted from house to house around the Blenhollow neighborhood, forming and breaking alliances based on an attachment to babies, animals, children her own age, adolescents, and sometimes adults. Opening your front door in the morning, you would find Gertrude sitting on your stoop. Going into the bathroom to shave, you would find Gertrude using the toilet. Looking into your son's crib, you would find it empty, and, looking further, you would find that Gertrude had pushed him in his baby carriage into the next village. She was helpful, pervasive, honest, hungry, and loyal. She never went home of her own choice. When the time to go arrived, she was indifferent to all its signs. "Go home, Gertrude," people could be heard saying in one house or another, night after night. "Go home, Gertrude. It's time for you to go home now, Gertrude." "You had better go home and get your supper, Gertrude." "I told you to go home twenty minutes ago, Gertrude." "Your mother will be worrying about you, Gertrude." "Go home, Gertrude, go home."

There are times when the lines around the human eye seem like shelves of eroded stone and when the staring eye itself strikes us with such a wilderness of animal feeling that we are at a loss. The look Francis gave the little girl was ugly and queer, and it frightened her. He reached into his pocket—his hands were shaking—and took out a quarter. "Go home, Gertrude, go home, and don't tell anyone, Gertrude. Don't—" He choked and ran into the living room as Julia called down to him from upstairs to hurry and dress.

The thought that he would drive Anne Murchison home later that night ran like a golden thread through the events of the party that Francis and Julia went to, and he laughed uproariously at dull jokes, dried a tear when Mabel Mercer told him about the death of her kitten, and stretched, yawned, sighed, and grunted like any other man with a rendezvous at the back of his mind. The bracelet was in his pocket. As he sat talking, the smell of grass was in his nose, and he was wondering where he would park the car. Nobody lived in the old Parker mansion, and the driveway was used as a lovers' lane. Townsend Street was a dead end, and he could park there, beyond the last house. The old lane that used to connect Elm Street to the riverbanks was overgrown, but he had walked there with his children, and he could drive his car deep enough into the brushwoods to be concealed.

The Weeds were the last to leave the party, and their host and hostess spoke of their own married happiness while they all four stood in the hallway saying good night. "She's my girl," their host said, squeezing his wife. "She's my blue sky. After sixteen years, I still bite her shoulders. She makes me feel like Hannibal crossing the Alps."

The Weeds drove home in silence. Francis brought the car up the driveway and sat still, with the motor running. "You can put the car in the garage," Julia said as she got out. "I told the Murchison girl she could leave at eleven. Someone drove her home." She shut the door, and Francis sat in the dark. He would be spared nothing then, it seemed, that a fool was not spared: ravening lewdness, jealousy, this hurt to his feelings that put tears in his eyes, even scorn—for he could see clearly the image he now presented, his arms spread over the steering wheel and his head buried in them for love.

Francis had been a dedicated Boy Scout when he was young, and, remembering the precepts.of his youth, he left his office early the next afternoon and played some round-robin squash, but, with his body toned up by exercise and a shower, he realized that he might better have stayed at his desk. It was a frosty night when he got home. The air smelled sharply of change. When he stepped into the house, he sensed an unusual stir. The children were in their best clothes, and when Julia came down, she was wearing a lavender dress and her diamond sunburst. She explained the stir: Mr. Hubber was coming at seven to take their photograph for the Christmas card. She had put out Francis' blue suit and a tie with some color in it, because the picture was

going to be in color this year. Julia was lighthearted at the thought of being photographed for Christmas. It was the kind of ceremony she enjoyed.

Francis went upstairs to change his clothes. He was tired from the day's work and tired with longing, and sitting on the edge of the bed had the effect of deepening his weariness. He thought of Anne Murchison, and the physical need to express himself, instead of being restrained by the pink lamps on Julia's dressing table, engulfed him. He went to Julia's desk, took a piece of writing paper, and began to write on it. "Dear Anne, I love you, I love you, I love you . . ." No one would see the letter, and he used no restraint. He used phrases like "heavenly bliss," and "love nest." He salivated, sighed, and trembled. When Julia called him to come down, the abyss between his fantasy and the practical world opened so wide that he felt it affect the muscles of his heart.

Julia and the children were on the stoop, and the photographer and his assistant had set up a double battery of floodlights to show the family and the architectural beauty of the entrance to their house. People who had come home on a late train slowed their cars to see the Weeds being photographed for their Christmas card. A few waved and called to the family. It took half an hour of smiling and wetting their lips before Mr. Hubber was satisfied. The heat of the lights made an unfresh smell in the frosty air, and when they were turned off, they lingered on the retina of Francis' eyes.

Later that night, while Francis and Julia were drinking their coffee in the living room, the doorbell rang. Julia answered the door and let in Clayton Thomas. He had come to pay her for some theater tickets that she had given his mother some time ago, and that Helen Thomas had scrupulously insisted on paying for, though Julia had asked her not to. Julia invited him in to have a cup of coffee. "I won't have any coffee," Clayton said, "but I will come in for a minute." He followed her into the living room, said good evening to Francis, and sat awkwardly in a chair.

Clayton's father had been killed in the war, and the young man's fatherlessness surrounded him like an element. This may have been conspicuous in Shady Hill because the Thomases were the only family that lacked a piece; all the other marriages were intact and productive. Clayton was in his second or third year of college, and he and his mother lived alone in a large house, which she hoped to sell. Clayton had once made some trouble. Years ago, he had stolen some money and run away; he had got to California before they caught up with him. He was tall and homely, wore horn-rimmed glasses, and spoke in a deep voice.

"When do you go back to college, Clayton?" Francis asked.

"I'm not going back," Clayton said. "Mother doesn't have the money, and there's no sense in all this pretense. I'm going to get a job, and if we sell the house, we'll take an apartment in New York."

"Won't you miss Shady Hill?" Julia asked.

"No," Clayton said. "I don't like it."

"Why not?" Francis asked.

"Well, there's a lot here I don't approve of," Clayton said gravely. "Things like the club dances. Last Saturday night, I looked in toward the end and saw Mr. Granner trying to put Mrs. Minot into the trophy case. They were both drunk. I disapprove of so much drinking."

"It was Saturday night," Francis said.

"And all the dovecotes are phony," Clayton said. "And the way people clutter up their lives. I've thought about it a lot, and what seems to me to be really wrong with Shady Hill is that it doesn't have any future. So much energy is spent in perpetuating the place—in keeping out undesirables, and so forth—that the only idea of the future anyone has is just more and more commuting trains and more parties. I don't think that's healthy. I think people ought to be able to dream big dreams about the future. I think people ought to be able to dream great dreams."

"It's too bad you couldn't continue with college," Julia said.

"I wanted to go to divinity school," Clayton said.

"What's your church?" Francis asked.

"Unitarian, Theosophist, Transcendentalist, Humanist," Clayton said.

"Wasn't Emerson a transcendentalist?" Julia asked.

"I mean the English transcendentalists," Clayton said. "All the American transcendentalists were goops."

"What kind of job do you expect to get?" Francis asked.

"Well, I'd like to work for a publisher," Clayton said, "but everyone tells me there's nothing doing. But it's the kind of thing I'm interested in. I'm writing a long verse play about good and evil. Uncle Charlie might get me into a bank, and that would be good for me. I need the discipline. I have a long way to go in forming my character. I have some terrible habits. I talk too much. I think I ought to take vows of silence. I ought to try not to speak for a week, and discipline myself. I've thought of making a retreat at one of the Episcopalian monasteries, but I don't like Trinitarianism."

"Do you have any girl friends?" Francis asked.

"I'm engaged to be married," Clayton said. "Of course, I'm not old enough or rich enough to have my engagement observed or respected or anything, but I bought a simulated emerald for Anne Murchison with the money I made cutting lawns this summer. We're going to be married as soon as she finishes school."

Francis recoiled at the mention of the girl's name. Then a dingy light seemed to emanate from his spirit, showing everything—Julia, the boy, the chairs—in their true colorlessness. It was like a bitter turn of the weather.

"We're going to have a large family," Clayton said. "Her father's a terrible rummy, and I've had my hard times, and we want to have lots of children. Oh, she's wonderful, Mr. and Mrs. Weed, and we have so much in common. We like all the same things. We sent out the same Christmas card last year without planning it, and we both have an allergy to tomatoes, and our eyebrows grow together in the middle. Well, good night."

Julia went to the door with him. When she returned, Francis said that Clayton was lazy, irresponsible, affected, and smelly. Julia said that Francis seemed to be getting intolerant; the Thomas boy was young and should be given a chance. Julia had noticed other cases where Francis had been short-tempered. "Mrs. Wrightson has asked everyone in Shady Hill to her anniversary party but us," she said.

"I'm sorry, Julia."

"Do you know why they didn't ask us?"

"Why?"

"Because you insulted Mrs. Wrightson."

"Then you know about it?"

"June Masterson told me. She was standing behind you."

Julia walked in front of the sofa with a small step that expressed, Francis knew, a feeling of anger.

"I did insult Mrs. Wrightson, Julia, and I meant to. I've never liked her parties, and I'm glad she's dropped us."

"What about Helen?"

"How does Helen come into this?"

"Mrs. Wrightson's the one who decides who goes to the assemblies."

"You mean she can keep Helen from going to the dances?"

"Yes."

"I hadn't thought of that."

"Oh, I knew you hadn't thought of it," Julia cried, thrusting hilt-deep into this chink of his armor. "And it makes me furious to see this kind of stupid thoughtlessness wreck everyone's happiness."

"I don't think I've wrecked anyone's happiness."

"Mrs. Wrightson runs Shady Hill and has run it for the last forty years. I don't know what makes you think that in a community like this you can indulge every impulse you have to be insulting, vulgar, and offensive."

"I have very good manners," Francis said, trying to give the evening a turn toward the light.

"Damn you, Francis Weed!" Julia cried, and the spit of her words struck him in the face. "I've worked hard for the social position we enjoy in this place, and I won't stand by and see you wreck it. You must have understood when you settled here that you couldn't expect to live like a bear in a cave."

"I've got to express my likes and dislikes."

"You can conceal your dislikes. You don't have to meet everything head-on, like a child. Unless you're anxious to be a social leper. It's no accident that we get asked out a great deal. It's no accident that Helen has so many friends. How would you like to spend your Saturday nights at the movies? How would you like tó spend your Sundays raking up dead leaves? How would you like it if your daughter spent the assembly nights sitting at her window, listening to the music from the club? How would you like it—" He did something then that was, after all, not so unaccountable, since her words seemed to raise up between them a wall so deadening that he gagged: He struck her full in the face. She staggered and then, a moment later, seemed composed. She went up the stairs to their room. She didn't slam the door. When Francis followed, a few minutes later, he found her packing a suitcase.

"Julia, I'm very sorry."

"It doesn't matter," she said. She was crying.

"Where do you think you're going?"

"I don't know. I just looked at a timetable. There's an eleven-sixteen into New York. I'll take that."

"You can't go, Julia."

"I can't stay. I know that."

"I'm sorry about Mrs. Wrightson, Julia, and I'm—"

"It doesn't matter about Mrs. Wrightson. That isn't the trouble."

"What is the trouble?"

"You don't love me."

"I do love you, Julia."

"No, you don't."

"Julia, I do love you, and I would like to be as we were—sweet and bawdy and dark—but now there are so many people."

"You hate me."

"I don't hate you, Julia."

"You have no idea of how much you

hate me. I think it's subconscious. You don't realize the cruel things you've done."

"What cruel things, Julia?"

"The cruel acts your subconscious drives you to in order to express your hatred of me."

"What, Julia?"

"I've never complained."

"Tell me."

"You don't know what you're doing."

"Tell me."

"Your clothes."

"What do you mean?"

"I mean the way you leave your dirty clothes around in order to express your subconscious hatred of me."

"I don't understand."

"I mean your dirty socks and your dirty pajamas and your dirty underwear and your dirty shirts!" She rose from kneeling by the suitcase and faced him, her eyes blazing and her voice ringing with emotion. "I'm talking about the fact that you've never learned to hang up anything. You just leave your clothes all over the floor where they drop, in order to humiliate me. You do it on purpose!" She fell on the bed, sobbing.

"Julia, darling!" he said, but when she felt his hand on her shoulder she got up.

"Leave me alone," she said. "I have to go." She brushed past him to the closet and came back with a dress. "I'm not taking any of the things you've given me," she said. "I'm leaving my pearls and the fur jacket."

"Oh, Julia!" Her figure, so helpless in its self-deceptions, bent over the suitcase made him nearly sick with pity. She did not understand how desolate her life would be without him. She didn't understand the hours that working women have to keep. She didn't understand that most of her friendships existed within the framework of their marriage, and that without this she would find herself alone. She didn't understand about travel, about hotels, about money. "Julia, I can't let you go! What you don't understand, Julia, is that you've come to be dependent on me."

She tossed her head back and covered her face with her hands. "Did you say that *I* was dependent on *you*?" she asked. "Is that what you said? And who is it that tells you what time to get up in the morning and when to go to bed at night? Who is it that prepares your meals and picks up your dirty closet and invites your friends to dinner? If it weren't for me, your neckties would be greasy and your clothing would be full of moth holes. You were alone when I met you, Francis Weed, and you'll be alone when I leave. When Mother asked you for a list to send out invitations to our wedding, how many names did you have to give her? Fourteen!"

"Cleveland wasn't my home, Julia."

"And how many of your friends came to the church? Two!"

"Cleveland wasn't my home, Julia."

"Since I'm not taking the fur jacket," she said quietly, "you'd better put it back into storage. There's an insurance policy on the pearls that comes due in January. The name of the laundry and the maid's telephone number—all those things are in my desk. I hope you won't drink too much, Francis. I hope that nothing bad will happen to you. If you do get into serious trouble, you can call me."

"Oh, my darling, I can't let you go!" Francis said. "I can't let you go, Julia!" He took her in his arms.

"I guess I'd better stay and take care of you for a little while longer," she said.

Riding to work in the morning, Francis saw the girl walk down the aisle of the coach. He was surprised; he hadn't realized that the school she went to was in the city, but she was carrying books, she seemed to be going to school. His surprise delayed his reaction, but then he got up clumsily and stepped into the aisle. Several people had come between them, but he could see her ahead of him, waiting for someone to open the car door, and then, as the train swerved, putting out her hand to support herself as she crossed the platform into the next car. He followed her through that car and halfway through another before calling her name—"Anne! Anne!"—but she didn't turn. He followed her into still another car, and she sat down in an aisle seat. Coming up to her, all his feelings warm and bent in her direction, he put his hand on the back of her seat—even this touch warmed him—and, leaning down to speak to her, he saw that it was not Anne. It was an older woman wearing glasses. He went on deliberately into another car, his face red with embarrassment and the much deeper feeling of having his good sense challenged; for if he couldn't tell one person from another, what evidence was there that his life with Julia and the children had as much reality as his dreams of iniquity in Paris or the litter, the grass smell, and the cave-shaped trees in Lovers' Lane.

Late that afternoon, Julia called to remind Francis that they were going out for dinner. A few minutes later, Trace Bearden called. "Look, fellar," Trace said, "I'm calling for Mrs. Thomas. You know? Clayton, that boy of hers, doesn't seem able to get a job, and I wondered if you could help. If you'd call Charlie Bell—I know he's indebted to you—and say a good word for the kid, I think Charlie would—"

"Trace, I hate to say this," Francis said, "but I don't feel that I can do anything for that boy. The kid's worthless. I know it's a harsh thing to say, but it's a fact. Any kindness done for him would backfire in everybody's face. He's just a worthless kid, Trace, and there's nothing to be done about it. Even if we got him a job, he wouldn't be able to keep it for a week. I know that to be a fact. It's an awful thing, Trace, and I know it is, but instead of recommending that kid, I'd feel obliged to warn people against him—people who knew his father and would naturally want to step in and do something. I'd feel obliged to warn them. He's a thief . . ."

The moment this conversation was finished, Miss Rainey came in and stood by his desk. "I'm not going to be able to work for you any more, Mr. Weed," she said. "I can stay until the seventeenth if you need me, but I've been offered a whirlwind of a job, and I'd like to leave as soon as possible."

She went out leaving him to face alone the wickedness of what he had done to the Thomas boy. His children in their photograph laughed and laughed, glazed with all the bright colors of summer, and he remembered that they had met a bagpiper on the beach that day and he had paid the piper a dollar to play them a battle song of the Black Watch. The girl would be at the house when he got home. He would spend another evening among his kind neighbors, picking and choosing dead-end streets, cart tracks, and the driveways of abandoned houses. There was nothing to mitigate his feeling—nothing that laughter or a game of softball with the children would change—and, thinking back over the plane crash, the Farquarsons' new maid, and Anne Murchison's difficulties with her drunken father, he wondered how he could have avoided arriving at just where he was. He was in trouble. He had been lost once in his life, coming back from a trout stream in the north woods, and he had now the same bleak realization that no amount of cheerfulness or hopefulness or valor or perseverance could help him find, in the gathering dark, the path that he'd lost. He smelled the forest. The feeling of bleakness was intolerable, and he saw clearly that he had reached the point where he would have to make a choice.

He could go to a psychiatrist, like Miss Rainey; he could go to church and confess his lusts; he could go to a Danish massage parlor in the West Seventies that had been recommended by a salesman; he could rape the girl or trust that he would somehow be prevented from doing this; or he could get drunk. It was his life, his boat, and, like every other man, he was made to be the father of thousands, and what harm could there be in a tryst that would make them both feel more kindly toward the world? This was the wrong train of thought, and he came back to the first, the psychiatrist. He had the telephone number of Miss Rainey's doctor, and he called and asked for an immediate appointment. He was insistent with the doctor's secretary—it was his manner in business—and when she said that the doctor's schedule was full for the next few weeks, Francis demanded an appointment that day and was told to come at five.

The psychiatrist's office was in a building that was used mostly by doctors and dentists, and the hallways were filled with the candy smell of mouthwash and memories of pain. Francis' character had been formed upon a series of private resolves—resolves about cleanliness, about going off the high diving board or repeating any other feat that challenged his courage, about punctuality, honesty, and virtue. To abdicate the perfect loneliness in which he had made his most vital decisions shattered his concept of character and left him now in a condition that felt like shock. He was stupefied. The scene for his *miserere mei Deus* was, like the waiting room of so many doctors' offices, a crude token gesture toward the sweets of domestic bliss: a place arranged with antiques, coffee tables, potted plants, and etchings of snow-covered bridges and geese in flight, although there were no children, no marriage bed, no stove, even, in this travesty of a house, where no one had ever spent the night and where the curtained windows looked straight onto a dark air shaft. Francis gave his name and address to a secretary and then saw, at the side of the room, a policeman moving toward him. "Hold it, hold it," the policeman said. "Don't move. Keep your hands where they are."

"I think it's all right, officer," the secretary began. "I think it will be—"

"Let's make sure," the policeman said, and he began to slap Francis' clothes, looking for what—pistols, knives, an icepick? Finding nothing, he went off, and the secretary began a nervous apology: "When you called on the telephone, Mr. Weed, you seemed very excited, and one of the doctor's patients has been threatening his life, and we have to be careful. If you want to go in now?" Francis pushed open a door connected to an electrical chime, and in the doctor's lair sat down heavily, blew his nose into a handkerchief, searched in his pockets for cigarettes, for matches, for something, and said hoarsely, with tears in his eyes, "I'm in love, Dr. Herzog."

It is a week or ten days later in Shady Hill. The seven-fourteen has come and gone, and here and there dinner is finished and the dishes are in the dishwashing machine. The village hangs, morally and economically, from a thread; but it hangs by its thread in the evening light. Donald Goslin has begun to worry the "Moonlight Sonata" again. *Marcato ma sempre pianissimo!* He seems to be wringing out a wet bath towel, but the housemaid does not heed him. She is writing a letter to Arthur Godfrey. In the cellar of his house, Francis Weed is building a coffee table. Dr. Herzog recommended woodwork as a therapy, and Francis finds some true consolation in the simple arithmetic involved and in the holy smell of new wood. Francis is happy. Upstairs, little Toby is crying, because he is tired. He puts off his cowboy hat, gloves, and fringed jacket, unbuckles the belt studded with gold and rubies, the silver bullets and holsters, slips off his suspenders, his checked shirt, and Levis, and sits on the edge of his bed to pull off his high boots. Leaving this equipment in a heap, he goes to the closet and takes his space suit off a nail. It is a struggle for him to get into the long tights, but he succeeds. He loops the magic cape over his shoulders and, climbing onto the footboard of his bed, he spreads his arms and flies the short distance to the floor, landing with a thump that is audible to everyone in the house but himself.

"Go home, Gertrude, go home," Mrs. Masterson says. "I told you to go home an hour ago, Gertrude. It's way past your suppertime, and your mother will be worried. Go home!" A door on the Babcock's terrace flies open, and out comes Mrs. Babcock without any clothes on, pursued by her naked husband. (Their children are away at boarding school, and their terrace is screened by a hedge.) Over the terrace they go and in at the kitchen door, as passionate and handsome a nymph and satyr as you will find on any wall in Venice. Cutting the last of the roses in her garden, Julia hears old Mr. Nixon shouting at the squirrels in his bird-feeding station. "Rapscallions! Varmints! Avaunt and quit my sight!" A miserable cat wanders into the garden, sunk in spiritual and physical discomfort. Tied to

its head is a small straw hat—a doll's hat
—and it is securely buttoned into a doll's
dress, from the skirts of which protrudes
its long, hairy tail. As it walks, it shakes
its feet, as if it had fallen into water.

"Here, pussy, pussy, pussy!" Julia calls.
"Here, pussy, here, poor pussy!" But
the cat gives her a skeptical look and
stumbles away in its skirts. The last to
come is Jupiter. He prances through the
tomato vines, holding in his generous
mouth the remains of an evening slipper.
Then it is dark; it is a night where kings
in golden suits ride elephants over the
mountains.

[1954]

QUESTIONS FOR STUDY

1. *How do each of the seemingly unrelated incidents at the beginning of
   the story serve to reveal the pattern of Francis Weed's life? What are
   the sources of his dissatisfaction?*
2. *What does Cheever mean when he says of Francis that "It was not his
   limitation at all to be unable to escape the past; it was perhaps his
   limitation that he had escaped it so successfully"?*
3. *Why is Francis so attracted to Anne Murchison?*
4. *Why is Weed deliberately rude to old Mrs. Wrightson? Why does he
   so willingly denounce Clayton Thomas?*
5. *How does Francis finally resolve his problem? Does he come to an
   understanding of himself? Why does the story conclude with a final
   panoramic glimpse of Shady Hill which comes to rest on Jupiter the
   dog? Why is Jupiter so "out of place" in Shady Hill?*
6. *To what extent is the story a satiric and humorous commentary on
   upper-middle-class American life? Is Francis Weed merely a stereo-
   type, or does Cheever manage to individualize him?*

ANTON CHEKHOV

The Bet

I

IT WAS a dark autumn night. The old banker was walking up and down his study and remembering how, fifteen years before, he had given a party one autumn evening. There had been many clever men there, and there had been interesting conversations. Among other things they had talked of capital punishment. The majority of the guests, among whom were many journalists and intellectual men, disapproved of the death penalty. They considered that form of punishment out of date, immoral, and unsuitable for Christian States. In the opinion of some of them the death penalty ought to be replaced everywhere by imprisonment for life.

"I don't agree with you," said their host the banker. "I have not tried either the death penalty or imprisonment for life, but if one may judge *à priori*, the death penalty is more moral and more humane than imprisonment for life. Capital punishment kills a man at once, but lifelong imprisonment kills him slowly. Which executioner is the more humane, he who kills you in a few minutes or he who drags the life out of you in the course of many years?"

"Both are equally immoral," observed one of the guests, "for they both have the same object—to take away life. The State is not God. It has not the right to take away what it cannot restore when it wants to."

Among the guests was a young lawyer, a young man of five-and-twenty. When he was asked his opinion, he said:

"The death sentence and the life sentence are equally immoral, but if I had to choose between the death penalty and imprisonment for life, I would certainly choose the second. To live anyhow is better than not at all."

A lively discussion arose. The banker, who was younger and more nervous in those days, was suddenly carried away by excitement; he struck the table with his fist and shouted at the young man:

"It's not true! I'll bet you two millions you wouldn't stay in solitary confinement for five years."

"If you mean that in earnest,'" said the young man, "I'll take the bet, but I would stay not five but fifteen years."

"Fifteen? Done!" cried the banker. "Gentlemen, I stake two millions!"

"Agreed! You stake your millions and I stake my freedom!" said the young man.

And this wild, senseless bet was carried out! The banker, spoilt and frivolous, with millions beyond his reckoning, was delighted at the bet. At supper he made fun of the young man, and said:

"Think better of it, young man, while there is still time. To me two millions are a trifle, but you are losing three or four of the best years of your life. I say three or four, because you won't stay longer. Don't forget either, you unhappy man, that voluntary confinement is a great deal harder to bear than compulsory. The thought that you have the right to step out in liberty at any moment will poison your whole existence in prison. I am sorry for you."

And now the banker, walking to and fro, remembered all this, and asked himself: "What was the object of that bet? What is the good of that man's losing fifteen years of his life·and my throwing away two millions? Can it prove that the death penalty is better or worse than imprisonment for life? No, no. It was all

Reprinted with permission of The Macmillan Company from *The Schoolmistress and Other Stories* by Anton Chekhov, translated from the Russian by Constance Garnett. Copyright 1921 by The Macmillan Company, renewed 1949 by David Garnett. Also used by permission of Mr. David Garnett and Chatto and Windus Ltd., London.

nonsensical and meaningless. On my part it was the caprice of a pampered man, and on his part simple greed for money. . . ."

Then he remembered what followed that evening. It was decided that the young man should spend the years of his captivity under the strictest supervision in one of the lodges in the banker's garden. It was agreed that for fifteen years he should not be free to cross the threshold of the lodge, to see human beings, to hear the human voice, or to receive letters and newspapers. He was allowed to have a musical instrument and books, and was allowed to write letters, to drink wine, and to smoke. By the terms of the agreement, the only relations he could have with the outer world were by a little window made purposely for that object. He might have anything he wanted—books, music, wine, and so on—in any quantity he desired by writing an order, but could only receive them through the window. The agreement provided for every detail and every trifle that would make his imprisonment strictly solitary, and bound the young man to stay there *exactly* fifteen years, beginning from twelve o'clock of November 14, 1870, and ending at twelve o'clock of November 14, 1885. The slightest attempt on his part to break the conditions, if only two minutes before the end, released the banker from the obligation to pay him two millions.

For the first year of his confinement, as far as one could judge from his brief notes, the prisoner suffered severely from loneliness and depression. The sounds of the piano could be heard continually day and night from his lodge. He refused wine and tobacco. Wine, he wrote, excites the desires, and desires are the worst foes of the prisoner; and besides, nothing could be more dreary than drinking good wine and seeing no one. And tobacco spoilt the air of his room. In the first year the books he sent for were principally of a light character; novels with a complicated love plot, sensational and fantastic stories, and so on.

In the second year the piano was silent in the lodge, and the prisoner asked only for the classics. In the fifth year music was audible again, and the prisoner asked for wine. Those who watched him through the window said that all that year he spent doing nothing but eating and drinking and lying on his bed, frequently yawning and angrily talking to himself. He did not read books. Sometimes at night he would sit down to write; he would spend hours writing, and in the morning tear up all that he had written. More than once he could be heard crying.

In the second half of the sixth year the prisoner began zealously studying languages, philosophy, and history. He threw himself eagerly into these studies —so much so that the banker had enough to do to get him the books he ordered. In the course of four years some six hundred volumes were procured at his request. It was during this period that the banker received the following letter from his prisoner:

"My dear Jailer, I write you these lines in six languages. Show them to people who know the languages. Let them read them. If they find not one mistake I implore you to fire a shot in the garden. That shot will show me that my efforts have not been thrown away. The geniuses of all ages and of all lands speak different languages, but the same flame burns in them all. Oh, if you only knew what unearthly happiness my soul feels now from being able to understand them!" The prisoner's desire was fulfilled. The banker ordered two shots to be fired in the garden.

Then after the tenth year, the prisoner sat immovably at the table and read nothing but the Gospel. It seemed strange to the banker that a man who in four years had mastered six hundred learned volumes should waste nearly a year over one thin book easy of comprehension. Theology and histories of religion followed the Gospels.

In the last two years of his confinement the prisoner read an immense quantity of books quite indiscriminately. At one time he was busy with the natural sciences, then he would ask for Byron or Shakespeare. There were notes in which he demanded at the same time books on chemistry, and a manual of medicine, and a novel, and some treatise on philosophy or theology. His reading suggested a man swimming in the sea among the wreckage of his ship, and trying to save his life by greedily clutching first at one spar and then at another.

II

The old banker remembered all this, and thought:

"To-morrow at twelve o'clock he will regain his freedom. By our agreement I ought to pay him two millions. If I do pay him, it is all over with me: I shall be utterly ruined."

Fifteen years before, his millions had been beyond his reckoning; now he was afraid to ask himself which were greater, his debts or his assets. Desperate gambling on the Stock Exchange, wild speculation, and the excitability which he could not get over even in advancing years, had by degrees led to the decline of his fortune, and the proud, fearless, self-confident millionaire had become a banker of middling rank, trembling at every rise and fall in his investments. "Cursed bet!" muttered the old man, clutching his head in despair. "Why didn't the man die? He is only forty now. He will take my last penny from me, he will marry, will enjoy life, will gamble on the Exchange; while I shall look at him with envy like a beggar, and hear from him every day the same sentence: 'I am indebted to you for the happiness of my life, let me help you!' No, it is too much! The one means of being saved from bankruptcy and disgrace is the death of that man!"

It struck three o'clock, the banker listened; everyone was asleep in the house, and nothing could be heard outside but the rustling of the chilled trees. Trying to make no noise, he took from a fireproof safe the key of the door which had not been opened for fifteen years, put on his overcoat, and went out of the house.

It was dark and cold in the garden. Rain was falling. A damp cutting wind was racing about the garden, howling and giving the trees no rest. The banker strained his eyes, but could see neither the earth nor the white statues, nor the lodge, nor the trees. Going to the spot where the lodge stood, he twice called the watch-

man. No answer followed. Evidently the watchman had sought shelter from the weather, and was now asleep somewhere either in the kitchen or in the greenhouse.

"If I had the pluck to carry out my intention," thought the old man, "suspicion would fall first upon the watchman."

He felt in the darkness for the steps and the door, and went into the entry of the lodge. Then he groped his way into a little passage and lighted a match. There was not a soul there. There was a bedstead with no bedding on it, and in the corner there was a dark cast-iron stove. The seals on the door leading to the prisoner's rooms were intact.

When the match went out the old man, trembling with emotion, peeped through the little window. A candle was burning dimly in the prisoner's room. He was sitting at the table. Nothing could be seen but his back, the hair on his head, and his hands. Open books were lying on the table, on the two easy-chairs, and on the carpet near the table.

Five minutes passed and the prisoner did not once stir. Fifteen years' imprisonment had taught him to sit still. The banker tapped at the window with his finger, and the prisoner made no movement whatever in response. Then the banker cautiously broke the seals off the door and put the key in the keyhole. The rusty lock gave a grating sound and the door creaked. The banker expected to hear at once footsteps and a cry of astonishment, but three minutes passed and it was as quiet as ever in the room. He made up his mind to go in.

At the table a man unlike ordinary people was sitting motionless. He was a skeleton with the skin drawn tight over his bones, with long curls like a woman's, and a shaggy beard. His face was yellow with an earthy tint in it, his cheeks were hollow, his back long and narrow, and the hand on which his shaggy head was propped was so thin and delicate that it was dreadful to look at it. His hair was already streaked with silver, and seeing his emaciated, aged-looking face, no one would have believed that he was only forty. He was asleep. . . . In front of his bowed head there lay on the table a sheet

of paper on which there was something
written in fine handwriting.

"Poor creature!" thought the banker,
"he is asleep and most likely dreaming of
the millions. And I have only to take this
half-dead man, throw him on the bed,
stifle him a little with the pillow, and the
most conscientious expert would find no
sign of a violent death. But let us first read
what he has written here. . . ."

The banker took the page from the
table and read as follows:

"To-morrow at twelve o'clock I regain
my freedom and the right to associate
with other men, but before I leave this
room and see the sunshine, I think it
necessary to say a few words to you. With
a clear conscience I tell you, as before
God, who beholds me, that I despise freedom and life and health, and all that in
your books is called the good things of the
world.

"For fifteen years I have been intently
studying earthly life. It is true I have not
seen the earth nor men, but in your books
I have drunk fragrant wine, I have sung
songs, I have hunted stags and wild boars
in the forests, have loved women. . . .
Beauties as ethereal as clouds, created by
the magic of your poets and geniuses,
have visited me at night, and have whispered in my ears wonderful tales that have
set my brain in a whirl. In your books I
have climbed to the peaks of Elburz and
Mont Blanc, and from there I have seen
the sun rise and have watched it at evening flood the sky, the ocean, and the
mountain-tops with gold and crimson. I
have watched from there the lightning
flashing over my head and cleaving the
storm-clouds. I have seen green forests,
fields, rivers, lakes, towns. I have heard
the singing of the sirens, and the strains
of the shepherds' pipes; I have touched the
wings of comely devils who flew down to
converse with me of God. . . . In your
books I have flung myself into the bottomless pit, performed miracles, slain, burned
towns, preached new religions, conquered
whole kingdoms. . . .

"Your books have given me wisdom.
All that the unresting thought of man has
created in the ages is compressed into a
small compass in my brain. I know that I
am wiser than all of you.

"And I despise your books, I despise
wisdom and the blessings of this world.
It is all worthless, fleeting, illusory, and
deceptive, like a mirage. You may be
proud, wise, and fine, but death will wipe
you off the face of the earth as though
you were no more than mice burrowing
under the floor, and your posterity, your
history, your immortal geniuses will burn
or freeze together with the earthly globe.

"You have lost your reason and taken
the wrong path. You have taken lies for
truth, and hideousness for beauty. You
would marvel if, owing to strange events
of some sorts, frogs and lizards suddenly
grew on apple and orange trees instead of
fruit, or if roses began to smell like a
sweating horse; so I marvel at you who
exchange heaven for earth. I don't want
to understand you.

"To prove to you in action how I despise all that you live by, I renounce the
two millions of which I once dreamed as
of paradise and which now I despise. To
deprive myself of the right to the money
I shall go out from here five hours before
the time fixed, and so break the compact. . . ."

When the banker had read this he laid
the page on the table, kissed the strange
man on the head, and went out of the
lodge, weeping. At no other time, even
when he had lost heavily on the Stock
Exchange, had he felt so great a contempt
for himself. When he got home he lay on
his bed, but his tears and emotion kept
him for hours from sleeping.

Next morning the watchmen ran in
with pale faces, and told him they had
seen the man who lived in the lodge climb
out of the window into the garden, go to
the gate, and disappear. The banker went
at once with the servants to the lodge and
made sure of the flight of his prisoner. To
avoid arousing unnecessary talk, he took
from the table the writing in which the
millions were renounced, and when he got
home locked it up in the fireproof safe.

[1888]

TRANSLATED BY
CONSTANCE GARNETT

QUESTIONS FOR STUDY

1. *What does the lawyer discover about knowledge and about life? Why are they apparently unsatisfactory? What clues to the changes taking place in the lawyer's mind are provided by the books he chooses to read?*
2. *Why does he willfully flee before the term of his confinement is officially over?*
3. *Does the banker also learn something from the bet? How does his decline compare to the change that takes place in the lawyer? Why does the banker kiss the lawyer's head? Why does he weep? Why does he lock the lawyer's letter in his safe?*
4. *What answer does the story provide to the initial question of whether life imprisonment is preferable to capital punishment?*

ANTON CHEKHOV

The Darling

OLENKA, the daughter of the retired collegiate assessor, Plemyanniakov, was sitting in her back porch, lost in thought. It was hot, the flies were persistent and teasing, and it was pleasant to reflect that it would soon be evening. Dark rainclouds were gathering from the east, and bringing from time to time a breath of moisture in the air.

Kukin, who was the manager of an open-air theatre called the Tivoli, and who lived in the lodge, was standing in the middle of the garden looking at the sky.

"Again!" he observed despairingly. "It's going to rain again! Rain every day, as though to spite me. I might as well hang myself! It's ruin! Fearful losses every day."

He flung up his hands, and went on, addressing Olenka:

"There! that's the life we lead, Olga Semyonovna. It's enough to make one cry. One works and does one's utmost, one wears oneself out, getting no sleep at night, and racks one's brain what to do for the best. And then what happens? To begin with, one's public is ignorant, boorish. I give them the very best operetta, a dainty masque, first rate music-hall artists. But do you suppose that's what they want! They don't understand anything of that sort. They want a clown; what they ask for is vulgarity. And then look at the weather! Almost every evening it rains. It started on the tenth of May, and it's kept it up all May and June. It's simply awful! The public doesn't come, but I've to pay the rent just the same, and pay the artists."

The next evening the clouds would gather again, and Kukin would say with an hysterical laugh:

"Well, rain away, then! Flood the garden, drown me! Damn my luck in this world and the next! Let the artists have me up! Send me to prison!—to Siberia!—the scaffold! Ha, ha, ha!"

And next day the same thing.

Olenka listened to Kukin with silent gravity, and sometimes tears came into her eyes. In the end his misfortunes touched her; she grew to love him. He was a small thin man, with a yellow face, and curls combed forward on his forehead. He spoke in a thin tenor; as he talked his mouth worked on one side, and there was always an expression of despair on his face; yet he aroused a deep and genuine affection in her. She was always fond of some one, and could not exist without loving. In earlier days she had loved her papa, who now sat in a darkened room, breathing with difficulty; she had loved her aunt who used to come every other year from Bryansk; and before that, when she was at school, she had loved her French master. She was a gentle, soft-hearted, compassionate girl, with mild, tender eyes and very good health. At the sight of her full rosy cheeks, her soft white neck with a little dark mole on it, and the kind, naïve smile, which came into her face when she listened to anything pleasant, men thought, "Yes, not half bad," and smiled too, while lady visitors could not refrain from seizing her hand in the middle of a conversation, exclaiming in a gush of delight, "You darling!"

The house in which she had lived from her birth upwards, and which was left her in her father's will, was at the extreme end of the town, not far from the Tivoli. In the evenings and at night she could hear the band playing, and the crackling and banging of fireworks, and it seemed to her

that it was Kukin struggling with his destiny, storming the entrenchments of his
chief foe, the indifferent public; there was
a sweet thrill at her heart, she had no
desire to sleep, and when he returned
home at day-break, she tapped softly at
her bedroom window, and showing him
only her face and one shoulder through
the curtain, she gave him a friendly
smile. . . .

He proposed to her, and they were
married. And when he had a closer view
of her neck and her plump, fine shoulders,
he threw up his hands, and said:

"You darling!"

He was happy, but as it rained on the
day and night of his wedding, his face
still retained an expression of despair.

They got on very well together. She
used to sit in his office, to look after things
in the Tivoli, to put down the accounts
and pay the wages. And her rosy cheeks,
her sweet, naïve, radiant smile, were to be
seen now at the office window, now in the
refreshment bar or behind the scenes of
the theatre. And already she used to say
to her acquaintants that the theatre was
the chief and most important thing in life,
and that it was only through the drama
that one could derive true enjoyment and
become cultivated and humane.

"But do you suppose the public understands that?" she used to say. "What they
want is a clown. Yesterday we gave 'Faust
Inside Out,' and almost all the boxes were
empty; but if Vanitchka and I had been
producing some vulgar thing, I assure you
the theatre would have been packed. To-
morrow Vanitchka and I are doing 'Or-
pheus in Hell.' Do come."

And what Kukin said about the theatre
and the actors she repeated. Like him she
despised the public for their ignorance
and their indifference to art; she took part
in the rehearsals, she corrected the actors,
she kept an eye on the behaviour of the
musicians, and when there was an un-
favourable notice in the local paper, she
shed tears, and then went to the editor's
office to set things right.

The actors were fond of her and used
to call her "Vanitchka and I," and "the
darling"; she was sorry for them and used
to lend them small sums of money, and if
they deceived her, she used to shed a few
tears in private, but did not complain to
her husband.

They got on well in the winter too.
They took the theatre in the town for the
whole winter, and let it for short terms to
a Little Russian company, or to a con-
jurer, or to a local dramatic society.
Olenka grew stouter, and was always
beaming with satisfaction, while Kukin
grew thinner and yellower, and continually complained of their terrible losses,
although he had not done badly all the
winter. He used to cough at night, and she
used to give him hot raspberry tea or lime-
flower water, to rub him with eau-de-
Cologne and to wrap him in her warm
shawls.

"You're such a sweet pet!" she used to
say with perfect sincerity, stroking his
hair. "You're such a pretty dear!"

Towards Lent he went to Moscow to
collect a new troupe, and without him she
could not sleep, but sat all night at her
window, looking at the stars, and she
compared herself with the hens, who are
awake all night and uneasy when the cock
is not in the hen-house. Kukin was detained in Moscow, and wrote that he
would be back at Easter, adding some instructions about the Tivoli. But on the
Sunday before Easter, late in the evening,
came a sudden ominous knock at the gate;
some one was hammering on the gate as
though on a barrel—boom, boom, boom!
The drowsy cook went flopping with her
bare feet through the puddles, as she ran
to open the gate.

"Please open," said some one outside in
a thick bass. "There is a telegram for
you."

Olenka had received telegrams from
her husband before, but this time for
some reason she felt numb with terror.
With shaking hands she opened the telegram and read as follows:

"Ivan Petrovitch died suddenly to-day.
Awaiting immate instructions fufuneral
Tuesday."

That was how it was written in the telegram—"fufuneral," and the utterly incomprehensible word "immate." It was

signed by the stage manager of the operatic company.

"My darling!" sobbed Olenka. "Vanitchka, my precious, my darling! Why did I ever meet you! Why did I know you and love you! Your poor heart-broken Olenka is all alone without you!"

Kukin's funeral took place on Tuesday in Moscow, Olenka returned home on Wednesday, and as soon as she got indoors she threw herself on her bed and sobbed so loudly that it could be heard next door, and in the street.

"Poor darling!" the neighbours said, as they crossed themselves. "Olga Semyonovna, poor darling! How she does take on!"

Three months later Olenka was coming home from mass, melancholy and in deep mourning. It happened that one of her neighbours, Vassily Andreitch Pustovalov, returning home from church, walked back beside her. He was the manager at Babakayev's, the timber merchant's. He wore a straw hat, a white waistcoat, and a gold watch-chain, and looked more like a country gentleman than a man in trade.

"Everything happens as it is ordained, Olga Semyonovna," he said gravely, with a sympathetic note in his voice; "and if any of our dear ones die, it must be because it is the will of God, so we ought to have fortitude and bear it submissively."

After seeing Olenka to her gate, he said good-bye and went on. All day afterwards she heard his sedately dignified voice, and whenever she shut her eyes she saw his dark beard. She liked him very much. And apparently she had made an impression on him too, for not long afterwards an elderly lady, with whom she was only slightly acquainted, came to drink coffee with her, and as soon as she was seated at table began to talk about Pustovalov, saying that he was an excellent man whom one could thoroughly depend upon, and that any girl would be glad to marry him. Three days later Pustovalov came himself. He did not stay long, only about ten minutes, and he did not say much, but when he left, Olenka loved him—loved him so much that she lay awake all night

in a perfect fever, and in the morning she sent for the elderly lady. The match was quickly arranged, and then came the wedding.

Pustovalov and Olenka got on very well together when they were married.

Usually he sat in the office till dinnertime, then he went out on business, while Olenka took his place, and sat in the office till evening, making up accounts and booking orders.

"Timber gets dearer every year; the price rises twenty per cent," she would say to her customers and friends. "Only fancy we used to sell local timber, and now Vassitchka always has to go for wood to the Mogilev district. And the freight!" she would add, covering her cheeks with her hands in horror. "The freight!"

It seemed to her that she had been in the timber trade for ages and ages, and that the most important and necessary thing in life was timber; and there was something intimate and touching to her in the very sound of words such as "baulk," "post," "beam," "pole," "scantling," "batten," "lath," "plank," etc.

At night when she was asleep she dreamed of perfect mountains of planks and boards, and long strings of wagons, carting timber somewhere far away. She dreamed that a whole regiment of six-inch beams forty feet high, standing on end, was marching upon the timber-yard; that logs, beams, and boards knocked together with the resounding crash of dry wood, kept falling and getting up again, piling themselves on each other. Olenka cried out in her sleep, and Pustovalov said to her tenderly: "Olenka, what's the matter, darling? Cross yourself!"

Her husband's ideas were hers. If he thought the room was too hot, or that business was slack, she thought the same. Her husband did not care for entertainments, and on holidays he stayed at home. She did likewise.

"You are always at home or in the office," her friends said to her. "You should go to the theatre, darling, or to the circus."

"Vassitchka and I have no time to go to theatres," she would answer sedately.

"We have no time for nonsense. What's the use of these theatres?"

On Saturdays Pustovalov and she used to go to the evening service; on holidays to early mass, and they walked side by side with softened faces as they came home from church. There was a pleasant fragrance about them both, and her silk dress rustled agreeably. At home they drank tea, with fancy bread and jams of various kinds, and afterwards they ate pie. Every day at twelve o'clock there was a savoury smell of beet-root soup and of mutton or duck in their yard, and on fast-days of fish, and no one could pass the gate without feeling hungry. In the office the samovar was always boiling, and customers were regaled with tea and cracknels. Once a week the couple went to the baths and returned side by side, both red in the face.

"Yes, we have nothing to complain of, thank God," Olenka used to say to her acquaintances. "I wish every one were as well off as Vassitchka and I."

When Pustovalov went away to buy wood in the Mogilev district, she missed him dreadfully, lay awake and cried. A young veterinary surgeon in the army, called Smirnin, to whom they had let their lodge, used sometimes to come in in the evening. He used to talk to her and play cards with her, and this entertained her in her husband's absence. She was particularly interested in what he told her of his home life. He was married and had a little boy, but was separated from his wife because she had been unfaithful to him, and now he hated her and used to send her forty roubles a month for the maintenance of their son. And hearing of all this, Olenka sighed and shook her head. She was sorry for him.

"Well, God keep you," she used to say to him at parting, as she lighted him down the stairs with a candle. "Thank you for coming to cheer me up, and may the Mother of God give you health."

And she always expressed herself with the same sedateness and dignity, the same reasonableness, in imitation of her husband. As the veterinary surgeon was disappearing behind the door below, she would say:

"You know, Vladimir Platonitch, you'd better make it up with your wife. You should forgive her for the sake of your son. You may be sure the little fellow understands."

And when Pustovalov came back, she told him in a low voice about the veterinary surgeon and his unhappy home life, and both sighed and shook their heads and talked about the boy, who, no doubt, missed his father, and by some strange connection of ideas, they went up to the holy ikons, bowed to the ground before them and prayed that God would give them children.

And so the Pustovalovs lived for six years quietly and peaceably in love and complete harmony.

But behold! one winter day after drinking hot tea in the office, Vassily Andreitch went out into the yard without his cap on to see about sending off some timber, caught cold and was taken ill. He had the best doctors, but he grew worse and died after four months' illness. And Olenka was a widow once more.

"I've nobody, now you've left me, my darling," she sobbed, after her husband's funeral. "How can I live without you, in wretchedness and misery! Pity me, good people, all alone in the world!"

She went about dressed in black with long "weepers," and gave up wearing hat and gloves for good. She hardly ever went out, except to church, or to her husband's grave, and led the life of a nun. It was not till six months later that she took off the weepers and opened the shutters of the windows. She was sometimes seen in the mornings, going with her cook to market for provisions, but what went on in her house and how she lived now could only be surmised. People guessed, from seeing her drinking tea in her garden with the veterinary surgeon, who read the newspaper aloud to her, and from the fact that, meeting a lady she knew at the post-office, she said to her:

"There is no proper veterinary inspection in our town, and that's the cause of all sorts of epidemics. One is always hearing of people's getting infection from the milk supply, or catching diseases from horses and cows. The health of domestic animals ought to be as well cared for as the health of human beings."

She repeated the veterinary surgeon's words, and was of the same opinion as he about everything. It was evident that she could not live a year without some attachment, and had found new happiness in the lodge. In any one else this would have been censured, but no one could think ill of Olenka; everything she did was so natural. Neither she nor the veterinary surgeon said anything to other people of the change in their relations, and tried, indeed, to conceal it, but without success, for Olenka could not keep a secret. When he had visitors, men serving in his regiment, and she poured out tea or served the supper, she would begin talking of the cattle plague, of the foot and mouth disease, and of the municipal slaughterhouses. He was dreadfully embarrassed, and when the guests had gone, he would seize her by the hand and hiss angrily:

"I've asked you before not to talk about what you don't understand. When we veterinary surgeons are talking among ourselves, please don't put your word in. It's really annoying."

And she would look at him with astonishment and dismay, and ask him in alarm: "But, Voioditchka, what *am* I to talk about?"

And with tears in her eyes she would embrace him, begging him not to be angry, and they were both happy.

But this happiness did not last long. The veterinary surgeon departed, departed for ever with his regiment, when it was transferred to a distant place—to Siberia, it may be. And Olenka was left alone.

Now she was absolutely alone. Her father had long been dead, and his armchair lay in the attic, covered with dust and lame of one leg. She got thinner and plainer, and when people met her in the street they did not look at her as they used to, and did not smile to her; evidently her best years were over and left behind, and now a new sort of life had begun for her, which did not bear thinking about. In the evening Olenka sat in the porch, and heard the band playing and the fireworks popping in the Tivoli, but now the sound stirred no response. She looked into her yard without interest, thought of nothing, wished for nothing, and afterwards, when night came on she went to bed and dreamed of her empty yard. She ate and drank as it were unwillingly.

And what was worst of all, she had no opinions of any sort. She saw the objects about her and understood what she saw, but could not form any opinion about them, and did not know what to talk about. And how awful it is not to have any opinions! One sees a bottle, for instance, or the rain, or a peasant driving in his cart, but what the bottle is for, or the rain, or the peasant, and what is the meaning of it, one can't say, and could not even for a thousand roubles. When she had Kukin, or Pustovalov, or the veterinary surgeon, Olenka could explain everything, and give her opinion about anything you like, but now there was the same emptiness in her brain and in her heart as there was in her yard outside. And it was as harsh and as bitter as wormwood in the mouth.

Little by little the town grew in all directions. The road became a street, and where the Tivoli and the timber-yard had been, there were new turnings and houses. How rapidly time passes! Olenka's house grew dingy, the roof got rusty, the shed sank on one side, and the whole yard was overgrown with docks and stinging-nettles. Olenka herself had grown plain and elderly; in summer she sat in the porch, and her soul, as before, was empty and dreary and full of bitterness. In winter she sat at her window and looked at the snow. When she caught the scent of spring, or heard the chime of the church bells, a sudden rush of memories from the past came over her, there was a tender ache in her heart, and her eyes brimmed over with tears; but this was only for a minute, and then came emptiness again and the sense of the futility of life. The black kitten, Briska, rubbed against her and purred softly, but Olenka was not touched by these feline caresses. That was not what she needed. She wanted a love that would absorb her whole being, her whole soul and reason—that would give her ideas and an object in life, and would warm her old blood. And she would shake the kitten off her skirt and say with vexation:

"Get along; I don't want you!"

And so it was, day after day and year after year, and no joy, and no opinions. Whatever Mavra, the cook, said she accepted.

One hot July day, towards evening, just as the cattle were being driven away, and the whole yard was full of dust, some one suddenly knocked at the gate. Olenka went to open it herself and was dumbfounded when she looked out: she saw Smirnin, the veterinary surgeon, greyheaded, and dressed as a civilian. She suddenly remembered everything. She could not help crying and letting her head fall on his breast without uttering a word, and in the violence of her feeling she did not notice how they both walked into the house and sat down to tea.

"My dear Vladimir Platonitch! What fate has brought you?" she muttered, trembling with joy.

"I want to settle here for good, Olga Semyonovna," he told her. "I have resigned my post, and have come to settle down and try my luck on my own account. Besides, it's time for my boy to go to school. He's a big boy. I am reconciled with my wife, you know."

"Where is she?" asked Olenka.

"She's at the hotel with the boy, and I'm looking for lodgings."

"Good gracious, my dear soul! Lodgings? Why not have my house? Why shouldn't that suit you? Why, my goodness, I wouldn't take any rent!" cried Olenka in a flutter, beginning to cry again. "You live here, and the lodge will do nicely for me. Oh dear! how glad I am!"

Next day the roof was painted and the walls were whitewashed, and Olenka, with her arms akimbo, walked about the yard giving directions. Her face was beaming with her old smile, and she was brisk and alert as though she had waked from a long sleep. The veterinary's wife arrived —a thin, plain lady, with short hair and a peevish expression. With her was her little Sasha, a boy of ten, small for his age, blue-eyed, chubby, with dimples in his cheeks. And scarcely had the boy walked into the yard when he ran after the cat, and at once there was the sound of his gay, joyous laugh.

"Is that your puss, auntie?" he asked Olenka. "When she has little ones, do give us a kitten. Mamma is awfully afraid of mice."

Olenka talked to him, and gave him tea. Her heart warmed and there was a sweet ache in her bosom, as though the boy had been her own child. And when he sat at the table in the evening, going over his lessons, she looked at him with deep tenderness and pity as she murmured to herself:

"You pretty pet! . . . my precious! . . . Such a fair little thing, and so clever."

" 'An island is a piece of land which is entirely surrounded by water,' " he read aloud.

"An island is a piece of land," she repeated, and this was the first opinion to which she gave utterance with positive conviction after so many years of silence and dearth of ideas.

Now she had opinions of her own, and at supper she talked to Sasha's parents, saying how difficult the lessons were at the high schools, but that yet the high school was better than a commercial one, since with a high-school education all careers were open to one, such as being a doctor or an engineer.

Sasha began going to the high school. His mother departed to Harkov to her sister's and did not return; his father used to go off every day to inspect cattle, and would often be away from home for three days together, and it seemed to Olenka as though Sasha was entirely abandoned, that he was not wanted at home, that he was being starved, and she carried him off to her lodge and gave him a little room there.

And for six months Sasha had lived in the lodge with her. Every morning Olenka came into his bedroom and found him fast asleep, sleeping noiselessly with his hand under his cheek. She was sorry to wake him.

"Sashenka," she would say mournfully, "get up, darling. It's time for school."

He would get up, dress and say his prayers, and then sit down to breakfast, drink three glasses of tea, and eat two large cracknels and a half a buttered roll. All this time he was hardly awake and a little ill-humoured in consequence.

"You don't quite know your fable, Sashenka," Olenka would say, looking at him as though he were about to set off on a long journey. "What a lot of trouble I have with you! You must work and do your best, darling, and obey your teachers."

"Oh, do leave me alone!" Sasha would say.

Then he would go down the street to school, a little figure, wearing a big cap and carrying a satchel on his shoulder. Olenka would follow him noiselessly.

"Sashenka!" she would call after him, and she would pop into his hand a date or a caramel. When he reached the street where the school was, he would feel ashamed of being followed by a tall, stout woman; he would turn round and say:

"You'd better go home, auntie. I can go the rest of the way alone."

She would stand still and look after him fixedly till he had disappeared at the school-gate.

Ah, how she loved him! Of her former attachments not one had been so deep; never had her soul surrendered to any feeling so spontaneously, so disinterestedly, and so joyously as now that her maternal instincts were aroused. For this little boy with the dimple in his cheek and the big school cap, she would have given her whole life, she would have given it with joy and tears of tenderness. Why? Who can tell why?

When she had seen the last of Sasha, she returned home, contented and serene, brimming over with love; her face, which had grown younger during the last six months, smiled and beamed; people meeting her looked at her with pleasure.

"Good-morning, Olga Semyonovna, darling. How are you, darling?"

"The lessons at the high school are very difficult now," she would relate at the market. "It's too much; in the first class yesterday they gave him a fable to learn by heart, and a Latin translation and a problem. You know it's too much for a little chap."

And she would begin talking about the teachers, the lessons, and the school books, saying just what Sasha said.

At three o'clock they had dinner together: in the evening they learned their lessons together and cried. When she put him to bed, she would stay a long time making the Cross over him and murmuring a prayer; then she would go to bed and dream of that far-away misty future when Sasha would finish his studies and become a doctor or an engineer, would have a big house of his own with horses and a carriage, would get married and have children. . . . She would fall asleep still thinking of the same thing, and tears would run down her cheeks from her closed eyes, while the black cat lay purring beside her: "Mrr, mrr, mrr."

Suddenly there would come a loud knock at the gate.

Olenka would wake up breathless with alarm, her heart throbbing. Half a minute later would come another knock.

"It must be a telegram from Harkov," she would think, beginning to tremble from head to foot. "Sasha's mother is sending for him from Harkov. . . . Oh, mercy on us!"

She was in despair. Her head, her hands, and her feet would turn chill, and she would feel that she was the most unhappy woman in the world. But another minute would pass, voices would be heard: it would turn out to be the veterinary surgeon coming home from the club.

"Well, thank God!" she would think.

And gradually the load in her heart would pass off, and she would feel at ease. She would go back to bed thinking of Sasha, who lay sound asleep in the next room, sometimes crying out in his sleep: "I'll give it you! Get away! Shut up!"

[1899]

TRANSLATED BY
CONSTANCE GARNETT

QUESTIONS FOR STUDY

1. *How does each of the four episodes of the story add to the reader's understanding of Olenka? How does the setting of each episode reflect Olenka's successive states of mind?*
2. *What is Chekhov's attitude toward Olenka? Is his treatment of her sympathetic, satiric, or somewhat ambivalent? What is his attitude toward the three men in the story: Kukin, Pustovalov, and Smirnin?*
3. *What does the story seem to be saying about a woman's capacity for love? Does Chekhov seem to imply that Olenka's love and devotion are excessive, or in any way parasitical and debilitating?*
4. *What is the significance of the words that Sasha calls out in his sleep: "I'll give it you! Get away! Shut up!"?*
5. *What is the significance of the story's title?*

ANTON CHEKHOV

Gooseberries

THE SKY had been covered with rain-clouds ever since the early morning; it was a still day, cool and dull, one of those misty days when the clouds have long been lowering overhead and you keep thinking it is just going to rain, and the rain holds off. Ivan Ivanich, the veterinary surgeon, and Burkin, the high-school teacher, had walked till they were tired, and the way over the fields seemed endless to them. Far ahead they could just make out the windmill of the village of Mironositskoye, and what looked like a range of low hills at the right extending well beyond the village, and they both knew that this range was really the bank of the river, and that further on were meadows, green willow-trees, country-estates; if they were on top of these hills, they knew they would see the same boundless fields and telegraph-posts, and the train, like a crawling caterpillar in the distance, while in fine weather even the town would be visible. On this still day, when the whole of nature seemed kindly and pensive, Ivan Ivanich and Burkin felt a surge of love for this plain, and thought how vast and beautiful their country was.

"The last time we stayed in Elder Prokofy's hut," said Burkin, "you said you had a story to tell me."

"Yes. I wanted to tell you the story of my brother."

Ivan Ivanich took a deep breath and lighted his pipe as a preliminary to his narrative, but just then the rain came. Five minutes later it was coming down in torrents and nobody could say when it would stop. Ivan Ivanich and Burkin stood still, lost in thought. The dogs, already soaked, stood with drooping tails, gazing at them wistfully.

"We must try and find shelter," said Burkin. "Let's go to Alekhin's. It's quite near."

"Come on, then."

They turned aside and walked straight across the newly reaped field, veering to the right till they came to a road. Very soon poplars, an orchard, and the red roofs of barns came into sight. The surface of a river gleamed, and they had a view of an extensive reach of water, a windmill and a whitewashed bathing-shed. This was Sofyino, where Alekhin lived.

The mill was working, and the noise made by its sails drowned the sound of the rain; the whole dam trembled. Horses, soaking wet, were standing near some carts, their heads drooping, and people were moving about with sacks over their heads and shoulders. It was wet, muddy, bleak, and the water looked cold and sinister. Ivan Ivanich and Burkin were already experiencing the misery of dampness, dirt, physical discomfort, their boots were caked with mud, and when, having passed the mill-dam, they took the upward path to the landowner's barns, they fell silent, as if vexed with one another.

The sound of winnowing came from one of the barns; the door was open, and clouds of dust issued from it. Standing in the door-way was Alekhin himself, a stout man of some forty years, with longish hair, looking more like a professor or an artist than a landed proprietor. He was wearing a white shirt, greatly in need of washing, belted with a piece of string, and long drawers with no trousers over them. His boots, too, were caked with mud and straw. His eyes and nose were ringed with dust. He recognized Ivan Ivanich and Burkin, and seemed glad to see them.

"Go up to the house, gentlemen," he said, smiling. "I'll be with you in a minute."

It was a large two-storey house. Alekhin occupied the ground floor, two rooms with vaulted ceilings and tiny windows, where the stewards had lived formerly. They were poorly furnished, and smelled of rye-bread, cheap vodka, and harness. He hardly ever went into the upstairs rooms, excepting when he had guests. Ivan Ivanich and Burkin were met by a maid-servant, a young woman of such beauty that they stood still involuntarily and exchanged glances.

"You have no idea how glad I am to see you here, dear friends," said Alekhin, overtaking them in the hall. "It's quite a surprise! Pelageya," he said, turning to the maid, "find the gentlemen a change of clothes. And I might as well change, myself. But I must have a wash first, for I don't believe I've had a bath since the spring. Wouldn't you like to go and have a bathe while they get things ready here?"

The beauteous Pelageya, looking very soft and delicate, brought them towels and soap, and Alekhin and his guests set off for the bathing-house.

"Yes, it's a long time since I had a wash," he said, taking off his clothes. "As you see I have a nice bathing-place, my father had it built, but somehow I never seem to get time to wash."

He sat on the step, soaping his long locks and his neck, and all round him the water was brown.

"Yes, you certainly . . ." remarked Ivan Ivanich, with a significant glance at his host's head.

"It's a long time since I had a wash . . ." repeated Alekhin, somewhat abashed, and he soaped himself again, and now the water was dark-blue, like ink.

Ivan Ivanich emerged from the shed, splashed noisily into the water, and began swimming beneath the rain, spreading his arms wide, making waves all round him, and the white water-lilies rocked on the waves he made. He swam into the very middle of the river and then dived, a moment later came up at another place and swam further, diving constantly, and trying to touch the bottom. "Ah, my God," he kept exclaiming in his enjoyment. "Ah, my God. . . ." He swam up to the mill, had a little talk with some peasants there and turned back, but when he got to the middle of the river, he floated, holding his face up to the rain. Burkin and Alekhin were dressed and ready to go, but he went on swimming and diving.

"God! God!" he kept exclaiming. "Dear God!"

"Come out!" Burkin shouted to him.

They went back to the house. And only after the lamp was lit in the great drawing-room on the upper floor, and Burkin and Ivan Ivanich, in silk dressing-gowns and warm slippers, were seated in arm-chairs, while Alekhin, washed and combed, paced the room in his new frock-coat, enjoying the warmth, the cleanliness, his dry clothes and comfortable slippers, while the fair Pelageya, smiling benevolently, stepped noiselessly over the carpet with her tray of tea and preserves, did Ivan Ivanich embark upon his yarn, the ancient dames, young ladies, and military gentlemen looking down at them severely from the gilded frames, as if they, too, were listening.

"There were two of us brothers," he began. "Ivan Ivanich (me), and my brother Nikolai Ivanich, two years younger than myself. I went in for learning and became a veterinary surgeon, but Nikolai started working in a government office when he was only nineteen. Our father, Chimsha-Himalaisky, was educated in a school for the sons of private soldiers, but was later promoted to officer's rank, and was made a hereditary nobleman and given a small estate. After his death the estate had to be sold for debts, but at least our childhood was passed in the freedom of the country-side, where we roamed the fields and the woods like peasant children, taking the horses to graze, peeling bark from the trunks of lime-trees, fishing, and all that sort of thing. And anyone who has once in his life fished for perch, or watched the thrushes fly south in the autumn, rising high over the village on clear, cool days, is spoilt for town life, and will long for the country-side for the rest of his days. My brother pined in his government office. The years passed and he sat in the same place every day, writing out the same documents and thinking all the time of the same thing—how to get back to the country. And these longings of his gradually turned into a definite desire, into a dream of purchasing a little estate somewhere on the bank of a river or the shore of a lake.

"He was a meek, good-natured chap, I was fond of him, but could feel no sympathy with the desire to lock oneself up for life in an estate of one's own. They say man only needs six feet of earth. But it is a corpse, and not man, which needs these six feet. And now people are actually saying that it is a good sign for our intellectuals to yearn for the land and try to obtain country-dwellings. And yet these estates are nothing but those same six feet of earth. To escape from the town, from the struggle, from the noise of life, to escape and hide one's head on a country-estate, is not life, but egoism, idleness, it is a sort of renunciation, but renunciation without faith. It is not six feet of earth, not a country-estate, that man needs, but the whole globe, the whole of nature, room to display his qualities and the individual characteristics of his soul.

"My brother Nikolai sat at his office-desk, dreaming of eating soup made from his own cabbages, which would spread a delicious smell all over his own yard, of eating out of doors, on the green grass, of sleeping in the sun, sitting for hours on a bench outside his gate, and gazing at the fields and woods. Books on agriculture, and all those hints printed on calendars were his delight, his favourite spiritual nourishment. He was fond of reading newspapers, too, but all he read in them was advertisements of the sale of so many acres of arable and meadowland, with residence attached, a river, an orchard, a mill, and ponds fed by springs. His head was full of visions of garden paths, flowers, fruit, nesting-boxes, carp-ponds, and all that sort of thing. These visions differed according to the advertisements he came across, but for some reason gooseberry bushes invariably figured in them. He could not picture to himself a single estate or picturesque nook that did not have gooseberry bushes in it.

" 'Country life has its conveniences,' he would say. 'You sit on the verandah, drinking tea, with your own ducks floating on the pond, and everything smells so nice, and . . . and the gooseberries ripen on the bushes.'

"He drew up plans for his estate, and every plan showed the same features: a) the main residence, b) the servant's wing, c) the kitchen-garden, d) gooseberry bushes. He lived thriftily, never ate or drank his fill, dressed anyhow, like a beggar, and saved up all his money in the bank. He became terribly stingy. I could hardly bear to look at him, and whenever I gave him a little money, or sent him a present on some holiday, he put that away, too. Once a man gets an idea into his head, there's no doing anything with him.

"The years passed, he was sent to another gubernia,[1] he was over forty, and was still reading advertisements in the papers, and saving up. At last I heard he had married. All for the same purpose, to buy himself an estate with gooseberry bushes on it, he married an ugly elderly widow, for whom he had not the slightest affection, just because she had some money. After his marriage he went on living as thriftily as ever, half-starving his wife, and putting her money in his own bank account. Her first husband had been a postmaster, and she was used to pies and cordials, but with her second husband she did not even get enough black bread to eat. She began to languish under such a regime, and three years later yielded up her soul to God. Of course my brother did not for a moment consider himself guilty of her death. Money, like vodka, makes a man eccentric. There was a merchant in our town who asked for a plate of honey on his deathbed and ate up all his bank-notes and lottery tickets with the honey, so that no one else should get it. And one day when I was examining a consignment of cattle at a railway station, a drover fell under the engine and his leg was severed from his body. We carried him all bloody into the waiting-room, a terrible sight, and he did nothing but beg us to look for his leg, worrying all the time—there were twenty rubles in the boot, and he was afraid they would be lost."

"You're losing the thread," put in Burkin.

Ivan Ivanich paused for a moment, and went on: "After his wife's death my brother began to look about for an estate. You can search for five years, of

---

1 province. (JHP)

course, and in the end make a mistake and buy something quite different from what you dreamed of. My brother Nikolai bought three hundred acres, complete with gentleman's house, servants' quarters, and a park, as well as a mortgage to be paid through an agent, but there were neither an orchard, gooseberry bushes, nor a pond with ducks on it. There was a river, but it was as dark as coffee, owing to the fact that there was a brick-works on one side of the estate, and bone-kilns on the other. Nothing daunted, however, my brother Nikolai Ivanich ordered two dozen gooseberry bushes and settled down as a landed proprietor.

"Last year I paid him a visit. I thought I would go and see how he was getting on there. In his letters my brother gave his address as Chumbaroklova Pustosh or Himalaiskoye. I arrived at Himalaiskoye in the afternoon. It was very hot. Everywhere were ditches, fences, hedges, rows of fir-trees, and it was hard to drive into the yard and find a place to leave one's carriage. As I went a fat ginger-coloured dog, remarkably like a pig, came out to meet me. It looked as if it would have barked if it were not so lazy. The cook, who was also fat and like a pig, came out of the kitchen, barefoot, and said her master was having his after-dinner rest. I made my way to my brother's room, and found him sitting up in bed, his knees covered by a blanket. He had aged, and grown stout and flabby. His cheeks, nose and lips protruded—I almost expected him to grunt into the blanket.

"We embraced and wept—tears of joy, mingled with melancholy—because we had once been young and were now both grey-haired and approaching the grave. He put on his clothes and went out to show me over his estate.

" 'Well, how are you getting on here?' I asked.

" 'All right, thanks be, I'm enjoying myself.' "

"He was no longer the poor, timid clerk, but a true proprietor, a gentleman. He had settled down, and was entering with zest into country life. He ate a lot, washed in the bath-house, and put on flesh. He had already got into litigation with the village commune, the brick-works and the bone-kilns, and took offence if the peasants failed to call him 'Your Honour.' He went in for religion in a solid, gentlemanly way, and there was nothing casual about his pretentious good works. And what were these good works? He treated all the diseases of the peasants with bicarbonate of soda and castor-oil, and had a special thanksgiving service held on his name-day, after which he provided half a pail of vodka, supposing that this was the right thing to do. Oh, those terrible half pails! Today the fat landlord hauls the peasants before the Zemstvo representative[2] for letting their sheep graze on his land, tomorrow, on the day of rejoicing, he treats them to half a pail of vodka, and they drink and sing and shout hurrah, prostrating themselves before him when they are drunk. Any improvement in his conditions, anything like satiety or idleness, develops the most insolent complacency in a Russian. Nikolai Ivanich, who had been afraid of having an opinion of his own when he was in the government service, was now continually coming out with axioms, in the most ministerial manner: 'Education is essential, but the people are not ready for it yet,' 'corporal punishment is an evil, but in certain cases it is beneficial and indispensable.'

" 'I know the people and I know how to treat them,' he said. 'The people love me. I only have to lift my little finger, and the people will do whatever I want.'

"And all this, mark you, with a wise, indulgent smile. Over and over again he repeated: 'We the gentry,' or 'speaking as a gentleman,' and seemed to have quite forgotten that our grandfather was a peasant, and our father a common soldier. Our very surname—Chimsha-Himalaisky —in reality so absurd, now seemed to him a resounding, distinguished, and euphonious name.

"But it is of myself, and not of him, that I wish to speak. I should like to describe to you the change which came over me in those few hours I spent on my brother's estate. As we were drinking tea

2 rural police officer. (JHP)

in the evening, the cook brought us a full plate of gooseberries. These were not gooseberries bought for money, they came from his own garden, and were the first fruits of the bushes he had planted. Nikolai Ivanich broke into a laugh and gazed at the gooseberries, in tearful silence for at least five minutes. Speechless with emotion, he popped a single gooseberry into his mouth, darted at me the triumphant glance of a child who has at last gained possession of a longed-for toy, and said:

" 'Delicious!'

"And he ate them greedily, repeating over and over again:

" 'Simply delicious! You try them.'

"They were hard and sour, but, as Pushkin says: 'The lie which elates us is dearer than a thousand sober truths.' I saw before me a really happy man, one whose dearest wish had come true, who had achieved his aim in life, got what he wanted, and was content with his lot and with himself. There had always been a tinge of melancholy in my conception of human happiness, and now, confronted by a happy man, I was overcome by a feeling of sadness bordering on desperation. This feeling grew strongest of all in the night. A bed was made up for me in the room next to my brother's bedroom, and I could hear him moving about restlessly, every now and then getting up to take a gooseberry from a plate. How many happy, satisfied people there are, after all, I said to myself! What an overwhelming force! Just consider this life— the insolence and idleness of the strong, the ignorance and bestiality of the weak, all around intolerable poverty, cramped dwellings, degeneracy, drunkenness, hypocrisy, lying. . . . And yet peace and order apparently prevail in all those homes and in the streets. Of the fifty thousand inhabitants of a town, not one will be found to cry out, to proclaim his indignation aloud. We see those who go to the market to buy food, who eat in the day-time and sleep at night, who prattle away, marry, grow old, carry their dead to the cemeteries. But we neither hear nor see those who suffer, and the terrible things in life are played out behind the scenes. All is calm and quiet, only statis-

tics, which are dumb, protest: so many have gone mad, so many barrels of drink have been consumed, so many children died of malnutrition. . . . And apparently this is as it should be. Apparently those who are happy can only enjoy themselves because the unhappy bear their burdens in silence, and but for this silence happiness would be impossible. It is a kind of universal hypnosis. There ought to be a man with a hammer behind the door of every happy man, to remind him by his constant knocks that there are unhappy people, and that happy as he himself may be, life will sooner or later show him its claws, catastrophe will overtake him— sickness, poverty, loss—and nobody will see it, just as he now neither sees nor hears the misfortunes of others. But there is no man with a hammer, the happy man goes on living and the petty vicissitudes of life touch him lightly, like the wind in an aspen-tree, and all is well.

"That night I understood that I, too, was happy and content," continued Ivan Ivanich, getting up. "I, too, while out hunting, or at the dinner table, have held forth on the right way to live, to worship, to manage the people. I, too, have declared that without knowledge there can be no light, that education is essential, but that bare literacy is sufficient for the common people. Freedom is a blessing, I have said, one can't get on without it, any more than without air, but we must wait. Yes, that is what I said, and now I ask: In the name of what must we wait?" Here Ivan Ivanich looked angrily at Burkin. "In the name of what must we wait, I ask you. What is there to be considered? Don't be in such a hurry, they tell me, every idea materializes gradually, in its own time. But who are they who say this? What is the proof that it is just? You refer to the natural order of things, to the logic of facts, but according to what order, what logic do I, a living, thinking individual, stand on the edge of a ditch and wait for it to be gradually filled up, or choked with silt, when I might leap across it or build a bridge over it? And again, in the name of what must we wait? Wait, when we have not the strength to live, though live we must and to live we desire!

"I left my brother early the next morning, and ever since I have found town life intolerable. The peace and order weigh on my spirits, and I am afraid to look into windows, because there is now no sadder spectacle for me than a happy family seated around the tea-table. I am old and unfit for the struggle, I am even incapable of feeling hatred. I can only suffer inwardly, and give way to irritation and annoyance, at night my head burns from the rush of thoughts, and I am unable to sleep. . . . Oh, if only I were young!"

Ivan Ivanich began pacing backwards and forwards, repeating:

"If only I were young still!"

Suddenly he went up to Alekhin and began pressing first one of his hands, and then the other.

"Pavel Konstantinich," he said in imploring accents. "Don't *you* fall into apathy, don't *you* let your conscience be lulled to sleep! While you are still young, strong, active, do not be weary of well-doing. There is no such thing as happiness, nor ought there to be, but if there is any sense or purpose in life, this sense and purpose are to be found not in our own happiness, but in something greater and more rational. Do good!"

Ivan Ivanich said all this with a piteous, imploring smile, as if he were asking for something for himself.

Then they all three sat in their armchairs a long way apart from one another, and said nothing. Ivan Ivanich's story satisfied neither Burkin or Alekhin. It was not interesting to listen to the story of a poor clerk who ate gooseberries, when from the walls generals and fine ladies, who seemed to come to life in the dark, were looking down from their gilded frames. It would have been much more interesting to hear about elegant people, lovely women. And the fact that they were sitting in a drawing-room in which everything—the swathed chandeliers, the arm-chairs, the carpet on the floor, proved that the people now looking out of the frames had once moved about here, sat in the chairs, drunk tea, where the fair Pelageya was now going noiselessly to and fro, was better than any story.

Alekhin was desperately sleepy. He had got up early, at three o'clock in the morning, to go about his work on the estate, and could now hardly keep his eyes open. But he would not go to bed, for fear one of his guests would relate something interesting after he was gone. He could not be sure whether what Ivan Ivanich had just told them was wise or just, but his visitors talked of other things besides grain, hay, or tar, of things which had no direct bearing on his daily life, and he liked this, and wanted them to go on. . . .

"Well, time to go to bed," said Burkin, getting up. "Allow me to wish you a good night."

Alekhin said good night and went downstairs to his own room, the visitors remaining on the upper floor. They were allotted a big room for the night, in which were two ancient bedsteads of carved wood, and an ivory crucifix in one corner. There was a pleasant smell of freshly laundered sheets from the wide, cool beds which the fair Pelageya made up for them.

Ivan Ivanich undressed in silence and lay down.

"Lord have mercy on us, sinners," he said, and covered his head with the sheet.

There was a strong smell of stale tobacco from his pipe, which he put on the table, and Burkin lay awake a long time, wondering where the stifling smell came from.

The rain tapped on the window-panes all night.

[1898]

TRANSLATED BY
IVY LITVINOV

QUESTIONS FOR STUDY

1. *How do the contradictions of Ivan's inner life reveal themselves? In what ways does he betray his own theory that happiness is a form of blindness and not a legitimate human goal?*
2. *What is the function of Ivan's anecdote? Why does he choose to tell it*

and to this particular audience? What ironies does it contain? How does it relate to the larger story which it frames? To which story, the inner or outer one, does Chekhov wish the reader's final attention to be directed?

3. *Can Alekhin be compared to Nikolai, Pelageya to Nikolai's cook?*
4. *Why does the story trouble Burkin? Is it significant that Ivan himself has no trouble falling asleep?*
5. *Why is "Gooseberries" an appropriate title for the story?*

AGATHA CHRISTIE
The Disappearance of Mr. Davenheim

POIROT and I were expecting our old friend Inspector Japp of Scotland Yard to tea. We were sitting around the tea table awaiting his arrival. Poirot had just finished carefully straightening the cups and saucers which our landlady was in the habit of throwing, rather than placing, on the table. He had also breathed heavily on the metal teapot, and polished it with a silk handkerchief. The kettle was on the boil, and a small enamel saucepan beside it contained some thick, sweet chocolate which was more to Poirot's palate than what he described as "your English poison."

A sharp "rat-tat" sounded below, and a few minutes afterward Japp entered briskly.

"Hope I'm not late," he said as he greeted us. "To tell the truth, I was yarning with Miller, the man who's in charge of the Davenheim case."

I pricked up my ears. For the last three days the papers had been full of the strange disappearance of Mr. Davenheim, senior partner of Davenheim and Salmon, the well-known bankers and financiers. On Saturday last he had walked out of his house, and had never been seen since. I looked forward to extracting some interesting details from Japp.

"I should have thought," I remarked, "that it would be almost impossible for anyone to 'disappear' nowadays."

Poirot moved a plate of bread and butter the eighth of an inch, and said sharply: "Be exact, my friend. What do you mean by 'disappear'? To which class of disappearance are you referring?"

"Are disappearances classified and labeled, then?" I laughed.

Japp smiled also. Poirot frowned at us both.

"But certainly they are! They fall into three categories: First, and most common, the voluntary disappearance. Second, the much abused 'loss of memory' case—rare, but occasionally genuine. Third, murder, and a more or less successful disposal of the body. Do you refer to all three as impossible of execution?"

"Very nearly so, I should think. You might lose your own memory, but someone would be sure to recognize you—especially in the case of a well-known man like Davenheim. Then 'bodies' can't be made to vanish into thin air. Sooner or later they turn up, concealed in lonely places, or in trunks. Murder will out. In the same way, the absconding clerk, or the domestic defaulter, is bound to be run down in these days of wireless telegraphy. He can be headed off from foreign countries; ports and railway stations are watched; and, as for concealment in this country, his features and appearance will be known to everyone who reads a daily newspaper. He's up against civilization."

"Mon ami," said Poirot, "you make one error. You do not allow for the fact that a man who had decided to make away with another man—or with himself in a figurative sense—might be that rare machine, a man of method. He might bring intelligence, talent, a careful calculation of detail to the task; and then I do not see why he should not be successful in baffling the police force."

"But not *you,* I suppose?" said Japp good-humoredly, winking at me. "He couldn't baffle *you,* eh, Monsieur Poirot?"

Poirot endeavored, with a marked lack of success, to look modest. "Me, also! Why not? It is true that I approach such problems with an exact science, a mathematical precision, which seems, alas, only too rare in the new generation of detectives!"

Japp grinned more widely.

"I don't know," he said. "Miller, the man who's on this case, is a smart chap. You may be very sure he won't overlook a footprint, or a cigar ash, or a crumb even. He's got eyes that see everything."

"So, *mon ami*," said Poirot, "has the London sparrow. But all the same, I should not ask the little brown bird to solve the problem of Mr. Davenheim."

"Come now, monsieur, you're not going to run down the value of details as clues?"

"By no means. These things are all good in their way. The danger is they may assume undue importance. Most details are insignificant; one or two are vital. It is the brain, the little gray cells————" he tapped his forehead————"on which one must rely. The senses mislead. One must seek the truth within—not without."

"You don't mean to say, Monsieur Poirot, that you would undertake to solve a case without moving from your chair, do you?"

"That is exactly what I do mean— granted the facts were placed before me. I regard myself as a consulting specialist."

Japp slapped his knee. "Hanged if I don't take you at your word. Bet you a fiver that you can't lay your hand—or rather tell me where to lay my hand—on Mr. Davenheim, dead or alive, before a week is out."

Poirot considered. *"Eh bien, mon ami,* I accept. *Le sport,*[1] it is the passion of you English. Now—the facts."

"On Saturday last, as is his usual custom, Mr. Davenheim took the 12:40 train from Victoria to Chingside, where his palatial country place, The Cedars, is situated. After lunch, he strolled around the grounds, and gave various directions to the gardeners. Everbody agrees that his manner was absolutely normal and as usual. After tea he put his head into his wife's boudoir, saying that he was going to stroll down to the village and post some letters. He added that he was ex-

pecting a Mr. Lowen, on business. If Lowen should come before he himself returned, he was to be shown into the study and asked to wait. Mr. Davenheim then left the house by the front door, passed leisurely down the drive, and out at the gate, and—was never seen again. From that hour, he vanished completely."

"Pretty—very pretty—altogether a charming little problem," murmured Poirot. "Proceed, my good friend."

"About a quarter of an hour later a tall, dark man with a thick black mustache rang the front-door bell, and explained that he had an appointment with Mr. Davenheim. He gave the name of Lowen, and in accordance with the banker's instructions was shown into the study. Nearly an hour passed. Mr. Davenheim did not return. Finally Mr. Lowen rang the bell, and explained that he was unable to wait any longer, as he must catch his train back to town. Mrs. Davenheim apologized for her husband's absence, which seemed unaccountable, as she knew him to have been expecting the visitor. Mr. Lowen reiterated his regrets and left.

"Well, as everyone knows, Mr. Davenheim did *not* return. Early on Sunday morning the police were communicated with, but could make neither head nor tail of the matter. Mr. Davenheim seemed literally to have vanished into thin air. He had not been to the post office; nor had he been seen passing through the village. At the station they were positive he had not departed by any train. His own motor had not left the garage. If he had hired a car to meet him in some lonely spot, it seems almost certain that by this time, in view of the large reward offered for information, the driver of it would have come forward to tell what he knew. True, there was a small race-meeting at Entfield, five miles away, and if he had walked to that station he might have passed unnoticed in the crowd. But since then his photograph and a full description of him have been circulated in every newspaper, and nobody has been able to give any news of him. We have, of course, received many letters from all over England, but each clue, so far, has ended in disappointment.

[1] "Oh well, my friend. . . . The sport."
(JHP)

"On Monday morning a further sensational discovery came to light. Behind a *portière* [2] in Mr. Davenheim's study stands a safe, and that safe had been broken into and rifled. The windows were fastened securely on the inside, which seems to put an ordinary burglary out of court, unless, of course, an accomplice within the house fastened them again afterwards. On the other hand, Sunday having intervened, and the household being in a state of chaos, it is likely that the burglary was committed on the Saturday, and remained undetected until Monday."

"*Précisément,*" said Poirot dryly. "Well, is he arrested, *ce pauvre M. Lowen?*" [3]

Japp grinned. "Not yet. But he's under pretty close supervision."

Poirot nodded. "What was taken from the safe? Have you any idea?"

"We've been going into that with the junior partner of the firm and Mrs. Davenheim. Apparently there was a considerable amount in bearer bonds, and a very large sum in notes, owing to some large transaction having been just carried through. There was also a small fortune in jewelry. All Mrs. Davenheim's jewels were kept in the safe. The purchasing of them had become a passion with her husband of late years, and hardly a month passed that he did not make her a present of some rare and costly gem."

"Altogether a good haul," said Poirot thoughtfully. "Now, what about Lowen? Is it known what his business was with Davenheim that evening?"

"Well, the two men were apparently not on very good terms. Lowen is a speculator in quite a small way. Nevertheless, he has been able once or twice to score a *coup* [4] off Davenheim in the market, though it seems they seldom or never actually met. It was a matter concerning some South American shares which led the banker to make his appointment."

"Had Davenheim interests in South America, then?"

"I believe so. Mrs. Davenheim happened to mention that he spent all last autumn in Buenos Aires."

"Any trouble in his home life? Were the husband and wife on good terms?"

"I should say his domestic life was quite peaceful and eventful. Mrs. Davenheim is a pleasant, rather unintelligent woman. Quite a nonentity, I think."

"Then we must not look for the solution of the mystery there. Had he any enemies?"

"He had plenty of financial rivals, and no doubt there are many people whom he has got the better of who bear him no particular good will. But there was no one likely to make away with him—and, if they had, where is the body?"

"Exactly. As Hastings says, bodies have a habit of coming to light with fatal persistency."

"By the way, one of the gardeners says he saw a figure going around to the side of the house toward the rose garden. The long French window of the study opens on to the rose garden, and Mr. Davenheim frequently entered and left the house that way. But the man was a good way off, at work on some cucumber frames, and cannot even say whether it was the figure of his master or not. Also, he cannot fix the time with any accuracy. It must have been before six, as the gardeners cease work at that time."

"And Mr. Davenheim left the house?"

"About half-past five or thereabouts."

"What lies beyond the rose garden?"

"A lake."

"With a boathouse?"

"Yes, a couple of punts are kept there. I suppose you're thinking of suicide, Monsieur Poirot? Well, I don't mind telling you that Miller's going down tomorrow expressly to see that piece of water dragged. That's the kind of man he is!"

Poirot smiled faintly, and turned to me. "Hastings, I pray you, hand me that copy of the *Daily Megaphone*. If I remember rightly, there is an unusually clear photograph there of the missing man."

I rose, and found the sheet required. Poirot studied the features attentively.

"H'm!" he murmured. "Wears his hair rather long and wavy, full mustache and

2 A door-curtain. (JHP)
3 "Precisely, . . . this poor Mr. Lowen?" (JHP)
4 A sudden, brilliant blow, or victory. (JHP)

pointed beard, bushy eyebrows. Eyes dark?"

"Yes."

"Hair and beard turning gray?"

The detective nodded. "Well, Monsieur Poirot, what have you got to say to it all? Clear as daylight, eh?"

"On the contrary, most obscure."

The Scotland Yard man looked pleased.

"Which gives me great hopes of solving it," finished Poirot placidly.

"Eh?"

"I find it a good sign when a case is obscure. If a thing is clear as daylight— *eh bien,* mistrust it! Someone has made it so."

Japp shook his head almost pityingly. "Well, each to their fancy. But it's not a bad thing to see your way clear ahead."

"I do not see," murmured Poirot. "I shut my eyes—and think."

Japp sighed. "Well, you've got a clear week to think in."

"And you will bring me any fresh developments that arise—the result of the labors of the hard-working and lynx-eyed Inspector Miller, for instance?"

"Certainly. That's in the bargain."

"Seems a shame, doesn't it?" said Japp to me as I accompanied him to the door. "Like robbing a child!"

I could not help agreeing with a smile. I was still smiling as I re-entered the room.

"Eh bien!" said Poirot immediately. "You make fun of Papa Poirot, is it not so?" He shook his finger at me. "You do not trust his gray cells? Ah, do not be confused! Let us discuss this little problem—incomplete as yet, I admit, but already showing one or two points of interest."

"The lake!" I said significantly.

"And even more than the lake, the boathouse!"

I looked sidewise at Poirot. He was smiling in his most inscrutable fashion. I felt that, for the moment, it would be quite useless to question him further.

We heard nothing of Japp until the following evening, when he walked in about nine o'clock. I saw at once by his expression that he was bursting with news of some kind.

"Eh bien, my friend," remarked Poirot.

"All goes well? But do not tell me that you have discovered the body of Mr. Davenheim in your lake, because I shall not believe you."

"We haven't found the body, but we did find his *clothes*—the identical clothes he was wearing that day. What do you say to that?"

"Any other clothes missing from the house?"

"No, his valet is quite positive on that point. The rest of his wardrobe is intact. There's more. We've arrested Lowen. One of the maids, whose business it is to fasten the bedroom windows, declares that she saw Lowen coming *toward* the study through the rose garden about a quarter past six. That would be about ten minutes before he left the house."

"What does he himself say to that?"

"Denied first of all that he had ever left the study. But the maid was positive and he pretended afterward that he had forgotten just stepping out of the window to examine an unusual species of rose. Rather a weak story! And there's fresh evidence against him come to light. Mr. Davenheim always wore a thick gold ring set with a solitaire diamond on the little finger of his right hand. Well, that ring was pawned in London on Saturday night by a man called Billy Kellett! He's already known to the police—did three months last autumn for lifting an old gentleman's watch. It seems he tried to pawn the ring at no less than five different places, succeeded at the last one, got gloriously drunk on the proceeds, assaulted a policeman, and was run in in consequence. I went to Bow Street with Miller and saw him. He's sober enough now, and I don't mind admitting we pretty well frightened the life out of him, hinting he might be charged with murder. This is his yarn, and a very queer one it is.

"He was at Entfield races on Saturday, though I dare say scarfpins was his line of business, rather than betting. Anyway, he had a bad day, and was down on his luck. He was tramping along the road to Chingside, and sat down in a ditch to rest just before he got into the village. A few minutes later he noticed a man coming along the road to the village, 'dark-complexioned gent, with a big mustache, one of them city toffs,' is his description of the man.

"Kellett was half concealed from the road by a heap of stones. Just before he got abreast of him, the man looked quickly up and down the road, and seeing it apparently deserted he took a small object from his pocket and threw it over the hedge. Then he went on toward the station. Now, the object he had thrown over the hedge had fallen with a slight 'chink' which aroused the curiosity of the human derelict in the ditch. He investigated and, after a short search, discovered the ring! That is Kellett's story. It's only fair to say that Lowen denies it utterly, and of course the word of a man like Kellett can't be relied upon in the slightest. It's within the bounds of possibility that he met Davenheim in the lane and robbed and murdered him."

Poirot shook his head.

"Very improbable, *mon ami*. He had no means of disposing of the body. It would have been found by now. Secondly, the open way in which he pawned the ring makes it unlikely that he did murder to get it. Thirdly, your sneak thief is rarely a murderer. Fourthly, as he has been in prison since Saturday, it would be too much of a coincidence that he is able to give an accurate description of Lowen."

Japp nodded. "I don't say you're not right. But all the same, you won't get a jury to take much note of a jailbird's evidence. What seems odd to me is that Lowen couldn't find a cleverer way of disposing of the ring."

Poirot shrugged his shoulders. "Well, after all, if it were found in the neighborhood, it might be argued that Davenheim himself had dropped it."

"But why remove it from the body at all?" I cried.

"There might be a reason for that," said Japp. "Do you know that just beyond the lake, a little gate leads out on to the hill, and not three minutes' walk brings you to—what do you think?—*a lime kiln*."

"Good heavens!" I cried. "You mean that the lime which destroyed the body would be powerless to affect the metal of the ring?"

"Exactly."

"It seems to me," I said, "that that explains everything. What a horrible crime!"

By common consent we both turned and looked at Poirot. He seemed lost in reflection, his brow knitted, as though with some supreme mental effort. I felt that at last his keen intellect was asserting itself. What would his first words be? We were not long left in doubt. With a sigh, the tension of his attitude relaxed, and turning to Japp, he asked:

"Have you any idea, my friend, whether Mr. and Mrs. Davenheim occupied the same bedroom?"

The question seemed so ludicrously inappropriate that for a moment we both stared in silence. Then Japp burst into a laugh. "Good Lord, Monsieur Poirot, I thought you were coming out with something startling. As to your question, I'm sure I don't know."

"You could find out?" asked Poirot with curious persistence.

"Oh, certainly—if you *really* want to know."

"Merci, mon ami. I should be obliged if you would make a point of it."

Japp stared at him a few minutes longer, but Poirot seemed to have forgotten us both. The detective shook his head sadly at me, and murmuring, "Poor old fellow! War's been too much for him!" gently withdrew from the room.

As Poirot still seemed sunk in a daydream, I took a sheet of paper, and amused myself by scribbling notes upon it. My friend's voice aroused me. He had come out of his reverie, and was looking brisk and alert.

"Que faites vous là, mon ami?" 5

"I was jotting down what occurred to me as the main points of interest in this affair."

"You become methodical—at last!" said Poirot approvingly. I concealed my pleasure. "Shall I read them to you?"

"By all means."

I cleared my throat.

5 "What are you doing there, my friend?" (JHP)

" 'One: All the evidence points to Lowen being the man who forced the safe.

" 'Two: He had a grudge against Davenheim.

" 'Three: He lied in his first statement that he had never left the study.

" 'Four: If you accept Billy Kellett's story as true, Lowen is unmistakably implicated.' "

I paused. "Well?" I asked, for I felt that I had put my finger on all the vital facts.

Poirot looked at me pityingly, shaking his head very gently. *"Mon pauvre ami!* But it is that you have not the gift! The important detail, you appreciate him never! Also, your reasoning is false."

"How?"

"Let me take your four points.

"One: Mr. Lowen could not possibly know that he would have the chance to open the safe. He came for a business interview. He could not know beforehand that Mr. Davenheim would be absent posting a letter, and that he would consequently be alone in the study!"

"He might have seized his opportunity," I suggested.

"And the tools? City gentlemen do not carry round housebreaker's tools on the off chance! And one could not cut into that safe with a penknife, *bien entendu!* [6]

"Well, what about Number Two?"

"You say Lowen had a grudge against Mr. Davenheim. What you mean is that he had once or twice got the better of him. And presumably those transactions were entered into with the view of benefiting himself. In any case you do not as a rule bear a grudge against a man you have got the better of—it is more likely to be the other way about. Whatever grudge there might have been would have been on Mr. Davenheim's side."

"Well, you can't deny that he lied about never having left the study?"

"No. But he may have been frightened. Remember, the missing man's clothes had just been discovered in the lake. Of course, as usual, he would have done better to speak the truth."

"And the fourth point?"

"I grant you that. If Kellett's story is true, Lowen is undeniably implicated. That is what makes the affair so very interesting."

"Then I did appreciate *one* vital fact?"

"Perhaps—but you have entirely overlooked the two most important points, the ones which undoubtedly hold the clue to the whole matter."

"And pray, what are they?"

"One, the passion which has grown upon Mr. Davenheim in the last few years for buying jewelry. Two, his trip to Buenos Aires last autumn."

"Poirot, you are joking!"

"I am most serious. Ah, sacred thunder, but I hope Japp will not forget my little commission."

But the detective, entering into the spirit of the joke, had remembered it so well that a telegram was handed to Poirot about eleven o'clock the next day. At his request I opened it and read it out:

HUSBAND AND WIFE HAVE OCCU-
PIED SEPARATE ROOMS SINCE
LAST WINTER

"Aha!" cried Poirot. "And now we are in mid-June! All is solved!"

I stared at him.

"You have no moneys in the bank of Davenheim and Salmon, *mon ami?*"

"No," I said, wondering. "Why?"

"Because I should advise you to withdraw it—before it is too late."

"Why, what do you expect?"

"I expect a big smash in a few days— perhaps sooner. Which reminds me, we will return the compliment of a *dépêche* [7] to Japp. A pencil, I pray you, and a form. *Voilà!* [8] 'Advise you to withdraw any money deposited with firm in question.' That will intrigue him, the good Japp! His eyes will open wide—wide! He will not comprehend in the slightest—until tomorrow, or the next day!"

I remained skeptical, but the morrow forced me to render tribute to my friend's remarkable powers. In every paper was a

---

6 "Of course!" or "naturally!" (JHP)

7 Telegram. (JHP)
8 "There you are!" (JHP)

huge headline telling of the sensational failure of the Davenheim bank. The disappearance of the famous financier took on a totally different aspect in the light of the revelation of the financial affairs of the bank.

Before we were halfway through breakfast, the door flew open and Japp rushed in. In his left hand was a paper; in his right was Poirot's telegram, which he banged down on the table in front of my friend.

"How did you know, Monsieur Poirot? How the blazes could you know?"

Poirot smiled placidly at him. "Ah, *mon ami,* after your wire, it was a certainty! From the commencement, see you, it struck me that the safe burglary was somewhat remarkable. Jewels, ready money, bearer bonds—all so conveniently arranged for—whom? Well, the good Monsieur Davenheim was of those who 'look after Number One' as your saying goes! It seemed almost certain that it was arranged for—himself! Then his passion of late years for buying jewelry! How simple! The funds he embezzled he converted into jewels, very likely replacing them in turn with paste duplicates, and so he put away in a safe place, under another name, a considerable fortune to be enjoyed all in good time when everyone has been thrown off the track. His arrangements completed, he makes an appointment with Mr. Lowen (who has been imprudent enough in the past to cross the great man once or twice), drills a hole in the safe, leaves orders that the guest is to be shown into the study, and walks out of the house—where?" Poirot stopped, and stretched out his hand for another boiled egg. He frowned. "It is really insupportable," he murmured, "that every hen lays an egg of a different size! What symmetry can there be on the breakfast table? At least they should sort them in dozens at the shop!"

"Never mind the eggs," said Japp impatiently. "Let 'em lay 'em square if they like. Tell us where our customer went to when he left The Cedars—that is, if you know!"

"*Eh bien,* he went to his hiding place. Ah, this Monsieur Davenheim, there may

be some malformation in his gray cells, but they are of the first quality!"

"Do you know where he is hiding?"

"Certainly! It is most ingenious."

"For the Lord's sake, tell us, then!"

Poirot gently collected every fragment of shell from his plate, placed them in the egg cup, and reversed the empty egg shell on top of them. This little operation concluded, he smiled at the neat effect, and then beamed affectionately on us both.

"Come, my friends, you are men of intelligence. Ask yourselves the question which I asked myself. 'If I were this man, where should *I* hide?' Hastings, what do you say?"

"Well," I said, "I'm rather inclined to think I'd not do a bolt at all. I'd stay in London—in the heart of things, travel by tubes and buses; ten to one I'd never be recognized. There's safety in a crowd."

Poirot turned inquiringly to Japp.

"I don't agree. Get clear away at once —that's the only chance. I would have had plenty of time to prepare things beforehand. I'd have a yacht waiting, with steam up, and I'd be off to one of the most out-of-the-way corners of the world before the hue and cry began!"

We both looked at Poirot. "What do *you* say, monsieur?"

For a moment he remained silent. Then a very curious smile flitted across his face.

"My friends, if *I* were hiding from the police, do you know *where* I should hide? *In a prison!*"

"*What?*"

"You are seeking Monsieur Davenheim in order to put him in prison, so you never dream of looking to see if he may not be already there!"

"What do you mean?"

"You tell me Madame Davenheim is not a very intelligent woman. Nevertheless I think that if you took her to Bow Street and confronted her with the man Billy Kellett, she would recognize him! In spite of the fact that he has shaved his beard and mustache and those bushy eyebrows, and has cropped his hair close. A woman nearly always knows her husband, though the rest of the world may be deceived!"

"Billy Kellett? But he's known to the police!"

"Did I not tell you Davenheim was a clever man? He prepared his alibi long beforehand. He was not in Buenos Aires last autumn—he was creating the character of Billy Kellett, 'doing three months,' so that the police should have no suspicions when the time came. He was playing, remember, for a large fortune, as well as liberty. It was worth while doing the thing thoroughly. Only————"

"Yes?"

"*Eh bien,* afterwards he had to wear a false beard and wig, had to *make up as himself* again, and to sleep with a false beard is not easy—it invites detection! He cannot risk continuing to share the chamber of madame his wife. You found out for me that for the last six months, or ever since his supposed return from Buenos Aires, he and Mrs. Davenheim occupied separate rooms. Then I was sure! Everything fitted in. The gardener who fancied he saw his master going around to the side of the house was quite right. He went to the boathouse, donned his 'tramp'

clothes, which you may be sure had been safely hidden from the eyes of his valet, dropped the others in the lake, and proceeded to carry out his plan by pawning the ring in an obvious manner, and then assaulting a policeman, getting himself safely into the haven of Bow Street, where nobody would ever dream of looking for him!"

"It's impossible," murmured Japp.

"Ask Madame," said my friend, smiling.

The next day a registered letter lay beside Poirot's plate. He opened it, and a five-pound note fluttered out. My friend's brow puckered.

"*Ah, sacré!* 9 But what shall I do with it? I have much remorse! *Ce pauvre Japp!* Ah, an idea! We will have a little dinner, we three! That consoles me. It was really too easy. I am ashamed. I, who would not rob a child—*mille tonnerres!* 10 *Mon ami,* what have you, that you laugh so heartily?"

[1924]

9 "Oh, damn!" (JHP)
10 "by thunder!" (JHP)

QUESTIONS FOR STUDY

1. *Agatha Christie has been called the "Mistress of Misdirection." What false clues does she insert in the story to throw off and confuse the reader? Does she also withhold any of the information essential to solving the crime?*

2. *Why should Miss Christie employ a Belgian detective—Hercule Poirot—to solve otherwise thoroughly English mysteries?*

3. *What qualities does Poirot associate with the best of detectives—and with the best of their criminal opponents?*

4. *What familiar elements of the "classic" detective story in the tradition of Edgar Allan Poe and Arthur Conan Doyle recur in this story?*

ARTHUR C. CLARKE

The Star

IT IS three thousand light-years to the
Vatican. Once, I believed that space
could have no power over faith, just
as I believed that the heavens declared
the glory of God's handiwork. Now I
have seen that handiwork, and my faith
is sorely troubled. I stare at the crucifix
that hangs on the cabin wall above the
Mark VI Computer, and for the first
time in my life I wonder if it is no more
than an empty symbol.

I have told no one yet, but the truth
cannot be concealed. The facts are there
for all to read, recorded on the countless miles of magnetic tape and the thousands of photographs we are carrying
back to Earth. Other scientists can interpret them as easily as I can, and I am
not one who would condone that tampering with the truth which often gave
my order a bad name in the olden days.

The crew were already sufficiently depressed: I wonder how they will take this
ultimate irony. Few of them have any
religious faith, yet they will not relish
using this final weapon in their campaign against me—that private, good-
natured, but fundamentally serious war
which lasted all the way from Earth. It
amused them to have a Jesuit [1] as chief
astrophysicist: Dr. Chandler, for instance, could never get over it. (Why are
medical men such notorious atheists?)
Sometimes he would meet me on the observation deck, where the lights are always low so that the stars shine with undiminished glory. He would come up to
me in the gloom and stand staring out
of the great oval port, while the heavens

1 A member of the Catholic religious order
for men founded in 1534 by Saint Ignatius
Loyola (1491–1556). (JHP)

crawled slowly around us as the ship
turned end over end with the residual
spin we had never bothered to correct.

"Well, Father," he would say at last,
"it goes on forever and forever, and perhaps *Something* made it. But how you
can believe that Something has a special
interest in us and our miserable little
world—that just beats me." Then the
argument would start, while the stars
and nebulae would swing around us in
silent, endless arcs beyond the flawlessly
clear plastic of the observation port.

It was, I think, the apparent incongruity of my position that caused most
amusement to the crew. In vain I would
point to my three papers in the *Astro-
physical Journal,* my five in the *Monthly
Notices of the Royal Astronomical Society.* I would remind them that my order has long been famous for its scientific works. We may be few now, but
ever since the eighteenth century we
have made contributions to astronomy
and geophysics out of all proportion to
our numbers. Will my report on the
Phoenix Nebula end our thousand years
of history? It will end, I fear, much more
than that.

I do not know who gave the nebula
its name, which seems to me a very bad
one. If it contains a prophecy, it is one
that cannot be verified for several billion
years. Even the word "nebula" is misleading: this is a far smaller object than
those stupendous clouds of mist—the
stuff of unborn stars—that are scattered
throughout the length of the Milky Way.
On the cosmic scale, indeed, the Phoenix
Nebula is a tiny thing—a tenuous shell
of gas surrounding a single star.

Or what is left of a star . . .

The Rubens engraving of Loyola

---

seems to mock me as it hangs there above the spectrophotometer tracings. What would *you,* Father, have made of this knowledge that has come into my keeping, so far from the little world that was all the Universe you knew? Would your faith have risen to the challenge, as mine has failed to do?

You gaze into the distance, Father, but I have traveled a distance beyond any that you could have imagined when you founded our order a thousand years ago. No other survey ship has been so far from Earth: we are at the very frontiers of the explored Universe. We set out to reach the Phoenix Nebula, we succeeded, and we are homeward bound with our burden of knowledge. I wish I could lift that burden from my shoulders, but I call to you in vain across the centuries and the light-years that lie between us.

On the book you are holding the words are plain to read. AD MAIOREM DEI GLORIAM,[2] the message runs, but it is a message I can no longer believe. Would you still believe it, if you could see what we have found?

We knew, of course, what the Phoenix Nebula was. Every year, in our Galaxy alone, more than a hundred stars explode, blazing for a few hours or days with thousands of times their normal brilliance before they sink back into death and obscurity. Such are the ordinary novae—the commonplace disasters of the Universe. I have recorded the spectrograms and light curves of dozens since I started working at the Lunar Observatory.

But three or four times in every thousand years occurs something beside which even a nova pales into total insignificance.

When a star becomes a *supernova,* it may for a little while outshine all the massed suns of the Galaxy. The Chinese astronomers watched this happen in A.D. 1054, not knowing what it was they saw. Five centuries later, in 1572, a supernova blazed in Cassiopeia so brilliantly

---

2 Latin: "To the greater glory of God." (JHP)

that it was visible in the daylight sky. There have been three more in the thousand years that have passed since then.

Our mission was to visit the remnants of such a catastrophe, to reconstruct the events that led up to it, and, if possible, to learn its cause. We came slowly in through the concentric shells of gas that had been blasted out six thousand years before, yet were expanding still. They were immensely hot, radiating even now with a fierce violet light, but were far too tenuous to do us any damage. When the star had exploded, its outer layers had been driven upward with such speed that they had escaped completely from its gravitational field. Now they formed a hollow shell large enough to engulf a thousand solar systems, and at its center burned the tiny, fantastic object which the star had now become—a White Dwarf, smaller than the Earth, yet weighing a million times as much.

The glowing gas shells were all around us, banishing the normal night of interstellar space. We were flying into the center of the cosmic bomb that had detonated millennia ago and whose incandescent fragments were still hurtling apart. The immense scale of the explosion, and the fact that the debris already covered a volume of space many billions of miles across, robbed the scene of any visible movement. It would take decades before the unaided eye could detect any motion in these tortured wisps and eddies of gas, yet the sense of turbulent expansion was overwhelming.

We had checked our primary drive hours before, and were drifting slowly toward the fierce little star ahead. Once it had been a sun like our own, but it had squandered in a few hours the energy that should have kept it shining for a million years. Now it was a shrunken miser, hoarding its resources as if trying to make amends for its prodigal youth.

No one seriously expected to find planets. If there had been any before the explosion, they would have been boiled into puffs of vapor, and their substance lost in the greater wreckage of the star itself. But we made the automatic search, as we always do when approaching an unknown sun, and presently we found a single small world circling the star at an immense distance. It must have been the Pluto of this vanished Solar System, orbiting on the frontiers of the night. Too far from the central sun ever to have known life, its remoteness had saved it from the fate of all its lost companions.

The passing fires had seared its rocks and burned away the mantle of frozen gas that must have covered it in the days before the disaster. We landed, and we found the Vault.

Its builders had made sure that we should. The monolithic marker that stood above the entrance was now a fused stump, but even the first long-range photographs told us that here was the work of intelligence. A little later we detected the continent-wide pattern of radioactivity that had been buried in the rock. Even if the pylon above the vault had been destroyed, this would have remained, an immovable and all but eternal beacon calling to the stars. Our ship fell toward this gigantic bull's-eye like an arrow into its target.

The pylon must have been a mile high when it was built, but now it looked like a candle that had melted down into a puddle of wax. It took us a week to drill through the fused rock, since we did not have the proper tools for a task like this. We were astronomers, not archaeologists, but we could improvise. Our original purpose was forgotten: this lonely monument, reared with such labor at the greatest possible distance from the doomed sun, could have only one meaning. A civilization that knew it was about to die had made its last bid for immortality.

It will take us generations to examine all the treasures that were placed in the Vault. They had plenty of time to prepare, for their sun must have given its first warnings many years before the final detonation. Everything that they wished to preserve, all the fruit of their genius, they brought here to this distant world in the days before the end, hoping that some other race would find it and that they would not be utterly forgotten. Would we have done as well, or would

we have been too lost in our own misery to give thought to a future we could never see or share?

If only they had had a little more time! They could travel freely enough between the planets of their own sun, but they had not yet learned to cross the interstellar gulfs, and the nearest Solar System was a hundred light-years away. Yet even had they possessed the secret of the Transfinite Drive, no more than a few millions could have been saved. Perhaps it was better thus.

Even if they had not been so disturbingly human as their sculpture shows, we could not have helped admiring them and grieving for their fate. They left thousands of visual records and the machines for projecting them, together with elaborate pictorial instructions from which it will not be difficult to learn their written language. We have examined many of these records, and brought to life for the first time in six thousand years the warmth and beauty of a civilization that in many ways must have been superior to our own. Perhaps they only showed us the best, and one can hardly blame them. But their worlds were very lovely, and their cities were built with a grace that matches anything of man's. We have watched them at work and play, and listened to their musical speech sounding across the centuries. One scene is still before my eyes—a group of children on a beach of strange blue sand, playing in the waves as children play on Earth. Curious whiplike trees line the shore, and some very large animal is wading in the shallows yet attracting no attention at all.

And sinking into the sea, still warm and friendly and life-giving, is the sun that will soon turn traitor and obliterate all this innocent happiness.

Perhaps if we had not been so far from home and so vulnerable to loneliness, we should not have been so deeply moved. Many of us had seen the ruins of ancient civilizations on other worlds, but they had never affected us so profoundly. This tragedy was unique. It is one thing for a race to fail and die, as nations and cultures have done on Earth.

But to be destroyed so completely in the full flower of its achievement, leaving no survivors—how could that be reconciled with the mercy of God?

My colleagues have asked me that, and I have given what answers I can. Perhaps you could have done better, Father Loyola, but I have found nothing in the *Exercitia Spiritualia* 3 that helps me here. They were not an evil people: I do not know what gods they worshiped, if indeed they worshiped any. But I have looked back at them across the centuries, and have watched while the loveliness they used their last strength to preserve was brought forth again into the light of their shrunken sun. They could have taught us much: why were they destroyed?

I know the answers that my colleagues will give when they get back to Earth. They will say that the Universe has no purpose and no plan, that since a hundred suns explode every year in our Galaxy, at this very moment some race is dying in the depths of space. Whether that race has done good or evil during its lifetime will make no difference in the end: there is no divine justice, for there is no God.

Yet, of course, what we have seen proves nothing of the sort. Anyone who argues thus is being swayed by emotion,

3 The name given to a series of religious meditations by Saint Ignatius published in Rome in 1548. (JHP)

not logic. God has no need to justify His actions to man. He who built the Universe can destroy it when He chooses. It is arrogance—it is perilously near blasphemy—for us to say what He may or may not do.

This I could have accepted, hard though it is to look upon whole worlds and peoples thrown into the furnace. But there comes a point when even the deepest faith must falter, and now, as I look at the calculations lying before me, I know I have reached that point at last.

We could not tell, before we reached the nebula, how long ago the explosion took place. Now, from the astronomical evidence and the record in the rocks of that one surviving planet, I have been able to date it very exactly. I know in what year the light of this colossal conflagration reached our Earth. I know how brilliantly the supernova whose corpse now dwindles behind our speeding ship once shone in terrestrial skies. I know how it must have blazed low in the east before sunrise, like a beacon in that oriental dawn.

There can be no reasonable doubt: the ancient mystery is solved at last. Yet, oh God, there were so many stars you could have used. What was the need to give these people to the fire, that the symbol of their passing might shine above Bethlehem?

[1955]

QUESTIONS FOR STUDY

1. *What is the major source of conflict in the story?*
2. *The story is told in retrospect by its troubled narrator. Could it have been told dramatically in the present? How would the story then be different? Could it have been as effectively narrated from a third person point of view? What might then be gained and/or lost?*
3. *What basic questions does the story raise about the existence and nature of God and the limitations of human wisdom?*
4. *What devices does Clarke use to make his science fiction believable and acceptable to the reader?*
5. *How do you account for the strong effect that the story has upon most of its readers?*

SAMUEL L. CLEMENS

The Man That Corrupted Hadleyburg

IT WAS many years ago. Hadleyburg was the most honest and upright town in all the region round about. It had kept that reputation unsmirched during three generations, and was prouder of it than of any other of its possessions. It was so proud of it, and so anxious to insure its perpetuation, that it began to teach the principles of honest dealing to its babies in the cradle, and made the like teachings the staple of their culture thenceforward through all the years devoted to their education. Also, throughout the formative years temptations were kept out of the way of the young people, so that their honesty could have every chance to harden and solidify, and become a part of their very bone. The neighboring towns were jealous of this honorable supremacy, and affected to sneer at Hadleyburg's pride in it and call it vanity; but all the same they were obliged to acknowledge that Hadleyburg was in reality an incorruptible town; and if pressed they would also acknowledge that the mere fact that a young man hailed from Hadleyburg was all the recommendation he needed when he went forth from his natal town to seek for responsible employment.

But at last, in the drift of time, Hadleyburg had the ill luck to offend a passing stranger—possibly without knowing it, certainly without caring, for Hadleyburg was sufficient unto itself, and cared not a rap for strangers or their opinions. Still, it would have been well to make an exception in this one's case, for he was a bitter man and revengeful. All through his wanderings during a whole year he kept his injury in mind, and gave all his leisure moments to trying to invent a compensating satisfaction for it. He contrived many plans, and all of them were good, but none of them was quite sweeping enough; the poorest of them would hurt a great many individuals, but what he wanted was a plan which would compre- hend the entire town, and not let so much as one person escape unhurt. At last he had a fortunate idea, and when it fell into his brain it lit up his whole head with an evil joy. He began to form a plan at once, saying to himself, "That is the thing to do —I will corrupt the town."

Six months later he went to Hadleyburg, and arrived in a buggy at the house of the old cashier of the bank about ten at night. He got a sack out of the buggy, shouldered it, and staggered with it through the cottage yard, and knocked at the door. A woman's voice said "Come in," and he entered, and set his sack behind the stove in the parlor, saying politely to the old lady who sat reading the *Missionary Herald* by the lamp:

"Pray keep your seat, madam, I will not disturb you. There—now it is pretty well concealed; one would hardly know it was there. Can I see your husband a moment, madam?"

No, he was gone to Brixton, and might not return before morning.

"Very well, madam, it is no matter. I merely wanted to leave that sack in his care, to be delivered to the rightful owner when he shall be found. I am a stranger; he does not know me; I am merely passing through the town to-night to discharge a matter which has been long in my mind. My errand is now completed, and I go pleased and a little proud, and you will never see me again. There is a paper attached to the sack which will explain everything. Good night, madam."

The old lady was afraid of the mysterious big stranger, and was glad to see him go. But her curiosity was roused, and she went straight to the sack and brought away the paper. It began as follows:

To be published; or, the right man sought out by private inquiry—either will answer. This sack contains gold coin weighing a hundred and sixty pounds four ounces—

"Mercy on us, and the door not locked!"

Mrs. Richards flew to it all in a tremble and locked it, then pulled down the window-shades and stood frightened, worried, and wondering if there was anything else she could do toward making herself and the money more safe. She listened awhile for burglars, then surrendered to curiosity and went back to the lamp and finished reading the paper:

I am a foreigner, and am presently going back to my own country, to remain there permanently. I am grateful to America for what I have received at her hands during my long stay under her flag; and to one of her citizens—a citizen of Hadleyburg—I am especially grateful for a great kindness done me a year or two ago. Two great kindnesses, in fact. I will explain. I was a gambler. I say I *was*. I was a ruined gambler. I arrived in this village at night, hungry and without a penny. I asked for help—in the dark; I was ashamed to beg in the light. I begged of the right man. He gave me twenty dollars—that is to say, he gave me life, as I considered it. He also gave me fortune; for out of that money I have made myself rich at the gaming-table. And finally, a remark which he made to me has remained with me to this day, and has at last conquered me; and in conquering has saved the remnant of my morals; I shall gamble no more. Now I have no idea who that man was, but I want him found, and I want him to have this money, to give away, throw away, or keep, as he pleases. It is merely my way of testifying my gratitude to him. If I could stay, I would find him myself; but no matter, he will be found. This is an honest town, an incorruptible town, and I know I can trust it without fear. This man can be identified by the remark which he made to me; I feel persuaded that he will remember it.

And now my plan is this: If you prefer to conduct the inquiry privately, do so. Tell the contents of this present writing to any one who is likely to be the right man. If he shall answer, 'I am the man; the remark I made was so-and-so,' apply the test —to wit: open the sack, and in it you will find a sealed envelope containing that remark. If the remark mentioned by the candidate tallies with it give him the money, and ask no further questions, for he is certainly the right man.

But if you shall prefer a public inquiry,

then publish this present writing in the local paper—with these instructions added, to wit: Thirty days from now, let the candidate appear at the town-hall at eight in the evening (Friday), and hand his remark, in a sealed envelope, to the Rev. Mr. Burgess (if he will be kind enough to act); and let Mr. Burgess there and then destroy the seals of the sack, open it, and see if the remark is correct; if correct, let the money be delivered, with my sincere gratitude, to my benefactor thus identified.

Mrs. Richards sat down, gently quivering with excitement, and was soon lost in thinkings—after this pattern: "What a strange thing it is! . . . And what a fortune for that kind man who set his bread afloat upon the waters! . . . If it had only been my husband that did it!—for we are so poor, so old and poor! . . ." Then, with a sigh—"but it was not my Edward; no, it was not he that gave a stranger twenty dollars. It is a pity, too; I see it now. . . ." Then, with a shudder—"But it is *gambler's* money! the wages of sin: we couldn't take it; we couldn't touch it. I don't like to be near it; it seems a defilement." She moved to a farther chair. . . ." I wish Edward would come and take it to the bank; a burglar might come at any moment; it is dreadful to be here all alone with it."

At eleven Mr. Richards arrived, and while his wife was saying, "I am *so* glad you've come!" he was saying, "I'm so tired—tired clear out; it is dreadful to be poor, and have to make these dismal journeys at my time of life. Always at the grind, grind, grind, on a salary—another man's slave, and he sitting at home in his slippers, rich and comfortable."

"I am so sorry for you, Edward, you know that; but be comforted: we have our livelihood; we have our good name—"

"Yes, Mary, and that is everything. Don't mind my talk—it's just a moment's irritation and doesn't mean anything. Kiss me—there, it's all gone now, and I am not complaining any more. What have you been getting? What's in the sack?"

Then his wife told him the great secret. It dazed him for a moment; then he said: "It weighs a hundred and sixty pounds? Why, Mary, it's for-ty thousand dollars— think of it—a whole fortune! Not ten men in this village are worth that much. Give me the paper."

He skimmed through it and said:

"Isn't it an adventure! Why it's a romance; it's like the impossible things one reads about in books, and never sees in life." He was well stirred up now; cheerful, even gleeful. He tapped his old wife on the cheek, and said, humorously, "Why, we're rich, Mary, rich; all we've got to do is to bury the money and burn the papers. If the gambler ever comes to inquire, we'll merely look coldly upon him and say: 'What is this nonsense you are talking? We have never heard of you and your sack of gold before'; and then he would look foolish, and—"

"And in the meantime, while you are running on with your jokes, the money is still here, and it is fast getting along toward burglar-time."

"True. Very well, what shall we do—make the inquiry private? No, not that: it would spoil the romance. The public method is better. Think what a noise it will make! And it will make all the other towns jealous; for no stranger would trust such a thing to any town but Hadleyburg, and they know it. It's a great card for us. I must get to the printing-office now, or I shall be too late."

"But stop—stop—don't leave me here alone with it, Edward!"

But he was gone. For only a little while, however. Not far from his own house he met the editor-proprietor of the paper, and gave him the document, and said, "Here is a good thing for you, Cox—put it in."

"It may be too late, Mr. Richards, but I'll see."

At home again he and his wife sat down to talk the charming mystery over; they were in no condition for sleep. The first question was, Who could the citizen have been who gave the stranger the twenty dollars? It seemed a simple one; both answered it in the same breath:

"Barclay Goodson."

"Yes," said Richards, "he could have done it, and it would have been like him, but there's not another in the town."

"Everybody will grant that, Edward—grant it privately, anyway. For six months, now, the village has been its own proper self once more—honest, narrow, self-righteous, and stingy."

"It is what he always called it, to the day of his death—said it right out publicly, too."

"Yes, and he was hated for it."

"Oh, of course; but he didn't care. I reckon he was the best-hated man among us, except the Reverend Burgess."

"Well, Burgess deserves it—he will never get another congregation here. Mean as the town is, it knows how to estimate *him*. Edward, doesn't it seem odd that the stranger should appoint Burgess to deliver the money?"

"Well, yes—it does. That is—that is—"

"Why so much that-*is*-ing? Would *you* select him?"

"Mary, maybe the stranger knows him better than this village does."

"Much *that* would help Burgess!"

The husband seemed perplexed for an answer; the wife kept a steady eye upon him, and waited. Finally Richards said, with the hesitancy of one who is making a statement which is likely to encounter doubt:

"Mary, Burgess is not a bad man."

His wife was certainly surprised.

"Nonsense!" she exclaimed.

"He is not a bad man. I know. The whole of his unpopularity had its foundation in that one thing—the thing that made so much noise."

"That 'one thing,' indeed! As if that 'one thing' wasn't enough, all by itself."

"Plenty. Plenty. Only he wasn't guilty of it."

"How you talk! Not guilty of it! Everybody knows he *was* guilty."

"Mary, I give you my word—he was innocent."

"I can't believe it, and I don't. How do you know?"

"It is a confession. I am ashamed, but I will make it. I was the only man who knew he was innocent. I could have saved him, and—and—well, you know how the town was wrought up—I hadn't the pluck to do it. I would have turned everybody against me. I felt mean, ever so mean; but I didn't dare; I hadn't the manliness to face that."

Mary looked troubled, and for a while was silent. Then she said, stammeringly:

"I—I don't think it would have done for you to—to—One musn't—er—public opinion—one has to be so careful—so—" It was a difficult road, and she got mired; but after a little she got started again. "It was a great pity, but—Why, we couldn't afford it, Edward—we couldn't indeed. Oh, I wouldn't have had you do it for anything!"

"It would have lost us the good will of so many people, Mary; and then—and then—"

"What troubles me now is, what *he* thinks of us, Edward."

"He? *He* doesn't suspect that I could have saved him."

"Oh," exclaimed the wife, in a tone of relief, "I am glad of that! As long as he doesn't know that you could have saved him, he—he—well, that makes it a great deal better. Why, I might have known he didn't know, because he is always trying to be friendly with us, as little encouragement as we give him. More than once people have twitted me with it. There's the Wilsons, and Wilcoxes, and the Harknesses, they take a mean pleasure in saying, '*Your friend* Burgess,' because they know it pesters me. I wish he wouldn't persist in liking us so; I can't think why he keeps it up."

"I can explain it. It's another confession. When the thing was new and hot, and the town made a plan to ride him on a rail, my conscience hurt me so that I couldn't stand it, and went privately and gave him notice, and he got out of the town and staid out till it was safe to come back."

"Edward! If the town had found it out—"

"*Don't!* It scares me yet, to think of it. I repented of it the minute it was done; and I was even afraid to tell you, lest your face might betray it to somebody. I didn't sleep any that night, for worrying. But after a few days I saw that no one was going to suspect me, and after that I got to feeling glad I did it. And I feel glad yet, Mary—glad through and through."

"So do I, now, for it would have been a dreadful way to treat him. Yes, I'm glad; for really you did owe him that, you know. But, Edward, suppose it should come out yet, some day!"

"It won't."

"Why?"

"Because everybody thinks it was Goodson."

"Of course they would!"

"Certainly. And of course *he* didn't care. They persuaded poor old Sawlsberry to go and charge it on him, and he went blustering over there and did it. Goodson looked him over, like as if he was hunting for a place on him that he could despise the most, then he says, 'So you are the Committee of Inquiry, are you?' Sawlsberry said that was about what he was. 'Hm. Do they require particulars, or do you reckon a kind of a *general* answer will do?' 'If they require particulars, I will come back, Mr. Goodson; I will take the general answer first.' 'Very well, then, tell them to go to hell—I reckon that's general enough. And I'll give you some advice, Sawlsberry; when you come back for the particulars, fetch a basket to carry the relics of yourself home in.' "

"Just like Goodson; it's got all the marks. He had only one vanity: he thought he could give advice better than any other person."

"It settled the business, and saved us, Mary. The subject was dropped."

"Bless you, I'm not doubting *that*."

Then they took up the gold-sack mystery again, with strong interest. Soon the conversation began to suffer breaks—interruptions caused by absorbed thinkings. The breaks grew more and more frequent. At last Richards lost himself wholly in thought. He sat long, gazing vacantly at the floor, and by and by he began to punctuate his thoughts with little nervous movements of his hands that seemed to indicate vexation. Meantime his wife too had relapsed into a thoughtful silence, and her movements were beginning to show a troubled discomfort. Finally Richards got up and strode aimlessly about the room, plowing his hands through his hair, much as a somnambulist might do who was having a bad dream. Then he seemed to arrive at a definite purpose; and without a word he put on his hat and passed quickly out of the house. His wife sat brooding, with a drawn face, and did not seem to be aware that she was alone. Now and then she murmured. "Lead us not into t- . . . but-but-we are so poor, so poor! . . . Lead us not into . . . Ah, who would be hurt by it?—and no one would ever know . . . Lead us . . ." The voice died out in mumblings. After a little while she glanced up and muttered in a half-frightened, half-glad way:

"He is gone! But, oh dear, he may be too late—too late. . . . Maybe not—maybe there is still time." She rose and stood thinking, nervously clasping and unclasping her hands. A slight shudder shook her frame, and she said, out of a dry throat, "God forgive me—it's awful to think such things—but . . . Lord, how we are made —how strangely we are made!"

She turned the light low, and slipped stealthily over and kneeled down by the sack and felt of its ridgy sides with her hands, and fondled them lovingly; and there was a gloating light in her poor old eyes. She fell into fits of absence; and came half out of them at times to mutter, "If we had only waited!—oh, if we had only waited a little, and not been in such a hurry!"

Meantime Cox had gone home from his office and told his wife all about the strange thing that had happened, and they had talked it over eagerly, and guessed that the late Goodson was the only man in the town who could have helped a suffering stranger with so noble a sum as twenty dollars. Then there was a pause, and the two became thoughtful and silent. And by and by nervous and fidgety. At last the wife said, as if to herself:

"Nobody knows this secret but the Richardses . . . and us . . . nobody."

The husband came out of his thinkings with a slight start, and gazed wistfully at his wife, whose face was become very pale; then he hesitatingly rose, and glanced furtively at his hat, then at his wife—a sort of mute inquiry. Mrs. Cox swallowed once or twice, with her hand at her throat, then in place of speech she nodded her head. In a moment she was alone, and mumbling to herself.

And now Richards and Cox were hurrying through the deserted streets, from opposite directions. They met, panting, at the foot of the printing-office stairs; by the night light there they read each other's face. Cox whispered:

"Nobody knows about this but us?"

The whispered answer was,

"Not a soul—on honor, not a soul!"

"If it isn't too late to—"

The men were starting up-stairs; at this moment they were overtaken by a boy, and Cox asked:

"Is that you, Johnny?"

"Yes, sir."

"You needn't ship the early mail—nor *any* mail; wait till I tell you."

"It's already gone, sir."

"*Gone?*" It had the sound of unspeakable disappointment in it.

"Yes, sir. Time-table for Brixton and all the towns beyond changed to-day, sir —had to get the papers in twenty minutes earlier than common. I had to rush; if I had been two minutes later—"

The men turned and walked slowly away, not waiting to hear the rest. Neither of them spoke during ten minutes; then Cox said, in a vexed tone:

"What possessed you to be in such a hurry, *I* can't make out."

The answer was humble enough:

"I see it now, but somehow I never thought, you know, until it was too late. But the next time—"

"Next time be hanged! It won't come in a thousand years."

Then the friends separated without a good night, and dragged themselves home with a gait of mortally stricken men. At their homes their wives sprang up with an eager "Well?"—then saw the answer with their eyes and sank down sorrowing, without waiting for it to come in words. In both houses a discussion followed of a heated sort—a new thing; there had been discussions before, but not heated ones, not ungentle ones. The discussions to-night were a sort of seeming plagiarisms of each other. Mrs. Richards said,

"If you had only waited, Edward—if you had only stopped to think; but no, you must run straight to the printing-office and spread it all over the world."

"It *said* publish it."

"That is nothing; it also said do it privately, if you liked. There, now—is that true, or not?"

"Why, yes—yes, it is true; but when I thought what a stir it would make, and what a compliment it was to Hadleyburg that a stranger should trust it so—"

"Oh, certainly, I know all that; but if you had only stopped to think, you would have seen that you *couldn't* find the right man, because he is in his grave, and hasn't left chick nor child nor relation behind him; and as long as the money went to somebody that awfully needed it, and nobody would be hurt by it, and—and—"

She broke down, crying. Her husband tried to think of some comforting thing to say, and presently came out with this:

"But after all, Mary, it must be for the best—it *must* be; we know that. And we must remember that it was so ordered—"

"Ordered! Oh, everything's *ordered*, when a person has to find some way out when he has been stupid. Just the same, it was *ordered* that the money should come to us in this special way, and it was you that must take it on yourself to go meddling with the designs of Providence—and who gave you the right? It was wicked, that is what it was—just blasphemous presumption, and no more becoming to a meek and humble professor of—"

"But, Mary, you know how we have been trained all our lives long, like the whole village, till it is absolutely second nature to us to stop not a single moment to think when there's an honest thing to be done—"

"Oh, I know it, I know it—it's been one everlasting training and training and training in honesty—honesty shielded, from the very cradle, against every possible temptation, and so it's *artificial* honesty, and weak as water when temptation comes, as we have seen this night. God knows I never had shade nor shadow of a doubt of my petrified and indestructible honesty until now—and now, under the very first big and real temptation, I— Edward, it is my belief that this town's honesty is as rotten as mine is; as rotten as yours is. It is a mean town, a hard, stingy town, and hasn't a virtue in the world but this honesty it is so celebrated for and so conceited about; and so help me, I do believe that if ever the day comes that its honesty falls under great temptation, its grand reputation will go to ruin like a house of cards. There, now, I've made confession, and I feel better; I am a humbug, and I've been one all my life, without knowing it. Let no man call me honest again—I will not have it."

"I—well, Mary, I feel a good deal as you do; I certainly do. It seems strange, too, so strange. I never could have believed it—never."

A long silence followed; both were sunk in thought. At last the wife looked up and said:

"I know what you are thinking, Edward."

Richards had the embarrassed look of a person who is caught.

"I am ashamed to confess it, Mary, but—"

"It's no matter, Edward, I was thinking the same question myself."

"I hope so. State it."

"You were thinking, if a body could only guess out *what the remark was* that Goodson made to the stranger."

"It's perfectly true. I feel guilty and ashamed. And you?"

"I'm past it. Let us make a pallet here; we've got to stand watch till the bank vault opens in the morning and admits the sack. . . . Oh dear, oh dear—if we hadn't made the mistake!"

The pallet was made, and Mary said:

"The open sesame—what could it have been? I do wonder what that remark could have been? But come; we will get to bed now."

"And sleep?"

"No: think."

"Yes, think."

By this time the Coxes too had completed their spat and their reconciliation, and were turning in—to think, to think, and toss, and fret, and worry over what the remark could possibly have been which Goodson made to the stranded derelict; that golden remark; that remark worth forty thousand dollars, cash.

The reason that the village telegraph-office was open later than usual that night was this: The foreman of Cox's paper was the local representative of the Associated Press. One might say its honorary representative, for it wasn't four times a year that he could furnish thirty words that would be accepted. But this time it was different. His despatch stating what he had caught got an instant answer:

Send the whole thing—all the details— twelve hundred words.

A colossal order! The foreman filled the bill; and he was the proudest man in the State. By breakfast-time the next morning the name of Hadleyburg the Incorruptible was on every lip in America, from Montreal to the Gulf, from the glaciers of Alaska to the orange-groves of Florida; and millions and millions of people were discussing the stranger and his money-sack, and wondering if the right man would be found, and hoping some more news about the matter would come soon—right away.

II

Hadleyburg village woke up world-celebrated — astonished — happy — vain. Vain beyond imagination. Its nineteen principal citizens and their wives went about shaking hands with each other, and beaming, and smiling, and congratulating, and saying *this* thing adds a new word to the dictionary—*Hadleyburg*, synonym for *incorruptible*—destined to live in dictionaries forever! And the minor and unimportant citizens and their wives went around acting in much the same way. Everybody ran to the bank to see the gold-sack; and before noon grieved and envious crowds began to flock in from Brixton and all neighboring towns; and that afternoon and next day reporters began to arrive from everywhere to verify the sack and its history and write the whole thing up anew, and make dashing free-hand pictures of the sack, and of Richards's house, and the bank, and the Presbyterian church, and the Baptist church, and the public square, and the town-hall where the test would be applied and the money delivered; and damnable portraits of the Richardses, and Pinkerton the banker, and Cox, and the foreman, and Reverend

Burgess, and the postmaster—and even of Jack Halliday, who was the loafing, good-natured, no-account, irreverent fisherman, hunter, boys' friend, stray-dogs' friend, typical "Sam Lawson" of the town. The little, mean, smirking, oily Pinkerton showed the sack to all comers, and rubbed his sleek palms together pleasantly, and enlarged upon the town's fine old reputation for honesty and upon this wonderful indorsement of it, and hoped and believed that the example would now spread far and wide over the American world, and be epoch-making in the matter of moral regeneration. And so on, and so on.

By the end of a week things had quieted down again; the wild intoxication of pride and joy had sobered to a soft, sweet, silent delight—a sort of deep, nameless, unutterable content. All faces bore a look of peaceful, holy happiness.

Then a change came. It was a gradual change: so gradual that its beginnings were hardly noticed; maybe were not noticed at all, except by Jack Halliday, who always noticed everything; and always made fun of it, too, no matter what it was. He began to throw out chaffing remarks about people not looking quite so happy as they did a day or two ago; and next he claimed that the new aspect was deepening to positive sadness; next, that it was taking on a sick look; and finally he said that everybody was become so moody, thoughtful, and absent-minded that he could rob the meanest man in town of a cent out of the bottom of his breeches pocket and not disturb his revery.

At this stage—or about this stage—a saying like this was dropped at bedtime —with a sigh, usually—by the head of each of the nineteen principal households: "Ah, what *could* have been the remark that Goodson made?"

And straightaway—with a shudder— came this, from the man's wife:

"Oh, *don't!* What horrible thing are you mulling in your mind? Put it away from you, for God's sake!"

But that question was wrung from those men again the next night—and got the same retort. But weaker.

And the third night the men uttered the

question yet again—with anguish, and absently. This time—and the following night—the wives fidgeted feebly, and tried to say something. But didn't.

And the night after that they found their tongues and responded longingly:

"Oh, if we *could* only guess!"

Halliday's comments grew daily more and more sparkingly disagreeable and disparaging. He went diligently about, laughing at the town, individually and in mass. But his laugh was the only one left in the village: it fell upon a hollow and mournful vacancy and emptiness. Not even a smile was findable anywhere. Halliday carried a cigar-box around on a tripod, playing that it was a camera, and halted all passers and aimed the thing and said, "Ready!—now look pleasant, please," but not even this capital joke could surprise the dreary faces into any softening.

So three weeks passed—one week was left. It was Saturday evening—after supper. Instead of the aforetime Saturday-evening flutter and bustle and shopping and larking, the streets were empty and desolate. Richards and his old wife sat apart in their little parlor—miserable and thinking. This was become their evening habit now: the lifelong habit which had preceded it, of reading, knitting, and contented chat, or receiving or paying neighborly calls, was dead and gone and forgotten, ages ago—two or three weeks ago; nobody talked now, nobody read, nobody visited—the whole village sat at home, sighing, worrying, silent. Trying to guess out that remark.

The postman left a letter. Richards glanced listlessly at the superscription and the postmark—unfamiliar, both—and tossed the letter on the table and resumed his might-have-beens and his hopeless dull miseries where he had left them off. Two or three hours later his wife got wearily up and was going away to bed without a good night—custom now—but she stopped near the letter and eyed it awhile with a dead interest, then broke it open, and began to skim it over. Richards, sitting there with his chair tilted back against the wall and his chin between his knees, heard something fall. It was his wife. He sprang to her side, but she cried out:

"Leave me alone, I am too happy. Read the letter—read it!"

He did. He devoured it, his brain reeling. The letter was from a distant state, and it said:

I am a stranger to you, but no matter: I have something to tell. I have just arrived home from Mexico, and learned about that episode. Of course you do not know who made that remark, but I know, and I am the only person living who does know. It was *Goodson*. I knew him well, many years ago. I passed through your village that very night, and was his guest till the midnight train came along. I overheard him make that remark to the stranger in the dark—it was in Hale Alley. He and I talked of it the rest of the way home, and while smoking in his house. He mentioned many of your villagers in the course of his talk—most of them in a very uncomplimentary way, but two or three favorably; among these latter yourself. I say "favorably"—nothing stronger. I remember his saying he did not actually *like* any person in the town—not one; but that you—I *think* he said you—am almost sure—had done him a very great service once, possibly without knowing the full value of it, and he wished he had a fortune, he would leave it to you when he died, and a curse apiece for the rest of the citizens. Now, then, if it was you that did him that service, you are his legitimate heir, and entitled to the sack of gold. I know that I can trust to your honor and honesty, for in a citizen of Hadleyburg these virtues are an unfailing inheritance, and so I am going to reveal to you the remark, well satisfied that if you are not the right man you will seek and find the right one and see that poor Goodson's debt of gratitude for the service referred to is paid. This is the remark: "*You are far from being a bad man: go, and reform.*"

Howard L. Stephenson

"Oh, Edward, the money is ours and I am so grateful, *oh*, so grateful—kiss me, dear, it's forever since we kissed—and we needed it so—the money—and now you are free of Pinkerton and his bank, and nobody's slave any more; it seems to me I could fly for joy."

It was a happy half-hour that the couple spent there on the settee caressing each other; it was the old days come again—days that had begun with their courtship and lasted without a break till the stranger brought the deadly money. By and by the wife said:

"Oh, Edward, how lucky it was you did him that grand service, poor Goodson! I never liked him, but I love him now. And it was fine and beautiful of you never to mention it or brag about it." Then, with a touch of reproach, "But you ought to have told *me*, Edward, you ought to have told your wife, you know."

"Well, I—er—well, Mary, you see—"

"Now stop hemming and hawing, and tell me about it, Edward. I always loved you, and now I'm proud of you. Everybody believes there was only one good generous soul in this village, and now it turns out that you—Edward, why don't you tell me?"

"Well—er—er—Why, Mary, I can't!"

"You *can't*? *Why* can't you?"

"You see, he—well, he—he made me promise I wouldn't."

The wife looked him over, and said, very slowly:

"Made—you—promise? Edward, what do you tell me that for?"

"Mary, do you think I would lie?"

She was troubled and silent for a moment, then she laid her hand within his and said:

"No . . . no. We have wandered far enough from our bearings—God spare us that! In all your life you have never uttered a lie. But now—now that the foundations of things seem to be crumbling from under us, we—we—" She lost her voice for a moment, then said, brokenly, "Lead us not into temptation. . . . I think you made the promise, Edward. Let it rest so. Let us keep away from that ground. Now—that is all gone by; let us be happy again; it is no time for clouds."

Edward found it something of an effort to comply, for his mind kept wandering —trying to remember what the service was that he had done Goodson.

The couple lay awake the most of the night, Mary happy and busy, Edward busy but not so happy. Mary was planning what she would do with the money. Edward was trying to recall that service. At first his conscience was sore on account of the lie he had told Mary—if it was a lie. After much reflection—suppose it *was* a lie? What then? Was it such a great matter? Aren't we always *acting* lies? Then why not *tell* them? Look at Mary— look what she had done. While he was hurrying off on his honest errand, what was she doing? Lamenting because the papers hadn't been destroyed and the money kept! Is theft better than lying?

That point lost its sting—the lie dropped into the background and left comfort behind it. The next point came to the front: *Had* he rendered that service? Well, here was Goodson's own evidence as reported in Stephenson's letter; there could be no better evidence than that— it was even *proof* that he had rendered it. Of course. So that point was settled. . . . No, not quite. He recalled with a wince that this unknown Mr. Stephenson was just a trifle unsure as to whether the performer of it was Richards or some other —and, oh dear, he had put Richards on his honor! He must himself decide whither that money must go—and Mr. Stephenson was not doubting that if he was the wrong man he would go honorably and find the right one. Oh, it was odious to put a man in such a situation—ah, why couldn't Stephenson have left out that doubt! What did he want to intrude that for?

Further reflection. How did it happen that *Richards'* name remained in Stephenson's mind as indicating the right man, and not some other man's name? That looked good. Yes, that looked very good. In fact, it went on looking better and better, straight along—until by and by it grew into positive *proof*. And then Richards put the matter at once out of his mind, for he had a private instinct that a proof once established is better left so.

He was feeling reasonably comfortable now, but there was still one other detail that kept pushing itself on his notice: of course he had done that service—that was settled; but what *was* that service? He must recall it—he would not go to sleep till he had recalled it; it would make his peace of mind perfect. And so he thought and thought. He thought of a dozen things —possible services, even probable services —but none of them seemed adequate, none of them seemed large enough, none of them seemed worth the money—worth the fortune Goodson had wished he could leave in his will. And besides, he couldn't remember having done them, anyway. Now, then—now, then—what *kind* of a service would it be that would make a man so inordinately grateful? Ah—the saving of his soul! That must be it. Yes, he could remember, now, how he once set himself the task of converting Goodson, and labored at it as much as—he was going to say three months; but upon closer examination it shrunk to a month, then to a week, then to a day, then to nothing. Yes, he remembered now, and with unwelcome vividness, that Goodson had told him to go to thunder and mind his own business—*he* wasn't hankering to follow Hadleyburg to heaven!

So that solution was a failure—he hadn't saved Goodson's soul. Richards was discouraged. Then after a little came another idea: had he saved Goodson's property? No, that wouldn't do—he hadn't any. His life? That is it! Of course. Why, he might have thought of it before. This time he was on the right track, sure. His imagination-mill was hard at work in a minute, now.

Thereafter during a stretch of two exhausting hours he was busy saving Goodson's life. He saved it in all kinds of difficult and perilous ways. In every case he got it saved satisfactorily up to a certain point; then, just as he was beginning to get well persuaded that it had really happened, a troublesome detail would turn up which made the whole thing impossible. As in the matter of drowning, for instance. In that case he had swum out and tugged Goodson ashore in an unconscious state with a great crowd looking on and applauding, but when he had got it all thought out and was just beginning to remember all about it, a whole swarm of disqualifying details arrived on the ground: the town would have known of the circumstance, Mary would have known of it, it would glare like a limelight in his own memory instead of being an inconspicuous service which he had possibly rendered "without knowing its full value." And at this point he remembered that he couldn't swim, anyway.

Ah—*there* was a point which he had been overlooking from the start: it had to be a service which he had rendered "possibly without knowing the full value of it." Why, really, that ought to be an easy hunt—much easier than those others. And sure enough, by and by he found it. Goodson, years and years ago, came near marrying a very sweet and pretty girl, named Nancy Hewitt, but in some way or other the match had been broken off; the girl died, Goodson remained a bachelor, and by and by became a soured one and a frank despiser of the human species. Soon after the girl's death the village found out, or thought it had found out, that she carried a spoonful of negro blood in her veins. Richards worked at these details a good while, and in the end he thought he remembered things concerning them which must have gotten mislaid in his memory through long neglect. He seemed to dimly remember that it was *he* that found out about the negro blood; that it was he that told the village; that the village told Goodson where they got it; that he thus saved Goodson from marrying the tainted girl; that he had done him this great service "without knowing the full value of it," in fact without knowing that he was doing it; but that Goodson knew the value of it, and what a narrow escape he had had, and so went to his grave grateful to his benefactor and wishing he had a fortune to leave him. It was all clear and simple now, and the more he went over it the more luminous and certain it grew; and at last, when he nestled to sleep satisfied and happy, he remembered the whole thing just as if it had been yesterday. In fact, he dimly remembered Goodson's *telling* him his gratitude once. Meantime Mary had spent six thousand dollars on a new house for herself and a pair of slippers for her pastor, and then had fallen peacefully to rest.

That same Saturday evening the postman had delivered a letter to each of the other principal citizens—nineteen letters in all. No two of the envelopes were alike, and no two of the superscriptions were in the same hand, but the letters inside were just like each other in every detail but one. They were exact copies of the letter received by Richards—handwriting and all—and were all signed by Stephenson, but in place of Richards's name each receiver's own name appeared.

All night long eighteen principal citizens did what their caste-brother Richards was doing at the same time—they put in their energies trying to remember what notable service it was that they had unconsciously done Barclay Goodson. In no case was it a holiday job; still they succeeded.

And while they were at this work, which was difficult, their wives put in the night spending the money, which was easy. During that one night the nineteen wives spent an average of seven thousand dollars each out of the forty thousand in the sack—a hundred and thirty-three thousand altogether.

Next day there was a surprise for Jack Halliday. He noticed that the faces of the nineteen chief citizens and their wives bore that expression of peaceful and holy happiness again. He could not understand it, neither was he able to invent any remarks about it that could damage it or disturb it. And so it was his turn to be dissatisfied with life. His private guesses at the reasons for the happiness failed in all instances, upon examination. When he met Mrs. Wilcox and noticed the placid ecstasy in her face, he said to himself, "Her cat has had kittens"—and went and asked the cook: it was not so; the cook had detected the happiness, but did not know the cause. When Halliday found the duplicate ecstasy in the face of "Shadbelly" Billson (village nickname), he was sure some neighbor of Billson's had broken his leg, but inquiry showed that this had not happened. The subdued ecstasy in Gregory Yates's face could mean but one thing—he was a mother-in-law short: it was another mistake. "And Pinkerton—Pinkerton—he has collected ten cents that he thought he was going to lose." And so on, and so on. In some cases the guesses had to remain in doubt, in the others they proved distinct errors. In the end Halliday said to himself, "Anyway it foots up that there's nineteen Hadleyburg families temporarily in heaven:

I don't know how it happened; I only know Providence is off duty to-day."

An architect and builder from the next state had lately ventured to set up a small business in this unpromising village, and his sign had now been hanging out a week. Not a customer yet; he was a discouraged man, and sorry he had come. But his weather changed suddenly now. First one and then another chief citizen's wife said to him privately:

"Come to my house Monday week—but say nothing about it for the present. We think of building."

He got eleven invitations that day. That night he wrote his daughter and broke off her match with her student. He said she could marry a mile higher than that.

Pinkerton the banker and two or three other well-to-do men planned country-seats—but waited. That kind don't count their chickens until they are hatched.

The Wilsons devised a grand new thing —a fancy-dress ball. They made no actual promises, but told all their acquaintanceship in confidence that they were thinking the matter over and thought they should give it—"and if we do, you will be invited, of course." People were surprised, and said, one to another, "Why, they are crazy, those poor Wilsons, they can't afford it." Several among the nineteen said privately to their husbands, "It is a good idea: we will keep still till their cheap thing is over, then *we* will give one that will make it sick."

The days drifted along, and the bill of future squandering rose higher and higher, wilder and wilder, more and more foolish and reckless. It began to look as if every member of the nineteen would not only spend his whole forty thousand dollars before receiving-day, but be actually in debt by the time he got the money. In some cases light-headed people did not stop with planning to spend, they really spent—on credit. They bought land, mortgages, farms, speculative stocks, fine clothes, horses, and various other things, paid down the bonus, and made themselves liable for the rest—at ten days. Presently the sober second thought came, and Halliday noticed a ghastly anxiety was beginning to show up in a good many faces. Again he was puzzled, and didn't know what to make of it. "The Wilcox kittens aren't dead, for they weren't born; nobody's broken a leg; there's no shrinkage in mother-in-laws; *nothing* has happened—it is an unsolvable mystery."

There was another puzzled man, too —the Rev. Mr. Burgess. For days, wherever he went, people seemed to follow him or to be watching out for him; and if he ever found himself in a retired spot, a member of the nineteen would be sure to appear, thrust an envelope privately into his hand, whisper "To be opened at the town-hall Friday evening," then vanish away like a guilty thing. He was expecting that there might be one claimant for the sack—doubtful, however, Goodson being dead—but it never occurred to him that all this crowd might be claimants. When the great Friday came at last, he found that he had nineteen envelopes.

III

The town hall had never looked finer. The platform at the end of it was backed by a showy draping of flags; at intervals along the walls were festoons of flags; the gallery fronts were clothed in flags; the supporting columns were swathed in flags; all this was to impress the stranger, for he would be there in considerable force, and in a large degree he would be connected with the press. The house was full. The 412 fixed seats were occupied; also the 68 extra chairs which had been packed into the aisles; the steps of the platform were occupied; some distinguished strangers were given seats on the platform; at the horseshoe of tables which fenced the front and sides of the platform sat a strong force of special correspondents who had come from everywhere. It was the best-dressed house the town had ever produced. There were some tolerably expensive toilets there, and in several cases the ladies who wore them had the look of being unfamiliar with that kind of clothes. At least the town thought they had that look, but the notion could have arisen from the town's knowledge of

the fact that these ladies had never inhabited such clothes before.

The gold sack stood on a little table at the front of the platform where all the house could see it. The bulk of the house gazed at it with a burning interest, a mouth-watering interest, a wistful and pathetic interest; a minority of nineteen couples gazed at it tenderly, lovingly, proprietarily, and the male half of this minority kept saying over to themselves the moving little impromptu speeches of thankfulness for the audience's applause and congratulations which they were presently going to get up and deliver. Every now and then one of these got a piece of paper out of his vest pocket and privately glanced at it to refresh his memory.

Of course there was a buzz of conversation going on—there always is; but at last when the Rev. Mr. Burgess rose and laid his hand on the sack he could hear his microbes gnaw, the place was so still. He related the curious history of the sack, then went on to speak in warm terms of Hadleyburg's old and well-earned reputation for spotless honesty, and of the town's just pride in this reputation. He said that this reputation was a treasure of priceless value; that under Providence its value had now become inestimably enhanced, for the recent episode had spread this fame far and wide, and thus had focused the eyes of the American world upon this village, and made its name for all time, as he hoped and believed, a synonym for commercial incorruptibility. [*Applause.*] "And who is to be the guardian of this noble treasure—the community as a whole? No! The responsibility is individual, not communal. From this day forth each and every one of you is in his own person its special guardian, and individually responsible that no harm shall come to it. Do you—does each of you—accept this great trust? [*Tumultuous assent.*] Then all is well. Transmit it to your children and to your children's children. To-day your purity is beyond reproach—see to it that it shall remain so. To-day there is not a person in your community who could be beguiled to touch a penny not his own—see to it that you abide in this grace. [*"We will! we will!"*] This is not the place to make comparisons between ourselves and other communities—some of them ungracious toward us; they have their ways, we have ours; let us be content. [*Applause.*] I am done. Under my hand, my friends, rests a stranger's eloquent recognition of what we are; through him the world will always henceforth know what we are. We do not know who he is, but in your name I utter your gratitude, and ask you to raise your voices in indorsement."

The house rose in a body and made the walls quake with the thunders of its thankfulness for the space of a long minute. Then it sat down, and Mrs. Burgess took an envelope out of his pocket. The house held its breath while he slit the envelope open and took from it a slip of paper. He read its contents—slowly and impressively—the audience listening with tranced attention to this magic document, each of whose words stood for an ingot of gold:

" *The remark which I made to the distressed stranger was this: "You are very far from being a bad man: go, and reform."* ' " Then he continued:

"We shall know in a moment now whether the remark here quoted corresponds with the one concealed in the sack; and if that shall prove to be so—and it undoubtedly will—this sack of gold belongs to a fellow-citizen who will henceforth stand before the nation as the symbol of the special virtue which has made our town famous throughout the land—Mr. Billson!"

The house had gotten itself all ready to burst into the proper tornado of applause; but instead of doing it, it seemed stricken with a paralysis; there was a deep hush for a moment or two, then a wave of whispered murmurs swept the place—of about this tenor: "*Billson!* oh, come, this is *too* thin! Twenty dollars to a stranger —or *anybody*—*Billson!* Tell it to the marines!" And now at this point the house caught its breath all of a sudden in a new access of astonishment, for it discovered that whereas in one part of the hall Deacon Billson was standing up with his head meekly bowed, in another part of it

Lawyer Wilson was doing the same. There was a wondering silence now for a while.

Everybody was puzzled, and nineteen couples were surprised and indignant.

Billson and Wilson turned and stared at each other. Billson asked, bitingly:

"Why do *you* rise, Mr. Wilson?"

"Because I have a right to. Perhaps you will be good enough to explain to the house why *you* rise?"

"With great pleasure. Because I wrote that paper."

"It is an impudent falsity! I wrote it myself."

It was Burgess's turn to be paralyzed. He stood looking vacantly at first one of the men and then the other, and did not seem to know what to do. The house was stupefied. Lawyer Wilson spoke up, now, and said:

"I asked the Chair to read the name signed to that paper."

That brought the Chair to itself, and it read out the name:

" 'John Wharton *Billson*.' "

"There!" shouted Billson, "what have you got to say for yourself, now? And what kind of apology are you going to make to me and to this insulted house for the imposture which you have attempted to play here?"

"No apologies are due, sir; and as for the rest of it, I publicly charge you with pilfering my note from Mr. Burgess and substituting a copy of it signed with your own name. There is no other way by which you could have gotten hold of the test-remark; I alone, of living men, possessed the secret of its wording."

There was likely to be a scandalous state of things if this went on; everybody noticed with distress that the short-hand scribes were scribbling like mad; many people were crying "Chair, Chair! Order! order!" Burgess rapped with his gavel and said:

"Let us not forget the proprieties due. There has evidently been a mistake somewhere, but surely that is all. If Mr. Wilson gave me an envelope—and I remember now that he did—I still have it."

He took one out of his pocket, opened it, glanced at it, looked surprised and worried, and stood silent a few moments.

Then he waved his hand in a wandering and mechanical way, and made an effort or two to say something, then gave it up, despondently. Several voices cried out: "Read it! read it! What is it?"

So he began in a dazed and sleep-walker fashion:

" 'The remark which I made to the unhappy stranger was this: "You are far from being a bad man. [The house gazed at him, marvelling.] Go, and reform." ' [Murmurs: "Amazing! what can this mean?"] This one," said the Chair, "is signed Thurlow G. Wilson."

"There!" cried Wilson. "I reckon that settles it! I knew perfectly well my note was purloined."

"Purloined!" retorted Billson. "I'll let you know that neither you nor any man of your kidney must venture to—"

The Chair: "Order, gentlemen, order! Take your seats, both of you, please."

They obeyed, shaking their heads and grumbling angrily. The house was profoundly puzzled; it did not know what to do with this curious emergency. Presently Thompson got up. Thompson was the hatter. He would have liked to be a Nineteener; but such was not for him: his stock of hats was not considerable enough for the position. He said:

"Mr. Chairman, if I may be permitted to make a suggestion, can both of these gentlemen be right? I put it to you, sir, can both have happened to say the very same words to the stranger? It seems to me—"

The tanner got up and interrupted him. The tanner was a disgruntled man; he believed himself entitled to be a Nineteener, but he couldn't get recognition. It made him a little unpleasant in his ways and speech. Said he:

"Sho, that's not the point! That could happen—twice in a hundred years—but not the other thing. Neither of them gave the twenty dollars!"

[A ripple of applause.]

Billson: "I did!"

Wilson: "I did!"

Then each accused the other of pilfering.

The Chair: "Order! Sit down, if you please—both of you. Neither of the notes

has been out of my possession at any moment."

A Voice: "Good—that settles that!"

The Tanner: "Mr. Chairman, one thing is now plain: one of these men has been eavesdropping under the other one's bed, and filching family secrets. If it is not unparliamentary to suggest it, I will remark that both are equal to it. [The Chair. "Order! order!"] I withdraw the remark, sir, and will confine myself to suggesting that if one of them has overheard the other reveal the test-remark to his wife, we shall catch him now."

A Voice: "How?"

The Tanner: "Easily. The two have not quoted the remark in exactly the same words. You would have noticed that, if there hadn't been a considerable stretch of time and an exciting quarrel inserted between the two readings."

A Voice: "Name the difference."

The Tanner: "The word very is in Billson's note, and not in the other."

Many Voices: "That's so—he's right!"

The Tanner: "And so, if the Chair will examine the test-remark in the sack, we shall know which of these two frauds—[The Chair. "Order!"]—which of these two adventurers—[The Chair. "Order! order!"]—which of these two gentlemen [laughter and applause]—is entitled to wear the belt as being the first dishonest blatherskite ever bred in this town—which he has dishonored, and which will be a sultry place for him from now out!" [Vigorous applause.]

Many Voices: "Open it!—Open the sack!"

Mr. Burgess made a slit in the sack, slid his hand in and brought out an envelope. In it were a couple of folded notes. He said:

"One of these is marked, 'Not to be examined until all written communications which have been addressed to the Chair—if any—shall have been read.' The other is marked 'The Test.' Allow me. It is worded—to wit:

" 'I do not require that the first half of the remark which was made to me by my benefactor shall be quoted with exactness, for it was not striking, and could be forgotten; but its closing fifteen words are quite striking, and I think easily rememberable; unless *these* shall be accurately reproduced, let the applicant be regarded as an impostor. My benefactor began by saying he seldom gave advice to any one, but that it always bore the hall-mark of high value when he did give it. Then he said this—and it has never faded from my memory: "*You are far from being a bad man*—"' "

Fifty Voices: "That settles it—the money's Wilson's! Wilson! Wilson! Speech! Speech!"

People jumped up and crowded around Wilson, wringing his hand and congratulating fervently—meantime the Chair was hammering with the gavel and shouting:

"Order, gentlemen! Order! Order! Let me finish reading, please." When quiet was restored, the reading was resumed— as follows:

"'"Go, and reform—or, mark my words—some day, for your sins, you will die and go to hell or Hadleyburg—try and make it the former."'"

A ghastly silence followed. First an angry cloud began to settle darkly upon the faces of the citizenship; after a pause the cloud began to rise, and a tickled expression tried to take its place; tried so hard that it was only kept under with great and painful difficulty; the reporters, the Brixtonites, and other strangers bent their heads down and shielded their faces with their hands, and managed to hold in by main strength and heroic courtesy. At this most inopportune time burst upon the stillness the roar of a solitary voice— Jack Halliday's:

"*That's* got the hall-mark on it!"

Then the house let go, strangers and all. Even Mr. Burgess's gravity broke down presently, then the audience considered itself officially absolved from all restraint, and it made the most of its privilege. It was a good long laugh, and a tempestuously whole-hearted one, but it ceased at last—long enough for Mr. Burgess to try to resume, and for the people to get their eyes partially wiped; then it broke out again; and afterward yet again; then at last Burgess was able to get out these serious words:

"It is useless to try to disguise the fact —we find ourselves in the presence of a matter of grave import. It involves the honor of your town, it strikes at the town's good name. The difference of a single word between the test-remarks offered by Mr. Wilson and Mr. Billson was itself a serious thing, since it indicated that one or the other of these gentlemen had committed a theft—"

The two men were sitting limp, nerveless, crushed; but at these words, both were electrified into movement, and started to get up—

"Sit down!" said the Chair, sharply, and they obeyed. "That, as I have said, was a serious thing. And it was—but for only one of them. But the matter has become graver; for the honor of *both* is now in formidable peril. Shall I go even further, and say in inextricable peril? *Both* left out the crucial fifteen words." He paused. During several moments he allowed the pervading stillness to gather and deepen its impressive effects, then added: "There would seem to be but one way whereby this could happen. I ask these gentlemen—Was there *collusion?— agreement?*"

A low murmur sifted through the house; its import was, "He's got them both."

Billson was not used to emergencies; he sat in a helpless collapse. But Wilson was a lawyer. He struggled to his feet, pale and worried, and said:

"I ask the indulgence of the house while I explain this most painful matter. I am sorry to say what I'm about to say, since it must inflict irreparable injury upon Mr. Billson, whom I have always esteemed and respected until now, and in whose invulnerability to temptation I entirely believed—as did you all. But for the preservation of my own honor I must speak—and with frankness. I confess with shame—and I now beseech your pardon for it—that I said to the ruined stranger all of the words contained in the test-remark, including the disparaging fifteen. [*Sensation.*] When the late publication was made I recalled them, and I resolved to claim the sack of coin, for by every right I was entitled to it. Now I will ask you to consider this point, and weigh it well: that stranger's gratitude to me that night knew no bounds; he said himself that he could find no words for it that were adequate, and that if he should ever be able he would repay me a thousandfold. Now, then, I ask you this: Could I expect—could I believe—could I even remotely imagine—that, feeling as he did, he would do so ungrateful a thing as to add those quite unnecessary fifteen words to his test?—set a trap for me?—expose me as a slanderer of my own town before my own people assembled in a public hall? It was preposterous; it was impossible. His test would contain only the kindly opening clause of my remark. Of that I had no shadow of doubt. You would have thought as I did. You would not have expected a base betrayal from one whom you had befriended and against whom you had committed no offense. And so, with perfect confidence, perfect trust, I wrote on a piece of paper the opening words—ending with 'Go, and reform,'—and signed it. When I was about to put it in an envelope I was called into my back office, and without thinking I left the paper lying open on my desk." He stopped, turned his head slowly toward Billson, waited a moment, then added: "I ask you to note this: when I returned, a little later, Mr. Billson was retiring by my street door." [*Sensation.*]

In a moment Billson was on his feet and shouting:

"It's a lie! It's an infamous lie!"

The Chair: "Be seated, sir! Mr. Wilson has the floor."

Billson's friends pulled him into his seat and quieted him, and Wilson went on:

"Those are the simple facts. My note was now lying in a different place on the table from where I had left it. I noticed that, but attached no importance to it, thinking a draught had blown it there. That Mr. Billson would read a private paper was a thing which could not occur to me; he was an honorable man, and he would be above that. If you will allow me to say it, I think his extra word '*very*' stands explained; it is attributable to a defect of memory. I was the only man in the world who could furnish here any detail of the test remark—by *honorable* means. I have finished."

There is nothing in the world like a persuasive speech to fuddle the mental apparatus and upset the convictions and debauch the emotions of an audience not practised in the tricks and delusions of oratory. Wilson sat down victorious. The house submerged him in tides of approving applause; friends swarmed to him and shook him by the hand and congratulated him, and Billson was shouted down and not allowed to say a word. The Chair hammered and hammered with its gavel, and kept shouting:

"But let us proceed, gentlemen, let us proceed!"

⁕ At last there was a measurable degree of quiet, and the hatter said: "But what is there to proceed with, sir, but to deliver the money?"

Voices: "That's it! That's it! Come forward, Wilson!"

The Hatter: "I move three cheers for Mr. Wilson, Symbol of the special virtue which—"

The cheers burst forth before he could finish; and in the midst of them—and in the midst of the clamor of the gavel also—some enthusiasts mounted Wilson on a big friend's shoulder and were going to fetch him in triumph to the platform. The Chair's voice now rose above the noise—

"Order! To your places! You forget that there is still a document to be read." When quiet had been restored he took up the document, and was going to read it, but laid it down again, saying: "I forgot; this is not to be read until all written communications received by me have first been read." He took an envelope out of his pocket, removed its inclosure, glanced at it—seemed astonished—held it out and gazed at it—stared at it.

Twenty or thirty voices cried out:

"What is it? Read it! read it!"

And he did—slowly, and wondering:

" '*The remark which I made to the stranger—*[*Voices.* "Hello! how's this?"] *—was this: "You are far from being a bad man. [Voices. "Great Scott!"] Go, and reform."* ' [*Voices.* "Oh, saw my leg off!"] Signed by Mr. Pinkerton, the banker."

The pandemonium of delight which turned itself loose now was of a sort to make the judicious weep. Those whose withers were unwrung laughed till the tears ran down; the reporters, in throes of laughter, set down disordered pot-hooks which would never in the world be decipherable; and a sleeping dog jumped up, scared out of its wits, and barked itself crazy at the turmoil. All manner of cries were scattered through the din: "We're getting rich—*two* Symbols of Incorruptibility!—without counting Billson!" "*Three!*—count Shadbelly in—we can't have too many!" "All right—Billson's elected!" "Alas, poor Wilson—victim of *two* thieves!"

A Powerful Voice: "Silence! The Chair's fished up something more out of his pocket."

Voices: "Hurrah! Is it something fresh? Read it! read it! read!"

The Chair [*reading*]: " 'The remark which I made,' etc.: ' "You are far from being a bad man. Go," ' etc. Signed, 'Gregory Yates.' "

Tornado of Voices: "Four Symbols!" " 'Rah for Yates!" "Fish again!"

The house was in a roaring humor now, and ready to get all the fun out of the occasion that might be in it. Several Nineteeners, looking pale and distressed, got up and began to work their way toward the aisles, but a score of shouts went up:

"The doors, the doors—close the doors; no Incorruptible shall leave this place! Sit down, everybody!"

The mandate was obeyed.

"Fish again! Read! read!"

The Chair fished again, and once more the familiar words began to fall from its lips—" '*You are far from being a bad man.*' "

"Name! name! What's his name?"

" 'L. Ingoldsby Sargent.' "

"Five elected! Pile up the Symbols! Go on, go on!"

" '*You are far from being a bad—*' "

"Name! name!"

" 'Nicholas Whitworth.' "

"Hooray! hooray! it's a symbolical day!"

Somebody wailed in, and began to sing this rhyme (leaving out "it's") to the lovely "Mikado" tune of "When a man's afraid, a beautiful maid—"; the audience joined in, with joy; then, just in time, somebody contributed another line—

And don't you this forget—

The house roared it out. A third line was at once furnished—

Corruptibles far from Hadleyburg are—

The house roared that one too. As the last note died, Jack Halliday's voice rose high and clear, freighted with a final line—

But the Symbols are here, you bet!

That was sung, with booming enthusiasm. Then the happy house started in at the beginning and sang the four lines through twice, with immense swing and dash, and finished up with a crashing three-times-three and a tiger for "Hadleyburg the Incorruptible and all Symbols of it which we shall find worthy to receive the hallmark to-night."

Then the shoutings at the Chair began again, all over the place:

"Go on! go on! Read! read some more! Read all you've got!"

"That's it—go on! We are winning eternal celebrity!"

A dozen men got up now and began to protest. They said that this farce was the work of some abandoned joker, and was an insult to the whole community. Without a doubt these signatures were all forgeries—

"Sit down! sit down! Shut up! You are confessing. We'll find *your* names in the lot."

"Mr. Chairman, how many of those envelopes have you got?"

The chair counted.

"Together with those that have been already examined, there are nineteen."

A storm of derisive applause broke out.

"Perhaps they all contain the secret. I move that you open them all and read every signature that is attached to a note of that sort—and read also the first eight words of the note."

"Second the motion!"

It was put and carried—uproariously. Then poor old Richards got up, and his wife rose and stood at his side. Her head was bent down, so that none might see that she was crying. Her husband gave her his arm, and so supporting her, he began to speak in a quavering voice:

"My friends, you have known us two

—Mary and me—all our lives, and I think you have liked us and respected us—"

The Chair interrupted him:

"Allow me. It is quite true—that which you are saying Mr. Richards: this town *does* know you two; it *does* like you; it *does* respect you; more—it honors you and *loves* you—"

Halliday's voice rang out:

"That's the hall-marked truth, too! If the Chair is right, let the house speak up and say it. Rise! Now, then—hip! hip! hip!—all together!"

The house rose in mass, faced toward the old couple eagerly, filled the air with a snow-storm of waving handkerchiefs, and delivered the cheers with all its affectionate heart.

The Chair then continued:

"What I was going to say is this: We know your good heart, Mr. Richards, but this is not a time for the exercise of charity toward offenders. [*Shouts of "Right! right!"*] I see your generous purpose in your face, but I cannot allow you to plead for these men—"

"But I was going to—"

"Please take your seat, Mr. Richards. We must examine the rest of these notes —simple fairness to the men who have already been exposed requires this. As soon as that has been done—I give you my word for this—you shall be heard."

Many Voices: "Right—the Chair is right—no interruption can be permitted at this stage! Go on!—the names! the names!—according to the terms of the motion!"

The old couple sat reluctantly down, and the husband whispered to the wife, "It is pitifully hard to have to wait; the shame will be greater than ever when they find we were only going to plead for *ourselves*."

Straightaway the jollity broke loose again with the reading of the names.

" '*You are far from being a bad man*—' Signature, 'Robert J. Titmarsh.'

" '*You are far from being a bad man*—' Signature, 'Eliphalet Weeks.'

" '*You are far from being a bad man*—' Signature, 'Oscar B. Wilder.' "

At this point the house lit upon the idea of taking the eight words out of the Chair-

man's hands. He was not unthankful for that. Thenceforward he held up each note in its turn and waited. The house droned out the eight words in a massed and measured and musical deep volume of sound (with a daringly close resemblance to a well-known church chant)— " 'You are f-a-r from being a b-a-a-a-d man.' " Then the Chair said, "Signature, 'Archibald Wilcox.' " And so on, and so on, name after name, and everybody had an increasingly and gloriously good time except the wretched Nineteen. Now and then, when a particularly shining name was called, the house made the Chair wait while it chanted the whole of the test-remark from the beginning to the closing words, "And go to hell or Hadleyburg—try and make it the for-or-m-e-r!" and in these special cases they added a grand and agonized and imposing "*A-a-a-a-men!*"

The list dwindled, dwindled, dwindled, poor old Richards keeping tally of the count, wincing when a name resembling his own was pronounced, and waiting in miserable suspense for the time to come when it would be his humiliating privilege to rise with Mary and finish his plea, which he was intending to word thus: ". . . for until now we have never done any wrong thing, but have gone our humble way unreproached. We are very poor, we are old, and have no chick nor child to help us; we were sorely tempted, and we fell. It was my purpose when I got up before to make confession and beg that my name might not be read out in this public place, for it seemed to us that we could not bear it; but I was prevented. It was just; it was our place to suffer with the rest. It has been hard for us. It is the first time we have ever heard our name fall from any one's lips—sullied. Be merciful—for the sake of the better days; make our shame as light to bear as in your charity you can." At this point in his revery Mary nudged him, perceiving that his mind was absent. The house was chanting, "You are f-a-r," etc.

"Be ready," Mary whispered. "Your name comes now; he has read eighteen."

The chant ended.

"Next! next! next!" came volleying from all over the house.

Burgess put his hand into his pocket.

The old couple, trembling, began to rise. Burgess fumbled a moment, then said, "I find I have read them all."

Faint with joy and surprise, the couple sank into their seats, and Mary whispered: "Oh, bless God, we are saved!—he has lost ours—I wouldn't give this for a hundred of those sacks!"

The house burst out with its "Mikado" travesty, and sang it three times with ever-increasing enthusiasm, rising to its feet when it reached for the third time the closing line—

But the Symbols are here, you bet!

and finishing up with cheers and a tiger for "Hadleyburg purity and our eighteen immortal representatives of it."

Then Wingate, the saddler, got up and proposed cheers "for the cleanest man in town, the one solitary important citizen in it who didn't try to steal that money—Edward Richards."

They were given with great and moving heartiness; then somebody proposed that Richards be elected sole guardian and Symbol of the now Sacred Hadleyburg Tradition, with power and right to stand up and look the whole sarcastic world in the face.

Passed, by acclamation; then they sang the "Mikado" again, and ended it with:

And there's *one* Symbol left, you bet!

There was a pause; then—

A Voice: "Now, then, who's to get the sack?"

The Tanner: [*with bitter sarcasm*] "That's easy. The money has to be divided among the eighteen Incorruptibles. They gave the suffering stranger twenty dollars apiece—and that remark—each in his turn—it took twenty-two minutes for the procession to move past. Staked the stranger—total contribution, $360. All they want is just the loan back—and interest—forty thousand dollars altogether."

Many Voices: [*derisively*] "That's it! Divvy! divvy! Be kind to the poor—don't keep them waiting!"

The Chair: "Order! I now offer the stranger's remaining document. It says: 'If no claimant shall appear [*grand chorus of groans*] I desire that you open the sack and count out the money to the prin-

cipal citizens of your town, they to take it in trust [*cries of "Oh! Oh! Oh"*], and use it in such ways as to them shall seem best for the propagation and preservation of your community's noble reputation for incorruptible honesty [*more cries*]—a reputation to which their names and their efforts will add a new and far-reaching luster.' [*Enthusiastic outburst of sarcastic applause.*] That seems to be all. No—here is a postscript:

'P.S.—Citizens of Hadleyburg. There *is* no test-remark—nobody made one. [*Great sensation.*] There wasn't any pauper stranger, nor any twenty-dollar contribution, nor any accompanying benediction and compliment—these are all inventions. [*General buzz and hum of astonishment and delight.*] Allow me to tell my story—it will take but a word or two. I passed through your town at a certain time, and received a deep offense which I had not earned. Any other man would have been content to kill one or two of you and call it square, but to me that would have been a trivial revenge, and inadequate; for the dead do not *suffer*. Besides, I could not kill you all—and, anyway, made as I am, even that would not have satisfied me. I wanted to damage every man in the place, and every woman—and not in their bodies or in their estate, but in their vanity—the place where feeble and foolish people are most vulnerable. So I disguised myself and came back and studied you. You were easy game. You had an old and lofty reputation for honesty, and naturally you were proud of it—it was your treasure of treasures, the very apple of your eye. As soon as I found out that you carefully and vigilantly kept yourselves and your children *out of temptation*, I knew how to proceed. Why, you simple creatures, the weakest of all weak things is a virtue which has not been tested in the fire. I laid a plan, and gathered a list of names. My project was to corrupt Hadleyburg the Incorruptible. My idea was to make liars and thieves of nearly half a hundred smirchless men and women who had never in their lives uttered a lie or stolen a penny. I was afraid of Goodson. He was neither born nor reared in Hadleyburg. I was afraid that if I started to operate my scheme by getting my letter laid before you, you would say to yourselves, "Goodson is the only man among us who would give away twenty dollars to a poor devil"—and then you might not bite at my bait. But Heaven took Goodson; then I knew I was safe, and I set my trap and baited it. It may be that I shall not catch all the men to whom I mailed the pretended test secret, but I shall catch the most of them, if I know Hadleyburg nature. [*Voices.* "Right—he got every last one of them."] I believe they will even steal ostensible *gamble*-money, rather than miss, poor, tempted, and mistrained fellows. I am hoping to eternally and everlastingly squelch your vanity and give Hadleyburg a new renown—one that will *stick*—and spread far. If I have succeeded, open the sack and summon the Committee on Propagation and Preservation of the Hadleyburg Reputation.'

A Cyclone of Voices: "Open it! Open it! The Eighteen to the front! Committee on Propagation of the Tradition! Forward —the Incorruptibles!"

The Chair ripped the sack wide, and gathered up a handful of bright, broad, yellow coins, shook them together, then examined them—

"Friends they are only gilded disks of lead!"

There was a crashing outbreak of delight over this news, and when the noise had subsided, the tanner called out:

"By right of apparent seniority in this business, Mr. Wilson is Chairman of the Committee on Propagation of the Tradition. I suggest that he step forward on behalf of his pals, and receive in trust the money."

A Hundred Voices: "Wilson! Wilson! Wilson! Speech! Speech!"

Wilson: [*in a voice trembling with anger*] "You will allow me to say, and without apologies for my language, *damn the money!*"

A Voice: "Oh, and him a Baptist!"

A Voice: "Seventeen Symbols left! Step up, gentlemen, and assume your trust!"

There was a pause—no response.

The Saddler: "Mr. Chairman, we've got *one* clean man left, anyway, out of the late aristocracy; and he needs money, and deserves it. I move that you appoint Jack Halliday to get up there and auction off that sack of gilt twenty-dollar pieces, and give the result to the right man—the man whom Hadleyburg delights to honor —Edward Richards."

This was received with great enthusiasm, the dog taking a hand again; the saddler started the bids at a dollar, the Brixton folk and Barnum's representative fought hard for it, the people cheered every jump that the bids made, the excitement climbed moment by moment higher and higher, the bidders got on their mettle and grew steadily more and more daring, more and more determined, the jumps went from a dollar up to five, then to ten, then to twenty, then fifty, then to a hundred, then—

At the beginning of the auction Richards whispered in distress to his wife: "O Mary, can we allow it? It—it—you see, it is an honor-reward, a testimonial to purity of character, and—and—can we allow it? Hadn't I better get up and—O Mary, what ought we to do?—what do you think we—[*Halliday's voice. "Fifteen I'm bid—fifteen for the sack!—twenty!— ah, thanks!—thirty—thanks again! Thirty, thirty, thirty!—do I hear forty?—forty it is! Keep the ball rolling gentlemen, keep it rolling!—fifty! thanks, noble Roman! going at fifty, fifty, fifty!—seventy! ninety! splendid!—a hundred! pile it up, pile it up!—hundred and twenty—forty!—just in time!—hundred and fifty!—Two hundred!—superb! Do I hear two h— thanks! —two hundred and fifty!—"*]

"It is another temptation, Edward— I'm all in a tremble—but, oh, we've escaped one temptation, and that ought to warn us to— [*"Six did I hear?—thanks! —six-fifty, six-f— seven hundred!"*] And yet, Edward, when you think—nobody susp— [*"Eight hundred dollars!—hurrah! —make it nine!—Mr. Parsons, did I hear you say—thanks—nine!—this noble sack of virgin lead going at only nine hundred dollars, gilding and all—come! do I hear —a thousand!—gratefully yours!—did someone say eleven?—a sack which is going to be the most celebrated in the whole Uni—"*] O Edward" (beginning to sob), "we are *so* poor!—but—but do as you think best—do as you think best."

Edward fell—that is, he sat still; sat with a conscience which was not satisfied, but which was overpowered by circumstances.

Meantime a stranger, who looked like an amateur detective gotten up as an impossible English earl, had been watching the evening's proceedings with manifest interest, and with a contented expression in his face; and he had been privately commenting to himself. He was now soliloquizing somewhat like this: "None of the Eighteen are bidding; that is not satisfactory; I must change that—the dramatic unities require it; they must buy the sack they tried to steal; they must pay a heavy price, too—some of them are rich. And another thing, when I make a mistake in Hadleyburg nature the man that puts that error upon me is entitled to a high honorarium, and some one must pay it. This poor old Richards has brought my judgment to shame; he is an honest man:—I don't understand it, but I acknowledge it. Yes, he saw my deuces *and* with a straight flush, and by rights the pot is his. And it shall be a jackpot, too, if I can manage it. He disappointed me, but let that pass."

He was watching the bidding. At a thousand, the market broke; the prices tumbled swiftly. He waited—and still watched. One competitor dropped out; then another, and another. He put in a bid or two now. When the bids had sunk to ten dollars, he added a five; some one raised him a three; he waited a moment, then flung in a fifty-dollar jump, and the sack was his—at $1,282. The house broke out in cheers—then stopped; for he was on his feet, and had lifted his hand. He began to speak.

"I desire to say a word, and ask a favor. I am a speculator in rarities, and I have dealings with persons interested in numismatics all over the world. I can make a profit on this purchase, just as it stands; but there is a way, if I can get your approval, whereby I can make every one of these leaden twenty-dollar pieces worth its face in gold, and perhaps more. Grant me that approval, and I will give part of my gains to your Mr. Richards, whose invulnerable probity you have so justly and so cordially recognized to-night; his share shall be ten thousand dollars, and I will hand him the money to-morrow. [*Great applause from the house.* But the "invulnerable probity" made the Richardses blush prettily; however, it went for modesty, and did no harm.] If you will pass my proposition by a good majority—I would like a two-thirds vote—I will re-

gard that as the town's consent, and that is all I ask. Rarities are always helped by any device which will rouse curiosity and compel remark. Now if I may have your permission to stamp upon the faces of each of these ostensible coins the names of the eighteen gentlemen who—"

Nine-tenths of the audience were on their feet in a moment—dog and all—and the proposition was carried with a whirlwind of approving applause and laughter.

They sat down, and all the Symbols except "Dr." Clay Harkness got up, violently protesting against the proposed outrage, and threatening to—

"I beg you not to threaten me," said the stranger calmly. "I know my legal rights, and am not accustomed to being frightened at bluster." [*Applause.*] He sat down. "Dr." Harkness saw an opportunity here. He was one of the two very rich men of the place, and Pinkerton was the other. Harkness was proprietor of a mint; that is to say, a popular patent medicine. He was running for the legislature on one ticket, and Pinkerton on the other. It was a close race and a hot one, and getting hotter every day. Both had strong appetites for money; each had bought a great tract of land, with a purpose; there was going to be a new railway, and each wanted to be in the legislature and help locate the route to his own advantage; a single vote might make the decision, and with it two or three fortunes. The stake was large, and Harkness was a daring speculator. He was sitting close to the stranger. He leaned over while one or another of the other Symbols was entertaining the house with protests and appeals, and asked, in a whisper.

"What is your price for the sack?"

"Forty thousand dollars."

"I'll give you twenty."

"No."

"Twenty-five."

"No."

"Say Thirty."

The price is forty thousand dollars; not a penny less."

"All right, I'll give it. I will come to the hotel at ten in the morning. I don't want it known: will see you privately."

"Very good." Then the stranger got up and said to the house:

"I find it late. The speeches of these gentlemen are not without merit, not without interest, not without grace; yet if I may be excused I will take my leave. I thank you for the great favor which you have shown me in granting my petition. I ask the Chair to keep the sack for me until to-morrow, and to hand these three five-hundred-dollar notes to Mr. Richards." They were passed up to the Chair. "At nine I will call for the sack, and at eleven will deliver the rest of the ten thousand to Mr. Richards in person, at his home. Good night."

Then he slipped out, and left the audience making a vast noise, which was composed of a mixture of cheers, the "Mikado" song, dog-disapproval, and the chant, "You are f-a-r from being a b-a-a-d man—a-a-a-men!"

IV

At home the Richardses had to endure congratulations and compliments until midnight. Then they were left to themselves. They looked a little sad, and they sat silent and thinking. Finally Mary sighed and said:

"Do you think we are to blame, Edward —*much* to blame?" and her eyes wandered to the accusing triplet of big banknotes lying on the table, where the congratulators had been gloating over them and reverently fingering them. Edward did not answer at once; then he brought out with a sigh and said, hesitatingly:

"We—we couldn't help it, Mary. It—well, it was ordered. *All* things are."

Mary glanced up and looked at him steadily, but he didn't return the look. Presently she said:

"I thought congratulations and praises always tasted good. But—it seems to me, now—Edward?"

"Well?"

"Are you going to stay in the bank?"

"N-n-o-no."

"Resign?"

"In the morning—by note."

"It does seem best."

Richards bowed his head in his hands and muttered:

"Before, I was not afraid to let oceans of people's money pour through my hands, but—Mary, I am so tired, so tired—"

"We will go to bed."

At nine in the morning the stranger called for the sack and took it to the hotel in a cab. At ten Harkness had a talk with him privately. The stranger asked for and got five checks on a metropolitan bank—drawn to "Bearer"—four for $1,500 each, and one for $34,000. He put one of the former in his pocketbook, and the remainder, representing $38,500, he put in an envelope, and with these he added a note, which he wrote after Harkness was gone. At eleven he called at the Richards house and knocked. Mrs. Richards peeped through the shutters, then went and received the envelope, and the stranger disappeared without a word. She came back flushed and a little unsteady on her legs, and gasped out:

"I am sure I recognized him! Last night it seemed to me that maybe I had seen him somewhere before."

"He is the man that brought the sack here?"

"I am almost sure of it."

"Then he is the ostensible Stephenson, too, and sold every important citizen in this town with his bogus secret. Now if he has sent checks instead of money, we are sold, too, after we thought we had escaped. I was beginning to feel fairly comfortable once more, after my night's rest, but the look of that envelope makes me sick. It isn't fat enough; $8,500 in even the largest bank-notes makes more bulk than that."

"Edward, why do you object to checks?"

"Checks signed by Stephenson! I am resigned to take the $8,500 if it could come in bank-notes—for it does seem that it was so ordered, Mary—but I have never had much courage, and I have not the pluck to try to market a check signed with that disastrous name. It would be a trap. That man tried to catch me; we escaped somehow or other; and now he is trying a new way. If it is checks—"

"Oh, Edward, it is *too* bad!" and she held up the checks and began to cry.

"Put them in the fire! quick! we musn't be tempted. It is a trick to make the world laugh at *us*, along with the rest, and—

Give them to *me*, since you can't do it!" He snatched them and tried to hold his grip till he could get to the stove; but he was human, he was a cashier, and he stopped a moment to make sure of the signature. Then he came near to fainting.

"Fan me, Mary, fan me! They are the same as gold!"

"Oh, how lovely, Edward! Why?"

"Signed by Harkness. What can the mystery of that be, Mary?"

"Edward, do you think—"

"Look here—look at this! Fifteen—fifteen—fifteen—thirty-four. Thirty-eight thousand five hundred! Mary, the sack isn't worth twelve dollars, and Harkness—apparently—has paid about par for it."

"And does it all come to us, do you think—instead of the ten thousand?"

"Why, it looks like it. And the checks are made to 'Bearer,' too."

"Is that good, Edward? What is it for?"

"A hint to collect them at some distant bank, I reckon. Perhaps Harkness doesn't want the matter known. What is that—a note?"

"Yes. It was with the checks."

It was in the "Stephenson" handwriting, but there was no signature. It said:

"I am a disappointed man. Your honesty is beyond the reach of temptation. I had a different idea about it, but I wronged you in that, and I beg pardon, and do it sincerely. I honor you—and that is sincere too. This town is not worthy to kiss the hem of your garment. Dear sir, I made a square bet with myself that there were nineteen debauchable men in your self-righteous community. I have lost. Take the whole pot, you are entitled to it."

Richards drew a deep sigh, and said:

"It seems written with fire—it burns so. Mary—I am miserable again."

"I, too. Ah, dear, I wish—"

"To think, Mary—he *believes* in me."

"Oh, don't Edward—I can't bear it."

"If those beautiful words were deserved, Mary—and God knows I believed I deserved them once—I think I could give the forty thousand dollars for them. And I would put that paper away, as representing more than gold and jewels, and keep it always. But now— We could not live in the shadow of its accusing presence, Mary."

He put it in the fire.

A messenger arrived and delivered an envelope.

Richards took from it a note and read it; it was from Burgess.

"You saved me, in a difficult time. I saved you last night. It was at cost of a lie, but I made the sacrifice freely, and out of a grateful heart. None in this village knows so well as I know how brave and good and noble you are. At bottom you cannot respect me, knowing as you do of that matter of which I am accused, and by the general voice condemned; but I beg that you will at least believe that I am a grateful man; it will help me to bear my burden."

[Signed] *Burgess*

"Saved, once more. And on such terms!" He put the note in the fire. "I—I wish I were dead, Mary, I wish I were out of it all."

"Oh, these are bitter, bitter days, Edward. The stabs, through their generosity, are so deep—and they come so fast!"

Three days before the election each of two thousand voters suddenly found himself in possession of a prized memento—one of the renowned bogus double-eagles. Around one of its faces was stamped these words: "The Remark I Made To The Poor Stranger Was—" Around the other face was stamped these: "Go, And Reform. [Signed] Pinkerton." Thus the entire remaining refuse of the renowned joke was emptied upon a single head, and with calamitous effect. It revived the recent vast laugh and concentrated it upon Pinkerton; and Harkness's election was a walkover.

Within twenty-four hours after the Richardses had received their checks their consciences were quieting down, discouraged; the old couple were learning to reconcile themselves to the sin which they had committed. But they were to learn, now, that a sin takes on new and real terrors when there seems a chance that it is going to be found out. This gives it a fresh and most substantial and important aspect. At church the morning sermon was of the usual pattern; it was the same old things said in the same old way; they had heard them a thousand times and found them innocuous, next to meaningless, and easy to sleep under; but now it was different: the sermon seemed to bristle with accusations; it seemed aimed straight and specially at people who were concealing deadly sins. After church they got away from the mob of congratulators as soon as they could, and hurried homeward, chilled to the bone at they did not know what—vague, shadowy, indefinite fears. And by chance they caught a glimpse of Mr. Burgess as he turned a corner. He paid no attention to their nod of recognition! He hadn't seen it; but they did not know that. What could his conduct mean? It might mean—it might mean—oh, a dozen dreadful things. Was it possible that he knew that Richards could have cleared him of guilt in that bygone time, and had been silently waiting for a chance to even up accounts? At home, in their distress they got to imagining that their servant might have been in the next room listening when Richards revealed the secret to his wife that he knew of Burgess's innocence; next, Richards began to imagine that he had heard the swish of a gown in there at that time; next, he was sure he *had* heard it. They would call Sarah in, on a pretext, and watch her face: if she had been betraying them to Mr. Burgess, it would show in her manner. They asked her some questions—questions which were so random and incoherent and seemingly purposeless that the girl felt sure that the old people's minds had been affected by their sudden good fortune; the sharp and watchful gaze which they bent upon her frightened her, and that completed the business. She blushed, she became nervous and confused, and to the old people these were plain signs of guilt—guilt of some fearful sort or other—without doubt she was a spy and a traitor. When they were alone again they began to piece many unrelated things together and get horrible results out of the combination. When things had got about to the worst, Richards was delivered of a sudden gasp, and his wife asked:

"Oh, what is it?—what is it?"

"The note—Burgess's note! Its language was sarcastic, I see it now." He quoted: " 'At bottom you cannot respect me, *knowing,* as you do, of *that matter* of

which I am accused'—oh, it is perfectly plain, now, God help me! He knows that I know! You see the ingenuity of the phrasing. It was a trap—and like a fool, I walked into it. And Mary—?"

"Oh, it is dreadful—I know what you are going to say—he didn't return your transcript of the pretended test-remark."

"No—kept it to destroy us with. Mary, he has exposed us to some already. I know it—I know it well. I saw it in a dozen faces after church. Ah, he wouldn't answer our nod of recognition—*he* knew what he had been doing!"

In the night the doctor was called. The news went around in the morning that the old couple were rather seriously ill—prostrated by the exhausting excitement growing out of their great windfall, the congratulations, and the late hours, the doctor said. The town was sincerely distressed; for these old people were about all it had left to be proud of, now.

Two days later the news was worse. The old couple were delirious, and were doing strange things. By witness of the nurses, Richards had exhibited checks—for $8,500? No—for an amazing sum—$38,500! What could be the explanation of this gigantic piece of luck?

The following day the nurses had more news—and wonderful. They had concluded to hide the checks, lest harm come to them; but when they searched they were gone from under the patient's pillow—vanished away. The patient said:

"Let the pillow alone; what do you want?"

"We thought it best that the checks—"

"You will never see them again—they are destroyed. They came from Satan. I saw the hell-brand on them, and I knew they were sent to betray me to sin." Then he fell to gabbling strange and dreadful things which were not clearly understandable, and which the doctor admonished them to keep to themselves.

Richards was right; the checks were never seen again.

A nurse must have talked in her sleep, for within two days the forbidden gabblings were the property of the town; and they were of a surprising sort. They seemed to indicate that Richards had been a claimant for the sack himself, and that

Burgess had concealed that fact and then maliciously betrayed it.

Burgess was taxed with this and stoutly denied it. And he said it was not fair to attach weight to the chatter of a sick old man who was out of his mind. Still, suspicion was in the air, and there was much talk.

After a day or two it was reported that Mrs. Richards' delirious deliveries were getting to be duplicates of her husband's. Suspicion flamed up into conviction, now, and the town's pride in the purity of its one undiscredited important citizen began to dim down and flicker toward extinction.

Six days passed, then came more news. The old couple were dying. Richards' mind cleared in his latest hour, and he sent for Burgess. Burgess said:

"Let the room be cleared. I think he wishes to say something in privacy."

"No!" said Richards: "I want witnesses. I want you all to hear my confession, so that I may die a man, and not a dog. I was clean—artificially—like the rest; and like the rest I fell when temptation came. I signed a lie, and claimed the miserable sack. Mr. Burgess remembered that I had done him a service, and in gratitude (and ignorance) he suppressed my claim and saved me. You know the thing that was charged against Burgess years ago. My testimony, and mine alone, could have cleared him, and I was a coward, and left him to suffer disgrace—"

"No—no—Mr. Richards, you—"

"My servant betrayed my secret to him—"

"No one has betrayed anything to me—"

—"and then he did a natural and justifiable thing, he repented of the saving kindness which he had done me, and he *exposed* me—as I deserved—"

"Never!—I make oath—"

"Out of my heart I forgive him."

Burgess's impassioned protestations fell upon deaf ears; the dying man passed away without knowing that once more he had done poor Burgess a wrong. The old wife died that night.

The last of the sacred Nineteen had fallen a prey to the fiendish sack; the town was stripped of the last rag of its ancient glory. Its mourning was not showy, but it was deep.

By act of the Legislature—upon prayer and petition—Hadleyburg was allowed to change its name to (never mind what —I will not give it away), and leave one word out of the motto that for many generations had graced the town's official seal.

It is an honest town once more, and the man will have to rise early that catches it napping again.

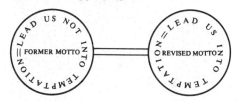

FORMER MOTTO: LEAD US NOT INTO TEMPTATION

REVISED MOTTO: LEAD US INTO TEMPTATION

[1899]

QUESTIONS FOR STUDY

1. *What fundamental mistakes in assessing human behavior do the citizens of Hadleyburg make in their efforts to keep the town uncorrupted? Why is the stranger's scheme for corrupting Hadleyburg so successful?*

2. *To what extent does the need for public approval motivate Edward Richards' actions; to what extent is he motivated by conscience? Which force is stronger?*

3. *What do Barclay Goodson, the Reverend Burgess, and Jack Halliday all share in common?*

4. *Why do the citizens of Hadleyburg react so joyfully to the destruction of the town's long-prized reputation?*

5. *What is significant in the fact that the townspeople ("with great enthusiasm") nominate Jack Halliday to auction off the coins on behalf of Edward Richards?*
6. *What new recognition about human nature and about the relationship between innocence and evil does Hadleyburg's altered motto suggest?*
7. *Does Mark Twain intend the reader to admire the stranger? If so, what makes him admirable?*

WILKIE COLLINS

The Traveler's Story of a Terribly Strange Bed

SHORTLY after my education at college was finished, I happened to be staying at Paris with an English friend. We were both young men then, and lived, I am afraid, rather a wild life, in the delightful city of our sojourn. One night we were idling about the neighborhood of the Palais Royal, doubtful to what amusement we should next betake ourselves. My friend proposed a visit to Frascati's; but his suggestion was not to my taste. I knew Frascati's, as the French saying is, by heart; had lost and won plenty of five-franc pieces there, merely for amusement's sake, until it was amusement no longer, and was thoroughly tired, in fact, of all the ghastly respectabilities of such a social anomaly as a respectable gambling-house. "For Heaven's sake," said I to my friend, "let us go somewhere where we can see a little genuine, blackguard, poverty-stricken gaming, with no false gingerbread glitter thrown over it at all. Let us get away from fashionable Frascati's, to a house where they don't mind letting in a man with a ragged coat, or a man with no coat, ragged or otherwise." "Very well," said my friend, "we needn't go out of the Palais Royal to find the sort of company you want. Here's the place just before us; as blackguard a place, by all report, as you could possibly wish to see." In another minute we arrived at the door, and entered the house, the back of which you have drawn in your sketch.[1]

When we got up stairs, and had left our hats and sticks with the door-keeper, we were admitted into the chief gambling-room. We did not find many people assembled there. But, few as the men were who looked up at us on our entrance, they were all types—lamentably true types—of their respective classes.

We had come to see blackguards; but these men were something worse. There is a comic side, more or less appreciable, in all blackguardism—here there was nothing but tragedy—mute, weird tragedy. The quiet in the room was horrible. The thin, haggard, long-haired young man, whose sunken eyes fiercely watched the turning up of the cards, never spoke; the flabby, fat-faced, pimply player, who pricked his piece of pasteboard perseveringly, to register how often black won, and how often red—never spoke; the dirty, wrinkled old man, with the vulture eyes and the darned great-coat, who had lost his last *sou*, and still looked on desperately, after he could play no longer—never spoke. Even the voice of the croupier sounded as if it were strangely dulled and thickened in the atmosphere of the room. I had entered the place to laugh, but the spectacle before me was something to weep over. I soon found it necessary to take refuge in excitement from the depression of spirits which was fast stealing on me. Unfortunately I sought the nearest excitement, by going to the table and beginning to play. Still more unfortunately, as the event will show, I won—won prodigiously; won incredibly; won at such a rate that the regular players at the table crowded round me; and staring at my stakes with hungry, superstitious eyes, whispered to one another that the English stranger was going to break the bank.

The game was *Rouge et Noir*. I had played at it in every city in Europe, without, however, the care or the wish to study the Theory of Chances—that philosopher's stone of all gamblers! And a

[1] In the lengthy and rambling prologue to the story Mr. Faulkner, the narrator, has happened upon a sketch of the house in the Palais Royal where his adventure took place. His discovery provides the occasion for him to tell his story to the artist. (JHP)

gambler, in the strict sense of the word, I had never been. I was heart-whole from the corroding passion for play. My gaming was a mere idle amusement. I never resorted to it by necessity, because I never knew what it was to want money. I never practiced it so incessantly as to lose more than I could afford, or to gain more than I could coolly pocket without being thrown off my balance by my good luck. In short, I had hitherto frequented gambling-tables—just as I frequented ball-rooms and opera-houses—because they amused me, and because I had nothing better to do with my leisure hours.

But on this occasion it was very different—now, for the first time in my life, I felt what the passion for play really was. My success first bewildered, and then, in the most literal meaning of the word, intoxicated me. Incredible as it may appear, it is nevertheless true, that I only lost when I attempted to estimate chances, and played according to previous calculation. If I left every thing to luck, and staked without any care or consideration, I was sure to win—to win in the face of every recognized probability in favor of the bank. At first some of the men present ventured their money safely enough on my color; but I speedily increased my stakes to sums which they dared not risk. One after another they left off playing, and breathlessly looked on at my game.

Still, time after time, I staked higher and higher, and still won. The excitement in the room rose to fever pitch. The silence was interrupted by a deep-muttered chorus of oaths and exclamations in different languages, every time the gold was shoveled across to my side of the table— even the imperturbable croupier dashed his rake on the floor in a (French) fury of astonishment at my success. But one man present preserved his self-possession, and that man was my friend. He came to my side, and whispering in English, begged me to leave the place, satisfied with what I had already gained. I must do him the justice to say that he repeated his warnings and entreaties several times, and only left me and went away, after I had rejected his advice (I was to all intents and purposes gambling drunk) in terms which rendered it impossible for him to address me again that night.

Shortly after he had gone, a hoarse voice behind me cried, "Permit me, my dear sir—permit me to restore to their proper place two napoleons which you have dropped. Wonderful luck, sir! I pledge you my word of honor, as an old soldier, in the course of my long experience in this sort of thing, I never saw such luck as yours—never! Go on, sir—*Sacré mille bombes!* Go on boldly, and break the bank!"

I turned round and saw, nodding and smiling at me with inveterate civility, a tall man, dressed in a frogged and braided surtout.

If I had been in my senses, I should have considered him, personally, as being rather a suspicious specimen of an old soldier. He had goggling, blood-shot eyes, mangy mustaches, and a broken nose. His voice betrayed a barrack-room intonation of the worst order, and he had the dirtiest pair of hands I ever saw—even in France. These little personal peculiarities exercised, however, no repelling influence on me. In the mad excitement, the reckless triumph of that moment, I was ready to "fraternize" with any body who encouraged me in my game. I accepted the old soldier's offered pinch of snuff; clapped him on the back, and swore he was the honestest fellow in the world—the most glorious relic of the Grand Army that I had ever met with. "Go on!" cried my military friend, snapping his fingers in ecstasy—"Go on, and win! Break the bank—*Mille tonnerres!* my gallant English comrade, break the bank!"

And I *did* go on—went on at such a rate, that in another quarter of an hour the croupier called out, "Gentlemen, the bank has discontinued for to-night." All the notes, and all the gold in that "bank," now lay in a heap under my hands; the whole floating capital of the gambling-house was waiting to pour into my pockets!

"Tie up the money in your pocket-handkerchief, my worthy sir!" said the old soldier, as I wildly plunged my hands into my heap of gold. "Tie it up, as we used to tie up a bit of dinner in the Grand

Army; your winnings are too heavy for any breeches-pockets that ever were sewed. There! that's it—shovel them in, notes and all! *Credié!* what luck! Stop! another napoleon on the floor! *Ah! sacré petit polisson de Napoleon!* have I found thee at last? Now then, sir—two tight double knots each way with your honorable permission, and the money's safe. Feel it! feel it, fortunate sir! hard and round as a cannon-ball— *Ah, bah!* if they had only fired such cannon-balls at us at Austerlitz—*nom d'une pipe!* if they only had! And now, as an ancient grenadier, as an ex-brave of the French army, what remains for me to do? I ask what? Simply this, to entreat my valued English friend to drink a bottle of Champagne with me, and toast the goddess Fortune in foaming goblets before we part!"

"Excellent ex-brave! Convivial ancient grenadier! Champagne by all means! An English cheer for an old soldier! Hurra! hurra! Another English cheer for the goddess Fortune! Hurra! hurra! hurra!"

"Bravo! the Englishman; the amiable, gracious Englishman, in whose veins circulates the vivacious blood of France! Another glass? *Ah, bah!*—the bottle is empty! Never mind! *Vive le vin!* I, the old soldier, order another bottle, and half a pound of *bonbons* with it!"

"No, no, ex-brave; never—ancient grenadier! *Your* bottle last time; *my* bottle this! Behold it! Toast away! The French Army! the great Napoleon! the present company! the croupier! the honest croupier's wife and daughters—if he has any! the Ladies generally! every body in the world!"

By the time the second bottle of Champagne was emptied, I felt as if I had been drinking liquid fire—my brain seemed all aflame. No excess in wine had ever had this effect on me before in my life. Was it the result of a stimulant acting upon my system when I was in a highly excited state? Was my stomach in a particularly disordered condition? Or was the Champagne amazingly strong?

"Ex-brave of the French Army!" cried I, in a mad state of exhilaration, "*I* am on fire! how are *you?* You have set me on fire! Do you hear, my hero of Austerlitz?

Let us have a third bottle of Champagne to put the flame out!"

The old soldier wagged his head, rolled his goggle-eyes, until I expected to see them slip out of their sockets; placed his dirty forefinger by the side of his broken nose; solemnly ejaculated "Coffee!" and immediately ran off into an inner room.

The word pronounced by the eccentric veteran seemed to have a magical effect on the rest of the company present. With one accord they all rose to depart. Probably they had expected to profit by my intoxication; but finding that my new friend was benevolently bent on preventing me from getting dead drunk, had now abandoned all hope of thriving pleasantly on my winnings. Whatever their motive might be, at any rate they went away in a body. When the old soldier returned, and sat down again opposite to me at the table, we had the room to ourselves. I could see the croupier, in a sort of vestibule which opened out of it, eating his supper in solitude. The silence was now deeper than ever.

A sudden change, too, had come over the "ex-brave." He assumed a portentously solemn look; and when he spoke to me again, his speech was ornamented by no oaths, enforced by no finger-snapping, enlivened by no apostrophes or exclamations.

"Listen, my dear sir," said he, in mysteriously confidential tones—"listen to an old soldier's advice. I have been to the mistress of the house (a very charming woman, with a genius for cookery!) to impress on her the necessity of making us some particularly strong and good coffee. You must drink this coffee in order to get rid of your little amiable exaltation of spirits before you think of going home— you *must*, my good and gracious friend! With all that money to take home tonight, it is a sacred duty to yourself to have your wits about you. You are known to be a winner to an enormous extent by several gentlemen present to-night, who, in a certain point of view, are very worthy and excellent fellows; but they are mortal men, my dear sir, and they have their amiable weaknesses! Need I say more? Ah, no, no! you understand me! Now, this is what you must do—send for a cabriolet when you feel quite well again—draw up all the windows when you get into it—and tell the driver to take you home only through the large and well-lighted thoroughfares. Do this; and you and your money will be safe. Do this; and to-morrow you will thank an old soldier for giving you a word of honest advice."

Just as the ex-brave ended his oration in very lachrymose tones, the coffee came in, ready poured out in two cups. My attentive friend handed me one of the cups with a bow. I was parched with thirst, and drank it off at a draught. Almost instantly afterward, I was seized with a fit of giddiness, and felt more completely intoxicated than ever. The room whirled round and round furiously; the old soldier seemed to be regularly bobbing up and down before me like the piston of a steam-engine. I was half deafened by a violent singing in my ears; a feeling of utter bewilderment, helplessness, idiocy, overcame me. I rose from my chair, holding on by the table to keep my balance; and stammered out that I felt dreadfully unwell—so unwell that I did not know how I was to get home.

"My dear friend," answered the old soldier—and even his voice seemed to be bobbing up and down as he spoke—"my dear friend, it would be madness to go home in *your* state; you would be sure to lose your money; you might be robbed and murdered with the greatest ease. *I* am going to sleep here: do *you* sleep here, too—they make up capital beds in this house—take one; sleep off the effects of the wine, and go home safely with your winnings to-morrow—to-morrow, in broad daylight."

I had but two ideas left: one, that I must never let go hold of my handkerchief full of money; the other, that I must lie down somewhere immediately, and fall off into a comfortable sleep. So I agreed to the proposal about the bed, and took the offered arm of the old soldier, carrying my money with my disengaged hand. Preceded by the croupier, we passed along some passages and up a flight of stairs into the bedroom which I was to occupy. The ex-brave shook me

warmly by the hand, proposed that we should breakfast together, and then, followed by the croupier, left me for the night.

I ran to the wash-hand stand; drank some of the water in my jug; poured the rest out, and plunged my face into it; then sat down in a chair and tried to compose myself. I soon felt better. The change for my lungs, from the fetid atmosphere of the gambling-room to the cool air of the apartment I now occupied, the almost equally refreshing change for my eyes, from the glaring gas-lights of the "salon" to the dim, quiet flicker of one bedroom-candle, aided wonderfully the restorative effects of cold water. The giddiness left me, and I began to feel a little like a reasonable being again. My first thought was of the risk of sleeping all night in a gambling-house; my second, of the still greater risk of trying to get out after the house was closed, and of going home alone at night through the streets of Paris with a large sum of money about me. I had slept in worse places than this on my travels; so I determined to lock, bolt, and barricade my door, and take my chance till the next morning.

Accordingly, I secured myself against all intrusion; looked under the bed, and into the cupboard; tried the fastening of the window; and then, satisfied that I had taken every proper precaution, pulled off my upper clothing, put my light, which was a dim one, on the hearth among a feathery litter of wood-ashes, and got into bed, with the handkerchief full of money under my pillow.

I soon felt not only that I could not go to sleep, but that I could not even close my eyes. I was wide awake, and in a high fever. Every nerve in my body trembled —every one of my senses seemed to be preternaturally sharpened. I tossed and rolled, and tried every kind of position, and perseveringly sought out the cold corners of the bed, and all to no purpose. Now I thrust my arms over the clothes; now I poked them under the clothes; now I violently shot my legs straight out down to the bottom of the bed; now I convulsively coiled them up as near my chin as they would go; now I shook out my crumpled pillow, changed it to the cool side, patted it flat, and lay down quietly on my back; now I fiercely doubled it in two, set it up on end, thrust it against the board of the bed, and tried a sitting posture. Every effort was in vain; I groaned with vexation as I felt that I was in for a sleepless night.

What could I do? I had no book to read. And yet, unless I found out some method of diverting my mind, I felt certain that I was in the condition to imagine all sorts of horrors; to rack my brain with forebodings of every possible and impossible danger; in short, to pass the night in suffering all conceivable varieties of nervous terror.

I raised myself on my elbow, and looked about the room—which was brightened by a lovely moonlight pouring straight through the window—to see if it contained any pictures or ornaments that I could at all clearly distinguish. While my eyes wandered from wall to wall, a remembrance of Le Maistre's delightful little book, "Voyage autour de ma Chambre," occurred to me. I resolved to imitate the French author, and find occupation and amusement enough to relieve the tedium of my wakefulness, by making a mental inventory of every article of furniture I could see, and by following up to their sources the multitude of associations which even a chair, a table, or a wash-hand stand may be made to call forth.

In the nervous unsettled state of my mind at that moment, I found it much easier to make my inventory than to make my reflections, and thereupon soon gave up all hope of thinking in Le Maistre's fanciful track—or, indeed, of thinking at all. I looked about the room at the different articles of furniture, and did nothing more.

There was, first, the bed I was lying in; a four-post bed, of all things in the world to meet with in Paris—yes, a thorough clumsy British four-poster, with a regular top lined with chintz—the regular fringed valance all round—the regular stifling, unwholesome curtains, which I remembered having mechanically drawn back against the posts without particularly noticing the bed when I first got into the

room. Then there was the marble-topped wash-hand stand, from which the water I had spilled, in my hurry to pour it out, was still dripping, slowly and more slowly, on to the brick floor. Then two small chairs, with my coat, waistcoat, and trowsers flung on them. Then a large elbow-chair covered with dirty white dimity, with my cravat and shirt collar thrown over the back. Then a chest of drawers with two of the brass handles off, and a tawdry, broken china inkstand placed on it by way of ornament for the top. Then the dressing-table, adorned by a very small looking-glass, and a very large pincushion. Then the window—an unusually large window. Then a dark old picture, which the feeble candle dimly showed me. It was the picture of a fellow in a high Spanish hat, crowned with a plume of towering feathers. A swarthy, sinister ruffian, looking upward, shading his eyes with his hand, and looking intently upward—it might be at some tall gallows at which he was going to be hanged. At any rate, he had the appearance of thoroughly deserving it.

This picture put a kind of constraint upon me to look upward too—at the top of the bed. It was a gloomy and not an interesting object, and I looked back at the picture. I counted the feathers in the man's hat—they stood out in relief—three white, two green. I observed the crown of his hat, which was of a conical shape, according to the fashion supposed to have been favored by Guido Fawkes. I wondered what he was looking up at. It couldn't be at the stars; such a desperado was neither astrologer nor astronomer. It must be at the high gallows, and he was going to be hanged presently. Would the executioner come into possession of his conical crowned hat and plume of feathers? I counted the feathers again—three white, two green.

While I still lingered over this very improving and intellectual employment, my thoughts insensibly began to wander. The moonlight shining into the room reminded me of a certain moonlight night in England—the night after a picnic party in a Welsh valley. Every incident of the drive homeward, through lovely scenery, which the moonlight made lovelier than ever, came back to my remembrance, though I had never given the picnic a thought for years; though, if I had *tried* to recollect it, I could certainly have recalled little or nothing of that scene long past. Of all the wonderful faculties that help to tell us we are immortal, which speaks the sublime truth more eloquently than memory? Here was I, in a strange house of the most suspicious character, in a situation of uncertainty, and even of peril, which might seem to make the cool exercise of my recollection almost out of the question; nevertheless, remembering, quite involuntarily, places, people, conversations, minute circumstances of every kind, which I had thought forgotten forever; which I could not possibly have recalled at will, even under the most favorable auspices. And what cause had produced in a moment the whole of this strange, complicated, mysterious effect? Nothing but some rays of moonlight shining in at my bedroom window.

I was still thinking of the picnic—of our merriment on the drive home—of the sentimental young lady who *would* quote "Childe Harold" because it was moonlight. I was absorbed by these past scenes and past amusements, when, in an instant, the thread on which my memories hung snapped asunder; my attention immediately came back to present things more vividly than ever, and I found myself, I neither knew why nor wherefore, looking hard at the picture again.

Looking for what?

Good God! the man had pulled his hat down on his brows! No! the hat itself was gone! Where was the conical crown? Where the feathers—three white, two green? Not there! In place of the hat and feathers, what dusky object was it that now hid his forehead, his eyes, his shading hand?

Was the bed moving?

I turned on my back and looked up. Was I mad? drunk? dreaming? giddy again? or was the top of the bed really moving down—sinking slowly, regularly, silently, horribly, right down throughout the whole of its length and breadth—right down upon me, as I lay underneath?

My blood seemed to stand still. A deadly, paralyzing coldness stole all over

me as I turned my head round on the pillow and determined to test whether the bed-top was really moving or not, by keeping my eye on the man in the picture.

The next look in that direction was enough. The dull, black, frowzy outline of the valance above me was within an inch of being parallel with his waist. I still looked breathlessly. And steadily and slowly—very slowly—I saw the figure, and the line of frame below the figure, vanish, as the valance moved down before it.

I am, constitutionally, any thing but timid. I have been on more than one occasion in peril of my life, and have not lost my self-possession for an instant; but when the conviction first settled on my mind that the bed-top was really moving, was steadily and continuously sinking down upon me, I looked up shuddering, helpless, panic-stricken, beneath the hideous machinery for murder, which was advancing closer and closer to suffocate me where I lay.

I looked up, motionless, speechless, breathless. The candle, fully spent, went out; but the moonlight still brightened the room. Down and down, without pausing and without sounding, came the bed-top, and still my panic terror seemed to bind me faster and faster to the mattress on which I lay—down and down it sank, till the dusty odor from the lining of the canopy came stealing into my nostrils.

At that final moment the instinct of self-preservation startled me out of my trance, and I moved at last. There was just room for me to roll myself sideways off the bed. As I dropped noiselessly to the floor, the edge of the murderous canopy touched me on the shoulder.

Without stopping to draw my breath, without wiping the cold sweat from my face, I rose instantly on my knees to watch the bed-top. I was literally spellbound by it. If I had heard footsteps behind me, I could not have turned round; if a means of escape had been miraculously provided for me, I could not have moved to take advantage of it. The whole life in me was, at that moment, concentrated in my eyes.

It descended—the whole canopy, with the fringe round it, came down—down—

close down; so close that there was not room now to squeeze my finger between the bed-top and the bed. I felt at the sides, and discovered that what had appeared to me from beneath to be the ordinary light canopy of a four-post bed was in reality a thick, broad mattress, the substance of which was concealed by the valance and its fringe. I looked up and saw the four posts rising hideously bare. In the middle of the bed-top was a huge wooden screw that had evidently worked it down through a hole in the ceiling, just as ordinary presses are worked down on the substance selected for compression. The frightful apparatus moved without making the faintest noise. There had been no creaking as it came down; there was now not the faintest sound from the room above. Amidst a dead and awful silence I beheld before me—in the nineteenth century, and in the civilized capital of France —such a machine for secret murder by suffocation as might have existed in the worst days of the Inquisition, in the lonely inns among the Hartz Mountains, in the mysterious tribunals of Westphalia! Still, as I looked on it, I could not move, I could hardly breathe, but I began to recover the power of thinking, and in a moment I discovered the murderous conspiracy framed against me in all its horror.

My cup of coffee had been drugged, and drugged too strongly. I had been saved from being smothered by having taken an overdose of some narcotic. How I had chafed and fretted at the fever fit which had preserved my life by keeping me awake! How recklessly I had confided myself to the two wretches who had led me into this room, determined, for the sake of my winnings, to kill me in my sleep by the surest and most horrible contrivance for secretly accomplishing my destruction! How many men, winners like me, had slept, as I had proposed to sleep, in that bed, and had never been seen or heard of more! I shuddered at the bare idea of it.

But ere long all thought was again suspended by the sight of the murderous canopy moving once more. After it had remained on the bed—as nearly as I could guess—about ten minutes, it began to move up again. The villains who worked it from above evidently believed that their purpose was now accomplished. Slowly and silently, as it had descended, that horrible bed-top rose toward its former place. When it reached the upper extremities of the four posts, it reached the ceiling too. Neither hole nor screw could be seen; the bed became in appearance an ordinary bed again—the canopy an ordinary canopy—even to the most suspicious eyes.

Now, for the first time, I was able to move—to rise from my knees—to dress myself in my upper clothing—and to consider of how I should escape. If I betrayed by the smallest noise that the attempt to suffocate me had failed, I was certain to be murdered. Had I made any noise already? I listened intently, looking toward the door.

No! no footsteps in the passage outside —no sound of a tread, light or heavy, in the room above—absolute silence everywhere. Besides locking and bolting my door, I had moved an old wooden chest against it, which I had found under the bed. To remove this chest (my blood ran cold as I thought of what its contents *might* be!) without making some disturbance was impossible; and, moreover, to think of escaping through the house, now barred up for the night, was sheer insanity. Only one chance was left me—the window. I stole to it on tiptoe.

My bedroom was on the first floor, above an *entresol*, and looked into the back street, which you have sketched in your view. I raised my hand to open the window, knowing that on that action hung, by the merest hair-breadth, my chance of safety. They keep vigilant watch in a House of Murder. If any part of the frame cracked, if the hinge creaked, I was a lost man! It must have occupied me at least five minutes, reckoning by time— five *hours*, reckoning by suspense—to open that window. I succeeded in doing it silently—in doing it with all the dexterity of a house-breaker—and then looked down into the street. To leap the distance beneath me would be almost certain destruction! Next, I looked round at the sides of the house. Down the left side ran the thick water-pipe which you have drawn—it passed close by the outer edge of the window. The moment I saw the pipe, I knew I was saved. My breath came and went freely for the first time since I had seen the canopy of the bed moving down upon me!

To some men the means of escape which I had discovered might have seemed difficult and dangerous enough— to *me* the prospect of slipping down the pipe into the street did not suggest even a thought of peril. I had always been accustomed, by the practice of gymnastics, to keep up my school-boy powers as a daring and expert climber; and knew that my head, hands, and feet would serve me faithfully in any hazards of ascent or descent. I had already got one leg over the window-sill, when I remembered the handkerchief filled with money under my pillow. I could well have afforded to leave it behind me, but I was revengefully determined that the miscreants of the gambling-house should miss their plunder as well as their victim. So I went back to the bed and tied the heavy handkerchief at my back by my cravat.

Just as I had made it tight and fixed it in a comfortable place, I thought I heard a sound of breathing outside the door. The chill feeling of horror ran through me again as I listened. No! dead silence still in the passage—I had only heard the night air blowing softly into the room. The next moment I was on the window-sill—and the next I had a firm grip on the water-pipe with my hands and knees.

I slid down into the street easily and quietly, as I thought I should, and immediately set off at the top of my speed to a branch "Prefecture" of Police, which I knew was situated in the immediate neighborhood. A "Sub-prefect," and several picked men among his subordinates, happened to be up, maturing, I believe, some scheme for discovering the perpetrator of a mysterious murder which all Paris was talking of just then. When I began my story, in a breathless hurry and in very bad French, I could see that the Sub-prefect suspected me of being a drunken Englishman who had robbed somebody; but he soon altered his opinion as I went

on, and before I had any thing like concluded, he shoved all the papers before him into a drawer, put on his hat, supplied me with another (for I was bare-headed), ordered a file of soldiers, desired his expert followers to get ready all sorts of tools for breaking open doors and ripping up brick flooring, and took my arm, in the most friendly and familiar manner possible, to lead me with him out of the house. I will venture to say that when the Sub-prefect was a little boy, and was taken for the first time to the play, he was not half as much pleased as he was now at the job in prospect for him at the gambling-house!

Away we went through the streets, the Sub-prefect cross-examining and congratulating me in the same breath as we marched at the head of our formidable *posse comitatus*. Sentinels were placed at the back and front of the house the moment we got to it; a tremendous battery of knocks was directed against the door; a light appeared at a window; I was told to conceal myself behind the police—then came more knocks, and a cry of "Open in the name of the law!" At that terrible summons bolts and locks gave way before an invisible hand, and the moment after the Sub-prefect was in the passage, confronting a waiter half dressed and ghastly pale. This was the short dialogue which immediately took place:

"We want to see the Englishman who is sleeping in this house?"

"He went away hours ago."

"He did no such thing. His friend went away; *he* remained. Show us to his bedroom!"

"I swear to you, Monsieur le Sous-prefect, he is not here! he—"

"I swear to you, Monsieur le Garçon, he is. He slept here—he didn't find your bed comfortable—he came to us to complain of it—here he is among my men— and here am I ready to look for a flea or two in his bedstead. Renaudin! (calling to one of the subordinates, and pointing to the waiter), collar that man, and tie his hands behind him. Now, then, gentlemen, let us walk up stairs!"

Every man and woman in the house was secured—the "Old Soldier" the first.

Then I identified the bed in which I had slept, and then we went into the room above.

No object that was at all extraordinary appeared in any part of it. The Sub-prefect looked round the place, commanded every body to be silent, stamped twice on the floor, called for a candle, looked attentively at the spot he had stamped on, and ordered the flooring there to be carefully taken up. This was done in no time. Lights were produced, and we saw a deep raftered cavity between the floor of this room and the ceiling of the room beneath. Through this cavity there ran perpendicularly a sort of case of iron thickly greased; and inside the case appeared the screw, which communicated with the bed-top below. Extra lengths of screw, freshly oiled; levers covered with felt; all the complete upper works of a heavy press—constructed with infernal ingenuity so as to join the fixtures below, and when taken to pieces again to go into the smallest possible compass—were next discovered and pulled out on the floor. After some little difficulty the Sub-prefect succeeded in putting the machinery together, and, leaving his men to work it, descended with me to the bedroom. The smothering canopy was then lowered, but not so noiselessly as I had seen it lowered. When I mentioned this to the Sub-prefect, his answer, simple as it was, had a terrible significance. "My men," said he, "are working down the bed-top for the first time—the men whose money you won were in better practice."

We left the house in the sole possession of two police agents—every one of the inmates being removed to prison on the spot. The Sub-prefect, after taking down my "*procès verbal*" in his office, returned with me to my hotel to get my passport. "Do you think," I asked, as I gave it to him, "that any men have really been smothered in that bed, as they tried to smother *me?*"

"I have seen dozens of drowned men laid out in the Morgue," answered the Sub-prefect, "in whose pocket-books were found letters stating that they had committed suicide in the Seine, because they had lost every thing at the gaming-table.

Do I know how many of those men entered the same gambling-house that *you* entered? won as *you* won? took that bed as *you* took it? slept in it? were smothered in it? and were privately thrown into the river, with a letter of explanation written by the murderers and placed in their pocket-books? No man can say how many or how few have suffered the fate from which you have escaped. The people of the gambling-house kept their bedstead machinery a secret from *us*—even from the police! The dead kept the rest of the secret for them. Good-night, or rather good-morning, Monsieur Faulkner! Be at my office again at nine o'clock—in the mean time, *au revoir!*"

The rest of my story is soon told. I was examined and re-examined; the gambling-house was strictly searched all through from top to bottom; the prisoners were separately interrogated; and two of the less guilty among them made a confession. I discovered that the Old Soldier was the master of the gambling-house—*justice* discovered that he had been drummed out of the army as a vagabond years ago; that he had been guilty of all sorts of villainies since; that he was in possession of stolen property, which the owners identified; and that he, the croupier, another accomplice, and the woman who had made my cup of coffee, were all in the secret of the bedstead. There appeared some reason to doubt whether the inferior persons attached to the house knew any thing of the suffocating machinery; and they received the benefit of that doubt, by being treated simply as thieves and vagabonds. As for the Old Soldier and his two head myrmidons, they went to the galleys; the woman who had drugged my coffee was imprisoned for I forget how many years; the regular attendants at the gambling-house were considered "suspicious," and placed under "surveillance;" and I became, for one whole week (which is a long time), the head "lion" in Parisian society. My adventure was dramatized by three illustrious play-makers, but never saw theatrical daylight; for the censorship forbade the introduction on the stage of a correct copy of the gambling-house bedstead.

One good result was produced by my adventure, which any censorship must have approved: it cured me of ever again trying *"Rouge et Noir"* as an amusement. The sight of a greencloth, with packs of cards and heaps of money on it, will henceforth be forever associated in my mind with the sight of a bed canopy descending to suffocate me in the silence and darkness of the night.

[1852]

QUESTIONS FOR STUDY

1. *How does the choice of point of view aid in the creation of suspense and terror?*
2. *How does Collins establish an appropriate atmosphere for his story? How does he go about giving his story plausibility?*
3. *What warning hints and clues does the narrator fail to recognize early in the evening?*
4. *What are the relative strengths and weaknesses of plot, characterization, and style?*
5. *Why does Collins choose to end his story with the visit by the police?*
6. *What seems to have been Collins' principal aim in writing the story? Has he been successful?*

JOSEPH CONRAD

The Secret Sharer

I

ON MY right hand there were lines of fishing-stakes resembling a mysterious system of half-submerged bamboo fences, incomprehensible in its division of the domain of tropical fishes, and crazy of aspect as if abandoned for ever by some nomad tribe of fishermen now gone to the other end of the ocean; for there was no sign of human habitation as far as the eye could reach. To the left a group of barren islets, suggesting ruins of stone walls, towers, and blockhouses, had its foundations set in a blue sea that itself looked solid, so still and stable did it lie below my feet; even the track of light from the westering sun shone smoothly, without that animated glitter which tells of an imperceptible ripple. And when I turned my head to take a parting glance at the tug which had just left us anchored outside the bar, I saw the straight line of the flat shore joined to the stable sea, edge to edge, with a perfect and unmarked closeness, in one levelled floor half brown, half blue under the enormous dome of the sky. Corresponding in their insignificance to the islets of the sea, two small clumps of trees, one on each side of the only fault in the impeccable joint, marked the mouth of the river Meinam we had just left on the first preparatory stage of our homeward journey; and, far back on the inland level, a larger and loftier mass, the grove surrounding the great Paknam pagoda, was the only thing on which the eye could rest from the vain task of exploring the monotonous sweep of the horizon. Here and there gleams as of a few scattered pieces of silver marked the windings of the great river; and on the nearest of them, just within the bar, the tug steaming right into the land became lost to my sight, hull and funnel and masts, as though the impassive earth had swallowed her up without an effort, without a tremor. My eye followed the light cloud of her smoke, now here, now there, above the plain, according to the devious curves of the stream, but always fainter and farther away, till I lost it at last behind the mitre-shaped hill of the great pagoda. And then I was left alone with my ship, anchored at the head of the Gulf of Siam.

She floated at the starting-point of a long journey, very still in an immense stillness, the shadows of her spars flung far to the eastward by the setting sun. At that moment I was alone on her decks. There was not a sound in her—and around us nothing moved, nothing lived, not a canoe on the water, not a bird in the air, not a cloud in the sky. In this breathless pause at the threshold of a long passage we seemed to be measuring our fitness for a long and arduous enterprise, the appointed task of both our existences to be carried out, far from all human eyes, with only sky and sea for spectators and for judges.

There must have been some glare in the air to interfere with one's sight, because it was only just before the sun left us that my roaming eyes made out beyond the highest ridge of the principal islet of the group something which did away with the solemnity of perfect solitude. The tide of darkness flowed on swiftly; and with tropical suddenness a swarm of stars came out above the shadowy earth, while I lingered yet, my hand resting lightly on my ship's rail as if on the shoulder of a trusted friend. But, with all that multitude of celestial bodies staring down at one, the comfort of quiet communion with her was gone for good. And there were also disturbing sounds by this time—voices,

From *'Twixt Land and Sea* by Joseph Conrad. Reprinted by permission of J. M. Dent & Sons Ltd., London, and the Trustees of the Joseph Conrad Estate.

footsteps forward; the steward flitted along the main-deck, a busily ministering spirit; a hand-bell tinkled urgently under the poop-deck. . . .

I found my two officers waiting for me near the supper table, in the lighted cuddy. We sat down at once, and as I helped the chief mate, I said:

"Are you aware that there is a ship anchored inside the islands? I saw her mastheads above the ridge as the sun went down."

He raised sharply his simple face, overcharged by a terrible growth of whisker, and emitted his usual ejaculations: "Bless my soul, sir! You don't say so!"

My second mate was a round-cheeked, silent young man, grave beyond his years, I thought; but as our eyes happened to meet I detected a slight quiver on his lips. I looked down at once. It was not my part to encourage sneering on board my ship. It must be said, too, that I knew very little of my officers. In consequence of certain events of no particular significance, except to myself, I had been appointed to the command only a fortnight before. Neither did I know much of the hands forward. All these people had been together for eighteen months or so, and my position was that of the only stranger on board. I mention this because it has some bearing on what is to follow. But what I felt most was my being a stranger to the ship; and if all the truth must be told, I was somewhat of a stranger to myself. The youngest man on board (barring the second mate), and untried as yet by a position of the fullest responsibility, I was willing to take the adequacy of the others for granted. They had simply to be equal to their tasks; but I wondered how far I should turn out faithful to that ideal conception of one's own personality every man sets up for himself secretly.

Meantime the chief mate, with an almost visible effect of collaboration on the part of his round eyes and frightful whiskers, was trying to evolve a theory of the anchored ship. His dominant trait was to take all things into earnest considera tion. He was of a painstaking turn of mind. As he used to say, he "liked to ac-count to himself" for practically everything that came in his way, down to a miserable scorpion he had found in his cabin a week before. The why and the wherefore of that scorpion—how it got on board and came to select his room rather than the pantry (which was a dark place and more what a scorpion would be partial to), and how on earth it managed to drown itself in the inkwell of his writing-desk—had exercised him infinitely. The ship within the islands was much more easily accounted for; and just as we were about to rise from table he made his pronouncement. She was, he doubted not, a ship from home lately arrived. Probably she drew too much water to cross the bar except at the top of spring tides. Therefore she went into that natural harbour to wait for a few days in preference to remaining in an open roadstead.

"That's so," confirmed the second mate, suddenly, in his slightly hoarse voice. "She draws over twenty feet. She's the Liverpool ship *Sephora* with a cargo of coal. Hundred and twenty-three days from Cardiff."

We looked at him in surprise.

"The tugboat skipper told me when he came on board for your letters, sir," explained the young man. "He expects to take her up the river the day after to-morrow."

After thus overwhelming us with the extent of his information he slipped out of the cabin. The mate observed regretfully that he "could not account for that young fellow's whims." What prevented him telling us all about it at once, he wanted to know.

I detained him as he was making a move. For the last two days the crew had had plenty of hard work, and the night before they had very little sleep. I felt painfully that I—a stranger—was doing something unusual when I directed him to let all hands turn in without setting an anchor-watch. I proposed to keep on deck myself till one o'clock or thereabouts. I would get the second mate to relieve me at that hour.

"He will turn out the cook and the steward at four," I concluded, "and then give you a call. Of course at the slightest sign of any sort of wind we'll have the hands up and make a start at once."

He concealed his astonishment. "Very well, sir." Outside the cuddy he put his head in the second mate's door to inform him of my unheard-of caprice to take a five hours' anchor-watch on myself. I heard the other raise his voice incredulously—"What? The Captain himself?" Then a few more murmurs, a door closed, then another. A few moments later I went on deck.

My strangeness, which had made me sleepless, had prompted that unconventional arrangement, as if I had expected in those solitary hours of the night to get on terms with the ship of which I knew nothing, manned by men of whom I knew very little more. Fast alongside a wharf, littered like any ship in port with a tangle of unrelated things, invaded by unrelated shore people, I had hardly seen her yet properly. Now, as she lay cleared for sea, the stretch of her main-deck seemed to me very fine under the stars. Very fine, very roomy for her size, and very inviting. I descended the poop and paced the waist, my mind picturing to myself the coming passage through the Malay Archipelago, down the Indian Ocean, and up the Atlantic. All its phases were familiar enough to me, every characteristic, all the alternatives which were likely to face me on the high seas—everything! . . . except the novel responsibility of command. But I took heart from the reasonable thought that the ship was like other ships, the men like other men, and that the sea was not likely to keep any special surprises expressly for my discomfiture.

Arrived at that comforting conclusion, I bethought myself of a cigar and went below to get it. All was still down there. Everybody at the after end of the ship was sleeping profoundly. I came out again on the quarter-deck, agreeably at ease in my sleeping-suit on that warm breathless night, barefooted, a glowing cigar in my teeth, and, going forward, I was met by the profound silence of the fore end of the ship. Only as I passed the door of the forecastle I heard a deep, quiet, trustful sigh of some sleeper inside. And suddenly I rejoiced in the great security of the sea as compared with the unrest of the land, in my choice of that untempted life presenting no disquieting problems, invested with an elementary moral beauty by the absolute straightforwardness of its appeal and by the singleness of its purpose.

The riding-light in the fore-rigging burned with a clear, untroubled, as if symbolic, flame, confident and bright in the mysterious shades of the night. Passing on my way aft along the other side of the ship, I observed that the rope side-ladder, put over, no doubt, for the master of the tug when he came to fetch away our letters, had not been hauled in as it should have been. I became annoyed at this, for exactitude in small matters is the very soul of discipline. Then I reflected that I had myself peremptorily dismissed my officers from duty, and by my own act had prevented the anchor-watch being formally set and things properly attended to. I asked myself whether it was wise ever to interfere with the established routine of duties even from the kindest of motives. My action might have made me appear eccentric. Goodness only knew how that absurdly whiskered mate would "account" for my conduct, and what the whole ship thought of that informality of their new captain. I was vexed with myself.

Not from compunction certainly, but, as it were mechanically, I proceeded to get the ladder in myself. Now a side-ladder of that sort is a light affair and comes in easily, yet my vigorous tug, which should have brought it flying on board, merely recoiled upon my body in a totally unexpected jerk. What the devil! . . . I was so astounded by the immovableness of that ladder that I remained stock-still, trying to account for it to myself like that imbecile mate of mine. In the end, of course, I put my head over the rail.

The side of the ship made an opaque belt of shadow on the darkling glassy shimmer of the sea. But I saw at once something elongated and pale floating very close to the ladder. Before I could form a guess a faint flash of phosphorescent light, which seemed to issue suddenly from the naked body of a man, flickered in the sleeping water with the elusive, silent play of summer lightning in a night sky. With a gasp I saw revealed to my stare a pair of feet, the long legs, a broad livid back immersed right up to the neck in a greenish cadaverous glow. One hand, awash, clutched the botttom rung of the ladder. He was complete but for the head. A headless corpse! The cigar dropped out of my gaping mouth with a tiny plop and a short hiss quite audible in the absolute stillness of all things under heaven. At that I suppose he raised up his face, a dimly pale oval in the shadow of the ship's side. But even then I could only barely make out down there the shape of his black-haired head. However, it was enough for the horrid, frost-bound sensation which had gripped me about the chest to pass off. The moment of vain exclamations was past, too. I only climbed on the spare spar and leaned over the rail as far as I could, to bring my eyes nearer to that mystery floating alongside.

As he hung by the ladder, like a resting swimmer, the sea-lightning played about his limbs at every stir; and he appeared in it ghastly, silvery, fish-like. He remained as mute as a fish, too. He made no motion to get out of the water, either. It was inconceivable that he should not attempt to come on board, and strangely troubling to suspect that perhaps he did not want to. And my first words were prompted by just that troubled incertitude.

"What's the matter?" I asked in my ordinary tone, speaking down to the face upturned exactly under mine.

"Cramp," it answered, no louder. Then slightly anxious, "I say, no need to call any one."

"I was not going to," I said.

"Are you alone on deck?"

"Yes."

I had somehow the impression that he was on the point of letting go the ladder to swim away beyond my ken—mysterious as he came. But, for the moment, this being appearing as if he had risen from the bottom of the sea (it was certainly the nearest land to the ship) wanted only to know the time. I told him. And he, down there, tentatively:

"I suppose your captain's turned in?"

"I am sure he isn't," I said.

He seemed to struggle with himself, for I heard something like the low, bitter murmur of doubt. "What's the good?" His next words came out with a hesitating effort.

"Look here, my man. Could you call him out quietly?"

I thought the time had come to declare myself.

"I am the captain."

I heard a "By Jove!" whispered at the level of the water. The phosphorescence flashed in the swirl of the water all about his limbs, his other hand seized the ladder.

"My name's Leggatt."

The voice was calm and resolute. A good voice. The self-possession of that man had somehow induced a corresponding state in myself. It was very quietly that I remarked:

"You must be a good swimmer."

"Yes. I've been in the water practically since nine o'clock. The question for me now is whether I am to let go this ladder and go on swimming till I sink from exhaustion, or—to come on board here."

I felt this was no mere formula of desperate speech, but a real alternative in the view of a strong soul. I should have gathered from this that he was young; indeed, it is only the young who are ever confronted by such clear issues. But at the time it was pure intuition on my part. A mysterious communication was established already between us two—in the face of that silent, darkened tropical sea. I was young, too; young enough to make no comment. The man in the water began suddenly to climb up the ladder, and I hastened away from the rail to fetch some clothes.

Before entering the cabin I stood still, listening in the lobby at the foot of the stairs. A faint snore came through the closed door of the chief mate's room. The second mate's door was on the hook, but the darkness in there was absolutely soundless. He, too, was young and could sleep like a stone. Remained the steward, but he was not likely to wake up before he was called. I got a sleeping-suit out of my room and, coming back on deck, saw the naked man from the sea sitting on the main-hatch, glimmering white in the darkness, his elbows on his knees and his head in his hands. In a moment he had concealed his damp body in a sleeping-suit of the same grey-stripe pattern as the one I was wearing and followed me like my double on the poop. Together we moved right aft, barefooted, silent.

"What is it?" I asked in a deadened voice, taking the lighted lamp out of the binnacle, and raising it to his face.

"An ugly business."

He had rather regular features; a good mouth; light eyes under somewhat heavy, dark eyebrows; a smooth, square forehead; no growth on his cheeks; a small, brown moustache, and a well-shaped, round chin. His expression was concentrated, meditative, under the inspecting light of the lamp I held up to his face; such as a man thinking hard in solitude might wear. My sleeping-suit was just right for his size. A well-knit young fellow of twenty-five at most. He caught his lower lip with the edge of white, even teeth.

"Yes," I said, replacing the lamp in the binnacle. The warm, heavy tropical night closed upon his head again.

"There's a ship over there," he murmured.

"Yes, I know. The *Sephora*. Did you know of us?"

"Hadn't the slightest idea. I am the mate of her——" He paused and corrected himself. "I should say I *was*."

"Aha! Something wrong?"

"Yes. Very wrong indeed. I've killed a man."

"What do you mean? Just now?"

"No, on the passage. Weeks ago. Thirty-nine south. When I say a man——"

"Fit of temper," I suggested, confidently.

The shadowy, dark head, like mine, seemed to nod imperceptibly above the ghostly grey of my sleeping-suit. It was, in the night, as though I had been faced by my own reflection in the depths of a sombre and immense mirror.

"A pretty thing to have to own up to for a Conway boy," murmured my double, distinctly.

"You're a Conway boy?"

"I am," he said, as if startled. Then, slowly . . . "Perhaps you too——"

It was so; but being a couple of years older I had left before he joined. After a quick interchange of dates a silence fell; and I thought suddenly of my absurd mate with his terrific whiskers and the "Bless my soul—you don't say so" type of intellect. My double gave me an inkling of his thoughts by saying: "My father's a parson in Norfolk. Do you see me before a judge and jury on that charge? For myself I can't see the necessity. There are fellows that an angel from heaven—— And I am not that. He was one of those creatures that are just simmering all the time with a silly sort of wickedness. Miserable devils that have no business to live at all. He wouldn't do his duty and wouldn't let anybody else do theirs. But what's the good of talking! You know well enough the sort of ill-conditioned snarling cur——"

He appealed to me as if our experiences had been as identical as our clothes. And I knew well enough the pestiferous danger of such a character where there are no means of legal repression. And I knew well enough also that my double there was no homicidal ruffian. I did not think of asking him for details, and he told me the story roughly in brusque, disconnected sentences. I needed no more. I saw it all going on as though I were myself inside that other sleeping-suit.

"It happened while we were setting a reefed foresail, at dusk. Reefed foresail! You understand the sort of weather. The only sail we had left to keep the ship running; so you may guess what it had been like for days. Anxious sort of job, that. He gave me some of his cursed insolence at the sheet. I tell you I was overdone with this terrific weather that seemed to have no end to it. Terrific, I tell you—and a deep ship. I believe the fellow himself was half crazed with funk. It was no time for gentlemanly reproof, so I turned round and felled him like an ox. He up and at me. We closed just as an awful sea made for the ship. All hands saw it coming and took to the rigging, but I had him by the throat, and went on shaking him like a rat, the men above us yelling. 'Look out! look out!' Then a crash as if the sky had fallen on my head. They say that for over ten minutes hardly anything was to be seen of the ship—just the three masts and a bit of the forecastle head and of the poop all awash driving along in a smother of foam. It was a miracle that they found us, jammed together behind the forebits. It's clear that I meant business, because I was holding him by the throat still when they picked us up. He was black in the face. It was too much for them. It seems they rushed us aft together, gripped as we were, screaming 'Murder!' like a lot of lunatics, and broke into the cuddy. And the ship running for her life, touch and go all the time, any minute her last in a sea fit to turn your hair grey only a-looking at it. I understand that the skipper, too, started raving like the rest of them. The man had been deprived of sleep for more than a week, and to have this sprung on him at the height of a furious gale nearly drove him out of his mind. I wonder they didn't fling me overboard after getting the carcass of their precious ship-mate out of my fingers. They had rather a job to separate us, I've been told. A sufficiently fierce story to make an old judge and a respectable jury sit up a bit. The first thing I heard when I came to myself was the maddening howling of that endless gale, and on that the voice of the old man. He was hanging on to my bunk, staring into my face out of his sou'wester.

" 'Mr. Leggatt, you have killed a man. You can act no longer as chief mate of this ship.' "

His care to subdue his voice made it sound monotonous. He rested a hand on the end of the skylight to steady himself with, and all that time did not stir a limb, so far as I could see. "Nice little tale for a quiet tea-party," he concluded in the same tone.

One of my hands, too, rested on the end of the skylight; neither did I stir a limb, so far as I knew. We stood less than a foot from each other. It occurred to me that if old "Bless my soul—you don't say so" were to put his head up the companion and catch sight of us, he would think he was seeing double, or imagine himself

come upon a scene of weird witchcraft; the strange captain having a quiet confabulation by the wheel with his own grey ghost. I became very much concerned to prevent anything of the sort. I heard the other's soothing undertone.

"My father's a parson in Norfolk," it said. Evidently he had forgotten he had told me this important fact before. Truly a nice little tale.

"You had better slip down into my stateroom now," I said, moving off stealthily. My double followed my movements; our bare feet made no sound; I let him in, closed the door with care, and, after giving a call to the second mate, returned on deck for my relief.

"Not much sign of any wind yet," I remarked when he approached.

"No, sir. Not much," he assented, sleepily, in his hoarse voice, with just enough deference, no more, and barely suppressing a yawn.

"Well, that's all you have to look out for. You have got your orders."

"Yes, sir."

I paced a turn or two on the poop and saw him take up his position face forward with his elbow in the ratlines of the mizzen-rigging before I went below. The mate's faint snoring was still going on peacefully. The cuddy lamp was burning over the table on which stood a vase with flowers, a polite attention from the ship's provision merchant—the last flowers we should see for the next three months at the very least. Two bunches of bananas hung from the beam symmetrically, one on each side of the rudder-casing. Everything was as before in the ship—except that two of her captain's sleeping-suits were simultaneously in use, one motionless in the cuddy, the other keeping very still in the captain's stateroom.

It must be explained here that my cabin had the form of the capital letter L the door being within the angle and opening into the short part of the letter. A couch was to the left, the bed-place to the right; my writing-desk and the chronometers' table faced the door. But any one opening it, unless he stepped right inside, had no view of what I call the long (or vertical) part of the letter. It contained some lockers surmounted by a bookcase; and a few clothes, a thick jacket or two, caps, oilskin coat, and such like, hung on hooks. There was at the bottom of that part a door opening into my bath-room, which could be entered also directly from the saloon. But that way was never used.

The mysterious arrival had discovered the advantage of this particular shape. Entering my room, lighted strongly by a big bulkhead lamp swung on gimbals above my writing-desk, I did not see him anywhere till he stepped out quietly from behind the coats hung in the recessed part.

"I heard somebody moving about, and went in there at once," he whispered.

I, too, spoke under my breath.

"Nobody is likely to come in here without knocking and getting permission."

He nodded. His face was thin and the sunburn faded, as though he had been ill. And no wonder. He had been, I heard presently, kept under arrest in his cabin for nearly seven weeks. But there was nothing sickly in his eyes or in his expression. He was not a bit like me, really; yet, as we stood leaning over my bed-place, whispering side by side, with our dark heads together and our backs to the door, anybody bold enough to open it stealthily would have been treated to the uncanny sight of a double captain busy talking in whispers with his other self.

"But all this doesn't tell me how you came to hang on to our side-ladder," I inquired, in the hardly audible murmurs we used, after he had told me something more of the proceedings on board the *Sephora* once the bad weather was over.

"When we sighted Java Head I had had time to think all those matters out several times over. I had six weeks of doing nothing else, and with only an hour or so every evening for a tramp on the quarter-deck."

He whispered, his arms folded on the side of my bed-place, staring through the open port. And I could imagine perfectly the manner of this thinking out—a stubborn if not a steadfast operation; something of which I should have been perfectly incapable.

"I reckoned it would be dark before we closed with the land," he continued, so low that I had to strain my hearing, near as we were to each other, shoulder touching shoulder almost. "So I asked to speak to the old man. He always seemed very sick when he came to see me—as if he could not look me in the face. You know, that foresail saved the ship. She was too deep to have run long under bare poles. And it was I that managed to set it for him. Anyway, he came. When I had him in my cabin—he stood by the door looking at me as if I had the halter round my neck already—I asked him right away to leave my cabin door unlocked at night while the ship was going through Sunda Straits. There would be the Java coast within two or three miles, off Angier Point. I wanted nothing more. I've had a prize for swimming my second year in the Conway."

"I can believe it," I breathed out.

"God only knows why they locked me in every night. To see some of their faces you'd have thought they were afraid I'd go about at night strangling people. Am I a murdering brute? Do I look it? By Jove! if I had been he wouldn't have trusted himself like that into my room. You'll say I might have chucked him aside and bolted out, there and then—it was dark already. Well, no. And for the same reason I wouldn't think of trying to smash the door. There would have been a rush to stop me at the noise, and I did not mean to get into a confounded scrimmage. Somebody else might have got killed—for I would not have broken out only to get chucked back, and I did not want any more of that work. He refused, looking more sick than ever. He was afraid of the men, and also of that old second mate of his who had been sailing with him for years—a grey-headed old humbug; and his steward, too, had been with him devil knows how long—seventeen years or more—a dogmatic sort of loafer who hated me like poison, just because I was the chief mate. No chief mate ever made more than one voyage in the *Sephora*, you know. Those two old chaps ran the ship. Devil only knows what the skipper wasn't afraid of (all his nerve went to pieces altogether in that hellish

spell of bad weather we had)—of what
the law would do to him—of his wife,
perhaps. Oh, yes! she's on board. Though
I don't think she would have meddled.
She would have been only too glad to
have me out of the ship in any way. The
'brand of Cain' business, don't you see.
That's all right. I was ready enough to go
off wandering on the face of the earth—
and that was price enough to pay for an
Abel of that sort. Anyhow, he wouldn't
listen to me. 'This thing must take its
course. I represent the law here.' He was
shaking like a leaf. 'So you won't?' 'No!'
'Then I hope you will be able to sleep on
that,' I said, and turned my back on him.
'I wonder that *you* can,' cries he, and
locks the door.

"Well, after that, I couldn't. Not very
well. That was three weeks ago. We have
had a slow passage through the Java Sea;
drifted about Carimata for ten days.
When we anchored here they thought, I
suppose, it was all right. The nearest land
(and that's five miles) is the ship's destination; the consul would soon set about
catching me; and there would have been
no object in bolting to these islets there. I
don't suppose there's a drop of water on
them. I don't know how it was, but to-
night that steward, after bringing me my
supper, went out to let me eat it, and left
the door unlocked. And I ate it—all there
was, too. After I had finished I strolled
out on the quarter-deck. I don't know
that I meant to do anything. A breath of
fresh air was all I wanted, I believe. Then
a sudden temptation came over me. I
kicked off my slippers and was in the
water before I had made up my mind
fairly. Somebody heard the splash and
they raised an awful hullabaloo. 'He's
gone! Lower the boats! He's committed
suicide! No, he's swimming.' Certainly I
was swimming. It's not so easy for a
swimmer like me to commit suicide by
drowning. I landed on the nearest islet
before the boat left the ship's side. I heard
them pulling about in the dark, hailing,
and so on, but after a bit they gave up.
Everything quieted down and the anchorage became as still as death. I sat down
on a stone and began to think. I felt certain they would start searching for me at

daylight. There was no place to hide on
those stony things—and if there had
been, what would have been the good?
But now I was clear of that ship, I was
not going back. So after a while I took off
all my clothes, tied them up in a bundle
with a stone inside, and dropped them in
the deep water on the outer side of that
islet. That was suicide enough for me.
Let them think what they liked, but I
didn't mean to drown myself. I meant to
swim till I sank—but that's not the same
thing. I struck out for another of these
little islands, and it was from that one
that I first saw your riding-light. Something to swim for. I went on easily, and
on the way I came upon a flat rock a foot
or two above the water. In the daytime, I
dare say, you might make it out with a
glass from your poop. I scrambled up on
it and rested myself for a bit. Then I
made another start. That last spell must
have been over a mile."

His whisper was getting fainter and
fainter, and all the time he stared straight
out through the port-hole, in which there
was not even a star to be seen. I had not
interrupted him. There was something
that made comment impossible in his narrative, or perhaps in himself; a sort of
feeling, a quality, which I can't find a
name for. And when he ceased, all I
found was a futile whisper: "So you
swam for our light?"

"Yes—straight for it. It was something
to swim for. I couldn't see any stars low
down because the coast was in the way,
and I couldn't see the land, either. The
water was like glass. One might have been
swimming in a confounded thousand-feet
deep cistern with no place for scrambling
out anywhere; but what I didn't like was
the notion of swimming round and round
like a crazed bullock before I gave out;
and as I didn't mean to go back . . . No.
Do you see me being hauled back, stark
naked, off one of these little islands by
the scruff of the neck and fighting like a
wild beast? Somebody would have got
killed for certain, and I did not want any
of that. So I went on. Then your ladder——"

"Why didn't you hail the ship?" I
asked, a little louder.

He touched my shoulder lightly. Lazy foosteps came right over our heads and stopped. The second mate had crossed from the other side of the poop and might have been hanging over the rail, for all we knew.

"He couldn't hear us talking—could he?" My double breathed into my very ear, anxiously.

His anxiety was an answer, a sufficient answer, to the question I had put to him. An answer containing all the difficulty of that situation. I closed the porthole quietly, to make sure. A louder word might have been overheard.

"Who's that?" he whispered then.

"My second mate. But I don't know much more of the fellow than you do."

And I told him a little about myself. I had been appointed to take charge while I least expected anything of the sort, not quite a fortnight ago. I didn't know either the ship or the people. Hadn't had the time in port to look about me or size anybody up. And as to the crew, all they knew was that I was appointed to take the ship home. For the rest, I was almost as much of a stranger on board as himself, I said. And at the moment I felt it most acutely. I felt that it would take very little to make me a suspect person in the eyes of the ship's company.

He had turned about meantime; and we, the two strangers in the ship, faced each other in identical attitudes.

"Your ladder——" he murmured, after a silence. "Who'd have thought of finding a ladder hanging over at night in a ship anchored out here! I felt just then a very unpleasant faintness. After the life I've been leading for nine weeks, anybody would have got out of condition. I wasn't capable of swimming round as far as your rudder-chains. And, lo and behold! there was a ladder to get hold of. After I gripped it I said to myself, 'What's the good?' When I saw a man's head looking over I thought I would swim away presently and leave him shouting—in whatever language it was. I didn't mind being looked at. I—I liked it. And then you speaking to me so quietly—as if you had expected me—made me hold on a little longer. It had been a confounded lonely time—I don't mean while swimming. I was glad to talk a little to somebody that didn't belong to the *Sephora*. As to asking for the captain, that was a mere impulse. It could have been no use, with all the ship knowing about me and the other people pretty certain to be round here in the morning. I don't know—I wanted to be seen, to talk with somebody, before I went on. I don't know what I would have said. . . . 'Fine night, isn't it?' or something of the sort."

"Do you think they will be round here presently?" I asked with some incredulity. "Quite likely," he said, faintly.

He looked extremely haggard all of a sudden. His head rolled on his shoulders.

"H'm. We shall see then. Meantime get into that bed," I whispered. "Want help? There."

It was a rather high bed-place with a set of drawers underneath. This amazing swimmer really needed the lift I gave him by seizing his leg. He tumbled in, rolled over on his back, and flung one arm across his eyes. And then, with his face nearly hidden, he must have looked exactly as I used to look in that bed. I gazed upon my other self for a while before drawing across carefully the two green serge curtains which ran on a brass rod. I thought for a moment of pinning them together for greater safety, but I sat down on the couch, and once there I felt unwilling to rise and hunt for a pin. I would do it in a moment. I was extremely tired, in a peculiarly intimate way, by the strain of stealthiness, by the effort of whispering and the general secrecy of his excitement. It was three o'clock by now and I had been on my feet since nine, but I was not sleepy; I could not have gone to sleep. I sat there, fagged out, looking at the curtains, trying to clear my mind of the confused sensation of being in two places at once, and greatly bothered by an exasperating knocking in my head. It was a relief to discover suddenly that it was not in my head at all, but on the outside of the door. Before I could collect myself the words "Come in" were out of my mouth, and the steward entered with a tray, bringing in my morning coffee. I had slept, after all, and I was so frightened that I shouted, "This way! I am here, steward," as though he had been miles away. He put down the tray on the table next the couch and only then said, very quietly, "I can see you are here, sir." I felt him give me a keen look, but I dared not meet his eyes just then. He must have wondered why I had drawn the curtains of my bed before going to sleep on the couch. He went out, hooking the door open as usual.

I heard the crew washing decks above me. I knew I would have been told at once if there had been any wind. Calm, I thought, and I was doubly vexed. Indeed, I felt dual more than ever. The steward reappeared suddenly in the doorway. I jumped up from the couch so quickly that he gave a start.

"What do you want here?"

"Close your port, sir—they are washing decks."

"It is closed," I said, reddening.

"Very well, sir." But he did not move from the doorway and returned my stare in an extraordinary, equivocal manner for a time. Then his eyes wavered, all his expression changed, and in a voice unusually gentle, almost coaxingly:

"May I come in to take the empty cup away, sir?"

"Of course!" I turned my back on him while he popped in and out. Then I unhooked and closed the door and even pushed the bolt. This sort of thing could not go on very long. The cabin was as hot as an oven, too. I took a peep at my double, and discovered that he had not moved, his arm was still over his eyes; but his chest heaved; his hair was wet; his chin glistened with perspiration. I reached over him and opened the port.

"I must show myself on deck," I reflected.

Of course, theoretically, I could do what I liked, with no one to say nay to me within the whole circle of the horizon; but to lock my cabin door and take the key away I did not dare. Directly I put my head out of the companion I saw the group of my two officers, the second mate barefooted, the chief mate in long india-rubber boots, near the break of the poop, and the steward half-way down the poop-ladder talking to them eagerly. He happened to catch sight of me and dived, the second ran down on the main-deck shouting some order or other, and the chief mate came to meet me, touching his cap.

There was a sort of curiosity in his eye that I did not like. I don't know whether the steward had told them that I was "queer" only, or downright drunk, but I know the man meant to have a good look at me. I watched him coming with a smile which, as he got into point-blank range, took effect and froze his very whiskers. I did not give him time to open his lips.

"Square the yards by lifts and braces before the hands go to breakfast."

It was the first particular order I had given on board that ship; and I stayed on deck to see it executed, too. I had felt the need of asserting myself without loss of time. That sneering young cub got taken down a peg or two on that occasion, and I also seized the opportunity of having a good look at the face of every foremast man as they filed past me to go to the after braces. At breakfast time, eating nothing myself, I presided with such frigid dignity that the two mates were only too glad to escape from the cabin as soon as decency permitted; and all the time the dual working of my mind distracted me almost to the point of insanity. I was constantly watching myself, my secret self, as dependent on my actions as my own personality, sleeping in that bed, behind that door which faced me as I sat at the head of the table. It was very much like being mad, only it was worse because one was aware of it.

I had to shake him for a solid minute, but when at last he opened his eyes it was in the full possession of his senses, with an inquiring look.

"All's well so far," I whispered. "Now you must vanish into the bath-room."

He did so, as noiseless as a ghost, and then I rang for the steward, and facing him boldly, directed him to tidy up my stateroom while I was having my bath—"and be quick about it." As my tone admitted of no excuses, he said, "Yes, sir," and ran off to fetch his dust-pan and brushes. I took a bath and did most of my dressing, splashing, and whistling softly for the steward's edification, while the secret sharer of my life stood drawn up bolt upright in that little space, his face looking very sunken in daylight, his eyelids lowered under the stern, dark line of his eyebrows drawn together by a slight frown.

When I left him there to go back to my room the steward was finishing dusting. I sent for the mate and engaged him in some insignificant conversation. It was, as it were, trifling with the terrific character of his whiskers; but my object was to give him an opportunity for a good look at my cabin. And then I could at last shut, with a clear conscience, the door of my stateroom and get my double back into the recessed part. There was nothing else for it. He had to sit still on a small folding stool, half smothered by the heavy coats hanging there. We listened to the steward going into the bath-room out of the saloon, filling the water-bottles there, scrubbing the bath, setting things to rights, whisk, bang, clatter—out again into the saloon—turn the key—click. Such was my scheme for keeping my second self invisible. Nothing better could be contrived under the circumstances. And there we sat; I at my writing-desk ready to appear busy with some papers, he behind me out of sight of the door. It would not have been prudent to talk in daytime; and I could not have stood the excitement of that queer sense of whispering to myself. Now and then, glancing over my shoulder, I saw him far back there, sitting rigidly on the low stool, his bare feet close together, his arms folded, his head hanging on his breast—and perfectly still. Anybody would have taken him for me.

I was fascinated by it myself. Every moment I had to glance over my shoulder. I was looking at him when a voice outside the door said:

"Beg pardon, sir."

"Well!" . . . I kept my eyes on him, and so when the voice outside the door announced, "There's a ship's boat coming our way, sir," I saw him give a start—the first movement he had made for hours. But he did not raise his bowed head.

'All right. Get the ladder over."

I hesitated. Should I whisper something to him? But what? His immobility seemed to have been never disturbed. What could I tell him he did not know already? . . . Finally I went on deck.

II

The skipper of the *Sephora* had a thin red whisker all round his face, and the sort of complexion that goes with hair of that colour; also the particular, rather smeary shade of blue in the eyes. He was not exactly a showy figure; his shoulders were high, his stature but middling—one leg slightly more bandy than the other. He shook hands, looking vaguely around. A spiritless tenacity was his main characteristic, I judged. I behaved with a politeness which seemed to disconcert him. Perhaps he was shy. He mumbled to me as if he were ashamed of what he was saying; gave his name (it was something like Archbold—but at this distance of years I hardly am sure), his ship's name, and a few other particulars of that sort, in the manner of a criminal making a reluctant and doleful confession. He had had terrible weather on the passage out—terrible—terrible—wife aboard, too.

By this time we were seated in the cabin and the steward brought in a tray with a bottle and glasses. "Thanks! No." Never took liquor. Would have some water, though. He drank two tumblerfuls. Terrible thirsty work. Ever since daylight had been exploring the islands round his ship.

"What was that for—fun?" I asked, with an appearance of polite interest.

"No!" He sighed. "Painful duty."

As he persisted in his mumbling and I wanted my double to hear every word, I hit upon the notion of informing him that I regretted to say I was hard of hearing.

"Such a young man, too!" he nodded, keeping his smeary blue, unintelligent eyes fastened upon me. What was the cause of it—some disease? he inquired, without the least sympathy and as if he thought that, if so, I'd got no more than I deserved.

"Yes; disease," I admitted in a cheerful tone which seemed to shock him. But my point was gained, because he had to raise his voice to give me his tale. It is not worth while to record that version. It was just over two months since all this had happened, and he had thought so much about it that he seemed completely muddled as to its bearings, but still immensely impressed.

"What would you think of such a thing happening on board your own ship? I've had the *Sephora* for these fifteen years. I am a well-known shipmaster."

He was densely distressed—and perhaps I should have sympathised with him if I had been able to detach my mental vision from the unsuspected sharer of my cabin as though he were my second self. There he was on the other side of the bulkhead, four or five feet from us, no more, as we sat in the saloon. I looked politely at Captain Archbold (if that was his name), but it was the other I saw; in a grey sleeping-suit, seated on a low stool, his bare feet close together, his arms folded, and every word said between us falling into the ears of his dark head bowed on his chest.

"I have been at sea now, man and boy, for seven-and-thirty years, and I've never heard of such a thing happening in an English ship. And that it should be my ship. Wife on board, too."

I was hardly listening to him.

"Don't you think," I said, "that the heavy sea which, you told me, came aboard just then might have killed the man? I have seen the sheer weight of a sea kill a man very neatly, by simply breaking his neck."

"Good God!" he uttered, impressively, fixing his smeary blue eyes on me. "The sea! No man killed by the sea ever looked like that." He seemed positively scandalised at my suggestion. And as I gazed at him, certainly not prepared for anything original on his part, he advanced his head close to mine and thrust his tongue out at me so suddenly that I couldn't help starting back.

After scoring over my calmness in this graphic way he nodded wisely. If I had seen the sight, he assured me, I would never forget it as long as I lived. The weather was too bad to give the corpse a proper sea burial. So next day at dawn they took it up on the poop, covering its face with a bit of bunting; he read a short prayer, and then, just as it was, in its oil-skins and long boots, they launched it amongst those mountainous seas that seemed ready every moment to swallow up the ship herself and the terrified lives on board of her.

"That reefed foresail saved you," I threw in.

"Under God—it did," he exclaimed fervently. "It was by a special mercy, I firmly believe, that it stood some of those hurricane squalls."

"It was the setting of that sail which ——" I began.

"God's own hand in it," he interrupted me. "Nothing less could have done it. I don't mind telling you that I hardly dared give the order. It seemed impossible that we could touch anything without losing it, and then our last hope would have been gone."

The terror of that gale was on him yet. I let him go on for a bit, then said, casually—as if returning to a minor subject:

"You were very anxious to give up your mate to the shore people, I believe?"

He was. To the law. His obscure tenacity on that point had in it something incomprehensible and a little awful; something, as it were, mystical, quite apart from his anxiety that he should not be suspected of "countenancing any doings of that sort." Seven-and-thirty virtuous years at sea, of which over twenty of immaculate command, and the last fifteen in the *Sephora*, seemed to have laid him under some pitiless obligation.

"And you know," he went on, groping shamefacedly amongst his feelings, "I did not engage that young fellow. His people had some interest with my owners. I was in a way forced to take him on. He looked very smart, very gentlemanly, and all that. But do you know—I never liked him, somehow. I am a plain man. You see, he wasn't exactly the sort for the chief mate of a ship like the *Sephora*."

I had become so connected in thoughts and impressions with the secret sharer of my cabin that I felt as if I, personally, were being given to understand that I, too, was not the sort that would have done for the chief mate of a ship like the *Sephora*. I had no doubt of it in my mind.

"Not at all the style of man. You understand," he insisted, superfluously, looking hard at me.

I smiled urbanely. He seemed at a loss for a while.

"I suppose I must report a suicide."

"Beg pardon?"

"Sui-cide! That's what I'll have to write to my owners directly I get in."

"Unless you manage to recover him before to-morrow," I assented, dispassionately. . . . "I mean, alive."

He mumbled something which I really did not catch, and I turned my ear to him in a puzzled manner. He fairly bawled:

"The land—I say, the mainland is at least seven miles off my anchorage."

"About that."

My lack of excitement, of curiosity, of surprise, of any sort of pronounced interest, began to arouse his distrust. But except for the felicitous pretence of deafness I had not tried to pretend anything. I had felt utterly incapable of playing the part of ignorance properly, and therefore was afraid to try. It is also certain that he had brought some ready-made suspicions with him, and that he viewed my politeness as a strange and unnatural phenomenon. And yet how else could I have received him? Not heartily! That was impossible for psychological reasons, which I need not state here. My only object was to keep off his inquiries. Surlily? Yes, but surliness might have provoked a point-blank question. From its novelty to him and from its nature, punctilious courtesy was the manner best calculated to restrain the man. But there was the danger of his breaking through my defence bluntly. I could not, I think, have met him by a direct lie, also for psychological (not moral) reasons. If he had only known how afraid I was of his putting my feeling of identity with the other to the test! But, strangely enough—(I thought of it only afterwards)—I believe that he was not a little disconcerted by the reverse side of that weird situation, by something in me that reminded him of the man he

was seeking—suggested a mysterious similitude to the young fellow he had distrusted and disliked from the first.

However that might have been, the silence was not very prolonged. He took another oblique step.

"I reckon I had no more than a two-mile pull to your ship. Not a bit more."

"And quite enough, too, in this awful heat," I said.

Another pause full of mistrust followed. Necessity, they say, is mother of invention, but fear, too, is not barren of ingenious suggestions. And I was afraid he would ask me point-blank for news of my other self.

"Nice little saloon, isn't it?" I remarked, as if noticing for the first time the way his eyes roamed from one closed door to the other. "And very well fitted out, too. Here, for instance," I continued, reaching over the back of my seat negligently and flinging the door open, "is my bath-room."

He made an eager movement, but hardly gave it a glance. I got up, shut the door of the bath-room, and invited him to have a look round, as if I were very proud of my accommodation. He had to rise and be shown round, but he went through the business without any raptures whatever.

"And now we'll have a look at my stateroom," I declared, in a voice as loud as I dared to make it, crossing the cabin to the starboard side with purposely heavy steps.

He followed me in and gazed around. My intelligent double had vanished. I played my part.

"Very convenient—isn't it?"

"Very nice. Very comf . . ." He didn't finish and went out brusquely as if to escape from some unrighteous wiles of mine. But it was not to be. I had been too frightened not to feel vengeful; I felt I had him on the run, and I meant to keep him on the run. My polite insistence must have had something menacing in it, because he gave in suddenly. And I did not let him off a single item; mate's room, pantry, storerooms, the very sail-locker which was also under the poop—he had to look into them all. When at last I showed him out on the quarter-deck he drew a long, spiritless sigh, and mumbled dismally that he must really be going back to his ship now. I desired my mate, who had joined us, to see to the captain's boat.

The man of whiskers gave a blast on the whistle which he used to wear hanging round his neck, and yelled, "*Sephora's* away!" My double down there in my cabin must have heard, and certainly could not feel more relieved than I. Four fellows came running out from somewhere forward and went over the side, while my own men, appearing on deck too, lined the rail. I escorted my visitor to the gangway ceremoniously, and nearly overdid it. He was a tenacious beast. On the very ladder he lingered, and in that unique, guiltily conscientious manner of sticking to the point:

"I say . . . you . . . you don't think that——"

I covered his voice loudly:

"Certainly not. . . . I am delighted. Good-bye."

I had an idea of what he meant to say, and just saved myself by the privilege of defective hearing. He was too shaken generally to insist, but my mate, close witness of that parting, looked mystified and his face took on a thoughtful cast. As I did not want to appear as if I wished to avoid all communication with my officers, he had the opportunity to address me.

"Seems a very nice man. His boat's crew told our chaps a very extraordinary story, if what I am told by the steward is true. I suppose you had it from the captain, sir?"

"Yes. I had a story from the captain."

"A very horrible affair—isn't it, sir?"

"It is."

"Beats all these tales we hear about murders in Yankee ships."

"I don't think it beats them. I don't think it resembles them in the least."

"Bless my soul—you don't say so! But of course I've no acquaintance whatever with American ships, not I, so I couldn't go against your knowledge. It's horrible enough for me. . . . But the queerest part is that those fellows seemed to have some

idea the man was hidden aboard here. They had really. Did you ever hear of such a thing?"

"Preposterous—isn't it?"

We were walking to and fro athwart the quarter-deck. No one of the crew forward could be seen (the day was Sunday), and the mate pursued:

"There was some little dispute about it. Our chaps took offence. 'As if we would harbour a thing like that,' they said. 'Wouldn't you like to look for him in our coalhole?' Quite a tiff. But they made it up in the end. I suppose he did drown himself. Don't you, sir?"

"I don't suppose anything."

"You have no doubt in the matter, sir?"

"None whatever."

I left him suddenly. I felt I was producing a bad impression, but with my double down there it was most trying to be on deck. And it was almost as trying to be below. Altogether a nerve-trying situation. But on the whole I felt less torn in two when I was with him. There was no one in the whole ship whom I dared take into my confidence. Since the hands had got to know his story, it would have been impossible to pass him off for any one else, and an accidental discovery was to be dreaded now more than ever. . . .

The steward being engaged in laying the table for dinner, we could talk only with our eyes when I first went down. Later in the afternoon we had a cautious try at whispering. The Sunday quietness of the ship was against us; the stillness of air and water around her was against us; the elements, the men were against us—everything was against us in our secret partnership; time itself—for this could not go on forever. The very trust in Providence was, I suppose, denied to his guilt. Shall I confess that this thought cast me down very much? And as to the chapter of accidents which counts for so much in the book of success, I could only hope that it was closed. For what favourable accident could be expected?

"Did you hear everything?" were my first words as soon as we took up our position side by side, leaning over my bed-place.

He had. And the proof of it was his

earnest whisper, "The man told you he hardly dared to give the order."

I understood the reference to be to that saving foresail.

"Yes. He was afraid of it being lost in the setting."

"I assure you he never gave the order. He may think he did, but he never gave it. He stood there with me on the break of the poop after the maintopsail blew away, and whimpered about our last hope —positively whimpered about it and nothing else—and the night coming on! To hear one's skipper go on like that in such weather was enough to drive any fellow out of his mind. It worked me up into a sort of desperation. I just took it into my own hands and went away from him, boiling, and—— But what's the use telling you? *You* know! . . . Do you think that if I had not been pretty fierce with them I should have got the men to do anything? Not it! The bo's'n perhaps? Perhaps! It wasn't a heavy sea—it was a sea gone mad! I suppose the end of the world will be something like that; and a man may have the heart to see it coming once and be done with it—but to have to face it day after day—— I don't blame anybody. I was precious little better than the rest. Only—I was an officer of that old coal-wagon, anyhow——"

"I quite understand," I conveyed that sincere assurance into his ear. He was out of breath with whispering; I could hear him pant slightly. It was all very simple. The same strung-up force which had given twenty-four men a chance, at least, for their lives, had, in a sort of recoil, crushed an unworthy mutinous existence.

But I had no leisure to weigh the merits of the matter—footsteps in the saloon, a heavy knock. "There's enough wind to get under way with, sir." Here was the call of a new claim upon my thoughts and even upon my feelings.

"Turn the hands up," I cried through the door. "I'll be on deck directly."

I was going out to make the acquaintance of my ship. Before I left the cabin our eyes met—the eyes of the only two strangers on board. I pointed to the recessed part where the little camp-stool awaited him and laid my finger on my lips. He made a gesture—somewhat vague—a little mysterious, accompanied by a faint smile, as if of regret.

This is not the place to enlarge upon the sensations of a man who feels for the first time a ship move under his feet to his own independent word. In my case they were not unalloyed. I was not wholly alone with my command; for there was that stranger in my cabin. Or rather, I was not completely and wholly with her. Part of me was absent. That mental feeling of being in two places at once affected me physically as if the mood of secrecy had penetrated my very soul. Before an hour had elapsed since the ship had begun to move, having occasion to ask the mate (he stood by my side) to take a compass bearing of the Pagoda, I caught myself reaching up to his ear in whispers. I say I caught myself, but enough had escaped to startle the man. I can't describe it otherwise than by saying that he shied. A grave, preoccupied manner, as though he were in possession of some perplexing intelligence, did not leave him henceforth. A little later I moved away from the rail to look at the compass with such a stealthy gait that the helmsman noticed it —and I could not help noticing the unusual roundness of his eyes. These are trifling instances, though it's to no commander's advantage to be suspected of ludicrous eccentricities. But I was also more seriously affected. There are to a seaman certain words, gestures, that should in given conditions come as naturally, as instinctively as the winking of a menaced eye. A certain order should spring on to his lips without thinking; a certain sign should get itself made, so to speak, without reflection. But all unconscious alertness had abandoned me. I had to make an effort of will to recall myself back (from the cabin) to the conditions of the moment. I felt that I was appearing an irresolute commander to those people who were watching me more or less critically.

And, besides, there were the scares. On the second day out, for instance, coming off the deck in the afternoon (I had straw slippers on my bare feet) I stopped at the open pantry door and spoke to the steward. He was doing something there with his back to me. At the sound of my voice he nearly jumped out of his skin, as the saying is, and incidentally broke a cup.

"What on earth's the matter with you?" I asked, astonished.

He was extremely confused. "Beg your pardon, sir. I made sure you were in your cabin."

"You see I wasn't."

"No, sir. I could have sworn I had heard you moving in there not a moment ago. It's most extraordinary . . . very sorry, sir."

I passed on with an inward shudder. I was so identified with my secret double that I did not even mention the fact in those scanty, fearful whispers we exchanged. I suppose he had made some slight noise of some kind or other. It would have been miraculous if he hadn't at one time or another. And yet, haggard as he appeared, he looked always perfectly self-controlled, more than calm—almost invulnerable. On my suggestion he remained almost entirely in the bathroom, which, upon the whole, was the safest place. There could be really no shadow of an excuse for any one ever wanting to go in there, once the steward had done with it. It was a very tiny place. Sometimes he reclined on the floor, his legs bent, his head sustained on one elbow. At others I would find him on the camp-stool, sitting in his grey sleeping-suit and with his cropped dark hair like a patient, unmoved convict. At night I would smuggle him into my bed-place, and we would whisper together, with the regular footfalls of the officer of the watch passing and repassing over our heads. It was an infinitely miserable time. It was lucky that some tins of fine preserves were stowed in a locker in my stateroom; hard bread I could always get hold of; and so he lived on stewed chicken, paté de foie gras, asparagus, cooked oysters, sardines—on all sorts of abominable sham delicacies out of tins. My early morning coffee he always drank; and it was all I dared do for him in that respect.

Every day there was the horrible manœuvring to go through so that my room

and then the bath-room should be done in the usual way. I came to hate the sight of the steward, to abhor the voice of that harmless man. I felt that it was he who would bring on the disaster of discovery. It hung like a sword over our heads.

The fourth day out, I think (we were then working down the east side of the Gulf of Siam, tack for tack, in light winds and smooth water)—the fourth day, I say, of this miserable juggling with the unavoidable, as we sat at our evening meal, that man, whose slightest movement I dreaded, after putting down the dishes ran up on deck busily. This could not be dangerous. Presently he came down again; and then it appeared that he remembered a coat of mine which I had thrown over a rail to dry after having been wetted in a shower which had passed over the ship in the afternoon. Sitting stolidly at the head of the table I became terrified at the sight of the garment on his arm. Of course he made for my door. There was no time to lose.

"Steward," I thundered. My nerves were so shaken that I could not govern my voice and conceal my agitation. This was the sort of thing that made my terrifically whiskered mate tap his forehead with his forefinger. I had detected him using that gesture while talking on deck with a confidential air to the carpenter. It was too far to hear a word, but I had no doubt that this pantomime could only refer to the strange new captain.

"Yes, sir," the pale-faced steward turned resignedly to me. It was this maddening course of being shouted at, checked without rhyme or reason, arbitrarily chased out of my cabin, suddenly called into it, sent flying out of his pantry on incomprehensible errands, that accounted for the growing wretchedness of his expression.

"Where are you going with that coat?"

"To your room, sir."

"Is there another shower coming?"

"I'm sure I don't know, sir. Shall I go up again and see, sir?"

"No! never mind."

My object was attained, as of course my other self in there would have heard everything that passed. During this interlude my two officers never raised their eyes off their respective plates; but the lip of that confounded cub, the second mate, quivered visibly.

I expected the steward to hook my coat on and come out at once. He was very slow about it; but I dominated my nervousness sufficiently not to shout after him. Suddenly I became aware (it could be heard plainly enough) that the fellow for some reason or other was opening the door of the bath-room. It was the end. The place was literally not big enough to swing a cat in. My voice died in my throat and I went stony all over. I expected to hear a yell of surprise and terror, and made a movement, but had not the strength to get on my legs. Everything remained still. Had my second self taken the poor wretch by the throat? I don't know what I could have done next moment if I had not seen the steward come out of my room, close the door, and then stand quietly by the sideboard.

"Saved," I thought. "But, no! Lost! Gone! He was gone!"

I laid my knife and fork down and leaned back in my chair. My head swam. After a while, when sufficiently recovered to speak in a steady voice, I instructed my mate to put the ship round at eight o'clock himself.

"I won't come on deck," I went on. "I think I'll turn in, and unless the wind shifts I don't want to be disturbed before midnight. I feel a bit seedy."

"You did look middling bad a little while ago," the chief mate remarked without showing any great concern.

They both went out, and I stared at the steward clearing the table. There was nothing to be read on that wretched man's face. But why did he avoid my eyes I asked myself. Then I thought I should like to hear the sound of his voice.

"Steward!"

"Sir!" Startled as usual.

"Where did you hang up that coat?"

"In the bath-room, sir." The usual anxious tone. "It's not quite dry yet, sir."

For some time longer I sat in the cuddy. Had my double vanished as he had come? But of his coming there was an explanation, whereas his disappearance would be inexplicable. . . . I went slowly into my dark room, shut the door, lighted the lamp, and for a time dared not turn round. When at last I did I saw him standing bolt-upright in the narrow recessed part. It would not be true to say I had a shock, but an irresistible doubt of his bodily existence flitted through my mind. Can it be, I asked myself, that he is not visible to other eyes than mine? It was like being haunted. Motionless, with a grave face, he raised his hands slightly at me in a gesture which meant clearly, "Heavens! what a narrow escape!" Narrow indeed. I think I had come creeping quietly as near insanity as any man who has not actually gone over the border. That gesture restrained me, so to speak.

The mate with the terrific whiskers was now putting the ship on the other tack. In the moment of profound silence which follows upon the hands going to their stations I heard on the poop his raised voice: "Hard alee!" and the distant shout of the order repeated on the maindeck. The sails, in that light breeze, made but a faint fluttering noise. It ceased. The ship was coming round slowly; I held my breath in the renewed stillness of expectation; one wouldn't have thought that there was a single living soul on her decks. A sudden brisk shout, "Mainsail haul!" broke the spell, and in the noisy cries and rush overhead of the men running away with the main-brace we two, down in my cabin, came together in our usual position by the bed-place.

He did not wait for my question. "I heard him fumbling here and just managed to squat myself down in the bath," he whispered to me. "The fellow only opened the door and put his arm in to hang the coat up. All the same——"

"I never thought of that," I whispered back, even more appalled than before at the closeness of the shave, and marvelling at that something unyielding in his character which was carrying him through so finely. There was no agitation in his whisper. Whoever was being driven distracted, it was not he. He was sane. And the proof of his sanity was continued when he took up the whispering again.

"It would never do for me to come to life again."

It was something that a ghost might

have said. But what he was alluding to was his old captain's reluctant admission of the theory of suicide. It would obviously serve his turn—if I had understood at all the view which seemed to govern the unalterable purpose of his action.

"You must maroon me as soon as ever you can get amongst these islands off the Cambodje shore," he went on.

"Maroon you! We are not living in a boy's adventure tale," I protested. His scornful whispering took me up.

"We aren't indeed! There's nothing of a boy's tale in this. But there's nothing else for it. I want no more. You don't suppose I am afraid of what can be done to me? Prison or gallows or whatever they may please. But you don't see me coming back to explain such things to an old fellow in a wig and twelve respectable tradesmen, do you? What can they know whether I am guilty or not—or of *what* I am guilty, either? That's my affair. What does the Bible say? 'Driven off the face of the earth.' Very well. I am off the face of the earth now. As I came at night so I shall go."

"Impossible!" I murmured. "You can't."

"Can't? . . . Not naked like a soul on the Day of Judgment. I shall freeze on to this sleeping-suit. The Last Day is not yet —and . . . you have understood thoroughly. Didn't you?"

I felt suddenly ashamed of myself. I may say truly that I understood—and my hesitation in letting that man swim away from my ship's side had been a mere sham sentiment, a sort of cowardice.

"It can't be done now till next night," I breathed out. "The ship is on the off-shore tack and the wind may fail us."

"As long as I know that you understand," he whispered. "But of course you do. It's a great satisfaction to have got somebody to understand. You seem to have been there on purpose." And in the same whisper, as if we two whenever we talked had to say things to each other which were not fit for the world to hear, he added, "It's very wonderful."

We remained side by side talking in our secret way—but sometimes silent or just exchanging a whispered word or two at long intervals. And as usual he stared through the port. A breath of wind came now and again into our faces. The ship might have been moored in dock, so gently and on an even keel she slipped through the water, that did not murmur even at our passage, shadowy and silent like a phantom sea.

At midnight I went on deck, and to my mate's great surprise put the ship round on the other tack. His terrible whiskers flitted round me in silent criticism. I certainly should not have done it if it had been only a question of getting out of that sleepy gulf as quickly as possible. I believe he told the second mate, who relieved him, that it was a great want of judgment. The other only yawned. That intolerable cub shuffled about so sleepily and lolled against the rails in such a slack, improper fashion that I came down on him sharply.

"Aren't you properly awake yet?"

"Yes, sir! I am awake."

"Well, then, be good enough to hold yourself as if you were. And keep a lookout. If there's any current we'll be closing with some islands before daylight."

The east side of the gulf is fringed with islands, some solitary, others in groups. On the blue background of the high coast they seem to float on silvery patches of calm water, arid and grey, or dark green and rounded like clumps of evergreen bushes, with the larger ones, a mile or two long, showing the outlines of ridges, ribs of grey rock under the dank mantle of matted leafage. Unknown to trade, to travel, almost to geography, the manner of life they harbour is an unsolved secret. There must be villages—settlements of fishermen at least—on the largest of them, and some communication with the world is probably kept up by native craft. But all that forenoon, as we headed for them, fanned along by the faintest of breezes, I saw no sign of man or canoe in the field of the telescope I kept on pointing at the scattered group.

At noon I gave no orders for a change of course, and the mate's whiskers became much concerned and seemed to be offering themselves unduly to my notice. At last I said:

"I am going to stand right in. Quite in —as far as I can take her."

The stare of extreme surprise imparted an air of ferocity also to his eyes, and he looked truly terrific for a moment.

"We're not doing well in the middle of the gulf," I continued, casually. "I am going to look for the land breezes to-night."

"Bless my soul! Do you mean, sir, in the dark amongst the lot of all them islands and reefs and shoals?"

"Well—if there are any regular land breezes at all on this coast one must get close inshore to find them, mustn't one?"

"Bless my soul!" he exclaimed again under his breath. All that afternoon he wore a dreamy, contemplative appearance which in him was a mark of perplexity. After dinner I went into my stateroom as if I meant to take some rest. There we two bent our dark heads over a half-unrolled chart lying on my bed.

"There," I said. "It's got to be Koh-ring. I've been looking at it ever since sunrise. It has got two hills and a low point. It must be inhabited. And on the coast opposite there is what looks like the mouth of a biggish river—with some town, no doubt, not far up. It's the best chance for you that I can see."

"Anything. Koh-ring let it be."

He looked thoughtfully at the chart as if surveying chances and distances from a lofty height—and following with his eyes his own figure wandering on the blank land of Cochin-China, and then passing off that piece of paper clean out of sight into uncharted regions. And it was as if the ship had two captains to plan her course for her. I had been so worried and restless running up and down that I had not had the patience to dress that day. I had remained in my sleeping-suit, with straw slippers and a soft floppy hat. The closeness of the heat in the gulf had been most oppressive, and the crew were used to see me wandering in that airy attire.

"She will clear the south point as she heads now," I whispered into his ear. "Goodness only knows when, though, but certainly after dark. I'll edge her in to half a mile, as far as I may be able to judge in the dark——"

"Be careful," he murmured, warningly —and I realised suddenly that all my future, the only future for which I was fit, would perhaps go irretrievably to pieces in any mishap to my first command.

I could not stop a moment longer in the room. I motioned him to get out of sight and made my way on the poop. That unplayful cub had the watch. I walked up and down for a while thinking things out, then beckoned him over.

"Send a couple of hands to open the two quarter-deck ports," I said, mildly.

He actually had the impudence, or else so forgot himself in his wonder at such an incomprehensible order, as to repeat:

"Open the quarter-deck ports! What for, sir?"

"The only reason you need concern yourself about is because I tell you to do so. Have them open wide and fastened properly."

He reddened and went off, but I believe made some jeering remark to the carpenter as to the sensible practice of ventilating a ship's quarter-deck. I know he popped into the mate's cabin to impart the fact to him because the whiskers came on deck, as it were by chance, and stole glances at me from below—for signs of lunacy or drunkenness, I suppose.

A little before supper, feeling more restless than ever, I rejoined, for a moment, my second self. And to find him sitting so quietly was surprising, like something against nature, inhuman.

I developed my plan in a hurried whisper.

"I shall stand in as close as I dare and then put her round. I will presently find means to smuggle you out of here into the sail-locker, which communicates with the lobby. But there is an opening, a sort of square for hauling the sails out, which gives straight on the quarter-deck and which is never closed in fine weather, so as to give air to the sails. When the ship's way is deadened in stays and all the hands are aft at the main-braces you will have a clear road to slip out and get overboard through the open quarter-deck port. I've had them both fastened up. Use a rope's end to lower yourself into the water so as to avoid a splash—you know. It could be heard and cause some beastly complication."

He kept silent for a while, then whispered, "I understand."

"I won't be there to see you go," I began with an effort. "The rest . . . I only hope I have understood, too."

"You have. From first to last"—and for the first time there seemed to be a faltering, something strained in his whisper. He caught hold of my arm, but the ringing of the supper bell made me start. He didn't, though; he only released his grip.

After supper I didn't come below again till well past eight o'clock. The faint, steady breeze was loaded with dew; and the wet, darkened sails held all there was of propelling power in it. The night, clear and starry, sparkled darkly, and the opaque, lightless patches shifting slowly against the low stars were the drifting islets. On the port bow there was a big one more distant and shadowily imposing by the great space of sky it eclipsed.

On opening the door I had a back view of my very own self looking at a chart. He had come out of the recess and was standing near the table.

"Quite dark enough," I whispered.

He stepped back and leaned against my bed with a level, quiet glance. I sat on the couch. We had nothing to say to each other. Over our heads the officer of the watch moved here and there. Then I heard him move quickly. I knew what that meant. He was making for the companion; and presently his voice was outside my door.

"We are drawing in pretty fast, sir. Land looks rather close."

"Very well," I answered. "I am coming on deck directly."

I waited till he was gone out of the cuddy, then rose. My double moved too. The time had come to exchange our last whispers, for neither of us was ever to hear each other's natural voice.

"Look here!" I opened a drawer and took out three sovereigns. "Take this anyhow. I've got six and I'd give you the lot, only I must keep a little money to buy some fruit and vegetables for the crew from native boats as we go through Sunda Straits."

He shook his head.

"Take it," I urged him, whispering desperately. "No one can tell what——"

He smiled and slapped meaningly the only pocket of the sleeping-jacket. It was not safe, certainly. But I produced a large old silk handkerchief of mine, and tying the three pieces of gold in a corner, pressed it on him. He was touched, I suppose, because he took it at last and tied it quickly round his waist under the jacket, on his bare skin.

Our eyes met; several seconds elapsed, till, our glances still mingled, I extended my hand and turned the lamp out. Then I passed through the cuddy, leaving the door of my room wide open. . . . "Steward!"

He was still lingering in the pantry in the greatness of his zeal, giving a rub-up to a plated cruet stand the last thing before going to bed. Being careful not to wake up the mate, whose room was opposite, I spoke in an undertone.

He looked round anxiously. "Sir!"

"Can you get me a little hot water from the galley?"

"I am afraid, sir, the galley fire's been out for some time now."

"Go and see."

He flew up the stairs.

"Now," I whispered, loudly, into the saloon—too loudly, perhaps, but I was afraid I couldn't make a sound. He was by my side in an instant—the double captain slipped past the stairs—through a tiny dark passage . . . a sliding door. We were in the sail-locker, scrambling on our knees over the sails. A sudden thought struck me. I saw myself wandering barefooted, bareheaded, the sun beating on my dark poll. I snatched off my floppy hat and tried hurriedly in the dark to ram it on my other self. He dodged and fended off silently. I wonder what he thought had come to me before he understood and suddenly desisted. Our hands met gropingly, lingered united in a steady, motionless clasp for a second. . . . No word was breathed by either of us when they separated.

I was standing quietly by the pantry door when the steward returned.

"Sorry, sir. Kettle barely warm. Shall I light the spirit-lamp?"

"Never mind."

I came out on deck slowly. It was now a matter of conscience to shave the land as close as possible—for now he must go overboard whenever the ship was put in stays. Must! There could be no going back for him. After a moment I walked over to leeward and my heart flew into my mouth at the nearness of the land on the bow. Under any other circumstances I would not have held on a minute longer. The second mate had followed me anxiously.

I looked on till I felt I could command my voice.

"She may weather," I said then in a quiet tone.

"Are you going to try that, sir?" he stammered out incredulously.

I took no notice of him and raised my tone just enough to be heard by the helmsman.

"Keep her good full."

"Good full, sir."

The wind fanned my cheek, the sails slept, the world was silent. The strain of watching the dark loom of the land grow bigger and denser was too much for me. I had shut my eyes—because the ship must go closer. She must! The stillness was intolerable. Were we standing still?

When I opened my eyes the second view started my heart with a thump. The black southern hill of Koh-ring seemed to hang right over the ship like a towering fragment of the everlasting night. On that enormous mass of blackness there was not a gleam to be seen, not a sound to be heard. It was gliding irresistibly towards us and yet seemed already within reach of the hand. I saw the vague figures of the watch grouped in the waist, gazing in awed silence.

"Are you going on, sir?" inquired an unsteady voice at my elbow.

I ignored it. I had to go on.

"Keep her full. Don't check her way. That won't do now," I said, warningly.

"I can't see the sails very well," the helmsman answered me, in strange, quavering tones.

Was she close enough? Already she was, I won't say in the shadow of the land, but in the very blackness of it, already swallowed up as it were, gone too close to be recalled, gone from me altogether.

"Give the mate a call," I said to the young man who stood at my elbow as still as death. "And turn all hands up."

My tone had a borrowed loudness reverberated from the height of the land. Several voices cried out together: "We are all on deck, sir."

Then stillness again, with the great shadow gliding closer, towering higher, without light, without a sound. Such a hush had fallen on the ship that she might have been a bark of the dead floating in slowly under the very gate of Erebus.

"My God! Where are we?"

It was the mate moaning at my elbow. He was thunderstruck, and as it were deprived of the moral support of his whiskers. He clapped his hands and absolutely cried out, "Lost!"

"Be quiet," I said, sternly.

He lowered his tone, but I saw the shadowy gesture of his despair. "What are we doing here?"

"Looking for the land wind."

He made as if to tear his hair, and addressed me recklessly.

"She will never get out. You have done it, sir. I knew it'd end in something like this. She will never weather, and you are too close now to stay. She'll drift ashore before she's round. O my God!"

I caught his arm as he was raising it to batter his poor devoted head, and shook it violently.

"She's ashore already," he wailed, trying to tear himself away.

"Is she? . . . Keep good full there!"

"Good full, sir," cried the helmsman in a frightened, thin, child-like voice.

I hadn't let go the mate's arm and went on shaking it. "Ready about, do you hear? You go forward"—shake—"and stop there"—shake—"and hold your noise"—shake—"and see these head-sheets properly overhauled"—shake, shake—shake.

And all the time I dared not look towards the land lest my heart should fail me. I released my grip at last and he ran forward as if fleeing for dear life.

I wondered what my double there in

the sail-locker thought of this commotion. He was able to hear everything—and perhaps he was able to understand why, on my conscience, it had to be thus close—no less. My first order "Hard alee!" re-echoed ominously under the towering shadow of Koh-ring as if I had shouted in a mountain gorge. And then I watched the land intently. In that smooth water and light wind it was impossible to feel the ship coming-to. No! I could not feel her. And my second self was making now ready to slip out and lower himself overboard. Perhaps he was gone already . . . ?

The great black mass brooding over our very mastheads began to pivot away from the ship's side silently. And now I forgot the secret stranger ready to depart, and remembered only that I was a total stranger to the ship. I did not know her. Would she do it? How was she to be handled?

I swung the mainyard and waited helplessly. She was perhaps stopped, and her very fate hung in the balance, with the black mass of Koh-ring like the gate of the everlasting night towering over her taffrail. What would she do now? Had she way on her yet? I stepped to the side swiftly, and on the shadowy water I could see nothing except a faint phosphorescent flash revealing the glassy smoothness of the sleeping surface. It was impossible to tell—and I had not learned yet the feel of my ship. Was she moving? What I needed was something easily seen, a piece of paper, which I could throw overboard and watch. I had nothing on me. To run down for it I didn't dare. There was no time. All at once my strained, yearning stare distinguished a white object floating within a yard of the ship's side. White on the black water. A phosphorescent flash passed under it. What was that thing? . . . I recognised my own floppy hat. It must have fallen off his head . . . and he didn't bother. Now I had what I wanted—the saving mark for my eyes. But I hardly thought of my other self, now gone from the ship, to be hidden for ever from all

friendly faces, to be a fugitive and a vagabond on the earth, with no brand of the curse on his sane forehead to stay a slaying hand . . . too proud to explain.

And I watched the hat—the expression of my sudden pity for his mere flesh. It had been meant to save his homeless head from the dangers of the sun. And now—behold—it was saving the ship, by serving me for a mark to help out the ignorance of my strangeness. Ha! It was drifting forward, warning me just in time that the ship had gathered sternway.

"Shift the helm," I said in a low voice to the seaman standing still like a statue.

The man's eyes glistened wildly in the binnacle light as he jumped round to the other side and spun round the wheel.

I walked to the break of the poop. On the overshadowed deck all hands stood by the forebraces waiting for my order. The stars ahead seemed to be gliding from right to left. And all was so still in the world that I heard the quiet remark "She's round," passed in a tone of intense relief between two seamen.

"Let go and haul."

The foreyards ran round with a great noise, amidst cheery cries. And now the frightful whiskers made themselves heard giving various orders. Already the ship was drawing ahead. And I was alone with her. Nothing! no one in the world should stand now between us, throwing a shadow on the way of silent knowledge and mute affection, the perfect communion of a seaman with his first command.

Walking to the taffrail, I was in time to make out, on the very edge of a darkness thrown by a towering black mass like the very gateway of Erebus—yes, I was in time to catch an evanescent glimpse of my white hat left behind to mark the spot where the secret sharer of my cabin and of my thoughts, as though he were my second self, had lowered himself into the water to take his punishment: a free man, a proud swimmer striking out for a new destiny.

[1910]

QUESTIONS FOR STUDY

1. *What is the Captain's problem as the story begins? What is the source of his misgivings and self-doubts? How are these misgivings and self-doubts projected by the descriptive paragraphs that open the story?*
2. *In what ways is Captain Archbold of the* Sephora *similar to the narrator? In what ways does he differ?*
3. *Why must the Captain rid himself of Leggatt?*
4. *To what extent are both men free at the end of the story?*
5. *What is the function of the Captain's floppy hat? What is its symbolic value?*
6. *The chief debate by critics of "The Secret Sharer" turns on the question of whether Leggatt has an objective existence of his own apart from the mind of the Captain. What details and evidence support either view? Does the acceptance of one view or the other really change the meaning of the story?*

HUBERT CRACKANTHORPE
Anthony Garstin's Courtship

I

A STAMPEDE of huddled sheep, wildly scampering over the slaty shingle, emerged from the leaden mist that muffled the fell-top, and a shrill shepherd's whistle broke the damp stillness of the air. And presently a man's figure appeared, following the sheep down the hillside. He halted a moment to whistle curtly to his two dogs, who, laying back their ears, chased the sheep at top-speed beyond the brow; then, his hands deep in his pockets, he strode vigorously forward. A streak of white smoke from a toiling train was creeping silently across the distance: the great, grey, desolate undulations of treeless country showed no other sign of life.

The sheep hurried in single file along a tiny track worn threadbare amid the brown, lumpy grass: and, as the man came round the mountain's shoulder, a narrow valley opened out beneath him— a scanty patchwork of green fields, and, here and there, a whitewashed farm, flanked by a dark cluster of sheltering trees.

The man walked with a loose, swinging gait. His figure was spare and angular: he wore a battered, black felt hat and clumsy, iron-bound boots: his clothes were dingy from long exposure to the weather. He had close-set, insignificant eyes, much wrinkled, and stubbly eyebrows streaked with grey. His mouth was close-shaven, and drawn by his abstraction into hard and taciturn lines; beneath his chin bristled an unkempt fringe of sandy-coloured hair.

When he reached the foot of the fell, the twilight was already blurring the distance. The sheep scurried, with a noisy rustling, across a flat, swampy stretch, over-grown with rushes, while the dogs headed them towards a gap in a low, ragged wall built of loosely-heaped boulders. The man swung the gate to after them, and waited, whistling peremptorily, recalling the dogs. A moment later, the animals re-appeared, cringing as they crawled through the bars of the gate. He kicked out at them contemptuously, and mounting a stone stile a few yards further up the road, dropped into a narrow lane.

Presently, as he passed a row of lighted windows, he heard a voice call to him. He stopped, and perceived a crooked, white-bearded figure, wearing clerical clothes, standing in the garden gateway.

"Good-evening, Anthony. A raw evening this."

"Ay, Mr. Blencarn, it's a bit frittish," he answered. "I've jest bin gittin' a few lambs off t' fell. I hope ye're keepin' fairly, an' Miss Rosa too." He spoke briefly, with a loud, spontaneous cordiality.

"Thank ye, Anthony, thank ye. Rosa's down at the church, playing over the hymns for to-morrow. How's Mrs. Garstin?"

"Nicely, thank ye, Mr. Blencarn. She's wonderful active, is mother."

"Well, good-night to ye, Anthony," said the old man, clicking the gate.

"Good-night, Mr. Blencarn," he called back.

A few minutes later the twinkling lights of the village came in sight, and from within the sombre form of the square-towered church, looming by the roadside, the slow, solemn strains of the organ floated out on the evening air. Anthony lightened his tread: then paused, listening; but, presently, becoming aware that a man stood, listening also, on the bridge some few yards distant, he moved forward again. Slackening his pace, as he approached, he eyed the figure keenly; but the man paid no heed to him, remaining, with his back turned, gazing over the parapet into the dark, gurgling stream.

Anthony trudged along the empty village street, past the gleaming squares of ruddy gold, starting on either side out of the darkness. Now and then he looked furtively backwards. The straight open road lay behind him, glimmering wanly: the organ seemed to have ceased: the figure on the bridge had left the parapet, and appeared to be moving away towards the church. Anthony halted, watching it till it had disappeared into the blackness beneath the churchyard trees. Then, after a moment's hesitation, he left the road, and mounted an upland meadow towards his mother's farm.

It was a bare, oblong house. In front, a whitewashed porch, and a narrow garden-plot, enclosed by a low iron railing, were dimly discernible: behind, the steep fell-side loomed like a monstrous, mysterious curtain hung across the night. He passed round the back into the twilight of a wide yard, cobbled and partially grass-grown, vaguely flanked by the shadowy outlines of long, low farm-buildings. All was wrapped in darkness: somewhere overhead a bat fluttered, darting its puny scream.

Inside, a blazing peat-fire scattered capering shadows across the smooth, stone floor, flickered among the dim rows of hams suspended from the ceiling and on the panelled cupboards of dark, glistening oak. A servant-girl, spreading the cloth for supper, clattered her clogs in and out of the kitchen: old Mrs. Garstin was stooping before the hearth, tremulously turning some girdle-cakes that lay roasting in the embers.

At the sound of Anthony's heavy tread in the passage, she rose, glancing sharply at the clock above the chimney-piece. She was a heavy-built woman, upright, stalwart almost, despite her years. Her face was gaunt and sallow; deep wrinkles accentuated the hardness of her features. She wore a black widow's cap above her iron-grey hair, gold-rimmed spectacles, and a soiled, chequered apron.

"Ye're varra late, Tony," she remarked querulously.

He unloosened his woollen neckerchief, and when he had hung it methodically with his hat behind the door, answered:

" 'Twas terrible thick on t' fell-top, an' them two bitches be that senseless."

She caught his sleeve, and, through her spectacles, suspiciously scrutinized his face.

"Ye did na meet wi' Rosa Blencarn?"

"Nay, she was in church, hymn-playin', wi' Luke Stock hangin' roond door," he retorted bitterly, rebuffing her with rough impatience.

She moved away, nodding sententiously to herself. They began supper: neither spoke: Anthony sat slowly stirring his tea, and staring moodily into the flames: the bacon on his plate lay untouched. From time to time his mother, laying down her knife and fork, looked across at him in unconcealed asperity, pursing her wide, ungainly mouth. At last, abruptly setting down her cup, she broke out:

"I wonder ye hav'na mare pride, Tony. For hoo lang are ye goin' t' continue settin' mopin' and broodin' like a seck sheep? Ye'll jest mak yesself ill, an' then I reckon what ye'll prove satisfied. Ay, but I wonder ye hav'na more pride."

But he made no answer, remaining unmoved, as if he had not heard.

Presently, half to himself, without raising his eyes, he murmured:

"Luke be goin' South, Monday."

"Well, ye canna tak' oop wi' his leavin's anyways. It hasna coom t' that, has it? Ye doan't intend settin' all t' parish a laughin' at ye a second occasion?"

He flushed dully, and bending over his plate, mechanically began his supper.

"Wa dang it," he broke out a minute later, "d'ye think I heed the cacklin' o' fifty parishes? Na, not I," and, with a short, grim laugh, he brought his fist down heavily on the oak table.

"Ye're daft, Tony," the old woman blurted.

"Daft or na daft, I tell ye this, mother, that I be forty-six year o' age this backend, and there be some things I will na listen to. Rosa Blencarn's bonny enough for me."

"Ay, bonny enough—I've na patience wi' ye. Bonny enough—tricked oot in her furbelows, gallivantin' wi' every royster fra Pe'rith. Bonny enough—that be all ye think on. She's bin a proper parson's niece—the giddy, feckless creature, an she'd mak' ye a proper sort o' wife, Tony Garstin, ye great, fond booby."

She pushed back her chair, and, hurriedly clattering the crockery, began to clear away the supper.

"T' hoose be mine, t' Lord be praised," she continued in a loud, hard voice, "an' as long as he spare me, Tony, I'll na see Rosa Blencarn set foot inside it."

Anthony scowled, without replying, and drew his chair to the hearth. His mother bustled about the room behind him. After a while she asked:

"Did ye pen t' lambs in t' back field?"

"Na, they're in Hullam bottom," he answered curtly.

The door closed behind her, and by and by he could hear her moving overhead. Meditatively blinking, he filled his pipe clumsily, and pulling a crumpled newspaper from his pocket, sat on over the smouldering fire, reading and stolidly puffing.

II

The music rolled through the dark, empty church. The last, leaden flicker of daylight glimmered in through the pointed windows, and beyond the level rows of dusky pews, tenanted only by a litter of prayer-books, two guttering candles revealed the organ pipes, and the young girl's swaying figure.

She played vigorously. Once or twice the tune stumbled, and she recovered it impatiently, bending over the key-board, showily flourishing her wrists as she touched the stops. She was bare-headed (her hat and cloak lay beside her on a stool). She had fair, fluffy hair, cut short behind her neck; large, round eyes, heightened by a fringe of dark lashes; rough, ruddy cheeks, and a rosy, full-lipped, unstable mouth. She was dressed quite simply, in a black, close-fitting bodice, a little frayed at the sleeves. Her hands and neck were coarsely fashioned: her comeliness was brawny, literal, unfinished, as it were.

When at last the ponderous chords of the Amen faded slowly into the twilight, flushed, breathing a little quickly, she paused, listening to the stillness of the church. Presently a small boy emerged from behind the organ.

"Good-evenin', Miss Rosa," he called, trotting briskly away down the aisle.

"Good-night, Robert," she answered, absently.

After a while, with an impatient gesture, as if to shake some importunate thought from her mind, she rose abruptly, pinned on her hat, threw her cloak round her shoulders, blew out the candles, and groped her way through the church, towards the half-open door. As she hurried along the narrow pathway that led across the churchyard, of a sudden, a figure started out of the blackness.

"Who's that?" she cried, in a loud, frightened voice.

A man's uneasy laugh answered her.

"It's only me, Rosa. I didna think t' scare ye. I've bin waitin' for ye, this hoor past."

She made no reply, but quickened her pace. He strode on beside her.

"I'm off, Monday, ye know," he continued. And, as she said nothing,

"Will ye na stop jest a minnit? I'd like t' speak a few words wi' ye before I go, an to-morrow I hev t' git over t' Scarsdale betimes," he persisted.

"I don't want t' speak wi' ye: I don't want ever to see ye agin. I jest hate the sight o' ye." She spoke with a vehement, concentrated hoarseness.

"Nay, but ye must listen to me. I will na be put off wi' fratchin speeches."

And gripping her arm, he forced her to stop.

"Loose me, ye great beast," she broke out.

"I'll na hould ye, if ye'll jest stand quiet-like. I meant t' speak fair t' ye, Rosa."

They stood at a bend in the road, face to face, quite close together. Behind his burly form stretched the dimness of a grey, ghostly field.

"What is't ye hev to say to me? Hev done wi' it quick," she said sullenly.

"It be jest this, Rosa," he began with dogged gravity. "I want t' tell ye that ef any trouble comes t' ye after I'm gone— ye know t' what I refer—I want t' tell ye that I'm prepared t' act square by ye. I've written out on an envelope my address in London. Luke Stock, care o' Purcell & Co., Smithfield Market, London."

"Ye're a bad, sinful man. I jest hate t' sight o' ye. I wish ye were dead."

"Ay, but I reckon what ye'd ha best thought o' that before. Ye've changed yer whistle considerably since Tuesday. Nay, hould on," he added, as she struggled to push past him. "Here's t' envelope."

She snatched the paper, and tore it passionately, scattering the fragments on to the road. When she had finished, he burst out angrily:

"Ye cussed, unreasonable fool."

"Let me pass, ef ye've nought mare t' say," she cried.

"Nay, I'll na part wi' ye this fashion. Ye can speak soft enough when ye choose. And seizing her shoulders, he forced her backwards against the wall.

"Ye do look fine, an' na mistake, when ye're jest ablaze wi' ragin'," he laughed bluntly, lowering his face to hers.

"Loose me, loose me, ye great coward," she gasped, striving to free her arms.

Holding her fast, he expostulated:

"Coom, Rosa, can we na part friends?"

"Part friends, indeed," she retorted bitterly. "Friends wi' the likes o' you. What d'ye tak me for? Let me git home, I tell ye. An' please God I'll never set eyes on ye again. I hate t' sight o' ye."

"Be off wi' ye, then," he answered, pushing her roughly back into the road. "Be off wi' ye, ye silly. Ye canna say I hav na spak fair t' ye, an', by goom, ye'll na see me shally-wallyin this fashion agin. Be off wi' ye: ye can jest shift for yerself, since ye canna keep a civil tongue in yer head."

The girl, catching at her breath, stood as if dazed, watching his retreating figure; then starting forward at a run, disappeared up the hill, into the darkness.

III

Old Mr. Blencarn concluded his husky sermon. The scanty congregation, who had been sitting, stolidly immobile in their stiff, Sunday clothes, shuffled to their feet, and the pewful of school children, in clamorous chorus, intoned the final hymn. Anthony stood near the organ, absently contemplating, while the rude melody resounded through the church, Rosa's deft manipulation of the key-board. The rugged lines of his face were relaxed to a vacant, thoughtful limpness, that aged his expression not a little: now and then, as if for reference, he glanced questioningly at the girl's profile.

A few minutes later the service was over, and the congregation sauntered out down the aisle. A gawky group of men remained loitering by the church door: one of them called to Anthony; but, nodding curtly, he passed on, and strode away down the road, across the grey upland meadows, towards home. As soon as he had breasted the hill, however, and was no longer visible from below, he turned abruptly to the left, along a small swampy hollow, till he had reached the lane that led down from the fellside.

He clambered over a rugged, moss-grown wall, and stood, gazing expectantly down the dark, disused roadway; then, after a moment's hesitation, perceiving nobody, seated himself beneath the wall, on a projecting slab of stone.

Overhead hung a sombre, drifting sky. A gusty wind rollicked down from the fell —huge masses of chilly grey, stripped of the last night's mist. A few dead leaves fluttered over the stones, and from off the fellside there floated the plaintive, quavering rumour of many bleating sheep.

Before long, he caught sight of two figures coming towards him, slowly climbing the hill. He sat awaiting their approach, fidgeting with his sandy beard, and abstractedly grinding the ground beneath his heel. At the brow they halted: plunging his hands deep into his pockets, he strolled sheepishly towards them.

"Ah! good day t' ye, Anthony," called the old man, in a shrill, breathless voice. "'Tis a long hill, an' my legs are not what they were. Time was when I'd think nought o' a whole day's tramp on t' fells. Ay, I'm gittin' feeble, Anthony, that's what 'tis. And if Rosa here wasn't the great, strong lass she is, I don't know how her old uncle 'd manage;" and he turned to the girl with a proud, tremulous smile.

"Will ye tak my arm a bit, Mr. Blencarn? Miss Rosa 'll be tired, likely," Anthony asked.

"Nay, Mr. Garstin, but I can manage nicely," the girl interrupted sharply.

Anthony looked up at her as she spoke.

She wore a straw hat, trimmed with crimson velvet, and a black, fur-edged cape, that seemed to set off mightily the fine whiteness of her neck. Her large, dark eyes were fixed upon him. He shifted his feet uneasily, and dropped his glance.

She linked her uncle's arm in hers, and the three moved slowly forward. Old Mr. Blencarn walked with difficulty, pausing at intervals for breath. Anthony, his eyes bent on the ground, sauntered beside him, clumsily kicking at the cobbles that lay in his path.

When they reached the vicarage gate, the old man asked him to come inside.

"Not jest now, thank ye, Mr. Blencarn. I've that lot o' lambs t' see to before dinner. It's a grand marnin', this," he added, inconsequently.

"Uncle's bought a nice lot o' Leghorns, Tuesday," Rosa remarked. Anthony met her gaze; there was a grave, subdued expression on her face this morning, that made her look more of a woman, less of a girl.

"Ay, do ye show him the birds, Rosa. I'd be glad to have his opinion on 'em."

The old man turned to hobble into the house, and Rosa, as she supported his arm, called back over her shoulder:

"I'll not be a minute, Mr. Garstin."

Anthony strolled round to the yard behind the house, and waited, watching a flock of glossy-white poultry that strutted, perkily pecking, over the grass-grown cobbles.

"Ay, Miss Rosa, they're a bonny lot," he remarked, as the girl joined him.

"Are they not?" she rejoined, scattering a handful of corn before her.

The birds scuttled across the yard with greedy, outstretched necks. The two stood, side by side, gazing at them.

"What did he give for 'em?" Anthony asked.

"Fifty-five shillings."

"Ay," he assented, nodding absently.

"Was Dr. Sanderson na seein' o' yer father yesterday?" he asked, after a moment.

"He came in t' forenoon. He said he was jest na worse."

"Ye knaw, Miss Rosa, as I'm still thinkin' on ye," he began abruptly, without looking up.

"I reckon it ain't much use," she answered shortly, scattering another handful of corn towards the birds. "I reckon I'll never marry. I'm jest weary o' bein' courted——"

"I would na weary ye wi' courtin'," he interrupted.

She laughed noisily.

"Ye are a queer customer, an' na mistake."

"I'm a match for Luke Stock anyway," he continued fiercely. "Ye think nought o' taking oop wi' him—about as ranty, wild a young feller as ever stepped."

The girl reddened, and bit her lip.

"I don't know what you mean, Mr. Garstin. It seems to me ye're mighty hasty in jumpin' t' conclusions."

"Mabbe I kin see a thing or two," he retorted doggedly.

"Luke Stock's gone to London, anyway."

"Ay, an' a powerful good job too, in t' opinion o' some folks."

"Ye're jest jealous," she exclaimed, with a forced titter. "Ye're jest jealous o' Luke Stock."

"Nay, but ye need na fill yer head wi' that nonsense. I'm too deep set on ye t' feel jealousy," he answered, gravely.

The smile faded from her face, as she murmured:

"I canna mak ye out, Mr. Garstin."

"Nay, that ye canna. An' I suppose it's natural, considerin' ye're little more than a child, an' I'm a'most old enough to be yer father," he retorted, with blunt bitterness.

"But ye know yer mother's took that dislike t' me. She'd never abide the sight o' me at Hootsey."

He remained silent a moment, moodily reflecting.

"She'd jest ha' t' git ower it. I see nought in that objection," he declared.

"Nay, Mr. Garstin, it canna be. Indeed it canna be at all. Ye'd best jest put it right from yer mind, once and for all."

"I'd jest best put it off my mind, had I? Ye talk like a child!" he burst out scornfully. "I intend ye t' coom t' love me, an' I will no take ye till ye do. I'll jest go on waitin' for ye, an', mark my words, my day 'ull coom at last."

He spoke loudly, in a slow, stubborn

voice, and stepped suddenly towards her. With a faint, frightened cry she shrank back into the doorway of the hen-house.

"Ye talk like a prophet. Ye sort o' skeer me."

He laughed grimly, and paused, reflectively scanning her face. He seemed about to continue in the same strain; but, instead turned abruptly on his heel, and strode away through the garden gate.

IV

For three hundred years there had been a Garstin at Hootsey: generation after generation had tramped the grey stretch of upland, in the spring-time scattering their flocks over the fell-sides, and, at the "back-end," on dark, winter afternoons, driving them home again, down the broad bridle-path that led over the "raise." They had been a race of few words, "keeping themselves to themselves," as the phrase goes; beholden to no man, filled with a dogged, churlish pride—an upright, old-fashioned race, stubborn, long-lived, rude in speech, slow of resolve.

Anthony had never seen his father, who had died one night, upon the fell-top, he and his shepherd, engulfed in the great snowstorm of 1849. Folks had said that he was the only Garstin who had failed to make old man's bones.

After his death, Jake Atkinson, from Ribblehead in Yorkshire, had come to live at Hootsey. Jake was a fine farmer, a canny bargainer, and very handy among the sheep, till he took to drink, and roystering every week with the town wenches up at Carlisle. He was a corpulent, deep-voiced, free-handed fellow: when his time came, though he died very hardly, he remained festive and convivial to the last. And for years afterwards in the valley, his memory lingered: men spoke of him regretfully, recalling his quips, his feats of strength, and his choice breed of Herdwicke rams. But he left behind him a host of debts up at Carlisle, in Penrith, and in almost every market town—debts that he had long ago pretended to have paid with money that belonged to his sister. The widow Garstin sold the twelve Herdwicke rams, and nine acres of land: within six

weeks she had cleared off every penny, and for thirteen months, on Sundays, wore her mourning with a mute, forbidding grimness: the bitter thought that, unbeknown to her, Jake had acted dishonestly in money matters, and that he had ended his days in riotous sin, soured her pride, imbued her with a rancorous hostility against all the world. For she was a very proud woman, independent, holding her head high, so folks said, like a Garstin bred and born; and Anthony, although some reckoned him quiet and of little account, came to take after her as he grew into manhood.

She took into her own hands the management of the Hootsey farm, and set the boy to work for her along with the two farm servants. It was twenty-five years now since his uncle Jake's death: there were grey hairs in his sandy beard; but he still worked for his mother, as he had done when a growing lad.

And now that times were grown to be bad (of late years the price of stock had been steadily falling; and the hay harvests had drifted from bad to worse) the widow Garstin no longer kept any labouring men; but lived, she and her son, year in and year out, in a close parsimonious way.

That had been Anthony Garstin's life—a dull, eventless sort of business, the sluggish incrustation of monotonous years. And until Rosa Blencarn had come to keep house for her uncle, he had never thought twice on a woman's face.

The Garstins had always been good church-goers, and Anthony, for years, had acted as churchwarden. It was one summer evening, up at the vicarage, whilst he was checking the offertory account, that he first set eyes upon her. She was fresh back from school at Leeds: she was dressed in a white dress: she looked, he thought, like a London lady.

She stood by the window, tall and straight and queenly, dreamily gazing out into the summer twilight, whilst he and her uncle sat over their business. When he rose to go, she glanced at him with quick curiosity; he hurried away, muttering a sheepish good-night.

The next time that he saw her was in

church on Sunday. He watched her shyly, with a hesitating, reverential discretion: her beauty seemed to him wonderful, distant, enigmatic. In the afternoon, young Mrs. Forsyth, from Longscale, dropped in for a cup of tea with his mother, and the two set off gossiping of Rosa Blencarn, speaking of her freely, in tones of acrimonious contempt. For a long while he sat silent, puffing at his pipe; but at last, when his mother concluded with, "She looks t' me fair stuck-oop, full o' toonish airs an' graces," despite himself, he burst out: "Ye're just wastin' yer breath wi' that cackle. I reckon Miss Blencarn's o' a different clay to us folks." Young Mrs. Forsyth tittered immoderately, and the next week it was rumoured about the valley that "Tony Garstin was gone luny over t' parson's niece."

But of all this he knew nothing—keeping to himself, as was his wont, and being, besides, very busy with the hay harvest—until one day, at dinner-time, Henry Sisson asked if he'd started his courting; Jacob Sowerby cried that Tony'd been too slow in getting to work, for that the girl had been seen spooning in Crosby Shaws with Curbison the auctioneer, and the others (there were half-a-dozen of them lounging round the hay-waggon) burst into a boisterous guffaw. Anthony flushed dully, looking hesitatingly from the one to the other; then slowly put down his beer-can, and of a sudden, seizing Jacob by the neck, swung him heavily on the grass. He fell against the waggon-wheel, and when he rose the blood was streaming from an ugly cut in his forehead. And henceforward Tony Garstin's courtship was the common jest of all the parish.

As yet, however, he had scarcely spoken to her, though twice he had passed her in the lane that led up to the vicarage. She had given him a frank, friendly smile; but he had not found the resolution to do more than lift his hat. He and Henry Sisson stacked the hay in the yard behind the house; there was no further mention made of Rosa Blencarn; but all day long Anthony, as he knelt thatching the rick, brooded over the strange sweetness of her face, and on the fell-top, while he tramped after the ewes over the dry, crackling heather, and as he jogged along the narrow, rickety road, driving his cartload of lambs into the auction mart.

Thus, as the weeks slipped by, he was content with blunt, wistful ruminations upon her indistinct image. Jacob Sowerby's accusation, and several kindred innuendoes let fall by his mother, left him cooly incredulous; the girl still seemed to him altogether distant; but from the first sight of her face he had evolved a stolid, unfaltering conception of her difference from the ruck of her sex.

But one evening, as he passed the vicarage on his way down from the fells, she called to him, and with a childish, confiding familiarity asking for advice concerning the feeding of the poultry. In his eagerness to answer her as best he could, he forgot his customary embarrassment, and grew, for the moment, almost voluble, and quite at his ease in her presence. Directly her flow of questions ceased, however, the returning perception of her rosy, hesitating smile, and of her large, deep eyes looking straight into his face, perturbed him strangely and, reddening, he remembered the quarrel in the hay-field and the tale of Crosby Shaws.

After this, the poultry became a link between them—a link which he regarded in all seriousness, blindly unconscious that there was aught else to bring them together, only feeling himself in awe of her, because of her schooling, her townish manners, her ladylike mode of dress. And soon, he came to take a sturdy, secret pride in her friendly familiarity towards him. Several times a week he would meet her in the lane, and they would loiter a moment together; she would admire his dogs, though he assured her earnestly that they were but sorry curs; and once, laughing at his staidness, she nicknamed him "Mr. Churchwarden."

That the girl was not liked in the valley he suspected, curtly attributing her unpopularity to the women's senseless jealousy. Of gossip concerning her he heard no further hint; but instinctively, and partly from that rugged, natural reserve of his, shrank from mentioning her name, even incidentally, to his mother.

Now, on Sunday evenings, he often

strolled up to the vicarage, each time quitting his mother with the same awkward affectation of casualness; and, on his return, becoming vaguely conscious of how she refrained from any comment on his absence, and appeared oddly oblivious of the existence of parson Blencarn's niece.

She had always been a sour-tongued woman; but, as the days shortened with the approach of the long winter months, she seemed to him to grow more fretful than ever; at times it was almost as if she bore him some smouldering, sullen resentment. He was of stubborn fibre, however, toughened by long habit of a bleak, unruly climate; he revolved the matter in his mind deliberately, and when, at last, after much plodding thought, it dawned upon him that she resented his acquaintance with Rosa Blencarn, he accepted the solution with an unflinching phlegm, and merely shifted his attitude towards the girl, calculating each day the likelihood of his meeting her, and making, in her presence, persistent efforts to break down, once for all, the barrier of his own timidity. He was a man not to be clumsily driven, still less, so he prided himself, a man to be craftily led.

It was close upon Christmas time before the crisis came. His mother was just home from Penrith market. The springcart stood in the yard, the old grey horse was steaming heavily in the still, frosty air.

"I reckon ye've come fast. T' ould horse is over hot," he remarked bluntly, as he went to the animal's head.

She clambered down hastily, and, coming to his side, began breathlessly:

"Ye ought t' hev coom t' market, Tony. There's bin pretty goin's on in Pe'rith to-day. I was helpin' Anna Forsyth t' choose six yards o' sheetin' in Dockroy, when we sees Rosa Blencarn coom oot o' t' 'Bell and Bullock' in company wi' Curbison and young Joe Smethwick. Smethwick was fair reelin' drunk, and Curbison and t' girl were a-houldin' on to him, to keep him fra fallin'; and then, after a bit, he puts his arm round the girl t' stiddy hisself, and that fashion they goes off, right oop t' public street——"

He continued to unload the packages, and to carry them mechanically one by one into the house. Each time, when he re-appeared, she was standing by the steaming horse, busy with her tale.

"An' on t' road we passed t' three on' em in Curbison's trap, with Smethwick leein' in t' bottom, singin' maudlin' songs. They were passin' Dunscale village, an' t' folks coom runnin' oot o' houses t' see 'em go past——"

He led the cart away towards the stable, leaving her to cry the remainder after him across the yard.

Half-an-hour later he came in for his dinner. During the meal not a word passed between them, and directly he had finished he strode out of the house. About nine o'clock he returned, lit his pipe, and sat down to smoke it over the kitchen fire.

"Where've ye bin, Tony?" she asked.

"Oop t' vicarage, courtin'," he retorted defiantly, with his pipe in his mouth.

This was ten months ago; ever since he had been doggedly waiting. That evening he had set his mind on the girl, he intended to have her; and while his mother gibed, as she did now upon every opportunity, his patience remained grimly unflagging. She would remind him that the farm belonged to her, that he would have to wait till her death before he could bring the hussey to Hootsey: he would retort that as soon as the girl would have him, he intended taking a small holding over at Scarsdale. Then she would give way, and for a while piteously upbraid him with her old age, and with the memory of all the years she and he had spent together, and he would comfort her with a display of brusque, evasive remorse.

But, none the less, on the morrow, his thoughts would return to dwell on the haunting vision of the girl's face, while his own rude, credulous chivalry, kindled by the recollection of her beauty, stifled his misgivings concerning her conduct.

Meanwhile she dallied with him, and amused herself with the younger men. Her old uncle fell ill in the spring, and could scarcely leave the house. She declared that she found life in the valley intolerably dull, that she hated the quiet of the place, that she longed for Leeds, and the exciting bustle of the streets; and in the evenings she wrote long letters to the girl-friends she had left behind there, describing with petulant vivacity her tribe of rustic admirers. At the harvest-time she went back on a fortnight's visit to friends; the evening before her departure she promised Anthony to give him her answer on her return. But, instead, she avoided him, pretended to have promised in jest, and took up with Luke Stock, a cattle-dealer from Wigton.

V

It was three weeks since he had fetched his flock down from the fell.

After dinner he and his mother sat together in the parlour: they had done so every Sunday afternoon, year in and year out, as far back as he could remember.

A row of mahogany chairs, with shiny, horse-hair seats, were ranged round the room. A great collection of agricultural prize-tickets were pinned over the wall; and, on a heavy, highly-polished side-board stood several silver cups. A heap of gilt-edged shavings filled the unused grate: there were gaudily-tinted roses along the mantelpiece, and, on a small table by the window, beneath a glass-case, a gilt basket filled with imitation flowers. Every object was disposed with a scrupulous precision: the carpet and the red-patterned cloth on the centre table were much faded. The room was spotlessly clean, and wore, in the chilly winter sunlight, a rigid, comfortless air.

Neither spoke, or appeared conscious of the other's presence. Old Mrs. Garstin, wrapped in a woollen shawl, sat knitting: Anthony dozed fitfully on a stiff-backed chair.

Of a sudden, in the distance, a bell started tolling. Anthony rubbed his eyes drowsily, and taking from the table his Sunday hat, strolled out across the dusky fields. Presently, reaching a rude wooden seat, built beside the bridle-path, he sat down and relit his pipe. The air was very still; below him a white filmy mist hung across the valley: the fell sides, vaguely grouped, resembled hulking masses of sombre shadow; and, as he looked back, three squares of glimmering gold revealed the lighted windows of the square-towered church.

He sat smoking; pondering, with placid and reverential contemplation, on the Mighty Maker of the world—a world majestically and inevitably ordered; a world where, he argued, each object—each fissure in the fells, the winding course of each tumbling stream—possesses its mysterious purport, its inevitable signification. . . .

At the end of the field two rams were fighting; retreating, then running together, and leaping from the ground, butting head to head and horn to horn. Anthony watched them absently, pursuing his rude meditations.

. . . And the succession of bad seasons, the slow ruination of the farmers throughout the country, were but punishment meted out for the accumulated wickedness of the world. In the olden time God rained plagues upon the land: now-a-days, in His wrath, He spoiled the produce of the earth, which, with His own hands, He had fashioned and bestowed upon men.

He rose and continued his walk along the bridle-path. A multitude of rabbits scuttled up the hill at his approach; and a great cloud of plovers, rising from the rushes, circled overhead, filling the air with a profusion of their querulous cries. All at once he heard a rattling of stones, and perceived a number of small pieces of shingle bounding in front of him down the grassy slope.

A woman's figure was moving among the rocks above him. The next moment, by the trimming of crimson velvet on her hat, he had recognized her. He mounted the slope with springing strides, wondering the while how it was she came to be there, that she was not in church playing the organ at afternoon service.

Before she was aware of his approach, he was beside her.

"I thought ye'd be in church——" he began.

She started: then, gradually regaining her composure, answered, weakly smiling:

"Mr. Jenkinson, the new school-master, wanted to try the organ."

He came towards her impulsively: she saw the odd flickers in his eyes as she stepped back in dismay.

"Nay, but I will na harm ye," he said. "Only I reckon what 'tis a special turn o' Providence, meetin' wi' ye oop here. I reckon what ye'll hev t' give me a square answer noo. Ye canna dilly-dally everlastingly."

He spoke almost brutally; and she stood, white and grasping, staring at him with large, frightened eyes. The sheepwalk was but a tiny threadlike track: the slope of the shingle on either side was very steep: below them lay the valley; distant, lifeless, all blurred by the evening dusk. She looked about her helplessly for a means of escape.

"Miss Rosa," he continued, in a husky voice, "can ye na coom t' think on me? Think ye, I've bin waitin' nigh upon two year for ye. I've watched ye tak oop, first wi' this young fellar, and then wi' that, till soomtimes my heart's fit t' burst. Many a day, oop on t' fell-top, t' thought o' ye's nigh driven me daft, and I've left my shepherdin' jest t'set on a cairn in t' mist, picturin' an' broodin' on yer face. Many an evening' I've started oop t' vicarage, wi' t' resolution t' speak right oot t' ye; but when it coomed t' point, a sort o' timidity seemed t' hould me back, I was that feared t' displease ye. I knaw I'm na scholar, an' mabbe ye think I'm rough-mannered. I knaw I've spoken sharply to ye once or twice lately. But it's jest because I'm that mad wi' love for ye: I jest canna help myself soomtimes——"

He waited, peering into her face. She could see the beads of sweat above his bristling eyebrows: the damp had settled on his sandy beard: his horny fingers were twitching at the buttons of his black Sunday coat.

She struggled to summon a smile; but her underlip quivered, and her large dark eyes filled slowly with tears.

And he went on:

"Ye've coom t' mean jest everything to me. Ef ye will na hev me, I care for nought else. I canna speak t' ye in phrases: I'm jest a plain, unscholarly man: I canna wheedle ye, wi' cunnin' after t' fashion o' toon folks. But I can love ye wi' all my might, an' watch over ye, and work for ye better than any one o' em——"

She was crying to herself, silently, while he spoke. He noticed nothing, however: the twilight hid her face from him.

"There's nought against me," he persisted. "I'm as good a man as any one on 'em. Ay, as good a man as any one on 'em," he repeated defiantly, raising his voice.

"It's impossible, Mr. Garstin, it's impossible. Ye've been very kind to me——" she added, in a choking voice.

"Wa dang it, I didna mean t' mak ye cry, lass," he exclaimed, with a softening of his tone. "There's nought for ye t' cry ower."

She sank on to the stones, passionately sobbing in hysterical and defenceless despair. Anthony stood a moment, gazing at her in clumsy perplexity: then, coming close to her, put his hand on her shoulder, and said gently:

"Coom, lass, what's trouble? Ye can trust me."

She shook her head faintly.

"Ay, but ye can though," he asserted, firmly. "Come, what is 't?"

Heedless of him, she continued to rock herself to and fro, crooning in her distress:

"Oh! I wish I were dead! . . . I wish I could die!"

—"Wish ye could die?" he repeated. "Why, whatever can 't be that's troublin' ye like this? There, there, lassie, give ower: it 'ull all coom right, whatever it be——"

"No, no," she wailed. "I wish I could die! . . . I wish I could die!"

Lights were twinkling in the village below; and across the valley darkness was draping the hills. The girl lifted her face from her hands, and looked up at him with a scared bewildered expression.

"I must go home: I must be getting home," she muttered.

"Nay, but there's sommut mighty amiss wi' ye."

"No, it's nothing . . . I don't know—I'm not well . . . I mean it's nothing . . . it'll pass over . . . you mustn't think anything of it."

"Nay, but I canna stand by an see ye in sich trouble."

"It's nothing, Mr. Garstin, indeed it's nothing," she repeated.

"Ay, but I canna credit that," he objected stubbornly.

She sent him a shifting, hunted glance.

"Let me get home . . . you must let me get home."

She made a tremulous, pitiful attempt at firmness. Eyeing her keenly, he barred her path: she flushed scarlet, and looked hastily away across the valley.

"If ye'll tell me yer distress, mabbe I can help ye."

"No, no, it's nothing . . . it's nothing."

"If ye'll tell me yer distress, mabbe I can help ye," he repeated, with a solemn, deliberate sternness. She shivered, and looked away again, vaguely, across the valley.

"You can do nothing: there's nought to be done," she murmured drearily.

"There's a man in this business," he declared.

"Let me go! Let me go!" she pleaded desperately.

"Who is't that's bin puttin' ye into this distress?" His voice sounded loud and harsh.

"No one, no one. I canna tell ye, Mr. Garstin. . . . It's no one," she protested weakly. The white, twisted look on his face frightened her.

"My God!" he burst out, gripping her wrist, "an' a proper soft fool ye've made o' me. Who is't, I tell you? Who's t' man?"

"Ye're hurtin' me. Let me go. I canna tell ye."

"And ye're fond o' him?"

"No, no. He's a wicked, sinful man. I pray God I may never set eyes on him again. I told him so."

"But ef he's got ye into trouble, he'll hev t' marry ye," he persisted with a brutal bitterness.

"I will not. I hate him!" she cried fiercely.

"But is he *willin'* t' marry ye?"

"I don't know . . . I don't care . . . he said so before he went away . . . But I'd kill myself sooner than live with him."

He let her hands fall and stepped back from her. She could only see his figure, like a sombre cloud, standing before her.

The whole fell-side seemed still and dark and lonely. Presently she heard his voice again:

"I reckon what there's one road oot o' yer distress."

She shook her head drearily.

"There's none. I'm a lost woman."

"An' ef ye took me instead?" he said eagerly.

"I—I don't understand——"

"Ef ye married me instead of Luke Stock?"

"But that's impossible—the—the——"

"Ay, t' child. I know. But I'll tak t' child as mine."

She remained silent. After a moment he heard her voice answer in a queer, distant tone:

"You mean that—that ye're ready to marry me, and adopt the child?"

"I do," he answered doggedly.

"But people—your mother——?"

"Folks 'ull jest know nought about it. It's none o' their business. T' child 'ull pass as mine. Ye'll accept that?"

"Yes," she answered, in a low, rapid voice.

"Ye'll consent t' hev me, ef I git ye oot o' yer trouble?"

"Yes," she repeated, in the same tone.

She heard him draw a long breath.

"I said 't was a turn o' Providence, meetin' wi' ye oop here," he exclaimed, with half-suppressed exultation.

Her teeth began to chatter a little: she felt that he was peering at her, curiously, through the darkness.

"An' noo," he continued briskly, "ye'd best be gettin' home. Give me ye're hand, an' I'll stiddy ye ower t' stones."

He helped her down the bank of shingle, exclaiming: "By goom, ye're stony cauld." Once or twice she slipped: he supported her, roughly gripping her knuckles. The stones rolled down the steps, noisily, disappearing into the night.

Presently they struck the turf bridle-path, and, as they descended silently towards the lights of the village, he said gravely:

"I always reckoned what my day 'ud coom."

She made no reply; and he added grimly:

"There'll be terrible work wi' mother over this."

He accompanied her down the narrow lane that led past her uncle's house. When the lighted windows came in sight he halted.

"Good-night, lassie," he said kindly. "Do ye give ower distressin' yeself."

"Good-night, Mr. Garstin," she answered, in the same low, rapid voice in which she had given him her answer up on the fell.

"We're man an' wife plighted now, are we not?" he blurted timidly.

She held her face to his, and he kissed her on the cheek, clumsily.

VI

The next morning the frost had set in. The sky was still clear and glittering: the whitened fields sparkled in the chilly sunlight: here and there, on high, distant peaks, gleamed dainty caps of snow. All the week Anthony was to be busy at the fell-foot, wall-building against the coming of the winter storms: the work was heavy, for he was single-handed, and the stone had to be fetched from off the fell-side. Two or three times a day he led his rickety, lumbering cart along the lane that passed the vicarage gate, pausing on each journey to glance furtively up at the windows. But he saw no sign of Rosa Blencarn; and, indeed, he felt no longing to see her: he was grimly exultant over the remembrance of his wooing of her, and over the knowledge that she was his. There glowed within him a stolid pride in himself: he thought of the others who had courted her, and the means by which he had won her seemed to him a fine stroke of cleverness.

And so he refrained from any mention of the matter; relishing, as he worked, all alone, the days through, the consciousness of his secret triumph, and anticipating, with inward chucklings, the discomforted cackle of his mother's female friends. He foresaw, without misgiving, her bitter opposition: he felt himself strong; and his heart warmed towards the girl. And when, at intervals, the brusque realization that, after all, he was to possess her swept over

him, he gripped the stones, and swung them almost fiercely into their places.

All around him the white, empty fields seemed slumbering breathlessly. The stillness stiffened the leafless trees. The frosty air flicked his blood: singing vigorously to himself he worked with a stubborn, unflagging resolution, methodically postponing, till the length of the wall should be completed, the announcement of his betrothal.

After his reticent, solitary fashion, he was very happy, reviewing his future prospects, with a plain and stead assurance, and, as the week-end approached, coming to ignore the irregularity of the whole business: almost to assume, in the exultation of his pride, that he had won her honestly; and to discard, stolidly, all thought of Luke Stock, of his relations with her, of the coming child that was to pass for his own.

And there were moments too, when, as he sauntered homewards through the dusk at the end of his day's work, his heart grew full to overflowing of a rugged, superstitious gratitude towards God in Heaven who had granted his desires.

About three o'clock on the Saturday afternoon he finished the length of wall. He went home, washed, shaved, put on his Sunday coat; and, avoiding the kitchen, where his mother sat knitting by the fireside, strode up to the vicarage.

It was Rosa who opened the door to him. On recognizing him she started, and he followed her into the dining-room. He seated himself, and began, brusquely:

"I've coom, Miss Rosa, t' speak t' Mr. Blencarn."

Then added, eyeing her closely:

"Ye're lookin' sick, lass."

Her faint smile accentuated the worn, white look on her face.

"I reckon ye've been frettin' yeself," he continued gently, "leein' awake o' nights, hev'n't yee, noo?"

She smiled vaguely.

"Well, but ye see I'm coom t' settle t' whole business for ye. Ye thought mabbe that I was na a man o' my word."

"No, no, not that," she protested, "but —but——"

"But what then?"

"Ye must not do it, Mr. Garstin . . . I must just bear my own trouble the best I can——" she broke out.

"D'ye fancy I'm takin' ye oot of charity? Ye little reckon the sort o' stuff my love for ye's made of. Nay, Miss Rosa, but ye canna draw back noo."

"But ye cannot do it, Mr. Garstin. Ye know your mother will na have me at Hootsey. . . . I could na live there with your mother. . . . I'd sooner bear my trouble alone, as best I can. . . . She's that stern is Mrs. Garstin. I couldn't look her in the face. . . . I can go away somewhere. . . . I could keep it all from uncle."

Her colour came and went: she stood before him, looking away from him, dully, out of the window.

"I intend ye t' coom t' Hootsey. I'm na lad: I reckon I can choose my own wife. Mother'll hev ye at t' farm, right enough: ye need na distress yeself on that point ——"

"Nay, Mr. Garstin, but indeed she will not, never. . . . I know she will not. . . . She always set herself against me, right from the first."

"Ay, but that was different. T' case is all changed noo," he objected doggedly.

"She'll support the sight of me all the less," the girl faltered.

"Mother'll hev ye at Hootsey—receive ye willin' of her own free wish—of her own free wish, d'ye hear? I'll answer for that."

He struck the table with his fist heavily. His tone of determination awed her: she glanced at him hurriedly, struggling with her irresolution.

"I knaw hoo t' manage mother. An' now," he concluded, changing his tone, "is yer uncle about t' place?"

"He's up the paddock, I think," she answered.

"Well, I'll jest step oop and hev a word wi' him."

"Ye're . . . . ye will na tell him."

"Tut, tut, na harrowin' tales, ye need na fear, lass. I reckon ef I can tackle mother, I can accommodate myself t' parson Blencarn."

He rose, and coming close to her, scanned her face.

"Ye must git t' roses back t' yer cheeks," he exclaimed, with a short laugh, "I canna be takin' a ghost t' church."

She smiled tremulously, and he continued, laying one hand affectionately on her shoulder:

"Nay, but I was but jestin'. Roses or na roses, ye'll be t' bonniest bride in all Coomberland. I'll meet ye in Hullam lane, after church time, to-morrow," he added, moving towards the door.

After he had gone, she hurried to the backdoor furtively. His retreating figure was already mounting the grey upland field. Presently, beyond him, she perceived her uncle, emerging through the paddock gate. She ran across the poultry yard, and mounting a tub, stood watching the two figures as they moved towards one another along the brow, Anthony vigorously trudging, with his hands thrust deep in his pockets; her uncle, his wideawake tilted over his nose, hobbling, and leaning stiffly on his pair of sticks. They met; she saw Anthony take her uncle's arm: the two, turning together, strolled away towards the fell.

She went back into the house. Anthony's dog came towards her, slinking along the passage. She caught the animal's head in her hands, and bent over it caressingly, in an impulsive outburst of almost hysterical affection.

VII

The two men returned towards the vicarage. At the paddock gate they halted, and the old man concluded:

"I could not have wished a better man for her, Anthony. Mabbe the Lord'll not be minded to spare me much longer. After I'm gone Rosa'll hev all I possess. She was my poor brother Isaac's only child. After her mother was taken, he, poor fellow, went altogether to the bad, and until she came here she mostly lived among strangers. It's been a wretched sort of childhood for her—a wretched sort of childhood. Ye'll take care of her, Anthony, will ye not? . . . Nay, but I could not hev wished for a better man for her, and there's my hand on 't."

"Thank ee, Mr. Blencarn, thank ee,"

Anthony answered huskily, gripping the old man's hand.

And he started off down the lane homewards.

His heart was full of a strange, rugged exaltation. He felt with a swelling pride that God had entrusted to him this great charge—to tend her; to make up to her, tenfold, for all that loving care, which, in her childhood, she had never known. And together with a stubborn confidence in himself, there welled up within him a great pity for her—a tender pity, that, chastening with his passion, made her seem to him, as he brooded over that lonely childhood of hers, the more distinctly beautiful, the more profoundly precious. He pictured to himself, tremulously, almost incredulously, their married life—in the winter, his return home at nightfall to find her awaiting him with a glad, trustful smile; their evenings, passed together, sitting in silent happiness over the smouldering logs; or, in summertime, the mid-day rest in the hay-fields when, wearing perhaps a large-brimmed hat fastened with a red ribbon, beneath her chin, he would catch sight of her, carrying his dinner, coming across the upland.

She had not been brought up to be a farmer's wife: she was but a child still, as the old parson had said. She should not have to work as other men's wives worked: she should dress like a lady, and on Sundays, in church, wear fine bonnets, and remain, as she had always been, the belle of all the parish.

And, meanwhile, he would farm as he had never farmed before, watching his opportunities, driving cunning bargains, spending nothing on himself, hoarding every penny that she might have what she wanted. . . . And, as he strode through the village, he seemed to foresee a general brightening of prospects, a sobering of the fever of speculation in sheep, a cessation of the insensate glutting, year after year, of the great winter marts throughout the North, a slackening of the foreign competition followed by a steady revival of the price of fatted stocks—a period of prosperity in store for the farmer at last. . . . And the future years appeared to open out before him, spread like a distant, glit-

tering plain, across which, he and she, hand in hand, were called to travel together. . . .

And then, suddenly, as his iron-bound boots clattered over the cobbled yard, he remembered, with brutal determination, his mother, and the stormy struggle that awaited him.

He waited till supper was over, till his mother had moved from the table to her place by the chimney corner. For several minutes he remained debating with himself the best method of breaking the news to her. Of a sudden he glanced up at her: her knitting had slipped on to her lap: she was sitting, bunched of a heap in her chair, nodding with sleep. By the flickering light of the wood fire, she looked worn and broken: he felt a twinge of clumsy compunction. And then he remembered the piteous, hunted look in the girl's eyes, and the old man's words when they had parted at the paddock gate, and he blurted out:

"I doot but what I'll hev t' marry Rosa Blencarn after all."

She started, and blinking her eyes, said:

"I was jest takin' a wink o' sleep. What was 't ye were saying, Tony?"

He hesitated a moment, puckering his forehead into coarse rugged lines, and fidgeting noisily with his tea-cup. Presently he repeated:

"I doot but what I'll hev t' marry Rosa Blencarn after all."

She rose stiffly, and stepping down from the hearth, came towards him.

"Mabbe I did na hear ye aright, Tony." She spoke hurriedly, and though she was quite close to him, steadying herself with one hand clutching the back of his chair, her voice sounded weak, distant almost.

"Look oop at me. Look oop into my face," she commanded fiercely.

He obeyed sullenly.

"No oot wi' 't. What's yer meanin', Tony?"

"I mean what I say," he retorted doggedly, averting his gaze.

"What d'ye mean by sayin' that ye've *got* t' marry her?"

"I tell yer I mean what I say," he repeated dully.

"Ye mean ye've bin an' put t' girl in trouble?"

He said nothing; but sat staring stupidly at the floor.

"Look oop at me, and answer," she commanded, gripping his shoulder and shaking him.

He raised his face slowly, and met her glance.

"Ay, that's aboot it," he answered.

"This 'll na be truth. It 'll be jest a piece o' wanton trickery!" she cried.

"Nay, but 't is truth," he answered deliberately.

"Ye will na swear t' it?" she persisted.

"I see na necessity for swearin'."

"Then ye canna swear t' it," she burst out triumphantly.

He paused an instant; then said quietly: "Ay, but I'll swear t' it easy enough. Fetch t' Book."

She lifted the heavy, tattered Bible from the chimney-piece, and placed it before him on the table. He laid his lumpish fist on it.

"Say," she continued with a tense tremulousness, "say, I swear t' ye, mother, that 't is t' truth, t' whole truth, and noat but t' truth, s'help me God."

"I swear t' ye, mother, it's truth, t' whole truth, and nothin' but t' truth, s'help me God," he repeated after her.

"Kiss t' Book," she ordered.

He lifted the Bible to his lips. As he replaced it on the table, he burst out into a short laugh:

"Be ye satisfied noo?"

She went back to the chimney corner without a word. The logs on the hearth hissed and crackled. Outside, amid the blackness the wind was rising, hooting through the firs, and past the windows.

After a long while he roused himself, and drawing his pipe from his pocket almost steadily, proceeded leisurely to pare in the palm of his hand a lump of black tobacco.

"We'll be asked in church Sunday," he remarked bluntly.

She made no answer.

He looked across at her.

Her mouth was drawn tight at the corners: her face wore a queer, rigid aspect. She looked, he thought, like a figure of stone.

"Ye're not feeling poorly, are ye, mother?" he asked.

She shook her head grimly: then, hobbling out into the room, began to speak in a shrill, tuneless voice.

"Ye talked at one time o' takin' a farm over Scarsdale way. But ye'd best stop here. I'll no hinder ye. Ye can have t' large bedroom in t' front, and I'll move ower to what used to be my brother Jake's room. Ye knaw I've never had no opinion of t' girl, but I'll do what's right by her, ef I breah my sperrit in t' doin' on't. I'll mak' t' girl welcome here: I'll stand by her proper-like: mebbe I'll finish by findin' soom good in her. But from this day forward, Tony, ye're na son o' mine. Ye've dishonoured yeself: ye've laid a trap for me—ay, laid a trap, that's t' word. Ye've brought shame and bitterness on yer ould mother in her ould age. Ye've made me despise t' varra seet o' ye. Ye can stop on here, but ye shall niver touch a penny of my money; every shillin' of 't shall go t' yer child, or to your child's children. Ay," she went on, raising her voice, "ay, ye've got yer way at last, and mebbe ye reckon ye've chosen a mighty smart way. But time 'ull coom when ye'll regret this day, when ye eat oot yer repentance in doost an' ashes. Ay, Lord 'ull punish ye, Tony, chastise ye properly. Ye'll learn that marriage begun in sin can end in nought but sin. Ay," she concluded, as she reached the door, raising her skinny hand prophetically, "ay, after I'm deed and gone, ye mind ye o' t' words o' t' apostle—'For them that hev sinned without t' law, shall also perish without t' law.' "

And she slammed the door behind her.

[1897]

QUESTIONS FOR STUDY

1. *What kind of man is Anthony Garstin? To what extent does his character seem to be an extension of his environment? How does he go about his courting? Why does he succeed?*

2. *Why does Mrs. Garstin so dislike Rosa? Is Rosa herself effectively portrayed?*
3. *What effect does Crackanthorpe gain by interrupting the chronology of his narrative to insert the background of Anthony and Rosa's early meetings?*
4. *What techniques does Crackanthorpe employ to give his story realism?*
5. *What is the function of the many specific references to religion in the story?*

STEPHEN CRANE

The Blue Hotel

I

THE PALACE Hotel at Fort Romper was painted a light blue, a shade that is on the legs of a kind of heron, causing the bird to declare its position against any background. The Palace Hotel, then, was always screaming and howling in a way that made the dazzling winter landscape of Nebraska seem only a grey swampish hush. It stood alone on the prairie, and when the snow was falling the town two hundred yards away was not visible. But when the traveller alighted at the railway station he was obliged to pass the Palace Hotel before he could come upon the company of low clapboard houses which composed Fort Romper, and it was not to be thought that any traveller could pass the Palace Hotel without looking at it. Pat Scully, the proprietor, had proved himself a master of strategy when he chose his paints. It is true that on clear days, when the great transcontinental expresses, long lines of swaying Pullmans, swept through Fort Romper, passengers were overcome at the sight, and the cult that knows the brown-reds and the subdivisions of the dark greens of the East expressed shame, pity, horror, in a laugh. But to the citizens of this prairie town and to the people who would naturally stop there, Pat Scully had performed a feat. With this opulence and splendour, these creeds, classes, egotisms, that streamed through Romper on the rails day after day, they had no colour in common.

As if the displayed delights of such a blue hotel were not sufficiently enticing, it was Scully's habit to go every morning and evening to meet the leisurely trains that stopped at Romper and work his seductions upon any man that he might see wavering, gripsack in hand.

One morning, when a snow-crusted engine dragged its long string of freight cars and its one passenger coach to the station, Scully performed the marvel of catching three men. One was a shaky and quick-eyed Swede, with a great shining cheap valise; one was a tall bronzed cowboy, who was on his way to a ranch near the Dakota line; one was a little silent man from the East, who didn't look it, and didn't announce it. Scully practically made them prisoners. He was so nimble and merry and kindly that each probably felt it would be the height of brutality to try to escape. They trudged off over the creaking board sidewalks in the wake of the eager little Irishman. He wore a heavy fur cap squeezed tightly down on his head. It caused his two red ears to stick out stiffly, as if they were made of tin.

At last, Scully, elaborately, with boisterous hospitality, conducted them through the portals of the blue hotel. The room which they entered was small. It seemed to be merely a proper temple for an enormous stove, which, in the centre, was humming with godlike violence. At various points on its surface the iron had become luminous and glowed yellow from the heat. Beside the stove Scully's son Johnnie was playing High-Five with an old farmer who had whiskers both grey and sandy. They were quarrelling. Frequently the old farmer turned his face toward a box of sawdust—coloured brown from tobacco juice—that was behind the stove, and spat with an air of great impatience and irritation. With a loud flourish of words Scully destroyed the game of cards, and bustled his son upstairs with part of the baggage of the new guests. He himself conducted them to three basins of the coldest water in the world. The cowboy and the Easterner burnished themselves fiery red with this water, until it seemed to be some kind of metal-polish. The Swede, however, merely dipped his fingers gingerly and with trepidation. It was notable that throughout this series of small ceremonies the three travellers were made to feel that Scully was very benevolent. He was conferring great favours upon them. He handed the towel from one to another with an air of philanthropic impulse.

Afterward they went to the first room, and, sitting about the stove, listened to Scully's officious clamour at his daughters, who were preparing the midday meal. They reflected in the silence of experienced men who tread carefully amid new people. Nevertheless, the old farmer, stationary, invincible in his chair near the warmest part of the stove, turned his face from the sawdust-box frequently and addressed a glowing commonplace to the strangers. Usually he was answered in short but adequate sentences by either the cowboy or the Easterner. The Swede said nothing. He seemed to be occupied in making furtive estimates of each man in the room. One might have thought that he had the sense of silly suspicion which comes to guilt. He resembled a badly frightened man.

Later, at dinner, he spoke a little, addressing his conversation entirely to Scully. He volunteered that he had come from New York, where for ten years he had worked as a tailor. These facts seemed to strike Scully as fascinating, and afterward he volunteered that he had lived at Romper for fourteen years. The Swede asked about the crops and the price of labour. He seemed barely to listen to Scully's extended replies. His eyes continued to rove from man to man.

Finally, with a laugh and a wink, he said that some of these Western communities were very dangerous; and after his statement he straightened his legs under the table, tilted his head, and laughed again, loudly. It was plain that the demonstration had no meaning to the others. They looked at him wondering and in silence.

II

As the men trooped heavily back into the front room, the two little windows presented views of a turmoiling sea of snow. The huge arms of the wind were making attempts—mighty, circular, futile

—to embrace the flakes as they sped. A gate-post like a still man with a blanched face stood aghast amid this profligate fury. In a hearty voice Scully announced the presence of a blizzard. The guests of the blue hotel, lighting their pipes, assented with grunts of lazy masculine contentment. No island of the sea could be exempt in the degree of this little room with its humming stove. Johnnie, son of Scully, in a tone which defined his opinion of his ability as a card-player, challenged the old farmer of both grey and sandy whiskers to a game of High-Five. The farmer agreed with a contemptuous and bitter scoff. They sat close to the stove, and squared their knees under a wide board. The cowboy and the Easterner watched the game with interest. The Swede remained near the window, aloof, but with a countenance that showed signs of an inexplicable excitement.

The play of Johnnie and the grey-beard was suddenly ended by another quarrel. The old man arose while casting a look of heated scorn at his adversary. He slowly buttoned his coat, and then stalked with fabulous dignity from the room. In the discreet silence of all other men the Swede laughed. His laughter rang somehow childish. Men by this time had begun to look at him askance, as if they wished to inquire what ailed him.

A new game was formed jocosely. The cowboy volunteered to become the partner of Johnnie, and they all then turned to ask the Swede to throw in his lot with the little Easterner. He asked some questions about the game, and, learning that it wore many names, and that he had played it when it was under an alias, he accepted the invitation. He strode toward the men nervously, as if he expected to be assaulted. Finally, seated, he gazed from face to face and laughed shrilly. This laugh was so strange that the Easterner looked up quickly, the cowboy sat intent and with his mouth open, and Johnnie paused, holding the cards with still fingers.

Afterward there was a short silence. Then Johnnie said, "Well, let's get at it. Come on now!" They pulled their chairs forward until their knees were bunched under the board. They began to play, and their interest in the game caused the others to forget the manner of the Swede.

The cowboy was a board-whacker. Each time that he held superior cards he whanged them, one by one, with exceeding force, down upon the improvised table, and took the tricks with a glowing air of prowess and pride that sent thrills of indignation into the hearts of his opponents. A game with a board-whacker in it is sure to become intense. The countenances of the Easterner and the Swede were miserable whenever the cowboy thundered down his aces and kings, while Johnnie, his eyes gleaming with joy, chuckled and chuckled.

Because of the absorbing play none considered the strange ways of the Swede. They paid strict heed to the game. Finally, during a lull caused by a new deal, the Swede suddenly addressed Johnnie: "I suppose there have been a good many men killed in this room." The jaws of the others dropped and they looked at him.

"What in hell are you talking about?" said Johnnie.

The Swede laughed again his blatant laugh, full of a kind of false courage and defiance. "Oh, you know what I mean all right," he answered.

"I'm a liar if I do!" Johnnie protested. The card was halted, and the men stared at the Swede. Johnnie evidently felt that as the son of the proprietor he should make a direct inquiry. "Now, what might you be drivin' at, mister?" he asked. The Swede winked at him. It was a wink full of cunning. His fingers shook on the edge of the board. "Oh, maybe you think I have been to nowheres. Maybe you think I'm a tenderfoot?"

"I don't know nothin' about you," answered Johnnie, "and I don't give a damn where you've been. All I got to say is that I don't know what you're driving at. There hain't never been nobody killed in this room."

The cowboy, who had been steadily gazing at the Swede, then spoke: "What's wrong with you, mister?"

Apparently it seemed to the Swede that he was formidably menaced. He shivered and turned white near the corners of his mouth. He sent an appealing glance in the direction of the little Easterner. During these moments he did not forget to wear his air of advanced pot-valour. "They say they don't know what I mean," he remarked mockingly to the Easterner.

The latter answered after prolonged and cautious reflection. "I don't understand you," he said, impassively.

The Swede made a movement then which announced that he thought he had encountered treachery from the only quarter where he had expected sympathy, if not help. "Oh, I see you are all against me. I see——"

The cowboy was in a state of deep stupefaction. "Say," he cried, as he tumbled the deck violently down upon the board, "say, what are you gittin' at, hey?"

The Swede sprang up with the celerity of a man escaping from a snake on the floor. "I don't want to fight!" he shouted. "I don't want to fight!"

The cowboy stretched his long legs indolently and deliberately. His hands were in his pockets. He spat into the sawdust-box. "Well, who the hell thought you did?" he inquired.

The Swede backed rapidly toward a corner of the room. His hands were out protectingly in front of his chest, but he was making an obvious struggle to control his fright. "Gentlemen," he quavered, "I suppose I am going to be killed before I can leave this house! I suppose I am going to be killed before I can leave this house!" In his eyes was the dying-swan look. Through the windows could be seen the snow turning blue in the shadow of dusk. The wind tore at the house, and some loose thing beat regularly against the clap-boards like a spirit tapping.

A door opened, and Scully himself entered. He paused in surprise as he noted the tragic attitude of the Swede. Then he said, "What's the matter here?"

The Swede answered him swiftly and eagerly: "These men are going to kill me."

"Kill you!" ejaculated Scully. "Kill you! What are you talkin'?"

The Swede made the gesture of a martyr.

Scully wheeled sternly upon his son. "What is this, Johnnie?"

The lad had grown sullen. "Damned if

I know," he answered. "I can't make no sense to it." He began to shuffle the cards, fluttering them together with an angry snap. "He says a good many men have been killed in this room, or something like that. And he says he's goin' to be killed here too. I don't know what ails him. He's crazy, I shouldn't wonder."

Scully then looked for explanation to the cowboy, but the cowboy simply shrugged his shoulders.

"Kill you?" said Scully again to the Swede. "Kill you? Man, you're off your nut."

"Oh, I know," burst out the Swede. "I know what will happen. Yes, I'm crazy—yes. Yes, of course, I'm crazy—yes. But I know one thing——" There was a sort of sweat of misery and terror upon his face. "I know I won't get out of here alive."

The cowboy drew a deep breath, as if his mind was passing into the last stages of dissolution. "Well, I'm doggoned," he whispered to himself.

Scully wheeled suddenly and faced his son. "You've been troublin' this man!"

Johnnie's voice was loud with its burden of grievance. "Why, good Gawd, I ain't done nothin' to 'im."

The Swede broke in. "Gentlemen, do not disturb yourselves. I will leave this house. I will go away, because"—he accused them dramatically with his glance—"because I do not want to be killed."

Scully was furious with his son. "Will you tell me what is the matter, you young divil? What's the matter, anyhow? Speak out!"

"Blame it!" cried Johnnie in despair, "don't I tell you I don't know? He—he says we want to kill him, and that's all I know. I can't tell what ails him."

The Swede continued to repeat: "Never mind, Mr. Scully; never mind. I will leave this house. I will go away, because I do not wish to be killed. Yes, of course, I am crazy—yes. But I know one thing! I will go away. I will leave this house. Never mind, Mr. Scully; never mind. I will go away."

"You will not go 'way," said Scully. "You will not go 'way until I hear the reason of this business. If anybody has troubled you I will take care of him.

This is my house. You are under my roof, and I will not allow any peaceable man to be troubled here." He cast a terrible eye upon Johnnie, the cowboy, and the Easterner.

"Never mind, Mr. Scully; never mind. I will go away. I do not wish to be killed." The Swede moved toward the door which opened upon the stairs. It was evidently his intention to go at once for his baggage.

"No, no," shouted Scully peremptorily; but the white-faced man slid by him and disappeared. "Now," said Scully severely, "what does this mean?"

Johnnie and the cowboy cried together: "Why, we didn't do nothin' to 'im!"

Scully's eyes were cold. "No," he said, "you didn't?"

Johnnie swore a deep oath. "Why, this is the wildest loon I ever see. We didn't do nothin' at all. We were jest sittin' here playin' cards, and he——"

The father suddenly spoke to the Easterner. "Mr. Blanc," he asked, "what has these boys been doin'?"

The Easterner reflected again. "I didn't see anything wrong at all," he said at last, slowly.

Scully began to howl. "But what does it mane?" He stared ferociously at his son. "I have a mind to lather you for this, me boy."

Johnnie was frantic. "Well, what have I done?" he bawled at his father.

III

"I think you are tongue-tied," said Scully finally to his son, the cowboy, and the Easterner; and at the end of this scornful sentence he left the room.

Upstairs the Swede was swiftly fastening the straps of his great valise. Once his back happened to be half turned toward the door, and, hearing a noise there, he wheeled and sprang up, uttering a loud cry. Scully's wrinkled visage showed grimly in the light of the small lamp he carried. This yellow effulgence, streaming upward, coloured only his prominent features, and left his eyes, for instance, in mysterious shadow. He resembled a murderer.

"Man! man!" he exclaimed, "have you gone daffy?"

"Oh, no! Oh, no!" rejoined the other. "There are people in this world who know pretty nearly as much as you do—understand?"

For a moment they stood gazing at each other. Upon the Swede's deathly pale cheeks were two spots brightly crimson and sharply edged, as if they had been carefully painted. Scully placed the light on the table and sat himself on the edge of the bed. He spoke ruminatively. "By cracky, I never heard of such a thing in my life. It's a complete muddle. I can't, for the soul of me, think how you ever got this idea into your head." Presently he lifted his eyes and asked: "And did you sure think they were going to kill you?"

The Swede scanned the old man as if he wished to see into his mind. "I did," he said at last. He obviously suspected that this answer might precipitate an outbreak. As he pulled on a strap his whole arm shook, the elbow wavering like a bit of paper.

Scully banged his hand impressively on the footboard of the bed. "Why, man, we're goin' to have a line of ilictric streetcars in this town next spring."

" 'A line of electric street cars,' " repeated the Swede, stupidly.

"And," said Scully, "there's a new railroad goin' to be built down from Broken Arm to here. Not to mintion the four churches and the smashin' big brick schoolhouse. Then there's the big factory, too. Why, in two years Romper'll be a met-tro-*pol*-is."

Having finished the preparation of his baggage, the Swede straightened himself. "Mr. Scully," he said, with sudden hardihood, "how much do I owe you?"

"You don't owe me anythin'," said the old man, angrily.

"Yes, I do," retorted the Swede. He took seventy-five cents from his pocket and tendered it to Scully; but the latter snapped his fingers in disdainful refusal. However, it happened that they both stood gazing in a strange fashion at three silver pieces on the Swede's open palm.

"I'll not take your money," said Scully at last. "Not after what's been goin' on here." Then a plan seemed to strike him. "Here," he cried, picking up his lamp and moving toward the door. "Here! Come with me a minute."

"No," said the Swede, in overwhelming alarm.

"Yes," urged the old man. "Come on! I want you to come and see a picter—just across the hall—in my room."

The Swede must have concluded that his hour was come. His jaw dropped and his teeth showed like a dead man's. He ultimately followed Scully across the corridor, but he had the step of one hung in chains.

Scully flashed the light high on the wall of his own chamber. There was revealed a ridiculous photograph of a little girl. She was leaning against a balustrade of gorgeous decoration, and the formidable bang to her hair was prominent. The figure was as graceful as an upright sledstake, and, withal, it was of the hue of lead. "There," said Scully, tenderly, "that's the picter of my little girl that died. Her name was Carrie. She had the purtiest hair you ever saw! I was that fond of her, she——"

Turning then, he saw that the Swede was not contemplating the picture at all, but, instead, was keeping keen watch on the gloom in the rear.

"Look man!" cried Scully, heartily. "That's the picter of my little gal that died. Her name was Carrie. And then here's the picter of my oldest boy, Michael. He's a lawyer in Lincoln, an' doin' well. I gave that boy a grand eddication, and I'm glad for it now. He's a fine boy. Look at 'im now. Ain't he bold as blazes, him there in Lincoln, an honoured an' respicted gintleman! An honoured and respicted gintleman," concluded Scully with a flourish. And, so saying, he smote the Swede jovially on the back.

The Swede faintly smiled.

"Now," said the old man, "there's only one more thing." He dropped suddenly to the floor and thrust his head beneath the bed. The Swede could hear his muffled voice. "I'd keep it under me piller if it wasn't for that boy Johnnie. Then there's the old woman—— Where is it now? I never put it twice in the same place. Ah, now come out with you!"

Presently he backed clumsily from under the bed, dragging with him an old coat rolled into a bundle. "I've fetched him," he muttered. Kneeling on the floor, he unrolled the coat and extracted from its heart a large yellow-brown whisky-bottle.

His first manœuvre was to hold the bottle up to the light. Reassured, apparently, that nobody had been tampering with it, he thrust it with a generous movement toward the Swede.

The weak-kneed Swede was about to eagerly clutch this element of strength, but he suddenly jerked his hand away and cast a look of horror upon Scully.

"Drink," said the old man affectionately. He had risen to his feet, and now stood facing the Swede.

There was a silence. Then again Scully said: "Drink!"

The Swede laughed wildly. He grabbed the bottle, put it to his mouth; and as his lips curled absurdly around the opening and his throat worked, he kept his glance, burning with hatred, upon the old man's face.

IV

After the departure of Scully the three men, with the cardboard still upon their knees, preserved for a long time an astounded silence. Then Johnnie said: "That's the dod-dangedest Swede I ever see."

"He ain't no Swede," said the cowboy scornfully.

"Well, what is he then?" cried Johnnie. "What is he then?"

"It's my opinion," replied the cowboy deliberately, "he's some kind of a Dutchman." It was a venerable custom of the country to entitle as Swedes all light-haired men who spoke with a heavy tongue. In consequence the idea of the cowboy was not without its daring. "Yes, sir," he repeated. "It's my opinion this feller is some kind of a Dutchman."

"Well, he says he's a Swede, anyhow," muttered Johnnie, sulkily. He turned to the Easterner: "What do you think, Mr. Blanc?"

"Oh, I don't know," replied the Easterner.

"Well, what do you think makes him act that way?" asked the cowboy.

"Why, he's frightened." The Easterner knocked his pipe against a rim of the stove. "He's clear frightened out of his boots."

"What at?" cried Johnnie and the cowboy together.

The Easterner reflected over his answer.

"What at?" cried the others again.

"Oh, I don't know, but it seems to me this man has been reading dime novels, and he thinks he's right out in the middle of it—the shootin' and stabbin' and all."

"But," said the cowboy, deeply scandalized, "this ain't Wyoming, ner none of them places. This is Nebrasker."

"Yes," added Johnnie, "an' why don't he wait till he gits *out West?*"

The travelled Easterner laughed. "It isn't different there even—not in these days. But he thinks he's right in the middle of hell."

Johnnie and the cowboy mused along.

"It's awful funny," remarked Johnnie at last.

"Yes," said the cowboy. "This is a queer game. I hope we don't git snowed in, because then we'd have to stand this here man bein' around with us all the time. That wouldn't be no good."

"I wish pop would throw him out," said Johnnie.

Presently they heard a loud stamping on the stairs, accompanied by ringing jokes in the voice of old Scully, and laughter, evidently from the Swede. The men around the stove stared vacantly at each other: "Gosh!" said the cowboy. The door flew open, and old Scully, flushed and anecdotal, came into the room. He was jabbering at the Swede, who followed him, laughing bravely. It was the entry of two roisterers from a banquet hall.

"Come now," said Scully sharply to the three seated men, "move up and give us a chance at the stove." The cowboy and the Easterner obediently sidled their chairs to make room for the new-comers. Johnnie, however, simply arranged himself in a more indolent attitude, and then remained motionless.

"Come! Git over, there," said Scully.

"Plenty of room on the other side of the stove," said Johnnie.

"Do you think we want to sit in the draught?" roared the father.

But the Swede had interposed with a grandeur of confidence. "No, no. Let the boy sit where he likes," he cried in a bullying voice to the father.

"All right! All right!" said Scully, deferentially. The cowboy and the Easterner exchanged glances of wonder.

The five chairs were formed in a crescent about one side of the stove. The Swede began to talk; he talked arrogantly, profanely, angrily. Johnnie, the cowboy, and the Easterner maintained a morose silence, while old Scully appeared to be receptive and eager, breaking in constantly with sympathetic ejaculations.

Finally the Swede announced that he was thirsty. He moved in his chair, and said that he would go for a drink of water.

"I'll git it for you," cried Scully at once.

"No," said the Swede, contemptuously. "I'll get it for myself." He arose and stalked with the air of an owner off into the executive parts of the hotel.

As soon as the Swede was out of hearing Scully sprang to his feet and whispered intensely to the others: "Upstairs he thought I was tryin' to poison 'im."

"Say," said Johnnie, "this makes me sick. Why don't you throw 'im out in the snow?"

"Why, he's all right now," declared Scully. "It was only that he was from the East, and he thought this was a tough place. That's all. He's all right now."

The cowboy looked with admiration upon the Easterner. "You were straight," he said. "You were on to that there Dutchman."

"Well," said Johnnie to his father, "he may be all right now, but I don't see it. Other time he was scared, but now he's too fresh."

Scully's speech was always a combination of Irish brogue and idiom, Western twang and idiom, and scraps of curiously formal diction taken from the story-books and newspapers. He now hurled a strange mass of language at the head of his son. "What do I keep? What do I keep? What do I keep?" he demanded, in a voice of thunder. He slapped his knee impressively, to indicate that he himself was going to make reply, and that all should heed. "I keep a hotel," he shouted. "A hotel, do you mind? A guest under my roof has sacred privileges. He is to be intimidated by none. Not one word shall he hear that would prijudice him in favour of goin' away. I'll not have it. There's no place in this here town where they can say they iver took in a guest of mine because he was afraid to stay here." He wheeled suddenly upon the cowboy and the Easterner. "Am I right?"

"Yes," Mr. Scully," said the cowboy, "I think you're right."

"Yes, Mr. Scully," said the Easterner, "I think you're right."

V

At six-o'clock supper, the Swede fizzed like a fire-wheel. He sometimes seemed on the point of bursting into riotous song, and in all his madness he was encouraged by old Scully. The Easterner was encased in reserve; the cowboy sat in wide-mouthed amazement, forgetting to eat, while Johnnie wrathily demolished great plates of food. The daughters of the house, when they were obliged to replenish the biscuits, approached as warily as Indians, and, having succeeded in their purpose, fled with ill-concealed trepidation. The Swede domineered the whole feast, and he gave it the appearance of a cruel bacchanal. He seemed to have grown suddenly taller; he gazed, brutally disdainful, into every face. His voice rang through the room. Once when he jabbed out harpoon-fashion with his fork to pinion a biscuit, the weapon nearly impaled the hand of the Easterner, which had been stretched quietly out for the same biscuit.

After supper, as the men filed toward

the other room, the Swede smote Scully ruthlessly on the shoulder. "Well, old boy, that was a good, square meal." Johnnie looked hopefully at his father; he knew that shoulder was tender from an old fall; and, indeed, it appeared for a moment as if Scully was going to flame out over the matter, but in the end he smiled a sickly smile and remained silent. The others understood from his manner that he was admitting his responsibility for the Swede's new view-point.

Johnnie, however, addressed his parent in an aside. "Why don't you license somebody to kick you downstairs?" Scully scowled darkly by way of reply.

When they were gathered about the stove, the Swede insisted on another game of High-Five. Scully gently deprecated the plan at first, but the Swede turned a wolfish glare upon him. The old man subsided, and the Swede canvassed the others. In his tone there was always a great threat. The cowboy and the Easterner both remarked indifferently that they would play. Scully said that he would presently have to go to meet the 6.58 train, and so the Swede turned menacingly upon Johnnie. For a moment their glances crossed like blades, and then Johnnie smiled and said, "Yes, I'll play."

They formed a square, with the little board on their knees. The Easterner and the Swede were again partners. As the play went on, it was noticeable that the cowboy was not board-whacking as usual. Meanwhile, Scully, near the lamp, had put on his spectacles and, with an appearance curiously like an old priest, was reading a newspaper. In time he went out to meet the 6.58 train, and, despite his precautions, a gust of polar wind whirled into the room as he opened the door. Besides scattering the cards, it chilled the players to the marrow. The Swede cursed frightfully. When Scully returned, his entrance disturbed a cosy and friendly scene. The Swede again cursed. But presently they were once more intent, their heads bent forward and their hands moving swiftly. The Swede had adopted the fashion of board-whacking.

Scully took up his paper and for a long time remained immersed in matters which were extraordinarily remote from him. The lamp burned badly, and once he stopped to adjust the wick. The newspaper, as he turned from page to page, rustled with a slow and comfortable sound. Then suddenly he heard three terrible words: "You are cheatin'!"

Such scenes often prove that there can be little of dramatic import in environment. Any room can present a tragic front; any room can be comic. This little den was now hideous as a torture-chamber. The new faces of the men themselves had changed it upon the instant. The Swede held a huge fist in front of Johnnie's face, while the latter looked steadily over it into the blazing orbs of his accuser. The Easterner had grown pallid; the cowboy's jaw had dropped in that expression of bovine amazement which was one of his important mannerisms. After the three words, the first sound in the room was made by Scully's paper as it floated forgotten to his feet. His spectacles had also fallen from his nose, but by a clutch he had saved them in air. His hand, grasping the spectacles, now remained poised awkwardly and near his shoulder. He stared at the card-players.

Probably the silence was while a second elapsed. Then, if the floor had been suddenly twitched out from under the men they could not have moved quicker. The five had projected themselves headlong toward a common point. It happened that Johnnie, in rising to hurl himself upon the Swede, had stumbled slightly because of his curiously instinctive care for the cards and the board. The loss of the moment allowed time for the arrival of Scully, and also allowed the cowboy time to give the Swede a great push which sent him staggering back. The men found tongue together, and hoarse shouts of rage, appeal, or fear burst from every throat. The cowboy pushed and jostled feverishly at the Swede, and the Easterner and Scully clung wildly to Johnnie; but through the smoky air, above the swaying bodies of the peace-compellers, the eyes of the two warriors ever sought each other in glances of challenge that were at once hot and steely.

Of course the board had been overturned, and now the whole company of cards was scattered over the floor, where the boots of the men trampled the fat and painted kings and queens as they gazed with their silly eyes at the war that was waging above them.

Scully's voice was dominating the yells. "Stop now! Stop, I say! Stop, now——"

Johnnie, as he struggled to burst through the rank formed by Scully and the Easterner, was crying, "Well, he says I cheated! He says I cheated! I won't allow no man to say I cheated! If he says I cheated, he's a —— ——!"

The cowboy was telling the Swede, "Quit, now! Quit, d'ye hear——"

The screams of the Swede never ceased: "He did cheat! I saw him! I saw him——"

As for the Easterner, he was importuning in a voice that was not heeded: "Wait a moment, can't you? Oh, wait a moment. What's the good of a fight over a game of cards? Wait a moment——"

In this tumult no complete sentences were clear. "Cheat"—"Quit"—"He says" —these fragments pierced the uproar and rang out sharply. It was remarkable that, whereas Scully undoubtedly made the most noise, he was the least heard of any of the riotous band.

Then suddenly there was a great cessation. It was as if each man had paused for breath; and although the room was still lighted with the anger of men, it could be seen that there was no danger of immediate conflict, and at once Johnnie, shouldering his way forward, almost succeeded in confronting the Swede. "What did you say I cheated for? What did you say I cheated for? I don't cheat, and I won't let no man say I do!"

The Swede said, "I saw you! I saw you!"

"Well," cried Johnnie, "I'll fight any man what says I cheat!"

"No, you won't," said the cowboy. "Not here."

"Ah, be still, can't you?" said Scully, coming between them.

The quiet was sufficient to allow the Easterner's voice to be heard. He was repeating, "Oh, wait a moment, can't you? What's the good of a fight over a game of cards? Wait a moment!"

Johnnie, his red face appearing above his father's shoulder, hailed the Swede again. "Did you say I cheated?"

The Swede showed his teeth. "Yes."

"Then," said Johnnie, "we must fight."

"Yes, fight," roared the Swede. He was like a demoniac. "Yes, fight! I'll show you what kind of a man I am! I'll show you who you want to fight! Maybe you think I can't fight! Maybe you think I can't! I'll show you, you skin, you card-sharp! Yes, you cheated! You cheated! You cheated!"

"Well, let's go at it, then, mister," said Johnnie, coolly.

The cowboy's brow was beaded with sweat from his efforts in intercepting all sorts of raids. He turned in despair to Scully. "What are you goin' to do now?"

A change had come over the Celtic visage of the old man. He now seemed all eagerness; his eyes glowed.

"We'll let them fight," he answered, stalwartly. "I can't put up with it any longer. I've stood this damned Swede till I'm sick. We'll let them fight."

VI

The men prepared to go out of doors. The Easterner was so nervous that he had great difficulty in getting his arms into the sleeves of his new leather coat. As the cowboy drew his fur cap down over his ears his hands trembled. In fact, Johnnie and old Scully were the only ones who displayed no agitation. These preliminaries were conducted without words.

Scully threw open the door. "Well, come on," he said. Instantly a terrific wind caused the flame of the lamp to struggle at its wick, while a puff of black smoke sprang from the chimney-top. The stove was in mid-current of the blast, and its voice swelled to equal the roar of the storm. Some of the scarred and bedabbled cards were caught up from the floor and dashed helplessly against the farther wall. The men lowered their heads and plunged into the tempest as into a sea.

No snow was falling, but great whirls and clouds of flakes, swept up from the ground by the frantic winds, were streaming southward with the speed of bullets. The covered land was blue with the sheen of an unearthly satin, and there was no other hue save where, at the low, black railway station—which seemed incredibly distant—one light gleamed like a tiny jewel. As the men floundered into a thigh-deep drift, it was known that the Swede was bawling out something. Scully went to him, put a hand on his shoulder, and projected an ear. "What's that you say?" he shouted.

"I say," bawled the Swede again, "I won't stand much show against this gang. I know you'll all pitch on me."

Scully smote him reproachfully on the arm. "Tut, man!" he yelled. The wind tore the words from Scully's lips and scattered them far alee.

"You are all a gang of——" boomed the Swede, but the storm also seized the remainder of this sentence.

Immediately turning their backs upon the wind, the men had swung around a corner to the sheltered side of the hotel. It was the function of the little house to preserve here, amid this great devastation of snow, an irregular V-shape of heavily encrusted grass, which crackled beneath the feet. One could imagine the great drifts piled against the windward side. When the party reached the comparative peace of this spot it was found that the Swede was still bellowing.

"Oh, I know what kind of a thing this is! I know you'll all pitch on me. I can't lick you all!"

Scully turned upon him panther-fashion. "You'll not have to whip all of us. You'll have to whip my son Johnnie. An' the man what troubles you durin' that time will have me to dale with."

The arrangements were swiftly made. The two men faced each other, obedient to the harsh commands of Scully, whose face, in the subtly luminous gloom, could be seen set in the austere impersonal lines that are pictured on the countenances of the Roman veterans. The Easterner's teeth were chattering, and he was hopping up and down like a mechanical toy. The cowboy stood rock-like.

The contestants had not stripped off any clothing. Each was in his ordinary attire. Their fists were up, and they eyed each other in a calm that had the elements of leonine cruelty in it.

During this pause, the Easterner's mind, like a film, took lasting impressions of three men—the iron-nerved master of the ceremony; the Swede, pale, motionless, terrible; and Johnnie, serene yet ferocious, brutish yet heroic. The entire prelude had in it a tragedy greater than the tragedy of action, and this aspect was accentuated by the long, mellow cry of the blizzard, as it sped the tumbling and wailing flakes into the black abyss of the south.

"Now!" said Scully.

The two combatants leaped forward and crashed together like bullocks. There was heard the cushioned sound of blows, and of a curse squeezing out from between the tight teeth of one.

As for the spectators, the Easterner's pent-up breath exploded from him with a pop of relief, absolute relief from the tension of the preliminaries. The cowboy bounded into the air with a yowl. Scully was immovable as from supreme amazement and fear at the fury of the fight which he himself had permitted and arranged.

For a time the encounter in the darkness was such a perplexity of flying arms that it presented no more detail than would a swiftly revolving wheel. Occasionally a face, as if illumined by a flash of light, would shine out, ghastly and marked with pink spots. A moment later, the men might have been known as shadows, if it were not for the involuntary utterance of oaths that came from them in whispers.

Suddenly a holocaust of warlike desire caught the cowboy, and he bolted forward with the speed of a broncho. "Go it, Johnnie! Go it! Kill him! Kill him!"

Scully confronted him. "Kape back," he said; and by his glance the cowboy could tell that this man was Johnnie's father.

To the Easterner there was a monotony of unchangeable fighting that was an abomination. This confused mingling was eternal to his sense, which was concentrated in a longing for the end, the priceless end. Once the fighters lurched near him, and as he scrambled hastily backward he heard them breathe like men on the rack.

"Kill him, Johnnie! Kill him! Kill him!

Kill him!" The cowboy's face was contorted like one of those agony masks in museums.

"Keep still," said Scully, icily.

Then there was a sudden loud grunt, incomplete, cut short, and Johnnie's body swung away from the Swede and fell with sickening heaviness to the grass. The cowboy was barely in time to prevent the mad Swede from flinging himself upon his prone adversary. "No, you don't," said the cowboy, interposing an arm. "Wait a second."

Scully was at his son's side. "Johnnie! Johnnie, me boy!" His voice had a quality of melancholy tenderness. "Johnnie! Can you go on with it?" He looked anxiously down into the bloody, pulpy face of his son.

There was a moment of silence, and then Johnnie answered in his ordinary voice, "Yes, I—it—yes."

Assisted by his father he struggled to his feet. "Wait a bit now till you git your wind," said the old man.

A few paces away the cowboy was lecturing the Swede. "No, you don't! Wait a second!"

The Easterner was plucking at Scully's sleeve. "Oh, this is enough," he pleaded. "This is enough! Let it go as it stands. This is enough!"

"Bill," said Scully, "git out of the road." The cowboy stepped aside. "Now." The combatants were actuated by a new caution as they advanced toward collision. They glared at each other, and then the Swede aimed a lightning blow that carried with it his entire weight. Johnnie was evidently half stupid from weakness, but he miraculously dodged, and his fist sent the over-balanced Swede sprawling.

The cowboy, Scully, and the Easterner burst into a cheer that was like a chorus of triumphant soldiery, but before its conclusion the Swede had scuffled agilely to his feet and come in berserk abandon at his foe. There was another perplexity of flying arms, and Johnnie's body again swung away and fell, even as a bundle might fall from a roof. The Swede instantly staggered to a little wind-waved tree and leaned upon it, breathing like an engine, while his savage and flamelit eyes roamed from face to face as the men bent over Johnnie. There was a splendour of isolation in his situation at this time which the Easterner felt once when, lifting his eyes from the man on the ground, he beheld that mysterious and lonely figure, waiting.

"Are you any good yet, Johnnie?" asked Scully in a broken voice.

The son gasped and opened his eyes languidly. After a moment he answered, "No—I ain't—any good—any—more." Then, from shame and bodily ill, he began to weep, the tears furrowing down through the blood-stains on his face. "He was too—too—too heavy for me."

Scully straightened and addressed the waiting figure. "Stranger," he said, evenly, "it's all up with our side." Then his voice changed into that vibrant huskiness which is commonly the tone of the most simple and deadly announcements. "Johnnie is whipped."

Without replying, the victor moved off on the route to the front door of the hotel.

The cowboy was formulating new and unspellable blasphemies. The Easterner was startled to find that they were out in a wind that seemed to come direct from the shadowed arctic floes. He heard again the wail of the snow as it was flung to its grave in the south. He knew now that all this time the cold had been sinking into him deeper and deeper, and he wondered that he had not perished. He felt indifferent to the condition of the vanquished man.

"Johnnie, can you walk?" asked Scully.

"Did I hurt—hurt him any?" asked the son.

"Can you walk, boy? Can you walk?"

Johnnie's voice was suddenly strong. There was a robust impatience in it. "I asked you whether I hurt him any!"

"Yes, yes, Johnnie," answered the cowboy, consolingly; "he's hurt a good deal."

They raised him from the ground, and as soon as he was on his feet he went tottering off, rebuffing all attempts at assistance. When the party rounded the corner they were fairly blinded by the pelting of the snow. It burned their faces like fire. The cowboy carried Johnnie through the drift to the door. As they entered, some cards again rose from the floor and beat against the wall.

The Easterner rushed to the stove. He was so profoundly chilled that he almost dared to embrace the glowing iron. The Swede was not in the room. Johnnie sank into a chair and, folding his arms on his knees, buried his face in them. Scully, warming one foot and then the other at a rim of the stove, muttered to himself with Celtic mournfulness. The cowboy had removed his fur cap, and with a dazed and rueful air he was running one hand through his tousled locks. From overhead they could hear the creaking of boards, as the Swede tramped here and there in his room.

The sad quiet was broken by the sudden flinging open of a door that led toward the kitchen. It was instantly followed by an inrush of women. They precipitated themselves upon Johnnie amid a chorus of lamentation. Before they carried their prey off to the kitchen, there to be bathed and harangued with that mixture of sympathy and abuse which is a feat of their sex, the mother straightened herself and fixed old Scully with an eye of stern reproach. "Shame be upon you, Patrick Scully!" she cried. "Your own son, too. Shame be upon you!"

"There, now! Be quiet, now!" said the old man, weakly.

"Shame be upon you, Patrick Scully!" The girls, rallying to this slogan, sniffed disdainfully in the direction of those trembling accomplices, the cowboy and the Easterner. Presently they bore Johnnie away, and left the three men to dismal reflection.

VII

"I'd like to fight this here Dutchman myself," said the cowboy, breaking a long silence.

Scully wagged his head sadly. "No, that wouldn't do. It wouldn't be right. It wouldn't be right."

"Well, why wouldn't it?" argued the cowboy. "I don't see no harm in it."

"No," answered Scully, with mournful heroism. "It wouldn't be right. It was

Johnnie's fight, and now we mustn't whip the man just because he whipped Johnnie."

"Yes, that's true enough," said the cowboy; "but—he better not get fresh with me, because I couldn't stand no more of it."

"You'll not say a word to him," commanded Scully, and even then they heard the tread of the Swede on the stairs. His entrance was made theatric. He swept the door back with a bang and swaggered to the middle of the room. No one looked at him. "Well," he cried, insolently, at Scully, "I s'pose you'll tell me now how much I owe you?"

The old man remained stolid. "You don't owe me nothin'."

"Huh!" said the Swede, "huh! Don't owe 'im nothin'."

The cowboy addressed the Swede. "Stranger, I don't see how you come to be so gay around here."

Old Scully was instantly alert. "Stop!" he shouted, holding his hand forth, fingers upward. "Bill, you shut up!"

The cowboy spat carelessly into the sawdust-box. "I didn't say a word, did I?" he asked.

"Mr. Scully," called the Swede, "how much do I owe you?" It was seen that he was attired for departure, and that he had his valise in his hand.

"You don't owe me nothin'," repeated Scully in the same imperturbable way.

"Huh!" said the Swede. "I guess you're right. I guess if it was any way at all, you'd owe me somethin'. That's what I guess." He turned to the cowboy. " 'Kill him! Kill him! Kill him!' " he mimicked, and then guffawed victoriously. " 'Kill him!' " He was convulsed with ironical humour.

But he might have been jeering the dead. The three men were immovable and silent, staring with glassy eyes at the stove.

The Swede opened the door and passed into the storm, giving one derisive glance backward at the still group.

As soon as the door was closed, Scully and the cowboy leaped to their feet and began to curse. They trampled to and fro, waving their arms and smashing into the air with their fists. "Oh, but that was a hard minute!" wailed Scully. "That was a hard minute! Him there leerin' and scoffin'!' One bang at his nose was worth forty dollars to me that minute! How did you stand it, Bill?"

"How did I stand it?" cried the cowboy in a quivering voice. "How did I stand it? Oh!"

The old man burst into sudden brogue. "I'd loike to take that Swade," he wailed, "and hould 'im down on a shtone flure and bate 'im to a jelly wid a shtick!"

The cowboy groaned in sympathy. "I'd like to git him by the neck and ha-ammer him"—he brought his hand down on a chair with a noise like a pistol-shot—"hammer that there Dutchman until he couldn't tell himself from a dead coyote!"

"I'd bate 'im until he——"

"I'd show *him* some things——"

And then together they raised a yearning, fanatic cry—"Oh-o-oh! if we only could——"

"Yes!"

"Yes!"

"And then I'd——"

"O-o-oh!"

VIII

The Swede, tightly gripping his valise, tacked across the face of the storm as if he carried sails. He was following a line of little naked, gasping trees which, he knew, must mark the way of the road. His face, fresh from the pounding of Johnnie's fists, felt more pleasure than pain in the wind and the driving snow. A number of square shapes loomed upon him finally, and he knew them as the houses of the main body of the town. He found a street and made travel along it, leaning heavily upon the wind whenever, at a corner, a terrific blast caught him.

He might have been in a deserted village. We picture the world as thick with conquering and elate humanity, but here, with the bugles of the tempest pealing, it was hard to imagine a peopled earth. One viewed the existence of man then as a marvel, and conceded a glamour of wonder to these lice which were caused to cling to a whirling, fire-smitten, ice-

locked, disease-stricken, space-lost bulb. The conceit of man was explained by this storm to be the very engine of life. One was a coxcomb not to die in it. However, the Swede found a saloon.

In front of it an indomitable red light was burning, and the snowflakes were made blood-colour as they flew through the circumscribed territory of the lamp's shining. The Swede pushed open the door of the saloon and entered. A sanded expanse was before him, and at the end of it four men sat about a table drinking. Down one side of the room extended a radiant bar, and its guardian was leaning upon his elbows listening to the talk of the men at the table. The Swede dropped his valise upon the floor and, smiling fraternally upon the barkeeper, said, "Gimme some whisky, will you?" The man placed a bottle, a whisky-glass, and a glass of ice-thick water upon the bar. The Swede poured himself an abnormal portion of whisky and drank it in three gulps. "Pretty bad night," remarked the bartender, indifferently. He was making the pretension of blindness which is usually a distinction of his class; but it could have been seen that he was furtively studying the half-erased blood-stains on the face of the Swede. "Bad night," he said again.

"Oh, it's good enough for me," replied the Swede, hardily, as he poured himself some more whisky. The barkeeper took his coin and manœuvred it through its reception by the highly nickelled cash-machine. A bell rang; a card labelled "20 cts." had appeared.

"No," continued the Swede, "this isn't too bad weather. It's good enough for me."

"So?" murmured the barkeeper, languidly.

The copious drams made the Swede's eyes swim, and he breathed a trifle heavier. "Yes, I like this weather. I like it. It suits me." It was apparently his design to impart a deep significance to these words.

"So?" murmured the bartender again. He turned to gaze dreamily at the scroll-like birds and bird-like scrolls which had been drawn with soap upon the mirrors in back of the bar.

"Well, I guess I'll take another drink," said the Swede, presently. "Have something?"

"No, thanks; I'm not drinkin'," answered the bartender. Afterwards he asked, "How did you hurt your face?"

The Swede immediately began to boast loudly. "Why, in a fight. I thumped the soul out of a man down here at Scully's hotel."

The interest of the four men at the table was at last aroused.

"Who was it?" said one.

"Johnnie Scully," blustered the Swede. "Son of the man what runs it. He will be pretty near dead for some weeks, I can tell you. I made a nice thing of him, I did. He couldn't get up. They carried him in the house. Have a drink?"

Instantly the men in some subtle way encased themselves in reserve. "No, thanks," said one. The group was of curious formation. Two were prominent local business men; one was the district attorney; and one was a professional gambler of the kind known as "square." But a scrutiny of the group would not have enabled an observer to pick the gambler from the men of more reputable pursuits. He was, in fact, a man so delicate in manner, when among people of fair class, and so judicious in his choice of victims, that in the strictly masculine part of the town's life he had come to be explicitly trusted and admired. People called him a thoroughbred. The fear and contempt with which his craft was regarded were undoubtedly the reason why his quiet dignity shone conspicuous above the quiet dignity of men who might be merely hatters, billiard-markers, or grocery clerks. Beyond an occasional unwary traveller who came by rail, this gambler was supposed to prey solely upon reckless and senile farmers, who, when flush with good crops, drove into town in all the pride and confidence of an absolutely invulnerable stupidity. Hearing at times in circuitous fashion of the despoilment of such a farmer, the important men of Romper invariably laughed in contempt of the victim, and if they thought of the wolf at all, it was with a kind of pride at the knowledge that he would never dare think of attacking their wisdom and cour-

age. Besides, it was popular that this gambler had a real wife and two real children in a neat cottage in a suburb, where he led an exemplary home life; and when any one even suggested a discrepancy in his character, the crowd immediately vociferated descriptions of this virtuous family circle. Then men who led exemplary home lives, and men who did not lead exemplary home lives, all subsided in a bunch, remarking that there was nothing more to be said.

However, when a restriction was placed upon him—as, for instance, when a strong clique of members of the new Pollywog Club refused to permit him, even as a spectator, to appear in the rooms of the organization—the candour and gentleness with which he accepted the judgment disarmed many of his foes and made his friends more desperately partisan. He invariably distinguished between himself and a respectable Romper man so quickly and frankly that his manner actually appeared to be a continual broadcast compliment.

And one must not forget to declare the fundamental fact of his entire position in Romper. It is irrefutable that in all affairs outside his business, in all matters that occur eternally and commonly between man and man, this thieving card-player was so generous, so just, so moral, that, in a contest, he could have put to flight the consciences of nine tenths of the citizens of Romper.

And so it happened that he was seated in this saloon with the two prominent local merchants and the district attorney.

The Swede continued to drink raw whisky, meanwhile babbling at the barkeeper and trying to induce him to indulge in potations. "Come on. Have a drink. Come on. What—no? Well, have a little one, then. By gawd, I've whipped a man to-night, and I want to celebrate. I whipped him good, too. Gentlemen," the Swede cried to the men at the table, "have a drink?"

"Ssh!" said the barkeeper.

The group at the table, although furtively attentive, had been pretending to be deep in talk, but now a man lifted his eyes toward the Swede and said, shortly, "Thanks. We don't want any more."

At this reply the Swede ruffled out his chest like a rooster. "Well," he exploded, "it seems I can't get anybody to drink with me in this town. Seems so, don't it? Well!"

"Ssh!" said the barkeeper.

"Say," snarled the Swede, "don't you try to shut me up. I won't have it. I'm a gentleman, and I want people to drink with me. And I want 'em to drink with me now. *Now*—do you understand?" He rapped the bar with his knuckles.

Years of experience had calloused the bartender. He merely grew sulky. "I hear you," he answered.

"Well," cried the Swede, "listen hard then. See those men over there? Well, they're going to drink with me, and don't you forget it. Now you watch."

"Hi!" yelled the barkeeper, "this won't do!"

"Why won't it?" demanded the Swede. He stalked over to the table, and by chance laid his hand upon the shoulder of the gambler. "How about this?" he asked wrathfully. "I asked you to drink with me."

The gambler simply twisted his head and spoke over his shoulder. "My friend, I don't know you."

"Oh, hell!" answered the Swede, "come and have a drink."

"Now, my boy," advised the gambler, kindly, "take your hand off my shoulder and go 'way and mind your own business." He was a little, slim man, and it seemed strange to hear him use this tone of heroic patronage to the burly Swede. The other men at the table said nothing.

"What! You won't drink with me, you little dude? I'll make you, then! I'll make you!" The Swede had grasped the gambler frenziedly at the throat, and was dragging him from his chair. The other men sprang up. The barkeeper dashed around the corner of his bar. There was a great tumult, and then was seen a long blade in the hand of the gambler. It shot forward, and a human body, this citadel of virtue, wisdom, power, was pierced as easily as if it had been a melon. The Swede fell with a cry of supreme astonishment.

The prominent merchants and the district attorney must have at once tumbled out of the place backward. The bartender found himself hanging limply to the arm of a chair and gazing into the eyes of a murderer.

"Henry," said the latter, as he wiped his knife on one of the towels that hung beneath the bar rail, "you tell 'em where to find me. I'll be home, waiting for 'em." Then he vanished. A moment afterward the barkeeper was in the street dinning through the storm for help and, moreover, companionship.

The corpse of the Swede, alone in the saloon, had its eyes fixed upon a dreadful legend that dwelt atop of the cash-machine: "This registers the amount of your purchase."

IX

Months later, the cowboy was frying pork over the stove of a little ranch near the Dakota line, when there was a quick thud of hoofs outside, and presently the Easterner entered with the letters and the papers.

"Well," said the Easterner at once, "the chap that killed the Swede has got three years. Wasn't much, was it?"

"He has? Three years?" The cowboy poised his pan of pork, while he ruminated upon the news. "Three years. That ain't much."

"No. It was a light sentence," replied the Easterner as he unbuckled his spurs. "Seems there was a good deal of sympathy for him in Romper."

"If the bartender had been any good," observed the cowboy, thoughtfully, "he would have gone in and cracked that there Dutchman on the head with a bottle in the beginnin' of it and stopped all this here murderin'."

"Yes, a thousand things might have happened," said the Easterner, tartly.

The cowboy returned his pan of pork to the fire, but his philosophy continued. "It's funny, ain't it? If he hadn't said Johnnie was cheatin' he'd be alive this minute. He was an awful fool. Game played for fun, too. Not for money. I believe he was crazy."

"I feel sorry for that gambler," said the Easterner.

"Oh, so do I," said the cowboy. "He

don't deserve none of it for killin' who he did."

"The Swede might not have been killed if everything had been square."

"Might not have been killed?" exclaimed the cowboy. "Everythin' square? Why, when he said that Johnnie was cheatin' and acted like such a jackass? And then in the saloon he fairly walked up to git hurt?" With these arguments the cowboy browbeat the Easterner and reduced him to rage.

"You're a fool!" cried the Easterner, viciously. "You're a bigger jackass than the Swede by a million majority. Now let me tell you one thing. Let me tell you something. Listen! Johnnie *was* cheating!"

" 'Johnnie,' " said the cowboy, blankly. There was a minute of silence, and then he said, robustly, "Why, no. The game was only for fun."

"Fun or not," said the Easterner, "Johnnie was cheating. I saw him. I know it. I saw him. And I refused to stand up and be a man. I let the Swede fight it out alone. And you—you were simply puffing around the place and wanting to fight. And then old Scully himself! We are all in it! This poor gambler isn't even a noun. He is kind of an adverb. Every sin is the result of a collaboration. We, five of us, have collaborated in the murder of this Swede. Usually there are from a dozen to forty women really involved in every murder, but in this case it seems to be only five men—you, I, Johnnie, old Scully; and that fool of an unfortunate gambler came merely as a culmination, the apex of a human movement, and gets all the punishment."

The cowboy, injured and rebellious, cried out blindly into this fog of mysterious theory: "Well, I didn't do anythin', did I?"

[1898]

QUESTIONS FOR STUDY

1. *What is the source of the Swede's fear? To what extent does it spring from a distorted view of reality and his own preconceived ideas? Is his subsequent courage ("conceit") just as irrational?*

2. *What seems to be Crane's view of man and his relationship to the universe? On what does man's survival depend?*

3. *What is ironic about the "dreadful legend that dwelt atop of the cashmachine: 'This registers the amount of your purchase' "?*

4. *How does the natural setting reinforce the theme and meaning of the story? What other kinds of imagery does Crane employ?*

5. *What does Crane mean at the end of the story when he has the Easterner say that "Every sin is the result of a collaboration"? How are all five of the major characters implicated in the Swede's death? Which are most guilty? To what extent does this statement shift the blame from the Swede himself?*

CHARLES DICKENS

The Signal-Man

"HALLOA! Below there!"
When he heard a voice thus calling to him, he was standing at the door of his box, with a flag in his hand, furled round its short ·pole. One would have thought, considering the nature of the ground, that he could not have doubted from what quarter the voice came; but, instead of looking up to where I stood on the top of the steep cutting nearly over his head, he turned himself about, and looked down the Line. There was something remarkable in his manner of doing so, though I could not have said for my life what. But I know it was remarkable enough to attract my notice, even though his figure was foreshortened and shadowed, down in the deep trench, and mine was high above him, so steeped in the glow of an angry sunset, that I had shaded my eyes with my hand before I saw him at all.

"Halloa! Below!"

From looking down the Line, he turned himself about again, and, raising his eyes, saw my figure high above him.

"Is there any path by which I can come down and speak to you?"

He looked up at me without replying, and I looked down at him without pressing him too soon with a repetition of my idle question. Just then there came a vague vibration in the earth and air, quickly changing into a violent pulsation, and an on-coming rush that caused me to start back, as though it had force to draw me down. When such vapor as rose to my height from this rapid train had passed me, and was skimming away over the landscape, I looked down again, and saw him refurling the flag he had shown while the train went by.

I repeated my inquiry. After a pause, during which he seemed to regard me with fixed attention, he motioned with his rolled-up flag towards a point on my level, some two or three hundred yards distant. I called down to him, "All right!" and made for that point. There, by dint of looking closely about me, I found a rough zigzag descending path notched out, which I followed.

The cutting was extremely deep, and unusually precipitate. It was made through a clammy stone, that became oozier and wetter as I went down. For these reasons I found the way long enough to give me time to recall a singular air of reluctance or compulsion with which he had pointed out the path.

When I came down low enough upon the zigzag descent to see him again, I saw that he was standing between the rails on the way by which the train had lately passed, in an attitude as if he were waiting for me to appear. He had his left hand at his chin, and that left elbow rested on his right hand, crossed over his breast. His attitude was one of such expectation and watchfulness, that I stopped a moment wondering at it.

I resumed my downward way, and stepping out upon the level of the railroad, and drawing nearer to him, saw that he was a dark sallow man, with a dark beard and rather heavy eyebrows. His post was in as solitary and dismal a place as ever I saw. On either side, a dripping-wet wall of jagged stone, excluding all view but a strip of sky; the perspective one way only a crooked prolongation of this great dungeon; the shorter perspective in the other direction terminating in a gloomy red light, and the gloomier entrance to a black tunnel, in whose massive architecture there was a barbarous, depressing, and forbidding air. So little sunlight ever found its way to this spot, that it had an earthy, deadly smell; and so much cold wind rushed through it, that it struck chill to me, as if I had left the natural world.

Before he stirred, I was near enough to him to have touched him. Not even then removing his eyes from mine, he stepped back one step, and lifted his hand.

This was a lonesome post to occupy (I said), and it had riveted my attention when I looked down from up yonder. A visitor was a rarity, I should suppose; not an unwelcome rarity, I hoped? In me he merely saw a man who had been shut up within narrow limits all his life, and who, being at last set free, had a newly awakened interest in these great works. To such purpose I spoke to him; but I am far from sure of the terms I used; for, besides that I am not happy in opening any conversation, there was something in the man that daunted me.

He directed a most curious look towards the red light near the tunnel's mouth, and looked all about it, as if something were missing from it, and then looked at me.

That light was part of his charge? Was it not?

He answered in a low voice, "Don't you know it is?"

The monstrous thought came into my mind, as I perused the fixed eyes and the saturnine face, that this was a spirit, not a man. I have speculated since whether there may have been infection in his mind.

In my turn, I stepped back. But, in making the action, I detected in his eyes some latent fear of me. This put the monstrous thought to flight.

"You look at me," I said, forcing a smile, "as if you had a dread of me."

"I was doubtful," he returned, "whether I had seen you before."

"Where?"

He pointed to the red light he had looked at.

"There?" I said.

Intently watchful of me, he replied (but without sound), "Yes."

"My good fellow, what should I do there? However, be that as it may, I never was there, you may swear."

"I think I may," he rejoined. "Yes; I am sure I may."

His manner cleared, like my own. He replied to my remarks with readiness, and in well-chosen words. Had he much to do there? Yes; that was to say, he had enough responsibility to bear; but exact-ness and watchfulness were what was required of him, and of actual work—manual labor—he had next to none. To change that signal, to trim those lights, and to turn this iron handle now and then, was all he had to do under that head. Regarding those many long and lonely hours of which I seemed to make so much, he could only say that the routine of his life had shaped itself into that form, and he had grown used to it. He had taught himself a language down here, —if only to know it by sight, and to have formed his own crude ideas of its pronunciation, could be called learning it. He had also worked at fractions and decimals, and tried a little algebra; but he was, and had been as a boy, a poor hand at figures. Was it necessary for him when on duty always to remain in that channel of damp air, and could he never rise into the sunshine from between those high stone walls? Why, that depended upon times and circumstances. Under some conditions there would be less upon the Line than under others, and the same held good as to certain hours of the day and night. In bright weather he did choose occasions for getting a little above these lower shadows; but, being at all times liable to be called by his electric bell, and at such times listening for it with redoubled anxiety, the relief was less than I would suppose.

He took me into his box, where there was a fire, a desk for an official book in which he had to make certain entries, a telegraphic instrument with its dial, face, and needles, and the little bell of which he had spoken. On my trusting that he would excuse the remark that he had been well educated, and (I hoped I might say without offence), perhaps educated above that station, he observed that instances of slight incongruity in such wise would rarely be found wanting among large bodies of men; that he had heard it was so in workhouses, in the police force, even in that last desperate resource, the army; and that he knew it was so, more or less, in any great railway staff. He had been, when young (if I could believe it, sitting in that hut,—he scarcely could), a student of natural philosophy, and had attended lectures; but he had run wild, misused his opportunities, gone down, and never risen again. He had no complaint to offer about that. He had made his bed, and he lay upon it. It was far too late to make another.

All that I have here condensed he said in a quiet manner, with his grave dark regards divided between me and the fire. He threw in the word "Sir" from time to time, and especially when he referred to his youth,—as though to request me to understand that he claimed to be nothing but what I found him. He was several times interrupted by the little bell, and had to read off messages and send replies. Once he had to stand without the door, and display a flag as a train passed, and make some verbal communication to the driver. In the discharge of his duties, I observed him to be remarkably exact and vigilant, breaking off his discourse at a syllable, and remaining silent until what he had to do was done.

In a word, I should have set this man down as one of the safest of men to be employed in that capacity, but for the circumstance that while he was speaking to me he twice broke off with a fallen color, turned his face towards the little bell when it did NOT ring, opened the door of the hut (which was kept shut to exclude the unhealthy damp), and looked out towards the red light near the mouth of the tunnel. On both of those occasions, he came back to the fire with the inexplicable air upon him which I had remarked, without being able to define, when we were so far asunder.

Said I, when I rose to leave him, "You almost make me think that I have met with a contented man."

(I am afraid I must acknowledge that I said it to lead him on.)

"I believe I used to be so," he rejoined in the low voice in which he had first spoken; "but I am troubled, sir, I am troubled."

He would have recalled the words if he could. He had said them, however, and I took them up quickly.

"With what? What is your trouble?"

"It is very difficult to impart, sir. It is very, very difficult to speak of. If ever you make me another visit, I will try to tell you."

"But I expressly intend to make you another visit. Say, when shall it be?"

"I go off early in the morning, and I shall be on again at ten to-morrow night, sir."

"I will come at eleven."

He thanked me, and went out at the door with me. "I'll show my white light, sir," he said in his peculiar low voice, "till you have found the way up. When you have found it, don't call out! And when you are at the top, don't call out!"

His manner seemed to make the place strike colder to me, but I said no more than, "Very well."

"And when you come down to-morrow night don't call out! Let me ask you a parting question. What made you cry, 'Halloa! Below there!' to-night?"

"Heaven knows," said I. "I cried something to that effect—"

"Not to that effect, sir. Those were the very words. I know them well."

"Admit those were the very words. I said them, no doubt, because I saw you below."

"For no other reason?"

"What other reason could I possibly have?"

"You had no feeling that they were conveyed to you in any supernatural way?"

"No."

He wished me good-night, and held up his light. I walked by the side of the down Line of rails (with a very disagreeable sensation of a train coming behind me) until I found the path. It was easier to mount than to descend, and I got back to my inn without any adventure.

Punctual to my appointment, I placed my foot on the first notch of the zigzag next night as the distant clocks were striking eleven. He was waiting for me at the bottom, with his white light on. "I have not called out," I said when we came close together; "may I speak now?" "By all means, sir." "Good-night, then, and here's my hand." "Good-night, sir, and here's mine." With that we walked side by side to his box, entered it, closed the door, and sat down by the fire.

"I have made up my mind, sir," he began, bending forward as soon as we were seated, and speaking in a tone but a little above a whisper, "that you shall not have to ask me twice what troubles me. I took you for some one else yesterday evening. That troubles me."

"That mistake?"

"No. That some one else."

"Who is it?"

"I don't know."

"Like me?"

"I don't know. I never saw the face. The left arm is across the face, and the right arm is waved,—violently waved. This way."

I followed his action with my eyes, and it was the action of an arm gesticulating, with the utmost passion and vehemence, "For God's sake, clear the way!"

"One moonlight night," said the man, "I was sitting here, when I heard a voice cry, 'Halloa! Below there!' I started up, looked from that door, and saw this Some one else standing by the red light near the tunnel, waving as I just now showed you. The voice seemed hoarse with shouting, and it cried, 'Look out! Look out!' And then again, 'Halloa! Below there! Look out!' I caught up my lamp, turned it on red, and ran towards the figure, calling, 'What's wrong? What has happened? Where?' It stood just outside the blackness of the tunnel. I advanced so close upon it that I wondered at its keeping the sleeve across its eyes. I ran right up at it, and had my hand stretched out to pull the sleeve away, when it was gone."

"Into the tunnel?" said I.

"No. I ran on into the tunnel, five hundred yards. I stopped and held my lamp above my head, and saw the figures of the measured distance, and saw the wet stains stealing down the walls and trickling through the arch. I ran out again faster than I had run in (for I had a mortal abhorrence of the place upon me), and I looked all round the red light with my own red light, and I went up the iron ladder to the gallery atop of it, and I came down again, and ran back here. I telegraphed both ways, 'An Alarm has been given. Is anything wrong?' The answer came back, both ways, 'All well.' "

Resisting the slow touch of a frozen finger tracing out my spine, I showed him how that this figure must be a deception of his sense of sight; and how that figures, originating in disease of the delicate nerves that minister to the functions of the eye, were known to have often troubled patients, some of whom had become conscious of the nature of their affliction, and had even proved it by experiments upon themselves. "As to an imaginary cry," I said, "do but listen for a moment to the wind in this unnatural valley while we speak so low, and to the wild harp it makes of the telegraph wires!"

That was all very well, he returned, after we had sat listening for a while, and he ought to know something of the wind and the wires,—he who so often passed long winter nights there, alone and watching. But he would beg to remark that he had not finished.

I asked his pardon, and he slowly added these words, touching my arm:

"Within six hours after the Appearance, the memorable accident on this Line happened, and within ten hours the dead and wounded were brought along through the tunnel over the spot where the figure had stood."

A disagreeable shudder crept over me, but I did my best against it. It was not to be denied, I rejoined, that this was a remarkable coincidence, calculated deeply to impress his mind. But it was unquestionable that remarkable coincidences did continually occur, and they must be taken into account in dealing with such a subject. Though to be sure I must admit, I added (for I thought I saw that he was going to bring the objection to bear upon me), men of common sense did not allow much for coincidences in making the ordinary calculations of life.

He again begged to remark that he had not finished.

I again begged his pardon for being betrayed into interruptions.

"This," he said, again laying his hand upon my arm, and glancing over his shoulder with hollow eyes, "was just a year ago. Six or seven months passed, and I had recovered from the surprise and shock, when one morning, as the day was breaking, I, standing at the door, looked towards the red light, and saw the spectre

again." He stopped with a fixed look at
me.

"Did it cry out?"

"No. It was silent."

"Did it wave its arm?"

"No. It leaned against the shaft of the
light, with both hands before the face.
Like this."

Once more I followed his action with
my eyes. It was an action of mourning. I
have seen such an attitude in stone figures
on tombs.

"Did you go up to it?"

"I came in and sat down, partly to collect my thoughts, partly because it had
turned me faint. When I went to the door
again, daylight was above me, and the
ghost was gone."

"But nothing followed? Nothing came
of this?"

He touched me on the arm with his
forefinger twice or thrice, giving a ghastly
nod each time:

"That very day, as a train came out of
the tunnel, I noticed, at a carriage window on my side, what looked like a confusion of hands and heads, and something
waved. I saw it just in time to signal the
driver, Stop! He shut off, and put his
brake on, but the train drifted past here a
hundred and fifty yards or more. I ran
after it, and, as I went along, heard terrible screams and cries. A beautiful young
lady had died instantaneously in one of
the compartments, and was brought in
here, and laid down on this floor between
us."

Involuntarily I pushed my chair back,
as I looked from the boards at which he
pointed to himself.

"True, sir. True. Precisely as it happened, so I tell it you."

I could think of nothing to say to any
purpose, and my mouth was very dry.
The wind and the wires took up the story
with a long lamenting wail.

He resumed. "Now, sir, mark this, and
judge how my mind is troubled. The
spectre came back a week ago. Ever
since, it has been there, now and again,
by fits and starts."

"At the light?"

"At the Danger-light."

"What does it seem to do?"

He repeated, if possible with increased
passion and vehemence, that former gesticulation of, "For God's sake, clear the
way!"

Then he went on. "I have no peace or
rest for it. It calls to me, for many minutes together, in an agonized manner,
'Below there! Look out! Look out!' It
stands waving to me. It rings my little
bell—"

I caught at that. "Did it ring your bell
yesterday evening when I was here, and
you went to the door?"

"Twice."

"Why, see," said I, "how your imagination misleads you! My eyes were on
the bell, and my ears were open to the
bell, and, if I am a living man, it did NOT
ring at those times. No, nor at any other
time, except when it was rung in the natural course of physical things by the station communicating with you."

He shook his head. "I have never made
a mistake as to that yet, sir. I have never
confused the spectre's ring with the
man's. The ghost's ring is a strange vibration in the bell that it derives from nothing else, and I have not asserted that the
bell stirs to the eye. I don't wonder that
you failed to hear it. But *I* heard it."

"And did the spectre seem to be there
when you looked out?"

"It WAS there."

"Both times?"

He repeated firmly: "Both times."

"Will you come to the door with me,
and look for it now?"

He bit his under lip as though he were
somewhat unwilling, but arose. I opened
the door, and stood on the step, while he
stood in the doorway. There was the
Danger-light. There was the dismal
mouth of the tunnel. There were the high,
wet stone walls of the cutting. There were
the stars above them.

"Do you see it?" I asked him, taking
particular note of his face. His eyes were
prominent and strained, but not very
much more so, perhaps, than my own
had been when I had directed them ear-
'nestly towards the same spot.

"No," he answered. "It is not there."

"Agreed," said I.

We went in again, shut the door, and

resumed our seats. I was thinking how best to improve this advantage, if it might be called one, when he took up the conversation in such a matter-of-course way, so assuming that there could be no serious question of fact between us, that I felt myself placed in the weakest of positions.

"By this time you will fully understand, sir," he said, "that what troubles me so dreadfully is the question, What does the spectre mean?"

I was not sure, I told him, that I did fully understand.

"What is its warning against?" he said, ruminating, with his eyes on the fire, and only by times turning them on me. "What is the danger? Where is the danger? There is danger overhanging somewhere on the Line. Some dreadful calamity will happen. It is not to be doubted this third time after what has gone before. But surely this is a cruel haunting of *me*. What can *I* do?"

He pulled out his handkerchief, and wiped the drops from his heated forehead.

"If I telegraph Danger on either side of me, or on both, I can give no reason for it," he went on, wiping the palms of his hands. "I should get into trouble, and do no good. They would think I was mad. This is the way it would work,—Message: 'Danger! Take care!' Answer: 'What Danger? Where?' Message: 'Don't know. But, for God's sake, take care!' They would displace me. What else could they do?"

His pain of mind was most pitiable to see. It was the mental torture of a conscientious man, oppressed beyond endurance by an unintelligible responsibility involving life.

"When it first stood under the Danger-light," he went on, putting his dark hair back from his head, and drawing his hands outward across and across his temples in an extremity of feverish distress, "why not tell me where that accident was to happen,—if it must happen? Why not tell me how it could be averted,—if it could have been averted? When on its second coming it hid its face, why not tell me, instead, 'She is going to die. Let them keep her at home'? If it came, on those

two occasions, only to show me that its warnings were true, and so to prepare me for the third, why not warn me plainly now? And I, Lord help me! A mere poor signal-man on this solitary station! Why not go to somebody with credit to be believed, and power to act?"

When I saw him in this state, I saw that for the poor man's sake, as well as for the public safety, what I had to do for the time was to compose his mind. Therefore, setting aside all question of reality or unreality between us, I represented to him that whoever thoroughly discharged his duty must do well, and that at least it was his comfort that he understood his duty, though he did not understand these confounding Appearances. In this effort I succeeded far better than in the attempt to reason him out of his conviction. He became calm; the occupations incidental to his post as the night advanced began to make larger demands on his attention: and I left him at two in the morning. I had offered to stay through the night, but he would not hear of it.

That I more than once looked back at the red light as I ascended the pathway, that I did not like the red light, and that I should have slept but poorly if my bed had been under it, I see no reason to conceal. Nor did I like the two sequences of the accident and the dead girl. I see no reason to conceal that either.

But what ran most in my thoughts was the consideration, how ought I to act, having become the recipient of this disclosure? I had proved the man to be intelligent, vigilant, pains-taking, and exact; but how long might he remain so, in his state of mind? Though in a subordinate position, still he held a most important trust, and would I (for instance) like to stake my own life on the chances of his continuing to execute it with precision?

Unable to overcome a feeling that there would be something treacherous in my communicating what he had told me to his superiors in the Company, without first being plain with himself and proposing a middle course to him, I ultimately resolved to offer to accompany him (otherwise keeping his secret for the present) to the wisest medical practitioner we could hear of in those parts, and to take his opinion. A change in his time of duty would come round next night, he had apprised me, and he would be off an hour or two after sunrise, and on again soon after sunset. I had appointed to return accordingly.

Next evening was a lovely evening, and I walked out early to enjoy it. The sun was not yet quite down when I traversed the field-path near the top of the deep cutting. I would extend my walk for an hour, I said to myself, half an hour on and half an hour back, and it would then be time to go to my signal-man's box.

Before pursuing my stroll, I stepped to the brink, and mechanically looked down, from the point from which I had first seen him. I cannot describe the thrill that seized upon me when, close at the mouth of the tunnel, I saw the appearance of a man, with his left sleeve across his eyes, passionately waving his right arm.

The nameless horror that oppressed me passed in a moment, for in a moment I saw that this appearance of a man was a man indeed, and that there was a little group of other men, standing at a short distance, to whom he seemed to be rehearsing the gesture he made. The Danger-light was not yet lighted. Against its shaft, a little low hut, entirely new to me, had been made of some wooden supports and tarpaulin. It looked no bigger than a bed.

With an irresistible sense that something was wrong,—with a flashing self-reproachful fear that fatal mischief had come of my leaving the man there, and causing no one to be sent to overlook or correct what he did,—I descended the notched path with all the speed I could make.

"What is the matter?" I asked the men.

"Signal-man killed this morning, sir."

"Not the man belonging to that box?"

"Yes, sir."

"Not the man I know?"

"You will recognize him, sir, if you knew him," said the man who spoke for the others, solemnly uncovering his own head, and raising an end of the tarpaulin, "for his face is quite composed."

"Oh, how did this happen, how did this happen?" I asked, turning from one to another as the hut closed in again.

"He was cut down by an engine, sir. No man in England knew his work better. But somehow he was not clear of the outer rail. It was just at broad day. He had struck the light, and had the lamp in his hand. As the engine came out of the tunnel, his back was towards her, and she cut him down. That man drove her, and was showing how it happened. Show the gentleman, Tom."

The man, who wore a rough dark dress, stepped back to his former place at the mouth of the tunnel.

"Coming round the curve in the tunnel, sir," he said, "I saw him at the end, like as if I saw him down a perspective-glass. There was no time to check speed, and I knew him to be very careful. As he didn't seem to take heed of the whistle, I shut it off when we were running down upon him, and called to him as loud as I could call."

"What did you say?"

"I said, 'Below there! Look out! Look out! For God's sake clear the way!' "

I started.

"Ah! it was a dreadful time, sir. I never left off calling to him. I put this arm before my eyes not to see, and I waved this arm to the last; but it was no use."

Without prolonging the narrative to dwell on any one of its curious circumstances more than on any other, I may, in closing it, point out the coincidence that the warning of the Engine-Driver included, not only the words which the unfortunate Signal-man had repeated to me as haunting him, but also the words which I myself—not he—had attached, and that only in my own mind, to the gesticulation he had imitated.

[1866]

QUESTIONS FOR STUDY

1. Is "The Signal-Man" an effective ghost story? How well does Dickens succeed in handling such elements as setting, mood, and plot?
2. How does Dickens go about establishing the character of the narrator? What kind of man is he?
3. Is it important to the success of the story that the reader never sees the "ghost" directly or that he comes to learn relatively little about the signal-man?
4. What instances of foreshadowing does Dickens employ?

FËDOR DOSTOEVSKI

The Grand Inquisitor

"Do you know, Alyosha—don't laugh! I made a poem about a year ago. If you can waste another ten minutes on me, I'll tell it to you."

"You wrote a poem?"

"Oh, no, I didn't write it," laughed Ivan, "and I've never written two lines of poetry in my life. But I made up this poem in prose and I remembered it. I was carried away when I made it up. You will be my first reader—that is, listener. Why should an author forgo even one listener?" smiled Ivan. "Shall I tell it to you?"

"I am all attention," said Alyosha.

"My poem is called 'The Grand Inquisitor'; it's a ridiculous thing, but I want to tell it to you.

"Even this must have a preface—that is, a literary preface," laughed Ivan, "and I am a poor hand at making one. You see, my action takes place in the sixteenth century, and at that time, as you probably learnt at school, it was customary in poetry to bring down heavenly powers on earth. Not to speak of Dante, in France, clerks, as well as the monks in the monasteries, used to give regular performances in which the Madonna, the saints, the angels, Christ, and God Himself were brought on the stage. In those days it was done in all simplicity. In Victor Hugo's 'Notre Dame de Paris' an edifying and gratuitous spectacle was provided for the people in the Hôtel de Ville of Paris in the reign of Louis XI in honour of the birth of the dauphin. It was called *Le bon jugement de la très sainte et gracieuse Vierge Marie*;[1] and she appears herself on the stage and pronounces her *bon jugement*. Similar plays, chiefly from the Old Testament, were occasionally performed in Moscow too, up to the times of Peter the Great. But besides plays there were all sorts of legends and ballads scattered about the world, in which the saints and angels and all the powers of Heaven took part when required. In our monasteries the monks busied themselves in translating, copying, and even composing such poems—and even under the Tatars. There is, for instance, one such poem (of course, from the Greek), 'The Wanderings of Our Lady through Hell', with descriptions as bold as Dante's. Our Lady visits Hell, and the Archangel Michael leads her through the torments. She sees the sinners and their punishments. There she sees among others one noteworthy set of sinners in a burning lake; some of them sink to the bottom of the lake so that they can't swim out, and 'these God forgets' —an expression of extraordinary depth and force. And so Our Lady, shocked and weeping, falls before the throne of God and begs for mercy for all in Hell—for all she has seen there, indiscriminately. Her conversation with God is immensely interesting. She beseeches Him, she will not desist, and when God points to the hands and feet of her Son, nailed to the Cross, and asks: 'How can I forgive His tormentors?' she bids all the saints, all the martyrs, all the angels and archangels to fall down with her and pray for mercy on all without distinction. It ends by her winning from God a respite of suffering every year from Good Friday till Trinity day, and the sinners at once raise a cry of thankfulness from Hell, chanting: 'Thou art just, O Lord, in this judgment.' Well, my poem would have been of that kind if it had appeared at that time. He comes on the scene in my poem, but He says

[1] The sound judgment of the most holy and gracious Virgin Mary. (JHP)

Reprinted with permission of The Macmillan Company from *The Brothers Karamazov* by Fëdor Dostoevski. Translated by Constance Garnett. Also used by permission of William Heinemann Ltd., London, the British publishers. Printed in Great Britain.

nothing, only appears and passes on. Fifteen centuries have passed since He promised to come in His glory, fifteen centuries since His prophet wrote, 'Behold, I come quickly'; 'Of that day and that hour knoweth no man, neither the Son, but the Father,' as He Himself predicted on earth. But humanity awaits him with the same faith and with the same love. Oh, with greater faith, for it is fifteen centuries since man has ceased to see signs from Heaven.

> No signs from Heaven come to-day
> To add to what the heart doth say.

There was nothing left but faith in what the heart doth say. It is true there were many miracles in those days. There were saints who performed miraculous cures; some holy people, according to their biographies, were visited by the Queen of Heaven herself. But the devil did not slumber, and doubts were already arising among men of the truth of these miracles. And just then there appeared in the north of Germany a terrible new heresy. 'A huge star like to a torch' (that is, to a church) 'fell on the sources of the waters and they became bitter.' These heretics began blasphemously denying miracles. But those who remained faithful were all the more ardent in their faith. The tears of humanity rose up to Him as before, awaited His coming, loved Him, hoped for Him, yearned to suffer and die for Him as before. And so many ages mankind had prayed with faith and fervour: 'O Lord our God, hasten Thy coming,' so many ages called upon Him, that in His infinite mercy He deigned to come down to His servants. Before that day He had come down, He had visited some holy men, martyrs and hermits, as is written in their 'Lives'. Among us, Tyutchev, with absolute faith in the truth of his words, bore witness that:

> Bearing the Cross, in slavish dress
> Weary and worn, the Heavenly King
> Our mother, Russia, came to bless
> And through our land went wandering.

And that certainly was so, I assure you.

"And behold, He deigned to appear for a moment to the people, to the tortured, suffering people, sunk in iniquity but loving Him like children. My story is laid in Spain, in Seville, in the most terrible time of the Inquisition, when fires were lighted every day to the glory of God, and 'in the splendid *auto da fé* the wicked heretics were burnt'. Oh, of course, this was not the coming in which He will appear according to His promise at the end of time in all His heavenly glory, and which will be sudden 'as lightning flashing from east to west'. No, He visited His children only for a moment, and there where the flames were crackling round the heretics. In His infinite mercy He came once more among men in that human shape in which He walked among men for three years fifteen centuries ago. He came down to the 'hot pavements' of the southern town in which on the day before almost a hundred heretics had, *ad majorem gloriam Dei*,[2] been burnt by the cardinal, the Grand Inquisitor, in a magnificent *auto da fé*, in the presence of the king, the court, the knights, the cardinals, the most charming ladies of the court, and the whole population of Seville.

"He came softly, unobserved, and yet, strange to say, everyone recognised Him. That might be one of the best passages in the poem. I mean, why they recognised Him. The people are irresistibly drawn to Him, they surround Him, they flock about Him, follow Him. He moves silently in their midst with a gentle smile of infinite compassion. The sun of love burns in His heart, light and power shine from His eyes, and their radiance, shed on the people, stirs their hearts with responsive love. He holds out His hands to them, blesses them, and a healing virtue comes from contact with Him, even with His garments. An old man in the crowd, blind from childhood, cries out, 'O Lord, heal me and I shall see Thee!' and, as it were, scales fall from his eyes and the blind man sees Him. The crowd weeps and kisses the earth under His feet. Children throw flowers before Him, sing, and cry hosannah. 'It is He—it is He!' all repeat. 'It must be He, it can be no one but Him!' He stops at the steps of the Seville cathe-

---

2 "to the greater glory of God." (JHP)

dral at the moment when the weeping mourners are bringing in a little open white coffin. In it lies a child of seven, the only daughter of a prominent citizen. The dead child lies hidden in flowers. 'He will raise your child,' the crowd shouts to the weeping mother. The priest, coming to meet the coffin, looks perplexed, and frowns, but the mother of the dead child throws herself at His feet with a wail. 'If it is Thou, raise my child!' she cries holding out her hands to Him. The procession halts, the coffin is laid on the steps at His feet. He looks with compassion, and His lips once more softly pronounce, 'Maiden, arise!' and the maiden arises. The little girl sits up in the coffin and looks round, smiling with wide-open wondering eyes, holding a bunch of white roses they had put in her hand.

"There are cries, sobs, confusion among the people, and at that moment, the cardinal himself, the Grand Inquisitor, passes by the cathedral. He is an old man, almost ninety, tall and erect, with a withered face and sunken eyes, in which there is still a gleam of light. He is not dressed in his gorgeous cardinal's robes, as he was the day before, when he was burning the enemies of the Roman Church—at that moment he was wearing his coarse, old, monk's cassock. At a distance behind him come his gloomy assistants and slaves and the 'holy guard'. He stops at the sight of the crowd and watches it from a distance. He sees everything; he sees them set the coffin down at His feet, sees the child rise up, and his face darkens. He knits his thick grey brows and his eyes gleam with a sinister fire. He holds out his finger and bids the guards take Him. And such is his power, so completely are the people cowed into submission and trembling obedience to him, that the crowd immediately make way for the guards, and in the midst of deathlike silence they lay hands on Him and lead Him away. The crowd instantly bows down to the earth, like one man, before the old inquisitor. He blesses the people in silence and passes on. The guards lead their prisoner to the close, gloomy vaulted prison in the ancient palace of the Holy Inquisition and shut Him in it. The day passes and is followed by the dark, burning 'breathless' night of Seville. The air is 'fragrant with laurel and lemon'. In the pitch darkness the iron door of the prison is suddenly opened and the Grand Inquisitor himself comes in with a light in his hand. He is alone; the door is closed at once behind him. He stands in the doorway and for a minute or two gazes into His face. At last he goes up slowly, sets the light on the table and speaks.

" 'Is it Thou? Thou?' but receiving no answer, he adds at once: 'Don't answer, be silent. What canst Thou say, indeed? I know too well what Thou wouldst say. And Thou hast no right to add anything to what Thou hadst said of old. Why, then, art Thou come to hinder us? For Thou hast come to hinder us, and Thou knowest that. But dost Thou know what will be to-morrow? I know not who Thou art and care not to know whether it is Thou or only a semblance of Him, but to-morrow I shall condemn Thee and burn Thee at the stake as the worst of heretics. And the very people who have to-day kissed Thy feet, to-morrow at the faintest sign from me will rush to heap up the embers of Thy fire. Knowest Thou that? Yes, maybe Thou knowest it,' he added with thoughtful penetration, never for a moment taking his eyes off the Prisoner."

"I don't quite understand, Ivan. What does it mean?" Alyosha, who had been listening in silence, said with a smile. "Is it simply a wild fantasy, or a mistake on the part of the old man—some impossible *quid pro quo*?"

"Take it as the last," said Ivan, laughing, "if you are so corrupted by modern realism and can't stand anything fantastic. If you like it to be a case of mistaken identity, let it be so. It is true," he went on, laughing, "the old man was ninety, and he might well be crazy over his set idea. He might have been struck by the appearance of the Prisoner. It might, in fact, be simply his ravings, the delusion of an old man of ninety, over-excited by the *auto da fé* of a hundred heretics the day before. But does it matter to us, after all, whether it was a mistake of identity or a wild fantasy? All that matters is that the old man should speak out, should speak openly of what he has thought in silence for ninety years."

"And the Prisoner too is silent? Does He look at him and not say a word?"

"That's inevitable in any case," Ivan laughed again. "The old man has told H:m He hasn't the right to add anything to what He has said of old. One may say it is the most fundamental feature of Roman Catholicism, in my opinion at least. 'All has been given by Thee to the Pope,' they say, 'and all, therefore, is still in the Pope's hands, and there is no need for Thee to come now at all. Thou must not meddle for the time, at least.' That's how they speak and write too—the Jesuits, at any rate. I have read it myself in the works of their theologians. 'Hast Thou the right to reveal to us one of the mysteries of that world from which Thou hast come?' my old man asks Him, and answers the question for Him. 'No, Thou hast not; that Thou mayest not add to what has been said of old, and mayest not take from men the freedom which Thou didst exalt when Thou wast on earth. Whatsoever Thou revealest anew will encroach on men's freedom of faith; for it will be manifest as a miracle, and the freedom of their faith was dearer to Thee than anything in those days fifteen hundred years ago. Didst Thou not often say then, "I will make you free"? But now Thou hast seen these "free" men,' the old man adds suddenly, with a pensive smile. 'Yes, we've paid dearly for it,' he goes on, looking sternly at Him, 'but at last we have completed that work in Thy name. For fifteen centuries we have been wrestling with Thy freedom, but now it is ended and over for good. Dost Thou not believe that it's over for good? Thou lookest meekly at me and deignest not even to be wroth with me. But let me tell Thee that now, to-day, people are more persuaded than ever that they have perfect freedom, yet they have brought their freedom to us and laid it humbly at our feet. But that has been our doing. Was this what Thou didst? Was this Thy freedom?' "

"I don't understand again," Alyosha broke in. "Is he ironical, is he jesting?"

"Not a bit of it! He claims it as a merit for himself and his Church that at last they have vanquished freedom and have done so to make men happy. 'For now' (he is speaking of the Inquisition, of course) 'for the first time it has become possible to think of the happiness of men. Man was created a rebel; and how can rebels be happy? Thou wast warned,' he says to Him. 'Thou hast had no lack of admonitions and warnings, but Thou didst not listen to those warnings; Thou didst reject the only way by which men might be made happy. But, fortunately, departing Thou didst hand on the work to us. Thou hast promised, Thou hast established by Thy word, Thou hast given to us the right to bind and to unbind, and now, of course, Thou canst not think of taking it away. Why, then, hast Thou come to hinder us?' "

"And what's the meaning of 'no lack of admonitions and warnings'?" asked Alyosha.

"Why, that's the chief part of what the old man must say.

" 'The wise and dread Spirit, the spirit of self-destruction and non-existence,' the old man goes on, 'the great spirit talked with Thee in the wilderness, and we are told in the books that he "tempted" Thee. Is that so? And could anything truer be said than what he revealed to Thee in three questions and what Thou didst reject, and what in the books is called "the temptation"? And yet if there has ever been on earth a real stupendous miracle, it took place on that day, on the day of the three temptations. The statement of those three questions was itself a miracle. If it were possible to imagine simply for the sake of argument that those three questions of the dread spirit had perished utterly from the books, and that we had to restore them and to invent them anew, and to do so had gathered together all the wise men of the earth—rulers, chief priests, learned men, philosophers, poets—and had set them the task to invent three questions, such as would not only fit the occasion but express in three words, three human phrases, the whole future history of the world and of humanity—dost Thou believe that all the wisdom of the earth united could have invented anything in depth and force equal to the three questions which were actually put to Thee then by the wise and mighty spirit in the wilderness? From those questions alone, from the miracle of their statement, we can see that we have here to do not with the fleeting human intelligence but with the absolute and eternal. For in those three questions the whole subsequent history of mankind is, as it were, brought together into one whole, and foretold, and in them are united all the unsolved historical contradictions of human nature. At the time it could not be so clear, since the future was unknown; but now that fifteen hundred years have passed, we see that everything in those three questions was so justly divined and foretold, and has been so truly fulfilled, that nothing can be added to them or taken from them.

" 'Judge Thyself who was right—Thou or he who questioned Thee then? Remember the first question; its meaning, in other words, was this: "Thou wouldst go into the world, and art going with empty hands, with some promise of freedom, which men in their simplicity and their natural unruliness cannot even understand, which they fear and dread—for nothing has ever been more insupportable for a man and a human society than freedom. But seest Thou these stones in this parched and barren wilderness? Turn them into bread, and mankind will run after Thee like a flock of sheep, grateful and obedient, though for ever trembling, lest Thou withdraw Thy hand and deny them Thy bread." But Thou wouldst not deprive man of freedom and didst reject the offer, thinking, what is that freedom worth, if obedience is bought with bread? Thou didst reply that man lives not by bread alone. But dost Thou know that for the sake of that earthly bread the spirit of the earth will rise up against Thee and will strive with Thee and overcome Thee, and all will follow him, crying, "Who can compare with this beast? He has given us fire from heaven!" Dost Thou know that the ages will pass, and humanity will proclaim by the lips of their sages that there is no crime, and therefore no sin; there is only hunger? "Feed men, and then ask of them virtue!" that's what they'll write on the banner, which they will raise against Thee, and with which they will destroy Thy temple. Where Thy temple stood will rise a new building; the terrible tower of Babel will be built again, and though, like the one of old, it will not be finished, yet Thou mightest have prevented that new tower and have cut short the sufferings of men for a thousand years; for they will come back to us after a thousand years of agony with their tower. They will seek us again, hidden underground in the catacombs, for we shall be again persecuted and tortured. They will find us and cry to us, "Feed us, for those who have promised us fire from heaven haven't given it!" And then we shall finish building their tower, for he finishes the building who feeds them. And we alone shall feed them in Thy name, declaring falsely that it is Thy name. Oh, never, never can they feed themselves without us! No science will give them bread so long as they remain free. In the end they will lay their freedom at our feet, and say to us, "Make us your slaves, but feed us". They will understand themselves, at last, that freedom and bread enough for all are inconceivable together, for never, never will they be able to share between them! They will be convinced, too, that they can never be free, for they are weak, vicious, worthless and rebellious. Thou didst promise them the bread of Heaven, but, I repeat again, can it compare with earthly bread in the eyes of the weak, ever-sinful and ignoble race of man? And if for the sake of the bread of Heaven thousands and ten of thousands shall follow Thee, what is to become of the millions and tens of thousands of millions of creatures who will not have the strength to forgo the earthly bread for the sake of the heavenly? Or dost Thou care only for the tens of thousands of the great and strong, while the millions, numerous as the sands of the sea, who are weak but love Thee, must exist only for the sake of the great and strong? No, we care for the weak too. They are sinful and rebellious, but in the end they too will become obedient. They will marvel at us and look on us as gods, because we are ready to endure the freedom which they have found so dreadful and to rule over them—so awful it will seem to them to be free. But we shall tell them that we are Thy servants and rule them in Thy name. We shall deceive them again, for we will not let Thee come to us again. That deception will be our suffering, for we shall be forced to lie.

" 'This is the significance of the first question in the wilderness, and this is what Thou hast rejected for the sake of that freedom which Thou hast exalted above everything. Yet in this question lies hid the great secret of this world. Choosing "bread", Thou wouldst have satisfied the universal and everlasting craving of humanity—to find someone to worship. So long as man remains free he strives for nothing so incessantly and so painfully as to find someone to worship. But man seeks to worship what is established beyond dispute, so that all men would agree at once to worship it. For these pitiful creatures are concerned not only to find what one or the other can worship, but to find something that all would believe in and worship; what is essential is that all may be *together* in it. This craving for *community* of worship is the chief misery of every man individually and of all humanity from the beginning of time. For the sake of common worship they've slain each other with the sword. They have set up gods and challenged one another, "Put away your gods and come and worship ours, or we will kill you and your gods!" And so it will be to the end of the world, even when gods disappear from the earth; they will fall down before idols just the same. Thou didst know, Thou couldst not but have known, this fundamental secret of human nature, but Thou didst reject the one infallible banner which was offered Thee to make all men bow down to Thee alone—the banner of earthly bread; and Thou hast rejected it for the sake of freedom and the bread of Heaven. Behold what Thou didst further. And all again in the name of freedom! I tell Thee that man is tormented by no greater anxiety than to find someone quickly to whom he can hand over that gift of freedom with which the ill-fated creature is born. But only one who can appease their conscience can take over their freedom. In bread there was offered Thee an invinc-

ible banner; give bread, and man will worship thee, for nothing is more certain than bread. But if someone else gains possession of his conscience—oh! then he will cast away Thy bread and follow after him who has ensnared his conscience. In that Thou wast right. For the secret of man's being is not only to live but to have something to live for. Without a stable conception of the object of life, man would not consent to go on living, and would rather destroy himself than remain on earth, though he had bread in abundance. That is true. But what happened? Instead of taking men's freedom from them, Thou didst make it greater than ever! Didst Thou forget that man prefers peace, and even death, to freedom of choice in the knowledge of good and evil? Nothing is more seductive for man than his freedom of conscience, but nothing is a greater cause of suffering. And behold, instead of giving a firm foundation for setting the conscience of man at rest for ever, Thou didst choose all that is exceptional, vague and enigmatic; Thou didst choose what was utterly beyond the strength of men, acting as though Thou didst not love them at all—Thou who didst come to give Thy life for them! Instead of taking possession of men's freedom, Thou didst increase it, and burdened the spiritual kingdom of mankind with its sufferings for ever. Thou didst desire man's free love, that he should follow Thee freely, enticed and taken captive by Thee. In place of the rigid ancient law, man must hereafter with free heart decide for himself what is good and what is evil, having only Thy image before him as his guide. But didst Thou not know that he would at last reject even Thy image and Thy truth, if he is weighed down with the fearful burden of free choice? They will cry aloud at last that the truth is not in Thee, for they could not have been left in greater confusion and suffering than Thou hast caused, laying upon them so many cares and unanswerable problems.

" 'So that, in truth, Thou didst Thyself lay the foundation for the destruction of Thy kingdom, and no one is more to blame for it. Yet what was offered Thee?

There are three powers, three powers alone, able to conquer and to hold captive for ever the conscience of these impotent rebels for their happiness—those forces are miracle, mystery and authority. Thou hast rejected all three and hast set the example for doing so. When the wise and dread spirit set Thee on the pinnacle of the temple and said to Thee, "If Thou wouldst know whether Thou art the Son of God then cast Thyself down, for it is written: the angels shall hold him up lest he fall and bruise himself, and Thou shalt know then whether Thou art the Son of God and shalt prove then how great is Thy faith in Thy Father." But Thou didst refuse and wouldst not cast Thyself down. Oh! of course, Thou didst proudly and well, like God; but the weak, unruly race of men, are they gods? Oh, Thou didst know then that in taking one step, in making one movement to cast Thyself down, Thou wouldst be tempting God and have lost all Thy faith in Him, and wouldst have been dashed to pieces against that earth which Thou didst come to save. And the wise spirit that tempted Thee would have rejoiced. But I ask again, are there many like Thee? And couldst Thou believe for one moment that men, too, could face such a temptation? Is the nature of men such, that they can reject miracle, and at the great moments of their life, the moments of their deepest, most agonising spiritual difficulties, cling only to the free verdict of the heart? Oh, Thou didst know that Thy deed would be recorded in books, would be handed down to remote times and the utmost ends of the earth, and Thou didst hope that man, following Thee, would cling to God and not ask for a miracle. But Thou didst not know that when man rejects miracle he rejects God too; for man seeks not so much God as the miraculous. And as man cannot bear to be without the miraculous, he will create new miracles of his own for himself, and will worship deeds of sorcery and witchcraft, though he might be a hundred times over a rebel, heretic and infidel. Thou didst not come down from the Cross when they shouted to Thee, mocking and reviling Thee, "Come down from the Cross and we will believe that Thou art He". Thou didst not come down, for again Thou wouldst not enslave man by a miracle, and didst crave faith given freely, not based on miracle. Thou didst crave for free love and not the base raptures of the slave before the might that has overawed him for ever. But Thou didst think too highly of men therein, for they are slaves, of course, though rebellious by nature. Look round and judge; fifteen centuries have passed, look upon them. Whom hast Thou raised up to Thyself? I swear, man is weaker and baser by nature than Thou hast believed him! Can he, can he do what Thou didst? By showing him so much respect, Thou didst, as it were, cease to feel for him, for Thou didst ask far too much from him—Thou who hast loved him more than Thyself! Respecting him less, Thou wouldst have asked less of him. That would have been more like love, for his burden would have been lighter. He is weak and vile. What though he is everywhere now rebelling against our power, and proud of his rebellion? It is the pride of a child and a schoolboy. They are little children rioting and barring out the teacher at school. But their childish delight will end; it will cost them dear. They will cast down temples and drench the earth with blood. But they will see at last, the foolish children, that, though they are rebels, they are impotent rebels, unable to keep up their own rebellion. Bathed in their foolish tears, they will recognise at last that He who created them rebels must have meant to mock at them. They will say this in despair, and their utterance will be a blasphemy which will make them more unhappy still, for man's nature cannot bear blasphemy, and in the end always avenges it on itself. And so unrest, confusion and unhappiness—that is the present lot of man after Thou didst bear so much for their freedom! Thy great prophet tells, in vision and in image, that he saw all those who took part in the first resurrection and that there were of each tribe twelve thousand. But if there were so many of them, they must have been no men but gods. They had borne Thy cross, they had endured scores of years in the barren, hungry wilderness, living upon locusts and roots—and Thou mayest indeed point with pride at those children of freedom, of free love, of free and splendid sacrifice for Thy name. But remember that they were only some thousands; and what of the rest? And how are the other weak ones to blame, because they could not endure what the strong have endured? How is the weak soul to blame that it is unable to receive such terrible gifts? Canst Thou have simply come to the elect and for the elect? But if so, it is a mystery and we cannot understand it. And if it is a mystery, we too have a right to preach a mystery, and to teach them that it's not the free judgment of their hearts, not love that matters, but a mystery which they must follow blindly, even against their conscience. So we have done. We have corrected Thy work and have founded it upon *miracle, mystery* and *authority*. And men rejoiced that they were again led like sheep, and that the terrible gift that had brought them such suffering was, at last, lifted from their hearts. Were we right teaching them this? Speak! Did we not love mankind, so meekly acknowledging their feebleness, lovingly lightening their burden, and permitting their weak nature even sin with our sanction? Why hast Thou come now to hinder us? And why dost Thou look silently and searchingly at me with Thy mild eyes? Be angry. I don't want Thy love, for I love Thee not. And what use is it for me to hide anything from Thee? Don't I know to Whom I am speaking? All that I can say is known to Thee already. And is it for me to conceal from Thee our mystery? Perhaps it is Thy will to hear it from my lips. Listen, then. We are not working with Thee but with *him* —that is our mystery. It's long—eight centuries—since we have been on *his* side and not on Thine. Just eight centuries ago we took from him what Thou didst reject with scorn, that last gift he offered Thee, showing Thee all the kingdoms of the earth. We took from him Rome and the sword of Cæsar, and proclaimed ourselves sole rulers of the earth, though hitherto we have not been able to complete our work. But whose fault is that? Oh, the work is only beginning, but it has begun. It has long to await completion and the earth has yet much to suffer, but we shall triumph and shall be Cæsars, and then we shall plan the universal happiness of man. But Thou mightest have taken even then the sword of Cæsar. Why didst Thou reject that last gift? Hadst Thou accepted that last counsel of the mighty spirit, Thou wouldst have accomplished all that man seeks on earth—that is, someone to worship, someone to keep his conscience, and some means of uniting all in one unanimous and harmonious ant-heap, for the craving for universal unity is the third and last anguish of men. Mankind as a whole has always striven to organise a universal state. There have been many great nations with great histories, but the more highly they were developed the more unhappy they were, for they felt more acutely than other people the craving for world-wide union. The great conquerors, Timours and Genghis Khans, whirled like hurricanes over the face of the earth striving to subdue its people, and they too were but the unconscious expression of the same craving for universal unity. Hadst Thou taken the world and Cæsar's purple, Thou wouldst have founded the universal state and have given universal peace. For who can rule men if not he who holds their conscience and their bread in his hands? We have taken the sword of Cæsar, and in taking it, of course have rejected Thee and followed *him*. Oh, ages are yet to come of the confusion of free thought, of their science and cannibalism. For having begun to build their tower of Babel without us, they will end, of course, with cannibalism. But then the beast will crawl to us and lick our feet and spatter them with tears of blood. And we shall sit upon the beast and raise the cup, and on it will be written, "Mystery". But then, and only then, the reign of peace and happiness will come for men. Thou art proud of Thine elect, but Thou hast only the elect, while we give rest to all. And besides, how many of those elect, those mighty ones who could become elect, have grown weary waiting for Thee, and have transferred and will transfer the powers of their spirit and the warmth of their heart to the other camp, and end by raising their *free* banner against Thee! Thou didst Thyself lift up that banner. But with us all will be happy and will no more rebel nor destroy one another as under Thy freedom. Oh, we shall persuade them that they will only become free when they renounce their freedom to us and submit to us. And shall we be right or shall we be lying? They will be convinced that we are right, for they will remember the horrors of slavery and confusion to which Thy freedom brought them. Freedom, free thought and science will lead them into such straits and will bring them face to face with such marvels and insoluble mysteries, that some of them, the fierce and rebellious, will destroy themselves; others, rebellious but weak, will destroy one another, while the rest, weak and unhappy, will crawl fawning to our feet and whine to us: "Yes, you were right, you alone possess His mystery, and we come back to you, save us from ourselves!"

" 'Receiving bread from us, they will see clearly that we take the bread made by their hands from them, to give it to them, without any miracle. They will see that we do not change the stones to bread, but in truth they will be more thankful for taking it from our hands than for the bread itself! For they will remember only too well that in old days, without our help, even the bread they made turned to stones in their hands, while since they have come back to us, the very stones have turned to bread in their hands. Too, too well they know the value of complete submission! And until men know that, they will be unhappy. Who is most to blame for their not knowing it, speak? Who scattered the flock and sent it astray on unknown paths? But the flock will come together again and will submit once more, and then it will be once for all. Then we shall give them the quiet humble happiness of weak creatures such as they are by nature. Oh, we shall persuade them at last not to be proud, for Thou didst lift them up and thereby taught them to be proud. We shall show them that they are weak, that they are only pitiful children, but that childlike happiness is the sweetest of all. They will become timid and will look to us and huddle close to us in fear, as chicks to the hen. They will marvel at us and will be awe-stricken before us, and

will be proud at our being so powerful and clever, that we have been able to subdue such a turbulent flock of thousands of millions. They will tremble impotently before our wrath, their minds will grow fearful, they will be quick to shed tears like women and children, but they will be just as ready at a sign from us to pass to laughter and rejoicing, to happy mirth and childish song. Yes, we shall set them to work, but in their leisure hours we shall make their life like a child's game, with children's songs and innocent dance. Oh, we shall allow them even sin, they are weak and helpless, and they will love us like children because we allow them to sin. We shall tell them that every sin will be expiated, if it is done with our permission, that we allow them to sin because we love them, and the punishment for these sins we take upon ourselves. And we shall take it upon ourselves, and they will adore us as their saviours who have taken on themselves their sins before God. And they will have no secrets from us. We shall allow or forbid them to live with their wives and mistresses, to have or not to have children—according to whether they have been obedient or disobedient—and they will submit to us gladly and cheerfully. The most painful secrets of their conscience, all, all they will bring to us, and we shall have an answer for all. And they will be glad to believe our answer, for it will save them from the great anxiety and terrible agony they endure at present in making a free decision for themselves. And all will be happy, all the millions of creatures except the hundred thousand who rule over them. For only we, we who guard the mystery, shall be unhappy. There will be thousands of millions of happy babes, and a hundred thousand sufferers who have taken upon themselves the curse of the knowledge of good and evil. Peacefully they will die, peacefully they will expire in Thy name, and beyond the grave they will find nothing but death. But we shall keep the secret, and for their happiness we shall allure them with the reward of heaven and eternity. Though if there were anything in the other world, it certainly would not be for such as they. It is prophesied that Thou wilt come again in victory,

Thou wilt come with Thy chosen, the proud and strong, but we will say that they have only saved themselves, but we have saved all. We are told that the harlot who sits upon the beast, and holds in her hands the *mystery*, shall be put to shame, that the weak will rise up again, and will rend her royal purple and will strip naked her loathsome body. But then I will stand up and point out to Thee the thousand millions of happy children who have known no sin. And we who have taken their sins upon us for their happiness will stand up before Thee and say: "Judge us if Thou canst and darest." Know that I fear Thee not. Know that I too have been in the wilderness, I too have lived on roots and locusts, I too prized the freedom with which Thou hast blessed men, and I too was striving to stand among Thy elect, among the strong and powerful, thirsting "to make up the number". But I awakened and would not serve madness. I turned back and joined the ranks of those *who have corrected Thy work.* I left the proud and went back to the humble, for the happiness of the humble. What I say to Thee will come to pass, and our dominion will be built up. I repeat, to-morrow Thou shalt see that obedient flock who at a sign from me will hasten to heap up the hot cinders about the pile on which I shall burn Thee for coming to hinder us. For if anyone has ever deserved our fires, it is Thou. To-morrow I shall burn Thee. Dixi.' " [3]

Ivan stopped. He was carried away as he talked and spoke with excitement; when he had finished, he suddenly smiled.

Alyosha had listened in silence; towards the end he was greatly moved and seemed several times on the point of interrupting, but restrained himself. Now his words came with a rush.

"But . . . that's absurd!" he cried, flushing. "Your poem is in praise of Jesus, not in blame of Him— as you meant it to be. And who will believe you about freedom? Is that the way to understand it? That's not the idea of it in the Orthodox Church . . . That's Rome, and not even the whole of Rome, it's false—those are the worst of the Catholics, the Inquisitors, the

3 Dixi: I have spoken. (JHP)

Jesuits! . . . And there could not be such a fantastic creature as your Inquisitor. What are these sins of mankind they take on themselves? Who are these keepers of the mystery who have taken some curse upon themselves for the happiness of mankind? When have they been seen? We know the Jesuits, they are spoken ill of, but surely they are not what you describe? They are not that at all, not at all. . . . They are simply the Romish army for the earthly sovereignty of the world in the future, with the Pontiff of Rome for Emperor . . . that's their ideal, but there's no sort of mystery or lofty melancholy about it. . . . It's simple lust of power, of filthy earthly gain, of domination—something like a universal serfdom with them as masters—that's all they stand for. They don't even believe in God, perhaps. Your suffering inquisitor is a mere fantasy."

"Stay, stay," laughed Ivan, "how hot you are! A fantasy, you say, let it be so! Of course it's a fantasy. But allow me to say: do you really think that the Roman Catholic movement of the last centuries is actually nothing but the lust of power, of filthy earthly gain? Is that Father Païssy's teaching?"

"No, no, on the contrary, Father Païssy did once say something rather the same as you . . . but of course it's not the same, not a bit the same," Alyosha hastily corrected himself.

"A precious admission, in spite of your 'not a bit the same'. I ask you why your Jesuits and Inquisitors have united simply for vile material gain? Why can there not be among them one martyr oppressed by great sorrow and loving humanity? You see, only suppose that there was one such man among all those who desire nothing but filthy material gain—if there's only one like my old inquisitor, who had himself eaten roots in the desert and made frenzied efforts to subdue his flesh to make himself free and perfect. But yet all his life he loved humanity, and suddenly his eyes were opened, and he saw that it is no great moral blessedness to attain perfection and freedom, if at the same time one gains the conviction that millions of God's creatures have been created as a mockery, that they will never be capable of using their freedom, that these poor rebels can never turn into giants to complete the tower, that it was not for such geese that the great idealist dreamt his dream of harmony. Seeing all that he turned back and joined—the clever people. Surely that could have happened?"

"Joined whom, what clever people?" cried Alyosha, completely carried away. "They have no such great cleverness and no mysteries and secrets. . . . Perhaps nothing but Atheism, that's all their secret. Your inquisitor does not believe in God, that's his secret!"

"What if it is so? At last you have guessed it. It's perfectly true, it's true that that's the whole secret, but isn't that suffering, at least for a man like that, who has wasted his whole life in the desert and yet could not shake off his incurable love of humanity? In his old age he reached the clear conviction that nothing but the advice of the great dread spirit could build up any tolerable sort of life for the feeble, unruly, 'incomplete, empirical creatures created in jest.' And so, convinced of this, he sees that he must follow the council of the wise spirit, the dread spirit of death and destruction, and therefore accept lying and deception, and lead men consciously to death and destruction, and yet deceive them all the way so that they may not notice where they are being led, that the poor blind creatures may at least, on the way, think themselves happy. And note, the deception is in the name of Him in Whose ideal the old man had so fervently believed all his life long. Is not that tragic? And if only one such stood at the head of the whole army 'filled with the lust of power only for the sake of filthy gain'—would not one such be enough to make a tragedy? More than that, one such standing at the head is enough to create the actual leading idea of the Roman Church, with all its armies and Jesuits, its highest idea. I tell you frankly that I firmly believe that there has always been such a man among those who stood at the head of the movement. Who knows, there may have been some such even among the Roman Popes. Who knows, perhaps the spirit of that accursed old man who loves mankind so obstinately in his own way, is to be found even now in a whole multitude of such old men, existing not by chance but by agreement, as a secret league formed long ago for the guarding of the mystery, to guard it from the weak and the unhappy, so as to make them happy. No doubt it is so, and so it must be indeed. I fancy that even among the Masons there's something of the same mystery at the bottom, and that that's why the Catholics so detest the Masons as their rivals breaking up the unity of the idea, while it is so essential that there should be one flock and one shepherd. . . . But from the way I defend my idea I might be an author impatient of your criticism. Enough of it."

"You are perhaps a Mason yourself!" broke suddenly from Alyosha. "You don't believe in God," he added, speaking this time very sorrowfully. He fancied besides that his brother was looking at him ironically. "How does your poem end?" he asked, suddenly looking down. "Or was it the end?"

"I meant to end it like this. When the Inquisitor ceased speaking he waited some time for his Prisoner to answer him. His silence weighed down upon him. He saw that the Prisoner had listened intently all the time, looking gently in his face and evidently not wishing to reply. The old man longed for Him to say something, however bitter and terrible. But He suddenly approached the old man in silence and softly kissed him on his bloodless aged lips. That was all his answer. The old man shuddered. His lips moved. He went to the door, opened it, and said to Him: 'Go, and come no more . . . come not at all, never, never!' And he let Him out into the dark alleys of the town. The Prisoner went away."

"And the old man?"

"The kiss glows in his heart, but the old man adheres to his idea."

"And you with him, you too?" cried Alyosha, mournfully.

Ivan laughed.

"Why, it's all nonsense, Alyosha. It's only a senseless poem of a senseless student, who could never write two lines of verse. Why do you take it so seriously?"

[1879]

TRANSLATED BY
CONSTANCE GARNETT

QUESTIONS FOR STUDY

1. *Why does Ivan call his story a "poem in prose"?*
2. *What charges does the Grand Inquisitor level against Christ? How has the Church "corrected" his errors? What has the Church substituted for the freedom which Christ offered mankind? Why?*
3. *What motivates the Grand Inquisitor's repudiation of Christ? What may be said in support of his position?*
4. *Why does Christ refuse to answer the Grand Inquisitor? What is the significance of his kiss? Why does the Grand Inquisitor let Christ go?*
5. *How does Dostoevski manage to make the silent Christ a powerful and convincing character?*

ARTHUR CONAN DOYLE

The Adventure of the Speckled Band

IN GLANCING over my notes of the seventy odd cases in which I have during the last eight years studied the methods of my friend Sherlock Holmes, I find many tragic, some comic, a large number merely strange, but none commonplace; for, working as he did rather for the love of his art than for the acquirement of wealth, he refused to associate himself with any investigation which did not tend towards the unusual, and even the fantastic. Of all these varied cases, however, I cannot recall any which presented more singular features than that which was associated with the well-known Surrey family of the Roylotts of Stoke Moran. The events in question occurred in the early days of my association with Holmes, when we were sharing rooms as bachelors, in Baker Street. It is possible that I might have placed them upon record before, but a promise of secrecy was made at the time, from which I have only been freed during the last month by the untimely death of the lady to whom the pledge was given. It is perhaps as well that the facts should now come to light, for I have reasons to know there are widespread rumours as to the death of Dr. Grimesby Roylott which tend to make the matter even more terrible than the truth.

It was early in April, in the year '83, that I woke one morning to find Sherlock Holmes standing, fully dressed, by the side of my bed. He was a late riser as a rule, and, as the clock on the mantelpiece showed me that it was only a quarter past seven, I blinked up at him in some surprise, and perhaps just a little resentment, for I was myself regular in my habits.

"Very sorry to knock you up, Watson," said he, "but it's the common lot this morning. Mrs. Hudson has been knocked up, she retorted upon me, and I on you."

"What is it, then? A fire?"

"No, a client. It seems that a young lady has arrived in a considerable state of excitement, who insists upon seeing me. She is waiting now in the sitting-room. Now, when young ladies wander about the metropolis at this hour of the morning, and knock sleepy people up out of their beds, I presume that it is something very pressing which they have to communicate. Should it prove to be an interesting case, you would, I am sure, wish to follow it from the outset. I thought at any rate that I should call you, and give you the chance."

"My dear fellow, I would not miss it for anything."

I had no keener pleasure than in following Holmes in his professional investigations, and in admiring the rapid deductions, as swift as intuitions, and yet always founded on a logical basis, with which he unravelled the problems which were submitted to him. I rapidly threw on my clothes, and was ready in a few minutes to accompany my friend down to the sitting-room. A lady dressed in black and heavily veiled, who had been sitting in the window, rose as we entered.

"Good morning, madam," said Holmes cheerily. "My name is Sherlock Holmes. This is my intimate friend and associate, Dr. Watson, before whom you can speak as freely as before myself. Ha, I am glad to see that Mrs. Hudson has had the good sense to light the fire. Pray draw up to it, and I shall order you a cup of hot coffee, for I observe that you are shivering."

Reprinted from Arthur Conan Doyle's *The Adventures of Sherlock Holmes,* by permission of John Murray (Publishers) Ltd./Jonathan Cape Ltd. and by permission of Baskervilles Investments Ltd.

"It is not cold which makes me shiver," said the woman in a low voice, changing her seat as requested.

"What then?"

"It is fear, Mr. Holmes. It is terror." She raised her veil as she spoke, and we could see that she was indeed in a pitiable state of agitation, her face all drawn and grey, with restless, frightened eyes, like those of some hunted animal. Her features and figure were those of a woman of thirty, but her hair was shot with premature grey, and her expression was weary and haggard. Sherlock Holmes ran her over with one of his quick, all-comprehensive glances.

"You must not fear," said he soothingly, bending forward and patting her forearm. "We shall soon set matters right, I have no doubt. You have come in by train this morning, I see."

"You know me, then?"

"No, but I observe the second half of a return ticket in the palm of your left glove. You must have started early, and yet you had a good drive in a dog-cart, along heavy roads, before you reached the station."

The lady gave a violent start, and stared in bewilderment at my companion.

"There is no mystery, my dear madam," said he, smiling. "The left arm of your jacket is spattered with mud in no less than seven places. The marks are perfectly fresh. There is no vehicle save a dog-cart which throws up mud in that way, and then only when you sit on the left-hand side of the driver."

"Whatever your reasons may be, you are perfectly correct," said she. "I started from home before six, reached Leatherhead at twenty past, and came in by the first train to Waterloo.[1] Sir, I can stand this strain no longer, I shall go mad if it continues. I have no one to turn to— none, save only one, who cares for me, and he, poor fellow, can be of little aid. I have heard of you, Mr. Holmes; I have heard of you from Mrs. Farintosh, whom you helped in the hour of her sore need. It was from her that I had

[1] Waterloo Station, London. (JHP)

your address. Oh, sir, do you not think you could help me too, and at least throw a little light through the dense darkness which surrounds me? At present it is out of my power to reward you for your services, but in a month or two I shall be married, with the control of my own income, and then at least you shall not find me ungrateful."

Holmes turned to his desk, and unlocking it, drew out a small case-book which he consulted.

"Farintosh," said he. "Ah, yes, I recall the case; it was concerned with an opal tiara. I think it was before your time, Watson. I can only say, madam, that I shall be happy to devote the same care to your case as I did to that of your friend. As to reward, my profession is its reward; but you are at liberty to defray whatever expenses I may be put to, at the time which suits you best. And now I beg that you will lay before us everything that may help us in forming an opinion upon the matter."

"Alas!" replied our visitor. "The very horror of my situation lies in the fact that my fears are so vague, and my suspicions depend so entirely upon small points, which might seem trivial to another, that even he to whom of all others I have a right to look for help and advice looks upon all that I tell him about it as the fancies of a nervous woman. He does not say so, but I can read it from his soothing answers and averted eyes. But I have heard, Mr. Holmes, that you can see deeply into the manifold wickedness of the human heart. You may advise me how to walk amid the dangers which encompass me."

"I am all attention, madam."

"My name is Helen Stoner, and I am living with my stepfather, who is the last survivor of one of the oldest Saxon families in England, the Roylotts of Stoke Moran, on the western border of Surrey."

Holmes nodded his head. "The name is familiar to me," said he.

"The family was at one time among the richest in England, and the estate extended over the borders into Berkshire in the north, and Hampshire in the west.

In the last century, however, four successive heirs were of a dissolute and wasteful disposition, and the family ruin was eventually completed by a gambler, in the days of the Regency.[2] Nothing was left save a few acres of ground and the two-hundred-year-old house, which is itself crushed under a heavy mortgage. The last squire dragged out his existence there, living the horrible life of an aristocratic pauper; but his only son, my stepfather, seeing that he must adapt himself to the new conditions, obtained an advance from a relative, which enabled him to take a medical degree, and went out to Calcutta, where, by his professional skill and his force of character, he established a large practice. In a fit of anger, however, caused by some robberies which had been perpetrated in the house, he beat his native butler to death, and narrowly escaped a capital sentence. As it was, he suffered a long term of imprisonment, and afterwards returned to England a morose and disappointed man.

"When Dr. Roylott was in India he married my mother, Mrs. Stoner, the young widow of Major-General Stoner, of the Bengal Artillery. My sister Julia and I were twins, and we were only two years old at the time of my mother's re-marriage. She had a considerable sum of money, not less than a thousand a year, and this she bequeathed to Dr. Roylott entirely whilst we resided with him, with a provision that a certain annual sum should be allowed to each of us in the event of our marriage. Shortly after our return to England my mother died—she was killed eight years ago in a railway accident near Crewe. Dr. Roylott then abandoned his attempts to establish himself in practice in London, and took us to live with him in the ancestral house at Stoke Moran. The money which my mother had left was enough for all our wants, and there seemed no obstacle to our happiness.

"But a terrible change came over our stepfather about this time. Instead of making friends and exchanging visits with our neighbours, who had at first been overjoyed to see a Roylott of Stoke Moran back in the old family seat, he shut himself up in his house, and seldom came out save to indulge in ferocious quarrels with whoever might cross his path. Violence of temper approaching to mania has been hereditary in the men of the family, and in my stepfather's case it had, I believe, been intensified by his long residence in the tropics. A series of disgraceful brawls took place, two of which ended in the police-court, until at last he became the terror of the village, and the folks would fly at his approach, for he is a man of immense strength, and absolutely uncontrollable in his anger.

"Last week he hurled the local blacksmith over a parapet into a stream and it was only by paying over all the money that I could gather together that I was able to avert another public exposure. He had no friends at all save the wandering gipsies, and he would give these vagabonds leave to encamp upon the few acres of bramble-covered land which represent the family estate, and would accept in return the hospitality of their tents, wandering away with them sometimes for weeks on end. He has a passion also for Indian animals, which are sent over to him by a correspondent, and he has at this moment a cheetah and a baboon, which wander freely over his grounds, and are feared by the villagers almost as much as their master.

"You can imagine from what I say that my poor sister Julia and I had no great pleasure in our lives. No servant would stay with us, and for a long time we did all the work of the house. She was but thirty at the time of her death, and yet her hair had already begun to whiten, even as mine has."

"Your sister is dead, then?"

"She died just two years ago, and it is of her death that I wish to speak to you. You can understand that, living the life which I have described, we were little likely to see anyone of our own age and position. We had, however, an aunt, my mother's maiden sister, Miss Honoria

2 1811–1820, the years of George III's incapacity, when the government was run by the Prince of Wales, later George IV. (JHP)

Westphail, who lives near Harrow, and we were occasionally allowed to pay short visits at this lady's house. Julia went there at Christmas two years ago, and met there a half-pay Major of Marines, to whom she became engaged. My stepfather learned of the engagement when my sister returned, and offered no objection to the marriage; but within a fortnight of the day which had been fixed for the wedding, the terrible event occurred which has deprived me of my only companion."

Sherlock Holmes had been leaning back in his chair with his eyes closed, and his head sunk in a cushion, but he half opened his lids now, and glanced across at his visitor.

"Pray be precise as to details," said he.

"It is easy for me to be so, for every event of that dreadful time is seared into my memory. The manor house is, as I have already said, very old, and only one wing is now inhabited. The bedrooms in this wing are on the ground floor, the sitting-rooms being in the central block of the buildings. Of these bedrooms, the first is Dr. Roylott's, the second my sister's, and the third my own. There is no communication between them, but they all open out into the same corridor. Do I make myself plain?"

"Perfectly so."

"The windows of the three rooms open out upon the lawn. That fatal night Dr. Roylott had gone to his room early, though we knew that he had not retired to rest, for my sister was troubled by the smell of the strong Indian cigars which it was his custom to smoke. She left her room, therefore, and came into mine, where she sat for some time, chatting about her approaching wedding. At eleven o'clock she rose to leave me, but she paused at the door and looked back.

" 'Tell me, Helen,' said she, 'have you ever heard anyone whistle in the dead of the night?'

" 'Never,' said I.

" 'I suppose that you could not possibly whistle yourself in your sleep?'

" 'Certainly not. But why?'

" 'Because during the last few nights I have always, about three in the morn-ing, heard a low clear whistle. I am a light sleeper, and it has awakened me. I cannot tell where it came from—perhaps from the next room, perhaps from the lawn. I thought that I would just ask you whether you had heard it.'

" 'No, I have not. It must be those wretched gipsies in the plantation.'

" 'Very likely. And yet if it were on the lawn I wonder that you did not hear it also.'

" 'Ah, but I sleep more heavily than you.'

" 'Well, it is of no great consequence, at any rate,' she smiled back at me, closed my door, and a few moments later I heard her key turn in the lock."

"Indeed," said Holmes. "Was it your custom always to lock yourselves in at night?"

"Always."

"And why?"

"I think that I mentioned to you that the Doctor kept a cheetah and a baboon. We had no feeling of security unless our doors were locked."

"Quite so. Pray proceed with your statement."

"I could not sleep that night. A vague feeling of impending misfortune impressed me. My sister and I, you will recollect, were twins, and you know how subtle are the links which bind two souls which are so closely allied. It was a wild night. The wind was howling outside, and the rain was beating and splashing against the windows. Suddenly, amidst all the hubbub of the gale, there burst forth the wild scream of a terrified woman. I knew that it was my sister's voice. I sprang from my bed, wrapped a shawl round me, and rushed into the corridor. As I opened my door I seemed to hear a low whistle, such as my sister described, and a few moments later a clanging sound, as if a mass of metal had fallen. As I ran down the passage my sister's door was unlocked, and revolved slowly upon its hinges. I stared at it horror-stricken, not knowing what was about to issue from it. By the light of the corridor lamp I saw my sister appear at the opening, her face blanched with terror, her hands groping for help, her whole figure swaying to and fro like that of a drunkard. I ran to her and threw my arms round her, but at that moment her knees seemed to give way and she fell to the ground. She writhed as one who is in terrible pain, and her limbs were dreadfully convulsed. At first I thought that she had not recognized me, but as I bent over her she suddenly shrieked out in a voice which I shall never forget, 'O, my God! Helen! It was the band! The speckled band!' There was something else which she would fain have said, and she stabbed with her finger into the air in the direction of the Doctor's room, but a fresh convulsion seized her and choked her words. I rushed out, calling loudly for my stepfather, and I met him hastening from his room in his dressing-gown. When he reached my sister's side she was unconscious, and though he poured brandy down her throat, and sent for medical aid from the village, all efforts were in vain, for she slowly sank and died without having recovered her consciousness. Such was the dreadful end of my beloved sister."

"One moment," said Holmes; "are you sure about this whistle and metallic sound? Could you swear to it?"

"That was what the county coroner asked me at the inquiry. It is my strong impression that I heard it, and yet among the crash of the gale, and the creaking of an old house, I may possibly have been deceived."

"Was your sister dressed?"

"No, she was in her nightdress. In her right hand was found the charred stump of a match, and in her left a matchbbox."

"Showing that she had struck a light and looked about her when the alarm took place. That is important. And what conclusions did the coroner come to?"

"He investigated the case with great care, for Dr. Roylott's conduct had long been notorious in the county, but he was unable to find any satisfactory cause of death. My evidence showed that the door had been fastened upon the inner side, and the windows were blocked by old-fashioned shutters with broad iron bars, which were secured every night. The walls were carefully sounded, and were shown to be quite solid all round, and the flooring was also thoroughly examined, with the same result. The chimney is wide, but is barred up by four large staples. It is certain, therefore, that my sister was quite alone when she met her end. Besides, there were no marks of any violence upon her."

"How about poison?"

"The doctors examined her for it, but without success."

"What do you think that this unfortunate lady died of, then?"

"It is my belief that she died of pure fear and nervous shock, though what it was which frightened her I cannot imagine."

"Were there gipsies in the plantation at the time?"

"Yes, there are nearly always some there."

"Ah, and what did you gather from this allusion to a band—a speckled band?"

"Sometimes I have thought that it was merely the wild talk of delirium, sometimes that it may have referred to some band of people, perhaps to these very gipsies in the plantation. I do not know whether the spotted handkerchiefs which so many of them wear over their heads might have suggested the strange adjective which she used."

Holmes shook his head like a man who is far from being satisfied.

"These are very deep waters," said he; "pray go on with your narrative."

"Two years have passed since then, and my life has been until lately lonelier than ever. A month ago, however, a dear friend, whom I have known for many years, has done me the honour to ask my hand in marriage. His name is Armitage—Percy Armitage—the second son of Mr. Armitage, of Crane Water, near. Reading. My stepfather has offered no opposition to the match, and we are to be married in the course of the spring. Two days ago some repairs were started in the west wing of the building, and my bedroom wall has been pierced, so that I have had to move into the chamber in which my sister died, and to sleep in the very bed in which she slept. Imagine, then, my thrill of terror when last night, as I lay awake, thinking over her terrible fate, I suddenly heard in the silence of the night the low whistle which had been the herald of her own death. I sprang up and lit the lamp, but nothing was to be seen in the room. I was too shaken to go to bed again, however, so I dressed, and as soon as it was daylight I slipped down, got a dog-cart at the Crown Inn, which is opposite, and drove to Leatherhead, from whence I have come on this morning, with the one object of seeing you and asking your advice."

"You have done wisely," said my friend. "But have you told me all?"

"Yes, all."

"Miss Stoner, you have not. You are screening your stepfather."

"Why, what do you mean?"

For answer Holmes pushed back the frill of black lace which fringed the hand that lay upon our visitor's knee. Five little livid spots, the marks of four fingers and a thumb, were printed upon the white wrist.

"You have been cruelly used," said Holmes.

The lady coloured deeply, and covered over her injured wrist. "He is a hard man," she said, "and perhaps he hardly knows his own strength."

There was a long silence, during which Holmes leaned his chin upon his hands and stared into the crackling fire.

"This is a very deep business," he said at last. "There are a thousand details which I should desire to know before I decide upon our course of action. Yet we have not a moment to lose. If we were to come to Stoke Moran to-day, would it be possible for us to see over these rooms without the knowledge of your stepfather?"

"As it happens, he spoke of coming into town to-day upon some most important business. It is probable that he will be away all day, and that there would be nothing to disturb you. We have a housekeeper now, but she is old and foolish, and I could easily get her out of the way."

"Excellent. You are not averse to this trip, Watson?"

"By no means."

"Then we shall both come. What are you going to do yourself?"

"I have one or two things which I would wish to do now that I am in town. But I shall return by the twelve o'clock train, so as to be there in time for your coming."

"And you may expect us early in the afternoon. I have myself some small business matters to attend to. Will you not wait and breakfast?"

"No, I must go. My heart is lightened already since I have confided my trouble to you. I shall look forward to seeing you again this afternoon." She dropped her thick black veil over her face, and glided from the room.

"And what do you think of it all, Watson?" asked Sherlock Holmes, leaning back in his chair.

"It seems to me to be a most dark and sinister business."

"Dark enough and sinister enough."

"Yet if the lady is correct in saying that the flooring and walls are sound, and that the door, window, and chimney are impassable, then her sister must have been undoubtedly alone when she met her mysterious end."

"What becomes, then, of these nocturnal whistles, and what of the very peculiar words of the dying woman?"

"I cannot think."

"When you combine the ideas of whistles at night, the presence of a band of gipsies who are on intimate terms with this old doctor, the fact that we have every reason to believe that the doctor has an interest in preventing his stepdaughter's marriage, the dying allusion to a band, and finally, the fact that Miss Helen Stoner heard a metallic clang, which might have been caused by one of those metal bars which secured the shutters falling back into their place, I think there is good ground to think that the mystery may be cleared along those lines."

"But what, then, did the gipsies do?"

"I cannot imagine."

"I see many objections to any such a theory."

"And so do I. It is precisely for that

reason that we are going to Stoke Moran this day. I want to see whether the objections are fatal, or if they may be explained away. But what, in the name of the devil!"

The ejaculation had been drawn from my companion by the fact that our door had been suddenly dashed open, and that a huge man framed himself in the aperture. His costume was a peculiar mixture of the professional and of the agricultural, having a black top-hat, a long frock-coat, and a pair of high gaiters, with a hunting-crop swinging in his hand. So tall was he that his hat actually brushed the cross-bar of the doorway, and his breadth seemed to span it across from side to side. A large face, seared with a thousand wrinkles, burned yellow with the sun, and marked with every evil passion, was turned from one to the other of us, while his deep-set, bile-shot eyes, and the high thin fleshless nose, gave him somewhat the resemblance to a fierce old bird of prey.

"Which of you is Holmes?" asked this apparition.

"My name, sir, but you have the advantage of me," said my companion quietly.

"I am Dr. Grimesby Roylott, of Stoke Moran."

"Indeed, Doctor," said Holmes blandly. "Pray take a seat."

"I will do nothing of the kind. My stepdaughter has been here. I have traced her. What has she been saying to you?"

"It is a little cold for the time of the year," said Holmes.

"What has she been saying to you?" screamed the old man furiously.

"But I have heard that the crocuses promise well," continued my companion imperturbably.

"Ha! You put me off, do you?" said our new visitor, taking a step forward, and shaking his hunting-crop. "I know you, you scoundrel! I have heard of you before. You are Holmes the meddler."

My friend smiled.

"Holmes the busybody!"

His smile broadened.

"Holmes the Scotland Yard jack-in-office."

Holmes chuckled heartily. "Your conversation is most entertaining," said he. "When you go out close the door, for there is a decided draught."

"I will go when I have had my say. Don't you dare to meddle with my affairs. I know that Miss Stoner has been here—I traced her! I am a dangerous man to fall foul of! See here." He stepped swiftly forward, seized the poker, and bent it into a curve with his huge brown hands.

"See that you keep yourself out of my grip," he snarled, and hurling the twisted poker into the fireplace, he strode out of the room.

"He seems a very amiable person," said Holmes, laughing. "I am not quite so bulky, but if he had remained I might have shown him that my grip was not much more feeble than his own." As he spoke he picked up the steel poker, and with a sudden effort straightened it out again.

"Fancy his having the insolence to confound me with the official detective force! This incident gives zest to our investigation, however, and I only trust that our little friend will not suffer from her imprudence in allowing this brute to trace her. And now, Watson, we shall order breakfast, and afterwards I shall walk down to Doctors' Commons,3 where I hope to get some data which may help us in this matter."

It was nearly one o'clock when Sherlock Holmes returned from his excursion. He held in his hand a sheet of blue paper, scrawled over with notes and figures.

"I have seen the will of the deceased wife," said he. "To determine its exact meaning I have been obliged to work out the present prices of the investments with which it is concerned. The total income, which at the time of the wife's death was little short of £1,100, is now

3 Holmes is obviously speaking in a general sense of the will office, for in 1874—nine years previous to the time of the story—the will office was moved from "Doctor's Common" (the College of Doctors of Civil Law) to Somerset House, its present location. (JHP)

through the fall in agricultural prices not more than £750. Each daughter can claim an income of £250, in case of marriage. It is evident, therefore, that if both girls had married this beauty would have had a mere pittance, while even one of them would cripple him to a serious extent. My morning's work has not been wasted, since it has proved that he has the very strongest motives for standing in the way of anything of the sort. And now, Watson, this is too serious for dawdling, especially as the old man is aware that we are interesting ourselves in his affairs, so if you are ready we shall call a cab and drive to Waterloo. I should be very much obliged if you would slip your revolver into your pocket. An Eley's No. 2 is an excellent argument with gentlemen who can twist steel pokers into knots. That and a toothbrush are, I think, all that we need."

At Waterloo we were fortunate in catching a train for Leatherhead, where we hired a trap at the station inn, and drove for four or five miles through the lovely Surrey lanes. It was a perfect day, with a bright sun and a few fleecy clouds in the heavens. The trees and wayside hedges were just throwing out their first green shoots, and the air was full of the pleasant smell of the moist earth. To me at least there was a strange contrast between the sweet promise of the spring and this sinister quest upon which we were engaged. My companion sat in front of the trap, his arms folded, his hat pulled down over his eyes, and his chin sunk upon his breast, buried in the deepest thought. Suddenly, however, he started, tapped me on the shoulder, and pointed over the meadows.

"Look there!" said he.

A heavily timbered park stretched up in a gentle slope, thickening into a grove at the highest point. From amidst the branches there jutted out the grey gables and high roof-tree of a very old mansion.

"Stoke Moran?" said he.

"Yes, sir, that be the house of Dr. Grimesby Roylott," remarked the driver.

"There is some building going on there," said Holmes; "that is where we are going."

"There's the village," said the driver, pointing to a cluster of roofs some distance to the left; "but if you want to get to the house, you'll find it shorter to go over this stile, and so by the footpath over the fields. There it is, where the lady is walking."

"And the lady, I fancy, is Miss Stoner," observed Holmes, shading his eyes. "Yes, I think we had better do as you suggest."

We got off, paid our fare, and the trap rattled back on its way to Leatherhead.

"I thought it as well," said Holmes, as we climbed the stile, "that this fellow should think we had come here as architects, or on some definite business. It may stop his gossip. Good afternoon, Miss Stoner. You see that we have been as good as our word."

Our client of the morning had hurried forward to meet us with a face which spoke her joy. "I have been waiting so eagerly for you," she cried, shaking hands with us warmly. "All has turned out splendidly. Dr. Roylott has gone to town, and it is unlikely that he will be back before evening."

"We have had the pleasure of making the Doctor's acquaintance," said Holmes, and in a few words he sketched out what had occurred. Miss Stoner turned white to the lips as she listened.

"Good heavens!" she cried, "he has followed me, then."

"So it appears."

"He is so cunning that I never know when I am safe from him. What will he say when he returns?"

"He must guard himself, for he may find that there is someone more cunning than himself upon his track. You must lock yourself from him to-night. If he is violent, we shall take you away to your aunt's at Harrow. Now, we must make the best use of our time, so kindly take us at once to the rooms which we are to examine."

The building was of grey, lichen-blotched stone, with a high central portion, and two curving wings, like the claws of a crab, thrown out on each side. In one of these wings the windows were broken, and blocked with wooden boards, while the roof was partly caved in, a picture of ruin. The central portion was in little better repair, but the right-hand block was comparatively modern, and the blinds in the windows, with the blue smoke curling up from the chimneys, showed that this was where the family resided. Some scaffolding had been erected against the end wall, and the stonework had been broken into, but there were no signs of any workmen at the moment of our visit. Holmes walked slowly up and down the ill-trimmed lawn, and examined with deep attention the outsides of the windows.

"This, I take it, belongs to the room in which you used to sleep, the centre one to your sister's, and the one next to the main building to Dr. Roylott's chamber?"

"Exactly so. But I am now sleeping in the middle one."

"Pending the alterations, as I understand. By the way, there does not seem to be any very pressing need for repairs at that end wall."

"There were none. I believe that it was an excuse to move me from my room."

"Ah! that is suggestive. Now, on the other side of this narrow wing runs the corridor from which these three rooms open. There are windows in it, of course?"

"Yes, but very small ones. Too narrow for anyone to pass through."

"As you both locked your doors at night, your rooms were unapproachable from that side. Now, would you have the kindness to go into your room, and to bar your shutters."

Miss Stoner did so, and Holmes, after a careful examination through the open window, endeavoured in every way to force the shutter open, but without success. There was no slit through which a knife could be passed to raise the bar. Then with his lens he tested the hinges, but they were of solid iron, built firmly into the massive masonry. "Hum!" said he, scratching his chin in some perplexity, "my theory certainly presents some difficulties. No one could pass these shutters

if they were bolted. Well, we shall see if the inside throws any light upon the matter."

A small side-door led into the whitewashed corridor from which the three bedrooms opened. Holmes refused to examine the third chamber, so we passed at once to the second, that in which Miss Stoner was now sleeping, and in which her sister had met her fate. It was a homely little room, with a low ceiling and a gaping fireplace, after the fashion of old country houses. A brown chest of drawers stood in one corner, a narrow white-counterpaned bed in another, and a dressing-table on the left-hand side of the window. These articles, with two small wickerwork chairs, made up all the furniture in the room, save for a square of Wilton carpet in the centre. The boards round and the panelling of the walls were brown, wormeaten oak, so old and discoloured that it may have dated from the original building of the house. Holmes drew one of the chairs into a corner and sat silent, while his eyes travelled round and round and up and down, taking in every detail of the apartment.

"Where does that bell communicate with?" he asked at last, pointing to a thick bell-rope which hung down beside the bed, the tassel actually lying upon the pillow.

"It goes to the housekeeper's room."

"It looks newer than the other things?"

"Yes, it was only put there a couple of years ago."

"Your sister asked for it, I suppose?"

"No, I never heard of her using it. We used always to get what we wanted for ourselves."

"Indeed, it seemed unnecessary to put so nice a bell-pull there. You will excuse me for a few minutes while I satisfy myself as to this floor." He threw himself down upon his face with his lens in his hand, and crawled swiftly backwards and forwards, examining minutely the cracks between the boards. Then he did the same with the woodwork with which the chamber was panelled. Finally he walked over to the bed and spent some time in staring at it, and in running his eye up and down the wall. Finally he took the bell-rope in his hand and gave it a brisk tug.

"Why, it's a dummy," said he.

"Won't it ring?"

"No, it is not even attached to a wire. This is very interesting. You can see now that it is fastened to a hook just above where the little opening of the ventilator is."

"How very absurd! I never noticed that before."

"Very strange!" muttered Holmes, pulling at the rope. "There are one or two very singular points about this room. For example, what a fool a builder must be to open a ventilator in another room, when, with the same trouble, he might have communicated with the outside air!"

"That is also quite modern," said the lady.

"Done about the same time as the bell-rope," remarked Holmes.

"Yes, there were several little changes carried out about that time."

"They seem to have been of a most interesting character—dummy bell-ropes, and ventilators which do not ventilate. With your permission, Miss Stoner, we shall now carry our researches into the inner apartment."

Dr. Grimesby Roylott's chamber was larger than that of his stepdaughter, but was as plainly furnished. A camp bed, a small wooden shelf full of books, mostly of a technical character, an arm-chair beside the bed, a plain wooden chair against the wall, a round table, and a large iron safe were the principal things which met the eye. Holmes walked slowly round and examined each and all of them with the keenest interest.

"What's in here?" he asked, tapping the safe.

"My stepfather's business papers."

"Oh! you have seen inside, then?"

"Only once, some years ago. I remember that it was full of papers."

"There isn't a cat in it, for example?"

"No. What a strange idea!"

"Well, look at this!" He took up a small saucer of milk which stood on the top of it.

"No; we don't keep a cat. But there is a cheetah and a baboon."

"Ah, yes, of course! Well, a cheetah is just a big cat, and yet a saucer of milk does not go very far in satisfying its wants, I daresay. There is one point which I should wish to determine." He squatted down in front of the wooden chair, and examined the seat of it with the greatest attention.

"Thank you. That is quite settled," said he, rising and putting his lens in his pocket. "Hullo! here is something interesting!"

The object which had caught his eye was a small dog lash hung on one corner of the bed. The lash, however, was curled upon itself, and tied so as to make a loop of whipcord.

"What do you make of that, Watson?"

"It's a common enough lash. But I don't know why it should be tied."

"That is not quite so common, is it? Ah, me! it's a wicked world, and when a clever man turns his brain to crime it is the worst of all. I think that I have seen enough now, Miss Stoner, and, with your permission, we shall walk out upon the lawn."

I had never seen my friend's face so grim, or his brow so dark, as it was when we turned from the scene of this investigation. We had walked several times up and down the lawn, neither Miss Stoner nor myself liking to break in upon his thoughts before he roused himself from his reverie.

"It is very essential, Miss Stoner," said he, "that you should absolutely follow my advice in every respect."

"I shall most certainly do so."

"The matter is too serious for any hesitation. Your life may depend upon your compliance."

"I assure you that I am in your hands."

"In the first place, both my friend and I must spend the night in your room."

Both Miss Stoner and I gazed at him in astonishment.

"Yes, it must be so. Let me explain. I believe that that is the village inn over there?"

"Yes, that is the 'Crown.'"

"Very good. Your windows would be visible from there?"

"Certainly."

"You must confine yourself to your room, on pretence of a headache, when your stepfather comes back. Then when you hear him retire for the night, you must open the shutters of your window, undo the hasp, put your lamp there as a signal to us, and then withdraw with everything which you are likely to want into the room which you used to occupy. I have no doubt that, in spite of the repairs, you could manage there for one night."

"Oh, yes, easily."

"The rest you will leave in our hands."

"But what will you do?"

"We shall spend the night in your room, and we shall investigate the cause of this noise which has disturbed you."

"I believe, Mr. Holmes, that you have already made up your mind," said Miss Stoner, laying her hand upon my companion's sleeve.

"Perhaps I have."

"Then for pity's sake tell me what was the cause of my sister's death."

"I should prefer to have clearer proofs before I speak."

"You can at least tell me whether my own thought is correct, and if she died from some sudden fright."

"No, I do not think so. I think that there was probably some more tangible cause. And now, Miss Stoner, we must leave you, for if Dr. Roylott returned and saw us, our journey would be in vain. Good-bye, and be brave, for if you will do what I have told you, you may rest assured that we shall soon drive away the dangers that threaten you."

Sherlock Holmes and I had no difficulty in engaging a bedroom and sitting-room at the Crown Inn. They were on the upper floor, and from our window we could command a view of the avenue gate, and of the inhabited wing of Stoke Moran Manor House. At dusk we saw Dr. Grimesby Roylott drive past, his huge form looming up beside the little figure of the lad who drove him. The boy had some slight difficulty in undoing the heavy iron gates, and we heard the hoarse roar of the Doctor's voice, and saw the fury with which he shook his clenched fists at him. The trap drove on, and a few minutes later we saw a sudden light spring up among the trees as the lamp was lit in one of the sitting rooms.

"Do you know, Watson," said Holmes, as we sat together in the gathering darkness, "I have really some scruples as to taking you to-night. There is a distinct element of danger."

"Can I be of assistance?"

"Your presence might be invaluable."

"Then I shall certainly come."

"It is very kind of you."

"You speak of danger. You have evidently seen more in these rooms than was visible to me."

"No, but I fancy that I may have deduced a little more. I imagine that you saw all that I did."

"I saw nothing remarkable save the bell-rope, and what purpose that could answer I confess is more than I can imagine."

"You saw the ventilator, too?"

"Yes, but I do not think that it is such a very unusual thing to have a small opening between two rooms. It was so small that a rat could hardly pass through."

"I knew that we should find a ventilator before ever we came to Stoke Moran."

"My dear Holmes!"

"Oh, yes, I did. You remember in her statement she said that her sister could smell Dr. Roylott's cigar. Now, of course that suggests at once that there must be a communication between the two rooms. It could only be a small one, or it would have been remarked upon at the coroner's inquiry. I deduced a ventilator."

"But what harm can there be in that?"

"Well, there is at least a curious coincidence of dates. A ventilator is made, a cord is hung, and a lady who sleeps in the bed dies. Does not that strike you?"

"I cannot as yet see any connection."

"Did you observe anything very peculiar about that bed?"

"No."

"It was clamped to the floor. Did you

ever see a bed fastened like that before?"

"I cannot say that I have."

"The lady could not move her bed. It must always be in the same relative position to the ventilator and to the rope—for so we may call it, since it was clearly never meant for a bell-pull."

"Holmes," I cried. "I seem to see dimly what you are hitting at. We are only just in time to prevent some subtle and horrible crime."

"Subtle enough and horrible enough. When a doctor does go wrong he is the first of criminals. He has nerve and he has knowledge. Palmer and Pritchard [4] were among the heads of their profession. This man strikes even deeper, but I think, Watson, that we shall be able to strike deeper still. But we shall have horrors enough before the night is over: for goodness' sake let us have a quiet pipe, and turn our minds for a few hours to something more cheerful."

About nine o'clock the light among the trees was extinguished, and all was dark in the direction of the Manor House. Two hours passed slowly away, and then, suddenly, just at the stroke of eleven, a single bright light shone out right in front of us.

"That is our signal," said Holmes, springing to his feet; "it comes from the middle window."

As we passed out he exchanged a few words with the landlord, explaining that we were going on a late visit to an acquaintance, and that it was possible that we might spend the night there. A moment later we were out on the dark road, a chill wind blowing in our faces, and one yellow light twinkling in front of us through the gloom to guide us on our sombre errand.

There was little difficulty in entering the grounds, for unrepaired breaches gaped in the old park wall. Making our way among the trees, we reached the lawn, crossed it, and were about to enter through the window, when out from a clump of laurel bushes there darted what

seemed to be a hideous and distorted child, who threw itself on the grass with writhing limbs, and then ran swiftly across the lawn into the darkness.

"My God!" I whispered, "did you see it?"

Holmes was for the moment as startled as I. His hand closed like a vice upon my wrist in his agitation. Then he broke into a low laugh, and put his lips to my ear.

"It is a nice household," he murmured, "that is the baboon."

I had forgotten the strange pets which the Doctor affected. There was a cheetah, too; perhaps we might find it upon our shoulders at any moment. I confess that I felt easier in my mind when, after following Holmes' example and slipping off my shoes, I found myself inside the bedroom. My companion noiselessly closed the shutters, moved the lamp onto the table, and cast his eyes round the room. All was as we had seen it in the day-time. Then creeping up to me and making a trumpet of his hand, he whispered into my ear again so gently that it was all that I could do to distinguish the words:

"The least sound would be fatal to our plans."

I nodded to show that I had heard.

"We must sit without a light. He would see it through the ventilator."

I nodded again.

"Do not go to sleep; your very life may depend upon it. Have your pistol ready in case we should need it. I will sit on the side of the bed, and you in that chair."

I took out my revolver and laid it on the corner of the table.

Holmes had brought up a long thin cane, and this he placed upon the bed beside him. By it he laid the box of matches and the stump of a candle. Then he turned down the lamp and we were left in darkness.

How shall I ever forget that dreadful vigil? I could not hear a sound, not even the drawing of a breath, and yet I knew that my companion sat open-eyed, within a few feet of me, in the same state of nervous tension in which I was myself.

4 Two doctors executed for murder in 1856 and 1865, respectively. (JHP)

The shutters cut off the least ray of light, and we waited in absolute darkness. From outside came the occasional cry of a night-bird, and once at our very window a long drawn, cat-like whine, which told us that the cheetah was indeed at liberty. Far away we could hear the deep tones of the parish clock, which boomed out every quarter of an hour. How long they seemed, those quarters! Twelve o'clock, and one, and two, and three, and still we sat waiting silently for whatever might befall.

Suddenly there was the momentary gleam of a light up in the direction of the ventilator, which vanished immediately, but was succeeded by a strong smell of burning oil and heated metal. Someone in the next room had lit a dark lantern. I heard a gentle sound of movement, and then all was silent once more, though the smell grew stronger. For half an hour I sat with straining ears. Then suddenly another sound became audible —a very gentle, soothing sound, like that of a small jet of steam escaping continually from a kettle. The instant that we heard it, Holmes sprang from the bed, struck a match, and lashed furiously with his cane at the bell-pull.

"You see it, Watson?" he yelled. "You see it?"

But I saw nothing. At the moment when Holmes struck the light I heard a low, clear whistle, but the sudden glare flashing into my weary eyes made it impossible for me to tell what it was at which my friend lashed so savagely. I could, however, see that his face was deadly pale, and filled with horror and loathing.

He had ceased to strike, and was gazing up at the ventilator, when suddenly there broke from the silence of the night the most horrible cry to which I have ever listened. It swelled up louder and louder, a hoarse yell of pain and fear and anger all mingled in the one dreadful shriek. They say that away down in the village, and even in the distant parsonage, that cry raised the sleepers from their beds. It struck cold to our hearts, and I stood gazing at Holmes, and he at me, until the last echoes of it had died away into the silence from which it rose.

"What can it mean?" I gasped.

"It means that it is all over," Holmes answered. "And perhaps, after all, it is for the best. Take your pistol, and we shall enter Dr. Roylott's room."

With a grave face he lit the lamp, and led the way down the corridor. Twice he struck at the chamber door without any reply from within. Then he turned the handle and entered, I at his heels, with the cocked pistol in my hand.

It was a singular sight which met our eyes. On the table stood a dark lantern with the shutter half open, throwing a brilliant beam of light upon the iron safe, the door of which was ajar. Beside this table, on the wooden chair, sat Dr. Grimesby Roylott, clad in a long grey dressing-gown, his bare ankles protruding beneath, and his feet thrust into red heelless Turkish slippers. Across his lap lay the short stock with the long lash which we had noticed during the day. His chin was cocked upwards, and his eyes were fixed in a dreadful rigid stare at the corner of the ceiling. Round his brow he had a peculiar yellow band, with brownish speckles, which seemed to be bound tightly round his head. As we entered he made neither sound nor motion.

"The band! the speckled band!" whispered Holmes.

I took a step forward. In an instant his strange head-gear began to move, and there reared itself from among his hair the squat diamond-shaped head and puffed neck of a loathsome serpent.

"It is a swamp adder!" cried Holmes —"the deadliest snake in India. He has died within ten seconds of being bitten. Violence does, in truth, recoil upon the violent, and the schemer falls into the pit which he digs for another. Let us thrust this creature back into its den, and we can then remove Miss Stoner to some place of shelter, and let the county police know what has happened."

As he spoke he drew the dog whip swiftly from the dead man's lap, and throwing the noose round the reptile's neck, he drew it from its horrid perch, and, carrying it at arm's length, threw it into the iron safe, which he closed upon it.

Such are the true facts of the death of Dr. Grimesby Roylott, of Stoke Moran. It is not necessary that I should prolong a narrative which has already run to too great a length, by telling how we broke the sad news to the terrified girl, how we conveyed her by the morning train to the care of her good aunt at Harrow, of how the slow process of official inquiry came to the conclusion that the Doctor met his fate while indiscreetly playing with a dangerous pet. The little which I had yet to learn of the case was told me by Sherlock Holmes as we travelled back next day.

"I had," said he, "come to an entirely erroneous conclusion, which shows, my dear Watson, how dangerous it always is to reason from insufficient data. The presence of the gipsies, and the use of the word 'band,' which was used by the poor girl, no doubt, to explain the appearance which she had caught a horrid glimpse of by the light of her match, were sufficient to put me upon an entirely wrong scent. I can only claim the merit that I instantly reconsidered my position when, however, it became clear to me that whatever danger threatened an occupant of the room could not come either from the window or the door. My attention was speedily drawn, as I have already remarked to you, to this ventilator, and to the bell-rope which hung down to the bed. The discovery that this was a dummy, and that the bed was clamped to the floor, instantly gave rise to the suspicion that the rope was there as a bridge for something passing through the hole, and coming to the bed. The idea of a snake instantly occurred to me, and when I coupled it with my knowledge that the Doctor was furnished with a supply of creatures from India, I felt that I was probably on the right track. The idea of using a form of poison which could not possibly be discovered by any chemical test was just such a one as would occur to a clever and ruthless man who had had an Eastern train-

ing. The rapidity with which such a poison would take effect would also, from his point of view, be an advantage. It would be a sharp-eyed coroner indeed who could distinguish the two little dark punctures which would show where the poison fangs had done their work. Then I thought of the whistle. Of course, he must recall the snake before the morning light revealed it to the victim. He had trained it, probably by the use of the milk which we saw, to return to him when summoned. He would put it through the ventilator at the hour that he thought best, with the certainty that it would crawl down the rope, and land on the bed. It might or might not bite the occupant, perhaps she might escape every night for a week, but sooner or later she must fall a victim.

"I had come to these conclusions before ever I had entered his room. An inspection of his chair showed me that he had been in the habit of standing on it, which, of course, would be necessary in order that he should reach the ventilator. The sight of the safe, the saucer of milk, and the loop of whipcord were enough to finally dispel any doubts which may have remained. The metallic clang heard by Miss Stoner was obviously caused by her father hastily closing the door of his safe upon its terrible occupant. Having once made up my mind, you know the steps which I took in order to put the matter to the proof. I heard the creature hiss, as I have no doubt that you did also, and I instantly lit the light and attacked it."

"With the result of driving it through the ventilator."

"And also with the result of causing it to turn upon its master at the other side. Some of the blows of my cane came home, and roused its snakish temper, so that it flew upon the first person it saw. In this way I am no doubt indirectly responsible for Dr. Grimesby Roylott's death, and I cannot say that it is likely to weigh very heavily upon my conscience."

[1892]

QUESTIONS FOR STUDY

1. *What factors would seem to account for the continuing popularity of the Sherlock Holmes stories? To what extent does their appeal have to do with the reader's own nostalgia?*

2. *Why are most detective stories—including those by Arthur Conan Doyle—narrated in the first person by someone other than the detective-hero himself? What are the advantages of such a narrative technique? What are its limitations?*

3. *Aside from providing the story's narrative voice, what other useful functions does Dr. Watson serve?*

4. *What methods or techniques does Conan Doyle employ in the story to build up the reader's interest?*

5. *Dr. Grimesby Roylott actually appears in the story just once, and then briefly. How does Doyle succeed in making him a convincing villain, worthy of taking on a Sherlock Holmes?*

ALBERT DRAKE

The Chicken Which Became a Rat

HE AIN'T eating the eggs," Uncle Boswick said. His voice carried that same amazed indignation as when he had asked my father, "Yer *paid* for the window?" or when he had reported to me, "He did it with the *sam-yer-eye*." His world had its own practical logic, of survival; these were acts which left him confounded. "The Jap ain't eating the eggs and he won't sell them."

"What's he plan to do?" I asked.

"No plans." Uncle Boswick shook the beads of dew from his slacks, and pointed his whangee cane across the tall grass which stretched from our house to the Jap's tarpaper shack: within the wire I could imagine the gaunt, long-necked hens eyeing each other suspiciously. "Nothing—the chickens are getting wild, the eggs are piling up, the garden's full of weeds—I don't get it."

And then, after picking out the grass kernels which jutted from his perforated two-tone shoes, Uncle Boswick was off to the USO [1] club. To build the boys' morale.

I was surprised that his attitude toward the Jap had changed from hatred to amazed indignation. The Jap had disappointed him. Eggs were rationed and Uncle Boswick saw the Jap's reluctance to sell his not as a foreign plot but rather as evidence of the humorless intensity of a backward race: Uncle Boswick would know how to make money here, somehow, if the Jap would only work *with* him.

What surprised me most was the change in the Jap's property: weeds choked the garden, the corn stalks were stunted and brown, the chicken coop was a box of rusty wire, a small concentration camp. If Uncle Boswick was baffled, how could I be expected to understand? But it seemed that after V-E Day [2] the Jap had given up, as if he knew the Allies would win, and now the land was reverting to the desolation it had been a year ago—a wasteland beyond the city's limits, marshy in winter, baked hard in summer. It now resembled the useless landscape of before last spring, when one night the Jap had infiltrated our neighborhood. He had sneaked in without noise or luggage, and the next morning, when I peeked through the gun-slot of venetian blinds, he was on the flatlands, bent to his hoe, against the rising sun.

It was the third year of the War.

His blade flashed like a bayonet into American soil. Silhouetted against the sun which spilled red across the tips of furrows, his insect shape reminded me of something I had seen or read—something thin, creepy, and utterly evil.

Then I recalled the source. On the coffee table was the current *Liberty:* on the cover Hitler assumed the body of a jackass, his hoofs kicking Europe; beside him Mussolini was a baboon, dangling mindlessly from a stripped, war-wrecked tree; and in the upper-right corner Tojo [3] was a furry, menacing spider whose web, like the land around our Jap, was stained blood-red.

The pavement ended at our house, and Home Front defenses honey-combed the neighborhood's perimeter. The day after the sneak attack on Pearl Harbor we had marched into this wasteland and each

---

[1] United Service Organization: a club, actually a network of clubs, catering to the off-hour needs of servicemen. (JHP)

[2] Victory in Europe Day (May 8, 1945), marking the formal end of the war in Europe. (JHP)

[3] The wartime leaders of Germany, Italy, and Japan. (JHP)

Reprinted by permission of the author. The story first appeared in *Northwest Review.*

boy had dug a foxhole, a hiding place against the bombing raids which seemed imminent. The only bombs to fall were random fire-balloons which fizzled out in the wet forests west of Portland; but as weeks turned to months into years, all our young muscle was directed at the War Effort. We dug a gridwork of slit trenches, pillboxes, and tunnels, and for armament we had stacks of dirt clods, stones, bags of smoke dust, apples drilled to accept a firecracker, and of course our B-B guns. Uncle Boswick had often said that we could expect a Presidential E flag.4

Into these trenches we crawled—Piggy, Slats, Mike, The MacGregor, and myself —soot streaked across our faces, like Commandos in movies; and we moved out, sinking low until the last observation post, where smooth throwing rocks and solid dirt clods were piled. For we were children of war, and had been taught to hate.

"I can smell him," The MacGregor said.

I crawled to the rim and partly turned, one eye on the Jap and the other on The MacGregor, who braced a foot against the dirt wall, his arm cocked. When I raised my finger he fired a distance round. It sailed across the broken landscape and dropped so far behind the Jap did not pause in his stroke.

"Correct elevation," I whispered.

The MacGregor sent off another stone, which arced white against the blue, until, falling, it became a black speck lost in the weeds. Still the enemy hoed on.

I realized that if The MacGregor, our strongest gunner, couldn't make the distance, none of us could. But I whispered, "Harrassment rounds," and raised two fingers, which meant to fire at will.

Our hate spun five clods upward, where they teetered against the sky, to fall in uneven arcs on the dull ground. The Jap, untouched, continued his insidious ground work, chopping treacherously at this piece of the United States, knocking crystals of dew from the weeds as he enlarged his claim.

4 Awarded for effort in wartime production. (JHP)

Over our heads a whistle pierced the sky.

The black speck seemed to travel forever in its swift, guided flight, diminishing until it reached an invisible peak; with a flash of white, the gesture of a wingtip, it peeled off, screaming earthward, to crash through the window of the Jap's shanty. The enemy jumped, dropped his hoe, and ran, flapping his wings like a chicken attempting flight.

We cheered, and as I turned to see who our supporting artillery might be, a volley of laughter strafed the field. At the edge of the pavement Uncle Boswick flipped a heavy stone from hand to hand; he looked more than ever like the posters of Uncle Sam.

It was toward the Jap that he pointed: I want you.

I could not understand why my father, when he learned of our victory, carefully folded the evening paper, hitched up his pants, and strode down the street, off the pavement, and across the field.

He was gone a long time, and dinner was halfway through before he returned. In fact, Uncle Boswick was well into seconds, his mouth so full he could barely exclaim: "Yer *paid* for the window?"

"But why?" I asked. Was he a traitor? Aiding the enemy. I almost believed this in spite of the signs on our front door glass: We Bought Our Quota. We Have A Boy in the NAVY; the blue cloth with the gold star. V for Victory . . . —

"Because your Uncle broke it," he said, spreading white margarine on his bread, digging into the Relief gravy over cereal-laden hamburger. "And because what that Jap does on that gawd-forsaken land is none of your business."

Now I could not believe it. I felt sick, confused, as shattered as the Jap's window. I looked to Uncle Boswick, but he was smiling as he snubbed out his cigarette—smoked as usual to the middle. Another wasteful habit which aggravated my mother.

"Just leave him alone," my father said quietly, always chewing. "Stay away from his place."

Uncle Boswick could not tolerate the

sight of my father calmly eating supper, asking us to leave the Jap alone. "But he's the ENEMY!" he shouted, fists clenched on the table.

"How do you know?" my father asked.

"Well . . . he's a gawdamn Jap, ain't he?"

"There," I said, jumping up, pointing to the wall. "There." On the kitchen wall were two pages my mother had torn from *Life* magazine: *How To Tell Japs From The Chinese.* The photos had an overlay to show that Chinese have long, fine-boned faces, parchment yellow complexion, and never have rosy cheeks; Japs have squat faces with the nose a flat blob, earthy yellow complexion, and sometimes rosy cheeks. I read: *An often sounder clue is facial expression, shaped by cultural, not anthropological factors. Chinese wear rational calm of tolerant realists. Japs, like General Tojo, show humorless intensity of ruthless mystics.* The other page showed Tall Chinese brothers and Short Japanese admirals— our allies and our enemies.

"He looked just like the Short Japanese admirals, and . . . ."

"Did he have rosy cheeks?" my father asked, smiling.

"Yes," I said, although I really wasn't sure. I hadn't been able to see my enemy's face.

"I don't like that Jap any better than you do," my father said, looking at me, Uncle Boswick, my mother. "But he's had a rough row to hoe." As he cleaned his plate with a final slice of bread, he repeated the story the Jap had told him: there had been a large farm near Gresham, where the fields sloped off toward the sun, and where seeds would not stay in the ground—in spring the strawberries grew big as a boy's fist, and in fall the corn was so large and tender that a single ear would make a meal. My father told the story in the dreamy, tragic tone of a man who has not owned anything himself—saying that in only two more years the farm would have been paid off, but after Pearl Harbor it was confiscated by the government and sold at auction, and the Jap—a Nisei,[5] who had been born on the farm, and was therefore an American citizen—had spent

the past two and a half years in an internment camp near Pendelton. Now released, he had no family, no farm, no money. "So I think you—everybody— ought to lay off him."

"Whadda think the Nips're doing to our boys?" Uncle Boswick shouted. "Wake Island, Bataan, the Death March. And don't forget Pearl Harbor: those jokers didn't pay us for any broken windows there. I wish. . . ."

My mother got up and began to clear the table. No doubt she was thinking of Grant on the *USS Plymouth,* now a month out of Hawaii. My father rolled Bugler into tan, wheat-straw paper, touched his tongue to the edge and flattened the ends. He always enjoyed one of Uncle Boswick's real cigarettes after dinner, but he would not ask; nor was one offered tonight.

The last thing I heard as I got up and went to sit on the front porch was Uncle Boswick finishing his sentence: ". . . I could get my licks in."

Uncle Boswick was our hero. The Declaration of War was being read over a million radio speakers when Uncle Boswick's foot missed a tailgate at Fort Ord; he lay screaming in pain as Roosevelt's voice called for unlimited sacrifices from our fighting men. The truck had been barely moving, but something had happened to Uncle Boswick's back. He was given a medical discharge and a fifty per cent disability pension, which meant he did not need to work even if he could. In the confusion of that December the papers officially honoring him as the first casualty of the war were lost in channels, but Uncle Boswick got the pension, a Purple Heart, and freedom from rationing: he had unlimited supplies at the airbase PX.[6] It was unfortunate, my mother often said, that the PX did not stock eggs and meat, but only cigarettes and liquor.

With my father it was different: he was 4-F.[7]

At times I felt that he was letting us

---

5 The son or daughter of Japanese immigrant parents, born and educated in America; hence a first generation Japanese-American. (JHP)

6 Post Exchange—a military base store. (JHP)

down by not being in uniform. Oh sure, building Liberty Ships 8 was pretty important work, but I could not get too excited about it—not even on those days when we would go to Swan Island for a launching, when after the speeches and free lunch he would show us the whirly crane he drove, a tiny cab sitting a hundred feet high on delicate girder legs. But seeing it sail down the tracks, with a bulkhead dangling from the long cables, just wasn't the same as seeing those thin, censored V-letters 9 that The MacGregor's father sent from North Africa.

So I could not understand why he had paid for the Jap's window. Although we were not so poor as we had been before the war, there was no money to spend foolishly. Oh, perhaps I had a vague idea why my father had paid off: because he believed that every man should own a piece of ground and a house, and that all others should respect the limits of ownership—even if it was a house no better than ours, where the wind whipped through the ivy covered lattice-work which was its foundation.

As I looked through dusk across the field I could see the Jap, his hoe flashing in the dim light. The sight made me furious. How were we to leave him alone? He was the Enemy: newspapers, magazines, our teachers, had taught us to hate him. And we learned well to hate. Oh, how we hated him—deeply, intensely. He was the grinning monkey-pilot who gleefully leaned into his gunsight to machinegun parachutists. He was the spidery Nip who saved bullets by using his bayonet on the wounded. We knew too well of his exquisite tortures—bamboo splinters ignited under toe-nails, fingernails removed by pliers, the eye-lid lifted off by the knife's thin whisper.

These thoughts were bothering me when Uncle Boswick came out to sit on the porch. "What I'd like to know is

how he got *released*. With a war on."

"Maybe he escaped," I suggested.

"He's up to something," Uncle Boswick whispered. "Keep your eye on him, kid. That slant-eyed devil is a spy or a saboteur."

Our eyes were on him all right. Every day after breakfast Piggy, Slats, Mike, The MacGregor, and I gathered in the farthest observation post. We pushed Uncle Boswick's binoculars over the rim of the hole until the lenses were full of yellow skin—earthy yellow, I was sure. We harrassed the Jap with random shots. We saluted him with raised middle-fingers and screamed *Banzai,*10 and asked how the hell Tojo was.

But the Jap refused to notice us, and anyway, we saw nothing suspicious. Just the hoe striking the ground and weeds flung from the tiny green shoots which were beginning to appear. This went on for a week, and suddenly the eighth day was Summer. By ten o'clock it was seventy, the flatlands shimmered, and the Jap, slashing with his hoe or carrying buckets of water, looked like a movie mirage.

The OP was an oven. When Piggy refused to drink the brackish canteen water, he went home. Then Mike remembered the bandoliers of ice in his mother's refrigerator. Soon only The MacGregor and myself sweated in the hole, pouring water over our heads, swearing, hating the Jap for keeping us there.

And at noon, when the sun was straight up, erasing any shade, we went swimming.

But the War, glorious and dreadful, near and distant, continued to touch us in many ways. Every day my mother scanned the paper fearfully:

TODAYS
ARMY-NAVY
CASUALTY LIST

Washington—Following are the latest casualties in the military services, including next of kin.
ARMY-NAVY DEAD

7 Exempted from the draft for physical reasons. (JHP)

8 The name given to World War II transport ships. (JHP)

9 Wartime letters designed to be easily opened by a military censor. (JHP)

10 The Japanese cheer of triumph. (JHP)

Her finger would tremble through the list to where Grant's last name, first name, rank, might be; then the newspaper would collapse in her folded hands and she would cry or pray or both. Sometimes, in the afternoon when the house was empty, I would burst in from play to find her at the writing desk, sobbing over a stack of tissue-thin V-letters; they were all postmarked San Francisco, Censor's Office, and she was wondering, no doubt, where in the wide Pacific her oldest boy might be.

Elsewhere, Captain America turned bullets off his shield, the Green Lantern sought truth, and even the Submariner [11] turned to the side of good: another ring of filthy rotten Nazi spies and saboteurs was broken. The Axis shed their animal skins in defeat. In our comics we fought the war, and in the papers we read of its progress: June 6th was D-Day; [12] during that month V-1 bombs, [13] a terrible undreamed of weapon, began to fall on England; the Marianas Campaign pushed ahead. The pleasant summer advanced, and so did our boys: troops landed at Saipan, and during July the big drive began through Normandy; Guam and Paris were liberated in August.

At home the war controlled us. Our battles were fought every day: we could buy comic books, but few fireworks and no bubblegum. The B-B's for our guns turned to lead. The currency of conversation was ration discs and coupon books. In our driveway my father's 1934 Terraplane sat without tires, graded by the C sticker on its windshield. Now he drove only the sedan, a 1930 Hudson; it was an immense, magnificent car, dark and square; and when he placed an ironing board across the jump seats he was able to haul nine people every day to the shipyard. However essential this was to the war effort, he could not get the red and white B sticker changed to the coveted grade A—so the coupe rested on its rims and the sedan eased around town at 35

mph on ancient patched rubber and there was not enough extra gas that summer to even go to the beach.

But we fought on: we flattened tons of tin cans for tanks and salvaged kitchen fat for munitions and bundled high stacks of newspapers and magazines for who knows what. We bought a twenty-five cent savings stamp a week, and when the book was full it became a War Bond. On walks and walls we chalked our beliefs—*Hitler is a Heel*—and assertions of evolution—*Tojo is a Monkey's Uncle*. We said prayers, pledged allegiance, saluted the flag; and a thousand times our razored hate cheered John Wayne's single-handed assault against the Japs on Friday nights.

One bright morning, when even the haze of war could not hide the sun, I came from behind the humped, tireless coupe in the driveway and suddenly noticed the marshland had become a profuse garden. The corn was a screen, thick as any bamboo grove, and below the tomatoes glowed red: tiny suns of nippon. Bayonets of onion greens stabbed upward; potatoes, peppers, lettuce, carrots camouflaged the ground. Even the tarpaper shack seemed to stand a little straighter in the chaos of flowers, and its shutters and front door were painted bright yellow.

Sneaking through the foliage was the Jap: he was building tripods, small tent skeletons, for the beans.

Behind me Uncle Boswick came out, stretched, and surveyed the changed, technicolor landscape. He sported a new panama hat and two-tone perforated shoes, and I guessed that he was on his way to the USO club, although it was pretty early.

"Poppies," he said. "And not the kind the Legion sells."

I admired Uncle Boswick—I would never have thought of *opium*—and so I said yes, when he asked me to reconnoiter the area and to get some fresh vegetables, to be sent to his friends in Washington, D.C., for analysis. In spite of my father's order that the Jap be left alone, I wanted to get in the fight. Our fight.

---

11 Comic book heroes. (JHP)
12 The Allied invasion of Europe at Normandy, June 6, 1944. (JHP)
13 The Germans' jet-propelled flying bomb. (JHP)

The rest of the day was spent with the Gang mapping out a plan of action. It was only after the details were settled that Slats mentioned it didn't get dark until nine, his bedtime. Our hoots and jeers at Slats were suddenly silenced when we realized that there wasn't one of us could stay out that late.

Therefore, at nine, as the sun fell beyond the muted, blacked out neon of Portland, I crawled from my bedroom window and slipped into the high grass. In the near-darkness I groped along the trench-work, and at the farthest OP I began to inch toward that garden on my stomach, a hunting knife clenched between my teeth. Near my face the *chiirrruup* of crickets was deafening, and at every shift of my body the gas-mask bag slipped noisily; I paused to look back, and through the summer mists I saw the dull yellow cracks around blackout curtains in our frontroom, far away.

Crickets chirped nearby, an echo of bullfrogs farther out in the marsh, and along Johnson Creek the Galloping Goose cried into the night. A veil of wind blew a pungent, acrid green and then I saw the oiled, metallic sides of vegetables: cucumbers lay like small surface mines, aimed in every direction.

I waited, staring into the blackness at the tar-paper shack. Then the knife blade slipped across prickly stalks and three large specimens were in the bag. I crouched among the corrugated sides of squash, knife slashing, and moved quickly into the bayonets of green onions. Beyond were tomato plants, the hard black balls swimming in metallic greenness. Among the wide, sharp leaves of corn I was shielded, and it was not until the fourth ear had been split from its stalk that I felt a pang of fear. In the terror of silence leaf rasped on leaf. The knife was in my hand when I stood to stare into the silent, black night.

Not three plants away the Jap waited, arms folded, hat tipped to conceal his inscrutable face.

Even as I jumped I knew it must be a *scarecrow*—but I threw the knife overhand and flung away the gas-mask bag and ran across the misty, deep grass, the uneven ground falling away under my racing feet. Only when I was again in bed, rubbing my legs to stop their trembling, did I realize that the Jap had my knife—that he was now *armed*.

I slept with this fear and in a dream I heard voices at the back steps: *well they are lovely* and *let me pay* and *I may keep the bag?*

I heard the screen door open and my mother say *Thankew*—it was a trick, no doubt—but then the door slammed shut and a figure passed outside my window. It shuffled under that same loose, flowing shirt and broad hat I had seen last night —but again *I could not see any feature of the face.*

"Well, you're awake," my mother said. She was running water into a dishpan at the sink, and on the table, the gas-mask bag spilled out vegetables like a horn of plenty. "The Jap man *gave* us these," she said. "He wouldn't take any money, but I asked him to bring us some every week and I said I'd pay him a quarter—does that sound fair? He said he wants to buy some chickens."

Once a week until November the Jap came with a bag of produce, to accept my mother's money (as if there was no war on!) and to pass so close beneath the window that he must have felt the glow of my hatred.

He never did return my knife, either.

In what seemed the middle of summer, school began again.

No matter that Paris and Guam and Palau had been liberated, or that bombs were falling on Manila, Luzon, and Okinawa, we marched into dull classrooms, carrying new notebooks already marked A.A.F.: [14] we were all destined to become pilots, wearing white scarfs, chamois helmets, and leather jackets with the Flying Tiger patch on the back,[15] like Errol Flynn. School for us was the twice-weekly War Communique film, where in the fluttering light we saw Patton tanks smash hedgerows, and

14 Army Air Force. (JHP)
15 The Flying Tigers were a group of volunteer American pilots helping Chiang Kai-shek fight the Japanese in China; the "patch" was a message in Chinese for use in case the pilot was shot down or forced to land. (JHP)

bombs tumble like eggs toward the ultimate explosion. We squirmed with excitement as infantry charged across beaches strewn with dead and debris, as a flame-thrower sucked burning Japanese from caves, ending their ruthless mysticism. When the narrator's voice and the marching music ground to a halt and the projector stopped and the olive drab blinds were raised, the boys would turn to look at one another and even Ellie Chombrake, the skinniest kid in the class, wore a sense of purpose on his face. The war was a common bond, holding us together; we all knew our role in this struggle for freedom.

Besides Christmas, only two things happened that school year.

One night in December, shortly before vacation, I was doing homework when I heard shouting in the field: it was The MacGregor.

From my front porch I heard him shouting crazily at the Jap and there was a distant crash of glass. I ran across the field, leaping trenches, until I saw the blurred outline of The MacGregor lobbing rock after rock at the tar-paper shanty; through the dark mist came the report of splintering boards. He was screaming and falling forward with every rock he threw, and I waited a minute before placing a hand on his shoulder. The face that turned was distorted into a crazy mask, and I stepped back, but not quickly enough—his throwing fist, clutching a rock, came from the night to smash into my face.

It was my father who helped us both home, and when he returned from The MacGregor's house, to hold an ice pack against my bleeding cheek, he told us that Mr. MacGregor had been killed in what the newspapers celebrated as the Battle of the Bulge—where General McAuliffe said "nuts" to the Nazis. The telegram from the War Department assured Mrs. MacGregor that her husband had died a Hero.

My cheek no longer hurt: I felt good, and I wanted to shake The MacGregor's hand. But it was too late that night, my father said, and for the rest of the week The MacGregor's desk at school was empty, and by Saturday the mother and son had moved to Seattle, leaving a dark, lifeless house.

The next week, as if to replace our loss, Piggy's uncle sent home a large, olive drab box from the Pacific. Piggy was certain it was a Christmas present for him but Gussie, his aunt, who was staying for the duration, said the box contained souvenirs, and that she had been instructed *not* to open it until Jed came home.

And within five minutes she had a crowbar against the lid, splintering wood; inside lay three long, dark rifles, a pistol wrapped in tan, oil-slick paper, and two Jap officer swords. Everything was coated with a thick rancid grease, but the guns were beautiful and the swords were works of art: they had scabbards crafted with inlaid wood and pearl, into which the delicate blade whispered. Gussie, who no doubt expected silks, hammered the lid back and from then on the basement door was kept locked.

But for us, knowing those weapons were there, the war seemed much closer.

School was a huge wheel, grinding toward Spring. Its monotonous progress was interrupted only by the excitement of paper drives and tin can collections, practice blackouts and marches to the basement, which was now called the Air Raid Shelter. Here we huddled until the All Clear bell, discussing how we would fight the war when called, even though we could not see how it would last another eight years: the newspaper maps showed wide arrows, and by April the Americans and Russians were shaking hands in a defeated Berlin, while most of Europe was occupied by our boys. Although the Japanese were using *kamikazes* and Baka Bombs,[16] Iwo Jima and Okinawa had been captured and it was only a matter of time before we would invade Japan itself.

16 Kamikazes were airplanes filled with explosives and flown on suicide missions by pilots without parachutes; Baka Bombs were engineless, manually piloted flying bombs, which were towed to the target area, released, and then guided by their pilots toward the target. Both were used by the Japanese in desperation toward the end of the war. (JHP)

Our winter had been mild and the spring rains turned the ground an energetic green. The trenches were hip-high in water, but from my bedroom window I watched the Jap at work seeding and hoeing. I wondered what he thought—surely he knew now that his country was defeated. A hundred short Japanese admirals were no match for one tall John Wayne marine. Why had he come here? What did he want? What was he working so hard for? No matter if he should again transform that wasteland into a blooming paradise, the whole neighborhood blotted him out with hate. Yet he foolishly worked on: feet bare, pants rolled to the knee, he dashed along the furrows in a lurching, forward-slanting crouch under the wide straw hat. When he was not working the land he was building the chicken coop. He had scrounged fragments of wood and wire; and the coop, a temporary, tottering structure, made the tar-paper shack seem a palace. Apparently he had sold enough vegetables the previous summer, because one morning the fenced area was filled with small puffs of yellow, like frantic flowers. His dream was coming true, and I wanted to cross that field to make sure he understood that this could only happen in America—this was free enterprise, democracy.

The Jap had his chicks, V-E Day was celebrated, my dad was talking about the new car he would buy when this war was over, the neighborhood grew green, and school would soon end. It was into this spirit of optimism that Piggy's uncle returned.

If I had not seen him in uniform for a fleeting minute, as he walked from the car to the house that first day, I would not have believed that he had been in battle: all day, every day, he sat on the front porch in a rocking chair, wearing faded bib overalls and a brown shirt, and bearing no visible wound. He was a strange man with small, dull eyes and skin which became red without tanning; when he spoke his voice faded through short sentences, and he refused to talk about the War, even to Uncle Boswick.

"All he wants," said Uncle Boswick,

"is to get back to that Alabama dirt farm, and sit."

"That's okay," my father said. "A man ought to own a bit of land."

"Gussie, now she's cut from a different bolt," Uncle Boswick said, winking. "I know her pretty well. She likes it here—plenty of ocean and forests and no niggers. Bet you five dollars she don't leave with him."

"Oh, now," my mother said, but her protest was weak for she had the gossip about Gussie straight from Piggy's mother: how Gussie had worked at Oregon Shipyard for two weeks after Jed had been shipped overseas. She had been back only for launchings, when the company gave out free beer and food, and we were told that any Saturday night she could be found along Harbor Drive, where ships on the Willamette tied up. Gussie, my mother said, was "wild" and "needed a baby to keep her home." Now that Jed was back she was sure that Gussie would "straighten out." Uncle Boswick, who seemed to know an awful lot about Gussie, said he wasn't so sure.

But rain or shine Jed remained in his rocking chair on the front porch, surveying the neighborhood with dull eyes. His uniform remained in the closet, and Piggy reported that Jed had gone into the basement only once to check the heavy box of souvenirs.

So we were surprised to see Gussie with the big samurai sword.

That late June sun was already an explosion of fire, burning life from the grass, but Piggy, Slats, Mike, and I worked in the trenches anyway; we felt needed, for after V-E Day the war focused on the Pacific, our ocean. We repaired trench walls where the rains had worn them away, and filled sandbags, piled our rocks, and sometimes lobbed an occasional missile at the Jap's chicken coop—but half-heartedly, for now that we knew Tojo was finished our Jap seemed more like a docile intruder: unwanted, but harmless. Uncle Boswick had even taken to crossing the field two or three times a week, to "interrogate" the Jap about when the hens would start laying. For eggs were still rationed.

I trained Uncle Boswick's binoculars on the Jap's shack, then slowly swept them across the chicken coop, the vast garden—for I wanted to see my enemy's face, to see if in these last days of the war that face could maintain its humorless intensity—when at my elbow Slats said: "What's that noise?"

All I heard was Gussie's radio. Whenever she was sunbathing her radio blared hot hillbilly music into the quiet neighborhood. But today she was not sunbathing. When I swung the binoculars past our house to Piggy's backyard, I saw Gussie in the far corner wearing tiny shorts and halter.

The noise that Slats heard was the blackberry vines being chopped, and what Gussie was using was the big Jap sword.

She was working, and I recalled what my mother had said about Gussie "straightening out" with Jed home. It was the first time I had ever seen her do work of any kind. Like Uncle Boswick, she did not need to work.

We charged from the trench, knowing that long wooden box of war souvenirs was lying open in an unlocked basement. But Piggy said: "If we wait for Jed, *he'll* show them to us."

Under the hot sun we waited while on that porch Jed rocked, his eyes focused on something above the rooftops, and in the far corner of the yard the sword flashed like a mirror. We waited, wondering how many American boys' heads that long blade had lopped off. We shuddered, for the courageous blood spilled on Bataan, Corrigedor, Wake Island, and for the blade each time that Gussie hit a rock. Through the binoculars I watched Jed's face, dull and impassive, and finally I saw the lips tighten slowly, pulling his eyes narrow. Suddenly the field of vision was filled with his striped bib-overalls. I lowered the glasses to see Jed stand up; he spit once over the porch rail, scratched his seat, and started down the steps as we charged from the trench.

Jed walked slowly past the basement door, down the driveway, and was blotted from sight by our house. We were halfway to the road when Jed re-appeared, to take the sword from Gussie.

Later I was unsure exactly what I saw —we were still a good distance away, and it happened very fast. She had the sword raised overhead in both hands, to assault the tenacious blackberry vines, when Jed stepped from behind and grabbed the blade. The surprise of his movement sent her spinning off balance, and she fell among the daggers of the vines. We heard her cry once—a single, abrupt noise—and saw the blade flash, an arc of sunlight across our eyes, forever impressed. An irregular, stunned line of boys watched in horror as Jed came from behind the trees and the obstructing house; he lurched toward that cool dark basement.

We retreated to the trench, where I exchanged one nervous glance with Piggy: Gussie lay in the vines, pumping her blood out, and beyond that dark, recessed doorway Jed had the guns. We gripped the lip of turf, not even pretending to arm ourselves with throwing stones, until we heard the thin siren droning from Loaner's Corner, an insect in the hot afternoon; and at the same instant a muffled explosion churned up from that basement, growing like a cloud to envelop the neighborhood.

A few minutes after Uncle Boswick jumped the fence which separated Piggy's yard from mine, the police car rocked to the curb. As the officers moved up the driveway, guns thrust into the yard's calm, we raced to the road and saw Uncle Boswick point to that far corner. Blood smudged his shirt, and his eyes slanted against tears—at the time, it was my impression that he had cut himself coming over the fence.

And before the policemen came back from viewing Gussie's slim, decapitated body, and before Uncle Boswick chased us into the street, we gathered at the small, dirt spattered basement window: Jed was sitting in the corner, propped against the dirt wall by the Jap rifle. The big toe of his right foot was hooked into the trigger-guard; the barrel pointed into the darkness where half his head was missing. Behind him a fan-shaped stain drew flies.

The deaths were not mentioned that evening at supper, a meal eaten in silence; but later, on the front steps, Uncle Boswick announced, as if I did not already know: "He did it with the *sam-yer-eye* sword. Can you believe that? Ahhhh, she was a beautiful girl." He went on, in a voice charged with amazed indignation, to tell how he had seen the blade flash once across the sun from the chaise lounge in our back yard; he thought it was a dream. From that moment his world was one of missing pieces, of edges that never did quite meet, and when I asked him again what *really* had happened all he could say was: "He did it with the *sam-yer-eye*."

But that was not what I wanted to know.

Nor did the Jap make any sense to him. A few days after the deaths Uncle Boswick crossed that wasteland to "interrogate" the Jap, and when he returned his voice was charged with amazed fury. "The hens are finally laying, but *he ain't eating the eggs*. The Jap ain't eating the eggs and he won't sell them. I'm telling you the whole world's gone nuts."

After Uncle Boswick left for the USO club, I got out his binoculars and my plane spotter's manual—for four years I had been searching the skies for a Zero or Mitsubitsi bomber.[17] From the blue skies I lowered the glasses to focus on the Jap's shack, and for the first time I noticed that the profusion of flowers had shrunk back into the mud. The shack leaned to its own shadow; a yellowed newspaper fluttered from the window broken long ago by The MacGregor's stone. I shifted to the garden out back, and saw corn burned by the sun fold into stiff stalks, diminishing like candle wax.

The glasses focused on the slanting assemblage of wood and wire, and although the nests were concealed I could see the clumps of dirty white which flashed from corners: the hens had begun to lay their eggs in any depression. I slowly swung the glasses across the Jap's property—scanning every inch of

peeling paint, broken glass, and browned foliage—but I saw no sign of the Jap. The chickens milled about the dusty arena, without food or water, eyeing one another suspiciously. The eggs began to pile up, dropped from the starving, wiry hens, and I knew this was another fiendish, exquisite eastern torture. I pictured the Jap hiding in a corner of the shack, drunk on sake, giggling his sharp-toothed, rat-faced fanaticism.

The eggs piled up, delicate and white, and every day Uncle Boswick crossed that wasteland to beg, plead, argue the Jap into selling him some eggs. I would watch Uncle Boswick cross the field and stand by the bottom step of the porch; I could see his mouth moving, hands flying—*but I never saw the Jap*. Only a shadow across the broken window, a faint movement which might have been the curtain blowing. On any day during the past year he would have been running on short admiral legs across the tilled soil, a water bucket in each hand, or he would have been leaning on his shovel, or kneeling over seeds, as if in prayer. Now he did not come out of the tar-paper shack, not even to feed the chickens.

It was not until two weeks later, when the heat of summer shifted into August, that Uncle Boswick was able to learn *why* the Jap refused to part with his eggs.

Uncle Boswick was trying to talk my mother into going across that field to plead with the Jap. "You've got to go—the egg route is all sewn up, I've got the customers. We've got to make some money soon, before this war is over. Gawd knows every businessman has lined *his* nest: the junk-yards selling gas stamps and tires from wrecks at black-market prices, the gas stations, the meat markets—they're getting rich!"

We had never had any money, and he was trying to appeal to her only fear: poverty. But apparently she feared the Jap even more, for she would not go—not even when he told her what he had learned.

"Do you know *why* he won't do anything with them?" Uncle Boswick asked. "He bought the chickens so he could have some eggs—and now he tells me he

17 Japanese warplanes: a single-engine fighter and a bomber. (JHP)

can't eat the eggs of hens he knows *personally.* That he has fed with his own hands. *Hens he knows personally!"*

For Uncle Boswick this was the ultimate puzzle, and he abandoned his attempt to collaborate with the enemy. Other afternoons would be spent in the chaise lounge, warming his war wounds against the sun, clipping money-making advertisements from magazines.

But I continued to watch the drama of torture with a strange fascination: every morning I went to the foxhole and focused binoculars on the chicken coop, where lean hens milled, eyeing each other suspiciously. Their high wiry bodies bobbed and crowded as they rotated in an endless circle under the blazing sun. I saw those near the fence stretch through the wire, their hysterical beaks reaching for any green leaf.

One day toward noon, just as I was about to return home for lunch, I saw a hen squat in the dust and when it rose, the quizzical eye aimed at the sun, its dusty, hoarse clucking was suddenly strangled. The hen's head darted like a wedge; the sharp beak smashed the shell, and the hen began to devour her own egg.

From the side another hen kicked high into the air, wings flapping, mad with the smell of food. A cloud of feathers exploded over the oily yolk as the two fought—others jumped in, and mass hysteria spread like the rising dust cloud. I watched with excited horror, for I had been waiting for something like this— the dust, torn feathers, the savage choked cries. From behind the wire a gas cloud rose, and the smell of rotten eggs drifted on the wind, an ominous yellow cloud which would stain every house, touch every life.

Fifteen minutes later, when the air was fairly clear, I could see that every egg had been pecked open.

Again the tide rotated wing to wing, hungry for food, space, the freedom of flight. They pressed together tightly accelerating in a small circle within the confines of the wire until motion became a brown blur. Their movement held no hope for escape, but the smell of food had driven them mad and this was a kind of direct action—in desperation their yellow feet raced across the baked earth, the head at the end of the arched neck in pursuit of something. I waited, watching with that same sense of excited horror I had known the day Jed walked off the porch and the morning the Jap had first appeared on our horizon.

Then, near the wire, one stumbled with exhaustion. Her wings fanned the dust, but before she could rise the beak of her neighbor slashed out. She struggled, her chalky *cluuuuk* filled with urgency and alarm, but from the circle's momentum a dozen hens peeled off and were on her, necks extended, beaks chopping at her eyes.

When two of the attackers drew back, their dusty feathers were speckled with blood. Through binoculars I could see the stained hens lift their wings, crane their necks at a difficult angle to dink off the beads of blood. Behind them the circle began to disintegrate, and the smell of blood carried to my foxhole as hens surrounded to attack the attackers.

Originally there were perhaps thirty chickens, and the next day when I returned there were half that number. On the third day their were ten, and then five walked among the debris of feathers and bones. These five had grown heavy, nourished by the fallen, and they waddled grotesque and wary. One stayed in each corner of the coop, and one paced a small circle in the center.

Later there were only two left, and these had been changed until they looked more like buzzards—their necks were plucked bare, and what lower feathers remained had turned black from the blood and dust. Seen through the binoculars the birds looked arrogant, fierce, and utterly mad. Their feet were claws and their heads like hatchets, topped by the blood-filled comb. Each preened and arched in her space, proud that she had survived. I wondered whether inside the shack the Jap was giggling or filled with revulsion—after all, these were hens he had known personally.

And suddenly the War was over.

On our small street people spilled from houses, cheering and shouting, touching one another. My mother, after saying a prayer to God, even smoked a cigarette in her excitement, and there was cold beer on the table. The cloud of War had lifted. Relief and happiness passed through our house like a seismic wave.

From the radio came the official details: *At 12:01 The Great Artiste dropped the second bomb . . . a pillar of purple fire, 10,000 feet high, shot skyward with enormous speed, moving to become a mushroom shaped cloud which eventually attained a height of 60,000 feet . . . officials estimate that the blast caused extensive damage. . . .*

The War had ended. In that room I sensed a curious mixture of gladness and despair, as if we were suddenly released from what had held us together. I could not remember a time before Pearl Harbor, I could only recall a world at war, and all my energy for four years had been consumed by the war effort—I'd spent hundreds of hours digging the home defenses, scanning the sky for enemy aircraft, watching war communique films at school. I had collected tons of waste paper, tin cans, old cooking fat. I had grown Victory gardens, stayed up nights watching for tire thieves, helped my mother to keep the OPA Consumer's Pledge.[18]

"Jesus." Uncle Boswick heard the news and his hand reached for another cold beer.

My father had his bank book out, and was searching the columns with a scowl. The War had killed the Depression, moving him into the only prosperity he'd ever known. He wet the pencil tip against his tongue and began to figure on an old envelope, moving into peace half-heartedly.

I walked to the street's edge and looked both ways, as if I might see that cresting mushroom cloud, or be touched by its gigantic shadow. For the war *had* touched us all: I thought of The Mac-Gregor, Gussie, and Jed—in the dark

enigma of that basement, that stained wall, I later realized we had viewed every casualty.

And in the field where we had labored hard and well, grass already grew in our trenches.

Perhaps because the Jap was no longer my enemy, but more likely because I was curious of the face I had never seen, I walked slowly through the yielding high grass toward the leaning tarpaper shack. Against the broken window the old newspaper floated, the type erased by sun and wind. Closer, I saw that the shutters threatened to fall from rusty hinges, and that their bright yellow paint had now curdled into rivulets. My knock was timid, and unanswered, but the door was ajar and I could see through the single room to the back yard.

The house was empty. Any furniture the Jap might have had was gone, and so was he. There was not even the smell of soy sauce, nor the odor of yellow; not even a grain of rice captured in the floor's parallel cracks remained as evidence. I stood in the tiny room, where dust motes drifted like dandelion fuzz across the sun's scorching shafts, and I wondered where he had gone. I wanted him to see my triumph—we had won, Japan was conquered. Also, I wanted to see his face—just once, up close, to see if he wasn't an exact copy of the grinning monkey the magazines had shown us. Where was he? Had he committed hari-kari [19] in the garden?

The only evidence that the empty room had been lived in recently were the newspapers covering one wall. Bold headlines jumped from the yellow paper; the print faded into blurred words, columns of statistics, tracing the war's progress—down to the two day old newspaper taped at a crazy angle in the corner, its ink still firm.

Under the low ceiling the August heat collected; thick blue flies hummed furiously in the hot air, and as I walked out the back door it occurred to me that the Jap's departure would *really* baffle Uncle Boswick.

18 Office of Price Administration, the governmental agency in charge of controlling wartime prices. (JHP)

19 Japanese ritualistic suicide. (JHP)

The garden was levelled; except for the small, open dirt mound, a row of scabs where the corn had been, all traces of the Jap's industry were sucked into the baked earth. A few loose feathers drifted across the space where last year cucumbers had lain in profusion, like surface mines, and the night air had been green with the metallic darkness of hard, fist-sized tomatoes. The feathers drifted from the rotting pile within the chicken coop, mute testimony to the destruction. The ground within the wire was perforated with the puck marks of claws, littered with bleached, dry bones. From inside the shed came a brittle noise, and I wondered if there could be a survivor—I had imagined those last two hens fighting by moonlight until each had driven a slashing, crescent beak into the other. The noise—a chewing, tearing sound—continued, and I searched the baked earth for a handful of grass, to throw over the wire fence. As the grass drifted down, each blade flashing like a knife, the burlap cover at the small doorway moved. Then the single remaining chicken emerged. She dashed across the enclosure on thick legs to where the blades were still falling; cautiously, she sniffed at my offering but did not touch it—she had acquired a taste for blood.

The angular, massive head turned and behind deep folds her fierce eyes were fixed on me; with a crouching run she accelerated, to crash heavily into the wire. Her thick, short neck absorbed the impact, and she moved back, grunting, to try again. Her rush had carried the terrific odor of fowl, blood, dung, dust; and with this stink in my nose I now saw that she had lost all of her feathers and the skin was a silky black, broken only by the white scars. Grown short and fat, the crescent beak hooked like a primitive tooth, she had metamorphosed into a kind of rat.

Of the flock, this was the Victor.

[1970]

QUESTIONS FOR STUDY

1. *Identify the story's narrator? Why is his age important? Does his perception of the adult world change? If so, how?*
2. *In what respects does the opening paragraph serve as the story's topic paragraph?*
3. *Contrast the attitudes expressed by Uncle Boswick and the narrator's father.*
4. *The incident between Gussie and Jed is purposely de-emphasized. How is it important to the story?*
5. *What does the story have to say about war? How does it go about making that statement?*
6. *What is the symbolic value of the chickens? What is the meaning of the story's title? Explain the metamorphosis that occurs at the end of the story.*

HARLAN ELLISON

"Repent, Harlequin!" Said the Ticktockman

THERE are always those who ask, what is it all about? For those who need points sharply made, who need to know "where it's at," this:

The mass of men serve the state thus, not as men mainly, but as machines, with their bodies. They are the standing army, and the militia, jailors, constables, posse comitatus, etc. In most cases there is no free exercise whatever of the judgment or of the moral sense; but they put themselves on a level with wood and earth and stones; and wooden men can perhaps be manufactured that will serve the purpose as well. Such command no more respect than men of straw or a lump of dirt. They have the same sort of worth only as horses and dogs. Yet such as these even are commonly esteemed good citizens. Others—as most legislators, politicians, lawyers, ministers, and officeholders—serve the state chiefly with their heads; and, as they rarely make any moral distinctions, they are as likely to serve the Devil, without intending it, as God. A very few, as heroes, patriots, martyrs, reformers in the great sense, and men, serve the state with their consciences also, and so necessarily resist it for the most part; and they are commonly treated as enemies by it.
       Henry David Thoreau,
       CIVIL DISOBEDIENCE 1

That is the heart of it. Now begin in the middle, and later learn the beginning; the end will take care of itself.

But because it was the very world it was, the very world they had allowed it to *become*, for months his activities did

1 In "Civil Disobedience" (1849) Henry David Thoreau (1817–1862) presented his classic statement of passive resistance in defense of his refusal to pay his poll tax in support of the Mexican War four years earlier. (JHP)

not come to the alarmed attention of The Ones Who Kept The Machine Functioning Smoothly, the ones who poured the very best butter 2 over the cams and mainsprings of the culture. Not until it had become obvious that somehow, someway, he had become a notoriety, a celebrity, perhaps even a hero for (what Officialdom inescapably tagged) "an emotionally disturbed segment of the populace," did they turn it over to the Ticktockman and his legal machinery. But by then, because it was the very world it was, and they had no way to predict he would happen—possibly a strain of disease long-defunct, now, suddenly, reborn in a system where immunity had been forgotten, had lapsed—he had been allowed to become too real. Now he had form and substance.

He had become a *personality*, something they had filtered out of the system many decades before. But there it was, and there *he* was, a very definitely imposing personality. In certain circles—middle-class circles—it was thought disgusting. Vulgar ostentation. Anarchistic. Shameful. In others, there was only sniggering: those strata where thought is subjugated to form and ritual, niceties, proprieties. But down below, ah, down below, where the people always needed their saints and sinners, their bread and circuses, their heroes and villains, he was considered a Bolivar; a Napoleon; a

2 "The very best butter" is a phrase taken from the Mad Hatter's Tea Party in Lewis Carroll's *Alice in Wonderland* (1865). Ellison notes that "this and subsequent swipes from Carroll [see footnote 7] are intended to convey an undertone that the world of this story is quite logically mad, as was the world Carroll described." (JHP)

Robin Hood; a Dick Bong (Ace of Aces); a Jesus; a Jomo Kenyatta.3

And at the top—where, like socially-attuned Shipwreck Kellys,4 every tremor and vibration threatens to dislodge the wealthy, powerful and titled from their flagpoles—he was considered a menace; a heretic; a rebel; a disgrace; a peril. He was known down the line, to the very heartmeat core, but the important reactions were high above and far below. At the very top, at the very bottom.

So his file was turned over, along with his time-card and his cardioplate, to the office of the Ticktockman.

The Ticktockman: very much over six feet tall, often silent, a soft purring man when things went timewise. The Ticktockman.

Even in the cubicles of the hierarchy, where fear was generated, seldom suffered, he was called the Ticktockman. But no one called him that to his mask.

You don't call a man a hated name, not when that man, behind his mask, is capable of revoking the minutes, the hours, the days and nights, the years of your life. He was called the Master Timekeeper to his mask. It was safer that way.

"This is *what* he is," said the Ticktockman with genuine softness, "but not *who* he is. This time-card I'm holding in my left hand has a name on it, but it is the name of *what* he is, not *who* he is. The cardioplate here in my right hand is also named, but not whom named, merely what named. Before I can exercise proper revocation, I have to know who this what is."

3 The allusions are as follows: Simon Bolivar (1783–1830), the South American liberator; Napoleon Bonaparte (1769–1821), the military emperor of France; Robin Hood of Sherwood Forest, the legendary outlaw of medieval England; Dick Bong (1921–1945), the American flying "ace" of World War II; Jesus of Nazareth (4 B.C.–A.D. 29?), the source of the Christian faith, who challenged the Jewish and Roman authorities of his time; and Jomo Kenyatta (1893–   ), the leader of Kenya's independence movement and first president of the new republic of Kenya. (JHP)

4 Shipwreck Kelly—Alvin Kelly (1892?–1952), a famous flagpole sitter of the 1920s and 1930s. (JHP)

To his staff, all the ferrets, all the loggers, all the finks, all the commex, even the mineez, he said, "Who is this Harlequin?"

He was not purring smoothly. Timewise, it was jangle.

However, it *was* the longest speech they had ever heard him utter at one time, the staff, the ferrets, the loggers, the finks, the commex, but not the mincez, who usually weren't around to know, in any case. But even they scurried to find out.

Who is the Harlequin?

High above the third level of the city, he crouched on the humming aluminum-frame platform of the air-boat (foof! air-boat, indeed! swizzleskid is what it was, with a tow-rack jerry-rigged) and stared down at the neat Mondrian 5 arrangement of the buildings.

Somewhere nearby, he could hear the metronomic left-right-left of the 2:47 P.M. shift, entering the Timkin roller-bearing plant in their sneakers. A minute later, precisely, he heard the softer right-left-right of the 5:00 A.M. formation, going home.

An elfin grin spread across his tanned features, and his dimples appeared for a moment. Then, scratching at his thatch of auburn hair, he shrugged within his motley, as though girding himself for what came next, and threw the joystick forward, and bent into the wind as the air-boat dropped. He skimmed over a slidewalk, purposely dropping a few feet to crease the tassels of the ladies of fashion, and—inserting thumbs in large ears —he stuck out his tongue, rolled his eyes and went wugga-wugga-wugga. It was a minor diversion. One pedestrian skittered and tumbled, sending parcels everywhichway, another wet herself, a third keeled slantwise and the walk was stopped automatically by the servitors till

5 According to Harlan Ellison, "A reference to the 'geometric' abstractions of the Dutch painter Piet Mondrian (Pieter Cornelis Mondriaan, 1872–1944), characterized by solid blocks of contrasting colors, sharply divided by straight lines." (JHP)

she could be resuscitated. It was a minor diversion.

Then he swirled away on a vagrant breeze, and was gone. Hi-ho.

As he rounded the cornice of the Time-Motion Study Building, he saw the shift, just boarding the slidewalk. With practiced motion and an absolute conservation of movement, they side-stepped up onto the slow-strip and (in a chorus line reminiscent of a Busby Berkeley film 6 of the antediluvian 1930's) advanced across the strips ostrich-walking till they were lined up on the expresstrip.

Once more, in anticipation, the elfin grin spread, and there was a tooth missing back there on the left side. He dipped, skimmed, and swooped over them; and then, scrunching about on the air-boat, he released the holding pins that fastened shut the ends of the home-made pouring troughs that kept his cargo from dumping prematurely. And as he pulled the trough-pins, the air-boat slid over the factory workers and one hundred and fifty thousand dollars worth of jelly beans cascaded down on the expresstrip.

Jelly beans! Millions and billions of purples and yellows and greens and licorice and grape and raspberry and mint and round and smooth and crunchy outside and soft-mealy inside and sugary and bouncing jouncing tumbling clittering clattering skittering fell on the heads and shoulders and hard-hats and carapaces of the Timkin workers, tinkling on the slidewalk and bouncing away and rolling about underfoot and filling the sky on their way down with all the colors of joy and childhood and holidays, coming down in a steady rain, a solid wash, a torrent of color and sweetness out of the sky from above, and entering a universe of sanity and metronomic order with quite-mad coocoo newness. Jelly beans!

The shift workers howled and laughed and were pelted, and broke ranks, and the jelly beans managed to work their

way into the mechanism of the slidewalks after which there was a hideous scraping as the sound of a million fingernails rasped down a quarter of a million blackboards, followed by a coughing and a sputtering, and then the slidewalks all stopped and everyone was dumped thisawayandthataway in a jackstraw tumble, still laughing and popping little jelly bean eggs of childish color into their mouths. It was a holiday, and a jollity, an absolute insanity, a giggle. But . . .

The shift was delayed seven minutes.

They did not get home for seven minutes.

The master schedule was thrown off by seven minutes.

Quotas were delayed by inoperative slidewalks for seven minutes.

He had tapped the first domino in the line, and one after another, like chik chik chik, the others had fallen.

The System had been seven minutes worth of disrupted. It was a tiny matter, one hardly worthy of note, but in a society where the single driving force was order and unity and promptness and clocklike precision and attention to the clock, reverence of the gods of the passage of time, it was a disaster of major importance.

So he was ordered to appear before the Ticktockman. It was broadcast across every channel of the communications web. He was ordered to be *there* at 7:00 dammit on time. And they waited, and they waited, but he didn't show up till almost ten-thirty, at which time he merely sang a little song about moonlight in a place no one had ever heard of, called Vermont, and vanished again. But they had all been waiting since seven, and it wrecked *hell* with their schedules. So the question remained: Who is the Harlequin?

But the *unasked* question (more important of the two) was: how did we get *into* this position, where a laughing, irresponsible japer of jabberwocky and jive 7 could disrupt our entire economic

6 Busby Berkeley—William Berkeley Enos (1895–1976), the director responsible for developing the complicated, lockstep dance numbers in many of the movies of the 1930s and early 1940s. (JHP)

7 "Jabberwocky and jive"—a phrase adapted from Lewis Carroll's *Through the Looking-Glass* (1871). (JHP)

and cultural life with a hundred and fifty thousand dollars worth of jelly beans . . .

Jelly for God's sake beans! This is madness! Where did he get the money to buy a hundred and fifty thousand dollars worth of jelly beans? (They knew it would have cost that much, because they had a team of Situation Analysts pulled off another assignment, and rushed to the slidewalk scene to sweep up and count the candies, and produce findings, which disrupted *their* schedules and threw their entire branch at least a day behind.) Jelly beans! Jelly . . . *beans?* Now wait a second—a second accounted for—no one has manufactured jelly beans for over a hundred years. Where did he get jelly beans?

That's another good question. More than likely it will never be answered to your complete satisfaction. But then, how many questions ever are?

The middle you know. Here is the beginning. How it starts:

A desk pad. Day for day, and turn each day. 9:00—open the mail. 9:45—appointment with planning commission board. 10:30—discuss installation progress charts with J. L. 11:45—pray for rain. 12:00—lunch. *And so it goes.*

"I'm sorry, Miss Grant, but the time for interviews was set at 2:30, and it's almost five now. I'm sorry you're late, but those are the rules. You'll have to wait till next year to submit application for this college again." *And so it goes.*

The 10:10 local stops at Cresthaven, Galesville, Tonawanda Junction, Selby and Farnhurst, but not at Indiana City, Lucasville and Colton, except on Sunday. The 10:35 express stops at Galesville, Selby and Indiana City, except on Sundays & Holidays, at which time it stops at . . . *and so it goes.*

"I couldn't wait, Fred. I had to be at Pierre Cartain's 8 by 3:00, and you said you'd meet me under the clock in the terminal at 2:45, and you weren't there,

8 "Simply a made-up name": Harlan Ellison. (JHP)

so I had to go on. You're always late, Fred. If you'd been there, we could have sewed it up together, but as it was, well, I took the order alone . . ." *And so it goes.*

Dear Mr. and Mrs. Atterley: in reference to your son Gerold's constant tardiness, I am afraid we will have to suspend him from school unless some more reliable method can be instituted guaranteeing he will arrive at his classes on time. Granted he is an exemplary student, and his marks are high, his constant flouting of the schedules of this school makes it impractical to maintain him in a system where the other children seem capable of getting where they are supposed to be on time *and so it goes.*

YOU CANNOT VOTE UNLESS YOU APPEAR AT 8:45 A.M.

"I don't care if the script is *good,* I need it Thursday!"

CHECK-OUT TIME IS 2:00 P.M.

"You got here late. The job's taken. Sorry."

YOUR SALARY HAS BEEN DOCKED FOR TWENTY MINUTES TIME LOST.

"God, what time is it, I've gotta run!"

And so it goes. And so it goes. And so it goes goes goes goes goes tick tock tick tock tick tock and one day we no longer let time serve us, we serve time and we are slaves of the schedule, worshippers of the sun's passing, bound into a life predicated on restrictions because the system will not function if we don't keep the schedule tight.

Until it becomes more than a minor inconvenience to be late. It becomes a sin. Then a crime. Then a crime punishable by this:

EFFECTIVE 15 JULY 2389 12:00:00 midnight, the office of the Master Timekeeper will require all citizens to submit their time-cards and cardioplates for processing. In accordance with Statute 555-7-SGH-999 governing the revocation of time per capita, all cardioplates will be keyed to the individual holder and—

What they had done, was to devise a

method of curtailing the amount of life a person could have. If he was ten minutes late, he lost ten minutes of his life. An hour was proportionately worth more revocation. If someone was consistently tardy, he might find himself, on a Sunday night, receiving a communique from the Master Timekeeper that his time had run out, and he would be "turned off" at high noon on Monday, please straighten your affairs, sir, madame or bisex.

And so, by this simple scientific expedient (utilizing a scientific process held dearly secret by the Ticktockman's office) the System was maintained. It was the only expedient thing to do. It was, after all, patriotic. The schedules had to be met. After all, there *was* a war on!

But, wasn't there always?

"Now that is really disgusting," the Harlequin said, when Pretty Alice showed him the wanted poster. "Disgusting and *high*ly improbable. After all, this isn't the days of desperadoes. A *wanted* poster!"

"You know," Alice noted, "you speak with a great deal of inflection."

"I'm sorry," said the Harlequin, humbly.

"No need to be sorry. You're always saying 'I'm sorry.' You have such massive guilt, Everett, it's really very sad."

"I'm sorry," he repeated, then pursed his lips so the dimples appeared momentarily. He hadn't wanted to say that at all. "I have to go out again. I have to *do* something."

Alice slammed her coffee-bulb down on the counter. "Oh for God's *sake*, Everett, can't you stay home just *one* night! Must you always be out in that ghastly clown suit, running around an*noy*ing people?"

"I'm—" he stopped, and clapped the jester's hat onto his auburn thatch with a tiny tingling of bells. He rose, rinsed out his coffee-bulb at the spray, and put it into the drier for a moment. "I have to go."

She didn't answer. The faxbox was purring, and she pulled a sheet out, read it, threw it toward him on the counter.

"It's about you. Of course. You're ridiculous."

He read it quickly. It said the Ticktockman was trying to locate him. He didn't care, he was going out to be late again. At the door, dredging for an exit line, he hurled back petulantly, "Well, *you* speak with inflection, *too!*"

Alice rolled her pretty eyes heavenward. "You're ridiculous." The Harlequin stalked out, slamming the door, which sighed shut softly, and locked itself.

There was a gentle knock, and Alice got up with an exhalation of exasperated breath, and opened the door. He stood there. "I'll be back about ten-thirty, okay?"

She pulled a rueful face. "Why do you tell me that? Why? You *know* you'll be late! You *know it!* You're *always* late, so why do you tell me these dumb things?" She closed the door.

On the other side, the Harlequin nodded to himself. *She's right. She's always right. I'll be late. I'm always late. Why do I tell her these dumb things?*

He shrugged again, and went off to be late once more.

He had fired off the firecracker rockets that said: I will attend the 115th annual International Medical Association Invocation at 8:00 P.M. precisely. I do hope you will all be able to join me.

The words had burned in the sky, and of course the authorities were there, lying in wait for him. They assumed, naturally, that he would be late. He arrived twenty minutes early, while they were setting up the spiderwebs to trap and hold him. Blowing a large bullhorn, he frightened and unnerved them so, their own moisturized encirclement webs sucked closed, and they were hauled up, kicking and shrieking, high above the amphitheater's floor. The Harlequin laughed and laughed, and apologized profusely. The physicians, gathered in solemn conclave, roared with laughter, and accepted the Harlequin's apologies with exaggerated bowing and posturing, and a merry time was had by all, who thought the Harlequin was a regular foofaraw in fancy pants; all, that is, but the authorities, who had been sent out by the office of the Ticktockman; they hung there like so much dockside cargo, hauled up above the floor of the amphitheater in a most unseemly fashion.

(In another part of the same city where the Harlequin carried on his "activities," totally unrelated in every way to what concerns us here, save that it illustrates the Ticktockman's power and import, a man named Marshall Delahanty received his turn-off notice from the Ticktockman's office. His wife received the notification from the gray-suited minee who delivered it, with the traditional "look of sorrow" plastered hideously across his face. She knew what it was, even without unsealing it. It was a billet-doux 9 of immediate recognition to everyone these days. She gasped, and held it as though it were a glass slide tinged with botulism, and prayed it was not for her. Let it be for Marsh, she thought, brutally, realistically; or one of the kids, but not for me, please dear God, not for me. And then she opened it, and it *was* for Marsh, and she was at one and the same time horrified and relieved. The next trooper in the line had caught the bullet. "Marshall," she screamed, "Marshall! Termination, Marshall! OhmiGod, Marshall, whattl we do, whattl we do, Marshall omigodmarshall . . ." and in their home that night there was the sound of tearing paper and fear, and the stink of madness went up the flue and there was nothing, absolutely nothing they could do about it.

(But Marshall Delahanty tried to run. And early the next day, when turn-off time came, he was deep in the Canadian forest two hundred miles away, and the office of the Ticktockman blanked his cardioplate, and Marshall Delahanty keeled over, running, and his heart stopped, and the blood dried up on its way to his brain, and he was dead that's all. One light went out on the sector map in the office of the Master Timekeeper, while notification was entered for fax

9 A French term for "love letter." (JHP)

reproduction, and Georgette Delahanty's name was entered on the dole roles till she could remarry. Which is the end of the footnote, and all the point that need be made, except don't laugh, because that is what would happen to the Harlequin if ever the Ticktockman found out his real name. It isn't funny.)

The shopping level of the city was thronged with the Thursday-colors of the buyers. Women in canary yellow chitons and men in pseudo-Tyrolean outfits that were jade and leather and fit very tightly, save for the balloon pants.

When the Harlequin appeared on the still-being-constructed shell of the new Efficiency Shopping Center, his bullhorn to his elfishly-laughing lips, everyone pointed and stared, and he berated them:

"Why let them order you about? Why let them tell you to hurry and scurry like ants or maggots? Take your time! Saunter a while! Enjoy the sunshine, enjoy the breeze, let life carry you at your own pace! Don't be slaves of time, it's a helluva way to die, slowly, by degrees . . . down with the Ticktockman!"

Who's the nut? most of the shoppers wanted to know. Who's the nut oh wow I'm gonna be late I gotta run . . .

And the construction gang on the Shopping Center received an urgent order from the office of the Master Timekeeper that the dangerous criminal known as the Harlequin was atop their spire, and their aid was urgently needed in apprehending him. The work crew said no, they would lose time on their construction schedule, but the Ticktockman managed to pull the proper threads of governmental webbing, and they were told to cease work and catch that nitwit up there on the spire; up there with the bullhorn. So a dozen and more burly workers began climbing into their construction platforms, releasing the a-grav plates, and rising toward the Harlequin.

After the debacle (in which, through the Harlequin's attention to personal safety, no one was seriously injured), the workers tried to reassemble, and assault him again, but it was too late. He had vanished. It had attracted quite a crowd, however, and the shopping cycle was thrown off by hours, simply hours. The purchasing needs of the system were therefore falling behind, and so measures were taken to accelerate the cycle for the rest of the day, but it got bogged down and speeded up and they sold too many float-valves and not nearly enough wegglers, which meant that the popli ratio was off, which made it necessary to rush cases and cases of spoiling Smash-O to stores that usually needed a case only every three or four hours. The shipments were bollixed, the transshipments were misrouted, and in the end, even the swizzleskid industries felt it.

"Don't come back till you have him!" the Ticktockman said, very quietly, very sincerely, extremely dangerously.

They used dogs. They used probes. They used cardioplate crossoffs. They used teepers. They used bribery. They used stiktytes. They used intimidation. They used torment. They used torture. They used finks. They used cops. They used search&seizure. They used fallaron. They used betterment incentive. They used fingerprints. They used Bertillon.[10] They used cunning. They used guile. They used treachery. They used Raoul Mitgong,[11] but he didn't help much. They used applied physics. They used techniques of criminology

[10] Alphonse Bertillon (1853–1914), the French anthropologist and criminologist. Harlan Ellison notes as follows: "This is a reference not only to Alphonse Bertillon, but to the system of identifying criminals he devised using anthropometric measurements—the shape and size and placement of eyes, nose, mouth, hairline, hands, feet, etc. In common usage it was not referred to as "the Bertillon system" but merely as Bertillon. It was the traditional identification system for police departments throughout the world until the advent of fingerprinting, which was less fallible and wieldier." (JHP)

[11] Harlan Ellison notes: "Merely a made-up name, thrown in to add a bit of nonsense background with a futuristic feel to it, as with 'cardioplate crossoffs,' 'teepers' (which is slang for telepathic persons), 'stiktytes,' and 'fallaron.' " (JHP)

And what the hell: they caught him.

After all, his name was Everett C. Marm, and he wasn't much to begin with, except a man who had no sense of time.

"Repent, Harlequin!" said the Ticktockman.

"Get stuffed!" the Harlequin replied, sneering.

"You've been late a total of sixty-three years, five months, three weeks, two days, twelve hours, forty-one minutes, fifty-nine seconds, point oh three six one one one microseconds. You've used up everything you can, and more. I'm going to turn you off."

"Scare someone else. I'd rather be dead than live in a dumb world with a bogeyman like you."

"It's my job."

"You're full of it. You're a tyrant. You have no right to order people around and kill them if they show up late."

"You can't adjust. You can't fit in."

"Unstrap me, and I'll fit my fist into your mouth."

"You're a non-conformist."

"That didn't used to be a felony."

"It is now. Live in the world around you."

"I hate it. It's a terrible world."

"Not everyone thinks so. Most people enjoy order."

"I don't, and most of the people I know don't."

"That's not true. How do you think we caught you?"

"I'm not interested."

"A girl named Pretty Alice told us who you were."

"That's a lie."

"It's true. You unnerve her. She wants to belong, she wants to conform, I'm going to turn you off."

"Then do it already, and stop arguing with me."

"I'm not going to turn you off."

"You're an idiot!"

"Repent, Harlequin!" said the Ticktockman.

"Get stuffed."

So they sent him to Coventry. And in Coventry they worked him over. It was just like what they did to Winston Smith [12] in "1984," which was a book none of them knew about, but the techniques are really quite ancient, and so they did it to Everett C. Marm, and one day quite a long time later, the Harlequin appeared on the communications web, appearing elfin and dimpled and bright-eyed, and not at all brainwashed, and he said he had been wrong, that it was a good, a very good thing indeed, to belong, to be right on time hip-ho and away we go, and everyone stared up at him on the public screens that covered an entire city block, and they said to themselves, well, you see, he was just a nut after all, and if that's the way the system is run, then let's do it that way,

[12] The "hero" who rebels against a totalitarian state in George Orwell's antiutopian novel *1984* (1949). (JHP)

because it doesn't pay to fight city hall, or in this case, the Ticktockman. So Everett C. Marm was destroyed, which was a loss, because of what Thoreau said earlier, but you can't make an omelet without breaking a few eggs, and in every revolution a few die who shouldn't, but they have to, because that's the way it happens, and if you make only a little change, then it seems to be worthwhile. Or, to make the point lucidly:

"Uh, excuse me, sir, I, uh, don't know how to uh, to uh, tell you this, but you were three minutes late. The schedule is a little, uh, bit off."

He grinned sheepishly.

"That's ridiculous!" murmured the Ticktockman behind his mask. "Check your watch." And then he went into his office, going mrmee, mrmee, mrmee, mrmee.

[1965]

QUESTIONS FOR STUDY

1. *How does Ellison manage to engage the reader's sympathy on behalf of the Harlequin? To what extent do the author's tone and style contribute to such a reaction? In what ways do his carefully inserted allusions also help?*
2. *Why is it appropriate that Everett Marm carry out his rebellion disguised as a harlequin?*
3. *What opposing values do the Harlequin and the Ticktockman come to represent?*
4. *Why doesn't the Ticktockman simply "turn off" Everett Marm the same way he "turns off" misfits such as Marshall Delahanty?*
5. *What are the implications of the story's concluding incident?*
6. *What comment does the story finally make about conformity and rebellion?*

RALPH ELLISON

King of the Bingo Game

THE WOMAN in front of him was eating roasted peanuts that smelled so good that he could barely contain his hunger. He could not even sleep and wished they'd hurry and begin the bingo game. There, on his right, two fellows were drinking wine out of a bottle wrapped in a paper bag, and he could hear soft gurgling in the dark. His stomach gave a low, gnawing growl. "If this was down South," he thought, "all I'd have to do is lean over and say, 'Lady, gimme a few of those peanuts, please ma'am,' and she'd pass me the bag and never think nothing of it." Or he could ask the fellows for a drink in the same way. Folks down South stuck together that way; they didn't even have to know you. But up here it was different. Ask somebody for something, and they'd think you were crazy. Well, I ain't crazy. I'm just broke, 'cause I got no birth certificate to get a job, and Laura 'bout to die 'cause we got no money for a doctor. But I ain't crazy. And yet a pinpoint of doubt was focused in his mind as he glanced toward the screen and saw the hero stealthily entering a dark room and sending the beam of a flashlight along a wall of bookcases. This is where he finds the trapdoor, he remembered. The man would pass abruptly through the wall and find the girl tied to a bed, her legs and arms spread wide, and her clothing torn to rags. He laughed softly to himself. He had seen the picture three times, and this was one of the best scenes.

On his right the fellow whispered wide-eyed to his companion, "Man, look a-yonder!"

"Damn!"

"Wouldn't I like to have her tied up like that . . ."

"Hey! That fool's letting her loose!"

"Aw, man, he loves her."

"Love or no love!"

The man moved impatiently beside him, and he tried to involve himself in the scene. But Laura was on his mind. Tiring quickly of watching the picture he looked back to where the white beam filtered from the projection room above the balcony. It started small and grew large, specks of dust dancing in its whiteness as it reached the screen. It was strange how the beam always landed right on the screen and didn't mess up and fall somewhere else. But they had it all fixed. Everything was fixed. Now suppose when they showed that girl with her dress torn the girl started taking off the rest of her clothes, and when the guy came in he didn't untie her but kept her there and went to taking off his own clothes? *That* would be something to see. If a picture got out of hand like that those guys up there would go nuts. Yeah, and there'd be so many folks in here you couldn't find a seat for nine months! A strange sensation played over his skin. He shuddered. Yesterday he'd seen a bedbug on a woman's neck as they walked out into the bright street. But exploring his thigh through a hole in his pocket he found only goose pimples and old scars.

The bottle gurgled again. He closed his eyes. Now a dreamy music was accompanying the film and train whistles were sounding in the distance, and he was a boy again walking along a railroad trestle down South, and seeing the train coming, and running back as fast as he could go, and hearing the whistle blowing, and getting off the trestle to solid ground just in time, with the earth trembling beneath his feet, and feeling relieved as he ran down the cinder-strewn embankment onto the highway, and looking back and seeing with terror that the train had left the track and was following him right down the middle of the street, and all the white people laughing as he ran screaming . . .

"Wake up there, buddy! What the hell do you mean hollering like that? Can't you see we trying to enjoy this here picture?"

He stared at the man with gratitude.

"I'm sorry, old man," he said. "I musta been dreaming."

"Well, here, have a drink. And don't be making no noise like that, damn!"

His hands trembled as he tilted his head. It was not wine, but whiskey. Cold rye whiskey. He took a deep swoller, decided it was better not to take another, and handed the bottle back to its owner.

"Thanks, old man," he said.

Now he felt the cold whiskey breaking a warm path straight through the middle of him, growing hotter and sharper as it moved. He had not eaten all day, and it made him light-headed. The smell of the peanuts stabbed him like a knife, and he got up and found a seat in the middle aisle. But no sooner did he sit than he saw a row of intense-faced young girls, and got up again, thinking, "You chicks musta been Lindy-hopping somewhere." He found a seat several rows ahead as the lights came on, and he saw the screen disappear behind a heavy red and gold curtain; then the curtain rising, and the man with the microphone and a uniformed attendant coming on the stage.

He felt for his bingo cards, smiling. The guy at the door wouldn't like it if he knew about his having *five* cards. Well, not everyone played the bingo game; and even with five cards he didn't have much of a chance. For Laura, though, he had to have faith. He studied the cards, each with its different numerals, punching the free center hole in each and spreading them neatly across his lap; and when the lights faded he sat slouched in his seat so that he could look from his cards to the bingo wheel with but a quick shifting of his eyes.

Ahead, at the end of the darkness, the man with the microphone was pressing a button attached to a long cord and spinning the bingo wheel and calling out the number each time the wheel came to rest. And each time the voice rang out his finger raced over the cards for the number. With five cards he had to move fast. He became nervous; there were too many cards, and the man went too fast with his grating voice. Perhaps he should just select one and throw the others away. But he was afraid. He became warm. Wonder how much Laura's doctor would cost? Damn that, watch the cards! And with despair he heard the man call three in a row which he missed on all five cards. This way he'd never win . . .

When he saw the row of holes punched across the third card, he sat paralyzed and heard the man call three more numbers before he stumbled forward, screaming.

"Bingo! Bingo!"

"Let that fool up there," someone called.

"Get up there, man!"

He stumbled down the aisle and up the steps to the stage into a light so sharp and bright that for a moment it blinded him, and he felt that he had moved into the spell of some strange, mysterious power. Yet it was as familiar as the sun, and he knew it was the perfectly familiar bingo.

The man with the microphone was saying something to the audience as he held out his card. A cold light flashed from the man's finger as the card left his hand. His knees trembled. The man stepped closer, checking the card against the numbers chalked on the board. Suppose he had made a mistake? The pomade on the man's hair made him feel faint, and he backed away. But the man was checking the card over the microphone now, and he had to stay. He stood tense, listening.

"Under the O, forty-four," the man chanted. "Under the I, seven. Under the G, three. Under the B, ninety-six. Under the N, thirteen!"

His breath came easier as the man smiled at the audience.

"Yessir, ladies and gentlemen, he's one of the chosen people!"

The audience rippled with laughter and applause.

"Step right up to the front of the stage."

He moved slowly forward, wishing that the light was not so bright.

"To win to-night's jackpot of $36.90 the wheel must stop between the double zero, understand?"

He nodded, knowing the ritual from the many days and nights he had watched the winners march across the stage to press the button that controlled the spinning wheel and receive the prizes. And now he followed the instructions as though he'd crossed the slippery stage a million prize-winning times.

The man was making some kind of a joke, and he nodded vacantly. So tense had he become that he felt a sudden desire to cry and shook it away. He felt vaguely that his whole life was determined by the bingo wheel; not only that which would happen now that he was at last before it, but all that had gone before, since his birth, and his mother's birth and the birth of his father. It had always been there, even though he had not been aware of it, handing out the unlucky cards and numbers of his days. The feeling persisted, and he started quickly away. I better get down from here before I make a fool of myself, he thought.

'Here, boy," the man called. "You haven't started yet."

Someone laughed as he went hesitantly back.

"Are you all reet?"

He grinned at the man's jive talk, but no words would come, and he knew it was not a convincing grin. For suddenly he knew that he stood on the slippery brink of some terrible embarrassment.

"Where are you from, boy?" the man asked.

"Down South."

"He's from down South, ladies and gentlemen," the man said. "Where from? Speak right into the mike."

"Rocky Mont," he said. "Rock' Mont, North Car'lina."

"So you decided to come down off that mountain to the U. S.," the man laughed. He felt that the man was making a fool of him, but then something cold was placed in his hand, and the lights were no longer behind him.

Standing before the wheel he felt alone, but that was somehow right, and he remembered his plan. He would give the wheel a short quick twirl. Just a touch of the button. He had watched it many times, and always it came close to double zero when it was short and quick. He steeled himself; the fear had left, and he felt a profound sense of promise, as though he were about to be repaid for all the things he'd suffered all his life. Trembling, he pressed the button. There was a whirl of lights, and in a second he realized with finality that though he wanted to, he could not stop. It was as though he held a high-powered line in his naked hand. His nerves tightened. As the wheel increased its speed it seemed to draw him more and more into its power, as though it held his fate; and with it came a deep need to submit, to whirl, to lose himself in its swirl of color. He could not stop it now. So let it be.

The button rested snugly in his palm where the man had placed it. And now he became aware of the man beside him, advising him through the microphone, while behind the shadowy audience hummed with noisy voices. He shifted his feet. There was still that feeling of helplessness within him, making part of him desire to turn back, even now that the jackpot was right in his hand. He squeezed the button until his fist ached. Then, like the sudden shriek of a subway whistle, a doubt tore through his head. Suppose he did not spin the wheel long enough? What could he do, and how could he tell? And then he knew, even as he wondered, that as long as he pressed the button, he could control the jackpot. He and only he could determine whether or not it was to be his. Not even the man with the microphone could do anything about it now. He felt drunk. Then, as though he had come down from a high hill into a valley of people, he heard the audience yelling.

"Come down from there, you jerk!"

"Let somebody else have a chance . . ."

"Ole Jack thinks he done found the end of the rainbow . . ."

The last voice was not unfriendly, and he turned and smiled dreamily into the yelling mouths. Then he turned his back squarely on them.

"Don't take too long, boy," a voice said.

He nodded. They were yelling behind him. Those folks did not understand what had happened to him. They had been playing the bingo game day in and night out for years, trying to win rent money or hamburger change. But not one of those wise guys had discovered this wonderful thing. He watched the wheel whirling past the numbers and experienced a burst of exaltation: This is God! This is the really truly God! He said it aloud, "This is God!"

He said it with such absolute conviction that he feared he would fall fainting into the footlights. But the crowd yelled so loud that they could not hear. Those fools, he thought. I'm here trying to tell them the most wonderful secret in the world, and they're yelling like they gone crazy. A hand fell upon his shoulder.

"You'll have to make a choice now, boy. You've taken too long."

He brushed the hand violently away.

"Leave me alone, man. I know what I'm doing!"

The man looked surprised and held on to the microphone for support. And because he did not wish to hurt the man's feelings he smiled, realizing with a sudden pang that there was no way of explaining to the man just why he had to stand there pressing the button forever.

"Come here," he called tiredly.

The man approached, rolling the heavy microphone across the stage.

"Anybody can play this bingo game, right?" he said.

"Sure, but . . ."

He smiled, feeling inclined to be patient with this slick looking white man with his blue shirt and his sharp gabardine suit.

"That's what I thought," he said. "Anybody can win the jackpot as long as they get the lucky number, right?"

"That's the rule, but after all . . ."

"That's what I thought," he said. "And the big prize goes to the man who knows how to win it?"

The man nodded speechlessly.

"Well then, go on over there and watch me win like I want to. I ain't going to hurt nobody," he said, "and I'll show you how to win. I mean to show the whole world how it's got to be done."

And because he understood, he smiled again to let the man know that he held

nothing against him for being white and impatient. Then he refused to see the man any longer and stood pressing the button, the voices of the crowd reaching him like sounds in distant streets. Let them yell. All the Negroes down there were just ashamed because he was black like them. He smiled inwardly, knowing how it was. Most of the time he was ashamed of what Negroes did himself. Well, let them be ashamed for something this time. Like him. He was like a long thin black wire that was being stretched and wound upon the bingo wheel; wound until he wanted to scream; wound, but this time himself controlling the winding and the sadness and the shame, and because he did, Laura would be all right. Suddenly the lights flickered. He staggered backwards. Had something gone wrong? All this noise. Didn't they know that although he controlled the wheel, it also controlled him, and unless he pressed the button forever and forever and ever it would stop, leaving him high and dry, dry and high on this hard high slippery hill and Laura dead? There was only one chance; he had to do whatever the wheel demanded. And gripping the button in despair, he discovered with surprise that it imparted a nervous energy. His spine tingled. He felt a certain power.

Now he faced the raging crowd with defiance, its screams penetrating his eardrums like trumpets shrieking from a juke-box. The vague faces glowing in the bingo lights gave him a sense of himself that he had never known before. He was running the show, by God! They had to react to him, for he was their luck. This is *me*, he thought. Let the bastards yell. Then someone was laughing inside him, and he realized that somehow he had forgotten his own name. It was a sad, lost feeling to lose your name, and a crazy thing to do. That name had been given him by the white man who had owned his grandfather a long lost time ago down South. But maybe those wise guys knew his name.

"Who am I?" he screamed.

"Hurry up and bingo, you jerk!"

They didn't know either, he thought sadly. They didn't even know their own names, they were all poor nameless bastards. Well, he didn't need that old name; he was reborn. For as long as he pressed the button he was The-man-who-pressed-the - button - who - held - the - prize - who - was-the-King-of-Bingo. That was the way it was, and he'd have to press the button even if nobody understood, even though Laura did not understand.

"Live!" he shouted.

The audience quieted like the dying of a huge fan.

"Live, Laura, baby. I got holt of it now, sugar. Live!"

He screamed it, tears streaming down his face. "I got nobody but YOU!"

The screams tore from his very guts. He felt as though the rush of blood to his head would burst out in baseball seams of small red droplets, like a head beaten by police clubs. Bending over he saw a trickle of blood splashing the toe of his shoe. With his free hand he searched his head. It was his nose. God, suppose something has gone wrong? He felt that the whole audience had somehow entered him and was stamping its feet in his stomach and he was unable to throw them out. They wanted the prize, that was it. They wanted the secret for themselves. But they'd never get it; he would keep the bingo wheel whirling forever, and Laura would be safe in the wheel. But would she? It had to be, because if she were not safe the wheel would cease to turn; it could not go on. He had to get away, *vomit* all, and his mind formed an image of himself running with Laura in his arms down the tracks of the subway just ahead of an A train, running desperately *vomit* with people screaming for him to come out but knowing no way of leaving the tracks because to stop would bring the train crushing down upon him and to attempt to leave across the other tracks would mean to run into a hot third rail as high as his waist which threw blue sparks that blinded his eyes until he could hardly see.

He heard singing and the audience was clapping its hands.

> Shoot the liquor to him, Jim, boy!
> Clap-clap-clap
> Well a-calla the cop
> He's blowing his top!
> Shoot the liquor to him, Jim, boy!

Bitter anger grew within him at the singing. They think I'm crazy. Well let 'em laugh. I'll do what I got to do.

He was standing in an attitude of intense listening when he saw that they were watching something on the stage behind him. He felt weak. But when he turned he saw no one. If only his thumb did not ache so. Now they were applauding. And for a moment he thought that the wheel had stopped. But that was impossible, his thumb still pressed the button. Then he saw them. Two men in uniform beckoned from the end of the stage. They were coming toward him, walking in step, slowly, like a tap-dance team returning for a third encore. But their shoulders shot forward, and he backed away, looking wildly about. There was nothing to fight them with. He had only the long black cord which led to a plug somewhere back stage, and he couldn't use that because it operated the bingo wheel. He backed slowly, fixing the men with his eyes as his lips stretched over his teeth in a tight, fixed grin; moved toward the end of the stage and realizing that he couldn't go much further, for suddenly the cord became taut and he couldn't afford to break the cord. But he had to do something. The audience was howling. Suddenly he stopped dead, seeing the men halt, their legs lifted as in an interrupted step of a slow-motion dance. There was nothing to do but run in the other direction and he dashed forward, slipping and sliding. The men fell back, surprised. He struck out violently going past.

"Grab him!"

He ran, but all too quickly the cord tightened, resistingly, and he turned and ran back again. This time he slipped them, and discovered by running in a circle before the wheel he could keep the cord from tightening. But this way he had to flail his arms to keep the men away. Why couldn't they leave a man alone? He ran, circling.

"Ring down the curtain," someone yelled. But they couldn't do that. If they did the wheel flashing from the projection room would be cut off. But they had him before he could tell them so, trying to pry open his fist, and he was wrestling and trying to bring his knees into the fight and holding on to the button, for it was his life. And now he was down, seeing a foot coming down, crushing his wrist cruelly, down, as he saw the wheel whirling serenely above.

"I can't give it up," he screamed. Then quietly, in a confidential tone, "Boys, I really can't give it up."

It landed hard against his head. And in the blank moment they had it away from him, completely now. He fought them trying to pull him up from the stage as he watched the wheel spin slowly to a stop. Without surprise he saw it rest at double-zero.

"You see," he pointed bitterly.

"Sure, boy, sure, it's O. K.," one of the men said smiling.

And seeing the man bow his head to someone he could not see, he felt very, very happy; he would receive what all the winners received.

But as he warmed in the justice of the man's tight smile he did not see the man's slow wink, nor see the bow-legged man behind him step clear of the swiftly descending curtain and set himself for a blow. He only felt the dull pain exploding in his skull, and he knew even as it slipped out of him that his luck had run out on the stage.

[1944]

QUESTIONS FOR STUDY

1. *What is the situation of Ellison's nameless protagonist at the beginning of the story? What is his background? What are his aspirations and fears?*
2. *What does the bingo wheel come to represent to him? What happens to the protagonist when he pushes the button? Why does he fight so hard to keep hold of the wire?*
3. *Why is the ending of the story ironic?*
4. *What is the appropriateness of the story's setting and its surrealistic and nightmarish imagery?*
5. *What are the larger implications of Ellison's story? To what extent is it about the "invisibility" of black men in white America?*

WILLIAM FAULKNER

Dry September

I

THROUGH the bloody September twilight, aftermath of sixty-two rainless days, it had gone like a fire in dry grass—the rumor, the story, whatever it was. Something about Miss Minnie Cooper and a Negro. Attacked, insulted, frightened: none of them, gathered in the barber shop on that Saturday evening where the ceiling fan stirred, without freshening it, the vitiated air, sending back upon them, in recurrent surges of stale pomade and lotion, their own stale breath and odors, knew exactly what had happened.

"Except it wasn't Will Mayes," a barber said. He was a man of middle age; a thin, sand-colored man with a mild face, who was shaving a client. "I know Will Mayes. He's a good nigger. And I know Miss Minnie Cooper, too."

"What do you know about her?" a second barber said.

"Who is she?" the client said. "A young girl?"

"No," the barber said. "She's about forty, I reckon. She aint married. That's why I don't believe—"

"Believe, hell!" a hulking youth in a sweat-stained silk shirt said. "Wont you take a white woman's word before a nigger's?"

"I dont believe Will Mayes did it," the barber said. "I know Will Mayes."

"Maybe you know who did it, then. Maybe you already got him out of town, you damn niggerlover."

"I dont believe anybody did anything. I dont believe anything happened. I leave it to you fellows if them ladies that get old without getting married dont have notions that a man cant—"

"Then you are a hell of a white man," the client said. He moved under the cloth. The youth had sprung to his feet.

"You dont?" he said. "Do you accuse a white woman of lying?"

The barber held the razor poised above the half-risen client. He did not look around.

"It's this durn weather," another said. "It's enough to make a man do anything. Even to her."

Nobody laughed. The barber said in his mild, stubborn tone: "I aint accusing nobody of nothing. I just know and you fellows know how a woman that never—"

"You damn niggerlover!" the youth said.

"Shut up, Butch," another said. "We'll get the facts in plenty of time to act."

"Who is? Who's getting them?" the youth said. "Facts, hell! I—"

"You're a fine white man," the client said. "Aint you?" In his frothy beard he looked like a desert rat in the moving pictures. "You tell them, Jack," he said to the youth. "If there aint any white men in this town, you can count on me, even if I aint only a drummer and a stranger."

"That's right, boys," the barber said. "Find out the truth first. I know Will Mayes."

"Well, by God!" the youth shouted. "To think that a white man in this town—"

"Shut up, Butch," the second speaker said. "We got plenty of time."

The client sat up. He looked at the speaker. "Do you claim that anything excuses a nigger attacking a white woman? Do you mean to tell me you are a white man and you'll stand for it? You better go back North where you came from. The South dont want your kind here."

"North what?" the second said. "I was born and raised in this town."

"Well, by God!" the youth said. He looked about with a strained, baffled gaze, as if he was trying to remember what it was he wanted to say or to do. He drew his sleeve across his sweating face. "Damn if I'm going to let a white woman—"

"You tell them, Jack," the drummer said. "By God, if they—"

The screen door crashed open. A man stood in the floor, his feet apart and his heavy-set body poised easily. His white shirt was open at the throat; he wore a felt hat. His hot, bold glance swept the group. His name was McLendon. He had commanded troops at the front in France and had been decorated for valor.

"Well," he said, "are you going to sit there and let a black son rape a white woman on the streets of Jefferson?"

Butch sprang up again. The silk of his shirt clung flat to his heavy shoulders. At each armpit was a dark halfmoon. "That's what I been telling them! That's what I—"

"Did it really happen?" a third said. "This aint the first man scare she ever had, like Hawkshaw says. Wasn't there something about a man on the kitchen roof, watching her undress, about a year ago?"

"What?" the client said. "What's that?" The barber had been slowly forcing him back into the chair; he arrested himself reclining, his head lifted, the barber still pressing him down.

McLendon whirled on the third speaker. "Happen? What the hell difference does it make? Are you going to let the black sons get away with it until one really does it?"

"That's what I'm telling them!" Butch shouted. He cursed, long and steady, pointless.

"Here, here," a fourth said. "Not so loud. Dont talk so loud."

"Sure," McLendon said; "no talking necessary at all. I've done my talking. Who's with me?" He poised on the balls of his feet, roving his gaze.

The barber held the drummer's face down, the razor poised. "Find out the facts first, boys. I know Willy Mayes. It wasn't him. Let's get the sheriff and do this thing right."

McLendon whirled upon him his furious, rigid face. The barber did not look away. They looked like men of different

races. The other barbers had ceased also above their prone clients. "You mean to tell me," McLendon said, "that you'd take a nigger's word before a white woman's? Why, you damn niggerloving—"

The third speaker rose and grasped McLendon's arm; he too had been a soldier. "Now, now. Let's figure this thing out. Who knows anything about what really happened?"

"Figure out hell!" McLendon jerked his arm free. "All that're with me get up from there. The ones that aint—" He roved his gaze, dragging his sleeve across his face.

Three men rose. The drummer in the chair sat up. "Here," he said, jerking at the cloth about his neck; "get this rag off me. I'm with him. I dont live here, but by God, if our mothers and wives and sisters—" He smeared the cloth over his face and flung it to the floor. McLendon stood in the floor and cursed the others. Another rose and moved toward him. The remainder sat uncomfortable, not looking at one another, then one by one they rose and joined him.

The barber picked the cloth from the floor. He began to fold it neatly. "Boys, dont do that. Will Mayes never done it. I know."

"Come on," McLendon said. He whirled. From his hip pocket protruded the butt of a heavy automatic pistol. They went out. The screen door crashed behind them reverberant in the dead air.

The barber wiped the razor carefully and swiftly, and put it away, and ran to the rear, and took his hat from the wall. "I'll be back as soon as I can," he said to the other barbers. "I cant let—" He went out, running. The two other barbers followed him to the door and caught it on the rebound, leaning out and looking up the street after him. The air was flat and dead. It had a metallic taste at the base of the tongue.

"What can he do?" the first said. The second one was saying "Jees Christ, Jees Christ" under his breath. "I'd just as lief be Will Mayes as Hawk, if he gets McLendon riled."

"Jees Christ, Jees Christ," the second whispered.

"You reckon he really done it to her?" the first said.

II

She was thirty-eight or thirty-nine. She lived in a small frame house with her invalid mother and a thin, sallow, unflagging aunt, where each morning between ten and eleven she would appear on the porch in a lace-trimmed boudoir cap, to sit swinging in the porch swing until noon. After dinner she lay down for a while, until the afternoon began to cool. Then, in one of the three or four new voile dresses which she had each summer, she would go downtown to spend the afternoon in the stores with the other ladies, where they would handle the goods and haggle over the prices in cold, immediate voices, without any intention of buying.

She was of comfortable people—not the best in Jefferson, but good people enough—and she was still on the slender side of ordinary looking, with a bright, faintly haggard manner and dress. When she was young she had had a slender, nervous body and a sort of hard vivacity which had enabled her for a time to ride upon the crest of the town's social life as exemplified by the high school party and church social period of her contemporaries while still children enough to be unclassconscious.

She was the last to realize that she was losing ground; that those among whom she had been a little brighter and louder flame than any other were beginning to learn the pleasure of snobbery—male—and retaliation—female. That was when her face began to wear that bright, haggard look. She still carried it to parties on shadowy porticoes and summer lawns, like a mask or a flag, with that bafflement of furious repudiation of truth in her eyes. One evening at a party she heard a boy and two girls, all schoolmates, talking. She never accepted another invitation.

She watched the girls with whom she had grown up as they married and got homes and children, but no man ever called on her steadily until the children of the other girls had been calling her "aunty" for several years, the while their mothers told them in bright voices about how popular Aunt Minnie had been as a girl. Then the town began to see her driving on Sunday afternoons with the cashier in the bank. He was a widower of about forty—a high-colored man, smelling always faintly of the barber shop or of whisky. He owned the first automobile in town, a red runabout; Minnie had the first motoring bonnet and veil the town ever saw. Then the town began to say: "Poor Minnie." "But she is old enough to take care of herself," others said. That was when she began to ask her old schoolmates that their children call her "cousin" instead of "aunty."

It was twelve years now since she had been relegated into adultery by public opinion, and eight years since the cashier had gone to a Memphis bank, returning for one day each Christmas, which he spent at an annual bachelors' party at a hunting club on the river. From behind their curtains the neighbors would see the party pass, and during the over-the-way Christmas day visiting they would tell her about him, about how well he looked, and how they heard that he was prospering in the city, watching with bright, secret eyes her haggard, bright face. Usually by that hour there would be the scent of whisky on her breath. It was supplied her by a youth, a clerk at the soda fountain: "Sure; I buy it for the old gal. I reckon she's entitled to a little fun."

Her mother kept to her room altogether now; the gaunt aunt ran the house. Against that background Minnie's bright dresses, her idle and empty days, had a quality of furious unreality. She went out in the evenings only with women now, neighbors, to the moving pictures. Each afternoon she dressed in one of the new dresses and went downtown alone, where her young "cousins" were already strolling in the late afternoons with their delicate, silken heads and thin, awkward arms and conscious hips, clinging to one another or shrieking and giggling with paired boys in the soda fountain when she passed and went on along the serried store fronts, in the doors of which the sitting and lounging men did not even follow her with their eyes any more.

III

The barber went swiftly up the street where the sparse lights, insect-swirled, glared in rigid and violent suspension in the lifeless air. The day had died in a pall of dust; above the darkened square, shrouded by the spent dust, the sky was as clear as the inside of a brass bell. Below the east was a rumor of the twice-waxed moon.

When he overtook them McLendon and three others were getting into a car parked in an alley. McLendon stooped his thick head, peering out beneath the top. "Changed your mind, did you?" he said. "Damn good thing; by God, tomorrow when this town hears about how you talked tonight—"

"Now, now," the other ex-soldier said. "Hawkshaw's all right. Come on, Hawk; jump in."

"Will Mayes never done it, boys," the barber said. "If anybody done it. Why, you all know well as I do there aint any town where they got better niggers than us. And you know how a lady will kind of think things about men when there aint reason to, and Miss Minnie anyway—"

"Sure, sure," the soldier said. "We're just going to talk to him a little; that's all."

"Talk hell!" Butch said. "When we're through with the—"

"Shut up, for God's sake!" the soldier said. "Do you want everybody in town—"

"Tell them, by God!" McLendon said. "Tell every one of the sons that'll let a white woman—"

"Let's go; let's go: here's the other car." The second car slid squealing out of a cloud of dust at the alley mouth. McLendon started his car and took the lead. Dust lay like fog in the street. The street lights hung nimbused as in water. They drove on out of town.

A rutted lane turned at right angles. Dust hung above it too, and above all the land. The dark bulk of the ice plant, where the Negro Mayes was night watch-man, rose against the sky. "Better stop here, hadn't we?" the soldier said. McLendon did not reply. He hurled the car up and slammed to a stop, the headlights glaring on the blank wall.

"Listen here, boys," the barber said; "if he's here, dont that prove he never done it? Dont it? If it was him, he would run. Dont you see he would?" The second car came up and stopped. McLendon got down; Butch sprang down beside him. "Listen, boys," the barber said.

"Cut the lights off!" McLendon said. The breathless dark rushed down. There was no sound in it save their lungs as they sought air in the parched dust in which for two months they had lived; then the diminishing crunch of McLendon's and Butch's feet, and a moment later McLendon's voice:

"Will! . . . Will!"

Below the east the wan hemorrhage of the moon increased. It heaved above the ridge, silvering the air, the dust, so that they seemed to breathe, live, in a bowl of molten lead. There was no sound of night-bird nor insect, no sound save their breathing and a faint ticking of contracting metal about the cars. Where their bodies touched one another they seemed to sweat dryly, for no more moisture came. "Christ!" a voice said; "let's get out of here."

But they didn't move until vague noises began to grow out of the darkness ahead; then they got out and waited tensely in the breathless dark. There was another sound: a blow, a hissing expulsion of breath and McLendon cursing in undertone. They stood a moment longer, then they ran forward. They ran in a stumbling clump, as though they were fleeing something. "Kill him, kill the son," a voice whispered. McLendon flung them back.

"Not here," he said. "Get him into the car." "Kill him, kill the black son!" the voice murmured. They dragged the Negro to the car. The barber had waited beside the car. He could feel himself sweating and he knew he was going to be sick at the stomach.

"What is it, captains?" the Negro said. "I aint done nothing. 'Fore God, Mr.

John." Someone produced handcuffs. They worked busily about the Negro as though he were a post, quiet, intent, getting in one another's way. He submitted to the handcuffs, looking swiftly and constantly from dim face to dim face. "Who's here, captains?" he said, leaning to peer into the faces until they could feel his breath and smell his sweaty reek. He spoke a name or two. "What you all say I done, Mr. John?"

McLendon jerked the car door open. "Get in!" he said.

The Negro did not move. "What you all going to do with me, Mr. John? I aint done nothing. White folks, captains, I aint done nothing: I swear 'fore God." He called another name.

"Get in!" McLendon said. He struck the Negro. The others expelled their breath in a dry hissing and struck him with random blows and he whirled and cursed them, and swept his manacled hands across their faces and slashed the barber upon the mouth, and the barber struck him also. "Get him in there," McLendon said. They pushed at him. He ceased struggling and got in and sat quietly as the others took their places. He sat between the barber and the soldier, drawing his limbs in so as not to touch them, his eyes going swiftly and constantly from face to face. Butch clung to the running board. The car moved on. The barber nursed his mouth with his handkerchief.

"What's the matter, Hawk?" the soldier said.

"Nothing," the barber said. They regained the highroad and turned away from town. The second car dropped back out of the dust. They went on, gaining speed; the final fringe of houses dropped behind.

"Goddamn, he stinks!" the soldier said.

"We'll fix that," the drummer in front beside McLendon said. On the running board Butch cursed into the hot rush of air. The barber leaned suddenly forward and touched McLendon's arm.

"Let me out, John," he said.

"Jump out, niggerlover," McLendon said without turning his head. He drove swiftly. Behind them the sourceless lights of the second car glared in the dust. Presently McLendon turned into a narrow road. It was rutted with disuse. It led back to an abandoned brick kiln—a series of reddish mounds and weed- and vine-choked vats without bottom. It had been used for pasture once, until one day the owner missed one of his mules. Although he prodded carefully in the vats with a long pole, he could not even find the bottom of them.

"John," the barber said.

"Jump out, then," McLendon said, hurling the car along the ruts. Beside the barber the Negro spoke:

"Mr. Henry."

The barber sat forward. The narrow tunnel of the road rushed up and past. Their motion was like an extinct furnace blast: cooler, but utterly dead. The car bounded from rut to rut.

"Mr. Henry," the Negro said.

The barber began to tug furiously at the door. "Look out, there!" the soldier said, but the barber had already kicked the door open and swung onto the running board. The soldier leaned across the Negro and grasped at him, but he had already jumped. The car went on without checking speed.

The impetus hurled him crashing through dust-sheathed weeds, into the ditch. Dust puffed about him, and in a thin, vicious crackling of sapless stems he lay choking and retching until the second car passed and died away. Then he rose and limped on until he reached the high-road and turned toward town, brushing at his clothes with his hands. The moon was higher, riding high and clear of the dust at last, and after a while the town began to glare beneath the dust. He went on, limping. Presently he heard cars and the glow of them grew in the dust behind him and he left the road and crouched again in the weeds until they passed. McLendon's car came last now. There were four people in it and Butch was not on the running board.

They went on; the dust swallowed them; the glare and the sound died away. The dust of them hung for a while, but soon the eternal dust absorbed it again. The barber climbed back onto the road and limped on toward town.

IV

As she dressed for supper on that Saturday evening, her own flesh felt like fever. Her hands trembled among the hooks and eyes, and her eyes had a feverish look, and her hair swirled crisp and crackling under the comb. While she was still dressing the friends called for her and sat while she donned her sheerest underthings and stockings and a new voile dress. "Do you feel strong enough to go out?" they said, their eyes bright too, with a dark glitter. "When you have had time to get over the shock, you must tell us what happened. What he said and did; everything."

In the leafed darkness, as they walked toward the square, she began to breathe deeply, something like a swimmer preparing to dive, until she ceased trembling, the four of them walking slowly because of the terrible heat and out of solicitude for her. But as they neared the square she began to tremble again, walking with her head up, her hands clenched at her sides, their voices about her murmurous, also with that feverish, glittering quality of their eyes.

They entered the square, she in the center of the group, fragile in her fresh dress. She was trembling worse. She walked slower and slower, as children eat ice cream, her head up and her eyes bright in the haggard banner of her face, passing the hotel and the coatless drummers in chairs along the curb looking around at her: "That's the one: see? The one in pink in the middle." "Is that her? What did they do with the nigger? Did they—?" "Sure. He's all right." "All right, is he?" "Sure. He went on a little trip." Then the drug store, where even the young men lounging in the doorway tipped their hats and followed with their eyes the motion of her hips and legs when she passed.

They went on, passing the lifted hats of the gentlemen, the suddenly ceased voices, deferent, protective. "Do you see?" the friends said. Their voices sounded like long, hovering sighs of hissing exultation. "There's not a Negro on the square. Not one."

They reached the picture show. It was like a miniature fairyland with its lighted lobby and colored lithographs of life caught in its terrible and beautiful mutations. Her lips began to tingle. In the dark, when the picture began, it would be all right; she could hold back the laughing so it would not waste away so fast and so soon. So she hurried on before the turning faces, the undertones of low astonishment, and they took their accustomed places where she could see the aisle against the silver glare and the young men and girls coming in two and two against it.

The lights flicked away; the screen glowed silver, and soon life began to unfold, beautiful and passionate and sad, while still the young men and girls entered, scented and sibilant in the half dark, their paired backs in silhouette delicate and sleek, their slim, quick bodies awkward, divinely young, while beyond them the silver dream accumulated, inevitably on and on. She began to laugh. In trying to suppress it, it made more noise than ever; heads began to turn. Still laughing, her friends raised her and led her out, and she stood at the curb, laughing on a high, sustained note, until the taxi came up and they helped her in.

They removed the pink voile and the sheer underthings and the stockings, and put her to bed, and cracked ice for her temples, and sent for the doctor. He was hard to locate, so they ministered to her with hushed ejaculations, renewing the ice and fanning her. While the ice was fresh and cold she stopped laughing and lay still for a time, moaning only a little. But soon the laughing welled again and her voice rose screaming.

"Shhhhhhhhhhh! Shhhhhhhhhhhhhhh!" they said, freshening the icepack, smoothing her hair, examining it for gray: "poor girl!" Then to one another: "Do you suppose anything really happened?" their eyes darkly aglitter, secret and passionate. "Shhhhhhhhhh! Poor girl! Poor Minnie!"

V

It was midnight when McLendon drove up to his neat new house. It was trim and fresh as a birdcake and almost as small, with its clean, green-and-white paint. He locked the car and mounted the porch and entered. His wife rose from a chair beside the reading lamp. McLendon stopped in the floor and stared at her until she looked down.

"Look at that clock," he said, lifting his arm, pointing. She stood before him, her face lowered, a magazine in her hands. Her face was pale, strained, and weary-looking. "Haven't I told you about sitting up like this, waiting to see when I come in?"

"John," she said. She laid the magazine down. Poised on the balls of his feet, he glared at her with his hot eyes, his sweating face.

"Didn't I tell you?" He went toward her. She looked up then. He caught her shoulder. She stood passive, looking at him.

"Don't, John. I couldn't sleep . . . The heat; something. Please, John. You're hurting me."

"Didn't I tell you?" He released her and half struck, half flung her across the chair, and she lay there and watched him quietly as he left the room.

He went on through the house, ripping off his shirt, and on the dark, screened porch at the rear he stood and mopped his head and shoulders with the shirt and flung it away. He took the pistol from his hip and laid it on the table beside the bed, and sat on the bed and removed his shoes, and rose and slipped his trousers off. He was sweating again already, and he stooped and hunted furiously for the shirt. At last he found it and wiped his body again, and, with his body pressed against the dusty screen, he stood panting. There was no movement, no sound, not even an insect. The dark world seemed to lie stricken beneath the cold moon and the lidless stars.

[1931]

QUESTIONS FOR STUDY

1. *How do setting and atmosphere serve to explain and reinforce the events of the story? What images and image patterns keep recurring? What is their symbolic value?*

2. *Why does Faulkner choose to focus two of the five sections on Miss Minnie Cooper, and how does the mood of those sections differ from the other three? What psychological and social tensions help explain the "furious repudiation of truth" in Minnie's eyes? What is the significance of her laughter?*

3. *What is the purpose of the final scene between McLendon and his wife? Why does he strike her? Does the apparent failure of their relationship help to explain McLendon's cruel and sadistic behavior?*

4. *Why does Faulkner include the barber in the story? Why does Hawkshaw strike Will Mayes? Why does he jump from the car?*

5. *Why doesn't Faulkner dramatize the actual murder?*

WILLIAM FAULKNER

The Old People

I

AT FIRST there was nothing. There was the faint, cold, steady rain, the gray and constant light of the late November dawn, with the voices of the hounds converging somewhere in it and toward them. Then Sam Fathers, standing just behind the boy as he had been standing when the boy shot his first running rabbit with his first gun and almost with the first load it ever carried, touched his shoulder and he began to shake, not with any cold. Then the buck was there. He did not come into sight; he was just there, looking not like a ghost but as if all of light were condensed in him and he were the source of it, not only moving in it but disseminating it, already running, seen first as you always see the deer, in that split second after he has already seen you, already slanting away in that first soaring bound, the antlers even in that dim light looking like a small rocking-chair balanced on his head.

"Now," Sam Fathers said, "shoot quick, and slow."

The boy did not remember that shot at all. He would live to be eighty, as his father and his father's twin brother and their father in his turn had lived to be, but he would never hear that shot nor remember even the shock of the gun-butt. He didn't even remember what he did with the gun afterward. He was running. Then he was standing over the buck where it lay on the wet earth still in the attitude of speed and not looking at all dead, standing over it shaking and jerking, with Sam Fathers beside him, extending the knife. "Dont walk up to him in front," Sam said. "If he aint dead, he will cut you all to pieces with his feet. Walk up to him from behind and take him by the horn first, so you can hold his head down until you can jump away. Then slip your other hand down and hook your fingers in his nostrils."

The boy did that—drew the head back and the throat taut and drew Sam Fathers' knife across the throat and Sam stooped and dipped his hands in the hot smoking blood and wiped them back and forth across the boy's face. Then Sam's horn rang in the wet gray woods and again and again; there was a boiling wave of dogs about them, with Tennie's Jim and Boon Hogganbeck whipping them back after each had had a taste of the blood, then the men, the true hunters—Walter Ewell whose rifle never missed, and Major de Spain and old General Compson and the boy's cousin, McCaslin Edmonds, grandson of his father's sister, sixteen years his senior and, since both he and McCaslin were only children and the boy's father had been nearing seventy when he was born, more his brother than his cousin and more his father than either—sitting their horses and looking down at them: at the old man of seventy who had been a negro for two generations now but whose face and bearing were still those of the Chickasaw chief who had been his father; and the white boy of twelve with the prints of bloody hands on his face, who had nothing to do now but stand straight and not let the trembling show.

"Did he do all right, Sam?" his cousin McCaslin said.

"He done all right," Sam Fathers said.

They were the white boy, marked forever, and the old dark man sired on both sides by savage kings, who had marked him, whose bloody hands had merely formally consecrated him to that which, under the man's tutelage, he had already accepted, humbly and joyfully, with abnegation and with pride too; the hands, the touch, the first worthy blood which he had been found at last worthy to draw, joining him and the man forever, so that the man would continue to live past the boy's seventy years and then eighty years, long after the man himself had entered the earth as chiefs and kings entered it;—the child, not yet a man, whose grandfather had lived in the same country and in almost the same manner as the boy himself would grow up to live, leaving his descendants in the land in his turn as his grandfather had done, and the old man past seventy whose grandfathers had owned the land long before the white men ever saw it and who had vanished from it now with all their kind, what of blood they left behind them running now in another race and for a while even in bondage and now drawing toward the end of its alien and irrevocable course, barren, since Sam Fathers had no children.

His father was Ikkemotubbe himself, who had named himself Doom. Sam told the boy about that—how Ikkemotubbe, old Issetibbeha's sister's son, had run away to New Orleans in his youth and returned seven years later with a French companion calling himself the Chevalier Soeur-Blonde de Vitry, who must have been the Ikkemotubbe of his family too and who was already addressing Ikkemotubbe as *Du Homme*;—returned, came home again, with his foreign Aramis and the quadroon slave woman who was to be Sam's mother, and a gold-laced hat and coat and a wicker wine-hamper containing a litter of month-old puppies and a gold snuff-box filled with a white powder resembling fine sugar. And how he was met at the River landing by three or four companions of his bachelor youth, and while the light of a smoking torch gleamed on the glittering braid of the hat and coat Doom squatted in the mud of the land and took one of the puppies from the hamper and put a pinch of the white powder on its tongue and the puppy died before the one who was holding it could cast it away. And how they returned to the Plantation where Issetibbeha, dead

now, had been succeeded by his son, Doom's fat cousin Moketubbe, and the next day Moketubbe's eight-year-old son died suddenly and that afternoon, in the presence of Moketubbe and most of the others (the People, Sam Fathers called them) Doom produced another puppy from the wine-hamper and put a pinch of the white powder on its tongue and Moketubbe abdicated and Doom became in fact The Man which his French friend already called him. And how on the day after that, during the ceremony of accession, Doom pronounced a marriage between the pregnant quadroon and one of the slave men which he had just inherited (that was how Sam Fathers got his name, which in Chickasaw had been Had-Two-Fathers) and two years later sold the man and woman and the child who was his own son to his white neighbor, Carothers McCaslin.

That was seventy years ago. The Sam Fathers whom the boy knew was already sixty—a man not tall, squat rather, almost sedentary, flabby-looking though he actually was not, with hair like a horse's mane which even at seventy showed no trace of white and a face which showed no age until he smiled, whose only visible trace of negro blood was a slight dullness of the hair and the fingernails, and something else which you did notice about the eyes, which you noticed because it was not always there, only in repose and not always then—something not in their shape nor pigment but in their expression, and the boy's cousin McCaslin told him what that was: not the heritage of Ham, not the mark of servitude but of bondage; the knowledge that for a while that part of his blood had been the blood of slaves. "Like an old lion or a bear in a cage," McCaslin said. "He was born in the cage and has been in it all his life; he knows nothing else. Then he smells something. It might be anything, any breeze blowing past anything and then into his nostrils. But there for a second was the hot sand or the cane-brake that he never even saw himself, might not even know if he did see it and probably does know he couldn't hold his own with it if he got back to it. But that's not what he smells then. It was the cage he smelled. He hadn't smelled the cage until that minute. Then the hot sand or the brake blew into his nostrils and blew away, and all he could smell was the cage. That's what makes his eyes look like that."

"Then let him go!" the boy cried. "Let him go!"

His cousin laughed shortly. Then he stopped laughing, making the sound that is. It had never been laughing. "His cage aint McCaslins," he said. "He was a wild man. When he was born, all his blood on both sides, except the little white part, knew things that had been tamed out of our blood so long ago that we have not only forgotten them, we have to live together in herds to protect ourselves from our own sources. He was the direct son not only of a warrior but of a chief. Then he grew up and began to learn things, and all of a sudden one day he found out that he had been betrayed, the blood of the warriors and chiefs had been betrayed. Not by his father," he added quickly. "He probably never held it against old Doom for selling him and his mother into slavery, because he probably believed the damage was already done before then and it was the same warriors' and chiefs' blood in him and Doom both that was betrayed through the black blood which his mother gave him. Not betrayed by the black blood and not wilfully betrayed by his mother, but betrayed by her all the same, who had bequeathed him not only the blood of slaves but even a little of the very blood which had enslaved it; himself his own battleground, the scene of his own vanquishment and the mausoleum of his defeat. His cage aint us," McCaslin said. "Did you ever know anybody yet, even your father and Uncle Buddy, that ever told him to do or not do anything that he ever paid any attention to?"

That was true. The boy first remembered him as sitting in the door of the plantation blacksmith-shop, where he sharpened plow-points and mended tools and even did rough carpenter-work when he was not in the woods. And sometimes, even when the woods had not drawn him, even with the shop cluttered with work

which the farm waited on, Sam would sit there, doing nothing at all for half a day or a whole one, and no man, neither the boy's father and twin uncle in their day nor his cousin McCaslin after he became practical though not yet titular master, ever to say to him, "I want this finished by sundown" or "why wasn't this done yesterday?" And once each year, in the late fall, in November, the boy would watch the wagon, the hooped canvas top erected now, being loaded—the food, hams and sausage from the smokehouse, coffee and flour and molasses from the commissary, a whole beef killed just last night for the dogs until there would be meat in camp, the crate containing the dogs themselves, then the bedding, the guns, the horns and lanterns and axes, and his cousin McCaslin and Sam Fathers in their hunting clothes would mount to the seat and with Tennie's Jim sitting on the dog-crate they would drive away to Jefferson, to join Major de Spain and General Compson and Boon Hogganbeck and Walter Ewell and go on into the big bottom of the Tallahatchie where the deer and bear were, to be gone two weeks. But before the wagon was even loaded the boy would find that he could watch no longer. He would go away, running almost, to stand behind the corner where he could not see the wagon and nobody could see him, not crying, holding himself rigid except for the trembling, whispering to himself: "Soon now. Soon now. Just three more years" (or two more or one more) "and I will be ten. Then Cass said I can go."

White man's work, when Sam did work. Because he did nothing else: farmed no allotted acres of his own, as the other ex-slaves of old Carothers McCaslin did, performed no field-work for daily wages as the younger and newer negroes did—and the boy never knew just how that had been settled between Sam and old Carothers, or perhaps with old Carothers' twin sons after him. For, although Sam lived among the negroes, in a cabin among the other cabins in the quarters, and consorted with negroes (what of consorting with anyone Sam did after the boy got big enough to walk alone from the house to the blacksmith-shop and then to carry a gun) and dressed like them and talked like them and even went with them to the negro church now and then, he was still the son of that Chickasaw chief and the negroes knew it. And, it seemed to the boy, not only negroes. Boon Hogganbeck's grand-mother had been a Chickasaw woman too, and although the blood had run white since and Boon was a white man, it was not chief's blood. To the boy at least, the difference was apparent immediately you saw Boon and Sam together, and even Boon seemed to know it was there— even Boon, to whom in his tradition it had never occurred that anyone might be better born than himself. A man might be smarter, he admitted that, or richer (luckier, he called it) but not bet-ter born. Boon was a mastiff, absolutely faithful, dividing his fidelity equally be-tween Major de Spain and the boy's cousin McCaslin, absolutely dependent for his very bread and dividing that im-partially too between Major de Spain and McCaslin, hardy, generous, coura-geous enough, a slave to all the appetites and almost unratiocinative. In the boy's eyes at least it was Sam Fathers, the negro, who bore himself not only toward his cousin McCaslin and Major de Spain but toward all white men, with gravity and dignity and without servility or recourse to that impenetrable wall of ready and easy mirth which negroes sustain between themselves and white men, bearing him-self toward his cousin McCaslin not only as one man to another but as an older man to a younger.

He taught the boy the woods, to hunt, when to shoot and when not to shoot, when to kill and when not to kill, and better, what to do with it afterward. Then he would talk to the boy, the two of them sitting beneath the close fierce stars on a summer hilltop while they waited for the hounds to bring the fox back within hear-ing, or beside a fire in the November or December woods while the dogs worked out a coon's trail along the creek, or fire-less in the pitch dark and heavy dew of April mornings while they squatted be-neath a turkey-roost. The boy would never question him; Sam did not react to questions. The boy would just wait and then listen and Sam would begin, talking about the old days and the People whom he had not had time ever to know and so could not remember (he did not remem-ber ever having seen his father's face), and in place of whom the other race into which his blood had run supplied him with no substitute.

And as he talked about those old times and those dead and vanished men of another race from either that the boy knew, gradually to the boy those old times would cease to be old times and would become a part of the boy's present, not only as if they had happened yesterday but as if they were still happening, the men who walked through them actually walking in breath and air and casting an actual shadow on the earth they had not quitted. And more: as if some of them had not happened yet but would occur tomorrow, until at last it would seem to the boy that he himself had not come into existence yet, that none of his race nor the other subject race which his people had brought with them into the land had come here yet; that although it had been his grandfather's and then his father's and uncle's and was now his cousin's and someday would be his own land which he and Sam hunted over, their hold upon it actually was as trivial and without reality as the now faded and ar-chaic script in the chancery book in Jef-ferson which allocated it to them and that it was he, the boy, who was the guest here and Sam Father's voice the mouth-piece of the host.

Until three years ago there had been two of them, the other a full-blood Chickasaw, in a sense even more in-credibly lost than Sam Fathers. He called himself Jobaker, as if it were one word. Nobody knew his history at all. He was a hermit, living in a foul little shack at the forks of the creek five miles from the plantation and about that far from any other habitation. He was a market hunter and fisherman and he consorted with no-body, black or white; no negro would even cross his path and no man dared ap-proach his hut except Sam. And perhaps once a month the boy would find them in Sam's shop—two old men squatting on their heels on the dirt floor, talking in a mixture of negroid English and flat hill dialect and now and then a phrase of that old tongue which as time went on and the boy squatted there too listening, he began to learn. Then Jobaker died. That is, nobody had seen him in some time. Then one morning Sam was missing, nobody, not even the boy, knew when nor where, until that night when some negroes hunting in the creek bottom saw the sudden burst of flame and approached. It was Jobaker's hut, but before they got anywhere near it, someone shot at them from the shadows beyond it. It was Sam who fired, but nobody ever found Jobaker's grave.

The next morning, sitting at breakfast with his cousin, the boy saw Sam pass the dining-room window and he remembered then that never in his life before had he seen Sam nearer the house than the blacksmith-shop. He stopped eating even; he sat there and he and his cousin both heard the voices from beyond the pantry door, then the door opened and Sam entered, carrying his hat in his hand but without knocking as anyone else on the place except a house servant would have done, entered just far enough for the door to close behind him and stood looking at neither of them—the Indian face above the nigger clothes, looking at something over their heads or at something not even in the room.

"I want to go," he said. "I want to go to the Big Bottom to live."

"To live?" the boy's cousin said.

"At Major de Spain's and your camp, where you go to hunt," Sam said. "I could take care of it for you all while you aint there. I will build me a little house in the woods, if you rather I didn't stay in the big one."

"What about Isaac here?" his cousin said. "How will you get away from him? Are you going to take him with you?" But still Sam looked at neither of them, standing just inside the room with that face which showed nothing, which showed that he was an old man only when it smiled.

"I want to go," he said. "Let me go."

"Yes," the cousin said quietly. "Of course. I'll fix it with Major de Spain. You want to go soon?"

"I'm going now," Sam said. He went out. And that was all. The boy was nine then; it seemed perfectly natural that nobody, not even his cousin McCaslin should argue with Sam. Also, since he was nine now, he could understand that Sam could leave him and their days and nights in the woods together without any wrench. He believed that he and Sam both knew that this was not only temporary but that the exigencies of his maturing, of that for which Sam had been training him all his life some day to dedicate himself, required it. They had settled that one night last summer while they listened to the hounds bringing a fox back up the creek valley; now the boy discerned in that very talk under the high, fierce August stars a presage, a warning, of this moment today. "I done taught you all there is of this settled country," Sam said. "You can hunt it good as I can now. You are ready for the Big Bottom now, for bear and deer. Hunter's meat," he said. "Next year you will be ten. You will write your age in two numbers and you will be ready to become a man. Your pa" (Sam always referred to the boy's cousin as his father, establishing even before the boy's orphanhood did that relation between them not of the ward to his guardian and kinsman and chief and head of his blood, but of the child to the man who sired his flesh and his thinking too.) "promised you can go with us then." So the boy could understand Sam's going. But he couldn't understand why now, in March, six months before the moon for hunting.

"If Jobaker's dead like they say," he said, "and Sam hasn't got anybody but us at all kin to him, why does he want to go to the Big Bottom now, when it will be six months before we get there?"

"Maybe that's what he wants," McCaslin said. "Maybe he wants to get away from you a little while."

But that was all right. McCaslin and other grown people often said things like that and he paid no attention to them, just as he paid no attention to Sam saying he wanted to go to the Big Bottom to live. After all, he would have to live there for six months, because there would be no use in going at all if he was going to turn right around and come back. And, as Sam himself had told him, he already knew all about hunting in this settled country that Sam or anybody else could teach him. So it would be all right. Summer, then the bright days after the first frost, then the cold and himself on the wagon with McCaslin this time and the moment would come and he would draw the blood, the big blood which would make him a man, a hunter, and Sam would come back home with them and he too would have outgrown the child's pursuit of rabbits and 'possums. Then he too would make one before the winter fire, talking of the old hunts and the hunts to come as hunters talked.

So Sam departed. He owned so little that he could carry it. He walked. He would neither let McCaslin send him in the wagon, nor take a mule to ride. No one saw him go even. He was just gone one morning, the cabin which had never had very much in it, vacant and empty, the shop in which there never had been very much done, standing idle. Then November came at last, and now the boy made one—himself and his cousin Mc-Caslin and Tennie's Jim, and Major de Spain and General Compson and Walter Ewell and Boon and old Uncle Ash to do the cooking, waiting for them in Jefferson with the other wagon, and the surrey in which he and McCaslin and General Compson and Major de Spain would ride.

Sam was waiting at the camp to meet them. If he was glad to see them, he did not show it. And if, when they broke camp two weeks later to return home, he was sorry to see them go, he did not show that either. Because he did not come back with them. It was only the boy who returned, returning solitary and alone to the settled familiar land, to follow for eleven months the childish business of rabbits and such while he waited to go back, having brought with him, even from his brief first sojourn, an unforgettable sense of the big woods—not a

quality dangerous or particularly inimical, but profound, sentient, gigantic and brooding, amid which he had been permitted to go to and fro at will, unscathed, why he knew not, but dwarfed and, until he had drawn honorably blood worthy of being drawn, alien.

Then November, and they would come back. Each morning Sam would take the boy out to the stand allotted him. It would be one of the poorer stands of course, since he was only ten and eleven and twelve and he had never even seen a deer running yet. But they would stand there, Sam a little behind him and without a gun himself, as he had been standing when the boy shot the running rabbit when he was eight years old. They would stand there in the November dawns, and after a while they would hear the dogs. Sometimes the chase would sweep up and past quite close, belling and invisible; once they heard the two heavy reports of Boon Hogganbeck's old gun with which he had never killed anything larger than a squirrel and that sitting, and twice they heard the flat unreverberant clap of Walter Ewell's rifle, following which you did not even wait to hear his horn.

"I'll never get a shot," the boy said. "I'll never kill one."

"Yes you will," Sam said. "You wait. You'll be a hunter. You'll be a man."

But Sam wouldn't come out. They would leave him there. He would come as far as the road where the surrey waited, to take the riding horses back, and that was all. The men would ride the horses and Uncle Ash and Tennie's Jim and the boy would follow in the wagon with Sam, with the camp equipment and the trophies, the meat, the heads, the antlers, the good ones, the wagon winding on among the tremendous gums and cypresses and oaks where no axe save that of the hunter had ever sounded, between the impenetrable walls of cane and brier —the two changing yet constant walls just beyond which the wilderness whose mark he had brought away forever on his spirit even from that first two weeks seemed to lean, stooping a little, watching them and listening, not quite inimical because they were too small, even those such as Walter and Major de Spain and old General

Compson who had killed many deer and bear, their sojourn too brief and too harmless to excite to that, but just brooding, secret, tremendous, almost inattentive.

Then they would emerge, they would be out of it, the line as sharp as the demarcation of a doored wall. Suddenly skeleton cotton- and corn-fields would flow away on either hand, gaunt and motionless beneath the gray rain; there would be a house, barns, fences, where the hand of man had clawed for an instant, holding, the wall of the wilderness behind them now, tremendous and still and seemingly impenetrable in the gray and fading light, the very tiny orifice through which they had emerged apparently swallowed up. The surrey would be waiting, his cousin McCaslin and Major de Spain and General Compson and Walter and Boon dismounted beside it. Then Sam would get down from the wagon and mount one of the horses and, with the others on a rope behind him, he would turn back. The boy would watch him for a while against that tall and secret wall, growing smaller and smaller against it, never looking back. Then he would enter it, returning to what the boy believed, and thought that his cousin McCaslin believed, was his loneliness and solitude.

II

So the instant came. He pulled trigger and Sam Fathers marked his face with the hot blood which he had spilled and he ceased to be a child and became a hunter and a man. It was the last day. They broke camp that afternoon and went out, his cousin and Major de Spain and General Compson and Boon on the horses, Walter Ewell and the negroes in the wagon with him and Sam and his hide and antlers. There could have been (and were) other trophies in the wagon. But for him they did not exist, just as for all practical purposes he and Sam Fathers were still alone together as they had been that morning. The wagon wound and jolted between the slow and shifting yet constant walls from beyond and above which the wilderness watched them pass,

less than inimical now and never to be inimical again since the buck still and forever leaped, the shaking gun-barrels coming constantly and forever steady at last, crashing, and still out of his instant of immortality the buck sprang, forever immortal;—the wagon jolting and bouncing on, the moment of the buck, the shot, Sam Fathers and himself and the blood with which Sam had marked him forever one with the wilderness which had accepted him since Sam said that he had done all right, when suddenly Sam reined back and stopped the wagon and they all heard the unmistakable and unforgettable sound of a deer breaking cover.

Then Boon shouted from beyond the bend of the trail and while they sat motionless in the halted wagon, Walter and the boy already reaching for their guns, Boon came galloping back, flogging his mule with his hat, his face wild and amazed as he shouted down at them. Then the other riders came around the bend, also spurring.

"Get the dogs!" Boon cried. "Get the dogs! If he had a nub on his head, he had fourteen points! Laying right there by the road in that pawpaw thicket! If I'd a knowed he was there, I could have cut his throat with my pocket knife!"

"Maybe that's why he run," Walter said. "He saw you never had your gun." He was already out of the wagon with his rifle. The boy was out too with his gun, and the other riders came up and Boon got off his mule somehow and was scrabbling and clawing among the duffel in the wagon, still shouting, "Get the dogs! Get the dogs!" And it seemed to the boy too that it would take them forever to decide what to do—the old men in whom the blood ran cold and slow, in whom during the intervening years between them and himself the blood had become a different and colder substance from that which ran in him and even in Boon and Walter.

"What about it, Sam?" Major de Spain said. "Could the dogs bring him back?"

"We wont need the dogs," Sam said. "If he dont hear the dogs behind him, he will circle back in here about sundown to bed."

"All right," Major de Spain said. "You boys take the horses. We'll go on out to

the road in the wagon and wait there."
He and General Compson and McCaslin
got into the wagon and Boon and Walter
and Sam and the boy mounted the horses
and turned back and out of the trail. Sam
led them for an hour through the gray
and unmarked afternoon whose light was
little different from what it had been at
dawn and which would become darkness
without any graduation between. Then
Sam stopped them.

"This is far enough," he said. "He'll
be coming upwind, and he dont want to
smell the mules." They tied the mounts
in a thicket. Sam led them on foot now,
unpathed through the markless afternoon,
the boy pressing close behind him, the two
others, or so it seemed to the boy, on his
heels. But they were not. Twice Sam
turned his head slightly and spoke back
to him across his shoulder, still walking:
"You got time. We'll get there fore he
does."

So he tried to go slower. He tried deliberately to decelerate the dizzy rushing
of time in which the buck which he had
not even seen was moving, which it
seemed to him must be carrying the buck
farther and farther and more and more
irretrievably away from them even
though there were no dogs behind him
now to make him run, even though, according to Sam, he must have completed
his circle now and was heading back toward them. They went on; it could have
been another hour or twice that or less
than half, the boy could not have said.
Then they were on a ridge. He had never
been in here before and he could not see
that it was a ridge. He just knew that the
earth had risen slightly because the underbrush had thinned a little, the ground
sloping invisibly away toward a dense
wall of cane. Sam stopped. "This is it,"
he said. He spoke to Walter and Boon:
"Follow this ridge and you will come to
two crossings. You will see the tracks. If
he crosses, it will be at one of these
three."

Walter looked about for a moment. "I
know it," he said. "I've even seen your
deer. I was in here last Monday. He aint
nothing but a yearling."

"A yearling?" Boon said. He was panting from the walking. His face still looked
a little wild. "If the one I saw was any
yearling, I'm still in kindergarten."

"Then I must have seen a rabbit," Walter said. "I always heard you quit school
altogether two years before the first
grade."

Boon glared at Walter. "If you dont
want to shoot him, get out of the way,"
he said. "Set down somewhere. By God,
I——"

"Aint nobody going to shoot him
standing here," Sam said quietly.

"Sam's right," Walter said. He moved,
slanting the worn, silver-colored barrel of
his rifle downward to walk with it again.
"A little more moving and a little more
quiet too. Five miles is still Hogganbeck
range, even if we wasn't downwind."
They went on. The boy could still hear
Boon talking, though presently that
ceased too. Then once more he and Sam
stood motionless together against a tremendous pin oak in a little thicket, and
again there was nothing. There was only
the soaring and sombre solitude in the
dim light, there was the thin murmur of
the faint cold rain which had not ceased
all day. Then, as if it had waited for
them to find their positions and become
still, the wilderness breathed again. It
seemed to lean inward above them, above
himself and Sam and Walter and Boon in
their separate lurking-places, tremendous,
attentive, impartial and omniscient, the
buck moving in it somewhere, not running yet since he had not been pursued,
not frightened yet and never fearsome
but just alert also as they were alert, perhaps already circling back, perhaps quite
near, perhaps conscious also of the eye
of the ancient immortal Umpire. Because
he was just twelve then, and that morning
something had happened to him: in less
than a second he had ceased forever to
be the child he was yesterday. Or perhaps that made no difference, perhaps
even a city-bred man, let alone a child,
could not have understood it; perhaps
only a country-bred one could comprehend loving the life he spills. He began
to shake again.

"I'm glad it's started now," he whispered. He did not move to speak; only

his lips shaped the expiring words: "Then it will be gone when I raise the gun——"

Nor did Sam. "Hush," he said.

"Is he that near?" the boy whispered. "Do you think——"

"Hush," Sam said. So he hushed. But he could not stop the shaking. He did not try, because he knew it would go away when he needed the steadiness— had not Sam Fathers already consecrated and absolved him from weakness and regret too?—not from love and pity for all which lived and ran and then ceased to live in a second in the very midst of splendor and speed, but from weakness and regret. So they stood motionless, breathing deep and quiet and steady. If there had been any sun, it would be near to setting now; there was a condensing, a densifying, of what he had thought was the gray and unchanging light until he realised suddenly that it was his own breathing, his heart, his blood—something, all things, and that Sam Fathers had marked him indeed, not as a mere hunter, but with something Sam had had in his turn of his vanished and forgotten people. He stopped breathing then; there was only his heart, his blood, and in the following silence the wilderness ceased to breathe also, leaning, stooping overhead with its breath held, tremendous and impartial and waiting. Then the shaking stopped too, as he had known it would, and he drew back the two heavy hammers of the gun.

Then it had passed. It was over. The solitude did not breathe again yet; it had merely stopped watching him and was looking somewhere else, even turning its back on him, looking on away up the ridge at another point, and the boy knew as well as if he had seen him that the buck had come to the edge of the cane and had either seen or scented them and faded back into it. But the solitude did not breathe again. It should have suspired again then but it did not. It was still facing, watching, what it had been watching and it was not here, not where he and Sam stood; rigid, not breathing himself, he thought, cried *No! No!*, knowing already that it was too late, thinking with the old despair of two and three years ago: *I'll*

never get a shot. Then he heard it—the flat single clap of Walter Ewell's rifle which never missed. Then the mellow sound of the horn came down the ridge and something went out of him and he knew then he had never expected to get the shot at all.

"I reckon that's it," he said. "Walter got him." He had raised the gun slightly without knowing it. He lowered it again and had lowered one of the hammers and was already moving out of the thicket when Sam spoke.

"Wait."

"Wait?" the boy cried. And he would remember that—how he turned upon Sam in the truculence of a boy's grief over the missed opportunity, the missed luck. "What for? Dont you hear that horn?"

And he would remember how Sam was standing. Sam had not moved. He was not tall, squat rather and broad, and the boy had been growing fast for the past year or so and there was not much difference between them in height, yet Sam was looking over the boy's head and up the ridge toward the sound of the horn and the boy knew that Sam did not even see him; that Sam knew he was still there beside him but he did not see the boy. Then the boy saw the buck. It was coming down the ridge, as if it were walking out of the very sound of the horn which related its death. It was not running, it was walking, tremendous, unhurried, slanting and tilting its head to pass the antlers through the undergrowth, and the boy standing with Sam beside him now instead of behind him as Sam always stood, and the gun still partly aimed and one of the hammers still cocked.

Then it saw them. And still it did not begin to run. It just stopped for an instant, taller than any man, looking at them; then its muscles suppled, gathered. It did not even alter its course, not fleeing, not even running, just moving with that winged and effortless ease with which deer move, passing within twenty feet of them, its head high and the eye not proud and not haughty but just full and wild and unafraid, and Sam standing beside the boy now, his right arm raised at full length, palm-outward, speaking in that tongue which the boy had learned from listening to him and Jobaker in the blacksmith shop, while up the ridge Walter Ewell's horn was still blowing them in to a dead buck.

"Oleh, Chief," Sam said. "Grandfather."

When they reached Walter, he was standing with his back toward them, quite still, bemused almost, looking down at his feet. He didn't look up at all.

"Come here, Sam," he said quietly. When they reached him he still did not look up, standing above a little spike buck which had still been a fawn last spring. "He was so little I pretty near let him go," Walter said. "But just look at the track he was making. It's pretty near big as a cow's. If there were any more tracks here besides the ones he is laying in, I would swear there was another buck here that I never even saw."

III

It was dark when they reached the road where the surrey waited. It was turning cold, the rain had stopped, and the sky was beginning to blow clear. His cousin and Major de Spain and General Compson had a fire going. "Did you get him?" Major de Spain said.

"Got a good-sized swamp-rabbit with spike horns," Walter said. He slid the little buck down from his mule. The boy's cousin McCaslin looked at it.

"Nobody saw the big one?" he said.

"I dont even believe Boon saw it," Walter said. "He probably jumped somebody's straw cow in that thicket." Boon started cursing, swearing at Walter and at Sam for not getting the dogs in the first place and at the buck and all.

"Never mind," Major de Spain said. "He'll be here for us next fall. Let's get started home."

It was after midnight when they let Walter out at his gate two miles from Jefferson and later still when they took General Compson to his house and then returned to Major de Spain's, where he and McCaslin would spend the rest of the night, since it was still seventeen miles home. It was cold, the sky was clear now; there would be a heavy frost by sunup and the ground was already frozen beneath the horses' feet and the wheels and beneath their own feet as they crossed Major de Spain's yard and entered the house, the warm dark house, feeling their way up the dark stairs until Major de Spain found a candle and lit it, and into the strange room and the big deep bed, the still cold sheets until they began to warm to their bodies and at last the shaking stopped and suddenly he was telling McCaslin about it while McCaslin listened quietly until he had finished. "You dont believe it," the boy said. "I know you dont——"

"Why not?" McCaslin said. "Think of all that has happened here, on this earth. All the blood hot and strong for living, pleasuring, that has soaked back into it. For grieving and suffering too, of course, but still getting something out of it for all that, getting a lot out of it, because after all you dont have to continue to bear what you believe is suffering, you can always choose to stop that, put an end to that. And even suffering and grieving is better than nothing; there is only one thing worse than not being alive, and that's shame. But you can't be alive forever, and you always wear out life long before you have exhausted the possibilities of living. And all that must be somewhere; all that could not have been invented and created just to be thrown away. And the earth is shallow; there is not a great deal of it before you come to the rock. And the earth dont want to just keep things, hoard them; it wants to use them again. Look at the seed, the acorns, at what happens even to carrion when you try to bury it: it refuses too, seethes and struggles too until it reaches light and air again, hunting the sun still. And they——" the boy saw his hand in silhouette for a moment against the window beyond which, accustomed to the darkness now, he could see sky where the scoured and icy stars glittered "——they dont want it, need it. Besides, what would it want, itself, knocking around out there, when it never had enough time about the earth as it was, when there is plenty of room about the earth, plenty of places still unchanged from what they were when the blood used and pleasured in them while it was still blood?"

"But we want them," the boy said. "We want them too. There is plenty of room for us and them too."

"That's right," McCaslin said. "Suppose they dont have substance, cant cast a shadow ——"

"But I saw it!" the boy cried. "I saw him!"

"Steady," McCaslin said. For an instant his hand touched the boy's flank beneath the covers. "Steady. I know you did. So did I. Sam took me in there once after I killed my first deer."

[1940]

QUESTIONS FOR STUDY

1. *What is Sam Fathers' ancestral heritage? What is his past and present relationship to the other major characters of the story? What values does he typify and represent?*

2. *Why does Sam return to the Big Bottom to live? Why does he go there only after the death of Jobaker?*

3. *Why is it appropriate that Sam should initiate Isaac to the wilderness? What is the ritualistic significance of Sam's act of smearing blood on Isaac's face?*

4. *What is the significance of Isaac's confrontation with the great buck? Is the deer real? Why does Sam greet him as "Grandfather"?*

5. *How does McCaslin clarify for Isaac the meaning of the episode? What does he tell Isaac about the unity and continuity of life?*

6. *What is the appropriateness of Faulkner's lyrical style?*

WILLIAM FAULKNER
That Evening Sun

I

MONDAY is no different from any other weekday in Jefferson now. The streets are paved now, and the telephone and electric companies are cutting down more and more of the shade trees—the water oaks, the maples and locusts and elms—to make room for iron poles bearing clusters of bloated and ghostly and bloodless grapes, and we have a city laundry which makes the rounds on Monday morning, gathering the bundles of clothes into bright-colored, specially-made motor cars: the soiled wearing of a whole week now flees apparitionlike behind alert and irritable electric horns, with a long diminishing noise of rubber and asphalt like tearing silk, and even the Negro women who still take in white people's washing after the old custom, fetch and deliver it in automobiles.

But fifteen years ago, on Monday morning the quiet, dusty, shady streets would be full of Negro women with, balanced on their steady, turbaned heads, bundles of clothes tied up in sheets, almost as large as cotton bales, carried so without touch of hand between the kitchen door of the white house and the blackened washpot beside a cabin door in Negro Hollow.

Nancy would set her bundle on the top of her head, then upon the bundle in turn she would set the black straw sailor hat which she wore winter and summer. She was tall, with a high, sad face sunken a little where her teeth were missing. Sometimes we would go a part of the way down the lane and across the pasture with her, to watch the balanced bundle and the hat that never bobbed nor wavered, even when she walked down into the ditch and up the other side and stooped through the fence. She would go down on her hands and knees and crawl through the gap, her head rigid, uptilted, the bundle steady as a rock or a balloon, and rise to her feet again and go on.

Sometimes the husbands of the washing women would fetch and deliver the clothes, but Jesus never did that for Nancy, even before father told him to stay away from our house, even when Dilsey was sick and Nancy would come to cook for us.

And then about half the time we'd have to go down the lane to Nancy's cabin and tell her to come on and cook breakfast. We would stop at the ditch, because father told us to not have anything to do with Jesus—he was a short black man, with a razor scar down his face—and we would throw rocks at Nancy's house until she came to the door, leaning her head around it without any clothes on.

"What yawl mean, chunking my house?" Nancy said. "What you little devils mean?"

"Father says for you to come on and get breakfast," Caddy said. "Father says it's over a half an hour now, and you've got to come this minute."

"I aint studying no breakfast," Nancy said. "I going to get my sleep out."

"I bet you're drunk," Jason said. "Father says you're drunk. Are you drunk, Nancy?"

"Who says I is?" Nancy said. "I got to get my sleep out. I aint studying no breakfast."

So after a while we quit chunking the cabin and went back home. When she finally came, it was too late for me to go to school. So we thought it was whisky until that day they arrested her again and they were taking her to jail and they passed Mr Stovall. He was the cashier in the bank and a deacon in the Baptist church, and Nancy began to say:

"When you going to pay me, white man? When you going to pay me, white man? It's been three times now since you paid me a cent—" Mr Stovall knocked her down, but she kept on saying, "When you going to pay me, white man? It's been three times now since—" until Mr Stovall kicked her in the mouth with his heel and the marshal caught Mr Stovall back, and Nancy lying in the street, laughing. She turned her head and spat out some blood and teeth and said, "It's been three times now since he paid me a cent."

That was how she lost her teeth, and all that day they told about Nancy and Mr Stovall, and all that night the ones that passed the jail could hear Nancy singing and yelling. They could see her hands holding to the window bars, and a lot of them stopped along the fence, listening to her and to the jailer trying to make her stop. She didn't shut up until almost daylight, when the jailer began to hear a bumping and scraping upstairs and he went up there and found Nancy hanging from the window bar. He said that it was cocaine and not whisky, because no nigger would try to commit suicide unless he was full of cocaine, because a nigger full of cocaine wasn't a nigger any longer.

The jailer cut her down and revived her; then he beat her, whipped her. She had hung herself with her dress. She had fixed it all right, but when they arrested her she didn't have on anything except a dress and so she didn't have anything to tie her hands with and she couldn't make her hands let go of the window ledge. So the jailer heard the noise and ran up there and found Nancy hanging from the window, stark naked, her belly already swelling out a little, like a little balloon.

When Dilsey was sick in her cabin and Nancy was cooking for us, we could see her apron swelling out; that was before father told Jesus to say away from the house. Jesus was in the kitchen, sitting behind the stove, with his razor scar on his black face like a piece of dirty string. He said it was a watermelon that Nancy had under her dress.

"It never come off of your vine, though," Nancy said.

"Off of what vine?" Caddy said.

"I can cut down the vine it did come off of," Jesus said.

"What makes you want to talk like that before these chillen?" Nancy said. "Whynt you go on to work? You done et. You want Mr Jason to catch you hanging around his kitchen, talking that way before these chillen?"

"Talking what way?" Caddy said. "What vine?"

"I cant hang around white man's kitchen," Jesus said. "But white man can hang around mine. White man can come in my house, but I cant stop him. When white man want to come in my house, I aint got no house. I cant stop him, but he cant kick me outen it. He cant do that."

Dilsey was still sick in her cabin. Father told Jesus to stay off our place. Dilsey was still sick. It was a long time. We were in the library after supper.

"Isn't Nancy through in the kitchen yet?" mother said. "It seems to me that she has had plenty of time to have finished the dishes."

"Let Quentin go and see," father said. "Go and see if Nancy is through, Quentin. Tell her she can go on home."

I went to the kitchen. Nancy was through. The dishes were put away and the fire was out. Nancy was sitting in a chair, close to the cold stove. She looked at me.

"Mother wants to know if you are through," I said.

"Yes," Nancy said. She looked at me. "I done finished." She looked at me.

"What is it?" I said. "What is it?"

"I aint nothing but a nigger," Nancy said. "It aint none of my fault."

She looked at me, sitting in the chair before the cold stove, the sailor hat on her head. I went back to the library. It was the cold stove and all, when you think of a kitchen being warm and busy and cheerful. And with a cold stove and the dishes all put away, and nobody wanting to eat at that hour.

"Is she through?" mother said.

"Yessum," I said.

"What is she doing?" mother said.

"She's not doing anything. She's through."

"I'll go and see," father said.

"Maybe she's waiting for Jesus to come and take her home," Caddy said.

"Jesus is gone," I said. Nancy told us how one morning she woke up and Jesus was gone.

"He quit me," Nancy said. "Done gone to Memphis, I reckon. Dodging them city *po*-lice for a while, I reckon."

"And a good riddance," father said. "I hope he stays there."

"Nancy's scaired of the dark," Jason said.

"So are you," Caddy said.

"I'm not," Jason said.

"Scairy cat," Caddy said.

"I'm not," Jason said.

"You, Candace!" mother said. Father came back.

"I am going to walk down the lane with Nancy," he said. "She says that Jesus is back."

"Has she seen him?" mother said.

"No. Some Negro sent her word that he was back in town. I wont be long."

"You'll leave me alone, to take Nancy home?" mother said. "Is her safety more precious to you than mine?"

"I wont be long," father said.

"You'll leave these children unprotected, with that Negro about?"

"I'm going too," Caddy said. "Let me go, Father."

"What would he do with them, if he were unfortunate enough to have them?" father said.

"I want to go, too," Jason said.

"Jason!" mother said. She was speaking to father. You could tell that by the way she said the name. Like she believed that all day father had been trying to think of doing the thing she wouldn't like the most, and that she knew all the time that after a while he would think of it. I stayed quiet, because father and I both knew that mother would want him to make me stay with her if she just thought of it in time. So father didn't look at me. I was the oldest. I was nine and Caddy was seven and Jason was five.

"Nonsense," father said. "We wont be long."

Nancy had her hat on. We came to the lane. "Jesus always been good to me," Nancy said. "Whenever he had two dollars, one of them was mine." We walked in the lane. "If I can just get through the lane," Nancy said, "I be all right then."

The lane was always dark. "This is where Jason got scared on Hallowe'en," Caddy said.

"I didn't," Jason said.

"Cant Aunt Rachel do anything with him?" father said. Aunt Rachel was old. She lived in a cabin beyond Nancy's, by herself. She had white hair and she smoked a pipe in the door, all day long; she didn't work any more. They said she was Jesus' mother. Sometimes she said she was and sometimes she said she wasn't any kin to Jesus.

"Yes, you did," Caddy said. "You were scairder than Frony. You were scairder than T.P. even. Scairder than niggers."

"Cant nobody do nothing with him," Nancy said. "He say I done woke up the devil in him and aint but one thing going to lay it down again."

"Well, he's gone now," father said. "There's nothing for you to be afraid of now. And if you'd just let white men alone."

"Let what white men alone?" Caddy said. "How let them alone?"

"He aint gone nowhere," Nancy said. "I can feel him. I can feel him now, in this lane. He hearing us talk, every word, hid somewhere, waiting. I aint seen him, and I aint going to see him again but once more, with that razor in his mouth. That razor on that string down his back, inside his shirt. And then I aint going to be even surprised."

"I wasn't scaired," Jason said.

"If you'd behave yourself, you'd have kept out of this," father said. "But it's all right now. He's probably in St. Louis now. Probably got another wife by now and forgot all about you."

"If he has, I better not find out about it," Nancy said. "I'd stand there right over them, and every time he wropped her, I'd cut that arm off. I'd cut his head off and I'd slit her belly and I'd shove—"

"Hush," father said.

"Slit whose belly, Nancy?" Caddy said.

"I wasn't scaired," Jason said. "I'd walk right down this lane by myself."

"Yah," Caddy said. "You wouldn't dare to put your foot down in it if we were not here too."

II

Dilsey was still sick, so we took Nancy home every night until mother said, "How much longer is this going on? I to be left alone in this big house while you take home a frightened Negro?"

We fixed a pallet in the kitchen for Nancy. One night we waked up, hearing the sound. It was not singing and it was not crying, coming up the dark stairs. There was a light in mother's room and we heard father going down the hall, down the back stairs, and Caddy and I went into the hall. The floor was cold. Our toes curled away from it while we listened to the sound. It was like singing and it wasn't like singing, like the sounds that Negroes make.

Then it stopped and we heard father going down the back stairs, and we went to the head of the stairs. Then the sound began again, in the stairway, not loud, and we could see Nancy's eyes halfway up the stairs, against the wall. They looked like cat's eyes do, like a big cat against the wall, watching us. When we came down the steps to where she was, she quit making the sound again, and we stood there until father came back up from the kitchen, with his pistol in his hand. He went back down with Nancy and they came back with Nancy's pallet.

We spread the pallet in our room. After the light in mother's room went off, we could see Nancy's eyes again. "Nancy," Caddy whispered, "are you asleep, Nancy?"

Nancy whispered something. It was oh or no, I dont know which. Like nobody had made it, like it came from nowhere and went nowhere, until it was like Nancy was not there at all; that I had looked so hard at her eyes on the stairs that they had got printed on my eyeballs, like the sun does when you have closed your eyes and there is no sun. "Jesus," Nancy whispered. "Jesus."

"Was it Jesus?" Caddy said. "Did he try to come into the kitchen?"

"Jesus," Nancy said. Like this: Jeeeeee-eeeeeeeeeesus, until the sound went out, like a match or a candle does.

"It's the other Jesus she means," I said.

"Can you see us, Nancy?" Caddy whispered. "Can you see our eyes too?"

"I aint nothing but a nigger," Nancy said. "God knows. God knows."

"What did you see down there in the kitchen?" Caddy whispered. "What tried to get in?"

"God knows," Nancy said. We could see her eyes. "God knows."

Dilsey got well. She cooked dinner. "You'd better stay in bed a day or two longer," father said.

"What for?" Dilsey said. "If I had been a day later, this place would be to rack and ruin. Get on out of here now, and let me get my kitchen straight again."

Dilsey cooked supper too. And that night, just before dark, Nancy came into the kitchen.

"How do you know he's back?" Dilsey said. "You aint seen him."

"Jesus is a nigger," Jason said.

"I can feel him," Nancy said. "I can feel him laying yonder in the ditch."

"Tonight?" Dilsey said. "Is he there tonight?"

"Dilsey's a nigger too," Jason said.

"You try to eat something," Dilsey said.

"I dont want nothing," Nancy said.

"I aint a nigger," Jason said.

"Drink some coffee," Dilsey said. She poured a cup of coffee for Nancy. "Do you know he's out there tonight? How come you know it's tonight?"

"I know," Nancy said. "He's there, waiting. I know. I done lived with him too long. I know what he is fixing to do fore he know it himself."

"Drink some coffee," Dilsey said. Nancy held the cup to her mouth and blew into the cup. Her mouth pursed out like a spreading adder's, like a rubber mouth, like she had blown all the color out of her lips with blowing the coffee.

"I aint a nigger," Jason said. "Are you a nigger, Nancy?"

"I hellborn, child," Nancy said. "I wont be nothing soon. I going back where I come from soon."

III

She began to drink the coffee. While she was drinking, holding the cup in both hands, she began to make the sound again.

She made the sound into the cup and the coffee sploshed out onto her hands and her dress. Her eyes looked at us and she sat there, her elbows on her knees, holding the cup in both hands, looking at us across the wet cup, making the sound. "Look at Nancy," Jason said. "Nancy cant cook for us now. Dilsey's got well now."

"You hush up," Dilsey said. Nancy held the cup in both hands, looking at us, making the sound, like there were two of them: one looking at us and the other making the sound. "Whyn't you let Mr Jason telefoam the marshal?" Dilsey said. Nancy stopped then, holding the cup in her long brown hands. She tried to drink some coffee again, but it sploshed out of the cup, onto her hands and her dress, and she put the cup down. Jason watched her.

"I cant swallow it," Nancy said. "I swallows but it wont go down me."

"You go down to the cabin," Dilsey said. "Frony will fix you a pallet and I'll be there soon."

"Wont no nigger stop him," Nancy said.

"I aint a nigger," Jason said. "Am I, Dilsey?"

"I reckon not," Dilsey said. She looked at Nancy. "I dont reckon so. What you going to do, then?"

Nancy looked at us. Her eyes went fast, like she was afraid there wasn't time to look, without hardly moving at all. She looked at us, at all three of us at one time. "You member that night I stayed in yawls' room?" she said. She told about how we waked up early the next morning, and played. We had to play quiet, on her pallet, until father woke up and it was time to get breakfast. "Go and ask your maw to let me stay here tonight," Nancy said. "I wont need no pallet. We can play some more."

Caddy asked mother. Jason went too. "I cant have Negroes sleeping in the bedrooms," mother said. Jason cried. He cried until mother said he couldn't have any dessert for three days if he didn't stop. Then Jason said he could stop if Dilsey would make a chocolate cake. Father was there.

"Why dont you do something about it?" mother said. "What do we have officers for?"

"Why is Nancy afraid of Jesus?" Caddy said. "Are you afraid of father, mother?"

"What could the officers do?" father said. "If Nancy hasn't seen him, how could the officers find him?"

"Then why is she afraid?" mother said.

"She says he is there. She says she knows he is there tonight."

"Yet we pay taxes," mother said. "I must wait here alone in this big house while you take a Negro woman home."

"You know that I am not lying outside with a razor," father said.

"I'll stop if Dilsey will make a chocolate cake," Jason said. Mother told us to go out and father said he didn't know if Jason would get a chocolate cake or not, but he knew what Jason was going to get in about a minute. We went back to the kitchen and told Nancy.

"Father said for you to go home and lock the door, and you'll be all right," Caddy said. "All right from what, Nancy? Is Jesus mad at you?" Nancy was holding the coffee cup in her hands again, her elbows on her knees and her hands holding the cup between her knees. She was looking into the cup. "What have you done that made Jesus mad?" Caddy said. Nancy let the cup go. It didn't break on the floor, but the coffee spilled out, and Nancy sat there with her hands still making the shape of the cup. She began to make the sound again, not loud. Not singing and not unsinging. We watched her.

"Here," Dilsey said. "You quit that, now. You get aholt of yourself. You wait here. I going to get Versh to walk home with you." Dilsey went out.

We looked at Nancy. Her shoulders kept shaking, but she quit making the sound. We watched her. "What's Jesus going to do to you?" Caddy said. "He went away."

Nancy looked at us. "We had fun that night I stayed in yawls' room, didn't we?"

"I didn't," Jason said. "I didn't have any fun."

"You were asleep in mother's room," Caddy said. "You were not there."

"Let's go down to my house and have some more fun," Nancy said.

"Mother wont let us," I said "It's too late now."

"Dont bother her," Nancy said. "We can tell her in the morning. She wont mind."

"She wouldn't let us," I said.

"Dont ask her now," Nancy said. "Dont bother her now."

"She didn't say we couldn't go," Caddy said.

"We didn't ask," I said.

"If you go, I'll tell," Jason said.

"We'll have fun," Nancy said. "They won't mind, just to my house. I been working for yawl a long time. They won't mind."

"I'm not afraid to go," Caddy said. "Jason is the one that's afraid. He'll tell."

"I'm not," Jason said.

"Yes, you are," Caddy said. "You'll tell."

"I won't tell," Jason said. "I'm not afraid."

"Jason ain't afraid to go with me," Nancy said. "Is you, Jason?"

"Jason is going to tell," Caddy said. The lane was dark. We passed the pasture gate. "I bet if something was to jump out from behind that gate, Jason would holler."

"I wouldn't," Jason said. We walked down the lane. Nancy was talking loud.

"What are you talking so loud for, Nancy?" Caddy said.

"Who; me?" Nancy said. "Listen at Quentin and Caddy and Jason saying I'm talking loud."

"You talk like there was five of us here," Caddy said. "You talk like father was here too."

"Who; me talking loud, Mr Jason?" Nancy said.

"Nancy called Jason 'Mister,'" Caddy said.

"Listen how Caddy and Quentin and Jason talk," Nancy said.

"We're not talking loud," Caddy said. "You're the one that's talking like father—"

"Hush," Nancy said; "hush, Mr Jason."

"Nancy called Jason 'Mister' aguh—"

"Hush," Nancy said. She was talking loud when we crossed the ditch and stooped through the fence where she used to stoop through with the clothes on her head. Then we came to her house. We were going fast then. She opened the door. The smell of the house was like the lamp and the smell of Nancy was like the wick, like they were waiting for one another to begin to smell. She lit the lamp and closed the door and put the bar up. Then she quit talking loud, looking at us.

"What're we going to do?" Caddy said.

"What do yawl want to do?" Nancy said.

"You said we would have some fun," Caddy said.

There was something about Nancy's house; something you could smell besides Nancy and the house. Jason smelled it, even. "I don't want to stay here," he said. "I want to go home."

"Go home, then," Caddy said.

"I don't want to go by myself," Jason said.

"We're going to have some fun," Nancy said.

"How?" Caddy said.

Nancy stood by the door. She was looking at us, only it was like she had emptied her eyes, like she had quit using them. "What do you want to do?" she said.

"Tell us a story," Caddy said. "Can you tell a story?"

"Yes," Nancy said.

"Tell it," Caddy said. We looked at Nancy. "You don't know any stories."

"Yes," Nancy said. "Yes, I do."

She came and sat in a chair before the hearth. There was a little fire there. Nancy built it up, when it was already hot inside. She built up a good blaze. She told a story. She talked like her eyes looked, like her eyes watching us and her voice talking to us did not belong to her. Like she was living somewhere else, waiting somewhere else. She was outside the cabin. Her voice was inside and the shape of her, the Nancy that could stoop under a barbed wire fence with a bundle of clothes balanced on her head as though without weight, like a balloon, was there. But that was all. "And so this here queen come walking up to the ditch, where that bad man was hiding. She was walking up to the ditch, and she say, 'If I can just get past this here ditch,' was what she say . . .'"

"What ditch?" Caddy said. "A ditch like that one out there? Why did a queen want to go into a ditch?"

"To get to her house," Nancy said. She looked at us. "She had to cross the ditch to get into her house quick and bar the door."

"Why did she want to go home and bar the door?" Caddy said.

IV

Nancy looked at us. She quit talking. She looked at us. Jason's legs stuck straight out of his pants where he sat on Nancy's lap. "I don't think that's a good story," he said. "I want to go home."

"Maybe we had better," Caddy said. She got up from the floor. "I bet they are looking for us right now." She went toward the door.

"No," Nancy said. "Don't open it." She got up quick and passed Caddy. She didn't touch the door, the wooden bar.

"Why not?" Caddy said.

"Come back to the lamp," Nancy said. "We'll have fun. You don't have to go."

"We ought to go," Caddy said. "Unless we have a lot of fun." She and Nancy came back to the fire, the lamp.

"I want to go home," Jason said. "I'm going to tell."

"I know another story," Nancy said. She stood close to the lamp. She looked at Caddy, like when your eyes look up at a stick balanced on your nose. She had to look down to see Caddy, but her eyes looked like that, like when you are balancing a stick.

"I won't listen to it," Jason said. "I'll bang on the floor."

"It's a good one," Nancy said. "It's better than the other one."

"What's it about?" Caddy said. Nancy was standing by the lamp. Her hand was on the lamp, against the light, long and brown.

"Your hand is on that hot globe," Caddy said. "Don't it feel hot to your hand?"

Nancy looked at her hand on the lamp chimney. She took her hand away, slow.

She stood there, looking at Caddy, wringing her long hand as though it were tied to her wrist with a string.

"Let's do something else," Caddy said.

"I want to go home," Jason said.

"I got some popcorn," Nancy said. She looked at Caddy and then at Jason and then at me and then at Caddy again. "I got some popcorn."

"I don't like popcorn," Jason said. "I'd rather have candy."

Nancy looked at Jason. "You can hold the popper." She was still wringing her hand; it was long and limp and brown.

"All right," Jason said. "I'll stay a while if I can do that. Caddy can't hold it. I'll want to go home again if Caddy holds the popper."

Nancy built up the fire. "Look at Nancy putting her hands in the fire," Caddy said. "What's the matter with you, Nancy?"

"I got popcorn," Nancy said. "I got some." She took the popper from under the bed. It was broken. Jason began to cry.

"Now we can't have any popcorn," he said.

"We ought to go home, anyway," Caddy said. "Come on, Quentin."

"Wait," Nancy said; "wait. I can fix it. Don't you want to help me fix it?"

"I don't think I want any," Caddy said. "It's too late now."

"You help me, Jason," Nancy said. "Don't you want to help me?"

"No," Jason said. "I want to go home."

"Hush," Nancy said; "hush. Watch. Watch me. I can fix it so Jason can hold it and pop the corn." She got a piece of wire and fixed the popper.

"It won't hold good," Caddy said.

"Yes, it will," Nancy said. "Yawl watch. Yawl help me shell some corn."

The popcorn was under the bed too. We shelled it into the popper and Nancy helped Jason hold the popper over the fire.

"It's not popping," Jason said. "I want to go home."

"You wait," Nancy said. "It'll begin to pop. We'll have fun then." She was sitting close to the fire. The lamp was turned up so high it was beginning to smoke.

"Why don't you turn it down some?" I said.

"It's all right," Nancy said. "I'll clean it. Yawl wait. The popcorn will start in a minute."

"I don't believe it's going to start," Caddy said. "We ought to start home, anyway. They'll be worried."

"No," Nancy said. "It's going to pop. Dilsey will tell um yawl with me. I been working for yawl long time. They won't mind if yawl at my house. You wait, now. It'll start popping any minute now."

Then Jason got some smoke in his eyes and he began to cry. He dropped the popper into the fire. Nancy got a wet rag and wiped Jason's face, but he didn't stop crying.

"Hush," she said. "Hush." But he didn't hush. Caddy took the popper out of the fire.

"It's burned up," she said. "You'll have to get some more popcorn, Nancy."

"Did you put all of it in?" Nancy said.

"Yes," Caddy said. Nancy looked at Caddy. Then she took the popper and opened it and poured the cinders into her apron and began to sort the grains, her hands long and brown, and we watching her.

"Haven't you got any more?" Caddy said.

"Yes," Nancy said; "yes. Look. This here ain't burnt. All we need to do is—"

"I want to go home," Jason said. "I'm going to tell."

"Hush," Caddy said. We all listened. Nancy's head was already turned toward the barred door, her eyes filled with red lamplight. "Somebody is coming," Caddy said.

Then Nancy began to make that sound again, not loud, sitting there above the fire, her long hands dangling between her knees; all of a sudden water began to come out on her face in big drops, running down her face, carrying in each one a little turning ball of firelight like a spark until it dropped off her chin. "She's not crying," I said.

"I ain't crying," Nancy said. Her eyes were closed. "I ain't crying. Who is it?"

"I don't know," Caddy said. She went to the door and looked out. "We've got to go now," she said. "Here comes father."

"I'm going to tell," Jason said. "Yawl made me come."

The water still ran down Nancy's face. She turned in her chair. "Listen. Tell him. Tell him we going to have fun. Tell him I take good care of yawl until in the morning. Tell him to let me come home with yawl and sleep on the floor. Tell him I won't need no pallet. We'll have fun. You member last time how we had so much fun?"

"I didn't have fun," Jason said. "You hurt me. You put smoke in my eyes. I'm going to tell."

V

Father came in. He looked at us. Nancy did not get up.

"Tell him," she said.

"Caddy made us come down here," Jason said. "I didn't want to."

Father came to the fire. Nancy looked up at him. "Can't you go to Aunt Rachel's and stay?" he said. Nancy looked up at father, her hands between her knees. "He's not here," father said. "I would have seen him. There's not a soul in sight."

"He in the ditch," Nancy said. "He waiting in the ditch yonder."

"Nonsense," father said. He looked at Nancy. "Do you know he's there?"

"I got the sign," Nancy said.

"What sign?"

"I got it. It was on the table when I come in. It was a hogbone, with blood meat still on it, laying by the lamp. He's out there. When yawl walk out that door, I gone."

"Gone where, Nancy?" Caddy said.

"I'm not a tattletale," Jason said.

"Nonsense," father said.

"He out there," Nancy said. "He looking through that window this minute, waiting for yawl to go. Then I gone."

"Nonsense," father said. "Lock up your house and we'll take you on to Aunt Rachel's."

" 'Twont do no good," Nancy said. She

didn't look at father now, but he looked down at her, at her long, limp, moving hands. "Putting it off wont do no good."

"Then what do you want to do?" father said.

"I don't know," Nancy said. "I can't do nothing. Just put it off. And that don't do no good. I reckon it belong to me. I reckon what I going to get ain't no more than mine."

"Get what?" Caddy said. "What's yours?"

"Nothing," father said. "You all must get to bed."

"Caddy made me come," Jason said.

"Go on to Aunt Rachel's," father said.

"It won't do no good," Nancy said. She sat before the fire, her elbows on her knees, her long hands between her knees. "When even your own kitchen wouldn't do no good. When even if I was sleeping on the floor in the room with your chillen, and the next morning there I am, and blood—"

"Hush," father said. "Lock the door and put out the lamp and go to bed."

"I scared of the dark," Nancy said. "I scared for it to happen in the dark."

"You mean you're going to sit right here with the lamp lighted?" father said. Then Nancy began to make the sound again, sitting before the fire, her long hands between her knees. "Ah, damnation," father said. "Come along, chillen. It's past bedtime."

"When yawl go home, I gone," Nancy said. She talked quieter now, and her face looked quiet, like her hands. "Anyway, I got my coffin money saved up with Mr. Lovelady." Mr. Lovelady was a short, dirty man who collected the Negro insurance, coming around to the cabins or the kitchens every Saturday morning, to collect fifteen cents. He and his wife lived at the hotel. One morning his wife committed suicide. They had a child, a little girl. He and the child went away. After a week or two he came back alone. We would see him going along the lanes and the back streets on Saturday mornings.

"Nonsense," father said. "You'll be the first thing I'll see in the kitchen tomorrow morning."

"You'll see what you'll see, I reckon," Nancy said. "But it will take the Lord to say what that will be."

VI

We left her sitting before the fire.

"Come and put the bar up," father said. But she didn't move. She didn't look at us again, sitting quietly there between the lamp and the fire. From some distance down the lane we could look back and see her through the open door.

"What, Father?" Caddy said. "What's going to happen?"

"Nothing," father said. Jason was on father's back, so Jason was the tallest of all of us. We went down into the ditch. I looked at it, quiet. I couldn't see much where the moonlight and the shadows tangled.

"If Jesus is hid here, he can see us, cant he?" Caddy said.

"He's not there," father said. "He went away a long time ago."

"You made me come," Jason said, high; against the sky it looked like father had two heads, a little one and a big one. "I didn't want to."

We went up out of the ditch. We could still see Nancy's house and the open door, but we couldn't see Nancy now, sitting before the fire with the door open, because she was tired. "I just done got tired," she said. "I just a nigger. It ain't no fault of mine."

But we could hear her, because she began just after we came up out of the ditch, the sound that was not singing and not unsinging. "Who will do our washing now, Father?" I said.

"I'm not a nigger," Jason said, high and close above father's head.

"You're worse," Caddy said, "you are a tattletale. If something was to jump out, you'd be scarier than a nigger."

"I wouldn't," Jason said.

"You'd cry," Caddy said.

"Caddy," father said.

"I wouldn't!" Jason said.

"Scairy cat," Caddy said.

"Candace!" father said.

[1931]

QUESTIONS FOR STUDY

1. *Why does Faulkner choose to reveal the adult world through the eyes of nine-year-old Quentin Compson? How does the point of view affect what the reader sees and how he sees it? How does it serve to heighten the story's impact?*

2. *Why is Nancy afraid of Jesus? How does her fear manifest itself? Why is she so helpless in her terror?*

3. *What is the function of the other major characters: Mr. and Mrs. Compson, Caddy, and Jason? How does each regard Nancy and her suffering? How do their attitudes toward fear differ?*

4. *What is the significance of Quentin's final question to his father? Why does Faulkner choose to leave Nancy's fate unresolved?*

F. SCOTT FITZGERALD

Winter Dreams

SOME of the caddies were poor as sin and lived in one-room houses with a neurasthenic cow in the front yard, but Dexter Green's father owned the second best grocery-store in Black Bear —the best one was "The Hub," patronized by the wealthy people from Sherry Island—and Dexter caddied only for pocket-money.

In the fall when the days became crisp and gray, and the long Minnesota winter shut down like the white lid of a box, Dexter's skis moved over the snow that hid the fairways of the golf course. At these times the country gave him a feeling of profound melancholy—it offended him that the links should lie in enforced fallowness, haunted by ragged sparrows for the long season. It was dreary, too, that on the tees where the gay colors fluttered in summer there were now only the desolate sand-boxes knee-deep in crusted ice. When he crossed the hills the wind blew cold as misery, and if the sun was out he tramped with his eyes squinted up against the hard dimensionless glare.

In April the winter ceased abruptly. The snow ran down into Black Bear Lake scarcely tarrying for the early golfers to brave the season with red and black balls. Without elation, without an interval of moist glory, the cold was gone.

Dexter knew that there was something dismal about this Northern spring, just as he knew there was something gorgeous about the fall. Fall made him clinch his hands and tremble and repeat idiotic sentences to himself, and make brisk abrupt gestures of command to imaginary audiences and armies. October filled him with hope which November raised to a sort of ecstatic triumph, and in this mood the fleeting brilliant impressions of the summer at Sherry Island were ready grist to his mill. He became a golf champion and defeated Mr. T. A. Hedrick in a marvellous match played a hundred times over the fairways of his imagination, a match each detail of which he changed about untiringly— sometimes he won with almost laughable ease, sometimes he came up magnificently from behind. Again, stepping from a Pierce-Arrow automobile, like Mr. Mortimer Jones, he strolled frigidly into the lounge of the Sherry Island Golf Club—or perhaps, surrounded by an admiring crowd, he gave an exhibition of fancy diving from the spring-board of the club raft. . . . Among those who watched him in open-mouthed wonder was Mr. Mortimer Jones.

And one day it came to pass that Mr. Jones—himself and not his ghost—came up to Dexter with tears in his eyes and said that Dexter was the — — best caddy in the club, and wouldn't he decide not to quit if Mr. Jones made it worth his while, because every other — — caddy in the club lost one ball a hole for him—regularly——

"No sir," said Dexter decisively, "I don't want to caddy any more." Then, after a pause: "I'm too old."

"You're not more than fourteen. Why the devil did you decide just this morning that you wanted to quit? You promised that next week you'd go over to the state tournament with me."

"I decided I was too old."

Dexter handed in his "A Class" badge, collected what money was due him from the caddy master, and walked home to Black Bear Village.

"The best — — caddy I ever saw," shouted Mr. Mortimer Jones over a drink that afternoon. "Never lost a ball! Willing! Intelligent! Quiet! Honest! Grateful!"

The little girl who had done this was eleven—beautifully ugly as little girls are apt to be who are destined after a few years to be inexpressibly lovely and bring no end of misery to a great number of men. The spark, however, was perceptible. There was a general ungodliness in the way her lips twisted down at the corners when she smiled, and in the— Heaven help us!—in the almost passionate quality of her eyes. Vitality is born in such women. It was utterly in evidence now, shining through her thin frame in a sort of glow.

She had come eagerly out on to the course at nine o'clock with a white linen nurse and five small new golf-clubs in a white canvas bag which the nurse was carrying. When Dexter first saw her she was standing by the caddy house, rather ill at ease and trying to conceal the fact by engaging her nurse in an obviously unnatural conversation graced by startling and irrelevant grimaces from herself.

"Well, it's certainly a nice day, Hilda," Dexter heard her say. She drew down the corners of her mouth, smiled, and glanced furtively around, her eyes in transit falling for an instant on Dexter.

Then to the nurse:

"Well, I guess there aren't very many people out here this morning, are there?"

The smile again—radiant, blatantly artificial—convincing.

"I don't know what we're supposed to do now," said the nurse, looking nowhere in particular.

"Oh, that's all right. I'll fix it up."

Dexter stood perfectly still, his mouth slightly ajar. He knew that if he moved forward a step his stare would be in her line of vision—if he moved backward he would lose his full view of her face. For a moment he had not realized how young she was. Now he remembered having seen her several times the year before—in bloomers.

Suddenly, involuntarily, he laughed, a short abrupt laugh—then, startled by himself, he turned and began to walk quickly away.

"Boy!"

Dexter stopped.

"Boy——"

Beyond question he was addressed. Not only that, but he was treated to that absurd smile, that preposterous smile— the memory of which at least a dozen men were to carry into middle age.

"Boy, do you know where the golf teacher is?"

"He's giving a lesson."

"Well, do you know where the caddy-master is?"

"He isn't here yet this morning."

"Oh." For a moment this baffled her. She stood alternately on her right and left foot.

"We'd like to get a caddy," said the nurse. "Mrs. Mortimer Jones sent us out to play golf, and we don't know how without we get a caddy."

Here she was stopped by an ominous glance from Miss Jones, followed immediately by the smile.

"There aren't any caddies here except me," said Dexter to the nurse, "and I got to stay here in charge until the caddy-master gets here."

"Oh."

Miss Jones and her retinue now withdrew, and at a proper distance from Dexter became involved in a heated conversation, which was concluded by Miss Jones taking one of the clubs and hitting it on the ground with violence. For further emphasis she raised it again and was about to bring it down smartly upon the nurse's bosom, when the nurse seized the club and twisted it from her hands.

"You damn little mean old *thing!*" cried Miss Jones wildly.

Another argument ensued. Realizing that the elements of the comedy were implied in the scene, Dexter several times began to laugh, but each time restrained the laugh before it reached audibility. He could not resist the monstrous conviction that the little girl was justified in beating the nurse.

The situation was resolved by the fortuitous appearance of the caddy-master, who was appealed to immediately by the nurse.

"Miss Jones is to have a little caddy, and this one says he can't go."

"Mr. McKenna said I was to wait here till you came," said Dexter quickly.

"Well, he's here now." Miss Jones smiled cheerfully at the caddy-master. Then she dropped her bag and set off at a haughty mince toward the first tee.

"Well?" The caddy-master turned to Dexter. "What you standing there like a dummy for? Go pick up the young lady's clubs."

"I don't think I'll go out to-day," said Dexter.

"You don't—"

"I think I'll quit."

The enormity of his decision frightened him. He was a favorite caddy, and the thirty dollars a month he earned through the summer were not to be made elsewhere around the lake. But he had received a strong emotional shock, and his perturbation required a violent and immediate outlet.

It is not so simple as that, either. As so frequently would be the case in the future, Dexter was unconsciously dictated to by his winter dreams.

II

Now, of course, the quality and the seasonability of these winter dreams varied, but the stuff of them remained. They persuaded Dexter several years later to pass up a business course at the State university—his father, prospering now, would have paid his way—for the precarious advantage of attending an older and more famous university in the East, where he was bothered by his scanty funds. But do not get the impression, because his winter dreams happened to be concerned at first with musings on the rich, that there was anything merely snobbish in the boy. He wanted not association with glittering things and glittering people—he wanted the glittering things themselves. Often he reached out for the best without knowing why he wanted it—and sometimes he ran up

against the mysterious denials and prohibitions in which life indulges. It is with one of those denials and not with his career as a whole that this story deals.

He made money. It was rather amazing. After college he went to the city from which Black Bear Lake draws its wealthy patrons. When he was only twenty-three and had been there not quite two years, there were already people who liked to say: "Now *there's* a boy—" All about him rich men's sons were peddling bonds precariously, or investing patrimonies precariously, or plodding through the two dozen volumes of the "George Washington Commercial Course," but Dexter borrowed a thousand dollars on his college degree and his confident mouth, and bought a partnership in a laundry.

It was a small laundry when he went into it, but Dexter made a specialty of learning how the English washed fine woolen golf-stockings without shrinking them, and within a year he was catering to the trade that wore knickerbockers. Men were insisting that their Shetland hose and sweaters go to his laundry, just as they had insisted on a caddy who could find golf-balls. A little later he was doing their wives' lingerie as well—and running five branches in different parts of the city. Before he was twenty-seven he owned the largest string of laundries in his section of the country. It was then that he sold out and went to New York. But the part of his story that concerns us goes back to the days when he was making his first big success.

When he was twenty-three Mr. Hart —one of the gray-haired men who like to say "Now there's a boy"—gave him a guest card to the Sherry Island Golf Club for a week-end. So he signed his name one day on the register, and that afternoon played golf in a foursome with Mr. Hart and Mr. Sandwood and Mr. T. A. Hedrick. He did not consider it necessary to remark that he had once carried Mr. Hart's bag over this same links, and that he knew every trap and gully with his eyes shut—but he found himself glancing at the four caddies who trailed them, trying to catch a gleam or gesture that would remind him of himself, that would lessen the gap which lay between his present and his past.

It was a curious day, slashed abruptly with fleeting, familiar impressions. One minute he had the sense of being a trespasser—in the next he was impressed by the tremendous superiority he felt toward Mr. T. A. Hedrick, who was a bore and not even a good golfer any more.

Then, because of a ball Mr. Hart lost near the fifteenth green, an enormous thing happened. While they were searching the stiff grasses of the rough there was a clear call of "Fore!" from behind a hill in their rear. And as they all turned abruptly from their search a bright new ball sliced abruptly over the hill and caught Mr. T. A. Hedrick in the abdomen.

"By Gad!" cried Mr. T. A. Hedrick, "they ought to put some of these crazy women off the course. It's getting to be outrageous."

A head and a voice came up together over the hill:

"Do you mind if we go through?"

"You hit me in the stomach!" declared Mr. Hedrick wildly.

"Did I?" The girl approached the group of men. "I'm sorry. I yelled 'Fore!' "

Her glance fell casually on each of the men—then scanned the fairway for her ball.

"Did I bounce into the rough?"

It was impossible to determine whether this question was ingenuous or malicious. In a moment, however, she left no doubt, for as her partner came up over the hill she called cheerfully:

"Here I am! I'd have gone on the green except that I hit something."

As she took her stance for a short mashie shot, Dexter looked at her closely. She wore a blue gingham dress, rimmed at throat and shoulders with a white edging that accentuated her tan. The quality of exaggeration, of thinness, which had made her passionate eyes and down-turning mouth absurd at eleven, was gone now. She was arrestingly beautiful. The color in her cheeks was centered like the color in a picture—it was

not a "high" color, but a sort of fluctuating and feverish warmth, so shaded that it seemed at any moment it would recede and disappear. This color and the mobility of her mouth gave a continual impression of flux, of intense life, of passionate vitality—balanced only partially by the sad luxury of her eyes.

She swung her mashie impatiently and without interest, pitching the ball into a sand-pit on the other side of the green. With a quick, insincere smile and a careless "Thank you!" she went on after it.

"That Judy Jones!" remarked Mr. Hedrick on the next tee, as they waited —some moments—for her to play on ahead. "All she needs is to be turned up and spanked for six months and then to be married off to an old-fashioned cavalry captain."

"My God, she's good-looking!" said Mr. Sandwood, who was just over thirty.

"Good-looking!" cried Mr. Hedrick contemptuously. "She always looks as if she wanted to be kissed! Turning those big cow-eyes on every calf in town!"

It was doubtful if Mr. Hedrick intended a reference to the maternal instinct.

"She'd play pretty good golf if she'd try," said Mr. Sandwood.

"She has no form," said Mr. Hedrick solemnly.

"She has a nice figure," said Mr. Sandwood.

"Better thank the Lord she doesn't drive a swifter ball," said Mr. Hart, winking at Dexter.

Later in the afternoon the sun went down with a riotous swirl of gold and varying blues and scarlets, and left the dry, rustling night of Western summer. Dexter watched from the veranda of the Golf Club, watched the even overlap of the waters in the little wind, silver molasses under the harvest-moon. Then the moon held a finger to her lips and the lake became a clear pool, pale and quiet. Dexter put on his bathing-suit and swam out to the farthest raft, where he stretched dripping on the wet canvas of the springboard.

There was a fish jumping and a star shining and the lights around the lake were gleaming. Over on a dark peninsula a piano was playing the songs of last summer and of summers before that —songs from "Chin-Chin" and "The Count of Luxemburg" and "The Chocolate Soldier" ¹—and because the sound of a piano over a stretch of water had always seemed beautiful to Dexter he lay perfectly quiet and listened.

The tune the piano was playing at that moment had been gay and new five years before when Dexter was a sophomore at college. They had played it at a prom once when he could not afford the luxury of proms, and he had stood outside the gymnasium and listened. The sound of the tune precipitated in him a sort of ecstasy and it was with that ecstasy he viewed what happened to him now. It was a mood of intense appreciation, a sense that, for once, he was magnificently attune to life and that everything about him was radiating a brightness and a glamour he might never know again.

A low, pale oblong detached itself suddenly from the darkness of the Island, spitting forth the reverberate sound of a racing motorboat. Two white streamers of cleft water rolled themselves out behind it and almost immediately the boat was beside him, drowning out the hot tinkle of the piano in the drone of its spray. Dexter raising himself on his arms was aware of a figure standing at the wheel, of two dark eyes regarding him over the lengthening space of water— then the boat had gone by and was sweeping in an immense and purposeless circle of spray round and round in the middle of the lake. With equal eccentricity one of the circles flattened out and headed back toward the raft.

"Who's that?" she called, shutting off her motor. She was so near now that Dexter could see her bathing-suit, which consisted apparently of pink rompers.

The nose of the boat bumped the raft, and as the latter tilted rakishly he was precipitated toward her. With different

¹ Popular Broadway musicals of the day. (JHP)

degrees of interest they recognized each other.

"Aren't you one of those men we played through this afternoon?" she demanded.

He was.

"Well, do you know how to drive a motor-boat? Because if you do I wish you'd drive this one so I can ride on the surf-board behind. My name is Judy Jones"—she favored him with an absurd smirk—rather, what tried to be a smirk, for, twist her mouth as she might, it was not grotesque, it was merely beautiful— "and I live in a house over there on the Island, and in that house there is a man waiting for me. When he drove up at the door I drove out of the dock because he says I'm his ideal."

There was a fish jumping and a star shining and the lights around the lake were gleaming. Dexter sat beside Judy Jones and she explained how her boat was driven. Then she was in the water, swimming to the floating surf-board with a sinuous crawl. Watching her was without effort to the eye, watching a branch waving or a sea-gull flying. Her arms, burned to butternut, moved sinuously among the dull platinum ripples, elbow appearing first, casting the forearm back with a cadence of falling water, then reaching out and down, stabbing a path ahead.

They moved out into the lake; turning. Dexter saw that she was kneeling on the low rear of the now uptilted surf-board.

"Go faster," she called, "fast as it'll go."

Obediently he jammed the lever forward and the white spray mounted at the bow. When he looked around again the girl was standing up on the rushing board, her arms spread wide, her eyes lifted toward the moon.

"It's awful cold," she shouted. "What's your name?"

He told her.

"Well, why don't you come to dinner tomorrow night?"

His heart turned over like the fly-wheel of the boat, and, for the second time, her casual whim gave a new direction to his life.

III

Next evening while he waited for her to come down-stairs, Dexter peopled the soft deep summer room and the sun-porch that opened from it with the men who had already loved Judy Jones. He knew the sort of men they were—the men who when he first went to college had entered from the great prep schools with graceful clothes and the deep tan of healthy summers. He had seen that, in one sense, he was better than these men. He was newer and stronger. Yet in acknowledging to himself that he wished his children to be like them he was admitting that he was but the rough, strong stuff from which they eternally sprang.

When the time had come for him to wear good clothes, he had known who were the best tailors in America, and the best tailors in America had made him the suit he wore this evening. He had acquired that particular reserve peculiar to his university, that set it off from other universities. He recognized the value to him of such a mannerism and he had adopted it; he knew that to be careless in dress and manner required more confidence than to be careful. But carelessness was for his children. His mother's name had been Krimplich. She was a Bohemian of the peasant class and she had talked broken English to the end of her days. Her son must keep to the set patterns.

At a little after seven Judy Jones came down-stairs. She wore a blue silk afternoon dress, and he was disappointed at first that she had not put on something more elaborate. This feeling was accentuated when, after a brief greeting, she went to the door of a butler's pantry and pushing it open called: "You can serve dinner, Martha." He had rather expected that a butler would announce dinner, that there would be a cocktail. Then he put these thoughts behind him as they sat down side by side on a lounge and looked at each other.

"Father and mother won't be here," she said thoughtfully.

He remembered the last time he had seen her father, and he was glad the parents were not to be here to-night—they might wonder who he was. He had been born in Keeble, a Minnesota village fifty miles farther north, and he always gave Keeble as his home instead of Black Bear Village. Country towns were well enough to come from if they weren't inconveniently in sight and used as footstools by fashionable lakes.

They talked of his university, which she had visited frequently during the past two years, and of the near-by city which supplied Sherry Island with its patrons, and whither Dexter would return next day to his prospering laundries.

During dinner she slipped into a moody depression which gave Dexter a feeling of uneasiness. Whatever petulance she uttered in her throaty voice worried him. Whatever she smiled at—at him, at a chicken liver, at nothing—it disturbed him that her smile could have no root in mirth, or even in amusement. When the scarlet corners of her lips curved down, it was less a smile than an invitation to a kiss.

Then, after dinner, she led him out on the dark sun-porch and deliberately changed the atmosphere.

"Do you mind if I weep a little?" she said.

"I'm afraid I'm boring you," he responded quickly.

"You're not. I like you. But I've just had a terrible afternoon. There was a man I cared about, and this afternoon he told me out of a clear sky that he was poor as a churchmouse. He'd never even hinted it before. Does this sound horribly mundane?"

"Perhaps he was afraid to tell you."

"Suppose he was," she answered. "He didn't start right. You see, if I'd thought of him as poor—well, I've been mad about loads of poor men, and fully intended to marry them all. But in this case, I hadn't thought of him that way, and my interest in him wasn't strong enough to survive the shock. As if a girl calmly informed her fiancé that she was a widow. He might not object to widows, but—

"Let's start right," she interrupted herself suddenly. "Who are you, anyhow?"

For a moment Dexter hesitated. Then: "I'm nobody," he announced. "My career is largely a matter of futures."

"Are you poor?"

"No," he said frankly, "I'm probably making more money than any man my age in the Northwest. I know that's an obnoxious remark, but you advised me to start right."

There was a pause. Then she smiled and the corners of her mouth drooped and an almost imperceptible sway brought her closer to him, looking up into his eyes. A lump rose in Dexter's throat, and he waited breathless for the experiment, facing the unpredictable compound that would form mysteriously from the elements of their lips. Then he saw—she communicated her excitement to him, lavishly, deeply, with kisses that were not a promise but a fulfilment. They aroused in him not hunger demanding renewal but surfeit that would demand more surfeit . . . kisses that were like charity, creating want by holding back nothing at all.

It did not take him many hours to decide that he had wanted Judy Jones ever since he was a proud, desirous little boy.

IV

It began like that—and continued, with varying shades of intensity, on such a note right up to the dénouement. Dexter surrendered a part of himself to the most direct and unprincipled personality with which he had ever come in contact. Whatever Judy wanted, she went after with the full pressure of her charm. There was no divergence of method, no jockeying for position or premeditation of effects—there was a very little mental side to any of her affairs. She simply made men conscious to the highest degree of her physical loveliness. Dexter had no desire to change her. Her deficiencies were knit up with a passionate energy that transcended and justified them.

When, as Judy's head lay against his shoulder that first night, she whispered, "I don't know what's the matter with me.

Last night I thought I was in love with a man and to-night I think I'm in love with you——"—it seemed to him a beautiful and romantic thing to say. It was the exquisite excitability that for the moment he controlled and owned. But a week later he was compelled to view this same quality in a different light. She took him in her roadster to a picnic supper, and after supper she disappeared, likewise in her roadster, with another man. Dexter became enormously upset and was scarcely able to be decently civil to the other people present. When she assured him that she had not kissed the other man, he knew she was lying—yet he was glad that she had taken the trouble to lie to him.

He was, as he found before the summer ended, one of a varying dozen who circulated about her. Each of them had at one time been favored above all others —about half of them still basked in the solace of occasional sentimental revivals. Whenever one showed signs of dropping out through long neglect, she granted him a brief honeyed hour, which encouraged him to tag along for a year or so longer. Judy made these forays upon the helpless and defeated without malice, indeed half unconscious that there was anything mischievous in what she did.

When a new man came to town every one dropped out—dates were automatically cancelled.

The helpless part of trying to do anything about it was that she did it all herself. She was not a girl who could be "won" in the kinetic sense—she was proof against cleverness, she was proof against charm; if any of these assailed her too strongly she would immediately resolve the affair to a physical basis, and under the magic of her physical splendor the strong as well as the brilliant played her game and not their own. She was entertained only by the gratification of her desires and by the direct exercise of her own charm. Perhaps from so much youthful love, so many youthful lovers, she had come, in self-defense, to nourish herself wholly from within.

Succeeding Dexter's first exhilaration came restlessness and dissatisfaction. The helpless ecstasy of losing himself in her was opiate rather than tonic. It was fortunate for his work during the winter that those moments of ecstasy came infrequently. Early in their acquaintance it had seemed for a while that there was a deep and spontaneous mutual attraction —that first· August, for example—three days of long evenings on her dusky veranda, of strange wan kisses through the late afternoon, in shadowy alcoves or behind the protecting trellises of the garden arbors, of mornings when she was fresh as a dream and almost shy at meeting him in the clarity of the rising day. There was all the ecstasy of an engagement about it, sharpened by his realization that there was no engagement. It was during those three days that, for the first time, he had asked her to marry him. She said "maybe some day," she said "kiss me," she said "I'd like to marry you," she said "I love you"—she said— nothing.

The three days were interrupted by the arrival of a New York man who visited at her house for half September. To Dexter's agony, rumor engaged them. The man was the son of the president of a great trust company. But at the end of a month it was reported that Judy was yawning. At a dance one night she sat all evening in a motor-boat with a local beau, while the New Yorker searched the club for her frantically. She told the local beau that she was bored with her visitor, and two days later he left. She was seen with him at the station, and it was reported that he looked very mournful indeed.

On this note the summer ended. Dexter was twenty-four, and he found himself increasingly in a position to do as he wished. He joined two clubs in the city and lived at one of them. Though he was by no means an integral part of the stag-lines at these clubs, he managed to be on hand at dances where Judy Jones was likely to appear. He could have gone out socially as much as he liked—he was an eligible young man, now, and popular with down-town fathers. His confessed devotion to Judy Jones had rather solidified his position. But he had no social

aspirations and rather despised the dancing men who were always on tap for the Thursday or Saturday parties and who filled in at dinners with the younger married set. Already he was playing with the idea of going East to New York. He wanted to take Judy Jones with him. No disillusion as to the world in which she had grown up could cure his illusion as to her desirability.

Remember that—for only in the light of it can what he did for her be understood.

Eighteen months after he first met Judy Jones he became engaged to another girl. Her name was Irene Scheerer, and her father was one of the men who had always believed in Dexter. Irene was light-haired and sweet and honorable, and a little stout, and she had two suitors whom she pleasantly relinquished when Dexter formally asked her to marry him.

Summer, fall, winter, spring, another summer, another fall—so much he had given of his active life to the incorrigible lips of Judy Jones. She had treated him with interest, with encouragement, with malice, with indifference, with contempt. She had inflicted on him the innumerable little slights and indignities possible in such a case—as if in revenge for having ever cared for him at all. She had beckoned him and yawned at him and beckoned him again and he had responded often with bitterness and narrowed eyes. She had brought him ecstatic happiness and intolerable agony of spirit. She had caused him untold inconvenience and not a little trouble. She had insulted him, and she had ridden over him, and she had played his interest in her against his interest in his work—for fun. She had done everything to him except to criticise him—this she had not done—it seemed to him only because it might have sullied the utter indifference she manifested and sincerely felt toward him.

When autumn had come and gone again it occurred to him that he could not have Judy Jones. He had to beat this into his mind but he convinced himself at last. He lay awake at night for a while and argued it over. He told himself the trouble and the pain she had caused him, he enumerated her glaring deficiencies as a wife. Then he said to himself that he loved her, and after a while he fell asleep. For a week, lest he imagined her husky voice over the telephone or her eyes opposite him at lunch, he worked hard and late, and at night he went to his office and plotted out his years.

At the end of a week he went to a dance and cut in on her once. For almost the first time since they had met he did not ask her to sit out with him or tell her that she was lovely. It hurt him that she did not miss these things— that was all. He was not jealous when he saw that there was a new man tonight. He had been hardened against jealousy long before.

He stayed late at the dance. He sat for an hour with Irene Scheerer and talked about books and about music. He knew very little about either. But he was beginning to be master of his own time now, and he had a rather priggish notion that he—the young and already fabulously successful Dexter Green— should know more about such things.

That was in October, when he was twenty-five. In January, Dexter and Irene became engaged. It was to be announced in June, and they were to be married three months later.

The Minnesota winter prolonged itself interminably, and it was almost May when the winds came soft and the snow ran down into Black Bear Lake at last. For the first time in over a year Dexter was enjoying a certain tranquility of spirit. Judy Jones had been in Florida, and afterward in Hot Springs, and somewhere she had been engaged, and somewhere she had broken it off. At first, when Dexter had definitely given her up, it had made him sad that people still linked them together and asked for news of her, but when he began to be placed at dinner next to Irene Scheerer people didn't ask him about her any more—they told him about her. He ceased to be an authority on her.

May at last. Dexter walked the streets at night when the darkness was damp as rain, wondering that so soon, with so little done, so much of ecstasy had gone from him. May one year back had been marked by Judy's poignant, unforgivable, yet forgiven turbulence—it had been one of those rare times when he fancied she had grown to care for him. That old penny's worth of happiness he had spent for this bushel of content. He knew that Irene would be no more than a curtain spread behind him, a hand moving among gleaming teacups, a voice calling to children . . . fire and loveliness were gone, the magic of nights and the wonder of the varying hours and seasons . . . slender lips, down-turning, dropping to his lips and bearing him up into a heaven of eyes. . . . The thing was deep in him. He was too strong and alive for it to die lightly.

In the middle of May when the weather balanced for a few days on the thin bridge that led to deep summer he turned in one night at Irene's house. Their engagement was to be announced in a week now—no one would be surprised at it. And to-night they would sit together on the lounge at the University Club and look on for an hour at the dancers. It gave him a sense of solidity to go with her—she was so sturdily popular, so intensely "great."

He mounted the steps of the brownstone house and stepped inside.

"Irene," he called.

Mrs. Scheerer came out of the livingroom to meet him.

"Dexter," she said, "Irene's gone upstairs with a splitting headache. She wanted to go with you but I made her go to bed."

"Nothing serious, I——"

"Oh, no. She's going to play golf with you in the morning. You can spare her for just one night, can't you, Dexter?"

Her smile was kind. She and Dexter liked each other. In the livingroom he talked for a moment before he said goodnight.

Returning to the University Club, where he had rooms, he stood in the doorway for a moment and watched the dancers. He leaned against the door-post, nodded at a man or two—yawned.

"Hello, darling."

The familiar voice at his elbow startled

him. Judy Jones had left a man and crossed the room to him—Judy Jones, a slender enamelled doll in cloth of gold: gold in a band at her head, gold in two slipper points at her dress's hem. The fragile glow of her face seemed to blossom as she smiled at him. A breeze of warmth and light blew through the room. His hands in the pockets of his dinner-jacket tightened spasmodically. He was filled with a sudden excitement.

"When did you get back?" he asked casually.

"Come here and I'll tell you about it."

She turned and he followed her. She had been away—he could have wept at the wonder of her return. She had passed through enchanted streets, doing things that were like provocative music. All mysterious happenings, all fresh and quickening hopes, had gone away with her, come back with her now.

She turned in the doorway.

"Have you a car here? If you haven't, I have."

"I have a coupé."

In then, with a rustle of golden cloth. He slammed the door. Into so many cars she had stepped—like this—like that— her back against the leather, so—her elbow resting on the door—waiting. She would have been soiled long since had there been anything to soil her—except herself—but this was her own self outpouring.

With an effort he forced himself to start the car and back into the street. This was nothing, he must remember. She had done this before, and he had put her behind him, as he would have crossed a bad account from his books.

He drove slowly down-town and, affecting abstraction, traversed the deserted streets of the business section, peopled here and there where a movie was giving out its crowd or where consumptive or pugilistic youth lounged in front of pool halls. The clink of glasses and the slap of hands on the bars issued from saloons, cloisters of glazed glass and dirty yellow light.

She was watching him closely and the silence was embarrassing, yet in this crisis he could find no casual word with which to profane the hour. At a convenient turning he began to zigzag back toward the University Club.

"Have you missed me?" she asked suddenly.

"Everybody missed you."

He wondered if she knew of Irene Scheerer. She had been back only a day —her absence had been almost contemporaneous with his engagement.

"What a remark!" Judy laughed sadly —without sadness. She looked at him searchingly. He became absorbed in the dashboard.

"You're handsomer than you used to be," she said thoughtfully. "Dexter, you have the most rememberable eyes."

He could have laughed at this, but he did not laugh. It was the sort of thing that was said to sophomores. Yet it stabbed at him.

"I'm awfully tired of everything, darling." She called every one darling, endowing the endearment with careless, individual camaraderie. "I wish you'd marry me."

The directness of this confused him. He should have told her now that he was going to marry another girl, but he could not tell her. He could as easily have sworn that he had never loved her.

"I think we'd get along," she continued, on the same note, "unless probably you've forgotten me and fallen in love with another girl."

Her confidence was obviously enormous. She had said, in effect, that she found such a thing impossible to believe, that if it were true he had merely committed a childish indiscretion—and probably to show off. She would forgive him, because it was not a matter of any moment but rather something to be brushed aside lightly.

"Of course you could never love anybody but me," she continued, "I like the way you love me. Oh, Dexter, have you forgotten last year?"

"No, I haven't forgotten."

"Neither have I!"

Was she sincerely moved—or was she carried along by the wave of her own acting?

"I wish we could be like that again,"

she said, and he forced himself to answer:

"I don't think we can."

"I suppose not. . . . I hear you're giving Irene Scheerer a violent rush."

There was not the faintest emphasis on the name, yet Dexter was suddenly ashamed.

"Oh, take me home," cried Judy suddenly; "I don't want to go back to that idiotic dance—with those children."

Then, as he turned up the street that led to the residence district, Judy began to cry quietly to herself. He had never seen her cry before.

The dark street lightened, the dwellings of the rich loomed up around them, he stopped his coupé in front of the great white bulk of the Mortimer Joneses' house, somnolent, gorgeous, drenched with the splendor of the damp moonlight. Its solidity startled him. The strong walls, the steel of the girders, the breadth and beam and pomp of it were there only to bring out the contrast with the young beauty beside him. It was sturdy to accentuate her slightness—as if to show what a breeze could be generated by a butterfly's wing.

He sat perfectly quiet, his nerves in wild clamor, afraid that if he moved he would find her irresistibly in his arms. Two tears had rolled down her wet face and trembled on her upper lip.

"I'm more beautiful than anybody else," she said brokenly, "why can't I be happy?" Her moist eyes tore at his stability—her mouth turned slowly downward with an exquisite sadness: "I'd like to marry you if you'll have me, Dexter. I suppose you think I'm not worth having, but I'll be so beautiful for you, Dexter."

A million phrases of anger, pride, passion, hatred, tenderness fought on his lips. Then a perfect wave of emotion washed over him, carrying off with it a sediment of wisdom, of convention, of doubt, of honor. This was his girl who was speaking, his own, his beautiful, his pride.

"Won't you come in?" He heard her draw in her breath sharply.

Waiting.

"All right," his voice was trembling, "I'll come in."

V

It was strange that neither when it was over nor a long time afterward did he regret that night. Looking at it from the perspective of ten years, the fact that Judy's flare for him endured just one month seemed of little importance. Nor did it matter that by his yielding he subjected himself to a deeper agony in the end and gave serious hurt to Irene Scheerer and to Irene's parents, who had befriended him. There was nothing sufficiently pictorial about Irene's grief to stamp itself on his mind.

Dexter was at bottom hard-minded. The attitude of the city on his action was of no importance to him, not because he was going to leave the city, but because any outside attitude on the situation seemed superficial. He was completely indifferent to popular opinion. Nor, when he had seen that it was no use, that he did not possess in himself the power to move fundamentally or to hold Judy Jones, did he bear any malice toward her. He loved her, and he would love her until the day he was too old for loving—but he could not have her. So he tasted the deep pain that is reserved only for the strong, just as he had tasted for a little while the deep happiness.

Even the ultimate falsity of the grounds upon which Judy terminated the engagement that she did not want to "take him away" from Irene—Judy who had wanted nothing else—did not revolt him. He was beyond any revulsion or any amusement.

He went East in February with the intention of selling out his laundries and settling in New York—but the war came to America in March and changed his plans. He returned to the West, handed over the management of the business to his partner, and went into the first officers' training-camp in late April. He was one of those young thousands who greeted the war with a certain amount of relief, welcoming the liberation from webs of tangled emotion.

VI

This story is not his biography, remember, although things creep into it which have nothing to do with those dreams he had when he was young. We are almost done with them and with him now. There is only one more incident to be related here, and it happens seven years farther on.

It took place in New York, where he had done well—so well that there were no barriers too high for him. He was thirty-two years old, and, except for one flying trip immediately after the war, he had not been West in seven years. A man named Devlin from Detroit came into his office to see him in a business way, and then and there this incident occurred, and closed out, so to speak, this particular side of his life.

"So you're from the Middle West," said the man Devlin with careless curiosity. "That's funny—I thought men like you were probably born and raised on Wall Street. You know—wife of one of my best friends in Detroit came from your city. I was an usher at the wedding."

Dexter waited with no apprehension of what was coming.

"Judy Simms," said Devlin with no particular interest; "Judy Jones she was once."

"Yes, I knew her." A dull impatience spread over him. He had heard, of course, that she was married—perhaps deliberately he had heard no more.

"Awfully nice girl," brooded Devlin meaninglessly, "I'm sort of sorry for her."

"Why?" Something in Dexter was alert, receptive, at once.

"Oh, Lud Simms has gone to pieces in a way. I don't mean he ill-uses her, but he drinks and runs around——"

"Doesn't she run around?"

"No. Stays at home with her kids."

"Oh."

"She's a little too old for him," said Devlin.

"Too old!" cried Dexter. "Why, man, she's only twenty-seven."

He was possessed with a wild notion of rushing out into the streets and taking a train to Detroit. He rose to his feet spasmodically.

"I guess you're busy," Devlin apologized quickly. "I didn't realize——"

"No, I'm not busy," said Dexter, steadying his voice. "I'm not busy at all. Not busy at all. Did you say she was—twenty-seven? No, I said she was twenty-seven."

"Yes, you did," agreed Devlin dryly.

"Go on, then. Go on."

"What do you mean?"

"About Judy Jones."

Devlin looked at him helplessly.

"Well, that's—I told you all there is to it. He treats her like the devil. Oh, they're not going to get divorced or anything. When he's particularly outrageous she forgives him. In fact, I'm inclined to think she loves him. She was a pretty girl when she first came to Detroit."

A pretty girl! The phrase struck Dexter as ludicrous.

"Isn't she—a pretty girl, any more?"

"Oh, she's all right."

"Look here," said Dexter, sitting down suddenly. "I don't understand. You say she was a 'pretty girl' and now you say she's 'all right.' I don't understand what you mean—Judy Jones wasn't a pretty girl, at all. She was a great beauty. Why, I knew her, I knew her. She was——"

Devlin laughed pleasantly.

"I'm not trying to start a row," he said. "I think Judy's a nice girl and I like her. I can't understand how a man like Lud Simms could fall madly in love with her, but he did." Then he added: "Most of the women like her."

Dexter looked closely at Devlin, thinking wildly that there must be a reason for this, some insensitivity in the man or some private malice.

"Lots of women fade just like *that*," Devlin snapped his fingers. "You must have seen it happen. Perhaps I've forgotten how pretty she was at her wedding. I've seen her so much since then, you see. She has nice eyes."

A sort of dullness settled down upon Dexter. For the first time in his life he felt like getting very drunk. He knew that he was laughing loudly at something Devlin had said, but he did not know what it was or why it was funny. When, in a few minutes, Devlin went he lay down on his lounge and looked out the window at the New York sky-line into which the sun was sinking in dull lovely shades of pink and gold.

He had thought that having nothing else to lose he was invulnerable at last—but he knew that he had just lost something more, as surely as if he had married Judy Jones and seen her fade away before his eyes.

The dream was gone. Something had been taken from him. In a sort of panic he pushed the palms of his hands into his eyes and tried to bring up a picture of the waters lapping on Sherry Island and the moonlit veranda, and gingham on the golf-links and the dry sun and the gold color of her neck's soft down. And her mouth damp to his kisses and her eyes plaintive with melancholy and her freshness like new fine linen in the morning. Why, these things were no longer in the world! They had existed and they existed no longer.

For the first time in years the tears were streaming down his face. But they were for himself now. He did not care about mouth and eyes and moving hands. He wanted to care, and he could not care. For he had gone away and he could never go back any more. The gates were closed, the sun was gone down, and there was no beauty but the gray beauty of steel that withstands all time. Even the grief he could have borne was left behind in the country of illusion, of youth, of the richness of life, where his winter dreams had flourished.

"Long ago," he said, "long ago, there was something in me, but now that thing is gone. Now that thing is gone, that thing is gone. I cannot cry. I cannot care. That thing will come back no more."

[1922]

QUESTIONS FOR STUDY

1. *What are Dexter's "winter dreams"? How does he set about to realize them? How do they relate to his love for Judy Jones?*

2. *Each of the story's six episodes dramatizes a different stage in Dexter Green's development. What changes take place? What remains essentially the same?*

3. *Why does Dexter react so emotionally to the news about Judy that he learns from the man from Detroit? What precisely is the nature of Dexter's loss? What does he discover about his "winter dreams" and about himself?*

4. *How would you describe the story's chosen point of view? In what ways is it appropriate?*

5. *What comment does the story make about the rich? What comment does it offer about American society at large?*

E. M. FORSTER

The Celestial Omnibus

THE BOY who resided at Agathox Lodge, 28, Buckingham Park Road, Surbiton, had often been puzzled by the old sign-post that stood almost opposite. He asked his mother about it, and she replied that it was a joke, and not a very nice one, which had been made many years back by some naughty young men, and that the police ought to remove it. For there were two strange things about this sign-post: firstly, it pointed up a blank alley, and, secondly, it had painted on it, in faded characters, the words, "To Heaven."

"What kind of young men were they?" he asked.

"I think your father told me that one of them wrote verses, and was expelled from the University and came to grief in other ways. Still, it was a long time ago. You must ask your father about it. He will say the same as I do, that it was put up as a joke."

"So it doesn't mean anything at all?"

She sent him up-stairs to put on his best things, for the Bonses were coming to tea, and he was to hand the cake-stand.

It struck him, as he wrenched on his tightening trousers, that he might do worse than ask Mr. Bons about the sign-post. His father, though very kind, always laughed at him—shrieked with laughter whenever he or any other child asked a question or spoke. But Mr. Bons was serious as well as kind. He had a beautiful house and lent one books, he was a churchwarden, and a candidate for the County Council; he had donated to the Free Library enormously, he presided over the Literary Society, and had Members of Parliament to stop with him—in short, he was probably the wisest person alive.

Yet even Mr. Bons could only say that

the sign-post was a joke—the joke of a person named Shelley.

"Of course!" cried the mother; "I told you so, dear. That was the name."

"Had you never heard of Shelley?" asked Mr. Bons.

"No," said the boy, and hung his head.

"But is there no Shelley in the house?"

"Why, yes!" exclaimed the lady, in much agitation. "Dear Mr. Bons, we aren't such Philistines as that. Two at the least. One a wedding present, and the other, smaller print, in one of the spare rooms."

"I believe we have seven Shelleys," said Mr. Bons, with a slow smile. Then he brushed the cake crumbs off his stomach, and, together with his daughter, rose to go.

The boy, obeying a wink from his mother, saw them all the way to the garden gate, and when they had gone he did not at once return to the house, but gazed for a little up and down Buckingham Park Road.

His parents lived at the right end of it. After No. 39 the quality of the houses dropped very suddenly, and 64 had not even a separate servants' entrance. But at the present moment the whole road looked rather pretty, for the sun had just set in splendour, and the inequalities of rent were drowned in a saffron afterglow. Small birds twittered, and the bread-winners' train shrieked musically down through the cutting—that wonderful cutting which has drawn to itself the whole beauty out of Surbiton, and clad itself, like any Alpine valley, with the glory of the fir and the silver birch and the primrose. It was this cutting that had first stirred desires within the boy—desires for something just a little different, he knew not what, desires that would return when-

Published 1947 by Alfred A. Knopf, Inc. From *The Collected Tales of E. M. Forster*. Reprinted by permission of the publisher. Also by permission of Sidgwick & Jackson Ltd., London.

ever things were sunlit, as they were this evening, running up and down inside him, up and down, up and down, till he would feel quite unusual all over, and as likely as not would want to cry. This evening he was even sillier, for he slipped across the road towards the sign-post and began to run up the blank alley.

The alley runs between high walls— the walls of the gardens of "Ivanhoe" and "Belle Vista" respectively. It smells a little all the way, and is scarcely twenty yards long, including the turn at the end. So not unnaturally the boy soon came to a standstill. "I'd like to kick that Shelley," he exclaimed, and glanced idly at a piece of paper which was pasted on the wall. Rather an odd piece of paper, and he read it carefully before he turned back. This is what he read:

S. AND C. R. C. C.

Alteration in Service.

Owing to lack of patronage the Company are regretfully compelled to suspend the hourly service, and to retain only the

Sunrise and Sunset Omnibuses,

which will run as usual. It is to be hoped that the public will patronize an arrangement which is intended for their convenience. As an extra inducement, the Company will, for the first time, now issue

Return Tickets!

(available one day only), which may be obtained of the driver. Passengers are again reminded that *no tickets are issued at the other end*, and that no complaints in this connection will receive consideration from the Company. Nor will the Company be responsible for any negligence or stupidity on the part of Passengers, nor for Hailstorms, Lightning, Loss of Tickets, nor for any Act of God.

For the Direction

Now he had never seen this notice before, nor could he imagine where the omnibus went to. S. of course was for Surbiton, and R.C.C. meant Road Car Company. But what was the meaning of the other C.? Coombe and Malden, perhaps, or possibly "City." Yet it could not hope to compete with the South-Western. The whole thing, the boy reflected, was

run on hopelessly unbusiness-like lines. Why no tickets from the other end? And what an hour to start! Then he realized that unless the notice was a hoax, an omnibus must have been starting just as he was wishing the Bonses good-bye. He peered at the ground through the gathering dusk, and there he saw what might or might not be the marks of wheels. Yet nothing had come out of the alley. And he had never seen an omnibus at any time in the Buckingham Park Road. No: it must be a hoax, like the sign-posts, like the fairy tales, like the dreams upon which he would wake suddenly in the night. And with a sigh he stepped from the alley—right into the arms of his father.

Oh, how his father laughed! "Poor, poor Popsey!" he cried. "Diddums! Diddums! Diddums think he'd walky-palky up to Evvink!" And his mother, also convulsed with laughter, appeared on the steps of Agathox Lodge. "Don't Bob!" she gasped. "Don't be so naughty! Oh, you'll kill me! Oh, leave the boy alone!"

But all the evening the joke was kept up. The father implored to be taken too. Was it a very tiring walk? Need one wipe one's shoes on the door-mat? And the boy went to bed feeling faint and sore, and thankful for only one thing—that he had not said a word about the omnibus. It was a hoax, yet through his dreams it grew more and more real, and the streets of Surbiton, through which he saw it driving, seemed instead to become hoaxes and shadows. And very early in the morning he woke with a cry, for he had had a glimpse of its destination.

He struck a match, and its light fell not only on his watch but also on his calendar, so that he knew it to be half-an-hour to sunrise. It was pitch dark, for the fog had come down from London in the night, and all Surbiton was wrapped in its embraces. Yet he sprang out and dressed himself, for he was determined to settle once for all which was real: the omnibus or the streets. "I shall be a fool one way or the other," he thought, "until I know." Soon he was shivering in the road under the gas lamp that guarded the entrance to the alley.

To enter the alley itself required some courage. Not only was it horribly dark, but he now realized that it was an impossible terminus for an omnibus. If it had not been for a policeman, whom he heard approaching through the fog, he would never have made the attempt. The next moment he had made the attempt and failed. Nothing. Nothing but a blank alley and a very silly boy gaping at its dirty floor. It *was* a hoax. "I'll tell papa and mamma," he decided. "I deserve it. I deserve that they should know. I am too silly to be alive." And he went back to the gate of Agathox Lodge.

There he remembered that his watch was fast. The sun was not risen; it would not rise for two minutes. "Give the bus every chance," he thought cynically, and returned into the alley.

But the omnibus was there.

II

It had two horses, whose sides were still smoking from their journey, and its two great lamps shone through the fog against the alley's walls, changing their cobwebs and moss into tissues of fairyland. The driver was huddled up in a cape. He faced the blank wall, and how he had managed to drive in so neatly and so silently was one of the many things that the boy never discovered. Nor could he imagine how ever he would drive out.

"Please," his voice quavered through the foul brown air, "Please, is that an omnibus?"

"Omnibus est," said the driver, without turning round. There was a moment's silence. The policeman passed, coughing, by the entrance of the alley. The boy crouched in the shadow, for he did not want to be found out. He was pretty sure, too, that it was a Pirate; nothing else, he reasoned, would go from such odd places and at such odd hours.

"About when do you start?" He tried to sound nonchalant.

"At sunrise."

"How far do you go?"

"The whole way."

"And can I have a return ticket which will bring me all the way back?"

"You can."

"Do you know, I half think I'll come." The driver made no answer. The sun must have risen, for he unhitched the brake. And scarcely had the boy jumped in before the omnibus was off.

How? Did it turn? There was no room. Did it go forward? There was a blank wall. Yet it was moving—moving at a stately pace through the fog, which had turned from brown to yellow. The thought of warm bed and warmer breakfast made the boy feel faint. He wished he had not come. His parents would not have approved. He would have gone back to them if the weather had not made it impossible. The solitude was terrible; he was the only passenger. And the omnibus, though well-built, was cold and somewhat musty. He drew his coat round him, and in so doing chanced to feel his pocket. It was empty. He had forgotten his purse.

"Stop!" he shouted. "Stop!" And then, being of a polite disposition, he glanced up at the painted notice-board so that he might call the driver by name. "Mr. Browne! stop; O, do please stop!"

Mr. Browne did not stop, but he opened a little window, and looked in at the boy. His face was a surprise, so kind it was and modest.

"Mr. Browne, I've left my purse behind. I've not got a penny. I can't pay for the ticket. Will you take my watch, please? I am in the most awful hole."

"Tickets on this line," said the driver, "whether single or return, can be purchased by coinage from no terrene mint. And a chronometer, though it had solaced the vigils of Charlemagne, or measured the slumbers of Laura, can acquire by no mutation the double-cake that charms the fangless Cerberus of Heaven!" So saying, he handed in the necessary ticket, and, while the boy said "Thank you," continued: "Titular pretensions, I know it well, are vanity. Yet they merit no censure when uttered on a laughing lip, and in an homonymous world are in some sort useful, since they do serve to distinguish one Jack from his fellow. Remember me, therefore, as Sir Thomas Browne."

"Are you a Sir? Oh, sorry!" He had heard of these gentlemen drivers. "It *is* good of you about the ticket. But if you go on at this rate, however does your bus pay?"

"It does not pay. It was not intended to pay. Many are the faults of my equipage; it is compounded too curiously of foreign woods; its cushions tickle erudition rather than promote repose; and my horses are nourished not on the evergreen pastures of the moment, but on the dried bents and clovers of Latinity. But that it pays!—that error at all events was never intended and never attained."

"Sorry again," said the boy rather hopelessly. Sir Thomas looked sad, fearing that, even for a moment, he had been the cause of sadness. He invited the boy to come up and sit beside him on the box, and together they journeyed on through the fog, which was now changing from yellow to white. There were no houses by the road; so it must be either Putney Heath or Wimbledon Common.

"Have you been a driver always?"

"I was a physician once."

"But why did you stop? Weren't you good?"

"As a healer of bodies I had scant success, and several score of my patients preceded me. But as a healer of the spirit I have succeeded beyond my hopes and my deserts. For though my draughts were not better nor subtler than those of other men, yet, by reason of the cunning goblets wherein I offered them, the queasy soul was ofttimes tempted to sip and be refreshed."

"The queasy soul," he murmured; "if the sun sets with trees in front of it, and you suddenly come strange all over, is that a queasy soul?"

"Have you felt that?"

"Why yes."

After a pause he told the boy a little, a very little, about the journey's end. But they did not chatter much, for the boy, when he liked a person, would as soon sit silent in his company as speak, and this, he discovered, was also the mind of Sir Thomas Browne and of many others with whom he was to be acquainted. He heard, however, about the young man Shelley, who was now quite a famous person, with a carriage of his own, and about some of the other drivers who are in the service of the Company. Meanwhile the light grew stronger, though the fog did not disperse. It was now more like mist than fog, and at times would travel quickly across them, as if it was part of a cloud. They had been ascending, too, in a most puzzling way; for over two hours the horses had been pulling against the collar, and even if it were Richmond Hill they ought to have been at the top long ago. Perhaps it was Epsom, or even the North Downs; yet the air seemed keener than that which blows on either. And as to the name of their destination, Sir Thomas Browne was silent.

Crash!

"Thunder, by Jove!" said the boy, "and not so far off either. Listen to the echoes! It's more like mountains."

He thought, not very vividly, of his father and mother. He saw them sitting down to sausages and listening to the storm. He saw his own empty place. Then there would be questions, alarms, theories, jokes, consolations. They would expect him back at lunch. To lunch he would not come, nor tea, but he would be in for dinner, and so his day's truancy would be over. If he had had his purse he would have bought them presents—not that he should have known what to get them.

Crash!

The peal and the lightning came together. The cloud quivered as if it were alive, and torn streamers of mist rushed past. "Are you afraid?" asked Sir Thomas Browne.

"What is there to be afraid of? Is it much farther?"

The horses of the omnibus stopped just as a ball of fire burst up and exploded with a ringing noise that was deafening but clear, like the noise of a blacksmith's forge. All the cloud was shattered.

"Oh, listen, Sir Thomas Browne! No, I mean look; we shall get a view at last. No, I mean listen; that sounds like a rainbow!"

The noise had died into the faintest murmur, beneath which another murmur grew, spreading stealthily, steadily, in a curve that widened but did not vary. And in widening curves a rainbow was spreading from the horses' feet into the dissolving mists.

"But how beautiful! What colours! Where will it stop? It is more like the rainbows you can tread on. More like dreams."

The colour and the sound grew together. The rainbow spanned an enormous gulf. Clouds rushed under it and were pierced by it, and still it grew, reaching forward, conquering the darkness, until it touched something that seemed more solid than a cloud.

The boy stood up "What is that out there?" he called. "What does it rest on, out at that other end?"

In the morning sunshine a precipice shone forth beyond the gulf. A precipice —or was it a castle? The horses moved. They set their feet upon the rainbow.

"Oh, look!" the boy shouted. "Oh, listen! Those caves—or are they gateways? Oh, look between those cliffs at those ledges. I see people! I see trees!"

"Look also below," whispered Sir Thomas. "Neglect not the diviner Acheron."

The boy looked below, past the flames of the rainbow that licked against their wheels. The gulf also had cleared, and in its depths there flowed an everlasting river. One sunbeam entered and struck a green pool, and as they passed over he saw three maidens rise to the surface of the pool, singing, and playing with something that glistened like a ring.

"You down in the water——" he called.

They answered, "You up on the bridge——" There was a burst of music. "You up on the bridge, good luck to you. Truth in the depth, truth on the height."

"You down in the water, what are you doing?"

Sir Thomas Browne replied: "They sport in the manciipary possession of their gold"; and the omnibus arrived.

III

The boy was in disgrace. He sat locked up in the nursery of Agathox Lodge, learning poetry for a punishment. His father had said, "My boy! I can pardon anything but untruthfulness," and had

caned him, saying at each stroke, "There is *no* omnibus, *no* driver, *no* bridge, *no* mountain; you are a *truant*, a *gutter snipe*, a *liar*." His father could be very stern at times. His mother had begged him to say he was sorry. But he could not say that. It was the greatest day of his life, in spite of the caning and the poetry at the end of it.

He had returned punctually at sunset —driven not by Sir Thomas Browne, but by a maiden lady who was full of quiet fun. They had talked of omnibuses and also of barouche landaus. How far away her gentle voice seemed now! Yet it was scarcely three hours since he had left her up the alley.

His mother called through the door. "Dear, you are to come down and to bring your poetry with you."

He came down, and found that Mr. Bons was in the smoking-room with his father. It had been a dinner party.

"Here is the great traveller!" said his father grimly. "Here is the young gentleman who drives in an omnibus over rainbows, while young ladies sing to him." Pleased with his wit, he laughed.

"After all," said Mr. Bons, smiling, "there is something a little like it in Wagner. It is odd how, in quite illiterate minds, you will find glimmers of Artistic Truth. The case interests me. Let me plead for the culprit. We have all romanced in our time, haven't we?"

"Hear how kind Mr. Bons is," said his mother, while his father said, "Very well. Let him say his Poem, and that will do. He is going away to my sister on Tuesday, and *she* will cure him of this alley-slopering." (Laughter.) "Say your Poem."

The boy began. " 'Standing aloof in giant ignorance.' "

His father laughed again—roared. "One for you, my son! 'Standing aloof in giant ignorance!' I never knew these poets talked sense. Just describes you. Here, Bons, you go in for poetry. Put him through it, will you, while I fetch up the whisky?"

"Yes, give me the Keats," said Mr. Bons. "Let him say his Keats to me."

So for a few moments the wise man and the ignorant boy were left alone in the smoking-room.

" 'Standing aloof in giant ignorance, of thee I dream and of the Cyclades, as one who sits ashore and longs perchance to visit——' "

"Quite right. To visit what?"

" 'To visit dolphin coral in deep seas,' " said the boy, and burst into tears.

"Come, come! why do you cry?"

"Because—because all these words that only rhymed before, now that I've come back they're me."

Mr. Bons laid the Keats down. The case was more interesting than he had expected. *"You?"* he exclaimed. "This sonnet, *you?"*

"Yes—and look further on: 'Aye, on the shores of darkness there is light, and precipices show untrodden green.' It *is* so, sir. All these things are true."

"I never doubted it," said Mr. Bons, with closed eyes.

"You—then you believe me? You believe in the omnibus and the driver and the storm and that return ticket I got for nothing and——"

"Tut, tut! No more of your yarns, my boy. I meant that I never doubted the essential truth of Poetry. Some day, when you have read more, you will understand what I mean."

"But Mr. Bons, it *is* so. There *is* light upon the shores of darkness. I have seen it coming. Light and a wind."

"Nonsense," said Mr. Bons.

"If I had stopped! They tempted me. They told me to give up my ticket—for you cannot come back if you lose your ticket. They called from the river for it, and indeed I was tempted, for I have never been so happy as among those precipices. But I thought of my mother and father, and that I must fetch them. Yet they will not come, though the road starts opposite our house. It has all happened as the people up there warned me, and Mr. Bons has disbelieved me like every one else. I have been caned. I shall never see that mountain again."

"What's that about me?" said Mr. Bons, sitting up in his chair very suddenly.

"I told them about you, and how clever you were, and how many books you had, and they said, 'Mr. Bons will certainly disbelieve you.' "

"Stuff and nonsense, my young friend. You grow impertinent. I—well—I will settle the matter. Not a word to your father. I will cure you. To-morrow evening I will myself call here to take you for a walk, and at sunset we will go up this alley opposite and hunt for your omnibus, you silly little boy."

His face grew serious, for the boy was not disconcerted, but leapt about the room singing, "Joy! joy! I told them you would believe me. We will drive together over the rainbow. I told them that you would come." After all, could there be anything in the story? Wagner? Keats? Shelley? Sir Thomas Browne? Certainly the case was interesting.

And on the morrow evening, though it was pouring with rain, Mr. Bons did not omit to call at Agathox Lodge.

The boy was ready, bubbling with excitement, and skipping about in a way that rather vexed the President of the Literary Society. They took a turn down Buckingham Park Road, and then—having seen that no one was watching them—slipped up the alley. Naturally enough (for the sun was setting) they ran straight against the omnibus.

"Good heavens!" exclaimed Mr. Bons. "Good gracious heavens!"

It was not the omnibus in which the boy had driven first, nor yet that in which he had returned. There were three horses —black, gray, and white, the gray being the finest. The driver, who turned round at the mention of goodness and of heaven, was a sallow man with terrifying jaws and sunken eyes. Mr. Bons, on seeing him, gave a cry as if of recognition, and began to tremble violently.

The boy jumped in.

"Is it possible?" cried Mr. Bons. "Is the impossible possible?"

"Sir; come in, sir. It is such a fine omnibus. Oh, here is his name—Dan some one."

Mr. Bons sprang in too. A blast of wind immediately slammed the omnibus door, and the shock jerked down all the omnibus blinds, which were very weak on their springs.

"Dan . . . Show me. Good gracious heavens! we're moving."

"Hooray!" said the boy.

Mr. Bons became flustered. He had not intended to be kidnapped. He could not find the door-handle, nor push up the blinds. The omnibus was quite dark, and by the time he had struck a match, night had come on outside also. They were moving rapidly.

"A strange, a memorable adventure," he said, surveying the interior of the omnibus, which was large, roomy, and constructed with extreme regularity, every part exactly answering to every other part. Over the door (the handle of which was outside) was written, "Lasciate ogni baldanza voi che entrate" [1]—at least, that was what was written, but Mr. Bons said that it was Lashy arty something, and that baldanza was a mistake for speranza.[2] His voice sounded as if he was in church. Meanwhile, the boy called to the cadaverous driver for two return tickets. They were handed in without a word. Mr. Bons covered his face with his hands and again trembled. "Do you know who that is!" he whispered, when the little window had shut upon them. "It is the impossible."

"Well, I don't like him as much as Sir Thomas Browne, though I shouldn't be surprised if he had even more in him."

"More in him?" He stamped irritably. "By accident you have made the greatest discovery of the century, and all you can say is that there is more in this man. Do you remember those vellum books in my library, stamped with red lilies, This—*sit still, I bring you stupendous news!—this is the man who wrote them.*"

The boy sat quite still. "I wonder if we shall see Mrs. Gamp?" he asked, after a civil pause.

"Mrs.——?"

"Mrs. Gamp and Mrs. Harris. I like Mrs. Harris. I came upon them quite suddenly. Mrs. Gamp's bandboxes have moved over the rainbow so badly. All the bottoms have fallen out, and two of the pippins off her bedstead tumbled into the stream."

"Out there sits the man who wrote my vellum books!" thundered Mr. Bons,

1 "Abandon all pride, ye who enter here." (JHP)
2 "hope." (JHP)

"and you talk to me of Dickens and of Mrs. Gamp?"

"I know Mrs. Gamp so well," he apologized. "I could not help being glad to see her. I recognized her voice. She was telling Mrs. Harris about Mrs. Prig."

"Did you spend the whole day in her elevating company?"

"Oh, no. I raced. I met a man who took me out beyond to a race-course. You run, and there are dolphins out at sea."

"Indeed. Do you remember the man's name?"

"Achilles. No; he was later. Tom Jones."

Mr. Bons sighed heavily. "Well, my lad, you have made a miserable mess of it. Think of a cultured person with your opportunities! A cultured person would have known all these characters and known what to have said to each. He would not have wasted his time with a Mrs. Gamp or a Tom Jones. The creations of Homer, of Shakespeare, and of Him who drives us now, would alone have contented him. He would not have raced. He would have asked intelligent questions."

"But, Mr. Bons," said the boy humbly, "you will be a cultured person. I told them so."

"True, true, and I beg you not to disgrace me when we arrive. No gossiping. No running. Keep close to my side, and never speak to these Immortals unless they speak to you. Yes, and give me the return tickets. You will be losing them."

The boy surrendered the tickets, but felt a little sore. After all, he had found the way to this place. It was hard first to be disbelieved and then to be lectured. Meanwhile, the rain had stopped, and moonlight crept into the omnibus through the cracks in the blinds.

"But how is there to be a rainbow?" cried the boy.

"You distract me," snapped Mr. Bons. "I wish to meditate on beauty. I wish to goodness I was with a reverent and sympathetic person."

The lad bit his lip. He made a hundred good resolutions. He would imitate Mr. Bons all the visit. He would not laugh, or run, or sing, or do any of the vulgar things that must have disgusted his new friends last time. He would be very careful to pronounce their names properly, and to remember who knew whom. Achilles did not know Tom Jones—at least, so Mr. Bons said. The Duchess of Malfi was older than Mrs. Gamp—at least, so Mr. Bons said. He would be self-conscious, reticent, and prim. He would never say he liked any one. Yet, when the blind flew up at a chance touch of his head, all these good resolutions went to the winds, for the omnibus had reached the summit of a moonlit hill, and there was the chasm, and there, across it, stood the old precipices, dreaming, with their feet in the everlasting river. He exclaimed, "The mountain! Listen to the new tune in the water! Look at the camp fires in the ravines," and Mr. Bons, after a hasty glance, retorted, "Water? Camp fires? Ridiculous rubbish. Hold your tongue. There is nothing at all."

Yet, under his eyes, a rainbow formed, compounded not of sunlight and storm, but of moonlight and the spray of the river. The three horses put their feet upon it. He thought it the finest rainbow he had seen, but did not dare say so, since Mr. Bons said that nothing was there. He leant out—the window had opened—and sang the tune that rose from the sleeping waters.

"The prelude to Rhinegold?" said Mr. Bons suddenly. "Who taught you these *leit motifs?*" He, too, looked out of the window. Then he behaved very oddly. He gave a choking cry, and fell back on to the omnibus floor. He writhed and kicked. His face was green.

"Does the bridge make you dizzy?" the boy asked.

"Dizzy!" gasped Mr. Bons. "I want to go back. Tell the driver."

But the driver shook his head.

"We are nearly there," said the boy. "They are asleep. Shall I call? They will be so pleased to see you, for I have prepared them."

Mr. Bons moaned. They moved over the lunar rainbow, which ever and ever broke away behind their wheels. How still the night was! Who would be sentry at the Gate?

"I am coming," he shouted, again forgetting the hundred resolutions. "I am returning—I, the boy."

"The boy is returning," cried a voice to other voices, who repeated, "The boy is returning."

"I am bringing Mr. Bons with me."

Silence.

"I should have said Mr. Bons is bringing me with him."

Profound silence.

"Who stands sentry?"

"Achilles."

And on the rocky causeway, close to the springing of the rainbow bridge, he saw a young man who carried a wonderful shield.

"Mr. Bons, it is Achilles, armed."

"I want to go back," said Mr. Bons.

The last fragment of the rainbow melted, the wheels sang upon the living rock, the door of the omnibus burst open. Out leapt the boy—he could not resist—and sprang to meet the warrior, who, stooping suddenly, caught him on his shield.

"Achilles!" he cried, "let me get down, for I am ignorant and vulgar, and I must wait for that Mr. Bons of whom I told you yesterday."

But Achilles raised him aloft. He crouched on the wonderful shield, on heroes and burning cities, on vineyards graven in gold, on every dear passion, every joy, on the entire image of the Mountain that he had discovered, encircled, like it, with an everlasting stream. "No, no," he protested, "I am not worthy. It is Mr. Bons who must be up here."

But Mr. Bons was whimpering, and Achilles trumpeted and cried, "Stand upright upon my shield!"

"Sir, I did not mean to stand! something made me stand. Sir, why do you delay? Here is only the great Achilles, whom you knew."

Mr. Bons screamed, "I see no one. I see nothing. I want to go back." Then he cried to the driver, "Save me! Let me stop in your chariot. I have honoured you. I have quoted you. I have bound you in vellum. Take me back to my world."

The driver replied, "I am the means and not the end. I am the food and not the life. Stand by yourself, as that boy has stood. I cannot save you. For poetry is a spirit; and they that would worship it must worship in spirit and in truth."

Mr. Bons—he could not resist—crawled out of the beautiful omnibus. His face appeared, gaping horribly. His hands followed, one gripping the step, the other beating the air. Now his shoulders emerged, his chest, his stomach. With a shriek of "I see London," he fell—fell against the hard, moonlit rock, fell into it as if it were water, fell through it, vanished, and was seen by the boy no more.

"Where have you fallen to, Mr. Bons? Here is a procession arriving to honour you with music and torches. Here come the men and women whose names you know. The mountain is awake, the river is awake, over the race-course the sea is awaking those dolphins, and it is all for you. They want you——"

There was the touch of fresh leaves on his forehead. Some one had crowned him.

TEΛOΣ [3]

From the *Kingston Gazette,*
Surbiton Times,
and *Raynes Park Observer.*

The body of Mr. Septimus Bons has been found in a shockingly mutilated condition in the vicinity of the Bermondsey gas-works. The deceased's pockets contained a sovercign-purse, a silver cigar-case, a bijou pronouncing dictionary, and a couple of omnibus tickets. The unfortunate gentleman had apparently been hurled from a considerable height. Foul play is suspected, and a thorough investigation is pending by the authorities.

[1908]

3 TELOS: THE END. (JHP)

QUESTIONS FOR STUDY

1. *What contrasting values toward literature are established by the beginning section of the story?*
2. *Why is the celestial omnibus so seldom used? Why are no tickets issued at the other end? Why has the company been forced to issue return tickets? Why does the omnibus depart at sunrise and return at sunset?*
3. *Why is the boy accepted into heaven while Mr. Bons is rejected? Where has Mr. Bons been revealed to be lacking? (Note his name, spelled backwards.) How does the motto displayed in the coach— "Abandon ye all pride, ye who enter here"—apply to him?*
4. *What is the significance of Mr. Bons' plea to the driver (Dante?): "I have honoured you. I have quoted you. I have bound you in vellum. Take me back to my world"?*
5. *What is the significance of the driver's reply: "I am the means and not the end. . . . I cannot save you. For poetry is a spirit; and they that would worship it must worship in spirit and in truth"?*

WILLIAM H. GASS

In the Heart of the Heart of the Country

A PLACE

SO I HAVE sailed the seas and come . . . to B . . . a small town fastened to a field in Indiana. Twice there have been twelve hundred people here to answer to the census. The town is outstandingly neat and shady, and always puts its best side to the highway. On one lawn there's even a wood or plastic iron deer.

You can reach us by crossing a creek. In the spring the lawns are green, the forsythia is singing, and even the railroad that guts the town has straight bright rails which hum when the train is coming, and the train itself has a welcome horning sound.

Down the back streets the asphalt crumbles into gravel. There's Westbrook's, with the geraniums, Horsefall's, Mott's. The sidewalk shatters. Gravel dust rises like breath behind the wagons. And I am in retirement from love.

WEATHER

In the Midwest, around the lower Lakes, the sky in the winter is heavy and close, and it is a rare day, a day to remark on, when the sky lifts and allows the heart up. I am keeping count, and as I write this page, it is eleven days since I have seen the sun.

MY HOUSE

There's a row of headless maples behind my house, cut to free the passage of electric wires. High stumps, ten feet tall, remain, and I climb these like a boy to watch the country sail away from me. They are ordinary fields, a little more uneven than they should be, since in the spring they puddle. The topsoil's thin, but

only moderately stony. Corn is grown one year, soybeans another. At dusk starlings darken the single tree—a larch—which stands in the middle. When the sky moves, fields move under it. I feel, on my perch, that I've lost my years. It's as though I were living at last in my eyes, as I have always dreamed of doing, and I think then I know why I've come here: to see, and so to go out against new things —oh god how easily—like air in a breeze. It's true there are moments—foolish moments, ecstasy on a tree stump—when I'm all but gone, scattered I like to think like seed, for I'm the sort now in the fool's position of having love left over which I'd like to lose; what good is it now to me, candy ungiven after Halloween?

A PERSON

There are vacant lots on either side of Billy Holsclaw's house. As the weather improves, they fill with hollyhocks. From spring through fall, Billy collects coal and wood and puts the lumps and pieces in piles near his door, for keeping warm is his one work. I see him most often on mild days sitting on his doorsill in the sun. I notice he's squinting a little, which is perhaps the reason he doesn't cackle as I pass. His house is the size of a single garage, and very old. It shed its paint with its youth, and its boards are a warped and weathered gray. So is Billy. He wears a short lumpy faded black coat when it's cold, otherwise he always goes about in the same loose, grease-spotted shirt and trousers. I suspect his galluses were yellow once, when they were new.

WIRES

These wires offend me. Three trees were maimed on their account, and now these wires deface the sky. They cross like a fence in front of me, enclosing the crows with the clouds. I can't reach in, but like a stick, I throw my feelings over. What is it that offends me? I am on my stump, I've built a platform there and the wires prevent my going out. The cut trees, the black wires, all the beyond birds therefore anger me. When I've wormed through a fence to reach a meadow, do I ever feel the same about the field?

THE CHURCH

The church has a steeple like the hat of a witch, and five birds, all doves, perch in its gutters.

MY HOUSE

Leaves move in the windows. I cannot tell you yet how beautiful it is, what it means. But they do move. They move in the glass.

POLITICS

. . . for all those not in love.

I've heard Batista described as a Mason. A farmer who'd seen him in Miami made this claim. He's as nice a fellow as you'd ever want to meet. Of Castro, of course, no one speaks.

For all those not in love there's law: to rule . . . to regulate . . . to rectify. I cannot write the poetry of such proposals, the poetry of politics, though sometimes —often—always now—I am in that uneasy peace of equal powers which makes a State; then I communicate by passing papers, proclamations, orders, through my bowels. Yet I was not a State with you, nor were we both together any Indiana. A squad of Pershing Rifles at the moment, I make myself Right Face! Legislation packs the screw of my intestines. Well, king of the classroom's king of the hill. You used to waddle when you walked because my sperm between your legs was draining to a towel. Teacher, poet, folded lover—like the politician, like those drunkards, ill, or those who faucet-off while pissing heartily to preach upon the force and fullness of that stream, or pause from vomiting to praise the purity and passion of their puke—I chant, I beg, I orate, I command, I sing—

Come back to Indiana—not too late!
   (Or will you be a ranger to the end?)
Good-bye . . . Good-bye . . . oh, I shall
   always wait
You, Larry, traveler—
            stranger,
                  son,
            —my friend—
my little girl, my poem by heart, my self, my childhood.

But I've heard Batista described as a Mason. That dries up my pity, melts my hate. Back from the garage where I have overheard it, I slap the mended fender of my car to laugh, and listen to the metal stinging tartly in my hand.

PEOPLE

Their hair in curlers and their heads wrapped in loud scarves, young mothers, fattish in trousers, lounge about in the speedwash, smoking cigarettes, eating candy, drinking pop, thumbing magazines, and screaming at their children above the whir and rumble of the machines.

At the bank a young man freshly pressed is letting himself in with a key. Along the street, delicately teetering, many grandfathers move in a dream. During the murderous heat of summer, they perch on window ledges, their feet dangling just inside the narrow shelf of shade the store has made, staring steadily into the street. Where their consciousness has gone I can't say. It's not in the eyes. Perhaps it's diffuse, all temperature and skin, like an infant's, though more mild. Near the corner there are several large overalled men employed in standing. A truck turns to be weighed on the scales at the Feed and Grain. Images drift on the drugstore window. The wind has blown the smell of cattle into town. Our eyes have been driven in like the eyes of the old men. And there's no one to have mercy on us.

VITAL DATA

There are two restaurants here and a tearoom, two bars, one bank, three barbers, one with a green shade with which he blinds his window. two groceries. a dealer in Fords. one drug, one hardware, and one appliance store. several that sell feed, grain, and farm equipment. an antique shop. a poolroom. a laundromat. three doctors. a dentist. a plumber. a vet. a funeral home in elegant repair the color of a buttercup. numerous beauty parlors which open and shut like night-blooming plants. a tiny dime and department store of no width but several floors. a hutch, home-made, where you can order, after lying down or squirming in, furniture that's been fashioned from bent lengths of stainless tubing, glowing plastic, metallic thread, and clear shellac. an American Legion Post and a root beer stand. little agencies for this and that: cosmetics, brushes, insurance, greeting cards and garden produce—anything—sample shoes—which do their business out of hats and satchels, over coffee cups and dissolving sugar. a factory for making paper sacks and pasteboard boxes that's lodged in an old brick building bearing the legend OPERA HOUSE, still faintly golden, on its roof. a library given by Carnegie. a post office. a school. a railroad station. fire station. lumberyard. telephone company. welding shop. garage . . . and spotted through the town from one end to the other in a line along the highway, gas stations to the number five.

EDUCATION

In 1833, Colin Goodykoontz, an itinerant preacher with a name from a fairy-tale, summed up the situation in one Indiana town this way:

Ignorance and her squalid brood. A universal dearth of intellect. Total abstinence from literature is very generally practiced. . . . There is not a scholar in grammar or geography, or a *teacher capable* of *instructing* in them, to my knowledge. . . . Others are supplied a few months of the year with the most antiquated & unreasonable forms of teaching reading, writing & cyphering. . . . Need I stop to remind you of the host of loathsome reptiles such a stagnant pool is fitted to breed! Croaking jealousy; bloated bigotry; coiling suspicion; wormish blindness; crocodile malice!

Things have changed since then, but in none of the respects mentioned.

BUSINESS

One side section of street is blocked off with sawhorses. Hard, thin, bitter men in blue jeans, cowboy boots and hats, untruck a dinky carnival. The merchants are promoting themselves. There will be free rides, raucous music, parades and coneys, pop, popcorn, candy, cones, awards and drawings, with all you can endure of pinch, push, bawl, shove, shout, scream, shriek, and bellow. Children pedal past on decorated bicycles, their wheels a blur of color, streaming crinkled paper and excited dogs. A little later, there's a pet show for a prize—dogs, cats, birds, sheep, ponies, goats—none of which wins. The whirlabouts whirl about. The Ferris wheel climbs dizzily into the sky as far as a tall man on tiptoe might be persuaded to reach, and the irritated operators measure the height and weight of every child with sour eyes to see if they are safe for the machines. An electrical megaphone repeatedly trumpets the names of the generous sponsors. The following day they do not allow the refuse to remain long in the street.

MY HOUSE, THIS PLACE AND BODY

I have met with some mischance, wings withering, as Plato says obscurely, and across the breadth of Ohio, like heaven on a table, I've fallen as far as the poet, to the sixth sort of body, this house in B, in Indiana, with its blue and gray bewitching windows, holy magical insides. Great thick evergreens protect its entry. And I live *in*.

Lost in the corn rows, I remember feeling just another stalk, and thus this country takes me over in the way I occupy myself when I am well . . . completely—to the edge of both my house and body. No one notices, when they walk by, that I am brimming in the doorways. My house, this place and body, I've come in mourning to be born in. To anybody else it's pretty silly: love. Why should I feel a loss? How am I bereft? She was never mine; she was a fiction, always a golden tomgirl, barefoot, with an adolescent's slouch and a boy's taste for sports and fishing, a figure out of Twain, or worse, in Riley. Age cannot be kind.

There's little hand-in-hand here . . . not in B. No one touches except in rage. Occasionally girls will twine their arms about each other and lurch along, school out, toward home and play. I dreamed my lips would drift down your back like a skiff on a river. I'd follow a vein with the point of my finger, hold your bare feet in my naked hands.

THE SAME PERSON

Billy Holsclaw lives alone—how alone it is impossible to fathom. In the post office he talks greedily to me about the weather. His head bobs on a wild flood of words, and I take this violence to be a measure of his eagerness for speech. He badly needs a shave, coal dust has layered his face, he spits when he speaks, and his fingers pick at his tatters. He wobbles out in the wind when I leave him, a paper sack mashed in the fold of his arm, the leaves blowing past him, and our encounter drives me sadly home to poetry— where there's no answer. Billy closes his door and carries coal or wood to his fire and closes his eyes, and there's simply no way of knowing how lonely and empty he is or whether he's as vacant and barren and loveless as the rest of us are— here in the heart of the country.

WEATHER

For we're always out of luck here. That's just how it is—for instance in the winter. The sides of the buildings, the roofs, the limbs of the trees are gray. Streets, sidewalks, faces, feelings—they are gray. Speech is gray, and the grass where it shows. Every flank and front, each top is gray. Everything is gray: hair, eyes, window glass, the hawkers' bills and touters' posters, lips, teeth, poles and metal signs—they're gray, quite gray. Cars are gray. Boots, shoes, suits, hats, gloves are gray. Horses, sheep, and cows, cats killed in the road, squirrels in the

same way, sparrows, doves, and pigeons, all are gray, everything is gray, and everyone is out of luck who lives here.

A similar haze turns the summer sky milky, and the air muffles your head and shoulders like a sweater you've got caught in. In the summer light, too, the sky darkens a moment when you open your eyes. The heat is pure distraction. Steeped in our fluids, miserable in the folds of our bodies, we can scarcely think of anything but our sticky parts. Hot cyclonic winds and storms of dust crisscross the country. In many places, given an indifferent push, the wind will still coast for miles, gathering resource and edge as it goes, cunning and force. According to the season, paper, leaves, field litter, seeds, snow, fill up the fences. Sometimes I think the land is flat because the winds have leveled it, they blow so constantly. In any case, a gale can grow in a field of corn that's as hot as a draft from hell, and to receive it is one of the most dismaying experiences of this life, though the smart of the same wind in winter is more humiliating, and in that sense even worse. But in the spring it rains as well, and the trees fill with ice.

PLACE

Many small Midwestern towns are nothing more than rural slums, and this community could easily become one. Principally, during the first decade of the century, though there were many earlier instances, well-to-do farmers moved to town and built fine homes to contain them in their retirement. Others desired a more social life, and so lived in, driving to their fields like storekeepers to their businesses. These houses are now dying like the bereaved who inhabit them; they are slowly losing their senses—deafness, blindness, forgetfulness, mumbling, an insecure gait, an uncontrollable trembling has overcome them. Some kind of Northern Snopes will occupy them next: large-familied, Catholic, Democratic, scrambling, vigorous, poor; and since the parents will work in larger, nearby towns, the children will be loosed upon themselves and upon the hapless neighbors much as the fabulous Khan loosed his legendary horde. These Snopes will undertake makeshift repairs with materials that other people have thrown away; paint halfway round their house, then quit; almost certainly maintain an ugly loud cantankerous dog and underfeed a pair of cats to keep the rodents down. They will collect piles of possibly useful junk in the back yard, park their cars in the front, live largely leaning over engines, give not a hoot for the land, the old community, the hallowed ways, the established clans. Weakening widow ladies have already begun to hire large rude youths from families such as these to rake and mow and tidy the grounds they will inherit.

PEOPLE

In the cinders at the station boys sit smoking steadily in darkened cars, their arms bent out the windows, white shirts glowing behind the glass. Nine o'clock is the best time. They sit in a line facing the highway—two or three or four of them —idling their engines. As you walk by a machine may growl at you or a pair of headlights flare up briefly. In a moment one will pull out, spinning cinders behind it, to stalk impatiently up and down the dark streets or roar half a mile into the country before returning to its place in line and pulling up.

MY HOUSE, MY CAT, MY COMPANY

I must organize myself. I must, as they say, pull myself together, dump this cat from my lap, stir—yes, resolve, move, do. But do what? My will is like the rosy dust-like light in this room: soft, diffuse, and gently comforting. It lets me do . . . anything . . . nothing. My ears hear what they happen to; I eat what's put before me; my eyes see what blunders into them; my thoughts are not thoughts, they are dreams. I'm empty or I'm full . . . depending; and I cannot choose. I sink my claws in Tick's fur and scratch the bones of his back until his rear rises amorously. Mr. Tick, I murmur, I must organize myself. I must pull myself together. And Mr. Tick rolls over on his belly, all ooze.

I spill Mr. Tick when I've rubbed his stomach. Shoo. He steps away slowly, his long tail rhyming with his paws. How beautifully he moves, I think; how beautifully he accepts. So I rise and wander from room to room, up and down, gazing through most of my forty-one windows. How well this house receives its loving too. Let out like Mr. Tick, my eyes sink in the shrubbery. I am not here; I've passed the glass, passed second-story spaces, flown by branches, brilliant berries, to the ground, grass high in seed and leafage every season; and it is the same as when I passed above you in my aged, ardent body; it's, in short, a kind of love; and I am learning to restore myself, my house, my body, by paying court to gardens, cats, and running water, and with neighbors keeping company.

Mrs. Desmond is my right-hand friend; she's eighty-five. A thin white mist of hair, fine and tangled, manifests the climate of her mind. She is habitually suspicious, fretful, nervous. Burglars break in at noon. Children trespass. Even now they are shaking the pear tree, stealing rhubarb, denting lawn. Flies caught in the screen and numbed by frost awake in the heat to buzz and scrape the metal cloth and frighten her, though she is deaf to me, and consequently cannot hear them. Boards creak, the wind whistles across the chimney mouth, drafts cruise like fish through the hollow rooms. It is herself she hears, her own flesh failing, for only death will preserve her from those daily chores she climbs like stairs, and all that anxious waiting. Is it now, she wonders. No? Then: is it now?

We do not converse. She visits me to talk. My task to murmur. She talks about her grandson, her daughter who lives in Delphi, her sister or her husband—both gone—obscure friends—dead—obscurer aunts and uncles—lost—ancient neighbors, members of her church or of her clubs—passed or passing on; and in this way she brings the ends of her life together with a terrifying rush: she is a girl, a wife, a mother, widow, all at once. All at once—appalling—but I believe it; I wince in expectation of the clap. Her talk's a fence—a shade drawn, window fastened, door that's locked—for no one dies taking tea in a kitchen; and as her years compress and begin to jumble, I really believe in the brevity of life; I sweat in my wonder; death is the dog down the street, the angry gander, bedroom spider, goblin who's come to get her; and it occurs to me that in my listening posture I'm the boy who suffered the winds of my grandfather with an exactly similiar politeness, that I am, right now, all my ages, out in elbows, as angular as badly stacked cards. Thus was I, when I loved you, every man I could be, youth and child—far from enough—and you, so strangely ambiguous a being, met me, heart for spade, play after play, the whole run of our suits.

Mr. Tick, you do me honor. You not only lie in my lap, but you remain alive there, coiled like a fetus. Through your deep nap, I feel you hum. You are, and are not, a machine. You are alive, alive exactly, and it means nothing to you— much to me. You are a cat—you cannot understand—you are a cat so easily. Your nature is not something you must rise to. You, not I, live in: in house, in skin, in shrubbery. Yes. I think I shall hat my head with a steeple; turn church; devour people. Mr. Tick, though, has a tail he can twitch, he need not fly his Fancy. Claws, not metrical schema, poetry his paws; while smoothing . . . smoothing . . . smoothing roughly, his tongue laps its neatness. O Mr. Tick, I know you; you are an electrical penis. Go on now, shoo. Mrs. Desmond doesn't like you. She thinks you will tangle yourself in her legs and she will fall. You murder her birds, she knows, and walk upon her roof with death in your jaws. I must gather myself together for a bound. What age is it I'm at right now, I wonder. The heart, don't they always say, keeps the true time. Mrs. Desmond is knocking. Faintly, you'd think, but she pounds. She's brought me a cucumber. I believe she believes I'm a woman. Come in, Mrs. Desmond, thank you, be my company, it looks lovely, and have tea. I'll slice it, crisp, with cream, for luncheon, each slice as thin as me.

POLITICS

O all ye isolate and separate powers, Sing! Sing, and sing in such a way that from a distance it will seem a harmony, a a Strindberg play, a friendship ring . . . so happy—happy, happy, happy—as here we go hand in handling, up and down. Our union was a singing, though we were silent in the songs we sang like single notes are silent in a symphony. In no sense sober, we barbershopped together and never heard the discords in our music or saw ourselves as dirty, cheap, or silly. Yet cats have worn out better shoes than those thrown through our love songs at us. Hush. Be patient—prudent—politic. Still, Cleveland killed you, Mr. Crane. Were you not politic enough and fond of being beaten? Like a piece of sewage, the city shat you from its stern three hundred miles from history—beyond the loving reach of sailors. Well, I'm not a poet who puts Paris to his temple in his youth to blow himself from Idaho, or—fancy that—Missouri. My god, I said, this is my country, but must my country go so far as Terre Haute or Whiting, go so far as Gary?

When the Russians first announced the launching of their satellite, many people naturally refused to believe them. Later others were outraged that they had sent a dog around the earth. I wouldn't want to take that mutt from out that metal flying thing if he's still living when he lands, our own dog catcher said; anybody knows you shut a dog up by himself to toss around the first thing he'll be setting on to do you let him out is bite somebody.

This Midwest. A dissonance of parts and people, we are a consonance of Towns. Like a man grown fat in everything but heart, we overlabor; our outlook never really urban, never rural either, we enlarge and linger at the same time. As Alice both changed and remained in her story. You are a blond. I put my hand upon your belly; feel it tremble from my trembling. We always drive large cars in my section of the country. How could you be a comfort to me now?

MORE VITAL DATA

The town is exactly fifty houses, trailers, stores, and miscellaneous buildings long, but in places no streets deep.

It takes on width as you drive south, always adding to the east. Most of the dwellings are fairly spacious farm houses in the customary white, with wide wraparound porches and tall narrow windows, though there are many of the grander kind—fretted, scalloped, turreted, and decorated with clapboards set at angles or on end, with stained-glass windows at the stair landings and lots of wrought iron full of fancy curls—and a few of these look like castles in their rarer brick. Old stables serve as garages now, and the lots are large to contain them and the vegetable and flower gardens which, ultimately, widows plant and weed and then entirely disappear in. The shade is ample, the grass is good, the sky a glorious fall violet; the apple trees are heavy and red, the roads are calm and empty; corn has sifted from the chains of tractored wagons to speckle the streets with gold and with the russet fragments of the cob, and a man would be a fool who wanted, blessed with this, to live anywhere else in the world.

EDUCATION

Buses like great orange animals move through the early light to school. There the children will be taught to read and warned against Communism. By Miss Janet Jakes. That's not her name. Her name is Helen something—Scott or James. A teacher twenty years. She's now worn fine and smooth, and has a face, Wilfred says, like a mail-order ax. Her voice is hoarse, and she has a cough. For she screams abuse. The children stare, their faces blank. This is the thirteenth week. They are used to it. You will all, she shouts, you will all draw pictures of me. No. She is a Mrs.—someone's missus. And in silence they set to work while Miss Jakes jabs hairpins in her hair. Wilfred says an ax, but she has those rimless tinted glasses, graying hair, an almost dimpled chin. I must concentrate. I must stop making up things. I must give myself to life; let it mold me: that's what they say in *Wisdom's Monthly Digest* every day. Enough, enough—you've been at it long enough; and the children rise formally a row at a time to present their work to her

desk. No, she wears rims; it's her chin that's dimpleless. Well, it will take more than a tablespoon of features to sweeten that face. So she grimly shuffles their sheets, examines her reflection crayoned on them. I would not dare . . . allow a child . . . to put a line around me. Though now and then she smiles like a nick in the blade, in the end these drawings depress her. I could not bear it—how can she ask?—that anyone . . . draw me. Her anger's lit. That's why she does it: flame. There go her eyes; the pink in her glasses brightens, dims. She is a pumpkin, and her rage is breathing like the candle in. No, she shouts, no—the cartoon trembling—no, John Mauck, John Stewart Mauck, this will not do. The picture flutters from her fingers. You've made me too muscular.

I work on my poetry. I remember my friends, associates, my students, by their names. Their names are Maypop, Dormouse, Upsydaisy. Their names are Gladiolus, Callow Bladder, Prince and Princess Oleo, Hieronymus, Cardinal Mummum, Mr. Fitchew, The Silken Howdah, Spot. Sometimes you're Tom Sawyer, Huckleberry Finn; it is perpetually summer; your buttocks are my pillow; we are adrift on a raft; your back is our river. Sometimes you are Major Barbara, sometimes a goddess who kills men in battle, sometimes you are soft like a shower of water; you are bread in my mouth.

I do not work on my poetry. I forget my friends, associates, my students, and their names: Gramophone, Blowgun, Pickle, Serenade . . . Marge the Barge, Arena, Uberhaupt . . . Doctor Dildoe, The Fog Machine. For I am now in B, in Indiana: out of job and out of patience, out of love and time and money, out of bread and out of body, in a temper, Mrs. Desmond, out of tea. So shut your fist up, bitch, you bag of death; go bang another door; go die, my dearie. Die, life-deaf old lady. Spill your breath. Fall over like a frozen board. Gray hair grows from the nose of your mind. You are a skull already—*memento mori*—the foreskin retracts from your teeth. Will your plastic gums last longer than your bones, and color their grinning? And is your twot still hazel-hairy, or are you bald as a ditch? . . . bitch . . . . . . bitch . . . . bitch. I wanted to be famous, but you bring me age—my emptiness. Was it *that* which I thought would balloon me above the rest? Love? where are you? . . . love me. I want to rise so high, I said, that when I shit I won't miss anybody.

BUSINESS

For most people, business is poor. Nearby cities have siphoned off all but a neighborhood trade. Except for feed and grain and farm supplies, you stand a chance to sell only what runs out to buy. Chevrolet has quit, and Frigidaire. A locker plant has left its afterimage. The lumberyard has been, so far, six months about its going. Gas stations change hands clumsily, a restaurant becomes available, a grocery closes. One day they came and knocked the cornices from the watch repair and pasted campaign posters on the windows. Torn across, by now, by boys, they urge you still to vote for half an orange beblazoned man who as a whole one failed two years ago to win at his election. Everywhere, in this manner, the past speaks, and it mostly speaks of failure. The empty stores, the old signs and dusty fixtures, the debris in alleys, the flaking paint and rusty gutters, the heavy locks and sagging boards: they say the same disagreeable things. What do the sightless windows see, I wonder, when the sun throws a passerby against them? Here a stair unfolds toward the street—dark, rickety, and treacherous—and I always feel, as I pass it, that if I just went carefully up and turned the corner at the landing, I would find myself out of the world. But I've never had the courage.

THAT SAME PERSON

The weeds catch up with Billy. In pursuit of the hollyhocks, they rise in coarse clumps all around the front of his house. Billy has to stamp down a circle by his door like a dog or cat does turning round to nest up, they're so thick. What particularly troubles me is that winter will find the weeds still standing stiff and tin-dery to take the sparks which Billy's little mortarless chimney spouts. It's true that fires are fun here. The town whistle, which otherwise only blows for noon (and there's no noon on Sunday), signals the direction of the fire by the length and number of its blasts, the volunteer firemen rush past in their cars and trucks, houses empty their owners along the street every time like an illustration in a children's book. There are many bikes, too, and barking dogs, and sometimes—halleluiah—the fire's right here in town—a vacant lot of weeds and stubble flaming up. But I'd rather it weren't Billy or Billy's lot or house. Quite selfishly, I want him to remain the way he is—counting his sticks and logs, sitting on his sill in the soft early sun—though I'm not sure what his presence means to me . . . or to anyone. Nevertheless, I keep wondering whether, given time, I might not someday find a figure in our language which would serve him faithfully, and furnish his poverty and loneliness richly out.

WIRES

Where sparrows sit like fists. Doves fly the steeple. In mist the wires change perspective, rise and twist. If they led to you, I would know what they were. Thoughts passing often, like the starlings who flock these fields at evening to sleep in the trees beyond, would form a family of paths like this; they'd foot down the natural height of air to just about a bird's perch. But they do not lead to you.

> Of whose beauty it was sung
> She shall make the old man young.

They fasten me.

If I walked straight on, in my present mood, I would reach the Wabash. It's not a mood in which· I'd choose to conjure you. Similes dangle like baubles from me. This time of year the river is slow and shallow, the clay banks crack in the sun, weeds surprise the sandbars. The air is moist and I am sweating. It's impossible to rhyme in this dust. Everything—sky, the cornfield, stump, wild daisies, my old clothes and pressless feelings—seem fabricated for installment purchase. Yes.

Christ. I am suffering a summer Christmas; and I cannot walk under the wires. The sparrows scatter like handfuls of gravel. Really, wires are voices in thin strips. They are words wound in cables. Bars of connection.

WEATHER

I would rather it were the weather that was to blame for what I am and what my friends and neighbors are—we who live here in the heart of the country. Better the weather, the wind, the pale dying snow . . . the snow—why not the snow? There's never much really, not around the lower Lakes anyway, not enough to boast about, not enough to be useful. My father tells how the snow in the Dakotas would sweep to the roofs of the barns in the old days, and he and his friends could sled on the crust that would form because the snow was so fiercely driven. In Bemidji trees have been known to explode. That would be something—if the trees in Davenport or Francisville or Carbondale or Niles were to go blam some winter—blam! blam! blam! all the way down the gray, cindery, snowsick streets.

A cold fall rain is blackening the trees or the air is like lilac and full of parachuting seeds. Who cares to live in any season but his own? Still I suspect the secret's in this snow, the secret of our sickness, if we could only diagnose it, for we are all dying like the elms in Urbana. This snow —like our skin it covers the country. Later dust will do it. Right now—snow. Mud presently. But it is snow without any laughter in it, a pale gray pudding thinly spread on stiff toast, and if that seems a strange description, it's accurate all the same. Of course soot blackens everything, but apart from that, we are never sufficiently cold here. The flakes as they come, alive and burning, we cannot retain, for if our temperatures fall, they rise promptly again, just as, in the summer, they bob about in the same feckless way. Suppose though . . . suppose they were to rise some August, climb and rise, and then hang in the hundreds like a hawk through December, what a desert we could make of ourselves—from Chicago to Cairo, from Hammond to Columbus—what beautiful Death Valleys.

PLACE

I would rather it were the weather. It drives us in upon ourselves—an unlucky fate. Of course there is enough to stir our wonder anywhere: there's enough to love, anywhere, if one is strong enough, if one is diligent enough, if one is perceptive, patient, kind enough—whatever it takes; and surely it's better to live in the country, to live on a prairie by a drawing of rivers, in Iowa or Illinois or Indiana, say, than in any city, in any stinking fog of human beings, in any blooming orchard of machines. It ought to be. The cities are swollen and poisonous with people. It ought to be better. Man has never been a fit environment for man— for rats, maybe, rats do nicely, or for dogs or cats and the household beetle.

And how long the street is, nowadays. These endless walls are fallen to keep back the tides of earth. Brick could be beautiful but we have covered it gradually with gray industrial vomits. Age does not make concrete genial, and asphalt is always—like America—twenty-one, until it breaks up in crumbs like stale cake. The brick, the asphalt, the concrete, the dancing signs and garish posters, the feed and excrement of the automobile, the litter of its inhabitants: they compose, they decorate, they line our streets, and there is nowhere, nowadays, our streets can't reach.

A man in the city has no natural thing by which to measure himself. His parks are potted plants. Nothing can live and remain free where he resides but the pigeon, starling, sparrow, spider, cockroach, mouse, moth, fly and weed, and he laments the existence of even these and makes his plans to poison them. The zoo? There *is* the zoo. Through its bars the city man stares at the great cats and dully sucks his ice. Living, alas, among men and their marvels, the city man supposes that his happiness depends on establishing, somehow, a special kind of harmonious accord with others. The novelists of the city, of slums and crowds, they call it love—and break their pens.

Wordsworth feared the accumulation of men in cities. He foresaw their "degrading thirst after outrageous stimulation,," and some of their hunger for love. Living in a city, among so many, dwelling in the heat and tumult of incessant movement, a man's affairs are touch and go—that's all. It's not surprising that the novelists of the slums, the cities, and the crowds, should find that sex is but a scratch to ease a tickle, that we're most human when we're sitting on the john, and that the justest image of our life is in full passage through the plumbing.

> That man, immur'd in cities, still retains
> His inborn inextinguishable thirst
> Of rural scenes, compensating his loss
> By supplemental shifts, the best he may.

Come into the country, then. The air nimbly and sweetly recommends itself unto our gentle senses. Here, growling tractors tear the earth. Dust roils up behind them. Drivers sit jouncing under bright umbrellas. They wear refrigerated hats and steer by looking at the tracks they've cut behind them, their transistors blaring. Close to the land, are they? good companions to the soil? Tell me: do they live in harmony with the alternating seasons?

It's a lie of old poetry. The modern husbandman uses chemicals from cylinders and sacks, spike-ball-and-claw machines, metal sheds, and cost accounting. Nature in the old sense does not matter. It does not exist. Our farmer's only mystical attachment is to parity. And if he does not realize that cows and corn are simply different kinds of chemical engine, he cannot expect to make a go of it.

It isn't necessary to suppose our cows have feelings; our neighbor hasn't as many as he used to have either; but think of it this way a moment, you can correct for the human imputations later: how would it feel to nurse those strange tentacled calves with their rubber, glass, and metal lips, their stainless eyes?

PEOPLE

Aunt Pet's still able to drive her car—a high square Ford—even though she walks with difficulty and a stout stick. She has a watery gaze, a smooth plump face despite her age, and jet black hair in a bun. She has the slowest smile of anyone I ever saw, but she hates dogs, and not very long ago cracked the back of one she cornered in her garden. To prove her vigor she will tell you this, her smile breaking gently while she raises the knob of her stick to the level of your eyes.

HOUSE, MY BREATH AND WINDOW

My window is a grave, and all that lies within it's dead. No snow is falling. There's no haze. It is not still, not silent. Its images are not an animal that waits, for movement is no demonstration. I have seen the sea slack, life bubble through a body without a trace, its spheres impervious as soda's. Downwound, the whore at wagtag clicks and clacks. Leaves wiggle. Grass sways. A bird chirps, pecks the ground. An auto wheel in penning circles keeps its rigid spokes. These images are stones; they are memorials. Beneath this sea lies sea: god rest it . . . rest the world beyond my window, me in front of my reflection, above this page, my shade. Death is not so still, so silent, since silence implies a falling quiet, stillness a stopping, containing, holding in; for death is time in a clock, like Mr. Tick, electric . . . like wind through a windup poet. And my blear floats out to visible against the, glass, befog its country and bespill myself. The mist lifts slowly from the fields in the morning. No one now would say: the Earth throws back its covers; it is rising from sleep. Why is the feeling foolish? The image is too Greek. I used to gaze at you so wantonly your body blushed. Imagine: wonder: that my eyes could cause such flowering. Ah, my friend, your face is pale, the weather cloudy; a street has been felled through your chin, bare trees do nothing, houses take root in their rectangles, a steeple stands up in your head. You speak of loving; then give me a kiss. The pane is cold. On icy mornings the fog rises to greet me (as you always did); the barns and other buildings, rather than ghostly, seem all the more substantial for looming, as if they grew in themselves while I watched (as you always did). Oh my approach, I suppose, was like breath in a rubber monkey. Nevertheless, on the road along the Wabash in the morning, though the trees are sometimes obscured by fog, their reflection floats serenely on the river, reasoning the banks, the sycamores in French rows. Magically, the world tips. I'm led to think that only those who grow down live (which will scarcely win me twenty-five from *Wisdom's Monthly Digest*), but I find I write that only those who live down grow; and what I write, I hold, whatever I really know. My every word's inverted, or reversed—or I am. I held you, too, that way. You were so utterly provisional, subject to my change. I could inflate your bosom with a kiss, disperse your skin with gentleness, enter your vagina from within, and make my love emerge like a fresh sex. The pane is cold. Honesty is cold, my inside lover. The sun looks, through the mist, like a plum on the tree of heaven, or a bruise on the slope of your belly. Which? The grass crawls with frost. We meet on this window, the world and I, inelegantly, swimmers of the glass; and swung wrong way round to one another, the world seems in. The world—how grand, how monumental, grave and deadly, that word is: the world, my house and poetry. All poets have their inside lovers. Wee penis does not belong to me, or any of this fog-gery. It is *his* property which he's thrust through what's womanly of me to set down this. These wooden houses in their squares, gray streets and fallen sidewalks, standing trees, your name I've written sentimentally across my breath into the whitening air, pale birds: they exist in me now because of him. I gazed with what intensity . . . A bush in the excitement of its roses could not have bloomed so beautifully as you did then. It was a look I'd like to give this page. For that is poetry: to bring within about, to change.

POLITICS

Sports, politics, and religion are the three passions of the badly educated. They are the Midwest's open sores. Ugly to see, a source of constant discontent, they sap the body's strength. Appalling

quantities of money, time, and energy are wasted on them. The rural mind is narrow, passionate, and reckless on these matters. Greed, however shortsighted and direct, will not alone account for it. I have known men, for instance, who for years have voted squarely against their interests. Nor have I ever noticed that their surly Christian views prevented them from urging forward the smithereening, say, of Russia, China, Cuba, or Korea. And they tend to back their country like they back their local team: they have a fanatical desire to win; yelling is their forte; and if things go badly, they are inclined to sack the coach. All in all, then, Birch is a good name. It stands for the bigot's stick, the wild-child-tamer's cane.

Forgetfulness—is that their object?

Oh, I was new, I thought. A fresh start; new cunt, new climate, and new country—there you were, and I was pioneer, and had no history. That language hurts me, too, my dear. You'll never hear it.

FINAL VITAL DATA

The Modern Homemakers' Demonstration Club. The Prairie Home Demonstration Club. The Night-outer's Home Demonstration Club. The IOOF, FFF, VFW, WCTU, WSCS, 4-H, 40 and 8, Psi Iota Chi, and PTA. The Boy and Girl Scouts, Rainbows, Masons, Indians and Rebekah Lodge. Also the Past Noble Grand Club of the Rebekah Lodge. As well as the Moose and the Ladies of the Moose. The Elks, the Eagles, the Jay-nettes and the Eastern Star. The Women's Literary Club, the Hobby Club, the Art Club, the Sunshine Society, the Dorcas Society, the Pythian Sisters, the Pilgrim Youth Fellowship, the American Legion, the American Legion Auxiliary, the American Legion Junior Auxiliary, the Garden Club, the Bridge for Fun Club, the What-can-you-do? Club, the Get To-gether Club, the Coterie Club, the Worth-while Club, the Let's Help Our Town Club, the No Name Club, the Forget-me-not Club, the Merry-go-round Club . . .

EDUCATION

Has a quarter disappeared from Paula Frosty's pocket book? Imagine the landscape of that face: no crayon could engender it; soft wax is wrong; thin wire in trifling snips might do the trick. Paula Frosty and Christopher Roger accuse the pale and splotchy Cheryl Pipes. But Miss Jakes, I *saw* her. Miss Jakes is so extremely vexed she snaps her pencil. What else is missing? I appoint you a detective, John: search her desk. Gum, candy, paper, pencils, marble, round eraser—whose? A thief. I can't watch her all the time, I'm here to teach. Poor pale fossetted Cheryl, it's determined, can't return the money because she took it home and spent it. Cindy, Janice, John, and Pete—you four who sit around her—you will be detectives this whole term to watch her. A thief. In all my time. Miss Jakes turns, unfists, and turns again. I'll handle you, she cries. To think. A thief. In all my years. Then she writes on the blackboard the name of Cheryl Pipes and beneath that the figure twenty-five with a large sign for cents. Now Cheryl, she says, this won't be taken off until you bring that money out of home, out of home straight up to here, Miss Jakes says, tapping her desk.

Which is three days.

ANOTHER PERSON

I was raking leaves when Uncle Halley introduced himself to me. He said his name came from the comet, and that his mother had borne him prematurely in her fright of it. I thought of Hobbes, whom fear of the Spanish Armada had hurried into birth, and so I believed Uncle Halley to honor the philosopher, though Uncle Halley is a liar, and neither the one hundred twenty-nine nor the fifty-three he ought to be. That fall the leaves had burned themselves out on the trees, the leaf lobes had curled, and now they flocked noisily down the street and were broken in the wires of my rake. Uncle Halley was himself (like Mrs. Desmond and history generally) both deaf and implacable, and he shooed me down his

basement stairs to a room set aside there for stacks of newspapers reaching to the ceiling, boxes of leaflets and letters and programs, racks of photo albums, scrapbooks, bundles of rolled-up posters and maps, flags and pennants and slanting piles of dusty magazines devoted mostly to motoring and the Christian ethic. I saw a bird cage, a tray of butterflies, a bugle, a stiff straw boater and all kinds of tassels tied to a coat tree. He still possessed and had on display the steering lever from his first car, a linen duster, driving gloves and goggles, photographs along the wall of himself, his friends, and his various machines, a shell from the first war, a record of "Ramona" nailed through its hole to a post, walking sticks and fanciful umbrellas, shoes of all sorts (his baby shoes, their counters broken, were held in sorrow beneath my nose—they had not been bronzed, but he might have them done someday before he died, he said), countless boxes of medals, pins, beads, trinkets, toys, and keys (I scarcely saw—they flowed like jewels from his palms), pictures of downtown when it was only a path by the railroad station, a brightly colored globe of the world with a dent in Poland, antique guns, belt buckles, buttons, souvenir plates and cups and saucers (I can't remember all of it—I won't), but I recall how shamefully, how rudely, how abruptly, I fled, a good story in my mouth but death in my nostrils; and how afterward I busily, righteously, burned my leaves as if I were purging the world of its years. I still wonder if this town—its life, and mine now—isn't really a record like the one of "Ramona" that I used to crank around on my grandmother's mahogany Victrola through lonely rainy days as a kid.

THE FIRST PERSON

Billy's like the coal he's found: spilled, mislaid, discarded. The sky's no comfort. His house and his body are dying together. His windows are boarded. And now he's reduced to his hands. I suspect he has glaucoma. At any rate he can scarcely see, and weeds his yard of rubble on his hands and knees. Perhaps he's a surgeon cleansing a wound or an ardent and tactile lover. I watch, I must say, apprehensively. Like mine-war detectors, his hands graze in circles ahead of him. Your nipples were the color of your eyes. Pebble. Snarl of paper. Length of twine. He leans down closely, picks up something silvery, holds it near his nose. Foil? cap? coin? He has within him—what, I wonder? Does he know more now because he fingers everything and has to sniff to see? It would be romantic cruelty to think so. He bends the down on your arms like a breeze. You wrote me: something is strange when we don't understand. I write in return: I think when I loved you I fell to my death.

Billy, I could read to you from Beddoes; he's your man perhaps; he held with dying, freed his blood of its arteries; and he said that there were many wretched love-ill fools like me lying alongside the last bone of their former selves, as full of spirit and speech, nonetheless, as Mrs. Desmond, Uncle Halley and the Ferris wheel, Aunt Pet, Miss Jakes, Ramona or the megaphone; yet I reverse him finally, Billy, on no evidence but braggadocio, and I declare that though my inner organs were devoured long ago, the worm which swallowed down my parts still throbs and glows like a crystal palace.

Yes, you were younger. I was Uncle Halley, the museum man and infrequent meteor. Here is my first piece of ass. They weren't so flat in those days, had more round, more juice. And over here's the sperm I've spilled, nicely jarred and clearly labeled. Look at this tape like lengths of intestine where I've stored my spew, the endless worm of words I've written, a hundred million emissions or more: oh I was quite a man right from the start; even when unconscious in my cradle, from crotch to cranium, I was erectile tissue; though mostly, after the manner approved by Plato, I had intercourse by eye. Never mind, old Holsclaw, you are blind. We pull down darkness when we go to bed; put out like Oedipus the actually offending organ, and train our touch to lies. All cats are gray, says Mr. Tick; so under cover of glaucoma you are sack gray too, and cannot be distinguished from a stallion.

I must pull myself together, get a grip, just as they say, but I feel spilled, bewildered, quite mislaid. I did not restore my house to its youth, but to its age. Hunting, you hitch through the hollyhocks. I'm inclined to say you aren't half the cripple I am, for there is nothing left of me but mouth. However, I resist the impulse. It is another lie of poetry. My organs are all there, though it's there where I fail—at the roots of my experience. Poet of the spiritual, Rilke, weren't you? yet that's what you said. Poetry, like love, is—in and out—a physical caress. I can't tolerate any more of my sophistries about spirit, mind, and breath. Body equals being, and if your weight goes down, you are the less.

HOUSEHOLD APPLES

I knew nothing about apples. Why should I? My country came in my childhood, and I dreamed of sitting among the blooms like the bees. I failed to spray the pear tree too. I doubled up under them at first, admiring the sturdy low branches I should have pruned, and later I acclaimed the blossoms. Shortly after the fruit formed there were falls—not many— apples the size of goodish stones which made me wobble on my ankles when I walked about the yard. Sometimes a piece crushed by a heel would cling on the shoe to track the house. I gathered a few and heaved them over the wires. A slingshot would have been splendid. Hard, an unattractive green, the worms had them. Before long I realized the worms had them all. Even as the apples reddened, lit their tree, they were being swallowed. The birds preferred the pears, which were small—sugar pears I think they're called —with thick skins of graying green that ripen on toward violet. So the fruit fell, and once I made some applesauce by quartering and paring hundreds; but mostly I did nothing, left them, until suddenly, overnight it seemed, in that ugly late September heat we often have in Indiana, my problem was upon me.

My childhood came in the country. I remember, now, the flies on our snowy luncheon table. As we cleared away they would settle, fastidiously scrub themselves and stroll to the crumbs to feed where I would kill them in crowds with a swatter. It was quite a game to catch them taking off. I struck heavily since I didn't mind a few stains; they'd wash. The swatter was a square of screen bound down in red cloth. It drove no air ahead of it to give them warning. They might have thought they'd flown headlong into a summered window. The faint pink dot where they had died did not rub out as I'd supposed, and after years of use our luncheon linen would faintly, pinkly, speckle.

The country became my childhood. Flies braided themselves on the flypaper in my grandmother's house. I can smell the bakery and the grocery and the stables and the dairy in that small Dakota town I knew as a kid; knew as I dreamed I'd know your body, as I've known nothing, before or since; knew as the flies knew, in the honest, unchaste sense: the burned house, hose-wet, which drew a mist of insects like the blue smoke of its smolder, and gangs of boys, moist-lipped, destructive as its burning. Flies have always impressed me; they are so persistently alive. Now they were coating the ground beneath my trees. Some were ordinary flies; there were the large blue-green ones; there were swarms of fruit flies too, and the red-spotted scavenger beetle; there were a few wasps, several sorts of bees and butterflies—checkers, sulphurs, monarchs, commas, question marks—and delicate dragonflies . . . but principally houseflies and horseflies and bottleflies, flies and more flies in clusters around the rotting fruit. They loved the pears. Inside, they fed. If you picked up a pear, they flew, and the pear became skin and stem. They were everywhere the fruit was: in the tree still—apples like a hive for them —or where the fruit littered the ground, squashing itself as you stepped . . . there was no help for it. The flies droned, feasting on the sweet juice. No one could go near the trees; I could not climb; so I determined at last to labor like Hercules. There were fruit baskets in the barn. Collecting them and kneeling under the branches, I began to gather remains. Deep in the strong rich smell of the fruit, I began to hum myself. The fruit caved in

at the touch. Glistening red apples, my lifting disclosed, had families of beetles, flies, and bugs, devouring their rotten undersides. There were streams of flies; there were lakes and cataracts and rivers of flies, seas and oceans. The hum was heavier, higher, than the hum of the bees when they came to the blooms in the spring, though the bees were there, among the flies, ignoring me—ignoring everyone. As my work went on and juice covered my hands and arms, they would form a sleeve, black and moving, like knotty wool. No caress could have been more indifferently complete. Still I rose fearfully, ramming my head in the branches, apples bumping against me before falling, bursting with bugs. I'd snap my hand sharply but the flies would cling to the sweet. I could toss a whole cluster into a basket from several feet. As the pear or apple lit, they would explosively rise, like monads for a moment, windowless, certainly, with respect to one another, sugar their harmony. I had to admit, though, despite my distaste, that my arm had never been more alive, oftener or more gently kissed. Those hundreds of feet were light. In washing them off, I pretended the hose was a pump. What have I missed? Childhood is a lie of poetry.

THE CHURCH

Friday night. Girls in dark skirts and white blouses sit in ranks and scream in concert. They carry funnels loosely stuffed with orange and black paper which they shake wildly, and small megaphones through which, as drilled, they direct and magnify their shouting. Their leaders, barely pubescent girls, prance and shake and whirl their skirts above their bloomers. The young men, leaping, extend their arms and race through puddles of amber light, their bodies glistening. In a lull, though it rarely occurs, you can hear the squeak of tennis shoes against the floor. Then the yelling begins again, and then continues; fathers, mothers, neighbors joining in to form a single pulsing ululation—a cry of the whole community—for in this gymnasium each body becomes the bodies beside it, pressed as they are together, thigh to thigh, and the same shudder runs through all of them, and runs toward the same release. Only the ball moves serenely through this dazzling din. Obedient to law it scarcely speaks but caroms quietly and lives at peace.

BUSINESS

It is the week of Christmas and the stores, to accommodate the rush they hope for, are remaining open in the evening. You can see snow falling in the cones of the street lamps. The roads are filling —undisturbed. Strings of red and green lights droop over the principal highway, and the water tower wears a star. The windows of the stores have been bedizened. Shamelessly they beckon. But I am alone, leaning against a pole—no . . . there is no one in sight. They're all at home, perhaps by their instruments, tuning in on their evenings, and like Ramona, tirelessly playing and replaying themselves. There's a speaker perched in the tower, and through the boughs of falling snow and over the vacant streets, it drapes the twisted and metallic strains of a tune that can barely be distinguished—yes, I believe it's one of the jolly ones, it's "Joy to the World." There's no one to hear the music but myself, and though I'm listening, I'm no longer certain. Perhaps the record's playing something else.

[1968]

QUESTIONS FOR STUDY

1. *What kind of man is the narrator? Why has he come to live in the small Indiana town? What is his psychological state of mind?*
2. *How does the narrator characterize the town? Is the description important in its own right? To what extent does it mirror the life and mood of the narrator himself?*
3. *Why does Gass divide his story into thirty-two separate sections? What kind of "whole" do the several parts add up to?*
4. *What, in the final analysis, is the subject of the story? What clue to the author's intention is provided by the opening invocation from William Butler Yeats' poem "Sailing to Byzantium"? What is the significance of the story's title?*

CHARLOTTE PERKINS GILMAN
The Yellow Wall-Paper

IT IS very seldom that mere ordinary people like John and myself secure ancestral halls for the summer.

A colonial mansion, a hereditary estate, I would say a haunted house, and reach the height of romantic felicity—but that would be asking too much of fate!

Still I will proudly declare that there is something queer about it.

Else, why should it be let so cheaply? And why have stood so long untenanted?

John laughs at me, of course, but one expects that in marriage.

John is practical in the extreme. He has no patience with faith, an intense horror of superstition, and he scoffs openly at any talk of things not to be felt and seen and put down in figures.

John is a physician, and *perhaps*—(I would not say it to a living soul, of course, but this is dead paper and a great relief to my mind—) *perhaps* that is one reason I do not get well faster.

You see he does not believe I am sick! And what can one do?

If a physician of high standing, and one's own husband, assures friends and relatives that there is really nothing the matter with one but temporary nervous depression—a slight hysterical tendency—what is one to do?

My brother is also a physician, and also of high standing, and he says the same thing.

So I take phosphates or phosphites—whichever it is, and tonics, and journeys, and air, and exercise, and am absolutely forbidden to "work" until I am well again.

Personally, I disagree with their ideas.

Personally, I believe that congenial work, with excitement and change, would do me good.

But what is one to do?

I did write for a while in spite of them; but it *does* exhaust me a good deal—having to be so sly about it, or else meet with heavy opposition.

I sometimes fancy that in my condition if I had less opposition and more society and stimulus—but John says the very worst thing I can do is to think about my condition, and I confess it always makes me feel bad.

So I will let it alone and talk about the house.

The most beautiful place! It is quite alone, standing well back from the road, quite three miles from the village. It makes me think of English places that you read about, for there are hedges and walls and gates that lock, and lots of separate little houses for the gardeners and people.

There is a *delicious* garden! I never saw such a garden—large and shady, full of box-bordered paths, and lined with long grape-covered arbors with seats under them.

There were greenhouses, too, but they are all broken now.

There was some legal trouble, I believe, something about the heirs and co-heirs; anyhow, the place has been empty for years.

That spoils my ghostliness, I am afraid, but I don't care—there is something strange about the house—I can feel it.

I even said so to John one moonlight evening, but he said what I felt was a *draught,* and shut the window.

I get unreasonably angry with John sometimes. I'm sure I never used to be so sensitive. I think it is due to this nervous condition.

But John says if I feel so, I shall neglect proper self-control; so I take pains to control myself—before him, at least, and that makes me very tired.

I don't like our room a bit. I wanted

one downstairs that opened on the piazza and had roses all over the window, and such pretty old-fashioned chintz hangings! but John would not hear of it.

He said there was only one window and not room for two beds, and no near room for him if he took another.

He is very careful and loving, and hardly lets me stir without special direction.

I have a schedule prescription for each hour in the day; he takes all care from me, and so I feel basely ungrateful not to value it more.

He said we came here soley on my account, that I was to have perfect rest and all the air I could get. "Your exercise depends on your strength, my dear," said he, "and your food somewhat on your appetite; but air you can absorb all the time." So we took the nursery at the top of the house.

It is a big, airy room, the whole floor nearly, with windows that look all ways, and air and sunshine galore. It was nursery first and then playroom and gymnasium, I should judge; for the windows are barred for little children, and there are rings and things in the walls.

The paint and paper look as if a boys' school had used it. It is stripped off—the paper—in great patches all around the head of my bed, about as far as I can reach, and in a great place on the other side of the room low down. I never saw a worse paper in my life.

One of those sprawling flamboyant patterns committing every artistic sin.

It is dull enough to confuse the eye in following, pronounced enough to constantly irritate and provoke study, and when you follow the lame uncertain curves for a little distance they suddenly commit suicide—plunge off at outrageous angles, destroy themselves in unheard of contradictions.

The color is repellent, almost revolting; a smouldering unclean yellow, strangely faded by the slow-turning sunlight.

It is a dull yet lurid orange in some places, a sickly sulphur tint in others.

No wonder the children hated it! I should hate it myself if I had to live in this room long.

There comes John, and I must put this away,—he hates to have me write a word.

*

We have been here two weeks, and I haven't felt like writing before, since that first day.

I am sitting by the window now, up in this atrocious nursery, and there is nothing to hinder my writing as much as I please, save lack of strength.

John is away all day, and even some nights when his cases are serious.

I am glad my case is not serious!

But these nervous troubles are dreadfully depressing.

John does not know how much I really suffer. He knows there is no *reason* to suffer, and that satisfies him.

Of course it is only nervousness. It does weigh on me so not to do my duty in any way!

I meant to be such a help to John, such a real rest and comfort, and here I am a comparative burden already!

Nobody would believe what an effort it is to do what little I am able,—to dress and entertain, and order things.

It is fortunate Mary is so good with the baby. Such a dear baby!

And yet I *cannot* be with him, it makes me so nervous.

I suppose John never was nervous in his life. He laughs at me so about this wall-paper!

At first he meant to repaper the room, but afterwards he said that I was letting it get the better of me, and that nothing was worse for a nervous patient than to give way to such fancies.

He said that after the wall-paper was changed it would be the heavy bedstead, and then the barred windows, and then that gate at the head of the stairs, and so on.

"You know the place is doing you good," he said, "and really, dear, I don't care to renovate the house just for a three months' rental."

"Then do let us go downstairs," I said, "there are such pretty rooms there."

Then he took me in his arms and called me, a blessed little goose, and said he would go down cellar, if I wished, and have it whitewashed into the bargain.

But he is right enough about the beds and windows and things.

It is an airy and comfortable room as any one need wish, and, of course, I would not be so silly as to make him uncomfortable just for a whim.

I'm really getting quite fond of the big room, all but that horrid paper.

Out of one window I can see the garden, those mysterious deep-shaded arbors, the riotous old-fashioned flowers, and bushes and gnarly trees.

Out of another I get a lovely view of the bay and a little private wharf belonging to the estate. There is a beautiful shaded lane that runs down there from the house. I always fancy I see people walking in these numerous paths and arbors, but John has cautioned me not to give way to fancy in the least. He says that with my imaginative power and habit of story-making, a nervous weakness like mine is sure to lead to all manner of excited fancies, and that I ought to use my will and good sense to check the tendency. So I try.

I think sometimes that if I were only well enough to write a little it would relieve the press of ideas and rest me.

But I find I get pretty tired when I try.

It is so discouraging not to have any advice and companionship about my work. When I get really well, John says we will ask Cousin Henry and Julia down for a long visit; but he says he would as soon put fireworks in my pillow-case as to let me have those stimulating people about now.

I wish I could get well faster.

But I must not think about that. This paper looks to me as if it *knew* what a vicious influence it had!

There is a recurrent spot where the pattern lolls like a broken neck and two bulbous eyes stare at you upside down.

I get positively angry with the impertinence of it and the everlastingness. Up and down and sideways they crawl, and those absurd, unblinking eyes are everywhere. There is one place where two breadths didn't match, and the eyes go all up and down the line, one a little higher than the other.

I never saw so much expression in an inanimate thing before, and we all know how much expression they have! I used to lie awake as a child and get more entertainment and terror out of blank walls and plain furniture than most children could find in a toy-store.

I remember what a kindly wink the knobs of our big, old bureau used to have, and there was one chair that always seemed like a strong friend.

I used to feel that if any of the other things looked too fierce I could always hop into that chair and be safe.

The furniture in this room is no worse than inharmonious, however, for we had to bring it all from downstairs. I suppose when this was used as a playroom they had to take the nursery things out, and no wonder! I never saw such ravages as the children have made here.

The wall-paper, as I said before, is torn off in spots, and it sticketh closer than a brother—they must have had perseverance as well as hatred.

Then the floor is scratched and gouged and splintered, the plaster itself is dug out here and there, and this great heavy bed which is all we found in the room, looks as if it had been through the wars.

But I don't mind it a bit—only the paper.

There comes John's sister. Such a dear girl as she is, and so careful of me! I must not let her find me writing.

She is a perfect and enthusiastic housekeeper, and hopes for no better profession. I verily believe she thinks it is the writing which made me sick!

But I can write when she is out, and see her a long way off from these windows.

There is one that commands the road, a lovely shaded winding road, and one that just looks off over the country. A lovely country, too, full of great elms and velvet meadows.

This wall-paper has a kind of subpattern in a different shade, a particularly irritating one, for you can only see it in certain lights, and not clearly then.

But in the places where it isn't faded and where the sun is just so—I can see a strange, provoking, formless sort of figure, that seems to skulk about behind that silly and conspicuous front design.

There's sister on the stairs!

*

Well, the Fourth of July is over! The people are all gone and I am tired out. John thought it might do me good to see a little company, so we just had mother and Nellie and the children down for a week.

Of course I didn't do a thing. Jennie sees to everything now.

But it tired me all the same.

John says if I don't pick up faster he shall send me to Weir Mitchell 1 in the fall.

But I don't want to go there at all. I had a friend who was in his hands once, and she says he is just like John and my brother, only more so!

Besides, it is such an undertaking to go so far.

I don't feel as if it was worth while to turn my hand over for anything, and I'm getting dreadfully fretful and querulous.

I cry at nothing, and cry most of the time.

Of course I don't when John is here, or anybody else, but when I am alone.

And I am alone a good deal just now. John is kept in town very often by serious cases, and Jennie is good and lets me alone when I want her to.

So I walk a little in the garden or down that lovely lane, sit on the porch under the roses, and lie down up here a good deal.

I'm getting really fond of the room in spite of the wall-paper. Perhaps *because* of the wall-paper.

It dwells in my mind so!

I lie here on this great immovable bed —it is nailed down, I believe—and follow that pattern about by the hour. It is as good as gymnastics, I assure you. I start, we'll say, at the bottom, down in the corner over there where it has not been touched, and I determine for the thousandth time that I *will* follow that

pointless pattern to some sort of a conclusion.

I know a little of the principle of design, and I know this thing was not arranged on any laws of radiation, or alternation, or repetition, or symmetry, or anything else that I ever heard of.

It is repeated, of course, by the breadths, but not otherwise.

Looked at in one way each breadth stands alone, the bloated curves and flourishes—a kind of "debased Romanesque" with *delirium tremens* 2 go waddling up and down in isolated columns of fatuity.

But, on the other hand, they connect diagonally, and the sprawling outlines run off in great slanting waves of optic horror, like a lot of wallowing seaweeds in full chase.

The whole thing goes horizontally, too, at least it seems so, and I exhaust myself in trying to distinguish the order of its going in that direction.

They have used a horizontal breadth for a frieze, and that adds wonderfully to the confusion.

There is one end of the room where it is almost intact, and there, when the crosslights fade and the low sun shines directly upon it, I can almost fancy radiation after all,—the interminable grotesques seems to form around a common centre and rush off in headlong plunges of equal distraction.

It makes me tired to follow it. I will take a nap I guess.

*

I don't know why I should write this.

I don't want to.

I don't feel able.

And I know John would think it absurd. But I *must* say what I feel and think in some way—it is such a relief!

But the effort is getting to be greater than the relief.

Half the time now I am awfully lazy, and lie down ever so much.

John says I mustn't lose my strength, and has me take cod liver oil and lots of

1 Silas Weir Mitchell (1829–1914), the Philadelphia neurologist-psychologist who introduced "rest cure" for nervous diseases. His medical books include *Diseases of the Nervous System, Especially of Women* (1881). (JHP)

2 Mental disorientation caused by excessive use of alcohol and characterized by physical tremors. (JHP)

tonics and things, to say nothing of ale and wine and rare meat.

Dear John! He loves me very dearly, and hates to have me sick. I tried to have a real earnest reasonable talk with him the other day, and tell him how I wish he would let me go and make a visit to Cousin Henry and Julia.

But he said I wasn't able to go, nor able to stand it after I got there; and I did not make out a very good case for myself, for I was crying before I had finished.

It is getting to be a great effort for me to think straight. Just this nervous weakness I suppose.

And dear John gathered me up in his arms, and just carried me upstairs and laid me on the bed, and sat by me and read to me till it tired my head.

He said I was his darling and his comfort and all he had, and that I must take care of myself for his sake, and keep well.

He says no one but myself can help me out of it, that I must use my will and self-control and not let any silly fancies run away with me.

There's one comfort, the baby is well and happy, and does not have to occupy this nursery with the horrid wall-paper.

If we had not used it, that blessed child would have! What a fortunate escape! Why, I wouldn't have a child of mine, an impressionable little thing, live in such a room for worlds.

I never thought of it before, but it is lucky that John kept me here after all, I can stand it so much easier than a baby, you see.

Of course I never mention it to them any more,—I am too wise,—but I keep watch of it all the same.

There are things in that paper that nobody knows but me, or ever will.

Behind that outside pattern the dim shapes get clearer every day.

It is always the same shape, only very numerous.

And it is like a woman stooping down and creeping about behind that pattern. I don't like it a bit. I wonder—I begin to think—I wish John would take me away from here!

*

It is so hard to talk with John about my case, because he is so wise, and because he loves me so.

But I tried it last night.

It was moonlight. The moon shines in all around just as the sun does.

I hate to see it sometimes, it creeps so slowly, and always comes in by one window or another.

John was asleep and I hated to waken him, so I kept still and watched the moonlight on that undulating wall-paper till I felt creepy.

The faint figure behind seemed to shake the pattern, just as if she wanted to get out.

I got up softly and went to feel and see if the paper *did* move, and when I came back John was awake.

"What is it, little girl?" he said. "Don't go walking about like that—you'll get cold."

I thought it was a good time to talk, so I told him that I really was not gaining here, and that I wished he would take me away.

"Why, darling!" said he, "our lease will be up in three weeks, and I can't see how to leave before.

"The repairs are not done at home, and I cannot possibly leave town just now. Of course if you were in any danger, I could and would, but you really are better, dear, whether you can see it or not. I am a doctor, dear, and I know. You are gaining flesh and color, your appetite is better, I feel really much easier about you."

"I don't weigh a bit more," said I, "nor as much; and my appetite may be better in the evening when you are here, but it is worse in the morning when you are away!"

"Bless her little heart!" said he with a big hug, "she shall be as sick as she pleases! But now let's improve the shining hours by going to sleep, and talk about it in the morning!"

"And you won't go away?" I asked gloomily.

"Why, how can I, dear? It is only three weeks more and then we will take a nice little trip of a few days while Jennie is getting the house ready. Really dear you are better!"

"Better in body perhaps—" I began, and stopped short, for he sat up straight and looked at me with such a stern, reproachful look that I could not say another word.

"My darling," said he, "I beg of you, for my sake and for our child's sake, as well as for your own, that you will never for one instant let that idea enter your mind! There is nothing so dangerous, so fascinating, to a temperament like yours. It is a false and foolish fancy. Can you not trust me as a physician when I tell you so?"

So of course I said no more on that score, and we went to sleep before long. He thought I was asleep first, but I wasn't, and lay there for hours trying to decide whether that front pattern and the back pattern really did move together or separately.

*

On a pattern like this, by daylight, there is a lack of sequence, a defiance of law, that is a constant irritant to a normal mind.

The color is hideous enough, and unreliable enough, and infuriating enough, but the pattern is torturing.

You think you have mastered it, but just as you get well underway in following, it turns a back-somersault and there you are. It slaps you in the face, knocks you down, and tramples upon you. It is like a bad dream.

The outside pattern is a florid arabesque, reminding one of a fungus. If you can imagine a toadstool in joints, an interminable string of toadstools, budding and sprouting in endless convolutions—why, that is something like it.

That is, sometimes!

There is one marked peculiarity about this paper, a thing nobody seems to notice but myself, and that is that it changes as the light changes.

When the sun shoots in through the east window—I always watch for that first long, straight ray—it changes so

quickly that I never can quite believe it.

That is why I watch it always.

By moonlight—the moon shines in all night when there is a moon—I wouldn't know it was the same paper.

At night in any kind of light, in twilight, candlelight, lamplight, and worst of all by moonlight, it becomes bars! The outside pattern I mean, and the woman behind it is as plain as can be.

I didn't realize for a long time what the thing was that showed behind, that dim sub-pattern, but now I am quite sure it is a woman.

By daylight she is subdued, quiet. I fancy it is the pattern that keeps her so still. It is so puzzling. It keeps me quiet by the hour.

I lie down ever so much now. John says it is good for me, and to sleep all I can.

Indeed he started the habit by making me lie down for an hour after each meal.

It is a very bad habit I am convinced, for you see I don't sleep.

And that cultivates deceit, for I don't tell them I'm awake—O no!

The fact is I am getting a little afraid of John.

He seems very queer sometimes, and even Jennie has an inexplicable look.

It strikes me occasionally, just as a scientific hypothesis,—that perhaps it is the paper!

I have watched John when he did not know I was looking, and come into the room suddenly on the most innocent excuses, and I've caught him several times *looking at the paper!* And Jennie too. I caught Jennie with her hand on it once.

She didn't know I was in the room, and when I asked her in a quiet, a very quiet voice, with the most restrained manner possible, what she was doing with the paper—she turned around as if she had been caught stealing, and looked quite angry—asked me why I should frighten her so!

Then she said that the paper stained everything it touched, that she had found yellow smooches on all my clothes and John's, and she wished we would be more careful!

Did not that sound innocent? But I

know she was studying that pattern, and I am determined that nobody shall find it out but myself!

*

Life is very much more exciting now than it used to be. You see I have something more to expect, to look forward to, to watch. I really do eat better, and am more quiet than I was.

John is so pleased to see me improve! He laughed a little the other day, and said I seemed to be flourishing in spite of my wall-paper.

I turned it off with a laugh. I had no intention of telling him it was *because* of the wall-paper—he would make fun of me. He might even want to take me away.

I don't want to leave now until I have found it out. There is a week more, and I think that will be enough.

*

I'm feeling ever so much better! I don't sleep much at night, for it is so interesting to watch developments; but I sleep a good deal in the daytime.

In the daytime it is tiresome and perplexing.

There are always new shoots on the fungus, and new shades of yellow all over it. I cannot keep count of them, though I have tried conscientiously.

It is the strangest yellow, that wallpaper! It makes me think of all the yellow things I ever saw—not beautiful ones like buttercups, but old foul, bad yellow things.

But there is something else about that paper—the smell! I noticed it the moment we came into the room, but with so much air and sun it was not bad. Now we have had a week of fog and rain, and whether the windows are open or not, the smell is here.

It creeps all over the house.

I find it hovering in the dining-room, skulking in the parlor, hiding in the hall, lying in wait for me on the stairs.

It gets into my hair.

Even when I go to ride, if I turn my head suddenly and surprise it—there is that smell!

Such a peculiar odor, too! I have spent hours in trying to analyze it, to find what it smelled like.

It is not bad—at first, and very gentle, but quite the subtlest, most enduring odor I ever met.

In this damp weather it is awful, I wake up in the night and find it hanging over me.

It used to disturb me at first. I thought seriously of burning the house—to reach the smell.

But now I am used to it. The only thing I can think of that it is like is the *color* of the paper! A yellow smell.

There is a very funny mark on this wall, low down, near the mopboard. A streak that runs round the room. It goes behind every piece of furniture, except the bed, a long, straight, even *smooch,* as if it had been rubbed over and over.

I wonder how it was done and who did it, and what they did it for. Round and round and round—round and round and round!—it makes me dizzy!

*

I really have discovered something at last.

Through watching so much at night, when it changes so, I have finally found out.

The front pattern *does* move—and no wonder! The woman behind shakes it!

Sometimes I think there are a great many women behind, and sometimes only one, and she crawls around fast, and her crawling shakes it all over.

Then in the very bright spots she keeps still, and in the very shady spots she just takes hold of the bars and shakes them hard.

And she is all the time trying to climb through. But nobody could climb through that pattern—it strangles so; I think that is why it has so many heads.

They get through, and then the pattern strangles them off and turns them upside down, and makes their eyes white!

If those heads were covered or taken off it would not be half so bad.

*

I think that woman gets out in the daytime!

And I'll tell you why—privately—I've seen her!

I can see her out of every one of my windows!

It is the same woman, I know, for she is always creeping, and most women do not creep by daylight.

I see her in that long shaded lane, creeping up and down. I see her in those dark grape arbors, creeping all around the garden.

I see her on that long road under the trees, creeping along, and when a carriage comes she hides under the blackberry vines.

I don't blame her a bit. It must be very humiliating to be caught creeping by daylight!

I always lock the door when I creep by daylight. I can't do it at night, for I know John would suspect something at once.

And John is so queer now, that I don't want to irritate him. I wish he would take another room! Besides, I don't want anybody to get that woman out at night but myself.

I often wonder if I could see her out of all the windows at once.

But, turn as fast as I can, I can only see out of one at one time.

And though I always see her, she *may* be able to creep faster than I can turn!

I have watched her sometimes away off in the open country, creeping as fast as a cloud shadow in a high wind.

*

If only that top pattern could be gotten off from the under one! I mean to try it, little by little.

I have found out another funny thing, but I shan't tell it this time! It does not do to trust people too much.

There are only two more days to get this paper off, and I believe John is beginning to notice. I don't like the look in his eyes.

And I heard him ask Jennie a lot of professional questions about me. She had a very good report to give.

She said I slept a good deal in the daytime.

John knows I don't sleep very well at night, for all I'm so quiet!

He asked me all sorts of questions, too, and pretended to be very loving and kind.

As if I couldn't see through him!

Still, I don't wonder he acts so, sleeping under this paper for three months.

It only interests me, but I feel sure John and Jennie are secretly affected by it.

*

Hurrah! This is the last day, but it is enough. John to stay in town over night, and won't be out until this evening.

Jennie wanted to sleep with me—the sly thing! but I told her I should undoubtedly rest better for a night all alone.

That was clever, for really I wasn't alone a bit! As soon as it was moonlight and that poor thing began to crawl and shake the pattern, I got up and ran to help her.

I pulled and she shook, I shook and she pulled, and before morning we had peeled off yards of that paper.

A strip about as high as my head and half around the room.

And then when the sun came and that awful pattern began to laugh at me, I declared I would finish it to-day!

We go away to-morrow, and they are moving all my furniture down again to leave things as they were before.

Jennie looked at the wall in amazement, but I told her merrily that I did it out of pure spite at the vicious thing.

She laughed and said she wouldn't mind doing it herself, but I must not get tired.

How she betrayed herself that time!

But I am here, and no person touches this paper but me,—not *alive!*

She tried to get me out of the room—it was too patent! But I said it was so quiet and empty and clean now that I believed I would lie down again and sleep all I could; and not to wake me even for dinner—I would call when I woke.

So now she is gone, and the servants are gone, and the things are gone, and there is nothing left but that great bedstead nailed down, with the canvas mattress we found on it.

We shall sleep downstairs to-night, and take the boat home to-morrow.

I quite enjoy the room, now it is bare again.

How those children did tear about here!

This bedstead is fairly gnawed!

But I must get to work.

I have locked the door and thrown the key down into the front path.

I don't want to go out, and I don't want to have anybody come in, till John comes.

I want to astonish him.

I've got a rope up here that even Jennie did not find. If that woman does get out, and tries to get away, I can tie her!

But I forgot I could not reach far without anything to stand on!

This bed will *not* move!

I tried to lift and push it until I was lame, and then I got so angry I bit off a little piece at one corner—but it hurt my teeth.

Then I peeled off all the paper I could reach standing on the floor. It sticks horribly and the pattern just enjoys it! All those strangled heads and bulbous eyes and waddling fungus growths just shriek with derision!

I am getting angry enough to do something desperate. To jump out of the window would be admirable exercise, but the bars are too strong even to try.

Besides I wouldn't do it. Of course not. I know well enough that a step like that is improper and might be misconstrued.

I don't like to *look* out of the windows even—there are so many of those creeping women, and they creep so fast.

I wonder if they all come out of that wall-paper as I did?

But I am securely fastened now by my well-hidden rope—you don't get *me* out in the road there!

I suppose I shall have to get back behind the pattern when it comes night, and that is hard!

It is so pleasant to be out in this great room and creep around as I please!

I don't want to go outside. I won't, even if Jennie asks me to.

For outside you have to creep on the ground, and everything is green instead of yellow.

But here I can creep smoothly on the floor, and my shoulder just fits in that long smooch around the wall, so I cannot lose my way.

Why there's John at the door!

It is no use, young man, you can't open it!

How he does call and pound!

Now he's crying for an axe.

It would be a shame to break down that beautiful door!

"John dear!" said I in the gentlest voice, "the key is down by the front steps, under a plaintain leaf!"

That silenced him for a few moments.

Then he said—very quietly indeed, "Open the door, my darling!"

"I can't," said I. "The key is down by the front door under a plaintain leaf!"

And then I said it again, several times, very gently and slowly, and said it so often that he had to go and see, and he got it of course, and came in. He stopped short by the door.

"What is the matter?" he cried. "For God's sake, what are you doing!"

I kept on creeping just the same, but I looked at him over my shoulder.

"I've got out at last," said I, "in spite of you and Jane? And I've pulled off most of the paper, so you can't put me back!"

Now why should that man have fainted? But he did, and right across my path by the wall, so that I had to creep over him every time!

[1892]

QUESTIONS FOR STUDY

1. Early in the story the narrator describes her husband as follows: "John is practical in the extreme. He has no patience with faith, an intense horror of superstition, and he scoffs openly at any talk of things not to be felt and seen and put down in figures." Does the rest of the story seem to confirm this view? What other attitudes characterize the husband's view of his wife? How do such attitudes contribute to the situation in which the wife finds herself?

2. How does the narrator's attitude toward her husband change in the course of the story?

3. What are the successive stages in the narrator's psychological breakdown? How are these stages reflected in her obsession with the yellow wallpaper? What does the wallpaper finally come to represent for her?

4. In what ways do the author's chosen point of view and style contribute to the story's emotional effect or impact?

5. Compare this story with Elizabeth Bowen's "The Demon Lover." What similarities and differences do you detect in the two stories?

GEORGE GISSING

The House of Cobwebs

IT WAS five o'clock on a June morning. The dirty-buff blind of the lodging-house bedroom shone like cloth of gold as the sun's unclouded rays poured through it, transforming all they illumined, so that things poor and mean seemed to share in the triumphant glory of new-born day. In the bed lay a young man who had already been awake for an hour. He kept stirring uneasily, but with no intention of trying to sleep again. His eyes followed the slow movement of the sunshine on the wallpaper, and noted, as they never had done before, the details of the flower pattern, which represented no flower wherewith botanists are acquainted, yet, in this summer light, turned the thoughts to garden and field and hedgerow. The young man had a troubled mind, and his thoughts ran thus:—

'I must have three months at least, and how am I to live? . . . Fifteen shillings a week—not quite that, if I spread my money out. Can one live on fifteen shillings a week—rent, food, washing? . . . I shall have to leave these lodgings at once. They're not luxurious, but I can't live here under twenty-five, that's clear. . . . Three months to finish my book. It's good; I'm hanged if it isn't! This time I shall find a publisher. All I have to do is to stick at my work and keep my mind easy. . . . Lucky that it's summer; I don't need fires. Any corner would do for me where I can be quiet and see the sun. . . . Wonder whether some cottager in Surrey would house and feed me for fifteen shillings a week? . . . No use lying here. Better get up and see how things look after an hour's walk.'

So the young man arose and clad himself, and went out into the shining street. His name was Goldthorpe. His years were not yet three-and-twenty. Since the age of legal independence he had been living alone in London, solitary and poor, very proud of a whole-hearted devotion to the career of authorship. As soon as he slipped out of the stuffy house, the live air, perfumed with freshness from meadows and hills afar, made his blood pulse joyously. He was at the age of hope, and something within him, which did not represent mere youthful illusion, supported his courage in the face of calculations such as would have damped sober experience. With boyish step, so light and springy that it seemed anxious to run and leap, he took his way through a suburb south of Thames, and pushed on towards the first rising of the Surrey hills. And as he walked resolve strengthened itself in his heart. Somehow or other he would live independently through the next three months. If the worst came to the worst, he could earn bread as clerk or labourer, but as long as his money lasted he would pursue his purpose, and that alone. He sang to himself in this gallant determination, happy as if some one had left him a fortune.

In an ascending road, quiet and tree-shadowed, where the dwellings on either side were for the most part old and small, though here and there a brand-new edifice on a larger scale showed that the neighbourhood was undergoing change such as in our time destroys the picturesque in all London suburbs, the cheery dreamer chanced to turn his eyes upon a spot of desolation which aroused his curiosity and set his fancy at work. Before him stood three deserted houses, a little row once tenanted by middle-class folk, but now for some time unoccupied and unrepaired. They were of brick, but the fronts had a stucco facing cut into imitation of ashlar, and weathered to the sombrest grey. The windows of the ground floor and of that above, and the fanlights above the doors, were boarded up, a guard against unlicensed intrusion; the top story had not been thought to stand in need of this protection, and a few panes were broken. On

these dead frontages could be traced the
marks of climbing plants, which once
hung their leaves about each doorway;
dry fragments of the old stem still adhered
to the stucco. What had been the narrow
strip of fore-garden, railed from the pavement, was now a little wilderness of coarse
grass, docks, nettles, and degenerate
shrubs. The paint on the doors had lost all
colour, and much of it was blistered off;
the three knockers had disappeared, leaving indications of rough removal, as if—
which was probably the case—they had
fallen a prey to marauders. Standing full
in the brilliant sunshine, this spectacle of
abandonment seemed sadder, yet less
ugly, than it would have looked under a
gloomy sky. Goldthorpe began to weave
stories about its musty squalor. He
crossed the road to make a nearer inspection; and as he stood gazing at the dishonoured thresholds, at the stained and
cracked boarding of the blind windows,
at the rusty paling and the broken gates,
there sounded from somewhere near a
thin, shaky strain of music, the notes of a
concertina played with uncertain hand.
The sound seemed to come from within
the houses, yet how could that be? Assuredly no one lived under these crazy
roofs. The musician was playing 'Home,
Sweet Home,' and as Goldthorpe listened
it seemed to him that the sound was not
stationary. Indeed, it moved; it became
more distant, then again the notes
sounded more distinctly, and now as if the
player were in the open air. Perhaps he
was at the back of the houses?

On either side ran a narrow passage,
which parted the spot of desolation from
inhabited dwellings. Exploring one of
these, Goldthorpe found that there lay in
the rear a tract of gardens. Each of the
three lifeless houses had its garden of
about twenty yards long. The bordering
wall along the passage allowed a man of
average height to peer over it, and Goldthorpe searched with curious eye the piece
of ground which was nearest to him.
Many a year must have gone by since any
gardening was done here. Once upon a
time the useful and ornamental had both
been represented in this modest space;
now, flowers and vegetables, such of them

as survived in the struggle for existence,
mingled together, and all alike were
threatened by a wild, rank growth of
grasses and weeds, which had obliterated
the beds, hidden the paths, and made of
the whole garden plot a green jungle. But
Goldthorpe gave only a glance at this still
life; his interest was engrossed by a human
figure, seated on a campstool near the
back wall of the house, and holding a
concertina, whence, at this moment, in
slow, melancholy strain, 'Home, Sweet
Home' began to wheeze forth. The player
was a middle-aged man, dressed like a
decent clerk or shopkeeper, his head
shaded with an old straw hat rather too
large for him, and on his feet—one of
which swung as he sat with legs crossed—
a pair of still more ancient slippers, also
too large. With head aside, and eyes looking upward, he seemed to listen in a mild
ecstasy to the notes of his instrument. He
had a round face of much simplicity
and good-nature, semicircular eyebrows,
pursed little mouth with abortive moustache, and short thin beard fringing the
chinless lower jaw. Having observed this
unimposing person for a minute or two,
himself unseen, Goldthorpe surveyed the
rear of the building, anxious to discover
any sign of its still serving as human
habitation; but nothing spoke of tenancy.
The windows on this side were not
boarded, and only a few panes were
broken; but the chief point of contrast
with the desolate front was made by a
Virginia creeper, which grew luxuriantly
up to the eaves, hiding every sign of decay
save those dim, dusty apertures which
seemed to deny all possibility of life within. And yet, on looking steadily, did he
not discern something at once of the windows on the top story—something like a
curtain or a blind? And had not that same
window the appearance of having been
more recently cleaned than the others?
He could not be sure; perhaps he only
fancied these things. With neck aching
from the strained position in which he had
made his survey over the wall, the young
man turned away. In the same moment
'Home, Sweet Home' came to an end, and,
but for the cry of a milkman, the early-
morning silence was undisturbed.

Goldthorpe pursued his walk, thinking of what he had seen, and wondering what it all meant. On his way back he made a point of again passing the deserted houses, and again he peered over the wall of the passage. The man was still there, but no longer seated with the concertina; wearing a round felt hat instead of the straw, he stood almost knee-deep in vegetation, and appeared to be examining the various growths about him. Presently he moved forward, and, with head still bent, approached the lower end of the garden, where, in a wall higher than that over which Goldthorpe made his espial, there was a wooden door. This the man opened with a key, and, having passed out, could be heard to turn a lock behind him. A minute more, and this short, respectable figure came into sight at the end of the passage. Goldthorpe could not resist the opportunity thus offered. Affecting to turn a look of interest towards the nearest roof, he waited until the stranger was about to pass him, then, with civil greeting, ventured upon a question.

'Can you tell me how these houses come to be in this neglected state?'

The stranger smiled; a soft, modest, deferential smile such as became his countenance, and spoke in a corresponding voice, which had a vaguely provincial accent.

'No wonder it surprises you, sir. I should be surprised myself. It comes of quarrels and lawsuits.'

'So I supposed. Do you know who the property belongs to?'

'Well, yes, sir. The fact is—it belongs to me.'

The avowal was made apologetically, and yet with a certain timid pride. Goldthorpe exhibited all the interest he felt. An idea had suddenly sprung up in his mind; he met the stranger's look, and spoke with the easy good-humour natural to him.

'It seems a great pity that houses should be standing empty like that. Are they quite uninhabitable? Couldn't one camp here during this fine summer weather? To tell you the truth, I'm looking for a room —as cheap a room as I can get. Could you let me one for the next three months?'

The stranger was astonished. He regarded the young man with an uneasy smile.

'You are joking, sir.'

"Not a bit of it. Is the thing quite impossible? Are all the rooms in too bad a state?'

'I won't say *that*,' replied the other cautiously, still eyeing his interlocutor with surprised glances. 'The upper rooms are really not so bad—that is to say, from a humble point of view. I—I have been looking at them just now. You really mean, sir——?'

'I'm quite in earnest, I assure you,' cried Goldthorpe cheerily. 'You see I'm tolerably well dressed still, but I've precious little money, and I want to eke out the little I've got for about three months. I'm writing a book. I think I shall manage to sell it when it's done, but it'll take me about three months yet. I don't care what sort of place I live in, so long as it's quiet. Couldn't we come to terms?'

The listener's visage seemed to grow rounder in progressive astonishment; his eyes declared an emotion akin to awe; his little mouth shaped itself as if about to whistle.

'A book, sir? You are writing a book? You are a literary man?'

'Well, a beginner. I have poverty on my side, you see.'

'Why, it's like Dr. Johnson!' cried the other, his face glowing with interest. 'It's like Chatterton!—though I'm sure I hope you won't end like him, sir. It's like Goldsmith!—indeed it is!'

'I've got half Oliver's name, at all events,' laughed the young man. 'Mine is Goldthorpe.'

'You don't say so, sir! What a strange coincidence! Mine, sir, is Spicer. I—I don't know whether you'd care to come into my garden? We might talk there—'

In a minute or two they were standing amid the green jungle, which Goldthorpe viewed with delight. He declared it the most picturesque garden he had ever seen.

'Why, there are potatoes growing there. And what are those things? Jerusalem artichokes? And look at that magnificent thistle; I never saw a finer thistle in my life! And poppies—and marigolds—and broad-beans—and isn't that lettuce?'

Mr. Spicer was red with gratification.

'I feel that something might be done with the garden, sir,' he said. 'The fact is, sir, I've only lately come into this property, and I'm sorry to say it'll only be mine for a little more than a year—a year from next midsummer day, sir. There's the explanation of what you see. It's leasehold property, and the lease is just coming to its end. Five years ago, sir, an uncle of mine inherited the property from his brother. The houses were then in a very bad state, and only one of them let, and there had been lawsuits going on for a long time between the leaseholder and the ground-landlord—I can't quite understand these matters, they're not at all in my line, sir; but at all events there were quarrels and lawsuits, and I'm told one of the tenants was somehow mixed up in it. The fact is, my uncle wasn't a very well-to-do man, and perhaps he didn't feel able to repair the houses, especially as the lease was drawing to its end. Would you like to go in and have a look round?'

They entered by the back door, which admitted them to a little wash-house. The window was overspun with cobwebs, thick, hoary; each corner of the ceiling was cobweb-packed; long, dusty filaments depended along the walls. Notwithstanding, Goldthorpe noticed that the house had a water-supply; the sink was wet, the tap above it looked new. This confirmed a suspicion in his mind, but he made no remark. They passed into the kitchen. Here again the work of the spider showed thick on every hand. The window, however, though uncleaned for years, had recently been opened; one knew that by the torn and ragged condition of the webs where the sashes joined. And lo! on the window-sill stood a plate, a cup and saucer, a knife, a fork, a spoon—all of them manifestly new-washed. Goldthorpe affected not to see these objects; he averted his face to hide an involuntary smile.

'I must light a candle,' said Mr. Spicer. 'The staircase is quite dark.'

A candle stood ready, with a box of matches, on the rusty cooking-stove. No fire had burned in the grate for many a long day; of that the visitor assured himself. Save the objects on the window-sill, no evidence of human occupation was discoverable. Having struck a light, Mr. Spicer advanced. In the front passage, on the stairs, on the landing, every angle and every projection had its drapery of cobwebs. The stuffy, musty air smelt of cobwebs; so, at all events, did Goldthorpe explain to himself a peculiar odour which he seemed never to have smelt. It was the same in the two rooms on the first floor. Through the boarded windows of that in front penetrated a few thin rays from the golden sky; they gleamed upon dust and web, on faded, torn wall-paper and a fireplace in ruins.

'I shouldn't recommend you to take either of *these* rooms,' said Mr. Spicer, looking nervously at his companion. 'They really can't be called attractive.'

'Those on the top are healthier, no doubt,' was the young man's reply. 'I noticed that some of the window-glass is broken. That must have been good for airing.'

Mr. Spicer grew more and more nervous. He opened his little round mouth, very much like a fish gasping, but seemed unable to speak. Silently he led the way to the top story, still amid cobwebs; the atmosphere was certainly purer up here, and when they entered the first room they found themselves all at once in such a flood of glorious sunshine that Goldthorpe shouted with delight.

'Ah, I could live here! Would it cost much to have the panes put in? An old woman with a broom would do the rest.' He added in a moment, 'But the back windows are not broken, I think?'

'No—I think not—I—no——'

Mr. Spicer gasped and stammered. He stood holding the candle (its light invisible) so that the grease dripped steadily on his trousers.

'Let's have a look at the other,' cried Goldthorpe. 'It gets the afternoon sun, no doubt. And one would have a view of the garden.'

'Stop, sir!' broke from his companion, who was red and perspiring. 'There's something I should like to tell you before you go into that room. I—it—the fact is, sir, that—temporarily—I am occupying it myself.'

'Oh, I beg your pardon, Mr. Spicer!'

'Not at all, sir! Don't mention it, sir. I have a reason—it seemed to me—I've merely put in a bed and a table, sir, that's all—a temporary arrangement.'

'Yes, yes; I quite understand. What could be more sensible? If the house were mine, I should do the same. What's the good of owning a house, and making no use of it?'

Great was Mr. Spicer's satisfaction.

'See what it is, sir,' he exclaimed, 'to have to do with a literary man! You are large-minded, sir; you see things from an intellectual point of view. I can't tell you how it gratifies me, sir, to have made your acquaintance. Let us go into the back room.'

With nervous boldness he threw the door open. Goldthorpe, advancing respectfully, saw that Mr. Spicer had not exaggerated the simplicity of his arrangements. In a certain measure the room had been cleaned, but along the angle of walls and ceiling there still clung a good many cobwebs, and the state of the paper was deplorable. A blind hung at the window, but the floor had no carpet. In one corner stood a little camp bed, neatly made for the day; a table and a chair, of the cheapest species, occupied the middle of the floor, and on the hearth was an oil cooking-stove.

'It's wonderful how little one really wants,' remarked Mr. Spicer, 'at all events in weather such as this. I find that I get along here very well indeed. The only expense I had was the water-supply. And really, sir, when one comes to think of it, the situation is pleasant. If one doesn't mind loneliness—and it happens that I don't. I have my books, sir——'

He opened the door of a cupboard containing several shelves. The first thing Goldthorpe's eye fell upon was the concertina; he saw also sundry articles of clothing, neatly disposed, a little crockery, and, ranged on the two top shelves, some thirty volumes, all of venerable aspect.

'Literature, sir,' pursued Mr. Spicer modestly, 'has always been my comfort. I haven't had very much time for reading, but my motto, sir, has been *nulla dies sine linea*.' [1]

[1] "never a day without a line." (JHP)

It appeared from his pronunciation that Mr. Spicer was no classical scholar, but he uttered the Latin words with infinite gusto, and timidly watched their effect upon the listener.

'This is delightful,' cried Mr. Goldthorpe. 'Will you let me have the front room? I could work here splendidly—splendidly! What rent do you ask, Mr. Spicer?'

'Why really, sir, to tell you the truth I don't know what to say. Of course the windows must be seen to. The fact is, sir, if you felt disposed to do that at your own expense, and—and to have the room cleaned, and—and, let us say, to bear half the water-rate whilst you are here, why, really, I hardly feel justified in asking anything more.'

It was Goldthorpe's turn to be embarrassed, for, little as he was prepared to pay, he did not like to accept a stranger's generosity. They discussed the matter in detail, with the result that for the arrangement which Mr. Spicer had proposed there was substituted a weekly rent of two shillings, the lease extending over a period of three months. Goldthorpe was to live quite independently, asking nothing in the way of domestic service; moreover, he was requested to introduce no other person to the house, even as casual visitor. These conditions Mr. Spicer set forth, in a commercial hand, on a sheet of note-paper, and the agreement was solemnly signed by both contracting parties.

On the way home to breakfast Goldthorpe reviewed his position now that he had taken this decisive step. It was plain that he must furnish his room with the articles which Mr. Spicer found indispensable, and this outlay, be as economical as he might, would tell upon the little capital which was to support him for three months. Indeed, when all had been done, and he found himself, four days later, dwelling on the top story of the house of cobwebs, a simple computation informed him that his total expenditure, after payment of rent, must not exceed fifteenpence a day. What matter? He was in the highest spirits, full of energy and hope. His landlord had been kind and helpful in all sorts of ways, helping him to clean the room, to remove his property from the old lodgings, to make purchases at the lowest possible rate, to established himself as comfortably as circumstances permitted. And when, on the first morning of his tenancy, he was awakened by a brilliant sun, the young man had a sensation of comfort and satisfaction quite new in his experience; for he was really at home; the bed he slept on, the table he ate at and wrote upon, were his own possessions; he thought with pity of his lodging-house life, and felt a joyous assurance that here he would do better work than ever before.

In less than a week Mr. Spicer and he were so friendly that they began to eat together, taking it in turns to prepare the meal. Now and then they walked in company, and every evening they sat smoking (very cheap tobacco) in the wild garden. Little by little Mr. Spicer revealed the facts of his history. He had begun life, in a midland town, as a chemist's errand-boy, and by steady perseverance, with a little pecuniary help from relatives, had at length risen to the position of chemist's assistant. For five-and-twenty years he practised such rigid economy that, having no one but himself to provide for, he began to foresee a possibility of passing his old age elsewhere than in the workhouse. Then befell the death of his uncle, which was to have important consequences for him. Mr. Spicer told the story of this exciting moment late one evening, when, kept indoors by rain, the companions sat together upstairs, one on each side of the rusty and empty fireplace.

'All my life, Mr. Goldthorpe, I've thought what a delightful thing it must be to have a house of one's own. I mean, really of one's own; not only a rented house, but one in which you could live and die, feeling that no one had a right to turn you out. Often and often I've dreamt of it, and tried to imagine what the feeling would be like. Not a large, fine house—oh dear, no! I didn't care how small it might be; indeed, the smaller the better for a man of my sort. Well, then, you can imagine how it came upon me when I heard—— But let me tell you first that I hadn't seen my uncle for fifteen years or more. I had always thought him a well-to-do man, and I knew he wasn't

married, but the truth is, it never came into my head that he might leave me something. Picture me, Mr. Goldthorpe—you have imagination, sir—standing behind the counter and thinking about nothing but business, when in comes a young gentleman—I see him now—and asks for Mr. Spicer. "Spicer is my name, sir," I said. "And you are the nephew," were his next words, "of the late Mr. Isaac Spicer, of Clapham, London?" That shook me, sir, I assure you it did, but I hope I behaved decently. The young gentleman went on to tell me that my uncle had left no will, and that I was believed to be his next-of-kin, and that if so, I inherited all his property, the principal part of which was three houses in London. Now try and think, Mr. Goldthorpe, what sort of state I was in after hearing that. You're an intellectual man, and you can enter into another's mind. Three houses! Well, sir, you know what houses those were. I came up to London at once (it was last autumn), and I saw my uncle's lawyer, and he told me all about the property, and I saw it for myself. Ah, Mr. Goldthorpe! If ever a man suffered a bitter disappointment, sir!'

He ended on a little laugh, as if excusing himself for making so much of his story, and sat for a moment with head bowed.

'Fate played you a nasty trick there,' said Goldthorpe. 'A knavish trick.'

'One felt almost justified in using strong language, sir—though I always avoid it on principle. However, I must tell you that the houses weren't all. Luckily there was a little money as well, and, putting it with my own savings, sir, I found it would yield me an income. When I say an income, I mean, of course, for a man in my position. Even when I have to go into lodgings, when my houses become the property of the ground-landlord—to my mind, Mr. Goldthorpe, a very great injustice, but I don't set myself up against the law of the land—I shall just be able to live. And that's no small blessing, sir, as I think you'll agree.'

'Rather! It's the height of human felicity, Mr. Spicer. I envy you vastly.

'Well, sir, I'm rather disposed to look

at it in that light myself. My nature is not discontented, Mr. Goldthorpe. But, sir, if you could have seen me when the lawyer began to explain about the houses! I was absolutely ignorant of the leasehold system; and at first I really couldn't understand. The lawyer thought me a fool, I fear, sir. And when I came down here and saw the houses themselves! I'm afraid, Mr. Goldthorpe, I'm really afraid, sir, I was weak enough to shed a tear.'

They were sitting by the light of a very small lamp, which did not tend to cheerfulness.

'Come,' cried Goldthorpe, 'after all, the houses are yours for a twelvemonth. Why shouldn't we both live on here all the time? It'll be a little breezy in winter, but we could have the fireplaces knocked into shape, and keep up good fires. When I've sold my book I'll pay a higher rent, Mr. Spicer. I like the old house, upon my word I do! Come, let us have a tune before we go to bed.'

Smiling and happy, Mr. Spicer fetched from the cupboard his concertina, and after the usual apology for what he called his 'imperfect mastery of the instrument,' sat down to play 'Home, Sweet Home.' He had played it for years, and evidently would never improve in his execution. After 'Home, Sweet Home' came 'The Bluebells of Scotland,' after that 'Annie Laurie'; and Mr. Spicer's repertory was at an end. He talked of learning new pieces, but there was not the slightest hope of this achievement.

Mr. Spicer's mental development had ceased more than twenty years ago, when, after extreme efforts, he had attained the qualification of chemist's assistant. Since then the world had stood still with him. Though a true lover of books, he knew nothing of any that had been published during his own lifetime. His father, though very poor, had possessed a little collection of volumes, the very same which now stood in Mr. Spicer's cupboard. The authors represented in this library were either English classics or obscure writers of the early part of the nineteenth century. Knowing these books very thoroughly, Mr. Spicer sometimes indulged in a quotation which would have

puzzled even the erudite. His favourite poet was Cowper, whose moral sentiments greatly soothed him. He spoke of Byron like some contemporary who, whilst admitting his lordship's genius, felt an abhorrence of his life. He judged literature solely from the moral point of view, and was incapable of understanding any other. Of fiction he had read very little indeed, for it was not regarded with favour by his parents. Scott was hardly more than a name to him. And though he avowed acquaintance with one or two works of Dickens, he spoke of them with an uneasy smile, as if in some doubt as to their tendency. With these intellectual characteristics, Mr. Spicer naturally found it difficult to appreciate the attitude of his literary friend, a young man whose brain thrilled in response to modern ideas, and who regarded himself as the destined leader of a new school of fiction. Not indiscreet, Goldthorpe soon became aware that he had better talk as little as possible of the work which absorbed his energies. He had enough liberality and sense of humour to understand and enjoy his landlord's conversation, and the simple goodness of the man inspired him with no little respect. Thus they got along together remarkably well. Mr. Spicer never ceased to feel himself honoured by the presence under his roof of one who—as he was wont to say—wielded the pen. The tradition of Grub Street was for him a living fact. He thought of all authors as struggling with poverty, and continued to cite eighteenth-century examples by way of encouraging Goldthorpe and animating his zeal. Whilst the young man was at work Mr. Spicer moved about the house with soundless footsteps. When invited into his tenant's room he had a reverential demeanour, and the sight of manuscript on the bare deal table caused him to subdue his voice.

The weeks went by, and Goldthorpe's novel steadily progressed. In London he had only two or three acquaintances, and from them he held aloof, lest necessity or temptation should lead to his spending money which he could not spare. The few letters which he received were addressed to a post-office—impossible to shock the nerves of a postman by requesting him to deliver correspondence at this dead house, of which the front door had not been opened for years. The weather was perfect; a great deal of sunshine, but as yet no oppressive heat, even in the chambers under the roof. Towards the end of June Mr. Spicer began to amuse himself with a little gardening. He had discovered in the coal-hole an ancient fork, with one prong broken and the others rusting away. This implement served him in his slow, meditative attack on that part of the jungle which seemed to offer least resistance. He would work for a quarter of an hour, then, resting on his fork, contemplate the tangled mass of vegetation which he had succeeded in tearing up.

'Our aim should be,' he said gravely, when Goldthorpe came to observe his progress, 'to clear the soil round about those vegetables and flowers which seem worth preserving. These broad-beans, for instance—they seem to be a very fine sort. And the Jerusalem artichokes. I've been making inquiry about the artichokes, and I'm told they are not ready to eat till the autumn. The first frost is said to improve them. They're fine plants—very fine plants.'

Already the garden had supplied them with occasional food, but they had to confess that, for the most part, these wild vegetables lacked savour. The artichokes, now shooting up into a leafy grove, were the great hope of the future. It would be deplorable to quit the house before this tuber came to maturity.

'The worst of it is,' remarked Mr. Spicer one day, when he was perspiring freely, 'that I can't help thinking of how different it would be if this garden was really my own. The fact is, Mr. Goldthorpe, I can't put much heart into the work; no, I can't. The more I reflect, the more indignant I become. Really now, Mr. Goldthorpe, speaking as an intellectual man, as a man of imagination, could anything be more cruelly unjust than this leasehold system? I assure you, it keeps me awake at night; it really does.'

The tenor of his conversation proved that Mr. Spicer had no intention of leaving the house until he was legally obliged

to do so. More than once he had an interview with his late uncle's solicitor, and each time he came back with melancholy brow. All the details of the story were now familiar to him; he knew all about the lawsuits which had ruined the property. Whenever he spoke of the ground-landlord, known to him only by name, it was with a severity such as he never permitted himself on any other subject. The ground-landlord was, to his mind, an embodiment of social injustice.

'Never in my life, Mr. Goldthorpe, did I grudge any payment of money as I grudge the ground-rent of these houses. I feel it as robbery, sir, as sheer robbery, though the sum is so small. When, in my ignorance, the matter was first explained to me, I wondered why my uncle had continued to pay this rent, the houses being of no profit to him. But now I understand, Mr. Goldthorpe; the sense of possession is very sweet. Property's property, even when it's leasehold and in ruins. I grudge the ground-rent bitterly, but I feel, sir, that I couldn't bear to lose my houses until the fatal moment, when lose them I must.'

In August the thermometer began to mark high degrees. Goldthorpe found it necessary to dispense with coat and waistcoat when he was working, and at times a treacherous languor whispered to him of the delights of idleness. After one particularly hot day, he and his landlord smoked together in the dusking garden, both unusually silent. Mr. Spicer's eye dwelt upon the great heap of weeds which was resulting from his labour; an odour somewhat too poignant arose from it upon the close air. Goldthorpe, who had been rather headachy all day, was trying to think into perfect clearness the last chapters of his book, and found it difficult.

'You know,' he said all at once, with an impatient movement, 'we ought to be at the seaside.'

'The seaside?' echoed his companion, in surprise. 'Ah, it's a long time since I saw the sea, Mr. Goldthorpe. Why, it must be —yes, it is at least twenty years.'

'Really? I've been there every year of my life till this. One gets into the way of thinking of luxuries as necessities. I tell you what it is. If I sell my book as soon as it's done, we'll have a few days somewhere on the south coast together.'

Mr. Spicer betrayed uneasiness.

'I should like it much,' he murmured, 'but I fear, Mr. Goldthorpe, I greatly fear I can't afford it.'

'Oh, but I mean that you shall go with me as my guest! But for you, Mr. Spicer, I might never have got my book written at all.'

'I feel it an honour, sir, I assure you, to have a literary man in my house,' was the genial reply. 'And you think the *work* will soon be finished, sir?'

Mr. Spicer always spoke of his tenant's novel as 'the work'—which on his lips had a very large and respectful sound.

'About a fortnight more,' answered Goldthorpe with grave intensity.

The heat continued. As he lay awake before getting up, eager to finish his book, yet dreading the torrid temperature of his room, which made the brain sluggish and the hand slow, Goldthorpe saw how two or three energetic spiders had begun to spin webs once more at the corners of the ceiling; now and then he heard the long buzzing of a fly entangled in one of these webs. The same thing was happening in Mr. Spicer's chamber. It did not seem worth while to brush the new webs away.

'When you come to think of it, sir,' said the landlord, 'it's the spiders who are the real owners of these houses. When I go away, they'll be pulled down; they're not fit for human habitation. Only the spiders are really at home here, and the fact is, sir, I don't feel I have the right to disturb them. As a man of imagination, Mr. Goldthorpe, you'll understand my thoughts!'

Only with a great effort was the novel finished. Goldthorpe had lost his appetite (not, perhaps, altogether a disadvantage), and he could not sleep; a slight fever seemed to be constantly upon him. But this work was a question of life and death to him, and he brought it to an end only a few days after the term he had set himself. The complete manuscript was exhibited to Mr. Spicer, who expressed his profound sense of the privilege. Then, without delay, Goldthorpe took it to the publishing house in which he had most hope.

The young author could now do nothing but wait, and, under the circumstances, waiting meant torture. His money was all but exhausted; if he could not speedily sell the book, his position would be that of a mere pauper. Supported thus long by the artist's enthusiasm, he fell into despondency, saw the dark side of things. To be sure, his mother (a widow in narrow circumstances) had written pressing him to take a holiday 'at home,' but he dreaded the thought of going penniless to his mother's house, and there, perchance, receiving bad news about his book. An ugly feature of the situation was that he continued to feel anything but well; indeed, he felt sure that he was getting worse. At night he suffered severely; sleep had almost forsaken him. Hour after hour he lay listening to mysterious noises, strange crackings and creakings through the desolate house; sometimes he imagined the sound of footsteps in the bare rooms below; even hushed voices, from he knew not where, chilled his blood at midnight. Since crumbs had begun to lie about, mice were common; they scampered as if in revelry above the ceiling, and under the floor, and within the walls. Goldthorpe began to dislike this strange abode. He felt that under any circumstances it would be impossible for him to dwell here much longer.

When his last coin was spent, and he had no choice but to pawn or sell something for a few days' subsistence, the manuscript came back upon his hands. It had been judged—declined.

That morning he felt seriously unwell. After making known the catastrophe to Mr. Spicer—who was stricken voiceless—he stood silent for a minute or two, then said with quiet resolve:

'It's all up. I've no money, and I feel as if I were going to have an illness. I must say good-bye to you, old friend.'

'Mr. Goldthorpe!' exclaimed the other solemnly; 'I entreat you, sir, to do nothing rash! Take heart, sir! Think of Samuel Johnson, think of Goldsmith——'

'The extent of my rashness, Mr. Spicer,

will be to raise enough money on my watch to get down into Derbyshire. I must go home. If I don't, you'll have the pleasant job of taking me to a hospital.'

Mr. Spicer insisted on lending him the small sum he needed. An hour or two later they were at St. Pancras Station, and before sunset Goldthorpe had found harbourage under his mother's roof. There he lay ill for more than a month, and convalescent for as long again. His doctor declared that he must have been living in some very unhealthy place, but the young man preferred to explain his illness by overwork. It seemed to him sheer ingratitude to throw blame on Mr. Spicer's house, where he had been so contented and worked so well until the hot days of latter August. Mr. Spicer himself wrote kind and odd little letters, giving an account of the garden, and earnestly hoping that his literary friend would be back in London to taste the Jerusalem artichokes. But Christmas came and went, and Goldthorpe was still at his mother's house.

Meanwhile the manuscript had gone from publisher to publisher, and at length, on a day in January—date ever memorable in Goldthorpe's life—there arrived a short letter in which a certain firm dryly intimated their approval of the story offered them, and their willingness to purchase the copyright for a sum of fifty pounds. The next morning the triumphant author travelled to London. For two or three days a violent gale had been blowing, with much damage throughout the country; on his journey Goldthorpe saw many great trees lying prostrate, beaten, as though scornfully, by the cold rain which now descended in torrents. Arrived in town, he went to the house where he had lodged in the time of comparative prosperity, and there was lucky enough to find his old rooms vacant. On the morrow he called upon the gracious publishers, and after that, under a sky now become more gentle, he took his way towards the abode of Mr. Spicer.

Eager to communicate the joyous news, glad in the prospect of seeing his simple-hearted friend, he went at a great pace up the ascending road. There were the three houses, looking drearier than ever in a faint gleam of winter sunshine. There

were his old windows. But—what had happened to the roof? He stood in astonishment and apprehension, for, just above the room where he had dwelt, the roof was an utter wreck, showing a great hole, as if something had fallen upon it with crushing weight. As indeed was the case; evidently the chimney-stack had come down, and doubtless in the recent gale. Seized with anxiety on Mr. Spicer's account, he ran round to the back of the garden and tried the door; but it was locked as usual. He strained to peer over the garden wall, but could discover nothing that threw light on his friend's fate; he noticed, however, a great grove of dead, brown artichoke stems, seven or eight feet high. Looking up at the back windows, he shouted Mr. Spicer's name; it was useless. Then, in serious alarm, he betook himself to the house on the other side of the passage, knocked at the door, and asked of the woman who presented herself whether anything was known of a gentleman who dwelt where the chimney-stack had just fallen. News was at once forthcoming; the event had obviously caused no small local excitement. It was two days since the falling of the chimney, which happened towards evening, when the gale blew its hardest. Mr. Spicer was at that moment sitting before the fire, and only by a miracle had he escaped destruction, for an immense weight of material came down through the rotten roof, and even broke a good deal of the flooring. Had the occupant been anywhere but close by the fireplace, he must have been crushed to a mummy; as it was, only a few bricks struck him, inflicting severe bruises on back and arms. But the shock had been serious. When his shouts from the window at length attracted attention and brought help, the poor man had to be carried downstairs, and in a thoroughly helpless state was removed to the nearest hospital.

'Which room was he in?' inquired Goldthorpe. 'Back or front?'

'In the front room. The back wasn't touched.'

Musing on Mr. Spicer's bad luck—for it seemed as if he had changed from the back to the front room just in order that the chimney might fall on him—Goldthorpe hastened away to the hospital. He could not be admitted to-day, but heard that his friend was doing very well; on the morrow he would be allowed to see him.

So at the visitors' hour Goldthorpe returned. Entering the long accident ward, he searched anxiously for the familiar face, and caught sight of it just as it began to beam recognition. Mr. Spicer was sitting up in bed; he looked pale and meagre, but not seriously ill; his voice quivered with delight as he greeted the young man.

'I heard of your inquiring for me yesterday, Mr. Goldthorpe, and I've hardly been able to live for impatience to see you. How are you, sir? How are you? And what news about the *work*, sir?'

'We'll talk about that presently, Mr. Spicer. Tell me all about your accident. How came you to be in the front room?'

'Ah, sir,' replied the patient, with a little shake of the head, 'that indeed was singular. Only a few days before, I had made a removal from my room into yours. I call it yours, sir, for I always thought of it as yours; but thank heaven you were not there. Only a few days before. I took that step, Mr. Goldthorpe, for two reasons: first, because water was coming through the roof at the back in rather unpleasant quantities, and secondly, because I hoped to get a little morning sun in the front. The fact is, sir, my room had been just a little depressing. Ah, Mr. Goldthorpe, if you knew how I have missed you, sir! But the *work*—what news of the *work*?'

Smiling as though carelessly, the author made known his good fortune. For a quarter of an hour Mr. Spicer could talk of nothing else.

'This has completed my cure!' he kept repeating. 'The work was composed under my roof, my own roof, sir! Did I not tell you to take heart?'

'And where are you going to live?' asked Goldthorpe presently. 'You can't go back to the old house.'

'Alas! no, sir. All my life I have dreamt of the joy of owning a house. You know how the dream was realised, Mr. Goldthorpe, and you see what has come of it at last. Probably it is a chastisement for overweening desires, sir. I should have remembered my position, and kept my wishes within bounds. But, Mr. Goldthorpe, I shall continue to cultivate the garden, sir. I shall put in spring lettuces, and radishes, and mustard and cress. The property is mine till midsummer day. You shall eat a lettuce of my growing, Mr. Goldthorpe; I am bent on that. And how I grieve that you were not with me at the time of the artichokes—just at the moment when they were touched by the first frost!'

'Ah! They were really good, Mr. Spicer?'

'Sir, they seemed good to *me*, very good. Just at the moment of the first frost!'

[1906]

QUESTIONS FOR STUDY

1. *What are the successive stages in Goldthorpe's relationship with Mr. Spicer and his house? How do they both come to affect him?*
2. *To what extent are Mr. Spicer's values, tastes, and aspirations antithetical to those of a would-be novelist?*
3. *Why is it significant that the vegetables from Mr. Spicer's garden "lacked savour"?*
4. *What is the importance of the fact that the roof of the house collapses simultaneously with the publisher's acceptance of Goldthorpe's novel?*
5. *What does the house of cobwebs finally seem to represent for Goldthorpe?*
6. *Does Goldthorpe seem to learn anything from his experience?*

NIKOLAI GOGOL

The Overcoat

IN THE department of . . . but I had better not mention in what department. There is nothing in the world more readily moved to wrath than a department, a regiment, a government office, and in fact any sort of official body. Nowadays every private individual considers all society insulted in his person. I have been told that very lately a petition was handed in from a police-captain of what town I don't recollect, and that in this petition he set forth clearly that the institutions of the State were in danger and that its sacred name was being taken in vain; and, in proof thereof, he appended to his petition an enormously long volume of some work of romance in which a police-captain appeared on every tenth page, occasionally, indeed, in an intoxicated condition. And so, to avoid any unpleasantness, we had better call the department of which we are speaking a certain department.

And so, in a certain department there was a government clerk; a clerk of whom it cannot be said that he was very remarkable; he was short, somewhat pockmarked, with rather reddish hair and rather dim, bleary eyes, with a small bald patch on the top of his head, with wrinkles on both sides of his cheeks and the sort of complexion which is usually associated with hæmorrhoids . . . no help for that, it is the Petersburg climate. As for his grade in the service (for among us the grade is what must be put first), he was what is called a perpetual titular councillor, a class at which, as we all know, various writers who indulge in the praiseworthy habit of attacking those who cannot defend themselves jeer and jibe to their hearts' content. This clerk's surname was Bashmatchkin. From the very name it is

clear that it must have been derived from a shoe (*bashmak*); but when and under what circumstances it was derived from a shoe, it is impossible to say. Both his father and his grandfather and even his brother-in-law, and all the Bashmatchkins without exception wore boots, which they simply re-soled two or three times a year. His name was Akaky Akakyevitch. Perhaps it may strike the reader as a rather strange and far-fetched name, but I can assure him that it was not far-fetched at all, that the circumstances were such that it was quite out of the question to give him any other name. Akaky Akakyevitch was born towards nightfall, if my memory does not deceive me, on the twenty-third of March. His mother, the wife of a government clerk, a very good woman, made arrangements in due course to christen the child. She was still lying in bed, facing the door, while on her right hand stood the godfather, an excellent man called Ivan Ivanovitch Yeroshkin, one of the head clerks in the Senate, and the godmother, the wife of a police official, and a woman of rare qualities, Arina Semyonovna Byelobryushkov. Three names were offered to the happy mother for selection—Moky, Sossy, or the name of the martyr Hozdazat. "No," thought the poor lady, "they are all such names!" To satisfy her, they opened the calendar at another place, and the names which turned up were: Trifily, Dula, Varahasy. "What an infliction!" said the mother. "What names they all are! I really never heard such names. Varadat or Varuh would be bad enough, but Trifily and Varahasy!" They turned over another page and the names were: Pavsikahy and Vahtisy. "Well, I see," said the mother, "it is clear that it is his fate. Since that is how it is, he had better be called after his father, his father is Akaky, let the son be Akaky, too." This was how he came to be Akaky Akakyevitch. The baby was christened and cried and made wry faces during the ceremony, as though he foresaw that he would be a titular councillor. So that was how it all came to pass. We have recalled it here so that the reader may see for himself that it happened quite inevitably and that to give him any other name was out of the question. No one has been able to remember when and how long ago he entered the department, nor who gave him the job. However many directors and higher officials of all sorts came and went, he was always seen in the same place, in the same position, at the very same duty, precisely the same copying clerk, so that they used to declare that he must have been born a copying clerk in uniform all complete and with a bald patch on his head. No respect at all was shown him in the department. The porters, far from getting up from their seats when he came in, took no more notice of him than if a simple fly had flown across the vestibule. His superiors treated him with a sort of domineering chilliness. The head clerk's assistant used to throw papers under his nose without even saying: "Copy this" or "Here is an interesting, nice little case" or some agreeable remark of the sort, as is usually done in well-behaved offices. And he would take it, gazing only at the paper without looking to see who had put it there and whether he had the right to do so; he would take it and at once set to work to copy it. The young clerks jeered and made jokes at him to the best of their clerkly wit, and told before his face all sorts of stories of their own invention about him; they would say of his landlady, an old woman of seventy, that she beat him, would enquire when the wedding was to take place, and would scatter bits of paper on his head, calling them snow. Akaky Akakyevitch never answered a word, however, but behaved as though there were no one there. It had no influence on his work even; in the midst of all this teasing, he never made a single mistake in his copying. Only when the jokes were too

unbearable, when they jolted his arm and prevented him from going on with his work, he would bring out: "Leave me alone! Why do you insult me?" and there was something strange in the words and in the voice in which they were uttered. There was a note in it of something that aroused compassion, so that one young man, new to the office, who, following the example of the rest, had allowed himself to mock at him, suddenly stopped as though cut to the heart, and from that time forth everything was, as it were, changed and appeared in a different light to him. Some unnatural force seemed to thrust him away from the companions with whom he had become acquainted, accepting them as well-bred, polished people. And long afterwards, at moments of the greatest gaiety, the figure of the humble little clerk with a bald patch on his head rose before him with his heart-rending words: "Leave me alone! Why do you insult me?" and in those heart-rending words he heard others: "I am your brother." And the poor young man hid his face in his hands, and many times afterwards in his life he shuddered, seeing how much inhumanity there is in man, how much savage brutality lies hidden under refined, cultured politeness, and, my God! even in a man whom the world accepts as a gentleman and a man of honour. . . .

It would be hard to find a man who lived in his work as did Akaky Akakyevitch. To say that he was zealous in his work is not enough; no, he loved his work. In it, in that copying, he found a varied and agreeable world of his own. There was a look of enjoyment on his face; certain letters were favourites with him, and when he came to them he was delighted; he chuckled to himself and winked and moved his lips, so that it seemed as though every letter his pen was forming could be read in his face. If rewards had been given according to the measure of zeal in the service, he might to his amazement have even found himself a civil councillor; but all he gained in the service, as the wits, his fellow-clerks expressed it, was a buckle in his button-hole and a pain in his back. It cannot be said, however, that no notice had ever been taken of him. One director, being a good-natured man and anxious to reward him for his long service, sent him something a little more important than his ordinary copying; he was instructed from a finished document to make some sort of report for another office, the work consisted only of altering the headings and in places changing the first person into the third. This cost him such an effort that it threw him into a regular perspiration: he mopped his brow and said at last, "No, better let me copy something."

From that time forth they left him to go on copying for ever. It seemed as though nothing in the world existed for him outside his copying. He gave no thought at all to his clothes; his uniform was—well, not green but some sort of rusty, muddy colour. His collar was very short and narrow, so that, although his neck was not particularly long, yet, standing out of the collar, it looked as immensely long as those of the plaster kittens that wag their heads and are carried about on trays on the heads of dozens of foreigners living in Russia. And there were always things sticking to his uniform, either bits of hay or threads; moreover, he had a special art of passing under a window at the very moment when various rubbish was being flung out into the street, and so was continually carrying off bits of melon rind and similar litter on his hat. He had never once in his life noticed what was being done and going on in the street, all those things at which, as we all know, his colleagues, the young clerks, always stare, carrying their sharp sight so far even as to notice any one on the other side of the pavement with a trouser strap hanging loose—a detail which always calls forth a sly grin. Whatever Akaky Akakyevitch looked at, he saw nothing anywhere but his clear, evenly written lines, and only perhaps when a horse's head suddenly appeared from nowhere just on his shoulder, and its nostrils blew a perfect gale upon his cheek, did he notice that he was not in the middle of his writing, but rather in the middle of the street.

On reaching home, he would sit down at once to the table, hurriedly sup his soup and eat a piece of beef with an onion; he did not notice the taste at all, but ate it all up together with the flies and anything else that Providence chanced to send him. When he felt that his stomach was beginning to be full, he would rise up from the table, get out a bottle of ink and set to copying the papers he had brought home with him. When he had none to do, he would make a copy expressly for his own pleasure, particularly if the document were remarkable not for the beauty of its style but for the fact of its being addressed to some new or important personage.

Even at those hours when the grey Petersburg sky is completely overcast and the whole population of clerks have dined and eaten their fill, each as best he can, according to the salary he receives and his personal tastes; when they are all resting after the scratching of pens and bustle of the office, their own necessary work and other people's, and all the tasks that an over-zealous man voluntarily sets himself even beyond what is necessary; when the clerks are hastening to devote what is left of their time to pleasure; some more enterprising are flying to the theatre, others to the street to spend their leisure, staring at women's hats, some to spend the evening paying compliments to some attractive girl, the star of a little official circle, while some—and this is the most frequent of all—go simply to a fellow-clerk's flat on the third or fourth storey, two little rooms with an entry or a kitchen, with some pretentions to style, with a lamp or some such article that has cost many sacrifices of dinners and excursions —at the time when all the clerks are scattered about the little flats of their friends, playing a tempestuous game of whist, sipping tea out of glasses to the accompaniment of farthing rusks, sucking in smoke from long pipes, telling, as the cards are dealt, some scandal that has floated down from higher circles, a pleasure which the Russian can never by any possibility deny himself, or, when there is nothing better to talk about, repeating the everlasting anecdote of the commanding officer who was told that the tail had been cut off the horse on the Falconet monument—in short, even when every one was eagerly seeking entertainment, Akaky Akakyevitch did not give himself up to any amusement. No one could say that they had ever seen him at an evening party. After working to his heart's content, he would go to bed, smiling at the thought of the next day and wondering what God would send him to copy! So flowed on the peaceful life of a man who knew how to be content with his fate on a salary of four hundred roubles, and so perhaps it would have flowed on to extreme old age, had it not been for the various calamities that bestrew the path through life, not only of titular, but even of privy, actual court and all other councillors, even those who neither give council to others nor accept it themselves.

There is in Petersburg a mighty foe of all who receive a salary of four hundred roubles or about that sum. That foe is none other than our northern frost, although it is said to be very good for the health. Between eight and nine in the morning, precisely at the hour when the streets are full of clerks going to their departments, the frost begins giving such sharp and stinging flips at all their noses indiscriminately that the poor fellows don't know what to do with them. At that time, when even those in the higher grade have a pain in their brows and tears in their eyes from the frost, the poor titular councillors are sometimes almost defence-less. Their only protection lies in running as fast as they can through five or six streets in a wretched, thin little overcoat and then warming their feet thoroughly in the porter's room, till all their faculties and qualifications for their various duties thaw again after being frozen on the way. Akaky Akakyevitch had for some time been feeling that his back and shoulders were particularly nipped by the cold, although he did try to run the regular distance as fast as he could. He wondered at last whether there were any defects in his overcoat. After examining it thoroughly in the privacy of his home, he discovered that in two or three places, to wit on the back and the shoulders, it had become a regular sieve; the cloth was so worn that

you could see through it and the lining was coming out. I must observe that Akaky Akakyevitch's overcoat had also served as a butt for the jibes of the clerks. It had even been deprived of the honourable name of overcoat and had been referred to as the "dressing jacket." It was indeed of rather a strange make. Its collar had been growing smaller year by year as it served to patch the other parts. The patches were not good specimens of the tailor's art, and they certainly looked clumsy and ugly. On seeing what was wrong, Akaky Akakyevitch decided that he would have to take the overcoat to Petrovitch, a tailor who lived on a fourth storey up a back staircase, and, in spite of having only one eye and being pock-marked all over his face, was rather successful in repairing the trousers and coats of clerks and others—that is, when he was sober, be it understood, and had no other enterprise in his mind. Of this tailor I ought not, of course, to say much, but since it is now the rule that the character of every person in a novel must be completely drawn, well, there is no help for it, here is Petrovitch too. At first he was called simply Grigory, and was a serf belonging to some gentleman or other. He began to be called Petrovitch from the time that he got his freedom and began to drink rather heavily on every holiday, at first only on the chief holidays, but afterwards on all church holidays indiscriminately, wherever there is a cross in the calendar. On that side he was true to the customs of his forefathers, and when he quarrelled with his wife used to call her "a worldly woman and a German." Since we have now mentioned the wife, it will be necessary to say a few words about her too, but unfortunately not much is known about her, except indeed that Petrovitch had a wife and that she wore a cap and not a kerchief, but apparently she could not boast of beauty; anyway, none but soldiers of the Guards peeped under her cap when they met her, and they twitched their moustaches and gave vent to a rather peculiar sound.

As he climbed the stairs, leading to Petrovitch's—which, to do them justice, were all soaked with water and slops and saturated through and through with that smell of spirits which makes the eyes smart, and is, as we all know, inseparable from the back-stairs of Petersburg houses —Akaky Akakyevitch was already wondering how much Petrovitch would ask for the job, and inwardly resolving not to give more than two roubles. The door was open, for Petrovitch's wife was frying some fish and had so filled the kitchen with smoke that you could not even see the black-beetles. Akaky Akakyevitch crossed the kitchen unnoticed by the good woman, and walked at last into a room where he saw Petrovitch sitting on a big, wooden, unpainted table with his legs tucked under him like a Turkish Pasha. The feet, as is usual with tailors when they sit at work, were bare; and the first object that caught Akaky Akakyevitch's eye was the big toe, with which he was already familiar, with a misshapen nail as thick and strong as the shell of a tortoise. Round Petrovitch's neck hung a skein of silk and another of thread and on his knees was a rag of some sort. He had for the last three minutes been trying to thread his needle, but could not get the thread into the eye and so was very angry with the darkness and indeed with the thread itself, muttering in an undertone: "It won't go in, the savage! You wear me out, you rascal." Akaky Akakyevitch was vexed that he had come just at the minute when Petrovitch was in a bad humour; he liked to give him an order when he was a little "elevated," or, as his wife expressed it, "had fortified himself on fizz, the one-eyed devil." In such circumstances Petrovitch was as a rule very ready to give way and agree, and invariably bowed and thanked him, indeed. Afterwards, it is true, his wife would come wailing that her husband had been drunk and so had asked too little, but adding a single ten-kopek piece would settle that. But on this occasion Petrovitch was apparently sober and consequently curt, unwilling to bargain, and the devil knows what price he would be ready to lay on. Akaky Akakyevitch perceived this, and was, as the saying is, beating a retreat, but things had gone too far, for Petrovitch was screwing up his solitary eye very attentively at him and Akaky Akakyevitch involuntarily

brought out: "Good day, Petrovitch!" "I wish you a good day, sir," said Petrovitch, and squinted at Akaky Akakyevitch's hands, trying to discover what sort of goods he had brought.

"Here I have come to you, Petrovitch, do you see . . . !"

It must be noticed that Akaky Akakyevitch for the most part explained himself by apologies, vague phrases, and particles which have absolutely no significance whatever. If the subject were a very difficult one, it was his habit indeed to leave his sentences quite unfinished, so that very often after a sentence had begun with the words, "It really is, don't you know . . ." nothing at all would follow and he himself would be quite oblivious, supposing he had said all that was necessary.

"What is it?" said Petrovitch, and at the same time with his solitary eye he scrutinized his whole uniform from the collar to the sleeves, the back, the skirts, the button-holes—with all of which he was very familiar, they were all his own work. Such scrutiny is habitual with tailors, it is the first thing they do on meeting one.

"It's like this, Petrovitch . . . the overcoat, the cloth . . . you see everywhere else it is quite strong; it's a little dusty and looks as though it were old, but it is new and it is only in one place just a little . . . on the back, and just a little worn on one shoulder and on this shoulder, too, a little . . . do you see? that's all, and it's not much work. . . ."

Petrovitch took the "dressing jacket," first spread it out over the table, examined it for a long time, shook his head and put his hand out to the window for a round snuff-box with a portrait on the lid of some general—which precisely I can't say, for a finger had been thrust through the spot where a face should have been, and the hole had been pasted up with a square piece of paper. After taking a pinch of snuff, Petrovitch held the "dressing jacket" up in his hands and looked at it against the light, and again he shook his head; then he turned it with the lining upwards and once more shook his head; again he took off the lid with the general pasted up with paper and stuffed a pinch into his nose, shut the box, put it away and at last said: "No, it can't be repaired;

a wretched garment!" Akaky Akakyevitch's heart sank at those words.

"Why can't it, Petrovitch?" he said, almost in the imploring voice of a child. "Why, the only thing is it is a bit worn on the shoulders; why, you have got some little pieces. . . ."

"Yes, the pieces will be found all right," said Petrovitch, "but it can't be patched, the stuff is quite rotten; if you put a needle in it, it would give way."

"Let it give way, but you just put a patch on it."

"There is nothing to put a patch on. There is nothing for it to hold on to; there is a great strain on it, it is not worth calling cloth, it would fly away at a breath of wind."

"Well, then, strengthen it with something—upon my word, really, this is . . . !"

"No," said Petrovitch resolutely, "there is nothing to be done, the thing is no good at all. You had far better, when the cold winter weather comes, make yourself leg wrappings out of it, for there is no warmth in stockings, the Germans invented them just to make money." (Petrovitch was fond of a dig at the Germans occasionally.) "And as for the overcoat, it is clear that you will have to have a new one."

At the word "new" there was a mist before Akaky Akakyevitch's eyes, and everything in the room seemed blurred. He could see nothing clearly but the general with the piece of paper over his face on the lid of Petrovitch's snuff-box. "A new one?" he said, still feeling as though he were in a dream; "why, I haven't the money for it."

"Yes, a new one," Petrovitch repeated with barbarous composure.

"Well, and if I did have a new one, how much would it . . . ?"

"You mean what will it cost?"

"Yes."

"Well, three fifty-rouble notes or more," said Petrovitch, and he compressed his lips significantly. He was very fond of making an effect, he was fond of suddenly disconcerting a man completely and then squinting sideways to see what sort of a face he made.

"A hundred and fifty roubles for an overcoat" screamed poor Akaky Akakyevitch—it was perhaps the first time he had screamed in his life, for he was always distinguished by the softness of his voice.

"Yes," said Petrovitch, "and even then it's according to the coat. If I were to put marten on the collar, and add a hood with silk linings, it would come to two hundred."

"Petrovitch, please," said Akaky Akakyevitch in an imploring voice, not hearing and not trying to hear what Petrovitch said, and missing all his effects, "do repair it somehow, so that it will serve a little longer."

"No, that would be wasting work and spending money for nothing," said Petrovitch, and after that Akaky Akakyevitch went away completely crushed, and when he had gone Petrovitch remained standing for a long time with his lips pursed up significantly before he took up his work again, feeling pleased that he had not demeaned himself nor lowered the dignity of the tailor's art.

When he got into the street, Akaky Akakyevitch was as though in a dream. "So that is how it is," he said to himself. "I really did not think it would be so . . ." and then after a pause he added, "So there it is! so that's how it is at last! and I really could never have supposed it would have been so. And there . . ." There followed another long silence, after which he brought out: "So there it is! well, it really is so utterly unexpected . . . who would have thought . . . what a circumstance. . . ." Saying this, instead of going home he walked off in quite the opposite direction without suspecting what he was doing. On the way a clumsy sweep brushed the whole of his sooty side against him and blackened all his shoulder; a regular hatful of plaster scattered upon him from the top of a house that was being built. He noticed nothing of this, and only after he had jostled against a sentry who had set his halberd down beside him and was shaking some snuff out of his horn into his rough fist, he came to himself a little and then only because the sentry said: "Why are you poking yourself right in one's face, haven't you the pavement to yourself?" This made him look round and turn homeward; only there he began to collect his thoughts, to see his position in a clear and true light and began talking to himself no longer incoherently but reasonably and openly as with a sensible friend with whom one can discuss the most intimate and vital matters. "No, indeed," said Akaky Akakyevitch, "it is no use talking to Petrovitch now; just now he really is . . . his wife must have been giving it to him. I had better go to him on Sunday morning; after the Saturday evening he will be squinting and sleepy, so he'll want a little drink to carry it off and his wife won't give him a penny. I'll slip ten kopecks into his hand and then he will be more accommodating and maybe take the overcoat. . . ."

So reasoning with himself, Akaky Akakyevitch cheered up and waited until the next Sunday; then, seeing from a distance Petrovitch's wife leaving the house, he went straight in. Petrovitch certainly was very tipsy after the Saturday. He could hardly hold his head up and was very drowsy: but, for all that, as soon as he heard what he was speaking about, it seemed as though the devil had nudged him. "I can't," he said, "you must kindly order a new one." Akaky Akakyevitch at once slipped a ten-kopeck piece into his hand. "I thank you, sir, I will have just a drop to your health, but don't trouble yourself about the overcoat; it is not a bit of good for anything. I'll make you a fine new coat, you can trust me for that."

Akaky Akakyevitch would have said more about repairs, but Petrovitch, without listening, said: "A new one now I'll make you without fail; you can rely upon that, I'll do my best. It could even be like the fashion that has come in with the collar to button with silver claws under appliqué."

Then Akaky Akakyevitch saw that there was no escape from a new overcoat and he was utterly depressed. How indeed, for what, with what money could he get it? Of course he could to some extent rely on the bonus for the coming holiday, but that money had long ago been appropriated and its use determined beforehand. It was needed for new trousers and to pay the cobbler an old debt for putting some new tops to some old boot-legs, and

he had to order three shirts from a seamstress as well as two specimens of an undergarment which it is improper to mention in print; in short, all that money absolutely must be spent, and even if the director were to be so gracious as to assign him a gratuity of forty-five or even fifty, instead of forty roubles, there would be still left a mere trifle, which would be but as a drop in the ocean beside the fortune needed for an overcoat. Though, of course, he knew that Petrovitch had a strange craze for suddenly putting on the devil knows what enormous price, so that at times his own wife could not help crying out: "Why, you are out of your wits, you idiot! Another time he'll undertake a job for nothing, and here the devil has bewitched him to ask more than he is worth himself." Though, of course, he knew that Petrovitch would undertake to make it for eighty roubles, still where would he get those eighty roubles? He might manage half of that sum; half of it could be found, perhaps even a little more; but where could he get the other half? . . . But, first of all, the reader ought to know where that first half was to be found. Akaky Akakyevitch had the habit every time he spent a rouble of putting aside two kopecks in a little locked-up box with a slit in the lid for slipping the money in. At the end of every half-year he would inspect the pile of coppers there and change them for small silver. He had done this for a long time, and in the course of many years the sum had mounted up to forty roubles and so he had half the money in his hands, but where was he to get the other half, where was he to get another forty roubles? Akaky Akakyevitch pondered and pondered and decided at last that he would have to diminish his ordinary expenses, at least for a year; give up burning candles in the evening, and if he had to do anything he must go into the landlady's room and work by her candle; that as he walked along the streets he must walk as lightly and carefully as possible, almost on tiptoe, on the cobbles and flagstones, so that his soles might last a little longer than usual; that he must send his linen to the wash less frequently, and that, to preserve it from being worn, he must take it off every day when he came home and sit in a thin cotton-shoddy dressing-gown, a very ancient garment which Time itself had spared. To tell the truth, he found it at first rather hard to get used to these privations, but after a while it became a habit and went smoothly enough—he even became quite accustomed to being hungry in the evening; on the other hand, he had spiritual nourishment, for he carried ever in his thoughts the idea of his future overcoat. His whole existence had in a sense become fuller, as though he had married, as though some other person were present with him, as though he were no longer alone, but an agreeable companion had consented to walk the path of life hand in hand with him, and that companion was no other than the new overcoat with its thick wadding and its strong, durable lining. He became, as it were, more alive, even more strong-willed, like a man who has set before himself a definite aim. Uncertainty, indecision, in fact all the hesitating and vague characteristics vanished from his face and his manners. At times there was a gleam in his eyes, indeed, the most bold and audacious ideas flashed through his mind. Why not really have marten on the collar? Meditation on the subject always made him absent-minded. On one occasion when he was copying a document, he very nearly made a mistake, so that he almost cried out "ough" aloud and crossed himself. At least once every month he went to Petrovitch to talk about the overcoat, where it would be best to buy the cloth, and what colour it should be, and what price, and, though he returned home a little anxious, he was always pleased at the thought that at last the time was at hand when everything would be bought and the overcoat would be made. Things moved even faster than he had anticipated. Contrary to all expectations, the director bestowed on Akaky Akakyevitch a gratuity of no less than sixty roubles. Whether it was that he had an inkling that Akaky Akakyevitch needed a greatcoat, or whether it happened so by chance, owing to this he found he had twenty roubles extra. This circumstance hastened the course of affairs. Another two or three months of partial fasting and Akaky Akakyevitch had actually saved up nearly eighty roubles. His heart, as a rule very tranquil, began to throb. The very first day he set off in company with Petrovitch to the shops. They bought some very good cloth, and no wonder, since they had been thinking of it for more than six months before, and scarcely a month had passed without their going to the shop to compare prices; now Petrovitch himself declared that there was no better cloth to be had. For the lining they chose calico, but of a stout quality, which in Petrovitch's words was even better than silk, and actually as strong and handsome to look at. Marten they did not buy, because it certainly was dear, but instead they chose cat fur, the best to be found in the shop—cat which in the distance might almost be taken for marten. Petrovitch was busy over the coat for a whole fortnight, because there were a great many button-holes, otherwise it would have been ready sooner. Petrovitch asked twelve roubles for the work; less than that it hardly could have been, everything was sewn with silk, with fine double seams, and Petrovitch went over every seam afterwards with his own teeth imprinting various figures with them. It was . . . it is hard to say precisely on what day, but probably on the most triumphant day of the life of Akaky Akakyevitch that Petrovitch at last brought the overcoat. He brought it in the morning, just before it was time to set off for the department. The overcoat could not have arrived more in the nick of time, for rather sharp frosts were just beginning and seemed threatening to be even more severe. Petrovitch brought the greatcoat himself as a good tailor should. There was an expression of importance on his face, such as Akaky Akakyevitch had never seen there before. He seemed fully conscious of having completed a work of no little moment and of having shown in his own person the gulf that separates tailors who only put in linings and do repairs from those who make up new materials. He took the greatcoat out of the pocket-handkerchief in which he had brought it (the pocket-handkerchief had just come home from the wash), he then folded it up and put it in his pocket for future use. After taking out the overcoat, he looked at it with much pride and, holding it in both hands, threw it very deftly over Akaky Akakyevitch's shoulders, then pulled it down and smoothed it out behind with his hands; then draped it about Akaky Akakyevitch with somewhat jaunty carelessness. The latter, as a man advanced in years, wished to try it with his arms in the sleeves. Petrovitch helped him to put it on, and it appeared that it looked splendid too with his arms in the sleeves. In fact it turned out that the overcoat was completely and entirely successful. Petrovitch did not let slip the occasion for observing that it was only because he lived in a small street and had no signboard, and because he had known Akaky Akakyevitch so long, that he had done it so cheaply, but on the Nevsky Prospect they would have asked him seventy-five roubles for the work alone. Akaky Akakyevitch had no inclination to discuss this with Petrovitch, besides he was frightened of the big sums that Petrovitch was fond of flinging airily about in conversation. He paid him, thanked him, and went off on the spot, with his new overcoat on, to the department. Petrovitch followed him out and stopped in the street, staring for a good time at the coat from a distance and then purposely turned off and, taking a short cut by a side street, came back into the street and got another view of the coat from the other side, that is, from the front.

Meanwhile Akaky Akakyevitch walked along with every emotion in its most holiday mood. He felt every second that he had a new overcoat on his shoulders, and several times he actually laughed from inward satisfaction. Indeed, it had two advantages, one that it was warm and the other that it was good. He did not notice the way at all and found himself all at once at the department; in the porter's room he took off the overcoat, looked it over and put it in the porter's special care. I cannot tell how it happened, but all at once every one in the department learned that Akaky Akakyevitch had a new overcoat and that the "dressing jacket" no

longer existed. They all ran out at once into the porter's room to look at Akaky Akakyevitch's new overcoat, they began welcoming him and congratulating him so that at first he could do nothing but smile and afterwards felt positively abashed. When, coming up to him, they all began saying that he must "sprinkle" the new overcoat and that he ought at least to stand them all a supper, Akaky Akakyevitch lost his head completely and did not know what to do, how to get out of it, nor what to answer. A few minutes later, flushing crimson, he even began assuring them with great simplicity that it was not a new overcoat at all, that it was just nothing, that it was an old overcoat. At last one of the clerks, indeed the assistant of the head clerk of the room, probably in order to show that he was not proud and was able to get on with those beneath him, said: "So be it, I'll give a party instead of Akaky Akakyevitch and invite you all to tea with me this evening; as luck would have it, it is my name-day." The clerks naturally congratulated the assistant head clerk and eagerly accepted the invitation. Akaky Akakyevitch was beginning to make excuses, but they all declared that it was uncivil of him, that it was simply a shame and a disgrace and that he could not possibly refuse. However, he felt pleased about it afterwards when he remembered that through this he would have the opportunity of going out in the evening, too, in his new overcoat. That whole day was for Akaky Akakyevitch the most triumphant and festive day in his life. He returned home in the happiest frame of mind, took off the overcoat and hung it carefully on the wall, admiring the cloth and lining once more, and then pulled out his old "dressing jacket," now completely coming to pieces, on purpose to compare them. He glanced at it and positively laughed, the difference was so immense! And long afterwards he went on laughing at dinner, as the position in which the "dressing jacket" was placed recurred to his mind. He dined in excellent spirits and after dinner wrote nothing, no papers at all, but just took his ease for a little while on his bed, till it got dark, then, without putting things off, he dressed, put on his overcoat, and went out into the street. Where precisely the clerk who had invited him lived we regret to say that we cannot tell; our memory is beginning to fail sadly, and everything there is in Petersburg, all the streets and houses, are so blurred and muddled in our head that it is a very difficult business to put anything in orderly fashion. However that may have been, there is no doubt that the clerk lived in the better part of the town and consequently a very long distance from Akaky Akakyevitch. At first the latter had to walk through deserted streets, scantily lighted, but as he approached his destination the streets became more lively, more full of people, and more brightly lighted; passers-by began to be more frequent, ladies began to appear, here and there, beautifully dressed, beaver collars were to be seen on the men. Cabmen with wooden trellis-work sledges, studded with gilt nails, were less frequently to be met; on the other hand, jaunty drivers in raspberry coloured velvet caps with varnished sledges and bearskin rugs appeared, and carriages with decorated boxes dashed along the streets, their wheels crunching through the snow.

Akaky Akakyevitch looked at all this as a novelty; for several years he had not gone out into the streets in the evening. He stopped with curiosity before a lighted shop-window to look at a picture in which a beautiful woman was represented in the act of taking off her shoe and displaying as she did so the whole of a very shapely leg, while behind her back a gentleman with whiskers and a handsome imperial on his chin was putting his head in at the door. Akaky Akakyevitch shook his head and smiled and then went on his way. Why did he smile? Was it because he had come across something quite unfamiliar to him, though every man retains some instinctive feeling on the subject, or was it that he reflected, like many other clerks, as follows: "Well, upon my soul, those Frenchmen! it's beyond anything! if they try on anything of the sort, it really is . . . !" Though possibly he did not even think that; there is no creeping into a man's soul and finding out all that he thinks. At last he reached the house in which the assistant head clerk lived in fine style; there was a lamp burning on the stairs, and the flat was on the second floor. As he went into the entry Akaky Akakyevitch saw whole rows of goloshes. Amongst them in the middle of the room stood a samovar hissing and letting off clouds of steam. On the walls hung coats and cloaks, among which some actually had beaver collars or velvet revers. The other side of the wall there was noise and talk, which suddenly became clear and loud when the door opened and the footman came out with a tray full of empty glasses, a jug of cream, and a basket of biscuits. It was evident that the clerks had arrived long before and had already drunk their first glass of tea. Akaky Akakyevitch, after hanging up his coat with his own hands, went into the room, and at the same moment there flashed before his eyes a vision of candles, clerks, pipes, and card tables, together with the confused sounds of conversation rising up on all sides and the noise of moving chairs. He stopped very awkwardly in the middle of the room, looking about and trying to think what to do, but he was observed and received with a shout and they all went at once into the entry and again took a look at his overcoat. Though Akaky Akakyevitch was somewhat embarrassed, yet, being a simple-hearted man, he could not help being pleased at seeing how they all admired his coat. Then of course they all abandoned him and his coat, and turned their attention as usual to the tables set for whist. All this—the noise, the talk, and the crowd of people—was strange and wonderful to Akaky Akakyevitch. He simply did not know how to behave, what to do with his arms and legs and his whole figure; at last he sat down beside the players, looked at the cards, stared first at one and then at another of the faces, and in a little while began to yawn and felt that he was bored—especially as it was long past the time at which he usually went to bed. He tried to take leave of his hosts, but they would not let him go, saying that he absolutely must have a glass of champagne in honour of the new coat. An hour later supper was served, consisting of salad, cold veal, a pasty, pies, and tarts from the confectioner's, and champagne. They made Akaky Akakyevitch drink two glasses, after which he felt that things were much more cheerful, though he could not forget that it was twelve o'clock and that he ought to have been home long ago. That his host might not take it into his head to detain him, he slipped out of the room, hunted in the entry for his greatcoat, which he found, not without regret, lying on the floor, shook it, removed some fluff from it, put it on, and went down the stairs into the street. It was still light in the streets. Some little general shops, those perpetual clubs for houseserfs and all sorts of people, were open; others which were closed showed, however, a long streak of light at every crack of the door, proving that they were not yet deserted, and probably maids and men-servants were still finishing their conversation and discussion, driving their masters to utter perplexity as to their whereabouts. Akaky Akakyevitch walked along in a cheerful state of mind; he was even on the point of running, goodness knows why, after a lady of some sort who passed by like lightning with every part of her frame in violent motion. He checked himself at once, however, and again walked along very gently, feeling positively surprised himself at the inexplicable impulse that had seized him. Soon the deserted streets, which are not particularly cheerful by day and even less so in the evening, stretched before him. Now they were still more dead and deserted; the light of street lamps was scantier, the oil was evidently running low; then came wooden houses and fences; not a soul anywhere; only the snow gleamed on the streets and the low-pitched slumbering hovels looked black and gloomy with their closed shutters. He approached the spot where the street was intersected by an endless square, which looked like a fearful desert with its houses scarcely visible on the further side.

In the distance, goodness knows where, there was a gleam of light from some sentry-box which seemed to be standing at the end of the world. Akaky Akakyevitch's light-heartedness grew somewhat sensibly less at this place. He stepped into the square, not without an involuntary uneasiness, as though his heart had a foreboding of evil. He looked behind him and to both sides—it was as though the sea were all round him. "No, better not look," he thought, and walked on, shutting his eyes, and when he opened them to see whether the end of the square were near, he suddenly saw standing before him, almost under his very nose, some men with moustaches; just what they were like he could not even distinguish. There was a mist before his eyes and a throbbing in his chest. "I say the overcoat is mine!" said one of them in a voice like a clap of thunder, seizing him by the collar. Akaky Akakyevitch was on the point of shouting "Help" when another put a fist the size of a clerk's head against his very lips, saying: "You just shout now." Akaky Akakyevitch felt only that they took the overcoat off, and gave him a kick with their knees, and he fell on his face in the snow and was conscious of nothing more. A few minutes later he came to himself and got on to his feet, but there was no one there. He felt that it was cold on the ground and that he had no overcoat, and began screaming, but it seemed as though his voice could not carry to the end of the square. Overwhelmed with despair and continuing to scream, he ran across the square straight to the sentry-box, beside which stood a sentry leaning on his halberd and, so it seemed, looking with curiosity to see who the devil the man was who was screaming and running towards him from the distance. As Akaky Akakyevitch reached him, he began breathlessly shouting that he was asleep and not looking after his duty not to see that a man was being robbed. The sentry answered that he had seen nothing, that he had only seen him stopped in the middle of the square by two men, and supposed that they were his friends, and that, instead of abusing him for nothing, he had better go the next day to the superintendent and that he would find out who had taken the overcoat. Akaky Akakyevitch ran home in a terrible state: his hair, which was still comparatively abundant on his temples and the back of his head, was completely dishevelled; his sides and chest and his trousers were all covered with snow. When his old landlady heard a fearful knock at the door she jumped hurriedly out of bed and, with only one slipper on, ran to open it, modestly holding her shift across her bosom; but when she opened it she stepped back, seeing what a state Akaky Akakyevitch was in. When he told her what had happened, she clasped her hands in horror and said that he must go straight to the superintendent, that the police constable of the quarter would deceive him, make promises and lead him a dance; that it would be best of all to go to the superintendent, and that she knew him indeed, because Anna the Finnish girl who was once her cook was now in service as a nurse at the superintendent's; and that she often saw him himself when he passed by their house, and that he used to be every Sunday at church too, saying his prayers and at the same time looking good-humouredly at every one, and that therefore by every token he must be a kind-hearted man. After listening to this advice, Akaky Akakyevitch made his way very gloomily to his room, and how he spent that night I leave to the imagination of those who are in the least able to picture the position of others. Early in the morning he set off to the police superintendent's, but was told that he was asleep. He came at ten o'clock, he was told again that he was asleep; he came at eleven and was told that the superintendent was not at home; he came at dinner-time, but the clerks in the ante-room would not let him in, and insisted on knowing what was the matter and what business had brought him and exactly what had happened; so that at last Akaky Akakyevitch for the first time in his life tried to show the strength of his character and said curtly that he must see the superintendent himself, that they dare not refuse to admit him, that he had come from the department on government business, and that if he made complaint of them they would see. The clerks dared say nothing to this, and one of them went to summon the superintendent. The latter received his story of being robbed of his overcoat in an extremely strange way. Instead of attending to the main point, he began asking Akaky Akakyevitch questions, why had he been coming home so late? wasn't he going, or hadn't he been, to some house of ill-fame? so that Akaky Akakyevitch was overwhelmed with confusion, and went away without knowing whether or not the proper measures would be taken in regard to his overcoat. He was absent from the office all that day (the only time that it had happened in his life). Next day he appeared with a pale face, wearing his old "dressing jacket" which had become a still more pitiful sight. The tidings of the theft of the overcoat—though they were clerks who did not let even this chance slip of jeering at Akaky Akakyevitch—touched many of them. They decided on the spot to get up a subscription for him, but collected only a very trifling sum, because the clerks had already spent a good deal on subscribing to the director's portrait and on the purchase of a book, at the suggestion of the head of their department, who was a friend of the author, and so the total realised was very insignificant. One of the clerks, moved by compassion, ventured at any rate to assist Akaky Akakyevitch with good advice, telling him not to go to the district police inspector, because though it might happen that the latter might be sufficiently zealous of gaining the approval of his superiors to succeed in finding the overcoat, it would remain in the possession of the police unless he presented legal proofs that it belonged to him; he urged that far the best thing would be to appeal to a Person of Consequence; that the Person of Consequence, by writing and getting into communication with the proper authorities, could push the matter through more successfully. There was nothing else for it. Akaky Akakyevitch made up his mind to go to the Person of Consequence. What precisely was the nature of the functions of the Person of Consequence has remained a matter of uncertainty. It must be noted that this Person of Consequence had only lately become a person of consequence, and until recently had been a person of no consequence. Though, indeed, his position even now was not reckoned of consequence in comparison with others of still greater consequence. But there is always to be found a circle of persons to whom a person of little consequence in the eyes of others is a person of consequence. It is true that he did his utmost to increase the consequence of his position in various ways, for instance by insisting that his subordinates should come out on to the stairs to meet him when he arrived at his office; that no one should venture to approach him directly but all proceedings should be by the strictest order of precedence, that a collegiate registration clerk should report the matter to the provincial secretary, and the provincial secretary to the titular councillor or whomsoever it might be, and that business should only reach him by this channel. Every one in Holy Russia has a craze for imitation, every one apes and mimics his superiors. I have actually been told that a titular councillor who was put in charge of a small separate office, immediately partitioned off a special room for himself, calling it the head office, and set special porters at the door with red collars and gold lace, who took hold of the handle of the door and opened it for every one who went in, though the "head office" was so tiny that it was with difficulty that an ordinary writing table could be put into it. The manners and habits of the Person of Consequence were dignified and majestic, but not complex. The chief foundation of his system was strictness, "strictness, strictness, and—strictness!" he used to say, and at the last word he would look very significantly at the person he was addressing, though, indeed, he had no reason to do so, for the dozen clerks who made up the whole administrative mechanism of his office stood in befitting awe of him; any clerk who saw him in the distance would leave his work and remain standing at attention till his superior had left the room. His conversation with his subordinates was usually marked by severity and almost confined to three phrases: "How dare you? Do you know to whom you are speaking? Do you understand who I am?" He was, however, at heart a good-natured man, pleasant and obliging with his colleagues; but the grade of general had completely turned his head. When he received it, he was perplexed, thrown off his balance, and quite at a loss how to behave. If he chanced to be with his equals, he was still quite a decent man, a very gentlemanly man, in fact, and in many ways even an intelligent man, but as soon as he was in company with men who were even one grade below him, there was simply no doing anything with him: he sat silent and his position excited compassion, the more so as he himself felt that he might have been spending his time to incomparably more advantage. At times there could be seen in his eyes an intense desire to join in some interesting conversation, but he was restrained by the doubt whether it would not be too much on his part, whether it would not be too great a familiarity and lowering of his dignity, and in consequence of these reflections he remained everlastingly in the same mute condition, only uttering from time to time monosyllabic sounds, and in this way he gained the reputation of being a very tiresome man.

So this was the Person of Consequence to whom our friend Akaky Akakyevitch appealed, and he appealed to him at a most unpropitious moment, very unfortunate for himself, though fortunate, indeed, for the Person of Consequence. The latter happened to be in his study, talking in the very best of spirits with an old friend of his childhood who had only just arrived and whom he had not seen for several years. It was at this moment that he was informed that a man called Bashmatchkin was asking to see him. He asked abruptly, "What sort of man is he?" and received the answer, "A government clerk." "Ah! he can wait, I haven't time now," said the Person of Consequence. Here I must observe that this was a complete lie on the part of the Person of Consequence: he had time; his friend and he had long ago said all they had to say to each other and their conversation had begun to be broken by very long pauses during which they merely slapped each other on the knee, saying, "So that's how things are, Ivan Abramovitch!"—"There it is, Stepan Varlamovitch!" but, for all that, he told the clerk to wait in order to show his friend, who had left the service years before and was living at home in the country how long clerks had to wait in his ante-room. At last after they had talked, or rather been silent to their heart's content and had smoked a cigar in very comfortable arm-chairs with sloping backs, he seemed suddenly to recollect, and said to the secretary, who was standing at the door with papers for his signature: "Oh, by the way, there is a clerk waiting, isn't there? tell him he can come in." When he saw Akaky Akakyevitch's meek appearance and old uniform, he turned to him at once and said: "What do you want?" in a firm and abrupt voice, which he had purposely practised in his own room in solitude before the looking-glass for a week before receiving his present post and the grade of a general. Akaky Akakyevitch, who was overwhelmed with befitting awe beforehand, was somewhat confused and, as far as his tongue would allow him, explained to the best of his powers, with even more frequent "ers" than usual, that he had had a perfectly new overcoat and now he had been robbed of it in the most inhuman way, and that now he had come to beg him by his intervention either to correspond with his honour the head policemaster or anybody else, and find the overcoat. This mode of proceeding struck the general for some reason as taking a great liberty. "What next, sir," he went on as abruptly, "don't you know the way to proceed? To whom are you addressing yourself? Don't you know how things are done? You ought first to have handed in a petition to the office; it would have gone to the head clerk of the room, and to the head clerk of the section, then it would have been handed to the secretary and the secretary would have brought it to me. . . ."

"But, your Excellency," said Akaky Akakyevitch, trying to collect all the small allowance of presence of mind he possessed and feeling at the same time that he was getting into a terrible perspiration, "I ventured, your Excellency, to trouble you because secretaries . . . er . . . are people you can't depend on. . . ."

"What? what? what?" said the Person of Consequence, "where did you get hold of that spirit? where did you pick up such ideas? What insubordination is spreading among young men against their superiors and betters." The Person of Consequence did not apparently observe that Akaky Akakyevitch was well over fifty, and therefore if he could have been called a young man it would only have been in comparison with a man of seventy. "Do you know to whom you are speaking? do you understand who I am? do you understand that, I ask you?" At this point he stamped, and raised his voice to such a powerful note that Akaky Akakyevitch was not the only one to be terrified. Akaky Akakyevitch was positively petrified; he staggered, trembling all over, and could not stand; if the porters had not run up to support him, he would have flopped upon the floor; he was led out almost unconscious. The Person of Consequence, pleased that the effect had surpassed his expectations and enchanted at the idea that his words could even deprive a man of consciousness, stole a sideway glance at his friend to see how he was taking it, and perceived not without satisfaction that his friend was feeling very uncertain and even beginning to be a little terrified himself.

How he got downstairs, how he went out into the street—of all that Akaky Akakyevitch remembered nothing, he had no feeling in his arms or his legs. In all his life he had never been so severely reprimanded by a general, and this was by one of another department, too. He went out into the snowstorm, that was whistling through the streets, with his mouth open, and as he went he stumbled off the pavement; the wind, as its way is in Petersburg, blew upon him from all points of the compass and from every side street. In an instant it had blown a quinsy into his throat, and when he got home he was not able to utter a word; with a swollen face and throat he went to bed. So violent is sometimes the effect of a suitable reprimand!

Next day he was in a high fever. Thanks to the gracious assistance of the Petersburg climate, the disease made more rapid progress than could have been expected, and when the doctor came, after feeling his pulse he could find nothing to do but prescribe a fomentation, and that simply that the patient might not be left without the benefit of medical assistance; however, two days later he informed him that his end was at hand, after which he turned to his landlady and said: "And you had better lose no time, my good woman, but order him now a deal coffin, for an oak one will be too dear for him." Whether Akaky Akakyevitch heard these fateful words or not, whether they produced a shattering effect upon him, and whether he regretted his pitiful life, no one can tell, for he was all the time in delirium and fever. Apparitions, each stranger than the one before, were continually haunting him: first, he saw Petrovitch and was ordering him to make a greatcoat trimmed with some sort of traps for robbers, who were, he fancied, continually under the bed, and he was calling his landlady every minute to pull out a thief who had even got under the quilt; then he kept asking why his old "dressing jacket" was hanging before him when he had a new overcoat, then he fancied he was standing before the general listening to the appropriate reprimand and saying "I am sorry, your Excellency," then finally he became abusive, uttering the most awful language, so that his old landlady positively crossed herself, having never heard anything of the kind from him before, and the more horrified because these dreadful words followed immediately upon the phrase "your Excellency." Later on, his talk was a mere medley of nonsense, so that it was quite unintelligible; all that could be seen was that his incoherent words and thoughts were concerned with nothing but the overcoat. At last poor Akaky Akakyevitch gave up the ghost. No seal was put upon his room nor upon his things, because, in the first place, he had no heirs and, in the second, the property left was very small, to wit, a bundle of goose-feathers, a quire of white government paper, three pairs of socks, two or three buttons that had come off his trousers, and the "dressing jacket" with which the reader is already familiar. Who

came into all this wealth God only knows, even I who tell the tale must own that I have not troubled to enquire. And Petersburg remained without Akaky Akakyevitch, as though, indeed, he had never been in the city. A creature had vanished and departed whose cause no one had championed, who was dear to no one, of interest to no one, who never even attracted the attention of the student of natural history, though the latter does not disdain to fix a common fly upon a pin and look at him under the microscope—a creature who bore patiently the jeers of the office and for no particular reason went to his grave, though even he at the very end of his life was visited by a gleam of brightness in the form of an overcoat that for one instant brought colour into his poor life—a creature on whom calamity broke as insufferably as it breaks upon the heads of the mighty ones of this world . . . !

Several days after his death, the porter from the department was sent to his lodgings with instructions that he should go at once to the office, for his chief was asking for him; but the porter was obliged to return without him, explaining that he could not come, and to the enquiry "Why?" he added, "Well, you see: the fact is he is dead, he was buried three days ago." This was how they learned at the office of the death of Akaky Akakyevitch, and the next day there was sitting in his seat a new clerk who was very much taller and who wrote not in the same upright hand but made his letters more slanting and crooked.

But who could have imagined that this was not all there was to tell about Akaky Akakyevitch, that he was destined for a few days to make a noise in the world after his death, as though to make up for his life having been unnoticed by any one? But so it happened, and our poor story unexpectedly finishes with a fantastic ending. Rumours were suddenly floating about Petersburg that in the neighbourhood of the Kalinkin Bridge and for a little distance beyond, a corpse had taken to appearing at night in the form of a clerk looking for a stolen overcoat, and stripping from the shoulders of all passers-by, regardless of grade and calling, overcoats of all descriptions—trimmed with cat fur, or beaver or wadded, lined with raccoon, fox and bear—made, in fact, of all sorts of skin which men have adapted for the covering of their own. One of the clerks of the department saw the corpse with his own eyes and at once recognised it as Akaky Akakyevitch; but it excited in him such terror, however, that he ran away as fast as his legs could carry him and so could not get a very clear view of him, and only saw him hold up his finger threateningly in the distance.

From all sides complaints were continually coming that backs and shoulders, not of mere titular councillors, but even of upper court councillors, had been exposed to taking chills, owing to being stripped of their greatcoats. Orders were given to the police to catch the corpse regardless of trouble or expense, alive or dead, and to punish him in the cruellest way, as an example to others, and, indeed, they very nearly succeeded in doing so. The sentry of one district police station in Kiryushkin Place snatched a corpse by the collar on the spot of the crime in the very act of attempting to snatch a frieze overcoat from a retired musician, who used in his day to play the flute. Having caught him by the collar, he shouted until he had brought two other comrades, whom he charged to hold him while he felt just a minute in his boot to get out a snuff-box in order to revive his nose which had six times in his life been frost-bitten, but the snuff was probably so strong that not even a dead man could stand it. The sentry had hardly had time to put his finger over his right nostril and draw up some snuff in the left when the corpse sneezed violently right into the eyes of all three. While they were putting their fists up to wipe them, the corpse completely vanished, so that they were not even sure whether he had actually been in their hands. From that time forward, the sentries conceived such a horror of the dead that they were even afraid to seize the living and confined themselves to shouting from the distance: "Hi, you there, be off!" and the dead clerk began to appear even on the other side of the Kalinkin Bridge, rousing no little terror in all timid people.

We have, however, quite deserted the Person of Consequence, who may in reality almost be said to be the cause of the fantastic ending of this perfectly true story. To begin with, my duty requires me to do justice to the Person of Consequence by recording that soon after poor Akaky Akakyevitch had gone away crushed to powder, he felt something not unlike regret. Sympathy was a feeling not unknown to him; his heart was open to many kindly impulses, although his exalted grade very often prevented them from being shown. As soon as his friend had gone out of his study, he even began brooding over poor Akaky Akakyevitch, and from that time forward, he was almost every day haunted by the image of the poor clerk who had succumbed so completely to the befitting reprimand. The thought of the man so worried him that a week later he actually decided to send a clerk to find out how he was and whether he really could help him in any way. And when they brought him word that Akaky Akakyevitch had died suddenly in delirium and fever, it made a great impression on him, his conscience reproached him and he was depressed all day. Anxious to distract his mind and to forget the unpleasant impression, he went to spend the evening with one of his friends, where he found a genteel company and, what was best of all, almost every one was of the same grade so that he was able to be quite free from restraint. This had a wonderful effect on his spirits, he expanded, became affable and genial—in short, spent a very agreeable evening. At supper he drank a couple of glasses of champagne—a proceeding which we all know has a happy effect in inducing good-humour. The champagne made him inclined to do something unusual, and he decided not to go home yet but to visit a lady of his acquaintance, one Karolina Ivanovna—a lady apparently of German extraction, for whom he entertained extremely friendly feelings. It must be noted that the Person of Consequence was a man no longer young, an excellent husband, and the respectable father of a family. He had two sons, one already serving in his office, and a nice-looking daughter of sixteen with a rather turned-up, pretty little nose, who used to come every morning to kiss his hand, saying: *"Bon jour, Papa."* His wife, who was still blooming and decidedly good-looking, indeed, used first to give him her hand to kiss and then would kiss his hand, turning it the other side upwards. But though the Person of Consequence was perfectly satisfied with the kind amenities of his domestic life, he thought it proper to have a lady friend in another quarter of the town. This lady friend was not a bit better looking nor younger than his wife, but these mysterious facts exist in the world and it is not our business to criticise them. And so the Person of Consequence went downstairs, got into his sledge, and said to his coachman, "To Karolina Ivan-ovna," while luxuriously wrapped in his warm fur coat he remained in that agreeable frame of mind sweeter to a Russian than anything that could be invented, that is, when one thinks of nothing while thoughts come into the mind of themselves, one pleasanter than the other, without the labour of following them or looking for them. Full of satisfaction, he recalled all the amusing moments of the evening he had spent, all the phrases that had set the little circle laughing; many of them he repeated in an undertone and found them as amusing as before, and so, very naturally, laughed very heartily at them again. From time to time, however, he was disturbed by a gust of wind which, blowing suddenly, God knows whence and wherefore, cut him in the face, pelting him with flakes of snow, puffing out his coat-collar like a sack, or suddenly flinging it with unnatural force over his head and giving him endless trouble to extricate himself from it. All at once, the Person of Consequence felt that some one had clutched him very tightly by the collar. Turning round he saw a short man in a shabby old uniform, and not without horror recognized him as Akaky Akakye-vitch. The clerk's face was white as snow and looked like that of a corpse, but the horror of the Person of Consequence was beyond all bounds when he saw the mouth of the corpse distorted into speech and,

breathing upon him the chill of the grave, it uttered the following words: "Ah, so here you are at last! At last I've . . . er . . . caught you by the collar. It's your overcoat I want, you refused to help me and abused me into the bargain! So now give me yours!" The poor Person of Consequence very nearly died. Resolute and determined as he was in his office and before subordinates in general, and though any one looking at his manly air and figure would have said: "Oh, what a man of character!" yet in this plight he felt, like very many persons of athletic appearance, such terror that not without reason he began to be afraid he would have some sort of fit. He actually flung his overcoat off his shoulders as fast as he could and shouted to his coachman in a voice unlike his own: "Drive home and make haste!" The coachman, hearing the tone which he had only heard in critical moments and then accompanied by something even more rousing, hunched his shoulders up to his ears in case of worse following, swung his whip and flew on like an arrow. In a little over six minutes the Person of Consequence was at the entrance of his own house. Pale, panic-stricken, and without his overcoat, he arrived home instead of at Karolina Ivan-ovna's, dragged himself to his own room and spent the night in great perturbation, so that next morning his daughter said to him at breakfast, "You look quite pale to-day, Papa": but her papa remained mute and said not a word to any one of what happened to him, where he had been, and where he had been going. The incident made a great impression upon him. Indeed, it happened far more rarely that he said to his subordinates, "How dare you? do you understand who I am?" and he never uttered those words at all until he had first heard all the rights of the case.

What was even more remarkable is that from that time the apparition of the dead clerk ceased entirely: apparently the general's overcoat had fitted him perfectly, anyway nothing more was heard of overcoats being snatched from any one. Many restless and anxious people refused, however, to be pacified, and still maintained that in remote parts of the town the ghost of the dead clerk went on appearing. One sentry in Kolomna, for instance, saw with his own eyes a ghost appear from behind a house; but, being by natural constitution somewhat feeble—so much so that on one occasion an ordinary, well-grown pig, making a sudden dash out of some building, knocked him off his feet to the vast entertainment of the cabmen standing round, from whom he exacted two kopecks each for snuff for such rudeness—he did not dare to stop it, and so followed it in the dark until the ghost suddenly looked round and, stopping, asked him: "What do you want?" displaying a fist such as you never see among the living. The sentry said: "Nothing," and turned back on the spot. This ghost, however, was considerably taller and adorned with immense moustaches, and directing its steps apparently towards Obuhov Bridge, vanished into the darkness of the night.

[1842]

TRANSLATED BY
CONSTANCE GARNETT

QUESTIONS FOR STUDY

1. *Why does the narrator adopt such a verbose, familiar, and comic tone in telling the story? What seems to be his attitude towards Akaky Akakyevitch?*
2. *How does the possession of the overcoat alter Akaky Akakyevitch and his way of life? What significance does it assume for him?*
3. *What is the purpose of the section of the story following Akaky Akakyevitch's death? Is it unnecessary? Is it logical and defensible?*
4. *To what extent may "The Overcoat" be read as a parable of the grotesqueness and absurdity of human life? Could it be recast in terms of the twentieth century? What significant changes or alterations in the story would be required by such a recasting?*
5. *What social criticism is implied in the story?*
6. *"The Overcoat" is often praised as a landmark in the development of Russian realism. What aspects of the story best support this claim?*

DASHIELL HAMMETT
They Can Only Hang You Once

SAMUEL SPADE said, "My name is Ronald Ames. I want to see Mr. Binnett—Mr. Timothy Binnett."

"Mr. Binnett is resting now, sir," the butler replied hesitantly.

"Will you find out when I can see him? It's important." Spade cleared his throat. "I'm—uh—just back from Australia, and it's about some of his properties there."

The butler turned on his heel while saying, "I'll see, sir," and was going up the front stairs before he had finished speaking.

Spade made and lit a cigarette.

The butler came downstairs again.

"I'm sorry; he can't be disturbed now, but Mr. Wallace Binnett—Mr. Timothy's nephew—will see you."

Spade said, "Thanks," and followed the butler upstairs.

Wallace Binnett was a slender, handsome, dark man of about Spade's age—thirty-eight—who rose smiling from a brocaded chair, said, "How do you do, Mr. Ames?" waved his hand at another chair, and sat down again. "You're from Australia?"

"Got in this morning."

"You're a business associate of Uncle Tim's?"

Spade smiled and shook his head. "Hardly that, but I've some information I think he ought to have—quick."

Wallace Binnett looked thoughtfully at the floor, then up at Spade.

"I'll do my best to persuade him to see you, Mr. Ames, but, frankly, I don't know."

Spade seemed mildly surprised. "Why?"

Binnett shrugged. "He's peculiar sometimes. Understand, his mind seems perfectly all right, but he has the testi-ness and eccentricity of an old man in ill health and—well—at times he can be difficult."

Spade asked slowly, "He's already refused to see me?"

"Yes."

Spade rose from his chair. His blond satan's face was expressionless.

Binnett raised a hand quickly.

"Wait, wait," he said, "I'll do what I can to make him change his mind. Perhaps if—" His dark eyes suddenly became wary. "You're not simply trying to sell him something, are you?"

"No."

The wary gleam went out of Binnett's eyes. "Well, then, I think I can—"

A young woman came in crying angrily, "Wally, that old fool has—"

She broke off with a hand to her breast when she saw Spade.

Spade and Binnett had risen together.

Binnett said suavely, "Joyce, this is Mr. Ames. My sister-in-law, Joyce Court."

Spade bowed.

Joyce Court uttered a short, embarrassed laugh and said, "Please excuse my whirlwind entrance."

She was a tall, blue-eyed, dark woman of twenty-four or -five with good shoulders and a strong, slim body. Her features made up in warmth what they lacked in regularity. She wore wide-legged, blue satin pajamas.

Binnett smiled good-naturedly at her and asked:

"Now what's all the excitement?"

Anger darkened her eyes again and she started to speak. Then she looked at Spade and said:

"But we shouldn't bore Mr. Ames with our stupid domestic affairs. If—" She hesitated.

Spade bowed again. "Sure," he said, "certainly."

"I won't be a minute," Binnett promised, and left the room with her.

Spade went to the open doorway through which they had vanished and, standing just inside, listened. Their footsteps became inaudible. Nothing else could be heard.

Spade was standing there—his yellow-gray eyes dreamy—when he heard the scream. It was a woman's scream, high and shrill with terror. Spade was through the doorway when he heard the shot.

It was a pistol shot, magnified, reverberated by walls and ceilings.

Twenty feet from the doorway Spade found a staircase, and went up it three steps at a time. He turned to the left. Halfway down the hallway a woman lay on her back on the floor.

Wallace Binnett knelt beside her, fondling one of her hands desperately, crying in a low, beseeching voice, "Darling, Molly, darling!"

Joyce Court stood behind him and wrung her hands while tears streaked her cheeks.

The woman on the floor resembled Joyce Court but was older, and her face had a hardness the younger one's had not.

"She's dead, she's been killed," Wallace Binnett said incredulously, raising his white face toward Spade.

When Binnett moved his head Spade could see the round hole in the woman's tan dress over her heart and the dark stain which was rapidly spreading below it.

Spade touched Joyce Court's arm.

"Police, emergency hospital—phone," he said.

As she ran toward the stairs he addressed Wallace Binnett: "Who did—"

A voice groaned feebly behind Spade.

He turned swiftly. Through an open doorway he could see an old man in white pajamas lying sprawled across a rumpled bed. His head, a shoulder, an arm dangled over the edge of the bed. His other hand held his throat tightly. He groaned again and his eyelids twitched, but did not open.

Spade lifted the old man's head and shoulders and put them up on the pillows. The old man groaned again and took his hand from his throat. His throat was red with half a dozen bruises. He was a gaunt man with a seamed face that probably exaggerated his age.

A glass of water was on a table beside the bed. Spade put water on the old man's face and, when the old man's eyes twitched again, leaned down and growled softly:

"Who did it?"

The twitching eyelids went up far enough to show a narrow strip of blood-shot gray eyes. The old man spoke painfully, putting a hand to his throat again:

"A man—he—" He coughed.

Spade made an impatient grimace. His lips almost touched the old man's ear.

"Where'd he go?" His voice was urgent.

A gaunt hand moved weakly to indicate the rear of the house and fell back on the bed.

The butler and two frightened female servants had joined Wallace Binnett beside the dead woman in the hallway.

"Who did it?" Spade asked them.

They stared at him blankly.

"Somebody look after the old man," he growled, and went down the hallway.

At the end of the hallway was a rear staircase. He descended two flights and went through a pantry into the kitchen. He saw nobody. The kitchen door was shut but, when he tried it, not locked. He crossed a narrow back yard to a gate that was shut, not locked. He opened the gate. There was nobody in the narrow alley behind it.

He sighed, shut the gate, and returned to the house.

Spade sat comfortably slack in a deep leather chair in a room that ran across the front second story of Wallace Binnett's house. There were shelves of books and the lights were on. The window showed outer darkness weakly diluted by a distant street lamp.

Facing Spade, Detective Sergeant Polhaus—a big, carelessly shaven, florid man in dark clothes that needed pressing —was sprawled in another chair; Lieutenant Dundy—smaller, compactly built, square-faced—stood with legs apart, head thrust a little forward, in the center of the room.

Spade was saying:

"—and the doctor would only let me talk to the old man a couple of minutes. We can try it again when he's rested a little, but it doesn't look like he knows much. He was catching a nap and he woke up with somebody's hands on his throat dragging him around the bed. The best he got was a one-eyed look at the fellow choking him. A big fellow, he says, with a soft hat pulled down over his eyes, dark, needing a shave. Sounds like Tom." Spade nodded at Polhaus.

The detective sergeant chuckled, but Dundy said, "Go on," curtly.

Spade grinned and went on:

"He's pretty far gone when he hears Mrs. Binnett scream at the door. The hands go away from his throat and he hears the shot and just before passing out he gets a flash of the big fellow heading for the rear of the house and Mrs. Binnett tumbling down on the hall floor. He says he never saw the big fellow before."

"What size gun was it?" Dundy asked.

"Thirty-eight. Well, nobody in the house is much more help. Wallace and his sister-in-law, Joyce, were in her room, so they say, and didn't see anything but the dead woman when they ran out, though they think they heard something that could've been somebody running downstairs—the back stairs.

"The butler—his name's Jarboe—was in here when he heard the scream and shot, so he says. Irene Kelly, the maid, was down on the ground floor, so she says. The cook, Margaret Finn, was in her room—third floor back—and didn't even hear anything, so she says. She's deaf as a post, so everybody else says. The back door and gate were unlocked, but are supposed to be kept locked, so everybody says. Nobody says they were in or around the kitchen or yard at the time." Spade spread his hands in a gesture of finality. "That's the crop."

Dundy shook his head. "Not exactly," he said. "How come you were here?"

Spade's face brightened.

"Maybe my client killed her," he said. "He's Wallace's cousin, Ira Binnett. Know him?"

Dundy shook his head. His blue eyes were hard and suspicious.

"He's a San Francisco lawyer," Spade said, "respectable and all that. A couple of days ago he came to me with a story about his uncle Timothy, a miserly old skinflint, lousy with money and pretty well broken up by hard living. He was the black sheep of the family. None of them had heard of him for years. But six or eight months ago he showed up in pretty bad shape every way except financially—he seems to have taken a lot of money out of Australia—wanting to spend his last days with his only living relatives, his nephews Wallace and Ira.

"That was all right with them. 'Only living relatives' meant 'only heirs' in their language. But by and by the nephews began to think it was better to be an heir than to be one of a couple of heirs—twice as good, in fact—and started fiddling for the inside track with the old man. At least, that's what Ira told me about Wallace, and I wouldn't be surprised if Wallace would say the same thing about Ira, though Wallace seems to be the harder up of the two. Anyhow, the nephews fell out, and then Uncle Tim, who had been staying at Ira's, came over here. That was a couple of months ago, and Ira hasn't seen Uncle Tim since, and hasn't been able to get in touch with him by phone or mail.

"That's what he wanted a private detective about. He didn't think Uncle Tim would come to any harm here—oh, no, he went to a lot of trouble to make that clear—but he thought maybe undue pressure was being brought to bear on the old boy, or he was being hornswoggled somehow, and at least being told lies about his loving nephew Ira. He wanted to know what was what. I waited until today, when a boat from Australia docked, and came up here as a Mr. Ames with some important information for Uncle Tim about his properties down there. All I wanted was fifteen minutes alone with him."

Spade frowned thoughtfully. "Well, I

didn't get them. Wallace told me the old man refused to see me. I don't know."

Suspicion had deepened in Dundy's cold blue eyes.

"And where is this Ira Binnett now?" he asked.

Spade's yellow-gray eyes were as guileless as his voice. "I wish I knew. I phoned his house and office and left word for him to come right over, but I'm afraid—"

Knuckles knocked sharply twice on the other side of the room's one door.

The three men in the room turned to face the door.

Dundy called, "Come in."

The door was opened by a sunburned blond policeman whose left hand held the right wrist of a plump man of forty or forty-five in well-fitting gray clothes. The policeman pushed the plump man into the room.

"Found him monkeying with the kitchen door," he said.

Spade looked up and said, "Ah!" His tone expressed satisfaction. "Mr. Ira Binnett, Lieutenant Dundy, Sergeant Polhaus."

Ira Binnett said rapidly, "Mr. Spade, will you tell this man that—"

Dundy addressed the policeman: "All right. Good work. You can leave him."

The policeman moved a hand vaguely toward his cap and went away.

Dundy glowered at Ira Binnett and demanded, "Well?"

Binnett looked from Dundy to Spade. "Has something—"

Spade said, "Better tell him why you were at the back door instead of the front."

Ira Binnett suddenly blushed. He cleared his throat in embarrassment.

He said, "I—uh—I should explain. It wasn't my fault, of course, but when Jarboe—he's the butler—phoned me that Uncle Tim wanted to see me he told me he'd leave the kitchen door unlocked, so Wallace wouldn't have to know I'd—"

"What'd he want to see you about?" Dundy asked.

"I don't know. He didn't say. He said it was very important."

"Didn't you get my message?" Spade asked.

Ira Binnett's eyes widened. "No. What was it? Has anything happened? What is—"

Spade was moving toward the door. "Go ahead," he said to Dundy. "I'll be right back."

He shut the door carefully behind him and went up to the third floor.

The butler Jarboe was on his knees at Timothy Binnett's door with an eye to the keyhole. On the floor beside him was a tray holding an egg in an egg-cup, toast, a pot of coffee, china, silver, and a napkin.

Spade said, "Your toast's going to get cold."

Jarboe, scrambling to his feet, almost upsetting the coffeepot in his haste, his face red and sheepish, stammered:

"I—er—beg your pardon, sir. I wanted to make sure Mr. Timothy was awake before I took this in." He picked up the tray. "I didn't want to disturb his rest if—"

Spade, who had reached the door, said "Sure, sure," and bent over to put his eye to the keyhole. When he straightened up he said in a mildly complaining tone, "You can't see the bed—only a chair and part of the window."

The butler replied quickly, "Yes, sir, I found that out."

Spade laughed.

The butler coughed, seemed about to say something, but did not. He hesitated, then knocked lightly on the door.

A tired voice said, "Come in."

Spade asked quickly in a low voice, "Where's Miss Court?"

"In her room, I think, sir, the second floor on the left," the butler said.

The tired voice inside the room said petulantly, "Well, come on in."

The butler opened the door and went in. Through the door, before the butler shut it, Spade caught a glimpse of Timothy Binnett propped up on pillows in his bed.

Spade went to the second door on the left and knocked. The door was opened almost immediately by Joyce Court. She stood in the doorway, not smiling, not speaking.

He said, "Miss Court, when you came into the room where I was with your brother-in-law you said, 'Wally, that old fool has—' Meaning Timothy?"

She stared at Spade for a moment. Then: "Yes."

"Mind telling me what the rest of the sentence would have been?"

She said slowly, "I don't know who you really are or why you ask, but I don't mind telling you. It would have been 'sent for Ira.' Jarboe had just told me."

"Thanks."

She shut the door before he had turned away.

He returned to Timothy Binnett's door and knocked on it.

"Who is it now?" the old man's voice demanded.

Spade opened the door. The old man was sitting up in bed. Spade said, "This Jarboe was peeping through your keyhole a few minutes ago," and returned to the library.

Ira Binnett, seated in the chair Spade had occupied, was saying to Dundy and Polhaus, "And Wallace got caught in the crash, like most of us, but he seems to have juggled accounts trying to save himself. He was expelled from the Stock Exchange."

Dundy waved a hand to indicate the room and its furnishings.

"Pretty classy layout for a man that's busted."

"His wife has some money," Ira Binnett said, "and he always lived beyond his means."

Dundy scowled at Binnett. "And you really think he and his missus weren't on good terms?"

"I don't think it," Binnett replied evenly. "I know it."

Dundy nodded. "And you know he's got a yen for the sister-in-law, this Court?"

"I don't know that. But I've heard plenty of gossip to the same effect."

Dundy made a growling noise in his throat, then asked sharply. "How does the old man's will read?"

"I don't know. I don't know whether he's made one." He addressed Spade, now earnestly: "I've told everything I know, every single thing."

Dundy said, "It's not enough." He jerked a thumb at the door. "Show him where to wait Tom, and let's have the widower in again."

Big Polhaus said, "Right," went out with Ira Binnett, and returned with Wallace Binnett, whose face was hard and pale.

Dundy asked, "Has your uncle made a will?"

"I don't know," Binnett replied.

Spade put the next question, softly: "Did your wife?"

Binnett's mouth tightened in a mirthless smile. He spoke deliberately:

"I'm going to say some things I'd rather not have to say. My wife, properly, had no money. When I got into financial trouble some time ago I made some property over to her, to save it. She turned it into money without my knowing about it till afterward. She paid our bills—our living expenses—out of it, but she refused to return it to me and she assured me that in no event—whether she lived or died or we stayed together or were divorced—would I ever be able to get hold of a penny of it. I believed her, and still do."

"You wanted a divorce?" Dundy asked.

"Yes."

"Why?"

"It wasn't a happy marriage."

"Joyce Court?"

Binnett's face flushed. He said stiffly, "I admire Joyce Court tremendously, but I'd've wanted a divorce anyway."

Spade said, "And you're sure—still absolutely sure—you don't know anybody who fits your uncle's description of the man who choked him?"

"Absolutely sure."

The sound of the doorbell ringing came faintly into the room. Dundy said sourly, "That'll do."

Binnett went out.

Polhaus said, "That guy's as wrong as they make them. And—"

From below came the heavy report of a pistol fired indoors. The lights went out.

In darkness the three detectives collided with one another going through the doorway into the dark hall.

Spade reached the stairs first. There

was a clatter of footsteps below him, but nothing could be seen until he reached a bend in the stairs. Then enough light came from the street through the open front door to show the dark figure of a man standing with his back to the open door.

A flashlight clicked in Dundy's hand —he was at Spade's heels—and threw a glaring white beam of light on the man's face.

He was Ira Binnett. He blinked in the light and pointed at something on the floor in front of him.

Dundy turned the beam of his light down on the floor. Jarboe lay there on his face, bleeding from a bullet hole in the back of his head.

Spade grunted softly.

Tom Polhaus came blundering down the stairs. Wallace Binnett close behind him. Joyce Court's frightened voice came from farther up:

"Oh, what's happened? Wally, what's happened?"

"Where's the light switch?" Dundy barked.

"Inside the cellar door, under these stairs," Wallace Binnett said. "What is it?"

Polhaus pushed past Binnett toward the cellar door.

Spade made an inarticulate sound in his throat and, pushing Wallace Binnett aside, sprang up the stairs. He brushed past Joyce Court and went on, heedless of her startled scream. He was halfway up the stairs to the third floor when the pistol went off up there.

He ran to Timothy Binnett's door. The door was open. He went in.

Something hard and angular struck him above his right ear, knocking him across the room, bringing him down on one knee. Something thumped and clattered on the floor just outside the door.

The lights came on.

On the floor, in the center of the room, Timothy Binnett lay on his back bleeding from a bullet wound in his left forearm. His pajama jacket was torn. His eyes were shut.

Spade stood up and put a hand to his head. He scowled at the old man on the floor, at the room, at the black automatic pistol lying on the hallway floor.

He said, "Come on, you old cutthroat. Get up and sit on a chair and I'll see if I can stop that bleeding till the doctor gets here."

The man on the floor did not move.

There were footsteps in the hallway and Dundy came in, followed by the two younger Binnetts. Dundy's face was dark and furious.

"Kitchen door wide open," he said in a choked voice. "They run in and out like—"

"Forget it," Spade said. "Uncle Tim is our meat." He paid no attention to Wallace Binnett's gasp, to the incredulous looks on Dundy's and Ira Binnett's faces. "Come on, get up," he said to the old man on the floor, "and tell us what it was the butler saw when he peeped through the keyhole."

The old man did not stir.

"He killed the butler because I told him the butler had peeped," Spade explained to Dundy. "I peeped, too, but didn't see anything except that chair and the window, though we'd made enough racket by then to scare him back to bed. Suppose you take the chair apart while I go over the window."

He went to the window and began to examine it carefully. He shook his head, put a hand out behind him, and said, "Give me the flashlight."

Dundy put the flashlight in his hand.

Spade raised the window and leaned out, turning the light on the outside of the building. Presently he grunted and put his other hand out, tugging at a brick a little below the sill. Presently the brick came loose. He put it on the window sill and stuck his hand into the hole its removal had made. Out of the opening, one at a time, he brought an empty black pistol holster, a partially filled box of cartridges, and an unsealed manila envelope.

Holding these things in his hands, he turned to face the others.

Joyce Court came in with a basin of water and a roll of gauze and knelt beside Timothy Binnett.

Spade put the holster and cartridges on a table and opened the manila envelope. Inside were two sheets of paper, covered on both sides with boldly penciled writing. Spade read a paragraph to himself, suddenly laughed, and began at the beginning again, reading aloud:

" 'I, Timothy Kieran Binnett, being sound of mind and body, do declare this to be my last will and testament. To my dear nephews, Ira Binnett and Wallace Bourke Binnett, in recognition of the loving kindness with which they have received me into their homes and attended my declining years, I give and bequeath, share and share alike, all my worldly possessions of whatever kind, to wit, my carcass and the clothes I stand in.

" 'I bequeath them, furthermore, the expense of my funeral and these memories: First, the memory of their credulity in believing that the fifteen years I spent in Sing Sing [1] were spent in Australia; second, the memory of their optimism in supposing that those fifteen years had brought me great wealth, and that if I lived on them, borrowed from them, and never spent any of my own money, it was because I was a miser whose hoard they would inherit; and not because I had no money except what I shook them down for; third, for their hopefulness in thinking that I would leave either of them anything if I had it; and, lastly, because their painful lack of any decent sense of humor will keep them from ever seeing how funny this has all been. Signed and sealed this—' "

Spade looked up to say, "There is no date, but it's signed Timothy Kieran Binnett with flourishes."

Ira Binnett was purple with anger.

Wallace's face was ghastly in its pallor and his whole body was trembling.

Joyce Court had stopped working on Timothy Binnett's arm.

The old man sat up and opened his eyes. He looked at his nephews and began to laugh. There was in his laughter neither hysteria nor madness: it was sane, hearty laughter, and subsided slowly.

Spade said, "All right, now you've had

your fun. Let's talk about the killings."

"I know nothing more about the first one than I've told you," the old man said, "and this one's not a killing, since I'm only—"

Wallace Binnett, still trembling violently, said painfully through his teeth:

"That's a lie. You killed Molly. Joyce and I came out of her room when we heard Molly scream, and heard the shot and saw her fall out of your room, and nobody came out afterward."

The old man said calmly, "Well, I'll tell you: it was an accident. They told me there was a fellow from Australia here to see me about some of my properties there. I knew there was something funny about that somewhere"—he grinned—"not ever having been there. I didn't know whether one of my dear nephews was getting suspicious and putting up a game on me or what, but I knew that if Wally wasn't in on it he'd certainly try to pump the gentleman from Australia about me and maybe I'd lose one of my free boarding houses."

He chuckled.

"So I figured I'd get in touch with Ira so I could go back to his house if things worked out bad here, and I'd try to get rid of this Australian. Wally's always thought I'm half-cracked"—he leered at his nephew—"and's afraid they'll lug me off to a madhouse before I could make a will in his favor, or they'll break it if I do. You see, he's got a pretty bad reputation, what with that Stock Exchange trouble and all, and he knows no court would appoint him to handle my affairs if I went screwy—not as long as I've got another nephew"—he turned his leer on Ira—"who's a respectable lawyer. So now I know that rather than have me kick up a row that might wind me up in the madhouse, he'll chase this visitor, and I put on a show for Molly, who happened to be the nearest one to hand. She took it too seriously, though.

"I had a gun and I did a lot of raving about being spied on by my enemies in Australia and that I was going down and shoot this fellow. But she got too excited and tried to take the gun away from me, and the first thing I knew it had gone off, and I had to make these marks on my neck and think up that story about the big dark man."

He looked contemptuously at Wallace. "I didn't know he was covering me up. Little as I thought of him, I never thought he'd be low enough to cover up his wife's murderer—even if he didn't like her—just for the sake of money."

Spade said "Never mind that. Now about the butler?"

"I don't know anything about the butler," the old man replied, looking at Spade with steady eyes.

Spade said, "You had to kill him quick, before he had time to do or say anything. So you slip down the back stairs, open the kitchen door to fool people, go to the front door, ring the bell, shut the door, and hide in the shadow of the cellar door under the front steps. When Jarboe answered the doorbell you shot him—the hole was in the back of his head—pulled the light switch, just inside the cellar door, and ducked up the back stairs in the dark and shot yourself carefully in the arm. I got up there too soon for you; so you smacked me with the gun, chucked it through the door, and spread yourself on the floor while I was shaking pinwheels out of my noodle."

The old man sniffed again. "You're just—"

"Stop it," Spade said patiently. "Don't let's argue. The first killing was an accident—all right. The second couldn't be. And it ought to be easy to show that both bullets, and the one in your arm, were fired from the same gun. What difference does it make which killing we can prove first-degree murder on? They can only hang you once." He smiled pleasantly. "And they will."

[1932]

QUESTIONS FOR STUDY

1. *What devices does Hammett use to engage and sustain the reader's interest?*
2. *What do we come to learn about Hammett's detective hero Sam Spade? What kind of values and attitudes does Spade seem to have? How does he differ from such predecessors as C. Auguste Dupin and Sherlock Holmes?*
3. *What differences do you note between Hammett's detective fiction and the other examples of the genre represented in* Fiction 100? *What conventions of the traditional detective story remain essentially unchanged?*
4. *One of the most identifiable characteristics of the "hard-boiled" school of detective fiction is its style. What are the most notable features of Hammett's prose syle? Compare the style of this story to the style of Ernest Hemingway's "The Killers." What do these stories have in common stylistically? What other qualities do they share?*

THOMAS HARDY

The Three Strangers

AMONG the few features of agricultural England which retain an appearance but little modified by the lapse of centuries, may be reckoned the long, grassy and furzy downs, coombs, or ewe-leases, as they are called according to their kind, that fill a large area of certain counties in the south and south-west. If any mark of human occupation is met with hereon, it usually takes the form of the solitary cottage of some shepherd.

Fifty years ago such a lonely cottage stood on such a down, and may possibly be standing there now. In spite of its loneliness, however, the spot, by actual measurement, was not three miles from a county-town. Yet that affected it little. Three miles of irregular upland, during the long inimical seasons, with their sleets, snows, rains, and mists, afford withdrawing space enough to isolate a Timon or a Nebuchadnezzar; much less, in fair weather, to please that less repellent tribe, the poets, philosophers, artists, and others who 'conceive and meditate of pleasant things.'

Some old earthen camp or barrow, some clump of trees, at least some starved fragment of ancient hedge is usually taken advantage of in the erection of these forlorn dwellings. But, in the present case, such a kind of shelter had been disregarded. Higher Crowstairs, as the house was called, stood quite detached and undefended. The only reason for its precise situation seemed to be the crossing of two footpaths at right angles hard by, which may have crossed there and thus for a good five hundred years. Hence the house was exposed to the elements on all sides. But, though the wind up here blew unmistakably when it did blow, and the rain hit hard whenever it fell, the various weathers of the winter season were not quite so formidable on the down as they were imagined to be by dwellers on low ground. The raw rimes were not so pernicious as in the hollows, and the frosts were scarcely so severe. When the shepherd and his family who tenanted the house were pitied for their sufferings from the exposure, they said that upon the whole they were less inconvenienced by 'wuzzes and flames' (hoarses and phlegms) than when they had lived by the stream of a snug neighbouring valley.

The night of March 28, 182—, was precisely one of the nights that were wont to call forth these expressions of commiseration. The level rainstorm smote walls, slopes, and hedges like the cloth-yard shafts of Senlac and Crecy. Such sheep and outdoor animals as had no shelter stood with their buttocks to the winds; while the tails of little birds trying to roost on some scraggy thorn were blown inside-out like umbrellas. The gable-end of the cottage was stained with wet, and the eavesdroppings flapped against the wall. Yet never was commiseration for the shepherd more misplaced. For that cheerful rustic was entertaining a large party in glorification of the christening of his second girl.

The guests had arrived before the rain began to fall, and they were all now assembled in the chief or living room of the dwelling. A glance into the apartment at eight o'clock on this eventful evening would have resulted in the opinion that it was as cosy and comfortable a nook as could be wished for in boisterous weather. The calling of its inhabitant was proclaimed by a number of highly-polished sheep-crooks without stems that were hung ornamentally over the fireplace, the curl of each shining crook varying from the antiquated type engraved in the patriarchal pictures of old family Bibles to the most approved fashion of the last local sheep-fair. The room was lighted by half-a-dozen candles, having wicks only a trifle smaller than the grease which enveloped them, in candlesticks that were never used but at highdays, holy-days, and family feasts. The lights were scattered about the room, two of them standing on the chimney-piece. This position of candles was in itself significant. Candles on the chimney-piece always meant a party.

On the hearth, in front of a back-brand to give substance, blazed a fire of thorns, that crackled 'like the laughter of the fool.'

Nineteen persons were gathered here. Of these, five women, wearing gowns of various bright hues, sat in chairs along the wall, girls shy and not shy filled the window-bench; four men, including Charley Jake the hedge-carpenter, Elijah New the parish-clerk, and John Pitcher, a neighbouring dairyman, the shepherd's father-in-law, lolled in the settle; a young man and maid, who were blushing over tentative *pourparlers* on a life-companionship, sat beneath the corner-cupboard; and an elderly engaged man of fifty or upward moved restlessly about from spots where his betrothed was not to the spot where she was. Enjoyment was pretty general, and so much the more prevailed in being unhampered by conventional restrictions. Absolute confidence in each other's good opinion begat perfect ease, while the finishing stroke of manner, amounting to a truly princely serenity, was lent to the majority by the absence of any expression or trait denoting that they wished to get on in the world, enlarge their minds, or do any eclipsing thing whatever—which nowadays so generally nips the bloom and *bonhomie* of all except the two extremes of the social scale.

Shepherd Fennel had married well, his wife being a dairyman's daughter from a vale at a distance, who brought fifty guineas in her pocket—and kept them there, till they should be required for ministering to the needs of a coming family. This frugal woman had been somewhat exercised as to the character that should be given to the gathering. A sit-still party had its advantages; but an undisturbed position of ease in chairs and settles was apt to lead on the men to such an unconscionable deal of toping that they would sometimes fairly drink the house dry. A dancing-party was the alternative; but this, while avoiding the foregoing objection on the score of good drink, had a counterbalancing disadvantage in the matter of good victuals, the ravenous appetites engendered by the exercise causing immense havoc in the buttery. Shepherdess Fennel fell back upon the intermediate plan of mingling short dances with short periods of talk and singing, so as to hinder any ungovernable rage in either. But this scheme was entirely confined to her own gentle mind: the shepherd himself was in the mood to exhibit the most reckless phases of hospitality.

The fiddler was a boy of those parts, about twelve years of age, who had a wonderful dexterity in jigs and reels, though his fingers were so small and short as to necessitate a constant shifting for the high notes, from which he scrambled back to the first position with sounds not of unmixed purity of tone. At seven the shrill tweedle-dee of this youngster had begun, accompanied by a booming ground-bass from Elijah New, the parish-clerk, who had thoughtfully brought with him his favourite musical instrument, the serpent. Dancing was instantaneous, Mrs. Fennel privately enjoining the players on no account to let the dance exceed the length of a quarter of an hour.

But Elijah and the boy in the excitement of their position quite forgot the injunction. Moreover, Oliver Giles, a man of seventeen, one of the dancers, who was enamoured of his partner, a fair girl of thirty-three rolling years, had recklessly handed a new crown-piece to the musicians, as a bribe to keep going as long as they had muscle and wind. Mrs. Fennel, seeing the steam begin to generate on the countenances of her guests, crossed over and touched the fiddler's elbow and put her hand on the serpent's mouth. But they took no notice, and fearing she might lose her character of genial hostess if she were to interfere too markedly, she retired and sat down helpless. And so the dance whizzed on with culmulative fury, the performers moving in their planet-like courses, direct and retrograde, from apogee to perigee, till the hand of the well-kicked clock at the bottom of the room had travelled over the circumference of an hour.

While these cheerful events were in course of enactment within Fennel's pastoral dwelling an incident having considerable bearing on the party had occurred in the gloomy night without. Mrs. Fennel's concern about the growing fierceness of the dance corresponded in point of time with the ascent of a human figure to the solitary hill of Higher Crowstairs from the direction of the distant town. This personage strode on through the rain without a pause, following the little-worn path which, further on in its course, skirted the shepherd's cottage.

It was nearly the time of full moon, and on this account, though the sky was lined with a uniform sheet of dripping cloud, ordinary objects out of doors were readily visible. The sad wan light revealed the lonely pedestrian to be a man of supple frame; his gait suggested that he had somewhat passed the period of perfect and instinctive agility, though not so far as to be otherwise than rapid of motion when occasion required. At a rough guess, he might have been about forty years of age. He appeared tall, but a recruiting sergeant, or other person accustomed to the judging of men's heights by the eye, would have discerned that this was chiefly owing to his gauntness, and that he was not more than five-feet-eight or nine.

Notwithstanding the regularity of his tread there was caution in it, as in that of one who mentally feels his way; and despite the fact that it was not a black coat nor a dark garment of any sort that he wore, there was something about him which suggested that he naturally belonged to the black-coated tribes of men. His clothes were of fustian, and his boots hobnailed, yet in his progress he showed not the mud-accustomed bearing of hobnailed and fustianed peasantry.

By the time that he had arrived abreast of the shepherd's premises the rain came down, or rather came along, with yet more determined violence. The outskirts of the little settlement partially broke the force of wind and rain, and this induced him to stand still. The most salient of the shepherd's domestic erections was an empty sty at the forward corner of his hedgeless garden, for in these latitudes the principle of masking the homelier features of your establishment by a conventional frontage was unknown. The traveller's eye was attracted to this small building by the pallid shine of the wet slates that covered it. He turned aside, and, finding it empty, stood under the pent-roof for shelter.

While he stood the boom of the serpent within the adjacent house, and the lesser strains of the fiddler, reached the spot as an accompaniment to the surging hiss of the flying rain on the sod, its louder beating on the cabbage-leaves of the garden, on the straw hackles of eight or ten bee-hives just discernible by the path, and its dripping from the eaves into a row of buckets and pans that had been placed under the walls of the cottage. For at Higher Crowstairs, as at all such elevated domiciles, the grand difficulty of housekeeping was an insufficiency of water; and a casual rainfall was utilized by turning out, as catchers, every utensil that the house contained. Some queer stories might be told of the contrivances for economy in suds and dish-waters that are absolutely necessitated in upland habitations during the droughts of summer. But at this season there were no such exigencies; a mere acceptance of what the skies bestowed was sufficient for an abundant store.

At last the notes of the serpent ceased and the house was silent. This cessation of activity aroused the solitary pedestrian from the reverie into which he had lapsed, and, emerging from the shed, with an apparently new intention, he walked up the path to the house-door. Arrived here, his first act was to kneel down on a large stone beside the row of vessels, and to drink a copious draught from one of them. Having quenched his thirst he rose and lifted his hand to knock, but paused with his eye upon the panel. Since the dark surface of the wood revealed absolutely nothing, it was evident that he must be mentally looking through the door, as if he wished to measure thereby all the possibilities that a house of this sort might include, and how they might bear upon the question of his entry.

In his indecision he turned and surveyed the scene around. Not a soul was anywhere visible. The garden-path stretched downward from his feet, gleaming like the track of a snail; the roof of the little well (mostly dry), the well-cover, the top rail of the garden-gate, were varnished with the same dull liquid glaze; while, far away in the vale, a faint whiteness of more than usual extent showed that the rivers were high in the meads. Beyond all this winked a few bleared lamplights through the beating drops—lights that denoted the situation of the county-town from which he had appeared to come. The absence of all notes of life in that direction seemed to clinch his intentions, and he knocked at the door.

Within, a desultory chat had taken the place of movement and musical sound. The hedge-carpenter was suggesting a song to the company, which nobody just then was inclined to undertake, so that the knock afforded a not unwelcome diversion.

'Walk in!' said the shepherd promptly.

The latch clicked upward, and out of the night our pedestrian appeared upon the door-mat. The shepherd arose, snuffed two of the nearest candles, and turned to look at him.

Their light disclosed that the stranger was dark in complexion and not unprepossessing as to feature. His hat, which for a moment he did not remove, hung low over his eyes, without concealing that they were large, open, and determined, moving with a flash rather than a glance round the room. He seemed pleased with his survey, and, baring his shaggy head, said, in a rich deep voice, 'The rain is so heavy, friends, that I ask leave to come in and rest awhile.'

'To be sure, stranger,' said the shepherd. 'And faith, you've been lucky in choosing your time, for we are having a bit of a fling for a glad cause—though, to be sure, a man could hardly wish that glad cause to happen more than once a year.'

'Nor less,' spoke up a woman. 'For 'tis best to get your family over and done with, as soon as you can, so as to be all the earlier out of the fag o't.'

'And what may be this glad cause?' asked the stranger.

'A birth and christening,' said the shepherd.

The stranger hoped his host might not be made unhappy either by too many or too few of such episodes, and being invited by a gesture to a pull at the mug, he readily acquiesced. His manner, which, before entering, had been so dubious, was now altogether that of a careless and candid man.

'Late to be traipsing athwart this coomb—hey?' said the engaged man of fifty.

'Late it is, master, as you say.—I'll take a seat in the chimney-corner, if you have nothing to urge against it, ma'am; for I am a little moist on the side that was next the rain.'

Mrs. Shepherd Fennel assented, and made room for the self-invited comer, who, having got completely inside the chimney-corner, stretched out his legs and his arms with the expansiveness of a person quite at home.

'Yes, I am rather cracked in the vamp,' he said freely, seeing that the eyes of the shepherd's wife fell upon his boots, 'and I am not well fitted either. I have had some rough times lately, and have been forced to pick up what I can get in the way of wearing, but I must find a suit better fit for working-days when I reach home.'

'One of hereabouts?' she inquired.

'Not quite that—further up the country.'

'I thought so. And so be I; and by your tongue you come from my neighbourhood.'

'But you would hardly have heard of me,' he said quickly. 'My time would be long before yours, ma'am, you see.'

This testimony to the youthfulness of his hostess had the effect of stopping her cross-examination.

'There is only one thing more wanted to make me happy,' continued the newcomer. 'And that is a little baccy, which I am sorry to say I am out of.'

'I'll fill your pipe,' said the shepherd.

'I must ask you to lend me a pipe likewise.'

'A smoker, and no pipe about 'ee?'

'I have dropped it somewhere on the road.'

The shepherd filled and handed him a new clay pipe, saying, as he did so, 'Hand me your baccy-box—I'll fill that too, now I am about it.'

The man went through the movement of searching his pockets.

'Lost that too?' said his entertainer, with some surprise.

'I am afraid so,' said the man with some confusion. 'Give it to me in a screw of paper.' Lighting his pipe at the candle with a suction that drew the whole flame into the bowl, he resettled himself in the corner and bent his looks upon the faint steam from his damp legs, as if he wished to say no more.

Meanwhile the general body of guests had been taking little notice of this visitor by reason of an absorbing discussion in which they were engaged with the band about a tune for the next dance. The matter being settled, they were about to stand up when an interruption came in the shape of another knock at the door.

At sound of the same the man in the chimney-corner took up the poker and began stirring the brands as if doing it thoroughly were the one aim of his existence; and a second time the shepherd said, "Walk in!' In a moment another man stood upon the straw-woven doormat. He too was a stranger.

This individual was one of a type radically different from the first. There was more of the commonplace in his manner, and a certain jovial cosmopolitanism sat upon his features. He was several years older than the first arrival, his hair being slightly frosted, his eyebrows bristly, and his whiskers cut back from his cheeks. His face was rather full and flabby, and yet it was not altogether a face without power. A few grog-blossoms marked the neighbourhood of his nose. He flung back his long drab greatcoat, revealing that beneath it he wore a suit of cinder-gray shade throughout, large heavy seals, of some metal or other that would take a polish, dangling from his fob as his only personal ornament. Shaking the water-drops from his low-crowned glazed hat, he said, "I must ask for a few minutes' shelter, comrades, or I shall be wetted to my skin before I get to Casterbridge.'

'Make yourself at home, master,' said the shepherd, perhaps a trifle less heartily than on the first occasion. Not that Fennel had the least tinge of niggardliness in his composition; but the room was far from large, spare chairs were not numerous, and damp companions were not altogether desirable at close quarters for the women and girls in their bright-coloured gowns.

However, the second comer, after taking off his greatcoat, and hanging his hat on a nail in one of the ceiling-beams as if he had been specially invited to put it there, advanced and sat down at the table. This had been pushed so closely into the chimney-corner, to give all available room to the dancers, that its inner edge grazed the elbow of the man who had ensconced himself by the fire; and thus the two strangers were brought into close companionship. They nodded to each other by way of breaking the ice of unacquaintance, and the first stranger handed his neighbour the family mug—a huge vessel of brown ware, having its upper edge worn away like a threshold by the rub of whole generations of thirsty lips that had gone the way of all flesh, and bearing the following inscription burnt upon its rotund side in yellow letters:—

THERE IS NO FUN
UNTiLL i CUM

The other man, nothing loth, raised the mug to his lips, and drank on, and on, and on—till a curious blueness overspread the countenance of the shepherd's wife, who had regarded with no little surprise the first stranger's free offer to the second of what did not belong to him to dispense.

'I knew it!' said the toper to the shepherd with much satisfaction. 'When I walked up your garden before coming in, and saw the hives all of a row, I said to myself, "Where there's bees there's honey, and where there's honey there's mead." But mead of such a truly comfortable sort as this I really didn't expect to meet in my older days.' He took yet another pull at the mug, till it assumed an ominous elevation.

'Glad you enjoy it!' said the shepherd warmly.

'It is goodish mead,' assented Mrs. Fennel, with an absence of enthusiasm which seemed to say that it was possible to buy praise for one's cellar at too heavy a price. 'It is trouble enough to make—and really I hardly think we shall make any more. For honey sells well, and we ourselves can make shift with a drop o' small mead and metheglin for common use from the comb-washings.'

'O, but you'll never have the heart!' reproachfully cried the stranger in cinder-gray, after taking up the mug a third time and setting it down empty. 'I love mead, when 'tis old like this, as I love to go to church o' Sundays, or to relieve the needy any day of the week.'

'Ha, ha, ha!' said the man in the chimney-corner, who, in spite of the taciturnity induced by the pipe of tobacco, could not or would not refrain from this slight testimony to his comrade's humour.

Now the old mead of those days, brewed of the purest first-year or maiden honey, four pounds to the gallon—with its due complement of white of eggs, cinnamon, ginger, cloves, mace, rosemary, yeast, and processes of working, bottling, and cellaring—tasted remarkably strong; but it did not taste so strong as it actually was. Hence, presently, the stranger in cinder-gray at the table, moved by its creeping influence, unbuttoned his waistcoat, threw himself back in his chair, spread his legs, and made his presence felt in various ways.

'Well, well, as I say,' he resumed, 'I am going to Casterbridge, and to Casterbridge I must go. I should have been almost there by this time; but the rain drove me into your dwelling, and I'm not sorry for it.'

'You don't live in Casterbridge?' said the shepherd.

'Not as yet; though I shortly mean to move there.'

'Going to set up in trade, perhaps?'

'No, no,' said the shepherd's wife. 'It is easy to see that the gentleman is rich, and don't want to work at anything.'

The cinder-gray stranger paused, as if to consider whether he would accept that definition of himself. He presently rejected it by answering, 'Rich is not quite the word for me, dame. I do work, and I must work. And even if I only get to Casterbridge by midnight I must begin work there at eight to-morrow morning. Yes, het or wet, blow or snow, famine or sword, my day's work to-morrow must be done.'

'Poor man! Then, in spite o' seeming, you be worse off than we?' replied the shepherd's wife.

' 'Tis the nature of my trade, men and maidens. 'Tis the nature of my trade more than my poverty. . . . But really and truly I must up and off, or I shan't get a lodging in the town.' However, the speaker did not move, and directly added, 'There's time for one more draught of friendship before I go; and I'd perform it at once if the mug were not dry.'

'Here's a mug o' small,' said Mrs. Fennel. 'Small, we call it, though to be sure 'tis only the first wash o' the combs.'

'No,' said the stranger disdainfully. 'I won't spoil your first kindness by partaking o' your second.'

'Certainly not,' broke in Fennel. 'We don't increase and multiply every day, and I'll fill the mug again.' He went away to the dark place under the stairs where the barrel stood. The shepherdess followed him.

'Why should you do this?' she said reproachfully, as soon as they were alone. 'He's emptied it once, though it held enough for ten people; and now he's not contented wi' the small, but must needs call for more o' the strong! And a stranger unbeknown to any of us. For my part, I don't like the look o' the man at all.'

'But he's in the house, my honey; and 'tis a wet night, and a christening. Daze it, what's a cup of mead more or less? There'll be plenty more next bee-burning.'

'Very well—this time, then,' she answered, looking wistfully at the barrel.

'But what is the man's calling, and where is he one of, that he should come in and join us like this?'

'I don't know. I'll ask him again.'

The catastrophe of having the mug drained dry at one pull by the stranger in cinder-gray was effectually guarded against this time by Mrs. Fennel. She poured out his allowance in a small cup, keeping the large one at a discreet distance from him. When he had tossed off his portion the shepherd renewed his inquiry about the stranger's occupation.

The latter did not immediately reply, and the man in the chimney-corner, with sudden demonstrativeness, said, 'Anybody may know my trade—I'm a wheelwright.'

'A very good trade for these parts,' said the shepherd.

'And anybody may know mine—if they've the sense to find it out,' said the stranger in cinder-gray.

'You may generally tell what a man is by his claws,' observed the hedge-carpenter, looking at his own hands. 'My fingers be as full of thorns as an old pin-cushion is of pins.'

The hands of the man in the chimney-corner instinctively sought the shade, and he gazed into the fire as he resumed his pipe. The man at the table took up the hedge-carpenter's remark, and added smartly, 'True; but the oddity of my trade is that, instead of setting a mark upon me, it sets a mark upon my customers.'

No observation being offered by anybody in elucidation of this enigma the shepherd's wife once more called for a song. The same obstacles presented themselves as at the former time—one had no voice, another had forgotten the first verse. The stranger at the table, whose soul had now risen to a good working temperature, relieved the difficulty by exclaiming that, to start the company, he would sing himself. Thrusting one thumb into the arm-hole of his waistcoat, he waved the other hand in the air, and, with an extemporizing gaze at the shining sheep-crooks above the mantelpiece, began:—

'O my trade it is the rarest one,
          Simple shepherds all—

My trade is a sight to see;
For my customers I tie, and take them up
          on high,
     And waft 'em to a far countree!'

The room was silent when he had finished the verse—with one exception, that of the man in the chimney-corner, who, at the singer's word, 'Chorus!' joined him in a deep voice of musical relish—

'And waft 'em to a far countree!'

Oliver Giles, John Pitcher the dairyman, the parish-clerk, the engaged man of fifty, the row of young women against the wall, seemed lost in thought not of the gayest kind. The shepherd looked meditatively on the ground, the shepherdess gazed keenly at the singer, and with some suspicion; she was doubting whether this stranger were merely singing an old song from recollection, or was composing one there and then for the occasion. All were as perplexed at the obscure revelation as the guests at Belshazzar's Feast, except the man in the chimney-corner, who quietly said, 'Second verse, stranger,' and smoked on.

The singer thoroughly moistened himself from his lips inwards, and went on with the next stanza as requested:—

'My tools are but common ones,
          Simple shepherds all—

My tools are no sight to see:
A little hempen string, and a post where-
          on to swing,
     Are implements enough for me!'

Shepherd Fennel glanced round. There was no longer any doubt that the stranger was answering his question rhythmically. The guests one and all started back with suppressed exclamations. The young woman engaged to the man of fifty fainted half-way, and would have proceeded, but finding him wanting in alacrity for catching her she sat down trembling.

'O, he's the——!' whispered the people in the background, mentioning the name of an ominous public officer. 'He's come to do it! 'Tis to be at Casterbridge jail tomorrow—the man for sheep-stealing—the poor clock-maker we heard of, who used to live away at Shottsford and had no work to do—Timothy Summers, whose family were a-starving, and so he went out of Shottsford by the high-road, and took a sheep in open daylight, defying the farmer and the farmer's wife and the farmer's lad, and every man jack among 'em. He' (and they nodded towards the stranger of the deadly trade) 'is come from up the country to do it because there's not enough to do in his own county-town, and he's got the place here now our own county man's dead; he's going to live in the same cottage under the prison wall.'

The stranger in cinder-gray took no notice of this whispered string of observations, but again wetted his lips. Seeing that his friend in the chimney-corner was the only one who reciprocated his joviality in any way, he held out his cup towards that appreciative comrade, who also held out his own. They clinked together, the eyes of the rest of the room hanging upon the singer's actions. He parted his lips for the third verse; but at that moment another knock was audible upon the door. This time the knock was faint and hesitating.

The company seemed scared; the shepherd looked with consternation towards the entrance, and it was with some effort that he resisted his alarmed wife's deprecatory glance, and uttered for the third time the welcoming words, 'Walk in!'

The door was gently opened, and another man stood upon the mat. He, like those who had preceded him, was a stranger. This time it was a short, small personage, of fair complexion, and dressed in a decent suit of dark clothes.

'Can you tell me the way to——?' he began: when, gazing round the room to observe the nature of the company amongst whom he had fallen, his eyes lighted on the stranger in cinder-gray. It was just at the instant when the latter, who had thrown his mind into his song with such a will that he scarcely heeded the interruption, silenced all whispers and inquiries by bursting into his third verse:—

'Tomorrow is my working day,
　　　　　Simple shepherds all—
To-morrow is a working day for me:

For the farmer's sheep is slain, and the
　　　lad who did it ta'en,
And on his soul may God ha' merc-y!'

The stranger in the chimney-corner, waving cups with the singer so heartily that his mead splashed over on the hearth, repeated in his bass voice as before:—

'And on his soul may God ha' merc-y!'

All this time the third stranger had been standing in the doorway. Finding now that he did not come forward or go on speaking, the guests particularly regarded him. They noticed to their surprise that he stood before them the picture of abject terror—his knees trembling, his hand shaking so violently that the door-latch by which he supported himself rattled audibly: his white lips were parted, and his eyes fixed on the merry officer of justice in the middle of the room. A moment more and he had turned, closed the door, and fled.

'What a man can it be?' said the shepherd.

The rest, between the awfulness of their late discovery and the odd conduct of this third visitor, looked as if they knew not what to think, and said nothing. Instinctively they withdrew further and further from the grim gentleman in their midst, whom some of them seemed to take for the Prince of Darkness himself, till they formed a remote circle, an empty space of floor being left between them and him—

'. . . circulus, cujus centrum diabolus.'

The room was so silent—though there were more than twenty people in it—that nothing could be heard but the patter of the rain against the window-shutters, accompanied by the occasional hiss of a stray drop that fell down the chimney into the fire, and the steady puffing of the man in the corner, who had now resumed his pipe of long clay.

The stillness was unexpectedly broken. The distant sound of a gun reverberated through the air—apparently from the direction of the county-town.

'Be jiggered!' cried the stranger who had sung the song, jumping up.

'What does that mean?' asked several.

'A prisoner escaped from the jail—that's what it means.'

All listened. The sound was repeated, and none of them spoke but the man in the chimney-corner, who said quietly, 'I've often been told that in this county they fire a gun at such times; but I never heard it till now.'

'I wonder if it is *my* man?' murmured the personage in cinder-gray.

'Surely it is!' said the shepherd involuntarily. 'And surely we've zeed him! That little man who looked in at the door by now, and quivered like a leaf when he zeed ye and heard your song!'

'His teeth chattered, and the breath went out of his body,' said the dairyman.

'And his heart seemed to sink within him like a stone,' said Oliver Giles.

'And he bolted as if he'd been shot at,' said the hedge-carpenter.

'True—his teeth chattered, and his heart seemed to sink; and he bolted as if he'd been shot at,' slowly summed up the man in the chimney-corner.

'I didn't notice it,' remarked the hangman.

'We were all a-wondering what made him run off in such a fright,' faltered one of the women against the wall, 'and now 'tis explained!'

The firing of the alarm-gun went on at intervals, low and sullenly, and their suspicions became a certainty. The sinister gentleman in cinder-gray roused himself. 'Is there a constable here?' he asked, in thick tones. 'If so, let him step forward.'

The engaged man of fifty stepped quavering out from the wall, his betrothed beginning to sob on the back of the chair.

'You are a sworn constable?'

'I be, sir.'

'Then pursue the criminal at once, with assistance, and bring him back here. He can't have gone far.'

'I will, sir, I will—when I've got my staff. I'll go home and get it, and come sharp here, and start in a body.'

'Staff!—never mind your staff; the man'll be gone!'

'But I can't do nothing without my staff—can I, William, and John, and Charles Jake? No; for there's the king's royal crown a painted on en in yaller and gold, and the lion and the unicorn, so as when

I raise en up and hit my prisoner, 'tis made a lawful blow thereby. I wouldn't 'tempt to take up a man without my staff—no, not I. If I hadn't the law to gie me courage, why, instead o' my taking up him he might take up me!'

'Now, I'm a king's man myself, and can give you authority enough for this,' said the formidable officer in gray. 'Now then, all of ye, be ready. Have ye any lanterns?'

'Yes—have ye any lanterns?—I demand it!' said the constable.

'And the rest of you able-bodied——'

'Able-bodied men—yes—the rest of ye!' said the constable.

'Have you some good stout staves and pitchforks——'

'Staves and pitchforks—in the name o' the law! And take 'em in yer hands and go in quest, and do as we in authority tell ye!'

Thus aroused, the men prepared to give chase. The evidence was, indeed, though circumstantial, so convincing, that but little argument was needed to show the shepherd's guests that after what they had seen it would look very much like connivance if they did not instantly pursue the unhappy third stranger, who could not as yet have gone more than a few hundred yards over such uneven country.

A shepherd is always well provided with lanterns; and, lighting these hastily, and with hurdle-staves in their hands, they poured out of the door, taking a direction along the crest of the hill, away from the town, the rain having fortunately a little abated.

Disturbed by the noise, or possibly by unpleasant dreams of her baptism, the child who had been christened began to cry heart-brokenly in the room overhead. These notes of grief came down through the chinks of the floor to the ears of the women below, who jumped up one by one, and seemed glad of the excuse to ascend and comfort the baby, for the incidents of the last half-hour greatly oppressed them. Thus in the space of two or three minutes the room on the ground-floor was deserted quite.

But it was not for long. Hardly had the sound of footsteps died away when a man returned round the corner of the house from the direction the pursuers had taken. Peeping in at the door, and seeing nobody there, he entered leisurely. It was the stranger of the chimney-corner, who had gone out with the rest. The motive of his return was shown by his helping himself to a cut piece of skimmer-cake that lay on a ledge beside where he had sat, and which he had apparently forgotten to take with him. He also poured out half a cup more mead from the quantity that remained, ravenously eating and drinking these as he stood. He had not finished when another figure came in just as quietly—his friend in cinder-gray.

'O—you here?' said the latter, smiling. 'I thought you had gone to help in the capture.' And this speaker also revealed the object of his return by looking solicitously round for the fascinating mug of old mead.

'And I thought you had gone,' said the other, continuing his skimmer-cake with some effort.

'Well, on second thoughts, I felt there were enough without me,' said the first confidentially, 'and such a night as it is, too. Besides, 'tis the business o' the Government to take care of its criminals—not mine.'

'True; so it is. And I felt as you did, that there were enough without me.'

'I don't want to break my limbs running over the humps and hollows of this wild country.'

'Nor I neither, between you and me.'

'These shepherd-people are used to it —simple-minded souls, you know, stirred up to anything in a moment. They'll have him ready for me before the morning, and no trouble to me at all.'

'They'll have him, and we shall have saved ourselves all labour in the matter.'

'True, true. Well, my way is to Casterbridge; and 'tis as much as my legs will do to take me that far. Going the same way?'

'No, I am sorry to say! I have to get home over there' (he nodded indefinitely to the right), 'and I feel as you do, that it is quite enough for my legs to do before bedtime.'

The other had by this time finished the mead in the mug, after which, shaking hands heartily at the door, and wishing each other well, they went their several ways.

In the meantime the company of pursuers had reached the end of the hog's-back elevation which dominated this part of the down. They had decided on no particular plan of action; and, finding that the man of the baleful trade was no longer in their company, they seemed quite unable to form any such plan now. They descended in all directions down the hill, and straightway several of the party fell into the snare set by Nature for all misguided midnight ramblers over this part of the cretaceous formation. The 'lanchets,' or flint slopes, which belted the escarpment at intervals of a dozen yards, took the less cautious ones unawares, and losing their footing on the rubbly steep they slid sharply downwards, the lanterns rolling from their hands to the bottom, and there lying on their sides till the horn was scorched through.

When they had again gathered themselves together the shepherd, as the man who knew the country best, took the lead, and guided them round these treacherous inclines. The lanterns, which seemed rather to dazzle their eyes and warn the fugitive than to assist them in the exploration, were extinguished, due silence was observed; and in this more rational order they plunged into the vale. It was a grassy, briery, moist defile, affording some shelter to any person who had sought it; but the party perambulated it in vain, and ascended on the other side. Here they wandered apart, and after an interval closed together again to report progress. At the second time of closing in they found themselves near a lonely ash, the single tree on this part of the coomb, probably sown there by a passing bird some fifty years before. And here, standing a little to one side of the trunk, as motionless as the trunk itself, appeared the man they were in quest of, his outline being well defined against the sky beyond. The band noiselessly drew up and faced him.

'Your money or your life!' said the constable sternly to the still figure.

'No, no,' whispered John Pitcher. ' 'Tisn't our side ought to say that. That's the doctrine of vagabonds like him, and we be on the side of the law.'

'Well, well,' replied the constable impatiently; 'I must say something, mustn't I? and if you had all the weight o' this undertaking upon your mind, perhaps you'd say the wrong thing too!—Prisoner at the bar, surrender, in the name of the Father—the Crown, I mane!'

The man under the tree seemed now to notice them for the first time, and, giving them no opportunity whatever for exhibiting their courage, he strolled slowly towards them. He was, indeed, the little man, the third stranger; but his trepidation had in a great measure gone.

'Well, travellers,' he said, 'did I hear ye speak to me?'

'You did: you've got to come and be our prisoner at once!' said the constable. 'We arrest 'ee on the charge of not biding in Casterbridge jail in a decent proper manner to be hung to-morrow morning. Neighbours, do your duty, and seize the culprit!'

On hearing the charge the man seemed enlightened, and, saying not another word, resigned himself with preternatural civility to the search-party, who, with their staves in their hands, surrounded him on all sides, and marched him back towards the shepherd's cottage.

It was eleven o'clock by the time they arrived. The light was shining from the open door, a sound of men's voices within, proclaimed to them as they approached the house that some new events had arisen in their absence. On entering they discovered the shepherd's living room to be invaded by two officers from Casterbridge jail, and a well-known magistrate who lived at the nearest country-seat, intelligence of the escape having become generally circulated.

'Gentlemen,' said the constable, 'I have brought back your man—not without risk and danger; but every one must do his duty! He is inside this circle of able-bodied persons, who have lent me useful aid, considering their ignorance of Crown work. Men, bring forward your prisoner!' And the third stranger was led to the light.

'Who is this?' said one of the officials.

'The man,' said the constable.

'Certainly not,' said the turnkey; and the first corroborated his statement.

'But how can it be otherwise?' asked the constable. 'Or why was he so terrified at sight o' the singing instrument of the law who sat there?' Here he related the strange behaviour of the third stranger on entering the house during the hangman's song.

'Can't understand it,' said the officer coolly. 'All I know is that it is not the condemned man. He's quite a different character from this one; a gauntish fellow, with dark hair and eyes, rather good-looking, and with a musical bass voice that if you heard it once you'd never mistake as long as you lived.'

'Why, souls—'twas the man in the chimney-corner!'

'Hey—what?' said the magistrate, coming forward after inquiring particulars from the shepherd in the background. 'Haven't you got the man after all?'

'Well, sir,' said the constable, 'he's the man we were in search of, that's true; and yet he's not the man we were in search of. For the man we were in search of was not the man we wanted, sir, if you understand my every-day way; for 'twas the man in the chimney-corner!'

'A pretty kettle of fish altogether!' said the magistrate. 'You had better start for the other man at once.'

The prisoner now spoke for the first time. The mention of the man in the chimney-corner seemed to have moved him as nothing else could do. 'Sir,' he said, stepping forward to the magistrate, 'take no more trouble about me. The time is come when I may as well speak. I have done nothing; my crime is that the condemned man is my brother. Early this afternoon I left home at Shottsford to tramp it all the way to Casterbridge jail to bid him farewell. I was benighted, and called here to rest and ask the way. When I opened the door I saw before me the very man, my brother, that I thought to see in the condemned cell at Casterbridge. He was in this chimney-corner; and jammed close to him, so that he could not have got out if he had tried, was the executioner who'd come to take his life, singing a song about it and not knowing that it was his victim who was close by, joining in to save appearances. My brother threw a glance of agony at me, and I knew he meant, "Don't reveal what you see; my life depends on it." I was so terror-struck that I could hardly stand, and, not knowing what I did, I turned and hurried away.'

The narrator's manner and tone had the stamp of truth, and his story made a great impression on all around. 'And do you know where your brother is at the present time?' asked the magistrate.

'I do not. I have never seen him since I closed this door.'

'I can testify to that, for we've been between ye ever since,' said the constable.

'Where does he think to fly to?—what is his occupation?'

'He's a watch-and-clock-maker, sir.'

''A said 'a was a wheelwright—a wicked rogue,' said the constable.

'The wheels of clocks and watches he meant, no doubt,' said Shepherd Fennel. 'I thought his hands were palish for's trade.'

'Well, it appears to me that nothing can be gained by retaining this poor man in custody,' said the magistrate; 'your business lies with the other, unquestionably.'

And so the little man was released offhand; but he looked nothing the less sad on that account, it being beyond the power of magistrate or constable to raze out the written troubles in his brain, for they concerned another whom he regarded with more solicitude than himself. When this was done, and the man had gone his way, the night was found to be so far advanced that it was deemed useless to renew the search before the next morning.

Next day, accordingly, the quest for the clever sheep-stealer became general and keen, to all appearance at least. But the intended punishment was cruelly disproportioned to the transgression, and the sympathy of a great many country-folk in that district was strongly on the side of the fugitive. Moreover, his marvellous coolness and daring in hob-and-nobbing with the hangman, under the unprecedented circumstances of the shepherd's party, won their admiration. So that it may be questioned if all those who ostensibly made themselves so busy in exploring woods and fields and lanes were quite so thorough when it came to the private examination of their own lofts and outhouses. Stories were afloat of a mysterious figure being occasionally seen in some old overgrown trackway or other, remote from turnpike roads; but when a search was instituted in any of these suspected quarters nobody was found. Thus the days and weeks passed without tidings.

In brief, the bass-voiced man of the chimney-corner was never recaptured. Some said that he went across the sea, others that he did not, but buried himself in the depths of a populous city. At any rate, the gentleman in cinder-gray never did his morning's work at Casterbridge, nor met anywhere at all, for business purposes, the genial comrade with whom he had passed an hour of relaxation in the lonely house on the slope of the coomb.

The grass has long been green on the graves of Shepherd Fennel and his frugal wife; the guests who made up the christening party have mainly followed their entertainers to the tomb; the baby in whose honour they all had met is a matron in the sere and yellow leaf. But the arrival of the three strangers at the shepherd's that night, and the details connected therewith, is a story as well known as ever in the country about Higher Crowstairs.

[1883]

QUESTIONS FOR STUDY

1. *What hints and clues suggest the real relationship among the three strangers?*
2. *What is the function of the first four paragraphs? How do they prepare the reader for the story that follows?*

3. *Is the plot too contrived? Is Hardy's major concern with plot at all? If so, in what sense? If not, what is his major concern?*

4. *What are some of the major examples of Hardy's use of irony?*

5. *What are the underlying attitudes of the guests toward the convicted sheep-stealer?*

6. *Why should the story of the three strangers become a legend told and retold for fifty years? How do point of view, setting, and characterization all reflect the story's legendary quality? What elements and attitudes traditionally found in a legend or folk tale are present in "The Three Strangers"?*

BRET HARTE

Tennessee's Partner

I DO NOT think that we ever knew his real name. Our ignorance of it certainly never gave us any social inconvenience, for at Sandy Bar in 1854 most men were christened anew. Sometimes these appellatives were derived from some distinctiveness of dress, as in the case of "Dungaree Jack"; or from some peculiarity of habit, as shown in "Saleratus Bill," so called from an undue proportion of that chemical in his daily bread; or from some unlucky slip, as exhibited in "The Iron Pirate," a mild, inoffensive man, who earned that baleful title by his unfortunate mispronunciation of the term "iron pyrites." Perhaps this may have been the beginning of a rude heraldry; but I am constrained to think that it was because a man's real name in that day rested solely upon his own unsupported statement. "Call yourself Clifford, do you?" said Boston, addressing a timid new-comer with infinite scorn; "hell is full of such Cliffords!" He then introduced the unfortunate man, whose name happened to be really Clifford, as "Jaybird Charley,"—an unhallowed inspiration of the moment, that clung to him ever after.

But to return to Tennessee's Partner, whom we never knew by any other than this relative title; that he had ever existed as a separate and distinct individuality we only learned later. It seems that in 1853 he left Poker Flat to go to San Francisco, ostensibly to procure a wife. He never got any farther than Stockton. At that place he was attracted by a young person who waited upon the table at the hotel where he took his meals. One morning he said something to her which caused her to smile not unkindly, to somewhat coquettishly break a plate of toast over his upturned, serious, simple face, and to retreat to the kitchen. He followed her, and emerged a few moments later, covered with more toast and victory. That day

week they were married by a Justice of the Peace, and returned to Poker Flat. I am aware that something more might be made of this episode, but I prefer to tell it as it was current at Sandy Bar,—in the gulches and bar-rooms,—where all sentiment was modified by a strong sense of humor.

Of their married felicity but little is known, perhaps for the reason that Tennessee, then living with his partner, one day took occasion to say something to the bride on his own account, at which, it is said, she smiled not unkindly and chastely retreated,—this time as far as Marysville, where Tennessee followed her, and where they went to housekeeping without the aid of a Justice of the Peace. Tennessee's Partner took the loss of his wife simply and seriously, as was his fashion. But to everybody's surprise, when Tennessee one day returned from Marysville, without his partner's wife,—she having smiled and retreated with somebody else,—Tennessee's Partner was the first man to shake his hand and greet him with affection. The boys who had gathered in the cañon to see the shooting were naturally indignant. Their indignation might have found vent in sarcasm but for a certain look in Tennessee's Partner's eye that indicated a lack of humorous appreciation. In fact, he was a grave man, with a steady application to practical detail which was unpleasant in a difficulty.

Meanwhile a popular feeling against Tennessee had grown up on the Bar. He was known to be a gambler; he was suspected to be a thief. In these suspicions Tennessee's Partner was equally compromised; his continued intimacy with Tennessee after the affair above quoted could only be accounted for on the hypothesis of a copartnership of crime. At last Tennessee's guilt became flagrant. One day he overtook a stranger on his way to Red Dog. The stranger afterward related that Tennessee beguiled the time with interesting anecdote and reminiscence, but illogically concluded the interview in the following words: "And now, young man, I'll trouble you for your knife, your pistols, and your money. You see your weppings might get you into trouble at Red Dog, and your money's a temptation to the evilly disposed. I think you said your address was San Francisco. I shall endeavor to call." It may be stated here that Tennessee had a fine flow of humor, which no business preoccupation could wholly subdue.

This exploit was his last. Red Dog and Sandy Bar made common cause against the highwayman. Tennessee was hunted in very much the same fashion as his prototype, the grizzly. As the toils closed around him, he made a desperate dash through the Bar, emptying his revolver at the crowd before the Arcade Saloon, and so on up Grizzly Cañon; but at its farther extremity he was stopped by a small man on a gray horse. The men looked at each other a moment in silence. Both were fearless, both self-possessed and independent; and both types of a civilization that in the seventeenth century would have been called heroic, but, in the nineteenth, simply "reckless." "What have you got there?—I call," said Tennessee, quietly. 'Two bowers and an ace," said the stranger, as quietly, showing two revolvers and a bowie-knife. That takes me," returned Tennessee; and with this gamblers epigram, he threw away his useless pistol, and rode back with his captor.

It was a warm night. The cool breeze which usually sprang up with the going down of the sun behind the *chaparral*-crested mountain was that evening withheld from Sandy Bar. The little cañon was stifling with heated resinous odors, and the decaying driftwood on the Bar sent forth faint, sickening exhalations. The feverishness of day, and its fierce passions, still filled the camp. Lights moved restlessly along the bank of the river, striking no answering reflection from its tawny current. Against the blackness of the pines the windows of the old loft above the express-office stood out

staringly bright; and through their curtainless panes the loungers below could see the forms of those who were even then deciding the fate of Tennessee. And above all this, etched on the dark firmament, rose the Sierra, remote and passionless, crowned with remoter passionless stars.

The trial of Tennessee was conducted as fairly as was consistent with a judge and jury who felt themselves to some extent obliged to justify, in their verdict, the previous irregularities of arrest and indictment. The law of Sandy Bar was implacable, but not vengeful. The excitement and personal feeling of the chase were over; with Tennessee safe in their hands they were ready to listen patiently to any defence, which they were already satisfied was insufficient. There being no doubt in their own minds, they were willing to give the prisoner the benefit of any that might exist. Secure in the hypothesis that he ought to be hanged, on general principles, they indulged him with more latitude of defence than his reckless hardihood seemed to ask. The Judge appeared to be more anxious than the prisoner, who, otherwise unconcerned, evidently took a grim pleasure in the responsibility he had created. "I don't take any hand in this yer game," had been his invariable, but good-humored reply to all questions. The Judge—who was also his captor—for a moment vaguely regretted that he had not shot him "on sight," that morning, but presently dismissed this human weakness as unworthy of the judicial mind. Nevertheless, when there was a tap at the door, and it was said that Tennessee's Partner was there on behalf of the prisoner, he was admitted at once without question. Perhaps the younger members of the jury, to whom the proceedings were becoming irksomely thoughtful, hailed him as a relief.

For he was not, certainly, an imposing figure. Short and stout, with a square face sunburned into a preternatural redness, clad in a loose duck "jumper," and trousers streaked and splashed with red soil, his aspect under any circumstances would have been quaint, and was now even ridiculous. As he stooped to deposit at his feet a heavy carpet-bag he was carrying, it became obvious, from partially developed legends and inscriptions, that the material with which his trousers had been patched had been originally intended for a less ambitious covering. Yet he advanced with great gravity, and after having shaken the hand of each person in the room with labored cordiality, he wiped his serious, perplexed face on a red bandanna handkerchief, a shade lighter than his complexion, laid his powerful hand upon the table to steady himself, and thus addressed the Judge:—

"I was passin' by," he began, by way of apology, "and I thought I'd just step in and see how things was gittin' on with Tennessee thar,—my pardner. It's a hot night. I disremember any sich weather before on the Bar."

He paused a moment, but nobody volunteering any other meteorological recollection, he again had recourse to his pocket-handkerchief, and for some moments mopped his face diligently.

"Have you anything to say in behalf of the prisoner?" said the Judge, finally.

"Thet's it," said Tennessee's Partner, in a tone of relief. "I come yar as Tennessee's pardner,—knowing him nigh on four year, off and on, wet and dry, in luck and out o' luck. His ways ain't allers my ways, but thar ain't any p'ints in that young man, thar ain't any liveliness as he's been up to, as I don't know. And you sez to me, sez you,—confidential-like, and between man and man,—sez you, 'Do you know anything in his behalf?' and I sez to you, sez I,—confidential-like, as between man and man,—'What should a man know of his pardner?'"

"Is this all you have to say?" asked the Judge, impatiently, feeling, perhaps, that a dangerous sympathy of humor was beginning to humanize the Court.

"Thet's so," continued Tennessee's Partner. "It ain't for me to say anything agin' him. And now, what's the case? Here's Tennessee wants money, wants it bad, and does n't like to ask it of his old pardner. Well, what does Tennessee do? He lays for a stranger, and he fetches that stranger. And you lays for *him*, and you fetches *him;* and the honors is easy. And

I put it to you, bein' a far-minded man, and to you, gentlemen, all, as far-minded men, ef this is n't so."

"Prisoner," said the Judge, interrupting, "have you any questions to ask this man?"

"No! no!" continued Tennessee's Partner, hastily. "I play this yer hand alone. To come down to the bed-rock, it's just this: Tennessee, thar, has played it pretty rough and expensive-like on a stranger, and on this yer camp. And now, what's the fair thing? Some would say more; some would say less. Here's seventeen hundred dollars in coarse gold and a watch,—it's about all my pile,—and call it square!" And before a hand could be raised to prevent him, he had emptied the contents of the carpet-bag upon the table.

For a moment his life was in jeopardy. One or two men sprang to their feet, several hands groped for hidden weapons, and a suggestion to "throw him from the window" was only overridden by a gesture from the Judge. Tennessee laughed. And apparently oblivious of the excitement, Tennessee's Partner improved the opportunity to mop his face again with his handkerchief.

When order was restored, and the man was made to understand, by the use of forcible figures and rhetoric, that Tennessee's offence could not be condoned by money, his face took a more serious and sanguinary hue, and those who were nearest to him noticed that his rough hand trembled slightly on the table. He hesitated a moment as he slowly returned the gold to the carpet-bag, as if he had not yet entirely caught the elevated sense of justice which swayed the tribunal, and was perplexed with the belief that he had not offered enough. Then he turned to the Judge, and saying, "This yer is a lone hand, played alone, and without my pardner," he bowed to the jury and was about to withdraw, when the Judge called him back. "If you have anything to say to Tennessee, you had better say it now." For the first time that evening the eyes of the prisoner and his strange advocate met. Tennessee smiled, showed his white teeth, and, saying, "Euchred, old man!" held out his hand. Tennessee's Partner took it in his own, and saying, "I just dropped in as I was passin' to see how things was gettin' on," let the hand passively fall, and adding that "it was a warm night," again mopped his face with his handkerchief, and without another word withdrew.

The two men never again met each other alive. For the unparalleled insult of a bribe offered to Judge Lynch—who, whether bigoted, weak, or narrow, was at least incorruptible—firmly fixed in the mind of that mythical personage any wavering determination of Tennessee's fate; and at the break of day he was marched, closely guarded, to meet it at the top of Marley's Hill.

How he met it, how cool he was, how he refused to say anything, how perfect were the arrangements of the committee, were all duly reported, with the addition of a warning moral and example to all future evil-doers, in the Red Dog Clarion, by its editor, who was present, and to whose vigorous English I cheerfully refer the reader. But the beauty of that midsummer morning, the blessed amity of earth and air and sky, the awakened life of the free woods and hills, the joyous renewal and promise of Nature, and above all, the infinite Serenity that thrilled through each, was not reported, as not being a part of the social lesson. And yet, when the weak and foolish deed was done, and a life, with its possibilities and responsibilities, had passed out of the misshapen thing that dangled between earth and sky, the birds sang, the flowers bloomed, the sun shone, as cheerily as before; and possibly the Red Dog Clarion was right.

Tennessee's Partner was not in the group that surrounded the ominous tree. But as they turned to disperse attention was drawn to the singular appearance of a motionless donkey-cart halted at the side of the road. As they approached, they at once recognized the venerable "Jenny" and the two-wheeled cart as the property of Tennessee's Partner,—used by him in carrying dirt from his claim; and a few paces distant the owner of the equipage himself, sitting under a buckeye-tree, wiping the perspiration from his glowing face. In answer to an inquiry, he said he had come for the body of the "diseased," "if it was all the same to the committee." He did n't wish to "hurry anything"; he could "wait." He was not working that day; and when the gentlemen were done with the "diseased," he would take him. "Ef thar is any present," he added, in his simple, serious way, "as would care to jine in the fun'l, they kin come." Perhaps it was from a sense of humor, which I have already intimated was a feature of Sandy Bar,—perhaps it was from something even better than that; but two thirds of the loungers accepted the invitation at once.

It was noon when the body of Tennessee was delivered into the hands of his partner. As the cart drew up to the fatal tree, we noticed that it contained a rough, oblong box,—apparently made from a section of sluicing,—and half filled with bark and the tassels of pine. The cart was further decorated with slips of willow, and made fragrant with buckeye-blossoms. When the body was deposited in the box, Tennessee's Partner drew over it a piece of tarred canvas, and gravely mounting the narrow seat in front, with his feet upon the shafts, urged the little donkey forward. The equipage moved slowly on, at that decorous pace which was habitual with "Jenny" even under less solemn circumstances. The men—half curiously, half jestingly, but all good-humoredly—strolled along beside the cart; some in advance, some a little in the rear of the homely catafalque. But, whether from the narrowing of the road or some present sense of decorum, as the cart passed on, the company fell to the rear in couples, keeping step, and otherwise assuming the external show of a formal procession. Jack Folinsbee, who had at the outset played a funeral march in dumb show upon an imaginary trombone, desisted, from a lack of sympathy and appreciation,—not having, perhaps, your true humorist's capacity to be content with the enjoyment of his own fun.

The way led through Grizzly Cañon,—by this time clothed in funereal drapery and shadows. The redwoods, burying their moccasined feet in the red soil, stood in Indian-file along the track, trailing an uncouth benediction from their bending boughs upon the passing bier. A hare, surprised into helpless inactivity, sat upright and pulsating in the ferns by the roadside, as the *cortége* went by. Squirrels hastened to gain a secure outlook from higher boughs; and the blue-jays, spreading their wings, fluttered before them like outriders, until the outskirts of Sandy Bar were reached, and the solitary cabin of Tennessee's Partner.

Viewed under more favorable circumstances, it would not have been a cheerful place. The unpicturesque site, the rude and unlovely outlines, the unsavory details, which distinguish the nest-building of the California miner, were all here, with the dreariness of decay superadded. A few paces from the cabin there was a rough enclosure, which, in the brief days of Tennessee's Partner's matrimonial felicity, had been used as a garden, but was now overgrown with fern. As we approached it we were surprised to find that what we had taken for a recent attempt at cultivation was the broken soil about an open grave.

The cart was halted before the enclosure; and rejecting the offers of assistance with the same air of simple self-reliance he had displayed throughout, Tennessee's Partner lifted the rough coffin on his back, and deposited it, unaided, within the shallow grave. He then nailed down the board which served as a lid; and mounting the little mound of earth beside it, took off his hat, and slowly mopped his face with his handkerchief. This the crowd felt was a preliminary to speech; and they disposed themselves variously on stumps and boulders, and sat expectant.

"When a man," began Tennessee's Partner, slowly, "has been running free all day, what's the natural thing for him to do? Why, to come home. And if he ain't in a condition to go home, what can his best friend do? Why, bring him home! And here's Tennessee has been running free, and we brings him home from his wandering." He paused, and picked up a fragment of quartz, rubbed it thoughtfully on his sleeve, and went on: "It ain't

the first time that I've packed him on my back, as you see'd me now. It ain't the first time that I brought him to this yer cabin when he could n't help himself; it ain't the first time that I and 'Jinny' have waited for him on yon hill, and picked him up and so fetched him home, when he could n't speak, and did n't know me. And now that it's the last time, why—" he paused, and rubbed the quartz gently on his sleeve—"you see it's sort of rough on his pardner. And now, gentlemen," he added, abruptly, picking up his long-handled shovel, "the fun'l 's over; and my thanks, and Tennessee's thanks, to you for your trouble."

Resisting any proffers of assistance, he began to fill in the grave, turning his back upon the crowd, that after a few moments' hesitation gradually withdrew. As they crossed the little ridge that hid Sandy Bar from view, some, looking back, thought they could see Tennessee's Partner, his work done, sitting upon the grave, his shovel between his knees, and his face buried in his red bandanna handkerchief. But it was argued by others that you could n't tell his face from his handkerchief at that distance; and this point remained undecided.

In the reaction that followed the feverish excitement of that day, Tennessee's Partner was not forgotten. A secret investigation had cleared him of any complicity in Tennessee's guilt, and left only a suspicion of his general sanity. Sandy Bar made a point of calling on him, and proffering various uncouth, but well-meant kindnesses. But from that day his rude health and great strength seemed visibly to decline; and when the rainy season fairly set in, and the tiny grass-blades were beginning to peep from the rocky mound above Tennessee's grave, he took to his bed.

One night, when the pines beside the cabin were swaying in the storm, and trailing their slender fingers over the roof, and the roar and rush of the swollen river were heard below, Tennesse's Partner lifted his head from the pillow, saying, "It is time to go for Tennessee; I must put 'Jinny' in the cart"; and would have risen from his bed but for the restraint of his attendant. Struggling, he still pursued his singular fancy: "There, now, steady, 'Jinny,'—steady, old girl. How dark it is! Look out for the ruts,—and look out for him, too, old gal. Sometimes, you know, when he's blind drunk, he drops down right in the trail. Keep on straight up to the pine on the top of the hill. Thar—I told you so!—thar he is,—coming this way, too,—all by himself, sober, and his face a-shining. Tennessee! Pardner!"

And so they met.

[1870]

QUESTIONS FOR STUDY

1. *What does the story have to say about the nature of loyalty and friendship? Is Tennessee's Partner's loyalty credible? What seems to be its basis?*

2. *How is nature used in the story?*

3. *Why does the partner die?*

4. *At the end of the second paragraph Harte notes that in Sandy Bar "all sentiment was modified by a strong sense of humor." What kind of humor does Harte himself employ and to what end? Is it sufficient to blunt the story's sentimentality?*

5. *Does "Tennessee's Partner" fulfill the requirements of a successful and satisfying short story? If not, how is its lingering popularity to be explained?*

NATHANIEL HAWTHORNE

My Kinsman, Major Molineux

AFTER the kings of Great Britain had assumed the right of appointing the colonial governors, the measures of the latter seldom met with the ready and general approbation which had been paid to those of their predecessors, under the original charters. The people looked with most jealous scrutiny to the exercise of power which did not emanate from themselves, and they usually rewarded their rulers with slender gratitude for the compliances by which, in softening their instructions from beyond the sea, they had incurred the reprehension of those who gave them. The annals of Massachusetts Bay will inform us, that of six governors in the space of about forty years from the surrender of the old charter, under James II., two were imprisoned by a popular insurrection; a third, as Hutchinson inclines to believe, was driven from the province by the whizzing of a musket-ball; a fourth, in the opinion of the same historian, was hastened to his grave by continual bickerings with the House of Representatives; and the remaining two, as well as their successors, till the Revolution, were favored with few and brief intervals of peaceful sway. The inferior members of the court party, in times of high political excitement, led scarcely a more desirable life. These remarks may serve as a preface to the following adventures, which chanced upon a summer night, not far from a hundred years ago. The reader, in order to avoid a long and dry detail of colonial affairs, is requested to dispense with an account of the train of circumstances that had caused much temporary inflammation of the popular mind.

It was near nine o'clock of a moonlight evening, when a boat crossed the ferry with a single passenger, who had obtained his conveyance at that unusual hour by the promise of an extra fare. While he stood on the landing-place, searching in either pocket for the means of fulfilling his agreement, the ferryman lifted a lantern, by the aid of which, and the newly risen moon, he took a very accurate survey of the stranger's figure. He was a youth of barely eighteen years, evidently country-bred, and now, as it should seem, upon his first visit to town. He was clad in a coarse gray coat, well worn, but in excellent repair; his under garments were durably constructed of leather, and fitted tight to a pair of serviceable and well-shaped limbs; his stockings of blue yarn were the incontrovertible work of a mother or a sister; and on his head was a three-cornered hat, which in its better days had perhaps sheltered the graver brow of the lad's father. Under his left arm was a heavy cudgel formed of an oak sapling, and retaining a part of the hardened root; and his equipment was completed by a wallet, not so abundantly stocked as to incommode the vigorous shoulders on which it hung. Brown, curly hair, well-shaped features, and bright, cheerful eyes were nature's gifts, and worth all that art could have done for his adornment.

The youth, one of whose names was Robin, finally drew from his pocket the half of a little province bill of five shillings, which, in the depreciation in that sort of currency, did but satisfy the ferryman's demand, with the surplus of a sexangular piece of parchment, valued at three pence. He then walked forward into the town, with as light a step as if his day's journey had not already exceeded thirty miles, and with as eager an eye as if he were entering London city, instead of the little metropolis of a New England colony. Before Robin had proceeded far, however, it occurred to him that he knew not whither to direct his steps; so he paused, and looked up and down the narrow street, scrutinizing the small and mean wooden buildings that were scattered on either side.

"This low hovel cannot be my kinsman's dwelling," thought he, "nor yonder house, where the moonlight enters at the broken casement; and truly I see none hereabouts that might be worthy of him. It would have been wise to inquire my way of the ferryman, and doubtless he would have gone with me, and earned a shilling from the Major for his pains. But the next man I meet will do as well."

He resumed his walk, and was glad to perceive that the street now became wider, and the houses more respectable in their appearance. He soon discerned a figure moving on moderately in advance, and hastened his steps to overtake it. As Robin drew nigh, he saw that the passenger was a man in years, with a full periwig of gray hair, a wide-skirted coat of dark cloth, and silk stockings rolled above his knees. He carried a long and polished cane, which he struck down perpendicularly before him at every step; and at regular intervals he uttered two successive hems, of a peculiarly solemn and sepulchral intonation. Having made these observations, Robin laid hold of the skirt of the old man's coat, just when the light from the open door and windows of a barber's shop fell upon both their figures.

"Good evening to you, honored sir," said he, making a low bow, and still retaining his hold of the skirt. "I pray you tell me whereabouts is the dwelling of my kinsman, Major Molineux."

The youth's question was uttered very loudly; and one of the barbers, whose razor was descending on a well-soaped chin, and another who was dressing a Ramillies wig, left their occupations, and came to the door. The citizen, in the mean time, turned a long-favored countenance upon Robin, and answered him in a tone of excessive anger and annoyance. His two sepulchral hems, however, broke into the very centre of his rebuke, with most singular effect, like a thought of the cold grave obtruding among wrathful passions.

"Let go my garment, fellow! I tell you, I know not the man you speak of. What! I have authority, I have—hem, hem—authority; and if this be the respect you show for your betters, your feet shall be brought acquainted with the stocks by daylight, to-morrow morning!"

Robin released the old man's skirt, and hastened away, pursued by an ill-mannered roar of laughter from the barber's shop. He was at first considerably surprised by the result of his question, but, being a shrewd youth, soon thought himself able to account for the mystery.

"This is some country representative," was his conclusion, "who has never seen the inside of my kinsman's door, and lacks the breeding to answer a stranger civilly. The man is old, or verily—I might be tempted to turn back and smite him on the nose. Ah, Robin, Robin! even the barber's boys laugh at you for choosing such a guide! You will be wiser in time, friend Robin."

He now became entangled in a succession of crooked and narrow streets, which crossed each other, and meandered at no great distance from the water-side. The smell of tar was obvious to his nostrils, the masts of vessels pierced the moonlight above the tops of the buildings, and the numerous signs, which Robin paused to read, informed him that he was near the centre of business. But the streets were empty, the shops were closed, and lights were visible only in the second stories of a few dwelling-houses. At length, on the corner of a narrow lane, through which he was passing, he beheld the broad countenance of a British hero swinging before the door of an inn, whence proceeded the voices of many guests. The casement of one of the lower windows was thrown back, and a very thin curtain permitted Robin to distinguish a party at supper, round a well-furnished table. The fragrance of the good cheer steamed forth into the outer air, and the youth could not fail to recollect that the last remnant of his travelling stock of provision had yielded to his morning appetite, and that noon had found and left him dinnerless.

"Oh, that a parchment three-penny might give me a right to sit down at yonder table!" said Robin, with a sigh. "But the Major will make me welcome to the best of his victuals; so I will even step boldly in, and inquire my way to his dwelling."

He entered the tavern, and was guided

by the murmur of voices and the fumes of tobacco to the public-room. It was a long and low apartment, with oaken walls, grown dark in the continual smoke, and a floor which was thickly sanded, but of no immaculate purity. A number of persons —the larger part of whom appeared to be mariners, or in some way connected with the sea—occupied the wooden benches, or leather-bottomed chairs, conversing on various matters, and occasionally lending their attention to some topic of general interest. Three or four little groups were draining as many bowls of punch, which the West India trade had long since made a familiar drink in the colony. Others, who had the appearance of men who lived by regular and laborious handicraft, preferred the insulated bliss of an unshared potation, and became more taciturn under its influence. Nearly all, in short, evinced a predilection for the Good Creature in some of its various shapes, for this is a vice to which, as Fast Day sermons of a hundred years ago will testify, we have a long hereditary claim. The only guests to whom Robin's sympathies inclined him were two or three sheepish countrymen, who were using the inn somewhat after the fashion of a Turkish caravansary; they had gotten themselves into the darkest corner of the room, and heedless of the Nicotian atmosphere, were supping on the bread of their own ovens, and the bacon cured in their own chimney-smoke. But though Robin felt a sort of brotherhood with these strangers, his eyes were attracted from them to a person who stood near the door, holding whispered conversation with a group of ill-dressed associates. His features were separately striking almost to grotesqueness, and the whole face left a deep impression on the memory. The forehead bulged out into a double prominence, with a vale between; the nose came boldly forth in an irregular curve, and its bridge was of more than a finger's breadth; the eyebrows were deep and shaggy, and the eyes glowed beneath them like fire in a cave.

While Robin deliberated of whom to inquire respecting his kinsman's dwelling, he was accosted by the innkeeper, a little man in a stained white apron, who had come to pay his professional welcome to the stranger. Being in the second generation from a French Protestant, he seemed to have inherited the courtesy of his parent nation; but no variety of circumstances was ever known to change his voice from the one shrill note in which he now addressed Robin.

"From the country, I presume, sir?" said he, with a profound bow. "Beg leave to congratulate you on your arrival, and trust you intend a long stay with us. Fine town here, sir, beautiful buildings, and much that may interest a stranger. May I hope for the honor of your commands in respect to supper?"

"The man sees a family likeness! the rogue has guessed that I am related to the Major!" thought Robin, who had hitherto experienced little superfluous civility.

All eyes were now turned on the country lad, standing at the door, in his worn three-cornered hat, gray coat, leather breeches, and blue yarn stockings, leaning on an oaken cudgel, and bearing a wallet on his back.

Robin replied to the courteous innkeeper, with such an assumption of confidence as befitted the Major's relative. "My honest friend," he said, "I shall make it a point to patronize your house on some occasion, when"—here he could not help lowering his voice—"when I may have more than a parchment three-pence in my pocket. My present business," continued he, speaking with lofty confidence, "is merely to inquire my way to the dwelling of my kinsman, Major Molineux."

There was a sudden and general movement in the room, which Robin interpreted as expressing the eagerness of each individual to become his guide. But the innkeeper turned his eyes to a written paper on the wall, which he read, or seemed to read, with occasional recurrences to the young man's figure.

"What have we here?" said he, breaking his speech into little dry fragments. " 'Left the house of the subscriber, bounden servant, Hezekiah Mudge,—had on, when he went away, gray coat, leather breeches, master's third-best hat. One pound currency reward to whosoever shall lodge him in any jail of the province.' Better trudge, boy; better trudge!"

Robin had begun to draw his hand towards the lighter end of the oak cudgel, but a strange hostility in every countenance induced him to relinquish his purpose of breaking the courteous innkeeper's head. As he turned to leave the room, he encountered a sneering glance from the bold-featured personage whom he had before noticed; and no sooner was he beyond the door, than he heard a general laugh, in which the innkeeper's voice might be distinguished, like the dropping of small stones into a kettle.

"Now, is it not strange," thought Robin, with his usual shrewdness,—"is it not strange that the confession of an empty pocket should outweigh the name of my kinsman, Major Molineux? Oh, if I had one of those grinning rascals in the woods, where I and my oak sapling grew up together, I would teach him that my arm is heavy though my purse be light!"

On turning the corner of the narrow lane, Robin found himself in a spacious street, with an unbroken line of lofty houses on each side, and a steepled building at the upper end, whence the ringing of a bell announced the hour of nine. The light of the moon, and the lamps from the numerous shop-windows, discovered people promenading on the pavement, and amongst them Robin hoped to recognize his hitherto inscrutable relative. The result of his former inquiries made him unwilling to hazard another, in a scene of such publicity, and he determined to walk slowly and silently up the street, thrusting his face close to that of every elderly gentleman, in search of the Major's lineaments. In his progress, Robin encountered many gay and gallant figures. Embroidered garments of showy colors, enormous periwigs, gold-laced hats, and silver-hilted swords glided past him and dazzled his optics. Travelled youths, imitators of the European fine gentlemen of the period, trod jauntily along, half dancing to the fashionable tunes which they hummed, and making poor Robin ashamed of his quiet and natural gait. At length, after many pauses to examine the gorgeous display of goods in the shop-windows, and after suffering some re-

bukes for the impertinence of his scrutiny into people's faces, the Major's kinsman found himself near the steepled building, still unsuccessful in his search. As yet, however, he had seen only one side of the thronged street; so Robin crossed, and continued the same sort of inquisition down the opposite pavement, with stronger hopes than the philosopher seeking an honest man, but with no better fortune. He had arrived about midway towards the lower end, from which his course began, when he overheard the approach of some one who struck down a cane on the flag-stones at every step, uttering, at regular intervals, two sepulchral hems.

"Mercy on us!" quoth Robin, recognizing the sound.

Turning a corner, which chanced to be close at his right hand, he hastened to pursue his researches in some other part of the town. His patience now was wearing low, and he seemed to feel more fatigue from his rambles since he crossed the ferry, than from his journey of several days on the other side. Hunger also pleaded loudly within him, and Robin began to balance the propriety of demanding, violently, and with lifted cudgel, the necessary guidance from the first solitary passenger whom he should meet. While a resolution to this effect was gaining strength, he entered a street of mean appearance, on either side of which a row of ill-built houses was straggling towards the harbor. The moonlight fell upon no passenger along the whole extent, but in the third domicile which Robin passed there was a half-opened door, and his keen glance detected a woman's garment within.

"My luck may be better here," said he to himself.

Accordingly, he approached the door, and beheld it shut closer as he did so; yet an open space remained, sufficing for the fair occupant to observe the stranger, without a corresponding display on her part. All that Robin could discern was a strip of scarlet petticoat, and the occasional sparkle of an eye, as if the moonbeams were trembling on some bright thing.

"Pretty mistress," for I may call her so

almost ghostly indistinctness, just as his eye appeared to grasp them; and finally he took a minute survey of an edifice which stood on the opposite side of the street, directly in front of the church-door, where he was stationed. It was a large, square mansion, distinguished from its neighbors by a balcony, which rested on tall pillars, and by an elaborate Gothic window, communicating therewith.

"Perhaps this is the very house I have been seeking," thought Robin.

Then he strove to speed away the time, by listening to a murmur which swept continually along the street, yet was scarcely audible, except to an unaccustomed ear like his; it was a low, dull, dreamy sound, compounded of many noises, each of which was at too great a distance to be separately heard. Robin marvelled at this snore of a sleeping town, and marvelled more whenever its continuity was broken by now and then a distant shout, apparently loud where it originated. But altogether it was a sleep-inspiring sound, and, to shake off its drowsy influence, Robin arose, and climbed a window-frame, that he might view the interior of the church. There the moonbeams came trembling in, and fell down upon the deserted pews, and extended along the quiet aisles. A fainter yet more awful radiance was hovering around the pulpit, and one solitary ray had dared to rest upon the open page of the great Bible. Had nature, in that deep hour, become a worshipper in the house which man had builded? Or was that heavenly light the visible sanctity of the place,—visible because no earthly and impure feet were within the walls? The scene made Robin's heart shiver with a sensation of loneliness stronger than he had ever felt in the remotest depths of his native woods; so he turned away and sat down again before the door. There were graves around the church, and now an uneasy thought obtruded into Robin's breast. What if the object of his search, which had been so often and so strangely thwarted, were all the time mouldering in his shroud? What if his kinsman should glide through yonder gate, and nod and smile to him in dimly passing by?

"Oh that any breathing thing were here with me!" said Robin.

Recalling his thoughts from this uncomfortable track, he sent them over forest, hill, and stream, and attempted to imagine how that evening of ambiguity and weariness had been spent by his father's household. He pictured them assembled at the door, beneath the tree, the great old tree, which had been spared for its huge twisted trunk and venerable shade, when a thousand leafy brethren fell. There, at the going down of the summer sun, it was his father's custom to perform domestic worship, that the neighbors might come and join with him like brothers of the family, and that the wayfaring man might pause to drink at that fountain, and keep his heart pure by freshening the memory of home. Robin distinguished the seat of every individual of the little audience; he saw the good man in the midst, holding the Scriptures in the golden light that fell from the western clouds; he beheld him close the book and all rise up to pray. He heard the old thanksgivings for daily mercies, the old supplications for their continuance, to which he had so often listened in weariness, but which were now among his dear remembrances. He perceived the slight inequality of his father's voice when he came to speak of the absent one; he noted how his mother turned her face to the broad and knotted trunk; how his elder brother scorned, because the beard was rough upon his upper lip, to permit his features to be moved; how the younger sister drew down a low hanging branch before her eyes; and how the little one of all, whose sports had hitherto broken the decorum of the scene, understood the prayer for her playmate, and burst into clamorous grief. Then he saw them go in at the door; and when Robin would have entered also, the latch tinkled into its place, and he was excluded from his home.

"Am I here, or there?" cried Robin, starting; for all at once, when his thoughts had become visible and audible in a dream, the long, wide, solitary street shone out before him.

He aroused himself, and endeavored to

with a good conscience, thought the shrewd youth, since I know nothing to the contrary,—"my sweet pretty mistress, will you be kind enough to tell me whereabouts I must seek the dwelling of my kinsman, Major Molineux?"

Robin's voice was plaintive and winning, and the female, seeing nothing to be shunned in the handsome country youth, thrust open the door, and came forth into the moonlight. She was a dainty little figure, with a white neck, round arms, and a slender waist, at the extremity of which her scarlet petticoat jutted out over a hoop, as if she were standing in a balloon. Moreover, her face was oval and pretty, her hair dark beneath the little cap, and her bright eyes possessed a sly freedom, which triumphed over those of Robin.

"Major Molineux dwells here," said this fair woman.

Now, her voice was the sweetest Robin had heard that night, the airy counterpart of a stream of melted silver; yet he could not help doubting whether that sweet voice spoke Gospel truth. He looked up and down the mean street, and then surveyed the house before which they stood. It was a small, dark edifice of two stories, the second of which projected over the lower floor, and the front apartment had the aspect of a shop for petty commodities.

"Now, truly, I am in luck," replied Robin, cunningly, "and so indeed is my kinsman, the Major, in having so pretty a housekeeper. But I prithee trouble him to step to the door; I will deliver him a message from his friends in the country, and then go back to my lodgings at the inn."

"Nay, the Major has been abed this hour or more," said the lady of the scarlet petticoat; "and it would be to little purpose to disturb him to-night, seeing his evening draught was of the strongest. But he is a kind-hearted man, and it would be as much as my life's worth to let a kinsman of his turn away from the door. You are the good old gentleman's very picture, and I could swear that was his rainy-weather hat. Also he has garments very much resembling those leather small-clothes. But come in, I pray, for I bid you hearty welcome in his name."

So saying, the fair and hospitable dame took our hero by the hand; and the touch was light, and the force was gentleness, and though Robin read in her eyes what he did not hear in her words, yet the slender-waisted woman in the scarlet petticoat proved stronger than the athletic country youth. She had drawn his half-willing footsteps nearly to the threshold, when the opening of a door in the neighborhood startled the Major's housekeeper, and, leaving the Major's kinsman, she vanished speedily into her own domicile. A heavy yawn preceded the appearance of a man, who, like the Moonshine of Pyramus and Thisbe, carried a lantern, needlessly aiding his sister luminary in the heavens. As he walked sleepily up the street, he turned his broad, dull face on Robin, and displayed a long staff, spiked at the end.

"Home, vagabond, home!" said the watchman, in accents that seemed to fall asleep as soon as they were uttered. "Home, or we'll set you in the stocks by peep of day!"

"This is the second hint of the kind," thought Robin. "I wish they would end my difficulties, by setting me there to-night."

Nevertheless, the youth felt an instinctive antipathy towards the guardian of midnight order, which at first prevented him from asking his usual question. But just when the man was about to vanish behind the corner, Robin resolved not to lose the opportunity, and shouted lustily after him,—

"I say, friend! will you guide me to the house of my kinsman, Major Molineux?"

The watchman made no reply, but turned the corner and was gone; yet Robin seemed to hear the sound of drowsy laughter stealing along the solitary street. At that moment, also, a pleasant titter saluted him from the open window above his head; he looked up, and caught the sparkle of a saucy eye; a round arm beckoned to him, and next he heard light footsteps descending the staircase within. But Robin, being of the household of a New England clergyman, was a good youth, as well as a shrewd one; so he resisted temptation, and fled away.

He now roamed desperately, and at

random, through the town, almost ready to believe that a spell was on him, like that by which a wizard of his country had once kept three pursuers wandering, a whole winter night, within twenty paces of the cottage which they sought. The streets lay before him, strange and desolate, and the lights were extinguished in almost every house. Twice, however, little parties of men, among whom Robin distinguished individuals in outlandish attire, came hurrying along; but, though on both occasions they paused to address him, such intercourse did not at all enlighten his perplexity. They did but utter a few words in some language of which Robin knew nothing, and perceiving his inability to answer, bestowed a curse upon him in plain English and hastened away. Finally, the lad determined to knock at the door of every mansion that might appear worthy to be occupied by his kinsman, trusting that perseverance would overcome the fatality that had hitherto thwarted him. Firm in this resolve, he was passing beneath the walls of a church, which formed the corner of two streets, when, as he turned into the shade of its steeple, he encountered a bulky stranger, muffled in a cloak. The man was proceeding with the speed of earnest business, but Robin planted himself full before him, holding the oak cudgel with both hands across his body as a bar to further passage.

"Halt, honest man, and answer me a question," said he, very resolutely. "Tell me, this instant, whereabouts is the dwelling of my kinsman, Major Molineux!"

"Keep your tongue between your teeth, fool, and let me pass!" said a deep, gruff voice, which Robin partly remembered. "Let me pass, I say, or I'll strike you to the earth!"

"No, no, neighbor!" cried Robin, flourishing his cudgel, and then thrusting its larger end close to the man's muffled face. "No, no, I'm not the fool you take me for, nor do you pass till I have an answer to my question. Whereabouts is the dwelling of my kinsman, Major Molineux?"

The stranger, instead of attempting to force his passage, stepped back into the moonlight, unmuffled his face, and stared full into that of Robin.

"Watch here an hour, and Major Molineux will pass by," said he.

Robin gazed with dismay and astonishment on the unprecedented physiognomy of the speaker. The forehead with its double prominence, the broad hooked nose, the shaggy eyebrows, and fiery eyes were those which he had noticed at the inn, but the man's complexion had undergone a singular, or, more properly, a twofold change. One side of the face blazed an intense red, while the other was black as midnight, the division line being in the broad bridge of the nose; and a mouth which seemed to extend from ear to ear was black or red, in contrast to the color of the cheek. The effect was as if two individual devils, a fiend of fire and a fiend of darkness, had united themselves to form this infernal visage. The stranger grinned in Robin's face, muffled his party-colored features, and was out of sight in a moment.

"Strange things we travellers see!" ejaculated Robin.

He seated himself, however, upon the steps of the church-door, resolving to wait the appointed time for his kinsman. A few moments were consumed in philosophical speculations upon the species of man who had just left him; but having settled this point shrewdly, rationally, and satisfactorily, he was compelled to look elsewhere for his amusement. And first he threw his eyes along the street. It was of more respectable appearance than most of those into which he had wandered; and the moon, creating, like the imaginative power, a beautiful strangeness in familiar objects, gave something of romance to a scene that might not have possessed it in the light of day. The irregular and often quaint architecture of the houses, some of whose roofs were broken into numerous little peaks, while others ascended, steep and narrow, into a single point, and others again were square; the pure snow-white of some of their complexions, the aged darkness of others, and the thousand sparklings, reflected from bright substances in the walls of many; these matters engaged Robin's attention for a while, and then began to grow wearisome. Next he endeavored to define the forms of distant objects, starting away, with fix his attention steadily upon the large edifice which he had surveyed before. But still his mind kept vibrating between fancy and reality; by turns, the pillars of the balcony lengthened into the tall, bare stems of pines, dwindled down to human figures, settled again into their true shape and size, and then commenced a new succession of changes. For a single moment, when he deemed himself awake, he could have sworn that a visage—one which he seemed to remember, yet could not absolutely name as his kinsman's—was looking towards him from the Gothic window. A deeper sleep wrestled with and nearly overcame him, but fled at the sound of footsteps along the opposite pavement. Robin rubbed his eyes, discerned a man passing at the foot of the balcony, and addressed him in a loud, peevish, and lamentable cry.

"Hallo, friend! must I wait here all night for my kinsman, Major Molineux?"

The sleeping echoes awoke, and answered the voice; and the passenger, barely able to discern a figure sitting in the oblique shade of the steeple, traversed the street to obtain a nearer view. He was himself a gentleman in his prime, of open, intelligent, cheerful, and altogether prepossessing countenance. Perceiving a country youth, apparently homeless and without friends, he accosted him in a tone of real kindness, which had become strange to Robin's ears.

"Well, my good lad, why are you sitting here?" inquired he. "Can I be of service to you in any way?"

"I am afraid not, sir," replied Robin, despondingly; "yet I shall take it kindly, if you'll answer me a single question. I've been searching, half the night, for one Major Molineux; now, sir, is there really such a person in these parts, or am I dreaming?"

"Major Molineux! The name is not altogether strange to me," said the gentleman, smiling. "Have you any objection to telling me the nature of your business with him?"

Then Robin briefly related that his father was a clergyman, settled on a small salary, at a long distance back in the country, and that he and Major Molineux were brothers' children. The Major, having inherited riches, and acquired civil and military rank, had visited his cousin, in great pomp, a year or two before; had manifested much interest in Robin and an elder brother, and, being childless himself, had thrown out hints respecting the future establishment of one of them in life. The elder brother was destined to succeed to the farm which his father cultivated in the interval of sacred duties; it was therefore determined that Robin should profit by his kinsman's generous intentions, especially as he seemed to be rather the favorite, and was thought to possess other necessary endowments.

"For I have the name of being a shrewd youth," observed Robin, in this part of his story.

"I doubt not you deserve it," replied his new friend, good-naturedly; "but pray proceed."

"Well, sir, being nearly eighteen years old, and well grown, as you see," continued Robin, drawing himself up to his full height, "I thought it high time to begin the world. So my mother and sister put me in handsome trim, and my father gave me half the remnant of his last year's salary, and five days ago I started for this place, to pay the Major a visit. But, would you believe it, sir! I crossed the ferry a little after dark, and have yet found nobody that would show me the way to his dwelling; only, an hour or two since, I was told to wait here, and Major Molineux would pass by."

"Can you describe the man who told you this?" inquired the gentleman.

"Oh, he was a very ill-favored fellow, sir," replied Robin, "with two great bumps on his forehead, a hook nose, fiery eyes; and, what struck me as the strangest, his face was of two different colors. Do you happen to know such a man, sir?"

"Not intimately," answered the stranger, "but I chanced to meet him a little time previous to your stopping me. I believe you may trust his word, and that the Major will very shortly pass through this street. In the mean time, as I have a singular curiosity to witness your meeting, I will sit down here upon the steps and bear you company."

He seated himself accordingly, and soon engaged his companion in animated discourse. It was but of brief continuance, however, for a noise of shouting, which had long been remotely audible, drew so much nearer that Robin inquired its cause.

"What may be the meaning of this uproar?" asked he. "Truly, if your town be always as noisy, I shall find little sleep while I am an inhabitant."

"Why, indeed, friend Robin, there do appear to be three or four riotous fellows abroad to-night," replied the gentleman. "You must not expect all the stillness of your native woods here in our streets. But the watch will shortly be at the heels of these lads and"—

"Ay, and set them in the stocks by peep of day," interrupted Robin, recollecting his own encounter with the drowsy lantern-bearer. "But, dear sir, if I may trust my ears, an army of watchmen would never make head against such a multitude of rioters. There were at least a thousand voices went up to make that one shout."

"May not a man have several voices, Robin, as well as two complexions?" said his friend.

"Perhaps a man may; but Heaven forbid that a woman should!" responded the shrewd youth, thinking of the seductive tones of the Major's housekeeper.

The sounds of a trumpet in some neighboring street now became so evident and continual, that Robin's curiosity was strongly excited. In addition to the shouts, he heard frequent bursts from many instruments of discord, and a wild and confused laughter filled up the intervals. Robin rose from the steps, and looked wistfully towards a point whither people seemed to be hastening.

"Surely some prodigious merry-making is going on," exclaimed he. "I have laughed very little since I left home, sir, and should be sorry to lose an opportunity. Shall we step round the corner by that darkish house, and take our share of the fun?"

"Sit down again, sit down, good Robin," replied the gentleman, laying his hand on the skirt of the gray coat. "You forget that we must wait here for your kinsman; and there is reason to believe that he will pass by, in the course of a very few moments."

The near approach of the uproar had now disturbed the neighborhood; windows flew open on all sides; and many heads, in the attire of the pillow, and confused by sleep suddenly broken, were protruded to the gaze of whoever had leisure to observe them. Eager voices hailed each other from house to house, all demanding the explanation, which not a soul could give. Half-dressed men hurried towards the unknown commotion, stumbling as they went over the stone steps that thrust themselves into the narrow foot-walk. The shouts, the laughter, and the tuneless bray, the antipodes of music, came onwards with increasing din, till scattered individuals, and then denser bodies, began to appear round a corner at the distance of a hundred yards.

"Will you recognize your kinsman, if he passes in this crowd?" inquired the gentleman.

"Indeed, I can't warrant it, sir; but I'll take my stand here, and keep a bright lookout," answered Robin, descending to the outer edge of the pavement.

A mighty stream of people now emptied into the street, and came rolling slowly towards the church. A single horseman wheeled the corner in the midst of them, and close behind him came a band of fearful wind-instruments, sending forth a fresher discord now that no intervening buildings kept it from the ear. Then a redder light disturbed the moonbeams, and a dense multitude of torches shone along the street, concealing, by their glare, whatever object they illuminated. The single horseman, clad in a military dress, and bearing a drawn sword, rode onward as the leader, and, by his fierce and variegated countenance, appeared like war personified; the red of one cheek was an emblem of fire and sword; the blackness of the other betokened the mourning that attends them. In his train were wild figures in the Indian dress, and many fantastic shapes without a model, giving the whole march a visionary air, as if a dream had broken forth from some feverish brain, and were sweeping visibly through the midnight streets. A mass of people, inactive, except as applauding spectators, hemmed the procession in; and several women ran along the sidewalk, piercing the confusion of heavier sounds with their shrill voices of mirth or terror.

"The double-faced fellow has his eye upon me," muttered Robin, with an indefinite but an uncomfortable idea that he was himself to bear a part in the pageantry.

The leader turned himself in the saddle, and fixed his glance full upon the country youth, as the steed went slowly by. When Robin had freed his eyes from those fiery ones, the musicians were passing before him, and the torches were close at hand; but the unsteady brightness of the latter formed a veil which he could not penetrate. The rattling of wheels over the stones sometimes found its way to his ear, and confused traces of a human form appeared at intervals, and then melted into the vivid light. A moment more, and the leader thundered a command to halt: the trumpets vomited a horrid breath, and then held their peace; the shouts and laughter of the people died away, and there remained only a universal hum, allied to silence. Right before Robin's eyes was an uncovered cart. There the torches blazed the brightest, there the moon shone out like day, and there, in tar-and-feathery dignity, sat his kinsman, Major Molineux!

He was an elderly man, of large and majestic person, and strong, square features, betokening a steady soul; but steady as it was, his enemies had found means to shake it. His face was pale as death, and far more ghastly; the broad forehead was contracted in his agony, so that his eyebrows formed one grizzled line; his eyes were red and wild, and the foam hung white upon his quivering lip. His whole frame was agitated by a quick and continual tremor, which his pride strove to quell, even in those circumstances of overwhelming humiliation. But perhaps the bitterest pang of all was when his eyes met those of Robin; for he evidently knew him on the instant, as the youth stood witnessing the foul disgrace of a head grown

gray in honor. They stared at each other in silence, and Robin's knees shook, and his hair bristled, with a mixture of pity and terror. Soon, however, a bewildering excitement began to seize upon his mind; the preceding adventures of the night, the unexpected appearance of the crowd, the torches, the confused din and the hush that followed, the spectre of his kinsman reviled by that great multitude,—all this, and, more than all, a perception of tremendous ridicule in the whole scene, affected him with a sort of mental inebriety. At that moment a voice of sluggish merriment saluted Robin's ears; he turned instinctively, and just behind the corner of the church stood the lantern-bearer, rubbing his eyes, and drowsily enjoying the lad's amazement. Then he heard a peal of laughter like the ringing of silvery bells; a woman twitched his arm, a saucy eye met his, and he saw the lady of the scarlet petticoat. A sharp, dry cachinnation appealed to his memory, and, standing on tiptoe in the crowd, with his white apron over his head, he beheld the courteous little innkeeper. And lastly, there sailed over the heads of the multitude a great, broad laugh, broken in the midst by two sepulchral hems; thus, "Haw, haw, haw, —hem, hem,—haw, haw, haw, haw!"

The sound proceeded from the balcony of the opposite edifice, and thither Robin turned his eyes. In front of the Gothic window stood the old citizen, wrapped in a wide gown, his gray periwig exchanged for a nightcap, which was thrust back from his forehead, and his silk stockings hanging about his legs. He supported himself on his polished cane in a fit of convulsive merriment, which manifested itself on his solemn old features like a funny inscription on a tombstone. Then Robin seemed to hear the voices of the barbers, of the guests of the inn, and of all who had made sport of him that night. The contagion was spreading among the multitude, when all at once, it seized upon Robin, and he sent forth a shout of laughter that echoed through the street,—every man shook his sides, every man emptied his lungs, but Robin's shout was the loudest there. The cloud-spirits peeped from their silvery islands, as the congregated mirth went roaring up the sky! The Man in the Moon heard the far bellow. "Oho," quoth he, "the old earth is frolicsome to-night!"

When there was a momentary calm in that tempestuous sea of sound, the leader gave the sign, the procession resumed its march. On they went, like fiends that throng in mockery around some dead potentate, mighty no more, but majestic still in his agony. On they went, in counterfeited pomp, in senseless uproar, in frenzied merriment, trampling all on an old man's heart. On swept the tumult, and left a silent street behind.

"Well, Robin, are you dreaming?" inquired the gentleman, laying his hand on the youth's shoulder.

Robin started, and withdrew his arm from the stone post to which he had instinctively clung, as the living stream rolled by him. His cheek was somewhat pale, and his eye not quite as lively as in the earlier part of the evening.

"Will you be kind enough to show me the way to the ferry?" said he, after a moment's pause.

"You have, then, adopted a new subject of inquiry?" observed his companion, with a smile.

"Why, yes, sir," replied Robin, rather dryly. "Thanks to you, and to my other friends, I have at last met my kinsman, and he will scarce desire to see my face again. I begin to grow weary of a town life, sir. Will you show me the way to the ferry?"

"No, my good friend Robin,—not to-night, at least," said the gentleman. "Some few days hence, if you wish it, I will speed you on your journey. Or, if you prefer to remain with us, perhaps, as you are a shrewd youth, you may rise in the world without the help of your kinsman, Major Molineux."

[1832]

QUESTIONS FOR STUDY

1. *How do Hawthorne's brief introductory remarks in the first paragraph concerning the development of a growing resistance to British authority in colonial Massachusetts serve to explain many of the incidents of the story? Why is it appropriate that such an historical movement should parallel Robin's search for his kinsman and that both should have a common climax?*

2. *Why is Robin in search of Major Molineux? Why are Robin's age, background, and appearance important?*

3. *Why does Hawthorne refer to Robin as "a shrewd youth"?*

4. *In what ways are Hawthorne's setting and atmosphere appropriate for the story?*

5. *What is the significance of Robin's dream of being excluded from his own home? What is the role or function of the kindly gentleman who offers to wait and watch with him?*

6. *What is the meaning of Robin's "shout of laughter"? Why is it a fitting climax to the laughter heard throughout the story?*

7. *What does Robin learn from his experience?*

NATHANIEL HAWTHORNE

Roger Malvin's Burial

ONE OF the few incidents of Indian warfare naturally susceptible of the moonlight of romance was that expedition undertaken for the defence of the frontiers in the year 1725, which resulted in the well-remembered "Lovell's Fight." Imagination, by casting certain circumstances judicially into the shade, may see much to admire in the heroism of a little band who gave battle to twice their number in the heart of the enemy's country. The open bravery displayed by both parties was in accordance with civilised ideas of valor; and chivalry itself might not blush to record the deeds of one or two individuals. The battle, though so fatal to those who fought, was not unfortunate in its consequences to the country; for it broke the strength of a tribe and conduced to the peace which subsisted during several ensuing years. History and tradition are unusually minute in their memorials of this affair; and the captain of a scouting party of frontier men has acquired as actual a military renown as many a victorious leader of thousands. Some of the incidents contained in the following pages will be recognized, notwithstanding the substitution of fictitious names, by such as have heard, from old men's lips, the fate of the few combatants who were in a condition to retreat after "Lovell's Fight."

The early sunbeams hovered cheerfully upon the tree-tops, beneath which two weary and wounded men had stretched their limbs the night before. Their bed of withered oak leaves was strewn upon the small level space, at the foot of a rock, situated near the summit of one of the gentle swells by which the face of the country is there diversified. The mass of granite, rearing its smooth, flat surface fifteen or twenty feet above their heads, was not unlike a gigantic gravestone, upon which the veins seemed to form an inscription in forgotten characters. On a tract of several acres around this rock, oaks and other hard-wood trees had supplied the place of the pines, which were the usual growth of the land; and a young and vigorous sapling stood close beside the travellers.

The severe wound of the elder man had probably deprived him of sleep; for, so soon as the first ray of sunshine rested on the top of the highest tree, he reared himself painfully from his recumbent posture and sat erect. The deep lines of his countenance and the scattered gray of his hair marked him as past the middle age; but his muscular frame would, but for the effects of his wound, have been as capable of sustaining fatigue as in the early vigor of life. Languor and exhaustion now sat upon his haggard features; and the despairing glance which he sent forward through the depths of the forest proved his own conviction that his pilgrimage was at an end. He next turned his eyes to the companion who reclined by his side. The youth—for he had scarcely attained the years of manhood—lay, with his head upon his arm, in the embrace of an unquiet sleep, which a thrill of pain from his wounds seemed each moment on the point of breaking. His right hand grasped a musket; and, to judge from the violent action of his features, his slumbers were bringing back a vision of the conflict of which he was one of the few survivors. A shout—deep and loud in his dreaming fancy—found its way in an imperfect murmur to his lips; and, starting even at the slight sound of his own voice, he suddenly awoke. The first act of reviving recollection was to make anxious inquiries respecting the condition of his wounded fellow-traveller. The latter shook his head.

"Reuben, my boy," said he, "this rock beneath which we sit will serve for an old hunter's gravestone. There is many and many a long mile of howling wilderness before us yet; nor would it avail me anything if the smoke of my own chimney were but on the other side of that swell of land. The Indian bullet was deadlier than I thought."

"You are weary with our three days' travel," replied the youth, "and a little longer rest will recruit you. Sit you here while I search the woods for the herbs and roots that must be our sustenance; and, having eaten, you shall lean on me, and we will turn our faces homeward. I doubt not that, with my help, you can attain to some one of the frontier garrisons."

"There is not two days' life in me, Reuben," said the other calmly, "and I will no longer burden you with my useless body, when you can scarcely support your own. Your wounds are deep and your strength is failing fast; yet, if you hasten onward alone, you may be preserved. For me there is no hope, and I will await death here."

"If it must be so, I will remain and watch by you," said Reuben, resolutely.

"No, my son, no," rejoined his companion. "Let the wish of a dying man have weight with you; give me one grasp of your hand, and get you hence. Think you that my last moments will be eased by the thought that I leave you to die a more lingering death? I have loved you like a father, Reuben; and at a time like this I should have something of a father's authority. I charge you to be gone that I may die in peace."

"And because you have been a father to me, should I therefore leave you to perish and to lie unburied in the wilderness?" exclaimed the youth. "No; if your end be in truth approaching, I will watch by you and receive your parting words. I will dig a grave here by the rock, in which, if my weakness overcome me, we will rest together; or, if Heaven gives me strength, I will seek my way home."

"In the cities and wherever men dwell," replied the other, "they bury their dead in the earth; they hide them from the sight of the living; but here, where no step may pass perhaps for a hundred years, wherefore should I not rest beneath the open sky, covered only by the oak leaves when the autumn winds shall strew them? And for a monument, here is this gray rock, on which my dying hand shall carve the name of Roger Malvin; and the traveller in days to come will know that here sleeps a hunter and a warrior. Tarry not, then, for a folly like this, but hasten away, if not for your own sake, for hers who will else be desolate."

Malvin spoke the last few words in a faltering voice, and their effect upon his companion was strongly visible. They reminded him that there were other and less questionable duties than that of sharing the fate of a man whom his death could not benefit. Nor can it be affirmed that no selfish feeling strove to enter Reuben's heart, though the consciousness made him more earnestly resist his companion's entreaties.

"How terrible to wait the slow approach of death in this solitude!" exclaimed he. "A brave man does not shrink in the battle; and, when friends stand round the bed, even women may die composedly; but here"—

"I shall not shrink even here, Reuben Bourne," interrupted Malvin. "I am a man of no weak heart, and, if I were, there is a surer support than that of earthly friends. You are young, and life is dear to you. Your last moments will need comfort far more than mine; and when you have laid me in the earth, and are alone, and night is settling on the forest, you will feel all the bitterness of the death that may now be escaped. But I will urge no selfish motive to your generous nature. Leave me for my sake, that, having said a prayer for your safety, I may have space to settle my account undisturbed by worldly sorrows."

"And your daughter,—how shall I dare to meet her eye?" exclaimed Reuben. "She will ask the fate of her father, whose life I vowed to defend with my own. Must I tell her that he travelled three days' march with me from the field of battle and that then I left him to perish in the wilderness? Were it not better to lie down and die by your side than to return safe and say this to Dorcas?"

"Tell my daughter," said Roger Malvin,

"that, though yourself sore wounded, and weak, and weary, you led my tottering footsteps many a mile, and left me only at my earnest entreaty, because I would not have your blood upon my soul. Tell her that through pain and danger you were faithful, and that, if your lifeblood could have saved me, it would have flowed to its last drop; and tell her that you will be something dearer than a father, and that my blessing is with you both, and that my dying eyes can see a long and pleasant path in which you will journey together."

As Malvin spoke he almost raised himself from the ground, and the energy of his concluding words seemed to fill the wild and lonely forest with a vision of happiness; but, when he sank exhausted upon his bed of oak leaves, the light which had kindled in Reuben's eye was quenched. He felt as if it were both sin and folly to think of happiness at such a moment. His companion watched his changing countenance, and sought with generous art to wile him to his own good.

"Perhaps I deceive myself in regard to the time I have to live," he resumed. "It may be that, with speedy assistance, I might recover of my wound. The foremost fugitives must, ere this, have carried tidings of our fatal battle to the frontiers, and parties will be out to succor those in like condition with ourselves. Should you meet one of these and guide them hither, who can tell but that I may sit by my own fireside again?"

A mournful smile strayed across the features of the dying man as he insinuated that unfounded hope,—which, however, was not without its effect on Reuben. No merely selfish motive, nor even the desolate condition of Dorcas, could have induced him to desert his companion at such a moment—but his wishes seized on the thought that Malvin's life might be preserved, and his sanguine nature heightened almost to certainty the remote possibility of procuring human aid.

"Surely there is reason, weighty reason, to hope that friends are not far distant," he said, half aloud. "There fled one coward, unwounded, in the beginning of the fight, and most probably he made

good speed. Every true man on the frontier would shoulder his musket at the news; and, though no party may range so far into the woods as this, I shall perhaps encounter them in one day's march. Counsel me faithfully," he added, turning to Malvin, in distrust of his own motives. "Were your situation mine, would you desert me while life remained?"

"It is now twenty years," replied Roger Malvin,—sighing, however, as he secretly acknowledged the wide dissimilarity between the two cases,—"it is now twenty years since I escaped with one dear friend from Indian captivity near Montreal. We journeyed many days through the woods, till at length overcome with hunger and weariness, my friend lay down and besought me to leave him; for he knew that, if I remained, we both must perish; and, with but little hope of obtaining succor, I heaped a pillow of dry leaves beneath his head and hastened on."

"And did you return in time to save him?" asked Reuben, hanging on Malvin's words as if they were to be prophetic of his own success.

"I did," answered the other. "I came upon the camp of a hunting party before sunset of the same day. I guided them to the spot where my comrade was expecting death; and he is now a hale and hearty man upon his own farm, far within the frontiers, while I lie wounded here in the depths of the wilderness."

This example, powerful in affecting Reuben's decision, was aided, unconsciously to himself, by the hidden strength of many another motive. Roger Malvin perceived that the victory was nearly won.

"Now, go, my son, and Heaven prosper you!" he said. "Turn not back with your friends when you meet them, lest your wounds and weariness overcome you; but send hitherward two or three, that may be spared, to search for me; and believe me, Reuben, my heart will be lighter with every step you take towards home." Yet there was, perhaps, a change both in his countenance and voice as he spoke thus; for, after all, it was a ghastly fate to be left expiring in the wilderness.

Reuben Bourne, but half convinced that he was acting rightly, at length raised himself from the ground and prepared himself for his departure. And first, though contrary to Malvin's wishes, he collected a stock of roots and herbs, which had been their only food during the last two days. This useless supply he placed within reach of the dying man, for whom, also, he swept together a bed of dry oak leaves. Then climbing to the summit of the rock, which on one side was rough and broken, he bent the oak sapling downward, and bound his handkerchief to the topmost branch. This precaution was not unnecessary to direct any who might come in search of Malvin; for every part of the rock, except its broad smooth front, was concealed at a little distance by the dense undergrowth of the forest. The handkerchief had been the bandage of a wound upon Reuben's arm; and, as he bound it to the tree, he vowed by the blood that stained it that he would return, either to save his companion's life or to lay his body in the grave. He then descended, and stood, with downcast eyes, to receive Roger Malvin's parting words.

The experience of the latter suggested much and minute advice respecting the youth's journey through the trackless forest. Upon this subject he spoke with calm earnestness, as if he were sending Reuben to the battle or the chase while he himself remained secure at home, and not as if the human countenance that was about to leave him were the last he would ever behold. But his firmness was shaken before he concluded.

"Carry my blessing to Dorcas, and say that my last prayer shall be for her and you. Bid her to have no hard thoughts because you left me here,"—Reuben's heart smote him,—"for that your life would not have weighed with you if its sacrifice could have done me good. She will marry you after she has mourned a little while for her father; and Heaven grant you long and happy days, and may your children's children stand round your death bed! And, Reuben," added he, as the weakness of mortality made its way at last, "return, when your wounds are healed and your weariness refreshed,—return to this wild rock, and lay my bones in the grave, and say a prayer over them."

An almost superstitious regard, arising perhaps from the customs of the Indians, whose war was with the dead as well as the living, was paid by the frontier inhabitants to the rites of sepulture; and there are many instances of the sacrifice of life in the attempt to bury those who had fallen by the "sword of the wilderness." Reuben, therefore, felt the full importance of the promise which he most solemnly made to return and perform Roger Malvin's obsequies. It was remarkable that the latter, speaking his whole heart in his parting words, no longer endeavored to persuade the youth that even the speediest succor might avail to the preservation of his life. Reuben was internally convinced that he should see Malvin's living face no more. His generous nature would fain have delayed him, at whatever risk, till the dying scene were past; but the desire of existence and the hope of happiness had strengthened in his heart, and he was unable to resist them.

"It is enough," said Roger Malvin, having listened to Reuben's promise. "Go, and God speed you!"

The youth pressed his hand in silence, turned, and was departing. His slow and faltering steps, however, had borne him but a little way before Malvin's voice recalled him.

"Reuben, Reuben," said he, faintly; and Reuben returned and knelt down by the dying man.

"Raise me, and let me lean against the rock," was his last request. "My face will be turned towards home, and I shall see you a moment longer as you pass among the trees."

Reuben, having made the desired alteration in his companion's posture, again began his solitary pilgrimage. He walked more hastily at first than was consistent with his strength; for a sort of guilty feeling, which sometimes torments men in their most justifiable acts, caused him to seek concealment from Malvin's eyes; but after he had trodden far upon the rustling forest leaves he crept back, impelled by a wild and painful curiosity, and, sheltered by the earthy roots of an uptorn tree, gazed earnestly at the desolate man. The morning sun was unclouded, and the trees and shrubs imbibed the sweet air of the month of May; yet there seemed a gloom on Nature's face, as if she sympathized with mortal pain and sorrow. Roger Malvin's hands were uplifted in a fervent prayer, some of the words of which stole through the stillness of the woods and entered Reuben's heart, torturing it with an unutterable pang. They were the broken accents of a petition for his own happiness and that of Dorcas; and, as the youth listened, conscience, or something in its similitude, pleaded strongly with him to return and lie down again by the rock. He felt how hard was the doom of the kind and generous being whom he had deserted in his extremity. Death would come like the slow approach of a corpse, stealing gradually towards him through the forest, and showing its ghastly and motionless features from behind a nearer and yet a nearer tree. But such must have been Reuben's own fate had he tarried another sunset; and who shall impute blame to him if he shrink from so useless a sacrifice? As he gave a parting look, a breeze waved the little banner upon the sapling oak and reminded Reuben of his vow.

Many circumstances combined to retard the wounded traveller in his way to the frontiers. On the second day the clouds, gathering densely over the sky, precluded the possibility of regulating his course by the position of the sun: and he knew not but that every effort of his almost exhausted strength was removing him farther from the home he sought. His scanty sustenance was supplied by the berries and other spontaneous products of the forest. Herds of deer, it is true, sometimes bounded past him, and partridges frequently whirred up before his footsteps; but his ammunition had been expended in the fight, and he had no means of slaying them. His wounds, irritated by the constant exertion in which lay the only hope of life, wore away his strength and at intervals confused his reason. But, even in the wanderings of intellect, Reuben's young heart clung strongly to existence; and it was only through absolute incapacity of motion that he at last sank down beneath a tree, compelled there to await death.

In this situation he was discovered by a party who, upon the first intelligence of the fight, had been despatched to the relief of the survivors. They conveyed him to the nearest settlement, which chanced to be that of his own residence.

Dorcas, in the simplicity of the olden time, watched by the bedside of her wounded lover, and administered all those comforts that are in the sole gift of woman's heart and hand. During several days Reuben's recollection strayed drowsily among the perils and hardships through which he had passed, and he was incapable of returning definite answers to the inquiries with which many were eager to harass him. No authentic particulars of the battle had yet been circulated; nor could mothers, wives, and children tell whether their loved ones were detained by captivity or by the stronger chain of death. Dorcas nourished her apprehensions in silence till one afternoon when Reuben awoke from an unquiet sleep, and seemed to recognize her more perfectly than at any previous time. She saw that his intellect had become composed, and she could no longer restrain her filial anxiety.

"My father, Reuben?" she began; but the change in her lover's countenance made her pause.

The youth shrank as if with a bitter pain, and the blood gushed vividly into his wan and hollow cheeks. His first impulse was to cover his face; but, apparently with a desperate effort, he half raised himself and spoke vehemently, defending himself against an imaginary accusation.

"Your father was sore wounded in the battle, Dorcas; and he bade me not burden myself with him, but only to lead him to the lakeside, that he might quench his thirst and die. But I would not desert the old man in his extremity, and, though bleeding myself, I supported him; I gave him half my strength, and led him away with me. For three days we journeyed on together, and your father was sustained beyond my hopes, but, awaking at sunrise on the fourth day, I found him faint and exhausted; he was unable to proceed; his life had ebbed away fast; and"—

"He died!" exclaimed Dorcas, faintly.

Reuben felt it impossible to acknowledge that his selfish love of life had hurried him away before her father's fate was decided. He spoke not; he only bowed his head; and, between shame and exhaustion, sank back and hid his face in the pillow. Dorcas wept when her fears were thus confirmed; but the shock, as it had been long anticipated, was on that account the less violent.

"You dug a grave for my poor father in the wilderness, Reuben?" was the question by which her filial piety manifested itself.

"My hands were weak; but I did what I could," replied the youth in a smothered tone. "There stands a noble tombstone above his head; and I would to Heaven I slept as soundly as he!"

Dorcas, perceiving the wildness of his latter words, inquired no further at the time; but her heart found ease in the thought that Roger Malvin had not lacked such funeral rites as it was possible to bestow. The tale of Reuben's courage and fidelity lost nothing when she communicated it to her friends; and the poor youth, tottering from his sick chamber to breathe the sunny air, experienced from every tongue the miserable and humiliating torture of unmerited praise. All acknowledged that he might worthily demand the hand of the fair maiden to whose father he had been "faithful unto death;" and, as my tale is not of love, it shall suffice to say that in the space of a few months Reuben became the husband of Dorcas Malvin. During the marriage ceremony the bride was covered with blushes, but the bridegroom's face was pale.

There was now in the breast of Reuben Bourne an incommunicable thought—something which he was to conceal most heedfully from her whom he most loved and trusted. He regretted, deeply and bitterly, the moral cowardice that had restrained his words when he was about to disclose the truth to Dorcas; but pride, the fear of losing her affection, the dread of universal scorn, forbade him to rectify this falsehood. He felt that for leaving Roger Malvin he deserved no censure. His presence, the gratuitous sacrifice of his own life, would have added only another and a needless agony to the last moments of the dying man; but concealment had imparted to a justifiable act much of the secret effect of guilt; and Reuben, while reason told him that he had done right, experienced in no small degree the mental horrors which punish the perpetrator of undiscovered crime. By a certain association of ideas, he at times almost imagined himself a murderer. For years, also, a thought would occasionally recur, which, though he perceived all its folly and extravagance, he had not power to banish from his mind. It was a haunting and torturing fancy that his father-in-law was yet sitting at the foot of the rock, on the withered forest leaves, alive, and awaiting his pledged assistance. These mental deceptions, however, came and went, nor did he ever mistake them for realities; but in the calmest and clearest moods of his mind he was conscious that he had a deep vow unredeemed, and that an unburied corpse was calling to him out of the wilderness. Yet such was the consequence of his prevarication that he could not obey the call. It was now too late to require the assistance of Roger Malvin's friends in performing his long-deferred sepulture; and superstitious fears, of which none were more susceptible than the people of the outward settlements, forbade Reuben to go alone. Neither did he know where in the pathless and illimitable forest to seek that smooth and lettered rock at the base of which the body lay: his remembrance of every portion of his travel thence was indistinct, and the latter part had left no impression upon his mind. There was, however, a continual impulse, a voice audible only to himself, commanding him to go forth and redeem his vow; and he had a strange impression that, were he to make the trial, he would be led straight to Malvin's bones. But year after year that summons, unheard but felt, was disobeyed. His one secret thought became like a chain binding down his spirit and like a serpent gnawing into his heart; and he was transformed into a sad and downcast yet irritable man.

In the course of a few years after their marriage changes began to be visible in the external prosperity of Reuben and

Dorcas. The only riches of the former had been his stout heart and strong arm; but the latter, her father's sole heiress, had made her husband master of a farm, under older cultivation, larger, and better stocked than most of the frontier establishments. Reuben Bourne, however, was a neglectful husbandman; and, while the lands of the other settlers became annually more fruitful, his deteriorated in the same proportion. The discouragements to agriculture were greatly lessened by the cessation of Indian war, during which men held the plough in one hand and the musket in the other, and were fortunate if the products of their dangerous labor were not destroyed, either in the field or in the barn, by the savage enemy. But Reuben did not profit by the altered condition of the country; nor can it be denied that his intervals of industrious attention to his affairs were but scantily rewarded with success. The irritability by which he had recently become distinguished was another cause of his declining prosperity, as it occasioned frequent quarrels in his unavoidable intercourse with the neighboring settlers. The results of these were innumerable lawsuits; for the people of New England, in the earliest stages and wildest circumstances of the country, adopted, whenever attainable, the legal mode of deciding their differences. To be brief, the world did not go well with Reuben Bourne; and, though not till many years after his marriage, he was finally a ruined man, with but one remaining expedient against the evil fate that had pursued him. He was to throw sunlight into some deep recess of the forest, and seek subsistence from the virgin bosom of the wilderness.

The only child of Reuben and Dorcas was a son, now arrived at the age of fifteen years, beautiful in youth, and giving promise of a glorious manhood. He was peculiarly qualified for, and already began to excel in, the wild accomplishments of frontier life. His foot was fleet, his aim true, his apprehension quick, his heart glad and high; and all who anticipated the return of Indian war spoke of Cyrus Bourne as a future leader in the land. The boy was loved by his father with a deep

and silent strength, as if whatever was good and happy in his own nature had been transferred to his child, carrying his affections with it. Even Dorcas, though loving and beloved, was far less dear to him; for Reuben's secret thoughts and insulated emotions had gradually made him a selfish man, and he could no longer love deeply except where he saw or imagined some reflection or likeness of his own mind. In Cyrus he recognized what he had himself been in other days; and at intervals he seemed to partake of the boy's spirit, and to be revived with a fresh and happy life. Reuben was accompanied by his son in the expedition, for the purpose of selecting a tract of land and felling and burning the timber, which necessarily preceded the removal of the household goods. Two months of autumn were thus occupied, after which Reuben Bourne and his young hunter returned to spend their last winter in the settlements.

It was early in the month of May that the little family snapped asunder whatever tendrils of affections had clung to inanimate objects, and bade farewell to the few who, in the blight of fortune, called themselves their friends. The sadness of the parting moment had, to each of the pilgrims, its peculiar alleviations. Reuben, a moody man, and misanthropic because unhappy, strode onward with his usual stern brow and downcast eye, feeling few regrets and disdaining to acknowledge any. Dorcas, while she wept abundantly over the broken ties by which her simple and affectionate nature had bound itself to everything, felt that the inhabitants of her inmost heart moved on with her, and that all else would be supplied wherever she might go. And the boy dashed one tear-drop from his eye, and thought of the adventurous pleasures of the untrodden forest.

Oh, who, in the enthusiasm of a daydream, has not wished that he were a wanderer in a world of summer wilderness, with one fair and gentle being hanging lightly on his arm? In youth his free and exulting step would know no barrier but the rolling ocean or the snow-topped mountains; calmer manhood would choose a home where Nature had strewn a double wealth in the vale of some transparent stream; and when hoary age, after long, long years of that pure life, stole on and found him there, it would find him the father of a race, the patriarch of a people, the founder of a mighty nation yet to be. When death, like the sweet sleep which we welcome after a day of happiness, came over him, his far descendants would mourn over the venerated dust. Enveloped by tradition in mysterious attributes, the men of future generations would call him godlike; and remote posterity would see him standing, dimly glorious, far up the valley of a hundred centuries.

The tangled and gloomy forest through which the personages of my tale were wandering differed widely from the dreamer's land of fantasy; yet there was something in their way of life that Nature asserted as her own, and the gnawing cares which went with them from the world were all that now obstructed their happiness. One stout and shaggy steed, the bearer of all their wealth, did not shrink from the added weight of Dorcas; although her hardy breeding sustained her, during the latter part of each day's journey, by her husband's side. Reuben and his son, their muskets on their shoulders and their axes slung behind them kept an unwearied pace, each watching with a hunter's eye for the game that supplied their food. When hunger bade, they halted and prepared their meal on the bank of some unpolluted forest brook, which, as they knelt down with thirsty lips to drink, murmured a sweet unwillingness, like a maiden at love's first kiss. They slept beneath a hut of branches, and awoke at peep of light refreshed for the toils of another day. Dorcas and the boy went on joyously, and even Reuben's spirit shone at intervals with an outward gladness; but inwardly there was a cold, cold sorrow, which he compared to the snowdrifts lying deep in the glens and hollows of the rivulets while the leaves were brightly green above.

Cyrus Bourne was sufficiently skilled in the travel of the woods to observe that his father did not adhere to the course they had pursued in their expedition of the preceding autumn. They were now keeping farther to the north, striking out more directly from the settlements, and into a region of which savage beasts and savage men were as yet the sole possessors. The boy sometimes hinted his opinions upon the subject, and Reuben listened attentively, and once or twice altered the direction of their march in accordance with his son's counsel; but, having so done, he seemed ill at ease. His quick and wandering glances were sent forward, apparently in search of enemies lurking behind the tree trunks; and, seeing nothing there, he would cast his eyes backwards as if in fear of some pursuer. Cyrus, perceiving that his father gradually resumed the old direction, forbore to interfere; nor, though something began to weigh upon his heart, did his adventurous nature permit him to regret the increased length and the mystery of their way.

On the afternoon of the fifth day they halted, and made their simple encampment nearly an hour before sunset. The face of the country, for the last few miles, had been diversified by swells of land resembling huge waves of a petrified sea; and in one of the corresponding hollows, a wild and romantic spot, had the family reared their hut and kindled their fire. There is something chilling, and yet heartwarming, in the thought of these three, united by strong bands of love and insulated from all that breathe beside. The dark and gloomy pines looked down upon them, and, as the wind swept through their tops, a pitying sound was heard in the forest; or did those old trees groan in fear that men were come to lay the axe to their roots at last? Reuben and his son, while Dorcas made ready their meal, proposed to wander out in search of game, of which that day's march had afforded no supply. The boy, promising not to quit the vicinity of the encampment, bounded off with a step as light and elastic as that of the deer he hoped to slay; while his father, feeling a transient happiness as he gazed after him, was about to pursue an opposite direction. Dorcas, in the meanwhile, had seated herself near their fire of fallen branches, upon the moss-grown and mouldering trunk of a tree up-rooted years before. Her employment, diversified by an occasional glance at the pot, now beginning to simmer over the blaze, was the perusal of the current year's Massachusetts Almanac, which, with the exception of an old black-letter Bible, comprised all the literary wealth of the family. None pay a greater regard to arbitrary divisions of time than those who are excluded from society; and Dorcas mentioned, as if the information were of importance, that it was now the twelfth of May. Her husband started.

"The twelfth of May! I should remember it well," muttered he, while many thoughts occasioned a momentary confusion in his mind. "Where am I? Whither am I wandering? Where did I leave him?"

Dorcas, too well accustomed to her husband's wayward moods to note any peculiarity of demeanor, now laid aside the almanac and addressed him in that mournful tone which the tender hearted appropriate to griefs long cold and dead.

"It was near this time of the month, eighteen years ago, that my poor father left this world for a better. He had a kind arm to hold his head and a kind voice to cheer him, Reuben, in his last moments; and the thought of the faithful care you took of him has comforted me many a time since. Oh, death would have been awful to a solitary man in a wild place like this!"

"Pray Heaven, Dorcas," said Reuben, in a broken voice,—"pray Heaven that neither of us three dies solitary and lies unburied in this howling wilderness!" And he hastened away, leaving her to watch the fire beneath the gloomy pines.

Reuben Bourne's rapid pace gradually slackened as the pang, unintentionally inflicted by the words of Dorcas, became less acute. Many strange reflections, however, thronged upon him; and, straying onward rather like a sleep walker than a hunter, it was attributable to no care of his own that his devious course kept him in the vicinity of the encampment. His steps were imperceptibly led almost in a circle; nor did he observe that he was on the verge of a tract of land heavily timbered, but not with pine-trees. The place

of the latter was here supplied by oaks and other of the harder woods; and around their roots clustered a dense and bushy under-growth, leaving, however, barren spaces between the trees, thick strewn with withered leaves. Whenever the rustling of the branches or the creaking of the trunks made a sound, as if the forest were waking from slumber, Reuben instinctively raised the musket that rested on his arm, and cast a quick, sharp glance on every side; but, convinced by a partial observation that no animal was near, he would again give himself up to his thoughts. He was musing on the strange influence that had led him away from his premeditated course, and so far into the depths of the wilderness. Unable to penetrate to the secret place of his soul where his motives lay hidden, he believed that a supernatural voice had called him onward, and that a supernatural power had obstructed his retreat. He trusted that it was Heaven's intent to afford him an opportunity of expiating his sin; he hoped that he might find the bones so long unburied; and that, having laid the earth over them, peace would throw its sunlight into the sepulchre of his heart. From these thoughts he was aroused by a rustling in the forest at some distance from the spot to which he had wandered. Perceiving the motion of some object behind a thick veil of undergrowth, he fired, with the instinct of a hunter and the aim of a practised marksman. A low moan, which told his success, and by which even animals can express their dying agony, was unheeded by Reuben Bourne. What were the recollections now breaking upon him?

The thicket into which Reuben had fired was near the summit of a swell of land, and was clustered around the base of a rock, which, in the shape and smoothness of one of its surfaces, was not unlike a gigantic gravestone. As if reflected in a mirror, its likeness was in Reuben's memory. He even recognized the veins which seemed to form an inscription in forgotten characters: everything remained the same, except that a thick covert of bushes shrouded the lower part of the rock, and would have hidden Roger Malvin had he still been sitting there. Yet in the next moment Reuben's eye was caught by another change that time had effected since he last stood where he was now standing again behind the earthy roots of the uptorn tree. The sapling to which he had bound the bloodstained symbol of his vow had increased and strengthened into an oak, far indeed from its maturity, but with no mean spread of shadowy branches. There was one singularity observable in this tree which made Reuben tremble. The middle and lower branches were in luxuriant life, and an excess of vegetation had fringed the trunk almost to the ground; but a blight had apparently stricken the upper part of the oak, and the very topmost bough was withered, sapless, and utterly dead. Reuben remembered how the little banner had fluttered on that topmost bough, when it was green and lovely, eighteen years before. Whose guilt had blasted it?

Dorcas, after the departure of the two hunters, continued her preparations for their evening repast. Her sylvan table was the moss-covered trunk of a large fallen tree, on the broadest part of which she had spread a snow-white cloth and arranged what were left of the bright pewter vessels that had been her pride in the settlements. It had a strange aspect, that one little spot of homely comfort in the desolate heart of Nature. The sunshine yet lingered upon the higher branches of the trees that grew on rising ground; but the shadows of evening had deepened into the hollow where the encampment was made, and the firelight began to redden as it gleamed up the tall trunks of the pines or hovered on the dense and obscure mass of foliage that circled round the spot. The heart of Dorcas was not sad; for she felt that it was better to journey in the wilderness with two whom she loved than to be a lonely woman in a crowd that cared not for her. As she busied herself in arranging seats of mouldering wood, covered with leaves, for Reuben and her son, her voice danced through the gloomy forest in the measure of a song that she had learned in youth. The rude melody, the production of a bard who won no name, was descriptive of a winter evening in a frontier cottage, when, secured from savage inroad by the high-piled snow-drifts, the family rejoiced by their own fireside. The whole song possessed the nameless charm peculiar to unborrowed thought, but four continually-recurring lines shone out from the rest like the blaze of the hearth whose joys they celebrated. Into them, working magic with a few simple words, the poet had instilled the very essence of domestic love and household happiness, and they were poetry and picture joined in one. As Dorcas sang, the walls of her forsaken home seemed to encircle her; she no longer saw the gloomy pines, nor heard the wind which still, as she began each verse, sent a heavy breath through the branches, and died away in a hollow moan from the burden of the song. She was aroused by the report of a gun in the vicinity of the encampment; and either the sudden sound, or her loneliness by the glowing fire, caused her to tremble violently. The next moment she laughed in the pride of a mother's heart.

"My beautiful young hunter! My boy has slain a deer!" she exclaimed, recollecting that in the direction whence the shot proceeded Cyrus had gone to the chase.

She waited a reasonable time to hear her son's light step bounding over the rustling leaves to tell of his success. But he did not immediately appear; and she sent her cheerful voice among the trees in search of him.

"Cyrus! Cyrus!"

His coming was still delayed; and she determined, as the report had apparently been very near, to seek for him in person. Her assistance, also, might be necessary in bringing home the venison which she flattered herself he had obtained. She therefore set forward, directing her steps by the long-past sound, and singing as she went, in order that the boy might be aware of her approach and run to meet her. From behind the trunk of every tree, and from every hiding-place in the thick foliage of the undergrowth, she hoped to discover the countenance of her son, laughing with the sportive mischief that is born of affection. The sun was now beneath the horizon, and the light that came down among the leaves was sufficiently dim to create many illusions in her expecting fancy. Several times she seemed indistinctly to see his face gazing out from among the leaves; and once she imagined that he stood beckoning to her at the base of a craggy rock. Keeping her eyes on this object, however, it proved to be no more than the trunk of an oak fringed to the very ground with little branches, one of which, thrust out farther than the rest, was shaken by the breeze. Making her way round the root of the rock, she suddenly found herself close to her husband, who had approached in another direction. Leaning upon the butt of his gun, the muzzle of which rested upon the withered leaves, he was apparently absorbed in the contemplation of some object at his feet.

"How is this Reuben? Have you slain the deer and fallen asleep over him?" exclaimed Dorcas, laughing cheerfully, on her first slight observation of his posture and appearance.

He stirred not, neither did he turn his eyes towards her; and a cold, shuddering fear, indefinite in its source and object, began to creep into her blood. She now perceived that her husband's face was ghastly pale, and his features were rigid, as if incapable of assuming any other expression than the strong despair which had hardened upon them. He gave not the slightest evidence that he was aware of her approach.

"For the love of Heaven, Reuben, speak to me!" cried Dorcas; and the strange sound of her own voice affrighted her even more than the dead silence.

Her husband started, stared into her face, drew her to the front of the rock, and pointed with his finger.

Oh, there lay the boy, asleep, but dreamless, upon the fallen forest leaves! His cheek rested upon his arm—his curled locks were thrown back from his brow—his limbs were slightly relaxed. Had a sudden weariness overcome the youthful hunter? Would his mother's voice arouse him? She knew that it was death.

"This broad rock is the gravestone of your near kindred, Dorcas," said her husband. "Your tears will fall at once over your father and your son."

She heard him not. With one wild shriek, that seemed to force its way from the sufferer's inmost soul, she sank insensible by the side of her dead boy. At that moment the withered topmost bough of the oak loosened itself in the stilly air, and fell in soft, light fragments upon the rock, upon the leaves, upon Reuben, upon his wife and child, and upon Roger Malvin's bones. Then Reuben's heart was stricken, and the tears gushed out like water from a rock. The vow that the wounded youth had made the blighted man had come to redeem. His sin was expiated,—the curse was gone from him; and in the hour when he had shed blood dearer to him than his own, a prayer, the first for years, went up to Heaven from the lips of Reuben Bourne.

[1832]

QUESTIONS FOR STUDY

1. *Why does Reuben finally leave Roger Malvin in the forest?*
2. *What is the source of Reuben's guilt? Is it justified? How does Reuben compound it? In what ways does his guilt affect him?*
3. *What draws Reuben back to the site of Roger Malvin's grave?*
4. *Why is it necessary for Reuben to kill or sacrifice his dearest possession in order to remove his guilt? To what extent is Cyrus the symbolic extension of Reuben himself?*
5. *What other symbolic devices does Hawthorne employ in the story?*

NATHANIEL HAWTHORNE

Young Goodman Brown

YOUNG Goodman Brown came forth at sunset, into the street of Salem village, but put his head back, after crossing the threshold, to exchange a parting kiss with his young wife. And Faith, as the wife was aptly named, thrust her own pretty head into the street, letting the wind play with the pink ribbons of her cap, while she called to Goodman Brown.

"Dearest heart," whispered she, softly and rather sadly, when her lips were close to his ear, "prithee, put off your journey until sunrise, and sleep in your own bed to-night. A lone woman is troubled with such dreams and such thoughts, that she's afeard of herself, sometimes. Pray, tarry with me this night, dear husband, of all nights in the year!"

"My love and my Faith," replied young Goodman Brown, "of all nights in the year, this one night must I tarry away from thee. My journey, as thou callest it, forth and back again, must needs be done 'twixt now and sunrise. What, my sweet, pretty wife, dost thou doubt me already, and we but three months married!"

"Then God bless you!" said Faith with the pink ribbons, "and may you find all well, when you come back."

"Amen!" cried Goodman Brown. "Say thy prayers, dear Faith, and go to bed at dusk, and no harm will come to thee."

So they parted; and the young man pursued his way, until, being about to turn the corner by the meeting-house, he looked back and saw the head of Faith still peeping after him, with a melancholy air, in spite of her pink ribbons.

"Poor little Faith!" thought he, for his heart smote him. "What a wretch am I, to leave her on such an errand! She talks of dreams, too. Methought, as she spoke, there was trouble in her face, as if a dream had warned her what work is to be done to-night. But no, no! 't would kill her to think it. Well; she's a blessed angel on earth; and after this one night, I'll cling to her skirts and follow her to Heaven."

With this excellent resolve for the future, Goodman Brown felt himself justified in making more haste on his present evil purpose. He had taken a dreary road, darkened by all the gloomiest trees of the forest, which barely stood aside to let the narrow path creep through, and closed immediately behind. It was as lonely as could be; and there is this peculiarity in such a solitude, that the traveller knows not who may be concealed by the innumerable trunks and the thick boughs overhead; so that, with lonely footsteps, he may yet be passing through an unseen multitude.

"There may be a devilish Indian behind every tree," said Goodman Brown to himself; and he glanced fearfully behind him, as he added, "What if the devil himself should be at my very elbow!"

His head being turned back, he passed a crook of the road, and looking forward again, behind the figure of a man, in grave and decent attire, seated at the foot of an old tree. He arose at Goodman Brown's approach, and walked onward, side by side with him.

"You are late, Goodman Brown," said he. "The clock of the Old South was striking, as I came through Boston; and that is full fifteen minutes agone."

"Faith kept me back awhile," replied the young man, with a tremor in his voice, caused by the sudden appearance of his companion, though not wholly unexpected.

It was now deep dusk in the forest, and deepest in that part of it where these two were journeying. As nearly as could be discerned, the second traveller was about fifty years old, apparently in the same rank of life as Goodman Brown, and bearing a considerable resemblance to him, though perhaps more in expression than features. Still, they might have been taken for father and son. And yet, though the elder person was as simply clad as the younger, and as simple in manner too, he had an indescribable air of one who knew the world, and would not have felt abashed at the governor's dinner-table, or in King William's court, were it possible that his affairs should call him thither. But the only thing about him that could be fixed upon as remarkable, was his staff, which bore the likeness of a great black snake, so curiously wrought, that it might almost be seen to twist and wriggle itself like a living serpent. This, of course, must have been an ocular deception, assisted by the uncertain light.

"Come, Goodman Brown!" cried his fellow-traveller, "this is a dull pace for the beginning of a journey. Take my staff, if you are so soon weary."

"Friend," said the other, exchanging his slow pace for a full stop, "having kept covenant by meeting thee here, it is my purpose now to return whence I came. I have scruples, touching the matter thou wot'st of."

"Sayest thou so?" replied he of the serpent, smiling apart. "Let us walk on, nevertheless, reasoning as we go, and if I convince thee not, thou shalt turn back. We are but a little way in the forest, yet."

"Too far, too far!" exclaimed the goodman, unconsciously resuming his walk. "My father never went into the woods on such an errand, nor his father before him. We have been a race of honest men and good Christians, since the days of the martyrs. And shall I be the first of the name of Brown that ever took this path and kept—"

"Such company, thou wouldst say," observed the elder person, interrupting his pause. "Well said, Goodman Brown! I have been as well acquainted with your family as with ever a one among the Puritans; and that's no trifle to say. I helped your grandfather, the constable, when he lashed the Quaker woman so smartly through the streets of Salem. And it was I that brought your father a pitch-pine knot, kindled at my own hearth, to set fire to an Indian village, in King Philip's war. They were my good friends, both; and many a pleasant walk have we had along this path, and returned merrily after midnight. I would fain be friends with you, for their sake."

"If it be as thou sayest," replied Goodman Brown, "I marvel they never spoke of these matters. Or, verily, I marvel not, seeing that the least rumor of the sort would have driven them from New England. We are a people of prayer, and good works to boot, and abide no such wickedness."

"Wickedness or not," said the traveller with the twisted staff, "I have a very general acquaintance here in New England. The deacons of many a church have drunk the communion wine with me; the selectmen, of divers towns, make me their chairman; and a majority of the Great and General Court are firm supporters of my interest. The governor and I, too— but these are state secrets."

"Can this be so!" cried Goodman Brown, with a stare of amazement at his undisturbed companion. "Howbeit, I have nothing to do with the governor and council; they have their own ways, and are no rule for a simple husbandman like me. But, were I to go on with thee, how should I meet the eye of that good old man, our minister, at Salem village? Oh, his voice would make me tremble, both Sabbath-day and lecture-day!"

Thus far, the elder traveller had listened with due gravity, but now burst into a fit of irrepressible mirth, shaking himself so violently, that his snakelike staff actually seemed to wriggle in sympathy.

"Ha, ha, ha!" shouted he, again and again; then composing himself, "Well, go on, Goodman Brown, go on; but, prithee, don't kill me with laughing!"

"Well, then, to end the matter at once," said Goodman Brown, considerably nettled, "there is my wife, Faith. It would break her dear little heart; and I'd rather break my own!"

"Nay, if that be the case," answered the other, "e'en go thy ways, Goodman Brown. I would not, for twenty old women like the one hobbling before us, that Faith should come to any harm."

As he spoke, he pointed his staff at a

female figure on the path, in whom Goodman Brown recognized a very pious and exemplary dame, who had taught him his catechism in youth, and was still his moral and spiritual adviser, jointly with the minister and Deacon Gookin.

"A marvel, truly, that Goody Cloyse should be so far in the wilderness, at nightfall!" said he. "But, with your leave, friend, I shall take a cut through the woods, until we have left this Christian woman behind. Being a stranger to you, she might ask whom I was consorting with, and whither I was going."

"Be it so," said his fellow-traveller. "Betake you to the woods, and let me keep the path."

Accordingly, the young man turned aside, but took care to watch his companion, who advanced softly along the road, until he had come within a staff's length of the old dame. She, meanwhile, was making the best of her way, with singular speed for so aged a woman, and mumbling some indistinct words, a prayer, doubtless, as she went. The traveller put forth his staff, and touched her withered neck with what seemed the serpent's tail.

"The devil!" screamed the pious old lady.

"Then Goody Cloyse knows her old friend?" observed the traveller, confronting her, and leaning on his writhing stick.

"Ah, forsooth, and is it your worship, indeed?" cried the good dame. "Yea, truly is it, and in the very image of my old gossip, Goodman Brown, the grandfather of the silly fellow that now is. But, would your worship believe it? my broomstick hath strangely disappeared, stolen, as I suspect, by that unhanged witch, Goody Cory, and that, too, when I was all anointed with the juice of smallage and cinque-foil and wolf's-bane—"

"Mingled with fine wheat and the fat of a new-born babe," said the shape of old Goodman Brown.

"Ah, your worship knows the recipe," cried the old lady, cackling aloud. "So, as I was saying, being all ready for the meeting, and no horse to ride on, I made up my mind to foot it; for they tell me there is a nice young man to be taken into communion to-night. But now your good worship will lend me your arm, and we shall be there in a twinkling."

"That can hardly be," answered her friend. "I may not spare you my arm, Goody Cloyse, but here is my staff, if you will."

So saying, he threw it down at her feet, where, perhaps, it assumed life, being one of the rods which its owner had formerly lent to the Egyptian Magi. Of this fact, however, Goodman Brown could not take cognizance. He had cast his eyes in astonishment, and looking down again, beheld neither Goody Cloyse nor the serpentine staff, but his fellow-traveller alone, who waited for him as calmly as if nothing had happened.

"That old woman taught me my catechism!" said the young man; and there was a world of meaning in this simple comment.

They continued to walk onward, while the elder traveller exhorted his companion to make good speed and persevere in the path, discoursing so aptly, that his arguments seemed rather to spring up in the bosom of his auditor, than to be suggested by himself. As they went he plucked a branch of maple, to serve for a walking-stick, and began to strip it of the twigs and little boughs, which were wet with evening dew. The moment his fingers touched them, they became strangely withered and dried up, as with a week's sunshine. Thus the pair proceeded, at a good free pace, until suddenly, in a gloomy hollow of the road, Goodman Brown sat himself down on the stump of a tree, and refused to go any farther.

"Friend," said he, stubbornly, "my mind is made up. Not another step will I budge on this errand. What if a wretched old woman do choose to go to the devil, when I thought she was going to Heaven! Is that any reason why I should quit my dear Faith, and go after her?"

"You will think better of this by and by," said his acquaintance, composedly. "Sit here and rest yourself awhile; and when you feel like moving again, there is my staff to help you along."

Without more words, he threw his companion the maple stick, and was as speedily out of sight as if he had vanished into the deepening gloom. The young man sat a few moments by the roadside, applauding himself greatly, and thinking with how clear a conscience he should meet the minister, in his morning walk, nor shrink from the eye of good old Deacon Gookin. And what calm sleep would be his, that very night, which was to have been spent so wickedly, but purely and sweetly now, in the arms of Faith! Amidst these pleasant and praiseworthy meditations, Goodman Brown heard the tramp of horses along the road, and deemed it advisable to conceal himself within the verge of the forest, conscious of the guilty purpose that had brought him thither, though now so happily turned from it.

On came the hoof-tramps and the voices of the riders, two grave old voices, conversing soberly as they drew near. These mingled sounds appeared to pass along the road, within a few yards of the young man's hiding-place; but owing, doubtless, to the depth of the gloom, at that particular spot, neither the travellers nor their steeds were visible. Though their figures brushed the small boughs by the wayside, it could not be seen that they intercepted, even for a moment, the faint gleam from the strip of bright sky, athwart which they must have passed. Goodman Brown alternately crouched and stood on tiptoe, pulling aside the branches, and thrusting forth his head as far as he durst, without discerning so much as a shadow. It vexed him the more, because he could have sworn, were such a thing possible, that he recognized the voices of the minister and Deacon Gookin, jogging along quietly, as they were wont to do, when bound to some ordination or ecclesiastical council. While yet within hearing, one of the riders stopped to pluck a switch.

"Of the two, reverend Sir," said the voice like the deacon's, "I had rather miss an ordination dinner than to-night's meeting. They tell me that some of our community are to be here from Falmouth and beyond, and others from Connecticut and Rhode Island; besides several of the Indian powwows, who, after their fashion, know almost as much devlitry as the best of us. Moreover, there is a goodly young woman to be taken into communion."

"Mighty well, Deacon Gookin!" replied the solemn old tones of the minister. "Spur up, or we shall be late. Nothing can be done, you know, until I get on the ground."

The hoofs clattered again, and the voices, talking so strangely in the empty air, passed on through the forest, where no church had ever been gathered, nor solitary Christian prayed. Whither, then, could these holy men be journeying, so deep into the heathen wilderness? Young Goodman Brown caught hold of a tree, for support, being ready to sink down on the ground, faint and over-burthened with the heavy sickness of his heart. He looked up to the sky, doubting whether there really was a Heaven above him. Yet, there was the blue arch, and the stars brightening in it.

"With Heaven above, and Faith below, I will yet stand firm against the devil!" cried Goodman Brown.

While he still gazed upward, into the deep arch of the firmament, and had lifted his hands to pray, a cloud, though no wind was stirring, hurried across the zenith, and hid the brightening stars. The blue sky was still visible, except directly overhead, where this black mass of cloud was sweeping swiftly northward. Aloft in the air, as if from the depths of the cloud, came a confused and doubtful sound of voices. Once, the listener fancied that he could distinguish the accents of townspeople of his own, men and women, both pious and ungodly, many of whom he had met at the communion-table, and had seen others rioting at the tavern. The next moment, so indistinct were the sounds, he doubted whether he had heard aught but the murmur of the old forest, whispering without a wind. Then came a stronger swell of those familiar tones, heard daily in the sunshine, at Salem village, but never, until now, from a cloud at night. There was one voice, of a young woman, uttering lamentations, yet with an uncertain sorrow, and entreating for some favor, which, perhaps, it would grieve her to obtain. And all the unseen multitude, both saints and sinners, seemed to encourage her onward.

"Faith!" shouted Goodman Brown, in a voice of agony and desperation; and the echoes of the forest mocked him, crying—"Faith! Faith!" as if bewildered wretches were seeking her, all through the wilderness.

The cry of grief, rage, and terror was yet piercing the night, when the unhappy husband held his breath for a response. There was a scream, drowned immediately in a louder murmur of voices fading into far-off laughter, as the dark cloud swept away, leaving the clear and silent sky above Goodman Brown. But something fluttered lightly down through the air, and caught on the branch of a tree. The young man seized it and beheld a pink ribbon.

"My Faith is gone!" cried he, after one stupefied moment. "There is no good on earth, and sin is but a name. Come, devil! for to thee is this world given."

And maddened with despair, so that he laughed loud and long, did Goodman Brown grasp his staff and set forth again, at such a rate, that he seemed to fly along the forest path, rather than to walk or run. The road grew wilder and drearier, and more faintly traced, and vanished at length, leaving him in the heart of the dark wilderness, still rushing onward, with the instinct that guides mortal man to evil. The whole forest was peopled with frightful sounds: the creaking of the trees, the howling of wild beasts, and the yell of Indians; while, sometimes, the wind tolled like a distant church bell, and sometimes gave a broad roar around the traveller, as if all Nature was laughing him to scorn. But he was himself the chief horror of the scene, and shrank not from its other horrors.

"Ha! ha! ha!" roared Goodman Brown, when the wind laughed at him. "Let us hear which will laugh loudest! Think not to frighten me with your deviltry! Come witch, come wizard, come Indian powwow, come devil himself! and here comes Goodman Brown. You may as well fear him as he fear you!"

In truth, all through the haunted forest, there could be nothing more frightful than the figure of Goodman Brown. On he flew, among the black pines, brandishing his staff with frenzied gestures, now giving vent to an inspiration of horrid blasphemy, and now shouting forth such laughter, as set all the echoes of the forest laughing like demons around him. The fiend in his own shape is less hideous, than when he rages in the breast of man. Thus sped the demoniac on his course, until, quivering among the trees, he saw a red light before him, as when the felled trunks and branches of a clearing have been set on fire, and throw up their lurid blaze against the sky, at the hour of midnight. He paused, in a lull of the tempest that had driven him onward, and heard the swell of what seemed a hymn, rolling solemnly from a distance, with the weight of many voices. He knew the tune. It was a familiar one in the choir of the village meeting-house. The verse died heavily away, and was lengthened by a chorus, not of human voices, but of all the sounds of the benighted wilderness, pealing in awful harmony together. Goodman Brown cried out; and his cry was lost to his own ear, by its unison with the cry of the desert.

In the interval of silence, he stole forward, until the light glared full upon his eyes. At one extremity of an open space, hemmed in by the dark wall of the forest, arose a rock, bearing some rude, natural resemblance either to an altar or a pulpit, and surrounded by four blazing pines, their tops aflame, their stems untouched, like candles at an evening meeting. The mass of foliage, that had overgrown the summit of the rock, was all on fire, blazing high into the night, and fitfully illuminating the whole field. Each pendent twig and leafy festoon was in a blaze. As the red light arose and fell, a numerous congregation alternately shone forth, then disappeared in shadow, and again grew, as it were, out of the darkness, peopling the heart of the solitary woods at once.

"A grave and dark-clad company!" quoth Goodman Brown.

In truth, they were such. Among them, quivering to-and-fro, between gloom and splendor, appeared faces that would be seen, next day, at the council-board of the province, and others which, Sabbath after Sabbath, looked devoutly heavenward, and benignantly over the crowded pews, from the holiest pulpits in the land. Some affirm, that the lady of the governor was there. At least, there were high dames well known to her, and wives of honored husbands, and widows a great multitude, and ancient maidens, all of excellent repute, and fair young girls, who trembled lest their mothers should espy them. Either the sudden gleams of light, flashing over the obscure field, bedazzled Goodman Brown, or he recognized a score of the church members of Salem village, famous for their especial sanctity. Good old Deacon Gookin had arrived, and waited at the skirts of that venerable saint, his reverend pastor. But, irreverently consorting with these grave, reputable, and pious people, these elders of the church, these chaste dames and dewy virgins, there were men of dissolute lives and women of spotted fame, wretches given over to all mean and filthy vice, and suspected even of horrid crimes. It was strange to see, that the good shrank not from the wicked, nor were the sinners abashed by the saints. Scattered, also, among their pale-faced enemies, were the Indian priests, or powwows, who had often scared their native forest with more hideous incantations than any known to English witchcraft.

"But, where is Faith?" thought Goodman Brown; and, as hope came into his heart, he trembled.

Another verse of the hymn arose, a slow and mournful strain, such as the pious love, but joined to words which expressed all that our nature can conceive of sin, and darkly hinted at far more. Unfathomable to mere mortals is the lore of fiends. Verse after verse was sung, and still the chorus of the desert swelled between, like the deepest tone of a mighty organ. And, with the final peal of that dreadful anthem, there came a sound, as if the roaring wind, the rushing streams, the howling beasts, and every other voice of the unconverted wilderness were mingling and according with the voice of guilty man, in homage to the prince of all. The four blazing pines threw up a loftier

flame, and obscurely discovered shapes and visages of horror on the smoke-wreaths, above the impious assembly. At the same moment, the fire on the rock shot redly forth, and formed a glowing arch above its base, where now appeared a figure. With reverence be it spoken, the apparition bore no slight similitude, both in garb and manner, to some grave divine of the New England churches.

"Bring forth the converts!" cried a voice, that echoed through the field and rolled into the forest.

At the word, Goodman Brown stepped forth from the shadow of the trees, and approached the congregation, with whom he felt a loathful brotherhood, by the sympathy of all that was wicked in his heart. He could have well-nigh sworn, that the shape of his own dead father beckoned him to advance, looking downward from a smoke-wreath, while a woman, with dim features of despair, threw out her hand to warn him back. Was it his mother? But he had no power to retreat one step, nor to resist, even in thought, when the minister and good old Deacon Gookin seized his arms, and led him to the blazing rock. Thither came also the slender form of a veiled female, led between Goody Cloyse, that pious teacher of the catechism, and Martha Carrier, who had received the devil's promise to be queen of hell. A rampant hag was she! And there stood the proselytes, beneath the canopy of fire.

"Welcome, my children," said the dark figure, "to the communion of your race! Ye have found, thus young, your nature and your destiny. My children, look behind you!"

They turned; and flashing forth, as it were, in a sheet of flame, the fiend-worshippers were seen; the smile of welcome gleamed darkly on every visage.

"There," resumed the sable form, "are all whom ye have reverenced from youth. Ye deemed them holier than yourselves, and shrank from your own sin, contrasting it with their lives of righteousness and prayerful aspirations heavenward. Yet, here are they all, in my worshipping assembly! This night it shall be granted you to know their secret deeds; how hoary-bearded elders of the church have whispered wanton words to the young maids of their households; how many a woman, eager for widow's weeds, has given her husband a drink at bedtime, and let him sleep his last sleep in her bosom; how beardless youths have made haste to inherit their father's wealth; and how fair damsels—blush not, sweet ones!—have dug little graves in the garden, and bidden me, the sole guest, to an infant's funeral. By the sympathy of your human hearts for sin, ye shall scent out all the places—whether in church, bedchamber, street, field, or forest—where crime has been committed, and shall exult to behold the whole earth one stain of guilt, one mighty blood-spot. Far more than this! It shall be yours to penetrate, in every bosom, the deep mystery of sin, the fountain of all wicked arts, and which inexhaustibly supplies more evil impulses than human power—than my power, at its utmost!—can make manifest in deeds. And now, my children, look upon each other."

They did so; and, by the blaze of the hell-kindled torches, the wretched man beheld his Faith, and the wife her husband, trembling before that unhallowed altar.

"Lo! there ye stand, my children," said the figure, in a deep and solemn tone, almost sad, with its despairing awfulness, as if his once angelic nature could yet mourn for our miserable race. "Depending upon one another's hearts, ye had still hoped that virtue were not all a dream! Now are ye undeceived!—Evil is the nature of mankind. Evil must be your only happiness. Welcome, again, my children, to the communion of your race!"

"Welcome!" repeated the fiend-worshippers, in one cry of despair and triumph.

And there they stood, the only pair, as it seemed, who were yet hesitating on the verge of wickedness, in this dark world. A basin was hollowed, naturally, in the rock. Did it contain water, reddened by the lurid light? or was it blood? or, perchance, a liquid flame? Herein did the Shape of Evil dip his hand, and prepare to lay the mark of baptism upon their foreheads, that they might be partakers of the mystery of sin, more conscious of the secret guilt of others, both in deed and thought, than they could now be of their own. The husband cast one look at his pale wife, and Faith at him. What polluted wretches would the next glance show them to each other, shuddering alike at what they disclosed and what they saw!

"Faith! Faith!" cried the husband. "Look up to Heaven, and resist the Wicked One!"

Whether Faith obeyed, he knew not. Hardly had he spoken, when he found himself amid calm night and solitude, listening to a roar of the wind, which died heavily away through the forest. He staggered against the rock, and felt it chill and damp, while a hanging twig, that had been all on fire, besprinkled his cheek with the coldest dew.

The next morning, young Goodman Brown came slowly into the street of Salem village staring around him like a bewildered man. The good old minister was taking a walk along the grave-yard, to get an appetite for breakfast and meditate his sermon, and bestowed a blessing, as he passed, on Goodman Brown. He shrank from the venerable saint, as if to avoid an anathema. Old Deacon Gookin was at domestic worship, and the holy words of his prayer were heard through the open window. "What God doth the wizard pray to?" quoth Goodman Brown. Goody Cloyse, that excellent old Christian, stood in the early sunshine, at her own lattice, catechising a little girl, who had brought her a pint of morning's milk. Goodman Brown snatched away the child, as from the grasp of the fiend himself. Turning the corner by the meeting-house, he spied the head of Faith, with the pink ribbons, gazing anxiously forth, and bursting into such joy at sight of him that she skipt along the street, and almost kissed her husband before the whole village. But Goodman Brown looked sternly and sadly into her face, and passed on without a greeting.

Had Goodman Brown fallen asleep in the forest, and only dreamed a wild dream of a witch-meeting?

Be it so, if you will. But, alas! it was a dream of evil omen for young Goodman Brown. A stern, a sad, a darkly meditative, a distrustful, if not a desperate man did he become, from the night of that fearful dream. On the Sabbath day, when the congregation were singing a holy psalm, he could not listen, because an anthem of sin rushed loudly upon his ear, and drowned all the blessed strain. When the minister spoke from the pulpit, with power and fervid eloquence, and with his hand on the open Bible, of the sacred truths of our religion, and of saint-like lives and triumphant deaths, and of future bliss or misery unutterable, then did Goodman Brown turn pale, dreading lest the roof should thunder down upon the gray blasphemer and his hearers. Often, awaking suddenly at midnight, he shrank from the bosom of Faith, and at morning or eventide, when the family knelt down at prayer, he scowled, and muttered to himself, and gazed sternly at his wife, and turned away. And when he had lived long, and was borne to his grave, a hoary corpse, followed by Faith, an aged woman, and children and grand-children, a goodly procession, besides neighbors not a few, they carved no hopeful verse upon his tombstone; for his dying hour was gloom.

[1835]

QUESTIONS FOR STUDY

1. *How does a knowledge of seventeenth-century New England history and theology aid in understanding the story?*
2. *What important facts about Goodman Brown does the reader learn at the beginning of the story? What compels Brown to make his journey in the forest?*
3. *Who is the stranger "with the twisted staff" that Brown meets at the foot of the old tree? What is the significance of the fact that he bears "a considerable resemblance" to Young Goodman Brown, so much so that "they might have been taken for father and son"?*
4. *What effect do Deacon Gookin, Goody Cloyse, and the minister have upon Goodman Brown? What social institutions do they represent?*
5. *What is the function of Faith's pink ribbons? Why should their color be pink? How do they precipitate Goodman Brown's final undoing?*
6. *What effect does the conviction of sin have upon Young Goodman Brown?*
7. *What final ambiguity surrounds the story? How would the story be different had Hawthorne omitted the last three paragraphs?*

ERNEST HEMINGWAY

The Killers

THE DOOR of Henry's lunch-room opened and two men came in. They sat down at the counter.

"What's yours?" George asked them.

"I don't know," one of the men said. "What do you want to eat, Al?"

"I don't know," said Al. "I don't know what I want to eat."

Outside it was getting dark. The streetlight came on outside the window. The two men at the counter read the menu. From the other end of the counter Nick Adams watched them. He had been talking to George when they came in.

"I'll have a roast pork tenderloin with apple sauce and mashed potatoes," the first man said.

"It isn't ready yet."

"What the hell do you put it on the card for?"

"That's the dinner," George explained. "You can get that at six o'clock."

George looked at the clock on the wall behind the counter.

"It's five o'clock."

"The clock says twenty minutes past five," the second man said.

"It's twenty minutes fast."

"Oh, to hell with the clock," the first man said. "What have you got to eat?"

"I can give you any kind of sandwiches," George said. "You can have ham and eggs, bacon and eggs, liver and bacon, or a steak."

"Give me chicken croquettes with green peas and cream sauce and mashed potatoes."

"That's the dinner."

"Everything we want's the dinner, eh? That's the way you work it."

"I can give you ham and eggs, bacon and eggs, liver——"

"I'll take ham and eggs," the man called Al said. He wore a derby hat and a black overcoat buttoned across the chest. His face was small and white and he had tight lips. He wore a silk muffler and gloves.

"Give me bacon and eggs," said the other man. He was about the same size as Al. Their faces were different, but they were dressed like twins. Both wore overcoats too tight for them. They sat leaning forward, their elbows on the counter.

"Got anything to drink?" Al asked.

"Silver beer, bevo, ginger-ale," George said.

"I mean you got anything to *drink?*"

"Just those I said."

"This is a hot town," said the other. "What do they call it?"

"Summit."

"Ever heard of it?" Al asked his friend.

"No," said the friend.

"What do you do here nights?" Al asked.

"They eat the dinner," his friend said. "They all come here and eat the big dinner."

"That's right," George said.

"So you think that's right?" Al asked George.

"Sure."

"You're a pretty bright boy, aren't you?"

"Sure," said George.

"Well, you're not," said the other little man. "Is he, Al?"

"He's dumb," said Al. He turned to Nick. "What's your name?"

"Adams."

"Another bright boy," Al said. "Ain't he a bright boy, Max?"

"The town's full of bright boys," Max said.

George put the two platters, one of ham and eggs, the other of bacon and eggs, on the counter. He set down two side-dishes of fried potatoes and closed the wicket into the kitchen.

"Which is yours?" he asked Al.

"Don't you remember?"

"Ham and eggs."

"Just a bright boy," Max said. He leaned forward and took the ham and eggs. Both men ate with their gloves on. George watched them eat.

"What are *you* looking at?" Max looked at George.

"Nothing."

"The hell you were. You were looking at me."

"Maybe the boy meant it for a joke, Max," Al said.

George laughed.

"*You* don't have to laugh," Max said to him. "'*You* don't have to laugh at all, see?"

"All right," said George.

"So he thinks it's all right." Max turned to Al. "He thinks it's all right. That's a good one."

"Oh, he's a thinker," Al said. They went on eating.

"What's the bright boy's name down the counter?" Al asked Max.

"Hey, bright boy," Max said to Nick. "You go around on the other side of the counter with your boy friend."

"What's the idea?" Nick asked.

"There isn't any idea."

"You better go around, bright boy," Al said. Nick went around behind the counter.

"What's the idea?" George asked.

"None of your damn business," Al said. "Who's out in the kitchen?"

"The nigger."

"What do you mean the nigger?"

"The nigger that cooks."

"Tell him to come in."

"What's the idea?"

"Tell him to come in."

"Where do you think you are?"

"We know damn well where we are," the man called Max said. "Do we look silly?"

"You talk silly," Al said to him. "What the hell do you argue with this kid for? Listen," he said to George, "tell the nigger to come out here."

"What are you going to do to him?"

"Nothing. Use your head, bright boy. What would we do to a nigger?"

George opened the slit that opened back into the kitchen. "Sam," he called. "Come in here a minute."

The door to the kitchen opened and the nigger came in. "What was it?" he asked. The two men at the counter took a look at him.

"All right, nigger. You stand right there," Al said.

Sam, the nigger, standing in his apron, looked at the two men sitting at the counter. "Yes, sir," he said. Al got down from his stool.

"I'm going back to the kitchen with the nigger and bright boy," he said. "Go on back to the kitchen, nigger. You go with him, bright boy." The little man walked after Nick and Sam, the cook, back into the kitchen. The door shut after them. The man called Max sat at the counter opposite George. He didn't look at George but looked in the mirror that ran along back of the counter. Henry's had been made over from a saloon into a lunch-counter.

"Well, bright boy," Max said, looking into the mirror, "why don't you say something?"

"What's it all about?"

"Hey, Al," Max called, "bright boy wants to know what it's all about."

"Why don't you tell him?" Al's voice came from the kitchen.

"What do you think it's all about?"

"I don't know."

"What do you think?"

Max looked into the mirror all the time he was talking.

"I wouldn't say."

"Hey, Al, bright boy says he wouldn't say what he thinks it's all about."

"I can hear you, all right," Al said from the kitchen. He had propped open the slit that dishes passed through into the kitchen with a catsup bottle. "Listen, bright boy," he said from the kitchen to George. "Stand a little further along the bar. You move a little to the left, Max." He was like a photographer arranging for a group picture.

"Talk to me, bright boy," Max said. "What do you think's going to happen?"

George did not say anything.

"I'll tell you," Max said. "We're going to kill a Swede. Do you know a big Swede named Ole Andreson?"

"Yes."

"He comes here to eat every night, don't he?"

"Sometimes he comes here."

"He comes here at six o'clock, don't he?"

"If he comes."

"We know all that, bright boy," Max said. "Talk about something else. Ever go to the movies?"

"Once in a while."

"You ought to go to the movies more. The movies are fine for a bright boy like you."

"What are you going to kill Ole Andreson for? What did he ever do to you?"

"He never had a chance to do anything to us. He never even seen us."

"And he's only going to see us once." Al said from the kitchen.

"What are you going to kill him for, then?" George asked.

"We're killing him for a friend. Just to oblige a friend, bright boy."

"Shut up," said Al from the kitchen. "You talk too goddam much."

"Well, I got to keep bright boy amused. Don't I, bright boy?"

"You talk too damn much," Al said. "The nigger and my bright boy are amused by themselves. I got them tied up like a couple of girl friends in the convent."

"I suppose you were in a convent?"

"You never know."

"You were in a kosher convent. That's where you were."

George looked up at the clock.

"If anyone comes in you tell them the cook is off, and if they keep after it, you tell them you'll go back and cook yourself. Do you get that, bright boy?"

"All right," George said. "What you going to do with us afterward?"

"That'll depend," Max said. "That's one of those things you never know at the time."

George looked up at the clock. It was a quarter past six. The door from the street opened. A street-car motorman came in.

"Hello, George," he said. "Can I get supper?"

"Sam's gone out," George said. "He'll be back in about half an hour."

"I'd better go up the street," the motorman said. George looked at the clock. It was twenty minutes past six.

"That was nice, bright boy," Max said. "You're a regular little gentleman."

"He knew I'd blow his head off," Al said from the kitchen.

"No," said Max. "It ain't that. Bright boy is nice. He's a nice boy. I like him."

At six-fifty-five George said: "He's not coming."

Two other people had been in the lunch-room. Once George had gone out to the kitchen and made a ham-and-egg sandwich "to go" that a man wanted to take with him. Inside the kitchen he saw Al, his derby hat tipped back, sitting on a stool beside the wicket with the muzzle of a sawed-off shotgun resting on the ledge. Nick and the cook were back to back in the corner, a towel tied in each of their mouths. George had cooked the sandwich, wrapped it up in oiled paper, put it in a bag, brought it in, and the man had paid for it and gone out.

"Bright boy can do everything," Max said. "He can cook and everything. You'd make some girl a nice wife, bright boy."

"Yes?" George said. "Your friend, Ole Andreson, isn't going to come."

"We'll give him ten minutes," Max said.

Max watched the mirror and the clock. The hands of the clock marked seven o'clock, and then five minutes past seven.

"Come on, Al," said Max. "We better go. He's not coming."

"Better give him five minutes," Al said from the kitchen.

In the five minutes a man came in, and George explained that the cook was sick.

"Why the hell don't you get another cook?" the man asked. "Aren't you running a lunch-counter?" He went out.

"Come on, Al," Max said.

"What about the two bright boys and the nigger?"

"They're all right."

"You think so?"

"Sure. We're through with it."

"I don't like it," said Al. "It's sloppy. You talk too much."

"Oh, what the hell," said Max. "We got to keep amused, haven't we?"

"You talk too much all the same," Al said. He came out from the kitchen. The cut-off barrels of the shotgun made a slight bulge under the waist of his too tight-fitting overcoat. He straightened his coat with his gloved hands.

"So long, bright boy," he said to George. "You got a lot of luck."

"That's the truth," Max said. "You ought to play the races, bright boy."

The two of them went out the door. George watched them, through the window, pass under the arc-light and cross the street. In their tight overcoats and derby hats they looked like a vaudeville team. George went back through the swinging-door into the kitchen and untied Nick and the cook.

"I don't want any more of that," said Sam, the cook. "I don't want any more of that."

Nick stood up. He had never had a towel in his mouth before.

"Say," he said. "What the hell?" He was trying to swagger it off.

"They were going to kill Ole Andreson," George said. "They were going to shoot him when he came in to eat."

"Ole Andreson?"

"Sure."

The cook felt the corners of his mouth with his thumbs.

"They all gone?" he asked.

"Yeah," said George. "They're gone now."

"I don't like it," said the cook. "I don't like any of it at all."

"Listen," George said to Nick. "You better go see Ole Andreson."

"All right."

"You better not have anything to do with it at all," Sam, the cook, said. "You better stay way out of it."

"Don't go if you don't want to," George said.

"Mixing up in this ain't going to get you anywhere," the cook said. "You stay out of it."

"I'll go see him," Nick said to George. "Where does he live?"

The cook turned away.

"Little boys always know what they want to do," he said.

"He lives up at Hirsch's rooming-house," George said to Nick.

"I'll go up there."

Outside the arc-light shone through the bare branches of a tree. Nick walked up the street beside the car-tracks and turned at the next arc-light down a side-street. Three houses up the street was Hirsch's rooming-house. Nick walked up the two steps and pushed the bell. A woman came to the door.

"Is Ole Andreson here?"

"Do you want to see him?"

"Yes, if he's in."

Nick followed the woman up a flight of stairs and back to the end of a corridor. She knocked on the door.

"Who is it?"

"It's somebody to see you, Mr. Andreson," the woman said.

"It's Nick Adams."

"Come in."

Nick opened the door and went into the room. Ole Andreson was lying on the bed with all his clothes on. He had been a heavyweight prizefighter and he was too long for the bed. He lay with his head on two pillows. He did not look at Nick.

"What was it?" he asked.

"I was up at Henry's," Nick said, "and two fellows came in and tied up me and the cook, and they said they were going to kill you."

It sounded silly when he said it. Ole Andreson said nothing.

"They put us out in the kitchen," Nick went on. "They were going to shoot you when you came in to supper."

Ole Andreson looked at the wall and did not say anything.

"George thought I better come and tell you about it."

"There isn't anything I can do about it," Ole Andreson said.

"I'll tell you what they were like."

"I don't want to know what they were like," Ole Andreson said. He looked at the wall. "Thanks for coming to tell me about it."

"That's all right."

Nick looked at the big man lying on the bed.

"Don't you want me to go and see the police?"

"No," Ole Andreson said. "That wouldn't do any good."

"Isn't there something I could do?"

"No. There ain't anything to do."

"Maybe it was just a bluff."

"No. It ain't just a bluff."

Ole Andreson rolled over toward the wall.

"The only thing is," he said, talking toward the wall, "I just can't make up my mind to go out. I been in here all day."

"Couldn't you get out of town?"

"No," Ole Andreson said. "I'm through with all that running around."

He looked at the wall.

"There ain't anything to do now."

"Couldn't you fix it up some way?"

"No. I got in wrong." He talked in the same flat voice. "There ain't anything to do. After a while I'll make up my mind to go out."

"I better go back and see George," Nick said.

"So long," said Ole Andreson. He did not look toward Nick. "Thanks for coming around."

Nick went out. As he shut the door he saw Ole Andreson with all his clothes on, lying on the bed looking at the wall.

"He's been in his room all day," the landlady said down-stairs. "I guess he don't feel well. I said to him: 'Mr. Andreson, you ought to go out and take a walk on a nice fall day like this,' but he didn't feel like it."

"He doesn't want to go out."

"I'm sorry he don't feel well," the woman said. "He's an awfully nice man. He was in the ring, you know."

"I know it."

"You'd never know it except from the way his face is," the woman said. They stood talking just inside the street door. "He's just as gentle."

"Well, good-night, Mrs. Hirsch," Nick said.

"I'm not Mrs. Hirsch," the woman said. "She owns the place. I just look after it for her. I'm Mrs. Bell."

"Well, good-night, Mrs. Bell," Nick said.

"Good-night," the woman said.

Nick walked up the dark street to the corner under the arc-light, and then along the car-tracks to Henry's eating-house. George was inside, back of the counter.

"Did you see Ole?"

"Yes," said Nick. "He's in his room and he won't go out."

The cook opened the door from the kitchen when he heard Nick's voice.

"I don't even listen to it," he said and shut the door.

"Did you tell him about it?" George asked.

"Sure. I told him but he knows what it's all about."

"What's he going to do?"

"Nothing."

"They'll kill him."

"I guess they will."

"He must have got mixed up in something in Chicago."

"I guess so," said Nick.

"It's a hell of a thing."

"It's an awful thing," Nick said.

They did not say anything. George reached down for a towel and wiped the counter.

"I wonder what he did?" Nick said.

"Double-crossed somebody. That's what they kill them for."

"I'm going to get out of this town," Nick said.

"Yes," said George. "That's a good thing to do."

"I can't stand to think about him waiting in the room and knowing he's going to get it. It's too damned awful."

"Well," said George, "you better not think about it."

[1927]

QUESTIONS FOR STUDY

1. *How are the two gangsters characterized? How does that characterization together with the bored and banal quality of their dialogue reinforce the underlying horror of the story?*

2. *What hints does the story offer that might provide a possible explanation for Ole Andreson's murder? Why doesn't Hemingway choose to be more specific?*

3. *Why does Ole Andreson refuse to attempt to escape? What is significant in the fact that he lies with his face to the wall?*

4. *What is the function of Mrs. Bell? Is it significant that Nick should mistake her for Mrs. Hirsch?*

5. *How do George, Sam, and Nick differ in their attitudes toward the incident? What does Nick appear to learn? Why does he say at the end "I'm going to get out of this town"?*

6. *Who is the story's focal character? Why?*

WASHINGTON IRVING

Rip Van Winkle

WHOEVER has made a voyage up the Hudson must remember the Kaatskill Mountains. They are a dismembered branch of the great Appalachian family, and are seen away to the west of the river, swelling up to a noble height and lording it over the surrounding country. Every change of season, every change of weather, indeed every hour of the day, produces some change in the magical hues and shapes of these mountains, and they are regarded by all the good wives, far and near, as perfect barometers. When the weather is fair and settled, they are clothed in blue and purple, and print their bold outlines on the clear evening sky; but sometimes, when the rest of the landscape is cloudless, they will gather a hood of gray vapor about their summits, which in the last rays of the setting sun will glow and light up like a crown of glory.

At the foot of these fairy mountains the voyager may have descried the light smoke curling up from a village, whose shingle roofs gleam among the trees just where the blue tints of the upland melt away into the fresh green of the nearer landscape. It is a little village of great antiquity, having been founded by some of the Dutch colonists in the early times of the province, just about the beginning of the government of the good Peter Stuyvesant (may he rest in peace!), and there were some of the houses of the original settlers standing within a few years, built of small yellow bricks brought from Holland, having latticed windows and gable fronts surmounted with weathercocks.

In that same village, and in one of these very houses (which, to tell the precise truth, was sadly time-worn and weather-beaten), there lived many years since, while the country was yet a province of Great Britain, a simple good-natured fellow of the name of Rip Van Winkle. He was a descendant of the Van Winkles who figured so gallantly in the chivalrous days of Peter Stuyvesant and accompanied him to the siege of Fort Christina. He inherited, however, but little of the martial character of his ancestors. I have observed that he was a simple good-natured man; he was, moreover, a kind neighbor and an obedient henpecked husband. Indeed, to the latter circumstance might be owing that meekness of spirit which gained him such universal popularity; for those men are most apt to be obsequious and conciliating abroad who are under the discipline of shrews at home. Their tempers, doubtless, are rendered pliant and malleable in the fiery furnace of domestic tribulation, and a curtain lecture is worth all the sermons in the world for teaching the virtues of patience and long-suffering. A termagant wife may, therefore, in some respects, be considered a tolerable blessing; and if so, Rip Van Winkle was thrice blessed.

Certain it is that he was a great favorite among all the good wives of the village, who, as usual with the amiable sex, took his part in all family squabbles, and never failed, whenever they talked those matters over in their evening gossips, to lay all the blame on Dame Van Winkle. The children of the village, too, would shout with joy whenever he approached. He assisted at their sports, made their playthings, taught them to fly kites and shoot marbles, and told them long stories of ghosts, witches, and Indians. Whenever he went dodging about the village he was surrounded by a troop of them, hanging on his skirts, clambering on his back, and playing a thousand tricks on him with impunity; and not a dog would bark at him throughout the neighborhood.

The great error in Rip's composition was an insuperable aversion to all kinds of profitable labor. It could not be from the want of assiduity or perseverance; for he would sit on a wet rock, with a rod as long and heavy as a Tartar's lance, and fish all day without a murmur, even though he should not be encouraged by a single nibble. He would carry a fowling-piece on his shoulder for hours together, trudging through woods and swamps and up hill and down dale, to shoot a few squirrels or wild pigeons. He would never refuse to assist a neighbor even in the roughest toil, and was a foremost man at all country frolics for husking Indian corn or building stone fences; the women of the village, too, used to employ him to run their errands, and to do such little odd jobs as their less obliging husbands would not do for them. In a word, Rip was ready to attend to anybody's business but his own; but as to doing family duty and keeping his farm in order, he found it impossible.

In fact, he declared it was of no use to work on his farm; it was the most pestilent little piece of ground in the whole country; everything about it went wrong, and would go wrong in spite of him. His fences were continually falling to pieces; his cow would either go astray or get among the cabbages; weeds were sure to grow quicker in his fields than anywhere else; the rain always made a point of setting in just as he had some out-door work to do; so that, though his patrimonial estate had dwindled away under his management, acre by acre, until there was little more left than a mere patch of Indian corn and potatoes, yet it was the worst-conditioned farm in the neighborhood.

His children, too, were as ragged and wild as if they belonged to nobody. His son Rip, an urchin begotten in his own likeness, promised to inherit the habits with the old clothes of his father. He was generally seen trooping like a colt at his mother's heels, equipped in a pair of his father's cast-off galligaskins, which he had much ado to hold up with one hand, as a fine lady does her train in bad weather.

Rip Van Winkle, however, was one of those happy mortals, of foolish, well-oiled disposition, who take the world easy, eat white bread or brown, whichever can be got with least thought or trouble, and would rather starve on a penny than work for a pound. If left to himself, he would have whistled life away in perfect contentment; but his wife kept continually dinning in his ears about his idleness, his carelessness, and the ruin he was bringing on his family. Morning, noon, and night her tongue was incessantly going, and everything he said or did was sure to produce a torrent of household eloquence. Rip had but one way of replying to all lectures of the kind, and that, by frequent use, had grown into a habit. He shrugged his shoulders, shook his head, cast up his eyes, but said nothing. This, however, always provoked a fresh volley from his wife; so that he was fain to draw off his forces and take to the outside of the house—the only side which, in truth, belongs to a henpecked husband.

Rip's sole domestic adherent was his dog Wolf, who was as much henpecked as his master; for Dame Van Winkle regarded them as companions in idleness, and even looked upon Wolf with an evil eye, as the cause of his master's going so often astray. True, it is, in all points of spirit befitting an honorable dog he was as courageous an animal as ever scoured the woods; but what courage can withstand the ever-during and all-besetting terrors of a woman's tongue? The moment Wolf entered the house his crest fell, his tail drooped to the ground or curled between his legs, he sneaked about with a gallows air, casting many a sidelong glance at Dame Van Winkle, and at the least flourish of a broomstick or ladle he would fly to the door with yelping precipitation.

Times grew worse and worse with Rip Van Winkle as years of matrimony rolled on; a tart temper never mellows with age, and a sharp tongue is the only edged tool that grows keener with constant use. For a long while he used to console himself, when driven from home, by frequenting a kind of perpetual club of the sages, philosophers, and other idle personages of the village which held its sessions on a bench before a small inn, designated by a rubicund portrait of His Majesty George the Third. Here they used to sit in the shade through a long lazy summer's day, talking listlessly over village gossip or telling endless sleepy stories about nothing. But it would have been worth any statesman's money to have heard the profound discussions that sometimes took place when by chance an old newspaper fell into their hands from some passing traveller. How solemnly they would listen to the contents, as drawled out by Derrick Van Bummel, the schoolmaster, a dapper learned little man, who was not to be daunted by the most gigantic word in the dictionary, and how sagely they would deliberate upon public events some months after they had taken place!

The opinions of this junto were completely controlled by Nicholas Vedder, a patriarch of the village and landlord of the inn, at the door of which he took his seat from morning till night, just moving sufficiently to avoid the sun and keep in the shade of a large tree; so that the neighbors could tell the hour by his movements as accurately as by a sun-dial. It is true he was rarely heard to speak, but smoked his pipe incessantly. His adherents, however (for every great man has his adherents), perfectly understood him, and knew how to gather his opinions. When anything that was read or related displeased him, he was observed to smoke his pipe vehemently, and to send forth short, frequent, and angry puffs; but when pleased, he would inhale the smoke slowly and tranquilly, and emit it in light and placid clouds; and sometimes, taking the pipe from his mouth and letting the fragrant vapor curl about his nose, would gravely nod his head in token of perfect approbation.

From even this stronghold the unlucky Rip was at length routed by his termagant wife, who would suddenly break in upon the tranquility of the assemblage and call the members all to naught; nor was that august personage, Nicholas Vedder himself, sacred from the daring tongue of this terrible virago, who charged him outright with encouraging her husband in habits of idleness.

Poor Rip was at last reduced almost to despair, and his only alternative, to escape from the labor of the farm and clamor of his wife, was to take gun in hand and stroll away into the woods. Here he would sometimes seat himself at the foot of a tree, and share the contents of his wallet with Wolf, with whom he sympathized as a fellow-sufferer in persecution. "Poor Wolf!" he would say, "thy mistress leads thee a dog's life of it; but never mind, my lad—whilst I live thou shalt never want a friend to stand by thee!" Wolf would wag his tail, look wistfully in his master's face, and, if dogs can feel pity, I verily believe he reciprocated the sentiment with all his heart.

In a long ramble of the kind on a fine autumnal day Rip had unconsciously scrambled to one of the highest parts of the Kaatskill Mountains. He was after his favorite sport of squirrel-shooting, and the still solitudes had echoed and re-echoed with the reports of his gun. Panting and fatigued, he threw himself, late in the afternoon, on a green knoll, covered with mountain-herbage, that crowned the brow of a precipice. From an opening between the trees he could overlook all the lower country for many a mile of rich woodland. He saw at a distance the lordly Hudson, far, far below him, moving on its silent but majestic course, with the reflection of a purple cloud or the sail of a lagging bark here and there sleeping on its glassy bosom, and at last losing itself in the huge highlands.

On the other side he looked down into a deep mountain-glen, wild, lonely, and shagged, the bottom filled with fragments from the impending cliffs, and scarcely lighted by the reflected rays of the setting sun. For some time Rip lay musing on this scene; evening was gradually advancing; the mountains began to throw their long blue shadows over the valleys; he saw that it would be dark long before he could reach the village, and he heaved a heavy sigh when he thought of encountering the terrors of Dame Van Winkle.

As he was about to descend, he heard a voice from a distance hallooing, "Rip Van Winkle! Rip Van Winkle!" He looked round, but could see nothing but a crow winging its solitary flight across the mountain. He thought his fancy must have deceived him, and turned again to descend, when he heard the same cry ring through the still evening air: "Rip Van Winkle! Rip Van Winkle!"—at the same time Wolf bristled up his back, and giving a low growl, skulked to his master's side, looking fearfully down into the glen. Rip now felt a vague apprehension stealing over him; he looked anxiously in the same direction, and perceived a strange figure slowly toiling up the rocks and bending under the weight of something he carried on his back. He was surprised to see any human being in this lonely and unfrequented place, but supposing it to be some one of the neighborhood in need of his assistance, he hastened down to yield it.

On nearer approach he was still more surprised at the singularity of the stranger's appearance. He was a short, square-built old fellow, with thick bushy hair and a grizzled beard. His dress was of the antique Dutch fashion—a cloth jerkin strapped round the waist—several pair of breeches, the outer one of ample volume, decorated with rows of buttons down the sides, and bunches at the knees. He bore on his shoulder a stout keg that seemed full of liquor, and made signs for Rip to approach and assist him with the load. Though rather shy and distrustful of this new acquaintance, Rip complied with his usual alacrity; and, mutually relieving each other, they clambered up a narrow gully, apparently the dry bed of a mountain-torrent. As they ascended, Rip every now and then heard long rolling peals, like distant thunder, that seemed to issue out of a deep ravine, or rather cleft, between lofty rocks, toward which their rugged path conducted. He paused for an instant, but supposing it to be the muttering of one of those transient thunder-showers which often take place in mountain-heights, he proceeded. Passing through the ravine, they came to a hollow, like a small amphitheatre, surrounded by perpendicular precipices, over the brinks of which impending trees shot their branches, so that you only caught glimpses of the azure sky and the bright evening cloud. During the whole time Rip and his companion had labored on in silence; for though the former marvelled greatly what could be the object of carrying a keg of liquor up this wild mountain, yet there was something strange and incomprehensible about the unknown that inspired awe and checked familiarity.

On entering the amphitheatre, new objects of wonder presented themselves. On a level spot in the centre was a company of odd-looking personages playing at nine-pins. They were dressed in a quaint outlandish fashion: some wore short doublets, others jerkins, with long knives in their belts, and most of them had enormous breeches, of similar style with that of the guide's. Their visages, too, were peculiar: one had a large head, broad face, and small piggish eyes: the face of another seemed to consist entirely of nose, and was surmounted by a white sugar-loaf hat, set off with a little red cock's tail. They all had beards, of various shapes and colors. There was one who seemed to be the commander. He was a stout old gentleman, with a weatherbeaten countenance; he wore a laced doublet, broad belt and hanger, high-crowned hat and feather, red stockings, and high-heeled shoes with roses in them. The whole group reminded Rip of the figures in an old Flemish painting in the parlor of Dominie Van Shaick, the village parson, and which had been brought over from Holland at the time of the settlement.

What seemed particularly odd to Rip was, that though these folks were evidently amusing themselves, yet they maintained the gravest faces, the most mysterious silence, and were, withal, the most melancholy party of pleasure he had ever witnessed. Nothing interrupted the stillness of the scene but the noise of the balls, which, whenever they were rolled, echoed along the mountains like rumbling peals of thunder.

As Rip and his companion approached them they suddenly desisted from their play, and stared at him with such fixed statue-like gaze, and such strange, uncouth, lack-lustre countenances, that his heart turned within him and his knees smote together. His companion now emptied the contents of the keg into large flagons, and made signs to him to wait upon the company. He obeyed with fear and trembling; they quaffed the liquor in profound silence, and then returned to their game.

By degrees Rip's awe and apprehension subsided. He even ventured, when no eye was fixed upon him, to taste the beverage, which he found had much of the flavor of excellent Hollands. He was naturally a thirsty soul, and was soon tempted to repeat the draught. One taste provoked another, and he reiterated his visits to the flagon so often that at length his senses were overpowered, his eyes swam in his head, his head gradually declined, and he fell into a deep sleep.

On waking, he found himself on the green knoll whence he had first seen the old man of the glen. He rubbed his eyes —it was a bright sunny morning. The birds were hopping and twittering among the bushes, and the eagle was wheeling aloft and breasting the pure mountain-breeze. "Surely," thought Rip, "I have not slept here all night." He recalled the occurrences before he fell asleep. The strange man with a keg of liquor—the mountain-ravine—the wild retreat among the rocks—the woebegone party at nine-pins—the flagon. "Oh, that flagon! that wicked flagon!" thought Rip—"what excuse shall I make to Dame Van Winkle?"

He looked round for his gun, but in place of the clean, well-oiled fowling-piece, he found an old firelock lying by him, the barrel encrusted with rust, the lock falling off, and the stock worm-eaten. He now suspected that the grave roysterers of the mountain had put a trick upon him, and, having dosed him with liquor, had robbed him of his gun. Wolf, too, had disappeared, but he might have strayed away after a squirrel or partridge. He whistled after him and shouted his name, but all in vain; the echoes repeated his whistle and shout, but no dog was to be seen.

He determined to revisit the scene of the last evening's gambol, and if he met with any of the party to demand his dog and gun. As he rose to walk, he found himself stiff in the joints and wanting in his usual activity. "These mountain-beds do not agree with me," thought Rip, "and if this frolic should lay me up with a fit of the rheumatism, I shall have a blessed time with Dame Van Winkle. With some difficulty he got down into the glen: he found the gully up which he and his companion had ascended the preceding evening; but to his astonishment a mountain-stream was now foaming down it, leaping from rock to rock and filling the glen with babbling murmurs. He, however, made shift to scramble up its sides, working his toilsome way through thickets of birch, sassafras, and witch-hazel, and sometimes tripped up or entangled by the wild grape-vines that twisted their coils or tendrils from tree to tree and spread a kind of net-work in his path.

At length he reached to where the ravine had opened through the cliffs to the amphitheatre; but no traces of such opening remained. The rocks presented a high impenetrable wall, over which the torrent came tumbling in a sheet of feathering foam, and fell into a broad, deep basin, black from the shadows of the surrounding forest. Here, then, poor Rip was brought to a stand. He again called and whistled after his dog; he was only answered by the cawing of a flock of idle crows sporting high in air about a dry tree that overhung a sunny precipice, and who, secure in their elevation, seemed to look down and scoff at the poor man's perplexities. What was to be done? The morning was passing away, and Rip felt famished for want of his breakfast. He grieved to give up his dog and gun; he dreaded to meet his wife; but it would not do to starve among the mountains. He shook his head, shouldered the rusty firelock, and with a heart full of trouble and anxiety turned his steps homeward.

As he approached the village he met a number of people but none whom he knew, which somewhat surprised him, for he had thought himself acquainted with every one in the country round. Their dress, too, was of a different fashion from that to which he was accustomed. They all stared at him with equal marks of surprise, and whenever they cast their eyes upon him, invariably stroked their chins. The constant recurrence of this gesture induced Rip, involuntarily, to do the same, when, to his astonishment, he found his beard had grown a foot long!

He had now entered the skirts of the village. A troop of strange children ran at his heels, hooting after him and pointing at his gray beard. The dogs, too, not one of which he recognized for an old acquaintance, barked at him as he passed. The very village was altered; it was larger and more populous. There were rows of houses which he had never seen before, and those which had been his familiar haunts had disappeared. Strange names were over the doors—strange faces at the windows—everything was strange. His mind now misgave him; he began to doubt whether both he and the world around him were not bewitched. Surely this was his native village, which he had left but the day before. There stood the Kaatskill Mountains—there ran the silver Hudson at a distance—there was every hill and dale precisely as it had always been. Rip was sorely perplexed. "That flagon last night," thought he, "has addled my poor head sadly."

It was with some difficulty that he found the way to his own house, which he approached with silent awe, expecting every moment to hear the shrill voice of Dame Van Winkle. He found the house gone to decay—the roof fallen in, the windows shattered, and the doors off the hinges. A half-starved dog that looked like Wolf was skulking about it. Rip called him by name, but the cur snarled, showed his teeth, and passed on. This was an unkind cut indeed. "My very dog," sighed poor Rip, "has forgotten me!"

He entered the house, which, to tell the truth, Dame Van Winkle had always kept in neat order. It was empty, forlorn, and apparently abandoned. This desolateness overcame all his connubial fears—he called loudly for his wife and children—the lonely chambers rang for a moment with his voice, and then all again was silence.

He now hurried forth, and hastened to his old resort, the village inn, but it too was gone. A large rickety wooden building stood in its place, with great gaping windows, some of them broken and mended with old hats and petticoats, and

over the door was painted, "The Union Hotel, by Jonathan Doolittle." Instead of the great tree that used to shelter the quiet little Dutch inn of yore, there now was reared a tall, naked pole, with something on the top that looked like a red nightcap, and from it was fluttering a flag, on which was a singular assemblage of stars and stripes. All this was strange and incomprehensible. He recognized on the sign, however, the ruby face of King George, under which he had smoked so many a peaceful pipe; but even this was singularly metamorphosed. The red coat was changed for one of blue and buff, a sword was held in the hand instead of a sceptre, the head was decorated with a cocked hat, and underneath was painted in large characters, GENERAL WASHINGTON.

There was, as usual, a crowd of folk about the door, but none that Rip recollected. The very character of the people seemed changed. There was a busy, bustling, disputatious tone about it, instead of the accustomed phlegm and drowsy tranquility. He looked in vain for the sage Nicholas Vedder, with his broad face, double chin, and fair long pipe, uttering clouds of tobacco-smoke instead of idle speeches; or Van Bummel, the schoolmaster, doling forth the contents of an ancient newspaper. In place of these, a lean, bilious-looking fellow, with his pockets full of handbills, was haranguing vehemently about rights of citizens—elections—members of Congress —liberty—Bunker's Hill—heroes of Seventy-six—and other words, which were a perfect Babylonish jargon to the bewildered Van Winkle.

The appearance of Rip, with his long, grizzled beard, his rusty fowling-piece, his uncouth dress, and an army of women and children at his heels, soon attracted the attention of the tavern politicians. They crowded round him, eyeing him from head to foot with great curiosity. The orator bustled up to him, and, drawing him partly aside, inquired "on which side he voted." Rip stared in vacant stupidity. Another short but busy little fellow pulled him by the arm, and, rising on tiptoe, inquired in his ear, "Whether he was Federal or Democrat." Rip was equally at a loss to comprehend the question; when a knowing, self-important old gentleman, in a sharp cocked hat, made his way through the crowd, putting them to the right and left with his elbows as he passed, and, planting himself before Van Winkle, with one arm akimbo, the other resting on his cane, his keen eyes and sharp hat penetrating, as it were, into his very soul, demanded in an austere tone, "What brought him to the election with a gun on his shoulder and a mob at his heels, and whether he meant to breed a riot in the village?"—"Alas! gentlemen," cried Rip, somewhat dismayed, "I am a poor, quiet man, a native of the place, and a loyal subject of the king, God bless him!"

Here a general shout burst from the bystanders—"A Tory! a Tory! a spy! a refugee! hustle him! away with him!" It was with great difficulty that the self-important man in the cocked hat restored order; and, having assumed a tenfold austerity of brow, demanded again of the unknown culprit what he came there for, and whom he was seeking. The poor man humbly assured him that he meant no harm, but merely came there in search of some of his neighbors, who used to keep about the tavern.

"Well—who are they?—name them."

Rip bethought himself a moment, and inquired, "Where's Nicholas Vedder?"

There was a silence for a little while, when an old man replied in a thin piping voice, "Nicholas Vedder! why, he is dead and gone these eighteen years! There was a wooden tombstone in the churchyard that used to tell all about him, but that's rotten and gone too."

"Where's Brom Dutcher?"

"Oh, he went off to the army in the beginning of the war; some say he was killed at the storming of Stony Point—others say he was drowned in a squall at the foot of Antony's Nose. I don't know —he never came back again."

"Where's Van Bummel, the schoolmaster?"

"He went off to the wars too, was a great militia general, and is now in Congress."

Rip's heart died away at hearing of these sad changes in his home and friends and finding himself thus alone in the world. Every answer puzzled him, too, by treating of such enormous lapses of time, and of matters which he could not understand: war—Congress—Stony Point. He had no courage to ask after any more friends, but cried out in despair, "Does nobody here know Rip Van Winkle?"

"Oh, Rip Van Winkle!" exclaimed two or three. "Oh, to be sure! that's Rip Van Winkle yonder, leaning against the tree."

Rip looked and beheld a precise counterpart of himself as he went up the mountain, apparently as lazy, and certainly as ragged. The poor fellow was now completely confounded. He doubted his own identity, and whether he was himself or another man. In the midst of his bewilderment the man in the cocked hat demanded who he was, and what was his name.

"God knows," exclaimed he, at his wit's end; "I'm not myself—I'm somebody else —that's me yonder—no—that's somebody else got into my shoes. I was myself last night, but I fell asleep on the mountain, and they've changed my gun, and everything's changed, and I'm changed, and I can't tell what's my name, or who I am!"

The bystanders began now to look at each other, nod, wink significantly, and tap their fingers against their foreheads. There was a whisper, also, about securing the gun and keeping the old fellow from doing mischief, at the very suggestion of which the self-important man in the cocked hat retired with some precipitation. At this critical moment a fresh comely woman passed through the throng to get a peep at the gray-bearded man. She had a chubby child in her arms, which, frightened at his looks, began to cry. "Hush, Rip," cried she, "hush, you little fool! the old man won't hurt you." The name of the child, the air of the mother, the tone of her voice, all awakened a train of recollections in his mind. "What is your name, my good woman?" asked he.

"Judith Gardenier."

"And your father's name?"

"Ah, poor man! Rip Van Winkle was his name, but it's twenty years since he went away from home with his gun, and never has been heard of since—his dog came home without him; but whether he shot himself, or was carried away by the Indians, nobody can tell. I was then but a little girl."

Rip had but one question more to ask, but he put it with a faltering voice:

"Where's your mother?"

"Oh, she, too, had died but a short time since; she broke a blood-vessel in a fit of passion at a New England peddler."

There was a drop of comfort, at least, in this intelligence. This honest man could contain himself no longer. He caught his daughter and her child in his arms. "I am your father!" cried he— "young Rip Van Winkle once—old Rip Van Winkle now! Does nobody know poor Rip Van Winkle?"

All stood amazed, until an old woman, tottering out from among the crowd, put her hand to her brow, and peering under it in his face for a moment, exclaimed, "Sure enough! it is Rip Van Winkle—it is himself! Welcome home again, old neighbor! Why, where have you been these twenty long years?"

Rip's story was soon told, for the whole twenty years had been to him but as one night. The neighbors stared when they heard it; some were seen to wink at each other, and put their tongues in their cheeks: and the self-important man in the cocked hat, who, when the alarm was over, had returned to the field, screwed down the corners of his mouth and shook his head—upon which there was a general shaking of the head throughout the assemblage.

It was determined, however, to take the opinion of old Peter Vanderdonk, who was seen slowly advancing up the road. He was a descendant of the historian of that name, who wrote one of the earliest accounts of the province. Peter was the most ancient inhabitant of the village, and well versed in all the wonderful events and traditions of the neighborhood. He recollected Rip at once, and corroborated his story in the most satisfactory manner. He assured the company that it was a fact, handed down from his ancestor the historian, that the Kaatskill Mountains had always been haunted by strange beings. That it was affirmed that the great Hendrick Hudson, the first discoverer of the river and country, kept a kind of vigil there every twenty years, with his crew of the Half-moon, being permitted in this way to revisit the scenes of his enterprise and keep a guardian eye upon the river and the great city called by his name. That his father had once seen them in their old Dutch dresses playing at nine-pins in a hollow of the mountain; and that he himself had heard, one summer afternoon, the sound of their balls, like distant peals of thunder.

To make a long story short, the company broke up, and returned to the more important concerns of the election. Rip's daughter took him home to live with her; she had a snug, well-furnished house, and a stout cheery farmer for a husband, whom Rip recollected for one of the urchins that used to climb upon his back. As to Rip's son and heir, who was the ditto of himself, seen leaning against the tree, he was employed to work on the farm, but evinced an hereditary disposition to attend to anything else but his business.

Rip now resumed his old walks and habits; he soon found many of his former cronies, though all rather the worse for the wear and tear of time; and preferred making friends among the rising generation, with whom he soon grew into great favor.

Having nothing to do at home, and being arrived at that happy age when a man can be idle with impunity, he took his place once more on the bench at the inn-door, and was reverenced as one of the patriarchs of the village and a chronicle of the old times "before the war." It was some time before he could get into the regular track of gossip, or could be made to comprehend the strange events that had taken place during his torpor. How that there had been a Revolutionary war— that the country had thrown off the yoke of old England—and that, instead of being a subject of his Majesty George the Third, he was now a free citizen of the

United States. Rip, in fact, was no politician; the changes of states and empires made but little impression on him; but there was one species of despotism under which he had long groaned, and that was —petticoat government. Happily, that was at an end; he had got his neck out of the yoke of matrimony, and could go in and out whenever he pleased, without dreading the tyranny of Dame Van Winkle. Whenever her name was mentioned, however, he shook his head, shrugged his shoulders, and cast up his eyes; which might pass either for an expression of resignation to his fate or joy at his deliverance.

He used to tell his story to every stranger that arrived at Mr. Doolittle's hotel. He was observed, at first, to vary on some points every time he told it, which was, doubtless, owing to his having so recently awaked. It at last settled down precisely to the tale I have related, and not a man, woman, or child in the neighborhood but knew it by heart. Some always pretended to doubt the reality of it, and insisted that Rip had been out of his head, and that this was one point on which he always remained flighty. The old Dutch inhabitants, however, almost universally gave it full credit. Even to this day they never hear a thunderstorm of a summer afternoon about the Kaatskill but they say Hendrick Hudson and his crew are at their game of nine-pins; and it is a common wish of all henpecked husbands in the neighborhood, when life hangs heavy on their hands, that they might have a quieting draught out of Rip Van Winkle's flagon.

[1819]

QUESTIONS FOR STUDY

1. *How does Irving go about establishing the mood of magic and fantasy which helps prepare the reader for Rip's strange experience in the mountains?*
2. *It has been said that Rip Van Winkle is Benjamin Franklin turned inside out. To what extent is Rip's character a burlesque of traditional American values? What contrasting values does Dame Van Winkle represent?*
3. *Can "Rip Van Winkle" be characterized as a case study of arrested development and adolescent behavior?*
4. *How does Rip avert the potential loss of his identity? How does that potential loss become a positive gain?*
5. *How does Irving illustrate Rip's confusion and disorientation as he returns to the village? What prevents the scene from being wholly comic and humorous?*

SHIRLEY JACKSON

The Lottery

THE MORNING of June 27th was clear and sunny, with the fresh warmth of a full-summer day; the flowers were blossoming profusely and the grass was richly green. The people of the village began to gather in the square, between the post office and the bank, around ten o'clock; in some towns there were so many people that the lottery took two days and had to be started on June 26th, but in this village, where there were only about three hundred people, the whole lottery took less than two hours, so it could begin at ten o'clock in the morning and still be through in time to allow the villagers to get home for noon dinner.

The children assembled first, of course. School was recently over for the summer, and the feeling of liberty sat uneasily on most of them; they tended to gather together quietly for a while before they broke into boisterous play, and their talk was still of the classroom and the teacher, of books and reprimands. Bobby Martin had already stuffed his pockets full of stones, and the other boys soon followed his example, selecting the smoothest and roundest stones; Bobby and Harry Jones and Dickie Delacroix— the villagers pronounced this name "Dellacroy"—eventually made a great pile of stones in one corner of the square and guarded it against the raids of the other boys. The girls stood aside, talking among themselves, looking over their shoulders at the boys, and the very small children rolled in the dust or clung to the hands of their older brothers or sisters.

Soon the men began to gather, surveying their own children, speaking of planting and rain, tractors and taxes. They stood together, away from the pile of stones in the corner, and their jokes were quiet and they smiled rather than laughed. The women, wearing faded house dresses and sweaters, came shortly after their menfolk. They greeted one another and exchanged bits of gossip as they went to join their husbands. Soon the women, standing by their husbands, began to call to their children, and the children came reluctantly, having to be called four or five times. Bobby Martin ducked under his mother's grasping hand and ran, laughing, back to the pile of stones. His father spoke up sharply, and Bobby came quickly and took his place between his father and his oldest brother.

The lottery was conducted—as were the square dances, the teen-age club, the Halloween program—by Mr. Summers, who had time and energy to devote to civic activities. He was a round-faced, jovial man and he ran the coal business, and people were sorry for him, because he had no children and his wife was a scold. When he arrived in the square, carrying the black wooden box, there was a murmur of conversation among the villagers, and he waved and called, "Little late today, folks." The postmaster, Mr. Graves, followed him, carrying a three-legged stool, and the stool was put in the center of the square and Mr. Summers set the black box down on it. The villagers kept their distance, leaving a space between themselves and the stool, and when Mr. Summers said, "Some of you fellows want to give me a hand?" there was a hesitation before two men, Mr. Martin and his oldest son, Baxter, came forward to hold the box steady on the stool while Mr. Summers stirred up the papers inside it.

The original paraphernalia for the lottery had been lost long ago, and the black box now resting on the stool had been put into use even before Old Man Warner, the oldest man in town, was born. Mr. Summers spoke frequently to the villagers about making a new box, but no one liked to upset even as much tradition as was represented by the black box. There was a story that the present box had been made with some pieces of the box that had preceded it, the one that had been constructed when the first people settled down to make a village here. Every year, after the lottery, Mr. Summers began talking again about a new box, but every year the subject was allowed to fade off without anything's being done. The black box grew shabbier each year; by now it was no longer completely black but splintered badly along one side to show the original wood color, and in some places faded or stained.

Mr. Martin and his oldest son, Baxter, held the black box securely on the stool until Mr. Summers had stirred the papers thoroughly with his hand. Because so much of the ritual had been forgotten or discarded, Mr. Summers had been successful in having slips of paper substituted for the chips of wood that had been used for generations. Chips of wood, Mr. Summers had argued, had been all very well when the village was tiny, but now that the population was more than three hundred and likely to keep on growing, it was necessary to use something that would fit more easily into the black box. The night before the lottery, Mr. Summers and Mr. Graves made up the slips of paper and put them in the box, and it was then taken to the safe of Mr. Summers' coal company and locked up until Mr. Summers was ready to take it to the square next morning. The rest of the year, the box was put away, sometimes one place, sometimes another; it had spent one year in Mr. Graves's barn and another year underfoot in the post office, and sometimes it was set on a shelf in the Martin grocery and left there.

There was a great deal of fussing to be done before Mr. Summers declared the lottery open. There were the lists to make up—of heads of families, heads of households in each family, members of each household in each family. There was the proper swearing-in of Mr. Summers by the postmaster, as the official of the lottery; at one time, some people remembered, there had been a recital of some sort, performed by the official of the lottery, a perfunctory, tuneless chant that had been rattled off duly each year; some people believed that the official of the lottery used to stand just so when he said or sang it, others believed that he was supposed to walk among the people, but years and years ago this part of the ritual had been allowed to lapse. There had been, also, a ritual salute, which the official of the lottery had had to use in addressing each person who came up to draw from the box, but this also had changed with time, until now it was felt necessary only for the official to speak to each person approaching. Mr. Summers was very good at all this; in his clean white shirt and blue jeans, with one hand resting carelessly on the black box, he seemed very proper and important as he talked interminably to Mr. Graves and the Martins.

Just as Mr. Summers finally left off talking and turned to the assembled villagers, Mrs. Hutchinson came hurriedly along the path to the square, her sweater thrown over her shoulders, and slid into place in the back of the crowd. "Clean forgot what day it was," she said to Mrs. Delacroix, who stood next to her, and they both laughed softly. "Thought my old man was out back stacking wood," Mrs. Hutchinson went on, "and then I looked out the window and the kids was gone, and then I remembered it was the twenty-seventh and came a-running." She dried her hands on her apron, and Mrs. Delacroix said, "You're in time, though. They're still talking away up there."

Mrs. Hutchinson craned her neck to see through the crowd and found her husband and children standing near the front. She tapped Mrs. Delacroix on the arm as a farewell and began to make her way through the crowd. The people separated good-humoredly to let her through; two or three people said, in voices just loud enough to be heard across the crowd, "Here comes your Missus, Hutchinson," and "Bill, she made it after all." Mrs. Hutchinson reached her husband, and Mr. Summers, who had been waiting, said cheerfully, "Thought we were going to have to get on without you, Tessie." Mrs. Hutchinson said, grinning, "Wouldn't have me leave m'dishes in the sink, now, would you, Joe?," and soft laughter ran through the crowd as the people stirred back into position after Mrs. Hutchinson's arrival.

"Well, now," Mr. Summers said soberly, "guess we better get started, get this over with, so's we can go back to work. Anybody ain't here?"

"Dunbar," several people said. "Dunbar, Dunbar."

Mr. Summers consulted his list. "Clyde Dunbar," he said. "That's right. He's broke his leg, hasn't he? Who's drawing for him?"

"Me, I guess," a woman said, and Mr. Summers turned to look at her. "Wife draws for her husband," Mr. Summers said. "Don't you have a grown boy to do it for you, Janey?" Although Mr. Summers and everyone else in the village knew the answer perfectly well, it was the business of the official of the lottery to ask such questions formally. Mr. Summers waited with an expression of polite interest while Mrs. Dunbar answered.

"Horace's not but sixteen yet," Mrs. Dunbar said regretfully. "Guess I gotta fill in for the old man this year."

"Right," Mr. Summers said. He made a note on the list he was holding. Then he asked, "Watson boy drawing this year?"

A tall boy in the crowd raised his hand. "Here," he said. "I'm drawing for m'mother and me." He blinked his eyes nervously and ducked his head as several voices in the crowd said things like "Good fellow, Jack," and "Glad to see your mother's got a man to do it."

"Well," Mr. Summers said, "guess that's everyone. Old Man Warner make it?"

"Here," a voice said, and Mr. Summers nodded.

A sudden hush fell on the crowd as

Mr. Summers cleared his throat and looked at the list. "All ready?" he called. "Now, I'll read the names—heads of families first—and the men come up and take a paper out of the box. Keep the paper folded in your hand without looking at it until everyone has had a turn. Everything clear?"

The people had done it so many times that they only half listened to the directions; most of them were quiet, wetting their lips, not looking around. Then Mr. Summers raised one hand high and said, "Adams." A man disengaged himself from the crowd and came forward. "Hi, Steve," Mr. Summers said, and Mr. Adams said, "Hi, Joe." They grinned at one another humorlessly and nervously. Then Mr. Adams reached into the black box and took out a folded paper. He held it firmly by one corner as he turned and went hastily back to his place in the crowd, where he stood a little apart from his family, not looking down at his hand.

"Allen," Mr. Summers said. "Anderson. . . . Bentham."

"Seems like there's no time at all between lotteries any more," Mrs. Delacroix said to Mrs. Graves in the back row. "Seems like we got through with the last one only last week."

"Time sure goes fast," Mrs. Graves said.

"Clark. . . . Delacroix."

"There goes my old man," Mrs. Delacroix said. She held her breath while her husband went forward.

"Dunbar," Mr. Summers said, and Mrs. Dunbar went steadily to the box while one of the women said, "Go on, Janey," and another said, "There she goes."

"We're next," Mrs. Graves said. She watched while Mr. Graves came around from the side of the box, greeted Mr. Summers gravely, and selected a slip of paper from the box. By now, all through the crowd there were men holding the small folded papers in their large hands, turning them over and over nervously. Mrs. Dunbar and her two sons stood together, Mrs. Dunbar holding the slip of paper.

"Harburt. . . . Hutchinson."

"Get up there, Bill," Mrs. Hutchinson said, and the people near her laughed.

"Jones."

"They do say," Mr. Adams said to Old Man Warner, who stood next to him, "that over in the north village they're talking of giving up the lottery."

Old Man Warner snorted. "Pack of crazy fools," he said. "Listening to the young folks, nothing's good enough for *them*. Next thing you know, they'll be wanting to go back to living in caves, nobody work any more, live *that* way for a while. Used to be a saying about 'Lottery in June, corn be heavy soon.' First thing you know, we'd all be eating stewed chickweed and acorns. There's *always* been a lottery," he added petulantly. "Bad enough to see young Joe Summers up there joking with everybody."

"Some places have already quit lotteries," Mrs. Adams said.

"Nothing but trouble in *that*," Old Man Warner said stoutly. "Pack of young fools."

"Martin." And Bobby Martin watched his father go forward. "Overdyke. . . . Percy."

"I wish they'd hurry," Mrs. Dunbar said to her older son. "I wish they'd hurry."

"They're almost through," her son said.

"You get ready to run tell Dad," Mrs. Dunbar said.

Mr. Summers called his own name and then stepped forward precisely and selected a slip from the box. Then he called, "Warner."

"Seventy-seventh year I been in the lottery," Old Man Warner said as he went through the crowd. "Seventy-seventh time."

"Watson." The tall boy came awkwardly through the crowd. Someone said, "Don't be nervous, Jack," and Mr. Summers said, "Take your time, son."

"Zanini."

After that, there was a long pause, a breathless pause, until Mr. Summers, holding his slip of paper in the air, said, "All right, fellows." For a minute, no one moved, and then all the slips of paper were opened. Suddenly, all the women began to speak at once, saying, "Who is it?," "Who's got it?," "Is it the Dunbars?," "It it the Watsons?" Then the voices began to say, 'It's Hutchinson. It's Bill," "Bill Hutchinson's got it."

"Go tell you father," Mrs. Dunbar said to her older son.

People began to look around to see the Hutchinsons. Bill Hutchinson was standing quiet, staring down at the paper in his hand. Suddenly, Tessie Hutchinson shouted to Mr. Summers, "You didn't give him time enough to take any paper he wanted. I saw you. It wasn't fair!"

"Be a good sport, Tessie," Mrs. Delacroix called, and Mrs. Graves said, "All of us took the same chance."

"Shut up, Tessie," Bill Hutchinson said.

"Well, everyone," Mr. Summers said, "that was done pretty fast, and now we've got to be hurrying a little more to get done in time." He consulted his next list. "Bill," he said, "you draw for the Hutchinson family. You got any other households in the Hutchinsons?"

"There's Don and Eva," Mrs. Hutchinson yelled. "Make *them* take their chance!"

"Daughters draw with their husbands' families, Tessie," Mr. Summers said gently. "You know that as well as anyone else."

"It wasn't *fair*," Tessie said.

"I guess not, Joe," Bill Hutchinson said regretfully. "My daughter draws with her husband's family, that's only fair. And I've got no other family except the kids."

"Then, as far as drawing for families is concerned, it's you," Mr. Summers said in explanation, "and as far as drawing for households is concerned, that's you, too. Right?"

"Right," Bill Hutchinson said.

"How many kids, Bill?" Mr. Summers asked formally.

"Three," Bill Hutchinson said. "There's Bill, Jr., and Nancy, and little Dave. And Tessie and me."

"All right, then," Mr. Summers said. "Harry, you got their tickets back?"

Mr. Graves nodded and held up the slips of paper. "Put them in the box, then," Mr. Summers directed. "Take Bill's and put it in."

"I think we ought to start over," Mrs. Hutchinson said, as quietly as she could. "I tell you it wasn't *fair*. You didn't give him time enough to choose. *Every*body saw that."

Mr. Graves had selected the five slips and put them in the box, and he dropped all the papers but those onto the ground, where the breeze caught them and lifted them off.

"Listen, everybody," Mrs. Hutchinson was saying to the people around her.

"Ready, Bill?" Mr. Summers asked, and Bill Hutchinson, with one quick glance around at his wife and children, nodded.

"Remember," Mr. Summers said, "take the slips and keep them folded until each person has taken one. Harry, you help little Dave." Mr. Graves took the hand of the little boy, who came willingly with him up to the box. "Take a paper out of the box, Davy," Mr. Summers said. Davy put his hand into the box and laughed. "Take just *one* paper," Mr. Summers said. "Harry, you hold it for him." Mr. Graves took the child's hand and removed the folded paper from the tight fist and held it while little Dave stood next to him and looked up at him wonderingly.

"Nancy next," Mr. Summers said. Nancy was twelve, and her school friends breathed heavily as she went forward, switching her skirt, and took a slip daintily from the box. "Bill, Jr.," Mr. Summers said, and Billy, his face red and his feet overlarge, nearly knocked the box over as he got a paper out. "Tessie," Mr. Summers said. She hesitated for a minute, looking around defiantly, and then set her lips and went up to the box. She snatched a paper out and held it behind her.

"Bill," Mr. Summers said, and Bill Hutchinson reached into the box and felt around, bringing his hand out at last with the slip of paper in it.

The crowd was quiet. A girl whispered, "I hope it's not Nancy," and the sound of the whisper reached the edges of the crowd.

"It's not the way it used to be," Old Man Warner said clearly. "People ain't the way they used to be."

"All right," Mr. Summers said. "Open the papers. Harry, you open little Dave's."

Mr. Graves opened the slip of paper and there was a general sigh through the crowd as he held it up and everyone could see that it was blank. Nancy and Bill, Jr., opened theirs at the same time, and both beamed and laughed, turning around to the crowd and holding their slips of paper above their heads.

"Tessie," Mr. Summers said. There was a pause, and then Mr. Summers looked at Bill Hutchinson, and Bill unfolded his paper and showed it. It was blank.

"It's Tessie," Mr. Summers said, and his voice was hushed. "Show us her paper, Bill."

Bill Hutchinson went over to his wife and forced the slip of paper out of her hand. It had a black spot on it, the black spot Mr. Summers had made the night before with the heavy pencil in the coal-company office. Bill Hutchinson held it up, and there was a stir in the crowd.

"All right, folks," Mr. Summers said. "Let's finish quickly."

Although the villagers had forgotten the ritual and lost the original black box, they still remembered to use stones. The pile of stones the boys had made earlier was ready; there were stones on the ground with the blowing scraps of paper that had come out of the box. Mrs. Delacroix selected a stone so large she had to pick it up with both hands and turned to Mrs. Dunbar. "Come on," she said. "Hurry up."

Mr. Dunbar had small stones in both hands, and she said, gasping for breath, "I can't run at all. You'll have to go ahead and I'll catch up with you."

The children had stones already, and someone gave little Davy Hutchinson a few pebbles.

Tessie Hutchinson was in the center

of a cleared space by now, and she held her hands out desperately as the villagers moved in on her. "It isn't fair," she said. A stone hit her on the side of the head.

Old Man Warner was saying, "Come on, come on, everyone." Steve Adams was in the front of the crowd of villagers, with Mrs. Graves beside him.

"It isn't fair, it isn't right," Mrs. Hutchinson screamed, and then they were upon her.

[1948]

QUESTIONS FOR STUDY

1. *Discuss the ways in which point of view, characterization, plot, setting, atmosphere, and style each contribute to the story's effectiveness. Which of these elements are most highly developed and which are least developed? Why?*

2. *What seems to have been the original purpose of the lottery?*

3. *How do the attitudes toward ritual and tradition of Mr. Summers, Old Man Warner, and the Adamses differ? What do their attitudes have in common? What comments about tradition and ritual does the author herself seem to be making?*

4. *What is the significance of Tessie's final scream, " 'It isn't fair, it isn't right' "? What aspect of the lottery does she explicitly challenge; what aspect goes unquestioned?*

5. *Many readers have commented upon the hypnotic power and emotional impact of the story. How does Shirley Jackson manage to achieve this effect? Do you feel that your response has been unfairly manipulated in any way?*

6. *Some critics insist that the story has an added symbolic or allegorical dimension. Do you agree? If so, what is Shirley Jackson trying to tell us about ourselves?*

HENRY JAMES

The Beast in the Jungle

I

WHAT determined the speech that startled him in the course of their encounter scarcely matters, being probably but some words spoken by himself quite without intention—spoken as they lingered and slowly moved together after their renewal of acquaintance. He had been conveyed by friends an hour or two before to the house at which she was staying; the party of visitors at the other house, of whom he was one, and thanks to whom it was his theory, as always, that he was lost in the crowd, had been invited over to luncheon. There had been after luncheon much dispersal, all in the interest of the original motive, a view of Weatherend itself and the fine things, intrinsic features, pictures, heirlooms, treasures of all the arts, that made the place almost famous; and the great rooms were so numerous that guests could wander at their will, hang back from the principal group and in cases where they took such matters with the least seriousness give themselves up to mysterious appreciations and measurements. There were persons to be observed, singly or in couples, bending toward objects in out-of-the-way corners with their hands on their knees and their heads nodding quite as with the emphasis of an excited sense of smell. When they were two they either mingled their sounds of ecstasy or melted into silences of even deeper import, so that there were aspects of the occasion that gave it for Marcher much the air of the "look round," previous to a sale highly advertised, that excites or quenches, as may be, the dream of acquisition. The dream of acquisition at Weatherend would have had to be wild indeed, and John Marcher found himself, among such suggestions, disconcerted almost equally by the presence of those who knew too much and by that of those who knew nothing.

The great rooms caused so much poetry and history to press upon him that he needed some straying apart to feel in a proper relation with them, though this impulse was not, as happened, like the gloating of some of his companions, to be compared to the movements of a dog sniffing a cupboard. It had an issue promptly enough in a direction that was not to have been calculated.

It led, briefly, in the course of the October afternoon, to his closer meeting with May Bartram, whose face, a reminder, yet not quite a remembrance, as they sat much separated at a very long table, had begun merely by troubling him rather pleasantly. It affected him as the sequel of something of which he had lost the beginning. He knew it, and for the time quite welcomed it, as a continuation, but didn't know what it continued, which was an interest or an amusement the greater as he was also somehow aware—yet without a direct sign from her—that the young woman herself hadn't lost the thread. She hadn't lost it, but she wouldn't give it back to him, he saw, without some putting forth of his hand for it; and he not only saw that, but saw several things more, things odd enough in the light of the fact that at the moment some accident of grouping brought them face to face he was still merely fumbling with the idea that any contact between them in the past would have had no importance. If it had had no importance he scarcely knew why his actual impression of her should so seem to have so much; the answer to which, however, was that in such a life as they all appeared to be leading for the moment one could but take things as they came. He was satisfied, without in the least being able to say why, that this young lady might roughly have ranked in the house as a poor relation; satisfied also that she was not there on a brief visit, but was more or less a part of the establishment—

almost a working, a remunerated part. Didn't she enjoy at periods a protection that she paid for by helping, among other services, to show the place and explain it, deal with the tiresome people, answer questions about the dates of the building, the styles of the furniture, the authorship of the pictures, the favourite haunts of the ghost? It wasn't that she looked as if you could have given her shillings—it was impossible to look less so. Yet when she finally drifted toward him, distinctly handsome, though ever so much older—older than when he had seen her before—it might have been as an effect of her guessing that she had, within the couple of hours, devoted more imagination to her than to all the others put together, and had thereby penetrated to a kind of truth that the others were too stupid for. She *was* there on harder terms than any one; she was there as a consequence of things suffered, one way and another, in the interval of years; and she remembered him very much as she was remembered—only a good deal better.

By the time they at last thus came to speech they were alone in one of the rooms—remarkable for a fine portrait over the chimney-place—out of which their friends had passed, and the charm of it was that even before they had spoken they had practically arranged with each other to stay behind for talk. The charm, happily, was in other things too—partly in there being scarce a spot at Weatherend without something to stay behind for. It was in the way the autumn day looked into the high windows as it waned; the way the red light, breaking at the close from under a low sombre sky, reached out in a long shaft and played over old wainscots, old tapestry, old gold, old colour. It was most of all perhaps in the way she came to him as if, since she had been turned on to deal with the simpler sort, he might, should he choose to keep the whole thing down, just take her mild attention for a part of her general business. As soon as he heard her voice, however, the gap was filled up and the missing link supplied; the slight irony he divined in her attitude lost its advantage. He almost jumped at it to get there before her.

"I met you years and years ago in Rome. I remember all about it." She confessed to disappointment—she had been so sure he didn't; and to prove how well he did he began to pour forth the particular recollections that popped up as he called for them. Her face and her voice, all at his service now, worked the miracle—the impression operating like the torch of a lamplighter who touches into flame, one by one, a long row of gas-jets. Marcher flattered himself the illumination was brilliant, yet he was really still more pleased on her showing him, with amusement, that in his haste to make everything right he had got most things rather wrong. It hadn't been at Rome—it had been at Naples; and it hadn't been eight years before—it had been more nearly ten. She hadn't been, either, with her uncle and aunt, but with her mother and her brother; in addition to which it was not with the Pembles *he* had been, but with the Boyers, coming down in their company from Rome—a point on which she insisted, a little to his confusion, and as to which she had her evidence in hand. The Boyers she had known, but didn't know the Pembles, though she had heard of them, and it was the people he was with who had made them acquainted. The incident of the thunderstorm that had raged round them with such violence as to drive them for refuge into an excavation—this incident had not occurred at the Palace of the Cæsars, but at Pompeii, on an occasion when they had been present there at an important find.

He accepted her amendments, he enjoyed her corrections, though the moral of them was, she pointed out, that he *really* didn't remember the least thing about her; and he only felt it as a drawback that when all was made strictly historic there didn't appear much of anything left. They lingered together still, she neglecting her office—for from the moment he was so clever she had no proper right to him—and both neglecting the house, just waiting as to see if a memory or two more wouldn't again breathe on them. It hadn't taken them many minutes, after all, to put down on the table, like the cards of a pack, those that constituted their respective hands; only what came out was that the pack was unfortunately not perfect—that the past, invoked, invited, encouraged, could give them, naturally, no more than it had. It had made them anciently meet—her at twenty, him at twenty-five; but nothing was so strange, they seemed to say to each other, as that, while so occupied, it hadn't done a little more for them. They looked at each other as with the feeling of an occasion missed; the present would have been so much better if the other, in the far distance, in the foreign land, hadn't been so stupidly meagre. There weren't apparently, all counted, more than a dozen little old things that had succeeded in coming to pass between them; trivialities of youth, simplicities of freshness, stupidities of ignorance, small possible germs, but too deeply buried—too deeply (didn't it seem?) to sprout after so many years. Marcher could only feel he ought to have rendered her some service—saved her from a capsized boat in the Bay or at least recovered her dressing-bag, filched from her cab in the streets of Naples by a lazzarone with a stiletto. Or it would have been nice if he could have been taken with fever all alone at his hotel, and she could have come to look after him, to write to his people, to drive him out in convalescence. *Then* they would be in possession of the something or other that their actual show seemed to lack. It yet somehow presented itself, this show, as too good to be spoiled; so that they were reduced for a few minutes more to wondering a little helplessly why—since they seemed to know a certain number of the same people—their reunion had been so long averted. They didn't use that name for it, but their delay from minute to minute to join the others was a kind of confession that they didn't quite want it to be a failure. Their attempted supposition of reasons for their not having met but showed how little they knew of each other. There came in fact a moment when Marcher felt a positive pang. It was vain to pretend she was an old friend, for all the communities were wanting, in spite of which it was as an old friend that he saw she would have suited him. He had new

ones enough—was surrounded with them for instance on the stage of the other house; as a new one he probably wouldn't have so much as noticed her. He would have liked to invent something, get her to make-believe with him that some passage of a romantic or critical kind *had* originally occurred. He was really almost reaching out in imagination—as against time—for something that would do, and saying to himself that if it didn't come this sketch of a fresh start would show for quite awkwardly bungled. They would separate, and now for no second or no third chance. They would have tried and not succeeded. Then it was, just at the turn, as he afterwards made it out to himself, that, everything else failing, she herself decided to take up the case and, as it were, save the situation. He felt as soon as she spoke that she had been consciously keeping back what she said and hoping to get on without it; a scruple in her that immensely touched him when, by the end of three or four minutes more, he was able to measure it. What she brought out, at any rate, quite cleared the air and supplied the link—the link it was so odd he should frivolously have managed to lose.

"You know you told me something I've never forgotten and that again and again has made me think of you since; it was that tremendously hot day when we went to Sorrento, across the bay, for the breeze. What I allude to was what you said to me, on the way back, as we sat under the awning of the boat enjoying the cool. Have you forgotten?"

He had forgotten and was even more surprised than ashamed. But the great thing was that he saw in this no vulgar reminder of any "sweet" speech. The vanity of women had long memories, but she was making no claim on him of a compliment or a mistake. With another woman, a totally different one, he might have feared the recall possibly even some imbecile "offer." So, in having to say that he had indeed forgotten, he was conscious rather of a loss than of a gain; he already saw an interest in the matter of her mention. "I try to think—but I give it up. Yet I remember the Sorrento day."

"I'm not very sure you do," May Bartram after a moment said; "and I'm not very sure I ought to want you to. It's dreadful to bring a person back at any time to what he was ten years before. If you've lived away from it," she smiled, "so much the better."

"Ah if *you* haven't why should I?" he asked.

"Lived away, you mean, from what I myself was?"

"From what *I* was. I was of course an ass," Marcher went on; "but I would rather know from you just the sort of ass I was than—from the moment you have something in your mind—not know anything."

Still, however, she hesitated. "But if you've completely ceased to be that sort—?"

"Why I can then all the more bear to know. Besides, perhaps I haven't."

"Perhaps. Yet if you haven't," she added, "I should suppose you'd remember. Not indeed that *I* in the least connect with my impression the invidious name you use. If I had only thought you foolish," she explained, "the thing I speak of wouldn't so have remained with me. It was about yourself." She waited as if it might come to him; but as, only meeting her eyes in wonder, he gave no sign, she burnt her ships. "Has it ever happened?"

Then it was that, while he continued to stare, a light broke for him and the blood slowly came to his face, which began to burn with recognition. "Do you mean I told you—?" But he faltered, lest what came to him shouldn't be right, lest he should only give himself away.

"It was something about yourself that it was natural one shouldn't forget—that is if one remembered you at all. That's why I ask you," she smiled, "if the thing you then spoke of has ever come to pass?"

Oh then he saw, but he was lost in wonder and found himself embarrassed. This, he also saw, made her sorry for him, as if her allusion had been a mistake. It took him but a moment, however, to feel it hadn't been, much as it had been a surprise. After the first little shock of it her knowledge on the contrary began, even if rather strangely, to taste sweet to him. She was the only other person in the world then who would have it, and she had had it all these years, while the fact of his having so breathed his secret had unaccountably faded from him. No wonder they couldn't have met as if nothing had happened. "I judge," he finally said, "that I know what you mean. Only I had strangely enough lost any sense of having taken you so far into my confidence."

"Is it because you've taken so many others as well?"

"I've taken nobody. Not a creature since then."

"So that I'm the only person who knows?"

"The only person in the world."

"Well," she quickly replied, "I myself have never spoken. I've never, never repeated of you what you told me." She looked at him so that he perfectly believed her. Their eyes met over it in such a way that he was without a doubt. "And I never will."

She spoke with an earnestness that, as if almost excessive, put him at ease about her possible derision. Somehow the whole question was a new luxury to him—that is from the moment she was in possession. If she didn't take the sarcastic view she clearly took the sympathetic, and that was what he had had, in all the long time, from no one whomsoever. What he felt was that he couldn't at present have begun to tell her, and yet could profit perhaps exquisitely by the accident of having done so of old. "Please don't then. We're just right as it is."

"Oh I am," she laughed, "if you are!" To which she added: "Then you do still feel in the same way?"

It was impossible he shouldn't take to himself that she was really interested, though it all kept coming as perfect surprise. He had thought of himself so long as abominably alone, and lo he wasn't alone a bit. He hadn't been, it appeared, for an hour—since those moments on the Sorrento boat. It was *she* who had been, he seemed to see as he looked at her—she who had been made so by the graceless fact of his lapse of fidelity. To tell her what he had told her—what had it been but to ask something of her? something that she had given, in her charity, without his having, by a remembrance, by a return of the spirit, failing another encounter, so much as thanked her. What he had asked of her had been simply at first not to laugh at him. She had beautifully not done so for ten years, and she was not doing so now. So he had endless gratitude to make up. Only for that he must see just how he had figured to her. "What, exactly, was the account I gave—?"

"Of the way you did feel? Well, it was very simple. You said you had had from your earliest time, as the deepest thing within you, the sense of being kept for something rare and strange, possibly prodigious and terrible, that was sooner or later to happen to you, that you had in your bones the foreboding and the conviction of, and that would perhaps overwhelm you."

"Do you call that very simple?" John Marcher asked.

She thought a moment. "It was perhaps because I seemed, as you spoke, to understand it."

"You do understand it?" he eagerly asked.

Again she kept her kind eyes on him. "You still have the belief?"

"Oh!" he exclaimed helplessly. There was too much to say.

"Whatever it's to be," she clearly made out, "it hasn't yet come."

He shook his head in complete surrender now. "It hasn't yet come. Only, you know, it isn't anything I'm to *do*, to achieve in the world, to be distinguished or admired for. I'm not such an ass as *that*. It would be much better, no doubt, if I were."

"It's to be something you're merely to suffer?"

"Well, say to wait for—to have to meet, to face, to see suddenly break out in my life; possibly destroying all further consciousness, possibly annihilating me; possibly, on the other hand, only altering everything, striking at the root of all my world and leaving me to the consequences, however they shape themselves."

She took this in, but the light in her eyes continued for him not to be that of mockery. "Isn't what you describe perhaps but the expectation—or at any rate the sense of danger, familiar to so many people—of falling in love?"

John Marcher wondered. "Did you ask me that before?"

"No—I wasn't so free-and-easy then. But it's what strikes me now."

"Of course," he said after a moment, "it strikes you. Of course it strikes *me*. Of course what's in store for me may be no more than that. The only thing is," he went on, "that I think if it had been that I should by this time know."

"Do you mean because you've *been* in love?" And then as he looked at her in silence: "You've been in love, and it hasn't meant such a cataclysm, hasn't proved the great affair?"

"Here I am, you see. It hasn't been overwhelming."

"Then it hasn't been love," said May Bartram.

"Well, I at least thought it was. I took it for that—I've taken it till now. It was agreeable, it was delightful, it was miserable," he explained. "But it wasn't strange. It wasn't what *my* affair's to be."

"You want something all to yourself —something that nobody else knows or *has* known?"

"It isn't a question of what I 'want'— God knows I don't want anything. It's only a question of the apprehension that haunts me—that I live with day by day."

He said this so lucidly and consistently that he could see it further impose itself. If she hadn't been interested before she'd have been interested now. "Is it a sense of coming violence?"

Evidently now too again he liked to talk of it. "I don't think of it as—when it does come—necessarily violent. I only think of it as natural and as of course above all unmistakeable. I think of it simply as *the* thing. *The* thing will of itself appear natural."

"Then how will it appear strange?"

Marcher bethought himself. "It won't —to *me*."

"To whom then?"

"Well," he replied, smiling at last, "say to you."

"Oh then I'm to be present?"

"Why you *are* present—since you know."

"I see." She turned it over. "But I mean at the catastrophe."

At this, for a minute, their lightness gave way to their gravity; it was as if the long look they exchanged held them together. "It will only depend on yourself— if you'll watch with me."

"Are you afraid?" she asked.

"Don't leave me *now*," he went on.

"Are you afraid?" she repeated.

"Do you think me simply out of my mind?" he pursued instead of answering. "Do I merely strike you as a harmless lunatic?"

"No," said May Bartram. "I understand you. I believe you."

"You mean you feel how my obsession —poor old thing!—may correspond to some possible reality?"

"To some possible reality."

"Then you *will* watch with me?"

She hesitated, then for the third time put her question. "Are you afraid?"

"Did I tell you I was—at Naples?"

"No, you said nothing about it."

"Then I don't know. And I should *like* to know," said John Marcher. "You'll tell me yourself whether you think so. If you'll watch with me you'll see."

"Very good then." They had been moving by this time across the room, and at the door, before passing out, they paused as for the full wind-up of their understanding. "I'll watch with you," said May Bartram.

II

The fact that she "knew"—knew and yet neither chaffed him nor betrayed him —had in a short time begun to constitute between them a goodly bond, which became more marked when, within the year that followed their afternoon at Weatherend, the opportunities for meeting multiplied. The event that thus promoted these occasions was the death of the ancient lady her great-aunt, under whose wing, since losing her mother, she had to such an extent found shelter, and who, though but the widowed mother of the new successor to the property, had succeeded— thanks to a high tone and a high temper —in not forfeiting the supreme position

at the great house. The deposition of this personage arrived but with her death, which, followed by many changes, made in particular a difference for the young woman in whom Marcher's expert attention had recognised from the first a dependent with a pride that might ache though it didn't bristle. Nothing for a long time had made him easier than the thought that the aching must have been much soothed by Miss Bartram's now finding herself able to set up a small home in London. She had acquired property, to an amount that made that luxury just possible, under her aunt's extremely complicated will, and when the whole matter began to be straightened out, which indeed took time, she let him know that the happy issue was at last in view. He had seen her again before that day, both because she had more than once accompanied the ancient lady to town and because he had paid another visit to the friends who so conveniently made of Weatherend one of the charms of their own hospitality. These friends had taken him back there; he had achieved there again with Miss Bartram some quiet detachment; and he had in London succeeded in persuading her to more than one brief absence from her aunt. They went together, on these latter occasions, to the National Gallery and the South Kensington Museum, where, among vivid reminders, they talked of Italy at large— not now attempting to recover, as at first, the taste of their youth and their ignorance. That recovery, the first day at Weatherend, had served its purpose well, had given them quite enough; so that they were, to Marcher's sense, no longer hovering about the headwaters of their stream, but had felt their boat pushed sharply off and down the current.

They were literally afloat together; for our gentleman this was marked, quite as marked as that the fortunate cause of it was just the buried treasure of her knowledge. He had with his own hands dug up this little hoard, brought to light—that is to within reach of the dim day constituted by their discretions and privacies—the object of value the hiding-place of which he had, after putting it into the ground himself, so strangely, so long forgotten. The rare luck of his having again just stumbled on the spot made him indifferent to any other question; he would doubtless have devoted more time to the odd accident of his lapse of memory if he hadn't been moved to devote so much to the sweetness, the comfort, as he felt, for the future, that this accident itself had helped to keep fresh. It had never entered into his plan than any one should "know," and mainly for the reason that it wasn't in him to tell any one. That would have been impossible, for nothing but the amusement of a cold world would have waited on it. Since, however, a mysterious fate had opened his mouth betimes, in spite of him, he would count that a compensation and profit by it to the utmost. That the right person *should* know tempered the asperity of his secret more even than his shyness had permitted him to imagine; and May Bartram was clearly right, because—well, because there she was. Her knowledge simply settled it; he would have been sure enough by this time had she been wrong. There was that in his situation, no doubt, that disposed him too much to see her as a mere confidant, taking all her light for him from the fact—the fact only—of her interest in his predicament; from her mercy, sympathy, seriousness, her consent not to regard him as the funniest of the funny. Aware, in fine, that her price for him was just in her giving him this constant sense of his being admirably spared, he was careful to remember that she had also a life of her own, with things that might happen to *her*, things that in friendship one should likewise take account of. Something fairly remarkable came to pass with him, for that matter, in this connexion—something represented by a certain passage of his consciousness, in the suddenest way, from one extreme to the other.

He had thought himself, so long as nobody knew, the most disinterested person in the world, carrying his concentrated burden, his perpetual suspense, ever so quietly, holding his tongue about it, giving others no glimpse of it nor of its effect upon his life, asking of them no allowance and only making on his side all those that were asked. He hadn't disturbed people with the queerness of their having to know a haunted man, though he had had moments of rather special temptation on hearing them say they were forsooth "unsettled." If they were as unsettled as he was—he who had never been settled for an hour in his life—they would know what it meant. Yet it wasn't, all the same, for him to make them, and he listened to them civilly enough. This was why he had such good—though possibly such rather colourless—manners; this was why, above all, he could regard himself, in a greedy world, as decently—as in fact perhaps even a little sublimely—unselfish. Our point is accordingly that he valued this character quite sufficiently to measure his present danger of letting it lapse, against which he promised himself to be much on his guard. He was quite ready, none the less, to be selfish just a little, since surely no more charming occasion for it had come to him. "Just a little," in a word, was just as much as Miss Bartram, taking one day with another, would let him. He never would be in the least coercive, and would keep well before him the lines on which consideration for her—the very highest—ought to proceed. He would thoroughly establish the heads under which her affairs, her requirements, her peculiarities —he went so far as to give them the latitude of that name—would come into their intercourse. All this naturally was a sign of how much he took the intercourse itself for granted. There was nothing more to be done about *that*. It simply existed; had sprung into being with her first penetrating question to him in the autumn light there at Weatherend. The real form it should have taken on the basis that stood out large was the form of their marrying. But the devil in this was that the very basis itself put marrying out of the question. His conviction, his apprehension, his obsession, in short, wasn't a privilege he could invite a woman to share; and that consequence of it was precisely what was the matter with him. Something or other lay in wait for him, amid the twists and the turns of the months and the years, like a crouching beast in the jungle. It signified little whether the crouching beast were destined to slay him or to be slain. The definite point was the inevitable spring of the creature; and the definite lesson from that was that a man of feeling didn't cause himself to be accompanied by a lady on a tiger-hunt. Such was the image under which he had ended by figuring his life.

They had at first, none the less, in the scattered hours spent together, made no allusion to that view of it; which was a sign he was handsomely alert to give that he didn't expect, that he in fact didn't care, always to be talking about it. Such a feature in one's outlook was really like a hump on one's back. The difference it made every minute of the day existed quite independently of discussion. One discussed of course *like* a hunchback, for there was always, if nothing else, the hunchback face. That remained, and she was watching him; but people watched best, as a general thing, in silence, so that such would be predominantly the manner of their vigil. Yet he didn't want, at the same time, to be tense and solemn; tense and solemn was what he imagined he too much showed for with other people. The thing to be, with the one person who knew, was easy and natural—to make the reference rather than be seeming to avoid it, to avoid it rather than be seeming to make it, and to keep it, in any case, familiar, facetious even, rather than pedantic and portentous. Some such consideration as the latter was doubtless in his mind for instance when he wrote pleasantly to Miss Bartram that perhaps the great thing he had so long felt as in the lap of the gods was no more than this circumstance, which touched him so nearly, of her acquiring a house in London. It was the first allusion they had yet again made, needing any other hitherto so little; but when she replied, after having given him the news, that she was by no means satisfied with such a trifle as the climax to so special a suspense, she almost set him wondering if she hadn't even a larger conception of singularity for him than he had for himself. He was at all events destined to become aware little by little, as time went by, that she was all the while looking at his life, judging it, measuring it, in the light of the thing she knew, which grew to be at last, with the consecration of the years, never mentioned between them save as "the real truth" about him. That had always been his own form of reference to it, but she adopted the form so quietly that, looking back at the end of a period, he knew there was no moment at which it was traceable that she had, as he might say, got inside his idea, or exchanged the attitude of beautifully indulging for that of still more beautifully believing him.

It was always open to him to accuse her of seeing him but as the most harmless of maniacs, and this, in the long run—since it covered so much ground—was his easiest description of their friendship. He had a screw loose for her, but she liked him in spite of it and was practically, against the rest of the world, his kind wise keeper, unremunerated but fairly amused and, in the absence of other near ties, not disreputably occupied. The rest of the world of course thought him queer, but she, she only, knew how, and above all why, queer; which was precisely what enabled her to dispose the concealing veil in the right folds. She took his gaiety from him—since it had to pass with them for gaiety—as she took everything else; but she certainly so far justified by her unerring touch his finer sense of the degree to which he had ended by convincing her. *She* at least never spoke of the secret of his life except as "the real truth about you," and she had in fact a wonderful way of making it seem, as such, the secret of her own life too. That was in fine how he so constantly felt her as allowing for him; he couldn't on the whole call it anything else. He allowed for himself, but she, exactly, allowed still more; partly because, better placed for a sight of the matter, she traced his unhappy perversion through reaches of its course into which he could scarce follow it. He knew how he felt, but, besides knowing that, she knew how he *looked* as well; he knew each of the things of importance he was insidiously kept from doing, but she could add up the amount they made, understand how much, with a lighter weight on his spirit, he might have done, and thereby establish how, clever as he was, he fell short. Above all she was in the secret of the difference between the forms he went through—those of his little office under Government, those of caring for his modest patrimony, for his library, for his garden in the country, for the people in London whose invitations he accepted and repaid —and the detachment that reigned beneath them and that made of all behaviour, all that could in the least be called behaviour, a long act of dissimulation. What it had come to was that he wore a mask painted with the social simper, out of the eye-holes of which there looked eyes of an expression not in the least matching the other features. This the stupid world, even after years, had never more than half-discovered. It was only May Bartram who had, and she achieved, by an art indescribable, the feat of at once —or perhaps it was only alternately— meeting the eyes from in front and mingling her own vision, as from over his shoulder, with their peep through the apertures.

So while they grew older together she did watch with him, and so she let this association give shape and colour to her own existence. Beneath *her* forms as well detachment had learned to sit, and behaviour had become for her, in the social sense, a false account of herself. There was but one account of her that would have been true all the while and that she could give straight to nobody, least of all to John Marcher. Her whole attitude was a virtual statement, but the perception of that only seemed called to take its place for him as one of the many things necessarily crowded out of his consciousness. If she had moreover, like himself, to make sacrifices to their real truth, it was to be granted that her compensation might have affected her as more prompt and more natural. They had long periods, in this London time, during which, when they were together, a stranger might have listened to them without in the least pricking up his ears; on the other hand the real truth was equally liable at any moment to rise to the surface, and the auditor would then have wondered indeed what they were talking about. They had from an

early hour made up their mind that society was, luckily, unintelligent, and the margin allowed them by this had fairly become one of their commonplaces. Yet there were still moments when the situation turned almost fresh—usually under the effect of some expression drawn from herself. Her expressions doubtless repeated themselves, but her intervals were generous. "What saves us, you know, is that we answer so completely to so usual an appearance: that of the man and woman whose friendship has become such a daily habit—or almost—as to be at last indispensable." That for instance was a remark she had frequently enough had occasion to make, though she had given it at different times different developments. What we are especially concerned with is the turn it happened to take from her one afternoon when he had come to see her in honour of her birthday. This anniversary had fallen on a Sunday, at a season of thick fog and general outward gloom; but he had brought her his customary offering, having known her now long enough to have established a hundred small traditions. It was one of his proofs to himself, the present he made her on her birthday, that he hadn't sunk into real selfishness. It was mostly nothing more than a small trinket, but it was always fine of its kind, and he was regularly careful to pay for it more than he thought he could afford. "Our habit saves you at least, don't you see? because it makes you, after all, for the vulgar, indistinguishable from other men. What's the most inveterate mark of men in general? Why the capacity to spend endless time with dull women—to spend it I won't say without being bored, but without minding that they are, without being driven off at a tangent by it; which comes to the same thing. I'm your dull woman, a part of the daily bread for which you pray at church. That covers your tracks more than anything."

"And what covers yours?" asked Marcher, whom his dull woman could mostly to this extent amuse. "I see of course what you mean by your saving me, in this way and that, so far as other people are concerned—I've seen it all along.

Only what is it that saves *you?* I often think, you know, of that."

She looked as if she sometimes thought of that too, but rather in a different way. "Where other people, you mean, are concerned?"

"Well, you're really so in with me, you know—as a sort of result of my being so in with yourself. I mean of my having such an immense regard for you, being so tremendously mindful of all you've done for me. I sometimes ask myself if it's quite fair. Fair I mean to have so involved and —since one may say it—interested you. I almost feel as if you hadn't really had time to do anything else."

"Anything else but be interested?" she asked. "Ah what else does one ever want to be? If I've been 'watching' with you, as we long ago agreed I was to do, watching's always in itself an absorption."

"Oh certainly," John Marcher said, "if you hadn't had your curiosity—! Only doesn't it sometimes come to you as time goes on that your curiosity isn't being particularly repaid?"

May Bartram had a pause. "Do you ask that, by any chance, because you feel at all that yours isn't? I mean because you have to wait so long."

Oh he understood what she meant! "For the thing to happen that never does happen? For the beast to jump out? No, I'm just where I was about it. It isn't a matter as to which I can *choose*, I can decide for a change. It isn't one as to which there *can* be a change. It's in the lap of the gods. One's in the hands of one's law—there one is. As to the form the law will take, the way it will operate, that's its own affair."

"Yes," Miss Bartram replied; "of course one's fate's coming, of course it *has* come in its own form and its own way, all the while. Only, you know, the form and the way in your case were to have been—well, something so exceptional and, as one may say, so particularly *your* own."

Something in this made him look at her with suspicion. "You say 'were to *have* been,' as if in your heart you had begun to doubt."

"Oh!" she vaguely protested.

"As if you believed," he went on, "that nothing will now take place."

She shook her head slowly but rather inscrutably. "You're far from my thought."

He continued to look at her. "What then is the matter with you?"

"Well," she said after another wait, "the matter with me is simply that I'm more sure than ever my curiosity, as you call it, will be but too well repaid."

They were frankly grave now; he had got up from his seat, had turned once more about the little drawing-room to which, year after year, he brought his inevitable topic; in which he had, as he might have said, tasted their intimate community with every sauce, where every object was as familiar to him as the things of his own house and the very carpets were worn with his fitful walk very much as the desks in the old counting-houses are worn by the elbows of generations of clerks. The generations of his nervous moods had been at work there, and the place was the written history of his whole middle life. Under the impression of what his friend had just said he knew himself, for some reason, more aware of these things; which made him, after a moment, stop again before her. "Is it possibly that you've grown afraid?"

"Afraid?" He thought, as she repeated the word, that his question had made her, a little, change colour; so that, lest he should have touched on a truth, he explained very kindly: "You remember that that was what you asked *me* long ago— that first day at Weatherend."

"Oh yes, and you told me you didn't know—that I was to see for myself. We've said little about it since, even in so long a time."

"Precisely," Marcher interposed— "quite as if it were too delicate a matter for us to make free with. Quite as if we might find, on pressure, that I *am* afraid. For then," he said, "we shouldn't, should we? quite know what to do."

She had for the time no answer to this question. "There have been days when I thought you were. Only, of course," she added, "there have been days when we have thought almost anything."

"Everything. Oh!" Marcher softly groaned as with a gasp, half-spent, at the face, more uncovered just then than it had been for a long while, of the imagination always with them. It had always had its incalculable moments of glaring out, quite as with the very eyes of the very Beast, and, used as he was to them, they could still draw from him the tribute of a sigh that rose from the depths of his being. All they had thought, first and last, rolled over him; the past seemed to have been reduced to mere barren speculation. This in fact was what the place had just struck him as so full of—the simplification of everything but the state of suspense. That remained only by seeming to hang in the void surrounding it. Even his original fear, if fear it had been, had lost itself in the desert. "I judge, however," he continued, "that you see I'm not afraid now."

"What I see, as I make it out, is that you've achieved something almost unprecedented in the way of getting used to danger. Living with it so long and so closely you've lost your sense of it; you know it's there, but you're indifferent, and you cease even, as of old, to have to whistle in the dark. Considering what the danger is," May Bartram wound up, "I'm bound to say I don't think your attitude could well be surpassed."

John Marcher faintly smiled. "It's heroic?"

"Certainly—call it that."

It was what he would have liked indeed to call it. "I *am* then a man of courage?"

"That's what you were to show me."

He still, however, wondered. "But doesn't the man of courage know what he's afraid of—or *not* afraid of? I don't know *that*, you see. I don't focus it. I can't name it. I only know I'm exposed."

"Yes, but exposed—how shall I say?— so directly. So intimately. That's surely enough."

"Enough to make you feel then—as what we may call the end and the upshot of our watch—that I'm not afraid?"

"You're not afraid. But it isn't," she said, "the end of our watch. That is it isn't the end of yours. You've everything still to see."

"Then why haven't *you*?" he asked. He had had, all along, to-day, the sense of her keeping something back, and he still had it. As this was his first impression of that it quite made a date. The case was the more marked as she didn't at first answer; which in turn made him go on. "You know something I don't." Then his voice, for that of a man of courage, trembled a little. "You know what's to happen." Her silence, with the face she showed, was almost a confession—it made him sure. "You know, and you're afraid to tell me. It's so bad that you're afraid I'll find out."

All this might be true, for she did look as if, unexpectedly to her, he had crossed some mystic line that she had secretly drawn round her. Yet she might, after all, not have worried; and the real climax was that he himself, at all events, needn't. "You'll never find out."

III

It was all to have made, none the less, as I have said, a date; which came out in the fact that again and again, even after long intervals, other things that passed between them wore in relation to this hour but the character of recalls and results. Its immediate effect had been indeed rather to lighten insistence—almost to provoke a reaction; as if their topic had dropped by its own weight and as if moreover, for that matter, Marcher had been visited by one of his occasional warnings against egotism. He had kept up, he felt, and very decently on the whole, his consciousness of the importance of not being selfish, and it was true that he had never sinned in that direction without promptly enough trying to press the scales the other way. He often repaired his fault, the season permitting, by inviting his friend to accompany him to the opera; and it not infrequently thus happened that, to show he didn't wish her to have but one sort of food for her mind, he was the cause of her appearing there with him a dozen nights in the month. It even happened that, seeing her home at such times, he occasionally went in with her to finish, as he called it, the evening, and, the better to make his point, sat down to the frugal but always careful little supper that awaited his pleasure. His point was made, he thought, by his not eternally insisting with her on himself; made for instance, at such hours, when it befell that, her piano at hand and each of them familiar with it, they went over passages of the opera together. It chanced to be on one of these occasions, however, that he reminded her of her not having answered a certain question he had put to her during the talk that had taken place between them on her last birthday. "What is it that saves *you?*"—saved her, he meant, from that appearance of variation from the usual human type. If he had practically escaped remark, as she pretended, by doing, in the most important particular, what most men do—find the answer to life in patching up an alliance of a sort with a woman no better than himself—how had she escaped it, and how could the alliance, such as it was, since they must suppose it had been more or less noticed, have failed to make her rather positively talked about?

"I never said," May Bartram replied, "that it hadn't made me a good deal talked about."

"Ah well then you're not 'saved.' "

"It hasn't been a question for me. If you've had your woman I've had," she said, "my man."

"And you mean that makes you all right?"

Oh it was always as if there were so much to say! "I don't know why it shouldn't make me—humanly, which is what we're speaking of—as right as it makes you."

"I see," Marcher returned. " 'Humanly,' no doubt, as showing that you're living for something. Not, that is, just for me and my secret."

May Bartram smiled. "I don't pretend it exactly shows that I'm not living for you. It's my intimacy with you that's in question."

He laughed as he saw what she meant. "Yes, but since, as you say, I'm only, so far as people make out, ordinary, you're —aren't you?—no more than ordinary either. You help me to pass for a man like another. So if I *am*, as I understand you, you're not compromised. Is that it?"

She had another of her waits, but she spoke clearly enough. "That's it. It's all that concerns me—to help you to pass for a man like another."

He was careful to acknowledge the remark handsomely. "How kind, how beautiful, you are to me! How shall I ever repay you?"

She had her last grave pause, as if there might be a choice of ways. But she chose. "By going on as you are."

It was into this going on as he was that they relapsed, and really for so long a time that the day inevitably came for a further sounding of their depths. These depths, constantly bridged over by a structure firm enough in spite of its lightness and of its occasional oscillation in the somewhat vertiginous air, invited on occasion, in the interest of their nerves, a dropping of the plummet and a measurement of the abyss. A difference had been made moreover, once for all, by the fact that she had all the while not appeared to feel the need of rebutting his charge of an idea within her that she didn't dare to express —a charge uttered just before one of the fullest of their later discussions ended. It had come up for him then that she "knew" something and that what she knew was bad—too bad to tell him. When he had spoken of it as visibly so bad that she was afraid he might find it out, her reply had left the matter too equivocal to be let alone and yet, for Marcher's special sensibility, almost too formidable again to touch. He circled about it at a distance that alternately narrowed and widened and that still wasn't much affected by the consciousness in him that there was nothing she could "know," after all, any better than he did. She had no source of knowledge he hadn't equally—except of course that she might have finer nerves. That was what women had where they were interested; they made out things, where people were concerned, that the people often couldn't have made out for themselves. Their nerves, their sensibility, their imagination, were conductors and revealers, and the beauty of May Bartram was in particular that she had given herself so to his case. He felt in these days what, oddly enough, he had never felt before, the growth of a dread of losing her by some catastrophe—some catastrophe that yet wouldn't at all be *the* catastrophe: partly because she had almost of a sudden begun to strike him as more useful to him than ever yet, and partly by reason of an appearance of uncertainty in her health, coincident and equally new. It was characteristic of the inner detachment he had hitherto so successfully cultivated and to which our whole account of him is a reference, it was characteristic that his complications, such as they were, had never yet seemed so as at this crisis to thicken about him, even to the point of making him ask himself if he were, by any chance, of a truth, within sight or sound, within touch or reach, within the immediate jurisdiction, of the thing that waited.

When the day came, as come it had to, that his friend confessed to him her fear of a deep disorder in her blood, he felt somehow the shadow of a change and the chill of a shock. He immediately began to imagine aggravations and disasters, and above all to think of her peril as the direct menace for himself of personal privation. This indeed gave him one of those partial recoveries of equanimity that were agreeable to him—it showed him that what was still first in his mind was the loss she herself might suffer. "What if she should have to die before knowing, before seeing—?" It would have been brutal, in the early stages of her trouble, to put that question to her; but it had immediately sounded for him to his own concern, and the possibility was what most made him sorry for her. If she did "know," moreover, in the sense of her having had some—what should he think?—mystical irresistible light, this would make the matter not better, but worse, inasmuch as her original adoption of his own curiosity had quite become the basis of her life. She had been living to see what would be to be seen, and it would quite lacerate her to have to give up before the accomplishment of the vision. These reflexions, as I say, quickened his generosity; yet, make them as he might, he saw himself, with the lapse of the period, more and more disconcerted. It lapsed for him with a strange steady sweep, and the oddest oddity was that it gave him, independently of the threat of much inconvenience, almost the only positive surprise his career, if career it could be called, had yet offered him. She kept the house as she had never done; he had

to go to her to see her—she could meet him nowhere now, though there was scarce a corner of their loved old London in which she hadn't in the past, at one time or another, done so; and he found her always seated by her fire in the deep old-fashioned chair she was less and less able to leave. He had been struck one day, after an absence exceeding his usual measure, with her suddenly looking much older to him than he had ever thought of her being; then he recognised that the suddenness was all on his side—he had just simply and suddenly noticed. She looked older because inevitably, after so many years, she *was* old, or almost; which was of course true in still greater measure of her companion. If she was old, or almost, John Marcher assuredly was, and yet it was her showing of the lesson, not his own, that brought the truth home to him. His surprises began here; when once they had begun they multiplied; they came rather with a rush: it was as if, in the oddest way in the world, they had all been kept back, sown in a thick cluster, for the late afternoon of life, the time at which for people in general, the unexpected has died out.

One of them was that he should have caught himself—for he *had* so done— *really* wondering if the great accident would take form now as nothing more than his being condemned to see this charming woman, this admirable friend, pass away from him. He had never so unreservedly qualified her as while confronted in thought with such a possibility; in spite of which there was small doubt for him that as answer to his long riddle the mere effacement of even so fine a feature of his situation would be an abject anticlimax. It would represent, as connected with his past attitude, a drop of dignity under the shadow of which his existence could only become the most grotesque of failures. He had been far from holding it a failure—long as he had waited for the appearance that was to make it a success. He had waited for quite another thing, not for such a thing as that. The breath of his good faith came short, however, as he recognised how long he had waited, or how long at least his companion had. That she, at all events, might be recorded as having waited in vain—this affected him sharply, and all the more because of his at first having done little more than amuse himself with the idea. It grew more grave as the gravity of her condition grew, and the state of mind it produced in him, which he himself ended by watching as if it had been some definite disfigurement of his outer person, may pass for another of his surprises. This conjoined itself still with another, the really stupefying consciousness of a question that he would have allowed to shape itself had he dared. What did everything mean—what, that is, did *she* mean, she and her vain waiting and her probable death and the soundless admonition of it all—unless that, at this time of day, it was simply, it was overwhelmingly too late? He had never at any stage of his queer consciousness admitted the whisper of such a correction; he had never till within these last few months been so false to his conviction as not to hold that what was to come to him had time, whether *he* struck himself as having it or not. That at last, at last, he certainly hadn't it, to speak of, or had it but in the scantiest measure—such, soon enough, as things went with him, became the inference with which his old obsession had to reckon: and this it was not helped to do by the more and more confirmed appearance that the great vagueness casting the long shadow in which he had lived had, to attest itself, almost no margin left. Since it was in Time that he was to have met his fate, so it was in Time that his fate was to have acted; and as he waked up to the sense of no longer being young, which was exactly the sense of being stale, just as that, in turn, was the sense of being weak, he waked up to another matter beside. It all hung together; they were subject, he and the great vagueness, to an equal and indivisible law. When the possibilities themselves had accordingly turned stale, when the secret of the gods had grown faint, had perhaps even quite evaporated, that, and that only, was failure. It wouldn't have been failure to be bankrupt, dishonoured, pilloried, hanged; it was failure not to be anything. And so, in the dark valley into which his path had taken its unlooked-for twist, he wondered not a little as he groped. He didn't care what awful crash might overtake him, with what ignominy or what monstrosity he might yet be associated—since he wasn't after all too utterly old to suffer—if it would only be decently proportionate to the posture he had kept, all his life, in the threatened presence of it. He had but one desire left—that he shouldn't have been "sold."

IV

Then it was that, one afternoon, while the spring of the year was young and new she met all in her own way his frankest betrayal of these alarms. He had gone in late to see her, but evening hadn't settled and she was presented to him in that long fresh light of waning April days which affects us often with a sadness sharper than the greyest hours of autumn. The week had been warm, the spring was supposed to have begun early, and May Bartram sat, for the first time in the year, without a fire, a fact that, to Marcher's sense, gave the scene of which she formed part a smooth and ultimate look, an air of knowing, in its immaculate order and cold meaningless cheer, that it would never see a fire again. Her own aspect—he could scarce have said why—intensified this note. Almost as white as wax, with the marks and signs in her face as numerous and as fine as if they had been etched by a needle, with soft white draperies relieved by a faded green scarf on the delicate tone of which the years had further refined, she was the picture of a serene and exquisite but impenetrable sphinx, whose head, or indeed all whose person, might have been powdered with silver. She was a sphinx, yet with her white petals and green fronds she might have been a lily too—only an artificial lily, wonderfully imitated and constantly kept, without dust or stain, though not exempt from a slight droop and a complexity of faint creases, under some clear glass bell. The perfection of household care, of high polish and finish, always reigned in her rooms, but they now looked most as if everything had been wound up, tucked in, put away, so that she might sit with folded hands and with nothing more to do. She was "out of it," to Marcher's vision; her work was over; she communicated with him as across some gulf or from some island of rest that she had already reached, and it made him feel strangely abandoned. Was it—or rather wasn't it—that if for so long she had been watching with him the answer to their question must have swum into her ken and taken on its name, so that her occupation was verily gone? He had as much as charged her with this in saying to her, many months before, that she even then knew something she was keeping from him. It was a point he had never since ventured to press, vaguely fearing as he did that it might become a difference, perhaps a disagreement, between them. He had in this later time turned nervous, which was what he in all the other years had never been; and the oddity was that his nervousness should have waited till he had begun to doubt, should have held off so long as he was sure. There was something, it seemed to him, that the wrong word would bring down on his head, something that would so at least ease off his tension. But he wanted not to speak the wrong word; that would make everything ugly. He wanted the knowledge he lacked to drop on him, if drop it could, by its own august weight. If she was to forsake him it was surely for her to take leave. This was why he didn't directly ask her again what she knew; but it was also why, approaching the matter from another side, he said to her in the course of his visit: "What do you regard as the very worst that at this time of day *can* happen to me?"

He had asked her that in the past often enough; they had, with the odd irregular rhythm of their intensities and avoidances, exchanged ideas about it and then had seen the ideas washed away by cool intervals, washed like figures traced in sea-sand. It had ever been the mark of their talk that the oldest allusions in it required but a little dismissal and reaction to come out again, sounding for the hour as new. She could thus at present meet his enquiry quite freshly and patiently. "Oh yes, I've repeatedly thought, only it always seemed to me of old that I couldn't quite make up my mind. I thought of dreadful things, between which it was difficult to choose; and so must you have done."

"Rather! I feel now as if I had scarce done anything else. I appear to myself to have spent my life in thinking of nothing *but* dreadful things. A great many of them I've at different times named to you, but there were others I couldn't name."

"They were too, too dreadful?"

"Too, too dreadful—some of them."

She looked at him a minute, and there came to him as he met it an inconsequent sense that her eyes, when one got their full clearness, were still as beautiful as they had been in youth, only beautiful with a strange cold light—a light that somehow was a part of the effect, if it wasn't rather a part of the cause, of the pale hard sweetness of the season and the hour. "And yet," she said at last, "there are horrors we've mentioned."

It deepened the strangeness to see her, as such a figure in such a picture, talk of "horrors," but she was to do in a few minutes something stranger yet—though even of this he was to take the full measure but afterwards—and the note of it already trembled. It was, for the matter of that, one of the signs that her eyes were having again the high flicker of their prime. He had to admit, however, what she said. "Oh yes, there were times when we did go far." He caught himself in the act of speaking as if it all were over. Well, he wished it were; and the consummation depended for him clearly more and more on his friend.

But she had now a soft smile. "Oh far—!"

It was oddly ironic. "Do you mean you're prepared to go further?"

She was frail and ancient and charming as she continued to look at him, yet it was rather as if she had lost the thread. "Do you consider that we went far?"

"Why I thought it the point you were just making—that we *had* looked most things in the face."

"Including each other?" She still smiled. "But you're quite right. We've had together great imaginations, often great fears; but some of them have been unspoken."

"Then the worst—we haven't faced that. I *could* face it, I believe, if I knew what you think it. I feel," he explained, "as if I had lost my power to conceive such things." And he wondered if he looked as blank as he sounded. "It's spent."

"Then why do you assume," she asked, "that mine isn't?"

"Because you've given me signs to the contrary. It isn't a question for you of conceiving, imagining, comparing. It isn't a question now of choosing." At last he came out with it. "You know something I don't. You've shown me that before."

These last words had affected her, he made out in a moment, exceedingly, and she spoke with firmness. "I've shown you, my dear, nothing."

He shook his head. "You can't hide it."

"Oh, oh!" May Bartram sounded over what she couldn't hide. It was almost a smothered groan.

"You admitted it months ago, when I spoke of it to you as of something you were afraid I should find out. Your answer was that I couldn't, that I wouldn't, and I don't pretend I have. But you had something therefore in mind, and I now see how it must have been, how it still is, the possibility that, of all possibilities, has settled itself for you as the worst. This," he went on, "is why I appeal to you. I'm only afraid of ignorance to-day—I'm not afraid of knowledge." And then as for a while she said nothing: "What makes me sure is that I see in your face and feel here, in this air and amid these appearances, that you're out of it. You've done. You've had your experience. You leave me to my fate."

Well, she listened, motionless and white in her chair, as on a decision to be made, so that her manner was fairly an avowal, though still, with a small fine inner stiffness, an imperfect surrender. "It *would* be the worst," she finally let herself say. "I mean the thing I've never said."

It hushed him a moment. "More monstrous than all the monstrosities we've named?"

"More monstrous. Isn't that what you

sufficiently express," she asked, "in calling it the worst?"

Marcher thought. "Assuredly—if you mean, as I do, something that includes all the loss and all the shame that are thinkable."

"It would if it *should* happen," said May Bartram. "What we're speaking of, remember, is only my idea."

"It's your belief," Marcher returned. "That's enough for me. I feel your beliefs are right. Therefore if, having this one, you give me no more light on it, you abandon me."

"No, no!" she repeated. "I'm with you—don't you see?—still." And as to make it more vivid to him she rose from her chair—a movement she seldom risked in these days—and showed herself, all draped and all soft, in her fairness and slimness. "I haven't forsaken you."

It was really, in its effort against weakness, a generous assurance, and had the success of the impulse not, happily, been great, it would have touched him to pain more than pleasure. But the cold charm in her eyes had spread, as she hovered before him, to all the rest of her person, so that it was for the minute almost a recovery of youth. He couldn't pity her for that; he could only take her as she showed—as capable even yet of helping him. It was as if, at the same time, her light might at any instant go out; wherefore he must make the most of it. There passed before him with intensity the three or four things he wanted most to know; but the question that came of itself to his lips really covered the others. "Then tell me if I shall consciously suffer."

She promptly shook her head. "Never!"

It confirmed the authority he imputed to her, and it produced on him an extraordinary effect. "Well, what's better than that? Do you call that the worst?"

"You think nothing is better?" she asked.

She seemed to mean something so special that he again sharply wondered, though still with the dawn of a prospect of relief. "Why not, if one doesn't *know*?" After which, as their eyes, over his question, met in a silence, the dawn deepened and something to his purpose came pro-

digiously out of her very face. His own,
as he took it in, suddenly flushed to the
forehead, and he gasped with the force of
a perception to which, on the instant,
everything fitted. The sound of his gasp
filled the air; then he became articulate.
"I see—if I don't suffer!"

In her own look, however, was doubt.
"You see what?"

"Why what you mean—what you've
always meant."

She again shook her head. "What I
mean isn't what I've always meant. It's
different."

"It's something new?"

She hung back from it a little. "Something new. It's not what you think. I see
what you think."

His divination drew breath then; only
her correction might be wrong. "It isn't
that I *am* a blockhead?" he asked between
faintness and grimness. "It isn't that it's
all a mistake?"

"A mistake?" she pityingly echoed.
That possibility, for her, he saw, would
be monstrous; and if she guaranteed him
the immunity from pain it would accordingly not be what she had in mind. "Oh
no," she declared; "it's nothing of that
sort. You've been right."

Yet he couldn't help asking himself if
she weren't, thus pressed, speaking but to
save him. It seemed to him he should be
most in a hole if his history should prove
all a platitude. "Are you telling me the
truth, so that I shan't have been a bigger
idiot than I can bear to know? I *haven't*
lived with a vain imagination, in the most
besotted illusion? I haven't waited but to
see the door shut in my face?"

She shook her head again. "However
the case stands *that* isn't the truth. Whatever the reality, it *is* a reality. The door
isn't shut. The door's open," said May
Bartram.

"Then something's to come?"

She waited once again, always with her
cold sweet eyes upon him. "It's never too
late." She had, with her gliding step,
diminished the distance between them,
and she stood nearer to him, close to him,
a minute, as if still charged with the unspoken. Her movement might have been
for some finer emphasis of what she was
at once hesitating and deciding to say. He
had been standing by the chimney-piece,
fireless and sparely adorned, a small perfect old French clock and two morsels of
rosy Dresden constituting all its furniture;
and her hand grasped the shelf while she
kept him waiting, grasped it a little as for
support and encouragement. She only
kept him waiting, however; that is he only
waited. It had become suddenly, from her
movement and attitude, beautiful and
vivid to him that she had something more
to give him; her wasted face delicately
shone with it—it glittered almost as with
the white lustre of silver in her expression.
She was right, incontestably, for what he
saw in her face was the truth, and strangely, without consequence, while their talk
of it as dreadful was still in the air, she
appeared to present it as inordinately soft.
This, prompting bewilderment, made him
but gape the more gratefully for her revelation, so that they continued for some
minutes silent, her face shining at him, her
contact imponderably pressing, and his
stare all kind but all expectant. The end,
none the less, was that what he had expected failed to come to him. Something
else took place instead, which seemed to
consist at first in the mere closing of her
eyes. She gave way at the same instant to
a slow fine shudder, and though he remained staring—though he stared in fact
but the harder—turned off and regained
her chair. It was the end of what she had
been intending, but it left him thinking
only of that.

"Well, you don't say—?"

She had touched in her passage a bell
near the chimney and had sunk back
strangely pale. "I'm afraid I'm too ill."

"Too ill to tell me?" It sprang up sharp
to him, and almost to his lips, the fear she
might die without giving him light. He
checked himself in time from so expressing his question, but she answered as if
she had heard the words.

"Don't you know—now?"

" 'Now'—?" She had spoken as if some
difference had been made within the moment. But her maid, quickly obedient to
her bell, was already with them. "I know
nothing." And he was afterwards to say
to himself that he must have spoken with

odious impatience, such an impatience as to show that, supremely disconcerted, he washed his hands of the whole question.

"Oh!" said May Bartram.

"Are you in pain?" he asked as the woman went to her.

"No," said May Bartram.

Her maid, who had put an arm round her as if to take her to her room, fixed on him eyes that appealingly contradicted her; in spite of which, however, he showed once more his mystification. "What then has happened?"

She was once more, with her companion's help, on her feet, and, feeling withdrawal imposed on him, he had blankly found his hat and gloves and had reached the door. Yet he waited for her answer. "What *was* to," she said.

v

He came back the next day, but she was then unable to see him, and as it was literally the first time this had occurred in the long stretch of their acquaintance he turned away, defeated and sore, almost angry—or feeling at least that such a break in their custom was really the beginning of the end—and wandered alone with his thoughts, especially with the one he was least able to keep down. She was dying and he would lose her; she was dying and his life would end. He stopped in the Park, into which he had passed, and stared before him at his recurrent doubt. Away from her the doubt pressed again; in her presence he had believed her, but as he felt his forlornness he threw himself into the explanation that, nearest at hand, had most of a miserable warmth for him and least of a cold torment. She had deceived him to save him—to put him off with something in which he should be able to rest. What could the thing that was to happen to him be, after all, but just this thing that had begun to happen? Her dying, her death, his consequent solitude —*that* was what he had figured as the Beast in the Jungle, that was what had been in the lap of the gods. He had had her word for it as he left her—what else on earth could she have meant? It wasn't a thing of a monstrous order; not a fate

rare and distinguished; not a stroke of fortune that overwhelmed and immortalised; it had only the stamp of the common doom. But poor Marcher at this hour judged the common doom sufficient. It would serve his turn, and even as the consummation of infinite waiting he would bend his pride to accept it. He sat down on a bench in the twilight. He hadn't been a fool. Something had *been*, as she had said, to come. Before he rose indeed it had quite struck him that the final fact really matched with the long avenue through which he had had to reach it. As sharing his suspense and as giving herself all, giving her life, to bring it to an end, she had come with him every step of the way. He had lived by her aid, and to leave her behind would be cruelly, damnably to miss her. What could be more overwhelming than that?

Well, he was to know within the week, for though she kept him a while at bay, left him restless and wretched during a series of days on each of which he asked about her only again to have to turn away, she ended his trial by receiving him where she had always received him. Yet she had been brought out at some hazard into the presence of so many of the things that were, consciously, vainly, half their past, and there was scant service left in the gentleness of her mere desire, all too visible, to check his obsession and wind up his long trouble. That was clearly what she wanted, the one thing more for her own peace while she could still put out her hand. He was so affected by her state that, once seated by her chair, he was moved to let everything go; it was she herself therefore who brought him back, took up again, before she dismissed him, her last word of the other time. She showed how she wished to leave their business in order. "I'm not sure you understood. You've nothing to wait for more. It *has* come."

Oh how he looked at her! "Really?"

"Really."

"The thing that, as you said, *was* to?"

"The thing that we began in our youth to watch for."

Face to face with her once more he believed her; it was a claim to which he had so abjectly little to oppose. "You mean that it has come as a positive definite occurrence, with a name and a date?"

"Positive. Definite. I don't know about the 'name,' but oh with a date!"

He found himself again too helplessly at sea. "But come in the night—come and passed me by?"

May Bartram had her strange faint smile. "Oh no, it hasn't passed you by!"

"But if I haven't been aware of it and it hasn't touched me—?"

"Ah your not being aware of it"—and she seemed to hesitate an instant to deal with this—"your not being aware of it is the strangeness *in* the strangeness. It's the wonder *of* the wonder." She spoke as with the softness almost of a sick child, yet now at last, at the end of all, with the perfect straightness of a sibyl. She visibly knew that she knew, and the effect on him was of something co-ordinate, in its high character, with the law that had ruled him. It was the true voice of the law; so on her lips would the law itself have sounded. "It *has* touched you," she went on. "It has done its office. It has made you all its own."

"So utterly without my knowing it?"

"So utterly without your knowing it." His hand, as he leaned to her, was on the arm of her chair, and, dimly smiling always now, she placed her own on it. "It's enough if *I* know it."

"Oh!" he confusedly breathed, as she herself of late so often had done.

"What I long ago said is true. You'll never know now, and I think you ought to be content. You've *had* it," said May Bartram.

"But had what?"

"Why what was to have marked you out. The proof of your law. It has acted. I'm too glad," she then bravely added, "to have been able to see what it's *not*."

He continued to attach his eyes to her, and with the sense that it was all beyond him, and that *she* was too, he would still have sharply challenged her hadn't he so felt it an abuse of her weakness to do more than take devoutly what she gave him, take it hushed as to a revelation. If he did speak, it was out of the foreknowledge of his loneliness to come. "If you're glad of what it's 'not' it might then have been worse?"

She turned her eyes away, she looked straight before her; with which after a moment: "Well, you know our fears."

He wondered. "It's something then we never feared?"

On this slowly she turned to him. "Did we ever dream, with all our dreams, that we should sit and talk of it thus?"

He tried for a little to make out that they had; but it was as if their dreams, numberless enough, were in solution in some thick cold mist through which thought lost itself. "It might have been that we couldn't talk?"

"Well"—she did her best for him—"not from this side. This, you see," she said, "is the *other* side."

"I think," poor Marcher returned, "that all sides are the same to me." Then, however, as she gently shook her head in correction: "We mightn't, as it were, have got across—?"

"To where we are—no. We're *here*"— she made her weak emphasis.

"And much good does it do us!" was her friend's frank comment.

"It does us the good it can. It does us the good that *it* isn't here. It's past. It's behind," said May Bartram. "Before—" but her voice dropped.

He had got up, not to tire her, but it was hard to combat his yearning. She after all told him nothing but that his light had failed—which he knew well enough without her. "Before—?" he blankly echoed.

"Before, you see, it was always to *come*. That kept it present."

"Oh I don't care what comes now! Besides," Marcher added, "it seems to me I liked it better present, as you say, than I can like it absent with *your* absence."

"Oh mine!"—and her pale hands made light of it.

"With the absence of everything." He had a dreadful sense of standing there before her for—so far as anything but this proved, this bottomless drop was concerned—the last time of their life. It rested on him with a weight he felt he could scarce bear, and this weight it apparently was that still pressed out what remained in him of speakable protest. "I believe you; but I can't begin to pretend I understand. *Nothing,* for me, is past; nothing *will* pass till I pass myself, which I pray my stars may. be as soon as possible. Say, however," he added, "that I've eaten my cake, as you contend, to the last crumb—how can the thing I've never felt at all be the thing I was marked out to feel?"

She met him perhaps less directly, but she met him unperturbed. "You take your 'feelings' for granted. You were to suffer your fate. That was not necessarily to know it."

"How in the world—when what is such knowledge but suffering?"

She looked up at him a while in silence. "No—you don't understand."

"I suffer," said John Marcher.

"Don't, don't!"

"How can I help at least *that?*"

"*Don't!*" May Bartram repeated.

She spoke it in a tone so special, in spite of her weakness, that he stared an instant —stared as if some light, hitherto hidden, had shimmered across his vision. Darkness again closed over it, but the gleam had already become for him an idea. "Because I haven't the right—?"

"Don't *know*—when you needn't," she mercifully urged. "You needn't—for we shouldn't."

"Shouldn't?" If he could but know what she meant!

"No—it's too much."

"Too much?" he still asked but, with a mystification that was the next moment of a sudden to give way. Her words, if they meant something, affected him in this light—the light also of her wasted face— as meaning *all,* and the sense of what knowledge had been for herself came over him with a rush which broke through into a question. "Is it of that then you're dying?"

She but watched him, gravely at first, as to see, with this, where he was, and she might have seen something or feared something that moved her sympathy. "I would live for you still—if I could." Her eyes closed for a little, as if, withdrawn into herself, she were for a last time trying. "But I can't!" she said as she raised them again to take leave of him.

She couldn't indeed, as but too promptly and sharply appeared, and he had no vision of her after this that was anything but darkness and doom. They had parted for ever in that strange talk; access to her chamber of pain, rigidly guarded, was almost wholly forbidden him; he was feeling now moreover, in the face of doctors, nurses, the two or three relatives attracted doubtless by the presumption of what she had to "leave," how few were the rights, as they were called in such cases, that he had to put forward, and how odd it might even seem that their intimacy shouldn't have given him more of them. The stupidest fourth cousin had more, even though she had been nothing in such a person's life. She had been a feature of features in *his,* for what else was it to have been so indispensable? Strange beyond saying were the ways of existence, baffling for him the anomaly of his lack, as he felt it to be, of producible claim. A woman might have been, as it were, everything to him, and it might yet present him in no connexion that any one seemed held to recognise. If this was the case in these closing weeks it was the case more sharply on the occasion of the last offices rendered, in the great grey London cemetery, to what had been mortal, to what had been precious, in his friend. The concourse at her grave was not numerous, but he saw himself treated as scarce more nearly concerned with it than if there had been a thousand others. He was in short from this moment face to face with the fact that he was to profit extraordinarily little by the interest May Bartram had taken in him. He couldn't quite have said what he expected, but he hadn't surely expected this approach to a double privation. Not only had her interest failed him, but he seemed to feel himself unattended— and for a reason he couldn't seize—by the distinction, the dignity, the propriety, if nothing else, of the man markedly bereaved. It was as if in the view of society he had not *been* markedly bereaved, as if there still failed some sign or proof of it, and as if none the less his character could never be affirmed nor the deficiency ever made up. There were moments as the weeks went by when he would have liked, by some almost aggressive act, to take his stand on the intimacy of his loss, in order that it *might* be questioned and his retort, to the relief of his spirit, so recorded; but the moments of an irritation more helpless followed fast on these, the moments during which, turning things over with a good conscience but with a bare horizon, he found himself wondering if he oughtn't to have begun, so to speak, further back.

He found himself wondering indeed at many things, and this last speculation had others to keep it company. What could he have done, after all, in her lifetime, without giving them both, as it were, away? He couldn't have made known she was watching him, for that would have published the superstition of the Beast. This was what closed his mouth now— now that the Jungle had been threshed to vacancy and that the Beast had stolen away. It sounded too foolish and too flat; the difference for him in this particular, the extinction in his life of the element of suspense, was such as in fact to surprise him. He could scarce have said what the effect resembled; the abrupt cessation, the positive prohibition, of music perhaps, more than anything else, in some place all adjusted and all accustomed to sonority and to attention. If he could at any rate have conceived lifting the veil from his image at some moment of the past (what had he done, after all, if not lift it to *her*?) so to do this to-day, to talk to people at large of the Jungle cleared and confide to them that he now felt it as safe, would have been not only to see them listen as to a goodwife's tale, but really to hear himself tell one. What it presently came to in truth was that poor Marcher waded through his beaten grass, where no life stirred, where no breath sounded, where no evil eye seemed to gleam from a possible lair, very much as if vaguely looking for the Beast, and still more as if acutely missing it. He walked about in an existence that had grown strangely more spacious, and, stopping fitfully in places where the undergrowth of life struck him as closer, asked himself yearningly, wondered secretly and sorely, if it would have lurked here or there. It would have at all events *sprung*; what was at least complete was his belief in the truth itself of the

assurance given him. The change from his old sense to his new was absolute and final: what was to happen *had* so absolutely and finally happened that he was as little able to know a fear for his future as to know a hope; so absent in short was any question of anything still to come. He was to live entirely with the other question, that of his unidentified past, that of his having to see his fortune impenetrably muffled and masked.

The torment of this vision became then his occupation; he couldn't perhaps have consented to live but for the possibility of guessing. She had told him, his friend, not to guess; she had forbidden him, so far as he might, to know, and she had even in a sort denied the power in him to learn: which were so many things, precisely, to deprive him of rest. It wasn't that he wanted, he argued for fairness, that anything past and done should repeat itself; it was only that he shouldn't, as an anticlimax, have been taken sleeping so sound as not to be able to win back by an effort of thought the lost stuff of consciousness. He declared to himself at moments that he would either win it back or have done with consciousness for ever; he made this idea his one motive in fine, made it so much his passion that none other, to compare with it, seemed ever to have touched him. The last stuff of consciousness became thus for him as a strayed or stolen child to an unappeasable father; he hunted it up and down very much as if he were knocking at doors and enquiring of the police. This was the spirit in which, inevitably, he set himself to travel; he started on a journey that was to be as long as he could make it; it danced before him that, as the other side of the globe couldn't possibly have less to say to him, it might, by a possibility of suggestion, have more. Before he quitted London, however, he made a pilgrimage to May Bartram's grave, took his way to it through the endless avenues of the grim suburban metropolis, sought it out in the wilderness of tombs, and, though he had come but for the renewal of the act of farewell, found himself, when he had at last stood by it, beguiled into long intensities. He stood for an hour, powerless to turn away and yet powerless to penetrate the darkness of death; fixing with his eyes her inscribed name and date, beating his forehead against the fact of the secret they kept, drawing his breath, while he waited, as if some sense would in pity of him rise from the stones. He kneeled on the stones, however, in vain; they kept what they concealed; and if the face of the tomb did become a face for him it was because her two names became a pair of eyes that didn't know him. He gave them a last long look, but no palest light broke.

VI

He stayed away, after this, for a year; he visited the depths of Asia, spending himself on scenes of romanic interest, of superlative sanctity; but what was present to him everywhere was that for a man who had known what *he* had known the world was vulgar and vain. The state of mind in which he had lived for so many years shone out to him, in reflexion, as a light that coloured and refined, a light beside which the glow of the East was garish cheap and thin. The terrible truth was that he had lost—with everything else —a distinction as well; the things he saw couldn't help being common when he had become common to look at them. He was simply now one of them himself—he was in the dust, without a peg for the sense of difference; and there were hours when, before the temples of gods and the sepulchres of kings, his spirit turned for nobleness of association to the barely discriminated slab in the London suburb. That had become for him, and more intensely with time and distance, his one witness of a past glory. It was all that was left to him for proof or pride, yet the past glories of Pharaohs were nothing to him as he thought of it. Small wonder then that he came back to it on the morrow of his return. He was drawn there this time as irresistibly as the other, yet with a confidence, almost, that was doubtless the effect of the many months that had elapsed. He had lived, in spite of himself, into his change of feeling, and in wandering over the earth had wandered, as might be said, from the circumference to the centre of his desert. He had settled to his safety and accepted perforce his extinction; figuring to himself, with some colour, in the likeness of certain little old men he remembered to have seen, of whom, all meagre and wizened as they might look, it was related that they had in their time fought twenty duels or been loved by ten princesses. They indeed had been wondrous for others while he was but wondrous for himself; which, however, was exactly the cause of his haste to renew the wonder by getting back, as he might put it, into his own presence. That had quickened his steps and checked his delay. If his visit was prompt it was because he had been separated so long from the part of himself that alone he now valued.

It's accordingly not false to say that he reached his goal with a certain elation and stood there again with a certain assurance. The creature beneath the sod *knew* of his rare experience, so that, strangely now, the place had lost for him its mere blankness of expression. It met him in mildness —not, as before, in mockery; it wore for him the air of conscious greeting that we find, after absence, in the things that have closely belonged to us and which seem to confess of themselves to the connexion. The plot of ground, the graven tablet, the tended flowers affected him so as belonging to him that he resembled for the hour a contented landlord reviewing a piece of property. Whatever had happened—well, had happened. He had not come back this time with the vanity of that question, his former worrying "What, *what?*" now practically so spent. Yet he would none the less never again so cut himself off from the spot; he would come back to it every month, for if he did nothing else by its aid he at least held up his head. It thus grew for him, in the oddest way, a positive resource; he carried out his idea of periodical returns, which took their place at last among the most inveterate of his habits. What it all amounted to, oddly enough, was that in his finally so simplified world this garden of death gave him the few square feet of earth on which he could still most live. It was as if, being nothing anywhere else for any one, nothing even for himself, he were just everything here, and if not for a crowd of witnesses or indeed for any witness but John Marcher, then by clear right of the register that he could scan like an open page. The open page was the tomb of his friend, and *there* were the facts of the past, there the truth of his life, there the backward reaches in which he could lose himself. He did this from time to time with such effect that he seemed to wander through the old years with his hand in the arm of a companion who was, in the most extraordinary manner, his other, his younger self; and to wander, which was more extraordinary yet, round and round a third presence—not wandering she, but stationary, still, whose eyes, turning with his revolution, never ceased to follow him, and whose seat was his point, so to speak, of orientation. Thus in short he settled to live—feeding all on the sense that he once *had* lived, and dependent on it not alone for a support but for an identity.

It sufficed him in its way for months and the year elapsed; it would doubtless even have carried him further but for an accident, superficially slight, which moved him, quite in another direction, with a force beyond any of his impressions of Egypt or of India. It was a thing of the merest chance—the turn, as he afterwards felt, of a hair, though he was indeed to live to believe that if light hadn't come to him in this particular fashion it would still have come in another. He was to live to believe this, I say, though he was not to live, I may not less definitely mention, to do much else. We allow him at any rate the benefit of the conviction, struggling up for him at the end, that, whatever might have happened or not happened, he would have come round of himself to the light. The incident of an autumn day had put the match to the train laid from of old by his misery. With the light before him he knew that even of late his ache had only been smothered. It was strangely drugged, but it throbbed; at the touch it began to bleed. And the touch, in the event, was the face of a fellow mortal. This face, one grey afternoon when the leaves were thick in the alleys, looked into Marcher's own, at the cemetery, with an expression like the cut of a blade. He felt

it, that is, so deep down that he winced at the steady thrust. The person who so mutely assaulted him was a figure he had noticed, on reaching his own goal, absorbed by a grave a short distance away, a grave apparently fresh, so that the emotion of the visitor would probably match it for frankness. This fact alone forbade further attention, though during the time he stayed he remained vaguely conscious of his neighbour, a middle-aged man apparently, in mourning, whose bowed back, among the clustered monuments and mortuary yews, was constantly presented. Marcher's theory that these were elements in contact with which he himself revived, had suffered, on this occasion, it may be granted, a marked, an excessive check. The autumn day was dire for him as none had recently been, and he rested with a heaviness he had not yet known on the low stone table that bore May Bartram's name. He rested without power to move, as if some spring in him, some spell vouchsafed, had suddenly been broken for ever. If he could have done that moment as he wanted he would simply have stretched himself on the slab that was ready to take him, treating it as a place prepared to receive his last sleep. What in all the wide world had he now to keep awake for? He stared before him with the question, and it was then that, as one of the cemetery walks passed near him, he caught the shock of the face.

His neighbour at the other grave had withdrawn, as he himself, with force enough in him, would have done by now, and was advancing along the path on his way to one of the gates. This brought him close, and his pace was slow, so that—and all the more as there was a kind of hunger in his look—the two men were for a minute directly confronted. Marcher knew him at once for one of the deeply stricken—a perception so sharp that nothing else in the picture comparatively lived, neither his dress, his age, nor his presumable character and class; nothing lived but the deep ravage of the features he showed. He *showed* them—that was the point; he was moved, as he passed, by some impulse that was either a signal for sympathy or, more possibly, a challenge to an opposed sorrow. He might already have been aware of our friend, might at some previous hour have noticed in him the smooth habit of the scene, with which the state of his own senses so scantly consorted, and might thereby have been stirred as by an overt discord. What Marcher was at all events conscious of was in the first place that the imaged of scarred passion presented to him was conscious too—of something that profaned the air; and in the second that, roused, startled, shocked, he was yet the next moment looking after it, as it went, with envy. The most extraordinary thing that had happened to him—though he had given that name to other matters as well—took place, after his immediate vague stare, as a consequence of this impression. The stranger passed, but the raw glare of his grief remained, making our friend wonder in pity what wrong, what wound it expressed, what injury not to be healed. What had the man *had*, to make him by the loss of it so bleed and yet live?

Something—and this reached him with a pang—that *he*, John Marcher, hadn't; the proof of which was precisely John Marcher's arid end. No passion had ever touched him, for this was what passion meant; he had survived and maundered and pined, but where had been *his* deep ravage? The extraordinary thing we speak of was the sudden rush of the result of this question. The sight that had just met his eyes named to him, as in letters of quick flame, something he had utterly, insanely missed, and what he had missed made these things a train of fire, made them mark themselves in an anguish of inward throbs. He had seen *outside* of his life, not learned it within, the way a woman was mourned when she had been loved for herself: such was the force of his conviction of the meaning of the stranger's face, which still flared for him as a smoky torch. It hadn't come to him, the knowledge, on the wings of experience; it had brushed him, jostled him, upset him, with the disrespect of chance, the insolence of accident. Now that the illumination had begun, however, it blazed to the zenith, and what he presently stood there gazing at was the sounded void of his life. He

gazed, he drew breath, in pain; he turned in his dismay, and, turning, he had before him in sharper incision than ever the open page of his story. The name on the table smote him as the passage of his neighbour had done, and what it said to him, full in the face, was that *she* was what he had missed. This was the awful thought, the answer to all the past, the vision at the dread clearness of which he grew as cold as the stone beneath him. Everything fell together, confessed, explained, overwhelmed; leaving him most of all stupefied at the blindness he had cherished. The fate he had been marked for he had met with a vengeance—he had emptied the cup to the lees; he had been the man of his time, *the* man, to whom nothing on earth was to have happened. That was the rare stroke—that was his visitation. So he saw it, as we say, in pale horror, while the pieces fitted and fitted. So *she* had seen it while he didn't, and so she served at this hour to drive the truth home. It was the truth, vivid and monstrous, that all the while he had waited the wait was itself his portion. This the companion of his vigil had at a given moment made out, and she had then offered him the chance to baffle his doom. One's doom, however, was never baffled, and on the day she told him his own had come down she had seen him but stupidly stare at the escape she offered him.

The escape would have been to love her; then, *then* he would have lived. *She* had lived—who could say now with what passion?—since she had loved him for himself; whereas he had never thought of her (ah how it hugely glared at him!) but in the chill of his egotism and the light of her use. Her spoken words came back to him—the chain stretched and stretched. The Beast had lurked indeed, and the Beast, at its hour, had sprung; it had sprung in that twilight of the cold April when, pale, ill, wasted, but all beautiful, and perhaps even then recoverable, she had risen from her chair to stand before him and let him imaginably guess. It had sprung as he didn't guess; it had sprung as she hopelessly turned from him, and the mark, by the time he left her, had fallen where it *was* to fall. He had justified his fear and achieved his fate; he had failed, with the last exactitude, of all he was to fail of; and a moan now rose to his lips as he remembered she had prayed he mightn't know. This horror of waking —*this* was knowledge, knowledge under the breath of which the very tears in his eyes seemed to freeze. Through them, none the less, he tried to fix it and hold it; he kept it there before him so that he might feel the pain. That at least, belated and bitter, had something of the taste of life. But the bitterness suddenly sickened him, and it was as if, horribly, he saw, in the truth, in the cruelty of his image, what had been appointed and done. He saw the Jungle of his life and saw the lurking Beast; then, while he looked, perceived it, as by a stir of the air, rise, huge and hideous, for the leap that was to settle him. His eyes darkened—it was close; and, instinctively turning, in his hallucination, to avoid it, he flung himself, face down, on the tomb.

[1903]

QUESTIONS FOR STUDY

1. *How do the six sections of the story relate to one another? What does each section add to the story? Are all of them essential?*
2. *Why did James choose the third person point of view? Why didn't he have John Marcher narrate his own story in the first person?*
3. *What efforts does May Bartram make to break through Marcher's ego? Why doesn't she choose to reveal to him directly the depths of her own understanding and love?*
4. *How does Marcher rationalize their relationship? Why doesn't he marry May?*
5. *What does Marcher finally learn from the stranger in the cemetery?*
6. *What are the major images and image patterns of the story, and how do they serve to reinforce its theme?*
7. *What are the major characteristics of James' literary style? In what ways is it appropriate to the story he is trying to tell?*

HENRY JAMES

Four Meetings

I SAW HER but four times, though I remember them vividly; she made her impression on me. I thought her very pretty and very interesting—a touching specimen of a type with which I had had other and perhaps less charming associations. I'm sorry to hear of her death, and yet when I think of it why *should* I be? The last time I saw her she was certainly not—! But it will be of interest to take our meetings in order.

I

The first was in the country, at a small tea-party, one snowy night of some seventeen years ago. My friend Latouche, going to spend Christmas with his mother, had insisted on my company, and the good lady had given in our honour the entertainment of which I speak. To me it was really full of savour—it had all the right marks: I had never been in the depths of New England at that season. It had been snowing all day and the drifts were knee-high. I wondered how the ladies had made their way to the house; but I inferred that just those general rigours rendered any assembly offering the attraction of two gentlemen from New York worth a desperate effort.

Mrs. Latouche in the course of the evening asked me if I "didn't want to" show the photographs to some of the young ladies. The photographs were in a couple of great portfolios, and had been brought home by her son, who, like myself, was lately returned from Europe. I looked round and was struck with the fact that most of the young ladies were provided with an object of interest more absorbing than the most vivid sun-picture. But there was a person alone near the mantel-shelf who looked round the room with a small vague smile, a discreet, a disguised yearning, which seemed somehow at odds with her isolation. I looked at her

a moment and then chose. "I should like to show them to that young lady."

"Oh yes," said Mrs. Latouche, "she's just the person. She doesn't care for flirting—I'll speak to her." I replied that if she didn't care for flirting she wasn't perhaps just the person; but Mrs. Latouche had already, with a few steps, appealed to her participation. "She's delighted," my hostess came back to report; "and she's just the person—so quiet and so bright." And she told me the young lady was by name Miss Caroline Spencer—with which she introduced me.

Miss Caroline Spencer was not quite a beauty, but was none the less, in her small odd way, formed to please. Close upon thirty, by every presumption, she was made almost like a little girl and had the complexion of a child. She had also the prettiest head, on which her hair was arranged as nearly as possible like the hair of a Greek bust, though indeed it was to be doubted if she had ever seen a Greek bust. She was "artistic," I suspected, so far as the polar influences of North Verona could allow for such yearnings or could minister to them. Her eyes were perhaps just too round and too inveterately surprised, but her lips had a certain mild decision and her teeth, when she showed them, were charming. About her neck she wore what ladies call, I believe, a "ruche" fastened with a very small pin of pink coral, and in her hand she carried a fan made of plaited straw and adorned with pink ribbon. She wore a scanty black silk dress. She spoke with slow soft neatness, even without smiles showing the prettiness of her teeth, and she seemed extremely pleased, in fact quite fluttered, at the prospect of my demonstrations. These went forward very smoothly after I had moved the portfolios out of their corner and placed a couple of chairs near a lamp. The photographs were usually things I knew—large views of Switzerland, Italy and Spain, landscapes, reproductions of famous buildings, pictures and statues. I said what I could for them, and my companion, looking at them as I held them up, sat perfectly still, her straw fan raised to her under-lip and gently, yet, as I could feel, almost excitedly, rubbing it. Occasionally, as I laid one of the pictures down, she said without confidence, which would have been too much: "Have you seen that place?" I usually answered that I had seen it several times—I had been a great traveller, though I was somehow particularly admonished not to swagger—and then I felt her look at me askance for a moment with her pretty eyes. I had asked her at the outset whether she had been to Europe; to this she had answered "No, no, no"—almost as much below her breath as if the image of such an event scarce, for solemnity, brooked phrasing. But after that, though she never took her eyes off the pictures, she said so little that I feared she was at last bored. Accordingly when we had finished one portfolio I offered, if she desired it, to desist. I rather guessed the exhibition really held her, but her reticence puzzled me and I wanted to make her speak. I turned round to judge better and then saw a faint flush in each of her cheeks. She kept waving her little fan to and fro. Instead of looking at me she fixed her eyes on the remainder of the collection, which leaned, in its receptacle, against the table.

"Won't you show me that?" she quavered, drawing the long breath of a person launched and afloat but conscious of rocking a little.

"With pleasure," I answered, "if you're really not tired."

"Oh I'm not tired a bit. I'm just fascinated." With which as I took up the other portfolio she laid her hand on it, rubbing it softly. "And have you been here too?"

On my opening the portfolio it appeared I had indeed been there. One of the first photographs was a large view of the Castle of Chillon by the Lake of Geneva. "Here," I said, "I've been many a time. Isn't it beautiful?" And I pointed to the perfect reflexion of the rugged rocks and pointed towers in the clear still water. She didn't say "Oh enchanting!"

and push it away to see the next picture. She looked a while and then asked if it weren't where Bonnivard, about whom Byron wrote, had been confined. I assented, trying to quote Byron's verses, but not quite bringing it off.

She fanned herself a moment and then repeated the lines correctly, in a soft flat voice but with charming conviction. By the time she had finished, she was nevertheless blushing. I complimented her and assured her she was perfectly equipped for visiting Switzerland and Italy. She looked at me askance again, to see if I might be serious, and I added that if she wished to recognise Byron's descriptions she must go abroad speedily—Europe was getting sadly dis-Byronised. "How soon must I go?" she thereupon enquired.

"Oh I'll give you ten years."

"Well, I guess I can go in *that* time," she answered as if measuring her words.

"Then you'll enjoy it immensely," I said; "you'll find it of the highest interest." Just then I came upon a photograph of some nook in a foreign city which I had been very fond of and which recalled tender memories. I discoursed (as I suppose) with considerable spirit; my companion sat listening breathless.

"Have you been *very* long over there?" she asked some time after I had ceased.

"Well, it mounts up, put all the times together."

"And have you travelled everywhere?"

"I've travelled a good deal. I'm very fond of it and happily have been able."

Again she turned on me her slow shy scrutiny. "Do you know the foreign languages?"

"After a fashion."

"Is it hard to speak them?"

"I don't imagine you'd find it so," I gallantly answered.

"Oh I shouldn't want to speak—I should only want to listen." Then on a pause she added: "They say the French theatre's so beautiful."

"Ah the best in the world."

"Did you go there very often?"

"When I was first in Paris I went every night."

"Every night!" And she opened her clear eyes very wide. "That to me is"—

and her expression hovered—"as if you tell me a fairy-tale." A few minutes later she put to me: "And which country do you prefer?"

"There's one I love beyond any. I think you'd do the same."

Her gaze rested as on a dim revelation and then she breathed "Italy?"

"Italy," I answered softly too; and for a moment we communed over it. She looked as pretty as if instead of showing her photographs I had been making love to her. To increase the resemblance she turned off blushing. It made a pause which she broke at last by saying: "That's the place which—in particular—I thought of going to."

"Oh that's the place—that's the place!' I laughed.

She looked at two or three more views in silence. "They say its not very dear."

"As some other countries? Well, one gets back there one's money. That's not the least of the charms."

"But it's *all* very expensive, isn't it?'

"Europe, you mean?"

"Going there and travelling. That has been the trouble. I've very little money. I teach, you know," said Miss Caroline Spencer.

"Oh of course one must have money,' I allowed; "but one can manage with a moderate amount judiciously spent."

"I think I should manage. I've saved and saved up, and I'm always adding a little to it. It's all for that." She paused a moment, and then went on with suppressed eagerness, as if telling me the story were a rare, but possibly an impure satisfaction. "You see it hasn't been only the money—it has been everything. Everything has acted against it. I've waited and waited. It has been my castle in the air. I'm almost afraid to talk about it. Two or three times it has come a little nearer, and then I've talked about it and it has melted away. I've talked about it too much," she said hypocritically—for I saw such talk was now a small tremulous ecstasy. "There's a lady who's a great friend of mine—she doesn't want to go, but I'm always at her about it. I think I must tire her dreadfully. She told me just the other day she didn't know what would

become of me. She guessed I'd go crazy if I didn't sail, and yet certainly I'd go crazy if I did."

"Well," I laughed, "you haven't sailed up to now—so I suppose you *are* crazy."

She took everything with the same seriousness. "Well, I guess I must be. It seems as if I couldn't think of anything else— and I don't require photographs to work me up! I'm always right *on* it. It kills any interest in things nearer home—things I ought to attend to. That's a kind of craziness."

"Well then the cure for it's just to go," I smiled—"I mean the cure for this kind. Of course you may have the other kind worse," I added—"the kind you get over there."

"Well, I've a faith that I'll go *some* time all right!" she quite elatedly cried. "I've a relative right there on the spot," she went on, "and I guess he'll know how to control me." I expressed the hope that he would, and I forget whether we turned over more photographs; but when I asked her if she had always lived just where I found her, "Oh no sir," she quite eagerly replied; "I've spent twenty-two months and a half in Boston." I met it with the inevitable joke that in this case foreign lands might prove a disappointment to her, but I quite failed to alarm her. "I know more about them than you might think"—her earnestness resisted even that. "I mean by reading—for I've really read considerable. In fact I guess I've prepared my mind about as much as you *can* —in advance. I've not only read Byron —I've read histories and guide-books and articles and lots of things. I know I shall rave about everything."

" 'Everything' is saying much, but I understand your case," I returned. "You've the great American disease, and you've got it 'bad'—the appetite, morbid and monstrous, for colour and form, for the picturesque and the romantic at any price. I don't know whether we come into the world with it—with the germs implanted and antecedent to experience; rather perhaps we catch it early, almost before developed consciousness—we *feel*, as we look about, that we're going (to save our souls, or at least our senses) to be thrown back on it hard. We're like travellers in the desert—deprived of water and subject to the terrible mirage, the torment of illusion, of the thirst-fever. They hear the plash of fountains, they see green gardens and orchards that are hundreds of miles away. So we with *our* thirst—except that with us it's *more* wonderful: we have before us the beautiful old things we've never seen at all, and when we do at last see them—if we're lucky!—we simply recognise them. What experience does is merely to confirm and consecrate our confident dream."

She listened with her rounded eyes. "The way you express it's too lovely, and I'm sure it will be just like that. I've dreamt of everything—I'll know it all!"

"I'm afraid," I pretended for harmless comedy, "that you've wasted a great deal of time."

"Oh yes, that has been my great wickedness!" The people about us had begun to scatter; they were taking their leave. She got up and put out her hand to me, timidly, but as if quite shining and throbbing.

"I'm going back there—one *has* to," I said as I shook hands with her. "I shall look out for you."

Yes, she fairly glittered with her fever of excited faith. "Well, I'll tell you if I'm disappointed." And she left me, fluttering all expressively her little straw fan.

II

A few months after this I crossed the sea eastward again and some three years elapsed. I had been living in Paris and, toward the end of October, went from that city to the Havre, to meet a pair of relatives who had written me they were about to arrive there. On reaching the Havre I found the steamer already docked—I was two or three hours late. I repaired directly to the hotel, where my travellers were duly established. My sister had gone to bed, exhausted and disabled by her voyage; she was the unsteadiest of sailors and her sufferings on this occasion had been extreme. She desired for the moment undisturbed rest and was able to see me but five minutes—long enough for

us to agree to stop over, restoratively, till the morrow. My brother-in-law, anxious about his wife, was unwilling to leave her room; but she insisted on my taking him a walk for aid to recovery of his spirits and his land-legs.

The early autumn day was warm and charming, and our stroll through the bright-coloured busy streets of the old French seaport beguiling enough. We walked along the sunny noisy quays and then turned into a wide pleasant street which lay half in sun and half in shade —a French provincial street that resembled an old water-colour drawing: tall grey steep-roofed red-gabled many-storied houses; green shutters on windows and old scroll-work above them; flowerpots in balconies and white-capped women in doorways. We walked in the shade; all this stretched away on the sunny side of the vista and made a picture. We looked at it as we passed along; then suddenly my companion stopped—pressing my arm and staring. I followed his gaze and saw that we had paused just before reaching a café where, under an awning, several tables and chairs were disposed upon the pavement. The windows were open behind; half a dozen plants in tubs were ranged beside the door; the pavement was besprinkled with clean bran. It was a dear little quiet old-world café; inside, in the comparative dusk, I saw a stout handsome woman, who had pink ribbons in her cap, perched up with a mirror behind her back and smiling at some one placed out of sight. This, to be exact, I noted afterwards; what I first observed was a lady seated alone, outside, at one of the little marble-topped tables. My brother-in-law had stopped to look at her. Something had been put before her, but she only leaned back, motionless and with her hands folded, looking down the street and away from us. I saw her but in diminished profile; nevertheless I was sure I knew on the spot that we must already have met.

"The little lady of the steamer!" my companion cried.

"Was she on your steamer?" I asked with interest.

"From morning till night. She was

never sick. She used to sit perpetually at the side of the vessel with her hands crossed that way, looking at the eastward horizon."

"And are you going to speak to her?"

"I don't know her. I never made acquaintance with her. I wasn't in form to make up to ladies. But I used to watch her and—I don't know why—to be interested in her. She's a dear little Yankee woman. I've an idea she's a school-mistress taking a holiday—for which her scholars have made up a purse."

She had now turned her face a little more into profile, looking at the steep grey house-fronts opposite. On this I decided. "I shall speak to her myself."

"I wouldn't—she's very shy," said my brother-in-law.

"My dear fellow, I know her. I once showed her photographs at a tea-party." With which I went up to her, making her, as she turned to look at me, leave me in no doubt of her identity. Miss Caroline Spencer had achieved her dream. But she was less quick to recognise me and showed a slight bewilderment. I pushed a chair to the table and sat down. "Well," I said, "I hope you're not disappointed!"

She stared, blushing a little—then gave a small jump and placed me. "It was you who showed me the photographs—at North Verona."

"Yes, it was I. This happens very charmingly, for isn't it quite for me to give you a formal reception here—the official welcome? I talked to you so much about Europe."

"You didn't say too much. I'm so intensely happy!" she declared.

Very happy indeed she looked. There was no sign of her being older; she was as gravely, decently, demurely pretty as before. If she had struck me then as a thin-stemmed mild-hued flower of Puritanism it may be imagined whether in her present situation this clear bloom was less appealing. Beside her an old gentleman was drinking absinthe; behind her the *dame de comptoir* in the pink ribbons called "Alcibiade, Alcibiade!" to the long-aproned waiter. I explained to Miss Spencer that the gentleman with me had lately been her shipmate, and my brother-in-

law came up and was introduced to her. But she looked at him as if she had never so much as seen him, and I remembered he had told me her eyes were always fixed on the eastward horizon. She had evidently not noticed him, and, still timidly smiling, made no attempt whatever to pretend the contrary. I staid with her on the little terrace of the café while he went back to the hotel and to his wife. I remarked to my friend that this meeting of ours at the first hour of her landing partook, among all chances, of the miraculous, but that I was delighted to be there and receive her first impressions.

"Oh I can't tell you," she said—"I feel so much in a dream. I've been sitting here an hour and I don't want to move. Everything's so delicious and romantic. I don't know whether the coffee has gone to my head—it's *so* unlike the coffee of my dead past."

"Really," I made answer, "if you're so pleased with this poor prosaic Havre you'll have no admiration left for better things. Don't spend your appreciation all the first day—remember it's your intellectual letter of credit. Remember all the beautiful places and things that are waiting for you. Remember that lovely Italy we talked about."

"I'm not afraid of running short," she said gaily, still looking at the opposite houses. "I could sit here all day—just saying to myself that here I am at last. It's so dark and strange—so old and different."

"By the way then," I asked, "how come you to be encamped in this odd place? Haven't you gone to one of the inns?" For I was half-amused, half-alarmed at the good conscience with which this delicately pretty woman had stationed herself in conspicuous isolation on the edge of the sidewalk.

"My cousin brought me here and—a little while ago—left me," she returned. "You know I told you I had a relation over here. He's still here—a real cousin. Well," she pursued with unclouded candour, "he met me at the steamer this morning."

It was absurd—and the case moreover none of my business; but I felt somehow disconcerted. "It was hardly worth his while to meet you if he was to desert you so soon."

"Oh he has only left me for half an hour," said Caroline Spencer. "He has gone to get my money."

I continued to wonder. "Where *is* your money?"

She appeared seldom to laugh, but she laughed for the joy of this. "It makes me feel very fine to tell you! It's in circular notes."

"And where are your circular notes?"

"In my cousin's pocket."

This statement was uttered with such clearness of candour that—I can hardly say why—it gave me a sensible chill. I couldn't at all at the moment have justified my lapse from ease, for I knew nothing of Miss Spencer's cousin. Since he stood in that relation to her—dear respectable little person—the presumption was in his favour. But I found myself wincing at the thought that half an hour after her landing her scanty funds should have passed into his hands. "Is he to travel with you?" I asked.

"Only as far as Paris. He's an art-student in Paris—I've always thought that so splendid. I wrote to him that I was coming, but I never expected him to come off to the ship. I supposed he'd only just meet me at the train in Paris. It's very kind of him. But he *is*," said Caroline Spencer, "very kind—and very bright."

I felt at once a strange eagerness to see this bright kind cousin who was an art-student. "He's gone to the banker's?" I enquired.

"Yes, to the banker's. He took me to an hotel—such a queer quaint cunning little place, with a court in the middle and a gallery all round, and a lovely landlady in such a beautifully fluted cap and such a perfectly fitting dress! After a while we came out to walk to the banker's, for I hadn't any French money. But I was very dizzy from the motion of the vessel and I thought I had better sit down. He found this place for me here—then he went off to the banker's himself. I'm to wait here till he comes back."

Her story was wholly lucid and my impression perfectly wanton, but it passed through my mind that the gentleman would never come back. I settled myself in a chair beside my friend and determined to await the event. She was lost in the vision and the imagination of everything near us and about us—she observed, she recognised and admired, with a touching intensity. She noticed everything that was brought before us by the movement of the street—the peculiarities of costume, the shapes of vehicles, the big Norman horses, the fat priests, the shaven poodles. We talked of these things, and there was something charming in her freshness of perception and the way her book-nourished fancy sallied forth for the revel.

"And when your cousin comes back what are you going to do?" I went on.

For this she had, a little oddly, to think. "We don't quite know."

"When do you go to Paris? If you go by the four o'clock train I may have the pleasure of making the journey with you."

"I don't think we shall do that." So far she was prepared. "My cousin thinks I had better stay here a few days."

"Oh!" said I—and for five minutes had nothing to add. I was wondering what our absentee was, in vulgar parlance, "up to." I looked up and down the street, but saw nothing that looked like a bright and kind American art-student. At last I took the liberty of observing that the Havre was hardly a place to choose as one of the æsthetic stations of a European tour. It was a place of convenience, nothing more; a place of transit, through which transit should be rapid. I recommended her to go to Paris by the afternoon train and meanwhile to amuse herself by driving to the ancient fortress at the mouth of the harbour—that remarkable circular structure which bore the name of Francis the First and figured a sort of small Castle of Saint Angelo. (I might really have foreknown that it was to be demolished.)

She listened with much interest—then for a moment looked grave. "My cousin told me that when he returned he should have something particular to say to me, and that we could do nothing or decide nothing till I should have heard it. But I'll make him tell me right off, and then we'll go to the ancient fortress. Francis the First, did you say? Why, that's lovely. There's no hurry to get to Paris; there's plenty of time."

She smiled with her softly severe little lips as she spoke those last words, yet, looking at her with a purpose, I made out in her eyes, I thought, a tiny gleam of apprehension. "Don't tell me," I said, "that this wretched man's going to give you bad news!"

She coloured as if convicted of a hidden perversity, but she was soaring too high to drop. "Well, I guess it's a *little* bad, but I don't believe it's *very* bad. At any rate I must listen to it."

I usurped an unscrupulous authority. "Look here; you didn't come to Europe to listen—you came to *see!*" But now I was sure her cousin would come back; since he had something disagreeable to say to her he'd infallibly turn up. We sat a while longer and I asked her about her plans of travel. She had them on her fingers' ends and told over the names as solemnly as a daughter of another faith might have told over the beads of a rosary: from Paris to Dijon and to Avignon, from Avignon to Marseilles and the Cornice road; thence to Genoa, to Spezia, to Pisa, to Florence, to Rome. It apparently had never occurred to her that there could be the least incommodity in her travelling alone; and since she was unprovided with a companion I of course civilly abstained from disturbing her sense of security.

At last her cousin came back. I saw him turn toward us out of a side-street, and from the moment my eyes rested on him I knew he could but be the bright, if not the kind, American art-student. He wore a slouch hat and a rusty black velvet jacket, such as I had often encountered in the Rue Bonaparte. His shirt-collar displayed a stretch of throat that at a distance wasn't strikingly statuesque. He was tall and lean, he had red hair and freckles. These items I had time to take in while he approached the café, staring at me with natural surprise from under his romantic brim. When he came up to us I immediately introduced myself as an old acquaintance of Miss Spencer's, a char-

acter she serenely permitted me to claim. He looked at me hard with a pair of small sharp eyes, then he gave me a solemn wave, in the "European" fashion, of his rather rusty sombrero.

"You weren't on the ship?" he asked.

"No, I wasn't on the ship. I've been in Europe these several years."

He bowed once more, portentously, and motioned me to be seated again. I sat down, but only for the purpose of observing him an instant—I saw it was time I should return to my sister. Miss Spencer's European protector was, by my measure, a very queer quantity. Nature hadn't shaped him for a Raphaelesque or Byronic attire, and his velvet doublet and exhibited though not columnar throat weren't in harmony with his facial attributes. His hair was cropped close to his head; his ears were large and ill-adjusted to the same. He had a lackadaisical carriage and a sentimental droop which were peculiarly at variance with his keen conscious strange-coloured eyes—of a brown that was almost red. Perhaps I was prejudiced, but I thought his eyes too shifty. He said nothing for some time; he leaned his hands on his stick and looked up and down the street. Then at last, slowly lifting the stick and pointing with it, "That's a very nice bit," he dropped with a certain flatness. He had his head to one side—he narrowed his ugly lids. I followed the direction of his stick; the object it indicated was a red cloth hung out of an old window. "Nice bit of colour," he continued; and without moving his head transferred his half-closed gaze to me. "Composes well. Fine old tone. Make a nice thing." He spoke in a charmless vulgar voice.

"I see you've a great deal of eye," I replied. "Your cousin tells me you're studying art." He looked at me in the same way, without answering, and I went on with deliberate urbanity: "I suppose you're at the studio of one of those great men." Still on this he continued to fix me, and then he named one of the greatest of that day; which led me to ask him if he liked his master.

"Do you understand French?" he returned.

"Some kinds."

He kept his little eyes on me; with which he remarked: "Je suis fou de la peinture!" [1]

"Oh I understand that kind!" I replied. Our companion laid her hand on his arm with a small pleased and fluttered movement; it was delightful to be among people who were on such easy terms with foreign tongues. I got up to take leave and asked her where, in Paris, I might have the honour of waiting on her. To what hotel would she go?

She turned to her cousin enquiringly and he favoured me again with his little languid leer. "Do you know the Hôtel des Princes?"

"I know where it is."

"Well, that's the shop."

"I congratulate you," I said to Miss Spencer. "I believe it's the best inn in the world; but, in case I should still have a moment to call on you here, where are you lodged?"

"Oh it's such a pretty name," she returned gleefully. "A la Belle Normande."

"I guess I know my way round!" her kinsman threw in; and as I left them he gave me with his swaggering head-cover a great flourish that was like the wave of a banner over a conquered field.

III

My relative, as it proved, was not sufficiently restored to leave the place by the afternoon train; so that as the autumn dusk began to fall I found myself at liberty to call at the establishment named to me by my friends. I must confess that I had spent much of the interval in wondering what the disagreeable thing was that the less attractive of these had been telling the other. The *auberge* of the Belle Normande proved an hostelry in a shady by-street, where it gave me satisfaction to think Miss Spencer must have encountered local colour in abundance. There was a crooked little court, where much of the hospitality of the house was carried on; there was a staircase climbing to bedrooms on the outer side of the wall; there was a small trickling fountain with a

stucco statuette set in the midst of it; there was a little boy in a white cap and apron cleaning copper vessels at a conspicuous kitchen door; there was a chattering landlady, neatly laced, arranging apricots and grapes into an artistic pyramid upon a pink plate. I looked about, and on a green bench outside of an open door labelled Salle-à-Manger, I distinguished Caroline Spencer. No sooner had I looked at her than I was sure something had happened since the morning. Supported by the back of her bench, with her hands clasped in her lap, she kept her eyes on the other side of the court where the landlady manipulated the apricots.

But I saw that, poor dear, she wasn't thinking of apricots or even of landladies. She was staring absently, thoughtfully; on a nearer view I could have certified she had been crying. I had seated myself beside her before she was aware; then, when she had done so, she simply turned round without surprise and showed me her sad face. Something very bad indeed had happened; she was completely changed, and I immediately charged her with it. "Your cousin has been giving you bad news. You've had a horrid time."

For a moment she said nothing, and I supposed her afraid to speak lest her tears should again rise. Then it came to me that even in the few hours since my leaving her she had shed them all—which made her now intensely, stoically composed. "My poor cousin has been having one," she replied at last. "He has had great worries. His news was bad." Then after a dismally conscious wait: "He was in dreadful want of money."

"In want of yours, you mean?"

"Of any he could get—honourably of course. Mine *is* all—well, that's available."

Ah it was as if I had been sure from the first! "And he has taken it from you?"

Again she hung fire, but her face meanwhile was pleading. "I gave him what I had."

I recall the accent of those words as the most angelic human sound I had ever listened to—which is exactly why I jumped up almost with a sense of personal outrage. "Gracious goodness, mad-

---

[1] "I am crazy about painting!" (JHP)

am, do you call that his getting it 'honourably'?"

I had gone too far—she coloured to her eyes. "We won't speak of it."

"We *must* speak of it," I declared as I dropped beside her again. "I'm your friend—upon my word I'm your protector; it seems to me you need one. What's the matter with this extraordinary person?"

She was perfectly able to say. "He's just badly in debt."

"No doubt he is! But what's the special propriety of your—in such tearing haste! —paying for that?"

"Well, he has told me all his story. I *feel* for him so much."

"So do I, if you come to that! But I hope," I roundly added, "he'll give you straight back your money."

As to this she was prompt. "Certainly he will—as soon as ever he can."

"And when the deuce will that be?"

Her lucidity maintained itself. "When he has finished his great picture."

It took me full in the face. "My dear young lady, damn his great picture! Where is this voracious man?"

It was as if she must let me feel a moment that I did push her!—though indeed, as appeared, he was just where he'd naturally be. "He's having his dinner."

I turned about and looked through the open door into the salle-à-manger. There, sure enough, alone at the end of a long table, was the object of my friend's compassion—the bright, the kind young artstudent. He was dining too attentively to notice me at first, but in the act of setting down a well-emptied wine-glass he caught sight of my air of observation. He paused in his repast and, with his head on one side and his meagre jaws slowly moving, fixedly returned my gaze. Then the landlady came brushing lightly by with her pyramid of apricots.

"And that nice little plate of fruit is for him?" I wailed.

Miss Spencer glanced at it tenderly. "They seem to arrange everything so nicely!" she simply sighed.

I felt helpless and irritated. "Come now, really," I said; "do you think it right, do you think it decent, that that long strong fellow should collar your

funds?" She looked away from me—I was evidently giving her pain. The case was hopeless; the long strong fellow had "interested" her.

"Pardon me if I speak of him so unceremoniously," I said. "But you're really too generous, and he hasn't, clearly, the rudiments of delicacy. He made his debts himself—he ought to pay them himself."

"He has been foolish," she obstinately said—"of course I know that. He has told me everything. We had a long talk this morning—the poor fellow threw himself on my charity. He has signed notes to a large amount."

"The more fool he!"

"He's in real distress—and it's not only himself. It's his poor young wife."

"Ah he has a poor young wife?"

"I didn't know—but he made a clean breast of it. He married two years since—secretly."

"Why secretly?"

My informant took precautions as if she feared listeners. Then with low impressiveness: "She was a Countess!"

"Are you very sure of that?"

"She has written me the most beautiful letter."

"Asking you—whom she has never seen—for money?"

"Asking me for confidence and sympathy"—Miss Spencer spoke now with spirit. "She has been cruelly treated by her family—in consequence of what she has done for him. My cousin has told me every particular, and she appeals to me in her own lovely way in the letter, which I've here in my pocket. It's such a wonderful old-world romance," said my prodigious friend. "She was a beautiful young widow—her first husband was a Count, tremendously high-born, but really most wicked, with whom she hadn't been happy and whose death had left her ruined after he had deceived her in all sorts of ways. My poor cousin, meeting her in that situation and perhaps a little too recklessly pitying her and charmed with her, found her, don't you see?" —Caroline's appeal on this head was amazing!—"but too ready to trust a better man after all she had been through. Only when her 'people,' as he says—and I do like the word!—understood she *would* have him, poor gifted young American art-student though he simply was, because she just adored him, her great-aunt, the old Marquise, from whom she had expectations of wealth which she could yet sacrifice for her love, utterly cast her off and wouldn't so much as speak to her, much less to *him*, in their dreadful haughtiness and pride. They *can* be haughty over here, it seems," she ineffably developed—"there's no mistake about that! It's like something in some famous old book. The family, my cousin's wife's," she by this time almost complacently wound up, "are of the oldest Provençal noblesse."

I listened half-bewildered. The poor woman positively found it so interesting to be swindled by a flower of that stock —if stock or flower or solitary grain of truth was really concerned in the matter —as practically to have lost the sense of what the forfeiture of her hoard meant for her. "My dear young lady," I groaned, "you don't want to be stripped of every dollar for such a rigmarole!"

She asserted, at this, her dignity— much as a small pink shorn lamb might have done. "It isn't a rigmarole, and I shan't be stripped. I shan't live any worse than I *have* lived, don't you see? And I'll come back before long to stay with them. The Countess—he still gives her, he says, her title, as they do to noble widows, that is to 'dowagers,' don't you know? in England—insists on a visit from me *some* time. So I guess for *that* I can start afresh —and meanwhile I'll have recovered my money."

It was all too heart-breaking. "You're going home then at once?"

I felt the faint tremor of voice she heroically tried to stifle. "I've nothing left for a tour."

"You gave it *all* up?"

"I've kept enough to take me back."

I uttered, I think, a positive howl, and at this juncture the hero of the situation, the happy proprietor of my little friend's sacred savings and of the infatuated *grande dame* just sketched for me, reappeared with the clear consciousness of a repast bravely earned and consistently enjoyed. He stood on the threshold an instant, extracting the stone from a plump apricot he had fondly retained; then he put the apricot into his mouth and, while he let it gratefully dissolve there, stood looking at us with his long legs apart and his hands thrust into the pockets of his velvet coat. My companion got up, giving him a thin glance that I caught in its passage and which expressed at once resignation and fascination—the last dregs of her sacrifice and with it an anguish of upliftedness. Ugly vulgar pretentious dishonest as I thought him, and destitute of every grace of plausibility, he had yet appealed successfully to her eager and tender imagination. I was deeply disgusted, but I had no warrant to interfere, and at any rate felt that it would be vain. He waved his hand meanwhile with a breadth of appreciation. "Nice old court. Nice mellow old place. Nice crooked old staircase. Several pretty things."

Decidedly I couldn't stand it, and without responding I gave my hand to my friend. She looked at me an instant with her little white face and rounded eyes, and as she showed her pretty teeth I suppose she meant to smile. "Don't be sorry for me," she sublimely pleaded; "I'm very sure I shall see something of this dear old Europe yet."

I refused however to take literal leave of her—I should find a moment to come back next morning. Her awful kinsman, who had put on his sombrero again, flourished it off at me by way of a bow—on which I hurried away.

On the morrow early I did return, and in the court of the inn met the landlady, more loosely laced than in the evening. On my asking for Miss Spencer, "*Partie*, monsieur," the good woman said. "She went away last night at ten o'clock, with her—her—not her husband, eh?—in fine her Monsieur. They went down to the American ship." I turned off—I felt the tears in my eyes. The poor girl had been some thirteen hours in Europe.

IV

I myself, more fortunate, continued to sacrifice to opportunity as I myself met it. During this period—of some five years— I lost my friend Latouche, who died of a malarious fever during a tour in the

Levant. One of the first things I did on my return to America was to go up to North Verona on a consolatory visit to his poor mother. I found her in deep affliction and sat with her the whole of the morning that followed my arrival—I had come in late at night—listening to her tearful descant and singing the praises of my friend. We talked of nothing else, and our conversation ended only with the arrival of a quick little woman who drove herself up to the door in a "carry-all" and whom I saw toss the reins to the horse's back with the briskness of a startled sleeper throwing off the bedclothes. She jumped out of the carry-all and she jumped into the room. She proved to be the minister's wife and the great town-gossip, and she had evidently, in the latter capacity, a choice morsel to communicate. I was as sure of this as I was that poor Mrs. Latouche was not absolutely too bereaved to listen to her. It seemed to me discreet to retire, and I described myself as anxious for a walk before dinner.

"And by the way," I added, "if you'll tell me where my old friend Miss Spencer lives I think I'll call on her."

The minister's wife immediately responded. Miss Spencer lived in the fourth house beyond the Baptist church; the Baptist church was the one on the right, with that queer green thing over the door; they called it portico, but it looked more like an old-fashioned bedstead swung in the air. "Yes, do look up poor Caroline," Mrs. Latouche further enjoined. "It will refresh her to see a strange face."

"I should think she had had enough of strange faces!" cried the minister's wife.

"To see, I mean, a charming visitor"— Mrs. Latouche amended her phrase.

"I should think she had had enough of charming visitors!" her companion returned. "But *you* don't mean to stay ten years," she added with significant eyes on me.

"Has she a visitor of that sort?" I asked in my ignorance.

"You'll make out the sort!" said the minister's wife. "She's easily seen; she generally sits in the front yard. Only take

care what you say to her, and be very sure you're polite."

"Ah she's so sensitive?"

The minister's wife jumped up and dropped me a curtsey—a most sarcastic curtsey. "That's what she is, if you please. 'Madame la Comtesse!' "

And pronouncing these titular words with the most scathing accent, the little woman seemed fairly to laugh in the face of the lady they designated. I stood staring, wondering, remembering.

"Oh I shall be very polite!" I cried; and, grasping my hat and stick, I went on my way.

I found Miss Spencer's residence without difficulty. The Baptist church was easily identified, and the small dwelling near it, of a rusty white, with a large central chimney-stack and a Virginia creeper, seemed naturally and properly the abode of a withdrawn old maid with a taste for striking effects inexpensively obtained. As I approached I slackened my pace, for I had heard that some one was always sitting in the front yard, and I wished to reconnoitre. I looked cautiously over the low white fence that separated the small garden-space from the unpaved street, but I descried nothing in the shape of a Comtesse. A small straight path led up to the crooked door-step, on either side of which was a little grass-plot fringed with currant-bushes. In the middle of the grass, right and left, was a large quince-tree, full of antiquity and contortions, and beneath one of the quince-trees were placed a small table and a couple of light chairs. On the table lay a piece of unfinished embroidery and two or three books in bright-coloured paper covers. I went in at the gate and paused halfway along the path, scanning the place for some further token of its occupant, before whom—I could hardly have said why—I hesitated abruptly to present myself. Then I saw the poor little house to be of the shabbiest and felt a sudden doubt of my right to penetrate, since curiosity had been my motive and curiosity here failed of confidence. While I demurred a figure appeared in the open doorway and stood there looking at me. I immediately recognised Miss Spencer, but she faced me as if we had never met. Gently, but gravely and timidly, I advanced to the door-step, where I spoke with an attempt at friendly banter.

"I waited for you over there to come back, but you never came."

"Waited where, sir?" she quavered, her innocent eyes rounding themselves as of old. She was much older; she looked tired and wasted.

"Well," I said, "I waited at the old French port."

She stared harder, then recognised me, smiling, flushing, clasping her two hands together. "I remember you now—I remember that day." But she stood there, neither coming out nor asking me to come in. She was embarrassed.

I too felt a little awkward while I poked at the path with my stick. "I kept looking out for you year after year."

"You mean in Europe?" she ruefully breathed.

"In Europe of course! Here apparently you're easy enough to find."

She leaned her hand against the unpainted doorpost and her head fell a little to one side. She looked at me thus without speaking, and I caught the expression visible in women's eyes when tears are rising. Suddenly she stepped out on the cracked slab of stone before her threshold and closed the door. Then her strained smile prevailed and I saw her teeth were as pretty as ever. But there had been tears too. "Have you been there ever since?" she lowered her voice to ask.

"Until three weeks ago. And you—you never came back?"

Still shining at me as she could, she put her hand behind her and reopened the door. "I'm not very polite," she said. "Won't you come in?"

"I'm afraid I incommode you."

"Oh no!"—she wouldn't hear of it now. And she pushed back the door with a sign that I should enter.

I followed her in. She led the way to a small room on the left of the narrow hall, which I supposed to be her parlour, though it was at the back of the house, and we passed the closed door of another apartment which apparently enjoyed a view of the quince-trees. This one looked out upon a small wood-shed and two clucking hens. But I thought it pretty until I saw its elegance to be of the most frugal kind; after which, presently, I thought it prettier still, for I had never seen faded chintz and old mezzotint engravings, framed in varnished autumn leaves, disposed with so touching a grace. Miss Spencer sat down on a very small section of the sofa, her hands tightly clasped in her lap. She looked ten years older, and I needn't now have felt called to insist on the facts of her person. But I still thought them interesting, and at any rate I was moved by them. She was peculiarly agitated. I tried to appear not to notice it; but suddenly, in the most inconsequent fashion—it was an irresistible echo of our concentrated passage in the old French port—I said to her: "I do incommode you. Again you're in distress."

She raised her two hands to her face and for a moment kept it buried in them. Then taking them away, "It's because you remind me," she said.

"I remind you, you mean, of that miserable day at the Havre?"

She wonderfully shook her head. "It wasn't miserable. It was delightful."

Ah, was it? my manner of receiving this must have commented. "I never was so shocked as when, on going back to your inn the next morning, I found you had wretchedly retreated."

She waited an instant, after which she said: "Please let us not speak of that."

"Did you come straight back here?" I nevertheless went on.

"I was back here just thirty days after my first start."

"And here you've remained ever since?"

"Every minute of the time."

I took it in; I didn't know what to say, and what I presently said had almost the sound of mockery. "When then are you going to make that tour?" It might be practically aggressive; but there was something that irritated me in her depths of resignation, and I wished to extort from her some expression of impatience.

She attached her eyes a moment to a small sunspot on the carpet; then she got up and lowered the window-blind a little to obliterate it. I waited, watching her with interest—as if she had still something more to give me. Well, presently, in answer to my last question, she gave it. "Never!"

"I hope at least your cousin repaid you that money," I said.

At this again she looked away from me. "I don't care for it now."

"You don't care for your money?"

"For ever going to Europe."

"Do you mean you wouldn't go if you could?"

"I can't—I can't," said Caroline Spencer. "It's all over. Everything's different. I never think of it."

"The scoundrel never repaid you then!" I cried.

"Please, please—!" she began.

But she had stopped—she was looking toward the door. There had been a rustle and a sound of steps in the hall.

I also looked toward the door, which was open and now admitted another person—a lady who paused just within the threshold. Behind her came a young man. The lady looked at me with a good deal of fixedness—long enough for me to rise to a vivid impression of herself. Then she turned to Caroline Spencer and, with a smile and a strong foreign accent, *"Pardon, ma chère!* I didn't know you had company," she said. "The gentleman came in so quietly." With which she again gave me the benefit of her attention. She was very strange, yet I was at once sure I had seen her before. Afterwards I rather put it that I had only seen ladies remarkably like her. But I had seen them very far away from North Verona, and it was the oddest of all things to meet one of them in that frame. To what quite other scene did the sight of her transport me? To some dusky landing before a shabby Parisian *quatrième*—to an open door revealing a greasy ante-chamber and to Madame leaning over the banisters while she holds a faded wrapper together and bawls down to the portress to bring up her coffee. My friend's guest was a very large lady, of middle age, with a plump dead-white face and hair drawn back *à la chinoise*. She had a small penetrating eye and what is called in French *le sourire*

*agréable.*² She wore an old pink cashmere dressing-gown covered with white embroideries, and, like the figure in my momentary vision, she confined it in front with a bare and rounded arm and a plump and deeply-dimpled hand.

"It's only to spick about my café," she said to her hostess with her *sourire agréable.* "I should like it served in the garden under the leetle tree."

The young man behind her had now stepped into the room, where he also stood revealed, though with rather less of a challenge. He was a gentleman of few inches but a vague importance, perhaps the leading man of the world of North Verona. He had a small pointed nose and a small pointed chin; also, as I observed, the most diminutive feet and a manner of no point at all. He looked at me foolishly and with his mouth open.

"You shall have your coffee," said Miss Spencer as if an army of cooks had been engaged in the preparation of it.

"C'est bien!" said her massive inmate. "Find your bouk"—and this personage turned to the gaping youth.

He gaped now at each quarter of the room. "My grammar, d'ye mean?"

The large lady however could but face her friend's visitor while persistently engaged with a certain laxity in the flow of her wrapper. "Find your bouk," she more absently repeated.

"My poetry, d'ye mean?" said the young man, who also couldn't take his eyes off me.

"Never mind your bouk"—his companion reconsidered. "To-day we'll just talk. We'll make some conversation. But we mustn't interrupt Mademoiselle's. Come, come"—and she moved off a step. "Under the leetle tree," she added for the benefit of Mademoiselle. After which she gave me a thin salutation, jerked a measured "Monsieur!" and swept away again with her swain following.

I looked at Miss Spencer, whose eyes never moved from the carpet, and I spoke, I fear, without grace. "Who in the world's that?"

"The Comtesse—that *was:* my *cousine* as they call it in French."

"And who's the young man?"

² "pleasant smile." (JHP)

"The Countess's pupil, Mr. Mixter." This description of the tie uniting the two persons who had just quitted us must certainly have upset my gravity; for I recall the marked increase of my friend's own as she continued to explain. "She gives lessons in French and music, the simpler sorts—"

"The simpler sorts of French?" I fear I broke in.

But she was still impenetrable, and in fact had now an intonation that put me vulgarly in the wrong. "She has had the worst reverses—with no one to look to. She's prepared for any exertion—and she takes her misfortunes with gaiety."

"Ah well," I returned—no doubt a little ruefully, "that's all I myself am pretending to do. If she's determined to be a burden to nobody, nothing could be more right and proper."

My hostess looked vaguely, though I thought quite wearily enough, about: she met this proposition in no other way. "I must go and get the coffee," she simply said.

"Has the lady many pupils?" I none the less persisted.

"She has only Mr. Mixter. She gives him all her time." It might have set me off again, but something in my whole impression of my friend's sensibility urged me to keep strictly decent. "He pays very well," she at all events inscrutably went on. "He's not very bright—as a pupil; but he's very rich and he's very kind. He has a buggy—with a back, and he takes the Countess to drive."

"For good long spells I hope," I couldn't help interjecting—even at the cost of her so taking it that she had still to avoid my eyes. "Well, the country's beautiful for miles," I went on. And then as she was turning away: "You're going for the Countess's coffee?"

"If you'll excuse me a few moments."

"Is there no one else to do it?"

She seemed to wonder who there should be. "I keep no servants."

"Then can't I help?" After which, as she but looked at me, I bettered it. "Can't she wait on herself?"

Miss Spencer had a slow headshake—as if that too had been a strange idea. "She isn't used to *manual* labour."

The discrimination was a treat, but I cultivated decorum. "I see—and you *are*." But at the same time I couldn't abjure curiosity. "Before you go, at any rate, please tell me this: who *is* this wonderful lady?"

"I told you just who in France—that extraordinary day. She's the wife of my cousin, whom you saw there."

"The lady disowned by her family in consequence of her marriage?"

"Yes; they've never seen her again. They've completely broken with her."

"And where's her husband?"

"My poor cousin's dead."

I pulled up, but only a moment. "And where's your money?"

The poor thing flinched—I kept her on the rack. "I don't know," she woefully said.

I scarce know what it didn't prompt me to—but I went step by step. "On her husband's death this lady at once came to you?"

It was as if she had had too often to describe it. "Yes, she arrived one day."

"How long ago?"

"Two years and four months."

"And has been here ever since?"

"Ever since."

I took it all in. "And how does she like it?"

"Well, not *very* much," said Miss Spencer divinely.

That too I took in. "And how do *you*—?"

She laid her face in her two hands an instant as she had done ten minutes before. Then, quickly, she went to get the Countess's coffee.

Left alone in the little parlour I found myself divided between the perfection of my disgust and a contrary wish to see, to learn more. At the end of a few minutes the young man in attendance on the lady in question reappeared as for a fresh gape at me. He was inordinately grave—to be dressed in such particoloured flannels; and he produced with no great confidence on his own side the message with which he had been charged. "She wants to know if you won't come right out."

"Who wants to know?"

"The Countess. That French lady."

"She has asked you to bring me?"

"Yes sir," said the young man feebly—for I may claim to have surpassed him in stature and weight.

I went out with him, and we found his instructress seated under one of the small quince-trees in front of the house; where she was engaged in drawing a fine needle with a very fat hand through a piece of embroidery not remarkable for freshness. She pointed graciously to the chair beside her and I sat down. Mr. Mixter glanced about him and then accommodated himself on the grass at her feet; whence he gazed upward more gapingly than ever and as if convinced that between us something wonderful would now occur.

"I'm sure you spick French," said the Countess, whose eyes were singularly protuberant as she played over me her agreeable smile.

"I do, madam—*tant bien que mal*," [3] I replied, I fear, more dryly.

"Ah *violà!*" she cried as with delight. "I knew it as soon as I looked at you. You've been in my poor dear country."

"A considerable time."

"You love it then, *mon pays de France?*"

"Oh it's an old affection." But I wasn't exuberant.

"And you know Paris well?"

"Yes, *sans me vanter*,[4] madam, I think I really do." And with a certain conscious purpose I let my eyes meet her own.

She presently, hereupon, moved her own and glanced down at Mr. Mixter. "What are we talking about?" she demanded of her attentive pupil.

He pulled his knees up, plucked at the grass, stared, blushed a little. "You're talking French," said Mr. Mixter.

"*La belle découverte!*" [5] mocked the Countess. "It's going on ten months," she explained to me, "since I took him in hand. Don't put yourself out not to say he's *la bêtise même*," [6] she added in fine style. "He won't in the least understand you."

A moment's consideration of Mr. Mixter, awkwardly sporting at our feet, quite assured me that he wouldn't. "I hope your other pupils do you more honour," I then remarked to my entertainer.

"I have no others. They don't know what French—or what anything else—is in this place; they don't want to know. You may therefore imagine the pleasure it is to me to meet a person who speaks it like yourself." I could but reply that my own pleasure wasn't less, and she continued to draw the stitches through her embroidery with an elegant curl of her little finger. Every few moments she put her eyes, near-sightedly, closer to her work—this as if for elegance too. She inspired me with no more confidence than her late husband, if husband he was, had done, years before, on the occasion with which this one so detestably matched: she was coarse, common, affected, dishonest—no more a Countess than I was a Caliph. She had an assurance—based clearly on experience; but this couldn't have been the experience of "race." Whatever it was indeed it did now, in a yearning fashion, flare out of her. "Talk to me of Paris, *mon beau Paris* that I'd give my eyes to see. The very name of it *me fait languir*.[7] How long since you were there?"

"A couple of months ago."

"*Vous avez de la chance!* [8] Tell me something about it. What were they doing? Oh for an hour of the Boulevard!"

"They were doing about what they're always doing—amusing themselves a good deal."

"At the theatres, *hein?*" sighed the Countess. "At the cafés-concerts? *sous ce beau ciel* [9]—at the little tables before the doors? *Quelle existence!* [10] You know I'm a Parisienne, monsieur," she added, "to my finger-tips."

"Miss Spencer was mistaken then," I ventured to return, "in telling me you're a Provençale."

She stared a moment, then put her nose to her embroidery, which struck me as having acquired even while we sat a dingier and more desultory air. "Ah I'm a Provençale by birth, but a Parisienne by—inclination." After which she pursued:

3 "after a fashion." (JHP)
4 "without boasting." (JHP)
5 "Quite a discovery!" (JHP)
6 "stupidity itself." (JHP)
7 "makes me pine." (JHP)
8 "How lucky you are!" (JHP)
9 "under the beautiful sky." (JHP)
10 "What a life!" (JHP)

"And by the saddest events of my life—as well as by some of the happiest, hélas!"

"In other words by a varied experience!" I now at last smiled.

She questioned me over it with her hard little salient eyes. "Oh experience! —I could talk of that, no doubt, if I wished. *On en a de toutes les sortes*[11]— and I never dreamed that mine, for example, would ever have *this* in store for me." And she indicated with her large bare elbow and with a jerk of her head all surrounding objects; the little white house, the pair of quince-trees, the rickety paling, even the rapt Mr. Mixter.

I took them all bravely in. "Ah if you mean you're decidedly in exile—!"

"You may imagine what it is. These two years of my *épreuve*—*elles m'en ont données, des heures, des heures!* [12] One gets used to things"—and she raised her shoulders to the highest shrug ever accomplished at North Verona; "so that I sometimes think I've got used to this. But there are some things that are always beginning again. For example my coffee."

I so far again lent myself. "Do you always have coffee at this hour?"

Her eyebrows went up as high as her shoulders had done. "At what hour would you propose to me to have it? I must have my little cup after breakfast."

"Ah you breakfast at this hour?"

"At mid-day—*comme cela se fair.*[13] Here they breakfast at a quarter past seven. That 'quarter past' is charming!"

"But you were telling me about your coffee," I observed sympathetically.

"My *cousine* can't believe in it; she can't understand it. "C'est une fille charmante, but that little cup of black coffee with a drop of '*fine*,' served at this hour —they exceed her comprehension. So I have to break the ice each day, and it takes the coffee the time you see to arrive. And when it does arrive, monsieur—! If I don't press it on *you*—though monsieur here sometimes joins me!—it's because you've drunk it on the Boulevard."

I resented extremely so critical a view of my poor friend's exertions, but I said

nothing at all—the only way to be sure of my civility. I dropped my eyes on Mr. Mixter, who, sitting cross-legged and nursing his knees, watched my companion's foreign graces with an interest that familiarity had apparently done little to restrict. She became aware, naturally, of my mystified view of him and faced the question with all her boldness. "He adores me, you know," she murmured with her nose again in her tapestry—"he dreams of becoming *mon amoureux*. Yes, *il me fait une cour acharnée*[14]—such as you see him. That's what we've come to. He has read some French novel—it took him six months. But ever since that he has thought himself a hero and me—such as I am, monsieur—*je ne sais quelle dévergondée!*" [15]

Mr. Mixter may have inferred that he was to that extent the object of our reference; but of the manner in which he was handled he must have had small suspicion—preoccupied as he was, as to my companion, with the ecstasy of contemplation. Our hostess moreover at this moment came out of the house, bearing a coffee-pot and three cups on a neat little tray. I took from her eyes, as she approached us, a brief but intense appeal— the mute expression, as I felt, conveyed in the hardest little look she had yet addressed me, of her longing to know what, as a man of the world in general and of the French world in particular, I thought of these allied forces now so encamped on the stricken field of her life. I could only "act" however, as they said at North Verona, quite impenetrably—only make no answering sign. I couldn't intimate, much less could I frankly utter, my inward sense of the Countess's probable past, with its measure of her virtue, value and accomplishments, and of the limits of the consideration to which she could properly pretend. I couldn't give my friend a hint of how I myself personally "saw" her interesting pensioner—whether as the runaway wife of a too-jealous hair-dresser or of a too-morose pastry-cook, say; whether as a very small

11 "One has all kinds—" (JHP)
12 "These two years have given me hours and hours of trial!" (JHP)
13 "as is the fashion." (JHP)
14 "Yes, he has courted me ardently—" (JHP)
15 "I know not what kind of shameless woman!" (JHP)

bourgeoise, in fine, who had vitiated her case beyond patching up, or even as some character, of the nomadic sort, less edifying still. I couldn't let in, by the jog of a shutter, as it were, a hard informing ray and then, washing my hands of the business, turn my back for ever. I could on the contrary but save the situation, my own at least, for the moment, by pulling myself together with a master hand and appearing to ignore everything but that the dreadful person between us *was* a "grande dame." This effort was possible indeed but as a retreat in good order and with all the forms of courtesy. If I couldn't speak, still less could I stay, and I think I must, in spite of everything, have turned black with disgust to see Caroline Spencer stand there like a waiting-maid. I therefore won't answer for the shade of success that may have attended my saying to the Countess, on my feet and as to leave her: "You expect to remain some time in these *parages?*" [16]

What passed between us, as from face to face, while she looked up at me, *that* at least our companion may have caught, that at least may have sown, for the after-time, some seed of revelation. The Countess repeated her terrible shrug. "Who knows? I don't see my way—! It isn't an existence, but when one's in misery—! *Chère belle,*" she added as an appeal to Miss Spencer, "you've gone and forgotten the '*fine*'!"

I detained that lady as, after considering a moment in silence the small array, she was about to turn off in quest of this article. I held out my hand in silence—I had to go. Her wan set little face, severely mild and with the question of a moment before now quite cold in it, spoke of extreme fatigue, but also of something else strange and conceived—whether a desperate patience still, or at last some other desperation, being more than I can say. What was clearest on the whole was that she was glad I was going. Mr. Mixter had risen to his feet and was pouring out the Countess's coffee. As I went back past the Baptist church I could feel how right my poor friend had been in her conviction at the other, the still intenser, the now historic crisis, that she should still see something of that dear old Europe.

[1877]

16 "parts." (JHP)

QUESTIONS FOR STUDY

1. *How is the narrator characterized? Are his observations reliable? Why does he come to take such an interest in Caroline Spencer?*

2. *What qualities are associated with Caroline Spencer? What does the narrator mean when he says to her: "You've the great American disease, and you've got it 'bad' "? Why does she so willingly befriend her cousin and the "countess"?*

3. *What clues suggest the true nature of the cousin and the Countess?*

4. *Why doesn't the narrator intervene more directly in Caroline Spencer's affairs?*

5. *Why is Caroline embarrassed by the narrator's final visit? Has she finally perceived the truth of the situation?*

6. *To what extent are all the characters stereotypes? What national qualities does James associate with each?*

HENRY JAMES

The Tree of Knowledge

I

IT WAS one of the secret opinions, such
as we all have, of Peter Brench that
his main success in life would have
consisted in his never having committed
himself about the work, as it was called,
of his friend Morgan Mallow. This was a
subject on which it was, to the best of his
belief, impossible with veracity to quote
him, and it was nowhere on record that
he had, in the connexion, on any occasion
and in any embarrassment, either lied or
spoken the truth. Such a triumph had its
honour even for a man of other triumphs
—a man who had reached fifty, who had
escaped marriage, who had lived within
his means, who had been in love with
Mrs. Mallow for years without breathing
it, and who, last not least, had judged
himself once for all. He had so judged
himself in fact that he felt an extreme and
general humility to be his proper portion;
yet there was nothing that made him
think so well of his parts as the course he
had steered so often through the shallows
just mentioned. It became thus a real
wonder that the friends in whom he had
most confidence were just those with
whom he had most reserves. He couldn't
tell Mrs. Mallow—or at least he supposed, excellent man, he couldn't—that
she was the one beautiful reason he had
never married; any more than he could
tell her husband that the sight of the multiplied marbles in that gentleman's studio
was an affliction of which even time had
never blunted the edge. His victory, however, as I have intimated, in regard to
these productions, was not simply in his
not having let it out that he deplored
them; it was, remarkably, in his not
having kept it in by anything else.

The whole situation, among these good
people, was verily a marvel, and there
was probably not such another for a long
way from the spot that engages us—the
point at which the soft declivity of Hamp-
stead began at that time to confess in
broken accents to Saint John's Wood. He
despised Mallow's statues and adored
Mallow's wife, and yet was distinctly
fond of Mallow, to whom, in turn, he
was equally dear. Mrs. Mallow rejoiced
in the statues—though she preferred,
when pressed, the busts; and if she was
visibly attached to Peter Brench it was
because of his affection for Morgan. Each
loved the other moreover for the love
borne in each case to Lancelot, whom the
Mallows respectively cherished as their
only child and whom the friend of their
fireside identified as the third—but decidedly the handsomest—of his godsons.
Already in the old years it had come to
that—that no one, for such a relation,
could possibly have occurred to any of
them, even to the baby itself, but Peter.
There was luckily a certain independence,
of the pecuniary sort, all round: the
Master could never otherwise have spent
his solemn *Wanderjahre* in Florence and
Rome, and continued by the Thames as
well as by the Arno and the Tiber to add
unpurchased group to group and model,
for what was too apt to prove in the event
mere love, fancy-heads of celebrities
either too busy or too buried—too much
of the age or too little of it—to sit.
Neither could Peter, lounging in almost
daily, have found time to keep the whole
complicated tradition so alive by his presence. He was massive but mild, the de-
positary of these mysteries—large and
loose and ruddy and curly, with deep
tones, deep eyes, deep pockets, to say
nothing of the habit of long pipes, soft
hats and brownish greyish weather-faded
clothes, apparently always the same.

He had "written," it was known, but
had never spoken, never spoken in particular of that; and he had the air (since,
as was believed, he continued to write) of
keeping it up in order to have something

more—as if he hadn't at the worst enough—to be silent about. Whatever his air, at any rate, Peter's occasional unmentioned prose and verse were quite truly the result of an impulse to maintain the purity of his taste by establishing still more firmly the right relation of fame to feebleness. The little green door of his domain was in a garden-wall on which the discoloured stucco made patches, and in the small detached villa behind it everything was old, the furniture, the servants, the books, the prints, the immemorial habits and the new improvements. The Mallows, at Carrara Lodge, were within ten minutes, and the studio there was on their little land, to which they had added, in their happy faith, for building it. This was the good fortune, if it was not the ill, of her having brought him in marriage a portion that put them in a manner at their ease and enabled them thus, on their side, to keep it up. And they did keep it up—they always had—the infatuated sculptor and his wife, for whom nature had refined on the impossible by relieving them of the sense of the difficult. Morgan had at all events everything of the sculptor but the spirit of Phidias—the brown velvet, the becoming *beretto*, the "plastic" presence, the fine fingers, the beautiful accent in Italian and the old Italian factotum. He seemed to make up for everything when he addressed Egidio with the "tu" and waved him to turn one of the rotary pedestals of which the place was full. They were tremendous Italians at Carrara Lodge, and the secret of the part played by this fact in Peter's life was in a large degree that it gave him, sturdy Briton as he was, just the amount of "going abroad" he could bear. The Mallows were all his Italy, but it was in a measure for Italy he liked them. His one worry was that Lance—to which they had shortened his godson—was, in spite of a public school, perhaps a shade too Italian. Morgan meanwhile looked like somebody's flattering idea of somebody's own person as expressed in the great room provided at the Uffizzi Museum for the general illustration of that idea by eminent hands. The Master's sole regret that he hadn't been born rather to the brush than to the chisel

sprang from his wish that he might have contributed to that collection.

It appeared with time at any rate to be to the brush that Lance had been born; for Mrs. Mallow, one day when the boy was turning twenty, broke it to their friend, who shared, to the last delicate morsel, their problems and pains, that it seemed as if nothing would really do but that he should embrace the career. It had been impossible longer to remain blind to the fact that he was gaining no glory at Cambridge, where Brench's own college had for a year tempered its tone to him as for Brench's own sake. Therefore why renew the vain form of preparing him for the impossible? The impossible—it had become clear—was that he should be anything but an artist.

"Oh dear, dear!" said poor Peter.

"Don't you believe in it?" asked Mrs. Mallow, who still, at more than forty, had her violet velvet eyes, her creamy satin skin and her silken chestnut hair.

"Believe in what?"

"Why in Lance's passion."

"I don't know what you mean by 'believing in it.' I've never been unaware, certainly, of his disposition, from his earliest time, to daub and draw; but I confess I've hoped it would burn out."

"But why should it," she sweetly smiled, "with his wonderful heredity? Passion is passion—though of course indeed *you*, dear Peter, know nothing of that. Has the Master's ever burned out?"

Peter looked off a little and, in his familiar formless way, kept up for a moment a sound between a smothered whistle and a subdued hum. "Do you think he's going to be another Master?"

She seemed scarce prepared to go that length, yet she had on the whole a marvellous trust. "I know what you mean by that. Will it be a career to incur the jealousies and provoke the machinations that have been at times almost too much for his father? Well—say it may be, since nothing but clap-trap, in these dreadful days, *can*, it would seem, make its way, and since, with the curse of refinement and distinction, one may easily find one's self begging one's bread. Put it at the worst—say he *has* the misfortune to wing his flight further than the vulgar taste of his stupid countrymen can follow. Think, all the same, of the happiness—the same the Master has had. He'll *know*."

Peter looked rueful. "Ah but *what* will he know?"

"Quiet joy!" cried Mrs. Mallow, quite impatient and turning away.

II

He had of course before long to meet the boy himself on it and to hear that practically everything was settled. Lance was not to go up again, but to go instead to Paris where, since the die was cast, he would find the best advantages. Peter had always felt he must be taken as he was, but had never perhaps found him so much of that pattern as on this occasion. "You chuck Cambridge then altogether? Doesn't that seem rather a pity?"

Lance would have been like his father, to his friend's sense, had he had less humour, and like his mother had he had more beauty. Yet it was a good middle way for Peter that, in the modern manner, he was, to the eye, rather the young stockbroker than the young artist. The youth reasoned that it was a question of time—there was such a mill to go through, such an awful lot to learn. He had talked with fellows and had judged. "One has got, to-day," he said, "don't you see? to know."

His interlocutor, at this, gave a groan. "Oh hang it, *don't* know!"

Lance wondered. " 'Don't'? Then what's the use—?"

"The use of what?"

"Why of anything. Don't you think I've talent?"

Peter smoked away for a little in silence; then went on: "It isn't knowledge, it's ignorance that—as we've been beautifully told—is bliss."

"Don't you think I've talent?" Lance repeated.

Peter, with his trick of queer kind demonstrations, passed his arm round his godson and held him a moment. "How do I know?"

"Oh," said the boy, "if it's your own ignorance you're defending—!"

Again, for a pause, on the sofa, his godfather smoked. "It isn't. I've the misfortune to be omniscient."

"Oh well," Lance laughed again, "if you know *too* much—!"

"That's what I do, and it's why I'm so wretched."

Lance's gaiety grew. "Wretched? Come, I say!"

"But I forgot," his companion went on—"you're not to know about that. It would indeed for you to make the too much. Only I'll tell you what I'll do." And Peter got up from the sofa. "If you'll go up again I'll pay your way at Cambridge."

Lance stared, a little rueful in spite of being still more amused. "Oh Peter! You disapprove so of Paris?"

"Well, I'm afraid of it."

"Ah I see!"

"No, you don't see—yet. But you will—that is you would. And you mustn't."

The young man thought more gravely. "But one's innocence, already—!"

"Is considerably damaged? Ah that won't matter," Peter persisted— "we'll patch it up here."

"Here? Then you want me to stay at home?"

Peter almost confessed to it. "Well, we're so right—we four together—just as we are. We're so safe. Come, don't spoil it."

The boy, who had turned to gravity, turned from this, on the real pressure in his friend's tone, to consternation. "Then what's a fellow to be?"

"My particular care. Come, old man" —and Peter now fairly pleaded—"*I'll* look out for you."

Lance, who had remained on the sofa with his legs out and his hands in his pockets, watched him with eyes that showed suspicion. Then he got up. "You think there's something the matter with me—that I can't make a success."

"Well, what do you call a success?"

Lance thought again. "Why the best sort, I suppose, is to please one's self. Isn't that the sort that, in spite of cabals and things, is—in his own peculiar line—the Master's?"

There were so much too many things in this question to be answered at once that they practically checked the discussion, which became particularly difficult in the light of such renewed proof that, though the young man's innocence might, in the course of his studies, as he contended, somewhat have shrunken, the finer essence of it still remained. That was indeed exactly what Peter had assumed and what above all he desired; yet perversely enough it gave him a chill. The boy believed in the cabals and things, believed in the peculiar line, believed, to be brief, in the Master. What happened a month or two later wasn't that he went up again at the expense of his godfather, but that a fortnight after he had got settled in Paris this personage sent him fifty pounds.

He had meanwhile at home, this personage, made up his mind to the worst; and what that might be had never yet grown quite so vivid to him as when, on his presenting himself one Sunday night, as he never failed to do, for supper, the mistress of Carrara Lodge met him with an appeal as to—of all things in the world —the wealth of the Canadians. She was earnest, she was even excited. "Are many of them *really* rich?"

He had to confess he knew nothing about them, but he often thought afterwards of that evening. The room in which they sat was adorned with sundry specimens of the Master's genius, which had the merit of being, as Mrs. Mallow herself frequently suggested, of an unusually convenient size. They were indeed of dimensions not customary in the products of the chisel, and they had the singularity that, if the objects and features intended to be small looked too large, the objects and features intended to be large looked too small. The Master's idea, either in respect to this matter or to any other, had in almost any case, even after years, remained undiscoverable to Peter Brench. The creations that so failed to reveal it stood about on pedestals and brackets, on tables and shelves, a little staring white population, heroic, idyllic, allegoric, mythic, symbolic, in which "scale" had so strayed and lost itself that the public square and the chimney-piece seemed to have changed places, the monumental being all diminutive and the diminutive all monumental; branches at any rate, markedly, of a

family in which stature was rather oddly irrespective of function, age and sex. They formed, like the Mallows themselves, poor Brench's own family—having at least to such a degree the note of familiarity. The occasion was one of those he had long ago learnt to know and to name—short flickers of the faint flame, soft gusts of a kinder air. Twice a year regularly the Master believed in his fortune, in addition to believing all the year round in his genius. This time it was to be made by a bereaved couple from Toronto, who had given him the handsomest order for a tomb to three lost children, each of whom they desired to see, in the composition, emblematically and characteristically represented.

Such was naturally the moral of Mrs. Mallow's question: if their wealth was to be assumed, it was clear, from the nature of their admiration, as well as from mysterious hints thrown out (they were a little odd!) as to other possibilities of the same mortuary sort, that their further patronage might be; and not less evident that should the Master become at all known in those climes nothing would be more inevitable than a run of Canadian custom. Peter had been present before at runs of custom, colonial and domestic— present at each of those of which the aggregation had left so few gaps in the marble company round him; but it was his habit never at these junctures to prick the bubble in advance. The fond illusion, while it lasted, eased the wound of elections never won, the long ache of medals and diplomas carried off, on every chance, by every one but the Master; it moreover lighted the lamp that would glimmer through the next eclipse. They lived, however, after all—as it was always beautiful to see—at a height scarce susceptible of ups and downs. They strained a point at times charmingly, strained it to admit that the public was here and there not too bad to buy; but they would have been nowhere without their attitude that the Master was always too good to sell. They were at all events deliciously formed, Peter often said to himself, for their fate; the Master had a vanity, his wife had a loyalty, of which success, depriving these things of innocence, would have diminished the merit and the grace. Any one could be charming under a charm, and as he looked about him at a world of prosperity more void of proportion even than the Master's museum he wondered if he knew another pair that so completely escaped vulgarity.

"What a pity Lance isn't with us to rejoice!" Mrs. Mallow on this occasion sighed at supper.

"We'll drink to the health of the absent," her husband replied, filling his friend's glass and his own and giving a drop to their companion; "but we must hope he's preparing himself for a happiness much less like this of ours this evening—excusable as I grant it to be!—than like the comfort we have always (whatever has happened or has not happened) been able to trust ourselves to enjoy. The comfort," the Master explained, leaning back in the pleasant lamplight and firelight, holding up his glass and looking round at his marble family, quartered more or less, a monstrous brood, in every room—"the comfort of art in itself!"

Peter looked a little shyly at his wine. "Well—I don't care what you may call it when a fellow doesn't—but Lance must learn to *sell*, you know. I drink to his acquisition of the secret of a base popularity!"

"Oh yes, *he* must sell," the boy's mother, who was still more, however, this seemed to give out, the Master's wife, rather artlessly allowed.

"Ah," the sculptor after a moment confidently pronounced, "Lance *will*. Don't be afraid. He'll have learnt."

"Which is exactly what Peter," Mrs. Mallow gaily returned—"why in the world were you so perverse, Peter?—wouldn't when he told him hear of."

Peter, when this lady looked at him with accusatory affection—a grace on her part not infrequent—could never find a word; but the Master, who was always all amenity and tact, helped him out now as he had often helped him before. "That's his old idea, you know—on which we've so often differed: his theory that the artist should be all impulse and instinct. *I* go in of course for a certain amount of school. Not too much—but a due propor-

tion. There's where his protest came in," he continued to explain to his wife, "as against what *might*, don't you see? be in question for Lance."

"Ah well"—and Mrs. Mallow turned the violet eyes across the table at the subject of this discourse—"he's sure to have meant of course nothing but good. Only that wouldn't have prevented him, if Lance *had* taken his advice, from being in effect horribly cruel."

They had a sociable way of talking to him to his face as if he had been in the clay or—at most—in the plaster, and the Master was unfailingly generous. He might have been waving Egidio to make him revolve. "Ah but poor Peter wasn't so wrong as to what it may after all come to that he *will* learn."

"Oh but nothing artistically bad," she urged—still, for poor Peter, arch and dewy.

"Why just the little French tricks," said the Master: on which their friend had to pretend to admit, when pressed by Mrs. Mallow, that these æsthetic vices had been the objects of his dread.

III

"I know now," Lance said to him the next year, "why you were so much against it." He had come back supposedly for a mere interval and was looking about him at Carrara Lodge, where indeed he had already on two or three occasions since his expatriation briefly reappeared. This had the air of a longer holiday. "Something rather awful has happened to me. It *isn't* so very good to know."

"I'm bound to say high spirits don't show in your face," Peter was rather ruefully forced to confess. "Still, are you very sure you do know?"

"Well, I at least know about as much as I can bear." These remarks were exchanged in Peter's den, and the young man, smoking cigarettes, stood before the fire with his back against the mantel. Something of his bloom seemed really to have left him.

Poor Peter wondered. "You're clear then as to what in particular I wanted you not to go for?"

"In particular?" Lance thought. "It seems to me that in particular there can have been only one thing."

They stood for a little sounding each other. "Are you quite sure?"

"Quite sure I'm a beastly duffer? Quite —by this time."

"Oh!"—and Peter turned away as if almost with relief.

"It's *that* that isn't pleasant to find out."

"Oh I don't care for 'that,' " said Peter, presently coming round again. "I mean I personally don't."

"Yet I hope you can understand a little that I myself should!"

"Well, what do you mean by it?" Peter sceptically asked.

And on this Lance had to explain— how the upshot of his studies in Paris had inexorably proved a mere deep doubt of his means. These studies had so waked him up that a new light was in his eyes; but what the new light did was really to show him too much. "Do you know what's the matter with me? I'm too horribly intelligent. Paris was really the last place for me. I've learnt what I can't do."

Poor Peter stared—it was a staggerer; but even after they had had, on the subject, a longish talk in which the boy brought out to the full the hard truth of his lesson, his friend betrayed less pleasure than usually breaks into a face to the happy tune of "I told you so!" Poor Peter himself made now indeed so little a point of having told him so that Lance broke ground in a different place a day or two after. "What was it then that— before I went—you were afraid I should find out?" This, however, Peter refused to tell him—on the ground that if he hadn't yet guessed perhaps he never would, and that in any case nothing at all for either of them was to be gained by giving the thing a name. Lance eyed him on this an instant with the bold curiosity of youth—with the air indeed of having in his mind two or three names, of which one or other would be right. Peter nevertheless, turning his back again, offered no encouragement, and when they parted afresh it was with some show of impatience on the side of the boy. Accord-

ingly on their next encounter Peter saw at a glance that he had now, in the interval, divined and that, to sound his note, he was only waiting till they should find themselves alone. This he had soon arranged and he then broke straight out. "Do you know your conundrum has been keeping me awake? But in the watches of the night the answer came over me—so that, upon my honour, I quite laughed out. Had you been supposing I had to go to Paris to learn *that*?" Even now, to see him still so sublimely on his guard, Peter's young friend had to laugh afresh. "You won't give a sign till you're sure? Beautiful old Peter!" But Lance at last produced it. "Why, hang it, the truth about the Master."

It made between them for some minutes a lively passage, full of wonder for each at the wonder of the other. "Then how long have you understood—"

"The true value of his work? I understood it," Lance recalled, "as soon as I began to understand anything. But I didn't begin fully to do that, I admit, till I got *là-bas*."

"Dear, dear!"—Peter gasped with retrospective dread.

"But for what have you taken me? I'm a hopeless muff—that I *had* to have rubbed in. But I'm not such a muff as the Master!" Lance declared.

"Then why did you never tell me—?"

"That I hadn't after all"—the boy took him up—"remained such an idiot? Just because I never dreamed *you* knew. But I beg your pardon. I only wanted to spare you. And what I don't now understand is how the deuce then for so long you've managed to keep bottled."

Peter produced his explanation, but only after some delay and with a gravity not void of embarrassment. "It was for your mother."

"Oh!" said Lance.

"And that's the great thing now— since the murder *is* out. I want a promise from you. I mean"—and Peter almost feverishly followed it up—"a vow from you, solemn and such as you owe me here on the spot, that you'll sacrifice anything rather than let her ever guess—"

"That *I've* guessed?"—Lance took it

in. "I see." He evidently after a moment had taken in much. "But what is it you've in mind that I may have a chance to sacrifice?"

"Oh one has always something."

Lance looked at him hard. "Do you mean that *you've* had—?" The look he received back, however, so put the question by that he found soon enough another. "Are you really sure my mother doesn't know?"

Peter, after renewed reflexion, was really sure. "If she does she's too wonderful."

"But aren't we all too wonderful?"

"Yes," Peter granted—"but in different ways. The thing's so desperately important because your father's little public consists only, as you know then," Peter developed—"well, of how many?"

"First of all," the Master's son risked, "of himself. And last of all too. I don't quite see of whom else."

Peter had an approach to impatience. "Of your mother, I say—*always*."

Lance cast it all up. "You absolutely feel that?"

"Absolutely."

"Well then with yourself that makes three."

"Oh *me!*"—and Peter, with a wag of his kind old head, modestly excused himself. "The number's at any rate small enough for any individual dropping out to be too dreadfully missed. Therefore, to put it in a nutshell, take care, my boy —that's all—that *you're* not!"

"I've got to keep on humbugging?" Lance wailed.

"It's just to warn you of the danger of your failing of that that I've seized this opportunity."

"And what do you regard in particular," the young man asked, "as the danger?"

"Why this certainty: that the moment your mother, who feels so strongly, should suspect your secret—well," said Peter desperately, "the fat would be on the fire."

Lance for a moment seemed to stare at the blaze. "She'd throw me over?"

"She'd throw *him* over."

"And come round to us?"

Peter, before he answered, turned away. "Come round to *you*." But he had said enough to indicate—and, as he evidently trusted, to avert—the horrid contingency.

IV

Within six months again, none the less, his fear was on more occasions than one all before him. Lance had returned to Paris for another trial; then had reappeared at home and had had, with his father, for the first time in his life, one of the scenes that strike sparks. He described it with much expression to Peter, touching whom (since they had never done so before) it was the sign of a new reserve on the part of the pair at Carrara Lodge that they at present failed, on a matter of intimate interest, to open themselves—if not in joy then in sorrow—to their good friend. This produced perhaps practically between the parties a shade of alienation and a slight intermission of commerce—marked mainly indeed by the fact that to talk at his ease with his old playmate Lance had in general to come to see him. The closest if not quite the gayest relation they had yet known together was thus ushered in. The difficulty for poor Lance was a tension at home—begotten by the fact that his father wished him to be at least the sort of success he himself had been. He hadn't "chucked" Paris—though nothing appeared more vivid to him than that Paris had chucked him: he would go back again because of the fascination in trying, in seeing, in sounding the depths —in learning one's lesson, briefly, even if the lesson were simply that of one's impotence in the presence of one's larger vision. But what did the Master, all aloft in his senseless fluency, know of impotence, and what vision—to be called such—had he in all his blind life ever had? Lance, heated and indignant, frankly appealed to his godparent on this score.

His father, it appeared, had come down on him for having, after so long, nothing to show, and hoped that on his next return this deficiency would be repaired. *The* thing, the Master complacently set forth was—for any artist, however inferior to himself—at least to "do" something. "What can you do? That's all I ask!" *He* had certainly done enough, and there was no mistake about what he had to show. Lance had tears in his eyes when it came thus to letting his old friend know how great the strain might be on the "sacrifice" asked of him. It wasn't so easy to continue humbugging —as from son to parent—after feeling one's self despised for not grovelling in mediocrity. Yet a noble duplicity was what, as they intimately faced the situation, Peter went on requiring; and it was still for a time what his young friend, bitter and sore, managed loyally to comfort him with. Fifty pounds more than once again, it was true, rewarded both in London and in Paris the young friend's loyalty; none the less sensibly, doubtless, at the moment, that the money was a direct advance on a decent sum for which Peter had long since privately prearranged an ultimate function. Whether by these arts or others, at all events, Lance's just resentment was kept for a season— at bay. The day arrived when he warned his companion that he could hold out— or hold in—no longer. Carrara Lodge had had to listen to another lecture delivered from a great height—an infliction really heavier at last than, without striking back or in some way letting the Master have the truth, flesh and blood could bear.

"And what I don't see is," Lance observed with a certain irritated eye for what was after all, if it came to that, owing to himself too; "what I don't see is, upon my honour, how *you*, as things are going, can keep the game up."

"Oh the game for me is only to hold my tongue," said placid Peter. "And I have my reason."

"Still my mother?"

Peter showed a queer face as he had often shown it before—that is by turning it straight away. "What will you have? I haven't ceased to like her."

"She's beautiful—she's a dear of course," Lance allowed; "but what is she to you, after all, and what is it to you

that, as to anything whatever, she should or she shouldn't?"

Peter, who had turned red, hung fire a little. "Well—it's all simply what I make of it."

There was now, however, in his young friend a strange, an adopted insistence. "What are you after all to *her*?"

"Oh nothing. But that's another matter."

"She cares only for my father," said Lance the Parisian.

"Naturally—and that's just why."

"Why you've wished to spare her?"

"Because she cares so tremendously much."

Lance took a turn about the room, but with his eyes still on his host. "How awfully—always—you must have liked her!"

"Awfully. Always," said Peter Brench.

The young man continued for a moment to muse—then stopped again in front of him. "Do you know how much she cares?" Their eyes met on it, but Peter, as if his own found something new in Lance's, appeared to hesitate, for the first time in an age, to say he did know. "*I've* only just found out," said Lance. "She came to my room last night, after being present, in silence and only with her eyes on me, at what I had had to take from him: she came—and she was with me an extraordinary hour."

He had paused again and they had again for a while sounded each other. Then something—and it made him suddenly turn pale—came to Peter. "She *does* know?"

"She does know. She let it all out to me—so as to demand of me no more than 'that,' as she said, of which she herself had been capable. She has always known," said Lance without pity.

Peter was silent a long time; during which his companion might have heard him gently breathe, and on touching him might have felt within him the vibration of a long low sound suppressed. By the time he spoke at last he had taken everything in. "Then I do see how tremendously much."

"Isn't it wonderful?" Lance asked.

"Wonderful," Peter mused.

"So that if your original effort to keep me from Paris was to keep me from knowledge—!" Lance exclaimed as if with a sufficient indication of this futility.

It might have been at the futility Peter appeared for a little to gaze. "I think it must have been—without my quite at the time knowing it—to keep *me*!" he replied at last as he turned away.

[1900]

QUESTIONS FOR STUDY

1. *What does James' story seem to be saying about knowledge, ignorance, and the awareness of awareness? Where do the author's sympathies seem to reside? With Peter Brench? With Mrs. Mallow? With Lancelot?*

2. *How does James characterize Peter Brench? Of what willful blindness has he himself been guilty? Why?*

3. *How do Peter Brench and Mrs. Mallow protect the Master's illusions? How does the Master protect himself? What indications are there early in the story that Mrs. Mallow understands perfectly the artistic abilities of her husband?*

4. *What advantages does James gain by restricting the point of view largely to the consciousness of Peter Brench?*

5. *What is the significance of the story's title? Of Lancelot's name?*

SARAH ORNE JEWETT

The Town Poor

Mrs. William Trimble and Miss Rebecca Wright were driving along Hampden east road, one afternoon in early spring. Their progress was slow. Mrs. Trimble's sorrel horse was old and stiff, and the wheels were clogged by clay mud. The frost was not yet out of the ground, although the snow was nearly gone, except in a few places on the north side of the woods, or where it had drifted all winter against a length of fence.

"There must be a good deal o' snow to the nor'ard of us yet," said weather-wise Mrs. Trimble. "I feel it in the air; 't is more than the ground-damp. We ain't goin' to have real nice weather till the up-country snow 's all gone."

"I heard say yesterday that there was good sleddin' yet, all up through Parsley," responded Miss Wright. "I should n't like to live in them northern places. My cousin Ellen's husband was a Parsley man, an' he was obliged, as you may have heard, to go up north to his father's second wife's funeral; got back day before yesterday. 'T was about twenty-one miles, an' they started on wheels; but when they 'd gone nine or ten miles, they found 't was no sort o' use, an' left their wagon an' took a sleigh. The man that owned it charged 'em four an' six, too. I should n't have thought he would; they told him they was goin' to a funeral; an' they had their own buffaloes an' everything."

"Well, I expect it's a good deal harder scratchin', up that way; they have to git money where they can; the farms is very poor as you go north," suggested Mrs. Trimble kindly. " 'T ain't none too rich a country where we be, but I've always been grateful I wa'n't born up to Parsley."

The old horse plodded along, and the sun, coming out from the heavy spring clouds, sent a sudden shine of light along the muddy road. Sister Wright drew her large veil forward over the high brim of her bonnet. She was not used to driving, or to being much in the open air; but Mrs. Trimble was an active business woman, and looked after her own affairs herself, in all weathers. The late Mr. Trimble had left her a good farm, but not much ready money, and it was often said that she was better off in the end than if he had lived. She regretted his loss deeply, however; it was impossible for her to speak of him, even to intimate friends, without emotion, and nobody had ever hinted that this emotion was insincere. She was most warm-hearted and generous, and in her limited way played the part of Lady Bountiful in the town of Hampden.

"Why, there's where the Bray girls lives, ain't it?" she exclaimed, as, beyond a thicket of witch-hazel and scrub-oak, they came in sight of a weather-beaten, solitary farmhouse. The barn was too far away for thrift or comfort, and they could see long lines of light between the shrunken boards as they came nearer. The fields looked both stony and sodden. Somehow, even Parsley itself could be hardly more forlorn.

"Yes 'm," said Miss Wright, "that's where they live now, poor things. I know the place, though I ain't been up here for years. You don't suppose, Mis' Trimble —I ain't seen the girls out to meetin' all winter. I've re'lly been covetin' "—

"Why, yes, Rebecca, of course we could stop," answered Mrs. Trimble heartily. "The exercises was over earlier 'n I expected, an' you 're goin' to remain over night long o' me, you know. There won't be no tea till we git there, so we can't be late. I'm in the habit o' sendin' a basket to the Bray girls when any o' our folks is comin' this way, but I ain't been to see 'em since they moved up here. Why, it must be a good deal over a year ago. I know 't was in the late winter they had to make the move. 'T was cruel hard, I must say, an' if I had n't been down with my pleurisy fever I'd have stirred round an' done somethin' about it. There was a good deal o' sickness at the time, an'—well, 't was kind o' rushed through, breakin' of 'em up, an' lots o' folks blamed the selec'*men;* but when 't was done, 't was done, an' nobody took holt to undo it. Ann an' Mandy looked same 's ever when they come to meetin', 'long in the summer,—kind o' wishful, perhaps. They've always sent me word they was gittin' on pretty comfortable."

"That would be their way," said Rebecca Wright. "They never was any hand to complain, though Mandy 's less cheerful than Ann. If Mandy 'd been spared such poor eyesight, an' Ann had n't got her lame wrist that wa'n't set right, they 'd kep' off the town fast enough. They both shed tears when they talked to me about havin' to break up, when I went to see 'em before I went over to brother Asa's. You see we was brought up neighbors, an' we went to school together, the Brays an' me. 'T was a special Providence brought us home this road, I 've been so covetin' a chance to git to see 'em. My lameness hampers me."

"I'm glad we come this way, myself," said Mrs. Trimble.

"I'd like to see just how they fare," Miss Rebecca Wright continued. "They give their consent to goin' on the town because they knew they'd got to be dependent, an' so they felt 't would come easier for all than for a few to help 'em. They acted real dignified an' right-minded, contrary to what most do in such cases, but they was dreadful anxious to see who would bid 'em off, town-meeting day; they did so hope 't would be somebody right in the village. I just sat down an' cried good when I found Abel Janes's folks had got hold of 'em. They always had the name of bein' slack an' poor-spirited, an' they did it just for what they got out o' the town. The selectmen this last year ain't what we have had. I hope they've been considerate about the Bray girls."

"I should have be'n more considerate about fetchin' of you over," apologized Mrs. Trimble. "I've got my horse, an' you 're lame-footed; 't is too far for you to come. But time does slip away with busy folks, an' I forgit a good deal I ought to remember."

"There 's nobody more considerate than you be," protested Miss Rebecca Wright.

Mrs. Trimble made no answer, but took out her whip and gently touched the sorrel horse, who walked considerably faster, but did not think it worth while to trot. It was a long, round-about way to the house, farther down the road and up a lane.

"I never had any opinion of the Bray girls' father, leavin' 'em as he did," said Mrs. Trimble.

"He was much praised in his time, though there was always some said his early life had n't been up to the mark," explained her companion. "He was a great favorite of our then preacher, the Reverend Daniel Longbrother. They did a good deal for the parish, but they did it their own way. Deacon Bray was one that did his part in the repairs without urging. You know 't was in his time the first repairs was made, when they got out the old soundin'-board an' them handsome square pews. It cost an awful sight o' money, too. They had n't done payin' up that debt when they set to alter it again an' git the walls frescoed. My grandmother was one that always spoke her mind right out, an' she was dreadful opposed to breakin' up the square pews where she 'd always set. They was countin' up what 't would cost in parish meetin', an' she riz right up an' said 't would n't cost nothin' to let 'em stay, an' there wa'n't a house carpenter left in the parish that could do such nice work, an' time would come when the great-grandchildren would give their eye-teeth to have the old meetin'-house look just as it did then. But haul the inside to pieces they would and did."

"There come to be a real fight over it, did n't there?" agreed Mrs. Trimble soothingly. "Well, 't wa'n't good taste. I remember the old house well. I come here as a child to visit a cousin o' mother's, an' Mr. Trimble's folks was neighbors, an' we was drawed to each other then, young 's we was. Mr. Trimble spoke of it many's the time,—that first time he ever see me, in a leghorn hat with a feather; 't was one that mother had, an' pressed over."

"When I think of them old sermons that used to be preached in that old meetin'-house of all, I'm glad it 's altered over, so 's not to remind folks," said Miss Rebecca Wright, after a suitable pause. "Them old brimstone discourses, you know, Mis' Trimble. Preachers is far more reasonable, nowadays. Why, I set an' thought, last Sabbath, as I listened, that if old Mr. Longbrother an' Deacon Bray could hear the difference they'd crack the ground over 'em like pole beans, an' come right up 'long side their headstones."

Mrs. Trimble laughed heartily, and shook the reins three or four times by way of emphasis. "There 's no gitting round you," she said, much pleased. "I should think Deacon Bray would want to rise, any way, if 't was so he could, an' knew how his poor girls was farin'. A man ought to provide for his folks he 's got to leave behind him, specially if they 're women. To be sure, they had their little home; but we 've seen how, with all their industrious ways, they had n't means to keep it. I s'pose he thought he'd got time enough to lay by, when he give so generous in collections; but he did n't lay by, an' there they be. He might have took lessons from the squirrels: even them little wild creatur's makes them their winter hoards, an' menfolks ought to know enough if squirrels does. 'Be just before you are generous:' that's what was always set for the B's in the copy-books, when I was to school, and it often runs through my mind."

" 'As for man, his days are as grass,'— that was for A; the two go well together," added Miss Rebecca Wright soberly. "My good gracious, ain't this a starved-lookin' place? It makes me ache to think them nice Bray girls has to brook it here."

The sorrel horse, though somewhat puzzled by an unexpected deviation from his homeward way, willingly came to a stand by the gnawed corner of the dooryard fence, which evidently served as hitching-place. Two or three ragged old hens were picking about the yard, and at last a face appeared at the kitchen window, tied up in a handkerchief, as if it were a case of toothache. By the time our friends reached the side door next this window, Mrs. Janes came disconsolately to open it for them, shutting it again as soon as possible, though the air felt more chilly inside the house.

"Take seats," said Mrs. Janes briefly. "You'll have to see me just as I be. I have been suffering these four days with the ague, and everything to do. Mr. Janes is to court, on the jury. 'T was inconvenient to spare him. I should be pleased to have you lay off your things."

Comfortable Mrs. Trimble looked about the cheerless kitchen, and could not think of anything to say; so she smiled blandly and shook her head in answer to the invitation. "We'll just set a few minutes with you, to pass the time o' day, an' then we must go in an' have a word with the Miss Brays, bein' old acquaintance. It ain't been so we could get to call on 'em before. I don't know 's you 're acquainted with Miss R'becca Wright. She 's been out of town a good deal."

"I heard she was stopping over to Plainfields with her brother's folks," replied Mrs. Janes, rocking herself with irregular motion, as she sat close to the stove. "Got back some time in the fall, I believe?"

"Yes 'm," said Miss Rebecca, with an undue sense of guilt and conviction. "We've been to the installation over to the East Parish, an' thought we'd stop in; we took this road home to see if 't was any better. How is the Miss Brays gettin' on?"

"They 're well 's common," answered Mrs. Janes grudgingly. "I was put out with Mr. Janes for fetchin' of 'em here, with all I 've got to do, an' I own I was kind o' surly to 'em 'long to the first of it. He gits the money from the town, an' it helps him out; but he bid 'em off for five dollars a month, an' we can't do much for 'em at no such price as that. I went an' dealt with the selec'men, an' made 'em promise to find their firewood an' some other things extra. They was glad to get rid o' the matter the fourth time I went, an' would ha' promised 'most anything. But Mr. Janes don't keep me half the time in oven-wood, he's off so much, an' we was cramped o' room, any way. I have to store things up garrit a good deal, an' that keeps me trampin' right through their room. I do the best for 'em I can, Mis' Trimble, but 't ain't so easy for me as 't is for you, with all your means to do with."

The poor woman looked pinched and miserable herself, though it was evident that she had no gift at house or home keeping. Mrs. Trimble's heart was wrung with pain, as she thought of the unwelcome inmates of such a place; but she held her peace bravely, while Miss Rebecca again gave some brief information in regard to the installation.

"You go right up them back stairs," the hostess directed at last. "I'm glad some o' you church folks has seen fit to come an' visit 'em. There ain't been nobody here this long spell, an' they've aged a sight since they come. They always send down a taste out of your baskets, Mis' Trimble, an' I relish it, I tell you. I'll shut the door after you, if you don't object. I feel every draught o' cold air."

"I've always heard she was a great hand to make a poor mouth. Wa'n't she from somewheres up Parsley way?" whispered Miss Rebecca, as they stumbled in the half-light.

"Poor meechin' body, wherever she come from," replied Mrs. Trimble, as she knocked at the door.

There was silence for a moment after this unusual sound; then one of the Bray sisters opened the door. The eager guests stared into a small, low room, brown with age, and gray, too, as if former dust and cobwebs could not be made wholly to disappear. The two elderly women who stood there looked like captives. Their withered faces wore a look of apprehension, and the room itself was more bare and plain than was fitting to their evident refinement of character and self-respect. There was an uncovered small table in the middle of the floor, with some crackers on a plate; and, for some reason or other, this added a great deal to the general desolation.

But Miss Ann Bray, the elder sister, who carried her right arm in a sling, with piteously drooping fingers, gazed at the

visitors with radiant joy. She had not seen them arrive.

The one window gave only the view at the back of the house, across the fields, and their coming was indeed a surprise. The next minute she was laughing and crying together. "Oh, sister!" she said, "if here ain't our dear Mis' Trimble!—an' my heart o' goodness, 't is 'Becca Wright, too! What dear good creatur's you be! I've felt all day as if something good was goin' to happen, an' was just sayin' to myself 't was most sundown now, but I would n't let on to Mandany I'd give up hope quite yet. You see, the scissors stuck in the floor this very mornin' an' it's always a reliable sign. There, I've got to kiss ye both again!"

"I don't know where we can all set," lamented sister Mandana. "There ain't but the one chair an' the bed; t' other chair's too rickety; an' we've been promised another these ten days; but first they 've forgot it, an' next Mis' Janes can't spare it,—one excuse an' another, I am goin' to git a stump o' wood an' nail a board on to it, when I can git outdoor again," said Mandana, in a plaintive voice. "There, I ain't goin' to complain o' nothin', now you've come," she added; as the guests sat down, Mrs. Trimble, as was proper, in the one chair.

"We've sat on the bed many's the time with you, 'Becca, an' talked over our girl nonsense, ain't we? You know where 't was—in the little back bedroom we had when we was girls, an' used to peek out at our beaux through the strings o' mornin'-glories," laughed Ann Bray delightedly, her thin face shining more and more with joy. "I brought some o' them mornin'-glory seeds along when we come away, we'd raised 'em so many years; an' we got 'em started all right, but the hens found 'em out. I declare I chased them poor hens, foolish as 't was; but the mornin'-glories I'd counted on a sight to remind me o' home. You see, our debts was so large, after my long sickness an' all, that we did n't feel 't was right to keep back anything we could help from the auction."

It was impossible for any one to speak for a moment or two; the sisters felt their own uprooted condition afresh, and their

guests for the first time really comprehended the piteous contrast between that
neat little village house, which now
seemed a palace of comfort, and this
cold, unpainted upper room in the remote
Janes farmhouse. It was an unwelcome
thought to Mrs. Trimble that the well-to-
do town of Hampden could provide no
better for its poor than this, and her
round face flushed with resentment and
the shame of personal responsibility. "The
girls shall be well settled in the village
before another winter, if I pay their board
myself," she made an inward resolution,
and took another almost tearful look at
the broken stove, the miserable bed, and
the sisters' one hair-covered trunk, on
which Mandana was sitting. But the poor
place was filled with a golden spirit of
hospitality.

Rebecca was again discoursing eloquently of the installation; it was so much
easier to speak of general subjects, and
the sisters had evidently been longing to
hear some news. Since the late summer
they had not been to church, and presently Mrs. Trimble asked the reason.

"Now, don't you go to pouring out our
woes, Mandy!" begged little old Ann,
looking shy and almost girlish, and as if
she insisted upon playing that life was still
all before them and all pleasure. "Don't
you go to spoilin' their visit with our complaints! They know well 's we do that
changes must come, an' we 'd been so
wonted to our home things that this come
hard at first; but then they felt for us, I
know just as well 's can be. 'T will soon be
summer again, an' 't is real pleasant right
out in the fields here, when there ain't too
hot a spell. I 've got to know a sight o'
singin' birds since we come."

"Give me the folks I've always known,"
sighed the younger sister, who looked
older than Miss Ann, and less even-tem-
pered. "You may have your birds, if you
want 'em. I do re'lly long to go to meetin'
an' see folks go by up the aisle. Now, I
will speak of it, Ann, whatever you say.
We need, each of us, a pair o' good stout
shoes an' rubbers,—ours are all wore out;
an' we 've asked an' asked, an' they never
think to bring 'em, an' "—

Poor old Mandana, on the trunk, cov-

ered her face with her arms and sobbed
aloud. The elder sister stood over her, and
patted her on the thin shoulder like a
child, and tried to comfort her. It crossed
Mrs. Trimble's mind that it was not the
first time one had wept and the other had
comforted. The sad scene must have been
repeated many times in that long, drear
winter. She would see them forever after
in her mind as fixed as a picture, and her
own tears fell fast.

"You did n't see Mis' Janes's cunning
little boy, the next one to the baby, did
you?" asked Ann Bray, turning round
quickly at last, and going cheerfully on
with the conversation. "Now, hush,
Mandy, dear; they'll think you're childish!
He's a dear, friendly little creatur', an'
likes to stay with us a good deal, though
we feel 's if it 't was too cold for him, now
we are waitin' to get us more wood."

"When I think of the acres o' woodland in this town!" groaned Rebecca
Wright. "I believe I'm goin' to preach
next Sunday, 'stead o' the minister, an' I'll
make the sparks fly. I've always heard the
saying, 'What's everybody's business is
nobody's business,' an' I've come to believe it."

"Now, don't you, 'Becca. You've happened on a kind of a poor time with us,
but we've got more belongings than you
see here, an' a good large cluset, where
we can store those things there ain't room
to have about. You an' Mis' Trimble have
happened on a kind of poor day, you
know. Soon's I git me some stout shoes
an' rubbers, as Mandy says, I can fetch
home plenty o' little dry boughs o' pine;
you remember I was always a great hand
to roam in the woods? If we could only
have a front room, so 't we could look
out on the road an' see passin', an' was
shod for meetin', I don' know 's we
should complain. Now we're just goin' to
give you what we've got, an' make out
with a good welcome. We make more tea
'n we want in the mornin', an' then let the
fire go down, since 't has been so mild.
We've got a *good* cluset" (disappearing as
she spoke) "an' I know this to be good
tea 'cause it's some o' yourn, Mis' Trimble.
An' here's our sprigged chiny cups that
R'becca knows by sight, if Mis' Trimble

don't. We kep' out four of 'em an' put the even half dozen with the rest of the auction stuff. I've often wondered who'd got 'em but I never asked for fear 't would be somebody that would distress us. They was mother's you know."

The four cups were poured and the little table pushed to the bed where Rebecca Wright still sat, and Mandana, wiping her eyes, came and joined her. Mrs. Trimble sat in her chair at the end, and Ann trotted about the room in pleased content for a while, and in and out of the closet, as if she still had much to do; then she came and stood opposite Mrs. Trimble. She was very short and small, and there was no painful sense of her being obliged to stand. The four cups were not quite full of cold tea, but there was a clean old tablecloth folded double, and a plate with three pairs of crackers neatly piled, and a small—it must be owned, a very small—piece of hard white cheese. Then, for a treat, in a glass dish, there was a little preserved peach, the last —Miss Rebecca knew it instinctively—of the household stores brought from their old home. It was very sugary, this bit of peach; and as she helped her guests and sister Mandy, Miss Ann Bray said, half unconsciously, as she often had said with less reason in the old days, "Our preserves ain't so good as usual this year; this is beginning to candy." Both the guests protested, while Rebecca added that the taste of it carried her back, and made her feel young again. The Brays had always managed to keep one or two peach-trees alive in their corner of a garden. "I've been keeping this preserve for a treat," said her friend. "I'm glad to have you eat some, 'Becca. Last summer I often wished you was home an' could come an' see us, 'stead o' being away off to Plainfields."

The crackers did not taste too dry. Miss Ann took the last of the peach on her own cracker; there could not have been quite a small spoonful, after the others were helped, but she asked them first if they would not have some more. Then there was a silence, and in the silence a wave of tender feeling rose high in the hearts of the four elderly women. At this moment the setting sun flooded the poor plain

room with light; the unpainted wood was all of a golden-brown, and Ann Bray, with her gray hair and aged face, stood at the head of the table in a kind of aureole. Mrs. Trimble's face was all aquiver as she looked at her; she thought of the text about two or three being gathered together, and was half afraid.

"I believe we ought to 've asked Mis' Janes if she would n't come up," said Ann. "She's real good feelin', but she's had it very hard, an gits discouraged. I can't find that she's ever had anything real pleasant to look back to, as we have. There, next time we'll make a good heartenin' time for her too."

The sorrel horse had taken a long nap by the gnawed fence-rail, and the cool air after sundown made him impatient to be gone. The two friends jolted homeward in the gathering darkness, through the stiffening mud, and neither Mrs. Trimble nor Rebecca Wright said a word until they were out of sight as well as out of sound of the Janes house. Time must elapse before they could reach a more familiar part of the road and resume conversation on its natural level.

"I consider myself to blame," insisted Mrs. Trimble at last. "I have n't no words of accusation for nobody else, an' I ain't one to take comfort in calling names to the board o' selec'men. I make no reproaches, an' I take it all on my own shoulders; but I'm goin' to stir about me, I tell you! I shall begin early to-morrow. They're goin' back to their own house,— it's been standin' empty all winter,—an' the town's goin' to give 'em the rent an' what firewood they need; it won't come to more than the board's payin' out now. An' you an' me'll take this same horse an' wagon, an' ride an go afoot by turns, an' git means enough together to buy back their furniture an' whatever was sold at that plaguey auction; an' we'll put it all back, an' tell 'em they've got to move to a new place, an' just carry 'em right back again where they come from. An' don't you never tell, R'becca, but here I be a widow woman, layin' up what I make from my farm for nobody knows who, an' I'm goin' to do for them Bray girls all

I'm a mind to. I should be sca't to wake up in heaven, an' hear anybody there ask how the Bray girls was. Don't talk to me about the town o' Hampden, an' don't ever let me hear the name o' town poor! I'm ashamed to go home an' see what's set out for supper. I wish I'd brought 'em right along."

"I was goin' to ask if we could n't git the new doctor to go up an' do somethin' for poor Ann's arm," said Miss Rebecca. "They say he's very smart. If she could get so 's to braid straw or hook rugs again, she'd soon be earnin' a little somethin'. An' may be he could do somethin' for Mandy's eyes. They did use to live so neat an' ladylike. Somehow I could n't speak to tell 'em there that 't was I bought them six best cups an' saucers, time of the auction; they went very low, as everything else did, an' I thought I could save it some other way. They shall have 'em back an' welcome. You're real whole-hearted, Mis' Trimble. I expect Ann'll be sayin' that her father's child'n wa'n't goin' to be left desolate, an' that all the bread he cast on the water's comin' back through you."

"I don't care what she says, dear creatur'!" exclaimed Mrs. Trimble. "I'm full o' regrets I took time for that installation, an' set there seepin' in a lot o' talk this whole day long, except for its kind of bringin' us to the Bray girls. I wish to my heart 't was to-morrow mornin' a'ready, an' I a-startin' for the selec'*men*."

[1890]

QUESTIONS FOR STUDY

1. *How does the author portray each of the major characters of the story and for what purpose (or purposes)? How does Mrs. Trimble differ from Rebecca Wright? How does Ann Bray differ from her sister Mandy?*

2. *What is the theme of the story, and how is it related to the story's ending (Mrs. Trimble's decision to help the Bray sisters)? Is the ending too sentimental? Does it serve to falsify or compromise the rest of the story?*

3. *As one of the so-called "local colorists"—the group of nineteenth-century American regional writers that includes Mark Twain and Bret Harte—Sarah Orne Jewett is noted for her ability to delineate the local manners, customs, dialect, scenery, and character types of her native Maine. How does this ability contribute to the success of "The Town Poor"? What role does nature play? In what way does Miss Jewett manipulate nature for symbolic purposes?*

JAMES JOYCE

Araby

NORTH RICHMOND STREET, being blind, was a quiet street except at the hour when the Christian Brothers' School set the boys free. An uninhabited house of two storeys stood at the blind end, detached from its neighbours in a square ground. The other houses of the street, conscious of decent lives within them, gazed at one another with brown imperturbable faces.

The former tenant of our house, a priest, had died in the back drawing-room. Air, musty from having been long enclosed, hung in all the rooms, and the waste room behind the kitchen was littered with old useless papers. Among these I found a few paper-covered books, the pages of which were curled and damp: *The Abbot*, by Walter Scott, *The Devout Communicant* and *The Memoirs of Vidocq*. I liked the last best because its leaves were yellow. The wild garden behind the house contained a central apple-tree and a few straggling bushes under one of which I found the late tenant's rusty bicycle-pump. He had been a very charitable priest; in his will he had left all his money to institutions and the furniture of his house to his sister.

When the short days of winter came dusk fell before we had well eaten our dinners. When we met in the street the houses had grown sombre. The space of sky above us was the colour of ever-changing violet and towards it the lamps of the street lifted their feeble lanterns. The cold air stung us and we played till our bodies glowed. Our shouts echoed in the silent street. The career of our play brought us through the dark muddy lanes behind the houses where we ran the gauntlet of the rough tribes from the cottages, to the back doors of the dark dripping gardens where odours arose from the ashpits, to the dark odorous stables where a coachman smoothed and combed the horse or shook music from the buckled harness. When we returned to the street light from the kitchen windows had filled the areas. If my uncle was seen turning the corner we hid in the shadow until we had seen him safely housed. Or if Mangan's sister came out on the doorstep to call her brother in to his tea we watched her from our shadow peer up and down the street. We waited to see whether she would remain or go in and, if she remained, we left our shadow and walked up to Mangan's steps resignedly. She was waiting for us, her figure defined by the light from the half-opened door. Her brother always teased her before he obeyed and I stood by the railings looking at her. Her dress swung as she moved her body and the soft rope of her hair tossed from side to side.

Every morning I lay on the floor in the front parlour watching her door. The blind was pulled down to within an inch of the sash so that I could not be seen. When she came out on the doorstep my heart leaped. I ran to the hall, seized my books and followed her. I kept her brown figure always in my eye and, when we came near the point at which our ways diverged, I quickened my pace and passed her. This happened morning after morning. I had never spoken to her, except for a few casual words, and yet her name was like a summons to all my foolish blood.

Her image accompanied me even in places the most hostile to romance. On Saturday evenings when my aunt went marketing I had to go to carry some of the parcels. We walked through the flaring streets, jostled by drunken men and bargaining women, amid the curse of labourers, the shrill litanies of shop-boys

---

who stood on guard by the barrels of pigs' cheeks, the nasal chanting of street-singers, who sang a *come-all-you* about O'Donovan Rossa, or a ballad about the troubles in our native land. These noises converged in a single sensation of life for me: I imagined that I bore my chalice safely through a throng of foes. Her name sprang to my lips at moments in strange prayers and praises which I myself did not understand. My eyes were often full of tears (I could not tell why) and at times a flood from my heart seemed to pour itself out into my bosom. I thought little of the future. I did not know whether I would ever speak to her or not or, if I spoke to her, how I could tell her of my confused adoration. But my body was like a harp and her words and gestures were like fingers running upon the wires.

One evening I went into the back drawing-room in which the priest had died. It was a dark rainy evening and there was no sound in the house. Through one of the broken panes I heard the rain impinge upon the earth, the fine incessant needles of water playing in the sodden beds. Some distant lamp or lighted window gleamed below me. I was thankful that I could see so little. All my senses seemed to desire to veil themselves and, feeling that I was about to slip from them, I pressed the palms of my hands together until they trembled, murmuring: "*O love! O love!*" many times.

At last she spoke to me. When she addressed the first words to me I was so confused that I did not know what to answer. She asked me was I going to *Araby*. I forgot whether I answered yes or no. It would be a splendid bazaar, she said she would love to go.

"And why can't you?" I asked.

While she spoke she turned a silver bracelet round and round her wrist. She could not go, she said, because there would be a retreat that week in her convent. Her brother and two other boys were fighting for their caps and I was alone at the railings. She held one of the spikes, bowing her head towards me. The light from the lamp opposite our door caught the white curve of her neck, lit up her hair that rested there and, falling, lit up the hand upon the railing. It fell over one side of her dress and caught the white border of a petticoat just visible as she stood at ease.

"It's well for you," she said.

"If I go," I said, "I will bring you something."

What innumerable follies laid waste my waking and sleeping thoughts after that evening! I wished to annihilate the tedious intervening days. I chafed against the work of school. At night in my bedroom and by day in the classroom her image came between me and the page I strove to read. The syllables of the word *Araby* were called to me through the silence in which my soul luxuriated and cast an Eastern enchantment over me. I asked for leave to go to the bazaar on Saturday night. My aunt was surprised and hoped it was not some Freemason affair. I answered few questions in class. I watched my master's face pass from amiability to sternness; he hoped I was not beginning to idle. I could not call my wandering thoughts together. I had hardly any patience with the serious work of life which, now that it stood between me and my desire, seemed to me child's play, ugly monotonous child's play.

On Saturday morning I reminded my uncle that I wished to go to the bazaar in the evening. He was fussing at the hallstand, looking for the hat-brush, and answered me curtly:

"Yes, boy, I know."

As he was in the hall I could not go into the front parlour and lie at the window. I left the house in bad humour and walked slowly towards the school. The air was pitilessly raw and already my heart misgave me.

When I came home to dinner my uncle had not yet been home. Still it was early. I sat staring at the clock for some time and, when its ticking began to irritate me, I left the room. I mounted the staircase and gained the upper part of the house. The high cold empty gloomy rooms liberated me and I went from room to room singing. From the front window I saw my companions playing below in the street. Their cries reached me weakened and indistinct and, leaning my forehead against the cool glass, I looked over at the dark house where she lived. I may have stood there for an hour, seeing nothing but the brown-clad figure cast by my imagination, touched discreetly by the lamplight at the curved neck, at the hand upon the railings and at the border below the dress.

When I came downstairs again I found Mrs. Mercer sitting at the fire. She was an old garrulous woman, a pawnbroker's widow, who collected used stamps for some pious purpose. I had to endure the gossip of the tea-table. The meal was prolonged beyond an hour and still my uncle did not come. Mrs. Mercer stood up to go: she was very sorry she couldn't wait any longer, but it was after eight o'clock and she did not like to be out late, as the night air was bad for her. When she had gone I began to walk up and down the room, clenching my fists. My aunt said:

"I'm afraid you may put off your bazaar for this night of Our Lord."

At nine o'clock I heard my uncle's latchkey in the halldoor. I heard him talking to himself and heard the hallstand rocking when it had received the weight of his overcoat. I could interpret these signs. When he was midway through his dinner I asked him to give me the money to go to the bazaar. He had forgotten.

"The people are in bed and after their first sleep now," he said.

I did not smile. My aunt said to him energetically:

"Can't you give him the money and let him go? You've kept him late enough as it is."

My uncle said he was very sorry he had forgotten. He said he believed in the old saying: "All work and no play makes Jack a dull boy." He asked me where I was going and, when I had told him a second time he asked me did I know *The Arab's Farewell to his Steed*. When I left the kitchen he was about to recite the opening lines of the piece to my aunt.

I held a florin tightly in my hand as I strode down Buckingham Street towards the station. The sight of the streets thronged with buyers and glaring with gas recalled to me the purpose of my journey. I took my seat in a third-class

carriage of a deserted train. After an intolerable delay the train moved out of the station slowly. It crept onward among ruinous houses and over the twinkling river. At Westland Row Station a crowd of people pressed to the carriage doors; but the porters moved them back, saying that it was a special train for the bazaar. I remained alone in the bare carriage. In a few minutes the train drew up beside an improvised wooden platform. I passed out on to the road and saw by the lighted dial of a clock that it was ten minutes to ten. In front of me was a large building which displayed the magical name.

I could not find any sixpenny entrance and, fearing that the bazaar would be closed, I passed quickly through a turnstile, handing a shilling to a weary-looking man. I found myself in a big hall girdled at half its height by a gallery. Nearly all the stalls were closed and the greater part of the hall was in darkness. I recognised a silence like that which pervades a church after a service. I walked into the centre of the bazaar timidly. A few people were gathered about the stalls which were still open. Before a curtain, over which the words *Café Chantant* were written in coloured lamps, two men were counting money on a salver. I listened to the fall of the coins.

Remembering with difficulty why I had come I went over to one of the stalls and examined porcelain vases and flowered tea-sets. At the door of the stall a young lady was talking and laughing with two young gentlemen. I remarked their English accents and listened vaguely to their conversation.

"O, I never said such a thing!"

"O, but you did!"

"O, but I didn't!"

"Didn't she say that?"

"Yes. I heard her."

"O, there's a . . . fib!"

Observing me the young lady came over and asked me did I wish to buy anything. The tone of her voice was not encouraging; she seemed to have spoken to me out of a sense of duty. I looked humbly at the great jars that stood like eastern guards at either side of the dark entrance to the stall and murmured:

"No, thank you."

The young lady changed the position of one of the vases and went back to the two young men. They began to talk of the same subject. Once or twice the young lady glanced at me over her shoulder.

I lingered before her stall, though I knew my stay was useless, to make my interest in her wares seem the more real. Then I turned away slowly and walked down the middle of the bazaar. I allowed the two pennies to fall against the sixpence in my pocket. I heard a voice call from one end of the gallery that the light was out. The upper part of the hall was now completely dark.

Gazing up into the darkness I saw myself as a creature driven and derided by vanity; and my eyes burned with anguish and anger.

[1914]

QUESTIONS FOR STUDY

1. *What does the reader learn about the boy from such apparent irrelevancies as the house in North Richmond Street, the surrounding neighborhood, and the dead priest's effects?*

2. *What kind of imagery is used to describe Mangan's sister? With what does the boy come to associate her and why? What other patterns of imagery are used in the story? How do they reinforce the story's theme?*

3. *What is the nature of the boy's sudden realization? How does Joyce help prepare the reader for this moment of illumination?*

4. *From what point of view is the story told? How far removed is the narrator from the events of the story? How does this distance serve to explain the narrator's harsh judgments upon himself? Is the chosen point of view an effective one?*

JAMES JOYCE

The Dead

LILY, the caretaker's daughter, was literally run off her feet. Hardly had she brought one gentleman into the little pantry behind the office on the ground floor and helped him off with his overcoat than the wheezy hall-door bell clanged again and she had to scamper along the bare hallway to let in another guest. It was well for her she had not to attend to the ladies also. But Miss Kate and Miss Julia had thought of that and had converted the bathroom upstairs into a ladies' dressing-room. Miss Kate and Miss Julia were there, gossiping and laughing and fussing, walking after each other to the head of the stairs, peering down over the banisters and calling down to Lily to ask her who had come.

It was always a great affair, the Misses Morkan's annual dance. Everybody who knew them came to it, members of the family, old friends of the family, the members of Julia's choir, any of Kate's pupils that were grown up enough, and even some of Mary Jane's pupils too. Never once had it fallen flat. For years and years it had gone off in splendid style, as long as anyone could remember; ever since Kate and Julia, after the death of their brother Pat, had left the house in Stoney Batter and taken Mary Jane, their only niece, to live with them in the dark, gaunt house on Usher's Island, the upper part of which they had rented from Mr. Fulham, the corn-factor on the ground floor. That was a good thirty years ago if it was a day. Mary Jane, who was then a little girl in short clothes, was now the main prop of the household, for she had the organ in Haddington Road. She had been through the Academy and gave a pupils' concert every year in the upper room of the Antient Concert Rooms. Many of her pupils belonged to the better-class families on the Kingstown and Dalkey line. Old as they were, her aunts also did their share. Julia, though she was quite grey, was still the leading soprano in Adam and Eve's, and Kate, being too feeble to go about much, gave music lessons to beginners on the old square piano in the back room. Lily, the caretaker's daughter, did housemaid's work for them. Though their life was modest, they believed in eating well; the best of everything: diamond-bone sirloins, three-shilling tea and the best bottled stout. But Lily seldom made a mistake in the orders, so that she got on well with her three mistresses. They were fussy, that was all. But the only thing they would not stand was back answers.

Of course, they had good reason to be fussy on such a night. And then it was long after ten o'clock and yet there was no sign of Gabriel and his wife. Besides they were dreadfully afraid that Freddy Malins might turn up screwed. They would not wish for worlds that any of Mary Jane's pupils should see him under the influence; and when he was like that it was sometimes very hard to manage him. Freddy Malins always came late, but they wondered what could be keeping Gabriel: and that was what brought them every two minutes to the banisters to ask Lily had Gabriel or Freddy come.

"O, Mr. Conroy," said Lily to Gabriel when she opened the door for him, "Miss Kate and Miss Julia thought you were never coming. Good-night, Mrs. Conroy."

"I'll engage they did," said Gabriel, "but they forget that my wife here takes three mortal hours to dress herself."

He stood on the mat, scraping the snow from his goloshes, while Lily led his wife to the foot of the stairs and called out:

"Miss Kate, here's Mrs. Conroy."

From *Dubliners* by James Joyce. Originally published by B. W. Huebsch, Inc., in 1916. Copyright © 1967 by the Estate of James Joyce. Reprinted by permission of The Viking Press, Inc.

Kate and Julia came toddling down the dark stairs at once. Both of them kissed Gabriel's wife, said she must be perished alive, and asked was Gabriel with her.

"Here I am as right as the mail, Aunt Kate! Go on up. I'll follow," called out Gabriel from the dark.

He continued scraping his feet vigorously while the three women went upstairs, laughing, to the ladies' dressing-room. A light fringe of snow lay like a cape on the shoulders of his overcoat and like toecaps on the toes of his goloshes; and, as the buttons of his overcoat slipped with a squeaking noise through the snow-stiffened frieze, a cold fragrant air from out-of-doors escaped from crevices and folds.

"Is it snowing again, Mr. Conroy?" asked Lily.

She had preceded him into the pantry to help him off with his overcoat. Gabriel smiled at the three syllables she had given his surname and glanced at her. She was a slim, growing girl, pale in complexion and with hay-coloured hair. The gas in the pantry made her look still paler. Gabriel had known her when she was a child and used to sit on the lowest step nursing a rag doll.

"Yes, Lily," he answered, "and I think we're in for a night of it."

He looked up at the pantry ceiling, which was shaking with the stamping and shuffling of feet on the floor above, listened for a moment to the piano and then glanced at the girl, who was folding his overcoat carefully at the end of a shelf.

"Tell me, Lily," he said in a friendly tone, "do you still go to school?"

"O no, sir," she answered. "I'm done schooling this year and more."

"O, then," said Gabriel gaily, "I suppose we'll be going to your wedding one of these fine days with your young man, eh?"

The girl glanced back at him over her shoulder and said with great bitterness:

"The men that is now is only all palaver and what they can get out of you."

Gabriel coloured, as if he felt he had made a mistake and, without looking at her, kicked off his goloshes and flicked actively with his muffler at his patent-leather shoes.

He was a stout, tallish young man. The high colour of his cheeks pushed upwards even to his forehead, where it scattered itself in a few formless patches of pale red; and on his hairless face there scintillated restlessly the polished lenses and the bright gilt rims of the glasses which screened his delicate and restless eyes. His glossy black hair was parted in the middle and brushed in a long curve behind his ears where it curled slightly beneath the groove left by his hat.

When he had flicked lustre into his shoes he stood up and pulled his waistcoat down more tightly on his plump body. Then he took a coin rapidly from his pocket.

"O Lily," he said, thrusting it into her hands, "it's Christmas-time, isn't it? Just ... here's a little. ..."

He walked rapidly towards the door.

"O no, sir!" cried the girl, following him. "Really, sir, I wouldn't take it."

"Christmas-time! Christmas-time!" said Gabriel, almost trotting to the stairs and waving his hand to her in deprecation.

The girl, seeing that he had gained the stairs, called out after him:

"Well, thank you, sir."

He waited outside the drawing-room door until the waltz should finish, listening to the skirts that swept against it and to the shuffling of feet. He was still discomposed by the girl's bitter and sudden retort. It had cast a gloom over him which he tried to dispel by arranging his cuffs and the bows of his tie. He then took from his waistcoat pocket a little paper and glanced at the headings he had made for his speech. He was undecided about the lines from Robert Browning, for he feared they would be above the heads of his hearers. Some quotation that they would recognise from Shakespeare or from the Melodies would be better. The indelicate clacking of the men's heels and the shuffling of their soles reminded him that their grade of culture differed from his. He would only make himself ridiculous by quoting poetry to them which they could not understand. They would think that he was airing his superior education. He would fail with them just as he had failed with the girl in the pantry. He had taken up a wrong tone. His whole speech was a mistake from first to last, an utter failure.

Just then his aunts and his wife came out of the ladies' dressing-room. His aunts were two small, plainly dressed old women. Aunt Julia was an inch or so the taller. Her hair, drawn low over the tops of her ears, was grey; and grey also, with darker shadows, was her large flaccid face. Though she was stout in build and stood erect, her slow eyes and parted lips gave her the appearance of a woman who did not know where she was or where she was going. Aunt Kate was more vivacious. Her face, healthier than her sister's, was all puckers and creases, like a shrivelled red apple, and her hair, braided in the same old-fashioned way, had not lost its ripe nut colour.

They both kissed Gabriel frankly. He was their favourite nephew, the son of their dead elder sister, Ellen, who had married T. J. Conroy of the Port and Docks.

"Gretta tells me you're not going to take a cab back to Monkstown tonight, Gabriel," said Aunt Kate.

"No," said Gabriel, turning to his wife, "we had quite enough of that last year, hadn't we? Don't you remember, Aunt Kate, what a cold Gretta got out of it? Cab windows rattling all the way, and the east wind blowing in after we passed Merrion. Very jolly it was. Gretta caught a dreadful cold."

Aunt Kate frowned severely and nodded her head at every word.

"Quite right, Gabriel, quite right," she said. "You can't be too careful."

"But as for Gretta there," said Gabriel, "she'd walk home in the snow if she were let."

Mrs. Conroy laughed.

"Don't mind him, Aunt Kate," she said. "He's really an awful bother, what with green shades for Tom's eyes at night and making him do the dumb-bells, and forcing Eva to eat the stir-about. The poor child! And she simply hates the sight of it! . . . O, but you'll never guess what he makes me wear now!"

She broke out into a peal of laughter and glanced at her husband, whose admiring and happy eyes had been wandering from her dress to her face and hair. The two aunts laughed heartily, too, for Gabriel's solicitude was a standing joke with them.

"Goloshes!" said Mrs. Conroy. "That's the latest. Whenever it's wet underfoot I must put on my goloshes. Tonight even, he wanted me to put them on, but I wouldn't. The next thing he'll buy me will be a diving suit."

Gabriel laughed nervously and patted his tie reassuringly, while Aunt Kate nearly doubled herself, so heartily did she enjoy the joke. The smile soon faded from Aunt Julia's face and her mirthless eyes were directed towards her nephew's face. After a pause she asked:

"And what are goloshes, Gabriel?"

"Goloshes, Julia!" exclaimed her sister. "Goodness me, don't you know what goloshes are? You wear them over your . . . over your boots, Gretta, isn't it?"

"Yes," said Mrs. Conroy. "Guttapercha things. We both have a pair now. Gabriel says everyone wears them on the Continent."

"O, on the Continent," murmured Aunt Julia, nodding her head slowly.

Gabriel knitted his brow and said, as if he were slightly angered:

"It's nothing very wonderful, but Gretta thinks it very funny because she says the word reminds her of Christy Minstrels."

"But tell me, Gabriel," said Aunt Kate, with brisk tact. "Of course, you've seen about the room. Gretta was saying . . ."

"O, the room is all right," replied Gabriel. "I've taken one in the Gresham."

"To be sure," said Aunt Kate, "by far the best thing to do. And the children, Gretta, you're not anxious about them?"

"O, for one night," said Mrs. Conroy. "Besides, Bessie will look after them."

"To be sure," said Aunt Kate again. "What a comfort it is to have a girl like that, one you can depend on! There's that Lily, I'm sure I don't know what has come over her lately. She's not the girl she was at all."

Gabriel was about to ask his aunt some

questions on this point, but she broke off suddenly to gaze after her sister, who had wandered down the stairs and was craning her neck over the banisters.

"Now, I ask you," she said almost testily, "where is Julia going? Julia! Julia! Where are you going?"

Julia, who had gone half way down one flight, came back and announced blandly:

"Here's Freddy."

At the same moment a clapping of hands and a final flourish of the pianist told that the waltz had ended. The drawing-room door was opened from within and some couples came out. Aunt Kate drew Gabriel aside hurriedly and whispered into his ear:

"Slip down, Gabriel, like a good fellow and see if he's all right, and don't let him up if he's screwed. I'm sure he's screwed. I'm sure he is."

Gabriel went to the stairs and listened over the banisters. He could hear two persons talking in the pantry. Then he recognised Freddy Malins' laugh. He went down the stairs noisily.

"It's such a relief," said Aunt Kate to Mrs. Conroy, "that Gabriel is here. I always feel easier in my mind when he's here. . . . Julia, there's Miss Daly and Miss Power will take some refreshment. Thanks for your beautiful waltz, Miss Daly. It made lovely time."

A tall wizen-faced man, with a stiff grizzled moustache and swarthy skin, who was passing out with his partner, said:

"And may we have some refreshment, too, Miss Morkan?"

"Julia," said Aunt Kate summarily, "and here's Mr. Browne and Miss Furlong. Take them in, Julia, with Miss Daly and Miss Power."

"I'm the man for the ladies," said Mr. Browne, pursing his lips until his moustache bristled and smiling in all his wrinkles. "You know, Miss Morkan, the reason they are so fond of me is——"

He did not finish his sentence, but, seeing that Aunt Kate was out of earshot, at once led the three young ladies into the back room. The middle of the room was occupied by two square tables placed end to end, and on these Aunt Julia and the caretaker were straightening and smoothing a large cloth. On the sideboard were arrayed dishes and plates, and glasses and bundles of knives and forks and spoons. The top of the closed square piano served also as a sideboard for viands and sweets. At a smaller sideboard in one corner two young men were standing, drinking hop-bitters.

Mr. Browne led his charges thither and invited them all, in jest, to some ladies' punch, hot, strong and sweet. As they said they never took anything strong, he opened three bottles of lemonade for them. Then he asked one of the young men to move aside, and, taking hold of the decanter, filled out for himself a goodly measure of whisky. The young men eyed him respectfully while he took a trial sip.

"God help me," he said, smiling, "it's the doctor's orders."

His wizened face broke into a broader smile, and the three young ladies laughed in musical echo to his pleasantry, swaying their bodies to and fro, with nervous jerks of their shoulders. The boldest said:

"O, now, Mr. Browne, I'm sure the doctor never ordered anything of the kind."

Mr. Browne took another sip of his whisky and said, with sidling mimicry:

"Well, you see, I'm like the famous Mrs. Cassidy, who is reported to have said: 'Now, Mary Grimes, if I don't take it, make me take it, for I feel I want it.' "

His hot face had leaned forward a little too confidentially and he had assumed a very low Dublin accent so that the young ladies, with one instinct, received his speech in silence. Miss Furlong, who was one of Mary Jane's pupils, asked Miss Daly what was the name of the pretty waltz she had played; and Mr. Browne, seeing that he was ignored, turned promptly to the two young men who were more appreciative.

A red-faced young woman, dressed in pansy, came into the room, excitedly clapping her hands and crying:

"Quadrilles! Quadrilles!"

Close on her heels came Aunt Kate, crying:

"Two gentlemen and three ladies, Mary Jane!"

"O, here's Mr. Bergin and Mr. Kerrigan," said Mary Jane. "Mr. Kerrigan, will you take Miss Power? Miss Furlong, may I get you a partner, Mr. Bergin. O, that'll just do now."

"Three ladies, Mary Jane," said Aunt Kate.

The two young gentlemen asked the ladies if they might have the pleasure, and Mary Jane turned to Miss Daly.

"O, Miss Daly, you're really awfully good, after playing for the last two dances, but really we're so short of ladies tonight."

"I don't mind in the least, Miss Morkan".

"But I've a nice partner for you, Mr. Bartell D'Arcy, the tenor. I'll get him to sing later on. All Dublin is raving about him."

"Lovely voice, lovely voice!" said Aunt Kate.

As the piano had twice begun the prelude to the first figure Mary Jane led her recruits quickly from the room. They had hardly gone when Aunt Julia wandered slowly into the room, looking behind her at something.

"What is the matter, Julia?" asked Aunt Kate anxiously. "Who is it?"

Julia, who was carrying in a column of table-napkins, turned to her sister and said, simply, as if the question had surprised her:

"It's only Freddy, Kate, and Gabriel with him."

In fact right behind her Gabriel could be seen piloting Freddy Malins across the landing. The latter, a young man of about forty, was of Gabriel's size and build, with very round shoulders. His face was fleshy and pallid, touched with colour only at the thick hanging lobes of his ears and at the wide wings of his nose. He had coarse features, a blunt nose, a convex and receding brow, tumid and protruded lips. His heavy-lidded eyes and the disorder of his scanty hair made him look sleepy. He was laughing heartily in a high key at a story which he had been telling Gabriel on the stairs and at the same time rubbing the knuckles of his left fist backwards and forwards into his left eye.

"Good-evening, Freddy," said Aunt Julia.

Freddy Malins bade the Misses Morkan good-evening in what seemed an offhand fashion by reason of the habitual catch in his voice and then, seeing that Mr. Browne was grinning at him from the sideboard, crossed the room on rather shaky legs and began to repeat in an undertone the story he had just told to Gabriel.

"He's not so bad, is he?" said Aunt Kate to Gabriel.

Gabriel's brows were dark but he raised them quickly and answered:

"O, no, hardly noticeable."

"Now, isn't he a terrible fellow!" she said. "And his poor mother made him take the pledge on New Year's Eve. But come on, Gabriel, into the drawing-room."

Before leaving the room with Gabriel she signalled to Mr. Browne by frowning and shaking her forefinger in warning to and fro. Mr. Browne nodded in answer and, when she had gone, said to Freddy Malins:

"Now, then, Teddy, I'm going to fill you out a good glass of lemonade just to buck you up."

Freddy Malins, who was nearing the climax of his story, waved the offer aside impatiently but Mr. Browne, having first called Freddy Malins' attention to a disarray in his dress, filled out and handed him a full glass of lemonade. Freddy Malins' left hand accepted the glass mechanically, his right hand being engaged in the mechanical readjustment of his dress. Mr. Browne, whose face was once more wrinkling with mirth, poured out for himself a glass of whisky while Freddy Malins exploded, before he had well reached the climax of his story, in a kink of high-pitched bronchitic laughter and, setting down his untasted and overflowing glass, began to rub the knuckles of his left fist backwards and forwards into his left eye, repeating words of his last phrase as well as his fit of laughter would allow him.

Gabriel could not listen while Mary Jane was playing her Academy piece, full of runs and difficult passages, to the hushed drawing-room. He liked music but the piece she was playing had no melody for him and he doubted whether it had any melody for the other listeners, though they had begged Mary Jane to play something. Four young men, who had come from the refreshment-room to stand in the doorway at the sound of the piano, had gone away quietly in couples after a few minutes. The only persons who seemed to follow the music were Mary Jane herself, her hands racing along the key-board or lifted from it at the pauses like those of a priestess in momentary imprecation, and Aunt Kate standing at her elbow to turn the page.

Gabriel's eyes, irritated by the floor, which glittered with beeswax under the heavy chandelier, wandered to the wall above the piano. A picture of the balcony scene in *Romeo and Juliet* hung there and beside it was a picture of the two murdered princes in the Tower which Aunt Julia had worked in red, blue and brown wools when she was a girl. Probably in the school they had gone to as girls that kind of work had been taught for one year. His mother had worked for him as a birthday present a waistcoat of purple tabinet, with little foxes' heads upon it, lined with brown satin and having round mulberry buttons. It was strange that his mother had had no musical talent though Aunt Kate used to call her the brains carrier of the Morkan family. Both she and Julia had always seemed a little proud of their serious and matronly sister. Her photograph stood before the pierglass. She held an open book on her knees and was pointing out something in it to Constantine who, dressed in a man-o'-war suit, lay at her feet. It was she who had chosen the name of her sons for she was very sensible of the dignity of family life. Thanks to her, Constantine was now senior curate in Balbriggan and, thanks to her, Gabriel himself had taken his degree in the Royal University. A shadow passed over his face as he remembered her sullen opposition to his marriage. Some slighting phrases she had used still rankled in his memory; she had once spoken of Gretta as being country cute and that was not true of Gretta at all. It was Gretta who had nursed her during all her last long illness in their house at Monkstown.

He knew that Mary Jane must be near the end of her piece for she was playing against the opening melody with runs of scales after every bar and while he waited for the end the resentment died down in his heart. The piece ended with a trill of octaves in the treble and a final deep octave in the bass. Great applause greeted Mary Jane as, blushing and rolling up her music nervously, she escaped from the room. The most vigorous clapping came from the four young men in the doorway who had gone away to the refreshment-room at the beginning of the piece but had come back when the piano had stopped.

Lancers were arranged. Gabriel found himself partnered with Miss Ivors. She was a frank-mannered talkative young lady, with a freckled face and prominent brown eyes. She did not wear a low-cut bodice and the large brooch which was fixed in the front of her collar bore on it an Irish device and motto.

When they had taken their places she said abruptly:

"I have a crow to pluck with you."

"With me?" said Gabriel.

She nodded her head gravely.

"What is it?" asked Gabriel, smiling at her solemn manner.

"Who is G. C.?" answered Miss Ivors, turning her eyes upon him.

Gabriel coloured and was about to knit his brows, as if he did not understand, when she said bluntly:

"O, innocent Amy! I have found out that you write for *The Daily Express*. Now, aren't you ashamed of yourself?"

"Why should I be ashamed of myself?" asked Gabriel, blinking his eyes and trying to smile.

"Well, I'm ashamed of you," said Miss Ivors frankly. "To say you'd write for a paper like that. I didn't think you were a West Briton."

A look of perplexity appeared on Gabriel's face. It was true that he wrote a literary column every Wednesday in *The Daily Express*, for which he was paid fifteen shillings. But that did not make him a West Briton surely. The books he received for review were almost more welcome than the paltry cheque. He loved to feel the covers and turn over the pages of newly printed books. Nearly every day when his teaching in the college was ended he used to wander down the quays to the second-hand booksellers, to Hickey's on Bachelor's Walk, to Web's or Massey's on Aston's Quay, or to O'Clohissey's in the by-street. He did not know how to meet her charge. He wanted to say that literature was above politics. But they were friends of many years' standing and their careers had been parallel, first at the University and then as teachers: he could not risk a grandiose phrase with her. He continued blinking his eyes and trying to smile and murmured lamely that he saw nothing political in writing reviews of books.

When their turn to cross had come he was still perplexed and inattentive. Miss Ivors promptly took his hand in a warm grasp and said in a soft friendly tone:

"Of course, I was only joking. Come, we cross now."

When they were together again she spoke of the University question and Gabriel felt more at ease. A friend of hers had shown her his review of Browning's poems. That was how she had found out the secret: but she liked the review immensely. Then she said suddenly:

"O, Mr. Conroy, will you come for an excursion to the Aran Isles this summer? We're going to stay there a whole month. It will be splendid out in the Atlantic. You ought to come. Mr. Clancy is coming, and Mr. Kilkelly and Kathleen Kearney. It would be splendid for Gretta too if she'd come. She's from Connacht, isn't she?"

"Her people are," said Gabriel shortly.

"But you will come, won't you?" said Miss Ivors, laying her warm hand eagerly on his arm.

"The fact is," said Gabriel, "I have just arranged to go——"

"Go where?" asked Miss Ivors.

"Well, you know, every year I go for a cycling tour with some fellows and so——"

"But where?" asked Miss Ivors.

"Well, we usually go to France or Belgium or perhaps Germany," said Gabriel awkwardly.

"And why do you go to France and Belgium," said Miss Ivors, "instead of visiting you own land?"

"Well," said Gabriel, "it's partly to keep in touch with languages and partly for a change."

"And haven't you your own language to keep in touch with—Irish?" asked Miss Ivors.

"Well," said Gabriel, "if it comes to that, you know, Irish is not my language."

Their neighbours had turned to listen to the cross examination. Gabriel glanced right and left nervously and tried to keep his good humour under the ordeal which was making a blush invade his forehead.

"And haven't you your own land to visit," continued Miss Ivors, "that you know nothing of, your own people, and your own country?"

"O, to tell you the truth," retorted Gabriel suddenly, "I'm sick of my own country, sick of it!"

"Why?" asked Miss Ivors.

Gabriel did not answer for his retort had heated him.

"Why?" repeated Miss Ivors.

They had to go visiting together and, as he had not answered her, Miss Ivors said warmly:

"Of course, you've no answer."

Gabriel tried to cover his agitation by taking part in the dance with great energy. He avoided her eyes for he had seen a sour expression on her face. But when they met in the long chain he was surprised to feel his hand firmly pressed. She looked at him from under her brows for a moment quizzically until he smiled. Then, just as the chain was about to start again, she stood on tiptoe and whispered into his ear:

"West Briton!"

When the lancers were over Gabriel went away to a remote corner of the room where Freddy Malins' mother was sitting. She was a stout feeble old woman with white hair. Her voice had a catch in it like her son's and she stuttered slightly. She had been told that Freddy had come and that he was nearly all right. Gabriel asked her whether she had had a good crossing. She lived with her married daughter in Glasgow and came to Dublin on a visit once a year. She answered placidly that she had had a beautiful crossing and that the captain had been most attentive to her. She spoke also of the beautiful house her daughter kept in Glasgow, and of all the friends they had there. While her tongue rambled on Gabriel tried to banish from his mind all memory of the unpleasant incident with Miss Ivors. Of course the girl or woman, or whatever she was, was an enthusiast but there was a time for all things. Perhaps he ought not to have answered her like that. But she had no right to call him a West Briton before people, even in joke. She had tried to make him ridiculous before people, heckling him and staring at him with her rabbit's eyes.

He saw his wife making her way towards him through the waltzing couples. When she reached him she said into his ear:

"Gabriel, Aunt Kate wants to know won't you carve the goose as usual. Miss Daly will carve the ham and I'll do the pudding."

"All right," said Gabriel.

"She's sending in the younger ones first as soon as this waltz is over so that we'll have the table to ourselves."

"Were you dancing?" asked Gabriel.

"Of course I was. Didn't you see me? What row had you with Molly Ivors?"

"No row. Why? Did she say so?"

"Something like that. I'm trying to get that Mr. D'Arcy to sing. He's full of conceit, I think."

"There was no row," said Gabriel moodily, "only she wanted me to go for a trip to the west of Ireland and I said I wouldn't."

His wife clasped her hands excitedly and gave a little jump.

"O, do go, Gabriel," she said. "I'd love to see Galway again."

"You can go if you like," said Gabriel coldly.

She looked at him for a moment, then turned to Mrs. Malins and said:

"There's a nice husband for you, Mrs. Malins."

While she was threading her way back across the room Mrs. Malins, without adverting to the interruption, went on to tell Gabriel what beautiful places there were in Scotland and beautiful scenery. Her son-in-law brought them every year to the lakes and they used to go fishing. Her son-in-law was a splendid fisher. One day he caught a beautiful big fish and the man in the hotel cooked it for their dinner.

Gabriel hardly heard what she said. Now that supper was coming near he began to think again about his speech and about the quotation. When he saw Freddy Malins coming across the room to visit his mother Gabriel left the chair free for him and retired into the embrasure of the window. The room had already cleared and from the back room came the clatter of plates and knives. Those who still remained in the drawing-room seemed tired of dancing and were conversing quietly in little groups. Gabriel's warm trembling fingers tapped the cold pane of the window. How cool it must be outside! How pleasant it would be to walk out alone, first along by the river and then through the park! The snow would be lying on the branches of the trees and forming a bright cap on the top of the Wellington Monument. How much more pleasant it would be there than at the supper-table!

He ran over the headings of his speech: Irish hospitality, sad memories, the Three Graces, Paris, the quotation from Browning. He repeated to himself a phrase he had written in his review: "One feels that one is listening to a thought-tormented music." Miss Ivors had praised the review. Was she sincere? Had she really any life of her own behind all her propagandism? There had never been any ill-feeling between them until that night. It unnerved him to think that she would be at the supper-table, looking up at him while he spoke with her critical quizzing eyes. Perhaps she would not be sorry to see him fail in his speech. An idea came into his mind and gave him courage. He would say, alluding to Aunt Kate and Aunt Julia: "Ladies and Gentlemen, the generation which is now on the wane among us may have had its faults but for my part I think it had certain qualities of hospitality, of humour, of humanity, which the new and very serious and hyper-educated generation that is growing up around us seems to me to lack." Very good: that was one for Miss Ivors. What did he care that his aunts were only two ignorant old women?

A murmur in the room attracted his attention. Mr. Browne was advancing from the door, gallantly escorting Aunt Julia, who leaned upon his arm, smiling and hanging her head. An irregular musketry of applause escorted her also as far as the piano and then, as Mary Jane seated herself on the stool, and Aunt Julia, no longer smiling, half turned so as to pitch her voice fairly into the room, gradually ceased. Gabriel recognised the prelude. It was that of an old song of Aunt Julia's—*Arrayed for the Bridal*. Her voice, strong and clear in tone, attacked with great spirit the runs which embellish the air and though she sang very rapidly she did not miss even the smallest of the grace notes. To follow the voice, without looking at the singer's face, was to feel and share the excitement of swift and secure flight. Gabriel applauded loudly with all the others at the close of the song and loud applause was borne in from the invisible supper-table. It sounded so genuine that a little colour struggled into Aunt Julia's face as she bent to replace in the music-stand the old leather-bound songbook that had her initials on the cover. Freddy Malins, who had listened with his head perched sideways to hear her better, was still applauding when everyone else had ceased and talking animatedly to his mother who nodded her head gravely and slowly in acquiescence. At last, when he could clap no more, he stood up suddenly and hurried across the room to Aunt Julia whose hand he seized and held in both his hands, shaking it when words failed him or the catch in his voice proved too much for him.

"I was just telling my mother," he said, "I never heard you sing so well, never. No, I never heard your voice so good as it is tonight. Now! Would you believe that now? That's the truth. Upon my word and honour that's the truth. I never heard your voice sound so fresh and so . . . so clear and fresh, never."

Aunt Julia smiled broadly and mur-mured something about compliments as she released her hand from his grasp. Mr. Browne extended his open hand to-wards her and said to those who were near him in the manner of a showman introducing a prodigy to an audience:

"Miss Julia Morkan, my latest dis-covery!"

He was laughing very heartily at this himself when Freddy Malins turned to him and said:

"Well, Browne, if you're serious you might make a worse discovery. All I can say is I never heard her sing half so well as long as I am coming here. And that's the honest truth."

"Neither did I," said Mr. Browne. "I think her voice has greatly improved."

Aunt Julia shrugged her shoulders and said with meek pride:

"Thirty years ago I hadn't a bad voice as voices go."

"I often told Julia," said Aunt Kate emphatically, "that she was simply thrown away in that choir. But she never would be said by me."

She turned as if to appeal to the good sense of the others against a refractory child while Aunt Julia gazed in front of her, a vague smile of reminiscence play-ing on her face.

"No," continued Aunt Kate, "she wouldn't be said or led by anyone, slav-ing there in that choir night and day, night and day. Six o'clock on Christmas morning! And all for what?"

"Well, isn't it for the honour of God, Aunt Kate?" asked Mary Jane, twisting round on the piano-stool and smiling.

Aunt Kate turned fiercely on her niece and said:

"I know all about the honour of God, Mary Jane, but I think it's not at all honourable for the pope to turn out the women out of the choirs that have slaved there all their lives and put little whipper-snappers of boys over their heads. I sup-pose it is for the good of the Church if the pope does it. But it's not just, Mary Jane, and it's not right."

She had worked herself into a passion and would have continued in defence of her sister for it was a sore subject with her but Mary Jane, seeing that all the dancers had come back, intervened pacifically:

"Now, Aunt Kate, you're giving scandal to Mr. Browne who is of the other persuasion."

Aunt Kate turned to Mr. Browne, who was grinning at this allusion to his religion, and said hastily:

"O, I don't question the pope's being right. I'm only a stupid old woman and I wouldn't presume to do such a thing. But there's such a thing as common everyday politeness and gratitude. And if I were in Julia's place I'd tell that Father Healey straight up to his face . . ."

"And besides, Aunt Kate," said Mary Jane, "we really are all hungry and when we are hungry we are all very quarrelsome."

"And when we are thirsty we are also quarrelsome," added Mr. Browne.

"So that we had better go to supper," said Mary Jane, "and finish the discussion afterwards."

On the landing outside the drawing-room Gabriel found his wife and Mary Jane trying to persuade Miss Ivors to stay for supper. But Miss Ivors, who had put on her hat and was buttoning her cloak, would not stay. She did not feel in the least hungry and she had already overstayed her time.

"But only for ten minutes, Molly," said Mrs. Conroy. "That won't delay you."

"To take a pick itself," said Mary Jane, "after all your dancing."

"I really couldn't," said Miss Ivors.

"I am afraid you didn't enjoy yourself at all," said Mary Jane hopelessly.

"Ever so much, I assure you," said Miss Ivors, "but you really must let me run off now."

"But how can you get home?" asked Mrs. Conroy.

"O, it's only two steps up the quay."

Gabriel hesitated a moment and said:

"If you will allow me, Miss Ivors, I'll see you home if you are really obliged to go."

But Miss Ivors broke away from them.

"I won't hear it," she cried. "For goodness' sake go in to your suppers and don't mind me. I'm quite well able to take care of myself."

"Well, you're the comical girl, Molly," said Mrs. Conroy frankly.

"*Beannacht libh*," cried Miss Ivors, with a laugh, as she ran down the staircase.

Mary Jane gazed after her, a moody puzzled expression on her face, while Mrs. Conroy leaned over the banisters to listen for the hall-door. Gabriel asked himself was he the cause of her abrupt departure. But she did not seem to be in ill humour: she had gone away laughing. He stared blankly down the staircase.

At the moment Aunt Kate came toddling out of the supper-room, almost wringing her hands in despair.

"Where is Gabriel?" she cried. "Where on earth is Gabriel? There's everyone waiting in there, stage to let, and nobody to carve the goose!"

"Here I am, Aunt Kate!" cried Gabriel, with sudden animation, "ready to carve a flock of geese, if necessary."

A fat brown goose lay at one end of the table and at the other end, on a bed of creased paper strewn with sprigs of parsley, lay a great ham, stripped of its outer skin and peppered over with crust crumbs, a neat paper frill round its shin and beside this was a round of spiced beef. Between these rival ends ran parallel lines of side-dishes: two little minsters of jelly, red and yellow; a shallow dish full of blocks of blancmange and red jam, a large green leaf-shaped dish with a stalk-shaped handle, on which lay bunches of purple raisins and peeled almonds, a companion dish on which lay a solid rectangle of Smyrna figs, a dish of custard topped with grated nutmeg, a small bowl full of chocolates and sweets wrapped in gold and silver papers and a glass vase in which stood some tall celery stalks. In the centre of the table there stood, as sentries to a fruit-stand which upheld a pyramid of oranges and American apples, two squat old-fashioned decanters of cut glass, one containing port and the other dark sherry. On the closed square piano a pudding in a huge yellow dish lay in waiting and behind it were three squads of bottles of stout and ale and minerals, drawn up according to the colours of their uniforms, the first two black, with brown and red labels, the third and smallest squad white, with transverse green sashes.

Gabriel took his seat boldly at the head of the table and, having looked to the edge of the carver, plunged his fork firmly into the goose. He felt quite at ease now for he was an expert carver and liked nothing better than to find himself at the head of a well-laden table.

"Miss Furlong, what shall I send you?" he asked. "A wing or a slice of the breast?"

"Just a small slice of the breast."

"Miss Higgins, what for you?"

"O, anything at all, Mr. Conroy."

While Gabriel and Miss Daly exchanged plates of goose and plates of ham and spiced beef Lily went from guest to guest with a dish of hot floury potatoes wrapped in a white napkin. This was Mary Jane's idea and she had also suggested apple sauce for the goose but Aunt Kate had said that plain roast goose without any apple sauce had always been good enough for her and she hoped she might never eat worse. Mary Jane waited on her pupils and saw that they got the best slices and Aunt Kate and Aunt Julia opened and carried across from the piano bottles of stout and ale for the gentlemen and bottles of minerals for the ladies. There was a great deal of confusion and laughter and noise, the noise of orders and counter-orders, of knives and forks, of corks and glass-stoppers. Gabriel began to carve second helpings as soon as he had finished the first round without serving himself. Everyone protested loudly so that he compromised by taking a long draught of stout for he had found the carving hot work. Mary Jane settled down quietly to her supper but Aunt Kate and Aunt Julia were still toddling round the table, walking on each other's heels, getting in each other's way and giving each other unheeded orders. Mr. Browne begged of them to sit down and eat their suppers and so did Gabriel but they said there was time enough, so that, at last Freddy Malins stood up and, capturing Aunt Kate, plumped her down on her chair amid general laughter.

When everyone had been well served Gabriel said, smiling:

"Now, if anyone wants a little more of what vulgar people call stuffing let him or her speak."

A chorus of voices invited him to begin his own supper and Lily came forward with three potatoes which she had reserved for him.

"Very well," said Gabriel amiably, as he took another preparatory draught, "kindly forget my existence, ladies and gentlemen, for a few minutes."

He set to his supper and took no part in the conversation with which the table covered Lily's removal of the plates. The subject of talk was the opera company which was then at the Theatre Royal. Mr. Bartell D'Arcy, the tenor, a dark-complexioned young man with a smart moustache, praised very highly the leading contralto of the company but Miss Furlong thought she had a rather vulgar style of production. Freddy Malins said there was a Negro chieftain singing in the second part of the Gaiety pantomime who had one of the finest tenor voices he had ever heard.

"Have you heard him?" he asked Mr. Bartell D'Arcy across the table.

"No," answered Mr. Bartell D'Arcy carelessly.

"Because," Freddy Malins explained, "now I'd be curious to hear your opinion of him. I think he has a grand voice."

"It takes Teddy to find out the really good things," said Mr. Browne familiarly to the table.

"And why couldn't he have a voice too?" asked Freddy Malins sharply. "Is it because he's only a black?"

Nobody answered this question and Mary Jane led the table back to the legitimate opera. One of her pupils had given her a pass for *Mignon*. Of course it was very fine, she said, but it made her think of poor Georgina Burns. Mr. Browne could go back farther still, to the old Italian companies that used to come to Dublin—Tietjens, Ilma de Murzka, Campanini, the great Trebelli, Giuglini, Ravelli, Aramburo. Those were the days, he said, when there was something like singing to be heard in Dublin. He told too of how the top gallery of the old Royal used to be packed night after night, of how one night an Italian tenor had sung five encores to *Let Me Like a Soldier Fall,* introducing a high C every time, and of how the gallery boys would sometimes in their enthusiasm unyoke the horses from the carriage of some great *prima donna* and pull her themselves through the streets to her hotel. Why did they never play the grand old operas now, he asked, *Dinorah, Lucrezia Borgia*? Because they could not get the voices to sing them: that was why.

"Oh, well," said Mr. Bartell D'Arcy, "I presume there are as good singers today as there were then."

"Where are they?" asked Mr. Browne defiantly.

"In London, Paris, Milan," said Mr. Bartell D'Arcy warmly. "I suppose Caruso, for example, is quite as good, if not better than any of the men you have mentioned."

"Maybe so," said Mr. Browne. "But I may tell you I doubt it strongly."

"O, I'd give anything to hear Caruso sing," said Mary Jane.

"For me," said Aunt Kate, who had been picking a bone, "there was only one tenor. To please me, I mean. But I suppose none of you ever heard of him."

"Who was he, Miss Morkan?" asked Mr. Bartell D'Arcy politely.

"His name," said Aunt Kate, "was Parkinson. I heard him when he was in his prime and I think he had then the purest tenor voice that was ever put into a man's throat."

"Strange," said Mr. Bartell D'Arcy. "I never even heard of him."

"Yes, yes, Miss Morkan is right," said Mr. Browne. "I remember hearing of old Parkinson but he's too far back for me."

"A beautiful, pure, sweet, mellow English tenor," said Aunt Kate with enthusiasm.

Gabriel having finished, the huge pudding was transferred to the table. The clatter of forks and spoons began again. Gabriel's wife served out spoonfuls of the pudding and passed the plates down the table. Midway down they were held up by Mary Jane, who replenished them with raspberry or orange jelly or with blancmange and jam. The pudding was of Aunt Julia's making and she received praises for it from all quarters. She herself said that it was not quite brown enough.

"Well, I hope, Miss Morkan," said Mr. Browne, "that I'm brown enough for you because, you know, I'm all brown."

All the gentlemen, except Gabriel, ate some of the pudding out of compliment to Aunt Julia. As Gabriel never ate sweets the celery had been left for him. Freddy Malins also took a stalk of celery and ate it with his pudding. He had been told that celery was a capital thing for the blood and he was just then under doctor's care. Mrs. Malins, who had been silent all through the supper, said that her son was going down to Mount Melleray in a week or so. The table then spoke of Mount Melleray, how bracing the air was down there, how hospitable the monks were and how they never asked for a penny-piece from their guests.

"And do you mean to say," asked Mr. Browne incredulously, "that a chap can go down there and put up there as if it were a hotel and live on the fat of the land and then come away without paying anything?"

"O, most people give some donation to the monastery when they leave," said Mary Jane.

"I wish we had an institution like that in our Church," said Mr. Browne candidly.

He was astonished to hear that the monks never spoke, got up at two in the morning and slept in their coffins. He asked what they did it for.

"That's the rule of the order," said Aunt Kate firmly.

"Yes, but why?" asked Mr. Browne.

Aunt Kate repeated that it was the rule that was all. Mr. Browne still seemed not to understand. Freddy Malins explained to him, as best he could, that the monks were trying to make up for the sins committed by all the sinners in the outside world. The explanation was not very clear for Mr. Browne grinned and said:

"I like that idea very much but wouldn't a comfortable spring bed do them as well as a coffin?"

"The coffin," said Mary Jane, "is to remind them of their last end."

As the subject had grown lugubrious it was buried in a silence of the table during which Mrs. Malins could be heard saying to her neighbour in an indistinct undertone:

"They are very good men, the monks, very pious men."

The raisins and almonds and figs and apples and oranges and chocolates and sweets were now passed about the table and Aunt Julia invited all the guests to have either port or sherry. At first Mr. Bartell D'Arcy refused to take either but one of his neighbours nudged him and whispered something to him upon which he allowed his glass to be filled. Gradually as the last glasses were being filled the conversation ceased. A pause followed, broken only by the noise of the wine and by unsettlings of chairs. The Misses Morkan, all three, looked down at the tablecloth. Someone coughed once or twice and then a few gentlemen patted the table gently as a signal for silence. The silence came and Gabriel pushed back his chair and stood up.

The patting at once grew louder in encouragement and then ceased altogether. Gabriel leaned his ten trembling fingers on the tablecloth and smiled nervously at the company. Meeting a row of unturned faces he raised his eyes to the chandelier. The piano was playing a waltz tune and he could hear the skirts sweeping against the drawing-room door. People, perhaps, were standing in the snow on the quay outside, gazing up at the lighted windows and listening to the waltz music. The air was pure there. In the distance lay the park where the trees were weighted with snow. The Wellington Monument wore a gleaming cap of snow that flashed westward over the white field of Fifteen Acres.

He began:

"Ladies and Gentlemen,

"It has fallen to my lot this evening, as in years past, to perform a very pleasing task but a task for which I am afraid my poor powers as a speaker are all too inadequate."

"No, no!" said Mr. Browne.

"But, however that may be, I can only ask you tonight to take the will for the deed and to lend me your attention for a few moments while I endeavour to express to you in words what my feelings are on this occasion.

"Ladies and Gentlemen, it is not the first time that we have gathered together under this hospitable roof, around this hospitable board. It is not the first time that we have been the recipients—or perhaps, I had better say, the victims—of the hospitality of certain good ladies."

He made a circle in the air with his arm and paused. Everyone laughed or smiled at Aunt Kate and Aunt Julia and Mary Jane who all turned crimson with pleasure. Gabriel went on more boldly:

"I feel more strongly with every recurring year that our country has no tradition which does it so much honour and which it should guard so jealously as that of its hospitality. It is a tradition that is unique as far as my experience goes (and I have visited not a few places abroad) among the modern nations. Some would say, perhaps, that with us it is rather a failing than anything to be boasted of. But granted even that, it is, to my mind, a princely failing, and one that I trust will long be cultivated among us. Of one thing, at least, I am sure. As long as this one roof shelters the good ladies aforesaid —and I wish from my heart it may do so for many and many a long year to come —the tradition of genuine warm-hearted courteous Irish hospitality, which our forefathers have handed down to us and which we in turn must hand down to our descendants, is still alive among us."

A hearty murmur of assent ran round the table. It shot through Gabriel's mind that Miss Ivors was not there and that she had gone away discourteously: and he said with confidence in himself:

"Ladies and Gentlemen,

"A new generation is growing up in our midst, a generation actuated by new ideas and new principles. It is serious and enthusiastic for these new ideas and its enthusiasm, even when it is misdirected, is, I believe, in the main sincere. But we are living in a sceptical and, if I may use the phrase, a thought-tormented age: and sometimes I fear that this new generation, educated or hypereducated as it is, will lack those qualities of humanity, or hospitality, of kindly humour which belonged to an older day. Listening tonight to the names of all those great singers of the past it seemed to me, I must confess, that we were living in a less spacious age. Those days might, without exaggeration, be called spacious days: and if they are gone beyond recall let us hope, at least, that in gatherings such as this we shall still speak of them with pride and affection, still cherish in our hearts the memory of those dead and gone great ones whose fame the world will not willingly let die."

"Hear, hear!" said Mr. Browne loudly.

"But yet," continued Gabriel, his voice falling into a softer inflection, "there are always in gatherings such as this sadder thoughts that will recur to our minds: thoughts of the past, of youth, of changes, of absent faces that we miss here tonight. Our path through life is strewn with many such sad memories: and were we to brood upon them always we could not find the heart to go on bravely with our work among the living. We have all of us living duties and living affections which claim, and rightly claim, our strenuous endeavours.

"Therefore, I will not linger on the past. I will not let any gloomy moralising intrude upon us here tonight. Here we are gathered together for a brief moment from the bustle and rush of our everyday routine. We are met here as friends, in the spirit of good-fellowship, as colleagues, also to a certain extent, in the true spirit of *camaraderie*, and as the guests of—what shall I call them— the Three Graces of the Dublin musical world."

The table burst into applause and laughter at this allusion. Aunt Julia vainly asked each of her neighbours in turn to tell her what Gabriel had said.

"He says we are the Three Graces, Aunt Julia," said Mary Jane.

Aunt Julia did not understand but she looked up, smiling, at Gabriel, who continued in the same vein:

"Ladies and Gentlemen,

"I will not attempt to play tonight the part that Paris played on another occasion. I will not attempt to choose between them. The task would be an invidious one and one beyond my poor powers. For when I view them in turn, whether it be our chief hostess herself, whose good heart, whose too good heart, has become a byword with all who know her, or her sister, who seems to be gifted with perennial youth and whose singing must have been a surprise and a revelation to us all tonight, or, last but not least, when I consider our youngest hostess, talented, cheerful, hard-working and the best of nieces, I confess, Ladies and Gentlemen, that I do not know to which of them I should award the prize."

Gabriel glanced down at his aunts and, seeing the large smile on Aunt Julia's face and the tears which had risen to Aunt Kate's eyes, hastened to his close. He raised his glass of port gallantly, while every member of the company fingered a glass expectantly, and said loudly:

"Let us toast them all three together. Let us drink to their health, wealth, long life, happiness and prosperity and may they long continue to hold the proud and self-won position which they hold in their profession and the position of honour and affection which they hold in our hearts."

All the guests stood up, glass in hand, and turning towards the three seated ladies, sang in unison, with Mr. Browne as leader:

> For they are jolly gay fellows,
> For they are jolly gay fellows,
> For they are jolly gay fellows,
> Which nobody can deny.

Aunt Kate was making frank use of her handkerchief and even Aunt Julia seemed moved. Freddy Malins beat time with his pudding-fork and the singers turned towards one another, as if in melodious conference, while they sang with emphasis:

> Unless he tells a lie,
> Unless he tells a lie,

Then, turning once more towards their hostesses, they sang:

For they are jolly gay fellows,
For they are jolly gay fellows,
For they are jolly gay fellows,
Which nobody can deny.

The acclamation which followed was taken up beyond the door of the supper-room by many of the other guests and renewed time after time, Freddy Malins acting as officer with his fork on high.

The piercing morning air came into the hall where they were standing so that Aunt Kate said:

"Close the door, somebody. Mrs. Malins will get her death of cold."

"Browne is out there, Aunt Kate," said Mary Jane.

"Browne is everywhere," said Aunt Kate, lowering her voice.

Mary Jane laughed at her tone.

"Really," she said archly, "he is very attentive."

"He has been laid on here like the gas," said Aunt Kate in the same tone, "all during the Christmas."

She laughed herself this time good-humouredly and then added quickly:

"But tell him to come in, Mary Jane, and close the door. I hope to goodness he didn't hear me."

At that moment the hall-door was opened and Mr. Browne came in from the doorstep, laughing as if his heart would break. He was dressed in a long green overcoat with mock astrakhan cuffs and collar and wore on his head an oval fur cap. He pointed down the snow-covered quay from where the sound of shrill prolonged whistling was borne in.

"Teddy will have all the cabs in Dublin out," he said.

Gabriel advanced from the little pantry behind the office, struggling into his overcoat and, looking round the hall, said:

"Gretta not down yet?"

"She's getting on her things, Gabriel," said Aunt Kate.

"Who's playing up there?" asked Gabriel.

"Nobody. They're all gone."

"O no, Aunt Kate," said Mary Jane. "Bartell D'Arcy and Miss O'Callaghan aren't gone yet."

"Someone is fooling at the piano anyhow," said Gabriel.

Mary Jane glanced at Gabriel and Mr. Browne and said with a shiver:

"It makes me feel cold to look at you two gentlemen muffled up like that. I wouldn't like to face your journey home at this hour."

"I'd like nothing better this minute," said Mr. Browne stoutly, "than a rattling fine walk in the country or a fast drive with a good spanking goer between the shafts."

"We used to have a very good horse and trap at home," said Aunt Julia sadly.

"The never-to-be-forgotten Johnny," said Mary Jane, laughing.

Aunt Kate and Gabriel laughed too.

"Why, what was wonderful about Johnny?" asked Mr. Browne.

"The late lamented Patrick Morkan, our grandfather, that is," explained Gabriel, "commonly known in his later years as the old gentleman, was a glue-boiler."

"O, now, Gabriel," said Aunt Kate, laughing, "he had a starch mill."

"Well, glue or starch," said Gabriel, "the old gentleman had a horse by the name of Johnny. And Johnny used to work in the old gentleman's mill, walking round and round in order to drive the mill. That was all very well; but now comes the tragic part about Johnny. One fine day the old gentleman thought he'd like to drive out with the quality to a military review in the park."

"The Lord have mercy on his soul," said Aunt Kate compassionately.

"Amen," said Gabriel. "So the old gentleman, as I said, harnessed Johnny and put on his very best tall hat and his very best stock collar and drove out in grand style from his ancestral mansion somewhere near Back Lane, I think."

Everyone laughed, even Mrs. Malins, at Gabriel's manner and Aunt Kate said:

"O, now, Gabriel, he didn't live in Back Lane, really. Only the mill was there."

"Out from the mansion of his forefathers," continued Gabriel, "he drove with Johnny. And everything went on beautifully until Johnny came in sight of King Billy's statue: and whether he fell in love with the horse King Billy sits on or whether he thought he was back again in the mill, anyhow he began to walk round the statue."

Gabriel paced in a circle round the hall in his goloshes amid the laughter of the others.

"Round and round he went," said Gabriel, "and the old gentleman, who was a very pompous old gentleman, was highly indignant. 'Go on, sir! What do you mean, sir? Johnny! Johnny! Most extraordinary conduct! Can't understand the horse!' "

The peal of laughter which followed Gabriel's imitation of the incident was interrupted by a resounding knock at the hall door. Mary Jane ran to open it and let in Freddy Malins. Freddy Malins, with his hat well back on his head and his shoulders humped with cold, was puffing and steaming after his exertions.

"I could only get one cab," he said.

"O, we'll find another along the quay," said Gabriel.

"Yes," said Aunt Kate. "Better not keep Mrs. Malins standing in the draught."

Mrs. Malins was helped down the front steps by her son and Mr. Browne and, after many manœuvres, hoisted into the cab. Freddy Malins clambered in after her and spent a long time settling her on the seat, Mr. Browne helping him with advice. At last she was settled comfortably and Freddy Malins invited Mr. Browne into the cab. There was a good deal of confused talk, and then Mr. Browne got into the cab. The cabman settled his rug over his knees, and bent down for the address. The confusion grew greater and the cabman was directed differently by Freddy Malins and Mr. Browne, each of whom had his head out through a window of the cab. The difficulty was to know where to drop Mr. Browne along the route, and Aunt Kate, Aunt Julia and Mary Jane helped the discussion from the doorstep with cross-directions and contradictions and abundance of laughter. As for Freddy Malins he was speechless with laughter. He popped his head in and out of the window every moment to the great danger of his hat, and told his mother how the discussion was progressing, till at last Mr.

Browne shouted to the bewildered cabman above the din of everybody's laughter:

"Do you know Trinity College?"

"Yes, sir," said the cabman.

"Well, drive bang up against Trinity College gates," said Mr. Browne, "and then we'll tell you where to go. You understand now?"

"Yes, sir," said the cabman,

"Make like a bird for Trinity College."

"Right, sir," said the cabman.

The horse was whipped up and the cab rattled off along the quay amid a chorus of laughter and adieus.

Gabriel had not gone to the door with the others. He was in a dark part of the hall gazing up the staircase. A woman was standing near the top of the first flight, in the shadow also. He could not see her face but he could see the terracotta and salmon-pink panels of her skirt which the shadow made appear black and white. It was his wife. She was leaning on the banisters, listening to something. Gabriel was surprised at her stillness and strained his ear to listen also. But he could hear little save the noise of laughter and dispute on the front steps, a few chords struck on the piano and a few notes of a man's voice singing.

He stood still in the gloom of the hall, trying to catch the air that the voice was singing and gazing up at his wife. There was grace and mystery in her attitude as if she were a symbol of something. He asked himself what is a woman standing on the stairs in the shadow, listening to distant music, a symbol of. If he were a painter he would paint her in that attitude. Her blue felt hat would show off the bronze of her hair against the darkness and the dark panels of her skirt would show off the light ones. *Distant Music* he would call the picture if he were a painter.

The hall-door was closed; and Aunt Kate, Aunt Julia and Mary Jane came down the hall, still laughing.

"Well, isn't Freddy terrible?" said Mary Jane. "He's really terrible."

Gabriel said nothing but pointed up the stairs towards where his wife was standing. Now that the hall-door was closed the voice and the piano could be heard more clearly. Gabriel held up his hand for them to be silent. The song seemed to be in the old Irish tonality and the singer seemed uncertain both of his words and of his voice. The voice, made plaintive by distance and by the singer's hoarseness, faintly illuminated the cadence of the air with words expressing grief:

O, the rain falls on my heavy locks
And the dew wets my skin,
My babe lies cold . . .

"O," exclaimed Mary Jane. "It's Bartell D'Arcy singing and he wouldn't sing all the night. O, I'll get him to sing a song before he goes."

"O, do, Mary Jane," said Aunt Kate.

Mary Jane brushed past the others and ran to the staircase, but before she reached it the singing stopped and the piano was closed abruptly.

"O, what a pity!" she cried. "Is he coming down, Gretta?"

Gabriel heard his wife answer yes and saw her come down towards them. A few steps behind her were Mr. Bartell D'Arcy and Miss O'Callaghan.

"O, Mr. D'Arcy," cried Mary Jane, "it's downright mean of you to break off like that when we were all in raptures listening to you."

"I have been at him all the evening," said Miss O'Callaghan, "and Mrs. Conroy, too, and he told us he had a dreadful cold and couldn't sing."

"O, Mr. D'Arcy," said Aunt Kate, "now that was a great fib to tell."

"Can't you see that I'm as hoarse as a crow?" said Mr. D'Arcy roughly.

He went into the pantry hastily and put on his overcoat. The others, taken aback by his rude speech, could find nothing to say. Aunt Kate wrinkled her brows and made signs to the others to drop the subject. Mr. D'Arcy stood swathing his neck carefully and frowning.

"It's the weather," said Aunt Julia, after a pause.

"Yes, everybody has colds," said Aunt Kate readily, "everybody."

"They say," said Mary Jane, "we haven't had snow like it for thirty years;

and I read this morning in the newspapers that the snow is general all over Ireland."

"I love the look of snow," said Aunt Julia sadly.

"So do I," said Miss O'Callaghan. "I think Christmas is never really Christmas unless we have the snow on the ground."

"But poor Mr. D'Arcy doesn't like the snow," said Aunt Kate, smiling.

Mr. D'Arcy came from the pantry, fully swathed and buttoned, and in a repentant tone told them the history of his cold. Everyone gave him advice and said it was a great pity and urged him to be very careful of his throat in the night air. Gabriel watched his wife, who did not join in the conversation. She was standing right under the dusty fanlight and the flame of the gas lit up the rich bronze of her hair, which he had seen her drying at the fire at few days before. She was in the same attitude and seemed unaware of the talk about her. At last she turned towards them and Gabriel saw that there was colour on her cheeks and that her eyes were shining. A sudden tide of joy went leaping out of his heart.

"Mr. D'Arcy," she said, "what is the name of that song you were singing?"

"It's called *The Lass of Aughrim*," said Mr. D'Arcy, "but I couldn't remember it properly. Why? Do you know it?"

"*The Lass of Aughrim*," she repeated. "I couldn't think of the name."

"It's a very nice air," said Mary Jane. "I'm sorry you were not in voice tonight."

"Now, Mary Jane," said Aunt Kate, "don't annoy Mr. D'Arcy. I won't have him annoyed."

Seeing that all were ready to start she shepherded them to the door, where goodnight was said:

"Well, good-night, Aunt Kate, and thanks for the pleasant evening."

"Good-night, Gabriel. Good-night, Gretta!"

"Good-night, Aunt Kate, and thanks ever so much. Good-night, Aunt Julia."

"O, good-night, Gretta, I didn't see you."

"Good-night, Mr. D'Arcy. Good-night, Miss O'Callaghan."

"Good-night, Miss Morkan."

"Good-night, again."

"Good-night, all. Safe home."

"Good-night. Good night."

The morning was still dark. A dull, yellow light brooded over the houses and the river; and the sky seemed to be descending. It was slushy underfoot; and only streaks and patches of snow lay on the roofs, on the parapets of the quay and on the area railings. The lamps were still burning redly in the murky air and, across the river, the palace of the Four Courts stood out menacingly against the heavy sky.

She was walking on before him with Mr. Bartell D'Arcy, her shoes in a brown parcel tucked under one arm and her hands holding her skirt up from the slush. She had no longer any grace of attitude, but Gabriel's eyes were still bright with happiness. The blood went bounding along his veins; and the thoughts went rioting through his brain, proud, joyful, tender, valorous.

She was walking on before him so lightly and so erect that he longed to run after her noiselessly, catch her by the shoulders and say something foolish and affectionate into her ear. She seemed to him so frail that he longed to defend her against something and then to be alone with her. Moments of their secret life together burst like stars upon his memory. A heliotrope envelope was lying beside his breakfast-cup and he was caressing it with his hand. Birds were twittering in the ivy and the sunny web of the curtain was shimmering along the floor: he could not eat for happiness. They were standing on the crowded platform and he was placing a ticket inside the warm palm of her glove. He was standing with her in the cold, looking in through a grated window at a man making bottles in a roaring furnace. It was very cold. Her face, fragrant in the cold air, was quite close to his; and suddenly he called out to the man at the furnace:

"Is the fire hot, sir?"

But the man could not hear with the noise of the furnace. It was just as well. He might have answered rudely.

A wave of yet more tender joy escaped from his heart and went coursing in warm flood along his arteries. Like the tender fire of stars moments of their life together, that no one knew of or would ever know of, broke upon and illumined his memory. He longed to recall to her those moments, to make her forget the years of their dull existence together and remember only their moments of ecstasy. For the years, he felt, had not quenched his soul or hers. Their children, his writing, her household cares had not quenched all their souls' tender fire. In one letter that he had written to her then he had said: "Why is it that words like these seem to me so dull and cold? Is it because there is no word tender enough to be your name?"

Like distant music these words that he had written years before were borne towards him from the past. He longed to be alone with her. When the others had gone away, when he and she were in the room in the hotel, then they would be alone together. He would call her softly:

"Gretta!"

Perhaps she would not hear at once: she would be undressing. Then something in his voice would strike her. She would turn and look at him. . . .

At the corner of Winetavern Street they met a cab. He was glad of its rattling noise as it saved him from conversation. She was looking out of the window and seemed tired. The others spoke only a few words, pointing out some building or street. The horse galloped along wearily under the murky morning sky, dragging his old rattling box after his heels, and Gabriel was again in a cab with her, galloping to catch the boat, galloping to their honeymoon.

As the cab drove across O'Connell Bridge Miss O'Callaghan said:

"They say you never cross O'Connell Bridge without seeing a white horse."

"I see a white man this time," said Gabriel.

"Where?" asked Mr. Bartell D'Arcy.

Gabriel pointed to the statue, on which lay patches of snow. Then he nodded familiarly to it and waved his hand.

"Good-night, Dan," he said gaily.

When the cab drew up before the hotel, Gabriel jumped out and, in spite of Mr.

Bartell D'Arcy's protest, paid the driver. He gave the man a shilling over his fare. The man saluted and said:

"A prosperous New Year to you, sir."

"The same to you," said Gabriel cordially.

She leaned for a moment on his arm in getting out of the cab and while standing at the curbstone, bidding the others good-night. She leaned lightly on his arm, as lightly at when she had danced with him a few hours before. He had felt proud and happy then, happy that she was his, proud of her grace and wifely carriage. But now, after the kindling again of so many memories, the first touch of her body, musical and strange and perfumed, sent through him a keen pang of lust. Under cover of her silence he pressed her closely to his side; and, as they stood at the hotel door, he felt that they had escaped from their lives and duties, escaped from home and friends and run away together with wild and radiant hearts to a new adventure.

An old man was dozing in a great hooded chair in the hall. He lit a candle in the office and went before them to the stairs. They followed him in silence, their feet falling in soft thuds on the thickly carpeted stairs. She mounted the stairs behind the porter, her head bowed in the ascent, her frail shoulders curved as with a burden, her skirt girt tightly about her. He could have flung his arms about her hips and held her still, for his arms were trembling with desire to seize her and only the stress of his nails against the palms of his hands held the wild impulse of his body in check. The porter halted on the stairs to settle his guttering candle. They halted, too, on the steps below him. In the silence Gabriel could hear the falling of the molten wax into the tray and the thumping of his own heart against his ribs.

The porter led them along a corridor and opened a door. Then he set his unstable candle down on a toilet-table and asked at what hour they were to be called in the morning.

"Eight," said Gabriel.

The porter pointed to the tap of the electric-light and began a muttered apology, but Gabriel cut him short.

"We don't want any light. We have light enough from the street. And I say," he added, pointing to the candle, "you might remove that handsome article, like a good man."

The porter took up his candle again, but slowly, for he was surprised by such a novel idea. Then he mumbled goodnight and went out. Gabriel shot the lock to.

A ghastly light from the street lamp lay in a long shaft from one window to the door. Gabriel threw his overcoat and hat on a couch and crossed the room towards the window. He looked down into the street in order that his emotion might calm a little. Then he turned and leaned against a chest of drawers with his back to the light. She had taken off her hat and cloak and was standing before a large swinging mirror, unhooking her waist. Gabriel paused for a few moments, watching her, and then said:

"Gretta!"

She turned away from the mirror slowly and walked along the shaft of light towards him. Her face looked so serious and weary that the words would not pass Gabriel's lips. No, it was not the moment yet.

"You looked tired," he said.

"I am a little," she answered.

"You don't feel ill or weak?"

"No, tired: that's all."

She went on to the window and stood there, looking out. Gabriel waited again and then, fearing that diffidence was about to conquer him, he said abruptly:

"By the way, Gretta!"

"What is it?"

"You know that poor fellow Malins?" he said quickly.

"Yes. What about him?"

"Well, poor fellow, he's a decent sort of chap, after all," continued Gabriel in a false voice. "He gave me back that sovereign I lent him, and I didn't expect it, really. It's a pity he wouldn't keep away from that Browne, because he's not a bad fellow, really."

He was trembling now with annoyance. Why did she seem so abstracted? He did not know how he could begin. Was she annoyed, too, about something? If she would only turn to him or come to him of her own accord! To take her as she was would be brutal. No, he must see some ardour in her eyes first. He longed to be master of her strange mood.

"When did you lend him the pound?" she asked, after a pause.

Gabriel strove to restrain himself from breaking out into brutal language about the sottish Malins and his pound. He longed to cry to her from his soul, to crush her body against his, to overmaster her. But he said:

"O, at Christmas, when he opened that little Christmas-card shop in Henry Street."

He was in such a fever of rage and desire that he did not hear her come from the window. She stood before him for an instant, looking at him strangely. Then, suddenly raising herself on tiptoe and resting her hands lightly on his shoulders, she kissed him.

"You are a very generous person, Gabriel," she said.

Gabriel, trembling with delight at her sudden kiss and at the quaintness of her phrase, put his hands on her hair and began smoothing it back, scarcely touching it with his fingers. The washing had made it fine and brilliant. His heart was brimming over with happiness. Just when he was wishing for it she had come to him of her own accord. Perhaps her thoughts had been running with his. Perhaps she had felt the impetuous desire that was in him, and then the yielding mood had come upon her. Now that she had fallen to him so easily, he wondered why he had been so diffident.

He stood, holding her head between his hands. Then, slipping one arm swiftly about her body and drawing her towards him, he said softly:

"Gretta, dear, what are you thinking about?"

She did not answer nor yield wholly to his arm. He said again, softly:

"Tell me what it is, Gretta. I think I know what is the matter. Do I know?"

She did not answer at once. Then she said in an outburst of tears:

"O, I am thinking about that song, *The Lass of Aughrim.*"

She broke loose from him and ran to the bed and, throwing her arms across the bed-rail, hid her face. Gabriel stood stock-still for a moment in astonishment and then followed her. As he passed in the way of the cheval-glass he caught sight of himself in full length, his broad, well-filled shirt-front, the face whose expression always puzzled him when he saw it in a mirror, and his glimmering gilt-rimmed eyeglasses. He halted a few paces from her and said:

"What about the song? Why does that make you cry?"

She raised her head from her arms and dried her eyes with the back of her hand like a child. A kinder note than he had intended went into his voice.

"Why, Gretta?" he asked.

"I am thinking about a person long ago who used to sing that song."

"And who was the person long ago?" asked Gabriel, smiling.

"It was a person I used to know in Galway when I was living with my grandmother," she said.

The smile passed away from Gabriel's face. A dull anger began to gather again at the back of his mind and the dull fires of his lust began to glow angrily in his veins.

"Someone you were in love with?" he asked ironically.

"It was a young boy I used to know," she answered, "named Michael Furey. He used to sing that song, *The Lass of Aughrim.* He was very delicate."

Gabriel was silent. He did not wish her to think that he was interested in this delicate boy.

"I can see him so plainly," she said, after a moment. "Such eyes as he had: big, dark eyes! And such an expression in them—an expression!"

"O, then, you are in love with him?" said Gabriel.

"I used to go out walking with him," she said, "when I was in Galway."

A thought flew across Gabriel's mind.

"Perhaps that was why you wanted to go to Galway with that Ivors girl?" he said coldly.

She looked at him and asked in surprise:

"What for?"

Her eyes made Gabriel feel awkward. He shugged his shoulders and said:

"How do I know? To see him, perhaps."

She looked away from him along the shaft of light towards the window in silence.

"He is dead," she said at length. "He died when he was only seventeen. Isn't it a terrible thing to die so young as that?"

"What was he?" asked Gabriel, still ironically.

"He was in the gasworks," she said.

Gabriel felt humiliated by the failure of his irony and by the evocation of this figure from the dead, a boy in the gasworks. While he had been full of memories of their secret life together, full of tenderness and joy and desire, she had been comparing him in her mind with another. A shameful consciousness of his own person assailed him. He saw himself as a ludicrous figure, acting as a pennyboy for his aunts, a nervous, well-meaning sentimentalist, orating to vulgarians and idealising his own clownish lusts, the pitiable fatuous fellow he had caught a glimpse of in the mirror. Instinctively he turned his back more to the light lest she might see the shame that burned upon his forehead.

He tried to keep up his tone of cold interrogation, but his voice when he spoke was humble and indifferent.

"I suppose you were in love with this Michael Furey, Gretta," he said.

"I was great with him at that time," she said.

Her voice was veiled and sad. Gabriel, feeling now how vain it would be to try to lead her whither he had purposed, caressed one of her hands and said, also sadly:

"And what did he die of so young, Gretta? Consumption, was it?"

"I think he died for me," she answered.

A vague terror seized Gabriel at this answer, as if, at that hour when he had hoped to triumph, some impalpable and vindictive being was coming against him, gathering forces against him in its vague world. But he shook himself free of it with an effort of reason and continued to caress her hand. He did not question her again, for he felt that she would tell him of herself. Her hand was warm and moist: it did not respond to his touch, but he continued to caress it just as he had caressed her first letter to him that spring morning.

"It was in the winter," she said, "about the beginning of the winter when I was going to leave my grandmother's and come up here to the convent. And he was ill at the time in his lodgings in Galway and wouldn't be let out, and his people in Oughterard were written to. He was in decline, they said, or something like that. I never knew rightly."

She paused for a moment and sighed.

"Poor fellow," she said. "He was very fond of me and he was such a gentle boy. We used to go out together, walking, you know, Gabriel, like the way they do in the country. He was going to study singing only for his health. He had a very good voice, poor Michael Furey."

"Well; and then?" asked Gabriel.

"And then when it came to the time for me to leave Galway and come up to the convent he was much worse and I wouldn't be let see him so I wrote him a letter saying I was going up to Dublin and would be back in the summer, and hoping he would be better then."

She paused for a moment to get her voice under control, and then went on:

"Then the night before I left, I was in my grandmother's house in Nuns' Island, packing up, and I heard gravel thrown up against the window. The window was so wet I couldn't see, so I ran downstairs as I was and slipped out the back into the garden and there was the poor fellow at the end of the garden, shivering."

"And did you not tell him to go back?" asked Gabriel.

"I implored of him to go home at once and told him he would get his death in the rain. But he said he did not want to live. I can see his eyes as well as well! He was standing at the end of the wall where there was a tree."

"And did he go home?" asked Gabriel.

"Yes, he went home. And when I was

only a week in the convent he died and he was buried in Oughterard, where his people came from. O, the day I heard that, that he was dead!"

She stopped, choking with sobs, and, overcome by emotion, flung herself face downward on the bed, sobbing in the quilt. Gabriel held her hand for a moment longer, irresolutely, and then, shy of intruding on her grief, let it fall gently and walked to the window.

She was fast asleep.

Gabriel, leaning on his elbow, looked for a few moments unresentfully on her tangled hair and half-open mouth, listening to her deep-drawn breath. So she had had that romance in her life: a man had died for her sake. It hardly pained him now to think how poor a part he, her husband, had played in her life. He watched her while she slept, as though he and she had never lived together as man and wife. His curious eyes rested long upon her face and on her hair: and, as he thought of what she must have been then, in that time of her first girlish beauty, a strange, friendly pity for her entered his soul. He did not like to say even to himself that her face was no longer beautiful, but he knew that it was no longer the face for which Michael Furey had braved death.

Perhaps she had not told him all the story. His eyes moved to the chair over which she had thrown some of her clothes. A petticoat string dangled to the floor. One boot stood upright, its limp upper fallen down: the fellow of it lay upon its side. He wondered at his riot of emotions of an hour before. From what had it proceeded? From his aunt's supper, from his own foolish speech, from the wine and dancing, the merry-making when saying good-night in the hall, the pleasure of the walk along the river in the snow. Poor Aunt Julia! She, too, would soon be a shade with the shade of Patrick Morkan and his horse. He had caught that haggard look upon her face for a moment when she was singing *Arrayed for the Bridal*. Soon, perhaps, he would be sitting in that same drawing-room, dressed in black, his silk hat on his knees. The blinds would be drawn down and Aunt Kate would be sitting beside him, crying and blowing her nose and telling him how Julia had died. He would cast about in his mind for some words that might console her, and would find only lame and useless ones. Yes, yes: that would happen very soon.

The air of the room chilled his shoulders. He stretched himself cautiously along under the sheets and lay down beside his wife. One by one, they were all becoming shades. Better pass boldly into that other world, in the full glory of some passion, than fade and wither dismally with age. He thought of how she who lay beside him had locked in her heart for so many years that image of her lover's eyes when he had told her that he did not wish to live.

Generous tears filled Gabriel's eyes. He had never felt like that himself towards any woman, but he knew that such a feeling must be love. The tears gathered more thickly in his eyes and in the partial darkness he imagined he saw the form of a young man standing under a dripping tree. Other forms were near. His soul had approached that region where dwell the vast hosts of the dead. He was conscious of, but could not apprehend, their wayward and flickering existence. His own identity was fading out into a grey impalpable world: the solid world itself, which these dead had one time reared and lived in, was dissolving and dwindling.

A few light taps upon the pane made him turn to the window. It had begun to snow again. He watched sleepily the flakes, silver and dark, falling obliquely against the lamplight. The time had come for him to set out on his journey westward. Yes, the newspapers were right: snow was general all over Ireland. It was falling on every part of the dark central plain, on the treeless hills, falling softly upon the Bog of Allen and, farther westward, softly falling into the dark mutinous Shannon waves. It was falling, too, upon every part of the lonely churchyard on the hill where Michael Furey lay buried. It lay thickly drifted on the crooked crosses and headstones, on the spears of the little gate, on the barren thorns. His soul swooned slowly as he heard the snow falling faintly through the universe and faintly falling, like the descent of their last end, upon all the living and the dead.

[1914]

QUESTIONS FOR STUDY

1. *What aspects of Gabriel's character are revealed by the successive events of the party? What are the sources of his insecurity, agitation, and discomfort? How does his mood progressively change?*
2. *What is at issue in the contention between Gabriel and Miss Ivors? What associations cluster around the West of Ireland?*
3. *What antithetical aspects of life are associated in Gretta's mind and emotions with Michael Furey and with Gabriel?*
4. *What are the ironies of the final scene in the hotel room? What does Gabriel learn about Gretta and about himself? How is Gabriel's moment of self-knowledge and self-awareness prepared for earlier in the story? What are the implications of Joyce's lyrical ending? For example, what is implied by the statement that "The time had come for him to set out on his journey westward"?*
5. *What are the primary patterns of imagery that recur throughout the story? What is their function?*

JAMES JOYCE

Ivy Day in the Committee Room

OLD JACK raked the cinders together with a piece of cardboard and spread them judiciously over the whitening dome of coals. When the dome was thinly covered his face lapsed into darkness but, as he set himself to fan the fire again, his crouching shadow ascended the opposite wall and his face slowly re-emerged into light. It was an old man's face, very bony and hairy. The moist blue eyes blinked at the fire and the moist mouth fell open at times, munching once or twice mechanically when it closed. When the cinders had caught he laid the piece of cardboard against the wall, sighed and said:

"That's better now, Mr. O'Connor."

Mr. O'Connor, a grey-haired young man, whose face was disfigured by many blotches and pimples, had just brought the tobacco for a cigarette into a shapely cylinder but when spoken to he undid his handiwork meditatively. Then he began to roll the tobacco again meditatively and after a moment's thought decided to lick the paper.

"Did Mr. Tierney say when he'd be back?" he asked in a husky falsetto.

"He didn't say."

Mr. O'Connor put his cigarette into his mouth and began to search his pockets. He took out a pack of thin pasteboard cards.

"I'll get you a match," said the old man.

"Never mind, this'll do," said Mr. O'Connor.

He selected one of the cards and read what was printed on it:

MUNICIPAL ELECTIONS

ROYAL EXCHANGE WARD

Mr. Richard J. Tierney, P.L.G., respect-fully solicits the favour of your vote and influence at the coming election in the Royal Exchange Ward.

Mr. O'Connor had been engaged by Tierney's agent to canvass one part of the ward but, as the weather was inclement and his boots let in the wet, he spent a great part of the day sitting by the fire in the Committee Room in Wicklow Street with Jack the old caretaker. They had been sitting thus since the short day had grown dark. It was the sixth of October, dismal and cold out of doors.

Mr. O'Connor tore a strip off the card and, lighting it, lit his cigarette. As he did so the flame lit up a leaf of dark glossy ivy in the lapel of his coat. The old man watched him attentively and then, taking up the piece of cardboard again, began to fan the fire slowly while his companion smoked.

"Ah, yes," he said, continuing, "it's hard to know what way to bring up children. Now who'd think he'd turn out like that! I sent him to the Christian Brothers and I done what I could for him, and there he goes boosing about. I tried to make him someway decent."

He replaced the cardboard wearily.

"Only I'm an old man now I'd change his tune for him. I'd take the stick to his back and beat him while I could stand over him—as I done many a time before. The mother, you know, she cocks him up with this and that. . . ."

"That's what ruins children," said Mr. O'Connor.

"To be sure it is," said the old man. "And little thanks you get for it, only impudence. He takes th'upper hand of me whenever he sees I've a sup taken. What's the world coming to when sons speak that way to their fathers?"

"What age is he?" said Mr. O'Connor.

"Nineteen," said the old man.

"Why don't you put him to something?"

"Sure, amn't I never done at the drunken bowsy ever since he left school? 'I won't keep you,' I says. 'You must get a job for yourself.' But, sure, it's worse whenever he gets a job; he drinks it all."

Mr. O'Connor shook his head in sympathy, and the old man fell silent, gazing into the fire. Someone opened the door of the room and called out:

"Hello! Is this a Freemason's meeting?"

"Who's that?" said the old man.

"What are you doing in the dark?" asked a voice.

"Is that you, Hynes?" asked Mr. O'Connor.

"Yes. What are you doing in the dark?" said Mr. Hynes, advancing into the light of the fire.

He was a tall, slender young man with a light brown moustache. Imminent little drops of rain hung at the brim of his hat and the collar of his jacket-coat was turned up.

"Well, Mat," he said to Mr. O'Connor, "how goes it?"

Mr. O'Connor shook his head. The old man left the hearth, and after stumbling about the room returned with two candlesticks which he thrust one after the other into the fire and carried to the table. A denuded room came into view and the fire lost all its cheerful colour. The walls of the room were bare except for a copy of an election address. In the middle of the room was a small table on which papers were heaped.

Mr. Hynes leaned against the mantelpiece and asked:

"Has he paid you yet?"

"Not yet," said Mr. O'Connor. "I hope to God he'll not leave us in the lurch tonight."

Mr. Hynes laughed.

"O, he'll pay you. Never fear," he said.

"I hope he'll look smart about it if he means business," said Mr. O'Connor.

"What do you think, Jack?" said Mr. Hynes satirically to the old man.

The old man returned to his seat by the fire, saying:

"It isn't but he has it, anyway. Not like the other tinker."

"What other tinker?" said Mr. Hynes.

"Colgan," said the old man scornfully.

"It is because Colgan's a working-man you say that? What's the difference between a good honest bricklayer and a publican—eh? Hasn't the working-man as good a right to be in the Corporation as anyone else—ay, and a better right than those shoneens that are always hat in hand before any fellow with a handle to his name? Isn't that so, Mat?" said Mr. Hynes, addressing Mr. O'Connor.

"I think you're right," said Mr. O'Connor.

"One man is a plain honest man with no hunker-sliding about him. He goes in to represent the labour classes. This fellow you're working for only wants to get some job or other."

"Of course, the working-classes should be represented," said the old man.

"The working-man," said Mr. Hynes, "gets all kicks and no halfpence. But it's labour produces everything. The working-man is not looking for fat jobs for his sons and nephews and cousins. The working-man is not going to drag the honour of Dublin in the mud to please a German monarch."

"How's that?" said the old man.

"Don't you know they want to present an address of welcome to Edward Rex if he comes here next year? What do we want kowtowing to a foreign king?"

"Our man won't vote for the address," said Mr. O'Connor. "He goes in on the Nationalist ticket."

"Won't he?" said Mr. Hynes. "Wait till you see whether he will or not. I know him. Is it Tricky Dicky Tierney?"

"By God! perhaps you're right, Joe," said Mr. O'Connor. "Anyway, I wish he'd turn up with the spondulics."

The three men fell silent. The old man began to rake more cinders together. Mr. Hynes took off his hat, shook it and then turned down the collar of his coat, displaying, as he did so, an ivy leaf in the lapel.

"If this man was alive," he said, pointing to the leaf, "we'd have no talk of an address of welcome."

"That's true," said Mr. O'Connor.

"Musha, God be with them times!" said the old man. "There was some life in it then."

The room was silent again. Then a bustling little man with a snuffling nose and very cold ears pushed in the door. He walked over quickly to the fire, rubbing his hands as if he intended to produce a spark from them.

"No money, boys," he said.

"Sit down here, Mr. Henchy," said the old man, offering him his chair.

"O, don't stir, Jack, don't stir," said Mr. Henchy.

He nodded curtly to Mr. Hynes and sat down on the chair which the old man vacated.

"Did you serve Aungier Street?" he asked Mr. O'Connor.

"Yes," said Mr. O'Connor, beginning to search his pockets for memoranda.

"Did you call on Grimes?"

"I did."

"Well? How does he stand?"

"He wouldn't promise. He said: 'I won't tell anyone what way I'm going to vote.' But I think he'll be all right."

"Why so?"

"He asked me who the nominators were; and I told him. I mentioned Father Burke's name. I think it'll be all right."

Mr. Henchy began to snuffle and to rub his hands over the fire at a terrific speed. Then he said:

"For the love of God, Jack, bring us a bit of coal. There must be some left."

The old man went out of the room.

"It's no go," said Mr. Henchy, shaking his head. "I asked the little shoeboy, but he said: 'O, now, Mr. Henchy, when I see the work going on properly I won't forget you, you may be sure.' Mean little tinker! 'Usha, how could he be anything else?"

"What did I tell you, Mat?" said Mr. Hynes. "Tricky Dicky Tierney."

"O, he's as tricky as they make 'em," said Mr. Henchy. "He hasn't got those little pigs' eyes for nothing. Blast his soul! Couldn't he pay up like a man instead of: 'O, now, Mr. Henchy, I must speak to Mr. Fanning. . . . I've spent a lot of money'? Mean little schoolboy of hell! I suppose he forgets the time his little old father kept the hand-me-down shop in Mary's Lane."

"But is that a fact?" asked Mr. O'Connor.

"God, yes," said Mr. Henchy. "Did you never hear that? And the men used to go in on Sunday morning before the houses were open to buy a waistcoat or a trousers—moya! But Tricky Dicky's little old father always had a tricky little black bottle up in a corner. Do you mind now? That's that. That's where he first saw the light."

The old man returned with a few lumps of coal which he placed here and there on the fire.

"That's a nice how-do-you-do," said Mr. O'Connor. "How does he expect us to work for him if he won't stump up?"

"I can't help it," said Mr. Henchy. "I expect to find the bailiffs in the hall when I go home."

Mr. Hynes laughed and, shoving himself away from the mantelpiece with the aid of his shoulders, made ready to leave.

"It'll be all right when King Eddie comes," he said. "Well, boys, I'm off for the present. See you later. 'Bye, 'bye."

He went out of the room slowly. Neither Mr. Henchy nor the old man said anything, but, just as the door was closing, Mr. O'Connor, who had been staring moodily into the fire, called out suddenly:

"'Bye, Joe."

Mr. Henchy waited a few moments and then nodded in the direction of the door.

"Tell me," he said across the fire, "what brings our friend in here? What does he want?"

"'Usha, poor Joe!" said Mr. O'Connor, throwing the end of his cigarette into the fire, "he's hard up, like the rest of us."

Mr. Henchy snuffled vigorously and spat so copiously that he nearly put out the fire, which uttered a hissing protest.

"To tell you my private and candid opinion," he said, "I think he's a man from the other camp. He's a spy of Colgan's, if you ask me. Just go round and try and find out how they're getting on. They won't suspect you. Do you twig?"

"Ah, poor Joe is a decent skin," said Mr. O'Connor.

"His father was a decent, respectable man," Mr. Henchy admitted. "Poor old Larry Hynes! Many a good turn he did in his day! But I'm greatly afraid our friend is not nineteen carat. Damn it, I can understand a fellow being hard up, but what I can't understand is a fellow sponging. Couldn't he have some spark of manhood about him?"

"He doesn't get a warm welcome from me when he comes," said the old man. "Let him work for his own side and not come spying around here."

"I don't know," said Mr. O'Connor dubiously, as he took out cigarette-papers and tobacco. "I think Joe Hynes is a straight man. He's a clever chap, too, with the pen. Do you remember that thing he wrote . . . ?"

"Some of these hillsiders and fenians are a bit too clever if you ask me," said Mr. Henchy. "Do you know what my private and candid opinion is about some of those little jokers? I believe half of them are in the pay of the Castle."

"There's no knowing," said the old man.

"O, but I know it for a fact," said Mr. Henchy. "They're Castle hacks. . . . I don't say Hynes. . . . No, damn it, I think he's a stroke above that. . . . But there's a certain little nobleman with a cock-eye —you know the patriot I'm alluding to?"

Mr. O'Connor nodded.

"There's a lineal descendant of Major Sirr for you if you like! O, the heart's blood of a patriot! That's a fellow now that'd sell his country for fourpence—ay —and go down on his bended knees and thank the Almighty Christ he had a country to sell."

There was a knock at the door.

"Come in!" said Mr. Henchy.

A person resembling a poor clergyman or a poor actor appeared in the doorway. His black clothes were tightly buttoned on his short body and it was impossible to say whether he wore a clergyman's collar or a layman's, because the collar of his shabby frock-coat, the uncovered buttons of which reflected the candle-light, was turned up about his neck. He wore a round hat of hard black felt. His face, shining with raindrops, had the appearance of damp yellow cheese save where two rosy spots indicated the cheekbones. He opened his very long mouth suddenly to express disappointment and at the same time opened wide his very

bright blue eyes to express pleasure and surprise.

"O Father Keon!" said Mr. Henchy, jumping up from his chair. "Is that you? Come in!"

"O, no, no, no!" said Father Keon quickly, pursing his lips as if he were addressing a child.

"Won't you come in and sit down?"

"No, no, no!" said Father Keon, speaking in a discreet, indulgent, velvety voice. "Don't let me disturb you now! I'm just looking for Mr. Fanning. . . ."

"He's round at the *Black Eagle*," said Mr. Henchy. "But won't you come in and sit down a minute?"

"No, no, thank you. It was just a little business matter," said Father Keon. "Thank you, indeed."

He retreated from the doorway and Mr. Henchy, seizing one of the candle-sticks, went to the door to light him downstairs.

"O, don't trouble, I beg!"

"No, but the stairs is so dark."

"No, no, I can see. . . . Thank you, indeed."

"Are you right now?"

"All right, thanks. . . . Thanks."

Mr. Henchy returned with the candle-stick and put it on the table. He sat down again at the fire. There was silence for a few moments.

"Tell me, John," said Mr. O'Connor, lighting his cigarette with another pasteboard card.

"Hm?"

"What he is exactly?"

"Ask me an easier one," said Mr. Henchy.

"Fanning and himself seem to me very thick. They're often in Kavanagh's together. Is he a priest at all?"

"Mmmyes, I believe so. . . . I think he's what you call a black sheep. We haven't many of them, thank God! but we have a few. . . . He's an unfortunate man of some kind. . . ."

"And how does he knock it out?" asked Mr. O'Connor.

"That's another mystery."

"Is he attached to any chapel or church or institution or——"

"No," said Mr. Henchy, "I think he's travelling on his own account. . . . God

forgive me," he added, "I thought he was
the dozen of stout."

"Is there any chance of a drink itself?"
asked Mr. O'Connor.

"I'm dry too," said the old man.

"I asked that little shoeboy three
times," said Mr. Henchy, "would he send
us a dozen of stout. I asked him again
now, but he was leaning on the counter
in his shirt-sleeves having a deep goster
with Alderman Cowley."

"Why didn't you remind him?" said
Mr. O'Connor.

"Well, I couldn't go over while he was
talking to Alderman Cowley. I just waited
till I caught his eye, and said: 'About
that little matter I was speaking to you
about. . . .' 'That'll be all right, Mr. H.,'
he said. Yerra, sure the little hop-o'-my-
thumb has forgotten all about it."

"There's some deal on in that quarter,"
said Mr. O'Connor thoughtfully. "I saw
the three of them hard at it yesterday at
Suffolk Street corner."

"I think I know the little game they're
at," said Mr. Henchy. "You must owe
the City Fathers money nowadays if you
want to be made Lord Mayor. Then
they'll make you Lord Mayor. By God!
I'm thinking seriously of becoming a City
Father myself. What do you think? Would
I do for the job?"

Mr. O'Connor laughed.

"So far as owing money goes. . . ."

"Driving out of the Mansion House,"
said Mr. Henchy, "in all my vermin, with
Jack here standing up behind me in a
powdered wig—eh?"

"And make me your private secretary,
John."

"Yes. And I'll make Father Keon my
private chaplain. We'll have a family
party."

"Faith, Mr. Henchy," said the old man,
"you'd keep up better style than some of
them. I was talking one day to old
Keegan, the porter. 'And how do you
like your new master, Pat?' says I to him.
'You haven't much entertaining now,'
says I. 'Entertaining!' says he. 'He'd live
on the smell of an oil-rag.' And do you
know what he told me? Now, I declare to
God I didn't believe him."

"What?" said Mr. Henchy and Mr.
O'Connor.

"He told me: 'What do you think of a
Lord Mayor of Dublin sending out for a
pound of chops for his dinner? How's that
for high living?' says he. 'Wisha! wisha,'
says I. 'A pound of chops,' says he, 'coming into the Mansion House.' 'Wisha!'
says I, 'what kind of people is going at all
now?' "

At this point there was a knock at the
door, and a boy put in his head.

"What is it?" said the old man.

"From the *Black Eagle*," said the boy,
walking in sideways and depositing a basket on the floor with a noise of shaken
bottles.

The old man helped the boy to transfer
the bottles from the basket to the table
and counted the full tally. After the transfer the boy put his basket on his arm and
asked:

"Any bottles?"

"What bottles?" said the old man.

"Won't you let us drink them first?"
said Mr. Henchy.

"I was told to ask for bottles."

"Come back to-morrow," said the old
man.

"Here, boy!" said Mr. Henchy, "will
you run over to O'Farrell's and ask him
to lend us a corkscrew—for Mr. Henchy,
say. Tell him we won't keep it a minute.
Leave the basket there."

The boy went out and Mr. Henchy began to rub his hands cheerfully, saying:

"Ah, well, he's not so bad after all.
He's as good as his word, anyhow."

"There's no tumblers," said the old
man.

"O, don't let that trouble you, Jack,"
said Mr. Henchy. "Many's the good man
before now drank out of the bottle."

"Anyway, it's better than nothing," said
Mr. O'Connor.

"He's not a bad sort," said Mr. Henchy,
"only Fanning has such a loan of him.
He means well, you know, in his own tin-
pot way."

The boy came back with the corkscrew. The old man opened three bottles
and was handing back the corkscrew
when Mr. Henchy said to the boy,

"Would you like a drink, boy?"

"If you please, sir," said the boy.

The old man opened another bottle
grudgingly, and handed it to the boy.

"What age are you?" he asked.

"Seventeen," said the boy.

As the old man said nothing further, the boy took the bottle, said: "Here's my best respects, sir, to Mr. Henchy," drank the contents, put the bottle back on the table and wiped his mouth with his sleeve. Then he took up the corkscrew and went out of the door sideways, muttering some form of salutation.

"That's the way it begins," said the old man.

"The thin edge of the wedge," said Mr. Henchy.

The old man distributed the three bottles which he had opened and the men drank from them simultaneously. After having drank each placed his bottle on the mantelpiece within hand's reach and drew in a long breath of satisfaction.

"Well, I did a good day's work to-day," said Mr. Henchy, after a pause.

"That so, John?"

"Yes. I got him one or two sure things in Dawson Street, Crofton and myself. Between ourselves, you know, Crofton (he's a decent chap, of course), but he's not worth a damn as a canvasser. He hasn't a word to throw to a dog. He stands and looks at the people while I do the talking."

Here two men entered the room. One of them was a very fat man, whose blue serge clothes seemed to be in danger of falling from his sloping figure. He had a big face which resembled a young ox's face in expression, staring blue eyes and a grizzled moustache. The other man, who was much younger and frailer, had a thin, clean-shaven face. He wore a very high double collar and a wide-brimmed bowler hat.

"Hello, Crofton!" said Mr. Henchy to the fat man. "Talk of the devil . . ."

"Where did the boose come from?" asked the young man. "Did the cow calve?"

"O, of course, Lyons spots the drink first thing!" said Mr. O'Connor, laughing.

"Is that the way you chaps canvass," said Mr. Lyons, "and Crofton and I out in the cold and rain looking for votes?"

"Why, blast your soul," said Mr. Henchy, "I'd get more votes in five minutes than you two'd get in a week."

"Open two bottles of stout, Jack," said Mr. O'Connor.

"How can I?" said the old man, "when there's no corkscrew?"

"Wait now, wait now!" said Mr. Henchy, getting up quickly. "Did you ever see this little trick?"

He took two bottles from the table and, carrying them to the fire, put them on the hob. Then he sat down again by the fire and took another drink from his bottle. Mr. Lyons sat on the edge of the table, pushed his hat towards the nape of his neck and began to swing his legs.

"Which is my bottle?" he asked.

"This, lad," said Mr. Henchy.

Mr. Crofton sat down on a box and looked fixedly at the other bottle on the hob. He was silent for two reasons. The first reason, sufficient in itself, was that he had nothing to say; the second reason was that he considered his companions beneath him. He had been a canvasser for Wilkins, the Conservative, but when the Conservatives had withdrawn their man and, choosing the lesser of two evils, given their support to the Nationalist candidate, he had been engaged to work for Mr. Tierney.

In a few minutes an apologetic "Pok!" was heard as the cork flew out of Mr. Lyons' bottle. Mr. Lyons jumped off the table, went to the fire, took his bottle and carried it back to the table.

"I was just telling them, Crofton," said Mr. Henchy, "that we got a good few votes to-day."

"Who did you get?" asked Mr. Lyons.

"Well, I got Parkes for one, and I got Atkinson for two, and I got Ward of Dawson Street. Fine old chap he is, too —regular old toff, old Conservative! 'But isn't your candidate a Nationalist?' said he. 'He's a respectable man,' said I. He's in favour of whatever will benefit this country. He's a big ratepayer,' I said. 'He has extensive house property in the city and three places of business and isn't it to his own advantage to keep down the rates? He's a prominent and respected citizen,' said I, 'and a Poor Law Guardian, and he doesn't belong to any party, good, bad, or indifferent.' That's the way to talk to 'em."

"And what about the address to the

King?" said Mr. Lyons after drinking and smacking his lips.

"Listen to me," said Mr. Henchy. "What we want in this country, as I said to old Ward, is capital. The King's coming here will mean an influx of money into this country. The citizens of Dublin will benefit by it. Look at all the factories down by the quays there, idle! Look at all the money there is in the country if we only worked the old industries, the mills, the ship-building yards and factories. It's capital we want."

"But look here, John," said Mr. O'Connor. "Why should we welcome the King of England? Didn't Parnell himself . . ."

"Parnell," said Mr. Henchy, "is dead. Now, here's the way I look at it. Here's this chap come to the throne after his old mother keeping him out of it till the man was grey. He's a man of the world, and he means well by us. He's a jolly fine decent fellow, if you ask me, and no damn nonsense about him. He just says to himself: 'The old one never went to see these wild Irish. By Christ, I'll go myself and see what they're like.' And are we going to insult the man when he comes over here on a friendly visit? Eh? Isn't that right, Crofton?"

Mr. Crofton nodded his head.

"But after all now," said Mr. Lyons argumentatively, "King Edward's life, you know, is not the very . . ."

"Let bygones be bygones," said Mr. Henchy. "I admire the man personally. He's just an ordinary knockabout like you and me. He's fond of his glass of grog and he's a bit of a rake, perhaps, and he's a good sportsman. Damn it, can't we Irish play fair?"

"That's all very fine," said Mr. Lyons. "But look at the case of Parnell now."

"In the name of God," said Mr. Henchy, "where's the analogy between the two cases?"

"What I mean," said Mr. Lyons, "is we have our ideals. Why, now, would we welcome a man like that? Do you think now after what he did Parnell was a fit man to lead us? And why, then, would we do it for Edward the Seventh?"

"This is Parnell's anniversary," said Mr. O'Connor, "and don't let us stir up any bad blood. We all respect him now that he's dead and gone—even the Conservatives," he added, turning to Mr. Crofton.

Pok! The tardy cork flew out of Mr. Crofton's bottle. Mr. Crofton got up from his box and went to the fire. As he returned with his capture he said in a deep voice:

"Our side of the house respects him, because he was a gentleman."

"Right you are, Crofton!" said Mr. Henchy fiercely. "He was the only man that could keep that bag of cats in order. 'Down, ye dogs! Lie down, ye curs!' That's the way he treated them. Come in Joe! Come in!" he called out, catching sight of Mr. Hynes in the doorway.

Mr. Hynes came in slowly.

"Open another bottle of stout, Jack," said Mr. Henchy. "O, I forgot there's no corkscrew. Here, show me one here and I'll put it at the fire."

The old man handed him another bottle and he placed it on the hob.

"Sit down, Joe," said Mr. O'Connor, "we're just talking about the Chief."

"Ay, ay!" said Mr. Henchy.

Mr. Hynes sat on the side of the table near Mr. Lyons but said nothing.

"There's one of them, anyhow," said Mr. Henchy, "that didn't renege him. By God, I'll say for you, Joe! No, by God, you stuck to him like a man!"

"O, Joe," said Mr. O'Connor suddenly. "Give us that thing you wrote—do you remember? Have you got it on you?"

"O, ay!" said Mr. Henchy. "Give us that. Did you ever hear that, Crofton? Listen to this, now: splendid thing."

"Go on," said Mr. O'Connor. "Fire away, Joe."

Mr. Hynes did not seem to remember at once the piece to which they were alluding, but, after reflecting a while, he said:

"O, that thing is it. . . . Sure, that's old now."

"Out with it, man!" said Mr. O'Connor.

"'Sh, 'sh," said Mr. Henchy. "Now, Joe!"

Mr. Hynes hesitated a little longer. Then amid the silence he took off his hat, laid it on the table and stood up. He seemed to be rehearsing the piece in his mind. After a rather long pause he announced:

THE DEATH OF PARNELL

6th October, 1891

He cleared his throat once or twice and then began to recite:

He is dead. Our Uncrowned King is dead.
 O, Erin, mourn with grief and woe
For he lies dead whom the fell gang
 Of modern hypocrites laid low.

He lies slain by the coward hounds
 He raised to glory from the mire;
And Erin's hopes and Erin's dreams
 Perish upon her monarch's pyre.

In palace, cabin or in cot
 The Irish heart where'er it be
Is bowed with woe—for he is gone
 Who would have wrought her destiny.

He would have had his Erin famed,
 The green flag gloriously unfurled,
Her statesmen, bards and warriors raised
 Before the nations of the World.

He dreamed (alas, 'twas but a dream!)
 Of Liberty: but as he strove
To clutch that idol, treachery
 Sundered him from the thing he loved.

Shame on the coward, caitiff hands
 That smote their Lord or with a kiss
Betrayed him to the rabble-rout
 Of fawning priests—no friends of his.

May everlasting shame consume
 The memory of those who tried

To befoul and smear the exalted name
 Of one who spurned them in his pride.

He fell as fall the mighty ones,
 Nobly undaunted to the last.
And death has now united him
 With Erin's heroes of the past.

No sound of strife disturb his sleep!
 Calmly he rests: no human pain
Or high ambition spurs him now
 The peaks of glory to attain.

They had their way: they laid him low.
 But Erin, list, his spirit may
Rise, like the Phœnix from the flames,
 When breaks the dawning of the day,

The day that brings us Freedom's reign.
 And on that day may Erin well
Pledge in the cup she lifts to Joy
 One grief—the memory of Parnell.

Mr. Hynes sat down again on the table. When he had finished his recitation there was a silence and then a burst of clapping: even Mr. Lyons clapped. The applause continued for a little time. When it had ceased all the auditors drank from their bottles in silence.

Pok! The cork flew out of Mr. Hynes' bottle, but Mr. Hynes remained sitting flushed and bare-headed on the table. He did not seem to have heard the invitation.

"Good man, Joe!" said Mr. O'Connor, taking out his cigarette papers and pouch the better to hide his emotion.

"What do you think of that, Crofton?" cried Mr. Henchy. "Isn't that fine? What?"

Mr. Crofton said that it was a very fine piece of writing.

[1914]

QUESTIONS FOR STUDY

1. *In what ways does Joyce's story suggest the political decay of "modern" Ireland? Why is it appropriate that it should take place on Ivy Day, October 6, the anniversary of the death of Irish nationalist leader Charles Parnell?*
2. *What qualities and concerns do Henchy, O'Connor, Lyons, and Crofton seem to share? In what ways does Joe Hynes differ from them? What qualities are associated with the dead Parnell?*
3. *What major themes of the story are stated in Mr. Hynes' poem?*
4. *What is the irony of Mr. Crofton's final comment?*
5. *What is suggested by the recurring references to fire and cinders? What other unifying motifs are also present in the story?*

FRANZ KAFKA

A Hunger Artist

DURING these last decades the interest in professional fasting has markedly diminished. It used to pay very well to stage such great performances under one's own management, but today that is quite impossible. We live in a different world now. At one time the whole town took a lively interest in the hunger artist; from day to day of his fast the excitement mounted; everybody wanted to see him at least once a day; there were people who bought season tickets for the last few days and sat from morning till night in front of his small barred cage; even in the nighttime there were visiting hours, when the whole effect was heightened by torch flares; on fine days the cage was set out in the open air, and then it was the children's special treat to see the hunger artist; for their elders he was often just a joke that happened to be in fashion, but the children stood open-mouthed, holding each other's hands for greater security, marvelling at him as he sat there pallid in black tights, with his ribs sticking out so prominently, not even on a seat but down among straw on the ground, sometimes giving a courteous nod, answering questions with a constrained smile, or perhaps stretching an arm through the bars so that one might feel how thin it was, and then again withdrawing deep into himself, paying no attention to anyone or anything, not even to the all-important striking of the clock that was the only piece of furniture in his cage, but merely staring into vacancy with half-shut eyes, now and then taking a sip from a tiny glass of water to moisten his lips.

Besides casual onlookers there were also relays of permanent watchers selected by the public, usually butchers, strangely enough, and it was their task to watch the hunger artist day and night, three of them at a time, in case he should have some secret recourse to nourishment. This was nothing but a formality, instituted to reassure the masses, for the initiates knew well enough that during his fast the artist would never in any circumstances, not even under forcible compulsion, swallow the smallest morsel of food; the honor of his profession forbade it. Not every watcher, of course, was capable of understanding this, there were often groups of night watchers who were very lax in carrying out their duties and deliberately huddled together in a retired corner to play cards with great absorption, obviously intending to give the hunger artist the chance of a little refreshment, which they supposed he could draw from some private hoard. Nothing annoyed the artist more than such watchers; they made him miserable; they made his fast seem unendurable; sometimes he mastered his feebleness sufficiently to sing during their watch for as long as he could keep going, to show them how unjust their suspicions were. But that was of little use; they only wondered at his cleverness in being able to fill his mouth even while singing. Much more to his taste were the watchers who sat close up to the bars, who were not content with the dim night lighting of the hall but focused him in the full glare of the electric pocket torch given them by the impresario. The harsh light did not trouble him at all. In any case he could never sleep properly, and he could always drowse a little, whatever the light, at any hour, even when the hall was thronged with noisy onlookers. He was quite happy at the prospect of spending a sleepless night with such watchers; he was ready to exchange jokes with them, to tell them stories out of his nomadic life, anything at all to keep them awake and demonstrate to them again that he had no eatables in his cage and that he was fasting as not one of them could fast. But his happiest moment was when the morning came and an enormous breakfast was brought them, at his expense, on which they flung themselves with the keen appetite of healthy men after a weary night of wakefulness. Of course there were people who argued that this breakfast was an unfair attempt to bribe the watchers, but that was going rather too far, and when they were invited to take on a night's vigil without a breakfast, merely for the sake of the cause, they made themselves scarce, although they stuck stubbornly to their suspicions.

Such suspicions, anyhow, were a necessary accompaniment to the profession of fasting. No one could possibly watch the hunger artist continuously, day and night, and so no one could produce first-hand evidence that the fast had really been rigorous and continuous; only the artist himself could know that; he was therefore bound to be the sole completely satisfied spectator of his own fast. Yet for other reasons he was never satisfied; it was not perhaps mere fasting that had brought him to such skeleton thinness that many people had regretfully to keep away from his exhibitions, because the sight of him was too much for them, perhaps it was dissatisfaction with himself that had worn him down. For he alone knew, what no other initiate knew, how easy it was to fast. It was the easiest thing in the world. He made no secret of this, yet people did not believe him; at the best they set him down as modest, most of them, however, thought he was out for publicity or else was some kind of cheat who found it easy to fast because he had discovered a way of making it easy, and then had the impudence to admit the fact, more or less. He had to put up with all that, and in the course of time had got used to it, but his inner dissatisfaction always rankled, and never yet, after any term of fasting—this must be granted to his credit—had he left the cage of his own free will. The longest period of fast-

ing was fixed by his impresario at forty days, beyond that term he was not allowed to go, not even in great cities, and there was good reason for it, too. Experience had proved that for about forty days the interest of the public could be stimulated by a steadily increasing pressure of advertisement, but after that the town began to lose interest, sympathetic support began notably to fall off; there were of course local variations as between one town and another or one country and another, but as a general rule forty days marked the limit. So on the fortieth day the flower-bedecked cage was opened, enthusiastic spectators filled the hall, a military band played, two doctors entered the cage to measure the results of the fast, which were announced through a megaphone, and finally two young ladies appeared, blissful at having been selected for the honor, to help the hunger artist down the few steps leading to a small table on which was spread a carefully chosen invalid repast. And at this very moment the artist always turned stubborn. True, he would entrust his bony arms to the outstretched helping hands of the ladies bending over him, but stand up he would not. Why stop fasting at this particular moment, after forty days of it? He had held out for a long time, an illimitably long time; why stop now, when he was in his best fasting form, or rather, not yet quite in his best fasting form? Why should he be cheated of the fame he would get for fasting longer, for being not only the record hunger artist of all time, which presumably he was already, but for beating his own record by a performance beyond human imagination, since he felt that there were no limits to his capacity for fasting? His public pretended to admire him so much, why should it have so little patience with him; if he could endure fasting longer, why shouldn't the public endure it? Besides, he was tired, he was comfortable sitting in the straw, and now he was supposed to lift himself to his full height and go down to a meal the very thought of which gave him a nausea that only the presence of the ladies kept him from betraying, and even that with an effort. And he looked up into the eyes of the ladies who were apparently so friendly and in reality so cruel, and shook his head, which felt too heavy on its strengthless neck. But then there happened yet again what always happened. The impresario came forward, without a word—for the band made speech impossible—lifted his arms in the air above the artist, as if inviting Heaven to look down upon its creature here in the straw, this suffering martyr, which indeed he was, although in quite another sense; grasped him round the emaciated waist, with exaggerated caution, so that the frail condition he was in might be appreciated; and committed him to the care of the blenching ladies, not without secretly giving him a shaking so that his legs and body tottered and swayed. The artist now submitted completely; his head lolled on his breast as if it had landed there by chance; his body was hollowed out; his legs in a spasm of self-preservation clung close to each other at the knees, yet scraped on the ground as if it were not really solid ground, as if they were only trying to find solid ground; and the whole weight of his body, a featherweight after all, relapsed onto one of the ladies, who, looking round for help and panting a little— this post of honor was not at all what she had expected it to be—first stretched her neck as far as she could to keep her face at least free from contact with the artist, then finding this impossible, and her more fortunate companion not coming to her aid but merely holding extended on her own trembling hand the little bunch of knucklebones that was the artist's, to the great delight of the spectators burst into tears and had to be replaced by an attendant who had long been stationed in readiness. Then came the food, a little of which the impresario managed to get between the artist's lips, while he sat in a kind of half-fainting trance, to the accompaniment of cheerful patter designed to distract the public's attention from the artist's condition; after that, a toast was drunk to the public, supposedly prompted by a whisper from the artist in the impresario's ear; the band confirmed it with a mighty flourish, the spectators melted away, and no one had any cause to be dissatisfied with the proceedings, no one except the hunger artist himself, he only, as always.

So he lived for many years, with small regular intervals of recuperation, in visible glory, honored by the world, yet in spite of that troubled in spirit, and all the more troubled because no one would take his trouble seriously. What comfort could he possibly need? What more could he possibly wish for? And if some good-natured person, feeling sorry for him, tried to console him by pointing out that his melancholy was probably caused by fasting, it could happen, especially when he had been fasting for some time, that he reacted with an outburst of fury and to the general alarm began to shake the bars of his cage like a wild animal. Yet the impresario had a way of punishing these outbreaks which he rather enjoyed putting into operation. He would apologize publicly for the artist's behavior, which was only to be excused, he admitted, because of the irritability caused by fasting; a condition hardly to be understood by well-fed people; then by natural transition he went on to mention the artist's equally incomprehensible boast that he could fast for much longer than he was doing; he praised the high ambition, the good will, the great self-denial undoubtedly implicit in such a statement; and then quite simply countered it by bringing out photographs, which were also on sale to the public, showing the artist on the fortieth day of a fast lying in bed almost dead from exhaustion. This perversion of the truth, familiar to the artist though it was, always unnerved him afresh and proved too much for him. What was a consequence of the premature ending of his fast was here presented as the cause of it! To fight against this lack of understanding, against a whole world of non-understanding, was impossible. Time and again in good faith he stood by the bars listening to the impresario, but as soon as the photographs appeared he always let go and sank with a groan back on to his straw, and the reassured public could once more come close and gaze at him.

A few years later when the witnesses of such scenes called them to mind, they often failed to understand themselves at all. For meanwhile the aforementioned change in public interest had set in; it seemed to happen almost overnight; there may have been profound causes for it, but who was going to bother about that; at any rate the pampered hunger artist suddenly found himself deserted one fine day by the amusement seekers, who went streaming past him to other more favored attractions. For the last time the impresario hurried him over half Europe to discover whether the old interest might still survive here and there; all in vain; everywhere, as if by secret agreement, a positive revulsion from professional fasting was in evidence. Of course it could not really have sprung up so suddenly as all that, and many premonitory symptoms which had not been sufficiently remarked or suppressed during the rush and glitter of success now came retrospectively to mind, but it was now too late to take any countermeasures. Fasting would surely come into fashion again at some future date, yet that was no comfort for those living in the present. What, then, was the hunger artist to do? He had been applauded by thousands in his time and could hardly come down to showing himself in a street booth at village fairs, and as for adopting another profession, he was not only too old for that but too fanatically devoted to fasting. So he took leave of the impresario, his partner in an unparalleled career, and hired himself to a large circus; in order to spare his own feelings he avoided reading the conditions of his contract.

A large circus with its enormous traffic in replacing and recruiting men, animals and apparatus can always find a use for people at any time, even for a hunger artist, provided of course that he does not ask too much, and in this particular case anyhow it was not only the artist who was taken on but his famous and long-known name as well; indeed considering the peculiar nature of his performance, which was not impaired by advancing age, it could not be objected that here was an artist past his prime, no longer

at the height of his professional skill, seeking a refuge in some quiet corner of a circus; on the contrary, the hunger artist averred that he could fast as well as ever, which was entirely credible; he even alleged that if he were allowed to fast as he liked, and this was at once promised him without more ado, he could astound the world by establishing a record never yet achieved, a statement which certainly provoked a smile among the other professionals, since it left out of account the change in public opinion, which the hunger artist in his zeal conveniently forgot.

He had not, however, actually lost his sense of the real situation and took it as a matter of course that he and his cage should be stationed, not in the middle of the ring as a main attraction, but outside, near the animal cages, on a site that was after all easily accessible. Large and gaily painted placards made a frame for the cage and announced what was to be seen inside it. When the public came thronging out in the intervals to see the animals, they could hardly avoid passing the hunger artist's cage and stopping there for a moment, perhaps they might even have stayed longer had not those pressing behind them in the narrow gangway, who did not understand why they should be held up on their way towards the excitements of the menagerie, made it impossible for anyone to stand gazing quietly for any length of time. And that was the reason why the hunger artist, who had of course been looking forward to these visiting hours as the main achievement of his life, began instead to shrink from them. At first he could hardly wait for the intervals; it was exhilarating to watch the crowds come streaming his way, until only too soon—not even the most obstinate self-deception, clung to almost consciously, could hold out against the fact—the conviction was borne in upon him that these people, most of them, to judge from their actions, again and again, without exception, were all on their way to the menagerie. And the first sight of them from the distance remained the best. For when they reached his cage he was at once deafened by the storm of shouting and abuse that arose from the two contending factions, which renewed themselves continuously, of those who wanted to stop and stare at him—he soon began to dislike them more than the others—not out of real interest but only out of obstinate self-assertiveness, and those who wanted to go straight on to the animals. When the first great rush was past, the stragglers came along, and these, whom nothing could have prevented from stopping to look at him as long as they had breath, raced past with long strides, hardly even glancing at him, in their haste to get to the menagerie in time. And all too rarely did it happen that he had a stroke of luck, when some father of a family fetched up before him with his children, pointed a finger at the hunger artist and explained at length what the phenomenon meant, telling stories of earlier years when he himself had watched similar but much more thrilling performances, and the children, still rather uncomprehending, since neither inside nor outside school had they been sufficiently prepared for this lesson—what did they care about fasting?—yet showed by the brightness of their intent eyes that new and better times might be coming. Perhaps, said the hunger artist to himself many a time, things would be a little better if his cage were set not quite so near the menagerie. That made it too easy for people to make their choice, to say nothing of what he suffered from the stench of the menagerie, the animals' restlessness by night, the carrying past of raw lumps of flesh for the beasts of prey, the roaring at feeding times, which depressed him continually. But he did not dare to lodge a complaint with the management; after all, he had the animals to thank for the troops of people who passed his cage, among whom there might always be one here and there to take an interest in him, and who could tell where they might seclude him if he called attention to his existence and thereby to the fact that, strictly speaking, he was only an impediment on the way to the menagerie.

A small impediment, to be sure, one that grew steadily less. People grew familiar with the strange idea that they could be expected, in times like these, to take an interest in a hunger artist, and with this familiarity the verdict went out against him. He might fast as much as he could, and he did so; but nothing could save him now, people passed him by. Just try to explain to anyone the art of fasting! Anyone who has no feeling for it cannot be made to understand it. The fine placards grew dirty and illegible, they were torn down; the little notice board telling the number of fast days achieved, which at first was changed carefully every day, had long stayed at the same figure, for after the first few weeks even this small task seemed pointless to the staff; and so the artist simply fasted on and on, as he had once dreamed of doing, and it was no trouble to him, just as he had always foretold, but no one counted the days, no one, not even the artist himself, knew what records he was already breaking, and his heart grew heavy. And when once in a time some leisurely passer-by stopped, made merry over the old figure on the board and spoke of swindling, that was in its way the stupidest lie ever invented by indifference and inborn malice, since it was not the hunger artist who was cheating; he was working honestly, but the world was cheating him of his reward.

Many more days went by, however, and that too came to an end. An overseer's eye fell on the cage one day and he asked the attendants why this perfectly good stage should be left standing there unused with dirty straw inside it; nobody knew, until one man, helped out by the notice board, remembered about the hunger artist. They poked into the straw with sticks and found him in it. "Are you still fasting?" asked the overseer. "When on earth do you mean to stop?" "Forgive me, everybody," whispered the hunger artist; only the overseer, who had his ear to the bars, understood him. "Of course," said the overseer, and tapped his forehead with a finger to let the attendants know what state the man was in, "we forgive you." "I always wanted you to admire my fasting," said the hunger artist. "We do admire it," said the overseer, affably. "But you shouldn't admire it," said the hunger artist. "Well, then we don't admire it," said the overseer, "but why shouldn't we admire it?" "Because I have to fast, I can't help it," said the hunger artist. "What a fellow you are," said the overseer, "and why can't you help it?" "Because," said the hunger artist, lifting his head a little and speaking, with his lips pursed, as if for a kiss, right into the overseer's ear, so that no syllable might be lost, "because I couldn't find the food I liked. If I had found it, believe me, I should have made no fuss and stuffed myself like you or anyone else." These were his last words, but in his dimming eyes remained the firm though no longer proud persuasion that he was still continuing to fast.

"Well, clear this out now!" said the overseer, and they buried the hunger artist, straw and all. Into the cage they put a young panther. Even the most insensitive felt it refreshing to see this wild creature leaping around the cage that had so long been dreary. The panther was all right. The food he liked was brought him without hesitation by the attendants; he seemed not even to miss his freedom; his noble body, furnished almost to the bursting point with all that it needed, seemed to carry freedom around with it too; somewhere in his jaws it seemed to lurk; and the joy of life streamed with such ardent passion from his throat that for the onlookers it was not easy to stand the shock of it. But they braced themselves, crowded round the cage, and did not want ever to move away.

[1922]

TRANSLATED BY
WILLA AND EDWIN MUIR

QUESTIONS FOR STUDY

1. *To what extent is the protagonist in fact an artist? What values and attitudes does he embody? What motivates him? What is his attitude toward his audience? What is the source of his perpetual dissatisfaction?*

2. *How does the public react to the hunger artist? Do they appreciate the nature of his artistry? What is the significance of the audience's shift in attitude? How does it affect the hunger artist?*

3. *What is the significance of the hunger artist's final revelation and the fact that his place is taken by a young panther? How does the audience react to the hunger artist's successor? Why?*

4. *What details support the view that "A Hunger Artist" can be read as an allegory about the creative individual (the artist) and his relationship with society? In what sense is it also about the failure of the artist to come to terms with life? What other possible interpretations of the story suggest themselves?*

5. *In what sense is the story's title ironic? What other examples of irony does the story contain?*

6. *What is the story's point of view? In what ways is the chosen point of view appropriate and effective?*

RUDYARD KIPLING

"They"

ONE VIEW called me to another; one hill top to its fellow, half across the county, and since I could answer at no more trouble than the snapping forward of a lever, I let the country flow under my wheels. The orchid-studded flats of the East gave way to the thyme, ilex, and gray grass of the Downs; these again to the rich cornland and fig-trees of the lower coast, where you carry the beat of the tide on your left hand for fifteen level miles; and when at last I turned inland through a huddle of rounded hills and woods I had run myself clean out of my known marks. Beyond that precise hamlet which stands godmother to the capital of the United States, I found hidden villages where bees, the only things awake, boomed in eighty-foot lindens that overhung gray Norman churches; miraculous brooks diving under stone bridges built for heavier traffic than would ever vex them again; tithe-barns larger than their churches, and an old smithy that cried out aloud how it had once been a hall of the Knights of the Temple. Gipsies I found on a common where the gorse, bracken, and heath fought it out together up a mile of Roman road; and a little farther on I disturbed a red fox rolling dog-fashion in the naked sunlight.

As the wooded hills closed about me I stood up in the car to take the bearings of that great Down whose ringed head is a landmark for fifty miles across the low countries. I judged that the lie of the country would bring me across some westward-running road that went to his feet, but I did not allow for the confusing veils of the woods. A quick turn plunged me first into a green cutting brimful of liquid sunshine, next into a gloomy tunnel where last year's dead leaves whispered and scuffled about my tires. The strong hazel stuff meeting overhead had not been cut for a couple of generations at least, nor had any axe helped the moss-cankered oak and beech to spring above them. Here the road changed frankly into a carpeted ride on whose brown velvet spent primrose-clumps showed like jade, and a few sickly, white-stalked bluebells nodded together. As the slope favored I shut off the power and slid over the whirled leaves, expecting every moment to meet a keeper; but I only heard a jay, far off, arguing against the silence under the twilight of the trees.

Still the track descended. I was on the point of reversing and working my way back on the second speed ere I ended in some swamp, when I saw sunshine through the tangle ahead and lifted the brake.

It was down again at once. As the light beat across my face my fore-wheels took the turf of a great still lawn from which sprang horsemen ten feet high with leveled lances, monstrous peacocks, and sleek round-headed maids of honor—blue, black, and glistening—all of clipped yew. Across the lawn—the marshaled woods besieged it on three sides—stood an ancient house of lichened and weather-worn stone, with mullioned windows and roofs of rose-red tile. It was flanked by semi-circular walls, also rose-red, that closed the lawn on the fourth side, and at their feet a box hedge grew man-high. There were doves on the roof about the slim brick chimneys, and I caught a glimpse of an octagonal dove-house behind the screening wall.

Here, then, I stayed; a horseman's green spear laid at my breast; held by the exceeding beauty of that jewel in that setting.

"If I am not packed off for a trespasser, or if this knight does not ride a wallop at me," thought I, "Shakespeare and Queen Elizabeth at least must come out of that half-open garden door and ask me to tea."

A child appeared at an upper window, and I thought the little thing waved a friendly hand. But it was to call a companion, for presently another bright head showed. Then I heard a laugh among the yew-peacocks, and turning to make sure (till then I had been watching the house only) I saw the silver of a fountain behind a hedge thrown up against the sun. The doves on the roof cooed to the cooing water; but between the two notes I caught the utterly happy chuckle of a child absorbed in some light mischief.

The garden door—heavy oak sunk deep in the thickness of the wall—opened further: a woman in a big garden hat set her foot slowly on the time-hollowed stone step and as slowly walked across the turf. I was forming some apology when she lifted up her head and I saw that she was blind.

"I heard you," she said. "Isn't that a motor car?"

"I'm afraid I've made a mistake in my road. I should have turned off up above —I never dreamed——" I began.

"But I'm very glad. Fancy a motor car coming into the garden! It will be such a treat——" She turned and made as though looking about her. "You—you haven't seen any one have you—perhaps?"

"No one to speak to, but the children seemed interested at a distance."

"Which?"

"I saw a couple up at the window just now, and I think I heard a little chap in the grounds."

"Oh, lucky you!" she cried, and her face brightened. "I hear them, of course, but that's all. You've seen them and heard them?"

"Yes," I answered. "And if I know anything of children one of them's having a beautiful time by the fountain yonder. Escaped, I should imagine."

"You're fond of children?"

I gave her one or two reasons why I did not altogether hate them.

"Of course, of course," she said. "Then you understand. Then you won't think it foolish if I ask you to take your car through the gardens, once or twice—quite slowly. I'm sure they'd like to see it. They see so little, poor things. One tries to make their life pleasant, but——" she threw out her hands towards the woods. "We're so out of the world here."

"That will be splendid," I said. "But I can't cut up your grass."

She faced to the right. "Wait a minute," she said. "We're at the South gate, aren't we? Behind those peacocks there's a flagged path. We call it the Peacock's Walk. You can't see it from here, they tell me, but if you squeeze along by the edge of the wood you can turn at the first peacock and get on to the flags."

It was sacrilege to wake that dreaming house-front with the clatter of machinery, but I swung the car to clear the turf, brushed along the edge of the wood and turned in on the broad stone path where the fountain-basin lay like one star-sapphire.

"May I come too?" she cried. "No, please don't help me. They'll like it better if they see me."

She felt her way lightly to the front of the car, and with one foot on the step she called: "Children, oh, children! Look and see what's going to happen!"

The voice would have drawn lost souls from the Pit, for the yearning that underlay its sweetness, and I was not surprised to hear an answering shout behind the yews. It must have been the child by the fountain, but he fled at our approach, leaving a little toy boat in the water. I saw the glint of his blue blouse among the still horsemen.

Very disposedly we paraded the length of the walk and at her request backed again. This time the child had got the better of his panic, but stood far off and doubting.

"The little fellow's watching us," I said. "I wonder if he'd like a ride."

"They're very shy still. Very shy. But, oh, lucky you to be able to see them! Let's listen."

I stopped the machine at once, and the humid stillness, heavy with the scent of box, cloaked us deep. Shears I could hear where some gardener was clipping; a mumble of bees and broken voices that might have been the doves.

"Oh, unkind!" she said, weariedly.

"Perhaps they're only shy of the motor. The little maid at the window looks tremendously interested."

"Yes?" She raised her head. "It was wrong of me to say that. They are really fond of me. It's the only thing that makes life worth living—when they're fond of you, isn't it? I daren't think what the place would be without them. By the way, is it beautiful?"

"I think it is the most beautiful place I have ever seen."

•"So they all tell me. I can feel it, of course, but that isn't quite the same thing."

"Then have you. never——?" I began, but stopped abashed.

"Not since I can remember. It happened when I was only a few months old, they tell me. And yet I must remember something, else how could I dream about colors. I see light in my dreams, and colors, but I never see *them*. I only hear them just as I do when I'm awake."

"It's difficult to see faces in dreams. Some people can but most of us haven't the gift," I went on, looking up at the window where the child stood all but hidden.

"I've heard that too," she said. "And they tell me that one never sees a dead person's face in a dream. Is that true?"

"I believe it is—now I come to think of it."

"But how is it with yourself—yourself?" The blind eyes turned toward me.

"I have never seen the faces of my dead in any dream," I answered.

"Then it must be as bad as being blind."

The sun had dipped behind the woods and the long shades were possessing the insolent horsemen one by one. I saw the light die from off the top of a glossy-leaved lance and all the brave hard green turn to soft black. The house, accepting another day at end, as it had accepted an hundred thousand gone, seemed to settle deeper into its rest among the shadows.

"Have you ever wanted to?" she said after the silence.

"Very much sometimes," I replied. The child had left the window as the shadows closed upon it.

"Ah! So've I, but I don't suppose it's allowed. . . . Where d'you live?"

"Quite the other side of the county—sixty miles and more, and I must be going back. I've come without my big lamp."

"But it's not dark yet. I can feel it."

"I'm afraid it will be by the time I get home. Could you lend me someone to set me on my road at first? I've utterly lost myself."

"I'll send Madden with you to the cross-roads. We are so out of the world, I don't wonder you were lost! I'll guide you round to the front of the house; but you will go slowly, won't you, till you're out of the grounds? It isn't foolish, do you think?"

"I promise you I'll go like this," I said, and let the car start herself down the flagged path.

We skirted the left wing of the house, whose elaborately cast lead guttering alone was worth a day's journey; passed under a great rose-grown gate in the red wall, and so round to the high front of the house which in beauty and stateliness as much excelled the back as that all others I had seen.

"Is it so very beautiful?" she said wistfully when she heard my raptures. "And you like the lead-figures too? There's the old azalea garden behind. They say that this place must have been made for children. Will you help me out, please? I should like to come with you as far as the cross-roads, but I mustn't leave them. Is that you, Madden? I want you to show this gentleman the way to the cross-roads. He has lost his way but—he has seen them."

A butler appeared noiselessly at the miracle of old oak that must be called the front door, and slipped aside to put on his hat. She stood looking at me with open blue eyes in which no sight lay, and I saw for the first time that she was beautiful.

"Remember," she said quietly, "if you are fond of them you will come again," and disappeared within the house.

The butler in the car said nothing till we were nearly at the lodge gates, where catching a glimpse of a blue blouse in a shrubbery I swerved amply lest the devil that leads little boys to play should drag me into child-murder.

"Excuse me," he asked of a sudden, "but why did you do that, Sir?"

"The child yonder."

"Our young gentleman in blue?"

"Of course."

"He runs about a good deal. Did you see him by the fountain, Sir?"

"Oh yes, several times. Do we turn here?"

"Yes, Sir. And did you 'appen to see them upstairs too?"

"At the upper window? Yes."

"Was that before the mistress come out to speak to you, Sir?"

"A little before that. Why d'you want to know?"

He paused a little. "Only to make sure that—that they had seen the car, Sir, because with children running about, though I'm sure you're driving particularly careful, there might be an accident. That was all, Sir. Here are the cross-roads. You can't miss your way from now on. Thank you, Sir, but that isn't *our* custom, not with——"

"I beg your pardon," I said, and thrust away the British silver.

"Oh, it's quite right with the rest of 'em as a rule. Good-bye, Sir."

He retired into the armor-plated conning tower of his caste and walked away. Evidently a butler solicitous for the honor of his house, and interested, probably through a maid, in the nursery.

Once beyond the signposts at the cross-roads I looked back, but the crumpled hills interlaced so jealously that I could not see where the house had lain. When I asked its name at a cottage along the road, the fat woman who sold sweetmeats there gave me to understand that people with motor cars had small right to live —much less to "go about talking like carriage folk." They were not a pleasant-mannered community.

When I retraced my route on the map that evening I was little wiser. Hawkin's Old Farm appeared to be the survey title of the place, and the old County Gazetteer, generally so ample, did not allude to it. The big house of those parts was Hodnington Hall, Georgian with early Victorian embellishments, as an atrocious steel engraving attested. I carried my difficulty to a neighbor—a deep-rooted tree of that soil—and he gave me a name of a family which conveyed no meaning.

A month or so later—I went again, or it may have been that my car took the road of her own volition. She over-ran the fruitless Downs, threaded every turn of the maze of lanes below the hills, drew through the high-walled woods, impenetrable in their full leaf, came out at the cross-roads where the butler had left me, and a little farther on developed an internal trouble which forced me to turn her in on a grass way-waste that cut into a summer-silent hazel wood. So far as I could make sure by the sun and a six-inch Ordnance map, this should be the road flank of that wood which I had first explored from the heights above. I made a mighty serious business of my repairs and a glittering shop of my repair kit, spanners, pump, and the like, which I spread out orderly upon a rug. It was a trap to catch all childhood, for on such a day, I argued, the children would not be far off. When I paused in my work I listened, but the wood was so full of the noises of summer (though the birds had mated) that I could not at first distinguish these from the tread of small cautious feet stealing across the dead leaves. I rang my bell in an alluring manner, but the feet fled, and I repented, for to a child a sudden noise is very real terror. I must have been at work half an hour when I heard in the wood the voice of the blind woman crying: "Children, oh children, where are you?" and the stillness made slow to close on the perfection of that cry. She came toward me, half feeling her way between the tree-boles, and though a child it seemed clung to her skirt, it swerved into the leafage like a rabbit as she drew nearer.

"Is that you?" she said, "from the other side of the county?"

"Yes, it's me from the other side of the county."

"Then why didn't you come through the upper woods? They were there just now."

"They were here a few minutes ago. I expect they knew my car had broken down, and came to see the fun."

"Nothing serious, I hope? How do cars break down?"

"In fifty different ways. Only mine has chosen the fifty-first."

She laughed merrily at the tiny joke, cooed with delicious laughter, and pushed her hat back.

"Let me hear," she said.

"Wait a moment," I cried, "and I'll get you a cushion."

She set her foot on the rug all covered with spare parts, and stooped above it eagerly. "What delightful things!" The hands through which she saw glanced in the checkered sunlight. "A box here—another box! Why you've arranged them like playing shop!"

"I confess now that I put it out to attract them. I don't need half those things really."

"How nice of you! I heard your bell in the upper wood. You say they were here before that?"

"I'm sure of it. Why are they so shy? That little fellow in blue who was with you just now ought to have got over his fright. He's been watching me like a Red Indian."

"It must have been your bell," she said. "I heard one of them go past me in trouble when I was coming down. They're shy—so shy even with me." She turned her face over her shoulder and cried again: "Children! Oh, children! Look and see!"

"They must have gone off together on their own affairs," I suggested, for there was a murmur behind us of lowered voices broken by the sudden squeaking giggles of childhood. I returned to my tinkerings and she leaned forward, her chin on her hand, listening interestedly.

"How many are they?" I said at last.

The work was finished, but I saw no reason to go.

Her forehead puckered a little in thought. "I don't quite know," she said simply. "Sometimes more—sometimes less. They come and stay with me because I love them, you see."

"That must be very jolly," I said, replacing a drawer, and as I spoke I heard the inanity of my answer.

"You—you aren't laughing at me," she cried. "I—I haven't any of my own. I never married. People laugh at me sometimes about them because—because——"

"Because they're savages," I returned. "It's nothing to fret for. That sort laugh at everything that isn't in their own fat lives."

"I don't know. How should I? I only don't like being laughed at about *them*. It hurts; and when one can't see. . . I don't want to seem silly," her chin quivered like a child's as she spoke, "but we blindies have only one skin, I think. Everything outside hits straight at our souls. It's different with you. You've such good defences in your eyes—looking out —before any one can really pain you in your soul. People forget that with us."

I was silent reviewing that inexhaustible matter—the more than inherited (since it is also carefully taught) brutality of the Christian peoples, beside which the mere heathendom of the West Coast nigger is clean and restrained. It led me a long distance into myself.

"Don't do that!" she said of a sudden, putting her hands before her eyes.

"What?"

She made a gesture with her hand.

"That! It's—it's all purple and black. Don't! That color hurts."

"But, how in the world do you know about colors?" I exclaimed, for here was a revelation indeed.

"Colors as colors?" she asked.

"No. *Those* Colors which you saw just now."

"You know as well as I do," she laughed, "else you wouldn't have asked that question. They aren't in the world at all. They're in *you*—when you went so angry."

"D'you mean a dull purplish patch, like port wine mixed with ink?" I said.

"I've never seen ink or port wine, but the colors aren't mixed. They are separate—all separate."

"Do you mean black streaks and jags across the purple?"

She nodded. "Yes—if they are like this," and zigzagged her finger again, "but it's more red than purple that bad color."

"And what are the colors at the top of the—whatever you see?"

Slowly she leaned forward and traced on the rug the figure of the Egg itself.

"I see them so," she said, pointing with a grass stem, "white, green, yellow, red, purple, and when people are angry or bad, black across the red—as you were just now."

"Who told you anything about it—in the beginning?" I demanded.

"About the colors? No one. I used to ask what colors were when I was little—in table-covers and curtains and carpets, you see—because some colors hurt me and some made me happy. People told me; and when I got older that was how I saw people." Again she traced the outline of the Egg which it is given to very few of us to see.

"All by yourself?" I repeated.

"All by myself. There wasn't any one else. I only found out afterwards that other people did not see the Colors."

She leaned against the tree-bole plaiting and unplaiting chance-plucked grass stems. The children in the wood had drawn nearer. I could see them with the tail of my eye frolicking like squirrels.

"Now I am sure you will never laugh at me," she went on after a long silence. "Nor at *them*."

"Goodness! No!" I cried, jolted out of my train of thought. "A man who laughs at a child—unless the child is laughing too—is a heathen!"

"I didn't mean that of course. You'd never laugh *at* children, but I thought—I used to think—that perhaps you might laugh about *them*. So now I beg your pardon. . . . What are you going to laugh at?"

I had made no sound, but she knew.

"At the notion of your begging my pardon. If you had done your duty as a pillar of the state and a landed proprietress you ought to have summoned me for trespass when I barged through your woods the other day. It was disgraceful of me—inexcusable."

She looked at me, her head against the tree trunk—long and steadfastly—this woman who could see the naked soul.

"How curious," she half whispered. "How very curious."

"Why, what have I done?"

"You don't understand . . . and yet you understood about the Colors. Don't you understand?"

She spoke with a passion that nothing had justified, and I faced her bewilderedly as she rose. The children had gathered themselves in a roundel behind a bramble bush. One sleek head bent over something smaller, and the set of the little shoulders told me that fingers were on lips. They, too, had some child's tremendous secret. I alone was hopelessly astray there in the broad sunlight.

"No," I said, and shook my head as though the dead eyes could note. "Whatever it is, I don't understand yet. Perhaps I shall later—if you'll let me come again."

"You will come again," she answered. "You will surely come again and walk in the wood."

"Perhaps the children will know me well enough by that time to let me play with them—as a favor. You know what children are like."

"It isn't a matter of favor but of right," she replied, and while I wondered what she meant, a disheveled woman plunged round the bend of the road, loose-haired, purple, almost lowing with agony as she ran. It was my rude, fat friend of the sweetmeat shop. The blind woman heard and stepped forward. "What is it, Mrs. Madehurst?" she asked.

The woman flung her apron over her head and literally groveled in the dust, crying that her grandchild was sick to death, that the local doctor was away fishing, that Jenny the mother was at her wits' end, and so forth, with repetitions and bellowings.

"Where's the next nearest doctor?" I asked between paroxysms.

"Madden will tell you. Go round to the house and take him with you. I'll attend to this. Be quick!" She half-supported the fat woman into the shade. In two minutes I was blowing all the horns of Jericho under the front of the House Beautiful, and Madden, in the pantry, rose to the crisis like a butler and a man.

A quarter of an hour at illegal speeds caught us a doctor five miles away. Within the half-hour we had decanted him, much interested in motors, at the door of the sweetmeat shop, and drew up the road to await the verdict.

"Useful things, cars," said Madden, all man and no butler. "If I'd had one when mine took sick she wouldn't have died."

"How was it?" I asked.

"Croup. Mrs. Madden was away. No one knew what to do. I drove eight miles in a tax cart for the doctor. She was choked when we came back. This car'd ha' saved her. She'd have been close on ten now."

"I'm sorry," I said. "I thought you were rather fond of children from what you told me going to the cross-roads the other day."

"Have you seen 'em again, Sir—this mornin'?"

"Yes, but they're well broke to cars. I couldn't get any of them within twenty yards of it."

He looked at me carefully as a scout considers a stranger—not as a menial should lift his eyes to his divinely appointed superior.

"I wonder why," he said just above the breath that he drew.

We waited on. A light wind from the sea wandered up and down the long lines of the woods, and the wayside grasses, whitened already with summer dust, rose and bowed in sallow waves.

A woman, wiping the suds off her arms, came out of the cottage next the sweetmeat shop.

"I've be'n listenin' in de back-yard," she said cheerily. "He says Arthur's unaccountable bad. Did ye hear him shruck just now? Unaccountable bad. I reckon t'will come Jenny's turn to walk in de wood nex' week along, Mr. Madden."

"Excuse me, Sir, but your lap-robe is slipping," said Madden deferentially. The woman started, dropped a curtsey, and hurried away.

"What does she mean by 'walking in the wood'?" I asked.

"It must be some saying they use hereabouts. I'm from Norfolk myself," said Madden. "They're an independent lot in this county. She took you for a chauffeur, Sir."

I saw the Doctor come out of the cottage followed by a draggle-tailed wench who clung to his arm as though he could make treaty for her with Death. "Dat sort," she wailed—"dey're just as much to us dat has 'em as if dey was lawful born. Just as much—just as much! An' God he'd be just as pleased if you saved 'un, Doctor. Don't take it from me. Miss Florence will tell ye de very same. Don't leave 'im, Doctor!"

"I know. I know," said the man, "but he'll be quiet for a while now. We'll get the nurse and the medicine as fast as we can." He signaled me to come forward with the car, and I strove not to be privy to what followed; but I saw the girl's face, blotched and frozen with grief, and I felt the hand without a ring clutching at my knees when we moved away.

The Doctor was a man of some humor, for I remember he claimed my car under the Oath of Æsculapius, and used it and me without mercy. First we convoyed Mrs. Madehurst and the blind woman to wait by the sick bed till the nurse should come. Next we invaded a neat county town for prescriptions (the Doctor said the trouble was cerebrospinal meningitis), and when the County Institute, banked and flanked with scared market cattle, reported itself out of nurses for the moment we literally flung ourselves loose upon the county. We conferred with the owners of great houses—magnates at the ends of overarching avenues whose big-boned womenfolk strode away from their tea-tables to listen to the imperious Doctor. At last a white-haired lady sitting under a cedar of Lebanon and surrounded by a court of magnificent Borzois—all hostile to motors—gave the Doctor, who received them as from a princess, written orders which we bore many miles at top speed, through a park, to a French nunnery, where we took over in exchange a pallid-faced and trembling Sister. She knelt at the bottom of the tonneau telling her beads without pause till, by short cuts of the Doctor's invention, we had her to the sweetmeat shop once more. It was a long afternoon crowded with mad episodes that rose and dissolved like the dust of our wheels; cross-sections of remote and incomprehensible lives through which we raced at right angles; and I went home in the dusk, wearied out, to dream of the clashing horns of cattle; round-eyed nuns walking in a garden of graves; pleasant tea-parties beneath shaded trees; the carbolic-scented, gray-painted corridors of the County Institute; the steps of shy children in the wood, and the hands that clung to my knees as the motor began to move.

I had intended to return in a day or two, but it pleased Fate to hold me from that side of the county, on many pretexts, till the elder and the wild rose had fruited. There came at last a brilliant day, swept clear from the southwest, that brought the hills within hand's reach—a day of unstable airs and high filmy clouds. Through no merit of my own I was free, and set the car for the third time on that known road. As I reached the crest of the Downs I felt the soft air change, saw it glaze under the sun; and, looking down at the sea, in that instant beheld the blue of the Channel turn through polished silver and dulled steel to dingy pewter. A laden collier hugging the coast steered outward for deeper water and, across copper-colored haze, I saw sails rise one by one on the anchored fishing-fleet. In a deep dene behind me an eddy of sudden wind drummed through sheltered oaks, and spun aloft the first day sample of autumn leaves. When I reached the beach road the sea-fog fumed over the brick-fields, and the tide was telling all the groins of the gale beyond Ushant. In less than an hour summer England vanished in chill gray. We were again the shut island of the North, all the ships of the world bellowing at our perilous gates; and between their outcries ran the piping of

bewildered gulls. My cap dripped moisture, the folds of the rug held it in pools or sluiced it away in runnels, and the salt-rime stuck to my lips.

Inland the smell of autumn loaded the thickened fog among the trees, and the drip became a continuous shower. Yet the late flowers—mallow of the wayside, scabious of the field, and dahlia of the garden—showed gay in the mist, and beyond the sea's breath there was little sign of decay in the leaf. Yet in the villages the house doors were all open, and bare-legged, bare-headed children sat at ease on the damp doorsteps to shout "pip-pip" at the stranger.

I made bold to call at the sweetmeat shop, where Mrs. Madehurst met me with a fat woman's hospitable tears. Jenny's child, she said, had died two days after the nun had come. It was, she felt, best out of the way, even though insurance offices, for reasons which she did not pretend to follow, would not willingly insure such stray lives. "Not but what Jenny didn't tend to Arthur as though he'd come all proper at de end of de first year—like Jenny herself." Thanks to Miss Florence, the child had been buried with a pomp which, in Mrs. Madehurst's opinion, more than covered the small irregularity of its birth. She described the coffin, within and without, the glass hearse, and the ever-green lining of the grave.

"But how's the mother?" I asked.

"Jenny? Oh, she'll get over it. I've felt dat way with one or two o' my own. She'll get over. She's walkin' in de wood now."

"In this weather?"

Mrs. Madehurst looked at me with narrowed eyes across the counter.

"I dunno but it opens de' 'eart like. Yes, it opens de 'eart. Dat's where losin' and bearin' comes so alike in de long run, we do say."

Now the wisdom of the old wives is greater than that of all the Fathers, and this last oracle sent me thinking so extendedly as I went up the road, that I nearly ran over a woman and a child at the wooded corner by the lodge gates of the House Beautiful.

"Awful weather!" I cried, as I slowed dead for the turn.

"Not so bad," she answered placidly out of the fog. "Mine's used to 'un. You'll find yours indoors, I reckon."

Indoors, Madden received me with professional courtesy, and kind inquiries for the health of the motor, which he would put under cover.

I waited in a still, nut-brown hall, pleasant with late flowers and warmed with a delicious wood fire—a place of good influence and great peace. (Men and women may sometimes, after great effort, achieve a creditable lie; but the house, which is their temple, cannot say anything save the truth of those who have lived in it.) A child's cart and a doll lay on the black-and-white floor, where a rug had been kicked back. I felt that the children had only just hurried away—to hide themselves, most like—in the many turns of the great adzed staircase that climbed stately out of the hall, or to crouch at gaze behind the lions and roses of the carven gallery above. Then I heard her voice above me, singing as the blind sing —from the soul:—

In the pleasant orchard-closes.

And all my early summer came back at the call.

In the pleasant orchard-closes,
God bless all our gains say we—
But may God bless all our losses,
Better suits with our degree.

She dropped the marring fifth line, and repeated—

Better suits with our degree!

I saw her lean over the gallery, her linked hands white as pearl against the oak.

"Is that you—from the other side of the county?" she called.

"Yes, me—from the other side of the county," I answered, laughing.

"What a long time before you had to come here again." She ran down the stairs, one hand lightly touching the broad rail. "It's two months and four days. Summer's gone!"

"I meant to come before, but Fate prevented."

"I knew it. Please do something to that fire. They won't let me play with it, but I can feel it's behaving badly. Hit it!"

I looked on either side of the deep fireplace, and found but a half-charred hedge-stake with which I punched a black log into flame.

"It never goes out, day or night," she said, as though explaining. "In case any one comes in with cold toes, you see."

"It's even lovelier inside than it was out," I murmured. The red light poured itself along the age-polished dusky panels till the Tudor roses and lions of the gallery took color and motion. An old eagle-topped convex mirror gathered the picture into its mysterious heart, distorting afresh the distorted shadows, and curving the gallery lines into the curves of a ship. The day was shutting down in half a gale as the fog turned to stringy scud. Through the uncurtained mullions of the broad window I could see valiant horsemen of the lawn rear and recover against the wind that taunted them with legions of dead leaves.

"Yes, it must be beautiful," she said. "Would you like to go over it? There's still light enough upstairs."

I followed her up the unflinching, wagon-wide staircase to the gallery whence opened the thin fluted Elizabethan doors.

"Feel how they put the latch down for the sake of the children." She swung a light door inward.

"By the way, where are they?" I asked. "I haven't even heard them to-day."

She did not answer at once. Then, "I can only hear them," she replied softly. "This is one of their rooms—everything ready, you see."

She pointed into a heavily-timbered room. There were little low gate tables and children's chairs. A doll's house, its hooked front half open, faced a great dappled rocking-horse, from whose padded saddle it was but a child's scramble to the broad window-seat overlooking the lawn. A toy gun lay in a corner beside a gilt wooden cannon.

"Surely they've only just gone," I whispered. In the failing light a door creaked cautiously. I heard the rustle of a frock and the patter of feet—quick feet through a room beyond.

"I heard that," she cried triumphantly. "Did you? Children, O children, where are you?"

The voice filled the walls that held it lovingly to the last perfect note, but there came no answering shout such as I had heard in the garden. We hurried on from room to oak-floored room; up a step here, down three steps there; among a maze of passages; always mocked by our quarry. One might as well have tried to work an unstopped warren with a single ferret. There were bolt-holes innumerable—recesses in walls, embrasures of deep slitten windows now darkened, whence they could start up behind us; and abandoned fireplaces, six feet deep in the masonry, as well as the tangle of communicating doors. Above all, they had the twilight for their helper in our game. I had caught one or two joyous chuckles of evasion, and once or twice had seen the silhouette of a child's frock against some darkening window at the end of a passage; but we returned empty-handed to the gallery just as a middle-aged woman was setting a lamp in its niche.

"No, I haven't seen her either this evening, Miss Florence," I heard her say, "but that Turpin he says he wants to see you about his shed."

"Oh, Mr. Turpin must want to see me very badly. Tell him to come to the hall, Mrs. Madden."

I looked down into the hall whose only light was the dulled fire, and deep in the shadow I saw them at last. They must have slipped down while we were in the passages, and now thought themselves perfectly hidden behind an old gilt leather screen. By child's law, my fruitless chase was as good as an introduction, but since I had taken so much trouble I resolved to force them to come forward later by the simple trick, which children detest, of pretending not to notice them. They lay close, in a little huddle, no more than shadows except when a quick flame betrayed an outline.

"And now we'll have some tea," she said. "I believe I ought to have offered it to you at first, but one doesn't arrive at manners somehow when one lives alone and is considered—h'm—peculiar." Then with very pretty scorn, "Would you like a lamp to see to eat by?"

"The firelight's much pleasanter, I think." We descended into that delicious gloom and Madden brought tea.

I took my chair in the direction of the screen ready to surprise or be surprised as the game should go, and at her permission, since a hearth is always sacred, bent forward to play with the fire.

"Where do you get these beautiful short faggots from?" I asked, idly. "Why, they are tallies!"

"Of course," she said. "As I can't read or write I'm driven back on the early English tally for my accounts. Give me one and I'll tell you what it meant."

I passed her an unburned hazel-tally, about a foot long, and she ran her thumb down the nicks.

"This is the milk-record for the home farm for the month of April last year, in gallons," said she. "I don't know what I should have done without tallics. An old forester of mine taught me the system. It's out of date now for everyone else; but my tenants respect it. One of them's coming now to see me. Oh, it doesn't matter. He has no business here out of office hours. He's a greedy, ignorant man—very greedy or—he wouldn't come here after dark."

"Have you much land then?"

"Only a couple of hundred acres in hand, thank goodness. The other six hundred are nearly all let to folk who knew my folk before me, but this Turpin is quite a new man—and a highway robber."

"But are you sure I sha'n't be——?"

"Certainly not. You have the right. He hasn't any children."

"Ah, the children!" I said, and slid my low chair back till it nearly touched the screen that hid them. "I wonder whether they'll come out for me."

There was a murmur of voices—Madden's and a deeper note—at the low, dark side door, and a ginger-headed, canvas-gaitered giant of the unmistakable tenant farmer type stumbled or was pushed in.

"Come to the fire, Mr. Turpin," she said.

"If—if you please, Miss, I'll—I'll be quite as well by the door." He clung to the latch as he spoke like a frightened child. Of a sudden I realized that he was in the grip of some almost overpowering fear.

"Well?"

"About that new shed for the young stock—that was all. These first autumn storms settin' in . . . but I'll come again, Miss." His teeth did not chatter much more than the door latch.

"I think not," she answered, levelly. "The new shed—m'm. What did my agent write you on the 15th?"

"I—fancied p'raps that if I came to see you—ma—man to man like, Miss. But——"

His eyes rolled into every corner of the room wide with horror. He half opened the door through which he had entered, but I noticed it shut again—from without and firmly.

"He wrote what I told him," she went on. "You are overstocked already. Dunnett's Farm never carried more than fifty bullocks—even in Mr. Wright's time. And *he* used cake. You've sixty-seven and you don't cake. You've broken the lease in that respect. You're dragging the heart out of the farm."

"I'm—I'm getting some minerals—superphosphates—next week. I've as good as ordered a truck-load already. I'll go down to the station to-morrow about 'em. Then I can come and see you man to man like, Miss, in the daylight. . . . That gentleman's not going away, is he?" He almost shrieked.

I had only slid the chair a little farther back, reaching behind me to tap on the leather of the screen, but he jumped like a rat.

"No. Please attend to me, Mr. Turpin." She turned in her chair and faced him with his back to the door. It was an old and sordid little piece of scheming that she forced from him—his plea for the new cowshed at his landlady's expense, that he might with the covered manure pay his next year's rent out of the valuation after, as she made clear, he had bled the enriched pastures to the bone. I could not but admire the intensity of his greed,

when I saw him outfacing for its sake whatever terror it was that ran wet on his forehead.

I ceased to tap the leather—was, indeed, calculating the cost of the shed—when I felt my relaxed hand taken and turned softly between the soft hands of a child. So at last I had triumphed. In a moment I would turn and acquaint myself with those quick-footed wanderers. . . .

The little brushing kiss fell in the center of my palm—as a gift on which the fingers were, once, expected to close: as the all-faithful half-reproachful signal of a waiting child not used to neglect even when grown-ups were busiest—a fragment of the mute code devised very long ago.

Then I knew. And it was as though I had known from the firs day when I looked across the lawn at the high window.

I heard the door shut. The woman turned to me in silence, and I felt that she knew.

What time passed after this I cannot say. I was roused by the fall of a log, and mechanically rose to put it back. Then I returned to my place in the chair very close to the screen.

"Now you understand," she whispered, across the packed shadows.

"Yes, I understand—now. Thank you."

"I—I only hear them." She bowed her head in her hands. "I have no right, you know—no other right. I have neither borne nor lost—neither borne nor lost!"

"Be very glad then," said I, for my soul was torn open within me.

"Forgive me!"

She was still, and I went back to my sorrow and joy.

"It was because I loved them so," she said at last, brokenly. "*That* was why it was, even from the first—even before I knew that they—they were all I should ever have. And I loved them so!"

She stretched out her arms to the shadows and the shadows within the shadow.

"They came because I loved them—because I needed them. I—I must have made them come. Was that wrong, think you?"

"No—no."

"I—I grant you that the toys and—and all that sort of thing were nonsense, but —but I used to so hate empty rooms myself when I was little." She pointed to the gallery. "And the passages all empty. . . . And how could I ever bear the garden door shut? Suppose——"

"Don't! For pity's sake, don't!" I cried. The twilight had brought a cold rain with gusty squalls that plucked at the leaded windows.

"And the same thing with keeping the fire in all night. *I* don't think it so foolish —do you?"

I looked at the broad brick hearth, saw, through tears I believe, that there was no unpassable iron on or near it, and bowed my head.

"I did all that and lots of other things —just to make believe. Then they came. I heard them, but I didn't know that they were not mine by right till Mrs. Madden told me——"

"The butler's wife? What?"

"One of them—I heard—she saw. And knew. Hers! *Not* for me. I didn't know at first. Perhaps I was jealous. Afterwards, I began to understand that it was only because I loved them, not because—— . . . Oh, you *must* bear or lose," she said piteously. "There is no other way—and yet they love me. They must? Don't they?"

There was no sound in the room except the lapping voices of the fire, but we two listened intently, and she at least took comfort from what she heard. She recovered herself and half rose. I sat still in my chair by the screen.

"Don't think me a wretch to whine about myself like this, but—but I'm all in the dark, you know, and *you* can see."

In truth I could see, and my vision confirmed me in my resolve, though that was like the very parting of spirit and flesh. Yet a little longer I would stay since it was the last time.

"You think it is wrong, then?" she cried, sharply enough. I had said nothing.

"Not for you. A thousand times no. For you it is right. . . . I am grateful to you beyond words. For me it would be wrong. For me only. . . ."

"Why?" she said, but passed her hand before her face as she had done at our second meeting in the wood. "Oh, I see," she went on simply as a child. "For you it would be wrong." Then with a little indrawn laugh, "and, d'you remember, I called you lucky—once—at first. You who must never come here again!"

She left me to sit a little longer by the screen, and I heard the sound of her feet die out along the gallery above.

[1904]

QUESTIONS FOR STUDY

1. *What enables Miss Florence to "see" the children? Why does Kipling include the conversation between Miss Florence and Turpin? What side of her personality does it reveal?*

2. *What is suggested by the "little brushing kiss" that the unseen child bestows upon the narrator? What clues are provided by the dialogue that follows? What does the reader learn—or come to surmise— about the narrator's personal life?*

3. *Why does the narrator determine never to visit the house again? What emotional truth has he come to recognize?*

4. *In what way does the green spear of the horseman which arrests the narrator's progress as he first approaches the house anticipate the story's ending?*

5. *Why does the remoteness of the Hawkins farm provide an appropriate setting for the story?*

6. *What devices and techniques does Kipling use to make the supernatural plausible and acceptable (if only temporarily) to the reader?*

D. H. LAWRENCE
The Rocking-Horse Winner

THERE was a woman who was beautiful, who started with all the advantages, yet she had no luck. She married for love, and the love turned to dust. She had bonny children, yet she felt they had been thrust upon her, and she could not love them. They looked at her coldly, as if they were finding fault with her. And hurriedly she felt she must cover up some fault in herself. Yet what it was that she must cover up she never knew. Nevertheless, when her children were present, she always felt the centre of her heart go hard. This troubled her, and in her manner she was all the more gentle and anxious for her children, as if she loved them very much. Only she herself knew that at the centre of her heart was a hard little place that could not feel love, no, not for anybody. Everybody else said of her: "She is such a good mother. She adores her children." Only she herself, and her children themselves, knew it was not so. They read it in each other's eyes.

There were a boy and two little girls. They lived in a pleasant house, with a garden, and they had discreet servants, and felt themselves superior to anyone in the neighbourhood.

Although they lived in style, they felt always an anxiety in the house. There was never enough money. The mother had a small income, and the father had a small income, but not nearly enough for the social position which they had to keep up. The father went into town to some office. But though he had good prospects, these prospects never materialised. There was always the grinding sense of the shortage of money, though the style was always kept up.

At last the mother said: "I will see if

I can't make something." But she did not know where to begin. She racked her brains, and tried this thing and the other, but could not find anything successful. The failure made deep lines come into her face. Her children were growing up, they would have to go to school. There must be more money, there must be more money. The father, who was always very handsome and expensive in his tastes, seemed as if he never *would* be able to do anything worth doing. And the mother, who had a great belief in herself, did not succeed any better, and her tastes were just as expensive.

And so the house came to be haunted by the unspoken phrase: *There must be more money! There must be more money!* The children could hear it all the time, though nobody said it aloud. They heard it at Christmas, when the expensive and splendid toys filled the nursery. Behind the shining modern rocking-horse, behind the smart doll's house, a voice would start whispering: "There *must* be more money! There *must* be more money!" And the children would stop playing, to listen for a moment. They would look into each other's eyes, to see if they had all heard. And each one saw in the eyes of the other two that they too had heard. "There *must* be more money! There *must* be more money!"

It came whispering from the springs of the still-swaying rocking-horse, and even the horse, bending his wooden, champing head, heard it. The big doll, sitting so pink and smirking in her new pram, could hear it quite plainly, and seemed to be smirking all the more self-consciously because of it. The foolish puppy, too, that took the place of the teddybear, he was looking so extraordinarily foolish for no other reason but that he heard the secret whisper all over the house: "There *must* be more money!"

Yet nobody ever said it aloud. The whisper was everywhere, and therefore no one spoke it. Just as no one ever says: "We are breathing!" in spite of the fact that breath is coming and going all the time.

"Mother," said the boy Paul one day, "why don't we keep a car of our own? Why do we always use uncle's, or else a taxi?"

"Because we're the poor members of the family," said the mother.

"But why *are* we, mother?"

"Well—I suppose," she said slowly and bitterly, "it's because your father has no luck."

The boy was silent for some time.

"Is luck money, mother?" he asked, rather timidly.

"No, Paul. Not quite. It's what causes you to have money."

"Oh!" said Paul vaguely. "I thought when Uncle Oscar said *filthy lucker,* it meant money."

"*Filthy lucre* does mean money," said the mother. "But it's lucre, not luck."

"Oh!" said the boy. "Then what *is* luck, mother?"

"It's what causes you to have money. If you're lucky you have money. That's why it's better to be born lucky than rich. If you're rich, you may lose your money. But if you're lucky, you will always get more money."

"Oh! Will you? And is father not lucky?"

"Very unlucky, I should say," she said bitterly.

The boy watched her with unsure eyes.

"Why?" he asked.

"I don't know. Nobody ever knows why one person is lucky and another unlucky."

"Don't they? Nobody at all? Does *nobody* know?"

"Perhaps God. But He never tells."

"He ought to, then. And aren't you lucky either, mother?"

"I can't be, if I married an unlucky husband."

"But by yourself, aren't you?"

"I used to think I was, before I married. Now I think I am very unlucky indeed."

"Why?"

"Well—never mind! Perhaps I'm not really," she said.

The child looked at her to see if she meant it. But he saw, by the lines of her mouth, that she was only trying to hide something from him.

"Well, anyhow," he said stoutly, "I'm a lucky person."

"Why?" said his mother, with a sudden laugh.

He stared at her. He didn't even know why he had said it.

"God told me," he asserted, brazening it out.

"I hope He did, dear!" she said, again with a laugh, but rather bitter.

"He did, mother!"

"Excellent!" said the mother, using one of her husband's exclamations.

The boy saw she did not believe him; or rather, that she paid no attention to his assertion. This angered him somewhere, and made him want to compel her attention.

He went off by himself, vaguely, in a childish way, seeking for the clue to 'luck'. Absorbed, taking no heed of other people, he went about with a sort of stealth, seeking inwardly for luck. He wanted luck, he wanted it, he wanted it. When the two girls were playing dolls in the nursery, he would sit on his big rocking-horse, charging madly into space, with a frenzy that made the little girls peer at him uneasily. Wildly the horse careered, the waving dark hair of the boy tossed, his eyes had a strange glare in them. The little girls dared not speak to him.

When he had ridden to the end of his mad little journey, he climbed down and stood in front of his rocking-horse, staring fixedly into its lowered face. Its red mouth was slightly open, its big eye was wide and glassy-bright.

"Now!" he would silently command the snorting steed. "Now, take me to where there is luck! Now take me!"

And he would slash the horse on the

neck with the little whip he had asked Uncle Oscar for. He *knew* the horse could take him to where there was luck, if only he forced it. So he would mount again and start on his furious ride, hoping at last to get there. He knew he could get there.

"You'll break your horse, Paul!" said the nurse.

"He's always riding like that! I wish he'd leave off!" said his elder sister Joan.

But he only glared down on them in silence. Nurse gave him up. She could make nothing of him. Anyhow, he was growing beyond her.

One day his mother and his Uncle Oscar came in when he was on one of his furious rides. He did not speak to them.

"Hallo, you young jockey! Riding a winner?" said his uncle.

"Aren't you growing too big for a rocking-horse? You're not a very little boy any longer, you know," said his mother.

But Paul only gave a blue glare from his big, rather close-set eyes. He would speak to nobody when he was in full tilt. His mother watched him with an anxious expression on her face.

At last he suddenly stopped forcing his horse into the mechanical gallop and slid down.

"Well, I got there!" he announced fiercely, his blue eyes still flaring, and his sturdy long legs straddling apart.

"Where did you get to?" asked his mother.

"Where I wanted to go," he flared back at her.

"That's right, son!" said Uncle Oscar. "Don't you stop till you get there. What's the horse's name?"

"He doesn't have a name," said the boy.

"Gets on without all right?" asked the uncle.

"Well, he has different names. He was called Sansovino last week."

"Sansovino, eh? Won the Ascot.[1] How did you know this name?"

"He always talks about horse-races with Bassett," said Joan.

The uncle was delighted to find that his small nephew was posted with all the racing news. Bassett, the young gardener, who had been wounded in the left foot in the war and had got his present job through Oscar Cresswell, whose batman he had been, was a perfect blade of the 'turf'. He lived in the racing events, and the small boy lived with him.

Oscar Cresswell got it all from Bassett.

"Master Paul comes and asks me, so I can't do more than tell him, sir," said Bassett, his face terribly serious, as if he were speaking of religious matters.

"And does he ever put anything on a horse he fancies?"

"Well—I don't want to give him away —he's a young sport, a fine sport, sir. Would you mind asking him himself? He sort of takes a pleasure in it, and perhaps he'd feel I was giving him away, sir, if you don't mind."

Bassett was serious as a church.

The uncle went back to his nephew and took him off for a ride in the car.

"Say, Paul, old man, do you ever put anything on a horse?" the uncle asked.

The boy watched the handsome man closely.

"Why, do you think I oughtn't to?" he parried.

"Not a bit of it! I thought perhaps you might give me a tip for the Lincoln." [2]

The car sped on into the country, going down to Uncle Oscar's place in Hampshire.

"Honour bright?" said the nephew.

"Honour bright, son!" said the uncle.

"Well, then, Daffodil."

"Daffodil! I doubt it, sonny. What about Mirza?"

"I only know the winner," said the boy. "That's Daffodil."

"Daffodil, eh?"

There was a pause. Daffodil was an obscure horse comparatively.

"Uncle!"

"Yes, son?"

1 The famous horse race run at the Ascot Heath racetrack near Ascot, England. (JHP)

2 The Lincolnshire Handicap run at Lincoln Downs. (JHP)

"You won't let it go any further, will you? I promised Bassett."

"Bassett be damned, old man! What's he got to do with it?"

"We're partners. We've been partners from the first. Uncle, he lent me my first five shillings, which I lost. I promised him, honour bright, it was only between me and him; only you gave me that ten-shilling note I started winning with, so I thought you were lucky. You won't let it go any further, will you?"

The boy gazed at his uncle from those big, hot, blue eyes, set rather close together. The uncle stirred and laughed uneasily.

"Right you are, son! I'll keep your tip private. Daffodil, eh? How much are you putting on him?"

"All except twenty pounds," said the boy. "I keep that in reserve."

The uncle thought it a good joke.

"You keep twenty pounds in reserve, do you, you young romancer? What are you betting, then?"

"I'm betting three hundred," said the boy gravely. "But it's between you and me, Uncle Oscar! Honour bright?"

The uncle burst into a roar of laughter.

"It's between you and me all right, you young Nat Gould," [3] he said, laughing. "But where's your three hundred?"

"Bassett keeps it for me. We're partners."

"You are, are you! And what is Bassett putting on Daffodil?"

"He won't go quite as high as I do, I expect. Perhaps he'll go a hundred and fifty."

"What, pennies?" laughed the uncle.

"Pounds," said the child, with a surprised look at his uncle. "Bassett keeps a bigger reserve than I do."

Between wonder and amusement Uncle Oscar was silent. He pursued the matter no further, but he determined to take his nephew with him to the Lincoln races.

"Now, son," he said, "I'm putting twenty on Mirza, and I'll put five on for

you on any horse you fancy. What's your pick?"

"Daffodil, uncle."

"No, not the fiver on Daffodil!"

"I should if it was my own fiver," said the child.

"Good! Good! Right you are! A fiver for me and a fiver for you on Daffodil."

The child had never been to a race-meeting before, and his eyes were blue fire. He pursed his mouth tight and watched. A Frenchman just in front had put his money on Lancelot. Wild with excitement, he flayed his arms up and down, yelling *"Lancelot! Lancelot!"* in his French accent.

Daffodil came in first, Lancelot second, Mirza third. The child, flushed and with eyes blazing, was curiously serene. His uncle brought him four five-pound notes, four to one.

"What am I to do with these?" he cried, waving them before the boy's eyes.

"I suppose we'll talk to Bassett," said the boy. "I expect I have fifteen hundred now; and twenty in reserve; and this twenty."

His uncle studied him for some moments.

"Look here, son!" he said. "You're not serious about Bassett and that fifteen hundred, are you?"

"Yes, I am. But it's between you and me, uncle. Honour bright?"

"Honour bright all right, son! But I must talk to Bassett."

"If you'd like to be a partner, uncle, with Bassett and me, we could all be partners. Only, you'd have to promise, honour bright, uncle, not to let it go beyond us three. Bassett and I are lucky, and you must be lucky, because it was your ten shillings I started winning with. . . ."

Uncle Oscar took both Bassett and Paul into Richmond Park for an afternoon, and there they talked.

"It's like this, you see, sir," Bassett said. "Master Paul would get me talking about racing events, spinning yarns, you know, sir. And he was always keen on knowing if I'd made or if I'd lost. It's about a year since, now, that I put five shillings on Blush of Dawn for him: and

3 Nathaniel Gould (1857–1919), a well-known writer who used horse racing as the subject for his journalism and fiction. (JHP)

we lost. Then the luck turned, with that ten shillings he had from you: that we put on Singhalese. And since that time, it's been pretty steady, all things considering. What do you say, Master Paul?"

"We're all right when we're sure," said Paul. "It's when we're not quite sure that we go down."

"Oh, but we're careful then," said Bassett.

"But when are you *sure?*" smiled Uncle Oscar.

"It's Master Paul, sir," said Bassett in a secret, religious voice. "It's as if he had it from heaven. Like Daffodil, now, for the Lincoln. That was as sure as eggs."

"Did you put anything on Daffodil?" asked Oscar Cresswell.

"Yes, sir. I made my bit."

"And my nephew?"

Bassett was obstinately silent, looking at Paul.

"I made twelve hundred, didn't I, Bassett? I told uncle I was putting three hundred on Daffodil."

"That's right," said Bassett, nodding.

"But where's the money?" asked the uncle.

"I keep it safe locked up, sir. Master Paul he can have it any minute he likes to ask for it."

"What, fifteen hundred pounds?"

"And twenty! And *forty,* that is, with the twenty he made on the course."

"It's amazing!" said the uncle.

"If Master Paul offers you to be partners, sir, I would, if I were you: if you'll excuse me," said Bassett.

Oscar Cresswell thought about it. "I'll see the money," he said.

They drove home again, and, sure enough, Bassett came round to the garden-house with fifteen hundred pounds in notes. The twenty pounds reserve was left with Joe Glee, in the Turf Commission deposit.

"You see, it's all right, uncle, when I'm *sure!* Then we go strong, for all we're worth. Don't we, Bassett?"

"We do that, Master Paul."

"And when are you sure?" said the uncle, laughing.

"Oh, well, sometimes I'm *absolutely* sure, like about Daffodil," said the boy;

"and sometimes I have an idea; and sometimes I haven't even an idea, have I, Bassett? Then we're careful, because we mostly go down."

"You do, do you! And when you're sure, like about Daffodil, what makes you sure, sonny?"

"Oh, well, I don't know," said the boy uneasily. "I'm sure, you know, uncle; that's all."

"It's as if he had it from heaven, sir," Bassett reiterated.

"I should say so!" said the uncle.

But he became a partner. And when the Leger [4] was coming on Paul was "sure' about Lively Spark, which was a quite inconsiderable horse. The boy insisted on putting a thousand on the horse, Bassett went for five hundred, and Oscar Cresswell two hundred. Lively Spark came in first, and the betting had been ten to one against him. Paul had made ten thousand.

"You see," he said, "I was absolutely sure of him."

Even Oscar Cresswell had cleared two thousand.

"Look here, son," he said, "this sort of thing makes me nervous."

"It needn't, uncle! Perhaps I shan't be sure again for a long time."

"But what are you going to do with your money?" asked the uncle.

"Of course," said the boy, "I started it for mother. She said she had no luck, because father is unlucky, so I thought if *I* was lucky, it might stop whispering."

"What might stop whispering?"

"Our house. I *hate* our house for whispering."

"What does it whisper?"

"Why—why"—the boy fidgeted—"why, I don't know. But it's always short of money, you know, uncle."

"I know it, son, I know it."

"You know people send mother writs,[5] don't you, uncle?"

"I'm afraid I do," said the uncle.

"And then the house whispers, like

4 The St. Leger Stakes run at Doncaster. (JHP)

5 Presumably, dunning letters from creditors. (JHP)

people laughing at you behind your back. It's awful, that is! I thought if I was lucky————"

"You might stop it," added the uncle.

The boy watched him with big blue eyes, that had an uncanny cold fire in them, and he said never a word.

"Well, then!" said the uncle. "What are we doing?"

"I shouldn't like mother to know I was lucky," said the boy.

"Why not, son?"

"She'd stop me."

"I don't think she would."

"Oh!"—and the boy writhed in an odd way—"I *don't* want her to know, uncle."

"All right, son! We'll manage it without her knowing."

They managed it very easily. Paul, at the other's suggestion, handed over five thousand pounds to his uncle, who deposited it with the family lawyer, who was then to inform Paul's mother that a relative had put five thousand pounds into his hands, which sum was to be paid out a thousand pounds at a time, on the mother's birthday, for the next five years.

"So she'll have a birthday present of a thousand pounds for five successive years," said Uncle Oscar. "I hope it won't make it all the harder for her later."

Paul's mother had her birthday in November. The house had been 'whispering' worse than ever lately, and, even in spite of his luck, Paul could not bear up against it. He was very anxious to see the effect of the birthday letter, telling his mother about the thousand pounds.

When there were no visitors, Paul now took his meals with his parents, as he was beyond the nursery control. His mother went into town nearly every day. She had discovered that she had an odd knack of sketching furs and dress materials, so she worked secretly in the studio of a friend who was the chief 'artist' for the leading drapers. She drew the figures of ladies in furs and ladies in silk and sequins for the newspaper advertisements. This young woman artist earned several thousand pounds a year, but Paul's mother only made several hundreds, and she was again dissatisfied.

She so wanted to be first in something, and she did not succeed, even in making sketches for drapery advertisements.

She was down to breakfast on the morning of her birthday. Paul watched her face as she read her letters. He knew the lawyer's letter. As his mother read it, her face hardened and became more expressionless. Then a cold, determined look came on her mouth. She hid the letter under the pile of others, and said not a word about it.

"Didn't you have anything nice in the post for your birthday, mother?" said Paul.

"Quite moderately nice," she said, her voice cold and absent.

She went away to town without saying more.

But in the afternoon Uncle Oscar appeared. He said Paul's mother had had a long interview with the lawyer, asking if the whole five thousand could not be advanced at once, as she was in debt.

"What do you think, uncle?" asked the boy.

"I leave it to you, son."

"Oh, let her have it, then! We can get some more with the other," said the boy.

"A bird in the hand is worth two in the bush, laddie!" said Uncle Oscar.

"But I'm sure to *know* for the Grand National; or the Lincolnshire; or else the Derby.[6] I'm sure to know for *one* of them," said Paul.

So Uncle Oscar signed the agreement, and Paul's mother touched the whole five thousand. Then something very curious happened. The voices in the house suddenly went mad, like a chorus of frogs on a spring evening. There were certain new furnishings, and Paul had a tutor. He was *really* going to Eton, his father's school, in the following autumn. There were flowers in the winter, and a blossoming of the luxury Paul's mother had been used to. And yet the voices in the house, behind the sprays of mimosa and almond-blossom, and from under the piles of iridescent cushions, simply trilled and screamed in a sort of ecstasy: "There

6 Well-known British horse races: the Grand National run at Aintree, the Lincolnshire run at Lincoln Downs, and the Derby run at Epsom Downs. (JHP).

must be more money! Oh-h-h; there *must* be more money. Oh, now, now-w! Now-w-w—there *must* be more money! —more than ever! More than ever!"

It frightened Paul terribly. He studied away at his Latin and Greek with his tutor. But his intense hours were spent with Bassett. The Grand National had gone by: he had not 'known,' and had lost a hundred pounds. Summer was at hand. He was in agony for the Lincoln. But even for the Lincoln he didn't 'know,' and he lost fifty pounds. He became wild-eyed and strange, as if something were going to explode in him.

"Let it alone, son! Don't you bother about it!" urged Uncle Oscar. But it was as if the boy couldn't really hear what his uncle was saying.

"I've got to know for the Derby! I've got to know for the Derby!" the child reiterated, his big blue eyes blazing with a sort of madness.

His mother noticed how overwrought he was.

"You'd better go to the seaside. Wouldn't you like to go now to the seaside, instead of waiting? I think you'd better," she said, looking down at him anxiously, her heart curiously heavy because of him.

But the child lifted his uncanny blue eyes.

"I couldn't possibly go before the Derby, mother!" he said. "I couldn't possibly!"

"Why not?" she said, her voice becoming heavy when she was opposed. "Why not? You can still go from the seaside to see the Derby with your Uncle Oscar, if that's what you wish. No need for you to wait here. Besides, I think you care too much about these races. It's a bad sign. My family has been a gambling family, and you won't know till you grow up how much damage it has done. But it has done damage. I shall have to send Bassett away, and ask Uncle Oscar not to talk racing to you, unless you promise to be reasonable about it: go away to the seaside and forget it. You're all nerves!"

"I'll do what you like, mother, so long as you don't send me away till after the Derby," the boy said.

"Send you away from where? Just from this house?"

"Yes," he said, gazing at her.

"Why, you curious child, what makes you care about this house so much, suddenly? I never knew you loved it."

He gazed at her without speaking. He had a secret within a secret, something he had not divulged, even to Bassett or to his Uncle Oscar.

But his mother, after standing undecided and a little bit sullen for some moments, said:

"Very well, then! Don't go to the seaside till after the Derby, if you don't wish it. But promise me you won't let your nerves go to pieces. Promise you won't think so much about horse-racing and *events*, as you call them!"

"Oh no," said the boy casually. "I won't think much about them, mother. You needn't worry. I wouldn't worry, mother, if I were you."

"If you were me and I were you," said his mother, "I wonder what we *should* do!"

"But you know you needn't worry, mother, don't you?" the boy repeated.

"I should be awfully glad to know it," she said wearily.

"Oh, well, you *can,* you know. I mean, you *ought* to know you needn't worry," he insisted.

"Ought I? Then I'll see about it," she said.

Paul's secret of secrets was his wooden horse, that which had no name. Since he was emancipated from a nurse and a nursery-governess, he had had his rocking-horse removed to his own bedroom at the top of the house.

"Surely you're too big for a rocking-horse!" his mother had remonstrated.

"Well, you see, mother, till I can have a *real* horse, I like to have *some* sort of animal about," had been his quaint answer.

"Do you feel he keeps you company?" she laughed.

"Oh yes! He's very good, he always keeps me company, when I'm there," said Paul.

So the horse, rather shabby, stood in an arrested prance in the boy's bedroom. The Derby was drawing near, and the boy grew more and more tense. He hardly heard what was spoken to him, he was very frail, and his eyes were really uncanny. His mother had sudden strange seizures of uneasiness about him. Sometimes, for half an hour, she would feel a sudden anxiety about him that was almost anguish. She wanted to rush to him at once, and know he was safe.

Two nights before the Derby, she was at a big party in town, when one of her rushes of anxiety about her boy, her firstborn, gripped her heart till she could hardly speak. She fought with the feeling, might and main, for she believed in common sense. But it was too strong. She had to leave the dance and go downstairs to telephone to the country. The children's nursery-governess was terribly surprised and startled at being rung up in the night.

"Are the children all right, Miss Wilmot?"

"Oh yes, they are quite all right."

"Master Paul? Is he all right?"

"He went to bed as right as a trivet. Shall I run up and look at him?"

"No," said Paul's mother reluctantly. "No! Don't trouble. It's all right. Don't sit up. We shall be home fairly soon." She did not want her son's privacy intruded upon.

"Very good," said the governess.

It was about one o'clock when Paul's mother and father drove up to their house. All was still. Paul's mother went to her room and slipped off her white fur cloak. She had told her maid not to wait up for her. She heard her husband downstairs, mixing a whisky and soda.

And then, because of the strange anxiety at her heart, she stole upstairs to her son's room. Noiselessly she went along the upper corridor. Was there a faint noise? What was it?

She stood, with arrested muscles, outside his door, listening. There was a strange, heavy, and yet not loud noise. Her heart stood still. It was a soundless noise, yet rushing and powerful. Something huge, in violent, hushed motion. What was it? What in God's name was it? She ought to know. She felt that she knew the noise. She knew what it was.

Yet she could not place it. She couldn't say what it was. And on and on it went, like a madness.

Softly, frozen with anxiety and fear, she turned the door-handle.

The room was dark. Yet in the space near the window, she heard and saw something plunging to and fro. She gazed in fear and amazement.

Then suddenly she switched on the light, and saw her son, in his green pyjamas, madly surging on the rocking-horse. The blaze of light suddenly lit him up, as he urged the wooden horse, and lit her up, as she stood, blonde, in her dress of pale green and crystal, in the doorway.

"Paul!" she cried. "Whatever are you doing?"

"It's Malabar!" he screamed in a powerful, strange voice. "It's Malabar!"

His eyes blazed at her for one strange and senseless second, as he ceased urging his wooden horse. Then he fell with a crash to the ground, and she, all her tormented motherhood flooding upon her, rushed to gather him up.

But he was unconscious, and unconscious he remained, with some brainfever. He talked and tossed, and his mother sat stonily by his side.

"Malabar! It's Malabar! Bassett, Bassett, I *know!* It's Malabar!"

So the child cried, trying to get up and urge the rocking-horse that gave him his inspiration.

"What does he mean by Malabar?" asked the heart-frozen mother.

"I don't know," said the father stonily.

"What does he mean by Malabar?" she asked her brother Oscar.

"It's one of the horses running for the Derby," was the answer.

And, in spite of himself, Oscar Cresswell spoke to Bassett, and himself put a thousand on Malabar: at fourteen to one.

The third day of the illness was critical: they were waiting for a change. The boy, with his rather long, curly hair, was tossing ceaselessly on the pillow. He neither slept nor regained consciousness, and his eyes were like blue stones. His mother sat, feeling her heart had gone, turned actually into a stone.

In the evening, Oscar Cresswell did not come, but Bassett sent a message, saying could he come up for one moment, just one moment? Paul's mother was very angry at the intrusion, but on second thoughts she agreed. The boy was the same. Perhaps Bassett might bring him to consciousness.

The gardener, a shortish fellow with a little brown moustache and sharp little brown eyes, tiptoed into the room, touched his imaginary cap to Paul's mother, and stole to the bedside, staring with glittering, smallish eyes at the tossing, dying child.

"Master Paul!" he whispered. "Master Paul! Malabar came in first all right, a clean win. I did as you told me. You've made over seventy thousand pounds, you have; you've got over eighty thousand. Malabar came in all right, Master Paul."

"Malabar! Malabar! Did I say Malabar, mother? Did I say Malabar? Do you think I'm lucky, mother? I knew Malabar, didn't I? Over eighty thousand pounds! I call that lucky, don't you, mother? Over eighty thousand pounds! I knew, didn't I know I knew? Malabar came in all right. If I ride my horse till I'm sure, then I tell you, Bassett, you can go as high as you like. Did you go for all you were worth, Bassett?"

"I went a thousand on it, Master Paul."

"I never told you, mother, that if I can ride my horse, and *get there*, then I'm absolutely sure—oh, absolutely! Mother, did I ever tell you? I *am* lucky!"

"No, you never did," said his mother.

But the boy died in the night.

And even as he lay dead, his mother heard her brother's voice saying to her: "My God, Hester, you're eighty-odd thousand to the good, and a poor devil of a son to the bad. But, poor devil, poor devil, he's best gone out of a life where he rides his rocking-horse to find a winner."

[1932]

QUESTIONS FOR STUDY

1. *What essential information about Paul and his mother do we learn from their initial conversation? What does "luck" represent for Paul? For his mother? How would you describe their characters?*
2. *Who is the focal character of the story and why?*
3. *What are the voices in the house? Why do they go "mad" after Paul's mother gets her five thousand pounds?*
4. *What role or function does Uncle Oscar have?*
5. *What is the cause of Paul's death? Where does Lawrence seem to place the responsibility and blame? What is the irony of Uncle Oscar's final comment?*
6. *What is the theme of Lawrence's story? To what extent can it be viewed as a criticism of upper-middle-class English life and, by extension, of modern society as a whole?*

DORIS LESSING

One off the Short List

WHEN he had first seen Barbara Coles, some years before, he only noticed her because someone said: "That's Johnson's new girl." He certainly had not used of her the private erotic formula: *Yes, that one.* He even wondered what Johnson saw in her. "She won't last long," he remembered thinking, as he watched Johnson, a handsome man, but rather flushed with drink, flirting with some unknown girl while Barbara stood by a wall looking on. He thought she had a sullen expression.

She was a pale girl, not slim, for her frame was generous, but her figure could pass as good. Her straight yellow hair was parted on one side in a way that struck him as gauche. He did not notice what she wore. But her eyes were all right, he remembered: large, and solidly green, square-looking because of some trick of the flesh at their corners. Emeraldlike eyes in the face of a schoolgirl, or young schoolmistress who was watching her lover flirt and would later sulk about it.

Her name sometimes cropped up in the papers. She was a stage decorator, a designer, something on those lines.

Then a Sunday newspaper had a competition for stage design and she won it. Barbara Coles was one of the "names" in the theatre, and her photograph was seen about. It was always serious. He remembered having thought her sullen.

One night he saw her across the room at a party. She was talking with a well-known actor. Her yellow hair was still done on one side, but now it looked sophisticated. She wore an emerald ring on her right hand that seemed deliberately to invite comparison with her eyes. He walked over and said: "We have met before, Graham Spence." He noted, with discomfort, that he sounded abrupt. "I'm sorry, I don't remember, but how do you do?" she said, smiling. And continued her conversation.

He hung around a bit, but soon she went off with a group of people she was inviting to her home for a drink. She did not invite Graham. There was about her an assurance, a carelessness, that he recognised as the signature of success. It was then, watching her laugh as she went off with her friends, that he used the formula: *"Yes, that one."* And he went home to his wife with enjoyable expectation, as if his date with Barbara Coles were already arranged.

His marriage was twenty years old. At first it had been stormy, painful, tragic—full of partings, betrayals and sweet reconciliations. It had taken him at least a decade to realise that there was nothing remarkable about this marriage that he had lived through with such surprise of the mind and the senses. On the contrary, the marriages of most of the people he knew, whether they were first, second or third attempts, were just the same. His had run true to form even to the serious love affair with the young girl for whose sake he had *almost* divorced his wife—yet at the last moment had changed his mind, letting the girl down so that he must have her for always (not unpleasurably) on his conscience. It was with humiliation that he had understood that this drama was not at all the unique thing he had imagined. It was nothing more than the experience of everyone in his circle. And presumably in everybody else's circle too?

Anyway, round about the tenth year of his marriage he had seen a good many things clearly, a certain kind of emotional adventure went from his life, and the marriage itself changed.

His wife had married a poor youth with a great future as a writer. Sacrifices had been made, chiefly by her, for that future. He was neither unaware of them, nor ungrateful; in fact he felt permanently guilty about it. He at last published a decently successful book, then a second which now, thank God, no one remembered. He had drifted into radio, television, book reviewing.

He understood he was not going to make it; that he had become—not a hack, no one could call him that—but a member of that army of people who live by their wits on the fringes of the arts. The moment of realisation was when he was in a pub one lunchtime near the B.B.C. where he often dropped in to meet others like himself: he understood that was why he went there—they *were* like him. Just as that melodramatic marriage had turned out to be like everyone else's—except that it had been shared with one woman instead of two or three—so it had turned out that his unique talent, his struggles as a writer had led him here, to this pub and the half dozen pubs like it, where all the men in sight had the same history. They all had their novel, their play, their book of poems, a moment of fame, to their credit. Yet here they were, running television programmes about which they were cynical (to each other or to their wives) or writing reviews about other people's books. Yes, that's what he had become, an impresario of other people's talent. These two moments of clarity, about his marriage and about his talent, had roughly coincided; and (perhaps not by chance) had coincided with his wife's decision to leave him for a man younger than himself who had a future, she said, as a playwright. Well, he had talked her out of it. For her part she had to understand he was not going to be the T. S. Eliot or Graham Greene of our time—but after all, how many were? She must finally understand this, for he could no longer bear her awful bitterness. For his part he must stop coming home drunk at five in the morning, and starting a new romantic affair every six months which

he took so seriously that he made her miserable because of her implied deficiencies. In short he was to be a good husband. (He had always been a dutiful father.) And she a good wife. And so it was; the marriage became stable, as they say.

The formula: *Yes, that one* no longer implied a necessarily sexual relationship. In its more mature form, it was far from being something he was ashamed of. On the contrary, it expressed a humorous respect for what he was, for his real talents and flair, which had turned out to be not artistic after all, but to do with emotional life, hard-earned experience. It expressed an ironical dignity, a proving to himself not only: I can be honest about myself, but also: I have earned the best in *that* field whenever I want it.

He watched the field for the women who were well known in the arts, or in politics; looked out for photographs, listened for bits of gossip. He made a point of going to see them act, or dance, or orate. He built up a not unshrewd picture of them. He would either quietly pull strings to meet her or—more often, for there was a gambler's pleasure in waiting —bide his time until he met her in the natural course of events, which was bound to happen sooner or later. He would be seen out with her a few times in public, which was in order, since his work meant he had to entertain well-known people, male and female. His wife always knew, he told her. He might have a brief affair with this woman, but more often than not it was the appearance of an affair. Not that he didn't get pleasure from other people envying him—he would make a point, for instance, of taking this woman into the pubs where his male colleagues went. It was that his real pleasure came when he saw her surprise at how well she was understood by him. He enjoyed the atmosphere he was able to set up between an intelligent woman and himself: a humorous complicity which had in it much that was unspoken, and which almost made sex irrelevant.

Onto the list of women with whom he planned to have this relationship went Barbara Coles. There was no hurry. Next week, next month, next year, they would meet at a party. The world of well-known people in London is a small one. Big and little fishes, they drift around, nose each other, flirt their fins, wriggle off again. When he bumped into Barbara Coles, it would be time to decide whether or not to sleep with her.

Meanwhile he listened. But he didn't discover much. She had a husband and children, but the husband seemed to be in the background. The children were charming and well brought up, like everyone else's children. She had affairs, they said; but while several men he met sounded familiar with her, it was hard to determine whether they had slept with her, because none directly boasted of her. She was spoken of in terms of her friends, her work, her house, a party she had given, a job she had found someone. She was liked, she was respected, and Graham Spence's self-esteem was flattered because he had chosen her. He looked forward to saying in just the same tone: "Barbara Coles asked me what I thought about the set and I told her quite frankly. . . ."

Then by chance he met a young man who did boast about Barbara Coles; he claimed to have had the great love affair with her, and recently at that; and he spoke of it as something generally known. Graham realised how much he had already become involved with her in his imagination because of how perturbed he was now, on account of the character of this youth, Jack Kennaway. He had recently become successful as a magazine editor—one of those young men who, not as rare as one might suppose in the big cities, are successful from sheer impertinence, effrontery. Without much talent or taste, yet he had the charm of his effrontery. "Yes, I'm going to succeed, because I've decided to; yes, I may be stupid, but not so stupid that I don't know my deficiencies. Yes, I'm going to be successful because you people with integrity, etc., etc., simply don't believe in the possibility of people like me. You are too cowardly to stop me. Yes, I've taken your measure and I'm going to succeed because I've got the courage, not only to be unscrupulous, but to be quite frank about it. And besides, you admire me, you must, or other-

wise you'd stop me. . . ." Well, that was young Jack Kennaway, and he shocked Graham. He was a tall, languishing young man, handsome in a dark melting way, and, it was quite clear, he was either asexual or homosexual. And this youth boasted of the favours of Barbara Coles; boasted, indeed, of her love. Either she was a raving neurotic with a taste for neurotics; or Jack Kennaway was a most accomplished liar; or she slept with anyone. Graham was intrigued. He took Jack Kennaway out to dinner in order to hear him talk about Barbara Coles. There was no doubt the two were pretty close—all those dinners, theatres, weekends in the country—Graham Spence felt he had put his finger on the secret pulse of Barbara Coles; and it was intolerable that he must wait to meet her; he decided to arrange it.

It became unnecessary. She was in the news again, with a run of luck. She had done a successful historical play, and immediately afterwards a modern play, and then a hit musical. In all three, the sets were remarked on. Graham saw some interviews in newspapers and on television. These all centered around the theme of her being able to deal easily with so many different styles of theatre; but the real point was, of course, that she was a woman, which naturally added piquancy to the thing. And now Graham Spence was asked to do a half-hour radio interview with her. He planned the questions he would ask her with care, drawing on what people had said of her, but above all on his instinct and experience with women. The interview was to be at nine-thirty at night; he was to pick her up at six from the theatre where she was currently at work, so that there would be time, as the letter from the B.B.C. had put it, "for you and Miss Coles to get to know each other."

At six he was at the stage door, but a message from Miss Coles said she was not quite ready, could he wait a little. He hung about, then went to the pub opposite for a quick one, but still no Miss Coles. So he made his way backstage, directed by voices, hammering, laughter. It was badly lit, and the group of people at work did not see him. The director, James

Poynter, had his arm around Barbara's shoulders. He was newly well-known, a carelessly good-looking young man reputed to be intelligent. Barbara Coles wore a dark blue overall, and her flat hair fell over her face so that she kept pushing it back with the hand that had the emerald on it. These two stood close, side by side. Three young men, stagehands, were on the other side of a trestle which had sketches and drawings on it. They were studying some sketches. Barbara said, in a voice warm with energy: "Well, so I thought if we did *this*—do you see, James? What do you think, Steven?" "Well, love," said the young man she called Steven, "I see your idea, but I wonder if . . ." "I think you're right, Babs," said the director. "Look," said Barbara, holding one of the sketches towards Steven, "look, let me show you." They all leaned forward, the five of them, absorbed in the business.

Suddenly Graham couldn't stand it. He understood he was shaken to his depths. He went off stage, and stood with his back against a wall in the dingy passage that led to the dressing rooms. His eyes were filled with tears. He was seeing what a long way he had come from the crude, uncompromising, admirable young egomaniac he had been when he was twenty. That group of people there—working, joking, arguing, yes, that's what he hadn't known for years. What bound them was the democracy of respect for each other's work, a confidence in themselves and in each other. They looked like people banded together against a world which they—no, not despised, but which they measured, understood, would fight to the death, out of respect for what *they* stood for, for what *it* stood for. It was a long time since he felt part of that balance. And he understood that he had seen Barbara Coles when she was most herself, at ease with a group of people she worked with. It was then, with the tears drying on his eyelids, which felt old and ironic, that he decided he would sleep with Barbara Coles. It was a necessity for him. He went back through the door onto the stage, burning with this single determination.

The five were still together. Barbara had a length of blue gleaming stuff which she was draping over the shoulder of Steven, the stagehand. He was showing it off, and the others watched. "What do you think, James?" she asked the director. "We've got that sort of dirty green, and I thought . . ." "Well," said James, not sure at all, "well, Babs, well . . ."

Now Graham went forward so that he stood beside Barbara, and said: "I'm Graham Spence, we've met before." For the second time she smiled socially and said: "Oh I'm sorry, I don't remember." Graham nodded at James, whom he had known, or at least had met off and on, for years. But it was obvious James didn't remember him either.

"From the B.B.C.," said Graham to Barbara again sounding abrupt, against his will. "Oh I'm sorry, I'm so sorry, I forgot all about it. I've got to be interviewed," she said to the group. "Mr. Spence is a journalist." Graham allowed himself a small smile ironical of the word journalist, but she was not looking at him. She was going on with her work. "We should decide tonight," she said. "Steven's right." "Yes, I am right," said the stagehand. "She's right, James, we need that blue with that sludge-green everywhere." "James," said Barbara, "James, what's wrong with it? You haven't said." She moved forward to James, passing Graham. Remembering him again, she became contrite. "I'm sorry," she said, "we can none of us agree. Well, look"—she turned to Graham—"you advise us, we've got so involved with it that . . ." At which James laughed, and so did the stagehands. "No, Babs," said James, "of course Mr. Spence can't advise. He's just this moment come in. We've got to decide. Well I'll give you till tomorrow morning. Time to go home, it must be six by now."

"It's nearly seven," said Graham, taking command.

"It isn't!" said Barbara, dramatic. "My God, how terrible, how appalling, how could I have done such a thing. . . ." She was laughing at herself. "Well, you'll have to forgive me, Mr. Spence, because you haven't got any alternative."

They began laughing again: this was clearly a group joke. And now Graham took his chance. He said firmly, as if he were her director, in fact copying James Poynter's manner with her: "No, Miss Coles, I won't forgive you, I've been kicking my heels for nearly an hour." She grimaced, then laughed and accepted it. James said: "There, Babs, that's how you ought to be treated. We spoil you." He kissed her on the cheek, she kissed him on both his, the stagehands moved off. "Have a good evening, Babs," said James, going, and nodding to Graham, who stood concealing his pleasure with difficulty. He knew, because he had had the courage to be firm, indeed, peremptory, with Barbara, that he had saved himself hours of maneuvering. Several drinks, a dinner—perhaps two or three evenings of drinks and dinners—had been saved because he was now on this footing with Barbara Coles, a man who could say: "No, I won't forgive you, you've kept me waiting."

She said: "I've just got to . . ." and went ahead of him. In the passage she hung her overall on a peg. She was thinking, it seemed, of something else, but seeing him watching her, she smiled at him, companionably: he realised with triumph it was the sort of smile she would offer one of the stagehands, or even James. She said again: "Just one second . . ." and went to the stage-door office. She and the stage doorman conferred. There was some problem. Graham said, taking another chance: "What's the trouble, can I help?"—as if he could help, as if he expected to be able to. "Well . . ." she said, frowning. Then, to the man: "No, it'll be all right. Good night." She came to Graham. "We've got ourselves into a bit of a fuss because half the set's in Liverpool and half's here and—but it will sort itself out." She stood, at ease, chatting to him, one colleague to another. All this was admirable, he felt; but there would be a bad moment when they emerged from the special atmosphere of the theatre into the street. He took another decision, grasped her arm firmly, and said: "We're going to have a drink before we do anything at all, it's a terrible evening out." Her arm felt resistant, but remained within his. It was raining outside, luckily. He directed her, authorita-

tive: "No, not that pub, there's a nicer one around the corner." "Oh, but I like this pub," said Barbara, "we always use it."

"Of course you do," he said to himself. But in that pub there would be the stagehands, and probably James, and he'd lose contact with her. He'd become a *journalist* again. He took her firmly out of danger around two corners, into a pub he picked at random. A quick look around—no, they weren't there. At least, if there were people from the theatre, she showed no sign. She asked for a beer. He ordered her a double Scotch, which she accepted. Then, having won a dozen preliminary rounds already, he took time to think. Something was bothering him—what? Yes, it was what he had observed backstage, Barbara and James Poynter. Was she having an affair with him? Because if so, it would all be much more difficult. He made himself see the two of them together, and thought with a jealousy surprisingly strong: *Yes, that's it.* Meantime he sat looking at her, seeing himself look at her, *a man gazing in calm appreciation at a woman*: waiting for her to feel it and respond. She was examining the pub. Her white woollen suit was belted, and had a not unprovocative suggestion of being a uniform. Her flat yellow hair, hastily pushed back after work, was untidy. Her clear white skin, without any colour, made her look tired. Not very exciting, at the moment, thought Graham, but maintaining his appreciative pose for when she would turn and see it. He knew what she would see: he was relying not only on the "warm kindly" beam of his gaze, for this was merely a reinforcement of the impression he knew he made. He had black hair, a little greyed. His clothes were loose and bulky—masculine. His eyes were humorous and appreciative. He was not, never had been, concerned to lessen the impression of being settled, dependable: the husband and father. On the contrary, he knew women found it reassuring.

When she at last turned she said, almost apologetic: "Would you mind if we sat down? I've been lugging great things around all day." She had spotted two empty chairs in a corner. So had he, but rejected them, because there were other people at the table. "But my dear, of course!" They took the chairs, and then Barbara said: "If you'll excuse me a moment." She had remembered she needed makeup. He watched her go off, annoyed with himself. She was tired; and he could have understood, protected, sheltered. He realised that in the other pub, with the people she had worked with all day, she would not have thought: "I must make myself up, I must be on show." That was for outsiders. She had not, until now, considered Graham an outsider, because of his taking his chance to seem one of the working group in the theatre; but now he had thrown this opportunity away. She returned armoured. Her hair was sleek, no longer defenceless. And she had made up her eyes. Her eyebrows were untouched, pale gold streaks above the brilliant green eyes whose lashes were blackened. Rather good, he thought, the contrast. Yes, but the moment had gone when he could say: Did you know you had a smudge on your cheek? Or—my dear girl!—pushing her hair back with the edge of a brotherly hand. In fact, unless he was careful, he'd be back at starting point.

He remarked: "That emerald is very cunning"—smiling into her eyes.

She smiled politely, and said: "It's not cunning, it's an accident, it was my grandmother's." She flirted her hand lightly by her face, though, smiling. But that was something she had done before, to a compliment she had had before, and often. It was all social, she had become social entirely. She remarked: "Didn't you say it was half past nine we had to record?"

"My dear Barbara, we've got two hours. We'll have another drink or two, then I'll ask you a couple of questions, then we'll drop down to the studio and get it over, and then we'll have a comfortable supper."

"I'd rather eat now, if you don't mind. I had no lunch, and I'm really hungry."

"But my dear, of course." He was angry. Just as he had been surprised by his real jealousy over James, so now he was thrown off balance by his anger: he

had been counting on the long quiet dinner afterwards to establish intimacy. "Finish your drink and I'll take you to Nott's." Nott's was expensive. He glanced at her assessingly as he mentioned it. She said: "I wonder if you know Butler's? It's good and it's rather close." Butler's was good, and it was cheap, and he gave her a good mark for liking it. But Nott's it was going to be. "My dear, we'll get into a taxi and be at Nott's in a moment, don't worry."

She obediently got to her feet: the way she did it made him understand how badly he had slipped. She was saying to herself: Very well, he's like that, then all right, I'll do what he wants and get it over with. . . .

Swallowing his own drink he followed her, and took her arm in the pub doorway. It was polite within his. Outside it drizzled. No taxi. He was having bad luck now. They walked in silence to the end of the street. There Barbara glanced into a side street where a sign said: BUTLER'S. Not to remind him of it, on the contrary, she concealed the glance. And here she was, entirely at his disposal, they might never have shared the comradely moment in the theatre.

They walked half a mile to Nott's. No taxis. She made conversation: this was, he saw, to cover any embarrassment he might feel because of a half-mile walk through rain when she was tired. She was talking about some theory to do with the theatre, with designs for theatre building. He heard himself saying, and repeatedly: Yes, yes, yes. He thought about Nott's, how to get things right when they reached Nott's. There he took the headwaiter aside, gave him a pound, and instructions. They were put in a corner. Large Scotches appeared. The menus were spread. "And now, my dear," he said, "I apologise for dragging you here, but I hope you'll think it's worth it."

"Oh, it's charming, I've always liked it. It's just that . . ." She stopped herself saying: it's such a long way. She smiled at him, raising her glass, and said: "It's one of my very favourite places, and I'm glad you dragged me here." Her voice was flat with tiredness. All this was appalling;

he knew it; and he sat thinking how to retrieve his position. Meanwhile she fingered the menu. The headwaiter took the order, but Graham made a gesture which said: Wait a moment. He wanted the Scotch to take effect before she ate. But she saw his silent order; and, without annoyance or reproach, leaned forward to say, sounding patient: "Graham, please, I've got to eat, you don't want me drunk when you interview me, do you?"

"They are bringing it as fast as they can," he said, making it sound as if she were greedy. He looked neither at the headwaiter nor at Barbara. He noted in himself, as he slipped further and further away from contact with her, a cold determination growing in him; one apart from, apparently, any conscious act of will, that come what may, if it took all night, he'd be in her bed before morning. And now, seeing the small pale face, with the enormous green eyes, it was for the first time that he imagined her in his arms. Although he had said: *Yes, that one*, weeks ago, it was only now that he imagined her as a sensual experience. Now he did, so strongly that he could only glance at her, and then away towards the waiters who were bringing food.

"Thank the Lord," said Barbara, and all at once her voice was gay and intimate. "Thank heavens. Thank every power that is. . . ." She was making fun of her own exaggeration; and, as he saw, because she wanted to put him at his ease after his boorishness over delaying the food. (She hadn't been taken in, he saw, humiliated, disliking her.) "Thank all the gods of Nott's," she went on, "because if I hadn't eaten inside five minutes I'd have died, I tell you." With which she picked up her knife and fork and began on her steak. He poured wine, smiling with her, thinking that *this* moment of closeness he would not throw away. He watched her frank hunger as she ate, and thought: Sensual—it's strange I hadn't wondered whether she would be or not.

"Now," she said, sitting back, having taken the edge off her hunger: "Let's get to work."

He said: "I've thought it over very carefully—how to present you. The first thing seems to me, we must get away from

that old chestnut: Miss Coles, how extraordinary for a woman to be so versatile in her work . . . I hope you agree?" This was his trump card. He had noted, when he had seen her on television, her polite smile when this note was struck. (The smile he had seen so often tonight.) This smile said: All right, if you *have* to be stupid, what can I do?

Now she laughed and said: "What a relief. I was afraid you were going to do the same thing."

"Good, now you eat and I'll talk."

In his carefully prepared monologue he spoke of the different styles of theatre she had shown herself mistress of, but not directly: he was flattering her on the breadth of her experience; the complexity of her character, as shown in her work. She ate, steadily, her face showing nothing. At last she asked: "And how did you plan to introduce this?"

He had meant to spring that on her as a surprise, something like: Miss Coles, a surprisingly young woman for what she has accomplished (she was thirty? thirty-two?) and a very attractive one. . . . "Perhaps I can give you an idea of what she's like if I say she could be taken for the film star Marie Carletta. . . ." The Carletta was a strong earthy blonde, known to be intellectual. He now saw he could not possibly say this: he could imagine her cool look if he did. She said: "Do you mind if we get away from all that—my manifold talents, et cetera. . . ." He felt himself stiffen with annoyance: particularly because this was not an accusation, he saw she did not think him worth one. She had assessed him: This is the kind of man who uses this kind of flattery and therefore. . . . It made him angrier that she did not even trouble to say: Why did you do exactly what you promised you wouldn't? She was being invincibly polite, trying to conceal her patience with his stupidity.

"After all," she was saying, "it is a stage designer's job to design what comes up. Would anyone take, let's say Johnnie Cranmore (another stage designer) "onto the air or television and say: How very versatile you are because you did that musical about Java last month and a modern play about Irish labourers this?"

He battened down his anger. "My dear Barbara, I'm sorry. I didn't realise that what I said would sound just like the mixture as before. So what shall we talk about?"

"What I was saying as we walked to the restaurant: can we get away from the personal stuff?"

Now he almost panicked. Then, thank God, he laughed from nervousness, for she laughed and said: "You didn't hear one word I said."

"No, I didn't. I was frightened you were going to be furious because I made you walk so far when you were tired."

They laughed together, back to where they had been in the theatre. He leaned over, took her hand, kissed it. He said: "Tell me again." He thought: Damn, now she's going to be earnest and intellectual.

But he understood he had been stupid. He had forgotten himself at twenty—or, for that matter, at thirty; forgotten one could live inside an idea, a set of ideas, with enthusiasm. For in talking about her ideas (also the ideas of the people she worked with) for a new theatre, a new style of theatre, she was as she had been with her colleagues over the sketches or the blue material. She was easy, informal, almost chattering. This was how, he remembered, one talked about ideas that were a breath of life. The ideas, he thought, were intelligent enough; and he would agree with them, with her, if he believed it mattered a damn one way or another, if any of these enthusiasms mattered a damn. But at least he now had the key, he knew what to do. At the end of not more than half an hour, they were again two professionals, talking about ideas they shared, for he remembered caring about all this himself once. *When? How many years ago was it that he had been able to care?*

At last he said: "My dear Barbara, do you realise the impossible position you're putting me in? Margaret Ruyen who runs this programme is determined to do you personally, the poor woman hasn't got a serious thought in her head."

Barbara frowned. He put his hand on hers, teasing her for the frown: "No, wait, trust me, we'll circumvent her." She smiled. In fact Margaret Ruyen had left

it all to him, had said nothing about Miss Coles.

"They aren't very bright—the brass," he said. "Well, never mind: we'll work out what we want, do it, and it'll be a *fait accompli*."

"Thank you, what a relief. How lucky I was to be given you to interview me." She was relaxed now, because of the whisky, the food, the wine, above all because of this new complicity against Margaret Ruyen. It would all be easy. They worked out five or six questions, over coffee, and took a taxi through rain to the studios. He noted that the cold necessity to have her, to make her, to beat her down, had left him. He was even seeing himself, as the evening ended, kissing her on the cheek and going home to his wife. This comradeship was extraordinarily pleasant. It was balm to the wound he had not known he carried until that evening, when he had had to accept the justice of the word *journalist*. He felt he could talk forever about the state of the theatre, its finances, the stupidity of the government, the philistinism of . . .

At the studios he was careful to make a joke so that they walked in on the laugh. He was careful that the interview began at once, without conversation with Margaret Ruyen; and that from the moment the green light went on, his voice lost its easy familiarity. He made sure that not one personal note was struck during the interview. Afterwards, Margaret Ruyen, who was pleased, came forward to say so; but he took her aside to say that Miss Coles was tired and needed to be taken home at once: for he knew this must look to Barbara as if he were squaring a producer who had been expecting a different interview. He led Barbara off, her hand held tight in his against his side. "Well," he said, "we've done it, and I don't think she knows what hit her."

"Thank you," she said, "it really was pleasant to talk about something sensible for once."

He kissed her lightly on the mouth. She returned it, smiling. By now he felt sure that the mood need not slip again, he could hold it.

"There are two things we can do," he said. "You can come to my club and have a drink. Or I can drive you home and you can give me a drink. I have to go past you."

"Where do you live?"

"Wimbledon." He lived, in fact, at Highgate; but she lived in Fulham. He was taking another chance, but by the time she found out, they would be in a position to laugh over his ruse.

"Good," she said. "You can drop me home then. I have to get up early." He made no comment. In the taxi he took her hand; it was heavy in his, and he asked: "Does James slave-drive you?"

"I didn't realize you knew him—no, he doesn't."

"Well I don't know him intimately. What's he like to work with?"

"Wonderful," she said at once. "There's no one I enjoy working with more."

Jealousy spurted in him. He could not help himself: "Are you having an affair with him?"

She looked: what's it to do with you? but said: "No, I'm not."

"He's very attractive," he said with a chuckle of worldly complicity. She said nothing, and he insisted: "If I were a woman I'd have an affair with James."

It seemed she might very well say nothing. But she remarked: "He's married."

His spirits rose in a swoop. It was the first stupid remark she had made. It was a remark of such staggering stupidity that . . . he let out a humoring snort of laughter, put his arm around her, kissed her, said: "My dear little Babs."

She said: "Why Babs?"

"Is that the prerogative of James. And of the stagehands?" he could not prevent himself adding.

"I'm only called that at work." She was stiff inside his arm.

"My dear Barbara, then . . ." He waited for her to enlighten and explain, but she said nothing. Soon she moved out of his arm, on the pretext of lighting a cigarette. He lit it for her. He noted that his determination to lay her, and at all costs, had come back. They were outside her house. He said quickly: "And now, Barbara, you can make me a cup of coffee and give me a brandy." She hesitated; but he

was out of the taxi, paying, opening the door for her. The house had no lights on, he noted. He said: "We'll be very quiet so as not to wake the children."

She turned her head slowly to look at him. She said, flat, replying to his real question: "My husband is away. As for the children, they are visiting friends to-night." She now went ahead of him to the door of the house. It was a small house, in a terrace of small and not very pretty houses. Inside a little, bright, intimate hall, she said: "I'll go and make some coffee. Then, my friend, you must go home because I'm very tired."

The *my friend* struck him deep, because he had become vulnerable during their comradeship. He said, gabbling: "You're annoyed with me—oh, please don't, I'm sorry."

She smiled, from a cool distance. He saw, in the small light from the ceiling, her extraordinary eyes. "Green" eyes are hazel, are brown with green flecks, are even blue. Eyes are chequered, flawed, changing. Hers were solid green, but really, he had never seen anything like them before. They were like very deep water. They were like—well, emeralds; or the absolute clarity of green in the depths of a tree in summer. And now, as she smiled almost perpendicularly up at him, he saw a darkness come over them. Darkness, swallowed the clear green. She said: "I'm not in the least annoyed." It was as if she had yawned with boredom. "And now I'll get the things . . . in there." She nodded at a white door and left him. He went into a long, very tidy white room, that had a narrow bed in one corner, a table covered with drawings, sketches, pencils. Tacked to the walls with drawing pins were swatches of coloured stuffs. Two small chairs stood near a low round table: an area of comfort in the working room. He was thinking: I wouldn't like it if my wife had a room like this. I wonder what Barbara's husband . . . ? He had not thought of her till now in relation to her husband, or to her children. Hard to imagine her with a frying pan in her hand, or for that matter, cosy in the double bed.

A noise outside: he hastily arranged

himself, leaning with one arm on the mantelpiece. She came in with a small tray that had cups, glasses, brandy, coffeepot. She looked abstracted. Graham was on the whole flattered by this: it probably meant she was at ease in his presence. He realised he was a little tight and rather tired. Of course, she was tired too, that was why she was vague. He remembered that earlier that evening he had lost a chance by not using her tiredness. Well now, if he were intelligent . . . She was about to pour coffee. He firmly took the coffeepot out of her hand, and nodded at a chair. Smiling, she obeyed him. "That's better," he said. He poured coffee, poured brandy, and pulled the table towards her. She watched him. Then he took her hand, kissed it, patted it, laid it down gently. Yes, he thought, I did that well.

Now, a problem. He wanted to be closer to her, but she was fitted into a damned silly little chair that had arms. If he were to sit by her on the floor . . . ? But no, for him, the big bulky reassuring man, there could be no casual gestures, no informal postures. Suppose I scoop her out of the chair onto the bed? He drank his coffee as he plotted. Yes, he'd carry her to the bed, but not yet.

"Graham," she said, setting down her cup. She was, he saw with annoyance, looking tolerant. "Graham, in about half an hour I want to be in bed and asleep."

As she said this, she offered him a smile of amusement at this situation—man and woman maneuvering, the great comic situation. And with part of himself he could have shared it. Almost, he smiled with her, laughed. (Not till days later he exclaimed to himself: Lord what a mistake I made, not to share the joke with her then: that was where I went seriously wrong.) But he could not smile. His face was frozen, with a stiff pride. Not because she had been watching him plot; the amusement she now offered him took the sting out of that; but because of his revived determination that he was going to have his own way, that he was going to have her. He was not going home. But he felt that he held a bunch of keys, and did not know which one to choose.

He lifted the second small chair oppo-site to Barbara, moving aside the coffee table for this purpose. He sat in this chair, leaned forward, took her two hands, and said: "My dear, don't make me go home yet, don't, I beg you." The trouble was, nothing had happened all evening that could be felt to lead up to these words and his tone—simple, dignified, human being pleading with human being for surcease. He saw himself leaning forward, his big hands swallowing her small ones; he saw his face, warm with the appeal. And he realised he had meant the words he used. They were nothing more than what he felt. He wanted to stay with her because she wanted him to, because he was her colleague, a fellow worker in the arts. He needed this desperately. But she was examining him, curious rather than surprised, and from a critical distance. He heard himself saying: "If James were here, I wonder what you'd do?" His voice was aggrieved; he saw the sudden dark descent over her eyes, and she said: "Graham, would you like some more coffee before you go?"

He said: "I've been wanting to meet you for years. I know a good many people who know you."

She leaned forward, poured herself a little more brandy, sat back, holding the glass between her two palms on her chest. An odd gesture: Graham felt that this vessel she was cherishing between her hands was herself. A patient, long-suffering gesture. He thought of various men who had mentioned her. He thought of Jack Kennaway, wavered, panicked, said: "For instance, Jack Kennaway."

And now, at the name, an emotion lit her eyes—what was it? He went on, deliberately testing this emotion, adding to it: "I had dinner with him last week—oh, quite by chance!—and he was talking about you."

"Was he?"

He remembered he had thought her sullen, all those years ago. Now she seemed defensive, and she frowned. He said: "In fact he spent most of the evening talking about you."

She said in short, breathless sentences, which he realised were due to anger: "I can very well imagine what he says. But

surely you can't think I enjoy being reminded that . . ." She broke off, resenting
him, he saw, because he forced her down
onto a level she despised. But it was not
his level either: it was all her fault, all
hers! He couldn't remember not being in
control of a situation with a woman for
years. Again he felt like a man teetering
on a tightrope. He said, trying to make
good use of Jack Kennaway, even at this
late hour: "Of course, he's a charming
boy, but not a man at all."

She looked at him, silent, guarding her
brandy glass against her breasts.

"Unless appearances are totally deceptive, of course." He could not resist probing, even though he knew it was fatal.

She said nothing.

"Do you know you are supposed to
have had the great affair with Jack Kennaway?" he exclaimed, making this an
amused expostulation against the fools
who could believe it.

"So I am told." She set down her glass.
"And now," she said, standing up, dismissing him. He lost his head, took a step
forward, grabbed her in his arms, and
groaned: "Barbara!"

She turned her face this way and that
under his kisses. He snatched a diagnostic
look at her expression—it was still patient. He placed his lips against her neck,
groaned "Barbara" again, and waited.
She would have to do something. Fight
free, respond, something. She did nothing
at all. At last she said: "For the Lord's
sake, Graham!" She sounded amused: he
was again being offered amusement. But
if he shared it with her, it would be the
end of this chance to have her. He
clamped his mouth over hers, silencing
her. She did not fight him off so much as
blow him off. Her mouth treated his
attacking mouth as a woman blows and
laughs in water, puffing off waves or spray
with a laugh, turning aside her head. It
was a gesture half annoyance, half
humour. He continued to kiss her while
she moved her head and face about under
the kisses as if they were small attacking
waves.

And so began what, when he looked
back on it afterwards, was the most embarrassing experience of his life. Even at
the time he hated her for his ineptitude.
For he held her there for what must have
been nearly half an hour. She was much
shorter than he, he had to bend, and his
neck ached. He held her rigid, his thighs
on either side of hers, her arms clamped
to her side in a bear's hug. She was unable
to move, except for her head. When his
mouth ground hers open and his tongue
moved and writhed inside it, she still remained passive. And he could not stop
himself. While with his intelligence he
watched this ridiculous scene, he was
determined to go on, because sooner or
later her body must soften in wanting his.
And he could not stop because he could
not face the horror of the moment when
he set her free and she looked at him.
And he hated her more, every moment.
Catching glimpses of her great green eyes,
open and dismal beneath his, he knew
he had never disliked anything more than
those "jewelled" eyes. They were repulsive to him. It occurred to him at last that
even if by now she wanted him, he would-
n't know it, because she was not able to
move at all. He cautiously loosened his
hold so that she had an inch or so leeway.
She remained quite passive. As if, he
thought derisively, she had read or been
told that the way to incite men maddened
by lust was to fight them. He found he
was thinking: Stupid cow, so you imagine
I find you attractive, do you? You've got
the conceit to think that!

The sheer, raving insanity of this
thought hit him, opened his arms, his
thighs, and lifted his tongue out of her
mouth. She stepped back, wiping her
mouth with the back of her hand, and
stood dazed with incredulity. The embarrassment that lay in wait for him nearly
engulfed him, but he let anger postpone
it. She said positively apologetic, even, at
this moment, humorous: "You're crazy,
Graham. What's the matter, are you
drunk? You don't seem drunk. You don't
even find me attractive."

The blood of hatred went to his head
and he gripped her again. Now she had
got her face firmly twisted away so that
he could not reach her mouth, and she
repeated steadily as he kissed the parts of
her cheeks and neck that were available

to him: "Graham, let me go, do let me go, Graham." She went on saying this; he went on squeezing, grinding, kissing and licking. It might go on all night: it was a sheer contest of wills, nothing else. He thought: It's only a really masculine woman who wouldn't have given in by now out of sheer decency of the flesh! One thing he knew, however: that she would be in that bed, in his arms, and very soon. He let her go, but said: "I'm going to sleep with you tonight, you know that, don't you?"

She leaned with hand on the mantelpiece to steady herself. Her face was colourless, since he had licked all the makeup off. She seemed quite different: small and defenceless with her large mouth pale now, her smudged green eyes fringed with gold. And now, for the first time, he felt what it might have been supposed (certainly by her) he felt hours ago. Seeing the small damp flesh of her face, he felt kinship, intimacy with her, he felt intimacy of the flesh, the affection and good humour of sensuality. He felt she was flesh of his flesh, his sister in the flesh. He felt desire for her, instead of the will to have her; and because of this, was ashamed of the farce he had been playing. Now he desired simply to take her into bed in the affection of his senses.

She said: "What on earth am I supposed to do? Telephone for the police, or what?" He was hurt that she still addressed the man who had ground her into sulky apathy; she was not addressing *him* at all.

She said: "Or scream for the neighbours, is that what you want?"

The gold-fringed eyes were almost black, because of the depth of the shadow of boredom over them. She was bored and weary to the point of falling to the floor, he could see that.

He said: "'I'm going to sleep with you."

"But how can you possibly want to?" —a reasonable, a civilised demand addressed to a man who (he could see) she believed would respond to it. She said: "You know I don't want to, and I know you don't really give a damn one way or the other."

He was stung back into being the boor because she had not the intelligence to see that the boor no longer existed; because she could not see that this was a man who wanted her in a way which she must respond to.

There she stood, supporting herself with one hand, looking small and white and exhausted, and utterly incredulous. She was going to turn and walk off out of simple incredulity, he could see that. "Do you think I don't mean it?" he demanded, grinding this out between his teeth. She made a movement—she was on the point of going away. His hand shot out on its own volition and grasped her wrist. She frowned. His other hand grasped her other wrist. His body hove up against hers to start the pressure of a new embrace. Before it could, she said: " Oh Lord, no, I'm not going through all that again. Right, then."

"What do you mean—right, then?" he demanded.

She said: "You're going to sleep with me. O.K. Anything rather than go through that again. Shall we get it over with?"

He grinned, saying in silence: "No darling, oh no you don't, I don't care what words you use, I'm going to have you now and that's all there is to it."

She shrugged. The contempt, the weariness of it, had no effect on him, because he was now again hating her so much that wanting her was like needing to kill something or someone.

She took her clothes off, as if she were going to bed by herself: her jacket, skirt, petticoat. She stood in white bra and panties, a rather solid girl, brown-skinned still from the summer. He felt a flash of affection for the brown girl with her loose yellow hair as she stood naked. She got into bed and lay there, while the green eyes looked at him in civilised appeal: Are you really going through with this? Do you have to? Yes, his eyes said back: I do have to. She shifted her gaze aside, to the wall, saying silently: Well, if you want to take me without any desire at all on my part, then go ahead, if you're not ashamed. He was not ashamed, because he was maintaining the flame of hate for her which he knew quite well was all that stood between him and shame. He took off his clothes, and got into bed beside her. As he did so, knowing he was putting himself in the position of raping a woman who was making it elaborately clear he bored her, his flesh subsided completely, sad, and full of reproach because a few moments ago it was reaching out for his sister whom he could have made happy. He lay on his side by her, secretly at work on himself, while he supported himself across her body on his elbow, using the free hand to manipulate her breasts. He saw that she gritted her teeth against his touch. At least she could not know that after all this fuss he was not potent.

In order to incite himself, he clasped her again. She felt his smallness, writhed free of him, sat up and said: "Lie down."

While she had been lying there, she had been thinking: The only way to get this over with is to make him big again, otherwise I've got to put up with him all night. His hatred of her was giving him a clairvoyance: he knew very well what went on through her mind. She had switched on, with the determination to *get it all over with*, a sensual good humour, a patience. He lay down. She squatted beside him, the light from the ceiling blooming on her brown shoulders, her flat fair hair falling over her face. But she would not look at his face. Like a bored, skilled wife, she was; or like a prostitute. She administered to him, she was setting herself to please him. Yes, he thought, she's sensual, or she could be. Meanwhile she was succeeding in defeating the reluctance of his flesh, which was the tender token of a possible desire for her, by using a cold skill that was the result of her contempt for him. Just as he decided: Right, it's enough, now I shall have her properly, she made him come. It was not a trick, to hurry or cheat him, what defeated him was her transparent thought: Yes, that's what he's worth.

Then, having succeeded, and waited for a moment or two, she stood up, naked, the fringes of gold at her loins and in her armpits speaking to him a language quite different from that of her green, bored

eyes. She looked at him and thought, showing it plainly: What sort of a man is it who . . .? He watched the slight movement of her shoulders: a just-checked shrug. She went out of the room, then the sound of running water. Soon she came back in a white dressing gown, carrying a yellow towel. She handed him the towel, looking away in politeness as he used it. "Are you going home now?" she enquired hopefully, at this point.

"No, I'm not." He believed that now he would have to start fighting her again, but she lay down beside him, not touching him (he could feel the distaste of her flesh for his) and he thought: Very well, my dear, but there's a lot of the night left yet. He said aloud: "I'm going to have you properly tonight." She said nothing, lay silent, yawned. Then she remarked consolingly, and he could have laughed outright from sheer surprise: "Those were hardly conducive circumstances for making love." She was *consoling* him. He hated her for it. A proper little slut: I force her into bed, she doesn't want me, but she still has to make me feel good, like a prostitute. But even while he hated her he responded in kind, from the habit of sexual generosity. "It's because of my admiration for you, because . . . after all, I was holding in my arms one of the thousand women."

A pause. "The thousand?" she enquired, carefully.

"The thousand especial women."

"In Britain or in the world? You choose them for their brains, their beauty—what?"

"Whatever it is that makes them outstanding," he said, offering her a compliment.

"Well," she remarked at last, inciting him to be amused again: "I hope that at least there's a short list you can say I am on, for politeness' sake."

He did not reply for he understood he was sleepy. He was still telling himself that he must stay awake when he was slowly waking and it was morning. It was about eight. Barbara was not there. He thought: My God! What on earth shall I tell my wife? Where was Barbara? He remembered the ridiculous scenes of last night and nearly succumbed to shame. Then he thought, reviving anger: If she didn't sleep beside me here I'll never forgive her. . . . He sat up, quietly, determined to go through the house until he found her and, having found her, to possess her, when the door opened and she came in. She was fully dressed in a green suit, her hair done, her eyes made up. She carried a tray of coffee, which she set down beside the bed. He was conscious of his big loose hairy body, half uncovered. He said to himself that he was not going to lie in bed, naked, while she was dressed. He said: "Have you got a gown of some kind?" She handed him, without speaking, a towel, and said: "The bathroom's second on the left." She went out. He followed, the towel around him. Everything in this house was gay, intimate—not at all like her efficient working room. He wanted to find out where she had slept, and opened the first door. It was the kitchen, and she was in it, putting a brown earthenware dish into the oven. "The next door," said Barbara. He went hastily past the second door, and opened (he hoped quietly) the third. It was a cupboard full of linen. "This door," said Barbara, behind him.

"So all right then, where did you sleep?"

"What's it to do with you? Upstairs, in my own bed. Now, if you have everything, I'll say goodbye, I want to get to the theatre."

"I'll take you," he said at once.

He saw again the movement of her eyes, the dark swallowing the light in deadly boredom. "I'll take you," he insisted.

"I'd prefer to go by myself," she remarked. Then she smiled: "However, you'll take me. Then you'll make a point of coming right in, so that James and everyone can see—that's what you want to take me for, isn't it?"

He hated her, finally, and quite simply, for her intelligence; that not once had he got away with anything, that she had been watching, since they had met yesterday, every movement of his campaign for her. However, some fate or inner urge over which he had no control made him say sentimentally: "My dear, you must see that I'd like at least to take you to your work."

"Not at all, have it on me," she said, giving him the lie direct. She went past him to the room he had slept in. "I shall be leaving in ten minutes," she said.

He took a shower, fast. When he returned, the workroom was already tidied, the bed made, all signs of the night gone. Also, there were no signs of the coffee she had brought in for him. He did not like to ask for it, for fear of an outright refusal. Besides, she was ready, her coat on, her handbag under her arm. He went, without a word, to the front door, and she came after him, silent.

He could see that every fibre of her body signalled a simple message: Oh God, for the moment when I can be rid of this boor! She was nothing but a slut, he thought.

A taxi came. In it she sat as far away from him as she could. He thought of what he should say to his wife.

Outside the theatre she remarked: "You could drop me here, if you liked." It was not a plea, she was too proud for that. "I'll take you in," he said, and saw her thinking: Very well, I'll go through with it to shame him. He was determined to take her in and hand her over to her colleagues, he was afraid she would give him the slip. But far from playing it down, she seemed determined to play it his way. At the stage door, she said to the doorman: "This is Mr. Spence, Tom —do you remember, Mr. Spence from last night?" "Good morning, Babs," said the man, examining Graham, politely, as he had been ordered to do.

Barbara went to the door to the stage, opened it, held it open for him. He went in first, then held it open for her. Together they walked into the cavernous, littered, badly lit place and she called out: "James, James!" A man's voice called out from the front of the house: "Here, Babs, why are you so late?"

The auditorium opened before them, darkish, silent, save for an early-morning busyness of charwomen. A vacuum cleaner roared, smally, somewhere close. A couple of stagehands stood looking up at a drop which had a design of blue and green spirals. James stood with his back to the auditorium, smoking. "You're late, Babs," he said again. He saw Graham behind her, and nodded. Barbara and James kissed. Barbara said, giving allowance to every syllable: "You remember Mr. Spence from last night?" James nodded: How do you do? Barbara stood beside him, and they looked together up at the blue-and-green backdrop. Then Barbara looked again at Graham, asking silently: All right now, isn't that enough? He could see her eyes, sullen with boredom.

He said: "Bye, Babs. Bye, James. I'll ring you, Babs." No response, she ignored him. He walked off slowly, listening for what might be said. For instance: "Babs, for God's sake, what are you doing with him?" Or she might say: "Are you won-dering about Graham Spence? Let me explain."

Graham passed the stagehands who, he could have sworn, didn't recognise him. Then at last he heard James's voice to Barbara: "It's no good, Babs, I know you're enamoured of that particular shade of blue, but do have another look at it, there's a good girl. . . ." Graham left the stage, went past the office where the stage doorman sat reading a newspaper. He looked up, nodded, went back to his paper. Graham went to find a taxi, thinking: I'd better think up something convincing, then I'll telephone my wife.

Luckily he had an excuse not to be at home that day, for this evening he had to interview a young man (for television) about his new novel.

[1963]

QUESTIONS FOR STUDY

1. *What sort of man is Graham Spence? What is his private formula: "Yes, that one"? Why does he determine to seduce Barbara Coles? Why does he fail?*
2. *To what extent is Barbara aware of his motives and tactics? How does she respond to his advances? Why?*
3. *Why does the evening become for Graham Spence "the most embarrassing experience of his life"?*
4. *How might the story be different if told exclusively from Barbara's point of view?*

JACK LONDON
To Build a Fire

DAY HAD broken cold and grey, exceedingly cold and grey, when the man turned aside from the main Yukon trail and climbed the high earth-bank, where a dim and little-travelled trail led eastward through the fat spruce timberland. It was a steep bank, and he paused for breath at the top, excusing the act to himself by looking at his watch. It was nine o'clock. There was no sun nor hint of sun, though there was not a cloud in the sky. It was a clear day, and yet there seemed an intangible pall over the face of things, a subtle gloom that made the day dark, and that was due to the absence of sun. This fact did not worry the man. He was used to the lack of sun. It had been days since he had seen the sun, and he knew that a few more days must pass before that cheerful orb, due south, would just peep above the skyline and dip immediately from view.

The man flung a look back along the way he had come. The Yukon lay a mile wide and hidden under three feet of ice. On top of this ice were as many feet of snow. It was all pure white, rolling in gentle undulations where the ice jams of the freeze-up had formed. North and south, as far as his eye could see, it was unbroken white, save for a dark hairline that curved and twisted from around the spruce-covered island to the south, and that curved and twisted away into the north, where it disappeared behind another spruce-covered island. This dark hairline was the trail—the main trail—that led south five hundred miles to the Chilcoot Pass, Dyea, and salt water; and that led north seventy miles to Dawson, and still on to the north a thousand miles to Nulato, and finally to St. Michael, on Bering Sea, a thousand miles and half a thousand more.

But all this—the mysterious, far-reaching hairline trail, the absence of sun from the sky, the tremendous cold, and the strangeness and weirdness of it all—made no impression on the man. It was not because he was long used to it. He was a newcomer in the land, a *chechaquo,*[1] and this was his first winter. The trouble with him was that he was without imagination. He was quick and alert in the things of life, but only in the things, and not in the significances. Fifty degrees below zero meant eighty-odd degrees of frost. Such fact impressed him as being cold and uncomfortable, and that was all. It did not lead him to meditate upon his frailty as a creature of temperature, and upon man's frailty in general, able only to live within certain narrow limits of heat and cold; and from there on it did not lead him to the conjectural field of immortality and man's place in the universe. Fifty degrees below zero stood for a bite of frost that hurt and that must be guarded against by the use of mittens, ear flaps, warm moccasins, and thick socks. Fifty degrees below zero. That there should be anything more to it than that was a thought that never entered his head.

As he turned to go on, he spat speculatively. There was a sharp explosive crackle that startled him. He spat again. And again, in the air, before it could fall to the snow, the spittle crackled. He knew that at fifty below spittle crackled on the snow, but this spittle had crackled in the air. Undoubtedly it was colder than fifty below—how much colder he did not know. But the temperature did not matter. He was bound for the old claim on the left fork of Henderson Creek, where the boys were already. They had come over across the divide from the Indian Creek country, while he had come the roundabout way to take a look at the possibilities of getting out

1 A tenderfoot. (JHP)

logs in the spring from the islands in the Yukon. He would be in to camp by six o'clock; a bit after dark, it was true, but the boys would be there, a fire would be going, and a hot supper would be ready. As for lunch, he pressed his hand against the protruding bundle under his jacket. It was also under his shirt, wrapped up in a handkerchief and lying against the naked skin. It was the only way to keep the biscuits from freezing. He smiled agreeably to himself as he thought of those biscuits, each cut open and sopped in bacon grease, and each enclosing a generous slice of fried bacon.

He plunged in among the big spruce trees. The trail was faint. A foot of snow had fallen since the last sled had passed over, and he was glad he was without a sled, travelling light. In fact, he carried nothing but the lunch wrapped in the handkerchief. He was surprised, however, at the cold. It certainly was cold, he concluded, as he rubbed his numb nose and cheekbones with his mittened hand. He was a warm-whiskered man, but the hair on his face did not protect the high cheekbones and the eager nose that thrust itself aggressively into the frosty air.

At the man's heels trotted a dog, a big native husky, the proper wolf-dog, grey-coated and without any visible or temperamental difference from its brother, the wild wolf. The animal was depressed by the tremendous cold. It knew that it was no time for travelling. Its instinct told it a truer tale than was told to the man by the man's judgment. In reality, it was not merely colder than fifty below zero; it was colder than sixty below, than seventy below. It was seventy-five below zero. Since the freezing point is thirty-two above zero, it meant that one hundred and seven degrees of frost obtained. The dog did not know anything about thermometers. Possibly in its brain there was no sharp consciousness of a condition of very cold such as was in the man's brain. But the brute had its instinct. It experienced a vague but menacing apprehension that subdued it and made it slink along at the man's heels, and that made it question eagerly every unwonted movement of the man as if expecting him to go into camp or to seek shelter somewhere and build a fire. The dog had learned fire, and it wanted fire, or else to burrow under the snow and cuddle its warmth away from the air.

The frozen moisture of its breathing had settled on its fur in a fine powder of frost, and especially were its jowls, muzzle, and eyelashes whitened by its crystal breath. The man's red beard and moustache were likewise frosted, but more solidly, the deposit taking the form of ice and increasing with every warm, moist breath he exhaled. Also, the man was chewing tobacco, and the muzzle of ice held his lips so rigidly that he was unable to clear his chin when he expelled the juice. The result was a crystal beard of the colour and solidity of amber was increasing its length on his chin. If he fell down it would shatter itself, like glass, into brittle fragments. But he did not mind the appendage. It was the penalty all tobacco chewers paid in that country, and he had been out before in two cold snaps. They had not been so cold as this, he knew, but by the spirit thermometer at Sixty Mile he knew they had been registered at fifty below and at fifty-five.

He held on through the level stretch of woods for several miles, crossed a wide flat of nigger heads, and dropped down a bank to the frozen bed of a small stream. This was Henderson Creek, and he knew he was ten miles from the forks. He looked at his watch. It was ten o'clock. He was making four miles an hour, and he calculated that he would arrive at the forks at half-past twelve. He decided to celebrate that event by eating his lunch there.

The dog dropped in again at his heels, with a tail drooping discouragement, as the man swung along the creek bed. The furrow of the old sled trail was plainly visible, but a dozen inches of snow covered up the marks of the last runners. In a month no man had come up or down that silent creek. The man held steadily on. He was not much given to thinking, and just then particularly he had nothing to think about save that he would eat lunch at the forks and that at six o'clock he would be in camp with the boys. There was nobody to talk to; and, had there been, speech would have been impossible because of the ice muzzle on his mouth. So he continued monotonously to chew tobacco and to increase the length of his amber beard. ·

Once in a while the thought reiterated itself that it was very cold and that he had never experienced such cold. As he walked along he rubbed his cheekbones and nose with the back of his mittened hand. He did this automatically, now and again changing hands. But, rub as he would, the instant he stopped his cheekbones went numb, and the following instant the end of his nose went numb. He was sure to frost his cheeks; he knew that, and experienced a pang of regret that he had not devised a nose strap of the sort Bud wore in cold snaps. Such a strap passed across the cheeks, as well, and saved them. But it didn't matter much, after all. What were frosted cheeks? A bit painful, that was all; they were never serious.

Empty as the man's mind was of thoughts, he was keenly observant, and he noticed the changes in the creeks, the curves and bends and timber jams, and always he sharply noted where he placed his feet. Once, coming round a bend, he shied abruptly, like a startled horse, curved away from the place where he had been walking, and retreated several paces back along the trail. The creek he knew was frozen clear to the bottom—no creek could contain water in that arctic winter—but he knew also that there were springs that bubbled out from the hillsides and ran along under the snow and on top of the ice of the creek. He knew that the coldest snaps never froze these springs, and he knew likewise their danger. They were traps. They hid pools of water under the snow that might be three inches deep, or three feet. Sometimes a skin of ice half an inch thick covered them, and in turn was covered by the snow. Sometimes there were alternate layers of water and ice skin, so that when one broke through he kept on breaking through for a while, sometimes wetting himself to the waist.

That was why he had shied in such a panic. He had felt the give under his feet and heard the crackle of a snow-hidden ice skin. And to get his feet wet in such a temperature meant trouble and danger. At the very least it meant delay, for he would be forced to stop and build a fire, and under its protection to bare his feet while he dried his socks and moccasins. He stood and studied the creek bed and its banks, and decided that the flow of water came from the right. He reflected awhile, rubbing his nose and cheeks, then skirted to the left, stepping gingerly and testing the footing for each step. Once clear of the danger, he took a fresh chew of tobacco and swung along at his four-mile gait.

In the course of the next two hours he came upon several similar traps. Usually the snow above the hidden pools had a sunken, candied appearance that advertised the danger. Once again, however, he compelled the dog to go on in front. The dog did not want to go. It hung back until the man shoved it forward, and then it went quickly across the white, unbroken surface. Suddenly it broke through, floundered to one side, and got away to firmer footing. It had wet its forefeet and legs, and almost immediately the water that clung to it turned to ice. It made quick efforts to lick the ice off its legs, then dropped down in the snow and began to bite out the ice that had formed between the toes. This was a matter of instinct. To permit the ice to remain would mean sore feet. It did not know this. It merely obeyed the mysterious prompting that arose from the deep crypts of its being. But the man knew, having achieved a judgment on the subject, and he removed the mitten from his right hand and helped to tear out the ice particles. He did not expose his fingers more than a minute, and was astonished at the swift numbness that smote them. It certainly was cold. He pulled on the mitten hastily, and beat the hand savagely across the chest.

At twelve o'clock the day was at its brightest. Yet the sun was too far south on its winter journey to clear the horizon. The bulge of the earth intervened between it and Henderson Creek, where the man walked under a clear sky at noon and cast no shadow. At half-past twelve, to the minute, he arrived at the forks of the creek. He was pleased at the speed he had made. If he kept it up, he would certainly be with the boys by six. He unbuttoned his jacket and shirt and drew forth his lunch. The action consumed no more than a quarter of a minute, yet in that brief moment the numbness laid hold of the exposed fingers. He did not put the mitten on, but, instead, struck the fingers a dozen sharp smashes against his leg. Then he sat down on a snow-covered log to eat. The sting that followed upon the striking of his fingers against his leg ceased so quickly that he was startled. He had had no chance to take a bite of biscuit. He struck the fingers repeatedly and returned them to the mitten, baring the other hand for the purpose of eating. He tried to take a mouthful, but the ice muzzle prevented. He had forgotten to build a fire and thaw out. He chuckled at his foolishness, and as he chuckled he noted the numbness creeping into the exposed fingers. Also, he noted that the stinging which had first come to his toes when he sat down was already passing away. He wondered whether the toes were warm or numb. He moved them inside the moccasins and decided that they were numb.

He pulled the mitten on hurriedly and stood up. He was a bit frightened. He stamped up and down until the stinging returned into the feet. It certainly was cold, was his thought. That man from Sulphur Creek had spoken the truth when telling how cold it sometimes got in the country. And he had laughed at him at the time! That showed one must not be too sure of things. There was no mistake about it, it *was* cold. He strode up and down, stamping his feet and threshing his arms, until reassured by the returning warmth. Then he got out matches and proceeded to make a fire. From the undergrowth, where high water of the previous spring had lodged a supply of seasoned twigs, he got his firewood. Working carefully from a small beginning, he soon had a roaring fire, over which he thawed the ice from his face and in the protection of which he ate his biscuits. For the moment the cold of space was outwitted. The dog took satisfaction in the fire, stretching out close enough for warmth and far enough away to escape being singed.

When the man had finished, he filled his pipe and took his comfortable time over a smoke. Then he pulled on his mittens, settled the ear-flaps of his cap firmly about his ears, and took the creek trail up the left fork. The dog was disappointed and yearned back towards the fire. This man did not know cold. Possibly all the generations of his ancestry had been ignorant of cold, of real cold, of cold one hundred and seven degrees below freezing point. But the dog knew; all its ancestry knew, and it had inherited the knowledge. And it knew that it was not good to walk abroad in such fearful cold. It was the time to lie snug in a hole in the snow and wait for a curtain of cloud to be drawn across the face of outer space whence this cold came. On the other hand, there was no keen intimacy between the dog and the man. The one was the toil slave of the other, and the only caresses it had ever received were the caresses of the whip lash and of harsh and menacing throat sounds that threatened the whip lash. So the dog made no effort to communicate its apprehension to the man. It was not concerned in the welfare of the man; it was for its own sake that it yearned back towards the fire. But the man whistled, and spoke to it with the sound of whip lashes, and the dog swung in at the man's heels and followed after.

The man took a chew of tobacco and proceeded to start a new amber beard. Also, his moist breath quickly powdered with white his moustache, eyebrows, and lashes. There did not seem to be so many springs on the left fork of the Henderson, and for half an hour the man saw no signs of any. And then it happened. At a place where there were no signs, where the soft, unbroken snow seemed to advertise solidity beneath, the man broke through. It was not deep. He wet himself half-way to the knees before he floundered out to the firm crust.

He was angry, and cursed his luck

aloud. He had hoped to get into camp with the boys at six o'clock, and this would delay him an hour, for he would have to build a fire and dry out his footgear. This was imperative at that low temperature—he knew that much; and he turned aside to the bank, which he climbed. On top, tangled in the underbrush about the trunks of several small spruce trees, was a highwater deposit of dry firewood—sticks and twigs, principally, but also larger portions of seasoned branches and fine, dry, last year's grasses. He threw down several large pieces on top of the snow. This served for a foundation and prevented the young flame from drowning itself in the snow it otherwise would melt. The flame he got by touching a match to a small shred of birch bark that he took from his pocket. This burned even more readily than paper. Placing it on the foundation, he fed the young flame with wisps of dry grass and with the tiniest dry twigs.

He worked slowly and carefully, keenly aware of his danger. Gradually, as the flame grew stronger, he increased the size of the twigs with which he fed it. He squatted in the snow pulling the twigs out from their entanglement in the brush and feeding directly to the flame. He knew there must be no failure. When it is seventy-five below zero, a man must not fail in his first attempt to build a fire—that is, if his feet are wet. If his feet are dry, and he fails, he can run along the trail for half a mile and restore his circulation. But the circulation of wet and freezing feet cannot be restored by running when it is seventy-five below. No matter how fast he runs, the wet feet will freeze the harder.

All this the man knew. The old-timer on Sulphur Creek had told him about it the previous fall, and now he was appreciating the advice. Already all sensation had gone out of his feet. To build the fire he had been forced to remove his mittens, and the fingers had quickly gone numb. His pace of four miles an hour had kept his heart pumping blood to the surface of his body and to all the extremities. But the instant he stopped, the action of the pump eased down. The cold of space smote the unprotected tip of the planet, and he, being on that unprotected tip, received the full force of the blow. The blood of his body recoiled before it. The blood was alive, like the dog, and like the dog it wanted to hide away and cover itself up from the fearful cold. So long as he walked four miles an hour, he pumped that blood, willy-nilly, to the surface; but now it ebbed away and sank down into the recesses of his body. The extremities were the first to feel its absence. His wet feet froze the faster, and his exposed fingers numbed the faster, though they had not yet begun to freeze. Nose and cheeks were already freezing, while the skin of all his body chilled as it lost its blood.

But he was safe. Toes and nose and cheeks would be only touched by the frost, for the fire was beginning to burn with strength. He was feeding it with twigs the size of his finger. In another minute he would be able to feed it with branches the size of his wrist, and then he could remove his wet footgear, and, while it dried, he could keep his naked feet warm by the fire, rubbing them at first, of course, with snow. The fire was a success. He was safe. He remembered the advice of the old-timer on Sulphur Creek, and smiled. The old-timer had been very serious in laying down the law that no man must travel alone in the Klondike after fifty below. Well, here he was; he had had the accident; he was alone; and he had saved himself. Those old-timers were rather womanish, some of them, he thought. All a man had to do was to keep his head, and he was all right. Any man who was a man could travel alone. But it was surprising, the rapidity with which his cheeks and nose were freezing. And he had not thought his fingers could go lifeless in so short a time. Lifeless they were, for he could scarcely make them move together to grip a twig, and they seemed remote from his body and from him. When he touched a twig, he had to look and see whether or not he had hold of it. The wires were pretty well down between him and his finger ends.

All of which counted for little. There was the fire, snapping and crackling and promising life with every dancing flame.

He started to untie his moccasins. They were coated with ice; the thick German socks were like sheaths of iron halfway to the knees; and the moccasin strings were like rods of steel all twisted and knotted as by some conflagration. For a moment he tugged with his numb fingers, then, realizing the folly of it, he drew his sheath knife.

But before he could cut the strings, it happened. It was his own fault or, rather, his mistake. He should not have built the fire under the spruce tree. He should have built it in the open. But it had been easier to pull the twigs from the brush and drop them directly on the fire. Now the tree under which he had done this carried a weight of snow on its boughs. No wind had blown for weeks, and each bough was fully freighted. Each time he had pulled a twig he had communicated a slight agitation to the tree—an imperceptible agitation, so far as he was concerned, but an agitation sufficient to bring about the disaster. High up in the tree one bough capsized its load of snow. This fell on the boughs beneath, capsizing them. This process continued, spreading out and involving the whole tree. It grew like an avalanche, and it descended without warning upon the man and the fire, and the fire was blotted out! Where it had burned was a mantle of fresh and disordered snow.

The man was shocked. It was as though he had just heard his own sentence of death. For a moment he sat and stared at the spot where the fire had been. Then he grew very calm. Perhaps the old-timer on Sulphur Creek was right. If he had only had a trail mate he would have been in no danger now. The trail mate could have built the fire. Well, it was up to him to build the fire over again, and this second time there must be no failure. Even if he succeeded, he would most likely lose some toes. His feet must be badly frozen by now, and there would be some time before the second fire was ready.

Such were his thoughts, but he did not sit and think them. He was busy all the time they were passing through his mind. He made a new foundation for a fire, this time in the open, where no treacherous tree could blot it out. Next he gathered dry grasses and tiny twigs from the high-water flotsam. He could not bring his fingers together to pull them out, but he was able to gather them by the handful. In this way he got many rotten twigs and bits of green moss that were undesirable, but it was the best he could do. He worked methodically, even collecting an armful of the larger branches to be used later when the fire gathered strength. And all the while the dog sat and watched him, a certain yearning wistfulness in its eyes, for it looked upon him as the fire provider, and the fire was slow in coming.

When all was ready, the man reached in his pocket for a second piece of birch bark. He knew the bark was there, and, though he could not feel it with his fingers, he could hear its crisp rustling as he fumbled for it. Try as he would, he could not clutch hold of it. And all the time, in his consciousness, was the knowledge that each instant his feet were freezing. This thought tended to put him in a panic, but he fought against it and kept calm. He pulled on his mittens with his teeth, and threshed his arms back and forth, beating his hands with all his might against his sides. He did this sitting down, and he stood up to do it; and all the while the dog sat in the snow, its wolf brush of a tail curled around warmly over its forefront, its sharp wolf ears pricked forward intently as it watched the man. And the man, as he beat and threshed with his arms and hands, felt a great surge of envy as he regarded the creature that was warm and secure in its natural covering.

After a time he was aware of the first faraway signals of sensation in his beaten fingers. The faint tingling grew stronger till it evolved into a stinging ache that was excruciating, but which the man hailed with satisfaction. He stripped the mitten from his right hand and fetched forth the birch bark. The exposed fingers were quickly going numb again. Next he brought out his bunch of sulphur matches. But the tremendous cold had already driven the life out of his fingers.

In his effort to separate one match from the others, the whole bunch fell in the snow. He tried to pick it out of the snow, but failed. The dead fingers could neither touch nor clutch. He was very careful. He drove the thought of his freezing feet, and nose, and cheeks, out of his mind, devoting his whole soul to the matches. He watched, using the sense of vision in place of that touch, and when he saw his fingers on each side of the bunch, he closed them—that is, he willed to close them, for the wires were down, and the fingers did not obey. He pulled the mitten on the right hand, and beat it fiercely against his knee. Then with both mittened hands, he scooped the bunch of matches, along with much snow, into his lap. Yet he was no better off.

After some manipulation he managed to get the bunch between the heels of his mittened hands. In this fashion he carried it to his mouth. The ice crackled and snapped when by a violent effort he opened his mouth. He drew the lower jaw in, curled the upper lip out of the way, and scraped the bunch with his upper teeth in order to separate a match. He succeeded in getting one, which he dropped on his lap. He was no better off. He could not pick it up. Then he devised a way. He picked it up in his teeth and scratched it on his leg. Twenty times he scratched before he succeeded in lighting it. As it flamed he held it with his teeth to the birch bark. But the burning brimstone went up his nostrils and into his lungs, causing him to cough spasmodically. The match fell into the snow and went out.

The old-timer on Sulphur Creek was right, he thought in the moment of controlled despair that ensued: after fifty below, a man should travel with a partner. He beat his hands, but failed in exciting any sensation. Suddenly he bared both hands, removing the mittens with his teeth. He caught the whole bunch between the heels of his hands. His arm muscles not being frozen enabled him to press the hand heels tightly against the matches. Then he scratched the bunch along his leg. It flared into flame, seventy sulphur matches at once! There was no wind to blow them out. He kept his head to one side to escape the strangling fumes, and held the blazing bunch to the birch bark. As he so held it, he became aware of sensation in his hand. His flesh was burning. He could smell it. Deep down below the surface he could feel it. The sensation developed into pain that grew acute. And still he endured it, holding the flame of the matches clumsily to the bark that would not light readily because his own burning hands were in the way, absorbing most of the flame.

At last, when he could endure no more, he jerked his hands apart. The blazing matches fell sizzling into the snow, but the birch bark was alight. He began laying dry grasses and the tiniest twigs on the flame. He could not pick and choose, for he had to lift the fuel between the heels of his hands. Small pieces of rotten wood and green moss clung to the twigs, and he bit them off as well as he could with his teeth. He cherished the flame carefully and awkwardly. It meant life, and it must not perish. The withdrawal of blood from the surface of his body now made him begin to shiver, and he grew more awkward. A large piece of green moss fell squarely on the little fire. He tried to poke it out with his fingers, but his shivering frame made him poke too far, and he disrupted the nucleus of the little fire, the burning grasses and tiny twigs separating and scattering. He tried to poke them together again, but in spite of the tenseness of the effort, his shivering got away with him, and the twigs were hopelessly scattered. Each twig gushed a puff of smoke and went out. The fire provider had failed. As he looked apathetically about him, his eyes chanced on the dog, sitting across the ruins of the fire from him, in the snow, making restless, hunching movements, slightly lifting one forefoot and then the other, shifting its weight back and forth on them with wistful eagerness.

The sight of the dog put a wild idea into his head. He remembered the tale of the man, caught in a blizzard, who killed a steer and crawled inside the carcass, and so was saved. He would kill the dog and bury his hands in the warm body un-til the numbness went out of them. Then he could build another fire. He spoke to the dog, calling it to him; but in his voice was a strange note of fear that frightened the animal, who had never known the man to speak in such a way before. Something was the matter, and its suspicious nature sensed danger—it know not what danger, but somewhere, somehow, in its brain arose an apprehension of the man. It flattened its ears down at the sound of the man's voice, and its restless, hunch-ing movements and the liftings and shift-ings of its forefeet became more pro-nounced; but it would not come to the man. He got on his hands and knees and crawled towards the dog. This unusual posture again excited suspicion, and the animal sidled mincingly away.

The man sat up in the snow for a mo-ment and struggled for calmness. Then he pulled on his mittens, by means of his teeth, and got upon his feet. He glanced down at first in order to assure himself that he was really standing up, for the absence of sensation in his feet left him unrelated to the earth. His erect position in itself started to drive the webs of sus-picion from the dog's mind; and when he spoke peremptorily, with the sound of whip lashes in his voice, the dog rendered its customary allegiance and came to him. As it came within reaching distance, the man lost his control. His arms flashed out to the dog, and he experienced genu-ine surprise when he discovered that his hands could not clutch, that there was neither bend nor feeling in the fingers. He had forgotten for the moment that they were frozen and that they were freezing more and more. All this hap-pened quickly, and before the animal could get away, he encircled its body with his arms. He sat down in the snow, and in this fashion held the dog, while it snarled and whined and struggled.

But it was all he could do, hold its body encircled in his arms and sit there. He realized he could not kill the dog. There was no way to do it. With his help-less hands he could neither draw nor hold his sheath knife nor throttle the animal. He released it, and it plunged wildly away, with tail between its legs, and still snarling. It halted forty feet away and surveyed him curiously, with ears sharply pricked forward.

The man looked down at his hands in order to locate them, and found them hanging on the ends of his arms. It struck him as curious that one should have to use his eyes in order to find out where his hands were. He began threshing his arms back and forth, beating the mit-tened hands against his sides. He did this for five minutes, violently, and his heart pumped enough blood up to the surface to put a stop to his shivering. But no sensation was aroused in the hands. He had an impression that they hung like weights on the ends of his arms, but when he tried to run the impression down, he could not find it.

A certain fear of death, dull and op-pressive, came to him. This fear quickly became poignant as he realized that it was no longer a mere matter of freezing his fingers and toes, or of losing his hands and feet, but that it was a matter of life and death with the chances against him. This threw him into a panic, and he turned and ran up the creek bed along the old, dim trail. The dog joined in be-hind him and kept up with him. He ran blindly, without intention, in fear such as he had never known in his life. Slowly, as he ploughed and floundered through the snow, he began to see things again— the banks of the creek, the old timber jams, the leafless aspens, and the sky. The running made him feel better. He did not shiver. Maybe, if he ran on, his feet would thaw out; and, anyway, if he ran far enough, he would reach camp and the boys. Without doubt he would lose some fingers and toes and some of his face; but the boys would take care of him, and save the rest of him when he got there. And at the same time there was another thought in his mind that said he would never get to the camp and the boys; that it was too many miles away, that the freezing had too great a start on him, and that he would soon be stiff and dead. This thought he kept in the back-ground and refused to consider. Some-times it pushed itself forward and demanded to be heard, but he thrust it back and strove to think of other things.

It struck him as curious that he could run at all on feet so frozen that he could not feel them when they struck the earth and took the weight of his body. He seemed to himself to skim along above the surface, and to have no connection with the earth. Somewhere he had once seen a winged Mercury, and he wondered if Mercury felt as he felt when skimming over the earth.

His theory of running until he reached camp and the boys had one flaw in it: he lacked the endurance. Several times he stumbled, and finally he tottered, crumpled up, and fell. When he tried to rise, he failed. He must sit and rest, he decided, and next time he would merely walk and keep on going. As he sat and regained his breath, he noted that he was feeling quite warm and comfortable. He was not shivering, and it even seemed that a warm glow had come to his chest and trunk. And yet, when he touched his nose or cheeks, there was no sensation. Running would not thaw them out. Nor would it thaw out his hands and feet. Then the thought came to him that the frozen portions of his body must be extending. He tried to keep this thought down, to forget it, to think of something else; he was aware of the panicky feeling that it caused, and he was afraid of the panic. But the thought asserted itself, and persisted, until it produced a vision of his body totally frozen. This was too much, and he made another wild run along the trail. Once he slowed down to a walk, but the thought of the freezing extending itself made him run again.

And all the time the dog ran with him, at his heels. When he fell down a second time, it curled its tail over its forefeet and sat in front of him, facing him, curiously eager and intent. The warmth and security of the animal angered him, and he cursed it till it flattened down its ears appeasingly. This time the shivering came more quickly upon the man. He was losing in his battle with the frost. It was creeping into his body from all sides. The thought of it drove him on, but he ran no more than a hundred feet, when he

staggered and pitched headlong. It was his last panic. When he had recovered his breath and control, he sat up and entertained in his mind the conception of meeting death with dignity. However, the conception did not come to him in such terms. His idea of it was that he had been making a fool of himself, running around like a chicken with its head cut off—such was the simile that occurred to him. Well, he was bound to freeze anyway, and he might as well take it decently. With this new-found peace of mind came the first glimmerings of drowsiness. A good idea, he thought, to sleep off to death. It was like taking an anaesthetic. Freezing was not so bad as people thought. There were lots worse ways to die.

He pictured the boys finding his body next day. Suddenly he found himself with them, coming along the trail looking for himself. And, still with them, he came around a turn in the trail and found himself lying in the snow. He did not belong with himself any more, for even then he was out of himself, standing with the boys and looking at himself in the snow. It certainly was cold, was his thought. When he got back to the States he could tell the folks what real cold was. He drifted on from this to a vision of the old-timer on Sulphur Creek. He could see him quite clearly, warm and comfortable, and smoking a pipe.

'You were right, old hoss; you were right,' the man mumbled to the old-timer of Sulphur Creek.

Then the man drowsed off into what seemed to him the most comfortable and satisfying sleep he had even known. The dog sat facing him and waiting. The brief day drew to a close in a long, slow twilight. There were no signs of a fire to be made, and, besides, never in the dog's experience had it known a man to sit like that in the snow and make no fire. As the twilight drew on, its eager yearning for the fire mastered it, and with a great lifting and shifting of forefeet, it whined softly, then flattened its ears down in anticipation of being chidden by the man. But the man remained silent. Later the dog whined loudly. And still later it crept close to the man and caught the scent of death. This made the animal bristle and back away. A little longer it delayed, howling under the stars that leaped and danced and shone brightly in the cold sky. Then it turned and trotted up the trail in the direction of the camp it knew, where were the other food providers and fire providers.

[1908]

QUESTIONS FOR STUDY

1. *What does London mean when he writes of his nameless protagonist that "The trouble with him was that he was without imagination"? How does this fact contribute to the man's death? Are there other contributing factors as well?*

2. *The dog and the "old timer" are both able to survive the cold of a Klondike winter. Why? In what ways do they serve as foils to the tenderfoot?*

3. *What is the dominant mood of the story? How does London's prose style (particularly his use of imagery) serve to establish and then to intensify that mood?*

4. *What comment does the story make about the relationship between man and nature?*

5. *Does the story have a theme? If it does, describe it.*

CARSON McCULLERS

A Tree, A Rock, A Cloud

IT WAS raining that morning, and still very dark. When the boy reached the streetcar café he had almost finished his route and he went in for a cup of coffee. The place was an all-night café owned by a bitter and stingy man called Leo. After the raw, empty street the café seemed friendly and bright: along the counter there were a couple of soldiers, three spinners from the cotton mill, and in a corner a man who sat hunched over with his nose and half his face down in a beer mug. The boy wore a helmet such as aviators wear. When he went into the café he unbuckled the chin strap and raised the right flap up over his pink little ear; often as he drank his coffee someone would speak to him in a friendly way. But this morning Leo did not look into his face and none of the men were talking. He paid and was leaving the café when a voice called out to him:

'Son! Hey Son!'

He turned back and the man in the corner was crooking his finger and nodding to him. He had brought his face out of the beer mug and he seemed suddenly very happy. The man was long and pale, with a big nose and faded orange hair.

'Hey Son!'

The boy went toward him. He was an undersized boy of about twelve, with one shoulder drawn higher than the other because of the weight of the paper sack. His face was shallow, freckled, and his eyes were round child eyes.

'Yeah Mister?'

The man laid one hand on the paper boy's shoulders, then grasped the boy's chin and turned his face slowly from one side to the other. The boy shrank back uneasily.

'Say! What's the big idea?'

The boy's voice was shrill; inside the café it was suddenly very quiet.

The man said slowly: 'I love you.'

All along the counter the men laughed. The boy, who had scowled and sidled away, did not know what to do. He looked over the counter at Leo, and Leo watched him with a weary, brittle jeer. The boy tried to laugh also. But the man was serious and sad.

'I did not mean to tease you, Son,' he said. 'Sit down and have a beer with me. There is something I have to explain.'

Cautiously, out of the corner of his eye, the paper boy questioned the men along the counter to see what he should do. But they had gone back to their beer or their breakfast and did not notice him. Leo put a cup of coffee on the counter and a little jug of cream.

'He is a minor,' Leo said.

The paper boy slid himself up onto the stool. His ear beneath the upturned flap of the helmet was very small and red. The man was nodding at him soberly. 'It is important,' he said. Then he reached in his hip pocket and brought out something which he held up in the palm of his hand for the boy to see.

'Look very carefully,' he said.

The boy stared, but there was nothing to look at very carefully. The man held in his big, grimy palm a photograph. It was the face of a woman, but blurred, so that only the hat and the dress she was wearing stood out clearly.

'See?' the man asked.

The boy nodded and the man placed another picture in his palm. The woman was standing on a beach in a bathing suit. The suit made her stomach very big, and that was the main thing you noticed.

'Got a good look?' He leaned over

closer and finally asked: 'You ever seen her before?'

The boy sat motionless, staring slantwise at the man. 'Not so I know of.'

'Very well.' The man blew on the photographs and put them back into his pocket. 'That was my wife.'

'Dead?' the boy asked.

Slowly the man shook his head. He pursed his lips as though about to whistle and answered in a long-drawn way: 'Nuuu—' he said. 'I will explain.'

The beer on the counter before the man was in a large brown mug. He did not pick it up to drink. Instead he bent down and, putting his face over the rim, he rested there for a moment. Then with both hands he tilted the mug and sipped.

'Some night you'll go to sleep with your nose in a mug and drown,' said Leo. 'Prominent transient drowns in beer. That would be a cute death.'

The paper boy tried to signal to Leo. While the man was not looking he screwed up his face and worked his mouth to question soundlessly: 'Drunk?' But Leo only raised his eyebrows and turned away to put some pink strips of bacon on the grill. The man pushed the mug away from him, straightened himself, and folded his loose crooked hands on the counter. His face was sad as he looked at the paper boy. He did not blink, but from time to time the lids closed down with delicate gravity over his pale green eyes. It was nearing dawn and the boy shifted the weight of the paper sack.

'I am talking about love,' the man said. 'With me it is a science.'

The boy half slid down from the stool. But the man raised his forefinger, and there was something about him that held the boy and would not let him go away.

'Twelve years ago I married the woman in the photograph. She was my wife for one year, nine months, three days, and two nights. I loved her. Yes . . .' He tightened his blurred, rambling voice and said again: 'I loved her. I thought also that she loved me. I was a railroad engineer. She had all home comforts and luxuries. It never crept into my brain that she was not satisfied. But do you know what happened?'

'Mgneeow!' said Leo.

The man did not take his eyes from the boy's face. 'She left me. I came in one night and the house was empty and she, was gone. She left me.'

'With a fellow?' the boy asked.

Gently the man placed his palm down on the counter. 'Why naturally, Son. A woman does not run off like that alone.'

The café was quiet, the soft rain black and endless in the street outside. Leo pressed down the frying bacon with the prongs of his long fork. 'So you have been chasing the floozie for eleven years. You frazzled old rascal!'

For the first time the man glanced at Leo. 'Please don't be vulgar. Besides, I was not speaking to you.' He turned back to the boy and said in a trusting and secretive undertone: 'Let's not pay any attention to him. O.K.?'

The paper boy nodded doubtfully.

'It was like this,' the man continued. 'I am a person who feels many things. All my life one thing after another has impressed me. Moonlight. The leg of a pretty girl. One thing after another. But the point is that when I had enjoyed anything there was a peculiar sensation as though it was laying around loose in me. Nothing seemed to finish itself up or fit in with the other things. Women? I had my portion of them. The same. Afterwards laying around loose in me. I was a man who had never loved.'

Very slowly he closed his eyelids, and the gesture was like a curtain drawn at the end of a scene in a play. When he spoke again his voice was excited and the words came fast—the lobes of his large, loose ears seemed to tremble.

'Then I met this woman. I was fifty-one and she always said she was thirty. I met her at a filling station and we were married within three days. And do you know what it was like? I just can't tell you. All I had ever felt was gathered together around this woman. Nothing lay loose in me any more but was finished up by her.'

The man stopped suddenly and stroked his long nose. His voice sank down to a steady and reproachful undertone: 'I'm not explaining this right. What happened was this. There were these beautiful feelings and loose little pleasures inside me. And this woman was something like an assembly line for my soul. I run these little pieces of myself through her and I come out complete. Now do you follow me?'

'What was her name?' the boy asked.

'Oh,' he said. 'I called her Dodo. But that is immaterial.'

'Did you try to make her come back?'

The man did not seem to hear. 'Under the circumstances you can imagine how I felt when she left me.'

Leo took the bacon from the grill and folded two strips of it between a bun. He had a gray face, with slitted eyes, and a pinched nose saddled by faint blue shadows. One of the mill workers signaled for more coffee and Leo poured it. He did not give refills on coffee free. The spinner ate breakfast there every morning, but the better Leo knew his customers the stingier he treated them. He nibbled his own bun as though he grudged it to himself.

'And you never got hold of her again?'

The boy did not know what to think of the man, and his child's face was uncertain with mingled curiosity and doubt. He was new on the paper route; it was still strange to him to be out in the town in the black, queer early morning.

'Yes,' the man said. 'I took a number of steps to get her back. I went around trying to locate her. I went to Tulsa where she had folks. And to Mobile. I went to every town she had ever mentioned to me, and I hunted down every man she had formerly been connected with. Tulsa, Atlanta, Chicago, Cheehaw, Memphis. . . . For the better part of two years I chased around the country trying to lay hold of her.'

'But the pair of them had vanished from the face of the earth!' said Leo.

'Don't listen to him,' the man said confidentially. 'And also just forget those two years. They are not important. What matters is that around the third year a curious thing begun to happen to me.'

'What?' the boy asked.

The man leaned down and tilted his mug to take a sip of beer. But as he hovered over the mug his nostrils fluttered slightly; he sniffed the staleness of the beer and did not drink. 'Love is a curious thing to begin with. At first 1 thought only of getting her back. It was a kind of mania. But then as time went on I tried to remember her. But do you know what happened?'

'No,' the boy said.

'When I laid myself down on a bed and tried to think about her my mind became a blank. I couldn't see her. I would take out her pictures and look. No good. Nothing doing. A blank. Can you imagine it?'

'Say Mac!' Leo called down the counter. 'Can you imagine this bozo's mind a blank!'

Slowly, as though fanning away flies, the man waved his hand. His green eyes were concentrated and fixed on the shallow little face of the paper boy.

'But a sudden piece of glass on a sidewalk. Or a nickel tune in a music box. A shadow on a wall at night. And I would remember. It might happen in a street and I would cry or bang my head against a lamppost. You follow me?'

'A piece of glass . . .' the boy said.

'Anything. I would walk around and I had no power of how and when to remember her. You think you can put up a kind of shield. But remembering don't come to a man face forward—it corners around sideways. I was at the mercy of everything I saw and heard. Suddenly instead of me combing the countryside to find her she begun to chase me around in my very soul. *She* chasing *me*, mind you! And in my soul.'

The boy asked finally: 'What part of the country were you in then?'

'Ooh,' the man groaned. 'I was a sick mortal. It was like smallpox. I confess, Son, that I boozed. I fornicated. I committed any sin that suddenly appealed to me. I am loath to confess it but I will do so. When I recall that period it is all curdled in my mind, it was so terrible.'

The man leaned his head down and tapped his forehead on the counter. For a few seconds he stayed bowed over in this position, the back of his stringy neck covered with orange furze, his hands with their long warped fingers held palm to palm in an attitude of prayer. Then the man straightened himself; he was smiling and suddenly his face was bright and tremulous and old.

'It was in the fifth year that it happened,' he said. 'And with it I started my science.'

Leo's mouth jerked with a pale, quick grin. 'Well none of we boys are getting any younger,' he said. Then with sudden anger he balled up a dishcloth he was holding and threw it down hard on the floor. 'You draggle-tailed old Romeo!'

'What happened?' the boy asked.

The old man's voice was high and clear: 'Peace,' he answered.

'Huh?'

'It is hard to explain scientifically, Son,' he said. 'I guess the logical explanation is that she and I had fleed around from each other for so long that finally we just got tangled up together and lay down and quit. Peace. A queer and beautiful blankness. It was spring in Portland and the rain came every afternoon. All evening I just stayed there on my bed in the dark. And that is how the science come to me.'

The windows in the streetcar were pale blue with light. The two soldiers paid for their beers and opened the door —one of the soldiers combed his hair and wiped off his muddy puttees before they went outside. The three mill workers bent silently over their breakfasts. Leo's clock was ticking on the wall.

'It is this. And listen carefully. I meditated on love and reasoned it out. I reasoned it out. I realized what is wrong with us. Men fall in love for the first time. And what do they fall in love with?'

The boy's soft mouth was partly open and he did not answer.

'A woman,' the old man said. 'Without science, with nothing to go by, they undertake the most dangerous and sacred experience in God's earth. They fall in love with a woman. Is that correct, Son?'

'Yeah,' the boy said faintly.

'They start at the wrong end of love. They begin at the climax. Can you wonder it is so miserable? Do you know how men should love?'

The old man reached over and grasped the boy by the collar of his leather jacket. He gave him a gentle little shake and his green eyes gazed down unblinking and grave.

'Son, do you know how love should be begun?'

The boy sat small and listening and still. Slowly he shook his head. The old man leaned closer and whispered:

'A tree. A rock. A cloud.'

It was still raining outside in the street: a mild, gray, endless rain. The mill whistle blew for the six o'clock shift and the three spinners paid and went away. There was no one in the café but Leo, the old man, and the little paper boy.

'The weather was like this in Portland,' he said. 'At the time my science was begun. I meditated and I started very cautious. I would pick up something from the street and take it home with me. I bought a goldfish and I concentrated on the goldfish and I loved it. I graduated from one thing to another. Day by day I was getting this technique. On the road from Portland to San Diego————'

'Aw shut up!' screamed Leo suddenly. 'Shut up! Shut up!'

The old man still held the collar of the boy's jacket; he was trembling and his face was earnest and bright and wild. 'For six years now I have gone around by myself and built up my science. And now I am a master. Son. I can love anything. No longer do I have to think about it even. I see a street full of people and a beautiful light comes in me. I watch a bird in the sky. Or I meet a traveler on the road. Everything, Son. And anybody. All stranger and all loved! Do you realize what a science like mine can mean?'

The boy held himself stiffly, his hands curled tight around the counter edge. Finally he asked: 'Did you ever really find that lady?'

'What? What say, Son?'

'I mean,' the boy asked timidly. 'Have you fallen in love with a woman again?'

The old man loosened his grasp on the boy's collar. He turned away and for the first time his green eyes had a vague and scattered look. He lifted the mug from the counter, drank down the yellow beer. His head was shaking slowly from side to side. Then finally he answered: 'No, Son. You see that is the last step in my science. I go cautious. And I am not quite ready yet.'

'Well!' said Leo. 'Well well well!'

The old man stood in the open doorway. 'Remember,' he said. Framed there in the gray damp light of the early morning he looked shrunken and seedy and frail. But his smile was bright. 'Remember I love you,' he said with a last nod. And the door closed quietly behind him.

The boy did not speak for a long time. He pulled down the bangs on his forehead and slid his grimy little forefinger around the rim of his empty cup. Then without looking at Leo he finally asked: 'Was he drunk?'

'No,' said Leo shortly.

The boy raised his clear voice higher. 'Then was he a dope fiend?'

'No.'

The boy looked up at Leo, and his flat little face was desperate, his voice urgent and shrill. 'Was he crazy? Do you think he was a lunatic?' The paper boy's voice dropped suddenly with doubt. 'Leo? Or not?'

But Leo would not answer him. Leo had run a night café for fourteen years, and he held himself to be a critic of craziness. There were the town characters and also the transients who roamed in from the night. He knew the manias of all of them. But he did not want to satisfy the questions of the waiting child. He tightened his pale face and was silent.

So the boy pulled down the right flap of his helmet and as he turned to leave he made the only comment that seemed safe to him, the only remark that could not be laughed down and despised:

'He sure has done a lot of traveling.'

[1942]

QUESTIONS FOR STUDY

1. *What is the primary function of the boy in the story? How does Carson McCullers go about establishing his innocence and naiveté?*

2. *What kind of attitudes and values does Leo seem to embody? How does he differ from the old man? Why does Leo react so strongly to the old man's story of "scientific" love? Why does he stubbornly refuse to answer the boy's questions?*

3. *What is the story's theme? (Remember that* theme *and* subject *are not always one and the same.) How do characterization, setting, and plot each contribute to defining and developing the theme?*

4. *What are the implications of the boy's final comment and the story's conclusion?*

5. *In what respects can this story be compared with Ernest Hemingway's "The Killers"?*

JAMES ALAN McPHERSON

Gold Coast

THAT spring, when I had a great deal of potential and no money at all, I took a job as a janitor. That was when I was still very young and spent money very freely, and when, almost every night, I drifted off to sleep lulled by sweet anticipation of that time when my potential would suddenly be realized and there would be capsule biographies of my life on dust jackets of many books, all proclaiming: ". . . He knew life on many levels. From shoeshine boy, freelance waiter, 3rd cook, janitor, he rose to . . ." I had never been a janitor before and I did not really have to be one and that is why I did it. But now, much later, I think it might have been because it is possible to be a janitor without really becoming one, and at parties or at mixers when asked what it was I did for a living, it was pretty good to hook my thumbs in my vest pockets and say comfortably: "Why, I am an apprentice janitor." The hippies would think it degenerate and really dig me and it made me feel good that people in Philosophy and Law and Business would feel uncomfortable trying to make me feel better about my station while wondering how the hell I had managed to crash the party.

"What's an apprentice janitor?" they would ask.

"I haven't got my card yet," I would reply. "Right now I'm just taking lessons. There's lots of complicated stuff you have to learn before you get your card and your own building."

"What kind of stuff?"

"Human nature, for one thing. *Race* nature, for another."

"Why race?"

"Because," I would say in a low voice looking around lest someone else should overhear, "you have to be able to spot Jews and Negroes who are passing."

"That's terrible," would surely be said then with a hint of indignation.

"It's an art," I would add masterfully.

After a good pause I would invariably be asked: "But you're a Negro yourself, how can you keep your own people out?"

At which point I would look terribly disappointed and say: "*I* don't keep them out. But if they get in it's my job to make their stay just as miserable as possible. Things are changing."

Now the speaker would just look at me in disbelief.

"It's Janitorial Objectivity," I would say to finish the thing as the speaker began to edge away. "Don't hate me," I would call after him to his considerable embarrassment. "Somebody has to do it."

It was an old building near Harvard Square. Conrad Aiken had once lived there and in the days of the Gold Coast, before Harvard built its great Houses, it had been a very fine haven for the rich; but that was a world ago, and this building was one of the few monuments of that era which had survived. The lobby had a high ceiling with thick redwood beams and it was replete with marble floor, fancy ironwork, and an old-fashioned house telephone that no longer worked. Each apartment had a small fireplace, and even the large bathtubs and chain toilets, when I was having my touch of nature, made me wonder what prominent personage of the past had worn away all the newness. And, being there, I felt a certain affinity toward the rich.

It was a funny building: because the people who lived there made it old. Conveniently placed as it was between the Houses and Harvard Yard, I expected to find it occupied by a company of hippies, hopeful working girls, and assorted graduate students. Instead, there were a majority of old maids, dowagers, asexual middle-aged men, homosexual young men, a few married couples and a teacher. No one was shacking up there, and walking through the quiet halls in the early evening, I sometimes had the urge to knock on a door and expose myself just to hear someone breathe hard for once.

It was a Cambridge spring: down by the Charles happy students were making love while sad-eyed middle-aged men watched them from the bridge. It was a time of activity: Law students were busy sublimating, Business School people were making records of the money they would make, the Harvard Houses were clearing out, and in the Square bearded pot-pushers were setting up their restaurant tables in anticipation of the Summer School faithfuls. There was a change of season in the air, and to comply with its urgings, James Sullivan, the old superintendent, passed his three beaten garbage cans on to me with the charge that I should take up his daily rounds of the six floors, and with unflinching humility, gather whatever scraps the old-maid tenants had refused to husband.

I then became very rich, with my own apartment, a sensitive girl, a stereo, two speakers, one tattered chair, one fork, a job, and the urge to acquire. Having all this and youth besides made me pity Sullivan: he had been in that building thirty years and had its whole history recorded in the little folds of his mind, as his own life was recorded in the wrinkles of his face. All he had to show for his time there was a berserk dog, a wife almost as mad as the dog, three cats, bursitis, acute myopia, and a drinking problem. He was well over seventy and could hardly walk, and his weekly check of twenty-two dollars from the company that managed the building would not support anything. So, out of compromise, he was retired to superintendent of my labor.

My first day as a janitor, while I skillfully lugged my three overflowing cans of garbage out of the building, he sat on his bench in the lobby, faded and old and smoking in patched, loose blue pants. He watched me. He was a chain smoker and I noticed right away that he very carefully

dropped all of the ashes and butts on the floor and crushed them under his feet until there was a yellow and gray smear. Then he laboriously pushed the mess under the bench with his shoe, all the while eyeing me like a cat in silence as I hauled the many cans of muck out to the big disposal unit next to the building. When I had finished, he gave me two old plates to help stock my kitchen and his first piece of advice.

"Sit down, for Chrissake, and take a load off your feet," he told me.

I sat on the red bench next to him and accepted the wilted cigarette he offered me from the crushed package he kept in his sweater pocket.

"Now I'll tell you something to help you get along in the building," he said.

I listened attentively.

"If any of these sons-of-bitches ever ask you to do something extra, be sure to charge them for it."

I assured him that I absolutely would.

"If they can afford to live here, they can afford to pay. The bastards."

"Undoubtedly," I assured him again.

"And another thing," he added. "Don't let any of these girls shove any cat shit under your nose. That ain't your job. You tell them to put it in a bag and take it out themselves."

I reminded him that I knew very well my station in life, and that I was not about to haul cat shit or anything of that nature. He looked at me through his thick-lensed glasses. He looked like a cat himself. "That's right," he said at last. "And if they still try to sneak it in the trash be sure to make the bastards pay." They can afford it." He crushed his seventh butt on the floor and scattered the mess some more while he lit up another. "I never hauled out no cat shit in the thirty years I been here and you don't do it either."

"I'm going up to wash my hands," I said.

"Remember," he called after me, "don't take no shit from any of them."

I protested once more that, upon my life, I would never, never do it, not even for the prettiest girl in the building. Going up in the elevator, I felt comfortably resolved that I would never do it. There were no pretty girls in the building.

I never found out what he had done before he came there, but I do know that being a janitor in that building was as high as he ever got in life. He had watched two generations of the rich pass the building on their way to the Yard, and he had seen many governors ride white horses thirty times into that same Yard to send sons and daughters of the rich out into life to produce, to acquire, to procreate and to send back sons and daughters so that the cycle would continue. He had watched the cycle from when he had been able to haul the cans out for himself, and now he could not, and he was bitter.

He was Irish, of course, and he took pride in Irish accomplishments when he could have none of his own. He had known Frank O'Connor when that writer had been at Harvard. He told me on many occasions how O'Connor had stopped to talk every day on his way to the Yard. He had also known James Michael Curley, and his most colorful memory of the man was a long ago day when he and James Curley sat in a Boston bar and one of Curley's runners had come in and said: "Hey Jim, Sol Bernstein the Jew wants to see you." And Curley, in his deep, memorial voice had said to James Sullivan: "Let us go forth and meet this Israelite Prince." These were his memories, and I would obediently put aside my garbage cans and laugh with him over the hundred or so colorful, insignificant little details which made up a whole lifetime of living in the basement of Harvard. And although they were of little value to me then, I knew that they were the reflections of a lifetime and the happiest moments he would ever have, being sold to me cheap, as youthful time is cheap, for as little time and interest as I wanted to spend. It was a buyer's market.

II

In those days I believed myself gifted with a boundless perception and attacked my daily garbage route with a gusto superreinforced by the happy knowledge that behind each of the fifty or so doors in our building lived a story which could, if I chose to grace it with the magic of my pen, become immortal. I watched my tenants fanatically, noting their perversions, their visitors, and their eating habits. So intense was my search for material that I had to restrain myself from going through their refuse scrap by scrap; but at the topmost layers of muck, without too much hand-soiling in the process, I set my perceptions to work. By late June, however, I had discovered only enough to put together a skimpy, rather naïve Henry Miller novel. The most colorful discoveries being:

(1) The lady in # 24 was an alumna of Paducah College.
(2) The couple in # 55 made love at least five hundred times a week and the wife had not yet discovered the pill.
(3) The old lady in # 36 was still having monthly inconvenience.
(4) The two fatsos in # 56 consumed nightly an extraordinary amount of chili.
(5) The fat man in # 54 had two dogs that were married to each other, but he was not married to anyone at all.
(6) The middle-aged single man in # 63 threw out an awful lot of flowers.

Disturbed by the snail's progress I was making, I confessed my futility to James one day as he sat on his bench chain-smoking and smearing butts on my newly waxed lobby floor. "So you want to know about the tenants?" he said, his cat's eyes flickering over me.

I nodded.

"Well the first thing to notice is how many Jews there are."

"I haven't noticed many Jews," I said.

He eyed me in amazement.

"Well, a few," I said quickly to prevent my treasured perception from being dulled any further.

"A few, hell," he said. "There's more Jews here than anybody."

"How can you tell?"

He gave me that undecided look again. "Where do you think all that garbage comes from?" He nodded feebly toward my bulging cans. I looked just in time to prevent a stray noodle from slipping over the brim. "That's right," he continued. "Jews are the biggest eaters in the world. They eat the best too."

I confessed then that I was of the chicken-soup generation and believed that Jews ate only enough to muster strength for their daily trips to the bank.

"Not so!" he replied emphatically. "You never heard the expression: 'Let's get to the restaurant before the Jews get there'?"

I shook my head sadly.

"You don't know that in certain restaurants they take the free onions and pickles off the tables when they see Jews coming?"

I held my head down in shame over the bounteous heap.

He trudged over to my can and began to turn back the leaves of noodles and crumpled tissues from # 47 with his hand. After a few seconds of digging he unmucked an empty paté can. "Look at that," he said triumphantly. "Gourmet stuff, no less."

"That's from # 44," I said.

"What else?" he said all-knowingly. "In 1946 a Swedish girl moved in up there and took a Jewish girl for her roommate. Then the Swedish girl moved out and there's been a Jewish Dynasty up there ever since."

I recalled that # 44 was occupied by a couple that threw out a good number of S. S. Pierce cans, Chivas Regal bottles, assorted broken records, and back issues of *Evergreen* and the *Realist*.

"You're right," I said.

"Of course," he replied as if there was never any doubt. "I can spot them anywhere, even when they think they're passing." He leaned closer and said in a you-and-me voice: "But don't ever say anything bad about them in public, the Anti-Defamation League will get you."

Just then his wife screamed for him from the second floor, and the dog joined her and beat against the door. He got into the elevator painfully and said: "Don't ever talk about them in public. You don't know who they are and that Defamation League will take everything you got."

Sullivan did not really hate Jews. He was just bitter toward anyone better off than himself. He liked me because I seemed to like hauling garbage and because I listened to him and seemed to respect what he said and seemed to imply, by lingering on even when he repeated himself, that I was eager to take what wisdom he had for no other reason than that I needed it in order to get along.

He lived with his wife on the second floor and his apartment was dirty because both of them were sick and old, and neither could move very well. His wife swept dirt out into the hall, and two hours after I had mopped and waxed their section of the floor, there was sure to be a layer of dirt, grease, and crushed-scattered tobacco from their door to the end of the hall. There was a smell of dogs and cats and age and death about their door, and I did not ever want to have to go in there for any reason because I feared something about it I cannot name.

Mrs. Sullivan, I found out, was from South Africa. She loved animals much more than people and there was a great deal of pain in her face. She kept little pans of meat posted at strategic points about the building, and I often came across her in the early morning or late at night throwing scraps out of the second-floor window to stray cats. Once, when James was about to throttle a stray mouse in their apartment, she had screamed at him to give the mouse a sporting chance. Whenever she attempted to walk she had to balance herself against a wall or a rail, and she hated the building because it confined her. She also hated James and most of the tenants. On the other hand, she loved the *Johnny Carson Show*, she loved to sit outside on the front steps (because she could get no further unassisted), and she loved to talk to anyone who would stop to listen. She never spoke coherently except when she was cursing James, and then she had a vocabulary like a sailor. She had great, shrill lungs, and her screams, accompanied by the rabid barks of the dog, could be heard all over the building. She was never really clean, her teeth were bad, and the first most pathetic thing in the world was to see her sitting on the steps in the morning watching the world pass, in a stained smock and a fresh summer blue hat she kept just to wear downstairs, with no place in the world to go. James told me, on the many occasions of her screaming, that she was mentally disturbed and could not control herself. The admirable thing about him was that he never lost his temper with her, no matter how rough her curses became and no matter who heard them. And the second most pathetic thing in the world was to see them slowly making their way in Harvard Square, he supporting her, through the hurrying crowds of miniskirted summer girls, J-Pressed Ivy Leaguers, beatniks, and bused Japanese tourists, decked in cameras, who would take pictures of every inch of Harvard Square except them. Once, he told me, a hippie had brushed past them and called back over his shoulder: "Don't break any track records, Mr. and Mrs. Speedy Molasses."

Also on the second floor lived Miss O'Hara, a spinster who hated Sullivan as only an old maid can hate an old man. Across from her lived a very nice, gentle, celibate named Murphy who had once served with Montgomery in North Africa and who was now spending the rest of his life cleaning his little apartment and gossiping with Miss O'Hara. It was an Irish floor.

I never found out just why Miss O'Hara hated the Sullivans with such a passion. Perhaps it was because they were so unkempt and she was so superciliously clean. Perhaps it was because Miss O'Hara had a great deal of Irish pride and they were stereotyped Irish. Perhaps it was because she merely had no reason to like them. She was a fanatic about cleanliness and put out her little bit of garbage wrapped very neatly in yesterday's *Christian Science Monitor* and tied in a bow with a fresh piece of string. Collecting all those little neat packages, I would wonder where she got the string and imagined her at night picking meat-market locks with a hairpin and hobbling off with yards and yards of white cord concealed under

the gray sweater she always wore. I could even imagine her back in her little apartment chuckling and rolling the cord into a great white ball by candlelight. Then she would stash it away in her breadbox. Miss O'Hara kept her door slightly open until late at night, and I suspected that she heard everything that went on in the building. I had the feeling that I should never dare to make love with gusto for fear that she would overhear and write down all my happy-time phrases, to be maliciously recounted to me if she were ever provoked.

She had been in the building longer than Sullivan, and I suppose that her greatest ambition in life was to outlive him and then attend his wake with a knitting ball and needles. She had been trying to get him fired for twenty-five years or so and did not know when to quit. On summer nights when I painfully mopped the second floor, she would offer me root beer, apples, or cupcakes while trying to pump me for evidence against him.

'He's just a filthy old man, Robert," she would declare in a little-old-lady whisper. "And don't think you have to clean up those dirty old butts of his. Just report him to the Company."

"Oh, I don't mind," I would tell her, gulping the root beer as fast as possible.

"Well, they're both a couple of lushes, if you ask me. They haven't been sober a day in twenty-five years."

"Well, she's sick too, you know."

"Ha!" She would throw up her hands in disgust. "She's only sick when he doesn't give her the booze."

I fought to keep down a burp. "How long have *you* been here?"

She motioned for me to step out of the hall and into her dark apartment. "Don't tell him,"—she nodded towards Sullivan's door—"but I've been here for thirty-four years." She waited for me to be taken aback. Then she added: "And it was a better building before those two lushes came.

She then offered me an apple, asked five times if the dog's barking bothered me, forced me to take a fudge brownie, said that the cats had wet the floor again last night, got me to dust the top of a large chest too high for her to reach, had me pick up the minute specks of dust which fell from my dustcloth, pressed another root beer on me, and then showed me her family album. As an afterthought, she had me take down a big old picture of her great-grandfather, also too high for her to reach, so that I could dust that too. Then together we picked up the dust from it which might have fallen to the floor. "He's really a filthy old man, Robert," she said in closing, "and don't be afraid to report him to the property manager any time you want."

I assured her that I would do it at the slightest provocation from Sullivan, finally accepted an apple but refused the money she offered, and escaped back to my mopping. Even then she watched me, smiling, from her half-opened door.

"Why does Miss O'Hara hate you?" I asked James once.

He lifted his cigaretted hand and let the long ash fall elegantly to the floor. "That old bitch has been an albatross around my neck ever since I got here," he said. "Don't trust her, Robert. It was her kind that sat around singing hymns and watching them burn saints in this state."

There was never an adequate answer to my question. And even though the dog was noisy and would surely kill someone if it ever got loose, no one could really dislike the old man because of it. The dog was all they had. In his garbage each night, for every wine bottle, there would be an equally empty can of dog food. Some nights he took the brute out for a long walk, when he could barely walk himself, and both of them had to be led back to the building.

III

In those days I had forgotten that I was first of all a black and I had a very lovely girl who was not first of all a black. We were both young and optimistic then, and she believed with me in my potential and liked me partly because of it; and I was happy because she belonged to me and not to the race, which made her special. It made me special too because I did not have to wear a beard or hate or be especially hip or ultra-Ivy Leaguish. I

did not have to smoke pot or supply her with it, or be for any other cause at all except myself. I only had to be myself, which pleased me; and I only had to produce, which pleased both of us. Like many of the artistically inclined rich, she wanted to own in someone else what she could not own in herself. But this I did not mind, and I forgave her for it because she forgave me moods and the constant smell of garbage and a great deal of latent hostility. She only minded James Sullivan and all the valuable time I was wasting listening to him rattle on and on. His conversations, she thought, were useless, repetitious, and promised nothing of value to me. She was accustomed to the old-rich whose conversations meandered around a leitmotiv of how well off they were and how much they would leave behind very soon. She was not at all cold, but she had been taught how to tolerate the old-poor and perhaps toss them a greeting in passing. But nothing more.

Sullivan did not like her when I first introduced them because he saw that she was not a hippie and could not be dismissed. It is in the nature of things that liberal people will tolerate two interracial hippies more than they will an intelligent, serious-minded mixed couple. The former liaison is easy to dismiss as the dregs of both races, deserving of each other and the contempt of both races; but the latter poses a threat because there is no immediacy or overpowering sensuality or "you-pick-my-fleas-I'll pick-yours" apparent on the surface of things, and people, even the most publicly liberal, cannot dismiss it so easily.

"That girl is Irish, isn't she?" he had asked one day in my apartment soon after I had introduced them.

"No," I said definitely.

"What's her name again?"

"Judy Smith," I said, which was not her name at all.

"Well, I can spot it," he said. "She's got Irish blood, all right."

"Everybody's got a little Irish blood," I told him.

He looked at me cattily and craftily from behind his thick lenses. "Well, she's from a good family, I suppose."

"I suppose," I said.

He paused to let some ashes fall to the rug. "They say the Colonel's lady and Nelly O'Grady are sisters under the skin." Then he added: "Rudyard Kipling."

"That's true," I said with equal innuendo, "that's why you have to maintain a distinction by marrying the Colonel's Lady."

An understanding passed between us then, and we never spoke more on the subject.

Almost every night the cats wet the second floor while Meg Sullivan watched the *Johnny Carson Show* and the dog howled and clawed the door. During commercials Meg would curse James to get out and stop dropping ashes on the floor or to take the dog out or something else, totally unintelligible to those of us on the fourth, fifth and sixth floors. Even after the *Carson Show* she would still curse him to get out, until finally he would go down to the basement and put away a bottle or two of wine. There was a steady stench of cat functions in the basement, and with all the grease and dirt, discarded trunks, beer bottles, chairs, old tools and the filthy sofa on which he sometimes slept, seeing him there made me want to cry. He drank the cheapest sherry, the wino kind, straight from the bottle; and on many nights that summer at 2:00 A.M. my phone would ring me out of bed.

"Rob? Jimmy Sullivan here. What are you doing?"

There was nothing suitable to say.

"Come on down to the basement for a drink."

"I have to be at work at eight-thirty," I would protest.

"Can't you have just one drink?" he would say pathetically.

I would carry down my own glass so that I would not have to drink out of the bottle. Looking at him on the sofa, I could not be mad because now I had many records for my stereo, a story that was going well, a girl who believed in me and belonged to me and not to the race, a new set of dishes, and a tomorrow morning with younger people.

"I don't want to burden you unduly," he would always preface.

I would force myself not to look at my watch and say: "Of course not."

"My Meg is not in the best health, you know," he would say, handing the bottle to me.

"She's just old."

"The doctors say she should be in an institution."

"That's no place to me."

"I'm a sick man myself, Rob. I can't take much more. She's crazy."

"Anybody who loves animals can't be crazy."

He took another long draw from the bottle. "I won't live another year. I'll be dead in a year.

"You don't know that."

He looked at me closely, without his glasses, so that I could see the desperation in his eyes. "I just hope Meg goes before I do. I don't want them to put her in an institution after I'm gone."

At 2:00 A.M. with the cat stench in my nose and a glass of bad sherry standing still in my hand because I refused in my mind to touch it, and when all my dreams of greatness were above him and the basement and the building itself, I did not know what to say. The only way I could keep from hating myself was to talk about the AMA or the Medicare program or hippies. He was pure hell on all three. To him, the medical profession was "morally bankrupt," Medicare was a great farce which deprived oldsters like himself of their "rainy-day dollars," and hippies were "dropouts from the human race." He could rage on and on in perfect phrases about all three of his major dislikes, and I had the feeling that because the sentences were so well constructed and well turned, he might have memorized them from something he had read. But then he was extremely well read and it did not matter if he had borrowed a phrase or two from someone else. The ideas were still his own.

It would be 3:00 A.M. before I knew it, and then 3:30, and still he would go on. He hated politicians in general and liked to recount, at these times, his private catalogue of political observations. By the time he got around to Civil Rights it would be 4:00 A.M., and I could not feel sorry or responsible for him at that hour.

I would begin to yawn and at first he would just ignore it. Then I would start to edge toward the door, and he would see that he could hold me no longer, not even by declaring that he wanted to be an honorary Negro because he loved the race so much.

"I hope I haven't burdened you unduly," he would say again.

"Of course not," I would say, because it was over then and I could leave him and the smell of the cats there and sometimes I would go out in the cool night and walk around the Yard and be thankful that I was only an assistant janitor, and a transient one at that. Walking in the early dawn and seeing the Summer School fellows sneak out of the girls' dormitories in the Yard gave me a good feeling, and I thought that tomorrow night it would be good to make love myself so that I could be busy when he called.

IV

"Why don't you tell that old man your job doesn't include baby-sitting with him?" Jean told me many times when she came over to visit during the day and found me sleeping.

I would look at her and think to myself about social forces and the pressures massing and poised, waiting to attack us. It was still July then. It was hot and I was working good. "He's just an old man," I said. "Who else would listen to him?"

"You're too soft. As long as you do your work you don't have to be bothered with him."

"He could be a story if I listened long enough."

"There are too many stories about old people."

"No," I said, thinking about us again, "there are just too many people who have no stories."

Sometimes he would come up and she would be there, but I would let him come in anyway, and he would stand in the room looking dirty and uncomfortable, offering some invented reason for having intruded. At these times something silent would pass between them, something I cannot name, which would reduce him to exactly what he was: an old man,

come out of his basement to intrude where he was not wanted. But all the time this was being communicated, there would be a surface, friendly conversation between them. And after five minutes or so of being unwelcome, he would apologize for having come, drop a few ashes on the rug and back out the door. Downstairs we could hear his wife screaming.

We endured and aged and August was almost over. Inside the building the cats were still wetting, Meg was still screaming, the dog was getting madder, and Sullivan began to drink during the day. Outside it was hot and lush and green, and the summer girls were wearing shorter miniskirts and no panties and the middle-aged men down by the Charles were going wild on their bridge. Everyone was restless for change, for August is the month when undone summer things must be finished or regretted all through the winter.

V

Being imaginative people, Jean and I played a number of original games. One of them we called "Social Forces," the object of which was to see which side could break us first. We played it with the unknown nightriders who screamed obscenities from passing cars. And because that was her side I would look at her expectantly, but she would laugh and say: "No." We played it at parties with unaware blacks who attempted to enchant her with skillful dances and hip vocabulary, believing her to be community property. She would be polite and aloof, and much later, it then being my turn, she would look at me expectantly. And I would force a smile and say: "No." The last round was played while taking her home in a subway car, on a hot August night, when one side of the car was black and tense and hating and the other side was white and of the same mind. There was not enough room on either side for the two of us to sit and we would not separate; and so we stood, holding on to a steel post through all the stops, feeling all the eyes, between the two sides of the car and the two sides of the world. We aged. And, getting off finally at the stop which was no longer ours, we looked at each other, again expectantly, and there was nothing left to say.

I began to avoid the old man, would not answer the door when I knew it was he who was knocking, and waited until very late at night, when he could not possibly be awake, to haul the trash down. I hated the building then; and I was really a janitor for the first time. I slept a lot and wrote very little. And I did not give a damn about Medicare, the AMA, the building, Meg or the crazy dog. I began to consider moving out.

In that same month, Miss O'Hara finally succeeded in badgering Murphy, the celibate Irishman, and a few other tenants into signing a complaint about the dog. No doubt Murphy signed because he was a nice fellow and women like Miss O'Hara had always dominated him. He did not really mind the dog: he did not really mind anything. She called him "Frank Dear," and I had the feeling that when he came to that place, fresh from Montgomery's Campaign, he must have had a will of his own; but she had drained it all away, year by year, so that now he would do anything just to be agreeable.

One day soon after the complaint, the Property Manager came around to tell Sullivan that the dog had to be taken away. Miss O'Hara told me the good news later, when she finally got around to my door.

"Well, that crazy dog is gone now, Robert. Those two are enough."

"Where is the dog?" I asked.

"I don't know, but Albert Rustin made them get him out. You should have seen the old drunk's face," she said. "That dirty useless old man."

"You should be at peace now," I said.

"Almost," was her reply. "The best thing would be to get rid of those two old boozers along with the dog."

I congratulated Miss O'Hara again and then went out. I knew that the old man would be drinking and would want to talk. I did not want to talk. But very late that evening he called on the telephone and caught me in.

"Rob?" he said. "James Sullivan here. Would you come down to my apartment

like a good fellow? I want to ask you something important."

I had never been in his apartment before and did not want to go then. But I went down anyway.

They had three rooms, all grimy from corner to corner. There was a peculiar odor in that place I did not want to ever smell again, and his wife was dragging herself around the room talking in mumbles. When she saw me come in the door, she said: "I can't clean it up. I just can't. Look at that window. I can't reach it. I can't keep it clean." She threw up both her hands and held her head down and to the side. "The whole place is dirty and I can't clean it up."

"What do you want?" I said to Sullivan.

"Sit down." He motioned me to a kitchen chair. "Have you changed that bulb on the fifth floor?"

"It's done."

He was silent for a while, drinking from a bottle of sherry, and he offered me some and a dirty glass. "You're the first person who's been in here in years," he said. "We couldn't have company because of the dog."

Somewhere in my mind was a note that I should never go into his apartment. But the dog had not been the reason. "Well, he's gone now," I said, fingering the dirty glass of sherry.

He began to cry. "They took my dog away," he said. "It was all I had. How can they take a man's dog away from him?"

There was nothing I could say.

"I couldn't do nothing," he continued. After a while he added: "But I know who it was. It was that old bitch O'Hara. Don't ever trust her, Rob. She smiles in your face but it was her kind that laughed when they burned Joan of Arc in this state."

Seeing him there, crying and making me feel unmanly because I wanted to touch him or say something warm, also made me eager to be far away and running hard. "Everybody's got problems," I said. "I don't have a girl now."

He brightened immediately, and for a while he looked almost happy in his old cat's eyes. Then he staggered over to my chair and held out his hand. I did not touch it, and he finally pulled it back. "I know how you feel," he said. "I know just how you feel."

"Sure," I said.

"But you're a young man, you have a future. But not me. I'll be dead inside of a year."

Just then his wife dragged in to offer me a cigar. They were being hospitable and I forced myself to drink a little of the sherry.

"They took my dog away today," she mumbled. "That's all I had in the world, my dog."

I looked at the old man. He was drinking from the bottle.

VI

During the first week of September one of the middle-aged men down by the Charles got tired of looking and tried to take a necking girl away from her boyfriend. The police hauled him off to jail, and the girl pulled down her dress tearfully. A few days later another man exposed himself near the same spot. And that same week a dead body was found on the banks of the Charles.

The miniskirted brigade had moved out of the Yard and it was quiet and green and peaceful there. In our building another Jewish couple moved into # 44. They did not eat gourmet stuff and, on occasion, threw out pork-and-beans cans. But I had lost interest in perception. I now had many records for my stereo, loads of S. S. Pierce stuff, and a small bottle of Chivas Regal which I never opened. I was working good again and did not miss other things as much; or at least I told myself that.

The old man was coming up steadily now, at least three times a day, and I had resigned myself to it. If I refused to let him in he would always come back later with a missing bulb on the fifth floor. We had taken to buying cases of beer together, and when he had finished his half, which was very frequently, he would come up to polish off mine. I began to enjoy talking about politics, the AMA, Medicare, and hippies, and listening to him recite from books he had read. I discovered that he was very well read in history, philosophy, literature and law. He was extraordinarily fond of saying: "I am really a cut above being a building superintendent. Circumstances made me what I am." And even though he was drunk and dirty and it was very late at night, I believed him and liked him anyway because having him there was much better than being alone. After he had gone I could sleep and I was not lonely in sleep; and it did not really matter how late I was at work the next morning, because when I really thought about it all, I discovered that nothing really matters except not being old and being alive and having potential to dream about, and not being alone.

Whenever I passed his wife on the steps she would say: "That no-good bastard let them take my dog away." And whenever her husband complained that he was sick she said: "That's good for him. He took my dog away."

Sullivan slept in the basement on the sofa almost every night because his wife would think about the dog after the *Carson Show* and blame him for letting it be taken away. He told her, and then me, that the dog was on a farm in New Hampshire; but that was unlikely because the dog had been near mad, and it did not appease her. It was nearing autumn and she was getting violent. Her screams could be heard for hours through the halls and I knew that beyond her quiet door Miss O'Hara was plotting again. Sullivan now had little cuts and bruises on his face and hands, and one day he said: "Meg is like an albatross around my neck. I wish she was dead. I'm sick myself and I can't take much more. She blames me for the dog and I couldn't help it."

"Why don't you take her out to see the dog?" I said.

"I couldn't help it Rob," he went on. "I'm old and I couldn't help it."

"You ought to just get her out of here for a while."

He looked at me, drunk as usual. "Where would we go? We can't even get past the Square."

There was nothing left to say.

"Honest to God, I couldn't help it," he said. He was not saying it to me.

That night I wrote a letter from a mythical New Hampshire farmer telling them that the dog was very fine and missed them a great deal because he kept trying to run off. I said that the children and all the other dogs liked him and that he was not vicious any more. I wrote that the open air was doing him a lot of good and added that they should feel absolutely free to come up to visit the dog at any time. That same night I gave him the letter.

One evening, some days later, I asked him about it.

"I tried to mail it, I really tried," he said.

"What happened?"

"I went down to the Square and looked for cars with New Hampshire license plates. But I never found anybody."

"That wasn't even necessary, was it?"

"It had to have a New Hampshire postmark. You don't know my Meg."

"Listen," I said. "I have a friend who goes up there. Give me the letter and I'll have him mail it."

He held his head down. "I'll tell you the truth. I carried that letter in my pocket so much it got ragged and dirty and I got tired of carrying it. I finally just tore it up."

Neither one of us said anything for a while.

"If I could have sent it off it would have helped some," he said at last. "I know it would have helped."

"Sure," I said.

"I wouldn't have to ask anybody if I had my strength."

"I know."

"If I had my strength I would have mailed it myself."

"I know," I said.

That night we both drank from his bottle of sherry and it did not matter at all that I did not provide my own glass.

VII

In late September the Cambridge police finally picked up the bearded pot-pusher in the Square. He had been in a restaurant all summer, at the same table, with the same customers flocking around him; but now that summer was over, they picked him up. The leaves were changing. In the early evening students passed the building and Meg, blue-hatted and waiting on the steps, carrying sofas and chairs and coffee tables to their suites in the Houses. Down by the Charles the middle-aged men were catching the last phases of summer sensuality before the grass grew cold and damp, and before the young would be forced indoors to play. I wondered what those hungry, spying men did in the winter or at night when it was too dark to see. Perhaps, I thought, they just stood there and listened.

In our building Miss O'Hara was still listening. She had never stopped. When Meg was outside on the steps it was very quiet and I felt good that Miss O'Hara had to wait a long, long time before she heard anything. The company gave the halls and ceilings a new coat of paint, but it was still old in the building. James Sullivan got his yearly two-week vacation and they went to the Boston Common for six hours: two hours going, two hours sitting on the benches, and two hours coming back. Then they both sat on the steps, watching and waiting.

At first I wanted to be kind because he was old and dying in a special way and I was young and ambitious. But at night, in my apartment, when I heard his dragging feet in the hall outside and knew that he would be drunk and repetitious and imposing on my privacy, I did not want to be kind any more. There were girls outside and I knew that I could have one now because that desperate look had finally gone somewhere deep inside. I was young and now I did not want to be bothered.

"Did you read about the lousy twelve per cent Social Security increase those bastards in Washington gave us?"

"No."

He would force himself past me, trying to block the door with my body, and into the room. "When those old pricks tell me to count my blessings, I tell them, 'You're not one of them.' " He would seat himself at the table without meeting my eyes. "The cost of living's gone up more than twelve per cent in the last six months."

"I know."

"What unmitigated bastards."

I would try to be busy with something on my desk.

"But the Texas Oil Barons got another depletion allowance."

"They can afford to bribe politicians," I would mumble.

"They tax away our rainy-day dollars and give us a lousy twelve per cent."

"It's tough."

He would know that I did not want to hear any more and he would know that he was making a burden of himself. It made me feel bad that it was so obvious to him, but I could not help myself. It made me feel bad that I disliked him more every time I heard a girl laugh on the street far below my window. So I would nod occasionally and say half-phrases and smile slightly at something witty he was saying for the third time. If I did not offer him a drink he would go sooner and so I gave him Coke when he hinted at how dry he was. Then, when he had finally gone, saying, "I hope I haven't burdened you unduly," I went to bed and hated myself.

VIII

If I am a janitor it is either because I have to be a janitor or because I want to be a janitor. And if I do not have to do it, and if I no longer want to do it, the easiest thing in the world, for a young man, is to step up to something else. Any move away from it is a step up because there is no job more demeaning than that of a janitor. One day I made myself suddenly realize that the three dirty cans would never contain anything of value to me, unless, of course, I decided to gather material for Harold Robbins or freelance for the *Realist*. Neither alternative appealed to me.

Toward dawn one day, during the first part of October, I rented a U-Haul truck and took away two loads of things I had accumulated. The records I packed very carefully, and the stereo I placed on the front seat of the truck beside me. I slipped the Chivas Regal and a picture of Jean under some clothes in a trunk I will not open for a long time. And I left the rug on the floor because it was dirty and too large for my new apartment. I also left the two plates given to me by James Sullivan, for no reason at all. Sometimes I want to go back to get them, but I do not know how to ask for them or explain why I left them in the first place. But sometimes at night, when there is a sleeping girl beside me, I think that I cannot have them again because I am still young and do not want to go back into that building.

I saw him once in the Square walking along very slowly with two shopping bags, and they seemed very heavy. As I came up behind him I saw him put them down and exercise his arms while the crowd moved in two streams around him. I had an instant impulse to offer help and I was close enough to touch him before I stopped. I will never know why I stopped. And after a few seconds of standing behind him and knowing that he was not aware of anything at all except the two heavy bags waiting to be lifted after his arms were sufficiently rested, I moved back into the stream of people which passed on the left of him. I never looked back.

[1968]

QUESTIONS FOR STUDY

1. *In what ways is the following statement central to the story's meaning: "nothing really matters except not being old and being alive and having potential to dream about, and not being alone"?*
2. *What does Robert mean when he says at the beginning of the story that "it is possible to be a janitor without becoming one"?*

3. *How do James Sullivan and Miss O'Hara reveal the despair and lone-liness of their old age? Why does Robert befriend James?*
4. *What does Robert dislike so much about the Sullivan's apartment ("I feared something about it I cannot name")?*
5. *Why does Robert begin to avoid James? Why does his attitude temporarily change when he loses Jean? What does Robert mean when he says of James, "I disliked him more every time I heard a girl laugh on the street far below my window"?*
6. *What is the significance of McPherson's repeated references to the middle-aged men on the bridge?*

BERNARD MALAMUD

The Magic Barrel

NOT LONG ago there lived in uptown New York, in a small, almost meager room, though crowded with books, Leo Finkle, a rabbinical student in the Yeshivah University. Finkle, after six years of study, was to be ordained in June and had been advised by an acquaintance that he might find it easier to win himself a congregation if he were married. Since he had no present prospects of marriage, after two tormented days of turning it over in his mind, he called Pinye Salzman, a marriage broker whose two-line advertisement he had read in the *Forward*.

The matchmaker appeared one night out of the dark fourth-floor hallway of the graystone rooming house where Finkle lived, grasping a black, strapped portfolio that had been worn thin with use. Salzman, who had been long in the business, was of slight but dignified build, wearing an old hat, and an overcoat too short and tight for him. He smelled frankly of fish, which he loved to eat, and although he was missing a few teeth, his presence was not displeasing, because of an amiable manner curiously contrasted with mournful eyes. His voice, his lips, his wisp of beard, his bony fingers were animated, but give him a moment of repose and his mild blue eyes revealed a depth of sadness, a characteristic that put Leo a little at ease although the situation, for him, was inherently tense.

He at once informed Salzman why he had asked him to come, explaining that his home was in Cleveland, and that but for his parents, who had married comparatively late in life, he was alone in the world. He had for six years devoted himself almost entirely to his studies, as a result of which, understandably, he had found himself without time for a social life and the company of young women. Therefore he thought it the better part of

trial and error—of embarrassing fumbling—to call in an experienced person to advise him on these matters. He remarked in passing that the function of the marriage broker was ancient and honorable, highly approved in the Jewish community, because it made practical the necessary without hindering joy. Moreover, his own parents had been brought together by a matchmaker. They had made, if not a financially profitable marriage—since neither had possessed any worldly goods to speak of—at least a successful one in the sense of their everlasting devotion to each other. Salzman listened in embarrassed surprise, sensing a sort of apology. Later, however, he experienced a glow of pride in his work, an emotion that had left him years ago, and he heartily approved of Finkle.

The two went to their business. Leo had led Salzman to the only clear place in the room, a table near a window that overlooked the lamp-lit city. He seated himself at the matchmaker's side but facing him, attempting by an act of will to suppress the unpleasant tickle in his throat. Salzman eagerly unstrapped his portfolio and removed a loose rubber band from a thin packet of much-handled cards. As he flipped through them, a gesture and sound that physically hurt Leo, the student pretended not to see and gazed steadfastly out the window. Although it was still February, winter was on its last legs, signs of which he had for the first time in years begun to notice. He now observed the round white moon, moving high in the sky through a cloud menagerie, and watched with half-open mouth as it penetrated a huge hen, and dropped out of her like an egg laying itself. Salzman, though pretending through eyeglasses he had just slipped on, to be engaged in scanning the writing on the cards, stole occasional glances at the young man's distinguished face, noting with pleasure the long, severe scholar's nose, brown eyes heavy with learning, sensitive yet ascetic lips, and a certain, almost hollow quality of the dark cheeks. He gazed around at shelves upon shelves of books and let out a soft, contented sigh.

When Leo's eyes fell upon the cards, he counted six spread out in Salzman's hand.

"So few?" he asked in disappointment.

"You wouldn't believe me how much cards I got in my office," Salzman replied. "The drawers are already filled to the top, so I keep them now in a barrel, but is every girl good for a new rabbi?"

Leo blushed at this, regretting all he had revealed of himself in a curriculum vitae he had sent to Salzman. He had thought it best to acquaint him with his strict standards and specifications, but in having done so, felt he had told the marriage broker more than was absolutely necessary.

He hesitantly inquired, "Do you keep photographs of your clients on file?"

"First comes family, amount of dowry, also what kind promises," Salzman replied, unbuttoning his tight coat and settling himself in the chair. "After comes pictures, rabbi."

"Call me Mr. Finkle. I'm not yet a rabbi."

Salzman said he would, but instead called him doctor, which he changed to rabbi when Leo was not listening too attentively.

Salzman adjusted his horn-rimmed spectacles, gently cleared his throat and read in an eager voice the contents of the top card:

"Sophie P. Twenty four years. Widow one year. No children. Educated high school and two years college. Father promises eight thousand dollars. Has wonderful wholesale business. Also real estate. On the mother's side comes teachers, also one actor. Well known on Second Avenue."

Leo gazed up in surprise. "Did you say a widow?"

"A widow don't mean spoiled, rabbi. She lived with her husband maybe four months. He was a sick boy she made a mistake to marry him."

"Marrying a widow has never entered my mind."

"This is because you have no experience. A widow, especially if she is young and healthy like this girl, is a wonderful person to marry. She will be thankful to you the rest of her life. Believe me, if I was looking now for a bride, I would marry a widow."

Leo reflected, then shook his head.

Salzman hunched his shoulders in an almost imperceptible gesture of disappointment. He placed the card down on the wooden table and began to read another:

"Lily H. High school teacher. Regular. Not a substitute. Has savings and new Dodge car. Lived in Paris one year. Father is successful dentist thirty-five years. Interested in professional man. Well Americanized family. Wonderful opportunity."

"I knew her personally," said Salzman. "I wish you could see this girl. She is a doll. Also very intelligent. All day you could talk to her about books and theyater and what not. She also knows current events."

"I don't believe you mentioned her age?"

"Her age?" Salzman said, raising his brows. "Her age is thirty-two years."

Leo said after a while, "I'm afraid that seems a little too old."

Salzman let out a laugh. "So how old are you, rabbi?"

"Twenty-seven."

"So what is the difference, tell me, between twenty-seven and thirty-two? My own wife is seven years older than me. So what did I suffer?—nothing. If Rothschild's a daughter wants to marry you, would you say on account her age, no?"

"Yes," Leo said dryly.

Salzman shook off the no in the yes. "Five years don't mean a thing. I give you my word that when you will live with her for one week you will forget her age. What does it mean five years—that she lived more and knows more than somebody who is younger? On this girl, God bless her, years are not wasted. Each one that it comes makes better the bargain."

"What subject does she teach in high school?"

"Languages. If you heard the way she speaks French, you will think it is music. I am in the business twenty-five years, and I recommend her with my whole heart. Believe me, I know what I'm talking, rabbi."

"What's on the next card?" Leo said abruptly.

Salzman reluctantly turned up the third card:

"Ruth K. Nineteen years. Honor student. Father offers thirteen thousand cash to the right bridegroom. He is a medical doctor. Stomach specialist with marvelous practice. Brother in law owns own garment business. Particular people."

Salzman looked as if he had read his trump card.

"Did you say nineteen?" Leo asked with interest.

"On the dot."

"Is she attractive?" He blushed. "Pretty?"

Salzman kissed his finger tips. "A little doll. On this I give you my word. Let me call the father tonight and you will see what means pretty."

But Leo was troubled. "You're sure she's that young?"

"This I am positive. The father will show you the birth certificate."

"Are you positive there isn't something wrong with her?" Leo insisted.

"Who says there is wrong?"

"I don't understand why an American girl her age should go to a marriage broker."

A smile spread over Salzman's face.

"So for the same reason you went, she comes."

Leo flushed. "I am pressed for time."

Salzman, realizing he had been tactless, quickly explained. "The father came, not her. He wants she should have the best, so he looks around himself. When we will locate the right boy he will introduce him and encourage. This makes a better marriage than if a young girl without experience takes for herself. I don't have to tell you this."

"But don't you think this young girl believes in love?" Leo spoke uneasily.

Salzman was about to guffaw but caught himself and said soberly, "Love comes with the right person, not before."

Leo parted dry lips but did not speak. Noticing that Salzman had snatched a glance at the next card, he cleverly asked, "How is her health?"

"Perfect," Salzman said, breathing with difficulty. "Of course, she is a little lame on her right foot from an auto accident that it happened to her when she was twelve years, but nobody notices on account she is so brilliant and also beautiful."

Leo got up heavily and went to the window. He felt curiously bitter and upbraided himself for having called in the marriage broker. Finally, he shook his head.

"Why not?" Salzman persisted, the pitch of his voice rising.

"Because I detest stomach specialists."

"So what do you care what is his business? After you marry her do you need him? Who says he must come every Friday night in your house?"

Ashamed of the way the talk was going, Leo dismissed Salzman, who went home with heavy, melancholy eyes.

Though he had felt only relief at the marriage broker's departure, Leo was in low spirits the next day. He explained it as arising from Salzman's failure to produce a suitable bride for him. He did not care for his type of clientele. But when Leo found himself hesitating whether to seek out another matchmaker, one more polished than Pinye, he wondered if it could be—his protestations to the contrary, and although he honored his father and mother—that he did not, in essence, care for the matchmaking institution? This thought he quickly put out of mind yet found himself still upset. All day he ran around in the woods—missed an important appointment, forgot to give out his laundry, walked out of a Broadway cafeteria without paying and had to run back with the ticket in his hand; had even not recognized his landlady in the street when she passed with a friend and courteously called out, "A good evening to you,

Doctor Finkle." By nightfall, however, he had regained sufficient calm to sink his nose into a book and there found peace from his thoughts.

Almost at once there came a knock on the door. Before Leo could say enter, Salzman, commercial cupid, was standing in the room. His face was gray and meager, his expression hungry, and he looked as if he would expire on his feet. Yet the marriage broker managed, by some trick of the muscles, to display a broad smile.

"So good evening. I am invited?"

Leo nodded, disturbed to see him again, yet unwilling to ask the man to leave.

Beaming still, Salzman laid his portfolio on the table. "Rabbi, I got for you tonight good news."

"I've asked you not to call me rabbi. I'm still a student."

"Your worries are finished. I have for you a first-class bride."

"Leave me in peace concerning this subject." Leo pretended lack of interest.

"The world will dance at your wedding."

"Please, Mr. Salzman, no more."

"But first must come back my strength," Salzman said weakly. He fumbled with the portfolio straps and took out of the leather case an oily paper bag, from which he extracted a hard, seeded roll and a small, smoked white fish. With a quick motion of his hand he stripped the fish out of its skin and began ravenously to chew. "All day in a rush," he muttered.

Leo watched him eat.

"A sliced tomato you have maybe?" Salzman hesitantly inquired.

"No."

The marriage broker shut his eyes and ate. When he had finished he carefully cleaned up the crumbs and rolled up the remains of the fish, in the paper bag. His spectacled eyes roamed the room until he discovered, amid some piles of books, a one-burner gas stove. Lifting his hat he humbly asked, "A glass tea you got, rabbi?"

Conscience-stricken, Leo rose and brewed the tea. He served it with a chunk of lemon and two cubes of lump sugar, delighting Salzman.

After he had drunk his tea, Salzman's strength and good spirits were restored.

"So tell me, rabbi," he said amiably, "you considered some more the three clients I mentioned yesterday?"

"There was no need to consider."

"Why not?"

"None of them suits me."

"What then suits you?"

Leo let it pass because he could give only a confused answer.

Without waiting for a reply, Salzman asked, "You remember this girl I talked to you—the high school teacher?"

"Age thirty-two?"

But, surprisingly, Salzman's face lit in a smile. "Age twenty-nine."

Leo shot him a look. "Reduced from thirty-two?"

"A mistake," Salzman avowed. "I talked today with the dentist. He took me to his safety deposit box and showed me the birth certificate. She was twenty-nine years last August. They made her a party in the mountains where she went for her vacation. When her father spoke to me the first time I forgot to write the age and I told you thirty-two, but now I remember this was a different client, a widow."

"The same one you told me about? I thought she was twenty-four?"

"A different. Am I responsible that the world is filled with widows?"

"No, but I'm not interested in them, nor for that matter, in school teachers."

Salzman pulled his clasped hands to his breast. Looking at the ceiling he devoutly exclaimed, "Yiddishe kinder, what can I say to somebody that he is not interested in high school teachers? So what then you are interested?"

Leo flushed but controlled himself.

"In what else will you be interested," Salzman went on, "if you not interested in this fine girl that she speaks four languages and has personally in the bank ten thousand dollars? Also her father guarantees further twelve thousand. Also she has a new car, wonderful clothes, talks on all subjects, and she will give you a first-class home and children. How near do we come in our life to paradise?"

"If she's so wonderful, why wasn't she married ten years ago?"

"Why?" said Salzman with a heavy laugh. "—Why? Because she is *partikiler*. This is why. She wants the *best*."

Leo was silent, amused at how he had entangled himself. But Salzman had aroused his interest in Lily H., and he began seriously to consider calling on her. When the marriage broker observed how intently Leo's mind was at work on the facts he had supplied, he felt certain they would soon come to an agreement.

Late Saturday afternoon, conscious of Salzman, Leo Finkle walked with Lily Hirschorn along Riverside Drive. He walked briskly and erectly, wearing with distinction the black fedora he had that morning taken with trepidation out of the dusty hat box on his closet shelf, and the heavy black Saturday coat he had thoroughly whisked clean. Leo also owned a walking stick, a present from a distant relative, but quickly put temptation aside and did not use it. Lily, petite and not unpretty, had on something signifying the approach of spring. She was au courant, animatedly, with all sorts of subjects, and he weighed her words and found her surprisingly sound—score another for Salzman, whom he uneasily sensed to be somewhere around, hiding perhaps high in a tree along the street, flashing the lady signals with a pocket mirror; or perhaps a cloven-hoofed Pan, piping nuptial ditties as he danced his invisible way before them, strewing wild buds on the walk and purple grapes in their path, symbolizing fruit of a union, though there was of course still none.

Lily startled Leo by remarking, "I was thinking of Mr. Salzman, a curious figure, wouldn't you say?"

Not certain what to answer, he nodded.

She bravely went on, blushing, "I for one am grateful for his introducing us. Aren't you?"

He courteously replied, "I am."

"I mean," she said with a little laugh—and it was all in good taste, or at least gave the effect of being not in bad—"do you mind that we came together so?"

He was not displeased with her honesty, recognizing that she meant to set the relationship aright, and understanding that it took a certain amount of experience in life, and courage, to want to do it quite that way. One had to have some sort of past to make that kind of beginning.

He said that he did not mind. Salzman's function was traditional and honorable—valuable for what it might achieve, which, he pointed out, was frequently nothing.

Lily agreed with a sigh. They walked on for a while and she said after a long silence, again with a nervous laugh, "Would you mind if I asked you something a little bit personal? Frankly I find the subject fascinating." Although Leo shrugged, she went on half embarrassedly, "How was it that you came to your calling? I mean was it a sudden passionate inspiration?"

Leo, after a time, slowly replied, "I was always interested in the Law."

"You saw revealed in it the presence of the Highest?"

He nodded and changed the subject. "I understand that you spent a little time in Paris, Miss Hirschorn?"

"Oh, did Mr. Salzman tell you, Rabbi Finkle?" Leo winced but she went on, "It was ages ago and almost forgotten. I remember I had to return for my sister's wedding."

And Lily would not be put off. "When," she asked in a trembly voice, "did you become enamored of God?"

He stared at her. Then it came to him that she was talking not about Leo Finkle, but of a total stranger, some mystical figure, perhaps even passionate prophet that Salzman had dreamed up for her—no relation to the living or dead. Leo trembled with rage and weakness. The trickster had obviously sold her a bill of goods, just as he had him, who'd expected to become acquainted with a young lady of twenty-nine, only to behold, the moment he laid eyes upon her strained and anxious face, a woman past thirty-five and aging rapidly. Only his self control had kept him this long in her presence.

"I am not," he said gravely, "a talented religious person," and in seeking words to go on, found himself possessed by shame and fear. "I think," he said in a strained manner, "that I came to God not because I loved Him, but because I did not."

This confession he spoke harshly because its unexpectedness shook him.

Lily wilted. Leo saw a profusion of loaves of bread go flying like ducks high over his head, not unlike the winged loaves by which he had counted himself to sleep last night. Mercifully, then, it snowed, which he would not put past Salzman's machinations.

He was infuriated with the marriage broker and swore he would throw him out of the room the minute he reappeared. But Salzman did not come that night, and when Leo's anger had subsided, an unaccountable despair grew in its place. At first he thought this was caused by his disappointment in Lily, but before long it became evident that he had involved himself with Salzman without a true knowledge of his own intent. He gradually realized—with an emptiness that seized him with six hands—that he had called in the broker to find him a bride because he was incapable of doing it himself. This terrifying insight he had derived as a result of his meeting and conversation with Lily Hirschorn. Her probing questions had somehow irritated him into revealing—to himself more than her—the true nature of his relationship to God, and from that it had come upon him, with shocking force, that apart from his parents, he had never loved anyone. Or perhaps it went the other way, that he did not love God so well as he might, because he had not loved man. It seemed to Leo that his whole life stood starkly revealed and he saw himself for the first time as he truly was—unloved and loveless. This bitter but somehow not fully unexpected revelation brought him to a point of panic, controlled only by extraordinary effort. He covered his face with his hands and cried.

The week that followed was the worst of his life. He did not eat and lost weight. His beard darkened and grew ragged. He stopped attending seminars and almost never opened a book. He seriously considered leaving the Yeshivah, although he was deeply troubled at the thought of the loss of all his years of study—saw them like pages torn from a book, strewn over the city—and at the devastating effect of this decision upon his parents. But he had lived without knowledge of himself, and never in the Five Books and all the Commentaries—mea culpa—had the truth been revealed to him. He did not know where to turn, and in all this desolating loneliness there was no *to whom*, although he often thought of Lily but not once could bring himself to go downstairs and make the call. He became touchy and irritable, especially with his landlady, who asked him all manner of personal questions; on the other hand, sensing his own disagreeableness, he waylaid her on the stairs and apologized abjectly, until mortified, she ran from him. Out of this, however, he drew the consolation that he was a Jew and that a Jew suffered. But gradually, as the long and terrible week drew to a close, he regained his composure and some idea of purpose in life: to go on as planned. Although he was imperfect, the ideal was not. As for his quest of a bride, the thought of continuing afflicted him with anxiety and heartburn, yet perhaps with this new knowledge of himself he would be more successful than in the past. Perhaps love would now come to him and a bride to that love. And for this sanctified seeking who needed a Salzman?

The marriage broker, a skeleton with haunted eyes, returned that very night. He looked, withal, the picture of frustrated expectancy—as if he had steadfastly waited the week at Miss Lily Hirschorn's side for a telephone call that never came.

Casually coughing, Salzman came immediately to the point: "So how did you like her?"

Leo's anger rose and he could not refrain from chiding the matchmaker: "Why did you lie to me, Salzman?"

Salzman's pale face went dead white, the world had snowed on him.

"Did you not state that she was twenty-nine?" Leo insisted.

"I give you my word—"

"She was thirty-five, if a day. *At least* thirty-five."

"Of this don't be too sure. Her father told me—"

"Never mind. The worst of it was that you lied to her."

"How did I lie to her, tell me?"

"You told her things about me that

weren't true. You made me out to be more, consequently less than I am. She had in mind a totally different person, a sort of semimystical Wonder Rabbi."

"All I said, you was a religious man."

"I can imagine."

Salzman sighed. "This is my weakness that I have," he confessed. "My wife says to me I shouldn't be a salesman, but when I have two fine people that they would be wonderful to be married, I am so happy that I talk too much." He smiled wanly. "This is why Salzman is a poor man."

Leo's anger left him. "Well, Salzman, I'm afraid that's all."

The marriage broker fastened hungry eyes on him.

"You don't want any more a bride?"

"I do," said Leo, "but I have decided to seek her in a different way. I am no longer interested in an arranged marriage. To be frank, I now admit the necessity of premarital love. That is, I want to be in love with the one I marry."

"Love?" said Salzman, astounded. After a moment he remarked, "For us, our love is our life, not for the ladies. In the ghetto they—"

"I know, I know," said Leo. "I've thought of it often. Love, I have said to myself, should be a by-product of living and worship rather than its own end. Yet for myself I find it necessary to establish the level of my need and fulfill it."

Salzman shrugged but answered, "Listen, rabbi, if you want love, this I can find for you also. I have such beautiful clients that you will love them the minute your eyes will see them."

Leo smiled unhappily. "I'm afraid you don't understand."

But Salzman hastily unstrapped his portfolio and withdrew a manila packet from it.

"Pictures," he said, quickly laying the envelope on the table.

Leo called after him to take the pictures away, but as if on the wings of the wind, Salzman had disappeared.

March came. Leo had returned to his regular routine. Although he felt not quite himself yet—lacked energy—he was making plans for a more active social life. Of course it would cost something, but he was an expert in cutting corners; and

when there were no corners left he would make circles rounder. All the while Salzman's pictures had lain on the table, gathering dust. Occasionally as Leo sat studying, or enjoying a cup of tea, his eyes fell on the manila envelope, but he never opened it.

The days went by and no social life to speak of developed with a member of the opposite sex—it was difficult, given the circumstances of his situation. One morning Leo toiled up the stairs to his room and stared out of the window at the city. Although the day was bright his view of it was dark. For some time he watched the people in the street below hurrying along and then turned with a heavy heart to his little room. On the table was the packet. With a sudden relentless gesture he tore it open. For a half-hour he stood by the table in a state of excitement, examining the photographs of the ladies Salzman had included. Finally, with a deep sigh he put them down. There were six, of varying degrees of attractiveness, but look at them long enough and they all became Lily Hirschorn: all past their prime, all starved behind bright smiles, not a true personality in the lot. Life, despite their frantic yoohooings, had passed them by; they were pictures in a brief case that stank of fish. After a while, however, as Leo attempted to return the photographs into the envelope, he found in it another, a snapshot of the type taken by a machine for a quarter. He gazed at it a moment and let out a cry.

Her face deeply moved him. Why, he could at first not say. It gave him the impression of youth—spring flowers, yet age —a sense of having been used to the bone, wasted; this came from the eyes, which were hauntingly familiar, yet absolutely strange. He had a vivid impression that he had met her before, but try as he might he could not place her although he could almost recall her name, as if hé had read it in her own handwriting. No, this couldn't be; he would have remembered her. It was not, he affirmed, that she had an extraordinary beauty—no, though her face was attractive enough; it was that *something* about her moved him. Feature for feature, even some of the ladies of the photographs could do better; but she leaped forth to his heart—had *lived*, or wanted to—more than just wanted, perhaps regretted how she had lived—had somehow deeply suffered: it could be seen in the depths of those reluctant eyes, and from the way the light enclosed and shone from her, and within her, opening realms of possibility: this was her own. Her he desired. His head ached and eyes narrowed with the intensity of his gazing, then as if an obscure fog had blown up in the mind, he experienced fear of her and was aware that he had received an impression, somehow, of evil. He shuddered, saying softly, it is thus with us all. Leo brewed some tea in a small pot and sat sipping it without sugar, to calm himself. But before he had finished drinking, again with excitement he examined the face and found it good: good for Leo Finkle. Only such a one could understand him and help him seek whatever he was seeking. She might, perhaps, love him. How she had happened to be among the discards in Salzman's barrel he could never guess, but he knew he must urgently go find her.

Leo rushed downstairs, grabbed up the Bronx telephone book, and searched for Salzman's home address. He was not listed, nor was his office. Neither was he in the Manhattan book. But Leo remembered having written down the address on a slip of paper after he had read Salzman's advertisement in the "personals" column of the *Forward*. He ran up to his room and tore through his papers, without luck. It was exasperating. Just when he needed the matchmaker he was nowhere to be found. Fortunately Leo remembered to look in his wallet. There on a card he found his name written and a Bronx address. No phone number was listed, the reason—Leo now recalled—he had originally communicated with Salzman by letter. He got on his coat, put a hat on over his skull cap and hurried to the subway station. All the way to the far end of the Bronx he sat on the edge of his seat. He was more than once tempted to take out the picture and see if the girl's face was as he remembered it, but he refrained, allowing the snapshot to remain in his inside coat pocket, content to have

her so close. When the train pulled into the station he was waiting at the door and bolted out. He quickly located the street Salzman had advertised.

The building he sought was less than a block from the subway, but it was not an office building, nor even a loft, nor a store in which one could rent office space. It was a very old tenement house. Leo found Salzman's name in pencil on a soiled tag under the bell and climbed three dark flights to his apartment. When he knocked, the door was opened by a thin, asthmatic, gray-haired woman, in felt slippers.

"Yes?" she said, expecting nothing. She listened without listening. He could have sworn he had seen her, too, before but knew it was an illusion.

"Salzman—does he live here? Pinye Salzman," he said, "the matchmaker?"

She stared at him a long minute. "Of course."

He felt embarrassed. "Is he in?"

"No." Her mouth, though left open, offered nothing more.

"The matter is urgent. Can you tell me where his office is?"

"In the air." She pointed upward.

"You mean he has no office?" Leo asked.

"In his socks."

He peered into the apartment. It was sunless and dingy, one large room divided by a half-open curtain, beyond which he could see a sagging metal bed. The near side of a room was crowded with rickety chairs, old bureaus, a three-legged table, racks of cooking utensils, and all the apparatus of a kitchen. But there was no sign of Salzman or his magic barrel, probably also a figment of the imagination. An odor of frying fish made Leo weak to the knees.

"Where is he?" he insisted. "I've got to see your husband."

At length she answered, "So who knows where he is? Every time he thinks a new thought he runs to a different place. Go home, he will find you."

"Tell him Leo Finkle."

She gave no sign she had heard.

He walked downstairs, depressed.

But Salzman, breathless, stood waiting at his door.

Leo was astounded and overjoyed. "How did you get here before me?"

"I rushed."

"Come inside."

They entered. Leo fixed tea, and a sardine sandwich for Salzman. As they were drinking he reached behind him for the packet of pictures and handed them to the marriage broker.

Salzman put down his glass and said expectantly, "You found somebody you like?"

"Not among these."

The marriage broker turned away.

"Here is the one I want." Leo held forth the snapshot.

Salzman slipped on his glasses and took the picture into his trembling hand. He turned ghastly and let out a groan.

"What's the matter?" cried Leo.

"Excuse me. Was an accident this picture. She isn't for you."

Salzman frantically shoved the manila packet into his portfolio. He thrust the snapshot into his pocket and fled down the stairs.

Leo, after momentary paralysis, gave chase and cornered the marriage broker in the vestibule. The landlady made hysterical outcries but neither of them listened.

"Give me back the picture, Salzman."

"No." The pain in his eyes was terrible.

"Tell me who she is then."

"This I can't tell you. Excuse me."

He made to depart, but Leo, forgetting himself, seized the matchmaker by his tight coat and shook him frenziedly.

"Please," sighed Salzman. *"Please."*

Leo ashamedly let him go. "Tell me who she is," he begged. "It's very important for me to know."

"She is not for you. She is a wild one —wild, without shame. This is not a bride for a rabbi."

"What do you mean wild?"

"Like an animal. Like a dog. For her to be poor was a sin. This is why to me she is dead now."

"In God's name, what do you mean?"

"Her I can't introduce to you," Salzman cried.

"Why are you so excited?"

"Why, he asks," Salzman said, bursting into tears. "This is my baby, my Stella, she should burn in hell."

Leo hurried up to bed and hid under the covers. Under the covers he thought his life through. Although he soon fell asleep he could not sleep her out of his mind. He woke, beating his breast. Though he prayed to be rid of her, his prayers went unanswered. Through days of torment he endlessly struggled not to love her; fearing success, he escaped it. He then concluded to convert her to goodness, himself to God. The idea alternately nauseated and exalted him.

He perhaps did not know that he had come to a final decision until he encountered Salzman in a Broadway cafeteria. He was sitting alone at a rear table, sucking the bony remains of a fish. The marriage broker appeared haggard, and transparent to the point of vanishing.

Salzman looked up at first without recognizing him. Leo had grown a pointed beard and his eyes were weighted with wisdom.

"Salzman," he said, "love has at last come to my heart."

"Who can love from a picture?" mocked the marriage broker.

"It is not impossible."

"If you can love her, then you can love anybody. Let me show you some new clients that they just sent me their photographs. One is a little doll."

"Just her I want," Leo murmured.

"Don't be a fool, doctor. Don't bother with her."

"Put me in touch with her, Salzman," Leo said humbly. "Perhaps I can be of service."

Salzman had stopped eating and Leo understood with emotion that it was now arranged.

Leaving the cafeteria, he was, however, afflicted by a tormenting suspicion that Salzman had planned it all to happen this way.

Leo was informed by letter that she would meet him on a certain corner, and she was there one spring night, waiting

under a street lamp. He appeared, carrying a small bouquet of violets and rose-
buds. Stella stood by the lamp post,
smoking. She wore white with red shoes,
which fitted his expectations, although in
a troubled moment he had imagined the
dress red, and only the shoes white. She
waited uneasily and shyly. From afar he
saw that her eyes—clearly her father's—
were filled with desperate innocence. He
pictured, in her, his own redemption.
Violins and lit candles revolved in the sky.
Leo ran forward with flowers outthrust.

Around the corner, Salzman, leaning
against a wall, chanted prayers for the
dead.

[1954]

QUESTIONS FOR STUDY

1. *What does Leo come to learn about himself and about his capacity to love?*
2. *What role does Lily Hirschorn play in this process of self-discovery? What role does Stella play? What is there in Stella's picture that so attracts Leo?*
3. *Why is Salzman so reluctant to introduce Leo to Stella? Why does Malamud choose to conclude his story with their first meeting? In what ways is the ending ambiguous?*
4. *Is there any evidence to suggest that Salzman is a con artist who has manipulated the whole affair for his own benefit? How does such an interpretation change the meaning of the story?*
5. *Why does Salzman lean against the wall, chanting prayers for the dead?*

THOMAS MANN

Mario and the Magician

THE ATMOSPHERE of Torre di Venere remains unpleasant in the memory. From the first moment the air of the place made us uneasy, we felt irritable, on edge; then at the end came the shocking business of Cipolla, that dreadful being who seemed to incorporate, in so fateful and so humanly impressive a way, all the peculiar evilness of the situation as a whole. Looking back, we had the feeling that the horrible end of the affair had been preordained and lay in the nature of things; that the children had to be present at it was an added impropriety, due to the false colours in which the weird creature presented himself. Luckily for them, they did not know where the comedy left off and the tragedy began; and we let them remain in their happy belief that the whole thing had been a play up till the end.

Torre di Venere lies some fifteen kilometres from Portoclemente, one of the most popular summer resorts on the Tyrrhenian Sea. Portoclemente is urban and elegant and full to overflowing for months on end. Its gay and busy main street of shops and hotels runs down to a wide sandy beach covered with tents and pennanted sand-castles and sunburnt humanity, where at all times a lively social bustle reigns, and much noise. But this same spacious and inviting fine-sanded beach, this same border of pine grove and near, presiding mountains, continues all the way along the coast. No wonder then that some competition of a quiet kind should have sprung up further on. Torre di Venere—the tower that gave the town its name is gone long since, one looks for it in vain—is an offshoot of the larger resort, and for some years remained an idyll for the few, a refuge for more unworldly spirits. But the usual history of such places repeated itself: peace has had to retire further along the coast, to Marina Petriera and dear knows where else. We all know how the world at once seeks peace and puts her to flight—rushing upon her in the fond idea that they two will wed, and where she is, there it can be at home. It will even set up its Vanity Fair in a spot and be capable of thinking that peace is still by its side. Thus Torre—though its atmosphere so far is more modest and contemplative than that of Portoclemente—has been quite taken up, by both Italians and foreigners. It is no longer the thing to go to Portoclemente —though still so much the thing that it is as noisy and crowded as ever. One goes next door, so to speak: to Torre. So much more refined, even, and cheaper to boot. And the attractiveness of these qualities persists, though the qualities themselves long ago ceased to be evident. Torre has got a Grand Hotel. Numerous pensions have sprung up, some modest, some pretentious. The people who own or rent the villas and pinetas overlooking the sea no longer have it all their own way on the beach. In July and August it looks just like the beach at Portoclemente: it swarms with a screaming, squabbling, merrymaking crowd, and the sun, blazing down like mad, peels the skin off their necks. Garish little flat-bottomed boats rock on the glittering blue, manned by children, whose mothers hover afar and fill the air with anxious cries of Nino! and Sandro! and Bice! and Maria! Pedlars step across the legs of recumbent sun-bathers, selling flowers and corals, oysters, lemonade, and *cornetti al burro*, and crying their wares in the breathy, full-throated southern voice.

Such was the scene that greeted our arrival in Torre: pleasant enough, but after all, we thought, we had come too soon. It was the middle of August, the Italian season was still at its height, scarcely the moment for strangers to learn to love the special charms of the place. What an afternoon crowd in the cafés on the front! For instance, in the Esquisito, where we sometimes sat and were served by Mario, that very Mario of whom I shall have presently to tell. It is well-nigh impossible to find a table; and the various orchestras contend together in the midst of one's conversation with bewildering effect. Of course, it is in the afternoon that people come from Portoclemente. The excursion is a favourite one for the restless denizens of that pleasure resort, and a Fiat motorbus plies to and fro, coating inch-thick with dust the oleander and laurel hedges along the highroad—a notable if repulsive sight.

Yes, decidedly one should go to Torre in September, when the great public has left. Or else in May, before the water is warm enough to tempt the Southerner to bathe. Even in the before and after seasons Torre is not empty, but life is less national and more subdued. English, French, and German prevail under the tent-awnings and in the pension diningrooms; whereas in August—in the Grand Hotel, at least, where, in default of private addresses, we had engaged rooms—the stranger finds the field so occupied by Florentine and Roman society that he feels quite isolated and even temporarily déclassé.

We had, rather to our annoyance, this experience on the evening we arrived, when we went in to dinner and were shown to our table by the waiter in charge. As a table, it had nothing against it, save that we had already fixed our eyes upon those on the veranda beyond, built out over the water, where little red-shaded lamps glowed—and there were still some tables empty, though it was as full as the dining-room within. The children went into raptures at the festive sight, and without more ado we announced our intention to take our meals by preference in the veranda. Our words, it appeared, were prompted by ignorance; for we were informed, with somewhat embarrassed politeness, that the cosy nook outside was reserved for the clients of the hotel: *ai nostri clienti*. Their clients? But we were their clients. We were not tourists or trippers, but boarders for a stay of some three or four weeks. However, we forbore to press for an explanation of the difference between the likes of us and that clientèle to whom it was vouchsafed to eat out there in the glow of the red lamps, and took our dinner by the prosaic common light of the dining-room chandelier —a thoroughly ordinary and monotonous hotel bill of fare, be it said. In Pensione Eleonora, a few steps landward, the table, as we were to discover, was much better.

And thither it was that we moved, three or four days later, before we had had time to settle in properly at the Grand Hotel. Not on account of the veranda and the lamps. The children, straightway on the best of terms with waiters and pages, absorbed in the joys of life on the beach, promptly forgot those colourful seductions. But now there arose, between ourselves and the veranda clientèle—or perhaps more correctly with the compliant management—one of those little unpleasantnesses which can quite spoil the pleasure of a holiday. Among the guests were some high Roman aristocracy, a Principe X and his family. These grand folk occupied rooms close to our own, and the Principessa, a great and a passionately maternal lady, was thrown into a panic by the vestiges of a whoopingcough which our little ones had lately got over, but which now and then still faintly troubled the unshatterable slumbers of our youngest-born. The nature of this illness is not clear, leaving some play for the imagination. So we took no offence at our elegant neighbour for clinging to the widely held view that whoopingcough is acoustically contagious and quite simply fearing lest her children yield to the bad example set by ours. In the fullness of her feminine self-confidence she protested to the management, which then, in the person of the proverbial frockcoated manager, hastened to represent to us, with many expressions of regret, that under the circumstances they were obliged to transfer us to the annexe. We did our best to assure him that the disease was in its very last stages, that it was actually over, and presented no danger of infection to anybody. All that we gained was permission to bring the case before the hotel physician—not one chosen by us—by whose verdict we must then abide. We agreed, convinced that thus we should at once pacify the Princess and escape the trouble of moving. The doctor appeared, and behaved like a faithful and honest servant of science. He examined the child and gave his opinion: the disease was quite over, no danger of contagion was present. We drew a long breath and considered the incident closed—until the manager announced that despite the doctor's verdict it would still be necessary for us to give up our rooms and retire to the *dépendance*. Byzantinism like this outraged us. It is not likely that the Principessa was responsible for the wilful breach of faith. Very likely the fawning management had not even dared to tell her what the physician said. Anyhow, we made it clear to his understanding that we preferred to leave the hotel altogether and at once—and packed our trunks. We could do so with a light heart, having already set up casual friendly relations with Casa Eleonora. We had noticed its pleasant exterior and formed the acquaintance of its proprietor, Signora Angiolieri, and her husband: she slender and black-haired, Tuscan in type, probably at the beginning of the thirties, with the dead ivory complexion of the southern woman, he quiet and bald and carefully dressed. They owned a larger establishment in Florence and presided only in summer and early autumn over the branch in Torre di Venere. But earlier, before her marriage, our new landlady had been companion, fellow-traveller, wardrobe mistress, yes, friend, of Eleonora Duse and manifestly regarded that period as the crown of her career. Even at our first visit she spoke of it with animation. Numerous photographs of the great actress, with affectionate inscriptions, were displayed about the drawing-room, and other souvenirs of their life together adorned the little tables and étagères. This cult of a so interesting past was calculated, of course, to heighten the advantages of the signora's present business. Nevertheless our pleasure and interest were quite genuine as we were conducted through the house by its owner and listened to her sonorous and staccato Tuscan voice relating anecdotes of that immortal mistress, depicting her suffering saintliness, her genius, her profound delicacy of feeling.

Thither, then, we moved our effects, to the dismay of the staff of the Grand Hotel, who, like all Italians, were very good to children. Our new quarters were retired and pleasant, we were within easy reach of the sea through the avenue of young plane trees that ran down to the esplanade. In the clean, cool dining-room Signora Angiolieri daily served the soup with her own hands, the service was attentive and good, the table capital. We even discovered some Viennese acquaintances, and enjoyed chatting with them after luncheon, in front of the house. They, in turn, were the means of our finding others—in short, all seemed for the best, and we were heartily glad of the change we had made. Nothing was now wanting to a holiday of the most gratifying kind.

And yet no proper gratification ensued. Perhaps the stupid occasion of our change of quarters pursued us to the new ones we had found. Personally, I admit that I do not easily forget these collisions with ordinary humanity, the naïve misuse of power, the injustice, the sycophantic corruption. I dwelt upon the incident too much, it irritated me in retrospect—quite futilely, of course, since such phenomena are only all too natural and all too much the rule. And we had not broken off relations with the Grand Hotel. The children were as friendly as ever there, the porter mended their toys, and we sometimes took tea in the garden. We even saw the Principessa. She would come out, with her firm and delicate tread, her lips emphatically corallined, to look after her children, playing under the supervision of their English governess. She did not dream that we were anywhere near, for so soon as she appeared in the offing we sternly forbade our little one even to clear his throat.

The heat—if I may bring it in evidence—was extreme. It was African. The power of the sun, directly one left the border of the indigo-blue wave, was so frightful, so relentless, that the mere thought of the few steps between the beach and luncheon was a burden, clad though one might be only in pyjamas. Do you care for that sort of thing? Weeks on end? Yes, of course, it is proper to the south, it is classic weather, the sun of Homer, the climate wherein human culture came to flower—and all the rest of it. But after a while it is too much for me, I reach a point where I begin to find it dull. The burning void of the sky, day after day, weighs one down; the high coloration, the enormous naïveté of the unrefracted light—they do, I dare say, induce light-heartedness, a carefree mood born of immunity from downpours and other meterological caprices. But slowly, slowly, there makes itself felt a lack: the deeper, more complex needs of the northern soul remain unsatisfied. You are left barren—even, it may be, in time, a little contemptuous. True, without that stupid business of the whooping-cough I might not have been feeling these things. I was annoyed, very likely I wanted to feel them and so half-consciously seized upon an idea lying ready to hand to induce, or if not to induce, at least to justify and strengthen, my attitude. Up to this point, then, if you like, let us grant some ill will on our part. But the sea; and the mornings spent extended upon the fine sand in face of its eternal splendours— no, the sea could not conceivably induce such feelings. Yet it was none the less true that, despite all previous experience, we were not at home on the beach, we were not happy.

It was too soon, too soon. The beach, as I have said, was still in the hands of the middle-class native. It is a pleasing breed to look at, and among the young we saw much shapeliness and charm. Still, we were necessarily surrounded by a great deal of very average humanity— a middle-class mob, which, you will admit, is not more charming under this sun than under one's own native sky. The voices these women have! It was sometimes hard to believe that we were in the land which is the western cradle of the art of song. *"Fuggièro!"* I can still hear

that cry, as for twenty mornings long I heard it close behind me, breathy, full-throated, hideously stressed, with a harsh open *e*, uttered in accents of mechanical despair. *"Fuggièro! Rispondi almeno!"* Answer when I call you! The *sp* in *rispondi* was pronounced like *shp*, as Germans pronounce it; and this, on top of what I felt already, vexed my sensitive soul. The cry was addressed to a repulsive youngster whose sunburn had made disgusting raw sores on his shoulders. He outdid anything I have ever seen for illbreeding, refractoriness, and temper and was a great coward to boot, putting the whole beach in an uproar, one day, because of his outrageous sensitiveness to the slightest pain. A sand-crab had pinched his toe in the water, and the minute injury made him set up a cry of heroic proportions—the shout of an antique hero in his agony—that pierced one to the marrow and called up visions of some frightful tragedy. Evidently he considered himself not only wounded, but poisoned as well; he crawled out on the sand and lay in apparently intolerable anguish, groaning *"Ohi!"* and *"Ohimè!"* and threshing about with arms and legs to ward off his mother's tragic appeals and the questions of the bystanders. An audience gathered round. A doctor was fetched—the same who had pronounced objective judgment on our whoopingcough—and here again acquitted himself like a man of science. Good-naturedly he reassured the boy, telling him that he was not hurt at all, he should simply go into the water again to relieve the smart. Instead of which, Fuggièro was borne off the beach, followed by a concourse of people. But he did not fail to appear next morning, nor did he leave off spoiling our children's sand-castles. Of course, always by accident. In short, a perfect terror.

And this twelve-year-old lad was prominent among the influences that, imperceptibly at first, combined to spoil our holiday and render it unwholesome. Somehow or other, there was a stiffness, a lack of innocent enjoyment. These people stood on their dignity—just why, and in what spirit, it was not easy at first to tell. They displayed much self-respectingness; towards each other and towards the foreigner their bearing was that of a person newly conscious of a sense of honour. And wherefore? Gradually we realized the political implications and understood that we were in the presence of a national ideal. The beach, in fact, was alive with patriotic children—a phenomenon as unnatural as it was depressing. Children are a human species and a society apart, a nation of their own, so to speak. On the basis of their common form of life, they find each other out with the greatest ease, no matter how different their small vocabularies. Ours soon played with natives and foreigners alike. Yet they were plainly both puzzled and disappointed at times. There were wounded sensibilities, displays of assertiveness —or rather hardly assertiveness, for it was too self-conscious and too didactic to deserve the name. There were quarrels over flags, disputes about authority and precedence. Grown-ups joined in, not so much to pacify as to render judgment and enunciate principles. Phrases were dropped about the greatness and dignity of Italy, solemn phrases that spoilt the fun. We saw our two little ones retreat, puzzled and hurt, and were put to it to explain the situation. These people, we told them, were just passing through a certain stage, something rather like an illness, perhaps; not very pleasant, but probably unavoidable.

We had only our own carelessness to thank that we came to blows in the end with this "stage"—which, after all, we had seen and sized up long before now. Yes, it came to another "cross-purposes," so evidently the earlier ones had not been sheer accident. In a word, we became an offence to the public morals. Our small daughter—eight years old, but in physical development a good year younger and thin as a chicken—had had a good long bathe and gone playing in the warm sun in her wet costume. We told her that she might take off her bathing-suit, which was stiff with sand, rinse it in the sea, and put it on again, after which she must take care to keep it cleaner. Off goes the costume and she runs down naked to the sea, rinses her little jersey, and comes

back. Ought we to have foreseen the outburst of anger and resentment which her conduct, and thus our conduct, called forth? Without delivering a homily on the subject, I may say that in the last decade our attitude towards the nude body and our feelings regarding it have undergone, all over the world, a fundamental change. There are things we "never think about" any more, and among them is the freedom we had permitted to this by no means provocative little childish body. But in these parts it was taken as a challenge. The patriotic children hooted. Fuggièro whistled on his fingers. The sudden buzz of conversation among the grown people in our neighbourhood boded no good. A gentleman in city togs, with a not very apropos bowler hat on the back of his head, was assuring his outraged womenfolk that he proposed to take punitive measures; he stepped up to us, and a philippic descended on our unworthy heads, in which all the emotionalism of the sense-loving south spoke in the service of morality and discipline. The offence against decency of which we had been guilty was, he said, the more to be condemned because it was also a gross ingratitude and an insulting breach of his country's hospitality. We had criminally injured not only the letter and spirit of the public bathing regulations, but also the honour of Italy; he, the gentleman in the city togs, knew how to defend that honour and proposed to see to it that our offence against the national dignity should not go unpunished.

We did our best, bowing respectfully, to give ear to this eloquence. To contradict the man, overheated as he was, would probably be to fall from one error into another. On the tips of our tongues we had various answers: as, that the word "hospitality," in its strictest sense, was not quite the right one, taking all the circumstances into consideration. We were not literally the guests of Italy, but of Signora Angiolieri, who had assumed the rôle of dispenser of hospitality some years ago on laying down that of familiar friend to Eleonora Duse. We longed to say that surely this beautful country had not sunk so low as to be reduced to a state of hypersensitive prudishness. But we confined ourselves to assuring the gentleman that any lack of respect, any provocation on our parts, had been the furthest from our thoughts. And as a mitigating circumstance we pointed out the tender age and physical slightness of the little culprit. In vain. Our protests were waved away, he did not believe in them; our defence would not hold water. We must be made an example of. The authorities were notified, by telephone, I believe, and their representative appeared on the beach. He said the case was "*molto grave.*" We had to go with him to the Municipio up in the Piazza, where a higher official confirmed the previous verdict of "*molto grave,*" launched into a stream of the usual didactic phrases—the selfsame tune and words as the man in the bowler hat—and levied a fine and ransom of fifty lire. We felt that the adventure must willy-nilly be worth to us this much of a contribution to the economy of the Italian government; paid, and left. Ought we not at this point to have left Torre as well?

If we only had! We should thus have escaped that fatal Cipolla. But circumstances combined to prevent us from making up our minds to a change. A certain poet says that it is indolence that makes us endure uncomfortable situations. The *aperçu* may serve as an explanation for our inaction. Anyhow, one dislikes voiding the field immediately upon such an event. Especially if sympathy from other quarters encourages one to defy it. And in the Villa Eleonora they pronounced as with one voice upon the injustice of our punishment. Some Italian after-dinner acquaintances found that the episode put their country in a very bad light, and proposed taking the man in the bowler hat to task, as one fellow-citizen to another. But the next day he and his party had vanished from the beach. Not on our account, of course. Though it might be that the consciousness of his impending departure had added energy to his rebuke; in any case his going was a relief. And, furthermore, we stayed because our stay had by now become remarkable in our own eyes, which is worth something in itself, quite apart from the

comfort or discomfort involved. Shall we strike sail, avoid a certain experience so soon as it seems not expressly calculated to increase our enjoyment or our self-esteem? Shall we go away whenever life looks like turning in the slightest uncanny, or not quite normal, or even rather painful and mortifying? No, surely not. Rather stay and look matters in the face, brave them out; perhaps precisely in so doing lies a lesson for us to learn. We stayed on and reaped as the awful reward of our constancy the unholy and staggering experience with Cipolla.

I have not mentioned that the after season had begun, almost on the very day we were disciplined by the city authorities. The worshipful gentleman in the bowler hat, our denouncer, was not the only person to leave the resort. There was a regular exodus, on every hand you saw luggage-carts on their way to the station. The beach denationalized itself. Life in Torre, in the cafés and the pinetas, became more homelike and more European. Very likely we might even have eaten at a table in the glass veranda, but we refrained, being content at Signora Angiolieri's—as content, that is, as our evil star would let us be. But at the same time with this turn for the better came a change in the weather: almost to an hour it showed itself in harmony with the holiday calendar of the general public. The sky was overcast; not that it grew any cooler, but the unclouded heat of the entire eighteen days since our arrival, and probably long before that, gave place to a stifling sirocco air, while from time to time a little ineffectual rain sprinkled the velvety surface of the beach. Add to which, that two-thirds of our intended stay at Torre had passed. The colourless, lazy sea, with sluggish jellyfish floating in its shallows, was at least a change. And it would have been silly to feel retrospective longings after a sun that had caused us so many sighs when it burned down in all its arrogant power.

At this juncture, then, it was that Cipolla announced himself. Cavaliere Cipolla he was called on the posters that appeared one day stuck up everywhere, even in the dining-room of Pensione

Eleonora. A travelling virtuoso, as entertainer, "*forzatore, illusionista, prestidigatore*," as he called himself, who proposed to wait upon the highly respectable population of Torre di Venere with a display of extraordinary phenomena of a mysterious and staggering kind. A conjuror! The bare announcement was enough to turn our children's heads. They had never seen anything of the sort, and now our present holiday was to afford them this new excitement. From that moment on they besieged us with prayers to take tickets for the performance. We had doubts, from the first, on the score of the lateness of the hour, nine o'clock; but gave way, in the idea that we might see a little of what Cipolla had to offer, probably no great matter, and then go home. Besides, of course, the children could sleep late the next day. We bought four tickets of Signora Angiolieri herself, she having taken a number of the stalls on commission to sell them to her guests. She could not vouch for the man's performance, and we had no great expectations. But we were conscious of a need for diversion, and the children's violent curiosity proved catching.

The Cavaliere's performance was to take place in a hall where during the season there had been a cinema with a weekly programme. We had never been there. You reached it by following the main street under the wall of the "*palazzo*," a ruin with a "For sale" sign, that suggested a castle and had obviously been built in lordlier days. In the same street were the chemist, the hairdresser, and all the better shops; it led, so to speak, from the feudal past the bourgeois into the proletarian, for it ended off between two rows of poor fishing-huts, where old women sat mending nets before the doors. And here, among the proletariat, was the hall, not much more, actually, than a wooden shed, though a large one, with a turreted entrance, plastered on either side with layers of gay placards. Some while after dinner, then, on the appointed evening, we wended our way thither in the dark, the children dressed in their best and blissful with the sense of so much irregularity. It was sultry,

as it had been for days; there was heat lightning now and then, and a little rain; we proceeded under umbrellas. It took us a quarter of an hour.

Our tickets were collected at the entrance, our places we had to find ourselves. They were in the third row left, and as we sat down we saw that, late though the hour was for the performance, it was to be interpreted with even more laxity. Only very slowly did an audience —who seemed to be relied upon to come late—begin to fill the stalls. These comprised the whole auditorium; there were no boxes. This tardiness gave us some concern. The children's cheeks were already flushed as much with fatigue as with excitement. But even when we entered, the standing-room at the back and in the side aisles was already well occupied. There stood the manhood of Torre di Venere, all and sundry, fisherfolk, rough-and-ready youths with bare forearms crossed over their striped jerseys. We were well pleased with the presence of this native assemblage, which always adds colour and animation to occasions like the present; and the children were frankly delighted. For they had friends among these people—acquaintances picked up on afternoon strolls to the further ends of the beach. We would be turning homeward, at the hour when the sun dropped into the sea, spent with the huge effort it had made and gilding with reddish gold the oncoming surf; and we would come upon bare-legged fisherfolk standing in rows, bracing and hauling with long-drawn cries as they drew in the nets and harvested in dripping baskets their catch, often so scanty, of *frutta di mare*. The children looked on, helped to pull, brought out their little stock of Italian words, made friends. So now they exchanged nods with the "standing-room" clientèle; there was Guiscardo, there Antonio, they knew them by name and waved and called across in half-whispers, getting answering nods and smiles that displayed rows of healthy white teeth. Look, there is even Mario, Mario from the Esquisito, who brings us the chocolate. He wants to see the conjuror, too, and he must have come early, for he is almost in front; but he does not see us, he is not paying attention; that is a way he has, even though he is a waiter. So we wave instead to the man who lets out the little boats on the beach; he is there too, standing at the back.

It had got to a quarter past nine, it got to almost half past. It was natural that we should be nervous. When would the children get to bed? It had been a mistake to bring them, for now it would be very hard to suggest breaking off their enjoyment before it had got well under way. The stalls had filled in time; all Torre, apparently, was there: the guests of the Grand Hotel, the guests of Villa Eleonora, familiar faces from the beach. We heard English and German and the sort of French that Rumanians speak with Italians. Madame Angiolieri herself sat two rows behind us, with her quiet, bald-headed spouse, who kept stroking his moustache with the two middle fingers of his right hand. Everybody had come late, but nobody too late. Cipolla made us wait for him.

He made us wait. That is probably the way to put it. He heightened the suspense by his delay in appearing. And we could see the point of this, too—only not when it was carried to extremes. Towards half past nine the audience began to clap—an amiable way of expressing justifiable impatience, evincing as it does an eagerness to applaud. For the little ones, this was a joy in itself—all children love to clap. From the popular sphere came loud cries of *"Pronti!"* *"Cominciamo!"* And lo, it seemed now as easy to begin as before it had been hard. A gong sounded, greeted by the standing rows with a many-voiced "Ah-h!" and the curtains parted. They revealed a platform furnished more like a schoolroom than like the theatre of a conjuring performance—largely because of the blackboard in the left foreground. There was a common yellow hat-stand, a few ordinary straw-bottomed chairs, and further back a little round table holding a water carafe and glass, also a tray with a liqueur glass and a flask of pale yellow liquid. We had still a few seconds of time to let these things sink in. Then, with no darkening of the house, Cavaliere Cipolla made his entry.

He came forward with a rapid step that expressed his eagerness to appear before his public and gave rise to the illusion that he had already come a long way to put himself at their service—whereas, of course, he had only been standing in the wings. His costume supported the fiction. A man of an age hard to determine, but by no means young; with a sharp, ravaged face, piercing eyes, compressed lips, small black waxed moustache, and a so-called imperial in the curve between mouth and chin. He was dressed for the street with a sort of complicated evening elegance, in a wide black pelerine with velvet collar and satin lining; which, in the hampered state of his arms, he held together in front with his white-gloved hands. He had a white scarf round his neck; a top hat with a curving brim sat far back on his head. Perhaps more than anywhere else the eighteenth century is still alive in Italy, and with it the charlatan and mountebank type so characteristic of the period. Only there, at any rate, does one still encounter really well-preserved specimens. Cipolla had in his whole appearance much of the historic type; his very clothes helped to conjure up the traditional figure with its blatantly, fantastically foppish air. His pretentious costume sat upon him, or rather hung upon him, most curiously, being in one place drawn too tight, in another a mass of awkward folds. There was something not quite in order about his figure, both front and back—that was plain later on. But I must emphasize the fact that there was not a trace of personal jocularity or clownishness in his pose, manner, or behaviour. On the contrary, there was complete seriousness, an absence of any humorous appeal; occasionally even a cross-grained pride, along with that curious, self-satisfied air so characteristic of the deformed. None of all this, however, prevented his appearance from being greeted with laughter from more than one quarter of the hall.

All the eagerness had left his manner. The swift entry had been merely an expression of energy, not of zeal. Standing at the footlights he negligently drew off his gloves, to display long yellow hands, one of them adorned with a seal ring with a lapis-lazuli in a high setting. As he stood there, his small hard eyes, with flabby pouches beneath them, roved appraisingly about the hall, not quickly, rather in a considered examination, pausing here and there upon a face with his lips clipped together, not speaking a word. Then with a display of skill as surprising as it was casual, he rolled his gloves into a ball and tossed them across a considerable distance into the glass on the table. Next from an inner pocket he drew forth a packet of cigarettes; you could see by the wrapper that they were the cheapest sort the government sells. With his fingertips he pulled out a cigarette and lighted it, without looking, from a quick-firing benzine lighter. He drew the smoke deep into his lungs and let it out again, tapping his foot, with both lips drawn in an arrogant grimace and the grey smoke streaming out between broken and saw-edged teeth.

With a keenness equal to his own his audience eyed him. The youths at the rear scowled as they peered at this cocksure creature to search out his secret weaknesses. He betrayed none. In fetching out and putting back the cigarettes his clothes got in his way. He had to turn back his pelerine, and in so doing revealed a riding-whip with a silver claw-handle that hung by a leather thong from his left forearm and looked decidedly out of place. You could see that he had on not evening clothes but a frock-coat, and under this, as he lifted it to get at his pocket, could be seen a striped sash worn about the body. Somebody behind me whispered that this sash went with his title of Cavaliere. I give the information for what it may be worth—personally, I never heard that the title carried such insignia with it. Perhaps the sash was sheer pose, like the way he stood there, without a word, casually and arrogantly puffing smoke into his audience's face.

People laughed, as I said. The merriment had become almost general when somebody in the "standing seats," in a loud, dry voice, remarked: "*Buona sera.*"

Cipolla cocked his head. "Who was that?" asked he, as though he had been dared. "Who was that just spoke? Well? First so bold and now so modest? *Paura,*

eh?" He spoke with a rather high, asthmatic voice, which yet had a metallic quality. He waited.

"That was me," a youth at the rear broke into the stillness, seeing himself thus challenged. He was not far from us, a handsome fellow in a woollen shirt, with his coat hanging over one shoulder. He wore his curly, wiry hair in a high, dishevelled mop, the style affected by the youth of the awakened Fatherland; it gave him an African appearance that rather spoiled his looks. "*Bè!* That was me. It was your business to say it first, but I was trying to be friendly."

More laughter. The chap had a tongue in his head. "*Ha sciolto la scilinguágnolo,*" [1] I heard near me. After all, the retort was deserved.

"Ah, bravo!" answered Cipolla. "I like you, *giovanotto.* Trust me, I've had my eye on you for some time. People like you are just in my line. I can use them. And you are the pick of the lot, that's plain to see. You do what you like. Or is it possible you have ever not done what you liked—or even, maybe, what you didn't like? What somebody else liked, in short? Hark ye, my friend, that might be a pleasant change for you, to divide up the willing and the doing and stop tackling both jobs at once. Division of labour, *sistema americano, sa'!* For instance, suppose you were to show your tongue to this select and honourable audience here— your whole tongue, right down to the roots?"

"No, I won't," said the youth hostilely. "Sticking out your tongue shows a bad bringing-up."

"Nothing of the sort, retorted Cipolla. "You would only be *doing* it. With all due respect to your bringing-up, I suggest that before I count ten, you will perform a right turn and stick out your tongue at the company here further than you knew yourself that you could stick it out."

He gazed at the youth, and his piercing eyes seemed to sink deeper into their sockets. "*Uno!*" said he. He had let his riding-whip slide down his arm and made it whistle once through the air. The boy faced about and put out his tongue, so

[1] "He has a glib tongue." (JHP)

long, so extendedly, that you could see it was the very uttermost in tongue which he had to offer. Then turned back, stony-faced, to his former position.

"That was me," mocked Cipolla, with a jerk of his head towards the youth. "*Bè!* That was me." Leaving the audience to enjoy its sensations, he turned towards the little round table, lifted the bottle, poured out a small glass of what was obviously cognac, and tipped it up with a practised hand.

The children laughed with all their hearts. They had understood practically nothing of what had been said, but it pleased them hugely that something so funny should happen, straightaway, between that queer man up there and somebody out of the audience. They had no preconception of what an "evening" would be like and were quite ready to find this a priceless beginning. As for us, we exchanged a glance and I remember that involuntarily I made with my lips the sound that Cipolla's whip had made when it cut the air. For the rest, it was plain that people did not know what to make of a preposterous beginning like this to a sleight-of-hand performance. They could not see why the *giovanotto*, who after all in a way had been their spokesman, should suddenly have turned on them to vent his incivility. They felt that he had behaved like a silly ass and withdrew their countenances from him in favour of the artist, who now came back from his refreshment table and addressed them as follows:

"Ladies and gentlemen," said he, in his wheezing, metallic voice, "you saw just now that I was rather sensitive on the score of the rebuke this hopeful young linguist saw fit to give me"—"*questo linguista di belle speranze*" [2] was what he said, and we all laughed at the pun. "I am a man who sets some store by himself, you may take it from me. And I see no point in being wished a good-evening unless it is done courteously and in all seriousness. For anything else there is no occasion. When a man wishes me a good-evening he wishes himself one, for the

audience will have one only if I do. So this lady-killer of Torre di Venere" (another thrust) "did well to testify that I have one tonight and that I can dispense with any wishes of his in the matter. I can boast of having good evenings almost without exception. One not so good does come my way now and again, but very seldom. My calling is hard and my health not of the best. I have a little physical defect which prevented me from doing my bit in the war for the greater glory of the Fatherland. It is perforce with my mental and spiritual parts that I conquer life—which after all only means conquering oneself. And I flatter myself that my achievements have aroused interest and respect among the educated public. The leading newspapers have lauded me, the *Corriere della Sera* did me the courtesy of calling me a phenomenon, and in Rome the brother of the *Duce* honoured me by his presence at one of my evenings. I should not have thought that in a relatively less important place" (laughter here, at the expense of poor little Torre) "I should have to give up the small personal habits which brilliant and elevated audiences had been ready to overlook. Nor did I think I had to stand being heckled by a person who seems to have been rather spoilt by the favours of the fair sex." All this of course at the expense of the youth whom Cipolla never tired of presenting in the guise of *donnaiuolo* and rustic Don Juan. His persistent thin-skinnedness and animosity were in striking contrast to the self-confidence and the worldly success he boasted of. One might have assumed that the *giovanotto* was merely the chosen butt of Cipolla's customary professional sallies, had not the very pointed witticisms betrayed a genuine antagonism. No one looking at the physical parts of the two men need have been at a loss for the explanation, even if the deformed man had not constantly played on the other's supposed success with the fair sex. "Well," Cipolla went on, "before beginning our entertainment this evening, perhaps you will permit me to make myself comfortable."

And he went towards the hat-stand to take off his things.

2 "this linguist of great hope." (JHP)

"*Parla benissimo,*" [3] asserted somebody in our neighbourhood. So far, the man had done nothing; but what he had said was accepted as an achievement, by means of that he had made an impression. Among southern peoples speech is a constituent part of the pleasure of living, it enjoys far livelier social esteem than in the north. The national cement, the mother tongue, is paid symbolic honours down here, and there is something blithely symbolical in the pleasure people take in their respect for its forms and phonetics. They enjoy speaking, they enjoy listening; and they listen with discrimination. For the way a man speaks serves as a measure of his personal rank; carelessness and clumsiness are greeted with scorn, elegance and mastery are rewarded with social éclat. Wherefore the small man too, where it is a question of getting his effect, chooses his phrase nicely and turns it with care. On this count, then, at least, Cipolla had won his audience; though he by no means belonged to the class of men which the Italian, in a singular mixture of moral and æsthetic judgments, labels "*simpatico.*"

After removing his hat, scarf, and mantle he came to the front of the stage, settling his coat, pulling down his cuffs with their large cuff-buttons, adjusting his absurd sash. He had very ugly hair; the top of his head, that is, was almost bald, while a narrow, black-varnished frizz of curls ran from front to back as though stuck on; the side hair, likewise blackened, was brushed forward to the corners of the eyes—it was, in short, the hairdressing of an old-fashioned circus-director, fantastic, but entirely suited to his outmoded personal type and worn with so much assurance as to take the edge off the public's sense of humour. The little physical defect of which he had warned us was now all too visible, though the nature of it was even now not very clear: the chest was too high, as is usual in such cases; but the corresponding malformation of the back did not sit between the shoulders, it took the form of a sort of hips or buttocks hump, which did not indeed hinder

his movements but gave him a grotesque and dipping stride at every step he took. However, by mentioning his deformity beforehand he had broken the shock of it, and a delicate propriety of feeling appeared to reign throughout the hall.

"At your service," said Cipolla. "With your kind permission, we will begin the evening with some arithmetical tests."

Arithmetic? That did not sound much like sleight-of-hand. We began to have our suspicions that the man was sailing under a false flag, only we did not yet know which was the right one. I felt sorry on the children's account; but for the moment they were content simply to be there.

The numerical test which Cipolla now introduced was as simple as it was baffling. He began by fastening a piece of paper to the upper right-hand corner of the blackboard; then lifting it up, he wrote something underneath. He talked all the while, relieving the dryness of his offering by a constant flow of words, and showed himself a practised speaker, never at a loss for conversational turns of phrase. It was in keeping with the nature of his performance, and at the same time vastly entertained the children, that he went on to eliminate the gap between stage and audience, which had already been bridged over by the curious skirmish with the fisher lad: he had representatives from the audience mount the stage, and himself descended the wooden steps to seek personal contact with his public. And again, with individuals, he fell into his former taunting tone. I do not know how far that was a deliberate feature of his system; he preserved a serious, even a peevish air, but his audience, at least the more popular section, seemed convinced that that was all part of the game. So then, after he had written something and covered the writing by the paper, he desired that two persons should come up on the platform and help to perform the calculations. They would not be difficult, even for people not clever at figures. As usual, nobody volunteered, and Cipolla took care not to molest the more select portion of his audience. He kept to the populace. Turning to two sturdy young louts standing behind us, he beckoned them to the

3 "He speaks well." (JHP)

front, encouraging and scolding by turns. They should not stand there gaping, he said, unwilling to oblige the company. Actually, he got them in motion; with clumsy tread they came down the middle aisle, climbed the steps, and stood in front of the blackboard, grinning sheepishly at their comrades' shouts and applause. Cipolla joked with them for a few minutes, praised their heroic firmness of limb and the size of their hands, so well calculated to do this service for the public. Then he handed one of them the chalk and told him to write down the numbers as they were called out. But now the creature declared that he could not write! *"Non so scrivere,"* said he in his gruff voice, and his companion added that neither did he.

God knows whether they told the truth or whether they wanted to make game of Cipolla. Anyhow, the latter was far from sharing the general merriment which their confession aroused. He was insulted and disgusted. He sat there on a straw-bottomed chair in the centre of the stage with his legs crossed, smoking a fresh cigarette out of his cheap packet; obviously it tasted the better for the cognac he had indulged in while the yokels were stumping up the steps. Again he inhaled the smoke and let it stream out between curling lips. Swinging his leg, with his gaze sternly averted from the two shamelessly chuckling creatures and from the audience as well, he stared into space as one who withdraws himself and his dignity from the contemplation of an utterly despicable phenomenon.

"Scandalous," said he, in a sort of icy snarl. "Go back to your places! In Italy everybody can write—in all her greatness there is no room for ignorance and unenlightenment. To accuse her of them, in the hearing of this international company, is a cheap joke, in which you yourselves cut a very poor figure and humiliate the government and the whole country as well. If it is true that Torre di Venere is indeed the last refuge of such ignorance, then I must blush to have visited the place —being, as I already was, aware of its inferiority to Rome in more than one respect—"

Here Cipolla was interrupted by the youth with the Nubian coiffure and his jacket across his shoulder. His fighting spirit, as we now saw, had only abdicated temporarily, and he now flung himself into the breach in defence of his native heath. "That will do," said he loudly. "That's enough jokes about Torre. We all come from the place and we won't stand strangers making fun of it. These two chaps are our friends. Maybe they are no scholars, but even so they may be straighter than some folks in the room who are so free with their boasts about Rome, though they did not build it either."

That was capital. The young man had certainly cut his eyeteeth. And this sort of spectacle was good fun, even though it still further delayed the regular performance. It is always fascinating to listen to an altercation. Some people it simply amuses, they take a sort of kill-joy pleasure in not being principals. Others feel upset and uneasy, and my sympathies are with these latter, although on the present occasion I was under the impression that all this was part of the show—the analphabetic yokels no less than the *giovanotto* with the jacket. The children listened well pleased. They understood not at all, but the sound of the voices made them hold their breath. So this was a "magic evening"—at least it was the kind they have in Italy. They expressly found it "lovely."

Cipolla had stood up and with two of his scooping strides was at the footlights.

"Well, well, see who's here!" said he with grim cordiality. "An old acquaintance! A young man with his heart at the end of his tongue" (he used the word *linguaccia*, which means a coated tongue, and gave rise to much hilarity). "That will do, my friends," he turned to the yokels. "I do not need you now, I have business with this deserving young man here, *con questo torregiano di Venere,* this tower of Venus, who no doubt expects the gratitude of the fair as a reward for his prowess—"

"Ah, non scherziamo!" [4] We're talking earnest," cried out the youth. His eyes

4 "Let's not joke!" (JHP)

flashed, and he actually made as though to pull off his jacket and proceed to direct methods of settlement.

Cipolla did not take him too seriously. We had exchanged apprehensive glances; but he was dealing with a fellow-countryman and had his native soil beneath his feet. He kept quite cool and showed complete mastery of the situation. He looked at his audience, smiled, and made a sideways motion of the head towards the young cockerel as though calling the public to witness how the man's bumptiousness only served to betray the simplicity of his mind. And then, for the second time, something strange happened, which set Cipolla's calm superiority in an uncanny light, and in some mysterious and irritating way turned all the explosiveness latent in the air into matter for laughter.

Cipolla drew still nearer to the fellow, looking him in the eye with a peculiar gaze. He even came half-way down the steps that led into the auditorium on our left, so that he stood directly in front of the trouble-maker, on slightly higher ground. The riding-whip hung from his arm.

"My son, you do not feel much like joking," he said. "It is only too natural, for anyone can see that you are not feeling too well. Even your tongue, which leaves something to be desired on the score of cleanliness, indicates acute disorder of the gastric system. An evening entertainment is no place for people in your state; you yourself, I can tell, were of several minds whether you would not do better to put on a flannel bandage and go to bed. It was not good judgment to drink so much of that very sour white wine this afternoon. Now you have such a colic you would like to double up with the pain. Go ahead, don't be embarrassed. There is a distinct relief that comes from bending over, in cases of intestinal cramp."

He spoke thus, word for word, with quiet impressiveness and a kind of stern sympathy, and his eyes, plunged the while deep in the young man's, seemed to grow very tired and at the same time burning above their enlarged tear-ducts—they were the strangest eyes, you could tell that

not manly pride alone was preventing the young adversary from withdrawing his gaze. And presently, indeed, all trace of its former arrogance was gone from the bronzed young face. He looked openmouthed at the Cavaliere and the open mouth was drawn in a rueful smile.

"Double over," repeated Cipolla. "What else can you do? With a colic like that you *must* bend. Surely you will not struggle against the performance of a perfectly natural action just because somebody suggests it to you?"

Slowly the youth lifted his forearms, folded and squeezed them across his body; it turned a little sideways, then bent, lower and lower, the feet shifted, the knees turned inward, until he had become a picture of writhing pain, until he all but grovelled upon the ground. Cipolla let him stand for some seconds thus, then made a short cut through the air with his whip and went with his scooping stride back to the little table, where he poured himself out a cognac.

"Il boit beaucoup," [5] asserted a lady behind us. Was that the only thing that struck her? We could not tell how far the audience grasped the situation. The fellow was standing upright again, with a sheepish grin—he looked as though he scarcely knew how it had all happened. The scene had been followed with tense interest and applauded at the end; there were shouts of *"Bravo, Cipolla!"* and *"Bravo, giovanotto!"* Apparently the issue of the duel was not looked upon as a personal defeat for the young man. Rather the audience encouraged him as one does an actor who succeeds in an unsympathetic rôle. Certainly his way of screwing himself up with cramp had been highly picturesque, its appeal was directly calculated to impress the gallery—in short, a fine dramatic performance. But I am not sure how far the audience were moved by that natural tactfulness in which the south excels, or how far it penetrated into the nature of what was going on.

The Cavaliere, refreshed, had lighted another cigarette. The numerical tests

5 "He's a heavy drinker." (JHP)

might now proceed. A young man was easily found in the back row who was willing to write down on the blackboard the numbers as they were dictated to him. Him too we knew; the whole entertainment had taken on an intimate character through our acquaintance with so many of the actors. This was the man who worked at the greengrocer's in the main street; he had served us several times, with neatness and dispatch. He wielded the chalk with clerkly confidence, while Cipolla descended to our level and walked with his deformed gait through the audience, collecting numbers as they were given, in two, three, and four places, and calling them out to the grocer's assistant, who wrote them down in a column. In all this, everything on both sides was calculated to amuse, with its jokes and its oratorical asides. The artist could not fail to hit on foreigners, who were not ready with their figures, and with them he was elaborately patient and chivalrous, to the great amusement of the natives, whom he reduced to confusion in their turn, by making them translate numbers that were given in English or French. Some people gave dates concerned with great events in Italian history. Cipolla took them up at once and made patriotic comments. Somebody shouted "Number one!" The Cavaliere, incensed at this as at every attempt to make game of him, retorted over his shoulder that he could not take less than two-place figures. Whereupon another joker cried out "Number two!" and was greeted with the applause and laughter which every reference to natural functions is sure to win among southerners.

When fifteen numbers stood in a long straggling row on the board, Cipolla called for a general adding-match. Ready reckoners might add in their heads, but pencil and paper were not forbidden. Cipolla, while the work went on, sat on his chair near the blackboard, smoked and grimaced, with the complacent, pompous air cripples so often have. The five-place addition was soon done. Somebody announced the answer, somebody else confirmed it, a third had arrived at a slightly different result, but the fourth agreed with the first and second. Cipolla got up, tapped some ash from his coat, and lifted the paper at the upper right-hand corner of the board to display the writing. The correct answer, a sum close on a million, stood there; he had written it down beforehand.

Astonishment, and loud applause. The children were overwhelmed. How had he done that, they wanted to know. We told them it was a trick, not easily explainable offhand. In short, the man was a conjuror. This was what a sleight-of-hand evening was like, so now they knew. First the fisherman had cramp, and then the right answer was written down beforehand—it was all simply glorious, and we saw with dismay that despite the hot eyes and the hand of the clock at almost half past ten, it would be very hard to get them away. There would be tears. And yet it was plain that this magician did not "magick"—at least not in the accepted sense, of manual dexterity—and that the entertainment was not at all suitable for children. Again, I do not know, either, what the audience really thought. Obviously there was grave doubt whether its answers had been given of "free choice"; here and there an individual might have answered of his own motion, but on the whole Cipolla certainly selected his people and thus kept the whole procedure in his own hands and directed it towards the given result. Even so, one had to admire the quickness of his calculations, however much one felt disinclined to admire anything else about the performance. Then his patriotism, his irritable sense of dignity—the Cavaliere's own countrymen might feel in their element with all that and continue in a laughing mood; but the combination certainly gave us outsiders food for thought.

Cipolla himself saw to it—though without giving them a name—that the nature of his powers should be clear beyond a doubt to even the least-instructed person. He alluded to them, of course, in his talk —and he talked without stopping—but only in vague, boastful, self-advertising phrases. He went on awhile with experiments on the same lines as the first, merely making them more complicated by introducing operations in multiplying, subtracting, and dividing; then he simplified them to the last degree in order to bring out the method. He simply had numbers "guessed" which were previously written under the paper; and the guess was nearly always right. One guesser admitted that he had had in mind to give a certain number, when Cipolla's whip went whistling through the air, and a quite different one slipped out, which proved to be the "right" one. Cipolla's shoulders shook. He pretended admiration for powers of the people he questioned. But in all his compliments there was something fleering and derogatory; the victims could scarcely have relished them much, although they smiled, and although they might easily have set down some part of the applause to their own credit. Moreover, I had not the impression that the artist was popular with his public. A certain ill will and reluctance were in the air, but courtesy kept such feelings in check, as did Cipolla's competency and his stern self-confidence. Even the riding-whip, I think, did much to keep rebellion from becoming overt.

From tricks with numbers he passed to tricks with cards. There were two packs, which he drew out of his pockets, and so much I still remember, that the basis of the tricks he played with them was as follows: from the first pack he drew three cards and thrust them without looking at them inside his coat. Another person then drew three out of the second pack, and these turned out to be the same as the first three—not invariably all the three, for it did happen that only two were the same. But in the majority of cases Cipolla triumphed, showing his three cards with a little bow in acknowledgment of the applause with which his audience conceded his possession of strange powers—strange whether for good or evil. A young man in the front row, to our right, an Italian, with proud, finely chiselled features, rose up and said that he intended to assert his own will in his choice and consciously to resist any influence, of whatever sort. Under these circumstances, what did Cipolla think would be the result? "You will," answered the Cavaliere, "make my task somewhat more difficult thereby. As for the result, your resistance will not alter it in the least. Freedom exists, and also the will exists; but freedom of the will does not exist, for a will that aims at its own freedom aims at the unknown. You are free to draw or not to draw. But if you draw, you will draw the right cards —the more certainly, the more wilfully obstinate your behaviour."

One must admit that he could not have chosen his words better, to trouble the waters and confuse the mind. The refractory youth hesitated before drawing. Then he pulled out a card and at once demanded to see if it was among the chosen three. "But why?" queried Cipolla. "Why do things by halves?" Then, as the other defiantly insisted, *"E servito,"* said the juggler, with a gesture of exaggerated servility; and held out the three cards fanwise, without looking at them himself. The left-hand card was the one drawn.

Amid general applause, the apostle of freedom sat down. How far Cipolla employed small tricks and manual dexterity to help out his natural talents, the deuce only knew. But even without them the result would have been the same: the curiosity of the entire audience was unbounded and universal, everybody both enjoyed the amazing character of the entertainment and unanimously conceded the professional skill of the performer. *"Lavora bene,"* [6] we heard, here and there in our neighbourhood; it signified the triumph of objective judgment over antipathy and repressed resentment.

After his last, incomplete, yet so much the more telling success, Cipolla had at once fortified himself with another cognac. Truly he did "drink a lot," and the fact made a bad impression. But obviously he needed the liquor and the cigarettes for the replenishment of his energy, upon which, as he himself said, heavy demands were made in all directions. Certainly in the intervals he looked very ill, exhausted and hollow-eyed. Then the little glassful would redress the balance, and the flow of lively, self-confident chatter run on, while the smoke he inhaled gushed out grey from his lungs. I clearly recall that he passed from the card-tricks to parlour

6 "He works well." (JHP)

games—the kind based on certain powers which in human nature are higher or else lower than human reason: on intuition and "magnetic" transmission; in short, upon a low type of manifestation. What I do not remember is the precise order things came in. And I will not bore you with a description of these experiments; everybody knows them, everybody has at one time or another taken part in this finding of hidden articles, this blind carrying out of a series of acts, directed by a force that proceeds from organism to organism by unexplored paths. Everybody has had his little glimpse into the equivocal, impure, inexplicable nature of the occult, has been conscious of both curiosity and contempt, has shaken his head over the human tendency of those who deal in it to help themselves out with humbuggery, though, after all, the humbuggery is no disproof whatever of the genuineness of the other elements in the dubious amalgam. I can only say here that each single circumstance gains in weight and the whole greatly in impressiveness when it is a man like Cipolla who is the chief actor and guiding spirit in the sinister business. He sat smoking at the rear of the stage, his back to the audience while they conferred. The object passed from hand to hand which it was his task to find, with which he was to perform some action agreed upon beforehand. Then he would start to move zigzag through the hall, with his head thrown back and one hand outstretched, the other clasped in that of a guide who was in the secret but enjoined to keep himself perfectly passive, with his thoughts directed upon the agreed goal. Cipolla moved with the bearing typical in these experiments: now groping upon a false start, now with a quick forward thrust, now pausing as though to listen and by sudden inspiration correcting his course. The rôles seemed reversed, the stream of influence was moving in the contrary direction, as the artist himself pointed out, in his ceaseless flow of discourse. The suffering, receptive, performing part was now his, the will he had before imposed on others was shut out, he acted in obedience to a voiceless common will which was in the air. But he made it perfectly clear that it all

came to the same thing. The capacity for self-surrender, he said, for becoming a tool, for the most unconditional and utter self-abnegation, was but the reverse side of that other power to will and to command. Commanding and obeying formed together one single principle, one indissoluble unity; he who knew how to obey knew also how to command, and conversely; the one idea was comprehended in the other, as people and leader were comprehended in one another. But that which was *done*, the highly exacting and exhausting performance, was in every case his, the leader's and mover's, in whom the will became obedience, the obedience will, whose person was the cradle and womb of both, and who thus suffered enormous hardship. Repeatedly he emphasized the fact that his lot was a hard one—presumably to account for his need of stimulant and his frequent recourse to the little glass.

Thus he groped his way forward, like a blind seer, led and sustained by the mysterious common will. He drew a pin set with a stone out of its hiding-place in an Englishwoman's shoe, carried it, halting and pressing on by turns, to another lady —Signora Angiolieri—and handed it to her on bended knee, with the words it had been agreed he was to utter. "I present you with this in token of my respect," was the sentence. Their sense was obvious, but the words themselves not easy to hit upon, for the reason that they had been agreed on in French; the language complication seemed to us a little malicious, implying as it did a conflict between the audience's natural interest in the success of the miracle, and their desire to witness the humiliation of this presumptuous man. It was a strange sight: Cipolla on his knees before the signora, wrestling, amid efforts at speech, after knowledge of the preordained words. "I must say something," he said, "and I feel clearly what it is I must say. But I also feel that if it passed my lips it would be wrong. Be careful not to help me unintentionally!" he cried out, though very likely that was precisely what he was hoping for. *"Pensez très fort,"* [7] he cried all at once, in bad French, and

7 "Think very hard." (JHP)

then burst out with the required words—in Italian, indeed, but with the final substantive pronounced in the sister tongue, in which he was probably far from fluent: he said *vénération* instead of *venerazione*, with an impossible nasal. And this partial success, after the complete success before it, the finding of the pin, the presentation of it on his knees to the right person—was almost more impressive than if he had got the sentence exactly right, and evoked bursts of admiring applause.

Cipolla got up from his knees and wiped the perspiration from his brow. You understand that this experiment with the pin was a single case, which I describe because it sticks in my memory. But he changed his method several times and improvised a number of variations suggested by his contact with his audience; a good deal of time thus went by. He seemed to get particular inspiration from the person of our landlady; she drew him on to the most extraordinary displays of clairvoyance. "It does not escape me, madame," he said to her, "that there is something unusual about you, some special and honourable distinction. He who has eyes to see descries about your lovely brow an aureola—if I mistake not, it once was stronger than now—a slowly paling radiance . . . hush, not a word! Don't help me. Beside you sits your husband—yes?" He turned towards the silent Signor Angiolieri. "You are the husband of this lady, and your happiness is complete. But in the midst of this happiness memories rise . . . the past, signora, so it seems to me, plays an important part in your present. You knew a king . . . has not a king crossed your path in bygone days?"

"No," breathed the dispenser of our midday soup, her golden-brown eyes gleaming in the noble pallor of her face.

"No? No, not a king; I meant that generally, I did not mean literally a king. Not a king, not a prince, and a prince after all, a king of a loftier realm; it was a great artist, at whose side you once—you would contradict me, and yet I am not wholly wrong. Well, then! It was a woman, a great, a world-renowned woman artist, whose friendship you enjoyed in your tender years, whose sacred memory overshadows and transfigures your whole existence. Her name? Need I utter it, whose fame has long been bound up with the Fatherland's, immortal as its own? Eleonora Duse," he finished, softly and with much solemnity.

The little woman bowed her head, overcome. The applause was like a patriotic demonstration. Nearly everyone there knew about Signora Angiolieri's wonderful past; they were all able to confirm the Cavaliere's intuition—not least the present guests of Casa Eleonora. But we wondered how much of the truth he had learned as the result of professional inquiries made on his arrival. Yet I see no reason at all to cast doubt, on rational grounds, upon powers which, before our very eyes, became fatal to their possessor.

At this point there was an intermission. Our lord and master withdrew. Now I confess that almost ever since the beginning of my tale I have looked forward with dread to this moment in it. The thoughts of men are mostly not hard to read; in this case they are very easy. You are sure to ask why we did not choose this moment to go away—and I must continue to owe you an answer. I do not know why. I cannot defend myself. By this time it was certainly eleven, probably later. The children were asleep. The last series of tests had been too long, nature had had her way. They were sleeping in our laps, the little one on mine, the boy on his mother's. That was, in a way, a consolation; but at the same time it was also ground for compassion and a clear leading to take them home to bed. And I give you my word that we wanted to obey this touching admonition, we seriously wanted to. We roused the poor things and told them it was now high time to go. But they were no sooner conscious than they began to resist and implore—you know how horrified children are at the thought of leaving before the end of a thing. No cajoling has any effect, you have to use force. It was so lovely, they wailed. How did we know what was coming next? Surely we could not leave until after the intermission; they liked a little nap now and again—only not go home, only not go to bed, while the beautiful evening was still going on!

We yielded, but only for the moment,

of course—so far as we knew—only for a little while, just a few minutes longer. I cannot excuse our staying, scarcely can I even understand it. Did we think, having once said A, we had to say B—having once brought the children hither we had to let them stay? No, it is not good enough. Were we ourselves so highly entertained? Yes, and no. Our feelings for Cavaliere Cipolla were of a very mixed kind, but so were the feelings of the whole audience, if I mistake not, and nobody left. Were we under the sway of a fascination which emanated from this man who took so strange a way to earn his bread; a fascination which he gave out independently of the programme and even between the tricks and which paralysed our resolve? Again, sheer curiosity may account for something. One was curious to know how such an evening turned out; Cipolla in his remarks having all along hinted that he had tricks in his bag stranger than any he had yet produced.

But all that is not it—or at least it is not all of it. More correct it would be to answer the first question with another. Why had we not left Torre di Venere itself before now? To me the two questions are one and the same, and in order to get out of the impasse I might simply say that I had answered it already. For, as things had been in Torre in general: queer, uncomfortable, troublesome, tense, oppressive, so precisely they were here in this hall tonight. Yes, more than precisely. For it seemed to be the fountainhead of all the uncanniness and all the strained feelings which had oppressed the atmosphere of our holiday. This man whose return to the stage we were awaiting was the personification of all that; and, as we had not gone away in general, so to speak, it would have been inconsistent to do it in the particular case. You may call this an explanation, you may call it inertia, as you see fit. Any argument more to the purpose I simply do not know how to adduce.

Well, there was an interval of ten minutes, which grew into nearly twenty. The children remained awake. They were enchanted by our compliance, and filled the break to their own satisfaction by renew-

ing relations with the popular sphere, with Antonio, Guiscardo, and the canoe man. They put their hands to their mouths and called messages across, appealing to us for the Italian words. "Hope you have a good catch tomorrow, a whole netful!" They called to Mario, Esquisito Mario: *"Mario, una cioccolata e biscotti!"* [8] And this time he heeded and answered with a smile: *"Subito, signorini!"* [9] Later we had reason to recall this kindly, if rather absent and pensive smile.

Thus the interval passed, the gong sounded. The audience, which had scattered in conversation, took their places again, the children sat up straight in their chairs with their hands in their laps. The curtain had not been dropped. Cipolla came forward again, with his dipping stride, and began to introduce the second half of the programme with a lecture.

Let me state once for all that this self-confident cripple was the most powerful hypnotist I have ever seen in my life. It was pretty plain now that he threw dust in the public eye and advertised himself as a prestidigitator on account of police regulations which would have prevented him from making his living by the exercise of his powers. Perhaps this eye-wash is the usual thing in Italy; it may be permitted or even connived at by the authorities. Certainly the man had from the beginning made little concealment of the actual nature of his operations; and this second half of the programme was quite frankly and exclusively devoted to one sort of experiment. While he still practised some rhetorical circumlocutions, the tests themselves were one long series of attacks upon the will-power, the loss or compulsion of volition. Comic, exciting, amazing by turns, by midnight they were still in full swing; we ran the gamut of all the phenomena this natural-unnatural field has to show, from the unimpressive at one end of the scale to the monstrous at the other. The audience laughed and applauded as they followed the grotesque details; shook their heads, clapped their knees, fell very frankly under the spell of

8 "Mario, a chocolate and biscuits!" (JHP)
9 "Right away, gentlemen!" (JHP)

this stern, self-assured personality. At the same time I saw signs that they were not quite complacent, not quite unconscious of the peculiar ignominy which lay, for the individual and for the general, in Cipolla's triumphs.

Two main features were constant in all the experiments: the liquor glass and the claw-handled riding-whip. The first was always invoked to add fuel to his demoniac fires; without it, apparently, they might have burned out. On this score we might even have felt pity for the man; but the whistle of his scourge, the insulting symbol of his domination, before which we all cowered, drowned out every sensation save a dazed and outbraved submission to his power. Did he then lay claim to our sympathy to boot? I was struck by a remark he made—it suggested no less. At the climax of his experiments, by stroking and breathing upon a certain young man who had offered himself as a subject and already proved himself a particularly susceptible one, he had not only put him into the condition known as deep trance and extended his insensible body by neck and feet across the backs of two chairs, but had actually sat down on the rigid form as on a bench, without making it yield. The sight of this unholy figure in a frock-coat squatted on the stiff body was horrible and incredible; the audience, convinced that the victim of this scientific diversion must be suffering, expressed its sympathy: *"Ah, poveretto!"* Poor soul, poor soul! *"Poor soul!"* Cipolla mocked them, with some bitterness. "Ladies and gentlemen, you are barking up the wrong tree. *Sono io il poveretto.* I am the person who is suffering, I am the one to be pitied." We pocketed the information. Very good. Maybe the experiment was at his expense, maybe it was he who had suffered the cramp when the *giovanotto* over there had made the faces. But appearances were all against it; and one does not feel like saying *poveretto* to a man who is suffering to bring about the humiliation of others.

I have got ahead of my story and lost sight of the sequence of events. To this day my mind is full of the Cavaliere's feats of endurance; only I do not recall them in their order—which does not matter. So much I do know: that the longer and more circumstantial tests, which got the most applause, impressed me less than some of the small ones which passed quickly over. I remember the young man whose body Cipolla converted into a board, only because of the accompanying remarks which I have quoted. An elderly lady in a cane-seated chair was lulled by Cipolla in the delusion that she was on a voyage to India and gave a voluble account of her adventures by land and sea. But I found this phenomenon less impressive than one which followed immediately after the intermission. A tall, well-built, soldierly man was unable to lift his arm, after the hunchback had told him that he could not and given a cut through the air with his whip. I can still see the face of that stately, mustachioed colonel smiling and clenching his teeth as he struggled to regain his lost freedom of action. A staggering performance! He seemed to be exerting his will, and in vain; the trouble, however, was probably simply that he could not will. There was involved here that recoil of the will upon itself which paralyses choice—as our tyrant had previously explained to the Roman gentleman.

Still less can I forget the touching scene, at once comic and horrible, with Signora Angiolieri. The Cavaliere, probably in his first bold survey of the room, had spied out her ethereal lack of resistance to his power. For actually he bewitched her, literally drew her out of her seat, out of her row, and away with him whither he willed. And in order to enhance his effect, he bade Signor Angiolieri call upon his wife by her name, to throw, as it were, all the weight of his existence and his rights in her into the scale, to rouse by the voice of her husband everything in his spouse's soul which could shield her virtue against the evil assaults of magic. And how vain it all was! Cipolla was standing at some distance from the couple, when he made a single cut with his whip through the air. It caused our landlady to shudder violently and turn her face towards him. "Sofronia!" cried Signor Angiolieri—we had not known that Signora Angiolieri's name was Sofronia. And he did well to call, everybody saw that there was no time to lose. His wife kept her face turned in the direction of the diabolical Cavaliere, who with his ten long yellow fingers was making passes at his victim, moving backwards as he did so, step by step. Then Signora Angiolieri, her pale face gleaming, rose up from her seat, turned right round, and began to glide after him. Fatal and forbidding sight! Her face as though moonstruck, stiff-armed, her lovely hands lifted a little at the wrists, the feet as it were together, she seemed to float slowly out of her row and after the tempter. "Call her, sir, keep on calling," prompted the redoubtable man. And Signor Angiolieri, in a weak voce, called: "Sofronia!" Ah, again and again he called; as his wife went further off he even curved one hand round his lips and beckoned with the other as he called. But the poor voice of love and duty echoed unheard, in vain, behind the lost one's back; the signora swayed along, moonstruck, deaf, enslaved; she glided into the middle aisle and down it towards the fingering hunchback, towards the door. We were convinced, we were driven to the conviction, that she would have followed her master, had he so willed it, to the ends of the earth.

"*Accidente!*" cried out Signor Angiolieri, in genuine affright, springing up as the exit was reached. But at the same moment the Cavaliere put aside, as it were, the triumphal crown and broke off. "Enough, signora, I thank you," he said, and offered his arm to lead her back to her husband. "Signor," he greeted the latter, "here is your wife. Unharmed, with my compliments, I give her into your hands. Cherish with all the strength of your manhood a treasure which is so wholly yours, and let your zeal be quickened by knowing that there are powers stronger than reason or virtue, and not always so magnanimously ready to relinquish their prey!"

Poor Signor Angiolieri, so quiet, so bald! He did not look as though he would know how to defend his happiness, even against powers much less demoniac than these which were now adding mockery to frightfulness. Solemnly and pompously the Cavaliere retired to the stage, amid applause to which his eloquence gave double strength. It was this particular episode, I feel sure, that set the seal upon his ascendancy. For now he made them dance, yes, literally; and the dancing lent a dissolute, abandoned, topsy-turvy air to the scene, a drunken abdication of the critical spirit which had so long resisted the spell of this man. Yes, he had had to fight to get the upper hand—for instance against the animosity of the young Roman gentleman, whose rebellious spirit threatened to serve others as a rallying-point. But it was precisely upon the importance of example that the Cavaliere was so strong. He had the wit to make his attack at the weakest point and to choose as his first victim that feeble, ecstatic youth whom he had previously made into a board. The master had but to look at him, when this young man would fling himself back as though struck by lightning, place his hands rigidly at his sides, and fall into a state of military somnambulism, in which is was plain to any eye that he was open to the most absurd suggestion that might be made to him. He seemed quite content in his abject state, quite pleased to be relieved of the burden of voluntary choice. Again and again he offered himself as a subject and gloried in the model facility he had in losing consciousness. So now he mounted the platform, and a single cut of the whip was enough to make him dance to the Cavaliere's orders, in a kind of complacent ecstasy, eyes closed, head nodding, lank limbs flying in all directions.

It looked unmistakably like enjoyment, and other recruits were not long in coming forward: two other young men, one humbly and one well dressed, were soon jigging alongside the first. But now the gentleman from Rome bobbed up again, asking defiantly if the Cavaliere would engage to make him dance too, even against his will.

"Even against your will," answered Cipolla, in unforgettable accents. That frightful *"anche se non vuole"* still rings in my ears. The struggle began. After Cipolla had taken another little glass and lighted a fresh cigarette he stationed the Roman at a point in the middle aisle and himself took up a position some distance behind him, making his whip whistle through the air as he gave the order: *"Balla!"* His opponent did not stir. *"Balla!"* repeated the Cavaliere incisively, and snapped his whip. You saw the young man move his neck round in his collar; at the same time one hand lifted slightly at the wrist, one ankle turned outward. But that was all, for the time at least; merely a tendency to twitch, now sternly repressed, now seeming about to get the upper hand. It escaped nobody that here a heroic obstinacy, a fixed resolve to resist, must needs be conquered; we were beholding a gallant effort to strike out and save the honour of the human race. He twitched but danced not; and the struggle was so prolonged that the Cavaliere had to divide his attention between it and the stage, turning now and then to make his riding-whip whistle in the direction of the dancers, as it were to keep them in leash. At the same time he advised the audience that no fatigue was involved in such activities, however long they went on, since it was not the automatons up there who danced, but himself. Then once more his eye would bore itself into the back of the Roman's neck and lay siege to the strength of purpose which defied him.

One saw it waver, that strength of purpose, beneath the repeated summons and whip-crackings. Saw with an objective interest which yet was not quite free from traces of sympathetic emotion—from pity, even from a cruel kind of pleasure. If I understand what was going on, it was the negative character of the young man's fighting position which was his undoing. It is likely that *not* willing is not a practicable state of mind; *not* to want to do something may be in the long run a mental content impossible to subsist on. Between not willing a certain thing and not willing at all—in other words, yielding to another person's will—there may lie too small a space for the idea of freedom to squeeze into. Again, there were the Cavaliere's persuasive words, woven in among the whip-crackings and commands, as he mingled effects that were his own secret with others of a bewilderingly psychological kind. *"Balla!"* said he. "Who wants to torture himself like that? Is forcing yourself your idea of freedom? *Una ballatina!* [10] Why, your arms and legs are aching for it. What a relief to give way to them—there, you are dancing already! That is no struggle any more, it is a pleasure!" And so it was. The jerking and twitching of the refractory youth's limbs had at last got the upper hand; he lifted his arms, then his knees, his joints quite suddenly relaxed, he flung his legs and danced, and amid bursts of applause the Cavaliere led him to join the row of puppets on the stage. Up there we could see his face as he "enjoyed" himself; it was clothed in a broad grin and the eyes were half-shut. In a way, it was consoling to see that he was having a better time than he had had in the hour of his pride.

His "fall" was, I may say, an epoch. The ice was completely broken, Cipolla's triumph had reached its height. The Circe's wand, that whistling leather whip with the claw handle, held absolute sway. At one time—it must have been well after midnight—not only were there eight or ten persons dancing on the little stage, but in the hall below a varied animation reigned, and a long-toothed Anglo-Saxoness in a pince-nez left her seat of her own motion to perform a tarantella in the centre aisle. Cipolla was lounging in a cane-seated chair at the left of the stage, gulping down the smoke of a cigarette and breathing it impudently out through his bad teeth. He tapped his foot and shrugged his shoulders, looking down upon the abandoned scene in the hall; now and then he snapped his whip backwards at a laggard upon the stage. The children were awake at the moment. With shame I speak of them. For it was not good to be here, least of all for them; that we had not taken them away can only be explained by saying that we had caught the general devil-may-careness of the hour. By that time it was all one. Anyhow, thank goodness, they lacked understanding for the disreputable side of the entertainment, and in their innocence

10 "A dance!" (JHP)

were perpetually charmed by the unheard-of indulgence which permitted them to be present at such a thing as a magician's "evening." Whole quarter-hours at a time they drowsed on our laps, waking refreshed and rosy-cheeked, with sleep-drunken eyes, to laugh to bursting at the leaps and jumps the magician made those people up there make. They had not thought it would be so jolly; they joined with their clumsy little hands in every round of applause. And jumped for joy upon their chairs, as was their wont, when Cipolla beckoned to their friend Mario from the Esquisito, beckoned to him just like a picture in a book, holding his hand in front of his nose and bending and straightening the forefinger by turns.

Mario obeyed. I can see him now going up the stairs to Cipolla, who continued to beckon him, in that droll, picture-book sort of way. He hesitated for a moment at first; that, too, I recall quite clearly. During the whole evening he had lounged against a wooden pillar at the side entrance, with his arms folded, or else with his hands thrust into his jacket pockets. He was on our left, near the youth with the militant hair, and had followed the performance attentively, so far as we had seen, if with no particular animation and God knows how much comprehension. He could not much relish being summoned thus, at the end of the evening. But it was only too easy to see why he obeyed. After all, obedience was his calling in life; and then, how should a simple lad like him find it within his human capacity to refuse compliance to a man so throned and crowned as Cipolla at that hour? Willy-nilly he left his column and with a word of thanks to those making way for him he mounted the steps with a doubtful smile on his full lips.

Picture a thickset youth of twenty years, with clipt hair, a low forehead, and heavy-lidded eyes of an indefinite grey, shot with green and yellow. These things I knew from having spoken with him, as we often had. There was a saddle of freckles on the flat nose, the whole upper half of the face retreated behind the lower, and that again was dominated by thick lips that parted to show the salivated teeth. These thick lips and the veiled look

of the eyes lent the whole face a primitive melancholy—it was that which had drawn us to him from the first. In it was not the faintest trace of brutality—indeed, his hands would have given the lie to such an idea, being unusually slender and delicate even for a southerner. They were hands by which one liked being served.

We knew him humanly without knowing him personally, if I may make that distinction. We saw him nearly every day, and felt a certain kindness for his dreamy ways, which might at times be actual inattentiveness, suddenly transformed into a redeeming zeal to serve. His mien was serious, only the children could bring a smile to his face. It was not sulky, but uningratiating, without intentional effort to please—or, rather, it seemed to give up being pleasant in the conviction that it could not succeed. We should have remembered Mario in any case, as one of those homely recollections of travel which often stick in the mind better than more important ones. But of his circumstances we knew no more than that his father was a petty clerk in the Municipio and his mother took in washing.

His white waiter's-coat became him better than the faded striped suit he wore, with a gay coloured scarf instead of a collar, the ends tucked into his jacket. He neared Cipolla, who however did not leave off that motion of his finger before his nose, so that Mario had to come still closer, right up to the chair-seat and the master's legs. Whereupon the latter spread out his elbows and seized the lad, turning him so that we had a view of his face. Then gazed him briskly up and down, with a careless, commanding eye.

"Well, *ragazzo mio*,[11] how comes it we make acquaintance so late in the day? But believe me, I made yours long ago. Yes, yes, I've had you in my eye this long while and known what good stuff you were made of. How could I go and forget you again? Well, I've had a good deal to think about. . . . Now tell me, what is your name? The first name, that's all I want."

"My name is Mario," the young man answered, in a low voice.

"Ah, Mario. Very good. Yes, yes, there

11 "my boy."

is such a name, quite a common name, a classic name too, one of those which preserve the heroic traditions of the Fatherland. *Bravo! Salve!*" And he flung up his arm slantingly above his crooked shoulder, palm outward, in the Roman salute. He may have been slightly tipsy by now, and no wonder; but he spoke as before, clearly, fluently, and with emphasis. Though about this time there had crept into his voice a gross, autocratic note, and a kind of arrogance was in his sprawl.

"Well, now, Mario *mio*," he went on, "it's a good thing you came this evening, and that's a pretty scarf you've got on; it is becoming to your style of beauty. It must stand you in good stead with the girls, the pretty pretty girls of Torre—"

From the row of youths, close by the place where Mario had been standing, sounded a laugh. It came from the youth with the militant hair. He stood there, his jacket over his shoulder, and laughed outright, rudely and scornfully.

Mario gave a start. I think it was a shrug, but he may have started and then hastened to cover the movement by shrugging his shoulders, as much as to say that the neckerchief and the fair sex were matters of equal indifference to him.

The Cavaliere gave a downward glance. "We needn't trouble about him," he said. "He is jealous, because your scarf is so popular with the girls, maybe partly because you and I are so friendly up here. Perhaps he'd like me to put him in mind of his colic—I could do it free of charge. Tell me, Mario. You've come here this evening for a bit of fun—and in the daytime you work in an ironmonger's shop?"

"In a café," corrected the youth.

"Oh, in a café. That's where Cipolla nearly came a cropper! What you are is a cup-bearer, a Ganymede—I like that, it is another classical allusion—*Salvietta!*" Again the Cavaliere saluted, to the huge gratification of his audience.

Mario smiled too. "But before that," he interpolated, in the interest of accuracy, "I worked for a while in a shop in Portoclemente." He seemed visited by a natural desire to assist the prophecy by dredging out its essential features.

"There, didn't I say so? In an ironmonger's shop?"

"They kept combs and brushes," Mario got round it.

"Didn't I say that you were not always a Ganymede? Not always at the sign of the serviette? Even when Cipolla makes a mistake, it is a kind that makes you believe in him. Now tell me: Do you believe in me?"

An indefinite gesture.

"A half-way answer," commented the Cavaliere. "Probably it is not easy to win your confidence. Even for me, I can see, it is not so easy. I see in your features a reserve, a sadness, *un tratto di malinconia* . . . tell me" (he seized Mario's hand persuasively) "have you troubles?"

"Nossignore," answered Mario, promptly and decidedly.

"You *have* troubles," insisted the Cavaliere, bearing down the denial by the weight of his authority. "Can't I see? Trying to pull the wool over Cipolla's eyes, are you? Of course, about the girls—it is a girl, isn't it? You have love troubles?"

Mario gave a vigorous head-shake. And again the *giovanotto's* brutal laugh rang out. The Cavaliere gave heed. His eyes were roving about somewhere in the air; but he cocked an ear to the sound, then swung his whip backwards, as he had once or twice before in his conversation with Mario, that none of his puppets might flag in their zeal. The gesture had nearly cost him his new prey: Mario gave a sudden start in the direction of the steps. But Cipolla had him in his clutch.

"Not so fast," said he. "That would be fine, wouldn't it? So you want to skip, do you, Ganymede, right in the middle of the fun, or, rather, when it is just beginning? Stay with me, I'll show you something nice. I'll convince you. You have no reason to worry, I promise you. This girl —you know her and others know her too —what's her name? Wait! I read the name in your eyes, it is on the tip of my tongue and yours too—"

"Silvestra!" shouted the *giovanotto* from below.

The Cavaliere's face did not change.

"Aren't there the forward people?" he asked, not looking down, more as in undisturbed converse with Mario. "Aren't there the young fighting-cocks that crow in season and out? Takes the word out of your mouth, the conceited fool, and seems to think he has some special right to it. Let him be. But Silvestra, your Silvestra—ah, what a girl that is! What a prize! Brings your heart into your mouth to see her walk or laugh or breathe, she is so lovely. And her round arms when she washes, and tosses her head back to get the hair out of her eyes! An angel from paradise!"

Mario stared at him, his head thrust forward. He seemed to have forgotten the audience, forgotten where he was. The red rings round his eyes had got larger, they looked as though they were painted on. His thick lips parted.

"And she makes you suffer, this angel," went on Cipolla, "or, rather, you make yourself suffer for her—there is a difference, my lad, a most important difference, let me tell you. There are misunderstandings in love, maybe nowhere else in the world are there so many. I know what you are thinking: what does this Cipolla, with his little physical defect, know about love? Wrong, all wrong, he knows a lot. He has a wide and powerful understanding of its workings, and it pays to listen to his advice. But let's leave Cipolla out, cut him out altogether and think only of Silvestra, your peerless Silvestra! What! Is she to give any young gamecock the preference, so that he can laugh while you cry? To prefer him to a chap like you, so full of feeling and so sympathetic? Not very likely, is it? It is impossible—we know better, Cipolla and she. If I were to put myself in her place and choose between the two of you, a tarry lout like that—a codfish, a sea-urchin—and a Mario, a knight of the serviette, who moves among gentlefolk and hands round refreshments with an air—my word, but my heart would speak in no uncertain tones—it knows to whom I gave it long ago. It is time that he should see and understand, my chosen one! It is time that you see me and recognize me, Mario, my beloved! Tell me, who am I?"

It was grisly, the way the betrayer made himself irresistible, wreathed and coquetted with his crooked shoulder, languished with the puffy eyes, and showed his splintered teeth in a sickly smile. And alas, at his beguiling words, what was come of our Mario? It is hard for me to tell, hard as it was for me to see; for here was nothing less than an utter abandonment of the inmost soul, a public exposure of timid and deluded passion and rapture. He put his hands across his mouth, his shoulders rose and fell with his pantings. He could not, it was plain, trust his eyes and ears for joy, and the one thing he forgot was precisely that he could not trust them. "Silvestra!" he breathed, from the very depths of his vanquished heart.

"Kiss me!" said the hunchback. "Trust me, I love thee. Kiss me here." And with the tip of his index finger, hand, arm, and little finger outspread, he pointed to his cheek, near the mouth. And Mario bent and kissed him.

It had grown very still in the room. That was a monstrous moment, grotesque and thrilling, the moment of Mario's bliss. In that evil span of time, crowded with a sense of the illusiveness of all joy, one sound became audible, and that not quite at once, but on the instant of the melancholy and ribald meeting between Mario's lips and the repulsive flesh which thrust itself forward for his caress. It was the sound of a laugh, from the *giovanotto* on our left. It broke into the dramatic suspense of the moment, coarse, mocking, and yet—or I must have been grossly mistaken—with an undertone of compassion for the poor bewildered, victimized creature. It had a faint ring of that *"Poveretto"* which Cipolla had declared was wasted on the wrong person, when he claimed the pity for his own.

The laugh still rang in the air when the recipient of the caress gave his whip a little swish, low down, close to his chair-leg, and Mario started up and flung himself back. He stood in that posture staring, his hands one over the other on those desecrated lips. Then he beat his temples with his clenched fists, over and over; turned and staggered down the steps, while the audience applauded, and Cipolla sat there with his hands in his lap, his shoulders shaking. Once below, and even while in full retreat, Mario hurled himself round with legs flung wide apart; one arm flew up, and two flat shattering detonations crashed through applause and laughter.

There was instant silence. Even the dancers came to a full stop and stared about, struck dumb. Cipolla bounded from his seat. He stood with his arms spread out, slanting as though to ward everybody off, as though next moment he would cry out: "Stop! Keep back! Silence! What was that?" Then, in that instant, he sank back in his seat, his head rolling on his chest; in the next he had fallen sideways to the floor, where he lay motionless, a huddled heap of clothing, with limbs awry.

The commotion was indescribable. Ladies hid their faces, shuddering, on the breasts of their escorts. There were shouts for a doctor, for the police. People flung themselves on Mario in a mob, to disarm him, to take away the weapon that hung from his fingers—that small, dull-metal, scarcely pistol-shaped tool with hardly any barrel—in how strange and unexpected a direction had fate levelled it!

And now—now finally, at last—we took the children and led them towards the exit, past the pair of *carabinieri* just entering. Was that the end, they wanted to know, that they might go in peace? Yes, we assured them, that was the end. An end of horror, a fatal end. And yet a liberation—for I could not, and I cannot, but find it so!

[1929]

TRANSLATED BY
H. T. LOWE-PORTER

QUESTIONS FOR STUDY

1. *"Mario and the Magician," which first appeared in 1929 during the period that witnessed Mussolini's rise to power in Italy and Hitler's in Germany, has been called a political allegory about fascism. What aspects of the story would seem to support such an interpretation? In what ways is such a view too limiting?*

2. *What is the function of the opening scenes? What kind of atmosphere characterizes Torre di Venere? To what extent is such an atmosphere a necessary precondition to Cipolla's later success?*

3. *How does Cipolla manipulate his audience? What is the significance of his deformity, his use of a whip, his frequent recourse to cognac and cigarettes?*

4. *What is the function of the children? Why can't the narrator bring himself to leave the hall?*

5. *Why does Cipolla choose Mario? What kind of man is he? In what sense is his demand of Mario the logical climax to the demands he has been making upon his audience all evening? Why does Mario shoot Cipolla? Is the act heroic?*

6. *What comments does Mann seem to be making about the nature of the human will?*

KATHERINE MANSFIELD

The Man Without a Temperament

HE STOOD at the hall door turning the ring, turning the heavy signet ring upon his little finger while his glance travelled cooly, deliberately, over the round tables and basket chairs scattered about the glassed-in verandah. He pursed his lips—he might have been going to whistle—but he did not whistle—only turned the ring—turned the ring on his pink, freshly washed hands.

Over in the corner sat The Two Topknots, drinking a decoction they always drank at this hour—something whitish, greyish, in glasses, with little husks floating on the top—and rooting in a tin full of paper shavings for pieces of speckled biscuit, which they broke, dropped into the glasses and fished for with spoons. Their two coils of knitting, like two snakes, slumbered beside the tray.

The American Woman sat where she always sat against the glass wall, in the shadow of a great creeping thing with wide open purple eyes that pressed—that flattened itself against the glass, hungrily watching her. And she knoo it was there —she knoo it was looking at her just that way. She played up to it; she gave herself little airs. Sometimes she even pointed at it, crying: "Isn't that the most terrible thing you've ever seen! Isn't that ghoulish!" It was on the other side of the verandah, after all . . . and besides it couldn't touch her, could it, Klaymongso? She was an American Woman, wasn't she Klaymongso, and she'd just go right away to her Consul. Klaymongso, curled in her lap, with her torn antique brocade bag, a grubby handkerchief, and a pile of letters from home on top of him, sneezed for reply.

The other tables were empty. A glance passed between the American and the Topknots. She gave a foreign little shrug; they waved an understanding biscuit. But he saw nothing. Now he was still, now from his eyes you saw he listened. "Hoo-e-zip-zoo-oo!" sounded the lift. The iron cage clanged open. Light dragging steps sounded across the hall, coming towards him. A hand, like a leaf, fell on his shoulder. A soft voice said: "Let's go and sit over there—where we can see the drive. The trees are so lovely." And he moved forward with the hand still on his shoulder, and the light, dragging steps beside his. He pulled out a chair and she sank into it, slowly, leaning her head against the back, her arms falling along the sides.

"Won't you bring the other up closer? It's such miles away." But he did not move.

"Where's your shawl?" he asked.

"Oh!" She gave a little groan of dismay. "How silly I am. I've left it upstairs on the bed. Never mind. Please don't go for it. I shan't want it, I know I shan't."

"You'd better have it." And he turned and swiftly crossed the verandah into the dim hall with its scarlet plush and gilt furniture—conjuror's furniture—its Notice of Services at the English Church, its green baize board with the unclaimed letters climbing the black lattice, huge "Presentation" clock that struck the hours at the half-hours, bundles of sticks and umbrellas and sunshades in the clasp of a brown wooden bear, past the two crippled palms, two ancient beggars at the foot of the staircase, up the marble stairs three at a time, past the life-size group on the landing of two stout peasant children with their marble pinnies full of marble grapes, and along the corridor, with its piled-up wreckage of old tin boxes, leather trunks, canvas hold-alls, to their room.

The servant girl was in their room, singing loudly while she emptied soapy water into a pail. The windows were open wide, the shutters put back, and the light glared in. She had thrown the carpets and the big white pillows over the balcony rails; the nets were looped up from the beds; on the writing table there stood a pan of fluff and match-ends. When she saw him her small impudent eyes snapped and her singing changed to humming. But he gave no sign. His eyes searched the glaring room. Where the devil was the shawl!

"Vous desirez, Monsieur?" [1] mocked the servant girl.

No answer. He had seen it. He strode across the room, grabbed the grey cobweb and went out, banging the door. The servant girl's voice at its loudest and shrillest followed him along the corridor.

"Oh, there you are. What happened? What kept you? The tea's here, you see. I've just sent Antonio off for the hot water. Isn't it extraordinary? I must have told him about it sixty times at least, and still he doesn't bring it. Thank you. That's very nice. One does just feel the air when one bends forward."

"Thanks." He took his tea and sat down in the other chair. "No, nothing to eat."

"Oh do! Just one, you had so little at lunch and it's hours before dinner."

Her shawl dropped off as she bent forward to hand him the biscuits. He took one and put it in his saucer.

"Oh, those trees along the drive," she cried, "I could look at them for ever. They are like the most exquisite huge ferns. And you see that one with the grey-silver bark and the clusters of cream coloured flowers, I pulled down a head of them yesterday to smell and the scent" —she shut her eyes at the memory and her voice thinned away, faint, airy—"was like freshly ground nutmegs." A little pause. She turned to him and smiled. "You do know what nutmegs smell like —do you, Robert?"

And he smiled back at her. "Now how am I going to prove to you that I do?"

Back came Antonio with not only the hot water—with letters on a salver and three rolls of paper.

"Oh, the post! Oh, how lovely! Oh, Robert, they mustn't be all for you! Have they just come, Antonio?" Her thin hands flew up and hovered over the letters that Antonio offered her, bending forward.

"Just this moment, Signora," grinned Antonio. "I took-a them from the postman myself. I made-a the postman give them for me."

"Noble Antonio!" laughed she. "There —those are mine, Robert; the rest are yours."

Antonio wheeled sharply, stiffened, the grin went out of his face. His striped linen jacket and his flat gleaming fringe made him look like a wooden doll.

Mr. Salesby put the letters into his pocket; the papers lay on the table. He turned the ring, turned the signet ring on his little finger and stared in front of him, blinking, vacant.

But she—with her teacup in one hand, the sheets of thin paper in the other, her head tilted back, her lips open, a brush of bright colour on her cheek-bones, sipped, sipped, drank . . . drank. . . .

"From Lottie," came the soft murmur. "Poor dear . . . such trouble . . . left foot. She thought . . . neuritis . . . Doctor Blyth . . . flat foot . . . massage. So many robins this year . . . maid most satisfactory . . . Indian Colonel . . . every grain. of rice separate . . . very heavy fall of snow." And her wide lighted eyes looked up from the letter. "Snow, Robert! Think of it!" And she touched the little dark violets pinned on her thin bosom and went back to the letter.

. . . Snow. Snow in London. Millie with the early morning cup of tea. "There's been a terrible fall of snow in the night, Sir." "Oh, has there, Millie?" The curtains ring apart, letting in the pale, reluctant light. He raises himself in the bed; he catches a glimpse of the solid houses opposite framed in white, of their window boxes full of great sprays of white coral. . . . In the bathroom—overlooking the

[1] "Is there something you want, sir?" (JHP)

back garden. Snow—heavy snow over everything. The lawn is covered with a wavy pattern of cat's paws; there is a thick, icing on the garden table; the withered pods of the laburnum tree are white tassels; only here and there in the ivy is a dark leaf showing. . . . Warming his back at the dining-room fire, the paper drying over a chair. Millie with the bacon. "Oh, if you please, Sir, there's two little boys come as will do the steps and front for a shilling, shall I let them?" . . . And then flying lightly, lightly down the stairs —Jinnie. "Oh, Robert, isn't it wonderful! Oh, what a pity it has to melt. Where's the pussy-wee?" "I'll get him from Millie" . . . "Millie, you might just hand me up the kitten if you've got him down there." "Very good, Sir." He feels the little beating heart under his hand. "Come on old chap, your Missus wants you." "Oh, Robert, do show him the snow—his first snow. Shall I open the window and give him a little piece on his paw to hold? . . ."

"Well, that's very satisfactory on the whole—very. Poor Lottie! Darling Anne! How I wish I could send them something of this," she cried, waving her letters at the brilliant, dazzling garden. "More tea, Robert? Robert dear, more tea."

"No, thanks, no. It was very good," he drawled.

"Well mine wasn't. Mine was just like chopped hay. Oh, here comes the Honeymoon Couple."

Half striding, half running, carrying a basket between them and rods and lines, they came up the drive, up the shallow steps.

"My! have you been out fishing?" cried the American Woman.

They were out of breath, they panted: "Yes, yes, we have been out in a little boat all day. We have caught seven. Four are good to eat. But three we shall give away. To the children."

Mrs. Salesby turned her chair to look; the Topknots laid the snakes down. They were a very dark young couple—black hair, olive skin, brilliant eyes and teeth. He was dressed "English fashion" in a flannel jacket, white trousers and shoes. Round his neck he wore a silk scarf; his head, with his hair brushed back, was bare. And he kept mopping his forehead, rubbing his hands with a brilliant handkerchief. Her white skirt had a patch of wet; her neck and throat were stained a deep pink. When she lifted her arms big half-loops of perspiration showed under her armpits; her hair clung in wet curls to her cheeks. She looked as though her young husband had been dipping her in the sea, and fishing her out again to dry in the sun and then—in with her again— all day.

"Would Klaymongso like a fish?" they cried. Their laughing voices charged with excitement beat against the glassed-in verandah like birds, and a strange saltish smell came from the basket.

"You will sleep well to-night," said a Topknot, picking her ear with a knitting needle while the other Topknot smiled and nodded.

The Honeymoon Couple looked at each other. A great wave seemed to go over them. They gasped, gulped, staggered a little and then came up laughing —laughing.

"We cannot go upstairs, we are too tired. We must have tea just as we are. Here—coffee. No—tea. No—coffee. Tea —coffee, Antonio!" Mrs. Salesby turned.

"Robert! Robert!" Where was he? He wasn't there. Oh, there he was at the other end of the verandah; with his back turned, smoking a cigarette. "Robert, shall we go for our little turn?"

"Right." He stumped the cigarette into an ash-tray and sauntered over, his eyes on the ground. "Will you be warm enough?"

"Oh, quite."

"Sure?"

"Well," she put her hand on his arm, "perhaps"—and gave his arm the faintest pressure—"it's not upstairs, it's only in the hall—perhaps you'd get me my cape. Hanging up."

He came back with it and she bent her small head while he dropped it on her shoulders. Then, very stiff, he offered her his arm. She bowed sweetly to the people on the verandah while he just covered a yawn, and they went down the steps together.

"*Vous avez voo ça!*" [2] said the American Woman.

"He is not a man," said the Two Top-knots, "he is an ox. I say to my sister in the morning and at night when we are in bed, I tell her—*No* man is he, but an ox!"

Wheeling, tumbling, swooping, the laughter of the Honeymoon Couple dashed against the glass of the verandah.

The sun was still high. Every leaf, every flower in the garden lay open, motionless, as if exhausted, and a sweet, rich, rank smell filled the quivering air. Out of the thick, fleshy leaves of a cactus there rose an aloe stem loaded with pale flowers that looked as though they had been cut out of butter; light flashed upon the lifted spears of the palms; over a bed of scarlet waxen flowers some big black insects "zoom-zoomed"; a great, gaudy creeper, orange splashed with jet, sprawled against a wall.

"I don't need my cape after all," said she. "It's really too warm." So he took it off and carried it over his arm. "Let us go down this path here. I feel so well to-day—marvellously better. Good heavens—look at those children! And to think it's November!"

In a corner of the garden there were two brimming tubs of water. Three little girls, having thoughtfully taken off their drawers and hung them on a bush, their skirts clasped to their waists, were standing in the tubs and tramping up and down. They screamed, their hair fell over their faces, they splashed one another. But suddenly, the smallest, who had a tub to herself, glanced up and saw who was looking. For a moment she seemed overcome with terror, then clumsily she struggled and strained out of her tub, and still holding her clothes above her waist. "The Englishman! The Englishman!" she shrieked and fled away to hide. Shrieking and screaming, the other two followed her. In a moment they were gone; in a moment there was nothing but the two brimming tubs and their little drawers on the bush.

"How—very—extraordinary!" said she. "What made them so frightened? Surely

2 "There you have it!" (JHP)

they were much too young to . . ." She looked up at him. She thought he looked pale—but wonderfully handsome with that great tropical tree behind him with its long, spiked thorns.

For a moment he did not answer. Then he met her glance, and smiling his slow smile, "*Très* rum!" said he.

Très rum! Oh, she felt quite faint. Oh, why should she love him so much just because he said a thing like that. *Très* rum! That was Robert all over. Nobody else but Robert could ever say such a thing. To be so wonderful, so brilliant, so learned, and then to say in that queer, boyish voice. . . . She could have wept.

"You know you're very absurd, sometimes," said she.

"I am," he answered. And they walked on.

But she was tired. She had had enough. She did not want to walk any more.

"Leave me here and go for a little constitutional, won't you? I'll be in one of these long chairs. What a good thing you've got my cape; you won't have to go upstairs for a rug. Thank you, Robert, I shall look at that delicious heliotrope. . . . You won't be gone long?"

"No—no. You don't mind being left?"

"Silly! I want you to go. I can't expect you to drag after your invalid wife every minute. . . . How long will you be?"

He took out his watch. "It's just after half-past four. I'll be back at a quarter past five."

"Back at a quarter past five," she repeated, and she lay still in the long chair and folded her hands.

He turned away. Suddenly he was back again. "Look here, would you like my watch?" And he dangled it before her.

"Oh!" She caught her breath. "Very, very much." And she clasped the watch, the warm watch, the darling watch in her fingers. "Now go quickly."

The gates of the Pension Villa Excelsior were open wide, jammed open against some bold geraniums. Stooping a little, staring straight ahead, walking swiftly, he passed through them and began climbing the hill that wound behind the town like a great rope looping the villas together.

The dust lay thick. A carriage came bowling along driving towards the Excelsior. In it sat the General and the Countess; they had been for his daily airing. Mr. Salesby stepped to one side but the dust beat up, thick, white, stifling like wool. The Countess just had time to nudge the General.

"There he goes," she said spitefully.

But the General gave a loud caw and refused to look.

"It is the Englishman," said the driver, turning round and smiling. And the Countess threw up her hands and nodded so amiably that he spat with satisfaction and gave the stumbling horse a cut.

On—on—past the finest villas in the town, magnificent palaces, palaces worth coming any distance to see, past the public gardens with the carved grottoes and statues and stone animals drinking at the fountain, into a poorer quarter. Here the road ran narrow and foul between high lean houses, the ground floors of which were scooped and hollowed into stables and carpenters' shops. At a fountain ahead of him two old hags were beating linen. As he passed them they squatted back on their haunches, stared, and then their "A-hak-kak-kak!" with the slap, slap, of the stone on the linen sounded after him.

He reached the top of the hill; he turned a corner and the town was hidden. Down he looked into a deep valley with a dried up river bed at the bottom. This side and that was covered with small dilapidated houses that had broken stone verandahs where the fruit lay drying, tomato lanes in the garden, and from the gates to the doors a trellis of vines. The late sunlight, deep, golden, lay in the cup of the valley; there was a smell of charcoal in the air. In the gardens the men were cutting grapes. He watched a man standing in the greenish shade, raising up, holding a black cluster in one hand, taking the knife from his belt, cutting, laying the bunch in a flat boat-shaped basket. The man worked leisurely, silently, taking hundreds of years over the job. On the hedges on the other side of the road there were grapes small as berries, growing wild, growing among the stones.

He leaned against a wall, filled his pipe, put a match to it. . . .

Leaned across a gate, turned up the collar of his mackintosh. It was going to rain. It didn't matter, he was prepared for it. You didn't expect anything else in November. He looked over the bare field. From the corner by the gate there came the smell of swedes, a great stack of them, wet, rank coloured. Two men passed walking towards the straggling village. "Good day!" "Good day!" By Jove! he had to hurry if he was going to catch that train home. Over the gate, across the field, over the stile, into the lane, swinging along in the drifting rain and dusk. . . . Just home in time for a bath and a change before supper. . . . In the drawing-room; Jinnie is sitting pretty nearly in the fire. "Oh, Robert, I didn't hear you come in. Did you have a good time? How nice you smell! A present?" "Some bits of blackberry I picked for you. Pretty colour." "Oh, lovely, Robert! Dennis and Beaty are coming to supper." Supper—cold beef, potatoes in their jackets, claret, household bread. They are gay—everybody's laughing. "Oh, we all know Robert," says Dennis, breathing on his eye-glasses and polishing them. "By the way, Dennis, I picked up a very jolly little edition of . . ."

A clock struck. He wheeled sharply. What time was it. Five? A quarter past? Back, back the way he came. As he passed through the gates he saw her on the lookout. She got up, waved and slowly she came to meet him, dragging the heavy cape. In her hand she carried a spray of heliotrope.

"You're late," she cried gaily. "You're three minutes late. Here's your watch, it's been very good while you were away. Did you have a nice time? Was it lovely? Tell me. Where did you go?"

"I say—put this on," he said, taking the cape from her.

"Yes, I will. Yes, it's getting chilly. Shall we go up to our room?"

When they reached the lift she was coughing. He frowned.

"It's nothing. I haven't been out too

late. Don't be cross." She sat down on one of the red plush chairs while he rang and rang, and then, getting no answer, kept his finger on the bell.

"Oh, Robert, do you think you ought to?"

"Ought to what?"

The door of the *salon* opened. "What is that? Who is making that noise?" sounded from within. Klaymongso began to yelp. "Caw! Caw! Caw!" came from the General. A Topknot darted out with one hand to her ear, opened the staff door, "Mr. Queet! Mr. Queet!" she bawled. That brought the manager up at a run.

"Is that you ringing the bell, Mr. Salesby? Do you want the lift? Very good, Sir. I'll take you up myself. Antonio wouldn't have been a minute, he was just taking off his apron—" And having ushered them in, the oily manager went to the door of the *salon*. "Very sorry you should have been troubled, ladies and gentlemen." Salesby stood in the cage, sucking in his cheeks, staring at the ceiling and turning the ring, turning the signet ring on his little finger. . . .

Arrived in their room he went swiftly over to the washstand, shook the bottle, poured her out a dose and brought it across.

"Sit down. Drink it. And don't talk." And he stood over her while she obeyed. Then he took the glass, rinsed it and put it back in its case. "Would you like a cushion?"

"No, I'm quite all right. Come over here. Sit down by me just a minute, will you, Robert? Ah, that's very nice." She turned and thrust the piece of heliotrope in the lapel of his coat. "That," she said, "is most becoming." And then she leaned her head against his shoulder, and he put his arm round her.

"Robert—" her voice like a sigh—like a breath.

"Yes—"

They sat there for a long while. The sky flamed, paled; the two white beds were like two ships. . . . At last he heard the servant girl running along the corridor with the hot water cans, and gently he released her and turned on the light.

"Oh, what time is it? Oh, what a heavenly evening. Oh, Robert, I was thinking while you were away this afternoon . . ."

They were the last couple to enter the dining-room. The Countess was there with her lorgnette and her fan, the General was there with his special chair and the air cushion and the small rug over his knees. The American Woman was there showing Klaymongso a copy of the *Saturday Evening Post*. . . . "We're having a feast of reason and a flow of soul." The Two Topknots were there feeling over the peaches and the pears in their dish of fruit, and putting aside all they considered unripe or overripe to show to the manager, and the Honeymoon Couple leaned across the table, whispering, trying not to burst out laughing.

Mr. Queet, in everyday clothes and white canvas shoes, served the soup, and Antonio, in full evening dress, handed it round.

"No," said the American Woman, "take it away, Antonio. We can't eat soup. We can't eat anything mushy, can we, Klaymongso?"

"Take them back and fill them to the rim!" said the Topknots, and they turned and watched while Antonio delivered the message.

"What is it? Rice? Is it cooked?" The Countess peered through her lorgnette. "Mr. Queet, the General can have some of this soup if it is cooked."

"Very good, Countess."

The Honeymoon Couple had their fish instead.

"Give me that one. That's the one I caught. No. it's not. Yes, it is. No, it's not. Well, it's looking at me with its eye so it must be. Tee! Hee! Hee!" Their feet were locked together under the table.

"Robert, you're not eating again. Is anything the matter?"

"No. Off food, that's all."

"Oh, what a bother. There are eggs and spinach coming. You don't like spinach, do you. I must tell them in future . . ."

An egg and mashed potatoes for the General.

"Mr. Queet! Mr. Queet!"

"Yes, Countess."

"The General's egg's too hard again."

"Caw! Caw! Caw!"

"Very sorry, Countess. Shall I have you another cooked, General?"

. . . They are the first to leave the dining-room. She rises, gathering her shawl and he stands aside waiting for her to pass, turning the ring, turning the signet ring on his little finger. In the hall Mr. Queet hovers. "I thought you might not want to wait for the lift. Antonio's just serving the finger bowls. And I'm sorry the bell won't ring, it's out of order. I can't think what's happened."

"Oh, I do hope . . ." from her.

"Get in," says he.

Mr. Queet steps after them and slams the door. . . .

. . . "Robert, do you mind if I go to bed very soon? Won't you go down to the *salon* or out into the garden? Or perhaps you might smoke a cigar on the balcony. It's lovely out there. And I like cigar smoke. I always did. But if you'd rather . . ."

"No, I'll sit here."

He takes a chair and sits on the balcony. He hears her moving about in the room, lightly, lightly, moving and rustling. Then she comes over to him. "Good night, Robert."

"Good night." He takes her hand and kisses the palm. "Don't catch cold."

The sky is the colour of jade. There are a great many stars; an enormous white moon hangs over the garden. Far away lightning flutters—flutters like a wing— flutters like a broken bird that tries to fly and sinks again and again struggles.

The lights from the *salon* shine across the garden path and there is the sound of a piano. And once the American Woman, opening the French window to let Klaymongso into the garden, cries: "Have you seen this moon?" But nobody answers.

He gets very cold sitting there, staring at the balcony rail. Finally he comes inside. The moon—the room is painted white with moonlight. The light trembles in the mirrors; the two beds seem to float. She is asleep. He sees her through the nets, half sitting, banked up with pillows, her white hands crossed on the sheet. Her white cheeks, her fair hair pressed against the pillow, are silvered over. He undresses quickly, stealthily and gets into bed. Lying there, his hands clasped behind his head. . . .

. . . In his study. Late summer. The virginia creeper just on the turn. . . .

"Well, my dear chap, that's the whole story. That's the long and short of it. If she can't cut away for the next two years and give a decent climate a chance she don't stand a dog's—h'm—show. Better be frank about these things." "Oh, certainly. . . ." "And hang it all, old man, what's to prevent you going with her? It isn't as though you've got a regular job like us wage earners. You can do what you do wherever you are—" "Two years." "Yes, I should give it two years. You'll have no trouble about letting this house you know. As a matter of fact . . ."

. . . He is with her. "Robert, the awful thing is—I suppose it's my illness—I simply feel I could not go alone. You see—you're everything. You're bread and wine, Robert, bread and wine. Oh, my darling—what am I saying? Of course I could, of course I won't take you away. . . ."

He hears her stirring. Does she want something?

"Boogles?"

Good Lord! She is talking in her sleep. They haven't used that name for years.

"Boogles. Are you awake?"

"Yes, do you want anything?"

"Oh, I'm going to be a bother. I'm so sorry. Do you mind? There's a wretched mosquito inside my net—I can hear him singing. Would you catch him? I don't want to move because of my heart."

"No, don't move. Stay where you are." He switches on the light, lifts the net. "Where is the little beggar? Have you spotted him?"

"Yes, there, over by the corner. Oh, I do feel such a fiend to have dragged you out of bed. Do you mind dreadfully?"

"No, of course not." For a moment he hovers in his blue and white pyjamas. Then, "got him," he said.

"Oh, good. Was he a juicy one?"

"Beastly." He went over to the washstand and dipped his fingers in water.

"Are you all right now? Shall I switch off the light?"

"Yes, please. No. Boogles! Come back here a moment. Sit down by me. Give me your hand." She turns his signet ring. "Why weren't you asleep? Boogles, listen. Come closer. I sometimes wonder—do you mind awfully being out here with me?"

He bends down. He kisses her. He tucks her in, he smoothes the pillow.

"Rot!" he whispers.

[1920]

QUESTIONS FOR STUDY

1. *How does Robert Salesby reveal his real attitudes toward his wife? What is the significance of his name, the signet ring which he continually turns, his reminiscences, his lack of appetite, his final statement, "Rot!"? Why do the maid and the three little girls react to Robert in the way they do?*
2. *Why does Mansfield choose to reveal Mrs. Salesby only indirectly, and chiefly through dialogue? What images are associated with her?*
3. *What is the function of the various minor characters—the Two Top-knots, the American Woman, the Honeymoon Couple, the Countess, and the General?*
4. *Why does Mansfield provide the story with a lush, tropical setting?*
5. *What sexual symbolism is employed in the story?*

GUY DE MAUPASSANT
Little Soldier

EVERY Sunday, as soon as they were free, the two little soldiers set off.

On leaving the barracks they turned to the right; went through Courbevoie with long quick steps, as though they were on a march; then, having left the houses behind them, they followed at a calmer gait the bare and dusty highroad which leads to Bezons.

Being little and thin, they looked quite lost in their coats, which were too big and too long. The sleeves hung down over their hands, and they were much bothered by their enormous red breeches, which compelled them to walk wide. Under their stiff, high shakos their faces seemed like mere nothings—two poor, hollow Breton faces, simple in an almost animal simplicity, and with blue eyes which were gentle and calm.

During the walk they never spoke. They went straight on, each with the same idea in his head as the other. It stood them in place of conversation, for the fact is that just inside the little wood near Les Champioux they had found a place which reminded them of their own country, and it was only there that they felt happy.

When they came under the trees where the roads from Colombes and from Chatou cross, they would take off their heavy shakos and wipe their foreheads.

They always stopped a little while on the Bezons bridge to look at the Seine. They would remain there two or three minutes, bent double, leaning on the parapet. Or sometimes they would gaze out over the great basin of Argenteuil, where the skiffs might be seen scudding, with their white, slanted sails, recalling perhaps the look of the Breton water, the harbor of Vannes, near which they lived, and the fishing-boats standing out across the Morbihan to the open sea.

As soon as they had crossed the Seine they bought their provisions from the sausage merchant, the baker, and the seller of the wine of the country. A piece of blood-pudding, four sous' worth of bread, and a litre of "petit bleu" constituted the provisions, which they carried off in their handkerchiefs. But after they had left this village they now went very slowly forward, and they began to talk.

In front of them a barren plain strewn with clumps of trees led to the wood, to the little wood which had seemed to them to resemble the one at Kermarivan. Grain-fields and hay-fields bordered the narrow path, which lost itself in this young greenness of the crops, and Jean Kerderen would always say to Luc le Ganidec:

"It looks like it does near Plounivon."

"Yes; exactly."

They went onward, side by side, their spirits suffused with vague memories of their own country, filled with awakened images—images as naïve as the pictures on the colored broadsheets which you buy for a penny. And they kept recognizing, as it were, now a corner of a field, a hedge, a bit of moorland, now a crossroads, now a granite cross.

Then, too, they would always stop beside a certain landmark, a great stone, because it looked something like the cromlech at Locneuven.

On arriving at the first clump of trees Luc le Ganidec every Sunday cut a switch, a hazel switch, and began gently to peel off the bark, thinking meanwhile of the folk there at home.

Jean Kerderen carried the provisions.

From time to time Luc mentioned a name, or recalled some doing of their childhood in a few brief words, which caused long thoughts. And their own country, their dear distant country, repossessed them little by little, seized upon them, and sent to them from afar her shapes, her sounds, her well-known prospects, her odors—odors of the green lands where the salt sea-air was blowing.

They were no longer conscious of the exhalations of the Parisian stables on which the earth of the *banlieue* fattens, but of the perfume of the flowering broom, which the salt breeze of the open sea plucks and bears away. And the sails of the boats, appearing above the river-banks, seemed to them the sails of the coasting vessels perceived beyond the great plain which extended from their homes to the very margin of the waves.

They went with short steps, Luc le Ganidec and Jean Kerderen, content and sad, haunted by a sweet melancholy, by the lingering, penetrating sorrow of a caged animal who remembers.

And by the time that Luc had stripped the slender wand of its bark they arrived at the corner of the wood where every Sunday they took breakfast.

They found the two bricks which they had hidden in the thicket, and they kindled a little fire of branches, over which to roast their blood-pudding at the end of a bayonet.

And when they had breakfasted, eaten their bread to the last crumb, and drunk their wine to the last drop, they remained seated side by side upon the grass, saying nothing, their eyes on the distance, their eyelids drooping, their fingers crossed as at mass, their red legs stretched out beside the poppies of the field. And the leather of their shakos and the brass of their buttons glittered in the ardent sun, and made the larks, which sang and hovered above their heads, stop short.

About mid-day they began to turn their eyes from time to time in the direction of the village of Bezons, because the girl with the cow was coming.

She passed by them every Sunday on her way to milk and change the position of her cow—the only cow of this district which ever went out of the stable to grass. It pastured in a narrow field along the edge of wood a little farther on.

They soon perceived the girl, the only human being who came walking across the land. And they felt themselves rejoiced by the brilliant reflections thrown off by her tin milk-pail under the flame of the sun. They never talked about her. They were simply glad to see her, without understanding why.

She was a great strong wench with red hair, burned by the heat of sunny days, a great sturdy wench of the environs of Paris.

Once, finding them again seated in the same place, she said:

"Good-morning. You two are always here, aren't you?"

Luc le Ganidec, the bolder, stammered:

"Yes; we come to rest."

That was all. But the next Sunday she laughed with a protecting benevolence and a feminine keenness which knew well enough that they were bashful. And she asked:

"What are you doing there? Are you trying to see the grass grow?"

Luc was cheered up by this, and smiled likewise: "Maybe we are."

She continued: "*Hein!* That's pretty slow work."

He answered, still laughing: "Well, yes, it is."

She went on. But coming back with a milk-pail full of milk, she stopped again before them, and said:

"Would you like a drop? It will taste like home."

With her instinctive feeling that they were of the same peasant race as she, being herself also far away from home perhaps, she had divined and touched the spot.

They were both touched. Then, with some difficulty, she managed to make a little milk run into the neck of the glass bottle in which they carried their wine. And Luc drank first, with little swallows, stopping every minute to see whether he had drunk more than his half. Then he handed the bottle to Jean.

She stood upright before them, her hands on her hips, her pail on the ground at her feet, glad at the pleasure which she had given.

Then she departed, shouting: "Allons! Adieu! Till next Sunday!"

And as long as they could see her at all, they followed with their eyes her tall silhouette, which withdrew itself, growing smaller and smaller, and seeming to sink into the verdure of the fields.

When they were leaving the barracks the week after, Jean said to Luc:

"Oughtn't we to buy her something good?"

And they remained in great embarrassment before the problem of the choice of a delicacy for the girl with the cow.

Luc was of the opinion that a bit of tripe would be the best, but Jean preferred some *berlingots*, because he was fond of sweets. His choice fairly made him enthusiastic, and they bought at a grocer's two sous' worth of candies white and red.

They ate their breakfast more rapidly than usual, being nervous with expectation.

Jean saw her the first. "There she is!" said he. Luc continued: "Yes, there she is."

While yet some distance off she laughed at seeing them. She cried:

"Is everything going as you like it?"

They answered together:

"Are you getting on all right?"

Then she conversed, talked to them of simple things in which they felt an interest—of the weather, of the crops, and of her master.

They were afraid to offer her their candies, which were slowly melting away in Jean's pocket.

At last Luc grew bold, and murmured: "We have brought you something."

She demanded, "What is it? Tell me!"

Then Jean, blushing up to his ears, managed to get at the little paper cornucopia, and held it out.

She began to eat the little pieces of sugar, rolling them from one cheek to the other. And they made lumps beneath her flesh. The two soldiers, seated before her, regarded her with emotion and delight.

Then she went to milk her cow, and once more gave them some milk on coming back.

They thought of her all the week; several times they even spoke of her. The next Sunday she sat down with them for a little longer talk; and all three, seated side by side, their eyes lost in the distance, clasping their knees with their hands, told the small doings, the minute details of their life in the villages where they had been born, while over there the cow, seeing that the milk-maid had stopped on her way, stretched out towards her its

heavy head with the dripping nostrils, and gave a long low to call her back.

Soon the girl consented to eat a bit of bread with them and drink a mouthful of wine. She often brought them plums in her pocket; for the season of plums had come. Her presence sharpened the wits of the two little Breton soldiers, and they chattered like two birds.

But, one Tuesday, Luc le Ganidec asked for leave—a thing which had never happened before—and he did not return until ten o'clock at night.

Jean racked his brains uneasily for a reason for his comrade's going out in this way.

The next Thursday Luc, having borrowed ten sous from his bed-fellow, again asked and obtained permission to leave the barracks for several hours.

And when he set off with Jean on their Sunday walk his manner was very queer, quite restless and quite changed. Kerderen did not understand, but he vaguely suspected something without divining what it could be.

They did not say a word to one another until they reached their usual stopping-place, where, from their constant sitting in the same spot, the grass was quite worn away. And they ate their breakfast slowly. Neither of them felt hungry.

Before long the girl appeared. As on every Sunday, they watched her coming. When she was quite near, Luc rose and made two steps forward. She put her milk-pail on the ground, and kissed him. She kissed him passionately, throwing her arms about his neck, without noticing Jean, without remembering that he was there, without even seeing him.

And he sat there desperate, he the poor Jean, so desperate that he did not understand, his soul quite overwhelmed, his heart bursting, not yet expressing it all to himself.

Then the girl seated herself beside Luc, and they began to chatter.

Jean did not look at them: he now divined why his comrade had gone out twice during the week, and he felt within him a burning grief, a kind of wound, that sense of rending which is caused by a treason.

Luc and the girl got up together to go and change the position of the cow.

Jean followed them with his eyes. He saw them departing side by side. The red breeches of his comrade made a bright spot on the road. It was Luc who picked up the mallet and hammered down the stake to which they tied the beast.

The girl stooped to milk her, while he stroked the cow's sharp spine with a careless hand. Then they left the milk-pail on the grass, and they went deep into the wood.

Jean saw nothing more but the wall of leaves where they had entered; and he felt himself so troubled that if he had tried to rise he would certainly have fallen.

He sat motionless, stupefied by astonishment and suffering, by a suffering which was simple but which was deep. He wanted to cry, to run away, to hide himself, never to see anybody any more.

Suddenly he saw them issuing from the thicket. They returned gently, holding each other's hands, as in the villages do those who are promised. It was Luc who carried the pail.

They kissed one another again before they separated, and the girl went off after having thrown Jean a friendly "good-evening" and a smile which was full of meaning. To-day she no longer thought of offering him any milk.

The two little soldiers sat side by side, motionless as usual, silent and calm, their placid faces betraying nothing of all which troubled their hearts. The sun fell on them. Sometimes the cow lowed, looking at them from afar.

At their usual hour they rose to go back.

Luc cut a switch. Jean carried the empty bottle. He returned it to the wine-seller at Bezons. Then they sallied out upon the bridge, and, as they did every Sunday, they stopped several minutes in the middle to watch the water flowing.

Jean leaned, leaned more and more, over the iron railing, as though he saw in the current something which attracted him. Luc said: "Are you trying to drink?" Just as he uttered the last word Jean's head overbalanced his body, his legs described a circle in the air, and the little blue and red soldier fell in a lump, entered the water, and disappeared.

Luc, his throat paralyzed with anguish, tried in vain to shout. Farther down he saw something stir; then the head of his comrade rose to the surface of the river and re-entered it as soon.

Farther still he again perceived a hand, a single hand which issued from the stream and then plunged back. That was all.

The barge-men who ran up did not find the body that day.

Luc returned alone to the barracks, running, his head filled with madness; and he told of the accident, with tears in his eyes and voice, blowing his nose again and again: "He leaned over . . . he . . . he leaned over . . . so far . . . so far that his head turned a somersault; and . . . and . . . so he fell . . . he fell. . . ."

He was strangled by emotion, he could say no more. If he had only known!

[1885]

TRANSLATED BY
JOHN STURGES

QUESTIONS FOR STUDY

1. *In what ways are Jean Kerderen and Luc le Ganidec alike? In what ways are they different? What is the bond that constitutes their friendship? What is the significance of their littleness, of the fact that their uniforms are much too large for them?*
2. *What significance does the girl with the cow assume for the two soldiers? Is it appropriate that Luc should win her?*
3. *Is Jean's death an accident or is it suicide? If the latter, why should Jean choose to kill himself?*
4. *What is it that Luc le Ganidec should have "known"?*
5. *To what extent is "Little Soldier" a conventional love story? To what extent is it unconventional?*

HERMAN MELVILLE

Bartleby the Scrivener

I AM A rather elderly man. The nature of my avocations, for the last thirty years, has brought me into more than ordinary contact with what would seem an interesting and somewhat singular set of men, of whom, as yet, nothing, that I know of, has ever been written—I mean, the law-copyists, or scriveners. I have known very many of them, professionally and privately, and, if I pleased, could relate divers histories, at which good-natured gentlemen might smile, and sentimental souls might weep. But I waive the biographies of all other scriveners, for a few passages in the life of Bartleby, who was a scrivener, the strangest I ever saw, or heard of. While, of other law-copyists, I might write the complete life, of Bartleby nothing of that sort can be done. I believe that no materials exist, for a full and satisfactory biography of this man. It is an irreparable loss to literature. Bartleby was one of those beings of whom nothing is ascertainable, except from the original sources, and, in his case, those are very small. What my own astonished eyes saw of Bartleby, *that* is all I know of him, except, indeed, one vague report, which will appear in the sequel.

Ere introducing the scrivener, as he first appeared to me, it is fit I make some mention of myself, my employés, my business, my chambers, and general surroundings; because some such description is indispensable to an adequate understanding of the chief character about to be presented. Imprimis: I am a man who, from his youth upward, has been filled with a profound conviction that the easiest way of life is the best. Hence, though I belong to a profession proverbially energetic and nervous, even to turbulence, at times, yet nothing of that sort have I ever suffered to invade my peace. I am one of those unambitious lawyers who never addresses a jury, or in any way draws down public applause; but, in the cool tranquillity of a snug retreat, do a snug business among rich men's bonds, and mortgages, and title-deeds. All who know me, consider me an eminently *safe* man. The late John Jacob Astor, a personage little given to poetic enthusiasm, had no hesitation in pronouncing my first grand point to be prudence; my next, method. I do not speak it in vanity, but simply record the fact, that I was not unemployed in my profession by the late John Jacob Astor; a name which, I admit, I love to repeat; for it hath a rounded and orbicular sound to it, and rings like unto bullion. I will freely add, that I was not insensible to the late John Jacob Astor's good opinion.

Some time prior to the period at which this little history begins, my avocations had been largely increased. The good old office, now extinct in the State of New York, of a Master in Chancery, had been conferred upon me. It was not a very arduous office, but very pleasantly remunerative. I seldom lose my temper; much more seldom indulge in dangerous indignation at wrongs and outrages; but, I must be permitted to be rash here, and declare, that I consider the sudden and violent abrogation of the office of Master in Chancery, by the new Constitution, as a—premature act; inasmuch as I had counted upon a life-lease of the profits, whereas I only received those of a few short years. But this is by the way.

My chambers were upstairs, at No. — Wall Street. At one end, they looked upon the white wall of the interior of a spacious skylight shaft, penetrating the building from top to bottom.

This view might have been considered rather tame than otherwise, deficient in what landscape painters call 'life.' But, if so, the view from the other end of my chambers offered, at least, a contrast, if nothing more. In that direction, my windows commanded an unobstructed view of a lofty brick wall, black by age and everlasting shade; which wall required no spy-glass to bring out its lurking beauties, but, for the benefit of all near-sighted spectators, was pushed up to within ten feet of my window panes. Owing to the great height of the surrounding buildings, and my chambers being on the second floor, the interval between this wall and mine not a little resembled a huge square cistern.

At the period just preceding the advent of Bartleby, I had two persons as copyists in my employment, and a promising lad as an office-boy. First, Turkey; second, Nippers; third, Ginger Nut. These may seem names, the like of which are not usually found in the Directory. In truth, they were nicknames, mutually conferred upon each other by my three clerks, and were deemed expressive of their respective persons or characters. Turkey was a short, pursy Englishman, of about my own age —that is, somewhere not far from sixty. In the morning, one might say, his face was of a fine florid hue, but after twelve o'clock, meridian—his dinner hour—it blazed like a grate full of Christmas coals; and continued blazing—but, as it were, with a gradual wane—till six o'clock, P.M., or thereabouts; after which, I saw no more of the proprietor of the face, which, gaining its meridian with the sun, seemed to set with it, to rise, culminate, and decline the following day, with the like regularity and undiminished glory. There are many singular coincidences I have known in the course of my life, not the least among which was the fact, that, exactly when Turkey displayed his fullest beams from his red and radiant countenance, just then, too, at that critical moment, began the daily period when I considered his business capacities as seriously disturbed for the remainder of the twenty-four hours. Not that he was absolutely idle, or averse to business, then; far from it. The difficulty was, he was apt to be altogether too energetic. There was a strange, inflamed, flurried, flighty recklessness of activity about him. He would be incautious in dipping his pen into his inkstand. All his blots upon my documents were dropped there after twelve o'clock, meridian. Indeed, not only would he be reckless, and sadly given to making blots in the afternoon, but, some days, he went further, and was rather noisy. At

such times, too, his face flamed with augmented blazonry, as if cannel coal had been heaped on anthracite. He made an unpleasant racket with his chair; spilled his sand-box; in mending his pens, impatiently split them all to pieces, and threw them on the floor in a sudden passion; stood up, and leaned over his table, boxing his papers about in a most indecorous manner, very sad to behold in an elderly man like him. Nevertheless, as he was in many ways a most valuable person to me, and all the time before twelve o'clock, meridian, was the quickest, steadiest creature, too, accomplishing a great deal of work in a style not easily to be matched—for these reasons, I was willing to overlook his eccentricities, though, indeed, occasionally, I remonstrated with him. I did this very gently, however, because, though the civilest, nay, the blandest and most reverential of men in the morning, yet, in the afternoon, he was disposed, upon provocation, to be slightly rash with his tongue—in fact, insolent. Now, valuing his morning services as I did, and resolved not to lose them—yet, at the same time, made uncomfortable by his inflamed ways after twelve o'clock—and being a man of peace, unwilling by my admonitions to call forth unseemly retorts from him, I took upon me, one Saturday noon (he was always worse on Saturdays) to hint to him, very kindly, that, perhaps, now that he was growing old, it might be well to abridge his labours; in short, he need not come to my chambers after twelve o'clock, but, dinner over, had best go home to his lodgings, and rest himself till tea-time. But no; he insisted upon his afternoon devotions. His countenance became intolerably fervid, as he oratorically assured me—gesticulating with a long ruler at the other end of the room—that if his services in the morning were useful, how indispensable, then, in the afternoon?

'With submission, sir,' said Turkey, on this occasion, 'I consider myself your right-hand man. In the morning I but marshal and deploy my columns; but in the afternoon I put myself at their head, and gallantly charge the foe, thus'—and he made a violent thrust with the ruler.

'But the blots, Turkey,' intimated I.

'True; but, with submission, sir, behold these hairs! I am getting old. Surely, sir, a blot or two of a warm afternoon is not to be severely urged against gray hairs. Old age—even if it blot the page—is honourable. With submission, sir, we *both* are getting old.'

This appeal to my fellow-feeling was hardly to be resisted. At all events, I saw that go he would not. So, I made up my mind to let him stay, resolving, nevertheless, to see to it that, during the afternoon, he had to do with my less important papers.

Nippers, the second on my list, was a whiskered, sallow, and, upon the whole, rather piratical-looking young man, of about five-and-twenty. I always deemed him the victim of two evil powers—ambition and indigestion. The ambition was evinced by a certain impatience of the duties of a mere copyist, an unwarrantable usurpation of strictly professional affairs, such as the original drawing up of legal documents. The indigestion seemed betokened in an occasional nervous testiness and grinning irritability, causing the teeth to audibly grind together over mistakes committed in copying; unnecessary maledictions, hissed, rather than spoken, in the heat of business; and especially by a continual discontent with the height of the table where he worked. Though of a very ingenious mechanical turn, Nippers could never get this table to suit him. He put chips under it, blocks of various sorts, bits of pasteboard, and at last went so far as to attempt an exquisite adjustment, by final pieces of folded blotting-paper. But no invention would answer. If, for the sake of easing his back, he brought the table lid at a sharp angle well up toward his chin, and wrote there like a man using the steep roof of a Dutch house for his desk, then he declared that it stopped the circulation in his arms. If now he lowered the table to his waistbands, and stooped over it in writing, then there was a sore aching in his back. In short, the truth of the matter was, Nippers knew not what he wanted. Or, if he wanted anything, it was to be rid of a scrivener's table altogether. Among the manifestations of his diseased ambition was a fondness he had for receiving visits from certain ambiguous-looking fellows in seedy coats, whom he called his clients. Indeed, I was aware that not only was he, at times, considerable of a ward-politician, but he occasionally did a little business at the Justices' courts, and was not unknown on the steps of the Tombs. I have good reason to believe, however, that one individual who called upon him at my chambers, and who, with a grand air, he insisted was his client, was no other than a dun, and the alleged title-deed, a bill. But, with all his failings, and the annoyances he caused me, Nippers, like his compatriot Turkey, was a very useful man to me; wrote a neat, swift hand; and, when he chose, was not deficient in a gentlemanly sort of deportment. Added to this, he always dressed in a gentlemanly sort of way; and so, incidentally, reflected credit upon my chambers. Whereas, with respect to Turkey, I had much ado to keep him from being a reproach to me. His clothes were apt to look oily, and smell of eating-houses. He wore his pantaloons very loose and baggy in summer. His coats were execrable; his hat not to be handled. But while the hat was a thing of indifference to me, inasmuch as his natural civility and deference, as a dependent Englishman, always led him to doff it the moment he entered the room, yet his coat was another matter. Concerning his coats, I reasoned with him; but with no effect. The truth was, I suppose, that a man with so small an income could not afford to sport such a lustrous face and a lustrous coat at one and the same time. As Nippers once observed, Turkey's money went chiefly for red ink. One winter day, I presented Turkey with a highly respectable-looking coat of my own—a padded gray coat, of a most comfortable warmth, and which buttoned straight up from the knee to the neck. I thought Turkey would appreciate the favour, and abate his rashness and obstreperousness of afternoons. But no; I verily believe that buttoning himself up in so downy and blanket-like a coat had a pernicious effect upon him—upon the same principle that too much oats are bad for horses. In fact, precisely as a rash, restive horse is said to feel his oats, so Turkey felt his coat. It made him insolent. He was a man whom prosperity harmed.

Though, concerning the self-indulgent habits of Turkey, I had my own private surmises, yet, touching Nippers, I was well persuaded that, whatever might be his faults in other respects, he was, at least, a temperate young man. But, indeed, nature herself seemed to have been his vintner, and, at his birth, charged him so thoroughly with an irritable, brandy-like disposition, that all subsequent potations were needless. When I consider how, amid the stillness of my chambers, Nippers would sometimes impatiently rise from his seat, and stooping over his table, spread his arms wide apart, seize the whole desk, and move it, and jerk it, with a grim, grinding motion on the floor, as if the table were a perverse voluntary agent, intent on thwarting and vexing him, I plainly perceive that, for Nippers, brandy-and-water were altogether superfluous.

It was fortunate for me that, owing to its peculiar cause—indigestion—the irritability and consequent nervousness of Nippers were mainly observable in the morning, while in the afternoon he was comparatively mild. So that, Turkey's paroxysms only coming on about twelve o'clock, I never had to do with their eccentricities at one time. Their fits relieved each other, like guards. When Nippers's was on, Turkey's was off; and *vice versa*. This was a good natural arrangement, under the circumstances.

Ginger Nut, the third on my list, was a lad, some twelve years old. His father was a carman, ambitious of seeing his son on the bench instead of a cart, before he died. So he sent him to my office, as student at law, errand-boy, cleaner and sweeper, at the rate of one dollar a week. He had a little desk to himself, but he did not use it much. Upon inspection, the drawer exhibited a great array of the shells of various sorts of nuts. Indeed, to this quick-witted youth, the whole noble science of the law was contained in a nutshell. Not the least among the employments of Ginger Nut, as well as one which he discharged with the most alacrity, was his duty as cake and apple purveyor for Turkey and Nippers. Copying law-papers being proverbially a dry, husky sort of business, my two scriveners were fain to moisten their mouths very often with Spitzenbergs, to be had at the numerous stalls nigh the Custom House and Post Office. Also, they sent Ginger Nut very frequently for that peculiar cake—small, flat, round, and very spicy—after which he had been named by them. Of a cold morning, when business was but dull, Turkey would gobble up scores of these cakes, as if they were mere wafers—indeed, they sell them at the rate of six or eight for a penny—the scrape of his pen blending with the crunching of the crisp particles in his mouth. Of all the fiery afternoon blunders and flurried rashnesses of Turkey, was his once moistening a ginger-cake between his lips, and clapping it on to a mortgage, for a seal. I came within an ace of dismissing him then. But he mollified me by making an oriental bow, and saying—'With submission, sir, it was generous of me to find you in stationery on my own account.'

Now my original business—that of a conveyancer and title-hunter, and drawer-up of recondite documents of all sorts—was considerably increased by receiving the master's office. There was now great work for scriveners. Not only must I push the clerks already with me, but I must have additional help.

In answer to my advertisement, a motionless young man one morning stood upon my office threshold, the door being open, for it was summer. I can see that figure now—pallidly neat, pitiably respectable, incurably forlorn! It was Bartleby.

After a few words touching his qualifications, I engaged him, glad to have among my corps of copyists a man of so singularly sedate an aspect, which I thought might operate beneficially upon the flighty temper of Turkey, and the fiery one of Nippers.

I should have stated before that ground-glass folding doors divided my premises into two parts, one of which was occupied by my scriveners, the other by myself. According to my humour, I threw open these doors, or closed them. I resolved to assign Bartleby a corner by the folding-doors, but on my side of them, so as to have this quiet man within easy call, in case any trifling thing was to be done. I placed his desk close up to a small side-window in that part of the room, a window which originally had afforded a lateral view of certain grimy back-yards and bricks, but which, owing to subsequent erections, commanded at present no view at all, though it gave some light. Within three feet of the panes was a wall, and the light came down from far above, between two lofty buildings, as from a very small opening in a dome. Still further to a satisfactory arrangement, I procured a high green folding-screen, which might entirely isolate Bartleby from my sight, though not remove him from my voice. And thus, in a manner, privacy and society were conjoined.

At first, Bartleby did an extraordinary quantity of writing. As if long famishing for something to copy, he seemed to gorge himself on my documents. There was no pause for digestion. He ran a day and night line, copying by sun-light and by candle-light. I should have been quite delighted with his application, had he been cheerfully industrious. But he wrote on silently, palely, mechanically.

It is, of course, an indispensable part of a scrivener's business to verify the accuracy of his copy, word by word. Where there are two or more scriveners in an office, they assist each other in this examination, one reading from the copy, the other holding the original. It is a very dull, wearisome, and lethargic affair. I can readily imagine that, to some sanguine temperaments, it would be altogether intolerable. For example, I cannot credit that the mettlesome poet, Byron, would have contentedly sat down with Bartleby to examine a law document, of say, five hundred pages, closely written in a crimpy hand.

Now and then, in the haste of business, it had been my habit to assist in comparing some brief document myself, calling Turkey or Nippers for this purpose. One object I had, in placing Bartleby so handy to me behind the screen, was, to avail myself of his services on such trivial occasions. It was on the third day, I think, of his being with me, and before any necessity had arisen for having his own writing examined, that, being much hurried to complete a small affair I had in hand, I abruptly called to Bartleby. In my haste and natural expectancy of instant compliance, I sat with my head bent over the original on my desk, and my right hand sideways, and somewhat nervously extended with the copy, so that, immediately upon emerging from his retreat, Bartleby might snatch it and proceed to business without the least delay.

In this very attitude did I sit when I called to him, rapidly stating what it was I wanted him to do—namely, to examine a small paper with me. Imagine my surprise, nay, my consternation, when, without moving from his privacy, Bartleby, in a singularly mild, firm voice, replied, 'I would prefer not to.'

I sat a while in perfect silence, rallying my stunned faculties. Immediately it occurred to me that my ears had deceived me, or Bartleby had entirely misunderstood my meaning. I repeated my request in the clearest tone I could assume; but in quite as clear a one came the previous reply, 'I would prefer not to.'

'Prefer not to,' echoed I, rising in high excitement, and crossing the room with a stride. 'What do you mean? Are you moon-struck? I want you to help me compare this sheet here—take it,' and I thrust it toward him.

'I would prefer not to,' said he.

I looked at him steadfastly. His face was leanly composed; his gray eye dimly calm. Not a wrinkle of agitation rippled him. Had there been the least uneasiness, anger, impatience, or impertinence in his manner; in other words, had there been anything ordinarily human about him, doubtless I should have violently dismissed him from the premises. But as it was, I should have as soon thought of turning my pale plaster-of-paris bust of Cicero out of doors. I stood gazing at him a while, as he went on with his own writing, and then reseated myself at my desk. This is very strange, thought I. What had one best do? But my business hurried me. I concluded to forget the matter for the present, reserving it for my future leisure. So calling Nippers from the other room, the paper was speedily examined.

A few days after this, Bartleby concluded four lengthy documents, being quadruplicates of a week's testimony taken before me in my High Court of Chancery. It became necessary to examine them. It was an important suit, and great accuracy was imperative. Having all things arranged, I called Turkey, Nippers, and Ginger Nut, from the next room, meaning to place the four copies in the hands of my four clerks, while I should read from the original. Accordingly, Turkey, Nippers, and Ginger Nut had taken their seats in a row, each with his document in his hand, when I called to Bartleby to join this interesting group.

'Bartleby! quick, I am waiting.'

I heard a slow scrape of his chair legs on the uncarpeted floor, and soon he appeared standing at the entrance of his hermitage.

'What is wanted?' said he mildly.

'The copies, the copies,' said I hurriedly. 'We are going to examine them. There'—and I held toward him the fourth quadruplicate.

'I would prefer not to,' he said, and gently disappeared behind the screen.

For a few moments I was turned into a pillar of salt, standing at the head of my seated column of clerks. Recovering myself, I advanced toward the screen, and demanded the reason for such extraordinary conduct.

'*Why* do you refuse?'

'I would prefer not to.'

With any other man I should have flown outright into a dreadful passion, scorned all further words, and thrust him ignominiously from my presence. But there was something about Bartleby that not only strangely disarmed me, but, in a wonderful manner, touched and disconcerted me. I began to reason with him.

'These are your own copies we are about to examine. It is labour saving to you, because one examination will answer for your four papers. It is common usage. Every copyist is bound to help examine his copy. Is it not so? Will you not speak? Answer!'

'I prefer not to,' he replied in a flute-like tone. It seemed to me that, while I had been addressing him, he carefully revolved every statement that I made; fully comprehended the meaning; could not gainsay the irresistible conclusion; but, at the same time, some paramount consideration prevailed with him to reply as he did.

'You are decided, then, not to comply with my request—a request made according to common usage and common sense?'

He briefly gave me to understand, that on that point my judgment was sound. Yes: his decision was irreversible.

It is not seldom the case that, when a man is browbeaten in some unprecedented and violently unreasonable way, he begins to stagger in his own plainest faith. He begins, as it were, vaguely to surmise that, wonderful as it may be, all the justice and all the reason is on the other side. Accordingly, if any disinterested persons are present, he turns to them for some reinforcement for his own faltering mind.

'Turkey,' said I, 'what do you think of this? Am I not right?'

'With submission, sir,' said Turkey, in his blandest tone, 'I think that you are.'

'Nippers,' said I, 'what do *you* think of it?'

'I think I should kick him out of the office.'

(The reader, of nice perceptions, will here perceive that, it being morning, Turkey's answer is couched in polite and tranquil terms, but Nippers's replies in ill-tempered ones. Or, to repeat a previous sentence, Nippers's ugly mood was on duty, and Turkey's off.)

'Ginger Nut,' said I, willing to enlist the smallest suffrage in my behalf, 'what do *you* think of it?'

'I think, sir, he's a little *luny*,' replied Ginger Nut, with a grin.

'You hear what they say,' said I, turning toward the screen, 'come forth and do your duty.'

But he vouchsafed no reply. I pondered a moment in sore perplexity. But once more business hurried me. I determined again to postpone the consideration of this dilemma to my future leisure. With a little trouble we made out to examine the papers without Bartleby, though at every page or two Turkey deferentially dropped his opinion, that this proceeding was quite out of the common; while Nippers, twitching in his chair with a dyspeptic nervousness, ground out, between his set teeth, occasional hissing maledictions against the stubborn oaf behind the screen. And for his (Nippers's) part, this was the first and the last time he would do another man's business without pay.

Meanwhile Bartleby sat in his hermitage, oblivious to everything but his own peculiar business there.

Some days passed, the scrivener being employed upon another lengthy work. His late remarkable conduct led me to regard his ways narrowly. I observed that he never went to dinner; indeed, that he never went anywhere. As yet I had never, of my personal knowledge, known him to be outside of my office. He was a perpetual sentry in the corner. At about eleven o'clock though, in the morning, I noticed that Ginger Nut would advance toward the opening in Bartleby's screen, as if silently beckoned thither by a gesture invisible to me where I sat. The boy would then leave the office, jingling a few pence, and reappear with a handful of ginger-nuts, which he delivered in the hermitage, receiving two of the cakes for his trouble.

He lives, then, on ginger-nuts, thought I; never eats a dinner, properly speaking; he must be a vegetarian, then; but no; he never eats even vegetables, he eats nothing but ginger-nuts. My mind then ran on in reveries concerning the probable effects upon the human constitution of living entirely on ginger-nuts. Ginger-nuts are so called, because they contain ginger as one of their peculiar constituents, and the final flavouring one. Now, what was ginger? A hot, spicy thing. Was Bartleby hot and spicy? Not at all. Ginger, then, had no effect upon Bartleby. Probably he preferred it should have none.

Nothing so aggravates an earnest person as a passive resistance. If the individual so resisted be of a not inhumane temper, and the resisting one perfectly harmless in his passivity, then, in the better moods of the former, he will endeavour charitably to construe to his imagination what proves impossible to be solved by his judgment. Even so, for the most part, I regarded Bartleby and his

ways. Poor fellow! thought I, he means no mischief; it is plain he intends no insolence; his aspect sufficiently evinces that his eccentricities are involuntary. He is useful to me. I can get along with him. If I turn him away, the chances are he will fall in with some less-indulgent employer, and then he will be rudely treated, and perhaps driven forth miserably to starve. Yes. Here I can cheaply purchase a delicious self-approval. To befriend Bartleby; to humour him in his strange wilfulness, will cost me little or nothing, while I lay up in my soul what will eventually prove a sweet morsel for my conscience. But this mood was not invariable with me. The passiveness of Bartleby sometimes irritated me. I felt strangely goaded on to encounter him in new opposition—to elicit some angry spark from him answerable to my own. But, indeed, I might as well have essayed to strike fire with my knuckles against a bit of Windsor soap. But one afternoon the evil impulse in me mastered me, and the following little scene ensued:—

'Bartleby,' said I, 'when those papers are all copied, I will compare them with you.'

'I would prefer not to.'

'How? Surely you do not mean to persist in that mulish vagary?'

No answer.

I threw open the folding-doors near by, and, turning upon Turkey and Nippers, exclaimed:

'Bartleby a second time says, he won't examine his papers. What do you think of it, Turkey?'

It was afternoon, be it remembered. Turkey sat glowing like a brass boiler; his bald head steaming; his hands reeling among his blotted papers.

'Think of it?' roared Turkey; 'I think I'll just step behind his screen, and black his eyes for him!'

So saying, Turkey rose to his feet and threw his arms into a pugilistic position. He was hurrying away to make good his promise, when I detained him, alarmed at the effect of incautiously rousing Turkey's combativeness after dinner.

'Sit down, Turkey,' said I, 'and hear what Nippers has to say. What do you think of it, Nippers? Would I not be justified in immediately dismissing Bartleby?'

'Excuse me, that is for you to decide, sir. I think his conduct quite unusual, and, indeed, unjust, as regards Turkey and myself. But it may only be a passing whim.'

'Ah,' exclaimed I, 'you have strangely changed your mind, then—you speak very gently of him now.'

'All beer,' cried Turkey; 'gentleness is effects of beer—Nippers and I dined together to-day. You see how gentle *I* am, sir. Shall I go and black his eyes?'

'You refer to Bartleby, I suppose. No, not to-day, Turkey,' I replied; 'pray, put up your fists.'

I closed the doors, and again advanced toward Bartleby. I felt additional incentives tempting me to my fate. I burned to be rebelled against again. I remembered that Bartleby never left the office.

'Bartleby,' said I, 'Ginger Nut is away; just step around to the Post Office, won't you? (it was but a three minutes' walk), and see if there is anything for me.'

'I would prefer not to.'

'You *will* not?'

'I *prefer* not.'

I staggered to my desk, and sat there in a deep study. My blind inveteracy returned. Was there any other thing in which I could procure myself to be ignominiously repulsed by this lean, penniless wight?—my hired clerk? What added thing is there, perfectly reasonable, that he will be sure to refuse to do?

'Bartleby!'

No answer.

'Bartleby,' in a louder tone.

No answer.

'Bartleby,' I roared.

Like a very ghost, agreeably to the laws of magical invocation, at the third summons, he appeared at the entrance of his hermitage.

'Go to the next room, and tell Nippers to come to me.'

'I prefer not to,' he respectfully and slowly said, and mildly disappeared.

'Very good, Bartleby,' said I, in a quiet sort of serenely-severe self-possessed tone, intimating the unalterable purpose of some terrible retribution very close at hand. At the moment I half intended something of the kind. But upon the whole, as it was drawing toward my dinner-hour, I thought it best to put on my hat and walk home for the day, suffering much from perplexity and distress of mind.

Shall I acknowledge it? The conclusion of this whole business was, that it soon became a fixed fact of my chambers, that a pale young scrivener, by the name of Bartleby, had a desk there; that he copied for me at the usual rate of four cents a folio (one hundred words); but he was permanently exempt from examining the work done by him, that duty being transferred to Turkey and Nippers, out of compliment, doubtless, to their superior acuteness; moreover, said Bartleby was never, on any account, to be dispatched on the most trivial errand of any sort; and that even if entreated to take upon him such a matter, it was generally understood that he would 'prefer not to'—in other words, that he would refuse point-blank.

As days passed on, I became considerably reconciled to Bartleby. His steadiness, his freedom from all dissipation, his incessant industry (except when he chose to throw himself into a standing revery behind his screen), his great stillness, his unalterableness of demeanour under all circumstances, made him a valuable acquisition. One prime thing was this— *he was always there*—first in the morning, continually through the day, and the last at night. I had a singular confidence in his honesty. I felt my most precious papers perfectly safe in his hands. Sometimes, to be sure, I could not, for the very soul of me, avoid falling into sudden spasmodic passions with him. For it was exceeding difficult to bear in mind all the time those strange peculiarities, privileges, and unheard-of exemptions, forming the tacit stipulations on Bartleby's part under which he remained in my office. Now and then, in the eagerness of dispatching pressing business, I would inadvertently summon Bartleby, in a short, rapid tone, to put his finger, say, on the incipient tie of a bit of red tape with which I was about compressing some papers. Of course, from behind the screen the usual answer, 'I prefer not to,' was sure to come; and then, how could a human creature, with the common infirmities of our nature, refrain from bitterly exclaiming upon such perverseness—such unreasonableness. However, every added repulse of this sort which I received only tended to lessen the probability of my repeating the inadvertence.

Here it must be said, that according to the custom of most legal gentlemen occupying chambers in densely populated lawbuildings, there were several keys to my door. One was kept by a woman residing in the attic, which person weekly scrubbed and daily swept and dusted my apartments. Another was kept by Turkey for convenience sake. The third I sometimes carried in my own pocket. The fourth I knew not who had.

Now, one Sunday morning I happened to go to Trinity Church, to hear a celebrated preacher, and finding myself rather early on the ground I thought I would walk round to my chambers for a while. Luckily I had my key with me; but upon applying it to the lock, I found it resisted by something inserted from the inside. Quite surprised, I called out; when to my consternation a key was turned from within; and thrusting his lean visage at me, and holding the door ajar, the apparition of Bartleby appeared, in his shirt-sleeves, and otherwise in a strangely tattered dishabille, saying quietly that he was sorry, but he was deeply engaged just then, and—preferred not admitting me at present. In a brief word or two, he moreover added, that perhaps I had better walk round the block two or three times, and by that time he would probably have concluded his affairs.

Now, the utterly unsurmised appearance of Bartleby, tenanting my lawchambers of a Sunday morning, with his cadaverously gentlemanly nonchalance, yet withal firm and self-possesed, had such a strange effect upon me, that incontinently I slunk away from my own door, and did as desired. But not without sundry twinges of impotent rebellion against the mild effrontery of this unaccountable scrivener. Indeed, it was his wonderful mildness chiefly, which not only disarmed me, but unmanned me as it were. For I consider that one, for the time, is a sort of unmanned when he tranquilly permits his hired clerk to dictate to him, and order him away from his own premises. Furthermore, I was full of uneasiness as to what Bartleby could possibly be doing in my office in his shirtsleeves, and in an otherwise dismantled condition of a Sunday morning. Was anything amiss going on? Nay, that was out of the question. It was not to be thought of for a moment that Bartleby was an immoral person. But what could he be doing there?—copying? Nay again, whatever might be his eccentricities, Bartleby was an eminently decorous person. He would be the last man to sit down to his desk in any state approaching to nudity. Besides, it was Sunday; and there was something about Bartleby that forbade the supposition that he would by any secular occupation violate the proprieties of the day.

Nevertheless, my mind was not pacified; and full of a restless curiosity, at last I returned to the door. Without hindrance I inserted my key, opened it, and entered. Bartleby was not to be seen. I looked round anxiously, peeped behind his screen; but it was very plain that he was gone. Upon more closely examining the place, I surmised that for an indefinite period Bartleby must have ate, dressed, and slept in my office, and that, too, without plate, mirror, or bed. The cushioned seat of a rickety old sofa in one corner bore the faint impress of a lean, reclining form. Rolled away under his desk, I found a blanket; under the empty grate a blacking box and brush; on a chair, a tin basin, with soap and a ragged towel; in a newspaper a few crumbs of ginger-nuts and a morsel of cheese. Yes, thought I, it is evident enough that Bartleby has been making his home here, keeping bachelor's hall all by himself. Immediately then the thought came sweeping across me, what miserable friendlessness and loneliness are here revealed! His poverty is great; but his solitude, how horrible! Think of it. Of a Sunday, Wall Street is deserted as Petra; and every night of every day it is an emptiness. This building, too, which of week-days hums with industry and life, at nightfall echoes with sheer vacancy, and all through Sunday is forlorn. And here Bartleby makes his home; sole spectator of a solitude which he has seen all-populous—a sort of innocent and transformed Marius brooding among the ruins of Carthage!

For the first time in my life a feeling of overpowering stinging melancholy seized me. Before, I had never experienced aught but a not unpleasing sadness. The bond of a common humanity now drew me irresistibly to gloom. A fraternal melancholy! For both I and Bartleby were sons of Adam. I remembered the bright silks and sparkling faces I had seen that day, in gala trim, swan-like sailing down the Mississippi of Broadway; and I contrasted them with the pallid copyist, and thought to myself, Ah, happiness courts the light, so we deem the world is gay; but misery hides aloof, so we deem that misery there is none. These sad fancyings—chimeras, doubtless, of a sick and silly brain—led on to other and more special thoughts, concerning the eccentricities of Bartleby. Presentiments of strange discoveries hovered round me. The scrivener's pale form appeared to me laid out, among uncaring strangers, in its shivering winding-sheet.

Suddenly I was attracted by Bartleby's closed desk, the key in open sight left in the lock.

I mean no mischief, seek the gratification of no heartless curiosity, thought I; besides, the desk is mine, and its contents, too, so I will make bold to look within. Everything was methodically arranged, the papers smoothly placed. The pigeon-holes were deep, and removing the files of documents, I groped into their recesses. Presently I felt something there, and dragged it out. It was an old bandanna handkerchief, heavy and knotted. I opened it, and saw it was a savings-bank.

I now recalled all the quiet mysteries which I had noted in the man. I remembered that he never spoke but to answer; that, though at intervals he had considerable time to himself, yet I had never seen him reading—no, not even a newspaper; that for long periods he would stand looking out, at his pale window behind the screen, upon the dead brick wall; I was quite sure he never visited any refectory or eating-house; while his pale face clearly indicated that he never drank beer like Turkey, or tea and coffee even, like other men; that he never went anywhere in particular that I could learn; never went out for a walk, unless, indeed, that was the case at present; that he had declined telling who he was, or whence he came, or whether he had any relatives in the world; that though so thin and pale, he never complained of ill health. And more than all, I remembered a certain unconscious air of pallid—how shall I call it?—of pallid haughtiness, say, or rather an austere reserve about him, which had positively awed me into my tame compliance with his eccentricities, when I had feared to ask him to do the slightest incidental thing for me, even though I might know, from his long-continued motionlessness, that behind his screen he must be standing in one of those dead-wall reveries of his.

Revolving all these things, and coupling them with the recently discovered fact, that he made my office his constant abiding-place and home, and not forgetful of his morbid moodiness; revolving all these things, a prudential feeling began to steal over me. My first emotions had been those of pure melancholy and sincerest pity; but just in proportion as the forlornness of Bartleby grew and grew to my imagination, did that same melancholy merge into fear, that pity into repulsion. So true it is, and so terrible, too, that up to a certain point the thought or sight of misery enlists our best affections; but, in certain special cases, beyond that point it does not. They err who would assert that invariably this is owing to the inherent selfishness of the human heart. It rather proceeds from a certain hopelessness of remedying excessive and organic ill. To a sensitive being, pity is not seldom pain. And when at last it is perceived that such pity cannot lead to effectual succour, commonsense bids the soul be rid of it. What I saw that morning persuaded me that the scrivener was the victim of innate and incurable disorder. I might give alms to his body; but his body did not pain him; it was his soul that suffered, and his soul I could not reach.

I did not accomplish the purpose of going to Trinity Church that morning. Somehow, the things I had seen disqualified me for the time from church-going. I walked homeward, thinking what I would do with Bartleby. Finally, I resolved upon this—I would put certain calm questions to him the next morning, touching his history, etc., and if he declined to answer them openly and unreservedly (and I supposed he would prefer not), then to give him a twenty-dollar bill over and above whatever I might owe him, and tell him his services were no longer required; but that if in any other way I could assist him, I would be happy to do so, especially if he desired to return to his native place, wherever that might be, I would willingly help to defray the expenses. Moreover, if, after reaching home, he found himself at any time in want of aid, a letter from him would be sure of a reply.

The next morning came.

'Bartleby,' said I, gently calling to him behind his screen.

No reply.

'Bartleby,' said I, in a still gentler tone, 'come here; I am not going to ask you to do anything you would prefer not to do— I simply wish to speak to you.'

Upon this he noiselessly slid into view.

'Will you tell me, Bartleby, where you were born?'

'I would prefer not to.'

'Will you tell me *anything* about yourself?'

'I would prefer not to.'

'But what reasonable objection can you have to speak to me? I feel friendly toward you.'

He did not look at me while I spoke, but kept his glance fixed upon my bust of Cicero, which, as I then sat, was directly behind me, some six inches above my head.

'What is your answer, Bartleby?' said I, after waiting a considerable time for a reply, during which his countenance remained immovable, only there was the faintest conceivable tremor of the white attenuated mouth.

'At present I prefer to give no answer,' he said, and retired into his hermitage.

It was rather weak in me, I confess, but his manner, on this occasion, nettled me. Not only did there seem to lurk in it a certain calm disdain, but his perverseness seemed ungrateful, considering the undeniable good usage and indulgence he had received from me.

Again I sat ruminating what I should do. Mortified as I was at his behaviour, and resolved as I had been to dismiss him when I entered my office, nevertheless I strangely felt something superstitious knocking at my heart, and forbidding me to carry out my purpose, and denouncing me for a villain if I dared to breathe one bitter word against this forlornest of mankind. At last, familiarly drawing my chair behind his screen, I sat down and said: 'Bartleby, never mind, then, about revealing your history; but let me entreat you, as a friend, to comply as far as may be with the usages of this office. Say now, you will help to examine papers to-morrow or next day: in short, say now, that in a day or two you will begin to be a little reasonable:—say so, Bartleby.'

'At present I would prefer not to be a little reasonable," was his mildly cadaverous reply.

Just then the folding doors opened, and Nippers approached. He seemed suffering from an unusually bad night's rest, induced by severer indigestion than common. He overheard those final words of Bartleby.

'*Prefer not*, eh?' gritted Nippers—'I'd *prefer* him, if I were you, sir,' addressing me—'I'd *prefer* him; I'd give him preferences, the stubborn mule! What is it, sir, pray, that he *prefers* not to do now?'

Bartleby moved not a limb.

'Mr. Nippers,' said I, 'I'd prefer that you would withdraw for the present.'

Somehow, of late, I had got into the way of involuntarily using this word 'prefer' upon all sorts of not exactly suitable occasions. And I trembled to think that my contact with the scrivener had already and seriously affected me in a mental way. And what further and deeper aberration might it not yet produce? This apprehension had not been without efficacy in determining me to summary measures.

As Nippers, looking very sour and sulky, was departing, Turkey blandly and deferentially approached.

'With submission, sir,' said he, 'yesterday I was thinking about Bartleby here, and I think that if he would but prefer to take a quart of good ale every day, it would do much toward mending him, and enabling him to assist in examining his papers.'

'So you have got the word too,' said I, slightly excited.

'With submission, what word, sir,' asked Turkey, respectfully crowding himself into the contracted space behind the screen, and by so doing, making me jostle the scrivener. 'What word, sir?'

'I would prefer to be left alone here,' said Bartleby, as if offended at being mobbed in his privacy.

'That's the word, Turkey,' said I— *'that's* it.'

'Oh, *prefer?* oh yes—queer word. I never use it myself. But, sir, as I was saying, if he would but prefer——'

'Turkey,' interrupted I, 'you will please withdraw.'

'Oh certainly, sir, if you prefer that I should.'

As he opened the folding-door to retire, Nippers at his desk caught a glimpse of me, and asked whether I would prefer to have a certain paper copied on blue paper or white. He did not in the least roguishly accent the word prefer. It was plain that it involuntarily rolled from his tongue. I thought to myself, surely I must get rid of a demented man, who already has in some degree turned the tongues, if not the heads of myself and clerks. But I thought it prudent not to break the dismission at once.

The next day I noticed that Bartleby did nothing but stand at his window in his dead-wall revery. Upon asking him why he did not write, he said that he had decided upon doing no more writing.

'Why, how now? what next?' exclaimed I, 'do no more writing?'

'No more.'

'And what is the reason?'

'Do you not see the reason for yourself?' he indifferently replied.

I looked steadfastly at him, and perceived that his eyes looked dull and glazed. Instantly it occurred to me, that his unexampled diligence in copying by his dim window for the first few weeks of his stay with me might have temporarily impaired his vision.

I was touched. I said something in condolence with him. I hinted that of course he did wisely in abstaining from writing for a while; and urged him to embrace that opportunity of taking wholesome exercise in the open air. This, however, he did not do. A few days after this, my other clerks being absent, and being in a great hurry to dispatch certain letters by the mail, I thought that having nothing else earthly to do, Bartleby would surely be less inflexible than usual, and carry these letters to the Post Office. But he blankly declined. So, much to my inconvenience, I went myself.

Still added days went by. Whether Bartleby's eyes improved or not, I could not say. To all appearance, I though they did. But when I asked him if they did, he vouchsafed no answer. At all events, he would do no copying. At last, in reply to my urgings, he informed me that he had permanently given up copying.

'What!' exclaimed I; 'suppose your eyes should get entirely well—better than ever before—would you not copy then?'

'I have given up copying,' he answered, and slid aside.

He remained as ever, a fixture in my chamber. Nay—if that were possible—he became still more of a fixture than before. What was to be done? He would do nothing in the office; why should he stay there? In plain fact, he had now become a millstone to me, not only useless as a necklace, but afflictive to bear. Yet I was sorry for him. I speak less than truth when I say that, on his own account, he occasioned me uneasiness. If he would but have named a single relative or friend, I would instantly have written, and urged their taking the poor fellow away to some convenient retreat. But he seemed alone, absolutely alone in the universe. A bit of wreck in the mid-Atlantic. At length, necessities connected with my business tyrannised over all other considerations. Decently as I could, I told Bartleby that in six days' time he must unconditionally leave the office. I warned him to take measures, in the interval, for procuring some other abode. I offered to assist him in this endeavour, if he himself would but take the first step toward a removal. 'And when you finally quit me, Bartleby,' added I, 'I shall see that you go not away entirely unprovided. Six days from this hour, remember.'

At the expiration of that period, I peeped behind the screen, and lo! Bartleby was there.

I buttoned up my coat, balanced myself; advanced slowly toward him, touched his shoulder, and said, 'The time has come; you must quit this place; I am sorry for you; here is money; but you must go.'

'I would prefer not,' he replied, with his back still toward me.

'You *must*.'

He remained silent.

Now I had an unbounded confidence in this man's common honesty. He had frequently restored to me sixpences and shillings carelessly dropped upon the floor, for I am apt to be very reckless in such shirt-button affairs. The proceeding, then, which followed will not be deemed extraordinary.

'Bartleby,' said I, 'I owe you twelve dollars on account; here are thirty-two; the odd twenty are yours—Will you take it?' and I handed the bills toward him.

But he made no motion.

'I will leave them here, then,' putting them under a weight on the table. Then taking my hat and cane and going to the door, I tranquilly turned and added— 'After you have removed your things from these offices, Bartleby, you will of course lock the door—since everyone is now gone for the day but you—and if you please, slip your key underneath the mat, so that I may have it in the morning. I shall not see you again; so good-bye to you. If, hereafter, in your new place of abode, I can be of any service to you, do not fail to advise me by letter. Good-bye, Bartleby, and fare you well.'

But he answered not a word; like the last column of some ruined temple, he remained standing mute and solitary in the middle of the otherwise deserted room.

As I walked home in a pensive mood, my vanity got the better of my pity. I could not but highly plume myself on my masterly management in getting rid of Bartleby. Masterly I call it, and such it must appear to any dispassionate thinker. The beauty of my procedure seemed to consist in its perfect quietness. There was no vulgar bullying, no bravado of any sort, no choleric hectoring, and striding to and fro across the apartment, jerking out vehement commands for Bartleby to bundle himself off with his beggarly traps. Nothing of the kind. Without loudly bidding Bartleby depart—as an inferior genius might have done—I *assumed* the ground that depart he must; and upon that assumption built all I had to say. The more I thought over my procedure, the more I was charmed with it. Nevertheless, next morning, upon awakening, I had my doubts—I had somehow slept off the fumes of vanity. One of the coolest and wisest hours a man has, is just after he awakes in the morning. My procedure seemed as sagacious as ever—but only in theory. How it would prove in practice—there was the rub. It was truly a beautiful thought to have assumed Bartleby's departure; but, after all, that assumption was simply my own, and none of Bartleby's. The great point was, not whether I had assumed that he would quit me, but whether he would prefer so to do. He was more a man of preferences than assumptions.

After breakfast, I walked down town, arguing the probabilities *pro* and *con*. One moment I thought it would prove a miserable failure, and Bartleby would be found all alive at my office as usual; the next moment it seemed certain that I should find his chair empty. And so I kept veering about. At the corner of Broadway and Canal Street, I saw quite an excited group of people standing in earnest conversation.

'I'll take odds he doesn't,' said a voice as I passed.

'Doesn't go?—done!' said I; 'put up your money.'

I was instinctively putting my hand in my pocket to produce my own, when I remembered that this was an election day. The words I had overheard bore no reference to Bartleby, but to the success or non-success of some candidate for the mayoralty. In my intent frame of mind, I had, as it were, imagined that all Broadway shared in my excitement, and were debating the same question with me. I passed on, very thankful that the uproar of the street screened my momentary absent-mindedness.

As I had intended, I was earlier than usual at my office door. I stood listening for a moment. All was still. He must be gone. I tried the knob. The door was locked. Yes, my procedure had worked to a charm; he indeed must be vanished. Yet a certain melancholy mixed with this: I was almost sorry for my brilliant success. I was fumbling under the door-mat for the key, which Bartleby was to have left there for me, when accidentally my knee knocked against a panel, producing a summoning sound, and in response a voice came to me from within— 'Not yet; I am occupied.'

It was Bartleby.

I was thunderstruck. For an instant I stood like the man who, pipe in mouth, was killed one cloudless afternoon long ago in Virginia, by summer lightning; at his own warm open window he was killed, and remained leaning out there upon the dreamy afternoon, till someone touched him, when he fell.

'Not gone!' I murmured at last. But again obeying that wondrous ascendency which the inscrutable scrivener had over me, and from which ascendency, for all my chafing, I could not completely escape, I slowly went downstairs and out into the street, and while walking round the block, considered what I should next do in this unheard-of perplexity. Turn the man out by an actual thrusting I could not; to drive him away by calling him hard names would not do; calling in the police was an unpleasant idea; and yet, permit him to enjoy his cadaverous triumph over me—this, too, I could not think of. What was to be done? or, if

nothing could be done, was there anything further that I could *assume* in the matter? Yes, as before I had prospectively assumed that Bartleby would depart, so now I might retrospectively assume that departed he was. In the legitimate carrying out of this assumption, I might enter my office in a great hurry, and pretending not to see Bartleby at all, walk straight against him as if he were air. Such a proceeding would in a singular degree have the appearance of a home-thrust. It was hardly possible that Bartleby could withstand such an application of the doctrine of assumptions. But upon second thoughts the success of the plan seemed rather dubious. I resolved to argue the matter over with him again.

'Bartleby,' said I, entering the office, with a quietly severe expression, 'I am seriously displeased. I am pained, Bartleby. I had thought better of you. I had imagined you of such a gentlemanly organisation, that in any delicate dilemma a slight hint would suffice—in short, an assumption. But it appears I am deceived. Why,' I added, unaffectedly starting, 'you have not even touched that money yet,' pointing to it, just where I had left it the evening previous.

He answered nothing.

'Will you, or will you not, quit me?' I now demanded in a sudden passion, advancing close to him.

'I would prefer *not* to quit you,' he replied, gently emphasising the *not*.

'What earthly right have you to stay here? Do you pay any rent? Do you pay my taxes? Or is this property yours?'

He answered nothing.

'Are you ready to go on and write now? Are your eyes recovered? Could you copy a small paper for me this morning? or help examine a few lines? or step round to the Post Office? In a word, will you do anything at all, to give a colouring to your refusal to depart the premises?'

He silently retired into his hermitage.

I was now in such a state of nervous resentment that I thought it but prudent to check myself at present from further demonstrations. Bartleby and I were alone. I remembered the tragedy of the unfortunate Adams and the still more unfortunate Colt in the solitary office of the latter; and how poor Colt, being dreadfully incensed by Adams, and imprudently permitting himself to get wildly excited, was at unawares hurried into his fatal act—an act which certainly no man could possibly deplore more than the actor himself. Often it had occurred to me in my ponderings upon the subject, that had that altercation taken place in the public street, or at a private residence, it would not have terminated as it did. It was the circumstance of being alone in a solitary office, upstairs, of a building entirely unhallowed by humanising domestic associations—an uncarpeted office, doubtless, of a dusty, haggard sort of appearance—this it must have been, which greatly helped to enhance the irritable desperation of the hapless Colt.

But when this old Adam of resentment rose in me and tempted me concerning Bartleby, I grappled him and threw him. How? Why, simply by recalling the divine injunction: 'A new commandment give I unto you, that ye love one another.' Yes, this it was that saved me. Aside from higher considerations, charity often operates as a vastly wise and prudent principle—a great safeguard to its possessor. Men have committed murder for jealousy's sake, and anger's sake, and hatred's sake, and selfishness' sake, and spiritual pride's sake; but no man, that ever I heard of, ever committed a diabolical murder for sweet charity's sake. Mere self-interest, then, if no better motive can be enlisted, should, especially with high-tempered men, prompt all beings to charity and philanthropy. At any rate, upon the occasion in question, I strove to drown my exasperated feelings toward the scrivener by benevolently construing his conduct. Poor fellow, poor fellow! thought I, he don't mean anything; and besides, he has seen hard times, and ought to be indulged.

I endeavoured, also, immediately to occupy myself, and at the same time to comfort my despondency. I tried to fancy, that in the course of the morning, at such time as might prove agreeable to him, Bartleby, of his own free accord, would emerge from his hermitage and take up some decided line of march in the direction of the door. But no. Half-past twelve o'clock came; Turkey began to glow in the face, overturn his inkstand, and become generally obstreperous; Nippers abated down into quietude and courtesy; Ginger Nut munched his noon apple; and Bartleby remained standing at his window in one of his profoundest dead-wall reveries. Will it be credited? Ought I to acknowledge it? That afternoon I left the office without saying one further word to him.

Some days now passed, during which, at leisure intervals, I looked a little into 'Edwards on the Will,' and 'Priestley on Necessity.' Under the circumstances, those books induced a salutary feeling. Gradually I slid into the persuasion that these troubles of mine, touching the scrivener, had been all predestinated from eternity, and Bartleby was billeted upon me for some mysterious purpose of an all-wise Providence, which it was not for a mere mortal like me to fathom. Yes, Bartleby, stay there behind your screen, thought I; I shall persecute you no more; you are harmless and noiseless as any of these old chairs; in short, I never feel so private as when I know you are here. At last I see it, I feel it; I penetrate to the predestinated purpose of my life. I am content. Others may have loftier parts to enact; but my mission in this world, Bartleby, is to furnish you with office-room for such period as you may see fit to remain.

I believe that this wise and blessed frame of mind would have continued with me, had it not been for the unsolicited and uncharitable remarks obtruded upon me by my professional friends who visited the rooms. But thus it often is, that the constant friction of illiberal minds wears out at last the best resolves of the more generous. Though to be sure, when I reflected upon it, it was not strange that people entering my office should be struck by the peculiar aspect of the unaccountable Bartleby, and so be tempted to throw out some sinister observations concerning him. Sometimes an attorney, having business with me, and calling at my office, and finding no one but the scrivener there, would undertake to obtain some sort of precise information from him touching my whereabouts; but without heeding his idle talk, Bartleby would remain standing immovable in the middle of the room. So after contemplating him in that position for a time, the attorney would depart, no wiser than he came.

Also, when a reference was going on, and the room full of lawyers and witnesses, and business driving fast, some deeply occupied legal gentleman present, seeing Bartleby wholly unemployed, would request him to run round to his (the legal gentleman's) office and fetch some papers for him. Thereupon, Bartleby would tranquilly decline, and yet remain idle as before. Then the lawyer would give a great stare, and turn to me. And what could I say? At last I was made aware that all through the circle of my professional acquaintance, a whisper of wonder was running round, having reference to the strange creature I kept at my office. This worried me very much. And as the idea came upon me of his possibly turning out a long-lived man, and keep occupying my chambers, and denying my authority; and perplexing my visitors; and scandalising my professional reputation; and casting a general gloom over the premises; keeping soul and body together to the last upon his savings (for doubtless he spent but half a dime a day), and in the end perhaps outlive me, and claim possession of my office by right of his perpetual occupancy: as all these dark anticipations crowded upon me more and more, and my friends continually intruded their relentless remarks upon the apparition in my room; a great change was wrought in me. I resolved to gather all my faculties together, and forever rid me of this intolerable incubus.

Ere revolving any complicated project, however, adapted to this end, I first simply suggested to Bartleby the propriety of his permanent departure. In a calm and serious tone, I commended the idea to his careful and mature consideration. But, having taken three days to meditate upon it, he apprised me, that his original determination remained the same; in short, that he still preferred to abide with me.

What shall I do? I now said to myself, buttoning up my coat to the last button. What shall I do? what ought I to do? what does conscience say I *should* do with this man, or, rather, ghost. Rid myself of him, I must; go, he shall. But how? You will not thrust him, the poor, pale, passive mortal—you will not thrust such a helpless creature out of your door? you will not dishonour yourself by such cruelty? No, I will not, I cannot do that. Rather would I let him live and die here, and then mason up his remains in the wall. What, then, will you do? For all your coaxing, he will not budge. Bribes he leaves under your own paperweight on your table; in short, it is quite plain that he prefers to cling to you.

Then something severe, something unusual must be done. What! surely you will not have him collared by a constable, and commit his innocent pallor to the common jail? And upon what ground could you procure such a thing to be done?—a vagrant, is he? What! he a vagrant, a wanderer, who refuses to budge? It is because he will *not* be a vagrant, then, that you seek to count him *as* a vagrant. That is too absurd. No visible means of support; there I have him. Wrong again: for indubitably he *does* support himself, and that is the only unanswerable proof that any man can show of his possessing the means so to do. No more, then. Since he will not quit me, I must quit him. I will change my offices; I will move elsewhere, and give him fair notice, that if I find him on my new premises I will then proceed against him as a common trespasser.

Acting accordingly, next day I thus addressed him: 'I find these chambers too far from the City Hall; the air is unwholesome. In a word, I propose to remove my offices next week, and shall no longer require your services. I tell you this now, in order that you may seek another place.'

He made no reply, and nothing more was said.

On the appointed day I engaged carts and men, proceeded to my chambers, and, having but little furniture, everything was removed in a few hours. Throughout, the scrivener remained standing behind the screen, which I directed to be removed the last thing. It was withdrawn; and, being folded up like

a huge folio, left him the motionless occupant of a naked room. I stood in the
entry watching him a moment, while
something from within me upbraided me.

I re-entered, with my hand in my
pocket—and—and my heart in my
mouth.

'Good-bye, Bartleby; I am going—
good-bye, and God some way bless you;
and take that,' slipping something in his
hand. But it dropped upon the floor, and
then—strange to say—I tore myself from
him whom I had so longed to be rid of.

Established in my new quarters, for a
day or two I kept the door locked, and
started at every footfall in the passages.
When I returned to my rooms, after any
little absence, I would pause at the threshold for an instant, and attentively listen
ere applying my key. But these fears were
needless. Bartleby never came nigh me.

I thought all was going well, when a
perturbed-looking stranger visited me, inquiring whether I was the person who
had recently occupied rooms at No. —
Wall Street.

Full of forebodings, I replied that I
was.

'Then, sir,' said the stranger, who
proved a lawyer, 'you are responsible for
the man you left there. He refuses to do
any copying; he refuses to do anything;
he says he prefers not to; and he refuses
to quit the premises.'

'I am very sorry, sir,' said I, with
assumed tranquillity, but an inward
tremor, 'but, really, the man you allude
to is nothing to me—he is no relation or
apprentice of mine, that you should hold
me responsible for him.'

'In mercy's name, who is he?'

'I certainly cannot inform you. I know
nothing about him. Formerly I employed
him as a copyist; but he has done nothing
for me now for some time past.'

'I shall settle him, then—good morning, sir.'

Several days passed, and I heard nothing more; and, though I often felt a
charitable prompting to call at the place
and see poor Bartleby, yet a certain
squeamishness, of I know not what, withheld me.

All is over with him, by this time,
thought I at last, when, through another

week, no further intelligence reached me.
But, coming to my room the day after, I
found several persons waiting at my door
in a high state of nervous excitement.

'That's the man—here he comes,' cried
the foremost one, whom I recognised as
the lawyer who had previously called
upon me alone.

'You must take him away, sir, at once,'
cried a portly person among them, advancing upon me, and whom I knew to
be the landlord of No. — Wall Street.
'These gentlemen, my tenants, cannot
stand it any longer; Mr. B——,' pointing
to the lawyer, 'has turned him out of his
room, and he now persists in haunting
the building generally, sitting upon the
banisters of the stairs by day, and sleeping
in the entry by night. Everybody is concerned; clients are leaving the offices;
some fears are entertained of a mob;
something you must do, and that without
delay.'

Aghast at this torrent, I fell back before it, and would fain have locked myself
in my new quarters. In vain I persisted
that Bartleby was nothing to me—no
more than to anyone else. In vain—I was
the last person known to have anything to
do with him, and they held me to the
terrible account. Fearful, then, of being
exposed in the papers (as one person
present obscurely threatened), I considered the matter, and, at length, said,
that if the lawyer would give me a confidential interview with the scrivener, in
his (the lawyer's) own room, I would,
that afternoon, strive my best to rid them
of the nuisance they complained of.

Going upstairs to my old haunt, there
was Bartleby silently sitting upon the
banister at the landing.

'What are you doing here, Bartleby?'
said I.

'Sitting upon the bannister,' he mildly
replied.

I motioned him into the lawyer's room,
who then left us.

'Bartleby,' said I, 'are you aware that
you are the cause of great tribulation to
me, by persisting in occupying the entry
after being dismissed from the office?'

No answer.

'Now one of two things must take
place. Either you must do something, or

something must be done to you. Now what sort of business would you like to engage in? Would you like to re-engage in copying for someone?'

'No; I would prefer not to make any change.'

'Would you like a clerkship in a dry-goods store?'

'There is too much confinement about that. No, I would not like a clerkship; but I am not particular.'

'Too much confinement,' I cried, 'why, you keep yourself confined all the time!'

'I would prefer not to take a clerkship,' he rejoined, as if to settle that little item at once.

'How would a bar-tender's business suit you? There is no trying of the eyesight in that.'

'I would not like it at all; though, as I said before, I am not particular.'

His unwonted wordiness inspirited me. I returned to the charge.

'Well, then, would you like to travel through the country collecting bills for the merchants? That would improve your health.'

'No, I would prefer to be doing something else.'

'How, then, would going as a companion to Europe, to entertain some young gentleman with your conversation —how would that suit you?'

'Not at all. It does not strike me that there is anything definite about that. I like to be stationary. But I am not particular.'

'Stationary you shall be, then,' I cried, now losing all patience, and, for the first time in all my exasperating connection with him, fairly flying into a passion. 'If you do not go away from these premises before night, I shall feel bound—indeed, I *am* bound—to—to quit the premises myself!' I rather absurdly concluded, knowing not with what possible threat to try to frighten his immobility into compliance. Despairing of all further efforts, I was precipitately leaving him, when a final thought occurred to me—one which had not been wholly unindulged before.

'Bartleby,' said I, in the kindest tone I could assume under such exciting circumstances, 'will you go home with me now —not to my office, but my dwelling—and remain there till we can conclude upon some convenient arrangement for you at our leisure? Come, let us start now, right away.'

'No; at present I would prefer not to make any change at all.'

I answered nothing; but, effectually dodging everyone by the suddenness and rapidity of my flight, rushed from the building, ran up Wall Street toward Broadway, and, jumping into the first omnibus, was soon removed from pursuit. As soon as tranquillity returned, I distinctly perceived that I had now done all that I possibly could, both in respect to the demands of the landlord and his tenants, and with regard to my own desire and sense of duty, to benefit Bartleby, and shield him from rude persecution. I now strove to be entirely carefree and quiescent; and my conscience justified me in the attempt; though, indeed, it was not so successful as I could have wished. So fearful was I of being again hunted out by the incensed landlord and his exasperated tenants, that, surrendering my business to Nippers, for a few days, I drove about the upper part of the town and through the suburbs, in my rockaway; crossed over to Jersey City and Hoboken, and paid fugitive visits to Manhattanville and Astoria. In fact, I almost lived in my rockaway for the time.

When again I entered my office, lo, a note from the landlord lay upon the desk. I opened it with trembling hands. It informed me that the writer had sent to the police, and had Bartleby removed to the Tombs as a vagrant. Moreover, since I knew more about him than anyone else, he wished me to appear at that place, and make a suitable statement of the facts. These tidings had a conflicting effect upon me. At first I was indignant; but, at last, almost approved. The landlord's energetic summary disposition had led him to adopt a procedure which I do not think I would have decided upon myself; and yet, as a last resort, under such peculiar circumstances, it seemed the only plan.

As I afterward learned, the poor scrivener, when told that he must be conducted to the Tombs, offered not the slightest obstacle, but, in his pale, unmoving way, silently acquiesced.

Some of the compassionate and curious bystanders joined the party; and headed by one of the constables arm in arm with Bartleby, the silent procession filed its way through all the noise, and heat, and joy of the roaring thoroughfares at noon.

The same day I received the note, I went to the Tombs, or, to speak more properly, the Halls of Justice. Seeking the right officer, I stated the purpose of my call, and was informed that the individual I described was, indeed, within. I then assured the functionary that Bartleby was a perfectly honest man, and greatly to be compassionated, however unaccountably eccentric. I narrated all I knew, and closed by suggesting the idea óf letting him remain in as indulgent confinement as possible, till something less harsh might be done—though, indeed, I hardly knew what. At all events, if nothing else could be decided upon, the almshouse must receive him. I then begged to have an interview.

Being under no disgraceful charge, and quite serene and harmless in all his ways, they had permitted him freely to wander about the prison, and, especially, in the enclosed grass-platted yards thereof. And so I found him there, standing all alone in the quietest of the yards, his face toward a high wall, while all around, from the narrow slits of the jail windows, I thought I saw peering out upon him the eyes of murderers and thieves.

'Bartleby!'

'I know you,' he said, without looking round—'and I want nothing to say to you.'

'It was not I that brought you here, Bartleby,' said I, keenly pained at his implied suspicion. 'And to you, this should not be so vile a place. Nothing reproachful attaches to you by being here. And see, it is not so sad a place as one might think. Look, there is the sky, and here is the grass.'

'I know where I am,' he replied, but would say nothing more, and so I left him.

As I entered the corridor again, a broad meat-like man, in an apron, accosted me,

and, jerking his thumb over his shoulder, said, 'Is that your friend?'

'Yes.'

'Does he want to starve? If he does, let him live on the prison fare, that's all.'

'Who are you?' asked I, not knowing what to make of such an unofficially speaking person in such a place.

'I am the grub-man. Such gentlemen as have friends here, hire me to provide them with something good to eat.'

'Is this so?' said I, turning to the turnkey.

He said it was.

'Well, then,' said I, slipping some silver into the grub-man's hands (for so they called him), 'I want you to give particular attention to my friend there; let him have the best dinner you can get. And you must be as polite to him as possible.'

'Introduce me, will you?' said the grubman, looking at me with an expression which seemed to say he was all impatience for an opportunity to give a specimen of his breeding.

Thinking it would prove of benefit to the scrivener, I acquiesced; and, asking the grub-man his name, went up with him to Bartleby.

'Bartleby, this is a friend; you will find him very useful to you.'

'Your sarvant, sir, your sarvant,' said the grub-man, making a low salutation behind his apron. 'Hope you find it pleasant here, sir; nice grounds—cool apartments—hope you'll stay with us some time—try to make it agreeable. What will you have for dinner to-day?'

'I prefer not to dine to-day,' said Bartleby, turning away. 'It would disagree with me; I am unused to dinners.' So saying, he slowly moved to the other side of the enclosure, and took up a position fronting the dead-wall.

'How's this?' said the grub-man, addressing me with a stare of astonishment. 'He's odd, ain't he?'

'I think he is a little deranged,' said I sadly.

'Deranged? deranged is it? Well, now, upon my word, I thought that friend of yourn was a gentleman forger; they are always pale and genteel-like, them forgers. I can't help pity 'em—can't help

it, sir. Did you know Monroe Edwards?'
he added touchingly, and paused. Then,
laying his hand piteously on my shoulder,
sighed, 'he died of consumption at Sing-
Sing. So you weren't acquainted with
Monroe?'

'No, I was never socially acquainted
with any forgers. But I cannot stop
longer. Look to my friend yonder. You
will not lose by it. I will see you again.'

Some few days after this, I again obtained admission to the Tombs, and went
through the corridors in quest of Bartleby; but without finding him.

'I saw him coming from his cell not
long ago,' said a turnkey, 'maybe he's
gone to loiter in the yards.'

So I went in that direction.

'Are you looking for the silent man?'
said another turnkey, passing me. 'Yonder he lies—sleeping in the yard there.
'Tis not twenty minutes since I saw him
lie down.'

The yard was entirely quiet. It was not
accessible to the common prisoners. The
surrounding walls, of amazing thickness,
kept off all sounds behind them. The
Egyptian character of the masonry
weighed upon me with its gloom. But a
soft imprisoned turf grew under foot. The
heart of the eternal pyramids, it seemed,
wherein, by some strange magic, through
the clefts, grass-seed, dropped by birds,
had sprung.

Strangely huddled at the base of the
wall, his knees drawn up, and lying on
his side, his head touching the cold
stones, I saw the wasted Bartleby. But
nothing stirred. I paused; then went close
up to him; stooped over, and saw that his
dim eyes were open; otherwise he seemed
profoundly sleeping. Something prompted
me to touch him. I felt his hand, when a
tingling shiver ran up my arm and down
my spine to my feet.

The round face of the grub-man peered
upon me now. 'His dinner is ready. Won't
he dine to-day, either? Or does he live
without dining?'

'Lives without dining,' said I, and
closed the eyes.

'Eh!—He's asleep, ain't he?'

'With kings and counsellors,' murmured I.

*

There would seem little need for proceeding further in this history. Imagination will readily supply the meagre recital
of poor Bartleby's interment. But, ere
parting with the reader, let me say, that if
this little narrative has sufficiently interested him, to awaken curiosity as to
who Bartleby was, and what manner of
life he led prior to the present narrator's
making his acquaintance, I can only
reply, that in such curiosity I fully share,
but am wholly unable to gratify it. Yet
here I hardly know whether I should
divulge one little item of rumour, which
came to my ear a few months after the
scrivener's decease. Upon what basis it
rested I could never ascertain; and hence,
how true it is I cannot now tell. But, inasmuch as this vague report has not been
without a certain suggestive interest to
me, however sad, it may prove the same
with some others; and so I will briefly
mention it. The report was this: that
Bartleby had been a subordinate clerk in
the Dead Letter Office at Washington,
from which he had been suddenly removed by a change in the administration.
When I think over this rumour, hardly
can I express the emotions which seize
me. Dead letters! does it not sound like
dead men? Conceive a man by nature and
misfortune prone to a pallid hopelessness,
can any business seem more fitted to
heighten it than that of continually handling these dead letters, and assorting them
for the flames? For by the cartload they
are annually burned. Sometimes from out
the folded paper the pale clerk takes a
ring—the finger it was meant for, perhaps, moulders in the grave; a bank-note
sent in swiftest charity—he whom it
would relieve, nor eats nor hungers any
more; pardon for those who died despairing; hope for those who died unhoping;
good tidings for those who died stifled by
unrelieved calamities. On errands of life,
these letters speed to death.

Ah, Bartleby! Ah, humanity!

[1853]

QUESTIONS FOR STUDY

1. *What is the effect of the lawyer-narrator's slightly humorous, slightly cynical tone? Why does he insist upon introducing himself in such elaborate detail?*
2. *What do Bartleby's "dead-wall reveries" and his persistent "I would prefer not to" indicate about his fundamental attitude or outlook on life? How does this attitude contrast with the narrator's own? How does Bartleby retain the integrity of his own point of view?*
3. *What are the stages in Bartleby's progressive withdrawal from the world?*
4. *What is the function of Nippers, Turkey, and Ginger Nut?*
5. *What is the narrator's attitude toward Bartleby? How does it change? Why does he refuse to abandon him in the end? What is the meaning of the narrator's "Ah, Bartleby! Ah, humanity!"? Does it indicate that he has reached some form of understanding?*
6. *What is the significance of the discovery that Bartleby has been a subordinate clerk in the Dead Letter Office?*
7. *Which character is in fact the story's protagonist?*

YUKIO MISHIMA

Patriotism

ON THE twenty-eighth of February, 1936 (on the third day, that is, of the February 26 Incident), Lieutenant Shinji Takeyama of the Konoe Transport Battalion—profoundly disturbed by the knowledge that his closest colleagues had been with the mutineers from the beginning, and indignant at the imminent prospect of Imperial troops attacking Imperial troops—took his officer's sword and ceremonially disemboweled himself in the eight-mat room of his private residence in the sixth block of Aoba-chō, in Yotsuya Ward. His wife, Reiko, followed him, stabbing herself to death. The lieutenant's farewell note consisted of one sentence: "Long live the Imperial Forces." His wife's, after apologies for her unfilial conduct in thus preceding her parents to the grave, concluded: "The day which, for a soldier's wife, had to come, has come. . . ." The last moments of this heroic and dedicated couple were such as to make the gods themselves weep. The lieutenant's age, it should be noted, was thirty-one, his wife's twenty-three; and it was not half a year since the celebration of their marriage.

II

Those who saw the bride and bridegroom in the commemorative photograph —perhaps no less than those actually present at the lieutenant's wedding—had exclaimed in wonder at the bearing of this handsome couple. The lieutenant, majestic in military uniform, stood protectively beside his bride, his right hand resting upon his sword, his officer's cap held at his left side. His expression was severe, and his dark brows and wide-gazing eyes well conveyed the clear integrity of youth.

For the beauty of the bride in her white over-robe no comparisons were adequate. In the eyes, round beneath soft brows, in the slender, finely shaped nose, and in the full lips, there was both sensuousness and refinement. One hand, emerging shyly from a sleeve of the over-robe, held a fan, and the tips of the fingers, clustering delicately, were like the bud of a moonflower.

After the suicide, people would take out this photograph and examine it, and sadly reflect that too often there was a curse on these seemingly flawless unions. Perhaps it was no more than imagination, but looking at the picture after the tragedy it almost seemed as if the two young people before the gold-lacquered screen were gazing, each with equal clarity, at the deaths which lay before them.

Thanks to the good offices of their go-between, Lieutenant General Ozeki, they had been able to set themselves up in a new home at Aoba-chō in Yotsuya. "New home" is perhaps misleading. It was an old three-room rented house backing onto a small garden. As neither the six- nor the four-and-a-half-mat room downstairs was favored by the sun, they used the upstairs eight-mat room as both bedroom and guest room. There was no maid, so Reiko was left alone to guard the house in her husband's absence.

The honeymoon trip was dispensed with on the grounds that these were times of national emergency. The two of them had spent the first night of their marriage at this house. Before going to bed, Shinji, sitting erect on the floor with his sword laid before him, had bestowed upon his wife a soldierly lecture. A woman who had become the wife of a soldier should know and resolutely accept that her husband's death might come at any moment.

It could be tomorrow. It could be the day after. But, no matter when it came—he asked—was she steadfast in her resolve to accept it? Reiko rose to her feet, pulled open a drawer of the cabinet, and took out what was the most prized of her new possessions, the dagger her mother had given her. Returning to her place, she laid the dagger without a word on the mat before her, just as her husband had laid his sword. A silent understanding was achieved at once, and the lieutenant never again sought to test his wife's resolve.

In the first few months of her marriage Reiko's beauty grew daily more radiant, shining serene like the moon after rain.

As both were possessed of young, vigorous bodies, their relationship was passionate. Nor was this merely a matter of the night. On more than one occasion, returning home straight from maneuvers, and begrudging even the time it took to remove his mud-splashed uniform, the lieutenant had pushed his wife to the floor almost as soon as he had entered the house. Reiko was equally ardent in her response. For a little more or a little less than a month, from the first night of their marriage Reiko knew happiness, and the lieutenant, seeing this, was happy too.

Reiko's body was white and pure, and her swelling breasts conveyed a firm and chaste refusal; but, upon consent, those breasts were lavish with their intimate, welcoming warmth. Even in bed these two were frighteningly and awesomely serious. In the very midst of wild, intoxicating passions, their hearts were sober and serious.

By day the lieutenant would think of his wife in the brief rest periods between training; and all day long, at home, Reiko would recall the image of her husband. Even when apart, however, they had only to look at the wedding photograph for their happiness to be once more confirmed. Reiko felt not the slightest surprise that a man who had been a complete stranger until a few months ago should now have become the sun about which her whole world revolved.

All these things had a moral basis, and were in accordance with the Education Rescript's injunction that "husband and wife should be harmonious." Not once did Reiko contradict her husband, nor did the lieutenant ever find reason to scold his wife. On the god shelf below the stairway, alongside the tablet from the Great Ise Shrine, were set photographs of their Imperial Majesties, and regularly every morning, before leaving for duty, the lieutenant would stand with his wife at this hallowed place and together they would bow their heads low. The offering water was renewed each morning, and the sacred sprig of *sasaki* was always green and fresh. Their lives were lived beneath the solemn protection of the gods and were filled with an intense happiness which set every fiber in their bodies trembling.

III

Although Lord Privy Seal Saitō's house was in their neighborhood, neither of them heard any noise of gunfire on the morning of February 26. It was a bugle, sounding muster in the dim, snowy dawn, when the ten-minute tragedy had already ended, which first disrupted the lieutenant's slumbers. Leaping at once from his bed, and without speaking a word, the lieutenant donned his uniform, buckled on the sword held ready for him by his wife, and hurried swiftly out into the snow-covered streets of the still darkened morning. He did not return until the evening of the twenty-eighth.

Later, from the radio news, Reiko learned the full extent of this sudden eruption of violence. Her life throughout the subsequent two days was lived alone, in complete tranquillity, and behind locked doors.

In the lieutenant's face, as he hurried silently out into the snowy morning, Reiko had read the determination to die. If her husband did not return, her own decision was made: she too would die. Quietly she attended to the disposition of her personal possessions. She chose her sets of visiting kimonos as keepsakes for friends of her schooldays, and she wrote a name and address on the stiff paper wrapping in which each was folded. Constantly admonished by her husband never to think of the morrow, Reiko had not even kept a diary and was now denied the pleasure of assiduously rereading her record of the happiness of the past few months and consigning each page to the fire as she did so. Ranged across the top of the radio were a small china dog, a rabbit, a squirrel, a bear, and a fox. There were also a small vase and a water pitcher. These comprised Reiko's one and only collection. But it would hardly do, she imagined, to give such things as keepsakes. Nor again would it be quite proper to ask specifically for them to be included in the coffin. It seemed to Reiko, as these thoughts passed through her mind, that the expressions on the small animals' faces grew even more lost and forlorn.

Reiko took the squirrel in her hand and looked at it. And then, her thoughts turning to a realm far beyond these child-like affections, she gazed up into the distance at the great sunlike principle which her husband embodied. She was ready, and happy, to be hurtled along to her destruction in that gleaming sun chariot—but now, for these few moments of solitude, she allowed herself to luxuriate in this innocent attachment to trifles. The time when she had genuinely loved these things, however, was long past. Now she merely loved the memory of having once loved them, and their place in her heart had been filled by more intense passions, by a more frenzied happiness. . . . For Reiko had never, even to herself, thought of those soaring joys of the flesh as a mere pleasure. The February cold, and the icy touch of the china squirrel, had numbed Reiko's slender fingers; yet, even so, in her lower limbs, beneath the ordered repetition of the pattern which crossed the skirt of her trim *meisen* kimono, she could feel now, as she thought of the lieutenant's powerful arms reaching toward her, a hot moistness of the flesh which defied the snows.

She was not in the least afraid of the death hovering in her mind. Waiting alone at home, Reiko firmly believed that everything her husband was feeling or thinking now, his anguish and distress, was leading her—just as surely as the power in his flesh—to a welcome death. She felt as if her body could melt away with ease and be transformed to the merest fraction of her husband's thought.

Listening to the frequent announcements on the radio, she heard the names of several of her husband's colleagues mentioned among those of the insurgents. This was news of death. She followed the developments closely, wondering anxiously, as the situation became daily more irrevocable, why no Imperial ordinance was sent down, and watching what had at first been taken as a movement to restore the nation's honor come gradually to be branded with the infamous name of mutiny. There was no communication from the regiment. At any moment, it seemed, fighting might commence in the city streets, where the remains of the snow still lay.

Toward sundown on the twenty-eighth Reiko was startled by a furious pounding on the front door. She hurried downstairs. As she pulled with fumbling fingers at the bolt, the shape dimly outlined beyond the frosted-glass panel made no sound, but she knew it was her husband. Reiko had never known the bolt on the sliding door to be so stiff. Still it resisted. The door just would not open.

In a moment, almost before she knew she had succeeded, the lieutenant was standing before her on the cement floor inside the porch, muffled in a khaki greatcoat, his top boots heavy with slush from the street. Closing the door behind him, he returned the bolt once more to its socket. With what significance, Reiko did not understand.

"Welcome home."

Reiko bowed deeply, but her husband made no response. As he had already unfastened his sword and was about to remove his greatcoat, Reiko moved around behind to assist. The coat, which was cold and damp and had lost the odor of horse dung it normally exuded when exposed to the sun, weighed heavily upon her arm. Draping it across a hanger, and cradling the sword and leather belt in her sleeves, she waited while her husband removed his top boots and then followed behind him into the "living room." This was the six-mat room downstairs.

Seen in the clear light from the lamp, her husband's face, covered with a heavy growth of bristle, was almost unrecognizably wasted and thin. The cheeks were hollow, their luster and resilience gone. In his normal good spirits he would have changed into old clothes as soon as he was home and have pressed her to get supper at once, but now he sat before the table still in his uniform, his head drooping dejectedly. Reiko refrained from asking whether she should prepare the supper.

After an interval the lieutenant spoke.

"I knew nothing. They hadn't asked me to join. Perhaps out of consideration, because I was newly married. Kanō, and Homma too, and Yamaguchi."

Reiko recalled momentarily the faces of high-spirited young officers, friends of her husband, who had come to the house occasionally as guests.

"There may be an Imperial ordinance sent down tomorrow. They'll be posted as rebels, I imagine. I shall be in command of a unit with orders to attack them. . . . I can't do it. It's impossible to do a thing like that."

He spoke again.

"They've taken me off guard duty, and I have permission to return home for one night. Tomorrow morning, without question, I must leave to join the attack. I can't do it, Reiko."

Reiko sat erect with lowered eyes. She understood clearly that her husband had spoken of his death. The lieutenant was resolved. Each word, being rooted in death, emerged sharply and with powerful significance against this dark, unmovable background. Although the lieutenant was speaking of his dilemma, already there was no room in his mind for vacillation.

However, there was a clarity, like the clarity of a stream fed from melting snows, in the silence which rested between them. Sitting in his own home after the long two-day ordeal, and looking across at the face of his beautiful wife, the lieutenant was for the first time experiencing true peace of mind. For he had at once known, though she said nothing, that his wife divined the resolve which lay beneath his words.

"Well, then . . ." The lieutenant's eyes opened wide. Despite his exhaustion they were strong and clear, and now for the first time they looked straight into the eyes of his wife. "To-night I shall cut my stomach."

Reiko did not flinch.

Her round eyes showed tension, as taut as the clang of a bell.

"I am ready," she said. "I ask permission to accompany you."

The lieutenant felt almost mesmerized by the strength in those eyes. His words flowed swiftly and easily, like the utterances of a man in delirium, and it was beyond his understanding how permission in a matter of such weight could be expressed so casually.

"Good. We'll go together. But I want you as a witness, first, for my own suicide. Agreed?"

When this was said a sudden release of abundant happiness welled up in both their hearts. Reiko was deeply affected by the greatness of her husband's trust in her. It was vital for the lieutenant, whatever else might happen, that there should be no irregularity in his death. For that reason there had to be a witness. The fact that he had chosen his wife for this was the first mark of his trust. The second, and even greater mark, was that though he had pledged that they should die together he did not intend to kill his wife first—he had deferred her death to a time when he would no longer be there to verify it. If the lieutenant had been a suspicious husband, he would doubtless, as in the usual suicide pact, have chosen to kill his wife first.

When Reiko said, "I ask permission to accompany you," the lieutenant felt these words to be the final fruit of the education which he had himself given his wife, starting on the first night of their marriage, and which had schooled her, when the moment came, to say what had to be said without a shadow of hesitation. This flattered the lieutenant's opinion of himself as a self-reliant man. He was not so romantic or conceited as to imagine that the words were spoken spontaneously, out of love for her husband.

With happiness welling almost too abundantly in their hearts, they could not help smiling at each other. Reiko felt as if she had returned to her wedding night.

Before her eyes was neither pain nor death. She seemed to see only a free and limitless expanse opening out into vast distances.

"The water is hot. Will you take your bath now?"

"Ah yes, of course."

"And supper . . . ?"

The words were delivered in such level, domestic tones that the lieutenant came near to thinking, for the fraction of a second, that everything had been a hallucination.

"I don't think we'll need supper. But perhaps you could warm some sake?"

"As you wish."

As Reiko rose and took a *tanzen* gown from the cabinet for after the bath, she purposely directed her husband's attention to the opened drawer. The lieutenant rose, crossed to the cabinet, and looked inside. From the ordered array of paper wrappings he read, one by one, the addresses of the keepsakes. There was no grief in the lieutenant's response to this demonstration of heroic resolve. His heart was filled with tenderness. Like a husband who is proudly shown the childish purchases of a young wife, the lieutenant, overwhelmed by affection, lovingly embraced his wife from behind and implanted a kiss upon her neck.

Reiko felt the roughness of the lieutenant's unshaven skin against her neck. This sensation, more than being just a thing of this world, was for Reiko almost the world itself, but now—with the feeling that it was soon to be lost forever—it had freshness beyond all her experience. Each moment had its own vital strength, and the senses in every corner of her body were reawakened. Accepting her husband's caresses from behind, Reiko raised herself on the tips of her toes, letting the vitality seep through her entire body.

"First the bath, and then, after some sake . . . lay out the bedding upstairs, will you?"

The lieutenant whispered the words into his wife's ear. Reiko silently nodded.

Flinging off his uniform, the lieutenant went to the bath. To faint background noises of slopping water Reiko tended the charcoal brazier in the living room and began the preparations for warming the sake.

Taking the *tanzen*, a sash, and some underclothes, she went to the bathroom to ask how the water was. In the midst of a coiling cloud of steam the lieutenant was sitting cross-legged on the floor, shaving, and she could dimly discern the rippling movements of the muscles on his damp, powerful back as they responded to the movement of his arms.

There was nothing to suggest a time of any special significance. Reiko, going busily about her tasks, was preparing side dishes from odds and ends in stock. Her hands did not tremble. If anything, she managed even more efficiently and smoothly than usual. From time to time, it is true, there was a strange throbbing deep within her breast. Like distant lightning, it had a moment of sharp intensity and then vanished without trace. Apart from that, nothing was in any way out of the ordinary.

The lieutenant, shaving in the bathroom, felt his warmed body miraculously healed at last of the desperate tiredness of the days of indecision and filled—in spite of the death which lay ahead—with pleasurable anticipation. The sound of his wife going about her work came to him faintly. A healthy physical craving, submerged for two days, reasserted itself.

The lieutenant was confident there had been no impurity in that joy they had experienced when resolving upon death. They had both sensed at that moment—though not, of course, in any clear and conscious way—that those permissible pleasures which they shared in private were once more beneath the protection of Righteousness and Divine Power, and of a complete and unassailable morality. On looking into each other's eyes and discovering there an honorable death, they had felt themselves safe once more behind steel walls which none could destroy, encased in an impenetrable armor of Beauty and Truth. Thus, so far from seeing any inconsistency or conflict between the urges of his flesh and the sincerity of his patriotism, the lieutenant was even able to regard the two as parts of the same thing.

Thrusting his face close to the dark,

cracked, misted wall mirror, the lieutenant shaved himself with great care. This would be his death face. There must be no unsightly blemishes. The clean-shaven face gleamed once more with a youthful luster, seeming to brighten the darkness of the mirror. There was a certain elegance, he even felt, in the association of death with this radiantly healthy face.

Just as it looked now, this would become his death face! Already, in fact, it had half departed from the lieutenant's personal possession and had become the bust above a dead soldier's memorial. As an experiment he closed his eyes tight. Everything was wrapped in blackness, and he was no longer a living, seeing creature.

Returning from the bath, the traces of the shave glowing faintly blue beneath his smooth cheeks, he seated himself beside the now well-kindled charcoal brazier. Busy though Reiko was, he noticed, she had found time lightly to touch up her face. Her cheeks were gay and her lips moist. There was no shadow of sadness to be seen. Truly, the lieutenant felt, as he saw this mark of his young wife's passionate nature, he had chosen the wife he ought to have chosen.

As soon as the lieutenant had drained his sake cup he offered it to Reiko. Reiko had never before tasted sake, but she accepted without hesitation and sipped timidly.

"Come here," the lieutenant said.

Reiko moved to her husband's side and was embraced as she leaned backward across his lap. Her breast was in violent commotion, as if sadness, joy, and the potent sake were mingling and reacting within her. The lieutenant looked down into his wife's face. It was the last face he would see in this world, the last face he would see of his wife. The lieutenant scrutinized the face minutely, with the eyes of a traveler bidding farewell to splendid vistas which he will never revisit. It was a face he could not tire of looking at—the features regular yet not cold, the lips lightly closed with a soft strength. The lieutenant kissed those lips, unthinkingly. And suddenly, though there was not the slightest distortion of the face into the unsightliness of sobbing, he noticed that tears were welling slowly from beneath the long lashes of the closed eyes and brimming over into a glistening stream.

When, a little later, the lieutenant urged that they should move to the upstairs bedroom, his wife replied that she would follow after taking a bath. Climbing the stairs alone to the bedroom, where the air was already warmed by the gas heater, the lieutenant lay down on the bedding with arms outstretched and legs apart. Even the time at which he lay waiting for his wife to join him was no later and no earlier than usual.

He folded his hands beneath his head and gazed at the dark boards of the ceiling in the dimness beyond the range of the standard lamp. Was it death he was now waiting for? Or a wild ecstasy of the senses? The two seemed to overlap, almost as if the object of this bodily desire was death itself. But, however that might be, it was certain that never before had the lieutenant tasted such total freedom.

There was the sound of a car outside the window. He could hear the screech of its tires skidding in the snow piled at the side of the street. The sound of its horn re-echoed from near-by walls. . . . Listening to these noises he had the feeling that this house rose like a solitary island in the ocean of a society going as restlessly about its business as ever. All around, vastly and untidily, stretched the country for which he grieved. He was to give his life for it. But would that great country, with which he was prepared to remonstrate to the extent of destroying himself, take the slightest heed of his death? He did not know; and it did not matter. His was a battlefield without glory, a battlefield where none could display deeds of valor: it was the front line of the spirit.

Reiko's footsteps sounded on the stairway. The steep stairs in this old house creaked badly. There were fond memories in that creaking, and many a time, while waiting in bed, the lieutenant had listened to its welcome sound. At the thought that he would hear it no more he listened with intense concentration, striving for every corner of every moment of this precious time to be filled with the sound of those soft footfalls on the creaking stairway. The moments seemed transformed to jewels, sparkling with inner light.

Reiko wore a Nagoya sash about the waist of her *yukata*, but as the lieutenant reached toward it, its redness sobered by the dimness of the light, Reiko's hand moved to his assistance and the sash fell away, slithering swiftly to the floor. As she stood before him, still in her *yukata*, the lieutenant inserted his hands through the side slits beneath each sleeve, intending to embrace her as she was; but at the touch of his finger tips upon the warm naked flesh, and as the armpits closed gently about his hands, his whole body was suddenly aflame.

In a few moments the two lay naked before the glowing gas heater.

Neither spoke the thought, but their hearts, their bodies, and their pounding breasts blazed with the knowledge that this was the very last time. It was as if the words "The Last Time" were spelled out, in invisible brushstrokes, across every inch of their bodies.

The lieutenant drew his wife close and kissed her vehemently. As their tongues explored each other's mouths, reaching out into the smooth, moist interior, they felt as if the still-unknown agonies of death had tempered their senses to the keenness of red-hot steel. The agonies they could not yet feel, the distant pains of death, had refined their awareness of pleasure.

"This is the last time I shall see your body," said the lieutenant. "Let me look at it closely." And, tilting the shade on the lampstand to one side, he directed the rays along the full length of Reiko's outstretched form.

Reiko lay still with her eyes closed. The light from the low lamp clearly revealed the majestic sweep of her white flesh. The lieutenant, not without a touch of egocentricity, rejoiced that he would never see this beauty crumble in death.

At his leisure, the lieutenant allowed the unforgettable spectacle to engrave itself upon his mind. With one hand he fondled the hair, with the other he softly stroked the magnificent face, implanting kisses here and there where his eyes lingered. The quiet coldness of the high, tapering forehead, the closed eyes with their long lashes beneath faintly etched brows, the set of the finely shaped nose, the gleam of teeth glimpsed between full, regular lips, the soft cheeks and the small, wise chin . . . these things conjured up in the lieutenant's mind the vision of a truly radiant death face, and again and again he pressed his lips tight against the white throat—where Reiko's own hand was soon to strike—and the throat reddened faintly beneath his kisses. Returning to the mouth he laid his lips against it with the gentlest of pressures, and moved them rhythmically over Reiko's with the light rolling motion of a small boat. If he closed his eyes, the world became a rocking cradle.

Wherever the lieutenant's eyes moved his lips faithfully followed. The high, swelling breasts, surmounted by nipples like the buds of a wild cherry, hardened as the lieutenant's lips closed about them. The arms flowed smoothly downward from each side of the breast, tapering toward the wrists, yet losing nothing of their roundness or symmetry, and at their tips were those delicate fingers which had held the fan at the wedding ceremony. One by one, as the lieutenant kissed them, the fingers withdrew behind their neighbor as if in shame. . . . The natural hollow curving between the bosom and the stomach carried in its lines a suggestion not only of softness but of resilient strength, and while it gave forewarning of the rich curves spreading outward from here to the hips it had, in itself, an appearance only of restraint and proper discipline. The whiteness and richness of the stomach and hips was like milk brimming in a great bowl, and the sharply shadowed dip of the navel could have been the fresh impress of a raindrop, fallen there that very moment. Where the shadows gathered more thickly, hair clustered, gentle and sensitive, and as the agitation mounted in the now no longer passive body there hung over this region a scent like the smoldering of fragrant blossoms, growing steadily more pervasive.

At length, in a tremulous voice, Reiko spoke.

"Show me. . . . Let me look too, for the last time."

Never before had he heard from his wife's lips so strong and unequivocal a request. It was as if something which her modesty had wished to keep hidden to the end had suddenly burst its bonds of constraint. The lieutenant obediently lay back and surrendered himself to his wife. Lithely she raised her white, trembling body, and—burning with an innocent desire to return to her husband what he had done for her—placed two white fingers on the lieutenant's eyes, which gazed fixedly up at her, and gently stroked them shut.

Suddenly overwhelmed by tenderness, her cheeks flushed by a dizzying uprush of emotion, Reiko threw her arms about the lieutenant's close-cropped head. The bristly hairs rubbed painfully against her breast, the prominent nose was cold as it dug into her flesh, and his breath was hot. Relaxing her embrace, she gazed down at her husband's masculine face. The severe brows, the closed eyes, the splendid bridge of the nose, the shapely lips drawn firmly together . . . the blue, clean-shaven cheeks reflecting the light and gleaming smoothly. Reiko kissed each of these. She kissed the broad nape of the neck, the strong, erect shoulders, the powerful chest with its twin circles like shields and its russet nipples. In the armpits, deeply shadowed by the ample flesh of the shoulders and chest, a sweet and melancholy odor emanated from the growth of hair, and in the sweetness of this odor was contained, somehow, the essence of young death. The lieutenant's naked skin glowed like a field of barley, and everywhere the muscles showed in sharp relief, converging on the lower abdomen about the small, unassuming navel. Gazing at the youthful, firm stomach, modestly covered by a vigorous growth of hair, Reiko thought of it as it was soon to be, cruelly cut by the sword, and she laid her head upon it, sobbing in pity, and bathed it with kisses.

At the touch of his wife's tears upon his stomach the lieutenant felt ready to endure with courage the cruelest agonies of his suicide.

What ecstasies they experienced after these tender exchanges may well be imagined. The lieutenant raised himself and enfolded his wife in a powerful embrace, her body now limp with exhaustion after her grief and tears. Passionately they held their faces close, rubbing cheek against cheek. Reiko's body was trembling. Their breasts, moist with sweat, were tightly joined, and every inch of the young and beautiful bodies had become so much one with the other that it seemed impossible there should ever again be a separation. Reiko cried out. From the heights they plunged into the abyss, and from the abyss they took wing and soared once more to dizzying heights. The lieutenant panted like the regimental standard-bearer on a route march. . . . As one cycle ended, almost immediately a new wave of passion would be generated, and together—with no trace of fatigue—they would climb again in a single breathless movement to the very summit.

IV

When the lieutenant at last turned away, it was not from weariness. For one thing, he was anxious not to undermine the considerable strength he would need in carrying out his suicide. For another, he would have been sorry to mar the sweetness of these last memories by overindulgence.

Since the lieutenant had clearly desisted, Reiko too, with her usual compliance, followed his example. The two lay naked on their backs, with fingers interlaced, staring fixedly at the dark ceiling. The room was warm from the heater, and even when the sweat had ceased to pour from their bodies they felt no cold. Outside, in the hushed night, the sounds of passing traffic had ceased. Even the noises of the trains and streetcars around Yotsuya station did not penetrate this far. After echoing through the region bounded by the moat, they were lost in the heavily wooded park fronting the broad driveway before Akasaka Palace. It was hard to believe in the tension gripping this whole quarter, where the two factions of the bitterly divided Imperial Army now confronted each other, poised for battle.

Savoring the warmth glowing within themselves, they lay still and recalled the ecstasies they had just known. Each moment of the experience was relived. They remembered the taste of kisses which had never wearied, the touch of naked flesh, episode after episode of dizzying bliss. But already, from the dark boards of the ceiling, the face of death was peering down. These joys had been final, and their bodies would never know them again. Not that joy of this intensity—and the same thought had occurred to them both —was ever likely to be reexperienced, even if they should live on to old age.

The feel of their fingers intertwined— this too would soon be lost. Even the wood-grain patterns they now gazed at on the dark ceiling boards would be taken from them. They could feel death edging in, nearer and nearer. There could be no hesitation now. They must have the courage to reach out to death themselves, and to seize it.

"Well, let's make our preparations," said the lieutenant. The note of determination in the words was unmistakable, but at the same time Reiko had never heard her husband's voice so warm and tender.

After they had risen, a variety of tasks awaited them.

The lieutenant, who had never once before helped with the bedding, now cheerfully slid back the door of the closet, lifted the mattress across the room by himself, and stowed it away inside.

Reiko turned off the gas heater and put away the lamp standard. During the lieutenant's absence she had arranged this room carefully, sweeping and dusting it to a fresh cleanness, and now—if one overlooked the rosewood table drawn into one corner—the eight-mat room gave all the appearance of a reception room ready to welcome an important guest.

"We've seen some drinking here, haven't we? With Kanō and Homma and Noguchi . . ."

"Yes, they were great drinkers, all of them."

"We'll be meeting them before long, in the other world. They'll tease us, I imagine, when they find I've brought you with me."

Descending the stairs, the lieutenant turned to look back into this calm, clean room, now brightly illuminated by the ceiling lamp. There floated across his mind the faces of the young officers who had drunk there, and laughed, and innocently bragged. He had never dreamed then that he would one day cut open his stomach in this room.

In the two rooms downstairs husband and wife busied themselves smoothly and serenely with their respective preparations. The lieutenant went to the toilet, and then to the bathroom to wash. Meanwhile Reiko folded away her husband's padded robe, placed his uniform tunic, his trousers, and a newly cut bleached loincloth in the bathroom, and set out sheets of paper on the living-room table for the farewell notes. Then she removed the lid from the writing box and began rubbing ink from the ink tablet. She had already decided upon the wording of her own note.

Reiko's fingers pressed hard upon the cold gilt letters of the ink tablet, and the water in the shallow well at once darkened, as if a black cloud had spread across it. She stopped thinking that this repeated action, this pressure from her fingers, this rise and fall of faint sound, was all and solely for death. It was a routine domestic task, a simple paring away of time until death should finally stand before her. But somehow, in the increasingly smooth motion of the tablet rubbing on the stone, and in the scent from the thickening ink, there was unspeakable darkness.

Neat in his uniform, which he now wore next to his skin, the lieutenant emerged from the bathroom. Without a word he seated himself at the table, bolt upright, took a brush in his hand, and stared undecidedly at the paper before him.

Reiko took a white silk kimono with her and entered the bathroom. When she reappeared in the living room, clad in the white kimono and with her face lightly made up, the farewell note lay completed on the table beneath the lamp. The thick black brushstrokes said simply:

"Long Live the Imperial Forces— Army Lieutenant Takeyama Shinji."

While Reiko sat opposite him writing her own note, the lieutenant gazed in silence, intensely serious, at the controlled movement of his wife's pale fingers as they manipulated the brush.

With their respective notes in their hands—the lieutenant's sword strapped to his side, Reiko's small dagger thrust into the sash of her white kimono—the two of them stood before the god shelf and silently prayed. Then they put out all the downstairs lights. As he mounted the stairs the lieutenant turned his head and gazed back at the striking, white-clad figure of his wife, climbing behind him, with lowered eyes, from the darkness beneath.

The farewell notes were laid side by side in the alcove of the upstairs room. They wondered whether they ought not to removed the hanging scroll, but since it had been written by their go-between, Lieutenant General Ozeki, and consisted, moreover, of two Chinese characters signifying "Sincerity," they left it where it was. Even if it were to become stained with splashes of blood, they felt that the lieutenant general would understand.

The lieutenant, sitting erect with his back to the alcove, laid his sword on the floor before him.

Reiko sat facing him, a mat's width away. With the rest of her so severely white the touch of rouge on her lips seemed remarkably seductive.

Across the dividing mat they gazed intently into each other's eyes. The lieutenant's sword lay before his knees. Seeing it, Reiko recalled their first night and was overwhelmed with sadness. The lieutenant spoke, in a hoarse voice:

"As I have no second to help me I shall cut deep. It may look unpleasant, but please do not panic. Death of any sort is a fearful thing to watch. You must not be discouraged by what you see. Is that all right?"

"Yes."

Reiko nodded deeply.

Looking at the slender white figure of his wife the lieutenant experienced a bizarre excitement. What he was about to perform was an act in his public capacity as a soldier, something he had never previously shown his wife. It called for a resolution equal to the courage to enter battle; it was a death of no less degree and quality than death in the front line. It was his conduct on the battlefield that he was now to display.

Momentarily the thought led the lieutenant to a strange fantasy. A lonely death on the battlefield, a death beneath the eyes of his beautiful wife . . . in the sensation that he was now to die in these two dimensions, realizing an impossible union of them both, there was sweetness beyond words. This must be the very pinnacle of good fortune, he thought. To have every moment of his death observed by those beautiful eyes—it was like being borne to death on a gentle, fragrant breeze. There was some special favor here. He did not understand precisely what it was, but it was a domain unknown to others: a dispensation granted to no one else had been permitted to himself. In the radiant, bridelike figure of his white-robed wife the lieutenant seemed to see a vision of all those things he had loved and for which he was to lay down his life—the Imperial Household, the Nation, the Army Flag. All these, no less than the wife who sat before him, were presences observing him closely with clear and never-faltering eyes.

Reiko too was gazing intently at her husband, so soon to die, and she thought that never in this world had she seen anything so beautiful. The lieutenant always looked well in uniform, but now, as he contemplated death with severe brows and firmly closed lips, he revealed what was perhaps masculine beauty at its most superb.

"It's time to go," the lieutenant said at last.

Reiko bent her body low to the mat in a deep bow. She could not raise her face. She did not wish to spoil her make-up with tears, but the tears could not be held back.

When at length she looked up she saw hazily through the tears that her husband had wound a white bandage around the blade of his now unsheathed sword, leaving five or six inches of naked steel showing at the point.

Resting the sword in its cloth wrapping on the mat before him, the lieutenant rose from his knees, resettled himself cross-legged, and unfastened the hooks of his uniform collar. His eyes no longer saw his wife. Slowly, one by one, he undid the flat brass buttons. The dusky brown chest was revealed, and then the stomach. He unclasped his belt and undid the buttons of his trousers. The pure whiteness of the thickly coiled loincloth showed itself. The lieutenant pushed the cloth down with both hands, further to ease his stomach, and then reached for the white-bandaged blade of his sword. With his left hand he massaged his abdomen, glancing downward as he did so.

To reassure himself on the sharpness of his sword's cutting edge the lieutenant folded back the left trouser flap, exposing a little of his thigh, and lightly drew the blade across the skin. Blood welled up in the wound at once, and several streaks of red trickled downward, glistening in the strong light.

It was the first time Reiko had ever seen her husband's blood, and she felt a violent throbbing in her chest. She looked at her husband's face. The lieutenant was looking at the blood with calm appraisal. For a moment—though thinking at the same time that it was hollow comfort—Reiko experienced a sense of relief.

The lieutenant's eyes fixed his wife with an intense, hawk-like stare. Moving the sword around to his front, he raised himself slightly on his hips and let the upper half of his body lean over the sword point. That he was mustering his whole strength was apparent from the angry tension of the uniform at his shoulders. The lieutenant aimed to strike deep into the left of his stomach. His sharp cry pierced the silence of the room.

Despite the effort he had himself put into the blow, the lieutenant had the impression that someone else had struck the side of his stomach agonizingly with a thick rod of iron. For a second or so his head reeled and he had no idea what had happened. The five or six inches of naked point had vanished completely into his flesh, and the white bandage, gripped in his clenched fist, pressed directly against his stomach.

He returned to consciousness. The blade had certainly pierced the wall of the stomach, he thought. His breathing was difficult, his chest thumped violently, and in some far deep region, which he could hardly believe was a part of himself, a fearful and excruciating pain came welling up as if the ground had split open to disgorge a boiling stream of molten rock. The pain came suddenly nearer, with terrifying speed. The lieutenant bit his lower lip and stifled an instinctive moan.

Was this *seppuku?*—he was thinking. It was a sensation of utter chaos, as if the sky had fallen on his head and the world was reeling drunkenly. His will power and courage, which had seemed so robust before he made the incision, had now dwindled to something like a single hair-like thread of steel, and he was assailed by the uneasy feeling that he must advance along this thread, clinging to it with desperation. His clenched fist had grown moist. Looking down, he saw that both his hand and the cloth about the blade were drenched in blood. His loincloth too was dyed a deep red. It struck him as incredible that, amidst this terrible agony, things which could be seen could still be seen, and existing things existed still.

The moment the lieutenant thrust the sword into his left side and she saw the deathly pallor fall across his face, like an abruptly lowered curtain, Reiko had to struggle to prevent herself from rushing to his side. Whatever happened, she must watch. She must be a witness. That was the duty her husband had laid upon her. Opposite her, a mat's space away, she could clearly see her husband biting his lip to stifle the pain. The pain was there, with absolute certainty, before her eyes. And Reiko had no means of rescuing him from it.

The sweat glistened on her husband's forehead. The lieutenant closed his eyes, and then opened them again, as if experimenting. The eyes had lost their luster, and seemed innocent and empty like the eyes of a small animal.

The agony before Reiko's eyes burned as strong as the summer sun, utterly remote from the grief which seemed to be tearing herself apart within. The pain grew steadily in stature, stretching upward. Reiko felt that her husband had already become a man in a separate world, a man whose whole being had been resolved into pain, a prisoner in a cage of pain where no hand could reach out to him. But Reiko felt no pain at all. Her grief was not pain. As she thought about this, Reiko began to feel as if someone had raised a cruel wall of glass high between herself and her husband.

Ever since her marriage her husband's existence had been her own existence, and every breath of his had been a breath drawn by herself. But now, while her husband's existence in pain was a vivid reality, Reiko could find in this grief of hers no certain proof at all of her own existence.

With only his right hand on the sword the lieutenant began to cut sideways across his stomach. But as the blade became entangled with the entrails it was pushed constantly outward by their soft resilience; and the lieutenant realized that it would be necessary, as he cut, to use both hands to keep the point pressed deep into his stomach. He pulled the blade across. It did not cut as easily as he had expected. He directed the strength of his whole body into his right hand and pulled again. There was a cut of three or four inches.

The pain spread slowly outward from the inner depths until the whole stomach reverberated. It was like the wild clanging of a bell. Or like a thousand bells which jangled simultaneously at every breath he breathed and every throb of his pulse, rocking his whole being. The lieutenant could no longer stop himself from moaning. But by now the blade had cut its way through to below the navel, and when he noticed this he felt a sense of satisfaction, and a renewal of courage.

The volume of blood had steadily increased, and now it spurted from the wound as if propelled by the beat of the pulse. The mat before the lieutenant was drenched red with splattered blood, and more blood overflowed onto it from pools which gathered in the folds of the lieutenant's khaki trousers. A spot, like a bird, came flying across to Reiko and settled on the lap of her white silk kimono.

By the time the lieutenant had at last drawn the sword across to the right side of his stomach, the blade was already cutting shallow and had revealed its naked tip, slippery with blood and grease. But, suddenly stricken by a fit of vomiting, the lieutenant cried out hoarsely. The vomiting made the fierce pain fiercer still, and the stomach, which had thus far remained firm and compact, now abruptly heaved, opening wide its wound, and the entrails burst through, as if the wound too were vomiting. Seemingly ignorant of their master's suffering, the entrails gave an impression of robust health and almost disagreeable vitality as they slipped smoothly out and spilled over into the crotch. The lieutenant's head drooped, his shoulders heaved, his eyes opened to narrow slits, and a thin trickle of saliva dribbled from his mouth. The gold markings on his epaulettes caught the light and glinted.

Blood was scattered everywhere. The lieutenant was soaked in it to his knees, and he sat now in a crumpled and listless posture, one hand on the floor. A raw smell filled the room. The lieutenant, his head drooping, retched repeatedly, and the movement showed vividly in his shoulders. The blade of the sword, now pushed back by the entrails and exposed to its tip, was still in the lieutenant's right hand.

It would be difficult to imagine a more heroic sight than that of the lieutenant at this moment, as he mustered his strength and flung back his head. The movement was performed with sudden violence, and the back of his head struck with a sharp crack against the alcove pillar. Reiko had been sitting until now with her face lowered, gazing in fascination at the tide of blood advancing toward her knees, but the sound took her by surprise and she looked up.

The lieutenant's face was not the face of a living man. The eyes were hollow, the skin parched, the once so lustrous cheeks and lips the color of dried mud. The right hand alone was moving. Laboriously gripping the sword, it hovered shakily in the air like the hand of a marionette and strove to direct the point at the base of the lieutenant's throat. Reiko watched her husband make this last, most heart-rending, futile exertion. Glistening with blood and grease, the point was thrust at the throat again and again. And each time it missed its aim. The strength to guide it was no longer there. The straying point struck the collar and the collar badges. Although its hooks had been unfastened, the stiff military collar had closed together again and was protecting the throat.

Reiko could bear the sight no longer. She tried to go to her husband's help, but she could not stand. She moved through the blood on her knees, and her white skirts grew deep red. Moving to the rear of her husband, she helped no more than by loosening the collar. The quivering blade at last contacted the naked flesh of the throat. At that moment Reiko's impression was that she herself had propelled her husband forward; but that was not the case. It was a movement planned by the lieutenant himself, his last exertion of strength. Abruptly he threw his body at the blade, and the blade pierced his neck, emerging at the nape. There was a tremendous spurt of blood and the lieutenant lay still, cold blue-tinged steel protruding from his neck at the back.

v

Slowly, her socks slippery with blood, Reiko descended the stairway. The upstairs room was now completely still.

Switching on the ground-floor lights, she checked the gas jet and the main gas plug and poured water over the smoldering, half-buried charcoal in the brazier. She stood before the upright mirror in the four-and-a-half mat room and held up her skirts. The bloodstains made it seem as if a bold, vivid pattern was printed across the lower half of her white kimono. When she sat down before the mirror, she was conscious of the dampness and coldness of her husband's blood in the region of her thighs, and she shivered. Then, for a long while, she lingered over her toilet preparations. She applied the rouge generously to her cheeks, and her lips too she painted heavily. This was no longer make-up to please her husband. It was make-up for the world which she would leave behind, and there was a touch of the magnificent and the spectacular in her brushwork. When she rose, the mat before the mirror was wet with blood. Reiko was not concerned about this.

Returning from the toilet, Reiko stood finally on the cement floor of the porchway. When her husband had bolted the door here last night it had been in preparation for death. For a while she stood immersed in the consideration of a simple problem. Should she now leave the bolt drawn? If she were to lock the door, it could be that the neighbors might not notice their suicide for several days. Reiko did not relish the thought of their two corpses putrefying before discovery. After all, it seemed, it would be best to leave it open. . . . She released the bolt, and also drew open the frosted-glass door a fraction. . . . At once a chill wind blew in. There was no sign of anyone in the midnight streets, and stars glittered ice-cold through the trees in the large house opposite.

Leaving the door as it was, Reiko mounted the stairs. She had walked here and there for some time and her socks were no longer slippery. About halfway up, her nostrils were already assailed by a peculiar smell.

The lieutenant was lying on his face in a sea of blood. The point protruding from his neck seemed to have grown even more prominent than before. Reiko walked heedlessly across the blood. Sitting beside the lieutenant's corpse, she stared intently at the face, which lay on one cheek on the mat. The eyes were opened wide, as if the lieutenant's attention had been attracted by something. She raised the head, folding it in her sleeve, wiped the blood from the lips, and bestowed a last kiss.

Then she rose and took from the closet a new white blanket and a waist cord. To prevent any derangement of her skirts, she wrapped the blanket about her waist and bound it there firmly with the cord.

Reiko sat herself on a spot about one foot distant from the lieutenant's body. Drawing the dagger from her sash, she examined its dully gleaming blade intently, and held it to her tongue. The taste of the polished steel was slightly sweet.

Reiko did not linger. When she thought how the pain which had previously opened such a gulf between herself and her dying husband was now to become a part of her own experience, she saw before her only the joy of herself entering a realm her husband had already made his own. In her husband's agonized face there had been something inexplicable which she was seeing for the first time. Now she would solve that riddle. Reiko sensed that at last she too would be able to taste the true bitterness and sweetness of that great moral principle in which her husband believed. What had until now been tasted only faintly through her husband's example she was about to savor directly with her own tongue.

Reiko rested the point of the blade against the base of her throat. She thrust hard. The wound was only shallow. Her head blazed, and her hands shook uncontrollably. She gave the blade a strong pull sideways. A warm substance flooded into her mouth, and everything before her eyes reddened, in a vision of spouting blood. She gathered her strength and plunged the point of the blade deep into her throat.

[1966]

TRANSLATED BY
GEOFFREY W. SARGENT

QUESTIONS FOR STUDY

1. *What does Mishima gain in exchange for the suspense he throws away by providing a concise synopsis of the story in section one?*

2. *Why is the author so careful to detail the patterns of ritual that dominate the lives of Takeyama and Reiko? Why does he introduce the episode of love-making which directly precedes the couple's suicide? Why does he present such a remarkably detailed picture of the ritual disemboweling? What comment on tradition and ritual is made by each of these scenes?*

3. *What comments does "Patriotism" seem to make about past and present, nature and society, emotion and intellect?*

4. *What is the significance of the story's title? What seems to be the author's attitude toward the kind of patriotism exhibited by Takeyama?*

5. *Is there any indication that the young lieutenant is guilty of self-deception? What is the significance of the fact that Takeyama misinterprets (or, rather, fails to comprehend) Reiko's willingness to die with him?*

6. *What is significant in the fact that Takeyama's suicide is not as neat and precise as the ritual of hari-kiri dictates?*

H. H. MUNRO

Sredni Vashtar

CONRADIN was ten years old, and the doctor had pronounced his professional opinion that the boy would not live another five years. The doctor was silky and effete, and counted for little, but his opinion was endorsed by Mrs. de Ropp, who counted for nearly everything. Mrs. de Ropp was Conradin's cousin and guardian, and in his eyes she represented those three-fifths of the world that are necessary and disagreeable and real; the other two-fifths, in perpetual antagonism to the foregoing, were summed up in himself and his imagination. One of these days Conradin supposed he would succumb to the mastering pressure of wearisome necessary things—such as illnesses and coddling restrictions and drawn-out dullness. Without his imagination, which was rampant under the spur of loneliness, he would have succumbed long ago.

Mrs. de Ropp would never, in her honestest moments, have confessed to herself that she disliked Conradin, though she might have been dimly aware that thwarting him "for his good" was a duty which she did not find particularly irksome. Conradin hated her with a desperate sincerity which he was perfectly able to mask. Such few pleasures as he could contrive for himself gained an added relish from the likelihood that they would be displeasing to his guardian, and from the realm of his imagination she was locked out—an unclean thing, which should find no entrance.

In the dull, cheerless garden, overlooked by so many windows that were ready to open with a message not to do this or that, or a reminder that medicines were due, he found little attraction. The few fruit-trees that it contained were set jealously apart from his plucking, as though they were rare specimens of their kind blooming in an arid waste; it would probably have been difficult to find a market-gardener who would have offered ten shillings for their entire yearly produce. In a forgotten corner, however, almost hidden behind a dismal shrubbery, was a disused tool-shed of respectable proportions, and within its walls Conradin found a haven, something that took on the varying aspects of a playroom and a cathedral. He had peopled it with a legion of familiar phantoms, evoked partly from fragments of history and partly from his own brain, but it also boasted two inmates of flesh and blood. In one corner lived a ragged-plumaged Houdan hen, on which the boy lavished an affection that had scarcely another outlet. Further back in the gloom stood a large hutch, divided into two compartments, one of which was fronted with close iron bars. This was the abode of a large polecat-ferret, which a friendly butcher-boy had once smuggled, cage and all, into its present quarters, in exchange for a long-secreted hoard of small silver. Conradin was dreadfully afraid of the lithe, sharp-fanged beast, but it was his most treasured possession. Its very presence in the tool-shed was a secret and fearful joy, to be kept scrupulously from the knowledge of the Woman, as he privately dubbed his cousin. And one day, out of Heaven knows what material, he spun the beast a wonderful name, and from that moment it grew into a god and a religion. The Woman indulged in religion once a week at a church near by, and took Conradin with her, but to him the church service was an alien rite in the House of Rimmon. Every Thursday, in the dim and musty silence of the tool-shed, he worshipped with mystic and elaborate ceremonial before the wooden hutch where dwelt Sredni Vashtar, the great ferret. Red flowers in their season and scarlet berries in the winter-time were offered at his shrine, for he was a god who laid some special stress on the fierce impatient side of things, as opposed to the Woman's religion, which, as far as Conradin could observe, went to great lengths in the contrary direction. And on great festivals powdered nutmeg was strewn in front of his hutch, an important feature of the offering being that the nutmeg had to be stolen. These festivals were of irregular occurrence, and were chiefly appointed to celebrate some passing event. On one occasion, when Mrs. de Ropp suffered from acute toothache for three days, Conradin kept up the festival during the entire three days, and almost succeeded in persuading himself that Sredni Vashtar was personally responsible for the toothache. If the malady had lasted for another day the supply of nutmeg would have given out.

The Houdan hen was never drawn into the cult of Sredni Vashtar. Conradin had long ago settled that she was an Anabaptist. He did not pretend to have the remotest knowledge as to what an Anabaptist was, but he privately hoped that it was dashing and not very respectable. Mrs. de Ropp was the ground plan on which he based and detested all respectability.

After a while Conradin's absorption in the tool-shed began to attract the notice of his guardian. "It is not good for him to be pottering down there in all weathers," she promptly decided, and at breakfast one morning she announced that the Houdan hen had been sold and taken away overnight. With her short-sighted eyes she peered at Conradin, waiting for an outbreak of rage and sorrow, which she was ready to rebuke with a flow of excellent precepts and reasoning. But Conradin said nothing: there was nothing to be said. Something perhaps in his white set face gave her a momentary qualm, for at tea that afternoon there was toast on the table, a delicacy which she usually banned on the ground that it was bad for him; also because the making of it "gave trouble," a deadly offence in the middle-class feminine eye.

"I thought you liked toast," she exclaimed, with an injured air, observing that he did not touch it.

"Sometimes," said Conradin.

In the shed that evening there was an innovation in the worship of the hutch-god. Conradin had been wont to chant his praises, to-night he asked a boon.

"Do one thing for me, Sredni Vashtar."

The thing was not specified. As Sredni Vashtar was a god he must be supposed to know. And choking back a sob as he looked at that other empty corner, Conradin went back to the world he so hated.

And every night, in the welcome darkness of his bedroom, and every evening in the dusk of the tool-shed, Conradin's bitter litany went up: "Do one thing for me, Sredni Vashtar."

Mrs. de Ropp noticed that the visits to the shed did not cease, and one day she made a further journey of inspection.

"What are you keeping in that locked hutch?" she asked. "I believe it's guinea-pigs. I'll have them all cleared away."

Conradin shut his lips tight, but the Woman ransacked his bedroom till she found the carefully hidden key, and forthwith marched down to the shed to complete her discovery. It was a cold afternoon, and Conradin had been bidden to keep to the house. From the furthest window of the dining-room the door of the shed could just be seen beyond the corner of the shrubbery, and there Conradin stationed himself. He saw the Woman enter, and then he imagined her opening the door of the sacred hutch and peering down with her short-sighted eyes into the thick straw bed where his god lay hidden. Perhaps she would prod at the straw in her clumsy impatience. And Conradin fervently breathed his prayer for the last time. But he knew as he prayed that he did not believe. He knew that the Woman would come out presently with that pursed smile he loathed so well on her face, and that in an hour or two the gardener would carry away his wonderful god, a god no longer, but a simple brown ferret in a hutch. And he knew that the Woman would triumph always as she triumphed now, and that he would grow ever more sickly under her pestering and domineering and superior wisdom, till one day nothing would matter much more with him, and the doctor would be proved right. And in the sting and misery of his defeat, he began to chant loudly and defiantly the hymn of his threatened idol:

Sredni Vashtar went forth,
His thoughts were red thoughts and his teeth were white.
His enemies called for peace, but he brought them death.
Sredni Vashtar the Beautiful.

And then of a sudden he stopped his chanting and drew closer to the window-pane. The door of the shed still stood ajar as it had been left, and the minutes were slipping by. They were long minutes, but they slipped by nevertheless. He watched the starlings running and flying in little parties across the lawn; he counted them over and over again, with one eye always on that swinging door. A sour-faced maid came in to lay the table for tea, and still Conradin stood and waited and watched. Hope had crept by inches into his heart, and now a look of triumph began to blaze in his eyes that had only known the wistful patience of defeat. Under his breath, with a furtive exultation, he began once again the pæan of victory and devastation. And presently his eyes were rewarded: out through that doorway came a long, low, yellow-and-brown beast, with eyes a-blink at the waning daylight, and dark wet stains around the fur of jaws and throat. Conradin dropped on his knees.

The great polecat-ferret made its way down to a small brook at the foot of the garden, drank for a moment, then crossed a little plank bridge and was lost to sight in the bushes. Such was the passing of Sredni Vashtar.

"Tea is ready," said the sour-faced maid; "where is the mistress?"

"She went down to the shed some time ago," said Conradin.

And while the maid went to summon her mistress to tea, Conradin fished a toasting-fork out of the sideboard drawer and proceeded to toast himself a piece of bread. And during the toasting of it and the buttering of it with much butter and the slow enjoyment of eating it, Conradin listened to the noises and silences which fell in quick spasms beyond the dining-room door. The loud foolish screaming of the maid, the answering chorus of wondering ejaculations from the kitchen region, the scuttering footsteps and hurried embassies for outside help, and then, after a lull, the scared sobbings and the shuffling tread of those who bore a heavy burden into the house.

"Whoever will break it to the poor child? I couldn't for the life of me!" exclaimed a shrill voice. And while they debated the matter among themselves, Conradin made himself another piece of toast.

[1911]

QUESTIONS FOR STUDY

1. *Why does Conradin "hate" Mrs. de Ropp and her "flow of excellent precepts and reasoning"? Is his dislike justified? What values does she embody? What contrasting values does Conradin represent? What is his defense against her?*
2. *What is the significance of Mrs. de Ropp's shortsightedness?*
3. *Is Sredni Vashtar really a god? To what extent is he responsible for Mrs. de Ropp's death? Why is her death ironic?*
4. *How does Conradin celebrate his triumph?*
5. *Many recent critics seem inclined to dismiss Munro's stories as "superficial." Does such a verdict seem justified in the case of "Sredni Vashtar"?*

JOYCE CAROL OATES

Four Summers

IT IS SOME kind of special day. "Where's Sissie?" Ma says. Her face gets sharp, she is frightened. When I run around her chair she laughs and hugs me. She is pretty when she laughs. Her hair is long and pretty.

We are sitting at the best table of all, out near the water. The sun is warm and the air smells nice. Daddy is coming back from the building with some glasses of beer, held in his arms. He makes a grunting noise when he sits down.

"Is the lake deep?" I ask them.

They don't hear me, they're talking. A woman and a man are sitting with us. The man marched in the parade we saw just awhile ago; he is a volunteer fireman and is wearing a uniform. Now his shirt is pulled open because it is hot. I can see the dark curly hair way up by his throat; it looks hot and prickly.

A man in a soldier's uniform comes over to us. They are all friends, but I can't remember him. We used to live around here, Ma told me, and then we moved away. The men are laughing. The man in the uniform leans back against the railing, laughing, and I am afraid it will break and he will fall into the water.

"Can we go out in a boat, Dad?" says Jerry.

He and Frank keep running back and forth. I don't want to go with them, I want to stay by Ma. She smells nice. Frank's face is dirty with sweat. "Dad," he says, whining, "can't we go out in a boat? Them kids are going out."

A big lake is behind the building and the open part where we are sitting. Some people are rowing on it. This tavern is noisy and everyone is laughing; it is too noisy for Dad to think about what Frank said.

"Harry," says Ma, "the kids want a boat ride. Why don't you leave off drinking and take them?"

"What?" says Dad.

He looks up from laughing with the men. His face is damp with sweat and he is happy. "Yeah, sure, in a few minutes. Go over there and play and I'll take you out in a few minutes."

The boys run out back by the rowboats, and I run after them. I have a bag of potato chips.

An old man with a white hat pulled down over his forehead is sitting by the boats, smoking. "You kids be careful," he says.

Frank is leaning over and looking at one of the boats. "This here is the best one," he says.

"Why's this one got water in it?" says Jerry.

"You kids watch out. Where's your father?" the man says.

"He's gonna take us for a ride," says Frank.

"Where is he?"

The boys run along, looking at the boats that are tied up. They don't bother with me. The boats are all painted dark green, but the paint is peeling off some of them in little pieces. There is water inside some of them. We watch two people come in, a man and a woman. The woman is giggling. She has on a pink dress and she leans over to trail one finger in the water. "What's all this filthy stuff by the shore?" she says. There is some scum in the water. It is colored a light brown, and there are little seeds and twigs and leaves in it.

The man helps the woman out of the boat. They laugh together. Around their rowboat little waves are still moving; they make a churning noise that I like.

"Where's Dad?" Frank says.

"He ain't coming," says Jerry.

They are tossing pebbles out into the water. Frank throws his sideways, twisting his body. He is ten and very big. "I bet he ain't coming," Jerry says, wiping his nose with the back of his hand.

After awhile we go back to the table. Behind the table is the white railing, and then the water, and then the bank curves out so that the weeping willow trees droop over the water. More men in uniforms, from the parade, are walking by.

"Dad," says Frank, "can't we go out? Can't we? There's a real nice boat there—"

"For Christ's sake, get them off me," Dad says. He is angry with Ma. "Why don't you take them out?"

"Honey, I can't row."

"Should we take out a boat, us two?" the other woman says. She has very short, wet-looking hair. It is curled in tiny little curls close to her head and is very bright. "We'll show them, Lenore. Come on, let's give your kids a ride. Show these guys how strong we are."

"That's all you need, to sink a boat," her husband says.

They all laugh.

The table is filled with brown beer bottles and wrappers of things. I can feel how happy they all are together, drawn together by the round table. I lean against Ma's warm leg and she pats me without looking down. She lunges forward and I can tell even before she says something that she is going to be loud.

"You guys're just jealous! Afraid we'll meet some soldiers!" she says.

"Can't we go out, Dad? Please?" Frank says. "We won't fight. . . ."

"Go and play over there. What're those kids doing—over there?" Dad says, frowning. His face is damp and loose, the way it is sometimes when he drinks. "In a little while, okay? Ask your mother."

"She can't do it," Frank says.

"They're just jealous," Ma says to the other woman, giggling. "They're afraid we might meet somebody somewhere."

"Just who's gonna meet this one here?" the other man says, nodding with his head at his wife.

Frank and Jerry walk away. I stay by Ma. My eyes burn and I want to sleep,

but they won't be leaving for a long time. It is still daylight. When we go home from places like this it is always dark and getting chilly and the grass by our house is wet.

"Duane Dorsey's in jail," Dad says. "You guys heard about that?"

"Duane? Yeah, really?"

"It was in the newspaper. His mother-in-law or somebody called the police, he was breaking windows in her house."

"That Duane was always a nut!"

"Is he out now, or what?"

"I don't know, I don't see him these days. We had a fight," Dad says.

The woman with the short hair looks at me. "She's a real cute little thing," she says, stretching her mouth. "She drink beer, Lenore?"

"I don't know."

"Want some of mine?"

She leans toward me and holds the glass by my mouth. I can smell the beer and the warm stale smell of perfume. There are pink lipstick smudges on the glass.

"Hey, what the hell are you doing?" her husband says.

When he talks rough like that I remember him: we were with him once before.

"Are you swearing at me?" the woman says.

"Leave off the kid, you want to make her a drunk like yourself?"

"It don't hurt, one little sip. . . ."

"It's okay," Ma says. She puts her arm around my shoulders and pulls me closer to the table.

"Let's play cards. Who wants to?" Dad says.

"Sissie wants a little sip, don't you?" the woman says. She is smiling at me and I can see that her teeth are darkish, not nice like Ma's.

"Sure, go ahead," says Ma.

"I said leave off that, Sue, for Christ's sake," the man says. He jerks the table. He is a big man with a thick neck; he is bigger than Dad. His eyebrows are blond, lighter than his hair, and are thick and tufted. Dad is staring at something out on the lake without seeing it. "Harry, look, my goddam wife is trying to make your kid drink beer."

"Who's getting hurt?" Ma says angrily.

Pa looks at me all at once and smiles. "Do you want it, baby?"

I have to say yes. The woman grins and holds the glass down to me, and it clicks against my teeth. They laugh. I stop swallowing right away because it is ugly, and some of the beer drips down on me. "Honey, you're so clumsy," Ma says, wiping me with a napkin.

"She's a real cute girl," the woman says, sitting back in her chair. "I wish I had a nice little girl like that."

"Lay off that," says her husband.

"Hey, did you bring any cards?" Dad says to the soldier.

"They got some inside."

"Look, I'm sick of cards," Ma says.

"Yeah, why don't we all go for a boat ride?" says the woman. "Be real nice, something new. Every time we get together we play cards. How's about a boat ride?"

"It better be a big boat, with you in it," her husband says. He is pleased when everyone laughs, even the woman. The soldier lights a cigarette and laughs. "How come your cousin here's so skinny and you're so fat?"

"She isn't fat," says Ma. "What the hell do you want? Look at yourself."

"Yes, the best days of my life are behind me," the man says. He wipes his face and then presses a beer bottle against it. "Harry, you're lucky you moved out. It's all going downhill, back in the neighborhood."

"You should talk, you let our house look like hell," the woman says. Her face is blotched now, some parts pale and some red. "Harry don't sit out in his back yard all weekend drinking. He gets something done."

"Harry's younger than me."

Ma reaches over and touches Dad's arm. "Harry, why don't you take the kids out? Before it gets dark."

Dad lifts his glass and finishes his beer. "Who else wants more?" he says.

"I'll get them, you went last time," the soldier says.

"Get a chair for yourself," says Dad. "We can play poker."

"I don't want to play poker, I want to play rummy," the woman says.

"At church this morning Father Reilly was real mad," says Ma. "He said some kids or somebody was out in the cemetery and left some beer bottles. Isn't that awful?"

"Duane Dorsey used to do worse than that," the man says, winking.

"Hey, who's that over there?"

"You mean that fat guy?"

"Isn't that the guy at the lumberyard that owes all that money?"

Dad turns around. His chair wobbles and he almost falls; he is angry.

"This goddamn place is too crowded," he says.

"This is a real nice place," the woman says. She is taking something out of her purse. "I always liked it, didn't you, Lenore?"

"Sue and me used to come here a lot," says Ma. "And not just with you two, either."

"Yeah, we're real jealous," the man says.

"You should be," says the woman.

The soldier comes back. Now I can see that he is really a boy. He runs to the table with the beer before he drops anything. He laughs.

"Jimmy, your ma wouldn't like to see you drinking!" the woman says happily.

"Well, she ain't here."

"Are they still living out in the country?" Ma says to the woman.

"Sure. No electricity, no running water, no bathroom—same old thing. What can you do with people like that?"

"She always talks about going back to the Old Country," the soldier says. "Thinks she can save up money and go back."

"Poor old bastards don't know there was a war," Dad says. He looks as if something tasted bad in his mouth. "My old man died thinking he could go back in a year or two. Stupid old bastards!"

"Your father was real nice. . . ." Ma says.

"Yeah, real nice," says Dad. "Better off dead."

Everybody is quiet.

"June Dieter's mother's got the same thing," the woman says in a low voice to Ma. "She's had it a year now and don't weigh a hundred pounds—you remember how big she used to be."

"She was big, all right," Ma says.

"Remember how she ran after June and slapped her? We were there—some guys were driving us home."

"Yeah. So she's got it too."

"Hey," says Dad, "why don't you get a chair, Jimmy? Sit down here."

The soldier looks around. His face is raw in spots, broken out. But his eyes are nice. He never looks at me.

"Get a chair from that table," Dad says.

"Those people might want it."

"Hell, just take it. Nobody's sitting on it."

"They might—"

Dad reaches around and yanks the chair over. The people look at him but don't say anything. Dad is breathing hard. "Here, sit here," he says. The soldier sits down.

Frank and Jerry come back. They stand by Dad, watching him. "Can we go out now? Frank says.

"What?"

"Out for a boat ride."

"What? No, next week. Do it next week. We're going to play cards."

"You said—"

"Shut up, we'll do it next week." Dad looks up and shades his eyes. "The lake don't look right anyway."

"Lot's of people are out there—"

"I said shut up."

"Honey," Ma whispers, "let him alone. Go and play by yourselves."

"Can we sit in the car?"

"Okay, but don't honk the horn."

"Ma, can't we go for a ride?"

"Go and play by yourselves, stop bothering us," she says. "Hey, will you take Sissie?"

They look at me. They don't like me, I can see it, but they take me with them. We run through the crowd and somebody spills a drink—he yells at us. "Oops, got to watch it!" Frank giggles.

We run along the walk by the boat. A woman in a yellow dress is carrying a baby. She looks at us like she doesn't like us.

Down at the far end some kids are standing together.

"Hey, lookit that," Frank says.

A blackbird is caught in the scum, by one of the boats. It can't fly up. One of the kids, a long-legged girl in a dirty dress, is poking at it with a stick.

The bird's wings keep fluttering but it can't get out. If it could get free it would fly and be safe, but the scum holds it down.

One of the kids throws a stone at it. "Stupid old goddamn bird," somebody says. Frank throws a stone. They are all throwing stones. The bird doesn't know enough to turn away. Its feathers are all wet and dirty. One of the stones hits the bird's head.

"Take that!" Frank says, throwing a rock. The water splashes up and some of the girls scream.

I watch them throwing stones. I am standing at the side. If the bird dies, then everything can die, I think. Inside the tavern there is music from the jukebox.

II

We are at the boathouse tavern again. It is a mild day, a Sunday afternoon. Dad is talking with some men; Jerry and I are waiting by the boats. Mommy is at home with the new baby. Frank has gone off with some friends of his, to a stock-car race. There are some people here, sitting out at the tables, but they don't notice us.

"Why doesn't he hurry up?" Jerry says.

Jerry is twelve now. He has pimples on his forehead and chin.

He pushes one of the rowboats with his foot. He is wearing sneakers that are dirty. I wish I could get in that boat and sit down, but I am afraid. A boy not much older than Jerry is squatting on the boardwalk, smoking. You can tell he is in charge of the boats.

"Daddy, come on. Come on," Jerry says, whining. Daddy can't hear him.

I have mosquito bites on my arms and legs. There are mosquitoes and flies around here; the flies crawl around the sticky mess left on tables. A car over in the parking lot has its radio on loud. You can hear the music all this way. "He's coming," I tell Jerry so he won't be mad. Jerry is like Dad, the way his eyes look.

"Oh, that fat guy keeps talking to him," Jerry says.

The fat man is one of the bartenders;

he has on a dirty white apron. All these men are familiar. We have been seeing them for years. He punches Dad's arm, up by the shoulder, and Dad pushes him. They are laughing, though. Nobody is mad.

"I'd sooner let a nigger—" the bartender says. We can't hear anything more, but the men laugh again.

"All he does is drink," Jerry says. "I hate him."

At school, up on the sixth-grade floor, Jerry got in trouble last month. The principal slapped him. I am afraid to look at Jerry when he's mad.

"I hate him, I wish he'd die," Jerry says.

Dad is trying to come to us, but every time he takes a step backward and gets ready to turn, one of the men says something. There are three men beside him. Their stomachs are big, but Dad's isn't. He is wearing dark pants and a white shirt; his tie is in the car. He wears a tie to church, then takes it off. He has his shirt sleeves rolled up and you can see how strong his arms must be.

Two women cross over from the parking lot. They are wearing high-heeled shoes and hats and bright dresses—orange and yellow—and when they walk past the men look at them. They go into the tavern. The men laugh about something. The way they laugh makes my eyes focus on something away from them—a bird flying in the sky—and it is hard for me to look anywhere else. I feel as if I'm falling asleep.

"Here he comes!" Jerry says.

Dad walks over to us, with his big steps. He is smiling and carrying a bottle of beer. "Hey, kid," he says to the boy squatting on the walk, "how's about a boat?"

"This one is the best," Jerry says.

"The best, huh? Great." Dad grins at us. "Okay, Sissie, let's get you in. Be careful now." He picks me up even though I am too heavy for it, and sets me in the boat. It hurts a little where he held me, under the arms, but I don't care.

Jerry climbs in. Dad steps and something happens—he almost slips, but he catches himself. With the wet oar he pushes us off from the boardwalk.

Dad can row fast. The sunlight is gleaming on the water. I sit very still, facing him, afraid to move. The boat goes fast, and Dad is leaning back and forth and pulling on the oars, breathing hard, doing everything fast like he always does. He is always in a hurry to get things done. He has set the bottle of beer down by his leg, pressed against the side of the boat so it won't fall.

"There's the guys we saw go out before," Jerry says. Coming around the island is a boat with three boys in it, older than Jerry. "They went on the island. Can we go there too?"

"Sure," says Dad. His eyes squint in the sun. He is suntanned, and there are freckles on his forehead. I am sitting close to him, facing him, and it surprises me what he looks like—he is like a stranger, with his eyes narrowed. The water beneath the boat makes me feel funny. It keeps us up now, but if I fell over the side I would sink and drown.

"Nice out here, huh?" Dad says. He is breathing hard.

"We should go over that way to get on the island," Jerry says.

"This goddamn oar has splinters in it," Dad says. He hooks the oar up and lets us glide. He reaches down to get the bottle of beer. Though the lake and some trees and the buildings back on shore are in front of me, what makes me look at it is my father's throat, the way it bobs when he swallows. He wipes his forehead. "Want to row, Sissie?" he says.

"Can I?"

"Let me do it," says Jerry.

"Naw, I was just kidding," Dad says.

"I can do it. It ain't hard."

"Stay where you are," Dad says.

He starts rowing again, faster. Why does he go so fast? His face is getting red, the way it does at home when he has trouble with Frank. He clears his throat and spits over the side; I don't like to see that but I can't help but watch. The other boat glides past us, heading for shore. The boys don't look over at us.

Jerry and I look to see if anyone else is on the island, but no one is. The island is very small. You can see around it.

"Are you going to land on it, Dad?" Jerry says.

"Sure, okay." Dad's face is flushed and looks angry.

The boat scrapes bottom and bumps. "Jump out and pull it in," Dad says. Jerry jumps out. His shoes and socks are wet now, but Dad doesn't notice. The boat bumps; it hurts me. I am afraid. But then we're up on the land and Dad is out and lifting me. "Nice ride, sugar?" he says.

Jerry and I run around the island. It is different from what we thought, but we don't know why. There are some trees on it, some wild grass, and then bare caked mud that goes down to the water. The water looks dark and deep on the other side, but when we get there it's shallow. Lily pads grow there; everything is thick and tangled. Jerry wades in the water and gets his pants legs wet. "There might be money in the water," he says.

Some napkins and beer cans are nearby. There is part of a hotdog bun, with flies buzzing around it.

When we go back by Dad, we see him squatting over the water doing something. His back jerks. Then I see that he is being sick. He is throwing up in the water and making a noise like coughing.

Jerry turns around right away and runs back. I follow him, afraid. On the other side we can look back at the boathouse and wish we were there.

III

Marian and Betty went to the show, but I couldn't. She made me come along here with them. "And cut out that snippy face," Ma said, to let me know she's watching. I have to help her take care of Linda—poor fat Linda, with her runny nose! So here we are inside the tavern. There's too much smoke, I hate smoke. Dad is smoking a cigar. I won't drink any more root beer, it's flat, and I'm sick of potato chips. Inside me there is something that wants to run away, that hates them. How loud they are, my parents! My mother spilled something on the front of her dress, but does she notice? And my aunt Lucy and uncle Joe, they're here. Try to avoid them. Lucy has false teeth that make everyone stare at her. I know that everyone is staring at us. I could hide my head in my arms and turn away, I'm

so tired and my legs hurt from sunburn and I can't stand them any more.

"So did you ever hear from them? That letter you wrote?" Ma says to Lucy.

"I'm still waiting. Somebody said you got to have connections to get on the show. But I don't believe it. That Howie Masterson that's the emcee, he's a real nice guy. I can tell."

"It's all crap," Dad says. "You women believe anything."

"I don't believe it," I say.

"Phony as hell," says my uncle.

"You do too believe it, Sissie," says my mother. "Sissie thinks he's cute. I know she does."

"I hate that guy!" I tell her, but she and my aunt are laughing. "I said I hate him! He's greasy."

"All that stuff is phony as hell," says my Uncle Joe. He is tired all the time, and right now he sits with his head bowed. I hate his bald head with the little fringe of gray hair on it. At least my father is still handsome. His jaws sag and there are lines in his neck—edged with dirt, I can see, embarrassed—and his stomach is bulging a little against the table, but still he is a handsome man. In a place like this women look at him. What's he see in *her?* they think. My mother had her hair cut too short last time; she looks queer. There is a photograph taken of her when she was young, standing by someone's motorcycle, with her hair long. In the photograph she was pretty, almost beautiful, but I don't believe it. Not really. I can't believe it, and I hate her. Her forehead gathers itself up in little wrinkles whenever she glances down at Linda, as if she can't remember who Linda is.

"Well, nobody wanted you, kid," she once said to Linda. Linda was a baby then, one year old. Ma was furious, standing in the kitchen where she was washing the floor, screaming: "Nobody wanted you, it was a goddamn accident! An accident!" That surprised me so I didn't know what to think, and I didn't know if I hated Ma or not; but I kept it all a secret . . . only my girl friends know, and I won't tell the priest either. Nobody can make me tell. I narrow my eyes and watch my mother leaning forward to say something—it's like she's going to toss something out on the table—and think that maybe she isn't my mother after all, and she isn't that pretty girl in the photograph, but someone else.

"A woman was on the show last night that lost two kids in a fire. Her house burned down," my aunt says loudly. "And she answered the questions right off and got a lot of money and the audience went wild. You could see she was a real lady. I love that guy, Howie Masterson. He's real sweet."

"He's a bastard," Dad says.

"Harry, what the hell? You never even seen him," Ma says.

"I sure as hell never did. Got better things to do at night." Dad turns to my uncle and his voice changes. "I'm on the night shift, now."

"Yeah, I hate that, I—"

"I can sleep during the day. What's the difference?"

"I hate those night shifts."

"What's there to do during the day?" Dad says flatly. His eyes scan us at the table as if he doesn't see anything, then they seem to fall off me and go behind me, looking at nothing.

"Not much," says my uncle, and I can see his white scalp beneath his hair. Both men are silent.

Dad pours beer into his glass and spills some of it. I wish I could look away. I love him, I think, but I hate to be here. Where would I rather be? With Marian and Betty at the movies, or in my room, lying on the bed and staring at the photographs of movie stars on my walls—those beautiful people that never say anything —while out in the kitchen my mother is waiting for my father to come home so they can continue their quarrel. It never stops, that quarrel. Sometimes they laugh together, kid around, they kiss. Then the quarrel starts up again in a few minutes.

"Ma, can I go outside and wait in the car?" I say. "Linda's asleep."

"What's so hot about the car?" she says, looking at me.

"I'm tired. My sunburn hurts."

Linda is sleeping in Ma's lap, with her mouth open and drooling on the front of her dress. "Okay, go on," Ma says. "But we're not going to hurry just for you." When she has drunk too much there is a struggle in her between being angry and being affectionate; she fights both of them, as if standing with her legs apart and her hands on her hips, bracing a strong wind.

When I cross through the crowded tavern I'm conscious of people looking at me. My hair lost its curl because it was so humid today, my legs are too thin, my figure is flat and not nice like Marian's— I want to hide somewhere, hide my face from them. I hate this noisy place and these people. Even the music is ugly because it belongs to them. Then, when I'm outside, the music gets faint right away and it doesn't sound so bad. It's cooler out here. No one is around. Out back, the old rowboats are tied up. Nobody's on the lake. There's no moon, the sky is overcast, it was raining earlier.

When I turn around, a man is standing by the door watching me.

"What're you doing?" he says.

"Nothing."

He has dark hair and a tanned face, I think, but everything is confused because the light from the door is pinkish—there's a neon sign there. My heart starts to pound. The man leans forward to stare at me. "Oh, I thought you were somebody else," he says.

I want to show him I'm not afraid. "Yeah, really? Who did you think I was?" When we ride on the school bus we smile out the windows at strange men, just for fun. We do that all the time. I'm not afraid of any of them.

"You're not her," he says.

Some people come out the door and he has to step out of their way. I say to him, "Maybe you seen me around here before. We come here pretty often."

"Who do you come with?" He is smiling as if he thinks I'm funny. "Anybody I know?"

"That's my business."

It's a game. I'm not afraid. When I think of my mother and father inside, something makes me want to step closer to this man—why should I be afraid? I could be wild like some of the other girls. Nothing surprises me.

We keep on talking. At first I can tell he wants me to come inside the tavern with him, but then he forgets about it; he keeps talking. I don't know what we say, but we talk in drawling voices, smiling at each other but in a secret, knowing way, as if each one of us knew more than the other. My cheeks start to burn. I could be wild like Betty is sometimes—like some of the other girls. Why not? Once before I talked with a man like this, on the bus. We were both sitting in the back. I wasn't afraid. This man and I keep talking and we talk about nothing, he wants to know how old I am, but it makes my heart pound so hard that I want to touch my chest to calm it. We are walking along the old boardwalk and I say: "Somebody took me out rowing once here."

"Is that so?" he says. "You want me to take you out?"

He has a hard, handsome face. I like that face. Why is he alone? When he smiles I know he's laughing at me, and this makes me stand taller, walk with my shoulders raised.

"Hey, are you with somebody inside there?" he says.

"I left them."

"Have a fight?"

"A fight, yes."

He looks at me quickly. "How old are you anyway?"

"That's none of your business."

"Girls your age are all alike."

"We're not all alike!" I arch my back and look at him in a way I must have learned somewhere—where?—with my lips not smiling but ready to smile, and my eyes narrowed. One leg is turned as if I'm ready to jump from him. He sees all this. He smiles.

"Say, you're real cute."

We're walking over by the parking lot now. He touches my arm. Right away my heart trips, but I say nothing, I keep walking. High above us the tree branches are moving in the wind. It's cold for June. It's late—after eleven. The man is wearing a jacket, but I have on a sleeveless dress and there are goose-pimples on my arms.

"Cold, huh?" he says.

He takes hold of my shoulders and leans toward me. This is to show me he's no kid, he's grown-up, this is how they do things; when he kisses me his grip on my shoulders gets tighter. "I better go back," I say to him. My voice is queer.

"What?" he says.

I am wearing a face like one of those faces pinned up in my room, and what if I lose it? This is not my face. I try to turn away from him.

He kisses me again. His breath smells like beer, maybe, it's like my father's breath, and my mind is empty; I can't think what to do. Why am I here? My legs feel numb, my fingers are cold. The man rubs my arms and says, "You should have a sweater or something. . . ."

He is waiting for me to say something, to keep on the way I was before. But I have forgotten how to do it. Before, I was Marian or one of the older girls; now I am just myself. I am fourteen. I think of Linda sleeping in my mother's lap, and something frightens me.

"Hey, what's wrong?" the man says.

He sees I'm afraid but pretends he doesn't. He comes to me again and embraces me, his mouth presses against my neck and shoulder, I feel as if I'm suffocating. "My car's over here," he says, trying to catch his breath. I can't move. Something dazzling and icy rises up in me, an awful fear, but I can't move and can't say anything. He is touching me with his hands. His mouth is soft but wants too much from me. I think, What is he doing? Do they all do this? Do I have to have it done to me too?

"You cut that out," I tell him.

He steps away. His chest is heaving and his eyes look like a dog's eyes, surprised and betrayed. The last thing I see of him is those eyes, before I turn and run back to the tavern.

IV

Jesse says, "Let's stop at this place. I been here a few times before."

It's the Lakeside Bar. That big old building with the grubby siding, and a big pink neon sign in front, and the cinder driveway that's so bumpy. Yes, everything the same. But different too—smaller, dirtier. There is a custard stand nearby with a glaring orange roof, and people are crowded around it. That's new. I haven't been here for years.

"I feel like a beer," he says.

He smiles at me and caresses my arm.

He treats me as if I were something that might break; in my cheap linen maternity dress I feel ugly and heavy. My flesh is so soft and thick that nothing could hurt it.

"Sure, honey. Pa used to stop in here too."

We cross through the parking lot to the tavern. Wild grass grows along the sidewalk and in the cracks of the sidewalk. Why is this place so ugly to me? I feel as if a hand were pressing against my chest, shutting off my breath. Is there some secret here? Why am I afraid?

I catch sight of myself in a dusty window as we pass. My hair is long, down to my shoulders. I am pretty, but my secret is that I am pretty like everyone is. My husband loves me for this but doesn't know it. I have a pink mouth and plucked darkened eyebrows and soft bangs over my forehead; I know everything, I have no need to learn from anyone else now. I am one of those girls younger girls study closely, to learn from. On buses, in five-and-tens, thirteen-year-old girls must look at me solemnly, learning, memorizing.

"Pretty Sissie!" my mother likes to say when we visit, though I told her how I hate that name. She is proud of me for being pretty, but thinks I'm too thin. "You'll fill out nice, after the baby," she says. Herself, she is fat and veins have begun to darken on her legs; she scuffs around the house in bedroom slippers. Who is my mother? When I think of her I can't think of anything—do I love her or hate her, or is there nothing there?

Jesse forgets and walks ahead of me, I have to walk fast to catch up. I'm wearing pastel-blue high heels—that must be because I am proud of my legs. I have little else. Then he remembers and turns to put out his hand for me, smiling to show he is sorry. Jesse is the kind of young man thirteen-year-old girls stare at secretly; he is not a man, not old enough, but not a boy either. He is a year older than I am, twenty. When I met him he was wearing a navy uniform and he was with a girl friend of mine.

Just a few people sitting outside at the tables. They're afraid of rain—the sky doesn't look good. And how bumpy the ground is here, bare spots and little holes and patches of crab grass, and every-where napkins and junk. Too many flies outside. Has this place changed hands? The screens at the window don't fit right; you can see why flies get inside. Jesse opens the door for me and I go in. All bars smell alike. There is a damp, dark odor of beer and something indefinable—spilled soft drinks, pretzels getting stale? This bar is just like any other. Before we were married we went to places like this, Jesse and me and other couples. We had to spend a certain amount of time doing things like that—and going to movies, playing miniature golf, bowling, dancing, swimming—then we got married, now we're going to have a baby. I think of the baby all the time, because my life will be changed then; everything will be different. Four months from now. I should be frightened, but a calm laziness has come over me. It was so easy for my mother. . . . But it will be different with me because my life will be changed by it, and nothing ever changed my mother. You couldn't change her! Why should I think? Why should I be afraid? My body is filled with love for this baby, and I will never be the same again.

We sit down at a table near the bar. Jesse is in a good mood. My father would have liked him, I think; when he laughs Jesse reminds me of him. Why is a certain kind of simple, healthy, honest man always destined to lose everything? Their souls are as clean and smooth as the muscular line of their arms. At night I hold Jesse, thinking of my father and what happened to him—all that drinking, then the accident at the factory—and I pray that Jesse will be different. I hope that his quick, open, loud way of talking is just a disguise, that really he is someone else—slower and calculating. That kind of man grows old without jerks and spasms. Why did I marry Jesse?

Someone at the bar turns around, and it's a man I think I know—I have known. Yes. That man outside, the man I met outside. I stare at him, my heart pounding, and he doesn't see me. He is dark, his hair is neatly combed but is thinner than before; he is wearing a cheap gray suit. But is it the same man? He is standing with a friend and looking around, as if he doesn't like what he sees. He is tired too. He has grown years older.

Our eyes meet. He glances away. He doesn't remember—that frightened girl he held in his arms.

I am tempted to put my hand on Jesse's arm and tell him about that man, but how can I? Jesse is talking about trading in our car for a new one. . . . I can't move, my mind seems to be coming to a stop. Is that the man I kissed, or someone else? A feeling of angry loss comes over me. Why should I lose everything? Everything? Is it the same man, and would he remember? My heart bothers me, it's stupid to be like this: here I sit, powdered and sweet, a girl safely married, pregnant and secured to the earth, with my husband beside me. He still loves me. Our love keeps on. Like my parents' love, it will subside someday, but nothing surprises me because I have learned everything.

The man turns away, talking to his friend. They are weary, tired of something. He isn't married yet, I think, and that pleases me. Good. But why are these men always tired? Is it the jobs they hold, the kind of men who stop in at this tavern? Why do they flash their teeth when they smile, but stop smiling so quickly? Why do their children cringe from them sometimes—an innocent upraised arm a frightening thing? Why do they grow old so quickly, sitting at kitchen tables with bottles of beer? They are everywhere, in every house. All the houses in this neighborhood and all neighborhoods around here. Jesse is young, but the outline of what he will be is already in his face; do you think I can't see it? Their lives are like hands dealt out to them in their innumerable card games. You pick up the sticky cards, and there it is: there it is. Can't change anything, all you can do is switch some cards around, stick one in here, one over here . . . pretend there is some sense, a secret scheme.

The man at the bar tosses some coins down and turns to go. I want to cry out to him, "Wait, wait!" But I cannot. I sit helplessly and watch him leave. Is it the same man? If he leaves I will be caught here, what can I do? I can almost hear my mother's shrill laughter coming in from outside, and some drawling remark of my father's—lifting for a moment above the music. Those little explosions of laughter, the slap of someone's hand on the damp table in anger, the clink of bottles accidentally touching—and there, there, my drunken aunt's voice, what is she saying? I am terrified at being left with them. I watch the man at the door and think that I could have loved him. I know it.

He has left, he and his friend. He is nothing to me, but suddenly I feel tears in my eyes. What's wrong with me? I hate everything that springs upon me and seems to draw itself down and oppress me in a way I could never explain to anyone. . . . I am crying because I am pregnant, but not with that man's child. It could have been his child, I could have gone with him to his car; but I did nothing, I ran away, I was afraid, and now I'm sitting here with Jesse, who is picking the label off his beer bottle with his thick squarish fingernails. I did nothing. I was afraid. Now he has left me here and what can I do?

I let my hand fall onto my stomach to remind myself that I am in love: with this baby, with Jesse, with everything. I am in love with our house and our life and the future and even this moment—right now—that I am struggling to live through.

[1967]

QUESTIONS FOR STUDY

1. *What similarities and differences exist in each of the four episodes? What changes take place? What remains the same?*

2. *How does the author organize each of the four sections? How old is Sissie in each? Is Oates' narrative technique in each section appropriate to Sissie's age and stage in life?*

3. *How do Sissie's responses to men and women change? What new awareness and widened understanding does she achieve as the story*

advances? How is her intuition of death and loss in the first episode
reinforced and expanded upon in the final three?

4. *What does Sissie come to realize about herself, her marriage, and her*
   life in the final episode? What does she mean when she says, "I am
   pretty, but my secret is that I am pretty like everyone is"? How does
   she rationalize her sudden fear? Why does she react so strongly to
   the men at the bar? What are the implications of the story's final
   sentence?

FLANNERY O'CONNOR

The Artificial Nigger

MR. HEAD awakened to discover that the room was full of moonlight. He sat up and stared at the floor boards—the color of silver—and then at the ticking on his pillow, which might have been brocade, and after a second, he saw half of the moon five feet away in his shaving mirror, paused as if it were waiting for his permission to enter. It rolled forward and cast a dignifying light on everything. The straight chair against the wall looked stiff and attentive as if it were awaiting an order and Mr. Head's trousers, hanging to the back of it, had an almost noble air, like the garment some great man had just flung to his servant; but the face on the moon was a grave one. It gazed across the room and out the window where it floated over the horsestall and appeared to contemplate itself with the look of a young man who sees his old age before him.

Mr. Head could have said to it that age was a choice blessing and that only with years does a man enter into that calm understanding of life that makes him a suitable guide for the young. This, at least, had been his own experience.

He sat up and grasped the iron posts at the foot of his bed and raised himself until he could see the face on the alarm clock which sat on an overturned bucket beside the chair. The hour was two in the morning. The alarm on the clock did not work but he was not dependent on any mechanical means to awaken him. Sixty years had not dulled his responses; his physical reactions, like his moral ones, were guided by his will and strong character, and these could be seen plainly in his features. He had a long tube-like face with a long rounded open jaw and a long depressed nose. His eyes were alert but quiet, and in the miraculous moonlight they had a look of composure and of ancient wisdom as if they belonged to one of the great guides of men. He might have been Vergil summoned in the middle of the night to go to Dante, or better, Raphael, awakened by a blast of God's light to fly to the side of Tobias. The only dark spot in the room was Nelson's pallet, underneath the shadow of the window.

Nelson was hunched over on his side, his knees under his chin and his heels under his bottom. His new suit and hat were in the boxes that they had been sent in and these were on the floor at the foot of the pallet where he could get his hands on them as soon as he woke up. The slop jar, out of the shadow and made snow-white in the moonlight, appeared to stand guard over him like a small personal angel. Mr. Head lay back down, feeling entirely confident that he could carry out the moral mission of the coming day. He meant to be up before Nelson and to have the breakfast cooking by the time he awakened. The boy was always irked when Mr. Head was the first up. They would have to leave the house at four to get to the railroad junction by five-thirty. The train was to stop for them at five forty-five and they had to be there on time for this train was stopping merely to accommodate them.

This would be the boy's first trip to the city though he claimed it would be his second because he had been born there. Mr. Head had tried to point out to him that when he was born he didn't have the intelligence to determine his whereabouts but this had made no impression on the child at all and he continued to insist that this was to be his second trip. It would be Mr. Head's third trip. Nelson had said, "I will've already been there twice and I ain't but ten."

Mr. Head had contradicted him.

"If you ain't been there in fifteen years, how you know you'll be able to find your way about?" Nelson had asked. "How you know it hasn't changed some?"

"Have you ever," Mr. Head had asked, "seen me lost?"

Nelson certainly had not but he was a child who was never satisfied until he had given an impudent answer and he replied, "It's nowhere around here to get lost at."

"The day is going to come," Mr. Head prophesied, "when you'll find you ain't as smart as you think you are." He had been thinking about this trip for several months but it was for the most part in moral terms that he conceived it. It was to be a lesson that the boy would never forget. He was to find out from it that he had no cause for pride merely because he had been born in a city. He was to find out that the city is not a great place. Mr. Head meant him to see everything there is to see in a city so that he would be content to stay at home for the rest of his life. He fell asleep thinking how the boy would at last find out that he was not as smart as he thought he was.

He was awakened at three-thirty by the smell of fatback frying and he leaped off his cot. The pallet was empty and the clothes boxes had been thrown open. He put on his trousers and ran into the other room. The boy had a corn pone on cooking and had fried the meat. He was sitting in the half-dark at the table, drinking cold coffee out of a can. He had on his new suit and his new gray hat pulled low over his eyes. It was too big for him but they had ordered it a size large because they expected his head to grow. He didn't say anything but his entire figure suggested satisfaction at having arisen before Mr. Head.

Mr. Head went to the stove and brought the meat to the table in the skillet. "It's no hurry," he said. "You'll get there soon enough and its no guarantee you'll like it when you do neither," and he sat down across from the boy whose hat teetered back slowly to reveal a fiercely expressionless face, very much the same shape as the old man's. They were grandfather and grandson but they looked enough alike to be brothers and brothers not too far apart in age, for Mr. Head had a youthful expression by daylight, while the boy's look was ancient, as if he knew everything already and would be pleased to forget it.

Mr. Head had once had a wife and daughter and when the wife died, the daughter ran away and returned after an interval with Nelson. Then one morning, without getting out of bed, she died and left Mr. Head with sole care of the year-old child. He had made the mistake of telling Nelson that he had been born in Atlanta. If he hadn't told him that, Nelson couldn't have insisted that this was going to be his second trip.

"You may not like it a bit," Mr. Head continued. "It'll be full of niggers."

The boy made a face as if he could handle a nigger.

"All right," Mr. Head said. "You ain't ever seen a nigger."

"You wasn't up very early," Nelson said.

"You ain't ever seen a nigger," Mr. Head repeated. "There hasn't been a nigger in this county since we run that one out twelve years ago and that was before you were born." He looked at the boy as if he were daring him to say he had ever seen a Negro.

"How you know I never saw a nigger when I lived there before?" Nelson asked. "I probably saw a lot of niggers."

"If you seen one you didn't know what he was," Mr. Head said, completely exasperated. "A six-month-old child don't know a nigger from anybody else."

"I reckon I'll know a nigger if I see one," the boy said and got up and straightened his slick sharply creased gray hat and went outside to the privy.

They reached the junction some time before the train was due to arrive and stood about two feet from the first set of tracks. Mr. Head carried a paper sack with some biscuits and a can of sardines in it for their lunch. A coarse-looking orange-colored sun coming up behind the east range of mountains was making the sky a dull red behind them, but in front of them it was still gray and they faced a gray transparent moon, hardly stronger than a thumbprint and completely without light. A small tin switch box and a black fuel tank were all there was to mark the place as a junction; the tracks were double and did not converge again until they were hidden behind the bends at either end of the clearing. Trains passing appeared to emerge from a tunnel of trees and, hit for a second by the cold sky, vanish terrified into the woods again. Mr. Head had had to make special arrangements with the ticket agent to have this train stop and he was secretly afraid it would not, in which case, he knew Nelson would say, "I never thought no train was going to stop for you." Under the useless morning moon the tracks looked white and fragile. Both the old man and the child stared ahead as if they were awaiting an apparition.

Then suddenly, before Mr. Head could make up his mind to turn back, there was a deep warning bleat and the train appeared, gliding very slowly, almost silently around the bend of trees about two hundred yards down the track, with one yellow front light shining. Mr. Head was still not certain it would stop and he felt it would make an even bigger idiot of him if it went by slowly. Both he and Nelson, however, were prepared to ignore the train if it passed them.

The engine charged by, filling their noses with the smell of hot metal and then the second coach came to a stop exactly where they were standing. A conductor with the face of an ancient bloated bulldog was on the step as if he expected them, though he did not look as if it mattered one way or the other to him if they got on or not. "To the right," he said.

Their entry took only a fraction of a second and the train was already speeding on as they entered the quiet car. Most of the travelers were still sleeping, some with their heads hanging off the chair arms, some stretched across two seats, and some sprawled out with their feet in the aisle. Mr. Head saw two unoccupied seats and pushed Nelson toward them. "Get in there by the winder," he said in his normal voice which was very loud at this hour of the morning. "Nobody cares if

you sit there because it's nobody in it. Sit right there."

"I heard you," the boy muttered. "It's no use in you yelling," and he sat down and turned his head to the glass. There he saw a pale ghost-like face scowling at him beneath the brim of a pale ghost-like hat. His grandfather, looking quickly too, saw a different ghost, pale but grinning, under a black hat.

Mr. Head sat down and settled himself and took out his ticket and started reading aloud everything that was printed on it. People began to stir. Several woke up and stared at him. "Take off your hat," he said to Nelson and took off his own and put it on his knee. He had a small amount of white hair that had turned tobacco-colored over the years and this lay flat across the back of his head. The front of his head was bald and creased. Nelson took off his hat and put it on his knee and they waited for the conductor to come ask for their tickets.

The man across the aisle from them was spread out over two seats, his feet propped on the window and his head jutting into the aisle. He had on a light blue suit and a yellow shirt unbuttoned at the neck. His eyes had just opened and Mr. Head was ready to introduce himself when the conductor came up from behind and growled, "Tickets."

When the conductor had gone, Mr. Head gave Nelson the return half of his ticket and said, "Now put that in your pocket and don't lose it or you'll have to stay in the city."

"Maybe I will," Nelson said as if this were a reasonable suggestion.

Mr. Head ignored him. "First time this boy has ever been on a train," he explained to the man across the aisle, who was sitting up now on the edge of his seat with both feet on the floor.

Nelson jerked his hat on again and turned angrily to the window.

"He's never seen anything before," Mr. Head continued. "Ignorant as the day he was born, but I mean for him to get his fill once and for all."

The boy leaned forward, across his grandfather and toward the stranger. "I was born in the city," he said. "I was born there. This is my second trip." He said it in a high positive voice but the man across the aisle didn't look as if he understood. There were heavy purple circles under his eyes.

Mr. Head reached across the aisle and tapped him on the arm. "The thing to do with a boy," he said sagely, "is to show him all it is to show. Don't hold nothing back."

"Yeah," the man said. He gazed down at his swollen feet and lifted the left one about ten inches from the floor. After a minute he put it down and lifted the other. All through the car people began to get up and move about and yawn and stretch. Separate voices could be heard here and there and then a general hum. Suddenly Mr. Head's serene expression changed. His mouth almost closed and a light, fierce and cautious both, came into his eyes. He was looking down the length of the car. Without turning, he caught Nelson by the arm and pulled him forward. "Look," he said.

A huge coffee-colored man was coming slowly forward. He had on a light suit and a yellow satin tie with a ruby pin in it. One of his hands rested on his stomach which rode majestically under his buttoned coat, and in the other he held the head of a black walking stick that he picked up and set down with a deliberate outward motion each time he took a step. He was proceeding very slowly, his large brown eyes gazing over the heads of the passengers. He had a small white mustache and white crinkly hair. Behind him there were two young women, both coffee-colored, one in a yellow dress and one in a green. Their progress was kept at the rate of his and they chatted in low throaty voices as they followed him.

Mr. Head's grip was tightening insistently on Nelson's arm. As the procession passed them, the light from a sapphire ring on the brown hand that picked up the cane reflected in Mr. Head's eye, but he did not look up nor did the tremendous man look at him. The group proceeded up the rest of the aisle and out of the car. Mr. Head's grip on Nelson's arm loosened. "What was that?" he asked.

"A man," the boy said and gave him an indignant look as if he were tired of having his intelligence insulted.

"What kind of a man?" Mr. Head persisted, his voice expressionless.

"A fat man," Nelson said. He was beginning to feel that he had better be cautious.

"You don't know what kind?" Mr. Head said in a final tone.

"An old man," the boy said and had a sudden foreboding that he was not going to enjoy the day.

"That was a nigger," Mr. Head said and sat back.

Nelson jumped up on the seat and stood looking backward to the end of the car but the Negro had gone.

"I'd of thought you'd know a nigger since you seen so many when you was in the city on your first visit," Mr. Head continued. "That's his first nigger," he said to the man across the aisle.

The boy slid down into the seat. "You said they were black,' he said in an angry voice. "You never said they were tan. How do you expect me to know anything when you don't tell me right?"

"You're just ignorant is all," Mr. Head said and he got up and moved over in the vacant seat by the man across the aisle.

Nelson turned backward again and looked where the Negro had disappeared. He felt that the Negro had deliberately walked down the aisle in order to make a fool of him and he hated him with a fierce raw fresh hate; and also, he understood now why his grandfather disliked them. He looked toward the window and the face there seemed to suggest that he might be inadequate to the day's exactions. He wondered if he would even recognize the city when they came to it.

After he had told several stories, Mr. Head realized that the man he was talking to was asleep and he got up and suggested to Nelson that they walk over the train and see the parts of it. He particularly wanted the boy to see the toilet so they went first to the men's room and examined the plumbing. Mr. Head demonstrated the ice-water cooler as if. he had invented it and showed Nelson the bowl with the single spigot where the travelers brushed their teeth. They went through several cars and came to the diner.

This was the most elegant car in the train. It was painted a rich egg-yellow and had a wine-colored carpet on the floor. There were wide windows over the tables and great spaces of the rolling view were caught in miniature in the sides of the coffee pots and in the glasses. Three very black Negroes in white suits and aprons were running up and down the aisle, swinging trays and bowing and bending over the travelers eating breakfast. One of them rushed up to Mr. Head and Nelson and said, holding up two fingers, "Space for two!" but Mr. Head replied in a loud voice, "We eaten before we left!"

The waiter wore large brown spectacles that increased the size of his eye whites. "Stan' aside then please," he said with an airy wave of the arm as if he were brushing aside flies.

Neither Nelson nor Mr. Head moved a fraction of an inch. "Look," Mr. Head said.

The near corner of the diner, containing two tables, was set off from the rest by a saffron-colored curtain. One table was set but empty but at the other, facing them, his back to the drape, sat the tremendous Negro. He was speaking in a soft voice to the two women while he buttered a muffin. He had a heavy sad face and his neck bulged over his white collar on either side. "They rope them off," Mr. Head explained. Then he said, "Let's go see the kitchen," and they walked the length of the diner but the black waiter was coming fast behind them.

"Passengers are not allowed in the kitchen!" he said in a haughty voice. "Passengers are N O T allowed in the kitchen!"

Mr. Head stopped where he was and turned. "And there's good reason for that," he shouted into the Negro's chest, "because the cockroaches would run the passengers out!"

All the travelers laughed and Mr. Head and Nelson walked out, grinning. Mr. Head was known at home for his quick wit and Nelson felt a sudden keen pride in him. He realized the old man would be his only support in the strange place they were approaching. He would be entirely alone in the world if he were ever lost from his grandfather. A terrible excitement shook him and he wanted to take hold of Mr. Head's coat and hold on like a child.

As they went back to their seats they could see through the passing windows that the countryside was becoming speckled with small houses and shacks and that a highway ran alongside the train. Cars sped by on it, very small and fast. Nelson felt that there was less breath in the air than there had been thirty minutes ago. The man across the aisle had left and there was no one near for Mr. Head to hold a conversation with so he looked out the window, through his own reflection, and read aloud the names of the buildings they were passing. "The Dixie Chemical Corp!" he announced. "Southern Maid Flour! Dixie Doors! Southern Belle Cotton Products! Patty's Peanut Butter! Southern Mammy Cane Syrup!"

"Hush up!" Nelson hissed.

All over the car people were beginning to get up and take their luggage off the overhead racks. Women were putting on their coats and hats. The conductor stuck his head in the car and snarled, "Firstoppppmry," and Nelson lunged out of his sitting position, trembling. Mr. Head pushed him down by the shoulder.

"Keep your seat," he said in dignified tones. "The first stop is on the edge of town. The second stop is at the main railroad station." He had come by this knowledge on his first trip when he had got off at the first stop and had had to pay a man fifteen cents to take him into the heart of town. Nelson sat back down, very pale. For the first time in his life, he understood that his grandfather was indispensable to him.

The train stopped and let off a few passengers and glided on as if it had never ceased moving. Outside, behind rows of brown rickety houses, a line of blue buildings stood up, and beyond them a pale rose-gray sky faded away to nothing. The train moved into the railroad yard. Looking down, Nelson saw lines and lines of silver tracks multiplying and criss-crossing. Then before he could start counting them, the face in the window started out at him, gray but distinct, and he looked the other way. The train was in the station. Both he and Mr. Head jumped up and ran to the door. Neither noticed that they had left the paper sack with the lunch in it on the seat.

They walked stiffly through the small station and came out of a heavy door into the squall of traffic. Crowds were hurrying to work. Nelson didn't know where to look. Mr. Head leaned against the side of the building and glared in front of him.

Finally Nelson said, "Well, how do you see what all it is to see?"

Mr. Head didn't answer. Then as if the sight of people passing had given him the clue, he said, "You walk," and started off down the street. Nelson followed, steadying his hat. So many sights and sounds were flooding in on him that for the first block he hardly knew what he was seeing. At the second corner, Mr. Head turned and looked behind him at the station they had left, a putty-colored terminal with a concrete dome on top. He thought that if he could keep the dome always in sight, he would be able to get back in the afternoon to catch the train again.

As they walked along Nelson began to distinguish details and take note of the store windows, jammed with every kind of equipment—hardware, drygoods, chicken feed, liquor. They passed one that Mr. Head called his particular attention to where you walked in and sat on a chair with your feet upon two rests and let a Negro polish your shoes. They walked slowly and stopped and stood at the entrances so he could see what went on in each place but they did not go into any of them. Mr. Head was determined not to go into any city store because on his first trip here, he had got lost in a large one and had found his way out only after many people had insulted him.

They came in the middle of the next block to a store that had a weighing machine in front of it and they both in turn stepped up on it and put in a penny and received a ticket. Mr. Head's ticket said, "You weigh 120 pounds. You are upright and brave and all your friends admire you." He put the ticket in his pocket, surprised that the machine should have got

his character correct but his weight wrong, for he had weighed on a grain scale not long before and knew he weighed 110. Nelson's ticket said, "You weigh 98 pounds. You have a great destiny ahead of you but beware of dark women." Nelson did not know any women and he weighed only 68 pounds but Mr. Head pointed out that the machine had probably printed the number upside-down, meaning the 9 for a 6.

They walked on and at the end of five blocks the dome of the terminal sank out of sight and Mr. Head turned to the left. Nelson could have stood in front of every store window for an hour if there had not been another more interesting one next to it. Suddenly he said, "I was born here!" Mr. Head turned and looked at him with horror. There was a sweaty brightness about his face. "This is where I come from!" he said.

Mr. Head was appalled. He saw the moment had come for drastic action. "Lemme show you one thing you ain't seen yet," he said and took him to the corner where there was a sewer entrance. "Squat down," he said, "and stick you head in there," and he held the back of the boy's coat while he got down and put his head in the sewer. He drew it back quickly, hearing a gurgling in the depths under the sidewalk. Then Mr. Head explained the sewer system, how the entire city was underlined with it, how it contained all the drainage and was full of rats and how a man could slide into it and be sucked along down endless pitchblack tunnels. At any minute any man in the city might be sucked into the sewer and never heard from again. He described it so well that Nelson was for some seconds shaken. He connected the sewer passages with the entrance to hell and understood for the first time how the world was put together in its lower parts. He drew away from the curb.

Then he said, "Yes, but you can stay away from the holes," and his face took on that stubborn look that was so exasperating to his grandfather. "This is where I come from!" he said.

Mr. Head was dismayed but he only muttered, "You'll get your fill," and they walked on. At the end of two more blocks he turned to the left, feeling that he was circling the dome; and he was correct for in a half-hour they passed in front of the railroad station again. At first Nelson did not notice that he was seeing the same stores twice but when they passed the one where you put your feet on the rests while the Negro polished your shoes, he perceived that they were walking in a circle.

"We done been here!" he shouted. "I don't believe you know where you're at!"

"The direction just slipped my mind for a minute," Mr. Head said and they turned down a different street. He still did not intend to let the dome get too far away and after two blocks in their new direction, he turned to the left. This street contained two- and three-story wooden dwellings. Anyone passing on the sidewalk could see into the rooms and Mr. Head, glancing through one window, saw a woman lying on an iron bed, looking out, with a sheet pulled over her. Her knowing expression shook him. A fierce-looking boy on a bicycle came driving down out of nowhere and he had to jump to the side to keep from being hit. "It's nothing to them if they knock you down," he said. "You better keep closer to me."

They walked on for some time on streets like this before he remembered to turn again. The houses they were passing now were all unpainted and the wood in them looked rotten; the street between was narrower. Nelson saw a colored man. Then another. Then another. "Niggers live in these houses," he observed.

"Well come on and we'll go somewheres else," Mr. Head said. "We didn't come to look at niggers," and they turned down another street but they continued to see Negroes everywhere. Nelson's skin began to prickle and they stepped along at a faster pace in order to leave the neighborhood as soon as possible. There were colored men in their undershirts standing in the doors and colored women rocking on the sagging porches. Colored children played in the gutters and stopped what they were doing to look at them. Before long they began to pass rows of stores with colored customers in them but they didn't pause at the entrances of these.

Black eyes in black faces were watching them from every direction. "Yes," Mr. Head said, "this is where you were born —right here with all these niggers."

Nelson scowled. "I think you done got us lost," he said.

Mr. Head swung around sharply and looked for the dome. It was nowhere in sight. "I ain't got us lost either," he said. "You're just tired of walking."

"I ain't tired, I'm hungry," Nelson said. "Give me a biscuit."

They discovered then that they had lost the lunch.

"You were the one holding the sack," Nelson said. "I would have kepaholt of it."

"If you want to direct this trip, I'll go on by myself and leave you right here," Mr. Head said and was pleased to see the boy turn white. However, he realized they were lost and drifting farther every minute from the station. He was hungry himself and beginning to be thirsty and since they had been in the colored neighborhood, they had both begun to sweat. Nelson had on his shoes and he was unaccustomed to them. The concrete sidewalks were very hard. They both wanted to find a place to sit down but this was impossible and they kept on walking, the boy muttering under his breath, "First you lost the sack and then you lost the way," and Mr. Head growling from time to time, "Anybody wants to be from this nigger heaven can be from it!"

By now the sun was well forward in the sky. The odor of dinners cooking drifted out to them. The Negroes were all at their doors to see them pass. "Whyn't you ast one of these niggers the way?" Nelson said. "You got us lost."

"This is where you were born," Mr. Head said. "You can ast one yourself if you want to."

Nelson was afraid of the colored men and he didn't want to be laughed at by the colored children. Up ahead he saw a large colored woman leaning in a doorway that opened onto the sidewalk. Her hair stood straight out from her head for about four inches all around and she was resting on bare brown feet that turned pink at the sides. She had on a pink dress that showed her exact shape. As they came abreast of her, she lazily lifted one hand to her head and her fingers disappeared into her hair.

Nelson stopped. He felt his breath drawn up by the woman's dark eyes. "How do you get back to town?" he said in a voice that did not sound like his own.

After a minute she said, "You in town now," in a rich low tone that made Nelson feel as if a cool spray had been turned on him.

"How do you get back to the train?" he said in the same reed-like voice.

"You can catch you a car," she said.

He understood she was making fun of him but he was too paralyzed even to scowl. He stood drinking in every detail of her. His eyes traveled up from her great knees to her forehead and then made a triangular path from the glistening sweat on her neck down and across her tremendous bosom and over her bare arm back to where her fingers lay hidden in her hair. He suddenly wanted her to reach down and pick him up and draw him against her and then he wanted to feel her breath on his face. He wanted to look down and down into her eyes while she held him tighter and tighter. He had never had such a feeling before. He felt as if he were reeling down through a pitchblack tunnel.

"You can go a block down yonder and catch you a car take you to the railroad station, Sugarpie," she said.

Nelson would have collapsed at her feet if Mr. Head had not pulled him roughly away. "You act like you don't have any sense!" the old man growled.

They hurried down the street and Nelson did not look back at the woman. He pushed his hat sharply forward over his face which was already burning with shame. The sneering ghost he had seen in the train window and all the foreboding feelings he had on the way returned to him and he remembered that his ticket from the scale had said to beware of dark women and that his grandfather's had said he was upright and brave. He took hold of the old man's hand, a sign of dependence that he seldom showed.

They headed down the street toward the car tracks where a long yellow rattling trolley was coming. Mr. Head had never boarded a streetcar and he let that one pass. Nelson was silent. From time to time his mouth trembled slightly but his grandfather, occupied with his own problems, paid him no attention. They stood on the corner and neither looked at the Negroes who were passing, going about their business just as if they had been white, except that most of them stopped and eyed Mr. Head and Nelson. It occurred to Mr. Head that since the streetcar ran on tracks, they could simply follow the tracks. He gave Nelson a slight push and explained that they would follow the tracks on into the railroad station, walking, and they set off.

Presently to their great relief they began to see white people again and Nelson sat down on the sidewalk against the wall of a building. "I got to rest myself some," he said. "You lost the sack and the direction. You can just wait on me to rest myself."

"There's the tracks in front of us," Mr. Head said. "All we got to do is keep them in sight and you could have remembered the sack as good as me. This is where you were born. This is your old home town. This is your second trip. You ought to know how to do," and he squatted down and continued in this vein but the boy, easing his burning feet out of his shoes, did not answer.

"And standing there grinning like a chim-pan-zee while a nigger woman gives you directions. Great Gawd!" Mr. Head said.

"I never said I was nothing but born here," the boy said in a shaky voice. "I never said I would or wouldn't like it. I never said I wanted to come. I only said I was born here and I never had nothing to do with that. I want to go home. I never wanted to come in the first place. It was all your big idea. How you know you ain't following the tracks in the wrong direction?"

This last had occurred to Mr. Head too. "All these people are white," he said.

"We ain't passed here before," Nelson said. This was a neighborhood of brick buildings that might have been lived in or might not. A few empty automobiles were parked along the curb and there was an occasional passerby. The heat of the pavement came up through Nelson's thin suit. His eyelids began to droop, and after a few minutes his head tilted forward. His shoulders twitched once or twice and then he fell over on his side and lay sprawled in an exhausted fit of sleep.

Mr. Head watched him silently. He was very tired himself but they could not both sleep at the same time and he could not have slept anyway because he did not know where he was. In a few minutes Nelson would wake up, refreshed by his sleep and very cocky, and would begin complaining that he had lost the sack and the way. You'd have a mighty sorry time if I wasn't here, Mr. Head thought; and then another idea occurred to him. He looked at the sprawled figure for several minutes; presently he stood up. He justified what he was going to do on the grounds that it is sometimes necessary to teach a child a lesson he won't forget, particularly when the child is always reasserting his position with some new impudence. He walked without a sound to the corner about twenty feet away and sat down on a covered garbage can in the alley where he could look out and watch Nelson wake up alone.

The boy was dozing fitfully, half conscious of vague noises and black forms moving up from some dark part of him into the light. His face worked in his sleep and he had pulled his knees up under his chin. The sun shed a dull dry light on the narrow street; everything looked like exactly what it was. After a while Mr. Head, hunched like an old monkey on the garbage can lid, decided that if Nelson didn't wake up soon, he would make a loud noise by bamming his foot against the can. He looked at his watch and discovered that it was two o'clock. Their train left at six and the possibility of missing it was too awful for him to think of. He kicked his foot backwards on the can and a hollow boom reverberated in the alley.

Nelson shot up onto his feet with a shout. He looked where his grandfather should have been and stared. He seemed to whirl several times and then, picking up his feet and throwing his head back, he dashed down the street like a wild mad-

dened pony. Mr. Head jumped off the can and galloped after but the child was almost out of sight. He saw a streak of gray disappearing diagonally a block ahead. He ran as fast as he could, looking both ways down every intersection, but without sight of him again. Then as he passed the third intersection, completely winded, he saw about half a block down the street a scene that stopped him altogether. He crouched behind a trash box to watch and get his bearings.

Nelson was sitting with both legs spread out and by his side lay an elderly woman, screaming. Groceries were scattered about the sidewalk. A crowd of women had already gathered to see justice done and Mr. Head distinctly heard the old woman on the pavement shout, "You've broken my ankle and your daddy'll pay for it! Every nickel! Police! Police!" Several of the women were plucking at Nelson's shoulder but the boy seemed too dazed to get up.

Something forced Mr. Head from behind the trash box and forward, but only at a creeping pace. He had never in his life been accosted by a policeman. The women were milling around Nelson as if they might suddenly all dive on him at once and tear him to pieces, and the old woman continued to scream that her ankle was broken and to call for an officer. Mr. Head came on so slowly that he could have been taking a backward step after each forward one, but when he was about ten feet away, Nelson saw him and sprang. The child caught him around the hips and clung panting against him.

The women all turned on Mr. Head. The injured one sat up and shouted, "You sir! You'll pay every penny of my doctor's bill that your boy has caused. He's a juve-nile delinquent! Where is an officer? Somebody take this man's name and address!"

Mr. Head was trying to detach Nelson's fingers from the flesh in the back of his legs. The old man's head had lowered itself into his collar like a turtle's; his eyes were glazed with fear and caution.

"Your boy has broken my ankle!" the old woman shouted. "Police!"

Mr. Head sensed the approach of the policeman from behind. He stared straight ahead at the women who were massed in their fury like a solid wall to block his escape. "This is not my boy," he said. "I never seen him before."

He felt Nelson's fingers fall out of his flesh.

The women dropped back, staring at him with horror, as if they were so repulsed by a man who would deny his own image and likeness that they could not bear to lay hands on him. Mr. Head walked on, through a space they silently cleared, and left Nelson behind. Ahead of him he saw nothing but a hollow tunnel that had once been the street.

The boy remained standing where he was, his neck craned forward and his hands hanging by his sides. His hat was jammed on his head so that there were no longer any creases in it. The injured woman got up and shook her fist at him and the others gave him pitying looks, but he didn't notice any of them. There was no policeman in sight.

In a minute he began to move mechanically, making no effort to catch up with his grandfather but merely following at about twenty paces. They walked on for five blocks in this way. Mr. Head's shoulders were sagging and his neck hung forward at such an angle that it was not visible from behind. He was afraid to turn his head. Finally he cut a short hopeful glance over his shoulder. Twenty feet behind him, he saw two small eyes piercing into his back like pitchfork prongs.

The boy was not of a forgiving nature but this was the first time he had ever had anything to forgive. Mr. Head had never disgraced himself before. After two more blocks, he turned and called over his shoulder in a high desperately gay voice, "Let's us go get us a Co' Cola somewheres!"

Nelson, with a dignity he had never shown before, turned and stood with his back to his grandfather.

Mr. Head began to feel the depth of his denial. His face as they walked on became all hollows and bare ridges. He saw nothing they were passing but he perceived that they had lost the car tracks. There was no dome to be seen anywhere and the afternoon was advancing. He knew that if dark overtook them in the city, they would be beaten and robbed. The speed of God's justice was only what he expected for himself, but he could not stand to think that his sins would be visited upon Nelson and that even now, he was leading the boy to his doom.

They continued to walk on block after block through an endless section of small brick houses until Mr. Head almost fell over a water spigot sticking up about six inches off the edge of a grass plot. He had not had a drink of water since early morning but he felt he did not deserve it now. Then he thought that Nelson would be thirsty and they would both drink and be brought together. He squatted down and put his mouth to the nozzle and turned a cold stream of water into his throat. Then he called out in the high desperate voice, "Come on and getcher some water!"

This time the child stared through him for nearly sixty seconds. Mr. Head got up and walked on as if he had drunk poison. Nelson, though he had not had water since some he had drunk out of a paper cup on the train, passed by the spigot, disdaining to drink where his grandfather had. When Mr. Head realized this, he lost all hope. His face in the waning afternoon light looked ravaged and abandoned. He could feel the boy's steady hate, traveling at an even pace behind him and he knew that (if by some miracle they escaped being murdered in the city) it would continue just that way for the rest of his life. He knew that now he was wandering into a black strange place where nothing was like it had ever been before, a long old age without respect and an end that would be welcome because it would be the end.

As for Nelson, his mind had frozen around his grandfather's treachery as if he were trying to preserve it intact to present at the final judgment. He walked without looking to one side or the other, but every now and then his mouth would twitch and this was when he felt, from some remote place inside himself, a black mysterious form reach up as if it would melt his frozen vision in one hot grasp.

The sun dropped down behind a row of houses and hardly noticing, they passed into an elegant suburban section where mansions were set back from the road by lawns with birdbaths on them. Here everything was entirely deserted. For blocks they didn't pass even a dog. The big white houses were like partially submerged icebergs in the distance. There were no sidewalks, only drives, and these wound around and around in endless ridiculous circles. Nelson made no move to come nearer to Mr. Head. The old man felt that if he saw a sewer entrance he would drop down into it and let himself be carried away; and he could imagine the boy standing by, watching with only a slight interest, while he disappeared.

A loud bark jarred him to attention and he looked up to see a fat man approaching with two bulldogs. He waved both arms like someone shipwrecked on a desert island. "I'm lost!" he called. "I'm lost and can't find my way and me and this boy have got to catch this train and I can't find the station. Oh Gawd I'm lost! Oh hep me Gawd I'm lost!"

The man, who was bald-headed and had on golf knickers, asked him what train he was trying to catch and Mr. Head began to get out his tickets, trembling so violently he could hardly hold them. Nelson had come up to within fifteen feet and stood watching.

"Well," the fat man said, giving him back the tickets, "you won't have time to get back to town to make this but you can catch it at the suburb stop. That's three blocks from here," and he began explaining how to get there.

Mr. Head stared as if he were slowly returning from the dead and when the man had finished and gone off with the dogs jumping at his heels, he turned to Nelson and said breathlessly, "We're going to get home!"

The child was standing about ten feet away, his face bloodless under the gray hat. His eyes were triumphantly cold. There was no light in them, no feeling, no interest. He was merely there, a small figure, waiting. Home was nothing to him.

Mr. Head turned slowly. He felt he knew now what time would be like without seasons and what heat would be like without light and what man would be like

without salvation. He didn't care if he never made the train and if it had not been for what suddenly caught his attention, like a cry out of the gathering dusk, he might have forgotten there was a station to go to.

He had not walked five hundred yards down the road when he saw, within reach of him, the plaster figure of a Negro sitting bent over on a low yellow brick fence that curved around a wide lawn. The Negro was about Nelson's size and he was pitched forward at an unsteady angle because the putty that held him to the wall had cracked. One of his eyes was entirely white and he held a piece of brown watermelon.

Mr. Head stood looking at him silently until Nelson stopped at a little distance. Then as the two of them stood there, Mr. Head breathed, "An artificial nigger!"

It was not possible to tell if the artificial Negro were meant to be young or old; he looked too miserable to be either. He was meant to look happy because his mouth was stretched up at the corners but the chipped eye and the angle he was cocked at gave him a wild look of misery instead.

"An artificial nigger!" Nelson repeated in Mr. Head's exact tone.

The two of them stood there with their necks forward at almost the same angle and their shoulders curved in almost exactly the same way and their hands trembling identically in their pockets. Mr. Head looked like an ancient child and Nelson like a miniature old man. They stood gazing at the artificial Negro as if they were faced with some great mystery, some monument to another's victory that brought them together in their common defeat. They could both feel it dissolving their differences like an action of mercy. Mr. Head had never known before what mercy felt like because he had been too good to deserve any, but he felt he knew now. He looked at Nelson and understood that he must say something to the child to show that he was still wise and in the look the boy returned he saw a hungry need for that assurance. Nelson's eyes seemed to implore him to explain once and for all the mystery of existence.

Mr. Head opened his lips to make a

lofty statement and heard himself say, "They ain't got enough real ones here. They got to have an artificial one."

After a second, the boy nodded with a strange shivering about his mouth, and said, "Let's go home before we get ourselves lost again."

Their train glided into the suburb stop just as they reached the station and they boarded it together, and ten minutes before it was due to arrive at the junction, they went to the door and stood ready to jump off it if it did not stop; but it did, just as the moon, restored to its full splendor, sprang from a cloud and flooded the clearing with light. As they stepped off, the sage grass was shivering gently in shades of silver and the clinkers under their feet glittered with a fresh black light. The treetops, fencing the junction like the protecting walls of a garden, were darker than the sky which was hung with gigantic white clouds illuminated like lanterns.

Mr. Head stood very still and felt the action of mercy touch him again but this time he knew that there were no words in the world that could name it. He understood that it grew out of agony, which is not denied to any man and which is given in strange ways to children. He under-

stood it was all a man could carry into death to give his Maker and he suddenly burned with shame that he had so little of it to take with him. He stood appalled, judging himself with the thoroughness of God, while the action of mercy covered his pride like a flame and consumed it. He had never thought himself a great sinner before but he saw now that his true depravity had been hidden from him lest it cause him despair. He realized that he was forgiven for sins from the beginning of time, when he had conceived in his own heart the sin of Adam, until the present, when he had denied poor Nelson. He saw that no sin was too monstrous for him to claim as his own, and since God loved in proportion as He forgave, he felt ready at that instant to enter Paradise.

Nelson, composing his expression under the shadow of his hat brim, watched him with a mixture of fatigue and suspicion, but as the train glided past them and disappeared like a frightened serpent into the woods, even his face lightened and he muttered, "I'm glad I've went once, but I'll never go back again!"

[1955]

QUESTIONS FOR STUDY

1. *At the beginning of the story Mr. Head complacently believes that he possesses "that calm understanding of life that makes him a suitable guide for the young." What does he come to discover about himself?*
2. *What does Nelson learn?*
3. *What is the "moral mission" on which Mr. Head embarks?*
4. *What does the city—with its black subterranean sewers, its maze of streets, and its crowded Negro section—seem to represent?*
5. *What does Nelson mean when he says "I was born here! . . . This is where I come from!"?*
6. *What significance seems to be attached to the plaster figure—the "artificial nigger"?*
7. *What does the story finally seem to imply about reason, sin, redemption, and man's need for faith and mercy?*
8. *Is it possible to read the conclusion of the story as ironic? If so, how does this affect the story's meaning?*

FLANNERY O'CONNOR

Everything That Rises Must Converge

HER DOCTOR had told Julian's mother that she must lose twenty pounds on account of her blood pressure, so on Wednesday nights Julian had to take her downtown on the bus for a reducing class at the Y. The reducing class was designed for working girls over fifty, who weighed from 165 to 200 pounds. His mother was one of the slimmer ones, but she said ladies did not tell their age or weight. She would not ride the buses by herself at night since they had been integrated, and because the reducing class was one of her few pleasures, necessary for her health, and *free*, she said Julian could at least put himself out to take her, considering all she did for him. Julian did not like to consider all she did for him, but every Wednesday night he braced himself and took her.

She was almost ready to go, standing before the hall mirror, putting on her hat, while he, his hands behind him, appeared pinned to the door frame, waiting like Saint Sebastian for the arrows to begin piercing him. The hat was new and had cost her seven dollars and a half. She kept saying, "Maybe I shouldn't have paid that for it. No, I shouldn't have. I'll take it off and return it tomorrow. I shouldn't have bought it."

Julian raised his eyes to heaven. "Yes, you should have bought it," he said. "Put it on and let's go." It was a hideous hat. A purple velvet flap came down on one side of it and stood up on the other; the rest of it was green and looked like a cushion with the stuffing out. He decided it was less comical than jaunty and pathetic. Everything that gave her pleasure was small and depressed him.

She lifted the hat one more time and set it down slowly on top of her head. Two wings of gray hair protruded on either side of her florid face, but her eyes, sky-blue, were as innocent and untouched by experience as they must have been when she was ten. Were it not that she was a widow who had struggled fiercely to feed and clothe and put him through school and who was supporting him still, "until he got on his feet," she might have been a little girl that he had to take to town.

"It's all right, it's all right," he said. "Let's go." He opened the door himself and started down the walk to get her going. The sky was a dying violet and the houses stood out darkly against it, bulbous liver-colored monstrosities of a uniform ugliness though no two were alike. Since this had been a fashionable neighborhood forty years ago, his mother persisted in thinking they did well to have an apartment in it. Each house had a narrow collar of dirt around it in which sat, usually, a grubby child. Julian walked with his hands in his pockets, his head down and thrust forward and his eyes glazed with the determination to make himself completely numb during the time he would be sacrificed to her pleasure.

The door closed and he turned to find the dumpy figure, surmounted by the atrocious hat, coming toward him. "Well," she said, "you only live once and paying a little more for it, I at least won't meet myself coming and going."

"Some day I'll start making money," Julian said gloomily—he knew he never would—"and you can have one of those jokes whenever you take the fit." But first they would move. He visualized a place where the nearest neighbors would be three miles away on either side.

"I think you're doing fine," she said, drawing on her gloves. "You've only been out of school a year. Rome wasn't built in a day."

She was one of the few members of

the Y reducing class who arrived in hat and gloves and who had a son who had been to college. "It takes time," she said, "and the world is in such a mess. This hat looked better on me than any of the others, though when she brought it out I said, 'Take that thing back. I wouldn't have it on my head,' and she said, 'Now wait till you see it on,' and when she put it on me, I said, 'We-ull,' and she said, 'If you ask me, that hat does something for you and you do something for the hat, and besides,' she said, 'with that hat, you won't meet yourself coming and going.' "

Julian thought he could have stood his lot better if she had been selfish, if she had been an old hag who drank and screamed at him. He walked along, saturated in depression, as if in the midst of his martyrdom he had lost his faith. Catching sight of his long, hopeless, irritated face, she stopped suddenly with a grief-stricken look, and pulled back on his arm. "Wait on me," she said. "I'm going back to the house and take this thing off and tomorrow I'm going to return it. I was out of my head. I can pay the gas bill with that seven-fifty."

He caught her arm in a vicious grip. "You are not going to take it back," he said. "I like it."

"Well," she said, "I don't think I ought. . . ."

"Shut up and enjoy it," he muttered, more depressed than ever.

"With the world in the mess it's in," she said, "it's a wonder we can enjoy anything. I tell you, the bottom rail is on the top."

Julian sighed.

"Of course," she said, "if you know who you are, you can go anywhere." She said this every time he took her to the reducing class. "Most of them in it are not our kind of people," she said, "but I can be gracious to anybody. I know who I am."

"They don't give a damn for your graciousness," Julian said savagely. "Knowing who you are is good for one generation only. You haven't the foggiest idea where you stand now or who you are."

She stopped and allowed her eyes to flash at him. "I most certainly do know who I am," she said, "and if you don't know who you are, I'm ashamed of you."

"Oh hell," Julian said.

"Your great-grandfather was a former governor of this state," she said. "Your grandfather was a prosperous landowner. Your grandmother was a Godhigh."

"Will you look around you," he said tensely, "and see where you are now?" and he swept his arm jerkily out to indicate the neighborhood, which the growing darkness at least made less dingy.

"You remain what you are," she said. "Your great-grandfather had a plantation and two hundred slaves."

"There are no more slaves," he said irritably.

"They were better off when they were," she said. He groaned to see that she was off on that topic. She rolled onto it every few days like a train on an open track. He knew every stop, every junction, every swamp along the way, and knew the exact point at which her conclusion would roll majestically into the station: "It's ridiculous. It's simply not realistic. They should rise, yes, but on their own side of the fence."

"Let's skip it," Julian said.

"The ones I feel sorry for," she said, "are the ones that are half white. They're tragic."

"Will you skip it?"

"Suppose we were half white. We would certainly have mixed feelings."

"I have mixed feelings now," he groaned.

"Well let's talk about something pleasant," she said. "I remember going to Grandpa's when I was a little girl. Then the house had double stairways that went up to what was really the second floor—all the cooking was done on the first. I used to like to stay down in the kitchen on account of the way the walls smelled. I would sit with my nose pressed against the plaster and take deep breaths. Actually the place belonged to the Godhighs but your grandfather Chestny paid the mortgage and saved it for them. They were in reduced circumstances," she said, "but reduced or not, they never forgot who they were."

"Doubtless that decayed mansion reminded them," Julian muttered. He never spoke of it without contempt or thought of it without longing. He had seen it once when he was a child before it had been sold. The double stairways had rotted and been torn down. Negroes were living in it. But it remained in his mind as his mother had known it. It appeared in his dreams regularly. He would stand on the wide porch, listening to the rustle of oak leaves, then wander through the high-ceilinged hall into the parlor that opened onto it and gaze at the worn rugs and faded draperies. It occurred to him that it was he, not she, who could have appreciated it. He preferred its threadbare elegance to anything he could name and it was because of it that all the neighborhoods they had lived in had been a torment to him—whereas she had hardly known the difference. She called her insensitivity "being adjustable."

"And I remember the old darky who was my nurse, Caroline. There was no better person in the world. I've always had a great respect for my colored friends," she said. "I'd do anything in the world for them and they'd. . . ."

"Will you for God's sake get off that subject?" Julian said. When he got on a bus by himself, he made it a point to sit down beside a Negro, in reparation as it were for his mother's sins.

"You're mighty touchy tonight," she said. "Do you feel all right?"

"Yes I feel all right," he said. "Now lay off."

She pursed her lips. "Well, you certainly are in a vile humor," she observed. "I just won't speak to you at all."

They had reached the bus stop. There was no bus in sight and Julian, his hands still jammed in his pockets and his head thrust forward, scowled down the empty street. The frustration of having to wait on the bus as well as ride on it began to creep up his neck like a hot hand. The presence of his mother was borne in upon him as she gave a pained sigh. He looked at her bleakly. She was holding herself very erect under the preposterous hat, wearing it like a banner of her imaginary dignity. There was in him an evil urge to break her spirit. He suddenly unloosened

his tie and pulled it off and put it in his pocket.

She stiffened. "Why must you look like *that* when you take me to town?" she said. "Why must you deliberately embarrass me?"

"If you'll never learn where you are," he said, "you can at least learn where I am."

"You look like a—thug," she said.

"Then I must be one," he murmured.

"I'll just go home," she said. "I will not bother you. If you can't do a little thing like that for me . . ."

Rolling his eyes upward, he put his tie back on. "Restored to my class," he muttered. He thrust his face toward her and hissed. "True culture is in the mind, the *mind*," he said, and tapped his head, "the mind."

"It's in the heart," she said, "and in how you do things and how you do things is because of who you *are*."

"Nobody in the damn bus cares who you are."

"I care who I am," she said icily.

The lighted bus appeared on top of the next hill and as it approached, they moved out into the street to meet it. He put his hand under her elbow and hoisted her up on the creaking step. She entered with a little smile, as if she were going into a drawing room where everyone had been waiting for her. While he put in the tokens, she sat down on one of the broad front seats for three which faced the aisle. A thin woman with protruding teeth and long yellow hair was sitting on the end of it. His mother moved up beside her and left room for Julian beside herself. He sat down and looked at the floor across the aisle where a pair of thin feet in red and white canvas sandals were planted.

His mother immediately began a general conversation meant to attract anyone who felt like talking. "Can it get any hotter?" she said and removed from her purse a folding fan, black with a Japanese scene on it, which she began to flutter before her.

"I reckon it might could," the woman with the protruding teeth said, "but I know for a fact my apartment couldn't get no hotter."

"It must get the afternoon sun," his

mother said. She sat forward and looked up and down the bus. It was half filled. Everybody was white. "I see we have the bus to ourselves," she said. Julian cringed.

"For a change," said the woman across the aisle, the owner of the red and white canvas sandals. "I come on one the other day and they were thick as fleas—up front and all through."

"The world is in a mess everywhere," his mother said. "I don't know how we've let it get in this fix."

"What gets my goat is all those boys from good families stealing automobile tires," the woman with the protruding teeth said. "I told my boy, I said you may not be rich but you been raised right and if I ever catch you in any such mess, they can send you on to the reformatory. Be exactly where you belong."

"Training tells," his mother said. "Is your boy in high school?"

"Ninth grade," the woman said.

"My son just finished college last year. He wants to write but he's selling typewriters until he gets started," his mother said.

The woman leaned forward and peered at Julian. He threw her such a malevolent look that she subsided against the seat. On the floor across the aisle there was an abandoned newspaper. He got up and got it and opened it out in front of him. His mother discreetly continued the conversation in a lower tone but the woman across the aisle said in a loud voice, "Well that's nice. Selling typewriters is close to writing. He can go right from one to the other."

"I tell him," his mother said, "that Rome wasn't built in a day."

Behind the newspaper Julian was withdrawing into the inner compartment of his mind where he spent most of his time. This was a kind of mental bubble in which he established himself when he could not bear to be a part of what was going on around him. From it he could see out and judge but in it he was safe from any kind of penetration from without. It was the only place where he felt free of the general idiocy of his fellows. His mother had never entered it but from it he could see her with absolute clarity.

The old lady was clever enough and he thought that if she had started from any of the right premises, more might have been expected of her. She lived according to the laws of her own fantasy world, outside of which he had never seen her set foot. The law of it was to sacrifice herself for him after she had first created the necessity to do so by making a mess of things. If he had permitted her sacrifices, it was only because her lack of foresight had made them necessary. All of her life had been a struggle to act like a Chestny without the Chestny goods, and to give him everything she thought a Chestny ought to have; but since, said she, it was fun to struggle, why complain? And when you had won, as she had won, what fun to look back on the hard times! He could not forgive her that she had enjoyed the struggle and that she thought *she* had won.

What she meant when she said she had won was that she had brought him up successfully and had sent him to college and that he had turned out so well—good looking (her teeth had gone unfilled so that his could be straightened), intelligent (he realized he was too intelligent to be a success), and with a future ahead of him (there was of course no future ahead of him). She excused his gloominess on the grounds that he was still growing up and his radical ideas on his lack of practical experience. She said he didn't yet know a thing about "life," that he hadn't even entered the real world—when already he was as disenchanted with it as a man of fifty.

The further irony of all this was that in spite of her, he had turned out so well. In spite of going to only a third-rate college, he had, on his own initiative, come out with a first-rate education; in spite of growing up dominated by a small mind, he had ended up with a large one; in spite of all her foolish views, he was free of prejudice and unafraid to face facts. Most miraculous of all, instead of being blinded by love for her as she was for him, he had cut himself emotionally free of her and could see her with complete objectivity. He was not dominated by his mother.

The bus stopped with a sudden jerk and shook him from his meditation. A woman from the back lurched forward with little steps and barely escaped falling in his newspaper as she righted herself. She got off and a large Negro got on. Julian kept his paper lowered to watch. It gave him a certain satisfaction to see injustice in daily operation. It confirmed his view that with a few exceptions there was no one worth knowing within a radius of three hundred miles. The Negro was well dressed and carried a briefcase. He looked around and then sat down on the other end of the seat where the woman with the red and white canvas sandals was sitting. He immediately unfolded a newspaper and obscured himself behind it. Julian's mother's elbow at once prodded insistently into his ribs. "Now you see why I won't ride on these buses by myself," she whispered.

The woman with the red and white canvas sandals had risen at the same time the Negro sat down and had gone further back in the bus and taken the seat of the woman who had got off. His mother leaned forward and cast her an approving look.

Julian rose, crossed the aisle, and sat down in the place of the woman with the canvas sandals. From this position, he looked serenely across at his mother. Her face had turned an angry red. He stared at her, making his eyes the eyes of a stranger. He felt his tension suddenly lift as if he had openly declared war on her.

He would have liked to get in conversation with the Negro and to talk with him about art or politics or any subject that would be above the comprehension of those around them, but the man remained entrenched behind his paper. He was either ignoring the change of seating or had never noticed it. There was no way for Julian to convey his sympathy.

His mother kept her eyes fixed reproachfully on his face. The woman with the protruding teeth was looking at him avidly as if he were a type of monster new to her.

"Do you have a light?" he asked the Negro.

Without looking away from his paper, the man reached in his pocket and handed him a packet of matches.

"Thanks," Julian said. For a moment he held the matches foolishly. A NO SMOKING sign looked down upon him from over the door. This alone would not have deterred him; he had no cigarettes. He had quit smoking some months before because he could not afford it. "Sorry," he muttered and handed back the matches. The Negro lowered the paper and gave him an annoyed look. He took the matches and raised the paper again.

His mother continued to gaze at him but she did not take advantage of his momentary discomfort. Her eyes retained their battered look. Her face seemed to be unnaturally red, as if her blood pressure had risen. Julian allowed no glimmer of sympathy to show on his face. Having got the advantage, he wanted desperately to keep it and carry it through. He would have liked to teach her a lesson that would last her a while, but there seemed no way to continue the point. The Negro refused to come out from behind his paper.

Julian folded his arms and looked stolidly before him, facing her but as if he did not see her, as if he had ceased to recognize her existence. He visualized a scene in which, the bus having reached their stop, he would remain in his seat and when she said, "Aren't you going to get off?" he would look at her as at a stranger who had rashly addressed him. The corner they got off on was usually deserted, but it was well lighted and it would not hurt her to walk by herself the four blocks to the Y. He decided to wait until the time came and then decide whether or not he would let her get off by herself. He would have to be at the Y at ten to bring her back, but he could leave her wondering if he was going to show up. There was no reason for her to think she could always depend on him.

He retired again into the high-ceilinged room sparsely settled with large pieces of antique furniture. His soul expanded momentarily but then he became aware of his mother across from him and the vision shriveled. He studied her coldly. Her feet in little pumps dangled like a child's and did not quite reach the floor. She was training on him an exaggerated look of reproach. He felt completely detached from her. At that moment he could with pleasure have slapped her as he would have slapped a particularly obnoxious child in his charge.

He began to imagine various unlikely ways by which he could teach her a lesson. He might make friends with some distinguished Negro professor or lawyer and bring him home to spend the evening. He would be entirely justified but her blood pressure would rise to 300. He could not push her to the extent of making her have a stroke, and moreover, he had never been successful at making any Negro friends. He had tried to strike up an acquaintance on the bus with some of the better types, with ones that looked like professors or ministers or lawyers. One morning he had sat down next to a distinguished-looking dark brown man who had answered his questions with a sonorous solemnity but who had turned out to be an undertaker. Another day he had sat down beside a cigar-smoking Negro with a diamond ring on his finger, but after a few stilted pleasantries, the Negro had rung the buzzer and risen, slipping two lottery tickets into Julian's hand as he climbed over him to leave.

He imagined his mother lying desperately ill and his being able to secure only a Negro doctor for her. He toyed with that idea for a few minutes and then dropped it for a momentary vision of himself participating as a sympathizer in a sit-in demonstration. This was possible but he did not linger with it. Instead, he approached the ultimate horror. He brought home a beautiful suspiciously Negroid woman. Prepare yourself, he said. There is nothing you can do about it. This is the woman I've chosen. She's intelligent, dignified, even good, and she's suffered and she hasn't thought it *fun*. Now persecute us, go ahead and persecute us. Drive her out of here, but remember, you're driving me too. His eyes were narrowed and through the indignation he had generated, he saw his mother across the aisle, purple-faced, shrunken to the dwarf-like proportions of her moral nature, sitting like a mummy beneath the ridiculous banner of her hat.

He was tilted out of his fantasy again as the bus stopped. The door opened with a sucking hiss and out of the dark a large, gaily dressed, sullen-looking colored woman got on with a little boy. The child, who might have been four, had on a short plaid suit and a Tyrolean hat with a blue feather in it. Julian hoped that he would sit down beside him and that the woman would push in beside his mother. He could think of no better arrangement.

As she waited for her tokens, the woman was surveying the seating possibilities—he hoped with the idea of sitting where she was least wanted. There was something familiar-looking about her but Julian could not place what it was. She was a giant of a woman. Her face was set not only to meet opposition but to seek it out. The downward tilt of her large lower lip was like a warning sign: DON'T TAMPER WITH ME. Her bulging figure was encased in a green crepe dress and her feet overflowed in red shoes. She had on a hideous hat. A purple velvet flap came down on one side of it and stood up on the other; the rest of it was green and looked like a cushion with the stuffing out. She carried a mammoth red pocketbook that bulged throughout as if it were stuffed with rocks.

To Julian's disappointment, the little boy climbed up on the empty seat beside his mother. His mother lumped all children, black and white, into the common category, "cute," and she thought little Negroes were on the whole cuter than little white children. She smiled at the little boy as he climbed on the seat.

Meanwhile the woman was bearing down upon the empty seat beside Julian. To his annoyance, she squeezed herself into it. He saw his mother's face change as the woman settled herself next to him and he realized with satisfaction that this was more objectionable to her than it was to him. Her face seemed almost gray and there was a look of dull recognition in her eyes, as if suddenly she had sickened at some awful confrontation. Julian saw that it was because she and the woman had, in a sense, swapped sons. Though his mother would not realize the symbolic significance of this, she would feel it. His amusement showed plainly on his face.

The woman next to him muttered something unintelligible to herself. He was conscious of a kind of bristling next to him, a muted growling like that of an angry cat. He could not see anything but the red pocketbook upright on the bulging green thighs. He visualized the woman as she had stood waiting for her tokens—the ponderous figure, rising from the red shoes upward over the solid hips, the mammoth bosom, the haughty face, to the green and purple hat.

His eyes widened.

The vision of the two hats, identical, broke upon him with the radiance of a brilliant sunrise. His face was suddenly lit with joy. He could not believe that Fate had thrust upon his mother such a lesson. He gave a loud chuckle so that she would look at him and see that he saw. She turned her eyes on him slowly. The blue in them seemed to have turned a bruised purple. For a moment he had an uncomfortable sense of her innocence, but it lasted only a second before principle rescued him. Justice entitled him to laugh. His grin hardened until it said to her as plainly as if he were saying aloud: Your punishment exactly fits your pettiness. This should teach you a permanent lesson.

Her eyes shifted to the woman. She seemed unable to bear looking at him and to find the woman preferable. He became conscious again of the bristling presence at his side. The woman was rumbling like a volcano about to become active. His mother's mouth began to twitch slightly at one corner. With a sinking heart, he saw incipient signs of recovery on her face and realized that this was going to strike her suddenly as funny and was going to be no lesson at all. She kept her eyes on the woman and an amused smile came over her face as if the woman were a monkey that had stolen her hat. The little Negro was looking up at her with large fascinated eyes. He had been trying to attract her attention for some time.

"Carver!" the woman said suddenly. "Come heah!"

When he saw that the spotlight was on him at last, Carver drew his feet up and turned himself toward Julian's mother and giggled.

"Carver!" the woman said. "You heah me? Come heah!"

Carver slid down from the seat but remained squatting with his back against the base of it, his head turned slyly around toward Julian's mother, who was smiling at him. The woman reached a hand across the aisle and snatched him to her. He righted himself and hung backwards on her knees, grinning at Julian's mother. "Isn't he cute?" Julian's mother said to the woman with the protruding teeth.

"I reckon he is," the woman said without conviction.

The Negress yanked him upright but he eased out of her grip and shot across the aisle and scrambled, giggling wildly, onto the seat beside his love.

"I think he likes me," Julian's mother said, and smiled at the woman. It was the smile she used when she was being particularly gracious to an inferior. Julian saw everything lost. The lesson had rolled off her like rain on a roof.

The woman stood up and yanked the little boy off the seat as if she were snatching him from contagion. Julian could feel the rage in her at having no weapon like his mother's smile. She gave the child a sharp slap across his leg. He howled once and then thrust his head into her stomach and kicked his feet against her shins. "Be-have," she said vehemently.

The bus stopped and the Negro who had been reading the newspaper got off. The woman moved over and set the little boy down with a thump between herself and Julian. She held him firmly by the knee. In a moment he put his hands in front of his face and peeped at Julian's mother through his fingers.

"I see yoooooooo!" she said and put her hand in front of her face and peeped at him.

The woman slapped his hand down. "Quit yo' foolishness," she said, "before I knock the living Jesus out of you!"

Julian was thankful that the next stop was theirs. He reached up and pulled the cord. The woman reached up and pulled it at the same time. Oh my God, he thought. He had the terrible intuition that when they got off the bus together, his mother would open her purse and give the little boy a nickel. The gesture would be as natural to her as breathing. The bus stopped and the woman got up and lunged to the front, dragging the child, who wished to stay on, after her. Julian and his mother got up and followed. As they neared the door, Julian tried to relieve her of her pocketbook.

"No," she murmured, "I want to give the little boy a nickel."

"No!" Julian hissed. "No!"

She smiled down at the child and opened her bag. The bus door opened and the woman picked him up by the arm and descended with him, hanging at her hip. Once in the street she set him down and shook him.

Julian's mother had to close her purse while she got down the bus step but as soon as her feet were on the ground, she opened it again and began to rummage inside. "I can't find but a penny," she whispered, "but it looks like a new one."

"Don't do it!" Julian said fiercely between his teeth. There was a streetlight on the corner and she hurried to get under it so that she could better see into her pocketbook. The woman was heading off rapidly down the street with the child still hanging backward on her hand.

"Oh little boy!" Julian's mother called and took a few quick steps and caught up with them just beyond the lamp-post. "Here's a bright new penny for you," and she held out the coin, which shone bronze in the dim light.

The huge woman turned and for a moment stood, her shoulders lifted and her face frozen with frustrated rage, and stared at Julian's mother. Then all at once she seemed to explode like a piece of machinery that had been given one ounce of pressure too much. Julian saw the black fist swing out with the red pocketbook. He shut his eyes and cringed as he heard the woman shout, "He don't take nobody's pennies!" When he opened his eyes, the woman was disappearing down the street with the little boy staring wide-eyed over her shoulder. Julian's mother was sitting on the sidewalk.

"I told you not to do that," Julian said angrily. "I told you not to do that!"

He stood over her for a minute, gritting his teeth. Her legs were stretched out in front of her and her hat was on her lap. He squatted down and looked her in the face. It was totally expressionless. "You got exactly what you deserved," he said. "Now get up."

He picked up her pocketbook and put what had fallen out back in it. He picked the hat up off her lap. The penny caught his eye on the sidewalk and he picked that up and let it drop before her eyes into the purse. Then he stood up and leaned over and held his hands out to pull her up. She remained immobile. He sighed. Rising above them on either side were black apartment buildings, marked with irregular rectangles of light. At the end of the block a man came out of a door and walked off in the opposite direction. "All right," he said, "suppose somebody happens by and wants to know why you're sitting on the sidewalk?"

She took the hand and, breathing hard, pulled heavily up on it and then stood for a moment, swaying slightly as if the spots of light in the darkness were circling around her. Her eyes, shadowed and confused, finally settled on his face. He did not try to conceal his irritation. "I hope this teaches you a lesson," he said. She leaned forward and her eyes raked his face. She seemed trying to determine his identity. Then, as if she found nothing familiar about him, she started off with a headlong movement in the wrong direction.

"Aren't you going on to the Y?" he asked.

"Home," she muttered.

"Well, are we walking?"

For answer she kept going. Julian followed along, his hands behind him. He saw no reason to let the lesson she had had go without backing it up with an explanation of its meaning. She might as well be made to understand what had happened to her. "Don't think that was just an uppity Negro woman," he said. "That was the whole colored race which will no longer take your condescending pennies. That was your black double. She can wear the same hat as you, and to be sure," he added gratuitously (because he thought it was funny), "it looked better on her than it did on you. What all this means," he said, "is that the old world is gone. The old manners are obsolete and your graciousness is not worth a damn." He thought bitterly of the house that had been lost for him. "You aren't who you think you are," he said.

She continued to plow ahead, paying no attention to him. Her hair had come undone on one side. She dropped her pocketbook and took no notice. He stooped and picked it up and handed it to her but she did not take it.

"You needn't act as if the world had come to an end," he said, "because it hasn't. From now on you've got to live in a new world and face a few realities for a change. Buck up," he said, "it won't kill you."

She was breathing fast.

"Let's wait on the bus," he said.

"Home," she said thickly.

"I hate to see you behave like this," he said. "Just like a child. I should be able to expect more of you." He decided to stop where he was and make her stop and wait for a bus. "I'm not going any farther," he said, stopping. "We're going on the bus."

She continued to go on as if she had not heard him. He took a few steps and caught her arm and stopped her. He looked into her face and caught his breath. He was looking into a face he had never seen before. "Tell Grandpa to come get me," she said.

He stared, stricken.

"Tell Caroline to come get me," she said.

Stunned, he let her go and she lurched forward again, walking as if one leg were shorter than the other. A tide of darkness seemed to be sweeping her from him. "Mother!" he cried. "Darling, sweetheart, wait!" Crumpling, she fell to the pavement. He dashed forward and fell at her side, crying, "Mamma, Mamma!" He turned her over. Her face was fiercely distorted. One eye, large and staring, moved slightly to the left as if it had become unmoored. The other remained fixed on him, raked his face again, found nothing and closed.

"Wait here, wait here!" he cried and jumped up and began to run for help toward a cluster of lights he saw in the distance ahead of him. "Help, help!" he shouted, but his voice was thin, scarcely a thread of sound. The lights drifted farther away the faster he ran and his feet moved numbly as if they carried him nowhere. The tide of darkness seemed to sweep him back to her, postponing from moment to moment his entry into the world of guilt and sorrow.

[1961]

QUESTIONS FOR STUDY

1. *How does Julian view himself at the beginning of the story? How does he view his mother?*
2. *To what extent are both mother and son tied to the past and living in a world of fantasy and illusion?*
3. *What is the "lesson" that Julian would like to teach his mother?*
4. *In what ways do Mrs. Chestny and the black woman resemble each other? Why does the black woman strike Mrs. Chestny?*
5. *What has risen and converged by the conclusion of the story? In what sense can the story be read as an allegory of the New South?*
6. *What (if anything) has Julian learned by the end of the story?*

FLANNERY O'CONNOR

A Good Man Is Hard to Find

THE GRANDMOTHER didn't want to go to Florida. She wanted to visit some of her connections in east Tennessee and she was seizing at every chance to change Bailey's mind. Bailey was the son she lived with, her only boy. He was sitting on the edge of his chair at the table, bent over the orange sports section of the *Journal.* "Now look here, Bailey," she said, "see here, read this," and she stood with one hand on her thin hip and the other rattling the newspaper at his bald head. "Here this fellow that calls himself The Misfit is aloose from the Federal Pen and headed toward Florida and you read here what it says he did to these people. Just you read it. I wouldn't take my children in any direction with a criminal like that aloose in it. I couldn't answer to my conscience if I did."

Bailey didn't look up from his reading so she wheeled around then and faced the children's mother, a young woman in slacks, whose face was as broad and innocent as a cabbage and was tied around with a green head-kerchief that had two points on the top like rabbit's ears. She was sitting on the sofa, feeding the baby his apricots out of a jar. "The children have been to Florida before," the old lady said. "You all ought to take them somewhere else for a change so they would see different parts of the world and be broad. They never have been to east Tennessee."

The children's mother didn't seem to hear her but the eight-year-old boy, John Wesley, a stocky child with glasses, said, "If you don't want to go to Florida, why dontcha stay at home?" He and the little girl, June Star, were reading the funny papers on the floor.

"She wouldn't stay at home to be queen for a day," June Star said without raising her yellow head.

"Yes and what would you do if this fellow, The Misfit, caught you?" the grandmother asked.

"I'd smack his face," John Wesley said.

"She wouldn't stay at home for a million bucks," June Star said. "Afraid she'd miss something. She has to go everywhere we go."

"All right, Miss," the grandmother said. "Just remember that the next time you want me to curl your hair."

June Star said her hair was naturally curly.

The next morning the grandmother was the first one in the car, ready to go. She had her big black valise that looked like the head of a hippopotamus in one corner, and underneath it she was hiding a basket with Pitty Sing, the cat, in it. She didn't intend for the cat to be left alone in the house for three days because he would miss her too much and she was afraid he might brush against one of the gas burners and accidentally asphyxiate himself. Her son, Bailey, didn't like to arrive at a motel with a cat.

She sat in the middle of the back seat with John Wesley and June Star on either side of her. Bailey and the children"s mother and the baby sat in front and they left Atlanta at eight forty-five with the mileage on the car at 55890. The grandmother wrote this down because she thought it would be interesting to say how many miles they had been when they got back. It took them twenty minutes to reach the outskirts of the city.

The old lady settled herself comfortably, removing her white cotton gloves and putting them up with her purse on the shelf in front of the back window. The children's mother still had on slacks and still had her head tied up in a green kerchief, but the grandmother had on a navy blue straw sailor hat with a bunch of white violets on the brim and a navy blue dress with a small white dot in the print. Her collars and cuffs were white organdy trimmed with lace and at her neckline she had pinned a purple spray of cloth violets containing a sachet. In case of an accident, anyone seeing her dead on the highway would know at once that she was a lady.

She said she thought it was going to be a good day for driving, neither too hot nor too cold, and she cautioned Bailey that the speed limit was fifty-five miles an hour and that the patrolmen hid themselves behind billboards and small clumps of trees and sped out after you before you had a chance to slow down. She pointed out interesting details of the scenery: Stone Mountain; the blue granite that in some places came up to both sides of the highway; the brilliant red clay banks slightly streaked with purple; and the various crops that made rows of green lace-work on the ground. The trees were full of silver-white sunlight and the meanest of them sparkled. The children were reading comic magazines and their mother had gone back to sleep.

"Let's go through Georgia fast so we won't have to look at it much," John Wesley said.

"If I were a little boy," said the grandmother, "I wouldn't talk about my native state that way. Tennessee has the mountains and Georgia has the hills."

"Tennessee is just a hillbilly dumping ground," John Wesley said, "and Georgia is a lousy state too."

"You said it," June Star said.

"In my time," said the grandmother, folding her thin veined fingers, "children were more respectful of their native states and their parents and everything else. People did right then. Oh look at the cute little pickaninny!" she said and pointed to a Negro child standing in the door of a shack. "Wouldn't that make a picture, now?" she asked and they all turned and looked at the little Negro out of the back window. He waved.

"He didn't have any britches on," June Star said.

"He probably didn't have any," the grandmother explained. "Little niggers in the country don't have things like we do. If I could paint, I'd paint that picture," she said.

The children exchanged comic books.

The grandmother offered to hold the baby and the children's mother passed him over the front seat to her. She set him on her knee and bounced him and told him about the things they were passing. She rolled her eyes and screwed up her mouth and stuck her leathery thin face into his smooth bland one. Occasionally he gave her a far-away smile. They passed a large cotton field with five or six graves fenced in the middle of it, like a small island. "Look at the graveyard!" the grandmother said, pointing it out. "That was the old family burying ground. That belonged to the plantation."

"Where's the plantation?" John Wesley asked.

"Gone With the Wind," said the grandmother. "Ha. Ha."

When the children finished all the comic books they had brought, they opened the lunch and ate it. The grandmother ate a peanut butter sandwich and an olive and would not let the children throw the box and the paper napkins out the window. When there was nothing else to do they played a game by choosing a cloud and making the other two guess what shape it suggested. John Wesley took one the shape of a cow and June Star guessed a cow and John Wesley said, no, an automobile, and June Star said he didn't play fair, and they began to slap each other over the grandmother.

The grandmother said she would tell them a story if they would keep quiet. When she told a story, she rolled her eyes and waved her head and was very dramatic. She said once when she was a maiden lady she had been courted by a Mr. Edgar Atkins Teagarden from Jasper, Georgia. She said he was a very good-looking man and a gentleman and that he brought her a watermelon every Saturday afternoon with his initials cut in it, E. A. T. Well, one Saturday, she said, Mr. Teagarden brought the watermelon and there was nobody at home and he left it on the front porch and returned in his buggy to Jasper, but she never got the watermelon, she said, because a nigger boy ate it when he saw the initials, E. A. T.! This story tickled John Wesley's funny bone and he giggled and giggled but June Star didn't think it was any good. She said she wouldn't marry a man that just brought her a watermelon on Saturday. The grandmother said she would have done well to marry Mr. Teagarden because he was a gentleman and had bought Coca-Cola stock when it first came out and that he had died only a few years ago, a very wealthy man.

They stopped at The Tower for barbecued sandwiches. The Tower was a part stucco and part wood filling station and dance hall set in a clearing outside of Timothy. A fat man named Red Sammy Butts ran it and there were signs stuck here and there on the building and for miles up and down the highway saying, TRY RED SAMMY'S FAMOUS BARBECUE. NONE LIKE FAMOUS RED SAMMY'S! RED SAM! THE FAT BOY WITH THE HAPPY LAUGH. A VETERAN! RED SAMMY'S YOUR MAN!

Red Sammy was lying on the bare ground outside The Tower with his head under a truck while a gray monkey about a foot high, chained to a small chinaberry tree, chattered nearby. The monkey sprang back into the tree and got on the highest limb as soon as he saw the children jump out of the car and run toward him.

Inside, The Tower was a long dark room with a counter at one end and tables at the other and dancing space in the middle. They all sat down at a board table next to the nickelodeon and Red Sam's wife, a tall burnt-brown woman with hair and eyes lighter than her skin, came and took their order. The children's mother put a dime in the machine and played "The Tennessee Waltz," and the grandmother said that tune always made her want to dance. She asked Bailey if he would like to dance but he only glared at her. He didn't have a naturally sunny disposition like she did and trips made him nervous. The grandmother's brown eyes were very bright. She swayed her head from side to side and pretended she was dancing in her chair. June Star said play something she could tap to so the children's mother put in another dime and played a fast number and June Star stepped out onto the dance floor and did her tap routine.

"Ain't she cute?" Red Sam's wife said, leaning over the counter. "Would you like to come be my little girl?"

"No I certainly wouldn't," June Star said. "I wouldn't live in a broken-down place like this for a million bucks!" and she ran back to the table.

"Ain't she cute?" the woman repeated, stretching her mouth politely.

"Arn't you ashamed?" hissed the grandmother.

Red Sam came in and told his wife to quit lounging on the counter and hurry up with these people's order. His khaki trousers reached just to his hip bones and his stomach hung over them like a sack of meal swaying under his shirt. He came over and sat down at a table nearby and let out a combination sigh and yodel. "You can't win," he said. "You can't win," and he wiped his sweating red face off with a gray handkerchief. "These days you don't know who to trust," he said. "Ain't that the truth?"

"People are certainly not nice like they used to be," said the grandmother.

"Two fellers come in here last week," Red Sammy said, "driving a Chrysler. It was a old beat-up car but it was a good one and these boys looked all right to me. Said they worked at the mill and you know I let them fellers charge the gas they bought? Now why did I do that?"

"Because you're a good man!" the grandmother said at once.

"Yes'm, I suppose so," Red Sam said as if he were struck with this answer.

His wife brought the orders, carrying the five plates all at once without a tray, two in each hand and one balanced on her arm. "It isn't a soul in this green world of God's that you can trust," she said. "And I don't count nobody out of that, not nobody," she repeated, looking at Red Sammy.

"Did you read about that criminal, The

Misfit, that's escaped?" asked the grand-mother.

"I wouldn't be a bit surprised if he didn't attact this place right here," said the woman. "If he hears about it being here, I wouldn't be none surprised to see him. If he hears it's two cent in the cash register, I wouldn't be a tall surprised if he . . ."

"That'll do," Red Sam said. "Go bring these people their Co'-Colas," and the woman went off to get the rest of the order.

"A good man is hard to find," Red Sammy said. "Everything is getting ter-rible. I remember the day you could go off and leave your screen door unlatched. Not no more."

He and the grandmother discussed better times. The old lady said that in her opinion Europe was entirely to blame for the way things were now. She said the way Europe acted you would think we were made of money and Red Sam said it was no use talking about it, she was exactly right. The children ran outside into the white sunlight and looked at the monkey in the lacy chinaberry tree. He was busy catching fleas on himself and biting each one carefully between his teeth as if it were a delicacy.

They drove off again into the hot after-noon. The grandmother took cat naps and woke up every few minutes with her own snoring. Outside of Toombsboro she woke up and recalled an old plantation that she had visited in this neighborhood once when she was a young lady. She said the house had six white columns across the front and that there was an avenue of oaks leading up to it and two little wooden trellis arbors on either side in front where you sat down with your suitor after a stroll in the garden. She re-called exactly which road to turn off to get to it. She knew that Bailey would not be willing to lose any time looking at an old house, but the more she talked about it, the more she wanted to see it once again and find out if the little twin arbors were still standing. "There was a secret panel in this house," she said craftily, not telling the truth but wishing that she were, "and the story went that all the

family silver was hidden in it when Sher-man came through but it was never found . . ."

"Hey!" John Wesley said. "Let's go see it! We'll find it! We'll poke all the wood-work and find it! Who lives there? Where do you turn off at? Hey Pop, can't we turn off there?"

"We never have seen a house with a secret panel!" June Star shrieked. "Let's go to the house with the secret panel! Hey Pop, can't we go see the house with the secret panel!"

"It's not far from here, I know," the grandmother said. "It wouldn't take over twenty minutes."

Bailey was looking straight ahead. His jaw was as rigid as a horseshoe. "No," he said.

The children began to yell and scream that they wanted to see the house with the secret panel. John Wesley kicked the back of the front seat and June Star hung over her mother's shoulder and whined desperately into her ear that they never had any fun even on their vacation, that they could never do what THEY wanted to do. The baby began to scream and John Wesley kicked the back of the seat so hard that his father could feel the blows in his kidney.

"All right!" he shouted and drew the car to a stop at the side of the road. "Will you all shut up? Will you all just shut up for one second? If you don't shut up, we won't go anywhere."

"It would be very educational for them," the grandmother murmured.

"All right," Bailey said, "but get this: this is the only time we're going to stop for anything like this. This is the one and only time."

"The dirt road that you have to turn down is about a mile back," the grand-mother directed. "I marked it when we passed."

"A dirt road," Bailey groaned.

After they had turned around and were headed toward the dirt road, the grand-mother recalled other points about the house, the beautiful glass over the front doorway and the candle-lamp in the hall. John Wesley said that the secret panel was probably in the fireplace.

"You can't go inside this house," Bailey said. "You don't know who lives there."

"While you all talk to the people in front, I'll run around behind and get in a window," John Wesley suggested.

"We'll all stay in the car," his mother said.

They turned onto the dirt road and the car raced roughly along in a swirl of pink dust. The grandmother recalled the times when there were no paved roads and thirty miles was a day's journey. The dirt road was hilly and there were sudden washes in it and sharp curves on dangerous embankments. All at once they would be on a hill, looking down over the blue tops of trees for miles around, then the next minute, they would be in a red depression with the dust-coated trees looking down on them.

"This place had better turn up in a minute," Bailey said, "or I'm going to turn around."

The road looked as if no one had traveled on it in months.

"It's not much farther," the grandmother said and just as she said it, a horrible thought came to her. The thought was so embarrassing that she turned red in the face and her eyes dilated and her feet jumped up, upsetting her valise in the corner. The instant the valise moved, the newspaper top she had over the basket under it rose with a snarl and Pitty Sing, the cat, sprang onto Bailey's shoulder.

· The children were thrown to the floor and their mother, clutching the baby, was thrown out the door onto the ground; the old lady was thrown into the front seat. The car turned over once and landed right-side-up in a gulch off the side of the road. Bailey remained in the driver's seat with the cat—gray-striped with a broad white face and an orange nose—clinging to his neck like a caterpillar.

As soon as the children saw they could move their arms and legs, they scrambled out of the car, shouting, "We've had an ACCIDENT!" The grandmother was curled up under the dashboard, hoping she was injured so that Bailey's wrath would not come down on her all at once. The horrible thought she had had before

the accident was that the house she had remembered so vividly was not in Georgia but in Tennessee.

Bailey removed the cat from his neck with both hands and flung it out the window against the side of a pine tree. Then he got out of the car and started looking for the children's mother. She was sitting against the side of the red gutted ditch, holding the screaming baby, but she only had a cut down her face and a broken shoulder. "We've had an ACCIDENT!" the children screamed in a frenzy of delight.

"But nobody's killed," June Star said with disappointment as the grandmother limped out of the car, her hat still pinned to her head but the broken front brim standing up at a jaunty angle and the violet spray hanging off the side. They all sat down in the ditch, except the children, to recover from the shock. They were all shaking.

"Maybe a car will come along," said the children's mother hoarsely.

"I believe I have injured an organ," said the grandmother, pressing her side, but no one answered her. Bailey's teeth were clattering. He had on a yellow sport shirt with bright blue parrots designed in it and his face was as yellow as the shirt. The grandmother decided that she would not mention that the house was in Tennessee.

The road was about ten feet above and they could see only the tops of the trees on the other side of it. Behind the ditch they were sitting in there were more woods, tall and dark and deep. In a few minutes they saw a car some distance away on top of a hill, coming slowly as if the occupants were watching them. The grandmother stood up and waved both arms dramatically to attract their attention. The car continued to come on slowly, disappeared around a bend and appeared again, moving even slower, on top of the hill they had gone over. It was a big black battered hearse-like automobile. There were three men in it.

It came to a stop just over them and for some minutes, the driver looked down with a steady expressionless gaze to where they were sitting, and didn't speak.

Then he turned his head and muttered something to the other two and they got out. One was a fat boy in black trousers and a red sweat shirt with a silver stallion embossed on the front of it. He moved around on the right side of them and stood staring, his mouth partly open in a kind of loose grin. The other had on khaki pants and a blue striped coat and a gray hat pulled down very low, hiding most of his face. He came around slowly on the left side. Neither spoke.

The driver got out of the car and stood by the side of it, looking down at them. He was an older man than the other two. His hair was just beginning to gray and he wore silver-rimmed spectacles that gave him a scholarly look. He had a long creased face and didn't have on any shirt or undershirt. He had on blue jeans that were too tight for him and was holding a black hat and a gun. The two boys also had guns.

"We've had an ACCIDENT!" the children screamed.

The grandmother had the peculiar feeling that the bespectacled man was someone she knew. His face was as familiar to her as if she had known him all her life but she could not recall who he was. He moved away from the car and began to come down the embankment, placing his feet carefully so that he wouldn't slip. He had on tan and white shoes and no socks, and his ankles were red and thin. "Good afternoon," he said. I see you all had you a little spill."

"We turned over twice!" said the grandmother.

"Oncet," he corrected. "We seen it happen. Try their car and see will it run, Hiram," he said quietly to the boy with the gray hat.

"What you got that gun for?" John Wesley asked. "Whatcha gonna do with that gun?"

"Lady," the man said to the children's mother, "would you mind calling them children to sit down by you? Children make me nervous. I want all you all to sit down right together there where you're at."

"What are you telling US what to do for?" June Star asked.

Behind them the line of woods gaped like a dark open mouth. "Come here," said their mother.

"Look here now," Bailey began suddenly, "we're in a predicament! We're in . . ."

The grandmother shrieked. She scrambled to her feet and stood staring. "You're The Misfit!" she said. "I recognized you at once!"

"Yes'm," the man said, smiling slightly as if he were pleased in spite of himself to be known, "but it would have been better for all of you, lady, if you hadn't of reckernized me."

Bailey turned his head sharply and said something to his mother that shocked even the children. The old lady began to cry and The Misfit reddened.

"Lady," he said, "don't you get upset. Sometimes a man says things he don't mean. I don't reckon he meant to talk to you thataway."

"You wouldn't shoot a lady, would you?" the grandmother said and removed a clean handkerchief from her cuff and began to slap at her eyes with it.

The Misfit pointed the toe of his shoe into the ground and made a little hole and then covered it up again. "I would hate to have to," he said.

"Listen," the grandmother almost screamed, "I know you're a good man. You don't look a bit like you have common blood. I know you must come from nice people!"

"Yes mam," he said, "finest people in the world." When he smiled he showed a row of strong white teeth. "God never made a finer woman than my mother and my daddy's heart was pure gold," he said. The boy with the red sweat shirt had come around behind them and was standing with his gun at his hip. The Misfit squatted down on the ground. "Watch them children, Bobby Lee," he said. "You know they make me nervous." He looked at the six of them huddled together in front of him and he seemed to be embarrassed as if he couldn't think of anything to say. "Ain't a cloud in the sky," he remarked, looking up at it. "Don't see no sun but don't see no cloud neither."

"Yes, it's a beautiful day," said the grandmother. "Listen," she said, "you shouldn't call yourself The Misfit because I know you're a good man at heart. I can just look at you and tell."

"Hush!" Bailey yelled. "Hush! Everybody shut up and let me handle this!" He was squatting in the position of a runner about to sprint forward but he didn't move.

"I pre-chate that, lady," The Misfit said and drew a little circle in the ground with the butt of his gun.

"It'll take a half a hour to fix this here car," Hiram called, looking over the raised hood of it.

"Well, first you and Bobby Lee get him and that little boy to step over yonder with you," The Misfit said, pointing to Bailey and John Wesley. "The boys want to ast you something," he said to Bailey. "Would you mind stepping back in them woods there with them?"

"Listen," Bailey began, "we're in a terrible predicament! Nobody realizes what this is," and his voice cracked. His eyes were as blue and intense as the parrots in his shirt and he remained perfectly still.

The grandmother reached up to adjust her hat brim as if she were going to the woods with him but it came off in her hand. She stood staring at it and after a second she let it fall on the ground. Hiram pulled Bailey up by the arm as if he were assisting an old man. John Wesley caught hold of his father's hand and Bobby Lee followed. They went off toward the woods and just as they reached the dark edge, Bailey turned and supporting himself against a gray naked pine trunk, he shouted, "I'll be back in a minute, Mamma, wait on me!"

"Come back this instant!" his mother shrilled but they all disappeared into the woods.

"Bailey Boy!" the grandmother called in a tragic voice but she found she was looking at The Misfit squatting on the ground in front of her. "I just know you're a good man," she said desperately. "You're not a bit common!"

"Nome, I ain't a good man," The Misfit said after a second as if he had considered her statement carefully, "but I ain't the worst in the world neither. My daddy said I was a different breed of dog from my brothers and sisters. 'You know,' Daddy said, 'it's some that can live their whole life out without asking about it and it's others has to know why it is, and this boy is one of the latters. He's going to be into everything!'" He put on his black hat and looked up suddenly and then away deep into the woods as if he were embarrassed again. "I'm sorry I don't have on a shirt before you ladies," he said, hunching his shoulders slightly. "We buried our clothes that we had on when we escaped and we're just making do until we can get better. We borrowed these from some folks we met," he explained.

"That's perfectly all right," the grandmother said. "Maybe Bailey has an extra shirt in his suitcase."

"I'll look and see terrectly," The Misfit said.

"Where are they taking him?" the children's mother screamed.

"Daddy was a card himself," The Misfit said. "You couldn't put anything over on him. He never got in trouble with the Authorities though. Just had the knack of handling them."

"You could be honest too if you'd only try," said the grandmother. "Think how wonderful it would be to settle down and live a comfortable life and not have to think about somebody chasing you all the time."

The Misfit kept scratching in the ground with the butt of his gun as if he were thinking about it. "Yes'm, somebody is always after you," he murmured.

The grandmother noticed how thin his shoulder blades were just behind his hat because she was standing up looking down on him. "Do you ever pray?" she asked.

He shook his head. All she saw was the black hat wiggle between his shoulder blades. "Nome," he said.

There was a pistol shot from the woods, followed closely by another. Then silence. The old lady's head jerked around. She could hear the wind move through the tree tops like a long satisfied insuck of breath. "Bailey Boy!" she called.

"I was a gospel singer for a while," The Misfit said. "I been most everything. Been in the arm service, both land and sea, at home and abroad, been twict married, been an undertaker, been with the railroads, plowed Mother Earth, been in a tornado, seen a man burnt alive oncet," and he looked up at the children's mother and the little girl who were sitting close together, their faces white and their eyes glassy; "I even seen a woman flogged," he said.

"Pray, pray," the grandmother began, "pray, pray . . ."

"I never was a bad boy that I remember of," The Misfit said in an almost dreamy voice, "but somewheres along the line I done something wrong and got sent to the penitentiary. I was buried alive," and he looked up and held her attention to him by a steady stare.

"That's when you should have started to pray," she said. "What did you do to get sent to the penitentiary that first time?"

"Turn to the right, it was a wall," The Misfit said, looking up again at the cloudless sky. "Turn to the left, it was a wall. Look up it was a ceiling, look down it was a floor. I forget what I done, lady. I set there and set there, trying to remember what it was I done and I ain't recalled it to this day. Oncet in a while, I would think it was coming to me, but it never come."

"Maybe they put you in by mistake," the old lady said vaguely.

"Nome," he said. "It wasn't no mistake. They had the papers on me."

"You must have stolen something," she said.

The Misfit sneered slightly. "Nobody had nothing I wanted," he said. "It was a head-doctor at the penitentiary said what I had done was kill my daddy but I known that for a lie. My daddy died in nineteen ought nineteen of the epidemic flu and I never had a thing to do with it. He was buried in the Mount Hopewell Baptist churchyard and you can go there and see for yourself."

"If you would pray," the old lady said, "Jesus would help you."

"That's right," The Misfit said.

"Well then, why don't you pray?" she asked trembling with delight suddenly.

"I don't want no hep," he said. "I'm doing all right by myself."

Bobby Lee and Hiram came ambling back from the woods. Bobby Lee was dragging a yellow shirt with bright blue parrots in it.

"Thow me that shirt, Bobby Lee," The Misfit said. The shirt came flying at him and landed on his shoulder and he put it on. The grandmother couldn't name what the shirt reminded her of. "No, lady," The Misfit said while he was buttoning it up, "I found out the crime don't matter. You can do one thing or you can do another, kill a man or take a tire off his car, because sooner or later you're going to forget what it was you done and just be punished for it."

The children's mother had begun to make heaving noises as if she couldn't get her breath. "Lady," he asked, "would you and that little girl like to step off yonder with Bobby Lee and Hiram and join your husband?"

"Yes, thank you," the mother said faintly. Her left arm dangled helplessly and she was holding the baby, who had gone to sleep, in the other. "Hep that lady up, Hiram," The Misfit said as she struggled to climb out of the ditch, "and Bobby Lee, you hold onto that little girl's hand."

"I don't want to hold hands with him," June Star said. "He reminds me of a pig."

The fat boy blushed and laughed and caught her by the arm and pulled her off into the woods after Hiram and her mother.

Alone with The Misfit, the grandmother found that she had lost her voice. There was not a cloud in the sky nor any sun. There was nothing around her but woods. She wanted to tell him that he must pray. She opened and closed her mouth several times before anything came out. Finally she found herself saying, "Jesus. Jesus," meaning, Jesus will help you, but the way she was saying it, it sounded as if she might be cursing.

"Yes'm," The Misfit said as if he agreed. "Jesus thown everything off balance. It was the same case with Him as with me except He hadn't committed any crime and they could prove I had committed one because they had the papers on me. Of course," he said, "they never shown me my papers. That's why I sign myself now. I said long ago, you get you a signature and sign everything you do and keep a copy of it. Then you'll know what you done and you can hold up the crime to the punishment and see do they match and in the end you'll have something to prove you ain't been treated right. I call myself The Misfit," he said, "because I can't make what all I done wrong fit what all I gone through in punishment."

There was a piercing scream from the woods, followed closely by a pistol report. "Does it seem right to you, lady, that one is punished a heap and another ain't punished at all?"

"Jesus!" the old lady cried. "You've got good blood! I know you wouldn't shoot a lady! I know you come from nice people! Pray! Jesus, you ought not to shoot a lady. I'll give you all the money I've got!"

"Lady," The Misfit said, looking beyond her far into the woods, "there never was a body that give the undertaker a tip."

There were two more pistol reports and the grandmother raised her head like a parched old turkey hen crying for water and called, "Bailey Boy, Bailey Boy!" as if her heart would break.

"Jesus was the only One that ever raised the dead," The Misfit continued, "and He shouldn't have done it. He thown everything off balance. If He did what He said, then it's nothing for you to do but thow away everything and follow Him, and if He didn't, then it's nothing for you to do but enjoy the few minutes you got left the best way you can—by killing somebody or burning down his house or doing some other meanness to him. No pleasure but meanness," he said and his voice had become almost a snarl.

"Maybe He didn't raise the dead," the old lady mumbled, not knowing what she was saying and feeling so dizzy that she sank down in the ditch with her legs twisted under her.

"I wasn't there so I can't say He didn't," The Misfit said. "I wisht I had of been there," he said, hitting the ground with his fist. "It ain't right I wasn't there because if I had of been there I would of known. Listen lady," he said in a high voice, "if I had of been there I would of known and I wouldn't be like I am now." His voice seemed about to crack and the grandmother's head cleared for an instant. She saw the man's face twisted close to her own as if he were going to cry and she murmured, "Why you're one of my babies. You're one of my own children!" She reached out and touched him on the shoulder. The Misfit sprang back as if a snake had bitten him and shot her three times through the chest. Then he put his gun down on the ground and took off his glasses and began to clean them.

Hiram and Bobby Lee returned from the woods and stood over the ditch, looking down at the grandmother who half sat and half lay in a puddle of blood with her legs crossed under her like a child's and her face smiling up at the cloudless sky.

Without his glasses, The Misfit's eyes were red-rimmed and pale and defenseless-looking. "Take her off and thow her where you thown the others," he said, picking up the cat that was rubbing itself against his leg.

"She was a talker, wasn't she?" Bobby Lee said, sliding down the ditch with a yodel.

"She would of been a good woman," The Misfit said, "if it had been somebody there to shoot her every minute of her life."

"Some fun!" Bobby Lee said.

"Shut up, Bobby Lee," The Misfit said. "It's no real pleasure in life."

[1953]

QUESTIONS FOR STUDY

1. *What conventional social and religious values does the grandmother represent? How are they exposed in the course of the story? What*

does *The Misfit* mean when he says of her: *"She would of been a good woman . . . if it had been somebody there to shoot her every minute of her life"? What is the function of the other members of the family?*

2. *What kind of philosophic position does The Misfit unknowingly give voice to in rationalizing his actions? What does he mean when he says that Jesus "thown everything off balance"? Whose view of reality is more honest, the grandmother's or The Misfit's?*

3. *How do the early episodes prepare for the meeting with The Misfit?*

4. *Is the chance meeting with The Misfit too contrived? To what extent are accident and chance an integral part of the story's meaning?*

5. *What final comment does the story seem to be making about "goodness" and about evil? What does the story seem to imply about the spiritual condition of modern man?*

FRANK O'CONNOR

Guests of the Nation

I

AT DUSK the big Englishman, Belcher, would shift his long legs out of the ashes and say, "Well, chums, what about it?" and Noble or me would say "All right, chum" (for we had picked up some of their curious expressions), and the little Englishman, Hawkins, would light the lamp and bring out the cards. Sometimes Jeremiah Donovan would come up and supervise the game and get excited over Hawkins's cards, which he always played badly, and shout at him as if he was one of our own "Ah, you divil, you, why didn't you play the tray?"

But ordinarily Jeremiah was a sober and contented poor devil like the big Englishman, Belcher, and was looked up to only because he was a fair hand at documents, though he was slow enough even with them. He wore a small cloth hat and big gaiters over his long pants, and you seldom saw him with his hands out of his pockets. He reddened when you talked to him, tilting from toe to heel and back, and looking down all the time at his big farmer's feet. Noble and me used to make fun of his broad accent, because we were from the town.

I couldn't at the time see the point of me and Noble guarding Belcher and Hawkins at all, for it was my belief that you could have planted that pair down anywhere from this to Claregalway and they'd have taken root there like a native weed. I never in my short experience seen two men to take to the country as they did.

They were handed on to us by the Second Battalion when the search for them became too hot, and Noble and myself, being young, took over with a natural feeling of responsibility, but Hawkins made us look like fools when he showed that he knew the country better than we did.

"You're the bloke they calls Bonaparte," he says to me. "Mary Brigid O'Connell told me to ask you what you done with the pair of her brother's socks you borrowed."

For it seemed, as they explained it, that the Second used to have little evenings, and some of the girls of the neighbourhood turned in, and, seeing they were such decent chaps, our fellows couldn't leave the two Englishmen out of them. Hawkins learned to dance "The Walls of Limerick," "The Siege of Ennis," and "The Waves of Tory" as well as any of them, though, naturally, he couldn't return the compliment, because our lads at that time did not dance foreign dances on principle.

So whatever privileges Belcher and Hawkins had with the Second they just naturally took with us, and after the first day or two we gave up all pretence of keeping a close eye on them. Not that they could have got far, for they had accents you could cut with a knife and wore khaki tunics and overcoats with civilian pants and boots. But it's my belief that they never had any idea of escaping and were quite content to be where they were.

It was a treat to see how Belcher got off with the old woman of the house where we were staying. She was a great warrant to scold, and cranky even with us, but before ever she had a chance of giving our guests, as I may call them, a lick of her tongue, Belcher had made her his friend for life. She was breaking sticks, and Belcher, who hadn't been more than ten minutes in the house, jumped up from his seat and went over to her.

"Allow me, madam," he says, smiling

From *Collection Two* by Frank O'Connor. Reprinted by permission of A. D. Peters and Company.

his queer little smile, "please allow me"; and he takes the bloody hatchet. She was struck too paralytic to speak, and after that, Belcher would be at her heels, carrying a bucket, a basket, or a load of turf, as the case might be. As Noble said, he got into looking before she leapt, and hot water, or any little thing she wanted, Belcher would have it ready for her. For such a huge man (and though I am five foot ten myself I had to look up at him) he had an uncommon shortness—or should I say lack?—of speech. It took us some time to get used to him, walking in and out, like a ghost, without a word. Especially because Hawkins talked enough for a platoon, it was strange to hear big Belcher with his toes in the ashes come out with a solitary "Excuse me, chum," or "That's right, chum." His one and only passion was cards, and I will say for him that he was a good card-player. He could have fleeced myself and Noble, but whatever we lost to him Hawkins lost to us, and Hawkins played with the money Belcher gave him.

Hawkins lost to us because he had too much old gab, and we probably lost to Belcher for the same reason. Hawkins and Noble would spit at one another about religion into the early hours of the morning, and Hawkins worried the soul out of Noble, whose brother was a priest, with a string of questions that would puzzle a cardinal. To make it worse, even in treating of holy subjects, Hawkins had a deplorable tongue. I never in all my career met a man who could mix such a variety of cursing and bad language into an argument. He was a terrible man, and a fright to argue. He never did a stroke of work, and when he had no one else to talk to, he fixed his claws into the old woman.

He met his match in her, for one day when he tried to get her to complain profanely of the drought, she gave him a great come-down by blaming it entirely on Jupiter Pluvius (a deity neither Hawkins nor I had ever heard of, though Noble said that among the pagans it was believed that he had something to do with the rain). Another day he was swearing at the capitalists for starting the German war when the old lady laid down her iron, puckered up her little crab's mouth, and said: "Mr. Hawkins, you can say what you like about the war, and think you'll deceive me because I'm only a simple poor countrywoman, but I know what started the war. It was the Italian Count that stole the heathen divinity out of the temple in Japan. Believe me, Mr. Hawkins, nothing but sorrow and want can follow the people that disturb the hidden powers."

A queer old girl, all right.

II

We had our tea one evening, and Hawkins lit the lamp and we all sat into cards. Jeremiah Donovan came in too, and sat down and watched us for a while, and it suddenly struck me that he had no great love for the two Englishmen. It came as a great surprise to me, because I hadn't noticed anything about him before.

Late in the evening a really terrible argument blew up between Hawkins and Noble, about capitalists and priests and love of your country.

"The capitalists," says Hawkins with an angry gulp, "pays the priests to tell you about the next world so as you won't notice what the bastards are up to in this."

"Nonsense, man!" says Noble, losing his temper. "Before ever a capitalist was thought of, people believed in the next world."

Hawkins stood up as though he was preaching a sermon.

"Oh, they did, did they?" he says with a sneer. "They believed all the things you believe, isn't that what you mean? And you believe that God created Adam, and Adam created Shem, and Shem created Jehoshophat. You believe all that silly old fairytale about Eve and Eden and the apple. Well, listen to me, chum. If you're entitled to hold a silly belief like that, I'm entitled to hold my silly belief—which is that the first thing your God created was a bleeding capitalist, with morality and Rolls-Royce complete. Am I right, chum?" he says to Belcher.

"You're right, chum," says Belcher

with his amused smile, and got up from the table to stretch his long legs into the fire and stroke his moustache. So, seeing that Jeremiah Donovan was going, and that there was no knowing when the argument about religion would be over, I went out with him. We strolled down to the village together, and then he stopped and started blushing and mumbling and saying I ought to be behind, keeping guard on the prisoners. I didn't like the tone he took with me, and anyway I was bored with life in the cottage, so I replied by asking him what the hell we wanted guarding them at all for. I told him I'd talked it over with Noble, and that we'd both rather be out with a fighting column.

"What use are those fellows to us?" says I.

He looked at me in surprise and said: "I thought you knew we were keeping them as hostages."

"Hostages?" I said.

"The enemy have prisoners belonging to us," he says, "and now they're talking of shooting them. If they shoot our prisoners, we'll shoot theirs."

"Shoot them?" I said.

"What else did you think we were keeping them for?" he says.

"Wasn't it very unforeseen of you not to warn Noble and myself of that in the beginning?" I said.

"How was it?" says he. "You might have known it."

"We couldn't know it, Jeremiah Donovan," says I. "How could we when they were on our hands so long?"

"The enemy have our prisoners as long and longer," says he.

"That's not the same thing at all," says I.

"What difference is there?" says he.

I couldn't tell him, because I knew he wouldn't understand. If it was only an old dog that was going to the vet's, you'd try and not get too fond of him, but Jeremiah Donovan wasn't a man that would ever be in danger of that.

"And when is this thing going to be decided?" says I.

"We might hear tonight," he says. "Or tomorrow or the next day at latest. So if it's only hanging round here that's a trouble to you, you'll be free soon enough."

It wasn't the hanging round that was a trouble to me at all by this time. I had worse things to worry about. When I got back to the cottage the argument was still on. Hawkins was holding forth in his best style, maintaining that there was no next world, and Noble was maintaining that there was; but I could see that Hawkins had had the best of it.

"Do you know what, chum?" he was saying with a saucy smile. "I think you're just as big a bleeding unbeliever as I am. You say you believe in the next world, and you know just as much about the next world as I do, which is sweet damn-all. What's heaven? You don't know. Where's heaven? You don't know. You know sweet damn-all! I ask you again, do they wear wings?"

"Very well, then," says Noble, "they do. Is that enough for you? They do wear wings."

"Where do they get them, then? Who makes them? Have they a factory for wings? Have they a sort of store where you hands in your chit and takes your bleeding wings?"

"You're an impossible man to argue with," says Noble. "Now, listen to me —" And they were off again.

It was long after midnight when we locked up and went to bed. As I blew out the candle I told Noble what Jeremiah Donovan was after telling me. Noble took it very quietly. When we'd been in bed about an hour he asked me did I think we ought to tell the Englishmen. I didn't think we should, because it was more than likely that the English wouldn't shoot our men, and even if they did, the brigade officers, who were always up and down with the Second Battalion and knew the Englishmen well, wouldn't be likely to want them plugged. "I think so too," says Noble. "It would be great cruelty to put the wind up them now."

"It was very unforseen of Jeremiah Donovan anyhow," says I.

It was next morning that we found it so hard to face Belcher and Hawkins. We went about the house all day scarcely saying a word. Belcher didn't seem to notice; he was stretched into the ashes as usual, with his usual look of waiting in quietness for something unforseen to happen, but Hawkins noticed and put it down to Noble's being beaten in the argument of the night before.

"Why can't you take a discussion in the proper spirit?" he says severely. "You and your Adam and Eve! I'm a Communist, that's what I am. Communist or anarchist, it all comes to much the same thing." And for hours he went round the house, muttering when the fit took him. "Adam and Eve! Adam and Eve! Nothing better to do with their time than picking bleeding apples!"

III

I don't know how we got through that day, but I was very glad when it was over, the tea things were cleared away, and Belcher said in his peaceable way: "Well, chums, what about it?" We sat round the table and Hawkins took out the cards, and just then I heard Jeremiah Donovan's footstep on the path and a dark presentiment crossed my mind. I rose from the table and caught him before he reached the door.

"What do you want?" I asked.

"I want those two soldier friends of yours," he says, getting red.

"Is that the way, Jeremiah Donovan?" I asked.

"That's the way. There were four of our lads shot this morning, one of them a boy of sixteen."

"That's bad," I said.

At that moment Noble followed me out, and the three of us walked down the path together, talking in whispers. Feeney, the local intelligence officer, was standing by the gate.

"What are you going to do about it?" I asked Jeremiah Donovan.

"I want you and Noble to get them out; tell them they're being shifted again; that'll be the quietest way."

"Leave me out of that," says Noble under his breath.

Jeremiah Donovan looks at him hard.

"All right," he says. "You and Feeney get a few tools from the shed and dig a hole by the far end of the bog. Bonaparte and myself will be after you. Don't let anyone see you with the tools. I wouldn't like it to go beyond ourselves."

We saw Feeney and Noble go round to the shed and went in ourselves. I left Jeremiah Donovan to do the explanations. He told them that he had orders to send them back to the Second Battalion. Hawkins let out a mouthful of curses, and you could see that though Belcher didn't say anything, he was a bit upset too. The old woman was for having them stay in spite of us, and she didn't stop advising them until Jeremiah Donovan lost his temper and turned on her. He had a nasty temper, I noticed. It was pitch-dark in the cottage by this time, but no one thought of lighting the lamp, and in the darkness the two Englishmen fetched their topcoats and said good-bye to the old woman.

"Just as a man makes a home of a bleeding place, some bastard at headquarters thinks you're too cushy and shunts you off," says Hawkins shaking her hand.

"A thousand thanks, madam," says Belcher. "A thousand thanks for everything"—as though he'd made it up.

We went round to the back of the house and down towards the bog. It was only then that Jeremiah Donovan told them. He was shaking with excitement.

"There were four of our fellows shot in Cork this morning and now you're to be shot as a reprisal."

"What are you talking about?" snaps Hawkins. "It's bad enough being mucked about as we are without having to put up with your funny jokes."

"It isn't a joke," says Donovan. "I'm sorry, Hawkins, but it's true," and begins on the usual rigmarole about duty and how unpleasant it is.

I never noticed that people who talk a lot about duty find it much of a trouble to them.

"Oh, cut it out!" says Hawkins.

"Ask Bonaparte," says Donovan, seeing that Hawkins isn't taking him seriously. "Isn't it true, Bonaparte?"

"It is," I say, and Hawkins stops.

"Ah, for Christ's sake, chum!"

"I mean it, chum," I say.

"You don't sound as if you meant it."

"If he doesn't mean it, I do," says Donovan, working himself up.

"What have you against me, Jeremiah Donovan?"

"I never said I had anything against you. But why did your people take out four of our prisoners and shoot them in cold blood?"

He took Hawkins by the arm and dragged him on, but it was impossible to make him understand that we were in earnest. I had the Smith and Wesson in my pocket and I kept fingering it and wondering what I'd do if they put up a fight for it or ran, and wishing to God they'd do one or the other. I knew if they did run for it, that I'd never fire on them. Hawkins wanted to know was Noble in it, and when we said yes, he asked us why Noble wanted to plug him. Why did any of us want to plug him? What had he done to us? Weren't we all chums? Didn't we understand him and didn't he understand us? Did we imagine for an instant that he'd shoot us for all the so-and-so officers in the so-and-so British Army?

By this time we'd reached the bog, and I was so sick I couldn't even answer him. We walked along the edge of it in the darkness, and every now and then Hawkins would call a halt and begin all over again, as if he was wound up, about our being chums, and I knew that nothing but the sight of the grave would convince him that we had to do it. And all the time I was hoping that something would happen; that they'd run for it or that Noble would take over the responsibility from me. I had the feeling that it was worse on Noble than on me.

IV

At last we saw the lantern in the distance and made towards it. Noble was carrying it, and Feeney was standing somewhere in the darkness behind him, and the picture of them so still and silent in the bogland brought it home to me that we were in earnest, and banished the last bit of hope I had.

Belcher, on recognizing Noble, said: "Hallo, chum," in his quiet way, but

Hawkins flew at him at once, and the argument began all over again, only this time Noble had nothing to say for himself and stood with his head down, holding the lantern between his legs.

It was Jeremiah Donovan who did the answering. For the twentieth time, as though it was haunting his mind, Hawkins asked if anybody thought he'd shoot Noble.

"Yes, you would," says Jeremiah Donovan.

"No, I wouldn't, damn you!"

"You would, because you'd know you'd be shot for not doing it."

"I wouldn't, not if I was to be shot twenty times over. I wouldn't shoot a pal. And Belcher wouldn't—isn't that right, Belcher?"

"That's right, chum," Belcher said, but more by way of answering the question than of joining in the argument. Belcher sounded as though whatever unforeseen thing he'd always been waiting for had come at last.

"Anyway, who says Noble would be shot if I wasn't? What do you think I'd do if I was in his place, out in the middle of a blasted bog?"

"What would you do?" asked Donovan.

"I'd go with him wherever he was going, of course. Share my last bob with him and stick by him through thick and thin. No one can ever say of me that I let down a pal."

"We've had enough of this," says Jeremiah Donovan, cocking his revolver. "Is there any message you want to send?"

"No, there isn't."

"Do you want to say your prayers?"

Hawkins came out with a cold-blooded remark that even shocked me and turned on Noble again.

"Listen to me, Noble," he says. "You and me are chums. You can't come over to my side, so I'll come over to your side. That show you I mean what I say? Give me a rifle and I'll go along with you and the other lads."

Nobody answered him. We knew there was no way out.

"Hear what I'm saying?" he says. "I'm through with it. I'm a deserter or anything else you like. I don't believe in your stuff, but it's no worse than mine. That satisfy you?"

Noble raised his head, but Donovan began to speak and he lowered it again without replying.

"For the last time, have you any messages to send?" says Donovan in a cold, excited sort of voice.

"Shut up, Donovan! You don't understand me, but these lads do. They're not the sort to make a pal and kill a pal. They're not the tools of any capitalist."

I alone of the crowd saw Donovan raise his Webley to the back of Hawkins's neck, and as he did so I shut my eyes and tried to pray. Hawkins had begun to say something else when Donovan fired, and as I opened my eyes at the bang, I saw Hawkins stagger at the knees and lie out flat at Noble's feet, slowly and as quiet as a kid falling asleep, with the lantern-light on his lean legs and bright farmer's boots. We all stood very still, watching him settle out in the last agony.

Then Belcher took out a handkerchief and began to tie it about his own eyes (in our excitement we'd forgotten to do the same for Hawkins), and, seeing it wasn't big enough, turned and asked for the loan of mine. I gave it to him and he knotted the two together and pointed with his foot at Hawkins.

"He's not quite dead," he says. "Better give him another."

Sure enough, Hawkins's left knee is beginning to rise. I bend down and put my gun to his head; then, recollecting myself, I get up again. Belcher understands what's in my mind.

"Give him his first," he says. "I don't mind. Poor bastard, we don't know what's happening to him now."

I knelt and fired. By this time I didn't seem to know what I was doing. Belcher, who was fumbling a bit awkwardly with the handkerchiefs, came out with a laugh as he heard the shot. It was the first time I had heard him laugh and it sent a shudder down my back; it sounded so unnatural.

"Poor bugger!" he said quietly. "And last night he was so curious about it all. It's very queer, chums, I always think. Now he knows as much about it as they'll

ever let him know, and last night he was all in the dark."

Donovan helped him to tie the handkerchiefs about his eyes. "Thanks, chum," he said. Donovan asked if there were any messages he wanted sent.

"No, chum," he says. "Not for me. If any of you would like to write to Hawkins's mother, you'll find a letter from her in his pocket. He and his mother were great chums. But my missus left me eight years ago. Went away with another fellow and took the kid with her. I like the feeling of a home, as you may have noticed, but I couldn't start again after that."

It was an extraordinary thing, but in those few minutes Belcher said more than in all the weeks before. It was just as if the sound of the shot had started a flood of talk in him and he could go on the whole night like that, quite happily, talking about himself. We stood round like fools now that he couldn't see us any longer. Donovan looked at Noble, and Noble shook his head. Then Donovan raised his Webley, and at that moment Belcher gives his queer laugh again. He may have thought we were talking about him, or perhaps he noticed the same thing I'd noticed and couldn't understand it.

"Excuse me, chums," he says. "I feel I'm talking the hell of a lot, and so silly, about my being so handy about a house and things like that. But this thing came on me suddenly. You'll forgive me, I'm sure."

"You don't want to say a prayer?" asks Donovan.

"No, chum," he says. "I don't think it would help. I'm ready, and you boys want to get it over."

"You understand that we're only doing our duty?" says Donovan.

Belcher's head was raised like a blind man's, so that you could only see his chin and the tip of his nose in the lantern-light.

"I never could make out what duty was myself," he said. "I think you're all good lads, if that's what you mean. I'm not complaining."

Noble, just as if he couldn't bear any more of it, raised his fist at Donovan, and in a flash Donovan raised his gun and fired. The big man went over like a sack of meal, and this time there was no need of a second shot.

I don't remember much about the burying, but that it was worse than all the rest because we had to carry them to the grave. It was all-mad lonely with nothing but a patch of lantern-light between ourselves and the dark, and birds hooting and screeching all round, disturbed by the guns. Noble went through Hawkins's belongings to find the letter from his mother, and then joined his hands together. He did the same with Belcher. Then, when we'd filled in the grave, we separated from Jeremiah Donovan and Feeney and took our tools back to the shed. All the way we didn't speak a word. The kitchen was dark and cold as we'd left it, and the old woman was sitting over the hearth, saying her beads. We walked past her into the room, and Noble struck a match to light the lamp. She rose quietly and came to the doorway with all her cantankerousness gone.

"What did ye do with them?" she asked in a whisper, and Noble started so that the match went out in his hand.

"What's that?" he asked without turning round.

"I heard ye," she said.

"What did you hear?" asked Noble.

"I heard ye. Do ye think I didn't hear ye, putting the spade back in the houseen?"

Noble struck another match and this time the lamp lit for him.

"Was that what ye did to them?" she asked.

Then, by God, in the very doorway, she fell on her knees and began praying, and after looking at her for a minute or two Noble did the same by the fireplace. I pushed my way out past her and left them at it. I stood at the door, watching the stars and listening to the shrieking of the birds dying out over the bogs. It is so strange what you feel at times like that that you can't describe it. Noble says he saw everything ten times the size, as though there were nothing in the whole world but that little patch of bog with the two Englishmen stiffening into it, but with me it was as if the patch of bog where the Englishmen were was a million miles away, and even Noble and the old woman, mumbling behind me, and the birds and the bloody stars were all far away, and I was somehow very small and very lost and lonely like a child astray in the snow. And anything that happened me afterwards, I never felt the same about again.

[1931]

QUESTIONS FOR STUDY

1. *How does the choice of a first person narrator add to the effectiveness of the story?*
2. *What are the chief identifying traits of the major characters? To what extent are they stereotypes? Does O'Connor succeed in individualizing them and in making them believable?*
3. *How is Jeremiah Donovan "different"?*
4. *What role does the old woman play? What is the significance of her speech blaming the war on the "Italian Count that stole the heathen divinity out of the temple in Japan"?*
5. *What does the narrator, Bonaparte, come to understand about himself and his relationship to others?*
6. *What comment does the story make about the relationship between patriotism and human decency?*

DOROTHY PARKER

Big Blonde

Hazel Morse was a large, fair woman of the type that incites some men when they use the word "blonde" to click their tongues and wag their heads roguishly. She prided herself upon her small feet and suffered for her vanity, boxing them in snub-toed, high-heeled slippers of the shortest bearable size. The curious things about her were her hands, strange terminations to the flabby white arms splattered with pale tan spots—long, quivering hands with deep and convex nails. She should not have disfigured them with little jewels.

She was not a woman given to recollections. At her middle thirties, her old days were a blurred and flickering sequence, an imperfect film, dealing with actions of strangers.

In her twenties, after the deferred death of a hazy widowed mother, she had been employed as a model in a wholesale dress establishment—it was still the day of the big woman, and she was then prettily colored and erect and high-breasted. Her job was not onerous, and she met numbers of men and spent numbers of evenings with them, laughing at their jokes and telling them she loved their neckties. Men liked her, and she took it for granted that the liking of many men was a desirable thing. Popularity seemed to her to be worth all the work that had to be put into its achievement. Men liked you because you were fun, and when they liked you they took you out, and there you were. So, and successfully, she was fun. She was a good sport. Men liked a good sport.

No other form of diversion, simpler or more complicated, drew her attention. She never pondered if she might not be better occupied doing something else. Her ideas, or, better, her acceptances, ran right along with those of the other substantially built blondes in whom she found her friends.

When she had been working in the dress establishment some years she met Herbie Morse. He was thin, quick, attractive, with shifting lines about his shiny, brown eyes and a habit of fiercely biting at the skin around his finger nails. He drank largely; she found that entertaining. Her habitual greeting to him was an allusion to his state of the previous night.

"Oh, what a peach you had," she used to say, through her easy laugh. "I thought I'd die, the way you kept asking the waiter to dance with you."

She liked him immediately upon their meeting. She was enormously amused at his fast, slurred sentences, his interpolations of apt phrases from vaudeville acts and comic strips; she thrilled at the feel of his lean arm tucked firm beneath the sleeve of her coat; she wanted to touch the wet, flat surface of his hair. He was as promptly drawn to her. They were married six weeks after they had met.

She was delighted at the idea of being a bride; coquetted with it, played upon it. Other offers of marriage she had had, and not a few of them, but it happened that they were all from stout, serious men who had visited the dress establishment as buyers; men from Des Moines and Houston and Chicago and, in her phrase, even funnier places. There was always something immensely comic to her in the thought of living elsewhere than New York. She could not regard as serious proposals that she share a western residence.

She wanted to be married. She was nearing thirty now, and she did not take the years well. She spread and softened, and her darkening hair turned her to in-expert dabblings with peroxide. There were times when she had little flashes of fear about her job. And she had had a couple of thousand evenings of being a good sport among her male acquaintances. She had come to be more conscientious than spontaneous about it.

Herbie earned enough, and they took a little apartment far uptown. There was a Mission-furnished dining-room with a hanging central light globed in liver-colored glass; in the living-room were an "over-stuffed suite," a Boston fern, and a reproduction of the Henner "Magdalene" with the red hair and the blue draperies; the bedroom was in gray enamel and old rose, with Herbie's photograph on Hazel's dressing-table and Hazel's likeness on Herbie's chest of drawers.

She cooked—and she was a good cook —and marketed and chatted with the delivery boys and the colored laundress. She loved the flat, she loved her life, she loved Herbie. In the first months of their marriage, she gave him all the passion she was ever to know.

She had not realized how tired she was. It was a delight, a new game, a holiday, to give up being a good sport. If her head ached or her arches throbbed, she complained piteously, babyishly. If her mood was quiet, she did not talk. If tears came to her eyes, she let them fall.

She fell readily into the habit of tears during the first year of her marriage. Even in her good sport days, she had been known to weep lavishly and disinterestedly on occasion. Her behavior at the theater was a standing joke. She could weep at anything in a play—tiny garments, love both unrequited and mutual, seduction, purity, faithful servitors, wedlock, the triangle.

"There goes Haze," her friends would say, watching her. "She's off again."

Wedded and relaxed, she poured her tears freely. To her who had laughed so much, crying was delicious. All sorrows became her sorrows; she was Tenderness. She would cry long and softly over newspaper accounts of kidnaped babies, deserted wives, unemployed men, strayed cats, heroic dogs. Even when the paper was no longer before her, her mind revolved upon these things and the drops slipped rhythmically over her plump cheeks.

"Honestly," she would say to Herbie, "all the sadness there is in the world when you stop to think about it!"

"Yeah," Herbie would say.

She missed nobody. The old crowd, the people who had brought her and Herbie together, dropped from their lives, lingeringly at first. When she thought of this at all, it was only to consider it fitting. This was marriage. This was peace.

But the thing was that Herbie was not amused.

For a time, he had enjoyed being alone with her. He found the voluntary isolation novel and sweet. Then it palled with a ferocious suddenness. It was as if one night, sitting with her in the steam-heated living-room, he would ask no more; and the next night he was through and done with the whole thing.

He became annoyed by her misty melancholies. At first, when he came home to find her softly tired and moody, he kissed her neck and patted her shoulder and begged her to tell her Herbie what was wrong. She loved that. But time slid by, and he found that there was never anything really, personally, the matter.

"Ah, for God's sake," he would say. "Crabbing again. All right, sit here and crab your head off. I'm going out."

And he would slam out of the flat and come back late and drunk.

She was completely bewildered by what happened to their marriage. First they were lovers; and then, it seemed without transition, they were enemies. She never understood it.

There were longer and longer intervals between his leaving his office and his arrival at the apartment. She went through agonies of picturing him run over and bleeding, dead and covered with a sheet. Then she lost her fears for his safety and grew sullen and wounded. When a person wanted to be with a person, he came as soon as possible. She desperately wanted him to want to be with her; her own hours only marked the time till he would come. It was often nearly nine o'clock before he came home to dinner. Always he had had many drinks, and their effect would die in him, leaving him loud and querulous and bristling for affronts.

He was too nervous, he said, to sit and do nothing for an evening. He boasted, probably not in all truth, that he had never read a book in his life.

"What am I expected to do—sit around this dump on my tail all night?" he would ask, rhetorically. And again he would slam out.

She did not know what to do. She could not manage him. She could not meet him.

She fought him furiously. A terrific domesticity had come upon her, and she would bite and scratch to guard it. She wanted what she called "a nice home." She wanted a sober, tender husband, prompt at dinner, punctual at work. She wanted sweet, comforting evenings. The idea of intimacy with other men was terrible to her; the thought that Herbie might be seeking entertainment in other women set her frantic.

It seemed to her that almost everything she read—novels from the drugstore lending library, magazine stories, women's pages in the papers—dealt with wives who lost their husbands' love. She could bear those, at that, better than accounts of neat, companionable marriage and living happily ever after.

She was frightened. Several times when Herbie came home in the evening, he found her determinedly dressed—she had had to alter those of her clothes that were not new, to make them fasten—and rouged.

"Let's go wild tonight, what do you say?" she would hail him. "A person's got lots of time to hang around and do nothing when they're dead."

So they would go out, to chop houses and the less expensive cabarets. But it turned out badly. She could no longer find amusement in watching Herbie drink. She could not laugh at his whimsicalities, she was so tensely counting his indulgences. And she was unable to keep back her remonstrances—"Ah, come on,

Herb, you've had enough, haven't you? You'll feel something terrible in the morning."

He would be immediately enraged. All right, crab; crab, crab, crab, crab, that was all she ever did. What a lousy sport *she* was! There would be scenes, and one or the other of them would rise and stalk out in fury.

She could not recall the definite day that she started drinking, herself. There was nothing separate about her days. Like drops upon a window-pane, they ran together and trickled away. She had been married six months; then a year; then three years.

She had never needed to drink, formerly. She could sit for most of a night at a table where the others were imbibing earnestly and never droop in looks or spirits, nor be bored by the doings of those about her. If she took a cocktail, it was so unusual as to cause twenty minutes or so of jocular comment. But now anguish was in her. Frequently, after a quarrel, Herbie would stay out for the night, and she could not learn from him where the time had been spent. Her heart felt tight and sore in her breast, and her mind turned like an electric fan.

She hated the taste of liquor. Gin, plain or in mixtures, made her promptly sick. After experiment, she found that Scotch whisky was best for her. She took it without water, because that was the quickest way to its effect.

Herbie pressed it on her. He was glad to see her drink. They both felt it might restore her high spirits, and their good times together might again be possible.

" 'Atta girl," he would approve her. "Let's see you get boiled, baby."

But it brought them no nearer. When she drank with him, there would be a little while of gaiety and then, strangely without beginning, they would be in a wild quarrel. They would wake in the morning not sure what it had all been about, foggy as to what had been said and done, but each deeply injured and bitterly resentful. There would be days of vengeful silence.

There had been a time when they had made up their quarrels, usually in bed.

There would be kisses and little names and assurances of fresh starts. . . . "Oh, it's going to be great now, Herb. We'll have swell times. I was a crab. I guess I must have been tired. But everything's going to be swell. You'll see."

Now there were no gentle reconciliations. They resumed friendly relations only in the brief magnanimity caused by liquor, before more liquor drew them into new battles. The scenes became more violent. There were shouted invectives and pushes, and sometimes sharp slaps. Once she had a black eye. Herbie was horrified next day at sight of it. He did not go to work; he followed her about, suggesting remedies and heaping dark blame on himself. But after they had had a few drinks—"to pull themselves together"—she made so many wistful references to her bruise that he shouted at her and rushed out and was gone for two days.

Each time he left the place in a rage, he threatened never to come back. She did not believe him, nor did she consider separation. Somewhere in her head or her heart was the lazy, nebulous hope that things would change and she and Herbie settle suddenly into soothing married life. Here were her home, her furniture, her husband, her station. She summoned no alternatives.

She could no longer bustle and potter. She had no more vicarious tears; the hot drops she shed were for herself. She walked ceaselessly about the rooms, her thoughts running mechanically round and round Herbie. In those days began the hatred of being alone that she was never to overcome. You could be by yourself when things were all right, but when you were blue you got the howling horrors.

She commenced drinking alone, little, short drinks all through the day. It was only with Herbie that alcohol made her nervous and quick in offense. Alone, it blurred sharp things for her. She lived in a haze of it. Her life took on a dream-like quality. Nothing was astonishing.

A Mrs. Martin moved into the flat across the hall. She was a great blonde woman of forty, a promise in looks of what Mrs. Morse was to be. They made acquaintance, quickly became inseparable. Mrs. Morse spent her days in the opposite apartment. They drank together, to brace themselves after the drinks of the nights before.

She never confided her troubles about Herbie to Mrs. Martin. The subject was too bewildering to her to find comfort in talk. She let it be assumed that her husband's business kept him much away. It was not regarded as important; husbands, as such, played but shadowy parts in Mrs. Martin's circle.

Mrs. Martin had no visible spouse; you were left to decide for yourself whether he was or was not dead. She had an admirer, Joe, who came to see her almost nightly. Often he brought several friends with him—"The Boys," they were called. The Boys were big, red, good-humored men, perhaps forty-five, perhaps fifty. Mrs. Morse was glad of invitations to join the parties—Herbie was scarcely ever at home at night now. If he did come home, she did not visit Mrs. Martin. An evening alone with Herbie meant inevitably a quarrel, yet she would stay with him. There was always her thin and wordless idea that, maybe, this night, things would begin to be all right.

The Boys brought plenty of liquor along with them whenever they came to Mrs. Martin's. Drinking with them, Mrs. Morse became lively and good-natured and audacious. She was quickly popular. When she had drunk enough to cloud her most recent battle with Herbie, she was excited by their approbation. Crab, was she? Rotten sport, was she? Well, there were some that thought different.

Ed was one of The Boys. He lived in Utica—had "his own business" there, was the awed report—but he came to New York almost every week. He was married. He showed Mrs. Morse the then current photographs of Junior and Sister, and she praised them abundantly and sincerely. Soon it was accepted by the others that Ed was her particular friend.

He staked her when they all played poker; sat next her and occasionally rubbed his knee against hers during the game. She was rather lucky. Frequently she went home with a twenty-dollar bill or a ten-dollar bill or a handful of crumpled dollars. She was glad of them. Herbie was getting, in her words, something awful about money. To ask him for it brought an instant row.

"What the hell do you do with it?" he would say. "Shoot it all on Scotch?"

"I try to run this house half-way decent," she would retort. "Never thought of that, did you? Oh, no, his lordship couldn't be bothered with that."

Again, she could not find a definite day, to fix the beginning of Ed's proprietorship. It became his custom to kiss her on the mouth when he came in, as well as for farewell, and he gave her little quick kisses of approval all through the evening. She liked this rather more than she disliked it. She never thought of his kisses when she was not with him.

He would run his hand lingeringly over her back and shoulders.

"Some dizzy blonde, eh?" he would say. "Some doll."

One afternoon she came home from Mrs. Martin's to find Herbie in the bedroom. He had been away for several nights, evidently on a prolonged drinking bout. His face was gray, his hands jerked as if they were on wires. On the bed were two old suitcases, packed high. Only her photograph remained on his bureau, and the wide doors of his closet disclosed nothing but coat-hangers.

"I'm blowing," he said. "I'm through with the whole works. I got a job in Detroit."

She sat down on the edge of the bed. She had drunk much the night before, and the four Scotches she had had with Mrs. Martin had only increased her fogginess.

"Good job?" she said.

"Oh, yeah," he said. "Looks all right."

He closed a suitcase with difficulty, swearing at it in whispers.

"There's some dough in the bank," he said. "The bank book's in your top drawer. You can have the furniture and stuff."

He looked at her, and his forehead twitched.

"God damn it, I'm through, I'm telling you," he cried. "I'm through."

"All right, all right," she said. "I heard you, didn't I?"

She saw him as if he were at one end of a cannon and she at the other. Her head was beginning to ache bumpingly, and her voice had a dreary, tiresome tone. She could not have raised it.

"Like a drink before you go?" she asked.

Again he looked at her, and a corner of his mouth jerked up.

"Cockeyed again for a change, aren't you?" he said. "That's nice. Sure, get a couple of shots, will you?"

She went to the pantry, mixed him a stiff highball, poured herself a couple of inches of whisky and drank it. Then she gave herself another portion and brought the glasses into the bedroom. He had strapped both suitcases and had put on his hat and overcoat.

He took his highball.

'Well," he said, and he gave a sudden, uncertain laugh. "Here's mud in your eye."

"Mud in your eye," she said.

They drank. He put down his glass and took up the heavy suitcases.

"Got to get a train around six," he said.

She followed him down the hall. There was a song, a song that Mrs. Martin played doggedly on the phonograph, running loudly through her mind. She had never liked the thing.

> *"Night and daytime,*
> *Always playtime.*
> *Ain't we got fun?"*

At the door he put down the bags and faced her.

"Well," he said. "Well, take care of yourself. You'll be all right, will you?"

"Oh, sure," she said.

He opened the door, then came back to her, holding out his hand.

" 'By, Haze," he said. "Good luck to you."

She took his hand and shook it.

"Pardon my wet glove," she said.

When the door had closed behind him, she went back to the pantry.

She was flushed and lively when she went in to Mrs. Martin's that evening. The Boys were there, Ed among them. He was glad to be in town, frisky and loud and full of jokes. But she spoke quietly to him for a minute.

"Herbie blew today," she said. "Going to live out west."

"That so?" he said. He looked at her and played with the fountain pen clipped to his waistcoat pocket.

"Think he's gone for good, do you?" he asked.

"Yeah," she said. "I know he is. I know. Yeah."

"You going to live on across the hall just the same?" he said. "Know what you're going to do?"

"Gee, I don't know," she said. "I don't give much of a damn."

"Oh, come on, that's no way to talk," he told her. "What you need—you need a little snifter. How about it?"

"Yeah," she said. "Just straight."

She won forty-three dollars at poker. When the game broke up, Ed took her back to her apartment.

"Got a little kiss for me?" he asked.

He wrapped her in his big arms and kissed her violently. She was entirely passive. He held her away and looked at her.

"Little tight, honey?" he asked, anxiously. "Not going to be sick, are you?"

"Me?" she said. "I'm swell."

II

When Ed left in the morning, he took her photograph with him. He said he wanted her picture to look at, up in Utica. "You can have that one on the bureau," she said.

She put Herbie's picture in a drawer, out of her sight. When she could look at it, she meant to tear it up. She was fairly successful in keeping her mind from racing around him. Whisky slowed it for her. She was almost peaceful, in her mist.

She accepted her relationship with Ed without question or enthusiasm. When he was away, she seldom thought definitely of him. He was good to her; he gave her frequent presents and a regular allowance. She was even able to save. She did not plan ahead of any day, but her wants were few, and you might as well put money in the bank as have it lying around.

When the lease of her apartment neared its end, it was Ed who suggested moving. His friendship with Mrs. Martin and Joe had become strained over a dispute at poker; a feud was impending.

"Let's get the hell out of here," Ed said. "What I want you to have is a place near the Grand Central. Make it easier for me."

So she took a little flat in the Forties. A colored maid came in every day to clean and to make coffee for her—she was "through with that housekeeping stuff," she said, and Ed, twenty years married to a passionately domestic woman, admired this romantic uselessness and felt doubly a man of the world in abetting it.

The coffee was all she had until she went out to dinner, but alcohol kept her fat. Prohibition she regarded only as a basis for jokes. You could always get all you wanted. She was never noticeably drunk and seldom nearly sober. It required a larger daily allowance to keep her misty-minded. Too little, and she was achingly melancholy.

Ed brought her to Jimmy's. He was proud, with the pride of the transient who would be mistaken for a native, in his knowledge of small, recent restaurants occupying the lower floors of shabby brownstone houses; places where, upon mentioning the name of an habitué friend, might be obtained strange whisky and fresh gin in many of their ramifications. Jimmy's place was the favorite of his acquaintances.

There, through Ed, Mrs. Morse met many men and women, formed quick friendships. The men often took her out when Ed was in Utica. He was proud of her popularity.

She fell into the habit of going to Jimmy's alone when she had no engagement. She was certain to meet some people she knew, and join them. It was a club for her friends, both men and women.

The women at Jimmy's looked remarkably alike, and this was curious, for, through feuds, removals, and opportunities of more profitable contacts, the personnel of the group changed constantly. Yet always the newcomers resembled those whom they replaced. They were all big women and stout, broad of shoulder and abundantly breasted, with faces thickly clothed in soft, high-colored flesh. They laughed loud and often, showing opaque and lusterless teeth like squares of crockery. There was about them the health of the big, yet a slight, unwholesome suggestion of stubborn preservation. They might have been thirty-six or forty-five or anywhere between.

They composed their titles of their own first names with their husbands' surnames—Mrs. Florence Miller, Mrs. Vera Riley, Mrs. Lilian Block. This gave at the same time the solidity of marriage and the glamour of freedom. Yet only one or two were actually divorced. Most of them never referred to their dimmed spouses; some, a shorter time separated, described them in terms of great biological interest. Several were mothers, each of an only child—a boy at school somewhere, or a girl being cared for by a grandmother. Often, well on toward morning, there would be displays of kodak portraits and of tears.

They were comfortable women, cordial and friendly and irrepressibly matronly. Theirs was the quality of ease. Become fatalistic, especially about money matters, they were unworried. Whenever their funds dropped alarmingly, a new donor appeared; this had always happened. The aim of each was to have one man, permanently, to pay all her bills, in return for which she would have immediately given up other admirers and probably would have become exceedingly fond of him; for the affections of all of them were, by now, unexacting, tranquil, and easily arranged. This end, however, grew increasingly difficult yearly. Mrs. Morse was regarded as fortunate.

Ed had a good year, increased her allowance and gave her a sealskin coat.

But she had to be careful of her moods with him. He insisted upon gaiety. He would not listen to admissions of aches or weariness.

"Hey, listen," he would say, "I got worries of my own, and plenty. Nobody wants to hear other people's troubles, sweetie. What you got to do, you got to be a sport and forget it. See? Well, slip us a little smile, then. That's my girl."

She never had enough interest to quarrel with him as she had with Herbie, but she wanted the privilege of occasional admitted sadness. It was strange. The other women she saw did not have to fight their moods. There was Mrs. Florence Miller who got regular crying jags, and the men sought only to cheer and comfort her. The others spent whole evenings in grieved recitals of worries and ills; their escorts paid them deep sympathy. But she was instantly undesirable when she was low in spirits. Once, at Jimmy's, when she could not make herself lively, Ed had walked out and left her.

"Why the hell don't you stay home and not go spoiling everybody's evening?" he had roared.

Even her slightest acquaintances seemed irritated if she were not conspicuously light-hearted.

"What's the matter with you, anyway?" they would say. "Be your age, why don't you? Have a little drink and snap out of it."

When her relationship with Ed had continued nearly three years, he moved to Florida to live. He hated leaving her; he gave her a large check and some shares of a sound stock, and his pale eyes were wet when he said good-by. She did not miss him. He came to New York infrequently, perhaps two or three times a year, and hurried directly from the train to see her. She was always pleased to have him come and never sorry to see him go.

Charley, an acquaintance of Ed's that she had met at Jimmy's, had long admired her. He had always made opportunities of touching her and leaning close to talk to her. He asked repeatedly of all their friends if they had ever heard such a fine laugh as she had. After Ed left, Charley became the main figure in her life. She classified him and spoke of him as "not so bad." There was nearly a year of Charley; then she divided her time between him and Sydney, another frequenter of Jimmy's; then Charley slipped away altogether.

Sydney was a little, brightly dressed, clever Jew. She was perhaps nearest contentment with him. He amused her always; her laughter was not forced.

He admired her completely. Her softness and size delighted him. And he thought she was great, he often told her, because she kept gay and lively when she was drunk.

"Once I had a gal," he said, "used to try and throw herself out of the window every time she got a can on. Jee-*zuss*," he added, feelingly.

Then Sydney married a rich and watchful bride, and then there was Billy. No—after Sydney came Ferd, then Billy. In her haze, she never recalled how men entered her life and left it. There were no surprises. She had no thrill at their advent, nor woe at their departure. She seemed to be always able to attract men. There was never another as rich as Ed, but they were all generous to her, in their means.

Once she had news of Herbie. She met Mrs. Martin dining at Jimmy's, and the old friendship was vigorously renewed. The still admiring Joe, while on a business trip, had seen Herbie. He had settled in Chicago, he looked fine, he was living with some woman—seemed to be crazy about her. Mrs. Morse had been drinking vastly that day. She took the news with mild interest, as one hearing of the sex peccadilloes of somebody whose name is, after a moment's groping, familiar.

"Must be damn near seven years since I saw him," she commented. "Gee. Seven years."

More and more, her days lost their individuality. She never knew dates, nor was sure of the day of the week.

"My God, was that a year ago!" she would exclaim, when an event was recalled in conversation.

She was tired so much of the time. Tired and blue. Almost everything could give her the blues. Those old horses she saw on Sixth Avenue—struggling and slipping along the car-tracks, or standing at the curb, their heads dropped level with their worn knees. The tightly stored tears would squeeze from her eyes as she teetered past on her aching feet in the stubby, champagne-colored slippers.

The thought of death came and stayed with her and lent her a sort of drowsy cheer. It would be nice, nice and restful, to be dead.

There was no settled, shocked moment when she first thought of killing herself; it seemed to her as if the idea had always been with her. She pounced upon all the accounts of suicides in the newspapers. There was an epidemic of self-killings—or maybe it was just that she searched for the stories of them so eagerly that she found many. To read of them roused reassurance in her; she felt a cozy solidarity with the big company of the voluntary dead.

She slept, aided by whisky, till deep into the afternoons, then lay abed, a bottle and glass at her hand, until it was time to dress and go out for dinner. She was beginning to feel toward alcohol a little puzzled distrust, as toward an old friend who has refused a simple favor. Whisky could still soothe her for most of the time, but there were sudden, inexplicable moments when the cloud fell treacherously away from her, and she was sawed by the sorrow and bewilderment and nuisance of all living. She played voluptuously with the thought of cool, sleepy retreat. She had never been troubled by religious belief and no vision of an after-life intimidated her. She dreamed by day of never again putting on tight shoes, of never having to laugh and listen and admire, of never more being a good sport. Never.

But how would you do it? It made her sick to think of jumping from heights. She could not stand a gun. At the theater, if one of the actors drew a revolver, she crammed her fingers into her ears and could not even look at the stage until after the shot had been fired. There was no gas in her flat. She looked long at the bright blue veins in her slim wrists—a cut with a razor blade, and there you'd be. But it would hurt, hurt like hell, and there would be blood to see. Poison—something tasteless and quick and painless—was the thing. But they wouldn't sell it to you in drugstores, because of the law.

She had few other thoughts.

There was a new man now—Art. He was short and fat and exacting and hard on her patience when he was drunk. But there had been only occasionals for some time before him, and she was glad of a little stability. Too, Art must be away for weeks at a stretch, selling silks, and that was restful. She was convincingly gay with him, though the effort shook her.

"The best sport in the world," he would murmur, deep in her neck. "The best sport in the world."

One night, when he had taken her to Jimmy's, she went into the dressing-room with Mrs. Florence Miller. There, while designing curly mouths on their faces with lip-rouge, they compared experiences of insomnia.

"Honestly," Mrs. Morse said, "I wouldn't close an eye if I didn't go to bed full of Scotch. I lie there and toss and turn and toss and turn. Blue! Does a person get blue lying awake that way!"

"Say, listen, Hazel," Mrs. Miller said, impressively, "I'm telling you I'd be awake for a year if I didn't take veronal. That stuff makes you sleep like a fool."

"Isn't it poison, or something?" Mrs. Morse asked.

"Oh, you take too much and you're out for the count," said Mrs. Miller. "I just take five grains—they come in tablets. I'd be scared to fool around with it. But five grains, and you cork off pretty."

"Can you get it anywhere?" Mrs. Morse felt superbly Machiavellian.

"Get all you want in Jersey," said Mrs. Miller. "They won't give it to you here without you have a doctor's prescription. Finished? We'd better go back and see what the boys are doing."

That night, Art left Mrs. Morse at the door of her apartment; his mother was in town. Mrs. Morse was still sober, and it happened that there was no whisky left in her cupboard. She lay in bed, looking up at the black ceiling.

She rose early, for her, and went to New Jersey. She had never taken the tube, and did not understand it. So she went to the Pennsylvania Station and bought a railroad ticket to Newark. She thought of nothing in particular on the trip out. She looked at the uninspired hats of the women about her and gazed through the smeared window at the flat, gritty scene.

In Newark, in the first drug-store she came to, she asked for a tin of talcum powder, a nailbrush, and a box of veronal tablets. The powder and the brush were to make the hypnotic seem also a casual need. The clerk was entirely unconcerned. "We only keep them in bottles," he said, and wrapped up for her a little glass vial containing ten white tablets, stacked one on another.

She went to another drug-store and bought a face-cloth, an orange-wood stick, and a bottle of veronal tablets. The clerk was also uninterested.

"Well, I guess I got enough to kill an ox," she thought, and went back to the station.

At home, she put the little vials in the drawer of her dressing-table and stood looking at them with a dreamy tenderness.

"There they are, God bless them," she said, and she kissed her finger-tip and touched each bottle.

The colored maid was busy in the living-room.

"Hey, Nettie," Mrs. Morse called. "Be an angel, will you? Run around to Jimmy's and get me a quart of Scotch."

She hummed while she awaited the girl's return.

During the next few days, whisky ministered to her as tenderly as it had done when she first turned to its aid. Alone, she was soothed and vague, at Jimmy's she was the gayest of the groups. Art was delighted with her.

Then, one night, she had an appointment to meet Art at Jimmy's for an early dinner. He was to leave afterward on a business excursion, to be away for a week. Mrs. Morse had been drinking all the afternoon; while she dressed to go out, she felt herself rising pleasurably from drowsiness to high spirits. But as she came out into the street the effects of the whisky deserted her completely, and she was filled with a slow, grinding wretchedness so horrible that she stood swaying on the pavement, unable for a moment to move forward. It was a gray night with spurts of mean, thin snow, and the streets shone with dark ice. As she slowly crossed Sixth Avenue, consciously dragging one foot past the other, a big, scarred horse pulling a rickety express-wagon crashed to his knees before her. The driver swore and screamed and lashed the beast insanely, bringing the whip back over his shoulder for every blow, while the horse struggled to get a footing on the slippery asphalt. A group gathered and watched with interest.

Art was waiting, when Mrs. Morse reached Jimmy's.

"What's the matter with you, for God's sake?" was his greeting to her.

"I saw a horse," she said. "Gee, I—a person feels sorry for horses. I—it isn't just horses. Everything's kind of terrible, isn't it? I can't help getting sunk."

"Ah, sunk, me eye," he said. "What's the idea of all the bellyaching? What have you got to be sunk about?"

"I can't help it," she said.

"Ah, help it, me eye," he said. "Pull yourself together, will you? Come on and sit down, and take that face off you."

She drank industriously and she tried hard, but she could not overcome her melancholy. Others joined them and commented on her gloom, and she could do no more for them than smile weakly. She made little dabs at her eyes with her handkerchief, trying to time her movements so they would be unnoticed, but several times Art caught her and scowled and shifted impatiently in his chair.

When it was time for him to go to his train, she said she would leave, too, and go home.

"And not a bad idea, either," he said.

"See if you can't sleep yourself out of it. I'll see you Thursday. For God's sake, try and cheer up by then, will you?"

"Yeah," she said. "I will."

In her bedroom, she undressed with a tense speed wholly unlike her usual slow uncertainty. She put on her nightgown, took off her hair-net and passed the comb quickly through her dry, vari-colored hair. Then she took the two little vials from the drawer and carried them into the bathroom. The splintering misery had gone from her, and she felt the quick excitement of one who is about to receive an anticipated gift.

She uncorked the vials, filled a glass with water and stood before the mirror, a tablet between her fingers. Suddenly she bowed graciously to her reflection, and raised the glass to it.

"Well, here's mud in your eye," she said.

The tablets were unpleasant to take, dry and powdery and sticking obstinately half-way down her throat. It took her a long time to swallow all twenty of them. She stood watching her reflection with deep, impersonal interest, studying the movements of the gulping throat. Once more she spoke aloud.

"For God's sake, try and cheer up by Thursday, will you?" she said. "Well, you know what he can do. He and the whole lot of them."

She had no idea how quickly to expect effect from the veronal. When she had taken the last tablet, she stood uncertainly, wondering, still with a courteous, vicarious interest, if death would strike her down then and there. She felt in no way strange, save for a slight stirring of sickness from the effort of swallowing the tablets, nor did her reflected face look at all different. It would not be immediate, then; it might even take an hour or so.

She stretched her arms high and gave a vast yawn.

"Guess I'll go to bed," she said. "Gee, I'm nearly dead."

That struck her as comic, and she turned out the bathroom light and went in and laid herself down in her bed, chuckling softly all the time.

"Gee, I'm nearly dead," she quoted. "That's a hot one!"

III

Nettie, the colored maid, came in late the next afternoon to clean the apartment, and found Mrs. Morse in her bed. But then, that was not unusual. Usually, though, the sounds of cleaning waked her, and she did not like to wake up. Nettie, an agreeable girl, had learned to move softly about her work.

But when she had done the living-room and stolen in to tidy the little square bedroom, she could not avoid a tiny clatter as she arranged the objects on the dressing-table. Instinctively, she glanced over her shoulder at the sleeper, and without warning a sickly uneasiness crept over her. She came to the bed and stared down at the woman lying there.

Mrs. Morse lay on her back, one flabby, white arm flung up, the wrist against her forehead. Her stiff hair hung untenderly along her face. The bed covers were pushed down, exposing a deep square of soft neck and a pink nightgown, its fabric worn uneven by many launderings; her great breasts, freed from their tight confiner, sagged beneath her arm-pits. Now and then she made knotted, snoring sounds, and from the corner of her opened mouth to the blurred turn of her jaw ran a lane of crusted spittle.

"Mis' Morse," Nettie called. "Oh, Mis' Morse! It's terrible late."

Mrs. Morse made no move.

"Mis' Morse," said Nettie. "Look, Mis' Morse. How'm I goin' get this bed made?"

Panic sprang upon the girl. She shook the woman's hot shoulder.

"Ah, wake up, will yuh?" she whined. "Ah, please wake up."

Suddenly the girl turned and ran out in the hall to the elevator door, keeping her thumb firm on the black, shiny button until the elderly car and its Negro attendant stood before her. She poured a jumble of words over the boy, and led him back to the apartment. He tiptoed creakingly in to the bedside; first gingerly, then so lustily that he left marks in the soft flesh, he prodded the unconscious woman.

"Hey, there!" he cried, and listened intently, as for an echo.

"Jeez. Out like a light," he commented.

At his interest in the spectacle, Nettie's panic left her. Importance was big in both of them. They talked in quick, unfinished whispers, and it was the boy's suggestion that he fetch the young doctor who lived on the ground floor. Nettie hurried along with him. They looked forward to the limelit moment of breaking their news of something untoward, something pleasurably unpleasant. Mrs. Morse had become the medium of drama. With no ill wish to her, they hoped that her state was serious, that she would not let them down by being awake and normal on their return. A little fear of this determined them to make the most, to the doctor, of her present condition. "Matter of life and death," returned to Nettie from her thin store of reading. She considered startling the doctor with the phrase.

The doctor was in and none too pleased at interruption. He wore a yellow and blue striped dressing-gown, and he was lying on his sofa, laughing with a dark girl, her face scaly with inexpensive powder, who perched on the arm. Half-emptied highball glasses stood beside them, and her coat and hat were neatly hung up with the comfortable implication of a long stay.

Always something, the doctor grumbled. Couldn't let anybody alone after a hard day. But he put some bottles and instruments into a case, changed his dressing-gown for his coat and started out with the Negroes.

"Snap it up there, big boy," the girl called after him. "Don't be all night."

The doctor strode loudly into Mrs. Morse's flat and on to the bedroom, Nettie and the boy right behind him. Mrs. Morse had not moved; her sleep was as deep, but soundless, now. The doctor looked sharply at her, then plunged his thumbs into the lidded pits above her eyeballs and threw his weight upon them. A high, sickened cry broke from Nettie.

"Look like he tryin' to push her right on th'ough the bed," said the boy. He chuckled.

Mrs. Morse gave no sign under the pressure. Abruptly the doctor abandoned it, and with one quick movement swept the covers down to the foot of the bed. With another he flung her nightgown back and lifted the thick, white legs, cross-hatched with blocks of tiny, iris-colored veins. He pinched them repeatedly, with long, cruel nips, back of the knees. She did not awaken.

"What's she been drinking?" he asked Nettie, over his shoulder.

With the certain celerity of one who knows just where to lay hands on a thing, Nettie went into the bathroom, bound for the cupboard where Mrs. Morse kept her whisky. But she stopped at the sight of the two vials, with their red and white labels, lying before the mirror. She brought them to the doctor.

"Oh, for the Lord Almighty's sweet sake!" he said. He dropped Mrs. Morse's legs, and pushed them impatiently across the bed. "What did she want to go taking that tripe for? Rotten yellow trick, that's what a thing like that is. Now we'll have to pump her out, and all that stuff. Nuisance, a thing like that is; that's what it amounts to. Here, George, take me down in the elevator. You wait here, maid. She won't do anything."

"She won't die on me, will she?" cried Nettie.

"No," said the doctor. "God, no. You couldn't kill her with an ax."

IV

After two days, Mrs. Morse came back to consciousness, dazed at first, then with a comprehension that brought with it the slow, saturating wretchedness.

"Oh, Lord, oh, Lord," she moaned and tears for herself and for life striped her cheeks.

Nettie came in at the sound. For two days she had done the ugly, incessant tasks in the nursing of the unconscious, for two nights she had caught broken bits of sleep on the living-room couch. She looked coldly at the big, blown woman in the bed.

"What you been tryin' to do, Mis' Morse?" she said. "What kine o' work is that, takin' all that stuff?"

"Oh, Lord," moaned Mrs. Morse, again, and she tried to cover her eyes with her arms. But the joints felt stiff and brittle, and she cried out at their ache.

"Tha's no way to ack, takin' them pills," said Nettie. "You can thank you' stars you heah at all. How you feel now?"

"Oh, I feel great," said Mrs. Morse. "Swell, I feel."

Her hot, painful tears fell as if they would never stop.

"Tha's no way to take on, cryin' like that," Nettie said. "After what you done. The doctor, he says he could have you arrested, doin' a thing like that. He was fit to be tied, here."

"Why couldn't he let me alone?" wailed Mrs. Morse. "Why the hell couldn't he have?"

"Tha's terr'ble, Mis' Morse, swearin' an' talkin' like that," said Nettie, "after what people done for you. Here I ain' had no sleep at all for two nights, an' had to give up goin' out to my other ladies!"

"Oh, I'm sorry, Nettie," she said. "You're a peach. I'm sorry I've given you so much trouble. I couldn't help it. I just got sunk. Didn't you ever feel like doing it? When everything looks just lousy to you?"

"I wouldn' think o' no such thing," declared Nettie. "You got to cheer up. Tha's what you got to do. Everybody's got their troubles."

"Yeah," said Mrs. Morse. "I know."

"Come a pretty picture card for you," Nettie said. "Maybe that will cheer you up."

She handed Mrs. Morse a post-card. Mrs. Morse had to cover one eye with her hand, in order to read the message; her eyes were not yet focusing correctly.

It was from Art. On the back of a view of the Detroit Athletic Club he had written: "Greeting and salutations. Hope you have lost that gloom. Cheer up and don't take any rubber nickels. See you on Thursday."

She dropped the card to the floor. Misery crushed her as if she were between great smooth stones. There passed before her a slow, slow pageant of days spent lying in her flat, of evenings at Jimmy's being a good sport, making herself laugh and coo at Art and other Arts; she saw a long parade of weary horses and shivering beggars and all beaten, driven, stumbling things. Her feet throbbed as if she had crammed them into the stubby champagne-colored slippers. Her heart seemed to swell and harden.

"Nettie," she cried, "for heaven's sake pour me a drink, will you?"

The maid looked doubtful.

"Now you know, Mis' Morse," she said, "you been near daid. I don' know if the doctor he let you drink nothin' yet."

"Oh, never mind him," she said. "You get me one, and bring in the bottle. Take one yourself."

"Well," said Nettie.

She poured them each a drink, deferentially leaving hers in the bathroom to be taken in solitude, and brought Mrs. Morse's glass in to her.

Mrs. Morse looked into the liquor and shuddered back from its odor. Maybe it would help. Maybe, when you had been knocked cold for a few days, your very first drink would give you a lift. Maybe whisky would be her friend again. She prayed without addressing a God, without knowing a God. Oh, please, please, let her be able to get drunk, please keep her always drunk.

She lifted the glass.

"Thanks, Nettie," she said. "Here's mud in your eye."

The maid giggled. "Tha's the way, Mis' Morse," she said. "You cheer up, now."

"Yeah," said Mrs. Morse. "Sure."

[1929]

QUESTIONS FOR STUDY

1. *How do the men of the story—including the doctor—regard and treat Hazel Morse? How does Hazel regard and treat herself? To what extent are the views of both Hazel and the men tied up with the idea of being a "good sport"?*
2. *What is the appropriateness of the story's title?*
3. *Describe the story's tone and style? How are both related to the story's theme?*
4. *What are the implications of the story's final sentences?*
5. *"Big Blonde" is obviously the story of Hazel Morse's decline and fall. Where does Dorothy Parker seem to lay the blame and the responsibility for Hazel's fate?*

EDGAR ALLAN POE

The Cask of Amontillado

THE THOUSAND injuries of Fortunato I had borne as I best could, but when he ventured upon insult I vowed revenge. You, who so well know the nature of my soul, will not suppose, however, that I gave utterance to a threat. *At length* I would be avenged; this was a point definitely settled—but the very definitiveness with which it was resolved precluded the idea of risk. I must not only punish but punish with impunity. A wrong is unredressed when retribution overtakes its redresser. It is equally unredressed when the avenger fails to make himself felt as such to him who has done the wrong.

It must be understood that neither by word nor deed had I given Fortunato cause to doubt my good will. I continued, as was my wont, to smile in his face, and he did not perceive that my smile *now* was at the thought of his immolation.

He had a weak point—this Fortunato —although in other regards he was a man to be respected and even feared. He prided himself on his connoisseurship in wine. Few Italians have the true virtuoso spirit. For the most part their enthusiasm is adopted to suit the time and opportunity, to practise imposture upon the British and Austrian *millionaires*. In painting and gemmary, Fortunato, like his countrymen, was a quack, but in the matter of old wines he was sincere. In this respect I did not differ from him materially;—I was skillful in the Italian vintages myself, and bought largely whenever I could.

It was about dusk, one evening during the supreme madness of the carnival season, that I encountered my friend. He accosted me with excessive warmth, for he had been drinking much. The man wore motley. He had on a tight-fitting parti-striped dress, and his head was surmounted by the conical cap and bells. I was so pleased to see him that I thought I should never have done wringing his hand.

I said to him—"My dear Fortunato, you are luckily met. How remarkably well you are looking to-day. But I have received a pipe of what passes for Amontillado, and I have my doubts."

"How?" said he. "Amontillado? A pipe? Impossible! And in the middle of the carnival!"

"I have my doubts," I replied; "and I was silly enough to pay the full Amontillado price without consulting you in the matter. You were not to be found, and I was fearful of losing a bargain."

"Amontillado!"

"I have my doubts."

"Amontillado!"

"And I must satisfy them."

"Amontillado!"

"As you are engaged, I am on my way to Luchresi. If any one has a critical turn it is he. He will tell me——"

"Luchresi cannot tell Amontillado from Sherry."

"And yet some fools will have it that his taste is a match for your own."

"Come, let us go."

"Whither?"

"To your vaults."

"My friend, no; I will not impose upon your good nature. I perceive you have an engagement. Luchresi——"

"I have no engagement;—come."

"My friend, no. It is not the engagement, but the severe cold with which I perceive you are afflicted. The vaults are insufferably damp. They are encrusted with nitre."

"Let us go, nevertheless. The cold is merely nothing. Amontillado! You have been imposed upon. And as for Luchresi, he cannot distinguish Sherry from Amontillado."

Thus speaking, Fortunato possessed himself of my arm; and putting on a mask of black silk and drawing a *roque-*

laire closely about my person, I suffered him to hurry me to my palazzo.

There were no attendants at home; they had absconded to make merry in honor of the time. I had told them that I should not return until the morning, and had given them explicit orders not to stir from the house. These orders were sufficient, I well knew, to insure their immediate disappearance, one and all, as soon as my back was turned.

I took from their sconces two flambeaux, and giving one to Fortunato, bowed him through several suites of rooms to the archway that led into the vaults. I passed down a long and winding staircase, requesting him to be cautious as he followed. We came at length to the foot of the descent, and stood together upon the damp ground of the catacombs of the Montresors.

The gait of my friend was unsteady, and the bells upon his cap jingled as he strode.

"The pipe," he said.

"It is farther on," said I; "but observe the white web-work which gleams from these cavern walls."

He turned towards me, and looked into my eyes with two filmy orbs that distilled the rheum of intoxication.

"Nitre?" he asked at length.

"Nitre," I replied. "How long have you had that cough?"

"Ugh! ugh! ugh!—ugh! ugh! ugh!—ugh! ugh! ugh!—ugh! ugh! ugh!—ugh! ugh! ugh!"

My poor friend found it impossible to reply for many minutes.

"It is nothing," he said at last.

"Come," I said, with decision, "we will go back; your health is precious. You are rich, respected, admired, beloved; you are happy, as once I was. You are a man to be missed. For me it is no matter. We will go back; you will be ill, and I cannot be responsible. Besides, there is Luchresi——"

"Enough," he said; "the cough is a mere nothing; it will not kill me. I shall not die of a cough."

"True—true," I replied; "and, indeed, I had no intention of alarming you unnecessarily—but you should use all proper caution. A draught of this Medoc will defend us from the damps."

Here I knocked off the neck of a bottle which I drew from a long row of its fellows that lay upon the mould.

"Drink," I said, presenting him the wine.

He raised it to his lips with a leer. He paused and nodded to me familiarly, while his bells jingled.

"I drink," he said, "to the buried that repose around us."

"And I to your long life."

He again took my arm, and we proceeded.

"These vaults," he said, "are extensive."

"The Montresors," I replied, "were a great and numerous family."

"I forget your arms."

"A huge human foot d'or, in a field azure; the foot crushes a serpent rampant whose fangs are imbedded in the heel."

"And the motto?"

"*Nemo me impune lacessit.*" [1]

"Good!" he said.

The wine sparkled in his eyes and the bells jingled. My own fancy grew warm with the Medoc. We had passed through long walls of piled skeletons, with casks and puncheons intermingling, into the inmost recesses of the catacombs. I paused again, and this time I made bold to sieze Fortunato by an arm above the elbow.

"The nitre!" I said; "see, it increases. It hangs like moss upon the vaults. We are below the river's bed. The drops of moisture trickle among the bones. Come, we will go back ere it is too late. Your cough——"

"It is nothing," he said; "let us go on. But first, another draught of the Medoc."

I broke and reached him a flagon of De Grâve. He emptied it at a breath. His eyes flashed with a fierce light. He laughed and threw the bottle upwards with a gesticulation I did not understand.

I looked at him in surprise. He repeated the movement—a grotesque one.

"You do not comprehend?" he said.

"Not I," I replied.

"Then you are not of the brotherhood."

"How?"

[1] "No one attacks me with impunity." (JHP)

"You are not of the masons."

"Yes, yes," I said; "yes, yes."

"You? Impossible! A mason?"

"A mason," I replied.

"A sign," he said, "a sign."

"It is this," I answered, producing from beneath the folds of my *roquelaire* a trowel.

"You jest," he exclaimed, recoiling a few paces. "But let us proceed to the Amontillado."

"Be it so," I said, replacing the tool beneath the cloak and again offering him my arm. He leaned upon it heavily. We continued our route in search of the Amontillado. We passed through a range of low arches, descended, passed on, and descending again, arrived at a deep crypt, in which the foulness of the air caused our flambeaux rather to glow than flame.

At the most remote end of the crypt there appeared another less spacious. Its walls had been lined with human remains, piled to the vault overhead, in the fashion of the great catacombs of Paris. Three sides of this interior crypt were still ornamented in this manner. From the fourth side the bones had been thrown down, and lay promiscuously upon the earth, forming at one point a mound of some size. Within the wall thus exposed by the displacing of the bones, we perceived a still interior crypt or recess, in depth about four feet, in width three, in height six or seven. It seemed to have been constructed for no especial use within itself, but formed merely the interval between two of the colossal supports of the roof of the catacombs, and was backed by one of their circumscribing walls of solid granite.

It was in vain that Fortunato, uplifting his dull torch, endeavored to pry into the depth of the recess. Its termination the feeble light did not enable us to see.

"Proceed," I said; "herein is the Amontillado. As for Luchresi——"

"He is an ignoramus," interrupted my friend, as he stepped unsteadily forward, while I followed immediately at his heels. In an instant he had reached the extremity of the niche, and finding his progress arrested by the rock, stood stupidly bewildered. A moment more and I had fettered him to the granite. In its surface were two iron staples, distant from each other about two feet, horizontally. From one of these depended a short chain, from the other a padlock. Throwing the links about his waist, it was but the work of a few seconds to secure it. He was too much astounded to resist. Withdrawing the key I stepped back from the recess.

"Pass your hand," I said, "over the wall; you cannot help feeling the nitre. Indeed, it is *very* damp. Once more let me *implore* you to return. No? Then I must positively leave you. But I must first render you all the little attentions in my power."

"The Amontillado!" ejaculated my friend, not yet recovered from his astonishment.

"True," I replied; "the Amontillado."

As I said these words I busied myself among the pile of bones of which I have before spoken. Throwing them aside, I soon uncovered a quantity of building stone and mortar. With these materials and with the aid of my trowel, I began vigorously to wall up the entrance of the niche.

I had scarcely laid the first tier of the masonry when I discovered that the intoxication of Fortunato had in a great measure worn off. The earliest indication I had of this was a low moaning cry from the depth of the recess. It was *not* the cry of a drunken man. There was a long and obstinate silence. I laid the second tier, and the third, and the fourth; and then I heard the furious vibrations of the chain. The noise lasted for several minutes, during which, that I might hearken to it with the more satisfaction, I ceased my labors and sat down upon the bones. When at last the clanking subsided, I resumed the trowel, and finished without interruption the fifth, the sixth, and the seventh tier. The wall was now nearly upon a level with my breast. I again paused, and holding the flambeaux over the mason-work, threw a few feeble rays upon the figure within.

A succession of loud and shrill screams, bursting suddenly from the throat of the chained form, seemed to thrust me violently back. For a brief moment I hesitated, I trembled. Unsheathing my rapier, I began to grope with it about the recess; but the thought of an instant reassured me. I placed my hand upon the solid fabric of the catacombs, and felt satisfied. I reapproached the wall; I replied to the yells of him who clamoured. I re-echoed, I aided, I surpassed them in volume and in strength. I did this, and the clamourer grew still.

It was now midnight, and my task was drawing to a close. I had completed the eighth, the ninth and the tenth tier. I had finished a portion of the last and the eleventh; there remained but a single stone to be fitted and plastered in. I struggled with its weight; I placed it partially in its destined position. But now there came from out the niche a low laugh that erected the hairs upon my head. It was succeeded by a sad voice, which I had difficulty in recognizing as that of the noble Fortunato. The voice said—

"Ha! ha! ha!—he! he! he!—a very good joke, indeed—an excellent jest. We will have many a rich laugh about it at the palazzo—he! he! he!—over our wine —he! he! he!"

"The Amontillado!" I said.

"He! he! he!—he! he! he!—yes, the Amontillado. But is it not getting late? Will not they be awaiting us at the palazzo, the Lady Fortunato and the rest? Let us be gone."

"Yes," I said, "let us be gone."

"For the love of God, Montresor!"

"Yes," I said, "for the love of God."

But to these words I hearkened in vain for a reply. I grew impatient. I called aloud—

"Fortunato!"

No answer. I called again—

"Fortunato!"

No answer still. I thrust a torch through the remaining aperture and let it fall within. There came forth in return only a jingling of the bells. My heart grew sick; it was the dampness of the catacombs that made it so. I hastened to make an end of my labour. I forced the last stone into its position; I plastered it up. Against the new masonry I re-erected the old rampart of bones. For the half of a century no mortal has disturbed them. *In pace requiescat!* [2]

2 May he rest in peace! (JHP)

[1846]

QUESTIONS FOR STUDY

1. *What hints does the story provide as to the "thousand injuries" that Fortunato has inflicted on Montresor? Do they serve to establish a* specific *motive for Montresor's revenge?*
2. *Why are the general setting of the story, "the supreme madness of carnival season," and the immediate setting, the catacombs, highly appropriate?*
3. *How does Montresor demonstrate his superior knowledge of human psychology?*
4. *What is the significance of (a) the names of the two major characters, (b) the costumes they wear, (c) Montresor's family motto and coat of arms, and (d) the flagon of De Grâve?*
5. *Why should the narrator's heart grow sick? What is the meaning of Montresor's own scream? Why does Montresor choose to retell his story some half century after the actual event?*

EDGAR ALLAN POE

The Man of the Crowd

Ce grand malheur, de ne pouvoir
être seul.

LA BRUYERE[1]

IT WAS well said of a certain German
book that *"es lässt sich nicht lesen"*—it
does not permit itself to be read. There
are some secrets which do not permit
themselves to be told. Men die nightly in
their beds, wringing the hands of ghostly
confessors, and looking them piteously in
the eyes—die with despair of heart and
convulsion of throat, on account of the
hideousness of mysteries which will not
suffer themselves to be revealed. Now and
then, alas, the conscience of man takes
up a burthen so heavy in horror that it
can be thrown down only into the grave.
And thus the essence of all crime is un-
divulged.

Not long ago, about the closing in of
an evening in autumn, I sat at the large
bow window of the D—— Coffee-House
in London. For some months I had been
ill in health, but was now convalescent,
and, with returning strength, found myself in one of those happy moods which
are so precisely the converse of *ennui*
—moods of the keenest appetency, when
the film from the mental vision departs
—the ἀχλὺς ἣ πρὶν ἐπῆεν[2]—and the intellect, electrified, surpasses as greatly
its everyday condition, as does the vivid
yet candid reason of Leibnitz, the mad
and flimsy rhetoric of Gorgias. Merely
to breathe was enjoyment; and I derived
positive pleasure even from many of the
legitimate sources of pain. I felt a calm
but inquisitive interest in every thing.
With a cigar in my mouth and a newspaper in my lap, I had been amusing myself for the greater part of the afternoon,

now in poring over advertisements, now
in observing the promiscuous company
in the room, and now in peering through
the smoky panes into the street.

This latter is one of the principal
thoroughfares of the city, and had been
very much crowded during the whole day.
But, as the darkness came on, the throng
momently increased; and, by the time the
lamps were well lighted, two dense and
continuous tides of population were rushing past the door. At this particular
period of the evening I had never before
been in a similar situation, and the
tumultuous sea of human heads filled
me, therefore, with a delicious novelty of
emotion. I gave up, at length, all care of
things within the hotel, and became absorbed in contemplation of the scene
without.

At first my observations took an
abstract and generalizing turn. I looked
at the passengers in masses, and thought
of them in their aggregate relations. Soon,
however, I descended to details, and regarded with minute interest the innumerable varieties of figure, dress, air, gait,
visage, and expression of countenance.

By far the greater number of those who
went by had a satisfied business-like demeanor, and seemed to be thinking of
only making their way through the press.
Their brows were knit, and their eyes
rolled quickly; when pushed against by
fellow-wayfarers they evinced no symp-
tom of impatience, but adjusted their
clothes and hurried on. Others, still a
numerous class, were restless in their
movements, had flushed faces, and talked
and gesticulated to themselves, as if feeling in solitude on account of the very
denseness of the company around. When
impeded in their progress, these people
suddenly ceased muttering, but redoubled
their gesticulations, and awaited, with an
absent and overdone smile upon the lips,
the course of the persons impeding them.

---

[1] The original passage from the writings of
Jean de la Bruyère (1645–1696) should be translated: "All our ills come from inability to be
alone." (JHP)

[2] *The Iliad:* "The mist that before was upon
it." (JHP)

If jostled, they bowed profusely to the jostlers, and appeared overwhelmed with confusion.—There was nothing very distinctive about these two large classes beyond what I have noted. Their habiliments belonged to that order which is pointedly termed the decent. They were undoubtedly noblemen, merchants, attorneys, tradesmen, stock-jobbers—the Eupatrids and the common-places of society—men of leisure and men actively engaged in affairs of their own—conducting business upon their own responsibility. They did not greatly excite my attention.

The tribe of clerks was an obvious one; and here I discerned two remarkable divisions. There were the junior clerks of flash houses—young gentlemen with tight coats, bright boots, well-oiled hair, and supercilious lips. Setting aside a certain dapperness of carriage, which may be termed *deskism* for want of a better word, the manner of these persons seemed to me an exact facsimile of what had been the perfection of *bon ton* about twelve or eighteen months before. They wore the cast-off graces of the gentry;—and this, I believe, involves the best definition of the class.

The division of the upper clerks of staunch firms, or of the "steady old fellows," it was not possible to mistake. These were known by their coats and pantaloons of black and brown, made to sit comfortably, with white cravats and waistcoats, broad solid-looking shoes, and thick hose or gaiters.—They had all slightly bald heads, from which the right ears, long used to pen-holding, had an odd habit of standing off on end. I observed that they always removed or settled their hats with both hands, and wore watches, with short gold chains of a substantial and ancient pattern. Theirs was the affectation of respectability;—if indeed there be an affectation so honorable.

There were many individuals of dashing appearance, whom I easily understood as belonging to the race of swell pickpockets, with which all great cities are infested. I watched these gentry with much inquisitiveness, and found it difficult to imagine how they should ever be mistaken for gentlemen by gentlemen themselves.

Their voluminousness of wristband, with an air of excessive frankness, should betray them at once.

The gamblers, of whom I descried not a few, were still more easily recognisable. They wore every variety of dress, from that of the desperate thimble-rig bully, with velvet waistcoat, fancy neckerchief, gilt chains, and filagreed buttons, to that of the scrupulously inornate clergyman than which nothing could be less liable to suspicion. Still all were distinguished by a certain sodden swarthiness of complexion, a filmy dimness of eye, and pallor and compression of lip. There were two other traits, moreover, by which I could always detect them;—a guarded lowness of tone in conversation, and a more than ordinary extension of the thumb in a direction at right angles with the fingers.—Very often, in company with these sharpers, I observed an order of men somewhat different in habits, but still birds of a kindred feather. They may be defined as the gentlemen who live by their wits. They seem to prey upon the public in two battalions—that of the dandies and that of the military men. Of the first grade the leading features are long socks and smiles; of the second frogged coats and frowns.

Descending in the scale of what is termed gentility, I found darker and deeper themes for speculation. I saw Jew pedlars, with hawk eyes flashing from countenances whose every other feature wore only an expression of abject humility; sturdy professional street beggars scowling upon mendicants of a better stamp, whom despair alone had driven forth into the night for charity; feeble and ghastly invalids, upon whom death had placed a sure hand, and who sidled and tottered through the mob, looking every one beseechingly in the face, as if in search of some chance consolation, some lost hope; modest young girls returning from long and late labor to a cheerless home, and shrinking more tearfully than indignantly from the glances of ruffians, whose direct contact, even, could not be avoided; women of the town of all kinds and of all ages—the unequivocal beauty in the prime of her womanhood, putting one in mind of the statue in Lucian, with the surface of Parian marble, and the interior filled with filth—the loathsome and utterly lost leper in rags—the wrinkled, bejewelled and paint-begrimed beldame, making a last effort at youth—the mere child of immature form, yet, from long association, an adept in the dreadful coquetries of her trade, and burning with a rabid ambition to be ranked the equal of her elders in vice; drunkards innumerable and indescribable—some in shreds and patches, reeling, inarticulate, with bruised visage and lack-lustre eyes—some in whole although filthy garments, with a slightly unsteady swagger, thick sensual lips, and hearty-looking rubicund faces —others clothed in materials which had once been good, and which even now were scrupulously well brushed—men who walked with a more than naturally firm and springy step, but whose countenances were fearfully pale, whose eyes hideously wild and red, and who clutched with quivering fingers, as they strode through the crowd, at every object which came within their reach; beside these, pie-men, porters, coal-heavers, sweeps; organ-grinders, monkey-exhibiters and ballad mongers, those who vended with those who sang; ragged artizans and exhausted laborers of every description, and all full of a noisy and inordinate vivacity which jarred discordantly upon the ear, and gave an aching sensation to the eye.

As the night deepened, so deepened to me the interest of the scene; for not only did the general character of the crowd materially alter (its gentler features retiring in the gradual withdrawal of the more elderly portion of the people, and its harsher ones coming out into bolder relief, as the late hour brought forth every species of infamy from its den,) but the rays of the gas-lamps, feeble at first in their struggle with the dying day, had now at length gained ascendancy, and threw over every thing a fitful and garish lustre. All was dark yet splendid—as that ebony to which has been likened the style of Tertullian.

The wild effects of the light enchained me to an examination of individual faces; and although the rapidity with which the world of light flitted before the window, prevented me from casting more than a glance upon each visage, still it seemed that, in my then peculiar mental state, I could frequently read, even in that brief interval of a glance, the history of long years.

With my brow to the glass, I was thus occupied in scrutinizing the mob, when suddenly there came into view a countenance (that of a decrepid old man, some sixty-five or seventy years of age,)—a countenance which at once arrested and absorbed my whole attention, on account of the absolute idiosyncrasy of its expression. Any thing even remotely resembling that expression I had never seen before. I well remember that my first thought, upon beholding it, was that Retzsch, had he viewed it, would have greatly preferred it to his own pictural incarnations of the fiend. As I endeavored, during the brief minute of my original survey, to form some analysis of the meaning conveyed, there arose confusedly and paradoxically within my mind, the ideas of vast mental power, of caution, of penuriousness, of avarice, of coolness, of malice, of blood-thirstiness, of triumph, of merriment, of excessive terror, of intense—of extreme despair. I felt singularly aroused, startled, fascinated. "How wild a history," I said to myself, "is written within that bosom!" Then came a craving desire to keep the man in view—to know more of him. Hurriedly putting on an overcoat, and seizing my hat and cane, I made my way into the street, and pushed through the crowd in the direction which I had seen him take; for he had already disappeared. With some little difficulty I at length came within sight of him, approached, and followed him closely, yet cautiously, so as not to attract his attention.

I had now a good opportunity of examining his person. He was short in stature, very thin, and apparently very feeble. His clothes, generally, were filthy and ragged; but as he came, now and then, within the strong glare of a lamp, I perceived that his linen, although dirty, was of beautiful texture; and my vision deceived me, or, through a rent in a closely-buttoned and evidently second-handed *roquelaire* which enveloped him, I caught a glimpse both of a diamond and of a dagger. These observations heightened my curiosity, and I resolved to follow the stranger whithersoever he should go.

It was now fully night-fall, and a thick humid fog hung over the city, soon ending in a settled and heavy rain. This change of weather had an odd effect upon the crowd, the whole of which was at once put into new commotion, and overshadowed by a world of umbrellas. The waver, the jostle, and the hum increased in a tenfold degree. For my own part I did not much regard the rain—the lurking of an old fever in my system rendering the moisture somewhat too dangerously pleasant. Tying a handkerchief about my mouth, I kept on. For half an hour the old man held his way with difficulty along the great thoroughfare; and I here walked close at his elbow through fear of losing sight of him. Never once turning his head to look back, he did not observe me. By and bye he passed into a cross street, which, although densely filled with people, was not quite so much thronged as the main one he had quitted. Here a change in his demeanor became evident. He walked more slowly and with less object than before—more hesitantly. He crossed and re-crossed the way repeatedly without apparent aim; and the press was still so thick, that, at every such movement, I was obliged to follow him closely. The street was a narrow and long one, and his course lay within it for nearly an hour, during which the passengers had gradually diminished to about that number which is ordinarily seen at noon in Broadway near the Park—so vast a difference is there between a London populace and that of the most frequented American city. A second turn brought us into a square, brilliantly lighted, and overflowing with life. The old manner of the stranger re-appeared. His chin fell upon his breast, while his eyes rolled wildly from under his knit brows, in every direction, upon those who hemmed him in. He urged his way steadily and perseveringly. I was surprised, however, to find, upon his having made the circuit of the square, that he turned and retraced his steps. Still more was I astonished to see him repeat the same walk several times—once nearly

detecting me as he came round with a sudden movement.

In this exercise he spent another hour, at the end of which we met with far less interruption from passengers than at first. The rain fell fast; the air grew cool, and the people were retiring to their homes. With a gesture of impatience, the wanderer passed into a by-street comparatively deserted. Down this, some quarter of a mile long, he rushed with an activity I could not have dreamed of seeing in one so aged, and which put me to much trouble in pursuit. A few minutes brought us to a large and busy bazaar, with the localities of which the stranger appeared well acquainted, and where his original demeanor again became apparent, as he forced his way to and fro, without aim, among the host of buyers and sellers.

During the hour and a half, or thereabouts, which we passed in this place, it required much caution on my part to keep him within reach without attracting his observation. Luckily I wore a pair of caoutchouc over-shoes, and could move about in perfect silence. At no moment did he see that I watched him. He entered shop after shop, priced nothing, spoke no word, and looked at all objects with a wild and vacant stare. I was now utterly amazed at his behavior, and firmly resolved that we should not part until I had satisfied myself in some measure respecting him.

A loud-toned clock struck eleven, and the company were fast deserting the bazaar. A shop-keeper, in putting up a shutter, jostled the old man, and at the instant I saw a strong shudder come over his frame. He hurried into the street, looked anxiously around him for an instant, and then ran with incredible swiftness through many crooked and peopleless lanes, until we emerged once more upon the great thoroughfare whence we had started—the street of the D—— Hotel. It no longer wore, however, the same aspect. It was still brilliant with gas; but the rain fell fiercely, and there were few persons to be seen. The stranger grew pale. He walked moodily some paces up the once populous avenue, then, with a heavy sigh, turned in the direction of the river, and, plunging through a great variety of devious ways, came out, at length, in view of one of the principal theatres. It was about being closed, and the audience were thronging from the doors. I saw the old man gasp as if for breath while he threw himself amid the crowd; but I thought that the intense agony of his countenance had, in some measure, abated. His head again fell upon his breast; he appeared as I had seen him at first. I observed that he now took the course in which had gone the greater number of the audience—but, upon the whole, I was at a loss to comprehend the waywardness of his actions.

As he proceeded, the company grew more scattered, and his old uneasiness and vacillation were resumed. For some time he followed closely a party of some ten or twelve roisterers; but from this number one by one dropped off, until three only remained together, in a narrow and gloomy lane little frequented. The stranger paused, and, for a moment, seemed lost in thought; then, with every mark of agitation, pursued rapidly a route which brought us to the verge of the city, amid regions very different from those we had hitherto traversed. It was the most noisome quarter of London, where everything wore the worst impress of the most deplorable poverty, and of the most desperate crime. By the dim light of an accidental lamp, tall, antique, worm-eaten, wooden tenements were seen tottering to their fall, in directions so many and capricious that scarce the semblance of a passage was discernible between them. The paving-stones lay at random, displaced from their beds by the rankly growing grass. Horrible filth festered in the dammed-up gutters. The whole atmosphere teemed with desolation. Yet, as we proceeded, the sound of human life revived by sure degrees, and at length large bands of the most abandoned of a London populace were seen reeling to and fro. The spirits of the old man again flickered up, as a lamp which is near its death-hour. Once more he strode onward with elastic tread. Suddenly a corner was turned, a blaze of light burst upon our sight, and we stood before one of the huge suburban temples of Intemperance—one of the palaces of the fiend, Gin.

It was now nearly day-break; but a number of wretched inebriates still pressed in and out of the flaunting entrance. With a half shriek of joy the old man forced a passage within, resumed at once his original bearing, and stalked backward and forward, without apparent object, among the throng. He had not been thus long occupied, however, before a rush to the doors gave token that the host was closing them for the night. It was something even more intense than despair that I then observed upon the countenance of the singular being whom I had watched so pertinaciously. Yet he did not hesitate in his career, but, with a mad energy, retraced his steps at once, to the heart of the mighty London. Long and swiftly he fled, while I followed him in the wildest amazement, resolute not to abandon a scrutiny in which I now felt an interest all-absorbing. The sun arose while we proceeded, and, when we had once again reached that most thronged mart of the populous town, the street of the D—— Hotel, it presented an appearance of human bustle and activity scarcely inferior to what I had seen on the evening before. And here, long, amid the momently increasing confusion, did I persist in my pursuit of the stranger. But, as usual, he walked to and fro, and during the day did not pass from out the turmoil of that street. And, as the shades of the second evening came on, I grew wearied unto death, and, stopping fully in front of the wanderer, gazed at him steadfastly in the face. He noticed me not, but resumed his solemn walk, while I, ceasing to follow, remained absorbed in contemplation. "This old man," I said at length, "is the type and the genius of deep crime. He refuses to be alone. *He is the man of the crowd.* It will be in vain to follow; for I shall learn no more of him, nor of his deeds. The worst heart of the world is a grosser book than the 'Hortulus Animæ,' [3] and perhaps it is but one of the great mercies of God that *es lässt sich nicht lesen.*"

3 The *Hortulus Animæ cum Oratiunculis Aliquibus Superadditis* of Grüninger. (Poe's own note)

[1840]

QUESTIONS FOR STUDY

1. *What is the function of the opening description of the passing throngs? Why does Poe make the narrator a convalescent? What attracts him to the decrepit old man?*

2. *What seems to be the object of the old man's search and the source (or sources) of his despair and agony? Do his wanderings reveal any recognizable pattern?*

3. *Who is the Man of the Crowd? The narrator refers to him as "the type and the genius of deep crime." Is he Everyman? If so, in what sense? Is he the embodiment of the narrator's own subjective projections, a kind of alter ego?*

4. *What final insight or illumination does the narrator seem to gain?*

5. *What is the significance of the story's epigraph from La Bruyère?*

EDGAR ALLAN POE

The Purloined Letter

Nil sapientiae odiosius acumine nimio.[1]

SENECA.

AT PARIS, just after dark one gusty evening in the autumn of 18—, I was enjoying the twofold luxury of meditation and a meerschaum, in company with my friend C. Auguste Dupin, in his little back library, or book-closet, *au troisième, No. 33, Rue Dunôt, Faubourg St. Germain.* For one hour at least we had maintained a profound silence; while each, to any casual observer, might have seemed intently and exclusively occupied with the curling eddies of smoke that oppressed the atmosphere of the chamber. For myself, however, I was mentally discussing certain topics which had formed matter for conversation between us at an earlier period of the evening; I mean the affair of the Rue Morgue, and the mystery attending the murder of Marie Rogêt.[2] I looked upon it, therefore, as something of a coincidence, when the door of our apartment was thrown open and admitted our old acquaintance, Monsieur G——, the Prefect of the Parisian police.

We gave him a hearty welcome; for there was nearly half as much of the entertaining as of the contemptible about the man, and we had not seen him for several years. We had been sitting in the dark, and Dupin now arose for the purpose of lighting a lamp, but sat down again, without doing so, upon G.'s saying that he had called to consult us, or rather to ask the opinion of my friend, about some official business which had occasioned a great deal of trouble.

"If it is any point requiring reflection," observed Dupin, as he forbore to enkindle the wick, "we shall examine it to better purpose in the dark."

"That is another of your odd notions," said the Prefect, who had a fashion of calling every thing "odd" that was beyond his comprehension, and thus lived amid an absolute legion of "oddities."

"Very true," said Dupin, as he supplied his visiter with a pipe, and rolled towards him a comfortable chair.

"And what is the difficulty now?" I asked. "Nothing more in the assassination way, I hope?"

"Oh no; nothing of that nature. The fact is, the business is *very* simple indeed, and I make no doubt that we can manage it sufficiently well ourselves; but then I thought Dupin would like to hear the details of it, because it is so excessively *odd.*"

"Simple and odd," said Dupin.

"Why, yes; and not exactly that, either. The fact is, we have all been a good deal puzzled because the affair *is* so simple, and yet baffles us altogether."

"Perhaps it is the very simplicity of the thing which puts you at fault," said my friend.

"What nonsense you *do* talk!" replied the Prefect, laughing heartily.

"Perhaps the mystery is a little *too* plain," said Dupin.

"Oh, good heavens! who ever heard of such an idea?"

"A little *too* self-evident."

"Ha! ha! ha!—ha! ha! ha!—ho! ho! ho!"—roared our visiter, profoundly amused, "oh, Dupin, you will be the death of me yet!"

"And what, after all, *is* the matter on hand?" I asked.

"Why, I will tell you," replied the Prefect, as he gave a long, steady, and contemplative puff, and settled himself in his chair. "I will tell you in a few words;

---

[1] "Nothing is more hateful to wisdom than too much cunning." (JHP)

[2] The allusion is to Poe's first two detective stories, "The Murders in the Rue Morgue" (1841) and "The Mystery of Marie Rogêt" (1842).

but, before I begin, let me caution you that this is an affair demanding the greatest secrecy, and that I should most probably lose the position I now hold, were it known that I confided it to any one."

"Proceed," said I.

"Or not," said Dupin.

"Well, then; I have received personal information, from a very high quarter, that a certain document of the last importance, has been purloined from the royal apartments. The individual who purloined it is known; this beyond a doubt; he was seen to take it. It is known, also, that it still remains in his possession."

"How is this known?" asked Dupin.

"It is clearly inferred," replied the Prefect, "from the nature of the document, and from the non-appearance of certain results which would at once arise from its passing *out* of the robber's possession; —that is to say, from his employing it as he must design in the end to employ it."

"Be a little more explicit," I said.

"Well, I may venture so far as to say that the paper gives its holder a certain power in a certain quarter where such power is immensely valuable." The Prefect was fond of the cant of diplomacy.

"Still I do not quite understand," said Dupin.

"No? Well; the disclosure of the document to a third person, who shall be nameless, would bring in question the honor of a personage of most exalted station; and this fact gives the holder of the document an ascendancy over the illustrious personage whose honor and peace are so jeopardized."

"But this ascendancy," I interposed, "would depend upon the robber's knowledge of the loser's knowledge of the robber. Who would dare—"

"The thief," said G., "is the Minister D——, who dares all things, those unbecoming as well as those becoming a man. The method of the theft was not less ingenious than bold. The document in question—a letter, to be frank—had been received by the personage robbed while alone in the royal *boudoir*. During its perusal she was suddenly interrupted by the entrance of the other exalted personage from whom especially it was her wish to conceal it. After a hurried and vain endeavor to thrust it in a drawer, she was forced to place it, open as it was, upon a table. The address, however, was uppermost, and, the contents thus unexposed, the letter escaped notice. At this juncture enters the Minister D——. His lynx eye immediately perceives the paper, recognises the handwriting of the address, observes the confusion of the personage addressed, and fathoms her secret. After some business transactions, hurried through in his ordinary manner, he produces a letter somewhat similar to the one in question, opens it, pretends to read it, and then places it in close juxtaposition to the other. Again he converses, for some fifteen minutes, upon the public affairs. At length, in taking leave, he takes also from the table the letter to which he had no claim. Its rightful owner saw, but, of course, dared not call attention to the act, in the presence of the third personage who stood at her elbow. The minister decamped; leaving his own letter—one of no importance—upon the table."

"Here, then," said Dupin to me, "you have precisely what you demand to make the ascendancy complete—the robber's knowledge of the loser's knowledge of the robber."

"Yes," replied the Prefect; "and the power thus attained has, for some months past, been wielded, for political purposes, to a very dangerous extent. The personage robbed is more thoroughly convinced, every day, of the necessity of reclaiming her letter. But this, of course, cannot be done openly. In fine, driven to despair, she has committed the matter to me."

"Than whom," said Dupin, amid a perfect whirlwind of smoke, "no more sagacious agent could, I suppose, be desired, or even imagined."

"You flatter me," replied the Prefect; "but it is possible that some such opinion may have been entertained."

"It is clear," said I, "as you observe, that the letter is still in possession of the minister; since it is in this possession, and not any employment of the letter, which bestows the power. With the employment the power departs."

"True," said G.; "and upon this conviction I proceeded. My first care was to make thorough search of the minister's hotel; 3 and here my chief embarrassment lay in the necessity of searching without his knowledge. Beyond all things, I have been warned of the danger which would result from giving him reason to suspect our design."

"But," said I, "you are quite *au fait* 4 in these investigations. The Parisian police have done this thing often before."

"O yes; and for this reason I did not despair. The habits of the minister gave me, too, a great advantage. He is frequently absent from home all night. His servants are by no means numerous. They sleep at a distance from their master's apartment, and, being chiefly Neapolitans, are readily made drunk. I have keys, as you know, with which I can open any chamber or cabinet in Paris. For three months a night has not passed, during the greater part of which I have not been engaged, personally, in ransacking the D—— Hôtel. My honor is interested, and, to mention a great secret, the reward is enormous. So I did not abandon the search until I had become fully satisfied that the thief is a more astute man than myself. I fancy that I have investigated every nook and corner of the premises in which it is possible that the paper can be concealed."

"But is it not possible," I suggested, "that although the letter may be in possession of the minister, as it unquestionably is, he may have concealed it elsewhere than upon his own premises?"

"This is barely possible," said Dupin. "The present peculiar condition of affairs at court, and especially of those intrigues in which D—— is known to be involved, would render the instant availability of the document—its susceptibility of being produced at a moment's notice—a point of nearly equal importance with its possession."

"Its susceptibility of being produced?" said I.

"That is to say, of being *destroyed,*" said Dupin.

"True," I observed; "the paper is clearly then upon the premises. As for its being upon the person of the minister, we may consider that as out of the question."

"Entirely," said the Prefect. "He has been twice waylaid, as if by footpads,5 and his person rigorously searched under my own inspection."

"You might have spared yourself this trouble," said Dupin. "D——, I presume, is not altogether a fool, and, if not, must have anticipated these waylayings, as a matter of course."

"Not *altogether* a fool," said G., "but then he's a poet, which I take to be only one remove from a fool."

"True," said Dupin, after a long and thoughtful whiff from his meerschaum, "although I have been guilty of certain doggerel myself."

"Suppose you detail," said I, "the particulars of your search."

"Why the fact is, we took our time, and we searched *every where*. I have had long experience in these affairs. I took the entire building, room by room; devoting the nights of a whole week to each. We examined, first, the furniture of each apartment. We opened every possible drawer; and I presume you know that, to a properly trained police agent, such a thing as a *secret* drawer is impossible. Any man is a dolt who permits a 'secret' drawer to escape him in a search of this kind. The thing is *so* plain. There is a certain amount of bulk—of space—to be accounted for in every cabinet. Then we have accurate rules. The fiftieth part of a line could not escape us. After the cabinets we took the chairs. The cushions we probed with the fine long needles you have seen me employ. From the tables we removed the tops."

"Why so?"

"Sometimes the top of a table, or

3 Mansion or townhouse. (JHP)
4 Skilled. (JHP)

5 Highwaymen who prey on pedestrians. (JHP)

other similarly arranged piece of furniture, is removed by the person wishing to conceal an article; then the leg is excavated, the article deposited within the cavity, and the top replaced. The bottoms and tops of bed-posts are employed in the same way."

"But could not the cavity be detected by sounding?" I asked.

"By no means, if, when the article is deposited, a sufficient wadding of cotton be placed around it. Besides, in our case, we were obliged to proceed without noise."

"But you could not have removed—you could not have taken to pieces *all* articles of furniture in which it would have been possible to make a deposit in the manner you mention. A letter may be compressed into a thin spiral roll, not differing much in shape or bulk from a large knitting-needle, and in this form it might be inserted into the rung of a chair, for example. You did not take to pieces all the chairs?"

"Certainly not; but we did better—we examined the rungs of every chair in the hotel, and, indeed, the jointings of every description of furniture, by the aid of a most powerful microscope.[6] Had there been any traces of recent disturbance we should not have failed to detect it instantly. A single grain of gimlet-dust, for example, would have been as obvious as an apple. Any disorder in the glueing—any unusual gaping in the joints—would have sufficed to insure detection."

"I presume you looked to the mirrors, between the boards and the plates, and you probed the beds and the bed-clothes, at well as the curtains and carpets."

"That of course; and when we had absolutely completed every particle of the furniture in this way, then we examined the house itself. We divided its entire surface into compartments, which we numbered, so that none might be missed; then we scrutinized each individual square inch throughout the premises, including the two houses immediately adjoining, with the microscope, as before."

"The two houses adjoining!" I ex-

claimed; "you must have had a great deal of trouble."

"We had; but the reward offered is prodigious."

"You include the *grounds* about the houses?"

"All the grounds are paved with brick. They gave us comparatively little trouble. We examined the moss between the bricks, and found it undisturbed."

"You looked among D——'s papers, of course, and into the books of the library?"

"Certainly; we opened every package and parcel; we not only opened every book, but we turned over every leaf in each volume, not contenting ourselves with a mere shake, according to the fashion of some of our police officers. We also measured the thickness of every book-*cover*, with the most accurate admeasurement, and applied to each the most jealous scrutiny of the microscope. Had any of the bindings been recently meddled with, it would have been utterly impossible that the fact should have escaped observation. Some five or six volumes, just from the hands of the binder, we carefully probed, longitudinally, with the needles."

"You explored the floors beneath the carpets?"

"Beyond doubt. We removed every carpet, and examined the boards with the microscope."

"And the paper on the walls?"

"Yes."

"You looked into the cellars?"

"We did."

"Then," I said, "you have been making a miscalculation, and the letter is *not* upon the premises, as you suppose."

"I fear you are right there," said the Prefect. "And now, Dupin, what would you advise me to do?"

"To make a thorough re-search of the premises."

"That is absolutely needless," replied G——. "I am not more sure that I breathe than I am that the letter is not at the Hôtel."

"I have no better advice to give you," said Dupin. "You have, of course, an accurate description of the letter?"

6 A magnifying glass. (JHP)

"Oh yes!"—And here the Prefect, producing a memorandum-book, proceeded to read aloud a minute account of the internal, and especially of the external appearance of the missing document. Soon after finishing the perusal of this description, he took his departure, more entirely depressed in spirits than I had ever known the good gentleman before.

In about a month afterwards he paid us another visit, and found us occupied very nearly as before. He took a pipe and a chair and entered into some ordinary conversation. At length I said,—

"Well, but G——, what of the purloined letter? I presume you have at last made up your mind that there is no such thing as overreaching the Minister?"

"Confound him, say I—yes; I made the re-examination, however, as Dupin suggested—but it was all labor lost, as I knew it would be."

"How much was the reward offered, did you say?" asked Dupin.

"Why, a very great deal—a *very* liberal reward—I don't like to say how much, precisely; but one thing I *will* say, that I wouldn't mind giving my individual check for fifty thousand francs to any one who could obtain me that letter. The fact is, it is becoming of more and more importance every day; and the reward has been lately doubled. If it were trebled, however, I could do no more than I have done."

"Why, yes," said Dupin, drawlingly, between the whiffs of his meerschaum, "I really—think, G——, you have not exerted yourself—to the utmost in this matter. You might—do a little more, I think, eh?"

"How?—in what way?"

"Why—puff, puff—you might—puff, puff—employ counsel in the matter, eh? —puff, puff, puff. Do you remember the story they tell of Abernethy?"

"No; hang Abernethy!"

"To be sure! hang him and welcome. But, once upon a time, a certain rich miser conceived the design of spunging upon this Abernethy for a medical opinion. Getting up, for this purpose, an ordinary conversation in a private company, he insinuated his case to the physician, as that of an imaginary individual.

" 'We will suppose,' said the miser, 'that his symptoms are such and such; now, doctor, what would *you* have directed him to take?' "

" 'Take!' said Abernethy,7 'why, take *advice,* to be sure.' "

"But," said the Prefect, a little discomposed, "I am *perfectly* willing to take advice, and to pay for it. I would *really* give fifty thousand francs to any one who would aid me in the matter."

"In that case," replied Dupin, opening a drawer, and producing a check-book, "you may as well fill me up a check for the amount mentioned. When you have signed it, I will hand you the letter."

I was astounded. The Prefect appeared absolutely thunder-stricken. For some minutes he remained speechless and motionless, looking incredulously at my friend with open mouth, and eyes that seemed starting from their sockets; then, apparently recovering himself in some measure, he seized a pen, and after several pauses and vacant stares, finally filled up and signed a check for fifty thousand francs, and handed it across the table to Dupin. The latter examined it carefully and deposited it in his pocket-book; then, unlocking an *escritoire,*8 took thence a letter and gave it to the Prefect. This functionary grasped it in a perfect agony of joy, opened it with a trembling hand, cast a rapid glance at its contents, and then, scrambling and struggling to the door, rushed at length unceremoniously from the room and from the house, without having uttered a syllable since Dupin had requested him to fill up the check.

When he had gone, my friend entered into some explanations.

"The Parisian police," he said, "are exceedingly able in their way. They are persevering, ingenious, cunning, and thoroughly versed in the knowledge which their duties seem chiefly to demand. Thus, when G—— detailed to us his mode of searching the premises at the Hôtel D——, I felt entire confidence

---

7 John Abernethy (1764–1831), a famous English surgeon. (JHP)

8 A writing desk. (JHP)

in his having made a satisfactory investigation—so far as his labors extended."

"So far as his labors etended?" said I.

"Yes," said Dupin. "The measures adopted were not only the best of their kind, but carried out to absolute perfection. Had the letter been deposited within the range of their search, these fellows would, beyond a question, have found it."

I merely laughed—but he seemed quite serious in all that he said.

"The measures, then," he continued, "were good in their kind, and well executed; their defect lay in their being inapplicable to the case, and to the man. A certain set of highly ingenious resources are, with the Prefect, a sort of Procrustean bed,9 to which he forcibly adapts his designs. But he perpetually errs by being too deep or too shallow, for the matter in hand; and many a schoolboy is a better reasoner than he. I knew one about eight years of age, whose success at guessing in the game of 'even and odd' attracted universal admiration. This game is simple, and is played with marbles. One player holds in his hand a number of these toys, and demands of another whether that number is even or odd. If the guess is right, the guesser wins one; if wrong, he loses one. The boy to whom I allude won all the marbles of the school. Of course he had some principle of guessing; and this lay in mere observation and admeasurement of the astuteness of his opponents. For example, an arrant simpleton is his opponent, and, holding up his closed hand, asks, 'are they even or odd?' Our schoolboy replies, 'odd,' and loses; but upon the second trial he wins, for he then says to himself, 'the simpleton had them even upon the first trial, and his amount of cunning is just sufficient to make him have them odd upon the second; I will therefore guess odd;'—he guesses odd, and wins. Now, with a simpleton a degree above the first, he would have reasoned thus: 'This fellow finds that in the first instance I guessed odd,

and, in the second, he will propose to himself upon the first impulse, a simple variation from even to odd, as did the first simpleton; but then a second thought will suggest that this is too simple a variation, and finally he will decide upon putting it even as before. I will therefore guess even;'—he guesses even, and wins. Now this mode of reasoning in the schoolboy, whom his fellows termed 'lucky,'—what, in its last analysis, is it?"

"It is merely," I said, "an identification of the reasoner's intellect with that of his opponent."

"It is," said Dupin; "and, upon inquiring of the boy by what means he effected the *thorough* identification in which his success consisted, I received answer as follows: 'When I wish to find out how wise, or how stupid, or how good, or how wicked is any one, or what are his thoughts at the moment, I fashion the expression of my face, as accurately as possible, in accordance with the expression of his, and then wait to see what thoughts or sentiments arise in my mind or heart, as if to match or correspond with the expression.' This response of the schoolboy lies at the bottom of all the spurious profundity which has been attributed to Rochefoucauld, to La Bougive, to Machiavelli, and to Campanella." 10

"And the identification," I said, "of the reasoner's intellect with that of his opponent, depends, if I understand you aright, upon the accuracy with which the opponent's intellect is admeasured."

"For its practical value it depends upon this," replied Dupin; "and the Prefect and his cohort fail so frequently, first, by default of this identification, and, secondly, by ill-admeasurement, or

---

9 Procrustes was a legendary Greek robber who fitted his victims to his bed by either stretching their legs or cutting them off. (JHP)

10 François de La Rochefoucauld (1613–1680) was the French author of *Moral Maxims and Reflections* (1665); Niccolò Machiavelli (1469–1527), an Italian, was the author of *The Prince* (1513), the classic treatise on the art of statecraft; Tommaso Campanella (1568–1639) was an Italian philosopher; "La Bougive," it has been suggested, is the result of an error in transcription—Poe intended an allusion to Jean de la Bruyère (1645–1696), the French author of *Characters* (1688), a study of human manners. All these writers saw selfishness as the chief motive for human behavior. (JHP)

rather through non-admeasurement, of the intellect with which they are engaged. They consider only their *own* ideas of ingenuity; and, in searching for anything hidden, advert only to the modes in which *they* would have hidden it. They are right in this much—that their own ingenuity is a faithful representative of that of *the mass;* but when the cunning of the individual felon is diverse in character from their own, the felon foils them, of course. This always happens when it is above their own, and very usually when it is below. They have no variation of principle in their investigations; at best, when urged by some unusual emergency—by some extraordinary reward—they extend or exaggerate their old modes of *practice,* without touching their principles. What, for example, in this case of D——, has been done to vary the principle of action? What is all this boring, and probing, and sounding, and scrutinizing with the microscope, and dividing the surface of the building into registered square inches— what is it all but an exaggeration *of the application* of the one principle or set of principles of search, which are based upon the one set of notions regarding human ingenuity, to which the Prefect, in the long routine of his duty, has been accustomed? Do you not see he has taken it for granted that *all* men proceed to conceal a letter,—not exactly in a gimlet-hole bored in a chair-leg—but, at least, in *some* out-of-the-way hole or corner suggested by the same tenor of thought which would urge a man to secrete a letter in a gimlet-hole bored in a chair-leg? And do you not see also, that such *recherchés* [11] nooks for concealment are adapted only for ordinary occasions, and would be adopted only by ordinary intellects; for, in all cases of concealment, a disposal of the article concealed—a disposal of it in this *recherché* [12] manner,—is, in the very first instance, presumable and presumed; and thus its discovery depends, not at all upon the acumen, but altogether upon

[11] Out of the way. (JHP)
[12] Clever. (JHP)

the mere care, patience, and determination of the seekers; and where the case is of importance—or, what amounts to the same thing in the political eyes, when the reward is of magnitude,—the qualities in question have *never* been known to fail. You will now understand what I meant in suggesting that, had the purloined letter been hidden any where within the limits of the Prefect's examination—in other words, had the principles of its concealment been comprehended within the principles of the Prefect—its discovery would have been a matter altogether beyond question. This functionary, however, has been thoroughly mystified; and the remote source of his defeat lies in the supposition that the Minister is a fool, because he has acquired renown as a poet. All fools are poets; this the Prefect *feels;* and he is merely guilty of a *non distributio medii* [13] in thence inferring that all poets are fools."

"But is this really the poet?" I asked. "There are two brothers, I know; and both have attained reputation in letters. The Minister I believe has written learnedly on the Differential Calculus. He is a mathematician, and no poet."

"You are mistaken; I know him well; he is both. As poet *and* mathematician, he would reason well; as mere mathematician, he could not have reasoned at all, and thus would have been at the mercy of the Prefect."

"You surprise me," I said, "by these opinions, which have been contradicted by the voice of the world. You do not mean to set at naught the well-digested idea of centuries. The mathematical reason has long been regarded as *the* reason *par excellence.*"

" 'Il y a à parier,' " replied Dupin, quoting from Chamfort, " 'que toute idée publique, toute convention reçue, est une sottise, car elle a convenu au plus grand nombre.' [14] The mathematicians, I grant you, have done their best to pro-

[13] In logic the "undistributed middle" is a syllogistic fallacy yielding a false conclusion. (JHP)

[14] "The chances are that every popular idea, every accepted convention, is nonsense, since it is acceptable to the majority." (JHP)

mulgate the popular error to which you allude, and which is none the less an error for its promulgation as truth. With an art worthy a better cause, for example, they have insinuated the term, 'analysis' into application to algebra. The French are the originators of this particular deception; but if a term is of any importance—if words derive any value from applicability—then 'analysis' conveys 'algebra' about as much as, in Latin, *'ambitus'* implies 'ambition,' *'religio'* 'religion,' or *'homines honesti,'* a set of *honorable* men."

"You have a quarrel on hand, I see," said I, "with some of the algebraists of Paris; but proceed."

"I dispute the availability, and thus the value, of that reason which is cultivated in any especial form other than the abstractly logical. I dispute, in particular, the reason educed by mathematical study. The mathematics are the science of form and quantity; mathematical reasoning is merely logic applied to observation upon form and quantity. The great error lies in supposing that even the truths of what is called *pure* algebra, are abstract or general truths. And this error is so egregious that I am confounded at the universality with which it has been received. Mathematical axioms are *not* axioms of general truth. What is true of *relation*—of form and quantity—is often grossly false in regard to morals, for example. In this latter science it is very usually *un*true that the aggregated parts are equal to the whole. In chemistry also the axiom fails. In the consideration of motive it fails; for two motives, each of a given value, have not, necessarily, a value when united, equal to the sum of their values apart. There are numerous other mathematical truths which are only truths within the limits of *relation*. But the mathematician argues, from his *finite truths,* through habit, as if they were of an absolutely general applicability—as the world indeed imagines them to be. Bryant, in his very learned 'Mythology,' 15 mentions an

analogous source of error, when he says that 'although the Pagan fables are not believed, yet we forget ouselves continually, and make inferences from them as existing realities.' With the algebraists, however, who are Pagans themselves, the 'Pagan fables' *are* believed, and the inferences are made, not so much through lapse of memory, as through an unaccountable addling of the brains. In short, I never yet encountered the mere mathematician who could be trusted out of equal roots, or one who did not clandestinely hold it as a point of his faith that $x^2 + px$ was absolutely and unconditionally equal to q. Say to one of these gentlemen, by way of experiment, if you please, that you believe occasions may occur where $x^2 + px$ is *not* altogether equal to q, and, having made him understand what you mean, get out of his reach as speedily as convenient, for, beyond doubt, he will endeavor to knock you down.

"I mean to say," continued Dupin, while I merely laughed at his last observations, "that if the Minister had been no more than a mathematician, the Prefect would have been under no necessity of giving me this check. I knew him, however, as both mathematician and poet, and my measures were adapted to his capacity, with reference to the circumstances by which he was surrounded. I knew him as a courtier, too, and as a bold *intriguant*.16 Such a man, I considered, could not fail to be aware of the ordinary policial modes of action. He could not have failed to anticipate—and events have proved that he did not fail to anticipate—the waylayings to which he was subjected. He must have foreseen, I reflected, the secret investigations of his premises. His frequent absences from home at night, which were hailed by the Prefect as certain aids to his success, I regarded only as *ruses,* to afford opportunity for thorough search to the police, and thus the sooner to impress them with the conviction to which G——, in fact, did finally arrive—the conviction that the letter was not upon

15 Jacob Bryant (1715–1804), the English author of *A New System or Analysis of Ancient Mythology* (1774–1776). (JHP)

16 Schemer. (JHP)

the premises. I felt, also, that the whole train of thought, which I was at some pains in detailing to you just now, concerning the invariable principle of policial action in searches for articles concealed—I felt that this whole train of thought would necessarily pass through the mind of the Minister. It would imperatively lead him to despise all the ordinary *nooks* of concealment. *He* could not, I reflected, be so weak as not to see that the most intricate and remote recess of his hotel would be as open as his commonest closets to the eyes, to the probes, to the gimlets, and to the microscopes of the Prefect. I saw, in fine, that he would be driven, as a matter of course, to *simplicity,* if not deliberately induced to it as a matter of choice. You will remember, perhaps, how desperately the Prefect laughed when I suggested, upon our first interview, that it was just possible this mystery troubled him so much on account of its being so *very* self-evident."

"Yes," said I, "I remember his merriment well. I really thought he would have fallen into convulsions."

"The material world," continued Dupin, "abounds with very strict analogies to the immaterial; and thus some color of truth has been given to the rhetorical dogma, that metaphor, or simile, may be made to strengthen an argument, as well as to embellish a description. The principle of the *vis inertiae,*[17] for example, seems to be identical in physics and metaphysics. It is not more true in the former, that a large body is with more difficulty set in motion than a smaller one, and that its subsequent *momentum* is commensurate with this difficulty, than it is, in the latter, that intellects of the vaster capacity, while more forcible, more constant, and more eventful in their movements than those of inferior grade, are yet the less readily moved, and more embarrassed and full of hesitation in the first few steps of their progress. Again: have you ever noticed which of the street signs, over the shop doors, are the most attractive of attention?"

[17] The power of inertia. (JHP)

"I have never given the matter a thought," I said.

"There is a game of puzzles," he resumed, "which is played upon a map. One party playing requires another to find a given word—the name of town, river, state or empire—any word, in short, upon the motley and perplexed surface of the chart. A novice in the game generally seeks to embarrass his opponents by giving them the most minutely lettered names; but the adept selects such words as stretch, in large characters, from one end of the chart to the other. These, like the over-largely lettered signs and placards of the street, escape observation by dint of being excessively obvious; and here the physical oversight is precisely analogous with the moral inapprehension by which the intellect suffers to pass unnoticed those considerations which are too obtrusively and too palpably self-evident. But this is a point, it appears, somewhat above or beneath the understanding of the Prefect. He never once thought it probable, or possible, that the Minister had deposited the letter immediately beneath the nose of the whole world, by way of best preventing any portion of that world from perceiving it.

"But the more I reflected upon the daring, dashing, and discriminating ingenuity of D——; upon the fact that the document must always have been *at hand,* if he intended to use it to good purpose; and upon the decisive evidence, obtained by the Prefect, that it was not hidden within the limits of that dignitary's ordinary search—the more satisfied I became that, to conceal this letter, the Minister had resorted to the comprehensive and sagacious expedient of not attempting to conceal it at all.

"Full of these ideas, I prepared myself with a pair of green spectacles, and called one fine morning, quite by accident, at the Ministerial hotel. I found D—— at home, yawning, lounging, and dawdling, as usual, and pretending to be in the last extremity of *ennui.* He is, perhaps, the most really energetic human being now alive—but that is only when nobody sees him.

"To be even with him, I complained

of my weak eyes, and lamented the necessity of the spectacles, under cover of which I cautiously and thoroughly surveyed the apartment, while seemingly intent only upon the conversation of my host.

"I paid special attention to a large writing-table near which he sat, and upon which lay confusedly, some miscellaneous letters and other papers, with one or two musical instruments and a few books. Here, however, after a long and very deliberate scrutiny, I saw nothing to excite particular suspicion.

"At length my eyes, in going the circuit of the room, fell upon a trumpery fillagree card-rack of paste-board, that hung dangling by a dirty blue ribbon, from a little brass knob just beneath the middle of the mantel-piece. In this rack, which had three or four compartments, were five or six visiting cards and a solitary letter. This last was much soiled and crumpled. It was torn nearly in two, across the middle—as if a design, in the first instance, to tear it entirely up as worthless, had been altered, or stayed, in the second. It had a large black seal, bearing the D—— cipher *very* conspicuously, and was addressed, in a diminutive female hand, to D——, the minister, himself. It was thrust carelessly, and even, as it seemed, contemptuously, into one of the upper divisions of the rack.

"No sooner had I glanced at this letter, than I concluded it to be that of which I was in search. To be sure, it was, to all appearance, radically different from the one of which the Prefect had read us so minute a description. Here the seal was large and black, with the D—— cipher; there it was small and red, with the ducal arms of the S—— family. Here, the address, to the Minister, was diminutive and feminine; there the superscription, to a certain royal personage, was markedly bold and decided; the size alone formed a point of correspondence. But, then, the *radicalness* of these differences, which was excessive; the dirt; the soiled and torn condition of the paper, so inconsistent with the *true* methodical habits of D——, and so suggestive of a design to delude the beholder into an idea of the worthlessness of the document; these things, together with the hyperobtrusive situation of this document, full in the view of every visiter, and thus exactly in accordance with the conclusions to which I had previously arrived; these things, I say, were strongly corroborative of suspicion, in one who came with the intention to suspect.

"I protracted my visit as long as possible, and, while I maintained a most animated discussion with the Minister, on a topic which I knew well had never failed to interest and excite him, I kept my attention really riveted upon the letter. In this examination, I committed to memory its external appearance and arrangement in the rack; and also fell, at length, upon a discovery which set at rest whatever trivial doubt I might have entertained. In scrutinizing the edges of the paper, I observed them to be more *chafed* than seemed necessary. They presented the *broken* appearance which is manifested when a stiff paper, having been once folded and pressed with a folder, is refolded in a reversed direction, in the same creases or edges which had formed the original fold. This discovery was sufficient. It was clear to me that the letter had been turned, as a glove, inside out, re-directed, and re-sealed. I bade the Minister good morning, and took my departure at once, leaving a gold snuff-box upon the table.

"The next morning I called for the snuff-box, when we resumed, quite eagerly, the conversation of the preceding day. While thus engaged, however, a loud report, as if of a pistol, was heard immediately beneath the windows of the hotel, and was succeeded by a series of fearful screams, and the shoutings of a mob. D—— rushed to a casement, threw it open, and looked out. In the meantime, I stepped to the card-rack, took the letter, put it in my pocket, and replaced it by a *fac-simile,* (so far as regards externals,) which I had carefully prepared at my lodgings; imitating the D—— cipher, very readily, by means of a seal formed of bread.

"The disturbance in the street had been occasioned by the frantic behavior of a man with a musket. He had fired it among a crowd of women and children. It proved, however, to have been without ball, and the fellow was suffered to go his way as a lunatic or a drunkard. When he had gone, D—— came from the window, whither I had followed him immediately upon securing the object in view. Soon afterwards I bade him farewell. The pretended lunatic was a man in my own pay."

"But what purpose had you," I asked, "in replacing the letter by a *fac-simile?* Would it not have been better, at the first visit, to have seized it openly, and departed?"

"D——," replied Dupin, "is a desperate man, and a man of nerve. His hotel, too, is not without attendants devoted to his interests. Had I made the wild attempt you suggest, I might never have left the Ministerial presence alive. The good people of Paris might have heard of me no more. But I had an object apart from these considerations. You know my political prepossessions. In this matter, I act as a partisan of the lady concerned. For eighteen months the Minister has had her in his power. She has now him in hers; since, being unaware that the letter is not in his possession, he will proceed with his exactions as if it was. Thus will he inevitably commit himself, at once, to his political destruction. His downfall, too, will not be more precipitate than awkward. It is all very well to talk about the *facilis descensus Averni;* [18] but in all kinds of climbing, as Catalani [19] said of singing, it is far more easy to get up than

to come down. In the present instance I have no sympathy—at least no pity—for him who descends. He is that *monstrum horrendum,* [20] an unprincipled man of genius. I confess, however, that I should like very well to know the precise character of his thoughts, when, being defied by her whom the Prefect terms 'a certain personage,' he is reduced to opening the letter which I left for him in the card-rack."

"How? did you put any thing particular in it?"

"Why—it did not seem altogether right to leave the interior blank—that would have been insulting. D——, at Vienna once, did me an evil turn, which I told him, quite good-humoredly, that I should remember. So, as I knew he would feel some curiosity in regard to the identity of the person who had outwitted him, I thought it a pity not to give him a clue. He is well acquainted with my MS., and I just copied into the middle of the blank sheet the words—

>   ———Un dessein si funeste,
> S'il n'est digne d'Atrée, est digne de
>   Thyeste. [21]

They are to be found in Crébillon's 'Atrée.' "

[1845]

18 "Easy is the descent to Hell"—Vergil's *Aeneid.* (JHP)

19 Angelica Catalini (1780–1849), a well-known Italian opera singer. (JHP)

20 Horrible monster. (JHP)

21 "A design so deadly, if unworthy of Atreus, is quite worthy of Thyestes." The lines are quoted from Crébillion's eighteenth-century French tragedy, *Atrée et Thyeste* (1707), in reference to Atreus, King of Mycenae, who murdered his nephews and served them up as a meal to their father Thyestes. Thyestes had previously seduced Atreus' wife and placed a curse on the house of Atreus. (JHP)

QUESTIONS FOR STUDY

1. *It is often said that the modern detective story was born with Edgar Allan Poe—and born in full bloom. Discuss the ways in which the following elements in Poe's story have become part of the stock in trade of later detective fiction: (a) the detective hero, C. Auguste Dupin; (b) his nameless companion; (c) his friendly rival, Monsieur G——, prefect of police; (d) the villain, Minister D——; (e) the crime; and (f) its solution.*

2. *Why did Poe, an American writer, choose to give his story French characters and a French setting?*

3. *In what sense is the quotation that introduces the story appropriate? To whom or to what does it refer?*

4. *Why does Poe choose to reveal the identity of the culprit from the beginning? How does this decision change the story's center of interest?*

5. *Why, at the story's conclusion, is Dupin content to allow Minister D———— to act as if the letter is still in his possession?*

6. *What are the implications of the final quotation from Crébillon that Dupin leaves for Minister D————?*

KATHERINE ANNE PORTER

The Grave

THE GRANDFATHER, dead for more than thirty years, had been twice disturbed in his long repose by the constancy and possessiveness of his widow. She removed his bones first to Louisiana and then to Texas as if she had set out to find her own burial place, knowing well she would never return to the places she had left. In Texas she set up a small cemetery in a corner of her first farm, and as the family connection grew, and oddments of relations came over from Kentucky to settle, it contained at last about twenty graves. After the grandmother's death, part of her land was to be sold for the benefit of certain of her children, and the cemetery happened to lie in the part set aside for sale. It was necessary to take up the bodies and bury them again in the family plot in the big new public cemetery, where the grandmother had been buried. At last her husband was to lie beside her for eternity, as she had planned.

The family cemetery had been a pleasant small neglected garden of tangled rose bushes and ragged cedar trees and cypress, the simple flat stones rising out of uncropped sweet-smelling wild grass. The graves were lying open and empty one burning day when Miranda and her brother Paul, who often went together to hunt rabbits and doves, propped their twenty-two Winchester rifles carefully against the rail fence, climbed over and explored among the graves. She was nine years old and he was twelve.

They peered into the pits all shaped alike with such purposeful accuracy, and looking at each other with pleased adventurous eyes, they said in solemn tones: "These were graves!" trying by words to shape a special, suitable emotion in their minds, but they felt nothing except an agreeable thrill of wonder: they were seeing a new sight, doing something they had not done before. In them both there was also a small disappointment at the entire commonplaceness of the actual spectacle. Even if it had once contained a coffin for years upon years, when the coffin was gone a grave was just a hole in the ground. Miranda leaped into the pit that had held her grandfather's bones. Scratching around aimlessly and pleasurably as any young animal, she scooped up a lump of earth and weighed it in her palm. It had a pleasantly sweet, corrupt smell, being mixed with cedar needles and small leaves, and as the crumbs fell apart, she saw a silver dove no larger than a hazel nut, with spread wings and a neat fan-shaped tail. The breast had a deep round hollow in it. Turning it up to the fierce sunlight, she saw that the inside of the hollow was cut in little whorls. She scrambled out, over the pile of loose earth that had fallen back into one end of the grave, calling to Paul that she had found something, he must guess what . . . His head appeared smiling over the rim of another grave. He waved a closed hand at her. "I've got something too!" They ran to compare treasures, making a game of it, so many guesses each, all wrong, and a final show-down with opened palms. Paul had found a thin wide gold ring carved with intricate flowers and leaves. Miranda was smitten at sight of the ring and wished to have it. Paul seemed more impressed by the dove. They made a trade, with some little bickering. After he had got the dove in his hand, Paul said, "Don't you know what this is? This is a screw head for a *coffin!* . . . I'll bet nobody else in the world has one like this!"

Miranda glanced at it without covetousness. She had the gold ring on her thumb; it fitted perfectly. "Maybe we ought to go now," she said, "Maybe one of the niggers 'll see us and tell somebody." They knew the land had been sold, the cemetery was no longer theirs, and they felt like trespassers. They climbed back over the fence, slung their rifles loosely under their arms—they had been shooting at targets with various kinds of firearms since they were seven years old—and set out to look for the rabbits and doves or whatever small game might happen along. On these expeditions Miranda always followed at Paul's heels along the path, obeying instructions about handling her gun when going through fences; learning how to stand it up properly so it would not slip and fire unexpectedly; how to wait her time for a shot and not just bang away in the air without looking, spoiling shots for Paul, who really could hit things if given a chance. Now and then, in her excitement at seeing birds whizz up suddenly before her face, or a rabbit leap across her very toes, she lost her head, and almost without sighting she flung her rifle up and pulled the trigger. She hardly ever hit any sort of mark. She had no proper sense of hunting at all. Her brother would be often completely disgusted with her. "You don't care whether you get your bird or not," he said. "That's no way to hunt." Miranda could not understand his indignation. She had seen him smash his hat and yell with fury when he had missed his aim. "What I like about shooting," said Miranda, with exasperating inconsequence, "is pulling the trigger and hearing the noise."

"Then, by golly," said Paul, "whyn't you go back to the range and shoot at bulls-eyes?"

"I'd just as soon," said Miranda, "only like this, we walk around more."

"Well, you just stay behind and stop spoiling my shots," said Paul, who, when he made a kill, wanted to be certain he had made it. Miranda, who alone brought down a bird once in twenty rounds, always claimed as her own any game they got when they fired at the same moment. It was tiresome and unfair and her brother was sick of it.

"Now, the first dove we see, or the first rabbit, is mine," he told her. "And the next will be yours. Remember that and don't get smarty."

"What about snakes?" asked Miranda idly. "Can I have the first snake?"

Waving her thumb gently and watching her gold ring glitter, Miranda lost interest in shooting. She was wearing her summer roughing outfit: dark blue overalls, a light blue shirt, a hired-man's straw hat, and thick brown sandals. Her brother had the same outfit except his was a sober hickory-nut color. Ordinarily Miranda preferred her overalls to any other dress, though it was making rather a scandal in the countryside, for the year was 1903, and in the back country the law of female decorum had teeth in it. Her father had been criticized for letting his girls dress like boys and go careering around astride barebacked horses. Big sister Maria, the really independent and fearless one, in spite of her rather affected ways, rode at a dead run with only a rope knotted around her horse's nose. It was said the motherless family was running down, with the grandmother no longer there to hold it together. It was known that she had discriminated against her son Harry in her will, and that he was in straits about money. Some of his old neighbors reflected with vicious satisfaction that now he would probably not be so stiff-necked, nor have any more high-stepping horses either. Miranda knew this, though she could not say how. She had met along the road old women of the kind who smoked corn-cob pipes, who had treated her grandmother with most sincere respect. They slanted their gummy old eyes side-ways at the granddaughter and said, "Ain't you ashamed of yoself, Missy? It's aginst the Scriptures to dress like that. Whut yo Pappy thinkin about?" Miranda, with her powerful social sense, which was like a fine set of antennae radiating from every pore of her skin, would feel ashamed because she knew well it was rude and ill-bred to shock anybody, even bad-tempered old crones, though she had faith in her father's judgment and was perfectly comfortable in the clothes. Her father had said, "They're just what you need, and they'll save your dresses for school . . ." This sounded quite simple and natural to her. She had been brought up in rigorous economy. Wastefulness was vulgar. It was also a sin. These were truths; she had heard them repeated many times and never once disputed.

Now the ring, shining with the serene purity of fine gold on her rather grubby thumb, turned her feelings against her overalls and sockless feet, toes sticking through the thick brown leather straps. She wanted to go back to the farmhouse, take a good cold bath, dust herself with plenty of Maria's violet talcum powder —provided Maria was not present to object, of course—put on the thinnest, most becoming dress she owned, with a big sash, and sit in a wicker chair under the trees . . . These things were not all she wanted, of course; she had vague stirrings of desire for luxury and a grand way of living which could not take precise form in her imagination but were founded on family legend of past wealth and leisure. These immediate comforts were what she could have, and she wanted them at once. She lagged rather far behind Paul, and once she thought of just turning back without a word and going home. She stopped, thinking that Paul would never do that to her, and so she would have to tell him. When a rabbit leaped, she let Paul have it without dispute. He killed it with one shot.

When she came up with him, he was already kneeling, examining the wound, the rabbit trailing from his hands. "Right through the head," he said complacently, as if he had aimed for it. He took out his sharp, competent bowie knife and started to skin the body. He did it very cleanly and quickly. Uncle Jimbilly knew how to prepare the skins so that Miranda always had fur coats for her dolls, for though she never cared much for her dolls she liked seeing them in fur coats. The children knelt facing each other over the dead animal. Miranda watched admiringly while her brother stripped the skin away as if he were taking off a glove. The flayed flesh emerged dark scarlet, sleek, firm; Miranda with thumb and finger felt the long fine muscles with the silvery flat strips binding them to the joints. Brother lifted the oddly bloated belly. "Look," he said, in a low amazed voice. "It was going to have young ones."

Very carefully he slit the thin flesh from the center ribs to the flanks, and a scarlet bag appeared. He slit again and pulled the bag open, and there lay a bundle of tiny rabbits, each wrapped in a thin scarlet veil. The brother pulled these off and there they were, dark gray, their sleek wet down lying in minute even ripples, like a baby's head just washed, their unbelievably small delicate ears folded close, their little blind faces almost featureless.

Miranda said, "Oh, I want to *see*," under her breath. She looked and looked— excited but not frightened, for she was accustomed to the sight of animals killed in hunting—filled with pity and astonishment and a kind of shocked delight in the wonderful little creatures for their own sakes, they were so pretty. She touched one of them ever so carefully, "Ah, there's blood running over them," she said and began to tremble without knowing why. Yet she wanted most deeply to see and to know. Having seen, she felt at once as if she had known all along. The very memory of her former ignorance faded, she had always known just this. No one had ever told her anything outright, she had been rather unobservant of the animal life around her because she was so accustomed to animals. They seemed simply disorderly and unaccountably rude in their habits, but altogether natural and not very interesting. Her brother had spoken as if he had known about everything all along. He may have seen all this before. He had never said a word to her, but she knew now a part at least of what he knew. She understood a little of the secret, formless intuitions in her own mind and body, which had been clearing up, taking form, so gradually and so steadily she had not realized that she was learning what she had to know. Paul said cautiously, as if he were talking about something forbidden: "They were just about ready to be born." His voice dropped on the last word. "I know," said Miranda, "like kittens. I know, like babies." She was quietly and terribly agitated, standing again with her rifle under her arm, looking down at the bloody heap. "I don't want the skin," she said, "I won't have it." Paul buried the young rabbits again in their mother's body, wrapped the skin around her, carried her to a clump of sage bushes, and hid her away. He came out again at once and said to Miranda, with an eager friendliness, a confidential tone quite unusual in him, as if he were taking her into an important secret on equal terms: "Listen now. Now you listen to me, and don't ever forget. Don't you ever tell a living soul that you saw this. Don't tell a soul. Don't tell Dad because I'll get into trouble. He'll say I'm leading you into things you ought not to do. He's always saying that. So now don't you go and forget and blab out sometime the way you're always doing . . . Now, that's a secret. Don't you tell."

Miranda never told, she did not even wish to tell anybody. She thought about the whole worrisome affair with confused unhappiness for a few days. Then it sank quietly into her mind and was heaped over by accumulated thousands of impressions, for nearly twenty years. One day she was picking her path among the puddles and crushed refuse of a market street in a strange city of a strange country, when without warning, plain and clear in its true colors as if she looked through a frame upon a scene that had not stirred nor changed since the moment it happened, the episode of that far-off day leaped from its burial place before her mind's eye. She was so reasonlessly horrified she halted suddenly staring, the scene before her eyes dimmed by the vision back of them. An Indian vendor had held up before her a tray of dyed sugar sweets, in the shapes of all kinds of small creatures: birds, baby chicks, baby rabbits, lambs, baby pigs. They were in gay colors and smelled of vanilla, maybe. . . . It was a very hot day and the smell in the market, with its piles of raw flesh and wilting flowers, was like the mingled sweetness and corruption she had smelled that other day in the empty cemetery at home: the day she had remembered always until now vaguely as the time she and her brother had found treasure in the opened graves. Instantly upon this thought the dreadful vision faded, and she saw clearly her brother, whose childhood face she had forgotten, standing again in the blazing sunshine, again twelve years old, a pleased sober smile in his eyes, turning the silver dove over and over in his hands.

[1944]

QUESTIONS FOR STUDY

1. *Why does Miranda want to trade the silver dove for the ring and what effect does the ring have on her? Why does Paul prefer the silver dove?*

2. *Why does Miranda react so strongly to the dead baby rabbits? What does she learn from the episode and how does it connect with "the secret, formless intuitions in her own mind and body"? What is Paul's reaction?*

3. *What triggers Miranda's sudden recollection in the market some twenty years later and what is the nature of her perception? What is significant in the fact that her "dreadful vision" gives way to the memory of Paul, a "pleased sober smile in his eyes, turning the silver dove over and over in his hands"?*

4. *How does the final episode relate to, illuminate, and complete the opening scene in the cemetery and the central episode with the rabbits?*

5. *What is the appropriateness of the story's title? What does Porter finally seem to be saying about the relationship between life and death, past and present, childhood and adolescence, and adolescence and maturity?*

ALAIN ROBBE-GRILLET

The Secret Room

THE FIRST thing to be seen is a red stain, of a deep, dark, shiny red, with almost black shadows. It is in the form of an irregular rosette, sharply outlined, extending in several directions in wide outflows of unequal length, dividing and dwindling afterward into single sinuous streaks. The whole stands out against a smooth, pale surface, round in shape, at once dull and pearly, a hemisphere joined by gentle curves to an expanse of the same pale color—white darkened by the shadowy quality of the place: a dungeon, a sunken room, or a cathedral—glowing with a diffused brilliance in the semidarkness.

Farther back, the space is filled with the cylindrical trunks of columns, repeated with progressive vagueness in their retreat toward the beginning of a vast stone stairway, turning slightly as it rises, growing narrower and narrower as it approaches the high vaults where it disappears.

The whole setting is empty, stairway and colonnades. Alone, in the foreground, the stretched-out body gleams feebly, marked with the red stain—a white body whose full, supple flesh can be sensed, fragile, no doubt, and vulnerable. Alongside the bloody hemisphere another identical round form, this one intact, is seen at almost the same angle of view; but the haloed point at its summit, of darker tint, is in this case quite recognizable, whereas the other one is entirely destroyed, or at least covered by the wound.

In the background, near the top of the stairway, a black silhouette is seen fleeing, a man wrapped in a long, floating cape, ascending the last steps without turning around, his deed accomplished. A thin smoke rises in twisting scrolls from a sort of incense burner placed on a high stand of ironwork with a silvery glint. Nearby lies the milkwhite body, with wide streaks of blood running from the left breast, along the flank and on the hip.

It is a fully rounded woman's body, but not heavy, completely nude, lying on its back, the bust raised up somewhat by thick cushions thrown down on the floor, which is covered with Oriental rugs. The waist is very narrow, the neck long and thin, curved to one side, the head thrown back into a darker area where, even so, the facial features may be discerned, the partly opened mouth, the wide-staring eyes, shining with a fixed brilliance, and the mass of long, black hair spread out in a complicated wavy disorder over a heavily folded cloth, of velvet perhaps, on which also rest the arm and shoulder.

It is a uniformly colored velvet of dark purple, or which seems so in this lighting. But purple, brown, blue also seem to dominate in the colors of the cushions— only a small portion of which is hidden beneath the velvet cloth, and which protrude noticeably, lower down, beneath the bust and waist—as well as in the Oriental patterns of the rugs on the floor. Farther on, these same colors are picked up again in the stone of the paving and the columns, the vaulted archways, the stairs, and the less discernible surfaces that disappear into the farthest reaches of the room.

The dimensions of this room are difficult to determine exactly; the body of the young sacrificial victim seems at first glance to occupy a substantial portion of it, but the vast size of the stairway leading down to it would imply rather that this is not the whole room, whose considerable space must in reality extend all around, right and left, as it does toward the far-away browns and blues among the columns standing in line, in every direction, perhaps toward other sofas, thick carpets, piles of cushions and fabrics, other tortured bodies, other incense burners.

It is also difficult to say where the light comes from. No clue, on the columns or on the floor, suggests the direction of the rays. Nor is any window or torch visible. The milkwhite body itself seems to light the scene, with its full breasts, the curve of its thighs, the rounded belly, the full buttocks, the stretched-out legs, widely spread, and the black tuft of the exposed sex, provocative, proffered, useless now.

The man has already moved several steps back. He is now on the first steps of the stairs, ready to go up. The bottom steps are wide and deep, like the steps leading up to some great building, a temple or theater; they grow smaller as they ascend, and at the same time describe a wide, helical curve, so gradually that the stairway has not yet made a half-turn by the time it disappears near the top of the vaults, reduced then to a steep, narrow flight of steps without handrail, vaguely outlined, moreover, in the thickening darkness beyond.

But the man does not look in this direction, where his movement nonetheless carries him; his left foot on the second step and his right foot already touching the third, with his knee bent, he has turned around to look at the spectacle for one last time. The long, floating cape thrown hastily over his shoulders, clasped in one hand at his waist, has been whirled around by the rapid circular motion that has just caused his head and chest to turn in the opposite direction, and a corner of the cloth remains suspended in the air as if blown by a gust of wind; this corner, twisting around upon itself in the form of a loose S, reveals the red silk lining with its gold embroidery.

The man's features are impassive, but tense, as if in expectation—or perhaps fear—of some sudden event, or surveying with one last glance the total immobility of the scene. Though he is looking backward, his whole body is turned slightly forward, as if he were continuing up the stairs. His right arm—not the one holding the edge of the cape—is bent sharply toward the left, toward a point in space where the balustrade should be, if this stairway had one, an interrupted gesture, almost incomprehensible, unless it arose from an instinctive movement to grasp the absent support.

As to the direction of his glance, it is certainly aimed at the body of the victim lying on the cushions, its extended members stretched out in the form of a cross, its bust raised up, its head thrown back. But the face is perhaps hidden from the man's eyes by one of the columns, standing at the foot of the stairs. The young woman's right hand touches the floor just at the foot of this column. The fragile wrist is encircled by an iron bracelet. The arm is almost in darkness, only the hand receiving enough light to make the thin, outspread fingers clearly visible against the circular protrusion at the base of the stone column. A black metal chain running around the column passes through a ring affixed to the bracelet, binding the wrist tightly to the column.

At the top of the arm a rounded shoulder, raised up by the cushions, also stands out well lighted, as well as the neck, the throat, and the other shoulder, the armpit with its soft hair, the left arm likewise pulled back with its wrist bound in the same manner to the base of another column, in the extreme foreground; here the iron bracelet and the chain are fully displayed, represented with perfect clarity down to the slightest details.

The same is true, still in the foreground but at the other side, for a similar chain, but not quite as thick, wound directly around the ankle, running twice around the column and terminating in a heavy iron ring embedded in the floor. About a yard further back, or perhaps slightly farther, the right foot is identically chained. But it is the left foot, and its chain, that are the most minutely depicted.

The foot is small, delicate, finely modeled. In several places the chain has broken the skin, causing noticeable if not extensive depressions in the flesh. The chain links are oval, thick, the size of an eye. The ring in the floor resembles those used to attach horses; it lies almost touching the stone pavement to which it is riveted by a massive iron peg. A few inches away is the edge of a rug; it is grossly wrinkled at this point, doubtless as a result of the convulsive, but necessarily very restricted, movements of the victim attempting to struggle.

The man is still standing about a yard away, half leaning over her. He looks at her face, seen upside down, her dark eyes made larger by their surrounding eyeshadow, her mouth wide open as if screaming. The man's posture allows his face to be seen only in a vague profile, but one senses in it a violent exaltation, despite the rigid attitude, the silence, the immobility. His back is slightly arched. His left hand, the only one visible, holds up at some distance from the body a piece of cloth, some dark-colored piece of clothing, which drags on the carpet, and which must be the long cape with its gold-embroidered lining.

This immense silhouette hides most of the bare flesh over which the red stain, spreading from the globe of the breast, runs in long rivulets that branch out, growing narrower, upon the pale background of the bust and the flank. One thread has reached the armpit and runs in an almost straight line along the arm; others have run down toward the waist and traced out, along one side of the belly, the hip, the top of the thigh, a more random network already starting to congeal. Three or four tiny veins have reached the hollow between the legs, meeting in a sinuous line, touching the point of the V formed by the outspread legs, and disappearing into the black tuft.

Look, now the flesh is still intact: the black tuft and the white belly, the soft curve of the hips, the narrow waist, and, higher up, the pearly breasts rising and falling in time with the rapid breathing, whose rhythm grows more accelerated.

The man, close to her, one knee on the floor, leans farther over. The head, with its long, curly hair, which alone is free to move somewhat, turns from side to side, struggling; finally the woman's mouth twists open, while the flesh is torn open, the blood spurts out over the tender skin, stretched tight, the carefully shadowed eyes grow abnormally larger, the mouth opens wider, the head twists violently, one last time, from right to left, then more gently, to fall back finally and become still, amid the mass of black hair spread out on the velvet.

At the very top of the stone stairway, the little door has opened, allowing a yellowish but sustained shaft of light to enter, against which stands out the dark silhouette of the man wrapped in his long cloak. He has but to climb a few more steps to reach the threshold.

Afterward, the whole setting is empty, the enormous room with its purple shadows and its stone columns proliferating in all directions, the monumental staircase with no handrail that twists upward, growing narrower and vaguer as it rises into the darkness, toward the top of the vaults where it disappears.

Near the body, whose wound has stiffened, whose brilliance is already growing dim, the thin smoke from the incense burner traces complicated scrolls in the still air: first a coil turned horizontally to the left, which then straightens out and rises slightly, then returns to the axis of its point of origin, which it crosses as it moves to the right, then turns back in the first direction, only to wind back again, thus forming an irregular sinusoidal curve, more and more flattened out, and rising vertically, toward the top of the canvas.

[1962]

TRANSLATED BY
BRUCE MORRISSETTE

QUESTIONS FOR STUDY

1. *What elements of the traditional short story does Robbe-Grillet dispense with? What does he emphasize in their place? Is this a short story at all? If so, in what sense?*
2. *What mood is established by the story?*

3. *How does Robbe-Grillet suggest movement or action? Is it chrono-logical? What cinematic techniques does he employ?*
4. *Why is the word "canvas" used at the end of the story? Is the author describing a painting (or a series of paintings), or is the word used in some other sense?*
5. *Can the story be interpreted? Need it be "interpreted" at all?*

PHILIP ROTH

Defender of the Faith

IN MAY of 1945, only a few weeks after the fighting had ended in Europe, I was rotated back to the States, where I spent the remainder of the war with a training company at Camp Crowder, Missouri. Along with the rest of the Ninth Army, I had been racing across Germany so swiftly during the late winter and spring that when I boarded the plane, I couldn't believe its destination lay to the west. My mind might inform me otherwise, but there was an inertia of the spirit that told me we were flying to a new front, where we would disembark and continue our push eastward—eastward until we'd circled the globe, marching through villages along whose twisting, cobbled streets crowds of the enemy would watch us take possession of what, up till then, they'd considered their own. I had changed enough in two years not to mind the trembling of the old people, the crying of the very young, the uncertainty and fear in the eyes of the once arrogant. I had been fortunate enough to develop an infantryman's heart, which, like his feet, at first aches and swells but finally grows horny enough for him to travel the weirdest paths without feeling a thing.

Captain Paul Barrett was my C.O. in Camp Crowder. The day I reported for duty, he came out of his office to shake my hand. He was short, gruff, and fiery, and—indoors or out—he wore his polished helmet liner pulled down to his little eyes. In Europe, he had received a battlefield commission and a serious chest wound, and he'd been returned to the States only a few months before. He spoke easily to me, and at the evening formation he introduced me to the troops. "Gentlemen," he said, "Sergeant

Thurston, as you know, is no longer with this company. Your new first sergeant is Sergeant Nathan Marx, here. He is a veteran of the European theater, and consequently will expect to find a company of soldiers here, and not a company of *boys*."

I sat up late in the orderly room that evening, trying half-heartedly to solve the riddle of duty rosters, personnel forms, and morning reports. The Charge of Quarters slept with his mouth open on a mattress on the floor. A trainee stood reading the next day's duty roster, which was posted on the bulletin board just inside the screen door. It was a warm evening, and I could hear radios playing dance music over in the barracks. The trainee, who had been staring at me whenever he thought I wouldn't notice, finally took a step in my direction.

"Hey, Sarge—we having a G.I. party tomorrow night?" he asked. A G.I. party is a barracks cleaning.

"You usually have them on Friday nights?" I asked him.

"Yes," he said, and then he added, mysteriously, "that's the whole thing."

"Then you'll have a G.I. party."

He turned away, and I heard him mumbling. His shoulders were moving, and I wondered if he was crying.

"What's your name, soldier?" I asked.

He turned, not crying at all. Instead, his green-speckled eyes, long and narrow, flashed like fish in the sun. He walked over to me and sat on the edge of my desk. He reached out a hand. "Sheldon," he said.

"Stand on your feet, Sheldon."

Getting off the desk, he said, "Sheldon Grossbart." He smiled at the familiarity into which he'd led me.

"You against cleaning the barracks

"Defender of the Faith" from *Goodbye Columbus* by Philip Roth. Reprinted by permission of Houghton Mifflin Company.

Friday night, Grossbart?" I said. "Maybe we shouldn't have G.I. parties. Maybe we should get a maid." My tone startled me. I felt I sounded like every top sergeant I had ever known.

"No, Sergeant." He grew serious, but with a seriousness that seemed to be only the stifling of a smile. "It's just—G.I. parties on Friday night, of all nights."

He slipped up onto the corner of the desk again—not quite sitting, but not quite standing, either. He looked at me with those speckled eyes flashing, and then made a gesture with his hand. It was very slight—no more than a movement back and forth of the wrist—and yet it managed to exclude from our affairs everything else in the orderly room, to make the two of us the center of the world. It seemed, in fact, to exclude everything even about the two of us except our hearts.

"Sergeant Thurston was one thing," he whispered, glancing at the sleeping C.Q., "but we thought that with you here things might be a little different."

"We?"

"The Jewish personnel."

"Why?" I asked, harshly. "What's on your mind?" Whether I was still angry at the "Sheldon" business, or now at something else, I hadn't time to tell, but clearly I was angry.

"We thought you—Marx, you know, like Karl Marx. The Marx Brothers. Those guys are all—M-a-r-x. Isn't that how *you* spell it, Sergeant?"

"M-a-r-x."

"Fishbein said—" He stopped. "What I mean to say, Sergeant—" His face and neck were red, and his mouth moved but no words came out. In a moment, he raised himself to attention, gazing down at me. It was as though he had suddenly decided he could expect no more sympathy from me than from Thurston, the reason being that I was of Thurston's faith, and not his. The young man had managed to confuse himself as to what my faith really was, but I felt no desire to straighten him out. Very simply, I didn't like him.

When I did nothing but return his gaze, he spoke, in an altered tone. "You

see, Sergeant," he explained to me, "Friday nights, Jews are supposed to go to services."

"Did Sergeant Thurston tell you you couldn't go to them when there was a G.I. party?"

"No."

"Did he say you had to stay and scrub the floors?"

"No, Sergeant."

"Did the Captain say you had to stay and scrub the floors?"

"That isn't it, Sergeant. It's the other guys in the barracks." He leaned toward me. "They think we're goofing off. But we're not. That's when Jews go to services, Friday night. We have to."

"Then go."

"But the other guys make accusations. They have no right."

"That's not the Army's problem, Grossbart. It's a personal problem you'll have to work out yourself."

"But it's *unfair.*"

I got up to leave. "There's nothing I can do about it," I said.

Grossbart stiffened and stood in front of me. "But this is a matter of *religion, sir.*"

"Sergeant," I said.

"I mean 'Sergeant,'" he said, almost snarling.

"Look, go see the chaplain. You want to see Captain Barrett, I'll arrange an appointment."

"No, no. I don't want to make trouble, Sergeant. That's the first thing they throw up to you. I just want my rights!"

"Damn it, Grossbart, stop whining. You have your rights. You can stay and scrub floors or you can go to shul—" [1]

The smile swam in again. Spittle gleamed at the corners of his mouth. "You mean church, Sergeant."

"I mean shul, Grossbart!"

I walked past him and went outside. Near me, I heard the scrunching of a guard's boots on gravel. Beyond the lighted windows of the barracks, young men in T shirts and fatigue pants were sitting on their bunks, polishing their rifles. Suddenly there was a light rustling

[1] Synagogue. (JHP)

behind me. I turned and saw Grossbart's dark frame fleeing back to the barracks, racing to tell his Jewish friends that they were right—that, like Karl and Harpo, I was one of them.

The next morning, while chatting with Captain Barrett, I recounted the incident of the previous evening. Somehow, in the telling, it must have seemed to the Captain that I was not so much explaining Grossbart's position as defending it. "Marx, I'd fight side by side with a nigger if the fella proved to me he was a man. I pride myself," he said, looking out the window, "that I've got an open mind. Consequently, Sergeant, nobody gets special treatment here, for the good *or* the bad. All a man's got to do is prove himself. A man fires well on the range, I give him a weekend pass. He scores high in P.T., he gets a weekend pass. He *earns* it." He turned from the window and pointed a finger at me. "You're a Jewish fella, am I right, Marx?"

"Yes, sir."

"And I admire you. I admire you because of the ribbons on your chest. I judge a man by what he shows me on the field of battle, Sergeant. It's what he's got *here*," he said, and then, though I expected he would point to his chest, he jerked a thumb toward the buttons straining to hold his blouse across his belly. "Guts," he said.

"O.K., sir. I only wanted to pass on to you how the men felt."

"Mr. Marx, you're going to be old before your time if you worry about how the men feel. Leave that stuff to the chaplain—that's his business, not yours. Let's us train these fellas to shoot straight. If the Jewish personnel feels the other men are accusing them of goldbricking—well, I just don't know. Seems awful funny that suddenly the Lord is calling so loud in Private Grossman's ear he's just got to run to church."

"Synagogue," I said.

"Synagogue is right, Sergeant. I'll write that down for handy reference. Thank you for stopping by."

That evening, a few minutes before the company gathered outside the or-

derly room for the chow formation, I called the C.Q., Corporal Robert LaHill, in to see me. LaHill was a dark, burly fellow whose hair curled out of his clothes wherever it could. He had a glaze in his eyes that made one think of caves and dinosaurs. "LaHill," I said, "when you take the formation, remind the men that they're free to attend church services *whenever* they are held, provided they report to the orderly room before they leave the area."

LaHill scratched his wrist, but gave no indication that he'd heard or understood.

"LaHill," I said, "*church*. You remember? Church, priest, Mass, confession."

He curled one lip into a kind of smile; I took it for a signal that for a second he had flickered back up into the human race.

"Jewish personnel who want to attend services this evening are to fall out in front of the orderly room at 1900," I said. Then, as an afterthought, I added, "By order of Captain Barrett."

A little while later, as the day's last light—softer than any I had seen that year—began to drop over Camp Crowder, I heard LaHill's thick, inflectionless voice outside my window: "Give me your ears, troopers. Toppie says for me to tell you that at 1900 hours all Jewish personnel is to fall out in front, here, if they want to attend the Jewish Mass."

At seven o'clock, I looked out the orderly-room window and saw three soldiers in starched khakis standing on the dusty quadrangle. They looked at their watches and fidgeted while they whispered back and forth. It was getting dimmer, and, alone on the otherwise deserted field, they looked tiny. When I opened the door, I heard the noises of the G.I. party coming from the surrounding barracks—bunks being pushed to the walls, faucets pounding water into buckets, brooms whisking at the wooden floors, cleaning the dirt away for Saturday's inspection. Big puffs of cloth moved round and round on the windowpanes. I walked outside, and the moment my foot hit the ground I thought I heard Grossbart call to the others, " 'Ten-*hut!*" Or maybe, when they all three jumped to attention, I imagined I heard the command.

Grossbart stepped forward, "Thank you, sir," he said.

" 'Sergeant,' Grossbart," I reminded him. "You call officers, 'sir.' I'm not an officer. You've been in the Army three weeks—you know that."

He turned his palms out at his sides to indicate that, in truth, he and I lived beyond convention. "Thank you anyway," he said.

"Yes," a tall boy behind him said. "Thanks a lot."

And the third boy whispered, "Thank you," but his mouth barely, fluttered, so that he did not alter by more than a lip's movement his posture of attention.

"For what?" I asked.

Grossbart snorted happily. "For the announcement. The Corporal's announcement. It helped. It made it—"

"Fancier." The tall boy finished Grossbart's sentence.

Grossbart smiled. "He means formal, sir. Public," he said to me. "Now it won't seem as though we're just taking off—goldbricking because the work has begun."

"It was by order of Captain Barrett," I said.

"Aaah, but you pull a little weight," Grossbart said. "So we thank you." Then he turned to his companions. "Sergeant Marx, I want you to meet Larry Fishbein."

The tall boy stepped forward and extended his hand. I shook it. "You from New York?" he asked.

"Yes."

"Me, too." He had a cadaverous face that collapsed inward from his cheekbone to his jaw, and when he smiled—as he did at the news of our communal attachment—revealed a mouthful of bad teeth. He was blinking his eyes a good deal, as though he were fighting back tears. "What borough?" he asked.

I turned to Grossbart. "It's five after seven. What time are services?"

"Shul," he said, smiling, "is in ten minutes. I want you to meet Mickey Halpern. This is Nathan Marx, our sergeant."

The third boy hopped forward. "Private Michael Halpern." He saluted.

"Salute officers, Halpern," I said. The boy dropped his hand, and, on its way down, in his nervousness, checked to see if his shirt pockets were buttoned.

"Shall I march them over, sir?" Grossbart asked. "Or are you coming along?"

From behind Grossbart, Fishbein piped up. "Afterward, they're having refreshments. A ladies auxiliary from St. Louis, the rabbi told us last week."

"The chaplain," Halpren whispered.

"You're welcome to come along," Grossbart said.

To avoid his plea, I looked away, and saw, in the windows of the barracks, a cloud of faces staring out at the four of us. "Hurry along, Grossbart," I said.

"O.K., then," he said. He turned to the others. "Double time, *march!*"

They started off, but ten feet away Grossbart spun around and, running backward, called to me, "Good *shabbus,*[2] sir!" And then the three of them were swallowed into the alien Missouri dusk.

Even after they had disappeared over the parade ground, whose green was now a deep blue, I could hear Grossbart singing the double-time cadence, and as it grew dimmer and dimmer, it suddenly touched a deep memory—as did the slant of the light—and I was remembering the shrill sounds of a Bronx playground where, years ago, beside the Grand Concourse, I had played on long spring evenings such as this. It was a pleasant memory for a young man so far from peace and home, and it brought so many recollections with it that I began to grow exceedingly tender about myself. In fact, I indulged myself in a reverie so strong that I felt as though a hand were reaching down inside me. It had to reach so very far to touch me! It had to reach past those days in the forests of Belgium, and past the dying I'd refused to weep over; past the nights in German farmhouses whose books we'd burned to warm us; past endless stretches when I had shut off all softness I might feel for

2 Sabbath. (JHP)

my fellows, and had managed even to deny myself the posture of a conqueror —the swagger that I, as a Jew, might well have worn as my boots whacked against the rubble of Wesel, Münster, and Braunschweig.

But now one night noise, one rumor of home and time past, and memory plunged down through all I had anesthetized, and came to what I suddenly remembered was myself. So it was not altogether curious that, in search of more of me, I found myself following Grossbart's tracks to Chapel No. 3, where the Jewish services were being held.

I took a seat in the last row, which was empty. Two rows in front of me sat Grossbart, Fishbein, and Halpern, holding little white Dixie cups. Each row of seats was raised higher than the one in front of it, and I could see clearly what was going on. Fishbein was pouring the contents of his cup into Grossbart's, and Grossbart looked mirthful as the liquid made a purple arc between Fishbein's hand and his. In the glaring yellow light, I saw the chaplain standing on the platform at the front; he was chanting the first line of the responsive reading. Grossbart's prayer book remained closed on his lap; he was swishing the cup around. Only Halpern responded to the chant by praying. The fingers of his right hand were spread wide across the cover of his open book. His cap was pulled down low onto his brow, which made it round, like a yarmulke.[3] From time to time, Grossbart wet his lips at the cup's edge; Fishbein, his long yellow face a dying light bulb, looked from here to there, craning forward to catch sight of the faces down the row, then of those in front of him, then behind. He saw me, and his eyelids beat a tattoo. His elbow slid into Grossbart's side, his neck inclined toward his friend, he whispered something, and then, when the congregation next responded to the chant, Grossbart's voice was among the others. Fishbein looked into his book now, too; his lips, however, didn't move.

Finally, it was time to drink the wine.

The chaplain smiled down at them as Grossbart swigged his in one long gulp, Halpern sipped, meditating, and Fishbein faked devotion with an empty cup. "As I look down amongst the congregation"—the chaplain grinned at the word —"this night, I see many new faces, and I want to welcome you to Friday-night services here at Camp Crowder. I am Major Leo Ben Ezra, your chaplain." Though an American, the chaplain spoke deliberately—syllable by syllable, almost —as though to communicate, above all, with the lip readers in his audience. "I have only a few words to say before we adjourn to the refreshment room, where the kind ladies of the Temple Sinai, St. Louis, Missouri, have a nice setting for you."

Applause and whistling broke out. After another momentary grin, the chaplain raised his hands, palms out, his eyes flicking upward a moment, as if to remind the troops where they were and Who Else might be in attendance. In the sudden silence that followed, I thought I heard Grossbart cackle, "Let the goyim [4] clean the floors!" Were those the words? I wasn't sure, but Fishbein, grinning, nudged Halpern. Halpern looked dumbly at him, then went back to his prayer book, which had been occupying him all through the rabbi's talk. One hand tugged at the black kinky hair that stuck out under his cap. His lips moved.

The rabbi continued. "It is about the food that I want to speak to you for a moment. I know, I know, I know," he intoned, wearily, "how in the mouths of most of you the *trafe* [5] food tastes like ashes. I know how you gag, some of you, and how your parents suffer to think of their children eating foods unclean and offensive to the palate. What can I tell you? I can only say, close your eyes and swallow as best you can. Eat what you must to live, and throw away the rest. I wish I could help more. For those of you who find this impossible, may I ask that you try and try, but then come to see me in private. If your revulsion is so

3 A skull cap. (JHP)

4 Gentiles. (JHP)
5 Nonkosher food. (JHP)

great, we will have to seek aid from those higher up."

A round of chatter rose and subsided. Then everyone sang "Ain Kelohainu"; after all those years, I discovered I still knew the words. Then, suddenly, the service over, Grossbart was upon me. "Higher up? He means the General?"

"Hey, Shelly," Fishbein said, "he means God." He smacked his face and looked at Halpern. "How high can you go!"

"Sh-h-h!" Grossbart said. "What do you think, Sergeant?"

"I don't know," I said. "You better ask the chaplain."

"I'm going to. I'm making an appointment to see him in private. So is Mickey."

Halpern shook his head. "No, no, Sheldon—"

"You have rights, Mickey," Grossbart said. "They can't push us around."

"It's O.K.," said Halpern. "It bothers my mother, not me."

Grossbart looked at me. "Yesterday he threw up. From the hash. It was all ham and God knows what else."

"I have a cold—that was why," Halpern said. He pushed his yarmulke back into a cap.

"What about you, Fishbein?" I asked. "You kosher, too?"

He flushed. "A little. But I'll let it ride. I have a very strong stomach, and I don't eat a lot anyway." I continued to look at him, and he held up his wrist to reinforce what he'd just said; his watch strap was tightened to the last hole, and he pointed that out to me.

"But services are important to you?" I asked him.

He looked at Grossbart. "Sure, sir."

" 'Sergeant.' "

"Not so much at home," said Grossbart, stepping between us, "but away from home it gives one a sense of his Jewishness."

"We have to stick together," Fishbein said.

I started to walk toward the door; Halpern stepped back to make way for me.

"That's what happened in Germany,"

Grossbart was saying, loud enough for me to hear. "They didn't stick together. They let themselves get pushed around."

I turned. "Look, Grossbart. This is the Army, not summer camp."

He smiled. "So?"

Halpern tried to sneak off, but Grossbart held his arm.

"Grossbart, how old are you?" I asked. "Nineteen."

"And you?" I said to Fishbein.

"The same. The same month, even."

"And what about him?" I pointed to Halpern, who had by now made it safely to the door.

"Eighteen," Grossbart whispered. "But like he can't tie his shoes or brush his teeth himself. I feel sorry for him."

"I feel sorry for all of us, Grossbart," I said, "but just act like a man. Just don't overdo it."

"Overdo what, sir?"

"The 'sir' business, for one thing. Don't overdo that," I said.

I left him standing there. I passed by Halpern, but he did not look at me. Then I was outside, but, behind, I heard Grossbart call, "Hey, Mickey, my *leben*,[6] come on back. Refreshments!"

"Leben!" My grandmother's word for me!

One morning a week later, while I was working at my desk, Captain Barrett shouted for me to come into his office. When I entered, he had his helmet liner squashed down so far on his head that I couldn't even see his eyes. He was on the phone, and when he spoke to me, he cupped one hand over the mouthpiece. "Who the hell is Grossbart?"

"Third platoon, Captain," I said. "A trainee."

"What's all this stink about food? His mother called a goddam congressman about the food." He uncovered the mouthpiece and slid his helmet up until I could see his bottom eyelashes. "Yes, sir," he said into the phone. "Yes, sir. I'm still here, sir. I'm asking Marx, here, right now—"

He covered the mouthpiece again and

6 Darling. (JHP)

turned his head back toward me. "Light-foot Harry's on the phone," he said, be-tween his teeth. "This congressman calls General Lyman, who calls Colonel Sousa, who calls the Major, who calls me. They're just dying to stick this thing on me. Whatsa matter?" He shook the phone at me. "I don't feed the troops? What is this?"

"Sir, Grossbart is strange—" Barrett greeted that with a mockingly indulgent smile. I altered my approach. "Captain, he's a very orthodox Jew, and so he's only allowed to eat certain foods."

"He throws up, the congressman said. Every time he eats something, his mother says, he throws up!"

"He's accustomed to observing the dietary laws, Captain."

"So why's his old lady have to call the White House?"

"Jewish parents, sir—they're apt to be more protective than you expect. I mean, Jews have a very close family life. A boy goes away from home, sometimes the mother is liable to get very upset. Prob-ably the boy mentioned something in a letter, and his mother misinterpreted."

"I'd like to punch him one right in the mouth," the Captain said. "There's a war on, and he wants a silver platter!"

"I don't think the boy's to blame, sir. I'm sure we can straighten it out by just asking him. Jewish parents worry—"

"*All* parents worry, for Christ's sake. But they don't get on their high horse and start pulling strings—"

I interrupted, my voice higher, tighter than before. "The home life, Captain, is very important—but you're right, it may sometimes get out of hand. It's a very wonderful thing, Captain, but because it's so close, this kind of thing . . ."

He didn't listen any longer to my at-tempt to present both myself and Light-foot Harry with an explanation for the letter. He turned back to the phone. "Sir?" he said. "Sir—Marx, here, tells me Jews have a tendency to be pushy. He says he thinks we can settle it right here in the company . . . Yes, sir . . . I *will* call back, sir, soon as I can." He hung up. "Where are the men, Sergeant?"

"On the range."

With a whack on the top of his hel-met, he crushed it down over his eyes again, and charged out of his chair. "We're going for a ride," he said.

The Captain drove, and I sat beside him. It was a hot spring day, and under my newly starched fatigues I felt as though my armpits were melting down onto my sides and chest. The roads were dry, and by the time we reached the firing range, my teeth felt gritty with dust, though my mouth had been shut the whole trip. The Captain slammed the brakes on and told me to get the hell out and find Grossbart.

I found him on his belly, firing wildly at the five-hundred-feet target. Waiting their turns behind him were Halpern and Fishbein. Fishbein, wearing a pair of steel-rimmed G.I. glasses I hadn't seen on him before, had the appearance of an old peddler who would gladly have sold you his rifle and the cartridges that were slung all over him. I stood back by the ammo boxes, waiting for Grossbart to finish spraying the distant targets. Fish-bein straggled back to stand near me.

"Hello, Sergeant Marx," he said.

"How are you?" I mumbled.

"Fine, thank you. Sheldon's really a good shot."

"I didn't notice."

"I'm not so good, but I think I'm get-ting the hang of it now. Sergeant, I don't mean to, you know, ask what I shouldn't—" The boy stopped. He was trying to speak intimately, but the noise of the shooting forced him to shout at me.

"What is it?" I asked. Down the range, I saw Captain Barrett standing up in the jeep, scanning the line for me and Gross-bart.

"My parents keep asking and asking where we're going," Fishbein said. "Everybody says the Pacific. I don't care, but my parents—If I could relieve their minds, I think I could concentrate more on my shooting."

"I don't know where, Fishbein. Try to concentrate anyway."

"Sheldon says you might be able to find out."

"I don't know a thing, Fishbein. You

just take it easy, and don't let Sheldon—"

"*I'm* taking it easy, Sergeant. It's at home—"

Grossbart had finished on the line, and was dusting his fatigues with one hand. I called to him. "Grossbart, the Captain wants to see you."

He came toward us. His eyes blazed and twinkled. "Hi!"

"Don't point that rifle!" I said.

"I wouldn't shoot you, Sarge." He gave me a smile as wide as a pumpkin, and turned the barrel aside.

"Damn you, Grossbart, this is no joke! Follow me."

I walked ahead of him, and had the awful suspicion that, behind me, Grossbart was *marching,* his rifle on his shoulder as though he were a one-man detachment. At the jeep, he gave the Captain a rifle salute. "Private Sheldon Grossbart, sir."

"At ease, Grossman." The Captain sat down, slid over into the empty seat, and, crooking a finger, invited Grossbart closer.

"Bart, sir. Sheldon Gross*bart.* It's a common error." Grossbart nodded at me; *I* understood, he indicated. I looked away just as the mess truck pulled up to the range, disgorging a half-dozen K.P.s with rolled-up sleeves. The mess sergeant screamed at them while they set up the chowline equipment.

"Grossbart, your mama wrote some congressman that we don't feed you right. Do you know that?" the Captain said.

"It was my father, sir. He wrote to Representative Franconi that my religion forbids me to eat certain foods."

"What religion is that, Grossbart?"

"Jewish."

" 'Jewish, *sir,*' " I said to Grossbart.

"Excuse me, sir, Jewish, sir."

"What have you been living on?" the Captain asked. "You've been in the Army a month already. You don't look to me like you're falling to pieces."

"I eat because I have to, sir. But Sergeant Marx will testify to the fact that I don't eat one mouthful more than I need to in order to survive."

"Is that so, Marx?" Barrett asked.

"I've never seen Grossbart eat, sir," I said.

"But you heard the rabbi," Grossbart said. "He told us what to do, and I listened."

The Captain looked at me. "Well, Marx?"

"I still don't know what he eats and doesn't eat, sir."

Grossbart raised his arms to plead with me, and it looked for a moment as though he were going to hand me his weapon to hold. "But, Sergeant—"

"Look, Grossbart, just answer the Captain's questions," I said sharply.

Barrett smiled at me, and I resented it. "All right, Grossbart," he said. "What is it you want? The little piece of paper? You want out?"

"No, sir. Only to be allowed to live as a Jew. And for the others, too."

"What others?"

"Fishbein, sir, and Halpern."

"They don't like the way we serve, either?"

"Halpern throws up, sir. I've seen it."

"I thought *you* throw up."

"Just once, sir. I didn't know the sausage was sausage."

"We'll give menus, Grossbart. We'll show training films about the food, so you can identify when we're trying to poison you."

Grossbart did not answer. The men had been organized into two long chow lines. At the tail end of one, I spotted Fishbein—or, rather, his glasses spotted me. They winked sunlight back at me. Halpern stood next to him, patting the inside of his collar with a khaki handkerchief. They moved with the line as it began to edge up toward the food. The mess sergeant was still screaming at the K.P.s. For a moment, I was actually terrified by the thought that somehow the mess sergeant was going to become involved in Grossbart's problem.

"Marx," the Captain said, "you're a Jewish fella—am I right?"

I played straight man. "Yes, sir."

"How long you been in the Army? Tell this boy."

"Three years and two months."

"A year in combat, Grossbart. Twelve

goddam months in combat all through Europe. I admire this man." The Captain snapped a wrist against my chest. "Do you hear him peeping about the food? Do you? I want an answer, Grossbart. Yes or no."

"No, sir."

"And why not? He's a Jewish fella."

"Some things are more important to some Jews than other things to other Jews."

Barrett blew up. "Look, Grossbart. Marx, here, is a good man—a goddam hero. When you were in high school, Sergeant Marx was killing Germans. Who does more for the Jews—you, by throwing up over a lousy piece of sausage, a piece of first-cut meat, or Marx, by killing those Nazi bastards? If I was a Jew, Grossbart, I'd kiss this man's feet. He's a goddam hero, and *he* eats what we give him. Why do you have to cause trouble is what I want to know! What is it you're buckin' for—a discharge?"

"No, sir."

"I'm talking to a wall! Sergeant, get him out of my way." Barrett swung himself back into the driver's seat. "I'm going to see the chaplain." The engine roared, the jeep spun around in a whirl of dust, and the Captain was headed back to camp.

For a moment, Grossbart and I stood side by side, watching the jeep. Then he looked at me and said, "I don't want to start trouble. That's the first thing they toss up to us."

When he spoke, I saw that his teeth were white and straight, and the sight of them suddenly made me understand that Grossbart actually did have parents —that once upon a time someone had taken little Sheldon to the dentist. He was their son. Despite all the talk about his parents, it was hard to believe in Grossbart as a child, an heir—as related by blood to anyone, mother, father, or, above all, to me. This realization led me to another.

"What does your father do, Grossbart?" I asked as we started to walk back toward the chow line.

"He's a tailor."

"An American?"

"Now, yes. A son in the Army," he said, jokingly.

"And your mother?" I asked.

He winked. "A *ballabusta*.[7] She practically sleeps with a dustcloth in her hand."

"She's also an immigrant?"

"All she talks is Yiddish, still."

"And your father, too?"

"A little English. 'Clean,' 'Press,' 'Take the pants in.' That's the extent of it. But they're good to me."

"Then, Grossbart—" I reached out and stopped him. He turned toward me, and when our eyes met, his seemed to jump back, to shiver in their sockets. "Grossbart—you were the one who wrote that letter, weren't you?"

It took only a second or two for his eyes to flash happy again. "Yes." He walked on, and I kept pace. "It's what my father *would* have written if he had known how. It was his name, though. *He* signed it. He even mailed it. I sent it home. For the New York postmark."

I was astonished, and he saw it. With complete seriousness, he thrust his right arm in front of me. "Blood is blood, Sergeant," he said, pinching the blue vein in his wrist.

"What the hell *are* you trying to do, Grossbart?" I asked. "I've seen you eat. Do you know that? I told the Captain I don't know what you eat, but I've seen you eat like a hound at chow."

"We work hard, Sergeant. We're in training. For a furnace to work, you've got to feed it coal."

"Why did you say in the letter that you threw up all the time?"

"I was really talking about Mickey there. I was talking *for* him. He would never write, Sergeant, though I pleaded with him. He'll waste away to nothing if I don't help. Sergeant, I used my name —my father's name—but it's Mickey, and Fishbein, too, I'm watching out for."

"You're a regular Messiah, aren't you?"

We were at the chow line now.

"That's a good one, Sergeant," he said,

7 A housekeeper or housewife. (JHP)

smiling. "But who knows? Who can tell? Maybe you're the Messiah—a little bit. What Mickey says is the Messiah is a collective idea. He went to Yeshiva,[8] Mickey, for a while. He says *together* we're the Messiah. Me a little bit, you a little bit. You should hear that kid talk, Sergeant, when he gets going."

"Me a little bit, you a little bit," I said. "You'd like to believe that, wouldn't you, Grossbart? That would make everything so clean for you."

"It doesn't seem too bad a thing to believe, Sergeant. It only means we should all *give* a little, is all."

I walked off to eat my rations with the other noncoms.

Two days later, a letter addressed to Captain Barrett passed over my desk. It had come through the chain of command—from the office of Congressman Franconi, where it had been received, to General Lyman, to Colonel Sousa, to Major Lamont, now to Captain Barrett. I read it over twice. It was dated May 14, the day Barrett had spoken with Grossbart on the rifle range.

Dear Congressman:

First let me thank you for your interest in behalf of my son, Private Sheldon Grossbart. Fortunately, I was able to speak with Sheldon on the phone the other night, and I think I've been able to solve our problem. He is, as I mentioned in my last letter, a very religious boy, and it was only with the greatest difficulty that I could persuade him that the religious thing to do—what God Himself would want Sheldon to do—would be to suffer the pangs of religious remorse for the good of his country and all mankind. It took some doing, Congressman, but finally he saw the light. In fact, what he said (and I wrote down the words on a scratch pad so as never to forget), what he said was "I guess you're right, Dad. So many millions of my fellow-Jews gave up their lives to the enemy, the least I can do is live for a while minus a bit of my heritage so as to help end this struggle and regain for all the children of God dignity and humanity." That, Congressman, would make any father proud.

By the way, Sheldon wanted me to know—and to pass on to you—the name of a soldier who helped him reach this decision: SERGEANT NATHAN MARX. Sergeant Marx is a combat veteran who is Sheldon's first sergeant. This man has helped Sheldon over some of the first hurdles he's had to face in the Army, and is in part responsible for Sheldon's changing his mind about the dietary laws. I know Sheldon would appreciate any recognition Marx could receive.

Thank you and good luck. I look forward to seeing your name on the next election ballot.

Respectfully,
Samuel E. Grossbart

Attached to the Grossbart communiqué was another, addressed to General Marshall Lyman, the post commander, and signed by Representative Charles E. Franconi, of the House of Representatives. The communiqué informed General Lyman that Sergeant Nathan Marx was a credit to the U.S. Army and the Jewish people.

What was Grossbart's motive in recanting? Did he feel he'd gone too far? Was the letter a strategic retreat—a crafty attempt to strengthen what he considered our alliance? Or had he actually changed his mind, via an imaginary dialogue between Grossbart *père* and Grossbart *fils*?[9] I was puzzled, but only for a few days—that is, only until I realized that, whatever his reasons, he had actually decided to disappear from my life; he was going to allow himself to become just another trainee. I saw him at inspection, but he never winked; at chow formations, but he never flashed me a sign. On Sunday, with the other trainees, he would sit around watching the noncoms' softball team, for which I pitched, but not once did he speak an unnecessary word to me. Fishbein and Halpern retreated, too—at Grossbart's command, I was sure. Apparently he had seen that wisdom lay in turning back before he plunged over into the ugliness of privilege undeserved. Our separation allowed me to forgive him our past encounters,

8 Jewish rabbinical seminary. (JHP)

9 Father and son. (JHP)

and, finally, to admire him for his good sense.

Meanwhile, free of Grossbart, I grew used to my job and my administrative tasks. I stepped on a scale one day, and discovered I had truly become a non-combatant; I had gained seven pounds. I found patience to get past the first three pages of a book. I thought about the future more and more, and wrote letters to girls I'd known before the war. I even got a few answers. I sent away to Columbia for a Law School catalogue. I continued to follow the war in the Pacific, but it was not my war. I thought I could see the end, and sometimes, at night, I dreamed that I was walking on the streets of Manhattan—Broadway, Third Avenue, 116th Street, where I had lived the three years I attended Columbia. I curled myself around these dreams and I began to be happy.

And then, one Sunday, when everybody was away and I was alone in the orderly room reading a month-old copy of the *Sporting News,* Grossbart reappeared.

"You a baseball fan, Sergeant?"

I looked up. "How are you?"

"Fine," Grossbart said. "They're making a soldier out of me."

"How are Fishbein and Halpern?"

"Coming along," he said. "We've got no training this afternoon. They're at the movies."

"How come you're not with them?"

"I wanted to come over and say hello."

He smiled—a shy, regular-guy smile, as though he and I well knew that our friendship drew its sustenance from unexpected visits, remembered birthdays, and borrowed lawnmowers. At first it offended me, and then the feeling was swallowed by the general uneasiness I felt at the thought that everyone on the post was locked away in a dark movie theater and I was here alone with Grossbart. I folded up my paper.

"Sergeant," he said, "I'd like to ask a favor. It is a favor, and I'm making no bones about it."

He stopped, allowing me to refuse him a hearing—which, of course, forced me into a courtesy I did not intend. "Go ahead."

"Well, actually, it's two favors."

I said nothing.

"The first one's about these rumors. Everybody says we're going to the Pacific."

"As I told your friend Fishbein, I don't know," I said. "You'll just have to wait to find out. Like everybody else."

"You think there's a chance of any of us going East?"

"Germany?" I said. "Maybe."

"I meant New York."

"I don't think so, Grossbart. Offhand."

"Thanks for the information, Sergeant," he said.

"It's not information, Grossbart. Just what I surmise."

"It certainly would be good to be near home. My parents—you know." He took a step toward the door and then turned back. "Oh, the other thing. May I ask the other?"

"What is it?"

"The other thing is—I've got relatives in St. Louis, and they say they'll give me a whole Passover dinner if I can get down there. God, Sergeant, that'd mean an awful lot to me."

I stood up. "No passes during basic, Grossbart."

"But we're off from now till Monday morning, Sergeant. I could leave the post and no one would even know."

"I'd know. You'd know."

"But that's all. Just the two of us. Last night, I called my aunt, and you should have heard her. 'Come—come,' she said. 'I got gefilte fish,[10] *chrain*— [11] the works!' Just a day, Sergeant. I'd take the blame if anything happened."

"The Captain isn't here to sign a pass."

"You could sign."

"Look, Grossbart—"

"Sergeant, for two months, practically, I've been eating *trafe* till I want to die."

"I thought you'd made up your mind to live with it. To be minus a little bit of heritage."

He pointed a finger at me. "You!" he said. "That wasn't for you to read."

10 A traditional Jewish dish of stewed or baked stuffed fish. (JHP)

11 Horseradish. (JHP)

"I read it. So what?"

"That letter was addressed to a congressman."

"Grossbart, don't feed me any baloney. You *wanted* me to read it."

"Why are you persecuting me, Sergeant?"

"Are you kidding!"

"I've run into this before," he said, "but never from my own!"

"Get out of here, Grossbart! Get the hell out of my sight!"

He did not move. "Ashamed, that's what you are," he said. "So you take it out on the rest of us. They say Hitler himself was half a Jew. Hearing you, I wouldn't doubt it."

"What are you trying to do with me, Grossbart?" I asked him. "What are you after? You want me to give you special privileges, to change the food, to find out about your orders, to give you weekend passes."

"You even talk like a goy!"[12] Grossbart shook his fist. "Is this just a weekend pass I'm asking for? Is a Seder[13] sacred, or not?"

Seder! It suddenly occurred to me that Passover had been celebrated weeks before. I said so.

"That's right," he replied. "Who says no? A month ago—and I was in the field eating hash! And now all I ask is a simple favor. A Jewish boy I thought would understand. My aunt's willing to go out of her way—to make a Seder a month later . . ." He turned to go, mumbling.

"Come back here!" I called. He stopped and looked at me. "Grossbart, why can't you be like the rest? Why do you have to stick out like a sore thumb?"

"Because I'm a Jew, Sergeant. I *am* different. Better, maybe not. But different."

"This is a war, Grossbart. For the time being *be* the same."

"I refuse."

"What?"

"I refuse. I can't stop being me, that's all there is to it." Tears came to his eyes. "It's a hard thing to be a Jew. But now

I understand what Mickey says—it's a harder thing to stay one." He raised a hand sadly toward me. "Look at *you*."

"Stop crying!"

"Stop this, stop that, stop the other thing! *You* stop, Sergeant. Stop closing your heart to your own!" And, wiping his face with his sleeve, he ran out the door. "The least we can do for one another—the least . . ."

An hour later, looking out of the window, I saw Grossbart headed across the field. He wore a pair of starched khakis and carried a little leather ditty bag. I went out into the heat of the day. It was quiet; not a soul was in sight except, over by the mess hall, four K.P.'s sitting around a pan, sloped forward from their waists, gabbing and peeling potatoes in the sun.

"Grossbart!" I called.

He looked toward me and continued walking.

"Grossbart, get over here!"

He turned and came across the field. Finally, he stood before me.

"Where are you going?" I asked.

"St. Louis. I don't care."

"You'll get caught without a pass."

"So I'll get caught without a pass."

"You'll go to the stockade."

"I'm *in* the stockade." He made an about-face and headed off.

I let him go only a step or two. "Come back here," I said, and he followed me into the office, where I typed out a pass and signed the Captain's name, and my own initials after it.

He took the pass and then, a moment later, reached out and grabbed my hand. "Sergeant, you don't know how much this means to me."

"O.K.," I said. "Don't get in any trouble."

"I wish I could show you how much this means to me."

"Don't do me any favors. Don't write any more congressmen for citations."

He smiled. "You're right. I won't. But let me do something."

"Bring me a piece of that gefilte fish. Just get out of here."

"I will!" he said. "With a slice of carrot and a little horseradish. I won't forget."

12 Gentile. (JHP)

13 Traditional Jewish ceremonial dinner held on the first evening of Passover. (JHP)

"All right. Just show your pass at the gate. And don't tell *anybody.*"

"I won't. It's a month late, but a good Yom Tov [14] to you."

"Good Yom Tov, Grossbart," I said.

"You're a good Jew, Sergeant. You like to think you have a hard heart, but underneath you're a fine, decent man. I mean that."

Those last three words touched me more than any words from Grossbart's mouth had the right to. "All right, Grossbart," I said. "Now call me 'sir,' and get the hell out of here."

He ran out the door and was gone. I felt very pleased with myself; it was a great relief to stop fighting Grossbart, and it had cost me nothing. Barrett would never find out, and if he did, I could manage to invent some excuse. For a while, I sat at my desk, comfortable in my decision. Then the screen door flew back and Grossbart burst in again. "Sergeant!" he said. Behind him I saw Fishbein and Halpern, both in starched khakis, both carrying ditty bags like Grossbart's.

"Sergeant, I caught Mickey and Larry coming out of the movies. I almost missed them."

"Grossbart—did I say to tell no one?" I said.

"But my aunt said I could bring friends. That I should, in fact."

"*I'm* the Sergeant, Grossbart—not your aunt!"

Grossbart looked at me in disbelief. He pulled Halpern up by his sleeve. "Mickey, tell the Sergeant what this would mean to you."

Halpern looked at me and, shrugging, said, "A lot."

Fishbein stepped forward without prompting. "This would mean a great deal to me and my parents, Sergeant Marx."

"No!" I shouted.

Grossbart was shaking his head. "Sergeant, I could see you denying me, but how you can deny Mickey, a Yeshiva boy—that's beyond me."

"I'm not denying Mickey anything,"

I said. "You just pushed a little too hard, Grossbart. *You* denied him."

"I'll give him my pass, then," Grossbart said. "I'll give him my aunt's address and a little note. At least let him go."

In a second, he had crammed the pass into Halpern's pants pocket. Halpern looked at me, and so did Fishbein. Grossbart was at the door, pushing it open. "Mickey, bring me a piece of gefilte fish, at least," he said, and then he was outside again.

The three of us looked at one another, and then I said, "Halpern, hand that pass over."

He took it from his pocket and gave it to me. Fishbein had now moved to the doorway, where he lingered. He stood there for a moment with his mouth slightly open, and then he pointed to himself. "And me?" he asked.

His utter ridiculousness exhausted me. I slumped down in my seat and felt pulses knocking at the back of my eyes. "Fishbein," I said, "you understand I'm not trying to deny you anything, don't you? If it was my Army, I'd serve gefilte fish in the mess hall. I'd sell *kugel* [15] in the PX, honest to God."

Halpern smiled.

"You understand, don't you, Halpern?"

"Yes, Sergeant."

"And you, Fishbein? I don't want enemies. I'm just like you—I want to serve my time and go home. I miss the same things you miss."

"Then, Sergeant," Fishbein said, "why don't you come, too?"

"Where?"

"To St. Louis. To Shelly's aunt. We'll have a regular Seder. Play hide-the-matzoh." [16] He gave me a broad, black-toothed smile.

I saw Grossbart again, on the other side of the screen.

"Pssst!" He waved a piece of paper. "Mickey, here's the address. Tell her I couldn't get away."

15 A pudding. (JHP)
16 Unleavened bread eaten at Passover. (JHP)

Halpern did not move. He looked at me, and I saw the shrug moving up his arms into his shoulders again. I took the cover off my typewriter and made out passes for him and Fishbein. "Go," I said. "The three of you."

I thought Halpern was going to kiss my hand.

That afternoon, in a bar in Joplin, I drank beer and listened with half an ear to the Cardinal game. I tried to look squarely at what I'd become involved in, and began to wonder if perhaps the struggle with Grossbart wasn't as much my fault as his. What was I that I had to *muster* generous feelings? Who was I to have been feeling so grudging, so tight-hearted? After all, I wasn't being asked to move the world. Had I a right, then, or a reason, to clamp down on Grossbart, when that meant clamping down on Halpern, too? And Fishbein— that ugly, agreeable soul? Out of the many recollections of my childhood that had tumbled over me these past few days I heard my grandmother's voice: "What are you making a *tsimmes?*" [17] It was what she would ask my mother when, say, I had cut myself while doing something I shouldn't have done, and her daughter was busy bawling me out. I needed a hug and a kiss, and my mother would moralize. But my grandmother knew—mercy overrides justice. I should have known it, too. Who was Nathan Marx to be such a penny pincher with kindness? Surely, I thought, the Messiah himself—if He should ever come—won't niggle over nickles and dimes. God willing, he'll hug and kiss.

The next day, while I was playing softball over on the parade ground, I decided to ask Bob Wright, who was noncom in charge of Classification and Assignment, where he thought our trainees would be sent when their cycle ended, in two weeks. I asked casually, between innings, and he said, "They're pushing them all into the Pacific. Shulman cut the orders on your boys the other day."

[17] A fuss or to-do. (JHP)

The news shocked me, as though I were the father of Halpern, Fishbein, and Grossbart.

That night, I was just sliding into sleep when someone tapped on my door. "Who is it?" I asked.

"Sheldon."

He opened the door and came in. For a moment, I felt his presence without being able to see him. "How was it?" I asked.

He popped into sight in the near-darkness before me. "Great, Sergeant." Then he was sitting on the edge of the bed. I sat up.

"How about you?" he asked. "Have a nice weekend?"

"Yes."

"The others went to sleep." He took a deep, paternal breath. We sat silent for a while, and a homey feeling invaded my ugly little cubicle; the door was locked, the cat was out, the children were safely in bed.

"Sergeant, can I tell you something? Personal?"

I did not answer, and he seemed to know why. "Not about me. About Mickey. Sergeant, I never felt for anybody like I feel for him. Last night I heard Mickey in the bed next to me. He was crying so, it could have broken your heart. Real sobs."

"I'm sorry to hear that."

"I had to talk to him to stop him. He held my hand, Sergeant—he wouldn't let it go. He was almost hysterical. He kept saying if he only knew where we were going. Even if he knew it *was* the Pacific, that would be bettter than nothing. Just to know."

Long ago, someone had taught Grossbart the sad rule that only lies can get the truth. Not that I couldn't believe in the fact of Halpern's crying; his eyes *always* seemed red-rimmed. But, fact or not, it became a lie when Grossbart uttered it. He was entirely strategic. But then—it came with the force of indictment—so was I! There are strategies of aggression, but there are strategies of retreat as well. And so, recognizing that

I myself had not been without craft and guile, I told him what I knew. "It is the Pacific."

He let out a small gasp, which was not a lie. "I'll tell him. I wish it was otherwise."

"So do I."

He jumped on my words. "You mean you think you could do something? A change, maybe?"

"No, I couldn't do a thing."

"Don't you know anybody over at C. and A.?"

"Grossbart, there's nothing I can do," I said. "If your orders are for the Pacific, then it's the Pacific."

"But Mickey—"

"Mickey, you, me—everybody, Grossbart. There's nothing to be done. Maybe the war'll end before you go. Pray for a miracle."

"But—"

"Good night, Grossbart." I settled back, and was relieved to feel the springs unbend as Grossbart rose to leave. I could see him clearly now; his jaw had dropped, and he looked like a dazed prizefighter. I noticed for the first time a little paper bag in his hand.

"Grossbart." I smiled. "My gift?"

"Oh, yes, Sergeant. Here—from all of us." He handed me the bag. "It's egg roll."

"Egg roll?" I accepted the bag and felt a damp grease spot on the bottom. I opened it, sure that Grossbart was joking.

"We thought you'd probably like it. You know—Chinese egg roll. We thought you'd probably have a taste for—"

"Your aunt served egg roll?"

"She wasn't home."

"Grossbart, she invited you. You told me she invited you and your friends."

"I know," he said. "I just reread the letter. *Next* week."

I got out of bed and walked to the window. "Grossbart," I said. But I was not calling to him.

"What?"

"What are you, Grossbart? Honest to God, what are you?"

I think it was the first time I'd asked him a question for which he didn't have an immediate answer.

"How can you do this to people?" I went on.

"Sergeant, the day away did us all a world of good. Fishbein, you should see him, he *loves* Chinese food."

"But the Seder," I said.

"We took second best, Sergeant."

Rage came charging at me. I didn't sidestep. "Grossbart, you're a liar!" I said. "You're a schemer and a crook. You've got no respect for anything. Nothing at all. Not for me, for the truth—not even for poor Halpern! You use us all—"

"Sergeant, Sergeant, I feel for Mickey. Honest to God, I do. I *love* Mickey. I try—"

"You try! You feel!" I lurched toward him and grabbed his shirt front. I shook him furiously. "Grossbart, get out! Get out and stay the hell away from me. Because if I see you, I'll make your life miserable. *You understand that?*"

"Yes."

I let him free, and when he walked from the room, I wanted to spit on the floor where he had stood. I couldn't stop the fury. It engulfed me, owned me, till it seemed I could only rid myself of it with tears or an act of violence. I snatched from the bed the bag Grossbart had given me and, with all my strength, threw it out the window. And the next morning, as the men policed the area around the barracks, I heard a great cry go up from one of the trainees, who had been anticipating only his morning handful of cigarette butts and candy wrappers. "Egg roll!" he shouted. "Holy Christ, Chinese goddam egg roll!"

A week later, when I read the orders that had come down from C. and A., I couldn't believe my eyes. Every single trainee was to be shipped to Camp Stoneman, California, and from there to the Pacific—every trainee but one. Private Sheldon Grossbart. He was to be sent to Fort Monmouth, New Jersey. I read the mimeographed sheet several times. Dee,

Farrell, Fishbein, Fuselli, Fylypowycz, Glinicki, Gromke, Gucwa, Halpern, Hardy, Helebrandt, right down to Anton Zygadlo—all were to be headed West before the month was out. All except Grossbart. He had pulled a string, and I wasn't it.

I lifted the phone and called C. and A. The voice on the other end said smartly, "Corporal Shulman, sir."

"Let me speak to Sergeant Wright."

"Who is this calling, sir?"

"Sergeant Marx."

And, to my surprise, the voice said, "*Oh!*" Then, "Just a minute, Sergeant."

Shulman's "*Oh!*" stayed with me while I waited for Wright to come to the phone. Why "*Oh!*"? Who was Shulman? And then, so simply, I knew I'd discovered the string that Grossbart had pulled. In fact, I could hear Grossbart the day he'd discovered Shulman in the PX, or in the bowling alley, or maybe even at services. "Glad to meet you. Where you from? Bronx? Me, too. Do you know So-and-So? And So-and-So? Me, too! You work at C. and A.? Really? Hey, how's chances of getting East? Could you do something? Change something? Swindle, cheat, lie? We gotta help each other, you know. If the Jews in Germany . . ."

Bob Wright answered the phone. "How are you, Nate? How's the pitching arm?"

"Good. Bob, I wonder if you could do me a favor." I heard clearly my own words, and they so reminded me of Grossbart that I dropped more easily than I could have imagined into what I had planned. "This may sound crazy, Bob, but I got a kid here on orders to Monmouth who wants them changed. He had a brother killed in Europe, and he's hot to go to the Pacific. Says he'd feel like a coward if he wound up Stateside. I don't know, Bob—can anything be done? Put somebody else in the Monmouth slot?"

"Who?" he asked cagily.

"Anybody. First guy in the alphabet. I don't care. The kid just asked if something could be done."

"What's his name?"

"Grossbart, Sheldon."

Wright didn't answer.

"Yeah," I said. "He's a Jewish kid, so he thought I could help him out. You know."

"I guess I can do something," he finally said. "The Major hasn't been around here for weeks. Temporary duty to the golf course. I'll try, Nate, that's all I can say."

"I'd appreciate it, Bob. See you Sunday." And I hung up, perspiring.

The following day, the corrected orders appeared: Fishbein, Fuselli, Fylypowycz, Glinicki, Gromke, Grossbart, Gucwa, Halpern, Hardy . . . Lucky Private Harley Alton was to go to Fort Monmouth, New Jersey, where, for some reason or other, they wanted an enlisted man with infantry training.

After chow that night, I stopped back at the orderly room to straighten out the guard-duty roster. Grossbart was waiting for me. He spoke first.

"You son of a bitch!"

I sat down at my desk, and while he glared at me, I began to make the necessary alterations in the duty roster.

"What do you have against me?" he cried. "Against my family? Would it kill you for me to be near my father, God knows how many months he has left to him?"

"Why so?"

"His heart," Grossbart said. "He hasn't had enough troubles in a lifetime, you've got to add to them. I curse the day I ever met you, Marx! Shulman told me what happened over there. There's no limit to your anti-Semitism, is there? The damage you've done here isn't enough. You have to make a special phone call! You really want me dead!"

I made the last few notations in the duty roster and got up to leave. "Good night, Grossbart."

"You owe me an explanation!" He stood in my path.

"Sheldon, you're the one who owes explanations."

He scowled. "To *you?*"

"To me, I think so—yes. Mostly to Fishbein and Halpern."

"That's right, twist things around. I owe nobody nothing. I've done all I could do for them. Now I think I've got the right to watch out for myself."

"For each other we have to learn to watch out, Sheldon. You told me yourself."

"You call this watching out for me—what you did?"

"No. For all of us."

I pushed him aside and started for the door. I heard his furious breathing behind me, and it sounded like steam rushing from an engine of terrible strength.

"You'll be all right," I said from the door. And, I thought, so would Fishbein and Halpern be all right, even in the Pacific, if only Grossbart continued to see—in the obsequiousness of the one, the soft spirituality of the other—some profit for himself.

I stood outside the orderly room, and I heard Grossbart weeping behind me. Over in the barracks, in the lighted windows, I could see the boys in their T shirts sitting on their bunks talking about their orders, as they'd been doing for the past two days. With a kind of quiet nervousness, they polished shoes, shined belt buckles, squared away underwear, trying as best they could to accept their fate. Behind me, Grossbart swallowed hard, accepting his. And then, resisting with all my will an impulse to turn and seek pardon for my vindictiveness, I accepted my own.

[1959]

QUESTIONS FOR STUDY

1. *Describe the dilemma in which Sergeant Marx finds himself. What conflicting claims or loyalties is he trying to reconcile? What wrong assumptions does Sheldon Grossbart make about him?*

2. *What evidence does the story provide that Nathan Marx really is the "hero" that Captain Barrett insists he is? Why is this fact important to the story?*

3. *At the height of his exasperation, Marx asks, "What are you, Grossbart? Honest to God, what are you?" How would you respond to the sergeant's query?*

4. *How does Grossbart justify his own behavior?*

5. *Why does Marx request that Grossbart be reassigned to the Pacific? What does Marx mean when he subsequently replies to Grossbart's charge of persecution that what he did was done "for all of us"?*

6. *What are the implications of Marx's final comment that "I accepted my own [fate]"?*

7. *To whom, in the end, does the story's title—"Defender of the Faith"—refer?*

DOROTHY L. SAYERS
Absolutely Elsewhere

LORD Peter Wimsey sat with Chief-Inspector Parker, of the C.I.D., and Inspector Henley, of the Baldock police, in the library at "The Lilacs."

"So you see," said Parker, "that all the obvious suspects were elsewhere at the time."

"What do you mean by 'elsewhere'?" demanded Wimsey, peevishly. Parker had hauled him down to Wapley, on the Great North Road, without his breakfast, and his temper had suffered. "Do you mean that they couldn't have reached the scene of the murder without travelling at over 186,000 miles a second? Because, if you don't mean that, they weren't absolutely elsewhere. They were only relatively and apparently elsewhere."

"For heaven's sake, don't go all Eddington. Humanly speaking, they were elsewhere, and if we're going to nail one of them we shall have to do it without going into their Fitzgerald contractions and coefficients of spherical curvature. I think, Inspector, we had better have them in one by one, so that I can hear all their stories again. You can check them up if they depart from their original statements at any point. Let's take the butler first."

The Inspector put his head out into the hall and said: "Hamworthy."

The butler was a man of middle age, whose spherical curvature was certainly worthy of consideration. His large face was pale and puffy, and he looked unwell. However, he embarked on his story without hesitation.

"I have been in the late Mr. Grimbold's service for twenty years, gentlemen, and have always found him a good master. He was a strict gentleman, but very just. I know he was considered very hard in business matters, but I suppose he had to be that. He was a bachelor, but he brought up his two nephews, Mr. Harcourt and Mr. Neville, and was very good to them. In his private life I should call him a kind and considerate man. His profession? Yes, I suppose you would call him a money-lender."

"About the events of last night, sir, yes. I shut up the house at 7.30 as usual. Everything was done exactly to time, sir, —Mr. Grimbold was very regular in his habits. I locked all the windows on the ground floor, as was customary during the winter months. I am quite sure I didn't miss anything out. They all have burglar-proof bolts and I should have noticed if they had been out of order. I also locked and bolted the front door and put up the chain."

"How about the conservatory door?"

"That, sir, is a Yale lock. I tried it, and saw that it was shut. No, I didn't fasten the catch. It was always left that way, sir, in case Mr. Grimbold had business which kept him in Town late, so that he could get in without disturbing the household."

"But he had no business in Town last night?"

"No, sir, but it was always left that way. Nobody could get in without the key, and Mr. Grimbold had that on his ring."

"Is there no other key in existence?"

"I believe"—the butler coughed—"I believe, sir, though I do not know, that there is *one,* sir,—in the possession of—of a lady, sir, who is at present in Paris."

"I see. Mr. Grimbold was about sixty years old, I believe. Just so. What is the name of this lady?"

"Mrs. Winter, sir. She lives at Wapley, but since her husband died last month, sir, I understand she has been residing abroad."

"I see. Better make a note of that, Inspector. Now, how about the upper rooms and the back door?"

"The upper-room windows were all fastened in the same way, sir, except Mr. Grimbold's bedroom and the cook's room and mine, sir; but they couldn't be reached without a ladder, and the ladder is locked up in the tool-shed."

"That's all right," put in Inspector Henley. "We went into that last night. The shed was locked and, what's more, there were unbroken cobwebs between the ladder and the wall."

"I went through all the rooms at half-past seven, sir, and there was nothing out of order."

"You may take it from me," said the Inspector, again, "that there was no interference with any of the locks. Carry on, Hamworthy."

"Yes, sir. While I was seeing to the house, Mr. Grimbold came down into the library for his glass of sherry. At 7.45 the soup was served and I called Mr. Grimbold to dinner. He sat at the end of the table as usual, facing the serving-hatch."

"With his back to the library door," said Parker, making a mark on a rough plan of the room, which lay before him. "Was that door shut?"

"Oh, yes, sir. All the doors and windows were shut."

"It looks a dashed draughty room," said Wimsey. "Two doors and a serving-hatch and two french windows."

"Yes, my lord; but they are all very well-fitting, and the curtains were drawn."

His lordship moved across to the connecting door and opened it.

"Yes," he said; "good and heavy and moves in sinister silence. I like these thick carpets, but the pattern's a bit fierce." He shut the door noiselessly and returned to his seat.

"Mr. Grimbold would take about five minutes over his soup, sir. When he had done, I removed it and put on the fish.

I did not have to leave the room; everything comes through the serving-hatch. The wine—that is, the Chablis—was already on the table. That course was only a small portion of turbot, and would take Mr. Grimbold about five minutes again. I removed that, and put on the roast pheasant. I was just about to serve Mr. Grimbold with the vegetables, when the telephone-bell rang. Mr. Grimbold said: 'You'd better see who it is. I'll help myself.' It was not the cook's business, of course, to answer the telephone."

"Are there no other servants?"

"Only the woman who comes in to clean during the day, sir. I went out to the instrument, shutting the door behind me."

"Was that this telephone or the one in the hall?"

"The one in the hall, sir. I always used that one, unless I happened to be actually in the library at the time. The call was from Mr. Neville Grimbold in Town, sir. He and Mr. Harcourt have a flat in Jermyn Street. Mr. Neville spoke, and I recognised his voice. He said: 'Is that you, Hamworthy? Wait a moment. Mr. Harcourt wants you.' He put the receiver down and then Mr. Harcourt came on. He said: 'Hamworthy, I want to run down to-night to see my uncle, if he's at home.' I said: 'Yes, sir, I'll tell him.' The young gentlemen often come down for a night or two, sir. We keep their bedrooms ready for them. Mr. Harcourt said he would be starting at once and expected to get down by about half-past nine. While he was speaking I heard the big grandfather-clock up in their flat chime the quarters and strike eight, and immediately after, our own hall-clock struck, and then I heard the Exchange say 'Three minutes.' So the call must have come through at three minutes to eight, sir."

"Then there's no doubt about the time. That's a comfort. What next, Hamworthy?"

"Mr. Harcourt asked for another call and said: 'Mr. Neville has got something to say,' and then Mr. Neville came back to the 'phone. He said he was going up to Scotland shortly, and wanted me to send up a country suit and some stockings and shirts that he had left down here. He wanted the suit sent to the cleaner's first, and there were various other instructions, so that he asked for another three minutes. That would be at 8.3, sir, yes. And about a minute after that, while he was still speaking, the front-door bell rang. I couldn't very well leave the 'phone, so the caller had to wait, and at five past eight he rang the bell again. I was just going to ask Mr. Neville to excuse me, when I saw Cook come out of the kitchen and go through the hall to the front door. Mr. Neville asked me to repeat his instructions, and then the Exchange interrupted us again, so he rang off, and when I turned round I saw Cook just closing the library door. I went to meet her, and she said: 'Here's that Mr. Payne again, wanting Mr. Grimbold. I've put him in the library, but I don't like the looks of him.' So I said: 'All right; I'll fix him,' and Cook went back to the kitchen."

"One moment," said Parker. "Who's Mr. Payne?"

"He's one of Mr. Grimbold's clients, sir. He lives about five minutes away, across the fields, and he's been here before, making trouble. I think he owes Mr. Grimbold money, sir, and wanted more time to pay."

"He's here, waiting in the hall," added Henley.

"Oh?" said Wimsey. "The unshaven party with the scowl and the ash-plant, and the blood-stained coat?"

"That's him, my lord," said the butler. "Well, sir,"—he turned to Parker again, "I started to go along to the library, when it come over me sudden-like that I'd never taken in the claret—Mr. Grimbold would be getting very annoyed. So I went back to my pantry—you see where that is, sir,—and fetched it from where it was warming before the fire. I had a little hunt then for the salver, sir, till I found I had put down my evening paper on top of it, but I wasn't more than a minute, sir, before I got back into the dining-room. And then, sir"—the butler's voice faltered—"then I saw Mr. Grimbold fallen forward on the table,

sir, all across his plate, like. I thought he must have been took ill, and I hurried up to him and found—I found he was dead, sir, with a dreadful wound in his back."

"No weapon anywhere?"

"Not that I could see, sir. There was a terrible lot of blood. It made me feel shockingly faint, sir, and for a minute I didn't hardly know what to do. As soon at I could think of anything, I rushed over to the serving-hatch and called Cook. She came hurrying in and let out an awful scream when she saw the master. Then I remembered Mr. Payne and opened the library door. He was standing there, and he began at once, asking how long he'd have to wait. So I said: 'Here's an awful thing! Mr. Grimbold has been murdered!' and he pushed past me into the dining-room, and the first thing he said was: 'How about those windows?' He pulled back the curtain of the one nearest the library, and there was the window standing open. 'This is the way he went,' he said, and started to rush out. I said, 'no, you don't'—thinking he meant to get away, and I hung on to him. He called me a lot of names, and then he said: 'Look here, my man, be reasonable. The fellow's getting away all this time. We must have a look for him.' So I said, 'Not without I go with you.' And he said, 'All right.' So I told Cook not to touch anything but to ring up the police, and Mr. Payne and I went out after I'd fetched my torch from the pantry."

"Did Payne go with you to fetch it?"

"Yes, sir. Well, him and me went out and we searched about in the garden, but we couldn't see any footprints or anything, because it's an asphalt path all round the house and down to the gate. And we couldn't see any weapon, either. So then he said: 'We'd better go back and get the car and search the roads,' but I said: 'No, he'll be away by then,' because it's only a quarter of a mile from our gate to the Great North Road, and it would take us five or ten minutes before we could start. So Mr. Payne said: 'Perhaps you're right,' and came back to the house with me. Well, then, sir, the constable came from Wapley, and after a bit, the Inspector here and Dr. Crofts from Baldock, and they made a search and asked a lot of questions, which I answered to the best of my ability, and I can't tell you no more, sir."

"Did you notice," asked Parker, "whether Mr. Payne had any stains of blood about him?"

"No, sir,—I can't say that he had. When I first saw him, he was standing in here, right under the light, and I think I should have seen it if there was anything, sir. I can't say fairer than that."

"Of course you've searched this room, Inspector, for bloodstains or a weapon or for anything such as gloves or a cloth, or anything that might have been used to protect the murderer from bloodstains?"

"Yes, Mr. Parker. We searched very carefully."

"Could anybody have come downstairs while you were in the dining-room with Mr. Grimbold?"

"Well, sir, I suppose they might. But they'd have to have got into the house before half-past seven, sir, and hidden themselves somewhere. Still, there's no doubt it might have happened that way. They couldn't come down by the back stairs, of course, because they'd have had to pass the kitchen, and Cook would have heard them, the passage being flagged, sir, but the front stairs—well, I don't know hardly what to say about that."

"That's how the man got in, depend upon it," said Parker. "Don't look so distressed, Hamworthy. You can't be expected to search all the cupboards in the house every evening for concealed criminals. Now I think I had better see the two nephews. I suppose they and their uncle got on together all right?"

"Oh, yes, sir. Never had a word of any sort. It's been a great blow to them, sir. They were terribly upset when Mr. Grimbold was ill in the summer————"

"He was ill, was he?"

"Yes, sir, with his heart, last July. He took a very bad turn, sir, and we had to send for Mr. Neville. But he pulled round wonderfully, sir,—only he never seemed to be quite such a cheerful gen-

tleman afterwards. I think it made him feel he wasn't getting younger, sir. But I'm sure nobody ever thought he'd be cut off like this."

"How is his money left?" asked Parker.

"Well, sir, that I don't know. I believe it would be divided between the two gentlemen, sir—not but what they have plenty of their own. But Mr. Harcourt would be able to tell you, sir. He's the executor."

"Very well, we'll ask him. Are the brothers on good terms?"

"Oh, yes, indeed, sir. Most devoted. Mr. Neville would do anything for Mr. Harcourt—and Mr. Harcourt for him, I'm sure. A very pleasant pair of gentlemen, sir. You couldn't have nicer."

"Thanks, Hamworthy. That will do for the moment, unless anybody else has anything to ask?"

"How much of the pheasant was eaten, Hamworthy?"

"Well, my lord, not a great deal of it —I mean, nothing like all of what Mr. Grimbold had on his plate. But he'd ate some of it. It might have taken three or four minutes or so to eat what he had done, my lord, judging by what I helped him to."

"There was nothing to suggest that he had been interrupted, for example, by somebody coming to the windows, or of his having got up to let the person in?"

"Nothing at all, my lord, that I could see."

"The chair was pushed in close to the table when I saw him," put in the Inspector, "and his napkin was on his knees and the knife and fork lying just under his hands, as though he had dropped them when the blow came. I understand that the body was not disturbed."

"No, sir. I never moved it—except, of course, to make sure that he was dead. But I never felt any doubt of that, sir, when I saw that dreadful wound in his back. I just lifted his head and let it fall forward again, same as before."

"All right, then, Hamworthy. Ask Mr. Harcourt to come in."

Mr. Harcourt Grimbold was a brisk-looking man of about thirty-five. He explained that he was a stockbroker and his brother Neville an official in the Ministry of Public Health, and that they had been brought up by their uncle from the ages of eleven and ten respectively. He was aware that his uncle had had many business enemies, but for his own part he had received nothing from him but kindness.

"I'm afraid I can't tell you much about this terrible business, as I didn't get here till 9.45 last night, when, of course, it was all over."

"That was a little later than you hoped to be here?"

"Just a little. My tail-lamp went out between Welwyn Garden City and Welwyn, and I was stopped by a bobby. I went to a garage in Welwyn, where they found that the lead had come loose. They put it right, and that delayed me for a few minutes more."

"It's about forty miles from here to London?"

"Just over. In the ordinary way, at that time of night, I should reckon an hour and a quarter from door to door. I'm not a speed merchant."

"Did you drive yourself?"

"Yes. I have a chauffeur, but I don't always bring him down here with me."

"When did you leave London?"

"About 8.20, I should think. Neville went round to the garage and fetched the car as soon as he'd finished telephoning, while I put my toothbrush and so on in my bag."

"You didn't hear about the death of your uncle before you left?"

"No. They didn't think of ringing me up, I gather, till after I had started. The police tried to get Neville later on, but he'd gone round to the club, or something. I 'phoned him myself after I got here, and he came down this morning."

"Well, now, Mr. Grimbold, can you tell us anything about your late uncle's affairs?"

"You mean his will? Who profits, and that kind of thing? Well, I do, for one, and Neville, for another. And Mrs.——— Have you heard of a Mrs. Winter?"

"Something, yes."

"Well, she does, for a third. And then, of course, old Hamworthy gets a nice little nest-egg, and the cook gets something, and there is a legacy of £500 to the clerk at my uncle's London office. But the bulk of it goes to us and to Mrs. Winter. I know what you're going to ask—how much is it? I haven't the faintest idea, but I know it must be something pretty considerable. The old man never let on to a soul how much he really was worth, and we never bothered about it. I'm turning over a good bit, and Neville's salary is a heavy burden on a long-suffering public, so we only had a mild, academic kind of interest in the question."

"Do you suppose Hamworthy knew he was down for a legacy?"

"Oh, yes—there was no secret about that. He was to get £100 and a life-interest in £200 a year, provided, of course, he was still in my uncle's service when he—my uncle, I mean—died."

"And he wasn't under notice, or anything?"

"N-no. No. Not more than usual. My uncle gave everybody notice about once a month, to keep them up to the mark. But it never came to anything. He was like the Queen of Hearts in *Alice*—he never executed nobody, you know."

"I see. We'd better ask Hamworthy about that, though. Now, this Mrs. Winter. Do you know anything about her?"

"Oh, yes. She's a nice woman. Of course, she was Uncle William's mistress for donkey's years, but her husband was practically potty with drink, and you could scarcely blame her. I wired her this morning and here's her reply, just come."

He handed Parker a telegram, despatched from Paris, which read: "Terribly shocked and grieved. Returning immediately. Love and sympathy. Lucy."

"You are on friendly terms with her, then?"

"Good Lord, yes. Why not? We were always damned sorry for her. Uncle William would have taken her away with him somewhere, only she wouldn't leave Winter. In fact, I think they had practically settled that they were to get mar-

ried now that Winter has had the grace
to peg out. She's only about thirty-eight,
and it's time she had some sort of show
in life, poor thing."

"So, in spite of the money, she hadn't
really very much to gain by your uncle's
death?"

"Not a thing. Unless, of course, she
wanted to marry somebody younger, and
was afraid of losing the cash. But I believe she was honestly fond of the old
boy. Anyhow, she couldn't have done
the murder, because she's in Paris."

"H'm!" said Parker. "I suppose she is.
We'd better make sure, though. I'll ring
through to the Yard and have her looked
out for at the ports. Is this 'phone
through to the Exchange?"

"Yes," said the Inspector. "It doesn't
have to go through the hall 'phone;
they're connected in parallel."

"All right. Well, I don't think we need
trouble you further, at the moment, Mr.
Grimbold. I'll put my call through, and
after that we'll send for the next witness.
. . . Give me Whitehall 1212, please. . . .
I suppose the time of Mr. Harcourt's call
from town has been checked, Inspector?"

"Yes, Mr. Parker. It was put in at
7.57 and renewed at 8 o'clock and 8.3.
Quite an expensive little item. And we've
also checked up on the constable who
spoke to him about his lights and the
garage that put them right for him. He
got into Welwyn at 9.5 and left again
about 9.15. The number of the car is
right, too."

"Well, he's out of it in any case, but
it's just as well to check all we can. . . .
Hullo, is that Scotland Yard? Put me
through to Chief-Inspector Hardy. Chief-
Inspector Parker speaking."

As soon as he had finished with his
call, Parker sent for Neville Grimbold.
He was rather like his brother, only a
little slimmer and a little more suave in
speech, as befitted a Civil Servant. He
had nothing to add, except to confirm his
brother's story and to explain that he
had gone to a cinema from 8.20 to about
10 o'clock, and then on to his club, so
that he had heard nothing about the
tragedy till later in the evening.

The cook was the next witness. She

had a great deal to say, but nothing very
convincing to tell. She had not happened
to see Hamworthy go to the pantry for
the claret, otherwise she confirmed his
story. She scouted the idea that somebody had been concealed in one of the
upper rooms, because the daily woman,
Mrs. Crabbe, had been in the house till
nearly dinner-time, putting camphor-
bags in all the wardrobes; and, anyhow,
she had no doubt but what "that Payne"
had stabbed Mr. Grimbold—"a nasty,
murdering beast." After which, it only
remained to interview the murderous
Mr. Payne.

Mr. Payne was almost aggressively
frank. He had been treated very harshly
by Mr. Grimbold. What with exorbitant
usury and accumulated interest added to
the principal, he had already paid back
about five times the original loan, and
now Mr. Grimbold had refused him any
more time to pay, and had announced
his intention of foreclosing on the security, namely, Mr. Payne's house and
land. It was all the more brutal because
Mr. Payne had every prospect of being
able to pay off the entire debt in six
months' time, owing to some sort of interest or share in something or other
which was confidently expected to turn
up trumps. In his opinion, old Grimbold
had refused to renew on purpose, so as
to prevent him from paying—what *he*
wanted was the property. Grimbold's
death was the saving of the situation, because it would postpone settlement till
after the confidently-expected trumps
had turned up. Mr. Payne would have
murdered old Grimbold with pleasure,
but he hadn't done so, and in any case
he wasn't the sort of man to stab anybody in the back, though, if the money-
lender had been a younger man, he,
Payne, would have been happy to break
all his bones for him. There it was, and
they could take it or leave it. If that
old fool, Hamworthy, hadn't got in his
way, he'd have laid hands on the murderer all right—if Hamworthy was a
fool, which he doubted. Blood? yes, there
was blood on his coat. He had got that
in struggling with Hamworthy at the
window. Hamworthy's hands had been

all over blood when he made his appearance in the library. No doubt he had got it from the corpse. He, Payne, had taken care not to change his clothes, because, if he had done so, somebody would have tried to make out that he was hiding something. Actually, he had not been home, or asked to go home, since the murder. Mr. Payne added that he objected strongly to the attitude taken up by the local police, who had treated him with undisguised hostility. To which Inspector Henley replied that Mr. Payne was quite mistaken.

"Mr. Payne," said Lord Peter, "will you tell me one thing? When you heard the commotion in the dining-room, and the cook screaming, and so on, why didn't you go in at once to find out what was the matter?"

"Why?" retorted Mr. Payne. "Because I never heard anything of the sort, that's why. The first thing I knew about it was seeing the butler-fellow standing there in the doorway, waving his bloody hands about and gibbering."

"Ah!" said Wimsey. "I thought it was a good, solid door. Shall we ask the lady to go in and scream for us now, with the dining-room window open?"

The Inspector departed on this errand, while the rest of the company waited anxiously to count the screams. Nothing happened, however, till Henley put his head in and asked, what about it?

"Nothing," said Parker.

"It's a well-built house," said Wimsey. "I suppose any sound coming through the window would be muffled by the conservatory. Well, Mr. Payne, if you didn't hear the screams it's not surprising that you didn't hear the murderer. Are those all your witnesses, Charles? Because I've got to get back to London to see a man about a dog. But I'll leave you two suggestions with my blessing. One is, that you should look for a car, which was parked within a quarter of a mile of this house last night, between 7.30 and 8.15; the second is, that you should all come and sit in the dining-room to-night, with the doors and windows shut, and watch the french windows. I'll give Mr. Parker a ring about

eight. Oh, and you might lend me the key of the conservatory door. I've got a theory about it."

The Chief Inspector handed over the key, and his lordship departed.

The party assembled in the dining-room was in no very companionable mood. In fact, all the conversation was supplied by the police, who kept up a chatty exchange of fishing reminiscences while Mr. Payne glowered, the two Grimbolds smoked cigarette after cigarette, and the cook and the butler balanced themselves nervously on the extreme edges of their chairs. It was a relief when the telephone-bell rang.

Parker glanced at his watch as he got up to answer it. "Seven-fifty-seven," he observed, and saw the butler pass his handkerchief over his twitching lips. "Keep your eye on the windows." He went out into the hall.

"Hullo!" he said.

"Is that Chief-Inspector Parker?" asked a voice he knew well. "This is Lord Peter Wimsey's man speaking from his lordship's rooms in London. Would you hold the line a moment? His lordship wishes to speak to you."

Parker heard the receiver set down and lifted again. Then Wimsey's voice came through: "Hullo, old man? Have you found that car yet?"

"We've heard of *a* car," replied the Chief Inspector cautiously, "at a Road-House on the Great North Road, about five minutes' walk from the house."

"Was the number A B J 28?"

"Yes. How did you know?"

"I thought it might be. It was hired from a London garage at five o'clock yesterday afternoon and brought back just before ten. Have you traced Mrs. Winter?"

"Yes, I think so. She landed from the Calais boat this evening. So apparently she's O.K."

"I thought she might be. Now, listen. Do you know that Harcourt Grimbold's affairs are in a bit of a mess? He nearly had a crisis last July, but somebody came to his rescue—possibly Uncle, don't you think? All rather fishy, my informant saith. And I'm told, very confidentially, that he's got badly caught over the Biggars-Whitlow crash. But of course he'll have no difficulty in raising money now, on the strength of Uncle's will. But I imagine the July business gave Uncle William a jolt. I expect————"

He was interrupted by a little burst of tinkling music, followed by the eight silvery strokes of a bell.

"Hear that? Recognise it? That's the big French clock in my sitting-room. . . . What? All right, Exchange, give me another three minutes. Bunter wants to speak to you again."

The receiver rattled, and the servant's suave voice took up the tale.

"His lordship asks me to ask you, sir, to ring off at once and go straight into the dining-room."

Parker obeyed. As he entered the room, he got an instantaneous impression of six people, sitting as he had left them, in an expectant semi-circle, their eyes strained towards the french windows. Then the library door opened noiselessly and Lord Peter Wimsey walked in.

"Good God!" exclaimed Parker, involuntarily. "How did you get here?" The six heads jerked round suddenly.

"On the back of the light waves." said Wimsey, smoothing back his hair. "I have travelled eighty miles to be with you, at 186,000 miles a second."

"It was rather obvious, really," said Wimsey, when they had secured Harcourt Grimbold (who fought desperately) and his brother Neville (who collapsed and had to be revived with brandy). "It had to be those two; they were so very much elsewhere—almost absolutely elsewhere. The murder could only have been committed between 7.57 and 8.6, and there had to be a reason for that prolonged 'phone-call about something that Harcourt could very well have explained when he came. And the murderer had to be in the library before 7.57, or he would have been seen in the hall—unless Grimbold had let him in by

the french window, which didn't appear likely.

"Here's how it was worked. Harcourt set off from Town in a hired car about six o'clock, driving himself. He parked the car at the Road-House, giving some explanation. I suppose he wasn't known there?"

"No; it's quite a new place; only opened last month."

"Ah! Then he walked the last quarter-mile on foot, arriving here at 7.45. It was dark, and he probably wore goloshes, so as not to make a noise coming up the path. He let himself into the conservatory with a duplicate key."

"How did he get that?"

"Pinched Uncle William's key off his ring last July, when the old boy was ill. It was probably the shock of hearing that his dear nephew was in trouble that caused the illness. Harcourt was here at the time—you remember it was only Neville that had to be 'sent for'—and I suppose Uncle paid up then, on conditions. But I doubt if he'd have done as much again—especially as he was thinking of getting married. And I expect, too, Harcourt thought that Uncle might easily alter his will after marriage. He might even have founded a family, and what would poor Harcourt do then, poor thing? From every point of view, it was better that Uncle should depart this life. So the duplicate key was cut and the plot thought out, and Brother Neville, who would 'do anything for Mr. Harcourt,' was roped in to help. I'm inclined to think that Harcourt must have done something rather worse than merely lose money, and Neville may have troubles of his own. But where was I?"

"Coming in at the conservatory door."

"Oh, yes—that's the way I came to-night. He'd take cover in the garden and would know when Uncle William went into the dining-room, because he'd see the library light go out. Remember, he knew the household. He came in, in the dark, locking the outer door after him, and waited by the telephone till Neville's call came through from London. When the bell stopped ringing, he lifted the receiver in the library. As soon as Neville had spoken his little piece, Harcourt chipped in. Nobody could hear him through these sound-proof doors, and Hamworthy couldn't possibly tell that his voice wasn't coming from London. In fact, it *was* coming from London, because, as the 'phones are connected in parallel, it could only come by way of the Exchange. At eight o'clock, the grandfather clock in Jermyn Street struck—further proof that the London line was open. The minute Harcourt heard that, he called on Neville to speak again, and hung up under cover of the rattle of Neville's receiver. Then Neville detained Hamworthy with a lot of rot about a suit, while Harcourt walked into the dining-room, stabbed his uncle and departed by the window. He had five good minutes in which to hurry back to his car and drive off—and Hamworthy and Payne actually gave him a few minutes more by suspecting and hampering one another."

"Why didn't he go back through the library and conservatory?"

"He hoped everybody would think that the murderer had come in by the window. In the meantime, Neville left London at 8.20 in Harcourt's car, carefully drawing the attention of a policeman and a garage man to the licence number as he passed through Welwyn. At an appointed place outside Welwyn he met Harcourt, primed him with his little story about tail-lights, and changed cars with him. Neville returned to town with the hired 'bus; Harcourt came back here with his own car. But I'm afraid you'll have a little difficulty in finding the weapon and the duplicate key and Harcourt's blood-stained gloves and coat. Neville probably took them back, and they may be anywhere. There's a good, big river in London."

[1939]

QUESTIONS FOR STUDY

1. *Dorothy Sayers, in a well-known essay of 1929, asserts that the skill of a modern detective writer is largely shown by his or her ability to manipulate point of view. What is the controlling point of view of this story? How does it contribute to the story's effectiveness?*

2. *What conventional techniques and devices of the detective story does Miss Sayers use?*

3. *Dorothy Sayers has also written that the writer of detective stories must "play fair." Does Miss Sayers herself "play fair" with the reader? Is any information essential to the murder's solution withheld?*

4. *Compare Dorothy Sayers' Lord Peter Wimsey to the other detective heroes in the anthology—Poe's C. Auguste Dupin; Doyle's Sherlock Holmes; Christie's Hercule Poirot; and Hammett's Sam Spade. What similarities and differences do you detect?*

ALAN SILLITOE

The Loneliness of the Long-Distance Runner

AS SOON as I got to Borstal they made me a long-distance cross-country runner. I suppose they thought I was just the build for it because I was long and skinny for my age (and still am) and in any case I didn't mind it much, to tell you the truth, because running had always been made much of in our family, especially running away from the police. I've always been a good runner, quick and with a big stride as well, the only trouble being that no matter how fast I run, and I did a very fair lick even though I do say so myself, it didn't stop me getting caught by the cops after that bakery job.

You might think it a bit rare, having long-distance cross-country runners in Borstal, thinking that the first thing a long-distance cross-country runner would do when they set him loose at them fields and woods would be to run as far away from the place as he could get on a bellyful of Borstal slumgullion—but you're wrong, and I'll tell you why. The first thing is that them bastards over us aren't as daft as they most of the time look, and for another thing I'm not so daft as I would look if I tried to make a break for it on my long-distance running, because to abscond and then get caught is nothing but a mug's game, and I'm not falling for it. Cunning is what counts in this life, and even that you've got to use in the slyest way you can; I'm telling you straight: they're cunning, and I'm cunning. If only 'them' and 'us' had the same ideas we'd get on like a house on fire, but they don't see eye to eye with us and we don't see eye to eye with them, so that's how it stands and how it will always stand. The one fact is that all of us are cunning, and because of this there's no love lost between us. So the thing is that they know I won't try to get away from them: they sit there like spiders in that crumbly manor house, perched like jumped-up jackdaws on the roof, watching out over the drives and fields like German generals from the tops of tanks. And even when I jog-trot on behind a wood and they can't see me anymore they know my sweeping-brush head will bob along that hedge-top in an hour's time and that I'll report to the bloke on the gate. Because when on a raw and frosty morning I get up at five o'clock and stand shivering my belly off on the stone floor and all the rest still have another hour to snooze before the bells go, I slink downstairs through all the corridors to the big outside door with a permit running-card in my fist, I feel like the first and last man on the world, both at once, if you can believe what I'm trying to say. I feel like the first man because I've hardly got a stitch on and am sent against the frozen fields in a shimmy and shorts—even the first poor bastard dropped on to the earth in midwinter knew how to make a suit of leaves, or how to skin a pterodactyl for a topcoat. But there I am, frozen stiff, with nothing to get me warm except a couple of hours' long-distance running before breakfast, not even a slice of bread-and-sheepdip. They're training me up fine for the big sports day when all the pig-faced snotty-nosed dukes and ladies—who can't add two and two together and would mess themselves like loonies if they didn't have slavies to beck-and-call—come and make speeches to us about sports being just the thing to get us leading an honest life and keep our itching finger-ends off them shop locks and safe handles and hairgrips to open gas meters. They give us a bit of blue ribbon and a cup for a prize after we've shagged ourselves out running or jumping, like race horses, only we don't get so well looked-after as race horses, that's the only thing.

So there I am, standing in the doorway in shimmy and shorts, not even a dry crust in my guts, looking out at frosty flowers on the ground. I suppose you think this is enough to make me cry? Not likely. Just because I feel like the first bloke in the world wouldn't make me bawl. It makes me feel fifty times better than when I'm cooped up in that dormitory with three hundred others. No, it's sometimes when I stand there feeling like the *last* man in the world that I don't feel so good. I feel like the last man in the world because I think that all those three hundred sleepers behind me are dead. They sleep so well I think that every scruffy head's kicked the bucket in the night and I'm the only one left, and when I look out into the bushes and frozen ponds I have the feeling that it's going to get colder and colder until everything I can see, meaning my red arms as well, is going to be covered with a thousand miles of ice, all the earth, right up to the sky and over every bit of land and sea. So I try to kick this feeling out and act like I'm the first man on earth. And that makes me feel good, so as soon as I'm steamed up enough to get this feeling in me, I take a flying leap out of the doorway, and off I trot.

I'm in Essex. It's supposed to be a good Borstal, at least that's what the governor said to me when I got here from Nottingham. "We want to trust you while you are in this establishment," he said, smoothing out his newspaper with lily-white workless hands, while I read the big words upside down: *Daily Telegraph.* "If you play ball with us, we'll play ball with you." (Honest to God, you'd have thought it was going to be one long tennis match.) "We want hard honest work and we want good athletics," he said as well. "And if you give us both these things

you can be sure we'll do right by you and send you back into the world an honest man." Well, I could have died laughing, especially when straight after this I hear the barking sergeant-major's voice calling me and two others to attention and marching us off like we was Grenadier Guards. And when the governor kept saying how 'we' wanted you to do this, and 'we' wanted you to do that, I kept looking round for the other blokes, wondering how many of them there was. Of course, I knew there were thousands of them, but as far as I knew only one was in the room. And there *are* thousands of them, all over the poxeaten country, in shops, offices, railway stations, cars, houses, pubs—In-law blokes like you and them, all on the watch for Out-law blokes like me and us—and waiting to 'phone for the coppers as soon as we make a false move. And it'll always be there, I'll tell you that now, because I haven't finished making all my false moves yet, and I dare say I won't until I kick the bucket. If the In-laws are hoping to stop me making false moves they're wasting their time. They might as well stand me up against a wall and let fly with a dozen rifles. That's the only way they'll stop me, and a few million others. Because I've been doing a lot of thinking since coming here. They can spy on us all day to see if we're pulling our puddings and if we're working good or doing our 'athletics' but they can't make an X-ray of our guts to find out what we're telling ourselves. I've been asking myself all sorts of questions, and thinking about my life up to now. And I like doing all this. It's a treat. It passes the time away and don't make Borstal seem half so bad as the boys in our street used to say it was. And this long-distance running lark is the best of all, because it makes me think so good that I learn things even better than when I'm on my bed at night. And apart from that, what with thinking so much while I'm running I'm getting to be one of the best runners in the Borstal. I can go my five miles round better than anybody else I know.

So as soon as I tell myself I'm the first man ever to be dropped into the world, and as soon as I take that first flying leap out into the frosty grass of an early morning when even birds haven't the heart to whistle, I get to thinking, and that's what I like. I go my rounds in a dream, turning at lane or footpath corners without knowing I'm turning, leaping brooks without knowing they're there, and shouting good morning to the early cow-milker without seeing him. It's a treat, being a long-distance runner, out in the world by yourself with not a soul to make you bad-tempered or tell you what to do or that there's a shop to break and enter a bit back from the next street. Sometimes I think that I've never been so free as during that couple of hours when I'm trotting up the path out of the gates and turning by that bare-faced, big-bellied oak tree at the lane end. Everything's dead, but good, because it's dead before coming alive, not dead after being alive. That's how I look at it. Mind you, I often feel frozen stiff at first. I can't feel my hands or feet or flesh at all, like I'm a ghost who wouldn't know the earth was under him if he didn't see it now and again through the mist. But even though some people would call this frost-pain suffering if they wrote about it to their mams in a letter, I don't, because I know that in half an hour I'm going to be warm, that by the time I get to the main road and am turning on to the wheatfield footpath by the bus stop I'm going to feel as hot as a potbellied stove and as happy as a dog with a tin tail.

It's a good life, I'm saying to myself, if you don't give in to coppers and Borstal-bosses and the rest of them bastard-faced In-laws. Trot-trot-trot. Puff-puff-puff. Slap-slap-slap go my feet on the hard soil. Swish-swish-swish as my arms and side catch the bare branches of a bush. For I'm seventeen now, and when they let me out of this—if I don't make a break and see that things turn out otherwise—they'll try to get me in the army, and what's the difference between the army and this place I'm in now? They can't kid me, the bastards. I've seen the barracks near where I live, and if there weren't swaddies on guard outside with rifles you wouldn't know the difference between their high walls and the place I'm in now.

Even though the swaddies come out at odd times a week for a pint of ale, so what? Don't I come out three mornings a week on my long-distance running, which is fifty times better than boozing? When they first said that I was to do my long-distance running without a guard pedalling beside me on a bike I couldn't believe it; but they called it a progressive and modern place, though they can't kid me because I know it's just like any other Borstal, going by the stories I've heard, except that they let me trot about like this. Borstal's Borstal no matter what they do; but anyway I moaned about it being a bit thick sending me out so early to run five miles on an empty stomach, until they talked me round to thinking it wasn't so bad—which I knew all the time —until they called me a good sport and patted me on the back when I said I'd do it and that I'd try to win them the Borstal Blue Ribbon Prize Cup for Long Distance Cross Country Running (All England). And now the governor talks to me when he comes on his rounds, almost as he'd talk to his prize race horse, if he had one.

"All right, Smith?" he asks.

"Yes, sir," I answer.

He flicks his grey moustache: "How's the running coming along?"

"I've set myself to trot round the grounds after dinner just to keep my hand in, sir," I tell him.

The pot-bellied pop-eyed bastard gets pleased at this: "Good show. I know you'll get us that cup," he says.

And I swear under my breath: "Like boggery, I will." No, I won't get them that cup, even though the stupid tash-twitching bastard has all his hopes in me. Because what does his barmy hope mean? I ask myself. Trot-trot-trot, slap-slap-slap, over the stream and into the wood where it's almost dark and frosty-dew twigs sting my legs. It won't mean a bloody thing to me, only to him, and it means as much to him as it would mean to me if I picked up the racing paper and put my bet on a hoss I didn't know, had never seen, and didn't care a sod if I ever did see. That's what it means to him. And I'll lose that race, because I'm not a race horse at all, and I'll let him know it when

I'm about to get out—if I don't sling my hook even before the race. By Christ I will. I'm a human being and I've got thoughts and secrets and bloody life inside me that he doesn't know is there, and he'll never know what's there because he's stupid. I suppose you'll laugh at this, me saying the governor's a stupid bastard when I know hardly how to write and he can read and write and add-up like a professor. But what I say is true right enough. He's stupid, and I'm not, because I can see further into the likes of him than he can see into the likes of me. Admitted, we're both cunning, but I'm more cunning and I'll win in the end even if I die in gaol at eighty-two, because I'll have more fun and fire out of my life than he'll ever get out of his. He's read a thousand books I suppose, and for all I know he might even have written a few, but I know for a dead cert, as sure as I'm sitting here, that what I'm scribbling down is worth a million to what he could ever scribble down. I don't care what anybody says, but that's the truth and can't be denied. I know when he talks to me and I look into his army mug that I'm alive and he's dead. He's as dead as a doornail. If he ran ten yards he'd drop dead. If he got ten yards into what goes on in my guts he'd drop dead as well—with surprise. At the moment it's dead blokes like him as have the whip-hand over blokes like me, and I'm almost dead sure it'll always be like that, but even so, by Christ, I'd rather be like I am—always on the run and breaking into shops for a packet of fags and a jar of jam—than have the whip-hand over somebody else and be dead from the toe nails up. Maybe as soon as you get the whip-hand over somebody you do go dead. By God, to say that last sentence has needed a few hundred miles of long-distance running. I could no more have said that at first than I could have took a million-pound note from my back pocket. But it's true, you know, now I think of it again, and has always been true, and always will be true, and I'm surer of it every time I see the governor open that door and say Goodmorning lads.

As I run and see my smoky breath going out into the air as if I had ten cigars stuck in different parts of my body I think more on the little speech the governor made when I first came. Honesty. Be honest. I laughed so much one morning I went ten minutes down in my timing because I had to stop and get rid of the stitch in my side. The governor was so worried when I got back late that he sent me to the doctor's for an X-ray and heart check. Be honest. It's like saying: Be dead, like me, and then you'll have no more pain of leaving your nice slummy house for Borstal or prison. Be honest and settle down in a cosy six pounds a week job. Well, even with all this long-distance running I haven't yet been able to decide what he means by this, although I'm just about beginning to—and I don't like what it means. Because after all my thinking I found that it adds up to something that can't be true about me, being born and brought up as I was. Because another thing people like the governor will never understand is that I *am* honest, that I've never been anything else but honest, and that I'll always be honest. Sounds funny. But it's true because I know what honest means according to me and he only knows what it means according to him. I think my honesty is the only sort in the world, and he thinks his is the only sort in the world as well. That's why this dirty great walled-up and fenced-up manor house in the middle of nowhere has been used to coop-up blokes like me. And if I had the whip-hand I wouldn't even bother to build a place like this to put all the cops, governors, posh whores, penpushers, army officers, Members of Parliament in; no, I'd stick them up against a wall and let them have it, like they'd have done with blokes like us years ago, that is, if they'd ever known what it means to be honest, which they don't and never will so help me God Almighty.

I was nearly eighteen months in Borstal before I thought about getting out. I can't tell you much about what it was like there because I haven't got the hang of describing buildings or saying how many crumby chairs and slatted windows make a room. Neither can I do much complaining, because to tell you the truth I didn't suffer in Borstal at all. I gave the same answer a pal of mine gave when someone asked him how much he hated it in the army. "I didn't hate it," he said. "They fed me, gave me a suit, and pocket-money, which was a bloody sight more than I ever got before, unless I worked myself to death for it, and most of the time they wouldn't let me work but sent me to the dole office twice a week." Well, that's more or less what I say. Borstal didn't hurt me in that respect, so since I've no complaints I don't have to describe what they gave us to eat, what the dorms were like, or how they treated us. But in another way Borstal does something to me. No, it doesn't get my back up, because it's always been up, right from when I was born. What it does do is show me what they've been trying to frighten me with. They've got other things as well, like prison and, in the end, the rope. It's like me rushing up to thump a man and snatch the coat off his back when, suddenly, I pull up because he whips out a knife and lifts it to stick me like a pig if I come too close. That knife is Borstal, clink, the rope. But once you've seen the knife you learn a bit of unarmed combat. You have to, because you'll never get that sort of knife in your own hands, and this unarmed combat doesn't amount to much. Still, there it is, and you keep on rushing up to this man, knife or not, hoping to get one of your hands on his wrist and the other on his elbow both at the same time, and press back until he drops the knife.

You see, by sending me to Borstal they've shown me the knife, and from now on I know something I didn't know before: that it's war between me and them. I always knew this, naturally, because I was in Remand Homes as well and the boys there told me a lot about their brothers in Borstal, but it was only touch and go then, like kittens, like boxing-gloves, like dobbie. But now that they've shown me the knife, whether I ever pinch another thing in my life again or not, I know who my enemies are and what war is. They can drop all the atom bombs they like for all I care: I'll never call it war and wear a soldier's uniform,

because I'm in a different sort of war, that they think is child's play. The war they think is war is suicide, and those that go and get killed in war should be put in clink for attempted suicide because that's the feeling in blokes' minds when they rush to join up or let themselves be called up. I know, because I've thought how good it would be sometimes to do myself in and the easiest way to do it, it occurred to me, was to hope for a big war so's I could join up and get killed. But I got past that when I knew I already was in a war of my own, that I was born into one, that I grew up hearing the sound of 'old soldiers' who'd been over the top at Dartmoor, half-killed at Lincoln, trapped in no-man's-land at Borstal, that sounded louder than any Jerry bombs. Government wars aren't my wars; they've got nowt to do with me, because my own war's all that I'll ever be bothered about. I remember when I was fourteen and I went out into the country with three of my cousins, all about the same age, who later went to different Borstals, and then to different regiments, from which they soon deserted, and then to different gaols where they still are as far as I know. But anyway, we were all kids then, and wanted to go out to the woods for a change, to get away from the roads of stinking hot tar one summer. We climbed over fences and went through fields, scrumping a few sour apples on our way, until we saw the wood about a mile off. Up Colliers' Pad we heard another lot of kids talking in high-school voices behind a hedge. We crept up on them and peeped through the brambles, and saw they were eating a picnic, a real posh spread out of baskets and flasks and towels. There must have been about seven of them, lads and girls sent out by their mams and dads for the afternoon. So we went on our bellies through the hedge like crocodiles and surrounded them, and then dashed into the middle, scattering the fire and batting their tabs and snatching up all there was to eat, then running off over Cherry Orchard fields into the wood, with a man chasing us who'd come up while we were ransacking their picnic. We got away all right, and had a good feed into the bargain, because we'd been clambed to death and couldn't wait long enough to get our chops ripping into them thin lettuce and ham sandwiches and creamy cakes.

Well, I'll always feel during every bit of my life like those daft kids should have felt before we broke them up. But they never dreamed that what happened was going to happen, just like the governor of this Borstal who spouts to us about honesty and all that wappy stuff don't know a bloody thing, while I know every minute of my life that a big boot is always likely to smash any nice picnic I might be barmy and dishonest enough to make for myself. I admit that there've been times when I've thought of telling the governor all this so as to put him on his guard, but when I've got as close as seeing him I've changed my mind, thinking to let him either find out for himself or go through the same mill as I've gone through. I'm not hard-hearted (in fact I've helped a few blokes in my time with the odd quid, lie, fag, or shelter from the rain when they've been on the run) but I'm boggered if I'm going to risk being put in the cells just for trying to give the governor a bit of advice he don't deserve. If my heart's soft I know the sort of people I'm going to save it for. And any advice I'd give the governor wouldn't do him the least bit of good; it'd only trip him up sooner than if he wasn't told at all, which I suppose is what I want to happen. But for the time being I'll let things go on as they are, which is something else I've learned in the last year or two. (It's a good job I can only think of these things as fast as I can write with this stub of pencil that's clutched in my paw, otherwise I'd have dropped the whole thing weeks ago.)

By the time I'm half-way through my morning course, when after a frost-bitten dawn I can see a phlegmy bit of sunlight hanging from the bare twigs of beech and sycamore, and when I've measured my half-way mark by the short-cut scrimmage down the steep bush-covered bank and into the sunken lane, when still there's not a soul in sight and not a sound except the neighing of a piebald foal in a cottage stable that I can't see, I get to thinking the deepest and daftest of all. The governor would have a fit if he could see me sliding down the bank because I could break my

neck or ankle, but I can't not do it because it's the only risk I take and the only excitement I ever get, flying flat-out like one of them pterodactyls from the 'Lost World' I once heard on the wireless, crazy like a cut-balled cockerel, scratching myself to bits and almost letting myself go but not quite. It's the most wonderful minute because there's not one thought or word or picture of anything in my head while I'm going down. I'm empty, as empty as I was before I was born, and I don't let myself go, I suppose, because whatever it is that's farthest down inside me don't want me to die or hurt myself bad. And it's daft to think deep, you know, because it gets you nowhere, though deep is what I am when I've passed this half-way mark because the long-distance run of an early morning makes me think that every run like this is a life—a little life, I know—but a life as full of misery and happiness and things happening as you can ever get really around yourself—and I remember that after a lot of these runs I thought that it didn't need much know-how to tell how a life was going to end once it had got well started. But as usual I was wrong, caught first by the cops and then by my own bad brain, I could never trust myself to fly scot-free over these traps, was always tripped up sooner or later no matter how many I got over to the good without even knowing it. Looking back I suppose them big trees put their branches to their snouts and gave each other the wink, and there I was whizzing down the bank and not seeing a bloody thing.

II

I don't say to myself: "You shouldn't have done the job and then you'd have stayed away from Borstal"; no, what I ram into my runner-brain is that my luck had no right to scram just when I was on my way to making the coppers think I hadn't done the job after all. The time was autumn and the night foggy enough to set me and my mate Mike roaming the streets when we should have been rooted in front of the telly or stuck into a plush posh seat at the pictures, but I was restless after six weeks away from any sort of work, and well you might ask me why I'd been bone-idle for so long because normally I sweated my thin guts out on a milling-machine with the rest of them, but you see, my dad died from cancer of the throat, and mam collected a cool five hundred in insurance and benefits from the factory where he'd worked, "for your bereavement," they said, or words like that.

Now I believe, and my mam must have thought the same, that a wad of crisp blue-back fixers ain't a sight of good to a living soul unless they're flying out of your hand into some shopkeeper's till, and the shopkeeper is passing you tip-top things in exchange over the counter, so as soon as she got the money, mam took me and my five brothers and sisters out to town and got us dolled-up in new clothes. Then she ordered a twenty-one-inch telly, a new carpet because the old one was covered with blood from dad's dying and wouldn't wash out, and took a taxi home with bags of grub and a new fur coat. And do you know—you wain't believe me when I tell you—she'd still near three hundred left in her bulging handbag the next day, so how could any of us go to work after that? Poor old dad, he didn't get a look in, and he was the one who'd done the suffering and dying for such a lot of lolly.

Night after night we sat in front of the telly with a ham sandwich in one hand, a bar of chocolate in the other, and a bottle of lemonade between our boots, while mam was with some fancy-man upstairs on the new bed she'd ordered, and I'd never known a family as happy as ours was in that couple of months when we'd got all the money we needed. And when the dough ran out I didn't think about anything much, but just roamed the streets—looking for another job. I told mam—hoping I suppose to get my hands on another five hundred nicker so's the nice life we'd got used to could go on and on for ever. Because it's surprising how quick you can get used to a different life. To begin with, the adverts on the telly had shown us how much more there was in the world to buy than we'd ever dreamed of when we'd looked into shop windows but hadn't seen all there was to see because we didn't have the money to buy it with anyway. And the telly made all these things seem twenty times better than we'd ever thought they were. Even adverts at the cinema were cool and tame, because now we were seeing them in private at home. We used to cock our noses up at things in shops that didn't move, but suddenly we saw their real value because they jumped and glittered around the screen and had some pasty-faced tart going head over heels to get her nail-polished grabbers on to them or her lipstick lips over them, not like the crumby adverts you saw on posters or in newspapers as dead as doornails; these were flickering around loose, half-open packets and tins, making you think that all you had to do was finish opening them before they were yours, like seeing an unlocked safe through a shop window with the man gone away for a cup of tea without thinking to guard his lolly. The films they showed were good as well, in that way, because we couldn't get our eyes unglued from the cops chasing the robbers who had satchel-bags crammed with cash and looked like getting away to spend it—until the last moment. I always hoped they would end up free to blow the lot, and could never stop wanting to put my hand out, smash into the screen (it only looked a bit of rag-screen like at the pictures) and get the copper in a half-nelson so's he'd stop following the bloke with the money-bags. Even when he'd knocked off a couple of bank clerks I hoped he wouldn't get nabbed. In fact then I wished more than ever he wouldn't because it meant the hot-chair if he did and I wouldn't wish that on anybody no matter what they'd done, because I'd read in a book where the hot-chair worn't a quick death at all, but that you just sat there scorching to death until you were dead. And it was when these cops were chasing the crooks that we played some good tricks with the telly, because when one of them opened his big gob to spout about getting their man I'd turn the sound down and see his mouth move like a goldfish or mackerel or a minnow mimicking what they were supposed to be acting—it was so funny the whole family nearly went into fits on the brand-new carpet that hadn't yet found its way to the bedroom. It was the best of all though when we did it to some Tory telling us about how good his government was going to be if we kept on voting for them—their slack chops rolling, opening and bumbling, hands lifting to twitch moustaches and touching their buttonholes to make sure the flower hadn't wilted, so that you could see they didn't mean a word they said, especially with not a murmur coming out because we'd cut off the sound. When the governor of the Borstal first talked to me I was reminded of those times so much that I nearly killed myself trying not to laugh. Yes, we played so many good stunts on the box of tricks that mam used to call us the Telly Boys, we got so clever at it.

My pal Mike got let off with probation because it was his first job—anyway the first they ever knew about—and because they said he would never have done it if it hadn't been for me talking him into it. They said I was a menace to honest lads like Mike—hands in his pockets so that they looked stone-empty, head bent forward as if looking for half-crowns to fill 'em with, a ripped jersey on and his hair falling into his eyes so that he could go up to women and ask them for a shilling because he was hungry—and that I was the brains behind the job, the guiding light when it came to making up anybody's mind, but I swear to God I worn't owt like that because really I ain't got no more brains than a gnat after hiding the money in the place I did. And I—being cranky like I am—got sent to Borstal because to tell you the honest truth I'd been to Remand Homes before—though that's another story and I suppose if ever I tell it it'll be just as boring as this one is. I was glad though that Mike got away with it, and I only hope he always will, not like silly bastard me.

So on this foggy night we tore ourselves away from the telly and slammed the front door behind us, setting off up our wide street like slow tugs on a river that'd broken their hooters, for we didn't know where the housefronts began what with the perishing cold mist all around. I was snatched to death without an overcoat: mam had forgotten to buy me one in the scrummage of shopping, and by the time I thought to remind her of it the dough was all gone. So we whistled 'The Teddy Boys Picnic' to keep us warm, and I told myself that I'd get a coat soon if it was the last thing I did. Mike said he thought the same about himself, adding that he'd also get some brand-new glasses with gold rims, to wear instead of the wire frames they'd given him at the school clinic years ago. He didn't twig it was foggy at first and cleaned his glasses every time I pulled him back from a lamp-post or car, but when he saw the lights on Alfreton Road looking like octopus eyes he put them in his pocket and didn't wear them again until we did the job. We hadn't got two ha-pennies between us, and though we weren't hungry we wished we'd got a bob or two when we passed the fish and chip shops because the delicious sniffs of salt and vinegar and frying fat made our mouths water. I don't mind telling you we walked the town from one end to the other and if our eyes worn't glued to the ground looking for lost wallets and watches they was swivelling around house windows and shop doors in case we saw something easy and worth nipping into.

Neither of us said as much as this to each other, but I know for a fact that that was what we was thinking. What I don't know—and as sure as I sit here I know I'll never know—is which of us was the first bastard to latch his peepers on to that baker's backyard. Oh yes, it's all right me telling myself it was me, but the truth is that I've never known whether it was Mike or not, because I do know that I didn't see the open window until he stabbed me in the ribs and pointed it out. "See it?" he said.

"Yes," I told him, "so let's get cracking."

"But what about the wall though?" he whispered, looking a bit closer.

"On your shoulders," I chipped in.

His eyes were already up there: "Will you be able to reach?" It was the only time he ever showed any life.

"Leave it to me," I said, ever-ready. "I can reach anywhere from your ham-hock shoulders."

Mike was a nipper compared to me, but underneath the scruffy draught-board jersey he wore were muscles as hard as iron, and you wouldn't think to see him walking down the street with glasses on and hands in pockets that he'd harm a fly, but I never liked to get on the wrong side of him in a fight because he's the sort that don't say a word for weeks on end—sits plugged in front of the telly, or reads a cowboy book, or just sleeps—when suddenly BIFF—half kills somebody for almost nothing at all, such as beating him in a race for the last Football Post on a Saturday night, pushing in before him at a bus stop, or bumping into him when he was day-dreaming about Dolly-on-the-Tub next door. I saw him set on a bloke once for no more than fixing him in a funny way with his eyes, and it turned out that the bloke was cockeyed but nobody knew it because he'd just that day come to live in our street. At other times none of these things would matter a bit, and I suppose the only reason why I was pals with him was because I didn't say much from one month's end to another either.

He puts his hands up in the air like he was being covered with a Gatling-Gun, and moved to the wall like he was going to be mowed down, and I climbed up him like he was a stile or step-ladder, and there he stood, the palms of his upshot maulers flat and turned out so's I could step on 'em like they was the adjustable jack-spanner under a car, not a sound of a breath nor the shiver of a flinch coming from him. I lost no time in any case, took my coat from between my teeth, chucked it up to the glass-topped wall (where the glass worn't too sharp because the jags had been worn down by years of accidental stones) and was sitting astraddle before I knew where I was. Then down the other side, with my legs rammed up into my throat when I hit the ground, the crack coming about as hard as when you fall after a high parachute drop, that one of my mates told me was like jumping off a twelve-foot wall, which this must have been. Then I picked up my bits and pieces and opened the gate for Mike, who was still grinning and full of life because the hardest part of the job was already done. "I came, I broke, I entered," like that clever-dick Borstal song.

I didn't think about anything at all, as usual, because I never do when I'm busy, when I'm draining pipes, looting sacks, yaling locks, lifting latches, forcing my bony hands and lanky legs into making something move, hardly feeling my lungs going in-whiff and out-whaff, not realizing whether my mouth is clamped tight or gaping, whether I'm hungry, itching from scabies, or whether my flies are open and flashing dirty words like muck and spit into the late-night final fog. And when I don't know anything about all this then how can I honest-to-God say I think of anything at such times? When I'm wondering what's the best way to get a window open or how to force a door, how can I be thinking or have anything on my mind? That's what the four-eyed white-smocked bloke with the note-book couldn't understand when he asked me questions for days and days after I got to Borstal; and I couldn't explain it to him then like I'm writing it down now; and even if I'd been able to maybe he still wouldn't have caught on because I don't know whether I can understand it myself even at this moment, though I'm doing my best you can bet.

So before I knew where I was I was inside the baker's office watching Mike picking up that cash box after he'd struck a match to see where it was, wearing a tailor-made fifty-shilling grin on his square crew-cut nut as his paws closed over the box like he'd squash it to nothing. "Out," he suddenly said, shaking it so's it rattled. "Let's scram."

"Maybe there's some more," I said, pulling half a dozen drawers out of a rollertop desk.

"No," he said, like he'd already been twenty years in the game, "this is the lot," patting his tin box, "this is it."

I pulled out another few drawers, full of bills, books and letters. "How do you know, you loony sod?"

He barged past me like a bull at a gate. "Because I do."

Right or wrong, we'd both got to stick together and do the same thing. I looked at an ever-loving babe of a brand-new typewriter, but I knew it was too traceable, so blew it a kiss, and went out after him. "Hang on," I said, pulling the door to, "we're in no hurry."

"Not much we aren't," he says over his shoulder.

"We've got months to splash the lolly," I whispered as we crossed the yard, "only don't let that gate creak too much or you'll have the narks tuning-in."

"You think I'm barmy?" he said, creaking the gate so that the whole street heard.

I don't know about Mike, but now I started to think, of how we'd get back safe through the streets with that money-box up my jumper. Because he'd clapped it into my hand as soon as we'd got to the main road, which might have meant that he'd started thinking as well, which only goes to show how you don't know what's in anybody else's mind unless you think about things yourself. But as far as my thinking went at that moment it wasn't up to much, only a bit of fright that wouldn't budge not even with a hot blow-lamp, about what we'd say if a copper asked us where we were off to with that hump in my guts.

"What is it?" he'd ask, and I'd say: "A growth." "What do you mean, a growth, my lad?" he'd say back, narky like. I'd cough and clutch myself like I was in the most tripe-twisting pain in the world, and screw my eyes up like I was on my way to the hospital, and Mike would take my arm like he was the best pal I'd got. "Cancer," I'd manage to say to Narker, which would make his slow punch-drunk brain suspect a thing or two. "A lad of your age?" So I'd groan again, and hope to make him feel a real bully of a bastard, which would be impossible, but anyway: "It's in the family. Dad died of it last month, and I'll die of it next month by the feel of it." "What, did he have it in the guts?" "No, in the throat. But it's got me in the stomach." Groan and cough. "Well, you shouldn't be out like this if you've got cancer, you should be in the hospital." I'd get ratty now: "That's where I'm trying to go if only you'd let me and stop asking so many questions. Aren't I, Mike?" Grunt from Mike as he unslung his cosh. Then just in time the copper would tell us to get on our way, kind and considerate all of a sudden, saying that

the outpatient department of the hospital closes at twelve, so hadn't he better call us a taxi? He would if we liked, he says, and he'd pay for it as well. But we tell him not to bother, that he's a good bloke even if he is a copper, that we know a short cut anyway. Then just as we're turning a corner he gets it into his big batchy head that we're going the opposite way to the hospital, and calls us back. So we'd start to run . . . if you can call all that thinking.

Up in my room Mike rips open that money-box with a hammer and chisel, and before we know where we are we've got seventy-eight pounds fifteen and fourpence ha'penny *each* lying all over my bed like tea spread out on Christmas Day: cake and trifle, salad and sandwiches, jam tarts and bars of chocolate: all shared and shared alike between Mike and me because we believed in equal work and equal pay, just like the comrades my dad was in until he couldn't do a stroke anymore and had no breath left to argue with. I thought how good it was that blokes like that poor baker didn't stash all his cash in one of the big marble-fronted banks that take up every corner of the town, how lucky for us that he didn't trust them no matter how many millions of tons of concrete or how many iron bars and boxes they were made of, or how many coppers kept their blue pop-eyed peepers glued on to them, how smashing it was that he believed in money-boxes when so many shopkeepers thought it old-fashioned and tried to be modern by using a bank, which wouldn't give a couple of sincere, honest, hard-working, conscientious blokes like Mike and me a chance.

Now you'd think, and I'd think, and anybody with a bit of imagination would think, that we'd done as clean a job as could ever be done, that, with the baker's shop being at least a mile from where we lived, and with not a soul having seen us, and what with the fog and the fact that we weren't more than five minutes in the place, that the coppers should never have been able to trace us. But then, you'd be wrong, I'd be wrong, and everybody else would be wrong, no matter how much imagination was diced out between us.

Even so, Mike and I didn't splash the

money about, because that would have made people think straightaway that we'd latched on to something that didn't belong to us. Which wouldn't do at all, because even in a street like ours there are people who love to do a good turn for the coppers, though I never know why they do. Some people are so mean-gutted that even if they've only got tuppence more than you and they think you're the sort that would take it if you have half the chance, they'd get you put inside if they saw you ripping lead out of a lavatory, even if it weren't their lavatory—just to keep their tuppence out of your reach. And so we didn't do anything to let on about how rich we were, nothing like going down town and coming back dressed in brand-new Teddy boy suits and carrying a set of skiffle-drums like another pal of ours who'd done a factory office about six months before. No, we took the odd bobs and pennies out and folded the notes into bundles and stuffed them up the drainpipe outside the door in the backyard. "Nobody'll ever think of looking for it there," I said to Mike. "We'll keep it doggo for a week or two, then take a few quid a week out till it's all gone. We might be thieving bastards, but we're not green."

Some days later a plain-clothes dick knocked at the door. And asked for me. I was still in bed, at eleven o'clock, and had to unroll myself from the comfortable black sheets when I heard mam calling me. "A man to see you," she said. "Hurry up, or he'll be gone."

I could hear her keeping him at the back door, nattering about how fine it had been but how it looked like rain since early this morning—and he didn't answer her except to snap out a snotty yes or no. I scrambled into my trousers and wondered why he'd come—knowing it was a copper because 'a man to see you' always meant just that in our house—and if I'd had any idea that one had gone to Mike's house as well at the same time I'd have twigged it to be because of that hundred and fifty quid's worth of paper stuffed up the drainpipe outside the back door about ten inches away from that plain-clothed copper's boot, where mam still talked to him thinking she was doing me a favour, and I wishing to God she'd ask him in, though on second thoughts realizing that that would seem more suspicious than keeping him outside, because they know we hate their guts and smell a rat if they think we're trying to be nice to them. Mam wasn't born yesterday, I thought, thumping my way down the creaking stairs.

I'd seen him before: Borstal Bernard in nicky-hat, Remand Home Ronald in rowing-boat boots, Probation Pete in a pit-prop mackintosh, three-months clink in collar and tie (all this out of a Borstal skiffle-ballad that my new mate made up, and I'd tell you it in full but it doesn't belong in this story), a 'tec who'd never had as much in his pockets as that drainpipe had up its jackses. He was like Hitler in the face, right down to the paint-brush tash, except that being six-foot tall made him seem worse. But I straightened my shoulders to look into his illiterate blue eyes—like I always do with any copper.

Then he started asking me questions, and my mother from behind said: "He's never left that television set for the last three months, so you've got nowt on him, mate. You might as well look for somebody else, because you're wasting the rates you get out of my rent and the income-tax that comes out of my pay-packet standing there like that"—which was a laugh because she'd never paid either to my knowledge, and never would, I hoped.

"Well, you know where Papplewick Street is, don't you?" the copper asked me, taking no notice of mam.

"Ain't it off Alfreton Road?" I asked him back, helpful and bright.

"You know there's a baker's half-way down on the left-hand side, don't you?"

"Ain't it next door to a pub, then?" I wanted to know.

He answered me sharp: "No, it bloody well ain't." Coppers always lose their tempers as quick as this, and more often than not they gain nothing by it. "Then I don't know it," I told him, saved by the bell.

He slid his big boot round and round on the doorstep. "Where were you last Friday night?" Back in the ring, but this was worse than a boxing match.

I didn't like him trying to accuse me of

something he wasn't sure I'd done. "Was I at that baker's you mentioned? Or in the pub next door?"

"You'll get five years in Borstal if you don't give me a straight answer," he said, unbuttoning his mac even though it was cold where he was standing.

"I was glued to the telly, like mam says," I swore blind. But he went on and on with his looney questions: "Have you got a television?"

The things he asked wouldn't have taken in a kid of two, and what else could I say to the last one except: "Has the aerial fell down? Or would you like to come in and see it?"

He was liking me even less for saying that. "We know you weren't listening to the television set last Friday, and so do you, don't you?"

"P'raps not, but I was *looking* at it, because sometimes we turn the sound down for a bit of fun." I could hear mam laughing from the kitchen, and I hoped Mike's mam was doing the same if the cops had gone to him as well.

"We know you weren't in the house," he said, starting up again, cranking himself with the handle. They always say 'We' 'We', never 'I' 'I'—as if they feel braver and righter knowing there's a lot of them against only one.

"I've got witnesses," I said to him. "Mam for one. Her fancy-man, for two. Ain't that enough? I can get you a dozen more, or thirteen altogether, if it was a baker's that got robbed."

"I don't want no lies," he said, not catching on about the baker's dozen. Where do they scrape cops up from anyway? "All I want is to get from you where you put that money."

Don't get mad, I kept saying to myself, don't get mad—hearing mam setting out cups and saucers and putting the pan on the stove for bacon. I stood back and waved him inside like I was a butler. "Come and search the house. If you've got a warrant."

"Listen, my lad," he said, like the dirty bullying jumped-up bastard he was, "I don't want too much of your lip, because if we get you down to the Guildhall you'll get a few bruises and black-eyes for your trouble." And I knew he wasn't kidding either, because I'd heard about all them sort of tricks. I hoped one day though that him and all his pals would be the ones to get the black-eyes and kicks; you never knew. It might come sooner than anybody thinks, like in Hungary. "Tell me where the money is, and I'll get you off with probation."

"What money?" I asked him, because I'd heard that one before as well.

"You know what money."

"Do I look as though I'd know owt about money?" I said, pushing my fist through a hole in my shirt.

"The money that was pinched, that you know all about," he said. "You can't trick me, so it's no use trying."

"Was it three-and-eightpence ha'-penny?" I asked.

"You thieving young bastard. We'll teach you to steal money that doesn't belong to you."

I turned my head around: "Mam," I called out, "get my lawyer on the blower, will you?"

"Clever, aren't you?" he said in a very unfriendly way, "but we won't rest until we clear all this up."

"Look," I pleaded, as if about to sob my socks off because he'd got me wrong, "it's all very well us talking like this, it's like a game almost, but I wish you'd tell me what it's all about, because honest-to-God I've just got out of bed and here you are at the door talking about me having pinched a lot of money, money that I don't know anything about."

He swung around now as if he'd trapped me, though I couldn't see why he might think so. "Who said anything about money? I didn't. What made you bring money into this little talk we're having?"

"It's you," I answered, thinking he was going barmy, and about to start foaming at the chops, "you've got money on the brain, like all policemen. Baker's shops as well."

He screwed his face up. "I want an answer from you: where's that money?"

But I was getting fed-up with all this. "I'll do a deal."

Judging by his flash-bulb face he

thought he was suddenly on to a good thing. "What sort of a deal?"

So I told him: "I'll give you all the money I've got, one and fourpence ha-penny, if you stop this third-degree and let me go in and get my breakfast. Honest, I'm clambed to death. I ain't had a bite since yesterday. Can't you hear my guts rollin'?"

His jaw dropped, but on he went, pumping me for another half hour. A routine check-up, as they say on the pictures. But I knew I was winning on points.

Then he left, but came back in the afternoon to search the house. He didn't find a thing, not a French farthing. He asked me questions again and I didn't tell him anything except lies, lies, lies, because I can go on doing that forever without batting an eyelid. He'd got nothing on me and we both of us knew it, otherwise I'd have been down at the Guildhall in no time, but he kept on keeping on because I'd been in a Remand Home for a high-wall job before; and Mike was put through the same mill because all the local cops knew he was my best pal.

When it got dark me and Mike were in our parlour with a low light on and the telly off, Mike taking it easy in the rocking chair and me slouched out on the settee, both of us puffing a packet of Woods. With the door bolted and curtains drawn we talked about the dough we'd crammed up the drainpipe. Mike thought we should take it out and both of us do a bunk to Skegness or Cleethorpes for a good time in the arcades, living like lords in a boarding house near the pier, then at least we'd both have had a big beano before getting sent down.

"Listen, you daft bleeder," I said, "we aren't going to get caught at all *and* we'll have a good time, later." We were so clever we didn't even go out to the pictures, though we wanted to.

In the morning old Hitler-face questioned me again, with one of his pals this time, and the next day they came, trying as hard as they could to get something out of me, but I didn't budge an inch. I know I'm showing off when I say this, but in me he'd met his match, and I'd never give in to questions no matter how long

it was kept up. They searched the house a couple of times as well, which made me think they thought they really had something to go by, but I know now that they hadn't, and that it was all buckshee speculation. They turned the house upside down and inside out like an old sock, went from top to bottom and front to back but naturally didn't find a thing. The copper even poked his face up the front-room chimney (that hadn't been used or swept for years) and came down looking like Al Jolson so that he had to swill himself clean at the scullery sink. They kept tapping and pottering around the big aspidistra plant that grandma had left to mam, lifting it up from the table to look under the cloth, putting it aside so's they could move the table and get at the boards under the rug—but the big headed stupid ignorant bastards never once thought of emptying the soil out of the plant pot, where they'd have found the crumpled-up money-box that we'd buried the night we did the job. I suppose it's still there, now I think about it, and I suppose mam wonders now and again why the plant don't prosper like it used to—as if it could with a fistful of thick black tin lapped around its guts.

The last time he knocked at our door was one wet morning at five minutes to nine and I was sleep-logged in my crumby bed as usual. Mam had gone to work that day so I shouted for him to hold on a bit, and then went down to see who it was. There he stood, six-feet tall and sopping wet, and for the first time in my life I did a spiteful thing I'll never forgive myself for: I didn't ask him to come in out of the rain, because I wanted him to get double pneumonia and die. I suppose he could have pushed by me and come in if he'd wanted, but maybe he'd got used to asking questions on the doorstep and didn't want to be put off by changing his ground even though it was raining. Not that I don't like being spiteful because of any barmy principle I've got, but this bit of spite, as it turned out, did me no good at all. I should have treated him as a brother I hadn't seen for twenty years and dragged him in for a cup of tea and a fag, told him about the picture I hadn't seen the night before, asked him how his wife was after her operation and whether they'd shaved her moustache off to make it, and then sent him happy and satisfied out by the front door. But no, I thought, let's see what he's got to say for himself now.

He stood a little to the side of the door, either because it was less wet there, or because he wanted to see me from a different angle, perhaps having found it monotonous to watch a bloke's face always tell lies from the same side. "You've been identified," he said, twitching raindrops from his tash. "A woman saw you and your mate yesterday and she swears blind you are the same chaps she saw going into that bakery."

I was dead sure he was still bluffing, because Mike and I hadn't even seen each other the day before, but I looked worried. "She's a menace then to innocent people, whoever she is, because the only bakery I've been in lately is the one up our street to get some cut-bread on tick for mam."

He didn't bite on this. "So now I want to know where the money is"—as if I hadn't answered him at all.

"I think mam took it to work this morning to get herself some tea in the canteen." Rain was splashing down so hard I thought he'd get washed away if he didn't come inside. But I wasn't much bothered, and went on: "I remember I put it in the telly-vase last night—it was my only one-and-three and I was saving it for a packet of tips this morning—and I nearly had a jibbering black fit just now when I saw it had gone. I was reckoning on it for getting me through today because I don't think life's worth living without a fag, do you?"

I was getting into my stride and began to feel good, twigging that this would be my last pack of lies, and that if I kept it up for long enough this time I'd have the bastards beat: Mike and me would be off to the coast in a few weeks time having the fun of our lives, playing at penny football and latching on to a couple of tarts that would give us all they were good for. "And this weather's no good for picking-up fag-ends in the street," I said,

"because they'd be sopping wet. Course, I know you could dry 'em out near the fire, but it don't taste the same you know, all said and done. Rainwater does summat to 'em that don't bear thinkin' about: it turns 'em back into hoss-tods without the taste though."

I began to wonder, at the back of my brainless eyes, why old copper-lugs didn't pull me up sharp and say he hadn't got time to listen to all this, but he wasn't looking at me anymore, and all my thoughts about Skegness went bursting to smithereens in my sludgy loaf. I could have dropped into the earth when I saw what he'd fixed his eyes on.

He was looking at *it*, an ever-loving fiver, and I could only jabber: "The one thing is to have some real fags because new hoss-tods is always better than stuff that's been rained on and dried, and I know how you feel about not being able to find money because one-and-three's one-and-three in anybody's pocket, and naturally if I see it knocking around I'll get you on the blower tomorrow straight-away and tell you where you can find it."

I thought I'd go down in a fit: three green-backs as well had been washed down by the water, and more were following, lying flat at first after their fall, then getting tilted at the corners by wind and rainspots as if they were alive and wanted to get back into the dry snug drainpipe out of the terrible weather, and you can't imagine how I wished they'd be able to. Old Hitler-face didn't know what to make of it but just kept staring down and down, and I thought I'd better keep on talking, though I knew it wasn't much good now.

"It's a fact, I know, that money's hard to come by and half-crowns don't get found on bus seats or in dustbins, and I didn't see any in bed last night because I'd 'ave known about it, wouldn't I? You can't sleep with things like that in the bed because they're too hard, and anyway at first they're. . . ." It took Hitler-boy a long time to catch on; they were beginning to spread over the yard a bit, reinforced by the third colour of a ten-bob note, before his hand clamped itself on to my shoulder.

III

The pop-eyed potbellied governor said to a pop-eyed pot-bellied Member of Parliament who sat next to his pop-eyed potbellied whore of a wife that I was his only hope for getting the Borstal Blue Ribbon Prize Cup For Long Distance Cross Country Running (All England), which I was, and it set me laughing to myself inside, and I didn't say a word to any potbellied pop-eyed bastard that might give them real hope, though I knew the governor anyway took my quietness to mean he'd got that cup already stuck on the bookshelf in his office among the few other mildewed trophies.

"He might take up running in a sort of professional way when he gets out," and it wasn't until he'd said this and I'd heard it with my own flap-tabs that I realized it might be possible to do such a thing, run for money, trot for wages on piece work at a bob a puff rising bit by bit to a guinea a gasp and retiring through old age at thirty-two because of lace-curtain lungs, a football heart, and legs like varicose beanstalks. But I'd have a wife and car and get my grinning long-distance clock in the papers and have a smashing secretary to answer piles of letters sent by tarts who'd mob me when they saw who I was as I pushed my way into Woolworth's for a packet of razor blades and a cup of tea. It was something to think about all right, and sure enough the governor knew he'd got me when he said, turning to me as if I would at any rate have to be consulted about it all: "How does this matter strike you, then, Smith, my lad?"

A line of potbellied pop-eyes gleamed at me and a row of goldfish mouths opened and wiggled gold teeth at me, so I gave them the answer they wanted because I'd hold my trump card until later. "It'd suit me fine, sir," I said.

"Good lad. Good show. Right spirit. Splendid."

"Well," the governor said, "get that cup for us today and I'll do all I can for you. I'll get you trained so that you whack every man in the Free World." And I had a picture in my brain of me running and beating everybody in the world, leaving them all behind until only I was trot-trotting across a big wide moor alone, doing a marvellous speed as I ripped between boulders and reed-clumps, when suddenly: CRACK! CRACK!—bullets that can go faster than any man running, coming from a copper's rifle planted in a tree, winged me and split my gizzard in spite of my perfect running, and down I fell.

The potbellies expected me to say something else. "Thank you, sir," I said.

Told to go, I trotted down the pavilion steps, out onto the field because the big cross-country was about to begin and the two entries from Gunthorpe had fixed themselves early at the starting line and were ready to move off like white kangaroos. The sports ground looked a treat: with big tea-tents all round and flags flying and seats for families—empty because no mam or dad had known what opening day meant—and boys still running heats for the hundred yards, and lords and ladies walking from stall to stall, and the Borstal Boys Brass Band in blue uniforms; and up on the stands the brown jackets of Hucknall as well as our own grey blazers, and then the Gunthorpe lot with shirt sleeves rolled. The blue sky was full of sunshine and it couldn't have been a better day, and all of the big show was like something out of Ivanhoe that we'd seen on the pictures a few days before.

"Come on, Smith," Roach the sports master called to me, "we don't want you to be late for the big race, eh? Although I dare say you'd catch them up if you were." The others cat-called and grunted at this, but I took no notice and placed myself between Gunthorpe and one of the Aylesham trusties, dropped on my knees and plucked a few grass blades to suck on the way round. So the big race it was, for them, watching from the grandstand under a fluttering Union Jack, a race for the governor, that he had been waiting for, and I hoped he and all the rest of his pop-eyed gang were busy placing big bets on me, hundred to one to win, all the money they had in their pockets, all the wages they were going to get for the next five years, and the more they placed the happier I'd be. Because here was a dead cert going to die on the big name they'd built for him, going to go down dying with laughter whether it choked him or not. My knees felt the cool soil pressing into them, and out of my eye's corner I saw Roach lift his hand. The Gunthorpe boy twitched before the signal was given; somebody cheered too soon; Medway bent forward; then the gun went; and I was away.

We went once around the field and then along a half-mile drive of elms, being cheered all the way, and I seemed to feel I was in the lead as we went out by the gate and into the lane, though I wasn't interested enough to find out. The five-mile course was marked by splashes of whitewash gleaming on gateposts and trunks and stiles and stones, and a boy with a waterbottle and bandage-box stood every half-mile waiting for those that dropped out or fainted. Over the first stile, without trying, I was still nearly in the lead but one; and if any of you want tips about running, never be in a hurry, and never let any of the other runners know you are in a hurry even if you are. You can always overtake on long-distance running without letting the others smell the hurry in you; and when you've used your craft like this to reach the two or three up front then you can do a big dash later that puts everybody else's hurry in the shade because you've not had to make haste up till then. I ran to a steady jog-trot rhythm, and soon it was so smooth that I forgot I was running, and I was hardly able to know that my legs were lifting and falling and my arms going in and out, and my lungs didn't seem to be working at all, and my heart stopped that wicked thumping I always get at the beginning of a run. Because you see I never race at all; I just run, and somehow I know that if I forget I'm racing and only jog-trot along until I don't know I'm running I always win the race. For when my eyes recognize that I'm getting near the end of the course— by seeing a stile or cottage corner—I put on a spurt, and such a fast big spurt it is because I feel that up till then I haven't been running and that I've used up no energy at all. And I've been able to do this because I've been thinking; and I

wonder if I'm the only one in the running business with this system of forgetting that I'm running because I'm too busy thinking; and I wonder if any of the other lads are on to the same lark, though I know for a fact that they aren't. Off like the wind along the cobbled footpath and rutted lane, smoother than the flat grass track on the field and better for thinking because it's not too smooth, and I was in my element that afternoon knowing that nobody could beat me at running but intending to beat myself before the day was over. For when the governor talked to me of being honest when I first came in he didn't know what the word meant or he wouldn't have had me here in this race, trotting along in shimmy and shorts and sunshine. He'd have had me where I'd have had him if I'd been in his place: in a quarry breaking rocks until he broke his back. At least old Hitler-face the plain-clothes dick was honester than the governor, because he at any rate had had it in for me and I for him, and when my case was coming up in court a copper knocked at our front door at four o'clock in the morning and got my mother out of bed when she was paralytic tired, reminding her she had to be in court at dead on half past nine. It was the finest bit of spite I've ever heard of, but I would call it honest, the same as my mam's words were honest when she really told that copper what she thought of him and called him all the dirty names she'd ever heard of, which took her half an hour and woke the terrace up.

I trotted on along the edge of a field bordered by the sunken lane, smelling green grass and honeysuckle, and I felt as though I came from a long line of whippets trained to run on two legs, only I couldn't see a toy rabbit in front and there wasn't a collier's cosh behind to make me keep up the pace. I passed the Gunthorpe runner whose shimmy was already black with sweat and I could just see the corner of the fenced-up copse in front where the only man I had to pass to win the race was going all out to gain the half-way mark. Then he turned into a tongue of trees and bushes where I couldn't see him anymore, and I couldn't see anybody, and

I knew what the loneliness of the long-distance runner running across country felt like, realizing that as far as I was concerned this feeling was the only honesty and realness there was in the world and knowing it would be no different ever, no matter what I felt at odd times, and no matter what anybody else tried to tell me. The runner behind me must have been a long way off because it was so quiet, and there was even less noise and movement than there had been at five o'clock of a frosty winter morning. It was hard to understand, and all I knew was that you had to run, run, run, without knowing why you were running, but on you went through fields you didn't understand and into woods that made you afraid, over hills without knowing you'd been up and down, and shooting across streams that would have cut the heart out of you had you fallen into them. And the winning post was no end to it, even though crowds might be cheering you in, because on you had to go before you got your breath back, and the only time you stopped really was when you tripped over a tree trunk and broke your neck or fell into a disused well and stayed dead in the darkness forever. So I thought: they aren't going to get me on this racing lark, this running and trying to win, this jog-trotting for a bit of blue ribbon, because it's not the way to go on at all, though they swear blind that it is. You should think about nobody and go your own way, not on a course marked out for you by people holding mugs of water and bottles of iodine in case you fall and cut yourself so that they can pick you up—even if you want to stay where you are—and get you moving again.

On I went, out of the wood, passing the man leading without knowing I was going to do so. Flip-flap, flip-flap, jog-trot, jog-trot, crunchslap-crunchslap, across the middle of a broad field again, rhythmically running in my greyhound effortless fashion, knowing I had won the race though it wasn't half over, won it if I wanted it, could go on for ten or fifteen or twenty miles if I had to and drop dead at the finish of it, which would be the same, in the end, as living an honest life like the governor wanted me to. It amounted to: win the race and be honest, and on trot-trotting I went, having the time of my life, loving my progress because it did me good and set me thinking which by now I liked to do, but not caring at all when I remembered that I had to win this race as well as run it. One of the two, I had to win the race or run it, and I knew I could do both because my legs had carried me well in front—now coming to the short cut down the bramble bank and over the sunken road—and carry me further because they seemed made of electric cable and easily alive to keep on slapping at those ruts and roots, but I'm not going to win because the only way I'd see I came in first would be if winning meant that I was going to escape the coppers after doing the biggest bank job of my life, but winning means the exact opposite, no matter how they try to kill or kid me, means running right into their white-gloved wall-barred hands and grinning mugs and staying there for the rest of my natural long life of stone-breaking anyway, but stone-breaking in the way I want to do it and not in the way they tell me.

Another honest thought that comes is that I could swing left at the next hedge of the field, and under its cover beat my slow retreat away from the sports ground winning post. I could do three or six or a dozen miles across the turf like this and cut a few main roads behind me so's they'd never know which one I'd taken; and maybe on the last one when it got dark I could thumb a lorry-lift and get a free ride north with somebody who might not give me away. But no, I said I wasn't daft didn't I? I won't pull out with only six months left, and besides there's nothing I want to dodge and run away from; I only want a bit of my own back on the In-laws and Potbellies by letting them sit up there on their big posh seats and watch me lose this race, though as sure as God made me I know that when I do lose I'll get the dirtiest crap and kitchen jobs in the months to go before my time is up. I won't be worth a threpp'ny-bit to anybody here, which will be all the thanks I get for being honest in the only way I know. For when the governor told me to be honest it was meant to be in his way not mine, and if I kept on being honest in the way he wanted and won my race for him he'd see I got the cushiest six months still left to run; but in my own way, well, it's not allowed, and if I find a way of doing it such as I've got now then I'll get what-for in every mean trick he can set his mind to. And if you look at it in my way, who can blame him? For this is war—and ain't I said so?—and when I hit him in the only place he knows he'll be sure to get his own back on me for not collaring that cup when his heart's been set for ages on seeing himself standing up at the end of the afternoon to clap me on the back as I take the cup from Lord Earwig or some such chinless wonder with a name like that. And so I'll hit him where it hurts a lot, and he'll do all he can to get his own back, tit for tat, though I'll enjoy it most because I'm hitting first, and because I planned it longer. I don't know why I think these thoughts are better than any I've ever had, but I do, and I don't care why. I suppose it took me a long time to get going on all this because I've had no time and peace in all my bandit life, and now my thoughts are coming pat and the only trouble is I often can't stop, even when my brain feels as if it's got cramp, frostbite and creeping paralysis all rolled into one and I have to give it a rest by slap-dashing down through the brambles of the sunken lane. And all this is another uppercut I'm getting in first at people like the governor, to show him—if I can— his races are never won even though some bloke always comes unknowingly in first, how in the end the governor is going to be doomed while blokes like me will take the pickings of his roasted bones and dance like maniacs around his Borstal's ruins. And so this story's like the race and once again I won't bring off a winner to suit the governor; no, I'm being honest like he told me to, without him knowing what he means, though I don't suppose he'll ever come in with a story of his own, even if he reads this one of mine and knows who I'm talking about.

I've just come up out of the sunken lane, kneed and elbowed, thumped and bramble-scratched, and the race is two-thirds over, and a voice is going like a wireless in my mind saying that when you've had enough of feeling good like the first man on earth of a frosty morning, and you've known how it is to be taken bad like the last man on earth on a summer's afternoon, then you get at last to being like the only man on earth and don't give a bogger about either good or bad, but just trot on with your slippers slapping the good dry soil that at least would never do you a bad turn. Now the words are like coming from a crystal-set that's broken down, and something's happening inside the shell-case of my guts that bothers me and I don't know why or what to blame it on, a grinding near my ticker as though a bag of rusty screws is loose inside me and I shake them up every time I trot forward. Now and again I break my rhythm to feel my left shoulderblade by swinging a right hand across my chest as if to rub the knife away that has somehow got stuck there. But I know it's nothing to bother about, that more likely it's caused by too much thinking that now and again I take for worry. For sometimes I'm the greatest worrier in the world I think (as you twigged I'll bet from me having got this story out) which is funny anyway because my mam don't know the meaning of the word so I don't take after her; though dad had a hard time of worry all his life up to when he filled his bedroom with hot blood and kicked the bucket that morning when nobody was in the house. I'll never forget it, straight I won't, because I was the one that found him and I often wished I hadn't. Back from a session on the fruit-machines at the fish-and-chip shop, jingling my three-lemon loot to a nail-dead house, as soon as I got in I knew something was wrong, stood leaning my head against the cold mirror above the mantelpiece trying not to open my eyes and see my stone-cold clock—because I knew I'd gone as white as a piece of chalk since coming in as if I'd been got at by a Dracula-vampire and even my penny-pocket winnings kept quiet on purpose.

Gunthorpe nearly caught me up. Birds were singing from the briar hedge, and a couple of thrushes flew like lightning into some thorny bushes. Corn had grown high in the next field and would be cut down soon with scythes and mowers; but I never wanted to notice much while running in case it put me off my stroke, so by the haystack I decided to leave it all behind and put on such a spurt, in spite of nails in my guts, that before long I'd left both Gunthorpe and the birds a good way off; I wasn't far now from going into that last mile and a half like a knife through margarine, but the quietness I suddenly trotted into between two pickets was like opening my eyes underwater and looking at the pebbles on a stream bottom, reminding me again of going back that morning to the house in which my old man had croaked, which is funny because I hadn't thought about it at all since it happened and even then I didn't brood much on it. I wonder why? I suppose that since I started to think on these long-distance runs I'm liable to have anything crop up and pester at my tripes and innards, and now that I see my bloody dad behind each grass-blade in my barmy runner-brain I'm not so sure I like to think and that it's such a good thing after all. I choke my phlegm and keep on running anyway and curse the Borstal-builders and their athletics—flappity-flap, slop-slop, crunchslap-crunchslap-crunchslap—who've maybe got their own back on me from the bright beginning by sliding magic-lantern slides into my head that never stood a chance before. Only if I take whatever comes like this in my runner's stride can I keep on keeping on like my old self and beat them back; and now I've thought on this far I know I'll win, in the crunchslap end. So anyway after a bit I went upstairs one step at a time not thinking anything about how I should find dad and what I'd do when I did. But now I'm making up for it by going over the rotten life mam led him ever since I can remember, knocking-on with different men even when he was alive and fit and she not caring whether he knew it or not, and most of the time he wasn't so blind as she thought and cursed and roared and threatened to punch her tab, and I had to stand up to stop him even though I knew she

deserved it. What a life for all of us. Well, I'm not grumbling, because if I did I might just as well win this bleeding race, which I'm not going to do, though if I don't lose speed I'll win it before I know where I am, and then where would I be?

Now I can hear the sportsground noise and music as I head back for the flags and the lead-in drive, the fresh new feel of underfoot gravel going against the iron muscles of my legs. I'm nowhere near puffed despite that bag of nails that rattles as much as ever, and I can still give a big last leap like gale-force wind if I want to, but everything is under control and I know now that there ain't another long-distance cross-country running runner in England to touch my speed and style. Our doddering bastard of a governor, our half-dead gangrened gaffer is hollow like an empty petrol drum, and he wants me and my running life to give him glory, to put in him blood and throbbing veins he never had, wants his potbellied pals to be his witnesses as I gasp and stagger up to his winning post so's he can say: "My Borstal gets that cup, you see. I win my bet, because it pays to be honest and try to gain the prizes I offer to my lads, and they know it, have known it all along. They'll always be honest now, because I made them so." And his pals will think: "He trains his lads to live right, after all; he deserves a medal but we'll get him made a Sir"—and at this very moment as the birds come back to whistling I can tell myself I'll never care a sod what any of the chinless spineless In-laws think or say. They've seen me and they're cheering now and loudspeakers set around the field like elephant's ears are spreading out the big news that I'm well in the lead, and can't do anything else but stay there. But I'm still thinking of the Out-law death my dad died, telling the doctors to scat from the house when they wanted him to finish up in hospital (like a bleeding guinea-pig, he raved at them). He got up in bed to throw them out and even followed them down the stairs in his shirt though he was no more than skin and stick. They tried to tell him he'd want some drugs but he didn't fall from it, and only took the pain-killer that mam and I got from a herb-seller in the next street. It's not till now that I know what guts he had, and when I went into the room that morning he was lying on his stomach with the clothes thrown back, looking like a skinned rabbit, his grey head resting just on the edge of the bed, and on the floor must have been all the blood he'd had in his body, right from his toe-nails up, for nearly all of the lino and carpet was covered in it, thin and pink.

And down the drive I went, carrying a heart blocked up like Boulder Dam across my arteries, the nail-bag clamped down tighter and tighter as though in a woodwork vice, yet with my feet like birdwings and arms like talons ready to fly across the field except that I didn't want to give anybody that much of a show, or win the race by accident. I smell the hot dry day now as I run towards the end, passing a mountain-heap of grass emptied from cans hooked on to the fronts of lawn-mowers pushed by my pals; I rip a piece of tree-bark with my fingers and stuff it in my mouth, chewing wood and dust and maybe maggots as I run until I'm nearly sick, yet swallowing what I can of it just the same because a little birdie whistled to me that I've got to go on living for at least a bloody sight longer yet but that for six months I'm not going to smell that grass or taste that dusty bark or trot this lovely path. I hate to have to say this but something bloody-well made me cry, and crying is a thing I haven't bloody-well done since I was a kid of two or three. Because I'm slowing down now for Gunthorpe to catch me up, and I'm doing it in a place just where the drive turns in to the sportsfield—where they can see what I'm doing, especially the governor and his gang from the grandstand, and I'm going so slow I'm almost marking time. Those on the nearest seats haven't caught on yet to what's happening and are still cheering like mad ready for when I make that mark, and I keep on wondering when the bleeding hell Gunthorpe behind me is going to nip by on to the field because I can't hold this up all day, and I think Oh Christ it's just my rotten luck that Gunthorpe's dropped out and that I'll be here for half an hour before the next bloke

comes up, but even so, I say, I won't budge, I won't go for that last hundred yards if I have to sit down cross-legged on the grass and have the governor and his chinless wonders pick me up and carry me there, which is against their rules so you can bet they'd never do it because they're not clever enough to break the rules—like I would be in their place—even though they are their own. No, I'll show him what honesty means if it's the last thing I do, though I'm sure he'll never understand because if he and all them like him did it'd mean they'd be on my side which is impossible. By God I'll stick this out like my dad stuck out his pain and kicked them doctors down the stairs: if he had guts for that then I've got guts for this and here I stay waiting for Gunthorpe or Aylesham to bash that turf and go right slap-up against that bit of clothes-line stretched across the winning post. As for me, the only time I'll hit that clothes-line will be when I'm dead and a comfortable coffin's been got ready on the other side. Until then I'm a long-distance runner, crossing country all on my own no matter how bad it feels.

The Essex boys were shouting themselves blue in the face telling me to get a move on, waving their arms, standing up and making as if to run at that rope themselves because they were only a few yards to the side of it. You cranky lot, I thought, stuck at that winning post, and yet I knew they didn't mean what they were shouting, were really on my side and always would be, not able to keep their maulers to themselves, in and out of cop-shops and clink. And there they were now having the time of their lives letting themselves go in cheering me which made the governor think they were heart and soul on his side when he wouldn't have thought any such thing if he'd had a grain of sense. And I could hear the lords and ladies now from the grandstand, and could see them standing up to wave me in: "Run!" they were shouting in their posh voices. "Run!" But I was deaf, daft and blind, and stood where I was, still tasting the bark in my mouth and still blubbing like a baby, blubbing now out of gladness that I'd got them beat at last.

Because I heard a roar and saw the Gunthorpe gang throwing their coats up in the air and I felt the pat-pat of feet on the drive behind me getting closer and closer and suddenly a smell of sweat and a pair of lungs on their last gasp passed me by and went swinging on towards that rope, all shagged out and rocking from side to side, grunting like a Zulu that didn't know any better, like the ghost of me at ninety when I'm heading for that fat upholstered coffin. I could have cheered him myself: "Go on, go on, get cracking. Knot yourself up on that piece of tape." But he was already there, and so I went on, trot-trotting after him until I got to the rope, and collapsed, with a murderous sounding roar going up through my ears while I was still on the wrong side of it.

It's about time to stop; though don't think I'm not still running, because I am, one way or another. The governor at Borstal proved me right; he didn't respect my honesty at all; not that I expected him to, or tried to explain it to him, but if he's supposed to be educated then he should have more or less twigged it. He got his own back right enough, or thought he did, because he had me carting dustbins about every morning from the big full-working kitchens to the garden-bottoms where I had to empty them; and in the afternoon I spread out slops over spuds and carrots growing in the allotments. In the evenings I scrubbed floors, miles and miles of them. But it wasn't a bad life for six months, which was another thing he could never understand and would have made it grimmer if he could, and it was worth it when I look back on it, considering all the thinking I did, and the fact that the boys caught on to me losing the race on purpose and never had enough good words to say about me, or curses to throw out (to themselves) at the governor.

The work didn't break me; if anything it made me stronger in many ways, and the governor knew, when I left, that his spite had got him nowhere, For since leaving Borstal they tried to get me in the army, but I didn't pass the medical and I'll tell you why. No sooner was I out, after that final run and six-months hard, that I went down with pleurisy, which means as far as I'm concerned that I lost the governor's race all right, and won my own twice over, because I know for certain that if I hadn't raced my race I wouldn't have got this pleurisy, which keeps me out of khaki but doesn't stop me doing the sort of work my itchy fingers want to do.

I'm out now and the heat's switched on again, but the rats haven't got me for the last big thing I pulled. I counted six hundred and twenty-eight pounds and am still living off it because I did the job all on my own, and after it I had the peace to write all this, and it'll be money enough to keep me going until I finish my plans for doing an even bigger snatch, something up my sleeve I wouldn't tell to a living soul. I worked out my systems and hiding-places while pushing scrubbing-brushes around them Borstal floors, planned my outward life of innocence and honest work, yet at the same time grew perfect in the razor-edges of my craft for what I knew I had to do once free; and what I'll do again if netted by the poaching coppers.

In the meantime (as they say in one or two books I've read since, useless though because all of them ended on a winning post and didn't teach me a thing) I'm going to give this story to a pal of mine and tell him that if I do get captured again by the coppers he can try and get it put into a book or something, because I'd like to see the governor's face when he reads it, if he does, which I don't suppose he will; even if he did read it though I don't think he'd know what it was all about. And if I don't get caught the bloke I give this story to will never give me away; he's lived in our terrace for as long as I can remember, and he's my pal. That I do know.

[1959]

QUESTIONS FOR STUDY

1. *What values and meanings does Smith attach to long-distance running? What fundamental distinction does he draw between "running" and "racing"? Why does he deliberately choose to lose the race?*

2. *What view of the human and social condition underlies Smith's rebellion against society? What does he mean when he says that "Cunning is what counts in this life" and "I haven't finished making all my false moves yet"?*

3. *Why does Smith claim that he is more "honest" than the Governor? Is he? What kind of "honesty" does the Governor stand for? Why does Smith consider him "dead"?*

4. *How do the scenes describing Smith's home life and the death of his father increase the reader's understanding of the story?*

5. *Where do Sillitoe's sympathies lie? Is he in any way ambivalent?*

ISAAC BASHEVIS SINGER

Gimpel the Fool

I

I AM GIMPEL the fool. I don't think myself a fool. On the contrary. But that's what folks call me. They gave me the name while I was still in school. I had seven names in all: imbecile, donkey, flax-head, dope, glump, ninny, and fool. The last name stuck. What did my foolishness consist of? I was easy to take in. They said, "Gimpel, you know the rabbi's wife has been brought to childbed?" So I skipped school. Well, it turned out to be a lie. How was I supposed to know? She hadn't had a big belly. But I never looked at her belly. Was that really so foolish? The gang laughed and heehawed, stomped and danced and chanted a good-night prayer. And instead of the raisins they give when a woman's lying in, they stuffed my hand full of goat turds. I was no weakling. If I slapped someone he'd see all the way to Cracow. But I'm really not a slugger by nature. I think to myself: Let it pass. So they take advantage of me.

I was coming home from school and heard a dog barking. I'm not afraid of dogs, but of course I never want to start up with them. One of them may be mad, and if he bites there's not a Tartar in the world who can help you. So I made tracks. Then I looked around and saw the whole market-place wild with laughter. It was no dog at all but Wolf-Leib the Thief. How was I supposed to know it was he? It sounded like a howling bitch.

When the pranksters and leg-pullers found that I was easy to fool, every one of them tried his luck with me. "Gimpel, the Czar is coming to Frampol; Gimpel, the moon fell down in Turbeen; Gimpel, little Hodel Furpiece found a treasure behind the bathhouse." And I like a golem[1] believed everyone. In the first place, everything is possible, as it is written in the Wisdom of the Fathers, I've forgotten just how. Second, I had to believe when the whole town came down on me! If I ever dared to say, "Ah, you're kidding!" there was trouble. People got angry. "What do you mean! You want to call everyone a liar?" What was I to do? I believed them, and I hope at least that did them some good.

I was an orphan. My grandfather who brought me up was already bent toward the grave. So they turned me over to a baker, and what a time they gave me there! Every woman or girl who came to bake a batch of noodles had to fool me at least once. "Gimpel, there's a fair in heaven; Gimpel, the rabbi gave birth to a calf in the seventh month; Gimpel, a cow flew over the roof and laid brass eggs." A student from the yeshiva[2] came once to buy a roll, and he said, "You, Gimpel, while you stand here scraping with your baker's shovel the Messiah has come. The dead have arisen." "What do you mean?" I said. "I heard no one blowing the ram's horn!" He said, "Are you deaf?" And all began to cry, "We heard it, we heard!" Then in came Rietze the Candle-dipper and called out in her hoarse voice, "Gimpel, your father and mother have stood up from the grave. They're looking for you."

To tell the truth, I knew very well that nothing of the sort had happened, but all the same, as folks were talking, I threw on my wool vest and went out. Maybe something had happened. What did I

[1] golem: a dunce or blockhead. (JHP)
[2] yeshiva: a seminary for rabbis. (JHP)

stand to lose by looking? Well, what a cat music went up! And then I took a vow to believe nothing more. But that was no go either. They confused me so that I didn't know the big end from the small.

I went to the rabbi to get some advice. He said, "It is written, better to be a fool all your days than for one hour to be evil. You are not a fool. They are the fools. For he who causes his neighbor to feel shame loses Paradise himself." Nevertheless the rabbi's daughter took me in. As I left the rabbinical court she said, "Have you kissed the wall yet?" I said, "No; what for?" She answered, "It's the law; you've got to do it after every visit." Well, there didn't seem to be any harm in it. And she burst out laughing. It was a fine trick. She put one over on me all right.

I wanted to go off to another town, but then everyone got busy matchmaking, and they were after me so they nearly tore my coat tails off. They talked at me and talked until I got water on the ear. She was no chaste maiden, but they told me she was a virgin pure. She had a limp, and they said it was deliberate, from coyness. She had a bastard, and they told me the child was her little brother. I cried, "You're wasting your time. I'll never marry that whore." But they said indignantly, "What a way to talk! Aren't you ashamed of yourself? We can take you to the rabbi and have you fined for giving her a bad name." I saw then that I wouldn't escape them so easily and I thought: They're set on making me their butt. But when you're married the husband's the master, and if that's all right with her it's agreeable to me too. Besides, you can't pass through life unscathed, nor expect to.

I went to her clay house, which was built on the sand, and the whole gang, hollering and chorusing, came after me. They acted like bear-baiters. When we came to the well they stopped all the same. They were afraid to start anything with Elka. Her mouth would open as if it were on a hinge, and she had a fierce tongue. I entered the house. Lines were strung from wall to wall and clothes were drying. Barefoot she stood by the tub, doing the wash. She was dressed in a worn hand-me-down gown of plush. She had her hair up in braids and pinned across her head. It took my breath away, almost, the reek of it all.

Evidently she knew who I was. She took a look at me and said, "Look who's here! He's come, the drip. Grab a seat."

I told her all; I denied nothing. "Tell me the truth," I said, "are you really a virgin, and is that mischievous Yechiel actually your little brother? Don't be deceitful with me, for I'm an orphan."

"I'm an orphan myself," she answered, "and whoever tries to twist you up, may the end of his nose take a twist. But don't let them think they can take advantage of me. I want a dowry of fifty guilders, and let them take up a collection besides. Otherwise they can kiss my you-know-what." She was very plainspoken. I said, "It's the bride and not the groom who gives a dowry." Then she said, "Don't bargain with me. Either a flat 'yes' or a flat 'no'—Go back where you came from."

I thought: No bread will ever be baked from *this* dough. But ours is not a poor town. They consented to everything and proceeded with the wedding. It so happened that there was a dysentery epidemic at the time. The ceremony was held at the cemetery gates, near the little corpse-washing hut. The fellows got drunk. While the marriage contract was being drawn up I heard the most pious high rabbi ask, "Is the bride a widow or a divorced woman?" And the sexton's wife answered for her, "Both a widow and divorced." It was a black moment for me. But what was I to do, run away from under the marriage canopy?

There was singing and dancing. An old granny danced opposite me, hugging a braided white *chalah*.[3] The master of revels made a "God 'a mercy" in memory of the bride's parents. The schoolboys threw burrs, as on Tishe b'Av[4] fast day. There were a lot of gifts after the sermon:

3 *chalah:* a loaf of bread eaten on the Sabbath. (JHP)
4 Tishe b'Av: a holiday commemorating the Roman destruction of the Second Temple in A.D. 70. (JHP)

a noodle board, a kneading trough, a bucket, brooms, ladles, household articles galore. Then I took a look and saw two strapping young men carrying a crib. "What do we need this for?" I asked. So they said, "Don't rack your brains about it. It's all right, it'll come in handy." I realized I was going to be rooked. Take it another way though, what did I stand to lose? I reflected: I'll see what comes of it. A whole town can't go altogether crazy.

II

At night I came where my wife lay, but she wouldn't let me in. "Say, look here, is this what they married us for?" I said. And she said, "My monthly has come." "But yesterday they took you to the ritual bath, and that's afterward, isn't it supposed to be?" "Today isn't yesterday," said she, "and yesterday's not today. You can beat it if you don't like it." In short, I waited.

Not four months later she was in childbed. The townsfolk hid their laughter with their knuckles. But what could I do? She suffered intolerable pains and clawed at the walls. "Gimpel," she cried, "I'm going. Forgive me!" The house filled with women. They were boiling pans of water. The screams rose to the welkin.

The thing to do was to go to the House of Prayer to repeat Psalms, and that was what I did.

The townsfolk liked that, all right. I stood in a corner saying Psalms and prayers, and they shook their heads at me. "Pray, pray!" they told me. "Prayer never made any woman pregnant." One of the congregation put a straw to my mouth and said, "Hay for the cows." There was something to that too, by God!

She gave birth to a boy. Friday at the synagogue the sexton stood up before the Ark, pounded on the reading table, and announced, "The wealthy Reb Gimpel invites the congregation to a feast in honor of the birth of a son." The whole House of Prayer rang with laughter. My face was flaming. But there was nothing I

could do. After all, I *was* the one responsible for the circumcision honors and rituals.

Half the town came running. You couldn't wedge another soul in. Women brought peppered chick-peas, and there was a keg of beer from the tavern. I ate and drank as much as anyone, and they all congratulated me. Then there was a circumcision, and I named the boy after my father, may he rest in peace. When all were gone and I was left with my wife alone, she thrust her head through the bed-curtain and called me to her.

"Gimpel," said she, "why are you silent? Has your ship gone and sunk?"

"What shall I say?" I answered. "A fine thing you've done to me! If my mother had known of it she'd have died a second time."

She said, "Are you crazy, or what?"

"How can you make such a fool," I said, "of one who should be the lord and master?"

"What's the matter with you?" she said. "What have you taken it into your head to imagine?"

I saw that I must speak bluntly and openly. "Do you think this is the way to use an orphan?" I said. "You have borne a bastard."

She answered, "Drive this foolishness out of your head. The child is yours."

"How can he be mine?" I argued. "He was born seventeen weeks after the wedding."

She told me then that he was premature. I said, "Isn't he a little too premature?" She said she had had a grandmother who carried just as short a time and she resembled this grandmother of hers as one drop of water does another. She swore to it with such oaths that you would have believed a peasant at the fair if he had used them. To tell the plain truth, I didn't believe her; but when I talked it over next day with the schoolmaster he told me that the very same thing had happened to Adam and Eve. Two they went up to bed, and four they descended.

"There isn't a woman in the world who is not the granddaughter of Eve," he said.

That was how it was; they argued me

dumb. But then, who really knows how such things are?

I began to forget my sorrow. I loved the child madly, and he loved me too. As soon as he saw me he'd wave his little hands and want me to pick him up, and when he was colicky I was the only one who could pacify him. I bought him a little bone teething ring and a little gilded cap. He was forever catching the evil eye from someone, and then I had to run to get one of those abracadabras for him that would get him out of it. I worked like an ox. You know how expenses go up when there's an infant in the house. I don't want to lie about it; I didn't dislike Elka either, for that matter. She swore at me and cursed, and I couldn't get enough of her. What strength she had! One of her looks could rob you of the power of speech. And her orations! Pitch and sulphur, that's what they were full of, and yet somehow also full of charm. I adored her every word. She gave me bloody wounds though.

In the evening I brought her a white loaf as well as a dark one, and also poppyseed rolls I baked myself. I thieved because of her and swiped everything I could lay hands on: macaroons, raisins, almonds, cakes. I hope I may be forgiven for stealing from the Saturday pots the women left to warm in the baker's oven. I would take out scraps of meat, a chunk of pudding, a chicken leg or head, a piece of tripe, whatever I could nip quickly. She ate and became fat and handsome.

I had to sleep away from home all during the week, at the bakery. On Friday nights when I got home she always made an excuse of some sort. Either she had heartburn, or a stitch in the side, or hiccups, or headaches. You know what women's excuses are. I had a bitter time of it. It was rough. To add to it, this little brother of hers, the bastard, was growing bigger. He'd put lumps on me, and when I wanted to hit back she'd open her mouth and curse so powerfully I saw a green haze floating before my eyes. Ten times a day she threatened to divorce me. Another man in my place would have taken French leave and disappeared. But I'm the type that bears it and says noth-

ing. What's one to do? Shoulders are from God, and burdens too.

One night there was a calamity in the bakery; the oven burst, and we almost had a fire. There was nothing to do but go home, so I went home. Let me, I thought, also taste the joy of sleeping in bed in mid-week. I didn't want to wake the sleeping mite and tiptoed into the house. Coming in, it seemed to me that I heard not the snoring of one but, as it were, a double snore, one a thin enough snore and the other like the snoring of a slaughtered ox. Oh, I didn't like that! I didn't like it at all. I went up to the bed, and things suddenly turned black. Next to Elka lay a man's form. Another in my place would have made an uproar, and enough noise to rouse the whole town, but the thought occurred to me that I might wake the child. A little thing like that—why frighten a little swallow, I thought. All right then, I went back to the bakery and stretched out on a sack of flour and till morning I never shut an eye. I shivered as if I had had malaria. "Enough of being a donkey," I said to myself. "Gimpel isn't going to be a sucker all his life. There's a limit even to the foolishness of a fool like Gimpel."

In the morning I went to the rabbi to get advice, and it made a great commotion in the town. They sent the beadle for Elka right away. She came, carrying the child. And what do you think she did? She denied it, denied everything, bone and stone! "He's out of his head," she said. "I know nothing of dreams or divinations." They yelled at her, warned her, hammered on the table, but she stuck to her guns: it was a false accusation, she said.

The butchers and the horse-traders took her part. One of the lads from the slaughterhouse came by and said to me, "We've got our eye on you, you're a marked man." Meanwhile the child started to bear down and soiled itself. In the rabbinical court there was an Ark of the Covenant, and they couldn't allow that, so they sent Elka away.

I said to the rabbi, "What shall I do?"

"You must divorce her at once," said he.

"And what if she refuses?" I asked.

He said, "You must serve the divorce. That's all you have to do."

I said, "Well, all right, Rabbi. Let me think about it."

"There's nothing to think about," said he. "You mustn't remain under the same roof with her."

"And if I want to see the child?" I asked.

"Let her go, the harlot," said he, "and her brood of bastards with her."

The verdict he gave was that I mustn't even cross her threshold—never again, as long as I should live.

During the day it didn't bother me so much. I thought: It was bound to happen, the abscess had to burst. But at night when I stretched out upon the sacks I felt it all very bitterly. A longing took me, for her and for the child. I wanted to be angry, but that's my misfortune exactly, I don't have it in me to be really angry. In the first place—this was how my thoughts went—there's bound to be a slip sometimes. You can't live without errors. Probably that lad who was with her led her on and gave her presents and what not, and women are often long on hair and short on sense, and so he got around her. And then since she denies it so, maybe I was only seeing things? Hallucinations do happen. You see a figure or a mannikin or something, but when you come up closer it's nothing, there's not a thing there. And if that's so, I'm doing her an injustice. And when I got so far in my thoughts I started to weep. I sobbed so that I wet the flour where I lay. In the morning I went to the rabbi and told him that I had made a mistake. The rabbi wrote on with his quill, and he said that if that were so he would have to reconsider the whole case. Until he had finished I wasn't to go near my wife, but I might send her bread and money by messenger.

III

Nine months passed before all the rabbis could come to an agreement. Letters went back and forth. I hadn't realized that there could be so much erudition about a matter like this.

Meanwhile Elka gave birth to still another child, a girl this time. On the Sabbath I went to the synagogue and invoked a blessing on her. They called me up to the Torah, and I named the child for my mother-in-law—may she rest in peace. The louts and loudmouths of the town who came into the bakery gave me a going over. All Frampol refreshed its spirits because of my trouble and grief. However, I resolved that I would always believe what I was told. What's the good of *not* believing? Today it's your wife you don't believe; tomorrow it's God Himself you won't take stock in.

By an apprentice who was her neighbor I sent daily a corn or a wheat loaf, or a piece of pastry, rolls or bagels, or, when I got the chance, a slab of pudding, a slice of honeycake, or wedding strudel —whatever came my way. The apprentice was a goodhearted lad, and more than once he added something on his own. He had formerly annoyed me a lot, plucking my nose and digging me in the ribs, but when he started to be a visitor to my house he became kind and friendly. "Hey, you, Gimpel," he said to me, "you have a very decent little wife and two fine kids. You don't deserve them."

"But the things people say about her," I said.

"Well, they have long tongues," he said, "and nothing to do with them but babble. Ignore it as you ignore the cold of last winter.

One day the rabbi sent for me and said, "Are you certain, Gimpel, that you were wrong about your wife?"

I said, "I'm certain."

"Why, but look here! You yourself saw it."

"It must have been a shadow," I said.

"The shadow of what?"

"Just one of the beams, I think."

"You can go home then. You owe thanks to the Yanover rabbi. He found an obscure reference in Maimonides that favored you."

I seized the rabbi's hand and kissed it

I wanted to run home immediately. It' no small thing to be separated for so lon a time from wife and child. Then I re flected: I'd better go back to work nov and go home in the evening. I said noth ing to anyone, although as far as my heart was concerned it was like one of the Holy Days. The women teased and twitted me as they did every day, but my thought was: Go on, with your loose talk. The truth is out, like the oil upon the water. Maimonides says it's right, and therefore it is right!

At night, when I had covered the dough to let it rise, I took my share of bread and a little sack of flour and started homeward. The moon was full and the stars were glistening, something to terrify the soul. I hurried onward, and before me darted a long shadow. It was winter, and a fresh snow had fallen. I had a mind to sing, but it was growing late and I didn't want to wake the householders. Then I felt like whistling, but I remembered that you don't whistle at night because it brings the demons out. So I was silent and walked as fast as I could.

Dogs in the Christian yards barked at me when I passed, but I thought: Bark your teeth out! What are you but mere dogs? Whereas I am a man, the husband of a fine wife, the father of promising children.

As I approached the house my heart started to pound as though it were the heart of a criminal. I felt no fear, but my heart went thump! thump! Well, no drawing back. I quietly lifted the latch and went in. Elka was asleep. I looked at the infant's cradle. The shutter was closed, but the moon forced its way through the cracks. I saw the newborn child's face and loved it as soon as I saw it—immediately—each tiny bone.

Then I came nearer to the bed. And what did I see but the apprentice lying there beside Elka. The moon went out all at once. It was utterly black, and I trembled. My teeth chattered. The bread fell from my hands, and my wife waked and said, "Who is that, ah?"

I muttered, "It's me."

"Gimpel?" she asked. "How come you're here? I thought it was forbidden."

"The rabbi said," I answered and shook as with a fever.

"Listen to me, Gimpel," she said, "go out to the shed and see if the goat's all right. It seems she's been sick." I have forgotten to say that we had a goat. When

I heard she was unwell I went into the yard. The nannygoat was a good little creature. I had a nearly human feeling for her.

With hesitant steps I went up to the shed and opened the door. The goat stood there on her four feet. I felt her everywhere, drew her by the horns, examined her udders, and found nothing wrong. She had probably eaten too much bark. "Good night, little goat," I said. "Keep well." And the little beast answered with a "Maa" as though to thank me for the good will.

I went back. The apprentice had vanished.

"Where," I asked, "is the lad?"

"What lad?" my wife answered.

"What do you mean?" I said. "The apprentice. You were sleeping with him."

"The things I have dreamed this night and the night before," she said, "may they come true and lay you low, body and soul! An evil spirit has taken root in you and dazzles your sight." She screamed out, "You hateful creature! You moon calf! You spook! You uncouth man! Get out, or I'll scream all Frampol out of bed!"

Before I could move, her brother sprang out from behind the oven and struck me a blow on the back of the head. I thought he had broken my neck. I felt that something about me was deeply wrong, and I said, "Don't make a scandal. All that's needed now is that people should accuse me of raising spooks and *dybbuks*." [5] For that was what she had meant. "No one will touch bread of my baking."

In short, I somehow calmed her.

"Well," she said, "that's enough. Lie down, and be shattered by wheels."

Next morning I called the apprentice aside. "Listen here, brother!" I said. And so on and so forth. "What do you say?" He stared at me as though I had dropped from the roof or something.

"I swear," he said, "you'd better go to an herb doctor or some healer. I'm afraid you have a screw loose, but I'll hush it up for you." And that's how the thing stood.

5 *dybbuks:* according to legend condemned souls which seek to escape their punishment by entering the bodies of religious persons. (JHP)

To make a long story short, I lived twenty years with my wife. She bore me six children, four daughters and two sons. All kinds of things happened, but I neither saw nor heard. I believed, and that's all. The rabbi recently said to me, "Belief in itself is beneficial. It is written that a good man lives by his faith."

Suddenly my wife took sick. It began with a trifle, a little growth upon the breast. But she evidently was not destined to live long; she had no years. I spent a fortune on her. I have forgotten to say that by this time I had a bakery of my own and in Frampol was considered to be something of a rich man. Daily the healer came, and every witch doctor in the neighborhood was brought. They decided to use leeches, and after that to try cupping. They even called a doctor from Lublin, but it was too late. Before she died she called me to her bed and said, "Forgive me, Gimpel."

I said, "What is there to forgive? You have been a good and faithful wife."

"Woe, Gimpel!" she said. "It was ugly how I deceived you all these years. I want to go clean to my Maker, and so I have to tell you that the children are not yours."

If I had been clouted on the head with a piece of wood it couldn't have bewildered me more.

"Whose are they?" I asked.

"I don't know," she said. "There were a lot . . . but they're not yours." And as she spoke she tossed her head to the side, her eyes turned glassy, and it was all up with Elka. On her whitened lips there remained a smile.

I imagined that, dead as she was, she was saying, "I deceived Gimpel. That was the meaning of my brief life."

IV

One night, when the period of mourning was done, as I lay dreaming on the flour sacks, there came the Spirit of Evil himself and said to me, "Gimpel, why do you sleep?"

I said, "What should I be doing? Eating *kreplach?*" [6]

6 *kreplach:* a pastry containing chopped meat. (JHP)

"The whole world deceives you," he said, "and you ought to deceive the world in your turn."

"How can I deceive all the world?" I asked him.

He answered, "You might accumulate a bucket of urine every day and at night pour it into the dough. Let the sages of Frampol eat filth."

"What about the judgment in the world to come?" I said.

"There is no world to come," he said. "They've sold you a bill of goods and talked you into believing you carried a cat in your belly. What nonsense!"

"Well then," I said, "and is there a God?"

He answered, "There is no God either."

"What," I said, "*is* there, then?"

"A thick mire."

He stood before my eyes with a goatish beard and horn, long-toothed, and with a tail. Hearing such words, I wanted to snatch him by the tail, but I tumbled from the flour sacks and nearly broke a rib. Then it happened that I had to answer the call of nature, and, passing, I saw the risen dough, which seemed to say to me, "Do it" In brief, I let myself be persuaded.

At dawn the apprentice came. We kneaded the bread, scattered caraway seeds on it, and set it to bake. Then the apprentice went away, and I was left sitting in the little trench by the oven on a pile of rags. Well, Gimpel, I thought, you've revenged yourself on them for all the shame they've put on you. Outside the frost glittered, but it was warm beside the oven. The flames heated my face. I bent my head and fell into a doze.

I saw in a dream at once, Elka in her shroud. She called to me, "What have you done, Gimpel?"

I said to her, "It's all your fault," and started to cry.

"You fool!" she said. "You fool! Because I was false is everything false too? I never deceived anyone but myself. I'm paying for it all, Gimpel. They spare you nothing here."

I looked at her face. It was black; I was startled and waked, and remained sitting dumb. I sensed that everything hung in the balance. A false step now and I'd lose Eternal Life. But God gave me His help. I seized the long shovel and took out the loaves, carried them into the yard, and started to dig a hole in the frozen earth.

My apprentice came back as I was doing it. "What are you doing boss?" he said, and grew pale as a corpse.

"I know what I'm doing," I said, and I buried it all before his very eyes.

Then I went home, and took my hoard from its hiding place, and divided it among the children. "I saw your mother tonight," I said. "She's turning black, poor thing.

They were so astounded they couldn't speak a word.

"Be well," I said, "and forget that such a one as Gimpel ever existed." I put on my short coat, a pair of boots, took the bag that held my prayer shawl in one hand, my stock in the other, and kissed the *mezzuzah*.[7] When people saw me in the street they were greatly surprised.

"Where are you going?" they said.

I answered, "Into the world." And so I departed from Frampol.

I wandered over the land, and good people did not neglect me. After many years I became old and white; I heard a great deal, many lies and falsehoods, but the longer I lived the more I understood that there were really no lies. Whatever doesn't really happen is dreamed at night. It happens to one if it doesn't happen to another, tomorrow if not today, or a century hence if not next year. What difference can it make? Often I heard tales of which I said, "Now this is a thing that cannot happen." But before a year had elapsed I heard that it actually had come to pass somewhere.

Going from place to place, eating at strange tables, it often happens that I spin yarns—improbable things that could never have happened—about devils, magicians, windmills, and the like. The children run after me, calling, "Grandfather, tell us a story." Sometimes they ask for particular stories, and I try to please them. A fat young boy once said to me, "Grandfather, it's the same story you told us before." The little rogue, he was right.

So it is with dreams too. It is many years since I left Frampol, but as soon as I shut my eyes I am there again. And whom do you think I see? Elka. She is standing by the washtub, as at our first encounter, but her face is shining and her eyes are as radiant as the eyes of a saint, and she speaks outlandish words to me, strange things. When I wake I have forgotten it all. But while the dream lasts I am comforted. She answers all my queries, and what comes out is that all is right. I weep and implore, "Let me be with you." And she consoles me and tells me to be patient. The time is nearer than it is far. Sometimes she strokes and kisses me and weeps upon my face. When I awaken I feel her lips and taste the salt of her tears.

No doubt the world is entirely an imaginary world, but it is only once removed from the true world. At the door of the hovel where I lie, there stands the plank on which the dead are taken away. The gravedigger Jew has his spade ready. The grave waits and the worms are hungry; the shrouds are prepared—I carry them in my beggar's sack. Another *shnorrer*[8] is waiting to inherit my bed of straw. When the time comes I will go joyfully. Whatever may be there, it will be real, without complication, without ridicule, without deception. God be praised: there even Gimpel cannot be deceived.

[1953]

TRANSLATED BY
SAUL BELLOW

---

7 *mezzuzah:* a piece of parchment inscribed on one side with the texts of Deut. vi. 4–9 and xi. 13–21 and on the other with the name of God, enclosed in a case and attached to a doorpost to ward off evil. (JHP)

8 *shnorrer:* a shameless beggar. (JHP)

QUESTIONS FOR STUDY

1. *Why does Gimpel continue to accept the fantastic stories of the villagers? How does he serve to expose their own foolishness?*

2. *Is Gimpel the fool he seems to be? Where does his wisdom lie? Why does he persist in believing in Elka? What kind of affirmation of life is implicit in his belief?*

3. *Why does Gimpel leave the village? Why does he tell his improbable tales to the children? How does his discovery that "there were really no lies" and that "the world is entirely an imaginary world, but it is only once removed from the true world" confirm and sanction his earlier behavior? Why does he look forward to death?*

4. *What does Singer finally seem to be saying about faith and skepticism?*

5. *Why is the choice of the first person point of view particularly effective in telling Gimpel's story?*

JOHN STEINBECK

The Chrysanthemums

THE HIGH gray-flannel fog of winter closed off the Salinas Valley from the sky and from all the rest of the world. On every side it sat like a lid on the mountains and made of the great valley a closed pot. On the broad, level land floor the gang plows bit deep and left the black earth shining like metal where the shares had cut. On the foothill ranches across the Salinas River, the yellow stubble fields seemed to be bathed in pale cold sunshine, but there was no sunshine in the valley now in December. The thick willow scrub along the river flamed with sharp and positive yellow leaves.

It was a time of quiet and of waiting. The air was cold and tender. A light wind blew up from the southwest so that the farmers were mildly hopeful of a good rain before long; but fog and rain do not go together.

Across the river, on Henry Allen's foothill ranch there was little work to be done, for the hay was cut and stored and the orchards were plowed up to receive the rain deeply when it should come. The cattle on the higher slopes were becoming shaggy and rough-coated.

Elisa Allen, working in her flower garden, looked down across the yard and saw Henry, her husband, talking to two men in business suits. The three of them stood by the tractor shed, each man with one foot on the side of the little Fordson. They smoked cigarettes and studied the machine as they talked.

Elisa watched them for a moment and then went back to her work. She was thirty-five. Her face was lean and strong and her eyes were as clear as water. Her figure looked blocked and heavy in her gardening costume, a man's black hat pulled down over her eyes, clodhopper shoes, a figured print dress almost completely covered by a big corduroy apron with four big pockets to hold the snips, the trowel and scratcher, the seeds and the knife she worked with. She wore heavy leather gloves to protect her hands while she worked.

She was cutting down the old year's chrysanthemum stalks with a pair of short and powerful scissors. She looked down toward the men by the tractor shed now and then. Her face was eager and mature and handsome; even her work with the scissors was over-eager, over-powerful. The chrysanthemum stems seemed too small and easy for her energy.

She brushed a cloud of hair out of her eyes with the back of her glove, and left a smudge of earth on her cheek in doing it. Behind her stood the neat white farm house with red geraniums close-banked around it as high as the windows. It was a hard-swept looking little house, with hard-polished windows, and a clean mud-mat on the front steps.

Elisa cast another glance toward the tractor shed. The strangers were getting into their Ford coupe. She took off a glove and put her strong fingers down into the forest of new green chrysanthemum sprouts that were growing around the old roots. She spread the leaves and looked down among the close-growing stems. No aphids were there, no sow-bugs or snails or cutworms. Her terrier fingers destroyed such pests before they could get started.

Elisa started at the sound of her husband's voice. He had come near quietly, and he leaned over the wire fence that protected her flower garden from cattle and dogs and chickens.

"At it again," he said. "You've got a strong new crop coming."

Elisa straightened her back and pulled

on the gardening glove again. "Yes. They'll be strong this coming year." In her tone and on her face there was a little smugness.

"You've got a gift with things," Henry observed. "Some of those yellow chrysanthemums you had this year were ten inches across. I wish you'd work out in the orchard and raise some apples that big."

Her eyes sharpened. "Maybe I could do it, too. I've a gift with things, all right. My mother had it. She could stick anything in the ground and make it grow. She said it was having planters' hands that knew how to do it."

"Well, it sure works with flowers," he said.

"Henry, who were those men you were talking to?"

"Why, sure, that's what I came to tell you. They were from the Western Meat Company. I sold them those thirty head of three-year-old steers. Got nearly my own price, too."

"Good," she said. "Good for you."

"And I thought," he continued, "I thought how it's Saturday afternoon, and we might go into Salinas for dinner at a restaurant, and then to a picture show—to celebrate, you see."

"Good," she repeated. "Oh, yes. That will be good."

Henry put on his joking tone. "There's fights tonight. How'd you like to go to the fights?"

"Oh, no," she said breathlessly. "No, I wouldn't like fights."

"Just fooling, Elisa. We'll go to a movie. Let's see. It's two now. I'm going to take Scotty and bring down those steers from the hill. It'll take us maybe two hours. We'll go in town about five and have dinner at the Cominos Hotel. Like that?"

"Of course I'll like it. It's good to eat away from home."

"All right, then. I'll go get up a couple of horses."

She said, "I'll have plenty of time to transplant some of these sets, I guess."

She heard her husband calling Scotty down by the barn. And a little later she saw the two men ride up the pale yellow hillside in search of the steers.

There was a little square sandy bed kept for rooting the chrysanthemums. With her trowel she turned the soil over and over, and smoothed it and patted it firm. Then she dug ten parallel trenches to receive the sets. Back at the chrysanthemum bed she pulled out the little crisp shoots, trimmed off the leaves of each one with her scissors and laid it on a small orderly pile.

A squeak of wheels and plod of hoofs came from the road. Elisa looked up. The country road ran along the dense bank of willows and cottonwoods that bordered the river, and up this road came a curious vehicle, curiously drawn. It was an old spring-wagon, with a round canvas top on it like the cover of a prairie schooner. It was drawn by an old bay horse and a little gray-and-white burro. A big stubble-bearded man sat between the cover flaps and drove the crawling team. Underneath the wagon, between the hind wheels, a lean and rangy mongrel dog walked sedately. Words were painted on the canvas, in clumsy, crooked letters. "Pots, pans, knives, sisors, lawn mores, Fixed." Two rows of articles, and the triumphantly definitive "Fixed" below. The black paint had run down in little sharp points beneath each letter.

Elisa, squatting on the ground, watched to see the crazy, loose-jointed wagon pass by. But it didn't pass. It turned into the farm road in front of her house, crooked old wheels skirling and squeaking. The rangy dog darted from between the wheels and ran ahead. Instantly the two ranch shepherds flew out at him. Then all three stopped and with stiff and quivering tails, with taut straight legs, with ambassadorial dignity, they slowly circled, sniffing daintily. The caravan pulled up to Elisa's wire fence and stopped. Now the newcomer dog, feeling out-numbered, lowered his tail and retired under the wagon with raised hackles and bared teeth.

The man on the wagon seat called out, "That's a bad dog in a fight when he gets started."

Elisa laughed. "I see he is. How soon does he generally get started?"

The man caught up her laughter and echoed it heartily. "Sometimes not for weeks and weeks," he said. He climbed stiffly down, over the wheel. The horse and the donkey drooped like unwatered flowers.

Elisa saw that he was a very big man. Although his hair and beard were graying, he did not look old. His worn black suit was wrinkled and spotted with grease. The laughter had disappeared from his face and eyes the moment his laughing voice ceased. His eyes were dark, and they were full of the brooding that gets in the eyes of teamsters and of sailors. The calloused hands he rested on the wire fence were cracked, and every crack was a black line. He took off his battered hat.

"I'm off my general road, ma'am," he said. "Does this dirt road cut over across the river to the Los Angeles highway?"

Elisa stood up and shoved the thick scissors in her apron pocket. "Well, yes, it does, but it winds around and then fords the river. I don't think your team could pull through the sand."

He replied with some asperity, "It might surprise you what them beasts can pull through."

"When they get started?" she asked.

He smiled for a second. "Yes. When they get started."

"Well," said Elisa, "I think you'll save time if you go back to the Salinas road and pick up the highway there."

He drew a big finger down the chicken wire and made it sing. "I ain't in any hurry, ma'am. I go from Seattle to San Diego and back every year. Takes all my time. About six months each way. I aim to follow nice weather."

Elisa took off her gloves and stuffed them in the apron pocket with the scissors. She touched the under edge of her man's hat, searching for fugitive hairs. "That sounds like a nice kind of way to live," she said.

He leaned confidentially over the fence. "Maybe you noticed the writing on my wagon. I mend pots and sharpen knives and scissors. You got any of them things to do?"

"Oh, no," she said quickly. "Nothing like that." Her eyes hardened with resistance.

"Scissors is the worst thing," he ex-plained. "Most people just ruin scissors trying to sharpen 'em, but I know how. I got a special tool. It's a little bobbit kind of thing, and patented. But it sure does the trick."

"No. My scissors are all sharp."

"All right, then. Take a pot," he continued earnestly, "a bent pot, or a pot with a hole. I can make it like new so you don't have to buy no new ones. That's a saving for you."

"No," she said shortly. "I tell you I have nothing like that for you to do."

His face fell to an exaggerated sadness. His voice took on a whining undertone. "I ain't had a thing to do today. Maybe I won't have no supper tonight. You see I'm off my regular road. I know folks on the highway clear from Seattle to San Diego. They save their things for me to sharpen up because they know I do it so good and save them money."

"I'm sorry," Elisa said irritably. "I haven't anything for you to do."

His eyes left her face and fell to searching the ground. They roamed about until they came to the chrysanthemum bed where she had been working. "What's them plants, ma'am?"

The irritation and resistance melted from Elisa's face. "Oh, those are chrysanthemums, giant whites and yellows. I raise them every year, bigger than anybody around here."

"Kind of a long-stemmed flower? Looks like a quick puff of colored smoke?" he asked.

"That's it. What a nice way to describe them."

"They smell kind of nasty till you get used to them," he said.

"It's a good bitter smell," she retorted, "not nasty at all."

He changed his tone quickly. "I like the smell myself."

"I had ten-inch blooms this year," she said.

The man leaned farther over the fence. "Look. I know a lady down the road a piece, has got the nicest garden you ever seen. Got nearly every kind of flower but no chrysanthemums. Last time I was mending a copper-bottom washtub for her (that's a hard job but I do it good), she said to me, 'If you ever run acrost some nice chrysanthemums I wish you'd try to get me a few seeds.' That's what she told me."

Elisa's eyes grew alert and eager. "She couldn't have known much about chrysanthemums. You *can* raise them from seed, but it's much easier to root the little sprouts you see there."

"Oh," he said. "I s'pose I can't take none to her, then."

"Why yes you can," Elisa cried. "I can put some in damp sand, and you can carry them right along with you. They'll take root in the pot if you keep them damp. And then she can transplant them."

"She'd sure like to have some, ma'am. You say they're nice ones?"

"Beautiful," she said. "Oh, beautiful." Her eyes shone. She tore off the battered hat and shook out her dark pretty hair. "I'll put them in a flower pot, and you can take them right with you. Come into the yard."

While the man came through the picket gate Elisa ran excitedly along the geranium-bordered path to the back of the house. And she returned carrying a big red flower pot. The gloves were forgotten now. She kneeled on the ground by the starting bed and dug up the sandy soil with her fingers and scooped it into the bright new flower pot. Then she picked up the little pile of shoots she had prepared. With her strong fingers she pressed them into the sand and tamped around them with her knuckles. The man stood over her. "I'll tell you what to do," she said. "You remember so you can tell the lady."

"Yes, I'll try to remember."

"Well, look. These will take root in about a month. Then she must set them out, about a foot apart in good rich earth like this, see?" She lifted a handful of dark soil for him to look at. "They'll grow fast and tall. Now remember this: In July tell her to cut them down, about eight inches from the ground."

"Before they bloom?" he asked.

"Yes, before they bloom." Her face was tight with eagerness. "They'll grow right up again. About the last of September the buds will start."

She stopped and seemed perplexed.

"It's the budding that takes the most care," she said hesitantly. "I don't know how to tell you." She looked deep into his eyes, searchingly. Her mouth opened a little, and she seemed to be listening. "I'll try to tell you," she said. "Did you ever hear of planting hands?"

"Can't say I have, ma'am."

"Well, I can only tell you what it feels like. It's when you're picking off the buds you don't want. Everything goes right down into your fingertips. You watch your fingers work. They do it themselves. You can feel how it is. They pick and pick the buds. They never make a mistake. They're with the plant. Do you see? Your fingers and the plant. You can feel that, right up your arm. They know. They never make a mistake. You can feel it. When you're like that you can't do anything wrong. Do you see that? Can you understand that?"

She was kneeling on the ground looking up at him. Her breast swelled passionately.

The man's eyes narrowed. He looked away self-consciously. "Maybe I know," he said. "Sometimes in the night in the wagon there——"

Elisa's voice grew husky. She broke in on him, "I've never lived as you do, but I know what you mean. When the night is dark—why, the stars are sharp-pointed, and there's quiet. Why, you rise up and up! Every pointed star gets driven into your body. It's like that. Hot and sharp and—lovely."

Kneeling there, her hand went out toward his legs in the greasy black trousers. Her hesitant fingers almost touched the cloth. Then her hand dropped to the ground. She crouched low like a fawning dog.

He said, "It's nice, just like you say. Only when you don't have no dinner, it ain't."

She stood up then, very straight, and her face was ashamed. She held the flower pot out to him and placed it gently in his arms. "Here. Put it in your wagon, on the seat, where you can watch it. Maybe I can find something for you to do."

At the back of the house she dug in the can pile and found two old and battered aluminum saucepans. She carried them back and gave them to him. "Here, maybe you can fix these."

His manner changed. He became professional. "Good as new I can fix them." At the back of his wagon he set a little anvil, and out of an oily tool box dug a small machine hammer. Elisa came through the gate to watch him while he pounded out the dents in the kettles. His mouth grew sure and knowing. At a difficult part of the work he sucked his underlip.

"You sleep right in the wagon?" Elisa asked.

"Right in the wagon, ma'am. Rain or shine I'm dry as a cow in there."

"It must be nice," she said. "It must be very nice. I wish women could do such things."

"It ain't the right kind of a life for a woman."

Her upper lip raised a little, showing her teeth. "How do you know? How can you tell?" she said.

"I don't know, ma'am," he protested. "Of course I don't know. Now here's your kettles, done. You don't have to buy no new ones."

"How much?"

"Oh, fifty cents'll do. I keep my prices down and my work good. That's why I have all them satisfied customers up and down the highway."

Elisa brought him a fifty-cent piece from the house and dropped it in his hand. "You might be surprised to have a rival some time. I can sharpen scissors, too. And I can beat the dents out of little pots. I could show you what a woman might do."

He put his hammer back in the oily box and shoved the little anvil out of sight. "It would be a lonely life for a woman, ma'am, and a scarey life, too, with animals creeping under the wagon all night." He climbed over the singletree, steadying himself with a hand on the burro's white rump. He settled himself in the seat, picked up the lines. "Thank you kindly, ma'am," he said. "I'll do like you told me; I'll go back and catch the Salinas road."

"Mind," she called, "if you're long in getting there, keep the sand damp."

"Sand, ma'am? . . . Sand? Oh, sure. You mean around the chrysanthemums. Sure I will." He clucked his tongue. The beasts leaned luxuriously into their collars. The mongrel dog took his place between the back wheels. The wagon turned and crawled out the entrance road and back the way it had come, along the river.

Elisa stood in front of her wire fence watching the slow progress of the caravan. Her shoulders were straight, her head thrown back, her eyes half-closed, so that the scene came vaguely into them. Her lips moved silently, forming the words "Good-bye—good-bye." Then she whispered, "That's a bright direction. There's a glowing there." The sound of her whisper startled her. She shook herself free and looked about to see whether anyone had been listening. Only the dogs had heard. They lifted their heads toward her from their sleeping in the dust, and then stretched out their chins and settled asleep again. Elisa turned and ran hurriedly into the house.

In the kitchen she reached behind the stove and felt the water tank. It was full of hot water from the noonday cooking. In the bathroom she tore off her soiled clothes and flung them into the corner. And then she scrubbed herself with a little block of pumice, legs and thighs, loins and chest and arms, until her skin was scratched and red. When she had dried herself she stood in front of a mirror in her bedroom and looked at her body. She tightened her stomach and threw out her chest. She turned and looked over her shoulder at her back.

After a while she began to dress slowly. She put on her newest underclothing and her nicest stockings and the dress which was the symbol of her prettiness. She worked carefully on her hair, penciled her eyebrows and rouged her lips.

Before she was finished she heard the little thunder of hoofs and the shouts of Henry and his helper as they drove the red steers into the corral. She heard the gate bang shut and set herself for Henry's arrival.

His steps sounded on the porch. He

entered the house calling, "Elisa, where are you?"

"In my room dressing. I'm not ready. There's hot water for your bath. Hurry up. It's getting late."

When she heard him splashing in the tub, Elisa laid his dark suit on the bed, and shirt and socks and tie beside it. She stood his polished shoes on the floor beside the bed. Then she went to the porch and sat primly and stiffly down. She looked toward the river road where the willow-line was still yellow with frosted leaves so that under the high gray fog they seemed a thin band of sunshine. This was the only color in the gray afternoon. She sat unmoved for a long time. Her eyes blinked rarely.

Henry came banging out of the door, shoving his tie inside his vest as he came. Elisa stiffened and her face grew tight. Henry stopped short and looked at her. "Why—why, Elisa. You look so nice!"

"Nice? You think I look nice? What do you mean by 'nice'?"

Henry blundered on. "I don't know. I mean you look different, strong and happy."

"I am strong? Yes, strong. What do you mean 'strong'?"

He looked bewildered. "You're playing some kind of a game," he said helplessly. "It's a kind of a play. You look strong enough to break a calf over your knee, happy enough to eat it like a watermelon."

For a second she lost her rigidity. "Henry! Don't talk like that. You didn't know what you said." She grew complete again. "I'm strong," she boasted. "I never knew before how strong."

Henry looked down toward the tractor shed, and when he brought his eyes back to her, they were his own again. "I'll get out the car. You can put on your coat while I'm starting."

Elisa went into the house. She heard him drive to the gate and idle down his motor, and then she took a long time to put on her hat. She pulled it here and pressed it there. When Henry turned the motor off she slipped into her coat and went out.

The little roadster bounced along on the dirt road by the river, raising the birds and driving the rabbits into the brush. Two cranes flapped heavily over the willow-line and dropped into the river-bed.

Far ahead on the road Elisa saw a dark speck. She knew.

She tried not to look as they passed it, but her eyes would not obey. She whispered to herself sadly, "He might have thrown them off the road. That wouldn't have been much trouble, not very much. But he kept the pot," she explained. "He had to keep the pot. That's why he couldn't get them off the road."

The roadster turned a bend and she saw the caravan ahead. She swung full around toward her husband so she could not see the little covered wagon and the mismatched team as the car passed them.

In a moment it was over. The thing was done. She did not look back.

She said loudly, to be heard above the motor, "It will be good, tonight, a good dinner."

"Now you're changed again," Henry complained. He took one hand from the wheel and patted her knee. "I ought to take you in to dinner oftener. It would be good for both of us. We get so heavy out on the ranch."

"Henry," she asked, "could we have wine at dinner?"

"Sure we could. Say! That will be fine."

She was silent for a while; then she said, "Henry, at those prize fights, do the men hurt each other very much?"

"Sometimes a little, not often. Why?"

"Well, I've read how they break noses, and blood runs down their chests. I've read how the fighting gloves get heavy and soggy with blood."

He looked around at her. "What's the matter, Elisa? I didn't know you read things like that." He brought the car to a stop, then turned to the right over the Salinas River bridge.

"Do any women ever go to the fights?" she asked.

"Oh, sure, some. What's the matter, Elisa? Do you want to go? I don't think you'd like it, but I'll take you if you really want to go."

She relaxed limply in the seat. "Oh, no. No. I don't want to go. I'm sure I don't." Her face was turned away from him. "It will be enough if we can have wine. It will be plenty." She turned up her coat collar so he could not see that she was crying weakly—like an old woman.

[1937]

QUESTIONS FOR STUDY

1. *What kind of marital relationship do Elisa Allen and her husband seem to enjoy?*
2. *How does Steinbeck's physical description of the Salinas Valley in December and his description of Elisa herself serve to reveal her character?*
3. *Why are the facts that Elisa is thirty-five and childless important to the story? What is the significance of her skill at gardening and the loving care that she bestows upon her flowers?*
4. *What is awakened or exposed in Elisa during her meeting with the tinker? Why does she respond so strongly to him? How are these newly aroused feelings reflected in the scene in her bedroom which immediately follows?*
5. *What effect does the discovery of the fate of her young plants have upon her? Why does Elisa ask her husband if fighters hurt each other very much? What is the significance of her final statement, "It will be enough if we can have wine. It will be plenty"?*
6. *Does the story manage to avoid sentimentality? How?*

ROBERT LOUIS STEVENSON

Markheim

"YES," SAID the dealer, "our wind-falls are of various kinds. Some customers are ignorant, and then I touch a dividend of my superior knowledge. Some are dishonest," and here he held up the candle, so that the light fell strongly on his visitor, "and in that case," he continued, "I profit by my virtue."

Markheim had but just entered from the daylight streets, and his eyes had not yet grown familiar with the mingled shine and darkness in the shop. At these pointed words, and before the near presence of the flame, he blinked painfully and looked aside.

The dealer chuckled. "You come to me on Christmas Day," he resumed, "when you know that I am alone in my house, put up my shutters, and make a point of refusing business. Well, you will have to pay for that; you will have to pay for my loss of time, when I should be balancing my books; you will have to pay, besides, for a kind of manner that I remark in you to-day very strongly. I am the essence of discretion, and ask no awkward questions; but when a customer cannot look me in the eye, he has to pay for it." The dealer once more chuckled; and then, changing to his usual business voice, though still with a note of irony, "You can give, as usual, a clear account of how you came into the possession of the object?" he continued. "Still your uncle's cabinet? A remarkable collector, sir!"

And the little pale, round-shouldered dealer stood almost on tiptoe, looking over the top of his gold spectacles, and nodding his head with every mark of disbelief. Markheim returned his gaze with one of infinite pity, and a touch of horror.

"This time," said he, "you are in error. I have not come to sell, but to buy. I have no curios to dispose of; my uncle's cabinet is bare to the wainscot; even were it still intact, I have done well on the Stock Exchange, and should more likely add to it than otherwise, and my errand to-day is simplicity itself. I seek a Christmas present for a lady," he continued, waxing more fluent as he struck into the speech he had prepared; "and certainly I owe you every excuse for thus disturbing you upon so small a matter. But the thing was neglected yesterday; I must produce my little compliment at dinner; and, as you very well know, a rich marriage is not a thing to be neglected."

There followed a pause, during which the dealer seemed to weigh this statement incredulously. The ticking of many clocks among the curious lumber of the shop, and the faint rushing of the cabs in a near thoroughfare, filled up the interval of silence.

"Well, sir," said the dealer, "be it so. You are an old customer after all; and if, as you say, you have the chance of a good marriage, far be it from me to be an obstacle.—Here is a nice thing for a lady now," he went on, "this hand glass—fifteenth century, warranted; comes from a good collection, too; but I reserve the name, in the interests of my customer, who was just like yourself, my dear sir, the nephew and sole heir of a remarkable collector."

The dealer, while he thus ran on in his dry and biting voice, had stooped to take the object from its place; and, as he had done so, a shock had passed through Markheim, a start both of hand and foot, a sudden leap of many tumultuous passions to the face. It passed as swiftly as it came, and left no trace beyond a certain trembling of the hand that now received the glass.

"A glass," he said hoarsely, and then paused, and repeated it more clearly. "A glass? For Christmas? Surely not?"

"And why not?" cried the dealer. "Why not a glass?"

Markheim was looking upon him with an indefinable expression. "You ask me why not?" he said. "Why, look here—look in it—look at yourself! Do you like to see it? No! nor I—nor any man."

The little man had jumped back when Markheim had so suddenly confronted him with the mirror; but now, perceiving there was nothing worse on hand, he chuckled. "Your future lady, sir, must be pretty hard-favoured," said he.

"I ask you," said Markheim, "for a Christmas present, and you give me this—this damned reminder of years, and sins and follies—this hand-conscience! Did you mean it? Had you a thought in your mind? Tell me. It will be better for you if you do. Come, tell me about yourself. I hazard a guess now, that you are in secret a very charitable man?"

The dealer looked closely at his companion. It was very odd, Markheim did not appear to be laughing; there was something in his face like an eager sparkle of hope, but nothing of mirth.

"What are you driving at?" the dealer asked.

"Not charitable?" returned the other, gloomily. "Not charitable; not pious; not scrupulous; unloving, unbeloved; a hand to get money, a safe to keep it. Is that all? Dear God, man, is that all?"

"I will tell you what it is," began the dealer, with some sharpness, and then broke off again into a chuckle. "But I see this is a love-match of yours, and you have been drinking the lady's health."

"Ah!" cried Markheim, with a strange curiosity. "Ah, have you been in love? Tell me about that."

"I," cried the dealer. "I in love! I never had the time, nor have I the time to-day for all this nonsense. Will you take the glass?"

"Where is the hurry?" returned Markheim. "It is very pleasant to stand here talking; and life is so short and insecure that I would not hurry away from any pleasure—no, not even from so mild a one as this. We should rather cling, cling to what little we can get, like a man at a cliff's edge. Every second is a cliff, if you think upon it—a cliff a mile high—high enough, if we fall, to dash us out of every feature of humanity. Hence it is best to talk pleasantly. Let us talk of each other; why should we wear this mask? Let us be confidential. Who knows we might become friends?"

"I have just one word to say to you," said the dealer. "Either make your purchase, or walk out of my shop."

"True, true," said Markheim. "Enough fooling. To business. Show me something else."

The dealer stooped once more, this time to replace the glass upon the shelf, his thin blond hair falling over his eyes as he did so. Markheim moved a little nearer, with one hand in the pocket of his great-coat; he drew himself up and filled his lungs; at the same time many different emotions were depicted together on his face—terror, horror, and resolve, fascination and a physical repulsion; and through a haggard lift of his upper lip, his teeth looked out.

"This, perhaps, may suit," observed the dealer; and then, as he began to re-arise, Markheim bounded from behind upon his victim. The long, skewer-like dagger flashed and fell. The dealer struggled like a hen, striking his temple on the shelf, and then tumbled on the floor in a heap.

Time had some score of small voices in that shop, some stately and slow as was becoming to their great age; others garrulous and hurried. All these told out the seconds in an intricate chorus of tickings. Then the passage of a lad's feet, heavily running on the pavement, broke in upon these smaller voices and startled Markheim into the consciousness of his surroundings. He looked about him awfully. The candle stood on the counter, its flame solemnly wagging in a draught; and by that inconsiderable movement, the whole room was filled with noiseless bustle and kept heaving like a sea: the tall shadows nodding, the gross blots of darkness swelling and dwindling as with respiration, the faces of the portraits and the china gods changing and wavering like images in water. The inner door stood ajar, and peered into that leaguer of shadows with a long slit of daylight like a pointing finger.

From these fear-stricken rovings, Markheim's eyes returned to the body of his victim, where it lay both humped and sprawling, incredibly small and strangely meaner than in life. In these poor, miserly clothes, in that ungainly attitude, the dealer lay like so much sawdust. Markheim had feared to see it, and, lo! it was nothing. And yet, as he gazed, this bundle of old clothes and pool of blood began to find eloquent voices. There it must lie; there was none to work the cunning hinges or direct the miracle of locomotion —there it must lie till it was found. Found! ay, and then? Then would this dead flesh lift up a cry that would ring over England, and fill the world with the echoes of pursuit. Ay, dead or not, this was still the enemy. "Time was that when the brains were out," he thought; and the first word struck into his mind. Time, now that the deed was accomplished—time, which had closed for the victim, had become instant and momentous for the slayer.

The thought was yet in his mind, when, first one and then another, with every variety of pace and voice—one deep as the bell from a cathedral turret, another ringing on its treble notes the prelude of a waltz—the clocks began to strike the hour of three in the afternoon.

The sudden outbreak of so many tongues in that dumb chamber staggered him. He began to bestir himself, going to and fro with the candle, beleaguered by moving shadows, and startled to the soul by chance reflections. In many rich mirrors, some of home designs, some from Venice or Amsterdam, he saw his face repeated and repeated, as it were an army of spies; his own eyes met and detected him; and the sound of his own steps, lightly as they fell, vexed the surrounding quiet. And still as he continued to fill his pockets, his mind accused him, with a sickening iteration, of the thousand faults of his design. He should have chosen a more quiet hour; he should have prepared an alibi; he should not have used a knife; he should have been more cautious, and only bound and gagged the dealer, and not killed him; he should have been more bold, and killed the servant also; he should have done all things otherwise; poignant regrets, weary, incessant toiling of the mind to change what was un-changeable, to plan what was now useless, to be the architect of the irrevocable past. Meanwhile, and behind all this activity, brute terrors, like the scurrying of rats in a deserted attic, filled the more remote chambers of his brain with riot; the hand of the constable would fall heavy on his shoulder, and his nerves would jerk like a hooked fish; or he beheld, in galloping defile, the dock, the prison, the gallows, and the black coffin.

Terror of the people in the street sat down before his mind like a besieging army. It was impossible, he thought, but that some rumour of the struggle must have reached their ears and set on edge their curiosity; and now, in all the neighbouring houses, he divined them sitting motionless and with uplifted ear—solitary people, condemned to spend Christmas dwelling alone on memories of the past, and now startlingly recalled from that tender exercise; happy family parties, struck into silence round the table, the mother still with raised finger: every degree and age and humour, but all, by their own hearts, prying and hearkening and weaving the rope that was to hang him. Sometimes it seemed to him he could not move too softly; the clink of the tall Bohemian goblets rang out loudly like a bell; and alarmed by the bigness of the ticking, he was tempted to stop the clocks. And then, again, with a swift transition of his terrors, the very silence of the place appeared a source of peril, and a thing to strike and freeze the passer-by; and he would step more boldly, and bustle aloud among the contents of the shop, and imitate, elaborate bravado, the movements of a busy man at ease in his own house.

But he was now so pulled about by different alarms that, while one portion of his mind was still alert and cunning, another trembled on the brink of lunacy. One hallucination in particular took a strong hold on his credulity. The neighbour hearkening with white face beside his window, the passer-by arrested by a horrible surmise on the pavement—these could at worst suspect, they could not know; through the brick walls and shuttered windows only sounds could penetrate. But here, within the house, was he alone? He knew he was; he had watched the servant set forth sweethearting, in her poor best, "out for the day" written in every ribbon and smile. Yes, he was alone, of course; and yet, in the bulk of empty house above him, he could surely hear a stir of delicate footing—he was surely conscious, inexplicably conscious of some presence. Ay, surely; to every room and corner of the house his imagination followed it; and now it was a faceless thing, and yet had eyes to see with; and again it was a shadow of himself; and yet again behold the image of the dead dealer, re-inspired with cunning and hatred.

At times, with a strong effort, he would glance at the open door which still seemed to repel his eyes. The house was tall, the skylight small and dirty, the day blind with fog; and the light that filtered down to the ground story was exceedingly faint, and showed dimly on the threshold of the shop. And yet, in that strip of doubtful brightness, did there not hang wavering a shadow?

Suddenly, from the street ouside, a very jovial gentleman began to beat with a staff on the shop-door, accompanying his blows with shouts and railleries in which the dealer was continually called upon by name. Markheim, smitten into ice, glanced at the dead man. But no! he lay quite still; he was fled away far beyond ear-shot of these blows and shoutings; he was sunk beneath seas of silence; and his name, which would once have caught his notice above the howling of a storm, had become an empty sound. And presently the jovial gentleman desisted from his knocking and departed.

Here was a broad hint to hurry what remained to be done, to get forth from this accusing neighbourhood, to plunge into a bath of London multitudes, and to reach, on the other side of the day, that haven of safety and apparent innocence—his bed. One visitor had come: at any moment another might follow and be more obstinate. To have done the deed, and yet not to reap the profit would be too abhorrent a failure. The money, that was now Markheim's concern; and as a means to that, the keys.

He glanced over his shoulder at the open door, where the shadow was still lingering and shivering; and with no conscious repugnance of the mind, yet with a tremor of the belly, he drew near the body of his victim. The human character had quite departed. Like a suit half stuffed with bran, the limbs lay scattered, the trunk doubled, on the floor; and yet the thing repelled him. Although so dingy and inconsiderable to the eye, he feared it might have more significance to the touch. He took the body by the shoulders, and turned it on its back. It was strangely light and supple, and the limbs, as if they had been broken, fell into the oddest postures. The face was robbed of all expression; but it was as pale as wax, and shockingly smeared with blood about one temple. That was, for Markheim, the one displeasing circumstance. It carried him back, upon the instant, to a certain fair day in a fishers' village: a grey day, a piping wind, a crowd upon the street, the blare of brasses, the booming of drums, the nasal voice of a ballad-singer; and a boy going to and fro, buried over head in the crowd and divided between interest and fear, until, coming out upon the chief place of concourse, he beheld a booth and a great screen with pictures, dismally de-signed, garishly coloured: Brownrigg with her apprentice; the Mannings with their murdered guest; Weare in the death-grip of Thurtell; and a score besides of famous crimes. The thing was as clear as an illu-sion; he was once again that little boy; he was looking once again, and with the same sense of physical revolt, at these vile pictures; he was still stunned by the thumping of the drums. A bar of that day's music returned upon his memory; and at that, for the first time, a qualm came over him, a breath of nausea, a sudden weakness of the joints, which he must instantly resist and conquer.

He judged it more prudent to confront than to flee from these considerations; looking the more hardily in the dead face, bending his mind to realise the nature and greatness of his crime. So little a while ago that face had moved with every change of sentiment, that pale mouth had spoken, that body had been all on fire with governable energies; and now, and by his act, that piece of life had been arrested, as the horologist, with interjected finger, arrests the beating of the clock. So he reasoned in vain; he could rise to no more remorseful consciousness; the same heart which had shuddered before the painted effigies of crime looked on its reality unmoved. At best, he felt a gleam of pity for one who had been endowed in vain with all those faculties that can make the world a garden of enchantment, one who had never lived and who was now dead. But of penitence, no, not a tremor.

With that, shaking himself clear of these considerations, he found the keys and advanced towards the open door of the shop. Outside, it had begun to rain smartly; and the sound of the shower upon the roof had banished silence. Like some dripping cavern, the chambers of the house were haunted by an incessant echoing, which filled the ear and mingled with the ticking of the clocks. And, as Markheim approached the door, he seemed to hear, in answer to his own cautious tread, the steps of another foot withdrawing up the stair. The shadow still palpitated loosely on the threshold. He threw a ton's weight of resolve upon his muscles, and drew back the door.

The faint, foggy daylight glimmered dimly on the bare floor and stairs; on the bright suit of armour posted, halbert in hand, upon the landing; and on the dark wood-carvings and framed pictures that hung against the yellow panels of the wainscot. So loud was the beating of the rain through all the house that, in Markheim's ears, it began to be distinguished into many different sounds. Footsteps and sighs, the tread of regiments marching in the distance, the chink of money in the counting, and the creaking of doors held stealthily ajar, appeared to mingle with the patter of the drops upon the cupola and the gushing of the water in the pipes. The sense that he was not alone grew upon him to the verge of madness. On every side he was haunted and begirt by presences. He heard them moving in the upper chambers; from the shop, he heard the dead man getting to his legs; and as he began with a great effort to mount the stairs, feet fled quietly before him and followed stealthily behind. If he were but deaf, he thought, how tranquilly he would possess his soul! And then again, and hearkening with ever fresh attention, he blessed himself for that unresting sense which held the outposts and stood a trusty sentinel upon his life. His head turned continually on his neck; his eyes, which seemed starting from their orbits, scouted on every side, and on every side were half rewarded as with the tail of something nameless vanishing. The four-and-twenty steps to the first floor were four-and-twenty agonies.

On that first story, the doors stood ajar, three of them like three ambushes, shaking his nerves like the throats of cannon. He could never again, he felt, be sufficiently immured and fortified from men's observing eyes; he longed to be home, girt in by walls, buried among bedclothes, and invisible to all but God. And at that thought he wondered a little, recollecting tales of other murderers and the fear they were said to entertain of heavenly avengers. It was not so, at least, with him. He feared the laws of nature, lest, in their callous and immutable procedure, they should preserve some damning evidence of his crime. He feared tenfold more, with a slavish, superstitious terror, some scission in the continuity of man's experience, some wilful illegality of nature. He played a game of skill, depending on the rules, calculating consequences from cause; and what if nature, as the defeated tyrant overthrew the chessboard, should break the mould of their succession? The like had befallen Napoleon (so writers said) when the winter changed the time of its appearance. The like might befall Markheim: the solid walls might become transparent and reveal his doings like those of bees in a glass hive; the stout planks might yield under his foot like quicksands and detain him in their clutch; ay, and there were soberer accidents that might destroy him: if, for instance, the house should fall and imprison him beside the body of his victim; or the house next door should fly on fire, and the firemen invade him from all sides. These things he feared; and, in a sense, these things might be called the hands of God reached forth against sin. But about God himself he was at ease; his act was doubtless exceptional, but so were his excuses, which God knew; it was there, and not among men, that he felt sure of justice.

When he had got safe into the drawing-room, and shut the door behind him, he was aware of a respite from alarms. The room was quite dismantled, uncarpeted besides, and strewn with packing-cases and incongruous furniture; several great pier-glasses, in which he beheld himself at various angles, like an actor on a stage; many pictures, framed and unframed, standing, with their faces to the wall; a fine Sheraton sideboard, a cabinet of marquetry, and a great old bed, with tapestry hangings. The windows opened to the floor; but by great good-fortune the lower part of the shutters had been closed, and this concealed him from the neighbours. Here, then, Markheim drew in a packing-case before the cabinet, and began to search among the keys. It was a long business, for there were many; and it was irksome, besides; for, after all, there might be nothing in the cabinet, and time was on the wing. But the closeness of the occupation sobered him. With the tail of his eye he saw the door—even glanced at it from time to time directly, like a besieged commander pleased to verify the good estate of his defences. But in truth he was at peace. The rain falling in the street sounded natural and pleasant. Presently, on the other side, the notes of a piano were wakened to the music of a hymn, and the voices of many children took up the air and words. How stately, how comfortable was the melody! How fresh the youthful voices! Markheim gave ear to it smilingly, as he sorted out the keys; and his mind was thronged with answerable ideas and images; church-going children and the pealing of the high organ; children afield, bathers by the brookside, ramblers on the brambly common, kite-fliers in the windy and cloud-navigated sky; and then, at another cadence of the hymn, back again to church, and the somnolence of summer Sundays, and the high genteel voice of the parson (which he smiled a little to recall) and the painted Jacobean tombs, and the dim lettering of the Ten Commandments in the chancel.

And as he sat thus, at once busy and absent, he was startled to his feet. A flash of ice, a flash of fire, a bursting gush of blood, went over him, and then he stood transfixed and thrilling. A step mounted the stair slowly and steadily, and presently a hand was laid upon the knob, and the lock clicked, and the door opened.

Fear held Markheim in a vice. What to expect he knew not, whether the dead man walking, or the official ministers of human justice, or some chance witness blindly stumbling in to consign him to the gallows. But when a face was thrust into the aperture, glanced round the room, looked at him, nodded and smiled as if in friendly recognition, and then withdrew again, and the door closed behind it, his fear broke loose from his control in a hoarse cry. At the sound of this the visitant returned.

"Did you call me?" he asked, pleasantly, and with that he entered the room and closed the door behind him.

Markheim stood and gazed at him with all his eyes. Perhaps there was a film upon his sight, but the outlines of the newcomer seemed to change and waver like those of the idols in the wavering candle-light of the shop; and at times he thought he knew him; and at times he thought he bore a likeness to himself; and always, like a lump of living terror, there lay in his bosom the conviction that this thing was not of the earth and not of God.

And yet the creature had a strange air of the commonplace, as he stood looking on Markheim with a smile; and when he added: "You are looking for the money, I believe?" it was in the tones of every-day politeness.

Markheim made no answer.

"I should warn you," resumed the other, "that the maid has left her sweetheart earlier than usual and will soon be here. If Mr. Markheim be found in this house, I need not describe to him the consequences."

"You know me?" cried the murderer.

The visitor smiled. "You have long

been a favourite of mine," he said; "and I have long observed and often sought to help you."

"What are you?" cried Markheim: "the devil?"

"What I may be," returned the other, "cannot affect the service I propose to render you."

"It can," cried Markheim; "it does! Be helped by you? No, never; not by you! You do not know me yet; thank God, you do not know me!"

"I know you," replied the visitant, with a sort of kind severity or rather firmness. "I know you to the soul."

"Know me!" cried Markheim. "Who can do so? My life is but a travesty and slander on myself. I have lived to belie my nature. All men do; all men are better than this disguise that grows about and stifles them. You see each dragged away by life, like one whom bravos have seized and muffled in a cloak. If they had their own control—if you could see their faces, they would be altogether different, they would shine out for heroes and saints! I am worse than most; my self is more overlaid; my excuse is known to me and God. But, had I the time, I could disclose myself."

"To me?" inquired the visitant.

"To you before all," returned the murderer. "I supposed you were intelligent. I thought—since you exist—you would prove a reader of the heart. And yet you would propose to judge me by my acts! Think of it; my acts; I was born and I have lived in a land of giants; giants have dragged me by the wrists since I was born out of my mother—the giants of circumstance. And you would judge me by my acts! But can you not look within? Can you not understand that evil is hateful to me? Can you not see within me the clear writing of conscience, never blurred by any wilful sophistry, although too often disregarded? Can you not read me for a thing that surely must be common as humanity—the unwilling sinner?"

"All this is very feelingly expressed," was the reply, "but it regards me not. These points of consistency are beyond my province, and I care not in the least by what compulsion you may have been dragged away, so as you are but carried in the right direction. But time flies; the servant delays, looking in the faces of the crowd and at the pictures on the hoardings, but still she keeps moving nearer; and remember, it is as if the gallows itself was striding towards you through the Christmas streets! Shall I help you; I, who know all? Shall I tell you where to find the money?"

"For what price?" asked Markheim.

"I offer you the service for a Christmas gift," returned the other.

Markheim could not refrain from smiling with a kind of bitter triumph. "No," said he, "I will take nothing at your hands; if I were dying of thirst, and it was your hand that put the pitcher to my lips, I should find the courage to refuse. It may be credulous, but I will do nothing to commit myself to evil."

"I have no objection to a death-bed repentance," observed the visitant.

"Because you disbelieve their efficacy!" Markheim cried.

"I do not say so," returned the other; "but I look on these things from a different side, and when the life is done my interest falls. The man has lived to serve me, to spread black looks under colour of religion, or to sow tares in the wheatfield, as you do, in a course of weak compliance with desire. Now that he draws so near to his deliverance, he can add but one act of service—to repent, to die smiling, and thus to build up in confidence and hope the more timorous of my surviving followers. I am not so hard a master. Try me. Accept my help. Please yourself in life as you have done hitherto; please yourself more amply; spread your elbows at the board; and when the night begins to fall and the curtains to be drawn, I tell you, for your greater comfort, that you will find it even easy to compound your quarrel with your conscience, and to make a truckling peace with God. I came but now from such a death-bed, and the room was full of sincere mourners, listening to the man's last words: and when I looked into that face, which had been set as a flint against mercy, I found it smiling with hope."

"And do you, then, suppose me such a

creature?" asked Markheim. "Do you think I have no more generous aspirations than to sin, and sin, and sin, and, at last, sneak into heaven? My heart rises at the thought. Is this, then, your experience of mankind? or is it because you find me with red hands that you presume such baseness? and is this crime of murder indeed so impious as to dry up the very springs of good?"

"Murder is to me no special category," replied the other. "All sins are murder, even as all life is war. I behold your race, like starving mariners on a raft, plucking crusts out of the hands of famine and feeding on each other's lives. I follow sins beyond the moment of their acting; I find in all that the last consequence is death; and to my eyes, the pretty maid who thwarts her mother with such taking graces on a question of a ball, drips no less visibly with human gore than such a murderer as yourself. Do I say that I follow sins? I follow virtues also; they differ not by the thickness of a nail, they are both scythes for the reaping angel of Death. Evil, for which I live, consists not in action but in character. The bad man is dear to me; not the bad act, whose fruits, if we would follow them far enough down the hurtling cataract of the ages, might yet be found more blessed than those of the rarest virtues. And it is not because you have killed a dealer, but because you are Markheim, that I offered to forward your escape."

"I will lay my heart open to you," answered Markheim. "This crime on which you find me is my last. On my way to it I have learned many lessons; itself is a lesson, a momentous lesson. Hitherto I have been driven with revolt to what I would not; I was a bond-slave to poverty, driven and scourged. There are robust virtues that can stand in these temptations; mine was not so: I had a thirst of pleasure. But to-day, and out of this deed, I pluck both warning and riches—both the power and a fresh resolve to be myself. I become in all things a free actor in the world; I begin to see myself all changed, these hands the agents of good, this heart at peace. Something comes over me out of the past; something of what I have dreamed on Sabbath evenings to the sound of the church organ, of what I forecast when I shed tears over noble books, or talked, an innocent child, with my mother. There lies my life; I have wandered a few years, but now I see once more my city of destination."

"You are to use this money on the Stock Exchange, I think?" remarked the visitor; "and there, if I mistake not, you have already lost some thousands?"

"Ah," said Markheim, "but this time I have a sure thing."

"This time, again, you will lose," replied the visitor quietly.

"Ah, but I keep back the half!" cried Markheim.

"That also you will lose," said the other.

The sweat started upon Markheim's brow. "Well, then, what matter?" he exclaimed. "Say it be lost, say I am plunged again in poverty, shall one part of me, and that the worst, continue until the end to over-ride the better? Evil and good run strong in me, haling me both ways. I do not love the one thing, I love all. I can conceive great deeds, renunciations, martyrdoms; and though I be fallen to such a crime as murder, pity is no stranger to my thoughts. I pity the poor; who knows their trials better than myself? I pity and help them; I prize love, I love honest laughter; there is no good thing nor true thing on earth but I love it from my heart. And are my vices only to direct my life, and my virtues to lie without effect, like some passive lumber of the mind? Not so; good, also, is a spring of acts."

But the visitant raised his finger. "For six-and-thirty years that you have been in the world," said he, "through many changes of fortune and varieties of humour, I have watched you steadily fall. Fifteen years ago you would have started at a theft. Three years back you would have blenched at the name of murder. Is there any crime, is there any cruelty or meanness, from which you still recoil?— five years from now I shall detect you in the fact! Downward, downward, lies your way; nor can anything but death avail to stop you."

"It is true," Markheim said huskily, "I

have in some degree complied with evil. But it is so with all: the very saints, in the mere exercise of living, grow less dainty and take on the tone of their surroundings."

"I will propound to you one simple question," said the other; "and as you answer, I shall read to you your moral horoscope. You have grown in many things more lax; possibly you do right to be so; and at any account, it is the same with all men. But granting that, are you in any one particular, however trifling, more difficult to please with your own conduct, or do you go in all things with a looser rein?"

"In any one?" repeated Markheim, with an anguish of consideration. "No," he added, with despair, "in none! I have gone down in all."

"Then," said the visitor, "content yourself with what you are, for you will never change; and the words of your part on this stage are irrevocably written down."

Markheim stood for a long while silent, and indeed it was the visitor who first broke the silence. "That being so," he said, "shall I show you the money?"

"And grace?" cried Markheim.

"Have you not tried it?" returned the other. "Two or three years ago, did I not see you on the platform of revival meetings, and was not your voice the loudest in the hymn?"

"It is true," said Markheim; "and I see clearly what remains for me by way of duty. I thank you for these lessons from my soul; my eyes are opened, and I behold myself at last for what I am."

At this moment, the sharp note of the doorbell rang through the house; and the visitant, as though this were some concerted signal for which he had been waiting, changed at once in his demeanour. "The maid!" he cried. "She has returned, as I forewarned you, and there is now before you one more difficult passage. Her master, you must say, is ill; you must let her in, with an assured but rather serious countenance—no smiles, no over-acting, and I promise you success! Once the girl within, and the door closed, the same dex-

terity that has already rid you of the dealer will relieve you of this last danger in your path. Thenceforward you have the whole evening—the whole night, if needful—to ransack the treasures of the house and to make good your safety. This is help that comes to you with the mask of danger. Up!" he cried: "up, friend; your life hangs trembling in the scales: up, and act!"

Markheim steadily regarded his counsellor. "If I be condemned to evil acts," he said, "there is still one door of freedom open—I can cease from action. If my life be an ill thing, I can lay it down. Though I be, as you say truly, at the beck of every small temptation, I can yet, by one decisive gesture, place myself beyond the reach of all. My love of good is damned to barrennness; it may, and let it be! But I have still my hatred of evil; and from that, to your galling disappointment, you shall see that I can draw both energy and courage."

The features of the visitor began to undergo a wonderful and lovely change: they brightened and softened with a tender triumph; and, even as they brightened, faded and dislimned. But Markheim did not pause to watch or understand the transformation. He opened the door and went down-stairs very slowly, thinking to himself. His past went soberly before him; he beheld it as it was, ugly and strenuous like a dream, random as chance-medley—a scene of defeat. Life, as he thus reviewed it, tempted him no longer; but on the further side he perceived a quiet haven for his bark. He paused in the passage, and looked into the shop, where the candle still burned by the dead body. It was strangely silent. Thoughts of the dealer swarmed into his mind, as he stood gazing. And then the bell once more broke out into impatient clamour.

He confronted the maid upon the threshold with something like a smile.

"You had better go for the police," said he: "I have killed your master."

[1885]

QUESTIONS FOR STUDY

1. *Why does Markheim react so strongly to the mirrors in the pawn-broker's shop?*
2. *How does Markheim initially justify to himself his act of murder? Why is it appropriate that the victim should be a pawnbroker and that the deed should take place in his shop?*
3. *Who (or what) is the stranger? What is significant in the time and place of the stranger's appearance and in the fact that he resembles Markheim himself?*
4. *What does Markheim learn from his dialogue with the stranger? What decision does it lead him to? Is his change of heart convincing?*
5. *What kind of imagery occurs most frequently in the story's descriptive passages? What functions does it serve?*
6. *Is the chosen point of view an effective one? Why?*

PETER TAYLOR

Miss Leonora When Last Seen

I

HERE in Thomasville we are all concerned over the whereabouts of Miss Leonora Logan. She has been missing for two weeks, and though a half dozen postcards have been received from her, stating that she is in good health and that no anxiety should be felt for her safety, still the whole town can talk of nothing else. She was last seen in Thomasville heading south on Logan Lane, which is the narrow little street that runs alongside her family property. At four-thirty on Wednesday afternoon—Wednesday before last, that is to say—she turned out of the dirt driveway that comes down from her house and drove south on the lane toward its intersection with the bypass of the Memphis-Chattanooga highway. She has not been seen since. Officially, she is away from home on a little trip. Unofficially, in the minds of the townspeople, she is a missing person, and because of events leading up to her departure none of us will rest easy until we know that the old lady is safe at home again.

Miss Leonora's half dozen postcards have come to us from points in as many states: Alabama, Georgia, North Carolina, West Virginia, Kentucky—in that order. It is considered a fair guess that her next card will come from Missouri or Arkansas, and that the one after that will be from Mississippi or Louisiana. She seems to be orbiting her native state of Tennessee. But, on the other hand, there is no proof that she has not crossed the state, back and forth, a number of times during the past two weeks. She is quite an old lady, and is driving a 1942 Dodge convertible. Anyone traveling in the region indicated should watch out for two

characteristics of her driving. First, she hates to be overtaken and passed by other vehicles—especially by trucks. The threat of such is apt to make her bear down on the accelerator and try to outdistance the would-be passer. Or, if passed, she can be counted on to try to overtake and pass the offender at first chance. The second characteristic is: when driving after dark, she invariably refuses to dim her lights unless an approaching car has dimmed its own while at least five hundred feet away. She is a good judge of distances, and she is not herself blinded by bright lights on the highway. And one ought to add that, out of long habit and for reasons best known to herself, Miss Leonora nearly always drives by night.

Some description will be due, presently, of this lady's person and of how she will be dressed while traveling. But that had better wait a while. It might seem prejudicial and even misleading with reference to her soundness of mind. And any question of that sort, no matter what the rest of the world may think, has no bearing upon the general consternation that her going away has created here.

Wherever Miss Leonora Logan is today, she knows in her heart that in the legal action recently taken against her in Thomasville there was no malice directed toward her personally. She knows this, and would say so. At this very moment she may be telling some new-found friend the history of the case—because I happen to know that when she is away from home she talks to people about herself and her forebears as she would never do to anyone here. And chances are she is giving a completely unbiased version of what has happened, since that is her way.

The cause of all our present tribulation is this: The Logan property, which Miss

Leonora inherited from one of her paternal great-uncles and which normally upon her death would have gone to distant relatives of hers in Chicago, has been chosen as the site for our county's new consolidated high school. A year and a half ago, Miss Leonora was offered a fair price for the three-acre tract and the old house, and she refused it. This summer, condemnation proceedings were begun, and two weeks ago the county court granted the writ. This will seem to you a bad thing for the town to have done, especially in view of the fact that Miss Leonora has given long years of service to our school system. She retired ten years ago after teaching for twenty-five years in the old high school. To be sure, four of us who are known hereabouts as Miss Leonora Logan's favorites among the male citizenry refused to have any part in the action. Two of us even preferred to resign from the school board. But still, times do change, and the interests of one individual cannot be allowed to hinder the progress of a whole community. Miss Leonora understands that. And she knows that her going away can only delay matters for a few weeks at most. Nevertheless, she is making it look very bad for Thomasville, and we want Miss Leonora to come home.

The kind of jaunt that she has gone off on isn't anything new for the old lady. During the ten years since her retirement she has been setting out on similar excursions rather consistently every month or so, and never, I believe, with a specific itinerary or destination in mind. Until she went away this time, people had ceased to bother themselves with the question of her whereabouts while she was gone or to be concerned about any harm that might come to her. We have been more inclined to think of the practical value her trips have for us. In the past, you see, she was never away for more than a week or ten days, and on her return she would gladly give anyone a full and accurate account of places visited and of the condition of roads traveled. It has, in fact, become the custom when you are planning an automobile trip to address yourself to Miss Leonora on the public

square one day and ask her advice on the best route to take. She is our authority not only on the main highways north, south, east, and west of here, in a radius of six or eight hundred miles, but even on the secondary and unimproved roads in places as remote as Brown County, Indiana, and the Outer Banks of North Carolina. Her advice is often very detailed, and will include warnings against "single-lane bridges" or "soft shoulders" or even "cops patrolling in unmarked cars."

It is only the facts she gives you, though. She doesn't express appreciation for the beauty of the countryside or her opinion of the character of towns she passes through. The most she is likely to say is that such-and-such a road is "regarded" as the scenic route, or that a certain town has a "well-worked-out traffic system." No one can doubt that while driving, Miss Leonora keeps her eyes and mind on the road. And that may be the reason why we have never worried about her. But one asks oneself, What pleasure can she ever have derived from these excursions? She declares that she hates the actual driving. And when giving advice on the roads somewhere she will always say that it is a dull and tedious trip and that the traveler will wish himself home in Thomasville a thousand times before he gets to wherever he is going.

Miss Leonora's motivation for taking these trips was always, until the present instance, something that it seemed pointless even to speculate on. It just seemed that the mood came on her and she was off and away. But if anything happens to her now, all the world will blame *us* and say we *sent* her on this journey, sent her out alone and possibly in a dangerous frame of mind. In particular, the blame will fall on the four timid male citizens who were the last to see her in Thomasville (for I do not honestly believe we will ever see her alive here again) and who, as old friends and former pupils of hers at the high school, ought to have prevented her going away. As a matter of fact, I am the one who opened the car door for the old lady that afternoon and politely assisted her into the driver's seat

—and without even saying I thought it unwise of her to go. I *thought* it unwise, but at the moment it was as if I were still her favorite pupil twenty years before, and as if I feared she might reprove me for any small failure of courtesy like not opening the car door.

That's how the old lady is—or was. Whatever your first relation to her might have been, she would never allow it to change, and some people even say that that is why she discourages us so about the trips we plan. She cannot bear to think of us away from Thomasville. She thinks this is where all of us belong. I remember one day at school when some boy said to her that he wished he lived in a place like Memphis or Chattanooga. She gave him the look she usually reserved for the people she caught cheating. I was seated in the first row of the class that day, and I saw the angry patches of red appear on her broad, flat cheeks and on her forehead. She paused a moment to rearrange the combs in her hair and to give the stern yank to her corset that was a sure sign she was awfully mad. (We used to say that, with her spare figure, she only wore a corset for the sake of that expressive gesture.) The class was silent, waiting. Miss Leonora looked out the window for a moment, squinting up her eyes as if she could actually make out the Memphis or even the Chattanooga skyline on the horizon. Then, turning back to the unfortunate boy, she said, grinding out her words to him through clenched teeth, "I wish I could *throw* you there!"

But it is ten years now since Miss Leonora retired, and, strange as it may sound, the fact of her having once taught in our school system was never introduced into the deliberations of the school board last spring—their deliberations upon whether or not they ought to sue for condemnation of the Logan home place. No doubt it was right that they didn't let this influence their decision. But what really seems to have happened is that nobody even recalled that the old lady had once been a teacher—or nobody but a very few, who did not want to remind the others.

What they remembered, to the exclu-sion of everything else, and what they always remember is that Miss Leonora is the last of the Logan family in Thomasville, a family that for a hundred years and more did all it could to impede the growth and progress of our town. It was a Logan, for instance, who kept the railroad from coming through town; it was another Logan who prevented the cotton mill and the snuff factory from locating here. They even kept us from getting the county seat moved here, until after the Civil War, when finally it became clear that nobody was ever going to buy lots up at Logan City, where they had put the first court-house. Their one idea was always to keep the town unspoiled, unspoiled by rail-roads or factories or even county politics. Perhaps they should not be blamed for wanting to keep the town unspoiled. Yet I am not quite sure about that. It is a question that even Miss Leonora doesn't feel sure about. Otherwise, why does she always go into that question with the people she meets away from home?

I must tell you about the kind of lodg-ing Miss Leonora takes when she stops for rest, and about the kind of people she finds to talk to. She wouldn't talk to you or me, and she wouldn't put up at a hotel like mine, here on the square, or even at a first-class motel like one of those out on the Memphis-Chattanooga bypass. I have asked her very direct questions about this, pleading a professional interest, and I have filled in with other material fur-nished by her friends of the road who have from time to time stopped in here at my place.

On a pretty autumn day like today, she will have picked a farmhouse that has one of those little home-lettered signs out by the mailbox saying "Clean Rooms for Tourists—Modern Conveniences." (She will, that is, unless she has changed her ways and taken to a different life, which is the possibility that I do not like to think of.) She stops only at places that are more or less in that category—old-fashioned tourist homes run by retired farm couples or, if the place is in town, by two old-maid sisters. Such an estab-lishment usually takes its name from whatever kind of trees happen to grow in the yard—Maple Lawn or Elmwood or

The Oaks. Or when there is a boxwood plant, it will be called Boxwood Manor. If the place is in the country, like the one today, it may be called Oak Crest.

You can just imagine how modern the modern conveniences at Oak Crest are. But it is cheap, which is a consideration for Miss Leonora. And the proprietors are probably good listeners, which is another consideration. She generally stops in the daytime, but since even in the daytime she can't sleep for long, she is apt to be found helping out with the chores. Underneath the Oak Crest "Clean Rooms for Tourists" sign there may be one that says "Sterile Day Old Eggs" or, during the present season, "Delicious Apples and Ripe Tomatoes." It wouldn't surprise me if you found Miss Leonora today out by the roadside assisting with the sale of Oak Crest's garden produce. And if that's the case she is happy in the knowledge that any passer-by will mistake her for the proprietress's mother or old-maid sister, and never suppose she is a paying guest. In her carefully got-up costume she sits there talking to her new friend. Or else she is in the house or in the chicken yard, talking away while she helps out with the chores . . . It is Miss Leonora's way of killing time—killing time until night falls and she can take to the road again.

Miss Leonora is an intellectual woman, and at the same time she is an extremely practical and simple kind of person. This makes it hard for any two people to agree on what she is really like. It is hard even for those of us who were her favorites when we went to school to her. For, in the end, we didn't really know her any better than anybody else did. Sometimes she would have one of us up to her house for coffee and cookies on a winter afternoon, but it was hardly a social occasion. We went up there strictly as her students. We never saw any of the house except the little front room that she called her "office" and that was furnished with a roll-top desk, oak bookcases, and three or four of the hardest chairs you ever sat in. It looked more like a schoolroom than her own classroom did, over at the high school. While you sat drinking coffee with her, she was still your English teacher or your history teacher or your Latin teacher, whichever she happened to be at the time, and you were supposed to make conversation with her about *Silas Marner* or Tom Paine or Cicero. If it was a good session and you had shown a little enthusiasm, then she would talk to you some about your future and say you ought to begin thinking about college—because she was always going to turn her favorites into professional men. That was how she was going to populate the town with the sort of people she thought it ought to have. She never got but one of us to college, however, and he came back home as a certified druggist instead of the doctor she had wanted him to be. (Our doctors are always men who have moved in here from somewhere else, and our lawyers are people Miss Leonora wouldn't pay any attention to when they were in school.) . . . I used to love to hear Miss Leonora talk, and I went along with her and did pretty well till toward the end of my last year, when I decided that college wasn't for me. I ought to have gone to college, and I had no better reason for deciding against it than any of the others did. It was just that during all the years when Miss Leonora was talking to you about making something of yourself and making Thomasville a more civilized place to live in, you were hearing at home and everywhere else about what the Logans had done to the town and how they held themselves above everybody else. I got to feeling ashamed of being known as her protégé.

As I said, Miss Leonora is an intellectual woman. She seldom comes out of the post office without a book under her arm that she has specially ordered or that has come to her from one of the national book clubs she belongs to; and she also reads all the cheapest kind of trash that's to be had at the drugstore. She is just a natural-born reader, and enjoys reading the way other people enjoy eating or sleeping. It used to be that she would bedevil all the preachers we got here, trying to talk theology with them, and worry the life out of the lawyers with talk about Hamilton and Jefferson and her theories about men like Henry Clay and John Marshall. But about the time she quit teaching she gave up all that, too.

Aside from the drugstore trash, nobody knows what she reads any more, though probably it is the same as always. We sometimes doubt that she knows herself what she reads nowadays. Her reading seems to mean no more to her than her driving about the country does, and one wonders why she goes on with it, and what she gets out of it. Every night, the light in her office burns almost all night, and when she comes out of the post office with a new book, she has the wrappings off before she is halfway across the square and is turning the pages and reading away—a mile a minute, so it seems—as she strolls through the square and then heads up High Street toward Logana, which is what the Logans have always called their old house. If someone speaks to her, she pretends not to hear the first time. If it is important, if you want some information about the roads somewhere, you have to call her name a second time. The first sign that she is going to give you her attention comes when she begins moving her lips, hurriedly finishing off a page or a paragraph. Then she slams the book closed, as though she is through with it for all time, and before you can phrase your question she begins asking you how you and all your family are. Nobody can give a warmer greeting and make you feel he is gladder to see you than she can. She stands there beating the new book against her thigh, as though the book were some worthless object that she would just as soon throw away, and when she has asked you about yourself and your family she is ready then to talk about any subject under the sun—anything, I ought to add, except herself. If she makes a reference to the book in her hand, it is only to comment on the binding or the print or the quality of the paper. Or she may say that the price of books has gotten all out of bounds and that the postal rate for books is too high. It's always something that any field hand could understand and is a far cry from the way she used to talk about books when we were in school.

I am reminded of one day six or eight years ago when I saw Miss Leonora stopped on the square by an old colored man named Hominy Atkinson. Or his name may really be Harmony Atkinson. I once asked him which it was, and at first he merely grinned and shrugged his shoulders. But then he said thoughtfully, as though it hadn't ever occurred to him before, "Some does call me the one, I s'pose, and some the other." He is a dirty old ignoramus, and the other Negroes say that in the summertime he has his own private swarm of flies that follows him around. His flies were with him that day when he stopped Miss Leonora. He was in his wagon, the way you always see him, and he managed to block the old lady's path when she stepped down off the curb and began to cross the street in front of the post office and had cut diagonally across the courthouse lawn. It was the street over there on the other side of the square that she was about to cross. I was standing nearby with a group of men, under the willow oak trees beside the goldfish pool. Twice before Miss Leonora looked up, Hominy Atkinson lifted a knobby hand to shoo the flies away from his head. In the wagon he was seated on a squat split-bottom chair; and on another chair beside him was his little son Albert. Albert was eight or nine years old at the the time, a plump little fellow dressed up in an old-fashioned Buster Brown outfit as tidy and clean as his daddy's rags were dirty.

This Albert is the son of Hominy and the young wife that Hominy took after he was already an old man. The three of them live on a worn-out piece of land three or four miles from town. Albert is a half-grown boy now, and there is nothing very remarkable about him except that they say he still goes to school more regularly than some of the other colored children do. But when he was a little fellow his daddy and mama spoiled and pampered him till, sitting up there in the wagon that day, he had the look of a fat little priss. The fact is, from the time he could sit up in a chair Hominy used never to go anywhere without him—he was so proud of the little pickaninny, and he was so mortally afraid something might happen to him when he was out of his sight. Somebody once asked Hominy why he didn't leave the child home with his mama, and Hominy replied that her hands were kept busy just washing and ironing and sewing for the boy. "It's no easy matter to raise up a clean child," he pronounced. Somebody else asked Hominy one time if he thought it right to take the boy to the square on First Monday, where he would be exposed to some pretty rough talk, or to the fairgrounds during Fair Week. Hominy replied, "What ain't fittin' for him to hear ain't fittin' for me." And it was true that you seldom saw Hominy on that corner of the square where the Negro men congregated or in the stable yard at the fairgrounds.

Before Miss Leonora looked up at Hominy that morning, he sat with his old rag of a hat in his lap, smiling down at her. Finally, she slammed her book shut and lifted her eyes. But Hominy didn't try to ask his question until she had satisfied herself that he, his young wife, and Albert there beside him were in good health, and several other of his relatives whose names she knew. Then he asked it.

"What does you need today, Miss Leonora?" he said. "Me, *I* needs a dollar bill."

She replied without hesitating, "I don't need anything I'd pay *you* a dollar for, Hominy." Hominy didn't bat an eye, only sat there gazing down at her while she spoke. "I have a full herd of your kind up at Logana, Hominy, who'll fetch and go for me without any dollar bill. You know that."

She was referring to the Negro families who live in the outbuildings up at her place. People say that some of them live right in the house with her, but when I used to go up there as a boy she kept them all out of sight. There was not even a sound of them on the place. She didn't even let her cook bring in the coffee things, and it gave you the queer feeling that either she was protecting you from them or them from you.

"What do you think you need a dollar for, Hominy?" she asked presently.

"I needs to buy the boy a book," he said.

"What book?" It was summertime, and she knew the boy wouldn't be in school.

"Why, most any book," said Hominy. "I jist can't seem to keep him in reading."

Miss Leonora peered around Hominy at Albert, who sat looking down at his own fat little washed-up hands, as if he might be ashamed of his daddy's begging. Then Miss Leonora glanced down at the book she had got in the mail. "Here, give him this," she said, handing the brand-new book up to that old tatterdemalion. It was as if she agreed with the old ignoramus that it didn't matter what kind of book the boy got so long as it was a book.

And now Albert himself couldn't resist raising his eyes to see the book that was coming his way. He gave Miss Leonora a big smile, showing a mouthful of teeth as white as his starched shirt collar. "Miss Leonora, you oughtn't to do—" he began in an airy little voice.

But his daddy put a stop to it. "Hush your mouth, honey. Miss Leonora knows what she's doing. Don't worry about that none." He handed the book over to Albert, hardly looking at it himself. Those of us over by the goldfish pool were never able to make out what the book was.

"I certainly thank you, Miss Leonora," Albert piped.

And Hominy said solemnly, "Yes'm, we are much obliged to you."

"Then move this conveyance of yours and let me pass," said Miss Leonora.

Hominy flipped the reins sharply on the rump of his mule and said, "Giddap, Bridesmaid." The old mule flattened its ears back on its head and pulled away with an angry jerk.

But even when the wagon was out of her way Miss Leonora continued to stand there for a minute or so, watching the receding figure of Albert perched on his chair in the wagon bed and bent over his book examining it the way an ordinary child would have examined a new toy. As long as she stood there the old lady kept her eyes on the little black boy. And before she finally set out across the street, we heard her cry aloud and almost as if for our benefit, "It may be . . . It may be . . . I suppose, yes, it may be."

II

School integration is not yet a burning issue in Thomasville. But some men in town were at first opposed to consolidation of our county high schools until it could be seen what kind of pressures are going to be put on us. In the past eighteen months, however, those men have more or less reversed their position. And they do not deny that their change of mind was influenced by the possibility that Logana might be acquired for the site of the new school. Nor do they pretend that it is because they think Logana such an ideal location. They have agreed to go along with the plan, so they say, because it is the only way of getting rid of the little colony of Negroes who have always lived up there and who would make a serious problem for us if it became a question of zoning the town, in some way, as a last barrier against integration. What they say sounds very logical, and any stranger would be apt to accept the explanation at face value. But the truth of the matter is that there are people here who dislike the memory of the Logans even more than they do the prospect of integration. They are willing to risk integration in order to see that last Logan dispossessed of his last piece of real estate in Thomasville. With them it is a matter of superstition almost that until this happens Thomasville will not begin to realize its immemorial aspirations to grow and become a citified place.

So that you will better understand this dislike of the Logan name, I will give you a few more details of their history here. In the beginning, and for a long while, the Logan family didn't seem to want to spoil Thomasville with their own presence even. General Logan laid out the town in 1816, naming it after a little son of his who died in infancy. But during the first generation the Logan wives stayed mostly over in Middle Tennessee, where they felt there were more people of their own kind. And the men came and went only as their interest in the cotton crops required. In those years, Logana was occupied by a succession of slave-driving overseers, as was also the Logans' other house, which used to stand five miles below here at Logan's Landing.

Now, we might have done without the Logan women and without the county

seat, which the women didn't want here, but when the Logans kept the railroad out everybody saw the handwriting on the wall. The general's grandson did that. He was Harwell Logan, for many years chief justice of the state, and a man so powerful that in one breath, so to speak, he could deny the railroad company a right of way through town and demand that it give the name Logan Station to our nearest flag stop . . . And what was it the chief justice's son did? Why, it was he who prevented the cotton mill and snuff factory from locating here. The snuff factory would have polluted the air. And the cotton mill would have drawn in the riff-raff from all over the county . . . Along about the turn of the century it looked as though we were going to get the insane asylum for West Tennessee, but one of the Logans was governor of the state; he arranged for it to go to Bolivar instead. Even by then, none of the Logan men was coming back here very much except to hunt birds in the fall. They had already scattered out and were living in the big cities where there was plenty of industry and railroads for them to invest their money in; and they had already sold off most of their land to get the money to invest. But they didn't forget Thomasville. No matter how far up in the world a Logan may advance, he seems to go on having sweet dreams about Thomasville. Even though he has never actually lived here himself, Thomasville is the one place he doesn't want spoiled.

Just after the First World War, there was talk of getting the new veterans' hospital. During the Depression, we heard about a CCC camp. At the beginning of the Second World War, people came down from Washington and took option on big tracts of land for "Camp Logan." Very mysteriously all of those projects failed to materialize. Like everything else, they would have spoiled the town. But what else is there, I ask you, for a town to have except the things that tend to spoil it? What else is there to give it life? We used to have a boys' academy here, and a girls' institute, which is where Miss Leonora did her first teaching. They were boarding schools, and boys and girls came here from everywhere, and spent their money on the public square. It wasn't much, but it was *something*.

The boys' academy closed down before I was born even, and there isn't a trace left of it. The Thomasville Female Institute burned in 1922, and nothing is left of it, either, except the crumbling shells of the old brick buildings. All we have now that you don't see on the square is the cotton gin and flour mill and the ice plant. We claim a population of eighteen hundred, counting white and colored, which is about five hundred short of what we claimed in the year 1880. It has been suggested that in the next census we count the trees in Thomasville instead of the people. They outnumber us considerably and they have more influence, too. It was to save the willow oaks on the public square and the giant sycamores along High Street that someone arranged to have the Memphis-Chattanooga bypass built in 1952 instead of bringing the new highway through town. It was some Logan who arranged that, you may be sure, and no doubt it gladdens his heart to see the new motels that have gone up out there and to know that the old hotel on the square is never overcrowded by a lot of silly tourists.

To my mind, Miss Leonora Logan is a very beautiful woman. But to think she is beautiful nowadays perhaps you would have to have first seen her as I did when I was not yet five years old. And perhaps you would have to have seen her under the same circumstances exactly.

I don't remember what the occasion was. We were on a picnic of some kind at Bennett's Wood, and it seems to me that half the town was there. Probably it was the Fourth of July, though I don't remember any flags or speeches. A band was playing in the bandstand, and as I walked along between my mother and father I noticed that the trunks of the walnut trees had been freshly white-washed. The bare earth at the roots of the trees was still dappled with the droppings from the lime buckets. My father pointed out a row of beehives on the far edge of the grove and said he hoped to God nobody would stir the bees up today as

some bad boys had once done when there was an outing at Bennett's Wood. My father smiled at Mother when he said this, and my guess is that he had been amongst the boys who did it. My mother smiled, too, and we continued our walk.

It was just before dusk. My impression is that the actual picnicking and the main events of the day were already over. I was holding my mother's hand as we came out from under the trees and into the clearing where Bennett's Pond is. Several groups were out on the pond in rowboats, drifting about among the lily pads. One boat had just drawn up to the grassy bank on the side where we were. My mother leaned toward my father and said in a quiet voice, "Look at Miss Leonora Logan. Isn't she beautiful!"

She was dressed all in white. She had stood up in the boat the moment it touched shore, and it seemed to me that she had risen out of the water itself and were about to step from one of the lily pads onto the bank. I was aware of her being taller than most women whose beauty I had heard admired, and I knew that she was already spoken of as an old maid—that she was older than my mother even; but when she placed the pointed toe of her white shoe on the green sod beside the pond, it was as if that lovely white point had pierced my soul and awakened me to a beauty I had not dreamed of. Her every movement was all lightness and grace, and her head of yellow hair dazzled.

The last rays of the sun were at that moment coming directly toward me across the pond, and presently I had to turn my face away from its glare. But I had the feeling that it was Miss Leonora's eyes and the burning beauty of her countenance that had suddenly blinded me, and when my mother asked me fretfully what was the matter and why I hung back so, I was ashamed. I imagined that Mother could read the thoughts in my head. I imagined also that my mother, who was a plain woman and who as the wife of the hotelkeeper made no pretension to elegance—I imagined that she was now jealous of my admiration for Miss Leonora. With my face still averted, I silently reproached her for having herself suggested the thoughts to me by her remark to my father. I was very angry, and my anger and shame must have brought a deep blush to my whole face and neck. I felt my mother's two fingers thrust under the collar of my middy, and then I was soothed by her sympathetic voice saying "Why, child, you're feverish. We'd better get you home."

I must have had many a glimpse of Miss Leonora when I was a small boy playing on the hotel porch. But the next profound impression she made on me was when I was nine years old. One of the boarding students at the Institute had been stealing the other girls' things. It fell to Miss Leonora to apprehend the thief, who proved to be none other than a member of the Logan clan itself—a sad-faced, unattractive girl, according to all reports, but from a very rich branch of the family. She had been sent back to Thomasville to school all the way from Omaha, Nebraska.

Several hours after Miss Leonora had obtained unmistakable evidence of the girl's guilt and had told her she was to be sent home, it was discovered that the girl had disappeared. Word got out in the town that they were dragging the moat around the old windmill on the Institute grounds for the girl's body. Soon a crowd of townspeople gathered on the lawn before the Institute, near to where the windmill stood. The windmill was no longer used to pump the school's water—the school had town water by then—and there was not even a shaft or any vanes in evidence. But the old brick tower had been left standing. With its moat of stagnant, mossy water around it, it was thought to be picturesque.

The crowd assembled on the lawn some fifty or sixty feet away from the tower, and from there we watched the two Negro men at their work in the moat. The moat was fed by a sluggish wet-weather spring. It was about twenty feet wide and was estimated to be from ten to fifteen feet deep. And so the two men had had to bring in a boat to do their work from. On the very edge of the moat stood Miss Leonora, alongside Dr. Perkins, the chancellor of the Institute, and with them were several other teachers in their dark-blue uniforms. They all kept staring up at the windows of the old brick residence hall, as if to make sure that none of the girls was peering out at the distressing scene.

Presently we heard one of the Negro men say something to the other and heard the other mumble something in reply. We couldn't make out what they said, but we knew that they had found the girl's body. In a matter of two or three minutes they were hauling it up, and all of the women teachers except Miss Leonora buried their faces in their hands. From where we were, the slimy object was hardly recognizable as anything human, but despite this, or because of it, the crowd sent up a chorus of gasps and groans.

Hearing our chorus, Miss Leonora whirled about. She glared at us across the stretch of lawn for a moment, and then she came striding toward us, waving both hands in the air and ordering us to leave. "Go away! Go away!" she called out. "What business have you coming here with your wailing and moaning? A lot you care about that dead girl!" As she drew nearer, I could see her glancing at the ground now and then as if looking for a stick to drive us away with. "Go away!" she cried. "Take your curious eyes away. What right have you to be curious about *our* dead?"

A general retreat began, down the lawn and through the open gateway in the spiked iron fence. I hurried along with the others, but I kept looking back at Miss Leonora, who now stood on the brow of the terraced lawn, watching the retreat with a proud, bemused expression, seeming for the moment to have forgotten the dead young woman in the moat.

How handsome she was standing there, with her high color and her thick yellow hair that seemed about to come loose on her head and fall down on the shoulders of her blue shirtwaist.

Beyond her I had glimpses of the two Negro men lifting the dead body out of the water. They moved slowly and cautiously, but after they had got the girl into the boat and were trying to move her out of the boat onto the lawn, I saw the girl's head fall back. Her wet hair hung down like Spanish moss beneath her, and when the winter sunlight struck it, all at once it looked as green as seaweed. It was very beautiful, and yet, of course, I didn't feel right in thinking it was. It is something I have never been able to forget.

One day when we were in high school, a girl in the class asked Miss Leonora to tell us about "the Institute girl who did away with herself"—because Miss Leonora did sometimes tell us about the old days at the Institute. She stood looking out the classroom window, and seemed to be going over the incident in her mind and trying to decide whether or not it was something we ought to know more about. Finally she said, "No, we'll go on with the lesson now."

But the class, having observed her moment of indecision, began to beg. "Please tell us, Miss Leonora. Please." I don't know how many of the others had been in the crowd that day when they pulled the girl out of the moat. I was not the only one, I'm sure. I think that everybody knew most of the details and only wanted to see if she would refer to the way it ended with her driving the crowd away. But Miss Leonora wouldn't have cared at all, even if she had thought that was our motive. She would have given us her version if she had wanted to.

"Open your books," she said.

But still we persisted, and I was bold enough to ask, "Why not?"

"I'll just tell you why not," she said, suddenly blazing out at me. "Because there is nothing instructive in the story for you."

After that day, I realized, as never before, that though she often seemed to wander from the subject in class, it was never really so. She was eternally instructing us. If only once she had let up on the instruction, we might have learned something—or I might have. I used to watch her for a sign—any sign—of her caring about what we thought of her, or of her *not* caring about her mission among us, if that's what it was. More and more it came to seem incredible to me that she

was the same woman I had gone feverish over at Bennett's Wood that time, which was probably before Miss Leonora had perceived her mission. And yet I have the feeling she was the same woman still. Looking back on those high-school days, I know that all along she was watching me and others like me for some kind of sign—any sign—that would make us seem worthy of knowing what we wanted to know about her.

I suppose that what we wanted to know, beyond any doubt, was that the old lady had suffered for being just what she was—for being born with her cold, rigid, intellectual nature, and for being born to represent something that had never taken root in Thomasville and that would surely die with her. But not knowing that that was what we wanted to know, we looked for other smaller things. She didn't, for instance, have lunch in the lunchroom with the other teachers, and she didn't go home for lunch. She had a Negro woman bring her lunch to her on a tray all the way from Logana, on the other side of town. Generally she ate alone in her classroom. Sometimes we made excuses to go back to the room during lunch hour, and when we came out we pretended to the others that we had had a great revelation—that we had caught Miss Leonora eating peas with her knife or sopping her plate with a biscuit. We never caught her doing anything so improper, of course, but it gave us a wonderful pleasure to imagine it.

It was while I was in high school that Miss Leonora inherited Logana. She had already been living in the house most of her life—all of it except for the years when she taught and lived at the Institute—but the house had really belonged to her grandfather's brother in St. Louis. The morning we heard she had inherited the place, we thought surely she would be in high spirits about her good fortune, and before she came into the room that morning one of the girls said she was going to ask her how it felt to be an heiress. It was a question that never got asked, however, because when our teacher finally appeared before us she was dressed in black. She had inherited the house where

she had lived most of her life as a poor
relation, but she was also in mourning for
the dead great-uncle away off in St. Louis.
For us it was impossible to detect either
the joy over the one event or grief over
the other. Perhaps she felt neither, or perhaps she had to hide her feelings because
she felt that it was really the great-uncle's
death in St. Louis she had inherited and
the house in Thomasville she had lost.
Our lessons went on that day as though
nothing at all had happened.

But before I ever started going to the
high school, and before Miss Leonora
went there to teach, I had seen her on yet
another memorable occasion up at the
Institute—the most memorable and dramatic of all, because it was the night that
the place burned down. I remember the
events of that night very clearly. It was
a February night in 1922. The temperature was in the low twenties, and no
doubt they had thrown open the drafts
in every one of the coal-burning heaters
up at the Institute.

The fire broke out in the refectory and
spread very rapidly to the residence hall
and the classrooms building. Like any big
fire, it quickly drew the whole town to
the scene. Before most of us got there it
was already out of hand. All over town the
sky looked like Judgment Day. On the way
to the fire, we could hear the floors of the
old buildings caving in, one after the
other; and so from the beginning there
was not much anybody could do. The
town waterworks couldn't get enough
pressure up there to be of any real use,
and after that girl drowned herself they
had filled in the old moat around the
windmill.

The first thing that happened after I
got in sight of the place was that the gingerbread porches, which were already on
fire, began to fall away from the buildings. There were porches on the second
and third floors of the residence hall, and
suddenly they fell away like flaming lad-
ders that somebody had given a kick to.
The banisters and posts and rafters fell
out into the evergreen shrubbery, and
pretty soon the smell of burning hemlock
and cedar filled the air . . . The teachers
had got all the girls out safely and the

first men to arrive even saved some
of the furniture and the books, but
beyond that there was nothing to be
done except to stand and watch the
flames devour the innards of the buildings. This was very fascinating to everybody, and the crowd shifted from one
point to another, always trying to get a
better view and to see into which room
or down which corridor the flames would
move next.

Miss Leonora was as fascinated as any
of the rest of us, and it was this about her
that impressed me that night. It was not
till later that I heard about how she behaved during the first phase of the fire.
She had dashed about from building to
building screaming orders to everyone,
even to the fire brigade when it arrived.
She would not believe it when the firemen
told her that the water pressure could not
be increased. She threw a bucket of water
in one man's face when he refused to take
the bucket and climb up a second-story
porch with it.

I didn't see any of that. When I arrived,
Miss Leonora was already resigned to the
total loss that was inevitable. On a little
knob of earth on the north side of the
lawn, which people used to call the Indian
Mound, she had taken her position all
alone and isolated from the general
crowd. The other teachers had been sent
off with the Institute girls to the hotel,
where my mother was waiting to receive
them. But wrapped in a black fur cape—
it was bearskin, I think, and must have
been a hand-me-down from some relative
—Miss Leonora was seated on one of the
iron benches that were grouped over there
on the mound. Her only companions
were two iron deer that stood nearby, one
with its head lowered as if grazing, the
other with its iron antlers lifted and its
blank iron eyes fixed on the burning
buildings.

She sat there very erect, looking
straight ahead. It was hard to tell
whether she was watching the flames or
watching the people watch the flames.
Perhaps she was fascinated equally by
both. It was all over for her. She knew
that practically nothing was going to be
saved, but still she wanted to see how it

would go. Now and then a shaft of flame would shoot up into the overcast sky, lighting up the mixture of cloud and smoke above us, and also lighting up the figure of Miss Leonora over on the mound. Some of the women whispered amongst themselves, "Poor Miss Leonora! The school was her life." But if you caught a glimpse of her in one of those moments when the brightest light was on her, it wasn't self-pity or despair you saw written on her face. You saw her awareness of what was going on around her, and a kind of curiosity about it all that seemed almost inhuman and that even a child was bound to resent somewhat. She looked dead herself, but at the same time very much alive to what was going on around her.

III

When Miss Leonora's house was condemned two weeks ago, *somebody* had to break the news to her. They couldn't just send the clerk up there with the notice, or, worse still, let her read it in the newspaper. The old lady had to be warned of how matters had gone . . . We left the courthouse at four o'clock that afternoon, and set out for the Logan place on foot. None of us wanted to go, but who else would go if we didn't? That was how Judge Potter had put it to us. I suppose we elected to go on foot merely because it would take longer to get up there that way.

It was while we walked along under the sycamores on High Street that I let the others talk me into doing the job alone. They said that I had, after all, been her very favorite—by which they meant only that I was her first favorite—and that if we went in a group she might take it as a sign of cowardice, might even tell us it was that to our faces. It was a funny business, and we laughed about it a little amongst ourselves, though not much. Finally, I agreed that the other three men should wait behind the sumac and elderberry down in the lane, while I went up to see Miss Leonora alone.

Once this was settled, the other three men turned to reminiscing about their ex-

periences with Miss Leonora when they were in high school. But I couldn't concentrate on what they said. It may have been because I knew their stories so well. Or maybe it wasn't that. At any rate, when we had walked two blocks up High Street I realized that I was out of cigarettes, and I told the others to wait a minute while I stepped into the filling station, on the corner there, to buy a package. When I paid for the cigarettes, Buck Wallace, who operates the station, looked at me and said, "Well, how did it go? Do we condemn?"

I nodded and said, "We're on the way up there to tell her, Buck."

"I guessed you were," he said. He glanced out the window at the others, and I looked out out at them, too. For a second it seemed that I was seeing them through Buck Wallace's eyes—them and myself. And the next second it seemed, for some reason, that I was seeing them through Miss Leonora's eyes—them and myself. We all had on our business suits, our lightweight topcoats, our gray fedoras; we were the innkeeper, the druggist, a bank clerk, and the rewrite man from the weekly paper. Our ages range from thirty to fifty—with me at the top —but we were every one of us decked out to look like the same kind of thing. We might have just that minute walked out of the Friday-noon meeting of the Exchange Club. In Buck Wallace's eyes, however, we were certainly not the cream of the Exchange Club crop—*not* the men who were going to get Thomasville its due. And in Miss Leonora's eyes we were a cut above the Exchange Club's ringleaders, though not enough above them to matter very much. To both her and Buck we were merely the go-betweens. It just happened that we were the last people left in town that the old lady would speak to, and so now we—or, rather, I—was going up to Logana and tell her she would have to accept the town's terms of unconditional surrender.

"You may be too late," Buck added as I was turning away. I looked back at him with lifted eyebrows. "She was in here a while ago," he went on to report, "getting her car gassed up. She said how she was about to take off on one of her trips. She said she might wait till she heard from the courthouse this afternoon and again she might not . . . She was got up kind of peculiar."

When I rejoined the other men outside, I didn't tell them what Buck had said. Suddenly I mistrusted them, and I didn't trust myself. Or rather I knew I *could* trust myself to let *them* have their way if they thought Miss Leonora was about to leave town. I was pretty sure she wouldn't leave without hearing from us, and I was pretty sure they would want to head us back to the courthouse immediately and send official word up there before she could get away. It would have been the wise thing to do, but I didn't let it happen.

In the filling station Buck Wallace had said to me that she was "got up kind of peculiar," and that meant, to my understanding, that Miss Leonora was dressed in one of two ways. Neither was a way that I had ever seen her dressed, and I wanted to see for myself. It meant either that she was got up in a lot of outmoded finery or she was wearing her dungarees! Because that is how, for ten years now, the old lady has been turning up at the tourist homes where she stops, and that is how, if you wanted to recognize her on the road, you would have to watch out for her. Either she would be in her finery —with the fox fur piece, and the diamond earrings, and the high-crowned velvet hat, and the kind of lace choker that even old ladies don't generally go in for any more and that Miss Leonora has never been seen to wear in Thomasville except by a very few—or she would be in her dungarees! The dungarees are the hardest to imagine, of course. With them she wears a home-knit, knee-length cardigan sweater. And for headgear she pulls on a big poke bonnet she has resurrected from somewhere, or sometimes she stuffs her long hair up under a man's hunting cap or an old broad-brimmed straw hat. A queer sight she must present riding about the countryside these autumn nights; and if she rides with the top of her convertible put back, as I've heard of her doing in the dead of winter even, why, it's enough to scare any children who may

see her and some grown people, too . . . Here in Thomasville, only Buck Wallace and a few others have seen her so garbed, and they only rarely, only sometimes when she was setting out on a trip. They say she looks like some inmate who has broken out of the asylum over at Bolivar.

But that's how she turns up at the tourist homes. If she is with the two old maids at Boxwood Manor or Maple Lawn, she affects the choker and the diamond earrings. She sits down in their parlor and removes the high-crowned velvet, and she talks about how the traditions and institutions of our country have been corrupted and says that soon not one stone will be left upon another. And, still using such terms and phrases, she will at last get round to telling them the story of her life and the history of the Logan family in Thomasville. She tells it all in the third person, pretending it is some friend of hers she has in mind, and the family of that friend. But the old maids know right along that it is herself she is speaking of, and they say she seems to know they know it and seems not to care . . . And if she is with the farm couple at Oak Crest, then she's in her dungarees. She at once sets about helping with the chores, if they will let her. She talks religion to them and says there is no religion left amongst the people in the town, says that they have forsaken the fountain of living waters and hewed them out broken cisterns that can hold no water—or something like that. And finally she gets round to telling *them* her story, again pretending that it is some friend of hers she is speaking of, and again with her listeners knowing it is herself. The farm couple won't like seeing an old woman wearing dungarees, but they will catch the spirit of her getup, and they understand what it means. For they have known other old women there in the country who, thrown entirely on their own, living alone and in desperate circumstances, have gotten so they dress in some such outrageous way. And the two old maids probably still have some eye for fashion and they find Miss Leonora pretty ridiculous. But they remember other old ladies who did once dress like that, and it seems somehow credible that there might still be one somewhere.

When Miss Leonora is at home in Thomasville, it is hard to believe she ever dresses herself up so. Here we are used to seeing her always in the most school-teacherish, ready-made-looking clothes. After the Institute burned, she changed from the uniform that the Institute teachers wore to what amounts to a uniform for our high-school teachers—the drab kind of street dresses that can be got through the mail-order catalogues. Right up till two weeks ago, that's how we were still seeing the old lady dressed. It was hard to realize that in her old age she had had a change of heart and was wishing that either she had played the role of the spinster great lady the way it is usually played or that she had married some dirt farmer and spent her life working alongside him in the fields.

I even used to think that perhaps Miss Leonora didn't really want to go off masquerading around the country—that it was a kind of madness and meant something that would be much more difficult to explain, and that all the time she was at home she was dreading her next seizure. Recently, however, I've come to realize that that wasn't the case. For years, her only satisfaction in life has been her periodic escapes into a reality that is scattered in bits and pieces along the highways and back roads of the country she travels. And what I hope above all else is that Miss Leonora *is* stopping today at Oak Crest or Boxwood Manor and *does* have on her dungarees or lace choker.

But now I must tell what makes me doubt that she is, after all, staying at one of those tourist homes she likes, and what makes me afraid that we may never see her here again.

I left the other men down at the corner of the lane and went up the dirt driveway to Logana alone. Her car was parked at the foot of the porch steps, and so there was no question about her being there. I saw her first through one of the side-lights at the front door and wasn't sure it was she. Then she opened the door, saying, "Dear boy, come in." I laughed,

it was so unlike her to call me that. That was not her line at all. She laughed, too, but it was a kind of laugh that was supposed to put me at my ease rather than to criticize or commend me, which would have been very much more in her line . . . I saw at a glance that this wasn't the Miss Leonora I had known, and wasn't one that I had heard about from her tourist-home friends, either.

She had done an awful thing to her hair. Her splendid white mane, with its faded yellow streaks and its look of being kept up on her head only by the two tortoise-shell combs at the back, was no more. She had cut it off, thinned it, and set it in little waves close to her head, and, worse still, she must have washed it in a solution of indigo bluing. She had powdered the shine off her nose, seemed almost to have powdered its sharpness and longness away. She may have applied a little rouge and lipstick, though hardly enough to be noticeable, only enough to make you realize it wasn't the natural coloring of an old lady and enough to make you *think* how old she was. And the dress she had on was exactly right with the hair and the face, though at first I couldn't tell why.

As I walked beside her from the center hall into her "office," her skirt made an unpleasant swishing sound that seemed out of place in Miss Leonora's house and that made me observe more closely what the dress was really like. It was of a dark silk stuff, very stiff, with a sort of middy-blouse collar, and sleeves that stopped a couple of inches above the wrists, and a little piece of belt in back, fastened on with two big buttons—very stylish, I think. For a minute I couldn't remember where it was I had seen this very woman before. Then it came to me. All that was lacking was a pair of pixie glasses with rhinestone rims, and a half dozen brace-lets on her wrists. She was one of those old women who come out here from Memphis looking for antiques and coun-try hams and who tell you how delighted they are to find a Southern town that is truly unchanged.

Even so, I half expected Miss Leonora to begin by asking me about my family and then about what kind of summer I had had. "Now, I know you have had a fine summer—all summers are fine to a boy your age," she would say. "So don't tell me what you have been doing. Tell me what you have been *thinking*, what you have been *reading*." It was the room that made me imagine she would still go on that way. Because the room was the same as it used to be. Even the same coffee cups and blue china coffeepot were set out on the little octagonal oak table, beside the plate of butter cookies. And for a moment I had the same guilty feeling I used always to have; because, of course, I hadn't been reading anything and hadn't been thinking anything she would want to hear about.

What she actually said was much kinder and was what anybody might have said under the circumstances. "I've felt so bad about your having to come here like this. I knew they would put it off on you. Even you must have dreaded coming, and you must hate me for putting you in such a position."

"Why, no. I wanted to come, Miss Leonora," I lied. "And I hope you have understood that I had no part in the proceedings." It was what, for months, I had known I would say, and it came out very easily.

"I do understand that," she said. "And we don't even need to talk about any of it."

But I said, "The county court has granted the writ condemning your property. They will send a notice up to you tomorrow morning. You ought to have had a lawyer represent you, and you ought to have come yourself."

I had said what I had promised Judge Potter I would say; she had her warning. And now I was on my own. She motioned me to sit down in a chair near the table where the coffee things were. When she poured out the coffee into our two cups, it was steaming hot. It smelled the way it used to smell in that room on winter afternoons, as fresh as if it were still brewing on the stove. I knew she hadn't made it herself, but, as in the old days, too, the Negro woman who had made it didn't appear or make a sound in the kit-

chen. You wouldn't have thought there was one of them on the place. There didn't seem to be another soul in the house but just herself and me. But *I* knew that the house was full of them, really. And there was still the feeling that either she was protecting me from them or them from me. I experienced the old uneasiness in addition to something new. And as for Miss Leonora, she seemed to sense from the start that the other three men were waiting down the lane—the three who had been even less willing than I to come, and who were that much nearer to the rest of the town in their feelings. Several times she referred to them, giving a little nod of her head in the direction of the very spot where I had left them waiting.

"When I think of the old days, the days when I used to have you up here—you and the others, too—I realize I was too hard on you. I asked too much of my pupils. I know that now."

It was nothing like the things the real Miss Leonora used to say. It was something anybody might have said.

And a little later: "I was unrealistic. I tried to be to you children what I thought you needed to have somebody be. That's a mistake, always. One has to try to be with people what they want one to be. Each of *you* tried to be that for me, to an admirable degree. Tim Hadley tried hardest—he went to college—but he didn't have your natural endowments." Then she took pains to say something good and something forgiving about each of the four. And, unless I imagined it, for each of those that hadn't come up with me she gave another nod in the direction of the elderberry and sumac thicket down at the corner.

"We were a dumb bunch, all along the line," I said, not meaning it—or not meaning it about myself.

"Nonsense. You were all fine boys, and *you* were my brightest hope," she said, with an empty cheerfulness.

"But you can't make a silk purse out of—" I began.

"Nonsense," she said again. "It was neither you nor I that failed." But she didn't care enough to make any further denial or explanation. She set her cup down on the table and rose from her chair. "It's been like old times, hasn't it," she said with a vague smile.

I looked away from her and sat gazing about the office, still holding my empty cup in my hand. It hadn't been like old times at all, of course. The room and the silence of the house were the same, but Miss Leonora was already gone, and without her the house was nothing but a heap of junk. I thought to myself that the best thing that could happen would be for them to begin moving out the furniture and moving out the Negroes and tearing the place down as soon as possible. Suddenly, I spied her black leather traveling bag over beside the doorway, and she must have seen my eyes light upon it. "I'm about to get off on a little trip," she said.

I set my cup down on the table and looked up at her. I could see she was expecting me to protest. "Will it be long?" I asked, not protesting.

"I don't know, dear boy. You know how I am."

I glanced at the traveling bag again, and this time I noticed her new cloth coat lying on the straight chair beside the bag. I got up and went over and picked up the coat and held it for her.

On the way out to the car, I kept reminding myself that this was really Miss Leonora Logan and that she was going away before receiving any official notice of the jury's verdict. Finally, when we were standing beside her car and she was waiting for me to put the bag, which I was carrying, inside the car, I looked squarely into her eyes. And there is no denying it; the eyes were still the same as always, not just their hazel color but their expression, their look of awareness— awareness of you, the individual before her, a very flattering awareness until presently you realized it was merely of you as an individual in her scheme of things for Thomasville. She was still looking at me as though I were one of the village children that she would like so much

to make something of. I opened the car door. I tossed the bag into the space behind the driver's seat. I even made sure I did the thing to her satisfaction by putting one hand out to her elbow as she slipped stiffly in under the steering wheel.

Neither of us made any pretense of saying goodbye. I stood there and watched the car as it bumped along down the driveway, raising a little cloud of dust in the autumn air. The last I saw of her was a glimpse of her bluinged head through the rear window of her convertible. When she turned out into the lane and headed away from town toward the bypass, I knew that the other three men would be watching. But they wouldn't be able to see how she was got up, and I knew they would hardly believe me when I told them.

I have told nearly everybody in town about it, and I think nobody really believes me. I have almost come to doubt it myself. And, anyway, I like to think that in her traveling bag she had the lace-choker outfit that she could change into along the way, and the dungarees, too; and that she is stopping at her usual kind of place today and is talking to the proprietors about Thomasville. Otherwise, there is no use in anyone's keeping an eye out for her. She will look too much like a thousand others, and no doubt will be driving on the highway the way everybody else does, letting other people pass her, dimming her lights for everyone. Maybe she even drives in the daytime, and maybe when she stops for the night it is at a big, modern motel with air conditioning and television in every room. The postcards she sends us indicate nothing about how she is dressed, of course, or about where and in what kind of places she is stopping. She says only that she is in good health, that it is wonderful weather for driving about the country, and that the roads have been improved everywhere. She says nothing about when we can expect her to come home.

[1960]

QUESTIONS FOR STUDY

1. *Why doesn't the narrator expect to see Miss Leonora alive again?*
2. *The narrator says that "in the end, we [her favorite students] didn't really know her any better than anybody else did." What essential facts about Miss Leonora and her life does the reader come to learn?*
3. *What has been Miss Leonora's self-appointed mission in Thomasville? What does she come to understand and admit about that role? How is that discovery mirrored in the clothes she chooses to wear for her final trip?*
4. *What seems to be the author's attitude toward Miss Leonora? Does the town's gain (a new school site) outweigh its loss (Miss Leonora herself)?*
5. *Describe the author's style. In what ways is it appropriate?*

JAMES THURBER

The Catbird Seat

M R. MARTIN bought the pack of Camels on Monday night in the most crowded cigar store on Broadway. It was theater time and seven or eight men were buying cigarettes. The clerk didn't even glance at Mr. Martin, who put the pack in his overcoat pocket and went out. If any of the staff at F & S had seen him buy the cigarettes, they would have been astonished, for it was generally known that Mr. Martin did not smoke, and never had. No one saw him.

It was just a week to the day since Mr. Martin had decided to rub out Mrs. Ulgine Barrows. The term "rub out" pleased him because it suggested nothing more than the correction of an error—in this case an error of Mr. Fitweiler. Mr. Martin had spent each night of the past week working out his plan and examining it. As he walked home now he went over it again. For the hundredth time he resented the element of imprecision, the margin of guesswork that entered into the business. The project as he had worked it out was casual and bold, the risks were considerable. Something might go wrong anywhere along the line. And therein lay the cunning of his scheme. No one would ever see in it the cautious, painstaking hand of Erwin Martin, head of the filing department at F & S, of whom Mr. Fitweiler had once said, "Man is fallible but Martin isn't." No one would see his hand, that is, unless it were caught in the act.

Sitting in his apartment, drinking a glass of milk, Mr. Martin reviewed his case against Mrs. Ulgine Barrows, as he had every night for seven nights. He began at the beginning. Her quacking voice and braying laugh had first profaned the halls of F & S on March 7, 1941 (Mr. Martin had a head for dates). Old Roberts, the personnel chief, had intro-duced her as the newly appointed special adviser to the president of the firm, Mr. Fitweiler. The woman had appalled Mr. Martin instantly, but he hadn't shown it. He had given her his dry hand, a look of studious concentration, and a faint smile. "Well," she had said, looking at the papers on his desk, "are you lifting the ox-cart out of the ditch?" As Mr. Martin recalled that moment, over his milk, he squirmed slightly. He must keep his mind on her crimes as a special adviser, not on her peccadillos as a personality. This he found difficult to do, in spite of entering an objection and sustaining it. The faults of the woman as a woman kept chattering on in his mind like an unruly witness. She had, for almost two years now, baited him. In the halls, in the elevator, even in his own office, into which she romped now and then like a circus horse, she was constantly shouting these silly questions at him. "Are you lifting the oxcart out of the ditch? Are you tearing up the pea patch? Are you hollering down the rain barrel? Are you scraping around the bottom of the pickle barrel? Are you sitting in the catbird seat?"

It was Joey Hart, one of Mr. Martin's two assistants, who had explained what the gibberish meant. "She must be a Dodger fan," he had said. "Red Barber announces the Dodger games over the radio and he uses those expressions—picked 'em up down South." Joey had gone on to explain one or two. "Tearing up the pea patch" meant going on a rampage; "sitting in the catbird seat" meant sitting pretty, like a batter with three balls and no strikes on him. Mr. Martin dismissed all this with an effort. It had been annoying, it had driven him near to distraction, but he was too solid a man to be moved to murder by anything so childish.

It was fortunate, he reflected as he passed on to the important charges against Mrs. Barrows, that he had stood up under it so well. He had maintained always an outward appearance of polite tolerance. "Why, I even believe you like the woman," Miss Paird, his other assistant, had once said to him. He had simply smiled.

A gavel rapped in Mr. Martin's mind and the case proper was resumed. Mrs. Ulgine Barrows stood charged with willful, blatant, and persistent attempts to destroy the efficiency and system of F & S. It was competent, material, and relevant to review her advent and rise to power. Mr. Martin had got the story from Miss Paird, who seemed always able to find things out. According to her, Mrs. Barrows had met Mr. Fitweiler at a party, where she had rescued him from the embraces of a powerfully built drunken man who had mistaken the president of F & S for a famous retired Middle Western football coach. She had led him to a sofa and somehow worked upon him a monstrous magic. The aging gentleman had jumped to the conclusion there and then that this was a woman of singular attainments, equipped to bring out the best in him and in the firm. A week later he had introduced her into F & S as his special adviser. On that day confusion got its foot in the door. After Miss Tyson, Mr. Brundage, and Mr. Bartlett had been fired and Mr. Munson had taken his hat and stalked out, mailing in his resignation later, old Roberts had been emboldened to speak to Mr. Fitweiler. He mentioned that Mr. Munson's department had been "a little disrupted" and hadn't they perhaps better resume the old system there? Mr. Fitweiler had said certainly not. He had the greatest faith in Mrs. Barrow's ideas. "They require a little seasoning, a little seasoning, is all," he had added. Mr. Roberts had given it up. Mr. Martin reviewed in detail all the changes wrought by Mrs. Barrows. She had begun chipping at the cornices of the firm's edifice and now she was swinging at the foundation stones with a pickaxe.

Mr. Martin came now, in his summing up, to the afternoon of Monday, November 2, 1942—just one week ago. On that day, at 3 P.M., Mrs. Barrows had bounced into his office. "Boo!" she had yelled. "Are you scraping around the bottom of the pickle barrel?" Mr. Martin had looked at her from under his green eyeshade, saying nothing. She had begun to wander about the office, taking it in with her great, popping eyes. "Do you really need *all* these filing cabinets?" she had demanded suddenly. Mr. Martin's heart had jumped. "Each of these files," he had said, keeping his voice even, "plays an indispensable part in the system of F & S." She had brayed at him, "Well, don't tear up the pea patch!" and gone to the door. From there she had bawled, "But you sure have got a lot of fine scrap in here!" Mr. Martin could no longer doubt that the finger was on his beloved department. Her pickaxe was on the upswing, poised for the first blow. It had not come yet; he had received no blue memo from the enchanted Mr. Fitweiler bearing nonsensical instructions deriving from the obscene woman. But there was no doubt in Mr. Martin's mind that one would be forthcoming. He must act quickly. Already a precious week had gone by. Mr. Martin stood up in his living room, still holding his milk glass. "Gentlemen of the jury," he said to himself, "I demand the death penalty for this horrible person."

The next day Mr. Martin followed his routine, as usual. He polished his glasses more often and once sharpened an already sharp pencil, but not even Miss Paird noticed. Only once did he catch sight of his victim; she swept past him in the hall with a patronizing "Hi!" At five-thirty he walked home, as usual, and had a glass of milk, as usual. He had never drunk anything stronger in his life—unless you could count ginger ale. The late Sam Schlosser, the S or F & S, had praised Mr. Martin at a staff meeting several years before for his temperate habits. "Our most efficient worker neither drinks nor smokes," he had said. "The results speak for themselves." Mr. Fitweiler had sat by, nodding approval.

Mr. Martin was still thinking about that red-letter day as he walked over to the Schrafft's on Fifth Avenue near Forty-sixth Street. He got there, as he always did, at eight o'clock. He finished his dinner and the financial page of the *Sun* at a quarter to nine, as he always did. It was his custom after dinner to take a walk. This time he walked down Fifth Avenue at a casual pace. His gloved hands felt moist and warm, his forehead cold. He transferred the Camels from his overcoat to a jacket pocket. He wondered, as he did so, if they did not represent an unnecessary note of strain. Mrs. Barrows' smoked only Luckies. It was his idea to puff a few puffs on a Camel (after the rubbing-out), stub it out in the ashtray holding her lipstick-stained Luckies, and thus drag a small red herring across the trail. Perhaps it was not a good idea. It would take time. He might even choke, too loudly.

Mr. Martin had never seen the house on West Twelfth Street where Mrs. Barrows lived, but he had a clear enough picture of it. Fortunately, she had bragged to everybody about her ducky first-floor apartment in the perfectly darling three-story red-brick. There would be no doorman or other attendants; just the tenants of the second and third floors. As he walked along, Mr. Martin realized that he would get there before nine-thirty. He had considered walking north on Fifth Avenue from Schrafft's to a point from which it would take him until ten o'clock to reach the house. At that hour people were less likely to be coming in or going out. But the procedure would have made an awkward loop in the straight thread of his casualness, and he had abandoned it. It was impossible to figure when people would be entering or leaving the house, anyway. There was a great risk at any hour. If he ran into anybody, he would simply have to place the rubbing-out of Ulgine Barrows in the inactive file forever. The same thing would hold true if there were someone in her apartment. In that case he would just say that he had been passing by, recognized her charming house and thought to drop in.

It was eighteen minutes after nine when Mr. Martin turned into Twelfth Street. A man passed him, and a man and a woman talking. There was no one within fifty paces when he came to the house, halfway down the block. He was up the steps and in the small vestibule in no time, pressing the bell under the card that said "Mrs. Ulgine Barrows." When the clicking in the lock started, he jumped forward against the door. He got inside fast, closing the door behind him. A bulb in a lantern hung from the hall ceiling on a chain seemed to give a monstrously bright light. There was nobody on the stair, which went up ahead of him along the left wall. A door opened down the hall in the wall on the right. He went toward it swiftly, on tiptoe.

"Well, for God's sake, look who's here!" bawled Mrs. Barrows, and her braying laugh rang out like the report of a shotgun. He rushed past her like a football tackle, bumping her. "Hey, quit shoving!" she said, closing the door behind them. They were in her living room, which seemed to Mr. Martin to be lighted by a hundred lamps. "What's after you?" she said. "You're as jumpy as a goat." He found he was unable to speak. His heart was wheezing in his throat. "I—yes," he finally brought out. She was jabbering and laughing as she started to help him off with his coat. "No, no," he said. "I'll put it here." He took it off and put it on a chair near the door. "Your hat and gloves, too," she said. "You're in a lady's house." He put his hat on top of the coat. Mrs. Barrows seemed larger than he had thought. He kept his gloves on. "I was passing by," he said. "I recognized—is there anyone here?" She laughed louder than ever. "No," she said, "we're all alone. You're as white as a sheet, you funny man. Whatever *has* come over you? I'll mix you a toddy." She started toward a door across the room. "Scotch-and-soda be all right? But say, you don't drink, do you?" She turned and gave him her amused look. Mr. Martin pulled himself together. "Scotch-and-soda will be all right," he heard himself say. He could hear her laughing in the kitchen.

Mr. Martin looked quickly around the living room for the weapon. He had counted on finding one there. There were andirons and a poker and something in a corner that looked like an Indian club.

None of them would do. It couldn't be that way. He began to pace around. He came to a desk. On it lay a metal paper knife with an ornate handle. Would it be sharp enough? He reached for it and knocked over a small brass jar. Stamps spilled out of it and it fell to the floor with a clatter. "Hey," Mrs. Barrows yelled from the kitchen, "are you tearing up the pea patch?" Mr. Martin gave a strange laugh. Picking up the knife, he tried its point against his left wrist. It was blunt. It wouldn't do.

When Mrs. Barrows reappeared, carrying two highballs, Mr. Martin, standing there with his gloves on, became acutely conscious of the fantasy he had wrought. Cigarettes in his pocket, a drink prepared for him—it was all too grossly improbable. It was more than that; it was impossible. Somewhere in the back of his mind a vague idea stirred, sprouted. "For heaven's sake, take off those gloves," said Mrs. Barrows. "I always wear them in the house," said Mr. Martin. The idea began to bloom, strange and wonderful. She put the glasses on a coffee table in front of a sofa and sat on the sofa. "Come over here, you odd little man," she said. Mr. Martin went over and sat beside her. It was difficult getting a cigarette out of the pack of Camels, but he managed it. She held a match for him, laughing. "Well," she said, handing him his drink, "this is perfectly marvelous. You with a drink and a cigarette."

Mr. Martin puffed, not too awkwardly, and took a gulp of the highball. "I drink and smoke all the time," he said. He clinked his glass against hers. "Here's nuts to that old windbag, Fitweiler," he said, and gulped again. The stuff tasted awful, but he made no grimace. "Really, Mr. Martin," she said, her voice and posture changing, "you are insulting our employer." Mrs. Barrows was now all special adviser to the president. "I am preparing a bomb," said Mr. Martin, "which will blow the old goat higher than hell." He had only had a little of the drink, which was not strong. It couldn't be that. "Do you take dope or something?" Mrs. Barrows asked coldly. "Heroin," said Mr.

Martin. "I'll be coked to the gills when I bump that old buzzard off." "Mr. Martin!" she shouted, getting to her feet. "That will be all of that. You must go at once." Mr. Martin took another swallow of his drink. He tapped his cigarette out in the ashtray and put the pack of Camels on the coffee table. Then he got up. She stood glaring at him. He walked over and put on his hat and coat. "Not a word about this," he said, and laid an index finger against his lips. All Mrs. Barrows could bring out was "Really!" Mr. Martin put his hand on the doorknob. "I'm sitting in the catbird seat," he said. He stuck his tongue out at her and left. Nobody saw him go.

Mr. Martin got to his apartment, walking, well before eleven. No one saw him go in. He had two glasses of milk after brushing his teeth, and he felt elated. It wasn't tipsiness, because he hadn't been tipsy. Anyway, the walk had worn off all effects of the whisky. He got in bed and read a magazine for a while. He was asleep before midnight.

Mr. Martin got to the office at eight-thirty the next morning, as usual. At a quarter to nine, Ulgine Barrows, who had never before arrived at work before ten, swept into his office. "I'm reporting to Mr. Fitweiler now!" she shouted. "If he turns you over to the police, it's no more than you deserve!" Mr. Martin gave her a look of shocked surprise. "I beg your pardon?" he said. Mrs. Barrows snorted and bounced out of the room, leaving Miss Paird and Joey Hart staring after her. "What's the matter with that old devil now?" asked Miss Paird. "I have no idea," said Mr. Martin, resuming his work. The other two looked at him and then at each other. Miss Paird got up and went out. She walked slowly past the closed door of Mr. Fitweiler's office. Mrs. Barrows was yelling inside, but she was not braying. Miss Paird could not hear what the woman was saying. She went back to her desk.

Forty-five minutes later, Mrs. Barrows left the president's office and went into her own, shutting the door. It wasn't until half an hour later that Mr. Fitweiler sent for

Mr. Martin. The head of the filing department, neat, quiet, attentive, stood in front of the old man's desk. Mr. Fitweiler was pale and nervous. He took his glasses off and twiddled them. He made a small, bruffing sound in his throat. "Martin," he said, "you have been with us more than twenty years." "Twenty-two, sir," said Mr. Martin. "In that time," pursued the president, "your work and your—uh—manner have been exemplary." "I trust so, sir," said Mr. Martin. "I have understood, Martin," said Mr. Fitweiler, "that you have never taken a drink or smoked." "That is correct, sir," said Mr. Martin. "Ah, yes." Mr. Fitweiler polished his glasses. "You may describe what you did after leaving the office yesterday, Martin," he said. Mr. Martin allowed less than a second for his bewildered pause. "Certainly, sir," he said. "I walked home. Then I went to Schrafft's for dinner. Afterward I walked home again. I went to bed early, sir, and read a magazine for a while. I was asleep before eleven." "Ah, yes," said Mr. Fitweiler again. He was silent for a moment, searching for the proper words to say to the head of the filing department. "Mrs. Barrows," he said finally, "Mrs. Barrows has worked hard, Martin, very hard. It grieves me to report that she has suffered a severe breakdown. It has taken the form of a persecution complex accompanied by distressing hallucinations." "I am very sorry, sir," said Mr. Martin. "Mrs. Barrows is under the delusion," continued Mr. Fitweiler, "that you visited her last evening and behaved yourself in an—uh—unseemly manner." He raised his hand to silence Mr. Martin's little pained outcry. "It is the nature of these psychological diseases," Mr. Fitweiler said, "to fix upon the least likely and most innocent party as the—uh—source of persecution. These matters are not for the lay mind to grasp, Martin. I've just had my psychiatrist, Dr. Fitch, on the phone. He would not, of course, commit himself, but he made enough generalizations to substantiate my suspicions. I suggested to Mrs. Barrows when she had completed her—uh—story to me this morning, that she visit Dr. Fitch, for I suspected a condition at once. She flew, I regret to say, into a rage, and demanded—uh—requested that I call you on the carpet. You may not know, Martin, but Mrs. Barrows had planned a reorganization of your department—subject to my approval, of course, subject to my approval. This brought you, rather than anyone else, to her mind—but again that is a phenomenon for Dr. Fitch and not for us. So, Martin, I am afraid Mrs. Barrows' usefulness here is at an end." "I am dreadfully sorry, sir," said Mr. Martin.

It was at this point that the door to the office blew open with the suddenness of a gas-main explosion and Mrs. Barrows catapulted through it. "Is the little rat denying it?" she screamed. "He can't get away with that!" Mr. Martin got up and moved discreetly to a point beside Mr. Fitweiler's chair. "You drank and smoked at my apartment," she bawled at Mr. Martin, "and you know it! You called Mr. Fitweiler an old windbag and said you were going to blow him up when you got coked to the gills on your heroin!" She stopped yelling to catch her breath and a new glint came into her popping eyes. "If you weren't such a drab, ordinary little man," she said, "I'd think you'd planned it all. Sticking your tongue out at me, saying you were sitting in the catbird seat, because you thought no one would believe me when I told it! My God, it's really too perfect!" She brayed loudly and hysterically, and the fury was on her again. She glared at Mr. Fitweiler. "Can't you see how he has tricked us, you old fool? Can't you see his little game?" But Mr. Fitweiler had been surreptitiously pressing all the buttons under the top of his desk and employees of F & S began pouring into the room. "Stockton," said Mr. Fitweiler, "you and Fishbein will take Mrs. Barrows to her home. Mrs. Powell, you will go with them." Stockton, who had played a little football in high school, blocked Mrs. Barrows as she made for Mr. Martin. It took him and Fishbein together to force her out of the door into the hall, crowded with stenographers and office boys. She was still screaming imprecations at Mr. Martin, tangled and contradictory imprecations. The hubbub finally died out down the corridor.

"I regret that this has happened," said Mr. Fitweiler. "I shall ask you to dismiss it from your mind, Martin." "Yes, sir," said Mr. Martin, anticipating his chief's "That will be all" by moving to the door. "I will dismiss it." He went out and shut the door, and his step was light and quick in the hall. When he entered his department he had slowed down to his customary gait, and he walked quietly across the room to the W20 file, wearing a look of studious concentration.

[1942]

QUESTIONS FOR STUDY

1. *What particular traits or characteristics make Mr. Martin, Mrs. Barrows, Mr. Fitweiler, Miss Paird, and Joey Hart familiar twentieth-century types?*
2. *In what ways does Thurber rely on contrast to establish the characters of Mr. Martin and Mrs. Barrows? What adjectives are used to describe Mr. Martin? What verbs are used to describe Mrs. Barrows? Why should adjectives be appropriate for one character and verbs for the other?*
3. *In what other ways does the author's use of language contribute to the story's effectiveness?*
4. *What enables Mr. Martin to triumph over Mrs. Barrows?*
5. *Is Thurber's intention in "The Catbird Seat" simply the creation of humor, or is there a discernible theme at work as well? If there is a theme, what is it?*

LEO TOLSTOY

The Death of Ivan Ilych

I

DURING an interval in the Melvinski trial in the large building of the Law Courts the members and public prosecutor met in Ivan Egorovich Shebek's private room, where the conversation turned on the celebrated Krasovski case. Fedor Vasilievich warmly maintained that it was not subject to their jurisdiction, Ivan Egorovich maintained the contrary, while Peter Ivanovich, not having entered into the discussion at the start, took no part in it but looked through the *Gazette* which had just been handed in.

'Gentlemen,' he said, 'Ivan Ilych has died!'

'You don't say so!'

'Here, read it yourself,' replied Peter Ivanovich, handing Fedor Vasilievich the paper still damp from the press. Surrounded by a black border were the words: 'Praskovya Fedorovna Golovina, with profound sorrow, informs relatives and friends of the demise of her beloved husband Ivan Ilych Golovin, Member of the Court of Justice, which occurred on February the 4th of this year 1882. The funeral will take place on Friday at one o'clock in the afternoon.'

Ivan Ilych had been a colleague of the gentlemen present and was liked by them all. He had been ill for some weeks with an illness said to be incurable. His post had been kept open for him, but there had been conjectures that in case of his death Alexeev might receive his appointment, and that either Vinnikov or Shtabel would succeed Alexeev. So on receiving the news of Ivan Ilych's death the first thought of each of the gentlemen in that private room was of the changes and promotions it might occasion among themselves or their acquaintances.

'I shall be sure to get Shtabel's place or Vinnikov's,' thought Fedor Vasilievich. 'I was promised that long ago, and the promotion means an extra eight hundred rubles a year for me besides the allowance.'

'Now I must apply for my brother-in-law's transfer from Kaluga,' thought Peter Ivanovich. 'My wife will be very glad, and then she won't be able to say that I never do anything for her relations.'

'I thought he would never leave his bed again,' said Peter Ivanovich aloud. 'It's very sad.'

'But what really was the matter with him?'

'The doctors couldn't say—at least they could, but each of them said something different. When last I saw him I thought he was getting better.'

'And I haven't been to see him since the holidays. I always meant to go.'

'Had he any property?'

'I think his wife had a little—but something quite trifling.'

'We shall have to go to see her, but they live so terribly far away.'

'Far away from you, you mean. Everything's far away from your place.'

'You see, he never can forgive my living on the other side of the river,' said Peter Ivanovich, smiling at Shebek. Then, still talking of the distances between different parts of the city, they returned to the Court.

Besides considerations as to the possible transfers and promotions likely to result from Ivan Ilych's death, the mere fact of the death of a near acquaintance aroused, as usual, in all who heard of it the complacent feeling that, 'it is he who is dead and not I'.

Each one thought or felt, 'Well, he's dead but I'm alive!' But the more intimate of Ivan Ilych's acquaintances, his so-

From *Ivan Ilych, Hadj Murad and Other Stories* by Leo Tolstoy. Translated from the Russian by Louise and Aylmer Maude and published by Oxford University Press, London.

called friends, could not help thinking also that they would now have to fulfil the very tiresome demands of propriety by attending the funeral service and paying a visit of condolence to the widow.

Fedor Vasilievich and Peter Ivanovich had been his nearest acquaintances. Peter Ivanovich had studied law with Ivan Ilych and had considered himself to be under obligations to him.

Having told his wife at dinner-time of Ivan Ilych's death, and of his conjecture that it might be possible to get her brother transferred to their circuit, Peter Ivanovich sacrificed his usual nap, put on his evening clothes, and drove to Ivan Ilych's house.

At the entrance stood a carriage and two cabs. Leaning against the wall in the hall downstairs near the cloak-stand was a coffin lid covered with cloth of gold, ornamented with gold cord and tassels, that had been polished up with metal powder. Two ladies in black were taking off their fur cloaks. Peter Ivanovich recognized one of them as Ivan Ilych's sister, but the other was a stranger to him. His colleague Schwartz was just coming downstairs, but on seeing Peter Ivanovich enter he stopped and winked at him, as if to say: 'Ivan Ilych has made a mess of things— not like you and me.'

Schwartz's face with his Piccadilly whiskers, and his slim figure in evening dress, had as usual an air of elegant solemnity which contrasted with the playfulness of his character and had a special piquancy here, or so it seemed to Peter Ivanovich.

Peter Ivanovich allowed the ladies to precede him and slowly followed them upstairs. Schwartz did not come down but remained where he was, and Peter Ivanovich understood that he wanted to arrange where they should play bridge that evening. The ladies went upstairs to the widow's room, and Schwartz with seriously compressed lips but a playful look in his eyes, indicated by a twist of his eyebrows the room to the right where the body lay.

Peter Ivanovich, like everyone else on such occasions, entered feeling uncertain what he would have to do. All he knew

was that at such times it is always safe to cross oneself. But he was not quite sure whether one should make obeisances while doing so. He therefore adopted a middle course. On entering the room he began crossing himself and made a slight movement resembling a bow. At the same time, as far as the motion of his head and arm allowed, he surveyed the room. Two young men—apparently nephews, one of whom was a high-school pupil—were leaving the room, crossing themselves as they did so. An old woman was standing motionless, and a lady with strangely arched eyebrows was saying something to her in a whisper. A vigorous, resolute Church Reader, in a frock-coat, was reading something in a loud voice with an expression that precluded any contradiction. The butler's assistant, Gerasim, stepping lightly in front of Peter Ivanovich, was strewing something on the floor. Noticing this, Peter Ivanovich was immediately aware of a faint odour of a decomposing body.

The last time he had called on Ivan Ilych, Peter Ivanovich had seen Gerasim in the study. Ivan Ilych had been particularly fond of him and he was performing the duty of a sick nurse.

Peter Ivanovich continued to make the sign of the cross slightly inclining his head in an intermediate direction between the coffin, the Reader, and the icons on the table in a corner of the room. Afterwards, when it seemed to him that this movement of his arm in crossing himself had gone on too long, he stopped and began to look at the corpse.

The dead man lay, as dead men always lie, in a specially heavy way, his rigid limbs sunk in the soft cushions of the coffin, with the head forever bowed on the pillow. His yellow waxen brow with bald patches over his sunken temples was thrust up in the way peculiar to the dead, the protruding nose seeming to press on the upper lip. He was much changed and had grown even thinner since Peter Ivanovich had last seen him, but, as is always the case with the dead, his face was handsomer and above all more dignified than when he was alive. The expression on the face said that what was necessary had been accomplished, and accomplished rightly. Besides this there was in that expression a reproach and a warning to the living. This warning seemed to Peter Ivanovich out of place, or at least not applicable to him. He felt a certain discomfort and so he hurriedly crossed himself once more and turned and went out of the door—too hurriedly and too regardless of propriety, as he himself was aware.

Schwartz was waiting for him in the adjoining room with legs spread wide apart and both hands toying with his top-hat behind his back. The mere sight of that playful, well-groomed, and elegant figure refreshed Peter Ivanovich. He felt that Schwartz was above all these happenings and would not surrender to any depressing influences. His very look said that this incident of a church service for Ivan Ilych could not be a sufficient reason for infringing the order of the session—in other words, that it would certainly not prevent his unwrapping a new pack of cards and shuffling them that evening while a footman placed four fresh candles on the table: in fact, that there was no reason for supposing that this incident would hinder their spending the evening agreeably. Indeed he said this in a whisper as Peter Ivanovich passed him, proposing that they should meet for a game at Fedor Vasilievich's. But apparently Peter Ivanovich was not destined to play bridge that evening. Praskovya Fedorovna (a short, fat woman who despite all efforts to the contrary had continued to broaden steadily from her shoulders downwards and who had the same extraordinarily arched eyebrows as the lady who had been standing by the coffin), dressed all in black, her head covered with lace, came out of her own room with some other ladies, conducted them to the room where the dead body lay, and said: 'The service will begin immediately. Please go in.'

Schwartz, making an indefinite bow, stood still, evidently neither accepting nor declining this invitation. Praskovya Fedorovna recognizing Peter Ivanovich, sighed, went close up to him, took his hand, and said: 'I know you were a true friend to Ivan Ilych . . .' and looked at him awaiting some suitable response. And Peter Ivanovich knew that, just as it had been the right thing to cross himself in that room, so what he had to do here was to press her hand, sigh, and say, 'Believe me . . .'. So he did all this and as he did it felt that the desired result had been achieved: that both he and she were touched.

'Come with me. I want to speak to you before it begins,' said the widow. 'Give me your arm.'

Peter Ivanovich gave her his arm and they went to the inner rooms, passing Schwartz who winked at Peter Ivanovich compassionately.

'That does for our bridge! Don't object if we find another player. Perhaps you can cut in when you do escape,' said his playful look.

Peter Ivanovich sighed still more deeply and despondently, and Praskovya Fedorovna pressed his arm gratefully. When they reached the drawing-room, upholstered in pink cretonne and lighted by a dim lamp, they sat down at the table—she on a sofa and Peter Ivanovich on a low pouffe, the springs of which yielded spasmodically under his weight. Praskovya Fedorovna had been on the point of warning him to take another seat, but felt that such a warning was out of keeping with her present condition and so changed her mind. As he sat down on the pouffe Peter Ivanovich recalled how Ivan Ilych had arranged this room and had consulted him regarding this pink cretonne with green leaves. The whole room was full of furniture and knick-knacks, and on her way to the sofa the lace of the widow's black shawl caught on the carved edge of the table. Peter Ivanovich rose to detach it, and the springs of the pouffe, relieved of his weight, rose also and gave him a push. The widow began detaching her shawl herself, and Peter Ivanovich again sat down, suppressing the rebellious springs of the pouffe under him. But the widow had not quite freed herself and Peter Ivanovich got up again, and again the pouffe rebelled and even creaked. When this was all over she took out a clean cambric handkerchief and began to weep. The episode with the shawl and the struggle with the pouffe had cooled Peter Ivanovich's emotions and he sat there with a sullen look on his face. This awkward situation was interrupted by Sokolov, Ivan Ilych's butler, who came to report that the plot in the cemetery that Praskovya Fedorovna had chosen would cost two hundred rubles. She stopped weeping and, looking at Peter Ivanovich with the air of a victim, remarked in French that it was very hard for her. Peter Ivanovich made a silent gesture signifying his full conviction that it must indeed be so.

'Please smoke,' she said in a magnanimous yet crushed voice, and turned to discuss with Sokolov the price of the plot for the grave.

Peter Ivanovich while lighting his cigarette heard her inquiring very circumstantially into the prices of different plots in the cemetery and finally decide which she would take. When that was done she gave instructions about engaging the choir. Sokolov then left the room.

'I look after everything myself,' she told Peter Ivanovich, shifting the albums that lay on the table; and noticing that the table was endangered by his cigarette-ash, she immediately passed him an ash-tray, saying as she did so: 'I consider it an affectation to say that my grief prevents my attending to practical affairs. On the contrary, if anything can—I won't say console me, but—distract me, it is seeing to everything concerning him.' She again took out her handkerchief as if preparing to cry, but suddenly, as if mastering her feeling, she shook herself and began to speak calmly. 'But there is something I want to talk to you about.'

Peter Ivanovich bowed, keeping control of the springs of the pouffe, which immediately began quivering under him.

'He suffered terribly the last few days.'

'Did he?' said Peter Ivanovich.

'Oh, terribly! He screamed unceasingly, not for minutes but for hours. For the last three days he screamed incessantly. It was unendurable. I cannot understand how I bore it; you could hear him three rooms off. Oh, what I have suffered!'

'Is it possible that he was conscious all that time?' asked Peter Ivanovich.

'Yes,' she whispered. 'To the last moment. He took leave of us a quarter of an hour before he died, and asked us to take Volodya away.'

The thought of the sufferings of this man he had known so intimately, first as a merry little boy, then as a school-mate, and later as a grown-up colleague, suddenly struck Peter Ivanovich with horror, despite an unpleasant consciousness of his own and this woman's dissimulation. He again saw that brow, and that nose pressing down on the lip, and felt afraid for himself.

'Three days of frightful suffering and then death! Why, that might suddenly, at any time, happen to me,' he thought, and for a moment felt terrified. But—he did not himself know how—the customary reflection at once occurred to him that this had happened to Ivan Ilych and not to him, and that it should not and could not happen to him, and that to think that it could would be yielding to depression which he ought not to do, as Schwartz's expression plainly showed. After which reflection Peter Ivanovich felt reassured, and began to ask with interest about the details of Ivan Ilych's death, as though death was an accident natural to Ivan Ilych but certainly not to himself.

After many details of the really dreadful physical sufferings Ivan Ilych had endured (which details he learnt only from the effect those sufferings had produced on Praskovya Fedorovna's nerves) the widow apparently found it necessary to get to business.

'Oh, Peter Ivanovich, how hard it is! How terribly, terribly hard!' and she again began to weep.

Peter Ivanovich sighed and waited for her to finish blowing her nose. When she had done so he said, 'Believe me . . .', and she again began talking and brought out what was evidently her chief concern with him—namely, to question him as to how she could obtain a grant of money from the government on the occasion of her husband's death. She made it appear that she was asking Peter Ivanovich's advice about her pension, but he soon saw that she already knew about that to the minutest detail, more even than he did himself. She knew how much could be got out of the government in consequence of her husband's death, but wanted to find out whether she could not possibly extract something more. Peter Ivanovich tried to think of some means of doing so, but after reflecting for a while and, out of propriety, condemning the government for its niggardliness, he said he thought that nothing more could be got. Then she sighed and evidently began to devise means of getting rid of her visitor. Noticing this, he put out his cigarette, rose, pressed her hand, and went out into the anteroom.

In the dining-room where the clock stood that Ivan Ilych had liked so much and had bought at an antique shop, Peter Ivanovich met a priest and a few acquaintances who had come to attend the service, and he recognized Ivan Ilych's daughter, a handsome young woman. She was in black and her slim figure appeared slimmer than ever. She had a gloomy, determined, almost angry expression, and bowed to Peter Ivanovich as though he were in some way to blame. Behind her, with the same offended look, stood a wealthy young man, an examining magistrate, whom Peter Ivanovich also knew and who was her fiancé, as he had heard. He bowed mournfully to them and was about to pass into the death-chamber, when from under the stairs appeared the figure of Ivan Ilych's schoolboy son, who was extremely like his father. He seemed a little Ivan Ilych, such as Peter Ivanovich remembered when they studied law together. His tear-stained eyes had in them the look that is seen in the eyes of boys of thirteen or fourteen who are not pure-minded. When he saw Peter Ivanovich he scowled morosely and shamefacedly. Peter Ivanovich nodded to him and entered the death-chamber. The service began: candles, groans, incense, tears, and sobs. Peter Ivanovich stood looking gloomily down at his feet. He did not look once at the dead man, did not yield to any depressing influence, and was one of the first to leave the room. There was no one in the anteroom, but Gerasim darted out of the dead man's room, rummaged with his strong hands among the fur coats

to find Peter Ivanovich's and helped him on with it.

'Well, friend Gerasim,' said Peter Ivanovich, so as to say something. 'It's a sad affair, isn't it?'

'It's God's will. We shall all come to it some day,' said Gerasim, displaying his teeth—the even, white teeth of a healthy peasant—and, like a man in the thick of urgent work, he briskly opened the front door, called the coachman, helped Peter Ivanovich into the sledge, and sprang back to the porch as if in readiness for what he had to do next.

Peter Ivanovich found the fresh air particularly pleasant after the smell of incense, the dead body, and carbolic acid.

'Where to, sir?' asked the coachman.

'It's not too late even now. . . . I'll call round on Fedor Vasilievich.'

He accordingly drove there and found them just finishing the first rubber, so that it was quite convenient for him to cut in.

II

Ivan Ilych's life had been most simple and most ordinary and therefore most terrible.

He had been a member of the Court of Justice, and died at the age of forty-five. His father had been an official who after serving in various ministries and departments in Petersburg had made the sort of career which brings men to positions from which by reason of their long service they cannot be dismissed, though they are obviously unfit to hold any responsible position, and for whom therefore posts are specially created, which though fictitious carry salaries of from six to ten thousand rubles that are not fictitious, and in receipt of which they live on to a great age.

Such was the Privy Councillor and superfluous member of various superfluous institutions, Ilya Epimovich Golovin.

He had three sons, of whom Ivan Ilych was the second. The eldest son was following in his father's footsteps only in another department, and was already approaching that stage in the service at which a similar sinecure would be reached. The third son was a failure. He had ruined his prospects in a number of positions and was now serving in the railway department. His father and brothers, and still more their wives, not merely disliked meeting him, but avoided remembering his existence unless compelled to do so. His sister had married Baron Greff, a Petersburg official of her father's type. Ivan Ilych was *le phénix de la famille* as people said. He was neither as cold and formal as his elder brother nor as wild as the younger, but was a happy mean between them—an intelligent, polished, lively and agreeable man. He had studied with his younger brother at the School of Law, but the latter had failed to complete the course and was expelled when he was in the fifth class. Ivan Ilych finished the course well. Even when he was at the School of Law he was just what he remained for the rest of his life: a capable, cheerful, good-natured, and sociable man, though strict in the fulfilment of what he considered to be his duty: and he considered his duty to be what was so considered by those in authority. Neither as a boy nor as a man was he a toady, but from early youth was by nature attracted to people of high station as a fly is drawn to the light, assimilating their ways and views of life and establishing friendly relations with them. All the enthusiasms of childhood and youth passed without leaving much trace on him; he succumbed to sensuality, to vanity, and latterly among the highest classes to liberalism, but always within limits which his instinct unfailingly indicated to him as correct.

At school he had done things which had formerly seemed to him very horrid and made him feel disgusted with himself when he did them; but when later on he saw that such actions were done by people of good position and that they did not regard them as wrong, he was able not exactly to regard them as right, but to forget about them entirely or not be at all troubled at remembering them.

Having graduated from the School of Law and qualified for the tenth rank of the civil service, and having received money from his father for his equipment, Ivan Ilych ordered himself clothes at Scharmer's, the fashionable tailor, hung a medallion inscribed *respice finem* on his watch-chain, took leave of his professor and the prince who was patron of the school, had a farewell dinner with his comrades at Donon's first-class restaurant, and with his new and fashionable portmanteau, linen, clothes, shaving and other toilet appliances, and a travelling rug, all purchased at the best shops, he set off for one of the provinces where, through his father's influence, he had been attached to the Governor as an official for special service.

In the province Ivan Ilych soon arranged as easy and agreeable a position for himself as he had had at the School of Law. He performed his official tasks, made his career, and at the same time amused himself pleasantly and decorously. Occasionally he paid official visits to country districts, where he behaved with dignity both to his superiors and inferiors, and performed the duties entrusted to him, which related chiefly to the sectarians, with an exactness and incorruptible honesty of which he could not but feel proud.

In official matters, despite his youth and taste for frivolous gaiety, he was exceedingly reserved, punctilious, and even severe; but in society he was often amusing and witty, and always good-natured, correct in his manner, and *bon enfant*, as the governor and his wife—with whom he was like one of the family—used to say of him.

In the province he had an affair with a lady who made advances to the elegant young lawyer, and there was also a milliner; and there were carousals with aides-de-camp who visited the district, and after-supper visits to a certain outlying street of doubtful reputation; and there was too some obsequiousness to his chief and even to his chief's wife, but all this was done with such a tone of good breeding that no hard names could be applied to it. It all came under the heading of the French saying: *'Il faut que jeunesse se passe.'*[1] It was all done with clean hands, in clean linen, with French phrases, and

[1] Youth must have its fling. (Translators' note)

above all among people of the best society and consequently with the approval of people of rank.

So Ivan Ilych served for five years and then came a change in his official life. The new and reformed judicial institutions were introduced, and new men were needed. Ivan Ilych became such a new man. He was offered the post of Examining Magistrate, and he accepted it though the post was in another province and obliged him to give up the connexions he had formed and to make new ones. His friends met to give him a send-off; they had a group-photograph taken and presented him with a silver cigarette-case, and he set off to his new post.

As examining magistrate Ivan Ilych was just as *comme il faut* and decorous a man, inspiring general respect and capable of separating his official duties from his private life, as he had been when acting as an official on special service. His duties now as examining magistrate were far more interesting and attractive than before. In his former position it had been pleasant to wear an undress uniform made by Scharmer, and to pass through the crowd of petitioners and officials who were timorously awaiting an audience with the governor, and who envied him as with free and easy gait he went straight into his chief's private room to have a cup of tea and a cigarette with him. But not many people had then been directly dependent on him—only police officials and the sectarians when he went on special missions—and he liked to treat them politely, almost as comrades, as if he were letting them feel that he who had the power to crush them was treating them in this simple, friendly way. There were then but few such people. But now, as an examining magistrate, Ivan Ilych felt that everyone without exception, even the most important and self-satisfied, was in his power, and that he need only write a few words on a sheet of paper with a certain heading, and this or that important, self-satisfied person would be brought before him in the role of an accused person or a witness, and if he did not choose to allow him to sit down, would have to stand before him and

answer his questions. Ivan Ilych never abused his power; he tried on the contrary to soften its expression, but the consciousness of it and of the possibility of softening its effect, supplied the chief interest and attraction of his office. In his work itself, especially in his examinations, he very soon acquired a method of eliminating all considerations irrelevant to the legal aspect of the case, and reducing even the most complicated case to a form in which it would be presented on paper only in its externals, completely excluding his personal opinion of the matter, while above all observing every prescribed formality. The work was new and Ivan Ilych was one of the first men to apply the new Code of 1864.[2]

On taking up the post of examining magistrate in a new town, he made new acquaintances and connexions, placed himself on a new footing, and assumed a somewhat different tone. He took up an attitude of rather dignified aloofness towards the provincial authorities, but picked out the best circle of legal gentlemen and wealthy gentry living in the town and assumed a tone of slight dissatisfaction with the government, of moderate liberalism, and of enlightened citizenship. At the same time, without at all altering the elegance of his toilet, he ceased shaving his chin and allowed his beard to grow as it pleased.

Ivan Ilych settled down very pleasantly in this new town. The society there, which inclined towards opposition to the Governor, was friendly, his salary was larger, and he began to play *vint* [a form of bridge], which he found added not a little to the pleasure of life, for he had a capacity for cards, played good-humouredly, and calculated rapidly and astutely, so that he usually won.

After living there for two years he met his future wife, Praskovya Fedorovna and relaxations from his labours as examining magistrate, Ivan Ilych established light and playful relations with her.

While he had been an official on special

---

2 The emancipation of the serfs in 1861 was followed by a thorough all-round reform of judicial proceedings. (Translators' note)

service he had been accustomed to dance, but now as an examining magistrate it was exceptional for him to do so. If he danced now, he did it as if to show that though he served under the reformed order of things, and had reached the fifth official rank, yet when it came to dancing he could do it better than most people. So at the end of an evening he sometimes danced with Praskovya Fedorovna, and it was chiefly during these dances that he captivated her. She fell in love with him. Ivan Ilych had at first no definite intention of marrying, but when the girl fell in love with him he said to himself: 'Really, why shouldn't I marry?'

Praskovya Fedorovna came of a good family, was not bad looking, and had some little property. Ivan Ilych might have aspired to a more brilliant match, but even this was good. He had his salary, and she, he hoped, would have an equal income. She was well connected, and was a sweet, pretty, and thoroughly correct young woman. To say that Ivan Ilych married because he fell in love with Praskovya Fedorovna and found that she sympathized with his views of life would be as incorrect as to say that he married because his social circle approved of the match. He was swayed by both these considerations: the marriage gave him personal satisfaction, and at the same time it was considered the right thing by the most highly placed of his associates.

So Ivan Ilych got married.

The preparations for marriage and the beginning of married life, with its conjugal caresses, the new furniture, new crockery, and new linen, were very pleasant until his wife became pregnant—so that Ivan Ilych had begun to think that marriage would not impair the easy, agreeable, gay and always decorous character of his life, approved of by society and regarded by himself as natural, but would even improve it. But from the first months of his wife's pregnancy, something new, unpleasant, depressing, and unseemly, and from which there was no way of escape, unexpectedly showed itself.

His wife, without any reason—*de gaieté de cœur* as Ivan Ilych expressed it

to himself—began to disturb the pleasure and propriety of their life. She began to be jealous without any cause, expected him to devote his whole attention to her, found fault with everything, and made coarse and ill-mannered scenes.

At first Ivan Ilych hoped to escape from the unpleasantness of this state of affairs by the same easy and decorous relation to life that had served him heretofore: he tried to ignore his wife's disagreeable moods, continued to live in his usual easy and pleasant way, invited friends to his house for a game of cards, and also tried going out to his club or spending his evenings with friends. But one day his wife began upbraiding him so vigorously, using such coarse words, and continued to abuse him every time he did not fulfil her demands, so resolutely and with such evident determination not to give way till he submitted—that is, till he stayed at home and was bored just as she was—that he became alarmed. He now realized that matrimony—at any rate with Praskovya Fedorovna—was not always conducive to the pleasures and amenities of life but on the contrary often infringed both comfort and propriety, and that he must therefore entrench himself against such infringement. And Ivan Ilych began to seek for means of doing so. His official duties were the one thing that imposed upon Praskovya Fedorovna, and by means of his official work and the duties attached to it he began struggling with his wife to secure his own independence.

With the birth of their child, the attempts to feed it and the various failures in doing so, and with the real and imaginary illnesses of mother and child, in which Ivan Ilych's sympathy was demanded but about which he understood nothing, the need of securing for himself an existence outside his family life became still more imperative.

As his wife grew more irritable and exacting and Ivan Ilych transferred the centre of gravity of his life more and more to his official work, so did he grow to like his work better and became more ambitious than before.

Very soon, within a year of his wedding, Ivan Ilych had realized that marriage, though it may add some comforts to life, is in fact a very intricate and difficult affair towards which in order to perform one's duty, that is, to lead a decorous life approved of by society, one must adopt a definite attitude just as towards one's official duties.

And Ivan Ilych evolved such an attitude toward married life. He only required of it those conveniences—dinner at home, housewife, and bed—which it could give him, and above all that propriety of external forms required by public opinion. For the rest he looked for light-hearted pleasure and propriety, and was very thankful when he found them, but if he met with antagonism and querulousness he at once retired into his separate fenced-off world of official duties, where he found satisfaction.

Ivan Ilych was esteemed a good official, and after three years was made Assistant Public Prosecutor. His new duties, their importance, the possibility of indicting and imprisoning anyone he chose, the publicity his speeches received, and the success he had in all these things, made his work still more attractive.

More children came. His wife became more and more querulous and ill-tempered, but the attitude Ivan Ilych had adopted towards his home life rendered him almost impervious to her grumbling.

After seven years' service in that town he was transferred to another province as Public Prosecutor. They moved, but were short of money and his wife did not like the place they moved to. Though the salary was higher the cost of living was greater, besides which two of their children died and family life became still more unpleasant for him.

Praskovya Fedorovna blamed her husband for every inconvenience they encountered in their new home. Most of the conversations between husband and wife, especially as to the children's education, led to topics which recalled former disputes, and those disputes were apt to flare up again at any moment. There remained only those rare periods of amorousness which still came to them at times but did not last long. These were islets at which they anchored for a while and then again set out upon that ocean of veiled hostility which showed itself in their aloofness from one another. This aloofness might have grieved Ivan Ilych had he considered that it ought not to exist, but he now regarded the position as normal, and even made it the goal at which he aimed in family life. His aim was to free himself more and more from those unpleasantnesses and to give them a semblance of harmlessness and propriety. He attained this by spending less and less time with his family, and when obliged to be at home he tried to safeguard his position by the presence of outsiders. The chief thing however was that he had his official duties. The whole interest of his life now centred in the official world and that interest absorbed him. The consciousness of his power, being able to ruin anybody he wished to ruin, the importance, even the external dignity of his entry into court, or meetings with his subordinates, his success with superiors and inferiors, and above all his masterly handling of cases, of which he was conscious—all this gave him pleasure and filled his life, together with chats with his colleagues, dinners, and bridge. So that on the whole Ivan Ilych's life continued to flow as he considered it should do—pleasantly and properly.

So things continued for another seven years. His eldest daughter was already sixteen, another child had died, and only one son was left, a schoolboy and a subject of dissension. Ivan Ilych wanted to put him in the School of Law, but to spite him Praskovya Fedorovna entered him at the High School. The daughter had been educated at home and had turned out well: the boy did not learn badly either.

III

So Ivan Ilych lived for seventeen years after his marriage. He was already a Public Prosecutor of long standing, and had declined several proposed transfers while awaiting a more desirable post, when an unanticipated and unpleasant occurrence quite upset the peaceful course of his life. He was expecting to be offered the post of presiding judge in a University town, but

Happe somehow came to the front and obtained the appointment instead. Ivan Ilych became irritable, reproached Happe, and quarrelled both with him and with his immediate superiors—who became colder to him and again passed him over when other appointments were made.

This was in 1880, the hardest year of Ivan Ilych's life. It was then that it became evident on the one hand that his salary was insufficient for them to live on, and on the other that he had been forgotten, and not only this, but that what was for him the greatest and most cruel injustice appeared to others a quite ordinary occurrence. Even his father did not consider it was his duty to help him. Ivan Ilych felt himself abandoned by everyone, and that they regarded his position with a salary of 3,500 roubles [about £350] as quite normal and even fortunate. He alone knew that with the consciousness of the injustices done him, with his wife's incessant nagging, and with the debts he had contracted by living beyond his means, his position was far from normal.

In order to save money that summer he obtained leave of absence and went with his wife to live in the country at her brother's place.

In the country, without his work, he experienced *ennui* for the first time in his life, and not only *ennui* but intolerable depression, and he decided that it was impossible to go on living like that, and that it was necessary to take energetic measures.

Having passed a sleepless night pacing up and down the veranda, he decided to go to Petersburg and bestir himself, in order to punish those who had failed to appreciate him and to get transferred to another ministry.

Next day, despite many protests from his wife and her brother, he started for Petersburg with the sole object of obtaining a post with a salary of five thousand rubles a year. He was no longer bent on any particular department, or tendency, or kind of activity. All he now wanted was an appointment to another post with a salary of five thousand rubles, either in the administration, in the banks, with the railways, in one of the Empress Marya's Institutions, or even in the customs—but it had to carry with it a salary of five thousand rubles and be in a ministry other than that in which they had failed to appreciate him.

And this quest of Ivan Ilych's was crowned with remarkable and unexpected success. At Kursk an acquaintance of his, F. I. Ilyin, got into the first-class carriage, sat down beside Ivan Ilych, and told him of a telegram just received by the Governor of Kursk announcing that a change was about to take place in the ministry: Peter Ivanovich was to be superseded by Ivan Semenovich.

The proposed change, apart from its significance for Russia, had a special significance for Ivan Ilych, because by bringing forward a new man, Peter Petrovich, and consequently his friend Zachar Ivanovich, it was highly favourable for Ivan Ilych, since Zachar Ivanovich was a friend and colleague of his.

In Moscow this news was confirmed, and on reaching Petersburg Ivan Ilych found Zachar Ivanovich and received a definite promise of an appointment in his former department of Justice.

A week later he telegraphed to his wife: 'Zachar in Miller's place. I shall receive appointment on presentation of report.'

Thanks to this change of personnel, Ivan Ilych had unexpectedly obtained an appointment in his former ministry which placed him two stages above his former colleagues besides giving him five thousand rubles salary and three thousand five hundred rubles for expenses connected with his removal. All his ill humour towards his former enemies and the whole department vanished, and Ivan Ilych was completely happy.

He returned to the country more cheerful and contented than he had been for a long time. Praskovya Fedorovna also cheered up and a truce was arranged between them. Ivan Ilych told of how he had been fêted by everybody in Petersburg, how all those who had been his enemies were put to shame and now fawned on him, how envious they were of his appointment, and how much everybody in Petersburg had liked him.

Praskovya Fedorovna listened to all

this and appeared to believe it. She did not contradict anything, but only made plans for their life in the town to which they were going. Ivan Ilych saw with delight that these plans were his plans, that he and his wife agreed, and that, after a stumble, his life was regaining its due and natural character of pleasant lightheartedness and decorum.

Ivan Ilych had come back for a short time only, for he had to take up his new duties on the 10th of September. Moreover, he needed time to settle into the new place, to move all his belongings from the province, and to buy and order many additional things: in a word, to make such arrangements as he had resolved on, which were almost exactly what Praskovya Fedorovna too had decided on.

Now that everything had happened so fortunately, and that he and his wife were at one in their aims and moreover saw so little of one another, they got on together better than they had done since the first years of marriage. Ivan Ilych had thought of taking his family away with him at once, but the insistence of his wife's brother and her sister-in-law, who had suddenly become particularly amiable and friendly to him and his family, induced him to depart alone.

So he departed, and the cheerful state of mind induced by his success and by the harmony between his wife and himself, the one intensifying the other, did not leave him. He found a delightful house, just the thing both he and his wife had dreamt of. Spacious, lofty reception rooms in the old style, a convenient and dignified study, rooms for his wife and daughter, a study for his son—it might have been specially built for them. Ivan Ilych himself superintended the arrangements, chose the wallpapers, supplemented the furniture (preferably with antiques which he considered particularly *comme il faut*), and supervised the upholstering. Everything progressed and progressed and approached the ideal he had set himself: even when things were only half completed they exceeded his expectations. He saw what a refined and elegant character, free from vulgarity, it would all have when it was ready. On fall-

ing asleep he pictured to himself how the reception-room would look. Looking at the yet unfinished drawing-room he could see the fireplace, the screen, the what-not, the little chairs dotted here and there, the dishes and plates on the walls, and the bronzes, as they would be when everything was in place. He was pleased by the thought of how his wife and daughter, who shared his taste in this matter, would be impressed by it. They were certainly not expecting as much. He had been particularly successful in finding, and buying cheaply, antiques which gave a particularly aristocratic character to the whole place. But in his letters he intentionally understated everything in order to be able to surprise them. All this so absorbed him that his new duties—though he liked his official work—interested him less than he expected. Sometimes he even had moments of absent-mindedness during the Court Sessions, and would consider whether he should have straight or curved cornices for his curtains. He was so interested in it all that he often did things himself, rearranging the furniture, or rehanging the curtains. Once when mounting a step-ladder to show the upholsterer, who did not understand, how he wanted the hangings draped, he made a false step and slipped, but being a strong and agile man he clung on and only knocked his side against the knob of the window frame. The bruised place was painful but the pain soon passed, and he felt particularly bright and well just then. He wrote: 'I feel fifteen years younger.' He thought he would have everything ready by September, but it dragged on till mid-October. But the result was charming not only in his eyes but to everyone who saw it.

In reality it was just what is usually seen in the houses of people of moderate means who want to appear rich, and therefore succeed only in resembling others like themselves: there were damasks, dark wood, plants, rugs, and dull and polished bronzes—all the things people of a certain class have in order to resemble other people of that class. His house was so like the others that it would never have been noticed, but to him it all seemed to be quite exceptional. He was very happy when he met his family at the station and brought them to the newly furnished house all lit up, where a footman in a white tie opened the door into the hall decorated with plants, and when they went on into the drawing-room and the study uttering exclamations of delight. He conducted them everywhere, drank in their praises eagerly, and beamed with pleasure. At tea that evening, when Praskovya Fedorovna among other things asked him about his fall, he laughed, and showed them how he had gone flying and had frightened the upholsterer.

'It's a good thing I'm a bit of an athlete. Another man might have been killed, but I merely knocked myself, just here; it hurts when it's touched, but it's passing off already—it's only a bruise.'

So they began living in their new home —in which, as always happens, when they got thoroughly settled in they found they were just one room short—and with the increased income, which as always was just a little (some five hundred rubles) too little, but it was all very nice.

Things went particularly well at first, before everything was finally arranged and while something had still to be done: this thing bought, that thing ordered, another thing moved, and something else adjusted. Though there were some disputes between husband and wife, they were both so well satisfied and had so much to do that it all passed off without any serious quarrels. When nothing was left to arrange it became rather dull and something seemed to be lacking, but they were then making acquaintances, forming habits, and life was growing fuller.

Ivan Ilych spent his mornings at the law court and came home to dinner, and at first he was generally in a good humour, though he occasionally became irritable just on account of his house. (Every spot on the tablecloth or the upholstery, and every broken window-blind string, irritated him. He had devoted so much trouble to arranging it all that every disturbance of it distressed him.) But on the whole his life ran its course as he believed life should do: easily, pleasantly, and decorously.

He got up at nine, drank his coffee, read the paper, and then put on his undress uniform and went to the law courts. There the harness in which he worked had already been stretched to fit him and he donned it without a hitch: petitioners, inquiries at the chancery, the chancery itself, and the sittings public and administrative. In all this the thing was to exclude everything fresh and vital, which always disturbs the regular course of official business, and to admit only official relations with people, and then only on official grounds. A man would come, for instance, wanting some information. Ivan Ilych, as one in whose sphere the matter did not lie, would have nothing to do with him: but if the man had some business with him in his official capacity, something that could be expressed on officially stamped paper, he would do everything, positively everything he could within the limits of such relations, and in doing so would maintain the semblance of friendly human relations, that is, would observe the courtesies of life. As soon as the official relations ended, so did everything else. Ivan Ilych possessed this capacity to separate his real life from the official side of affairs and not mix the two, in the highest degree, and by long practice and natural aptitude had brought it to such a pitch that sometimes, in the manner of a virtuoso, he would even allow himself to let the human and official relations mingle. He let himself do this just because he felt that he could at any time he chose resume the strictly official attitude again and drop the human relation. And he did it all easily, pleasantly, correctly, and even artistically. In the intervals between the sessions he smoked, drank tea, chatted a little about politics, a little about general topics, a little about cards, but most of all about official appointments. Tired, but with the feelings of a virtuoso—one of the first violins who has played his part in an orchestra with precision—he would return home to find that his wife and daughter had been out paying calls, or had a visitor, and that his son had been to school, had done his homework with his tutor, and was duly learning what is taught at High Schools. Everything was as it should be. After dinner, if they had no visitors, Ivan Ilych sometimes read a book that was being much discussed at the time, and in the evening settled down to work, that is, read official papers, compared the depositions of witnesses, and noted paragraphs of the Code applying to them. This was neither dull nor amusing. It was dull when he might have been playing bridge, but if no bridge was available it was at any rate better than doing nothing or sitting with his wife. Ivan Ilych's chief pleasure was giving little dinners to which he invited men and women of good social position, and just as his drawing-room resembled all other drawing-rooms so did his enjoyable little parties resemble all other such parties.

Once they even gave a dance. Ivan Ilych enjoyed it and everything went off well, except that it led to a violent quarrel with his wife about the cakes and sweets. Praskovya Fedorovna had made her own plans, but Ivan Ilych insisted on getting everything from an expensive confectioner and ordered too many cakes, and the quarrel occurred because some of those cakes were left over and the confectioner's bill came to forty-five rubles. It was a great and disagreeable quarrel. Praskovya Fedorovna called him 'a fool and an imbecile', and he clutched at his head and made angry allusions to divorce.

But the dance itself had been enjoyable. The best people were there, and Ivan Ilych had danced with Princess Trufonova, a sister of the distinguished founder of the Society 'Bear my Burden'.

The pleasures connected with his work were pleasures of ambition; his social pleasures were those of vanity; but Ivan Ilych's greatest pleasure was playing bridge. He acknowledged that whatever disagreeable incident happened in his life, the pleasure that beamed like a ray of light above everything else was to sit down to bridge with good players, not noisy partners, and of course to four-handed bridge (with five players it was annoying to have to stand out, though one pretended not to mind), to play a clever and serious game (when the cards allowed it) and then to have supper and drink a glass of wine. After a game of bridge, especially if he had won a little (to win a large sum was unpleasant), Ivan

Ilych went to bed in specially good humour.

So they lived. They formed a circle of acqua'ntances among the best people and were visited by people of importance and by young folk. In their views as to their acquaintances, husband and wife and daughter were entirely agreed, and tacitly and unanimously kept at arm's length and shook off the various shabby friends and relations who, with much show of affection, gushed into the drawing-room with its Japanese plates on the walls. Soon these shabby friends ceased to obtrude themselves and only the best people remained in the Golovins' set.

Young men made up to Lisa, and Petrischhev, an examining magistrate and Dmitri Ivanovich Petrischev's son and sole heir, began to be so attentive to her that Ivan Ilych had already spoken to Praskovya Fedorovna about it, and considered whether they should not arrange a party for them, or get up some private theatricals.

So they lived, and all went well, without change, and life flowed pleasantly.

IV

They were all in good health. It could not be called ill health if Ivan Ilych sometimes said that he had a queer taste in his mouth and felt some discomfort in his left side.

But this discomfort increased and, though not exactly painful, grew into a sense of pressure in his side accompanied by ill humour. And his irritability became worse and worse and began to mar the agreeable, easy, and correct life that had established itself in the Golovin family. Quarrels between husband and wife became more and more frequent, and soon the ease and amenity disappeared and even the decorum was barely maintained. Scenes again became frequent, and very few of those islets remained on which husband and wife could meet without an explosion. Praskovya Fedorovna now had good reason to say that her husband's temper was trying. With characteristic exaggeration she said he had always had a dreadful temper, and that it had needed all her good nature to put up with it for twenty years. It was true that now the quarrels were started by him. His bursts of temper always came just before dinner, often just as he began to eat his soup. Sometimes he noticed that a plate or dish was chipped, or the food was not right, or his son put his elbow on the table, or his daughter's hair was not done as he liked it, and for all this he blamed Praskovya Fedorovna. At first she retorted and said disagreeable things to him, but once or twice he fell into such a rage at the beginning of dinner that she realized it was due to some physical derangement brought on by taking food, and so she restrained herself and did not answer, but only hurried to get the dinner over. She regarded this self-restraint as highly praiseworthy. Having come to the conclusion that her husband had a dreadful temper and made her life miserable, she began to feel sorry for herself, and the more she pitied herself the more she hated her husband. She began to wish he would die; yet she did not want him to die because then his salary would cease. And this irritated her against him still more. She considered herself dreadfully unhappy just because not even his death could save her, and though she concealed her exasperation, that hidden exasperation of hers increased his irritation also.

After one scene in which Ivan Ilych had been particularly unfair and after which he had said in explanation that he certainly was irritable but that it was due to his not being well, she said that if he was ill it should be attended to, and insisted on his going to see a celebrated doctor.

He went. Everything took place as he had expected and as it always does. There was the usual waiting and the important air assumed by the doctor, with which he was so familiar (resembling that which he himself assumed in court), and the sounding and listening, and the questions which called for answers that were foregone conclusions and were evidently unnecessary, and the look of importance which implied that 'if only you put yourself in our hands we will arrange everything—we know indubitably how it has to be done, always in the same way for everybody alike.' It was all just as it was

in the law courts. The doctor put on just the same air towards him as he himself put on towards an accused person.

The doctor said that so-and-so indicated that there was so-and-so inside the patient, but if the investigation of so-and-so did not confirm this, then he must assume that and that. If he assumed that and that, then . . . and so on. To Ivan Ilych only one question was important: was his case serious or not? But the doctor ignored that inappropriate question. From his point of view it was not the one under consideration, the real question was to decide between a floating kidney, chronic catarrh, or appendicitis. It was not a question of Ivan Ilych's life or death, but one between a floating kidney and appendicitis. And that question the doctor solved brilliantly, as it seemed to Ivan Ilych, in favour of the appendix, with the reservation that should an examination of the urine give fresh indications the matter would be reconsidered. All this was just what Ivan Ilych had himself brilliantly accomplished a thousand times in dealing with men on trial. The doctor summed up just as brilliantly, looking over his spectacles triumphantly and even gaily at the accused. From the doctor's summing up Ivan Ilych concluded that things were bad, but that for the doctor, and perhaps for everybody else, it was a matter of indifference, though for him it was bad. And this conclusion struck him painfully, arousing in him a great feeling of pity for himself and of bitterness towards the doctor's indifference to a matter of such importance.

He said nothing of this, but rose, placed the doctor's fee on the table, and remarked with a sigh: 'We sick people probably often put inappropriate questions. But tell me, in general, is this complaint dangerous, or not? . . .'

The doctor looked at him sternly over his spectacles with one eye, as if to say: 'Prisoner, if you will not keep to the questions put to you, I shall be obliged to have you removed from the court.'

'I have already told you what I consider necessary and proper. The analysis may show something more.' And the doctor bowed.

Ivan Ilych went out slowly, seated himself disconsolately in his sledge, and drove home. All the way home he was going over what the doctor had said, trying to translate those complicated, obscure, scientific phrases into plain language and find in them an answer to the question: 'Is my condition bad? Is it very bad? Or is there as yet nothing much wrong?' And it seemed to him that the meaning of what the doctor had said was that it was very bad. Everything in the streets seemed depressing. The cabmen, the houses, the passers-by, and the shops, were dismal. His ache, this dull gnawing ache that never ceased for a moment, seemed to have acquired a new and more serious significance from the doctor's dubious remarks. Ivan Ilych now watched it with a new and oppressive feeling.

He reached home and began to tell his wife about it. She listened, but in the middle of his account his daughter came in with her hat on, ready to go out with her mother. She sat down reluctantly to listen to this tedious story, but could not stand it long, and her mother too did not hear him to the end.

'Well, I am very glad,' she said. 'Mind now to take your medicine regularly. Give me the prescription and I'll send Gerasim to the chemist's.' And she went to get ready to go out.

While she was in the room Ivan Ilych had hardly taken time to breathe, but he sighed deeply when she left it.

'Well,' he thought, 'perhaps it isn't so bad after all.'

He began taking his medicine and following the doctor's directions, which had been altered after the examination of the urine. But then it happened that there was a contradiction between the indications drawn from the examination of the urine and the symptoms that showed themselves. It turned out that what was happening differed from what the doctor had told him, and that he had either forgotten, or blundered, or hidden something from him. He could not, however, be blamed for that, and Ivan Ilych still obeyed his orders implicitly and at first derived some comfort from doing so.

From the time of his visit to the doctor, Ivan Ilych's chief occupation was the exact fulfilment of the doctor's instructions regarding hygiene and the taking of medicine, and the observation of his pain and his excretions. His chief interests came to be people's ailments and people's health. When sickness, deaths, or recoveries, were mentioned in his presence, especially when the illness resembled his own, he listened with agitation which he tried to hide, asked questions, and applied what he heard to his own case.

The pain did not grow less, but Ivan Ilych made efforts to force himself to think that he was better. And he could do this so long as nothing agitated him. But as soon as he had any unpleasantness with his wife, any lack of success in his official work, or held bad cards at bridge, he was at once acutely sensible of his disease. He had formerly borne such mischances, hoping soon to adjust what was wrong, to master it and attain success, or make a grand slam. But now every mischance upset him and plunged him into despair. He would say to himself: 'There now, just as I was beginning to get better and the medicine had begun to take effect, comes this accursed misfortune, or unpleasantness . . .' And he was furious with the mishap, or with the people who were causing the unpleasantness and killing him, for he felt that this fury was killing him but could not restrain it. One would have thought that it should have been clear to him that this exasperation with circumstances and people aggravated his illness, and that he ought therefore to ignore unpleasant occurrences. But he drew the very opposite conclusion: he said that he needed peace, and he watched for everything that might disturb it and became irritable at the slightest infringement of it. His condition was rendered worse by the fact that he read medical books and consulted doctors. The progress of his disease was so gradual that he could deceive himself when comparing one day with another—the difference was so slight. But when he consulted the doctors it seemed to him that he was getting worse, and even very rapidly. Yet despite this he was continually consulting them.

That month he went to see another celebrity, who told him almost the same as the first had done but put his questions rather differently, and the interview with this celebrity only increased Ivan Ilych's doubts and fears. A friend of a friend of his, a very good doctor, diagnosed his illness again quite differently from the others, and though he predicted recovery, his questions and suppositions bewildered Ivan Ilych still more and increased his doubts. A homoeopathist diagnosed the disease in yet another way, and prescribed medicine which Ivan Ilych took secretly for a week. But after a week, not feeling any improvement and having lost confidence both in the former doctor's treatment and in this one's, he became still more despondent. One day a lady acquaintance mentioned a cure effected by a wonder-working icon. Ivan Ilych caught himself listening attentively and beginning to believe that it had occurred. This incident alarmed him. 'Has my mind really weakened to such an extent?' he asked himself. 'Nonsense! It's all rubbish. I mustn't give way to nervous fears but having chosen a doctor must keep strictly to his treatment. That is what I will do. Now it's all settled. I won't think about it, but will follow the treatment seriously till summer, and then we shall see. From now there must be no more of this wavering!' This was easy to say but impossible to carry out. The pain in his side oppressed him and seemed to grow worse and more incessant, while the taste in his mouth grew stranger and stranger. It seemed to him that his breath had a disgusting smell, and he was conscious of a loss of appetite and strength. There was no deceiving himself: something terrible, new, and more important than anything before in his life, was taking place within him of which he alone was aware. Those about him did not understand or would not understand it, but thought everything in the world was going on as usual. That tormented Ivan Ilych more than anything. He saw that his household, especially his wife and daughter who were in a perfect whirl of visiting, did not understand anything of it and were annoyed that he was so depressed and exacting, as if he were to blame for it. Though they tried to disguise it he saw that he was an obstacle in their path, and that his wife had adopted a definite line in regard to his illness

and kept to it regardless of anything he said or did. Her attitude was this: 'You know,' she would say to her friends, 'Ivan Ilych can't do as other people do, and keep to the treatment prescribed for him. One day he'll take his drops and keep strictly to his diet and go to bed in good time, but the next day unless I watch him he'll suddenly forget his medicine, eat sturgeon—which is forbidden—and sit up playing cards until one o'clock in the morning.'

'Oh, come, when was that?' Ivan Ilych would ask in vexation. 'Only once at Peter Ivanovich's.'

'And yesterday with Shebek.'

'Well, even if I hadn't stayed up, this pain would have kept me awake.'

'Be that as it may you'll never get well like that, but will always make us wretched.'

Praskovya Fedorovna's attitude to Ivan Ilych's illness, as she expressed it both to others and to him, was that it was his own fault and was another of the annoyances he caused her. Ivan Ilych felt that this opinion escaped her involuntarily—but that did not make it easier for him.

At the law courts too, Ivan Ilych noticed, or thought he noticed, a strange attitude towards himself. It sometimes seemed to him that people were watching him inquisitively as a man whose place might soon be vacant. Then again, his friends would suddenly begin to chaff him in a friendly way about his low spirits, as if the awful, horrible, and unheard-of thing that was going on within him, incessantly gnawing at him and irresistably drawing him away, was a very agreeable subject for jests. Schwartz in particular irritated him by his jocularity, vivacity, and *savoir-faire*, which reminded him of what he himself had been ten years ago.

Friends came to make up a set and they sat down to cards. They dealt, bending the new cards to soften them, and he sorted the diamonds in his hand and found he had seven. His partner said 'No trumps' and supported him with two diamonds. What more could be wished for? It ought to be jolly and lively. They would make a grand slam. But suddenly Ivan Ilych was conscious of that gnawing pain, that taste in his mouth, and it seemed ridiculous that in such circumstances he should be pleased to make a grand slam.

He looked at his partner Mikhail Mikhaylovich, who rapped the table with his strong hand and instead of snatching up the tricks pushed the cards courteously and indulgently towards Ivan Ilych that he might have the pleasure of gathering them up without the trouble of stretching out his hand for them. 'Does he think I am too weak to stretch out my arm?' thought Ivan Ilych, and forgetting what he was doing he over-trumped his partner, missing the grand slam by three tricks. And what was most awful of all was that he saw how upset Mikhail Mikhaylovich was about it but did not himself care. And it was dreadful to realize why he did not care.

They all saw that he was suffering, and said: 'We can stop if you are tired. Take a rest.' Lie down? No, he was not at all tired, and he finished the rubber. All were gloomy and silent. Ivan Ilych felt that he had diffused this gloom over them and could not dispel it. They had supper and went away, and Ivan Ilych was left alone with the consciousness that his life was poisoned and was poisoning the lives of others, and that this poison did not weaken but penetrated more and more deeply into his whole being.

With this consciousness, and with physical pain besides the terror, he must go to bed, often to lie awake the greater part of the night. Next morning he had to get up again, dress, go to the law courts, speak, and write; or if he did not go out, spend at home those twenty-four hours a day each of which was a torture. And he had to live thus all alone on the brink of an abyss, with no one who understood or pitied him.

V

So one month passed and then another. Just before the New Year his brother-in-law came to town and stayed at their house. Ivan Ilych was at the law courts and Praskovya Fedorovna had gone shopping. When Ivan Ilych came home and entered his study he found his brother-in-law there—a healthy, florid man—unpacking his portmanteau himself. He raised his head on hearing Ivan Ilych's footsteps and looked up at him for a moment without a word. That stare told Ivan Ilych everything. His brother-in-law opened his mouth to utter an exclamation of surprise but checked himself, and that action confirmed all.

'I have changed, eh?'

'Yes, there is a change.'

And after that, try as he would to get his brother-in-law to return to the subject of his looks, the latter would say nothing about it. Praskovya Fedorovna came home and her brother went out to her. Ivan Ilych locked the door and began to examine himself in the glass, first full face, then in profile. He took up a portrait of himself taken with his wife, and compared it with what he saw in the glass. The change in him was immense. Then he bared his arms to the elbow, looked at them, drew the sleeves down again, sat down on an ottoman, and grew blacker than night.

'No, no, this won't do!' he said to himself, and jumped up, went to the table, took up some law papers and began to read them, but could not continue. He unlocked the door and went into the reception-room. The door leading to the drawing-room was shut. He approached it on tiptoe and listened.

'No, you are exaggerating!' Praskovya Fedorovna was saying.

'Exaggerating! Don't you see it? Why, he's a dead man! Look at his eyes—there's no light in them. But what is it that is wrong with him?'

'No one knows. Nikolaevich [that was another doctor] said something, but I don't know what. And Leschetitsky [this was the celebrated specialist] said quite the contrary . . .'

Ivan Ilych walked away, went to his own room, lay down, and began musing: 'The kidney, a floating kidney.' He recalled all the doctors had told him of how it detached itself and swayed about. And by an effort of imagination he tried to catch that kidney and arrest it and support it. So little was needed for this, it seemed to him. 'No, I'll go to see Peter Ivanovich again.' [That was the friend whose friend was a doctor.] He rang, ordered the carriage, and got ready to go.

'Where are you going, Jean?' asked his wife, with a specially sad and exceptionally kind look.

This exceptionally kind look irritated him. He looked morosely at her.

'I must go to see Peter Ivanovich.'

He went to see Peter Ivanovich, and together they went to see his friend, the doctor. He was in, and Ivan Ilych had a long talk with him.

Reviewing the anatomical and psychological details of what in the doctor's opinion was going on inside him, he understood it all.

There was something, a small thing, in the vermiform appendix. It might all come right. Only stimulate the energy of one organ and check the activity of another, then absorption would take place and everything would come right. He got home rather late for dinner, ate his dinner, and conversed cheerfully, but could not for a long time bring himself to go back to work in his room. At last, however, he went to his study and did what was necessary, but the consciousness that he had put something aside—an important, intimate matter which he would revert to when his work was done—never left him. When he had finished his work he remembered that this intimate matter was the thought of his vermiform appendix. But he did not give himself up to it, and went to the drawing-room for tea. There were callers there, including the examining magistrate who was a desirable match for his daughter, and they were conversing, playing the piano and singing. Ivan Ilych, as Praskovya Fedorovna remarked, spent that evening more cheerfully than usual, but he never for a moment forgot that he had postponed the important matter of the appendix. At eleven o'clock he said good-night and went to his bedroom. Since his illness he had slept in a small room next to his study. He undressed and took up a novel by Zola, but instead of reading it he fell into thought, and in his imagination that desired improvement in the vermiform

appendix occurred. There was the absorption and evacuation and the reestablishment of normal activity. 'Yes, that's it!' he said to himself. 'One need only assist nature, that's all.' He remembered his medicine, rose, took it, and lay down on his back watching for the beneficient action of the medicine and for it to lessen the pain. 'I need only take it regularly and avoid all injurious influences. I am already feeling better, much better.' He began touching his side: it was not painful to the touch. 'There, I really don't feel it. It's much better already.' He put out the light and turned on his side . . . 'The appendix is getting better, absorption is occurring.' Suddenly he felt the old, familiar, dull, gnawing pain, stubborn and serious. There was the same familiar loathsome taste in his mouth. His heart sank and he felt dazed. 'My God! My God!' he muttered. 'Again, again! And it will never cease.' And suddenly the matter presented itself in a quite different aspect. 'Vermiform appendix! Kidney!' he said to himself. 'It's not a question of appendix or kidney, but of life and . . . death. Yes, life was there and now it is going, going and I cannot stop it. Yes. Why deceive myself? Isn't it obvious to everyone but me that I'm dying, and that it's only a question of weeks, days . . . it may happen this moment. There was light and now there is darkness. I was here and now I'm going there! Where?' A chill came over him, his breathing ceased, and he felt only the throbbing of his heart.

'When I am not, what will there be? There will be nothing. Then where shall I be when I am no more? Can this be dying? No, I don't want to!' He jumped up and tried to light the candle, felt for it with trembling hands, dropped candle and candlestick on the floor, and fell back on his pillow.

'What's the use? It makes no difference,' he said to himself, staring with wide-open eyes into the darkness. Death. Yes, death. And none of them know or wish to know it, and they have no pity for me. Now they are playing.' (He heard through the door the distant sound of a song and its accompaniment.) 'It's all the same to them, but they will die too! Fools! I first, and they later, but it will be the same for them. And now they are merry . . . the beasts!'

Anger choked him and he was agonizingly, unbearably miserable. 'It is impossible that all men have been doomed to suffer this awful horror!' He raised himself.

'Something must be wrong. I must calm myself—must think it all over from the beginning.' And he again began thinking. 'Yes, the beginning of my illness: I knocked my side, but I was still quite well that day and the next. It hurt a little, then rather more. I saw the doctors, then followed despondency and anguish, more doctors, and I drew nearer to the abyss. My strength grew less and I kept coming nearer and nearer, and now I have wasted away and there is no light in my eyes. I think of the appendix—but this is death! I think of mending the appendix, and all the while here is death! Can it really be death?' Again terror seized him and he gasped for breath. He leant down and began feeling for the matches, pressing with his elbow on the stand beside the bed. It was in his way and hurt him, he grew furious with it, pressed on it still harder, and upset it. Breathless and in despair he fell on his back, expecting death to come immediately.

Meanwhile the visitors were leaving. Praskovya Fedorovna was seeing them off. She heard something fall and came in.

'What has happened?'

'Nothing. I knocked it over accidentally.'

She went out and returned with a candle. He lay there panting heavily, like a man who has run a thousand yards, and stared upwards at her with a fixed look.

'What is it, Jean?'

'No . . . o . . . thing. I upset it.' ('Why speak of it? She won't understand,' he thought.)

And in truth she did not understand. She picked up the stand, lit the candle, and hurried away to see another visitor off. When she came back he still lay on his back, looking upwards.

'What is it? Do you feel worse?'

'Yes.'

She shook her head and sat down.

'Do you know, Jean, I think we must ask Leshchetitsky to come and see you here.'

This meant calling in the famous specialist, regardless of expense. He smiled malignantly and said 'No'. She remained a little longer and then went up to him and kissed his forehead.

While she was kissing him he hated her from the bottom of his soul and with difficulty refrained from pushing her away.

'Good-night. Please God you'll sleep.'

'Yes.'

VI

Ivan Ilych saw that he was dying, and he was in continual despair.

In the depth of his heart he knew he was dying, but not only was he not accustomed to the thought, he simply did not and could not grasp it.

The syllogism he had learnt from Kiezewetter's Logic: 'Caius is a man, men are mortal, therefore Caius is mortal', had always seemed to him correct as applied to Caius, but certainly not as applied to himself. That Caius—man in the abstract—was mortal, was perfectly correct, but he was not Caius, not an abstract man, but a creature quite quite separate from all others. He had been little Vanya, with a mamma and a papa, with Mitya and Volodya, with the toys, a coachman and a nurse, afterwards with Katenka and with all the joys, griefs, and delights of childhood, boyhood, and youth. What did Caius know of the smell of that striped leather ball Vanya had been so fond of? Had Caius kissed his mother's hand like that, and did the silk of her dress rustle so for Caius? Had he rioted like that at school when the pastry was bad? Had Caius been in love like that? Could Caius preside at a session as he did? 'Caius really was mortal, and it was right for him to die; but for me, little Vanya, Ivan Ilych, with all my thoughts and emotions, it's altogether a different matter. It cannot be that I ought to die. That would be too terrible.'

Such was his feeling.

'If I had to die like Caius I should have known it was so. An inner voice would have told me so, but there was nothing of the sort in me and I and all my friends felt that our case was quite different from that of Caius. And now here it is!' he said to himself. 'It can't be. It's impossible! But here it is. How is this? How is one to understand it?'

He could not understand it, and tried to drive this false, incorrect, morbid thought away and to replace it by other proper and healthy thoughts. But that thought, and not the thought only but the reality itself, seemed to come and confront him.

And to replace that thought he called up a succession of others, hoping to find in them some support. He tried to get back into the former current of thoughts that had once screened the thought of death from him. But strange to say, all that had formerly shut off, hidden, and destroyed, his consciousness of death, no longer had that effect. Ivan Ilych now spent most of his time in attempting to re-establish that old current. He would say to himself: 'I will take up my duties again—after all I used to live by them.' And banishing all doubts he would go to the law courts, enter into conversation with his colleagues, and sit carelessly as was his wont, scanning the crowd with a thoughtful look and leaning both his emaciated arms on the arms of his oak chair; bending over as usual to a colleague and drawing his papers nearer he would interchange whispers with him, and then suddenly raising his eyes and sitting erect would pronounce certain words and open the proceedings. But suddenly in the midst of those proceedings the pain in his side, regardless of the stage the proceedings had reached, would begin its own gnawing work. Ivan Ilych would turn his attention to it and try to drive the thought of it away, but without success. It would come and stand before him and look at him, and he would be petrified and the light would die out of his eyes, and he would again begin asking himself whether It alone was true. And his colleagues and subordinates would see

with surprise and distress that he, the brilliant and subtle judge, was becoming confused and making mistakes. He would shake himself, try to pull himself together, manage somehow to bring the sitting to a close, and return home with the sorrowful consciousness that his judicial labours could not as formerly hide from him what he wanted them to hide, and could not deliver him from It. And what was worst of all was that It drew his attention to itself not in order to make him take some action but only that he should look at It, look it straight in the face: look at it and without doing anything, suffer inexpressibly.

And to save himself from this condition Ivan Ilych looked for consolations —new screens—and new screens were found and for a while seemed to save him, but then they immediately fell to pieces or rather became transparent, as if It penetrated them and nothing could veil It.

In these latter days he would go into the drawing-room he had arranged—that drawing-room where he had fallen and for the sake of which (how bitterly ridiculous it seemed) he had sacrificed his life—for he knew that his illness originated with that knock. He would enter and see that something had scratched the polished table. He would look for the cause of this and find that it was the bronze ornamentation of an album, that had got bent. He would take up the expensive album which he had lovingly arranged, and feel vexed with his daughter and her friends for their untidiness—for the album was torn here and there and some of the photographs turned upside down. He would put it carefully in order and bend the ornamentation back into position. Then it would occur to him to place all those things in another corner of the room, near the plants. He would call the footman, but his daughter or wife would come to help him. They would not agree, and his wife would contradict him, and he would dispute and grow angry. But that was all right, for then he did not think about It. It was invisible.

But then, when he was moving something himself, his wife would say: 'Let the servants do it. You will hurt yourself again.' And suddenly *It* would flash through the screen and he would see it. It was just a flash, and he hoped it would disappear, but he would involuntarily pay attention to his side. 'It sits there as before, gnawing just the same!' And he could no longer forget *It,* but could distinctly see it looking at him from behind the flowers. 'What is it all for?'

'It really is so! I lost my life over that curtain as I might have done when storming a fort. Is that possible? How terrible and how stupid. It can't be true! It can't, but it is.'

He would go to his study, lie down, and again be alone with *It*: face to face with *It.* And nothing could be done with *It* except to look at it and shudder.

VII

How it happened it is impossible to say because it came about step by step, unnoticed, but in the third month of Ivan Ilych's illness, his wife, his daughter, his son, his acquaintances, the doctors, the servants, and above all he himself, were aware that the whole interest he had for other people was whether he would soon vacate his place, and at last release the living from the discomfort caused by his presence and be himself released from his sufferings.

He slept less and less. He was given opium and hypodermic injections or morphine, but this did not relieve him. The dull depression he experienced in a somnolent condition at first gave him a little relief, but only as something new, afterwards it became as distressing as the pain itself or even more so.

Special foods were prepared for him by the doctors' orders, but all those foods became increasingly distasteful and disgusting to him.

For his excretions also special arrangements had to be made, and this was a torment to him every time—a torment from the uncleanliness, the unseemliness, and the smell, and from knowing that another person had to take part in it.

But just through this most unpleasant matter Ivan Ilych obtained comfort.

Gerasim, the butler's young assistant, always came in to carry the things out. Gerasim was a clean, fresh peasant lad, grown stout on town food and always cheerful and bright. At first the sight of him, in his clean Russian peasant costume, engaged on that disgusting task embarrassed Ivan Ilych.

Once when he got up from the commode too weak to draw up his trousers, he dropped into a soft armchair and looked with horror at his bare, enfeebled thighs with the muscles so sharply marked on them.

Gerasim with a firm light tread, his heavy boots emitting a pleasant smell of tar and fresh winter air, came in wearing a clean Hessian apron, the sleeves of his print shirt tucked up over his strong bare young arms and refraining from looking at his sick master out of consideration for his feelings, and restraining the joy of life that beamed from his face, he went up to the commode.

'Gerasim!' said Ivan Ilych in a weak voice.

Gerasim started, evidently afraid he might have committed some blunder, and with a rapid movement turned his fresh, kind, simple young face which just showed the first downy signs of a beard.

'Yes, sir?'

'That must be very unpleasant for you. You must forgive me. I am helpless.'

'Oh, why, sir,' and Gerasim's eyes beamed and he showed his glistening white teeth, 'what's a little trouble? It's a case of illness with you, sir.'

And his deft strong hands did their accustomed task, and he went out of the room stepping lightly. Five minutes later he as lightly returned.

Ivan Ilych was still sitting in the same position in the armchair.

'Gerasim,' he said when the latter had replaced the freshly-washed utensil. 'Please come here and help me.' Gerasim went up to him. 'Lift me up. It is hard for me to get up, and I have sent Dmitri away.'

Gerasim went up to him, grasped his master with his strong arms deftly but gently, in the same way that he stepped—lifted him, supported him with one hand,

and with the other drew up his trousers and would have set him down again, but Ivan Ilych asked to be led to the sofa. Gerasim, without an effort and without apparent pressure, led him, almost lifting him, to the sofa and placed him on it.

'Thank you. How easily and well you do it all!'

Gerasim smiled again and turned to leave the room. But Ivan Ilych felt his presence such a comfort that he did not want to let him go.

'One thing more, please move up that chair. No, the other one—under my feet. It is easier for me when my feet are raised.'

Gerasim brought the chair, set it down gently in place, and raised Ivan Ilych's legs on to it. It seemed to Ivan Ilych that he felt better while Gerasim was holding up his legs.

'It's better when my legs are higher,' he said. 'Place that cushion under them.'

Gerasim did so. He again lifted the legs and placed them, and again Ivan Ilych felt better while Gerasim held his legs. When he set them down Ivan Ilych fancied he felt worse.

'Gerasim,' he said. 'Are you busy now?'

'Not at all, sir,' said Gerasim, who had learnt from the townfolk how to speak to gentlefolk.

'What have you still to do?'

'What have I to do? I've done everything except chopping the logs for tomorrow.'

'Then hold my legs up a bit higher, can you?'

'Of course I can. Why not?' And Gerasim raised his master's legs higher and Ivan Ilych thought that in that position he did not feel any pain at all.

'And how about the logs?'

'Don't trouble about that, sir. There's plenty of time.'

Ivan Ilych told Gerasim to sit down and hold his legs, and began to talk to him. And strange to say it seemed to him that he felt better while Gerasim held his legs up.

After that Ivan Ilych would sometimes call Gerasim and get him to hold his legs on his shoulders, and he liked talking to him. Gerasim did it all easily, willingly, simply, and with a good nature that touched Ivan Ilych. Health, strength, and vitality in other people were offensive to him, but Gerasim's strength and vitality did not mortify but soothed him.

What tormented Ivan Ilych most was the deception, the lie, which for some reason they all accepted, that he was not dying but was simply ill, and that he only need keep quiet and undergo a treatment and then something very good would result. He however knew that do what they would nothing would come of it, only still more agonizing suffering and death. This deception tortured him—their not wishing to admit what they all knew and what he knew, but wanting to lie to him concerning his terrible condition, and wishing and forcing him to participate in that lie. Those lies—lies enacted over him on the eve of his death and destined to degrade this awful, solemn act to the level of their visitings, their curtains, their sturgeon for dinner—were a terrible agony for Ivan Ilych. And strangely enough, many times when they were going through their antics over him he had been within a hairbreadth of calling out to them: 'Stop lying! You know and I know that I am dying. Then at least stop lying about it!' But he had never had the spirit to do it. The awful terrible act of his dying was, he could see, reduced by those about him to the level of a casual, unpleasant, and almost indecorous incident (as if someone entered a drawing-room diffusing an unpleasant odor) and this was done by that very decorum which he had served all his life long. He saw that no one felt for him, because no one even wished to grasp his position. Only Gerasim recognized it and pitied him. And so Ivan Ilych felt at ease only with him. He felt comforted when Gerasim supported his legs (sometimes all night long) and refused to go to bed, saying: 'Don't you worry, Ivan Ilych. I'll get sleep enough later on,' or when he suddenly became familiar and exclaimed: 'If you weren't sick it would be another matter, but as it is, why should I grudge a little trouble?' Gerasim alone did not lie; everything showed that he alone understood the facts of the case and did not consider it necessary to disguise them, but simply felt sorry for his emaciated and enfeebled master. Once when Ivan Ilych was sending him away he even said straight out: 'We shall all of us die, so why should I grudge a little trouble?'—expressing the fact that he did not think his work burdensome, because he was doing it for a dying man and hoped someone would do the same for him when his time came.

Apart from this lying, or because of it, what most tormented Ivan Ilych was that no one pitied him as he wished to be pitied. At certain moments after prolonged suffering he wished most of all (though he would have been ashamed to confess it) for someone to pity him as a sick child is pitied. He longed to be petted and comforted. He knew he was an important functionary, that he had a beard turning grey, and that therefore what he longed for was impossible, but still he longed for it. And in Gerasim's attitude toward him there was something akin to what he wished for, and so that attitude comforted him. Ivan Ilych wanted to be petted and cried over, and then his colleague Shebek would come, and instead of weeping and being petted, Ivan Ilych would assume a serious, severe, and profound air, and by force of habit would express his opinion on a decision of the Court of Cassation and would stubbornly insist on that view. This falsity around him and within him did more than anything else to poison his last days.

VIII

It was morning. He knew it was morning because Gerasim had gone, and Peter the footman had come and put out the candles, drawn back one of the curtains, and began quietly to tidy up. Whether it was morning or evening, Friday or Sunday, made no difference, it was all just the same: the gnawing, unmitigated, agonizing pain, never ceasing for an instant, the consciousness of life inexorably waning but not yet extinguished, the approach of that ever dreaded and hateful Death which was the only reality, and always the same falsity. What were days, weeks, hours, in such a case?

'Will you have some tea, sir?'

'He wants things to be regular, and wishes the gentlefolk to drink tea in the morning,' thought Ivan Ilych, and only said 'No'.

'Wouldn't you like to move onto the sofa, sir?'

'He wants to tidy up the room, and I'm in the way. I am uncleanliness and disorder,' he thought, and said only:

'No, leave me alone.'

The man went on bustling about. Ivan Ilych stretched out his hand. Peter came up, ready to help.

'What is it, sir?'

'My watch.'

Peter took the watch which was close at hand and gave it to his master.

'Half-past eight. Are they up?'

'No sir, except Vladimir Ivanich' (the son) 'who has gone to school. Praskovya Fedorovna ordered me to wake her if you asked for her. Shall I do so?'

'No, there's no need to.' 'Perhaps I'd better have some tea,' he thought, and added aloud: 'Yes, bring me some tea.'

Peter went out. Left alone Ivan Ilych dreaded being left alone. 'How can I keep him here? Oh yes, my medicine.' 'Peter, give me my medicine.' 'Why not? Perhaps it may still do me some good.' He took a spoonful and swallowed it. 'No, it won't help. It's all tomfoolery, all deception,' he decided as soon as he became aware of the familiar, sickly, hopeless taste. 'No, I can't believe in it any longer. But the pain, why this pain? If it would only cease just for a moment!' And he moaned. Peter turned towards him. 'It's all right. Go and fetch me some tea.'

Peter went out. Left alone Ivan Ilych groaned not so much with pain, terrible though that was, as from mental anguish. Always and for ever the same, always these endless days and nights. If only it would come quicker! If only *what* would come quicker? Death, darkness? . . . No, no! Anything rather than death!

When Peter returned with the tea on a tray, Ivan Ilych stared at him for a time in perplexity, not realizing who and what he was. Peter was disconcerted by that look and his embarrassment brought Ivan Ilych to himself.

'Oh, tea! All right, put it down. Only help me to wash and put on a clean shirt.'

And Ivan Ilych began to wash. With pauses for rest, he washed his hands and then his face, cleaned his teeth, brushed his hair, and looked in the glass. He was terrified by what he saw, especially by the limp way in which his hair clung to his pallid forehead.

While his shirt was being changed he knew that he would be still more frightened at the sight of his body, so he avoided looking at it. Finally he was ready. He drew on a dressing-gown, wrapped himself in a plaid, and sat down in the armchair to take his tea. For a moment he felt refreshed, but as soon as he began to drink the tea he was again aware of the same taste, and the pain also returned. He finished it with an effort, and then lay down stretching out his legs, and dismissed Peter.

Always the same. Now a spark of hope flashes up, then a sea of despair rages, and always pain; always pain, always despair, and always the same. When alone he had a dreadful and distressing desire to call someone, but he knew beforehand that with others present it would be still worse. 'Another dose of morphine—to lose consciousness. I will tell him, the doctor, that he must think of something else. It's impossible, impossible, to go on like this.'

An hour and another pass like that. But now there is a ring at the door bell. Perhaps it's the doctor? It is. He comes in fresh, hearty, plump, and cheerful, with that look on his face that seems to say: 'There now, you're in a panic about something, but we'll arrange it all for you directly!' The doctor knows this expression is out of place here, but he has put it on once for all and can't take it off—like a man who has put on a frock-coat in the morning to pay a round of calls.

The doctor rubs his hands vigorously and reassuringly.

'Brr! How cold it is! There's such a sharp frost; just let me warm myself!' he says, as if it were only a matter of waiting till he was warm, and then he would put everything right.

'Well now, how are you?'

Ivan Ilych feels that the doctor would like to say: 'Well, how are our affairs?' but that even he feels that this would not do, and says instead: 'What sort of a night have you had?'

Ivan Ilych looks at him as much as to say: 'Are you really never ashamed of lying?' But the doctor does not wish to understand this question, and Ivan Ilych says: 'Just as terrible as ever. The pain never leaves me and never subsides. If only something . . .'

'Yes, you sick people are always like that. . . . There, now I think I am warm enough. Even Praskovya Fedorovna, who is so particular, could find no fault with my temperature. Well, now I can say good-morning,' and the doctor presses his patient's hand.

Then, dropping his former playfulness, he begins with a most serious face to examine the patient, feeling his pulse and taking his temperature, and then begins the sounding and auscultation.

Ivan Ilych knows quite well and definitely that all this is nonsense and pure deception, but when the doctor, getting down on his knee, leans over him, putting his ear first higher then lower, and performs various gymnastic movements over him with a significant expression on his face, Ivan Ilych submits to it all as he used to submit to the speeches of the lawyers, though he knew very well that they were all lying and why they were lying.

The doctor, kneeling on the sofa, is still sounding him when Praskovya Fedorovna's silk dress rustles at the door and she is heard scolding Peter for not having let her know of the doctor's arrival.

She comes in, kisses her husband, and at once proceeds to prove that she has been up a long time already, and only owing to a misunderstanding failed to be there when the doctor arrived.

Ivan Ilych looks at her, scans her all over, sets against her the whiteness and plumpness and cleanness of her hands and neck, the gloss of her hair, and the sparkle of her vivacious eyes. He hates her with his whole soul. And the thrill of hatred he feels for her makes him suffer from her touch.

Her attitude towards him and his disease is still the same. Just as the doctor had adopted a certain relation to his patient which he could not abandon, so had she formed one towards him—that he was not doing something he ought to do and was himself to blame, and that she reproached him lovingly for this—and she could not now change that attitude.

'You see he doesn't listen to me and doesn't take his medicine at the proper time. And above all he lies in a position that is no doubt bad for him—with his legs up.'

She described how he made Gerasim hold his legs up.

The doctor smiled with a contemptuous affability that said: 'What's to be done? These sick people do have foolish fancies of that kind, but we must forgive them.'

When the examination was over the doctor looked at his watch, and then Praskovya Fedorovna announced to Ivan Ilych that it was of course as he pleased, but she had sent to-day for a celebrated specialist who would examine him and have a consultation with Michael Danilovich (their regular doctor).

'Please don't raise any objections. I am doing this for my own sake,' she said ironically, letting it be felt that she was doing it all for his sake and only said this to leave him no right to refuse. He remained silent, knitting his brows. He felt that he was so surrounded and involved in a mesh of falsity that it was hard to unravel anything.

Everything she did for him was entirely for her own sake, and she told him she was doing for herself what she actually was doing for herself, as if that was so incredible that he must understand the opposite.

At half-past eleven the celebrated specialist arrived. Again the sounding began and the significant conversations in his presence and in another room, about the kidneys and the appendix, and the questions and answers, with such an air of importance that again, instead of the real question of life and death which now alone confronted him, the question arose of the kidney and appendix which were not behaving as they ought to and would now be attacked by Michael Danilovich

and the specialist and forced to amend their ways.

The celebrated specialist took leave of him with a serious though not hopeless look, and in reply to the timid question Ivan Ilych, with eyes glistening with fear and hope, put to him as to whether there was a chance of recovery, said that he could not vouch for it but there was a possibility. The look of hope with which Ivan Ilych watched the doctor out was so pathetic that Praskovya Fedorovna, seeing it, even wept as she left the room to hand the doctor his fee.

The gleam of hope kindled by the doctor's encouragement did not last long. The same room, the same pictures, curtains, wall-paper, medicine bottles, were all there, and the same aching suffering body, and Ivan Ilych began to moan. They gave him a subcutaneous injection and he sank into oblivion.

It was twilight when he came to. They brought his dinner and he swallowed some beef tea with difficulty, and then everything was the same again and night was coming on.

Aften dinner, at seven o'clock, Praskovya Fedorovna came into the room in evening dress, her full bosom pushed up by her corset, and with traces of powder on her face. She had reminded him in the morning that they were going to the theatre. Sarah Bernhardt was visiting the town and they had a box, which he had insisted on their taking. Now he had forgotten about it and her toilet offended him, but he concealed his vexation when he remembered that he had himself insisted on their securing a box and going because it would be an instructive and aesthetic pleasure for the children.

Praskovya Fedorovna came in, self-satisfied but yet with a rather guilty air. She sat down and asked how he was but, as he saw, only for the sake of asking and not in order to learn about it, knowing that there was nothing to learn—and then went on to what she really wanted to say: that she would not on any account have gone but that the box had been taken and Helen and their daughter were going, as well as Petrishchev (the examining magistrate, their daughter's fiancé) and that it was out of the question to let them go

alone; but that she would have much preferred to sit with him for a while; and he
must be sure to follow the doctor's orders
while she was away.

'Oh, and Fedor Petrovich' (the fiancé)
'would like to come in. May he? And
Lisa?'

'All right.'

Their daughter came in in full evening
dress, her fresh young flesh exposed (making a show of that very flesh which in his
own case caused so much suffering),
strong, healthy, evidently in love, and
impatient with illness, suffering, and death,
because they interfered with her happiness.

Fedor Petrovich came in too, in evening dress, his hair curled à la Capoul, a
tight stiff collar round his long sinewy
neck, an enormous white shirt-front and
narrow black trousers tightly stretched
over his strong thighs. He had one white
glove tightly drawn on, and was holding
his opera hat in his hand.

Following him the schoolboy crept in
unnoticed, in a new uniform, poor little
fellow, and wearing gloves. Terribly dark
shadows showed under his eyes, the
meaning of which Ivan Ilych knew well.

His son had always seemed pathetic to
him, and now it was dreadful to see the
boy's frightened look of pity. It seemed
to Ivan Ilych that Vasya was the only one
besides Gerasim who understood and
pitied him.

They all sat down and again asked how
he was. A silence followed. Lisa asked
her mother about the opera-glasses, and
there was an altercation between mother
and daughter as to who had taken them
and where they had been put. This occasioned some unpleasantness.

Fedor Petrovich inquired of Ivan Ilych
whether he had ever seen Sarah Bernhardt. Ivan Ilych did not at first catch the
question, but then replied: 'No, have you
seen her before?'

'Yes, in *Adrienne Lecouvreur*.'

Praskovya Fedorovna mentioned some
rôles in which Sarah Bernhardt was particularly good. Her daughter disagreed.
Conversation sprang up as to the elegance
and realism of her acting—the sort of
conversation that is always repeated and
is always the same.

In the midst of the conversation Fedor
Petrovich glanced at Ivan Ilych and became silent. The others also looked at him
and grew silent. Ivan Ilych was staring
with glittering eyes straight before him,
evidently indignant with them. This had
to be rectified, but it was impossible to do
so. The silence had to be broken, but for
a time no one dared to break it and they
all became afraid that the conventional
deception would suddenly become obvious and the truth become plain to all.
Lisa was the first to pluck up courage and
break that silence, but by trying to hide
what everybody was feeling, she betrayed
it.

'Well, if we are going it's time to start,'
she said, looking at her watch, a present
from her father, and with a faint and significant smile at Fedor Petrovich relating
to something known only to them. She
got up with a rustle of her dress.

They all rose, said good-night, and
went away.

When they had gone it seemed to Ivan
Ilych that he felt better; the falsity had
gone with them. But the pain remained—
that same pain and that same fear that
made everything monotonously alike,
nothing harder and nothing easier. Everything was worse.

Again minute followed minute and
hour followed hour. Everything remained
the same and there was no cessation. And
the inevitable end of it all became more
and more terrible.

'Yes, send Gerasim here,' he replied to
a question Peter asked.

IX

His wife returned late at night. She
came in on tiptoe, but he heard her,
opened his eyes, and made haste to close
them again. She wished to send Gerasim
away and to sit with him herself, but he
opened his eyes and said: 'No, go
away.'

'Are you in great pain?'

'Always the same.'

'Take some opium.'

He agreed and took some. She went
away.

Till about three in the morning he was
in a state of stupified misery. It seemed

to him that he and his pain were being thrust into a narrow, deep black sack, but though they were pushed further and further in they could not be pushed to the bottom. And this, terrible enough in itself, was accompanied by suffering. He was frightened yet wanted to fall through the sack, he struggled but yet co-operated. And suddenly he broke through, fell, and regained consciousness. Gerasim was sitting at the foot of the bed dozing quietly and patiently, while he himself lay with his emaciated stockinged legs resting on Gerasim's shoulders; the same shaded candle was there and the same unceasing pain.

'Go away, Gerasim,' he whispered.

'It's all right, sir. I'll stay a while.'

'No. Go away.'

He removed his legs from Gerasim's shoulders, turned sideways onto his arm, and felt sorry for himself. He only waited till Gerasim had gone into the next room and then restrained himself no longer but wept like a child. He wept on account of his helplessness, his terrible loneliness, the cruelty of man, the cruelty of God, and the absence of God.

'Why hast Thou done all this? Why hast Thou brought me here? Why, why dost Thou torment me so terribly?'

He did not expect an answer and yet wept because there was no answer and could be none. The pain again grew more acute, but he did not stir and did not call. He said to himself: 'Go on! Strike me! But what is it for? What have I done to Thee? What is it for?'

Then he grew quiet and not only ceased weeping but even held his breath and became all attention. It was as though he were listening not to an audible voice but to the voice of his soul, to the current of thoughts arising within him.

'What is it you want?' was the first clear conception capable of expression in words, that he heard.

'What do you want? What do you want?' he repeated to himself.

'What do I want? To live and not to suffer,' he answered.

And again he listened with such concentrated attention that even his pain did not distract him.

'To live? How?' asked his inner voice.

'Why, to live as I used to—well and pleasantly.'

'As you lived before, well and pleasantly?' the voice repeated.

And in imagination he began to recall the best moments of his pleasant life. But strange to say none of those best moments of his pleasant life now seemed at all what they had then seemed—none of them except the first recollections of childhood. There, in childhood, there had been something really pleasant with which it would be possible to live if it could return. But the child who had experienced that happiness existed no longer, it was like a reminiscence of somebody else.

As soon as the period began which had produced the present Ivan Ilych, all that had then seemed joys now melted before his sight and turned into something trivial and often nasty.

And the further he departed from childhood and the nearer he came to the present the more worthless and doubtful were the joys. This began with the School of Law. A little that was really good was still found there—there was light-heartedness, friendship, and hope. But in the upper classes there had already been fewer of such good moments. Then during the first years of his official career, when he was in the service of the Governor, some pleasant moments again occurred: they were the memories of love for a woman. Then all became confused and there was still less of what was good; later on again there was still less that was good, and the further he went the less there was. His marriage, a mere accident, then the disenchantment that followed it, his wife's bad breath and the sensuality and hypocrisy: then that deadly official life and those preoccupations about money, a year of it, and two, and ten, and twenty, and always the same thing. And the longer it lasted the more deadly it became. 'It is as if I had been going downhill while I imagined I was going up. And that is really what it was. I was going up in public opinion, but to the same extent life was ebbing away from me. And now it is all done and there is only death.'

'Then what does it mean? Why? It can't be that life is so senseless and horrible. But if it really has been so horrible and senseless, why must I die and die in agony? There is something wrong!'

'Maybe I did not live as I ought to have done,' it suddenly occurred to him. 'But how could that be, when I did everything properly?' he replied, and immediately dismissed from his mind this, the sole solution of all the riddles of life and death, as something quite impossible.

'Then what do you want now? To live? Live how? Live as you lived in the law courts when the usher proclaimed "The judge is coming!" The judge is coming, the judge!' he repeated to himself. 'Here he is, the judge. But I am not guilty!' he exclaimed angrily. 'What is it for?' And he ceased crying, but turning his face to the wall continued to ponder on the same question: Why, and for what purpose, is there all this horror? But however much he pondered he found no answer. And whenever the thought occurred to him, as it often did, that it all resulted from his not having lived as he ought to have done, he at once recalled the correctness of his whole life and dismissed so strange an idea.

x

Another fortnight passed. Ivan Ilych now no longer left his sofa. He would not lie in bed but lay on the sofa, facing the wall nearly all the time. He suffered ever the same unceasing agonies and in his loneliness pondered always on the same insoluble question: 'What is this? Can it be that it is Death?' And the inner voice answered: 'Yes, it is Death.'

'Why these sufferings?' And the voice answered, 'For no reason—they just are so.' Beyond and besides this there was nothing.

From the very beginning of his illness, ever since he had first been to see the doctor, Ivan Ilych's life had been divided between two contrary and alternating moods: now it was despair and the expectation of this uncomprehended and terrible death, and now hope and an intently interested observation of the functioning of his organs. Now before his eyes there was only a kidney or an intestine that temporarily evaded its duty, and now only

that incomprehensible and dreadful death from which it was impossible to escape.

These two states of mind had alternated from the very beginning of his illness, but the further it progressed the more doubtful and fantastic became the conception of the kidney, and the more real the sense of impending death.

He had but to call to mind what he had been three months before and what he was now, to call to mind with what regularity he had been going downhill, for every possibility of hope to be shattered.

Latterly during that loneliness in which he found himself as he lay facing the back of the sofa, a loneliness in the midst of a populous town and surrounded by numerous acquaintances and relations but that yet could not have been more complete anywhere—either at the bottom of the sea or under the earth—during that terrible loneliness Ivan Ilych had lived only in memories of the past. Pictures of his past rose before him one after another. They always began with what was nearest in time and then went back to what was most remote—to his childhood—and rested there. If he thought of the stewed prunes that had been offered him that day, his mind went back to the raw shrivelled French plums of his childhood, their peculiar flavour and the flow of saliva when he sucked their stones, and along with the memory of that taste came a whole series of memories of those day: his nurse, his brother, and their toys. 'No, I mustn't think of that. . . . It is too painful,' Ivan Ilych said to himself, and brought himself back to the present—to the button on the back of the sofa and the creases in its morocco. 'Morocco is expensive, but it does not wear well: there had been a quarrel about it. It was a different kind of quarrel and a different kind of morocco that time when we tore father's portfolio and were punished, and mamma brought us some tarts. . . .' And again his thoughts dwelt on his childhood, and again it was painful and he tried to banish them and fix his mind on something else.

Then again together with that chain of memories another series passed through his mind—of how his illness had progressed and grown worse. There also the further back he looked the more life there had been. There had been more of what was good in life and more of life itself. The two merged together. 'Just as the pain went on getting worse and worse so my life grew worse and worse,' he thought. 'There is one bright spot there at the back, at the beginning of life, and afterwards all becomes blacker and blacker and proceeds more and more rapidly —in inverse ratio to the square of the distance from death,' thought Ivan Ilych. And the example of a stone falling downwards with increasing velocity entered his mind. Life, a series of increasing sufferings, flies further and further towards its end—the most terrible suffering. 'I am flying. . . .' He shuddered, shifted himself, and tried to resist, but was already aware that resistance was impossible, and again with eyes weary of gazing but unable to cease seeing what was before them, he stared at the back of the sofa and waited —awaiting that dreadful fall and shock and destruction.

'Resistance is impossible!' he said to himself. 'If I could only understand what it is all for! But that too is impossible. An explanation would be possible if it could be said that I have not lived as I ought to. But it is impossible to say that,' and he remembered all the legality, correctitude, and propriety of his life. 'That at any rate can certainly not be admitted,' he thought, and his lips smiled ironically as if someone could see that smile and be taken in by it. 'There is no explanation! Agony, death. . . . What for?'

XI

Another two weeks went by in this way and during that fortnight an event occurred that Ivan Ilych and his wife had desired. Petrishchev formally proposed. It happened in the evening. The next day Praskovya Fedorovna came into her husband's room considering how best to inform him of it, but that very night there had been a fresh change for the worse in his condition. She found him still lying on the sofa but in a different position. He lay on his back, groaning and staring fixedly straight in front of him.

She began to remind him of his medicines, but he turned his eyes towards her with such a look that she did not finish what she was saying; so great an animosity, to her in particular, did that look express.

'For Christ's sake let me die in peace!' he said.

She would have gone away, but just then their daughter came in and went up to say good morning. He looked at her as he had done at his wife, and in reply to her inquiry about his health said dryly that he would soon free them all of himself. They were both silent and after sitting with him for a while went away.

'Is it our fault?' Lisa said to her mother. 'It's as if we were to blame! I am sorry for papa, but why should we be tortured?'

The doctor came at his usual time. Ivan Ilych answered 'Yes' and 'No', never taking his angry eyes from him, and at last said: 'You know you can do nothing for me, so leave me alone.'

'We can ease your sufferings.'

'You can't even do that. Let me be.'

The doctor went into the drawing-room and told Praskovya Fedorovna that the case was very serious and that the only resource left was opium to allay her husband's sufferings, which must be terrible.

It was true, as the doctor said, that Ivan Ilych's physical sufferings were terrible, but worse than the physical sufferings were his mental sufferings which were his chief torture.

His mental sufferings were due to the fact that that night, as he looked at Gerasim's sleepy, good-natured face with its prominent cheek-bones, the question suddenly occurred to him: 'What if my whole life has really been wrong?'

It occurred to him that what had appeared perfectly impossible before, namely that he had not spent his life as he should have done, might after all be true. It occurred to him that his scarcely perceptible attempts to struggle against what was considered good by the most highly placed people, those scarcely noticeable impulses which he had immediately suppressed, might have been the real thing, and all the rest false. And his professional duties and the whole arrangement of his life and of his family, and all his social and official interests, might all have been false. He tried to defend all those things to himself and suddenly felt the weakness of what he was defending. There was nothing to defend.

'But if that is so,' he said to himself, 'and I am leaving this life with the consciousness that I have lost all that was given me and it is impossible to rectify it —what then?'

He lay on his back and began to pass his life in review in quite a new way. In the morning when he saw first his footman, then his wife, then his daughter, and then the doctor, their every word and movement confirmed to him the awful truth that had been revealed to him during the night. In them he saw himself—all that for which he had lived—and saw clearly that it was not real at all, but a terrible and huge deception which had hidden both life and death. This consciousness intensified his physical suffering tenfold. He groaned and tossed about, and pulled at his clothing which choked and stifled him. And he hated them on that account.

He was given a large dose of opium and became unconscious, but at noon his sufferings began again. He drove everybody away and tossed from side to side.

His wife came to him and said:

'Jean, my dear, do this for me. It can't do any harm and often helps. Healthy people often do it.'

He opened his eyes wide.

'What? Take communion? Why? It's unnecessary! However. . . .'

She began to cry.

'Yes, do, my dear. I'll send for our priest. He is such a nice man.'

'All right. Very well,' he muttered.

When the priest came and heard his confession, Ivan Ilych was softened and seemed to feel a relief from his doubts and consequently from his sufferings, and for a moment there came a ray of hope. He again began to think of the vermiform appendix and the possibility of correcting it. He received the sacrament with tears in his eyes.

When they laid him down again afterwards he felt a moment's ease, and the hope that he might live awoke in him again. He began to think of the operation that had been suggested to him. 'To live! I want to live!' he said to himself.

His wife came in to congratulate him after his communion, and when uttering the usual conventional words she added:

'You feel better, don't you?'

Without looking at her he said 'Yes'.

Her dress, her figure, the expression of her face, the tone of her voice, all revealed the same thing. 'This is wrong, it is not as it should be. All you have lived for and still live for is falsehood and deception, hiding life and death from you.' And as soon as he admitted that thought, his hatred and his agonizing physical suffering again sprang up, and with that suffering a consciousness of the unavoidable, approaching end. And to this was added a new sensation of grinding shooting pain and a feeling of suffocation.

The expression of his face when he uttered that 'yes' was dreadful. Having uttered it, he looked her straight in the eyes, turned on his face with a rapidity extraordinary in his weak state and shouted:

'Go away! Go away and leave me alone!'

XII

From that moment the screaming began that continued for three days, and was so terrible that one could not hear it through two closed doors without horror. At the moment he answered his wife he realized that he was lost, that there was no return, that the end had come, the very end, and his doubts were still unsolved and remained doubts.

'Oh! Oh! Oh!' he cried in various intonations. He had begun by screaming 'I won't!' and continued screaming on the letter 'o'.

For three whole days, during which time did not exist for him, he struggled in that black sack into which he was being thrust by an invisible, resistless force. He struggled as a man condemned to death struggles in the hands of the executioner, knowing that he cannot save himself. And every moment he felt that despite all his efforts he was drawing nearer and nearer to what terrified him. He felt that his agony was due to his being thrust into that black hole and still more to his not being able to get right into it. He was hindered from getting into it by his conviction that his life had been a good one. That very justification of his life held him fast and prevented his moving forward, and it caused him most torment of all.

Suddenly some force struck him in the chest and side, making it still harder to breathe, and he fell through the hole and there at the bottom was a light. What had happened to him was like the sensation one sometimes experiences in a railway carriage when one thinks one is going backwards while one is really going forwards and suddenly becomes aware of the real direction.

'Yes, it was all not the right thing,' he said to himself, 'but that's no matter. It can be done. But what *is* the right thing?' he asked himself, and suddenly grew quiet.

This occurred at the end of the third day, two hours before his death. Just then his schoolboy son had crept softly in and gone up to the bedside. The dying man was still screaming desperately and waving his arms. His hand fell on the boy's head, and the boy caught it, pressed it to his lips, and began to cry.

At that very moment Ivan Ilych fell through and caught sight of the light, and it was revealed to him that though his life had not been what it should have been, this could still be rectified. He asked himself, 'What *is* the right thing?' and grew still, listening. Then he felt that someone was kissing his hand. He opened his eyes, looked at his son, and felt sorry for him. His wife came up to him and he glanced at her. She was gazing at him open-mouthed, with undried tears on her nose and cheek and a despairing look on her face. He felt sorry for her too.

'Yes, I am making them wretched,' he thought. 'They are sorry, but it will be better for them when I die.' He wished to say this but had not the strength to utter it. 'Besides, why speak? I must act,' he thought. With a look at his wife he indicated his son and said: 'Take him away . . . sorry for him . . . sorry for you too. . . .' He tried to add, 'forgive me', but said 'forego' and waved his hand, knowing that He whose understanding mattered would understand.

And suddenly it grew clear to him that what had been oppressing him and would not leave him was all dropping away at once from two sides, from ten sides, and from all sides. He was sorry for them, he must act so as not to hurt them: release them and free himself from these sufferings. 'How good and how simple!' he thought. 'And the pain?' he asked himself. 'What has become of it? Where are you, pain?'

He turned his attention to it.

'Yes, here it is. Well, what of it? Let the pain be.'

'And death . . . where is it?'

He sought his former accustomed fear of death and did not find it. 'Where is it? What death?' There was no fear because there was no death.

In place of death there was light.

'So that's what it is!' he suddenly exclaimed aloud. 'What joy!'

To him all this happened in a single instant, and the meaning of that instant did not change. For those present his agony continued for another two hours. Something rattled in his throat, his emaciated body twitched, then the gasping and rattle became less and less frequent.

'It is finished!' said someone near him.

He heard these words and repeated them in his soul.

'Death is finished,' he said to himself. 'It is no more!'

He drew in a breath, stopped in the midst of a sigh, stretched out, and died.

[1886]

TRANSLATED BY
LOUISE AND AYLMER MAUDE

QUESTIONS FOR STUDY

1. *What does Ivan Ilych come to understand about the meaning of his own life and death? What meaning does his death have for his friends? For his wife?*

2. *Why does Tolstoy choose to begin with Ivan's death and funeral and then work backwards? What kind of context does the opening section provide for the story that follows?*

3. *What kind of man is Ivan Ilych? How have the values which Ivan has chosen to live by shaped the kind of man that he is? Why doesn't Tolstoy make him a more sympathetic character?*

4. *What does Tolstoy mean when he says that "Ivan Ilych's death had been most simple and most ordinary and therefore most terrible"?*

5. *In what ways does the peasant servant Gerasim serve as a contrast or foil to Ivan and to the other characters in the story?*

LIONEL TRILLING

Of This Time, Of That Place

I T WAS a fine September day. By noon it would be summer again, but now it was true autumn with a touch of chill in the air. As Joseph Howe stood on the porch of the house in which he lodged, ready to leave for his first class of the year, he thought with pleasure of the long indoor days that were coming. It was a moment when he could feel glad of his profession.

On the lawn the peach tree was still in fruit and young Hilda Aiken was taking a picture of it. She held the camera tight against her chest. She wanted the sun behind her, but she did not want her own long morning shadow in the foreground. She raised the camera, but that did not help, and she lowered it, but that made things worse. She twisted her body to the left, then to the right. In the end she had to step out of the direct line of the sun. At last she snapped the shutter and wound the film with intense care.

Howe, watching her from the porch, waited for her to finish and called good morning. She turned, startled, and almost sullenly lowered her glance. In the year Howe had lived at the Aikens', Hilda had accepted him as one of her family, but since his absence of the summer she had grown shy. Then suddenly she lifted her head and smiled at him, and the humorous smile confirmed his pleasure in the day. She picked up her bookbag and set off for school.

The handsome houses on the streets to the college were not yet fully awake, but they looked very friendly. Howe went by the Bradby house where he would be a guest this evening at the first dinner party of the year. When he had gone the length of the picket fence, the whitest in town, he turned back. Along the path there was a fine row of asters and he went through the gate and picked one for his buttonhole. The Bradbys would be pleased if they happened to see him invading their lawn and the knowledge of this made him even more comfortable.

He reached the campus as the hour was striking. The students were hurrying to their classes. He himself was in no hurry. He stopped at his dim cubicle of an office and lit a cigarette. The prospect of facing his class had suddenly presented itself to him and his hands were cold; the lawful seizure of power he was about to make seemed momentous. Waiting did not help. He put out his cigarette, picked up a pad of theme paper, and went to his classroom.

As he entered, the rattle of voices ceased, and the twenty-odd freshmen settled themselves and looked at him appraisingly. Their faces seemed gross, his heart sank at their massed impassivity, but he spoke briskly.

'My name is Howe,' he said, and turned and wrote it on the blackboard. The carelessness of the scrawl confirmed his authority. He went on, 'My office is 412 Slemp Hall, and my office-hours are Monday, Wednesday and Friday from eleven-thirty to twelve-thirty."

He wrote, 'M., W., F., 11:30—12:30.' He said, 'I'll be very glad to see any of you at that time. Or if you can't come then, you can arrange with me for some other time.'

He turned again to the blackboard and spoke over his shoulder. 'The text for the course is Jarman's *Modern Plays*, revised edition. The Co-op has it in stock.' He wrote the name, underlined 'revised edition' and waited for it to be taken down in the new notebooks.

When the bent heads were raised again he began his speech of prospectus. 'It is hard to explain—' he said, and paused as they composed themselves. 'It is hard to explain what a course like this is intended to do. We are going to try to learn something about modern literature and something about prose composition.'

As he spoke, his hands warmed and he was able to look directly at the class. Last year on the first day the faces had seemed just as cloddish, but as the term wore on they became gradually alive and quite likable. It did not seem possible that the same thing could happen again.

'I shall not lecture in this course,' he continued. 'Our work will be carried on by discussion and we will try to learn by an exchange of opinion. But you will soon recognize that my opinion is worth more than anyone else's here.'

He remained grave as he said it, but two boys understood and laughed. The rest took permission from them and laughed too. All Howe's private ironies protested the vulgarity of the joke, but the laughter made him feel benign and powerful.

When the little speech was finished, Howe picked up the pad of paper he had brought. He announced that they would write an extemporaneous theme. Its subject was traditional, 'Who I am and why I came to Dwight College.' By now the class was more at ease and it gave a ritualistic groan of protest. Then there was a stir as fountain pens were brought out and the writing-arms of the chairs were cleared, and the paper was passed about. At last, all the heads bent to work, and the room became still.

Howe sat idly at his desk. The sun shone through the tall clumsy windows. The cool of the morning was already passing. There was a scent of autumn and of varnish and the stillness of the room was deep and oddly touching. Now and then a student's head was raised and scratched in the old, elaborate students' pantomime that calls the teacher to witness honest intellectual effort.

Suddenly a tall boy stood within the frame of the open door. 'Is this,' he said, and thrust a large nose into a college catalogue, 'is this the meeting place of English 1A? The section instructed by Dr. Joseph Howe?'

He stood on the very sill of the door, as if refusing to enter until he was perfectly sure of all his rights. The class looked up from work, found him absurd and gave a low mocking cheer.

The teacher and the new student, with equal pointedness, ignored the disturbance. Howe nodded to the boy, who pushed his head forward and then jerked it back in a wide elaborate arc to clear his brow of a heavy lock of hair. He advanced into the room and halted before Howe, almost at attention. In a loud, clear voice he announced, 'I am Tertan, Ferdinand R., reporting at the direction of Head of Department Vincent.'

The heraldic formality of this statement brought forth another cheer. Howe looked at the class with a sternness he could not really feel, for there was indeed something ridiculous about this boy. Under his displeased regard the rows of heads dropped to work again. Then he touched Tertan's elbow, led him up to the desk and stood so as to shield their conversation from the class.

'We are writing an extemporaneous theme,' he said. 'The subject is, "Who am I and why I came to Dwight College." '

He stripped a few sheets from the pad and offered them to the boy. Tertan hesitated and then took the paper, but he held it only tentatively. As if with the effort of making something clear, he gulped, and a slow smile fixed itself on his face. It was at once knowing and shy.

'Professor,' he said, 'to be perfectly fair to my classmates'—he made a large gesture over the room—'and to you'— he inclined his head to Howe—'this would not be for me an extemporaneous subject.'

Howe tried to understand. 'You mean you've already thought about it—you've heard we always give the same subject? That doesn't matter.'

Again the boy ducked his head and gulped. It was the gesture of one who wishes to make a difficult explanation with perfect candor. 'Sir,' he said, and made the distinction with great care, 'the topic I did not expect, but I have given much ratiocination to the subject.'

Howe smiled and said, 'I don't think that's an unfair advantage. Just go ahead and write.'

Tertan narrowed his eyes and glanced sidewise at Howe. His strange mouth smiled. Then in quizzical acceptance, he ducked his head, threw back the heavy, dank lock, dropped into a seat with a great loose noise and began to write rapidly.

The room fell silent again and Howe resumed his idleness. When the bell rang, the students who had groaned when the task had been set now groaned again because they had not finished. Howe took up the papers, and held the class while he made the first assignment. When he dismissed it, Tertan bore down on him, his slack mouth held ready for speech.

'Some professors,' he said, 'are pedants. They are Dryasdusts. However, some professors are free souls and creative spirits. Kant, Hegel and Nietzsche were all professors.' With this pronouncement he paused. 'It is my opinion,' he continued, 'that you occupy the second category.'

Howe looked at the boy in surprise and said with good-natured irony, 'With Kant, Hegel and Nietzsche?'

Not only Tertan's hand and head but his whole awkward body waved away the stupidity. 'It is the kind and not the quantity of the kind,' he said sternly.

Rebuked, Howe said as simply and seriously as he could, 'It would be nice to think so.' He added, 'Of course I am not a professor.'

This was clearly a disappointment but Tertan met it. 'In the French sense,' he said with composure. 'Generically, a teacher.'

Suddenly he bowed. It was such a bow, Howe fancied, as a stage director might teach an actor playing a medieval student who takes leave of Abelard—stiff, solemn, with elbows close to the body and feet together. Then, quite as suddenly, he turned and left.

A queer fish, and as soon as Howe reached his office, he sifted through the batch of themes and drew out Tertan's. The boy had filled many sheets with his unformed headlong scrawl. 'Who am I?' he had begun. 'Here, in a mundane, not to say commercialized academe, is asked the question which from time long immemorably out of mind has accreted doubts and thoughts in the psyche of man

to pester him as a nuisance. Whether in St. Augustine (or Austin as sometimes called) or Miss Bashkirtsieff or Frederic Amiel or Empedocles, or in less lights of the intellect than these, this posed question has been ineluctable.'

Howe took out his pencil. He circled 'academe' and wrote 'vocab.' in the margin. He underlined 'time long immemorably out of mind' and wrote 'Diction!' But this seemed inadequate for what was wrong. He put down his pencil and read ahead to discover the principle of error in the theme. "Today as ever, in spite of gloomy prophets of the dismal science (economics) the question is uninvalidated. Out of the starry depths of heaven hurtles this spear of query demanding to be caught on the shield of the mind ere it pierces the skull and the limbs be unstrung.'

Baffled but quite caught, Howe read on. 'Materialism, by which is meant the philosophic concept and not the moral idea, provides no aegis against the question which lies beyond the tangible (metaphysics). Existence without alloy is the question presented. Environment and heredity relegated aside, the rags and old clothes of practical life discarded, the name and the instrumentality of livelihood do not, as the prophets of the dismal science insist on in this connection, give solution to the interrogation which not from the professor merely but veritably from the cosmos is given. I think, therefore I am (cogito etc.) but who am I? Tertan I am, but what is Tertan? Of this time, of that place, of some parentage, what does it matter?'

Existence without alloy: the phrase established itself. Howe put aside Tertan's paper and at random picked up another. 'I am Arthur J. Casebeer, Jr.,' he read. 'My father is Arthur J. Casebeer and my grandfather was Arthur J. Casebeer before him. My mother is Nina Wimble Casebeer. Both of them are college graduates and my father is in insurance. I was born in St. Louis eighteen years ago and we still make our residence there.'

Arthur J. Casebeer, who knew who he was, was less interesting than Tertan, but more coherent. Howe picked up Tertan's paper again. It was clear that none of the routine marginal comments, no 'sent. str.' or 'punct.' or 'vocab.' could cope with this torrential rhetoric. He read ahead, contenting himself with underscoring the errors against the time when he should have the necessary 'conference' with Tertan.

It was a busy and official day of cards and sheets, arrangements and small decisions, and it gave Howe pleasure. Even when it was time to attend the first of the weekly Convocations he felt the charm of the beginning of things when intention is still innocent and uncorrupted by effort. He sat among the young instructors on the platform, and joined in their humorous complaints at having to assist at the ceremony, but actually he got a clear satisfaction from the ritual of prayer and prosy speech, and even from wearing his academic gown. And when the Convocation was over the pleasure continued as he crossed the campus, exchanging greetings with men he had not seen since the spring. They were people who did not yet, and perhaps never would, mean much to him, but in a year they had grown amiably to be part of his life. They were his fellow-townsmen.

The day had cooled again at sunset, and there was a bright chill in the September twilight. Howe carried his voluminous gown over his arm, he swung his doctoral hood by its purple neckpiece, and on his head he wore his mortarboard with its heavy gold tassel bobbing just over his eye. These were the weighty and absurd symbols of his new profession and they pleased him. At twenty-six Joseph Howe had discovered that he was neither so well off nor so bohemian as he had once thought. A small income, adequate when supplemented by a sizable cash legacy, was genteel poverty when the cash was all spent. And the literary life—the room at the Lafayette, or the small apartment without a lease, the long summers on the Cape, the long afternoons and the social evenings—began to weary him. His writing filled his mornings and should perhaps have filled his life, yet it did not. To the amusement of his friends, and with a certain sense that he was betraying his own freedom, he had used the last of his

legacy for a year at Harvard. The small but respectable reputation of his two volumes of verse had proved useful—he continued at Harvard on a fellowship and when he emerged as Doctor Howe he received an excellent appointment, with prospects, at Dwight.

He had his moments of fear when all that had ever been said of the dangers of the academic life had occurred to him. But after a year in which he had tested every possibility of corruption and seduction he was ready to rest easy. His third volume of verse, most of it written in his first year of teaching, was not only ampler but, he thought, better than its predecessors.

There was a clear hour before the Bradby dinner party, and Howe looked forward to it. But he was not to enjoy it, for lying with his mail on the hall table was a copy of this quarter's issue of *Life and Letters,* to which his landlord subscribed. Its severe cover announced that its editor, Frederic Woolley, had this month contributed an essay called 'Two Poets,' and Howe, picking it up, curious to see who the two poets might be, felt his own name start out at him with cabalistic power—Joseph Howe. As he continued to turn the pages his hand trembled.

Standing in the dark hall, holding the neat little magazine, Howe knew that his literary contempt for Frederic Woolley meant nothing, for he suddenly understood how he respected Woolley in the way of the world. He knew this by the trembling of his hand. And of the little world as well as the great, for although the literary groups of New York might dismiss Woolley, his name carried high authority in the academic world. At Dwight it was even a revered name, for it had been here at the college that Frederic Woolley had made the distinguished scholarly career from which he had gone on to literary journalism. In middle life he had been induced to take the editorship of *Life and Letters*, a literary monthly not widely read but heavily endowed, and in its pages he had carried on the defense of what he sometimes called the older values. He was not without wit, he had great knowledge and considerable taste, and even in the full movement of the 'new' literature he had won a certain respect for his refusal to accept it. In France, even in England, he would have been connected with a more robust tradition of conservatism, but America gave him an audience not much better than genteel. It was known in the college that to the subsidy of *Life and Letters* the Bradbys contributed a great part.

As Howe read, he saw that he was involved in nothing less than an event. When the Fifth Series of *Studies in Order and Value* came to be collected, this latest issue of Frederic Woolley's essays would not be merely another step in the old direction. Clearly and unmistakably, it was a turning point. All his literary life Woolley had been concerned with the relation of literature to morality, religion, and the private and delicate pieties, and he had been unalterably opposed to all that he had called 'inhuman humanitarianism.' But here, suddenly, dramatically late, he had made an about-face, turning to the public life and to the humanitarian politics he had so long despised. This was the kind of incident the histories of literature make much of. Frederic Woolley was opening for himself a new career and winning a kind of new youth. He contrasted the two poets, Thomas Wormser, who was admirable, Joseph Howe, who was almost dangerous. He spoke of the 'precious subjectivism' of Howe's verse. 'In times like ours,' he wrote, 'with millions facing penury and want, one feels that the qualities of the *tour d'ivoire* are well-nigh inhuman, nearly insulting. The *tour d'ivoire* becomes the *tour d'ivresse*, and it is not self-intoxicated poets that our people need.' The essay said more: 'The problem is one of meaning. I am not ignorant that the creed of the esoteric poets declares that a poem does not and should not *mean* anything, that it *is* something. But poetry is what the poet makes it, and if he is a true poet he makes what his society needs. And what is needed now is the tradition in which Mr. Wormser writes, the true tradition of poetry. The Howes do no harm, but they do no good

when positive good is demanded of all responsible men. Or do the Howes indeed do no harm? Perhaps Plato would have said they do, that in some ways theirs is the Phrygian music that turns men's minds from the struggle. Certainly it is true that Thomas Wormser writes in the lucid Dorian mode which sends men into battle with evil.'

It was easy to understand why Woolley had chosen to praise Thomas Wormser. The long, lilting lines of *Corn Under Willows* hymned, as Woolley put it, the struggle for wheat in the Iowa fields, and expressed the real lives of real people. But why out of the dozen more notable examples he had chosen Howe's little volume as the example of 'precious subjectivism' was hard to guess. In a way it was funny, this multiplication of himself into 'the Howes.' And yet this becoming the multiform political symbol by whose creation Frederic Woolley gave the sign of a sudden new life, this use of him as a sacrifice whose blood was necessary for the rites of rejuvenation, made him feel oddly unclean.

Nor could Howe get rid of a certain practical resentment. As a poet he had a special and respectable place in the college life. But it might be another thing to be marked as the poet of a wilful and selfish obscurity.

As he walked to the Bradby's, Howe was a little tense and defensive. It seemed to him that all the world knew of the 'attack' and agreed with it. And, indeed, the Bradbys had read the essay but Professor Bradby, a kind and pretentious man, said, 'I see my old friend knocked you about a bit, my boy,' and his wife Eugenia looked at Howe with her childlike blue eyes and said, 'I shall *scold* Frederic for the untrue things he wrote about you. You aren't the least obscure.' They beamed at him. In their genial snobbery they seemed to feel that he had distinguished himself. He was the leader of Howeism. He enjoyed the dinner party as much as he had thought he would.

And in the following days, as he was more preoccupied with his duties, the incident was forgotten. His classes had ceased to be mere groups. Student after student detached himself from the mass and required or claimed a place in Howe's awareness. Of them all it was Tertan who first and most violently signaled his separate existence. A week after classes had begun Howe saw his silhouette on the frosted glass of his office door. It was motionless for a long time, perhaps stopped by the problem of whether or not to knock before entering. Howe called, 'Come in!' and Tertan entered with his shambling stride.

He stood beside the desk, silent and at attention. When Howe asked him to sit down, he responded with a gesture of head and hand, as if to say that such amenities were beside the point. Nevertheless, he did take the chair. He put his ragged, crammed briefcase between his legs. His face, which Howe now observed fully for the first time, was confusing, for it was made up of florid curves, the nose arched in the bone and voluted in the nostril, the mouth loose and soft and rather moist. Yet the face was so thin and narrow as to seem the very type of asceticism. Lashes of unusual length veiled the eyes and, indeed, it seemed as if there were a veil over the whole countenance. Before the words actually came, the face screwed itself into an attitude of preparation for them.

'You can confer with me now?' Tertan said.

'Yes, I'd be glad to. There are several things in your two themes I want to talk to you about.' Howe reached for the packet of themes on his desk and sought for Tertan's. But the boy was waving them away.

'These are done perforce,' he said. 'Under the pressure of your requirement. They are not significant; mere duties.' Again his great hand flapped vaguely to dismiss his themes. He leaned forward and gazed at his teacher.

'You are,' he said, 'a man of letters? You are a poet?' It was more declaration than question.

'I should like to think so,' Howe said.

At first Tertan accepted the answer with a show of appreciation, as though the understatement made a secret between himself and Howe. Then he chose to mis-understand. With his shrewd and disconcerting control of expression, he presented to Howe a puzzled grimace. 'What does that mean?' he said.

Howe retracted the irony. 'Yes. I am a poet.' It sounded strange to say.

'That,' Tertan said, 'is a wonder.' He corrected himself with his ducking head. 'I mean that is wonderful.'

Suddenly, he dived at the miserable briefcase between his legs, put it on his knees, and began to fumble with the catch, all intent on the difficulty it presented. Howe noted that his suit was worn thin, his shirt almost unclean. He became aware, even, of a vague and musty odor of garments worn too long in unaired rooms. Tertan conquered the lock and began to concentrate upon a search into the interior. At last he held in his hand what he was after, a torn and crumpled copy of *Life and Letters*.

'I learned it from here,' he said, holding it out.

Howe looked at him sharply, his hackles a little up. But the boy's face was not only perfectly innocent, it even shone with a conscious admiration. Apparently nothing of the import of the essay had touched him except the wonderful fact that his teacher was a 'man of letters.' Yet this seemed too stupid, and Howe, to test it, said, 'The man who wrote that doesn't think it's wonderful.'

Tertan made a moist hissing sound as he cleared his mouth of saliva. His head, oddly loose on his neck, wove a pattern of contempt in the air. 'A critic,' he said, 'who admits *prima facie* that he does not understand.' Then he said grandly, 'It is the inevitable fate.'

It was absurd, yet Howe was not only aware of the absurdity but of a tension suddenly and wonderfully relaxed. Now that the 'attack' was on the table between himself and this strange boy, and subject to the boy's funny and absolutely certain contempt, the hidden force of his feeling was revealed to him in the very moment that it vanished. All unsuspected, there had been a film over the world, a transparent but discoloring haze of danger. But he had no time to stop over the brightened aspect of things. Tertan was going on. 'I also am a man of letters. Putative.'

'You have written a good deal?' Howe meant to be no more than polite, and he was surprised at the tenderness he heard in his words.

Solemnly the boy nodded, threw back the dank lock, and sucked in a deep, anticipatory breath. 'First, a word of homiletics, which is a defense of the principles of religious optimism against the pessimism of Schopenhauer and the humanism of Nietzsche.'

'Humanism? Why do you call it humanism?'

'It is my nomenclature for making a deity of man,' Tertan replied negligently. 'Then three fictional works, novels. And numerous essays in science, combating materialism. Is it your duty to read these if I bring them to you?'

Howe answered simply, 'No, it isn't exactly my duty, but I shall be happy to read them.'

Tertan stood up and remained silent. He rested his bag on the chair. With a certain compunction—for it did not seem entirely proper that, of two men of letters, one should have the right to bluepencil the other, to grade him or to question the quality of his 'sentence structure' —Howe reached for Tertan's papers. But before he could take them up, the boy suddenly made his bow-to-Abelard, the stiff inclination of the body with the hands seeming to emerge from the scholar's gown. Then he was gone.

But after his departure something was still left of him. The timbre of his curious sentences, the downright finality of so quaint a phrase as 'It is the inevitable fate' still rang in the air. Howe gave the warmth of his feeling to the new visitor who stood at the door announcing himself with a genteel clearing of the throat.

'Doctor Howe, I believe?' the student said. A large hand advanced into the room and grasped Howe's hand. 'Blackburn, sir, Theodore Blackburn, vice-president of the Student Council. A great pleasure, sir.'

Out of a pair of ruddy cheeks a pair of small eyes twinkled good-naturedly. The large face, the large body were not so much fat as beefy and suggested something 'typical'—monk, politician, or innkeeper.

Blackburn took the seat beside Howe's desk. 'I may have seemed to introduce myself in my public capacity, sir,' he said. 'But it is really as an individual that I came to see you. That is to say, as one of your students to be.'

He spoke with an English intonation and he went on, 'I was once an English major, sir.'

For a moment Howe was startled, for the roast-beef look of the boy and the manner of his speech gave a second's credibility to one sense of his statement. Then the collegiate meaning of the phrase asserted itself, but some perversity made Howe say what was not really in good taste even with so forward a student, 'Indeed? What regiment?'

Blackburn stared and then gave a little pouf-pouf of laughter. He waved the misapprehension away. *'Very* good, sir. It certainly is an ambiguous term.' He chuckled in appreciation of Howe's joke, then cleared his throat to put it aside. 'I look forward to taking your course in the romantic poets, sir,' he said earnestly. 'To me the romantic poets are the very crown of English literature.'

Howe made a dry sound, and the boy, catching some meaning in it, said, 'Little as I know them, of course. But even Shakespeare who is so dear to us of the Anglo-Saxon tradition is in a sense but the preparation for Shelley, Keats and Byron. And Wadsworth.'

Almost sorry for him, Howe dropped his eyes. With some embarrassment, for the boy was not actually his student, he said softly 'Wordsworth.'

'Sir?'

'Wordsworth, not Wadsworth. You said Wadsworth.'

'Did I, sir?' Gravely he shook his head to rebuke himself for the error. 'Wordsworth, of course—slip of the tongue.' Then, quite in command again, he went on. 'I have a favor to ask of you, Doctor Howe. You see, I began my college course as an English major,'—he smiled—'as I said.'

'Yes?'

'But after my first year I shifted. I shifted to the social sciences. Sociology and government—I find them stimulating and very *real*.' He paused, out of respect for reality. 'But now I find that perhaps I have neglected the other side.'

'The other side?' Howe said.

'Imagination, fancy, culture. A well-rounded man.' He trailed off as if there were perfect understanding between them. 'And so, sir, I have decided to end my senior year with your course in the romantic poets.'

His voice was filled with an indulgence which Howe ignored as he said flatly and gravely, 'But that course isn't given until the spring term.'

'Yes, sir, and that is where the favor comes in. Would you let me take your romantic prose course? I can't take it for credit, sir, my program is full, but just for background it seems to me that I ought to take it. I do hope,' he concluded in a manly way, 'that you will consent.'

'Well, it's no great favor, Mr. Blackburn. You can come if you wish, though there's not much point in it if you don't do the reading.'

The bell rang for the hour and Howe got up.

'May I begin with this class, sir?' Blackburn's smile was candid and boyish.

Howe nodded carelessly and together, silently, they walked to the classroom down the hall. When they reached the door Howe stood back to let his student enter, but Blackburn moved adroitly behind him and grasped him by the arm to urge him over the threshold. They entered together with Blackburn's hand firmly on Howe's biceps, the student inducting the teacher into his own room. Howe felt a surge of temper rise in him and almost violently he disengaged his arm and walked to the desk, while Blackburn found a seat in the front row and smiled at him.

II

The question was, At whose door must the tragedy be laid?

All night the snow had fallen heavily and only now was abating in sparse little flurries. The windows were valanced high with white. It was very quiet; something of the quiet of the world had reached the class, and Howe found that everyone was glad to talk or listen. In the room there was a comfortable sense of pleasure in being human.

Casebeer believed that the blame for the tragedy rested with heredity. Picking up the book he read, 'The sins of the fathers are visited on their children.' This opinion was received with general favor. Nevertheless, Johnson ventured to say that the fault was all Pastor Manders' because the Pastor had made Mrs. Alving go back to her husband and was always hiding the truth. To this Hibbard objected with logic enough, 'Well then, it was really all her husband's fault. He *did* all the bad things.' De Witt, his face bright with an impatient idea, said that the fault was all society's. 'By society I don't mean upper-crust society,' he said. He looked around a little defiantly, taking in any members of the class who might be members of upper-crust society. 'Not in that sense. I mean the social unit.'

Howe nodded and said, 'Yes, of course.'

'If the society of the time had progressed far enough in science,' De Witt went on, 'then there would be no problem for Mr. Ibsen to write about. Captain Alving plays around a little, gives way to perfectly natural biological urges, and he gets a social disease, a venereal disease. If the disease is cured, no problem. Invent salvarsan and the disease is cured. The problem of heredity disappears and li'l Oswald just doesn't get paresis. No paresis, no problem—no problem, no play.'

This was carrying the ark into battle, and the class looked at De Witt with respectful curiosity. It was his usual way and on the whole they were sympathetic with his struggle to prove to Howe that science was better than literature. Still, there was something in his reckless manner that alienated them a little.

'Or take birth-control, for instance,' De Witt went on. 'If Mrs. Alving had some knowledge of contraception, she wouldn't have had to have li'l Oswald at all. No li'l Oswald, no play.'

The class was suddenly quieter. In the

back row Stettenthover swung his great football shoulders in a righteous sulking gesture, first to the right, then to the left. He puckered his mouth ostentatiously. Intellect was always ending up by talking dirty.

Tertan's hand went up, and Howe said, 'Mr. Tertan.' The boy shambled to his feet and began his long characteristic gulp. Howe made a motion with his fingers, as small as possible, and Tertan ducked his head and smiled in apology. He sat down. The class laughed. With more than half the term gone, Tertan had not been able to remember that one did not rise to speak. He seemed unable to carry on the life of the intellect without this mark of respect for it. To Howe the boy's habit of rising seemed to accord with the formal shabbiness of his dress. He never wore the casual sweaters and jackets of his classmates. Into the free and comfortable air of the college classroom he brought the stuffy sordid strictness of some crowded, metropolitan high school.

'Speaking from one sense,' Tertan began slowly, 'there is no blame ascribable. From the sense of determinism, who can say where the blame lies? The preordained is the preordained and it cannot be said without rebellion against the universe, a palpable absurdity.'

In the back row Stettenhover slumped suddenly in his seat, his heels held out before him, making a loud, dry, disgusted sound. His body sank until his neck rested on the back of his chair. He folded his hands across his belly and looked significantly out of the window, exasperated not only with Tertan, but with Howe, with the class, with the whole system designed to encourage this kind of thing. There was a certain insolence in the movement and Howe flushed. As Tertan continued to speak, Howe stalked casually toward the window and placed himself in the line of Stettenhover's vision. He stared at the great fellow, who pretended not to see him. There was so much power in the big body, so much contempt in the Greek-athlete face under the crisp Greek-athlete curls, that Howe felt almost physical fear. But at last Stettenhover admitted him to focus and under his dis-

approving gaze sat up with slow indifference. His eyebrows raised high in resignation, he began to examine his hands. Howe relaxed and turned his attention back to Tertan.

'Flux of existence,' Tertan was saying, 'produces all things, so that judgment wavers. Beyond the phenomena, what? But phenomena are adumbrated and to them we are limited.'

Howe saw it for a moment as perhaps it existed in the boy's mind—the world of shadows which are cast by a great light upon a hidden reality as in the old myth of the Cave. But the little brush with Stettenhover had tired him, and he said irritably, 'But come to the point, Mr. Tertan.'

He said it so sharply that some of his class looked at him curiously. For three months he had gently carried Tertan through his verbosities, to the vaguely respectful surprise of the other students, who seemed to conceive that there existed between this strange classmate and their teacher some special understanding from which they were content to be excluded. Tertan looked at him mildly, and at once came brilliantly to the point. 'This is the summation of the play,' he said and took up his book and read, ' "Your poor father never found any outlet for the overmastering joy of life that was in him. And I brought no holiday into his home, either. Everything seemed to turn upon duty and I am afraid I made your poor father's home unbearable to him, Oswald." Spoken by Mrs. Alving.'

Yes that was surely the 'summation' of the play and Tertan had hit it, as he hit, deviously and eventually, the literary point of almost everything. But now, as always, he was wrapping it away from sight. 'For most mortals,' he said, 'there are only joys of biological urgings, gross and crass, such as the sensuous Captain Alving. For certain few there are the transmutations beyond these to a contemplation of the utter whole.'

Oh, the boy was mad. And suddenly the word, used in hyperbole, intended almost for the expression of exasperated admiration, became literal. Now that the word was used, it became simply apparent to Howe that Tertan was mad.

It was a monstrous word and stood like a bestial thing in the room. Yet it so completely comprehended everything that had puzzled Howe, it so arranged and explained what for three months had been perplexing him that almost at once its horror became domesticated. With this word Howe was able to understand why he had never been able to communicate to Tertan the value of a single criticism or correction of his wild, verbose themes. Their conferences had been frequent and long but had done nothing to reduce to order the splendid confusion of the boy's ideas. Yet, impossible though its expression was, Tertan's incandescent mind could always strike for a moment into some dark corner of thought.

And now it was suddenly apparent that it was not a faulty rhetoric that Howe had to contend with. With his new knowledge he looked at Tertan's face and wondered how he could have so long deceived himself. Tertan was still talking, and the class had lapsed into a kind of patient unconsciousness, a coma of respect for words which, for all that most of them knew, might be profound. Almost with a suffusion of shame, Howe believed that in some dim way the class had long ago had some intimation of Tertan's madness. He reached out as decisively as he could to seize the thread of Tertan's discourse before it should be entangled further.

'Mr. Tertan says that the blame must be put upon whoever kills the joy of living in another. We have been assuming that Captain Alving was a wholly bad man, but what if we assume that he became bad only because Mrs. Alving, when they were first married, acted toward him in the prudish way she says she did?'

It was a ticklish idea to advance to freshmen and perhaps not profitable. Not all of them were following.

'That would put the blame on Mrs. Alving herself, whom most of you admire. And she herself seems to think so.' He glanced at his watch. The hour was nearly over. 'What do you think, Mr. De Witt?'

De Witt rose to the idea; he wanted to know if society couldn't be blamed for educating Mrs. Alving's temperament in the wrong way. Casebeer was puzzled,

Stettenhover continued to look at his hands until the bell rang.

Tertan, his brows louring in thought, was making as always for a private word. Howe gathered his books and papers to leave quickly. At this moment of his discovery and with the knowledge still raw, he could not engage himself with Tertan. Tertan sucked in his breath to prepare for speech and Howe made ready for the pain and confusion. But at that moment Casebeer detached himself from the group with which he had been conferring and which he seemed to represent. His constituency remained at a tactful distance. The mission involved the time of an assigned essay. Casebeer's presentation of the plea—it was based on the freshmen's heavy duties at the fraternities during Carnival Week—cut across Tertan's preparations for speech. 'And so some of us fellows thought,' Casebeer concluded with heavy solemnity, 'that we could do a better job, give our minds to it more, if we had more time.'

Tertan regarded Casebeer with mingled curiosity and revulsion. Howe not only said that he would postpone the assignment but went on to talk about the Carnival, and even drew the waiting constituency into the conversation. He was conscious of Tertan's stern and astonished stare, then of his sudden departure.

Now that the fact was clear, Howe knew that he must act on it. His course was simple enough. He must lay the case before the Dean. Yet he hesitated. His feeling for Tertan must now, certainly, be in some way invalidated. Yet could he, because of a word, hurry to assign to official and reasonable solicitude what had been, until this moment, so various and warm? He could at least delay and, by moving slowly, lend a poor grace to the necessary, ugly act of making his report.

It was with some notion of keeping the matter in his own hands that he went to the Dean's office to look up Tertan's records. In the outer office the Dean's secretary greeted him brightly, and at his request brought him the manila folder with the small identifying photograph pasted in the corner. She laughed. 'He was looking for the birdie in the wrong place,' she said.

Howe leaned over her shoulder to look at the picture. It was as bad as all the Dean's-office photographs were, but it differed from all that Howe had ever seen. Tertan, instead of looking into the camera, as no doubt he had been bidden, had, at the moment of exposure, turned his eyes upward. His mouth, as though conscious of the trick played on the photographer, had the sly superior look that Howe knew.

The secretary was fascinated by the picture. 'What a funny boy,' she said. 'He looks like Tartuffe!'

And so he did, with the absurd piety of the eyes and the conscious slyness of the mouth and the whole face bloated by the bad lens.

'Is he *like* that?' the secretary said.

'Like Tartuffe? No.'

From the photograph there was little enough comfort to be had. The records themselves gave no clue to madness, though they suggested sadness enough. Howe read of a father, Stanislaus Tertan, born in Budapest and trained in engineering in Berlin, once employed by the Hercules Chemical Corporation—this was one of the factories that dominated the sound end of the town—but now without employment. He read of a mother Erminie (Youngfellow) Tertan, born in Manchester, educated at a Normal School at Leeds, now housewife by profession. The family lived on Greenbriar Street which Howe knew as a row of once elegant homes near what was now the factory district. The old mansion had long ago been divided into small and primitive apartments. Of Ferdinand himself there was little to learn. He lived with his parents, had attended a Detroit high school and had transferred to the local school in his last year. His rating for intelligence, as expressed in numbers, was high, his scholastic record was remarkable, he held a college scholarship for his tuition.

Howe laid the folder on the secretary's desk. 'Did you find what you wanted to know?' she asked.

The phrases from Tertan's momentous first theme came back to him. "Tertan I am, but what is Tertan? Of this time, of that place, of some parentage, what does it matter?'

'No, I didn't find it,' he said.

Now that he had consulted the sad, half-meaningless record he knew all the more firmly that he must not give the matter out of his own hands. He must not release Tertan to authority. Not that he anticipated from the Dean anything but the greatest kindness for Tertan. The Dean would have the experience and skill which he himself could not have. One way or another the Dean could answer the question, 'What is Tertan?' Yet this was precisely what he feared. He alone could keep alive—not forever but for a somehow important time—the question, 'What is Tertan?' He alone could keep it still a question. Some sure instinct told him that he must not surrender the question to a clean official desk in a clear official light to be dealt with, settled and closed.

He heard himself saying, 'Is the Dean busy at the moment? I'd like to see him.'

His request came thus unbidden, even forbidden, and it was one of the surprising and startling incidents of his life. Later when he reviewed the events, so disconnected in themselves, or so merely odd, of the story that unfolded for him that year, it was over this moment, on its face the least notable, that he paused longest. It was frequently to be with fear and never without a certainty of its meaning in his own knowledge of himself that he would recall this simple, routine request, and the feeling of shame and freedom it gave him as he sent everything down the official chute. In the end, of course, no matter what he did to 'protect' Tertan, he would have had to make the same request and lay the matter on the Dean's clean desk. But it would always be a landmark of his life that, at the very moment when he was rejecting the official way, he had been, without will or intention, so gladly drawn to it.

After the storm's last delicate flurry, the sun had come out. Reflected by the new snow, it filled the office with a golden light which was almost musical in the way it made all the commonplace objects of efficiency shine with a sudden sad and noble significance. And the light, now that he noticed it, made the utterance of his perverse and unwanted request even more momentous.

The secretary consulted the engagement pad. 'He'll be free any minute. Don't you want to wait in the parlor?'

She threw open the door of the large and pleasant room in which the Dean held his Committee meetings, and in which his visitors waited. It was designed with a homely elegance on the masculine side of the eighteenth-century manner. There was a small coal fire in the grate and the handsome mahogany table was strewn with books and magazines. The large windows gave on the snowy lawn, and there was such a fine width of window that the white casements and walls seemed at this moment but a continuation of the snow, the snow but an extension of casement and walls. The outdoors seemed taken in and made safe, the indoors seemed luxuriously freshened and expanded.

Howe sat down by the fire and lighted a cigarette. The room had its intended effect upon him. He felt comfortable and relaxed, yet nicely organized, some young diplomatic agent of the eighteenth century, the newly fledged Swift carrying out Sir William Temple's business. The rawness of Tertan's case quite vanished. He crossed his legs and reached for a magazine.

It was that famous issue of *Life and Letters* that his idle hand had found and his blood raced as he sifted through it, and the shape of his own name, Joseph Howe, sprang out at him, still cabalistic in its power. He tossed the magazine back on the table as the door of the Dean's office opened and the Dean ushered out Theodore Blackburn.

'Ah, Joseph!' the Dean said.

Blackburn said, 'Good morning, Doctor.' Howe winced at the title and caught the flicker of amusement over the Dean's face. The Dean stood with his hand high on the door-jamb and Blackburn, still in the doorway, remained standing almost under the long arm.

Howe nodded briefly to Blackburn, snubbing his eager deference. 'Can you give me a few minutes?' he said to the Dean.

'All the time you want. Come in.' Before the two men could enter the office, Blackburn claimed their attention with a long full 'er.' As they turned to him, Blackburn said, 'Can *you* give *me* a few minutes, Doctor Howe?' His eyes sparkled at the little audacity he had committed, the slightly impudent play with hierarchy. Of the three of them Blackburn kept himself the lowest, but he reminded Howe of his subaltern relation to the Dean.

'I mean, of course,' Blackburn went on easily, 'when you've finished with the Dean.'

'I'll be in my office shortly,' Howe said, turned his back on the ready 'Thank you, sir,' and followed the Dean into the inner room.

'Energetic boy,' said the Dean. 'A bit beyond himself but very energetic. Sit down.'

The Dean lighted a cigarette, leaned back in his chair, sat easy and silent for a moment, giving Howe no signal to go ahead with business. He was a young Dean, not much beyond forty, a tall handsome man with sad, ambitious eyes. He had been a Rhodes scholar. His friends looked for great things from him, and it was generally said that he had notions of education which he was not yet ready to try to put into practice.

His relaxed silence was meant as a compliment to Howe. He smiled and said, 'What's the business, Joseph?'

'Do you know Tertan—Ferdinand Tertan, a freshman?'

The Dean's cigarette was in his mouth and his hands were clasped behind his head. He did not seem to search his memory for the name. He said, 'What about him?'

Clearly the Dean knew something, and he was waiting for Howe to tell him more. Howe moved only tentatively. Now that he was doing what he had resolved to do, he felt more guilty at having been so long deceived by Tertan and more need to be loyal to his error.

'He's a strange fellow,' he ventured.

He said stubbornly, 'In a strange way he's very brilliant.' He concluded, 'But very strange.'

The springs of the Dean's swivel chair creaked as he came out of his sprawl and leaned forward to Howe. 'Do you mean he's so strange that it's something you could give a name to?'

Howe looked at him stupidly. 'What do you mean?' he said.

'What's his trouble?' the Dean said more neutrally.

'He's very brilliant, in a way. I looked him up and he has a top intelligence rating. But somehow, and it's hard to explain just how, what he says is always on the edge of sense and doesn't quite make it.'

The Dean looked at him and Howe flushed up. The Dean had surely read Woolley on the subject of 'the Howes' and the *tour d'ivresse*. Was that quick glance ironical?

The Dean picked up some papers from his desk, and Howe could see that they were in Tertan's impatient scrawl. Perhaps the little gleam in the Dean's glance had come only from putting facts together.

'He sent me this yesterday,' the Dean said. 'After an interview I had with him. I haven't been able to do more than glance at it. When you said what you did, I realized there was something wrong.'

Twisting his mouth, the Dean looked over the letter. 'You seem to be involved,' he said without looking up. 'By the way, what did you give him at mid-term?'

Flushing, setting his shoulders, Howe said firmly, 'I gave him A-minus.'

The Dean chuckled. 'Might be a good idea if some of our nicer boys went crazy—just a little.' He said, 'Well,' to conclude the matter and handed the papers to Howe. 'See if this is the same thing you've been finding. Then we can go into the matter again.'

Before the fire in the parlor, in the chair that Howe had been occupying, sat Blackburn. He sprang to his feet as Howe entered.

'I said my office, Mr. Blackburn.' Howe's voice was sharp. Then he was almost sorry for the rebuke, so clearly and naively did Blackburn seem to relish

his stay in the parlour, close to authority.

'I'm in a bit of a hurry, sir,' he said, 'and I did want to be sure to speak to you, sir.'

He was really absurd, yet fifteen years from now he would have grown up to himself, to the assurance and mature beefiness. In banks, in consular offices, in brokerage firms, on the bench, more seriously affable, a little sterner, he would make use of his ability to be administered by his job. It was almost reassuring. Now he was exercising his too-great skill on Howe. 'I owe you an apology, sir,' he said.

Howe knew that he did, but he showed surprise.

'I mean, Doctor, after your having been so kind about letting me attend your class, I stopped coming.' He smiled in deprecation. 'Extracurricular activities take up so much of my time. I'm afraid I undertook more than I could perform.'

Howe had noticed the absence and had been a little irritated by it after Blackburn's elaborate plea. It was an absence that might be interpreted as a comment on the teacher. But there was only one way for him to answer. 'You've no need to apologize,' he said. 'It's wholly your affair.'

Blackburn beamed. 'I'm so glad you feel that way about it, sir. I was worried you might think I had stayed away because I was influenced by—' he stopped and lowered his eyes.

Astonished, Howe said, 'Influenced by what?'

'Well, by—' Blackburn hesitated and for answer pointed to the table on which lay the copy of *Life and Letters*. Without looking at it, he knew where to direct his hand. 'By the unfavorable publicity, sir.' He hurried on. 'And that brings me to another point, sir. I am vice president of Quill and Scroll, sir, the student literary society, and I wonder if you would address us. You could read your own poetry, sir, and defend your own point of view. It would be very interesting.'

It was truly amazing. Howe looked long and cruelly into Blackburn's face, trying to catch the secret of the mind that could have conceived this way of manipulating him, this way so daring and inept —but not entirely inept—with its malice so without malignity. The face did not yield its secret. Howe smiled broadly and said, 'Of course I don't think you were influenced by the unfavorable publicity.'

'I'm still going to take—regularly, for credit—your romantic poets course next term,' Blackburn said.

'Don't worry, my dear fellow, don't worry about it.'

Howe started to leave and Blackburn stopped him with, 'But about Quill, sir?'

'Suppose we wait until next term? I'll be less busy then.'

And Blackburn said, 'Very good, sir, and thank you.'

In his office the little encounter seemed less funny to Howe, was even in some indeterminate way disturbing. He made an effort to put it from his mind by turning to what was sure to disturb him more, the Tertan letter read in the new interpretation. He found what he had always found, the same florid leaps beyond fact and meaning, the same headlong certainty. But as his eye passed over the familiar scrawl it caught his own name, and for the second time that hour he felt the race of his blood.

'The Paraclete,' Tertan had written to the Dean, 'from a Greek word meaning to stand in place of, but going beyond the primitive idea to mean traditionally the helper, the one who comforts and assists, cannot without fundamental loss be jettisoned. Even if taken no longer in the supernatural sense, the concept remains deeply in the human consciousness inevitably. Humanitarianism is no reply, for not every man stands in the place of every other man for this other comrade's comfort. But certain are chosen out of the human race to be the consoler of some other. Of these, for example, is Joseph Barker Howe, Ph.D. Of intellects not the first yet of true intellect and lambent instructions, given to that which is intuitive and irrational, not to what is logical in the strict word, what is judged by him is of the heart and not the head. Here is one chosen, in that he chooses himself to stand in the place of another for comfort and consolation. To him more than another I give my gratitude,

with all respect to our Dean who reads this, a noble man, but merely dedicated not consecrated. But not in the aspect of the Paraclete only is Dr. Joseph Barker Howe established, for he must be the Paraclete to another aspect of himself, that which is driven and persecuted by the lack of understanding in the world at large, so that he in himself embodies the full history of man's tribulations and, overflowing upon others, notably the present writer, is the ultimate end.'

This was love. There was no escape from it. Try as Howe might to remember that Tertan was mad and all his emotions invalidated, he could not destroy the effect upon him of his student's stern, affectionate regard. He had betrayed not only a power of mind but a power of love. And, however firmly he held before his attention the fact of Tertan's madness, he could do nothing to banish the physical sensation of gratitude he felt. He had never thought of himself as 'driven and persecuted' and he did not now. But still he could not make meaningless his sensation of gratitude. The pitiable Tertan sternly pitied him, and comfort came from Tertan's never-to-be-comforted mind.

III

In an academic community, even an efficient one, official matters move slowly. The term drew to a close with no action in the case of Tertan, and Joseph Howe had to confront a curious problem. How should he grade his strange student, Tertan?

Tertan's final examination had been no different from all his other writing, and what did one 'give' such a student? De Witt must have his A, that was clear. Johnson would get a B. With Casebeer it was a question of a B-minus or a C-plus, and Stettenhover, who had been crammed by the team tutor to fill half a blue-book with his thin feminine scrawl, would have his C-minus which he would accept with mingled indifference and resentment. But with Tertan it was not so easy.

The boy was still in the college process and his name could not be omitted from the grade sheet. Yet what should a mind under suspicion of madness be graded? Until the medical verdict was given, it was for Howe to continue as Tertan's teacher and to keep his judgment pedagogical. Impossible to give him an F: he had not failed. B was for Johnson's stolid mediocrity. He could not be put on the edge of passing with Stettenhover, for he exactly did not pass. In energy and richness of intellect he was perhaps even De Witt's superior, and Howe toyed grimly with the notion of giving him an A, but that would lower the value of the A De Witt had won with his beautiful and clear, if still arrogant, mind. There was a notation which the Registrar recognized—Inc., for Incomplete, and in the horrible comedy of the situation, Howe considered that. But really only a mark of M for Mad would serve.

In his perplexity, Howe sought the Dean, but the Dean was out of town. In the end, he decided to maintain the A-minus he had given Tertan at mid-term. After all, there had been no falling away from that quality. He entered it on the grade sheet with something like bravado.

Academic time moves quickly. A college year is not really a year, lacking as it does three months. And it is endlessly divided into units which, at their beginning, appear larger than they are—terms, half-terms, months, weeks. And the ultimate unit, the hour, is not really an hour, lacking as it does ten minutes. And so the new term advanced rapidly, and one day the fields about the town were all brown, cleared of even the few thin patches of snow which had lingered so long.

Howe, as he lectured on the romantic poets, became conscious of Blackburn emanating wrath. Blackburn did it well, did it with enormous dignity. He did not stir in his seat, he kept his eyes fixed on Howe in perfect attention, but he abstained from using his notebook, there was no mistaking what he proposed to himself as an attitude. His elbow on the writing-wing of the chair, his chin on the curled fingers of his hand, he was the embodiment of intellectual indignation. He was thinking his own thoughts, would give no public offense, yet would claim his due, was not to be intimidated. Howe knew that he would present himself at the end of the hour.

Blackburn entered the office without invitation. He did not smile; there was no cajolery about him. Without invitation he sat down beside Howe's desk. He did not speak until he had taken the blue-book from his pocket. He said, 'What does this mean, sir?'

It was a sound and conservative student tactic. Said in the usual way it meant, 'How could you have so misunderstood me?' or 'What does this mean for my future in the course?' But there were none of the humbler tones in Blackburn's way of saying it.

Howe made the established reply, 'I think that's for you to tell me.'

Blackburn continued icy. 'I'm sure I can't, sir.'

There was a silence between them. Both dropped their eyes to the blue-book on the desk. On its cover Howe had penciled: 'F. This is very poor work.'

Howe picked up the blue-book. There was always the possibility of injustice. The teacher may be bored by the mass of papers and not wholly attentive. A phrase, even the student's handwriting, may irritate him unreasonably. 'Well,' said Howe. 'Let's go through it.'

He opened the first page. 'Now here: you write, "In *The Ancient Mariner*, Coleridge lives in and transports us to a honey-sweet world where all is rich and strange, a world of charm to which we can escape from the humdrum existence of our daily lives, the world of romance. Here, in this warm and honey-sweet land of charming dreams we can relax and enjoy ourselves." '

Howe lowered the paper and waited with a neutral look for Blackburn to speak. Blackburn returned the look boldly, did not speak, sat stolid and lofty. At last Howe said, speaking gently, 'Did you mean that, or were you just at a loss for something to say?'

'You imply that I was just "bluffing"?' The quotation marks hung palpably in the air about the word.

'I'd like to know. I'd prefer believing that you were bluffing to believing that you really thought this.'

Blackburn's eyebrows went up. From the height of a great and firm-based idea he looked at his teacher. He clasped the crags for a moment and then pounced, craftily, suavely. 'Do you mean, Doctor Howe, that there aren't two opinions possible?'

It was superbly done in its air of putting all of Howe's intellectual life into the balance. Howe remained patient and simple. 'Yes,' many opinons are possible, but not this one. Whatever anyone believes of *The Ancient Mariner*, no one can in reason believe that it represents a —a honey-sweet world in which we can relax.'

'But that is what I *feel*, sir.'

This was well-done, too. Howe said, 'Look, Mr. Blackburn. Do you really relax with hunger and thirst, the heat and the sea-serpents, the dead men with staring eyes, Life in Death and the skeletons? Come now, Mr. Blackburn.'

Blackburn made no answer, and Howe pressed forward. 'Now, you say of Wordsworth, "Of peasant stock himself, he turned from the effete life of the salons and found in the peasant the hope of a flaming revolution which would sweep away all the old ideas. This is the subject of his best poems.",

Beaming at his teacher with youthful eagerness, Blackburn said, 'Yes, sir, a rebel, a bringer of light to suffering mankind. I see him as a kind of Prothemeus.'

'A kind of what?'

'Prothemeus, sir.'

'Think, Mr. Blackburn. We were talking about him only today and I mentioned his name a dozen times. You don't mean Prothemeus. You mean—' Howe waited, but there was no response.

'You mean Prometheus.'

Blackburn gave no assent, and Howe took the reins. 'You've done a bad job here, Mr. Blackburn, about as bad as could be done.' He saw Blackburn stiffen and his genial face harden again. 'It shows either a lack of preparation or a complete lack of understanding.' He saw Blackburn's face begin to go to pieces and he stopped.

'Oh, sir,' Blackburn burst out, 'I've never had a mark like this before, never

anything below a B, never. A thing like this has never happened to me before.'

It must be true, it was a statement too easily verified. Could it be that other instructors accepted such flaunting nonsense? Howe wanted to end the interview. 'I'll set it down to lack of preparation,' he said. 'I know you're busy. That's not an excuse, but it's an explanation. Now, suppose you really prepare, and then take another quiz in two weeks. We'll forget this one and count the other.'

Blackburn squirmed with pleasure and gratitude. 'Thank you, sir. You're really very kind, very kind.'

Howe rose to conclude the visit. 'All right, then—in two weeks.'

It was that day that the Dean imparted to Howe the conclusion of the case of Tertan. It was simple and a little anticlimactic. A physician had been called in, and had said the word, given the name.

'A classic case, he called it,' the Dean said. 'Not a doubt in the world,' he said. His eyes were full of miserable pity, and he clutched at a word. 'A classic case, a classic case.' To his aid and to Howe's there came the Parthenon and the form of the Greek drama, the Aristotelian logic, Racine and the Well-Tempered Clavichord, the blueness of the Aegean and its clear sky. Classic—that is to say, without a doubt, perfect in its way, a veritable model, and, as the Dean had been told, sure to take a perfectly predictable and inevitable course to a foreknown conclusion.

It was not only pity that stood in the Dean's eyes. For a moment there was fear too. 'Terrible,' he said, 'it is simply terrible.'

Then he went on briskly. 'Naturally, we've told the boy nothing. And, naturally, we won't. His tuition's paid by his scholarship, and we'll continue him on the rolls until the end of the year. That will be kindest. After that the matter will be out of our control. We'll see, of course, that he gets into the proper hands. I'm told there will be no change, he'll go on like this, be as good as this, for four to six months. And so we'll just go along as usual.'

So Tertan continued to sit in Section 5 of English 1A, to his classmates still a figure of curiously dignified fun, symbol to most of them of the respectable but absurd intellectual life. But to his teacher he was now very different. He had not changed—he was still the greyhound casting for the scent of ideas, and Howe could see that he was still the same Tertan, but he could not feel it. What he felt as he looked at the boy sitting in his accustomed place was the hard blank of a fact. The fact itself was formidable and depressing. But what Howe was chiefly aware of was that he had permitted the metamorphosis of Tertan from person to fact.

As much as possible he avoided seeing Tertan's upraised hand and eager eye. But the fact did not know of its mere factuality, it continued its existence as if it were Tertan, hand up and eye questioning, and one day it appeared in Howe's office with a document.

'Even the spirit who lives egregiously, above the herd, must have its relations with the fellowman,' Tertan declared. He laid the document on Howe's desk. It was headed 'Quill and Scroll Society of Dwight College. Application for Membership.'

'In most ways these are crass minds,' Tertan said, touching the paper. 'Yet as a whole, bound together in their common love of letters, they transcend their intellectual lacks since it is not a paradox that the whole is greater than the sum of its parts.'

'When are the elections?' Howe asked.

'They take place tomorrow.'

'I certainly hope you will be successful.'

'Thank you. Would you wish to implement that hope?' A rather dirty finger pointed to the bottom of the sheet. 'A faculty recommender is necessary,' Tertan said stiffly, and waited.

'And you wish me to recommend you?'

'It would be an honor.'

'You may use my name.'

Tertan's finger pointed again. 'It must be a written sponsorship, signed by the sponsor.' There was a large blank space on the form under the heading, 'Opinion of Faculty Sponsor.'

This was almost another thing and Howe hesitated. Yet there was nothing else to do and he took out his fountain pen. He wrote, 'Mr. Ferdinand Tertan is marked by his intense devotion to letters and by his exceptional love of all things of the mind.' To this he signed his name, which looked bold and assertive on the white page. It disturbed him, the strange affirming power of a name. With a business-like air, Tertan whipped up the paper, folding it with decision, and put it into his pocket. He bowed and took his departure, leaving Howe with the sense of having done something oddly momentous.

And so much now seemed odd and momentous to Howe that should not have seemed so. It was odd and momentous, he felt, when he sat with Blackburn's second quiz before him, and wrote in an excessively firm hand the grade of C-minus. The paper was a clear, an indisputable failure. He was carefully and consciously committing a cowardice. Blackburn had told the truth when he had pleaded his past record. Howe had consulted it in the Dean's office. It showed no grade lower than a B-minus. A canvass of some of Blackburn's previous instructors had brought vague attestations to the adequate powers of a student imperfectly remembered, and sometimes surprise that his abilities could be questioned at all.

As he wrote the grade, Howe told himself that his cowardice sprang from an unwillingness to have more dealings with a student he disliked. He knew it was simpler than that. He knew he feared Blackburn: that was the absurd truth. And cowardice did not solve the matter after all. Blackburn, flushed with a first success, attacked at once. The minimal passing grade had not assuaged his feelings and he sat at Howe's desk and again the blue-book lay between them. Blackburn said nothing. With an enormous impudence, he was waiting for Howe to speak and explain himself.

At last Howe said sharply and rudely, 'Well?' His throat was tense and the blood was hammering in his head. His mouth was tight with anger at himself for his disturbance.

Blackburn's glance was almost baleful. 'This is impossible, sir.'

'But there it is,' Howe answered.

'Sir?' Blackburn had not caught the meaning but his tone was still haughty.

Impatiently Howe said, 'There it is, plain as day. Are you here to complain again?'

'Indeed I am, sir.' There was surprise in Blackburn's voice that Howe should ask the question.

'I shouldn't complain if I were you. You did a thoroughly bad job on your first quiz. This one is a little, only a very little, better.' This was not true. If anything, it was worse.

'That might be a matter of opinion, sir.'

'It is a matter of opinion. Of my opinion.'

'Another opinion might be different, sir.'

'You really believe that?' Howe said.

'Yes.' The omission of the 'sir' was monumental.

'Whose, for example?'

'The Dean's, for example.' Then the fleshy jaw came forward a little. 'Or a certain literary critic's, for example.'

It was colossal and almost too much for Blackburn himself to handle. The solidity of his face almost crumpled under it. But he withstood his own audacity and went on. 'And the Dean's opinion might be guided by the knowledge that the person who gave me this mark is the man whom a famous critic, the most eminent judge of literature in this country, called a drunken man. The Dean might think twice about whether such a man is fit to teach Dwight students.'

Howe said in quiet admonition, 'Blackburn, you're mad,' meaning no more than to check the boy's extravagance.

But Blackburn paid no heed. He had another shot in the locker. 'And the Dean might be guided by the information, of which I have evidence, documentary evidence,'—he slapped his breast pocket twice—'that this same person personally recommended to the college literary society, the oldest in the country, that he personally recommended a student who is crazy, who threw the meeting into an uproar—a psychiatric case. The Dean might take that into account.'

Howe was never to learn the details of that 'uproar.' He had always to content himself with the dim but passionate picture which at that moment sprang into his mind, of Tertan standing on some abstract height and madly denouncing the multitude of Quill and Scroll who howled him down.

He sat quiet a moment and looked at Blackburn. The ferocity had entirely gone from the student's face. He sat regarding his teacher almost benevolently. He had played a good card and now, scarcely at all unfriendly, he was waiting to see the effect. Howe took up the blue-book and negligently sifted through it. He read a page, closed the book, struck out the C-minus and wrote an F.

'Now you may take the paper to the Dean,' he said. 'You may tell him that after reconsidering it, I lowered the grade.'

The gasp was audible. 'Oh, sir!' Blackburn cried. 'Please!' His face was agonized. 'It means my graduation, my livelihood, my future. Don't do this to me.'

'It's done already.'

Blackburn stood up, 'I spoke rashly, sir, hastily. I had no intention, no real intention, of seeing the Dean. It rests with you—entirely, entirely. I *hope* you will restore the first mark.'

'Take the matter to the Dean or not, just as you choose. The grade is what you deserve and it stands.'

Blackburn's head dropped. 'And will I be failed at mid-term, sir?'

'Of course.'

From deep out of Blackburn's great chest rose a cry of anguish. 'Oh, sir, if you want me to go down on my knees to you, I will, I will.'

Howe looked at him in amazement.

'I will, I will. On my knees, sir. This mustn't, mustn't happen.'

He spoke so literally, meaning so very truly that his knees and exactly his knees were involved and seeming to think that he was offering something of tangible value to his teacher, that Howe, whose head had become icy clear in the nonsensical drama, thought, 'The boy is mad,' and began to speculate fantastically whether something in himself attracted or developed aberration. He could see himself standing absurdly before the Dean and saying, 'I've found another. This time it's the Vice-president of the Council, the manager of the debating team and secretary of Quill and Scroll.'

One more such discovery, he thought, and he himself would be discovered! And there, suddenly, Blackburn was on his knees with a thump, his huge thighs straining his trousers, his hand outstretched in a great gesture of supplication.

With a cry, Howe shoved back his swivel chair and it rolled away on its casters half across the little room. Blackburn knelt for a moment to nothing at all, then got to his feet.

Howe rose abruptly. He said, 'Blackburn, you will stop acting like an idiot. Dust your knees off, take your paper and get out. You've behaved like a fool and a malicious person. You have half a term to do a decent job. Keep your silly mouth shut and try to do it. Now get out.'

Blackburn's head was low. He raised it and there was a pious light in his eyes. 'Will you shake hands, sir?' he said. He thrust out his hand.

'I will not,' Howe said.

Head and hand sank together. Blackburn picked up his blue-book and walked to the door. He turned and said, 'Thank you, sir.' His back, as he departed, was heavy with tragedy and stateliness.

IV

After years of bad luck with the weather, the College had a perfect day for Commencement. It was wonderfully bright, the air so transparent, the wind so brisk that no one could resist talking about it.

As Howe set out for the campus he heard Hilda calling from the back yard. She called, 'Professor, professor,' and came running to him.

Howe said, 'What's this "professor" business?'

'Mother told me,' Hilda said. 'You've been promoted. And I want to take your picture.'

'Next year,' said Howe. 'I won't be a professor until next year. And you know better than to call anybody "professor." '

'It was just in fun,' Hida said. She seemed disappointed.

'But you can take my picture if you want. I won't look much different next year.' Still, it was frightening. It might mean that he was to stay in this town all his life.

Hilda brightened. 'Can I take it in this?' she said, and touched the gown he carried over his arm.

Howe laughed. 'Yes, you can take it in this.'

'I'll get my things and meet you in front of Otis,' Hilda said. 'I have the background all picked out.'

On the campus the Commencement crowd was already large. It stood about in eager, nervous little family groups. As he crossed, Howe was greeted by a student, capped and gowned, glad of the chance to make an event for his parents by introducing one of his teachers. It was while Howe stood there chatting that he saw Tertan.

He had never seen anyone quite so alone, as though a circle had been woven about him to separate him from the gay crowd on the campus. Not that Tertan was not gay, he was the gayest of all. Three weeks had passed since Howe had last seen him, the weeks of examination, the lazy week before Commencement, and this was now a different Tertan. On his head he wore a panama hat, broadbrimmed and fine, of the shape associated with South American planters. He wore a suit of raw silk, luxurious, but yellowed with age and much too tight, and he sported a whangee cane. He walked sedately, the hat tilted at a devastating angle, the stick coming up and down in time to his measured tread. He had, Howe guessed, outfitted himself to greet the day in the clothes of that ruined father whose existence was on record in the Dean's office. Gravely and arrogantly he surveyed the scene—in it, his whole bearing seemed to say, but not of it. With his haughty step, with his flashing eye,

Tertan was coming nearer. Howe did not wish to be seen. He shifted his position slightly. When he looked again, Tertan was not in sight.

The chapel clock struck the quarter hour. Howe detached himself from his chat and hurried to Otis Hall at the far end of the campus. Hilda had not yet come. He went up into the high portico and, using the glass of the door for a mirror, put on his gown, adjusted the hood on his shoulders and set the mortarboard on his head. When he came down the steps, Hilda had arrived.

Nothing could have told him more forcibly that a year had passed than the development of Hilda's photographic possessions from the box camera of the previous fall. By a strap about her neck was hung a leather case, so thick and strong, so carefully stitched and so molded to its contents that it could only hold a costly camera. The appearance was deceptive, Howe knew, for he had been present at the Aikens' pre-Christmas conference about its purchase. It was only a fairly good domestic camera. Still, it looked very impressive. Hilda carried another leather case from which she drew a collapsible tripod. Decisively she extended each of its gleaming legs and set it up on the path. She removed the camera from its case and fixed it to the tripod. In its compact efficiency the camera almost had a life of its own, but Hilda treated it with easy familiarity, looked into its eye, glanced casually at its gauges. Then from a pocket she took still another leather case and drew from it a small instrument through which she looked first at Howe, who began to feel inanimate and lost, and then at the sky. She made some adjustment on the instrument, then some adjustment on the camera. She swept the scene with her eye, found a spot and pointed the camera in its direction. She walked to the spot, stood on it and beckoned to Howe. With each new leather case, with each new instrument, and with each new adjustment she had grown in ease and now she said, 'Joe, will you stand here?'

Obediently Howe stood where he was bidden. She had yet another instrument.

She took out a tape-measure on a mechanical spool. Kneeling down before Howe, she put the little metal ring of the tape under the tip of his shoe. At her request, Howe pressed it with his toe. When she had measured her distance, she nodded to Howe who released the tape. At a touch, it sprang back into the spool. 'You have to be careful if you're going to get what you want,' Hilda said. 'I don't believe in all this snap-snap-snapping,' she remarked loftily. Howe nodded in agreement, although he was beginning to think Hilda's care excessive.

Now at last the moment had come. Hilda squinted into the camera, moved the tripod slightly. She stood to the side, holding the plunger of the shutter-cable. 'Ready,' she said. 'Will you relax, Joseph, please?' Howe realized that he was standing frozen. Hilda stood poised and precise as a setter, one hand holding the little cable, the other extended with curled dainty fingers like a dancer's, as if expressing to her subject the precarious delicacy of the moment. She pressed the plunger and there was the click. At once she stirred to action, got behind the camera, turned a new exposure. 'Thank you,' she said. 'Would you stand under that tree and let me do a character study with light and shade?'

The childish absurdity of the remark restored Howe's ease. He went to the little tree. The pattern the leaves made on his gown was what Hilda was after. He had just taken a satisfactory position when he heard in the unmistakable voice, 'Ah, Doctor! Having your picture taken?'

Howe gave up the pose and turned to Blackburn who stood on the walk, his hands behind his back, a little too large for his bachelor's gown. Annoyed that Blackburn should see him posing for a character study in light and shade, Howe said irritably, 'Yes, having my picture taken.'

Blackburn beamed at Hilda. 'And the little photographer?' he said. Hilda fixed her eyes on the ground and stood closer to her brilliant and aggressive camera. Blackburn, teetering on his heels, his hands behind his back, wholly prelatical and benignly patient, was not abashed at the silence. At last Howe said, 'If you'll excuse us, Mr. Blackburn, we'll go on with the picture.'

'Go right ahead, sir. I'm running along.' But he only came closer. 'Doctor Howe,' he said fervently, 'I want to tell you how glad I am that I was able to satisfy your standards at last.'

Howe was surprised at the hard, insulting brightness of his own voice, and even Hilda looked up curiously as he said, 'Nothing you have ever done has satisfied me, and nothing you could ever do would satisfy me, Blackburn.'

With a glance at Hilda, Blackburn made a gesture as if to hush Howe—as though all his former bold malice had taken for granted a kind of understanding between himself and his teacher, a secret which must not be betrayed to a third person. 'I only meant, sir,' he said, 'that I was able to pass your course after all.'

Howe said, 'You didn't pass my course. I passed you out of my course. I passed you without even reading your paper. I wanted to be sure the college would be rid of you. And when all the grades were in and I did read your paper, I saw I was right not to have read it first.'

Blackburn presented a stricken face. 'It was very bad, sir?'

But Howe had turned away. The paper had been fantastic. The paper had been, if he wished to see it so, mad. It was at this moment that the Dean came up behind Howe and caught his arm. 'Hello, Joseph,' he said. 'We'd better be getting along, it's almost late.'

He was not a familiar man, but when he saw Blackburn, who approached to greet him, he took Blackburn's arm, too. 'Hello, Theodore,' he said. Leaning forward on Howe's arm and on Blackburn's, he said, 'Hello, Hilda dear.' Hilda replied quietly, 'Hello, Uncle George.'

Still clinging to their arms, still linking Howe and Blackburn, the Dean said, 'Another year gone, Joe, and we've turned out another crop. After you've been here a few years, you'll find it reasonably upsetting—you wonder how there can be so many graduating classes while you stay the same. But of course you don't stay the same.' Then he said, 'Well,' sharply, to dismiss the thought. He pulled Blackburn's arm and swung him around to Howe. 'Have you heard about Teddy Blackburn?' he asked. 'He has a job already, before graduation—the first man of his class to be placed.' Expectant of congratulations, Blackburn beamed at Howe. Howe remained silent.

'Isn't that good?' the Dean said. Still Howe did not answer and the Dean, puzzled and put out, turned to Hilda. 'That's a very fine-looking camera, Hilda.' She touched it with affectionate pride.

'Instruments of precision,' said a voice. 'Instruments of precision.' Of the three with joined arms, Howe was the nearest to Tertan, whose gaze took in all the scene except the smile and the nod which Howe gave him. The boy leaned on his cane. The broad-brimmed hat, canting jauntily over his eye, confused the image of his face that Howe had established, suppressed the rigid lines of the ascetic and brought out the baroque curves. It made an effect of perverse majesty.

'Instruments of precision,' said Tertan for the last time, addressing no one, making a casual comment to the universe. And it occurred to Howe that Tertan might not be referring to Hilda's equipment. The sense of the thrice-woven circle of the boy's loneliness smote him fiercely. Tertan stood in majestic jauntiness, superior to all the scene, but his isolation made Howe ache with a pity of which Tertan was more the cause than the object, so general and indiscriminate was it.

Whether in his sorrow he made some unintended movement toward Tertan which the Dean checked, or whether the suddenly tightened grip on his arm was the Dean's own sorrow and fear, he did not know. Tertan watched them in the incurious way people watch a photograph being taken, and suddenly the thought that, to the boy, it must seem that the three were posing for a picture together made Howe detach himself almost rudely from the Dean's grasp.

'I promised Hilda another picture,' he announced—needlessly, for Tertan was no longer there, he had vanished in the last sudden flux of visitors who, now that

the band had struck up, were rushing
nervously to find seats.

'You'd better hurry,' the Dean said.
'I'll go along, it's getting late for me.' He
departed and Blackburn walked stately
by his side.

Howe again took his position under
the little tree which cast its shadow over
his face and gown. 'Just hurry, Hilda,

won't you?' he said. Hilda held the cable
at arm's length, her other arm crooked
and her fingers crisped. She rose on her
toes and said 'Ready,' and pressed the
release. 'Thank you,' she said gravely and
began to dismantle her camera as he
hurried off to join the procession.

[1943]

QUESTIONS FOR STUDY

1. *What are the successive stages in Dr. Howe's relationship with Ferdinand Tertan? Why does Howe reject him and permit "the metamorphosis of Tertan from person to fact"? To what extent is Howe's rejection of Tertan a betrayal of Howe himself?*
2. *Is the verdict of Howe, the physician, and the Dean correct—is Tertan really "mad"? What does each mean by the term "mad"?*
3. *In what ways is Tertan like Howe himself? (Consider Woolley's criticism of Howe's poetry in* Life and Letters.*)*
4. *How does Howe's relationship with Tertan and Blackburn bring into focus his own anxieties over his role as teacher, poet, and human being?*
5. *What is the significance of the final scene with the camera and Tertan's thrice-repeated remark about "Instruments of precision"?*

IVAN TURGENEV

The Country Doctor

ONE AUTUMN, on the way back from an outlying property, I caught a heavy chill. Luckily I was in the local market-town, at the inn, when the fever came on. I sent for the doctor. After half an hour he appeared, a shortish, thinnish man, with black hair. He prescribed the usual sudorific, ordered a mustard-plaster to be applied, deftly tucked my five-rouble note away up his sleeve—meanwhile coughing loudly, it is true, and averting his gaze—and was on the point of going home, when somehow or other he got talking and stayed on. I was oppressed by my fever; I foresaw a sleepless night and was glad to have the chance of a talk with the good man. We had tea served. My friend the doctor let himself go. The little fellow was no fool. He had a lively and rather amusing way of expressing himself. It's strange how things happen in life: you live with someone for a long time, you are on the best of terms, yet you never once speak to them frankly and from the heart; with someone else, you've hardly even got acquainted—and there you are: as if at confession, one or other of you is blurting out all his most intimate secrets. I do not know what I did to deserve the confidence of my new friend—anyway, for no particular reason, he got going, as they say, and told me a rather remarkable story, which I will relate here for the benefit of my courteous reader. I will try to express myself in the doctor's own words.

"You don't happen to know," he began, in a voice that had grown suddenly faint and trembling (such is the effect of unadulterated "birch" snuff), "you don't happen to know our local judge, Pavel Lukich Mylov? You don't? . . . Well, it doesn't matter." He cleared his throat and wiped his eyes. "Anyway, this is the story.

Let me see, now—to be exact, it was in Lent, at the time of the thaw. I was sitting at the judge's, playing Preference. Our judge is a capital fellow and a great hand at Preference. Suddenly"—this was a word that the doctor often used—"a message comes that someone is asking for me. I say, 'What does he want?' 'He's brought a note'—doubtless from a patient. 'Give me the note,' I say. Yes: It's from a patient. . . . Well, all right—you know, it's our daily bread. . . . The note is from a land-owner's widow; she says: 'My daughter is dying, for God's sake come, I've sent horses to fetch you.' Well, that's all right . . . but the lady lives twenty versts from town, and night's upon us, and the roads are in such a state, my word! and the lady herself is not so well off as she was; two silver roubles is the most you can expect, and even that is doubtful. Perhaps all that I shall get out of it will be a piece of linen and a little flour. . . . However, duty first, you know: someone's dying. At once I pass my hand to Councillor Kalliopin and return home. I see a small cart standing outside my porch; real peasant's horses—enormous pot bellies, and woolly hair as thick as felt; and a coachman sitting bareheaded, as a sign of respect. Well, my friend, I think, it's plain that *your* masters don't eat off gold plate. . . . You, sir, may well smile, but I tell you: we are poor men in our profession and we have to notice all these things. . . . If the coachman sits up like a prince and doesn't take off his cap, if he sniggers at you in his beard and toys with his whip—you can rely on a couple of five-rouble notes. But this turn-out here is a very different pair of shoes. Well, I think, it can't be helped: duty first. I grab the essential medicines, and off I go. Believe me, it was all we could do to get there.

From *A Sportsman's Notebook* by Ivan Turgenev. Translated from the Russian by Charles and Natasha Hepburn. Reprinted by permission of Barrie & Jenkins Ltd., London.

The road was hellish: streams, snow, mud, ravines, then, suddenly, a burst dam. Chaos! At last I'm there. A little house with a thatched roof. The windows are lit up: they must be waiting for me. A dignified little old lady in a cap comes to meet me. 'Save her,' she says, 'she is dying.' I say: 'Pray calm yourself. . . . Where is the patient?' 'Here, please come this way.' I see a small, clean room, an oil-lamp in the corner, on the bed a girl of about twenty, unconscious, heat fairly blazing from her, breathing heavily: a high fever. There are two other girls there, too, her sisters—badly scared, and in tears. 'Yesterday,' they say, 'she was perfectly well and had a good appetite; this morning she complained of a headache, then suddenly in the evening she became like this.' I repeat again, 'Pray calm yourselves'—it's part of the doctor's job, you know—and I set to work. I bleed her, I order mustard-plasters, I prescribe a mixture. Meanwhile I look at her. I look and look; my goodness, never have I seen such a face before . . . an absolute beauty! I feel so sorry for the girl, it fairly tears me to pieces. Such lovely features, such eyes. . . . At last, thank God, she gets more comfortable; she begins to sweat, partly recovers consciousness; looks round, smiles, passes her hand over her face . . . The sisters bend over her and ask: 'What's the matter?' 'Nothing,' she says, and turns her head away. . . . I look—she's dropped off to sleep. 'Well,' I say, 'now we must leave the patient in peace.' We all tiptoe out; only the maid stays behind in case of emergencies. In the sitting-room the samovar's on the table and a bottle of rum beside it: in our job we can't get along without it. They gave me tea; they ask me to stay the night. I accepted: where else could I go at that hour! The old lady keeps up a steady groaning. 'What's the matter?' I ask. 'She'll live; calm yourself and go to bed: it's two o-clock.' 'You'll have me woken up if anything happens?' 'Of course I will.' The old lady retired and the girls went to their room; a bed was put up for me in the drawing-room. I lay down—but couldn't get to sleep, strangely enough. You'd have thought that I'd worried my head enough already. I couldn't get my patient out of my head. Finally I could stand it no longer and all of a sudden I got up; I thought I'd just go and see how she was. Her bedroom adjoined the drawing-room. Well, I got up, and quietly opened the door, and my heart was fairly beating away. I saw the maid asleep, with her mouth open, snoring away like an animal, and the patient lying with her face towards me, her arms moving restlessly, poor girl! I went up to her . . . and suddenly she opened her eyes and stared at me. 'Who are you?' I felt awkward. 'Don't be afraid,' I said; 'I am the doctor; I've come to see how you feel.' 'You're the doctor?' 'Yes, I am . . . your mother sent for me from town; we've bled you, and now, please, you must rest, and in two days, with God's help, we shall have you up and about.' 'Oh yes, yes, doctor, don't let me die . . . please, please.' 'Good Heavens, whatever next!' But, I thought to myself, the fever is on her again; I felt her pulse: yes, I was right. She looked at me—and suddenly she took me by the hand. 'I'll tell you why I don't want to die, I'll tell you . . . now that we're alone: only not a word, please . . . listen. . . .' I bent over her; her lips moved right against my ear, her hair touched my cheek —I admit, my head went round in circles —and she began to whisper. . . . I didn't understand a word. . . . Oh, of course, she must be delirious. She whispered and whispered, but so quickly, as if in a foreign language, and when she had done she shuddered, dropped her head on the pillow and raised a finger at me. 'Listen, doctor, not a word.' . . . Somehow or other I calmed her, gave her a drink, woke the maid and went out."

The doctor took another violent pinch of snuff and sat stock-still for a moment.

"Anyhow," he continued, "next day, contrary to my expectations, the patient was no better. I thought and thought and suddenly decided to stay on, although I had other patients waiting for me. . . . You know, one shouldn't neglect them: it's bad for one's practice. But, in the first place, the girl was really desperately ill; and secondly, to tell the truth, I felt myself strongly attracted to her. Besides, I liked the whole family. Although they were very hard up, they were extraordinarily cultivated people. . . . The father had been a scholar, a writer; he died a poor man, of course, but he'd managed to give his children an excellent education; he left them a lot of books, too. Whether it was because I put my whole heart into looking after the patient, or whether there were other reasons, anyway, I'd go so far as to say that they came to love me in that house like one of the family. . . . Meanwhile the thaw got worse and worse: communications were completely broken, I could hardly even get medicines sent out from town. . . . The girl got no better . . . day after day, day after day . . . but then . . . well . . ." The doctor paused. "The truth is that I don't know how to explain to you . . ." He took another pinch of snuff, sneezed, and swallowed a gulp of tea. . . . "I'll tell you straight out, my patient . . . how shall I put it? . . . fell in love with me, I suppose . . . or rather, she wasn't exactly in love . . . but anyway . . . it's certainly . . ." The doctor looked down and blushed.

"No," he continued with some animation, " 'Love' is the wrong word. One must see oneself at one's own worth, after all. She was a cultivated, intelligent, well-read girl, and I, well, I'd even forgotten my Latin, more or less completely. My figure, too"—and the doctor looked at himself with a smile—"is nothing to boast about, I think. But God didn't make me a fool either: I don't call white black; I've got a mind that works at times. For instance, I understood very well that what Alexandra Andreyevna—that was her name—felt towards me was not love, but affection, so to speak, regard, or what not. Although she herself probably misread her feelings towards me, her condition was such, as you can imagine . . . Anyhow," added the doctor, who had uttered all these disjointed statements without drawing breath, and with obvious embarrassment, "I think I've let my tongue run away with me . . . and the result is that you won't understand what happened . . . so I'll tell you the story in its proper order."

He finished his glass of tea and resumed in a calmer voice.

"This is how it was. My patient continued to get worse and worse. You, my good sir, are not a doctor; you have no idea of what goes on inside a doctor's head, especially in his early days, when it dawns on him that a patient's illness is defeating him. All his self-assurance vanishes into thin air. I can't tell you how scared he gets. It seems to him that he's forgotten everything he ever knew, that his patient has no confidence in him, that other people are beginning to notice that he's out of his depth, and don't want to describe the patient's symptoms, that they are looking at him strangely, and whispering . . . oh, it's terrible! He feels there must be some way of treating the case if only it could be found. Perhaps this is it? He tries—no, wrong after all. He leaves no time for the treatment to take its proper effect. . . . He snatches first at one method, then at another. He takes up his book of prescriptions . . . here it is, he thinks, this is it! To be quite honest, sometimes he opens the book at random: this, he thinks, must be the hand of fate. . . . Meanwhile there is someone dying; someone whom another doctor would have saved. I must have another opinion, you think; I won't take the whole responsibility myself. But what a fool you look on such occasions! Well, as time goes on, you get used to it, you say to yourself: never mind. The patient has died—it's not your fault; you only followed the rules. But what disturbs you still more is this: when other people have blind confidence in yourself, and all the time you know that you're helpless. It was exactly such confidence that all Alexandra Andreyevna's family felt towards me: they no longer even thought of her as in danger. And I, on my side, was assuring them that there was nothing to worry about, but really my heart was in my boots. To make things even worse, the thaw became so bad that the coachman spent whole days fetching medicines. Meanwhile I never left the patient's room; I simply couldn't tear myself away. I told her all sorts of funny stories; I played cards with her; I spent the nights at her bedside. The old lady would thank me with tears in her eyes; but I thought to myself: I don't deserve your gratitude. I confess to you frankly—there is no reason why I should conceal it now—I was in love with my patient. And Alexandra Andreyevna grew fonder and fonder of me: she would allow no one into her room except me. We would get talking; she would ask me where I studied, what sort of life I led, and about my parents and my friends. And I felt that we shouldn't be talking, but to stop her, stop her really firmly, was more than I could do. I would bury my head in my hands: what are you doing, scoundrel? . . . And then she would take my hand and hold it, look at me for a long, long time, turn away, sigh and say: 'How good you are!' Her hands were so feverish, her eyes so big and languid. 'Yes,' she would say. 'You're a good, kind man. You're not like our neighbours . . you're quite, quite different. . . . To think that I never knew you until now!' 'Alexandra Andreyevna, calm yourself,' I'd say. 'Believe me, I appreciate it; I don't know what I've done to . . . only calm yourself, for Heaven's sake, calm yourself . . . everything will be all right; you'll get quite well again.' By the way, I must tell you," added the doctor, leaning forward and lifting his eyebrows, "they had little to do with their neighbours, because the smaller people weren't up to them, and they were too proud to get to know the richer ones. I tell you, it was an extraordinarily cultivated family; so that, for me, it was quite flattering. Alexandra would only take her medicine from my hands . . . the poor girl would lift herself up, with my help, swallow the medicine and gaze at me . . . and my heart would fairly turn over. But all the time she was getting worse and worse: she will die, I thought, she will surely die. Believe me or not, I would gladly have lain in the coffin instead of her; but there were her mother and sisters watching me, looking into my eyes, and I could feel their confidence on the wane. 'Well, how is she?' 'Nothing to worry about, nothing at all'—but what did I mean, 'nothing at all'? My head was in a daze. There I was, one night, alone, as usual, sitting at the bedside. The maid was sitting in the room too, snoring for all she was worth . . . well, one couldn't find fault with the poor girl, she too was quite exhausted. Alexandra had been feeling very bad the whole evening; the fever gave her no rest. Right up to midnight she had been tossing away; at last she seemed to fall asleep; at any rate she stopped moving and lay still. The oil-lamp was burning in the corner in front of the icon. I sat there, my head dropped forward, you know, and I too dozed off. Suddenly it was as if someone had given me a push in the ribs; I looked around . . . God Almighty! Alexandra was staring at me wide-eyed . . . her lips parted, her cheeks aflame. 'What is it?' 'Doctor, am I going to die?' 'For Heaven's sake!' 'No, please, doctor, please, don't tell me that I'm going to live . . . don't tell me that . . . if only you knew . . . listen, for God's sake don't try to hide my condition from me.' I noticed how quickly she was breathing. 'If I can know for sure that I am going to die . . . then I can tell you everything I have to say.' 'Alexandra Andreyevna, for mercy's sake!' 'Listen, I haven't slept a wink, I've been looking and looking at you . . . for God's sake . . . I trust you, you're kind, you're honest, I implore you by everything that's holy on earth—tell me the truth! If only you knew how much it matters to me. . . . Doctor, tell me, for God's sake, am I in danger?' 'What can. I tell you, Alexandra Andreyevna?' 'For God's sake, I beseech you to tell me.' 'Alexandra Andreyevna, I can't hide the truth from you—you are in danger, but God is merciful . . .' 'I'm going to die, I'm going to die . . .' And it was as if she was overjoyed at the thought, her face lit up so; I was fairly terrified. 'Never fear, never fear, death has no terror for me.' All of a sudden she raised herself on one elbow. 'Now . . . well, now I can tell you that I'm grateful to you from all my heart; that you're good and kind; that I love you.' . . . I looked at her like a man possessed; I can tell you, I had quite a creepy feeling. . . . 'Listen to me. I love you.' 'Alexandra Andreyevna, what have I done to deserve this?' 'No, no, you don't understand me, my dear one . . .' And suddenly she reached out, took my head in her hands and kissed me. Believe me or not, it was all I could do not to cry out loud. . . . I fell on my knees and hid my head in the pillow. She said nothing; her fingers trembled on my hair; I could hear her crying. I began to comfort her, to assure her. . . . I really don't know what I said to her. 'You'll wake the maid . . . believe me when I say . . . how grateful I am . . . and calm yourself.' 'Don't . . . don't,' she kept repeating. 'Never mind any of them, let them wake, let them come—it doesn't signify: I'm dying anyway. . . . Why are you so shy and timid? Lift your head . . . Or can it be that you don't love me, that I was mistaken? . . . If that is so, please forgive me.' 'What are you saying? . . . I love you, Alexandra Andreyevna.' She gazed at me, straight in the eyes, and opened her arms. 'Then, put your arms around me.' . . . I tell you honestly: I don't understand how I got through that night without going out of my mind. I knew that my patient was killing herself; I saw that she was half delirious; I also understood that if she had not believed herself on the point of death, she would never have given me a thought; but, say what you like, there must be something appalling about dying at twenty-five without ever having loved; that was the thought that tormented her, that was why, in despair, she seized on me. Now do you see it all? She still held me tightly in her arms. 'Have pity on me, Alexandra Andreyevna, have pity on us both,' I said. 'Why?' she answered, 'what is there to pity? Don't you understand that I've got to die?' She kept on repeating this phrase. 'If I knew that I was going to live and turn into a well-brought-up young lady again, I should be ashamed, yes, ashamed . . . but, as it is? . . .' 'And who told you that you were going to die?' Oh, no, enough of that, you can't deceive me, you don't know how to lie, just look at yourself.' 'You will live, Alexandra Andreyevna; I will cure you; we will ask your mother for her blessing . . . nothing will part us; we shall be happy.' 'No, no, I have your word that I must die . . . you promised me . . . you told me I must . . .' It was a bitter moment for me, bitter for many reasons. You know, sometimes small things can happen: they amount to nothing, but they hurt all the same. It occurred to her to ask me my name, my Christian name, I mean. Of course it would be my ill-luck to be called Trifon.[1] Yes, sir; Trifon, Trifon Ivanich. In the house, all the family called me doctor. Well, there was nothing for it, so I answered: 'Trifon.' She screwed her eyes up, shook her head and whispered something in French—oh, it was something unflattering, and she laughed unkindly, too. Well, like this, I spent almost the whole night with her. At dawn I went out, like one possessed; it was midday when I returned to her room, after taking tea. God Almighty! You couldn't recognize her: I've seen prettier sights laid out in the coffin. Upon my word, I don't know to this day, I simply don't know how I stood the ordeal. For three days and three nights my patient's life still flickered on . . . and what nights they were! What things she told me! . . . On the last night of the three—just fancy—I was sitting beside her, praying now for one thing only: O, God, take her quickly, and take me as well . . . when suddenly the old lady, her mother, burst into the room. . . . I had already hold her the day before that there was little hope, that things were bad, and that it would be as well to send for the priest. As soon as she saw her mother, the sick girl said: 'I'm glad that you've come . . . look at us, we love each other, we are pledged to each other.' 'What's she saying, doctor, what's she saying?' I went pale as death. 'She's delirious,' I said, 'it's the fever.' But then, from Alexandra: 'Enough of that, just now you spoke to me quite differently and accepted my ring. . . . Why pretend? My mother is kind, she will forgive, she will understand, but I am dying—why should I lie? Give me your hand.' I jumped up and ran from the room. Of course, the old lady guessed the whole story.

"Anyway, I won't attempt to bore you further, and, what's more, to tell you the truth, it hurts me to remember. The following day my patient passed away. May God rest her soul!" added the doctor hurriedly, with a sigh. "Before she died, she asked that everyone should go out and

[1] "Trifon" is roughly the equivalent of "Cuthbert." (Translators' note)

leave me alone with her. 'Forgive me,' she said. 'Perhaps I've acted wrongly towards you . . . it's my illness . . . but, believe me, I've never loved anyone more than you . . . don't forget me . . . treasure my ring. . . .' "

The doctor turned away; I seized him by the hand.

"Och!" he said, "let's talk about something else, or perhaps you'd like a little game of Preference for low stakes? You know, in our profession we should never give way to such exalted sentiments. In our profession all we should think about is how to stop the children from yelling and the wife from nagging. For, since then, I have gone in for holy matrimony, as they call it . . . with a vengeance . . . I married a merchant's daughter: seven thousand roubles dowry. Her name is Akulina; it's on a par with Trifon. A spiteful hag, I must say, but luckily she sleeps all day. . . . What about that game of Preference?"

We got down to Preference for copeck stakes. Trifon Ivanich won two and a half roubles from me—and went home late, very pleased with his victory.

[1852]

TRANSLATED BY
CHARLES AND NATASHA HEPBURN

QUESTIONS FOR STUDY

1. *Why does Turgenev choose to build an external frame around his story? How does it help to further the reader's understanding of the doctor? Does he seem to have changed since the events of the story took place? What is significant in the fact that he has chosen to marry the ill-tempered daughter of a wealthy merchant?*

2. *Why does the doctor feel compelled to tell his story to his patient? Why does he continually feel the need to rationalize and justify his behavior? Why does he choose to bring his story to so abrupt a conclusion?*

3. *Why does the doctor pray that Alexandra will die quickly? Why doesn't he acknowledge at once to her mother that he and Alexandra are in love?*

4. *What final opinion of the doctor does Turgenev leave with the reader? Does Turgenev himself seem to have ambivalent feelings?*

MIGUEL DE UNAMUNO

Saint Emmanuel the Good, Martyr

> If with this life only in view we have
> had hope in Christ, we are of all men
> the most to be pitied.
> Saint Paul: 1 COR. 15:19

NOW THAT the bishop of the diocese of Renada, to which this my beloved village of Valverde de Lucerna belongs, is seeking (according to rumor), to initiate the process of beatification of our Don Manuel, or more correctly, Saint Emmanuel the Good, who was parish priest here, I want to state in writing, by way of confession (although to what end only God, and not I can say), all that I can vouch for and remember of that matriarchal man who pervaded the most secret life of my soul, who was my true spiritual father, the father of my spirit, the spirit of myself, Angela Carballino.

The other, my flesh-and-blood temporal father, I scarcely knew, for he died when I was still a very young girl. I know that he came to Valverde de Lucerna from the outside world—that he was a stranger—and that he settled here when he married my mother. He had brought a number of books with him: *Don Quixote,* some plays from the classic theatre, some novels; a few histories, the *Bertoldo,* everything all mixed together. From these books (practically the only ones in the entire village), I nurtured dreams as a young girl, dreams which in turn devoured me. My good mother gave me very little account either of the words or the deeds of my father. For the words and deeds of Don Manuel, whom she worshipped, of whom she was enamored, in common with all the rest of the village—in an exquisitely chaste manner, of course—had obliterated the memory of the words and deeds of her husband; him she commended to God, with full fervor, as she said her daily rosary.

Don Emmanuel I remember as if it were yesterday, from the time when I was a girl of ten, just before I was taken to the convent school in the cathedral city of Renada. At that time Don Emmanuel, our saint, must have been about thirty-seven years old. He was tall, slender, erect; he carried himself the way our Buitre Peak carries its crest, and his eyes had all the blue depth of our lake. As he walked he commanded all eyes, and not only the eyes but the hearts of all; gazing round at us he seemed to look through our flesh as through glass and penetrate our hearts. We all of us loved him, especially the children. And the things he said to us! Not words, things! The villagers could scent the odor of sanctity, they were intoxicated with it.

It was at this time that my brother Lazarus, who was in America, from where he regularly sent us money with which he lived in decent leisure, had my mother send me to the convent school, so that my education might be completed outside the village; he suggested this move despite the fact that he had no special fondness for the nuns. "But since, as far as I know," he wrote us, "there are no lay schools there yet,—especially not for young ladies—we will have to make use of the ones that do exist. The important thing is for Angelita to receive some polish and not be forced to continue among village girls." And so I entered the convent school. At one point I even thought I would become a teacher; but pedagogy soon palled upon me.

At school I met girls from the city and I made friends with some of them. But I still kept in touch with people in our village, and I received frequent reports and sometimes a visit.

And the fame of the parish priest reached as far as the school, for he was beginning to be talked of in the cathedral city. The nuns never tired of asking me about him.

Ever since early youth I had been endowed, I don't very well know from where, with a large degree of curiosity and restlessness, due at least in part to that jumble of books which my father had collected, and these qualities were stimulated at school, especially in the course of a relationship which I developed with a girl friend, who grew excessively attached to me. At times she proposed that we enter the same convent together, swearing to an everlasting "sisterhood"—and even that we seal the oath in blood. At other times she talked to me, with eyes half closed, of sweethearts and marriage adventures. Strangely enough, I have never heard of her since, or of what became of her, despite the fact that whenever our Don Manuel was spoken of, or when my mother wrote me something about him in her letters—which happened in almost every letter—and I read it to her, this girl would exclaim, as if in rapture: "What luck, my dear, to be able to live near a saint like that, a live saint, of flesh and blood, and to be able to kiss his hand; when you go back to your village write me everything, everything, and tell me about him."

Five years passed at school, five years which now have evanesced in memory like a dream at dawn, and when I became fifteen I returned to my own Valverde de Lucerna. By now everything revolved around Don Emmanuel: Don Emmanuel, the lake and the mountain. I arrived home anxious to know him, to place myself under his protection, and hopeful he would set me on my path in life.

It was rumored that he had entered the seminary to become a priest so that he might thus look after the sons of a sister recently widowed and provide for them in place of their father; that in the seminary his keen mind and his talents had distinguished him and that he had subsequently turned down opportunities for a brilliant career in the church because he wanted to remain exclusively a part of his Valverde de Lucerna, of his remote village which lay like a brooch between the lake and the mountain reflected in it.

How he did love his people! His life consisted in salvaging wrecked marriages, in forcing unruly sons to submit to their parents, or reconciling parents to their sons, and, above all, of consoling the embittered and the weary in spirit; meanwhile he helped everyone to die well.

I recall, among other incidents, the occasion when the unfortunate daughter of old aunt Rabona returned to our town. She had been in the city and lost her virtue there; now she returned unmarried and castoff, and she brought back a little son. Don Emmanuel did not rest until he had persuaded an old sweetheart, Perote by name, to marry the poor girl and, moreover, to legitimize the little creature with his own name. Don Emmanuel told Perote:

"Come now, give this poor waif a father, for he hasn't got one except in heaven."

"But, Don Emmanuel, it's not my fault . . . !"

"Who knows, my son, who knows . . . ! And besides, it's not a question of guilt."

And today, poor Perote, inspired on that occasion to saintliness by Don Emmanuel, and now a paralytic and invalid, has for staff and consolation of his life the son he accepted as his own when the boy was not his at all.

On Midsummer's Night, the shortest night of the year, it was a local custom here (and still is) for all the old crones, and a few old men, who thought they were possessed or bewitched (hysterics they were, for the most part, or in some cases epileptics) to flock to the lake. Don Emmanuel undertook to fulfill the same function as the lake, to serve as a pool of healing, to treat his charges and even, if possible, to cure them. And such was the effect of his presence, of his gaze, and above all of his voice—the miracle of his voice!—and the infinitely sweet authority of his words, that he actually did achieve some remarkable cures. Whereupon his fame increased, drawing all the sick of the environs to our lake and our priest. And yet once when a mother came to ask for a miracle in behalf of her son, he answered her with a sad smile:

"Ah, but I don't have my bishop's permission to perform miracles."

He was particularly interested in seeing that all the villagers kept themselves clean. If he chanced upon someone with a torn garment he would send him to the church: "Go and see the sacristan, and let him mend that tear." The sacristan was a tailor, and when, on the first day of the year, everyone went to congratulate him on his saint's day—his holy patron was Our Lord Jesus Himself—it was by Don Emmanuel's wish that everyone appeared in a new shirt, and those that had none received the present of a new one from Don Emmanuel himself.

He treated everyone with the greatest kindness; if he favored anyone, it was the most unfortunate, and especially those who rebelled. There was a congenital idiot in the village, the fool Blasillo, and it was toward him that Don Emmanuel chose to show the greatest love and concern; as a consequence he succeeded in miraculously teaching him things which had appeared beyond the idiot's comprehension. The fact was that the embers of understanding feebly glowing in the idiot were kindled whenever, like a pitiable monkey, he imitated his Don Emmanuel.

The marvel of the man was his voice; a divine voice which brought one close to weeping. Whenever he officiated at Solemn High Mass and intoned the prelude, a tremor ran through the congregation and all within sound of his voice were moved to the depths of their being. The sound of his chanting, overflowing the church, went on to float over the lake and settle at the foot of the mountain. And when on Good Friday he intoned "My God, my God, my God, why hast Thou forsaken me?" a profound shudder swept through the multitude, like the lash of a northeaster across the waters of the lake. It was as if these people heard the Lord Jesus Christ himself, as if the voice sprang from the ancient crucifix, at the foot of which generations of mothers had offered up their sorrows. And it happened that on one occasion his mother heard

him and was unable to contain herself, and cried out to him right in the church, "My son!," calling her child. And the entire congregation was visibly affected. It was as if the mother's cry had issued from the half-open lips of the Mater Dolorosa—her heart transfixed by seven swords—which stood in one of the chapels of the nave. Afterwards, the fool Blasillo went about piteously repeating, as if he were an echo, "My God, my God, my God, why hast Thou forsaken me?" with such effect that everyone who heard him was moved to tears, to the great satisfaction of the fool, who prided himself on this triumph of imitation.

The priest's effect on people was such that no one ever dared to tell him a lie, and everyone confessed themselves to him without need of a confessional. So true was this that on one occasion, when a revolting crime had been committed in a neighboring village, the judge—a dull fellow who badly misunderstood Don Emmanuel—called on the priest and said:

"Let us see, Don Manuel, if you can get this bandit to admit the truth."

"So that afterwards you may punish him?" asked the saintly man. "No, Judge, no; I will not extract from any man a truth which could be the death of him. That is a matter between him and his God. . . . Human justice is none of my affair. 'Judge not that ye be not judged,' said our Lord."

"But the fact is, Father, that I, a judge . . ."

"I understand. You, Judge, must render unto Caesar that which is Caesar's, while I shall render unto God that which is God's."

And, as Don Emmanuel departed, he gazed at the suspected criminal and said:

"Make sure, only, that God forgives you, for that is all that matters."

Everyone went to Mass in the village, even if it were only to hear him and see him at the altar, where he appeared to be transfigured, his countenance lit from within. He introduced one holy practice to the popular cult; it consisted in assembling the whole town inside the church, men and women, ancients and youths, some thousand persons; there we recited the Creed, in unison, so that it sounded like a single voice: "I believe in God, the Almighty Father, Creator of heaven and earth . . ." and all the rest. It was not a chorus, but a single voice, a simple united voice, all the voices based on one on which they formed a kind of mountain, whose peak, lost at times in the clouds, was Don Emmanuel. As we reached the section "I believe in the resurrection of the flesh and life everlasting," the voice of Don Emmanuel was submerged, drowned in the voice of the populace as in a lake. In truth, he was silent. And I could hear the bells of that city which is said hereabouts to be at the bottom of the lake—bells which are also said to be audible on Midsummer's Night—the bells of the city which is submerged in the spiritual lake of our populace; I was hearing the voice of our dead, resurrected in us by the communion of saints. Later, when I had learned the secret of our saint, I understood that it was as if a caravan crossing the desert lost its leader as they approached the goal of their trek, whereupon his people lifted him on their shoulders to bring his lifeless body into the promised land.

When it came to dying themselves, most of the villagers refused to die unless they were holding on to Don Emmanuel's hand, as if to an anchor chain.

In his sermons he never inveighed against unbelievers, Masons, liberals or heretics. What for, when there were none in the village? Nor did it occur to him to speak against the wickedness of the press. On the other hand, one of his most frequent themes was gossip, against which he lashed out.

"Envy," he liked to repeat, "envy is nurtured by those who prefer to think they are envied, and most persecutions are the result of a persecution complex rather than of an impulse to persecute."

"But Don Emmanuel, just listen to what that fellow was trying to tell me . . ."

"We should concern ourselves less with what people are trying to tell us than with what they tell us without trying . . ."

His life was active rather than contemplative, and he constantly fled from idleness, even from leisure. Whenever he heard it said that idleness was the mother of all the vices, he added: "And also of the greatest vice of them all, which is to think idly." Once I asked him what he meant and he answered: "Thinking idly is thinking as a substitute for doing, or thinking too much about what is already done instead of about what must be done. What's done is done and over with, and one must go on to something else, for there is nothing worse than remorse without possible relief." Action! Action! Even in those early days I had already begun to realize that Don Emmanuel fled from being left to think in solitude, and I guessed that some obsession haunted him.

And so it was that he was always occupied, sometimes even occupied in searching for occupations. He wrote very little on his own, so that he scarcely left us anything in writing, even notes; on the other hand, he acted as scrivener for everyone else, especially mothers, for whom he composed letters to their absent sons.

He also worked with his hands, pitching in to help with some of the village tasks. At threshing time he reported to the threshing floor, to flail and winnow, meanwhile teaching and entertaining the workers by turn. Sometimes he took the place of a worker who had fallen sick. One day in the dead of winter he came upon a child, shivering with the bitter cold. The child's father had sent him into the woods to bring back a strayed calf.

"Listen," he said to the child, "you go home and get warm, and tell your father that I am bringing back the calf." On the way back with the animal he ran into the father, who had come out to meet him, thoroughly ashamed of himself.

In winter he chopped wood for the poor. When a certain magnificent walnut tree died—"that matriarchal walnut," he called it, a tree under whose shade he had played as a boy and whose fruit he had eaten for so many years—he asked for the trunk, carried it to his house and, after he had cut six planks from it, which he put away at the foot of his bed, he made firewood of the rest to warm the poor. He also was in the habit of making handballs for the boys and a goodly number of toys for the younger children.

Often he used to accompany the doctor on his rounds, adding his presence and prestige to the doctor's prescriptions. Most of all he was interested in maternity cases and the care of children; it was his opinion that the old wives' sayings "from the cradle to heaven" and the other one about "little angels belong in heaven" were nothing short of blasphemy. The death of a child moved him deeply.

"A child stillborn," I once heard him say, "or one who dies soon after birth, is the most terrible of mysteries to me. It's as if it were a suicide. Or as if the child were crucified."

And once, when a man had taken his own life and the father of the suicide, an outsider, asked Don Emmanuel if his son could be buried in consecrated ground, the priest answered:

"Most certainly, for at the last moment, in the very last throes, he must certainly have repented. There is no doubt of it whatsoever in my mind."

From time to time he would visit the local school to help the teacher, to teach alongside him—and not only the catechism. The simple truth was that he fled relentlessly from idleness and from solitude. He went so far in this desire of his to mingle with the villagers, especially the youth and the children, that he even attended the village dances. And more than once he played the drum to keep time for the young men and women dancing; this kind of activity, which in another priest would have seemed like a grotesque mockery of his calling, in him somehow took on the appearance of a holy and religious exercise. When the Angelus would ring out, he would put down the drum and sticks, take off his hat (all the others doing the same) and pray: "The angel of the Lord declared unto Mary: Hail Mary . . ." And afterwards: "Now, let us rest until tomorrow."

"First of all," he would say, "the village must be happy; everyone must be happy to be alive. To be satisfied with life is of first importance. No one should want to die until it is God's will."

"I want to die now," a recently widowed woman once told him, "I want to be with my husband . . ."

"And why now?" he asked. "Stay here and pray God for his soul."

One of his well-loved remarks was made at a wedding: "Ah, if I could only change all the water in our lake into wine, into a dear little wine which, no matter how much of it one drank, would always make one joyful without intoxicating . . . or, if intoxicating, would make one joyfully drunk."

Once upon a time a band of poor acrobats came through the village. The leader—who arrived on the scene with a gravely ill and pregnant wife and three sons to help him—played the clown. While he was in the village square making all the children, and even some of the adults, laugh with glee, his wife suddenly fell desperately ill and had to leave; she went off accompanied by a look of anguish from the clown and a howl of laughter from the children. Don Emmanuel hurried after, and, a little later, in a corner of the inn's stable, he helped her give up her soul in a state of grace. When the performance was over and the villagers and the clown learned of the tragedy, they came to the inn, and there the poor bereaved clown, in a voice choked with tears, told Don Emmanuel, as he took his hand and kissed it: "They are quite right, Father, when they say you are a saint." Don Emmanuel took the clown's hand in his and replied before everyone:

"It's you who are the saint, good clown. I watched you at your work and understood that you do it not only to provide bread for your children, but also to give joy to the children of others. And I tell you now that your wife, the mother of your children, whom I sent to God while you worked to give joy, is at rest in the Lord, and that you will join her there, and that the angels, whom you will make laugh with happiness in heaven, will reward you with their laughter."

And everyone present wept, children and elders alike, as much from sorrow as from a mysterious joy in which all sorrow was drowned. Later, recalling that solemn hour, I have come to realize that the imperturbable joyousness of Don Emmanuel was merely the temporal, earthly form of an infinite, eternal sadness which the priest concealed from the eyes and ears of the world with heroic saintliness.

His constant activity, his ceaseless intervention in the tasks and diversions of everyone, had the appearance, in short, of a flight from himself, of a flight from solitude. He confirmed this suspicion: "I have a fear of solitude," he would say. And still, from time to time he would go off by himself, along the shores of the lake, to the ruins of the abbey where the souls of pious Cistercians seem still to repose, although history has long since buried them in oblivion. There, the cell of the so-called Father-Captain can still be found, and it is said that the drops of blood spattered on the walls as he flagellated himself can still be seen. What thoughts occupied our Don Emmanuel as he walked there? I remember a conversation we held once in which I asked him, as he was speaking of the abbey, why it had never occurred to him to enter a monastery, and he answered me:

"It is not at all because of the fact that my sister is a widow and I have her children and herself to support—for God looks after the poor—but rather because I simply was not born to be a hermit, an anchorite; the solitude would crush my soul; and, as far as a monastery is concerned, my monastery is Valverde de Lucerna. I was not meant to live alone, or die alone. I was meant to live for my village, and die for it too. How should I save my soul if I were not to save the soul of my village as well?"

"But there have been saints who were hermits, solitaries . . ." I said.

"Yes, the Lord gave them the grace of solitude which He has denied me, and I must resign myself. I must not throw away my village to win my soul. God made me that way. I would not be able to resist the temptations of the desert. I would not be able, alone, to carry the cross of birth . . ."

I have summoned up all these recollections, from which my faith was fed, in order to portray our Don Emmanuel as

he was when I, a young girl of sixteen, returned from the convent of Renada to our "monastery of Valverde de Lucerna," once more to kneel at the feet of our "abbot."

"Well, here is the daughter of Simona," he said as soon as he saw me, "made into a young woman, and knowing French, and how to play the piano, and embroider, and heaven knows what else besides! Now you must get ready to give us a family. And your brother Lazarus; when does he return? Is he still in the New World?"

"Yes, Father, he is still in the New World."

"The New World! And we in the Old. Well then, when you write him, tell him for me, on behalf of the parish priest, that I should like to know when he is returning from the New World to the Old, to bring us the latest from over there. And tell him that he will find the lake and the mountain as he left them."

When I first went to him for confession, I became so confused that I could not enunciate a word. I recited the "Forgive me, Father for I have sinned," in a stammer, almost a sob. And he, observing this, said:

"Good heavens, my dear, what are you afraid of, or of whom are you afraid? Certainly you're not trembling now under the weight of your sins, nor in fear of God. No, you're trembling because of me, isn't that so?"

At this point I burst into tears.

"What have they been telling you about me? What fairy tales? Was it your mother, perhaps? Come, come, please be calm; you must imagine you are talking to your brother . . ."

At this I plucked up courage and began to tell him of my anxieties, doubts and sorrows.

"Bah! Where did you read all this, Miss Intellectual. All this is literary nonsense. Don't succumb to everything you read just yet, not even to Saint Theresa. If you need to amuse yourself, read the *Bertoldo,* as your father before you did."

I came away from my first confession to that holy man deeply consoled. The initial fear—simple fright more than respect—with which I had approached him, turned into a profound pity. I was at that time a very young woman, almost a girl still; and yet, I was beginning to be a woman, in my innermost being I felt the juice and stirrings of maternity, and when I found myself in the confessional at the side of the saintly priest, I sensed a kind of unspoken confession on his part in the soft murmur of his voice. And I remembered how when he had intoned in the church the words of Jesus Christ: "My God, my God, why hast Thou forsaken me?" his own mother had cried out in the congregation: "My son!"; and I could hear the cry that had rent the silence of the temple. And I went to him again for confession—and to comfort him.

Another time in the confessional I told him of a doubt which assailed me, and he responded:

"As to that, you know what the catechism says. Don't question me about it, for I am ignorant; in Holy Mother Church there are learned doctors of theology who will know how to answer you."

"But you are the learned doctor here."

"Me? A learned doctor? Not even in thought! I, my little doctress, am only a poor country priest. And those questions, . . . do you know who whispers them into your ear? Well . . . the Devil does!"

Then, making bold, I asked him pointblank:

"And suppose he were to whisper these questions to you?"

"Who? To me? The Devil? No, we don't even know each other, my daughter, we haven't met .at all."

"But if he did whisper them? . . ."

"I wouldn't pay any attention. And that's enough of that; let's get on, for there are some people, really sick people, waiting for me."

I went away thinking, I don't know why, that our Don Emmanuel, so famous for curing the bedeviled, didn't really even believe in the Devil. As I started home, I ran into the fool Blasillo, who had probably been hovering around outside; as soon as he saw me, and by way of treating me to a display of his virtuosity, he began the business of repeating—and in what a manner!—"My God, my God,

why hast Thou forsaken me?" I arrived home utterly saddened and locked myself in my room to cry, until finally my mother arrived.

"With all these confessions, Angelita, you will end by going off to a nunnery."

"Don't worry, Mother," I answered her. "I have plenty to do here, in the village, and it will be my only convent."

"Until you marry."

"I don't intend to," I rejoined.

The next time I saw Don Emmanuel I asked him, looking straight into his eyes:

"Is there really a Hell, Don Emmanuel?"

And he, without altering his expression, answered:

"For you, my daughter, no."

"For others, then?"

"Does it matter to you, if you are not to go there?"

"It matters for the others, in any case. Is there a Hell?"

"Believe in Heaven, the Heaven we can see. Look at it there"—and he pointed to the heavens above the mountain, and then down into the lake, to the reflection.

"But we are supposed to believe in Hell as well as in Heaven," I said.

"That's true. We must believe everything believed and taught by our Holy Mother Church, Catholic, Apostolic, and Roman. And now, that will do!"

I thought I read a deep unknown sadness in his eyes, eyes which were as blue as the waters of the lake.

Those years passed as if in a dream. Within me, a reflected image of Don Emmanuel was unconsciously taking form. He was an ordinary enough man in many ways, of such daily use as the daily bread we asked for in our Paternoster. I helped him whenever I could with his tasks, visiting the sick, his sick, the girls at school, and helping, too, with the church linen and the vestments; I served in the role, as he said, of his deaconess. Once I was invited to the city for a few days by a school friend, but I had to hurry home, for the city stifled me—something was missing, I was thirsty for a sight of the waters of the lake, hungry for a sight of the peaks of the mountain; and even more, I missed my Don Emmanuel, as if his absence called to me, as if he were endangered by my being so far away, as if he were in need of me. I began to feel a kind of maternal affection for my spiritual father; I longed to help him bear the cross of birth.

My twenty-fourth birthday was approaching when my brother Lazarus came back from America with the small fortune he had saved up. He came back to Valverde de Lucerna with the intention of taking me and my mother to live in a city, perhaps even Madrid.

"In the country," he said, "in these villages, a person becomes stupefied, brutalized and spiritually impoverished." And he added: "Civilization is the very opposite of everything countryfied. The idiocy of village life! No, that's not for us; I didn't have you sent away to school so that later you might spoil here, among these ignorant peasants."

I said nothing, though I was disposed to resist emigration. But our mother, already past sixty, took a firm stand from the start: "Change pastures at my age?" she demanded at once. A little later she made it quite clear that she could not live out of sight of her lake, her mountain, and, above all, of her Don Emmanuel.

"The two of you are like those cats that get attached to houses," my brother muttered.

When he realized the complete sway exercised over the entire village—especially over my mother and myself—by the saintly priest, my brother began to resent him. He saw in this situation an example of the obscurantist theocracy which, according to him, smothered Spain. And he commenced to spout the old anti-clerical commonplaces, to which he added anti-religious and "progressive" propaganda brought back from the New World.

"In the Spain of sloth and flabby useless men, the priests manipulate the women, and the women manipulate the men. Not to mention the idiocy of the country, and this feudal backwater!"

"Feudal," to him, meant something frightful. "Feudal" and "medieval" were the epithets he employed to condemn something completely.

The failure of his diatribes to move us and their total lack of effect upon the village—where they were listened to with respectful indifference—disconcerted him no end. "The man does not exist who could move these clods." But, he soon began to understand—for he was an intelligent man, and therefore a good one—the kind of influence exercised over the village by Don Emmanuel, and he came to appreciate the effect of the priest's work in the village.

"This priest is not like the others," he announced. "He is, in fact, a saint."

"How do you know what the others are like," I asked. To which he answered:

"I can imagine."

In any case, he did not set foot inside the church nor did he miss an opportunity to parade his incredulity—though he always exempted Don Emmanuel from his scorning accusations. In the village, an unconscious expectancy began to build up, the anticipation of a kind of duel between my brother Lazarus and Don Emmanuel—in short, it was expected that Don Emmanuel would convert my brother. No one doubted but that in the end the priest would bring him into the fold. On his side, Lazarus was eager (he told me so himself, later) to go and hear Don Emmanuel, to see and hear him in the church, to get to know him and to talk with him, so that he might learn the secret of his spiritual hold over our souls. And he let himself be coaxed to this end, so that finally—"out of curiosity," as he said—he went to hear the preacher.

"Now, this is something else again," he told me as soon as he came from hearing Don Emmanuel for the first time. "He's not like the others; still, he doesn't fool me, he's too intelligent to believe everything he must teach."

"You mean you think he's a hypocrite?"

"A hypocrite . . . no! But he has a job by which he must live."

As for me, my brother undertook to see that I read the books he brought me, and others which he urged me to buy.

"So your brother Lazarus wants you to

read," Don Emmanuel queried. "Well, read, my daughter, read and make him happy by doing so. I know you will read only worthy books. Read even if only novels; they are as good as the books which deal with so-called 'reality.' You are better off reading than concerning yourself with village gossip and old wives' tales. Above all, though, you will do well to read devotional books which will bring you contentment in life, a quiet, gentle contentment, and peace."

And he, did he enjoy such contentment?

It was about this time that our mother fell mortally sick and died. In her last days her one wish was that Don Emmanuel should convert Lazarus, whom she expected to see again in heaven, in some little corner among the stars from where they could see the lake and the mountain of Valverde de Lucerna. She felt she was going there now, to see God.

"You are not going anywhere," Don Emmanuel would tell her; "you are staying right here. Your body will remain here, in this land, and your soul also, in this house, watching and listening to your children though they do not see or hear you."

"But, Father," she said, "I am going to see God."

"God, my daughter, is all around us, and you will see Him from here, right from here. And all of us in Him, and He in all of us."

"God bless you," I whispered to him.

"The peace in which your mother dies will be her eternal life," he told me.

And, turning to my brother Lazarus: "Her heaven is to go on seeing you, and it is at this moment that she must be saved. Tell her you will pray for her."

"But—"

"But what? . . . Tell her you will pray for her, to whom you owe your life. And I know that once you promise her, you *will* pray, and I know that once you pray . . ."

My brother, his eyes filled with tears, drew near our dying mother and gave her his solemn promise to pray for her.

"And I, in heaven, will pray for you, for all of you," my mother responded. And then, kissing the crucifix and fixing her eyes on Don Emmanuel, she gave up her soul to God.

"Into Thy hands I commend my spirit," prayed the priest.

My brother and I stayed on in the house alone. What had happened at the time of my mother's death had established a bond between Lazarus and Don Emmanuel. The latter seemed even to neglect some of his charges, his patients and his other needy to look after my brother. In the afternoons, they would go for a stroll together, walking along the lake or toward the ruins, overgrown with ivy, of the old Cistercian abbey.

"He's an extraordinary man," Lazarus told me. "You know the story they tell of how there is a city at the bottom of the lake, submerged beneath the water, and that on Midsummer's Night at midnight the sound of its church bells can be heard . . ."

"Yes, a city 'feudal and medieval' . . ."

"And I believe," he went on, "that at the bottom of Don Emmanuel's soul there is a city, submerged and inundated, and that sometimes the sound of its bells can be heard . . ."

"Yes . . . And this city submerged in Don Emmanuel's soul, and perhaps—why not?—in yours as well, is certainly the cemetery of the souls of our ancestors, the ancestors of our Valverde de Lucerna . . . 'feudal and medieval'!"

In the end, my brother began going to Mass. He went regularly to hear Don Emmanuel. When it became known that he was prepared to comply with his annual duty of receiving Communion, that he would receive when the others received, an intimate joy ran through the town, which felt that by this act he was restored to his people. The rejoicing was of such nature, moreover, so openhanded and honest, that Lazarus never did feel that he had been "vanquished" or "overcome."

The day of his Communion arrived; of Communion before the entire village, with the entire village. When it came time for my brother's turn, I saw Don Emmanuel—white as January snow on the mountain, and moving like the surface of the lake when it is stirred by the northeast wind—come up to him with the holy wafer in his hand, which trembled violently as it reached out to Lazarus's mouth; at that moment the priest had an instant of faintness and the wafer dropped to the ground. My brother himself recovered it and placed it in his mouth. The people saw the tears on Don Emmanuel's face, and everyone wept, saying: "What great love he bears!" and then, because it was dawn, a cock crowed.

On returning home I locked myself in with my brother; alone with him I put my arms around his neck and kissed him.

"Lazarus, Lazarus, what joy you have given us all today; the entire village, the living and the dead, and especially our mother. Did you see how Don Emmanuel wept for joy? What joy you have given us all!"

"It was for that reason that I did what I did," he answered me.

"For what? To give us pleasure? Surely you did it for your own sake, first of all; because of your conversion."

And then Lazarus, my brother, grown as pale and tremulous as Don Emmanuel when he was giving Communion, bade me sit down, in the very chair where our mother used to sit. He took a deep breath, and, in the intimate tone of a familiar and domestic confession, he told me:

"Angelita, the time has come when I must tell you the truth, the absolute truth, and I shall tell you because I must, because I cannot, I ought not, conceal it from you, and because, sooner or later, you are bound to intuit it anyway, if only halfway—which would be worse."

Thereupon, serenely and tranquilly, in a subdued voice, he recounted a tale that drowned me in a lake of sorrow. He told how Don Emmanuel had appealed to him, particularly during the walks to the ruins of the old Cistercian abbey, to set a good example, to avoid scandalizing the townspeople, to take part in the religious life of the community, to feign belief even if he did not feel any, to conceal his own ideas—all this without attempting in any way to catechize him, to instruct him in religion, or to effect a true conversion.

"But is it possible?" I asked in consternation.

"Possible and true. When I said to him: 'Is this you, the priest, who suggests I dissimulate?' he replied, hesitatingly: 'Dissimulate? Not at all! That is not dissimulation. "Dip your fingers in holy water, and you will end by believing," as someone said.' And I, gazing into his eyes, asked him: 'And you, celebrating the Mass, have you ended by believing?' He looked away and stared out at the lake, until his eyes filled with tears. And it was in this way that I came to understand his secret."

"Lazarus!" I cried out, incapable of another word.

At that moment the fool Blasillo came along our street, crying out his: "My God, my God, why hast Thou forsaken me?" And Lazarus shuddered, as if he had heard the voice of Don Emmanuel, or of Christ.

"It was then," my brother at length continued, "that I really understood his motives and his saintliness; for a saint he is, Sister, a true saint. In trying to convert me to his holy cause—for it is a holy cause, a most holy cause—he was not attempting to score a triumph, but rather was doing it to protect the peace, the happiness, the illusions, perhaps, of his charges. I understood that if he thus deceives them—if it *is* deceit—it is not for his own advantage. I submitted to his logic—and that was my conversion.

"I shall never forget the day on which I said to him: 'But, Don Emmanuel, the truth, the truth, above all!'; and he, all a-tremble, whispered in my ear—though we were all alone in the middle of the countryside—'The truth? The truth, Lazarus, is perhaps something so unbearable, so terrible, something so deadly, that simple people could not live with it!'

" 'And why do you show me a glimpse of it now, here, as if we were in the confessional?' I asked. And he said: 'Because if I did not, I would be so tormented by it, so tormented, that I would finally shout it in the middle of the plaza, which I must never, never, never do . . . I am put here to give life to thc souls of my charges, to make them happy, to make them dream they are immortal—and not to destroy them. The important thing is that they live sanely, in concord with each other,—and with the truth, with my truth, they could not live at all. Let them live. That is what the Church does, it lets them live. As for true religion, all religions are true as long as they give spiritual life to the people who profess them, as long as they console them for having been born only to die. And for each people the truest religion is their own, the religion that made them . . . And mine? Mine consists in consoling myself by consoling others, even though the consolation I give them is not ever mine.' I shall never forget his words."

"But then this Communion of yours has been a sacrilege," I dared interrupt, regretting my words as soon as I said them.

"Sacrilege? What about the priest who gave it to me? And his Masses?"

"What martyrdom!" I exclaimed.

"And now," said my brother, "there is one more person to console the people."

"To deceive them, you mean?" I said.

"Not at all," he replied, "but rather to confirm them in their faith."

"And they, the people, do they really believe, do you think?"

"About that, I know nothing! . . . They probably believe without trying, from force of habit, tradition. The important thing is not to stir them up. To let them live from their thin sentiments, without acquiring the torments of luxury. Blessed are the poor in spirit!"

"That then is the sentiment you have learned from Don Emmanuel. . . . And tell me, do you feel you have carried out your promise to our mother on her deathbed, when you promised to pay for her?"

"Do you think I *could* fail her? What do you take me for, sister? Do you think I would go back on my word, my solemn promise made at the hour of death to a mother?"

"I don't know. . . . You might have wanted to deceive her so she could die in peace."

"The fact is, though, that if I had not lived up to my promise, I would be totally miserable."

"And . . ."

"I carried out my promise and I have not neglected for a single day to pray for her."

"Only for her?"

"Well, now, for whom else?"

"For yourself! And now, for Don Emmanuel."

We parted and went to our separate rooms. I to weep through the night, praying for the conversion of my brother and of Don Emmanuel. And Lazarus, to what purpose, I know not.

From that day on I was fearful of finding myself alone with Don Emmanuel, whom I continued to aid in his pious works. And he seemed to sense my inner state and to guess at its cause. When at last I came to him in the confessional's penitential tribunal (who was the judge, and who the offender?) the two of us, he and I bowed our heads in silence and began to cry. It was he, finally, Don Emmanuel, who broke the terrible silence, with a voice which seemed to issue from the tomb:

"Angelita, you have the same faith you had when you were ten, don't you? You believe, don't you?"

"I believe, Father."

"Then go on believing. And if doubts come to torment you, suppress them utterly, even to yourself. The main thing is to live . . ."

I summoned up courage, and dared to ask, trembling:

"But, Father, do you believe?"

For a brief moment he hesitated, and then, mastering himself, he said:

"I believe!"

"In what, Father, in what? Do you believe in the after life? Do you believe that in dying we do not die in every way, completely? Do you believe that we will see each other again, that we will love each other in a world to come? Do you believe in another life?"

The poor saint was sobbing.

"My child, leave off, leave off!"

Now, when I come to write this memoir, I ask myself: Why did he not deceive me? Why did he not deceive me as he deceived the others? Why did he afflict himself? Why could he not deceive himself, or why could he not deceive me? And I want to believe that he was afflicted because he could not deceive himself into deceiving me.

"And now," he said, "pray for me, for your brother, and for yourself—for all of us. We must go on living. And giving life."

And, after a pause:

"Angelita, why don't you marry?"

"You know why I do not."

"No, no; you must marry. Lazarus and I will find you a suitor. For it would be good for you to marry, and rid yourself of these obsessions."

"Obsessions, Don Emmanuel?"

"I know well enough what I am saying. You should not torment yourself for the sake of others, for each of us has more than enough to do answering for himself."

"That it should be you, Don Emmanuel, who say this! That you should advise me to marry and answer for myself alone and not suffer over others! That it should be you!"

"Yes, you are right, Angelita. I am no longer sure of what I say. I am no longer sure of what I say since I began to confess to you. Only, one must go on living. Yes! One must live!"

And when I rose to leave the church, he asked me:

"Now, Angelita, in the name of the people, do you absolve me?"

I felt pierced by a mysterious and priestly prompting and said:

"In the name of the Father, the Son and the Holy Ghost, I absolve you, Father."

We quitted the church, and as I went out I felt the quickening of maternity within me.

My brother, now totally devoted to the work of Don Emmanuel, had become his closest and most zealous collaborator and companion. They were bound together, moreover, by their common secret. Lazarus accompanied the priest on his visits to the sick, and to schools, and he placed his resources at the disposition of the saintly man. A little more zeal, and he would have learned to help celebrate Mass. All the while he was sounding deeper in the unfathomable soul of the priest.

"What manliness!" he exclaimed to me once. "Yesterday, as we walked along the lake he said: 'There lies my direst temptation.' When I interrogated him with my eyes, he went on: 'My poor father, who was close to ninety when he died, was tormented all his life, as he confessed to me himself, by a temptation to suicide, by an instinct to self-destruction which had come to him from a time before memory—from birth, from his *nation,* as he said—and was forced to fight against it always. And this fight grew to be his life. So as not to succumb to this temptation he was forced to take precautions, to guard his life. He told me of terrible episodes. His urge was a form of madness,—and I have inherited it. How that water beckons me in its deep quiet! . . . an apparent quietude reflecting the sky like a mirror—and beneath it the hidden current! My life, Lazarus, is a kind of continual suicide, or a struggle against suicide, which is the same thing. . . . Just so long as our people go on living!' And then he added: 'Here the river eddies to form a lake, so that later, flowing down the plateau, it may form into cascades, waterfalls, and torrents, hurling itself through gorges and chasms. Thus does life eddy in the village; and the temptation to suicide is the greater beside the still waters which at night reflect the stars, than it is beside the crashing falls which drive one back in fear. Listen, Lazarus, I have helped poor villagers to die well, ignorant, illiterate villagers, who had scarcely ever been out of their village, and I have learned from their own lips, or divined it when they were silent, the real cause of their sickness unto death, and there at the head of their deathbed I have been able to see into the black abyss of their life-weariness. A weariness a thousand times worse than hunger! For our part, Lazarus, let us go on with our kind of suicide of working for the people, and let them dream their life as the lake dreams the heavens.'

"Another time," said my brother, "as we were coming back, we spied a country girl, a goatherd, standing erect on a height of the mountain slope overlooking the lake and she was singing in a voice fresher than its waters. Don Emmanuel took hold of me, and pointing to her said: 'Look, it's as though time had stopped, as though this country girl had always been there just as she is, singing in the way she is, and as though she would always be there, as she was before my consciousness began, as she will be when it is past. That girl is a part of nature—not of history—along with the rocks, the clouds, the trees, and the waters.' He has such a subtle feeling for nature, he infuses it with spirit!

"I shall not forget the day when snow was falling and he asked me: 'Have you ever seen a greater mystery, Lazarus, than the snow falling, and dying, in the lake, while a hood is laid upon the mountain?' "

Don Emmanuel had to moderate and temper my brother's zeal and his neophyte's rawness. As soon as he heard that Lazarus was going about inveighing against some of the popular superstitions he told him forcefully:

"Leave them alone! It's difficult enough making them understand where orthodox belief leaves off and where superstition begins. It's hard · enough, especially for us. Leave them alone, then, as long as they get some comfort. . . . It's better for them to believe everything, even things that contradict one another, than to believe nothing. The idea that someone who believes too much ends by not believing in anything is a Protestant notion. Let us not protest! Protestation destroys contentment and peace."

My brother told me, too, about one moonlit night when they were returning to town along the lake (whose surface a mountain breeze was stirring, so that the moonbeams topped the whitecaps), Don Emmanuel turned to him and said:

"Look, the water is reciting the litany and saying: *ianua caeli, ora pro nobis;* gate of heaven, pray for us."

Two evanescent tears fell from his lashes to the grass, where the light of the full moon shone upon them like dew.

And time went hurrying by, and my brother and I began to notice that Don Emmanuel's spirits were failing, that he could no longer control completely the deep rooted sadness which consumed him; perhaps some treacherous illness was undermining his body and soul. In an effort to rouse his interest, Lazarus spoke to him of the good effect the organization of a type of Catholic agrarian syndicate would have.

"A syndicate?" Don Emmanuel repeated sadly. "A syndicate? And what is that? The Church is the only syndicate I know. And you have certainly heard 'My kingdom is not of this world.' Our kingdom, Lazarus, is not of this world'. . ."

"And of the other?"

Don Emmanuel bowed his head:

"The other is here. Two kingdoms exist in this world. Or rather, the other world. . . . Ah, I don't really know what I'm saying. But as for the syndicate, that's a vestige from your days of 'progressivism.' No, Lazarus, no; religion does not exist to resolve the economic or political conflicts of this world, which God handed over to men for their disputes. Let men think and act as they will, let them console themselves for having been born, let them live as happily as possible in the illusion that all this has a purpose. I don't propose to advise the poor to submit to the rich, nor to suggest to the rich that they subordinate themselves to the poor; but rather to preach resignation in everyone, and charity toward everyone. For even the rich man must resign himself—to his riches, and to life; and the poor man must show charity—even to the rich. The Social Question? Ignore it, for it is none of our business. So, a new society is on the way, in which there will be neither rich nor poor, in which wealth will be justly divided, in which everything will belong to everyone—and so, what then? Won't this general well-being and comfort lead to even greater tedium and weariness of life? I know well enough that one of those chiefs of what they call the Social Revolution has already said that religion is the opium of the people. Opium . . . Opium . . . Yes, opium it is. We should give them opium, and help them sleep, and dream. I, myself, with my mad activity, give myself opium. And still I don't manage to sleep well, let alone dream well. . . . What a fearful nightmare! . . . I, too, can say, with the Divine Master: 'My soul is weary unto death.' No, Lazarus, no; no syndicates for us. If *they* organize them, well and good—they would be distracting themselves in that way. Let them play at syndicates, if that makes them happy."

The entire village began to realize that Don Emmanuel's spirit was weakening, that his strength was waning. His very voice—that miracle of a voice—acquired a kind of quaking. Tears came into his eyes for any reason whatever—or for no reason. Whenever he spoke to people about the other world, about the other life, he was compelled to pause at frequent intervals, and he would close his eyes. "It is a vision," people would say, "he has a vision of what lies ahead." At such moments the fool Blasillo was the first to break into tears. He wept copiously these days, crying now more than he laughed, and even his laughter had the sound of tears.

The last Easter Week which Don Emmanuel was to celebrate among us, in this world, in this village of ours, arrived, and all the village sensed the impending end of tragedy. And how the words did strike home when for the last time Don Emmanuel cried out before us: "My God, my God, why hast Thou forsaken me?"! And when he repeated the words of the Lord to the Good Thief ("All thieves are good," Don Emmanuel used to tell us): "Tomorrow shalt thou be with me in Paradise." . . . ! And then, the last general Communion which our saint was to give! When he came to my brother to give him the Host—his hand steady this

time—, just after the liturgical ". . . *in vitam aeternam,"* he bent down and whispered to him: "There is no other life but this, no life more eternal . . . let them dream it eternal . . . let it be eternal for a few years . . ."

And when he came to me he said: "Pray, my child, pray for us all." And then, something so extraordinary happened that I carry it now in my heart as the greatest of mysteries: he bent over and said, in a voice which seemed to belong to the other world: ". . . and pray, too, for our Lord Jesus Christ."

I stood up, going weak as I did so, like a somnambulist. Everything around me seemed dream-like. And I thought: "Am I to pray, too, for the lake and the mountain?" and next: "Am I bewitched, then?" Home at last, I took up the crucifix my mother had held in her hands when she had given up her soul to God, and, gazing at it through my tears and recalling the "My God, my God, why hast Thou forsaken me?" of our two Christs, the one of this earth and the other of this village, I prayed: "Thy will be done on earth as it is in heaven," and then, "And lead us not into temptation. Amen." After this I turned to the statue of the Mater Dolorosa—her heart transfixed by seven swords—which had been my poor mother's most sorrowful comfort, and I prayed again: "Holy Mary, Mother of God, pray for us sinners, now and in the hour of our death. Amen." I had scarcely finished the prayer, when I asked myself: "Sinners? Sinners are we? And what is our sin, what is it?" And all day I brooded over the question.

The next day I presented myself before Don Emmanuel—Don Emmanuel now in the full sunset of his magnificent religiosity—and I said to him:

"Do you remember, my Father, years ago when I asked you a certain question you answered: 'That question you must not ask me; for I am ignorant; there are learned doctors of the Holy Mother Church who will know how to answer you'?"

"Do I remember? . . . Of course. And I remember I told you those were questions put to you by the Devil."

"Well, then, Father, I have come again, bedeviled, to ask you another question put to me by my Guardian Devil."

"Ask it."

"Yesterday, when you gave me Communion, you asked me to pray for all of us, and even for . . ."

"That's enough! . . . Go on."

"I arrived home and began to pray; when I came to the part 'Pray for us sinners, now and at the hour of our death,' a voice in me asked: 'Sinners? Sinners are we? And what is our sin?' What is our sin, Father?"

"Our sin?" he replied. "A great doctor of the Spanish Catholic Apostolic Church has already explained it; the great doctor of *Life Is a Dream* has written 'The greatest sin of man is to have been born.' That, my child, is our sin; to have been born."

"Can it be atoned, Father?"

"Go and pray again. Pray once more for us sinners, now and at the hour of our death. . . . Yes, at length the dream is atoned . . . at length life is atoned . . . at length the cross of birth is expiated and atoned, and the drama comes to an end. . . . And as Calderón said, to have done good, to have feigned good, even in dreams, is something which is not lost."

The hour of his death arrived at last. The entire village saw it come. And he made it his finest lesson. For he would not die alone or at rest. He died preaching to his people in the church. But first, before being carried to the church (his paralysis made it impossible for him to move), he summoned Lazarus and me to his bedside. Alone there, the three of us together, he said:

"Listen to me: watch over these poor sheep; find some comfort for them in living, and let them believe what I could not. And Lazarus, when your hour comes, die as I die, as Angela will die, in the arms of the Holy Mother Church, Catholic, Apostolic, and Roman; that is to say, of the Holy Mother Church of Valverde de Lucerna. And now, farewell; until we never meet again, for this dream of life is coming to an end . . ."

"Father, Father," I cried out.

"Do not grieve, Angela, only go on praying for all sinners, for all who have been born. Let them dream, let them dream . . . O, what a longing I have to sleep, to sleep, sleep without end, sleep for all eternity, and never dream! Forgetting this dream! . . . When they go to bury me, let it be in a box made from the six planks I cut from the old walnut tree —poor old tree!—in whose shade I played as a child, when I began the dream. . . . In those days, I did really believe in life everlasting. That is to say, it seems to me now that I believed. For a child, to believe is the same as to dream. And for a people, too. . . . You'll find those six planks I cut at the foot of the bed."

He was seized by a sudden fit of choking, and then, composing himself once more, he went on:

"You will recall that when we prayed together, animated by a common sentiment, a community of spirit, and we came to the final verse of the Creed, you will remember that I would fall silent. . . . When the Israelites were coming to the end of their wandering in the desert, the Lord told Aaron and Moses that because they had not believed in Him they would not set foot in the Promised Land with their people; and he bade them climb the heights of Mount Hor, where Moses ordered Aaron stripped of his garments, so that Aaron died there, and then Moses went up from the plains of Moab to Mount Nebo, to the top of Pisgah, looking into Jericho, and the Lord showed him all of the land promised to His people, but said to him: 'You will not go there.' And there Moses died, and no one knew his grave. And he left Joshua to be chief in his place. You, Lazarus, must be my Joshua, and if you can make the sun stand still, make it stop, and never mind progress. Like Moses, I have seen the face of God—our supreme dream—face to face, and as you already know, and as the Scripture says, he who sees God's face, he who sees the eyes of the dream, the eyes with which He looks at us, will die inexorably and forever. And therefore, do not let our people, so long as they live, look into the face of God. Once dead, it will no longer matter, for then they will see nothing . . ."

"Father, Father, Father," I cried again.

And he said:

"Angela, you must pray always, so that all sinners may go on dreaming, until they die, of the resurrection of the flesh and the life everlasting . . ."

I was expecting "and who knows it might be . . ." But instead, Don Emmanuel had another attack of coughing.

"And now," he finally went on, "and now, in the hour of my death, it is high time to have me brought, in this very chair, to the church, so that I may take leave there of my people, who await me."

He was carried to the church and brought, in his armchair, into the chancel, to the foot of the altar. In his hands he held a crucifix. My brother and I stood close to him, but the fool Blasillo wanted to stand even closer. He wanted to grasp Don Emmanuel by the hand, so that he could kiss it. When some of the people nearby tried to stop him, Don Emmanuel rebuked them and said:

"Let him come closer. . . . Come, Blasillo, give me your hand."

The fool cried for joy. And then Don Emmanuel spoke:

"I have very few words left, my children; I scarcely feel I have strength enough left to die. And then, I have nothing new to tell you, either. I have already said everything I have to say. Live with each other in peace and contentment, in the hope that we will all see each other again some day, in the other Valverde de Lucerna up there among the nighttime stars, the stars which the lake reflects over the image of the reflected mountain. And pray, pray to the Most Blessed Mary, and to our Lord. Be good . . . that is enough. Forgive me whatever wrong I may have done you inadvertently or unknowingly. After I give you my blessing, let us pray together, let us say the Paternoster, the Ave Maria, the Salve, and the Creed."

Then he gave his blessing to the whole village, with the crucifix held in his hand, while the women and children cried and even some of the men wept softly. Almost at once the prayers were begun. Don Em-

manuel listened to them in silence, his hand in the hand of Blasillo the fool, who began to fall asleep to the sound of the praying. First the Paternoster, with its "Thy will be done on earth as it is in heaven"; then the Ave Maria, with its "Pray for us sinners, now and in hour of our death"; followed by the Salve, with its "mourning and weeping in his vale of tears"; and finally, the Creed. On reaching "The resurrection of the flesh and life everlasting" the people sensed that their saint had yielded up his soul to God. It was not necessary to close his eyes even, for he died with them closed. When an attempt was made to wake Blasillo, it was found that he, too, had fallen asleep in the Lord forever. So that later there were two bodies to be buried.

The village immediately repaired en masse to the house of the saint to carry away holy relics, to divide up pieces of his garments among themselves, to carry off whatever they could find as a memento of the blessed martyr. My brother preserved his breviary, between the pages of which he discovered a carnation, dried as in a herbarium and mounted on a piece of paper, and upon the paper a cross and a certain date.

No one in the village seemed able to believe that Don Emmanuel was dead; everyone expected to see him—perhaps some of them did—taking his daily walk along the side of the lake, his figure mirrored in the water, or silhouetted against the background of the mountain. They continued to hear his voice, and they all visited his grave, around which a veritable cult sprang up, old women "possessed by devils" came to touch the cross of walnut, made with his own hands from the tree which had yielded the six planks of his casket.

The ones who least of all believed in his death were my brother and I. Lazarus carried on the tradition of the saint, and he began to compile a record of the priest's words. Some of the conversations in this account of mine were made possible by his notes.

"It was he," said my brother, "who made me into a new man. I was a true

Lazarus whom he raised from the dead. He gave me faith."

"Ah, faith . . ."

"Yes, faith, faith in the charity of life, in life's joy. It was he who cured me of my delusion of 'progress,' of my belief in its political implications. For there are, Angela, two types of dangerous and harmful men: those who, convinced of life beyond the grave, of the resurrection of the flesh, torment other people—like the inquisitors they are—so that they will despise this life as a transitory thing and work for the other life; and then, there are those who, believe only in this life . . ."

"Like you, perhaps . . ."

"Yes, and like Don Emmanuel. Believing only in this world, this second group looks forward to some vague future society and exerts every effort to prevent the populace finding consoling joy from belief in another world . . ."

"And so . . ."

"The people should be allowed to live with their illusion."

The poor priest who came to the parish to replace Don Emmanuel found himself overwhelmed in Valverde de Lucerna by the memory of the saint, and he put himself in the hands of my brother and myself for guidance. He wanted only to follow in the footsteps of the saint. And my brother told him: "Very little theology, Father, very little theology. Religion, religion, religion." Listening to him, I smiled to myself, wondering if this was not a kind of theology, too.

I had by now begun to fear for my poor brother. From the time Don Emmanuel died it could scarcely be said that he lived. Daily he went to the priest's tomb; for hours on end he stood gazing into the lake. He was filled with nostalgia for deep, abiding peace.

"Don't stare into the lake so much," I begged him.

"Don't worry. It's not this lake which draws me, nor the mountain. Only, I cannot live without his help."

"And the joy of living, Lazarus, what about the joy of living?"

"That's for others. Not for those of us who have seen God's face, those of us on whom the Dream of Life has gazed with His eyes."

"What; are you preparing to go and see Don Emmanuel?"

"No, sister, no. Here at home now, between the two of us, the whole truth— bitter as it may be, bitter as the sea into which the sweet waters of our lake flow— the whole truth for you, who are so set against it . . ."

"No, no, Lazarus. You are wrong. Your truth is not the truth."

"It's my truth."

"Yours, perhaps, but surely not . . ."

"His, too."

"No, Lazarus. Not now, it isn't. Now, he must believe otherwise; now he must believe . . ."

"Listen, Angela, once Don Emmanuel told me that there are truths which, though one reveals them to oneself, must be kept from others; and I told him that telling me was the same as telling himself. And then he said, he confessed to me, that he thought that more than one of the great saints, perhaps the very greatest himself, had died without believing in the other life."

"Is it possible?"

"All too possible! And now, sister, you must be careful that here, among the people, no one even suspects our secret . . ."

"Suspect it?" I cried in amazement. "Why even if I were to try, in a fit of madness, to explain it to them, they wouldn't understand it. The people do not understand your words, they understand your actions much better. To try and explain all this to them would be like reading some pages from Saint Thomas Aquinas to eight-year-old children, in Latin."

"All the better. In any case, when I am gone, pray for me and for him and for all of us."

At length, his own time came. A sickness which had been eating away at his robust nature seemed to flare with the death of Don Emmanuel.

"I don't so much mind dying," he said to me in his last days, "as the fact that with me another piece of Don Emmanuel dies too. The remainder of him must live on with you. Until, one day, even we dead will die forever."

When he lay in the throes of death, the people of the village came in to bid him farewell (as is customary in our towns) and they commended his soul to the care of Don Emmanuel the Good, Martyr. My brother said nothing to them; he had nothing more to say. He had already said everything there was to say. He had become a link between the two Valverde de Lucernas—the one at the bottom of the lake and the one reflected in its surface. He was already one more of us who had died of life, and, in his way, one more of our saints.

I was desolate, more than desolate; but I was, at least, among my own people, in my own village. Now, having lost my Saint Emmanuel, the father of my soul, and my own Lazarus, my more than carnal brother, my spiritual brother, now it is I realize that I have aged. But, have I really lost them then? Have I grown old? Is my death approaching?

I must live! And he taught me to live, he taught us to live, to feel life, to feel the meaning of life, to merge with the soul of the mountain, with the soul of the lake, with the soul of the village, to lose ourselves in them so as to remain in them forever. He taught me by his life to lose myself in the life of the people of my village, and I no longer felt the passing of the hours, and the days, and the years, any more than I felt the passage of the water in the lake. It began to seem that my life would always be thus. I no longer felt myself growing old. I no longer lived in myself, but in my people, and my people lived in me. I tried to speak as they spoke, as they spoke without trying. I went into the street—it was the one highway—and, since I knew everyone, I lived in them and forgot myself (while, on the other hand, in Madrid, where I went once with my brother, I had felt a terrible loneliness, since I knew no one, and had been tortured by the sight of so many unknown people).

Now, as I write this memoir, this confession of my experience with saintliness, with a saint, I am of the opinion that Don Emmanuel the Good, my Don Emmanuel, and my brother, too, died believing they did not believe, but that, without believing in their belief, they actually believed, with resignation and in desolation.

But why, I have asked myself repeatedly, did not Don Emmanuel attempt to convert my brother deceitfully, with a lie, pretending to be a believer himself without being one? And I have finally come to think that Don Emmanuel realized he would not be able to delude him, that with him a fraud would not do, that only through the truth, with his truth, would he be able to convert him; that he knew he would accomplish nothing if he attempted to enact the comedy—the tragedy, rather—which he played out for the benefit of the people. And thus did he win him over, in effect, to his pious fraud; thus did he win him over to the cause of life with the truth of death. And thus did he win me, who never permitted anyone to see through his divine, his most saintly, game. For I believed then, and I believe now, that God—as part of I know not what sacred and inscrutable purpose—caused them to believe they were unbelievers. And that at the moment of their passing, perhaps, the blindfold was removed.

And I, do I believe?

As I write this—here in my mother's old house, and I past my fiftieth year and my memories growing as dim and blanched as my hair—outside it is snowing, snowing upon the lake, snowing upon the mountain, upon the memory of my father, the stranger, upon the memory of my mother, my brother Lazarus, my people, upon the memory of my Saint Emmanuel, and even on the memory of the poor fool Blasillo, my Saint Blasillo—and may he help me in heaven! The snow effaces corners and blots out shadows, for even in the night it shines and illuminates. Truly, I do not know what is true and what is false, nor what I saw and what I merely dreamt—or rather, what I dreamt and what I merely saw—, nor what I really knew or what I merely believed true. Neither do I know whether or not I am transferring to this paper, white as the snow outside, my consciousness, for it to remain in writing, leaving me without it. But why, any longer, cling to it?

Do I really understand any of it? Do I really believe in any of it? Did what I am writing about here actually take place, and did it take place in just the way I tell it? Is it possible for such things to happen? Is it possible that all this is more than a dream dreamed within another dream? Can it be that I, Angela Carballino, a woman in her fifties, am the only one in this village to be assailed by far-fetched thoughts, thoughts unknown to everyone else? And the others, those around me, do they believe? And what does it mean, to believe? At least they go on living. And now they believe in Saint Emmanuel the Good, Martyr, who, with no hope of immortality for himself, preserved their hope in it.

It appears that our most illustrious bishop, who set in motion the process for beatifying our saint from Valverde de Lucerna, is intent on writing an account of Don Emmanuel's life, something which would serve as a guide for the perfect parish priest, and with this end in mind he is gathering information of every sort. He has repeatedly solicited information from me; more than once he has come to see me; and I have supplied him with all sorts of facts. But I have never revealed the tragic secret of Don Emmanuel and my brother. And it is curious that he has never suspected. I trust that what I have set down here will never come to his knowledge. For, all temporal authorities are to be avoided; I fear all authorities on this earth—even when they are church authorities.

But this is an end to it. Let its fate be what it will . . .

How, you ask, did this document, this memoir of Angela Carballino fall into my hands? That, reader, is something I must keep secret. I have transcribed it for you just as it is written, just as it came to me, with only a few, a very few editorial emendations. It recalls to you other things I have written? This fact does not gainsay its objectivity, its originality. More-

over, for all I know, perhaps I created real, actual beings, independent of me, beyond my control, characters with immortal souls. For all I know, Augusto Perez in my novel *Mist* was right when he claimed to be more real, more objective than I myself, who had thought to have invented him. As for the reality of this Saint Emmanuel the Good, Martyr—as he is revealed to me by his disciple and spiritual daughter Angela Carballino—of his reality it has not occurred to me to doubt. I believe in it more than the saint himself did. I believe in it more than I do in my own reality.

And now, before I bring this epilogue to a close, I wish to recall to your mind, patient reader, the ninth verse of the Epistle of the forgotten Apostle, Saint Judas—what power in a name!—where we are told how my heavenly patron, St. Michael Archangel (Michael means "Who such as God?" and· archangel means archmessenger) disputed with the Devil (Devil means accuser, prosecutor) over the body of Moses, and would not allow him to carry it off as a prize, to damnation. Instead, he told the Devil: "May the Lord rebuke thee." And may he who wishes to understand, understand!

I would like also, since Angela Carballino injected her own feelings into her narrative—I don't know how it could have been otherwise—to comment on her statement to the effect that if Don Emmanuel and his disciple Lazarus had confessed their convictions to the people, they, the people, would not have understood. Nor, I should like to add, would they have believed the pair. They would have believed in their works and not their words. And works stand by themselves, and need no words to back them up. In a village like Valverde de Lucerna one makes one's confession by one's conduct.

And as for faith, the people scarce know what it is, and care less.

I am well aware of the fact that no action takes place in this narrative, this *novelistic* narrative, if you will—the novel is, after all, the most intimate, the truest history, so that I scarcely understand why some people are outraged to have the Bible called a novel, when such a designation actually sets it above some mere chronicle or other. In short, nothing happens. But I hope that this is because everything that takes place happens, and instead of coming to pass, and passing away, remains forever, like the lakes and the mountains and the blessed simple souls fixed firmly beyond faith and despair, the blessed souls who, in the lakes and the mountains, outside history, in their divine novel, take refuge.

[1930]
TRANSLATED BY
ANTHONY KERRIGAN

QUESTIONS FOR STUDY

1. *The names of the three major characters have important religious connotations (Angela—angel; Lazarus—the brother of Martha and Mary raised by Jesus from the dead; Don Emmanuel—Immanuel, "God with us," the name given to the Messiah by the prophet Isaiah). How do these names clarify the role that each character plays in the story? What other Biblical allusions are found in the story? What is their function?*

2. *What are the major tenets of Don Emmanuel's philosophy? In what sense is he a saint and a martyr?*

3. *Why does Unamuno continually compare Don Emmanuel to the mountain and lake that border the village of Valverde de Lucerna? How do such comparisons serve to increase the reader's understanding of Don Emmanuel's life and message?*

4. *What does Angela mean when she says that both Don Emmanuel and her brother "died believing they did not believe, but that, without believing in their belief, they actually believed, with resignation and in desolation"? What final serenity does Angela herself reach?*

5. *What is the purpose of Unamuno's epilogue?*

6. *What is the overall theme of the story?*

JOHN UPDIKE

A & P

IN WALKS these three girls in nothing but bathing suits. I'm in the third check-out slot, with my back to the door, so I don't see them until they're over by the bread. The one that caught my eye first was the one in the plaid green two-piece. She was a chunky kid, with a good tan and a sweet broad soft-looking can with those two crescents of white just under it, where the sun never seems to hit, at the top of the backs of her legs. I stood there with my hand on a box of HiHo crackers trying to remember if I rang it up or not. I ring it up again and the customer starts giving me hell. She's one of these cash-register-watchers, a witch about fifty with rouge on her cheekbones and no eye-brows, and I know it made her day to trip me up. She'd been watching cash registers for fifty years and probably never seen a mistake before.

By the time I got her feathers smoothed and her goodies into a bag—she gives me a little snort in passing, if she'd been born at the right time they would have burned her over in Salem—by the time I get her on her way the girls had circled around the bread and were coming back, without a pushcart, back my way along the counters, in the aisle between the checkouts and the Special bins. They didn't even have shoes on. There was this chunky one, with the two-piece—it was bright green and the seams on the bra were still sharp and her belly was still pretty pale so I guessed she just got it (the suit)—there was this one, with one of those chubby berry-faces, the lips all bunched together under her nose, this one, and a tall one, with black hair that hadn't quite frizzed right, and one of these sunburns right across under the eyes, and a chin that was too long—you know, the kind of girl other girls think is very "striking" and "attractive" but never quite makes it, as they very well know, which is why they like her so much—and then the third one, that wasn't quite so tall. She was the queen. She kind of led them, the other two peeking around and making their shoulders round. She didn't look around, not this queen, she just walked straight on slowly, on these long white prima-donna legs. She came down a little hard on her heels, as if she didn't walk in bare feet that much, putting down her heels and then letting the weight move along to her toes as if she was testing the floor with every step, putting a little deliberate extra action into it. You never know for sure how girls' minds work (do you really think it's a mind in there or just a little buzz like a bee in a glass jar?) but you got the idea she had talked the other two into coming in here with her, and now she was showing them how to do it, walk slow and hold yourself straight.

She had on a kind of dirty-pink—beige maybe, I don't know—bathing suit with a little nubble all over it and, what got me, the straps were down. They were off her shoulders looped loose around the cool tops of her arms, and I guess as a result the suit had slipped a little on her, so all around the top of the cloth there was this shining rim. If it hadn't been there you wouldn't have known there could have been anything whiter than those shoul-ders. With the straps pushed off, there was nothing between the top of the suit and the top of her head except just *her*, this clean bare plane of the top of her chest down from the shoulder bones like a dented sheet of metal tilted in the light. I mean, it was more than pretty.

She had a sort of oaky hair that the sun and salt had bleached, done up in a bun that was unravelling, and a kind of prim face. Walking into the A & P with your straps down, I suppose it's the only kind of face you *can* have. She held her head so high her neck, coming up out of those white shoulders, looked kind of stretched, but I didn't mind. The longer her neck was, the more of her there was.

She must have felt in the corner of her eye me and over my shoulder Stokesie in the second slot watching, but she didn't tip. Not this queen. She kept her eyes moving across the racks, and stopped, and turned so slow it made my stomach rub the inside of my apron, and buzzed to the other two, who kind of huddled against her for relief, and then they all three of them went up the cat-and-dog-food - breakfast - cereal - macaroni - rice - raisins - seasonings - spreads - spaghetti - soft-drinks - crackers - and - cookies aisle. From the third slot I look straight up this aisle to the meat counter, and I watched them all the way. The fat one with the tan sort of fumbled with the cookies, but on second thought she put the package back. The sheep pushing their carts down the aisle—the girls were walking against the usual traffic (not that we have one-way signs or anything)—were pretty hilarious. You could see them, when Queenie's white shoulders dawned on them, kind of jerk, or hop, or hiccup, but their eyes snapped back to their own baskets and on they pushed. I bet you could set off dynamite in an A & P and the people would by and large keep reaching and checking oatmeal off their lists and muttering "Let me see, there was a third thing, began with A, asparagus, no, ah, yes, applesauce!" or whatever it is they do mutter. But there was no doubt, this jiggled them. A few houseslaves in pin curlers even looked around after pushing their carts past to make sure what they had seen was correct.

You know, it's one thing to have a girl in a bathing suit down on the beach, where what with the glare nobody can look at each other much anyway, and another thing in the cool of the A & P, under the fluorescent lights, against all those stacked packages, with her feet paddling along naked over our checkerboard green-and-cream rubber-tile floor.

"Oh Daddy," Stokesie said beside me. "I feel so faint."

"Darling," I said. "Hold me tight." Stokesie's married, with two babies chalked up on his fuselage already, but as far as I can tell that's the only difference. He's twenty-two, and I was nineteen this April.

"Is it done?" he asks, the responsible married man finding his voice. I forgot to say he thinks he's going to be manager some sunny day, maybe in 1990 when it's called the Great Alexandrov and Petrooshki Tea Company or something.

What he meant was, our town is five miles from a beach, with a big summer colony out on the Point, but we're right in the middle of town, and the women generally put on a shirt or shorts or something before they get out of the car into the street. And anyway these are usually women with six children and varicose veins mapping their legs and nobody, including them, could care less. As I say, we're right in the middle of town, and if you stand at our front doors you can see two banks and the Congregational church and the newspaper store and three real-estate offices and about twenty-seven old freeloaders tearing up Central Street because the sewer broke again. It's not as if we're on the Cape; we're north of Boston and there's people in this town haven't seen the ocean for twenty years.

The girls had reached the meat counter and were asking McMahon something. He pointed, they pointed, and they shuffled out of sight behind a pyramid of Diet Delight peaches. All that was left for us to see was old McMahon patting his mouth and looking after them sizing up their joints. Poor kids, I began to feel sorry for them, they couldn't help it.

Now here comes the sad part of the story, at least my family says it's sad, but I don't think it's so sad myself. The store's pretty empty, it being Thursday afternoon, so there was nothing much to do except lean on the register and wait for the girls to show up again. The whole store was like a pinball machine and I didn't know which tunnel they'd come out of. After a while they come around out of the far aisle, around the light bulbs, records at discount of the Caribbean Six or Tony Martin Sings or some such gunk you wonder they waste the wax on, six-packs of candy bars, and plastic toys done up in cellophane that fall apart when a kid looks at them anyway. Around they come, Queenie still leading the way, and holding a little gray jar in her hand. Slots Three through Seven are unmanned and I could see her wondering between Stokes and me, but Stokesie with his usual luck draws an old party in baggy gray pants who stumbles up with four giant cans of pineapple juice (what do these bums *do* with all that pineapple juice? I've often asked myself) so the girls come to me. Queenie puts down the jar and I take it into my fingers icy cold. Kingfish Fancy Herring Snacks in Pure Sour Cream: 49¢. Now her hands are empty, not a ring or a bracelet, bare as God made them, and I wonder where the money's coming from. Still with that prim look she lifts a folded dollar bill out of the hollow at the center of her nubbled pink top. The jar went heavy in my hand. Really, I thought that was so cute.

Then everybody's luck begins to run out. Lengel comes in from haggling with a truck full of cabbages on the lot and is about to scuttle into that door marked MANAGER behind which he hides all day when the girls touch his eye. Lengel's pretty dreary, teaches Sunday school and the rest, but he doesn't miss that much. He comes over and says, "Girls, this isn't the beach."

Queenie blushes, though maybe it's just a brush of sunburn I was noticing for the first time, now that she was so close. "My mother asked me to pick up a jar of herring snacks." Her voice kind of startled me, the way voices do when you see the people first, coming out so flat and dumb yet kind of tony, too, the way it ticked over "pick up" and "snacks." All of a sudden I slid right down her voice into her living room. Her father and the other men were standing around in ice-cream coats and bow ties and the women were in sandals picking up herring snacks on toothpicks off a big glass plate and they were all holding drinks the color of water with olives and sprigs of mint in them. When my parents have somebody over they get lemonade and if it's a real racy affair Schlitz in tall glasses with "They'll Do It Every Time" cartoons stencilled on.

"That's all right," Lengel said. "But this isn't the beach." His repeating this struck me as funny, as if it had just occurred to him, and he had been thinking all these years the A & P was a great big dune and he was the head lifeguard. He didn't like my smiling—as I say he doesn't miss much—but he concentrates on giving the girls that sad Sunday-school-superintendent stare.

Queenie's blush is no sunburn now, and the plump one in plaid, that I liked better from the back—a really sweet can —pipes up, "We weren't doing any shopping. We just came in for the one thing."

"That makes no difference," Lengel tells her, and I could see from the way his eyes went that he hadn't noticed she was wearing a two-piece before. "We want you decently dressed when you come in here."

"We *are* decent," Queenie says suddenly, her lower lip pushing, getting sore now that she remembers her place, a place from which the crowd that runs the A & P must look pretty crummy. Fancy Herring Snacks flashed in her very blue eyes.

"Girls, I don't want to argue with you. After this come in here with your shoulders covered. It's our policy." He turns his back. That's policy for you. Policy is what the kingpins want. What the others want is juvenile delinquency.

All this while, the customers had been showing up with their carts but, you know, sheep, seeing a scene, they had all bunched up on Stokesie, who shook open a paper bag as gently as peeling a peach, not wanting to miss a word. I could feel in the silence everybody getting nervous, most of all Lengel, who asks me, "Sammy, have you rung up their purchase?"

I thought and said "No" but it wasn't about that I was thinking. I go through the punches, 4, 9, GROC, TOT—it's more complicated than you think, and after you do it often enough, it begins to make a little song, that you hear words to, in my case

"Hello (*bing*) there, you (*gung*) hap-py pee-pul (*splat*)!"— the *splat* being the drawer flying out. I increase the bill, tenderly as you may imagine, it just having come from between the two smoothest scoops of vanilla I had ever known there were, and pass a half and a penny into her narrow pink palm, and nestle the herrings in a bag and twist its neck and hand it over, all the time thinking.

The girls, and who'd blame them, are in a hurry to get out, so I say "I quit" to Lengel quick enough for them to hear, hoping they'll stop and watch me, their unsuspected hero. They keep right on going, into the electric eye; the door flies open and they flicker across the lot to their car, Queenie and Plaid and Big Tall Goony-Goony (not that as raw material she was so bad), leaving me with Lengel and a kink in his eyebrow.

"Did you say something, Sammy?"

"I said I quit."

"I thought you did."

"You didn't have to embarrass them."

"It was they who were embarrassing us."

I started to say something that came out "'Fiddle-de-do." It's a saying of my grandmother's, and I know she would have been pleased.

"I don't think you know what you're saying," Lengel said.

"I know you don't," I said. "But I do." I pull the bow at the back of my apron and start shrugging it off my shoulders. A couple of customers that had been heading for my slot begin to knock against each other, like scared pigs in a chute.

Lengel sighs and begins to look very patient and old and gray. He's been a friend of my parents for years. "Sammy, you don't want to do this to your Mom and Dad," he tells me. It's true, I don't. But it seems to me that once you begin a gesture it's fatal not to go through with it. I fold the apron, "Sammy" stitched in red on the pocket, and put it on the counter, and drop the bow tie on top of it. The bow tie is theirs, if you've ever wondered. "You'll feel this for the rest of your life," Lengel says, and I know that's true, too, but remembering how he made that pretty girl blush makes me so scrunchy inside I punch the No Sale tab and the machine whirs "pee-pul" and the drawer splats out. One advantage to this scene taking place in summer, I can follow this up with a clean exit, there's no fumbling around getting your coat and galoshes, I just saunter into the electric eye in my white shirt that my mother ironed the night before, and the door heaves itself open, and outside the sunshine is skating around on the asphalt.

I look around for my girls, but they're gone, of course. There wasn't anybody but some young married screaming with her children about some candy they didn't get by the door of a powder-blue Falcon station wagon. Looking back in the big windows, over the bags of peat moss and aluminum lawn furniture stacked on the pavement, I could see Lengel in my place in the slot, checking the sheep through. His face was dark gray and his back stiff, as if he's just had an injection of iron, and my stomach kind of fell as I felt how hard the world was going to be to me hereafter.

[1962]

QUESTIONS FOR STUDY

1. *What does Sammy reveal in the course of the story about his own values and attitudes?*

2. *What values and attitudes does Sammy impute to the fifty-year-old woman and the other "sheep," to Queenie and her family, to Mr. Lengel, to his own family? To what extent is he guilty of oversimplification?*

3. *What is the role of Stokesie? To what extent does he serve as a foil to Sammy?*

4. *What attitudes cause Mr. Lengel to reprimand the girls? Is his reprimand justified?*

5. *Why does Sammy quit his job so suddenly? Is his gesture genuinely heroic or is it merely the misguided idealism of a rebellious adolescent? How is it prepared for earlier in the story? Why is it ironic?*
6. *What is the relationship to the author's theme of Sammy's final statement: "I felt how hard the world was going to be to me hereafter"?*
7. *What are the major characteristics of Updike's style? In what ways is it appropriate and effective?*
8. *To what extent is Sammy aware of the implied humor in his narrative? What would happen to the story if Updike had chosen to make the humor more explicit?*

KURT VONNEGUT, JR.

Report on the Barnhouse Effect

ET ME begin by saying that I don't know any more about where Professor Arthur Barnhouse is hiding than anyone else does. Save for one short, enigmatic message left in my mailbox on Christmas Eve, I have not heard from him since his disappearance a year and a half ago.

What's more, readers of this article will be disappointed if they expect to learn how *they* can bring about the so-called "Barnhouse Effect." If I were able and willing to give away that secret, I would certainly be something more important than a psychology instructor.

I have been urged to write this report because I did research under the professor's direction and because I was the first to learn of his astonishing discovery. But while I was his student I was never entrusted with knowledge of how the mental forces could be released and directed. He was unwilling to trust anyone with that information.

I would like to point out that the term "Barnhouse Effect" is a creation of the popular press, and was never used by Professor Barnhouse. The name he chose for the phenomenon was *"dynamopsychism,"* or *force of the mind.*

I cannot believe that there is a civilized person yet to be convinced that such a force exists, what with its destructive effects on display in every national capital. I think humanity has always had an inkling that this sort of force does exist. It has been common knowledge that some people are luckier than others with inanimate objects like dice. What Professor Barnhouse did was to show that such "luck" was a measurable force, which in his case could be enormous.

By my calculations, the professor was about fifty-five times more powerful than a Nagasaki-type atomic bomb at the time he went into hiding. He was not bluffing when, on the eve of "Operation Brainstorm," he told General Honus Barker: "Sitting here at the dinner table, I'm pretty sure I can flatten anything on earth—from Joe Louis [1] to the Great Wall of China."

There is an understandable tendency to look upon Professor Barnhouse as a supernatural visitation. The First Church of Barnhouse in Los Angeles has a congregation numbering in the thousands. He is godlike in neither appearance nor intellect. The man who disarms the world is single, shorter than the average American male, stout, and averse to exercise. His I.Q. is 143, which is good but certainly not sensational. He is quite mortal, about to celebrate his fortieth birthday, and in good health. If he is alone now, the isolation won't bother him too much. He was quiet and shy when I knew him, and seemed to find more companionship in books and music than in his associations at the college.

Neither he nor his powers fall outside the sphere of Nature. His dynamopsychic radiations are subject to many known physical laws that apply in the field of radio. Hardly a person has not now heard the snarl of "Barnhouse static" on his home receiver. The radiations are affected by sunspots and variations in the ionosphere.

However, they differ from ordinary broadcast waves in several important ways. Their total energy can be brought

[1] Joe Louis (1914–), the world heavyweight boxing champion who retired undefeated in March 1949. (JHP)

---

to bear on any single point the professor chooses, and that energy is undiminished by distance. As a weapon, then, dynamopsychism has an impressive advantage over bacteria and atomic bombs, beyond the fact that it costs nothing to use: it enables the professor to single out critical individuals and objects instead of slaughtering whole populations in the process of maintaining international equilibrium.

As General Honus Barker told the House Military Affairs Committee: "Until someone finds Barnhouse, there is no defense against the Barnhouse Effect." Efforts to "jam" or block the radiations have failed. Premier Slezak could have saved himself the fantastic expense of his "Barnhouseproof" shelter. Despite the shelter's twelve-foot-thick lead armor, the premier has been floored twice while in it.

There is talk of screening the population for men potentially as powerful dynamopsychically as the professor. Senator Warren Foust demanded funds for this purpose last month, with the passionate declaration: "He who rules the Barnhouse Effect rules the world!" Commissar Kropotnik said much the same thing, so another costly armaments race, with a new twist, has begun.

This race at least has its comical aspects. The world's best gamblers are being coddled by governments like so many nuclear physicists. There may be several hundred persons with dynamopsychic talent on earth, myself included. But, without knowledge of the professor's technique, they can never be anything but dice-table despots. With the secret, it would probably take them ten years to become dangerous weapons. It took the professor that long. He who rules the Barnhouse Effect is Barnhouse and will be for some time.

Popularly, the "Age of Barnhouse" is said to have begun a year and a half ago, on the day of Operation Brainstorm. That was when dynamopsychism became significant politically. Actually, the phenomenon was discovered in May, 1942, shortly after the professor turned down a direct commission in the Army and enlisted as an artillery private. Like X-rays and vulcanized rubber, dynamopsychism was discovered by accident.

From time to time Private Barnhouse was invited to take part in games of chance by his barrack mates. He knew nothing about the games, and usually begged off. But one evening, out of social grace, he agreed to shoot craps. It was terrible or wonderful that he played, depending upon whether or not you like the world as it now is.

"Shoot sevens, Pop," someone said.

So "Pop" shot sevens—ten in a row to bankrupt the barracks. He retired to his bunk and, at a mathematical exercise, calculated the odds against his feat on the back of a laundry slip. His chances of doing it, he found, were one in almost ten million! Bewildered, he borrowed a pair of dice from the man in the bunk next to his. He tried to roll sevens again, but got only the usual assortment of numbers. He lay back for a moment, then resumed his toying with the dice. He rolled ten more sevens in a row.

He might have dismissed the phenomenon with a low whistle. But the professor instead mulled over the circumstances surrounding his two lucky streaks. There was one single factor in common: on both occasions, *the same thought train had flashed through his mind just before he threw the dice.* It was that thought train which aligned the professor's brain cells into what has since become the most powerful weapon on earth.

The soldier in the next bunk gave dynamopsychism its first token of respect. In an understatement certain to bring wry smiles to the faces of the world's dejected demagogues, the soldier said, "You're hotter'n a two-dollar pistol, Pop." Professor Barnhouse was all of that. The dice that did his bidding weighed but a few grams, so the forces involved were minute; but the unmistakable fact that there were such forces was earth-shaking.

Professional caution kept him from

revealing his discovery immediately. He wanted more facts and a body of theory to go with them. Later, when the atomic bomb was dropped on Hiroshima, it was fear that made him hold his peace. At no time were his experiments, as Premier Slezak called them, "a bourgeois plot to shackle the true democracies of the world." The professor didn't know where they were leading.

In time, he came to recognize another startling feature of dynamopsychism: *its strength increased with use*. Within six months, he was able to govern dice thrown by men the length of a barracks distant. By the time of his discharge in 1945, he could knock bricks loose from chimneys three miles away.

Charges that Professor Barnhouse could have won the last war in a minute, but did not care to do so, are perfectly senseless. When the war ended, he had the range and power of a 37-millimeter cannon, perhaps—certainly no more. His dynamopsychic powers graduated from the small-arms class only after his discharge and return to Wyandotte College.

I enrolled in the Wyandotte Graduate School two years after the professor had rejoined the faculty. By chance, he was assigned as my thesis adviser. I was unhappy about the assignment, for the professor was, in the eyes of both colleagues and students, a somewhat ridiculous figure. He missed classes or had lapses of memory during lectures. When I arrived, in fact, his shortcomings had passed from the ridiculous to the intolerable.

"We're assigning you to Barnhouse as a sort of temporary thing," the dean of social studies told me. He looked apologetic and perplexed. "Brilliant man, Barnhouse, I guess. Difficult to know since his return, perhaps, but his work before the war brought a great deal of credit to our little school."

When I reported to the professor's laboratory for the first time, what I saw was more distressing than the gossip. Every surface in the room was covered with dust; books and apparatus had not been disturbed for months. The professor sat napping at his desk when I entered. The only signs of recent activity were three overflowing ashtrays, a pair of scissors, and a morning paper with several items clipped from its front page.

As he raised his head to look at me, I saw that his eyes were clouded with fatigue. "Hi," he said, "just can't seem to get my sleeping done at night." He lighted a cigarette, his hands trembling slightly. "You the young man I'm supposed to help with a thesis?"

"Yes, sir," I said. In minutes he converted my misgivings to alarm.

"You an overseas veteran?" he asked.

"Yes, sir."

"Not much left over there, is there?" He frowned. "Enjoy the last war?"

"No, sir."

"Look like another war to you?"

"Kind of, sir."

"What can be done about it?"

I shrugged. "Looks pretty hopeless."

He peered at me intently. "Know anything about international law, the U.N., and all that?"

"Only what I pick up from the papers."

"Same here," he sighed. He showed me a fat scrapbook packed with newspaper clippings. "Never used to pay any attention to international politics. Now I study them the way I used to study rats in mazes. Everybody tells me the same thing—'Looks hopeless.'"

"Nothing short of a miracle—" I began.

"Believe in magic?" he asked sharply. The professor fished two dice from his vest pocket. "I will try to roll twos," he said. He rolled twos three times in a row. "One chance in about 47,000 of that happening. There's a miracle for you." He beamed for an instant, then brought the interview to an end, remarking that he had a class which had begun ten minutes ago.

He was not quick to take me into his confidence, and he said no more about his trick with the dice. I assumed they were loaded, and forgot about them. He set me the task of watching male rats cross electrified metal strips to get to food or female rats—an experiment that had been done to everyone's satisfaction in the nineteen-thirties. As though the pointlessness of my work were not bad enough, the professor annoyed me further with irrelevant questions. His favorites were: "Think we should have dropped the atomic bomb on Hiroshima?" and "Think every new piece of scientific information is a good thing for humanity?"

However, I did not feel put upon for long. "Give those poor animals a holiday," he said one morning, after I had been with him only a month. "I wish you'd help me look into a more interesting problem—namely, my sanity."

I returned the rats to their cages.

"What you must do is simple," he said, speaking softly. "Watch the inkwell on my desk. If you see nothing happen to it, say so, and I'll go quietly—relieved, I might add—to the nearest sanitarium."

I nodded uncertainly.

He locked the laboratory door and drew the blinds, so that we were in twilight for a moment. "I'm odd, I know," he said. "It's fear of myself that's made me odd."

"I've found you somewhat eccentric, perhaps, but certainly not—"

"If nothing happens to that inkwell, 'crazy as a bedbug' is the only description of me that will do," he interrupted, turning on the overhead lights. His eyes narrowed. "To give you an idea of how crazy, I'll tell you what's been running through my mind when I should have been sleeping. I think maybe I can save the world. I think maybe I can make every nation a *have* nation, and do away with war for good. I think maybe I can clear roads through jungles, irrigate deserts, build dams overnight."

"Yes, sir."

"Watch the inkwell!"

Dutifully and fearfully I watched. A high-pitched humming seemed to come from the inkwell; then it began to vibrate alarmingly, and finally to bound about the top of the desk, making two noisy circuits. It stopped, hummed again, glowed red, then popped in splinters with a blue-green flash.

Perhaps my hair stood on end. The professor laughed gently. "Magnets?" I managed to say at last.

"Wish to heaven it were magnets," he murmured. It was then that he told me of dynamopsychism. He knew only that there was such a force; he could not explain it. "It's me and me alone—and it's awful."

"I'd say it was amazing and wonderful!" I cried.

"If all I could do was make inkwells dance, I'd be tickled silly with the whole business." He shrugged disconsolately. "But I'm no toy, my boy. If you like, we can drive around the neighborhood, and I'll show you what I mean." He told me about pulverized boulders, shattered oaks, and abandoned farm buildings demolished within a fifty-mile radius of the campus. "Did every bit of it sitting right here, just thinking—not even thinking hard."

He scratched his head nervously. "I have never dared to concentrate as hard as I can for fear of the damage I might do. I'm to the point where a mere whim is a blockbuster." There was a depressing pause. "Up until a few days ago, I've thought it best to keep my secret for fear of what use it might be put to," he continued. "Now I realize that I haven't any more right to it than a man has a right to own an atomic bomb."

He fumbled through a heap of papers. "This says about all that needs to be said, I think." He handed me a draft of a letter to the Secretary of State.

Dear Sir:

I have discovered a new force which costs nothing to use, and which is probably more important than atomic energy. I should like to see it used most effectively in the cause of peace, and am, therefore, requesting your advice as to how this might best be done.

Yours truly,
A. Barnhouse.

"I have no idea what will happen next," said the professor.

There followed three months of perpetual nightmare, wherein the nation's political and military great came at all hours to watch the professor's tricks.

We were quartered in an old mansion near Charlottesville, Virginia, to which we had been whisked five days after the letter was mailed. Surrounded by barbed wire and twenty guards, we were labeled "Project Wishing Well," and were classified as Top Secret.

For companionship we had General Honus Barker and the State Department's William K. Cuthrell. For the professor's talk of peace-through-plenty they had indulgent smiles and much discourse on practical measures and realistic thinking. So treated, the professor, who had at first been almost meek, progressed in a matter of weeks toward stubbornness.

He had agreed to reveal the thought train by means of which he aligned his mind into a dynamopsychic transmitter. But, under Cuthrell's and Barker's nagging to do so, he began to hedge. At first he declared that the information could be passed on simply by word of mouth. Later he said that it would have to be written up in a long report. Finally, at dinner one night, just after General Barker had read the secret orders for Operation Brainstorm, the professor announced, "The report may take as long as five years to write." He looked fiercely at the general. "Maybe twenty."

The dismay occasioned by this flat announcement was offset somewhat by the exciting anticipation of Operation Brainstorm. The general was in a holiday mood. "The target ships are on their way to the Caroline Islands at this very moment," he declared ecstatically. "One hundred and twenty of them! At the same time, ten V-2s are being readied for firing in New Mexico, and fifty radio-controlled jet bombers are being equipped for a mock attack on the Aleutians. Just think of it!" Happily he reviewed his orders. "At exactly 1100 hours next Wednesday, I will give you the order to *concentrate;* and you, professor, will think as hard as you can about sinking the target ships, destroying the V-2s before they hit the ground, and knocking down the bombers before they reach the Aleutians! Think you can handle it?"

The professor turned gray and closed his eyes. "As I told you before, my friend, I don't know what I can do." He added bitterly, "As for this Operation Brainstorm, I was never consulted about it, and it strikes me as childish and insanely expensive."

General Barker bridled. "Sir," he said, "your field is psychology, and I wouldn't presume to give you advice in that field. Mine is national defense. I have had thirty years of experience and success, Professor, and I'll ask you not to criticize my judgment."

The professor appealed to Mr. Cuthrell. "Look," he pleaded, "isn't it war and military matters we're all trying to get rid of? Wouldn't it be a whole lot more significant and lots cheaper for me to try moving cloud masses into drought areas, and things like that? I admit I know next to nothing about international politics, but it seems reasonable to suppose that nobody would want to fight wars if there were enough of everything to go around. Mr. Cuthrell, I'd like to try running generators where there isn't any coal or water power, irrigating deserts, and so on. Why, you could figure out what each country needs to make the most of its resources, and I could give it to them without costing American taxpayers a penny."

"Eternal vigilance is the price of freedom," said the general heavily.

Mr. Cuthrell threw the general a look of mild distaste. "Unfortunately, the general is right in his own way," he said. "I wish to heaven the world were ready for ideals like yours, but it simply isn't. We aren't surrounded by brothers, but by enemies. It isn't a lack of food or resources that has us on the brink of war —it's a struggle for power. Who's going to be in charge of the world, our kind of people or theirs?"

The professor nodded in reluctant agreement and arose from the table. "I beg your pardon, gentlemen. You are, after all, better qualified to judge what is best for the country. I'll do whatever you say." He turned to me. "Don't forget to wind the restricted clock and put the confidential cat out," he said gloomily, and ascended the stairs to his bedroom.

For reasons of national security, Operation Brainstorm was carried on without the knowledge of the American citizenry which was paying the bill. The observers, technicians, and military men involved in the activity knew that a test was under way—a test of what, they had no idea. Only thirty-seven key men, myself included, knew what was afoot.

In Virginia, the day for Operation Brainstorm was unseasonably cool. Inside, a log fire crackled in the fireplace, and the flames were reflected in the polished metal cabinets that lined the living room. All that remained of the room's lovely old furniture was a Victorian love seat, set squarely in the center of the floor, facing three television receivers. One long bench had been brought in for the ten of us privileged to watch. The television screens showed, from left to right, the stretch of desert which was the rocket target, the guinea-pig fleet, and a section of the Aleutian sky through which the radio-controlled bomber formation would roar.

Ninety minutes before H-hour the radios announced that the rockets were ready, that the observation ships had backed away to what was thought to be a safe distance, and that the bombers were on their way. The small Virginia audience lined up on the bench in order of rank, smoked a great deal, and said little. Professor Barnhouse was in his bedroom. General Barker bustled about the house like a woman preparing Thanksgiving dinner for twenty.

At ten minutes before H-hour the general came in, shepherding the professor before him. The professor was comfortably attired in sneakers, gray flannels, a blue sweater, and a white shirt open at the neck. The two of them sat side by side on the love seat. The general was rigid and perspiring; the professor was cheerful. He looked at each of the screens, lighted a cigarette and settled back.

"Bombers sighted!" cried the Aleutian observers.

"Rockets away!" barked the New Mexico radio operator.

All of us looked quickly at the big elec-

tric clock over the mantel, while the professor, a half-smile on his face, continued to watch the television sets. In hollow tones, the general counted away the seconds remaining. "Five . . . four . . . three . . . two . . . one . . . *Concentrate!*"

Professor Barnhouse closed his eyes, pursed his lips, and stroked his temples. He held the position for a minute. The television images were scrambled, and the radio signals were drowned in the din of Barnhouse static. The professor sighed, opened his eyes, and smiled confidently.

"Did you give it everything you had?" asked the general dubiously.

"I was wide open," the professor replied.

The television images pulled themselves together, and mingled cries of amazement came over the radios tuned to the observers. The Aleutian sky was streaked with the smoke trails of bombers screaming down in flames. Simultaneously, there appeared high over the rocket target a cluster of white puffs, followed by faint thunder.

General Barker shook his head happily. "By George!" he crowed. "Well, sir, by George, by George, by George!"

"Look!" shouted the admiral seated next to me. "The fleet—it wasn't touched!"

"The guns seem to be drooping," said Mr. Cuthrell.

We left the bench and clustered about the television sets to examine the damage more closely. What Mr. Cuthrell had said was true. The ships' guns curved downward, their muzzles resting on the steel decks. We in Virginia were making such a hullabaloo that it was impossible to hear the radio reports. We were so engrossed, in fact, that we didn't miss the professor until two short snarls of Barnhouse static shocked us into sudden silence. The radios went dead.

We looked around apprehensively. The professor was gone. A harassed guard threw open the front door from the outside to yell that the professor had escaped. He brandished his pistol in the direction of the gates, which hung open, limp and twisted. In the distance, a speeding government station wagon topped a ridge and dropped from sight into the valley beyond. The air was filled with choking smoke, for every vehicle on the grounds was ablaze. Pursuit was impossible.

"What in God's name got into him?" bellowed the general.

Mr. Cuthrell, who had rushed out onto the front porch, now slouched back into the room, reading a penciled note as he came. He thrust the note into my hands. "The good man left this billet-doux under the door knocker. Perhaps our young friend will be kind enough to read it to you gentlemen, while I take a restful walk through the woods."

"*Gentlemen,*" I read aloud, "*As the first superweapon with a conscience, I am removing myself from your national defense stockpile. Setting a new precedent in the behavior of ordnance, I have humane reasons for going off. A. Barnhouse.*"

Since that day, of course, the professor has been systematically destroying the world's armaments, until there is now little with which to equip an army other than rocks and sharp sticks. His activities haven't exactly resulted in peace, but have, rather, precipitated a bloodless and entertaining sort of war that might be called the "War of the Tattletales." Every nation is flooded with enemy agents whose sole mission is to locate military equipment, which is promptly wrecked when it is brought to the professor's attention in the press.

Just as every day brings news of more armaments pulverized by dynamopsychism, so has it brought rumors of the professor's whereabouts. During last week alone, three publications carried articles proving variously that he was hiding in an Inca ruin in the Andes, in the sewers of Paris, and in the unexplored lower chambers of Carlsbad Caverns. Knowing the man, I am inclined to regard such hiding places as unnecessarily romantic and uncomfortable. While there are numerous persons eager to kill him, there must be millions who would care for him and hide him. I like

to think that he is in the home of such a person.

One thing is certain: at this writing, Professor Barnhouse is not dead. Barnhouse static jammed broadcasts not ten minutes ago. In the eighteen months since his disappearance, he has been reported dead some half-dozen times. Each report has stemmed from the death of an unidentified man resembling the professor, during a period free of the static. The first three reports were followed at once by renewed talk of rearmament and recourse to war. The saber-rattlers have learned how imprudent premature celebrations of the professor's demise can be.

Many a stouthearted patriot has found himself prone in the tangled bunting and timbers of a smashed reviewing stand, seconds after having announced that the arch-tyranny of Barnhouse was at an end. But those who would make war if they could, in every country in the world, wait in sullen silence for what must come—the passing of Professor Barnhouse.

To ask how much longer the professor will live is to ask how much longer we must wait for the blessings of another world war. He is of short-lived stock: his mother lived to be fifty-three, his father to be forty-nine; and the life-spans of his grandparents on both sides were of the same order. He might be expected to live, then, for perhaps fifteen years more, if he can remain hidden from his enemies. When one considers the number and vigor of these enemies, however, fifteen years seems an extraordinary length of time, which might better be revised to fifteen days, hours, or minutes.

The professor knows that he cannot live much longer. I say this because of the message left in my mailbox on Christmas Eve. Unsigned, typewritten on a soiled scrap of paper, the note consisted of ten sentences. The first nine of these, each a bewildering tangle of psychological jargon and references to obscure texts, made no sense to me at first reading. The tenth, unlike the rest, was simply constructed and contained no large words—but its irrational content made it the most puzzling and bizarre sentence of all. I nearly threw the note away, thinking it a colleague's warped notion of a practical joke. For some reason, though, I added it to the clutter on top of my desk, which included, among other mementos, the professor's dice.

It took me several weeks to realize that the message really meant something, that the first nine sentences, when unsnarled, could be taken as instructions. The tenth still told me nothing. It was only last night that I discovered how it fitted in with the rest. The sentence appeared in my thoughts last night, while I was toying absently with the professor's dice.

I promised to have this report on its way to the publishers today. In view of what has happened, I am obliged to break that promise, or release the report incomplete. The delay will not be a long one, for one of the few blessings accorded a bachelor like myself is the ability to move quickly from one abode to another, or from one way of life to another. What property I want to take with me can be packed in a few hours. Fortunately, I am not without substantial private means, which may take as long as a week to realize in liquid and anonymous form. When this is done, I shall mail the report.

I have just returned from a visit to my doctor, who tells me my health is excellent. I am young, and, with any luck at all, I shall live to a ripe old age indeed, for my family on both sides is noted for longevity.

Briefly, I propose to vanish.

Sooner or later, Professor Barnhouse must die. But long before then I shall be ready. So, to the saber-rattlers of today —and even, I hope, of tomorrow—I say: Be advised. Barnhouse will die. But not the Barnhouse Effect.

Last night, I tried once more to follow the oblique instructions on the scrap of paper. I took the professor's dice, and then, with the last, nightmarish sentence flitting through my mind, I rolled fifty consecutive sevens.

Good-by.

[1950]

QUESTIONS FOR STUDY

1. *How does Vonnegut use the first paragraphs of the story to engage and develop reader interest?*
2. *On what aspects of contemporary society does Vonnegut focus his satire?*
3. *What contrasting sets of human values are embodied in General Barker and Professor Barnhouse?*
4. *Why does Professor Barnhouse eventually decide to disappear? Why is the fact of his disappearance ironic?*
5. *What are the implications of the story's conclusion?*
6. *What are the advantages in having the story narrated in the first person by a young protégé of Professor Barnhouse's?*

H. G. WELLS

The Country of the Blind

THREE hundred miles and more from Chimborazo, one hundred from the snows of Cotopaxi, in the wildest wastes of Ecuador's Andes, there lies that mysterious mountain valley, cut off from the world of men, the Country of the Blind. Long years ago that valley lay so far open to the world that men might come at last through frightful gorges and over an icy pass into its equable meadows; and thither indeed men came, a family or so of Peruvian half-breeds fleeing from the lust and tyranny of an evil Spanish ruler. Then came the stupendous outbreak of Mindobamba, when it was night in Quito for seventeen days, and the water was boiling at Yaguachi and all the fish floating dying even as far as Guayaquil; everywhere along the Pacific slopes there were land-slips and swift thawings and sudden floods, and one whole side of the old Arauca crest slipped and came down in thunder, and cut off the Country of the Blind for ever from the exploring feet of men. But one of these early settlers had chanced to be on the hither side of the gorges when the world had so terribly shaken itself, and he perforce had to forget his wife and his child and all the friends and possessions he had left up there, and start life over again in the lower world. He started it again but ill, blindness overtook him, and he died of punishment in the mines; but the story he told begot a legend that lingers along the length of the Cordilleras of the Andes to this day.

He told of his reason for venturing back from that fastness, into which he had first been carried lashed to a llama, beside a vast bale of gear, when he was a child. The valley, he said, had in it all that the heart of man could desire—sweet water, pasture, and even climate, slopes of rich brown soil with tangles of a shrub that bore an excellent fruit, and on one side great hanging forests of pine that held the avalanches high. Far overhead, on three sides, vast cliffs of grey-green rock were capped by cliffs of ice; but the glacier stream came not to them but flowed away by the farther slopes, and only now and then huge ice masses fell on the valley side. In this valley it neither rained nor snowed, but the abundant springs gave a rich green pasture, that irrigation would spread over all the valley space. The settlers did well indeed there. Their beasts did well and multiplied, and but one thing marred their happiness. Yet it was enough to mar it greatly. A strange disease had come upon them, and had made all the children born to them there—and, indeed, several older children also—blind. It was to seek some charm or antidote against this plague of blindness that he had with fatigue and danger and difficulty returned down the gorge. In those days, in such cases, men did not think of germs and infections but of sins; and it seemed to him that the reason of this affliction must lie in the negligence of these priestless immigrants to set up a shrine so soon as they entered the valley. He wanted a shrine—a handsome, cheap, effectual shrine—to be erected in the valley; he wanted relics and such-like potent things of faith, blessed objects and mysterious medals and prayers. In his wallet he had a bar of native silver for which he would not account; he insisted there was none in the valley with something of the insistence of an inexpert liar. They had all clubbed their money and ornaments together, having little need for such treasure up there, he said, to buy them holy help against their ill. I figure this dim-eyed young mountaineer, sunburnt, gaunt, and anxious, hat-brim clutched feverishly, a man all unused to the ways of the lower world, telling this story to some keen-eyed, attentive priest before the great convulsion; I can picture him presently seeking to return with pious and infallible remedies against that trouble, and the infinite dismay with which he must have faced the tumbled vastness where the gorge had once come out. But the rest of his story of mischances is lost to me, save that I know of his evil death after several years. Poor stray from that remoteness! The stream that had once made the gorge now bursts from the mouth of a rocky cave, and the legend his poor, ill-told story set going developed into the legend of a race of blind men somewhere "over there" one may still hear to-day.

And amidst the little population of that now isolated and forgotten valley the disease ran its course. The old became groping and purblind, the young saw but dimly, and the children that were born to them saw never at all. But life was very easy in that snow-rimmed basin, lost to all the world, with neither thorns nor briars, with no evil insects nor any beasts save the gentle breed of llamas they had lugged and thrust and followed up the beds of the shrunken rivers in the gorges up which they had come. The seeing had become purblind so gradually that they scarcely noted their loss. They guided the sightless youngsters hither and thither until they knew the whole valley marvellously, and when at last sight died out among them the race lived on. They had even time to adapt themselves to the control of fire, which they made carefully in stoves of stone. They were a simple strain of people at the first, unlettered, only slightly touched with the Spanish civilisation, but with something of a tradition of the arts of old Peru and of its lost philosophy. Generation followed generation. They forgot many things; they devised many things. Their tradition of the greater world they came from became mythical in colour and uncertain. In all things save sight they were strong and able; and presently the chance

of birth and heredity sent one who had an original mind and who could talk and persuade among them, and then afterwards another. These two passed, leaving their effects, and the little community grew in numbers and in understanding, and met and settled social and economic problems that arose. Generation followed generation. Generation followed generation. There came a time when a child was born who was fifteen generations from that ancestor who went out of the valley with a bar of silver to seek God's aid, and who never returned. Thereabouts it chanced that a man came into this community from the outer world. And this is the story of that man.

He was a mountaineer from the country near Quito, a man who had been down to the sea and had seen the world, a reader of books in an original way, an acute and enterprising man, and he was taken on by a party of Englishmen who had come out to Ecuador to climb mountains, to replace one of their three Swiss guides who had fallen ill. He climbed here and he climbed there, and then came the attempt on Parascotopetl, the Matterhorn of the Andes, in which he was lost to the outer world. The story of the accident has been written a dozen times. Pointer's narrative is the best. He tells how the party worked their difficult and almost vertical way up to the very foot of the last and greatest precipice, and how they built a night shelter amidst the snow upon a little shelf of rock, and, with a touch of real dramatic power, how presently they found Nunez had gone from them. They shouted, and there was no reply; shouted and whistled, and for the rest of that night they slept no more.

As the morning broke they saw the traces of his fall. It seems impossible he could have uttered a sound. He had slipped eastward towards the unknown side of the mountain; far below he had struck a steep slope of snow, and ploughed his way down it in the midst of a snow avalanche. His track went straight to the edge of a frightful precipice, and beyond that everything was hidden. Far, far below, and hazy with distance, they could see trees rising out of a narrow, shut-in valley—the lost Country of the Blind. But they did not know it was the lost Country of the Blind, nor distinguish it in any way from any other narrow streak of upland valley. Unnerved by the disaster, they abandoned their attempt in the afternoon, and Pointer was called away to the war before he could make another attack. To this day Parascotopetl lifts an unconquered crest, and Pointer's shelter crumbles unvisited amidst the snows.

And the man who fell survived.

At the end of the slope he fell a thousand feet, and came down in the midst of a cloud of snow upon a snow slope even steeper than the one above. Down this he was whirled, stunned and insensible, but without a bone broken in his body; and then at last came to gentler slopes, and at last rolled out and lay still, buried amidst a softening heap of the white masses that had accompanied and saved him. He came to himself with a dim fancy that he was ill in bed; then realised his position with a mountaineer's intelligence and, after a rest or so, out until he saw the stars. He rested flat upon his chest for a space, wondering where he was and what had happened to him. He explored his limbs, and discovered that several of his buttons were gone and his coat turned over his head. His knife had gone from his pocket, and his hat was lost, though he had tied it under his chin. He recalled that he had been looking for loose stones to raise his piece of the shelter wall. His ice-axe had disappeared.

He decided he must have fallen, and looked up to see, exaggerated by the ghastly light of the rising moon, the tremendous flight he had taken. For a while he lay, gazing blankly at that vast pale cliff towering above, rising moment by moment out of a subsiding tide of darkness. Its phantasmal, mysterious beauty held him for a space, and then he was seized with a paroxysm of sobbing laughter. . . .

After a great interval of time he became aware that he was near the lower edge of the snow. Below, down what was now a moonlit and practicable slope, he saw the dark and broken appearance of rock-strewn turf. He struggled to his feet, aching in every joint and limb, got down painfully from the heaped loose snow about him, went downward until he was on the turf, and there dropped rather than lay beside a boulder, drank deep from the flask in his inner pocket, and instantly fell asleep. . . .

He was awakened by the singing of birds in the trees far below.

He sat up and perceived he was on a little alp at the foot of a vast precipice, that was grooved by the gully down which he and his snow had come. Over against him another wall of rock reared itself against the sky. The gorge between these precipices ran east and west and was full of the morning sunlight, which lit to the westward the mass of fallen mountain that closed the descending gorge. Below him it seemed there was a precipice equally steep, but behind the snow in the gully he found a sort of chimney-cleft dripping with snow-water down which a desperate man might venture. He found it easier than it seemed, and came at last to another desolate alp, and then after a rock climb of no particular difficulty to a steep slope of trees. He took his bearings and turned his face up the gorge, for he saw it opened out above upon green meadows, among which he now glimpsed quite distinctly a cluster of stone huts of unfamiliar fashion. At times his progress was like clambering along the face of a wall, and after a time the rising sun ceased to strike along the gorge, the voices of the singing birds died away, and the air grew cold and dark above him. But the distant valley with its houses was all the brighter for that. He came presently to talus, and among the rocks he noted—for he was an observant man—an unfamiliar fern that seemed to clutch out of the crevices with intense green hands. He picked a frond or so and gnawed its stalk and found it helpful.

About midday he came at last out of the throat of the gorge into the plain and the sunlight. He was stiff and weary; he sat down in the shadow of a rock, filled up his flask with water from a spring and drank it down, and remained for a time resting before he went on to the houses.

They were very strange to his eyes, and indeed the whole aspect of that valley became, as he regarded it, queerer and more unfamiliar. The greater part of its surface was lush green meadow, starred with many beautiful flowers, irrigated with extraordinary care, and bearing evidence of systematic cropping piece by piece. High up and ringing the valley about was a wall, and what appeared to be a circumferential water-channel, from which the little trickles of water that fed the meadow plants came, and on the higher slopes above this flocks of llamas cropped the scanty herbage. Sheds, apparently shelters or feeding-places for the llamas, stood against the boundary wall here and there. The irrigation streams ran together into a main channel down the centre of the valley, and this was enclosed on either side by a wall breast high. This gave a singularly urban quality to this secluded place, a quality that was greatly enhanced by the fact that a number of paths paved with black and white stones, and each with a curious little kerb at the side, ran hither and thither in an orderly manner. The houses of the central village were quite unlike the casual and higgledy-piggledy agglomeration of the mountain villages he knew; they stood in a continuous row on either side of a central street of astonishing cleanness; here and there their parti-coloured façade was pierced by a door, and not a solitary window broke their even frontage. They were parti-coloured with extraordinary irregularity; smeared with a sort of plaster that was sometimes grey, sometimes drab, sometimes slate-coloured or dark brown; and it was the sight of this wild plastering first brought the word "blind" into the thoughts of the explorer. "The good man who did that," he thought, "must have been as blind as a bat."

He descended a steep place, and so came to the wall and channel that ran about the valley, near where the latter spouted out its surplus contents into the deeps of the gorge in a thin and wavering thread of cascade. He could now see a number of men and women resting on piled heaps of grass, as if taking a siesta, in the remoter part of the meadow, and nearer the village a number of recumbent children, and then nearer at hand three men carrying pails on yokes along a little path that ran from the encircling wall towards the houses. These latter were clad in garments of llama cloth and boots and belts of leather, and they wore caps of cloth with back and ear flaps. They followed one another in single file, walking slowly and yawning as they walked, like men who have been up all night. There was something so reassuringly prosperous and respectable in their bearing that after a moment's hesitation Nunez stood forward as conspicuously as possible upon his rock, and gave vent to a mighty shout that echoed round the valley.

The three men stopped, and moved their heads as though they were looking about them. They turned their faces this way and that, and Nunez gesticulated with freedom. But they did not appear to see him for all his gestures, and after a time, directing themselves towards the mountains far away to the right, they shouted as if in answer. Nunez bawled again, and then once more, and as he gestured ineffectually the word "blind" came up to the top of his thoughts. "The fools must be blind," he said.

When at last, after much shouting and wrath, Nunez crossed the stream by a little bridge, came through a gate in the wall, and approached them, he was sure that they were blind. He was sure that this was the Country of the Blind of which the legends told. Conviction had sprung upon him, and a sense of great and rather enviable adventure. The three stood side by side, not looking at him, but with their ears directed towards him, judging him by his unfamiliar steps. They stood close together like men a little afraid, and he could see their eyelids closed and sunken, as though the very balls beneath had shrunk away. There was an expression near awe on their faces.

"A man," one said, in hardly recognisable Spanish—"a man it is—a man or a spirit—coming down from the rocks."

But Nunez advanced with the confident steps of a youth who enters upon life. All the old stories of the lost valley and the Country of the Blind had come back to his mind, and through his thoughts ran this old proverb, as if it were a refrain—

"In the Country of the Blind the One-eyed Man is King."

"In the Country of the Blind the One-eyed Man is King."

And very civilly he gave them greeting. He talked to them and used his eyes.

"Where does he come from, brother Pedro?" asked one.

"Down out of the rocks."

"Over the mountains I come," said Nunez, "out of the country beyond there—where men can see. From near Bogota, where there are a hundred thousands of people, and where the city passes out of sight."

"Sight?" muttered Pedro. "Sight?"

"He comes," said the second blind man, "out of the rocks."

The cloth of their coats Nunez saw was curiously fashioned, each with a different sort of stitching.

They startled him by a simultaneous movement towards him, each with a hand outstretched. He stepped back from the advance of these spread fingers.

"Come hither," said the third blind man, following his motion and clutching him neatly.

And they held Nunez and felt him over, saying no word further until they had done so.

"Carefully," he cried, with a finger in his eye, and found they thought that organ, with its fluttering lids, a queer thing in him. They went over it again.

"A strange creature, Correa," said the one called Pedro. "Feel the coarseness of his hair. Like a llama's hair."

"Rough he is as the rocks that begot him," said Correa, investigating Nunez's unshaven chin with a soft and slightly moist hand. "Perhaps he will grow finer." Nunez struggled a little under their examination, but they gripped him firm.

"Carefully," he said again.

"He speaks," said the third man. "Certainly he is a man."

"Ugh!" said Pedro, at the roughness of his coat.

"And you have come into the world?" asked Pedro.

"*Out* of the world. Over mountains and glaciers; right over above there, half-way to the sun. Out of the great big world that goes down, twelve days' journey to the sea."

They scarcely seemed to heed him. "Our fathers have told us men may be made by the forces of Nature," said Correa. "It is the warmth of things and moisture, and rottenness—rottenness."

"Let us lead him to the elders," said Pedro.

"Shout first," said Correa, "lest the children be afraid. This is a marvellous occasion."

So they shouted, and Pedro went first and took Nunez by the hand to lead him to the houses.

He drew his hand away. "I can see," he said.

"See?" said Correa.

"Yes, see," said Nunez, turning towards him, and stumbled against Pedro's pail.

"His senses are still imperfect," said the third blind man. "He stumbles, and talks unmeaning words. Lead him by the hand."

"As you will," said Nunez, and was led along, laughing.

It seemed they knew nothing of sight.

Well, all in good time he would teach them.

He heard people shouting, and saw a number of figures gathering together in the middle roadway of the village.

He found it taxed his nerve and patience more than he had anticipated, that first encounter with the population of the Country of the Blind. The place seemed larger as he drew near to it, and the smeared plasterings queerer, and a crowd of children and men and women (the women and girls, he was pleased to note, had some of them quite sweet faces, for all that their eyes were shut and sunken) came about him, holding on to him, touching him with soft, sensitive hands, smelling at him, and listening at every word he spoke. Some of the maidens and children, however, kept aloof as if afraid, and indeed his voice seemed coarse and rude beside their softer notes. They mobbed him. His three guides kept close to him with an effect of proprietorship, and said again and again, "A wild man out of the rocks."

"Bogota," he said. "Bogota. Over the mountain crests."

"A wild man—using wild words," said Pedro. "Did you hear that—*Bogota?* His mind is hardly formed yet. He has only the beginnings of speech."

A little boy nipped his hand. "Bogota!" he said mockingly.

"Ay! A city to your village. I come from the great world—where men have eyes and see."

"His name's Bogota," they said.

"He stumbled," said Correa; "stumbled twice as we came hither."

"Bring him to the elders."

And they thrust him suddenly through a doorway into a room as black as pitch, save at the end there faintly glowed a fire. The crowd closed in behind him and shut out all but the faintest glimmer of day, and before he could arrest himself he had fallen headlong over the feet of a seated man. His arm, outflung, struck the face of someone else as he went down; he felt the soft impact of features and heard a cry of anger, and for a moment he struggled against a number of hands that clutched him. It was a one-sided fight. An inkling of the situation came to him, and he lay quiet.

"I fell down," he said; "I couldn't see in this pitchy darkness."

There was a pause as if the unseen persons about him tried to understand his words. Then the voice of Correa said: "He is but newly formed. He stumbles as he walks and mingles words that mean nothing with his speech."

Others also said things about him that he heard or understood imperfectly.

"May I sit up?" he asked, in a pause. "I will not struggle against you again."

They consulted and let him rise.

The voice of an older man began to question him, and Nunez found himself trying to explain the great world out of which he had fallen, and the sky and mountains and sight and such-like marvels, to these elders who sat in darkness in the Country of the Blind. And they would believe and understand nothing whatever he told them, a thing quite outside his expectation. They would not even understand many of his words. For fourteen generations these people had been blind and cut off from all the seeing world; the names for all the things of sight had faded and changed; the story of the outer world was faded and changed to a child's story; and they had ceased to concern themselves with anything beyond the rocky slopes above their circling wall. Blind men of genius had arisen among them and questioned the shreds of belief and tradition they had brought with them from their seeing days, and had dismissed all these things as idle fancies, and replaced them with new and saner explanations. Much of their imagination had shrivelled with their eyes, and they had made for themselves new imaginations with their ever more sensitive ears and finger-tips. Slowly Nunez realised this; that his expectation of wonder and reverence at his origin and his gifts was not to be borne out; and after his poor attempt to explain sight to them had been set aside as the confused version of a new-made being describing the marvels of his incoherent sensations, he subsided, a little dashed, into listening to their instruction. And the eldest of the blind men explained to him life and philosophy and religion, how that the world (meaning their valley) had been first an empty hollow in the rocks, and then had come, first, inanimate things without the gift of touch, and llamas and a few other creatures that had little sense, and then men, and at last angels, whom one could hear singing and making fluttering sounds, but whom no one could touch at all, which puzzled Nunez greatly until he thought of the birds.

He went on to tell Nunez how this time had been divided into the warm and the cold, which are the blind equivalents of day and night, and how it was good to sleep in the warm and work during the cold, so that now, but for his advent, the whole town of the blind would have been asleep. He said Nunez must have been specially created to learn and serve the wisdom they had acquired, and for that all his mental incoherency and stumbling behaviour he must have courage, and do his best to learn, and at that all the people in the doorway murmured encouragingly. He said the night—for the blind call their day night—was now far gone, and it behoved every one to go back to sleep. He asked Nunez if he knew how to sleep, and Nunez said he did, but that before sleep he wanted food.

They brought him food—llama's milk in a bowl, and rough salted bread—and led him into a lonely place to eat out of their hearing, and afterwards to slumber until the chill of the mountain evening roused them to begin their day again. But Nunez slumbered not at all.

Instead, he sat up in the place where they had left him, resting his limbs and turning the unanticipated circumstances of his arrival over and over in his mind.

Every now and then he laughed, sometimes with amusement, and sometimes with indignation.

"Unformed mind!" he said. "Got no senses yet! They little know they've been insulting their heaven-sent king and master. I see I must bring them to reason. Let me think—let me think."

He was still thinking when the sun set.

Nunez had an eye for all beautiful things, and it seemed to him that the glow upon the snowfields and glaciers that rose about the valley on every side was the most beautiful thing he had ever seen. His eyes went from that inaccessible glory to the village and irrigated fields, fast sinking into the twilight, and suddenly a wave of emotion took him, and he thanked God from the bottom of his heart that the power of sight had been given him.

He heard a voice calling to him from out of the village.

"Ya ho there, Bogota! Come hither!"

At that he stood up smiling. He would show these people once and for all what sight would do for a man. They would seek him, but not find him.

"You move not, Bogota," said the voice.

He laughed noiselessly, and made two stealthy steps aside from the path.

"Trample not on the grass, Bogota; that is not allowed."

Nunez had scarcely heard the sound he made himself. He stopped amazed.

The owner of the voice came running up the piebald path towards him.

He stepped back into the pathway. "Here I am," he said.

"Why did you not come when I called you?" said the blind man. "Must you be led like a child? Cannot you hear the path as you walk?"

Nunez laughed. "I can see it," he said.

"There is no such word as *see,*" said the blind man, after a pause. "Cease this folly, and follow the sound of my feet."

Nunez followed, a little annoyed.

"My time will come," he said.

"You'll learn," the blind man answered. "There is much to learn in the world."

"Has no one told you, 'In the Country of the Blind the One-eyed Man is King'?"

"What is blind?" asked the blind man carelessly over his shoulder.

Four days passed, and the fifth found the King of the Blind still incognito, as a clumsy and useless stranger among his subjects.

It was, he found, much more difficult to proclaim himself than he had supposed, and in the meantime, while he meditated his *coup d'état,* he did what he was told and learned the manners and customs of the Country of the Blind. He found working and going about at night a particularly irksome thing, and he decided that that should be the first thing he would change.

They led a simple, laborious life, these people, with all the elements of virtue and happiness, as these things can be understood by men. They toiled, but not oppressively; they had food and clothing sufficient for their needs; they had days and seasons of rest; they made much of music and singing, and there was love among them, and little children.

It was marvellous with what confidence and precision they went about their ordered world. Everything, you see, had been made to fit their needs; each of the radiating paths of the valley area had a constant angle to the others, and was distinguished by a special notch upon its kerbing; all obstacles and irregularities of path or meadow had long since been cleared away; all their methods and procedure arose naturally from their special needs. Their senses had become marvellously acute; they could hear and judge the slightest gesture of a man a dozen paces away—could hear the very beating of his heart. Intonation had long replaced expression with them, and touches gesture, and their work with hoe and spade and fork was as free and confident as garden work can be. Their sense of smell was extraordinarily fine; they could distinguish individual differences as readily as a dog can, and they went about the tending of the llamas, who lived among the rocks above and came to the wall for food and shelter, with ease and confidence. It was only when at last Nunez sought to assert himself that he found how easy and confident their movements could be.

He rebelled only after he had tried persuasion.

He tried at first on several occasions to tell them of sight. "Look you here, you people," he said. "There are things you do not understand in me."

Once or twice one or two of them attended to him; they sat with faces downcast and ears turned intelligently towards him, and he did his best to tell them what it was to see. Among his hearers was a girl, with eyelids less red and sunken than the others, so that one could almost fancy she was hiding eyes, whom especially he hoped to persuade. He spoke of the beauties of sight, of watching the mountains, of the sky and the sunrise, and they heard him with amused incredulity that presently became condemnatory. They told him there were indeed no mountains at all, but that the end of the rocks where the llamas grazed was indeed the end of the world; thence sprang a cavernous roof of the universe, from which the dew and the avalanches fell; and when he maintained stoutly the world had neither end nor roof such as

they supposed, they said his thoughts were wicked. So far as he could describe sky and clouds and stars to them it seemed to them a hideous void, a terrible blankness in the place of the smooth roof to things in which they believed—it was an article of faith with them that the cavern roof was exquisitely smooth to the touch. He saw that in some manner he shocked them, and gave up that aspect of the matter altogether, and tried to show them the practical value of sight. One morning he saw Pedro in the path called Seventeen and coming towards the central houses, but still too far off for hearing or scent, and he told them as much. "In a little while," he prophesied, "Pedro will be here." An old man remarked that Pedro had no business on path Seventeen, and then, as if in confirmation, that individual as he drew near turned and went transversely into path Ten, and so back with nimble paces towards the outer wall. They mocked Nunez when Pedro did not arrive, and afterwards, when he asked Pedro questions to clear his character, Pedro denied and outfaced him, and was afterwards hostile to him.

Then he induced them to let him go a long way up the sloping meadows towards the wall with one complacent individual, and to him he promised to describe all that happened among the houses. He noted certain goings and comings, but the things that really seemed to signify to these people happened inside of or behind the windowless houses —the only things they took note of to test him by—and of these he could see or tell nothing; and it was after the failure of this attempt, and the ridicule they could not repress, that he resorted to force. He thought of seizing a spade and suddenly smiting one or two of them to earth, and so in fair combat showing the advantage of eyes. He went so far with that resolution as to seize his spade, and then he discovered a new thing about himself, and that was that it was impossible for him to hit a blind man in cold blood.

He hesitated, and found them all aware that he snatched up the spade. They stood alert, with their heads on one side, and bent ears towards him for what he would do next.

"Put that spade down," said one, and he felt a sort of helpless horror. He came near obedience.

Then he thrust one backwards against a house wall, and fled past him and out of the village.

He went athwart one of their meadows, leaving a track of trampled grass behind his feet, and presently sat down by the side of one of their ways. He felt something of the buoyancy that comes to all men in the beginning of a fight, but more perplexity. He began to realise that you cannot even fight happily with creatures who stand upon a different mental basis to yourself. Far away he saw a number of men carrying spades and sticks come out of the street of houses, and advance in a spreading line along the several paths towards him. They advanced slowly, speaking frequently to one another, and ever and again the whole cordon would halt and sniff the air and listen.

The first time they did this Nunez laughed. But afterwards he did not laugh.

One struck his trail in the meadow grass, and came stooping and feeling his way along it.

For five minutes he watched the slow extension of the cordon, and then his vague disposition to do something forthwith became frantic. He stood up, went a pace or so towards the circumferential wall, turned, and went back a little way. There they all stood in a crescent, still and listening.

He also stood still, gripping his spade very tightly in both hands. Should he charge them?

The pulse in his ears ran into the rhythm of "In the Country of the Blind the One-eyed Man is King!"

Should he charge them?

He looked back at the high and unclimbable wall behind—unclimbable because of its smooth plastering, but withal pierced with many little doors, and at the approaching line of seekers. Behind these, others were now coming out of the street of houses.

Should he charge them?

"Bogota!" called one. "Bogota! where are you?"

He gripped his spade still tighter, and advanced down the meadows towards the place of habitations, and directly he moved they converged upon him. "I'll hit them if they touch me," he swore; "by Heaven, I will. I'll hit." He called aloud, "Look here, I'm going to do what I like in this valley. Do you hear? I'm going to do what I like and go where I like!"

They were moving in upon him quickly, groping, yet moving rapidly. It was like playing blind man's buff, with everyone blindfolded except one. "Get hold of him!" cried one. He found himself in the arc of a loose curve of pursuers. He felt suddenly he must be active and resolute.

"You don't understand," he cried in a voice that was meant to be great and resolute, and which broke. "You are blind, and I can see. Leave me alone!"

"Bogota! Put down that spade, and come off the grass!"

The last order, grotesque in its urban familiarity, produced a gust of anger.

"I'll hurt you," he said, sobbing with emotion. "By Heaven, I'll hurt you. Leave me alone!"

He began to run, not knowing clearly where to run. He ran from the nearest blind man, because it was a horror to hit him. He stopped, and then made a dash to escape from their closing ranks. He made for where a gap was wide, and the men on either side, with a quick perception of the approach of his paces, rushed in on one another. He sprang forward, and then saw he must be caught, and *swish!* the spade had struck. He felt the soft thud of hand and arm, and the man was down with a yell of pain, and he was through.

Through! And then he was close to the street of houses again, and blind men, whirling spades and stakes, were running with a sort of reasoned swiftness hither and thither.

He heard steps behind him just in time, and found a tall man rushing forward and swiping at the sound of him. He lost his nerve, hurled his spade a yard wide at his antagonist, and whirled about and fled, fairly yelling as he dodged another.

He was panic-stricken. He ran furiously to and fro, dodging when there was no need to dodge, and in his anxiety to see on every side of him at once, stumbling. For a moment, he was down and they heard his fall. Far away in the circumferential wall a little doorway looked like heaven, and he set off in a wild rush for it. He did not even look round at his pursuers until it was gained, and he had stumbled across the bridge, clambered a little way among the rocks, to the surprise and dismay of a young llama, who went leaping out of sight, and lay down sobbing for breath.

And so his *coup d'état* came to an end.

He stayed outside the wall of the valley of the Blind for two nights and days without food or shelter, and meditated upon the unexpected. During these meditations he repeated very frequently and always with a profounder note of derision the exploded proverb: "In the Country of the Blind the One-eyed Man is King." He thought chiefly of ways of fighting and conquering these people, and it grew clear that for him no practicable way was possible. He had no weapons, and now it would be hard to get one.

The canker of civilisation had got to him even in Bogota, and he could not find it in himself to go down and assassinate a blind man. Of course, if he did that, he might then dictate terms on the threat of assassinating them all. But—sooner or later he must sleep! . . .

He tried also to find food among the pine trees, to be comfortable under pine boughs while the frost fell at night, and —with less confidence—to catch a llama by artifice in order to try to kill it—perhaps by hammering it with a stone—and so finally, perhaps, to eat some of it. But the llamas had a doubt of him and regarded him with distrustful brown eyes, and spat when he drew near. Fear came on him the second day and fits of shivering. Finally he crawled down to the wall of the Country of the Blind and tried to make terms. He crawled along by the stream, shouting, until two blind men came out to the gate and talked to him.

"I was mad," he said. "But I was only newly made."

They said that was better.

He told them he was wiser now, and repented of all he had done.

Then he wept without intention, for he was very weak and ill now, and they took that as a favourable sign.

They asked him if he still thought he could *"see."*

"No," he said. "That was folly. The word means nothing—less than nothing!"

They asked him what was overhead.

"About ten times ten the height of a man there is a roof above the world—of rock—and very, very smooth." . . . He burst again into hysterical tears. "Before you ask me any more, give me some food or I shall die."

He expected dire punishments, but these blind people were capable of toleration. They regarded his rebellion as but one more proof of his general idiocy and inferiority; and after they had whipped him they appointed him to do the simplest and heaviest work they had for anyone to do, and he, seeing no other way of living, did submissively what he was told.

He was ill for some days, and they nursed him kindly. That refined his submission. But they insisted on his lying in the dark, and that was a great misery. And blind philosophers came and talked to him of the wicked levity of his mind, and reproved him so impressively for his doubts about the lid of rock that covered their cosmic casserole that he almost doubted whether indeed he was not the victim of hallucination in not seeing it overhead.

So Nunez became a citizen of the Country of the Blind, and these people ceased to be a generalised people and became individualities and familiar to him, while the world beyond the mountains became more and more remote and unreal. There was Yacob, his master, a kindly man when not annoyed; there was Pedro, Yacob's nephew; and there was Medina-saroté, who was the youngest daughter of Yacob. She was little esteemed in the world of the blind, because she had a clear-cut face, and lacked that satisfying, glossy smoothness that is the blind man's ideal of feminine beauty; but Nunez thought her beautiful at first, and presently the most beautiful thing in the whole creation. Her closed eyelids were not sunken and red after the common way of the valley, but lay as though they might open again at any moment; and she had long eyelashes, which were considered a grave disfigurement. And her voice was strong, and did not satisfy the acute hearing of the valley swains. So that she had no lover.

There came a time when Nunez thought that, could he win her, he would be resigned to live in the valley for all the rest of his days.

He watched her; he sought opportunities of doing her little services, and presently he found that she observed him. Once at a rest-day gathering they sat side by side in the dim starlight, and the music was sweet. His hand came upon hers and he dared to clasp it. Then very tenderly she returned his pressure. And one day, as they were at their meal in the darkness, he felt her hand very softly seeking him, and as it chanced the fire leaped then and he saw the tenderness of her face.

He sought to speak to her.

He went to her one day when she was sitting in the summer moonlight spinning. The light made her a thing of silver and mystery. He sat down at her feet and told her he loved her, and told her how beautiful she seemed to him. He had a lover's voice, he spoke with a tender reverence that came near to awe, and she had never before been touched by adoration. She made him no definite answer, but it was clear his words pleased her.

After that he talked to her whenever he could take an opportunity. The valley became the world for him, and the world beyond the mountains where men lived in sunlight seemed no more than a fairy tale he would some day pour into her ears. Very tentatively and timidly he spoke to her of sight.

Sight seemed to her the most poetical of fancies, and she listened to his description of the stars and the mountains and her own sweet white-lit beauty as though it was a guilty indulgence. She did not believe, she could only half understand, but she was mysteriously delighted, and it seemed to him that she completely understood.

His love lost its awe and took courage. Presently he was for demanding her of Yacob and the elders in marriage, but she became fearful and delayed. And it was one of her elder sisters who first told Yacob that Medina-saroté and Nunez were in love.

There was from the first very great opposition to the marriage of Nunez and Medina-saroté; not so much because they valued her as because they held him as a being apart, an idiot, incompetent thing below the permissible level of a man. Her sisters opposed it bitterly as bringing discredit on them all; and old Yacob, though he had formed a sort of liking for his clumsy, obedient serf, shook his head and said the thing could not be. The young men were all angry at the idea of corrupting the race, and one went so far as to revile and strike Nunez. He struck back. Then for the first time he found an advantage in seeing, even by twilight, and after that fight was over no one was disposed to raise a hand against him. But they still found his marriage impossible.

Old Yacob had a tenderness for his last little daughter, and was grieved to have her weep upon his shoulder.

"You see, my dear, he's an idiot. He has delusions; he can't do anything right."

"I know," wept Medina-saroté. "But he's better than he was. He's getting better. And he's strong, dear father, and kind—stronger and kinder than any other man in the world. And he loves me—and, father, I love him."

Old Yacob was greatly distressed to find her inconsolable, and, besides—what made it more distressing—he liked Nunez for many things. So he went and sat in the windowless council-chamber with the other elders and watched the trend of the talk, and said, at the proper time, "He's better than he was. Very likely, some day, we shall find him as sane as ourselves."

Then afterwards one of the elders, who thought deeply, had an idea. He was the great doctor among these people, their medicine-man, and he had a very philosophical and inventive mind, and the idea of curing Nunez of his peculiarities appealed to him. One day when Yacob was present he returned to the topic of Nunez.

"I have examined Bogota," he said, "and the case is clearer to me. I think very probably he might be cured."

"That is what I have always hoped," said old Yacob.

"His brain is affected," said the blind doctor.

The elders murmured assent.

"Now, *what* affects it?"

"Ah!" said old Yacob.

"This," said the doctor, answering his own question. "Those queer things that are called the eyes, and which exist to make an agreeable soft depression in the face, are diseased, in the case of Bogota, in such a way as to affect his brain. They are greatly distended, he has eyelashes, and his eyelids move, and consequently his brain is in a state of constant irritation and destruction."

"Yes?" said old Yacob. "Yes?"

"And I think I may say with reasonable certainty that, in order to cure him completely, all that we need do is a simple and easy surgical operation— namely, to remove these irritant bodies."

"And then he will be sane?"

"Then he will be perfectly sane, and a quite admirable citizen."

"Thank Heaven for science!" said old Yacob, and went forth at once to tell Nunez of his happy hopes.

But Nunez's manner of receiving the good news struck him as being cold and disappointing.

"One might think," he said, "from the tone you take, that you did not care for my daughter."

It was Medina-saroté who persuaded Nunez to face the blind surgeons.

"You do not want me," he said, "to lose my gift of sight?"

She shook her head.

"My world is sight."

Her head drooped lower.

"There are the beautiful things, the beautiful little things—the flowers, the lichens among the rocks, the lightness and softness on a piece of fur, the far sky with its drifting down of clouds, the sunsets and the stars. And there is *you.* For you alone it is good to have sight, to see your sweet, serene face, your kindly lips, your dear, beautiful hands folded together. . . . It is these eyes of mine you won, these eyes that hold me to you, that these idiots seek. Instead, I must touch you, hear you, and never see you again. I must come under that roof of rock and stone and darkness, that horrible roof under which your imagination stoops. . . . No; you would not have me do that?"

A disagreeable doubt had arisen in him. He stopped, and left the thing a question.

"I wish," she said, "sometimes——" She paused.

"Yes?" said he, a little apprehensively.

"I wish sometimes—you would not talk like that."

"Like what?"

"I know it's pretty—it's your imagination. I love it, but *now*——"

He felt cold. *"Now?"* he said faintly.

She sat quite still.

"You mean—you think—I should be better, better perhaps——"

He was realising things very swiftly. He felt anger, indeed, anger at the dull course of fate, but also sympathy for her lack of understanding—a sympathy near akin to pity.

"Dear," he said, and he could see by her whiteness how intensely her spirit pressed against the things she could not say. He put his arms about her, he kissed her ear, and they sat for a time in silence.

"If I were to consent to this?" he said at last, in a voice that was very gentle.

She flung her arms about him, weeping wildly. "Oh, if you would," she sobbed, "if only you would!"

For a week before the operation that was to raise him from his servitude and inferiority to the level of a blind citizen, Nunez knew nothing of sleep, and all through the warm sunlit hours, while the others slumbered happily, he sat brooding or wandered aimlessly, trying to bring his mind to bear on his dilemma. He had given his answer, he had given his consent, and still he was not sure. And at last work-time was over, the sun rose in splendour over the golden crests, and his last day of vision began for him. He had a few minutes with Medina-saroté before she went apart to sleep.

"To-morrow," he said, "I shall see no more."

"Dear heart!" she answered, and pressed his hands with all her strength.

"They will hurt you but little," she said; "and you are going through this pain—you are going through it, dear lover, for *me*. . . . Dear, if a woman's heart and life can do it, I will repay you. My dearest one, my dearest with the tender voice, I will repay."

He was drenched in pity for himself and her.

He held her in his arms, and pressed his lips to hers, and looked on her sweet face for the last time. "Good-bye!" he whispered at that dear sight, "good-bye!"

And then in silence he turned away from her.

She could hear his slow retreating footsteps, and something in the rhythm of them threw her into a passion of weeping.

He had fully meant to go to a lonely place where the meadows were beautiful with white narcissus, and there remain until the hour of his sacrifice should come, but as he went he lifted up his eyes and saw the morning, the morning like an angel in golden armour, marching down the steeps. . . .

It seemed to him that before this splendour he, and this blind world in the valley, and his love, and all, were no more than a pit of sin.

He did not turn aside as he had meant to do, but went on, and passed through the wall of the circumference and out upon the rocks, and his eyes were always upon the sunlit ice and snow.

He saw their infinite beauty, and his imagination soared over them to the things beyond he was now to resign for ever.

He thought of that great free world he was parted from, the world that was his own, and he had a vision of those further slopes, distance beyond distance, with Bogota, a place of multitudinous stirring beauty, a glory by day, a luminous mystery by night, a place of palaces and fountains and statues and white houses, lying beautifully in the middle distance. He thought how for a day or so one might come down through passes, drawing ever nearer and nearer to its busy streets and ways. He thought of the river journey, day by day, from great Bogota to the still vaster world beyond, through towns and villages, forest and desert places, the rushing river day by day, until its banks receded and the big steamers came splashing by, and one had reached the sea—the limitless sea, with its thousand islands, its thousands of islands, and its ships seen dimly far away in their incessant journeyings round and about that greater world. And there, unpent by mountains, one saw the sky—the sky, not such a disc as one saw it here, but an arch of immeasurable blue, a deep of deeps in which the circling stars were floating. . . .

His eyes scrutinised the great curtain of the mountains with a keener inquiry.

For example, if one went so, up that gully and to that chimney there, then one might come out high among those stunted pines that ran round in a sort of shelf and rose still higher and higher as it passed above the gorge. And then? That talus might be managed. Thence perhaps a climb might be found to take him up to the precipice that came below the snow; and if that chimney failed, then another farther to the east might serve his purpose better. And then? Then one would be out upon the amber-lit snow there, and half-way up to the crest of those beautiful desolations.

He glanced back at the village, then turned right round and regarded it steadfastly.

He thought of Medina-saroté, and she had become small and remote.

He turned again towards the mountain

wall, down which the day had come to him.

Then very circumspectly he began to climb.

When sunset came he was no longer climbing, but he was far and high. He had been higher, but he was still very high. His clothes were torn, his limbs were blood-stained, he was bruised in many places, but he lay as if he were at his ease, and there was a smile on his face.

From where he rested the valley seemed as if it were in a pit and nearly a mile below. Already it was dim with haze and shadow, though the mountain summits around him were things of light and fire, and the little details of the rocks near at hand were drenched with subtle beauty—a vein of green mineral piercing the grey, the flash of crystal faces here and there, a minute, minutely beautiful orange lichen close beside his face. There were deep mysterious shadows in the gorge, blue deepening into purple, and purple into a luminous darkness, and overhead was the illimitable vastness of the sky. But he heeded these things no longer, but lay quite inactive there, smiling as if he were satisfied merely to have escaped from the valley of the Blind in which he had thought to be King.

The glow of the sunset passed, and the night came, and still he lay peacefully contented under the cold stars.

[1904]

QUESTIONS FOR STUDY

1. *How does Wells go about making his story seem credible?*
2. *What false assumptions does Nunez make when he first enters the valley? What significant changes does he undergo? Why does he finally decide to leave?*
3. *What are the implications of the story's final sentence? Do you find the ending satisfactory? If so, in what ways? If not, why not?*
4. *Read metaphorically, what does the story seem to say about tradition, conformity, and other forms of human "blindness"?*
5. *At least one critic has argued that Nunez actually dies during his initial fall, and that the remainder of the story is what flashes through his mind as he rolls down the mountainside toward his death. What details in the story might be cited in support of this thesis?*

EUDORA WELTY

The Demonstrators

NEAR eleven o'clock that Saturday night, the doctor stopped again by his office. He had recently got into playing a weekly bridge game at the club, but tonight it had been interrupted for the third time, and he'd just come from attending to Miss Marcia Pope. Now bedridden, scorning all medication and in particular tranquillizers, she had a seizure every morning before breakfast and often on Saturday night for some reason, but had retained her memory; she could amuse herself by giving out great wads of Shakespeare and *"Arma virumque cano,"* [1] or the like. The more forcefully Miss Marcia Pope declaimed, the more innocent grew her old face—the lines went right out.

"She'll sleep naturally now, I think," he'd told the companion, still in her rocker.

Mrs. Warrum did well, perhaps hadn't hit yet on an excuse to quit that suited her. She failed to be alarmed by Miss Marcia Pope, either in convulsions or in recitation. From where she lived, she'd never gone to school to this lady, who had taught three generations of Holden, Mississippi, its Latin, civics, and English, and who had carried, for forty years, a leather satchel bigger than the doctor's bag.

As he'd snapped his bag shut tonight, Miss Marcia had opened her eyes and spoken distinctly: "Richard Strickland? I have it on my report that Irene Roberts is not where she belongs. Now which of you wants the whipping?"

"It's all right, Miss Marcia. She's still my wife," he'd said, but could not be sure the answer got by her.

---

[1] "Arms and the man I sing"—the first words of Vergil's *Aeneid*. (JHP)

In the office, he picked up the city newspaper he subscribed to—seeing as he did so the picture on the front of a young man burning his draft card before a camera—and locked up, ready to face home. As he came down the stairway onto the street, his sleeve was plucked.

It was a Negro child. "We got to hurry," she said.

His bag was still in the car. She climbed into the back and stood there behind his ear as he drove down the hill. He met the marshal's car as both bounced over the railroad track—no passenger rode with the marshal that he could see—and the doctor asked the child, "Who got hurt? Whose house?" But she could only tell him how to get there, an alley at a time, till they got around the cottonseed mill.

Down here, the street lights were out tonight. The last electric light of any kind appeared to be the one burning in the vast shrouded cavern of the gin. His car lights threw into relief the dead goldenrod that stood along the road and made it look heavier than the bridge across the creek.

As soon as the child leaned on his shoulder and he had stopped the car, he heard men's voices; but at first his eyes could make out little but an assembly of white forms spaced in the air near a low roof—chickens roosting in a tree. Then he saw the reds of cigarettes. A dooryard was as packed with a standing crowd as if it were funeral time. They were all men. Still more people seemed to be moving from the nearby churchyard and joining onto the crowd in front of the house.

The men parted before them as he went following the child up broken steps and across a porch. A kerosene lamp was being held for him in the doorway. He stepped into a roomful of women. The child kept going, went to the foot of an iron bed and stopped. The lamp came up closer behind him and he followed a path of newspapers laid down on the floor from the doorway to the bed.

A dark quilt was pulled up to the throat of a girl alive on the bed. A pillow raised her at the shoulders. The dome of her forehead looked thick as a battering ram, because of the rolling of her eyes.

Dr. Strickland turned back the quilt. The young, very black-skinned woman lay in a white dress with her shoes on. A maid? Then he saw that of course the white was not the starched material of a uniform but shiny, clinging stuff, and there was a banner of some kind crossing it in a crumpled red line from the shoulder. He unfastened the knot at the waist and got the banner out of the way. The skintight satin had been undone at the neck already; as he parted it farther, the girl kicked at the foot of the bed. He exposed the breast and then, before her hand had pounced on his, the wound below the breast. There was a small puncture with little evidence of external bleeding. He had seen splashes of blood on the dress, now almost dry.

"Go boil me some water. Too much excitement to send for the doctor a little earlier?"

The girl clawed at his hand with her sticky nails.

"Have you touched her?" he asked.

"See there? And she don't want you trying it, either," said a voice in the room.

A necklace like sharp and pearly teeth was fastened around her throat. It was when he took that off that the little girl who had been sent for him cried out. "I bid that!" she said, but without coming nearer. He found no other wounds.

"Does it hurt you to breathe?" He spoke almost absently as he addressed the girl.

The nipples of her breasts cast shadows that looked like figs; she would not take a deep breath when he used the stethoscope. Sweat in the airless room, in the bed, rose and seemed to weaken and un-

stick the newspapered walls like steam from a kettle already boiling; it glazed his own white hand, his tapping fingers. It was the stench of sensation. The women's faces coming nearer were streaked in the hot lamplight. Somewhere close to the side of his head something glittered; hung over the knob of the bed-post, where a boy would have tossed his cap, was a tambourine. He let the stethoscope fall, and heard women's sighs travel around the room, domestic sounds like a broom being flirted about, women getting ready for company.

"Stand back," he said. "You got a fire on in here?" Warm as it was, crowded as it was in here, he looked behind him and saw the gas heater burning, half the radiants burning blue. The girl, with lips turned down, lay pulling away while he took her pulse.

The child who had been sent for him and then had been sent to heat the water brought the kettle in from the kitchen too soon and had to be sent back to make it boil. When it was ready and in the pan, the lamp was held closer; it was beside his elbow as if to singe his arm.

"Stand back," he said. Again and again the girl's hand had to be forced away from her breast. The wound quickened spasmodically as if it responded to light.

"Icepick?"

"You right this time," said voices in the room.

"Who did this to her?"

The room went quiet; he only heard the men in the yard laughing together. "How long ago?" He looked at the path of newspapers spread on the floor. "Where? Where did it happen? How did she get here?"

He had an odd feeling that somewhere in the room somebody was sending out beckoning smiles in his direction. He lifted, half turned his head. The elevated coal that glowed at regular intervals was the pipe of an old woman in a boiled white apron standing near the door.

He persisted. "Has she coughed up anything yet?"

"Don't you know her?" they cried, as if he never was going to hit on the right question.

He let go the girl's arm, and her hand started its way back again to her wound. Sending one glowing look at him, she covered it again. As if she had spoken, he recognized her.

"Why, it's Ruby," he said.

Ruby Gaddy *was* the maid. Five days a week she cleaned up on the second floor of the bank building where he kept his office and consulting rooms.

He said to her, "Ruby, this is Dr. Strickland. What have you been up to?"

"Nothin'!" everybody cried for her.

The girl's eyes stopped rolling and rested themselves on the expressionless face of the little girl, who again stood at the foot of the bed watching from this restful distance. Look equalled look: sisters.

"Am I supposed to just know?" The doctor looked all around him. An infant was sitting up on the splintery floor near his feet, he now saw, on a clean newspaper, a spoon stuck pipelike in its mouth. From out in the yard at that moment came a regular guffaw, not much different from the one that followed the telling of a dirty story or a race story by one of the clowns in the Elks' Club. He frowned at the baby; and the baby, a boy, looked back over his upsidedown spoon and gave it a long audible suck.

"She married? Where's her husband? That where the trouble was?"

Now, while the women in the room, too, broke out in sounds of amusement, the doctor stumbled where he stood. "What the devil's running in here? Rats?"

"You wrong there."

Guinea pigs were running underfoot, not only in this room but on the other side of the wall, in the kitchen where the water had finally got boiled. Somebody's head turned toward the leaf end of a stalk of celery wilting on top of the Bible on the table.

"Catch those things!" he exclaimed.

The baby laughed; the rest copied the baby.

"They lightning. Get away from you so fast!" said a voice.

"Them guinea pigs ain't been caught since they was born. Let you try."

"Know why? 'Cause they's Dove's."

Dove left 'em here when he move out, just to be in the way."

The doctor felt the weight recede from Ruby's fingers, and saw it flatten her arm where it lay on the bed. Her eyes had closed. A little boy with a sanctimonious face had taken the bit of celery and knelt down on the floor; there was scrambling about and increasing laughter until Dr. Strickland made himself heard in the room.

"All right. I heard you. Is Dove who did it? Go on. Say."

He heard somebody spit on the stove. Then:

"It's Dove."

"Dove."

"Dove."

"Dove."

"You got it right that time."

While the name went around, passed from one mouth to the other, the doctor drew a deep breath. But the sigh that filled the room was the girl's own, luxuriously uncontained.

"Dove Collins? I believe you. I've had to sew him up enough times on Sunday morning, you all know that," said the doctor. "I know Ruby, I know Dove, and if the lights would come back on I can tell you the names of the rest of you and you know it." While he was speaking, his eyes fell on Oree, a figure of the Holden square for twenty years, whom he had inherited—sitting here in the room in her express wagon, the flowered skirt spread down from her lap and tucked in over the stumps of her knees.

While he was preparing the hypodermic, he was aware that more watchers, a row of them dressed in white with red banners like Ruby's, were coming in to fill up the corners. The lamp was lifted—higher than the dipping shadows of their heads, a valentine tacked on the wall radiated color—and then, as he leaned over the bed, the lamp was brought down closer and closer to the girl, like something that would devour her.

"Now I can't see what I'm doing," the doctor said sharply, and as the light jumped and swung behind him he thought he recognized the anger as a mother's.

"Look to me like the fight's starting

to go out of Ruby mighty early," said a voice.

Still her eyes stayed closed. He gave the shot.

"Where'd he get to—Dove? Is the marshal out looking for him?" he asked.

The sister moved along the bed and put the baby down on it close to Ruby's face.

"Remove him," said the doctor.

"She don't even study him," said the sister. "Poke her," she told the baby.

"Take him out of here," ordered Dr. Strickland.

The baby opened one of his mother's eyes with his fingers. When she shut it on him he cried, as if he knew it to be deliberate of her.

"Get that baby out of here and all the kids, I tell you," Dr. Strickland said into the room. "This ain't going to be pretty."

"Carry him next door, Twosie," said a voice.

"I ain't. You all promised me if I leave long enough to get the doctor I could stand right here until." The child's voice was loud.

"O.K. Then you got to hold Roger."

The baby made a final reach for his mother's face, putting out a hand with its untrimmed nails, gray as the claw of a squirrel. The woman who had held the lamp set that down and grabbed the baby out of the bed herself. His legs began churning even before she struck him a blow on the side of the head.

"You trying to raise him an idiot?" the doctor flung out.

"*I* ain't going to raise him," the mother said toward the girl on the bed.

The deliberation had gone out of her face. She was drifting into unconsciousness. Setting her hand to one side, the doctor inspected the puncture once more. It was clean as the eye of a needle. While he stood there watching her, he lifted her hand and washed it—the wrist, horny palm, blood-caked fingers one by one.

But as he again found her pulse, he saw her eyes opening. As long as he counted he was aware of those eyes as if they loomed larger than the watch face. They were filled with the unresponding

gaze of ownership. She knew what she had. Memory did not make the further effort to close the lids when he replaced her hand, or when he took her shoes off and set them on the floor, or when he stepped away from the bed and again the full lamplight struck her face.

The twelve-year-old stared on, over the buttress of the baby she held to her chest.

"Can you ever hush that baby?"

A satisfied voice said, "He going to keep-a-noise till he learn better."

"Well, I'd like a little peace and consideration to be shown!" the doctor said. "Try to remember there's somebody in here with you that's going to be pumping mighty hard to breathe." He raised a finger and pointed it at the old woman in the boiled apron whose pipe had continued to glow with regularity by the door. "You stay. You sit here and watch Ruby," he called. "The rest of you clear out of here."

He closed his bag and straightened up. The woman stuck the lamp hot into his own face.

"Remember Lucille? I'm Lucille. I was washing for your mother when you was born. Let me see you do something," she said with fury. "You ain't even tied her up! You sure ain't your daddy!"

"Why, she's bleeding inside," he retorted. "What do you think *she's* doing?"

They hushed. For a minute all he heard was the guinea pigs racing. He looked back at the girl; her eyes were fixed with possession. "I gave her a shot. She'll just go to sleep. If she doesn't, call me and I'll come back and give her another one. One of you kindly bring me a drink of water," the doctor continued in the same tone.

With a crash, hushed off like cymbals struck by mistake, something was moved on the kitchen side of the wall. The little boy who had held the celery to catch the guinea pigs came in carrying a teacup. He passed through the room and out onto the porch, where he could be heard splashing fresh water from a pump. He came back inside and at arm's length held the cup out to the doctor.

Dr. Strickland drank with a thirst they

all could and did follow. The cup, though it held the whole smell of this house in it, was of thin china, was an old one.

Then he stepped across the gaze of the girl on the bed as he would have had to step over a crack yawning in the floor.

"Fixing to leave?" asked the old woman in the boiled white apron, who still stood up by the door, the pipe gone from her lips. He then remembered her. In the days when he travelled East to medical school, she used to be the sole factotum at the Holden depot when the passenger train came through sometime between two and three in the morning. It was always late. Circling the pewlike benches of the waiting rooms, she carried around coffee which she poured boiling hot into paper cups out of a white-en-amelled pot that looked as long as her arm. She wore then, in addition to the apron, a white and flaring head covering —something between a chef's cap and a sunbonnet. As the train at last steamed in, she called the stations. She didn't use a loudspeaker but just the power of her lungs. In all the natural volume of her baritone voice she thundered them out to the scattered and few who had waited under lights too poor to read by—first in the colored waiting room, then in the white waiting room, to echo both times from the vault of the roof: ". . . Meridian. Birmingham. Chattanooga. Bristol. Lynchburg. Washington. Baltimore. Philadelphia. And New York." Seizing all the bags, two by two, in her own hands, walking slowly in front of the passengers, she saw to it that they left.

He said to her, "I'm going, but you're not. You're keeping a watch on Ruby. Don't let her slide down in the bed. Call me if you need me." As a boy, had he never even wondered what her name was —this tyrant? He didn't know it now. He put the cup into her reaching hand. "Aren't you ready to leave?" he asked Oree, the legless woman. She still lived by the tracks where the train had cut off her legs.

"I ain't in no hurry," she replied and as he passed her she called her usual "Take it easy, Doc."

When he stepped outside onto the porch, he saw that there was moonlight everywhere. Uninterrupted by any lights from Holden, it filled the whole country lying out there in the haze of the long rainless fall. He himself stood on the edge of Holden. Just one house and one church farther, the Delta began, and the cotton fields ran into the scattered paleness of a dimmed-out Milky Way.

Nobody called him back, yet he turned his head and got a sideways glimpse all at once of a row of dresses hung up across the front of the house, starched until they could have stood alone (as his mother complained), and in an instant had recognized his mother's gardening dress, his sister Annie's golf dress, his wife's favorite duster that she liked to wear to the breakfast table, and more dresses, less substantial. Elevated across the front of the porch, they were hung again between him and the road. With sleeves spread wide, trying to scratch his forehead with the tails of their skirts, they were flying around this house in the moonlight.

The moment of vertigo passed, as a small black man came up the steps and across the porch wearing heeltaps on his shoes.

"Sister Gaddy entered yet into the gates of joy?"

"No, Preacher, you're in time," said the doctor.

As soon as he left the house, he heard it become as noisy as the yard had been, and the men in the yard went quiet to let him through. From the road, he saw the moon itself. It was above the tree with the chickens in it; it might have been one of the chickens flown loose. He scraped children off the hood of his car, pulled another from position at the wheel, and climbed inside. He turned the car around in the churchyard. There was a flickering light inside the church. Flat-roofed as a warehouse, it had its shades pulled down like a bedroom. This was the church where the sounds of music and dancing came from habitually on many another night besides Sunday, clearly to be heard on top of the hill.

He drove back along the road, across the creek, its banks glittering now with the narrow bottles, the size of harmonicas, in which paregoric was persistently sold under the name of Mother's Helper. The telephone wires along the road were hung with shreds of cotton, the sides of the road were strewn with them too, as if the doctor were out on a paper chase.

He passed the throbbing mill, working on its own generator. No lights ever shone through the windowless and now moonlit sheet iron, but the smell came out freely and spread over the town at large—a cooking smell, like a dish ordered by a man with an endless appetite. Pipes hung with streamers of lint fed into the moonlit gin, and wagons and trucks heaped up round as the gypsy caravans or circus wagons of his father's, or even his grandfather's, stories, stood this way and that, waiting in the yard outside.

Far down the railroad track, beyond the unlighted town, rose the pillow-shaped glow of a grass fire. It was gaseous, unveined, unblotted by smoke, a cloud with the November flush of the sedge grass by day, sparkless and nerveless, not to be confused with a burning church, but like anesthetic made visible.

Then a long beam of electric light came solid as a board from behind him to move forward along the long loading platform, to some bales of cotton standing on it, some of them tumbled one against the others as if pushed by the light; then it ran up the wall of the dark station so you could read the name, "Holden." The hooter sounded. This was a grade crossing with a bad record, and it seemed to the doctor that he had never started over it in his life that something was not bearing down. He stopped the car, and as the train in its heat began to pass in front of him he saw it to be a doubleheader, a loaded freight this time. It was going right on through Holden.

He cut off his motor. One of the sleepers rocked and complained with every set of wheels that rolled over it. Presently the regular, slow creaking reminded the doctor of an old-fashioned porch swing holding lovers in the dark.

He had been carried a cup tonight that might have been his own mother's china or his wife's mother's—the rim not a perfect round, a thin, porcelain cup his lips and his fingers had recognized. In that house of murder, comfort had been brought to him at his request. After drinking from it he had all but reeled into a flock of dresses stretched widesleeved across the porch of that house like a child's drawing of angels.

Faintly rocked by the passing train, he sat bent at the wheel of the car, and the feeling of well-being persisted. It increased, until he had come to the point of tears.

The doctor was the son of a doctor, practicing in his father's office; all the older patients, like Miss Marcia Pope—and like Lucille and Oree—spoke of his father, and some confused the young doctor with the old; but not they. The watch he carried was the gold one that had belonged to his father. Richard had grown up in Holden, married "the prettiest girl in the Delta." Except for his years at the university and then at medical school and during his interneship, he had lived here at home and had carried on the practice—the only practice in town. Now his father and his mother both were dead, his sister had married and moved away, a year ago his child had died. Then, back in the summer, he and his wife had separated, by her wish.

Sylvia had been their only child. Until her death from pneumonia last Christmas, at the age of thirteen, she had never sat up or spoken. He had loved her and mourned her all her life; she had been injured at birth. But Irene had done more; she had dedicated her life to Sylvia, sparing herself nothing, tending her, lifting her, feeding her, everything. What do you do after giving all your devotion to something that cannot be helped, and that has been taken away? You give all your devotion to something else that cannot be helped. But you shun all the terrible reminders, and turn not to a human being but to an idea.

Last June, there had come along a student, one of the civil-rights workers, calling at his office with a letter of introduction. For the sake of an old friend, the doctor had taken him home to dinner. (He had been reminded of him once tonight, already, by a photograph in the city paper.) He remembered that the young man had already finished talking about his work. They had just laughed around the table after Irene had quoted the classic question the governor-before-this-one had asked, after a prison break: "If you can't trust a trusty, who can you trust?" Then the doctor had remarked "Speaking of who can you trust, what's this I read in your own paper, Philip? It said some of your outfit over in the next county were forced at gunpoint to go into the fields at hundred-degree temperature and pick cotton. Well, that didn't happen—there isn't any cotton in June."

"I asked myself the same question you do. But I told myself, 'Well, they won't know the difference where the paper is read,' " said the young man.

"It's lying, though."

"We are dramatizing your hostility," the young bearded man had corrected him. "It's a way of reaching people. Don't forget—what they *might* have done to us is even worse."

"Still—you're not justified in putting a false front on things, in my opinion," Dr. Strickland had said. "Even for a good cause."

"*You* won't tell Herman Fairbrothers what's the matter with him," said his wife, and she jumped up from the table.

Later, as a result of this entertainment, he supposed, broken glass had been spread the length and breadth of his driveway. He hadn't seen in time what it wouldn't have occurred to him to look for, and Irene, standing in the door, had suddenly broken into laughter. . . .

He had eventually agreed that she have her wish and withdraw herself for as long as she liked. She was back now where she came from, where, he'd heard, they were all giving parties for her. He had offered to be the one to leave. "Leave Holden without its Dr. Strickland? You wouldn't to save your soul, would you?" she had replied. But as yet it was not divorce.

He thought he had been patient, but patience had made him tired. He was so increasingly tired, so sick and even bored with the bitterness, intractability that divided everybody and everything.

And suddenly, tonight, things had seemed just the way they used to seem.

He had felt as though someone had stopped him on the street and offered to carry his load for a while—had insisted on it—some old, trusted, half-forgotten family friend that he had lost sight of since youth. Was it the sensation, now returning, that there was still allowed to everybody on earth a *self*—savage, death-defying, private? The pounding of his heart was like the assault of hope, throwing itself against him without a stop, merciless.

It seemed a long time that he had sat there, but the cars were still going by. Here came the caboose. He had counted them without knowing it—seventy-two cars. The grass fire at the edge of town came back in sight.

The doctor's feeling gradually ebbed away, like nausea put down. He started up the car and drove across the track and on up the hill.

Candles, some of them in dining-room candelabra, burned clear across the upstairs windows in the Fairbrothers' house. His own house, next door, was of course dark, and while he was wondering where Irene kept candles for emergencies he had driven on past his driveway for the second time that night. But the last place he wanted to go now was back to the club. He'd only tried it anyway to please his sister Annie. Now that he'd got by Miss Marcia Pope's dark window, he smelled her sweet-olive tree, solid as the bank building.

Here stood the bank, with its doorway onto the stairs to Drs. Strickland & Strickland, their names in black and gilt on three windows. He passed it. The haze and the moonlight were one over the square, over the row of storefronts opposite with the line of poles thin as matchsticks rising to prop the one long strip of tin over the sidewalk, the drygoods store with its ornamental top that looked like opened paper fans held up by acrobats. He slowly started around the square. Behind its iron railings, the courthouse-and-jail stood barely emerging from its black cave of trees and only the slicked iron steps of the stile caught the moon. He drove on, past the shut-down movie house with all the light bulbs unscrewed from the sign that spelled out in empty sockets "BROADWAY." In front of the new post office the flagpole looked feathery, like the track of a jet that is already gone from the sky. From in front of the fire station, the fire chief's old Buick had gone home.

What was there, who was there, to keep him from going home? The doctor drove on slowly around. From the center of the deserted pavement, where cars and wagons stood parked helter-skelter by day, rose the water tank, pale as a balloon that might be only tethered here. A clanking came out of it, for the water supply too had been a source of trouble this summer—a hollow, irregular knocking now and then from inside, but the doctor no longer heard it. In turning his car, he saw a man lying prone and colorless in the arena of moonlight.

The lights of the car fastened on him and his clothes turned golden yellow. The man looked as if he had been sleeping all day in a bed of flowers and rolled in their pollen and were sleeping there still, with his face buried. He was covered his length in cottonseed meal.

Dr. Strickland stopped the car short and got out. His footsteps made the only sound in town. The man raised up on his hands and looked at him like a seal. Blood laced his head like a net through which he had broken. His wide tongue hung down out of his mouth. But the doctor knew the face.

"So you're alive, Dove, you're still alive?"

Slowly, hardly moving his tongue, Dove said: "Hide me." Then he hemorrhaged through the mouth.

Through the other half of the night, the doctor's calls came to him over the telephone—all chronic cases. Eva Duckett Fairbrothers telephoned at daylight.

"Feels low in his mind? Of course he feels low in his mind," he had finally shouted at her. "If I had what Herman has, I'd go down in the back yard and shoot myself!"

The *Sentinel,* owned and edited by Horatio Duckett, came out on Tuesdays. The next week's back-page headline read, "TWO DEAD, ONE ICE PICK. FREAK EPISODE AT NEGRO CHURCH." The subhead read, "No Racial Content Espied."

The doctor sat at the table in his dining room, finishing breakfast as he looked it over.

An employee of the Fairbrothers Cotton Seed Oil Mill and a Holden maid, both Negroes, were stabbed with a sharp instrument judged to be an ice pick in a crowded churchyard here Saturday night. Both later expired. The incident was not believed by Mayor Herman Fairbrothers to carry racial significance.

"It warrants no stir," the Mayor declared.

The mishap boosted Holden's weekend death toll to 3. Billy Lee Warrum Jr. died Sunday before reaching a hospital in Jackson where he was rushed after being thrown from his new motorcycle while on his way there. He was the oldest son of Mrs. Billy Lee Warrum, Rt. 1. Reputedly en route to see his fiance he was pronounced dead on arrival. Multiple injuries was listed as the cause, the motorcycle having speeded into an interstate truck loaded to capacity with holiday turkeys. (See eye-witness account, page 1.)

As Holden marshal Curtis "Cowboy" Stubblefield reconstructed the earlier mishap, Ruby Gaddy, 21, was stabbed in full view of the departing congregation of the Holy Gospel Tabernacle as she attempted to leave the church when services were concluded at approximately 9:30 P.M. Saturday.

Witnesses said Dave Collins, 25, appeared outside the church as early as 9:15 P.M. having come directly from his shift at the mill where he had been employed since 1959. On being invited to come in and be seated he joked and said he preferred to wait outdoors as he was only wearing work clothes until the Gaddy woman, said to be his common-law wife, came outside the frame structure.

In the ensuing struggle at the conclusion of the services, the woman, who was a member of the choir, is believed to have received fatal ice-pick injuries to a vital organ, then to have wrested the weapon from her assailant and paid him back in kind. The Gaddy woman then walked to her mother's house but later collapsed.

Members of the congregation said they chased Collins 13 or 14 yds. in the direction of Snake Creek on the South side of the church then he fell to the ground and rolled approximately ten feet down the bank, rolling over six or seven times. Those present believed him to have succumbed since it was said the pick while in the woman's hand had been seen to drive in and pierce either his ear or his eye, either of which is in close approximation to the brain. However, Collins later managed to crawl unseen from the creek and to make his way undetected up Railroad Avenue and to the Main St. door of an office occupied by Richard Strickland, M.D., above the Citizens Bank & Trust.

Witnesses were divided on which of the Negroes struck the first blow. Percy McAtee, pastor of the church, would not take sides but declared on being questioned by Marshal Stubblefield he was satisfied no outside agitators were involved and no arrests were made.

Collins was discovered on his own doorstep by Dr. Strickland who had been spending the evening at the Country Club. Collins is reported by Dr. Strickland to have expired shortly following his discovery, alleging his death to chest wounds.

"He offered no statement," Dr. Strickland said in response to a query.

Interviewed at home where he is recuperating from an ailment, Mayor Fairbrothers stated that he had not heard of there being trouble of any description at the Mill. "We are not trying to ruin our good reputation by inviting any, either," he said. "If the weatherman stays on our side we expect to attain capacity production in the latter part of next month," he stated. Saturday had been pay day as usual.

When Collins' body was searched by officers the pockets were empty however.

An ice pick, reportedly the property of the Holy Gospel Tabernacle, was later found by Deacon Gaddy, 8, brother of Ruby Gaddy, covered with blood and carried it to Marshal Stubblefield. Stubblefield said it had been found in the grounds of the new $100,000.00 Negro school. It is believed to have served as the instrument in the twin slayings, the victims thus virtually succeeding in killing each other.

"Well, I'm surprised didn't more of them get hurt," said Rev. Alonzo Duck-

ett, pastor of the Holden First Baptist Church. "And yet they expect to be seated in our churches." County Sheriff Vince Lasseter, reached fishing at Lake Bourne, said: "That's one they can't pin the blame on us for. That's how they treat their own kind. Please take note our conscience is clear."

Members of the Negro congregation said they could not account for Collins having left Snake Creek at the unspecified time. "We stood there a while and flipped some bottle caps down at him and threw his cap down after him right over his face and didn't get a stir out of him," stated an official of the congregation. "The way he acted, we figured he was dead. We would not have gone off and left him if we had known he was able to subsequently crawl up the hill." They stated Collins was not in the habit of worshipping at Holy Gospel Tabernacle.

The Gaddy woman died later this morning, also from chest wounds.

No cause was cited for the fracas.

The cook had refilled his cup without his noticing. The doctor dropped the paper and carried his coffee out onto the little porch; it was still his morning habit.

The porch was at the back of the house, screened on three sides. Sylvia's daybed used to stand here; it put her in the garden. No other houses were in sight; the gin could not be heard or even the traffic whining on the highway up off the bypass.

The roses were done for, the perennials too. But the surrounding crape-myrtle tree, the redbud, the dogwood, the Chinese tallow tree, and the pomegranate bush were bright as toys. The ailing pear tree had shed its leaves ahead of the rest. Past a falling wall of Michaelmas daisies that had not been tied up, a pair of flickers were rifling the grass, the cock in one part of the garden, the hen in another, picking at the devastation right through the bright leaves that appeared to have been left lying there just for them, probing and feeding. They stayed year round, he supposed, but it was only in the fall of the year that he ever noticed them. He was pretty sure that Sylvia had known the birds were there. Her eyes would follow birds when they flew across the garden. As he watched, the cock spread one wing, showy as a zebra's hide, and with a turn of his head showed his red seal.

Dr. Strickland swallowed the coffee and picked up his bag. It was all going to be just about as hard as seeing Her-man and Eva Fairbrothers through. He thought that in all Holden, as of now, only Miss Marcia Pope was still quite able to take care of herself—or such was her own opinion.

[1966]

QUESTIONS FOR STUDY

1. *Why does Eudora Welty choose Dr. Strickland as the story's center of consciousness? Is the choice a good one? How does Dr. Strickland apparently differ from the other white citizens of Holden? What impact do the events of the evening have upon him? Do they change him in any way?*

2. *What is the appropriateness of the title? How many "demonstrators" appear in the story? What are they demonstrating for or against?*

3. *What attitude(s) toward life does the story dramatize and seem to affirm? Are its final implications optimistic, pessimistic, or somewhere in between?*

4. *Note the names of the characters—Strickland, Pope, Fairbrothers, Duckett, Lasseter, Stubblefield, Warrum. In what ways are they fitting?*

5. *Why does Miss Welty conclude her story with the lengthy newspaper article? What is its relationship to the rest of the story?*

6. *Some critics have perceived the story, in part at least, as Eudora Welty's own personal comment on a writer's social responsibilities. To what extent does such an interpretation seem justified?*

EUDORA WELTY
Petrified Man

REACH in my purse and git me a cigarette without no powder in it if you kin, Mrs. Fletcher, honey," said Leota to her ten o'clock shampoo-and-set customer. "I don't like no perfumed cigarettes."

Mrs. Fletcher gladly reached over to the lavender shelf under the lavender-framed mirror, shook a hair net loose from the clasp of the patent-leather bag, and slapped her hand down quickly on a powder puff which burst out when the purse was opened.

"Why, look at the peanuts, Leota!" said Mrs. Fletcher. in her marvelling voice.

"Honey, them goobers has been in my purse a week if they's been in it a day. Mrs. Pike bought them peanuts."

"Who's Mrs. Pike?" asked Mrs. Fletcher, settling back. Hidden in this den of curling fluid and henna packs, separated by a lavender swing-door from the other customers, who were being gratified in other booths, she could give her curiosity its freedom. She looked expectantly at the black part in Leota's yellow curls as she bent to light the cigarette.

"Mrs. Pike is this lady from New Orleans," said Leota, puffing, and pressing into Mrs. Fletcher's scalp with strong red-nailed fingers. "A friend, not a customer. You see, like maybe I told you last time, me and Fred and Sal and Joe all had us a fuss, so Sal and Joe up and moved out, so we didn't do a thing but rent out their room. So we rented it to Mrs. Pike. And Mr. Pike." She flicked an ash into the basket of dirty towels. "Mrs. Pike is a very decided blonde. *She* bought me the peanuts."

"She must be cute," said Mrs. Fletcher.

"Honey, 'cute' ain't the word for what she is. I'm tellin' you, Mrs. Pike is attractive. She has her a good time. She's got a sharp eye out, Mrs. Pike has."

She dashed the comb through the air, and paused dramatically as a cloud of Mrs. Fletcher's hennaed hair floated out of the lavender teeth like a small storm-cloud.

"Hair fallin'."

"Aw, Leota."

"Uh-huh, commencin' to fall out," said Leota, combing again, and letting fall another cloud.

"Is it any dandruff in it?" Mrs. Fletcher was frowning, her hair-line eyebrows diving down toward her nose, and her wrinkled, beady-lashed eyelids batting with concentration.

"Nope." She combed again. "Just fallin' out."

"Bet it was that last perm'nent you gave me that did it," Mrs. Fletcher said cruelly. "Remember you cooked me fourteen minutes."

"You had fourteen minutes comin' to you," said Leota with finality.

"Bound to be somethin'," persisted Mrs. Fletcher. "Dandruff, dandruff. I couldn't of caught a thing like that from Mr. Fletcher, could I?"

"Well," Leota answered at last, "you know what I heard in here yestiddy, one of Thelma's ladies was settin' over yonder in Thelma's booth gittin' a machine-less, and I don't mean to insist or insinuate or anything, Mrs. Fletcher, but Thelma's lady just happ'med to throw out—I forgotten what she was talkin' about at the time—that you was p-r-e-g., and lots of times that'll make your hair do awful funny, fall out and God knows what all. It just ain't our fault, is the way I look at it."

There was a pause. The women stared at each other in the mirror.

"Who was it?" demanded Mrs. Fletcher.

"Honey, I really couldn't say," said Leota. "Not that you look it."

"Where's Thelma? I'll get it out of her," said Mrs. Fletcher.

"Now, honey, I wouldn't go and git mad over a little thing like that," Leota said, combing hastily, as though to hold Mrs. Fletcher down by the hair. "I'm sure it was somebody didn't mean no harm in the world. How far gone are you?"

"Just wait," said Mrs. Fletcher, and shrieked for Thelma, who came in and took a drag from Leota's cigarette.

"Thelma, honey, throw your mind back to yestiddy if you kin," said Leota, drenching Mrs. Fletcher's hair with a thick fluid and catching the overflow in a cold wet towel at her neck.

"Well, I got my lady half wound for a spiral," said Thelma doubtfully.

"This won't take but a minute," said Leota. "Who is it you got in there, old Horse Face? Just cast your mind back and try to remember who your lady was yestiddy who happ'm to mention that my customer was pregnant, that's all. She's dead to know."

Thelma drooped her blood-red lips and looked over Mrs. Fletcher's head into the mirror. "Why, honey, I ain't got the faintest," she breathed. "I really don't recollect the faintest. But I'm sure she meant no harm. I declare, I forgot my hair finally got combed and thought it was a stranger behind me."

"Was it that Mrs. Hutchinson?" Mrs. Fletcher was tensely polite.

"Mrs. Hutchinson? Oh, Mrs. Hutchinson." Thelma batted her eyes. "Naw, precious, she come on Thursday and didn't ev'm mention your name. I doubt if she ev'm knows you're on the way."

"Thelma!" cried Leota staunchly.

"All I know is, whoever it is 'll be sorry some day. Why, I just barely knew it myself!" cried Mrs. Fletcher. "Just let her wait!"

"Why? What're you gonna do to her?"

It was a child's voice, and the women looked down. A little boy was making tents with aluminum wave pinchers on the floor under the sink.

"Billy Boy, hon, mustn't bother nice ladies," Leota smiled. She slapped him brightly and behind her back waved Thelma out of the booth. "Ain't Billy Boy a sight? Only three years old and already just nuts about the beauty-parlor business."

"I never saw him here before," said Mrs. Fletcher, still unmollified.

"He ain't been here before, that's how come," said Leota. "He belongs to Mrs. Pike. She got her a job but it was Fay's Millinery. He oughtn't to try on those ladies' hats, they come down over his eyes like I don't know what. They just git to look ridiculous, that's what, an' of course he's gonna put 'em on: hats. They tole Mrs. Pike they didn't appreciate him hangin' around there. Here, he couldn't hurt a thing."

"Well! I don't like children that much," said Mrs. Fletcher.

"Well!" said Leota moodily.

"Well! I'm almost tempted not to have this one," said Mrs. Fletcher. "That Mrs. Hutchinson! Just looks straight through you when she sees you on the street and then spits at you behind your back."

"Mr. Fletcher would beat you on the head if you didn't have it now," said Leota reasonably. "After going this far."

Mrs. Fletcher sat up straight. "Mr. Fletcher can't do a thing with me."

"He can't!" Leota winked at herself in the mirror.

"No, siree, he can't. If he so much as raises his voice against me, he knows good and well I'll have one of my sick headaches, and then I'm just not fit to live with. And if I really look that pregnant already—"

"Well, now, honey, I just want you to know—I habm't told any of my ladies and I ain't goin' to tell 'em—even that you're losin' your hair. You just get you one of those Stork-a-Lure dresses and stop worryin'. What people don't know don't hurt nobody, as Mrs. Pike says."

"Did you tell Mrs. Pike?" asked Mrs. Fletcher sulkily.

"Well, Mrs. Fletcher, look, you ain't

ever goin' to lay eyes on Mrs. Pike or her lay eyes on you, so what diffunce does it make in the long run?"

"I knew it!" Mrs. Fletcher deliberately nodded her head so as to destroy a ringlet Leota was working on behind her ear. "Mrs. Pike!"

Leota sighed. "I reckon I might as well tell you. It wasn't any more Thelma's lady tole me you was pregnant than a bat."

"Not Mrs. Hutchinson?"

"Naw, Lord! It was Mrs. Pike."

"Mrs. Pike!" Mrs. Fletcher could only sputter and let curling fluid roll into her ear. "How could Mrs. Pike possibly know I was pregnant or otherwise, when she doesn't even know me? The nerve of some people!"

"Well, here's how it was. Remember Sunday?"

"Yes," said Mrs. Fletcher.

"Sunday, Mrs. Pike an' me was all by ourself. Mr. Pike and Fred had gone over to Eagle Lake, sayin' they was goin' to catch 'em some fish, but they didn't a course. So we was settin' in Mrs. Pike's car, it's a 1939 Dodge—"

"1939, eh," said Mrs. Fletcher.

"—An' we was gettin' us a Jax beer apiece—that's the beer that Mrs. Pike says in made right in N.O., so she won't drink no other kind. So I seen you drive up to the drugstore an' run in for just a secont, leavin' I reckon Mr. Fletcher in the car, an' come runnin' out with looked like a perscription. So I says to Mrs. Pike, just to be makin' talk, 'Right yonder's Mrs. Fletcher, and I reckon that's Mr. Fletcher—she's one of my regular customers,' I says."

"I had on a figured print," said Mrs. Fletcher tentatively.

"You sure did," agreed Leota. "So Mrs. Pike, she give you a good look— she's very observant, a good judge of character, cute as a minute, you know— and she says, 'I bet you another Jax that lady's three months on the way.' "

"What gall!" said Mrs. Fletcher. "Mrs. Pike!"

"Mrs. Pike ain't goin' to bite you," said Leota. "Mrs. Pike is a lovely girl, you'd be crazy about her, Mrs. Fletcher.

But she can't sit still a minute. We went to the travellin' freak show yestiddy after work. I got through early—nine o'clock. In the vacant store next door. What, you ain't been?"

"No, I despise freaks," declared Mrs. Fletcher.

"Aw. Well, honey, talkin' about bein' pregnant an' all, you ought to see those twins in a bottle, you really owe it to yourself."

"What twins?" asked Mrs. Fletcher out of the side of her mouth.

"Well, honey, they got these two twins in a bottle, see? Born joined plumb together—dead a course." Leota dropped her voice into a soft lyrical hum. "They was about this long—pardon—must of been full time, all right, wouldn't you say?—an' they had these two heads an' two faces an' four arms an' four legs, all kind of joined *here*. See, this face looked this-a-way, and the other face looked that-a-way, over their shoulder, see. Kinda pathetic."

"Glah!" said Mrs. Fletcher disapprovingly.

"Well, ugly? Honey, I mean to tell you —their parents was first cousins and all like that. Billy Boy, git me a fresh towel from off Teeny's stack—this 'n's wringin' wet—an' quit ticklin' my ankles with that curler. I declare! He don't miss nothin'."

"Me and Mr. Fletcher aren't one speck of kin, or he could never of had me," said Mrs. Fletcher placidly.

"Of course not!" protested Leota. "Neither is me an' Fred, not that we know of. Well, honey, what Mrs. Pike liked was the pygmies. They've got these pygmies down there, too, an' Mrs. Pike was just wild about 'em. You know, the teeniniest men in the universe? Well, honey, they can just rest back on their little bohunkus an' roll around an' you can't hardly tell if they're sittin' or standin'. That'll give you some idea. They're about forty-two years old. Just suppose it was your husband!"

"Well, Mr. Fletcher is five foot nine and one half," said Mrs. Fletcher quickly.

"Fred's five foot ten," said Leota, "but I tell him he's still a shrimp, account of

I'm so tall." She made a deep wave over Mrs. Fletcher's other temple with the comb. "Well, these pygmies are a kind of a dark brown, Mrs. Fletcher. Not bad-lookin' for what they are, you know."

"I wouldn't care for them," said Mrs. Fletcher. "What does that Mrs. Pike see in them?"

"Aw, I don't know," said Leota. "She's just cute, that's all. But they got this man, this petrified man, that ever'thing ever since he was nine years old, when it goes through his digestion, see, somehow Mrs. Pike says it goes to his joints and has been turning to stone."

"How awful!" said Mrs. Fletcher.

"He's forty-two too. That looks like a bad age."

"Who said so, that Mrs. Pike? I bet she's forty-two," said Mrs. Fletcher.

"Naw," said Leota, "Mrs. Pike's thirty-three, born in January, an Aquarian. He could move his head—like this. A course his head and mind ain't a joint, so to speak, and I guess his stomach ain't, either—not yet, anyways. But see—his food, he eats it, and it goes down, see, and then he digests it"—Leota rose on her toes for an instant—"and it goes out to his joints and before you can say 'Jack Robinson,' it's stone—pure stone. He's turning to stone. How'd you like to be married to a guy like that? All he can do, he can move his head just a quarter of an inch. A course he *looks* just *terrible*."

"I should think he would," said Mrs. Fletcher frostily. "Mr. Fletcher takes bending exercises every night of the world. I make him."

"All Fred does is lay around the house like a rug. I wouldn't be surprised if he woke up some day and couldn't move. The petrified man just sat there moving his quarter of an inch though," said Leota reminiscently.

"Did Mrs. Pike like the petrified man?" asked Mrs. Fletcher.

"Not as much as she did the others," said Leota deprecatingly. "And then she likes a man to be a good dresser, and all that."

"Is Mr. Pike a good dresser?" asked Mrs. Fletcher sceptically.

"Oh, well, yeah," said Leota, "but he's twelve or fourteen years older'n her. She ast Lady Evangeline about him."

"Who's Lady Evangeline?" asked Mrs. Fletcher.

"Well, it's this mind reader they got in the freak show," said Leota. "Was real good. Lady Evangeline is her name, and if I had another dollar I wouldn't do a thing but have my other palm read. She had what Mrs. Pike said was the 'sixth mind' but she had the worst manicure I ever saw on a living person."

"What did she tell Mrs. Pike?" asked Mrs. Fletcher.

"She told her Mr. Pike was as true to her as he could be and besides, would come into some money."

"Humph!" said Mrs. Fletcher. "What does he do?"

"I can't tell," said Leota, "because he don't work. Lady Evangeline didn't tell me enough about my nature or anything. And I would like to go back and find out some more about this boy. Used to go with this boy until he got married to this girl. Oh, shoot, that was about three and a half years ago, when you was still goin' to the Robert E. Lee Beauty Shop in Jackson. He married her for her money. Another fortune-teller tole me that at the time. So I'm not in love with him any more, anyway, besides being married to Fred, but Mrs. Pike thought, just for the hell of it, see, to ask Lady Evangeline was he happy."

"Does Mrs. Pike know everything about you already?" asked Mrs. Fletcher unbelievingly. "Mercy!"

"Oh, yeah, I tole her ever'thing about ever'thing, from now on back to I don't know when—to when I first started goin' out," said Leota. "So I ast Lady Evangeline for one of my questions, was he happily married, and she says, just like she was glad I ask her, 'Honey,' she says, 'naw, he idn't. You write down this day, March 8, 1941,' she says, 'and mock it down: three years from today him and her won't be occupyin' the same bed.' There it is, up on the wall with them other dates—see, Mrs. Fletcher? And she says, 'Child, you ought to be glad you didn't git him, because he's so mercenary.' So I'm glad I married Fred. He sure ain't mercenary, money don't mean a thing to him. But I sure would like to go back and have my other palm read."

"Did Mrs. Pike believe in what the fortune-teller said?" asked Mrs. Fletcher in a superior tone of voice.

"Lord, yes, she's from New Orleans. Ever'body in New Orleans believes ever'thing spooky. One of 'em in New Orleans before it was raided says to Mrs. Pike one summer she was goin' to go from State to State and meet some grey-headed men, and, sure enough, she says she went on a beautician convention up to Chicago. . . ."

"Oh!" said Mrs. Fletcher. "Oh, is Mrs. Pike a beautician too?"

"Sure she is," protested Leota. "She's a beautician. I'm goin' to git her in here if I can. Before she married. But it don't leave you. She says sure enough, there was three men who was a very large part of making her trip what it was, and they all three had grey in their hair and they went in six States. Got Christmas cards from 'em. Billy Boy, go see if Thelma's got any dry cotton. Look how Mrs. Fletcher's a-drippin'."

"Where did Mrs. Pike meet Mr. Pike?" asked Mrs. Fletcher primly.

"On another train," said Leota.

"I met Mr. Fletcher, or rather he met me, in a rental library," said Mrs. Fletcher with dignity, as she watched the net come down over her head.

"Honey, me an' Fred, we met in a rumble seat eight months ago and we was practically on what you might call the way to the altar inside of half an hour," said Leota in a guttural voice, and bit a bobby pin open. "Course it don't last. Mrs. Pike says nothin' like that ever lasts."

"Mr. Fletcher and myself are as much in love as the day we married," said Mrs. Fletcher belligerently as Leota stuffed cotton into her ears.

"Mrs. Pike says it don't last," repeated Leota in a louder voice. "Now go git under the dryer. You can turn yourself on, can't you? I'll be back to comb you out. Durin' lunch I promised to give Mrs. Pike a facial. You know—free. Her bein' in the business, so to speak."

"I bet she needs one," said Mrs. Fletcher, letting the swing-door fly back against Leota. "Oh, pardon me."

A week later, on time for her appointment, Mrs. Fletcher sank heavily into Leota's chair after first removing a drug-store rental book, called *Life Is Like That,* from the seat. She stared in a discouraged way into the mirror.

"You can tell it when I'm sitting down, all right," she said.

Leota seemed preoccupied and stood shaking out a lavender cloth. She began to pin it around Mrs. Fletcher's neck in silence.

"I said you sure can tell it when I'm sitting straight on and coming at you this way," Mrs. Fletcher said.

"Why, honey, naw you can't," said Leota gloomily. "Why, I'd never know. If somebody was to come up to me on the street and say, 'Mrs. Fletcher is pregnant!' I'd say, 'Heck, she don't look it to me.' "

"If a certain party hadn't found it out and spread it around, it wouldn't be too late even now," said Mrs. Fletcher frostily, but Leota was almost choking her with the cloth, pinning it so tight, and she couldn't speak clearly. She paddled her hands in the air until Leota wearily loosened her.

"Listen, honey, you're just a virgin compared to Mrs. Montjoy," Leota was going on, still absent-minded. She bent Mrs. Fletcher back in the chair and, sighing, tossed liquid from a teacup on to her head and dug both hands into her scalp. "You know Mrs. Montjoy—her husband's that premature-grey-headed fella?"

"She's in the Trojan Garden Club, is all I know," said Mrs. Fletcher.

"Well, honey," said Leota, but in a weary voice, "she come in here not the week before and not the day before she had her baby—she come in here the very selfsame day, I mean to tell you. Child, we was all plumb scared to death. There she was! Come for her shampoo an' set. Why, Mrs. Fletcher, in an hour an' twenty minutes she was layin' up there in the Babtist Hospital with a seb'm-pound son. It was that close a shave. I declare, if I hadn't been so tired I would of drank up a bottle of gin that night."

"What gall," said Mrs. Fletcher. "I never knew her at all well."

"See, her husband was waitin' outside in the car, and her bags was all packed an' in the back seat, an' she was all ready, 'cept she wanted her shampoo an' set. An' havin' one pain right after another. Her husband kep' comin' in here, scared-like, but couldn't do nothin' with her a course. She yelled bloody murder, too, but she always yelled her head off when I give her a perm'nent."

"She must of been crazy," said Mrs. Fletcher. "How did she look?"

"Shoot!" said Leota.

"Well, I can guess," said Mrs. Fletcher. "Awful."

"Just wanted to look pretty while she was havin' her baby, is all," said Leota airily. "Course, we was glad to give the lady what she was after—that's our motto—but I bet a hour later she wasn't payin' no mind to them little end curls. I bet she wasn't thinkin' about she ought to have on a net. It wouldn't of done her no good if she had."

"No, I don't suppose it would," said Mrs. Fletcher.

"Yeah man! She was a-yellin'. Just like when I give her perm'nent."

"Her husband ought to make her behave. Don't it seem that way to you?" asked Mrs. Fletcher. "He ought to put his foot down."

"Ha," said Leota. "A lot he could do. Maybe some women is soft."

"Oh, you mistake me, I don't mean for her to get soft—far from it! Women have to stand up for themselves, or there's just no telling. But now you take me—I ask Mr. Fletcher's advice now and then, and he appreciates it, especially on something important, like is it time for a permanent—not that I've told him about the baby. He says, 'Why, dear, go ahead!' Just ask their *advice*."

"Huh! If I ever ast Fred's advice we'd be floatin' down the Yazoo River on a houseboat or somethin' by this time,"

said Leota. "I'm sick of Fred. I told him to go over to Vicksburg."

"Is he going?" demanded Mrs. Fletcher.

"Sure. See, the fortune-teller—I went back and had my other palm read, since we've got to rent the room agin—said my lover was goin' to work in Vicksburg, so I don't know who she could mean, unless she meant Fred. And Fred ain't workin' here—that much is so."

"Is he going to work in Vicksburg?" asked Mrs. Fletcher. "And—"

"Sure. Lady Evangeline said so. Said the future is going to be brighter than the present. He don't want to go, but I ain't gonna put up with nothin' like that. Lays around the house an' bulls—did bull—with that good-for-nothin' Mr. Pike. He says if he goes who'll cook, but I says I never get to eat anyway—not meals. Billy Boy, take Mrs. Grover that *Screen Secrets* and leg it."

Mrs. Fletcher heard stamping feet go out the door.

"Is that that Mrs. Pike's little boy here again?" she asked, sitting up gingerly.

"Yeah, that's still him." Leota stuck out her tongue.

Mrs. Fletcher could hardly believe her eyes. "Well! How's Mrs. Pike, your attractive new friend with the sharp eyes who spreads it around town that perfect strangers are pregnant?" she asked in a sweetened tone.

"Oh, Mizziz Pike." Leota combed Mrs. Fletcher's hair with heavy strokes.

"You act like you're tired," said Mrs. Fletcher.

"Tired? Feel like it's four o'clock in the afternoon already," said Leota. "I ain't told you the awful luck we had, me and Fred? It's the worst thing you ever heard of. Maybe *you* think Mrs. Pike's got sharp eyes. Shoot, there's a limit! Well, you know, we rented out our room to this Mr. and Mrs. Pike from New Orleans when Sal an' Joe Fentress got mad at us 'cause they drank up some home-brew we had in the closet—Sal an' Joe did. So, a week ago Sat'day Mr. and Mrs. Pike moved in. Well, I kinda fixed up the room, you know—put a sofa pillow on the couch and picked some ragged robbins and put in a vase, but they never did say they appreciated it. Anyway, then I put some old magazines on the table."

"I think that was lovely," said Mrs. Fletcher.

"Wait. So, come night 'fore last, Fred and this Mr. Pike, who Fred just took up with, was back from they said they was fishin', bein' as neither one of 'em has got a job to his name, and we was all settin' around in their room. So Mrs. Pike was settin' there, readin' a old *Startling G-Man Tales* that was mine, mind you, I'd bought it myself, and all of a sudden she jumps!—into the air— you'd 'a' thought she'd set on a spider— an' says, 'Canfield'—ain't that silly, that's Mr. Pike—'Canfield, my God A'mighty,' she says, 'honey,' she says, 'we're rich, and you won't have to work.' Not that he turned one hand anyway. Well, me and Fred rushes over to her, and Mr. Pike, too, and there she sets, pointin' her finger at a photo in my copy of *Startling G-Man*. 'See that man?' yells Mrs. Pike. 'Remember him, Canfield?' 'Never forget a face,' says Mr. Pike. 'It's Mr. Petrie, that we stayed with him in the apartment next to ours in Toulouse Street in N.O. for six weeks. Mr. Petrie.' 'Well,' says Mrs. Pike, like she can't hold out one secont longer, 'Mr. Petrie is wanted for five hundred dollars cash, for rapin' four women in California, and I know where he is.' "

"Mercy!" said Mrs. Fletcher. "Where was he?"

At some time Leota had washed her hair and now she yanked her up by the back locks and sat her up.

"Know where he was?"

"I certainly don't," Mrs. Fletcher said. Her scalp hurt all over.

Leota flung a towel around the top of her customer's head. "Nowhere else but in that freak show! I saw him just as plain as Mrs. Pike. *He* was the petrified man!"

"Who would ever have thought that!" cried Mrs. Fletcher sympathetically.

"So Mr. Pike says, 'Well whatta you know about that,' an' he looks real hard at the photo and whistles. And she starts dancin' and singin' about their good luck. She meant our bad luck! I made a point of tellin' that fortune-teller the next time I saw her. I said, 'Listen, that magazine was layin' around the house for a month, and there was the freak show runnin' night an' day, not two steps away from my own beauty parlor, with Mr. Petrie just settin' there waitin'. An' it had to be Mr. and Mrs. Pike, almost perfect strangers.' "

"What gall," said Mrs. Fletcher. She was only sitting there, wrapped in a turban, but she did not mind.

"Fortune-tellers don't care. And Mrs. Pike, she goes around actin' like she thinks she was Mrs. God," said Leota. "So they're goin' to leave tomorrow, Mr. and Mrs. Pike. And in the meantime I got to keep that mean, bad little ole kid here, gettin' under my feet ever' minute of the day an' talkin' back too."

"Have they gotten the five hundred dollars' reward already?" asked Mrs. Fletcher.

"Well," said Leota, "at first Mr. Pike didn't want to do anything about it. Can you feature that? Said he kinda liked that ole bird and said he was real nice to 'em, lent 'em money or somethin'. But Mrs. Pike simply tole him he could just go to hell, and I can see her point. She says, 'You ain't worked a lick in six months, and here I make five hundred dollars in two seconts, and what thanks do I get for it? You go to hell, Canfield,' she says. So," Leota went on in a despondent voice, "they called up the cops and they caught the ole bird, all right, right there in the freak show where I saw him with my own eyes, thinkin' he was petrified. He's the one. Did it under his real name —Mr. Petrie. Four women in California, all in the month of August. So Mrs. Pike gits five hundred dollars. And my magazine, and right next door to my beauty parlor. I cried all night, but Fred said it wasn't a bit of use and to go to sleep, because the whole thing was just a sort of coincidence—you know: can't do nothin' about it. He says it put him clean out of the notion of goin' to Vicksburg for a few days till we rent out the room agin—no tellin' who we'll git this time."

"But can you imagine anybody knowing this old man, that's raped four women?" persisted Mrs. Fletcher, and she shuddered audibly. "Did Mrs. Pike *speak* to him when she met him in the freak show?"

Leota had begun to comb Mrs. Fletcher's hair. "I says to her, I says, 'I didn't notice you fallin' on his neck when he was the petrified man—don't tell me you didn't recognize your fine friend?' And she says, 'I didn't recognize him with that white powder all over his face. He just looked familiar.' Mrs. Pike says, 'and lots of people look familiar.' But she says that ole petrified man did put her in mind of somebody. She wondered who it was! Kep' her awake, which man she'd ever knew it reminded her of. So when she seen the photo, it all come to her. Like a flash. Mr. Petrie. The way he'd turn his head and look at her when she took him in his breakfast."

"Took him in his breakfast!" shrieked Mrs. Fletcher. "Listen—don't tell me. I'd 'a' felt something."

"Four women. I guess those women didn't have the faintest notion at the time they'd be worth a hundred an' twenty-five bucks a piece some day to Mrs. Pike. We ast her how old the fella was then, an' she says he musta had one foot in the grave, at least. Can you beat it?"

"Not really petrified at all, of course," said Mrs. Fletcher meditatively. She drew herself up. "I'd 'a' felt something," she said proudly.

"Shoot! I did feel somethin'," said Leota. "I tole Fred when I got home I felt so funny. I said, 'Fred, that ole petrified man sure did leave me with a funny feelin'.' He says, 'Funny-haha or funny-peculiar?' and I says, 'Funny-peculiar.' " She pointed her comb into the air emphatically.

"I'll bet you did," said Mrs. Fletcher.

They both heard a crackling noise.

Leota screamed, "Billy Boy! What you doin' in my purse?"

"Aw, I'm just eatin' these ole stale peanuts up," said Billy Boy.

"You come here to me!" screamed Leota, recklessly flinging down the comb, which scattered a whole ashtray full of bobby pins and knocked down a row of Coca-Cola bottles. "This is the last straw!"

"I caught him! I caught him!" giggled Mrs. Fletcher. "I'll hold him on my lap. You bad, bad boy, you! I guess I better learn how to spank little old bad boys," she said.

Leota's eleven o'clock customer pushed open the swing-door upon Leota paddling him heartily with the brush, while he gave angry but belittling screams which penetrated beyond the booth and filled the whole curious beauty parlor. From everywhere ladies began to gather round to watch the paddling. Billy Boy kicked both Leota and Mrs. Fletcher as hard as he could, Mrs. Fletcher with her new fixed smile.

Billy Boy stomped through the group of wild-haired ladies and went out the door, but flung back the words, "If you're so smart, why ain't you rich?"

[1939]

QUESTIONS FOR STUDY

1. *The story is often described as a study of the grotesqueness and vulgarity of modern life. To what extent do the story's setting, characterization, dialogue, plot, and imagery support such an interpretation?*

2. *What happens in the story to conventional male and female roles? What is implied about love, marriage, childbearing, and adult sexuality? To what extent have all of the men in the story become "petrified"?*

3. *In what ways does the episode about Mrs. Pike and the petrified man, Mr. Petrie, serve to focus and reinforce the story's theme?*

4. *How does Mr. Petrie differ from the other men in the story? In what sense, ironically, does the reader come to regard him as something of an admirable character?*

5. *Why is Billy Boy included in the story? Why do Leota and Mrs. Fletcher turn on him? What are the implications of his final taunt, "If you're so smart, why ain't you rich?"*

EUDORA WELTY

Powerhouse

POWERHOUSE is playing! He's here on tour from the city— "Powerhouse and His Keyboard"— "Powerhouse and His Tasmanians"— think of the things he calls himself! There's no one in the world like him. You can't tell what he is. "Nigger man"? —he looks more Asiatic, monkey, Jewish, Babylonian, Peruvian, fanatic, devil. He has pale gray eyes, heavy lids, maybe horny like a lizard's, but big glowing eyes when they're open. He has African feet of the greatest size, stomping, both together, on each side of the pedals. He's not coal black—beverage colored—looks like a preacher when his mouth is shut, but then it opens—vast and obscene. And his mouth is going every minute: like a monkey's when it looks for something. Improvising, coming on a light and childish melody—*smooch*—he loves it with his mouth.

Is it possible that he could be this! When you have him there performing for you, that's what you feel. You know people on a stage—and people of a darker race—so likely to be marvelous, frightening.

This is a white dance. Powerhouse is not a show-off like the Harlem boys, not drunk, not crazy—he's in a trance; he's a person of joy, a fanatic. He listens as much as he performs, a look of hideous, powerful rapture on his face. Big arched eyebrows that never stop traveling, like a Jew's—wandering-Jew eyebrows. When he plays he beats down piano and seat and wears them away. He is in motion every moment—what could be more obscene? There he is with his great head, fat stomach, and little round piston legs, and long yellow-sectioned strong big fingers, at rest about the size of bananas. Of course you know how he sounds— you've heard him on records—but still you need to see him. He's going all the time, like skating around the skating rink or rowing a boat. It makes everybody crowd around, here in this shadowless steel-trussed hall with the rose-like posters of Nelson Eddy and the testimonial for the mind-reading horse in handwriting magnified five hundred times. Then all quietly he lays his finger on a key with the promise and serenity of a sibyl touching the book.

Powerhouse is so monstrous he sends everybody into oblivion. When any group, any performers, come to town, don't people always come out and hover near, learning inward about them, to learn what it is? What is it? Listen. Remember how it was with the acrobats. Watch them carefully, hear the least word, especially what they say to one another, in another language—don't let them escape you; it's the only time for hallucination, the last time. They can't stay. They'll be somewhere else this time tomorrow.

Powerhouse has as much as possible done by signals. Everybody, laughing as if to hide a weakness, will sooner or later hand him up a written request. Powerhouse reads each one, studying with a secret face: that is the face which looks like a mask—anybody's; there is a moment when he makes a decision. Then a light slides under his eyelids, and he says, "92!" or some combination of figures—never a name. Before a number the band is all frantic, misbehaving, pushing, like children in a classroom, and he is the teacher getting silence. His hands over the keys, he says sternly. "You-all ready? You-all ready to do some serious walking?" —waits—then, STAMP. Quiet.

STAMP, for the second time. This is absolute. Then a set of rhythmic kicks
against the floor to communicate the
tempo. Then, O Lord! say the distended
eyes from beyond the boundary of the
trumpets, Hello and good-bye, and they
are all down the first note like a waterfall.

This note marks the end of any known
discipline. Powerhouse seems to abandon
them all—he himself seems lost—down
in the song, yelling up like somebody in
a whirlpool—not guiding them—hailing
them only. But he knows, really. He cries
out, but he must know exactly. "Mercy!
. . . What I say! . . . Yeah!" And then
drifting, listening—"Where that skin
beater?"—wanting drums, and starting
up and pouring it out in the greatest delight and brutality. On the sweet pieces
such a leer for everybody! He looks down
so benevolently upon all our faces and
whispers the lyrics to us. And if you
could hear him at this moment on "Marie,
the Dawn is Breaking"! He's going up the
keyboard with a few fingers in some very
derogatory triplet-routine, he gets higher
and higher, and then he looks over the
end of the piano, as if over a cliff. But not
in a show-off way—the song makes him
do it.

He loves the way they all play, too—
all those next to him. The far section of
the band is all studious, wearing glasses,
every one—they don't count. Only those
playing around Powerhouse are the real
ones. He has a bass fiddler from Vicksburg, black as pitch, named Valentine,
who plays with his eyes shut and talking
to himself, very young: Powerhouse has
to keep encouraging him. "Go on, go on,
give it up, bring it on out there!" When
you heard him like that on records, did
you know he was really pleading?

He calls Valentine out to take a solo.

"What you going to play?" Powerhouse
looks out kindly from behind the piano;
he opens his mouth and shows his tongue,
listening.

Valentine looks down, drawing against
his instrument, and says without a lip
movement, " 'Honeysuckle Rose.' "

He has a clarinet player named Little
Brother, and loves to listen to anything
he does. He'll smile and say, "Beautiful!"

Little Brother takes a step forward when
he plays and stands at the very front, with
the whites of his eyes like fishes swimming. Once when he played a low note,
Powerhouse muttered a dirty praise, "He
went clear downstairs to get that one!"

After a long time, he holds up the number of fingers to tell the band how many
choruses still to go—usually five. He
keeps his directions down to signals.

It's a bad night outside. It's a white
dance, and nobody dances, except a few
straggling jitterbugs and two elderly
couples. Everybody just stands around
the band and watches Powerhouse. Sometimes they steal glances at one another,
as if to say, Of course, you know how it
is with *them*—Negroes—band leaders—
they would play the same way, giving all
they've got, for an audience of one. . . .
When somebody, no matter who, gives
everything, it makes people feel ashamed
for him.

Late at night they play the one waltz
they will ever consent to play—by request, "Pagan Love Song." Powerhouse's
head rolls and sinks like a weight between
his waving shoulders. He groans, and
his fingers drag into the keys heavily,
holding on to the notes, retrieving. It is a
sad song.

"You know what happened to me?"
says Powerhouse.

Valentine hums a response, dreaming
at the bass.

"I got a telegram my wife is dead,"
says Powerhouse, with wandering fingers.

"Uh-huh?"

His mouth gathers and forms a barbarous O while his fingers walk up
straight, unwillingly, three octaves.

"Gypsy? Why how come her to die,
didn't you just phone her up in the night
last night long distance?"

"Telegram say—here the words: Your
wife is dead." He puts 4/4 over the 3/4.

"Not but four words?" This is the
drummer, an unpopular boy named
Scoot, a disbelieving maniac.

Powerhouse is shaking his vast cheeks.
"What the hell was she trying to do? What
was she up to?"

"What name has it got signed, if you

got a telegram?" Scoot is spitting away with those wire brushes.

Little Brother, the clarinet player, who cannot now speak, glares and tilts back.

"Uranus Knockwood is the name signed." Powerhouse lifts his eyes open. "Ever heard of him?" A bubble shoots out on his lip like a plate on a counter.

Valentine is beating slowly on with his palm and scratching the strings with his long blue nails. He is fond of a waltz, Powerhouse interrupts him.

"I don't know him. Don't know who he is." Valentine shakes his head with the closed eyes.

"Say it agin."

"Uranus Knockwood."

"That ain't Lenox Avenue."

"It ain't Broadway."

"Ain't ever seen it wrote out in any print, even for horse racing."

"Hell, that's on a star, boy, ain't it?" Crash of the cymbals.

"What the hell was she up to?" Powerhouse shudders. "Tell me, tell me, tell me." He makes triplets, and begins a new chorus. He holds three fingers up.

"You say you got a telegram." This is Valentine, patient and sleepy, beginning again.

Powerhouse is elaborate. "Yas, the time I go out, go way downstairs along a long cor-ri-dor to where they puts us: coming back along the cor-ri-dor: steps out and hands me a telegram: Your wife is dead."

"Gypsy?" The drummer like a spider over his drums.

"Aaaaaaaaa!" shouts Powerhouse, flinging out both powerful arms for three whole beats to flex his muscles, then kneading a dough of bass notes. His eyes glitter. He plays the piano like a drum sometimes—why not?

"Gypsy? Such a dancer?"

"Why you don't hear it straight from your agent? Why it ain't come from head-quarters? What you been doing, getting telegrams in the *corridor,* signed no-body?"

They all laugh. End of that chorus.

"What time is it?" Powerhouse calls. "What the hell place is this? Where is my watch and chain?"

"I hang it on you," whimpers Valentine. "It still there."

There it rides on Powerhouse's great stomach, down where he can never see it.

"Sure did hear some clock striking twelve while ago. Must be *midnight."*

"It going to be intermission," Power-house declares, lifting up his finger with the signet ring.

He draws the chorus to an end. He pulls a big Northern hotel towel out of the deep pocket in his vast, special-cut tux pants and pushes his forehead into it.

"If she went and killed herself!" he says with a hidden face. "If she up and jumped out that window!" He gets to his feet, turning vaguely, wearing the towel on his head.

"Ha, ha!"

"Sheik, sheik!"

"She wouldn't do that." Little Brother sets down his clarinet like a precious vase, and speaks. He still looks like an East Indian queen, implacable, divine, and full of snakes. "You ain't going to expect people doing what they says over long distance."

"Come on!" roars Powerhouse. He is already at the back door, he has pulled it wide open, and with a wild, gathered-up face is smelling the terrible night.

Powerhouse, Valentine, Scoot and Little Brother step outside into the drenching rain.

"Well, they emptying buckets," says Powerhouse in a modified voice. On the street he holds his hands out and turns up the blanched palms like sieves.

A hundred dark, ragged, silent, de-lighted Negroes have come around from under the eaves of the hall, and follow wherever they go.

"Watch out Little Brother don't shrink," says Powerhouse. "You just the right size now, clarinet don't suck you in. You got a dry throat, Little Brother, you in the desert?" He reaches into the pocket and pulls out a paper of mints. "Now hold 'em in your mouth—don't chew 'em. I don't carry around nothing without limit."

"Go in that joint and have beer," says Scoot, who walks ahead.

"Beer? Beer? You know what beer is?

What do they say is beer? What's beer?
Where I been?"

"Down yonder where it say World
Café—that do?" They are in Negrotown
now.

Valentine patters over and holds open
a screen door warped like a sea shell,
bitter in the wet, and they walk in, stained
darker with the rain and leaving footprints. Inside, sheltered dry smells stand
like screens around a table covered with
a red-checkered cloth, in the center of
which flies hang onto an obelisk-shaped
ketchup bottle. The midnight walls are
checkered again with admonishing "Not
Responsible" signs and black-figured,
smoky calendars. It is a waiting, silent,
limp room. There is a burned-out-looking
nickelodeon and right beside it a long-
necked wall instrument labeled "Business
Phone, Don't Keep Talking." Circled
phone numbers are written up every
where. There is a worn-out peacock
feather hanging by a thread to an old,
thin, pink, exposed light bulb, where it
slowly turns around and around, whoever
breathes.

A waitress watches.

"Come here, living statue, and get
all this big order of beer we fixing to
give."

"Never seen you before anywhere."
The waitress moves and comes forward
and slowly shows little gold leaves and
tendrils over her teeth. She shoves up her
shoulders and breasts. "How I going to
know who you might be? Robbers?
Coming in out of the black of night right
at midnight, setting down so big at my
table?"

"Boogers," says Powerhouse, his eyes
opening lazily as in a cave.

The girl screams delicately with
pleasure. O Lord, she likes talk and
scares.

"Where you going to find enough beer
to put out on this here table?"

She runs to the kitchen with bent
elbows and sliding steps.

"Here's a million nickels," says Powerhouse, pulling his hand out of his pocket
and sprinkling coins out, all but the last
one, which he makes vanish like a
magician.

Valentine and Scoot take the money
over to the nickelodeon, which looks as
battered as a slot machine, and read all
the names of the records out loud.

"Whose 'Tuxedo Junction'?" asks
Powerhouse.

"You know whose."

"Nickelodeon, I request you please to
play 'Empty Red Blues' and let Bessie
Smith sing."

Silence: they hold it like a measure.

"Bring me all those nickels on back
here," says Powerhouse. "Look at that!
What you tell me the name of this place?"

"White dance, week night, raining,
Alligator, Mississippi, long ways from
home."

"Uh-huh."

"Sent for You Yesterday and Here
You Come Today" plays.

The waitress, setting the tray of beer
down on a back table, comes up taut
and apprehensive as a hen. "Says in the
kitchen, back there putting their eyes to
little hole peeping out, that you is Mr.
Powerhouse. . . . They knows from a picture they seen."

"They seeing right tonight, that is him,"
says Little Brother.

"You him?"

"That is him in the flesh," says Scoot.

"Does you wish to touch him?" asks
Valentine. "Because he don't bite."

"You passing through?"

"Now you got everything right."

She waits like a drop, hands languishing together in front.

"Little-Bit, ain't you going to bring
the beer?"

She brings it, and goes behind the cash
register and smiles, turning different ways.
The little fillet of gold in her mouth is
gleaming.

"The Mississippi River's here," she
says once.

Now all the watching Negroes press in
gently and bright-eyed through the door,
as many as can get in. One is a little boy
in a straw sombrero which has been
coated with aluminum paint all over.

Powerhouse, Valentine, Scoot and
Little Brother drink beer, and their eyelids come together like curtains. The wall
and the rain and the humble beautiful

waitress waiting on them and the other Negroes watching enclose them.

"Listen!" whispers Powerhouse, looking into the ketchup bottle and slowly spreading his performer's hands over the damp, wrinkling cloth with the red squares. "Listen how it is. My wife gets missing me. Gypsy. She goes to the window. She looks out and sees you know what. Street. Sign saying Hotel. People walking. Somebody looks up. Old man. She looks down, out the window. Well? . . . *Ssssst! Plooey!* What she do? Jump out and burst her brains all over the world."

He opens his eyes.

"That's it," agrees Valentine. "You gets a telegram."

"Sure she misses you," Little Brother adds.

"No, it's night time." How softly he tells them! "Sure. It's the night time. She say, What do I hear? Footsteps walking up the hall? That him? Footsteps go on off. It's not me. I'm in Alligator, Mississippi, she's crazy. Shaking all over. Listens till her ears and all grow out like old music-box horns but still she can't hear a thing. She says, All right! I'll jump out the window then. Got on her nightgown. I know that nightgown, and her thinking there. Says, Ho hum, all right, and jumps out the window. Is she mad at me! Is she crazy! She don't leave *nothing* behind her!"

"Ya! Ha!"

"Brains and insides everywhere, Lord, Lord."

All the watching Negroes stir in their delight, and to their higher delight he says affectionately, "Listen! Rats in here."

"That must be the way, boss."

"Only, naw, Powerhouse, that ain't true. That sound too *bad*."

"Does I even know who finds her," cries Powerhouse. "That no-good pussy-footed crooning creeper, that creeper that follow around after me, coming up like weeds behind me, following around after me everything I do and messing around on the trail I leave. Bets my numbers, sings my songs, gets close to my agent like a Betsy-bug; when I going out

he just coming in. I got him now! I got my eye on him."

"Know who he is?"

"Why, it's that old Uranus Knockwood!"

"Ya! Ha!"

"Yeah, and he coming now, he going to find Gypsy. There he is, coming around that corner, and Gypsy kadoodling down, oh-oh, watch out! *Ssssst! Plooey!* See, there she is in her little old nightgown, and her insides and brains all scattered round."

A sigh fills the room.

"Hush about her brains. Hush about her insides."

"Ya! Ha! You talking about her brains and insides—old Uranus Knockwood," says Powerhouse, "look down and say Jesus! He say, Look here what I'm walking round in!"

They all burst into halloos of laughter. Powerhouse's face looks like a big hot iron stove.

"Why, he picks her up and carries her off!" he says.

"Ya! Ha!"

"Carries her *back* around the corner. . . ."

"Oh, Powerhouse!"

"You know him."

"Uranus Knockwood!"

"Yeahhh!"

"He take our wives when we gone!"

"He come in when we goes out!"

"Uh-huh!"

"He go out when we comes in!"

"Yeahhh!"

"He standing behind the door!"

"Old Uranus Knockwood."

"You know him."

"Middle-size man."

"Wears a hat."

"That's him."

Everybody in the room moans with pleasure. The little boy in the fine silver hat opens a paper and divides out a jelly roll among his followers.

And out of the breathless ring somebody moves forward like a slave, leading a great logy Negro with bursting eyes, and says, "This here is Sugar-Stick Thompson, that dove down to the bottom of July Creek and pulled up all those drownded white people fall out of a boat. Last summer, pulled up fourteen."

"Hello," says Powerhouse, turning and looking around at them all with his great daring face until they nearly suffocate.

Sugar-Stick, their instrument, cannot speak; he can only look back at the others.

"Can't even swim. Done it by holding his breath," says the fellow with the hero.

Powerhouse looks at him seekingly.

"I his half brother," the fellow puts in. They step back.

"Gypsy say," Powerhouse rumbles gently again, looking at *them*, " 'What is the use? I'm gonna jump out so far—so far. . . .' *Sssst—!*"

"Don't, boss, don't do it again," says Little Brother.

"It's awful," says the waitress. "I hates that Mr. Knockwoods. All that the truth?"

"Want to see the telegram I got from him?" Powerhouse's hand goes to the vast pocket.

"Now wait, now wait, boss." They all watch him.

"It must be the real truth," says the waitress, sucking in her lower lip, her luminous eyes turning sadly, seeking the windows.

"No, babe, it ain't the truth." His eyebrows fly up, and he begins to whisper to her out of his vast oven mouth. His hand stays in his pocket. "Truth is something worse, I ain't said what, yet. It's something hasn't come to me, but I ain't saying it won't. And when it does, then want me to tell you?" He sniffs all at once, his eyes come open and turn up, almost too far. He is dreamily smiling.

"Don't, boss, don't, Powerhouse!"

"Oh!" the waitress screams.

"Go on get out of here!" bellows Powerhouse, taking his hand out of his pocket and clapping after her red dress.

The ring of watchers breaks and falls away.

"*Look* at that! Intermission is up," says Powerhouse.

He folds money under a glass, and after they go out, Valentine leans back in and drops a nickel in the nickelodeon behind them, and it lights up and begins to play "The Goona Goo." The feather dangles still.

"Take a telegram!" Powerhouse shouts suddenly up into the rain over the street. "Take a answer. Now what was the name?"

They get a little tired.

"Uranus Knockwood."

"You ought to know."

"Yas? Spell it to me."

They spell it all the ways it could be spelled. It puts them in a wonderful humor.

"Here's the answer. I got it right here. 'What in the hell you talking about? Don't make any difference: I gotcha.' Name signed: Powerhouse."

"That going to reach him, Powerhouse?" Valentine speaks in a maternal voice.

"Yas, yas."

All hushing, following him up the dark street at a distance, like old rained-on black ghosts, the Negroes are afraid they will die laughing.

Powerhouse throws back his vast head into the streaming rain, and a look of hopeful desire seems to blow somehow like a vapor from his own dilated nostrils over his face and bring a mist to his eyes.

"Reach him and come out the other side."

"That's it, Powerhouse, that's it. You got him now."

Powerhouse lets out a long sigh.

"But ain't you going back there to call up Gypsy long distance, the way you did last night in that other place? I seen a telephone. . . . Just to see if she there at home?"

There is a measure of silence. That is one crazy drummer that's going to get his neck broken some day.

"No," growls Powerhouse. "No! How many thousand times tonight I got to say No?"

He holds up his arm in the rain.

"You sure-enough unroll your voice some night, it about reach up yonder to her," says Little Brother, dismayed.

They go on up the street, shaking the rain off and on them like birds.

Back in the dance hall, they play "San" (99). The jitterbugs start up like wind-mills stationed over the floor, and in their orbits—one circle, another, a long stretch and a zigzag—dance the elderly couples with old smoothness, undisturbed and stately.

When Powerhouse first came back from intermission, no doubt full of beer, they said, he got the band tuned up again in his own way. He didn't strike the piano keys for pitch—he simply opened his mouth and gave falsetto howls—in A, D and so on—they tuned by him. Then he took hold of the piano, as if he saw it for the first time in his life, and tested it for strength, hit it down in the bass, played an octave with his elbow, lifted the top, looked inside, and leaned against it with all his might. He sat down and played it for a few minutes with outrageous force and got it under his power—a bass deep and coarse as a sea net—then produced something glimmering and fragile, and smiled. And who could ever remember any of the things he says? They are just inspired remarks that roll out of his mouth like smoke.

They've requested "Somebody Loves Me," and he's already done twelve or fourteen choruses, piling them up nobody knows how, and it will be a wonder if he ever gets through. Now and then he calls and shouts. " 'Somebody loves me! Somebody loves me, I wonder who!' " His mouth gets to be nothing but a vol-cano. "I wonder who!"

"Maybe . . ." He uses all his right hand on a trill.

"Maybe . . ." He pulls back his spread fingers and looks out upon the place where he is. A vast, impersonal and yet furious grimace transfigures his wet face.

". . . Maybe it's you!"

[1941]

QUESTIONS FOR STUDY

1. *Who is the implied narrator of the story's opening paragraphs? What kind of picture or image of Powerhouse does he create?*

2. *To what extent does Powerhouse conceal his true emotions and real identity behind the mask of his public image? In what ways are his real character and personality revealed?*

3. *Is Gypsy really dead (is she even his wife)? If not, why does Power-house create and dwell upon this particular fantasy? Who (or what) is Uranus Knockwood?*

4. *What stylistic devices does Welty use to communicate the effect of Powerhouse's music?*

5. *Ralph Ellison has written of the blues: "The blues is an impulse to keep the painful details and episodes of a brutal experience alive in one's aching consciousness, to finger its jagged grain, and to tran-scend it, not by the consolation of philosophy, but by squeezing from it a near-tragic, near-comic lyricism." How might such a definition be applied to the story?*

E. B. WHITE

The Second Tree from the Corner

"EVER have any bizarre thoughts?" asked the doctor.

Mr. Trexler failed to catch the word. "What kind?" he said.

"Bizarre," repeated the doctor, his voice steady. He watched his patient for any slight change of expression, any wince. It seemed to Trexler that the doctor was not only watching him closely but was creeping slowly toward him, like a lizard toward a bug. Trexler shoved his chair back an inch and gathered himself for a reply. He was about to say "Yes" when he realized that if he said yes the next question would be unanswerable. Bizarre thoughts, bizarre thoughts? Ever have any bizarre thoughts? What kind of thoughts *except* bizarre had he had since the age of two?

Trexler felt the time passing, the necessity for an answer. These psychiatrists were busy men, overloaded, not to be kept waiting. The next patient was probably already perched out there in the waiting room, lonely, worried, shifting around on the sofa, his mind stuffed with bizarre thoughts and amorphous fears. Poor bastard, thought Trexler. Out there all alone in that misshapen antechamber, staring at the filing cabinet and wondering whether to tell the doctor about that day on the Madison Avenue bus.

Let's see, bizarre thoughts. Trexler dodged back along the dreadful corridor of the years to see what he could find. He felt the doctor's eyes upon him and knew that time was running out. Don't be so conscientious, he said to himself. If a bizarre thought is indicated here, just reach into the bag and pick anything at all. A man as well supplied with bizarre thoughts as you are should have no diffi-culty producing one for the record. Trexler darted into the bag, hung for a moment before one of his thoughts, as a hummingbird pauses in the delphinium. No, he said, not that one. He darted to another (the one about the rhesus monkey), paused, considered. No, he said, not that.

Trexler knew he must hurry. He had already used up pretty nearly four seconds since the question had been put. But it was an impossible situation—just one more lousy, impossible situation such as he was always getting himself into. When, he asked himself, are you going to quit maneuvering yourself into a pocket? He made one more effort. This time he stopped at the asylum, only the bars were lucite—fluted, retractable. Not here, he said. Not this one.

He looked straight at the doctor. "No," he said quietly. "I never have any bizarre thoughts."

The doctor sucked in on his pipe, blew a plume of smoke toward the rows of medical books. Trexler's gaze followed the smoke. He managed to make out one of the titles, "The Genito-Urinary System." A bright wave of fear swept cleanly over him, and he winced under the first pain of kidney stones. He remembered when he was a child, the first time he ever entered a doctor's office, sneaking a look at the titles of the books—and the flush of fear, the shirt wet under the arms, the book on t.b., the sudden knowledge that he was in the advanced stages of consumption, the quick vision of the hemorrhage. Trexler sighed wearily. Forty years, he thought, and I still get thrown by the title of a medical book. Forty years and I still can't stay on life's little bucky horse. No wonder I'm sitting here in this dreary joint at the end of this woebegone afternoon, lying about my bizarre thoughts to a doctor who looks, come to think of it, rather tired.

The session dragged on. After about twenty minutes, the doctor rose and knocked his pipe out. Trexler got up, knocked the ashes out of his brain, and waited. The doctor smiled warmly and stuck out his hand. "There's nothing the matter with you—you're just scared. Want to know how I know you're scared?"

"How?" asked Trexler.

"Look at the chair you've been sitting in! See how it has moved back away from my desk? You kept inching away from me while I asked you questions. That means you're scared."

"Does it?" said Trexler, faking a grin. "Yeah, I suppose it does."

They finished shaking hands. Trexler turned and walked out uncertainly along the passage, then into the waiting room and out past the next patient, a ruddy pin-striped man who was seated on the sofa twirling his hat nervously and staring straight ahead at the files. Poor, frightened guy, thought Trexler, he's probably read in the *Times* that one American male out of every two is going to die of heart disease by twelve o'clock next Thursday. It says that in the paper almost every morning. And he's also probably thinking about that day on the Madison Avenue bus.

A week later, Trexler was back in the patient's chair. And for several weeks thereafter he continued to visit the doctor, always toward the end of the afternoon, when the vapors hung thick above the pool of the mind and darkened the whole region of the East Seventies. He felt no better as time went on, and he found it impossible to work. He discovered that the visits were becoming routine and that although the routine was one to which he certainly did not look forward, at least he could accept it with cool resignation, as once, years ago, he had accepted a long spell with a dentist who had settled down to a steady fooling with a couple of dead teeth. The visits,

moreover, were now assuming a pattern recognizable to the patient.

Each session would begin with a résumé of symptoms—the dizziness in the streets, the constricting pain in the back of the neck, the apprehensions, the tightness of the scalp, the inability to concentrate, the despondency and the melancholy times, the feeling of pressure and tension, the anger at not being able to work, the anxiety over work not done, the gas on the stomach. Dullest set of neurotic symptoms in the world, Trexler would think, as he obediently trudged back over them for the doctor's benefit. And then, having listened attentively to the recital, the doctor would spring his question: "Have you ever found anything that gives you relief?" And Trexler would answer, "Yes. A drink." And the doctor would nod his head knowingly.

As he became familiar with the pattern Trexler found that he increasingly tended to identify himself with the doctor, transferring himself into the doctor's seat—probably (he thought) some rather slick form of escapism. At any rate, it was nothing new for Trexler to identify himself with other people. Whenever he got into a cab, he instantly became the driver, saw everything from the hackman's angle (and the reaching over with the right hand, the nudging of the flag, the pushing it down, all the way down along the side of the meter), saw everything—traffic, fare, everything—through the eyes of Anthony Rocco, or Isidore Freedman, or Matthew Scott. In a barbershop, Trexler was the barber, his fingers curled around the comb, his hand on the tonic. Perfectly natural, then, that Trexler should soon be occupying the doctor's chair, asking the questions, waiting for the answers. He got quite interested in the doctor, in this way. He liked him, and he found him a not too difficult patient.

It was on the fifth visit, about halfway through, that the doctor turned to Trexler and said, suddenly, "What do you want?" He gave the word "want" special emphasis.

"I d'know," replied Trexler uneasily. "I guess nobody knows the answer to that one."

"Sure they do," replied the doctor.

"Do *you* know what *you* want?" asked Trexler narrowly.

"Certainly," said the doctor. Trexler noticed that at this point the doctor's chair slid slightly backward, away from him. Trexler stifled a small, internal smile. Scared as a rabbit, he said to himself. Look at him scoot!

"What *do* you want?" continued Trexler, pressing his advantage, pressing it hard.

The doctor glided back another inch away from his inquisitor. "I want a wing on the small house I own in Westport. I want more money, and more leisure to do the things I want to do."

Trexler was just about to say, "And what are those things you want to do, Doctor?" when he caught himself. Better not go too far, he mused. Better not lose possession of the ball. And besides, he thought, what the hell goes on here, anyway—me paying fifteen bucks a throw for these séances and then doing the work myself, asking the questions, weighing the answers. So he wants a new wing! There's a fine piece of theatrical gauze for you! A new wing.

Trexler settled down again and resumed the role of patient for the rest of the visit. It ended on a kindly, friendly note. The doctor reassured him that his fears were the cause of his sickness, and that his fears were unsubstantial. They shook hands, smiling.

Trexler walked dizzily through the empty waiting room and the doctor followed along to let him out. It was late; the secretary had shut up shop and gone home. Another day over the dam. "Goodbye," said Trexler. He stepped into the street, turned west toward Madison, and thought of the doctor all alone there, after hours, in that desolate hole—a man who worked longer hours than his secretary. Poor, scared, overworked bastard, thought Trexler. And that new wing!

It was an evening of clearing weather, the Park showing green and desirable in the distance, the last daylight applying a high lacquer to the brick and brownstone walls and giving the street scene a luminous and intoxicating splendor. Trex-

ler meditated, as he walked, on what he wanted. "What do you want?" he heard again. Trexler knew what he wanted, and what, in general, all men wanted; and he was glad, in a way, that it was both inexpressible and unattainable, and that it wasn't a wing. He was satisfied to remember that it was deep, formless, enduring, and impossible of fulfillment, and that it made men sick, and that when you sauntered along Third Avenue and looked through the doorways into the dim saloons, you could sometimes pick out from the unregenerate ranks the ones who had not forgotten, gazing steadily into the bottoms of the glasses on the long chance that they could get another little peek at it. Trexler found himself renewed by the remembrance that what he wanted was at once great and microscopic, and that although it borrowed from the nature of large deeds and of youthful love and of old songs and early intimations, it was not any one of these things, and that it had not been isolated or pinned down, and that a man who attempted to define it in the privacy of a doctor's office would fall flat on his face.

Trexler felt invigorated. Suddenly his sickness seemed health, his dizziness stability. A small tree, rising between him and the light, stood there saturated with the evening, each gilt-edged leaf perfectly drunk with excellence and delicacy. Trexler's spine registered an ever so slight tremor as it picked up this natural disturbance in the lovely scene. "I want the second tree from the corner, just as it stands," he said, answering an imaginary question from an imaginary physician. And he felt a slow pride in realizing that what he wanted none could bestow, and that what he had none could take away. He felt content to be sick, unembarrassed at being afraid; and in the jungle of his fear he glimpsed (as he had so often glimpsed them before) the flashy tail feathers of the bird courage.

Then he thought once again of the doctor, and of his being left there all alone, tired, frightened. (The poor, scared guy, thought Trexler.) Trexler began humming "Moonshine Lullaby," his spirit reacting instantly to the hypodermic of Merman's healthy voice. He crossed Madison, boarded a downtown bus, and rode all the way to Fifty-second Street before he had a thought that could rightly have been called bizarre.

[1947]

QUESTIONS FOR STUDY

1. *What seems to be the "problem" that takes Trexler to the psychiatrist's office?*
2. *What is significant in the fact that Trexler "increasingly tended to identify himself with the doctor"? To what extent does such an identification seem justifiable?*
3. *What does Trexler mean when he says "I want the second tree from the corner, just as it stands"? Why the "second" tree?*
4. *What kind of resolution to Trexler's problem does the story offer?*
5. *The story is narrated in the third person. What are the advantages of such a point of view? Could it be told as effectively in the first person by Trexler himself?*
6. *Describe the tone of the story. Does it seem appropriate? Why?*

RICHARD WRIGHT

The Man Who Was Almost a Man

DAVE STRUCK OUT across the fields, looking homeward through paling light. Whut's the use talkin wid em niggers in the field? Anyhow, his mother was putting supper on the table. Them niggers can't understan nothing. One of these days he was going to get a gun and practice shooting, then they couldn't talk to him as though he were a little boy. He slowed, looking at the ground. Shucks, Ah ain scareda them even ef they are biggern me! Aw, Ah know whut Ahma do. Ahm going by ol Joe's sto n git that Sears Roebuck catlog n look at them guns. Mebbe Ma will lemme buy one when she gits mah pay from ol man Hawkins. Ahma beg her t gimme some money. Ahm ol ernough t hava gun. Ahm seventeen. Almost a man. He strode, feeling his long loose-jointed limbs. Shucks, a man oughta hava little gun aftah he done worked hard all day.

He came in sight of Joe's store. A yellow lantern glowed on the front porch. He mounted steps and went through the screen door, hearing it bang behind him There was a strong smell of coal oil and mackerel fish. He felt very confident until he saw fat Joe walk in through the rear door, then his courage began to ooze.

"Howdy, Dave! Whutcha want?"

"How yuh, Mistah Joe? Aw, Ah don wanna buy nothing. Ah jus wanted t see ef yuhd lemme look at tha catlog erwhile."

"Sure! You wanna see it here?"

"Nawsuh. Ah wans t take it home wid me. Ah'll bring it back termorrow when Ah come in from the fiels."

"You plannin on buying something?"

"Yessuh."

"Your ma lettin you have your own money now?"

"Shucks. Mistah Joe, Ahm gittin t be a man like anybody else!"

Joe laughed and wiped his greasy white face with a red bandanna.

"Whut you plannin on buyin?"

Dave looked at the floor, scratched his head, scratched his thigh, and smiled. Then he looked up shyly.

"Ah'll tell yuh, Mistah Joe, ef yuh promise yuh won't tell."

"I promise."

"Waal, Ahma buy a gun."

"A gun? Whut you want with a gun?"

"Ah wanna keep it."

"You ain't nothing but a boy. You don't need a gun."

"Aw, lemme have the catlog, Mistah Joe. Ah'll bring it back."

Joe walked through the rear door. Dave was elated. He looked around at barrels of sugar and flour. He heard Joe coming back. He craned his neck to see if he were bringing the book. Yeah, he's got it. Gawddog, he's got it!

"Here, but be sure you bring it back. It's the only one I got."

"Sho, Mistah Joe."

"Say, if you wanna buy a gun, why don't you buy one from me? I gotta gun to sell."

"Will it shoot?"

"Sure it'll shoot."

"Whut kind is it?"

"Oh, it's kinda old . . . a left-hand Wheeler. A pistol. A big one."

"Is it got bullets in it?"

"It's loaded."

"Kin Ah see it?"

"Where's your money?"

"Whut yuh wan fer it?"

"I'll let you have it for two dollars."

"Just two dollahs? Shucks, Ah could buy tha when Ah git mah pay."

"I'll have it here when you want it."

"Awright, suh. Ah be in fer it."

He went through the door, hearing it slam again behind him. Ahma git some money from Ma n buy me a gun! Only two dollahs! He tucked the thick catalogue under his arm and hurried.

"Where yuh been, boy?" His mother held a steaming dish of black-eyed peas.

"Aw, Ma, Ah jus stopped down the road t talk wid the boys."

"Yuh know bettah t keep suppah waitin."

He sat down, resting the catalogue on the edge of the table.

"Yuh git up from there and git to the well n wash yoself! Ah ain feedin no hogs in mah house!"

She grabbed his shoulder and pushed him. He stumbled out of the room, then came back to get the catalogue.

"Whut this?"

"Aw, Ma, it's jusa catlog."

"Who yuh git it from?"

"From Joe, down at the sto."

"Waal, thas good. We kin use it in the outhouse."

"Naw, Ma." He grabbed for it. "Gimme ma catlog, Ma."

She held onto it and glared at him.

"Quit hollerin at me! Whut's wrong wid yuh? Yuh crazy?"

"But Ma, please. It ain mine! It's Joe's! He tol me t bring it back t im termorrow."

She gave up the book. He stumbled down the back steps, hugging the thick book under his arm. When he had splashed water on his face and hands, he groped back to the kitchen and fumbled in a corner for the towel. He bumped into a chair; it clattered to the floor. The catalogue sprawled at his feet. When he had dried his eyes he snatched up the book and held it again under his arm. His mother stood watching him.

"Now, ef yuh gonna act a fool over that ol book, Ah'll take it n burn it up."

"Naw, Ma, please."

"Waal, set down n be still!"

He sat down and drew the oil lamp close. He thumbed page after page, unaware of the food his mother set on the table. His father came in. Then his small brother.

"Whutcha got there, Dave?" his father asked.

"Jusa catlog," he answered, not looking up.

"Yeah, here they is!" His eyes glowed

at blue-and-black revolvers. He glanced up, feeling sudden guilt. His father was watching him. He eased the book under the table and rested it on his knees. After the blessing was asked, he ate. He scooped up peas and swallowed fat meat without chewing. Buttermilk helped to wash it down. He did not want to mention money before his father. He would do much better by cornering his mother when she was alone. He looked at his father uneasily out of the edge of his eye.

"Boy, how come yuh don quit foolin wid tha book n eat yo suppah?"

"Yessuh."

"How you n ol man Hawkins gitten erlong?"

"Suh?"

"Can't yuh hear? Why don yuh lissen? Ah ast yu how wuz yuh n ol man Hawkins gittin erlong?"

"Oh, swell, Pa. Ah plows mo lan than anybody over there."

"Waal, yuh oughta keep yo mind on whut yuh doin."

"Yessuh."

He poured his plate full of molasses and sopped it up slowly with a chunk of cornbread. When his father and brother had left the kitchen, he still sat and looked again at the guns in the catalogue, longing to muster courage enough to present his case to his mother. Lawd, ef Ah only had tha pretty one! He could almost feel the slickness of the weapon with his fingers. If he had a gun like that he would polish it and keep it shining so it would never rust. N Ah'd keep it loaded, by Gawd!

"Ma?" His voice was hesitant.

"Hunh?"

"Ol man Hawkins give yuh mah money yit?"

"Yeah, but ain no usa yuh thinking bout throwin nona it erway. Ahm keepin tha money sos yuh kin have cloes t go to school this winter."

He rose and went to her side with the open catalogue in his palms. She was washing dishes, her head bent low over a pan. Shyly he raised the book. When he spoke, his voice was husky, faint.

"Ma, Gawd knows Ah wans one of these."

"One of whut?" she asked, not raising her eyes.

"One of these," he said again, not daring even to point. She glanced up at the page, then at him with wide eyes.

"Nigger, is yuh gone plumb crazy?"

"Aw, Ma—"

"Git outta here! Don yuh talk t me bout no gun! Yuh a fool!"

"Ma, Ah kin buy one fer two dollahs."

"Not ef Ah knows it, yuh ain!"

"But yuh promised me one—"

"Ah don care whut Ah promised! Yuh ain nothing but a boy yit!"

"Ma, ef yuh lemme buy one Ah'll *never* ast yuh fer nothing no mo'."

"Ah tol yuh t git outta here! Yuh ain gonna toucha penny of tha money fer no gun! Thas how come Ah has Mistah Hawkins t pay yo wages t me, cause Ah knows yuh ain got no sense."

"But, Ma, we needa gun. Pa ain got no gun. We needa gun in the house. Yuh kin never tell whut might happen."

"Now don yuh try to maka fool outta me, boy! Ef we did hava gun, yuh wouldn't have it!"

He laid the catalogue down and slipped his arm around her waist.

"Aw, Ma, Ah done worked hard alla summer n ain ast yuh fer nothin, is Ah, now?"

"Thas whut yuh spose t do!"

"But Ma, Ah wans a gun. Yuh kin lemme have two dollahs outta mah money. Please, Ma. I kin give it to Pa . . . Please, Ma! Ah loves yuh, Ma."

When she spoke her voice came soft and low.

"Whut yu wan wida gun, Dave? Yuh don need no gun. Yuh'll git in trouble. N ef yo pa jus thought Ah let yuh have money t buy a gun he'd hava fit."

"Ah'll hide it, Ma. It ain but two dollahs."

"Lawd, chil, whut's wrong wid yuh?"

"Ain nothin wrong, Ma. Ahm almos a man now. Ah wans a gun."

"Who gonna sell yuh a gun?"

"Ol Joe at the sto."

"N it don cos but two dollahs?"

"Thas all, Ma. Jus two dollahs. Please, Ma."

She was stacking the plates away; her hands moved slowly, reflectively. Dave kept an anxious silence. Finally, she turned to him.

"Ah'll let yuh git tha gun ef yuh promise me one thing."

"Whut's tha, Ma?"

"Yuh bring it straight back t me, yuh hear? It be fer Pa."

"Yessum! Lemme go now, Ma."

She stooped, turned slightly to one side, raised the hem of her dress, rolled down the top of her stocking, and came up with a slender wad of bills.

"Here," she said. "Lawd knows yuh don need no gun. But yer pa does. Yuh bring it right back t me, yuh hear? Ahma put it up. Now ef yuh don, Ahma have yuh pa lick yuh so hard yuh won fergit it."

"Yessum."

He took the money, ran down the steps, and across the yard.

"Dave! Yuuuuuh Daaaaave!"

He heard, but he was not going to stop now. "Naw, Lawd!"

The first movement he made the following morning was to reach under his pillow for the gun. In the gray light of dawn he held it loosely, feeling a sense of power. Could kill a man with a gun like this. Kill anybody, black or white. And if he were holding his gun in his hand, nobody could run over him; they would have to respect him. It was a big gun, with a long barrel and a heavy handle. He raised and lowered it in his hand, marveling at its weight.

He had not come straight home with it as his mother had asked; instead he had stayed out in the fields, holding the weapon in his hand, aiming it now and then at some imaginary foe. But he had not fired it; he had been afraid that his father might hear. Also he was not sure he knew how to fire it.

To avoid surrendering the pistol he had not come into the house until he knew that they were all asleep. When his mother had tiptoed to his bedside late that night and demanded the gun, he had first played possum; then he had told her that the gun was hidden outdoors, that he would bring it to her in the morning. Now he lay turning it slowly in his hands.

He broke it, took out the cartridges, felt them, and then put them back.

He slid out of bed, got a long strip of old flannel from a trunk, wrapped the gun in it, and tied it to his naked thigh while it was still loaded. He did not go in to breakfast. Even though it was not yet daylight, he started for Jim Hawkins' plantation. Just as the sun was rising he reached the barns where the mules and plows were kept.

"Hey! That you, Dave?"

He turned. Jim Hawkins stood eying him suspiciously.

"What're yuh doing here so early?"

"Ah didn't know Ah wuz gittin up so early, Mistah Hawkins. Ah wuz fixin t hitch up ol Jenny n take her t the fiels."

"Good. Since you're so early, how about plowing that stretch down by the woods?"

"Suits me, Mistah Hawkins."

"O.K. Go to it!"

He hitched Jenny to a plow and started across the fields. Hot dog! This was just what he wanted. If he could get down by the woods, he could shoot his gun and nobody would hear. He walked behind the plow, hearing the traces creaking, feeling the gun tied tight to his thigh.

When he reached the woods, he plowed two whole rows before he decided to take out the gun. Finally, he stopped, looked in all directions, then untied the gun and held it in his hand. He turned to the mule and smiled.

"Know whut this is, Jenny? Naw, yuh wouldn know! Yuhs jusa ol mule! Anyhow, this is a gun, n it kin shoot, by Gawd!"

He held the gun at arm's length. Whut t hell, Ahma shoot this thing! He looked at Jenny again.

"Lissen here, Jenny! When Ah pull this ol trigger, Ah don wan yuh t run n acka fool now!"

Jenny stood with head down, her short ears pricked straight. Dave walked off about twenty feet, held the gun far out from him at arm's length, and turned his head. Hell, he told himself, Ah ain afraid. The gun felt loose in his fingers; he waved it wildly for a moment. Then he shut his eyes and tightened his forefinger. Bloom!

A report half deafened him and he thought his right hand was torn from his arm. He heard Jenny whinnying and galloping over the field, and he found himself on his knees, squeezing his fingers hard between his legs. His hand was numb; he jammed it into his mouth, trying to warm it, trying to stop the pain. The gun lay at his feet. He did not quite know what had happened. He stood up and stared at the gun as though it were a living thing. He gritted his teeth and kicked the gun. Yuh almos broke mah arm! He turned to look for Jenny; she was far over the fields, tossing her head and kicking wildly.

"Hol on there, ol mule!"

When he caught up with her she stood trembling, walling her big white eyes at him. The plow was far away; the traces had broken. Then Dave stopped short, looking, not believing. Jenny was bleeding. Her left side was red and wet with blood. He went closer. Lawd, have mercy! Wondah did Ah shoot this mule? He grabbed for Jenny's mane. She flinched, snorted, whirled, tossing her head.

"Hol on now! Hol on."

Then he saw the hole in Jenny's side, right between the ribs. It was round, wet, red. A crimson stream streaked down the front leg, flowing fast. Good Gawd! Ah wuzn't shootin at tha mule. He felt panic. He knew he had to stop that blood, or Jenny would bleed to death. He had never seen so much blood in all his life. He chased the mule for half a mile, trying to catch her. Finally she stopped, breathing hard, stumpy tail half arched. He caught her mane and led her back to where the plough and gun lay. Then he stooped and grabbed handfuls of damp black earth and tried to plug the bullet hole. Jenny shuddered, whinnied, and broke from him.

"Hol on! Hol on now!"

He tried to plug it again, but blood came anyhow. His fingers were hot and sticky. He rubbed dirt into his palms, trying to dry them. Then again he attempted to plug the bullet hole, but Jenny shied away, kicking her heels high. He stood helpless. He had to do something. He ran at Jenny; she dodged him. He watched a red stream of blood flow down Jenny's leg and form a bright pool at her feet.

"Jenny . . . Jenny," he called weakly.

His lips trembled. She's bleeding t death! He looked in the direction of home, wanting to go back, wanting to get help. But he saw the pistol lying in the damp black clay. He had a queer feeling that if he only did something, this would not be; Jenny would not be there bleeding to death.

When he went to her this time, she did not move. She stood with sleepy, dreamy eyes; and when he touched her she gave a low-pitched whinny and knelt to the ground, her front knees slopping in blood.

"Jenny . . . Jenny . . ." he whispered.

For a long time she held her neck erect; then her head sank, slowly. Her ribs swelled with a mighty heave and she went over.

Dave's stomach felt empty, very empty. He picked up the gun and held it gingerly between his thumb and forefinger. He buried it at the foot of a tree. He took a stick and tried to cover the pool of blood with dirt—but what was the use? There was Jenny lying with her mouth open and her eyes walled and glassy. He could not tell Jim Hawkins he had shot his mule. But he had to tell something. Yeah, Ah'll tell em Jenny started gittin wil n fell on the joint of the plow. . . . But that would hardly happen to a mule. He walked across the field slowly, head down.

It was sunset. Two of Jim Hawkins' men were over near the edge of the woods digging a hole in which to bury Jenny. Dave was surrounded by a knot of people, all of whom were looking down at the dead mule.

"I don't see how in the world it happened," said Jim Hawkins for the tenth time.

The crowd parted and Dave's mother, father, and small brother pushed into the center.

"Where Dave?" his mother called.

"There he is," said Jim Hawkins.

His mother grabbed him.

"Whut happened, Dave? Whut yuh done?"

"Nothin."

"C mon, boy, talk," his father said.

Dave took a deep breath and told the story he knew nobody believed.

"Waal," he drawled. "Ah brung ol Jenny down here sos Ah could do mah plowin. Ah plowed bout two rows, just like yuh see." He stopped and pointed at the long rows of upturned earth. "Then somethin musta been wrong wid ol Jenny. She wouldn ack right a-tall. She started snortin n kickin her heels. Ah tried t hol her, but she pulled erway, rearin n goin in. Then when the point of the plow was stickin up in the air, she swung erroun n twisted herself back on it . . . She stuck herself n started t bleed. N fo Ah could do anything, she wuz dead."

"Did you ever hear of anything like that in all your life?" asked Jim Hawkins.

There were white and black standing in the crowd. They murmured. Dave's mother came close to him and looked hard into his face. "Tell the truth, Dave," she said.

"Looks like a bullet hole to me," said one man.

"Dave, whut yuh do wid the gun?" his mother asked.

The crowd surged in, looking at him. He jammed his hands into his pockets, shook his head slowly from left to right, and backed away. His eyes were wide and painful.

"Did he hava gun?" asked Jim Hawkins.

"By Gawd, Ah tol yuh tha wuz a gun wound," said a man, slapping his thigh.

His father caught his shoulders and shook him till his teeth rattled.

"Tell whut happened, yuh rascal! Tell whut . . ."

Dave looked at Jenny's stiff legs and began to cry.

"Whut yuh do wid tha gun?" his mother asked.

"Whut wuz he doin wida gun?" his father asked.

"Come on and tell the truth," said Hawkins. "Ain't nobody going to hurt you . . ."

His mother crowded close to him.

"Did yuh shoot tha mule, Dave?"

Dave cried, seeing blurred white and black faces.

"Ahh ddinn gggo tt sshooot hher . . . Ah sssswear ffo Gawd Ahh ddin. . . . Ah wuz a-tryin t sssee ef the old gggun would sshoot—"

"Where yuh git the gun from?" his father asked.

"Ah got it from Joe, at the sto."

"Where yuh git the money?"

"Ma give it t me."

"He kept worryin me, Bob. Ah had t. Ah tol im t bring the gun right back t me . . . It was fer yuh, the gun."

"But how yuh happen to shoot that mule?" asked Jim Hawkins.

"Ah wuzn shootin at the mule, Mistah Hawkins. The gun jumped when Ah pulled the trigger . . . N fo Ah knowed anythin Jenny was there a-bleedin."

Somebody in the crowd laughed. Jim Hawkins walked close to Dave and looked into his face.

"Well, looks like you have bought you a mule, Dave."

"Ah swear fo Gawd, Ah didn go t kill the mule, Mistah Hawkins!"

"But you killed her!"

All the crowd was laughing now. They stood on tiptoe and poked heads over one another's shoulders.

"Well, boy, looks like yuh done bought a dead mule! Hahaha!"

"Ain tha ershame."

"Hohohohoho."

Dave stood, head down, twisting his feet in the dirt.

"Well, you needn't worry about it, Bob," said Jim Hawkins to Dave's father. "Just let the boy keep on working and pay me two dollars a month."

"Whut yuh wan fer yo mule, Mistah Hawkins?"

Jim Hawkins screwed up his eyes.

"Fifty dollars."

"Whut yuh do wid tha gun?" Dave's father demanded.

Dave said nothing.

"Yuh wan me t take a tree n beat yuh till yuh talk!"

"Nawsuh!"

"Whut yuh do wid it?"

"Ah throwed it erway."

"Where?"

"Ah . . . Ah throwed it in the creek."

"Waal, c mon home. N firs thing in the mawnin git to tha creek n fin tha gun."

"Yessuh."

"Whut yuh pay fer it?"

"Two dollahs."

"Take tha gun n git yo money back n carry it t Mistah Hawkins, yuh hear? N don fergit Ahma lam you black bottom good fer this! Now march yosef on home, suh!"

Dave turned and walked slowly. He heard people laughing. Dave glared, his eyes welling with tears. Hot anger bubbled in him. Then he swallowed and stumbled on.

That night Dave did not sleep. He was glad that he had gotten out of killing the mule so easily, but he was hurt. Something hot seemed to turn over inside him each time he remembered how they had laughed. He tossed on his bed, feeling his hard pillow. N Pa says he's gonna beat me . . . He remembered other beatings, and his back quivered. Naw, naw, Ah sho don wan im t beat me tha way no mo. Dam em all! Nobody ever gave him anything. All he did was work. They treat me like a mule, n then they beat me. He gritted his teeth. N Ma had t tell on me.

Well, if he had to, he would take old man Hawkins that two dollars. But that meant selling the gun. And he wanted to keep that gun. Fifty dollars for a dead mule.

He turned over, thinking how he had fired the gun. He had an itch to fire it again. Ef other men kin shoota gun, by Gawd, Ah kin! He was still, listening. Mebbe they all sleepin now. The house was still. He heard the soft breathing of his brother. Yes, now! He would go down and get that gun and see if he could fire it! He eased out of bed and slipped into overalls.

The moon was bright. He ran almost all the way to the edge of the woods. He stumbled over the ground, looking for the spot where he had buried the gun. Yeah, here it is. Like a hungry dog scratching for a bone, he pawed it up.

He puffed his black cheeks and blew dirt from the trigger and barrel. He broke it and found four cartridges unshot. He looked around; the fields were filled with silence and moonlight. He clutched the gun stiff and hard in his fingers. But, as soon as he wanted to pull the trigger, he shut his eyes and turned his head. Naw, Ah can't shoot wid mah eyes closed n mah head turned. With effort he held his eyes open; then he squeezed. *Blooooom!* He was stiff, not breathing. The gun was still in his hands. Dammit, he'd done it! He fired again. *Blooooom!* He smiled. *Blooooom! Blooooom! Click, click.* There! It was empty. If anybody could shoot a gun, he could. He put the gun into his hip pocket and started across the fields.

When he reached the top of a ridge he stood straight and proud in the moonlight, looking at Jim Hawkins' big white house, feeling the gun sagging in his pocket. Lawd, ef Ah had just one mo bullet Ah'd taka shot at tha house. Ah'd like t scare ol man Hawkins jusa little . . . Jusa enough t let im know Dave Saunders is a man.

To his left the road curved, running to the tracks of the Illinois Central. He jerked his head, listening. From far off came a faint *hoooof-hoooof; hoooof-hoooof; hoooof-hoooof.* . . . He stood rigid. Two dollahs a mont. Les see now . . . Tha means it'll take bout two years. Shucks! Ah'll be dam!

He started down the road, toward the tracks. Yeah, here she comes! He stood beside the track and held himself stiffly. Here she comes, erroun the ben . . . C mon, yuh slow poke! C mon! He had his hand on his gun; something quivered in his stomach. Then the train thundered past, the gray and brown box cars rumbling and clinking. He gripped the gun tightly; then he jerked his hand out of his pocket. Ah betcha Bill wouldn't do it! Ah betcha . . . The cars slid past, steel grinding upon steel. Ahm ridin yuh ternight, so hep me Gawd! He was hot all over. He hesitated just a moment; then he grabbed, pulled atop of a car, and lay flat. He felt his pocket; the gun was still there. Ahead the long rails were glinting in the moonlight, stretching away, away to somewhere, somewhere where he could be a man . . .

[1940]

QUESTIONS FOR STUDY

1. *In what ways does Dave's gun serve to define the problems of his adolescence and his relationship to his family, Mr. Hawkins, and the blacks who work in the fields?*
2. *In what sense can Dave's accidental shooting of Jenny the mule be viewed as a subconscious act of rebellion? Does the story contain other signs of Dave's rebelliousness or hostility?*
3. *Is Dave's decision to climb aboard the freight train a convincing conclusion to the story?*
4. *How important is the story's setting?*

Biographical Notes

AICHINGER

ILSE AICHINGER (1921–   ) was born in Vienna, Austria, and was raised there and in nearby Linz. Following World War II, during which she and her family were persecuted by the Nazis, she briefly studied medicine before turning her attention to fiction. Her work, much of it reminiscent of Kafka, has attracted wide attention throughout Europe and has won her a number of important literary honors. Her much acclaimed first novel *Herod's Children* and her collection of stories *The Bound Man* have been available in English since 1963 and 1956 respectively. Married to the poet Gunther Eich, Ilse Aichinger currently makes her home in Bavaria.

ANDERSON

SHERWOOD ANDERSON (1876–1941) was born in Camden, Ohio, and was largely self-educated. After a succession of odd jobs—farm laborer, factory worker, copywriter—he enlisted in the Spanish American War, following which he made his way to Chicago, where he became a successful advertising writer. Anderson married in 1904, and two years later moved to Cleveland, acquired an interest in a factory in nearby Elyria, and spent the next years combining manufacturing, advertising, and the writing of fiction. Following a nervous breakdown in 1912, Anderson gave up his Ohio interests and their financial rewards to return to Chicago, where he used his income as an advertising writer to support his literary efforts. His first three published volumes—the novels *Windy McPherson's Son* (1916) and *Marching Men* (1917) and the volume of poems *Mid-American Chants* (1918)— were only mildly successful, but his fourth work, the collection of stories *Winesburg, Ohio* (1919), with its powerful psychological portraits of men and women trapped by the repressive atmosphere of small-town life, won deserved recognition and established Anderson's reputation. His later works include the novels *Poor White* (1920) and *Dark Laughter* (1925) and three volumes of short stories: *Triumph of the Egg* (1821), *Horses and Men* (1923), and *Death in the Woods* (1933).

BALDWIN

JAMES BALDWIN (1924–   ), the son of a revivalist minister, was born and raised in New York's Harlem. His early literary promise brought him to the attention of black expatriate writer Richard Wright, who helped Baldwin win a fellowship to forward work on his first novel, *Go Tell It on the Mountain,* published in 1953. Baldwin's other novels include *Giovanni's Room* (1956), *Another Country* (1962), *Tell Me How Long the Train's Been Gone* (1968), and *If Beale Street Could Talk* (1974). He has also published several volumes of essays, *Notes of a Native Son* (1955), *Nobody Knows My Name* (1961), *The Fire Next Time* (1963), *No Name in the Street* (1972), and *The Devil Finds Work* (1976); a volume of collected stories, *Going to Meet the Man* (1965); and two plays, *Blues for Mister Charlie* (1964) and *The Amen Corner* (1968).

BARTH

JOHN BARTH (1930–   ) was born and raised in Cambridge, Maryland, and after briefly attending the Julliard School of Music in New York received his B.A. from Johns Hopkins in 1951, followed by an M.A. in 1952. He published the first of his unconventional and increasingly experimental novels, *The Floating Opera,* in 1956, followed by *The End of the Road* (1958), *The Sot-Weed Factor* (1960), and *Giles Goat-Boy* (1966). His collection of short stories, *Lost in the Funhouse,* appeared in 1968. His most recent book, *Chimera,* composed of three long stories, was published in 1972. Barth taught English at the Pennsylvania State University before joining the English faculty of the State University of New York at Buffalo in 1965, is currently writer-in-residence and professor of English at Johns Hopkins.

BARTHELME

DONALD BARTHELME (1933–   ), one of the most exciting and strikingly innovative of America's younger generation of short story writers, was born in Philadelphia and raised in Houston, Texas, where he attended the University of Houston. His career to date has been a varied one: newspaper reporter, magazine editor, museum director, avante-garde author. Barthelme has published two novels, *Snow White* (1967) and *The Dead Father* (1975): four collections of short stories, *Come Back,*

Unspeakable Practices,
68), *City Life* (1970),
and a volume of non-
ures (1974). Many of
published in the *New*
the early 1960s. Bar-
.kes his home in New

SAUL BELLOW (1915–   ), the son of
Russian immigrants, was born in Quebec,
Canada, but grew up in the city of Chicago. He attended the University of Chicago, and then transferred to nearby Northwestern University, where he earned a B.S.
degree in anthropology and sociology in
1937. After briefly attending graduate school
at the University of Wisconsin, Bellow returned to Chicago to work for the Works
Progress Administration (WPA) and then
for the editorial staff of the *Encyclopedia
Britannica.* Following the publication of his
first novel, *Dangling Man* (1944), Bellow
joined the English faculty of the University
of Minnesota. He has subsequently taught
at New York University, Princeton University, Bard College, the University of
Puerto Rico, and since 1962 at the University of Chicago as a member of the
Committee on Social Thought. Bellow's
novels include *The Victim* (1947), *The
Adventures of Augie March* (1953), *Seize
the Day* (1956), *Henderson the Rain King*
(1959), *Herzog* (1964), *Mr. Sammler's
Planet* (1970), and *Humboldt's Gift* (1975).
Both *The Adventures of Augie March* and
Herzog earned for Bellow the much coveted National Book Award and in 1976 he
was awarded the Nobel Prize for Literature. Bellow has also authored a prize-
winning play, *The Last Analysis* (1965),
and a volume of collected short stories,
Mosby's Memoirs and Other Stories (1968).
The story here anthologized, "Looking for
Mr. Green," provides a good introduction
to Saul Bellow's fiction, particularly in its
concern for the experience of contemporary
man in search of his own identity.

BIERCE

AMBROSE BIERCE (1842–1914) was the
youngest of the nine children of a poverty-
stricken Ohio farmer, and as a result received little formal education. In 1861, at
the age of nineteen, he enlisted as a drummer boy in the Ninth Indiana Volunteers.
During the four years that followed, Bierce
rose steadily through the ranks, emerging
from the war as a brevet major. Wounded

twice, he saw action in some of the war's
most bloody engagements, unconsciously
gathering as he did so much of the material
for his later stories. Following the Civil
War Bierce began a journalistic and literary
career that took him to California, England,
and Washington. His bitterness and pessimism, attenuated by personal tragedy, increased through the years to its climax in
1913 when, having put his affairs in order,
Bierce disappeared into Mexico. His best
short stories appeared in two volumes:
Tales of Soldiers and Civilians (1891) and
Can Such Things Be? (1893).

BONTEMPS

ARNA BONTEMPS (1902–1973) was born
in Louisiana and grew up in California,
where he graduated from Pacific Union
College. In the early 1920s Bontemps came
to New York, where he discovered the impetus to write in the black cultural revival
known as the Harlem Renaissance. His subsequent writing and literary activities took
many directions: poetry, fiction, literary anthologies, children's literature, and essays.
For many years Bontemps served as librarian at Fisk University, in Nashville, Tennessee. His books include *God Sends Sunday* (1931), *Black Thunder* (1936), and *The
Story of the Negro* (1948). With fellow
writer Langston Hughes he edited two important anthologies of black American literature: *The Book of Negro Folklore*
(1948) and *The Poetry of the Negro*
(1949).

BORGES

JORGE LUIS BORGES (1899–   ), generally recognized as the greatest living
writer in Spanish, was born in Buenos
Aires, Argentina, and raised and educated
in Europe. Under the influence of avant-
garde writers Borges himself began to
write, and published his first book, a volume of poems, in 1923. During the decade
that followed, Borges expanded his hori-
zons to include the writing of essays, film
criticism, Spanish translations of the works
of such major literary figures as Kafka and
Joyce, and, almost by accident, short stories. From 1938 to 1946 he served as a
municipal librarian in his native Buenos
Aires until he was turned out by Argen-
tinian dictator Juan Perón. With the over-
throw of the Perónists in 1955, Borges became Director of the National Library of
Buenos Aires and, in 1956, professor of
English and American literature at the
University of Buenos Aires. Among the

volumes of his writings now available in English are *Labyrinths* (1962), *Ficciones* (1962), *Dreamtigers* (1964), *Other Inquisitions* (1965), *A Personal Anthology* (1967), *The Aleph* (1970), and *Doctor Brodie's Report* (1972). Borges' short stories, the products of his voluminous and encyclopedic reading, demonstrate through the medium of fantasy man's attempts to find order and meaning in an apparently chaotic universe.

BOWEN

ELIZABETH BOWEN (1899–1973) was born in Dublin, Ireland, but raised and educated in England. During World War I she worked as a nurse in a veteran's hospital in Dublin, and then returned to England where she briefly studied at the London Council of Art. She published her first volume of fiction, a collection of short stories titled *Encounter,* in 1923. For the next dozen years she made her home in Old Headington, outside Oxford, and it was from there that Elizabeth Bowen established her critical reputation as an accomplished prose stylist with such books as *The Hotel* (1927), *The Last September* (1929), *Friends and Relations* (1931), and *The House in Paris* (1935). In 1935 she and her husband, Alan Charles Cameron, moved to Regent's Park, London, where they remained throughout World War II and where she added to her literary activities the task of reviewer for and contributor to *The New Statesman.* She published *Death of the Heart,* perhaps her most famous novel, in 1938, followed by *Look at All Those Roses* (1941), *The Demon Lover* (1945), *The Heat of the Day* (1949), *A World of Love* (1955), *The Little Girls* (1964), and *Eva Trout* (1969).

BOYLE

KAY BOYLE (1903–   ) was born in St. Paul, Minnesota, and spent her childhood in a succession of different cities: Philadelphia, Atlantic City, Washington, and Cincinnati. She also traveled widely in Europe. Educated at the Shipley School, Bryn Mawr, the Ohio Mechanics Institute in Cincinnati, and at the Cincinnati Conservatory of Music, she then went to New York where she began her writing career. Following her marriage in 1922 to a French engineering student, she made her home abroad, in France, England, Austria, and Germany, before returning to America almost a quarter of a century later. Kay Boyle currently makes her residence in San Francisco. Her literary career has been a

productive one: more than a dozen novels, several volumes of poetry, and such collections of short stories as *Wedding Day* (1930), *The First Lover* (1933), *The White Horses of Vienna* (1937), *Crazy Hunter* (1940), and *Thirty Stories* (1946).

BRADBURY

RAY BRADBURY (1920–   ), one of America's best known and energetic writers of science fiction and fantasy, was born in Waukegan, Illinois, and attended school in Waukegan and in Los Angeles, California. By the age of twelve he had begun to write and illustrate his own stories and as a high school student founded and edited his own mimeographed quarterly, *Futuria Fantasia.* During the early years of his career, 1940–1943, Bradbury sold newspapers on the streets of Los Angeles to finance his writing. He sold his first story in 1941 and by the age of twenty-five was securely established as a published author. That Bradbury's science fiction (which is humanistic in its affirmations and notoriously unscientific) has won him the acclaim of literary critics is due in good measure to his prose style, which is at its best, as Gilbert Highet has noted, a "curious mixture of poetry and colloquialism." Bradbury's books include *Dark Carnival* (1947), *The Martian Chronicles* (1950), *The Illustrated Man* (1951), *The Golden Apples of the Sun* (1953), *Fahrenheit 451* (1953), *The October Country* (1955), *Dandelion Wine* (1957), *Something Wicked This Way Comes* (1962), *The Machineries of Joy* (1964), *I Sing the Body Electric* (1969), and *The Halloween Tree* (1972). Ray Bradbury currently makes his home in Los Angeles.

CAMUS

ALBERT CAMUS (1913–1960) was born and educated in Algeria, then still a colony of France, and as a college student at the University of Algiers devoted considerable time to fostering the activities of a small theatrical company which he organized and directed. Although active in the underground resistance movement which sprang up following the fall of France to the Germans in World War II, Camus nonetheless found time to write and publish *The Stranger* (1942) and *The Myth of Sisyphus* (1943), two works that became landmarks of postwar French existential thought. His later published works include the novels *The Plague* (1947) and *The Fall* (1956) and a collection of short stories, *The Exile and the Kingdom* (1957). These works helped to earn him the 1957 Nobel Prize in Literature. Camus died suddenly and tragically in 1960 as the result of an automobile accident.

CHEEVER

JOHN CHEEVER (1912–) was born in Quincy, Massachusetts, and educated at the exclusive Thayer Academy, from which he was expelled in his junior year. The record of his experiences at Thayer published in a series of sketches in the *New Republic* in October 1930 constituted Cheever's literary debut. Thereafter, short stories, many of them depicting upper-middle-class American life as it is lived in suburbia, began to appear regularly in such magazines as the *New Republic, Yale Review, Atlantic Monthly,* and the *New Yorker.* They have been collected in *The Way Some People Live* (1943), *The Enormous Radio* (1953), *The Housebreaker of Shady Hill* (1958), *Some People, Places and Things That Will Not Appear in My Next Novel* (1961), *The Brigadier and the Golf Widow* (1964), and *The World of Apples* (1973). Cheever's novels include *The Wapshot Chronicle* (1957), *The Wapshot Scandal* (1964), *Bullet Park* (1969), and *Falconer* (1977).

CHEKHOV

ANTON CHEKHOV (1860–1904), the grandson of a serf, was born in the southern Russian seaport town of Taganrog, but followed his family to Moscow in 1879 after the failure of his father's grocery business. Educated as a doctor, a profession he was to practice only as an adjunct to literature, he received his medical degree and published his first collection of short stories the same year (1884). Although Chekhov's early stories are uneven in quality—he wrote much and he wrote quickly—they won him respect, reputation, and, most important, financial independence. In the last dozen years of his life, by contrast, he wrote fewer than fifty stories, many of them classics. At their best, Chekhov's stories are subtle and complex mixtures of comedy and tragedy which illuminate his characters and their humanity in an objective, yet compassionate way. Incredible as it seems, considering the shortness of his life, Chekhov also produced such masterpieces of the drama as *The Sea Gull* (1896), *Uncle Vanya* (1899), *The Three Sisters* (1901), and *The Cherry Orchard* (1904).

CHRISTIE

AGATHA CHRISTIE (1890–1976) was born at Torquay, Devon, England. After the death of her American father, she was reared and educated by her English mother who also encouraged her in the writing of fiction. She published her first detective novel, *The Mysterious Affair at Styles,* in 1920, a novel that also celebrated the first appearance of her famous detective, the diminutive Belgian, Hercule Poirot. Its success encouraged other novels, and for the next half-century, through more than eighty books that sold in excess of 350 million copies, Agatha Christie reigned as the first lady of detective fiction. Among her better-known detective novels are *The Murder of Roger Ackroyd* (1926), *Murder on the Orient Express* (1934), *The A. B. C. Murders* (1935), *Death on the Nile* (1937), *Ten Little Indians* (1939), *Crooked House* (1949), *A Murder Is Announced* (1950), *Dead Man's Folly* (1956), *The Clocks* (1963), *Endless Night* (1967), and *Passenger to Frankfurt* (1970). Miss Christie's collections of shorter detective fiction include *Poirot Investigates* (1924), *Partners in Crime* (1929), *Thirteen Problems* (1932), *Hound of Death* (1933), *Dead Man's Mirror* (1937), *Witness for the Prosecution and Other Stories* (1948), *Three Blind Mice and Other Stories* (1950), and *Under Dog and Other Stories* (1952). In addition, Agatha Christie published a number of gothic romances under the pseudonym "Mary Westmacott," and two highly successful plays, *The Mousetrap* (1952) and *Witness for the Prosecution* (1953), both adaptations of her earlier short stories. The former has the distinction of being the longest-running play ever to take the British stage, and the latter was made into a classic film starring Charles Laughton, Elsa Lanchester, and Marlene Dietrich. Miss Christie's detective fictions are characterized by their idealized British middle-class settings, the attractiveness of their detective heroes (notably the mustachioed Poirot and the spinster Miss Jane Marple), and by the ingenuity of their plots.

CLARKE

ARTHUR C. CLARKE (1917–) was born in Minehead, Somerset, England. Even as a small boy, Clarke displayed a strong interest in things scientific, and by the age of fifteen was writing scientific fantasies for his school paper. Financially unable to attend a university, Clarke took a job in London as an auditor, where he also became involved as treasurer with the recently founded British Interplanetary Society. It was during this period—the years prior to World War II—that Clarke also began to write science fiction stories and technical articles dealing with scientific subjects. Clarke served with the Royal Air Force as a radar specialist, and then, in 1946, used the British version of the G.I. Bill to enter Kings College, London, where in two years he earned an honors degree in physics and mathematics. In the same year he published his first novel, *Against the Fall of Night*. Since that time Clarke has emerged as one of the two or three major contemporary science fiction writers. His novels, each of which turns on some serious concept or idea, include *Prelude to Space* (1951), *Childhood's End* (1953), *Earthlight* (1955), *The City and the Stars* (1956), *The Deep Range* (1957), *A Fall of Moondust* (1961), and *Imperial Earth* (1975). His more than 300 short stories have been brought together in such collections as *Expedition to Earth* (1953), *Tales from the White Hart* (1957), *Tales of Ten Worlds* (1962), *Prelude to Mars* (1965), *The Nine Billion Names of God* (1967), and *The Wind from the Sun* (1972). In addition, Clarke has written many volumes of nonfiction on scientific subjects, including *The Exploration of Space,* an early plea for space travel that became a Book-of-the-Month Club selection upon its publication in 1951. More recently Clarke collaborated with Stanley Kubrick on the film script for the widely acclaimed *2001: A Space Odyssey* (1968). Among his many other honors are the Kalinga Prize for 1962, presented by UNESCO for his popularization of science, the Hugo best story award, which came to him in 1956 for "The Star," and the Hugo and Nebula awards for the best novel, 1974, for *Rendezvous with Rama* (1973). For the past twenty years Clarke has made his home on the island of Sri Lanka (Ceylon).

CLEMENS

SAMUEL LANGHORNE CLEMENS (1835–1910), Mark Twain, was born in rural Missouri and raised in the Mississippi River town of Hannibal, a town that this fiction was to immortalize. As a boy of twelve he became an apprentice printer on the local newspaper and then struck out on his own as a journeyman printer, a trade that took him to St. Louis, Chicago, Philadelphia, and Cincinnati. After serving briefly as a river boat pilot, and even more briefly as a

Confederate soldier, Clemens accompanied his brother west to the Nevada Territory, where Samuel Clemens began his long career as journalist and writer. Even without his two classics of midwestern boyhood, *Tom Sawyer* (1876) and *Huckleberry Finn* (1885), he would be famous for such books as *The Innocents Abroad* (1869), *Roughing It* (1872), *The Gilded Age* (1873), *Life on the Mississippi* (1883), *A Connecticut Yankee in King Arthur's Court* (1889), *Pudd'nhead Wilson* (1894), and his *Autobiography* (1924).

COLLINS

WILKIE COLLINS (1824–1889) was a lifelong resident of London and a close friend of Charles Dickens, whose fiction he imitated and under whom he served as a member of the staff of the periodicals *Household Words* and, later, *All the Year Round*. Collins is best remembered for three novels—*The Woman in White* (1860), *Armadale* (1860), and *The Moonstone* (1868)—all of which demonstrate in their intricacies of plot Collins' mastery of climax and suspense. Collins brought his best short stories together in a volume titled *After Dark* (1856), from which "The Traveler's Story" is taken.

CONRAD

JOSEPH CONRAD (1857–1924) was born in Berdycezew, Poland, as Josef Teodor Konrad Nalecz Korzeniowski. As a young man he followed the sea, visiting such faraway and exotic places as Africa, South America, the Caribbean, Australia, and the Far East, surviving two shipwrecks, and eventually rising from ordinary seaman to captain in the British merchant marine. During this period, which lasted some twenty years (1874–1894), Conrad learned much about the world and about the drama of human existence, assimilating those materials that were eventually to make him one of the great masters of the novel in English. By the time he published his first novel *Almayer's Folly* in 1895, he had left the sea to devote his full attention to the pursuit of literature. Noted for his magnificent plots, subtle psychology of character, rich symbolism, and rhythmical prose style, Conrad published some twenty-seven volumes in all, including *Lord Jim* (1900), *Nostromo* (1904), *The Secret Agent* (1907), *Chance* (1914), and *Victory* (1915).

CRACKANTHORPE

HUBERT CRACKANTHORPE (1870–1895), though born with every possible advantage, rejected his upper-middle-class origins, following his dismissal from Cambridge University, in favor of the life of a London bohemian author. For a time he traveled on the Continent as a bareback rider with a circus, and then in 1892 became the co-editor of *Albemarle,* a London periodical noted for its concern with social and economic problems, in which he published some of his early stories. He married in 1893, and two years later, while visiting his parents in France, apparently committed suicide. His published writings, with their realistic, yet sympathetic, treatment of character, include three volumes of short stories, *Wreckage* (1893), *Sentimental Studies and a Set of Village Tales* (1895), and *Last Studies* (1897), and a small volume of sketches, *Vignettes* (1896).

CRANE

STEPHEN CRANE (1871–1900) was born in Newark, New Jersey, and briefly attended Lafayette College and Syracuse University before becoming a free-lance journalist in New York City. His real interests, however, were literary—he had written the first draft of *Maggie: A Girl of the Streets* while in college—and for several years, until the publication of *The Red Badge of Courage* in 1895 won him recognition, Crane existed on the brink of poverty with but few calls upon his journalistic talents. Once established, however, Crane was in demand as a special correspondent, and in that capacity he covered the Greco-Turkish and Spanish-American wars. *Maggie* was published in 1896, and other volumes followed: *George's Mother* (1896), *The Open Boat and Other Tales of Adventure* (1898), *The Monster* (1899), *Whilomville Stories* (1900), and *Wounds in the Rain: War Stories* (1900). Crane also published two volumes of poetry: *The Black Riders and Other Lines* (1895) and *War Is Kind* (1899). He died of tuberculosis in Badenweiler, Germany, in 1900.

DICKENS

CHARLES DICKENS (1812–1870) was born in Portsea, England, of lower-middle-class parents. A constant reader, even as a boy, Dickens' early education was haphazard and fragmented, and when his father was committed to debtor's prison Charles, then twelve, was forced for a time to take a job pasting labels on bottles in a blacking warehouse. In 1833 Dickens published the first of what eventually became *Sketches by Boz* in the *Monthly Magazine.* The first of his serialized novels, *Oliver Twist,* appeared in 1837–1838, and Dickens' writing future was secure. His major novels—which clearly demonstrate his sympathies for the downtrodden poor and his great talent for narrative and characterization—include *The Old Curiosity Shop* (1840–1841), *David Copperfield* (1849–1850), *Bleak House* (1852–1853), *Hard Times* (1854), and *Great Expectations* (1860–1861).

DOSTOEVSKI

FËDOR DOSTOEVSKI (1821–1881), one of the giants of nineteenth-century Russian literature, was born in Moscow. Never in very good health (he was an epileptic) and suffering from periods of psychological depression, Dostoevski attended a military engineering college in Petersburg, though he increasingly found in literature an antidote to the military and scientific studies that he hated. Receiving his degree in 1843, a year later he retired from the army in favor of literature and politics. Arrested by Czar Nicholas I for political conspiracy in 1849 and sentenced to death by firing squad, Dostoevski had his sentence commuted at the last moment to penal servitude in Siberia. The years in exile proved to be a period of profound intellectual and spiritual maturation, and prepared the way for the literary masterpieces that followed: *Notes from the Underground* (1864), *Crime and Punishment* (1866), *The Idiot* (1869), and *The Brothers Karamazov* (1880)—all demonstrating Dostoevski's concern for the moral and ethical problems of mankind and his great gift for probing the depths of the human spirit.

DOYLE

ARTHUR CONAN DOYLE (1859–1930) was born in Edinburgh and educated in Britain and elsewhere in Europe before taking up the study of medicine at Edinburgh's Royal Infirmary. Doyle began his practice in Southsea, near Portsmouth, in 1882, with but only modest success. With time on his hands, the young physician began to write short stories, which he published in minor magazines. Though Doyle's first novel met nothing but rejections, he began another, *A Study in Scarlet,* chronicling the adventures of an eccentric detective, Mr. Sherlock Holmes, 221-B, Baker Street, London, who was named after the American poet Oliver Wendell Holmes and modeled upon Doyle's former medical tutor Joseph Bell. Published in December 1887, the book attracted little notice; and it was only at the urging of *Lippincott's,* an American magazine, that Doyle was encouraged to bring back Holmes for a second time in *The Sign of Four* (1890). Published in London later that same year, the novel became a popular success and the amazing career of Sherlock Holmes— the most popular fictional detective hero of all time—was underway. For some forty years, and despite Doyle's own periodic attempts to turn his hand to more "important" fiction, the adventures of Holmes and Dr. Watson continued to delight an ever-growing audience. The fifty-six Holmes stories were collected in *The Adventures of Sherlock Holmes* (1892), *The Memoirs of Sherlock Holmes* (1894), *The Return of Sherlock Holmes* (1905), *His Last Bow* (1917), and *The Case-Book of Sherlock Holmes* (1927). Holmes is also featured in the full-length novels *The Hound of the Baskervilles* (1902) and *The Valley of Fear* (1915). In addition, Doyle wrote the fine historical novels *Micah Clarke* (1889) and *The White Company* (1890), and the science fiction novels *The Lost World* (1912) and *The Poison Belt* (1913), as well as various works of nonfiction.

DRAKE

ALBERT DEE DRAKE (1935–   ) was born and raised in Portland, Oregon, and educated at Portland State College and the University of Oregon. He has worked full time as a mechanic, grave-digger, warehouseman, laborer, and research assistant. More recently, he has taught English and creative writing at the University of Oregon and at Michigan State University, where he is an associate professor of English. Drake's poetry, essays, and reviews have been published in some 200 little magazines and literary journals; his fiction has appeared in nearly fifty magazines, including *Redbook, Chicago Review, Fiction International, December,* and *West Coast Review.* "The Chicken Which Became a Rat," which first appeared in *Northwest Review,* was selected by Martha Foley for inclusion in her prestigious anthology *The Best American Short Stories 1971.* Mr. Drake's first collection of fiction, *The Postcard Mysteries & Other Stories,* was published by the Red Cedar Press in 1976.

ELLISON

HARLAN ELLISON (1934–   ) was born in Cleveland, Ohio, and briefly attended Ohio State University. In the process of becoming one of America's best-known writers of imaginative fiction, Ellison has done just about everything, including working for a carnival and working as a department store floorwalker, crop-picker, logger, tuna fisherman, short-order cook in a diner, lithographer, copywriter, door-to-door brush salesman, truck driver, hired gun for a wealthy neurotic, television columnist, editor, free-lance writer (31 books, over 800 magazine stories and articles), and college lecturer. He has served as a film critic for *Cinema* magazine and has written motion-picture and television scripts for such popular series as "The Outer Limits," "Star Trek," "The Alfred Hitchcock Hour," "The Man From U.N.C.L.E." and "The Young Lawyers." Ellison's short stories have been published in the following collections: *The Deadly Streets* (1958), *A Touch of Infinity* (1960), *Children of the Streets* (1961), *Gentleman Junkie and Other Stories of the Hung-Up Generation* (1961), *Ellison Wonderland* (1962), *Paingod and Other Delusions* (1965), *I Have No Mouth and I Must Scream* (1967), *From the Land of Fear* (1967), *Love Ain't Nothing But Sex Misspelled* (1968), *The Beast That Shouted Love at the Heart of the World* (1969), *Over the Edge* (1970), *Partners in Wonder* (1971), *Alone Against Tomorrow* (1971), *Approaching Oblivion* (1974), *Deathbird Stories* (1975), *No Doors, No Windows* (1975), and *Shatterday* (1976). In addition, Ellison has edited the award winning trilogy of anthologies *Dangerous Visions* (1967), *Again, Dangerous Visions* (1972), and *The Last Dangerous Visions* (1977), "'Repent, Harlequin!' Said the Ticktockman" won both the World Science Fiction Convention's Hugo award for the best short story of 1965 and the Science Fiction Writers of America's Nebula award for the same year.

ELLISON

RALPH ELLISON (1914–   ) was born in Oklahoma City and studied music at Tuskegee Institute in Alabama before coming to New York City, where like James Baldwin, he fell under the influence of author Richard Wright. He studied sculpture for a time, worked with the Federal Writers Project, and then, in 1942, became editor of the *Negro Quarterly.* He has taught abroad, in Germany and Austria, and in this country at Bard College, the University of Chicago, Rutgers University, and at Yale University. His one novel, *The Invisible Man* (1952), a symbolic treatment of the black man in white America, won the National Book Award and has since established itself as something of an American classic. A collection of essays, *Shadow and Act,* appeared in 1964. Ellison's short stories remain uncollected.

FAULKNER

WILLIAM FAULKNER (1897–1962) was born in New Albany, Mississippi, but soon moved to Oxford, which he made his home for the rest of his life. In 1918 Faulkner enlisted in the Canadian Royal Flying Corps, but was soon back in Oxford, where he enrolled for two years at the University of Mississippi. Following a succession of odd jobs Faulkner lived for a time in New Orleans, where he made the friendship of author Sherwood Anderson and began to write himself. A collection of poems, *The Marble Faun,* appeared in 1924, followed by the novels *Soldier's Pay* (1926) *Mosquitoes* (1927), *Sartoris* (1929), *The Sound and the Fury* (1929), and *As I Lay Dying* (1930). With the publication of *Sartoris* Faulkner began his celebrated series of Yoknapatawpha stories, named for the fictitional Mississippi county whose past and present he peopled with characters cutting across the social and economic spectrum of the Old and New South. The cycle was continued in *Light in August* (1932), *Absalom, Absalom!* (1936), *The Hamlet* (1940), *Go Down, Moses* (1942), *Intruder in the Dust* (1948), *The Town* (1957), *The Mansion* (1959), and *The Reivers* (1962). Faulkner was awarded the 1949 Nobel Prize in Literature.

FITZGERALD

F. SCOTT FITZGERALD (1896–1940), whose name in synonymous with the Jazz Age of post-World War I America that he pictured so vividly in his novels and stories, was born in St. Paul, Minnesota, and educated at Princeton University. His first novel, *This Side of Paradise,* appeared in 1920 and its instant success launched his career. Other novels followed: *The Beautiful and Damned* (1922), *The Great Gatsby* (1925), *Tender Is the Night* (1934), and *The Last Tycoon* (1941). His best short stories were collected and published in *Flappers and Philosophers* (1921), *Tales of the Jazz Age* (1922), *All the Sad Young Men* (1926), and *Taps at Reveille* (1935). Fitzgerald's final years were marked by personal tragedy. His wife's mental breakdown in 1930 was followed by his own gradual decline, and Fitzgerald died in Hollywood at age forty-four, in debt and largely out of literary favor.

FORSTER

EDWARD MORGAN FORSTER (1879–1970) was born in London and educated at King's College, Cambridge. Following an extended trip to Italy and Greece, Forster returned to England, where he helped found the *Independent Review* and became one of its chief contributors. In 1905, at the age of only twenty-six, Forster published the first of his major novels, *Where Angels Fear to Tread.* Others appeared in rapid succession: *The Longest Journey* (1907), *A Room with a View* (1908), *Howards End* (1910), and in 1924, following two trips to India, his masterpiece, *A Passage to India.* Thereafter, Forster turned away from prose fiction, with its quiet humanism and its emphasis on the need for understanding and tolerance in human relationships. His subsequent writings included literary criticism, *Aspects of the Novel* (1927); biography, *Goldsworthy Lowes Dickinson* (1934) and *Marianne Thornton* (1956); personal reminiscence, *The Hill of Devi* (1953); and the prose essay, *Abinger Harvest* (1936) and *Two Cheers for Democracy* (1951). In 1946 Forster returned to King's College as an Honorary Fellow, an honor he continued to enjoy for the remainder of his life. His short stories are collected in two volumes: *The Celestial Omnibus* (1911) and *The Eternal Moment* (1928).

GASS

WILLIAM H. GASS (1924–) was born in Fargo, North Dakota, and educated at Kenyon College, Ohio Wesleyan University, and Cornell University, where he received his Ph.D. in 1954. He has taught philosophy at the College of Wooster, Purdue University, and is currently professor of philosophy at Washington University, in St. Louis. His stories have appeared in *Accent, Perspective, Minnesota Review, Art and Literature, New American Review,* and have been collected together in a volume entitled *In the Heart of the Heart of the Country* (1968). Mr. Gass has also published a novel, *Omensetter's Luck* (1966).

GISSING

GEORGE GISSING (1857–1903) won early recognition for his scholarly and academic abilities and in 1874, at the age of seventeen, received a scholarship to Owens College, University of Manchester. Dismissed from college and briefly imprisoned for stealing money to aid a prostitute with whom he had fallen in love, Gissing left England for the United States and a new start in life. He taught school for a time in Massachusetts and eventually found his way to Chicago, where he sold a few short stories to the Chicago *Tribune*. Returning to England in 1877, he married the woman he had befriended and embarked on a literary career with the publication of a novel *Workers in the Dawn* (1880). For twenty years, averaging a book a year and against a background of great personal tragedy, Gissing labored in the despair of obscurity, though he was not without friends among discerning critics. Gissing is perhaps best known for his novel *New Grub Street* (1891); his book of speculations on human experience, *The Private Papers of Henry Ryecroft* (1903); and two collections of short stories, *Human Odds and Ends* (1898) and *The House of Cobwebs* (1906).

GOGOL

NIKOLAI GOGOL (1809-1852) was born in Sorochintzy, in the Ukraine, and began his life as a civil servant in St. Petersburg. The literary life of the Russian capital and his friendship with the poet Alexander Pushkin turned him in the direction of literature, and in 1831-1832 Gogol published a two-volume collection of stories entitled *Evenings on a Farm Near Dikanka*. *Taras Bulba*, an historical novel, appeared in 1835, followed by the successful play *The Inspector General* in 1836, and the novel that Gogol himself considered his best work, *Dead Souls*, in 1842. "The Overcoat," Gogol's most famous and highly praised story was published in the collected edition of his writings in 1842. "We all came out of 'The Overcoat,'" Dostoevski is supposed to have remarked. Although no doubt apocryphal, such a statement correctly suggests the important place Gogol occupies in the development of that unique sensibility that runs throughout nineteenth-century Russian literature.

HAMMETT

DASHIELL HAMMETT (1894-1961) was born in St. Mary's County, Maryland, and grew up in Philadelphia and Baltimore. Leaving school at fourteen, Hammett pursued a variety of jobs before becoming a private detective for the famous Pinkerton Detective Agency. Following World War I, Hammett returned briefly to Pinkerton's before setting off on a whole new career—the writing of fiction. Like many ambitious young writers of the period, Hammett sold to the "pulps," then the leading vehicle for

popular fiction, with their garish covers, coarse, untrimmed paper, and cheap prices. Hammett's contribution was the "hardboiled" detective story, of which he quickly became a skillful and influential practitioner. The most famous of the detective pulps of the late 1920s was *Black Mask*, and it was there that Hammett's first detective hero, the cool, tough-minded and nameless Continental Op (he worked for the Continental Detective Agency), made his initial appearance in a series of stories notable for their rapid action, realistic detail, colloquial language, and violence. Hammett's four most important novels each first appeared serially in *Black Mask: Red Harvest* (1929), *The Dain Curse* (1929), *The Maltese Falcon* (1930)—the novel that featured the most famous of Hammett's private eyes, Sam Spade —and *The Glass Key* (1931). *The Thin Man*, which introduced Nick Charles, appeared in 1932. Hammett's short stories are collected in *The Adventures of Sam Spade* (1944) and *The Creeping Siamese and Other Stories* (1950). Though he lived until 1961, Hammett peaked as a writer in the late 1920s and the early 1930s, but not before his detectives—most notably the Continental Op and Sam Spade—had established the standard for a new breed of popular hero.

HARDY

THOMAS HARDY (1840-1928) was born in Dorset, England, amidst the Wessex countryside whose brooding landscape he was to celebrate in the pages of his novels. Trained as an architect, a career he practiced until his marriage in 1874, Hardy came to literature slowly and only after several false starts. His first major novel, *Far from the Madding Crowd*, appeared anonymously in 1874, to be followed by *The Return of the Native* (1878), *The Mayor of Casterbridge* (1886), *Tess of the D'Urbervilles* (1891), and *Jude the Obscure* (1896). The last two novels shocked Victorian sensibilities because of their emphasis on the tragedy of strong sexual passions. After the publication of *Jude the Obscure*, Hardy abandoned the novel and turned his attention to the writing of lyrical poetry. His best short stories were collected in three major volumes: *Wessex Tales* (1888), *A Group of Noble Dames* (1891), and *Life's Little Ironies* (1894).

HARTE

BRET HARTE (1836-1902) was born in Albany, New York, and at the age of eighteen travelled west with his widowed mother to California, where he held a variety of jobs: schoolteacher, Wells Fargo messenger, typesetter, and newspaper editor. In 1864 Harte became secretary of the California mint, a position that left him ample time to write. Four years later, in 1868, his short story "The Luck of Roaring Camp" appeared in the *Overland Monthly* and Harte's reputation was established almost overnight. His first volume of stories, *The Luck of Roaring Camp*, with their emphasis on local color, was published in 1870, and became a model for other regional writers of the post–Civil War period. His later years were spent abroad, as U.S. consul in Krefeld, Germany, in 1878, and in Glasgow, Scotland, 1880–1885, and as a contributor to British magazines. His stories, poems, essays, and sketches were brought together in a number of volumes, including *Tales of the Argonauts* (1875), *A Sappho of Green Springs* (1891), *Colonel Starbottle's Client* (1892), *A Protégée of Jack Hamlin's* (1894), *The Bell-Ringer of Angel's* (1894), and *Condensed Novels* (1902).

HAWTHORNE

NATHANIEL HAWTHORNE (1804–1864) was born in Salem, Massachusetts, and educated at Maine's Bowdoin College, where his classmates included the poet Henry Wadsworth Longfellow and Franklin Pierce, the future president. Following his graduation in 1825, Hawthorne returned home to Salem, where he spent the next twelve years in comparative seclusion, undergoing his literary apprenticeship. His first volume of allegorical and richly symbolic stories of moral responsibility and human guilt, *Twice-Told Tales* (1837), nonetheless attracted but little notice. After his marriage in 1842 Hawthorne lived for a time in the Old Manse at Concord, the neighbor of Emerson and Thoreau, until financial necessity forced him to return to Salem and a job as surveyor in the Custom House. The publication in 1850 of *The Scarlet Letter* marked a change in his literary fortunes; it was quickly followed by *The House of the Seven Gables* (1851) and *The Blithedale Romance* (1852). His final novel, *The Marble Faun*, appeared in 1860. Hawthorne's stories and sketches were published in *Twice-Told Tales* (1837), *Mosses from an Old Manse* (1846), and *The Snow Image and Other Twice-Told Tales* (1851).

HEMINGWAY

ERNEST HEMINGWAY (1898–1961) was born in Oak Park, Illinois. Following his graduation from the local high school, he became a reporter for the Kansas City *Star,*

prior to going to France as a volunteer ambulance driver in the early days of World War I. He returned to journalism after the war as a European correspondent for the Toronto *Star,* and while in Paris joined the many artists and intellectuals who comprised the so-called lost generation. Encouraged by his friendship with Ezra Pound, Gertrude Stein, and others, Hemingway published his first book, the collection of stories titled *In Our Time,* in 1924. Two years later, in 1926, his famous novel of the postwar generation, *The Sun Also Rises,* appeared, and his reputation began to grow. Another collection of stories, *Men Without Women,* appeared in 1927, followed by *A Farewell to Arms* (1929), *To Have and Have Not* (1937), *For Whom the Bell Tolls* (1940), *Across the River and into the Trees* (1950), and *The Old Man and the Sea* (1952). His code heroes, crisp staccato dialogue, and insistence on the active, strenuous life made Hemingway one of the most popular of all modern American writers and a veritable legend during his own lifetime. He was awarded the 1954 Nobel Prize in Literature.

IRVING

WASHINGTON IRVING (1783–1859) was born in New York City. Educated for the law and admitted to the bar, Irving turned instead to literature, then, at best, an uncertain vocation. His first major work, the comic history of his native city, *Diedrich Knickerbocker's History of New York,* appeared in 1809. Irving went to Europe in 1815 on family business, and it was there that he published in installments *The Sketch Book of Geoffrey Crayon* (1819–1820), a collection of stories and sketches that contained his two masterpieces, "Rip Van Winkle" and "The Legend of Sleepy Hollow." With the publication of *The Sketch Book* Irving became the first American writer to win the approbation of British literary critics. Other sketch books, drawn to much the same formula, followed: *Bracebridge Hall* (1822), *Tales of a Traveller* (1824), *The Alhambra* (1832). Irving returned to America in 1832, a writer with a truly international reputation. Irving also wrote a biography of Christopher Columbus (1828), a history of John Jacob Astor's fur trading empire in the Pacific northwest (1836), and a five-volume life of George Washington (1855–1859).

JACKSON

SHIRLEY JACKSON (1919–1965) was born in San Francisco and raised in Rochester,

New York. Shortly after her graduation in
1940 from Syracuse Universsity, where she
founded, edited, and was a contributor to
the university's literary magazine, she married the late literary critic Stanley Edgar
Hyman and settled in Bennington, Vermont,
where Mr. Hyman was on the faculty of
Bennington College. Though perhaps best
known for her short story of communal
brutality and ritualistic murder, "The Lottery," Shirley Jackson also wrote a number
of novels, including *Hangsaman* (1951), *The
Bird's Nest* (1954), *The Haunting of Hill
House* (1959), and *We Have Always Lived
in the Castle* (1962). Her short stories, with
their curious mixture of commonplace reality, the bizarre, and the supernatural, were
brought together in *The Lottery* (1944) and
in *The Magic of Shirley Jackson* (1966), the
latter volume a posthumous collection edited by her husband.

JAMES

HENRY JAMES (1843–1916) was born in
New York City of wealthy, patrician parents and privately tutored in New York
and abroad, in London, Switzerland, France,
and Germany. James was admitted to Harvard Law School in 1862, at the age of nineteen, but quickly turned his interests to literature. After 1875, the year that saw the
publication of his first collection of stories,
A Passionate Pilgrim, and the serialization
in the *Atlantic* of his first noteworthy novel,
Roderick Random, James made his home
in Europe, finally, toward the end of his
life, renouncing his American citizenship
altogether. His literary output in the years
that followed was prodigious, all of it bearing the increasingly sophisticated Jamesian
stylistic qualities and techniques that critics
have come to venerate more and more with
the passage of time. James' major novels
include *The American* (1877), *Daisy Miller*
(1879), *The Portrait of a Lady* (1881), *The
Princess Casamassima* (1886), *The Turn of
the Screw* (1898), *The Wings of the Dove*
(1902), *The Ambassadors* (1903), and *The
Golden Bowl* (1904). In addition, James
wrote dozens of short stories, many of them
classics in their own right.

JEWETT

SARAH ORNE JEWETT (1849–1909) was
born, raised, and passed most of her adult
life in South Berwick, Maine, a typical nineteenth-century New England village located
on the Piscataqua River, some twenty miles
above Portsmouth and the sea. Chronically
ill as a child, Miss Jewett's formal education was sporadic, though she early discovered the world of books and, by accompanying her doctor father on his rounds,
observed at firsthand the rural manners, customs, and inhabitants of her native region.
Inspired by the local color stories of her
neighbor Harriet Beecher Stowe, Sarah
Jewett began to write tales and poems, and
by the age of twenty had been accepted for
publication in the *Atlantic Monthly.* Her
stories and sketches of rural life, with their
objective though sympathetic portrayal of
human nature, their realistic settings, and
their faithful renderings of New England
dialect and folkways, were collected in such
volumes as *Deephaven* (1877), *A White
Heron and Other Stories* (1886), *Tales of
New England* (1890), *Strangers and Way-
farers* (1890), and *The Country of the
Pointed Firs* (1896). Her best known novel,
A Country Doctor, inspired by the life of
her father, was published in 1884.

JOYCE

JAMES JOYCE (1882–1941) was born,
raised, and educated in Dublin, Ireland, the
city that became through his literary art a
microcosm of all human experience. His
feelings for Dublin were nonetheless decidedly ambivalent, and Joyce spent much
of his adult life abroad in self-imposed exile, in Trieste, Paris, and Zurich, where he
supported himself as a teacher of foreign
languages. A volume of poetry, *Chamber
Music,* was published in 1907, followed by
Dubliners, his brilliant collection of stories
about the life and inhabitants of his native
city, in 1914; *A Portrait of the Artist as a
Young Man,* a semiautobiographical account
of the alienated artist, in 1916; *Ulysses,* his
magnificent major novel, in 1922; and *Fin-
negan's Wake* in 1939. His play, *Exiles,* was
published in 1918. Although largely ignored
and certainly misunderstood during his own
lifetime, Joyce has long since been recognized as one of the truly creative geniuses
of modern literature for his experiments
with the form and technique of prose fiction.

KAFKA

FRANZ KAFKA (1883–1924) was born in
Prague, Czechoslovakia, received a law degree from the German University there in
1906, and then became a civil servant for
the Austrian Government. Kafka's three
novels, with their dreamlike distorted sense
of reality—*The Trial* (1925), *The Castle*
(1926), and *America* (1927)—were all published posthumously by a literary executor

who defied Kafka's request that the manuscripts be destroyed. His short stories have been collected and translated into English in *The Great Wall of China* (1933), *A Franz Kafka Miscellany* (1940), and *Parables and Paradoxes* (1962).

KIPLING

RUDYARD KIPLING (1865–1936) was born in Bombay, India, where his father was a professor of architectural sculpture at the University of Bombay. Educated in England, Kipling returned to India at seventeen and became a subeditor of the *Civil and Military Gazette* at Lahore. There he wrote many of the famous poems and stories, later collected in *Departmental Ditties* (1886) and *Plain Tales from the Hills* (1887), that first introduced many in England to Anglo-Indian life. In 1887 he became a traveling correspondent for the Allahabad *Pioneer,* visiting such countries as Afghanistan, South Africa, Australia, and the United States before settling briefly in London. Following his marriage in 1892 to an American, Kipling lived for a time in Brattleboro, Vermont. There he wrote the *Jungle Books* (1894–1895) and many of the *Just So Stories* (1902). In 1896 he returned once again to England, where he made his home in Sussex. Kipling was awarded the 1907 Nobel Prize in Literature. His other better known works, in which he achieved a surprising diversity, include the novels *The Light That Failed* (1891), *Captains Courageous* (1897), and *Kim* (1901); the short stories collected in *Life's Handicap* (1891), *Many Inventions* (1893), *Puck of Pook's Hill* (1906), and *Debits and Credits* (1926); and his most famous collection of poems, *Barrack-Room Ballads* (1892).

LAWRENCE

DAVID HERBERT LAWRENCE (1885–1930), the son of a coal miner, was born and raised in Eastwood, a village near Nottingham, England. His experiences as a clerk, a schoolmaster, at Nottingham University, and with the industrial midlands, which surrounded him, persuaded Lawrence to turn his back on Britain and seek relief from its oppressive and dehumanizing industrial and class-oriented society in other countries: in Italy, Australia, Mexico, and the United States. His fiction, with its concern for the anxieties and frustrations of human relationships and its perceptive psychological insights, includes the novels *Son and Lovers* (1913), *The Rainbow* (1915), *Women in Love* (1920), *The Plumed Serpent* (1926), and *Lady Chatterley's Lover* (1928).

His short stories are most readily accessible in *The Complete Short Stories of D. H. Lawrence* (1961). The Lawrencian canon also includes criticism and nonfictional prose, *Psychoanalysis and the Unconscious* (1921), *Studies in Classic American Literature* (1923), *Pornography and Obscenity* (1929), and *Apocalypse* (1931); travel books, *Twilight in Italy* (1916), *Sea and Sardinia* (1921), *Mornings in Mexico* (1927), and *Etruscan Places* (1932); and poetry.

LESSING

DORIS LESSING (1919–   ) was born in Persia and raised on a large farm in Southern Rhodesia, Africa, then still a comparative wilderness just coming under cultivation. At eighteen she went to live in Salisbury, the capital, where she held a variety of jobs. In 1949 she left Africa for London, and a year later launched her literary career with the publication of the novel *The Grass Is Singing* (1950). Other works, many of them drawing on her early experiences in Africa and reflecting her concern with socialism and its dilemmas, followed in quick succession: *Martha Quest* (1952), *Five* (1953), *A Proper Marriage* (1954), *Retreat to Innocence* (1956), *A Ripple from the Storm* (1958), *The Golden Notebook* (1962), *Landlocked* (1965), *The Four-Gated City* (1969), *Briefing for a Descent into Hell* (1971), and *The Summer Before Dark* (1973). Doris Lessing's short stories have been collected in *This Was the Old Chief's Country* (1951), *The Habit of Loving* (1957), *A Man and Two Women* (1963), *African Stories* (1964), *The Black Madonna* (1966), *The Story of a Non-Marrying Man and Other Stories* (1972), *The Temptation of Jack Orkney and Other Stories* (1972), and *The Memoirs of a Survivor* (1975).

LONDON

JACK LONDON (1876–1916) was born in a poor section of San Francisco and spent his youth on a series of California farms and ranches and in the city of Oakland. At the age of thirteen, London bought a boat—the first of several—which became, along with reading, his first love. In 1893, London signed aboard a sailing vessel for a seven-month voyage to the Pacific. Upon his return he held a series of wretched jobs and then joined Coxey's Army of unemployed laborers in its celebrated march on Washington. Determined to improve himself, London returned to Oakland to finish high school in 1895, and then spent a semester at the University of California. From there he went to the gold fields of Alaska's Klondike,

and though London failed to strike it rich
he did gather sufficient material for a series
of stories that were published in such magazines as the *Overland Monthly* and the *Atlantic Monthly.* Collected and published in
book form in 1900 as *The Son of the Wolf,*
these stories were widely acclaimed and
served to launch London upon his writing
career. One book quickly followed another,
earning him fame and fortune, most of
which he squandered away on a large ranch
and upon his forty-five-foot boat the *Snark.*
At the age of forty, having turned his back
upon his earlier socialist idealism, sick and
in despair, London died of an overdose of
narcotics. London's best-known novels include *The Call of the Wild* (1903), *The Sea-
Wolf* (1904), *White Fang* (1906), *The Iron
Heel* (1908), *and Martin Eden* (1909). His
short stories were brought together in some
fifteen collections during his lifetime, including *The Son of the Wolf* (1900), *Children of the Frost* (1902), *When God Laughs*
(1911), and *South Sea Tales* (1911).

McCULLERS

CARSON McCULLERS (1917-1967) was
born and raised in Columbus, Georgia. Following her graduation from high school, she
worked for a time as a reporter on the Columbus *Enquirer,* and then set out for New
York City with the intention of studying at
the Juilliard School of Music. Once in New
York, however, she turned instead to writing, taking courses at Columbia University
by night and working at a variety of jobs
by day. In 1940, not yet twenty-three, she
published her first novel, *The Heart Is a
Lonely Hunter,* a book at once widely
praised by critics. A second novel, *Reflections In a Golden Eye,* appeared in 1941,
followed by a series of excellent short stories in such magazines as *Vogue, The New
Yorker, Harper's Bazaar,* and *Mademoiselle.*
A third highly acclaimed novel, *The Member of the Wedding,* was published in 1946
—it later became a successful Broadway
play (1951) and a musical (1971). *The Ballad of the Sad Café,* a collection of stories,
and the novel *Clock without Hands* were
published in 1951 and 1961, respectively.
Constitutionally weak from childhood, Mc-
Cullers suffered what was to be the first of
a series of strokes in 1941. From that time
on she lived and worked under the constant
threat of illness, finally dying of a cerebral
hemorrhage in 1967 at the age of fifty. Together with her two contemporaries Flannery O'Connor and Eudora Welty, McCullers belongs to the so-called school of
"Southern Gothic." Her fictional world is
one peopled by a series of physical and psychological grotesques and misfits, who in
their abject loneliness and spiritual isolation
are unable to communicate effectively with
others.

McPHERSON

JAMES ALAN McPHERSON (1943-   )
was born and raised in Savannah, Georgia,
and graduated from Morris Brown College
in Atlanta in 1965. The same year he received the combined *Reader's Digest*–United
Negro College Fund prize for literature. In
1968 he graduated from Harvard Law
School. Since that time he has worked in
Roxbury, Massachusetts, as a reporter for
the *Bay State Banner,* taught English and
Afro-American literature at the University
of Iowa, and served as a fellow of College
V, University of California at Santa Cruz.
Currently Mr. McPherson is a contributing
editor of the *Atlantic Monthly.* His short
story "Gold Coast" won an Atlantic Award
as the best new story of 1968 (it was also
selected for inclusion in Martha Foley's *The
Best American Short Stories, 1969*). "Gold
Coast" has been republished in McPhersons'
first collection of short stories, *Hue and Cry*
(1969).

MALAMUD

BERNARD MALAMUD (1914-   ) was
born in Brooklyn, New York, received a
B.A. from the City College of New York
in 1936 and an M.A. from Columbia Uni-
versity in 1942, and has taught English at
Oregon State University and at Vermont's
Bennington College. His first novel, *The
Natural,* appeared in 1952, followed by *The
Assistant* (1947), *A New Life* (1961), *The
Fixer* (1966), which was awarded a Pulitzer
Prize, and *The Tenants* (1971). His short
stories have been collected in *The Magic
Barrel* (1958), winner of the National Book
Award, *Idiots First* (1963), *Pictures of Fi-
delman* (1969), and *Rembrandt's Hat*
(1973). Unlike many of his contemporaries,
Malamud's works suggest modern man's
ability to affirm life, even in a world that
seems to deny its possibilities.

MANN

THOMAS MANN (1875-1955) was born in
Lübeck, Germany, the son of a well-to-do
grain merchant and senator and the heir to
a way of life whose decay at the hands of
twentieth-century materialism he was to
chronicle in his semiautobiographical novel
Buddenbrooks (1901). Mann worked for a
time for a fire insurance company before

turning his full attention to writing. Long at odds with contemporary culture and with the life and politics of his native Germany, Mann became an outspoken critic of the Nazi order, which in turn burned his books and revoked his citizenship. Between 1942 and 1952 Mann lived in California (he became an American citizen in 1944), and then returned to Europe, where he made his home near Zurich, Switzerland, until his death in 1955. Mann received the 1929 Nobel Prize in Literature. His major novels include *Buddenbrooks* (1901), *The Magic Mountain* (1924), the tetralogy *Joseph and His Brothers* (1933–1943), *Doctor Faustus* (1947), and *Confessions of Felix Krull, Confidence Man* (1954). Mann's short stories were brought together in *Stories of Three Decades* (1936).

MANSFIELD

KATHERINE MANSFIELD (1888–1923) was born in Wellington, New Zealand, and came to England to study music at Queen's College, London. Following a brief trip home, she returned to London and a career in journalism, which slowly gave way to the writing of short fiction. Her first volume of stories, *In a German Pension,* was published in 1911, though full recognition of her abilities as a writer had to wait upon the publication of *Bliss* (1920), *The Garden Party* (1922), and *The Dove's Nest* (1923), which fully reveal her Chekov-like mastery of the techniques of short fiction, particularly characterization. In 1918 Miss Mansfield married noted critic John Middleton Murry. Plagued by ill health and a weak constitution most of her life, Katherine Mansfield succumbed to tuberculosis in 1923 while convalescing in France.

MAUPASSANT

GUY DE MAUPASSANT (1850–1893), who wrote almost 300 short stories within a span of roughly ten years, 1880–1890, was born in Normandy near the French seacoast town of Dieppe. He received his early education from his highly cultured mother before being enrolled, at the age of thirteen, in a seminary, from which he was soon expelled for insubordination. From there he was sent to a school in Rouen, with the intention that he would eventually study law. Following the Franco-Prussian War of 1870–1871, in which he served with the French Army, Maupassant settled in Paris as a clerk in the naval ministry. There he was drawn into the famous literary circle which included Turgenev, Edmond Goncourt, Al-

phonse Daudet, Zola, and Flaubert. He became the special protégé of Flaubert himself, whose exacting standards prevented Maupassant from publishing anything in his own name for a period of seven years. With the publication of the short story *Boulle de Suif* ("*Ball of Fat*") in 1880, in an anthology edited by Zola, Maupassant's reputation was established almost overnight. His novels include *Une Vie* (1883), *Bel Ami* (1885), and *Pierre et Jean* (1888); the most famous of his short stories were collected in *La Maison Tellier* (1881), *Mademoiselle Fifi* (1882), *Contes de la Bécasse* (1883), *Contes et Nouvelles* (1885), and *L'Inutile Beauté* (1890). Although most of Maupassant's short stories appear at first to be nothing more than brief and rather transparent anecdotes, the best succeed in giving impressionistic but truthful insights into the hidden lives of people caught amidst the trials of everyday existence.

MELVILLE

HERMAN MELVILLE (1819–1891) was born in New York City, the son of fairly well-to-do parents. After the early death of his father, the family moved to Albany, to be close to relatives, and it was there that Herman went to school and found his first jobs. His initiation to the sea came in 1837, as a cabin boy on a Liverpool-bound merchantman, and was followed four years later by an extended voyage to the South Seas aboard the whaler *Acushnet*. His subsequent adventures in the Marquesas Islands, where he jumped ship, and in Tahiti provided the material for his first three published books, *Typee* (1846), *Omoo* (1847), and *Mardi* (1849). Returning home, Melville took up writing in earnest. *Redburn,* an account of his Liverpool voyage, appeared in 1849; and *White-Jacket,* based on his return voyage to Boston on a U.S. man-of-war, appeared in 1850. Melville lived for a time in Pittsfield, Massachusetts, in the Berkshires, where he cultivated a friendship with Hawthorne and finished his masterpiece of whaling, *Moby-Dick* (1851). Returning to New York, Melville spent some twenty years laboring in the obscurity of the U.S. Custom House. His other major works include *Pierre* (1852), *The Piazza Tales* (1856), *The Confidence Man* (1857), and the posthumously published *Billy Budd* (1924).

MISHIMA

YUKIO MISHIMA (1925–1970), the pseudonym of Kimitake Hiraoka, was born in

Tokyo, Japan. Educated at the aristocratic Peer's School and Tokyo Imperial University, Mishima worked briefly for the Japanese Finance Ministry before resigning to turn his full attention to literature and a host of other ancillary activities, including politics and acting (he played the role of the lieutenant in the film version of his short story "Patriotism"). A man of amazing versatility and almost frightening energy —he became a veritable legend in his own time—Mishima's prolific production of stories, poems, plays, and essays had established him by the time of his death as Japan's foremost man of letters. In 1968 Mishima became the founder and leader of the so-called Shield Society, a group of young men accused by their opponents of being proto-Fascists but whose avowed aim was to protect Japan from a leftist uprising. He committed suicide in 1970 in traditional hara-kiri style, apparently in protest against the "spinelessness" of Japan's military posture. Mishima's novels published in English include *Confessions of a Mask* (1949), *Temple of the Golden Pavilion* (1959), *After the Banquet* (1963), *The Sailor Who Fell from Grace with the Sea* (1965), and *Forbidden Colors* (1968). "Patriotism" appears in a collection of stories entitled *Death in Midsummer,* published in America in 1966.

MUNRO

HECTOR HUGH MUNRO (1870–1916), was born in Akyab, Burma, but was raised and educated in England. He returned to Burma in 1893, served for a time with the military police, and then returned once more to England, where he began to write short stories under the famous pseudonym of "Saki." Between 1902 and 1908 Munro again spent time abroad in the Balkans, Russia, and France. During the years prior to World War I he lived in London, where he continued to write his witty and urbane stories and novels in addition to political journalism. Enlisting in the army, Munro was killed on the battlefields of France in November 1916. His volumes of collected short stories include *Reginald* (1904), *The Chronicles of Clovis* (1911), *and Beasts and Super-Beasts* (1914).

OATES

JOYCE CAROL OATES (1938–   ), one of America's leading contemporary writers, was born in Lockport, New York, and educated at Syracuse University and the University of Wisconsin. She is presently on the English faculty of the University of Windsor, in Canada. Miss Oates' novels include *With Shuddering Fall* (1964), *A Garden of Earthly Delights* (1967), *Expensive People* (1968), *Them* (1969), winner of the National Book Award, *Wonderland* (1971), *Do with Me What You Will* (1973), *The Assassins* (1975) and *Childwold* (1976). Her short stories are collected in *By the North Gate* (1963), *Upon the Sweeping Flood* (1966), *The Wheel of Love* (1970), *Marriages and Infidelities* (1972), *The Goddess and Other Women* (1974), *The Hungry Ghost: Seven Allusive Comedies* (1974), *The Poisoned Kiss and Other Stories from the Portugese* (1975), *The Seduction and Other Stories* (1975) and *Crossing the Border* (1976). Joyce Carol Oates has also published three volumes of literary criticism: *The Edge of Impossibility: Tragic Forms in Literature* (1972), *The Hostile Sun: The Poetry of D. H. Lawrence* (1973), and *New Heaven, New Earth: The Visionary Experience in Literature* (1974).

O'CONNOR, FLANNERY

FLANNERY O'CONNOR (1925–1964) was born in Savannah, Georgia, attended Georgia State College for Women, and received an MFA in creative writing from the writer's workshop of the University of Iowa in 1947. Miss O'Connor lived briefly in New York and Connecticut, but returned to her mother's farm near Milledgeville, Georgia, in 1950 when she discovered that she had the same tubercular skin disease that took the life of her father. There she lived for the last fourteen years of her life, occasionally able to travel and give lectures during periods of the disease's remission. Flannery O'Connor's fiction, depicting hypocrisy, blindness, and inhumanity in a grotesque and absurd world won wide acclaim during her lifetime. Her published writing includes two novels, *Wise Blood* (1952), and *The Violent Bear It Away* (1960), and two collections of short stories, *A Good Man Is Hard to Find* (1955) and *Everything That Rises Must Converge* (1965).

O'CONNOR, FRANK

FRANK O'CONNOR (1903–1966), the pseudonym of Michael John O'Donovan, was born in Cork, Ireland. During the civil war of the early 1920s he fought with the Irish Republican Army (the IRA) against the British. These experiences, which included a year in a British prisoner of war camp, served as the basis for his first published collection of short stories, *The Guests of the Nation* (1931). Largely self-educated, O'Connor supported himself as a writer for a number of years by working as a librarian in Cork and Dublin. During the late 1930s he served as a director of the famous Abbey Theatre in Dublin, one of the vital centers of modern Irish cultural life. Best known as a writer of short fiction—O'Connor published more than twenty volumes of stories—he also wrote literary criticism, several plays, two novels, and two volumes of autobiography, *An Only Child* (1961) and *My Father's Son* (1968). During his later years O'Connor spent a good deal of time in the United States, where he taught at Harvard, Northwestern, and Stanford universities.

PARKER

DOROTHY PARKER (1893–1967) was born in West End, New Jersey, but grew up in Manhattan's West Side, before being sent to a private school in Morristown, New Jersey, where she completed her formal education in 1911. A woman of uncommon intelligence and wit, she began her literary career at *Vogue,* where she published her first verse in 1916. The next year she became a drama critic for *Vanity Fair,* an association that lasted until 1920 when her harsh and caustic reviews cost her her job. For a time she did free-lance work with Robert Benchley, and then joined Harold Ross's new magazine *The New Yorker,* where she wrote book and drama reviews. The first volume of her light, bittersweet poetry, *Enough Rope,* appeared in 1926, followed by *Sunset Gun* in 1928, and *Death and Taxes* in 1931. Her short stories, which originally had appeared in the leading magazines of the day, were collected in *Laments for the Living* (1930), *After Such Pleasures* (1933), and *Here Lies* (1939). Known for her urbanity and for a brand of wry and cynical humor that at times ran to the sardonic, Parker's reputation as an American writer belongs mainly to the late 1920s and early 1930s when, as her biographer John Keats has noted, "she was the most talked-about woman of her time," worshipped by an entire "college generation . . . for [whom] she mirrored, expressed, and helped to establish a new style in life and art." Her flirtation with radical politics in the 1930s led her to Spain where she reported on the Spanish Civil War. Returning to America she worked on a series of film scripts in Hollywood until being blacklisted in the early 1950s for her alleged Communist sympathies. "Big Blonde," her most

famous story, won the O'Henry Memorial Award as the best short story for 1929.

POE

EDGAR ALLAN POE (1809–1849), whose fiction occupies a key place in the early development of the short story, was born in Boston of theatrical parents. After the death of his mother in 1811, Poe was adopted by John Allan of Richmond, Virginia, who oversaw his early schooling in England and Richmond and then enrolled him in 1826 in the University of Virginia. Withdrawn by Allan after a single term, apparently because of the debts he had contracted, Poe then made his way to Boston. Three years in the army (including a year at the U.S. Military Academy at West Point) followed. Finally disowned entirely by Allan, Poe was forced to make his own way. Turning to writing—he had already published a volume of poetry, *Tamerlane and Other Poems,* in 1827—Poe made his home in New York and Baltimore, and in 1833 won a prize from the Baltimore *Saturday Visiter* for his story "MS. Found in a Bottle." Two years later, Poe became editor of the *Southern Literary Messenger,* the first of a succession of editorial positions that were to occupy his attention throughout the decade that followed. It was during this period, and against a background of poverty and increasing personal tragedy, that Poe published the great majority of his famous poems and stories. *Tales of the Grotesque and Arabesque* appeared in 1840, *Tales, The Raven and Other Poems* in 1845.

PORTER

KATHERINE ANNE PORTER (1890–   ) was born in Indian Creek, Texas, near San Antonio, and was educated in convent schools in Texas and Louisiana. Miss Porter began her writing career as a journalist and free-lance writer in New York, Dallas, and Denver. Her first collection of short stories, *Flowering Judas,* appeared in 1930 and won immediate recognition for its level of craftsmanship and rich prose style—the hallmarks of her fiction. Other collections of stories and short novels followed: *Hacienda* (1934), *Pale Horse Pale Rider* (1939), and *The Leaning Tower* (1944). Her long-awaited allegorical novel, *Ship of Fools,* was published in 1962 and has since been made into a movie. Miss Porter's short stories were brought together anew in 1965 in *The Collected Stories of Katherine Anne Porter,* a volume that won the National Book Award.

ROBBE-GRILLET

ALAIN ROBBE-GRILLET (1922–   ) was born in Brest, France, and educated as an agronomic engineer, a career that took him to Morocco, Equatorial Africa, and the French Antilles. Turning to literature, he published his first novel, *The Erasers*, in 1953. Since that time he has become a leading exponent of the so-called New Novel, a literary movement that eschews, among other things, many of the traditional techniques of fiction to concentrate its attention on an objective, detached portrayal of material objects. Robbe-Grillet's other works include the novels *The Voyeur* (1955), *Jealousy* (1957), *In the Labyrinth* (1959), *The House of Assignation* (1965), and *Project for a Revolution in New York* (English translation, 1972); a volume of experimental short fiction, *Snapshots* (1962); a collection of essays, *Towards a New Novel* (1963); and the film script for "Last Year at Marienbad" (1961).

ROTH

PHILIP ROTH (1933–   ) was born in Newark, New Jersey. Following his graduation from Bucknell University, Roth earned a master's degree at the University of Chicago, where he taught English from 1956 to 1958. He has subsequently been a visiting professor at a number of universities, among them Iowa, Harvard, Princeton, the State University of New York at Stony Brook, and the University of Pennsylvania. Since the publication of *Goodbye, Columbus* in 1959, Roth has become increasingly known as a versatile, prolific, and not infrequently controversial writer, well-attuned to the cultural predicaments and absurdities of contemporary American society, in general, and the mores and psychology of the Jewish-American, in particular. His published work includes novels written in the realistic tradition—*Letting Go* (1962), *When She Was Good* (1967), and *My Life as a Man* (1974), and imaginative departures into the world of social and political satire and fantasy—*Portnoy's Complaint* (1969), *Our Gang* (1971), *The Breast* (1972), and *The Great American Novel* (1973). Roth's most recent work, *Reading Myself and Others* (1975), combines a series of interviews with an attempt at critical self-appraisal. His short stories—many of which remain uncollected—first appeared in such places as *Chicago Review*, *Esquire*, *Epoch*, *The New Yorker*, *Playboy*, and *New American Review*. *Goodbye, Co-lumbus*, which includes five short stories and a novella, earned Roth the National Book Award in 1960.

SAYERS

DOROTHY L. SAYERS (1893–1957), the creator of Lord Peter Wimsey, was born at Oxford and educated at Somerville College, Oxford University where she graduated in 1915 (one of the first women ever to take an Oxford degree) with honors in medieval literature. While working as a copywriter for a London advertising agency, she took up the writing of stories, and in 1923 published the first of the novel's featuring the wealthy, witty, and erudite detective Lord Peter Wimsey. *Whose Body?* (1923) was followed in rapid succession by *Clouds of Witness* (1926), *Unnatural Death* (1927), *The Unpleasantness at the Bellona Club* (1928), *Strong Poison* (1930), *The Documents of the Case*, with Robert Eustace, (1930), *The Five Red Herrings* (1931), *Have His Carcase* (1932), *Murder Must Advertise* (1933), *The Nine Tailors* (1934), *Gaudy Night* (1935), and *Busman's Holiday* (1937), all displaying Miss Sayer's remarkable learning and exacting literary craftsmanship. She also published three collections of shorter detective fiction: *Lord Peter Views the Body* (1928), *Hangman's Holiday* (1933), and *In the Teeth of the Evidence* (1939), the final two volumes of which feature the exploits of Dorothy Sayers' other detective hero, Montague Egg, the middle-class wine salesman. After 1937, Miss Sayers turned from detective novels to the writing of religious plays, lecturing on Christianity and medieval studies, and translating Dante's *Divine Comedy* and also *The Song of Roland*.

SILLITOE

ALAN SILLITOE (1928–   ), the best known chronicler of contemporary British working-class life, was born in Nottingham, England, and left school at the age of fourteen to go to work in a bicycle factory. Encouraged to write by poet-novelist Robert Graves, Sillitoe published his first novel, *Saturday Night and Sunday Morning*, in 1958, and a year later, in 1959, his first collection of short stories, *The Loneliness of the Long-Distance Runner*. His subsequent work includes the novels *The General* (1960), *Key to the Door* (1961), *The Death of William Posters* (1965), *A Tree on Fire* (1967), *A Start in Life* (1970), *Travels in Nihilon* (1971) and *Raw Material* (1972); three collections of stories, *The Ragman's*

Daughter (1963), *Guzman Go Home* (1968), and *Men, Women, and Children* (1973); and several volumes of poetry.

SINGER

ISAAC BASHEVIS SINGER (1904–) was born in Radzymin, Poland, and grew up in Warsaw, where for a time he studied at the Rabbinical Seminary before turning to journalism in the 1920s as a writer for the Yiddish press. He came to the United States in 1935, and has since established himself as the foremost living writer of Yiddish novels, short stories, and essays, covering a wide range of ideas and themes. His novels include *The Family Muskat* (1950), *The Magician of Lublin* (1960), *The Slave* (1962), *The Manor* (1967), *The Estate* (1969), and *Enemies: A Love Story* (1972). Singer's short stories have been collected in *Gimpel the Fool* (1957), *The Spinoza of Market Street* (1961), *Short Friday* (1964), *The Séance* (1968), *A Friend of Kafka* (1970), *A Crown of Feathers* (1973), and *Passions* (1975).

STEINBECK·

JOHN STEINBECK (1902–1968) was born in Salinas, California, and grew up near Monterey, the country in which he was later to set so many of his short stories and novels. He worked his way through Stanford University, and following his graduation in 1925 tried to crack the literary market in New York City. Frustrated, he returned to California, where he supported himself through a succession of odd jobs— fruit picker, laboratory assistant, caretaker —while continuing to write. Steinbeck began to receive popular attention with the publication in 1935 of his fourth novel, *Tortilla Flat*. It was followed by *In Dubious Battle* (1936), *The Grapes of Wrath* (1939)—his classic story of the Joad family's losing battle with the Oklahoma dustbowl—and *Of Mice and Men* (1940). During World War II Steinbeck served as a correspondent in Italy. His later novels include *Cannery Row* (1945), *East of Eden* (1952), *Sweet Thursday* (1954), and *The Winter of Our Discontent* (1961). Steinbeck was awarded the 1962 Nobel Prize in Literature.

STEVENSON

ROBERT LOUIS STEVENSON (1850–1894) was born in Edinburgh, Scotland, and took a law degree at the University of Edinburgh. His impaired health took him to southern France, where he began to write; his quest for health led him to Switzerland, to California (where he married an American woman), and eventually to the South Seas, and provided the materials for many of his novels, short stories, and essays. Although perhaps best known for his romantic and swashbuckling novels— *Treasure Island* (1883), *Kidnapped* (1886), *The Strange Case of Dr. Jekyll and Mr. Hyde* (1886), and *The Master of Ballantrae* (1889)—Stevenson was also an accomplished writer of travel books and essays, *An Inland Voyage* (1878), *Travels with a Donkey in the Cevennes* (1879), and *Familiar Studies of Men and Books* (1882); of children's poetry, *A Child's Garden of Verses* (1885); and short stories, *The Merry Men* (1887). He died of a cerebral hemorrhage in Samoa in 1894.

TAYLOR

PETER TAYLOR (1917–) was born in Trenton, Tennessee, but grew up in Nashville, where he briefly attended Vanderbilt University. Taylor received his B.A. from Ohio's Kenyon College in 1940, and after serving in World War II entered the academic world as a professor of English, first at the University of North Carolina at Greensboro and then at Kenyon College, the University of Virginia, and the University of North Carolina at Chapel Hill. His first volume of short stories of the middle south, *A Long Fourth,* appeared in 1948, followed by *The Widows of Thornton* (1952), *Happy Families Are All Alike* (1959), and *Miss Leonora When Last Seen and Fifteen Other Stories* (1963). His novel, *A Woman of Means,* was published in 1950. Peter Taylor is married to poetnovelist Eleanor Ross.

THURBER

JAMES THURBER (1894–1961), perhaps the greatest American literary humorist of the twentieth century, was born and raised in Columbus, Ohio, where he attended Ohio State University. Leaving college without taking a degree, he worked for the State Department in Washington and Paris before returning to Columbus and a job as a reporter on the Columbus *Dispatch*. He also began writing and directing musical comedies for a theater group at Ohio State. Thurber married in 1922, and for the next five years continued his journalistic career before being hired by E. B. White and Harold Ross for the staff of *The New Yorker* magazine, where many of his essays, fables, and stories, with their accompanying cartoons, were to appear during an association of more than thirty years. In 1929 Thurber published his first book, *Is Sex Necessary?* in collaboration with E. B. White, followed by two books of humorous essays, *The Owl in the Attic and Other Perplexities* (1931) and *The Seal in the Bedroom and Other Predicaments* (1932). For the next three decades Thurber continued unabated, with writings that combined humor, social criticism, and satire with a steady and probing view of the essential nature of man himself. His other books include *The Middle-Aged Man on the Flying Trapeze* (1935), *Fables for Our Time and Famous Poems Illustrated* (1940), *The Thurber Carnival* (1945), *The Beast in Me and Other Animals* (1948), *Thurber Country* (1953), *Further Fables for Our Time* (1956), and *Lanterns and Lances* (1961).

TOLSTOY

LEO TOLSTOY (1828–1910) was born near Tula, Russia, of aristocratic parents. Brought up by an aunt following the early death of his parents, Tolstoy for a time entered upon the carefree, aimless life of a young man with money in Moscow and in St. Petersburg. He began to write while serving as an artillery officer in the Crimea and received the encouragement of Ivan Turgenev, already a published author. Tolstoy's two great novels of Russian aristocratic life, *War and Peace* and *Anna Karenina,* were published in 1869 and 1877, after which he passed through a deep personal and religious crisis. His later works, including *The Death of Ivan Ilych* (1886), *Master and Man* (1895), and *Resurrection* (1899), reflect his disenchantment with bourgeoise society and his own hard-won conception of Christian salvation. These beliefs and the struggle leading up to them led to the publication of such nonfiction as *What Men Live By* (1881), *My Confession* (1882), *What I Believe* (1884), and *The Kingdom of God Is Within You* (1893).

TRILLING

LIONEL TRILLING (1905–1975) was born, raised, and spent much of his adult life in New York City. He attended Columbia University, where he received his Ph.D. in 1938, after which he taught briefly at the University of Washington and Hunter College before joining the English faculty at his alma mater in 1941. In 1965 he became George Edward Woodberry Professor of Literature and Criticism. Professor Trilling's career was a distinguished and versatile

one. He wrote two full-length critical studies, *Matthew Arnold* (1939) and *E. M. Forster* (1943); several volumes of essays, including *The Liberal Imagination* (1950), *The Opposing Self* (1955), *A Gathering of Fugitives* (1956), and *Beyond Culture* (1965); a novel, *The Middle of the Journey* (1947); and served as an editor of the *Partisan Review* and as an advisory editor of the *Kenyon Review*. He was married to the noted critic Diana Trilling.

TURGENEV

IVAN TURGENEV (1818–1883) was born in Orel, Russia, of wealthy, landowning parents. He attended the universities at Moscow, St. Petersburg, and Berlin before entering the Russian civil service at the insistence of his mother (Turgenev had wanted to be a teacher). Shortly thereafter Turgenev struck out on his own and took up literature. A collection of his early stories, *A Sportsman's Notebook,* appeared in 1852. His later works include the novels *Fathers and Sons* (1862), *Smoke* (1867), and *Virgin Soil* (1876). Between 1856 and the time of his death, Turgenev lived abroad, for the most part in Paris, where he made the friendship of many Western writers including Henry James, who helped bring Turgenev's realism to the attention of American readers.

UNAMUNO

MIGUEL DE UNAMUNO (1864–1936) was born in Bilbao, Spain, earned a doctoral degree at the University of Madrid, and in 1891, at the age of twenty-seven, became a professor of Greek at the University of Salamanca. Ten years later he became Rector of the University, a position he held until 1914, when he was relieved for his outspoken political opinions. Reelected in 1931, the temperamental, quixotic Unamuno again lost his position in 1936, at the outset of the Spanish Civil War, for his opposition to Franco. He died shortly thereafter. A philosopher, poet, short story writer, novelist, dramatist, and essayist, Unamuno's reputation in Spain and throughout Europe grew rapidly during the early years of the twentieth century. As a philosopher he is perhaps best known for his *Tragic Sense of Life* (1913), an existential treatise on death. His best known fiction is found in *Abel Sanchez* (1917) and *Three Exemplary Novels* (1920).

UPDIKE

JOHN UPDIKE (1932–   ) now in his midforties, is firmly established as one of

America's leading writers. Born and raised in Pennsylvania, and educated at Harvard (he graduated *summa cum laude*), Updike spent a year studying art at the Ruskin School of Drawing and Fine Art in Oxford, England, prior to joining the staff of *The New Yorker* magazine, where he worked until 1957. He has published three volumes of poetry, *The Carpentered Hen and Other Tame Creatures,* (1958), *Telephone Poles* (1963), and *Midpoint* (1969), and several novels, including *The Poorhouse Fair* (1959), *Rabbit, Run* (1960), *The Centaur* (1963), *Of the Farm* (1965), *Couples* (1968), *Rabbit Redux* (1971), *A Month of Sundays* (1975), and *Marry Me* (1976). Updike's short stories, finely crafted vignettes of the frustrations and tensions of contemporary life, have been collected in *The Same Door* (1959), *Pigeon Feathers* (1962), *The Music School* (1966), *Bech: A Book* (1970), and *Museums & Women* (1972). Many of these stories originally appeared in the pages of *The New Yorker.* Updike has also published a play, *Buchanan Dying* (1974), and a volume of reviews, essays, introducions, and speeches, *Picked-Up Pieces* (1975).

VONNEGUT

KURT VONNEGUT, JR. (1922–   ), was born and raised in Indianapolis, Indiana. In 1942, following a year at Cornell where he majored in chemistry, Vonnegut joined the army and was shipped overseas. Taken prisoner by the Germans at the Battle of the Bulge in late 1944, Vonnegut was sent on to Dresden where he survived the devastating firebombing of February 1945, before being released two months later. The Dresden experience was to provide the subject matter for the novel *Slaughterhouse-Five* (1969), which subsequently was made into a film. Following the war, Vonnegut attended the University of Chicago as a graduate student in anthropology, and then went to work for General Electric as a publicist at its Schenectady, New York, research laboratory. This association lasted until 1950, when Vonnegut left G.E. to become a full-time writer. In the quarter of a century since, Kurt Vonnegut has clearly established himself as one of America's most important—and most popular writers. Vonnegut's novels—displaying his interest in science fiction, his hatred of war, and his insistence on the need to resist the dehumanizing pressures of our technological society, together with his gift for humor and satire—include *Player Piano* (1952), *The*

Sirens of Titan (1959), *Mother Night* (1961), *Cat's Cradle* (1963), *God Bless You, Mr. Rosewater* (1966), *Slaughterhouse-Five* (1969), *Breakfast of Champions* (1973), and *Slapstick. Or Lonesome No More* (1976). His short fiction, "work I sold in order to finance the writing of the novels," has been brought together in *Canary in a Cat House* (1961) and *Welcome to the Monkey House* (1968).

WELLS

H. G. WELLS (1866–1946) was born in Bromley, England. An avid reader from the age of eight, when a broken leg resulted in a long period of convalescence, Wells studied biology and zoology at the Normal School of Science in London under the direction of noted scientist Thomas H. Huxley, after which he taught science until poor health turned him toward the writing of fiction. In 1888 he published his first major work, an early version of his famous story "The Time Machine," followed by *The Stolen Bacillus and Other Incidents* (1895), *The Island of Dr. Moreau* (1896), *The Wheels of Chance* (1896), *The Plattner Story and Others* (1897), *The Invisible Man* (1897), and *The War of the Worlds* (1898). Although most often remembered as a writer of science fiction, Wells also produced a number of realistic novels depicting Edwardian life, including *Kipps* (1905), *Tono-Bungay* (1909), and *The History of Mr. Polly* (1910). During World War I he published *Mr. Britling Sees It Through* (1916), picturing the war as seen from the perspective of an average Englishman. It became a best seller in both England and America. His writings following the war revealed his optimistic hopes for peace based on world government, a faith that slowly soured as World War II became a reality.

WELTY

EUDORA WELTY (1909–   ) was born in Jackson, Mississippi, attended Mississippi State College for Women and the University of Wisconsin, where she received a B.A. in 1929, and then spent a year in New York City at Columbia University's School of Advertising. In 1932 she returned to Jackson and turned to a literary career. The quality of Miss Welty's writing has been consistently high, earning her a number of O. Henry Memorial Prizes and the prestigious Howells award of the American Academy of Arts and Letters. She has published four collections of short stories, *A*

Curtain of Green (1941), *The Wide Net* (1943), *The Golden Apples* (1949), and *The Bride of the Innisfallen* (1955); and five novels, *The Robber Bridegroom* (1942), *Delta Wedding* (1946). *The Ponder Heart* (1954), *Losing Battles* (1970), and *The Optimist's Daughter* (1972). Eudora Welty continues to make her home in Jackson, in the midst of the region that appears most frequently as the locale of her fiction.

WHITE

ELWIN BROOKS WHITE (1899–) was born and raised in Mount Vernon, New York, and attended Cornell University where he was editor-in-chief of the *Cornell Daily Sun*. Following his graduation in 1921, White began his long career as a writer, first as a reporter and advertising copywriter and then as the author of sensitive and humorous short stories, essays, and poems, most of which first appeared in the pages of *The New Yorker*. White began his association with that magazine in 1926, and for some three decades his name and *The New Yorker* were virtually synonymous. White's works have been collected in *Is Sex Necessary?* (on which he colaborated with James Thurber in 1929), *Every Day Is Saturday* (1934), *The Fox of Peapack* (1938), *Quo Vadimus?* (1939), *One Man's Meat* (1942), *The Wild Flag* (1946), *Here Is New York* (1949), *The Second Tree from the Corner* (1953) and *The Points of My Compass* (1962). In 1959, he edited and revised *The Elements of Style*, the writing textbook of his former teacher at Cornell, William Strunk, Jr. White's rendition has long since become a classic in its own right. White is also the author of three charming children's books,

Stuart Little (1945), *Charlotte's Web* (1952), and *The Trumpet of the Swan* (1970).

WRIGHT

RICHARD WRIGHT (1908–1960) was born on a cotton plantation near Natchez, Mississippi, into a childhood filled with transience and poverty. Abandoned by her tenant-farmer husband when Richard was five, Wright's mother supported the family by working as a domestic until her total paralysis dissolved the family unit completely and forced Richard into a series of foster homes and finally into an orphanage. From Memphis, where he eked out a living doing odd jobs, Wright went in 1927 to Chicago, where, in the midst of the Great Depression, he joined the Communist party and began to write. A Guggenheim Fellowship allowed him to complete his first novel, *Native Son* (1940), a brutally realistic story of alienation and murder that soon established Wright as America's leading black author. It was followed five years later, in 1945, by *Black Boy*, the autobiographical recounting of his own youth. Between 1947 and the time of his death in 1960 Wright made his home in France. His other books include *Uncle Tom's Children* (1938), a collection of four longish stories; *The God That Failed* (1950), the story of his own disenchantment with Communism; *The Outsider* (1953) and *The Long Dream* (1958), two novels influenced by his contact with French existentialism; *Black Power* (1954), an account of his travels among the emerging nations of West Africa; and *Eight Men* (1961), a posthumous collection of short stories.

A Glossary of Literary Terms

ACTION: The events or incidents that take place within a story. These events may be external (physical) as well as internal (psychological). The patterned arrangement of these events is usually referred to as the PLOT.

ALLEGORY: A type of narrative that attempts to reinforce its thesis by making its characters (and sometimes its events and setting as well) represent certain abstract ideas or qualities. See FABLE and PARABLE.

ALLUSION: A reference, generally brief, to a person, place, thing, or event beyond the work with which the reader is presumably familiar. An allusion may be explicit or implied; the referent real or imaginary. Appropriate allusions serve to clarify and add new meaning to a literary work.

AMBIGUITY: A word, phrase, event, or situation that may be understood or interpreted in two or more ways, each valid in the immediate context. The deliberate use of ambiguity can add to a work's effectiveness and richness; ambiguity that is not deliberate often reflects carelessness and results in obscurity.

ANACHRONISM: A person or thing that is chronologically out of place.

ANECDOTE: A brief, unadorned narrative about a particular person or incident. Short stories differ from anecdotes by virtue of their greater length and the deliberate, artistic arrangement of their elements.

ANTAGONIST: The rival or opponent against whom the major character (the hero or protagonist) is contending.

ANTICLIMAX: A sudden transition from the important (or serious) to the trivial (or ludicrous). In fiction we speak of something being anticlimatic when it occurs after the climax or turning point of the story has been reached. See CLIMAX.

ARCHETYPE: A term used in fictional analysis to describe certain basic and repeated patterns of plot, character, or theme. It enters literary criticism from the depth psychology of Swiss psychologist Carl Gustav Jung (1875–1961) and his concept that each individual retains the recollection of his racial past—what he calls the "collective unconscious." The presence of this collective memory allows us to respond to a group of "primordial images" or archetypes formed out of repeated, shared experiences in the lives of our ancestors.

ATMOSPHERE: The mood or feeling pervading a literary work. Atmosphere is established through the author's deliberate manipulation of the story's setting, characters, plot, and/or style.

BURLESQUE: A form of humor that ridicules persons, attitudes, actions, or things by means of distortion and exaggeration. Burlesque of a particular literary work or style is referred to as PARODY. CARICATURE, on the other hand, creates its humor by distorting or exaggerating an individual's prominent physical features. See also SATIRE.

CARICATURE: See BURLESQUE.

CATASTROPHE: A form of dénouement, usually tragic in its outcome. See DÉNOUEMENT.

CHARACTER: An individual within a literary work. The chief character of a given work is called the PROTAGONIST or HERO; his opponent is called the ANTAGONIST. Characters may be complex and well developed (round characters) or undifferentiated and one dimensional (flat characters); they may change in the course of the story (dynamic characters) or remain essentially the same (static characters). Characters who conventionally appear in certain forms of literature and are easily recognizable on that basis are referred to as STOCK CHARACTERS—for example, the rich uncle of domestic comedy; the hard-boiled detective of the pulps; the female confidante of soap opera; the cruel step-mother of the fairy tale; and the mus-tachioed villain of nineteenth-century melodrama.

CHARACTERIZATION: The process by which an author creates, develops, and presents a fictional character. Characterization can be achieved through direct comments by the author, through description, or, dramatically, through dialogue and action.

CLICHÉ: A phrase or expression that is trite, threadbare, and otherwise overused.

CLIMAX: That point during the plot when the action reaches its peak of intensity and its turning point. *See* ANTI-CLIMAX.

COMPLICATION: That part of the plot in which the conflict is developed and intensified.

CONFLICT: The struggle or encounter within the plot of two opposing forces that serves to create reader interest and suspense. Conflict may be *external,* between two characters (say, the *protagonist* and the *antagonist*) or between one character and some aspect of his or her environment; *internal,* between two opposing ideas, feelings, or tendencies struggling within a single character; or a combination of both.

CONNOTATION: The meaning suggested or implied by a given word or phrase, as opposed to its literal, dictionary meaning. *See* DENOTATION.

CONVENTION: Any literary device, technique, style, or form, or any aspect of subject matter, characterization, or theme that has become recognized and accepted by both authors and their audiences through repeated use. *See also* STOCK CHARACTER.

CRITICISM: The description, analysis, interpretation, or evaluation of a literary work of art.

DENOTATION: The literal, dictionary meaning of a given word or phrase. *See* CONNOTATION.

DÉNOUEMENT: From the French word meaning "unknotting" or "untying." The final resolution of the conflict or complications of the plot.

DEUS EX MACHINA: "God from the machine." Derived from a practice in Greek drama whereby an impersonation of a god was mechanically lowered onto the stage to intervene in and solve the issues of the play. Commonly used today to describe the intervention of fate, destiny, or any apparently contrived or improbable device used by an author to resolve the difficulties of plot.

DIALOGUE: The conversation that goes on between or among characters in a literary work.

DICTION: The author's choice or selection of words, his vocabulary. The artistic arangement of those words constitutes STYLE.

DIDACTIC: Literature designed more to teach a lesson or instruct the reader than to present an experience objectively. In a didactic work *theme* is generally the most important element.

DRAMATIC IRONY: *See* IRONY.

EMPATHY: The state of entering into and actually participating in the emotional, mental, and/or physical life of an object, person, or literary character. Empathy should not be confused with SYMPATHY, in which we feel for, or identify emotionally with, someone else and share his or her feelings.

EPIGRAPH: A quotation prefacing a literary work, often containing a clue to the writer's intention.

EPIPHANY: A term applied to literature by James Joyce to describe a sudden revelation, or "showing forth," of the essential truth about a character, situation, or experience.

EPISODE: A single, unified incident within a narrative that may or may not advance the plot. Plots may be composed of a single episode or several episodes; plots consisting of a series of loosely connected incidents that are arranged chronologically are said to be EPISODIC.

EXPLICATION: *See* CRITICISM.

EXPOSITION: The part of a work that provides necessary background information.

FABLE: A story with a moral lesson, usually employing animals who talk and act like human beings. *See* ALLEGORY.

FANTASY: A work of fiction that deliberately sets aside everyday reality.

FICTION: A prose narrative that is a product of the imagination.

FIGURATIVE LANGUAGE: Language used imaginatively and nonliterally. Figurative language is composed of such figures of speech (or *tropes*) as metaphor, simile, personification, metonymy, synecdoche, apostrophe, hyperbole, symbol, irony, and paradox.

FLASHBACK: The interruption of a story's narrative in order to present an earlier scene or episode. A method of *exposition.*

FLAT AND ROUND CHARACTERS: *See* CHARACTER.

FOIL. A character who provides a direct contrast to another character.

FORESHADOWING: A device by means of which the author hints at something to follow.

FORM: *See* GENRE.

GENRE: A *form,* class, or type of literary work—for example, the short story, novel, poem, play, or essay. Often the term is also used to denote such literary subclassifications as the detective story or the gothic novel.

HERO: The central character in a literary work. Also often referred to as the *protagonist.*

IMAGERY: Most commonly refers to the visual pictures within a work produced verbally through *figurative language,* though it is often defined more broadly to include sensory experiences other than the visual.

INITIATION STORY: A term commonly used to describe a narrative focusing on a young person's movement from innocence toward adult maturity through contact with experience.

IN MEDIAS RES: A Latin phrase used to describe a narrative that begins in the middle of things.

IRONY: A term that refers to the contrast or discrepancy between appearance and reality. Irony takes a number of special forms: in *verbal irony* there is a contrast between what is literally said and what is actually meant; in *dramatic irony* the state of affairs known to the audience (or reader) is the reverse of what its participants suppose it to be; in *situational irony* a set of circumstances turns out to be the reverse of what is expected or is appropriate.

METAPHOR: A figure of speech in which two unlike objects are explicitly compared with one another without the use of "like" or "as." *See* FIGURATIVE LANGUAGE.

MOOD: *See* ATMOSPHERE.

MOTIF: An idea, theme, character, situation, or element that recurs in literature or folklore. *See* ARCHETYPE, CONVENTION, STOCK CHARACTER.

MOTIVATION: The causes that move a character to act. In realistic literature we generally require that a character be properly motivated, that his actions or behavior be consistent with his personality and situation.

MYTH: In its widest sense, any idea or belief to which a number of people subscribe.

NARRATIVE: A series of unified events. *See* PLOT *and* ACTION.

NARRATIVE TECHNIQUE: The author's methods of presenting or telling a story.

NARRATOR: The character or voice that tells the story. *See* POINT OF VIEW.

NATURALISM: A post-Darwinian movement of the late nineteenth century that tried to apply the "laws" of scientific determinism to fiction. The Naturalist went beyond the Realist's insistence on the objective presentation of the details of everyday life to insist that the materials of literature should be arranged to reflect a deterministic universe in which man is a biological creature controlled by his environment and heredity. *See* REALISM.

NOVEL: The name generally applied to any long fictional prose narrative.

NOVELETTE: A longish prose narrative, not long enough to be regarded as a novel but too long to be a short story.

OMNISCIENT POINT OF VIEW: *See* POINT OF VIEW.

PARABLE: A story designed to convey or illustrate a moral lesson. *See* ALLEGORY *and* FABLE.

PARODY: *See* BURLESQUE.

PATHOS: The quality in a literary work that evokes a feeling of pity, tenderness, and sympathy from the reader or audience. Overdone or misused pathos becomes mere *sentimentality*.

PERSONA (Pl.: personae): A term applied to the voice or mask the author adopts for the purpose of telling the story. The term *persona* is a way of reminding us that the "I" voice of the story is not to be confused with the author himself; rather it is to be regarded as another of the author's creation or fictions.

PLOT: The patterned arrangement of the events in a narrative or play. *See also* ACTION, CONFLICT, COMPLICATION, CLIMAX, (ANTICLIMAX), CATASTROPHE, *and* DÉNOUEMENT.

POINT OF VIEW: The angle or perspective from which the story is told. There are two basic points of view—*first person* and *third person*. In *first person* point of view the story is told by one of the characters, who may or may not be the *protagonist;* in *third person* point of view the story is told by someone who is not a participant in the story at all. Third person points of view may be subdivided as follows: third person *omniscient*, in which the narrator is all-knowing, has access to the thoughts and feelings of all the characters, and moves freely among them to comment editorially on any aspect of the story; third person *limited*, in which the narrator restricts his access to one or more of the characters and what that character (or those characters) sees, thinks, feels, or hears; and third person *dramatic* (or scenic), in which the narrator adopts a neutral stance, stands back, and like a motion-picture camera simply records the action of the story without editorializing or entering the consciousness of any of the characters. By common agreement, no aspect of fiction is more important, more capable of variation and refinement, or more troublesome for the critic.

PREFACE: The author's introduction to his or her work.

PROTAGONIST: The chief character of a literary work. Also commonly referred to as the *hero*. *See* CHARACTER *and* ANTAGONIST.

REALISM: The nineteenth-century literary movement that reacted to romanticism by insisting upon a faithful, objective presentation of the details of everyday life. *See* NATURALISM.

RESOLUTION: *See* DÉNOUEMENT.

ROUND CHARACTER: *See* CHARACTER.

SATIRE: A type of writing that holds up persons, ideas, or things to varying degrees of amusement, ridicule, or contempt in order, presumably, to improve, correct, or bring about some desirable change.

SCENE: A self-contained segment of a work of fiction that is treated dramatically.

SENTIMENTALITY: The presence of emotion or feeling that seems excessive or unjustified in terms of the objective circumstances. *See* PATHOS.

SETTING: The time and place in which the action of a story or play occurs. *See* ATMOSPHERE.

SHORT STORY: A short work of narrative prose fiction. The distinction between the short story and novel is mainly one of length.

SITUATIONAL IRONY: *See* IRONY.

STOCK CHARACTER: *See* CHARACTER.

STREAM OF CONSCIOUSNESS: The narrative method of capturing and representing the inner workings of a character's mind. The pattern of thoughts and feelings thus presented may be logical and connected, or chaotic and disconnected, composed only of bits of apparently unrelated ideas, emotions, and sense impressions.

STRUCTURE: The overall pattern, design, or organization of a literary work.

STYLE: The author's characteristic manner of expression; style includes the author's diction, syntax, sentence patterns, punctuation, and spelling, as well as the use made of such devices as sound, rhythm, imagery, and figurative language.

SUSPENSE: The psychological tension or anxiety resulting from the reader's uncertainty of just how the work is likely to end.

SYMBOL: Literally, something that stands for something else. In literature, any word, image, object, action, or character that embodies and evokes a *range* of additional meaning and significance.

SYMPATHY: *See* EMPATHY.

THEME: The controlling idea or meaning of a work of art.

TONE: The author's attitude toward both his subject and audience.

VERISIMILITUDE: The quality of being lifelike or true to actuality.